The 1998
ESPN
Information Please®
Sports Almanac

With Year in Review Commentary from
ESPN anchors and analysts:

David Aldridge
on Pro Basketball

Chris Berman
on Pro Football

Linda Cohn
on Pro Hockey

Lee Corso
on College Football

Mike Durbin
on Bowling

Jack Edwards
on College Hockey
College Soccer
Pro Soccer and
International Sports

Rich Eisen
on the Top 40 Moments

Chris Fowler
on College Basketball
College Football and
College Sports

Peter Gamm
on Baseball

Hank Goldb
on Horse Racing

Mimi Griffin
on Women's College Basketball

Steve Levy
on Pro Hockey

Kenny Mayne
on Auto Racing

Chris Mortensen
on Pro Football

Sal Paolantonio
on Tennis

Dan Patrick
on the Top 40 Personalities

Karl Ravech
on Ballparks and Arenas
and Baseball

Stuart Scott
on the Top 40 Moments

Charley Steiner
on Boxing

The Champions of 1997

Auto Racing

NASCAR Circuit
Daytona 500 ....Jeff Gordon
Winston 500 ....Mark Martin
Coca-Cola 600 ....Jeff Gordon
Southern 500 ....Jeff Gordon
IndyCar Circuit
U.S. 500 ....Alex Zanardi
PPG Cup Champion ....Alex Zanardi
Indy Racing League Circuit
Indianapolis 500 ....Arie Luyendyk
Formula One Circuit
World Driving Championship ......Jacques Villeneuve

Baseball

World Series .....Florida def. Cleveland, 4 games to 3
MVP ....Livan Hernandez, Florida, P
All-Star Game ....AL 3, NL 1 in Cleveland
MVP ....Sandy Alomar Jr., Cleveland, C
College World Series ....LSU
MVP ....Brandon Larson, LSU, SS

College Basketball

Men's NCAA Final Four
Championship ....Arizona 84, Kentucky 79 (OT)
MVP ....Miles Simon, Arizona, G
Women's NCAA Final Four
Championship ....Tennessee 68, Old Dominion 59
MVP ....Chamique Holdsclaw, Tennessee, F

Pro Basketball

NBA Finals ....Chicago def. Utah 4 games to 2
MVP ....Michael Jordan, Chicago, G
Eastern Final ....Chicago def. Miami 4 games to 1
Western Final ....Utah def. Houston 4 games to 2
All-Star Game ......East 132, West 120 at Cleveland
MVP ....Glen Rice, Charlotte, G

Bowling

Men's Major Championships
PBA National ....Rick Steelsmith
Tournament of Champions ....John Gant
ABC Masters ....Jason Queen
Women's Major Championships
Sam's Town Invitational (1996) ....Carol Gianotti-Block
WIBC Queens ....Sandra Jo Odom
AMF Gold Cup ....Aleta Sill

College Football (1996)

National Champions
AP and Coaches ....Florida (12-1)
Major Bowls
Orange ....Nebraska 41, Virginia Tech 21
Rose ....Ohio St. 20, Arizona St. 17
Sugar ....Florida 52, Florida St. 20
Fiesta ....Penn St. 38, Texas 15
Heisman Trophy ....Danny Wuerffel, Florida, QB

Pro Football (1996)

Super Bowl XXXI ....Green Bay 35, New England 21
MVP ....Desmond Howard, Green Bay, KR
AFC Championship ...New England 20, Jacksonville 6
NFC Championship ....Green Bay 30, Carolina 13
Pro Bowl ....AFC 26, NFC 23
MVP ....Mark Brunell, Jacksonville, QB
CFL Grey Cup Final ....Toronto 43, Edmonton 37
MVP ....Doug Flutie, Toronto, QB

Golf

Men's Major Championships
Masters ....Tiger Woods
U.S. Open ....Ernie Els
British Open ....Justin Leonard
PGA Championship ....Davis Love III
Seniors Major Championships
The Tradition ....Gil Morgan
PGA Seniors ....Hale Irwin
U.S. Senior Open ....Graham Marsh
Senior Players Championship ....Larry Gilbert
Women's Major Championships
Nabisco Dinah Shore ....Betsy King
LPGA Championship ....Chris Johnson
U.S. Women's Open ....Alison Nicholas
du Marier Classic ....Colleen Walker
National Team Competition
Ryder Cup ....Europe 14½, United States 13½

Hockey

Stanley Cup .....Detroit def. Philadelphia 4 games to 0
MVP ....Mike Vernon, Detroit, G
Western Final ......Detroit def. Colorado 4 games to 2
Eastern Final .Philadelphia def. NY Rangers 4 games to 1
All-Star Game ....East 11, West 7 at San Jose
MVP ....Mark Recchi, Montreal, RW
NCAA Div. 1 Final ....North Dakota 6, Boston U. 4
MVP ....Matt Hederson, North Dakota F

Horse Racing

Triple Crown Champions
Kentucky Derby ....Silver Charm (Gary Sevens)
Preakness ....Silver Charm (Gary Stevens)
Belmont ....Touch Gold (Chris McCarron)
Harness Racing
Hambletonian ....Malabar Man (Mal Burroughs)
Little Brown Jug .....Western Dreamer (Mike Lachance)

Soccer

MLS Champ. Game .........D.C. United 2, Colorado 1
MVP ....Jaime Moreno, D.C. United, F
Copa America ....Brazil
World Youth Championships ....Argentina
Under 17 World Champs. ....Brazil
US Cup '97 ....Mexico

Tennis

Men's Grand Slam Championships
Australian Open ....Pete Sampras
French Open ....Gustavo Kuerten
Wimbledon ....Pete Sampras
U.S. Open ....Patrick Rafter
Women's Grand Slam Championships
Australian Open ....Martina Hingis
French Open ....Iva Majoli
Wimbledon ....Martina Hingis
U.S. Open ....Martina Hingis
National Team Competition
Fed Cup (Women) ....France 4, Netherlands 1

Miscellaneous Champions

Little League World Series ......Guadalupe, Mexico
Tour de France ....Jan Ullrich (GER)
Iditarod ....Martin Buser
U.S. Chess Championships ....Joel Benjamin

THE 1998
ESPn INFORMATION PLEASE®
SPORTS
ALMANAC

John Hassan
EDITOR

information please LLC

HYPERION
ESPn®
BOOKS

Editor
John Hassan
Associate Editors
Gerry Brown, Michael Morrison
Reporters
Gary Brown, John Bishop, John Gettings
Production Editors
Peggy Groppo, Elaine Rho
Production Assistant
Linda Bean-Pardee
Principal Database Manager
Susan Hyde
Database Developer
Paul Crook

Comments and suggestions from readers are invited. Because of the many letters received, however, it's not possible to respond personally to every correspondent. Nevertheless, all letters are welcome and each will be carefully considered. The **1998 ESPN Information Please Sports Almanac** does not rule on bets or wagers. Address all correspondence to: Sports, Information Please LLC, 31 St. James Avenue, Boston, MA 02116.
Email: ipsa@infoplease.com.

Information Please and Information Please Almanac are registered trademarks of Information Please LLC.

ISBN 0-7868-8296-4

FIRST EDITION

10 9 8 7 6 5 4 3 2 1

CONTENTS 5

6   **CONTENTS**

CONTENTS 7

Usually, it's best not to judge a book by its cover. In this case, however, I hope you do.

After eight years on our own, we here at the *Information Please® Sports Almanac* have joined forces with ESPN and Hyperion to bring you the *1998 ESPN Information Please® Sports Almanac*.

We may have added only four letters to our name but they are the four most important letters in sports.

The ESPN-ization of this almanac has resulted in many exciting changes. Most notably, each sport is covered by an expert who covers that sport on a daily basis for ESPN. You simply won't find better coverage. And I couldn't have found more friendly and professional people to work with. I want to thank each ESPN contributor for taking the time to ensure that each sport in this almanac received the same kind of authoritative treatment that is synonymous with ESPN's SportsCenter.

Another new feature: Each sport's essay section now ends with a few statistics from the "Inside the Numbers" staff at ESPN. I am indebted to coordinating producer Matthew Ipsan, a true star, and his crew for always coming through with a great selection of telling, informative numbers for every sport.

This synergy with ESPN could not have happened without the blessing of John Walsh, senior vice-president and executive editor of ESPN. I am grateful to John for his excellent editorial ideas and steadfast support. I received a lot of assistance from many other people at ESPN headquarters in Bristol, CT. Thanks, then, to Russell Baxter, Dennis Denninger, Diane Dillon, Vince Doria, Grace Gallo and Norby Williamson.

I reserve a special thanks for Sharyn Taymor at ESPN and Gretchen Young at Hyperion. Gretchen and Sharyn were my best pals and closest contacts at their respective companies. They were always there when I needed them and I couldn't have completed the job without their help and friendship.

Thanks also to Muriel Caplan, Adrian James, Kris Kliemann, Lesley Krauss, Jennifer Landers, Jennifer Lang, Bob Miller and Jennifer Morgan, all at Hyperion.

My colleagues at Information Please have my enduring gratitude for the support necessary to get another almanac into your hands. My sincere thanks to Liz Kubik, Jim Bryant, Scott Beatty, Nicole Guest, and Pam Greene. Susan Hyde, Paul Crook, Elaine Rho, Linda Bean-Pardee, and Peggy Groppo were tremendously helpful with every aspect of the book's production.

Gerry Brown and Michael Morrison were there for every pitch and every trip to the dentist. I am lucky to have them as colleagues and friends. John Gettings, Gary Brown and John Bishop provided invaluable reporting and fact-checking.

Outside assistance was graciously provided by Pam Reichmann of R.C. Ltd, Nat Andriani and the amazing Carolyn McMahon of the Associated Press, Rick Campbell, Gary Johnson and Sharon Tufano of the NCAA, Barbara Zidovsky of Nielsen Media Research, Greg Sharko of the ATP Tour, Paul Ramlow of the United States Trotting Association, Howard Bass of Thoroughbred Racing, Rusty Ingram of the Boston Bruins, and Shelley Youngblut of ESPN Magazine.

I also must acknowledge the help of Tom Farrey and Ted Bishop of ESPN SportsZone. After working with Tom and Ted, I know why SportsZone is the best sports web site around.

After we amassed all of this information, there was the tricky task of getting it on paper. I wish to thank Paul Schaefer and Jim Murphy of Western Graphic Communications and Arlene Cretella of Digital Fine Color for their gracious professionalism and expertise.

Finally, I want to thank my dear wife, Karen Mynatt. We were meant to be together for a myriad of reasons but, right now, two stand out. She loves Tennessee football and I am a Red Sox fan. But thanks to her, I always feel like a winner.

John Hassan
Boston
October 27, 1997

Major League Cities & Teams

As of Oct. 31, 1997, there were 127 major league teams playing or scheduled to play baseball, basketball, NFL football, hockey and soccer in 50 cities in the United States and Canada. Listed below are the cities and the teams that play there.

Anaheim
AL   Angels
NHL   Mighty Ducks of Anaheim

Atlanta
NL   Braves
NBA   Hawks
NFL   Falcons

Baltimore
AL   Orioles
NFL   Ravens

Boston
AL   Red Sox
NBA   Celtics
NFL   N.E. Patriots (Foxboro)
NHL   Bruins
MLS   N.E. Revolution (Foxboro)

Buffalo
NFL   Bills (Orchard Park)
NHL   Sabres

Calgary
NHL   Flames

Charlotte
NBA   Hornets
NFL   Carolina Panthers

Chicago
AL   White Sox
NL   Cubs
NBA   Bulls
NFL   Bears
NHL   Blackhawks
MLS   Fire

Cincinnati
NL   Reds
NFL   Bengals

Cleveland
AL   Indians
NBA   Cavaliers

Columbus
MLS   Crew

Dallas
AL   Texas Rangers (Arlington)
NBA   Mavericks
NFL   Cowboys (Irving)
NHL   Stars
MLS   Burn

Denver
NL   Colorado Rockies
NBA   Nuggets
NFL   Broncos
NHL   Colorado Avalanche
MLS   Colorado Rapids

Detroit
AL   Tigers
NBA   Pistons (Auburn Hills)
NFL   Lions (Pontiac)
NHL   Red Wings

East Rutherford
NBA   New Jersey Nets
NFL   New York Giants
NFL   New York Jets
NHL   New Jersey Devils
MLS   NY/NJ Metrostars

Edmonton
NHL   Oilers

Green Bay
NFL   Packers

Greensboro
NHL   Carolina Hurricanes

Houston
NL   Astros
NBA   Rockets

Indianapolis
NBA   Pacers
NFL   Colts

Jacksonville
NFL   Jaguars

Kansas City
AL   Royals
NFL   Chiefs
MLS   Wizards

Los Angeles
NL   Dodgers
NBA   Clippers
NBA   Lakers (Inglewood)
NHL   Kings (Inglewood)
MLS   Galaxy (Pasadena)

Memphis
NFL   Tennessee Oilers

Miami
NL   Florida Marlins
NBA   Heat
NFL   Dolphins
NHL   Florida Panthers
MLS   Fusion

Milwaukee
AL   Brewers
NBA   Bucks

Minneapolis
AL   Minn. Twins
NBA   Minn. Timberwolves
NFL   Minn. Vikings

Montreal
NL   Expos
NHL   Canadiens

New Orleans
NFL   Saints

New York
AL   Yankees
NL   Mets
NBA   Knicks
NHL   Rangers
NHL   N.Y. Islanders (Uniondale)

Oakland
AL   Athletics
NBA   Golden St. Warriors
NFL   Raiders

Orlando
NBA   Magic

Ottawa
NHL   Senators (Kanata)

Philadelphia
NL   Phillies
NBA   76ers
NFL   Eagles
NHL   Flyers

Phoenix
NBA   Suns
NFL   Arizona Cardinals (Tempe)
AL   Arizona DiamondBacks
NHL   Coyotes

Pittsburgh
NL   Pirates
NFL   Steelers
NHL   Penguins

Portland
NBA   Trail Blazers

Sacramento
NBA   Kings

St. Louis
NL   Cardinals
NFL   Rams
NHL   Blues

Salt Lake City
NBA   Utah Jazz

San Antonio
NBA   Spurs

San Diego
NL   Padres
NFL   Chargers

San Francisco
NL   Giants
NFL   49ers

San Jose
NHL   Sharks
MLS   Clash

Seattle
AL   Mariners
NBA   SuperSonics
NFL   Seahawks

Tampa
NFL   T.B. Buccaneers
NHL   T.B. Lightning
AL   T.B. Devil Rays
MLS   T.B. Mutiny

Toronto
AL   Blue Jays
NBA   Raptors
NHL   Maple Leafs

Vancouver
NBA   Grizzlies
NHL   Canucks

Washington
NBA   Wizards (Landover)
NFL   Redskins
NHL   Capitals (Landover)
MLS   D.C. United

Updates

Florida football coach **Steve Spurrier** calls out a helpful hint to his players on Sept. 27, 1997 during a game against Kentucky. The Gators started strong but a surprise loss to LSU on Oct. 11 had the defending national champions reeling.

Dean's Done

After 36 exemplary seasons, Dean Smith retired as the men's basketball coach at North Carolina.

On October 9, 1997 Dean Smith, with every bit of the expected dignity and class, stepped down as the coach of the men's basketball team at the University of North Carolina. In 36 years, Smith turned the Tar Heels into an annual powerhouse and developed an alumni association that reads like a Who's Who of college and professional basketball.

Larry Brown, Billy Cunningham, George Karl, Bobby Jones, Bob McAdoo, Mitch Kupchak, Charlie Scott, Phil Ford, James Worthy, Michael Jordan, Sam Perkins and Jerry Stackhouse, to name a few, are all graduates of Smith's program at North Carolina.

The announcement came as something of a surprise. Practice was to begin only a week later. But Smith seemed comfortable with his decision. As is so often the case in today's sports world, Smith had not tired of the actual work. "I enjoy basketball. I enjoy coaching basketball," he said. "It's the out of season stuff I didn't handle well." Smith had enjoyed one weekend with his family in seven months during and after the 1996–97 basketball season.

North Carolina named longtime Tar Heels assistant Bill Guthridge to succeed Smith. Guthridge had turned down many head coaching jobs during the 30 years he sat beside Smith, who seemed genuinely happy that his friend finally took a head coaching job. Smith displayed his legendary loyalty and generosity by leaving Guthridge with a team that is widely expected to contend for the national championship.

Former Tar Heel Phil Ford, the school's all-time leading scorer, is considered to be the school's choice as the long-term successor to Smith. Ford has been an assistant at North Carolina for nine seasons.

The accomplishments of Dean Smith at North Carolina speak loudly. He won two national championships, in 1982 and 1993. He went to the Final Four 11 times. He finished in the top three of the Atlantic Coast Conference for 33 consecutive seasons. He retired as the winningest coach in college basketball history with a record of 879–254.

He also created a sense of family and, like all good fathers, Smith did not play favorites as he cared as much

Dean Smith points to an admirer on his way to the podium to address the media after resigning as men's basketball coach at the University of North Carolina.

about his lesser players as he did about his All-Americans. This fairness led nearly all of his former players to stay in touch and never really leave Chapel Hill.

Smith also ran a clean program. Not one NCAA violation in 36 years.

Smith's stature is such that he coached his last few years in a building called the Dean Smith Center, an honor never given before to an active coach. But nobody thought it odd or self-serving. It just seemed right.

But perhaps Smith's legacy can be best summed up in the actions of his most accomplished student, Michael Jordan. During his legendary career in the NBA, Jordan has always worn North Carolina shorts under his Bulls uniform. ■

College Football

On October 20, the Associated Press college football poll had a top five of Nebraska, Penn State, Florida State and North Carolina. Defending champion Florida was ranked sixth due to a shocking upset at the hands of Louisiana State University on October 11.

Nebraska had jumped past Penn State due to the games of October 18 in which the Nittany Lions barely beat the poorly regarded Minnesota Gophers 16–15 and Nebraska smoked Texas Tech 29–0. As usual, there was some controversy with the poll results because many people felt that Penn State should not drop in the polls after a week in which they did not lose. The switch is important for Nebraska who

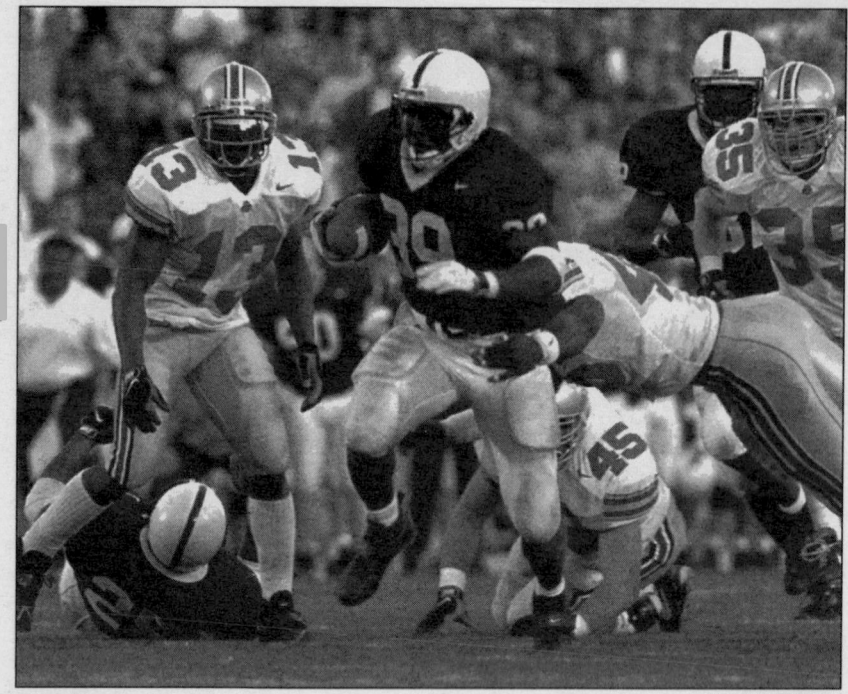

Penn State's **Curtis Enis** eludes the tackle of Ohio State's Matt LaVarr on his way to scoring the winning touchdown during the Nittany Lions 31–27 defeat of the Buckeyes on October 11, 1997. Enis finished the day with 211 yards.

looked able to maintain the top spot and an Orange Bowl bid by rolling through the rest of their relatively weak schedule.

Penn State was still in line for the Rose Bowl, although the rest of their schedule was considerably tougher than Nebraska's. Even after an unbeaten season and a Rose Bowl victory, Penn State could still remain number two behind Nebraska. Just like 1994, 1997 was shaping up as an example of why college football needs a playoff system. And just like in 1994, Penn State may lose the most.

Pro Football

At the midway point of the NFL season, the top team in the league was the Denver Broncos who were leading the AFC West at 6–1. Other than a loss to the Oakland Raiders, the Broncos had shown themselves to be a strong and balanced team, leading the league in scoring and having one of the stingier defenses.

The Jacksonville Jaguars and Pittsburgh Steelers were battling it out in the AFC Central, with Jacksonville showing that last season's appearance in the AFC title game was no fluke. The Jags were thriving despite having lost quarterback Mark Brunell for most of the pre-season and the first three games.

The disappointing New England Patriots were tied with the Miami Dolphins atop the AFC East at 5–2 but New England had been blown out by the Broncos and had lost a close one to Bill Parcells' Jets. Pete Carroll had yet to prove he was capable of leading the Patriots back to the Super Bowl as his team had trampled weak opponents but played poorly against real competition. Parcells had done a miraculous job in New York, leading the Jets to a 5–2 record, more wins than the Jets had been able to amass in the previous two seasons.

In the NFC, the San Francisco 49ers sported a 6–1 record to lead the West division. San Francisco was thriving despite having lost wide receiver Jerry Rice for the season to a knee injury. Garrison Hearst stepped up, though, and the Niners were enjoying their best running game in years. The 6–1 record was a bit flawed, though, because the NFC West was proving to be a rather weak division. The Carolina Panthers were at 3–4 and not playing like the team that had made it all the way to the NFC title game last season.

The New York Giants were in first place in the NFC East at 5–3 with Dallas and Washington tied at 4–3. The Cowboys were having trouble getting into the end zone and the offensive line was showing its age. After seven games, Emmitt Smith had one rushing touchdown.

Two of the biggest surprises of the year were in the NFC Central division. The Green Bay Packers, decimated by injuries, were playing very poorly on defense and quarterback Brett Favre was reverting to the careless style that he had abandoned during his two-year reign as the league's MVP. The Tampa Bay Buccaneers had started off strongly, led by a tough defense and rookie running back Warrick Dunn. The Packers and Bucs were tied with the Minnesota Vikings for the division lead at 5–2. ■

Auto Racing

When Jacques Villeneuve dropped the appeal of his disqualification at the Japanese Grand Prix, he lost two points in the standings. So, heading into the final race of the season, the European Grand Prix, Michael Schumacher held a one point lead over Villeneuve. In a dramatic finish, Villeneuve and Schumacher bumped during the 48th lap as Villeneuve tried to pass Schumacher who had led most of the way. Schumacher ended up off the track and Villeneuve finished third, good enough to win his first Formula One championship. ■

Pro Basketball

Injuries were the big story as NBA camps opened in October. The Miami Heat lost Alonzo Mourning for two to three months after Mourning had surgery to repair a partially torn patellar tendon in his left knee.

John Stockton of the Utah Jazz underwent knee surgery and would probably miss two to three months, ending a streak of seven consecutive seasons in which he played every game.

Scottie Pippen of the Chicago Bulls had surgery to remove a bone spur to correct a soft-tissue injury and was expected to be out until January of 1998. Michael Jordan also had foot surgery to remove ingrown toenails but he was not expected miss the season opener. ■

Police Blotter

——This report was compiled using information from ESPN's "Outside the Lines" and ESPN's SportsZone.

As we went to press, former NBA player Dennis Johnson was arrested on charges of aggravated assault and domestic abuse after a fight with his wife. A few days later, Oklahoma running back Bennie Butler was charged with similar crimes. Butler was the third Oklahoma football player charged with a crime that week as two players were accused of misdemeanor malicious injury to property for damage at an apartment complex. Unfortunately, that was just another week in the sports pages.

In the first week of September 1997, sports fans read about a weapons conviction of the NBA rookie of the year, an alleged assault of his wife by Riddick Bowe, more domestic violence involving a Denver Bronco, drunk driving by a Mississippi State basketball player, the latest arrest of an Ohio State basketball player and the latest crime-related suspension of a Florida State football player. As of September 3, 1997, 145 athletes and sports figures have been arrested in a total of 134 alleged crimes, according to research by ESPN's Outside the Lines and ESPN SportsZone.

Taken together, that means that a new incident of athlete crime emerged once every two days, not including crimes that went unreported in the media. Also excluded were those that involved long-retired athletes, civil actions, administrative actions, and violations of league drug policies that did not involve police.

The study of athlete crime revealed several key points:

Half of the incidents had a violent nature.

Half of the alleged incidents of violent crime were commited by men against women.

Substance abuse remains a problem.

In fairness, it must be reported that many allegations were ultimately dismissed. And it is clear that the high profile of the people involved sometimes invites spurious charges. Many athletes interviewed for the study stated that their group is no different from any other group— that every segment of society has a few individuals that step outside the law. Others insist that crime is a long-standing problem that has simply gotten worse as the money in sports has grown and athletes have become more detached from normal society. In today's society, however, less and less is being swept under the rug. Athletes are not protected like they used to be.

As Tom Farrey wrote on SportsZone, "The net effect is that fans know more than ever about their heroes, warts and all. Yet each new incident launches another miserable, mini-saga that often casts a pall over the related team— and detracts from the real reason fans turn to sports in the first place."

Mo Vaughn of the Boston Red Sox told SportsZone that "Every organization — baseball, basketball or football — has to look the situations that have happened. And the athletes involved have to be educated. There has to be some kind of seminar that looks at these facts and talks about how you're not going to get a slap on the hand like you used to." ■

TENNIS

Late 1997 Tournament Results
Men's Tour

Finals	Tournament	Winner	Earnings	Loser	Score
Oct. 5	Swiss Indoors (Basel)	Greg Rusedski	$137,000	M. Philippoussis	63 76 76
Oct. 5	China Open (Beijing)	Jim Courier	43,000	M. Gustafsson	76 36 63
Oct. 5	Int'l Championship of Sicily	Alberto Berasategui	43,000	D. Hrbaty	64 62
Oct. 12	Heineken Open (Singapore)	Magnus Gustafsson	102,000	N. Kiefer	46 63 63
Oct. 12	CA Tennis Trophy (Vienna)	Goran Ivanisevic	125,400	G. Rusedski	36 67 76 62 63
Oct. 19	Czech Indoor (Ostrava)	Karol Kucera	137,000	M. Norman	62 (ret.)
Oct. 19	Lyon Grand Prix	Fabrice Santoro	102,000	T. Haas	64 64
Oct. 26	Eurocard Open (Stuttgart)	Petr Korda	350,000	R. Krajicek	76 62 64
Oct. 26	Mexican Open (Mexico City)	Francisco Clavet	43,200	J. Albert Viloca	64 76

Remaining Events (8): Paris Open (Nov. 2); Colombian Open (Nov. 2); Kremlin Cup (Nov. 9); Hellmann's Cup (Nov. 9); Stockholm Open (Nov. 9); ATP Tour World Championship (Nov. 16); Phoenix/ATP Tour World Doubles Championship (Nov. 23); Davis Cup Final (Nov. 30).

Women's Tour

Finals	Tournament	Winner	Earnings	Loser	Score
Oct. 12	Porsche Grand Prix (Filderstadt)	Martina Hingis	$79,000	L. Raymond	64 62
Oct. 19	European Indoors (Zurich)	Lindsay Davenport	150,000	N. Tauziat	76 75
Oct. 26	Bell Challenge (Quebec)	B. Schultz-McCarthy	27,000	D. van Roost	64 67 75
Oct. 26	Seat Open (Luxembourg)	Amanda Coetzer	27,000	B. Paulus	64 36 75

Remaining Events (5): Ladies Kremlin Cup (Nov. 2); Ameritech Cup (Nov. 9); Advanta Championships (Nov. 16); WTA Tour Championships (Nov. 23); Volvo Women's Open (Nov. 23).

GOLF

Late 1997 Tournament Results
PGA Tour

Last Rd	Tournament	Winner	Earnings	Runner-Up
Oct. 12	Michelob Championship	David Duval (271)*	$279,000	G. Waite & D. Waldorf (271)
Oct. 19	Disney/Oldsmobile Classic	David Duval (270)*	270,000	D. Forsman (270)
Oct. 26	Las Vegas International	Bill Glasson (340)	324,000	B. Mayfair & D. Edwards (341)

*Playoffs: Michelob— Duval won on the first hole; **Disney/Oldsmobile**— Duval won on the first hole.
Remaining Events (11): The Tour Championship (Oct. 30-Nov. 2); Kapalua International (Nov. 6-9); Subaru Sarazen World Open (Nov. 6-9); Shark Shootout (Nov. 14-16); PGA Grand Slam (Nov. 17-18); World Cup of Golf (Nov. 20-23); Skins Game (Nov. 29-30); JC Penney Classic (Dec. 4-7); Diners Club Matches (Dec. 11-14); Wendy's Three-Tour Challenge (Nov. 20-21); Andersen Consulting World Champ. (Jan. 3-4, 1998).

European PGA Tour

Last Rd	Tournament	Winner	Earnings	Runner-Up
Oct. 12	Toyota World Matchplay	Vijay Singh (1-up)	£170,000	E. Els
Oct. 12	Open Novotel Perrier	Anders Forsbrand/ Michael Jonzon (343)*	35,000 (each)	S. Luna/ J. Rivero (343)
Oct. 19	Alfred Dunhill Cup	South Africa (2-1)	300,000	Sweden
Oct. 26	Oki Pro-Am	Paul McGinley (266)	75,000	I. Pyman (270)

*Playoffs: Novotel— Forsbrand/Jonzon won on the first hole.
Remaining Events (4): Volvo Masters (Oct. 30-Nov. 2); Subaru Sarazen World Open (Nov. 6-9); World Cup of Golf (Nov. 20-23); Andersen Consulting World Championship (Jan. 3-4, 1998).

Senior PGA Tour

Last Rd	Tournament	Winner	Earnings	Runner-Up
Oct. 12	The TransAmerica	Dave Eichelberger (205)	$120,000	4-way tie (209)
Oct. 19	Maui Kaanapali Classic	Hale Irwin (200)	127,500	M. Hill/ & B. Summerhays (203)
Oct. 26	Raley's Gold Rush	Bob Eastwood (204)	135,000	R. Acton (206)

Second place ties (3 players or more): 4-WAY— **TransAmerica** (F. Conner, T. Dill, J. Jacobs, D. Weaver).
Remaining Events (5): Ralph's Senior Classic (Oct. 31-Nov. 2); Energizer Senior Tour Championship (Nov. 6-9); Diners Club Matches (Dec. 11-14); Lexus Challenge (Dec. 20-21); Wendy's Three-Tour Challenge (Dec. 20-21).

LPGA Tour

Last Rd	Tournament	Winner	Earnings	Runner-Up
Oct. 19	World Championship of Golf	Juli Inkster (280)*	$131,000	H. Alfredsson/ K. Robbins (280)

*Playoffs: World Championship— Inkster won on the first hole.
Remaining Events (6): Nichirei International (Oct. 31-Nov.2); Toray Japan Queens Cup (Nov. 7-9); Tour Championship (Nov. 20-23); JC Penney Classic (Dec. 4-7); Diners Club Matches (Dec. 12-14); Wendy's Three-Tour Challenge (Dec. 20-21).

Late 1997 Tournament Results (Cont.)

Team Competition
Alfred Dunhill Cup
at St. Andrews, Scotland (Oct. 16-19)
South Africa def. Sweden, 2-1

Semifinals (Sweden def. United States, 2-1): Mark O'Meara (USA) def. Jesper Parnevik (SWE), 68-69; Joakim Haeggman (SWE) def. Justin Leonard (USA), 68-72; Per-Ulrik Johansson (SWE) def. Brad Faxon (USA), 71-74.

Semifinals (South Africa def. New Zealand, 2-1): Retief Goosen (S.AFR) def. Michael Long (NZ), 67-72; David Frost (S.AFR) def. Steven Alker (NZ), 72-76; Frank Nobilo (NZ) def. Ernie Els (S.AFR), 66-70.

Finals (South Africa def. Sweden, 2-1): Retief Goosen (S.AFR) def. Jesper Parnevik (SWE), 70-74; Per-Ulrik Johansson (SWE) def. David Frost (S.AFR), 71-74; Ernie Els (S.AFR) def. Joakim Haeggman (SWE), 69-72.

THOROUGHBRED RACING
Late 1997 Major Stakes Races
(Through Oct. 19)

Date	Race	Location	Miles	Winner	Jockey	Purse
Sept. 27	Vosburgh Stakes	Belmont	7 F	Victor Cooley	Jorge Chavez	$250,000
Sept. 27	Queen Elizabeth II Stakes	Ascot	1 (T)	Air Express	Olivier Peslier	498,566
Sept. 28	Super Derby	Louisiana Downs	1¼	Deputy Commander	Chris McCarron	500,000
Oct. 5	L'Arc De Triomphe	Longchamp	1⅛ (T)	Peintre Celebre	Olivier Peslier	1,114,400
Oct. 11	Goodwood Breeders Cup	Santa Anita	1⅛	Benchmark	Eddie Delahoussaye	248,700
Oct. 12	Spinster Stakes	Keeneland	1⅛	Clear Mandate	Pat Day	542,500
Oct. 12	Oak Tree Turf Champ.	Santa Anita	1¼ (T)	Rainbow Dancer	Alex Solis	300,000
Oct. 18	Jockey Club Gold Cup	Belmont	1¼	Skip Away	Jerry Bailey	1,000,000
Oct. 18	Turf Classic International	Belmont	1½ (T)	Val's Prince	Mike Smith	500,000
Oct. 18	Champagne Stakes	Belmont	1 1/16	Grand Slam	Gary Stevens	400,000
Oct. 19	Canadian International	Woodbine	1½ (T)	Chief Bearhart	Jose Santos	1,000,000
Oct. 19	Beldame Stakes	Belmont	1⅛	Hidden Lake	Richard Migliore	400,000
Oct. 19	Frizette Stakes	Belmont	1 1/16	Silver Maiden	Jerry Bailey	400,000

HARNESS RACING
Late 1997 Major Stakes Races

	Race	Raceway	Winner	Driver	Purse
Oct. 3	Kentucky Futurity	Lexington	Take Chances	Wally Hennessey	$144,200
Oct. 10	Messenger Stakes	Ladbroke	Western Dreamer*	Mike Lachance	414,126
Oct. 24	BC 3 Yr-Old C & G Trot	Mowhawk	Malabar Man	Mal Burroughs	440,000
Oct. 24	BC 3 Yr-Old C & G Pace	Mowhawk	Village Jasper	Paul Macdonell	440,000
Oct. 24	BC 3 Yr-Old Filly Pace	Mowhawk	Steinam's Place	Jack Moiseyev	365,000
Oct. 24	BC 3 Yr-Old Filly Trot	Mowhawk	No Nonsense Woman	Jim Doherty	325,000
Oct. 24	BC 2 Yr-Old Colt Trot	Mowhawk	Catch as Catch Can	Wally Hennessey	300,000
Oct. 24	BC 2 Yr-Old C & G Pace	Mowhawk	Artiscape	Mike Lachance	492,700
Oct. 24	BC 2 Yr-Old Filly Trot	Mowhawk	My Dolly	Wally Hennessey	300,000
Oct. 24	BC 2 Yr-Old Filly Pace	Mowhawk	Take Flight	Luc Ouellette	432,000

* By winning the Messenger Stakes, Western Dreamer became the first horse since Ralph Hanover in 1983 to win the pacing triple crown. Western Dreamer had previously won the Aug. 22 Cane Pace and the Little Brown Jug on Sept. 18.

STEEPLECHASE RACING
Late 1997 Major Stakes Races

Date	Race	Location	Miles	Winner	Jockey	Purse
Oct. 25	Grand National	Far Hills, NJ	2⅝	Rowdy Irishman	Sean Clancy	$150,000

AUTO RACING
Late 1997 Results
Formula One

Date	Grand Prix	Location	Winner	Time	Avg.mph	Pole	Qual.mph
Oct. 26	European	Jerez	Mika Hakkinen	1:38:57.771	115.145	J. Villeneuve	121.072

Winning Constructor: McLAREN MERCEDES (1)—Hakkinen.

Note: Going into this race, Michael Schumacher held a one point lead over Jacques Villeneuve in the F-1 season-long point standings. Schumacher could not finish the race after the two bumped on the 48th lap while Villeneuve went on to take third place and the F-1 championship, 81-78.

NASCAR

Date	Event	Location	Winner	Avg.mph	Earnings	Pole	Qual.mph
Oct. 27	AC Delco 400 ....Rockingham		Bobby Hamilton	121.730	$89,150	B. Labonte	156.696

Winning Car: PONTIAC GRAND PRIX (1)— Hamilton.
Remaining Races (2): Dura-Lube 500 in Phoenix (Nov. 2); NAPA 500 in Atlanta (Nov. 16).

NHRA

Date		Event	Winner	Time	MPH	2nd Place	Time	MPH
Oct. 5	Pennzoil Nationals	Top Fuel	Jim Head	4.677	308.53	L. Dixon	4.671	312.17
		Funny Car	John Force	5.172	296.34	C. Pedregon	7.002	127.94
		Pro Stock	Jim Yates	6.969	197.28	M. Osborne	7.047	196.12
Oct. 19	Revell Nationals	Top Fuel	Cory McClenathan	4.802	302.21	J. Amato	8.871	110.76
		Funny Car	Al Hofmann	5.083	251.60	J. Force	Foul	—
		Pro Stock	Jim Yates	7.028	197.41	W. Johnson	7.040	194.42

Remaining Events (2): Matco Tools Supernationals in Houston, Tex. (Oct. 23-27); Winston Finals in Pomona, Cal. (Nov. 6-9).

BOWLING

1997 Fall Tour Results

PBA

Final	Event	Winner	Earnings	Final	Runner-Up
Oct. 8	Ebonite-Windsor Locks	Norm Duke	$21,000	236-194	Pete Weber
Oct. 15	Ebonite-Rochester	Steve Hoskins*	21,000	226-216	Rick Steelsmith
Oct. 22	Mobil One Classic	Amleto Monacelli	25,000	213-191	Jason Couch

* Hoskins earned an additional $10,000 for bowling a 300 game.
Remaining Events (3): Ebonite Challenge – Indianapolis (Oct. 25-29); Ebonite Challenge – Chesapeake, Va. (Nov. 1-5); Bayer/Brunswick Touring Players Championship (Nov. 8-12).

Senior PBA

Final	Event	Winner	Earnings	Final	Runner-Up
Sept. 18	St. Pete Showboat Open	Teata Semiz	$10,000	227-224	Ron Winger
Sept. 25	Naples Senior Open	Gene Stus	10,000	226-205	Ron Winger

Remaining Events (1): PBA Senior World Open (Nov. 1-8).

LPBT

Final	Event	Winner	Earnings	Final	Runner-Up
Sept. 18	Baltimore Eastern Open	Wendy Macpherson	$9,000	221-203	C. Dorin-Ballard
Sept. 25	Three Rivers Open	Carolyn Dorin-Ballard	9,000	247-223	Dana Miller-Mackie
Oct. 2	Track Triton Open	Carol Gianotti-Block	11,000	180-157	Anne Marie Duggan

Remaining Events (1): Sam's Town Invitational (Nov. 15-22).

SOCCER

MLS Cup '97

D.C. United 2, Colorado Rapids 1
Oct. 26 at RFK Stadium, Washington, D.C.
Attendance: 57,431

	1	2	Final
Colorado	0	1	— 1
Washington D.C.	1	1	— 2

Scoring
1st Half: D.C.— Jaime Moreno (Tony Sanneh, David Vaudreuil) 37th minute.
2nd Half: D.C.— Sanneh (John Harkes, Richie Williams) 68th; COL— Adrian Paz (David Patino, Matt Kmosko) 75th.
MVP: Jaime Moreno, D.C. United, F.

MLS Annual Awards

MVP: Preki, Kansas City
Coach of the Year: Bruce Arena, D.C. United
Goalkeeper of the Year: Brad Friedel, Columbus
Defender of the Year: Eddie Pope, D.C. United
Rookie of the Year: Mike Duhaney, Tampa Bay
Executive of the Year: Kevin Payne, D.C. United

All MLS Team

G— Brad Friedel, Clb.
D— Eddie Pope, D.C.
D— Richard Gough, K.C.
D— Jeff Agoos, D.C.
D— Thomas Dooley, Clb
M— M. Etcheverry, D.C.

M— Preki, K.C.
M— Mark Chung, K.C.
M— C. Valderrama, T.B.
F— Ronald Cerritos, S.J.
F— Jaime Moreno, D.C.

Olympics
Winter Games

Year	No.	Host City	Dates
1998	XVIII	Nagano, Japan	Feb. 7-22
2002	XIX	Salt Lake City, Utah	Feb. 9-24

Summer Games

Year	No.	Host City	Dates
2000	XXVII	Sydney, Australia	Sept. 16-Oct. 1
2004	XXVIII	Athens, Greece	TBA

All-Star Games
Baseball

Year	Site	Date
1998	Coors Field, Denver	July 7
1999	Fenway Park, Boston	TBA

NBA Basketball

Year	Site	Date
1998	Madison Square Garden	Feb. 8
1999	CoreStates Center, Philadelphia	Feb. 11

NFL Pro Bowl

Year	Site	Date
1998	Aloha Stadium, Honolulu	Feb. 1
1999	Aloha Stadium, Honolulu	Feb. 7

NHL Hockey

Year	Site	Date
1998	GM Place, Vancouver	Jan. 18
1999	Ice Palace, Tampa Bay	Jan. 24

Auto Racing

The Daytona 500 stock car race is usually held on the Sunday before the third Monday in February, while the Indianapolis 500 is usually held on the Sunday of Memorial Day weekend in May. Except for 1998, the following dates are tentative.

Year	Daytona 500	Indianapolis 500
1998	Feb. 15	May 24
1999	Feb. 14	May 23
2000	Feb. 19	May 28

NCAA Basketball
Men's Final Four

Year	Site	Date
1998	Alamodome, San Antonio	March 28-30
1999	ThunderDome, St. Petersburg	March 27-29
2000	RCA Dome, Indianapolis	April 1-3
2001	Metrodome, Minneapolis	Mar. 31-Apr. 2
2002	Georgia Dome, Atlanta	Mar. 30-Apr. 1

Women's Final Four

Year	Site	Date
1998	Kemper Arena, Kansas City	March 28-29
1999	San Jose Arena, San Jose	March 26-28
2000	CoreStates Spectrum, Phila.	Mar. 31-Apr. 2
2001	Kiel Center, St. Louis	Mar. 30-Apr. 1
2002	Alamodome, San Antonio	March 29-31

NFL Football
Super Bowl

No.	Site	Date
XXXII	Qualcomm Stadium, San Diego	Jan. 25, 1998
XXXIII	Pro Player Stadium, Miami	Jan. 31, 1999
XXXIV	Georgia Dome, Atlanta	Jan. 30, 2000
XXXV	Stadium TBD, Tampa	Jan. 28, 2001

Golf
The Masters

Year	Site	Date
1998	Augusta National Ga	April 9-12
1999	Augusta National Ga	April 8-11

U.S. Open

Year	Site	Date
1998	Olympic Club, San Francisco	June 18-21
1999	Pinehurst CC, Pinehurst, N.J.	June 17-20
2000	Pebble Beach (Calif.) Golf Links.	June 15-18

U.S. Women's Open

Year	Site	Date
1998	Blackwolf Run GC, Kohler, Wisc.	July 2-5
1999	Old Waverly GC, West Point, Miss.	June 3-6
2000	Merit Club, Libertyville, Ill.	July 20-23

U.S. Senior Open

Year	Site	Date
1998	Riviera CC, Pacific Palisades, Calif.	July 9-12
1999	Des Moines GC, W. Des Moines, Iowa	July 8-11
2000	Saucon Valley GC, Bethlehem, Pa.	TBA

PGA Championship

Year	Site	Date
1998	Sahalee CC, Seattle	Aug. 13-16
1999	Medinah CC, Medinah, Ill.	Aug. 19-22

British Open

Year	Site	Date
1998	Royal Birkdale, England	July 16-19
1999	Carnoustie, Scotland	July 15-18
2000	Royal Lytham, England	July 20-23

Ryder Cup

Year	Site	Date
1999	The Country Club, Brookline, Mass.	TBA

Horse Racing
Triple Crown

The Kentucky Derby is always held at Churchill Downs in Louisville on the first Saturday in May, followed two weeks later by the Preakness Stakes at Pimlico Race Course in Baltimore and three weeks after that by the Belmont Stakes at Belmont Park in Elmont, N.Y.

Year	Ky Derby	Preakness	Belmont
1998	May 2	May 16	June 6
1999	May 1	May 15	June 5
2000	May 6	May 20	June 10

Tennis
U.S. Open

Usually held from the last Monday in August through the second Sunday in September, with Labor Day weekend the midway point in the tournament.

Year	Site	Dates
1998	Arthur Ashe Stadium, NYC	Aug. 31-Sept. 13
1999	Arthur Ashe Stadium, NYC	Aug. 30-Sept. 12
2000	Arthur Ashe Stadium, NYC	Aug. 28-Sept. 10

Personalities

Tiger Woods likes what he sees on the 14th green at Augusta National Golf Club during the final round of his record-setting victory in the 1997 Masters. ————

Wide World Photos

Top 40 Personalities of 1997

Our man at the anchor desk picks his Fab Forty.

by
Dan Patrick

What is it about certain athletes that makes them stand out?

What makes a person a "personality"?

Is it something they do? Is it something they say?

Some athletes have prodigious physical talents that must be recognized. Others achieve a sustained excellence that cannot be ignored. Others have stories that touch us, the stories that make sports so compelling on a human scale. Maybe that's part of it.

Whatever it is, we keep watching because while we may not be able to pin down some elusive "personality," we can see that, out there on the playing field, these athletes are, more than anything else, human. The only differ-

ence is that, unlike other humans, superstar athletes can hit 500–foot homeruns and buzzer-beating jump shots. Which is of course, the other reason we watch.

Here, then, is a list of people who caught our attention in 1997. And remember, books have deadlines that don't always fit the sports calendar. If Tino Martinez, who isn't on this list, hits five homers in a World Series game, don't call me.

40. Tracy McGrady

Is he an anomaly or a sign of the times? It's nice to sign a $12 million sneaker deal before your first pro dribble! Every player coming out of high school should be so fortunate. Isiah Thomas and the Toronto Raptors took a real chance on McGrady in the first round of the draft.

Dan Patrick is the co-anchor of ESPN's 11 PM *SportsCenter*.

Reggie White of the Green Bay Packers takes a break during his team's victory in the 1997 Super Bowl. The NFL championship capped a great year for the "Minister of Defense."

39. Carlos Valderrama

He is no less than *Mr.* MLS. Valderrama is quite a colorful sight on the field and the most important performer there as well.

38. Steve Spurrier

Not loved by his coaching peers, he got that elusive national championship ring. Give the man credit as one of the top coaches in college football as he has built the Gators into a consistent winner, strong now on *both* sides of the ball.

37. Lute Olson

After finishing out of the money in the Pac-10 during the regular season, he led the Wildcats to a surprising national title. Nobody mentioned the prior opening-round losses to East Tennessee State or Santa Clara during this year's Final Four.

36. Reggie White

Not only for his dominating Super Bowl performance, but his leadership and handling of issues off the field as well. All season long, the sack master didn't appear to have lost too many steps in terrorizing opposing quarterbacks.

35. Rick Pitino

Kentucky bluegrass took on a darker shade of green . . . hear that cash register going off? Author . . . Motivator . . . Businessman . . . Coach.

34. Bill Parcells

He'd disagree with any analogy that compares him to Vince Lombardi. But

Wlde World Photos

After four mediocre years in a row, the Boston Red Sox chose not to re-sign **Roger Clemens**, shown pitching to former teammate **Mo Vaughn**. Clemens became a Toronto Blue Jay and turned in the best season of his career. So there.

Parcells' success should tell you otherwise; he belongs in Lombardi-type company. Besides taking the Patriots to the Super Bowl, his battle with Robert Kraft and subsequent move to the Jets made news. The Tuna was a prized off-season catch.

33. Albert Belle

Is it him or is it us? Is he the most misunderstood athlete in sports? He has over 11 million reasons, right or wrong, to make this list.

32. Dean Smith

In the bottom line world of sports, only two national championships in 36 seasons would not be considered great. You can't measure his success on that. In 1997, the Tar Heels coach passed Adolph Rupp to become the winningest Division I coach. He also earned another trip to the Final Four.

31. Roger Clemens

We were wrong, Roger. Following four sub-par seasons, we the media wrote the Rocket off as nothing more than a sparkler. We fizzled and he blasted off, earning his first 20+ win season since 1990; we apologize!

30. Larry Walker/Tony Gwynn

For a good portion of the '96 season you couldn't mention one without the other. The two seemed joined at the hip as they pursued .400. Along the way, the 37-year-old Gwynn became the oldest player in history to record his first 100 RBI season while Walker showcased his arm, legs and triple crown-threatening bat almost on a daily basis.

29. Mark McGwire

In a game of inches, Big Red's was measured in feet. His tape measure home runs were Ruthian in length. But considering his age and health, McGwire may never make the serious run at the home run record everyone had hoped for.

28. Brett Favre

The kid from Southern Miss. was a hit in the 1996–97 campaign, earning both regular-season and Super Bowl MVP honors. His headlines were not confined to just his job. Favre wrote a book detailing his off-field problems.

27. Chamique Holdsclaw

She wasn't "at" the Final Four, she *was* the Final Four! In a performance to rekindle memories of Cheryl Miller's showcase days at USC, Holdsclaw proved that if asked, one for all can beat all for one.

26. Oscar De La Hoya

Staying unbeaten may not be his top priority; Oscar may need to save his sport from itself. Boxing has few true superstars and here's the one guy capable of redeeming the tawdriest sport. The Golden Boy's year included wins over Sweet Pea Whitaker and Macho Camacho. Now if he could only bulk up to become a heavyweight!

25. Mario Lemieux

One of the most dominating offensive talents in the sport's history. He didn't have enough energy left over to write a happier ending as the Penguins bowed out to the Flyers in the opening round of the playoffs. We may never know just how sick or how hurt he was during the latter portion of his career, which makes his accomplishments even more startling.

24. Phil Jackson

He will never be given the credit he is due, but that's the price you pay when you are blessed with Michael and Scottie. But as other NBA coaches will attest, with today's athlete, it is one thing to have talent, and quite another to keep it happy.

23. Michael Jordan

His highlight reel has turned into a video library. Will anyone forget his last-second heroics in Game 1 of the NBA Finals, or the back-from-the-dead performance in Game 5? At $36 million, Jordan is still the best bargain in sports.

22. Justin Leonard

Armed with a "don't try this at home without adult supervision" swing, Leonard swiped the Claret Jug and had his fingers on the Wanamaker Trophy. The win at the British Open and runner-up at the PGA paved the way for a season second only to you know who.

21. Tim Duncan

I shouldn't have to applaud an athlete for staying in school to get a degree, but Tim Duncan is a special

Chicago Bulls coach **Phil Jackson** holds the trophy he won as 1996–97 NBA Coach of the Year. Jackson's trademark as a coach has been his ability to get talented players to play together as a team, a talent much in evidence in 1997.

exception. During last year's ESPY ceremonies, the College Player of the Year wanted to know what time he could fly out of New York and still get back to classes the next day. Don't ever lose your perspective, Tim.

20. Matt Hartl

The Northwestern fullback didn't play in 1996 after being diagnosed with Hodgkin's Disease. After undergoing chemotherapy in the off-season, Hartl was back in the starting lineup for the 'Cats opening win over Oklahoma.

19. Cynthia Cooper

She stood in Cheryl Miller's shadow in college and emerged from the ones cast by Rebecca Lobo and Lisa Leslie in the pros. She turned in a Michael Jordan-like season . . . scoring title, regular season MVP, playoff MVP and championship.

18. Allen Iverson

If his nickname is "The Answer," then I don't want to know the question. Maybe Iverson should change the moniker to "Too," as in too much talent, too much trouble and too bad. He could be the most explosive point guard in both passing and scoring since Nate "Tiny" Archibald.

17. Mike Helfen

In a day and age when the media must constantly manufacture or fine

Boxing oddity **Don King** is surrounded by **Mike Tyson** (l) and **Evander Holyfield** (r) before the infamous "bite fight". No one was surprised that King was involved in the strangest sporting spectacle in recent memory.

tune images to create heroes, let me introduce you to this youngster from Dyer, Indiana. In between chemotherapy treatments last summer, Helfen found time to pitch in the 1997 Little League World Series.

16. Don King

It was anything but a glorious year for the self-absorbed yet resilient ring king. Fights like Tyson-Holyfield and Akinwande-Lewis seemed to bring out the annual cries to clean up the sport. A suggestion would be to stop buying what King is selling.

15. Jeff Gordon

He wrapped NASCAR around his steering wheel this year, producing the single greatest money-making season in the sport's history. He's been called the Tiger Woods of his sport but in fairness to Gordon, maybe Tiger is the Jeff Gordon of his sport!

14. Danny Wuerffel

The Heisman winner showed me a lot more in his lone loss in 1996 than he did in the Gators' 12 wins. I have not seen a quarterback absorb as much punishment as Wuerffel did during Florida's regular-season loss to Florida State. He never complained or flinched. His payback was just as painful for the Seminoles — a 52-20 loss in the national title game.

13. Larry Bird

Larry Legend made news again by going home again — it's not French Lick, but it is Indiana. Coach Bird's philosophy with the Pacers should be do as I say, or as I did!

12. Barry Sanders

He's one of the more frugal athletes I've ever met . . . so I'm not sure he needs $5 million per year to live. But it's not like he hasn't earned it. If he doesn't get bored first, Sanders will pass Walter Payton on the all-time career rushing list.

11. Michael Irvin

Considering his vices, Irvin was indeed a receiver on and off the field. Maybe for a change he'll keep his headlines on the sports page and not on the front page.

10. Donovan Bailey

He talked the talk, walked the walk and then ran, and finished the race. Canada's favorite son eclipsed Michael Johnson in their over-hyped match race in Toronto.

9. Dominik Hasek

He certainly lived up to his nickname in 1997. "The Dominator" not only brought home the MVP, he won the battle of wills with former coach Ted Nolan. However, Hasek's season has an asterisk attached due to his "mysterious" absence from most of the preseason.

8. Karl Malone

It only took the Mailman 12 years to become an overnight sensation. His MVP season included a trip to the Finals and his 10th straight season in the top five in scoring. During Utah's six-game series with the Bulls, Malone made no excuses in defeat.

7. Pete Sampras

Not even a classy loss in the Round of 16 at the U.S. Open could stain his remarkable year. His wins at Wimbledon and the Australian Open bring his Grand Slam total to 10 wins, second-best ever. And he's only 26 years old.

6. Martina Hingis

The similarities with Martina Navratilova aren't in name only. With Steffi Graf hurt and Monica Seles still recovering, Hingis gave the sport a fresh blast of exuberance. Her middle name should be Chrissie; Hingis possesses Navratilova's athleticism to play at the net and Evert's patience to linger on the baseline.

5. Hideki Irabu

Baseball's exchange student needs to go back to school. I have no sympathy for his struggles. He asked for the Yankee way of life, and that's what he got. Somebody owes Nolan Ryan an apology for making the laughable comparison.

4./3. Evander Holyfield/Mike Tyson

You can make all of the ear-related jokes you want to, but the bottom line is when the fighter couldn't solve the boxer, he bit, spit, quit and then split . . . at least for a year. As for Holyfield, he could be, according to *New York Times* columnist Dave Anderson- ". . .the sport's last gladiator."

2. Ken Griffey Jr.

Have we started to take Junior for granted at the ripe old age of 27? There's no more exciting player in baseball, with the bat or the glove, as he showed this season. He blasted through the 50 HR mark this year with 56. 60 is next.

1. Tiger Woods

I purposely left a blank so you can fill in your own adjectives to describe him. I've simply run out of words to describe Tiger's talents and impact on the sport. ∎

Moments

When **Tiger Woods** won the Masters and walked off the 18th green, he went straight to the man who had been with him from the beginning, his father **Earl Woods**.

Wide World Photos

Top 40 Moments of 1997

Stuart hits leadoff. Rich runs a nice anchor. Together, they deliver the magic moments of 1997.

by
Rich Eisen and Stuart Scott

I remember exactly where I was the moment Hank Aaron took Al Downing deep into the Atlanta night and notched his belt with the historic #715. My older brother, two cousins and I were watching in my cousins' kitchen in Chicago. I was just a kid, eight and a half years old, but that moment will be forever etched into my mind. We jumped up and down like *we* had hit the homer.

One moment, one in a thousand, yet one that will always be a part of who we are.

That's what makes sports moments unique. They are like permanent magic markers; even if you wanted to, you couldn't erase them.

I was excited, in large part, because Hank Aaron was a black baseball player to whom I could look up. Twenty-three years later came two more moments that will be significant for years to come. For our society, for all races but especially for African-Americans. I begin my list of moments from 1997 with these two.

1. Woods Wins the Masters

It's easy to be in complete awe because this 21-year-old kid beat the field, beat the course and beat both badly. Eldrick finished 18 under par, with second place being 12 strokes back. More important, though, Tiger made it cool to be young, gifted, black AND to enjoy hitting the links. Now, if we could just get more faces of color in those gallery shots.

Rich Eisen and **Stuart Scott** are anchor/reporters on ESPN's SportsCenter.

In 1997, major league baseball, in a rare moment of clarity and vision, honored one of its greatest players by retiring **Jackie Robinson's number 42** throughout the sport. At Shea Stadium, **President Bill Clinton** and Robinson's widow **Rachel Robinson** presided over the ceremonies announcing the honor.

2. The anniversary of Jackie Robinson's first game

He was an unprecedented man, worthy of an unprecedented act; the sport-wide retirement of a jersey number. Nobody in baseball will again wear the number 42. Nobody else should. Jackie held his tongue, held his fists and held his temper. He simply showed that he was one of the most talented players in the game, regardless of the color of his skin.

3. Packers win the Super Bowl

Glory restored. "Titletown" really becomes "Titletown" again. And what's all this fuss about the Heisman trophy jinx? A Heisman trophy-winning return man steals the show.

4. Gators win the Sugar Bowl

One Heisman winner coaching, another Heisman winner quarterbacking. That was a first for a national title winner and a first championship for Florida. The Gators sweetly avenged an early season loss to Florida State.

5. Boris Becker retires

At Wimbledon, a class act guy retires from a class act tournament after losing to Pete Sampras simply because the "retiree" wanted his last Wimbledon match to be against someone he admired and respected.

6. Game 5 NBA Finals

Michael Jordan could barely stand, he was so weak from the flu. So what!

The Bulls needed a win. Jordan delivered even though he was closer to dead than alive. He epitomized "leaving everything on the court." 38 points, 7 rebounds, 5 assists. For my money, as long as Jordan's heart beats, he's the NBA MVP.

7. White Sox deadline trade

Three-and-a-half games out of first place in late July and you trade your best starter and best reliever? Why? Jerry Reinsdorf.

8. Randy Johnson vs. Mark McGwire

Unreal, phat, monstrous. On June 24, 1997 the game's most feared pitcher faced its most feared hitter. The pitch came in at 98 mph and left at 103 mph. Over 500 feet later the ball landed.

9. USA sprinters rule

At the World Championships, Maurice Greene backed up his boast to 100-meter world record holder Donovan Bailey. Even more significant, Marion Jones began to unveil the talent that might make her the best sprinter . . . ever. Just think how good she'd be if she hadn't been leading UNC to a national basketball championship in 1994.

10. 4–Minute mile broken twice

Forty-three years after Roger Bannister broke the 4-minute mile barrier, Kenya's Daniel Komen did him one better by becoming the first person to run 2 miles in less than 8 minutes. His 7 minute 58.61 second performance doubled up Bannister. Obscure? Sure! But for those people who don't realize, this is a huge track record.

11. M.J.: The Endorser

Instead of the Endorsee? What? I'm taking a glamorized commercial and making it one of sport's Top 40 moments from 1997? You're probably thinking "Oh, it's Jordan, Stuart's North Carolina buddy. Stuart's just trying to kiss up to him." No! I'd list this even if it wasn't Michael. It's the significance of an athlete putting his name on an entire line of athletic wear, "Brand Jordan." And all at once, that brand is bigger than every other athletic brand except Nike and Reebok.

12. Big Unit: Part 1 and Part 2

No American League lefty had ever struck out 19 batters in one game, let alone twice in a career . . . let alone twice in a season. Leave it to the tallest player in big league history, Randy Johnson. That's 38 professional hitters shaking their heads and walking back to the dugout in just two games.

13. Hideki Irabu

OK, forget the demotion back to triple-A, then the demotion to the bullpen. Forget denting George Steinbrenner's car in the parking lot. (Wait, don't forget that; it was funny.) Hideki Irabu electrified the Bronx in his big league debut with over fifty-thousand strong watching him record nine "sanshin" which is Japanese for strikeout. Steinbrenner was a genius . . . or so it seemed. If we had a list for the 40 low moments in sports, we could wax on more about Irabu.

14. WNBA Debut

Lisa Leslie against Rebecca Lobo. L.A. against New York. Glitz, glamour . . . groovy! The beginning of an NBA-sponsored league for women but

Wide World Photos

Robbie Alomar and **John Hirschbeck** put their troubles behind them and shake hands during their first encounter since the infamous spitting incident at the end of the 1996 regular season.

would it work? Would the game be good? Would anyone care? Yes, not really and no. Lisa Leslie had a fast break, a chance for a slam dunk, which she can do . . . and muffed it. So what. Everybody had a blast.

15. WNBA Title Game

The Houston Comets won the first WNBA Championship. But it wasn't really about the game. It was about the courage of the game's best player. While Leslie, Lobo, and Sheryl Swoopes got all of the preseason press coverage, Cynthia Cooper emerged as the game's best player. She was the unanimous MVP and the league's leading scorer. Every time she scored at least 30 points, the Comets won and "Coop" did all of it while her mother

battled cancer and went for regular chemotherapy treatments with Cynthia by her side. Not bad for a girl who speaks Italian so fluently she dreams in that language.

16. Alomar — Hirschbeck

"I'm sorry." It was quick, but genuine. In the first game in which Robbie Alomar played and John Hirschbeck umpired, Alomar, on his way out to the field stopped by the first base line where Hirschbeck was and shook his hand. A nice ending to one of the uglier incidents in sports history.

Afterward Hirschbeck said, "He said he was sorry (for the spitting incident) and I told him 'Let's put it behind us.'"

17. The Comeback

26-to-nothing. 26-zip. 26-nada. And Buffalo came back. In the 4th game of the NFL season, the Colts, who had yet to score an offensive touchdown, get a 26-nothing lead on the Buffalo Bills . . . and blow it. Did somebody say something about a Frank Reich sighting? The Bills get the second biggest comeback in regular season history. Of course, they also have the biggest comeback in history, period. That playoff game back in '92 against the Oilers.

18. The Great One

Still Great. It was almost as if Wayne Gretzky heard the whispers. "PPSSSTT . . . Wayne might be losing it!" For all you doubters, how about a playoff hat trick against the Panthers on April 23rd. His 9th career playoff 3-goal game. Any more doubters? Didn't think so.

19. The Perfect Block

This one is all personal. Odds are no one will even care. But it was a thrill that brought back memories from yesteryear. In the full contact flag football league I play in, all blocking is full speed, above the waist and as hard as you can bring it. I play wide receiver. After running a pass pattern, I look back as a teammate catches a short pass. As he turns upfield, his defender is going full speed and is only three steps behind him. I've got an angle and the defensive back doesn't see me until a second before I nail him in the chest. His feet go up in the air. On the football field, it's known as a "decleater." He gets up . . . after a few seconds. I let out a yell. One moment . . . my moment.

20. IRL

That's right, auto racing. True Value 500 on June 8th. Who says racing's not a contact sport? Arie Luyendyk hadn't won. Or so we all thought. After the race, he walked into victory lane to protest the win by A.J. Foyt's driver. Foyt, who has a feisty side, walked over and smacked Luyendyk upside the head . . . and pushed him down. Arie's consolation prize? He was right. The laps had been counted wrong. Luyendyk declared the winner.

That's it. 20 of the Top 40 Moments in sports for 1997. *My* 20 Moments, of course. I'm just one man. For a second man, and a second man's opinion, I gotta give up some props for my late night partner in crime, RICH EISEN, who is still crying a little bit because I got to go first.

Alright, Stuart's had his say, a say, by the way, which he won by the flip of a coin. I said heads. It came up tails. So, there, I lost. And now I get all the leftover Top 40 Moments of the year. Thus, if my big moments sound a little stale, sound like they're a bit of a stretch, cut me some slack. And blame Stuart. Now, that I have covered myself, let's play ball.

1. Bite Night: Tyson-Holyfield, Part 2

Perhaps Iron Mike didn't have breakfast that day. We all knew he entered the ring hungry, but this was ridiculous. Did Tyson bite Evander Holyfield's ear on purpose because he thought he had no shot? Or did he do it out of a fit of rage, one that the ordinary person frankly can't understand? Either way, it was another of the proverbial black eyes on the sport of boxing. Millions of people at home

Any hopes the **New York Knicks** had of beating the **Miami Heat** and moving on in the 1997 NBA play-offs disappeared in the wake of this bench-clearing brawl. Suspensions resulted in the Knicks being severely undermanned for the final two games of the series and they lost.

spending millions of dollars to watch that crock. Even worse, Tyson got paid $27 million for the fight.

2. The Pool-Buster Tournament

Whose NCAA Tournament pool wasn't worth the piece of paper it was written on by, oh, the second round? The Mocs of U-T Chattanooga? The College of Charleston? The University of Arizona going the whole way? The same school that is a virtual lock to choke under pressure? The same Wildcat team whose fans had such confidence in them that, upon leaving for the Final Four, exactly two fans showed at the airport to see them off? If you won your pool, congrats. You earned it.

3. Alomar's All-Star Moment

The only thing missing from this moment was a bolt of lightning preceding it. All-Star Game, Jacobs Field, Cleveland, Ohio. Game tied at 1–1. Two outs. Bernie Williams on second base. Sandy Alomar of the Cleveland Indians steps to the plate. Crowd goes wild. Hometown hero, entering the game with a 30 game hitting streak. 44,916 fans expecting something big to happen. It does. 2-run homer off Shawn Estes. Sandy Alomar, an easy pick for All-Star Game MVP.

4. Knicks-Heat Brawl

How could one of the better title shots of Patrick Ewing's career go down in such unbelievably ludicrous flames? P.J. Brown uses Charlie Ward to mop the floor and all heck breaks loose. Unfortunately, for the Knicks, the fight occurred right in front of their bench. Fortunately, for everyone involved there were no litigious cameramen underneath the pigpile. Ewing just strolled off the bench and really didn't enter the fray. Technically, however, he left the bench. So did John Starks. And Allan Houston. And Larry Johnson. The Knicks could not beat the Heat without them. And they didn't.

5. Tino the Bambino

It all began on the second night of the season. A three home-run night for Tino Martinez in Seattle. It just had to be a fluke, right? Not at all. Who knew it was just the beginning? Just one year after facing the wrath of Yankees fans because he had the gall to enter the scene after Don Mattingly left it, Tino Martinez hits more home runs in a season than any Yankee since Roger Maris and Mickey Mantle.

6. The Detroit Red Wings

After 42 years of pure futility for the franchise, and 14 years for Steve Yzerman himself, the Wings and Stevie Y got to hoist the cup himself in front of a frenzied Joe Louis Arena crowd. Scottie Bowman had now won 7 of these things himself but this time he actually went into the locker room and laced up the skates so he could glide around the ice with the Cup. Who could blame him? Two days later, a crowd estimated at slightly more than a million showed up at Hart Plaza to bask in the glory.

7. The Accident

Sadly, the Wings were brought down to earth way too soon. Less than a week after wiping away the suffering, they really learned what suffering meant. A terrible car accident. A limo carrying Slava Fetisov, Vladimir Konstantinov and team masseur Sergei Mnatsakanov back from a picnic celebration wound up wrapped around a tree. Fetisov sustained minor injuries. Konstantinov and Mnatsakanov were still in the hospital as of this printing.

8. Mays or Edmonds?

Now there's a question we thought we'd never hear! Whose catch was better, Willie Mays in the '54 World Series or Jim Edmonds against the Kansas City Royals during the 1997 regular season? David Howard sent one deep to centerfield that had triple written all over it. Edmonds, running full speed, back to home plate, dove straight for the centerfield fence and made like a wide receiver in the back of the end zone. It's the centerpiece to the centerfielder's Gold Glove resume tape. The rest of the year on Sports-Center, whenever someone made a good catch during a highlight, we would say, "Nice, but not as good as Edmonds."

9. Arrivaderci, Mario

After 13 seasons, 683 goals, 1,649 points, 2 Stanley Cups and one courageous comeback from Hodgkin's disease, Mario Lemieux hung them up. A testament to his greatness, he got a lengthy standing ovation while making several solo trips around the ice in his final game . . . from Philadelphia Flyers fans. Why did Mario retire during his prime? After all, he amassed a

Hockey legend **Mario Lemieux** had many moments like this in 1997. Lemieux is shown waving goodbye to the Pittsburgh fans after his last home game, a playoff win over the Philadelphia Flyers on April 23.

league-leading 122 points this season. Mario was supposedly sick and tired of all the stick work and clutching and grabbing that was never called. He practically begged the league to do something about it. If that's true, then what a shame. At least we were able to enjoy it for 13 seasons. Said Mario: "I did it my way."

10. Michael Jordan's Game 1

The Utah Jazz actually had thoughts of taking a one-game-to-none lead in the 1997 NBA Finals. And on the Bulls' home floor, no less. Silly Jazz. Even sillier, with less than 10 seconds left and everyone in the building, let alone the planet, knowing who was going to take the last shot, the Jazz played Michael Jordan straight up. No double team. No problem. Jordan stuck the jumper with no time left and the Bulls won Game 1 by 1 point. Talk about your tone setter.

11. Parcells returns to New England

Less than 10 months after he took the Patriots to the Super Bowl, Bill Parcells brought his Jets into Foxboro Stadium and the New England fans were waiting. 60,292 of them to be exact. The words "Can the Tuna" couldn't be printed on more items: T-shirts, hats, towels . . . who knows? Maybe even underwear. But let's not go there. The Jets survived the first rush of emotion and actually made a game of it. But as it was with the pre-Parcells Jets, when it came to losing,

Mark McGwire had 58 moments that were pretty special in 1997 as he hit more home runs than anyone since Roger Maris hit 61 in 1961.

it wasn't a matter of when, it was a matter of how: John Hall had a chip shot, 29-yard field goal blocked in the final seconds of regulation. The Jets lost in overtime.

12. Davis Love III wins the PGA

This moment was so directly out of the movies, the only thing missing was a soundtrack. Davis Love III finally rids himself of the dreaded "Best Player to Never Win a Major" label by winning the PGA Championship. All throughout his final round of 66, Love thought of his mentor and father, Davis Jr, who died in a plane crash in 1988 and never saw his son win one of his 10 PGA Tour events. His brother Mark was caddying and at Davis' side as he strolled up 18 in a slight drizzle, soaking in the adoration from the gallery. Love sunk a 12-foot

birdie to win his first major with a flourish . . . and a rainbow appeared in the sky. He said it was his father. "I was choking up a lot of times out there," Love said.

13. Mark McGwire's 52nd Home Run

Why not 33? Why not 1? Why, of all of McGwire's home runs, choose 52? Because, earlier in the day, McGwire had just signed a three-year, $28 million dollar contract with the Cardinals, chicken feed compared to what Big Mac could have snagged on the open market. But McGwire said he fell in love with St. Louis and sounded sincere in saying so. That night, when McGwire stepped to the plate against LA's Ramon Martinez, Busch Stadium shook from the roar of the crowd. McGwire stepped out on a

2-0 count, specifically to soak it all in. He then clubbed a 517 foot home run, the longest ever recorded in Busch Stadium. "It was one of the greatest moments I've ever had in baseball," McGwire said. That's why home run No. 52.

14. Dallas 21, Philadelphia 20
The final score most definitely *should* have read Philadelphia 23, Dallas 21 but somehow, some way the Eagles muffed the snap on a game-winning 22-yard field goal with one second left. Eagles kicker Chris Boniol, who had made 46 consecutive field goals inside the 35-yard line, was all set to sink his former team. But, after a poor snap, holder Tom Hutton, the punter, made like Lucy to Boniol's Charlie Brown. He tried to set the ball up, but then, perhaps in a fit of panic, yanked it away and then made a feeble attempt to run the ball in. The Cowboys avoided a 1-2 start in one of the strangest endings you'll ever see in football. "I couldn't believe what happened," Dallas coach Barry Switzer said. "Somebody up there likes us."

15. Holy Comeback, Robin!
Chicago White Sox third baseman Robin Ventura's 1997 season got off to a horrible start. A compound fracture of his ankle while sliding into home plate during a spring training game. His foot was perpendicular to the rest of his leg. Teammate Ray Durham vomited at the sight. Forget about his '97 season, Ventura's career was in jeopardy. Amazingly, Ventura came back in four months. A remarkable return highlighted by the game-winning, 8th inning, 2-out double hit by Ventura to beat the Texas Rangers.

16. Coaching Comebacks
Rick Pitino lured out of Kentucky by the Celtics green, as in 10 years for a reported $70 million. Chuck Daly lured out of retirement by the Orlando Magic. Dick Vermeil lured out of the broadcast booth by the Rams offer and the call of the coaching siren. Mike Ditka lured out of the studio by the Saints, of all teams. Just when you thought the coaches carousel was broken down, everyone comes back. Who's next, Hank Stram?

17. Dodgers at Giants, September 17-18
Forget about interleague play, the best and most exciting baseball is good old-fashioned intra-league, intra-division play as this two-game series between two of baseball's oldest rivals showed us. Two taut one-run games with everything on the line. The Dodgers came in with a two game lead over San Francisco for the NL West lead. The Dodgers lost both games and then, one week later, went on to lose the division. The largest crowd in three years showed up at 3Com Park for Wednesday night's game. Almost 2,000 more fans showed for Thursday afternoon's series crescendo, a 12-inning, 6-5 Giants victory. Who says baseball needs to inject more excitement?

18. Peyton's Place . . . Not
He delayed the fortune that comes with NFL fame for one more year. Peyton Manning said he still had more to accomplish on the college level and one of the things, without question, was to beat Florida. Gators coach Steve Spurrier, as is his frequent wont, stirred the pot by tossing verbal barbs Manning's way. His best shot: You

In 1997, several young golfers made major statements. Ernie Els won the U.S. Open and Tiger Woods blew away the field at the Masters. **Justin Leonard** finished second in the PGA and won the British Open.

can't spell Citrus Bowl without UT. The Gators' dominance kept Tennessee out of the Sugar Bowl and in the Citrus Bowl. Get it? Anyway, Spurrier's Gators spanked Manning and the Vols . . . again. Manning's line: 29 of 51 for 353 yards, 3 touchdowns, 2 INTs and one loss . . . again.

19. Golf's Twentysomethings

Davis Love III's victory in the PGA Championship broke up quite a year for golf's 20 somethings: Tiger Woods (Masters), Ernie Els (U.S. Open) and Justin Leonard (British Open), winners of the the other majors. This breed of golfers has served notice on the rest of the PGA Tour. There's a new game in town.

20. Jeff Gordon wins the Winston Million

It's professional sports' most difficult play: NASCAR's Winston Million. All you have to do is win three of the following four races in the same year; the Daytona 500, the Coca Cola 600, the Winston 500 and the Southern 500. That's all. And you win $1 million. Bill Elliott did it back in 1985. No man had done it since- . . . until Jeff Gordon in 1997. And he did it with his usual flourish. After winning Daytona and the Coca-Cola, he won the Southern 500 for the third straight time. No driver had ever accomplished *that* triple-play. ■

CALENDAR

On April 15, 1997, the fiftieth anniversary of Jackie Robinson's first major league game, **President Clinton** (l), **Rachel Robinson** (c) and baseball commissioner **Bud Selig** (r) announce that Jackie Robinson's number 42 will be retired throughout baseball at a ceremony at Shea Stadium in New York.

Wide World Photos

NOV '96

Sun	Mon	Tue	Wed	Thu	Fri	Sat
					1	2
3	4	5	6	7	8	9
10	11	12	13	14	15	16
17	18	19	20	21	22	23
24	25	26	27	28	29	30

SNICKER SNICKER

Ken Caminiti of the San Diego Padres was the fourth unanimous NL MVP in History. His already good season turned great after he contracted a little Montezuma's Revenge during a three game series in Mexico with the Mets. With the help of an IV and a Snickers bar, Caminiti dragged himself out onto the field for the last game. That day he hit 2 homers and got 4 RBIs. The rest of his year is shown below.

	Before IV	After IV
Games	109	37
Average	.301	.399
HR	24	16
RBI	83	47
Slug. Pct.	.549	.833

STALLWART

In seven years at Alabama, **Gene Stallings** acquitted himself rather nicely. He won a national title in 1992 and beat Auburn a bunch. It should be noted that the NCAA recognizes Stallings' record as 61–24 after ruling that eight wins and one tie in 1993 came after using an ineligible player. Don't blame Gene, though. A player had improper conduct with an agent but Stallings never knew.

Gene Stallings at Alabama

Overall record	69-15-1
In bowl games	4-1
vs ranked teams	13-9-1
vs Auburn	5-2

1 **NBA season tips off** with the world-champion Bulls picking up where they left off the previous season, storming back from a 16 point deficit to trounce the hapless Celtics 107-98. Shaquille O'Neal scores 23 and grabs 14 rebounds in his debut with the Lakers, a 96-82 win over Phoenix. The NBA draft's first pick Allen Iverson scores 30 and dishes out six assists for the 76ers in a 111-103 loss to Milwaukee.

2 **Tommy Morrison** makes a controversial return to the ring for the first time since testing positive for HIV and polishes off an overmatched Marcus Rhode at 1:38 of the first round.

3 **Italy's Giacomo Leone** and Romania's Anuta Catuna break the tape at the 27th annual New York Marathon. Leone finishes in 2 hours, 9.54 minutes while Catuna wins in 2:28.18 after last year's winner Tegla Loroupe tires and falls to 7th.

4 **Derek Jeter** of the New York Yankees receives all 28 first-place votes and 140 points overall in running away with the AL Rookie of the Year award.

Terry Collins is hired as manager of the Anaheim Angels after being fired from the Houston Astros.

6 **Scandal rocks Boston College** for the second time in the past 20 years as 13 football players are suspended for sports betting, including two who bet against B.C. in a 45–17 loss to Syracuse.

UCLA fires men's basketball coach Jim Harrick for what the university considered unethical conduct. Harrick, just one year removed from winning the school's 11th national title, is replaced by assistant Steve Lavin.

Outfielder Todd Hollandsworth becomes the major league record fifth consecutive Los Angeles Dodger to win the National League Rookie of the Year award.

7 **Yankee manager Joe Torre** and Rangers manager Johnny Oates are named co-American League Managers of the Year, the first tie in the 14 year history of the award.

8 **San Diego's Bruce Bochy,** who guided the Padres to their first postseason appearance since 1984, is named NL Manager of the Year.

9 **Evander Holyfied shocks** the boxing world, registering a thrilling 11th round TKO over heavyweight champ Mike Tyson. At age 34, Holyfidy joins legend Muhammad Ali as the only two fighters to have won the belt three times.

10 **Terry Labonte** finishes fifth in the NAPA 500 to clinch his second Winston Cup title, 12 years after his first. Bobby Labonte holds off Dale Jarrett (2nd) and Jeff Gordon (3rd) to win the event and insure the overall championship for his brother.

Dan Marino reaches 50,000 yards passing in a milestone-filled day that includes Marcus Allen playing in his 200th career game, Morton Andersen scoring his 1,500th point and Dave Kreig being sacked an NFL record-tying 483rd time. Boomer Esiason steals some thunder by throwing for 522 yards in a 37-34 OT win vs. Washington.

11 **Atlanta fireballer John Smoltz** takes 26 first-place and two second-place votes in cruising to the NL Cy Young Award.

12 **Pot calling the kettle black** as San Francisco mayor Willie Brown calls 49er quarterback Elvis Grbac an "embarrassment to humankind" in response to the 49ers' 20-17 loss to Dallas. He later apologizes for his idiotic comments when informed that Grbac's son suffers from spina bifida.

Totonto Blue Jay Pat Hentgen edges Yankee Andy Pettitte to become the first pitcher from a Canadian team to win the AL Cy Young award. Hentgen receives 110 points to Pettitte's 104 in the second-closest vote in the history of the award.

Notre Dame football coach **Lou Holtz** addresses the media after announcing that he will step down at the end of the season, his 11th at the school.

13 Cleveland Indians acquire power-hitting third baseman Matt Williams from the San Francisco Giants for middle infielders Jeff Kent and Jose Vizcaino and reliever Julian Tavarez.

San Diego third baseman Ken Caminiti secures all 28 first place votes in becoming the fourth unanimous MVP in league history.

14 Danny Ainge takes over for Cotton Fitzsimmons as head coach of the Phoenix Suns after the team stumbles to an 0-8 start, their worst in 11 years.

Pittsburgh Pirates slash payroll further and continue to build for the future by sending all-star second baseman Carlos Garcia, Orlando Merced, and Dan Plesac to the Toronto Blue Jays for six minor league prospects.

Texas Rangers slugger Juan Gonzalez squeaks by Seattle shortstop Alex Rodriguez by three votes to win the AL MVP award. It matches the second-closest vote ever for the AL award.

16 Time flies in Buffalo when the Marine Midland Arena's brand new $3 million-plus clock/scoreboard crashes to the ice before the Sabres-Bruins game.

17 Denver Broncos establish themselves as the top regular season team in the AFC by thrashing the New England Patriots 34-8 in Foxboro. Terrell Davis runs for 154 yards and scores three times.

18 Lou Holtz announces his decision to step down from his 11 years as head coach of Notre Dame football following the 1996 season.

Dallas kicker Chris Boniol scores all of the Cowboys' points and ties an NFL record by booting seven field goals in a 21-6 victory over Green Bay. Many Packers take offense to the record-tying kick with 20 seconds left to play, accusing the Cowboys of running up the score.

19 Chicago White Sox make fiery slugger Albert Belle the highest paid player in baseball history, inking the outfielder to a five-year, $55 million contract.

Boston Red Sox choose former Toronto manager and Atlanta third base coach Jimy Williams to manage their club.

23 Michigan stuns second-ranked Ohio State for the second consecutive year with a 13-9 victory, ruining the Buckeyes' chances for a perfect season and a national title.

Tennessee women's basketball coach Pat Summitt wins her 600th career game as the Lady Vols upend Marquette 83-68.

Chicago Bulls lose their first game of the season after 12 consecutive wins, succumbing to the Utah Jazz 105-100.

24 Doug Flutie throws for 302 yards and scampers for 96 more to lead the Toronto Argonauts past the Edmonton Eskimos 43-37 in the CFL's Grey Cup. Flutie is named game MVP for the fifth time in his career.

25 Five 1-A football coaches either resign or are fired on a day some have dubbed "Black Monday". BC's Dan Henning and Pitt's Johnny Majors are the most prominent, both having resigned under duress.

26 Baseball owners ratify by a 26-4 margin a new collective bargaining agreement, assuring labor peace and uninterrupted play through the year 2000.

Denver Nuggets' Bernie Bickerstaff steps down from his head coaching position, resuming his old job as president and GM. Dick Motta, the third-winningest coach in NBA history, is hired to replace him.

30 No. 2 Florida St. jumps out to a 17-0 first quarter lead and holds on to upset No. 1 Florida 24-21 and grab the nation's top spot going into the bowls. Warrick Dunn rushes for 185 yards and the Seminole defense sacks Danny Wuerffel six times and picks off three of his passes.

DEC '96

Sun	Mon	Tue	Wed	Thu	Fri	Sat
1	2	3	4	5	6	7
8	9	10	11	12	13	14
15	16	17	18	19	20	21
22	23	24	25	26	27	28
29	30	31				

ROCKET RECORDS

When the Boston Red Sox let Roger Clemens head off to Toronto, they said goodbye to the best pitcher in team history, as the following table illustrates. In addition to leading the team in all these categories, Clemens is tied with Cy Young for career wins on the Red Sox with 192.

Roger Clemens's Red Sox Resumé

Cy Young awards	3
Single season strikeouts	291
10 strikeout games	68
20 strikeout games	2
200 strikeout seasons	8
Career strikeouts	2,590

TRIPLE PLAY

Detroit Lion Barry Sanders led the NFL in rushing in 1996 with 1,553 yards. That performance capped off one of the best three-year spans by a running back in league history.

Gimme Three Steps

	Rushing Yards
Eric Dickerson, 1984-86	5,160
Dickerson, 1983-85	5.147
Earl Campbell, 1978-80	5,081
Campbell, 1979-81	5,007
Orenthal J. Simpson, 1973-75	4,945
Barry Sanders, 1994-96	**4,936**

1 **Fred Couples** earns $240,000 and seven skins with a birdie of the 15th hole to give him his second consecutive victory at the Skins Game.

3 **Dallas Cowboys DT Leon Lett** is suspended without pay for a minimum of one year for violating the NFL's drug policy.

TNT is awarded cable rights to the 1998 Winter Olympics in Nagano. The cable giant pays approximately $10 million for 50 hours of coverage that includes hockey, speed skating and skiing.

4 **World Cup downhill champ** Picabo Street crashes in a training run at Vail, tearing cartilage and tendons in her left knee that will require season-ending surgery.

NASCAR team owner Rick Hendrick is indicted by a federal grand jury on charges of conspiring to bribe Honda executives for preferential treatment.

Orlando Magic tie the NBA record for fewest points in a game in an 84-57 rout at the hands of the Cleveland Cavaliers. Gerald Wilkins scorches the Cavs for ten points to lead the Magic.

5 **Ohio St. offensive tackle Orlando Pace,** master of the famed pancake block, wins the Lombardi Award as the nations top college lineman, becoming the only two-time recipient of the award

Catcher Terry Steinbach, in a move all too uncommon, decides to go home to play for the Minnesota Twins, accepting less money than was offered by three other teams.

6 **Pete Rozelle,** NFL commissioner from 1960-1989 and the father of the Super Bowl, dies of brain cancer at his home at the age of 70.

7 **Texas stuns** heavily favored Nebraska 37-27 in the Big 12 Championship game, knocking the Huskers out of the national title picture. Longhorn Quarterback James Brown, who had earlier predicted a 21-point Texas win, seals the victory with a daring 61-yard completion on fourth and one from his own 28.

8 **North Carolina** returns to the top of the women's soccer world with a 1-0 overtime win over defending champ Notre Dame for their 14th NCAA title in the past 16 years.

10 **Bob Hill is fired** as head coach of the 3-15 San Antonio Spurs and replaced wirh GM Gregg Popovich.

11 **Reggie White** agrees to a 5-year, $19 million deal to stay with the Green Bay Packers for what is likely the remainder of his career.

12 **Florida Marlins** continue their offseason free agent signing binge, inking outfielder Moises Alou to a five-year, $25 million contract. He joins fellow signees Bobby Bonilla, Alex Fernandez and Jim Eisenreich in boosting the club's payroll to $89 million.

13 **Toronto Blue Jays** come out of nowhere to win the Roger Clemens sweepstakes, signing the aging righthander to a four-year deal worth approximately $32 million. Clemens spurns offers from the Indians, Yankees and Red Sox to become baseball's highest paid pitcher.

14 **Florida QB Danny Wuerffel,** the most accurate passer in NCAA history, takes home the Heisman Trophy in the closest vote since 1989. Wuerffel garners 300 first place votes and 1,363 points, beating Iowa State running back Troy Davis (209 and 1,174).

Heavyweight Andrew Golota, proving once again that his considerable boxing talent is completely overmatched by his lack of intelligence, is disqualified for the second consecutive match for a low blow on Riddick Bowe. Golota knocks Bowe down twice and seemingly has the fight well in hand until his illegal punches DQ him late in the ninth round.

15 **World Seies MVP** John Wetteland agrees to a four-year, $21 million deal to pitch for the Texas Rangers.

Wide World Photos

In December of 1996, the Toronto Blue Jays signed **Roger Clemens** away from the Boston Red Sox with a contract that briefly made him the highest paid pitcher in baseball. The Blue Jays finished last but Clemens is shown pitching in his 20th win of the season.

St. John's routs Florida International 4-1 in the NCAA Division I men's soccer championship game, giving the Red Storm their first national championship in any sport.

17 Championship Auto Racing Teams (CART) agrees to relinquish the right to refer to itself as "Indy-Car", a trademark it had used for 17 years. The upstart Indy Racing League is given rights to the term.

19 Mike Keenan is fired as general manager/coach of the St. Louis Blues after making several deals which were unpopular with fans and engaging in a rift with club superstar Brett Hull.

Bowl season begins with Nevada beating Ball St. 18-15 in the Las Vegas Bowl behind two touchdown passes from quarterback Damond Wilkins. The game draws just 10,118 fans.

21 New England Patriots rally from a 22-0 halftime deficit and score 20 points in just under 11 minutes to defeat the Giants 23-22 and earn a first round bye in the AFC playoffs.

Top ranked Marshall whips Montana 49-29 to win the NCAA Division I-AA football title. Freshman Florida St. transfer Randy Moss grabs nine passes for 220 yards and four touchdowns to lead the Thundering Herd.

22 Atlanta kicker Morten Andersen unbelievably misses a 30-yard field goal with four seconds remaining to give the Jacksonville Jaguars a 19-17 win and a wildcard berth in the upcoming playoffs. It is his first miss from 30 yards or less after making 59 in a row.

St. Louis' Brett Hull notches a hat trick in the Blues' 7-4 win over Los Angeles to become the 24th NHL player to register 500 goals.

23 Lions RB Barry Sanders, needing 161 yards against a stingy 49er defense for the NFL rushing title, scampers for 175 in the Lions 24-14 loss.

24 Dom Capers is voted NFL Coach of the Year after leading the Carolina Panthers to a 12-4 record and the NFC West title in their second year in existence.

25 Houston running back Eddie George, who scored eight touchdowns and gained 1,368 yards, wins the NFL Rookie of the Year Award.

26 Detroit Lions end months, if not years, of speculation, firing long-time head coach Wayne Fontes after a 5-11 season. Fontes becomes the sixth coach fired since the end of the season.

Phoenix Suns acquire point guard Jason Kidd, Tony Dumas, and Loren Meyer from the Dallas Mavericks in exchange for Sam Cassell, A.C. Green, Michael Finley and a second-round pick.

29 Cleveland Indians reliever Jose Mesa is arrested in Cleveland on felony charges of carrying a concealed weapon and fondling a woman.

30 Green Bay Packer Brett Favre joins Joe Montana as the only NFL players to be selected league MVP in two consecutive seasons.

Boise St. football coach Pokey Allen dies from a form of muscle cancer at the age of 53.

31 No. 6 Nebraska reaches 11 wins for the fourth consecutive year with a 41-21 pasting of No. 10 Virginia Tech in the Orange Bowl.

Amy Van Dyken, winner of four gold medals at the 1996 Summer Olympics, is voted AP female athlete of the year.

JAN '97

Sun	Mon	Tue	Wed	Thu	Fri	Sat
			1	2	3	4
5	6	7	8	9	10	11
12	13	14	15	16	17	18
19	20	21	22	23	24	25
26	27	28	29	30	31	

TOP 20 **FINISHES**

January is college football bowl and poll time. In losing Lou Holtz, Notre Dame has lost a coach who has a knack for getting teams to the top. In 11 seasons in South Bend, Holtz delivered eight top 20 teams. Here is how Holtz ranks in top 20 finishes compared to other active coaching legends.

	Top 20 Finishes
Joe Paterno	23
Bobby Bowden	22
Tom Osborne	16
Lou Holtz	14

IRISH **BOWLS**

1997, Lou Holtz's last year with Notre Dame, marked the first time since 1986, Holtz's first year, that the Fighting Irish did not play in a bowl game. In between, Holtz clinched a national title with a victory in the 1989 Fiesta Bowl. Overall, Notre Dame is 13–8 in bowl games, dating back to a 27–10 Rose Bowl victory over Stanford in 1925.

Notre Dame's Bowl Record

Cotton	5-2
Sugar	2-1
Orange	2-3
Others	4-2
Lou Holtz	5-4

1 **No. 4 Ohio St.** ends Arizona St.'s bid for a perfect season and a national title with a 20-17 Rose Bowl win. Sophomore QB Joe Germaine's five-yard TD strike with 19 seconds to go lifts the Buckeyes. In other major bowl action, No. 9 Tennessee pounds No. 11 Northwestern in the Citrus Bowl, No. 5 BYU slips by No 14 Kansas St. for their 14th win of the season, and No. 7 Penn St. crushes No. 20 Texas.

2 **QB Danny Wuerffel leads** Florida to its first Division I national football title by avenging its earlier loss with a 52-20 dismantling of Florida St. Wuerffel throws for 306 yards and three touchdowns and runs for another. FSU suffers its first postseason loss since 1981.

Canadian Junior coach Graham James is sentenced to 3½ years in prison after pleading guilty to sexually abusing two of his former players, including current Boston Bruins winger Sheldon Kennedy.

LSU veteran coach Dale Brown announces he will retire at the end of the season after 25 seasons as head coach of the Tigers.

3 **San Diego head coach Bobby Ross,** who led the Chargers to the Super Bowl just two years ago, quits the team after differences with GM Bobby Beathard.

4 **Natrone Means rushes** for 140 yards to lead the Jacksonville Jaguars to a 30-27 upset over heavily favored Denver, earning the second-year club a spot in the AFC title game.

5 **Defending AFC and NFC champs** go down in defeat as the Dallas Cowboys fall to the upstart Carolina Panthers 26–17, and the Pittsburgh Steelers are throttled by New England 28–3.

6 **Pitcher Phil Niekro,** winner of 318 major league games, is finally elected to baseball's Hall of Fame on his fifth attempt. Dodgers pitcher Don Sutton and Reds slugger Tony Perez miss by nine and 43 votes, respectively.

Peter O'Malley, whose family has owned the Dodgers since 1950, announces his intentions to sell the team and Dodger Stadium.

8 **Maryland overcomes** a 22 point second half deficit to shock No. 12 ranked North Carolina 85-75 in Chapel Hill. The Terps shoot 56 percent from the field and outscore the Heels 41-9 in the second half.

11 **Legendary golfer Arnold Palmer** announces he has prostate cancer and will be taking a hiatus from the senior tour.

12 **Green Bay Packers return** to the Super Bowl for the first time since Super Bowl II in 1968 with a 30-13 demolition of the Carolina Panthers. They will face the New England Patriots who make it to the Big Show in New Orleans with a 20-6 win over the surprising Jacksonville Jaguars.

Tiger Woods wins his third PGA event in nine tries with a playoff victory over Tom Lehman in the Mercedes Championships. Woods shoots a final round 65, birdying the last four holes to force the playoff.

Olympic gold medal figure skater Oksana Baiul is hospitalized with a concussion after running her car off a Connecticut road. She is later found to have a blood-alcohol level of .168 percent.

Dallas Cowboys stars Michael Irvin and Erik Williams have their names cleared in regard to accusations that they assaulted a 23-year-old Nina Shahravan. The woman signs a confession admitting the story was a hoax.

15 **George Seifert,** the winningest head coach in San Francisco 49er history, resigns with a year remaining on his contract. Cal coach Steve Mariucci is later hired as his replacement.

Wide World Photos

American **Pete Sampras** started off 1997 with a bang by winning the Australian Open. Sampras also won Wimbledon in 1997. At 26, he is tied with Bill Tilden for fourth place on the all-time list of Grand Slam wins with ten.

Bulls' forward Dennis Rodman is at it again, kicking cameraman Eugene Amos in the groin after diving for a loose ball in the Bulls' 112-102 win in Minnesota. Amos, who is carried off on a stretcher, subsequently sues Rodman and settles out of court for $200,000. Rodman is suspended 11 games by the league, the second longest suspension in NBA history.

Pittsburgh Penguins' goalie Patrick Lalime shuts out the Hartford Whalers 3-0 for his 15th consecutive start without a loss (13-0-2), setting the NHL record for best start by a rookie goalie.

18 Canadiens' winger Mark Recchi leads the Eastern Conference to an 11-7 victory in the 47th NHL All-Star game. Recchi, named MVP, potted three goals for the East as did the West's Owen Nolan in a game where 27 of the 40 players figured in the scoring.

20 Curt Flood, baseball pioneer who opened the door for free agency, dies of throat cancer at the age of 59.

ABC analyst Dick Vermeil returns to the NFL as coach of the St. Louis Rams, 15 years after retiring as coach of the Philadelphia Eagles.

22 Yankee great Don Mattingly officially retires from baseball after 14 years, nine gold gloves and six all-star selections. He will be the 15th player to have his number retired by the Yankees.

24 Martina Hingis cruises to a 6-2, 6-2 victory over former champion Mary Pierce in the finals of the Australian Open. At 16 years, six months, she becomes the youngest woman to win a major in 110 years.

Bash brothers are reunited as the Boston Red Sox trade power hitting DH Jose Canseco back to the Oakland A's for pitcher John Wasdin.

Brian Winters is fired as head coach of the Vancouver Grizzlies after leading the club to a 23-102 mark in his 1½ year tenure. He is replaced by president/general manager Stu Jackson.

25 Top-ranked Pete Sampras grabs his 9th major title with a 6-2, 6-3, 6-3 triumph over No. 24 Carlos Moya at the Australian Open.

Chicago Blackhawks trade two-time Vezina Trophy winning goalie Ed Belfour to San Jose for Chris Terreri, Ulf Dahlen and Michal Sykora.

26 Green Bay Packers are annointed kings of the NFL with a 35-21 shootout victory over the New England Patriots in Super Bowl XXXI. Desmond Howard returns a kickoff 99 yards for a score to break the game open and take home the game's MVP. Brett Favre throws for 246 yards and no interceptions compared to Drew Bledsoe's four picks. Reggie White registers three second-half sacks.

Mario Lemieux ties an NHL record with four goals in the third period to lead the Pittsburgh Penguins to a 5-2 win over Montreal.

28 Former Super Bowl coach Mike Ditka signs a three-year contract to coach the troubled New Orleans Saints

29 Bill Parcells' struggle to leave the New England Patriots intensifies when NFL commissioner Paul Tagliabue rules that the the coach must obtain permission from Pats' owner Bob Kraft in order to coach another team.

31 Buffalo Bills' Jim Kelly announces his retirement from the NFL in an emotional press conference. Kelly, considered by many to be the greatest quarterback in Bills' history, had quarterbacked the Bills to four Super Bowl appearances in his 11 year NFL career.

FEB '97

Sun	Mon	Tue	Wed	Thu	Fri	Sat
						1
2	3	4	5	6	7	8
9	10	11	12	13	14	15
16	17	18	19	20	21	22
23	24	25	26	27	28	

HAPPY NEW YEAR

Starting on January 1, Glen Rice of the Charlotte Hornets went on a two-month tear. As of February 19, he had led his team in scoring in 22 of 25 games, topped 40 points in a game four times, topped 30 points 14 times and, for the whole season, was hitting on 45% of his three-pointers. Here is how Rice ranked with other top scorers over that time.

Winter Hot Streak

	Points PG	FG Pct.
Glen Rice	**30.8**	**49.6**
Michael Jordan	30.1	51.9
Mitch Richmond	28.8	46.9
Karl Malone	28.0	55.1
Latrell Sprewell	27.7	46.8

MINNESOTA MILESTONE

February 21, 1997 marked the latest in the year that the Minnesota Timberwolves reached the .500 mark. The T-Wolves had been at .500 two other times in their eight year history, going 1–1 in the 1990–91 season and 2–2 in the 1992–93 campaign.

Timberwolves after 54 games, 1992–97

1996-97	**27-27**
1995-96	16-38
1994-95	14-40
1993-94	16-38
1992-93	14-40

1 **Boston Bruins defenseman Ray Bourque** scores the team's first goal in a 3-0 win over Tampa to surpass Hall of Famer John Bucyk and become the Bruins' all-time leading scorer with 1,340 points.

2 **Colts' kicker Cary Blanchard** boots a 37 yard field goal in overtime to give the AFC a 26-23 victory over the NFC in the Pro Bowl. Investment banker Lance Alstodt kicks a 35 yarder during halftime to win $1 million.

Bowler Jeremy Sonnenfeld, a 20 year-old sophomore at Nebraska, rolls three consecutive 300 games, the first-ever sanctioned 900 series in history.

3 **New England Patriots,** in the midst of a bitter dispute with former coach Bill Parcells, hire ex-NY Jets coach and 49er defensive coordinator Pete Carroll to a five-year deal.

Legendary college coaches Don Haskins of UTEP and Pete Carrill of Princeton head a list of seven inducted into the Basketball Hall of Fame.

4 **Missouri hands No. 1 Kansas** its first loss of the season after 22 consecutive wins, stunning the Jayhawks 96-94 in double overtime.

NY Jets, searching for loopholes around the league's decision to keep Bill Parcells from becoming their coach without compensation given to the Patriots, hire him as "consultant." Bill Belichick is given head coaching duties for the upcoming season. Parcells promises to "sit silently."

Mario Lemieux scores an empty net goal in the final minute of the Penguins' 6-4 win over Vancouver to become the seventh NHL player to record 600 goals in a career.

5 **Washington Bullets fire** head coach Jim Lynam after a mediocre 22-24 start to the season. He is replaced on an interim basis by assistant Bob Staak.

7 **WBC heavyweight champ Oliver McCall** suffers an apparently-drug-induced mental breakdown in the fourth round of his title fight with Lennox Lewis. A sobbing McCall is disqualified in the fifth after he refuses help from his corner and refuses to defend himself or throw a punch.

Don Nelson is hired as general manager of the troubled and struggling Dallas Mavericks.

8 **Detroit Red Wing coach Scotty Bowman** becomes the first coach in NHL history to win 1,000 regular season games with the Wings' 6-5 overtime win over Pittsburgh.

9 **Michael Jordan** records the first triple-double in NBA All-Star game history but Glen Rice's 26 points are enough to earn MVP honors and lead the East to a 132-120 win. Rice pours in 20 points in the third quarter and 24 in the second half, both all-star records.

10 **Parcells-Kraft soap opera** comes to a conclusion as NFL commissioner Paul Tagliabue brokers an agreement whereby Parcells is allowed to coach the Jets in exchange for giving the Patriots a 1997 third and fourth draft choice, a 1998 second-round pick and a 1999 first rounder.

Heavyweight Riddick Bowe decides the Marines can't possibly be tougher than Andrew Golota's low blows and enters boot camp in South Carolina. Unfortunately his "dream" is shortlived as Bowe lasts only 11 days before returning to civilian status.

12 **White Sox slugger Albert Belle,** on trial for chasing egg-throwing kids with his car, admits to losing as much as $40,000 gambling on pro football and college basketball. He vehemently denies betting on baseball.

Lakers' star Shaquille O'Neal hyperextends his left knee in a 100-84 win over Miami, putting him out of commission for two to three months.

Jeff Gordon celebrates his victory in the 1997 Daytona 500. 25 at the time, Gordon is the youngest driver ever to win at Daytona.

15 **14-year-old Tara Lipinski** stuns world champion Michelle Kwan to become the youngest American figure skating champion. Two-time champ Nicole Bobek finishes third.

16 **Jeff Gordon takes** the checkered flag at the Daytona 500, becoming the youngest (25) winner in race history. Terry Labonte and Rickey Craven finish in second and third respectively to give owner Rick Hendrick, in the hospital with leukemia, the top three spots. Perennial bridesmaid Dale Earnhardt crashes with ten laps to go, insuring the victory for Gordon.

N.C. State upsets No. 2 Wake Forest, 60-59 on Clint Harrison's controversial 3-point overtime buzzer beater. Replays clearly show his foot inside the arc

17 **Dallas Mavericks and New Jersey Nets** exchange nine players in one of the biggest trades in league history. New Mavs' GM Don Nelson cleans house by trading guards Jimmy Jackson and Sam Cassell, forwards Chris Gatling and George McCloud, and center Eric Montross in exchange for center Shawn Bradley, guards Robert Pack and Khalid Reeves, and forward Ed O'Bannon.

18 **Brian Hill is fired** as coach of the Orlando Magic after a 24-25 start and amidst numerous player complaints. Assistant Richie Adubato takes over as interim coach.

19 **A second scandal rocks** the Canadian hockey world as allegations claim staff at Toronto's Maple Leaf

Gardens sexually abused boys in exchange for autographs and game tickets.

20 **San Francisco leftfielder Barry Bonds signs** a two-year deal worth $22.9 million, making him the highest paid player in 1999 and 2000, for the time being.

NBA trade deadline passes with several players exchanged but none of major consequence. Mark Jackson returns to Indiana from Denver and Charlotte acquires guard Rickey Pierce.

21 **Wayne Gretzky finally scores** in the Rangers' 7-2 loss to Hartford, ending the longest goal drought of his career at 21 games.

22 **Tonya Harding returns** to the ice for her first public routine since the 1994 Olympics, performing a two minute exhibition before a minor league hockey game in Reno, Nevada. She is greeted with several flower bouquets from the crowd – along with two collapsible batons.

23 **Jeff Gordon** makes it two for two to start the season as he chases down Dale Jarrett to win Nascar's Goodwrench 400 in Rockingham, N.C.

25 **New Jersey Devils strengthen** themselves for their upcoming playoff run by acquiring veteran star center Doug Gilmour and defenseman Dave Ellett from the Toronto Maple Leafs.

MAR '97

Sun	Mon	Tue	Wed	Thu	Fri	Sat
						1
2	3	4	5	6	7	8
9	10	11	12	13	14	15
16	17	18	19	20	21	22
23/30	24/31	25	26	27	28	29

YOU'RE **NUMBER ONE**

On March 15, when Dean Smith passed Adolph Rupp to become the winningest coach in college basketball history, we wondered who the other top coaches were in some of the other major sports. The totals for Wilkens, Shula and Smith reflect the day they took over the top spot. For Bowman and Robinson, the total reflects the most recent personal milestone since they are so far ahead of anyone else.

Coaching Milestones

	Wins	Passed
NCAA Basketball - Dean Smith	877	Adolph Rupp
NHL - Scotty Bowman	1000	First coach to reach 1000
NCAA Football - Eddie Robinson	400	First to 400
NBA - Lenny Wilkens	939	Red Auerbach
NHL - Don Shula	325	George Halas

MC**MAN** OF THE HOUR

NFL quarterback Jim McMahon retired in March of 1997. McMahon had a very strong run with the Bears, especially the 15–1 1985 regular season. He left the Bears after the 1988 season and played well if unspectacularly for the Chargers, Eagles, Vikings, Cardinals and Packers. He leaves the game with a solid reputation and a nifty uniform collection.

McMahon's Career Breakdown

	w/ Bears	w/other teams
Games	66	54
Yards Per Game	169.7	128.6
TDs	67	33
TD/Int Differential	+11	-1

1 **Boston Bruins unload** salary and most of its remaining talent by trading veteran stars Adam Oates, Rick Tocchet and Bill Ranford to the Washington Capitals for goalie Jim Carey, youngsters Jason Allison and Anson Carter, and two draft picks.

Hector "Macho" Camacho disposes of 40-year-old Sugar Ray Leonard with a fifth round TKO, ending the former middleweight champion's fourth comeback.

2 **Mary Slaney** records the world's sixth-fastest indoor 1,500 meter time with a 4:03.08 to take the title at the USA Indoor Track and Field Championships in Atlanta.

3 **Pittsburgh Penguins fire** head coach Eddie Johnston after the team loses eight of its last nine games. GM Craig Patrick will take over on an interim basis.

5 **Tennessee quarterback Peyton Manning**, potential No. 1 draft selection, decides to pass up the cash offered by the NFL and return to school for one more crack at the Heisman, the Florida Seminoles and the national championship.

Indiana's Bobby Knight becomes the seventh NCAA Division I coach to win 700 games with the Hoosiers' 70-66 win over Wisconsin.

Baseball's Veterans Selection Committee elects manager Tommy Lasorda, second baseman Nellie Fox and Negro League shortstop Willie Wells to join Phil Niekro to be inducted into the Hall of Fame.

Desmond Howard signs a four-year, $6 million contract with the Oakland Raiders, becoming the second consecutive Super Bowl MVP (Larry Brown) to don the black and silver.

9 **Nothing shocking** from the NCAA Tournament Selection Committee as Kansas, North Carolina and Minnesota join defending champ Kentucky as No. 1 seeds. Stanford, North Carolina, Old Dominion and UConn claim the top spots in the women's bracket.

11 **Columbus Quest rips** the Richmond Rage 77-64 to capture the first ABL championship, three games to two. Theresa Edwards nets 23 to lead the Quest and regular season MVP Nikki McCray adds 11 and sings the national anthem to boot.

12 **NFL owners** reject the proposal to bring back instant replay as an officiating tool. The proposal receives 20 votes from the 30 owners, shy of the required 23. Some owners reverse their vote after learning that a challenge would cost their team a time-out, even if a call is overturned.

13 **The America's Cup** is badly damaged when a protestor dressed in a suit and tie walks into the New Zealand yacht clubhouse with a sledgehammer and hacks away.

14 **15th ranked Coppin St.** provides the inevitable early upset of the NCAA tourney, shocking No. 2 South Carolina 78-65.

15 **Dean Smith wins no. 877,** a 73-56 second round blowout of Colorado to surpass the legendary Adolph Rupp and become the winningest Division I basketball coach of all time.

New Jersey's Dave Andreychuk follows Joey Mullen's lead and notches his 500th in the Devils' 3-2 win over Washington, becoming the 26th NHLer to reach the milestone.

19 **Pepsi signs** a five-year, $50 million deal with Major League Baseball to become the league's 12th national sponsor. The company will be limited to events encompassing all major league teams, however, since 24 of the 28 teams are already under contract with Coke. The deal comes on the heels of the Yankees' ten-year, $95 million deal with Adidas.

World and Olympic figure skating champion Scott Hamilton is diagnosed with testicular cancer after going to the hospital with severe stomach pains.

Gold medalist **Tara Lipinski** (c), silver medalist **Michelle Kwan** (l), and bronze winner **Vanessa Gusmeroli** display their winnings at the 1997 World Figure Skating Championships in Lausanne, Switzerland.

20 **Canada's Elvis Stojko** wins his third World Figure Skating Championship after landing four quadruple jumps, including the rare quad-triple toe combination. Defending champ Todd Eldredge of the United States finishes in second.

21 **Office pools** throughout the country take a beating as No. 1 seed and tournament favorite Kansas is shocked by Arizona 85-82 in the regional semifinals.

Light heavyweight champ Roy Jones Jr. "loses" his first professional fight after 34 consecutive victories when he is disqualified in the ninth round of his title match with challenger Montell Griffin. Jones nails Griffin with two shots after Griffin drops to one knee, forcing the DQ.

22 **Fourteen year old Tara Lipinski** becomes the youngest women's figure skating world champion, edging teammate Michelle Kwan for the title. It is the fifth time in history and first since 1992 that Americans finish 1-2 in the standings.

23 **Final four is set** as No. 4 seed Arizona's 96-92 overtime win over Providence puts them in the big dance with No. 1 seeds Kentucky, North Carolina and Minnesota.

24 **Tennessee Lady Vols beat UConn** 91-81 for the Huskies' only loss of the year. The win vaults Tennessee into its 10th Final Four in the past 17 years, joining Stanford, Old Dominion and Notre Dame.

Nets' coach John Calipari apologizes to beat writer Dan Garcia after calling him a "Mexican idiot" while arguing after a practice. He is later fined $25,000 by the NBA.

25 **Cleveland Indians and Atlanta Braves** conduct the blockbuster trade of the year with the Indians shipping all-star speedster Kenny Lofton and reliever Alan Embree to the Braves for outfielders Dave Justice and Marquis Grissom.

26 **Hartford Whalers' owner** Peter Karmanos announces he will pay $20.5 million to get out of his lease at the Hartford Civic Center and move his team out of Connecticut before the 1997-98 season.

Colorado Avalanche and Detroit Red Wings engage in a heated bloodbath that includes 148 minutes in penalties. Goalies Patrick Roy and Mike Vernon square off and the Red Wings' Darren McCarty slams nemesis Claude Lemieux's head into the boards in retaliation for last year's illegal hit on Kris Draper. On a side note, the Red Wings win 6-5 in overtime.

28 **Michigan senior Brendan Morrison** wins the Hobey Baker Award as the nation's top college hockey player.

29 **North Dakota scores** five goals in the second period to come from behind and beat Boston University 6-4 for their sixth NCAA Division I college hockey championship.

30 **Pat Summitt's Lady Vols do it again,** beating Old Dominion 68-59 for their second consecutive NCAA Division I women's basketball title. All-American sophomore Chamique Holdsclaw leads Tennessee with 24 points.

Betsey King cards a 12-under-par 276 to win the Nabisco Dinah Shore by two strokes over runner-up Kris Tschetter. It is her third Dinah Shore championship and 31st victory of her stellar career.

31 **Arizona completes** their stunning tournament run by finishing off Kentucky 84-79 in overtime to win the NCAA Division I basketball championship.

APR '97

Sun	Mon	Tue	Wed	Thu	Fri	Sat
		1	2	3	4	5
6	7	8	9	10	11	12
13	14	15	16	17	18	19
20	21	22	23	24	25	26
27	28	29	30			

EN FUEGO NOT!

On April 6, the Dallas Mavericks broke an NBA record for fewest points in a quarter when they only tickled the twine twice in the third quarter against the Lakers. Derek Harper helped the team avoid the unspeakable when he hit two free throws with just 1:51 left in the quarter. Here's a look at the other low moments in NBA scoring history.

Bad as They Wanna Be

Points	Teams	Date
2	Mavericks at Lakers	**April 6, 1997**
4	Kings at Lakers	Feb. 4, 1987
4	Buffalo Braves at Bucks	Oct. 21, 1972

MAJOR MARGINS

Tiger Woods won the 1997 Masters by a record 12 strokes. That is the largest margin of victory at the Masters and the second largest in majors overall. Woods' achievement is striking because there have been 60 previous Masters, 78 previous PGAs and both the U.S. and British Opens began play in the previous century.

Margins of Victory

Shots	Winner	Major
13	Old Tom Morris	1862 British Open
12	**Tiger Woods**	**1997 Masters**
12	Young Tom Morris	1870 British
11	Willie Smith	1899 US Open
9	Jack Nicklaus	1965 Masters
9	James Barnes	1921 US Open

1 Former heavyweight champ Oliver McCall is ordered to seek help at a mental hospital after his wife obtained an emergency custody order against him and says he is a danger to himself and others.

Arizona Wildcats finish number one in the college basketball USA Today/CNN Coaches Poll with a 25–9 record. Rounding out the top five are Kentucky (35–5), Minnesota (31–4), North Carolina (28–7) and Kansas (34–2).

Dallas Stars center Mike Modano is named NHL Player of the Month for March after leading his team to a 8–0–2 record during the month.

2 A fatal accident involving world-class triathlete Judith Marie Flannery and a car driven by an unlicensed man takes the life of the 57–year-old former four-time world champion and six-time U.S. champion as she rode her bike in the Washington D.C. suburbs.

3 Phillies pitcher Curt Schilling inks a $15.4 million contract extension good through the year 2000.

4 Colorado point guard Chauncey Billups announces he will skip his final two college seasons and enter the NBA draft.

5 Larry Walker's three home runs lead the way for the Colorado Rockies who go on to blast a team record seven homers in a 15–3 victory at Montreal.

The Cincinnati Bengals welcome back Boomer Esiason, signing the quarterback to a two-year contract. Esiason, who led the team to the Super Bowl in 1989, will back up Jeff Blake.

6 Legendary owner Jack Kent Cooke dies of cardiac arrest at the age of 84 at George Washington Hospital in Washington D.C.

Martina Hingis shows the world why she's number one, defeating Monica Seles in her first tournament atop the WTA rankings. It's Hingis' sixth-straight tournament title and the 31st consecutive match she has won.

Mario Lemieux makes it official by confirming that he will retire at the conclusion of the hockey season.

8 Mike Tyson announces his fight with Evander Holyfield scheduled for May 3rd will be postponed because of a cut Tyson sustained over his left eye during training. The fight is rescheduled for June 28.

9 Indians reliever Jose Mesa is acquitted of charges of rape, gross sexual imposition and theft, stemming from a Dec. 22 incident at a Cleveland—area hotel. Mesa, however, still faces weapons charges.

The MLS says it will expand in 1998, welcoming new teams from Miami and Chicago. Miami will play its home games at the Orange Bowl while Chicago will call Soldier Field its home.

The NFL signs an agreement with the CFL which will provide the struggling Canadian Football League with $3 million and marketing assistance. In return, NFL teams will be allowed to sign CFL players after the conclusion of the Grey Cup championship game.

11 Boxer Vinny Pazienza is awarded $1.5 million from a federal jury in Providence, R.I. for the broken neck he suffered in a 1991 car crash which almost ended his career.

12 The Ottawa Senators secure the franchise's first-ever playoff birth with a 1–0 victory over Buffalo.

13 Tiger Woods tames the mighty Augusta National GC and makes sports history by winning the Masters by a record 12 strokes with a final-round 69. The 21–year-old fueled his already mythical status by setting six tournament records and tying another.

14 Triathlete Paula Newby Frasier races to victory at the Ironman Australia competition and becomes the

Wide World Photos

At the 1997 Masters **Tiger Woods** justified every word of hype ever laid on him. He dominated the world's best players at one of the world's most hallowed courses, winning by 12 strokes, the biggest margin of victory ever in the Masters and the most in any major since 1862.

first person to win 20 Ironman competitions. The 34–year–old's first victory was in 1986.

76ers rookie Allen Iverson sets a new rookie record with his fifth consecutive game with 40 or more points by scoring 40 in a 113–110 loss to Washington. Philadelphia has lost all five games during the streak.

15 The 50th Anniversary of Jackie Robinson's major-league debut with the Brooklyn Dodgers. To commemorate this event Robinson's #42 is officially retired from baseball.

19 Ohio St. junior lineman Orlando Pace is chosen first in the 62nd annual NFL Draft by the St. Louis Rams.

The NY Knicks squash the Bulls hopes of consecutive 70–victory seasons by defeating them 103–101. The Bulls would finish the regular season 69–13.

Tennis star Andre Agassi marries actress Brooke Shields in Monterey, Calif.

20 A 14–game losing streak ends for the Cubs when they defeat the Mets 4–3.

21 Fatuma Roba of Ethiopia wins the 101st Boston Marathon with a time of 2:26.23. Lameck Aguta won the women's division with a time of 2:10:34.

Golfer Fuzzy Zoeller apologizes to Tiger Woods for remarks he made about the reigning Masters' champion. Zoeller reportedly called Woods "a little boy" and urged him not to request "fried chicken or collard greens or whatever they serve" at next year's Champions Dinner.

Bruce Baumgartner, who has won the freestyle competition at the U.S. National Wrestling Championships every year since 1983, announces he will not compete this year.

22 The Yankees obtain the rights to Japanese pitcher Hideki Irabu and three minor league players from the San Diego Padres in exchange for two top prospects

and $3 million in cash.

A hat trick of upsets highlights the first round of the Monte Carlo Open as Pete Sampras, Thomas Muster and Boris Becker all bow out early.

Roberto Alomar shakes the hand of umpire John Hirschbeck prior to the Orioles-White Sox game at Camden Yards where the two meet for the first time since last October when Alomar was suspended for spitting in Hirschbeck's face after a called third strike.

23 Wayne Gretzky's ninth career playoff hat trick helps the Rangers defeat the Panthers 3–2 and jump out to a 3–1 lead in the first-round playoff series.

24 The Orlando Magic tie a NBA record by scoring just 64 points in its opening round loss to Miami.

25 Ken Griffey Jr. hits three homers and sets a major league record for home runs in April with 13.

26 Mario Lemieux skates off the ice for the last time as the Pittsburgh Penguins are eliminated from the playoffs by the Philadelphia Flyers.

Heavyweight George Foreman, 48, continues his comeback, garnering a 12–round decision over previously undefeated Lou Savarese in Atlantic City.

27 Former UConn star Kara Wolters signs a three-year contract with the New England Blizzard of the American Basketball League.

29 Michael Jordan pumps in 55 points as the Bulls defeat the Washington Bullets 109–104 in game two of their best-of-five game series.

An era of NHL hockey comes to an end when the last player to go without a helmet, St. Louis Blues' forward Craig McTavish, announces his retirement after 16 NHL seasons.

30 Heavyweight Riddick Bowe announces he will retire from boxing and join the HBO broadcasting crew.

MAY '97

Sun	Mon	Tue	Wed	Thu	Fri	Sat
				1	2	3
4	5	6	7	8	9	10
11	12	13	14	15	16	17
18	19	20	21	22	23	24
25	26	27	28	29	30	31

STARTLING STARTS

On May 26, Toronto Blue Jays ace Roger Clemens raised his season record to 9-0 with a 8-1 Toronto win over Texas. He would go on to an 11-0 start before finally losing to the Seattle Mariners, 5-1, on June 11. In 1986, when Clemens played for the Boston Red Sox, he started the year 14-0 and went on to win the American League Cy Young and MVP awards with a final mark of 24-4. Major league pitchers with the most consecutive wins to start a season:

Player, team (year)	Start	Final record
Rube Marquard, N.Y. Giants (1912)	19-0	26-11
Roy Face, Pirates (1959)	17-0	18-1
Johnny Allen, Indians (1937)	15-0	15-1
Dave McNally, Orioles (1969)	15-0	20-7
Roger Clemens, Red Sox (1986)	14-0	24-4
Joe McGinnity, N.Y. Giants (1904)	14-0	35-8

LONG TIME COMING

Utah Jazz point guard John Stockton entered the 1997 NBA playoffs with 107 postseason games under his belt. By the time his Jazz were eliminated in six games by the Chicago Bulls he had played in 20 more and still has yet to capture his first NBA title. Players with the most career playoff games without winning a championship:

	Games
Elgin Baylor	134
John Stockton	127
Caldwell Jones	119
Charles Oakley	119
Sam Perkins	118
Charles Barkley	115

NOT FAVORED

Kentucky Derby favorite Captain Bodgit continued a recent trend, failing to win the 123rd Run For the Roses. He placed second. Lately, favorites have not fared especially well. The last to win the derby was Spectacular Bid in 1979. Since then only five, including Captain Bodgit, have finished in the money. Below is the all-time record for betting favorites in the Kentucky Derby:

Win	48
Place	26
Show	9
Other	39

1 Allen Iverson wins the NBA Rookie of the Year award after leading all rookies in scoring with 23.5 points a game. Iverson is the first Philadelphia player to win the award since Wilt Chamberlain in 1960.

Sabres goalie Dominik Hasek is suspended for the first three games of the playoffs and is fined $10,000 for attacking Buffalo News reporter Jim Kelley.

2 Shoulder problems force 1991 Wimbledon champion Michael Stich to call it quits at the end of the tennis season.

3 Silver Charm holds off 4–1 favorite Captain Bodgit to take the 123rd Kentucky Derby.

4 Mark Martin finally ends a 42–race drought by speeding to victory at the Save Mart 300 in Sonoma, Calif. Martin's last Winston Cup victory came in October 1995.

A screaming line drive hit by the Indians' Julio Franco clocked at 107 mph strikes Detroit pitcher Willie Blair in the face, breaking his jaw.

5 Larry Brown is named head coach of the Philadelphia 76ers and signs a 5–year $5 million contract.

Former UCLA basketball coach Jim Harrick who was fired for lying to cover up a recruiting violation was named head coach at the University of Rhode Island, signing a $250,000 contract.

6 Kentucky's Rick Pitino accepts the job to coach the Boston Celtics for a reported $70 million over 10 years.

The Hartford Whalers announce they will move to North Carolina and become the Carolina Hurricanes in time for the next NHL season. The team says it will play in Greensboro, N.C. for two years before moving to its permanent home in Raleigh.

7 Denny McLain, the last major league pitcher to win 30 games in a season, is sentenced to eight years in prison and ordered to pay $2.5 million for stealing from the pension plan of a company that went bankrupt 18 months after he bought it.

8 Larry Bird returns to his nesting ground. The former Indiana St. star accepts his first NBA head coaching assignment with the Indiana Pacers.

Toronto Raptors forward Marcus Camby says he intends to pay back the $151,617 the University of Massachusetts was ordered to return by the NCAA Executive Committee for allowing Camby to play despite his dealings with sports agents.

Free agent receiver Eric Metcalf signs a one-year deal with the San Diego Chargers.

11 The Boston Bruins, who failed to make the playoffs for the first time in 30 years, win the NHL Draft Lottery and will pick first in this year's draft.

12 NBA Hall of Famer K.C. Jones is picked to coach the New England Blizzard of the American Basketball League.

Tubby Smith is named as a replacement for Rick Pitino at Kentucky. The former Georgia coach had once been an assistant for the Wildcats.

13 George Steinbrenner is tossed off baseball's executive council by a unanimous vote because of his lawsuit against baseball which covers the Yankees 10–year, $95 million deal with adidas.

15 The NBA suspends five NY Knicks for one game and one Miami Heat player for two games for their actions in a brawl that interrupted game five of the Eastern Conference Semifinals.

Wide World Photos

New Boston Celtics head coach and president **Rick Pitino** is all smiles at the press conference that announced his affiliation with the team. The Celtics laid some serious green on Pitino, a reported $70 million over ten years.

Groundbreaking for the future home of the Cleveland Browns begins. The NFL has guaranteed the Browns will return to the city in 1999.

17 Silver Charm staves off Captain Bodgit again, this time in the Preakness, to capture the second title in the prestigious triple crown.

18 The San Antonio Spurs win the NBA Draft Lottery and will pick first overall on June 25.

Karl Malone is named the NBA's most valuable player, beating out Michael Jordan in the second-closest voting ever 986–957.

Maryland's women's lacrosse team wins its third consecutive Div. 1 title, while last year's Div. 2 champion College of New Jersey sees its 102–game victory streak halted by Middlebury, 14–9.

Tony Phillips returns to the Anaheim Angels by way of a four player deal with the Chicago White Sox.

20 Marv Albert, one of America's most recognized sports broadcasters, is indicted on sodomy and assault charges after a 42–year–old Virgina woman accuses him of forcing her to perform oral sex on Feb. 12 in his hotel room.

The NL suspends Reds manager Ray Knight and fines him $1,000 for his antics during a 6–2 loss to San Diego on May 17 when Knight kicked dirt on, and then removed and threw third base. It's the first discipline levied against a major league manager in two years.

21 Roger Clemens (8–0) captures his 200th career pitching victory, striking out 12 in a 4–1 triumph over the Yankees.

22 Tom Glavine becomes the highest-paid pitcher in baseball, agreeing to a four-year, $34 million contract extension with the Atlanta Braves.

Bryan Cox fires back at the NFL, filing a lawsuit against the league and its commissioner in retaliation for the $850,000 fine levied against the Bears linebacker for making an obscene gesture at an official.

25 The Philadelphia Flyers beat the NY Rangers 4–2 and advance to the NHL Finals.

27 Arie Luyendyk wins his second Indianapolis 500 after the race had been postponed two days due to heavy rain.

29 Utah guard John Stockton swishes a three-pointer as time expires, lifting the Jazz past Houston 103–100 in the Western Conference finals and into the NBA Finals for the first time in franchise history.

The NY Yankees think they have finally gotten their man and sign Japanese pitcher Hideki Irabu to a four-year deal worth $12.8 million and a signing bonus of $8.5 million.

30 Hall of Fame goalie Ken Dryden is named president of the Toronto Maple Leafs.

31 Ethiopia's Haile Gabrselassie sets a new world record in the two mile with a time of 8:01.08.

JUNE '97

Sun	Mon	Tue	Wed	Thu	Fri	Sat
1	2	3	4	5	6	7
8	9	10	11	12	13	14
15	16	17	18	19	20	21
22	23	24	25	26	27	28
29	30					

Team-by-team no-nos

June 10—Marlins' ace Kevin Brown throws the first no-hitter of the 1997 season and the second in the team's five-year history. Pretty impressive when you consider the Tigers have just five in their 97-year history and the Mets (born in 1962) are still awaiting their first. Below is the number of no-hitters for each major league team, the year in which the last one occurred and the pitcher that threw it. (nine innings or more)

American League	No.	Last	Pitcher
Chicago White Sox	15	1991	Wilson Alvarez
Cleveland Indians	14	1981	Len Barker
Boston Red Sox	14	1965	Dave Morehead
NY Yankees	10	1996	Dwight Gooden
Oakland A's	10	1990	Dave Stewart
Baltimore Orioles	9	1991	Milacki-Flanagan-Williamson-Olson
Anaheim Angels	8	1990	Langston-Witt
Minnesota Twins	5	1994	Scott Erickson
Texas Rangers	5	1994	Kenny Rogers
Detroit Tigers	5	1984	Jack Morris
Kansas City Royals	4	1991	Bret Saberhagen
Seattle Mariners	2	1993	Chris Bosio
Toronto Blue Jays	1	1990	Dave Steib
Milwaukee Brewers	1	1987	Juan Nieves

National League	No.	Last	Pitcher
LA Dodgers	20	1996	Hideo Nomo
Cincinnati Reds	14	1988	Tom Browning
Chicago Cubs	12	1972	Milt Pappas
Atlanta Braves	12	1994	Kent Mercker
SF Giants	12	1976	John Montefusco
Houston Astros	9	1993	Darryl Kile
Philadelphia Phillies	8	1991	Tommy Greene
St. Louis Cardinals	7	1983	Bob Forsch
Pittsburgh Pirates	6	1997	Cordova-Rincon
Montreal Expos	4	1991	Dennis Martinez
Florida Marlins	2	1997	Kevin Brown
Colorado Rockies	0	—	—
San Diego Padres	0	—	—
NY Mets	0	—	—

Note: Figures include all stats from previous teams or locations. For example, LA Dodgers' totals include their time in Brooklyn and Minnesota Twins' totals include old Washington Senators' numbers.

1 Donovan Bailey races to victory against Michael Johnson in the much anticipated 150–meter race to decide who is the world's fastest man. Bailey finishes in 14.99 seconds while Johnson pulls up lame with a left thigh injury.

Chris Humbert scores three goals to help USA defeat Greece 8–5 to win the Water Polo World Cup at Athens.

Race car driver Ricky Rudd wins his first race of the Winston Cup season. Rudd's victory at the Miller 500 is the 18th of his career and means he has won at least one race in each of the last 15 seasons.

Michael Jordan's jump shot at the buzzer, which followed two missed free-throws by Karl Malone, gives the Bulls an 84–82 victory and a 1–0 lead in the NBA Finals.

3 Former Detroit Piston and Olympic Dream Team coach Chuck Daly accepts the head coaching job at Orlando.

4 Former All-Pro linebacker Lawrence Taylor pleads guilty to the charge that he filed a false income tax return in 1990. Taylor faces up to three years in prison and a $100,000 fine.

5 Seattle SS Alex Rodriguez becomes the first Mariner to hit for the cycle in a nine-inning game. Teammate Jay Buhner hit for the cycle in a 14–inning affair in 1993.

7 The Detroit Red Wings end a 42–year dry spell by capturing the Stanley Cup with a 2–1 defeat of the Philadelphia Flyers.

LSU wins the College World Series for the fourth time this decade by defeating Alabama 13–6.

8 Twenty-year-old Brazilian Gustavo Kuerten, ranked number 66 in the world, beats two-time champ Sergi Bruguera 6–3,6–4,6–2 to capture the French Open. Kuerten is the lowest-ranked player ever to win a grand slam event.

10 Florida Marlins pitcher Kevin Brown throws the first no-hitter of the season, defeating the Giants 9–0.

11 In perhaps the "guttiest "performance of his career, Michael Jordan scores 15 of his game-high 38 points in the fourth quarter of the Bulls' 90–88 Game 5 victory over the Jazz despite suffering from nausea and dehydration due to a viral infection.

Roger Clemens's bid for a Blue Jays record for consecutive victories ends one short at 11 thanks to a 5–1 loss to the Mariners.

Red Sox outfielder Wilfredo Cordero is charged with assault and battery with a deadly weapon and threatening to commit a crime after an argument with his wife.

12 In the first regular season interleague game in MLB history, the San Francisco Giants defeat the Texas Rangers 4–3.

13 A serious limousine accident leaves Detroit Red Wings players Vladimir Konstantinov and Viachslav Fetisov, as well as a team masseur with serious injuries.

14 Oscar De La Hoya ups his professional record to 25–0 after needing less than two rounds to defeat challenger David Kamau.

15 South African golfer Ernie Els wins his second U.S. Open championship in four years.

Victory erases tragedy as NASCAR driver Ernie Irvan races to victory in the Miller 400 at Michigan Speedway in Brooklyn where Irvan almost lost his life in 1994 after sustaining massive head injuries in a crash during a practice session.

16 Tiger Woods knocks Greg Norman from the top spot in the world rankings and becomes the youngest golfer ever to hold that position.

Wide World Photos

Brazil's **Gustavo Kuerten** holds the trophy he won after defeating Spaniard Sergei Bruguera in the final of the 1997 French Open. The 21–year-old Kuerten, at 66th in the world, is the lowest-ranked player ever to win a grand slam tournament.

The NHL announces it has recommended expansion franchises in Nashville, Tenn., in 1998; Atlanta, Ga. in 1999; and St. Paul, Minn. and Columbus, Ohio in 2000.

17 Art Monk officially announces his retirement from the NFL after 16 seasons as a wide receiver.

18 The NHRA suspends driver Jerry Eckman and car owner Bill Orndorff for at least two years and fined them $25,000 for using nitrous oxide, a banned and volatile fuel additive.

Dominik Hasek wins the Hart Trophy as the NHL's most valuable player, becoming the first goalie to win the award since Jacques Plante in 1962. Hasek also takes home his third Vezina Trophy.

High school basketball player Tracy McGrady signs an endorsement deal with adidas for $12 million over six years.

20 Andre Agassi says he will miss his second-straight grand slam event, Wimbledon, because of an injured wrist.

21 Joe Thornton is selected number one overall by the Boston Bruins at the NHL draft.

The WNBA tips off its inaugural season as the NY Liberty beat the LA Sparks 67–57 in front of 14,284 fans.

22 Ernie Els successfully defends his title in the Buick Classic by two strokes, firing a 16–under-par 268.

Jeff Gordon has enough gas to win the first-ever California 500 at California Speedway, but not enough to get him to the winner's circle where he's supposed to pick up his trophy.

The Barcelona Dragons win their first World Bowl title by defeating the Rhein Fire 38–24 the WLAF championship.

24 Mariners left-hander Randy Johnson strikes out 19 Oakland A's, one short of the major league record. Seattle, however, loses the game 4–1.

Figure skater Scott Hamilton undergoes four hours of successful surgery to treat testicular cancer.

25 Tim Duncan is selected first overall in the NBA draft by the San Antonio Spurs. The former Wake Forest center will join an already talented frontcourt that includes David Robinson and Sean Elliot.

Chicago Blackhawk Denis Savard announces his retirement after scoring more than 1,300 points.

Track star Michael Johnson has his eight-year, 58–race victory streak snapped when he finishes fourth in Paris.

26 Brian Hill, fired as coach of the Orlando Magic Feb. 18, is named head coach of the Vancouver Grizzlies.

27 The Baltimore Orioles obtain outfielder Geronimo Berroa from the Oakland A's in exchange for pitcher Jimmy Haynes and a player to be named later.

28 Mike Tyson bites Evander Holyfield in the ear during round three of their world heavyweight match. Despite a warning from referee Mills Lane, Tyson then bites Holyfield's other ear in retaliation of what Tyson called an intentional headbutt by Holyfield. Tyson is disqualified and Holyfield retains his WBA heavyweight belt.

JULY '97

Sun	Mon	Tue	Wed	Thu	Fri	Sat
		1	2	3	4	5
6	7	8	9	10	11	12
13	14	15	16	17	18	19
20	21	22	23	24	25	26
27	28	29	30			

THE TEXAS TORNADO

Golfing legend Ben Hogan passed away on July 25, 1997. Hogan turned pro in 1929 and won his first tournament at the Hershey Four-Ball in 1938. He won 63 tournaments in his career including all of the majors; 2 PGAs, 4 U.S. Opens, 2 Masters and 1 British Open. He survived a near-fatal car crash on February 2, 1949. He won six of his majors after the crash which severely limited the number of tournaments he entered each year. Hogan's last career victory was at the 1959 Colonial Invitational and his last pro tournament was at the same event in 1971. The following chart indicates Hogan's stature as one of the all-time greats.

Heavy Hitters

Player	Career wins	Majors
Sam Snead	81	6
Jack Nicklaus	70	18
Ben Hogan	**63**	**9**
Arnold Palmer	60	7

SHULA'S WAY

Don Shula, who won 347 games as a coach in the NFL for the Baltimore Colts and Miami Dolphins, was inducted into the Pro Football Hall of Fame on July 26, 1997. Shula coached in six Super Bowls and won two. The following chart indicates Shula's remarkable consistency as a winner.

Shula by the Decade

	Record	Win %
1960's	71-23-4	.745
1970's	104-39-1	.726
1980's	94-57-1	.622
1990's	59-37	.614

1 Former San Antonio Spurs President Jack Diller is named president of Nashville's NHL expansion franchise.

2 NY Knicks center Patrick Ewing agrees with the team on a four-year deal one day after becoming a free agent.

Goalie Ed Belfour signs a three-year, $10 million contract with the Dallas Stars.

3 After losing to Pete Sampras at Wimbledon, Boris Becker announces it will be his last year playing in the event.

5 Martina Hingis becomes the youngest Wimbledon champion of the century by defeating Jana Novotna in the finals.

LA Lakers backup center Travis Knight signs a seven-year contract with the Boston Celtics worth $22 million.

6 Pete Sampras wraps up his fourth Wimbledon singles championship with a victory over Cedric Pioline, 6–4, 6–2, 6–4.

7 Denmark's Wilson Kipketer ties track and field's oldest record by finishing the 800–meter run in 1:41.73. Sebastian Coe set the record in 1981.

8 Sandy Alomar Jr. hits a seventh-inning two-run home run to help give the AL a 3–1 victory in baseball's All Star Game. Alomar, playing in front of his home crowd at Jacob's field in Cleveland takes home the MVP for his efforts.

9 Brian McBride's blast with less than two minutes left gives the Eastern Conference a 5–4 victory in the MLS All-Star game.

The Nevada Athletic Commission hands down its decision regarding the Tyson-Holyfield fight. The commission revokes Tyson's boxing license and takes 10 percent of his $30 million purse.

10 Hideki Irabu impresses as the Yankees' high-priced import makes his first start, striking out nine in a 10–3 victory at Yankee Stadium.

Redskins running back Terry Allen is arrested and charged with driving under the influence and speeding after police say Allen was driving up to 133 mph and hit a tree.

12 Toronto pitcher Roger Clemens returns to Fenway Park for the first time as a visitor, dazzling his former teammates with a 16–strikeout performance en route to his 14th victory of the season.

Pirate pitchers Francisco Cordova and Ricardo Rincon combine for a 10–inning no hitter against the Houston Astros. Pittsburgh won the game on a three-run homer by Mark Smith in the 10th.

13 Alison Nicholas wins the U.S. Open by carding a 10–under-par 274, the lowest winning score in the tournament's 52–year history.

Cuba calls off a tour by their national baseball team because officials fear many players may try to defect.

14 A tragedy mars the opening of the Maccabiah Games, an Olympic-style event in Tel Aviv, Israel, as two Australian athletes are killed and dozens more injured when a bridge to the stadium collapses.

Iowa wrestling coach Dan Gable announces he will take a year off from coaching which could become permanent. Gable has coached the Hawkeyes to 15 national championships.

15 A pair of Cowboys decide to ride off into the sunset. Defensive end Charles Haley and tight end Jay Novacek, who own a total of eight Super Bowl rings, announce their retirements.

Baseball's all-time save leader Lee Smith says he's calling it quits after amassing 478 saves for eight different teams over 18 seasons.

Baltimore's **Roberto Alomar** (c) yuks it up at the always hilarious American League All-Star team photo session in Cleveland. Randy Johnson is reported to have made a wickedly funny "height" joke.

16 **Kevin Brown just misses** his second no-hitter of the season by allowing one hit in a 5–1 victory over the Dodgers.

17 **Andy Moog**, the NHL's winningest active goalie signs a two-year contract with the Montreal Canadians.

19 **Daniel Komen** becomes the first person to break the eight-minute barrier, racing to a time of 7:58.61, in the 2-mile.

20 **Justin Leonard shoots** a 6-under-par 65, including six birdies on the first nine holes, giving the 25-year-old his first British Open title.

Detroit running back Barry Sanders becomes the NFL's highest paid player, signing a five-year contract with an option for a sixth that will pay him more than $34 million.

Dale Jarrett won his third Winston Cup race of the year, capturing the checkered flag at the Pennsylvania 500.

21 **The Philadelphia Phillies** trade Darren Daulton, who spent 17 years in the Phillies organization to the Marlins for a minor leaguer.

22 **Defensive end Darrell Russell** becomes the richest rookie in NFL history when the Oakland Raiders sign the second overall selection in the draft to a $22.05 million contract.

23 **Phil Jackson and the Chicago Bulls** come to an agreement on a one-year contract that will pay him $5.7 million. It's the most lucrative contract ever for a coach who does not also share GM duties.

Dallas businessman John Spano is arrested in Uniondale, N.Y. on bank and wire fraud charges stemming from his failed attempts to buy the NHL's NY Islanders.

25 **Golfing legend Ben Hogan** dies at the age of 84 from complications of cancer and Alzheimer's in Ft. Worth, Texas.

League MVP Brett Favre signs a seven-year deal worth up to $48 million. Just for signing the contract the Packers quarterback will receive a $12 million bonus.

The Cincinnati Reds fire manager Ray Knight.

26 **Don Shula**, Mike Haynes, Mike Webster and Wellington Mara are inducted into professional football's hall of fame in Canton, Ohio.

The Green Bay Packers lose running back Edgar Bennett for the season after he tears his Achilles tendon in the team's first exhibition game.

28 **Hideki Irabu is sent** to the minor leagues after garnering a 7.97 ERA and a record of 2–2 with the NY Yankees.

Mark Messier inks a three-year deal with the Vancouver Canucks that could pay him up to $20 million.

Jacksonville quarterback Mark Brunell re-signs with the team for $30 million, including a $10 million signing bonus.

29 **Tom Welch resigns** as head of the Salt Lake Organizing Committee because of battery charges filled against him by his wife.

30 **Steve Young ends** Brett Favre's five-day reign as the league's highest-paid player by signing a contract extension with the San Francisco 49ers worth $45 million.

NBA referee Jess Kersey resigns after pleading guilty in court to filing a false income tax report.

AUG '97

Sun	Mon	Tue	Wed	Thu	Fri	Sat
					1	2
3	4	5	6	7	8	9
10	11	12	13	14	15	16
17	18	19	20	21	22	23
24/31	25	26	27	28	29	30

LEAVING HIS **MARK**

Mark Messier is bringing a tremendous track record to the Vancouver Canucks, with whom he signed a free agent contract in late July. Messier brings 6 Stanley Cup rings with him and he is the only man to captain two Cup winners. He is making the big dollars but his playoffs numbers in goals and assists show that he is truly a money player.

Messier by the Numbers

		All-time rank
Playoff goals	109	2nd
Playoff assists	295	2nd
Career points	1,552	5th
Assists	977	6th
Goals	575	10th

CHIEF AMONG US

Robert Parish retired on August 25, 1997. The sure Hall of Famer played 21 years in the NBA, making his mark in 14 stellar seasons with the Boston Celtics, with whom he won three NBA championships.

The Parish Record

		All-Time Rank
Seasons	21	1st
Games	1,611	1st
Blocked shots	2,361	6th
Rebounds	14,715	6th
Points	23,334	12th

1 **All-Pro defensive end Bruce Smith** ends his 21–day holdout after announcing he will play out the final year of his contract with the Buffalo Bills worth $2.2 million.

2 **Ricky Rudd beats Bobby Labonte** in a three-lap dash to win NASCAR's Brickyard 400 at the Indianapolis Speedway.

3 **Tommy Lasorda**, Phil Niekro, Nellie Fox and Willie Wells are inducted into baseball's hall of fame in Cooperstown, Ohio.

NBA Rookie of the Year Allen Iverson is arrested in Virginia for drug and firearms possession. Iverson was in the passenger's seat of a car police say was traveling 93 mph in a 65 mph zone.

U.S. sprinters Marion Jones (10.83) and Maurice Greene (9.86) dash to victory in the women's and men's 100 respectively at the World Track and Field Championships.

4 **Cowboys head coach Barry Switzer** is arrested when officials at the Dallas-Ft. Worth International Airport find a loaded revolver in his carry-on baggage.

Minnesota Twins pitcher Brad Radke ties a club record by wining his 12th straight game.

Joe Thornton, the first player selected in this year's NHL draft, agrees to a three-year deal with the Boston Bruins.

5 **Track star Michael Johnson wins** his seventh World Track and Field Championship gold medal, finishing the 400 in a time of 44.12.

6 **A visibly upset Jerry Jones** fines Barry Switzer $75,000 for his arrest on gun charges two days earlier. It is the largest fine ever dished out to an NFL coach.

7 **Roy Jones Jr. reclaims** the WBC light-heavyweight title from Montell Griffin by knocking Griffin out at the 2:31 mark in the first round. Jones lost the title to Griffin in March after being disqualified for hitting Griffin while he was down on one knee.

8 **Gearing up for a playoff run**, the NY Mets acquire closer Mel Rojas, reliever Turk Wendell and outfielder Brian McRae from Chicago in exchange for outfielder Lance Johnson and two players to be named later.

9 **Malvern Burroughs becomes** only the second amateur driver in 72 years to win the Hambletonian when he guides Malabar Man to a one-lengh victory in East Rutherford, N.J.

10 **Braves pitcher Greg Maddux** becomes the league's highest-paid player when he signs a five-year, $57.5 million contract. The new extension means that Atlanta has its starting rotation of Maddux, Tom Glavine, John Smoltz and Denny Neagle signed through 2000 for $140 million.

Dana Quigley who made the field at the Senior PGA Tour Northville Classic as a Monday qualifier, made a 2½–foot par putt on the third playoff hole, giving the 50–year-old his first professional tournament victory. Quigley's jubilation was tempered however by the news his father, Wallace, had died of cancer only hours earlier.

12 **Timberwolves forward** Kevin Garnett, 21, rejects a six-year, $103 million dollar contract offer from the team.

13 **The Colorado Avalanche choose** to match the three-year $21 million deal offered to its star center Joe Sakic by the NY Rangers.

Denver linebacker Bill Romanowski is fined

Wide World Photos

Atlanta Braves pitcher **Greg Maddux** signed a five-year, $57.5 million contract that made him the highest paid player in the National League.

$20,000 by the NFL for a hit on Carolina's Kerry Collins that broke the quarterback's jaw.

15 Offensive lineman Orlando Pace, the number one pick overall in the NFL Draft, agrees to terms with the St. Louis Rams.

16 Oakland Raiders linebacker Pat Swilling announces his retirement.

18 Fred Couples and Lee Janzen nab spots on the 1997 U.S. Ryder Cup team captained by Tom Kite.

Tony Phillips is suspended indefinitely by the Anaheim Angels after he refuses to go on the disabled list and enter a rehabilitation program following his being charged with felony cocaine possession.

19 Redskins receiver Michael Westbrook attacks teammate Stephen Davis at a Washington practice. Westbrook and other teammates appeared to be involved in light conversation before Westbrook began pummeling Davis with his fists until (and after) he was face down on the ground.

20 Michelle Smith of Ireland, swimming under her married name — Michelle de Bruin, wins her second gold medal at the European Swimming Championships, following up a victory in the 200–meter freestyle with a win in the 400–meter individual medley.

A unique deal involving free agent Chris Gratton allows Tampa Bay to acquire Mikael Renberg and Karl Dykhuis from Philadelphia after Tampa sends the four compensatory picks they received for not matching Philly's offer sheet back to the Flyers in exchange for the two players.

21 In a dramatic return to the water, Russia's Aleksandr Popov wins a gold medal in the 100–meter freestyle at the European Swimming Championships. It was Popov's first race since being stabbed and seriously wounded by a watermelon vendor in his home country.

23 Mission Viejo, Calif. fails to hold on to a 4–1 lead over a team from Guadalupe, Mexico allowing four runs in the final inning and loses 5–4 at the Little League World Series in Williamsport, Pa.

College football returns for the 1997 season as Northwestern blanks Oklahoma 24–0 in the Pigskin Classic.

24 The Carolina Panthers cut veteran linebacker Kevin Greene who led the league in sacks last season but refused to show up at training camp under his current contract.

Kenyans continue to break track and field records at the Cologne Grand Prix meet in Germany. Wilson Kipketer and Bernard Barmasai set records in the 800 and the 3,000–meter steeplechase respectively, just two days after records were broken in the 5,000 and 10,000 events.

25 Veteran center Robert Parish announces his retirement from professional basketball after playing in more NBA games than any other player in basketball history and garnering four championship rings along the way.

26 Kevin Greene signs a six-year deal worth $13 million with Carolina's new division rival the San Francisco 49ers.

Carl Lewis ends his track and field career with a victory in his final race, running the anchor leg of the 400–meter relay which the U.S. captures with a time of 38.24.

Michael Jordan signs a $36 million contract to play the 1997–98 season with the Chicago Bulls.

30 Cynthia Cooper scores 25 points, helping the Houston Comets win the first WNBA Championship Game by defeating the New York Liberty, 65–51, before a sellout crowd at the Summit.

SEPT '97

Sun	Mon	Tue	Wed	Thu	Fri	Sat
	1	2	3	4	5	6
7	8	9	10	11	12	13
14	15	16	17	18	19	20
21	22	23	24	25	26	27
28	29	30				

LIKE **FATHER,** LIKE **SON**

When Pete Rose Jr. slapped a single on September 1, he and his dad shot to number two on the all-time list of hits by father/son combos. That is the most unbalanced pair and, as of September 1997, the Bonds, were the most equitable pair, with Bobby having 1,886 and Barry at 1,728. Hank Williams and Hank Jr. also had a lot of hits but that's another list.

A Family Tradition

	Hits
Gus and Buddy Bell	4,337
Pete and Pete Rose	4,257
Bobby and Barry Bonds	3,614
George and Dick Sisler	3,532
Ken and Ken Griffey	3,351

LITTLE **BIG RED MACHINE**

For another look at generational baseball stats, we wondered how the children of some of those great Reds teams of the 1970s were doing. Pedro Borbon Jr. didn't play in 1997 due to injury and Ed Sprague Sr. was too marginal a player for the Reds or we would have included his son's stats with the Blue Jays this year. Here's how they looked on September 1.

The Kids Are Alright

Stats on September 1, 1997

Ken Griffey Jr.	.306 BA, 44 HR
Eduardo Perez	.280 BA, 14 HR
Brian McRae	.241 BA, 15 SB
Pete Rose Jr.	1 for 3 with a walk

1 **Petr Korda, seeded 15th, stuns** No. 1 seed Pete Sampras at the U.S. Open, defeating the defending champion in five sets.

Pete Rose Jr. records his first major-league hit when he singles during his second at-bat for the Cincinnati Reds as his father watches from the stands.

2 **Irina Spirlea upsets** Monica Seles and advances to the semifinals of the U.S. Open where she will face Venus Williams.

3 **WBA Champion Evander Holyfield announces** he will fight IBF Champion Michael Moorer on Nov. 8.

Hockey legend Gordie Howe says he will attempt to become the only player to play professionally in six separate decades and plans to skate with the Detroit Vipers in their home opener Oct. 3.

5 **The International Olympic Committee** bestows Athens with the duty of hosting the 2004 Summer Games. Athens edges out Rome for the opportunity to host the games for first time since 1896.

6 **The U.S. captures three gold medals** in the single sculls, men's pairs with coxswain and the open sculls events at the World Rowing Championships in Cambery, France.

7 **Patrick Rafter becomes the first Australian man** in 24 years to win the U.S. Open, defeating Greg Rusedski in the finals, 6–3, 6–2, 4–6, 7–5.

Martina Hingis holds off Venus Williams in the U.S. Open womens' final, to earn her her third grand-slam victory of the year.

9 **The NHL announces** they will waive the three-year waiting period to induct Mario Lemieux into the Hall of Fame this year. Other inductees include, Bryan Trottier and Glen Sather.

Hall of Famer and Philadelphia icon Richie Ashburn, who spent 35 years in broadcasting after his baseball career ended, dies at the age of 70 of a heart attack.

10 **St. Louis' Mark McGwire** becomes the first baseball player since Babe Ruth (1927-28) to hit 50 or more home runs in back to back seasons after he smashes his 50th of the year in a 7-6 loss to the Giants.

13 **Oscar De La Hoya defeats** Hector "Macho" Camacho in a 12–round decision.

14 **The Washington Redskins need overtime** to defeat the Arizona Cardinals 19–13 in the first game played in Jack Kent Cooke Stadium.

15 **The NHL decides** to tinker with its annual All-Star Game, changing the teams to the North American All-Stars vs. the World All-Stars.

16 **Philadelphia pitcher Curt Schilling notches** his 300th strikeout of the season during a 3–2 complete-game victory over the NY Mets.

Nikki McCray, MVP of the American Basketball League signs with the WNBA — the ABL's rival league.

17 **The Atlanta Braves become** the first team in baseball history to clinch six straight playoff appearances, securing the honor with a 10-2 victory over the NY Mets.

20 **No. 3 Florida continues** its dominance over Tennessee, beating the Vols 33–20, highlighting a weekend in college football that sees three top 10 teams including Washington (#2) and Auburn (#10) lose games.

21 **Pete Sampras leads the US to a 4–1 victory** over Australia in Davis Cup semifinal-round action. On Nov. 28–30, the US will face Sweeden in the finals.

Only 17,737 "fans" show up to the 62,320-seat Liberty Bowl in Memphis, Tenn. to watch the Oilers lose

Wide World Photos

Sportscaster **Marv Albert** and his fiance **Heather Falkiner** briefly address the media at the end of his forcible sodomy trial in Virginia. On September 25, Albert ended the proceedings by pleading guilty to a lesser charge of misdemeanor assault and battery.

to the Baltimore Ravens 36–10.

The Buffalo Bills use the second-biggest comeback in NFL history to defeat the Colts 37–35. The Bills trailed by 26 points before stampeding over the Colts.

22 Jacksonville QB Mark Brunell returns from torn knee ligaments to lead the Jaguars to a 30-21 Monday night victory over Pittsburgh. It is the Jag's third consecutive victory under three different quarterbacks.

23 Injured Spanish golfer Miguel Angel Martin is reinstated to the European Ryder Cup team after threatening legal action. Martin had qualified for the squad but was unceremoniously thrown off due to an injured wrist.

24 Toronto Blue Jays fire their veteran skipper Cito Gaston with five games remaining in the season. Gaston led the Blue Jays to a world championship in 1992 and 1993 but the team struggled this year under his command, going 72-85 despite the signing of Roger Clemens.

25 Marv Albert pleads guilty to a misdemeanor assault and battery charge, ending a painful and embarrassing trial that exposed the seemier side of the legendary sportscaster. The guilty plea prompts prosecutors to drop the more serious charge of forcible sodomy but also prompts NBC to fire Albert.

Seattle Super Sonics deal whiny superstar Shawn Kemp to the Cleveland Cavaliers in a three-team bonanza that has the Sonics getting forward Vin Baker and Sherman Douglas from Milwaukee and the Bucks getting Terrell Brandon and Tyrone Hill from the Cavs.

26 United States and Europe tie 3-3 in opening day Ryder Cup action in Valderrama, Spain which also saw a 1 hour and 40 minute rain delay.

All-time hits leader Pete Rose applies for reinstatement to baseball in an attempt to end the lifetime ban that currently keeps him out of the Hall of Fame.

27 Europe takes a commanding 9–4 lead in the Ryder Cup amidst more delays due to terrential rain storms.

San Francisco Giants whip the San Diego Padres 6-1 to clinch their first National League West title since 1989. The Giants are the last division winner to clinch and will join Baltimore, Cleveland, Seattle, Atlanta, Houston and wildcard winners New York Yankees and Florida in the 1997 postseason.

Michigan beats Notre Dame 21-14, giving the Irish a 1-3 start to the season and a three-game losing streak for the first time in 12 years.

28 On the final day of baseball's regular season, Mark McGwire pounds homerun #58, three short of Roger Maris' coveted mark but equalling Jimmie Foxx and Hank Greenburg's record for homeruns by a right-handed batter. Ken Griffey Jr. ends the season with 56, the 7th-highest total in history.

USA scratches back but the Europeans take home their second consecutive Ryder Cup with a 14½–13½ win. Colin Montgomerie, Costantino Rocca and Bernhard Langer lead Europe with three wins each. PGA majors winners Tiger Woods (Masters) and Justin Leonard (British Open) finish a combined 1-5-3.

Pete Sampras crushes Australian Patrick Rafter 6-2, 6-4, 7-5 to win $2 million at the Grand Slam Cup in Munich, tennis' richest event.

30 Chicago White Sox fire manager Terry Bevington after an 80-81 season.

OCT '97

Sun	Mon	Tue	Wed	Thu	Fri	Sat
			1	2	3	4
5	6	7	8	9	10	11
12	13	14	15	16	17	18
19	20	21	22	23	24	25
26	27	28	29	30	31	

Prince **Albert** is the Man

In 1997, Albert Belle of the Chicago White Sox became only the fifth player in baseball history to hit 30 homeruns and knock in 100 runs in six consecutive seasons. Jimmie Foxx did it an amazing 12 years in a row. Hank Aaron did it from 1959–63 and missed this list by only 5 RBIs in 1958.

30 Homeruns/100 RBIs in consecutive seasons

	Number of seasons
Jimmie Foxx, 1929-40	12
Lou Gehrig, 1929-37	9
Babe Ruth, 1926-33	8
Willie Mays, 1961-66	6
Albert Belle, 1992-97	**6**

Put me in, coach!

For some reason, every year an observer of the baseball scene suggests that Cal Ripken Jr. of the Baltimore Orioles take a day off. Here is a guy who shows up every day, wanting only to perform the task he is paid for, and this annoys someone! Oh, well. Since breaking Lou Gehrig's record, Ripken's streak over that span would rank fourth on the active list.

Consecutive Games Played/ Active Streaks

	Games
Cal Ripken, Baltimore Orioles	2,478
Craig Biggio, Houston Astros	379
Jeff Bagwell, Houston Astros	350
Eric Karros, L.A. Dodgers	266

1 Kevin Garnett inks the richest deal in professional sports, signing a contract extension with the NBA's Minnesota Timberwolves that will pay the 21-year-old forward $125 million over the next six seasons.

Three-team trade in the NBA sends Denver Nuggets center Antonio McDyess to the Phoenix Suns who in turn ship Wesley Person and Tony Dumas to the Cleveland Cavaliers. The Nuggets receive a first round pick from the Cavs, two first round and two second round picks from the Suns as well as $500,000.

2 Wayne Gretzky signs a contract extension with the New York Rangers. The deal assures that the NHL's all-time leading scorer will finish his career in New York.

3 U.S. national soccer team manages only a 1-1 draw in its important World Cup qualifying match against Jamaica in front of 51,528 fans at a sold out RFK Stadium in Washington, D.C..

Gordie Howe, 69, fulfills his dream of playing professional hockey over six decades when he skates the opening shift with the Detroit Vipers in their IHL opener against Kansas City. He does not touch the puck with his stick in his 47 seconds on the ice, but does get hit in the leg with it once.

4 Lennox Lewis wins a stunning first-round TKO over Andrew Golota in their WBC heavyweight title fight in Atlantic City. The fight lasts 95 seconds as Lewis lands 30 of 36 shots to retain his belt. Golota suffers a concussion and later collapses and has a seizure in his dressing room following the bout.

6 Denver Broncos beat the New England Patriots, 34-13 in a highly anticipated match up of unbeatens on Monday Night Football. Bronco running back Terrell Davis runs 32 times for 171 yards and two touchdowns.

The New York Yankees, lose 4-3 to the Cleveland Indians in the final game of their best-of-five divisional series. The Tribe's ace rookie Jaret Wright gets his second win in the series to send the defending world champions packing.

7 Scottie Pippen undergoes foot surgery that will sideline him for up to the first two months of the upcoming NBA season. The Bulls' star forward suffered the injury in game five of the 1996 Eastern Conference finals against Miami.

9 Dean Smith retires as head coach at the University of North Carolina after 36 seasons at Chapel Hill. Smith won a record 879 games, two national titles, 17 ACC regular season crowns and 27 consecutive 20-win seasons.

11 Steve Fisher is fired as head basketball coach at Michigan. Fisher was canned two days after a law firm hired by the university found three minor NCAA violations and questioned his role in arranging free tickets for a Michigan booster.

12 Livan Hernandez whiffs 15 and shuts down the Braves in a 2–1 Marlins victory in the NLCS. Hernandez was forced into action when scheduled starter Kevin Brown becomes ill with a virus.

13 Gail Devers and Mia Hamm are honored by the Women's Sports Foundation as sportswomen of the year. Devers, a sprinter, receives the award in the individual category and Hamm, a star on the U.S. women's soccer team, receives the award in the team category.

14 Florida Marlins advance to the World Series, beating the Braves, 7-4, in game six of the NLCS. The Marlins are the first wild card team to play in the Fall Classic and although they finished nine games behind the Braves in the regular season, they won 12 of their 18 meetings.

Wide World Photos

Florida football coach **Steve Spurrier** greets Louisiana State University coach **Gerry DiNardo** after LSU beat the previously unbeaten and top ranked Gators 28–21.

John Stockton undergoes arthroscopic surgery on his left knee and will miss the first 6-8 weeks of the NBA season. The injury forces the Jazz point-guard to end his consecutive games-played streak at 609. It was the third-longest active streak in the NBA behind A.C. Green (696) and Michael Cage (657).

15 Cleveland Indians move on to the World Series when Tony Fernandez hits an 11th-inning home run to beat the Orioles, 1-0, in game six of the ALCS.

18 Marlins take game one of the Series, 7-4, behind back-to-back home runs by Moises Alou and Charles Johnson. Cuban rookie Livan Hernandez gets the win for the Marlins in front of 67,245 at Pro Player Stadium.

19 Cleveland evens the Series with a 6-1 victory in game two thanks largely to Chad Ogea's strong outing, who scattered seven hits over 6⅔ innings.

Tom Barrasso notches the 300th win in his distinguished 14–year career with a 4-1 victory over the Florida Panthers. The Pittsburgh goalie is the first American-born player to reach this mark.

21 Florida wins game three of the World Series, scoring seven runs in the ninth-inning to beat the Indians, 14-11 at Jacobs Field.

Dong Yanmei shatters the women's 5,000-meter record with her run of 14:31.27 at the Chinese National Games in Shanghai, breaking the mark of 14:36.45 set by Portugal's Fernanda Ribeiro in 1995.

22 Indians tie the Series again, taking game four, 10-3. The Indians are led by rookie pitcher Jaret Wright who goes six strong innings and Matt Williams who hit two singles and a home run.

Ben Crenshaw is named captain of the 1999 Ryder Cup team. Crenshaw, a two-time Masters champion, had played in four Ryder Cups.

New York Knicks ship Walter McCarty, Dontae' Jones, John Thomas and Scott Brooks to the Boston Celtics for veteran forward Chris Mills and two future second-round draft picks.

Janet Jones, wife of New York Ranger Wayne Gretzky, is knocked unconscious and suffers a cut lip when she is hit in the head by a pane of plexiglass following a collision along the boards during a game against Chicago at Madison Square Garden.

23 Florida jumps ahead three games to two in the World Series with an 8-7 victory over Cleveland in game five at Jacobs Field.

Jiang Bo shatters the two-day old women's 5,000 meter record set by her compatriot Dong Yanmei on Tuesday. Jiang's time of 14:28.09 knocks more than three seconds off Dong's time.

24 Marv Albert receives a 12-month delayed sentence and no jail time from an Arlington, Va. judge for his misdemeanor assault and battery charge. If Albert makes no violations and complies with counseling, the charges will be dropped in a year and his record will be cleared.

26 Florida Marlins win the World Series in the 11th inning of Game 7 at Pro Player Stadium when Edgar Renteria singles home Craig Counsell.

Jacques Villeneuve takes his first Formula One drivers championship, finishing third in the European GP at Jerez, Spain. Villeneuve enters the race one point behind Michael Schumacher, but Schumacher bumps into Villeneuve's car and goes flying off the track on the 48th lap.

D.C. United claim back-to-back MLS Cup titles with their 2-1 win over the Colorado Rapids at RFK Stadium. The United's Jaime Moreno, who scored in the 37th minute, is named the game's MVP.

JANUARY

1 Major bowl games (2): Sugar (New Orleans); Rose (Pasadena).
2 Orange Bowl (Miami).
3 NFL Playoffs (2): AFC/NFC semifinal games.
4 NFL Playoffs (2): AFC/NFC semifinal games.
4 U.S. Figure Skating Championships begin (Philadelphia).
10 NCAA Convention begins (Atlanta).
11 NFL playoffs (2): AFC/NFC championship games.
13 Australian Open tennis begins (Melbourne).
15 Winter X Games begin (Crested Butte, Co.).
17 NHL All-Star Game (Vancouver).
25 Super Bowl XXXII (San Diego).
31 24 Hours of Daytona begins (Daytona Beach).

FEBRUARY

1 NFL Pro Bowl (Honolulu).
7 Winter Olympics begin (Nagano).
8 NBA All-Star Game (New York).
9 ESPY Awards (New York).
15 Daytona 500 (Daytona Beach).
15 PBA National Championship begins (Toledo).
16 Westminster Dog Show begins (New York).

MARCH

7 NCAA Men's and Women's Basketball Tournament Selections.
7 Iditarod Trail Sled Dog race begins (Anchorage to Nome).
13 NCAA Indoor Track & Field Championships begin (TBD).
13 NCAA Men's Division I Basketball tournament begins.
13 NCAA Women's Division I Basketball tournament begins.
19 NCAA Women's Div. I Swimming & Diving finals begin (Minneapolis).
22 World Figure Skating Championships begin (Minneapolis).
22 NFL Annual Meeting begins (Orlando).
26 LPGA Dinah Shore golf begins (Rancho Mirage, Calif.).
26 NCAA Men's Div. I Swimming & Diving finals begin (Auburn).
28 NCAA Women's Basketball Final Four begins (Kansas City).
28 NCAA Men's Basketball Final Four begins (San Antonio).
31 Baseball opening night.

APRIL

2 NCAA Division I Hockey Final Four begins (Boston).
3 Davis Cup first round begins (8 different sites).
9 Masters golf begins (Augusta).
11 U.S. Open Women's Bowling Tournament (Milford, Ct.).
12 NHL regular season ends.
13 Women's Fed Cup tennis begins (various sites).
15 NHL Stanley Cup playoffs begin.
18 NFL Draft begins (New York).
19 NBA regular season ends.
20 Boston Marathon.
23 NBA playoffs begin.

MAY

2 Kentucky Derby (Louisville).
4 ABC Masters Bowling tournament begins (Reno).
14 LPGA McDonald's Championship golf begins (Wilmington, Del.).
16 Preakness Stakes (Baltimore).
17 NBA draft lottery.
23 NCAA Men's Div. I Lacrosse Final Four begins (New Brunswick, N.J.).
25 Indianapolis 500.
25 French Open tennis begins (Paris).
29 NCAA College World Series begins (Omaha, Neb.).
* tentative dates

JUNE

3 NCAA Men's and Women's Track & Field Championships begin (Buffalo).
6 Belmont Stakes (Elmont, N.Y.).
10 World Cup soccer begins (Paris).
18 U.S. Open golf begins (San Francisco).
19 Summer X Games begin (TBD).
22 Wimbledon tennis begins.
24 NBA Draft (Vancouver).
27 NHL Draft (Buffalo).

JULY

2 U.S. Women's Open golf begins (Kohler, Wisc.).
4 Tour de France cycling begins (through July 26).
7 Baseball All Star Game (Denver).
9 U.S. Senior Open golf begins (Pacific Palisades, Cal.).
12 World Cup soccer final (Paris).
16 British Open golf begins (Royal Birkdale).
17 Davis Cup second round begins (4 different sites).
20 Women's Fed Cup tennis semifinals begin.
26 U.S. 500 (Brooklyn, Mich.).
30 LPGA du Maurier Classic begins (Canada).

AUGUST

6 Bass Masters Classic begins.
8 All-American Soap Box Derby (Akron, Ohio).
13 PGA Championship golf begins (Seattle).
19 U.S. Gymnastics Championships begin (Indianapolis).
24 Little League World Series begins (Williamsport, Pa.).
24 U.S. Open tennis begins (Flushing, N.Y.).

SEPTEMBER

6 NFL regular season opens.
14 Women's Fed Cup tennis finals begin.
16 Women's golf Solheim Cup begins (Dublin, Ohio).
25 Davis Cup semifinals begin (2 different sites).
27 Baseball regular season ends.
30 Baseball playoffs begin.*

OCTOBER

3 Ironman Triathlon Championship (Hawaii).
7 Baseball League Championship Series begin.*
11 College Football: Oklahoma vs. Texas (Dallas).
16 ABL regular season begins.
17 World Series begins (in city of AL champion).
25 MLS World Cup '98 (Pasadena, Cal.).

NOVEMBER

1 New York City Marathon.
7 Breeders' Cup horse racing (TBD).
16 WTA Tour Tennis Championships begin (New York).
16 CFL Grey Cup (Edmonton).
18 PBA Tournament of Champions (Reno).
21 College Football: Michigan at Ohio St., UCLA at USC and Yale at Harvard.
23 ATP Men's Tennis Championship begins (Hannover, Ger.).
28 College Football: Notre Dame at USC and Auburn at Alabama.

DECEMBER

4 National Finals Rodeo begins (Las Vegas).
4 Davis Cup finals begin.
4 NCAA Women's Soccer Final Four begins (Greensboro, NC).
5 College Football: SEC Championship Game (Atlanta); Army vs. Navy (Philadelphia).
11 NCAA Men's Soccer Final Four (Richmond, Va.).
12 Heisman Trophy winner announced (New York).
19 NCAA Div. I-AA Football Championship (Chattanooga, TN).
28 NFL regular season ends.
2 (Jan.) NFL Playoffs begin.
* tentative dates

Baseball

In 1997, **Mark McGwire** hit 58 home runs while playing in both the National and American Leagues. McGwire's total was the highest since Roger Maris hit 61 in 1961.

Wide World Photos

Marlins Reel It In

The Florida Marlins beat the Cleveland Indians to win the World Series in their fifth year of existence.

by
Karl Ravech

In the end, we came full circle. As baseball always does, it started in Florida in March. But, as baseball never has, it ended in Florida in October. Such perfect symmetry for a sport that is so out of whack.

What does it say about baseball that, before the season started, most fans could probably have named six of the eight teams that eventually made the playoffs? It says revenue sharing is still not nearly enough to separate the haves from the have-nots. And that while money may not be the sole factor in ensuring a World Series trophy, without it you can't even consider playing in October.

In the end, though, the best team with the best manager but one of the worst baseball facilities won it all. The Marlins beat the Indians in a seven-game thriller that featured an exciting final game that went 11 innings, ended by Edgar Renteria's bases-loaded single off Charles Nagy just after midnight.

April began with the Marlins winning eight of their first nine and the Cubs losing their first 14. The May flowers led to a blooming of home runs unlike any we have seen. Ken Griffey, Jr. had gone deep 23 times by the end of the month and once again talk of Roger Maris' record being shattered was more than just a whisper. The point was moot by the end of September, again, although it was not Griffey leading the majors in dingers. It was Mark McGwire and his 58 home runs that had baseball's attention during the final weeks of the season. On the other side of the field, Roger Clemens was 11–0 in June and finished 21–7 with a 2.05 ERA and, believe it or not, a career-high 292 strikeouts.

1997 also saw a monumental change to the game: interleague play. A smashing success in most places but

---

Karl Ravech is the host of ESPN's *Baseball Tonight.*

The Florida Marlins' ride to a World Series victory featured many contributors, none more vital than **Livan Hernandez**, who won the MVP award in both the NLCS and the World Series.

a disappointment in others. Interleague play started with the Giants and the Rangers though it was highlighted by the Yankees-Mets and Cubs-White Sox series.

Cleveland was the home of the All-Star game in 1997 and it was also home to one of the most compelling individual stories of the season. Sandy Alomar Jr. had spent most of his career in the shadow of his brother Roberto. But in 1997, Sandy hit the game-winning homerun in the All-Star game, hit safely in 30 straight games and came up with countless other clutch hits during a dream season that saw him lead Cleveland back to the World Series for the second time in three years.

Alomar's offensive statistics were matched in the NL by Larry Walker of the Colorado Rockies. Dubbed the MVP by August, his .366 batting average, 49 homeruns, 130 RBIs and league-leading slugging percentage were the stuff of legends. For good measure, his 409 total bases were the highest since Stan Musial's 429 in 1948.

As for disappointments, certainly the Braves belong in that category. They had a new ballpark but it wasn't enough. The World's Best Starting Rotation still has just one championship.

As of this writing, the Marlins are the World Champions but may soon

In 1997, **Ken Griffey Jr.** of the Seattle Mariners hit 56 home runs and knocked in 147 runs. The Mariners won the AL West but lost in the first round of the playoffs to the Baltimore Orioles.

have a different owner and a far different outlook. The 1997 season may be remembered as the one in which Wayne Huizenga bought himself a championship. But the fact is that money buys talent, not heart, not character and certainly not luck. To win a World Series, you need them all and in 1997 the Marlins had plenty. ∎

Peter Gammons' Highlights of the 1997 Baseball Season.

10. **Omar Vizquel** — He turned in what is arguably the greatest defensive play ever in a World Series. Like Carlton Fisk's home run, it will forever be etched in the minds of baseball fans and it was made for the losing team.

9. **The Umpires** — It got so bad that the umpires tossed a trainer. The men in blue have developed such a bad attitude that instead of blending into the game they have become far too great a distraction.

8. **Mark McGwire** — He symbolizes everything good about the game. Off the field, a genuine, caring father and community leader. On the field, there were those 58 home runs.

7. **Paul Beeston** — In the long run, this may be the most significant move of year. In July, he became baseball's president. His talent for building consensus among owners

and his ability to communicate rationally with the players bodes well for the future of the game.

6. **Hideki Irabu** — George Steinbrenner's baseball people told him that this Japanese pitcher was the real deal. By the end of his first season, Irabu was in the minors and Steinbrenner was wondering why he has baseball people.

5. **The Florida Marlins** — This franchise became the first wild card, and fastest expansion, team to win a World Series. It took them five years and roughly $89 million in free agent spending. In the end, however, it was guys named Edgar Renteria, Craig Counsell, Livan Hernandez and Jim Leyland making all the difference.

4. **The Sale of the Dodgers** — The O'Malley family finally released its hold on the franchise in a sale to Rupert Murdoch and his Fox TV network. Further proof that baseball is as much about business and entertainment as it is about sports.

3. **The Handshake** — Roberto Alomar and John Hirschbeck put to rest one of the ugliest incidents in recent baseball memory when they shook hands before a game on April 22.

2. **Jackie Robinson** — 1997 will be remembered as the year baseball recognized the 50th anniversary of Robinson's first game. His courage, conviction, and impact on the game are nearly unsurpassed.

1. **Interleague Play** — For the first time in the history of the game, the American and National Leagues played each other during the regular season. Great if you saw the Yankees-Mets or the Cubs-White Sox. Not so great if you had to sit through Brewers-Astros. ■

THE NUMBERS

INSIDE

by

Todd Snyder, Kristen Micali and Craig Wachs

X **MARKS** THE SPOT

Odd as it may seem, before 1997 Mark McGwire had never officially hit a baseball over 500 feet. In 1997, he hit five. After a period of adjustment, McGwire really took to the National League as three of his 500–foot blasts came as a St. Louis Cardinal after his trade from the Oakland Athletics.

Mark McGwire's 500-Foot Homers in 1997

Date	Place	Feet
June 24	Seattle Kingdome	538*
September 16	Busch Stadium	517
April 20	Tiger Stadium	514
September 2	Busch Stadium	504
August 22	Pro Player Stadium	500

*off Randy Johnson; longest in the majors in 1997.

PIAZZA WITH EVERYTHING

Over the last three seasons, Mike Piazza has put together three of the best offensive seasons by a catcher

71

Sandy Alomar Jr. had a magical 1997. He was named the MVP of the All-Star game, had his best season offensively and delivered several key hits in the post season, including a ninth inning home run that tied Game 4 against the Yankees in the divisional playoffs.

since World War II. In batting average alone, his .362 in 1997 is the best over that span, beating Elston Howard's .348 in 1961. Since 1995, Piazza has also hit 108 home runs and knocked in 268. Not bad for someone originally drafted as a favor to Tommy Lasorda.

Highest BA by Catchers Since WWII

Mike Piazza, 1997	**.362**
Elston Howard, 1961	.348
Mike Piazza, 1995	.346
Mike Piazza, 1996	.336
Ted Simmons, 1975	.332

INTERLEAGUE TOTEBOARD

After getting off to a bad start in the first round of interleague play, in which the American League trounced them 48–36, the National League took over and won the next two rounds handily. One key advantage was the DH. The NL used the extra bat well, hitting 18 points higher than the AL in that spot.

Interleague Baseball Roundup

	American League	National League
Wins	97	117
ERA	4.29	4.28
DH BA	.245	.263
Pitchers' BA	.106	.165
Home runs	225	218

BASEBALL STATISTICS

THE 1998

ESPN INFORMATION PLEASE SPORTS ALMANAC

THE SEASON IN REVIEW
1997
LEAGUE LEADERS • POST SEASON

SEC A

PAGE 73

Final Major League Standings

Division champions (*) and Wild Card (†) winners are noted. Number of seasons listed after each manager refers to current tenure with club.

American League
East Division

	W	L	Pct	GB	Home	Road
* Baltimore	98	64	.605	—	46-35	52-29
† New York	96	66	.593	2	47-33	29-19
Detroit	79	83	.488	19	42-39	37-44
Boston	78	84	.481	20	39-42	39-42
Toronto	76	86	.469	22	42-39	34-47

1997 Managers: Bal– Davey Johnson (2nd season); **NY**–Joe Torre (2nd); **Det**– Buddy Bell (2nd); **Bos**– Jimy Williams (1st); **Tor**– replaced Cito Gaston (9th, 72-85) on Sept. 24 with Mel Queen (4-1).
1996 Standings: 1. New York (92–70); 2. Baltimore (88–74); 3. Boston (85–77); 4. Toronto (74–88); 5. Detroit (53–109).

Central Division

	W	L	Pct	GB	Home	Road
* Cleveland	86	75	.534	—	44-37	42-38
Chicago	80	81	.497	6	45-36	35-45
Milwaukee	78	83	.484	8	47-33	31-50
Minnesota	68	94	.420	18½	35-46	33-48
Kansas City	67	94	.416	19	33-47	34-47

1997 Managers: Cle– Mike Hargrove (7th season); **Chi**–Terry Bevington (3rd); **Mil**– Phil Garner (6th); **Min**– Tom Kelly (12th); **KC**– replaced Bob Boone (3rd, 36-46) with Tony Muser (1st, 31-48) on July 9.
1996 Standings: 1. Cleveland (99–62); 2. Chicago (85–77); 3. Milwaukee (80–82); 4. Minnesota (78–84); 5. Kansas City (75–86).

West Division

	W	L	Pct	GB	Home	Road
* Seattle	90	72	.556	—	45-36	45-36
Anaheim	84	78	.519	6	46-36	38-42
Texas	77	85	.475	13	39-42	38-43
Oakland	65	97	.401	25	35-46	30-51

1997 Managers: Sea– Lou Piniella (5th season); **Ana**–Terry Collins (1st); **Tex**– Johnny Oates (3rd); **Oak**– Art Howe (2nd).
1996 Standings: 1. Texas (90–72); 2. Seattle (85–76); 3. Oakland (78–84); 4. California (70–91). **Note:** The California Angels changed their name to the Anaheim Angels prior to the 1997 season.

National League
East Division

	W	L	Pct	GB	Home	Road
* Atlanta	101	61	.623	—	50-31	51-30
† Florida	92	70	.568	9	52-29	40-41
New York	88	74	.543	13	50-31	38-43
Montreal	78	84	.481	23	45-36	33-48
Philadelphia	68	94	.420	33	38-43	30-51

1997 Managers: Atl– Bobby Cox (8th season); **Fla**– Jim Leyland (1st); **NY**– Bobby Valentine (2nd); **Mon**– Felipe Alou (6th); **Phi**– Jim Fregosi (7th).
1996 Standings: 1. Atlanta (96–66); 2. Montreal (88–74); 3. Florida (80–82); 4. New York (71–91); 5. Philadelphia (67–95).

Central Division

	W	L	Pct	GB	Home	Road
* Houston	84	78	.519	—	46-35	38-43
Pittsburgh	79	83	.488	5	43-38	36-45
Cincinnati	76	86	.469	8	40-41	36-45
St. Louis	73	89	.451	11	41-40	32-49
Chicago	68	94	.420	16	42-39	26-55

1997 Managers: Hou– Larry Dierker (1st season); **Pit**–Gene Lamont (1st); **Cin**– replaced Ray Knight (2nd, 43-56) with Jack McKeon (38-25) on July 25; **St.L**– Tony La Russa (2nd); **Chi**– Jim Riggleman (3rd).
1996 Standings: 1. St. Louis (88–74); 2. Houston (82–80); 3. Cincinnati (81–81); 4. Chicago (76–86); 5. Pittsburgh (73–89).

West Division

	W	L	Pct	GB	Home	Road
* San Francisco	90	72	.556	—	48-33	42-39
Los Angeles	88	74	.543	2	47-34	41-40
Colorado	83	79	.512	7	47-34	36-45
San Diego	76	86	.469	14	39-42	37-44

1997 Managers: SF– Dusty Baker (5th season); **LA**– Bill Russell (2nd); **Col**– Don Baylor (5th); SD– Bruce Bochy (3rd).
1996 Standings: 1. San Diego (91–74); 2. Los Angeles (90–72); 3. Colorado (83–79); 4. San Francisco (68–94).

Baseball's Eight Work Stoppages

Year	Work Stoppage	Games Missed	Length	Dates	Issue
1972	Strike	86	13 days	April 1-13	Pensions
1973	Lockout	0	17 days	February 8-25	Salary arbitration
1976	Lockout	0	17 days	March 1-17	Free agency
1980	Strike	0	8 days	April 1-8	Free-agent compensation
1981	Strike	712	50 days	June 12-July 31	Free-agent compensation
1985	Strike	0	2 days	August 6-7	Salary arbitration
1990	Lockout	0	32 days	Feb. 15-March 18	Salary arbitration and salary cap
1994	Strike	920	232 days	Aug. 12-March 31	Salary cap and revenue sharing

Ken Griffey Jr.
Seattle Mariners
Home Runs, RBI, runs, Total Bases, Slugging Pct.

Nomar Garciaparra
Boston Red Sox
Hits, Triples

Brian Hunter
Detroit Tigers
Stolen Bases

Randy Myers
Baltimore Orioles
Saves

American League Leaders
Batting

	Bat	Gm	AB	R	H	Avg	TB	2B	3B	HR	RBI	BB	Int BB	SO	SB	Slg Pct	OB Pct
Frank Thomas, Chi	R	146	530	110	184	.347	324	35	0	35	125	109	9	69	1	.611	.456
Edgar Martinez, Sea	R	155	542	104	179	.330	300	35	1	28	108	119	11	86	2	.554	.330
Dave Justice, Cle	L	139	495	84	163	.329	295	31	1	33	101	80	11	79	3	.596	.329
Bernie Williams, NY	S	129	509	107	167	.328	277	35	6	21	100	73	6	80	15	.544	.408
Manny Ramirez, Cle	R	150	561	99	184	.328	302	40	0	26	88	79	4	115	2	.538	.415
Paul O'Neill, NY	L	149	553	89	179	.324	284	42	0	21	117	75	8	92	10	.514	.399
Rusty Greer, Tex	L	157	601	112	193	.321	319	42	3	26	87	83	4	87	9	.531	.405
Reggie Jefferson, Bos	L	136	489	74	156	.319	230	33	1	13	67	24	5	93	1	.470	.358
Mo Vaughn, Bos	L	141	527	91	166	.315	295	24	0	35	96	86	17	154	2	.560	.420
Ivan Rodriguez, Tex	R	150	597	98	187	.313	289	34	4	20	77	38	7	89	7	.484	.360
Troy O'Leary, Bos	L	146	499	65	154	.309	239	32	4	15	80	39	7	70	0	.479	.358
John Valentin, Bos	R	143	575	95	176	.306	287	47	5	18	77	58	5	66	7	.499	.372
Nomar Garciaparra*, Bos	R	153	684	122	209	.306	365	44	11	30	98	35	2	92	22	.534	.342
Paul Molitor, Min	R	135	538	63	164	.305	234	32	4	10	89	45	8	73	11	.435	.351
Ken Griffey Jr., Sea	L	157	608	125	185	.304	393	34	3	56	147	76	23	121	15	.646	.382

Home Runs

Griffey Jr., Sea	56
Martinez, NY	44
Gonzalez, Tex	42
Buhner, Sea	40
Thome, Cle	40
Palmeiro, Bal	38
Thomas, Chi	35
Vaughn, Bos	35
Salmon, Ana	33
Justice, Cle	33

Runs Batted In

Griffey, Jr., Sea	147
Martinez, NY	141
Gonzalez, Tex	131
Salmon, Ana	129
Thomas, Chi	125
O'Neill, NY	117
Clark, Det	117
Belle, Chi	116
King, KC	112
Palmeiro, Bal	110

Hits

Garciaparra*, Bos	209
Greer, Tex	193
Jeter, NY	190
Anderson, Ana	189
Rodriguez, Tex	192
Griffey Jr., Sea	185
Thomas, Chi	184
Ramirez, Cle	184
Martinez, Sea	179
O'Neill, NY	179

Stolen Bases

	SB	CS
Hunter, Det	74	18
Knoblauch, Min	62	10
Goodwin, Tex	50	16
Vizquel, Cle	43	12
Durham, Chi	33	16
Rodriguez, Sea	29	6
Easley, Det	28	13
Four tied with 23 each.		

Triples

Garciaparra*, Bos	11
Knoblauch, Min	10
Burnitz, Mil	8
Damon, KC	8
Anderson, Bal	7
Jeter, NY	7
Alicea, Ana	7
Hunter, Det	7
Stewart*, Tor	7

Doubles

Valentin, Bos	47
Cirillo, Mil	46
Belle, Chi	45
Garciaparra*, Bos	44
O'Neill, NY	42
Delgado, Tor	42
Greer, Tex	42
Giambi, Oak	41

Runs

Griffey Jr., Sea	125
Garciaparra*, Bos	122
Knoblauch, Min	117
Jeter, NY	116
Greer, Tex	116
Hunter, Det	112
Thomas, Chi	110
Williams, NY	107

Total Bases

Griffey Jr., Sea	393
Garciaparra*, Bos	365
Martinez, NY	343
Thomas, Chi	324
Greer, Tex	319
Gonzalez, Tex	314
Belle, Chi	311
Ramirez, Cle	302
Salmon, Ana	301

On Base Pct.

Thomas, Chi	.456
Martinez, Sea	.456
Thome, Cle	.423
Vaughn, Bos	.420
Justice, Cle	.418
Ramirez, Cle	.415
Williams, NY	.408

Slugging Pct.

Griffey Jr., Sea	.646
Thomas, Chi	.611
Justice, Cle	.596
Gonzalez, Tex	.589
Thome, Cle	.579
Martinez, NY	.577
Vaughn, Bos	.560

Walks

Thome, Cle	120
Martinez, Sea	119
Buhner, Sea	119
Thomas, Chi	109
Phillips, Ana	102
Salmon, Ana	95
Clark, Det	93

Strikeouts

Buhner, Sea	175
Nieves, Det	157
Vaughn, Bos	154
Thome, Cle	146
Clark, Det	144
Salmon, Ana	142
Palmer, KC	134
Delgado, Tor	133

Pitching

	Arm	W	L	ERA	Gm	GS	CG	ShO	Sv	IP	H	R	ER	HR	HB	BB	SO	WP
Roger Clemens, Tor	R	21	7	**2.05**	34	34	9	3	0	264.0	204	65	60	9	12	68	292	4
Randy Johnson, Sea	L	20	4	**2.28**	30	29	5	2	0	213.0	147	60	54	20	10	77	291	4
David Cone, NY	R	12	6	**2.82**	29	29	1	0	0	195.0	155	67	61	17	4	86	222	14
Andy Pettitte, NY	L	18	7	**2.88**	35	35	4	1	0	240.1	233	86	77	7	7	65	166	7
Justin Thompson, Det	L	15	11	**3.02**	32	32	4	0	0	223.1	188	82	75	20	2	66	151	4
Mike Mussina, Bal	R	15	8	**3.20**	33	33	4	1	0	224.2	197	87	80	27	3	54	218	5
Kevin Appier, KC	R	9	13	**3.40**	34	34	4	1	0	235.2	215	96	89	24	4	74	196	14
Jimmy Key, Bal	L	16	10	**3.43**	34	34	1	1	0	212.1	210	90	81	24	5	82	141	4
Jeff Fassero, Sea	L	16	9	**3.61**	35	35	2	1	0	234.1	226	108	94	21	3	84	189	13
Pat Hentgen, Tor	R	15	10	**3.68**	35	35	9	3	0	264.0	253	116	108	31	7	71	160	6
Scott Erickson, Bal	R	16	7	**3.69**	34	33	3	2	0	221.2	218	100	91	16	5	61	131	11
Tom Gordon, Bos	R	6	10	**3.74**	42	25	2	1	11	182.2	155	85	76	10	3	78	159	5
Jamie Moyer, Sea	L	17	5	**3.86**	30	30	2	0	0	188.2	187	82	81	21	7	43	113	3
Brad Radke, Min	R	20	10	**3.87**	35	35	4	1	0	239.2	238	114	103	28	3	42	174	1
Scott Kamieniecki, Bal	R	10	6	**4.01**	30	30	0	0	0	179.1	179	83	80	20	4	67	109	5

Wins

Clemens, Tor	21-7
Johnson, Sea	20-4
Radke, Min	20-10
Pettitte, NY	18-7
Moyer, Sea	17-5
Erickson, Bal	16-7
Blair, Det	16-8
Fassero, Sea	16-9
Key, Bal	16-10
Wells, NY	16-10

Losses

Wakefield, Bos	12-15
Baldwin, Chi	12-15
Eldred, Mil	13-15
Sanders, Det	6-14
Navarro, Chi	9-14
Williams, Tor	9-14
Smiley, Cle	11-14
Tewksbury, Min	8-13
Appier, KC	9-13
Karl, Tex	10-13

Saves

	SV	BS
Myers, Bal	45	1
Rivera, NY	43	9
Jones, Mil	36	2
Jones, Det	31	5
Wetteland, Tex	31	6
Percival, Ana	27	4
Slocumb, Bos-Sea	27	6
Aguilera, Min	26	7
Taylor, Oak	23	7
Mesa, Cle	16	5

Strikeouts

Clemens, Tor	292
Johnson, Sea	291
Cone, NY	222
Mussina, Bal	218
Appier, KC	196
Fassero, Sea	189
Radke, Min	174
Pettitte, NY	166
Hentgen, Tor	160
Gordon, Bos	159

Appearances

Myers, Det	88
Groom, Oak	78
Quantrill, Tor	77
Nelson, NY	77
Slocumb, Bos-Sea	76

Innings

Hentgen, Tor	264.0
Clemens, Tor	264.0
Pettitte, NY	240.1
Radke, Min	239.2
Appier, KC	235.2
Fassero, Sea	234.1
Nagy, Cle	227.0
Mussina, Bal	224.2
Thompson, Det	223.1

HRs Given Up

Watson, Ana	37
Witt, Tex	33
Dickson*, Ana	32
Springer, Ana	32
Eldred, Mil	31
Belcher, KC	31
Williams, Tor	31
Hentgen, Tor	31

Walks

Hill, Tex-Ana	95
Eldred, Mil	89
Wakefield, Bos	87
Cone, NY	86
Fassero, Sea	84
Baldwin, Chi	83

Complete Games

Hentgen, Tor	9
Clemens, Tor	9
Wells, NY	5
Johnson, Sea	5
Tewksbury, Min	5

Shutouts

Hentgen, Tor	3
Clemens, Tor	3
Erickson, Bal	2
Wells, NY	2
Johnson, Sea	2
Wakefield, Bos	2
Olivares, Sea	2
Tewksbury, Min	2

Wild Pitches

Baldwin, Chi	14
Cone, NY	14
Appier, KC	14
Navarro, Chi	14
Fassero, Sea	13

Hit Batters

Wakefield, Bos	16
Sele, Bos	15
Olivares, Sea	13
Clemens, Tor	12
Hershiser, Cle	11
Oliver, Tex	11

Team Leaders

Batting

Team	Avg	AB	R	H	HR	RBI	SB
Boston	.291	5781	851	1684	185	810	68
New York	.287	5710	891	1636	161	846	99
Cleveland	.286	5556	868	1589	220	810	118
Seattle	.280	5614	925	1574	264	890	89
Texas	.274	5651	807	1547	187	773	72
Chicago	.273	5491	779	1498	158	740	106
Anaheim	.272	5628	829	1531	161	775	126
Minnesota	.270	5634	772	1522	132	730	151
Baltimore	.268	5584	812	1498	196	780	63
Kansas City	.264	5599	747	1478	158	711	130
Milwaukee	.260	5444	681	1415	135	643	103
Oakland	.260	5589	764	1451	197	714	71
Detroit	.258	5481	784	1415	176	743	161
Toronto	.244	5473	654	1333	147	627	134

Pitching

	ERA	W	Sv	CG	ShO	HR	BB	SO
New York	3.84	96	51	11	3	144	532	1165
Baltimore	3.91	98	59	8	4	164	563	1139
Toronto	3.93	76	34	19	7	167	497	1150
Milwaukee	4.23	78	44	6	3	177	542	1016
Anaheim	4.52	84	39	9	3	202	605	1050
Detroit	4.56	79	42	13	5	178	552	982
Texas	4.70	77	33	8	1	169	541	925
Kansas City	4.71	67	29	11	2	186	531	961
Cleveland	4.73	86	39	4	1	181	575	1036
Chicago	4.74	80	52	6	1	175	575	961
Seattle	4.79	90	38	9	3	192	598	1207
Boston	4.85	78	40	7	3	149	611	987
Minnesota	5.02	68	30	10	3	187	495	908
Oakland	5.49	65	38	2	0	197	642	953

Colorado Rockies
Larry Walker
Home Runs, Total Bases,
Slugging Pct., OBP

San Diego Padres
Tony Gwynn
Batting Average

Colorado Rockies
Andres Galarraga
RBI

Montreal Expos
Pedro Martinez
ERA, CG

National League Leaders
Batting

	Bat	Gm	AB	R	H	Avg	TB	2B	3B	HR	RBI	BB	Int BB	SO	SB	Slg Pct	OB Pct
Tony Gwynn, SD	L	149	592	97	220	**.372**	324	49	2	17	119	43	12	28	12	.547	.409
Larry Walker, Col	L	153	568	143	208	**.366**	409	46	4	49	130	78	14	90	33	.720	.452
Mike Piazza, LA	R	152	556	104	201	**.362**	355	32	1	40	124	69	11	77	5	.638	.431
Kenny Lofton, Atl	L	122	493	90	164	**.333**	211	20	6	5	48	64	5	83	27	.428	.409
Wally Joyner, SD	L	135	455	59	149	**.327**	221	29	2	13	83	51	5	51	3	.486	.390
Mark Grace, Chi	L	151	555	87	177	**.319**	258	32	5	13	78	88	3	45	2	.465	.409
Andres Gallaraga, Col	R	154	600	120	191	**.318**	351	31	3	41	140	54	2	141	15	.585	.389
Edgardo Alfonzo, NY	R	151	518	84	163	**.315**	224	27	2	10	72	63	0	56	11	.432	.391
Raul Mondesi, LA	R	159	616	95	191	**.310**	333	42	5	30	87	44	7	105	32	.541	.360
Craig Biggio, Hou	R	162	619	146	191	**.309**	310	37	8	22	81	84	6	107	47	.501	.415
Dante Bichette, Col	R	151	561	81	173	**.308**	286	31	2	26	118	30	1	90	6	.510	.343
Jeff Blauser, Atl	R	151	519	90	160	**.308**	250	31	4	17	70	70	6	101	5	.482	.405
David Segui, Mon	S	125	459	75	141	**.307**	232	22	3	21	68	57	12	66	1	.505	.380
Vinny Castilla, Col	R	159	612	94	186	**.304**	335	25	2	10	113	44	9	108	2	.547	.356
Shawon Dunston, Chi-Pit	R	132	490	71	147	**.300**	221	22	5	14	57	8	0	75	32	.451	.312
Doug Glanville, Chi	R	146	474	79	142	**.300**	186	22	5	4	35	24	0	46	19	.392	.333
Bobby Bonilla, Fla	S	153	562	77	167	**.297**	263	39	3	17	96	73	8	94	6	.468	.378
Delino DeShields, St.L	L	150	572	92	169	**.295**	256	26	14	11	58	55	1	72	55	.448	.357
Chipper Jones, Atl	S	157	597	100	176	**.295**	286	41	3	21	111	76	8	88	20	.479	.371
Mickey Morandini, Phi	L	150	553	83	163	**.295**	210	40	2	1	39	62	0	91	16	.380	.371

Home Runs

Walker, Col 49
Bagwell, Hou 43
Galarraga, Col 41
Bonds, SF 40
Castilla, Col 40
Piazza, LA 40
Sosa, Chi 36
Burks, Col 32
Karros, LA 31
Lankford, St.L 31
Zeile, LA 31

Runs Batted In

Galarraga, Col 140
Bagwell, Hou 135
Walker, Col 130
Piazza, LA 124
Kent, SF 121
Gwynn, SD 119
Sosa, Chi 119
Bichette, Col 118
Alou, Fla 115
Castilla, Col 113
C. Jones, Atl 111

Hits

Johnson, NY 227
Gwynn, SD 220
Walker, Col 208
Piazza, LA 201
Biggio, Hou 191
Galarraga, Col 191
Mondesi, LA 191
Castilla, Col 186
Womack, Pit 178
Grace, Chi 177
Grudzielanek, Mon ...177

Stolen Bases

	SB	CS
Womack, Pit	.60	7
D. Sanders, Cin	.56	13
DeShields, St.L	.55	14
Biggio, Hou	.47	10
Young, Col-LA	.45	14
Bonds, SF	.37	6
Q. Veras, SD	.33	12
Walker, Col	.33	8
Mondesi, LA	.32	15
Dunston, Chi-Pit	.32	8
Renteria, Fla	.32	15

Triples

DeShields, St.L 14
Perez, Col 10
Guerrero, LA 9
Randa, Pit 9
Womack, Pit 9

Doubles

Grudzielanek, Mon 54
Gwynn, SD 49
Walker, Col 46
Lansing, Mon 45
Mondesi, LA 42
C. Jones, Atl 41

Runs

Biggio, Hou 146
Walker, Col 143
Bonds, SF 123
Galarraga, Col 120
Bagwell, Hou 109
Young, Col-LA 106
Piazza, LA 104

Total Bases

Walker, Col 409
Piazza, LA 355
Galarraga, Col 351
Bagwell, Hou 335
Castilla, Col 335
Mondesi, LA 333

On Base Pct.

Walker, Col .... .452
Bonds, SF 446
Piazza, LA 431
Bagwell, Hou 425
Sheffield, Fla 424
Biggio, Hou 415

Slugging Pct.

Walker, Col .... .720
Piazza, LA .... .638
Bagwell, Hou .... .592
Galarraga, Col ..... .585
Lankford, St.L ..... .585
Bonds, SF .... .585

Walks

Bonds, SF 145
Bagwell, Hou 127
Sheffield, Fla 121
Snow, SF 96
Lankford, St.L 95
Grace, Chi 88

Strikeouts

Sosa, Chi 174
Gant, St.L 162
Rodriguez, Mon 149
Galarraga, Col 141
Rolen*, Phi 138
Kent, SF 133

Pitching

	Arm	W	L	ERA	Gm	GS	CG	ShO	Sv	IP	H	R	ER	HR	HB	BB	SO	WP
Pedro Martinez, Mon	R	17	8	**1.90**	31	31	13	4	0	241.1	158	65	51	16	9	67	305	3
Greg Maddux, Atl	R	19	4	**2.20**	33	33	5	2	0	232.2	200	58	57	9	6	20	177	0
Daryl Kile, Hou	R	19	7	**2.57**	34	34	6	4	0	255.2	208	87	73	19	10	94	205	7
Ismael Valdes, LA	R	10	11	**2.65**	30	30	0	0	0	196.2	171	68	58	16	3	47	140	3
Kevin Brown, Fla	R	16	8	**2.69**	33	33	6	2	0	237.1	214	77	71	10	14	66	205	7
Rick Reed, NY	R	13	9	**2.89**	33	31	2	0	0	208.1	186	76	67	19	5	31	113	0
Tom Glavine, Atl	L	14	7	**2.96**	33	33	5	2	0	240.0	197	86	79	20	4	79	152	3
Denny Neagle, Atl	L	20	5	**2.97**	34	34	4	4	0	233.1	204	87	77	18	6	49	172	3
Curt Schilling, Phi	R	17	11	**2.97**	35	35	7	2	0	251.1	208	96	84	25	4	58	319	5
John Smoltz, Atl	R	15	12	**3.02**	35	35	7	2	0	256.0	234	97	86	21	1	63	241	10
Andy Benes, St.L	R	10	7	**3.10**	26	26	0	0	0	177.0	149	64	61	9	5	61	175	7
Shawn Estes, SF	L	19	5	**3.18**	32	32	3	2	0	201.0	162	80	71	12	8	100	181	10
Matt Morris*, St.L	R	12	9	**3.19**	33	33	3	0	0	217.0	208	88	77	12	7	69	149	5
Chan Ho Park, LA	R	14	8	**3.38**	32	29	2	0	0	192.0	149	80	72	24	8	70	166	4
Kirk Rueter, SF	L	13	6	**3.45**	32	32	0	0	0	190.2	194	83	73	17	1	51	115	3
Wilson Alvarez, SF	L	13	11	**3.48**	33	33	2	1	0	212.0	180	97	82	18	4	91	179	5
Chris Holt*, Hou	R	8	12	**3.52**	33	32	0	0	0	209.2	211	98	82	17	8	61	95	1
Alex Fernandez, Fla.	R	17	12	**3.59**	32	32	5	1	0	220.2	193	93	88	25	4	69	183	9
Francisco Cordova, Pit	R	11	8	**3.63**	29	29	2	2	0	178.2	175	80	72	14	9	49	121	4
Bobby Jones, NY	R	15	9	**3.63**	30	30	3	1	0	193.1	177	88	78	24	2	63	125	3

Wins
Neagle, Atl 20-5
Estes, SF 19-5
Kile, Hou 19-7
Maddux, Atl 19-4
Fernandez, Fla ...17-12
Martinez, Mon 17-8
Schilling, Phi 17-11
Brown, Fla 16-8
Hampton, Hou 15-10
Jones, NY 15-9
Smoltz, Atl 15-12

Appearances
Tavarez, SF 89
Belinda, Cin 84
Shaw, Cin 78
Rojas, Chi-NY 77
Patterson, Chi 76
Spradlin, Phi 76
Radinsky, LA 75
Henry, SF 75

Complete Games
Martinez, Mon 13
Perez, Mon 8
Hampton, Hou 7
Schilling, Phi 7
Smoltz, Atl 7
Brown, Fla 6
Kile, Hou 6

Losses
Leiter, Phi 10-17
Cooke, Pit 9-15
Lieber, Pit 11-14
Mulholland, Chi-SF ...6-13
Perez, Mon 12-13
Eleven tied with 12 each.

Innings
Smoltz, Atl 256.0
Kile, Hou 255.2
Schilling, Phi 254.1
Martinez, Mon 241.1
Glavine, Atl 240.0
Brown, Fla 237.1
Neagle, Atl 233.1
Maddux, Atl 232.2
Hampton, Hou 223.0
Fernandez, Fla 220.2

Shutouts
Perez, Mon 5
Kile, Hou 4
Martinez, Mon 4
Neagle, Atl 4
Ten tied with two each.

Saves
	SV	BS
Shaw, Cin	42	7
Beck, SF	37	8
Hoffman, SD	37	7
Eckersley, St.L	36	7
J. Franco, NY	36	6
Nen, Fla	35	7
Worrell, LA	35	9
Bottalico, Phi	34	7
Wohlers, Atl	33	7
Loiselle, Pit	29	5
Urbina, Mon	27	5

HRs Given Up
Trachsel, Chi 32
Gardner, SF 28
Bailey, Col 27
Foster, Chi 27
Five tied with 25 each.

Wild Pitches
Remlinger, Cin 12
Leiter, Phi 11
Estes, SF 10
Nomo, LA 10
Smoltz, Atl 10

Strikeouts
Schilling, Phi 319
Martinez, Mon 305
Smoltz, Atl 241
Nomo, LA 233
Brown, Fla 205
Kile, Hou 205
Fernandez, Fla 183
Estes, SF 181
Maddux, Atl 177
An. Benes, St.L 175
Neagle, Atl 172
Astacio, LA-Col 166
Park, LA 166

Walks
Estes, SF 100
Kile, Hou 94
Nomo, LA 92
Leiter, Fla 91
Alvarez, SF 91
Glavine, Atl 79
Hampton, Hou 77
Cooke, Pit 77

Hit Batters
Brown, Fla 14
Bailey, Col 13
Bullinger, Mon 12
Hamilton, SD 12
Leiter, Fla 12
Loaiza, Pit 12
Stottlemyre, St.L 12

Team Leaders

Batting

	AVG	AB	R	H	HR	RBI	SB
Colorado	.288	5603	923	1611	239	869	137
San Diego	.271	5609	795	1519	152	761	141
Atlanta	.270	5528	791	1490	174	755	108
Los Angeles	.268	5544	742	1488	174	706	131
Chicago	.263	5489	687	1444	127	642	116
New York	.262	5524	777	1448	153	741	95
Pittsburgh	.262	5507	724	1441	129	686	160
Florida	.259	5439	740	1410	136	703	115
Houston	.259	5502	777	1427	133	720	171
Montreal	.258	5526	691	1423	172	659	75
S. Francisco	.258	5480	784	1414	172	746	121
Philadelphia	.255	5443	668	1390	116	622	92
St. Louis	.255	5524	689	1409	144	653	164
Cincinnati	.253	5484	651	1386	142	615	190

Pitching

	ERA	W	SV	CG	ShO	HR	BB	SO
Atlanta	3.18	101	37	21	17	111	450	1196
Los Angeles	3.63	88	45	6	6	163	546	1232
Houston	3.67	84	37	16	12	134	511	1138
Florida	3.83	92	39	12	10	131	639	1188
St. Louis	3.90	73	39	5	3	124	535	1133
New York	3.95	88	49	7	8	160	504	982
Montreal	4.14	78	37	27	14	149	557	1138
Pittsburgh	4.28	79	41	6	8	143	560	1080
Cincinnati	4.42	76	86	5	8	173	558	1159
S. Francisco	4.42	90	45	5	9	160	579	1041
Chicago	4.44	68	37	6	4	185	590	1072
Philadelphia	4.87	68	35	13	7	171	616	1209
San Diego	4.99	76	43	5	2	172	596	1059
Colorado	5.25	83	38	9	5	196	566	870

1997 All-Star Game

68th Baseball All-Star Game. Date: July 8 at Jacobs Field in Cleveland, OH; **Managers:** Joe Torre, New York (AL) and Bobby Cox, Atlanta (NL); **Most Valuable Player:** C Sandy Alomar Jr., Cle. (AL): game-winning two-run HR.

National League

	AB	R	H	BI	BB	SO	Avg
Craig Biggio, Hou, 2b	3	0	0	0	0	1	.000
Tony Womack, Pit, 2b	1	0	0	0	0	0	.000
Tony Gwynn, SD, dh	3	0	0	0	0	0	.000
Andres Galarraga, Col, dh	1	0	0	0	0	1	.000
Barry Bonds, SF, lf	2	0	0	1	1	1	.000
Steve Finley, SD, lf	1	0	0	0	0	1	.000
Mike Piazza, LA, c	1	0	0	0	1	0	.000
Javy Lopez, Atl, c	1	1	1	1	0	0	1.000
Charles Johnson, Fla, c	1	0	0	0	0	1	.000
Jeff Bagwell, Hou, 1b	3	0	0	0	0	0	.000
Mark Grace, Chi, 1b	1	0	0	0	0	0	.000
Larry Walker, Col, rf	1	0	0	0	1	0	.000
Moises Alou, Fla, rf	2	0	1	0	0	0	.500
Ken Caminiti, SD, 3b	2	0	0	0	0	0	.000
Chipper Jones, Atl, 3b	1	0	0	0	0	0	.000
Ray Lankford, St.L, cf	2	0	0	1	0	1	.000
Jeff Blauser, Atl, ss	2	0	1	0	0	0	.000
Royce Clayton, St.L, ss	1	0	0	0	0	1	.000
TOTALS	29	1	3	1	4	7	.103

American League

	AB	R	H	BI	BB	SO	Avg
Brady Anderson, Bal, lf-rf	4	0	2	0	0	0	.500
Alex Rodriguez, Sea, ss	3	0	1	0	0	2	.333
Nomar Garciaparra, Bos, ss	1	0	0	0	0	0	.000
Ken Griffey Jr., Sea, cf	4	0	0	0	0	2	.000
Tino Martinez, NY, 1b	2	0	0	0	0	0	.000
Mark McGwire, Oak, 1b	2	0	0	0	0	2	.000
Edgar Martinez, Sea, dh	2	1	2	1	0	0	1.000
Jim Thome, Cle, dh	1	0	0	0	0	0	.000
Paul O'Neill, NY, rf	2	0	0	0	0	1	.000
Bernie Williams, NY, lf	0	1	0	0	1	0	.000
Cal Ripken, Bal, 3b	2	0	1	0	0	0	.500
Joey Cora, Sea, 2b	1	0	0	0	0	0	.000
Chuck Knoblauch, Min, 2b	0	0	0	0	0	0	.000
Ivan Rodriguez, Tex, c	2	0	0	0	0	0	.000
Sandy Alomar Jr., Cle, c	1	1	1	2	0	0	1.000
Roberto Alomar, Bal, 2b	2	0	0	0	0	0	.000
Jeff Cirillo, Mil, 3b	1	0	0	0	0	1	.000
TOTALS	30	3	7	3	1	8	.233

	1	2	3	4	5	6	7	8	9	R	H	E
National League	0	0	0	0	0	0	1	0	0	– 1	3	0
American League	0	1	0	0	0	0	0	2	0	X – 3	7	0

LOB—National 5, American 4. **2B**—Anderson (AL). **HR**—Lopez (NL, off Rosado), E. Martinez (AL, off Maddux), S. Alomar (AL, off Estes). **SB**—Bonds (NL, 2nd base off Cone/Rodriguez). **CS**—E. Martinez (AL, 2nd base by Schilling/Lopez). **PB**—Lopez (NL).

NL Pitching

	IP	H	R	ER	BB	SO	NP
Greg Maddux, Atl	2.0	2	1	1	0	0	34
Curt Schilling, Phi	2.0	2	0	0	0	3	40
Kevin Brown, Fla	1.0	1	0	0	0	0	19
Pedro Martinez, Mon	1.0	0	0	0	0	2	12
Shawn Estes, SF (L)	1.0	1	2	2	1	1	23
Bobby Jones, NY	1.0	1	0	0	0	2	25
TOTALS	8.0	7	3	3	1	8	153

AL Pitching

	IP	H	R	ER	BB	SO	NP
Randy Johnson, Sea	2.0	0	0	0	1	2	30
Roger Clemens, Tor	1.0	1	0	0	0	0	13
David Cone, NY	1.0	0	0	0	2	0	17
Justin Thompson, Det	1.0	0	0	0	0	1	13
Pat Hentgen, Tor	1.0	0	0	0	0	0	6
Jose Rosado, KC (W)	1.0	2	1	1	1	1	22
Randy Myers, Bal	1.0	0	0	0	0	2	16
Mariano Rivera, NY (S)	1.0	0	0	0	0	1	11
TOTALS	9.0	3	1	1	4	7	128

Umpires—Larry Barnett (AL) plate; Gerry Davis (NL) 1b; Drew Coble (AL) 2b; Jeffrey Kellogg (NL) 3b; Terry Craft (AL) lf; Wally Bell (NL) rf. **Attendance**—44,916. **Time**— 2:36. **TV Rating**—11.8/21 share (Fox).

Home Attendance

Overall 1997 regular season attendance in Major League Baseball was 63,196,222 in 2,234 games for an average per game crowd of 28,288; numbers in parentheses indicate ranking in 1996; HD indicates home dates; Attendance based on tickets sold.

American League

		Attendance	HD	Average
1	Baltimore (1)	3,711,132	81	45,816
2	Cleveland (2)	3,404,750	80	42,559
3	Seattle (4)	3,198,995	81	39,494
4	Texas (3)	2,945,228	80	36,815
5	New York (7)	2,580,445	78	33,083
6	Toronto (5)	2,589,297	81	31,967
7	Boston (6)	2,226,136	80	27,827
8	Chicago (9)	1,865,222	78	23,913
9	Anaheim (8)	1,767,324	81	21,819
10	Kansas City (11)	1,517,638	77	19,710
11	Milwaukee (12)	1,444,027	78	18,513
12	Minnesota (10)	1,411,064	81	17,421
13	Detroit (13)	1,365,157	79	17,280
14	Oakland (14)	1,261,219	79	15,965
	AL Totals	31,287,634	1,114	28,086

National League

		Attendance	HD	Average
1	Colorado (1)	3,888,453	81	48,006
2	Atlanta (3)	3,463,988	81	42,765
3	Los Angeles (2)	3,318,886	81	40,974
4	St. Louis (4)	2,658,357	81	32,819
5	Florida (10)	2,364,387	80	29,555
6	Chicago (5)	2,190,308	79	27,725
7	San Diego (6)	2,089,336	80	26,117
8	Houston (7)	2,046,811	81	25,269
9	New York (12)	1,766,174	78	22,643
10	Cincinnati (8)	1,785,788	80	22,322
11	S. Francisco (13)	1,690,831	80	21,135
12	Pittsburgh (14)	1,657,022	80	20,713
13	Philadelphia (9)	1,490,638	77	19,359
14	Montreal (11)	1,497,609	81	18,489
	NL Totals	31,908,588	1,120	28,490

AL Team by Team Statistics

At least 135 at bats or 40 innings pitched during the regular season, unless otherwise indicated. Players who competed for more than one AL team are listed with their final club. Players traded from the NL are listed with AL team only if they have 135 AB or 40 IP. Note that (*) indicates rookie and PTBN indicates player to be named.

Anaheim Angels

Batting (135 AB)	Avg	AB	R	H	HR	RBI	SB
Garret Anderson ...	303	624	76	189	8	92	10
Darin Erstad	299	539	99	161	16	77	23
Tim Salmon	296	582	95	172	33	129	9
Jim Edmonds	291	502	82	146	26	80	5
Dave Hollins	288	572	101	165	16	85	16
Tony Phillips	275	534	96	147	8	57	13
Jack Howell	259	174	25	45	14	34	1
Luis Alicea	253	388	59	98	5	37	22
Gary DiSarcina	246	549	52	135	4	47	7
Chad Kreuter	231	255	25	59	5	21	0

Acquired: P DeLucia from SF for PTBN (Apr. 14); OF Phillips and C Kreuter from ChW for P Chuck McElroy and C Jorge Fabregas (May 18); P Hill from Tex. for C Jim Leyritz and PTBN (July 29);

Pitching (40 IP)	ERA	W-L	Gm	IP	BB	SO
Mike Holtz	3.32	3-4	66	43.1	15	40
Troy Percival	3.46	5-5	55	52.0	22	72
Rich DeLucia	3.61	6-4	33	42.1	27	42
Pep Harris*	3.62	5-4	61	79.2	38	56
S. Hasegawa	3.93	3-7	50	116.2	46	83
Chuck Finley	4.23	13-6	25	164.0	65	155
Jason Dickson* ...	4.29	13-9	33	203.2	56	115
Mike James	4.31	5-5	58	62.2	28	57
Ken Hill	4.55	9-12	31	190.0	95	106
Allen Watson	4.93	12-12	35	199.0	73	141
Dennis Springer ...	5.18	9-9	32	194.2	73	75
Darrell May*	5.23	2-1	29	51.2	25	42
Mark Langston	5.85	2-4	9	47.2	29	30
Matt Perisho*	6.00	0-2	11	45.0	28	35

Saves: Percival (27); James (7); DeLucia (3); Holtz (2). **Complete games:** Finley and Springer (3); Dickson (2); Hill (1). **Shutouts:** Dickson, Finley and Springer (1).

Baltimore Orioles

Batting (135 AB)	Avg	AB	R	H	HR	RBI	SB
Roberto Alomar	333	412	64	137	14	60	9
Eric Davis	304	158	29	48	8	25	6
Harold Baines	301	452	55	136	16	67	0
Brady Anderson ...	288	590	97	170	18	73	18
B.J. Surhoff	284	528	80	150	18	88	1
Geronimo Berroa ...	283	561	88	159	26	90	4
Cal Ripken Jr.	270	615	79	166	17	84	1
Jeffrey Hammonds ..	264	397	71	105	21	55	15
Chris Hoiles	259	320	45	83	12	49	1
Lenny Webster	255	259	29	66	7	37	0
Rafael Palmeiro ...	254	614	95	156	38	110	5
Jeff Reboulet	237	228	26	54	4	27	3
Mike Bordick	236	509	55	120	7	46	0
Tony Tarasco	205	166	26	34	7	26	2

Acquired: OF Berroa from Oak. for P Jimmy Haynes and PTBN (June 27); DH Baines from ChW for PTBN (July 29).

Pitching (40 IP)	ERA	W-L	Gm	IP	BB	SO
Randy Myers	1.51	2-3	61	59.2	22	56
Jesse Orosco	2.32	6-3	71	50.1	30	46
Armando Benitez .	2.45	4-5	71	73.1	43	106
Arthur Rhodes	3.02	10-3	53	95.1	26	102
Mike Mussina	3.20	15-8	33	224.2	54	218
Jimmy Key	3.43	16-10	34	212.1	82	141
Scott Erickson	3.69	16-7	34	221.2	61	131
Scott Kamieniecki .	4.01	10-6	30	179.1	67	109
Terry Mathews	4.41	4-4	57	63.1	36	39
Rick Krivda	6.30	4-2	10	50.0	18	29
Shawn Boskie	6.43	6-6	28	77.0	26	50

Saves: Myers (45); Benitez (9); Boskie, Mathews and Rhodes (1). **Complete games:** Mussina (4); Erickson (3); Key (1). **Shutouts:** Erickson (2); Key and Mussina (1).

Boston Red Sox

Batting (135 AB)	Avg	AB	R	H	HR	RBI	SB
Reggie Jefferson ..	319	489	74	156	13	67	1
Mo Vaughn	315	527	91	166	35	96	2
Jeff Frye	312	404	56	126	3	51	19
Troy O'Leary	309	499	65	154	15	80	0
John Valentin	306	575	95	176	18	77	7
N. Garciaparra* ..	306	684	122	209	30	98	22
Tim Naehring	286	259	38	74	9	40	1
Wil Cordero	281	570	82	160	18	72	1
Scott Hatteberg* ..	277	350	46	97	10	44	0
Darren Bragg	257	513	65	132	9	57	10
Bill Haselman	236	212	22	50	6	26	0
Curtis Pride	213	164	22	35	3	20	6

Acquired: P Lowe and C Jason Varitek from Sea. for P Heathcliff Slocumb (July 31).
Signed: OF Pride (Aug. 30).

Pitching (40 IP)	ERA	W-L	Gm	IP	BB	SO
Jim Corsi	3.43	5-3	52	57.2	21	40
Butch Henry	3.52	7-3	36	84.1	19	51
Tom Gordon	3.74	6-10	42	182.2	78	159
Tim Wakefield ...	4.25	12-15	35	201.1	87	151
John Wasdin	4.40	4-6	53	124.2	38	84
Aaron Sele	5.38	13-12	33	177.1	80	122
Mark Brandenburg	5.49	0-2	31	41.0	16	34
Jeff Suppan	5.69	7-3	23	112.1	36	67
Chris Hammond ...	5.92	3-4	29	65.1	27	48
Kerry Lacy*	6.11	1-1	33	45.2	22	18
Derek Lowe*	6.13	2-6	20	69.0	23	52
Vaughn Eshelman .	6.33	3-3	21	42.2	17	18
Steve Avery	6.42	6-7	22	96.2	49	51

Saves: Gordon (11); Henry (6); Lacy (3); Corsi (2); Hammond (1). **Complete games:** Wakefield (4); Gordon (2); Sele (1). **Shutouts:** Wakefield (2); Gordon (1).

Chicago White Sox

Batting (135 AB)	Avg	AB	R	H	HR	RBI	SB
Frank Thomas	347	530	110	184	35	125	1
Norberto Martin ..	300	213	24	64	2	27	1
Dave Martinez	286	504	78	144	12	55	12
Albert Belle	274	634	90	174	30	116	4
Ray Durham	271	634	106	172	11	53	33
Lyle Mouton	269	242	26	65	5	23	4
Robin Ventura	262	183	27	48	6	26	0
Mike Cameron* ...	259	379	63	98	14	55	23
Jorge Fabregas ...	258	360	33	93	7	51	1
Ozzie Guillen	245	490	59	120	4	52	5
Chris Snopek	218	298	27	65	5	35	3
Ron Karkovice ...	181	138	10	25	6	18	0

Acquired: P McElroy and C Fabregas from Ana. for OF Tony Phillips and C Chad Kreuter (May 18).
Traded: P Hernandez, P Alvarez and P Darwin to SF for six minor leaguers (July 31).

Pitching (40 IP)	ERA	W-L	Gm	IP	BB	SO
Roberto Hernandez	2.44	5-1	46	48.0	24	47
Matt Karchner	2.91	3-1	52	52.2	26	30
Wilson Alvarez ...	3.03	9-8	22	145.2	55	110
Chuck McElroy ...	3.84	1-3	61	75.0	22	62
Danny Darwin	4.13	4-8	21	113.1	31	62
Bill Simas	4.33	3-1	40	41.1	24	38
Carlos Castillo* ..	4.48	2-1	37	66.1	33	43
Tony Castillo	4.91	4-4	64	62.1	23	42
Scott Eyre*	5.04	4-4	11	60.2	31	36
James Baldwin ...	5.27	12-15	32	200.0	83	140
Doug Drabek	5.74	12-11	31	169.1	69	85
Jaime Navarro ...	5.79	9-14	33	209.2	73	142

Saves: Hernandez (27); Karchner (15); T. Castillo (4); C. Castillo, McElroy and Simas (1). **Complete games:** Alvarez and Navarro (2); Baldwin and Darwin (1). **Shutouts:** Alvarez (1).

AL Team by Team Statistics (Cont.)

Cleveland Indians

Batting (135 AB)	Avg	AB	R	H	HR	RBI	SB
Dave Justice	.329	495	84	163	33	101	3
Manny Ramirez	.328	561	99	184	26	88	2
Sandy Alomar Jr.	.324	451	63	146	21	83	0
Bip Roberts	.302	431	63	130	4	44	18
Pat Borders	.296	159	17	47	4	15	0
Jim Thome	.286	496	104	142	40	102	1
Tony Fernandez	.286	409	55	117	11	44	6
Omar Vizquel	.280	565	89	158	5	49	43
Brian Giles	.268	377	62	101	17	61	13
Kevin Seitzer	.268	198	27	53	2	24	0
Matt Williams	.263	596	86	157	32	105	12
Marquis Grissom	.262	558	74	146	12	66	22

Acquired: IF Roberts from KC for P Roland de la Maza (Aug. 31).
Claimed: P Jacome on waivers from KC (May 8).

Pitching (40 IP)	ERA	W-L	Gm	IP	BB	SO
Jose Mesa	2.40	4-4	66	82.1	28	69
Paul Assenmacher	2.94	5-0	75	49.0	15	53
Mike Jackson	3.24	2-5	71	75.0	29	74
Charles Nagy	4.28	15-11	34	227.0	77	149
Jaret Wright*	4.38	8-3	16	90.1	35	63
Orel Hershiser	4.47	14-6	32	195.1	69	107
Eric Plunk	4.66	4-5	55	65.2	36	66
Brian Anderson	4.69	4-2	8	48.0	11	22
Chad Ogea	4.99	8-9	21	126.1	47	80
Jack McDowell	5.09	3-3	8	40.2	18	38
Bartolo Colon*	5.65	4-7	19	94.0	45	66
Jason Jacome	5.84	2-0	28	49.1	20	27
Paul Shuey	6.20	4-2	40	45.0	28	46
Albie Lopez	6.93	3-7	37	76.2	40	63

Saves: Mesa (16); Jackson (15); Assenmacher (4); Shuey (2).
Complete games: Colon, Hershiser, Nagy and Ogea (1).
Shutouts: Nagy (1).

Detroit Tigers

Batting (135 AB)	Avg	AB	R	H	HR	RBI	SB
Bobby Higginson	.299	546	94	163	27	101	12
Matt Walbeck	.277	137	18	38	3	10	3
Tony Clark	.276	580	105	160	32	117	1
Travis Fryman	.274	595	90	163	22	102	16
Bob Hamelin	.270	318	47	86	18	52	2
Brian L. Hunter	.269	658	112	177	4	45	74
Damion Easley	.264	527	97	139	22	72	28
Raul Casanova*	.243	304	27	74	5	24	1
Deivi Cruz*	.241	436	35	105	2	40	3
Brian Johnson	.237	139	13	33	2	18	1
Phil Nevin	.235	251	32	59	9	35	0
Melvin Nieves	.228	359	46	82	20	64	1

Acquired: P Sanders and two minor leaguers from Sea. for P Omar Olivares and P Felipe Lira (July 18).
Claimed: P Jarvis on waivers from Cin. (May 2) and then from Min. (June 17).
Signed: 1B/DH Hamelin (Apr. 8); P Bautista (Apr. 9).

Pitching (40 IP)	ERA	W-L	Gm	IP	BB	SO
Justin Thompson	3.02	15-11	32	223.1	66	151
Todd Jones	3.09	5-4	68	70.0	35	70
Doug Brocail	3.23	3-4	61	78.0	36	60
Willie Blair	4.17	16-8	29	175.0	46	90
A.J. Sager	4.60	3-4	38	84.0	24	53
Brian Moehler*	4.67	11-12	31	175.1	61	97
Dan Miceli	5.01	3-2	71	82.2	38	79
Mike Myers	5.70	0-4	88	53.2	25	50
Scott Sanders	5.86	6-14	47	139.2	62	120
Greg Keagle	6.55	3-5	11	45.1	18	33
Jose Bautista	6.69	2-2	21	40.1	12	19
Kevin Jarvis	7.08	0-3	23	54.2	22	36

Saves: Jones (31); Sager and Miceli (3); Brocail, Myers and Sanders (2). **Complete games:** Thompson (4); Blair and Moehler (2); Sanders (1). **Shutouts:** Moehler and Sanders (1).

Kansas City Royals

Batting (135 AB)	Avg	AB	R	H	HR	RBI	SB
Jose Offerman	.297	424	59	126	2	39	9
Jay Bell	.291	573	89	167	21	92	10
Chili Davis	.279	477	71	133	30	90	6
Johnny Damon	.275	472	70	130	8	48	16
Yamil Benitez*	.267	191	22	51	8	21	2
Dean Palmer	.256	542	70	139	23	86	2
Mike Sweeney	.242	240	30	58	7	31	3
David Howard	.241	162	24	39	1	13	2
Jeff King	.238	543	84	129	28	112	16
Mike Macfarlane	.237	257	34	61	8	35	0
Jermaine Dye	.236	263	26	62	7	22	2
Craig Paquette	.230	252	26	58	8	33	2
Scott Cooper	.201	159	12	32	3	15	1

Acquired: P Bones from Mil. for cash (June 26); IF Palmer from Tex. for OF Tom Goodwin (July 25).
Signed: P Olson (May 24).

Pitching (40 IP)	ERA	W-L	Gm	IP	BB	SO
Kevin Appier	.340	9-13	34	235.2	74	196
Jeff Montgomery	3.49	1-4	55	59.1	18	48
Hipolito Pichardo	4.22	3-5	47	49.0	24	34
Chris Haney	4.38	1-2	8	24.2	5	14
Jose Rosado	4.69	9-12	33	203.1	73	129
Tim Belcher	5.02	13-12	32	213.1	70	113
Jamie Walker*	5.44	3-3	50	43.0	20	24
Jim Pittsley*	5.46	5-8	21	112.0	54	52
Glendon Rusch*	5.50	6-9	30	170.1	52	116
Gregg Olson	5.58	4-3	45	50.0	28	34
Ricky Bones	5.97	4-7	21	78.1	25	36

Saves: Montgomery (14); Pichardo (11); Olson (1). **Complete games:** Appier (4); Belcher (3); Rosado (2); Rusch and Bones (1). **Shutouts:** Appier and Belcher (1).

Milwaukee Brewers

Batting (135 AB)	Avg	AB	R	H	HR	RBI	SB
Jeff Cirillo	.288	580	74	167	10	82	4
Mark Loretta	.287	418	56	120	5	47	5
Jesse Levis	.285	200	19	57	1	19	1
Jeromy Burnitz	.281	494	85	139	27	85	20
Dave Nilsson	.278	554	71	154	20	81	2
Fernando Vina	.275	324	37	89	4	28	8
Julio Franco	.270	430	68	116	7	44	15
Darrin Jackson	.261	211	26	55	5	36	4
Jose Valentin	.253	494	58	125	17	58	19
Gerald Williams	.253	566	73	143	10	41	23
Matt Mieske	.249	253	39	63	5	21	1
John Jaha	.247	162	25	40	11	26	1
Jack Voigt	.245	151	20	37	8	22	1
Mike Matheny	.244	320	29	78	4	32	0
Marc Newfield	.229	157	14	36	1	18	0
Jeff Huson	.203	143	12	29	0	11	3

Acquired: IF Huson from Col. for PTBN (Apr. 23); OF Jackson from Min. for PTBN (Aug. 31).
Signed: IF Franco (Aug. 13).

Pitching (40 IP)	ERA	W-L	Gm	IP	BB	SO
Doug Jones	2.02	6-6	75	80.1	9	82
Bob Wickman	2.73	7-6	74	95.2	41	78
Ron Villone	3.42	1-0	50	52.2	36	40
Mike Fetters	3.45	1-5	51	70.1	33	62
Joel Adamson*	3.54	5-3	30	76.1	19	56
Jose Mercedes	3.79	7-10	29	159.0	53	80
Ben McDonald	4.06	8-7	21	133.0	36	110
Bryce Florie	4.32	4-4	32	75.0	42	53
Scott Karl	4.47	10-13	32	193.1	67	119
Jeff D'Amico	4.71	9-7	23	135.2	43	94
Cal Eldred	4.99	13-15	34	202.0	89	122

Saves: Jones (36); Fetters (8); Wickman (1). **Complete games:** Mercedes (3); McDonald, Karl, D'Amico and Eldred. **Shutouts:** Mercedes, D'Amico and Eldred (1).

Minnesota Twins

Batting (135 AB)	Avg	AB	R	H	HR	RBI	SB
Paul Molitor	.305	538	63	164	10	89	11
Ron Coomer	.298	523	63	156	13	85	4
Chuck Knoblauch	.291	611	117	178	9	58	62
Greg Colbrunn	.281	217	24	61	5	26	1
Pat Meares	.276	439	63	121	10	60	7
Brent Brede*	.274	190	25	52	3	21	7
Greg Myers	.267	165	24	44	5	28	0
Rich Becker	.264	443	61	117	10	45	17
Denny Hocking	.257	253	28	65	2	25	3
Terry Steinbach	.248	447	60	111	12	54	6
Matt Lawton	.248	460	74	114	14	60	7
Marty Cordova	.246	378	44	93	15	51	5
Todd Walker*	.237	156	15	37	3	16	7
Scott Stahoviak	.229	275	33	63	10	33	5

Traded: IF Colbrunn to Atl. for PTBN (Aug. 14); C Myers to Atl. for PTBN (Sept. 5).

Pitching (40 IP)	ERA	W-L	Gm	IP	BB	SO
Greg Swindell	.3.58	7 4	65	115.2	25	75
Rick Aguilera	.3.82	5-4	61	68.1	22	68
Brad Radke	.3.87	20-10	35	239.2	48	174
Eddie Guardado	.3.91	0-4	69	46.0	17	54
Bob Tewksbury	.4.22	8-13	26	168.2	31	92
Mike Trombley	.4.37	2-3	67	82.1	31	74
Todd Ritchie*	.4.58	2-3	42	74.2	28	44
Frank Rodriguez	.4.62	3-6	43	142.1	60	65
Rich Robertson	.5.69	8-12	31	147.0	70	69
LaToy Hawkins	.5.84	6-12	20	103.1	47	58
Travis Miller*	.7.63	1-5	13	48.1	23	26
Scott Aldred	.7.68	2-10	17	77.1	28	33

Saves: Aguilera (26); Swindell, Guardado and Trombley (1). **Complete games:** Tewksbury (5); Radke (4). **Shutouts:** Tewksbury (2); Radke (1).

New York Yankees

Batting (135 AB)	Avg	AB	R	H	HR	RBI	SB
Bernie Williams	.328	509	107	167	21	100	15
Paul O'Neill	.324	553	89	179	21	117	10
Tim Raines	.321	271	56	87	4	38	8
Luis Sojo	.307	215	27	66	2	25	3
Mike Stanley	.297	347	61	103	16	65	0
Tino Martinez	.296	594	96	176	44	141	3
Wade Boggs	.292	353	55	103	4	28	0
Derek Jeter	.291	654	116	190	10	70	23
Chad Curtis	.284	349	59	99	15	55	12
Mark Whiten	.265	215	34	57	5	24	4
Joe Girardi	.264	398	38	105	1	50	2
Cecil Fielder	.260	361	40	94	13	61	0
Charlie Hayes	.258	353	39	91	11	53	3
Jorge Posada*	.250	188	29	47	6	25	1
Pete Incaviglia	.247	154	19	38	5	12	0

Acquired: P Irabu and three minor leaguers from SD for $3 million, OF Ruben Rivera and P Rafael Medina (Apr. 22); OF Curtis from Cle. for P David Weathers (Apr. 22); C/DH Stanley and minor leaguer from Bos. for minor leaguer and PTBN (Aug. 13); IF Sanchez from ChC for minor leaguer (Aug. 16); **Signed:** OF Incaviglia (July 25).

Pitching (50 IP)	ERA	W-L	Gm	IP	BB	SO
Mariano Rivera	.1.88	6-4	66	71.2	20	68
Mike Stanton	.2.57	6-1	64	66.2	34	70
David Cone	.2.82	12-6	29	195.0	86	222
Jeff Nelson	.2.86	3-7	77	78.2	37	81
Andy Pettitte	.2.88	18-7	35	240.1	65	166
David Wells	.4.21	16-10	32	218.0	45	156
Ramiro Mendoza	.4.24	8-6	39	133.2	28	82
Dwight Gooden	.4.91	9-5	20	106.1	53	66
Kenny Rogers	.5.65	6-7	31	145.0	62	78
Hideki Irabu	.7.09	5-4	13	53.1	20	56

Saves: Rivera (43); Stanton (3); Nelson and Mendoza (2); Lloyd (1). **Complete games:** Wells (5); Pettitte (4); Cone and Rogers (1). **Shutouts:** Wells (2); Pettitte (1).

Oakland Athletics

Batting (180 AB)	Avg	AB	R	H	HR	RBI	SB
Dave Magadan	.303	271	38	82	4	30	1
Matt Stairs	.298	352	62	105	27	73	3
Jason Giambi	.293	519	66	152	20	81	0
Brent Mayne	.289	256	29	74	6	22	1
George Williams	.289	201	30	58	3	22	0
Mark McGwire	.284	366	48	104	34	81	1
Rafael Bournigal	.279	222	29	62	1	20	2
Jason McDonald*	.263	236	47	62	4	14	13
Damon Mashore	.247	279	55	69	3	18	5
Scott Spiezio*	.243	538	58	131	14	65	9
Jose Canseco	.235	388	56	91	23	74	8
Mark Bellhorn*	.228	224	33	51	6	19	7
Scott Brosius	.203	479	59	97	11	41	9
Tony Batista	.202	188	22	38	4	18	2

Acquired: P Haynes and PTBN from Bal. for OF Geronimo Berroa (June 27); **Claimed:** IF Brito on waivers from Tor. (Aug. 8). **Traded:** IF McGwire to St.L for P T.J. Mathews and two minor leaguers (July 31).

Pitching (50 IP)	ERA	W-L	Gm	IP	BB	SO
Bill Taylor	.3.82	3-4	72	73.0	36	66
Aaron Small*	.4.28	9-5	71	96.2	40	57
Jimmy Haynes	.4.42	3-6	13	73.1	40	65
Brad Rigby	.4.87	1-7	14	77.2	22	34
Mike Oquist	.5.02	4-6	19	107.2	43	72
Ariel Prieto	.5.04	6-8	22	125.0	70	90
Mike Mohler	.5.13	1-10	62	101.2	54	66
Buddy Groom	.5.15	2-2	78	64.2	24	45
Steve Karsay	.5.77	3-12	24	132.2	47	92
Carlos Reyes	.5.82	3-4	37	77.1	25	43
Don Wengert	.6.04	5-11	49	134.0	41	68
Dave Telgheder	.6.06	4-6	20	101.0	35	55
Willie Adams	.8.18	3-5	13	58.1	32	37

Saves: Taylor (23); Small (4); Groom (3); Johnson and Wengert (2); Mohler (1). **Complete games:** Oquist and Wengert (1). **Shutouts:** none.

Seattle Mariners

Batting (150 AB)	Avg	AB	R	H	HR	RBI	SB
Edgar Martinez	.330	542	104	179	28	108	2
Ken Griffey Jr.	.304	608	125	185	56	147	15
Alex Rodriguez	.300	587	100	176	23	84	29
Joey Cora	.300	574	105	172	11	54	6
Mike Blowers	.293	150	22	44	5	20	0
Roberto Kelly	.291	368	58	107	12	59	9
Rich Amaral	.284	190	34	54	1	21	12
Russ Davis	.271	420	57	114	20	63	6
Dan Wilson	.270	508	66	137	15	74	7
Paul Sorrento	.269	457	68	123	31	80	0
Jay Buhner	.243	540	104	131	40	109	0
Brent Gates	.238	151	18	36	3	20	0

Acquired: P Olivares and P Lira from Det. for P Scott Sanders two minor leaguers (July 18); P Timlin and P Spoljaric from Tor. for OF Jose Cruz Jr. (July 31); P Slocumb from Bos. for P Derek Lowe and C Jason Varitek (July 31); OF Kelly from Min. for PTBN (Aug. 21).

Pitching (50 IP)	ERA	W- L	Gm	IP	BB	SO
Randy Johnson	.2.28	20-4	30	213.0	77	291
Mike Timlin	.3.22	6-4	64	72.2	20	45
Jeff Fassero	.3.61	16-9	35	234.1	84	189
Paul Spoljaric	.3.69	0-3	57	70.2	36	70
Bobby Ayala	.3.82	10-5	71	96.2	41	92
Jamie Moyer	.3.86	17-5	30	188.2	43	113
Omar Olivares	.4.97	6-10	32	177.1	81	103
Ken Cloude*	.5.12	4-2	10	51.0	26	46
H. Slocumb	.5.16	0-9	76	75.0	49	64
Bob Wells	.5.75	2-0	46	67.1	18	51
Bob Wolcott	.6.03	5-6	19	100.0	29	58
Felipe Lira	.6.34	5-11	28	110.2	55	73
Norm Charlton	.7.27	3-8	71	69.1	47	55

Saves: Slocumb (27); Charlton (14); Timlin (10); Ayala (8); Spoljaric (3); Wells (2). **Complete games:** Johnson (5); Olivares (3); Fassero and Moyer (2); Lira (1). **Shutouts:** Johnson and Olivares (2); Fassero and Lira (1).

AL Team by Team Statistics (Cont.)

Texas Rangers

Batting (140 AB)	Avg	AB	R	H	HR	RBI	SB
Will Clark	.326	393	56	128	12	51	0
Rusty Greer	.321	601	112	193	26	87	9
Ivan Rodriguez	.313	597	98	187	20	77	7
Lee Stevens	.300	426	58	128	21	74	1
Juan Gonzalez	.296	533	87	158	42	131	0
Domingo Cedeno	.282	365	49	103	4	36	3
Jim Leyritz	.277	379	58	105	11	64	2
Billy Ripken	.276	203	18	56	3	24	0
Mark McLemore	.261	349	47	91	1	25	7
Tom Goodwin	.260	574	90	149	2	39	50
Fernando Tatis*	.256	223	29	57	8	29	3
Damon Buford	.224	366	49	82	8	39	18
Benji Gil	.224	317	35	71	5	31	1
Warren Newson	.213	169	23	36	10	23	3

Acquired: OF Goodwin from KC for IF Dean Palmer (July 25); C Leyritz and PTBN from Ana. for P Ken Hill (July 29); P Helling from Fla. for P Vosberg (Aug. 12); **Claimed:** P Clark on waivers from Cle. (Aug. 5);

Pitching (45 IP)	ERA	W-L	Gm	IP	BB	SO
John Wetteland	1.94	7-2	61	65.0	21	63
Eric Gunderson	3.26	2-1	60	49.2	15	31
Danny Patterson*	3.42	10-6	54	71.0	23	69
Darren Oliver	4.20	13-12	32	201.1	82	104
Roger Pavlik	4.37	3-5	11	57.2	31	35
Xavier Hernandez	4.56	0-4	44	49.1	22	36
John Burkett	4.56	9-12	30	189.1	30	139
Rick Helling	4.58	3-3	10	55.0	21	46
Bobby Witt	4.82	12-12	34	209.0	74	121
Matt Whiteside	5.08	4-1	42	72.2	26	44
Terry Clark	6.00	1-7	13	57.0	23	24
Julio Santana*	6.75	4-6	30	104.0	49	64

Saves: Wetteland (31); Gunderson and Patterson (1). **Complete games:** Oliver and Witt (3); Burkett (2). **Shutouts:** Oliver (1).

Toronto Blue Jays

Batting (135 AB)	Avg	AB	R	H	HR	RBI	SB
Shawn Green	.287	429	57	123	16	53	14
Shannon Stewart*	.286	168	25	48	0	22	10
Orlando Merced	.266	368	45	98	9	40	7
Carlos Delgado	.262	519	79	136	30	91	0
Otis Nixon	.262	401	54	105	1	26	47
Jose Cruz Jr.*	.248	395	59	98	26	68	7
Benito Santiago	.243	341	31	83	13	42	1
Alex Gonzalez	.239	426	46	102	12	35	15
Mariano Duncan	.236	339	36	80	1	25	6
Joe Carter	.234	612	76	143	21	102	8
Ed Sprague	.228	504	63	115	14	48	0
Carlos Garcia	.220	350	29	77	3	23	11
Charlie O'Brien	.218	225	22	49	4	27	0
Jacob Brumfield	.207	174	22	36	2	20	4

Acquired: IF Duncan and cash from NYY for minor leaguer (July 29); OF Cruz Jr. from Sea. for P Mike Timlin and P Paul Spoljaric (July 31). **Traded:** OF Nixon to LA for C Bobby Cripps (Aug. 12).

Pitching (40 IP)	ERA	W-L	Gm	IP	BB	SO
Paul Quantrill	1.94	6-7	77	88.0	17	56
Roger Clemens	2.05	21-7	34	264.0	68	292
Dan Plesac	3.58	2-4	73	50.1	19	61
Pat Hentgen	3.68	15-10	35	264.2	71	160
Woody Williams	4.35	9-14	31	194.2	66	124
Juan Guzman	4.95	3-6	13	60.0	31	52
Chris Carpenter*	5.09	3-7	14	81.1	37	55
Robert Person	5.61	5-10	23	128.1	60	99
Luis Andujar	6.48	0-6	17	50.0	21	28
Tim Crabtree	7.08	3-3	37	40.2	17	26

Saves: Escobar (14); Quantrill (5); Crabtree (2); Plesac (1). **Complete games:** Clemens and Hentgen (9); Carpenter (1). **Shutouts:** Clemens and Hentgen (3); Carpenter (1).

Players Who Played in Both Leagues in 1997

While all individual major league statistics count on career records, players cannot transfer their stats from one league to the other if they are traded during the regular season. Here are the combined stats for batters with 235 at bats and pitchers with 80 innings pitched, who played in both leagues in 1997.

Batters (235 AB)

	Avg	AB	R	H	HR	RBI	SB
Greg Colbrunn	.280	271	27	76	7	35	1
MIN	.281	217	24	61	5	26	1
ATL	.278	54	3	15	2	9	0
Rickey Henderson	.248	403	84	100	8	34	45
S.D.	.274	288	63	79	6	27	29
ANA	.183	115	21	21	2	7	16
Brian Johnson	.261	318	32	83	13	45	1
DET	.237	139	13	33	2	18	1
S.F.	.279	179	19	50	11	27	0
Mark McGwire	.274	540	86	148	58	123	3
OAK	.284	366	48	104	34	81	1
ST.L	.253	174	38	44	24	42	2

	Avg	AB	R	H	HR	RBI	SB
Otis Nixon	.266	576	84	153	2	44	59
TOR	.262	401	54	105	1	26	47
L.A.	.274	175	30	48	1	18	12
Rey Sanchez	.274	343	35	94	2	27	4
CHI (NL)	.249	205	14	51	1	12	4
N.Y. (AL)	.312	138	21	43	1	15	0
Chuck Carr	.248	238	37	59	4	17	12
MIL	.130	46	3	6	0	0	1
HOU	.276	192	34	53	4	17	11

Pitchers (80 IP)

	ERA	W-L	Gm	IP	BB	SO
Wilson Alvarez	3.48	13-11	33	212.0	91	179
CHI (AL)	3.03	9-8	22	145.2	55	110
S.F.	4.48	4-3	11	66.1	36	69
Ricky Bones	6.75	4-8	30	96.0	36	44
CIN	10.19	0-1	9	17.2	11	8
K.C.	5.97	4-7	21	78.1	25	36
Hector Carrasco	4.40	2-8	66	86.0	41	76
CIN	3.68	1-2	38	51.1	25	46
K.C.	5.45	1-6	28	34.2	16	30
Danny Darwin	4.35	5-11	31	157.1	45	92
CHI (AL)	4.13	4-8	21	113.1	31	62
SF	4.91	1-3	10	44.0	14	30
Rick Helling	4.47	5-9	41	131.0	69	99
FLA	4.38	2-6	31	76.0	48	53
TEX	4.58	3-3	10	55.0	21	46

	ERA	W-L	Gm	IP	BB	SO
Roberto Hernandez	2.45	10-3	74	80.2	38	82
CHI (AL)	2.44	5-1	46	48.0	24	47
S.F.	2.48	5-2	28	32.2	14	35
Mike Johnson	6.83	2-6	25	89.2	37	57
BAL	7.94	0-1	14	39.2	16	29
MON	5.94	2-5	11	50.0	21	28
Jeff Juden	4.46	11-6	30	161.1	72	136
MON	4.22	11-5	22	130.0	57	107
CLE	5.46	0-1	8	31.1	15	29
John Smiley	5.31	11-14	26	154.1	41	120
CIN	5.23	9-10	20	117.0	31	94
CLE	5.54	2-4	6	37.1	10	26

NL Team by Team Statistics

At least 135 at bats or 40 innings pitched during the regular season unless otherwise indicated. Players who competed for more than one NL team are listed with their final club. Players traded from the AL are listed with NL team only if they have 135 AB or 40 IP. Note that (*) indicates rookie.

Atlanta Braves

Batting (135 AB)	Avg	AB	R	H	HR	RBI	SB
Kenny Lofton	.333	493	90	164	5	48	27
Jeff Blauser	.308	519	90	160	17	70	5
Chipper Jones	.295	597	100	176	21	111	20
Javier Lopez	.295	414	52	122	23	68	1
Michael Tucker	.283	499	80	141	14	56	12
Keith Lockhart	.279	147	25	41	6	32	0
Fred McGriff	.277	564	77	156	22	97	5
Ryan Klesko	.261	467	67	122	24	84	4
Tony Graffanino*	.258	186	33	48	8	20	6
Mark Lemke	.245	351	33	86	2	26	2
Andruw Jones*	.231	399	60	92	18	70	20
Eduardo Perez	.215	191	20	41	6	18	0

Pitching (40 IP)	ERA	W-L	Gm	IP	BB	SO
Greg Maddux	2.20	19-4	33	232.2	20	177
Alan Embree	2.54	3-1	66	46.0	20	45
Tom Glavine	2.96	14-7	33	240.0	79	152
Denny Neagle	2.97	20-5	34	233.1	49	172
John Smoltz	3.02	15-12	35	256.0	63	241
Mark Wohlers	3.50	5-7	71	69.1	38	92
Brad Clontz	3.75	5-1	51	48.0	18	42
Kevin Millwood*	4.03	5-3	12	51.1	21	42
Mike Bielecki	4.08	3-7	50	57.1	21	60
Paul Byrd	5.26	4-4	31	53.0	28	37
Terrell Wade	5.36	2-3	12	42.0	16	35

Saves: Wohlers (33); Bielecki (2); Clontz (1). **Complete games:** Smoltz (7); Maddux and Glavine (5); Neagle (4). **Shutouts:** Neagle (4); Maddux, Glavine and Smoltz (2).

Chicago Cubs

Batting (135 AB)	Avg	AB	R	H	HR	RBI	SB
Mark Grace	.319	555	87	177	13	78	2
Dave Hansen	.311	151	19	47	3	21	1
Lance Johnson	.307	410	60	126	5	39	20
Dave Clark	.301	143	19	43	5	32	1
Doug Glanville	.300	474	79	142	4	35	19
Kevin Orie*	.275	364	40	100	8	44	2
Jose Hernandez	.273	183	33	50	7	26	2
Manny Alexander	.266	248	37	66	3	22	13
Ryne Sandberg	.264	447	54	118	12	64	7
Tyler Houston	.260	196	15	51	2	28	1
Scott Servais	.260	385	36	100	6	45	0
Sammy Sosa	.251	642	90	161	36	119	22
Rey Sanchez	.249	205	14	51	1	12	4
Brant Brown*	.234	137	15	32	5	15	2

Acquired: OF Johnson, P Clark and IF Alexander from NYM for OF Brian McRae, P Mel Rojas and P Turk Wendell (Aug. 8). **Traded:** IF Sanchez to NYY for minor leaguer (Aug. 16).

Pitching (40 IP)	ERA	W-L	Gm	IP	BB	SO
Bob Patterson	3.34	1-6	76	59.1	10	58
Kevin Tapani	3.39	9-3	13	85.0	23	55
Mark Clark	3.82	14-8	32	205.0	59	123
Kent Bottenfield	3.86	2-3	64	84.0	35	74
Jeremi Gonzalez*	4.25	11-9	23	144.0	69	93
Steve Trachsel	4.51	8-12	34	201.1	69	160
Kevin Foster	4.61	10-7	26	146.1	66	119
Terry Adams	4.62	2-9	74	74.0	40	64
Ramon Tatis*	5.34	1-1	56	55.2	29	33

Saves: Adams (18); Bottenfield (2). **Complete games:** Clark (3); Tapani, Gonzalez and Foster (1). **Shutouts:** Tapani and Gonzalez (1).

Cincinnati Reds

Batting (145 AB)	Avg	AB	R	H	HR	RBI	SB
Chris Stynes	.348	198	31	69	6	28	11
Jon Nunnally	.318	201	38	64	13	35	7
Barry Larkin	.317	224	34	71	4	20	14
Hal Morris	.276	333	42	92	1	33	3
Deion Sanders	.273	465	53	127	5	23	56
Lenny Harris	.273	238	32	65	3	28	4
Eddie Taubensee	.268	254	26	68	10	34	0
Joe Oliver	.258	349	28	90	14	43	1
Reggie Sanders	.253	312	52	79	19	56	13
Curtis Goodwin	.253	265	27	67	1	12	22
Willie Greene	.253	495	62	125	26	91	6
Eduardo Perez	.253	297	44	75	16	52	5
Bret Boone	.223	443	40	99	7	46	5
Pokey Reese	.219	397	48	87	4	26	25

Acquired: OF Stynes and OF Nunnally from KC for P Carrasco and P Scott Service (July 15). **Traded:** P Smiley and IF Jeff Branson to Cle. for four minor leaguers (July 31).

Pitching (50 IP)	ERA	W-L	Gm	IP	BB	SO
Jeff Shaw	2.38	4-2	78	94.2	12	74
Scott Sullivan*	3.24	5-3	59	97.1	30	96
Brett Tomko*	3.43	11-7	22	126.0	47	95
Hector Carrasco	3.68	1-2	58	51.1	25	46
Stan Belinda	3.71	1-5	84	99.1	33	114
Kent Mercker	3.92	8-11	28	144.2	62	75
Mike Remlinger	4.14	8-8	69	124.0	60	145
Dave Burba	4.73	11-10	30	160.0	73	131
Mike Morgan	4.78	9-12	31	162.0	49	103
John Smiley	5.23	9-10	20	117.0	31	94
Pete Schourek	5.42	5-8	18	84.2	38	59

Saves: Shaw (42); Remlinger (2); Sullivan, Belinda and White (1). **Complete games:** Remlinger and Burba (2); Morgan (1). **Shutouts:** none.

Colorado Rockies

Batting (135 AB)	Avg	AB	R	H	HR	RBI	SB
Larry Walker	.366	568	143	208	49	130	33
Andres Galarraga	.318	600	120	191	41	140	15
Dante Bichette	.308	561	81	173	26	118	6
Vinny Castilla	.304	612	94	186	40	113	2
Jeff Reed	.297	256	43	76	17	47	2
Q. McCracken	.292	325	69	95	3	36	28
Neifi Perez*	.291	313	46	91	5	31	4
Ellis Burks	.290	424	91	123	32	82	7
Walt Weiss	.270	393	52	106	4	38	5
Kirt Manwaring	.226	337	22	76	1	27	1

Acquired: P Castillo from ChC for P Matt Pool (July 15); P Hutton from Fla. for P Craig Counsell (July 27); P Astacio from LA for IF Eric Young (Aug. 18).

Pitching (50 IP)	ERA	W-L	Gm	IP	BB	SO
Mike DeJean*	3.99	5-0	55	67.2	24	38
Steve Reed	4.04	4-6	63	62.1	27	43
Pedro Astacio	4.14	12-10	33	202.1	61	166
Roger Bailey	4.29	9-10	29	191.0	70	84
Mark Hutton	4.48	3-2	40	60.1	26	39
Jerry Dipoto	4.70	5-3	74	95.2	33	74
John Thomson*	4.71	7-9	27	166.1	51	106
Darren Holmes	5.34	9-2	42	89.1	36	70
Frank Castillo	5.42	12-13	34	184.1	69	126
Curtis Leskanic	5.55	4-0	55	58.1	24	53
Kevin Ritz	5.87	6-8	18	107.1	46	55
Jamey Wright	6.25	8-12	26	149.2	71	59
Bill Swift	6.34	4-6	14	65.1	26	29
John Burke*	6.56	2-5	17	59.0	26	39

Saves: Dipoto (16); Reed (6); Holmes (3); DeJean, Munoz and Leskanic (2). **Complete games:** Bailey (5); Astacio and Thomson (2); Ritz and Wright (1). **Shutouts:** Bailey (2); Astacio and Thomson (1).

NL Team by Team Statistics (Cont.)

Florida Marlins

Batting (135 AB)	Avg	AB	R	H	HR	RBI	SB
Gregg Zaun	.301	143	21	43	2	20	1
Craig Counsell*	.299	164	20	49	1	16	1
Bobby Bonilla	.297	562	77	167	17	96	6
Moises Alou	.292	538	88	157	23	115	9
Jim Eisenreich	.280	293	36	82	2	34	0
Edgar Renteria	.277	617	90	171	4	52	32
Kurt Abbott	.274	252	35	69	6	30	3
Darren Daulton	.263	395	68	104	14	63	6
Charles Johnson	.250	416	43	104	19	63	0
Gary Sheffield	.250	444	86	111	21	71	11
Devon White	.245	265	37	65	6	34	13
John Cangelosi	.245	192	28	47	1	12	5
Jeff Conine	.242	405	46	98	17	61	2
Luis Castillo	.240	263	27	63	0	8	16
Cliff Floyd	.234	137	23	32	6	19	6

Acquired: OF Daulton from Phi. for Billy McMillon (July 21); IF Counsell from Col. for P Mark Hutton (July 27). **Traded:** P Helling to Tex. for P Ed Vosberg (Aug. 12).

Pitching (40 IP)	ERA	W-L	Gm	IP	BB	SO
Kevin Brown	2.69	16-8	33	237.1	66	205
Livan Hernandez*	3.18	9-3	17	96.1	38	72
Jay Powell	3.28	7-2	74	79.2	30	65
Alex Fernandez	3.59	17-12	32	220.2	69	183
Robb Nen	3.89	9-3	73	74.0	40	81
Dennis Cook	3.90	1-2	59	62.1	28	63
Felix Heredia*	4.29	5-3	56	56.2	30	54
Al Leiter	4.34	11-9	27	151.1	91	132
Rick Helling	4.38	2-6	31	76.0	48	53
Rob Stanifer*	4.60	1-2	36	45.0	16	28
Tony Saunders*	4.61	4-6	22	111.1	64	102

Saves: Nen (35); Powell (2); Vosberg and Stanifer (1). **Complete games:** Brown (6); Fernandez (5). **Shutouts:** Brown (2); Fernandez (1).

Houston Astros

Batting (135 AB)	Avg	AB	R	H	HR	RBI	SB
Bill Spiers	.320	291	51	93	4	48	10
Craig Biggio	.309	619	146	191	22	81	47
Jeff Bagwell	.286	566	109	162	43	135	31
Chuck Carr	.276	192	34	53	4	17	11
Derek Bell	.276	493	67	136	15	71	15
Tony Eusebio	.274	164	12	45	1	18	0
Brad Ausmus	.266	425	45	113	4	44	14
Ricky Gutierrez	.261	303	33	79	3	34	5
Luis Gonzalez	.258	550	78	142	10	68	10
Sean Berry	.256	301	37	77	8	43	1
Bob Abreu*	.250	188	22	47	3	26	7
Tim Bogar	.249	241	30	60	4	30	4
Thomas Howard	.247	255	24	63	3	22	1
James Mouton	.211	180	24	38	3	23	9

Claimed: IF Bogar on waivers from NYM (Mar. 31). **Signed:** OF Carr (June 1).

Pitchers (40 IP)	ERA	W-L	Gm	IP	BB	SO
Tom Martin*	2.09	5-3	55	56.0	23	36
Mike Magnante	2.27	3-1	40	47.2	11	43
Darryl Kile	2.57	19-7	34	255.2	94	205
Billy Wagner	2.85	7-8	62	66.1	30	106
Chris Holt*	3.52	8-12	33	209.2	61	95
Ramon Garcia	3.69	9-8	42	158.2	52	120
Mike Hampton	3.83	15-10	34	223.0	77	139
Shane Reynolds	4.23	9-10	30	181.0	47	152
Russ Springer	4.23	3-3	54	55.1	27	74
Jose Lima	5.28	1-6	52	75.0	16	63
John Hudek	5.98	1-3	40	40.2	33	36
Donne Wall	6.26	2-5	8	41.2	16	25

Saves: Wagner (23); Hudek (4); Springer (3); Martin and Lima (2); Magnante and Garcia (1). **Complete games:** Hampton (7); Kile (6); Reynolds (2); Garcia (1). **Shutouts:** Kile (4); Hampton (2); Garcia (1).

Los Angeles Dodgers

Batting (135 AB)	Avg	AB	R	H	HR	RBI	SB
Mike Piazza	.362	556	104	201	40	124	5
Raul Mondesi	.310	616	95	191	30	87	32
Wilton Guerrero*	.291	357	39	104	4	32	6
Brett Butler	.283	343	52	97	0	18	15
Eric Young	.280	622	106	174	8	61	45
Otis Nixon	.274	175	30	48	1	18	12
Roger Cedeno	.273	194	31	53	3	17	9
Todd Zeile	.268	575	89	154	31	90	8
Eric Karros	.266	628	86	167	31	104	15
Greg Gagne	.251	514	49	129	9	57	2
T. Hollandsworth	.247	296	39	73	4	31	5

Acquired: OF Nixon from Tor. for C Bobby Cripps (Aug. 12); IF Young from Col. for P Pedro Astacio (Aug. 18).

Pitching (40 IP)	ERA	W-L	Gm	IP	BB	SO
Antonio Osuna	2.19	3-4	48	61.2	19	68
Darren Hall	2.30	3-2	63	54.2	26	39
Ismael Valdes	2.65	10-11	30	196.2	47	140
Darren Dreifort	2.86	5-2	48	63.0	34	63
Scott Radinsky	2.89	5-1	75	62.1	21	44
Chan Ho Park	3.38	14-8	32	192.0	70	166
Tom Candiotti	3.60	10-7	41	135.0	40	89
Ramon Martinez	3.64	10-5	22	133.2	68	120
Dennis Reyes*	3.83	2-3	14	47.0	18	36
Hideo Nomo	4.25	14-12	33	207.1	92	233
Todd Worrell	5.28	2-6	65	59.2	23	61
Mark Guthrie	5.32	1-4	62	69.1	30	42

Saves: Worrell (35); Dreifort (4); Radinsky (3); Hall (2); Guthrie (1). **Complete games:** Park (2); Martinez and Nomo (1). **Shutouts:** none.

Montreal Expos

Batting (135 AB)	Avg	AB	R	H	HR	RBI	SB
David Segui	.307	459	75	141	21	68	1
Vlad. Guerrero*	.302	325	44	98	11	40	3
Mike Lansing	.281	572	86	161	20	70	11
Darrin Fletcher	.277	310	39	86	17	55	1
M. Grudzielanek	.273	649	76	177	4	51	25
Rondell White	.270	592	84	160	28	82	16
Doug Strange	.257	327	40	84	12	47	0
Ryan McGuire*	.256	199	22	51	3	17	1
F.P. Santangelo	.249	350	56	87	5	31	8
Jose Vidro*	.249	169	19	42	2	17	1
Henry Rodriguez	.244	476	55	116	26	83	3
Chris Widger	.234	278	30	65	7	37	2
Joe Orsulak	.227	150	13	34	1	7	0

Pitching (40 IP)	ERA	W-L	Gm	IP	BB	SO
Pedro Martinez	1.90	17-8	31	241.1	67	305
Marc Valdes	3.13	4-4	48	95.0	39	54
Anthony Telford	3.24	4-6	65	89.0	33	61
Dave Veres	3.48	2-3	53	62.0	27	47
Dustin Hermanson	3.69	8-8	32	158.1	66	136
Ugueth Urbina*	3.78	5-8	63	64.1	29	84
Carlos Perez	3.88	12-13	33	206.2	48	110
Jeff Juden	4.22	11-5	22	130.0	57	107
Jim Bullinger	5.56	7-12	36	155.1	74	87
Mike Johnson*	5.94	2-5	11	50.0	21	28

Saves: Urbina (27); Valdes (2); Telford and Veres (1). **Complete games:** Martinez (13); Perez (8); Juden (3); Bullinger (2); Hermanson (1). **Shutouts:** Perez (5); Martinez (4); Bullinger (2); Hermanson (1).

New York Mets

Batting (135 AB)	Avg	AB	R	H	HR	RBI	SB
Edgardo Alfonzo ..315		518	84	163	10	72	11
John Olerud 294		524	90	154	22	102	0
Butch Huskey 287		471	61	135	24	81	8
Carlos Baerga 281		467	53	131	9	52	2
Matt Franco* 276		163	21	45	5	21	1
Todd Hundley 273		417	78	114	30	86	2
Luis Lopez 270		178	19	48	1	19	2
Bernard Gilkey 249		518	85	129	18	78	7
Carl Everett 248		443	58	110	14	57	17
Alex Ochoa 244		238	31	58	3	22	3
Brian McRae 242		562	86	136	11	43	17
Rey Ordonez 216		356	35	77	1	33	11

Acquired: P Kashiwada from Yomiuri of Japan for cash (Apr. 3); OF McRae, P Rojas and P Wendell from ChC for OF Lance Johnson, P Mark Clark and IF Manny Alexander (Aug. 6).
Claimed: IF Lopez in consideration for Houston signing IF Tim Bogar (Mar. 31).

Pitching (40 IP)	ERA	W-L	Gm	IP	BB	SO
John Franco 2.55		5-3	59	60.0	20	53
Rick Reed 2.89		13-9	33	208.1	31	113
Greg McMichael .2.98		7-10	73	87.2	27	81
Joe Crawford* ...3.30		4-3	19	46.1	13	25
Cory Lidle* 3.53		7-2	54	81.2	20	54
Juan Acevedo ...3.59		3-1	25	47.2	22	33
Bobby Jones 3.63		15-9	30	193.1	63	125
Brian Bohanon ...3.82		6-4	19	94.1	34	66
Dave Mlicki 4.00		8-12	32	193.2	76	157
T. Kashiwada 4.31		3-1	35	31.1	18	19
Turk Wendell 4.36		3-5	65	76.1	53	64
A. Reynoso 4.53		6-3	16	91.1	29	47
Mel Rojas 4.64		0-6	77	85.1	36	93

Saves: Franco (36); Rojas (15); McMichael (7); Wendell (5); Lidle (2). **Complete games:** Jones and Reed (2); Mlicki and Reynoso (1). **Shutouts:** Jones, Mlicki and Reynoso (1).

Philadelphia Phillies

Batting (135 AB)	Avg	AB	R	H	HR	RBI	SB
Mickey Morandini .295		553	83	163	1	39	16
Tony Barron* 286		189	22	54	4	24	0
Scott Rolen* 283		561	93	159	21	92	16
Kevin Stocker 266		504	51	134	4	40	11
Kevin Jordan 266		177	19	47	6	30	0
Midre Cummings .264		314	35	83	4	31	2
Gregg Jefferies ..256		476	68	122	11	48	12
Rico Brogna 252		543	68	137	20	81	12
Ricky Otero 252		151	20	38	0	3	0
Mike Lieberthal ..246		455	59	112	20	77	3
Ruben Amaro 234		175	18	41	2	21	1
Derrick May 228		149	8	34	1	13	4

Claimed: OF Cummings on waivers from Pit. (July 8).

Pitchers (40 IP)	ERA	W-L	Gm	IP	BB	SO
Curt Schilling 2.97		17-11	35	254.1	58	319
G. Stephenson* .3.15		8-6	20	117.0	38	81
Ricky Bottalico 3.65		2-5	69	74.0	42	89
Jerry Spradlin ...4.74		4-8	76	81.2	27	67
Tyler Green 4.93		4-4	14	76.2	45	58
Ron Blazier 5.03		1-1	36	53.2	21	42
Matt Beech* 5.07		4-9	24	136.2	57	120
Wayne Gomes* ..5.27		5-1	37	42.2	24	24
Reggie Harris 5.30		1-3	50	54.1	43	45
Mark Leiter 5.67		10-17	31	182.2	64	148
Calvin Maduro* ..7.23		3-7	15	71.0	41	31

Saves: Bottalico (34); Spradlin (1). **Complete games:** Schilling (7); Leiter (3); Stephenson (2). **Shutouts:** Schilling (2).

Pittsburgh Pirates

Batting (135 AB)	Avg	AB	R	H	HR	RBI	SB
Turner Ward 353		167	33	59	7	33	4
Joe Randa 302		443	58	134	7	60	4
Kevin Young 300		333	59	100	18	74	11
Shawon Dunston ..300		490	71	147	14	57	32
Jason Kendall 294		486	71	143	8	49	18
Al Martin 291		423	64	123	13	59	23
Mark Smith 285		193	29	55	9	35	3
Tony Womack 278		641	85	178	6	50	60
Kevin Polcovich* ..273		245	37	67	4	21	2
Jose Guillen* 267		498	58	133	14	70	1
Dale Sveum 261		306	30	80	12	47	0
J. Allensworth 255		369	55	94	3	43	14
Mark Johnson 215		219	30	47	4	29	1
Adrian Brown* 190		147	17	28	1	10	8

Acquired: IF Dunston from ChC for PTBN (Aug. 31).

Pitching (40 IP)	ERA	W-L	Gm	IP	BB	SO
Rich Loiselle* 3.10		1-5	72	72.2	24	66
Ricardo Rincon* .3.45		4-8	62	60.0	24	71
F. Cordova 3.63		11-8	29	178.2	49	121
Clint Sodowsky* .3.63		2-2	45	52.0	34	51
Marc Wilkins 3.69		9-5	70	75.2	33	47
Esteban Loaiza ..4.13		11-11	33	196.1	56	122
Steve Cooke 4.30		9-15	32	167.1	77	109
Jon Lieber 4.49		11-14	32	188.1	51	160
Jason Schmidt 4.60		10-9	32	187.2	76	136
Matt Ruebel 6.32		3-2	44	62.2	27	50

Saves: Loiselle (29); Rincon (4); Wilkins (2). **Complete games:** Cordova and Schmidt (2); Loaiza and Lieber (1). **Shutouts:** Cordova (2).

St. Louis Cardinals

Batting (135 AB)	Avg	AB	R	H	HR	RBI	SB
Willie McGee 300		300	29	90	3	38	8
Delino DeShields ..295		572	92	169	11	58	55
Ray Lankford 295		465	94	137	31	98	21
John Mabry 284		388	40	110	5	36	0
Royce Clayton 266		576	75	153	9	61	30
Dmitri Young* 258		333	38	86	5	34	6
Mark McGwire ...253		174	38	44	24	42	2
Gary Gaetti 251		502	63	126	17	69	7
Tom Lampkin 245		229	28	56	7	22	2
Mike Difelice* 238		260	16	62	4	30	1
Brian Jordan 234		145	17	34	0	10	6
Ron Gant 229		502	68	115	17	62	14
David Bell 211		142	9	30	1	12	1

Acquired: P Valenzuela, OF Phil Plantier and IF Scott Livingstone from SD for P Danny Jackson, P Rich Batchelor and OF Mark Sweeney (June 13); IF McGwire from Oak. for P Mathews and two minor leaguers (July 31).

Pitching (40 IP)	ERA	W-L	Gm	IP	BB	SO
T.J. Mathews 2.15		4-4	40	46.0	18	46
John Frascatore* ..2.48		5-2	59	80.0	33	58
Alan Benes 2.89		9-9	23	161.2	68	160
Andy Benes 3.10		10-7	26	177.0	61	175
Matt Morris* 3.19		12-9	33	217.0	69	149
Rigo Beltran* 3.48		1-2	35	54.1	17	50
Tony Fossas 3.83		2-7	71	51.2	26	41
Todd Stottlemyre .3.88		12-9	28	181.0	65	160
Dennis Eckersley .3.91		1-5	57	53.0	8	45
Manny Aybar* ...4.24		2-4	12	68.0	29	41
D. Osborne 4.93		3-7	14	80.1	23	51
F. Valenzuela 4.96		2-12	18	89.0	46	61
Mark Petkovsek ...5.06		4-7	55	96.0	31	51

Saves: Eckersley (36); Petkovsek (2); Beltran (1). **Complete games:** Morris (3); Al. Benes (2); Valenzuela (1). **Shutouts:** none.

NL Team by Team Statistics (Cont.)

San Diego Padres

Batting (140 AB)	Avg	AB	R	H	HR	RBI	SB
Tony Gwynn	.372	592	97	220	17	119	12
Wally Joyner	.327	455	59	149	13	83	3
Ken Caminiti	.290	486	92	141	26	90	11
Mark Sweeney	.280	164	16	46	2	23	2
Rickey Henderson	.274	288	63	79	6	27	29
John Flaherty	.273	439	38	120	9	46	4
Quilvio Veras	.265	539	74	143	3	45	33
Steve Finley	.261	560	101	146	28	92	15
Chris Gomez	.253	522	62	132	5	54	5
Archi Cianfrocco	.245	220	25	54	4	26	7
Chris Jones	.243	152	24	37	7	25	7
Greg Vaughn	.216	361	60	78	18	57	7

Acquired: P Menhart from Sea. for P Andres Berumen (June 10); P Jackson, P Rich Batchelor and OF Sweeney from St.L for P Fernando Valenzuela, OF Phil Plantier and IF Scott Livingstone (June 13). **Traded:** OF Henderson to Ana. for IF George Arias and two minor leaguers (Aug. 13).

Pitching (50 IP)	ERA	W- L	Gm	IP	BB	SO
Trevor Hoffman	2.66	6-4	70	81.1	24	111
Andy Ashby	4.13	9-11	30	200.2	49	144
Joey Hamilton	4.25	12-7	31	192.2	69	124
Doug Bochtler	4.77	3-6	54	60.1	50	46
Pete Smith	4.81	7-6	37	118.0	52	68
Tim Worrell	5.16	4-8	60	106.1	50	81
Sterling Hitchcock	5.20	10-11	32	161.0	55	106
Will Cunnane*	5.81	6-3	54	91.1	49	79
Sean Bergman	6.09	2-4	44	99.0	38	74
Danny Jackson	7.58	2-9	17	67.2	28	32

Saves: Hoffman (37); Worrell (3); Bochtler (2); Smith (1). **Complete games:** Ashby (2); Hamilton and Hitchcock (1). **Shutouts:** none.

San Francisco Giants

Batting (135 AB)	Avg	AB	R	H	HR	RBI	SB
Bill Mueller	.292	390	51	114	7	44	4
Barry Bonds	.291	532	123	155	40	101	37
Stan Javier	.286	440	69	126	8	50	25
J.T. Snow	.281	531	81	149	28	104	6
Brian Johnson	.279	179	19	50	11	27	0
Darryl Hamilton	.270	460	78	124	5	43	15
Mark Lewis	.267	341	50	91	10	42	3
Jose Vizcaino	.266	568	77	151	5	50	8
Glenallen Hill	.261	398	47	104	11	64	7
Damon Berryhill	.257	167	17	43	3	23	0
Jeff Kent	.250	580	90	145	29	121	11
Rick Wilkins	.195	190	18	37	6	23	0

Acquired: C Johnson from Det. for C Marcus Jensen (July 16); P Rapp from Fla. for two minor leaguers (July 18); P Alvarez, P Darwin and P Roberto Hernandez from ChW for P Foulke and five minor leaguers (July 31). **Claimed:** P Mulholland on waivers from ChC (Aug. 8).

Pitching (50 IP)	ERA	W-L	Gm	IP	BB	SO
Rich Rodriguez	3.17	4-3	71	65.1	21	32
Shawn Estes	3.18	19-5	32	201.0	100	181
Kirk Rueter	3.45	13-6	32	190.2	51	115
Rod Beck	3.47	7-4	73	70.0	8	53
Julian Tavarez	3.87	6-4	89	88.1	34	38
Terry Mulholland	4.24	6-13	40	186.2	51	99
Mark Gardner	4.29	12-9	30	180.1	57	136
Wilson Alvarez	4.48	4-3	11	66.1	36	69
Doug Henry	4.71	4-5	75	70.2	41	69
Pat Rapp	4.83	5-8	27	141.2	72	92
Osvaldo Fernandez	4.95	3-4	11	56.1	15	31
Wil VanLandingham	4.96	4-7	18	89.0	59	52
Joe Roa*	5.21	2-5	28	65.2	20	34

Saves: Beck (37); Henry (3); Rodriguez (1). **Complete games:** Estes (3); Gardner (2); Mulholland and Rapp (1). **Shutouts:** Estes (2); Gardner and Rapp (1).

58 Big Flies

St. Louis Cardinals

Mark McGwire

Fell short of Roger Maris' fabled mark of 61 home runs in a season but did club 58 to tie the mark for right-handers set by Jimmie Foxx in 1932 and matched by Hank Greenburg in 1938...became the first hitter since Babe Ruth in 1927-28 to hit 50 homers in two consecutive seasons.

Triple Crown

Toronto Blue Jays

Roger Clemens

Became the first pitcher since Dwight Gooden of the 1985 New York Mets to win the pitching "triple crown," leading the AL in ERA (2.05), wins (21) and strikeouts (292, a personal career high)...was the seventh AL pitcher to accomplish the feat and the first since Detroit's Hal Newhouser in 1945.

Without E's

Florida Marlins

Charles Johnson

Became the only NL starting catcher in history to play the entire season without committing an error...played 124 errorless games behind the plate for the Marlins in 1997, extending his regular-season streak to 171 games...Buddy Rosar went errorless for the AL Philadelphia Athletics in 117 games in 1946.

No DP's

Houston Astros

Craig Biggio

Played all 162 games for Houston without hitting into a double play...broke the previous major league mark for games played with no double plays (154) set in 1935 by Augie Galan of the Chicago Cubs...Detroit Tigers infielder Dick McAuliffe has the AL mark with 151 games in 1968.

Divisional Series Summaries

AMERICAN LEAGUE

Indians, 3–2

Date	Winner	Home Field
Sept. 30	Yankees, 8-6	at New York
Oct. 2	Indians, 7-5	at New York
Oct. 4	Yankees, 6-1	at Cleveland
Oct. 5	Indians, 3-2	at Cleveland
Oct. 6	Indians, 4-3	at Cleveland

Game 1
Tuesday, Sept. 30, at New York

	1	2	3	4	5	6	7	8	9	R	H	E
Cleveland ...	5	0	0	1	0	0	0	0	0 -	6	11	0
New York ..	0	1	0	1	1	5	0	0	x -	8	11	0

Win: Mendoza, NY (1-0). **Loss:** Plunk, Cle (0-1). **Save:** Rivera, NY (1).

2B: Cleveland— Justice; New York— Sanchez. **3B:** Cleveland— Grissom. **HR:** Cleveland— Alomar (1); New York— Martinez (1), Raines (1), Jeter (1), O'Neill (1). **RBI:** Cleveland— Ramirez, Alomar 3, Roberts; New York— Boggs, Martinez, Raines 3, Sanchez, Jeter, O'Neill. **SB:** Cleveland— Roberts 2 (2).
Attendance: 57,398. **Time:** 3:28.

Game 2
Thursday, Oct. 2, at New York

	1	2	3	4	5	6	7	8	9	R	H	E
Cleveland ..	0	0	0	5	2	0	0	0	0 -	7	11	1
New York ..	3	0	0	0	0	0	0	1	1 -	5	7	2

Win: Wright, Cle (1-0). **Loss:** Pettitte, NY (0-1).
2B: Cleveland— Fernandez; New York— Martinez, B. Williams. **HR:** Cleveland— M. Williams (1); New York— Jeter (2). **RBI:** Cleveland— Justice, Alomar, Thome, Fernandez 2, M. Williams 2; New York— Martinez 2, Hayes, Stanley, Jeter. **SB:** Cleveland— Vizquel (1).
Attendance: 57,360. **Time:** 3:32.

Game 3
Saturday, Oct. 4, at Cleveland

	1	2	3	4	5	6	7	8	9	R	H	E
New York ..	1	0	1	4	0	0	0	0	0 -	6	4	1
Cleveland ..	0	1	0	0	0	0	0	0	0 -	1	5	1

Win: Wells, NY (1-0). **Loss:** Nagy, Cle (0-1).
2B: Cleveland— Justice. **HR:** New York— O'Neill (2). **RBI:** New York— O'Neill 5, Martinez; Cleveland— Fernandez. **SB:** New York— Jeter (1).
Attendance: 50,860. **Time:** 3:09.

Game 4
Sunday, Oct. 5, at Cleveland

	1	2	3	4	5	6	7	8	9	R	H	E
New York ..	2	0	0	0	0	0	0	0	0 -	2	9	1
Cleveland ..	0	1	0	0	0	0	0	1	1 -	3	8	0

Win: Jackson, Cle (1-0). **Loss:** Mendoza, NY (1-1).
2B: New York— Jeter, O'Neill; Cleveland— M. Williams. **HR:** Cleveland— Justice (1), Alomar (2). **RBI:** New York— O'Neill, Fielder; Cleveland— Justice, Alomar, Vizquel. **SB:** Cleveland— Vizquel (2).
Attendance: 45,231. **Time:** 3:22.

Game 5
Monday, Oct. 6, at Cleveland

	1	2	3	4	5	6	7	8	9	R	H	E
New York ..	0	0	0	0	2	1	0	0	0 -	3	12	0
Cleveland ..	0	0	3	1	0	0	0	0	x -	4	7	2

Win: Wright, Cle (2-0). **Loss:** Pettitte, NY (0-2). **Save:** Mesa (1).
2B: New York— Stanley, O'Neill; Cleveland— Ramirez, Alomar. **RBI:** New York— B. Williams, Boggs; Cleveland— Ramirez 2, M. Williams, Fernandez. **SB:** New York— Raines 2 (2); Cleveland— Vizquel 2 (4).
Attendance: 45,203. **Time:** 3:29.

Orioles, 3-1

Date	Winner	Home Field
Oct. 1	Orioles, 9-3	at Seattle
Oct. 2	Orioles, 9-3	at Seattle
Oct. 4	Mariners, 4-2	at Baltimore
Oct. 5	Orioles, 3-1	at Baltimore

Game 1
Wednesday, Oct. 1, at Seattle

	1	2	3	4	5	6	7	8	9	R	H	E
Baltimore ...	0	0	1	0	4	4	0	0	0 -	9	13	0
Seattle	0	0	0	1	0	0	1	0	1 -	3	7	1

Win: Mussina, Bal. (1-0). **Loss:** Johnson, Sea. (0-1).
2B: Baltimore— Bordick, Palmeiro, Surhoff; Seattle— Kelly, Sorrento. **HR:** Baltimore— Berroa (1), Hoiles (1); Seattle— Martinez, Buhner, Rodriguez. **RBI:** Baltimore— Bordick 2, Anderson, Davis 2, Berroa, Hoiles, Surhoff 2; Seattle— Martinez, Buhner, Rodriguez. **SB:** Baltimore— Anderson (1), Hammonds (1).
Attendance: 59,579. **Time:** 3:14.

AMERICAN LEAGUE (Cont.)

Game 2
Thursday, Oct. 2, at Seattle

	1	2	3	4	5	6	7	8	9	R	H	E
Baltimore ...	0	1	0	0	2	0	2	4	0 -	9	14	0
Seattle	2	0	0	0	0	0	1	0	0 -	3	9	0

Win: Erickson, Bal. (1-0). **Loss:** Moyer, Sea. (0-1).
2B: Baltimore—Alomar, Ripken 2, Anderson, Palmeiro; Seattle—Kelly. **HR:** Baltimore— Baines (1), Anderson (1). **RBI:** Baltimore—Baines, Alomar 2, Anderson 3, Webster, Bordick 2; Seattle—Griffey, Martinez, Ducey. **SB:** Seattle— Griffey 2 (2).
Attendance: 59,309. **Time:** 3:25.

Game 3
Saturday, Oct. 4, at Baltimore

	1	2	3	4	5	6	7	8	9	R	H	E
Seattle	0	0	1	0	1	0	0	0	2 -	4	11	0
Baltimore ...	0	0	0	0	0	0	0	0	2 -	2	5	0

Win: Fassero, Sea. (1-0). **Loss:** Key, Bal. (0-1).
2B: Seattle— Kelly, Rodriguez; Baltimore— Alomar, Hammonds. **HR:** Seattle— Buhner (2), Sorrento (1). **RBI:** Seattle— Kelly, Griffey, Buhner, Sorrento; Baltimore— Hammonds 2.
Attendance: 49,137. **Time:** 3:26.

Game 4
Sunday, Oct. 5, at Baltimore

	1	2	3	4	5	6	7	8	9	R	H	E
Seattle	0	1	0	0	0	0	0	0	0 -	1	2	0
Baltimore ...	2	0	0	0	1	0	0	0	x -	3	7	0

Win: Mussina, Bal. (2-0). **Loss:** Johnson, Sea. (0-2). **Save:** Myers, Bal. (1).
2B: Baltimore— Berroa. **HR:** Seattle— Martinez (2); Baltimore— Reboulet (1), Berroa (1). **RBI:** Seattle— Martinez; Baltimore— Reboulet, Ripken, Berroa.
Attendance: 48,766. **Time:** 2:42.

Playoff Series
The AL and NL League Championship Series began in 1969 with a Best of 5 format, then changed to Best of 7 in 1985. The '95 season was the first year for wild card teams and the new Best of 3 Divisional Series.

NATIONAL LEAGUE

Braves, 3-0

Date	Winner	Home Field
Sept. 30	Braves, 2-1	at Atlanta
Oct. 1	Braves, 13-3	at Atlanta
Oct. 3	Braves, 4-1	at Houston

Game 1
Tuesday, Sept. 30, at Atlanta

	1	2	3	4	5	6	7	8	9	R	H	E
Houston	0	0	0	0	1	0	0	0	0 -	1	7	1
Atlanta	1	1	0	0	0	0	0	0	x -	2	2	0

Win: Maddux, Atl. (1-0). **Loss:** Kile, Hou. (0-1).
2B: Atlanta— Lofton. **HR:** Atlanta— Klesko (1). **RBI:** Houston— Kile; Atlanta— C. Jones, Klesko. **SB:** Houston— Eusebio (1), Abreu (1).
Attendance: 46,467. **Time:** 2:15.

Game 2
Wednesday, Oct. 1, at Atlanta

	1	2	3	4	5	6	7	8	9	R	H	E
Houston	0	0	0	3	0	0	0	0	0 -	3	6	2
Atlanta	0	0	3	0	3	5	0	2	x -	13	10	1

Win: Glavine, Atl. (1-0). **Loss:** Hampton, Hou. (0-1).
2B: Houston— Ausmus; Atlanta— Lopez. **HR:** Atlanta— Blauser (1). **RBI:** Houston— Ausmus 2, Hampton; Atlanta— Blauser 3, A. Jones, Colbrunn 2, McGriff, Bautista 2, Lopez. **SB:** C. Jones (1)
Attendance: 49,200. **Time:** 3:06.

Game 3
Friday, Oct. 3, at Houston

	1	2	3	4	5	6	7	8	9	R	H	E
Atlanta	1	1	0	0	0	0	1	1	0 -	4	8	2
Houston	0	0	0	0	0	0	1	0	0 -	1	3	1

Win: Smoltz, Atl. (1-0). **Loss:** Reynolds, Hou. (0-1).
2B: Atlanta— Klesko, Lopez. **HR:** Atlanta— C. Jones (1); Houston— Carr (1). **RBI:** Atlanta— C. Jones, Blauser, Tucker; Houston— Carr.
Attendance: 53,688. **Time:** 2:36.

Marlins, 3-0

Date	Winner	Home Field
Sept. 30	Marlins, 2-1	at Florida
Oct. 1	Marlins, 7-6	at Florida
Oct. 3	Marlins, 6-2	at San Francisco

Game 1
Tuesday, Sept. 30, at Florida

	1	2	3	4	5	6	7	8	9	R	H	E
S. Francisco	0	0	0	0	0	0	1	0	0 -	1	4	0
Florida	0	0	0	0	0	0	1	0	1 -	2	7	0

Win: Cook, Fla. (1-0). **Loss:** Tavarez, SF (0-1).
2B: San Francisco— Bonds; Florida— Sheffield. **HR:** San Francisco— Mueller (1); Florida— Johnson (1). **RBI:** San Francisco— Mueller; Florida— Johnson, Renteria.
Attendance: 42,167. **Time:** 2:48.

Game 2
Wednesday, Oct. 1, at Florida

	1	2	3	4	5	6	7	8	9	R	H	E
S. Francisco	1	1	1	1	0	0	1	0	1 -	6	11	0
Florida	2	0	1	2	0	1	0	0	1 -	7	10	2

Win: Nen, Fla. (1-0). **Loss:** Hernandez, SF (0-1).
2B: San Francisco— Javier, Vizcaino, Bonds; Florida— Conine. **HR:** San Francisco— Johnson (1); Floirda— Boniila (1), Sheffield (1). **RBI:** San Francisco— Lewis, Johnson, Bonds 2, Javier; Florida— Bonilla 3, Arias, Sheffield, Alou. **SB:** San Francisco— Javier (1), Bonds (1); Florida— Sheffield (1).
Attendance: 41,283. **Time:** 3:12.

Game 3
Friday, Oct. 3, at San Francisco

	1	2	3	4	5	6	7	8	9	R	H	E
Florida	0	0	0	0	0	4	0	2	0 -	6	10	2
S. Francisco	0	0	0	1	0	1	0	0	0 -	2	7	0

Win: Fernandez, Fla. (1-0). **Loss:** Alvarez, SF (0-1).
2B: Florida— Alou, Johnson, Counsell. **HR:** Florida— White (1); San Francisco— Kent 2 (2). **RBI:** Florida— White 4, Johnson, Counsell; San Francisco— Kents 2.
Attendance: 57,188. **Time:** 3:22.

American League Championship Series

Indians, 4–2

Date	Winner	Home Field
Oct. 8	Orioles, 3-0	at Baltimore
Oct. 9	Indians, 5-4	at Baltimore
Oct. 11	Indians, 2-1 (12 inn.)	at Cleveland
Oct. 12	Indians, 8-7	at Cleveland
Oct. 13	Orioles, 4-2	at Cleveland
Oct. 14	Indians, 1-0 (11 inn.)	at Baltimore

Most Valuable Player

Marquis Grissom, Cleveland, CF

Avg	AB	R	H	HR	RBI	BB	SO	SB
.261	23	2	6	1	4	1	9	3

Game 1

Wednesday, Oct. 8, at Baltimore

	1 2 3	4 5 6	7 8 9	R	H	E
Cleveland	0 0 0	0 0 0	0 0 0 -	0	4	1
Baltimore	1 0 2	0 0 0	0 0 x -	3	6	1

Win: Erickson, Bal. (2-0). **Loss:** Ogea, Cle. (0-1).
2B: Baltimore— Anderson, Alomar. **HR:** Baltimore— Anderson (2), Alomar (1). **RBI:** Baltimore— Anderson, Alomar 2. **SB:** Cleveland— Roberts (3).
Attendance: 49,029. **Time:** 2:33.

Game 2

Thursday, Oct. 9, at Baltimore

	1 2 3	4 5 6	7 8 9	R	H	E
Cleveland	2 0 0	0 0 0	0 3 0 -	5	6	3
Baltimore	0 2 0	0 0 2	0 0 0 -	4	8	1

Win: Assenmacher, Cle. (1-0). **Loss:** Benitez (0-1). **Save:** Mesa, Cle. (2).
2B: Baltimore— Palmeiro. **HR:** Cleveland— Ramirez (1), Grissom (1); Baltimore— Ripken (1). **RBI:** Cleveland— Ramirez 2, Grissom 3; Baltimore— Ripken 2, Bordick 2. **SB:** Cleveland— Williams (1), Grissom (1).
Attendance: 49,131. **Time:** 3:53.

Game 3

Saturday, Oct. 11, at Cleveland

	1 2 3 4 5 6 7 8 9 10 11 12	R	H	E
Baltimore	0 0 0 0 0 0 0 1 0 0 0 0	1	8	1
Cleveland	0 0 0 0 0 1 0 0 0 0 0 1	2	6	0

Win: Plunk, Cle. (1-1). **Loss:** Myers, Bal. (0-1).
2B: Baltimore— Anderson, Berroa. **RBI:** Baltimore— Anderson; Cleveland— Williams. **SB:** Baltimore— Anderson (2).
Attendance: 45,047. **Time:** 4:51.

Game 4

Sunday, Oct. 12, at Cleveland

	1 2 3	4 5 6	7 8 9	R	H	E
Baltimore	0 1 4	0 0 0	1 0 1 -	7	12	2
Cleveland	0 5 0	1 4 0	0 0 1 -	8	13	0

Win: Mesa, Cle. (1-0). **Loss:** Mills, Bal. (0-1).
2B: Baltimore— Surhoff 2; Cleveland— Giles 2, Ramirez. **HR:** Baltimore— Anderson (3), Baines (2), Palmeiro (1); Cleveland— Alomar (3), Ramirez (2). **RBI:** Baltimore— Surhoff, Anderson, Baines 2, Palmeiro 2, Berroa; Cleveland— Alomar 4, Grissom, Ramirez. **SB:** Anderson (3).
Attendance: 45,081. **Time:** 3:32.

Game 5

Monday, Oct. 13, at Cleveland

	1 2 3	4 5 6	7 8 9	R	H	E
Baltimore	0 0 2	0 0 0	0 0 2 -	4	10	0
Cleveland	0 0 0	0 0 0	0 0 2 -	2	8	1

Win: Kamieniecki, Bal. (1-0). **Loss:** Ogea, Bal. (0-2).
2B: Baltimore— Palmeiro; Cleveland— Roberts, Giles, Williams, Fernandez. **HR:** Baltimore— Davis (1). **RBI:** Baltimore— Berroa 2, Davis, Ripken; Cleveland— Williams, Fernandez. **SB:** Cleveland— Grissom (3).
Attendance: 45,086. **Time:** 3:08.

Game 6

Wednesday, Oct. 15, at Baltimore

	1 2 3 4 5 6 7 8 9 10 11	R	H	E
Cleveland	0 0 0 0 0 0 0 0 0 1 1	3	0
Baltimore	0 0 0 0 0 0 0 0 0 0 0	1 0 0

Win: Anderson, Cleveland (1-0). **Loss:** Benitez, Bal. (0-2).
2B: Cleveland— Justice; Baltimore— Berroa, Bordick, Ripken. **HR:** Cleveland— Fernandez (1). **RBI:** Cleveland— Fernandez. **SB:** Baltimore— Hammonds (2).
Attendance: 49,075. **Time:** 3:52.

ALCS Composite Box Score

Cleveland Indians

Batting	Avg	LCS vs. Baltimore							Overall AL Playoffs							
		AB	R	H	HR	RBI	BB	SO	Avg	AB	R	H	HR	RBI	BB	SO
Tony Fernandez, 2b	.357	14	1	5	1	2	1	2	.280	25	1	7	1	6	1	2
David Justice, dh	.333	21	3	7	0	0	2	4	.300	40	6	12	1	2	4	7
Manny Ramirez, rf	.286	21	3	6	2	3	5	5	.214	42	5	9	2	6	5	8
Marquis Grissom, cf	.261	23	2	6	1	4	1	9	.250	40	5	10	1	4	2	11
Matt Willams, 3b	.217	23	1	5	0	2	4	7	.225	40	5	9	0	5	7	10
Brian Giles, lf	.188	16	1	3	0	0	2	6	.174	23	1	4	0	0	2	7
Bip Roberts, 2b-lf	.150	20	0	3	0	0	0	8	.231	39	1	9	0	1	2	10
Sandy Alomar Jr., c	.125	24	3	3	1	4	1	3	.209	43	7	9	3	9	1	5
Jim Thome, 1b	.071	14	3	1	0	0	5	4	.138	29	4	4	0	1	5	9
Omar Vizquel, ss	.040	25	1	1	0	0	1	10	.233	43	4	10	0	1	3	11
Kevin Seitzer, 1b	.000	4	0	0	0	0	0	2	.000	6	0	0	0	0	1	2
Jeff Branson, dh	.000	2	0	0	0	0	0	2	.000	2	0	0	0	0	0	2
TOTALS	.193	207	18	40	5	15	23	62	.222	374	39	83	8	35	33	84

American League Championship Series (Cont.)

Pitching	ERA	W-L	SV	Gm	IP	H	BB	SO	ERA	W-L	Sv	Gm	IP	H	BB	SO
Orel Hershiser	0.00	0-0	0	1	7.0	4	1	7	2.45	0-0	0	3	18.1	18	3	11
Mike Jackson	0.00	0-0	0	5	4.1	1	1	7	0.00	1-0	0	8	8.2	3	2	11
Alvin Morman	0.00	0-0	0	2	1.1	0	0	1	0.00	0-0	0	3	1.1	0	1	1
Jeff Juden	0.00	0-0	0	3	1.0	2	2	2	0.00	0-0	0	3	1.0	2	2	2
Eric Plunk	0.00	1-0	0	1	0.2	1	0	0	18.00	1-1	0	2	2.0	3	6	1
Brian Anderson	1.42	1-0	0	3	6.1	1	3	7	1.42	1-0	0	3	6.1	1	3	7
Charles Nagy	2.77	0-0	0	2	13.0	17	5	5	4.32	0-1	0	3	16.2	19	11	6
Chad Ogea	3.21	0-2	0	2	14.0	12	5	7	2.79	0-2	0	3	19.1	14	3	6
Jose Mesa	3.38	1-0	2	4	5.1	5	3	5	3.18	1-0	3	6	8.2	10	4	7
Paul Assenmacher	9.00	1-0	0	5	2.0	5	1	3	6.75	1-0	0	9	5.1	7	3	5
Jaret Wright	15.00	0-0	0	1	3.0	6	2	3	6.28	2-0	0	3	14.1	17	9	13
TOTALS	2.95	4-2	2	6	58.0	54	23	47	3.62	7-4	3	11	102.0	94	47	70

Wild Pitches— LCS (none); OVERALL (none). **Hit Batters—** LCS (Nagy); OVERALL (Nagy).

Baltimore Orioles

Batting	LCS vs Cleveland								Overall AL Playoffs							
	Avg	AB	R	H	HR	RBI	BB	SO	Avg	AB	R	H	HR	RBI	BB	SO
Brady Anderson, cf	.360	25	5	9	2	3	4	4	.357	42	8	15	3	7	5	8
Harold Baines, dh	.353	17	1	6	1	2	2	1	.364	22	3	8	2	3	3	1
Cal Ripken, 3b	.348	23	3	8	1	3	4	6	.385	39	4	15	1	4	6	8
Geronimo Berroa, rf	.286	21	1	6	0	3	0	3	.324	34	5	11	2	5	2	5
Rafael Palmeiro, 1b	.280	25	3	7	1	2	0	10	.270	37	5	10	1	2	0	12
Lenny Webster, c	.222	9	0	2	0	0	0	1	.200	15	1	3	0	1	1	1
B.J. Surhoff, lf	.200	25	1	5	0	1	2	2	.222	36	1	8	0	3	2	4
Roberto Alomar, 2b	.182	22	2	4	1	2	7	3	.219	32	3	7	1	4	8	4
Mike Bordick, ss	.158	19	0	3	0	2	0	6	.241	29	4	7	0	6	4	8
Eric Davis, rf	.154	13	1	2	1	1	1	3	.181	22	1	4	1	3	1	8
Chris Hoiles, c	.143	14	1	2	0	0	2	5	.143	21	2	3	1	1	4	6
Jeffrey Hammonds, ph	.000	3	0	0	0	0	1	2	.077	13	3	1	0	2	3	4
Jeff Reboulet, pr-ss	.000	2	1	0	0	0	0	1	.143	7	2	1	1	1	0	3
Jerome Walton, rf	.000	0	0	0	0	0	0	0	.000	4	0	0	0	0	0	2
TOTALS	.248	218	19	54	7	19	23	47	.263	353	42	93	13	42	39	74

Pitching	ERA	W-L	Sv	Gm	IP	H	BB	SO	ERA	W-L	Sv	Gm	IP	H	BB	SO
Scott Kamieniecki	0.00	1-0	0	2	8.0	4	2	5	0.00	1-0	0	2	8.0	4	2	5
Arthur Rhodes	0.00	0-0	0	2	2.1	2	3	2	0.00	0-0	0	3	4.2	2	3	6
Jesse Orosco	0.00	0-0	0	2	1.1	0	1	1	0.00	0-0	0	4	2.2	1	1	2
Mike Mussina	0.60	0-0	0	2	15.0	4	4	25	1.24	2-0	0	4	29.0	11	7	41
Jimmy Key	2.57	0-0	0	2	7.0	5	3	7	3.09	0-1	0	4	11.2	13	3	11
Alan Mills	2.70	0-1	0	3	3.1	1	2	3	2.08	0-1	0	4	4.1	2	2	4
Scott Erickson	4.26	1-0	0	2	12.2	15	6	2	4.19	2-0	0	3	19.1	22	3	12
Randy Myers	5.06	0-1	1	4	5.1	6	3	7	3.68	0-1	2	3	7.1	6	3	12
Armando Benitez	12.00	0-2	0	4	3.0	3	4	6	7.50	0-2	0	7	6.0	6	6	10
Terry Mathews	0.00	0-0	0	0	0.0	0	0	0	18.00	0-0	0	1	1.0	2	0	1
TOTALS	2.64	2-4	1	6	58.0	40	23	62	2.68	5-5	2	10	94.0	69	30	104

Wild Pitches— LCS (Rhodes 2); OVERALL (Rhodes 2, Key). **Hit Batters—**LCS (Key 3, Kamieniecki); OVERALL (Key 3, Kamieniecki).

Score by Innings

	1	2	3	4	5	6	7	8	9	10	11	12		R	H	E
Cleveland	2	2	0	1	4	0	1	3	3	0	1	1	-	18	40	5
Baltimore	1	3	8	0	0	2	1	0	4	0	0	0	-	19	54	5

DP: Cleveland 11, Baltimore 4. **LOB:** Cleveland 44, Baltimore 50. **2B:** Cleveland— Giles (3), Fernandez, Justice, Ramirez, Roberts, Williams; Baltimore— Anderson (2), Berroa (2), Palmeiro (2), Ripken (2), Surhoff (2), Bordick. **SB:** Cleveland— Grissom (3), Roberts, Williams; Baltimore— Anderson (2), Hammonds. **CS:** Baltimore— Baines. **Picked Off:** Cleveland— Ramirez. **S:** Cleveland— Seitzer, Vizquel; Baltimore— Bordick. **GIDP:** Cleveland— 3; Baltimore— 10.
Umpires: Joe Brinkman, John Hirschbeck, Jim Joyce, Larry McCoy, Durwood Merrill, Mike Reilly.

National League Championship Series

Marlins, 4-2

Date	Winner	Home Field
Oct. 7	Marlins, 5-3	at Atlanta
Oct. 8	Braves, 7-1	at Atlanta
Oct. 10	Marlins, 5-2	at Florida
Oct. 11	Braves, 4-0	at Florida
Oct. 12	Marlins, 2-1	at Florida
Oct. 14	Marlins, 7-4	at Atlanta

Game 1
Tuesday, Oct. 7, at Atlanta

```
             1 2 3  4 5 6  7 8 9   R  H  E
Florida ..... 3 0 2  0 0 0  0 0 0 - 5  6  0
Atlanta ..... 1 0 1  0 0 1  0 0 0 - 3  5  2
```
Win: Brown, Fla. (1-0). **Loss:** Maddux, Atl. (1-1). **Save:** Nen, Fla. (1).
2B: Florida— Alou, Johnson; Atlanta— Lockhart. **HR:** Atlanta— C. Jones (2), Klesko (2). **RBI:** Florida— Alou 4, Johnson; Atlanta— McGriff, C. Jones, Klesko. **SB:** Florida— Renteria (1).
Attendance: 49,244 . **Time:** 3:04.

Game 2
Wednesday, Oct. 8, at Atlanta

```
             1 2 3  4 5 6  7 8 9   R  H  E
Florida ..... 0 0 0  0 0 0  0 1 0 - 1  3  1
Atlanta ..... 3 0 2  0 0 0  2 0 x - 7 13  0
```
Win: Glavine, Atl. (2-0). **Loss:** Fernandez, Fla. (1-1).
2B: Florida— Abbott, White; Atlanta— Lopez, Graffanino. **3B:** Atlanta— Lockhart. **HR:** Atlanta— Klesko (3), C. Jones (3). **RBI:** Florida— White; Atlanta— Lockhart, Klesko 2, C. Jones 3, Lopez.
Attendance: 48,933. **Time:** 2:51.

Game 3
Friday, Oct. 10, at Florida

```
             1 2 3  4 5 6  7 8 9   R  H  E
Atlanta ..... 0 0 0  1 0 1  0 0 0 - 2  6  1
Florida ..... 0 0 0  1 0 4  0 0 x - 5  8  1
```
Win: Hernandez, Fla. (1-0). **Loss:** Smoltz, Atl. (1-1). **Save:** Nen, Fla. (2).
2B: Florida— Renteria, Daulton, Johnson. **HR:** Florida— Sheffield (2). **RBI:** Atlanta— McGriff, Lopez; Florida— Sheffield, Daulton, Johnson 3.
Attendance: 53,857. **Time:** 2:59.

Most Valuable Player
Livan Hernandez, Florida, P

ERA	W-L	IP	H	R	BB	SO	HR
0.84	2-0	10.2	5	1	2	16	1

Game 4
Saturday, Oct. 11, at Florida

```
             1 2 3  4 5 6  7 8 9   R  H  E
Atlanta ..... 1 0 1  0 2 0  0 0 0 - 4 11  0
Florida ..... 0 0 0  0 0 0  0 0 0 - 0  4  0
```
Win: Neagle, Atl. (1-0). **Loss:** Leiter, Fla. (0-1).
2B: Atlanta— C. Jones, McGriff. **HR:** Atlanta— Blauser (2). **RBI:** Atlanta— McGriff 2, A. Jones, Blauser.
Attendance: 54,890. **Time:** 2:48.

Game 5
Sunday, Oct. 12, at Florida

```
             1 2 3  4 5 6  7 8 9   R  H  E
Atlanta ..... 0 1 0  0 0 0  0 0 0 - 1  3  0
Florida ..... 1 0 0  0 0 0  1 0 x - 2  5  0
```
Win: Hernandez, Fla. (2-0). **Loss:** Maddux, Atl. (1-2).
2B: Florida— Bonilla. **3B:** Atlanta— Lofton. **HR:** Atlanta— Tucker (1). **RBI:** Atlanta— Tucker; Florida— Bonilla, Conine.
SB: Florida— White (1).
Attendance: 51,982. **Time:** 2:27.

Game 6
Tuesday, Oct. 14, at Atlanta

```
             1 2 3  4 5 6  7 8 9   R  H  E
Florida ..... 4 0 0  0 0 3  0 0 0 - 7 10  1
Atlanta ..... 1 2 0  0 0 0  0 0 1 - 4 11  1
```
Win: Brown, Fla. (2-0). **Loss:** Glavine, Atl. (2-1).
RBI: Florida— Bonilla 3, Johnson, Counsell 2, Alou; Atlanta— Klesko, Lofton, Lockhart 2. **SB:** Atlanta— Lofton (1).
Attendance: 50,446. **Time:** 3:10.

NLCS Composite Box Score

Florida Marlins

Batting	Avg	LCS vs Atlanta							Overall NL Playoffs						
		AB	R	H	HR	RBI	BB	SO	Avg	AB	R	H	HR	RBI	BB	SO
Alex Arias, ph-3b	1.000	1	0	1	0	0	0	0	1.000	2	0	2	0	1	0	0
Craig Counsell, 2b	.429	14	0	6	0	2	1	3	.421	19	0	8	0	3	4	3
Kurt Abbott, 2b	.375	8	0	3	0	0	0	2	.313	16	0	5	0	0	0	2
Bobby Bonilla, 3b	.261	23	3	6	0	4	1	6	.286	35	4	10	1	7	3	7
Darren Daulton, ph-1b	.250	4	1	1	0	1	1	2	.250	4	1	1	0	1	1	2
Gary Sheffield, rf	.235	17	6	4	1	1	7	3	.346	26	9	9	2	2	12	3
Edgar Renteria, ss	.227	22	4	5	0	0	3	6	.200	35	5	7	0	1	5	10
John Cangelosi, ph-lf	.200	5	0	1	0	0	1	0	.167	6	0	1	0	0	1	0
Devon White, cf	.190	21	4	4	0	1	2	7	.188	32	5	6	1	5	4	10
Charles Johnson, c	.118	17	1	2	0	5	3	8	.160	25	6	4	1	7	6	10
Jeff Conine, 1b	.111	18	1	2	0	1	1	4	.207	29	4	6	0	1	2	4
Moises Alou, lf	.067	15	0	1	0	5	1	3	.138	29	1	4	0	6	1	6
Kevin Brown, p	.000	6	0	0	0	0	0	5	.000	8	0	0	0	0	0	5
Livan Hernandez, p	.000	3	0	0	0	0	0	1	.000	5	0	0	0	0	1	2
Jim Eisenreich, lf	.000	3	0	0	0	0	0	0	.000	3	0	0	0	0	2	0
Tony Saunders, p	.000	2	0	0	0	0	0	2	.000	2	0	0	0	0	0	2

National League Championship Series (Cont.)

Batting	Avg	LCS vs Atlanta							Overall NL Playoffs							
		AB	R	H	HR	RBI	BB	SO	Avg	AB	R	H	HR	RBI	BB	SO
Al Leiter, p	.000	1	0	0	0	0	0	1	.000	2	0	0	0	0	0	1
Alex Fernandez, p	.000	1	0	0	0	0	0	1	.000	1	0	0	0	0	0	1
Dennis Cook, p	.000	0	0	0	0	0	0	0	.000	0	0	0	0	0	0	0
Felix Heredia, p	.000	0	0	0	0	0	0	0	.000	0	0	0	0	0	0	0
Robb Nen, p	.000	0	0	0	0	0	0	0	.000	0	0	0	0	0	0	0
Ed Vosberg, p	.000	0	0	0	0	0	0	0	.000	0	0	0	0	0	0	0
Jay Powell, p	.000	0	0	0	0	0	0	0	.000	0	0	0	0	0	0	0
Gregg Zaun, c	.000	0	0	0	0	0	0	0	.000	0	0	0	0	0	0	0
John Wehner, pr-rf	—	—	—	—	—	—	—	—	.000	1	0	0	0	0	0	0
TOTALS	.199	181	20	36	1	20	23	52	.225	280	35	63	5	34	42	68

Pitching	ERA	W-L	Sv	Gm	IP	H	BB	SO	ERA	W-L	Sv	Gm	IP	H	BB	SO
Ed Vosberg	0.00	0-0	0	2	2.2	2	1	3	0.00	0-0	0	2	2.2	2	1	3
Dennis Cook	0.00	0-0	0	2	2.1	0	0	2	0.00	1-0	0	4	5.1	0	1	5
Robb Nen	0.00	0-0	0	2	2.0	0	0	0	0.00	1-0	2	4	4.0	1	2	2
Jay Powell	0.00	0-0	0	1	0.2	0	0	1	0.00	0-0	0	1	0.2	0	0	1
Livan Hernandez	0.84	2-0	0	2	10.2	5	2	16	1.23	2-0	0	3	14.2	8	2	19
Tony Saunders	3.38	0-0	0	1	5.1	4	3	3	3.38	0-0	0	1	5.1	4	3	3
Kevin Brown	4.20	2-0	0	2	15.0	16	5	11	3.27	2-0	0	3	22.0	20	5	16
Al Leiter	4.32	0-1	0	2	8.1	13	2	6	5.84	0-1	0	3	12.1	20	5	9
Felix Heredia	5.40	0-0	0	2	3.1	3	2	4	5.40	0-0	0	2	3.1	3	2	4
Alex Fernandez	16.88	0-1	0	1	2.2	6	1	3	6.75	1-1	0	2	9.2	13	1	8
TOTALS	3.57	4-2	2	6	53.0	49	16	49	3.26	7-2	2	9	80.0	71	22	70

Wild Pitches— LCS (none); OVERALL (Leiter, Nen). **Hit Batters—**LCS (Brown, Cook); OVERALL (Brown, Cook).

Atlanta Braves

Batting	Avg	LCS vs Florida							Overall NL Playoffs							
		AB	R	H	HR	RBI	BB	SO	Avg	AB	R	H	HR	RBI	BB	SO
Greg Colbrunn, ph	.667	3	0	2	0	0	0	0	.750	4	0	3	0	2	0	0
Keith Lockhart, 2b	.500	16	4	8	0	3	1	1	.364	22	4	8	0	3	1	2
Andruw Jones, ph-rf	.444	9	0	4	0	1	1	1	.286	14	1	4	0	2	2	2
Fred McGriff, 1b	.333	21	0	7	0	4	2	7	.300	30	4	9	0	5	5	9
Tom Glavine, p	.333	3	0	1	0	0	0	2	.500	6	2	3	0	0	0	2
Jeff Blauser, ss	.300	20	5	6	1	1	3	6	.300	30	7	9	2	5	5	8
Chipper Jones, 3b	.292	24	5	7	2	4	2	3	.344	32	8	11	2	6	5	5
Tony Graffanino, 2b	.250	8	1	2	0	0	0	3	.182	11	1	2	0	0	2	4
Danny Bautista, lf	.250	4	0	1	0	0	0	0	.286	7	0	2	0	2	0	1
Ryan Klesko, lf	.235	17	2	4	2	4	2	3	.240	25	4	6	3	5	2	5
Kenny Lofton, cf	.185	27	3	5	0	1	1	7	.175	40	5	7	0	1	2	9
Michael Tucker, rf	.100	10	1	1	1	1	3	4	.125	16	1	2	1	2	3	5
Javier Lopez, c	.059	17	0	1	0	2	1	7	.125	24	3	3	0	3	3	8
Tommy Gregg, ph	.000	4	0	0	0	0	0	0	.000	4	0	0	0	0	0	1
Greg Maddux, p	.000	3	0	0	0	0	0	2	.000	5	0	0	0	0	0	3
Denny Neagle, p	.000	3	0	0	0	0	0	1	.000	3	0	0	0	0	0	1
Eduardo Perez, c	.000	3	0	0	0	0	0	0	.000	6	0	0	0	0	0	1
John Smoltz, p	.000	2	0	0	0	0	0	1	.000	6	0	0	0	0	0	1
Mike Cather, p	.000	0	0	0	0	0	0	0	.000	1	0	0	0	0	0	1
TOTALS	.253	194	21	49	6	21	16	49	.241	286	40	69	8	36	31	69

Pitching	ERA	W-L	Sv	Gm	IP	H	BB	SO	ERA	W-L	Sv	Gm	IP	H	BB	SO
Denny Neagle	0.00	1-0	0	2	12.0	5	1	9	0.00	1-0	0	2	12.0	5	1	9
Kerry Ligtenberg	0.00	0-0	0	2	3.0	1	0	4	0.00	0-0	0	2	3.0	1	0	4
Mike Cather	0.00	0-0	0	4	2.2	3	0	3	0.00	0-0	0	5	4.2	3	1	5
Alan Embree	0.00	0-0	0	1	1.0	0	1	1	0.00	0-0	0	1	1.0	0	1	1
Mark Wohlers	0.00	0-0	0	1	1.0	0	1	1	0.00	0-0	0	2	2.0	1	1	2
Greg Maddux	1.38	0-2	0	2	13.0	9	4	16	1.23	1-2	0	3	22.0	16	5	22
Tom Glavine	5.40	1-1	0	2	13.1	13	11	9	5.13	2-1	0	3	19.1	18	16	13
John Smoltz	7.50	0-1	0	1	6.0	5	5	9	3.60	1-1	0	2	15.0	8	6	20
TOTALS	2.60	2-4	0	6	52.0	36	23	52	2.28	5-4	0	9	79.0	52	31	76

Wild Pitches— LCS (none); OVERALL (none). **Hit Batters—**LCS (Glavine, Neagle, Maddux); OVERALL (Glavine, Neagle, Maddux).

Score by Innings

	1	2	3	4	5	6	7	8	9		R	H	E
Florida	8	0	2	1	0	7	1	1	0	-	20	36	3
Atlanta	6	3	4	1	2	2	2	0	1	-	21	21	4

DP: Florida 4, Atlanta 7. **LOB:** Florida 36, Atlanta 40. **2B:**. Florida— Johnson (2), Abbott, Alou, Bonilla, Daulton, Renteria, White; Atlanta— Graffanino, C. Jones, Lockhart, Lopez, McGriff. **3B:** Atlanta— Lockhart, Lofton. **SB:** Florida— Renteria, White; Atlanta— Lofton. **CS:** Florida— Johnson; Atlanta— Lofton. **Picked Off:** Florida— Conine. **S:** Florida— Brown (2), Conine, Hernandez, Johnson; Atlanta— Glavine (2), C. Jones, Maddux, Neagle. **SF:** Atlanta— Lopez (2), McGriff. **GIDP:** Florida— 4; Atlanta— 3.

Umpires: Bruce Froemming, Eric Gregg, Jerry Layne, Frank Pulli, Charlie Williams, Mike Winters.

WORLD SERIES

Florida, 4-3

Date		Winner	Home Field
Oct. 18	......	Marlins, 7-4	at Florida
Oct. 19	......	Indians, 6-1	at Florida
Oct. 21	......	Marlins, 14-11	at Cleveland
Oct. 22	......	Indians, 10-3	at Cleveland
Oct. 23	......	Marlins, 8-7	at Cleveland
Oct. 25	......	Indians, 4-1	at Florida
Oct. 26	......	Marlins, 3-2 (11 inn.)	at Florida

Game 1

Saturday, Oct. 18, 1997, at Florida

	1	2	3	4	5	6	7	8	9	R	H	E
Cleveland	1	0	0	0	1	1	0	1	0	—4	11	0
Florida	0	0	1	4	2	0	0	0	x	—7	7	1

Win: Hernandez, Fla. (1-0). **Loss:** Hershiser, Cle. (0-1). **Save:** Nen, Fla. (1).

2B: Cleveland— Roberts 2, Grissom, Giles; Florida— Counsell. **HR:** Cleveland— Ramirez (1), Thome (1); Florida— Alou (1), Johnson (1). **RBI:** Cleveland— Justice (1), Ramirez (1), Thome (1), Giles (1). Florida— Renteria (1), Alou 3 (3), Johnson (1), Conine (1).

S: Cleveland— Vizquel; Florida— Hernandez.

Attendance: 67,245. **Time:** 3:19.

Game 2

Sunday, Oct. 19, at Florida

	1	2	3	4	5	6	7	8	9	R	H	E
Cleveland	1	0	0	3	2	0	0	0	0	—6	14	0
Florida	1	0	0	0	0	0	0	0	0	—1	8	0

Win: Ogea, Cle. (1-0). **Loss:** Brown, Fla. (0-1).

2B: Cleveland— Vizquel, Fernandez; Florida— Renteria, Alou 2, White. **HR:** Cleveland— Alomar (1). **RBI:** Cleveland— Justice (2), Grissom (1), Roberts 2 (2), Alomar 2 (2). **S:** Cleveland— Ogea. **CS:** Cleveland— Justice.

Attendance: 67,025. **Time:** 2:48.

Game 3

Tuesday, Oct. 21 at Cleveland

	1	2	3	4	5	6	7	8	9	R	H	E
Florida	1	0	1	1	0	2	2	0	7	—14	16	3
Cleveland	2	0	0	3	2	0	0	0	4	—11	10	3

Win: Cook, Fla.. (1-0). **Loss:** Plunk, Cle. (0-1).

2B: Florida— Sheffield; Cleveland— Roberts. **HR:** Florida— Sheffield (1), Daulton (1), Eisenreich (1); Cleveland— Thome (2). **RBI:** Florida— Sheffield 5 (5), Daulton (1), Eisenreich 2 (2), Renteria (2), Counsell (1), Bonilla 2 (2); Cleveland— Williams (1), Alomar (3), Vizquel (1), Ramirez (2), Thome 2 (3), Fernandez (1), Grissom (2), Robert 2 (4). **S:** Cleveland— Roberts. **SF:** Cleveland— Fernandez.

Attendance: 44,880. **Time:** 4:12.

Game 4

Wednesday, Oct. 22, at Cleveland

	1	2	3	4	5	6	7	8	9	R	H	E
Florida	0	0	0	1	0	2	0	0	0	—3	6	2
Cleveland	3	0	3	0	0	1	1	2	x	—10	15	0

Win: Wright, Cle. (1-0). **Loss:** Saunders, Fla. (0-1). **Save:** Anderson, Cle. (1)

2B: Florida— Daulton; Cleveland— Alomar. **HR:** Florida— Alou (2); Cleveland— Ramirez (2), Williams (1). **RBI:** Florida— Eisenreich (3), Alou 2 (5); Cleveland— Ramirez 2 (4), Alomar 3 (6), Fernandez (2), Giles (2), Williams 2 (3). **SB:** Florida— Counsell (1); Cleveland— Vizquel (1). **CS:** Cleveland— Giles.

Attendance: 44,877. **Time:** 3:15.

Game 5

Thursday, Oct. 23, at Cleveland

	1	2	3	4	5	6	7	8	9	R	H	E
Florida	0	2	0	0	0	4	0	1	1	—8	15	2
Cleveland	0	1	3	0	0	0	0	0	3	—7	9	0

Win: Hernandez, Fla. (2-0). **Loss:** Hershiser, Cle. (0-2). **Save:** Nen, Fla. (2).

2B: Florida— Daulton, White 2, Bonilla. **3B:** Cleveland— Thome. **HR:** Florida— Alou (3); Cleveland— Alomar (2). **RBI:** Florida— Johnson 2 (3), White 2 (2), Alou 4 (9); Cleveland— Alomar 4 (10), Justice 2 (4), Thome (4). **S:** Cleveland— Vizquel. **SB:** Florida— Alou, Daulton.

Attendance: 44,888. **Time:** 3:39.

Game 6

Saturday, Oct. 25, at Florida

	1	2	3	4	5	6	7	8	9	R	H	E
Cleveland	0	2	1	0	1	0	0	0	0	—4	7	0
Florida	0	0	0	0	1	0	0	0	0	—1	8	0

Win: Ogea, Cle. (2-0). **Loss:** Brown, Fla. (0-2). **Save:** Mesa, Cle. (1).

2B: Cleveland— Vizquel, Ogea, Williams. **3B:** Florida— White. **RBI:** Cleveland— Ogea 2 (2), Ramirez 2 (6); Florida— Daulton (2). **SF:** Cleveland— Ramirez 2; Florida— Daulton. **SB:** Cleveland— Vizquel 2 (3); Florida— White (1). **CS:** Cleveland— Roberts (1).

Attendance: 67,498. **Time:** 3:15.

World Series (Cont.)

Game 7
Sunday, Oct. 26, at Florida

	1	2	3	4	5	6	7	8	9	10	11	R	H	E
Cleveland ...	0	0	2	0	0	0	0	0	0	0	0	—2	6	2
Florida	0	0	0	0	0	0	1	0	1	0	1	—3	8	0

Win: Powell, Fla. (1-0). **Loss:** Nagy, Cle. (0-1).
2B: Florida— Renteria. **HR:** Florida— Bonilla. **RBI:**
Cleveland— Fernandez 2 (4); Florida— Bonilla (3), Counsell
(2), Renteria (3). **S:** Cleveland— Wright. **SF:** Florida—
Counsell. **SB:** Cleveland— Vizquel 2 (5).
Attendance: 67,204. **Time:** 4:10.

Most Valuable Player
Livan Hernandez, Florida, RHP

W-L	Svs	ERA	Gm	IP	H	BB	SO
2-0	0	5.27	2	13.2	15	10	7

World Series Composite Box Score

Florida Marlins

Batting		WS vs Cleveland							Overall Playoffs						
	Avg	AB	R	H	HR	RBI	BB	SO	Avg	AB	R	H	HR	RBI	BB	SO
Jim Eisenreich, ph-1b-dh ...	.500	8	1	4	1	3	3	1	.364	11	1	4	1	3	5	1
Darren Daulton, 1b	.389	18	7	7	1	2	3	0	.364	22	8	8	1	3	4	2
Charles Johnson, c	.357	28	4	10	1	3	1	6	.264	53	10	14	2	10	7	16
John Cangelosi, ph	.333	3	0	1	0	0	0	2	.222	9	0	2	0	0	1	2
Moises Alou, lf	.321	28	6	9	3	9	3	6	.228	57	7	13	3	15	4	12
Gary Sheffield, rf	.292	24	4	7	1	5	8	5	.320	50	13	16	3	7	20	8
Edgar Renteria, ss	.290	31	3	9	0	3	3	5	.230	61	8	14	0	3	8	14
Devon White, cf	.242	33	0	8	0	2	3	10	.215	65	5	14	1	7	7	20
Jeff Conine, 1b-ph	.231	13	1	3	0	2	0	4	.214	42	5	9	0	3	2	4
Bobby Bonilla, 3b	.207	29	5	6	1	3	3	5	.250	64	9	16	2	10	6	12
Craig Counsell, 2b	.182	22	4	4	0	2	7	3	.293	41	4	12	0	5	10	8
Kurt Abbott, ph-dh	.000	3	0	0	0	0	0	1	.263	19	0	5	0	0	0	3
Kevin Brown, p	.000	3	0	0	0	0	0	1	.000	11	0	0	0	0	0	6
Cliff Floyd, ph-dh	.000	2	1	0	0	0	1	1	.000	2	1	0	0	0	1	1
Gregg Zaun, ph-c	.000	2	0	0	0	0	0	0	.000	2	0	0	0	0	0	0
Livan Hernandez, p	.000	2	0	0	0	0	0	0	.000	6	0	0	0	0	0	0
Alex Arias, ph-dh	.000	1	1	0	0	0	0	0	.667	3	1	2	0	1	0	0
Al Leiter, p	—	—	—	—	—	—	—	—	.000	2	0	0	0	0	0	2
Alex Fernandez, p	—	—	—	—	—	—	—	—	.000	3	0	0	0	0	1	1
Tony Saunders, p	—	—	—	—	—	—	—	—	.000	2	0	0	0	0	0	2
TOTALS	.272	250	37	68	8	34	36	48	.246	525	72	129	13	67	78	115

Pitching															
	ERA	W-L	Sv	Gm	IP	H	BB	SO	ERA	W-L	Sv	Gm	IP	H	BB	SO
Antonio Alfonseca	0.00	0-0	0	3	6.1	6	1	5	0.00	0-0	0	3	6.1	6	1	5
Felix Heredia	0.00	0-0	0	4	5.1	2	1	5	2.08	0-0	0	6	8.2	5	3	9
Dennis Cook	0.00	1-0	0	3	3.2	1	1	5	0.00	2-0	0	7	9.0	1	2	10
Al Leiter	5.06	0-0	0	2	10.2	10	10	10	5.48	0-1	0	5	23.0	30	15	19
Livan Hernandez	5.27	2-0	0	2	13.2	15	10	7	3.18	4-0	0	5	28.1	23	11	10
Ed Vosberg	6.00	0-0	0	2	3.0	3	3	2	3.18	0-0	0	4	5.2	5	4	4
Jay Powell	7.36	1-0	0	4	3.2	5	4	2	6.23	1-0	0	5	4.1	5	4	3
Robb Nen	7.71	0-0	2	4	4.2	8	2	7	4.15	1-0	4	8	8.2	9	4	9
Kevin Brown	8.18	0-2	0	2	11.0	15	10	10	4.91	2-2	0	5	33.0	35	10	22
Tony Saunders	27.00	0-1	0	1	2.0	7	3	2	9.82	0-1	0	2	7.1	11	6	5
Alex Fernandez	—	—	—	—	—	—	—	—	6.52	1-1	0	2	9.2	13	1	8
TOTALS	5.48	4-3	2	7	64.0	72	40	51	4.25	11-5	4	16	144.0	143	62	121

Wild Pitches—WS (Hernandez); OVERALL (Hernandez, Nen, Leiter). **Hit Batters**—WS (None); OVERALL (Cook, Brown).
Balk—WS (none); OVERALL—(none).

Cleveland Indians

Batting		WS vs Florida							Overall Playoffs						
	Avg	AB	R	H	HR	RBI	BB	SO	Avg	AB	R	H	HR	RBI	BB	SO
Brian Giles	.500	4	1	2	0	2	4	1	.222	27	2	6	0	2	6	8
Chad Ogea, p	.500	4	1	2	0	2	0	1	.500	4	1	2	0	2	0	1
Tony Fernandez, ph-2b ...	.471	17	1	8	0	4	0	1	.357	42	2	15	1	10	1	3
Matt Williams, 3b	.385	17	1	8	1	3	7	6	.288	66	13	19	2	8	13	16
Sandy Alomar Jr., c	.367	30	5	11	2	10	2	3	.274	73	12	20	5	19	3	8
Marquis Grissom, cf	.360	25	5	9	0	2	4	4	.292	65	10	19	1	6	6	15
Jim Thome, 1b	.286	28	8	8	2	4	5	7	.211	57	12	12	2	5	10	16
Bip Roberts, 2b-lf	.273	22	3	6	0	4	3	5	.246	61	4	15	0	5	5	15
Omar Vizquel, ss	.233	30	5	7	0	1	3	5	.233	73	9	17	0	2	7	16
David Justice, lf-dh	.185	27	4	5	0	4	6	8	.254	67	10	17	1	6	10	15

Batting	Avg	AB	R	H	HR	RBI	BB	SO	Avg	AB	R	H	HR	RBI	BB	SO
			WS vs Florida									**Overall Playoffs**				
Manny Ramirez, ...	.154	26	3	4	2	6	6	5	.191	68	8	13	4	12	11	13
Mike Jackson, p	.000	2	0	0	0	0	0	1	.000	2	0	0	0	0	0	1
Orel Hershiser, p	.000	2	0	0	0	0	0	1	.000	2	0	0	0	0	0	1
Jaret Wright, p	.000	2	0	0	0	0	0	2	.000	2	0	0	0	0	0	2
Jeff Branson, ...	.000	1	0	0	0	0	0	0	.000	3	0	0	0	0	0	3
Kevin Seitzer	.000	1	0	0	0	0	0	0	.000	9	0	0	0	0	1	2
TOTALS	.291	247	44	72	7	42	40	51	.250	621	83	155	16	77	73	135

Pitching	ERA	W-L	Sv	Gm	IP	H	BB	SO	ERA	W-L	Sv	Gm	IP	H	BB	SO
Paul Assenmacher	0.00	0-0	0	5	4.0	5	0	6	3.86	1-0	0	14	9.1	12	3	11
Alvin Morman	0.00	0-0	0	2	0.1	0	2	1	0.00	0-0	0	5	1.2	0	3	2
Chad Ogea	1.54	2-0	0	2	11.2	11	3	5	2.32	2-2	0	5	31.0	25	8	13
Mike Jackson	1.93	0-0	0	4	4.2	5	3	4	0.67	1-0	0	13	13.1	9	5	16
Brian Anderson	2.45	0-0	0	3	3.2	2	0	2	1.80	0-0	1	6	10.0	3	3	9
Jaret Wright	2.92	1-0	0	2	12.1	7	10	12	4.73	3-0	0	5	26.2	24	19	25
Jeff Juden	4.50	0-0	0	2	2.0	2	2	0	3.00	0-0	0	5	3.0	4	4	2
Jose Mesa	5.40	0-0	1	5	5.0	10	1	5	3.95	1-0	4	11	13.2	20	5	12
Charles Nagy	6.43	0-1	0	2	7.0	8	5	5	4.94	0-2	0	5	23.2	27	16	11
Eric Plunk	9.00	0-1	0	3	3.0	3	4	3	12.60	1-2	0	5	5.0	8	4	4
Orel Hershiser	11.70	0-2	0	2	10.0	15	6	5	5.72	0-2	0	5	28.1	33	9	16
TOTALS	4.67	3-4	2	7	63.2	68	36	48	4.02	10-8	5	18	165.2	165	79	121

Wild Pitches—WS (Juden, Mesa, Wright); OVERALL (Juden, Mesa, Wright). **Hit Batters**—WS (Ogea); OVERALL (Ogea, Assenmacher, Mesa, Nagy, Hershiser). **Balk**—WS (none); OVERALL—(none).

Score by Innings

	1	2	3	4	5	6	7	8	9	10	11		R	H	E
Cleveland	7	3	9	3	7	4	1	3	7	0	0	—	44	72	5
Florida	2	2	2	6	3	8	3	1	9	0	1	—	37	68	8

DP: Cleveland 8, Florida 9. **LOB:** Cleveland 59, Florida 62. **2B:** Cleveland— Roberts (4), Vizquel (2), Alomar, Fernandez, Giles, Grissom, Ogea, Williams; Florida— White (3), Alou (2), Daulton (2), Renteria (2), Bonilla, Counsell, Sheffield. **3B:** Cleveland— Thome; Florida— White. **SB:** Cleveland— Vizquel (5); Florida— Alou, Counsell, Daulton, White. **CS:** Cleveland— Giles, Justice, Roberts. **S:** Cleveland— Vizquel (2), Ogea, Roberts, Wright; Florida— Hernandez. **SF:** Cleveland— Ramirez (2), Fernandez; Florida— Counsell, Daulton.

Umpires: Dale Ford (AL), Ken Kaiser (AL), Greg Kosc (AL), Randy Marsh (NL), Ed Montague (NL), Joe West (NL).

COLLEGE

Final *Baseball America* Top 25

Final 1997 Division I Top 25, voted on by the editors of *Baseball America* and released after the NCAA College World Series. Given are final records and winning percentage (including all postseason games); records in College World Series and team eliminated by (DNP indicates team did not play in tourney); head coach (career years and Division I record including 1997 postseason); preseason ranking and rank before start of CWS.

		Record	Pct	CWS Recap	Head Coach	Preseason Rank	Rank before CWS
1	LSU	57-13	.814	4-0	Skip Bertman (14 yrs: 685-248-1)	11	2
2	Alabama	56-14	.800	4-2 (LSU)	Jim Wells (8 yrs: 340-145)	19	1
3	Miami-FL	51-18	.739	2-2 (Alabama)	Jim Morris (16 yrs: 702-307-1)	4	3
4	Stanford	45-20	.692	2-2 (LSU)	Mark Marquess (21 yrs: 853-453-4)	1	5
5	UCLA	45-21	.682	0-2 (Miss. St.)	Gary Adams (28 yrs: 960-680-11)	5	4
6	Auburn	50-17	.746	1-2 (Stanford)	Hal Baird (18 yrs: 646-337)	NR	6
7	Mississippi St. ...	47-21	.691	1-2 (Alabama)	Ron Polk (26 yrs: 1,043-486)	9	9
8	Rice	47-16	.746	0-2 (Auburn)	Wayne Graham (6 yrs: 231-123)	10	7
9	Florida St.	50-17	.746	DNP	Mike Martin (18 yrs: 969-330-3)	2	8
10	USC	42-20	.677	DNP	Mike Gillespie (11 yrs: 434-250-2)	3	10
11	Arizona St.	39-22	.639	DNP	Pat Murphy (3 yrs: 481-235-3)	7	11
12	Texas Tech	46-14	.767	DNP	Larry Hays (27 yrs: 1,113-602-2)	NR	12
13	Washington	46-20	.697	DNP	Ken Knutson (5 yrs: 185-115)	24	13
14	Oklahoma St. ...	46-19	.708	DNP	Tom Holliday (1 yr: 46-19)	18	14
15	South Alabama ..	43-19	.694	DNP	Steve Kittrell (14 yrs: 561-302-1)	20	15
16	Florida	40-24	.625	DNP	Andy Lopez (15 yrs: 531-325-5)	15	16
17	Georgia Tech	46-15	.754	DNP	Danny Hall (10 yrs: 382-195)	6	17
18	Long Beach St. ..	39-26	.600	DNP	Dave Snow (13 yrs: 529-275-4)	23	18
19	Oklahoma	39-20	.661	DNP	Larry Cochell (32 yrs: 1,073-606-3)	NR	19
20	SW Louisiana	43-18	.705	DNP	Tony Robichaux (10 yrs: 332-223)	NR	20
21	N.C. State	43-20	.683	DNP	Elliott Avent (9 yrs: 300-252)	NR	21
22	Santa Clara	41-20	.672	DNP	John Oldham (13 yrs: 433-324)	NR	22
23	Fresno St.	40-28	.588	DNP	Bob Bennett (29 yrs: 1,124-627)	NR	23
24	CS-Fullerton	39-24	.619	DNP	CS-Fullerton (1 yr: 39-24)	12	24
25	Tennessee	42-19	.689	DNP	Rod Delmonico (8 yrs: 340-159)	17	25

College (Cont.)

College World Series

CWS Seeds: 1. Alabama (52-12); **2.** LSU (53-13); **3.** Stanford (43-18); **4.** UCLA (45-19); **5.** Miami (49-16); **6.** Auburn (49-15); **7.** Rice (47-14); **8.** Mississippi St. (46-19).

Bracket One

May 30—Stanford 8	....	Auburn 3
May 30—LSU 5	....	Rice 4
June 1—LSU 10	....	Stanford 5
June 1—Auburn 10	....	Rice 1 (out)
June 3—Stanford 11	....	Auburn 4 (out)
June 4—LSU 13	....	Stanford 7 (out)

Bracket Two

May 31—Miami 7	....	UCLA 3 (12 inn.)
May 31—Alabama 3	....	Mississippi St. 2
June 2—Miami 6	....	Alabama 1
June 2—Mississippi St. 7	....	UCLA 5 (out)
June 3—Alabama 9	....	Mississippi St. 5 (out)
June 5—Alabama 8	....	Miami 6
June 6—Alabama 8	....	Miami 2 (out)

Annual Awards

Chosen by *Baseball America*, *Collegiate Baseball*, National Collegiate Baseball Writers Association and the American Baseball Coaches Association.

Players of the Year

J.D. Drew, Florida St.	....	ABCA, *BA, CB*
Lance Berkman, Rice	....	NCBWA

Coaches of the Year

Skip Bertman, LSU	....	ABCA, *CB*
Jim Wells, Alabama	....	*BA*

CWS Championship Game

Saturday, June 7, at Rosenblatt Stadium in Omaha.

	1 2 3	4 5 6	7 8 9		R	H	E
Alabama	0 0 2	2 0 0	0 2 0	—	6	11	3
LSU	6 3 0	0 0 2	1 1 x	—	13	15	1

Win: LSU– Doug Thompson (12-3). **Loss:** Alabama– Michael Daniel (5-1). **Starters:** Alabama– Daniel; LSU– Patrick Coogan. **Strikeouts:** Alabama– Jarrod Kingrey 4, Heath Henderson 4, Doug Hurst 2; LSU– Coogan 8, Thompson 7. **WP:** LSU– Coogan 3, Thompson.

2B: Alabama– Joe Caruso, Andy Phillips, Robbie Tucker, Mark Peer; LSU– Tom Bernhardt, Wes Davis. **HR:** Alabama– Caruso (15); LSU– Danny Higgins (11), Bernhardt (17). **RBI:** Alabama– Caruso 4, Tucker 2; LSU– Higgins 3, Brandon Larson 3, Bernhardt 3, Davis 3, Mike Koerner 3. **SB:** Alabama– Caruso (13). **HBP:** Alabama– G.W. Keller (by Coogan); LSU– Trey McClure (by Henderson).

Attendance: 24,401. **Time** 3:15.

Most Outstanding Player

Brandon Larson, LSU, SS

Avg	AB	R	H	HR	RBI	SB
.389	18	6	7	3	8	1

All-Tournament Team

C– Matt Frick, Alabama. **1B**– Eddy Furniss, LSU. **2B**– Joe Caruso, Alabama. **3B**– Andy Phillips, Alabama. **SS**– Brandon Larson, LSU. **OF**– Mike Koerner and Tom Bernhardt, LSU; G.W. Keller, Alabama. **DH**– Mark Peer, Alabama. **P**– Jeff Austin, Stanford; Jarrod Kingrey, Alabama.

Head over Heels

It's deja vu all over again as the LSU Tigers celebrate their second consecutive Division I College World Series title with a 13-6 pasting of Alabama on June 7 at Rosenblatt Stadium in Omaha. No injuries were reported from the celebration.

World Wide Photos

Consensus All-America Team

NCAA Division I players cited most frequently by the following four selectors: the American Baseball Coaches Assn. (ABCA), *Baseball America*, *Collegiate Baseball*, and the National Collegiate Baseball Writers Assn. (NCBWA). Holdovers from the 1996 All-America first team are in **bold** type.

First Team

Pos		Cl	Avg	HR	RBI
C	G. Chiaramonte, Fresno St.	Jr.	.341	26	72
1B	Lance Berkman, Rice	Jr.	.431	41	134
2B	Keith Ginter, Texas Tech	Jr.	.426	17	77
SS	Brandon Larson, LSU	Jr.	.381	40	118
3B	Pat Burrell, Miami	So.	.409	21	76
OF	J.D. Drew, Florida St.	Jr.	.455	31	100
OF	Mike Marchiano, Fordham	Sr.	.493	29	85
OF	Jeremy Morris, Florida St.	Jr.	.356	25	116
UT	Tim Hudson, Auburn	Sr.	.396	18	95

		Cl	W-L	Sv	ERA
P	Matt Anderson, Rice	Jr.	10-2	7	2.05
P	Dan Reichert, Pacific	Jr.	13-4	0	2.30
P	Jason Gooding, Texas Tech	Jr.	11-0	0	3.49
P	Chris Enochs, West Virginia	Jr.	12-1	0	3.03
P	Jason Navarro, Tulane	Jr.	12-2	0	2.00
P	Jim Parque, UCLA	Jr.	13-2	0	3.08
P	Kyle Peterson, Stanford	Jr.	11-3	0	4.19

Second Team

Pos		Cl	Avg	HR	RBI
C	Matthew LeCroy, Clemson	Jr.	.359	24	79
1B	Joe Dillon, Texas Tech	Sr.	.393	33	89
2B	Tom Sergio, N.C. State	Sr.	.412	16	68
SS	Adam Kennedy, CS-Northridge	Jr.	.482	26	99
3B	Troy Glaus, UCLA	Jr.	.409	34	91
OF	Jeff Guiel, Oklahoma St.	Sr.	.418	23	79
OF	John Heinrichs, UCLA	Jr.	.358	28	79
OF	Dan McKinley, Arizona St.	Jr.	.423	15	70
UT	Brad Wilkerson, Florida	So.	.386	23	76
UT	Roberto Vaz, Alabama	Jr.	.400	22	73

		Cl	W-L	Sv	ERA
P	Patrick Coogan, LSU	Jr.	14-3	2	4.46
P	Kris Wilson, Georgia Tech	Jr.	12-2	2	3.12
P	Randy Choate, Florida St.	Jr.	13-3	0	3.61
P	Randy Wolf, Pepperdine	Jr.	9-4	1	1.79
P	Tod Lee, Ga. Southern	Jr.	6-2	7	3.92
P	Jeff Weaver, Fresno St.	Jr.	11-5	2	3.63

NCAA Division I Leaders

Batting
Average

(At least 75 AB)	Cl	Gm	AB	H	Avg
Mike Marchiano, Fordham	Sr.	53	207	102	.493
Adam Kennedy, CS-Northridge	Jr.	63	278	134	.482
Brian Nickerson, Dartmouth	Fr.	38	136	63	.463
J.D. Drew, Florida St.	Jr.	67	233	106	.455
Talmadge Nunnari, Jacksonville	Sr.	54	200	90	.450
Greg Ryan, Eastern Michigan	So.	54	197	88	.447
Elvis Hernandez, Ill.-Chicago	Fr.	38	137	61	.445
Dan Hummel, Seton Hall	Jr.	54	196	85	.434
Brian August, Delaware	Jr.	54	199	86	.432
Billy Rich, Connecticut	Jr.	47	190	82	.432

Home Runs (per game)

(At least 15)	Cl	Gm	HR	Avg
Lance Berkman, Rice	Jr.	63	41	0.65
Brandon Larson, LSU	Jr.	69	40	0.58
Joe Dillon, Texas Tech	Sr.	57	33	0.58
Mike Marchiano, Fordham	Sr.	53	29	0.55
Casey Child, Utah	Jr.	58	31	0.53
Troy Glaus, UCLA	Jr.	67	34	0.51
Andy Dominique, Nevada	Sr.	60	30	0.50
H. Hargrove, CS-Sacramento	Jr.	55	26	0.47
J.D. Drew, Florida St.	Jr.	67	31	0.46
Jamie Palmese, Cent. Conn. St.	Sr.	35	16	0.46

Runs Batted In

(At least 50)	Cl	Gm	RBI	Avg
Lance Berkman, Rice	Jr.	63	134	2.13
Jeremy Morris, Florida St.	Sr.	66	116	1.76
Brandon Larson, LSU	Jr.	69	118	1.71
Casey Child, Utah	Jr.	58	97	1.67
Mike Scioletti, Army	Jr.	41	67	1.63
Mark Fischer, Georgia Tech	Jr.	61	98	1.61
Mike Marchiano, Fordham	Sr.	53	85	1.60
Andy Dominique, Nevada	Sr.	60	96	1.60
Ryan Upshaw, N. Mex. St.	Jr.	53	84	1.58
Joe Dillon, Texas Tech	Sr.	57	90	1.58

Stolen Bases

(At least 25)	Cl	Gm	SB	SBA	Avg
Jason Maule, Cent. Conn. St.	So.	36	39	44	1.08
Brad Gorrie, Massachusetts	Jr.	46	43	48	0.93
Brian Harris, Indiana	Sr.	54	50	59	0.93
Clay Greene, Tennessee	Sr.	59	54	63	0.92
Kevin Fahy, Drexel	Sr.	51	45	48	0.88
Schuyler Doakes, Jackson St.	Jr.	34	30	36	0.88
Ryan Grimmett, Miami-FL	Sr.	62	53	67	0.85
Kent Brown, Austin Peay	Sr.	59	50	65	0.85
Tommy Lewis, Northeast La.	Sr.	50	42	48	0.84
Scott Lobaugh, Pittsburgh	Jr.	40	32	38	0.80

Pitching
Earned Run Avg.

(At least 50 inn.)	Cl	Gm	IP	ERA
Sonny Garcia, Texas Southern	Jr.	14	66.0	1.77
Randy Wolf, Pepperdine	Jr.	17	121.0	1.79
Andy Smith, Bowling Green	Sr.	16	87.1	1.85
Jay Akin, Arkansas St.	Sr.	18	110.1	1.96
Jason Navarro, Tulane	Jr.	17	112.1	2.00
Tyson Taplin, Alcorn St.	Sr.	12	71.2	2.01
Eddy Reyes, Miami-FL	Jr.	43	70.2	2.04
Matt Anderson, Rice	Jr.	30	79.0	2.05
Mark Newell, Oregon St.	So.	10	72.1	2.12
Eric Cammack, Lamar	Jr.	10	62.2	2.15

Wins

	Cl	Gm	IP	W-L
Jason Parsons, N.C.-Greensboro	Jr.	35	105.1	15-1
Tim Hudson, Auburn	Sr.	22	118.1	15-2
Patrick Coogan, LSU	Jr.	25	125.0	14-3
Heath Henderson, Alabama	Jr.	22	124.1	13-2
Jim Parque, UCLA	Jr.	19	120.0	13-2
Randy Choate, Florida St.	Jr.	19	134.2	13-3
Dan Reichert, Pacific	Jr.	20	133.1	13-4

Thirteen tied with 12 wins each.

NCAA Division I Leaders (Cont.)

Strikeouts (per 9 inn.)

(At least 50 inn.)	Cl	IP	SO	Avg
Tod Lee, Ga. Southern	Jr.	64.1	99	13.8
Jason Grilli, Seton Hall	Jr.	81.1	125	13.8
Barry Zito, UC Santa Barb.	Fr.	85.1	123	13.0
Ryan Saylor, Eastern Ky.	Sr.	68.1	98	12.9
Eric Cammack, Lamar	Jr.	62.2	89	12.8
Tim Hudson, Auburn	Sr.	118.1	165	12.5
Monty Ward, Texas Tech	So.	86.1	117	12.2
Chad Harville, Memphis	Jr.	101.2	136	12.0
Matt Anderson, Rice	Jr.	79.0	105	12.0
B. Williamson, Jacksonville St.	Jr.	66.0	87	11.9

Saves

	Cl	IP	ERA	Saves
Ara Petrosian, Long Beach St.	Jr.	78.1	3.91	15
Van Johnson, Mississippi St.	Jr.	83.1	4.21	13
Marc Bluma, Wichita St.	So.	39.2	3.63	12
Mark Squire, Wright St.	So.	59.2	2.56	11
Jack Krawczyk, USC	Jr.	39.1	3.20	11
David Johnson, Kansas St.	Jr.	29.0	5.28	11
Six tied with 10 each.				

Other College World Series

Participants' final records in parentheses.

NCAA Div. II
at Montgomery, Ala. (May 24-June 1)

Participants: Adelphi, NY (30-16); Cal State Chico (52-11); Central Missouri St. (39-13); Central Oklahoma (42-21); Kennesaw St., Ga. (48-14); Slippery Rock, Pa. (30-21); Southern Illinois-Edwardsville (37-19); Tampa (46-16).
Championship: Cal State Chico def. Central Oklahoma, 13-12.

NAIA
at Sioux City, Iowa (May 23-May 30)

Participants: Bellevue, Neb. (43-16); Brewton-Parker, GA (64-7); California Baptist (37-15); Cumberland, TN (49-13); Dallas Baptist, TX (55-15); Dominican, NY (38-13-1); Mt. Vernon Nazarene, Ohio (47-8); Southeastern Oklahoma (56-9).
Championship: Brewton Parker def. Bellevue, 8-4.

NCAA Div. III
at Salem, Va. (May 24-28)

Participants: Bridgewater St., Mass. (29-11-1); Carthage, Wis. (40-10); Chapman, Cal. (31-16); Cortland St., NY (31-10); N.C. Wesleyan (40-7); Southern Maine (39-9); Wisconsin-Stevens Point (31-13); Wooster, Ohio (46-8-1).
Championship: Southern Maine def. Wooster, 15-1.

NJCAA Div. I
at Grand Junction, Colo. (May 24-31)

Participants: Allegany, MD (38-8); Central Fla. (37-18); Columbia St., TN (40-18); Cowley County, KS (54-11); Hill, TX (46-15); Indian Hills, Iowa (41-15); San Jacinto, TX (43-26); Scottsdale CC (43-19); Seminole, OK (57-5); Wallace St., Ala. (42-14).
Championship: Cowley County def. Seminole, 4-2.

MLB Amateur Draft

Top 50 selections at the 33rd Amateur Draft held June 3-5, 1997. Selections 1-31 are first round picks and 32-50 are supplemental first round picks awarded for the loss of free agents.

Top 50 Picks

No		Pos
1	Detroit ....Matt Anderson, Rice	P
2	Philadelphia .........J.D. Drew, Florida St.	OF
3	Anaheim ....Troy Glaus, UCLA	3B-SS
4	San Francisco ...... Jason Grilli, Seton Hall	P
5	Toronto .....Vernon Wells, HS-Arlington, Tx.	OF
6	NY Mets ....Geoff Goetz, HS-Tampa, Fl.	P
7	Kansas City ....Dan Reichert, Pacific	P
8	Pittsburgh ... J.J. Davis, HS-Ponoma, Ca.	1B
9	Minnesota ... Michael Cuddyer, HS-Chesapeake, Va.	SS
10	Chicago-NL Jon Garland, HS-Granada Hills, Ca.	P
11	Oakland ....Chris Enochs, West Virginia	P
12	Florida ...Aaron Akin, Cowley County (Kan.) CC	P
13	Milwaukee ....Kyle Peterson, Stanford	P
14	Cincinnati ....Brandon Larson, LSU	SS
15	Chicago-AL ... Jason Dellaero, South Florida	SS
16	Houston ....Lance Berkman, Rice	1B
17	Boston ... John Curtice, HS-Chesapeake, Va.	P
18	Colorado .Mark Mangum, HS-Kingwood, Tx.	P
19	Seattle ..Ryan Anderson, HS-Westland, Mich.	P
20	St. Louis .....Adam Kennedy, CS-Northridge	SS
21	a-Oakland .....Eric Dubose, Mississippi St.	P
22	Baltimore ... Jayson Werth, HS-Chatham, Ill.	C
23	Montreal .Donnie Bridges, HS-Hattiesburg, Miss.	P
24	b-NY Yankees .Tyrell Godwin, HS-Elizabethtown, NC	OF
25	Los Angeles ....Glenn Davis, Vanderbilt	1B-OF

No		Pos
26	c-Baltimore ..Darnell McDonald, HS-Englewood, Col.	OF
27	San Diego ....Kevin Nicholson, Stetson	SS
28	Cleveland ....Tim Drew, HS-Hahira, Ga.	P
29	Atlanta ....Troy Cameron, HS-Ft. Lauderdale, Fla.	SS
30	Arizona ......Jack Cust, HS-Flemington, NJ	1B
31	Tampa Bay ..Jason Standridge, HS-Trussville, Ala.	P
32	Oakland ...Nathan Hayes, HS-Hercules, Cal.	OF
33	Chicago-AL ....Kyle Kane, Saddleback (Cal.) CC	P
34	Chicago-AL .Brett Caradonna, HS-San Diego, Cal.	OF
35	Boston ....Mark Fischer, Georgia Tech	OF
36	Baltimore .....Ntema Ndungidi, HS-Montreal	OF
37	Montreal ..Chris Stowe, HS-Fredricksburg, Va	P
38	Montreal ....Scott Hodges, HS-Lexington, Ky.	SS
39	Texas ....Jason Romano, HS-Tampa, Fla.	3B
40	NY Yankees ....Ryan Bradley, Arizona St.	P
41	Cleveland ....Jason Fitzgerald, Tulane	OF
42	Oakland .....Denny Wagner, Virginia Tech	P
43	Chicago-AL ...Aaron Myette, Central Arizona JC	P
44	Montreal ....Bryan Hebson, Auburn	P
45	Montreal ..Thomas Pittman, HS-Garyville, La.	1B
46	Chicago-AL ....Jim Parque, UCLA	P
47	Montreal ....T.J. Tucker, HS-New Port Richey, Fla.	P
48	Montreal .Shane Arthurs, HS-Oklahoma City, Ok.	P
49	San Francisco ....Dan McKinley, Arizona St.	OF
50	Minnesota ....Matthew LeCroy, Clemson	C

Acquired picks: a–from Baltimore for signing Mike Bordick; **b**–from Texas for signing John Wetteland; **c**–from NY Yankees for signing David Wells.

Tigers Take it Again

by Tim Scanlan

Baseball nirvana is in the heartland. In Omaha, Nebraska in late May, early June, a very special sporting event is played out like an annual school play, complete with leading characters, villains and heroes. This year's College World Series will be remembered for many things: a showcase for the Southeastern Conference with four teams advancing through the regionals, the end of the line for a champion of college baseball, a stage for some future big league stars and a championship featuring baseball's best rivalry.

The sights, sounds and smells of Rosenblatt Stadium in Omaha give one the sensation of being inside a Norman Rockwell painting. A record 204,309 people, many of them young kids, enjoyed sunshine, temperatures in the 80s and the smell of popcorn, brats on the grill and corn-on-the-cob, over eight days of the double elimination tournament.

The Southeastern Conference was well represented as the defending national champion Louisiana State Tigers, the Mississippi State Bulldogs, the Auburn Tigers and the Alabama Crimson Tide came rolling into Omaha.

The Pacific Ten Conference with its deep talent pool of California kids, was represented by Stanford and UCLA. The Rice Owls (WAC) and the Miami Hurricanes (Big East) filled in the brackets.

Skip Bertman, head coach at LSU, had reason to feel confident that his squad would win its fourth national championship in seven years. The Tigers scored runs in bunches throughout the 1997 season. They had homered in each of its 70 games, finishing with an NCAA record 188 for the year. To win the tournament Bertman figured that he would have to beat Alabama. The Tide, coached by Bertman's former assistant Jim Wells, won the conference tournament championship. The series between the teacher and the pupil has

developed into a terrific baseball rivalry.

Jim Wells has learned well from coach Bertman. The Crimson Tide was coming off a 4-23 conference mark in 1995 when Wells took the helm. Since then, Alabama has won three straight SEC tournaments and finished the 1997 season with a 56-14 record. Baseball America recognized Jim Wells as their Coach of the Year in 1997 .

The great weather provided for good defense, solid pitching and clutch hitting during the tournament. The stars came out to shine, with Brandon Larson slugging three home runs and 8 RBI for LSU, and Joe Caruso of Alabama knocking out 14 hits. Great pitching performances were put forth by Jarrod Kingery of Alabama, Jeff Austin of Stanford, Eddy Reyes of Miami and flame-throwing reliever Matt Anderson of Rice, who showcased his 98 mph fastball and was claimed number-one draft pick overall by the Detroit Tigers in the MLB amateur draft.

The rivalry that everyone envisioned took shape when LSU and Alabama advanced to the semifinal brackets and then advanced to the championship game on June 7th. The two teams had met five times prior to the championship, with the Crimson Tide holding a three games to two advantage, including a 28-2 thrashing in the final series of the regular season. This was the worst loss in the history of Louisiana State University.

So the stage was set, Bertman vs. Wells, conference, regional and national bragging rights at stake. One team that could hit home runs by the bundle, the other winning with great defense and timely hitting. The LSU Tigers scored six runs in the first inning and three more in the second, off of junior right-hander Mike Daniel. The Tigers held on to a 13-6 victory before a record 24,401 fans. The all-tournament team featured four LSU Tigers, five from Alabama, with LSU's Brandon Larson being voted the Most Outstanding Player.

Tim Scanlan is a producer for ESPN's college baseball coverage.

Minor League Triple A Final Standings

International League

Eastern Division	W	L	Pct	GB
Rochester (Orioles)	83	58	.589	—
Pawtucket (Red Sox)	81	60	.574	2
Scranton/W-B (Phillies)	66	76	.465	17½
Syracuse (Blue Jays)	55	87	.387	28½
Ottawa (Expos)	54	86	.386	28½
Western Division	W	L	Pct	GB
Columbus (Yankees)	79	63	.556	—
Charlotte (Marlins)	76	65	.539	2½
Norfolk (Mets)	75	67	.528	4
Richmond (Braves)	70	72	.493	9
Toledo (Tigers)	68	73	.482	10½

Playoffs

Division Finals (Best of 5): Rochester def. Pawtucket (3-1); Columbus def. Charlotte (3-1).

Championship (Best of Five)
Rochester vs. Columbus

Sept. 8	Rochester, 11-6	at Columbus
Sept. 9	Columbus, 8-4	at Columbus
Sept. 12	Rochester, 3-1	at Rochester
Sept. 13	Columbus, 4-3	at Rochester
Sept. 14	Rochester, 4-3	at Rochester

Rochester wins series, 3-2.

American Association

Eastern Division	W	L	Pct	GB
Buffalo (Indians)	87	57	.604	—
Indianapolis (Reds)	85	59	.590	2
Nashville (White Sox)	74	69	.517	12½
Louisville (Cardinals)	58	85	.406	28½
Western Division	W	L	Pct	GB
Iowa (Cubs)	74	69	.517	—
New Orleans (Astros)	74	70	.514	½
Oklahoma City (Rangers)	61	82	.427	13
Omaha (Royals)	61	83	.424	13½

Playoffs

Division Finals (Best of 5): Buffalo def. Indianapolis (3-2); Iowa def. New Orleans (3-0).

Championship (Best of Five)
Buffalo vs. Iowa

Sept. 8	Buffalo, 2-1	at Buffalo
Sept. 9	Buffalo, 6-3	at Buffalo
Sept. 10	Buffalo, 5-4 (10 inn.)	at Iowa

Buffalo wins series, 3-0.

Pacific Coast League

Northern Division	W	L	Pct	GB
† Edmonton (Athletics)	42	31	.575	—
Tacoma (Mariners)	40	31	.563	1
Salt Lake (Twins)	38	33	.535	3
* Vancouver (Angels)	36	36	.500	5½
Calgary (Pirates)	31	40	.437	10
Southern Division	W	L	Pct	GB
† Phoenix (Giants)	49	22	.690	—
Las Vegas (Padres)	31	39	.443	17½
* Colorado Springs (Rockies)	31	41	.431	18½
Tucson (Brewers)	30	41	.423	19
Albuquerque (Dodgers)	29	43	.403	20½

* first half divisional champ; † second half divisional champ

Playoffs

Division Finals (Best of 5): Phoenix def. Colorado Springs (3-0); Edmonton def. Vancouver (3-0).

Championship (Best of Five)
Phoenix vs. Edmonton

Sept. 8	Edmonton, 6-5 (11 inn.)	at Edmonton
Sept. 9	Edmonton, 4-2	at Edmonton
Sept. 10	Phoenix, 8-2	at Phoenix
Sept. 11	Edmonton, 7-1	at Phoenix

Edmonton wins series, 3-1.

Japan League

Final Standings

Central League	W	L	T	Pct	GB
Yakult Swallows	83	52	2	.615	—
Yokohama BayStars	72	63	0	.533	11
Hiroshima Carp	66	69	0	.489	17
Yomiuri Giants	63	72	0	.467	20
Hanshin Tigers	62	73	1	.459	21
Chunichi Dragons	59	76	1	.437	24

Pacific League	W	L	T	Pct	GB
Seibu Lions	76	56	3	.576	—
Orix Blue Wave	71	61	3	.538	5
Kintetsu Buffaloes	68	63	4	.519	7½
Nippon Ham Fighters	63	71	1	.470	14
Fukuoka Daiei Hawks	63	71	1	.470	14
Chiba Lotte Marines	57	76	2	.429	19½

Japan Series (Best of 7)

Oct. 18	Yakult, 1-0	at Seibu
Oct. 19	Seibu, 6-5 (10 inn.)	at Seibu
Oct. 21	Yakult, 5-3	at Yakult
Oct. 22	Yakult, 7-1	at Yakult
Oct. 23	Yakult, 3-0	at Yakult

Yakult wins Japan Series, 4-1

Japan League Leaders

Avg.	Ichiro Suzuki, Orix	.345
HR	Dwayne Hosey, Yak.	38
RBI	Hiroki Kokubo, Dai.	114
ERA	Satoru Komiyama, Lot.	2.49
Win Pct.	Daisuke Miura, Yok.	.769 (10-3)
SO	Fumiya Nishiguchi, Sei.	192

THE 1998 ESPN INFORMATION PLEASE SPORTS ALMANAC

B A S E B A L L
S T A T I S T I C S

THROUGH THE YEARS
1876-1997
WORLD SERIES • ALL-TIMERS

SEC
B

PAGE
101

The World Series

The World Series began in 1903 when Pittsburgh of the older National League (founded in 1876) invited Boston of the American League (founded in 1901) to play a best-of-9 game series to determine which of the two league champions was the best. Boston was the surprise winner, 5 games to 3. The 1904 NL champion New York Giants refused to play Boston the following year, so there was no series. Giants' owner John T. Brush and his manager John McGraw both despised AL president Ban Johnson and considered the junior circuit to be a minor league. By the following year, however, Brush and Johnson had smoothed out their differences and the Giants agreed to play Philadelphia in a best-of-7 game series. Since then the World Series has been a best-of-7 format, except from 1919-21 when it returned to best-of-9.

After surviving two world wars and an earthquake in 1989, the World Series was cancelled for only the second time in 1994 when the players went out on strike Aug. 12 to protest the owners' call for revenue sharing and a salary cap. On Sept. 14, with no hope of reaching a labor agreement to end the 34-day strike, the owners called off the remainder of the regular season and the entire postseason. The strike ended after 232 days on Mar. 31, 1995.

In the chart below, the National League teams are listed in CAPITAL letters. Also, each World Series champion's wins and losses are noted in parentheses after the Series score in games.

Multiple champions: New York Yankees (23); Philadelphia-Oakland A's and St. Louis Cardinals (9); Brooklyn-Los Angeles Dodgers (6); Boston Red Sox, Cincinnati Reds, New York-San Francisco Giants and Pittsburgh Pirates (5); Detroit Tigers (4); Baltimore Orioles, Boston-Milwaukee-Atlanta Braves and Washington Senators-Minnesota Twins (3); Chicago Cubs, Chicago White Sox, Cleveland Indians, New York Mets and Toronto Blue Jays (2).

Year	Winner	Manager	Series	Loser	Manager
1903	Boston Red Sox	Jimmy Collins	5-3 (LWLLWWWW)	PITTSBURGH	Fred Clarke
1904	Not held				
1905	NY GIANTS	John McGraw	4-1 (WLWWW)	Philadelphia A's	Connie Mack
1906	Chicago White Sox	Fielder Jones	4-2 (WLWLWW)	CHICAGO CUBS	Frank Chance
1907	CHICAGO CUBS	Frank Chance	4-0-1 (TWWWW)	Detroit	Hughie Jennings
1908	CHICAGO CUBS	Frank Chance	4-1 (WWLWW)	Detroit	Hughie Jennings
1909	PITTSBURGH	Fred Clarke	4-3 (WLWLWLW)	Detroit	Hughie Jennings
1910	Philadelphia A's	Connie Mack	4-1 (WWWLW)	CHICAGO CUBS	Frank Chance
1911	Philadelphia A's	Connie Mack	4-2 (LWWWLW)	NY GIANTS	John McGraw
1912	Boston Red Sox	Jake Stahl	4-3-1 (WTLWWLLW)	NY GIANTS	John McGraw
1913	Philadelphia A's	Connie Mack	4-1 (WLWWW)	NY GIANTS	John McGraw
1914	BOSTON BRAVES	George Stallings	4-0	Philadelphia A's	Connie Mack
1915	Boston Red Sox	Bill Carrigan	4-1 (LWWWW)	PHILA. PHILLIES	Pat Moran
1916	Boston Red Sox	Bill Carrigan	4-1 (WWLWW)	BKLN. DODGERS	Wilbert Robinson
1917	Chicago White Sox	Pants Rowland	4-2 (WWLLWW)	NY GIANTS	John McGraw
1918	Boston Red Sox	Ed Barrow	4-2 (WLWWLW)	CHICAGO CUBS	Fred Mitchell
1919	CINCINNATI	Pat Moran	5-3 (WWLWWLLW)	Chicago White Sox	Kid Gleason
1920	Cleveland	Tris Speaker	5-2 (WLLWWWW)	BKLN. DODGERS	Wilbert Robinson
1921	NY GIANTS	John McGraw	5-3 (LLWWLWWW)	NY Yankees	Miller Huggins
1922	NY GIANTS	John McGraw	4-0-1 (WTWWW)	NY Yankees	Miller Huggins
1923	NY Yankees	Miller Huggins	4-2 (LWLWWW)	NY GIANTS	John McGraw
1924	Washington	Bucky Harris	4-3 (LWLWLWW)	NY GIANTS	John McGraw
1925	PITTSBURGH	Bill McKechnie	4-3 (LWLLWWW)	Washington	Bucky Harris
1926	ST.L. CARDINALS	Rogers Hornsby	4-3 (LWWWLLWW)	NY Yankees	Miller Huggins
1927	NY Yankees	Miller Huggins	4-0	PITTSBURGH	Donie Bush
1928	NY Yankees	Miller Huggins	4-0	ST.L. CARDINALS	Bill McKechnie
1929	Philadelphia A's	Connie Mack	4-1 (WWLWW)	CHICAGO CUBS	Joe McCarthy
1930	Philadelphia A's	Connie Mack	4-2 (WWLLWW)	ST.L. CARDINALS	Gabby Street
1931	ST.L. CARDINALS	Gabby Street	4-3 (LWWLWLW)	Philadelphia A's	Connie Mack
1932	NY Yankees	Joe McCarthy	4-0	CHICAGO CUBS	Charlie Grimm
1933	NY Yankees	Bill Terry	4-1 (WWLWW)	Washington	Joe Cronin
1934	ST.L. CARDINALS	Frankie Frisch	4-3 (WLWLLWW)	Detroit	Mickey Cochrane
1935	Detroit	Mickey Cochrane	4-2 (LWWWLW)	CHICAGO CUBS	Charlie Grimm
1936	NY Yankees	Joe McCarthy	4-2 (LWWWLW)	NY GIANTS	Bill Terry
1937	NY Yankees	Joe McCarthy	4-1 (WWWLW)	NY GIANTS	Bill Terry
1938	NY Yankees	Joe McCarthy	4-0	CHICAGO CUBS	Gabby Hartnett
1939	NY Yankees	Joe McCarthy	4-0	CINCINNATI	Bill McKechnie
1940	CINCINNATI	Bill McKechnie	4-3 (LWLWLWW)	Detroit	Del Baker
1941	NY Yankees	Joe McCarthy	4-1 (WLWWW)	BKLN. DODGERS	Leo Durocher

Year	Winner	Manager	Series	Loser	Manager
1942	ST.L. CARDINALS	Billy Southworth	4-1 (LWWWW)	NY Yankees	Joe McCarthy
1943	NY Yankees	Joe McCarthy	4-1 (WLWWW)	ST.L. CARDINALS	Billy Southworth
1944	ST.L. CARDINALS	Billy Southworth	4-2 (LWLWWW)	St. Louis Browns	Luke Sewell
1945	Detroit	Steve O'Neill	4-3 (LWLWLWW)	CHICAGO CUBS	Charlie Grimm
1946	ST.L. CARDINALS	Eddie Dyer	4-3 (LWLWLWW)	Boston Red Sox	Joe Cronin
1947	NY Yankees	Bucky Harris	4-3 (WWLLWLW)	BKLN. DODGERS	Burt Shotton
1948	Cleveland	Lou Boudreau	4-2 (LWWWLW)	BOSTON BRAVES	Billy Southworth
1949	NY Yankees	Casey Stengel	4-1 (WLWWW)	BKLN. DODGERS	Burt Shotton
1950	NY Yankees	Casey Stengel	4-0	PHILA. PHILLIES	Eddie Sawyer
1951	NY Yankees	Casey Stengel	4-2 (LWLWWW)	NY GIANTS	Leo Durocher
1952	NY Yankees	Casey Stengel	4-3 (LWLWLWW)	BKLN. DODGERS	Charlie Dressen
1953	NY Yankees	Casey Stengel	4-2 (WWLLWW)	BKLN. DODGERS	Charlie Dressen
1954	NY GIANTS	Leo Durocher	4-0	Cleveland	Al Lopez
1955	BKLN. DODGERS	Walter Alston	4-3 (LLWWWLW)	NY Yankees	Casey Stengel
1956	NY Yankees	Casey Stengel	4-3 (LLWWWLW	BKLN. DODGERS	Walter Alston
1957	MILW. BRAVES	Fred Haney	4-3 (LWLWLWW)	NY Yankees	Casey Stengel
1958	NY Yankees	Casey Stengel	4-3 (LLWLWWW)	MILW. BRAVES	Fred Haney
1959	LA DODGERS	Walter Alston	4-2 (LWWWLW)	Chicago White Sox	Al Lopez
1960	PITTSBURGH	Danny Murtaugh	4-3 (WLLWWLW)	NY Yankees	Casey Stengel
1961	NY Yankees	Ralph Houk	4-1 (WLWWW)	CINCINNATI	Fred Hutchinson
1962	NY Yankees	Ralph Houk	4-3 (WLWLWLW)	SF GIANTS	Alvin Dark
1963	LA DODGERS	Walter Alston	4-0	NY Yankees	Ralph Houk
1964	ST.L. CARDINALS	Johnny Keane	4-3 (WLLWWLW)	NY Yankees	Yogi Berra
1965	LA DODGERS	Walter Alston	4-3 (LLWWWLW)	Minnesota	Sam Mele
1966	Baltimore	Hank Bauer	4-0	LA DODGERS	Walter Alston
1967	ST.L. CARDINALS	Red Schoendienst	4-3 (WLWWLLW)	Boston Red Sox	Dick Williams
1968	Detroit	Mayo Smith	4-3 (LWLLWWW)	ST.L. CARDINALS	Red Schoendienst
1969	NY METS	Gil Hodges	4-1 (LWWWW)	Baltimore	Earl Weaver
1970	Baltimore	Earl Weaver	4-1 (WWWLW)	CINCINNATI	Sparky Anderson
1971	PITTSBURGH	Danny Murtaugh	4-3 (LLWWWLW)	Baltimore	Earl Weaver
1972	Oakland A's	Dick Williams	4-3 (WWLWLLW)	CINCINNATI	Sparky Anderson
1973	Oakland A's	Dick Williams	4-3 (WLWLWLW)	NY METS	Yogi Berra
1974	Oakland A's	Alvin Dark	4-1 (WLWWW)	LA DODGERS	Walter Alston
1975	CINCINNATI	Sparky Anderson	4-3 (LWWLWLW)	Boston Red Sox	Darrell Johnson
1976	CINCINNATI	Sparky Anderson	4-0	NY Yankees	Billy Martin
1977	NY Yankees	Billy Martin	4-2 (WLWWLW)	LA DODGERS	Tommy Lasorda
1978	NY Yankees	Bob Lemon	4-2 (LLWWWW)	LA DODGERS	Tommy Lasorda
1979	PITTSBURGH	Chuck Tanner	4-3 (LWLLWWW)	Baltimore	Earl Weaver
1980	PHILA. PHILLIES	Dallas Green	4-2 (WWLLWW)	Kansas City	Jim Frey
1981	LA DODGERS	Tommy Lasorda	4-2 (LLWWWW)	NY Yankees	Bob Lemon
1982	ST.L. CARDINALS	Whitey Herzog	4-3 (LWWLLWW)	Milwaukee Brewers	Harvey Kuenn
1983	Baltimore	Joe Altobelli	4-1 (LWWWW)	PHILA. PHILLIES	Paul Owens
1984	Detroit	Sparky Anderson	4-1 (WWLWW)	SAN DIEGO	Dick Williams
1985	Kansas City	Dick Howser	4-3 (LLWLWWW)	ST.L. CARDINALS	Whitey Herzog
1986	NY METS	Davey Johnson	4-3 (LLWWLWW)	Boston Red Sox	John McNamara
1987	Minnesota	Tom Kelly	4-3 (WWLLLWW)	ST.L. CARDINALS	Whitey Herzog
1988	LA DODGERS	Tommy Lasorda	4-1 (WWLWW)	Oakland A's	Tony La Russa
1989	Oakland A's	Tony La Russa	4-0	SF GIANTS	Roger Craig
1990	CINCINNATI	Lou Piniella	4-0	Oakland A's	Tony La Russa
1991	Minnesota	Tom Kelly	4-3 (WWLLLWW)	ATLANTA BRAVES	Bobby Cox
1992	Toronto	Cito Gaston	4-2 (LWWWLW)	ATLANTA BRAVES	Bobby Cox
1993	Toronto	Cito Gaston	4-2 (WLWWLW)	PHILA. PHILLIES	Jim Fregosi
1994	Not held				
1995	ATLANTA BRAVES	Bobby Cox	4-2 (WWLWLW)	Cleveland	Mike Hargrove
1996	New York Yankees	Joe Torre	4-2 (LLWWWW)	ATLANTA BRAVES	Bobby Cox
1997	FLORIDA MARLINS	Jim Leyland	4-3 (WLWLWLW)	Cleveland	Mike Hargrove

Most Valuable Players

Currently selected by media panel made up of representatives of CBS Sports, CBS Radio, AP, UPI, and World Series official scorers. Presented by *Sport* magazine from 1955-88 and by Major League Baseball since 1989. Winner who did not play for World Series champions is in **bold** type.

Multiple winners: Bob Gibson, Reggie Jackson and Sandy Koufax (2).

Year		Year		Year	
1955	Johnny Podres, Bklyn, P	1961	Whitey Ford, NY, P	1967	Bob Gibson, St.L., P
1956	Don Larsen, NY, P	1962	Ralph Terry, NY, P	1968	Mickey Lolich, Det., P
1957	Lew Burdette, Mil., P	1963	Sandy Koufax, LA, P	1969	Donn Clendenon, NY, 1B
1958	Bob Turley, NY, P	1964	Bob Gibson, St.L., P	1970	Brooks Robinson, Bal., 3B
1959	Larry Sherry, LA, P	1965	Sandy Koufax, LA, P	1971	Roberto Clemente, Pit., OF
1960	**Bobby Richardson**, NY, 2B	1966	Frank Robinson, Bal., OF	1972	Gene Tenace, Oak., C

Year		Year		Year	
1973	Reggie Jackson, Oak., OF		Ron Cey, LA, 3B;	1989	Dave Stewart, Oak., P
1974	Rollie Fingers, Oak., P		& Steve Yeager, LA, C	1990	Jose Rijo, Cin., P
1975	Pete Rose, Cin., 3B	1982	Darrell Porter, St.L., C	1991	Jack Morris, Min., P
1976	Johnny Bench, Cin., C	1983	Rick Dempsey, Bal., C	1992	Pat Borders, Tor., C
1977	Reggie Jackson, NY, OF	1984	Alan Trammell, Det., SS	1993	Paul Molitor, Tor., DH/1B/3B
1978	Bucky Dent, NY, SS	1985	Bret Saberhagen, KC, P	1994	Series not held.
1979	Willie Stargell, Pit., 1B	1986	Ray Knight, NY, 3B	1995	Tom Glavine, Atl., P
1980	Mike Schmidt, Phi., 3B	1987	Frank Viola, Min., P	1996	John Wetteland, NY, P
1981	Pedro Guerrero, LA, OF;	1988	Orel Hershiser, LA, P	1997	Livan Hernandez, Fla., P

All-Time World Series Leaders
CAREER

World Series leaders through 1997. Years listed indicate number of World Series appearances.

Hitting

Games

	Yrs	Gm
Yogi Berra, NY Yankees	14	75
Mickey Mantle, NY Yankees	12	65
Elston Howard, NY Yankees-Boston	10	54
Hank Bauer, NY Yankees	9	53
Gil McDougald, NY Yankees	8	53

At Bats

	Yrs	AB
Yogi Berra, NY Yankees	14	259
Mickey Mantle, NY Yankees	12	230
Joe DiMaggio, NY Yankees	10	199
Frankie Frisch, NY Giants-St.L. Cards	8	197
Gil McDougald, NY Yankees	8	190

Batting Avg. (minimum 50 AB)

	AB	H	Avg
Pepper Martin, St.L. Cards	55	23	.418
Paul Molitor, Mil. Brewers-Tor. Blue Jays	55	23	.418
Lou Brock, St. Louis	87	34	.391
Marquis Grissom, Atl-Cle	77	30	.389
Thurman Munson, NY Yankees	67	25	.373
George Brett, Kansas City	51	19	.373
Hank Aaron, Milw. Braves	55	20	.364

Hits

	AB	H	Avg
Yogi Berra, NY Yankees	259	71	.274
Mickey Mantle, NY Yankees	230	59	.257
Frankie Frisch, NYG-St.L. Cards	197	58	.294
Joe DiMaggio, NY Yankees	199	54	.271
Hank Bauer, NY Yankees	188	46	.245
Pee Wee Reese, Brooklyn	169	46	.272

Runs

	Gm	R
Mickey Mantle, NY Yankees	65	42
Yogi Berra, NY Yankees	75	41
Babe Ruth, Boston Red Sox-NY Yankees	41	37
Lou Gehrig, NY Yankees	34	30
Joe DiMaggio, NY Yankees	51	27

Home Runs

	AB	HR
Mickey Mantle, NY Yankees	230	18
Babe Ruth, Boston Red Sox-NY Yankees	129	15
Yogi Berra, NY Yankees	259	12
Duke Snider, Brooklyn-LA	133	11
Lou Gehrig, NY Yankees	119	10
Reggie Jackson, Oakland-NY Yankees	98	10

Runs Batted In

	Gm	RBI
Mickey Mantle, NY Yankees	65	40
Yogi Berra, NY Yankees	75	39
Lou Gehrig, NY Yankees	34	35
Babe Ruth, Boston Red Sox-NY Yankees	41	33
Joe DiMaggio, NY Yankees	51	30

Stolen Bases

	Gm	SB
Lou Brock, St. Louis	21	14
Eddie Collins, Phi. A's-Chisox	34	14
Frank Chance, Chi. Cubs	20	10
Davey Lopes, Los Angeles	23	10
Phil Rizzuto, NY Yankees	52	10

Total Bases

	Gm	TB
Mickey Mantle, NY Yankees	65	123
Yogi Berra, NY Yankees	75	117
Babe Ruth, Boston Red Sox-NY Yankees	41	96
Lou Gehrig, NY Yankees	34	87
Joe DiMaggio, NY Yankees	51	84

Slugging Pct. (50 AB)

	AB	Pct
Reggie Jackson, Oakland-NY Yankees	98	.755
Babe Ruth, Boston Red Sox-NY Yankees	129	.744
Lou Gehrig, NY Yankees	119	.731
Al Simmons, Phi. A's-Cincinnati	73	.658
Lou Brock, St. Louis	87	.655

World Series Appearances

In the 92 years that the World Series has been contested, American League teams have won 54 championships while National League teams have won 38.

The following teams are ranked by number of appearances through the 1996 World Series; (*) indicates AL teams.

	App	W	L	Pct.	Last Series	Last Title
NY Yankees*	34	23	11	.676	1996	1996
Bklyn/LA Dodgers	18	6	12	.333	1988	1988
NY/SF Giants	16	5	11	.313	1989	1954
St.L. Cardinals	15	9	6	.600	1987	1982
Phi/KC/Oak.A's*	14	9	5	.643	1990	1989
Chicago Cubs	10	2	8	.200	1945	1908
Boston Red Sox*	9	5	4	.556	1986	1918
Cincinnati Reds	9	5	4	.556	1990	1990
Detroit Tigers*	9	4	5	.444	1984	1984
Bos/Mil/Atl.Braves	8	3	5	.375	1996	1995
Pittsburgh Pirates	7	5	2	.714	1979	1979
St.L/Bal.Orioles*	7	3	4	.429	1983	1983
Wash/Min.Twins*	6	3	3	.500	1991	1991
Phi.Phillies	5	1	4	.200	1993	1980
Chi.White Sox*	4	2	2	.500	1959	1917
Cle.Indians*	5	2	3	.400	1997	1948
NY Mets	3	2	1	.667	1986	1986
Tor. Blue Jays*	2	2	0	1.000	1993	1993
KC Royals*	2	1	1	.500	1985	1985
Fla. Marlins	1	1	0	1.000	1997	1997
Sea/Mil.Brewers*	1	0	1	.000	1982	—
SD Padres	1	0	1	.000	1984	—

Pitching

Games

	Yrs	Gm
Whitey Ford, NY Yankees	11	22
Rollie Fingers, Oakland	3	16
Allie Reynolds, NY Yankees	6	15
Bob Turley, NY Yankees	5	15
Clay Carroll, Cincinnati	3	14

Wins

	Gm	W-L
Whitey Ford, NY Yankees	22	10-8
Bob Gibson, St. Louis	9	7-2
Allie Reynolds, NY Yankees	15	7-2
Red Ruffing, NY Yankees	10	7-2
Lefty Gomez, NY Yankees	7	6-0
Chief Bender, Philadelphia A's	10	6-4
Waite Hoyt, NY Yankees-Phi. A's	12	6-4

ERA (minimum 25 IP)

	Gm	IP	ERA
Jack Billingham, Cincinnati	7	25	0.36
Harry Brecheen, St. Louis	7	33	0.83
Babe Ruth, Boston Red Sox	3	31	0.87
Sherry Smith, Brooklyn	3	30	0.89
Sandy Koufax, Los Angeles	8	57	0.95

Saves

	Gm	IP	Sv
Rollie Fingers, Oakland	16	33	6
Allie Reynolds, NY Yankees	15	77	4
Johnny Murphy, NY Yankees	8	16	4
John Wetteland, NY Yankees	5	4.1	4
Seven pitchers tied with 3 each.			

Shutouts

	GS	CG	ShO
Christy Mathewson, NY Giants	11	10	4
Three Finger Brown, Chi. Cubs	7	5	3
Whitey Ford, NY Yankees	22	7	3
Seven pitchers tied with 2 each.			

Innings Pitched

	Gm	IP
Whitey Ford, NY Yankees	22	146
Christy Mathewson, NY Giants	11	102
Red Ruffing, NY Yankees	10	86
Chief Bender, Philadelphia A's	10	85
Waite Hoyt, NY Yankees-Phi. A's	12	84

Complete Games

	GS	CG	W-L
Christy Mathewson, NY Giants	11	10	5-5
Chief Bender, Philadelphia A's	10	9	6-4
Bob Gibson, St. Louis	9	8	7-2
Whitey Ford, NY Yankees	22	7	10-8
Red Ruffing, NY Yankees	10	7	7-2

Strikeouts

	Gm	IP	SO
Whitey Ford, NY Yankees	22	146	94
Bob Gibson, St. Louis	9	81	92
Allie Reynolds, NY Yankees	15	77	62
Sandy Koufax, Los Angeles	8	57	61
Red Ruffing, NY Yankees	10	86	61

Bases on Balls

	Gm	IP	BB
Whitey Ford, NY Yankees	22	146	34
Allie Reynolds, NY Yankees	15	77	32
Art Nehf, NY Giants-Chi. Cubs	12	79	32
Jim Palmer, Baltimore	9	65	31
Bob Turley, NY Yankees	15	54	29

Losses

	Gm	W-L
Whitey Ford, NY Yankees	22	10-8
Christy Mathewson, NY Giants	11	5-5
Joe Bush, Phi. A's-Bosox-NY Yankees	9	2-5
Rube Marquard, NY Giants-Brooklyn	11	2-5
Eddie Plank, Philadelphia A's	7	2-5
Schoolboy Rowe, Detroit	8	2-5

League Championship Series

Division play came to the major leagues in 1969 when both the American and National Leagues expanded to 12 teams. With an East and West Division in each league, League Championship Series (LCS) became necessary to determine the NL and AL pennant winners. In 1994, teams were realigned into three divisions, the East, Central, and West with division winners and one wildcard team playing a best of five series to determine the LCS competitors. In the charts below, the East Division champions are noted by the letter E, the Central division champions by C and the West Division champions by W. A wildcard winner is noted by WC. Also, each playoff winner's wins and losses are noted in parentheses after the series score. The LCS changed from best-of-5 to best-of-7 in 1985. Each league's LCS was cancelled in 1994 due to the players' strike.

National League

Multiple champions: Cincinnati and LA Dodgers (5); Atlanta (4); NY Mets, Philadelphia and St. Louis (3); Pittsburgh (2).

Year	Winner	Manager	Series	Loser	Manager
1969	E- New York	Gil Hodges	3-0	W- Atlanta	Lum Harris
1970	W- Cincinnati	Sparky Anderson	3-0	E- Pittsburgh	Danny Murtaugh
1971	E- Pittsburgh	Danny Murtaugh	3-1 (LWWW)	W- San Francisco	Charlie Fox
1972	W- Cincinnati	Sparky Anderson	3-2 (LWLWW)	E- Pittsburgh	Bill Virdon
1973	E- New York	Yogi Berra	3-2 (LWWLW)	W- Cincinnati	Sparky Anderson
1974	W- Los Angeles	Walter Alston	3-1 (WWLW)	E- Pittsburgh	Danny Murtaugh
1975	W- Cincinnati	Sparky Anderson	3-0	E- Pittsburgh	Danny Murtaugh
1976	W- Cincinnati	Sparky Anderson	3-0	E- Philadelphia	Danny Ozark
1977	W- Los Angeles	Tommy Lasorda	3-1 (LWWW)	E- Philadelphia	Danny Ozark
1978	W- Los Angeles	Tommy Lasorda	3-1 (WWLW)	E- Philadelphia	Danny Ozark
1979	E- Pittsburgh	Chuck Tanner	3-0	W- Cincinnati	John McNamara
1980	E- Philadelphia	Dallas Green	3-2 (WLLWW)	W- Houston	Bill Virdon
1981	W- Los Angeles	Tommy Lasorda	3-2 (WLLWW)	E- Montreal	Jim Fanning
1982	E- St. Louis	Whitey Herzog	3-0	W- Atlanta	Joe Torre
1983	E- Philadelphia	Paul Owens	3-1 (LWWW)	W- Los Angeles	Tommy Lasorda
1984	W- San Diego	Dick Williams	3-2 (LLWWW)	E- Chicago	Jim Frey
1985	E- St. Louis	Whitey Herzog	4-2 (LLWWWW)	W- Los Angeles	Tommy Lasorda
1986	E- New York	Davey Johnson	4-2 (LWWLWW)	W- Houston	Hal Lanier
1987	E- St. Louis	Whitey Herzog	4-3 (WLWLLWW)	W- San Francisco	Roger Craig
1988	W- Los Angeles	Tommy Lasorda	4-3 (LWLWWLW)	E- New York	Davey Johnson

Year	Winner	Manager	Series	Loser	Manager
1989	W- San Francisco	Roger Craig	4-1 (WLWWW)	E- Chicago	Don Zimmer
1990	W- Cincinnati	Lou Piniella	4-2 (LWWWLW)	E- Pittsburgh	Jim Leyland
1991	W- Atlanta	Bobby Cox	4-3 (LWWLLWW)	E- Pittsburgh	Jim Leyland
1992	W- Atlanta	Bobby Cox	4-3 (WWLWLLW)	E- Pittsburgh	Jim Leyland
1993	E- Philadelphia	Jim Fregosi	4-2 (WLLWWW)	W- Atlanta	Bobby Cox
1994	Not held				
1995	E- Atlanta	Bobby Cox	4-0	C- Cincinnati	Davey Johnson
1996	E- Atlanta	Bobby Cox	4-3 (WLLLWWW)	C- St. Louis	Tony LaRussa
1997	E-Florida	Jim Leyland	4-2 (WLWLWW)	E-Atlanta	Bobby Cox

NLCS Most Valuable Players

Winners who did not play for NLCS champions are in **bold** type.

Multiple winner: Steve Garvey (2).

Year		Year		Year	
1977	Dusty Baker, LA, OF	1985	Ozzie Smith, St.L., SS	1992	John Smoltz, Atl., P
1978	Steve Garvey, LA, 1B	1986	**Mike Scott,** Hou., P	1993	Curt Schilling, Phi., P
1979	Willie Stargell, Pit., 1B	1987	**Jeff Leonard,** SF, OF	1994	LCS not held.
1980	Manny Trillo, Phi., 2B	1988	Orel Hershiser, LA, P	1995	Mike Devereaux, Atl., OF
1981	Burt Hooton, LA, P	1989	Will Clark, SF, 1B	1996	Javy Lopez, Atl., C
1982	Darrell Porter, St.L., C	1990	Rob Dibble, Cin., P	1997	Livan Hernandez, Fla., P
1983	Gary Matthews, Phi., OF		& Randy Myers, Cin., P		
1984	Steve Garvey, SD, 1B	1991	Steve Avery, Atl., P		

American League

Multiple champions: Oakland (6); Baltimore and NY Yankees (5); Boston, Cleveland, Kansas City, Minnesota and Toronto (2).

Year	Winner	Manager	Series	Loser	Manager
1969	E- Baltimore	Earl Weaver	3-0	W- Minnesota	Billy Martin
1970	E- Baltimore	Earl Weaver	3-0	W- Minnesota	Bill Rigney
1971	E- Baltimore	Earl Weaver	3-0	W- Oakland	Dick Williams
1972	W- Oakland	Dick Williams	3-2 (WWLLW)	E- Detroit	Billy Martin
1973	W- Oakland	Dick Williams	3-2 (LWWLW)	E- Baltimore	Earl Weaver
1974	W- Oakland	Alvin Dark	3-1 (LWWW)	E- Baltimore	Earl Weaver
1975	E- Boston	Darrell Johnson	3-0	W- Oakland	Alvin Dark
1976	E- New York	Billy Martin	3-2 (WLWLW)	W- Kansas City	Whitey Herzog
1977	E- New York	Billy Martin	3-2 (LWWLW)	W- Kansas City	Whitey Herzog
1978	E- New York	Bob Lemon	3-1 (WLWW)	W- Kansas City	Whitey Herzog
1979	E- Baltimore	Earl Weaver	3-1 (WWLW)	W- California	Jim Fregosi
1980	W- Kansas City	Jim Frey	3-0	E- New York	Dick Howser
1981	E- New York	Bob Lemon	3-0	W- Oakland	Billy Martin
1982	E- Milwaukee	Harvey Kuenn	3-2 (LLWWW)	W- California	Gene Mauch
1983	E- Baltimore	Joe Altobelli	3-1 (LWWW)	W- Chicago	Tony La Russa
1984	E- Detroit	Sparky Anderson	3-0	W- Kansas City	Dick Howser
1985	W- Kansas City	Dick Howser	4-3 (LLWLWWW)	E- Toronto	Bobby Cox
1986	E- Boston	John McNamara	4-3 (LWLLWWW)	W- California	Gene Mauch
1987	W- Minnesota	Tom Kelly	4-1 (WWLWW)	E- Detroit	Sparky Anderson
1988	W- Oakland	Tony La Russa	4-0	E- Boston	Joe Morgan
1989	W- Oakland	Tony La Russa	4-1 (WWLWW)	E- Toronto	Cito Gaston
1990	W- Oakland	Tony La Russa	4-0	E- Boston	Joe Morgan
1991	W- Minnesota	Tom Kelly	4-1 (WLWWW)	E- Toronto	Cito Gaston
1992	E- Toronto	Cito Gaston	4-2 (LWWWLW)	W- Oakland	Tony La Russa
1993	E- Toronto	Cito Gaston	4-2 (WWLLWW)	W- Chicago	Gene Lamont
1994	Not held				
1995	C- Cleveland	Mike Hargrove	4-2 (LWLWWW)	W-Seattle	Lou Piniella
1996	E- New York	Joe Torre	4-1 (WLWWW)	E-Baltimore	Davey Johnson
1997	C-Cleveland	Mike Hargrove	4-2 (LWWWLW)	E-Baltimore	Davey Johnson

ALCS Most Valuable Players

Winner who did not play for ALCS champions is in **bold** type.

Multiple winner: Dave Stewart (2).

Year		Year		Year	
1980	Frank White, KC, 2B	1986	Marty Barrett, Bos., 2B	1992	Roberto Alomar, Tor., 2B
1981	Graig Nettles, NY, 3B	1987	Gary Gaetti, Min., 3B	1993	Dave Stewart, Tor., P
1982	**Fred Lynn,** Cal., OF	1988	Dennis Eckersley, Oak., P	1994	LCS not held.
1983	Mike Boddicker, Bal., P	1989	Rickey Henderson, Oak., OF	1995	Orel Hershiser, Cle., P
1984	Kirk Gibson, Det., OF	1990	Dave Stewart, Oak., P	1996	Bernie Williams, NY, OF
1985	George Brett, KC, 3B	1991	Kirby Puckett, Min., OF	1997	Marquis Grissom, Cle., OF

Other Playoffs

Seven times from 1946-80, playoffs were necessary to decide league or division championships when two teams tied for first place at the end of the regular season. In the strike year of 1981, there were playoffs between the first and second half-season champions in both leagues. In 1995, the 1994-95 players' strike shortened the regular season to 144 games.

National League

Year	NL	W	L	Manager	Year	NL	W	L	Manager
1946	Brooklyn	96	58	Leo Durocher	1962	Los Angeles	101	61	Walter Alston
	St. Louis	96	58	Eddie Dyer		San Francisco	101	61	Alvin Dark
	Playoff: (Best-of-3) St. Louis, 2-0					Playoff: (Best-of-3) San Francisco, 2-1 (WLW)			

Year	NL	W	L	Manager	Year	NL West	W	L	Manager
1951	Brooklyn	96	58	Charlie Dressen	1980	Houston	92	70	Bill Virdon
	New York	96	58	Leo Durocher		Los Angeles	92	70	Tommy Lasorda
	Playoff: (Best-of-3) New York, 2-1 (WLW)					Playoff: (1 game) Houston, 7-1 (at LA)			

Year	NL	W	L	Manager	Year	NL East	W	L	Manager
1959	Milwaukee	86	68	Fred Haney	1981	(1st Half) Phila	34	21	Dallas Green
	Los Angeles	86	68	Walter Alston		(2nd Half) Montreal	30	23	Jim Fanning
	Playoff: (Best-of-3) Los Angeles, 2-0					Playoff: (Best-of-5) Montreal, 3-2 (WWLLW)			

Year	NL	W	L	Manager	Year	NL West	W	L	Manager
1959	Milwaukee	86	68	Fred Haney	1981	(1st Half) Los Ang	36	21	Tommy Lasorda
	Los Angeles	86	68	Walter Alston		(2nd Half) Houston	33	20	Bill Virdon
	Playoff: (Best-of-3) Los Angeles, 2-0					Playoff: (Best-of-5) Los Angeles, 3-2 (LLWWW)			

American League

Year	AL	W	L	Manager	Year	AL East	W	L	Manager
1948	Boston	96	58	Joe McCarthy	1981	(1st Half) N.Y.	34	22	Bob Lemon
	Cleveland	96	58	Lou Boudreau		(2nd Half) Milw.	31	22	Buck Rodgers
	Playoff: (1 game) Cleveland, 8-3 (at Boston)					Playoff: (Best-of-5) New York, 3-2 (WWLLW)			

Year	AL East	W	L	Manager	Year	AL West	W	L	Manager
1978	Boston	99	63	Don Zimmer	1981	(1st Half) Oakland	37	23	Billy Martin
	New York	99	63	Bob Lemon		(2nd Half) Kan.City	30	23	Jim Frey
	Playoff: (1 game) New York, 5-4 (at Boston)					Playoff: (Best-of-5), Oakland, 3-0			

Year	AL West	W	L	Manager
1995	Seattle	78	66	Lou Piniella
	California	78	66	M. Lachemann
	Playoff: (1 game) Seattle, 9-1 (at Seattle)			

Regular Season League & Division Winners

Regular season National and American League pennant winners from 1900-68, as well as West and East divisional champions from 1969-93. In 1994, both leagues went to three divisions—West, Central and East. However, due to the 1994 players' strike that resulted in the cancelling of the season after games played on Aug. 11, division leaders at the time of the strike are not considered official champions by either league. Note that (*) indicates 1994 divisional champion is unofficial and that **GA** column indicates games ahead of the second place club. See National League Pennant Winners from 1876-99 for NL Pennant winners before 1900.

National League

Multiple pennant winners: Brooklyn-LA (19); New York-SF Giants (17); St. Louis (15); Chicago (10); Cincinnati and Pittsburgh (9); Boston-Milwaukee-Atlanta (8); Philadelphia (5); New York Mets (3).

Multiple division winners: WEST—Los Angeles (8); Cincinnati (7); Atlanta (5); San Francisco (4); Houston and San Diego (2). CENTRAL—Cincinnati (2). EAST—Pittsburgh (9); Philadelphia (6); NY Mets (4); Atlanta and St. Louis (3); Chicago (2).

Year		W	L	Pct	GA	Year		W	L	Pct	GA
1900	Brooklyn	82	54	.603	4½	1920	Brooklyn	93	61	.604	7
1901	Pittsburgh	90	49	.647	7½	1921	New York	94	59	.614	4
1902	Pittsburgh	103	36	.741	27½	1922	New York	93	61	.604	7
1903	Pittsburgh	91	49	.650	6½	1923	New York	95	58	.621	4½
1904	New York	106	47	.693	13	1924	New York	93	60	.608	1½
1905	New York	105	48	.686	9	1925	Pittsburgh	95	58	.621	8½
1906	Chicago	116	36	.763	20	1926	St. Louis	89	65	.578	2
1907	Chicago	107	45	.704	17	1927	Pittsburgh	94	60	.610	1½
1908	Chicago	99	55	.643	1	1928	St. Louis	95	59	.617	2
1909	Pittsburgh	110	42	.724	6½	1929	Chicago	98	54	.645	10½
1910	Chicago	104	50	.675	13	1930	St. Louis	92	62	.597	2
1911	New York	99	54	.647	7½	1931	St. Louis	101	53	.656	13
1912	New York	103	48	.682	10	1932	Chicago	90	64	.584	4
1913	New York	101	51	.664	12½	1933	New York	91	61	.599	5
1914	Boston	94	59	.614	10½	1934	St. Louis	95	58	.621	2
1915	Philadelphia	90	62	.592	7	1935	Chicago	100	54	.649	4
1916	Brooklyn	94	60	.610	2½	1936	New York	92	62	.597	5
1917	New York	98	56	.636	10	1937	New York	95	57	.625	3
1918	Chicago	84	45	.651	10½	1938	Chicago	89	63	.586	2
1919	Cincinnati	96	44	.686	9	1939	Cincinnati	97	57	.630	4½

Year		W	L	Pct	GA
1940	Cincinnati	100	53	.654	12
1941	Brooklyn	100	54	.649	2½
1942	St. Louis	106	48	.688	2
1943	St. Louis	105	49	.682	18
1944	St. Louis	105	49	.682	14½
1945	Chicago	98	56	.636	3
1946	St. Louis†	98	58	.628	2
1947	Brooklyn	94	60	.610	5
1948	Boston	91	62	.595	6½
1949	Brooklyn	97	57	.630	1
1950	Philadelphia	91	63	.591	2
1951	New York†	98	59	.624	1
1952	Brooklyn	96	57	.627	4½
1953	Brooklyn	105	49	.682	13
1954	New York	97	57	.630	5
1955	Brooklyn	98	55	.641	13½
1956	Brooklyn	93	61	.604	1
1957	Milwaukee	95	59	.617	8
1958	Milwaukee	92	62	.597	8
1959	Los Angeles†	88	68	.564	2
1960	Pittsburgh	95	59	.617	7
1961	Cincinnati	93	61	.604	4
1962	San Francisco†	103	62	.624	1
1963	Los Angeles	99	63	.611	6
1964	St. Louis	93	69	.574	1
1965	Los Angeles	97	65	.599	2
1966	Los Angeles	95	67	.586	1½
1967	St. Louis	101	60	.627	10½
1968	St. Louis	97	65	.599	9
1969	West—Atlanta	93	69	.574	3
	East—N.Y. Mets	100	62	.617	8
1970	West—Cincinnati	102	60	.630	14½
	East—Pittsburgh	89	73	.549	5
1971	West—San Francisco	90	72	.556	1
	East—Pittsburgh	97	65	.599	7
1972	West—Cincinnati	95	59	.617	10½
	East—Pittsburgh	96	59	.619	11
1973	West—Cincinnati	99	63	.611	3½
	East—N.Y. Mets	82	79	.509	1½
1974	West—Los Angeles	102	60	.630	4
	East—Pittsburgh	88	74	.543	1½
1975	West—Cincinnati	108	54	.667	20
	East—Pittsburgh	92	69	.571	6½
1976	West—Cincinnati	102	60	.630	10
	East—Philadelphia	101	61	.623	9
1977	West—Los Angeles	98	64	.605	10

Year		W	L	Pct	GA
	East—Philadelphia	101	61	.623	5
1978	West—Los Angeles	95	67	.586	2½
	East—Philadelphia	90	72	.556	1½
1979	West—Cincinnati	90	71	.559	1½
	East—Pittsburgh	98	64	.605	2
1980	West—Houston	93	70	.571	1
	East—Philadelphia	91	71	.562	1
1981	West—Los Angeles†	63	47	.573	—
	East—Montreal†	60	48	.556	—
1982	West—Atlanta	89	73	.549	1
	East—St. Louis	92	70	.568	3
1983	West—Los Angeles	91	71	.562	3
	East—Philadelphia	90	72	.556	6
1984	West—San Diego	92	70	.568	12
	East—Chicago	96	65	.596	6½
1985	West—Los Angeles	95	67	.586	5½
	East—St. Louis	101	61	.623	3
1986	West—Houston	96	66	.593	10
	East—N.Y. Mets	108	54	.667	21½
1987	West—San Francisco	90	72	.556	6
	East—St. Louis	95	67	.586	3
1988	West—Los Angeles	94	67	.584	7
	East—N.Y. Mets	100	60	.625	15
1989	West—San Francisco	92	70	.568	3
	East—Chicago	93	69	.574	6
1990	West—Cincinnati	91	71	.562	5
	East—Pittsburgh	95	67	.586	4
1991	West—Atlanta	94	68	.580	1
	East—Pittsburgh	98	64	.605	14
1992	West—Atlanta	98	64	.605	8
	East—Pittsburgh	96	66	.593	9
1993	West—Atlanta	104	58	.642	1
	East—Philadelphia	97	65	.599	3
1994	West—Los Angeles*	58	56	.509	3½
	Central—Cincinnati*	66	48	.579	½
	East—Montreal*	74	40	.649	6
1995	West—Los Angeles	78	66	.542	1
	Central—Cincinnati	85	59	.590	9
	East—Atlanta	90	54	.625	21
1996	West—San Diego	91	71	.562	1
	Central—St. Louis	88	74	.543	6
	East—Atlanta	96	66	.593	8
1997	West—San Francisco	90	72	.556	2
	Central—Houston	84	78	.519	5
	East—Atlanta	101	61	.623	9

†Regular season playoffs: 1946—St. Louis def. Brooklyn (2 games to 1); 1951—New York def. Brooklyn (2 games to 1); 1959—Los Angeles def. Milwaukee (2 games to none); 1962—San Francisco def. Los Angeles (2 games to 1); 1981—East: Montreal def. Philadelphia (3 games to 2) and West: Los Angeles def. Houston (3 games to 2).

American League

Multiple pennant winners: NY Yankees (34); Philadelphia-Oakland A's (15); Boston (10); Detroit (9); Baltimore and Washington-Minnesota (6); Chicago (5); Cleveland (3); KC Royals and Toronto (2).

Multiple division winners: WEST—Oakland (10); Kansas City (6); Minnesota (4); California (3); Chicago (2). EAST—Baltimore (8); NY Yankees (6); Boston and Toronto (5); Detroit (3). CENTRAL—Cleveland (3).

Year		W	L	Pct	GA
1901	Chicago	83	53	.610	4
1902	Philadelphia	83	53	.610	5
1903	Boston	91	47	.659	14½
1904	Boston	95	59	.617	1½
1905	Philadelphia	92	56	.622	2
1906	Chicago	93	58	.616	3
1907	Detroit	92	58	.613	1½
1908	Detroit	90	63	.588	½
1909	Detroit	98	54	.645	3½
1910	Philadelphia	102	48	.680	14½
1911	Philadelphia	101	50	.669	13½
1912	Boston	105	47	.691	14
1913	Philadelphia	96	57	.627	6½
1914	Philadelphia	99	53	.651	8½

Year		W	L	Pct	GA
1915	Boston	101	50	.669	2½
1916	Boston	91	63	.591	2
1917	Chicago	100	54	.649	9
1918	Boston	75	51	.595	2½
1919	Chicago	88	52	.629	3½
1920	Cleveland	98	56	.636	2
1921	New York	98	55	.641	4½
1922	New York	94	60	.610	1
1923	New York	98	54	.645	16
1924	Washington	92	62	.597	2
1925	Washington	96	55	.636	8½
1926	New York	91	63	.591	3
1927	New York	110	44	.714	19
1928	New York	101	53	.656	2½

American League (Cont.)

Year		W	L	Pct	GA	Year		W	L	Pct	GA
1929	Philadelphia	104	46	.693	18		East—Baltimore	91	71	.562	2
1930	Philadelphia	102	52	.662	8	1975	West—Oakland	98	64	.605	7
1931	Philadelphia	107	45	.704	13½		East—Boston	95	65	.594	4½
1932	New York	107	47	.695	13	1976	West—Kansas City	90	72	.556	2½
1933	Washington	99	53	.651	7		East—New York	97	62	.610	10½
1934	Detroit	101	53	.656	7	1977	West—Kansas City	102	60	.630	8
1935	Detroit	93	58	.616	3		East—New York	100	62	.617	2½
1936	New York	102	51	.667	19½	1978	West—Kansas City	92	70	.568	5
1937	New York	102	52	.662	13		East—New York†	100	63	.613	1
1938	New York	99	53	.651	9½	1979	West—California	88	74	.543	3
1939	New York	106	45	.702	17		East—Baltimore	102	57	.642	8
1940	Detroit	90	64	.584	1	1980	West—Kansas City	97	65	.599	14
1941	New York	101	53	.656	17		East—New York	103	59	.636	3
1942	New York	103	51	.669	9	1981	West—Oakland†	64	45	.587	—
1943	New York	98	56	.636	13½		East—New York†	59	48	.551	—
1944	St. Louis	89	65	.578	1	1982	West—California	93	69	.574	3
1945	Detroit	88	65	.575	1½		East—Milwaukee	95	67	.586	1
1946	Boston	104	50	.675	12	1983	West—Chicago	99	63	.611	20
1947	New York	97	57	.630	12		East—Baltimore	98	64	.605	6
1948	Cleveland†	97	58	.626	1	1984	West—Kansas City	84	78	.519	3
1949	New York	97	57	.630	1		East—Detroit	104	58	.642	15
1950	New York	98	56	.636	3	1985	West—Kansas City	91	71	.562	1
1951	New York	98	56	.636	5		East—Toronto	99	62	.615	2
1952	New York	95	59	.617	2	1986	West—California	92	70	.568	5
1953	New York	99	52	.656	8½		East—Boston	95	66	.590	5½
1954	Cleveland	111	43	.721	8	1987	West—Minnesota	85	77	.525	2
1955	New York	96	58	.623	3		East—Detroit	98	64	.605	2
1956	New York	97	57	.630	9	1988	West—Oakland	104	58	.642	13
1957	New York	98	56	.636	8		East—Boston	89	73	.549	1
1958	New York	92	62	.597	10	1989	West—Oakland	99	63	.611	7
1959	Chicago	94	60	.610	5		East—Toronto	89	73	.549	2
1960	New York	97	57	.630	8	1990	West—Oakland	103	59	.636	9
1961	New York	109	53	.673	8		East—Boston	88	74	.543	2
1962	New York	96	66	.593	5	1991	West—Minnesota	95	67	.586	8
1963	New York	104	57	.646	10½		East—Toronto	91	71	.562	7
1964	New York	99	63	.611	1	1992	West—Oakland	96	66	.593	6
1965	Minnesota	102	60	.630	7		East—Toronto	96	66	.593	4
1966	Baltimore	97	63	.606	9	1993	West—Chicago	94	68	.580	8
1967	Boston	92	70	.568	1		East—Toronto	95	67	.586	7
1968	Detroit	103	59	.636	12	1994	West—Texas*	52	62	.456	1
1969	West—Minnesota	97	65	.599	9		Central—Chicago*	67	46	.593	1
	East—Baltimore	109	53	.673	19		East—New York*	70	43	.619	6½
1970	West—Minnesota	98	64	.605	9	1995	West—Seattle†	79	66	.545	1
	East—Baltimore	108	54	.667	15		Central—Cleveland	100	44	.694	30
1971	West—Oakland	101	60	.627	16		East—Boston	86	58	.597	7
	East—Baltimore	101	57	.639	12	1996	West—Texas	90	72	.556	4½
1972	West—Oakland	93	62	.600	5½		Central—Cleveland	99	62	.615	14½
	East—Detroit	86	70	.551	½		East—New York	92	70	.568	4
1973	West—Oakland	94	68	.580	6	1997	West—Seattle	90	72	.556	6
	East—Baltimore	97	65	.599	8		Central—Cleveland	86	75	.534	6
1974	West—Oakland	90	72	.556	5		East—Baltimore	98	64	.605	2

†**Regular season playoffs: 1948**—Cleveland def. Boston, 8-3 (one game); **1978**—New York def. Boston, 5-4 (one game); **1981**—East: New York def. Milwaukee (3 games to 2) and West: Oakland def. Kansas City (3 games to none); **1995**—Seattle def. California, 9-1 (one game).

The All-Star Game

Baseball's first All-Star Game was held on July 6, 1933, before 47,595 at Comiskey Park in Chicago. From that year on, the All-Star Game has matched the best players in the American League against the best in the National. From 1959-62, two All-Star Games were played. The only year an All-Star Game wasn't played was 1945, when World War II travel restrictions made it necessary to cancel the meeting. The NL leads the series, 40-27-1. In the chart below, the American League is listed in **bold** type.

The All-Star Game MVP Award is named after Arch Ward, the *Chicago Tribune* sports editor who founded the game in 1933. First given at the two All-Star games in 1962, the name of the award was changed to the Commissioner's Trophy in 1970 and back to the Ward Memorial Award in 1985.

Multiple winners: Gary Carter, Steve Garvey and Willie Mays (2).

Year		Host	AL Manager	NL Manager	MVP
1933	**American,** 4-2	Chicago (AL)	Connie Mack	John McGraw	No award
1934	**American,** 9-7	New York (NL)	Joe Cronin	Bill Terry	No award
1935	**American,** 4-1	Cleveland	Mickey Cochrane	Frankie Frisch	No award

Year		Host	AL Manager	NL Manager	MVP
1936	National, 4-3	Boston (NL)	Joe McCarthy	Charlie Grimm	No award
1937	**American,** 8-3	Washington	Joe McCarthy	Bill Terry	No award
1938	National, 4-1	Cincinnati	Joe McCarthy	Bill Terry	No award
1939	**American,** 3-1	New York (AL)	Joe McCarthy	Gabby Hartnett	No award
1940	National, 4-0	St. Louis (NL)	Joe Cronin	Bill McKechnie	No award
1941	**American,** 7-5	Detroit	Del Baker	Bill McKechnie	No award
1942	**American,** 3-1	New York (NL)	Joe McCarthy	Leo Durocher	No award
1943	**American,** 5-3	Philadelphia (AL)	Joe McCarthy	Billy Southworth	No award
1944	National, 7-1	Pittsburgh	Joe McCarthy	Billy Southworth	No award
1945	Not held				
1946	**American,** 12-0	Boston (AL)	Steve O'Neill	Charlie Grimm	No award
1947	**American,** 2-1	Chicago (NL)	Joe Cronin	Eddie Dyer	No award
1948	**American,** 5-2	St. Louis (AL)	Bucky Harris	Leo Durocher	No award
1949	**American,** 11-7	Brooklyn	Lou Boudreau	Billy Southworth	No award
1950	National, 4-3 (14)	Chicago (AL)	Casey Stengel	Burt Shotton	No award
1951	National, 8-3	Detroit	Casey Stengel	Eddie Sawyer	No award
1952	National, 3-2 (5, rain)	Philadelphia (NL)	Casey Stengel	Leo Durocher	No award
1953	National, 5-1	Cincinnati	Casey Stengel	Charlie Dressen	No award
1954	**American,** 11-9	Cleveland	Casey Stengel	Walter Alston	No award
1955	National, 6-5 (12)	Milwaukee	Al Lopez	Leo Durocher	No award
1956	National, 7-3	Washington	Casey Stengel	Walter Alston	No award
1957	**American,** 6-5	St. Louis	Casey Stengel	Walter Alston	No award
1958	**American,** 4-3	Baltimore	Casey Stengel	Fred Haney	No award
1959-a	National, 5-4	Pittsburgh	Casey Stengel	Fred Haney	No award
1959-b	**American,** 5-3	Los Angeles	Casey Stengel	Fred Haney	No award
1960-a	National, 5-3	Kansas City	Al Lopez	Walter Alston	No award
1960-b	National, 6-0	New York	Al Lopez	Walter Alston	No award
1961-a	National, 5-4 (10)	San Francisco	Paul Richards	Danny Murtaugh	No award
1961-b	TIE, 1-1 (9, rain)	Boston	Paul Richards	Danny Murtaugh	No award
1962-a	National, 3-1	Washington	Ralph Houk	Fred Hutchinson	Maury Wills, LA (NL), SS
1962-b	**American,** 9-4	Chicago (NL)	Ralph Houk	Fred Hutchinson	Leon Wagner, LA (AL), OF
1963	National, 5-3	Cleveland	Ralph Houk	Alvin Dark	Willie Mays, SF, OF
1964	National, 7-4	New York (NL)	Al Lopez	Walter Alston	Johnny Callison, Phi., OF
1965	National, 6-5	Minnesota	Al Lopez	Gene Mauch	Juan Marichal, SF, P
1966	National, 2-1 (10)	St. Louis	Sam Mele	Walter Alston	Brooks Robinson, Bal., 3B
1967	National, 2-1 (15)	California	Hank Bauer	Walter Alston	Tony Perez, Cin., 3B
1968	National, 1-0	Houston	Dick Williams	Red Schoendienst	Willie Mays, SF, OF
1969	National, 9-3	Washington	Mayo Smith	Red Schoendienst	Willie McCovey, SF, 1B
1970	National, 5-4 (12)	Cincinnati	Earl Weaver	Gil Hodges	Carl Yastrzemski, Bos., OF-1B
1971	**American,** 6-4	Detroit	Earl Weaver	Sparky Anderson	Frank Robinson, Bal., OF
1972	National, 4-3 (10)	Atlanta	Earl Weaver	Danny Murtaugh	Joe Morgan, Con., 2B
1973	National, 7-1	Kansas	Dick Williams	Sparky Anderson	Bobby Bonds, SF, OF
1974	National, 7-2	Pittsburgh	Dick Williams	Yogi Berra	Steve Garvey, LA, 1B
1975	National, 6-3	Milwaukee	Alvin Dark	Walter Alston	Bill Madlock, Chi. (NL), 3B & Jon Matlack, NY (NL), P
1976	National, 7-1	Philadelphia	Darrell Johnson	Sparky Anderson	George Foster, Cin., OF
1977	National, 7-5	New York (AL)	Billy Martin	Sparky Anderson	Don Sutton, LA, P
1978	National, 7-3	San Diego	Billy Martin	Tommy Lasorda	Steve Garvey, LA, 1B
1979	National, 7-6	Seattle	Bob Lemon	Tommy Lasorda	Dave Parker, Pit, OF
1980	National, 4-2	Los Angeles	Earl Weaver	Chuck Tanner	Ken Griffey, Cin., OF
1981	National, 5-4	Cleveland	Jim Frey	Dallas Green	Gary Carter, Mon., C
1982	National, 4-1	Montreal	Billy Martin	Tommy Lasorda	Dave Concepcion, Cin., SS
1983	**American,** 13-3	Chicago (AL)	Harvey Kuenn	Whitey Herzog	Fred Lynn, Cal., OF
1984	National, 3-1	San Francisco	Joe Altobelli	Paul Owens	Gary Carter, Mon., C
1985	National, 6-1	Minnesota	Sparky Anderson	Dick Williams	LaMarr Hoyt, SD, P
1986	**American,** 3-2	Houston	Dick Howser	Whitey Herzog	Roger Clemens, Bos., P
1987	National, 2-0 (13)	Oakland	John McNamara	Davey Johnson	Tim Raines, Mon., OF
1988	**American,** 2-1	Cincinnati	Tom Kelly	Whitey Herzog	Terry Steinbach, Oak., C
1989	**American,** 5-3	California	Tony La Russa	Tommy Lasorda	Bo Jackson, KC, OF
1990	**American,** 2-0	Chicago (NL)	Tony La Russa	Roger Craig	Julio Franco, Tex., 2B
1991	**American,** 4-2	Toronto	Tony La Russa	Lou Piniella	Cal Ripken Jr., Bal., SS
1992	**American,** 13-6	San Diego	Tom Kelly	Bobby Cox	Ken Griffey Jr., Sea., OF
1993	**American,** 9-3	Baltimore	Cito Gaston	Bobby Cox	Kirby Puckett, Min., OF
1994	National, 8-7 (10)	Pittsburgh	Cito Gaston	Jim Fregosi	Fred McGriff, Atl., 1B
1995	National, 3-2	Texas	Buck Showalter	Felipe Alou	Jeff Conine, Fla., PH
1996	National, 6-0	Philadelphia	Mike Hargrove	Bobby Cox	Mike Piazza, LA, C
1997	**American,** 3-1	Cleveland	Joe Torre	Bobby Cox	Sandy Alomar Jr., Cle., C

Major League Franchise Origins

Here is what the current 28 teams in Major League Baseball have to show for the years they have put in as members of the National League (NL) and American League (AL). Pennants and World Series championships are since 1901.

National League

	1st Year	Pennants & World Series	Franchise Stops

Atlanta Braves	1876	8 NL (1914,48,57-58,91-92,95,96)
		3 WS (1914,57,95)
			• Boston (1876-1952)
			  Milwaukee (1953-65)
			  Atlanta (1966—)

Chicago Cubs	1876	10 NL (1906-08,10,18,29,32,35,38,45) 2 WS (1907-08)	• Chicago (1876—)
Cincinnati Reds	1876	9 NL (1919,39-40,61,70,72,75-76,90) 5 WS (1919,40,75-76,90)	• Cincinnati (1876-80) Cincinnati (1890—)
Colorado Rockies	1993	None	• Denver (1993—)
Florida Marlins	1993	1 NL (1997) 1 WS (1997)	• Miami (1993—)
Houston Astros	1962	None	• Houston (1962—)
Los Angeles Dodgers	1890	18 NL (1916,20,41,47,49,52-53,55-56,59,63, 65-66,74,77-78, 81,88) 6 WS (1955,59,63,65,81,88)	• Brooklyn (1890-1957) Los Angeles (1958—)
Montreal Expos	1969	None	• Montreal (1969—)
New York Mets	1962	3 NL (1969,73,86) 2 WS (1969,86)	• New York (1962—)
Philadelphia Phillies	1883	5 NL (1915,50,80,83,93) 1 WS (1980)	• Philadelphia (1883—)
Pittsburgh Pirates	1887	7 NL (1903,09,25,27,60,71,79) 5 WS (1909,25,60,71,79)	• Pittsburgh (1887—)
St. Louis Cardinals	1892	15 NL (1926,28,30-31,34,42-44,46,64, 67-68,82,85,87) 9 WS (1926,31,34,42,44,46,64,67,82)	• St. Louis (1892—)
San Diego Padres	1969	1 NL (1984)	• San Diego (1969—)
San Francisco Giants	1883	16 NL (1905,11-13,17,21-24,33,36-37,51, 54,62,89) 5 WS (1905,21-22,33,54)	• New York (1883-1957) San Francisco (1958—)

American League

	1st Year	Pennants & World Series	Franchise Stops
Arizona Diamondbacks	1998	None	• Phoenix (1998—)

Baltimore Orioles	1901	7 AL (1944,66,69-71,79,83)
		3 WS (1966,70,83)
			• Milwaukee (1901)
			  St. Louis (1902-53)
			  Baltimore (1954—)

Boston Red Sox	1901	9 AL (1903,12,15-16,18,46,67,75,86) 5 WS (1903,12,15-16,18)	• Boston (1901—)
California Angels	1961	None	• Los Angeles (1961-65) Anaheim, CA (1966—)
Chicago White Sox	1901	4 AL (1906,17,19,59) 2 WS (1906,17)	• Chicago (1901—)
Cleveland Indians	1901	5 AL (1920,48,54,95,97) 2 WS (1920,48)	• Cleveland (1901—)
Detroit Tigers	1901	9 AL (1907-09,34-35,40,45,68,84) 4 WS (1935,45,68,84)	• Detroit (1901—)
Kansas City Royals	1969	2 AL (1980,85) 1 WS (1985)	• Kansas City (1969—)
Milwaukee Brewers	1969	1 AL (1982)	• Seattle (1969) Milwaukee (1970—)

Minnesota Twins	1901	6 AL (1924-25,33,65,87,91)
		3 WS (1924,87,91)
			• Washington, DC (1901-60)
			  Bloomington, MN (1961-81)
			  Minneapolis (1982—)

New York Yankees	1901	34 AL (1921-23,26-28,32,36-39,41-43,47, 49-53,55-58,60-64,76-78,81,96) 23 WS (1923,27-28,32,36-39,41,43,47,49-53, 56,58,61-62,77-78,96)	• Baltimore (1901-02) New York (1903—)

Oakland Athletics	1901	14 AL (1905,10-11,13-14,29-31,72-74,88-90)
		9 WS (1910-11,13,29-30,72-74,89)
			• Philadelphia (1901-54)
			  Kansas City (1955-67)
			  Oakland (1968—)

Seattle Mariners	1977	None	• Seattle (1977—)
Tampa Bay Devil Rays	1998	None	• Tampa (1998—)
Texas Rangers	1961	None	• Washington, DC (1961-71) Arlington, TX (1972—)
Toronto Blue Jays	1977	2 AL (1992-93) 2 WS (1992-93)	• Toronto (1977—)

The Growth of Major League Baseball

The National League (founded in 1876) and the American League (founded in 1901) were both eight-team circuits at the turn of the century and remained that way until expansion finally came to Major League Baseball in the 1960s. The AL added two teams in 1961 and the NL did the same a year later. Both leagues went to 12 teams and split into two divisions in 1969. The AL then grew by two more teams in 1977, but the NL didn't follow suit until adding its 13th and 14th clubs in 1993.

Expansion Timetable (Since 1901)

1961—Los Angeles Angels (now Anaheim) and Washington Senators (now Texas Rangers) join AL; **1962**—Houston Colt .45s (now Astros) and New York Mets join NL; **1969**—Kansas City Royals and Seattle Pilots (now Milwaukee Brewers) join AL, while Montreal Expos and San Diego Padres join NL; **1977**—Seattle Mariners and Toronto Blue Jays join AL; **1993**—Colorado Rockies and Florida Marlins join NL; **1998**—Arizona Diamondbacks and Tampa Bay Devil Rays join AL.

City and Nickname Changes

National League

1953—Boston Braves move to Milwaukee; **1958**—Brooklyn Dodgers move to Los Angeles and New York Giants move to San Francisco; **1965**—Houston Colt .45s renamed Astros; **1966**—Milwaukee Braves move to Atlanta.
Other nicknames: Boston (Beaneaters and Doves through 1908, and Bees from 1936-40); **Brooklyn** (Superbas through 1926, then Robins from 1927-31; then Dodgers from 1932-57); **Cincinnati** (Red Legs from 1944-45, then Redlegs from 1954-60, then Reds since 1961); **Philadelphia** (Blue Jays from 1943-44).

American League

1902—Milwaukee Brewers move to St. Louis and become Browns; **1903**—Baltimore Orioles move to New York and become Highlanders; **1913**—NY Highlanders renamed Yankees; **1954**—St. Louis Browns move to Baltimore and become Orioles; **1955**—Philadelphia Athletics move to Kansas City; **1961**—Washington Senators move to Bloomington, Minn., and become Minnesota Twins; **1965**—LA Angels renamed California Angels; **1966**—California Angels move to Anaheim; **1968**—KC Athletics move to Oakland and become A's; **1970**—Seattle Pilots move to Milwaukee and become Brewers; **1972**—Washington Senators move to Arlington, Texas, and become Rangers; **1982**—Minnesota Twins move to Minneapolis; **1987**—Oakland A's renamed Athletics; **1997**—California Angels renamed Anaheim Angels.
Other nicknames: Boston (Pilgrims, Puritans, Plymouth Rocks and Somersets through 1906); **Cleveland** (Broncos, Blues, Naps and Molly McGuires through 1914); **Washington** (Senators through 1904, then Nationals from 1905-44, then Senators again from 1945-60).

National League Pennant Winners from 1876-99

Founded in 1876, the National League played 24 seasons before the turn of the century and its eventual rivalry with the younger American League.
Multiple winners: Boston (8); Chicago (6); Baltimore (3); Brooklyn and New York (2).

Year		Year		Year		Year	
1876	Chicago	1882	Chicago	1888	New York	1894	Baltimore
1877	Boston	1883	Boston	1889	New York	1895	Baltimore
1878	Boston	1884	Providence	1890	Brooklyn	1896	Baltimore
1879	Providence	1885	Chicago	1891	Boston	1897	Boston
1880	Chicago	1886	Chicago	1892	Boston	1898	Boston
1881	Chicago	1887	Detroit	1893	Boston	1899	Brooklyn

Champions of Leagues That No Longer Exist

A Special Baseball Records Committee appointed by the commissioner found in 1968 that four extinct leagues qualified for major league status—the American Association (1882-91), the Union Association (1884), the Players' League (1890) and the Federal League (1914-15). The first years of the American League (1900) and Federal League (1913) were not recognized.

American Association

Year	Champion	Manager	Year	Champion	Manager	Year	Champion	Manager
1882	Cincinnati	Pop Snyder	1886	St. Louis	Charlie Comiskey	1889	Brooklyn	Bill McGunnigle
1883	Philadelphia	Lew Simmons	1887	St. Louis	Charlie Comiskey	1890	Louisville	Jack Chapman
1884	New York	Jim Mutrie	1888	St. Louis	Charlie Comiskey	1891	Boston	Arthur Irwin
1885	St. Louis	Charlie Comiskey						

Union Association			**Players' League**			**Federal League**		
Year	Champion	Manager	Year	Champion	Manager	Year	Champion	Manager
1884	St. Louis	Henry Lucas	1890	Boston	King Kelly	1914	Indianapolis	Bill Phillips
						1915	Chicago	Joe Tinker

Annual Batting Leaders (since 1900)
Batting Average
National League

Multiple winners: Tony Gwynn and Honus Wagner (8); Rogers Hornsby and Stan Musial (7); Roberto Clemente and Bill Madlock (4); Pete Rose and Paul Waner (3); Hank Aaron, Richie Ashburn, Jake Daubert, Tommy Davis, Ernie Lombardi, Willie McGee, Lefty O'Doul, Dave Parker and Edd Roush (2).

Year		Avg	Year		Avg	Year		Avg
1900	Honus Wagner, Pit	.381	1933	Chuck Klein, Phi	.368	1966	Matty Alou, Pit	.342
1901	Jesse Burkett, St.L	.382	1934	Paul Waner, Pit	.362	1967	Roberto Clemente, Pit	.357
1902	Ginger Beaumont, Pit	.357	1935	Arky Vaughan, Pit	.385	1968	Pete Rose, Cin	.335
1903	Honus Wagner, Pit	.355	1936	Paul Waner, Pit	.373	1969	Pete Rose, Cin	.348
1904	Honus Wagner, Pit	.349	1937	Joe Medwick, St.L	.374			
1905	Cy Seymour, Cin	.377	1938	Ernie Lombardi, Cin	.342	1970	Rico Carty, Atl	.366
1906	Honus Wagner, Pit	.339	1939	Johnny Mize, St.L	.349	1971	Joe Torre, St.L	.363
1907	Honus Wagner, Pit	.350				1972	Billy Williams, Chi	.333
1908	Honus Wagner, Pit	.354	1940	Debs Garms, Pit	.355	1973	Pete Rose, Cin	.338
1909	Honus Wagner, Pit	.339	1941	Pete Reiser, Bklyn	.343	1974	Ralph Garr, Atl	.353
			1942	Ernie Lombardi, Bos	.330	1975	Bill Madlock, Chi	.354
1910	Sherry Magee, Phi	.331	1943	Stan Musial, St.L	.357	1976	Bill Madlock, Chi	.339
1911	Honus Wagner, Pit	.334	1944	Dixie Walker, Bklyn	.357	1977	Dave Parker, Pit	.338
1912	Heinie Zimmerman, Chi	.372	1945	Phil Cavarretta, Chi	.355	1978	Dave Parker, Pit	.334
1913	Jake Daubert, Bklyn	.350	1946	Stan Musial, St.L	.365	1979	Keith Hernandez, St.L	.344
1914	Jake Daubert, Bklyn	.329	1947	Harry Walker, St.L-Phi	.363			
1915	Larry Doyle, NY	.320	1948	Stan Musial, St.L	.376	1980	Bill Buckner, Chi	.324
1916	Hal Chase, Cin	.339	1949	Jackie Robinson, Bklyn	.342	1981	Bill Madlock, Pit	.341
1917	Edd Roush, Cin	.341				1982	Al Oliver, Mon	.331
1918	Zack Wheat, Bklyn	.335	1950	Stan Musial, St.L	.346	1983	Bill Madlock, Pit	.323
1919	Edd Roush, Cin	.321	1951	Stan Musial, St.L	.355	1984	Tony Gwynn, SD	.351
			1952	Stan Musial, St.L	.336	1985	Willie McGee, St.L	.353
1920	Rogers Hornsby, St.L	.370	1953	Carl Furillo, Bklyn	.344	1986	Tim Raines, Mon	.334
1921	Rogers Hornsby, St.L	.397	1954	Willie Mays, NY	.345	1987	Tony Gwynn, SD	.370
1922	Rogers Hornsby, St.L	.401	1955	Richie Ashburn, Phi	.338	1988	Tony Gwynn, SD	.313
1923	Rogers Hornsby, St.L	.384	1956	Hank Aaron, Mil	.328	1989	Tony Gwynn, SD	.336
1924	Rogers Hornsby, St.L	.424	1957	Stan Musial, St.L	.351			
1925	Rogers Hornsby, St.L	.403	1958	Richie Ashburn, Phi	.350	1990	Willie McGee, St.L	.335
1926	Bubbles Hargrave, Cin	.353	1959	Hank Aaron, Mil	.355	1991	Terry Pendleton, Atl	.319
1927	Paul Waner, Pit	.380				1992	Gary Sheffield, SD	.330
1928	Rogers Hornsby, Bos	.387	1960	Dick Groat, Pit	.325	1993	Andres Galarraga, Col	.370
1929	Lefty O'Doul, Phi	.398	1961	Roberto Clemente, Pit	.351	1994	Tony Gwynn, SD	.394
			1962	Tommy Davis, LA	.346	1995	Tony Gwynn, SD	.368
1930	Bill Terry, NY	.401	1963	Tommy Davis, LA	.326	1996	Tony Gwynn, SD	.353
1931	Chick Hafey, St.L	.349	1964	Roberto Clemente, Pit	.339	1997	Tony Gwynn, SD	.372
1932	Lefty O'Doul, Bklyn	.368	1965	Roberto Clemente, Pit	.329			

American League

Multiple winners: Ty Cobb (12); Rod Carew (7); Ted Williams (6); Wade Boggs (5); Harry Heilmann (4); George Brett, Nap Lajoie, Tony Oliva and Carl Yastrzemski (3); Luke Appling, Joe DiMaggio, Ferris Fain, Jimmie Foxx, Edgar Martinez, Pete Runnels, Al Simmons, George Sisler and Mickey Vernon (2).

Year		Avg	Year		Avg	Year		Avg
1901	Nap Lajoie, Phi	.422	1923	Harry Heilmann, Det	.403	1945	Snuffy Stirnweiss, NY	.309
1902	Ed Delahanty, Wash	.376	1924	Babe Ruth, NY	.378	1946	Mickey Vernon, Wash	.353
1903	Nap Lajoie, Cle	.355	1925	Harry Heilmann, Det	.393	1947	Ted Williams, Bos	.343
1904	Nap Lajoie, Cle	.381	1926	Heinie Manush, Det	.378	1948	Ted Williams, Bos	.369
1905	Elmer Flick, Cle	.306	1927	Harry Heilmann, Det	.398	1949	George Kell, Det	.343
1906	George Stone, St.L	.358	1928	Goose Goslin, Wash	.379			
1907	Ty Cobb, Det	.350	1929	Lew Fonseca, Cle	.369	1950	Billy Goodman, Bos	.354
1908	Ty Cobb, Det	.324				1951	Ferris Fain, Phi	.344
1909	Ty Cobb, Det	.377	1930	Al Simmons, Phi	.381	1952	Ferris Fain, Phi	.327
			1931	Al Simmons, Phi	.390	1953	Mickey Vernon, Wash	.337
1910	Ty Cobb, Det	.385	1932	Dale Alexander, Det-Bos	.367	1954	Bobby Avila, Clev	.341
1911	Ty Cobb, Det	.420	1933	Jimmie Foxx, Phi	.356	1955	Al Kaline, Det	.340
1912	Ty Cobb, Det	.410	1934	Lou Gehrig, NY	.363	1956	Mickey Mantle, NY	.353
1913	Ty Cobb, Det	.390	1935	Buddy Myer, Wash	.349	1957	Ted Williams, Bos	.388
1914	Ty Cobb, Det	.368	1936	Luke Appling, Chi	.388	1958	Ted Williams, Bos	.328
1915	Ty Cobb, Det	.369	1937	Charlie Gehringer, Det	.371	1959	Harvey Kuenn, Det	.353
1916	Tris Speaker, Cle	.386	1938	Jimmie Foxx, Bos	.349			
1917	Ty Cobb, Det	.383	1939	Joe DiMaggio, NY	.381	1960	Pete Runnels, Bos	.320
1918	Ty Cobb, Det	.382	1940	Joe DiMaggio, NY	.352	1961	Norm Cash, Det	.361*
1919	Ty Cobb, Det	.384	1941	Ted Williams, Bos	.406	1962	Pete Runnels, Bos	.326
			1942	Ted Williams, Bos	.356	1963	Carl Yastrzemski, Bos	.321
1920	George Sisler, St.L	.407	1943	Luke Appling, Chi	.328	1964	Tony Oliva, Min	.323
1921	Harry Heilmann, Det	.394	1944	Lou Boudreau, Clev	.327	1965	Tony Oliva, Min	.321
1922	George Sisler, St.L	.420				1966	Frank Robinson, Bal	.316

*Norm Cash later admitted to using a corked bat the entire season. He played 16 other seasons and never hit better than .286.

Year		Avg	Year		Avg	Year		Avg
1967	Carl Yastrzemski, Bos	.326	1978	Rod Carew, Min	.333	1989	Kirby Puckett, Min	.339
1968	Carl Yastrzemski, Bos	.301	1979	Fred Lynn, Min	.333	1990	George Brett, KC	.329
1969	Rod Carew, Min	.332	1980	George Brett, KC	.390	1991	Julio Franco, Tex	.341
1970	Alex Johnson, Cal	.329	1981	Carney Lansford, Bos	.336	1992	Edgar Martinez, Sea	.343
1971	Tony Oliva, Min	.337	1982	Willie Wilson, KC	.332	1993	John Olerud, Tor	.363
1972	Rod Carew, Min	.318	1983	Wade Boggs, Bos	.361	1994	Paul O'Neill, NY	.359
1973	Rod Carew, Min	.350	1984	Don Mattingly, NY	.343	1995	Edgar Martinez, Sea	.356
1974	Rod Carew, Min	.364	1985	Wade Boggs, Bos	.368	1996	Alex Rodriguez, Sea	.358
1975	Rod Carew, Min	.359	1986	Wade Boggs, Bos	.357	1997	Frank Thomas, Chi	.347
1976	George Brett, KC	.333	1987	Wade Boggs, Bos	.363			
1977	Rod Carew, Min	.388	1988	Wade Boggs, Bos	.366			

Home Runs
National League

Multiple winners: Mike Schmidt (8); Ralph Kiner (7); Gavvy Cravath and Mel Ott (6); Hank Aaron, Chuck Klein, Willie Mays, Johnny Mize, Cy Williams and Hack Wilson (4); Willie McCovey (3); Ernie Banks, Johnny Bench, George Foster, Rogers Hornsby, Tim Jordan, Dave Kingman, Eddie Mathews, Dale Murphy, Bill Nicholson, Dave Robertson, Wildfire Schulte and Willie Stargell (2).

Year		HR	Year		HR	Year		HR
1900	Herman Long, Bos	12	1933	Chuck Klein, Phi	28	1966	Hank Aaron, Atl	44
1901	Sam Crawford, Cin	16	1934	Rip Collins, St.L	35	1967	Hank Aaron, Atl	39
1902	Tommy Leach, Pit	6		& Mel Ott, NY	35	1968	Willie McCovey, SF	36
1903	Jimmy Sheckard, Bklyn	9	1935	Wally Berger, Bos	34	1969	Willie McCovey, SF	45
1904	Harry Lumley, Bklyn	9	1936	Mel Ott, NY	33	1970	Johnny Bench, Cin	45
1905	Fred Odwell, Cin	9	1937	Joe Medwick, St.L	31	1971	Willie Stargell, Pit	48
1906	Tim Jordan, Bklyn	12		& Mel Ott, NY	31	1972	Johnny Bench, Cin	40
1907	Dave Brain, Bos	10	1938	Mel Ott, NY	36	1973	Willie Stargell, Pit	44
1908	Tim Jordan, Bklyn	12	1939	Johnny Mize, St.L	28	1974	Mike Schmidt, Phi	36
1909	Red Murray, NY	7	1940	Johnny Mize, St.L	43	1975	Mike Schmidt, Phi	38
1910	Fred Beck, Bos	10	1941	Dolf Camilli, Bklyn	34	1976	Mike Schmidt, Phi	38
	& Wildfire Schulte, Chi	10	1942	Mel Ott, NY	30	1977	George Foster, Cin	52
1911	Wildfire Schulte, Chi	21	1943	Bill Nicholson, Chi	29	1978	George Foster, Cin	40
1912	Heinie Zimmerman, Chi	14	1944	Bill Nicholson, Chi	33	1979	Dave Kingman, Chi	48
1913	Gavvy Cravath, Phi	19	1945	Tommy Holmes, Bos	28	1980	Mike Schmidt, Phi	48
1914	Gavvy Cravath, Phi	19	1946	Ralph Kiner, Pit	23	1981	Mike Schmidt, Phi	31
1915	Gavvy Cravath, Phi	24	1947	Ralph Kiner, Pit	51	1982	Dave Kingman, NY	37
1916	Cy Williams, Chi	12		& Johnny Mize, NY	51	1983	Mike Schmidt, Phi	40
	& Dave Robertson, NY	12	1948	Ralph Kiner, Pit	40	1984	Dale Murphy, Atl	36
1917	Gavvy Cravath, Phi	12		& Johnny Mize, NY	40		& Mike Schmidt, Phi	36
	& Dave Robertson, NY	12	1949	Ralph Kiner, Pit	54	1985	Dale Murphy, Atl	37
1918	Gavvy Cravath, Phi	8	1950	Ralph Kiner, Pit	47	1986	Mike Schmidt, Phi	37
1919	Gavvy Cravath, Phi	12	1951	Ralph Kiner, Pit	42	1987	Andre Dawson, Chi	49
1920	Cy Williams, Phi	15	1952	Ralph Kiner, Pit	37	1988	Darryl Strawberry, NY	39
1921	George Kelly, NY	23		& Hank Sauer, Chi	37	1989	Kevin Mitchell, SF	47
1922	Rogers Hornsby, St.L	42	1953	Eddie Mathews, Mil	47	1990	Ryne Sandberg, Chi	40
1923	Cy Williams, Phi	41	1954	Ted Kluszewski, Cin	49	1991	Howard Johnson, NY	38
1924	Jack Fournier, Bklyn	27	1955	Willie Mays, NY	51	1992	Fred McGriff, SD	35
1925	Rogers Hornsby, St.L	39	1956	Duke Snider, Bklyn	43	1993	Barry Bonds, SF	46
1926	Hack Wilson, Chi	21	1957	Hank Aaron, Mil	44	1994	Matt Williams, SF	43
1927	Cy Williams, Phi	30	1958	Ernie Banks, Chi	47	1995	Dante Bichette, Col	40
	& Hack Wilson, Chi	30	1959	Eddie Mathews, Mil	46	1996	Andres Galarraga, Col	47
1928	Jim Bottomley, St.L	31	1960	Ernie Banks, Chi	41	1997	Larry Walker, Col	49
	& Hack Wilson, Chi	31	1961	Orlando Cepeda, SF	46			
1929	Chuck Klein, Phi	43	1962	Willie Mays, SF	49			
1930	Hack Wilson, Chi	56	1963	Hank Aaron, Mil	44			
1931	Chuck Klein, Phi	31		& Willie McCovey, SF	44			
1932	Chuck Klein, Phi	38	1964	Willie Mays, SF	47			
	& Mel Ott, NY	38	1965	Willie Mays, SF	52			

Note: In 1997 Mark McGwire hit 58 home runs but hit 34 of them in the AL with Oakland before getting traded to St. Louis.

American League

Multiple winners: Babe Ruth (12); Harmon Killebrew (6); Home Run Baker, Harry Davis, Jimmie Foxx, Hank Greenberg, Reggie Jackson, Mickey Mantle and Ted Williams (4); Lou Gehrig and Jim Rice (3); Dick Allen, Tony Armas, Jose Canseco, Joe DiMaggio, Larry Doby, Cecil Fielder, Juan Gonzalez, Ken Griffey Jr., Mark McGwire, Wally Pipp, Al Rosen and Gorman Thomas (2).

Year		HR	Year		HR	Year		HR
1901	Nap Lajoie, Phi	14	1906	Harry Davis, Phi	12	1911	Home Run Baker, Phi	11
1902	Socks Seybold, Phi	16	1907	Harry Davis, Phi	8	1912	Home Run Baker, Phi	10
1903	Buck Freeman, Bos	13	1908	Sam Crawford, Det	7		& Tris Speaker, Bos	10
1904	Harry Davis, Phi	10	1909	Ty Cobb, Det	9	1913	Home Run Baker, Phi	12
1905	Harry Davis, Phi	8	1910	Jake Stahl, Bos	10	1914	Home Run Baker, Phi	9

Annual Batting Leaders (Cont.)

Year		HR	Year		HR	Year		HR
1915	Braggo Roth, Chi-Cle	7	1945	Vern Stephens, St.L	24		& George Scott, Mil	36
1916	Wally Pipp, NY	12	1946	Hank Greenberg, Det	44	1976	Graig Nettles, NY	32
1917	Wally Pipp, NY	9	1947	Ted Williams, Bos	32	1977	Jim Rice, Bos	39
1918	Babe Ruth, Bos	11	1948	Joe DiMaggio, NY	39	1978	Jim Rice, Bos	46
	& Tilly Walker, Phi	11	1949	Ted Williams, Bos	43	1979	Gorman Thomas, Mil	45
1919	Babe Ruth, Bos	29	1950	Al Rosen, Cle	37	1980	Reggie Jackson, NY	41
1920	Babe Ruth, NY	54	1951	Gus Zernial, Chi-Phi	33		& Ben Oglivie, Mil	41
1921	Babe Ruth, NY	59	1952	Larry Doby, Cle	32	1981	Tony Armas, Oak	22
1922	Ken Williams, St.L	39	1953	Al Rosen, Cle	43		Dwight Evans, Bos	22
1923	Babe Ruth, NY	41	1954	Larry Doby, Cle	32		Bobby Grich, Cal	22
1924	Babe Ruth, NY	46	1955	Mickey Mantle, NY	37		& Eddie Murray, Bal	22
1925	Bob Meusel, NY	33	1956	Mickey Mantle, NY	52	1982	Reggie Jackson, Cal	39
1926	Babe Ruth, NY	47	1957	Roy Sievers, Wash	42		& Gorman Thomas, Mil	39
1927	Babe Ruth, NY	60	1958	Mickey Mantle, NY	42	1983	Jim Rice, Bos	39
1928	Babe Ruth, NY	54	1959	Rocky Colavito, Cle	42	1984	Tony Armas, Bos	43
1929	Babe Ruth, NY	46		& Harmon Killebrew, Wash	42	1985	Darrell Evans, Det	40
1930	Babe Ruth, NY	49	1960	Mickey Mantle, NY	40	1986	Jesse Barfield, Tor	40
1931	Lou Gehrig, NY	46	1961	Roger Maris, NY	61	1987	Mark McGwire, Oak	49
	& Babe Ruth, NY	46	1962	Harmon Killebrew, Min	48	1988	Jose Canseco, Oak	42
1932	Jimmie Foxx, Phi	58	1963	Harmon Killebrew, Min	45	1989	Fred McGriff, Tor	36
1933	Jimmie Foxx, Phi	48	1964	Harmon Killebrew, Min	49	1990	Cecil Fielder, Det	51
1934	Lou Gehrig, NY	49	1965	Tony Conigliaro, Bos	32	1991	Jose Canseco, Oak	44
1935	Jimmie Foxx, Phi	36	1966	Frank Robinson, Bal	49		& Cecil Fielder, Det	44
	& Hank Greenberg, Det	36	1967	Harmon Killebrew, Min	44	1992	Juan Gonzalez, Tex	43
1936	Lou Gehrig, NY	49		& Carl Yastrzemski, Bos	44	1993	Juan Gonzalez, Tex	46
1937	Joe DiMaggio, NY	46	1968	Frank Howard, Wash	44	1994	Ken Griffey Jr., Sea	40
1938	Hank Greenberg, Det	58	1969	Harmon Killebrew, Min	49	1995	Albert Belle, Cle	50
1939	Jimmie Foxx, Bos	35	1970	Frank Howard, Wash	44	1996	Mark McGwire, Oak	52
1940	Hank Greenberg, Det	41	1971	Bill Melton, Chi	33	1997	Ken Griffey Jr., Sea	56
1941	Ted Williams, Bos	37	1972	Dick Allen, Chi	37			
1942	Ted Williams, Bos	36	1973	Reggie Jackson, Oak	32			
1943	Rudy York, Det	34	1974	Dick Allen, Chi	32			
1944	Nick Etten, NY	22	1975	Reggie Jackson, Oak	36			

Note: In 1997 Mark McGwire hit 58 home runs but hit 24 of them in the NL with St. Louis after getting traded from Oakland.

Runs Batted In
National League

Multiple winners: Hank Aaron, Rogers Hornsby, Sherry Magee, Mike Schmidt and Honus Wagner (4); Johnny Bench, George Foster, Joe Medwick, Johnny Mize and Heinie Zimmerman (3); Ernie Banks, Jim Bottomley, Orlando Cepeda, Gavvy Cravath, Andres Galarraga, George Kelly, Chuck Klein, Willie McCovey, Dale Murphy, Stan Musial, Bill Nicholson and Hack Wilson (2).

Year		RBI	Year		RBI	Year		RBI
1900	Elmer Flick, Phi	110	1924	George Kelly, NY	136	1949	Ralph Kiner, Pit	127
1901	Honus Wagner, Pit	126	1925	Rogers Hornsby, St.L	143	1950	Del Ennis, Phi	126
1902	Honus Wagner, Pit	91	1926	Jim Bottomley, St.L	120	1951	Monte Irvin, NY	121
1903	Sam Mertes, NY	104	1927	Paul Waner, Pit	131	1952	Hank Sauer, Chi	121
1904	Bill Dahlen, NY	80	1928	Jim Bottomley, St.L	136	1953	Roy Campanella, Bklyn	142
1905	Cy Seymour, Cin	121	1929	Hack Wilson, Chi	159	1954	Ted Kluszewski, Cin	141
1906	Jim Nealon, Pit	83	1930	Hack Wilson, Chi	190	1955	Duke Snider, Bklyn	136
	& Harry Steinfeldt, Chi	83	1931	Chuck Klein, Phi	121	1956	Stan Musial, St.L	109
1907	Sherry Magee, Phi	85	1932	Don Hurst, Phi	143	1957	Hank Aaron, Mil	132
1908	Honus Wagner, Pit	109	1933	Chuck Klein, Phi	120	1958	Ernie Banks, Chi	129
1909	Honus Wagner, Pit	100	1934	Mel Ott, NY	135	1959	Ernie Banks, Chi	143
1910	Sherry Magee, Phi	123	1935	Wally Berger, Bos	130	1960	Hank Aaron, Mil	126
1911	Wildfire Schulte, Chi	121	1936	Joe Medwick, St.L	138	1961	Orlando Cepeda, SF	142
1912	Heinie Zimmerman, Chi	103	1937	Joe Medwick, St.L	154	1962	Tommy Davis, LA	153
1913	Gavvy Cravath, Phi	128	1938	Joe Medwick, St.L	122	1963	Hank Aaron, Mil	130
1914	Sherry Magee, Phi	103	1939	Frank McCormick, Cin	128	1964	Ken Boyer, St.L	119
1915	Gavvy Cravath, Phi	115	1940	Johnny Mize, St.L	137	1965	Deron Johnson, Cin	130
1916	Heinie Zimmerman, Chi-NY	83	1941	Dolph Camilli, Bklyn	120	1966	Hank Aaron, Atl	127
1917	Heinie Zimmerman, NY	102	1942	Johnny Mize, NY	110	1967	Orlando Cepeda, St.L	111
1918	Sherry Magee, Cin	76	1943	Bill Nicholson, Chi	128	1968	Willie McCovey, SF	105
1919	Hy Myers, Bklyn	73	1944	Bill Nicholson, Chi	122	1969	Willie McCovey, SF	126
1920	Rogers Hornsby, St.L	94	1945	Dixie Walker, Bklyn	124	1970	Johnny Bench, Cin	148
	& George Kelly, NY	94	1946	Enos Slaughter, St.L	130	1971	Joe Torre, St.L	137
1921	Rogers Hornsby, St.L	126	1947	Johnny Mize, NY	138	1972	Johnny Bench, Cin	125
1922	Rogers Hornsby, St.L	152	1948	Stan Musial, St.L	131	1973	Willie Stargell, Pit	119
1923	Irish Meusel, NY	125				1974	Johnny Bench, Cin	129

Year		RBI	Year		RBI	Year		RBI
1975	Greg Luzinski, Phi	120	1983	Dale Murphy, Atl	121	1991	Howard Johnson, NY	117
1976	George Foster, Cin	121	1984	Gary Carter, Mon	106	1992	Darren Daulton, Phi	109
1977	George Foster, Cin	149		& Mike Schmidt, Phi	106	1993	Barry Bonds, SF	123
1978	George Foster, Cin	120	1985	Dave Parker, Cin	125	1994	Jeff Bagwell, Hou	116
1979	Dave Winfield, SD	118	1986	Mike Schmidt, Phi	119	1995	Dante Bichette, Col	128
			1987	Andre Dawson, Chi	137	1996	Andres Galarraga, Col	150
1980	Mike Schmidt, Phi	121	1988	Will Clark, SF	109	1997	Andres Galarraga, Col	140
1981	Mike Schmidt, Phi	91	1989	Kevin Mitchell, SF	125			
1982	Dale Murphy, Atl	109	1990	Matt Williams, SF	122			
	& Al Oliver, Mon	109						

American League

Multiple winners: Babe Ruth (6); Lou Gehrig (5); Ty Cobb, Hank Greenberg and Ted Williams (4); Albert Belle, Sam Crawford, Cecil Fielder, Jimmie Foxx, Jackie Jensen, Harmon Killebrew, Vern Stephens and Bobby Veach (3); Home Run Baker, Cecil Cooper, Harry Davis, Joe DiMaggio, Buck Freeman, Nap Lajoie, Roger Maris, Jim Rice, Al Rosen, and Bobby Veach (2).

Year		RBI	Year		RBI	Year		RBI
1901	Nap Lajoie, Phi	125	1934	Lou Gehrig, NY	165	1966	Frank Robinson, Bal	122
1902	Buck Freeman, Bos	121	1935	Hank Greenberg, Det	170	1967	Carl Yastrzemski, Bos	121
1903	Buck Freeman, Bos	104	1936	Hal Trosky, Cle	162	1968	Ken Harrelson, Bos	109
1904	Nap Lajoie, Cle	102	1937	Hank Greenberg, Det	183	1969	Harmon Killebrew, Min	140
1905	Harry Davis, Phi	83	1938	Jimmie Foxx, Bos	175			
1906	Harry Davis, Phi	96	1939	Ted Williams, Bos	145	1970	Frank Howard, Wash	126
1907	Ty Cobb, Det	116				1971	Harmon Killebrew, Min	119
1908	Ty Cobb, Det	108	1940	Hank Greenberg, Det	150	1972	Dick Allen, Chi	113
1909	Ty Cobb, Det	107	1941	Joe DiMaggio, NY	125	1973	Reggie Jackson, Oak	117
			1942	Ted Williams, Bos	137	1974	Jeff Burroughs, Tex	118
1910	Sam Crawford, Det	120	1943	Rudy York, Det	118	1975	George Scott, Mil	109
1911	Ty Cobb, Det	144	1944	Vern Stephens, St.L	109	1976	Lee May, Bal	109
1912	Home Run Baker, Phi	133	1945	Nick Etten, NY	111	1977	Larry Hisle, Min	119
1913	Home Run Baker, Phi	126	1946	Hank Greenberg, Det	127	1978	Jim Rice, Bos	139
1914	Sam Crawford, Det	104	1947	Ted Williams, Bos	114	1979	Don Baylor, Cal	139
1915	Sam Crawford, Det	112	1948	Joe DiMaggio, NY	155			
	& Bobby Veach, Det	112	1949	Ted Williams, Bos	159	1980	Cecil Cooper, Mil	122
1916	Del Pratt, St.L	103		& Vern Stephens, Bos	159	1981	Eddie Murray, Bal	78
1917	Bobby Veach, Det	103				1982	Hal McRae, KC	133
1918	Bobby Veach, Det	78	1950	Walt Dropo, Bos	144	1983	Cecil Cooper, Mil	126
1919	Babe Ruth, Bos	114		& Vern Stephens, Bos	144		& Jim Rice, Bos	126
			1951	Gus Zernial, Chi-Phi	129	1984	Tony Armas, Bos	123
1920	Babe Ruth, NY	137	1952	Al Rosen, Cle	105	1985	Don Mattingly, NY	145
1921	Babe Ruth, NY	171	1953	Al Rosen, Cle	145	1986	Joe Carter, Cle	121
1922	Ken Williams, St.L	155	1954	Larry Doby, Cle	126	1987	George Bell, Tor	134
1923	Babe Ruth, NY	131	1955	Ray Boone, Det	116	1988	Jose Canseco, Oak	124
1924	Goose Goslin, Wash	129		& Jackie Jensen, Bos	116	1989	Ruben Sierra, Tex	119
1925	Bob Meusel, NY	138	1956	Mickey Mantle, NY	130			
1926	Babe Ruth, NY	145	1957	Roy Sievers, Wash	114	1990	Cecil Fielder, Det	132
1927	Lou Gehrig, NY	175	1958	Jackie Jensen, Bos	122	1991	Cecil Fielder, Det	133
1928	Lou Gehrig, NY	142	1959	Jackie Jensen, Bos	112	1992	Cecil Fielder, Det	124
	& Babe Ruth, NY	142				1993	Albert Belle, Cle	129
1929	Al Simmons, Phi	157	1960	Roger Maris, NY	112	1994	Kirby Puckett, Min	112
			1961	Roger Maris, NY	142	1995	Albert Belle, Cle	126
1930	Lou Gehrig, NY	174	1962	Harmon Killebrew, Min	126		& Mo Vaughn, Bos	126
1931	Lou Gehrig, NY	184	1963	Dick Stuart, Bos	118	1996	Albert Belle, Cle	148
1932	Jimmie Foxx, Phi	169	1964	Brooks Robinson, Bal	118	1997	Ken Griffey Jr., Sea	147
1933	Jimmie Foxx, Phi	163	1965	Rocky Colavito, Cle	108			

Batting Triple Crown Winners

Players who led either league in Batting Average, Home Runs and Runs Batted In over a single season.

National League

	Year	Avg	HR	RBI
Paul Hines, Providence	1878	.358	4	50
Hugh Duffy, Boston	1894	.438	18	145
Heinie Zimmerman, Chicago	1912	.372	14	103
Rogers Hornsby, St. Louis	1922	.401	42	152
Rogers Hornsby, St. Louis	1925	.403	39	143
Chuck Klein, Philadelphia	1933	.368	28	120
Joe Medwick, St. Louis	1937	.374	31*	154

*Tied for league lead in HRs with Mel Ott, NY.

American League

	Year	Avg	HR	RBI
Nap Lajoie, Philadelphia	1901	.422	14	125
Ty Cobb, Detroit	1909	.377	9	115
Jimmie Foxx, Philadelphia	1933	.356	48	163
Lou Gehrig, New York	1934	.363	49	165
Ted Williams, Boston	1942	.356	36	137
Ted Williams, Boston	1947	.343	32	114
Mickey Mantle, New York	1956	.353	52	130
Frank Robinson, Baltimore	1966	.316	49	122
Carl Yastrzemski, Boston	1967	.326	44*	121

*Tied for league lead in HRs with Harmon Killebrew, Min.

Annual Batting Leaders (Cont.)

Stolen Bases
National League

Multiple winners: Max Carey (10); Lou Brock (8); Vince Coleman and Maury Wills (6); Honus Wagner (5); Bob Bescher, Kiki Cuyler, Willie Mays and Tim Raines (4); Bill Bruton, Frankie Frisch and Pepper Martin (3); George Burns, Frank Chance, Augie Galan, Marquis Grissom, Stan Hack, Sam Jethroe, Davey Lopes, Omar Moreno, Pete Reiser and Jackie Robinson (2).

Year		SB	Year		SB	Year		SB
1900	Patsy Donovan, St.L	.45	1932	Chuck Klein, Phi	.20	1966	Lou Brock, St.L	.74
	& George Van Haltren, NY	45	1933	Pepper Martin, St.L	.26	1967	Lou Brock, St.L	.52
1901	Honus Wagner, Pit	.49	1934	Pepper Martin, St.L	.23	1968	Lou Brock, St.L	.62
1902	Honus Wagner, Pit	.42	1935	Augie Galan, Chi	.22	1969	Lou Brock, St.L	.53
1903	Frank Chance, Chi	.67	1936	Pepper Martin, St.L	.23	1970	Bobby Tolan, Cin	.57
	& Jimmy Sheckard, Bklyn	.67	1937	Augie Galan, Chi	.23	1971	Lou Brock, St.L	.64
1904	Honus Wagner, Pit	.53	1938	Stan Hack, Chi	.16	1972	Lou Brock, St.L	.63
1905	Art Devlin, NY	.59	1939	Stan Hack, Chi	.17	1973	Lou Brock, St.L	.70
	& Billy Maloney, Chi	.59		& Lee Handley, Pit	.17	1974	Lou Brock, St.L	.118
1906	Frank Chance, Chi	.57	1940	Lonny Frey, Cin	.22	1975	Davey Lopes, LA	.77
1907	Honus Wagner, Pit	.61	1941	Danny Murtaugh, Phi	.18	1976	Davey Lopes, LA	.63
1908	Honus Wagner, Pit	.53	1942	Pete Reiser, Bklyn	.20	1977	Frank Taveras, Pit	.70
1909	Bob Bescher, Cin	.54	1943	Arky Vaughan, Bklyn	.20	1978	Omar Moreno, Pit	.71
1910	Bob Bescher, Cin	.70	1944	Johnny Barrett, Pit	.28	1979	Omar Moreno, Pit	.77
1911	Bob Bescher, Cin	.81	1945	Red Schoendienst, St.L	.26	1980	Ron LeFlore, Mon	.97
1912	Bob Bescher, Cin	.67	1946	Pete Reiser, Bklyn	.34	1981	Tim Raines, Mon	.71
1913	Max Carey, Pit	.61	1947	Jackie Robinson, Bklyn	.29	1982	Tim Raines, Mon	.78
1914	George Burns, NY	.62	1948	Richie Ashburn, Phi	.32	1983	Tim Raines, Mon	.90
1915	Max Carey, Pit	.36	1949	Jackie Robinson, Bklyn	.37	1984	Tim Raines, Mon	.75
1916	Max Carey, Pit	.63	1950	Sam Jethroe, Bos	.35	1985	Vince Coleman, St.L	.110
1917	Max Carey, Pit	.46	1951	Sam Jethroe, Bos	.35	1986	Vince Coleman, St.L	.107
1918	Max Carey, Pit	.58	1952	Pee Wee Reese, Bklyn	.30	1987	Vince Coleman, St.L	.109
1919	George Burns, NY	.40	1953	Bill Bruton, Mil	.26	1988	Vince Coleman, St.L	.81
1920	Max Carey, Pit	.52	1954	Bill Bruton, Mil	.34	1989	Vince Coleman, St.L	.65
1921	Frankie Frisch, NY	.49	1955	Bill Bruton, Mil	.25	1990	Vince Coleman, St.L	.77
1922	Max Carey, Pit	.51	1956	Willie Mays, NY	.40	1991	Marquis Grissom, Mon	.76
1923	Max Carey, Pit	.51	1957	Willie Mays, NY	.38	1992	Marquis Grissom, Mon	.78
1924	Max Carey, Pit	.49	1958	Willie Mays, SF	.31	1993	Chuck Carr, Fla	.58
1925	Max Carey, Pit	.46	1959	Willie Mays, SF	.27	1994	Craig Biggio, Hou	.39
1926	Kiki Cuyler, Pit	.35	1960	Maury Wills, LA	.50	1995	Quilvio Veras, Fla	.56
1927	Frankie Frisch, St.L	.48	1961	Maury Wills, LA	.35	1996	Eric Young, Col	.53
1928	Kiki Cuyler, Chi	.37	1962	Maury Wills, LA	.104	1997	Tony Womack, Pit	.60
1929	Kiki Cuyler, Chi	.43	1963	Maury Wills, LA	.40			
1930	Kiki Cuyler, Chi	.37	1964	Maury Wills, LA	.53			
1931	Frankie Frisch, St.L	.28	1965	Maury Wills, LA	.94			

30 Homers & 30 Stolen Bases in One Season
National League

	Year	Gm	HR	SB		Year	Gm	HR	SB
Willie Mays, NY Giants	1956	152	36	40	Barry Bonds, San Francisco	1996	158	42	40
Willie Mays, NY Giants	1957	152	35	38	Ellis Burks, Colorado	1996	156	40	32
Hank Aaron, Milwaukee	1963	161	44	31	Dante Bichette, Colorado	1996	159	31	31
Bobby Bonds, San Francisco	1969	158	32	45	Larry Walker, Colorado	1997	153	49	33
Bobby Bonds, San Francisco	1973	160	39	43	Barry Bonds, San Francisco	1997	159	40	37
Dale Murphy, Atlanta	1983	162	36	30	Raul Mondesi, Los Angeles	1997	159	30	32
Eric Davis, Cincinnati	1987	129	37	50	Jeff Bagwell, Houston	1997	162	43	31
Howard Johnson, NY Mets	1987	157	36	32					
Darryl Strawberry, NY Mets	1987	154	39	36					
Howard Johnson, NY Mets	1989	153	36	41	**American League**				
Ron Gant, Atlanta	1990	152	32	33		Year	Gm	HR	SB
Barry Bonds, Pittsburgh	1990	151	33	52	Kenny Williams, St. Louis	1922	153	39	37
Ron Gant, Atlanta	1991	154	32	34	Tommy Harper, Milwaukee	1970	154	31	38
Howard Johnson, NY Mets	1991	156	38	30	Bobby Bonds, New York	1975	145	32	30
Barry Bonds, Pittsburgh	1992	140	34	39	Bobby Bonds, California	1977	158	37	41
Sammy Sosa, Chicago	1993	159	33	36	Bobby Bonds, Chicago-Texas	1978	156	31	43
Barry Bonds, San Francisco	1995	144	33	31	Joe Carter, Cleveland	1987	149	32	31
Sammy Sosa, Chicago	1995	144	36	34	Jose Canseco, Oakland	1988	158	42	40

American League

Multiple winners: Rickey Henderson (11); Luis Aparicio (9); Bert Campaneris, George Case and Ty Cobb (6); Kenny Lofton (5); Ben Chapman, Eddie Collins and George Sisler (4); Bob Dillinger, Minnie Minoso and Bill Werber (3); Elmer Flick, Tommy Harper, Clyde Milan, Johnny Mostil, Bill North and Snuffy Stirnweiss (2).

Year		SB	Year		SB	Year		SB
1901	Frank Isbell, Chi	52	1933	Ben Chapman, NY	27	1965	Bert Campaneris, KC	51
1902	Topsy Hartsel, Phi	47	1934	Bill Werber, Bos	40	1966	Bert Campaneris, KC	52
1903	Harry Bay, Cle	45	1935	Bill Werber, Bos	29	1967	Bert Campaneris, KC	55
1904	Elmer Flick, Cle	42	1936	Lyn Lary, St.L	37	1968	Bert Campaneris, Oak	62
1905	Danny Hoffman, Phi	46	1937	Ben Chapman, Wash-Bos	35	1969	Tommy Harper, Sea	73
1906	John Anderson, Wash	39		& Bill Werber, Phi	35	1970	Bert Campaneris, Oak	42
	& Elmer Flick, Cle	39	1938	Frank Crosetti, NY	27	1971	Amos Otis, KC	52
1907	Ty Cobb, Det	49	1939	George Case, Wash	51	1972	Bert Campaneris, Oak	52
1908	Patsy Dougherty, Chi	47	1940	George Case, Wash	35	1973	Tommy Harper, Bos	54
1909	Ty Cobb, Det	76	1941	George Case, Wash	33	1974	Bill North, Oak	54
1910	Eddie Collins, Phi	81	1942	George Case, Wash	44	1975	Mickey Rivers, CA	70
1911	Ty Cobb, Det	83	1943	George Case, Wash	61	1976	Bill North, Oak	75
1912	Clyde Milan, Wash	88	1944	Snuffy Stirnweiss, NY	55	1977	Freddie Patek, KC	53
1913	Clyde Milan, Wash	75	1945	Snuffy Stirnweiss, NY	33	1978	Ron LeFlore, Det	68
1914	Fritz Maisel, NY	74	1946	George Case, Cle	28	1979	Willie Wilson, KC	83
1915	Ty Cobb, Det	96	1947	Bob Dillinger, St.L	34	1980	Rickey Henderson, Oak	100
1916	Ty Cobb, Det	68	1948	Bob Dillinger, St.L	28	1981	Rickey Henderson, Oak	56
1917	Ty Cobb, Det	55	1949	Bob Dillinger, St.L	20	1982	Rickey Henderson, Oak	130
1918	George Sisler, St.L	45	1950	Dom DiMaggio, Bos	15	1983	Rickey Henderson, Oak	108
1919	Eddie Collins, Chi	33	1951	Minnie Minoso, Cle-Chi	31	1984	Rickey Henderson, Oak	66
1920	Sam Rice, Wash	63	1952	Minnie Minoso, Chi	22	1985	Rickey Henderson, NY	80
1921	George Sisler, St.L	35	1953	Minnie Minoso, Chi	25	1986	Rickey Henderson, NY	87
1922	George Sisler, St.L	51	1954	Jackie Jensen, Bos	22	1987	Harold Reynolds, Sea	60
1923	Eddie Collins, Chi	47	1955	Jim Rivera, Chi	25	1988	Rickey Henderson, NY	93
1924	Eddie Collins, Chi	42	1956	Luis Aparicio, Chi	21	1989	R. Henderson, NY-Oak	77
1925	Johnny Mostil, Chi	43	1957	Luis Aparicio, Chi	28	1990	Rickey Henderson, Oak	65
1926	Johnny Mostil, Chi	35	1958	Luis Aparicio, Chi	29	1991	Rickey Henderson, Oak	58
1927	George Sisler, St.L	27	1959	Luis Aparicio, Chi	56	1992	Kenny Lofton, Cle	66
1928	Buddy Myer, Bos	30	1960	Luis Aparicio, Chi	51	1993	Kenny Lofton, Cle	70
1929	Charlie Gehringer, Det	28	1961	Luis Aparicio, Chi	53	1994	Kenny Lofton, Cle	60
1930	Marty McManus, Det	23	1962	Luis Aparicio, Chi	31	1995	Kenny Lofton, Cle	54
1931	Ben Chapman, NY	61	1963	Luis Aparicio, Bal	40	1996	Kenny Lofton, Cle	75
1932	Ben Chapman, NY	38	1964	Luis Aparicio, Bal	57	1997	Brian Hunter, Det	74

Consecutive Game Streaks

Regular season games through 1997.

Games Played

Active streak in **bold** type.

Gm		Dates of Streak
2478	**Cal Ripken Jr.,** Bal	5/30/82 to —
2130	Lou Gehrig, NY	6/1/25 to 4/30/39
1307	Everett Scott, Bos-NY	6/20/16 to 5/5/25
1207	Steve Garvey, LA-SD	9/3/75 to 7/29/83
1117	Billy Williams, Cubs	9/22/63 to 9/2/70
1103	Joe Sewell, Cle	9/13/22 to 4/30/30
895	Stan Musial, St.L	4/15/52 to 8/23/57
829	Eddie Yost, Wash	4/30/49 to 5/11/55
822	Gus Suhr, Pit	9/11/31 to 6/4/37
798	Nellie Fox, Chisox	8/8/55 to 9/3/60
745	Pete Rose, Cin-Phi	9/2/78 to 8/23/83
740	Dale Murphy, Atl	9/26/81 to 7/8/86
730	Richie Ashburn, Phi	6/7/50 to 4/13/55
717	Ernie Banks, Cubs	8/28/56 to 6/22/61
678	Pete Rose, Cin	9/28/73 to 5/7/78

Others

Gm		Gm	
673	Earl Averill	565	Aaron Ward
652	Frank McCormick	540	Candy LaChance
648	Sandy Alomar Sr.	535	Buck Freeman
618	Eddie Brown	533	Fred Luderus
585	Roy McMillan	511	Clyde Milan
577	George Pinckney	511	Charlie Gehringer
574	Steve Brodie	508	Vada Pinson

Hitting

		Gm	Year
Joe DiMaggio, New York (AL)		56	1941
Willie Keeler, Baltimore (NL)		44	1897
Pete Rose, Cincinnati (NL)		44	1978
Bill Dahlen, Chicago (NL)		42	1894
George Sisler, St. Louis (AL)		41	1922
Ty Cobb, Detroit (AL)		40	1911
Paul Molitor, Milwaukee (AL)		39	1987
Tommy Holmes, Boston (NL)		37	1945
Billy Hamilton, Philadelphia (NL)		36	1894
Fred Clarke, Louisville (NL)		35	1895
Ty Cobb, Detroit (AL)		35	1917
Ty Cobb, Detroit (AL)		34	1912
George Sisler, St. Louis (AL)		34	1925
George McQuinn, St. Louis (AL)		34	1938
Dom DiMaggio, Boston (AL)		34	1949
Benito Santiago, San Diego (NL)		34	1987
George Davis, New York (NL)		33	1893
Hal Chase, New York (AL)		33	1907
Rogers Hornsby, St. Louis (NL)		33	1922
Heinie Manush, Washington (AL)		33	1933
Ed Delahanty, Philadelphia (NL)		31	1899
Nap Lajoie, Cleveland (AL)		31	1906
Sam Rice, Washington, (AL)		31	1924
Willie Davis, Los Angeles (NL)		31	1969
Rico Carty, Atlanta (NL)		31	1970
Ken Landreaux, Minnesota (AL)		31	1980

Annual Pitching Leaders (since 1900)

Winning Percentage
At least 15 wins, except in strike years of 1981 and 1994 (when the minimum was 10).

National League
Multiple winners: Ed Reulbach and Tom Seaver (3); Larry Benton, Harry Brecheen, Jack Chesbro, Paul Derringer, Freddie Fitzsimmons, Don Gullett, Claude Hendrix, Carl Hubbell, Sandy Koufax, Bill Lee, Greg Maddux, Christy Mathewson, Don Newcombe and Preacher Roe (2).

Year		W-L	Pct	Year		W-L	Pct
1900	Jesse Tannehill, Pittsburgh	20-6	.769	1950	Sal Maglie, New York	18-4	.818
1901	Jack Chesbro, Pittsburgh	21-10	.677	1951	Preacher Roe, Brooklyn	22-3	.880
1902	Jack Chesbro, Pittsburgh	28-6	.824	1952	Hoyt Wilhelm, New York	15-3	.833
1903	Sam Leever, Pittsburgh	25-7	.781	1953	Carl Erskine, Brooklyn	20-6	.769
1904	Joe McGinnity, New York	35-8	.814	1954	Johnny Antonelli, New York	21-7	.750
1905	Christy Mathewson, New York	31-8	.795	1955	Don Newcombe, Brooklyn	20-5	.800
1906	Ed Reulbach, Chicago	19-4	.826	1956	Don Newcombe, Brooklyn	27-7	.794
1907	Ed Reulbach, Chicago	17-4	.810	1957	Bob Buhl, Milwaukee	18-7	.720
1908	Ed Reulbach, Chicago	24-7	.774	1958	Warren Spahn, Milwaukee	22-11	.667
1909	Howie Camnitz, Pittsburgh	25-6	.806		& Lew Burdette, Milwaukee	20-10	.667
	& Christy Mathewson, New York	25-6	.806	1959	Roy Face, Pittsburgh	18-1	.947
1910	King Cole, Chicago	20-4	.833	1960	Ernie Broglio, St. Louis	21-9	.700
1911	Rube Marquard, New York	24-7	.774	1961	Johnny Podres, Los Angeles	18-5	.783
1912	Claude Hendrix, Pittsburgh	24-9	.727	1962	Bob Purkey, Cincinnati	23-5	.821
1913	Bert Humphries, Chicago	16-4	.800	1963	Ron Perranoski, Los Angeles	16-3	.842
1914	Bill James, Boston	26-7	.788	1964	Sandy Koufax, Los Angeles	19-5	.792
1915	Grover Alexander, Phila.	31-10	.756	1965	Sandy Koufax, Los Angeles	26-8	.765
1916	Tom Hughes, Boston	16-3	.842	1966	Juan Marichal, San Francisco	25-6	.806
1917	Ferdie Schupp, New York	21-7	.750	1967	Dick Hughes, St. Louis	16-6	.727
1918	Claude Hendrix, Chicago	19-7	.731	1968	Steve Blass, Pittsburgh	18-6	.750
1919	Dutch Ruether, Cincinnati	19-6	.760	1969	Tom Seaver, New York	25-7	.781
1920	Burleigh Grimes, Brooklyn	23-11	.676	1970	Bob Gibson, St. Louis	23-7	.767
1921	Bill Doak, St. Louis	15-6	.714	1971	Don Gullett, Cincinnati	16-6	.727
1922	Pete Donohue, Cincinnati	18-9	.667	1972	Gary Nolan, Cincinnati	15-5	.750
1923	Dolf Luque, Cincinnati	27-8	.771	1973	Tommy John, Los Angeles	16-7	.696
1924	Emil Yde, Pittsburgh	16-3	.842	1974	Andy Messersmith, Los Angeles	20-6	.769
1925	Bill Sherdel, St. Louis	15-6	.714	1975	Don Gullett, Cincinnati	15-4	.789
1926	Ray Kremer, Pittsburgh	20-6	.769	1976	Steve Carlton, Philadelphia	20-7	.741
1927	Larry Benton, Boston-NY	17-7	.708	1977	John Candelaria, Pittsburgh	20-5	.800
1928	Larry Benton, New York	25-9	.735	1978	Gaylord Perry, San Diego	21-6	.778
1929	Charlie Root, Chicago	19-6	.760	1979	Tom Seaver, Cincinnati	16-6	.727
1930	Freddie Fitzsimmons, NY	19-7	.731	1980	Jim Bibby, Pittsburgh	19-6	.760
1931	Paul Derringer, St. Louis	18-8	.692	1981	Tom Seaver, Cincinnati	14-2	.875
1932	Lon Warneke, Chicago	22-6	.786	1982	Phil Niekro, Atlanta	17-4	.810
1933	Ben Cantwell, Boston	20-10	.667	1983	John Denny, Philadelphia	19-6	.760
1934	Dizzy Dean, St. Louis	30-7	.811	1984	Rick Sutcliffe, Chicago	16-1	.941
1935	Bill Lee, Chicago	20-6	.769	1985	Orel Hershiser, Los Angeles	19-3	.864
1936	Carl Hubbell, New York	26-6	.813	1986	Bob Ojeda, New York	18-5	.783
1937	Carl Hubbell, New York	22-8	.733	1987	Dwight Gooden, New York	15-7	.682
1938	Bill Lee, Chicago	22-9	.710	1988	David Cone, New York	20-3	.870
1939	Paul Derringer, Cincinnati	25-7	.781	1989	Mike Bielecki, Chicago	18-7	.720
1940	Freddie Fitzsimmons, Bklyn	16-2	.889	1990	Doug Drabek, Pittsburgh	22-6	.786
1941	Elmer Riddle, Cincinnati	19-4	.826	1991	John Smiley, Pittsburgh	20-8	.714
1942	Larry French, Brooklyn	15-4	.789		& Jose Rijo, Cincinnati	15-6	.714
1943	Mort Cooper, St. Louis	21-8	.724	1992	Bob Tewksbury, St. Louis	16-5	.762
1944	Ted Wilks, St. Louis	17-4	.810	1993	Mark Portugal, Houston	18-4	.818
1945	Harry Brecheen, St. Louis	14-4	.778	1994	Marvin Freeman, Colorado	10-2	.833
1946	Murray Dickson, St. Louis	15-6	.714	1995	Greg Maddux, Atlanta	19-2	.905
1947	Larry Jansen, New York	21-5	.808	1996	John Smoltz, Atlanta	24-8	.750
1948	Harry Brecheen, St. Louis	20-7	.741	1997	Greg Maddux, Atlanta	19-4	.826
1949	Preacher Roe, Brooklyn	15-6	.714				

Note: In 1984, Sutcliffe was also 4-5 with Cleveland for a combined AL-NL record of 20-6 (.769).

American League

Multiple winners: Lefty Grove (5); Chief Bender and Whitey Ford (3); Johnny Allen, Eddie Cicotte, Roger Clemens, Mike Cuellar, Lefty Gomez, Catfish Hunter, Randy Johnson, Walter Johnson, Jim Palmer, Pete Vuckovich and Smokey Joe Wood (2).

Year		W-L	Pct	Year		W-L	Pct
1901	Clark Griffith, Chicago	24-7	.774	1904	Jack Chesbro, New York	41-12	.774
1902	Bill Bernhard, Phila-Cleve	18-5	.783	1905	Andy Coakley, Philadelphia	20-7	.741
1903	Cy Young, Boston	28-9	.757	1906	Eddie Plank, Philadelphia	19-6	.760

Year		W-L	Pct	Year		W-L	Pct
1907	Wild Bill Donovan, Detroit	25-4	.862	1954	Sandy Consuegra, Chicago	16-3	.842
1908	Ed Walsh, Chicago	40-15	.727	1955	Tommy Byrne, New York	16-5	.762
1909	George Mullin, Detroit	29-8	.784	1956	Whitey Ford, New York	19-6	.760
1910	Chief Bender, Philadelphia	23-5	.821	1957	Dick Donovan, Chicago	16-6	.727
1911	Chief Bender, Philadelphia	17-5	.773		& Tom Sturdivant, New York	16-6	.727
1912	Smokey Joe Wood, Boston	34-5	.872	1958	Bob Turley, New York	21-7	.750
1913	Walter Johnson, Washington	36-7	.837	1959	Bob Shaw, Chicago	18-6	.750
1914	Chief Bender, Philadelphia	17-3	.850	1960	Jim Perry, Cleveland	18-10	.643
1915	Smokey Joe Wood, Boston	15-5	.750	1961	Whitey Ford, New York	25-4	.862
1916	Eddie Cicotte, Chicago	15-7	.682	1962	Ray Herbert, Chicago	20-9	.690
1917	Reb Russell, Chicago	15-5	.750	1963	Whitey Ford, New York	24-7	.774
1918	Sad Sam Jones, Boston	16-5	.762	1964	Wally Bunker, Baltimore	19-5	.792
1919	Eddie Cicotte, Chicago	29-7	.806	1965	Mudcat Grant, Minnesota	21-7	.750
1920	Jim Bagby, Cleveland	31-12	.721	1966	Sonny Siebert, Cleveland	16-8	.667
1921	Carl Mays, New York	27-9	.750	1967	Joe Horlen, Chicago	19-7	.731
1922	Joe Bush, New York	26-7	.788	1968	Denny McLain, Detroit	31-6	.838
1923	Herb Pennock, New York	19-6	.760	1969	Jim Palmer, Baltimore	16-4	.800
1924	Walter Johnson, Washington	23-7	.767	1970	Mike Cuellar, Baltimore	24-8	.750
1925	Stan Coveleski, Washington	20-5	.800	1971	Dave McNally, Baltimore	21-5	.808
1926	George Uhle, Cleveland	27-11	.711	1972	Catfish Hunter, Oakland	21-7	.750
1927	Waite Hoyt, New York	22-7	.759	1973	Catfish Hunter, Oakland	21-5	.808
1928	General Crowder, St. Louis	21-5	.808	1974	Mike Cuellar, Baltimore	22-10	.688
1929	Lefty Grove, Philadelphia	20-6	.769	1975	Mike Torrez, Baltimore	20-9	.690
1930	Lefty Grove, Philadelphia	28-5	.848	1976	Bill Campbell, Minnesota	17-5	.773
1931	Lefty Grove, Philadelphia	31-4	.886	1977	Paul Splittorff, Kansas City	16-6	.727
1932	Johnny Allen, New York	17-4	.810	1978	Ron Guidry, New York	25-3	.893
1933	Lefty Grove, Philadelphia	24-8	.750	1979	Mike Caldwell, Milwaukee	16-6	.727
1934	Lefty Gomez, New York	26-5	.839	1980	Steve Stone, Baltimore	25-7	.781
1935	Eldon Auker, Detroit	18-7	.720	1981	Pete Vuckovich, Milwaukee	14-4	.778
1936	Monte Pearson, New York	19-7	.731	1982	Pete Vuckovich, Milwaukee	18-6	.750
1937	Johnny Allen, Cleveland	15-1	.938		& Jim Palmer, Baltimore	15-5	.750
1938	Red Ruffing, New York	21-7	.750	1983	Rich Dotson, Chicago	22-7	.759
1939	Lefty Grove, Boston	15-4	.789	1984	Doyle Alexander, Toronto	17-6	.739
1940	Schoolboy Rowe, Detroit	16-3	.842	1985	Ron Guidry, New York	22-6	.786
1941	Lefty Gomez, New York	15-5	.750	1986	Roger Clemens, Boston	24-4	.857
1942	Ernie Bonham, New York	21-5	.808	1987	Roger Clemens, Boston	20-9	.690
1943	Spud Chandler, New York	20-4	.833	1988	Frank Viola, Minnesota	24-7	.774
1944	Tex Hughson, Boston	18-5	.783	1989	Bret Saberhagen, Kansas City	23-6	.793
1945	Hal Newhouser, Detroit	25-9	.735	1990	Bob Welch, Oakland	27-6	.818
1946	Boo Ferriss, Boston	25-6	.806	1991	Scott Erickson, Minnesota	20-8	.714
1947	Allie Reynolds, New York	19-8	.704	1992	Mike Mussina, Baltimore	18-5	.783
1948	Jack Kramer, Boston	18-5	.783	1993	Jimmy Key, New York	18-6	.750
1949	Ellis Kinder, Boston	23-6	.793	1994	Jason Bere, Chicago	12-2	.857
1950	Vic Raschi, New York	21-8	.724	1995	Randy Johnson, Seattle	18-2	.900
1951	Bob Feller, Cleveland	22-8	.733	1996	Charles Nagy, Cleveland	17-5	.773
1952	Bobby Shantz, Philadelphia	24-7	.774	1997	Randy Johnson, Seattle	20-4	.833
1953	Ed Lopat, New York	16-4	.800				

Earned Run Average

Earned Run Averages were based on at least 10 complete games pitched (1900-50), at least 154 innings pitched (1950-60), and at least 162 innings pitched since 1961 in the AL and 1962 in the NL. In the strike year of 1981, '94 and '95 qualifiers had to pitch at least as many innings as the total number of games their team played that season.

National League

Multiple winners: Grover Alexander, Sandy Koufax and Christy Mathewson (5); Carl Hubbell, Greg Maddux, Tom Seaver, Warren Spahn and Dazzy Vance (3); Bill Doak, Ray Kremer, Dolf Luque, Howie Pollet, Nolan Ryan, Bill Walker and Bucky Walters (2).

Year		ERA	Year		ERA	Year		ERA
1900	Rube Waddell, Pit	2.37	1911	Christy Mathewson, NY	1.99	1922	Rosy Ryan, NY	3.01
1901	Jesse Tannehill, Pit	2.18	1912	Jeff Tesreau, NY	1.96	1923	Dolf Luque, Cin	1.93
1902	Jack Taylor, Chi	1.33	1913	Christy Mathewson, NY	2.06	1924	Dazzy Vance, Bklyn	2.16
1903	Sam Leever, Pit	2.06	1914	Bill Doak, St.L	1.72	1925	Dolf Luque, Cin	2.63
1904	Joe McGinnity, NY	1.61	1915	Grover Alexander, Phi	1.22	1926	Ray Kremer, Pit	2.61
1905	Christy Mathewson, NY	1.27	1916	Grover Alexander, Phi	1.55	1927	Ray Kremer, Pit	2.47
1906	Three Finger Brown, Chi	1.04	1917	Grover Alexander, Phi	1.86	1928	Dazzy Vance, Bklyn	2.09
1907	Jack Pfiester, Chi	1.15	1918	Hippo Vaughn, Chi	1.74	1929	Bill Walker, NY	3.09
1908	Christy Mathewson, NY	1.43	1919	Grover Alexander, Chi	1.72	1930	Dazzy Vance, Bklyn	2.61
1909	Christy Mathewson, NY	1.14	1920	Grover Alexander, Chi	1.91	1931	Bill Walker, NY	2.26
1910	George McQuillan, Phi	1.60	1921	Bill Doak, St.L	2.59	1932	Lon Warneke, Chi	2.37

Earned Run Average (Cont.)

Year		ERA	Year		ERA	Year		ERA
1933	Carl Hubbell, NY	1.66	1955	Bob Friend, Pit	2.83	1977	John Candelaria, Pit	2.34
1934	Carl Hubbell, NY	2.30	1956	Lew Burdette, Mil	2.70	1978	Craig Swan, NY	2.43
1935	Cy Blanton, Pit	2.58	1957	Johnny Podres, Bklyn	2.66	1979	J.R. Richard, Hou	2.71
1936	Carl Hubbell, NY	2.31	1958	Stu Miller, SF	2.47			
1937	Jim Turner, Bos	2.38	1959	Sam Jones, SF	2.83	1980	Don Sutton, LA	2.21
1938	Bill Lee, Chi	2.66				1981	Nolan Ryan, Hou	1.69
1939	Bucky Walters, Cin	2.29	1960	Mike McCormick, SF	2.70	1982	Steve Rogers, Mon	2.40
			1961	Warren Spahn, Mil	3.02	1983	Atlee Hammaker, SF	2.25
1940	Bucky Walters, Cin	2.48	1962	Sandy Koufax, LA	2.54	1984	Alejandro Peña, LA	2.48
1941	Elmer Riddle, Cin	2.24	1963	Sandy Koufax, LA	1.88	1985	Dwight Gooden, NY	1.53
1942	Mort Cooper, St.L	1.78	1964	Sandy Koufax, LA	1.74	1986	Mike Scott, Hou	2.22
1943	Howie Pollet, St.L	1.75	1965	Sandy Koufax, LA	2.04	1987	Nolan Ryan, Hou	2.76
1944	Ed Heusser, Cin	2.38	1966	Sandy Koufax, LA	1.73	1988	Joe Magrane, St.L	2.18
1945	Hank Borowy, Chi	2.13	1967	Phil Niekro, Atl	1.87	1989	Scott Garrelts, SF	2.28
1946	Howie Pollet, St.L	2.10	1968	Bob Gibson, St.L	1.12			
1947	Warren Spahn, Bos	2.33	1969	Juan Marichal, SF	2.10	1990	Danny Darwin, Hou	2.21
1948	Harry Brecheen, St.L	2.24				1991	Dennis Martinez, Mon	2.39
1949	Dave Koslo, NY	2.50	1970	Tom Seaver, NY	2.81	1992	Bill Swift, SF	2.08
			1971	Tom Seaver, NY	1.76	1993	Greg Maddux, Atl	2.36
1950	Jim Hearn, St.L-NY	2.49	1972	Steve Carlton, Phi	1.97	1994	Greg Maddux, Atl	1.56
1951	Chet Nichols, Bos	2.88	1973	Tom Seaver, NY	2.08	1995	Greg Maddux, Atl	1.63
1952	Hoyt Wilhelm, NY	2.43	1974	Buzz Capra, Atl	2.28	1996	Kevin Brown, Fla	1.89
1953	Warren Spahn, Mil	2.10	1975	Randy Jones, SD	2.24	1997	Pedro Martinez, Mon	1.90
1954	Johnny Antonelli, NY	2.30	1976	John Denny, St.L	2.52			

Note: In 1945, Borowy had a 3.13 ERA in 18 games with New York (AL) for a combined ERA of 2.65.

American League

Multiple winners: Lefty Grove (9); Roger Clemens and Walter Johnson (5); Spud Chandler, Stan Coveleski, Red Faber, Whitey Ford, Lefty Gomez, Ron Guidry, Addie Joss, Hal Newhouser, Jim Palmer, Gary Peters, Luis Tiant and Ed Walsh (2).

Year		ERA	Year		ERA	Year		ERA
1901	Cy Young, Bos	1.62	1934	Lefty Gomez, NY	2.33	1967	Joe Horlen, Chi	2.06
1902	Ed Siever, Det	1.91	1935	Lefty Grove, Bos	2.70	1968	Luis Tiant, Cle	1.60
1903	Earl Moore, Cle	1.77	1936	Lefty Grove, Bos	2.81	1969	Dick Bosman, Wash	2.19
1904	Addie Joss, Cle	1.59	1937	Lefty Gomez, NY	2.33			
1905	Rube Waddell, Phi	1.48	1938	Lefty Grove, Bos	3.08	1970	Diego Segui, Oak	2.56
1906	Doc White, Chi	1.52	1939	Lefty Grove, Bos	2.54	1971	Vida Blue, Oak	1.82
1907	Ed Walsh, Chi	1.60				1972	Luis Tiant, Bos	1.91
1908	Addie Joss, Cle	1.16	1940	Bob Feller, Cle	2.61	1973	Jim Palmer, Bal	2.40
1909	Harry Krause, Phi	1.39	1941	Thornton Lee, Chi	2.37	1974	Catfish Hunter, Oak	2.49
			1942	Ted Lyons, Chi	2.10	1975	Jim Palmer, Bal	2.09
1910	Ed Walsh, Chi	1.27	1943	Spud Chandler, NY	1.64	1976	Mark Fidrych, Det	2.34
1911	Vean Gregg, Cle	1.81	1944	Dizzy Trout, Det	2.12	1977	Frank Tanana, Cal	2.54
1912	Walter Johnson, Wash	1.39	1945	Hal Newhouser, Det	1.81	1978	Ron Guidry, NY	1.74
1913	Walter Johnson, Wash	1.09	1946	Hal Newhouser, Det	1.94	1979	Ron Guidry, NY	2.78
1914	Dutch Leonard, Bos	1.01	1947	Spud Chandler, NY	2.46			
1915	Smokey Joe Wood, Bos	1.49	1948	Gene Bearden, Cle	2.43	1980	Rudy May, NY	2.47
1916	Babe Ruth, Bos	1.75	1949	Mel Parnell, Bos	2.77	1981	Steve McCatty, Oak	2.32
1917	Eddie Cicotte, Chi	1.53				1982	Rick Sutcliffe, Cle	2.96
1918	Walter Johnson, Wash	1.27	1950	Early Wynn, Cle	3.20	1983	Rick Honeycutt, Tex	2.42
1919	Walter Johnson, Wash	1.49	1951	Saul Rogovin, Det-Chi	2.78	1984	Mike Boddicker, Bal	2.79
			1952	Allie Reynolds, NY	2.06	1985	Dave Stieb, Tor	2.48
1920	Bob Shawkey, NY	2.45	1953	Ed Lopat, NY	2.42	1986	Roger Clemens, Bos	2.48
1921	Red Faber, Chi	2.48	1954	Mike Garcia, Cle	2.64	1987	Jimmy Key, Tor	2.76
1922	Red Faber, Chi	2.80	1955	Billy Pierce, Chi	1.97	1988	Allan Anderson, Min	2.45
1923	Stan Coveleski, Cle	2.76	1956	Whitey Ford, NY	2.47	1989	Bret Saberhagen, KC	2.16
1924	Walter Johnson, Wash	2.72	1957	Bobby Shantz, NY	2.45			
1925	Stan Coveleski, Wash	2.84	1958	Whitey Ford, NY	2.01	1990	Roger Clemens, Bos	1.93
1926	Lefty Grove, Phi	2.51	1959	Hoyt Wilhelm, Bal	2.19	1991	Roger Clemens, Bos	2.62
1927	Wiley Moore, NY	2.28				1992	Roger Clemens, Bos	2.41
1928	Garland Braxton, Wash	2.51	1960	Frank Baumann, Chi	2.67	1993	Kevin Appier, KC	2.56
1929	Lefty Grove, Phi	2.81	1961	Dick Donovan, Wash	2.40	1994	Steve Ontiveros, Oak	2.65
			1962	Hank Aguirre, Det	2.21	1995	Randy Johnson, Sea	2.48
1930	Lefty Grove, Phi	2.54	1963	Gary Peters, Chi	2.33	1996	Juan Guzman, Tor	2.93
1931	Lefty Grove, Phi	2.06	1964	Dean Chance, LA	1.65	1997	Roger Clemens, Tor	2.05
1932	Lefty Grove, Phi	2.84	1965	Sam McDowell, Cle	2.18			
1933	Monte Pearson, Cle	2.33	1966	Gary Peters, Chi	1.98			

Note: In 1940, Ernie Bonham of NY had a 1.90 ERA and 10 complete games, but appeared in only a total of 12 games and 99 innings.

Strikeouts
National League

Multiple winners: Dazzy Vance (7); Grover Alexander (6); Steve Carlton, Christy Mathewson and Tom Seaver (5); Dizzy Dean, Sandy Koufax and Warren Spahn (4); Don Drysdale, Sam Jones and Johnny Vander Meer (3); David Cone, Dwight Gooden, Bill Hallahan, J.R. Richard, Robin Roberts, Nolan Ryan, John Smoltz and Hippo Vaughn (2).

Year		SO	Year		SO	Year		SO
1900	Rube Waddell, Pit	.130	1934	Dizzy Dean, St.L	.195	1966	Sandy Koufax, LA	.317
1901	Noodles Hahn, Cin	.239	1935	Dizzy Dean, St.L	.190	1967	Jim Bunning, Phi	.253
1902	Vic Willis, Bos	.225	1936	Van Lingle Mungo, Bklyn	.238	1968	Bob Gibson, St.L	.268
1903	Christy Mathewson, NY	.267	1937	Carl Hubbell, NY	.159	1969	Ferguson Jenkins, Chi	.273
1904	Christy Mathewson, NY	.212	1938	Clay Bryant, Chi	.135			
1905	Christy Mathewson, NY	.206	1939	Claude Passeau, Phi-Chi	.137	1970	Tom Seaver, NY	.283
1906	Fred Beebe, Chi-St.L	.171		& Bucky Walters, Cin	.137	1971	Tom Seaver, NY	.289
1907	Christy Mathewson, NY	.178				1972	Steve Carlton, Phi	.310
1908	Christy Mathewson, NY	.259	1940	Kirby Higbe, Phi	.137	1973	Tom Seaver, NY	.251
1909	Orval Overall, Chi	.205	1941	John Vander Meer, Cin	.202	1974	Steve Carlton, Phi	.240
			1942	John Vander Meer, Cin	.186	1975	Tom Seaver, NY	.243
1910	Earl Moore, Phi	.185	1943	John Vander Meer, Cin	.174	1976	Tom Seaver, NY	.235
1911	Rube Marquard, NY	.237	1944	Bill Voiselle, NY	.161	1977	Phil Niekro, Atl	.262
1912	Grover Alexander, Phi	.195	1945	Preacher Roe, Pit	.148	1978	J.R. Richard, Hou	.303
1913	Tom Seaton, Phi	.168	1946	Johnny Schmitz, Chi	.135	1979	J.R. Richard, Hou	.313
1914	Grover Alexander, Phi	.214	1947	Ewell Blackwell, Cin	.193			
1915	Grover Alexander, Phi	.241	1948	Harry Brecheen, St.L	.149	1980	Steve Carlton, Phi	.286
1916	Grover Alexander, Phi	.167	1949	Warren Spahn, Bos	.151	1981	F. Valenzuela, LA	.180
1917	Grover Alexander, Phi	.201				1982	Steve Carlton, Phi	.286
1918	Hippo Vaughn, Chi	.148	1950	Warren Spahn, Bos	.191	1983	Steve Carlton, Phi	.275
1919	Hippo Vaughn, Chi	.141	1951	Don Newcombe, Bklyn	.164	1984	Dwight Gooden, NY	.276
				& Warren Spahn, Bos	.164	1985	Dwight Gooden, NY	.268
1920	Grover Alexander, Chi	.173	1952	Warren Spahn, Bos	.183	1986	Mike Scott, Hou	.306
1921	Burleigh Grimes, Bklyn	.136	1953	Robin Roberts, Phi	.198	1987	Nolan Ryan, Hou	.270
1922	Dazzy Vance, Bklyn	.134	1954	Robin Roberts, Phi	.185	1988	Nolan Ryan, Hou	.228
1923	Dazzy Vance, Bklyn	.197	1955	Sam Jones, Chi	.198	1989	Jose DeLeon, St.L	.201
1924	Dazzy Vance, Bklyn	.262	1956	Sam Jones, Chi	.176			
1925	Dazzy Vance, Bklyn	.221	1957	Jack Sanford, Phi	.188	1990	David Cone, NY	.233
1926	Dazzy Vance, Bklyn	.140	1958	Sam Jones, St.L	.225	1991	David Cone, NY	.241
1927	Dazzy Vance, Bklyn	.184	1959	Don Drysdale, LA	.242	1992	John Smoltz, Atl.	.215
1928	Dazzy Vance, Bklyn	.200				1993	Jose Rijo, Cin	.227
1929	Pat Malone, Chi	.166	1960	Don Drysdale, LA	.246	1994	Andy Benes, SD	.189
			1961	Sandy Koufax, LA	.269	1995	Hideo Nomo, LA	.236
1930	Bill Hallahan, St.L	.177	1962	Don Drysdale, LA	.232	1996	John Smoltz, Atl	.276
1931	Bill Hallahan, St.L	.159	1963	Sandy Koufax, LA	.306	1997	Curt Schilling, Phi	.319
1932	Dizzy Dean, St.L	.191	1964	Bob Veale, Pit	.250			
1933	Dizzy Dean, St.L	.199	1965	Sandy Koufax, LA	.382			

American League

Multiple winners: Walter Johnson (12); Nolan Ryan (9); Bob Feller and Lefty Grove (7); Rube Waddell (6); Sam McDowell (5); Roger Clemens and Randy Johnson (4); Lefty Gomez, Mark Langston and Camilo Pascual (3); Len Barker, Tommy Bridges, Jim Bunning, Hal Newhouser, Allie Reynolds, Herb Score, Ed Walsh and Early Wynn (2).

Year		SO	Year		SO	Year		SO
1901	Cy Young, Bos	.158	1923	Walter Johnson, Wash	.130	1944	Hal Newhouser, Det	.187
1902	Rube Waddell, Phi	.210	1924	Walter Johnson, Wash	.158	1945	Hal Newhouser, Det	.212
1903	Rube Waddell, Phi	.302	1925	Lefty Grove, Phi	.116	1946	Bob Feller, Cle	.348
1904	Rube Waddell, Phi	.349	1926	Lefty Grove, Phi	.194	1947	Bob Feller, Cle	.196
1905	Rube Waddell, Phi	.287	1927	Lefty Grove, Phi	.174	1948	Bob Feller, Cle	.164
1906	Rube Waddell, Phi	.196	1928	Lefty Grove, Phi	.183	1949	Virgil Trucks, Det	.153
1907	Rube Waddell, Phi	.232	1929	Lefty Grove, Phi	.170			
1908	Ed Walsh, Chi	.269				1950	Bob Lemon, Cle	.170
1909	Frank Smith, Chi	.177	1930	Lefty Grove, Phi	.209	1951	Vic Raschi, NY	.164
			1931	Lefty Grove, Phi	.175	1952	Allie Reynolds, NY	.160
1910	Walter Johnson, Wash	.313	1932	Red Ruffing, NY	.190	1953	Billy Pierce, Chi	.186
1911	Ed Walsh, Chi	.255	1933	Lefty Gomez, NY	.163	1954	Bob Turley, Bal	.185
1912	Walter Johnson, Wash	.303	1934	Lefty Gomez, NY	.158	1955	Herb Score, Cle	.245
1913	Walter Johnson, Wash	.243	1935	Tommy Bridges, Det	.163	1956	Herb Score, Cle	.263
1914	Walter Johnson, Wash	.225	1936	Tommy Bridges, Det	.175	1957	Early Wynn, Cle	.184
1915	Walter Johnson, Wash	.203	1937	Lefty Gomez, NY	.194	1958	Early Wynn, Chi	.179
1916	Walter Johnson, Wash	.228	1938	Bob Feller, Cle	.240	1959	Jim Bunning, Det	.201
1917	Walter Johnson, Wash	.188	1939	Bob Feller, Cle	.246			
1918	Walter Johnson, Wash	.162	1940	Bob Feller, Cle	.261	1960	Jim Bunning, Det	.201
1919	Walter Johnson, Wash	.147	1941	Bob Feller, Cle	.260	1961	Camilo Pascual, Min	.221
			1942	Tex Hughson, Bos	.113	1962	Camilo Pascual, Min	.206
1920	Stan Coveleski, Cle	.133		& Bobo Newsom, Wash	.113	1963	Camilo Pascual, Min	.202
1921	Walter Johnson, Wash	.143	1943	Allie Reynolds, Cle	.151	1964	Al Downing, NY	.217
1922	Urban Shocker, St.L	.149				1965	Sam McDowell, Cle	.325

Strikeouts (Cont.)

Year		SO	Year		SO	Year		SO
1966	Sam McDowell, Cle	225	1978	Nolan Ryan, Cal	260	1990	Nolan Ryan, Tex	232
1967	Jim Lonborg, Bos	246	1979	Nolan Ryan, Cal	223	1991	Roger Clemens, Bos	241
1968	Sam McDowell, Cle	283	1980	Len Barker, Cle	187	1992	Randy Johnson, Sea	241
1969	Sam McDowell, Cle	279	1981	Len Barker, Cle	127	1993	Randy Johnson, Sea	308
1970	Sam McDowell, Cle	304	1982	Floyd Bannister, Sea	209	1994	Randy Johnson, Sea	204
1971	Mickey Lolich, Det	308	1983	Jack Morris, Det	232	1995	Randy Johnson, Sea	294
1972	Nolan Ryan, Cal	329	1984	Mark Langston, Sea	204	1996	Roger Clemens, Bos	257
1973	Nolan Ryan, Cal	383	1985	Bert Blyleven, Cle-Min	206	1997	Roger Clemens, Tor	292
1974	Nolan Ryan, Cal	367	1986	Mark Langston, Sea	245			
1975	Frank Tanana, Cal	269	1987	Mark Langston, Sea	262			
1976	Nolan Ryan, Cal	327	1988	Roger Clemens, Bos	291			
1977	Nolan Ryan, Cal	341	1989	Nolan Ryan, Tex	301			

Pitching Triple Crown Winners

Pitchers who led either league in Earned Run Average, Wins and Strikeouts over a single season.

National League

	Year	ERA	W-L	SO
Tommy Bond, Bos	1877	2.11	40-17	170
Hoss Radbourne, Prov	1884	1.38	60-12	441
Tim Keefe, NY	1888	1.74	35-12	333
John Clarkson, Bos	1889	2.73	49-19	284
Amos Rusie, NY	1894	2.78	36-13	195
Christy Mathewson, NY	1905	1.27	31-8	206
Christy Mathewson, NY	1908	1.43	37-11	259
Grover Alexander, Phi	1915	1.22	31-10	241
Grover Alexander, Phi	1916	1.55	33-12	167
Grover Alexander, Phi	1917	1.86	30-13	201
Hippo Vaughn, Chi	1918	1.74	22-10	148
Grover Alexander, Chi	1920	1.91	27-14	173
Dazzy Vance, Bklyn	1924	2.16	28-6	262
Bucky Walters, Cin	1939	2.29	27-11	137
Sandy Koufax, LA	1963	1.88	25-5	306
Sandy Koufax, LA	1965	2.04	26-8	382
Sandy Koufax, LA	1966	1.73	27-9	317
Steve Carlton, Phi	1972	1.97	27-10	310
Dwight Gooden, NY	1985	1.53	24-4	268

Ties: In 1894, Rusie tied for league lead in wins with Jouett Meekin, NY (36-10); in 1939, Walters tied for league lead in strikeouts with Claude Passeau, Phi-Chi; in 1963, Koufax tied for the league lead in wins with Juan Marichal, SF.

American League

	Year	ERA	W-L	SO
Cy Young, Bos	1901	1.62	33-10	158
Rube Waddell, Phi	1905	1.48	26-11	287
Walter Johnson, Wash	1913	1.09	36-7	243
Walter Johnson, Wash	1918	1.27	23-13	162
Walter Johnson, Wash	1924	2.72	23-7	158
Lefty Grove, Phi	1930	2.54	28-5	209
Lefty Grove, Phi	1931	2.06	31-4	175
Lefty Gomez, NY	1934	2.33	26-5	158
Lefty Gomez, NY	1937	2.33	21-11	194
Hal Newhouser, Det	1945	1.81	25-9	212
Roger Clemens, Tor	1997	2.05	21-7	292

Perfect Games

Sixteen pitchers have thrown perfect games (27 up, 27 down) in major league history. However, the games pitched by Harvey Haddix and Ernie Shore are not considered to be official.

National League

	Game	Date	Score
Lee Richmond	Wor. vs Cle.	6/12/1880	1-0
Monte Ward	Prov. vs Bos.	6/17/1880	5-0
Harvey Haddix	Pit. at Mil.	5/26/1959	0-1*
Jim Bunning	Phi. at NY	6/21/1964	6-0
Sandy Koufax	LA vs Chi.	9/9/1965	1-0
Tom Browning	Cin. vs LA	9/16/1988	1-0
Dennis Martinez	Mon. at LA	7/28/1991	2-0

*Haddix pitched 12 perfect innings before losing in the 13th. Braves' lead-off batter Felix Mantilla reached on a throwing error by Pirates 3B Don Hoak, Eddie Mathews sacrificed Mantilla to 2nd, Hank Aaron was walked intentionally, and Joe Adcock hit a 3-run HR. Adcock, however, passed Aaron on the bases and was only credited with a 1-run double.

American League

	Game	Date	Score
Cy Young	Bos. vs Phi.	5/5/1904	3-0
Addie Joss	Cle. vs Chi.	10/2/1908	1-0
Ernie Shore	Bos. vs Wash.	6/23/1917	4-0*
Charlie Robertson	Chi. at Det.	4/30/1922	2-0
Catfish Hunter	Oak. vs Min.	5/8/1968	4-0
Len Barker	Cle. vs Tor.	5/15/1981	3-0
Mike Witt	Cal. at Tex.	9/30/1984	1-0
Kenny Rogers	Tex. vs Cal.	6/28/1994	4-0

*Babe Ruth started for Boston, walking Senators' lead-off batter Ray Morgan, then was thrown out of game by umpire Brick Owens for arguing the call: Shore came on in relief. Morgan was caught stealing and Shore retired the next 26 batters in a row. While technically not a perfect game—since he didn't start—Shore gets credit anyway.

World Series

Pitcher	Game	Date	Score
Don Larsen	NY vs Bklyn	10/8/1956	2-0

No-Hit Games

Nine innings or more, including perfect games, since 1876. Losing pitchers in **bold** type.

National League

Multiple no-hitters: Nolan Ryan (7); Sandy Koufax (4); Larry Cocoran, Bob Feller and Cy Young (3); Jim Bunning, Steve Busby, Carl Erskine, Bob Forsch, Pud Galvin, Ken Holtzman, Addie Joss, Hub Leonard, Jim Maloney, Christy Mathewson, Allie Reynolds, Warren Spahn, Bill Stoneham, Virgil Trucks and Johnny Vander Meer (2).

Year	Date	Pitcher	Result	Year	Date	Pitcher	Result
1876	7/15	George Bradley	St.L vs Har, 2-0	1956	5/12	Carl Erskine	Bklyn vs NY, 3-0
1880	6/12	Lee Richmond	Wor vs Cle,1-0 (perfect game)		9/25	Sal Maglie	Bklyn vs Phi, 5-0
	6/17	Monte Ward	Prov vs Buf, 5-0 (perfect game)	1960	5/15	Don Cardwell	Chi vs St.L, 4-0
					8/18	Lew Burdette	Mil vs Phi, 1-0
	8/19	Larry Corcoran	Chi vs Bos, 6-0		9/16	Warren Spahn	Mil vs Phi, 4-0
	8/20	Pud Galvin	Buf at Wor, 1-0	1961	4/28	Warren Spahn	Mil vs SF, 1-0
1882	9/20	Larry Corcoran	Chi vs Wor, 1-0	1962	6/30	Sandy Koufax	LA vs NY, 5-0
1883	7/25	Old Hoss Radbourne	Prov at Cle, 8-0	1963	5/11	Sandy Koufax	LA vs SF, 1-0
	9/13	Hugh Daily	Cle at Phi, 1-0		5/17	Don Nottebart	Hou vs Phi, 4-1
1884	6/27	Larry Cocoran	Chi vs Prov, 6-0		6/15	Juan Marichal	SF vs Hou, 1-0
	8/4	Pud Galvin	Buf at Det, 18-0	1964	4/23	**Ken Johnson**	Hou vs Cin, 0-1
1885	7/27	John Clarkson	Chi vs Prov, 6-0		6/4	Sandy Koufax	LA at Phi, 3-0
	8/29	Charlie Ferguson	Phi vs Prov, 1-0		6/21	Jim Bunning	Phi at NY, 6-0 (perfect game)
1891	6/22	Tom Lovett	Bklyn vs NY, 4-0	1965	8/19	Jim Maloney	Cin at Chi, 1-0 (10)
	7/31	Amos Rusie	NY vs Bklyn, 11-0		9/9	Sandy Koufax	LA vs Chi, 1-0 (perfect game)
1892	8/6	John Stivetts	Bos vs Bklyn, 11-0				
	8/22	Ben Sanders	Lou vs Bal, 6-2	1967	6/18	Don Wilson	Hou vs Atl, 2-0
	10/22	Bumpus Jones	Cin vs Pit, 7-1 (1st major league game)	1968	4/27	George Culver	Cin at Phi, 6-1
					9/17	Gaylord Perry	SF vs St.L, 1-0
1893	8/16	Bill Hawke	Bal vs Wash, 5-0		9/18	Ray Washburn	St.L at SF, 2-0 (next day, same park)
1897	9/18	Cy Young	Cle vs Cin, 6-0				
1898	4/22	Ted Breitenstein	Cin vs Pit, 11-0	1969	4/17	Bill Stoneman	Mon at Phi, 7-0
	4/22	Jim Hughes	Bal vs Bos, 8-0		4/30	Jim Maloney	Cin vs Hou, 10-0
	7/8	Frank Donahue	Phi vs Bos, 5-0		5/1	Don Wilson	Hou at Cin, 4-0
	8/21	Walter Thornton	Chi vs Bklyn, 2-0		8/19	Ken Holtzman	Chi vs Atl, 3-0
1899	5/25	Deacon Phillippe	Lou vs NY, 7-0		9/20	Bob Moose	Pit at NY, 4-0
1900	7/12	Noodles Hahn	Cin vs Phi, 4-0	1970	6/12	Dock Ellis	Pit at SD, 2-0
1901	7/15	Christy Mathewson	NY vs St.L, 5-0		7/20	Bill Singer	LA vs Phi, 5-0
1903	9/18	Chick Fraser	Phi at Chi, 10-0	1971	6/3	Ken Holtzman	Chi at Cin, 1-0
1905	6/13	Christy Mathewson	NY at Chi, 1-0		6/23	Rick Wise	Phi at Cin, 4-0
1906	5/1	John Lush	Phi at Bklyn, 1-0		8/14	Bob Gibson	St.L at Pit, 11-0
	7/20	Mal Eason	Bklyn at St.L, 2-0	1972	4/16	Burt Hooton	Chi vs Phi, 4-0
1907	5/8	Frank Pfeffer	Bos vs Cin, 6-0		9/2	Milt Pappas	Chi vs SD, 8-0
	9/20	Nick Maddox	Pit vs Bkn, 2-1		10/2	Bill Stoneman	Mon vs NY, 7-0
1908	7/4	Hooks Wiltse	NY vs Phi, 1-0 (10)	1973	8/5	Phil Niekro	Atl vs SD, 9-0
	9/5	Nap Rucker	Bklyn vs Bos, 6-0	1975	8/24	Ed Halicki	SF vs NY, 6-0
1912	9/6	Jeff Tesreau	NY at Phi, 3-0	1976	7/9	Larry Dierker	Hou vs Mon, 6-0
1914	9/9	George Davis	Bos vs Phi, 7-0		8/9	John Candelaria	Pit vs LA, 2-0
1915	4/15	Rube Marquard	NY vs Bklyn, 2-0		9/29	John Montefusco	SF vs Atl, 9-0
	8/31	Jimmy Lavender	Chi at N.Y, 2-0	1978	4/16	Bob Forsch	St.L vs Phi, 5-0
1916	6/16	Tom Hughes	Bos vs. Pit, 2-0		6/16	Tom Seaver	Cin vs St.L, 4-0
1917	5/2	Fred Toney	Cin at Chi, 1-0 (10)	1979	4/7	Ken Forsch	Hou vs Atl, 6-0
1919	5/11	Hod Eller	Cin at St.L, 6-0	1980	6/27	Jerry Reuss	LA at SF, 4-0
1922	5/7	Jesse Barnes	NY vs Phi, 6-0	1981	5/10	Charlie Lea	Mon vs SF, 4-0
1924	7/17	Jesse Haines	St.L vs Bos, 5-0		9/26	Nolan Ryan	Hou vs LA, 5-0
1925	9/17	Dazzy Vance	Bklyn vs Phi, 10-1	1983	9/26	Bob Forsch	St.L vs Mon, 3-0
1929	5/8	Carl Hubbell	NY vs Pit, 2-0	1986	9/25	Mike Scott	Hou vs SF, 2-0
1934	9/21	Paul Dean	St.L vs Bklyn, 3-0	1988	9/16	Tom Browning	Cin vs LA, 1-0 (perfect game)
1938	6/11	Johnny Vander Meer	Cin vs Bos, 3-0				
	6/15	Johnny Vander Meer	Cin at Bklyn, 6-0 (consecutive starts)	1990	6/29	Fernando Valenzuela	LA vs St.L, 6-0
					8/15	Terry Mulholland	Phi vs SF, 6-0
1940	4/30	Tex Carleton	Bklyn at Cin, 3-0	1991	5/23	Tommy Greene	Phi at Mon, 2-0
1941	8/30	Lon Warneke	St.L at Cin, 2-0		7/28	Dennis Martinez	Mon at LA, 2-0 (perfect game)
1944	4/27	Jim Tobin	Bos vs Bklyn, 2-0				
	5/15	Clyde Shoun	Cin vs Bos, 1-0		9/11	Kent Mercker (6), Mark Wohlers (2) & Alejandro Peña (1)	Atl vs SD, 1-0 (combined no-hitter)
1946	4/23	Ed Head	Bklyn at NY, 2-0				
1947	6/18	Ewell Blackwell	Cin vs Bos, 6-0				
1948	9/9	Rex Barney	Bklyn at NY, 2-0	1992	8/17	Kevin Gross	LA vs SF, 2-0
1950	8/11	Vern Bickford	Bos vs Bklyn, 7-0	1993	9/8	Darryl Kile	Hou vs NY, 7-1
1951	5/6	Cliff Chambers	Pit at Bos, 3-0	1994	4/8	Kent Mercker	Atl at LA, 6-0
1952	6/19	Carl Erskine	Bklyn vs Chi, 5-0	1995	7/14	Ramon Martinez	LA vs Fla, 7-0
1954	6/12	Jim Wilson	Mil vs Phi, 2-0	1996	5/11	Al Leiter	Fla vs Col, 11-0
1955	5/12	Sam Jones	Chi vs Pit, 4-0		9/17	Hideo Nomo	LA at Col, 9-0

No-Hit Games (Cont.)

Year	Date	Pitcher	Result	Year	Date	Pitcher	Result
1997	6/10	Kevin Brown	Fla at SF, 9-0		7/12	Francisco Cordova (9)	Pit vs. Hou, 3-0 (10 inn.)
						Ricardo Rincon (1)	(combined no-hitter)

American League

Year	Date	Pitcher	Result	Year	Date	Pitcher	Result
1902	9/20	Jimmy Callahan	Chi vs Det, 3-0		6/26	Earl Wilson	Bos vs LA, 2-0
1904	5/5	Cy Young	Bos vs Phi, 3-0		8/1	Bill Monbouquette	Bos at Chi, 1-0
			(perfect game)		8/26	Jack Kralick	Min vs KC, 1-0
	8/17	Jesse Tannehill	Bos vs Chi, 6-0	1965	9/16	Dave Morehead	Bos vs Cle, 2-0
1905	7/22	Weldon Henley	Phi at St. L, 6-0	1966	6/10	Sonny Siebert	Cle vs Wash, 2-0
	9/6	Frank Smith	Chi at Det, 15-0	1967	4/30	**Steve Barber** (8⅔)	Bal vs Det, 1-2
	9/27	Bill Dinneen	Bos vs Chi, 2-0			**& Stu Miller** (⅓)	(combined no-hitter)
1908	6/30	Cy Young	Bos at NY, 8-0		8/25	Dean Chance	Min at Cle, 2-1
	9/18	Dusty Rhoades	Cle vs Bos, 2-0		9/10	Joel Horlen	Chi vs Det, 6-0
	9/20	Frank Smith	Chi vs Phi, 1-0	1968	4/27	Tom Phoebus	Bal vs Bos, 6-0
	10/2	Addie Joss	Cle vs Chi, 1-0		5/8	Catfish Hunter	Oak vs Min, 4-0
			(perfect game)				(perfect game)
1910	4/20	Addie Joss	Cle at Chi, 1-0	1969	8/13	Jim Palmer	Bal vs Oak, 8-0
	5/12	Chief Bender	Phi vs Cle, 4-0	1970	7/3	Clyde Wright	Cal vs Oak, 4-0
1911	7/19	Smokey Joe Wood	Bos vs St. L, 5-0		9/21	Vida Blue	Oak vs Min, 6-0
	8/27	Ed Walsh	Chi vs Bos, 5-0	1973	4/27	Steve Busby	KC at Det, 3-0
1912	7/4	George Mullin	Det vs St. L, 7-0		5/15	Nolan Ryan	Cal at KC, 3-0
	8/30	Earl Hamilton	St. L at Det, 5-1		7/15	Nolan Ryan	Cal at Det, 6-0
1914	5/31	Joe Benz	Chi vs Cle, 6-1		7/30	Jim Bibby	Tex at Oak, 6-0
1916	6/16	Rube Foster	Bos vs NY, 2-0	1974	6/19	Steve Busby	KC at Mil, 2-0
	8/26	Joe Bush	Phi vs Cle, 5-0		7/19	Dick Bosman	Cle at Oak, 4-0
	8/30	Hub Leonard	Bos vs St. L, 4-0		9/28	Nolan Ryan	Cal at Min, 4-0
1917	4/14	Ed Cicotte	Chi at St. L, 11-0	1975	6/1	Nolan Ryan	Cal vs Bal, 1-0
	4/24	George Mogridge	NY at Bos, 2-1		9/28	Vida Blue (5),	Oak vs Cal, 5-0
	5/5	Ernie Koob	St. L vs Chi, 1-0			Glenn Abbott (1),	(combined no-hitter)
	5/6	Bob Groom	St. L vs Chi, 3-0			Paul Lindblad (1),	
	6/23	Babe Ruth (0)	Bos vs Wash, 4-0			& Rollie Fingers (2)	
		& Ernie Shore (9)	(combined no-hitter)	1976	7/28	John Odom (5) &	Chi at Oak, 2-1
1918	6/3	Hub Leonard	Bos at Det, 5-0			Francisco Barrios (4)	(combined no-hitter)
1919	9/10	Ray Caldwell	Cle at NY, 3-0	1977	5/14	Jim Colborn	KC vs Tex, 6-0
1920	7/1	Walter Johnson	Wash at Bos, 1-0		5/30	Dennis Eckersley	Cle vs Cal, 1-0
1922	4/30	Charlie Robertson	Chi at Det, 2-0		9/22	Bert Blyleven	Tex at Cal, 6-0
			(perfect game)	1981	5/15	Len Barker	Cle vs Tor, 3-0
1923	9/4	Sam Jones	NY at Phi, 2-0				(perfect game)
	9/7	Howard Ehmke	Bos at Phi, 4-0	1983	7/4	Dave Righetti	NY vs Bos, 4-0
1926	8/21	Ted Lyons	Chi at Bos, 6-0		9/29	Mike Warren	Oak vs Chi, 3-0
1931	4/29	Wes Ferrell	Cle vs St. L, 9-0	1984	4/7	Jack Morris	Det at Chi, 4-0
	8/8	Bob Burke	Wash vs Bos, 5-0		9/30	Mike Witt	Cal at Tex, 1-0
1935	8/31	Vern Kennedy	Chi vs Cle, 5-0				(perfect game)
1937	6/1	Bill Dietrich	Chi vs St. L, 8-0	1986	9/19	Joe Cowley	Chi at Cal, 7-1
1938	8/27	Monte Pearson	NY vs Cle, 13-0	1987	4/15	Juan Nieves	Mil at Bal, 7-0
1940	4/16	Bob Feller	Cle at Chi, 1-0	1990	6/2	Mark Langston (7)	Cal vs Sea, 1-0
			(Opening Day)			& Mike Witt (2)	(combined no-hitter)
1945	9/9	Dick Fowler	Phi vs St. L, 1-0		6/2	Randy Johnson	Sea vs Det, 2-0
1946	4/30	Bob Feller	Cle vs NY, 1-0		6/11	Nolan Ryan	Tex at Oak, 5-0
1947	7/10	Don Black	Cle vs Phi, 3-0		6/29	Dave Stewart	Oak at Tor, 5-0
	9/3	Bill McCahan	Phi vs Wash, 3-0		9/2	Dave Stieb	Tor at Cle, 3-0
1948	6/30	Bob Lemon	Cle at Det, 2-0	1991	5/1	Nolan Ryan	Tex vs Tor, 3-0
1951	7/1	Bob Feller	Cle vs Det, 2-1		7/13	Bob Milacki (6),	Bal at Oak, 2-0
	7/12	Allie Reynolds	NY vs Cle, 1-0			Mike Flanagan (1),	(combined no-hitter)
	9/28	Allie Reynolds	NY vs Bos, 8-0			Mark Williamson (1)	
1952	5/15	Virgil Trucks	Det vs Wash, 1-0			& Gregg Olson (1)	
	8/25	Virgil Trucks	Det at NY, 1-0		8/11	Wilson Alvarez	Chi at Bal, 7-0
1953	5/6	Bobo Holloman	St. L vs Phi, 6-0		8/26	Bret Saberhagen	KC vs Chi, 7-0
			(first major league start)	1993	4/22	Chris Bosio	Sea vs Bos, 7-0
1956	7/14	Mel Parnell	Bos vs Chi, 4-0		9/4	Jim Abbott	NY vs Cle, 4-0
	10/8	Don Larsen	NY vs Bklyn, 2-0	1994	4/27	Scott Erickson	Min vs Mil, 6-0
			(perfect W. Series game)		7/28	Kenny Rogers	Tex vs Cal, 4-0
1957	8/20	Bob Keegan	Chi vs Wash, 1-0				(perfect game)
1958	7/20	Jim Bunning	Det at Bos, 3-0	1996	5/14	Dwight Gooden	NY vs Sea, 2-0
	9/2	Hoyt Wilhelm	Bal vs NY, 1-0				
1962	5/5	Bo Belinsky	LA vs Bal, 2-0				

All-Time Major League Leaders

Based on statistics compiled by *The Baseball Encyclopedia* (9th ed.); through 1997 regular season.

CAREER

Players active in 1997 in **bold** type.

Batting

Note that (*) indicates left-handed hitter and (†) indicates switch-hitter.

Batting Average

		Yrs	AB	H	Avg
1	Ty Cobb*	24	11,429	4191	.367
2	Rogers Hornsby	23	8,137	2930	.358
3	Joe Jackson*	13	4,981	1774	.356
4	Ed Delahanty	16	7,509	2597	.346
5	Tris Speaker*	22	10,197	3514	.345
6	Ted Williams*	19	7,706	2654	.344
7	Billy Hamilton*	14	6,284	2163	.344
8	Willie Keeler*	19	8,585	2947	.343
9	Dan Brouthers*	19	6,711	2296	.342
10	Babe Ruth*	22	8,399	2873	.342
11	Harry Heilmann	17	7,787	2660	.342
12	Pete Browning	13	4,820	1646	.341
13	Bill Terry*	14	6,428	2193	.341
14	George Sisler*	15	8,267	2812	.340
15	Lou Gehrig*	17	8,001	2721	.340
16	**Tony Gwynn***	16	8,187	2780	.340
17	Jesse Burkett*	16	8,413	2853	.339
18	Nap Lajoie	21	9,592	3244	.338
19	Riggs Stephenson	14	4,508	1515	.336
20	Al Simmons	20	8,761	2927	.334
21	Paul Waner*	20	9,459	3152	.333
22	Eddie Collins*	25	9,951	3313	.333
23	**Wade Boggs***	16	8,453	2800	.331
24	Stan Musial*	22	10,972	3630	.331
25	Sam Thompson*	14	6,005	1986	.331

Hits

		Yrs	AB	H	Avg
1	Pete Rose†	24	14,053	**4256**	.303
2	Ty Cobb*	24	11,429	**4191**	.367
3	Hank Aaron	23	12,364	**3771**	.305
4	Stan Musial*	22	10,972	**3630**	.331
5	Tris Speaker*	22	10,197	**3514**	.345
6	Carl Yastrzemski*	23	11,988	**3419**	.285
7	Honus Wagner	21	10,443	**3418**	.327
8	Eddie Collins*	25	9,951	**3313**	.333
9	Willie Mays	22	10,881	**3283**	.302
10	**Eddie Murray†**	21	11,336	**3255**	.287
11	Nap Lajoie	21	9,592	**3244**	.338
12	**Paul Molitor**	20	10,333	**3178**	.308
13	George Brett*	21	10,349	**3154**	.305
14	Paul Waner*	20	9,459	**3152**	.333
15	Robin Yount	20	11,008	**3142**	.285
16	Dave Winfield	22	11,003	**3110**	.283
17	Rod Carew*	19	9,315	**3053**	.328
18	Lou Brock*	19	10,332	**3023**	.293
19	Al Kaline	22	10,116	**3007**	.297
20	Cap Anson	22	9,108	**3000**	.329
	Roberto Clemente	18	9,454	**3000**	.317
22	Sam Rice*	20	9,269	**2987**	.322
23	Sam Crawford*	19	9,580	**2964**	.309
24	Willie Keeler*	19	8,585	**2947**	.343
25	Frank Robinson	21	10,006	**2943**	.294

Players Active in 1997

		Yrs	AB	H	Avg
1	Tony Gwynn*	16	8,187	2780	.340
2	Mike Piazza	6	2,558	854	.334
3	Wade Boggs*	16	8,453	2800	.331
4	Frank Thomas	8	3,821	1261	.330
5	Edgar Martinez	11	3,818	1210	.317
6	Kenny Lofton*	7	3,314	1047	.316
7	Mark Grace*	10	5,458	1691	.310
8	Paul Molitor	20	10,333	3178	.308
9	Hal Morris*	10	3,255	994	.305
10	Jeff Bagwell	7	3,657	1112	.304
11	Chuck Knoblauch	7	3,939	1197	.304
12	Roberto Alomar†	10	5,460	1659	.304
13	Ken Griffey Jr.*	9	4,593	1389	.302

Players Active in 1997

		Yrs	AB	H	Avg
1	Eddie Murray†	21	11,336	**3255**	.287
2	Paul Molitor	20	10,333	**3178**	.308
3	Wade Boggs*	16	8,453	**2800**	.331
4	Tony Gwynn*	16	8,187	**2780**	.340
5	Cal Ripken Jr.	17	9,832	**2715**	.276
6	Harold Baines*	18	8,818	**2561**	.290
7	Rickey Henderson	19	8,846	**2550**	.288
8	Tim Raines+	19	8,238	**2439**	.296
9	Ryne Sandberg	16	8,385	**2386**	.285
10	Brett Butler*	17	8,180	**2375**	.290
11	Chili Davis†	17	8,094	**2222**	.275
12	Julio Franco	15	7,243	**2177**	.300
13	Willie McGee†	16	7109	**2118**	.298

Games Played

1	Pete Rose	3562
2	Carl Yastrzemski	3308
3	Hank Aaron	3298
4	Ty Cobb	3034
5	Stan Musial	3026
	Eddie Murray	3026
7	Willie Mays	2992
8	Dave Winfield	2973
9	Rusty Staub	2951
10	Brooks Robinson	2896
11	Robin Yount	2856
12	Al Kaline	2834
13	Eddie Collins	2826
14	Reggie Jackson	2820
15	Frank Robinson	2808
16	Tris Speaker	2789
	Honus Wagner	2789
18	Tony Perez	2777
19	Mel Ott	2734
20	George Brett	2707

At Bats

1	Pete Rose	14,053
2	Hank Aaron	12,364
3	Carl Yastrzemski	11,988
4	Ty Cobb	11,429
5	**Eddie Murray**	11,336
6	Robin Yount	11,008
7	Dave Winfield	11,003
8	Stan Musial	10,972
9	Willie Mays	10,881
10	Brooks Robinson	10,654
11	Honus Wagner	10,441
12	George Brett	10,349
13	**Paul Molitor**	10,333
14	Lou Brock	10,332
15	Luis Aparicio	10,230
16	Tris Speaker	10,197
17	Al Kaline	10,116
18	Rabbit Maranville	10,078
19	Frank Robinson	10,006
20	Eddie Collins	9,951

Total Bases

1	Hank Aaron	6856
2	Stan Musial	6134
3	Willie Mays	6066
4	Ty Cobb	5863
5	Babe Ruth	5793
6	Pete Rose	5752
7	Carl Yastrzemski	5539
8	**Eddie Murray**	5397
9	Frank Robinson	5373
10	Dave Winfield	5219
11	Tris Speaker	5103
12	Lou Gehrig	5059
13	George Brett	5044
14	Mel Ott	5041
15	Jimmie Foxx	4956
16	Ted Williams	4884
17	Honus Wagner	4868
18	Al Kaline	4852
19	Reggie Jackson	4834
20	Andre Dawson	4787

All-Time Major League Leaders (Cont.)

Home Runs

		Yrs	AB	HR	AB/HR
1	Hank Aaron	23	12,364	755	16.4
2	Babe Ruth*	22	8,399	714	11.8
3	Willie Mays	22	10,881	660	16.5
4	Frank Robinson	21	10,006	586	17.1
5	Harmon Killebrew	22	8,147	573	14.2
6	Reggie Jackson*	21	9,864	563	17.5
7	Mike Schmidt	18	8,352	548	15.2
8	Mickey Mantle†	18	8,102	536	15.1
9	Jimmie Foxx	20	8,134	534	15.2
10	Ted Williams*	19	7,706	521	14.8
	Willie McCovey*	22	8,197	521	15.7
12	Ed Mathews*	17	8,537	512	16.7
	Ernie Banks	19	9,421	512	18.4
14	Mel Ott*	22	9,456	511	18.5
15	**Eddie Murray†**	21	11,336	504	22.5
16	Lou Gehrig*	17	8,001	493	16.2
17	Willie Stargell*	21	7,927	475	16.7
	Stan Musial*	22	10,972	475	23.1
19	Dave Winfield	22	11,003	465	23.7
20	Carl Yastrzemski*	23	11,988	452	26.5
21	Dave Kingman	16	6,677	442	15.1
22	Andre Dawson	21	9,927	438	22.7
23	Billy Williams*	18	9,350	426	22.0
24	Darrell Evans	21	8,973	414	21.7
25	Duke Snider*	18	7,161	407	17.6

Players Active in 1997

		Yrs	AB	HR	AB/HR
1	Eddie Murray†	21	11,336	504	22.5
2	Mark McGwire	12	4,622	387	11.9
3	Joe Carter	15	8,034	378	21.3
4	Barry Bonds*	12	6,069	374	16.2
5	Cal Ripken Jr.	17	9,832	370	26.6
6	Jose Canseco	13	5,459	351	15.6
7	Harold Baines*	18	8,818	339	26.0
	Fred McGriff*	12	5,693	339	16.8
9	Gary Gaetti	17	8,227	332	24.8
10	Chili Davis†	17	8,094	328	24.7
11	Darryl Strawberry*	15	5,074	308	16.5
12	Cecil Fielder	12	4,741	302	15.7
13	Ken Griffey Jr.	9	4,593	294	15.6
14	Andres Galarraga	13	6,074	288	21.1
15	Ryne Sandberg	16	8,385	282	29.7

Runs Batted In

		Yrs	Gm	RBI	P/G
1	Hank Aaron	23	3298	2297	.70
2	Babe Ruth*	22	2503	2211	.88
3	Lou Gehrig*	17	2164	1990	.92
4	Ty Cobb*	24	3034	1961	.65
5	Stan Musial*	22	3026	1951	.64
6	Jimmie Foxx	20	2317	1921	.83
7	**Eddie Murray†**	21	2980	1917	.64
8	Willie Mays	22	2992	1903	.64
9	Mel Ott*	22	2732	1861	.68
10	Carl Yastrzemski*	23	3308	1844	.56
11	Ted Williams*	19	2292	1839	.80
12	Dave Winfield	22	2973	1833	.62
13	Al Simmons	20	2215	1827	.82
14	Frank Robinson	21	2808	1812	.65
15	Honus Wagner	21	2786	1732	.62
16	Cap Anson	22	2276	1715	.75
17	Reggie Jackson*	21	2820	1702	.60
18	Tony Perez	23	2777	1652	.59
19	Ernie Banks	19	2528	1636	.65
20	Goose Goslin*	18	2287	1609	.70
21	Nap Lajoie	21	2475	1599	.65
22	Mike Schmidt	18	2404	1595	.66
23	George Brett*	21	2707	1595	.59
24	Andre Dawson	21	2627	1591	.61
25	Rogers Hornsby	23	2259	1584	.70
	Harmon Killebrew	22	2435	1584	.65

Players Active in 1997

		Yrs	Gm	RBI	P/G
1	Eddie Murray†	21	2980	1917	.64
2	Cal Ripken Jr.	17	2543	1453	.57
3	Harold Baines*	18	2458	1423	.58
4	Joe Carter	15	2037	1382	.68
5	Chili Davis†	17	2253	1285	.57
6	Paul Molitor	20	2556	1238	.48
7	Gary Gaetti	17	2253	1224	.54
8	Jose Canseco	13	1445	1107	.77
9	Barry Bonds*	12	1742	1094	.63
10	Bobby Bonilla†	12	1746	1061	.61
	Ryne Sanberg	16	2164	1061	.49
12	Andres Galarraga	13	1621	1051	.65
13	Ruben Sierra†	12	1610	1029	.64
14	Fred McGriff*	12	1602	1007	.63
15	Will Clark*	12	1620	1004	.62

Runs

1	Ty Cobb	2245
2	Babe Ruth	2174
	Hank Aaron	2174
4	Pete Rose	2165
5	Willie Mays	2062
6	Stan Musial	1949
7	**Rickey Henderson**	1913
8	Lou Gehrig	1888
9	Tris Speaker	1882
10	Mel Ott	1859
11	Frank Robinson	1829
12	Eddie Collins	1820
13	**Paul Molitor**	1807
14	Carl Yastrzemski	1816
15	Ted Williams	1798
16	Charlie Gehringer	1774
17	Jimmie Foxx	1751
18	Honus Wagner	1735
19	Willie Keeler	1727
20	Cap Anson	1719

Extra Base Hits

1	Hank Aaron	1477
2	Stan Musial	1377
3	Babe Ruth	1356
4	Willie Mays	1323
5	Lou Gehrig	1190
6	Frank Robinson	1186
7	Carl Yastrzemski	1157
8	Ty Cobb	1139
9	Tris Speaker	1132
10	George Brett	1119
11	Ted Williams	1117
	Jimmie Foxx	1117
13	**Eddie Murray**	1099
14	Dave Winfield	1093
15	Reggie Jackson	1075
16	Mel Ott	1071
17	Pete Rose	1041
18	Andre Dawson	1039
19	Mike Schmidt	1015
20	Rogers Hornsby	1011

Slugging Percentage

1	Babe Ruth	.690
2	Ted Williams	.634
3	Lou Gehrig	.632
4	Jimmie Foxx	.609
5	Hank Greenberg	.605
6	Joe DiMaggio	.579
7	Rogers Hornsby	.577
8	Johnny Mize	.562
9	**Ken Griffey Jr.**	.562
10	Stan Musial	.559
11	Willie Mays	.557
12	Mickey Mantle	.557
13	**Mark McGwire**	.556
14	Hank Aaron	.555
15	**Barry Bonds**	.551
16	Ralph Kiner	.548
17	Hack Wilson	.545
18	Chuck Klein	.543
19	Duke Snider	.540
20	Frank Robinson	.537

Stolen Bases

1	**Rickey Henderson**	1231
2	Lou Brock	938
3	Billy Hamilton	915
4	Ty Cobb	892
5	**Tim Raines**	795
6	**Vince Coleman**	752
7	Eddie Collins	743
8	Max Carey	738
9	Honus Wagner	720
10	Joe Morgan	689
11	Arlie Latham	679
12	Willie Wilson	668
13	Bert Campaneris	649
14	Tom Brown	627
15	George Davis	615
16	Dummy Hoy	597
17	Maury Wills	586
18	Hugh Duffy	583
	George Van Haltren	583
20	Ozzie Smith	580

Walks

1	Babe Ruth	2056
2	Ted Williams	2019
3	Joe Morgan	1865
4	Carl Yastrzemski	1845
5	**Rickey Henderson**	1772
6	Mickey Mantle	1734
7	Mel Ott	1708
8	Eddie Yost	1614
9	Darrell Evans	1605
10	Stan Musial	1599
11	Pete Rose	1566
12	Harmon Killebrew	1559
13	Lou Gehrig	1508
14	Mike Schmidt	1507
15	Eddie Collins	1503
16	Willie Mays	1463
17	Jimmie Foxx	1452
18	Eddie Mathews	1444
19	Frank Robinson	1420
20	Hank Aaron	1402

Strikeouts

1	Reggie Jackson	2597
2	Willie Stargell	1936
3	Mike Schmidt	1883
4	Tony Perez	1867
5	Dave Kingman	1816
6	Bobby Bonds	1757
7	Dale Murphy	1748
8	Lou Brock	1730
9	Mickey Mantle	1710
10	Harmon Killebrew	1699
11	Dwight Evans	1697
12	Dave Winfield	1686
13	**Chili Davis**	1580
14	Lee May	1570
15	Dick Allen	1556
16	Willie McCovey	1550
17	Dave Parker	1537
18	Frank Robinson	1532
19	Lance Parrish	1527
20	Willie Mays	1526

Pitching

Note that (*) indicates left-handed pitcher. Active pitcher leaders are listed for wins, strikeouts and saves.

Wins

		Yrs	GS	W	L	Pct
1	Cy Young	22	815	511	316	.618
2	Walter Johnson	21	666	416	279	.599
3	Christy Mathewson	17	551	373	188	.665
	Grover Alexander	20	598	373	208	.642
4	Warren Spahn*	21	665	363	245	.597
6	Kid Nichols	15	561	361	208	.634
	Pud Galvin	14	682	361	308	.540
8	Tim Keefe	14	594	342	225	.603
9	Steve Carlton*	24	709	329	244	.574
10	Eddie Plank*	17	527	327	193	.629
11	John Clarkson	12	518	326	177	.648
12	Don Sutton	23	756	324	256	.559
13	Nolan Ryan	27	773	324	292	.526
14	Phil Niekro	24	716	318	274	.537
15	Gaylord Perry	22	690	314	265	.542
16	Old Hoss Radbourne	12	503	311	194	.616
	Tom Seaver	20	647	311	205	.603
18	Mickey Welch	13	549	308	209	.596
19	Lefty Grove*	17	456	300	141	.680
	Early Wynn	23	612	300	244	.551
21	Tommy John*	26	700	288	231	.555
22	Bert Blyleven	22	685	287	250	.534
23	Robin Roberts	19	609	286	245	.539
24	Tony Mullane	13	505	285	220	.564
25	Ferguson Jenkins	19	594	284	226	.557
26	Jim Kaat*	25	625	283	237	.544
27	Red Ruffing	22	536	273	225	.548
28	Burleigh Grimes	19	495	270	212	.560
29	Jim Palmer	19	521	268	152	.638
30	Bob Feller	18	484	266	162	.621

Strikeouts

		Yrs	IP	SO	P/9
1	Nolan Ryan	27	5387.0	5714	9.54
2	Steve Carlton*	24	5217.1	4136	7.13
3	Bert Blyleven	22	4970.1	3701	6.70
4	Tom Seaver	20	4782.2	3640	6.85
5	Don Sutton	23	5282.1	3574	6.09
6	Gaylord Perry	22	5350.1	3534	5.94
7	Walter Johnson	21	5923.2	3508	5.33
8	Phil Niekro	24	5404.1	3342	5.57
9	Ferguson Jenkins	19	4500.2	3192	6.38
10	Bob Gibson	17	3884.1	3117	7.22
11	**Roger Clemens**	14	3040.0	2882	8.53
12	Jim Bunning	17	3760.1	2855	6.83
13	Mickey Lolich*	16	3638.1	2832	7.01
14	Cy Young	22	7354.2	2796	3.42
15	Frank Tanana*	21	4186.2	2773	5.96
16	Warren Spahn*	21	5243.2	2583	4.43
17	Bob Feller	18	3827.0	2581	6.07
18	Jerry Koosman*	19	3839.1	2556	5.99
19	Tim Keefe	14	5061.1	2527	4.50
20	Christy Mathewson	17	4781.0	2502	4.71
21	Don Drysdale	14	3432.0	2486	6.52
22	Jack Morris	18	3824.2	2478	5.83
23	Jim Kaat*	25	4530.1	2461	4.89
24	Sam McDowell*	15	2492.1	2453	8.86
25	Luis Tiant	19	3486.1	2416	6.24
26	Sandy Koufax*	12	2324.1	2396	9.28
27	**Dennis Eckersley**	23	3246.0	2379	6.60
28	**Mark Langston***	14	2819.2	2365	7.55
29	Charlie Hough	25	3799.1	2363	5.60
30	Robin Roberts	19	4688.2	2357	4.52

Pitchers Active in 1997

		Yrs	GS	W	L	Pct
1	Dennis Martinez	22	556	241	187	.563
2	Roger Clemens	14	416	213	118	.644
3	Dennis Eckersley	23	361	193	170	.532
4	Greg Maddux	12	365	184	108	.630
5	Jimmy Key	14	378	180	114	.612
6	Orel Hershiser	15	394	179	123	.593
7	Dwight Gooden	13	353	177	97	.646
8	Mark Langston*	14	406	174	149	.539
9	Fernando Valenzuela*	17	424	173	153	.531
10	Danny Darwin	20	346	163	172	.487

Pitchers Active in 1997

		Yrs	IP	SO	P/9
1	Roger Clemens	14	3040.0	2882	8.53
2	Dennis Eckersley	23	3246.0	2379	6.60
3	Mark Langston*	14	2819.2	2365	7.55
4	Dennis Martinez	22	3909.1	2087	4.81
5	Fernando Valenzuela*	17	2930.0	2074	6.37
6	Dwight Gooden	13	2446.2	2067	7.60
7	David Cone	12	2139.0	2034	8.56
8	Randy Johnson*	10	1733.2	2000	10.38
9	Danny Darwin	20	2868.2	1861	5.84
10	Greg Maddux	12	2598.1	1820	6.30

All-Time Major League Leaders (Cont.)

Winning Pct.

		Yrs	W-L	Pct
1	Bob Caruthers	9	218-97	.692
2	Dave Foutz	11	147-66	.690
3	Whitey Ford*	16	236-106	.690
4	Lefty Grove*	17	300-141	.680
5	Vic Raschi	10	132-66	.667
6	Christy Mathewson	17	373-188	.665
7	Larry Corcoran	8	177-90	.663
8	Sam Leever	13	194-101	.658
9	Sal Maglie	10	119-62	.657
10	Sandy Koufax*	12	165-87	.655
11	Johnny Allen	13	142-75	.654
12	Ron Guidry*	14	170-91	.651
13	Lefty Gomez*	14	189-102	.649
14	**Dwight Gooden**	13	177-97	.646
15	**Randy Johnson***	10	124-68	.646

Losses

		Yrs	GS	W	L	Pct
1	Cy Young	22	815	511	**316**	.618
2	Pud Galvin	14	682	361	**308**	.540
3	Nolan Ryan	27	773	324	**292**	.526
4	Walter Johnson	21	666	416	**279**	.599
5	Phil Niekro	24	716	318	**274**	.537
6	Gaylord Perry	22	690	314	**265**	.542
7	Jack Powell	16	517	245	**256**	.489
	Don Sutton	23	756	324	**256**	.559
9	Eppa Rixey*	21	552	266	**251**	.515
10	Bert Blyleven	22	685	287	**250**	.534
11	Robin Roberts	19	609	286	**245**	.539
	Warren Spahn*	21	665	363	**245**	.597
13	Early Wynn	23	612	300	**244**	.551
	Steve Carlton*	24	709	329	**244**	.574
15	Jim Kaat*	25	625	283	**237**	.544

Appearances

1	Hoyt Wilhelm	1070
2	Kent Tekulve	1050
3	**Lee Smith**	1022
4	**Dennis Eckersley**	1021
5	Rich Gossage	1002
6	Lindy McDaniel	987
7	**Jesse Orosco**	956
8	Rollie Fingers	944
9	Gene Garber	931
10	Cy Young	906
11	Sparky Lyle	899
12	Jim Kaat	898
13	Jeff Reardon	880
14	Don McMahon	874
15	Phil Niekro	864

Innings Pitched

1	Cy Young	7356.0
2	Pud Galvin	5941.1
3	Walter Johnson	5923.2
4	Phil Niekro	5403.1
5	Nolan Ryan	5387.0
6	Gaylord Perry	5350.1
7	Don Sutton	5280.1
8	Warren Spahn	5243.2
9	Steve Carlton	5217.1
10	Grover Alexander	5189.2
11	Kid Nichols	5084.0
12	Tim Keefe	5061.1
13	Bert Blyleven	4970.1
14	Mickey Welch	4802.0
15	Tom Seaver	4782.2

Earned Run Avg.

1	Ed Walsh	1.82
2	Addie Joss	1.88
3	Three Finger Brown	2.06
4	Monte Ward	2.10
5	Christy Mathewson	2.13
6	Rube Waddell	2.16
7	Walter Johnson	2.17
8	Orval Overall	2.24
9	Tommy Bond	2.25
10	Will White	2.28
11	Ed Reulbach	2.28
12	Jim Scott	2.32
13	Eddie Plank	2.34
14	Larry Corcoran	2.36
15	Eddie Cicotte	2.37

Shutouts

1	Walter Johnson	110
2	Grover Alexander	90
3	Christy Mathewson	80
4	Cy Young	76
5	Eddie Plank	69
6	Warren Spahn	63
7	Nolan Ryan	61
	Tom Seaver	61
9	Bert Blyleven	60
10	Don Sutton	58
11	Three Finger Brown	57
	Pud Galvin	57
	Ed Walsh	57
14	Bob Gibson	56
15	Steve Carlton	55

Walks Allowed

1	Nolan Ryan	2795
2	Steve Carlton	1833
3	Phil Niekro	1809
4	Early Wynn	1775
5	Bob Feller	1764
6	Bobo Newsom	1732
7	Amos Rusie	1704
8	Charlie Hough	1665
9	Gus Weyhing	1566
10	Red Ruffing	1541
11	Bump Hadley	1442
12	Warren Spahn	1434
13	Earl Whitehill	1431
14	Tony Mullane	1409
15	Sad Sam Jones	1396

HRs Allowed

1	Robin Roberts	505
2	Ferguson Jenkins	484
3	Phil Niekro	482
4	Don Sutton	472
5	Frank Tanana	448
6	Warren Spahn	434
7	Bert Blyleven	430
8	Steve Carlton	414
9	Gaylord Perry	399
10	Jim Kaat	395
11	Jack Morris	389
12	Charlie Hough	383
13	Tom Seaver	380
14	Jim Hunter	374
15	Jim Bunning	372

Saves

1	**Lee Smith**	478	11	**Jeff Montgomery**	256
2	**Dennis Eckersley**	389		**Todd Worrell**	256
3	Jeff Reardon	367	13	Dave Righetti	252
4	**John Franco**	359	14	Dan Quisenberry	244
5	Rollie Fingers	341	15	Sparky Lyle	238
6	**Randy Myers**	319	16	**Rick Aguilera**	237
7	Tom Henke	311	17	Hoyt Wilhelm	227
8	Rich Gossage	310	18	Gene Garber	218
9	Bruce Sutter	300	19	Dave Smith	216
10	**Doug Jones**	278	20	**John Wetteland**	211
21	Bobby Thigpen	201			
22	**Rod Beck**	199			
23	Roy Face	193			
	Mike Henneman	193			
25	Mitch Williams	192			
26	Jeff Russell	186			
27	Steve Bedrosian	184			
	Kent Tekulve	184			
29	Tug McGraw	180			
30	Ron Perranoski	179			

SINGLE SEASON
Through 1997 regular season.
Batting

Home Runs

		Year	Gm	AB	HR
1	Roger Maris, NY-AL	1961	162	590	61
2	Babe Ruth, NY-AL	1927	151	540	60
3	Babe Ruth, NY-AL	1921	152	540	59
4	**Mark McGwire**, Oak-St.L	1997	156	540	58
	Hank Greenberg, Det	1938	155	556	58
	Jimmie Foxx, Phi-AL	1932	154	585	58
7	Hack Wilson, Chi-NL	1930	155	585	56
	Ken Griffey Jr., Sea	1997	157	608	56
9	Babe Ruth, NY-AL	1920	142	458	54
	Mickey Mantle, NY-AL	1961	153	514	54
	Babe Ruth, NY-AL	1928	154	536	54
	Ralph Kiner, Pit	1949	152	549	54
13	Mickey Mantle, NY-AL	1956	150	533	52
	Willie Mays, SF	1965	157	558	52
	George Foster, Cin	1977	158	615	52
	Mark McGwire, Oak	1996	130	423	52
17	Ralph Kiner, Pit	1947	152	565	51
	Cecil Fielder, Det	1990	159	573	51
	Willie Mays, NY-NL	1955	152	580	51
	Johnny Mize, NY-NL	1947	154	586	51
21	Jimmie Foxx, Bos-AL	1938	149	565	50
	Albert Belle, Cle	1995	143	546	50
	Brady Anderson, Bal	1996	149	579	50

Hits

		Year	AB	H	Avg
1	George Sisler, StL-AL	1920	631	257	.407
2	Bill Terry, NY-NL	1930	633	254	.401
	Lefty O'Doul, Phi-NL	1929	638	254	.398
4	Al Simmons, Phi-AL	1925	658	253	.384
5	Rogers Hornsby, StL-NL	1922	623	250	.401
6	Chuck Klein, Phi-NL	1930	648	250	.386
7	Ty Cobb, Det	1911	591	248	.420
8	George Sisler, StL-AL	1922	586	246	.420
9	Babe Herman, Bklyn	1930	614	241	.393
	Heinie Manush, StL-AL	1928	638	241	.378
11	Wade Boggs, Bos	1985	653	240	.368
12	Rod Carew, Min	1977	616	239	.388
13	Don Mattingly, NY-AL	1986	677	238	.352
14	Harry Heilmann, Det	1921	602	237	.394
	Paul Waner, Pit	1927	623	237	.380
	Joe Medwick, StL-NL	1937	633	237	.374
17	Jack Tobin, StL-AL	1921	671	236	.352
18	Rogers Hornsby, StL-NL	1921	592	235	.397
19	Lloyd Waner, Pit	1929	662	234	.353
	Kirby Puckett, Min	1988	657	234	.356
20	Joe Jackson, Cle	1911	571	233	.408

Batting Average

From 1900-49

		Year	AB	H	Avg
1	Rogers Hornsby, StL-NL	1924	536	227	.424
2	Nap Lajoie, Phi-AL	1901	543	229	.422
3	George Sisler, StL-AL	1922	586	246	.420
4	Ty Cobb, Det	1911	591	248	.420
5	Ty Cobb, Det	1912	533	227	.410
6	Joe Jackson, Cle	1911	571	233	.408
7	George Sisler, StL-AL	1920	631	257	.407
8	Ted Williams, Bos-AL	1941	456	185	.406
9	Rogers Hornsby, StL-NL	1925	504	203	.403
10	Harry Heilmann, Det	1923	524	211	.403

Since 1950

		Year	AB	H	Avg
1	Tony Gwynn, SD	1994	419	175	.394
2	George Brett, KC	1980	449	175	.390
3	Ted Williams, Bos	1957	420	163	.388
4	Rod Carew, Min	1977	616	239	.388
5	**Tony Gwynn**, SD	1997	592	220	.372
6	Andres Galarraga, Col	1993	470	174	.370
7	Tony Gwynn, SD	1987	589	218	.370
8	Tony Gwynn, SD	1995	535	197	.368
9	Wade Boggs, Bos	1985	653	240	.368
10	Wade Boggs, Bos	1988	584	214	.366

Total Bases

From 1900-49

		Year	TB
1	Babe Ruth, New York-AL	1921	457
2	Rogers Hornsby, St. Louis-NL	1922	450
3	Lou Gehrig, New York-AL	1927	447
4	Chuck Klein, Philadelphia-NL	1930	445
5	Jimmie Foxx, Philadelphia-AL	1932	438
6	Stan Musial, St. Louis-NL	1948	429
7	Hack Wilson, Chicago-NL	1930	423
8	Chuck Klein, Philadelphia-NL	1932	420
9	Lou Gehrig, New York-AL	1930	419
10	Joe DiMaggio, New York-AL	1937	418

Since 1950

		Year	TB
1	**Larry Walker**, Colorado	1997	409
2	Jim Rice, Boston	1978	406
3	Hank Aaron, Milwaukee	1959	400
4	**Ken Griffey Jr.**, Seattle	1997	393
5	Ellis Burks, Colorado	1996	392
6	George Foster, Cincinnati	1977	388
	Don Mattingly, New York-AL	1986	388
8	Willie Mays, New York-NL	1955	382
	Willie Mays, San Francisco	1962	382
	Jim Rice, Boston	1977	382

Runs Batted In

From 1900-49

		Year	Avg	HR	RBI
1	Hack Wilson, Chi-NL	1930	.356	56	190
2	Lou Gehrig, NY-AL	1931	.341	46	184
3	Hank Greenberg, Det	1937	.337	40	183
4	Lou Gehrig, NY-AL	1927	.373	47	175
	Jimmie Foxx, Bos-AL	1938	.349	50	175
6	Lou Gehrig, NY-AL	1930	.379	41	174
7	Babe Ruth, NY-AL	1921	.378	59	171
8	Chuck Klein, Phi-NL	1930	.386	40	170
	Hank Greenberg, Det	1935	.328	36	170
10	Jimmie Foxx, Phi-AL	1932	.364	58	169

Since 1950

		Year	Avg	HR	RBI
1	Tommy Davis, LA-NL	1962	.346	27	153
2	Andres Galarraga, Col	1996	.304	47	150
3	George Foster, Cin	1977	.320	52	149
4	Johnny Bench, Cin	1970	.293	45	148
5	Albert Belle, Cle	1996	.311	48	148
6	**Ken Griffey Jr.**, Sea	1997	.304	56	147
7	Al Rosen, Cle	1953	.336	43	145
	Don Mattingly, NY-AL	1985	.324	35	145
9	Walt Dropo, Bos-AL	1950	.322	34	144
	Juan Gonzalez, Tex	1996	.314	47	144
	Vern Stephens, Bos-AL	1950	.295	30	144

Runs

		Year	Runs
1	Babe Ruth, New York-AL	1921	177
2	Lou Gehrig, New York-AL	1936	167
3	Babe Ruth, New York-AL	1928	163
	Lou Gehrig, New York-AL	1931	163
5	Babe Ruth, New York-AL	1920	158
	Babe Ruth, New York-AL	1927	158
	Chuck Klein, Philadelphia-NL	1930	158
8	Rogers Hornsby, Chicago-NL	1929	156
9	Kiki Cuyler, Chicago-NL	1930	155
10	Lefty O'Doul, Philadelphia-NL	1929	152
	Woody English, Chicago-NL	1930	152
	Al Simmons, Philadelphia-AL	1930	152
	Chuck Klein, Philadelphia-NL	1932	152
14	Babe Ruth, New York-AL	1923	151
	Jimmie Foxx, Philadelphia-AL	1932	151
	Joe DiMaggio, New York-AL	1937	151
17	Babe Ruth, New York-AL	1930	150
	Ted Williams, Boston-AL	1940	150
19	Lou Gehrig, New York-AL	1927	149
	Babe Ruth, New York-AL	1931	149

Walks

		Year	BB
1	Babe Ruth, New York-AL	1923	170
2	Ted Williams, Boston-AL	1947	162
	Ted Williams, Boston-AL	1949	162
4	Ted Williams, Boston-AL	1946	156
5	Barry Bonds, San Francisco	1996	151
	Eddie Yost, Washington	1956	151
7	Eddie Joost, Philadelphia-AL	1949	149
8	Babe Ruth, New York-AL	1920	148
	Eddie Stanky, Brooklyn	1945	148
	Jimmy Wynn, Houston	1969	148

Extra Base Hits

		Year	EBH
1	Babe Ruth, New York-AL	1921	119
2	Lou Gehrig, New York-AL	1927	117
3	Chuck Klein, Philadelphia-NL	1930	107
4	Chuck Klein, Philadelphia-NL	1932	103
	Hank Greenberg, Detroit	1937	103
	Stan Musial, St. Louis-NL	1948	103
	Albert Belle, Cleveland	1995	103
8	Rogers Hornsby, St. Louis-NL	1922	102
9	Lou Gehrig, New York-AL	1930	100
	Jimmie Foxx, Philadelphia-AL	1933	100

Slugging Percentage From 1900-49

		Year	Pct
1	Babe Ruth, New York-AL	1920	.847
2	Babe Ruth, New York-AL	1921	.846
3	Babe Ruth, New York-AL	1927	.772
4	Lou Gehrig, New York-AL	1927	.765
5	Babe Ruth, New York-AL	1923	.764
6	Rogers Hornsby, St. Louis-NL	1925	.756
7	Jimmie Foxx, Philadelphia-AL	1932	.749
8	Babe Ruth, New York-AL	1924	.739
9	Babe Ruth, New York-AL	1926	.737
10	Ted Williams, Boston-AL	1941	.735

Since 1950

		Year	Pct
1	Jeff Bagwell, Houston	1994	.750
2	Ted Williams, Boston-AL	1957	.731
3	Mark McGwire, Oakland	1996	.730
4	Frank Thomas, Chicago-AL	1994	.729
5	**Larry Walker**, Colorado	1997	.720

Stolen Bases

		Year	SB
1	Rickey Henderson, Oakland	1982	130
2	Lou Brock, St. Louis	1974	118
3	Vince Coleman, St. Louis	1985	110
4	Vince Coleman, St. Louis	1987	109
5	Rickey Henderson, Oakland	1983	108
6	Vince Coleman, St. Louis	1986	107
7	Maury Wills, Los Angeles-NL	1962	104
8	Rickey Henderson, Oakland	1980	100
9	Ron LeFlore, Montreal	1980	97
10	Ty Cobb, Detroit	1915	96
11	Omar Moreno, Pittsburgh	1980	96
12	Maury Wills, Los Angeles	1965	94
13	Rickey Henderson, New York-AL	1988	93
14	Tim Raines, Montreal	1983	90
15	Clyde Milan, Washington	1912	88
16	Rickey Henderson, New York-AL	1986	87
17	Ty Cobb, Detroit	1911	83
	Willie Wilson, Kansas City	1979	83
19	Bob Bescher, Cincinnati	1911	81
	Eddie Collins, Philadelphia-AL	1910	81
	Vince Coleman, St. Louis	1988	81

Strikeouts

		Year	SO
1	Bobby Bonds, San Francisco	1970	189
2	Bobby Bonds, San Francisco	1969	187
3	Rob Deer, Milwaukee	1987	186
4	Pete Incaviglia, Texas	1986	185
5	Cecil Fielder, Detroit	1990	182
6	Mike Schmidt, Philadelphia	1975	180
7	Rob Deer, Milwaukee	1986	179
8	Dave Nicholson, Chicago-AL	1963	175
	Gorman Thomas, Milwaukee	1979	175
	Jose Canseco, Oakland	1986	175
	Rob Deer, Detroit	1991	175
	Jay Buhner, Seattle	1997	175

Pinch Hits

Career pinch hits in parentheses.

		Year	PH	
1	John Vander Wal, Colorado	1995	26	(64)
2	Jose Morales, Montreal	1976	25	(123)
3	Dave Philley, Baltimore	1961	24	(93)
	Vic Davalillo, St. Louis	1970	24	(95)
	Rusty Staub, New York-NL	1983	24	(100)

Four tied with 22 each.

Note: The all-time career pinch hit leader is Manny Mota (150).

Four Home Runs in One Game
National League

	Date	H/A	Inn
Bobby Lowe, Boston	5/30/1894	H	9
Ed Delahanty, Philadelphia	7/13/1896	A	9
Chuck Klein, Philadelphia	7/10/1936	A	10
Gil Hodges, Brooklyn	8/31/1950	H	9
Joe Adcock, Milwaukee	7/31/1954	A	9
Willie Mays, San Francisco	4/30/1961	A	9
Mike Schmidt, Philadelphia	4/17/1976	A	10
Bob Horner, Atlanta	7/6/1986	H	9
Mark Whiten, St. Louis	9/7/1993	A	9

American League

	Date	H/A	Inn
Lou Gehrig, New York	6/3/1932	A	9
Pat Seerey, Chicago	7/18/1948	A	11
Rocky Colavito, Cleveland	6/10/1959	A	9

Pitching
Wins

From 1900-49

		Year	W	L	Pct
1	Jack Chesbro, NY-AL	1904	41	12	.774
2	Ed Walsh, Chi-AL	1908	40	15	.727
3	Christy Mathewson, NY-NL	1908	37	11	.771
4	Walter Johnson, Wash	1913	36	7	.837
5	Joe McGinnity, NY-NL	1904	35	8	.814
6	Smokey Joe Wood, Bos-AL	1912	34	5	.872
7	Cy Young, Bos-AL	1901	33	10	.767
	Grover Alexander, Phi-NL	1916	33	12	.733
	Christy Mathewson, NY-NL	1904	33	12	.733
10	Cy Young, Bos-AL	1902	32	11	.744

Since 1950

		Year	W	L	Pct
1	Denny McLain, Det	1968	31	6	.838
2	Robin Roberts, Phi-NL	1952	28	7	.800
3	Bob Welch, Oak	1990	27	6	.818
	Don Newcombe, Bklyn	1956	27	7	.794
	Sandy Koufax, LA	1966	27	9	.750
	Steve Carlton, Phi	1972	27	10	.730
7	Sandy Koufax, LA	1965	26	8	.765
	Juan Marichal, SF	1968	26	9	.743

Note: 11 pitchers tied with 25 wins, including Marichal twice.

Earned Run Average

From 1900-49

		Year	ShO	ERA
1	Dutch Leonard, Bos-AL	1914	7	1.01
2	Three Finger Brown,	1906	10	1.04
3	Walter Johnson, Wash	1913	11	1.09
4	Christy Mathewson, NY-NL	1909	8	1.14
5	Jack Pfiester, Chi-NL	1907	3	1.15
6	Addie Joss, Cle	1908	9	1.16
7	Carl Lundgren, Chi-NL	1907	7	1.17
8	Grover Alexander, Phi-NL	1915	12	1.22
9	Cy Young, Bos-AL	1908	3	1.26
10	Three pitchers tied at 1.27			

Since 1950

		Year	ShO	ERA
1	Bob Gibson, St.L	1968	13	1.12
2	Dwight Gooden, NY-NL	1985	8	1.53
3	Greg Maddux, Atl.	1994	3	1.56
4	Luis Tiant, Cle	1968	9	1.60
5	Greg Maddux, Atl	1995	3	1.63
6	Dean Chance, LA-AL	1964	11	1.65
7	Nolan Ryan, Cal	1981	3	1.69
8	Sandy Koufax, LA	1966	5	1.73
	Sandy Koufax, LA	1964	7	1.74
9	Ron Guidry, NY-AL	1978	9	1.74
10	Tom Seaver, NY-NL	1971	4	1.76

Winning Pct.

		Year	W-L	Pct
1	Roy Face, Pit	1959	18-1	.947
2	Rick Sutcliffe, Chi-NL*	1984	16-1	.941
3	Johnny Allen, Cle	1937	15-1	.938
4	Greg Maddux, Atl	1995	19-2	.904
5	Randy Johnson, Sea	1995	18-2	.900
6	Ron Guidry, NY-AL	1978	25-3	.893
7	Freddie Fitzsimmons, Bklyn	1940	16-2	.889
8	Lefty Grove, Phi-AL	1931	31-4	.886
9	Bob Stanley, Bos	1978	15-2	.882
10	Preacher Roe, Bklyn	1951	22-3	.880
11	Tom Seaver, Cin	1981	14-2	.875
12	Smokey Joe Wood, Bos-AL	1912	34-5	.872

*Sutcliffe began 1984 with Cleveland and was 4-5 before being traded to the Cubs; his overall winning pct. was .769 (20-6).

Appearances

		Year	App	Sv
1	Mike Marshall, LA	1974	106	21
2	Kent Tekulve, Pit	1979	94	31
3	Mike Marshall, LA	1973	92	31
4	Kent Tekulve, Pit	1978	91	31
5	Wayne Granger, Cin	1969	90	27
	Mike Marshall, Min	1979	90	32
	Kent Tekulve, Phi	1987	90	3

Innings Pitched (since 1920)

		Year	IP	W-L
1	Wilbur Wood, Chi-AL	1972	377	24-17
2	Mickey Lolich, Det	1971	376	25-14
3	Bob Feller, Cle	1946	371	26-15
4	Grover Alexander, Chi-NL	1920	363	27-14
5	Wilbur Wood, Chi-AL	1973	359	24-20

Walks Allowed

		Year	BB	SO
1	Bob Feller, Cle	1938	208	240
2	Nolan Ryan, Cal	1977	204	341
3	Nolan Ryan, Cal	1974	202	367
4	Bob Feller, Cle	1941	194	260
5	Bobo Newsom, St.L-AL	1938	192	226

Strikeouts

		Year	SO	P/G
1	Nolan Ryan, Cal	1973	383	10.57
2	Sandy Koufax, LA	1965	382	10.24
3	Nolan Ryan, Cal	1974	367	9.92
4	Rube Waddell, Phi-AL	1904	349	8.12
5	Bob Feller, Cle	1946	348	8.45
6	Nolan Ryan, Cal	1977	341	10.26
7	Nolan Ryan, Cal	1972	329	10.43
8	Nolan Ryan, Cal	1976	327	10.36
9	Sam McDowell, Cle	1965	325	10.71
10	Curt Schilling, Phi	1997	319	9.11

Saves

		Year	App	Sv
1	Bobby Thigpen, Chi-AL	1990	77	57
2	Randy Myers, Chi-NL	1993	73	53
3	Dennis Eckersley, Oak	1992	69	51
4	Dennis Eckersley, Oak	1990	63	48
	Rod Beck, SF	1993	76	48
6	Lee Smith, St.L	1991	67	47

Shutouts

		Year	ShO	ERA
1	Grover Alexander, Phi-NL	1916	16	1.55
2	Jack Coombs, Phi-AL	1910	13	1.30
	Bob Gibson, St.L	1968	13	1.12
4	Christy Mathewson, NY-NL	1908	12	1.43
	Grover Alexander, Phi-NL	1915	12	1.22

Home Runs Allowed

		Year	HRs
1	Bert Blyleven, Minnesota	1986	50
2	Robin Roberts, Philadelphia	1956	46
	Bert Blyleven, Minnesota	1987	46
4	Pedro Ramos, Washington	1957	43
5	Denny McLain, Detroit	1966	42

Home Run in First Major League At-bat
* on first pitch

A.L. Luke Stuart, St. Louis, August 8, 1921.
Earl Averill, Cleveland, April 16, 1929.
Ace Parker, Philadelphia, April 30, 1937.
Gene Hasson, Philadelphia, September 9, 1937, first game.
Bill Lefebvre, Boston, June 10, 1938.*
Hack Miller, Detroit, April 23, 1944, second game.
Eddie Pellagrini, Boston, April 22, 1946.
George Vico, Detroit, April 20, 1948.*
Bob Nieman, St. Louis, September 14, 1951.
Bob Tillman, Boston, May 19, 1962.
John Kennedy, Washington, September 5, 1962, first game.
Buster Narum, Baltimore, May 3, 1963.
Gates Brown, Detroit, June 19, 1963.
Bert Campaneris, Kansas City, July 23, 1964.*
Bill Roman, Detroit, September 30, 1964, second game.
Brant Alyea, Washington, September 12, 1965.*
John Miller, New York, September 11, 1966.
Rick Renick, Minnesota, July 11, 1968.
Joe Keough, Oakland, August 7, 1968, second game.
Gene Lamont, Detroit, September 2, 1970, second game.
Don Rose, California, May 24, 1972.*
Reggie Sanders, Detroit, September 1, 1974.
Dave McKay, Minnesota, August 22, 1975.
Al Woods, Toronto, April 7, 1977.
Dave Machemer, California, June 21, 1978.
Gary Gaetti, Minnesota, September 20, 1981.
Andre David, Minnesota, June 29, 1984, first game.
Terry Steinbach, Oakland, September 12, 1986.
Jay Bell, Cleveland, September 29, 1986.*
Junior Felix, Toronto, May 4, 1989.*
Jon Nunnally, Kansas City, April 29, 1995.
Total number of players: 31

N.L. Joe Harrington, Boston, September 10, 1895.
Bill Duggleby, Philadelphia, April 21, 1898.
Johnny Bates, Boston, April 12, 1906.
Walter Mueller, Pittsburgh, May 7, 1922.
Clise Dudley, Brooklyn, April 27, 1929.*
Gordon Slade, Brooklyn, May 24, 1930.
Eddie Morgan, St. Louis, April 14, 1936.*
Ernie Koy, Brooklyn, April 19, 1938.
Emmett Mueller, Philadelphia, April 19, 1938.
Clyde Vollmer, Cincinnati, May 31, 1942, second game.*
Paul Gillespie, Chicago, September 11, 1942.
Buddy Kerr, New York, September 8, 1943.
Whitey Lockman, New York, July 5, 1945.
Dan Bankhead, Brooklyn, August 26, 1947.
Les Layton, New York, May 21, 1948.
Ed Sanicki, Philadelphia, September 14, 1949.
Ted Tappe, Cincinnati, September 14, 1950, first game.
Hoyt Wilhelm, New York, April 23, 1952.
Wally Moon, St. Louis, April 13, 1954.
Chuck Tanner, Milwaukee, April 12, 1955.*
Bill White, New York, May 7, 1956.
Frank Ernaga, Chicago, May 24, 1957.
Don Leppert, Pittsburgh, June 18, 1961, first game.
Cuno Barragan, Chicago, September 1, 1961.
Benny Ayala, New York, August 27, 1974.
John Montefusco, San Francisco, September 3, 1974.
Jose Sosa, Houston, July 30, 1975.
Johnnie LeMaster, San Francisco, September 2, 1975.
Tim Wallach, Montreal, September 6, 1980.
Carmelo Martinez, Chicago, August 22, 1983.
Mike Fitzgerald, New York, September 13, 1983.
Will Clark, San Francisco, April 8, 1986.
Ricky Jordan, Philadelphia, July 17, 1988.
Jose Offerman, Los Angeles, August 19, 1990.
Dave Eiland, San Diego, April 10, 1992.
Jim Bullinger, Chicago, June 8, 1992, first game.
Jay Gainer, Colorado, May 14, 1993.*
Mitch Lyden, Florida, June 16, 1993.
Garey Ingram, Los Angeles, May 19, 1994.
Total number of players: 39

Hitting home runs from both sides of plate, game
(Since 1986)

A.L. Roy Smalley, Minnesota, May 30, 1986.
Tony Bernazard, Cleveland, July 1, 1986.
Ruben Sierra, Texas, September 13, 1986.
Eddie Murray, Baltimore, May 8, 1987.
Eddie Murray, Baltimore, May 9, 1987.
Devon White, California, June 23, 1987.
Dale Sveum, Milwaukee, July 17, 1987
Dale Sveum, Milwaukee, June 12, 1988.
Mickey Tettleton, Baltimore, June 13, 1988.
Tim Raines, Chicago, August 31, 1993.
Chad Kreuter, Detroit, September 7, 1993.
Eddie Murray, Cleveland, April 21, 1994.
Chili Davis, California, May 11, 1994.
Bernie Williams, New York, June 6, 1994.
Ruben Sierra, Oakland, June 7, 1994.
Chili Davis, California, July 30, 1994.
Mickey Tettleton, Texas, April 28, 1995.
Roberto Alomar, Toronto, May 4, 1995
Luis Alicea, Boston, July 28, 1995.
N.L. Chili Davis, San Francisco, June 27, 1987.
Bobby Bonilla, Pittsburgh, July 3, 1987.
Kevin Bass, Houston, August 3, 1987, 13 innings.
Kevin Bass, Houston, September 2, 1987.
Chili Davis, San Francisco, September 15, 1987.

Bobby Bonilla, Pittsburgh, April 6, 1988, 14 innings.
Tim Raines, Montreal, July 16, 1988.
Steve Jeltz, Philadelphia, June 8, 1989.
Kevin Bass, Houston, August 20, 1989.
Eddie Murray, Los Angeles, April 18, 1990.
Eddie Murray, Los Angeles, June 9, 1990.
Bret Barberie, Montreal, August 2, 1991.
Howard Johnson, New York, August 31, 1991.
Kevin Bass, San Francisco, August 2, 1992, second game.
Bobby Bonilla, New York, April 23, 1993.
Bobby Bonilla, New York, June 10, 1993.
Todd Benzinger, San Francisco, August 30, 1993.
Mark Whiten, St. Louis, September 14, 1993.
Geronimo Pena, St. Louis, April 17, 1994.
Bobby Bonilla, New York, May 4, 1994.
Todd Hundley, New York, June 18, 1994.
Ken Caminiti, Houston, July 3, 1994.
Bobby Bonilla, New York, May 12, 1995.
Ken Caminiti, San Diego, September 16, 1995.
Ken Caminiti, San Diego, September 17, 1995.
Ken Caminiti, San Diego, September 19, 1995.

All-Time Winningest Managers

Top 20 Major League career victories through the 1997 season. Career, regular season and postseason (playoffs and World Series) records are noted along with AL and NL pennants and World Series titles won. Managers active during 1997 season in **bold** type.

		Career			Regular Season			Postseason			
		Yrs	W	L	Pct	W	L	Pct	W	L	Pct	Titles
1	Connie Mack	53	**3755**	3967	.486	3731	3948	.486	24	19	.558	9 AL, 5 WS
2	John McGraw	33	**2810**	1987	.586	2784	1959	.587	26	28	.482	10 NL, 3 WS
3	Sparky Anderson	26	**2238**	1855	.547	2194	1834	.545	34	21	.618	4 NL, 1 AL, 3 WS
4	Bucky Harris	29	**2168**	2228	.493	2157	2218	.493	11	10	.524	3 AL, 2 WS
5	Joe McCarthy	24	**2155**	1346	.616	2125	1333	.615	30	13	.698	1 NL, 8 AL, 7 WS
6	Walter Alston	23	**2063**	1634	.558	2040	1613	.558	23	21	.523	7 NL, 4 WS
7	Leo Durocher	24	**2015**	1717	.540	2008	1709	.540	7	8	.467	3 NL, 1 WS
8	Casey Stengel	25	**1942**	1868	.510	1905	1842	.508	37	26	.587	10 AL, 7 WS
9	Gene Mauch	26	**1907**	2044	.483	1902	2037	.483	5	7	.417	—None—
10	Bill McKechnie	25	**1904**	1737	.523	1896	1723	.524	8	14	.364	4 NL, 2 WS
11	Tommy Lasorda	21	**1630**	1469	.526	1599	1439	.526	31	30	.508	4 NL, 2 WS
12	Ralph Houk	20	**1627**	1539	.514	1619	1531	.514	8	8	.500	3 AL, 2 WS
13	Fred Clarke	19	**1609**	1189	.575	1602	1181	.576	7	8	.467	4 NL, 1 WS
14	Dick Williams	21	**1592**	1474	.519	1571	1451	.520	21	23	.477	3 AL, 1 NL, 2 WS
15	**Tony La Russa**	19	**1507**	1366	.525	1481	1346	.524	26	20	.565	3 AL, 1 WS
16	Earl Weaver	17	**1506**	1080	.582	1480	1060	.583	26	20	.565	4 AL, 1 WS
17	Clark Griffith	20	**1491**	1367	.522	1491	1367	.522	0	0	.000	1 AL (1901)
18	Miller Huggins	17	**1431**	1149	.555	1413	1134	.555	18	15	.545	6 AL, 3 WS
19	Al Lopez	17	**1412**	1012	.583	1410	1004	.584	2	8	.200	2 AL
20	Jimmy Dykes	21	**1406**	1541	.477	1406	1541	.477	0	0	.000	—None—

Notes: John McGraw's postseason record also includes two World Series tie games (1912,'22); Miller Huggins postseason record also includes one World Series tie game (1922).

Where They Managed

Alston—Brooklyn/Los Angeles NL (1954-76); **Anderson**—Cincinnati NL (1970-78), Detroit AL (1979-95); **Clarke**—Louisville NL (1897-99), Pittsburgh NL (1900-15); **Durocher**—Brooklyn NL (1939-46,48), New York NL (1948-55), Chicago NL (1966-72), Houston NL (1972-73); **Dykes**—Chicago AL (1934-46), Philadelphia AL (1951- 53), Baltimore AL (1954), Cincinnati (1958), Detroit AL (1959-60), Cleveland AL (1960-61); **Griffith**—Chicago AL (1901-02), New York AL (1903-08), Cincinnati NL (1909-11), Washington AL (1912-20); **Harris**—Washington AL (1924-28,35-42,50-54), Detroit AL (1929-33,55-56), Boston AL (1934), Philadelphia NL (1943), New York AL (1947-48); **Houk**—New York AL (1961-63,66-73), Detroit AL (1974-78), Boston AL (1981-84); **Huggins**—St. Louis NL (1913-17), New York AL (1918-29); **La Russa**—Chicago AL (1979-86), Oakland (1986-95); St. Louis (1996-) **Lasorda**—Los Angeles NL (1976-96); **Lopez**—Cleveland AL (1951-56), Chicago AL (1957-65,68-69).

Mack—Pittsburgh NL (1894-96), Philadelphia AL (1901-50); **Mauch**—Philadelphia NL (1960-68), Montreal NL (1969-75), Minnesota AL (1976-80), California AL (1981-82,85-87); **McCarthy**—Chicago NL (1926-30), New York AL (1931-46), Boston AL (1948-50); **McGraw**—Baltimore AL (1899), Baltimore AL (1901-02), New York NL (1902-32); **McKechnie**—Newark FL (1915), Pittsburgh NL (1922-26), St. Louis NL (1928-29), Boston NL (1930- 37), Cincinnati NL (1938-46); **Stengel**—Brooklyn NL (1934-36), Boston NL (1938-43), New York AL (1949-60), New York NL (1962-65); **Weaver**—Baltimore AL (1968-82,85-86); **Williams**—Boston AL (1967-69), Oakland NL (1971-73), California AL (1974-76), Montreal NL (1977-81), San Diego NL (1982-85), Seattle AL (1986-88).

Regular Season Winning Pct.

Minimum of 750 victories.

		Yrs	W	L	Pct	Pen
1	Joe McCarthy	24	2125	1333	**.615**	9
2	Charlie Comiskey	12	838	541	**.608**	4
3	Frank Selee	16	1284	862	**.598**	5
4	Billy Southworth	13	1044	704	**.597**	4
5	Frank Chance	11	946	648	**.593**	4
6	John McGraw	33	2784	1959	**.587**	10
7	Al Lopez	17	1410	1004	**.584**	2
8	Earl Weaver	17	1480	1060	**.583**	4
9	Cap Anson	20	1296	947	**.578**	5
10	Fred Clarke	19	1602	1181	**.576**	4
11	**Davey Johnson**	12	985	727	**.575**	1
12	Steve O'Neill	14	1040	821	**.559**	1
13	Walter Alston	23	2040	1613	**.558**	7
14	Bill Terry	10	823	661	**.555**	3
15	Miller Huggins	17	1413	1134	**.555**	6
16	Billy Martin	16	1253	1013	**.553**	2
17	Harry Wright	18	1000	825	**.548**	3
18	Charlie Grimm	19	1287	1067	**.547**	3
19	**Bobby Cox**	16	1312	1089	**.546**	4
20	Sparky Anderson	26	2194	1834	**.545**	5

World Series Victories

		App	W	L	T	Pct	WS
1	Casey Stengel	10	**37**	26	0	.587	7
2	Joe McCarthy	9	**30**	13	0	.698	7
3	John McGraw	9	**26**	28	2	.482	2
4	Connie Mack	8	**24**	19	0	.558	5
5	Walter Alston	7	**20**	20	0	.500	4
6	Miller Huggins	6	**18**	15	1	.544	3
7	Sparky Anderson	5	**16**	12	0	.571	3
8	Tommy Lasorda	4	**12**	11	0	.522	2
	Dick Williams	4	**12**	14	0	.462	2
10	Frank Chance	4	**11**	9	1	.548	2
	Bucky Harris	3	**11**	10	0	.524	2
	Billy Southworth	4	**11**	11	0	.500	2
	Earl Weaver	4	**11**	13	0	.458	2
	Bobby Cox	4	**11**	14	0	.440	1
15	Whitey Herzog	3	**10**	11	0	.476	1
16	Bill Carrigan	2	**8**	2	0	.800	2
	Danny Murtaugh	2	**8**	6	0	.571	2
	Ralph Houk	3	**8**	8	0	.500	2
	Bill McKechnie	4	**8**	14	0	.364	2
	Tom Kelly	2	**8**	6	0	.571	2

Active Managers' Records
Regular season games only; through 1997.

National League

		Yrs	W	L	Pct
1	Tony La Russa, St.L.	19	**1481**	1346	.524
2	Bobby Cox, Atl.	16	**1312**	1089	.546
3	Jim Leyland, Fla.	12	**943**	933	.503
4	Jim Fregosi, Phi	13	**861**	937	.479
5	Bobby Valentine, NY	10	**681**	698	.494
6	Felipe Alou, Mon.	6	**462**	407	.532
7	Dusty Baker, SF	5	**383**	362	.514
8	Don Baylor, Col.	5	**363**	384	.486
9	Gene Lamont, Pit.	5	**337**	293	.535
10	Jim Riggleman, Chi.	6	**329**	430	.433
11	Bruce Bochy, SD	3	**237**	231	.506
12	Bill Russell, LA	2	**137**	111	.552
13	Larry Dierker, Hou.	1	**84**	78	.519
14	Jack McKeon, Cin	1	**33**	27	.550

American League

		Yrs	W	L	Pct
1	Joe Torre, NY	14	**1062**	1112	.489
2	Davey Johnson, Bal.	12	**985**	727	.575
3	Lou Piniella, Sea.	11	**864**	781	.525
4	Tom Kelly, Min.	12	**853**	885	.491
5	Mike Hargrove, Cle.	7	**535**	453	.541
6	Johnny Oates, Tex.	6	**532**	497	.517
7	Phil Garner, Mil.	6	**437**	469	482
8	Jimy Williams, Bos	5	**359**	325	.525
9	Art Howe, Oak.	2	**143**	181	.441
10	Buddy Bell, Det.	2	**132**	192	.407
11	Terry Collins, Ana	1	**84**	78	.519
12	Tony Muser, KC	1	**31**	48	.392
13	Mel Queen, Tor	1	**4**	1	.800
14	Chicago				

Annual Awards

MOST VALUABLE PLAYER

There have been three different Most Valuable Player awards in baseball since 1911—the Chalmers Award (1911-14), presented by the Detroit-based automobile company; the League Award (1922-29), presented by the National and American Leagues; and the Baseball Writers' Award (since 1931), presented by the Baseball Writers' Association of America. Statistics for winning players are provided below. Stats for winning pitchers before advent of Cy Young Award are in MVP Pitchers' Statistics table.

Multiple winners: NL—Barry Bonds, Roy Campanella, Stan Musial and Mike Schmidt (3); Ernie Banks, Johnny Bench, Rogers Hornsby, Carl Hubbell, Willie Mays, Joe Morgan and Dale Murphy (2). **AL**—Yogi Berra, Joe DiMaggio, Jimmie Foxx and Mickey Mantle (3); Mickey Cochrane, Lou Gehrig, Hank Greenberg, Walter Johnson, Roger Maris, Hal Newhouser, Cal Ripken Jr., Frank Thomas, Ted Williams and Robin Yount (2). **NL & AL**—Frank Robinson (2, one in each).

Chalmers Award

National League

Year		Pos	HR	RBI	Avg
1911	Wildfire Schulte, Chi	OF	21	121	.300
1912	Larry Doyle, NY	2B	10	90	.330
1913	Jake Daubert, Bklyn	1B	2	52	.350
1914	Johnny Evers, Bos	2B	1	40	.279

American League

Year		Pos	HR	RBI	Avg
1911	Ty Cobb, Det	OF	8	144	.420
1912	Tris Speaker, Bos	OF	10	98	.383
1913	Walter Johnson, Wash	P			
1914	Eddie Collins, Phi	2B	2	85	.344

League Award

National League

Year		Pos	HR	RBI	Avg
1922	No selection				
1923	No selection				
1924	Dazzy Vance, Bklyn	P	—	—	—
1925	Rogers Hornsby, St.L	2B-Mgr	39	143	.403
1926	Bob O'Farrell, St.L	C	7	68	.293
1927	Paul Waner, Pit	OF	9	131	.380
1928	Jim Bottomley, St.L	1B	31	136	.325
1929	Rogers Hornsby, Chi	2B	39	149	.380

American League

Year		Pos	HR	RBI	Avg
1922	George Sisler, St.L	1B	8	105	.420
1923	Babe Ruth, NY	OF	41	131	.393
1924	Walter Johnson, Wash	P	—	—	—
1925	Roger Peckinpaugh, Wash	SS	4	64	.294
1926	George Burns, Cle	1B	4	114	.358
1927	Lou Gehrig, NY	1B	47	175	.373
1928	Mickey Cochrane, Phi	C	10	57	.293
1929	No selection				

Most Valuable Player

National League

Year		Pos	HR	RBI	Avg
1931	Frankie Frisch, St.L	2B	4	82	.311
1932	Chuck Klein, Phi	OF	38	137	.348
1933	Carl Hubbell, NY	P	—	—	—
1934	Dizzy Dean, St.L	P	—	—	—
1935	Gabby Hartnett, Chi.	C	13	91	.344
1936	Carl Hubbell, NY	P	—	—	—
1937	Joe Medwick, St.L	OF	31	154	.374
1938	Ernie Lombardi, Cin	C	19	95	.342
1939	Bucky Walters, Cin	P	—	—	—
1940	Frank McCormick, Cin	1B	19	127	.309
1941	Dolf Camilli, Bklyn	1B	34	120	.285
1942	Mort Cooper, St.L	P	—	—	—
1943	Stan Musial, St.L	OF	13	81	.357

Year		Pos	HR	RBI	Avg
1944	Marty Marion, St.L	SS	6	63	.267
1945	Phil Cavarretta, Chi	1B	6	97	.355
1946	Stan Musial, St.L	1B-OF	16	103	.365
1947	Bob Elliott, Bos	3B	22	113	.317
1948	Stan Musial, St.L	OF	39	131	.376
1949	Jackie Robinson, Bklyn	2B	16	124	.342
1950	Jim Konstanty, Phi	P	—	—	—
1951	Roy Campanella, Bklyn	C	33	108	.325
1952	Hank Sauer, Chi	OF	37	121	.270
1953	Roy Campanella, Bklyn	C	41	142	.312
1954	Willie Mays, NY	OF	41	110	.345
1955	Roy Campanella, Bklyn	C	32	107	.318
1956	Don Newcombe, Bklyn	P	—	—	—

Year		Pos	HR	RBI	Avg
1957	Hank Aaron, Mil	OF	44	132	.322
1958	Ernie Banks, Chi	SS	47	129	.313
1959	Ernie Banks, Chi	SS	45	143	.304
1960	Dick Groat, Pit	SS	2	50	.325
1961	Frank Robinson, Cin	OF	37	124	.323
1962	Maury Wills, LA	SS	6	48	.299
1963	Sandy Koufax, LA	P	—	—	—
1964	Ken Boyer, St.L	3B	24	119	.295
1965	Willie Mays, SF	OF	52	112	.317
1966	Roberto Clemente, Pit	OF	29	119	.317
1967	Orlando Cepeda, St.L	1B	25	111	.325
1968	Bob Gibson, St.L	P	—	—	—
1969	Willie McCovey, SF	1B	45	126	.320
1970	Johnny Bench, Cin	C	45	148	.293
1971	Joe Torre, St.L	3B	24	137	.363
1972	Johnny Bench, Cin	C	40	125	.270
1973	Pete Rose, Cin	OF	5	64	.338
1974	Steve Garvey, LA	1B	21	111	.312
1975	Joe Morgan, Cin	2B	17	94	.327
1976	Joe Morgan, Cin	2B	27	111	.320
1977	George Foster, Cin	OF	52	149	.320
1978	Dave Parker, Pit	OF	30	117	.334
1979	Keith Hernandez, St.L	1B	11	105	.344
	Willie Stargell, Pit	1B	32	82	.281
1980	Mike Schmidt, Phi	3B	48	121	.286
1981	Mike Schmidt, Phi	3B	31	91	.316
1982	Dale Murphy, Atl	OF	36	109	.281
1983	Dale Murphy, Atl	OF	36	121	.302
1984	Ryne Sandberg, Chi	2B	19	84	.314
1985	Willie McGee, St.L	OF	10	82	.353
1986	Mike Schmidt, Phi	3B	37	119	.290
1987	Andre Dawson, Chi	OF	49	137	.287
1988	Kirk Gibson, LA	OF	25	76	.290
1989	Kevin Mitchell, SF	OF	47	125	.291
1990	Barry Bonds, Pit	OF	33	114	.301
1991	Terry Pendleton, Atl	3B	22	86	.319
1992	Barry Bonds, Pit	OF	34	103	.311
1993	Barry Bonds, SF	OF	46	123	.336
1994	Jeff Bagwell, Hou	1B	39	116	.368
1995	Barry Larkin, Cin	SS	15	66	.319
1996	Ken Caminiti, SD	3B	40	130	.326

American League

Year		Pos	HR	RBI	Avg
1931	Lefty Grove, Phi	P	—	—	—
1932	Jimmie Foxx, Phi	1B	58	169	.364
1933	Jimmie Foxx, Phi	1B	48	163	.356
1934	Mickey Cochrane, Det	C-Mgr	2	76	.320
1935	Hank Greenberg, Det	1B	36	170	.328
1936	Lou Gehrig, NY	1B	49	152	.354
1937	Charlie Gehringer, Det	2B	14	96	.371
1938	Jimmie Foxx, Bos	1B	50	175	.349
1939	Joe DiMaggio, NY	OF	30	126	.381
1940	Hank Greenberg, Det	OF	41	150	.340
1941	Joe DiMaggio, NY	OF	30	125	.357

Year		Pos	HR	RBI	Avg
1942	Joe Gordon, NY	2B	18	103	.322
1943	Spud Chandler, NY	P	—	—	—
1944	Hal Newhouser, Det	P	—	—	—
1945	Hal Newhouser, Det	P	—	—	—
1946	Ted Williams, Bos	OF	38	123	.342
1947	Joe DiMaggio, NY	OF	20	97	.315
1948	Lou Boudreau, Cle	SS-Mgr	18	106	.355
1949	Ted Williams, Bos	OF	43	159	.343
1950	Phil Rizzuto, NY	SS	7	66	.324
1951	Yogi Berra, NY	C	27	88	.294
1952	Bobby Shantz, Phi	P	—	—	—
1953	Al Rosen, Cle	3B	43	145	.336
1954	Yogi Berra, NY	C	22	125	.307
1955	Yogi Berra, NY	C	27	108	.272
1956	Mickey Mantle, NY	OF	52	130	.353
1957	Mickey Mantle, NY	OF	34	94	.365
1958	Jackie Jensen, Bos	OF	35	122	.286
1959	Nellie Fox, Chi	2B	2	70	.306
1960	Roger Maris, NY	OF	39	112	.283
1961	Roger Maris, NY	OF	61	142	.269
1962	Mickey Mantle, NY	OF	30	89	.321
1963	Elston Howard, NY	C	28	85	.287
1964	Brooks Robinson, Bal	3B	28	118	.317
1965	Zoilo Versalles, Min	SS	19	77	.273
1966	Frank Robinson, Bal	OF	49	122	.316
1967	Carl Yastrzemski, Bos	OF	44	121	.326
1968	Denny McLain, Det	P	—	—	—
1969	Harmon Killebrew, Min	3B-1B	49	140	.276
1970	Boog Powell, Bal	1B	35	114	.297
1971	Vida Blue, Oak	P	—	—	—
1972	Dick Allen, Chi	1B	37	113	.308
1973	Reggie Jackson, Oak	OF	32	117	.293
1974	Jeff Burroughs, Tex	OF	25	118	.301
1975	Fred Lynn, Bos	OF	21	105	.331
1976	Thurman Munson, NY	C	17	105	.302
1977	Rod Carew, Min	1B	14	100	.388
1978	Jim Rice, Bos	OF-DH	46	139	.315
1979	Don Baylor, Cal	OF-DH	36	139	.296
1980	George Brett, KC	3B	24	118	.390
1981	Rollie Fingers, Mil	P	—	—	—
1982	Robin Yount, Mil	SS	29	114	.331
1983	Cal Ripken Jr., Bal	SS	27	102	.318
1984	Willie Hernandez, Det	P	—	—	—
1985	Don Mattingly, NY	1B	35	145	.324
1986	Roger Clemens, Bos	P	—	—	—
1987	George Bell, Tor	OF	47	134	.308
1988	Jose Canseco, Oak	OF	42	124	.307
1989	Robin Yount, Mil	OF	21	103	.318
1990	Rickey Henderson, Oak	OF	28	61	.325
1991	Cal Ripken Jr., Bal	SS	34	114	.323
1992	Dennis Eckersley, Oak	P	—	—	—
1993	Frank Thomas, Chi	1B	41	128	.317
1994	Frank Thomas, Chi	1B	38	101	.353
1995	Mo Vaughn, Bos	1B	39	126	.300
1996	Juan Gonzalez, Tex	OF-DH	47	144	.314

MVP Pitchers' Statistics

Pitchers have been named Most Valuable Player on 23 occasions, 10 times in the NL and 13 in the AL. Four have been relief pitchers—Jim Konstanty, Rollie Fingers, Willie Hernandez and Dennis Eckersley.

National League

Year		Gm	W-L	SV	ERA
1924	Dazzy Vance, Bklyn	35	28-6	0	2.16
1933	Carl Hubbell, NY	45	23-12	5	1.66
1934	Dizzy Dean, St.L	50	30-7	7	2.66
1936	Carl Hubbell, NY	42	26-6	3	2.31
1939	Bucky Walters, Cin	39	27-11	0	2.29
1942	Mort Cooper, St.L	37	22-7	0	1.78
1950	Jim Konstanty, Phi	74	16-7	22	2.66

American League

Year		Gm	W-L	SV	ERA
1913	Walter Johnson, Wash	47	36-7	2	1.09
1924	Walter Johnson, Wash	38	23-7	0	2.72
1931	Lefty Grove, Phi	41	31-4	5	2.06
1943	Spud Chandler, NY	30	20-4	0	1.64
1944	Hal Hewhouser, Det	47	29-9	2	2.22
1945	Hal Newhouser, Det	40	25-9	2	1.81
1952	Bobby Shantz, Phi	33	24-7	0	2.48

CY YOUNG AWARD

Voted on by the Baseball Writers Association of America. One award was presented from 1956-66, two since 1967. Pitchers who won the MVP and Cy Young awards in the same season are in **bold** type.
Multiple winners: NL—Steve Carlton and Greg Maddux (4); Sandy Koufax and Tom Seaver (3); Bob Gibson (2). **AL**—Jim Palmer and Roger Clemens (3); Denny McLain (2). **NL & AL**—Gaylord Perry (2, one in each).

NL and AL Combined

Year	National League	Gm	W-L	SV	ERA	Year	American League	Gm	W-L	SV	ERA
1956	**Don Newcombe**, Bklyn	...38	27-7	0	3.06	1958	Bob Turley, NY	...33	21-7	1	2.97
1957	Warren Spahn, Mil	39	21-11	3	2.69	1959	Early Wynn, Chi	37	22-10	0	3.17
1960	Vernon Law, Pit	35	20-9	0	3.08	1961	Whitey Ford, NY	39	25-4	0	3.21
1962	Don Drysdale, LA	43	25-9	1	2.83	1964	Dean Chance, LA	46	20-9	4	1.65
1963	**Sandy Koufax**, LA	40	25-5	0	1.88						
1965	Sandy Koufax, LA	43	26-8	2	2.04						
1966	Sandy Koufax, LA	41	27-9	0	1.73						

Separate League Awards

Year	National League	Gm	W-L	SV	ERA	Year	American League	Gm	W-L	SV	ERA
1967	Mike McCormick, SF	...40	22-10	0	2.85	1967	Jim Lonborg, Bos	39	22-9	0	3.16
1968	**Bob Gibson**, St.L	34	22-9	0	1.12	1968	**Denny McLain**, Det	41	31-6	0	1.96
1969	Tom Seaver, NY	36	25-7	0	2.21	1969	Denny McLain, Det	42	24-9	0	2.80
1970	Bob Gibson, St.L	34	23-7	0	3.12		Mike Cuellar, Bal	39	23-11	0	2.38
1971	Ferguson Jenkins, Chi	39	24-13	0	2.77	1970	Jim Perry, Min	40	24-12	0	3.03
1972	Steve Carlton, Phi	41	27-10	0	1.97	1971	**Vida Blue**, Oak	39	24-8	0	1.82
1973	Tom Seaver, NY	36	19-10	0	2.08	1972	Gaylord Perry, Cle	41	24-16	1	1.92
1974	Mike Marshall, LA	106	15-12	21	2.42	1973	Jim Palmer, Bal	38	22-9	1	2.40
1975	Tom Seaver, NY	36	22-9	0	2.38	1974	Catfish Hunter, Oak	41	25-12	0	2.49
1976	Randy Jones, SD	40	22-14	0	2.74	1975	Jim Palmer, Bal	39	23-11	1	2.09
1977	Steve Carlton, Phi	36	23-10	0	2.64	1976	Jim Palmer, Bal	40	22-13	0	2.51
1978	Gaylord Perry, SD	37	21-6	0	2.72	1977	Sparky Lyle, NY	72	13-5	26	2.17
1979	Bruce Sutter, Chi	62	6-6	37	2.23	1978	Ron Guidry, NY	35	25-3	0	1.74
1980	Steve Carlton, Phi	38	24-9	0	2.34	1979	Mike Flanagan, Bal	39	23-9	0	3.08
1981	Fernando Valenzuela, LA	...25	13-7	0	2.48	1980	Steve Stone, Bal	37	25-7	0	3.23
1982	Steve Carlton, Phi	38	23-11	0	3.10	1981	**Rollie Fingers**, Mil	47	6-3	28	1.04
1983	John Denny, Phi	36	19-6	0	2.37	1982	Pete Vuckovich, Mil	30	18-6	0	3.34
1984	Rick Sutcliffe, Chi	.......20*	16-1	0	2.69	1983	LaMarr Hoyt, Chi	36	24-10	0	3.66
1985	Dwight Gooden, NY	35	24-4	0	1.53	1984	**Willie Hernandez**, Det	80	9-3	32	1.92
1986	Mike Scott, Hou	37	18-10	0	2.22	1985	Bret Saberhagen, KC	32	20-6	0	2.87
1987	Steve Bedrosian, Phi	65	5-3	40	2.83	1986	**Roger Clemens**, Bos	33	24-4	0	2.48
1988	Orel Hershiser, LA	35	23-8	1	2.26	1987	Roger Clemens, Bos	36	20-9	0	2.97
1989	Mark Davis, SD	70	4-3	44	1.85	1988	Frank Viola, Min	35	24-7	0	2.64
1990	Doug Drabek, Pit	33	22-6	0	2.76	1989	Bret Saberhagen, KC	36	23-6	0	2.16
1991	Tom Glavine, Atl	34	20-11	0	2.55	1990	Bob Welch, Oak	35	27-6	0	2.95
1992	Greg Maddux, Chi	35	20-11	0	2.18	1991	Roger Clemens, Bos	35	18-10	0	2.62
1993	Greg Maddux, Atl	36	20-10	0	2.36	1992	**Dennis Eckersley**, Oak	...69	7-1	51	1.91
1994	Greg Maddux, Atl	25	16-6	0	1.56	1993	Jack McDowell, Chi	34	22-10	0	3.37
1995	Greg Maddux, Atl	28	19-2	0	1.63	1994	David Cone, KC	23	16-5	0	2.94
1996	John Smoltz, Atl	35	24-8	0	2.94	1995	Randy Johnson, Sea	30	18-2	0	2.48
						1996	Pat Hentgen, Tor	35	20-10	0	3.22

*NL games only, Sutcliffe pitched 15 games with Cleveland before being traded to the Cubs.

ROOKIE OF THE YEAR

Voted on by the Baseball Writers Assn. of America. One award was presented from 1947-48. Two awards (one for each league) have been presented since 1949. Winner who was also named MVP is in **bold** type.

NL and AL Combined

Year		Pos	Year		Pos
1947	Jackie Robinson, Brooklyn	....................1B	1948	Alvin Dark, Boston-NL	........................SS

National League

Year		Pos	Year		Pos	Year		Pos
1949	Don Newcombe, Bklyn	......P	1956	Frank Robinson, Cin	.......OF	1963	Pete Rose, Cin	.............2B
1950	Sam Jethroe, Bos	..........OF	1957	Jack Sanford, Phi	............P	1964	Richie Allen, Phi	...........2B
1951	Willie Mays, NY	..........OF	1958	Orlando Cepeda, SF	.......1B	1965	Jim Lefebvre, LA	...........2B
1952	Joe Black, Bklyn	...........P	1959	Willie McCovey, SF	.......1B	1966	Tommy Helms, Cin	.........3B
1953	Jim Gilliam, Bklyn	..........2B	1960	Frank Howard, LA	.........OF	1967	Tom Seaver, NY	.............P
1954	Wally Moon, St.L	..........OF	1961	Billy Williams, Chi	.........OF	1968	Johnny Bench, Cin	C
1955	Bill Virdon, St.L	..........OF	1962	Ken Hubbs, Chi	..........2B	1969	Ted Sizemore, LA	.........2B

Year	Pos	Year	Pos	Year	Pos
1970 Carl Morton, Mon	P	1979 Rick Sutcliffe, LA	P	1989 Jerome Walton, Chi	OF
1971 Earl Williams, Atl	C	1980 Steve Howe, LA	P	1990 David Justice, Atl	OF
1972 Jon Matlack, NY	P	1981 Fernando Valenzuela, LA	P	1991 Jeff Bagwell, Hou.	1B
1973 Gary Matthews, SF	OF	1982 Steve Sax, LA	2B	1992 Eric Karros, LA	1B
1974 Bake McBride, St.L	OF	1983 Darryl Strawberry, NY	OF	1993 Mike Piazza, LA	C
1975 John Montefusco, SF	P	1984 Dwight Gooden, NY	P	1994 Raul Mondesi, LA	OF
1976 Butch Metzger, SD	P	1985 Vince Coleman, St.L	OF	1995 Hideo Nomo, LA	P
& Pat Zachry, Cin	P	1986 Todd Worrell, St.L	P	1996 Todd Hollandsworth, LA	OF
1977 Andre Dawson, Mon	OF	1987 Benito Santiago, SD	C		
1978 Bob Horner, Atl	3B	1988 Chris Sabo, Cin	3B		

American League

Year	Pos	Year	Pos	Year	Pos
1949 Roy Sievers, St.L	OF	1965 Curt Blefary, Bal	OF	1981 Dave Righetti, NY	P
1950 Walt Dropo, Bos	1B	1966 Tommie Agee, Chi	OF	1982 Cal Ripken Jr., Bal	SS-3B
1951 Gil McDougald, NY	3B	1967 Rod Carew, Min	2B	1983 Ron Kittle, Chi	OF
1952 Harry Byrd, Phi	P	1968 Stan Bahnsen, NY	P	1984 Alvin Davis, Sea	1B
1953 Harvey Kuenn, Det	SS	1969 Lou Piniella, KC	OF	1985 Ozzie Guillen, Chi	SS
1954 Bob Grim, NY	P	1970 Thurman Munson, NY	C	1986 Jose Canseco, Oak	OF
1955 Herb Score, Cle	P	1971 Chris Chambliss, Cle	1B	1987 Mark McGwire, Oak	1B
1956 Luis Aparicio, Chi	SS	1972 Carlton Fisk, Bos	C	1988 Walt Weiss, Oak	SS
1957 Tony Kubek, NY	INF-OF	1973 Al Bumbry, Bal	OF	1989 Gregg Olson, Bal	P
1958 Albie Pearson, Wash	OF	1974 Mike Hargrove, Tex	1B	1990 Sandy Alomar Jr., Cle	C
1959 Bob Allison, Wash	OF	1975 Fred Lynn, Bos	OF	1991 Chuck Knoblauch, Min	2B
1960 Ron Hansen, Bal	SS	1976 Mark Fidrych, Det	P	1992 Pat Listach, Mil	SS
1961 Don Schwall, Bos	P	1977 Eddie Murray, Bal	DH-1B	1993 Tim Salmon, Cal	OF
1962 Tom Tresh, NY	SS-OF	1978 Lou Whitaker, Det	2B	1994 Bob Hamelin, KC	DH
1963 Gary Peters, Chi	P	1979 John Castino, Min	3B	1995 Marty Cordova, Min	OF
1964 Tony Oliva, Min	OF	1980 Joe Charboneau, Cle	OF-DH	1996 Derek Jeter, NY	SS

MANAGER OF THE YEAR

Voted on by the Baseball Writers Association of America. Two awards (one for each league) presented since 1983. Note that (*) indicates manager's team won division championship and (†) indicates unofficial division won in 1994.

Multiple winners: Tony La Russa (3); Sparky Anderson, Bobby Cox, Tommy Lasorda and Jim Leyland (2).

National League

Year		Improvement
1983 Tommy Lasorda, LA	88-74	to 91-71*
1984 Jim Frey, Chi	71-91	to 96-75*
1985 Whitey Herzog, St. L	84-78	to 101-61*
1986 Hal Lanier, Hou.	83-79	to 96-66*
1987 Buck Rodgers, Mon	78-83	to 91-71
1988 Tommy Lasorda, LA	73-89	to 94-67*
1989 Don Zimmer, Chi	77-85	to 93-69*
1990 Jim Leyland, Pit	74-88	to 95-67*
1991 Bobby Cox, Atl	65-97	to 94-68*
1992 Jim Leyland, Pit	98-64*	to 96-66*
1993 Dusty Baker, SF	72-90	to 103-59
1994 Felipe Alou, Mon	94-68	to 74-40†
1995 Don Baylor, Col	53-64	to 77-67
1996 Bruce Bochy, SD	70-74	to 91-71

American League

Year		Improvement
1983 Tony La Russa, Chi	87-75	to 99-63*
1984 Sparky Anderson, Det	92-70	to 104-58*
1985 Bobby Cox, Tor	89-73	to 99-62*
1986 John McNamara, Bos	81-81	to 95-66*
1987 Sparky Anderson, Det	87-75	to 98-64*
1988 Tony La Russa, Oak	81-81	to 104-58*
1989 Frank Robinson, Bal	54-107	to 87-75
1990 Jeff Torborg, Chi	69-92	to 94-68
1991 Tom Kelly, Min	74-88	to 95-67*
1992 Tony La Russa, Oak	84-78	to 96-66*
1993 Gene Lamont, Chi.	86-76	to 94-68*
1994 Buck Showalter, NY	88-74	to 70-43†
1995 Lou Piniella, Sea	49-63	to 79-66*
1996 Joe Torre, NY	79-65	to 92-70
& Johnny Oates, Tex	74-70	to 90-72

George Steinbrenner's Managerial Merry-Go-Round

As managing general partner of the New York Yankees since 1973, George Steinbrenner has changed managers 21 times in 24 years. In that time, the Yankees have won five AL pennants (1976-78, '81 and '96) and three World Series (1977-78, '96). Note that (*) indicates interim status. Managers with multiple hitches are Billy Martin (5), and Bob Lemon, Gene Michael and Lou Piniella (2).

	Tenure	W-L		Tenure	W-L		Tenure	W-L
Ralph Houk	1973	80-82	Bob Lemon	1981-82	17-22	Lou Piniella	1988	45-48
Bill Virdon	1974-75	142-124	Gene Michael	1982	44-42	Dallas Green	1989	56-65
Billy Martin	1975-78*	279-192	Clyde King	1982	29-33	Bucky Dent	1989-90	36-53
Dick Howser	1978	0-1	Billy Martin	1983	91-71	Stump Merrill	1990-91	120-155
Bob Lemon	1978-79	82-51	Yogi Berra	1984-85	93-85	Buck Showalter	1992-95	313-268
Billy Martin	1979	55-40	Billy Martin	1985	91-54	Joe Torre	1996—	188-136
Dick Howser	1980	103-59	Lou Piniella	1986-87	179-145			
Gene Michael	1981	48-34	Billy Martin	1988	40-28			

COLLEGE BASEBALL

College World Series

The NCAA Division I College World Series has been held in Kalamazoo, Mich. (1947-48), Wichita, Kan. (1949) and Omaha, Neb. (since 1950).

Multiple winners: USC (11); Arizona St. (5); Texas (4); Arizona, CS-Fullerton, LSU and Minnesota (3); California, Miami-FL, Michigan, Oklahoma and Stanford (2).

Year	Winner	Coach	Score	Runner-up	Year	Winner	Coach	Score	Runner-up
1947	California	Clint Evans	8-7	Yale	1973	USC	Rod Dedeaux	4-3	Ariz. St.
1948	USC	Sam Barry	9-2	Yale	1974	USC	Rod Dedeaux	7-3	Miami, FL
1949	Texas	Bibb Falk	10-3	W. Forest	1975	Texas	Cliff Gustafson	5-1	S. Carolina
1950	Texas	Bibb Falk	3-0	Wash. St.	1976	Arizona	Jerry Kindall	7-1	E. Michigan
1951	Oklahoma	Jack Baer	3-2	Tennessee	1977	Arizona St.	Jim Brock	2-1	S. Carolina
1952	Holy Cross	Jack Barry	8-4	Missouri	1978	USC	Rod Dedeaux	10-3	Ariz. St.
1953	Michigan	Ray Fisher	7-5	Texas	1979	CS-Fullerton	Augie Garrido	2-1	Arkansas
1954	Missouri	Hi Simmons	4-1	Rollins	1980	Arizona	Jerry Kindall	5-3	Hawaii
1955	Wake Forest	Taylor Sanford	7-6	W. Mich.	1981	Arizona St.	Jim Brock	7-4	Okla. St.
1956	Minnesota	Dick Siebert	12-1	Arizona	1982	Miami-FL	Ron Fraser	9-3	Wichita St.
1957	California	Geo. Wolfman	1-0	Penn St.	1983	Texas	Cliff Gustafson	4-3	Alabama
1958	USC	Rod Dedeaux	8-7	Missouri	1984	CS-Fullerton	Augie Garrido	3-1	Texas
1959	Oklahoma St.	Toby Greene	5-3	Arizona	1985	Miami-FL	Ron Fraser	10-6	Texas
1960	Minnesota	Dick Siebert	2-1	USC	1986	Arizona	Jerry Kindall	10-2	Fla. St.
1961	USC	Rod Dedeaux	1-0	Okla. St.	1987	Stanford	M. Marquess	9-5	Okla. St.
1962	Michigan	Don Lund	5-4	S. Clara	1988	Stanford	M. Marquess	9-4	Ariz. St.
1963	USC	Rod Dedeaux	5-2	Arizona	1989	Wichita St.	G.Stephenson	5-3	Texas
1964	Minnesota	Dick Siebert	5-1	Missouri	1990	Georgia	Steve Webber	2-1	Okla. St.
1965	Arizona St.	Bobby Winkles	2-1	Ohio St.	1991	LSU	Skip Bertman	6-3	Wichita St.
1966	Ohio St.	Marty Karow	8-2	Okla. St.	1992	Pepperdine	Andy Lopez	3-2	CS-Fullerton
1967	Arizona St.	Bobby Winkles	11-2	Houston	1993	LSU	Skip Bertman	8-0	Wichita St.
1968	USC	Rod Dedeaux	4-3	So. Ill.	1994	Oklahoma	Larry Cochell	13-5	Ga. Tech
1969	Arizona St.	Bobby Winkles	10-1	Tulsa	1995	CS-Fullerton	Augie Garrido	11-5	USC
1970	USC	Rod Dedeaux	2-1	Fla. St.	1996	LSU	Skip Bertman	9-8	Miami, FL
1971	USC	Rod Dedeaux	7-2	So. Ill.	1997	LSU	Skip Bertman	13-6	Alabama
1972	USC	Rod Dedeaux							

Most Outstanding Players

The Most Outstanding Player has been selected every year of the College World Series since 1949. Winners who did not play for the CWS champion are listed in **bold** type. No player has won the award more than once.

Year		Year		Year	
1949	**Charles Teague,** W. Forest, 2B	1965	Sal Bando, Ariz. St., 3B	1981	Stan Holmes, Ariz. St., LF
1950	**Ray VanCleef,** Rutgers, CF	1966	Steve Arlin, Ohio St., P	1982	Dan Smith, Miami-FL, P
1951	**Sidney Hatfield,** Tenn., P-1B	1967	Ron Davini, Ariz. St., C	1983	Calvin Schiraldi, Texas, P
1952	James O'Neill, Holy Cross, P	1968	Bill Seinsoth, USC, 1B	1984	John Fishel, CS-Fullerton, LF
1953	**J.L. Smith,** Texas, P	1969	John Dolinsek, Ariz. St., LF	1985	Greg Ellena, Miami-FL, LF
1954	**Tom Yewcic,** Mich. St., C	1970	**Gene Ammann,** Fla. St., P	1986	Mike Senne, Arizona, DH
1955	**Tom Borland,** Okla. St., P	1971	**Jerry Tabb,** Tulsa, 1B	1987	Paul Carey, Stanford, RF
1956	Jerry Thomas, Minn., P	1972	Russ McQueen, USC, P	1988	Lee Plemel, Stanford, P
1957	**Cal Emery,** Penn St., P-1B	1973	**Dave Winfield,** Minn., P-OF	1989	Greg Brummett, Wich. St., P
1958	Bill Thom, USC, P	1974	George Milke, USC, P	1990	Mike Rebhan, Georgia, P
1959	Jim Dobson, Okla. St., 3B	1975	Mickey Reichenbach, Texas, 1B	1991	Gary Hymel, LSU, C
1960	John Erickson, Minn., 2B	1976	Steve Powers, Arizona, P-DH	1992	**Phil Nevin,** CS-Fullerton, 3B
1961	**Littleton Fowler,** Okla. St., P	1977	Bob Horner, Ariz. St., 3B	1993	Todd Walker, LSU, 2B
1962	**Bob Garibaldi,** Santa Clara, P	1978	Rod Boxberger, USC, P	1994	Chip Glass, Oklahoma, OF
1963	Bud Hollowell, USC, C	1979	Tony Hudson, CS-Fullerton, P	1995	Mark Kotsay, CS-Fullerton, OF
1964	**Joe Ferris,** Maine, P	1980	Terry Francona, Arizona, LF	1996	**Pat Burrell,** Miami-FL, 3B
				1997	Brandon Larson, LSU, SS

Annual Awards

Golden Spikes Award

First presented in 1978 by USA Baseball, honoring the nation's best amateur player. Alex Fernandez, the 1990 winner, has been the only junior college player chosen.

Year		Year		Year	
1978	Bob Horner, Ariz. St, 2B	1985	Will Clark, Miss. St., 1B	1992	Phil Nevin, CS-Fullerton, 3B
1979	Tim Wallach, CS-Fullerton, 1B	1986	Mike Loynd, Fla. St., P	1993	Darren Dreifort, Wichita St., P
1980	Terry Francona, Arizona, OF	1987	Jim Abbott, Michigan, P	1994	Jason Varitek, Ga. Tech, C
1981	Mike Fuentes, Fla. St., OF	1988	Robin Ventura, Okla. St., 3B	1995	Mark Kotsay, CS-Fullerton, OF
1982	Augie Schmidt, N. Orleans, SS	1989	Ben McDonald, LSU, P	1996	Travis Lee, San Diego St., 1B
1983	Dave Magadan, Alabama, 1B	1990	Alex Fernandez, Miami-Dade, P		
1984	Oddibe McDowell, Ariz. St., OF	1991	Mike Kelly, Ariz. St., OF		

Baseball America Player of the Year

Presented to the College Player of the Year since 1981 by *Baseball America*.

Year		Year		Year	
1981	Mike Sodders, Ariz. St., 3B	1987	Robin Ventura, Okla. St., 3B	1993	Brooks Kieschnick, Texas, DH/P
1982	Jeff Ledbetter, Fla. St., OF/P	1988	John Olerud, Wash. St., 1B/P	1994	Jason Varitek, Ga. Tech, C
1983	Dave Magadan, Alabama, 1B	1989	Ben McDonald, LSU, P	1995	Todd Helton, Tenn., 1B/P
1984	Oddibe McDowell, Ariz. St., OF	1990	Mike Kelly, Ariz. St., OF	1996	Kris Benson, Clemson, P
1985	Pete Incaviglia, Okla. St., OF	1991	David McCarty, Stanford, 1B	1997	J.D. Drew, Florida St., OF
1986	Casey Close, Michigan, OF	1992	Phil Nevin, CS-Fullerton, 3B		

Dick Howser Trophy

Presented to the College Player of the Year since 1987 by the American Baseball Coaches Association. Named after the late two-time All-America shortstop and college coach at Florida St., Howser was also a major league manager with Kansas City and the New York Yankees.

Multiple winner: Brooks Kieschnick (2).

Year		Year		Year	
1987	Mike Fiore, Miami-FL, OF	1991	Bobby Jones, Fresno St., P	1995	Todd Helton, Tenn., 1B/P
1988	Robin Ventura, Okla. St., 3B	1992	Brooks Kieschnick, Texas, DH/P	1996	Kris Benson, Clemson, P
1989	Scott Bryant, Texas, DH	1993	Brooks Kieschnick, Texas, DH/P	1997	J.D. Drew, Florida St., OF
1990	Paul Ellis, UCLA, C	1994	Jason Varitek, Ga. Tech, C		

Baseball America Coach of the Year

Presented to the College Coach of the Year since 1981 by *Baseball America*.

Multiple winner: Skip Bertman, Dave Snow and Gene Stephenson (2).

1981	Ron Fraser, Miami-FL	1987	Mark Marquess, Stanford	1994	Jim Morris, Miami-FL
1982	Gene Stephenson, Wichita St.	1988	Jim Brock, Arizona St.	1995	Rob Delmonico, Tennessee
1983	Barry Shollenberger, Alabama	1989	Dave Snow, Long Beach St.	1996	Skip Bertman, LSU
1984	Augie Garrido, CS-Fullerton	1990	Steve Webber, Georgia	1997	Jim Wells, Alabama
1985	Ron Polk, Mississippi St.	1991	Jim Hendry, Creighton		
1986	Skip Bertman, LSU	1992	Andy Lopez, Pepperdine		
	& Dave Snow, Loyola-CA	1993	Gene Stephenson, Wichita St.		

All-Time Winningest Coaches

Coaches active in 1997 in **bold** type.

Top 30 Winning Percentage

(Minimum 10 years in Division I)

		Yrs	W	L	T	Pct
1	John Barry	40	619	147	6	.806
2	W.J. Disch	29	465	115	0	.802
3	Cliff Gustafson	29	1427	373	2	.792
4	Harry Carlson	17	143	41	0	.777
5	**Gene Stephenson**	20	1109	339	3	.765
6	Gary Ward	19	953	313	1	.753
7	George Jacobs	11	76	25	0	.752
8	Bobby Winkles	13	524	173	0	.752
9	**Mike Martin**	18	969	330	3	.745
10	Frank Sancet	23	831	283	8	.744
11	Ron Fraser	30	1,271	438	9	.742
12	Bob Wren	23	464	160	4	.742
13	Bibb Falk	25	435	152	0	.741
14	**Skip Bertman**	14	685	248	1	.734
15	Bud Middaugh	22	821	319	1	.720
16	J.F."Pop" McKale	30	302	118	7	.715
17	Jim Brock	28	1,100	440	0	.714
18	Toby Green	21	318	132	0	.707
19	Joe Arnold	18	750	313	2	.705
20	**Mark Johnson**	13	570	241	2	.702
21	Joe Bedenk	32	380	159	3	.701
22	Rod Dedeaux	45	1,332	571	11	.699
23	Enos Semore	22	851	370	1	.697
24	**Jim Morris**	16	702	307	1	.696
25	**Bob Hannah**	34	938	409	6	.695
26	Dave Keilitz	14	456	208	0	.692
27	Pete Beiden	21	600	268	0	.691
28	Brad Babcock	19	558	251	4	.689
29	Chuck Brayton	33	1,162	523	8	.689
30	Chuck Medlar	19	312	141	6	.686

Top 30 Victories

		Yrs	W	L	T	Pct
1	Cliff Gustafson	29	**1427**	373	2	.792
2	Rod Dedeaux	45	**1332**	571	11	.699
3	Ron Fraser	30	**1271**	438	9	.742
4	Al Ogletree	41	**1217**	713	1	.631
5	**Jack Stallings**	37	**1207**	737	5	.621
6	**Augie Garrido**	29	**1181**	546	7	.683
7	**Chuck Hartman**	38	**1172**	587	3	.666
8	Bobo Brayton	33	**1162**	523	8	.690
9	Bill Wilhelm	36	**1161**	536	10	.683
10	**Bob Bennett**	29	**1124**	627	7	.641
11	**Larry Hays**	27	**1,113**	603	2	.648
12	**Gene Stephenson**	20	**1,109**	339	3	.765
13	Jim Brock	23	**1,100**	440	0	.714
14	**Larry Cochell**	31	**1,073**	607	2	.639
15	**Jim Dietz**	26	**1,061**	616	18	.631
16	Ron Polk	26	**1,043**	486	0	.682
17	**Norm DeBriyn**	28	995	521	6	.656
18	**Les Murakami**	27	980	500	4	.662
19	**Richard Jones**	31	980	557	5	.637
20	**Mike Martin**	18	969	330	3	.745
21	Gary Adams	28	960	680	12	.585
22	Gary Ward	19	953	313	1	.753
23	**Bob Hannah**	34	938	409	6	.695
24	John Winkin	42	934	670	11	.582
25	Duane Banks	30	901	585	4	.606
26	Jerry Kindall	24	861	578	6	.598
27	**Gary Pullins**	21	858	409	6	.676
28	**James Wilson**	38	855	596	23	.588
29	**Mark Marquess**	21	853	453	4	.653
30	Enos Semore	22	851	370	1	.697

Other NCAA Champions
Division II

Multiple winner: Florida Southern (8); Cal Poly Pomona (3); CS-Northridge, Jacksonville St., Tampa, Troy St., UC-Irvine and UC-Riverside (2).

Year		Year		Year		Year	
1968	Chapman, CA	1976	Cal Poly Pomona	1984	CS-Northridge	1992	Tampa
1969	Illinois St.	1977	UC-Riverside	1985	Florida Southern	1993	Tampa
1970	CS-Northridge	1978	Florida Southern	1986	Troy St., AL	1994	Central Missouri St.
1971	Florida Southern	1979	Valdosta St., GA	1987	Troy St., AL	1995	Florida Southern
1972	Florida Southern	1980	Cal Poly Pomona	1988	Florida Southern	1996	Kennesaw St., GA
1973	UC-Irvine	1981	Florida Southern	1989	Cal Poly SLO	1997	CS-Chico
1974	UC-Irvine	1982	UC-Riverside	1990	Jacksonville St., AL		
1975	Florida Southern	1983	Cal Poly Pomona	1991	Jacksonville St., AL		

Division III

Multiple winner: Marietta (3); CS-Stanislaus, Eastern Conn. St., Glassboro St., Ithaca, Montclair St., Southern Maine and Wm. Paterson, NJ (2).

Year		Year		Year		Year	
1976	CS-Stanislaus	1982	Eastern Conn. St.	1988	Ithaca, NY	1994	Wisconsin-Oshkosh
1977	CS-Stanislaus	1983	Marietta, OH	1989	NC-Wesleyan	1995	La Verne, CA
1978	Glassboro St., NJ	1984	Ramapo, NJ	1990	Eastern Conn. St.	1996	Wm. Paterson, NJ
1979	Glassboro St., NJ	1985	Wisconsin-Oshkosh	1991	Southern Maine	1997	Southern Maine
1980	Ithaca, NY	1986	Marietta, OH	1992	Wm. Paterson, NJ		
1981	Marietta, OH	1987	Monclair St., NJ	1993	Montclair St., NJ		

Major League Number One Picks

Year		Pos	Team	Year		Pos	Team
1965	Rick Monday	OF	Kansas City Athletics	1982	Shawon Dunston	SS	Chicago Cubs
1966	Steve Chilcott	C	New York Mets	1983	Tim Belcher	P	Minnesota Twins
1967	Rom Blomberg	1B	New York Yankees	1984	Shawn Abner	OF	New York Mets
1968	Tim Foli	IF	New York Mets	1985	B.J. Surhoff	C	Milwaukee Brewers
1969	Jeff Burroughs	OF	Washington Senators	1986	Jeff King	IF	Pittsburgh Pirates
1970	Mike Ivie	C	San Diego Padres	1987	Ken Griffey Jr.	OF	Seattle Mariners
1971	Danny Goodwin	C	Chicago White Sox	1988	Andy Benes	P	San Diego Padres
1972	Dave Roberts	IF	San Diego Padres	1989	Ben McDonald	P	Baltimore Orioles
1973	David Clyde	P	Texas Rangers	1990	Chipper Jones	SS	Atlanta Braves
1974	Bill Almon	IF	San Diego Padres	1991	Brien Taylor	P	New York Yankees
1975	Danny Goodwin	C	California Angels	1992	Phil Nevin	3B	Houston Astros
1976	Floyd Bannister	P	Houston Astros	1993	Alex Rodriguez	SS	Seattle Mariners
1977	Harold Baines	OF	Chicago White Sox	1994	Paul Wilson	P	New York Mets
1978	Bob Horner	3B	Atlanta Braves	1995	Darin Erstad	OF/P	California Angels
1979	Al Chambers	OF	Seattle Mariners	1996	Kris Benson	P	Pittsburgh Pirates
1980	Darryl Strawberry	OF	New York Mets	1997	Matt Anderson	P	Detroit Tigers
1981	Mike Moore	P	Seattle Mariners				

Straight to the Majors

Since Major League baseball began its free agent draft in 1965, 17 selections have advanced directly to the major leagues without first playing in the minors

Draft		Pos	Team	Draft		Pos	Team
1967	Mike Adamson, South Carolina	P	Baltimore		Eddie Bane, Arizona St.	P	Minnesota
1969	Steve Dunning, Stanford	P	Cleveland	1978	Tim Conroy, Gateway HS (Pa.)	P	Oakland
1971	Pete Broberg, Dartmouth	P	Washington		Bob Horner, Arizona St.	IF	Atlanta
	Rob Ellis, Michigan St.	IF	Milwaukee		Brian Milner, Southwest HS (Tex.)	C	Toronto
	Burt Hooton, Texas	P	Chicago		Mike Morgan, Valley HS (Nev.)	P	Oakland
1972	Dave Roberts, Oregon	IF	San Diego .	1985	Pete Incaviglia, Oklahoma St.	OF	Montreal
1973	Dick Ruthven, Fresno St.	P	Philadelphia	1988	Jim Abbott, Michigan	P	California
1973	David Clyde, Westchester HS (Tex.)	P	Texas	1989	John Olerud, Washington St.	IF	Toronto
	Dave Winfield, Minnesota	OF	San Diego				

College Football

Florida coach **Steve Spurrier** allows himself the tiniest of smiles as the 1997 Sugar Bowl winds down and his Gators claim their first national championship.

Wide World Photos

One Tough Gator

The most enduring part of Danny Wuerffel's legacy may be his toughness

by
Chris Fowler

Fear flashed in the eyes of Danny Wuerffel as he sat on the Superdome's rug, gripping his right shoulder. Seconds before, he'd been sandwiched by one of college football's most fearsome pass rush tandems ever, Florida State's Peter Boulware and Reinard Wilson.

Boulware's helmet made a direct hit on Wuerffel's right triceps. Hot pain shot up and down his throwing arm. As he looked to the sideline, the calm command always present in his eyes was gone, replaced by a panicky look. He mouthed the words "Oh, shoot!" Not even this occasion could induce a Wuerffel curse, of course.

Backup quarterback Doug Johnson also had what players call "big eyes" because as Wuerffel came to the bench in the second quarter of the Gators' Sugar Bowl rematch with their enemies from upstate, he doubted his

Chris Fowler *is the host of ESPN's* College GameDay.

record-breaking arm could throw another pass.

Destiny had delivered them this chance at redemption—with Texas dethroning Nebraska on the decade's gutsiest call and Ohio State spoiling Arizona State's national championship claim with heart-stopping Rose Bowl heroics. But to the few who saw that rare fear in Wuerffel's eyes, Florida's quest for its first national title seemed in deep danger.

This was Steve Spurrier's nightmare. He'd made Wuerffel's security the focus of his game plan, even adopting the shotgun formation he had always stubbornly forsaken. Then for the three weeks leading up to the "The Battle on the Bayou", Spurrier's single-minded media agenda put the Seminoles' superb defense on the defensive by harping on the hits—both late and low—that FSU laid on Wuerffel in the Seminoles' late November win. Now a hit neither late

Reuters/Lee Celano/Archive Photos
Gator **Danny Wuerffel** stood tall in 1996, winning the national championship and the Heisman Trophy while setting a new standard for college quarterbacks.

nor low had Wuerffel's arm hanging lifelessly.

But not for long. When the Gators regained possession, Wuerffel was in there and the pain had been pushed aside. He absorbed further blows but dished out many more, as Florida exposed and demoralized an FSU defense built purely on punishing the quarterback. Wuerffel's wheels—heavily braced but deceptively nimble—even won a race to the pylon on the longest touchdown run of his career.

The morning after, his Florida career over, Wuerffel walked to a quiet corner of the press room as teammates posed with the crystal football symbolic of a national championship. He peeled back the right sleeve of his t-shirt to reveal his own trophy:

a nasty baseball-sized bruise. That morning he couldn't have thrown any ball ten feet. Weeks later, the injury kept him out of the Hula Bowl. But during the Sugar Bowl, few of his teammates even realized he was playing hurt.

Too often buried in the avalanche of stats, records and rhetoric about the "Spurrier" system is the essential truth about Wuerffel's success: the minister's kid with choir boy looks, unfailing politeness and unshakable faith is one the toughest, grittiest college football players we've ever seen.

So, in the end, it's for that ugly purple mark on the back of his arm—not all those beautiful bronze trophies—that I'll remember Danny Wuerffel's college days. ∎

Tennessee coach **Phillip Fulmer** (l) is all smiles as he and QB **Peyton Manning** preside over an unusual press conference in which a collegiate star announces that he is *not* turning pro.

Lee Corso's Top Ten Highlights of the 1996 College Football Season

10. **The Texas Longhorns upset of Nebraska** in the Big 12 title game pushed the Cornhuskers out of the national title picture and set up the rematch of Florida and Florida State in the Sugar Bowl as the acknowledged championship game.

9. The **Danny Wuerffel-Troy Davis Heisman trophy race** was one of the closest in years, involving two glamour positions. Wuerffel won after posting the greatest season by a college QB in history but Davis posted an unprecedented second straight season of 2,000 rushing yards.

8. **Academic standards** came under scrutiny, as well. Should these standards be raised or kept the same?

7. An **inordinate number of head coaches were fired,** including several well-regarded veterans. Reasons? New athletic directors and lack of support (read money).

6. The **continued abatement of Title IX programs** raised the question of whether the expansion of women's sports was viable economically. If a Division I men's football program can't break even, does it make sense for the same school to get into field hockey?

5. **The economic problems in college football** were highlighted when many schools dropped non-revenue generating sports that previously had been supported by football. Another pressing money question also emerged: Should athletes be paid?

4. When **Lou Holtz resigned from Notre Dame,** one nagging question remained unanswered: Why did he really leave?

3. **The Bowl Alliance** remained in the news because of Brigham Young's season. Should a one-loss team be in the alliance, no matter what their schedule looked like?

2. **Good things continued at Northwestern** as Gary Barnett led the Wildcats to their second straight Big Ten title.

1. The **rags to riches story of Arizona State** was very exciting as the Sun Devils went from unranked at the end of 1995 to an undefeated 1996 season, Pac Ten championship and a close loss to Ohio State in the Rose Bowl. ■

THE NUMBERS

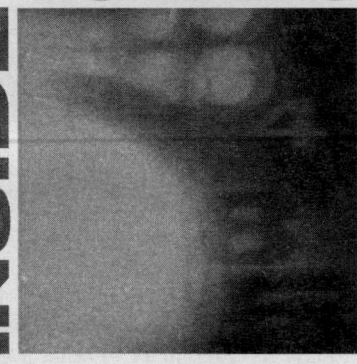

by
Chris Fallica

Heisman Hangover

The performance of Heisman Trophy Winners in National Title Games since 1970 has not been exactly award-winning. Perhaps it is fitting, though, since only Dorsett, Campbell and Walker were outstanding pros.

1996	**Danny Wuerffel (Florida)**	**W**
1993	**Charlie Ward (Florida St.)**	**W**
1992	Gino Torretta (Miami)	L
1986	Vinny Testaverde (Miami)	L
1983	Mike Rozier (Nebraska)	L
1982	Herschel Walker (Georgia)	L
1977	Earl Campbell (Texas)	L
1976	**Tony Dorsett (Pittsburgh)**	**W**
1975	Archie Griffin (Ohio State)	L

Semi-Rush

Florida State's defensive pressure on Danny Wuerffel was excellent in their first meeting in 1996, a Seminole victory. In the Sugar Bowl, however, a slight dropoff was enough to give Wuerffel the win and the Gators the national title.

FSU Defense	1st game	Nat. Champ.
Knockdowns	32	19
Sacks	6	5
Interceptions	3	1
Comp. Pct.	47.9	52.9
QB Rating	119.4	151.7

Great Dayne

In 1996, Ron Dayne shattered Herschel Walker's NCAA freshman rushing record. Other freshman running stars like Walker, Smith, Dorsett and Faulk were first round draft selections. So, with the lure of big money making college athletic careers shorter and shorter, Dayne is certainly making the most of his. One caveat: Alex Smith declared for the NFL draft after his junior season and went undrafted.

Top Freshman Rushers		
1996	**Ron Dayne (Wisconsin)**	**1,863 yds**
1980	Herschel Walker (Georgia)	1,616 yds
1973	Tony Dorsett (Pittsburgh)	1,586 yds
1994	Alex Smith (Indiana)	1,475 yds.
1991	Marshall Faulk (San Diego St.)	1,429 yds
1987	Emmitt Smith (Florida)	1,341 yds

Nothing Lately

John Cooper's career numbers at Ohio State are a respectable 75-29-4 but a look inside those numbers reveals a troubling, perhaps job-fatal, trend. When looking at Cooper's

In 1996, Wisconsin's **Ron Dayne** turned in the best rushing performance ever by a freshman, gaining over 1,800 yards. Since Dayne is unlikely to endure a sophomore slump, 2,000 yards could be the next milestone checked off on his resume.

record in the 1990's at Ohio State, there are three distinct periods: Before Michigan, which is the first ten games of the season, Cooper has a .845 winning percentage. During Michigan, Cooper's percentage drops to .214. After Michigan, which is bowl games, the tally is a tough .167.

John Cooper in the 1990s at Ohio State

First Ten Games	59-10-2
Vs Michigan	1-5-1
in Bowls	2-5

Troy Wonder

In 1995-96, Iowa State's **Troy Davis** put together the best two seasons in a row by a college running back. Thanks to Danny Wuerffel and Eddie George, however, Davis' college career doesn't include a Heisman trophy. As a reminder of what a great career Davis had, we offer a list of Division 1-A leading rushers for consecutive seasons. Yes, the other four won the Heisman. Timing is everything.

Leading Rushers in Consecutive Seasons

	Years	Yards
Troy Davis (Iowa State)	**1995-96**	**4,195**
Marcus Allen (USC)	1980-81	3,905
Mike Rozier (Nebraska)	1982-83	3,837
Herschel Walker (Georgia)	1981-82	3,643
Charles White (USC)	1978-79	3,563

COLLEGE FOOTBALL
S T A T I S T I C S

THE SEASON IN REVIEW
1996-1997

TOP 25 • BOWLS • STANDINGS

SEC **B**

PAGE **147**

THE 1998
ESPN INFORMATION PLEASE SPORTS ALMANAC

Final AP Top 25 Poll

Voted on by panel of 67 sportswriters & broadcasters and released on Jan. 3, 1997, following the Sugar Bowl: winning team receives the Bear Bryant Trophy, given since 1983; first place votes in parentheses, records, total points (based on 25 for 1st, 24 for 2nd, etc.) bowl game result, head coach and career record, preseason rank (released on Aug. 11, 1996) and final regular season rank (released Dec. 8, 1996).

		Final Record	Points	Bowl Game	Head Coach	Aug. 11 Rank	Dec. 8 Rank
1	Florida (65½)	12-1-0	1673½	won Sugar	Steve Spurrier (10 yrs: 93-27-2)	4	3
2	Ohio St. (1½)	11-1-0	1585½	won Rose	John Cooper (20 yrs: 157-70-6)	9	4
3	Florida St.	11-1-0	1529	lost Sugar	Bobby Bowden (31 yrs: 270-82-4)	3	1
4	Arizona St.	11-1-0	1486	lost Rose	Bruce Snyder (17 yrs: 100-85-5)	20	2
5	Brigham Young	14-1-0	1360	won Cotton	LaVell Edwards (25 yrs: 228-81-3)	NR	5
6	Nebraska	11-2-0	1316	won Orange	Tom Osborne (24 yrs: 242-49-3)	1	6
7	Penn St.	11-2-0	1293	won Fiesta	Joe Paterno (31 yrs: 289-74-3)	11	7
8	Colorado	10-2-0	1228	won Holiday	Rick Neuheisel (2 yrs: 20-4-0)	5	8
9	Tennessee	10-2-0	1172	won Citrus	Phillip Fulmer (5 yrs: 42-9-0)	2	9
10	North Carolina	10-2-0	1070	won Gator	Mack Brown (13 yrs: 76-73-1)	NR	12
11	Alabama	10-3-0	977	won Outback	Gene Stallings (14 yrs: 97-61-2)	15	16
12	LSU	10-2-0	849	won Peach	Gerry DiNardo (6 yrs: 36-31-1)	19	17
13	Virginia Tech	10-2-0	786	lost Orange	Frank Beamer (16 yrs: 103-74-4)	16	10
14	Miami-FL	9-3-0	690	won Carquest	Butch Davis (2 yrs: 17-6-0)	12	19
15	Northwestern	9-3-0	663	lost Citrus	Gary Barnett (7 yrs: 35-40-2)	18	11
16	Washington	9-3-0	643	lost Holiday	Jim Lambright (3 yrs: 30-14-1)	NR	13
17	Kansas St.	9-3-0	625	lost Cotton	Bill Snyder (8 yrs: 55-36-1)	21	14
18	Iowa	9-3-0	535	won Alamo	Hayden Fry (35 yrs: 222-165-10)	22	21
19	Notre Dame	8-3-0	511	no bowl	Lou Holtz (27 yrs: 216-95-7)	6	18
20	Michigan	8-4-0	466	lost Outback	Lloyd Carr (2 yrs: 17-8-0)	14	15
21	Syracuse	9-3-0	451	won Liberty	Paul Pasqualoni (11 yrs: 85-35-1)	10	23
22	Wyoming	10-2-0	314	no bowl	Joe Tiller (6 yrs: 39-30-1)	NR	22
23	Texas	8-5-0	169	lost Fiesta	John Mackovic (12 yrs: 81-57-3)	8	20
24	Auburn	8-4-0	130	won Independence	Terry Bowden (13 yrs: 101-44-2)	17	NR
25	Army	10-2-0	71	lost Independence	Bob Sutton (6 yrs: 34-32-1)	NR	24

Other teams receiving votes: 26. **West Virginia** (8-4-0, 43 points, lost Gator); 27. **East Carolina** (8-3-0, 37 pts, no bowl); 28. **Southern Mississippi** (8-3-0, 22 pts, no bowl); 29. **Stanford** (7-5-0, 16 pts, won Sun); 30. **Wisconsin** (8-5-0, 14 pts, won Copper); 31. **San Diego St.** (8-3-0, 4 pts, no bowl); 32. **Virginia** (7-5-0, 3 pts, lost Carquest); 33. **Clemson** (7-5-0, 2 pts, lost Peach).

AP Preseason and Final Regular Season Polls

First place votes in parentheses.

Top 25 (Aug. 11, 1996)

		Pts
1	Nebraska (50)	1644
2	Tennessee (7)	1538
3	Florida St. (5)	1529
4	Florida (1)	1490
5	Colorado (3)	1377
6	Notre Dame (1)	1295
7	USC	1171
8	Texas	1026
9	Ohio St.	987
10	Syracuse	982
11	Penn St.	981
12	Miami-FL	877
13	Texas A&M	803
14	Michigan	766
15	Alabama	601
16	Virginia Tech	563
17	Auburn	536
18	Northwestern	496
19	LSU	465
20	Arizona St.	380
21	Kansas St.	366
22	Iowa	356
23	Virginia	288
24	Kansas	217
25	Clemson	212

Top 25 (Dec. 8, 1996)

		Pts
1	Florida St. (62)	1670
2	Arizona St. (5)	1612
3	Florida	1539
4	Ohio St.	1454
5	Brigham Young	1322
6	Nebraska	1271
7	Penn St.	1259
8	Colorado	1248
9	Tennessee	1078
10	Virginia Tech	1037
11	Northwestern	1000
12	North Carolina	929
13	Washington	914
14	Kansas St.	838
15	Michigan	676
16	Alabama	655
17	LSU	645
18	Notre Dame	504
19	Miami	459
20	Texas	423
21	Iowa	291
22	Wyoming	288
23	Syracuse	242
24	Army	213
25	West Virginia	78

1996-97 Bowl Games

Listed by bowls matching highest-ranked teams as of final regular season AP poll (released Dec. 8, 1996). Attendance figures indicate tickets sold.

Bowl		Winner	Regular Season		Loser	Regular Season	Score	Date	Attendance
Sugar	#3	Florida	11-1-0	#1	Florida St.	11-0-0	52-20	Jan. 2	78,344
Rose	#4	Ohio St.	10-1-0	#2	Arizona St.	11-0-0	20-17	Jan. 1	100,645
Cotton	#5	Brigham Young	13-1-0	#14	Kansas St.	9-2-0	19-15	Jan. 1	71,928
Orange	#6	Nebraska	10-2-0	#10	Virginia Tech	10-1-0	41-21	Dec. 31	51,212
Fiesta	#7	Penn St.	10-2-0	#20	Texas	8-4-0	38-15	Jan. 1	65,106
Holiday	#8	Colorado	9-2-0	#13	Washington	9-2-0	33-21	Dec. 30	54,749
Citrus	#9	Tennessee	9-2-0	#11	Northwestern	9-2-0	48-28	Jan. 1	63,467
Gator	#12	North Carolina	9-2-0	#25	West Virginia	8-3-0	20-13	Jan. 1	52,103
Outback	#16	Alabama	9-3-0	#15	Michigan	8-3-0	17-14	Jan. 1	53,161
Peach	#17	LSU	9-2-0		Clemson	7-4-0	10-7	Dec. 28	63,622
Carquest	#19	Miami-FL	8-3-0		Virginia	7-4-0	31-21	Dec. 27	46,418
Alamo	#21	Iowa	8-3-0		Texas Tech	7-4-0	27-0	Dec. 29	55,677
Liberty	#23	Syracuse	8-3-0		Houston	7-4-0	30-17	Dec. 27	49,163
Independence		Auburn	7-4-0	#24	Army	10-1-0	32-29	Dec. 31	41,366
Aloha		Navy	8-3-0		California	6-5-0	42-38	Dec. 25	30,411
Copper		Wisconsin	7-5-0		Utah	8-3-0	38-10	Dec. 27	42,122
Las Vegas		Nevada	8-3-0		Ball St.	8-3-0	18-15	Dec. 19	10,118
Sun		Stanford	6-5-0		Michigan St.	6-5-0	38-0	Dec. 31	42,741

FAVORITES

Sugar (Florida by 3 points); **Rose** (Ohio St. by 2); **Cotton** (Kansas St. by 3½); **Orange** (Nebraska by 16½); **Fiesta** (Texas by 1); **Holiday** (Colorado by 5); **Citrus** (Tennessee by 8); **Gator** (North Carolina by 6½); **Outback** (Michigan by 1); **Peach** (LSU by 6½); **Carquest** (Miami by 3½); **Alamo** (Texas Tech by 3½); **Liberty** (Syracuse by 16½); **Independence** (Auburn by 9); **Aloha** (Navy by 1); **Copper** (Wisconsin by 7½); **Las Vegas** (Nevada by 5); **Sun** (Michigan St. by 7).

PER TEAM PAYOUTS

Nokia Sugar ($8.736 million); **FedEx Orange** and **Tostitos Fiesta** ($8.486 million); **Rose** ($8.25 million); **CompUSA Florida Citrus** ($3 million); **Southwestern Bell Cotton** ($2 million); **Outback** and **Toyota Gator** ($1.5 million); **Plymouth Holiday** ($1.4 million); **Peach** ($1.3 million); **Builders Square Alamo** and **Sun** ($1 million); **Poulan/Weed Eater Independence** and **St. Jude's Liberty** ($800,000); **Carquest**, **Jeep Eagle Aloha** and **Weiser Lock Copper** ($750,000); **Las Vegas** ($150,000).

Final Bowl Alliance Poll

Combined point totals of the final regular season AP media and USA Today/CNN coaches' polls to help determine bowl match-ups. Polls were released Dec. 8, 1996.

		AP Poll No. Pts		Coaches No. Pts		Total Pts
1	Florida St.	1	(1670)	1	(1545)	3215
2	Arizona St.	2	(1612)	2	(1491)	3103
3	Florida	3	(1539)	3	(1410)	2949
4	Ohio St.	4	(1454)	4	(1340)	2794
5	Brigham Young	5	(1322)	5	(1235)	2557
6	Nebraska	6	(1271)	6	(1185)	2456
7	Penn St.	7	(1259)	7	(1162)	2421
8	Colorado	8	(1248)	8	(1106)	2354
9	Virginia Tech	10	(1037)	9	(1098)	2135
10	Tennessee	9	(1078)	10	(989)	2067
11	Northwestern	11	(1000)	11	(889)	1889
12	Washington	13	(914)	12	(847)	1761
13	North Carolina	12	(929)	13	(815)	1744
14	Kansas St.	14	(838)	14	(727)	1565
15	Alabama	16	(655)	15	(651)	1306
16	LSU	17	(645)	16	(615)	1260
17	Michigan	15	(676)	17	(529)	1205
18	Notre Dame	18	(504)	18	(421)	925
19	Miami	19	(459)	19	(408)	867
20	Texas	20	(423)	20	(324)	747
21	Iowa	21	(291)	21	(312)	603
22	Wyoming	22	(288)	23	(246)	534
23	Syracuse	23	(242)	22	(251)	493
24	Army	24	(213)	24	(231)	444
25	West Virginia	25	(78)	25	(130)	208

Bowl MVPs

Most Valuable Player, Offensive and Defensive Players of the Game, and Team MVP selections in all 18 bowl games following the 1996 season.

		Pos
Alamo	Off— Sedrick Shaw, Iowa	RB
	Def— Jared DeVries, Iowa	DT
Aloha	Team— Chris McCoy, Navy	QB
	Team— Pat Barnes, California	QB
Carquest	MVP— Tremain Mack, Miami-FL	DB
Citrus	MVP— Peyton Manning, Tennessee	QB
Copper	MVP— Ron Dayne, Wisconsin	RB
Cotton	Off— Steve Sarkisian, BYU	QB
	& Kevin Lockett, Kansas St.	WR
	Def— Shay Muirbrook, BYU	LB
Fiesta	Off— Curtis Enis, Penn St.	RB
	Def— Brandon Noble, Penn St.	DT
Gator	Team— Oscar Davenport, N. Carolina	QB
	Team— David Saunders, W. Virginia	WR
Holiday	Off— Koy Detmer, Colorado	QB
	Def— Nick Ziegler, Colorado	DE
Independence	Off— Dameyune Craig, Auburn	QB
	Def— Takeo Spikes, Auburn	LB
Las Vegas	Team— Mike Crawford, Nevada	LB
	Team— Brad Maynard, Ball St.	P
Liberty	MVP— Malcolm Thomas, Syracuse	RB
Orange	Team— Damon Benning, Nebraska	RB
	Team— Ken Oxendine, Va. Tech	RB
Outback	MVP— Dwayne Rudd, Alabama	LB
Peach	Off— Herb Tyler, LSU	QB
	& Raymond Priester, Clemson	RB
	Def— Anthony McFarland, LSU	DT
	& Trevor Pryce, Clemson	DE
Rose	MVP— Joe Germaine, Ohio St.	QB
Sun	MVP— Chad Hutchinson, Stanford	QB
Sugar	MVP— Danny Wuerffel, Florida	QB

Bowl Alliance Championship Game

Florida St. and Florida, who ranked first and third in the final regular season AP poll, met in the Sugar Bowl on Jan. 2, 1997 to decide the national championship for the 1996 season. Opponents' records and AP rank listed below are day of game.

Florida St. Seminoles (11-1-0)

Date	AP Rank	Opponent	Result
Sept. 7	#3	Duke (0-0-0)	44-7
Sept. 19	#3	at N. Carolina St. (0-1-0)	51-17
Sept. 28	#2	#11 North Carolina (3-0-0)	13-0
Oct. 5	#2	Clemson (2-2-0)	34-3
Oct. 12	#3	at #6 Miami-FL (4-0-0)	34-16
Oct. 26	#3	#14 Virginia (5-1-0)	31-24
Nov. 2	#3	at Georgia Tech (5-2-0)	49-3
Nov. 9	#3	vs. Wake Forest (2-6-0)	44-7
Nov. 16	#3	#25 Southern Miss (8-2-0).	54-14
Nov. 23	#3	vs. Maryland (5-4-0)	48-10
Nov. 30	#2	#1 Florida (10-0-0)	24-21
Jan. 2	#1	vs. #3 Florida (11-1-0)†	20-52

†Sugar Bowl (at New Orleans)

Note: Five of the 11 teams on the Seminoles' 1996 regular season schedule went to bowl games– North Carolina (won Gator), Clemson (lost Peach), Miami–FL (won Carquest), Virginia (lost Carquest) and Florida (won Sugar).

Regular Season Statistics

Passing (5 Att)

	Att	Cmp	Pct.	Yds	TD	Rate
Thad Busby	243	134	55.1	1866	16	131.5
Dan Kendra	89	46	51.7	665	9	143.3

Interceptions: Busby 12, Kendra 2.

Top Receivers

	No	Yds	Avg	Long	TD
E.G. Green	34	662	19.5	60-td	7
Warrick Dunn	30	355	11.8	77-td	2
Andre Cooper	26	338	13.0	38-td	4
Peter Warrick	22	467	21.2	59	4
Wayne Messam	21	299	14.2	48-td	3
Laveranues Coles	10	104	10.4	15	2
Melvin Pearsall	8	77	9.6	21	2
Ron Dugans	7	66	9.4	16	1
Rock Preston	7	19	2.7	19	0

Top Rushers

	Car	Yds	Avg	Long	TD
Warrick Dunn	189	1180	6.2	80-td	12
Rock Preston	49	386	7.9	47	5
Laveranues Coles	14	91	6.5	13	0
Pooh Bear Williams	24	79	3.3	20	2
Khalid Abdullah	19	73	3.8	13	0
Dee Feaster	20	60	3.0	41	0
Dan Kendra	36	55	1.5	16	2
Lamarr Glenn	8	49	6.1	21	0
Peter Warrick	8	20	2.5	36	0

Most Touchdowns

	TD	Run	Rec	Ret	Pts
Warrick Dunn	14	12	2	0	84
E.G. Green	7	0	7	0	42
Rock Preston	5	5	0	0	30
Andre Cooper	4	0	4	0	24
Peter Warrick	4	0	4	0	24
Wayne Messam	3	0	3	0	18
Shevin Smith	3	0	0	3	18
Laveranues Coles	2	0	2	0	12
Dee Feaster	2	0	2	0	12
Dan Kendra	2	2	0	0	12
Pooh Bear Williams	2	2	0	0	12
Melvin Pearsall	2	0	2	0	12

Kicking

	FG/Att	Lg	PAT/Att	Pts
Scott Bentley	16/18	48*	52/53	100

*Did it twice.

Punting

	No	Yds	Long	Blk	Avg
Sean Liss	62	2670	76	0	43.1

Most Interceptions

Shevin Smith	3
James Colzie	3
Samari Rolle	2

Most Sacks

Peter Boulware	19
Reinard Wilson	12
Greg Spires	7

Florida Gators (12-1-0)

Date	AP Rank	Opponent	Result
Aug. 31	#4	SW Louisiana (0-0-0)	55-21
Sept. 7	#4	Georgia Southern (1-0-0)	62-14
Sept. 21	#4	at #2 Tennessee (2-0-0)	35-29
Sept. 28	#1	Kentucky (1-2-0)	65-0
Oct. 5	#1	at Arkansas (1-2-0)	42-7
Oct. 12	#1	#12 LSU (4-0-0)	56-13
Oct. 19	#1	#16 Auburn (5-1-0)	51-10
Nov. 2	#1	Georgia (3-4-0)	47-7
Nov. 9	#1	at Vanderbilt (2-6-0)	28-21
Nov. 16	#1	South Carolina (5-4-0)	52-25
Nov. 30	#1	at #2 Florida St. (10-0-0)	21-24
Dec. 7	#4	vs. #15 Alabama (9-2-0)*	45-30
Jan. 2	#3	vs. #1 Florida St. (11-0-0)†	52-20

* SEC title game at Atlanta
† Sugar Bowl (at New Orleans)

Note: Five of the 12 teams on the Gators' 1996 regular season schedule went to bowl games– Tennessee (won Citrus), LSU (won Peach), Auburn (won Independence), Florida St. (lost Sugar) and Alabama (won Outback).

Regular Season Statistics

Passing (5 Att)

	Att	Cmp	Pct.	Yds	TD	Rate
Danny Wuerffel	360	207	57.5	3625	39	170.6
B. Schottenheimer	21	13	61.9	194	1	155.2
Doug Johnson	27	12	44.4	171	2	99.9

Interceptions: Wuerffel 13, Johnson 3.

Top Receivers

	No	Yds	Avg	Long	TD
Reidel Anthony	72	1293	18.0	56-td	18
Ike Hilliard	47	900	19.2	46-td	10
Jacquez Green	33	626	19.0	85-td	9
Travis McGriff	14	167	11.9	27	0
Elijah Williams	14	253	18.1	45-td	1
Terry Jackson	13	163	12.5	43	1
Fred Taylor	8	120	15.0	38	0
Tremayne Allen	7	118	16.9	32	1
Jamie Richardson	5	75	15.0	34	1

Top Rushers

	Car	Yds	Avg	Long	TD
Elijah Williams	106	671	6.3	46	4
Fred Taylor	104	629	6.0	30	5
Terry Jackson	79	388	4.9	34	8
Eugene McCaslin	41	290	7.1	63-td	4
Tyrone Baker	16	80	5.0	18	0
Reidel Anthony	4	33	8.3	13	0
Jacquez Green	6	21	3.5	10	1
Dwayne Mobley	2	17	8.5	10	0
Jerome Evans	2	11	5.5	9	0

Most Touchdowns

	TD	Run	Rec	Ret	Pts
Reidel Anthony	18	0	18	0	108
Jacquez Green	12	1	9	2	72
Ike Hilliard	10	0	10	0	60
Terry Jackson	9	8	1	0	54
Fred Taylor	5	5	0	0	30
Elijah Williams	5	4	1	0	30
Eugene Mccaslin	4	4	0	0	24
Fred Weary	2	0	0	2	12
Danny Wuerffel	2	2	0	0	12

Kicking

	FG/Att	Lg	PAT/Att	Pts
Bart Edminston	9/17	39	64/66	91
Chris Cooper	1/1	35	7/9	10

Punting

	No	Yds	Long	Blk	Avg
Robby Stevenson	35	1475	64	0	42.1

Most Interceptions

Fred Weary	5
Teako Brown	3
Anthone Lott	3

Most Sacks

Tim Beauchamp	6
Cameron Davis	5½
Johnny Rutledge	5
Ed Chester	5

Sugar Bowl
Thursday, Jan. 2, 1997 at Sugar Bowl in New Orleans, La.

#3 **Florida** (SEC) 10   14   14   14   **—52**
#1 **Florida St.** (ACC) 3   14   3   0   **—20**

1st: FLA—Ike Hilliard 9-yd pass from Danny Wuerffel (Bart Edmiston kick), 5:12. Drive: 77 yards in 9 plays. FSU—Scott Bentley 43-yd FG, 7:11. Drive: 55 yards in 8 plays. FLA—Edmiston 32-yd FG, 12:16. Drive: 11 yards in 5 plays.
2nd: FLA—Fred Taylor 2-yd run (Edmiston kick), 3:32. Drive: 73 yards in 4 plays. FSU—E.G. Green 29-yd pass from Thad Busby (Bentley kick), 7:32. Drive: 63 yards in 7 plays. FLA—Hilliard 31-yd pass from Wuerffel (Edmiston kick), 9:42. Drive: 65 yards in 4 plays. FSU—Warrick Dunn 12-yd run (Bentley kick), 14:20. Drive: 66 yards in 5 plays.
3rd: FSU—Bentley 45-yd FG, 4:36. Drive: 30 yards in 6 plays. FLA—Hilliard 8-yd pass from Wuerffel (Edmiston kick), 9:17. Drive: 24 yards in 4 plays. FLA—Wuerffel 16-yd run (Edmiston kick), 14:47. Drive: 68 yards in 9 plays.
4th: FLA—Terry Jackson 42-yd run (Edmiston kick), 6:08. Drive: 62 yards in 5 plays. FLA—Jackson 1-yd run (Edmiston kick), 13:48. Drive: 70 yards in 10 plays.

Favorite: Florida by 3   **Attendance:** 78,344
Field: Turf   **Time:** 4:10
Weather: Dome   **TV Rating:** 17.9/29 share (ABC)
MVP: Danny Wuerffel, Florida, QB

Team Statistics

	Florida	Florida St.
Touchdowns	7	2
Rushing	4	1
Passing	3	1
Kick returns	0	0
Interception returns	0	0
Safeties	0	0
Time of possession	36:27	23:33
First downs	26	13
Rushing	8	2
Passing	12	9
Penalties	6	2
3rd down efficiency	5-16	5-18
4th down efficiency	1-1	0-1
Total offense (net yards)	474	313
Plays	77	63
Average gain	6.2	5.0
Carries/yards (includ. sacks)	43/168	21/42
Passing yards	306	271
Completions/attempts	18/34	17/42
Times sacked/yards lost	3/25	5/26
Return yardage	12/169	14/250
Punt returns/yards	6/69	5/74
Kickoff returns/yards	4/93	8/152
Interceptions/yards	2/7	1/24
Fumbles/lost	1/0	0/0
Penalties/yards	15/102	14/115
Punts/average	7/48.1	8/46.4
Punts blocked	0	0
PATs/attempts	7/7	2/2
Field goals/attempts	1/1	2/3

Individual Statistics
Florida

Passing	Att	Cmp	Pct.	Yds	TD	Int
Danny Wuerffel	34	18	52.9	306	3	1
TOTAL	34	18	52.9	306	3	1

Receiving	No	Yds	Avg	Long	TD
Ike Hilliard	7	150	21.4	47	3
Jacquez Green	5	79	15.8	40	0
Reidel Anthony	4	50	12.5	28	0
Dwayne Mobley	1	16	16.0	16	0
Fred Taylor	1	11	11.0	11	0
TOTAL	18	306	17.0	47	3

Rushing	Car	Yds	Avg	Long	TD
Terry Jackson	12	118	9.8	42-td	2
Fred Taylor	18	60	3.3	18	1
Elijah Williams	4	2	0.5	3	0
B. Schottenheimer	1	0	0.0	0	0
Eugene McCaslin	2	-2	-1.0	1	0
Danny Wuerffel	6	-10	-1.7	16-td	1
TOTAL	43	168	3.9	42-td	4

Field Goals	20-29	30-39	40-49	50-59	Total
Bart Edmiston	0-0	1-1	0-0	0-0	1-1

Punting	No	Yds	Long	Blk	Avg
Robby Stevenson	7	337	69	0	48.1

Punt Returns	FC	Ret	Yds	Long	Avg	TD
Jacquez Green	2	6	69	26	11.5	0
TOTAL	2	6	69	26	11.5	0

Kickoff Returns	No	Yds	Long	Avg	TD
Ike Hilliard	2	48	28	24.0	0
Reidel Anthony	1	31	31	31.0	0
Elijah Williams	1	14	14	14.0	0
TOTAL	4	93	31	23.3	0

Interceptions		Sacks	
Teako Brown	1	Ed Chester	2
Ernie Badeaux	1	Cameron Davis	1

Florida St.

Passing	Att	Cmp	Pct.	Yds	TD	Int
Thad Busby	41	17	41.5	271	1	1
Dan Kendra	1	0	0.0	0	0	1
TOTAL	42	17	40.5	271	1	2

Receiving	No	Yds	Avg	Long	TD
Wayne Messam	5	48	9.6	23	0
Andre Cooper	4	82	20.5	55	0
E.G. Green	3	86	28.7	34	1
Melvin Pearsall	1	25	25.0	25	0
Warrick Dunn	1	12	12.0	12	0
Khalid Abdullah	1	10	10.0	10	0
Peter Warrick	1	7	7.0	7	0
P.B. Williams	1	1	1.0	1	0
TOTAL	17	271	15.9	55	1

Rushing	Car	Yds	Avg	Long	TD
Warrick Dunn	9	28	3.1	12-td	1
Peter Warrick	1	12	12.0	12	0
P.B. Williams	2	7	3.5	7	0
Dee Feaster	2	1	0.5	2	0
Thad Busby	7	-6	-0.9	8	0
TOTAL	21	42	2.0	12	1

Field Goals	20-29	30-39	40-49	50-59	Total
Scott Bentley	0-0	0-0	2-2	0-1	2-3

Punting	No	Yds	Long	Blk	Avg
Sean Liss	8	371	57	0	46.4

Punt Returns	FC	Ret	Yds	Long	Avg	TD
Peter Warrick	0	3	32	19	10.7	0
Dee Feaster	0	2	42	24	21.0	0

Kickoff Returns	No	Yds	Long	Avg	TD
Laveranues Coles	4	73	22	18.3	0
Dee Feaster	2	45	23	22.5	0
Peter Warrick	1	19	19	19.0	0
Germaine Stringer	1	15	15	15.0	0

Interceptions		Sacks	
Vernon Crawford	1	Peter Boulware	2
		Three tied with one each.	

Other Final Division I-A Polls

USA Today/CNN Coaches Poll

Voted on by panel of 62 Division I-A head coaches; winning team receives the Sears Trophy (originally the McDonald's Trophy, 1991-93); first place votes in parentheses with total points (based on 25 for 1st, 24 for 2nd, etc.).

		Pts			Pts
1	Florida (58)	1546	14	Miami-FL	636
2	Ohio St. (4)	1466	15	Washington	622
3	Florida St.	1408	16	Northwestern	594
4	Arizona St.	1341	17	Kansas St.	564
5	BYU	1261	18	Iowa	549
6	Nebraska	1235	19	Syracuse	446
7	Penn St.	1205	20	Michigan	390
8	Colorado	1128	21	Notre Dame	381
9	Tennessee	1077	22	Wyoming	259
10	North Carolina	971	23	Texas	141
11	Alabama	906	24	Army	106
12	Virginia Tech	791	25	Auburn	103
13	LSU	746			

Other teams receiving votes: West Virginia (85 pts); Navy (76); Virginia (30); Stanford (24); East Carolina (19); Wisconsin (15); Southern Mississippi (13); Nevada and San Diego St. (5); Clemson (4); Texas Tech (2). **Teams on probation**: Mississippi.

NFF/Hall of Fame Poll

Voted on by panel of 62 members of the National Football Foundation and College Hall of Fame; winning team receives the NFF's MacArthur Bowl, given since 1959; first place votes in parentheses with total points (based on 25 for 1st, 24 for 2nd, etc.).

		Pts			Pts
1	Florida (63)	1646	14	Northwestern	710
2	Ohio St. (2)	1563	15	Washington	659
3	Florida St.	1507	16	Miami-FL	656
4	Arizona St.	1463	17	Kansas St.	614
5	BYU (1)	1320	18	Michigan	489
6	Nebraska	1318	19	Iowa	477
7	Penn St.	1271	20	Syracuse	453
8	Colorado	1208	21	Notre Dame	425
9	Tennessee	1156	22	Texas	247
10	North Carolina	1004	23	Wyoming	197
11	Alabama	959	24	Auburn	165
12	Virginia Tech	802	25	Army	124
13	LSU	790			

FWAA Poll

Voted on by a five-man panel comprised of Tim Layden of *Sports Illustrated*, Steve Weiberg of *USA Today*, Mark Blaudschun of the *Boston Globe*, Andy Bagnato of *The Chicago Tribune* and Tony Barnhart of the *Atlanta Constitution*. Each selector voted for one team.

Winning team receives the Grantland Rice Award, given since 1954.

Florida (5)

Winningest Teams of the 1990s

Division I-A schools with the best overall winning percentage from 1990-96, through the Jan. 1-2, 1997, bowl games. **National champions:** 1990—Colorado (AP, FWAA, NFF) and Georgia Tech (UPI); 1991—Miami-FL (AP) and Washington (FWAA, NFF, USA Today/CNN); 1992—Alabama; 1993—Florida St; 1994—Nebraska; 1995—Nebraska; 1996—Florida.

		Overall Record	Bowls W-L-T	Overall Win Pct.
1	Florida St	75-10-1	6-1-0	.878
2	Nebraska	74-11-1	3-4-0	.866
3	Florida	73-14-1	3-3-0	.835
4	Miami-FL	69-14-0	3-3-0	.831
5	Colorado	67-14-4	5-2-0	.812
6	Penn St.	69-17-0	5-2-0	.802
7	Tennessee	66-17-2	5-2-0	.788
8	Texas A&M	66-17-2	2-3-0	.788
9	Nevada†	66-20-0	1-2-0	.767
10	Notre Dame	63-19-2	3-3-0	.762
11	Ohio St.	64-19-3	2-5-0	.762
12	Washington	61-20-1	2-3-0	.750
13	Michigan	61-21-3	4-3-0	.735
14	Syracuse	58-22-3	5-0-0	.717
15	Alabama	62-25-0	5-1-0	.713
16	BYU	63-25-2	2-3-1	.711
17	Auburn	54-23-3	2-1-0	.694
18	North Carolina	57-25-1	3-2-0	.693
19	Kansas St.	54-26-1	2-2-0	.673
20	Virginia	55-28-1	2-4-0	.661
21	Toledo	50-25-3	1-0-0	.660
22	Clemson	53-28-1	2-3-0	.652
23	Bowling Green	48-26-4	2-0-0	.641
24	Texas	52-29-2	1-3-0	.639
25	Iowa	51-30-2	2-2-1	.627
26	Virginia Tech	50-30-1	2-2-0	.623
27	Central Fla.†	49-31-0	0-0-0	.613
28	Ala.-Birmingham†	37-24-2	0-0-0	.603
29	Ball St.	46-30-2	0-2-0	.603
30	Utah	49-33-0	1-2-0	.598

† Nevada joined I-A in 1992, Central Fla. and Ala.-Birmingham in 1996.

NY Times Computer Ratings

Based on an analysis of each team's scores with emphasis on three factors: who won, by what margin, and against what quality of opposition. Computer balances lop-sided scores, notes home field advantage and gives late-season games more weight than those played earlier in the schedule.

The top team is assigned a rating of 1.000, ratings of all other teams reflect their strength relative to strength of No.1 team. Rankings include all regular season games.

		Rating			Rating
1	Florida St.	1.000	14	Tennessee	.798
2	Arizona St.	.989	15	Kansas St.	.790
3	Florida	.965	16	Texas	.770
4	Nebraska	.930	17	Army	.757
5	Ohio St.	.921	18	Miami-FL	.739
6	Washington	.908	19	LSU	.735
7	Brigham Young	.906	20	Michigan	.735
8	Virginia Tech	.894	21	Iowa	.725
9	Colorado	.845	22	East Carolina	.724
10	Penn St.	.809	23	Rice	.721
11	Syracuse	.806	24	Texas Tech	.719
12	North Carolina	.801	25	Wyoming	.717
13	Notre Dame	.800			

☞ See pages 162-164 for list of all national championship teams since 1869. Also, see pages 166-180 for every Associated Press final Top 20 poll since 1936.

NCAA Division I-A Final Standings

Standings based on conference games only; overall records include postseason games.

Atlantic Coast Conference

	Conference				Overall			
	W	L	PF	PA	W	L	PF	PA
*Florida St.	8	0	314	71	11	1	446	174
*North Carolina ...	6	2	240	76	10	2	357	123
*Clemson	6	2	164	156	7	5	245	241
*Virginia	5	3	219	112	7	5	341	203
Georgia Tech	4	4	157	161	5	6	220	236
Maryland	3	5	118	205	5	6	187	239
N. C. State	3	5	199	285	3	8	268	401
Wake Forest	1	7	79	287	3	8	144	374
Duke	0	8	105	242	0	11	162	379

Bowls (1-3): Florida St. (lost Sugar); North Carolina (won Gator); Clemson (lost Peach); Virginia (lost Carquest).

Big East Conference

	Conference				Overall			
	W	L	PF	PA	W	L	PF	PA
*Virginia Tech ...	6	1	220	111	10	2	370	209
*Miami-FL	6	1	233	111	9	3	368	210
*Syracuse	6	1	291	105	9	3	437	208
*West Virginia ..	4	3	181	112	8	4	271	156
Pittsburgh	3	4	121	242	4	7	214	430
Boston College .	2	5	138	220	5	7	264	364
Rutgers	1	6	78	238	2	9	143	380
Temple	0	7	140	263	1	10	218	386

Bowls (2-2): Virginia Tech (lost Orange); Miami-FL (won Carquest); Syracuse (won Liberty); West Virginia (lost Gator).

Big Ten Conference

	Conference				Overall			
	W	L	PF	PA	W	L	PF	PA
*Ohio St.	7	1	264	91	11	1	455	131
*Northwestern ..	7	1	215	182	9	3	336	278
*Penn St.	6	2	224	174	11	2	400	203
*Iowa	6	2	233	183	9	3	339	243
*Michigan	5	3	185	131	8	4	277	184
*Michigan St. ...	5	3	277	179	6	6	358	302
*Wisconsin	3	5	190	203	8	5	377	243
Purdue	2	6	146	248	3	8	194	324
Minnesota	1	7	145	281	4	7	236	340
Indiana	1	7	181	268	3	8	242	291
Illinois	1	7	149	269	2	9	190	372

Rose Bowl tiebreaker: The first tiebreaker is head-to-head competition between the tied teams. Since Ohio St. and Northwestern did not play during the 1996 season, the second tiebreaker (overall winning percentage) was used. Ohio St. earned the Rose Bowl berth with a 10-1 mark while Northwestern ended the regular season at 9-2.

Bowls (4-3): Ohio St. (won Rose); Northwestern (lost Citrus); Penn St. (won Fiesta); Iowa (won Alamo); Michigan (lost Outback); Michigan St. (lost Sun); Wisconsin (won Copper).

Conference Bowling Results

Postseason records for 1996 season.

	W-L
SEC	5-0
Big West	1-0
Big Ten	4-3
Big East	2-2
Independents	1-1
WAC	1-1
Big 12	2-3
ACC	1-3
Pac-10	1-3
Conference USA	0-1
Mid-American	0-1

Big 12 Conference

	Conference				Overall			
North	W	L	PF	PA	W	L	PF	PA
*Nebraska	8	1	392	111	11	2	553	174
*Colorado	7	1	221	126	10	2	352	220
*Kansas St.	6	2	197	162	9	3	340	191
Missouri	3	5	197	307	5	6	278	376
Kansas	2	6	171	286	4	7	300	358
Iowa St.	1	7	221	299	2	9	314	401

	Conference				Overall			
South	W	L	PF	PA	W	L	PF	PA
*Texas	7	2	354	196	8	5	447	305
*Texas Tech	5	3	197	149	7	5	323	232
Texas A&M	4	4	174	174	6	6	351	257
Oklahoma	3	5	193	290	3	8	255	392
Oklahoma St. ..	2	6	159	281	5	6	243	327
Baylor	1	7	186	281	4	7	266	320

Big 12 championship game: Texas beat Nebraska, 37-27 (Dec. 7).

Bowls (2-3): Nebraska (won Orange); Colorado (won Holiday); Kansas St. (lost Cotton); Texas (lost Fiesta); Texas Tech (lost Alamo).

Big West Conference

	Conference				Overall			
	W	L	PF	PA	W	L	PF	PA
*Nevada	4	1	238	106	8	3	497	263
Utah St.	4	1	175	130	6	5	330	339
Idaho	3	2	167	112	6	5	374	296
North Texas	3	2	93	105	5	6	161	293
Boise St.	1	4	121	231	2	10	240	459
N. Mexico St. ..	0	5	86	196	1	10	166	396

Las Vegas Bowl tiebreaker: Nevada and Utah St. finished the regular season as Big West co-champions. Nevada earned the right to represent the conference in the Las Vegas Bowl by beating Utah St. 54-27 on Nov. 9.

Bowls (1-0): Nevada (won Las Vegas)

Conference USA

	Conference				Overall			
	W	L	PF	PA	W	L	PF	PA
Southern Miss.	4	1	141	108	8	3	287	247
*Houston	4	1	171	124	7	5	361	341
Cincinnati	2	3	88	100	6	5	228	212
Louisville	2	3	57	102	5	6	182	205
Memphis	2	3	65	92	4	7	141	219
Tulane	1	4	109	105	2	9	213	268

Liberty Bowl tiebreaker: Southern Miss. and Houston finished the season as conference co-champions. Houston earned the right to represent the conference in the Liberty Bowl by beating Southern Miss. 56-49 in overtime on Nov. 9.

Bowls (0-1): Houston (lost Liberty).

Mid-American Conference

	Conference				Overall			
	W	L	PF	PA	W	L	PF	PA
*Ball St.	7	1	217	121	8	4	296	210
Toledo	6	2	153	134	7	4	210	259
Miami-OH	6	2	229	90	6	5	273	168
Ohio	5	3	209	107	6	6	302	237
Central Michigan .	4	4	251	239	5	6	351	353
Akron	3	5	116	193	4	7	175	269
Bowling Green .	3	5	130	176	4	7	176	240
Eastern Michigan	3	5	183	185	3	8	210	284
Western Michigan .	2	6	151	200	2	9	208	304
Kent	1	7	171	365	2	9	255	492

Bowls (0-1): Ball St. (lost Las Vegas).

Pacific 10 Conference

	Conference				Overall			
	W	L	PF	PA	W	L	PF	PA
*Arizona St.	8	0	344	182	11	1	488	216
*Washington	7	1	268	140	9	3	391	254
*Stanford	5	3	174	196	7	5	247	229
UCLA	4	4	257	245	5	6	330	318
*California	3	5	224	288	6	6	382	407
Oregon	3	5	269	271	6	6	378	356
USC	3	5	210	211	6	6	325	267
Arizona	3	5	226	256	6	6	310	280
Washington St. .	3	5	205	230	5	6	314	317
Oregon St. ...	1	7	125	283	2	9	216	388

*Bowls (1-3): Arizona St. (lost Rose); Washington (lost Holiday); Stanford (won Sun); California (lost Aloha).

Southeastern Conference

	Conference				Overall			
Eastern	W	L	PF	PA	W	L	PF	PA
*Florida	9	0	421	142	12	1	611	221
*Tennessee	7	1	275	113	10	2	437	185
South Carolina ..	4	4	171	170	6	5	245	238
Georgia	3	5	189	224	5	6	230	257
Kentucky	3	5	118	260	4	7	138	322
Vanderbilt	0	8	65	198	2	9	122	234

	Conference				Overall			
Western	W	L	PF	PA	W	L	PF	PA
*LSU	6	2	192	145	10	2	335	210
*Alabama	6	3	234	145	10	3	316	195
*Auburn	4	4	247	224	8	4	398	277
Mississippi St. ..	3	5	136	181	5	6	249	229
Mississippi	2	6	96	228	5	6	203	270
Arkansas	2	6	88	202	4	7	174	267

SEC championship game: Florida beat Alabama, 45-30 (Dec. 7).

*Bowls (5-0): Florida (won Sugar); Tennessee (won Citrus); LSU (won Peach); Alabama (won Outback); Auburn (won Independence).

Western Athletic Conference

	Conference				Overall			
Pacific	W	L	PF	PA	W	L	PF	PA
Wyoming ...	7	2	341	180	10	2	464	284
San Diego St. ..	6	2	300	209	8	3	428	303
Colorado St. ...	6	2	248	169	7	5	380	336
Air Force	5	3	316	171	6	5	360	231
Fresno St.	3	5	199	245	4	7	267	344
San Jose St.	3	5	168	273	3	9	221	448
Hawaii	1	7	100	315	2	10	161	433
UNLV	1	7	211	320	1	11	276	551

	Conference				Overall			
Mountain	W	L	PF	PA	W	L	PF	PA
*BYU	9	0	347	142	14	1	590	277
*Utah	6	2	224	199	8	4	313	309
Rice	6	2	261	194	7	4	296	312
SMU	4	4	180	211	5	6	246	267
New Mexico ...	3	5	237	233	6	5	331	280
TCU	3	5	167	208	4	7	211	302
Tulsa	2	6	178	259	4	7	245	333
UTEP	0	8	129	278	2	9	183	314

WAC championship game: BYU beat Wyoming, 28-25 (Dec. 7).

*Bowls (1-1): BYU (won Cotton); Utah (lost Copper).

I-A Independents

	W	L	PF	PA
*Army	10	2	379	224
*Navy	9	3	392	309
East Carolina	8	3	316	214
Notre Dame	8	3	407	181
Louisiana Tech	6	5	351	342
Ala.-Birmingham	5	6	266	279
Central Florida	5	6	277	261
NE Louisiana	5	6	192	353
SW Louisiana	5	6	304	404
Arkansas St.	4	7	272	365
Northern Illinois	1	10	157	400

*Bowls (1-1): Army (lost Independence); Navy (won Aloha).

NCAA Division I-A Individual Leaders
REGULAR SEASON
Total Offense

		Rushing				Passing		Total Offense				
	Cl	Car	Gain	Loss	Net	Att	Yds	Plays	Yds	YdsPP	TDR*	YdsPG
Josh Wallwork, Wyoming ...	Sr.	67	257	138	119	458	4090	525	4209	8.02	35	350.75
Ryan Fien, Idaho	Sr.	59	133	198	-65	455	3662	514	3597	7.00	29	327.00
Pat Barnes, California	Sr.	86	208	291	-83	420	3499	506	3416	6.75	32	310.55
Jon Denton, UNLV	Fr.	88	344	306	38	506	3591	594	3629	6.11	28	302.42
Jason Martin, La. Tech	Sr.	25	58	97	-39	415	3360	440	3321	7.55	32	301.91
Danny Wuerffel, Florida	Sr.	63	126	226	-100	360	3625	423	3525	8.33	41	293.75
Billy Blanton, San Diego St. .	Sr.	70	208	268	-60	344	3221	414	3161	7.64	30	287.36
Peyton Manning, Tennessee .	Jr.	42	35	166	-131	380	3287	422	3156	7.48	23	286.91
Koy Detmer, Colorado	Sr.	36	108	114	-6	363	3156	399	3150	7.89	25	286.36
Steve Sarkisian, BYU	Sr.	82	216	260	-44	404	4027	486	3983	8.20	34	284.50

* Touchdowns responsible for include TD passes and TDs scored.

All-Purpose Yards

	Cl	Gm	Rush	Rec	PR	KOR	Total Yds	YdsPG
Troy Davis, Iowa St.	Jr.	11	2185	61	0	118	2364	214.91
Byron Hanspard, Texas Tech	Jr.	11	2084	192	0	0	2276	206.91
Corey Dillon, Washington	Jr.	11	1555	273	0	357	2185	198.64
Kevin Faulk, LSU	So.	11	1282	134	375	313	2104	191.27
Silas Massey, Central Mich.	So.	10	1544	103	0	159	1806	180.60
June Henley, Kansas	Sr.	10	1349	215	0	209	1773	177.30
Scott Harley, E. Carolina	So.	11	1745	199	0	0	1944	176.73
Tiki Barber, Virginia	Sr.	11	1360	258	241	0	1859	169.00
Leon Johnson, N. Carolina	Sr.	11	913	381	191	347	1832	166.55
Ron Dayne, Wisconsin	Fr.	12	1863	133	0	0	1996	166.33

Iowa St.   Brigham Young   Washington   Wyoming

Troy Davis   **Steve Sarkisian**   **Corey Dillon**   **Josh Wallwork**

Rushing, All-Purpose   Passing   Scoring   Total Offense

NCAA Division I-A Individual Leaders (Cont.)

Passing Efficiency

(Minimum 15 attempts per game)

	Cl	Gm	Att	Cmp	Cmp Pct	Int	Int Pct	Yds	Yds/ Att	TD	TD Pct	Rating Points
Steve Sarkisian, BYU	Sr.	14	404	278	68.81	12	2.97	4027	9.97	33	8.17	173.6
Danny Wuerffel, Florida	Sr.	12	360	207	57.50	13	3.61	3625	10.07	39	10.83	170.6
Billy Blanton, San Diego St. .	Sr.	11	344	227	65.99	5	1.45	3221	9.36	29	8.43	169.6
Josh Wallwork, Wyoming . . .	Sr.	12	458	286	62.45	15	3.28	4090	8.93	33	7.21	154.7
John Dutton, Nevada	So.	11	334	222	66.47	6	1.80	2750	8.23	22	6.59	153.8
Pat Barnes, California	Sr.	11	420	250	59.52	8	1.90	3499	8.33	31	7.38	150.1
Peyton Manning, Tennessee .	Jr.	11	380	243	63.95	12	3.16	3287	8.65	20	5.26	147.7
Mike Fouts, Utah	Sr.	11	302	177	58.61	7	2.32	2526	8.36	21	6.95	147.2
Ryan Clement, Miami-FL	Jr.	11	246	148	60.16	6	2.44	1983	8.06	18	7.32	147.1
Brent Baldwin, Ball St.	Sr.	11	205	121	59.02	5	2.44	1703	8.31	14	6.83	146.5
Jason Martin, Louisiana Tech .	Sr.	11	415	247	59.52	16	3.86	3360	8.10	32	7.71	145.3
Donovan McNabb, Syracuse .	So.	11	215	118	54.88	9	4.19	1776	8.26	19	8.84	145.1
Jim Druckenmiller, Va. Tech . .	Sr.	11	250	142	56.80	5	2.00	2071	8.28	17	6.80	144.8

Rushing

	Cl	Car	Yds	TD	YdsPG
Troy Davis, Iowa St.	Jr.	402	2185	21	198.64
Byron Hanspard, Texas Tech	Jr.	339	2084	13	189.45
Scott Harley, E. Carolina . .	So.	307	1745	14	158.64
Ron Dayne, Wisconsin . . .	Fr.	295	1863	18	155.25
Silas Massey, Central Mich.	So.	312	1544	16	154.40
Corey Dillon, Washington . .	Jr.	271	1555	22	141.36
Darnell Autry, Northwestern	Jr.	263	1386	15	138.60
David Thompson, Okla St. .	Sr.	293	1524	13	138.55
Beau Morgan, Air Force . .	Sr.	225	1494	18	135.82
June Henley, Kansas	Sr.	302	1349	17	134.90

Games: All played 11, except Dayne (12); Massey, Autry, and Henley (10).

Receptions

	Cl	No	Yds	TD	P/Gm
Damond Wilkins, Nevada . .	Sr.	114	1121	4	10.36
Marcus Harris, Wyoming . .	Sr.	109	1650	13	9.08
Geoffrey Noisy, Nevada . .	So.	98	1435	9	8.91
Chad Mackey, La. Tech	Sr.	85	1466	10	7.73
Nakia Jenkins, Utah St.	Jr.	82	1397	8	7.45
Brandon Stokley, SW La. . .	So.	81	1160	7	7.36
Brian Roberson, Fresno St. .	Sr.	78	1248	5	7.09
Will Blackwell, San Diego St. .	Sr.	60	1000	11	6.67
Reggie Allen, Central Mich. .	So.	66	1229	9	6.60
Kevin Lockett, Kansas St. . . .	Sr.	72	882	6	6.55
Tony Knox, Western Mich. . .	Sr.	71	754	6	6.45

Games: All played 11, except Harris (12); Allen (10); Blackwell (9).

Scoring

Non-Kickers

	Cl	TD	Pts	P/Gm
Corey Dillon, Washington	Jr.	23	138	12.55
Troy Davis, Iowa St.	Jr.	21	126	11.45
Calvin Branch, Colorado St. . . .	Sr.	22	132	11.00
Terry Battle, Arizona St.	Jr.	20	120	10.91
Skip Hicks, UCLA	Jr.	20	120	10.91
June Henley, Kansas	Sr.	18	108	10.80
Beau Morgan, Air Force	Sr.	18	108	9.82
Sedrick Irvin, Michigan St. . . .	Fr.	18	108	9.82
Silas Massey, Central Mich. . . .	So.	16	98*	9.80
Darnell Autry, Northwestern . . .	Jr.	16	96	9.60

*Includes one 2-point conversion.

Games: All played 11, except Branch (12); Henley, Massey and Autry (10).

Kickers

	FG/Att	PAT/Att	Pts	P/Gm
Damon Shea, Nevada . .	20/22	55/56	115	10.45
Scott Bentley, Florida St. .	16/18	52/53	100	9.09
Cory Wedel, Wyoming . .	20/27	48/48	108	9.00
Phil Dawson, Texas	19/24	51/51	108	9.00
Ethan Pochman, BYU . . .	20/28	63/65	123	8.79
Rafael Garcia, Virginia . .	21/25	33/33	96	8.73
Joseph Parker, Army	18/21	40/40	94	8.55
Robert Nycz, Arizona St. . .	11/16	60/60	93	8.45
Bart Edmiston, Florida . .	9/17	64/66	91	8.27
Peter Holt, San Diego St. .	15/19	41/44	86	7.82

Games: All played 11, except Pochman (14); Wedel and Dawson (12).

Field Goals

	Cl	FG/Att	Pct	Lg
Rafael Garcia, Virginia	Sr.	21/27	.778	46
Marc Primanti, NC State	Sr.	20/20	1.000	48
Damon Shea, Nevada	So.	20/22	.909	43
Corey Wedel, Wyoming	Jr.	20/27	.741	51
Ethan Pochman, BYU	Sr.	20/27	.741	51
James Anderson, Tulsa	Jr.	20/28	.714	53
Phil Dawson, Texas	Jr.	19/24	.792	53
J. Parker, Army	Sr.	18/21	.857	45
Kyle Bryant, Texas A&M	Jr.	18/23	.783	52
Brett Conway, Penn St.	Sr.	18/24	.750	52

Games: All played 11, except Pochman (14); Wedel, Bryant and Conway (12).

Longest FG of season: 57 yds by Michael Reeder, TCU vs. UTEP (Oct. 12).

Interceptions

	Cl	No	Yds	TD	Lg
Dre' Bly, N. Carolina	Fr.	11	141	1	51-td
Brian Lee, Wyoming	Jr.	8	68	0	41
Kim Herring, Penn St.	Sr.	7	64	0	28
Kevin Jackson, Alabama	Sr.	7	44	1	44-td

Eight tied with 6 each.

Games: All played 12, except Bly (11).

Punting

(Minimum of 3.6 per game)

	Cl	No	Yds	Avg
Bill Marinangel, Vanderbilt	Sr.	77	3586	46.57
Noel Prefontaine, San Diego St	Sr.	48	2234	46.54
Andy Russ, Mississippi St.	Sr.	53	2466	46.53
Ty Atteberry, Baylor	Sr.	60	2781	46.35
Tucker Phillips, Rice	Sr.	53	2433	45.91

	Cl	No	Yds	Avg
Brad Maynard, Ball St.	Sr.	59	2705	45.85
Jim Wren, USC	Jr.	66	3006	45.55
Marc Harris, Iowa St.	Sr.	51	2312	45.33
Ryan Longwell, California	Sr.	60	2714	45.23
John Krueger, Duke	Sr.	58	2619	45.16

Punt Returns

(Minimum of 1.2 per game)

	Cl	No	Yds	TD	Avg
Allen Rossum, Notre Dame	Jr.	15	344	3	22.93
Tim Dwight, Iowa	Jr.	22	417	2	18.95
James Dye, Brigham Young	Sr.	20	352	2	17.60
Kevin Faulk, LSU	So.	24	375	1	15.63
Keijuan Douglas, Eastern Mich.	Fr.	12	183	1	15.25
Leandrew Childs, San Diego St.	Jr.	22	332	0	15.09
Chad Smith, New Mexico	So.	14	200	1	14.29
Terry Fair, Tennessee	Jr.	29	400	2	13.79
Brian Roberson, Fresno St.	Sr.	24	330	1	13.75
Tremayne Banks, Miami-OH	Sr.	29	395	0	13.62

Kickoff Returns

(Minimum of 1.2 per game)

	Cl	No	Yds	TD	Avg
Tremain Mack, Miami-FL	Jr.	13	514	1	39.54
Terry Battle, Arizona St.	Jr.	17	528	2	31.06
Pat Johnson, Oregon	Jr.	12	368	1	30.67
Eric Booth, Southern Miss.	Jr.	12	352	0	29.33
Cedric Johnson, UTEP	Sr.	25	729	1	29.16
Rodnick Phillips, SMU	Fr.	22	618	1	28.09
John Avery, Mississippi	Jr.	17	473	2	27.82
Tony Knox, Western Mich.	Sr.	25	690	1	27.60
Jim Turner, Syracuse	Jr.	23	633	1	27.52
Tremayne Banks, Miami-OH	Sr.	19	518	1	27.26

NCAA Division I-A Team Leaders
REGULAR SEASON

Scoring Offense

	Gm	Record	Pts	Avg
Florida	12	11-1	559	46.6
Nevada	11	8-3	497	45.2
Arizona St.	11	11-0	471	42.8
Nebraska	12	10-2	512	42.7
BYU	14	13-1	571	40.8
Ohio St.	11	10-1	435	39.5
San Diego St.	11	8-3	428	38.9
Florida St.	11	11-0	426	38.7
Wyoming	12	10-2	464	38.7
Syracuse	11	9-3	407	37.0

Scoring Defense

	Gm	Record	Pts	Avg
N. Carolina	11	9-2	110	10.0
Ohio St.	11	10-1	114	10.4
Florida St.	11	11-0	122	11.1
W. Virginia	11	8-3	136	12.4
Nebraska	12	10-2	153	12.8
Tennessee	11	9-2	157	14.3
Alabama	12	9-3	181	15.1
Michigan	11	8-3	167	15.2
Virginia Tech	11	10-2	168	15.3
Miami-OH	11	6-5	168	15.3

Total Offense

	Gm	Plays	Yds	Avg	TD	YdsPG
Nevada	11	915	5800	6.3	57	527.27
Florida	12	854	6047	7.1	67	503.92
Wyoming	12	905	5987	6.6	54	498.92
Arizona St.	11	874	5417	6.2	54	492.45
Idaho	11	848	5294	6.2	48	481.27
BYU	14	1004	6692	6.7	67	478.00
Central Mich.	11	871	5252	6.0	45	477.45
San Diego St.	11	803	5241	6.5	51	476.45
Utah St.	11	835	5110	6.1	43	464.55
Notre Dame	11	817	5096	6.2	49	463.27

Note: Touchdowns scored by rushing and passing only.

Total Defense

	Gm	Plays	Yds	Avg	TD	YdsPG
W. Virginia	11	712	2392	3.4	15	217.5
N. Carolina	11	660	2482	3.8	12	225.6
Florida St.	11	776	2524	3.3	14	229.5
Louisville	11	765	2594	3.4	20	235.8
Tennessee	11	708	2602	3.7	16	236.5
Ohio St.	11	707	2676	3.8	12	243.3
Nebraska	12	776	3065	3.9	15	255.4
Alabama	12	711	3067	4.3	20	255.6
Army	11	626	2819	4.5	23	256.3
Syracuse	11	725	2875	4.0	17	261.4

Note: Opponents' TDs scored by rushing and passing only.

Single Game Highs
INDIVIDUAL

Rushing Yards

Yds
378   Troy Davis, Iowa St. vs. Missouri (Sept. 28)
351   Scott Harley, E. Carolina vs. N.C. State (Nov. 30)
339   Ron Dayne, Wisconsin at Hawaii (Nov. 30)
321   David Thompson, Oklahoma St. vs. Baylor (Nov. 23)
315   Robert Holcombe, Illinois vs. Minnesota (Nov. 16)

Rushing & Passing Yards

Yds
531   Ryan Fien, Idaho at Wyoming (Aug. 31)
529   Jason Martin, La. Tech vs. Toledo (Oct. 19)
519   Steve Sarkisian, BYU vs. Texas A&M (Aug. 24)
513   Jon Denton, UNLV vs. San Diego St. (Nov. 16)
503   Pat Barnes, California vs. Arizona (Nov. 2)

Passes Attempted

Att
65   Peyton Manning, Tennessee vs. Florida (Sept. 21)
64   Branndon Stewart, Texas A&M vs. Colorado (Sept. 28)
63   Chris Redman, Louisville vs. So. Miss. (Sept. 28)
62   Walt Church, E. Michigan at Cent. Michigan (Oct. 19)
61   Jon Denton, UNLV at San Jose St. (Nov. 23)

Receptions

No
18   Geoffery Noisy, Nevada vs. Arkansas St. (Nov. 16)
18   Albert Connell, Texas A&M vs. Colorado (Sept. 28)
16   Marcus Harris, Wyoming at Iowa St. (Sept. 7)
16   Marcus Harris, Wyoming at Colorado St. (Nov. 16)
15   Several Tied

Receiving Yards

Yds
310   Chad Mackey, La. Tech vs. Toledo (Oct. 19)
296   Geoffery Noisy, Nevada at Utah St. (Nov. 9)
283   Jeremy McDaniel, Arizona at California (Nov. 2)
280   Will Blackwell, San Diego St. at California (Sept. 14)
260   Jay Soward, USC at UCLA (Nov. 23)
260   Kendrick Lee, So. Miss. at Houston (Nov. 9)

Passing Yards

Yds
542   Jason Martin, La. Tech vs. Toledo (Oct. 19)
542   Ryan Fien, Idaho at Wyoming (Aug. 31)
536   Steve Sarkisian, BYU vs. Texas A&M (Aug. 24)
503   Pat Barnes, California vs. Arizona (Nov. 2)
503   Jon Denton, UNLV vs. San Diego St. (Nov. 16)

Passes Completed

No
37   Peyton Manning, Tennessee vs. Florida (Sept. 21)
36   Josh Wallwork, Wyoming at Iowa St. (Sept. 7)
36   Jason Martin, La. Tech at Arkansas St. (Nov. 9)
36   Ryan Fien, Idaho at Wyoming (Aug. 31)
35   Pat Barnes, California vs. Arizona (Nov. 2)
35   Chris Redman, Louisville vs. So. Miss (Sept. 28)

TEAM
Points Scored

Pts
76   W. Mich (76-27) vs. Kent St. (Nov. 16)
73   Nebraska (73-21) vs. Oklahoma (Nov. 2)
72   Ohio St. (72-0) vs. Pittsburgh (Sept. 21)
71   Texas (71-14) vs. Oklahoma St. (Oct. 5)
70   Ohio St. (70-7) vs. Rice (Sept. 7)
67   Oregon St. (67-28) vs. N. Illinois (Nov. 16)
66   Wyoming (66-0) vs. Hawaii (Sept. 14)
66   Nevada (66-28) vs. Boise St. (Oct. 12)
66   Nevada (66-14) vs. Arkansas St. (Nov. 16)
65   Air Force (65-17) vs. UNLV (Sept. 7)
65   Florida (65-0) vs, Kentucky (Sept. 28)
65   Nebraska (65-9) vs. Colorado St. (Sept. 28)

Annual Awards

Player of the Year

Danny Wuerffel ...Camp, Heisman, Maxwell, *The Sporting News*

Position Players of the Year

O'Brien Award (Quarterback) ....Danny Wuerffel, Florida
Unitas Award (Senior QB) ....Danny Wuerffel
Walker Award (Running Back) .Byron Hanspard, Texas Tech
Biletnikoff Award (Receiver) .....Marcus Harris, Wyoming
Groza Award (Kicker) ....Marc Primanti, N.C. State
Outland Trophy (Interior Lineman) ..Orlando Pace, Ohio St.
Lombardi Award (Lineman) ....Orlando Pace
Butkus Award (Linebacker) ....Matt Russell, Colorado
Thorpe Award (Defensive Back) ..Lawrence Wright, Florida
Nagurski Award (Defensive Player) ....Pat Fitzgerald,
                                            Northwestern

Payton Award
(IAA Player of the Year) ......Archie Amerson, N. Arizona
Buchanan Award
(IAA Defensive Player) ....Dexter Coakley, Appalachian St.
Hill Trophy
(Div. II Player of the Year) .... Jarrett Anderson, Truman St.

Coaches of the Year

Bruce Snyder, Arizona St. ......AFCA, Camp, FWAA, *The Sporting News*
Bob Sutton, Army ....Dodd

Heisman Trophy Vote

Presented since 1935 by the Downtown Athletic Club of New York City and named after former college coach and DAC athletic director John W. Heisman. Voting done by national media and former Heisman winners. Each ballot allows for three names (points based on 3 for 1st, 2 for 2nd and 1 for 3rd).

Top 10 Vote-Getters

	Pos	1st	2nd	3rd	Pts
Danny Wuerffel, Florida	QB	300	158	147	1363
Troy Davis, Iowa St.	RB	209	206	135	1174
Jake Plummer, Arizona St. ..	QB	116	113	111	685
Orlando Pace, Ohio St.	OT	87	101	136	599
Warrick Dunn, Florida St. ...	RB	40	76	69	341
Byron Hanspard, Texas Tech ..	RB	15	68	70	251
Darnell Autry, N'western	RB	9	19	20	85
Peyton Manning, Tenn.	QB	4	23	23	81
Marcus Harris, Wyoming ...	WR	7	7	18	53
Beau Morgan, Air Force ...	QB	3	3	11	26

Note: All players were seniors except juniors Autry, Davis, Hanspard, Manning and Pace.

Consensus All-America Team

NCAA Division I-A players cited most frequently by the following five selectors: AFCA, AP, FWAA, *The Sporting News* and Walter Camp Foundation. Holdovers from 1995 All-America team are in **bold** type; (*) indicates unanimous selection.

Offense

	Player	Class	Ht	Wt
WR	Marcus Harris, Wyoming	Sr.	6-2	215
WR	Reidel Anthony, Florida	Jr.	6-0	181
TE	Tony Gonzalez, California ...	Jr.	6-6	235
OL	**Orlando Pace***, Ohio St. ..	Jr.	6-5	320
OL	Dan Neil, Texas	Sr.	6-2	285
OL	Aaron Taylor, Nebraska	Jr.	6-1	305
OL	Chris Naeole, Colorado	Sr.	6-4	310
OL	Juan Roque, Arizona St.	Sr.	6-8	319
QB	Danny Wuerffel, Florida	Sr.	6-2	207
RB	Byron Hanspard*, Texas Tech .	Jr.	6-0	190
RB	**Troy Davis**, Iowa St.	Jr.	5-8	190
K	Marc Primanti, N.C. State ...	Sr.	5-7	158

Defense

	Player	Class	Ht	Wt
DL	Peter Boulware, Florida St...	Jr.	6-5	255
DL	Mike Vrabel, Ohio St.	Sr.	6-4	260
DL	Grant Wistrom, Nebraska	Jr.	6-5	250
LB	Jarrett Irons, Michigan	Sr.	6-2	234
LB	**Pat Fitzgerald**, Northwestern .	Sr.	6-2	245
LB	Matt Russell, Colorado	Sr.	6-2	245
LB	Canute Curtis, West Virginia ..	Sr.	6-2	250
DB	Dre' Bly, North Carolina	Fr.	5-10	190
DB	Chris Canty*, Kansas St.	Jr.	5-10	190
DB	Kevin Jackson*, Alabama	Sr.	6-2	200
DB	Shawn Springs, Ohio St.	Jr.	6-0	190
DB	Charles Woodson, Michigan ..	So.	6-1	192
P	**Brad Maynard**, Ball St.	Sr.	6-1	176

Underclassmen Who Declared for 1997 NFL Draft

Thirty-four players forfeited the remainder of their college eligibility and declared for the NFL draft in 1997. NFL teams drafted 25 underclassmen. Players listed in alphabetical order.

	Pos	Drafted by	Overall pick
Reidel Anthony, Florida ..	WR	Tampa Bay	16
Darnell Autry, Northwestern	RB	Chicago	105
Ronde Barber, Virginia ...	CB	Tampa Bay	66
Terry Battle, Arizona St. ..	RB	Detroit	206
Will Blackwell, San Diego St.	WR	Pittsburgh	53
Peter Boulware, Florida St.	DE	Baltimore	4
Chris Canty, Kansas St.	CB	New England	29
Jason Caudill, Ohio U.	OT	not selected	—
Tony Daniels, Texas Tech ..	DE	not selected	—
Troy Davis, Iowa St.	RB	New Orleans	62
Corey Dillon, Washington	RB	Cincinnati	43
Tony Gonzalez, California	TE	Kansas City	13
Yatil Green, Miami-FL	WR	Miami	15
Byron Hanspard, Texas Tech	RB	Atlanta	41
Ike Hilliard, Florida	WR	NY Giants	7
Hudhaifa Ismaeli, N'western	DB	Miami	203
Walter Jones, Florida St. ..	OT	Seattle	6

	Pos	Drafted by	Overall pick
Kenard Lang, Miami-FL ...	DE	Washington	17
Tremain Mack, Miami-FL ...	S	Cincinnati	111
LeVance McQueen, Duke ...	LB	not selected	—
Jamie Nails, Florida A&M ...	OT	Buffalo	120
Orlando Pace, Ohio St.	OT	St. Louis	1
Pearce Pegross, Baylor ...	WR	not selected	—
Trevor Pryce, Clemson	DE	Denver	28
Derrick Rodgers, Arizona St.	DE	Miami	92
Dwayne Rudd, Alabama ..	LB	Minnesota	20
Darrell Russell, USC	DT	Oakland	2
Alex Smith, Indiana	RB	not selected	—
Shawn Springs, Ohio St. ...	DB	Seattle	3
Maurice Staley, Tennessee ..	WR	not selected	—
Broderick Thomas, So. Miss.	DB	not selected	—
Rodney Wells, Florida St. ..	DB	not selected	—
Kenny Wheaton, Oregon .	DB	Dallas	94
C.J. Williams, Georgia Tech	RB	not selected	—

NCAA Division I-AA Final Standings

Standings based on conference games only; overall records include post-season games.

Big Sky Conference

	Conference				Overall			
	W	L	PF	PA	W	L	PF	PA
*Montana	8	0	325	164	14	1	638	264
*Northern Arizona .	7	1	324	229	9	3	506	333
CS-Northridge	5	3	291	225	7	4	407	313
Weber St.	5	3	235	208	7	4	325	262
Eastern Wash.	4	4	213	189	6	5	305	254
Montana St.	4	4	166	171	6	5	247	222
Idaho St.	2	6	224	246	4	7	320	316
Portland St.	1	7	117	292	3	8	196	359
CS-Sacramento	0	8	190	361	1	10	248	466

***Playoffs (3-2):** Montana (3-1); Northern Arizona (0-1).

Gateway Athletic Conference

	Conference				Overall			
	W	L	PF	PA	W	L	PF	PA
*Northern Iowa ..	5	0	182	73	12	2	457	255
SW Missouri St. ..	3	2	123	103	7	4	285	179
Indiana St.	3	2	88	88	6	5	256	233
*Western Ill.	3	2	90	87	9	3	270	185
Southern Ill.	1	4	94	142	5	6	302	302
Illinois St.	0	5	76	160	3	8	226	306

***Playoffs (2-2):** Northern Iowa (2-1); Western Ill. (0-1).

Ivy League

	Conference				Overall			
	W	L	PF	PA	W	L	PF	PA
Dartmouth	7	0	199	76	10	0	275	104
Columbia	5	2	119	133	8	2	181	159
Brown	4	3	171	160	5	5	238	246
Cornell	4	3	157	178	4	6	221	280
Pennsylvania	3	4	130	116	5	5	222	172
Harvard	2	5	98	115	4	6	163	164
Princeton	2	5	87	142	3	7	144	202
Yale	1	6	103	144	2	8	145	246

Playoffs: League does not play postseason games.

Metro-Atlantic Conference

	Conference				Overall			
	W	L	PF	PA	W	L	PF	PA
Duquesne	8	0	274	79	10	1	392	129
Georgetown	7	1	261	76	7	3	303	167
Marist	6	2	194	116	7	3	254	176
St. John's	5	3	227	185	6	4	260	209
Canisius	4	4	137	108	5	4	158	108
St. Peter's	2	6	119	229	2	7	131	270
Siena	2	6	146	213	2	7	156	256
Fairfield	1	7	93	271	1	8	112	313
Iona	1	7	63	237	1	9	83	290

Playoffs: No teams invited.

NCAA Division I-AA Final Standings (Cont.)

Mid-Eastern Athletic Conference

	Conference				Overall			
	W	L	PF	PA	W	L	PF	PA
*Florida A&M	7	0	320	181	9	3	437	238
†Howard	6	1	345	85	10	2	441	178
N. Car. A&T	4	3	209	137	8	3	312	194
S.Car. St.	4	3	139	115	4	6	187	208
Hampton	3	4	202	177	5	6	266	241
Morgan St.	2	5	89	277	4	7	172	365
Delaware St.	2	5	145	223	3	8	257	317
Bethune-Cookman	0	7	95	280	2	9	195	384

*Playoffs (0-1): Florida A&M (0-1).
†Heritage Bowl: Howard beat SWAC entrant Southern-BR, 27-24 (Dec. 31).

Northeast Conference

	Conference				Overall			
	W	L	PF	PA	W	L	PF	PA
Robert Morris ...	3	1	129	72	9	2	318	142
Monmouth (NJ) ...	3	1	108	97	7	3	247	170
Wagner	2	2	113	113	5	5	252	232
Cent. Conn. St. ..	2	2	117	123	3	7	230	344
St. Francis (Pa.) ..	0	4	52	114	3	7	165	261

Playoffs: No teams invited.

Ohio Valley Conference

	Conference				Overall			
	W	L	PF	PA	W	L	PF	PA
*Murray St.	8	0	272	87	11	2	463	206
Eastern Ky.	6	2	227	109	6	5	286	184
*Eastern Ill.	5	3	267	163	8	4	378	240
Mid. Tenn. St. ...	4	4	174	154	6	5	220	206
Tennessee Tech ..	4	4	142	190	5	6	180	242
Tennessee St.	3	4	163	167	4	7	258	268
SE Missouri St. ..	3	5	104	186	3	8	130	287
Austin Peay	1	7	137	269	1	10	149	339
Tenn-Martin	1	7	92	260	1	10	125	357

*Playoffs (1-2): Murray St. (1-1); Eastern Ill. (0-1).

Patriot League

	Conference				Overall			
	W	L	PF	PA	W	L	PF	PA
Bucknell	4	1	131	80	6	5	234	223
Colgate	3	2	152	111	6	5	285	256
Lehigh	3	2	92	80	5	6	208	264
Lafayette	2	2	89	91	5	5	192	214
Fordham	1	3	72	105	2	8	172	248
Holy Cross	1	4	76	145	2	9	209	351

Playoffs: League does not play postseason games.

Pioneer League

	Conference				Overall			
	W	L	PF	PA	W	L	PF	PA
Dayton	5	0	168	95	11	0	411	186
Drake	4	1	183	79	8	3	361	188
Evansville	2	3	130	188	5	5	270	330
Butler	2	3	113	165	3	7	164	307
Valparaiso	1	4	139	144	4	6	275	258
San Diego	1	4	77	139	4	6	197	257

Playoffs: No teams invited.

Southern Conference

	Conference				Overall			
	W	L	PF	PA	W	L	PF	PA
*Marshall	9	0	385	116	15	0	658	210
*East Tenn. St. ...	7	1	235	131	10	3	378	286
*Furman	6	3	230	235	9	4	335	301
Appalachian St. .	5	3	173	160	7	4	223	196
The Citadel	3	5	196	247	4	7	236	335
Ga. Southern	2	6	168	205	4	7	255	295
VMI	2	6	141	218	3	8	189	296
Tenn-Chatt	2	6	121	206	3	8	175	290
W. Carolina	1	7	143	274	4	7	232	318

*Playoffs (6-2): Marshall (4-0); East Tennessee St. (1-1); Furman (1-1).

Southland Conference

	Conference				Overall			
	W	L	PF	PA	W	L	PF	PA
*Troy St.	6	1	179	95	12	2	434	252
*Nicholls St.	5	2	144	151	8	4	212	235
Stephen F. Austin .	4	3	159	130	7	4	310	211
Northwestern St. .	3	3	137	96	6	5	241	166
Sam Houston St. .	3	3	118	145	4	7	238	309
SW Texas St.	2	4	113	183	5	6	221	310
McNeese St.	1	5	123	120	3	8	236	225
Jacksonville St. ..	0	3	39	94	1	9	177	290

*Playoffs (2-2): Troy St. (2-1); Nicholls St. (0-1).

Southwestern Athletic Conference

	Conference				Overall			
	W	L	PF	PA	W	L	PF	PA
*Jackson St.	6	1	281	91	10	2	396	183
†Southern-BR	5	2	196	92	7	5	270	195
Miss. Valley St. ..	5	2	116	119	7	4	180	203
Texas Southern ..	5	2	165	135	7	4	261	199
Alcorn State	3	4	143	105	4	7	199	216
Grambling	2	5	96	151	3	8	161	218
Alabama St.	2	5	77	142	3	8	135	248
Prarie View	0	7	71	310	0	10	117	419

*Playoffs (0-1): Jackson St. (0-1).
†Heritage Bowl: Southern-BR lost to MEAC entrant Howard, 27-24 (Dec. 31).

Yankee Conference

	Conference				Overall			
New England	W	L	PF	PA	W	L	PF	PA
New Hampshire .	7	3	269	186	8	3	311	213
Maine	5	3	221	157	7	4	285	212
Massachusetts ..	4	5	188	264	6	5	257	294
Connecticut	2	5	166	158	4	6	244	191
Rhode Island ...	2	5	183	221	4	6	260	258
Boston University .	0	9	80	337	1	10	119	373

	Conference				Overall			
Mid-Atlantic	W	L	PF	PA	W	L	PF	PA
*Wm. & Mary ...	7	1	194	110	10	3	394	214
*Villanova	7	2	272	178	8	4	378	261
*Delaware	6	2	192	131	8	4	293	244
James Madison .	5	4	205	205	7	4	259	215
Northeastern ...	5	5	212	198	6	5	248	204
Richmond	1	7	127	164	2	9	157	197

*Playoffs (1-3): Wm. & Mary (1-1); Villanova (0-1); Delaware (0-1).

NCAA I-AA Independents

	W	L	PF	PA
Buffalo	8	3	271	241
Youngstown St.	8	3	261	131
St. Mary's (Cal.)	7	3	312	224
Western Ky.	7	4	304	251
Davidson	6	4	223	216
Morehead St.	6	4	308	252
Towson St.	6	4	234	204
Samford	6	5	175	240
Wofford	6	5	264	220
Cal Poly-SLO	5	6	308	356
Hofstra	5	6	203	138
Liberty	5	6	251	261
Southern Utah	3	7	251	347
Charleston Southern	2	8	164	359

Playoffs: No teams invited.

N. Arizona   CS-Northridge   Wm & Mary   Montana

Archie Amerson   **David Romines**   **Darren Sharper**   **Brian Ah Yat**
Scoring   Receptions   Interceptions   Total Offense

NCAA Division I-AA Regular Season Leaders

INDIVIDUALS

Passing Efficiency

(Minimum 15 attempts per game)

	Cl	Gm	Att	Cmp	Cmp Pct	Int	Int Pct	Yds	Yds/ Att	TD	TD Pct	Rating Points
Ted White, Howard	So.	11	289	174	60.21	10	3.46	2814	9.74	36	12.46	176.2
Steven Beard, Northern Iowa ..	Sr.	11	238	140	58.82	9	3.78	2526	10.61	21	8.82	169.5
Sean Laird, St. Mary's (Cal.) ..	Jr.	10	256	161	62.89	4	1.56	2199	8.59	22	8.59	160.3
Braniff Bonaventure, Furman ...	Sr.	11	234	152	64.96	2	0.85	2012	8.60	16	6.84	158.0
Eric Kresser, Marshall	Sr.	10	276	170	61.59	7	2.54	2341	8.48	24	8.70	156.5
Brian Ah Yat, Montana	So.	11	432	265	61.34	16	3.70	3615	8.37	42	9.72	156.3
Eric Goebel, Evansville	Sr.	8	192	102	53.13	2	1.04	1641	8.55	19	9.90	155.5
Mike Simpson, Eastern Ill.	Jr.	11	247	163	65.99	7	2.83	1987	8.04	19	7.69	153.3
Kevin Johns, Dayton	Jr.	11	218	114	52.29	10	4.59	1980	9.08	21	9.63	151.2

Total Offense

	Cl	Rush	Pass	Yds	YdsPG
Brian Ah Yat, Montana ...	So.	129	3615	3744	340.36
Aaron Flowers, CS-N'ridge	Jr.	82	3540	3622	329.27
Travis Brown, N. Arizona .	Fr.	-62	3398	3336	303.27
Roger Cook, Weber St. ...	Sr.	-80	3207	3127	284.27
Oteman Sampson, Fla. A&M	Jr.	312	2814	3126	284.18
Ted White, Howard	So.	225	2814	3039	276.27
Jason McCullough, Brown .	Sr.	95	2609	2704	270.40
Grailyn Pratt, Jackson St. ..	Jr.	368	2597	2965	269.55
Kevin Smith, Towson	So.	1	2299	2300	255.56
Mike Cook, Wm. & Mary ..	So.	34	2515	2549	231.73

Rushing

	Cl	Car	Yds	TD	YdsPG
Reggie Greene, Siena	Jr.	280	1719	12	191.00
Archie Amerson, N. Ariz. ..	Sr.	333	2079	25	189.00
Kenny Bynum, S.Car. St. ...	Sr.	236	1649	14	164.90
Chad Levitt, Cornell	Sr.	267	1435	13	159.44
Thomas Haskins, VMI	Sr.	287	1704	15	154.91
Rick Sarille, Wagner	So.	279	1475	11	147.50
Claude Mathis, SW Texas St.	Jr.	294	1593	16	144.82
Damon Scott, Appalachian St.	Sr.	286	1466	14	133.27
Michael Cosey, SW Mo. St. ..	Sr.	293	1453	13	132.09
Brian Knuckles, Western Ill. .	Sr.	270	1310	14	131.00

Games: All played 11, except Bynum, Sarille and Knuckles (10); Greene and Levitt (9).

Receptions

	Cl	No	Yds	TD	P/Gm
David Romines, CS-N'ridge ..	Sr.	87	1300	12	8.70
Antwuan Wyatt, Beth.Cook. ..	Sr.	70	985	4	7.78
Thomas Lopusznick, Fairfield ..	Fr.	69	857	6	7.67
Joe Douglass, Montana	Sr.	82	1469	18	7.45
Brian Finneran, Villanova	Jr.	81	1207	8	7.36
Rameek Wright, Maine	Jr.	79	1143	5	7.18
Robert Wilson, Florida A&M ..	Sr.	78	1161	10	7.09
Juan Hall, Tennessee St.	Jr.	72	1021	5	6.55
Michael Tolbert, Valparaiso ..	Sr.	64	919	4	6.40
Blake Tuffli, St. Mary's (Cal.) .	Sr.	61	953	12	6.10

Games: All played 11, except Romines, Tolbert and Tuffli (10); Wyatt and Lopusznick (9).

Interceptions

	Cl	No	Yds	TD	LG
Darren Sharper, Wm. & Mary .	Sr.	10	228	1	88-td
Scott Shields, Weber St.	So.	10	101	0	35
Robert Taylor, Tenn. Tech	Sr.	9	24	0	13
Shane Hurd, Canisius	Jr.	7	198	2	90-td
Lloyd Lee, Dartmouth	Jr.	7	116	1	70-td
Sean Woodson, Jackson St. .	Sr.	7	79	0	40
Tyree Talton, Northern Iowa ..	So.	7	169	1	65-td
Dorrell Green, Delaware	Jr.	7	159	1	93-td
Jeff Morris, Samford	Sr.	7	75	0	30
Trevor Bell, Idaho St.	Jr.	7	55	0	49

Games: All played 11, except Lee and Woodson (10); Hurd (7).

NCAA Division I-AA Regular Season Leaders (Cont.)

Scoring
Non-Kickers

	Cl	TD	XPt	Pts	P/Gm
Archie Amerson, N. Ariz. ...	Sr.	26	0	156	14.18
Stan House, Cent. Conn. St. .	Jr.	20	0	120	12.00
Sean Bennett, Evansville	So.	19	4	118	11.80
Jerry Azumah, N. Hampshire .	So.	21	0	126	11.45
Joe Douglass, Montana	Sr.	19	2	116	10.55
Randy Moss, Marshall	Fr.	19	0	114	10.36

Games: All played 11, except House and Bennett (10).

Kickers

	Cl	FG/Att	PAT/Att	Pts
Rob Hart, Murray St.	Jr.	22/27	46/47	112
Wayne Boyer, SW Mo. St. ..	Sr.	25/30	28/28	103
Tim Openlander, Marshall ...	Sr.	11/14	58/58	91
Scott Shields, Weber St.	So.	18/24	35/38	89
Matt Huerkamp, Troy St.	Sr.	16/22	39/42	87

Games: All played 11.

Field Goals

	Cl	FG/Att	Pct	LG
Wayne Boyer, SW Mo. St. ...	Sr.	25/30	.833	57
Rob Hart, Murray St.	Jr.	22/27	.815	52
Scott Shields, Weber St.	So.	18/24	.750	52
Matt Huerkamp, Troy St.	Sr.	16/22	.727	48
James Ferrell, Idaho St.	Jr.	15/19	.789	52
Keith Jones, Western Ill.	Jr.	15/20	.750	52
Adam Diel, Nicholls St.	Sr.	15/23	.652	49

Games: All played 11. **Longest FG of season**: 57 yds by Boyer, SW Missouri St. vs. Truman St. (Sept. 14).

Punt/Kickoff Leaders

Punting	Cl	No	Yds		Avg
Mark Gagliano, Southern Ill. .	Sr.	54	2432		45.04

Punt Returns	Cl	No	Yds	TD	Avg
Ricky Pearsall, N. Ariz. ...	Jr.	29	490	2	16.90

Kickoff Returns	Cl	No	Yds	TD	Avg
Randy Moss, Marshall	Fr.	14	484	0	34.57

TEAMS

Scoring Offense

	Gm	Record	Pts	Avg			Gm	Record	Pts	Avg
Northern Ariz.	11	9-2	475	43.2		Northern Iowa	11	10-1	384	34.9
Marshall	11	11-0	465	42.3		Troy St.	11	10-1	367	33.4
Montana	11	11-0	447	40.6		Eastern Ill.	11	8-3	364	33.1
Murray St.	11	10-1	426	38.7		Drake	11	8-3	361	32.8
Howard	11	9-2	414	37.6		Villanova	11	8-3	349	31.7
Florida A&M	11	9-2	412	37.5		St. Mary's-CA	10	7-3	312	31.2
Dayton	11	11-0	411	37.4		Morehead St.	10	6-4	308	30.8
CS-Northridge	11	7-4	407	37.0		Georgetown	10	7-3	303	30.8
Duquesne	10	10-0	366	36.6		East Tenn. St.	11	9-2	329	29.9
Jackson St.	11	10-1	390	35.5		Weber St.	11	7-4	325	29.5

Scoring Defense

	Gm	Record	Pts	Avg			Gm	Record	Pts	Avg
Duquesne	10	10-0	101	10.1		Howard	11	9-2	154	14.0
Dartmouth	10	10-0	104	10.4		Northwestern St.	11	6-5	166	15.1
Robert Morris	10	8-2	116	11.6		Southern-BR.	11	7-4	168	15.3
Youngstown St.	11	8-3	131	11.9		Murray St.	11	10-1	169	15.4
Canisius	9	5-4	108	12.0		William & Mary	11	9-2	170	15.5
Hofstra	11	5-6	138	12.5		Columbia	10	8-2	159	15.9
Jackson St.	11	10-1	138	12.5		Northern Iowa	11	10-1	175	15.9
Western Ill.	11	9-2	151	13.7		SW Missouri St.	11	7-4	179	16.3
Marshall	11	11-0	153	13.9		Harvard	10	4-6	164	16.4
Troy St.	11	10-1	154	14.0		Georgetown	10	7-3	167	16.7

Total Offense

	Record	Plays	Yds	Avg			Record	Plays	Yds	Avg
Northern Ariz.	9-2	873	5751	522.82		Georgetown	7-3	603	2182	218.2
Montana	11-0	808	5332	484.73		William & Mary	9-2	728	2550	231.8
Marshall	11-0	743	5105	464.09		Duquesne	10-1	646	2444	244.4
CS-Northridge	7-4	813	5062	460.18		Youngstown St.	8-3	712	2785	253.2
Howard	9-2	719	5050	459.09		Hofstra	5-6	742	2847	258.8
Dayton	11-0	780	4887	444.27		Robert Morris	9-2	674	2590	259.0
Cal Poly-SLO	5-6	828	4872	442.91		Murray St.	10-1	727	2850	259.1
Jackson St.	10-1	854	4835	439.55		Howard	9-2	724	2909	264.5
Murray St.	10-1	796	4817	437.91		Jackson St.	10-1	729	2913	264.8
Florida A&M	9-2	736	4767	433.36		Northeastern	6-5	672	2932	266.5

Total Defense

NCAA Playoffs

Division I-AA
First Round (Nov. 30)

at Montana 48 . . . . .Nicholls St. 3
at East Tennessee St. 35 . . . . .Villanova 29
at Troy St. 29 . . . . .Florida A&M 25
at Murray St. 34 . . . . .Western Illinois 6
at Marshall 59 . . . . .Delaware 14
Furman 42 .at Northern Arizona 31
at Northern Iowa 21 . . . . .Eastern Illinois 14
at William & Mary 45 .Jackson St. 6

Quarterfinals (Dec. 7)

at Montana 44 . . . . .East Tennessee St. 14
at Troy St. 31 . . . . .Murray St. 3
at Marshall 54 . . . . .Furman 0
at Northern Iowa 38 . . . . .William & Mary 35

Semifinals (Dec. 14)

at Montana 70 . . . . .Troy St. 7
at Marshall 31 . . . . .Northern Iowa 14

Championship Game
Dec. 21 at Huntington, W. Va. (Att: 30,052)

Marshall 49 . . . . .Montana 29
(15-0)   (14-1)

Division II
First Round (Nov. 23)

at Clarion (Pa.) 42 . . . . .Bloomsburg (Pa.) 29
at Ferris St. (Mich.) 24 . . . . .Indiana (Pa.) 23
Northern Colorado 24 . . . . .at Pittsburg St. (Kan.) 21
Northwest Missouri St. 22 . . . . .at Nebraska-Omaha 21
at Valdosta St. (Ga.) 38 . . . . .Albany St. (Ga.) 28
at Carson-Newman (Tenn.) 41 . . . . .West Georgia 7
at Central Oklahoma 23 . . . . .Chadron St. (Neb.) 21
UC Davis 17 . . . . .at Texas A&M Kingsville 14

Quarterfinals (Nov. 30)

Clarion St. 23 . . . . .at Ferris St. 21
at Northern Colorado 27 . . . . . . .Northwest Missouri St. 26
at Carson-Newman 24 . . . . .Valdosta St. 19
at UC Davis 26 .Central Oklahoma 7

Semifinals (Dec. 7)

Northern Colorado 19 . . . . .at Clarion 18
at Carson-Newman 29 .UC Davis 26

Championship Game
Dec. 14 at Florence, Ala. (Att: 5,745)

Northern Colorado 23 . . . . .Carson-Newman 14
(12-3)   (12-2)

Division I-AA, II and III Awards
Players of the Year

Payton Award (Div. I-AA) . . . . . . .Archie Amerson, RB
                                    Northern Arizona (Sr.)
Hill Trophy (Div. II) . . . . .Jarrett Anderson, RB
                                         Truman St. (Sr.)
Gagliardi Trophy (Div. III) . . . . .Lon Erickson, QB
                                       Illinois Wesleyan (Sr.)

Coaches of the Year

AFCA (NCAA Div. I-AA) . . . . .Ray Tellier, Columbia
AFCA (College Div. II) . . . . .Joe Glenn, No. Colorado
AFCA (College Div. III) . . . . . .Larry Kehres, Mt. Union

Division III
First Round (Nov. 23)

at Mount Union (Ohio) 31 . . . . .Allegheny 26
Illinois Wesleyan 23 . . . . .at Albion (Mich.) 20
at Wisc.-La Crosse 44 . . . . .Wisc.-River Falls 0
at St. John's (Minn.) 21 . . . . .Simpson (Iowa) 18
at Lycoming (Pa.) 31 . . . . .Ursinus (Pa.) 24
Albright (Pa.) 31 . . . . .at Wash. & Jeff. (Pa.) 17
Rowan (NJ) 21 .at Buffalo St. 20
at Coll. of New Jersey 17 . . . . .Coast Guard 16

Quarterfinals (Nov. 30)

at Mount Union 49 . . . . .Illinois Wesleyan 14
at Wisc.-La Crosse 37 . . . . .St. John's 30
at Lycoming 31 . . . . .Albright 13
Rowan 7 . . . . .at Coll. of New Jersey 3

Semifinals (Dec. 7)

Mount Union 39 . . . . .at Wisc.-La Crosse 21
at Rowan 33 . . . . .Lycoming 14

Amos Alonzo Stagg Bowl
Dec. 14 at Salem, Va. (Att: 4,905)

Mount Union 56 . . . . .Rowan 24
(14-0)   (10-3)

NAIA Playoffs
Division I
Semifinals (Nov. 23)

Southwestern Okla. St. 17 . . . . . .Northwestern Okla. St. 7
Montana Tech 49 . . . . .Carroll College (Mont.) 28

Championship
Dec. 7 at Weatherford, Okla. (Att: 5,000)

Southwestern Okla. St. 33 . . . . .Montana Tech 31
(9-3)   (7-5)

Division II
First round (Nov. 23)

Westminster Coll. (Pa.) 27 . . . . .Clinch Valley Coll. (Va.) 20
Northwestern Coll. (Ia.) 14 . . . . .Valley City St. (ND) 7
Sioux Falls (SD) 56 . . . . .Mary (ND) 19
Lambuth (Tenn.) 34 . . . . .Benedictine Coll. (Kan.) 20
Evangel Coll. (Mo.) 45 . . . . .Hardin Simmons (Tex.) 23
Findlay (Ohio) 38 . . . . .Geneva (Pa.) 13
Western Washington 21 . . .Pacific Lutheran (Wash.) 20 OT
Willamette (Ore.) 56 . . . . .Bethany Coll. (Kan.) 35

Quarterfinals (Dec. 7)

Findlay 28 . . . . .Westminster Coll. 9
Evangel Coll. 28 . . . . .Lambuth 27
Sioux Falls 52 . . . . .Northwestern Coll. 21
Western Washington 13 . . . . .Willamette 12

Semifinals (Dec. 14)

Western Washington 28 .Findlay 21
Sioux Falls 28 . . . . .Evangel 22

Championship
Dec. 21 at Savannah, Tenn. (Att: 4,000 est.)

Sioux Falls 47 . . . . .Western Washington 25
(14-0)   (11-2)

COLLEGE FOOTBALL
S T A T I S T I C S

THE 1998 ESPN INFORMATION PLEASE SPORTS ALMANAC

THROUGH THE YEARS
1869-1997
BOWLS • ALL-TIME LEADERS

SEC B
PAGE 162

National Champions

Over the last 127 years, there have been 25 major selectors of national champions by way of polls (11), mathematical rating systems (10) and historical research (4). The best-known and most widely circulated of these surveys, the Associated Press poll of sportswriters and broadcasters, first appeared during the 1936 season. Champions prior to 1936 have been determined by retro polls, ratings, and historical research.

The Early Years (1869-1935)

National champions based on the Dickinson mathematical system (DS) and three historical retro polls taken by the College Football Researchers Association (CFRA), the National Championship Foundation (NCF) and the Helms Athletic Foundation (HF). The CFRA and NCF polls start in 1869, college football's inaugural year, while the Helms poll begins in 1883, the first season the game adopted a point system for scoring. Frank Dickinson, an economics professor at Illinois, introduced his system in 1926 and retro-picked winners in 1924 and '25. Bowl game results were counted in the Helms selections, but not in the other three.

Multiple champions: Yale (18); Princeton (17); Harvard (9); Michigan (7); Notre Dame and Penn (4); Alabama, Cornell, Illinois, Pittsburgh and USC (3); California, Georgia Tech, Minnesota and Penn St. (2).

Year		Record	Year		Record	Year		Record
1869	Princeton	1-1-0	1880	Yale (CFRA)	4-0-1	1891	Yale	13-0-0
1870	Princeton	1-0-0		& Princeton (NCF)	4-0-1	1892	Yale	13-0-0
1871	No games played		1881	Yale	5-0-1	1893	Princeton	11-0-0
1872	Princeton	1-0-0	1882	Yale	8-0-0	1894	Yale	16-0-0
1873	Princeton	1-0-0	1883	Yale	8-0-0	1895	Penn	14-0-0
1874	Yale	3-0-0	1884	Yale	8-0-1	1896	Princeton (CFRA)	10-0-1
1875	Princeton (CFRA)	2-0-0	1885	Princeton	9-0-0		& Lafayette (NCF)	11-0-1
	& Harvard (NCF)	4-0-0	1886	Yale	9-0-1	1897	Penn	15-0-0
1876	Yale	3-0-0	1887	Yale	9-0-0	1898	Harvard	11-0-0
1877	Yale	3-0-1	1888	Yale	13-0-0	1899	Princeton (CFRA)	12-1-0
1878	Princeton	6-0-0	1889	Princeton	10-0-0		& Harvard (NCF, HF)	10-0-1
1879	Princeton	4-0-1	1890	Harvard	11-0-0			

Year		Record	Bowl Game	Head Coach	Outstanding Player
1900	Yale	12-0-0	No bowl	Malcolm McBride	Perry Hale, HB
1901	Harvard (CFRA)	12-0-0	No bowl	Bill Reid	Bob Kernan, HB
	& Michigan (NCF, HF)	11-0-0	Won Rose	Hurry Up Yost	Neil Snow, E
1902	Michigan	11-0-0	No bowl	Hurry Up Yost	Boss Weeks, QB
1903	Princeton	11-0-0	No bowl	Art Hillebrand	John DeWitt, G
1904	Penn (CFRA, HF)	12-0-0	No bowl	Carl Williams	Andy Smith, FB
	& Michigan (NCF)	10-0-0	No bowl	Hurry Up Yost	Willie Heston, HB
1905	Chicago	10-0-0	No bowl	Amos Alonzo Stagg	Walter Eckersall, QB
1906	Princeton	9-0-1	No bowl	Bill Roper	Cap Wister, E
1907	Yale	9-0-1	No bowl	Bill Knox	Tad Jones, HB
1908	Penn (CFRA, HF)	11-0-1	No bowl	Sol Metzger	Hunter Scarlett, E
	& LSU (NCF)	10-0-0	No bowl	Edgar Wingard	Doc Fenton, QB
1909	Yale	12-1-0	No bowl	Howard Jones	Ted Coy, FB
1910	Harvard (CFRA, HF)	8-0-1	No bowl	Percy Haughton	Percy Wendell, HB
	& Pittsburgh (NCF)	9-0-0	No bowl	Joe Thompson	Ralph Galvin, C
1911	Princeton (CFRA, HF)	8-0-2	No bowl	Bill Roper	Sam White, E
	& Penn St. (NCF)	8-0-1	No bowl	Bill Hollenback	Dexter Very, E
1912	Harvard (CFRA, HF)	9-0-0	No bowl	Percy Haughton	Charley Brickley, HB
	& Penn St. (NCF)	8-0-0	No bowl	Bill Hollenback	Dexter Very, E
1913	Harvard	9-0-0	No bowl	Percy Haughton	Eddie Mahan, FB
1914	Army	9-0-0	No bowl	Charley Daly	John McEwan, C
1915	Cornell	9-0-0	No bowl	Al Sharpe	Charley Barrett, QB
1916	Pittsburgh	8-0-0	No bowl	Pop Warner	Bob Peck, C
1917	Georgia Tech	9-0-0	No bowl	John Heisman	Ev Strupper, HB
1918	Pittsburgh (CFRA, HF)	4-1-0	No bowl	Pop Warner	Tom Davies, HB
	& Michigan (NCF)	5-0-0	No bowl	Hurry Up Yost	Frank Steketee, FB
1919	Harvard (CFRA-tie, HF)	9-0-1	Won Rose	Bob Fisher	Eddie Casey, HB
	Illinois (CFRA-tie)	6-1-0	No bowl	Bob Zuppke	Chuck Carney, E
	& Notre Dame (NCF)	9-0-0	No bowl	Knute Rockne	George Gipp, HB

Year		Record	Bowl Game	Head Coach	Outstanding Player
1920	**California**	9-0-0	Won Rose	Andy Smith	Dan McMillan, T
1921	**California** (CFRA)	9-0-1	Tied Rose	Andy Smith	Brick Muller, E
	& **Cornell** (NCF, HF)	8-0-0	No bowl	Gil Dobie	Eddie Kaw, HB
1922	**Princeton** (CFRA)	8-0-0	No bowl	Bill Roper	Herb Treat, T
	California (NCF)	9-0-0	No bowl	Andy Smith	Brick Muller, E
	& **Cornell** (HF)	8-0-0	No bowl	Gil Dobie	Eddie Kaw, HB
1923	**Illinois** (CFRA, HF)	8-0-0	No bowl	Bob Zuppke	Red Grange, HB
	& **Michigan** (NCF)	8-0-0	No bowl	Hurry Up Yost	Jack Blott, C
1924	**Notre Dame**	10-0-0	Won Rose	Knute Rockne	The Four Horsemen*
1925	**Alabama** (CFRA, HF)	10-0-0	Won Rose	Wallace Wade	Johnny Mack Brown, HB
	& **Dartmouth** (DS)	8-0-0	No bowl	Jesse Hawley	Swede Oberlander, HB
1926	**Alabama** (CFRA, HF)	9-0-1	Tied Rose	Wallace Wade	Hoyt Winslett, E
	& **Stanford** (DS)	10-0-1	Tied Rose	Pop Warner	Ted Shipkey, E
1927	**Yale** (CFRA)	7-1-0	No bowl	Tad Jones	Bill Webster, G
	& **Illinois** (NCF, HF, DS)	7-0-1	No bowl	Bob Zuppke	Bob Reitsch, C
1928	**Georgia Tech** (CFRA, NCF, HF)	10-0-0	Won Rose	Bill Alexander	Pete Pund, C
	& **USC** (DS)	9-0-1	No bowl	Howard Jones	Jesse Hibbs, T
1929	**Notre Dame**	9-0-0	No bowl	Knute Rockne	Frank Carideo, QB
1930	**Alabama** (CFRA)	10-0-0	Won Rose	Wallace Wade	Fred Sington, T
	& **Notre Dame** (NCF, HF, DS)	10-0-0	No bowl	Knute Rockne	Marchy Schwartz, HB
1931	**USC**	10-1-0	Won Rose	Howard Jones	John Baker, G
1932	**USC** (CFRA, NCF, HF)	10-0-0	Won Rose	Howard Jones	Ernie Smith, T
	& **Michigan** (DS)	8-0-0	No bowl	Harry Kipke	Harry Newman, QB
1933	**Michigan**	8-0-0	No bowl	Harry Kipke	Chuck Bernard, C
1934	**Minnesota**	8-0-0	No bowl	Bernie Bierman	Pug Lund, HB
1935	**Minnesota** (CFRA, NCF, HF)	8-0-0	No bowl	Bernie Bierman	Dick Smith, T
	& **SMU** (DS)	12-1-0	Lost Rose	Matty Bell	Bobby Wilson, HB

*Notre Dame's **Four Horsemen** were Harry Stuhldreher (QB), Jim Crowley (HB), Don Miller (HB-P) and Elmer Layden (FB).

The Media Poll Years (since 1936)

National champions according to seven media and coaches' polls: Associated Press (since 1936), United Press (1950-57), International News Service (1952-57), United Press International (1958-92), Football Writers Association of America (since 1954), National Football Foundation and Hall of Fame (since 1959) and USA Today/CNN (since 1991). In 1991, the American Football Coaches Association switched outlets for its poll from UPI to USA Today/CNN.

After 29 years of releasing its final Top 20 poll in early December, AP named its 1965 national champion following that season's bowl games. AP returned to a pre-bowls final vote in 1966 and '67, but has polled its writers and broadcasters after the bowl games since the 1968 season. The FWAA has selected its champion after the bowl games since the 1955 season, the NFF-Hall of Fame since 1971, UPI after 1974 and USA Today/CNN since 1982.

The Associated Press changed the name of its national championship award from the AP Trophy to the Bear Bryant Trophy after the legendary Alabama coach's death in 1983. The Football Writers' trophy is called the Grantland Rice Award (after the celebrated sportswriter) and the NFF-Hall of Fame trophy is called the MacArthur Bowl (in honor of Gen. Douglas MacArthur).

Multiple champions: Notre Dame (9); Alabama (7); Ohio St. and Oklahoma (6); USC (5); Miami-FL, Minnesota and Nebraska (4); Michigan St. and Texas (3); Army, Georgia Tech, Penn St. and Pittsburgh (2).

Year		Record	Bowl Game	Head Coach	Outstanding Player
1936	**Minnesota**	7-1-0	No bowl	Bernie Bierman	Ed Widseth, T
1937	**Pittsburgh**	9-0-1	No bowl	Jock Sutherland	Marshall Goldberg, HB
1938	**TCU**	11-0-0	Won Sugar	Dutch Meyer	Davey O'Brien, QB
1939	**Texas A&M**	11-0-0	Won Sugar	Homer Norton	John Kimbrough, FB
1940	**Minnesota**	8-0-0	No Bowl	Bernie Bierman	George Franck, HB
1941	**Minnesota**	8-0-0	No bowl	Bernie Bierman	Bruce Smith, HB
1942	**Ohio St.**	9-1-0	No bowl	Paul Brown	Gene Fekete, FB
1943	**Notre Dame**	9-1-0	No bowl	Frank Leahy	Angelo Bertelli, QB
1944	**Army**	9-0-0	No bowl	Red Blaik	Glenn Davis, HB
1945	**Army**	9-0-0	No bowl	Red Blaik	Doc Blanchard, FB
1946	**Notre Dame**	8-0-1	No bowl	Frank Leahy	Johnny Lujack, QB
1947	**Notre Dame**	9-0-0	No bowl	Frank Leahy	Johnny Lujack, QB
1948	**Michigan**	9-0-0	No bowl	Bennie Oosterbaan	Dick Rifenburg, E
1949	**Notre Dame**	10-0-0	No bowl	Frank Leahy	Leon Hart, E
1950	**Oklahoma**	10-1-0	Lost Sugar	Bud Wilkinson	Leon Heath, FB
1951	**Tennessee**	10-1-0	Lost Sugar	Bob Neyland	Hank Lauricella, TB
1952	**Michigan St.** (AP, UP)	9-0-0	No bowl	Biggie Munn	Don McAuliffe, HB
	& **Georgia Tech** (INS)	12-0-0	Won Sugar	Bobby Dodd	Hal Miller, T
1953	**Maryland**	10-1-0	Lost Orange	Jim Tatum	Bernie Faloney, QB
1954	**Ohio St.** (AP, INS)	10-0-0	Won Rose	Woody Hayes	Howard Cassady, HB
	& **UCLA** (UP, FW)	9-0-0	No bowl	Red Sanders	Jack Ellena, T
1955	**Oklahoma**	11-0-0	Won Orange	Bud Wilkinson	Jerry Tubbs, C
1956	**Oklahoma**	10-0-0	No bowl	Bud Wilkinson	Tommy McDonald, HB

National Champions (Cont.)

Year	Team	Record	Bowl	Coach	Player
1957	**Auburn** (AP)	10-0-0	No bowl	Shug Jordan	Jimmy Phillips, E
	& Ohio St. (UP, FW, INS)	9-1-0	Won Rose	Woody Hayes	Bob White, FB
1958	**LSU** (AP, UPI)	11-0-0	Won Sugar	Paul Dietzel	Billy Cannon, HB
	& Iowa (FW)	8-1-1	Won Rose	Forest Evashevski	Randy Duncan, QB
1959	**Syracuse**	11-0-0	Won Cotton	Ben Schwartzwalder	Ernie Davis, HB
1960	**Minnesota** (AP, UPI, NFF)	8-2-0	Lost Rose	Murray Warmath	Tom Brown, G
	& Mississippi (FW)	10-0-1	Won Sugar	Johnny Vaught	Jake Gibbs, QB
1961	**Alabama** (AP, UPI, NFF)	11-0-0	Won Sugar	Bear Bryant	Billy Neighbors, T
	& Ohio St. (FW)	8-0-1	No bowl	Woody Hayes	Bob Ferguson, HB
1962	**USC**	11-0-0	Won Rose	John McKay	Hal Bedsole, E
1963	**Texas**	11-0-0	Won Cotton	Darrell Royal	Scott Appleton, T
1964	**Alabama** (AP, UPI),	10-1-0	Lost Orange	Bear Bryant	Joe Namath, QB
	Arkansas (FW)	11-0-0	Won Cotton	Frank Broyles	Ronnie Caveness, LB
	& Notre Dame (NFF)	9-1-0	No bowl	Ara Parseghian	John Huarte, QB
1965	**Alabama** (AP, FW-tie)	9-1-1	Won Orange	Bear Bryant	Paul Crane, C
	& Michigan St. (UPI, NFF, FW-tie)	10-1-0	Lost Rose	Duffy Daugherty	George Webster, LB
1966	**Notre Dame** (AP, UPI, FW, NFF-tie)	9-0-1	No bowl	Ara Parseghian	Jim Lynch, LB
	& Michigan St. (NFF-tie)	9-0-1	No bowl	Duffy Daugherty	Bubba Smith, DE
1967	**USC**	10-1-0	Won Rose	John McKay	O.J. Simpson, HB
1968	**Ohio St.**	10-0-0	Won Rose	Woody Hayes	Rex Kern, QB
1969	**Texas**	11-0-0	Won Cotton	Darrell Royal	James Street, QB
1970	**Nebraska** (AP, FW)	11-0-1	Won Orange	Bob Devaney	Jerry Tagge, QB
	Texas (UPI, NFF-tie),	10-1-0	Lost Cotton	Darrell Royal	Steve Worster, RB
	& Ohio St. (NFF-tie)	9-1-0	Lost Rose	Woody Hayes	Jim Stillwagon, MG
1971	**Nebraska**	13-0-0	Won Orange	Bob Devaney	Johnny Rodgers, WR
1972	**USC**	12-0-0	Won Rose	John McKay	Charles Young, TE
1973	**Notre Dame** (AP, FW, NFF)	11-0-0	Won Sugar	Ara Parseghian	Mike Townsend, DB
	& Alabama (UPI)	11-1-0	Lost Sugar	Bear Bryant	Buddy Brown, OT
1974	**Oklahoma** (AP)	11-0-0	No bowl	Barry Switzer	Joe Washington, RB
	& USC (UPI, FW, NFF)	10-1-1	Won Rose	John McKay	Anthony Davis, RB
1975	**Oklahoma**	11-1-0	Won Orange	Barry Switzer	Lee Roy Selmon, DT
1976	**Pittsburgh**	12-0-0	Won Sugar	Johnny Majors	Tony Dorsett, RB
1977	**Notre Dame**	11-1-0	Won Cotton	Dan Devine	Ross Browner, DE
1978	**Alabama** (AP, FW, NFF)	11-1-0	Won Sugar	Bear Bryant	Marty Lyons, DT
	& USC (UPI)	12-1-0	Won Rose	John Robinson	Charles White, RB
1979	**Alabama**	12-0-0	Won Sugar	Bear Bryant	Jim Bunch, OT
1980	**Georgia**	12-0-0	Won Sugar	Vince Dooley	Herschel Walker, RB
1981	**Clemson**	12-0-0	Won Orange	Danny Ford	Jeff Davis, LB
1982	**Penn St.**	11-1-0	Won Sugar	Joe Paterno	Todd Blackledge, QB
1983	**Miami-FL**	11-1-0	Won Orange	H. Schnellenberger	Bernie Kosar, QB
1984	**BYU**	13-0-0	Won Holiday	LaVell Edwards	Robbie Bosco, QB
1985	**Oklahoma**	11-1-0	Won Orange	Barry Switzer	Brian Bosworth, LB
1986	**Penn St.**	12-0-0	Won Fiesta	Joe Paterno	D.J. Dozier, RB
1987	**Miami-FL**	12-0-0	Won Orange	Jimmy Johnson	Steve Walsh, QB
1988	**Notre Dame**	12-0-0	Won Fiesta	Lou Holtz	Tony Rice, QB
1989	**Miami-FL**	11-1-0	Won Sugar	Dennis Erickson	Craig Erickson, QB
1990	**Colorado** (AP, FW, NFF)	11-1-1	Won Orange	Bill McCartney	Eric Bieniemy, RB
	& Georgia Tech (UPI)	11-0-1	Won Citrus	Bobby Ross	Shawn Jones, QB
1991	**Miami-FL** (AP)	12-0-0	Won Orange	Dennis Erickson	Gino Torretta, QB
	& Washington (USA, FW, NFF)	12-0-0	Won Rose	Don James	Steve Emtman, DT
1992	**Alabama**	13-0-0	Won Sugar	Gene Stallings	Eric Curry, DE
1993	**Florida St.**	12-1-0	Won Orange	Bobby Bowden	Charlie Ward, QB
1994	**Nebraska**	13-0-0	Won Orange	Tom Osborne	Zach Wiegert, OT
1995	**Nebraska**	12-0-0	Won Fiesta	Tom Osborne	Tommie Frazier, QB
1996	**Florida**	12-1-0	Won Sugar	Steve Spurrier	Danny Wuerffel, QB

Number 1 vs. Number 2

Since the Associated Press writers poll started keeping track of such things in 1936, the No.1 and No.2 ranked teams in the country have met 31 times; 20 during the regular season and 11 in bowl games. Since the first showdown in 1943, the No.1 team has beaten the No. 2 team 18 times, lost 11 and there have been two ties. Each showdown is listed below with the date, the match-up, each team's record going into the game, the final score, the stadium and site.

Date		Match-up			Stadium	Date		Match-up			Stadium
Oct. 9 1943	#1 #2	Notre Dame (2-0) Michigan (3-0)	...	35 12	Michigan (Ann Arbor)	Nov. 10 1945	#1 #2	Army (6-0) Notre Dame (5-0-1)	...	48 0	Yankee (New York)
Nov. 20 1943	#1 #2	Notre Dame (8-0) Iowa Pre-Flight (8-0)	...	14 13	Notre Dame (South Bend)	Dec. 1 1945	#1 #2	Army (8-0) Navy (7-0-1)	...	32 13	Municipal (Philadelphia)
Dec. 2 1944	#1 #2	Army (8-0) Navy (6-2)	...	23 7	Municipal (Baltimore)	Nov. 9 1946	#1 #2	Army (7-0) Notre Dame (5-0)	...	0 0	Yankee (New York)

Number 1 vs. Number 2 (Cont.)

Date	Match-up		Stadium
Jan. 1 #1	USC (10-0)	42	ROSE BOWL
1963 #2	Wisconsin (8-1)	37	(Pasadena)
Oct. 12 #2	Texas (3-0)	28	Cotton Bowl
1963 #1	Oklahoma (2-0)	7	(Dallas)
Jan. 1 #1	Texas (10-0)	28	COTTON BOWL
1964 #2	Navy (9-1)	6	(Dallas)
Nov. 19 #1	Notre Dame (8-0)	10	Spartan
1966 #2	Michigan St. (9-0)	10	(East Lansing)
Sept. 28 #1	Purdue (1-0)	37	Notre Dame
1968 #2	Notre Dame (1-0)	22	(South Bend)
Jan. 1 #1	Ohio St. (9-0)	27	ROSE BOWL
1969 #2	USC (9-0-1)	16	(Pasadena)
Dec. 6 #1	Texas (9-0)	15	Razorback
1969 #2	Arkansas (9-0)	14	(Fayetteville)
Nov. 25 #1	Nebraska (10-0)	35	Owen Field
1971 #2	Oklahoma (9-0)	31	(Norman)
Jan. 1 #1	Nebraska (12-0)	38	ORANGE BOWL
1972 #2	Alabama (11-0)	6	(Miami)
Jan. 1 #2	Alabama (10-1)	14	SUGAR BOWL
1979 #1	Penn St. (11-0)	7	(New Orleans)
Sept. 26 #1	USC (2-0)	28	Coliseum
1981 #2	Oklahoma (1-0)	24	(Los Angeles)
Jan. 1 #2	Penn St. (10-1)	27	SUGAR BOWL
1983 #1	Georgia (11-0)	23	(New Orleans)
Oct. 19 #1	Iowa (5-0)	12	Kinnick
1985 #2	Michigan (5-0)	10	(Iowa City)

Date	Match-up		Stadium
Sept. 27 #2	Miami-FL (3-0)	28	Orange Bowl
1986 #1	Oklahoma (2-0)	16	(Miami)
Jan. 2 #2	Penn St. (11-0)	14	FIESTA BOWL
1987 #1	Miami-FL (11-0)	10	(Tempe)
Nov. 21 #2	Oklahoma (10-0)	17	Memorial
1987 #1	Nebraska (10-0)	7	(Lincoln)
Jan. 1 #2	Miami-FL (11-0)	20	ORANGE BOWL
1988 #1	Oklahoma (11-0)	14	(Miami)
Nov. 26 #1	Notre Dame (10-0)	27	Coliseum
1988 #2	USC (10-0)	10	(Los Angeles)
Sept. 16 #1	Notre Dame (1-0)	24	Michigan
1989 #2	Michigan (0-0)	19	(Ann Arbor)
Nov. 16 #2	Miami-FL (8-0)	17	Doak Campbell
1991 #1	Florida St. (10-0)	16	(Tallahassee)
Jan. 1 #2	Alabama (12-0-0)	34	SUGAR BOWL
1993 #1	Miama-FL (11-0-0)	13	(New Orleans)
Nov. 13 #2	Notre Dame (9-0)	31	Notre Dame
1993 #1	Florida St. (9-0)	24	(South Bend)
Jan. 1 #1	Florida St. (11-1)	18	ORANGE BOWL
1994 #2	Nebraska (11-0)	16	(Miami)
Jan. 2 #1	Nebraska (11-0)	62	FIESTA BOWL
1996 #2	Florida (12-0)	24	(Tempe)
Nov. 30 #2	Florida St. (10-0)	24	Doak Campbell
1996 #1	Florida (10-0)	21	(Tallahassee)

Top 50 Rivalries

Top Division I-A and I-AA series records, including games through the 1996 season. All rivalries listed below are renewed annually with the following exceptions: **LSU-Tulane** began playing on even-numbered years only in 1995; **Michigan-Notre Dame** did not play in 1995 and 1996, but they are scheduled to meet in both 1997 and '98; **Penn St-Pitt** have not played since 1992, but are scheduled to meet again for four consecutive years from 1997-2000.

RECENTLY DISCONTINUED SERIES: **Arkansas vs Texas** in 1992 after 73 games (Texas ahead, 54-19-0); **Baylor vs TCU** in 1995 after 102 games (Baylor ahead 48-47-7); **Boston College vs Holy Cross** in 1986 after 79 games (BC ahead, 48-31-0); **Florida vs Miami-FL** in 1991 after 49 games (Florida ahead, 25-24); **Miami-FL vs Notre Dame** in 1990 after 23 games (ND ahead, 15-7-1).

	Gm	Series Leader		Gm	Series Leader
Air Force-Army	31	Air Force (18-12-1)	**Michigan-Notre Dame**	26	Michigan (15-10-1)
Air Force-Navy	29	Air Force (19-10-0)	**Michigan-Ohio St**	93	Michigan (53-34-6)
Alabama-Auburn	61	Alabama (35-25-1)	**Minnesota-Wisconsin**	106	Minnesota (57-41-8)
Alabama-Tennessee	79	Alabama (42-30-7)	**Mississippi-Miss. St.**	93	Ole Miss (53-34-6)
Arizona-Arizona St	70	Arizona (40-29-1)	**Missouri-Kansas**	105	Missouri (49-47-9)
Army-Navy	97	Army (47-43-7)	**Nebraska-Oklahoma**	77	Oklahoma (39-35-3)
Auburn-Georgia	100	Auburn (47-45-8)	**N. Mexico-N. Mexico St**	86	N. Mexico (56-25-5)
California-Stanford	99	Stanford (49-39-11)	**N. Carolina-N.C. State**	86	N. Carolina (56-24-6)
The Citadel-VMI	56	VMI (28-26-2)	**Notre Dame-Purdue**	68	Notre Dame (45-21-2)
Clemson-S. Carolina	94	Clemson (55-35-4)	**Notre Dame-USC**	68	Notre Dame (39-24-5)
Colorado-Nebraska	55	Nebraska (39-14-2)	**Oklahoma-Okla. St**	91	Oklahoma (72-12-7)
Colo. St.-Wyoming	86	Colorado St. (44-37-5)	**Oregon-Oregon St**	100	Oregon (50-40-10)
Duke-N. Carolina	82	N. Carolina (43-35-4)	**Penn-Cornell**	103	Penn (58-40-5)
Florida-Florida St	41	Florida (25-14-2)	**Penn St.-Pittsburgh**	92	Penn St. (47-41-4)
Florida-Georgia	75	Georgia (44-29-2)	**Pittsburgh-West Va**	89	Pitt (55-31-3)
Florida St.-Miami,FL	40	Miami (23-17-0)	**Princeton-Yale**	119	Yale (64-45-10)
Georgia-Georgia Tech	91	Georgia (51-35-5)	**Purdue-Indiana**	99	Purdue (59-34-6)
Grambling-Southern	45	Grambling (23-22-0)	**Richmond-Wm.& Mary**	106	Wm. & Mary (54-47-5)
Harvard-Yale	113	Yale (61-44-8)	**Tennessee-Vanderbilt**	90	Tennessee (59-26-5)
Kansas-Kansas St	94	Kansas (61-28-5)	**Texas-Oklahoma**	91	Texas (52-34-5)
Kentucky-Tennessee	92	Tennessee (60-23-9)	**Texas-Texas A&M**	103	Texas (66-32-5)
Lafayette-Lehigh	132	Lafayette (71-56-5)	**UCLA-USC**	66	USC (34-25-7)
LSU-Tulane	93	LSU (64-22-7)*	**Utah-BYU**	72	Utah (43-25-4)
Miami,OH-Cincinnati	101	Miami (54-40-7)	**Utah-Utah St**	94	Utah (62-28-4)
Michigan-Michigan St	89	Michigan (58-26-5)	**Washington-Wash. St**	89	Washington (57-26-6)

*Disputed series record: Tulane claims 23-61-7.

Associated Press Final Polls

The Associated Press introduced its weekly college football poll of sportswriters (later, sportswriters and broadcasters) in 1936. The final AP poll was released at the end of the regular season until 1965, when bowl results were included for one year. After a two-year return to regular season games only, the final poll has come out after the bowls since 1968.

1936

Final poll released Nov. 30. Top 20 regular season results after that: **Dec. 5**–#8 Notre Dame tied USC, 13-13; #17 Tennessee tied Ole Miss, 0-0; #18 Arkansas over Texas, 6-0. **Dec. 12**–#16 TCU over #6 Santa Clara, 9-0.

		As of Nov. 30	Head Coach	After Bowls
1	Minnesota	7-1-0	Bernie Bierman	same
2	LSU	9-0-1	Bernie Moore	9-1-1
3	Pittsburgh	7-1-1	Jock Sutherland	8-1-1
4	Alabama	8-0-1	Frank Thomas	same
5	Washington	7-1-1	Jimmy Phelan	7-2-1
6	Santa Clara	7-0-0	Buck Shaw	8-1-0
7	Northwestern	7-1-0	Pappy Waldorf	same
8	Notre Dame	6-2-0	Elmer Layden	6-2-1
9	Nebraska	7-2-0	Dana X. Bible	same
10	Penn	7-1-0	Harvey Harman	same
11	Duke	9-1-0	Wallace Wade	same
12	Yale	7-1-0	Ducky Pond	same
13	Dartmouth	7-1-1	Red Blaik	same
14	Duquesne	7-2-0	John Smith	8-2-0
15	Fordham	5-1-2	Jim Crowley	same
16	TCU	7-2-2	Dutch Meyer	9-2-2
17	Tennessee	6-2-1	Bob Neyland	6-2-2
18	Arkansas	6-3-0	Fred Thomsen	7-3-0
	Navy	6-3-0	Tom Hamilton	same
20	Marquette	7-1-0	Frank Murray	7-2-0

Key Bowl Games

Sugar–#6 Santa Clara over #2 LSU, 21-14; **Rose**– #3 Pitt over #5 Washington, 21-0; **Orange**–#14 Duquesne over Mississippi St., 13-12; **Cotton**–#16 TCU over #20 Marquette, 16-6.

1937

Final poll released Nov. 29. Top 20 regular season results after that: **Dec. 4**–#18 Rice over SMU, 15-7.

		As of Nov. 29	Head Coach	After Bowls
1	Pittsburgh	9-0-1	Jock Sutherland	same
2	California	9-0-1	Stub Allison	10-0-1
3	Fordham	7-0-1	Jim Crowley	same
4	Alabama	9-0-0	Frank Thomas	9-1-0
5	Minnesota	6-2-0	Bernie Bierman	same
6	Villanova	8-0-1	Clipper Smith	same
7	Dartmouth	7-0-2	Red Blaik	same
8	LSU	9-1-0	Bernie Moore	9-2-0
9	Notre Dame	6-2-1	Elmer Layden	same
	Santa Clara	8-0-0	Buck Shaw	9-0-0
11	Nebraska	6-1-2	Biff Jones	same
12	Yale	6-1-1	Ducky Pond	same
13	Ohio St.	6-2-0	Francis Schmidt	same
14	Holy Cross	8-0-2	Eddie Anderson	same
	Arkansas	6-2-2	Fred Thomsen	same
16	TCU	4-2-2	Dutch Meyer	same
17	Colorado	8-0-0	Bunnie Oakes	8-1-0
18	Rice	4-3-2	Jimmy Kitts	6-3-2
19	North Carolina	7-1-1	Ray Wolf	same
20	Duke	7-2-1	Wallace Wade	same

Key Bowl Games

Rose–#2 Cal over #4 Alabama, 13-0; **Sugar**–#9 Santa Clara over #8 LSU, 6-0; **Cotton**–#18 Rice over #17 Colorado, 28-14; **Orange**–Auburn over Michigan St., 6-0.

1938

Final poll released Dec. 5. Top 20 regular season results after that: **Dec. 26**–#14 Cal over Georgia Tech, 13-7.

		As of Dec. 5	Head Coach	After Bowls
1	TCU	10-0-0	Dutch Meyer	11-0-0
2	Tennessee	10-0-0	Bob Neyland	11-0-0
3	Duke	9-0-0	Wallace Wade	9-1-0
4	Oklahoma	10-0-0	Tom Stidham	10-1-0
5	Notre Dame	8-1-0	Elmer Layden	same
6	Carnegie Tech	7-1-0	Bill Kern	7-2-0
7	USC	8-2-0	Howard Jones	9-2-0
8	Pittsburgh	8-2-0	Jock Sutherland	same
9	Holy Cross	8-1-0	Eddie Anderson	same
10	Minnesota	6-2-0	Bernie Bierman	same
11	Texas Tech	10-0-0	Pete Cawthon	10-1-0
12	Cornell	5-1-1	Carl Snavely	same
13	Alabama	7-1-1	Frank Thomas	same
14	California	9-1-0	Stub Allison	10-1-0
15	Fordham	6-1-2	Jim Crowley	same
16	Michigan	6-1-1	Fritz Crisler	same
17	Northwestern	4-2-2	Pappy Waldorf	same
18	Villanova	8-0-1	Clipper Smith	same
19	Tulane	7-2-1	Red Dawson	same
20	Dartmouth	7-2-0	Red Blaik	same

Key Bowl Games

Sugar–#1 TCU over #6 Carnegie Tech, 15-7; **Orange**–#2 Tennessee over #4 Oklahoma, 17-0; **Rose**–#7 USC over #3 Duke, 7-3; **Cotton**–St. Mary's over #11 Texas Tech 20-13.

1939

Final poll released Dec. 11. Top 20 regular season results after that: None.

		As of Dec. 11	Head Coach	After Bowls
1	Texas A&M	10-0-0	Homer Norton	11-0-0
2	Tennessee	10-0-0	Bob Neyland	10-1-0
3	USC	7-0-2	Howard Jones	8-0-2
4	Cornell	8-0-0	Carl Snavely	same
5	Tulane	8-0-1	Red Dawson	8-1-1
6	Missouri	8-1-0	Don Faurot	8-2-0
7	UCLA	6-0-4	Babe Horrell	same
8	Duke	8-1-0	Wallace Wade	same
9	Iowa	6-1-1	Eddie Anderson	same
10	Duquesne	8-0-1	Buff Donelli	same
11	Boston College	9-1-0	Frank Leahy	9-2-0
12	Clemson	8-1-0	Jess Neely	9-1-0
13	Notre Dame	7-2-0	Elmer Layden	same
14	Santa Clara	5-1-3	Buck Shaw	same
15	Ohio St.	6-2-0	Francis Schmidt	same
16	Georgia Tech	7-2-0	Bill Alexander	8-2-0
17	Fordham	6-2-0	Jim Crowley	same
18	Nebraska	7-1-1	Biff Jones	same
19	Oklahoma	6-2-1	Tom Stidham	same
20	Michigan	6-2-0	Fritz Crisler	same

Key Bowl Games

Sugar–#1 Texas A&M over #5 Tulane, 14-13; **Rose**–#3 USC over #2 Tennessee, 14-0; **Orange**–#16 Georgia Tech over #6 Missouri, 21-7; **Cotton**–#12 Clemson over #11 Boston College, 6-3.

1940

Final poll released Dec. 2. Top 20 regular season results after that: **Dec. 7**–#16 SMU over Rice, 7-6.

		As of Dec. 2	Head Coach	After Bowls
1	Minnesota	8-0-0	Bernie Bierman	same
2	Stanford	9-0-0	Clark Shaughnessy	10-0-0
3	Michigan	7-1-0	Fritz Crisler	same
4	Tennessee	10-0-0	Bob Neyland	10-1-0
5	Boston College .	10-0-0	Frank Leahy	11-0-0
6	Texas A&M	8-1-0	Homer Norton	9-1-0
7	Nebraska	8-1-0	Biff Jones	8-2-0
8	Northwestern ..	6-2-0	Pappy Waldorf	same
9	Mississippi St. ..	9-0-1	Allyn McKeen	10-0-1
10	Washington	7-2-0	Jimmy Phelan	same
11	Santa Clara ...	6-1-1	Buck Shaw	same
12	Fordham	7-1-0	Jim Crowley	7-2-0
13	Georgetown ...	8-1-0	Jack Hagerty	8-2-0
14	Penn	6-1-1	George Munger	same
15	Cornell	6-2-0	Carl Snavely	same
16	SMU	7-1-1	Matty Bell	8-1-1
17	Hardin-Simmons .	9-0-0	Warren Woodson	same
18	Duke	7-2-0	Wallace Wade	same
19	Lafayette	9-0-0	Hooks Mylin	same
20	–			

Note: Only 19 teams ranked.

Key Bowl Games

Rose–#2 Stanford over #7 Nebraska, 21-13; **Sugar**– #5 Boston College over #4 Tennessee, 19-13; **Cotton**–#6 Texas A&M over #12 Fordham, 13-12; **Orange**–#9 Mississippi St. over #13 Georgetown, 14-7.

1941

Final poll released Dec. 1. Top 20 regular season results after that: **Dec. 6**–#4 Texas over Oregon, 71-7; #9 Texas A&M over #19 Washington St., 7-0; #16 Mississippi St. over San Francisco, 26-13.

		As of Dec. 1	Head Coach	After Bowls
1	Minnesota	8-0-0	Bernie Bierman	same
2	Duke	9-0-0	Wallace Wade	9-1-0
3	Notre Dame ...	8-0-1	Frank Leahy	same
4	Texas	7-1-1	Dana X. Bible	8-1-1
5	Michigan	6-1-1	Fritz Crisler	same
6	Fordham	7-1-0	Jim Crowley	8-1-0
7	Missouri	8-1-0	Don Faurot	8-2-0
8	Duquesne	8-0-0	Buff Donelli	same
9	Texas A&M	8-1-0	Homer Norton	9-2-0
10	Navy	7-1-1	Swede Larson	same
11	Northwestern ...	5-3-0	Pappy Waldorf	same
12	Oregon St.	7-2-0	Lon Stiner	8-2-0
13	Ohio St.	6-1-1	Paul Brown	same
14	Georgia	8-1-1	Wally Butts	9-1-1
15	Penn	7-1-1	George Munger	same
16	Mississippi St. ..	7-1-1	Allyn McKeen	8-1-1
17	Mississippi	6-2-1	Harry Mehre	same
18	Tennessee	8-2-0	John Barnhill	same
19	Washington St. .	6-3-0	Babe Hollingbery	6-4-0
20	Alabama	8-2-0	Frank Thomas	9-2-0

Note: 1942 Rose Bowl moved to Durham, N.C., for one year after outbreak of World War II.

Key Bowl Games

Rose–#12 Oregon St. over #2 Duke, 20-16; **Sugar**– #6 Fordham over #7 Missouri, 2-0; **Cotton**–#20 Alabama over #9 Texas A&M, 29-21; **Orange**–#14 Georgia over TCU, 40-26.

1942

Final poll released Nov. 30. Top 20 regular season results after that: **Dec. 5**–#6 Notre Dame tied Great Lakes Naval Station, 13-13; #13 UCLA over Idaho, 40-13; #14 William & Mary over Oklahoma, 14-7; #17 Washington St. lost to Texas A&M, 21-0; #18 Mississippi St. over San Francisco, 19-7. **Dec. 12**–#13 UCLA over USC, 14-7.

		As of Nov. 30	Head Coach	After Bowls
1	Ohio St.	9-1-0	Paul Brown	same
2	Georgia	10-1-0	Wally Butts	11-1-0
3	Wisconsin	8-1-1	Harry Stuhldreher	same
4	Tulsa	10-0-0	Henry Frnka	10-1-0
5	Georgia Tech ..	9-1-0	Bill Alexander	9-2-0
6	Notre Dame ...	7-2-1	Frank Leahy	7-2-2
7	Tennessee	8-1-1	John Barnhill	9-1-1
8	Boston College .	8-1-0	Denny Myers	8-2-0
9	Michigan	7-3-0	Fritz Crisler	same
10	Alabama	7-3-0	Frank Thomas	8-3-0
11	Texas	8-2-0	Dana X. Bible	9-2-0
12	Stanford	6-4-0	Marchie Schwartz	same
13	UCLA	5-3-0	Babe Horrell	7-4-0
14	William & Mary	8-1-1	Carl Voyles	9-1-1
15	Santa Clara ...	7-2-0	Buck Shaw	same
16	Auburn	6-4-1	Jack Meagher	same
17	Washington St.	6-1-2	Babe Hollingbery	6-2-2
18	Mississippi St. .	7-2-0	Allyn McKeen	8-2-0
19	Minnesota	5-4-0	George Hauser	same
	Holy Cross	5-4-1	Ank Scanlon	same
	Penn St.	6-1-1	Bob Higgins	same

Key Bowl Games

Rose–#2 Georgia over #13 UCLA, 9-0; **Sugar**–#7 Tennessee over #4 Tulsa, 14-7; **Cotton**–#11 Texas over #5 Georgia Tech, 14-7; **Orange**–#10 Alabama over #8 Boston College, 37-21.

1943

Final poll released Nov. 29. Top 20 regular season results after that: **Dec.11**–#10 March Field over #19 Pacific, 19-0.

		As of Nov. 29	Head Coach	After Bowls
1	Notre Dame	9-1-0	Frank Leahy	same
2	Iowa Pre-Flight ..	9-1-0	Don Faurot	same
3	Michigan	8-1-0	Fritz Crisler	same
4	Navy	8-1-0	Billick Whelchel	same
5	Purdue	9-0-0	Elmer Burnham	same
6	Great Lakes Naval Station .	10-2-0	Tony Hinkle	same
7	Duke	8-1-0	Eddie Cameron	same
8	DelMonte Pre-Flight	7-1-0	Bill Kern	same
9	Northwestern ...	6-2-0	Pappy Waldorf	same
10	March Field ...	8-1-0	Paul Schissler	9-1-0
11	Army	7-2-1	Red Blaik	same
12	Washington	4-0-0	Ralph Welch	4-1-0
13	Georgia Tech ...	7-3-0	Bill Alexander	8-3-0
14	Texas	7-1-0	Dana X. Bible	7-1-1
15	Tulsa	6-0-1	Henry Frnka	6-1-1
16	Dartmouth	6-1-0	Earl Brown	same
17	Bainbridge Navy Training School	7-0-0	Joe Maniaci	same
18	Colorado College	7-0-0	Hal White	same
19	Pacific	7-1-0	Amos A. Stagg	7-2-0
20	Penn	6-2-1	George Munger	same

Key Bowl Games

Rose–USC over #12 Washington, 29-0; **Sugar**–#13 Georgia Tech over #15 Tulsa, 20-18; **Cotton**–#14 Texas tied Randolph Field, 7-7; **Orange**–LSU over Texas A&M, 19-14.

Associated Press Final Polls (Cont.)

1944

Final poll released Dec. 4. Top 20 regular season results after that: **Dec. 10**–#3 Randolph Field over #10 March Field, 20-7; #18 Fort Pierce over Kessler Field, 34-7; Morris Field over #20 Second Air Force, 14-7.

		As of Dec. 4	Head Coach	After Bowls
1	Army	9-0-0	Red Blaik	same
2	Ohio St.	9-0-0	Carroll Widdoes	same
3	Randolph Field	10-0-0	Frank Tritico	12-0-0
4	Navy	6-3-0	Oscar Hagberg	same
5	Bainbridge Navy Training School	10-0-0	Joe Maniaci	same
6	Iowa Pre-Flight	10-1-0	Jack Meagher	same
7	USC	7-0-2	Jeff Cravath	8-0-2
8	Michigan	8-2-0	Fritz Crisler	same
9	Notre Dame	8-2-0	Ed McKeever	same
10	March Field	7-0-2	Paul Schissler	7-1-2
11	Duke	5-4-0	Eddie Cameron	6-4-0
12	Tennessee	7-0-1	John Barnhill	7-1-1
13	Georgia Tech	8-2-0	Bill Alexander	8-3-0
14	Norman Pre-Flight	6-0-0	John Gregg	same
15	Illinois	5-4-1	Ray Eliot	same
16	El Toro Marines	8-1-0	Dick Hanley	same
17	Great Lakes Naval Station	9-2-1	Paul Brown	same
18	Fort Pierce	8-0-0	Hamp Pool	9-0-0
19	St. Mary's Pre-Flight	4-4-0	Jules Sikes	same
20	Second Air Force	10-2-1	Bill Reese	10-4-1

Key Bowl Games

Treasury–#3 Randolph Field over #20 Second Air Force, 13-6; **Rose**–#7 USC over #12 Tennessee, 25-0; **Sugar**–#11 Duke over Alabama, 29-26; **Orange**–Tulsa over #13 Georgia Tech, 26-12; **Cotton**–Oklahoma A&M over TCU, 34-0.

1945

Final poll released Dec. 3. Top 20 regular season results after that: None.

		As of Dec. 3	Head Coach	After Bowls
1	Army	9-0-0	Red Blaik	same
2	Alabama	9-0-0	Frank Thomas	10-0-0
3	Navy	7-1-1	Oscar Hagberg	same
4	Indiana	9-0-1	Bo McMillan	same
5	Oklahoma A&M	8-0-0	Jim Lookabaugh	9-0-0
6	Michigan	7-3-0	Fritz Crisler	same
7	St. Mary's-CA	7-1-0	Jimmy Phelan	7-2-0
8	Penn	6-2-0	George Munger	same
9	Notre Dame	7-2-1	Hugh Devore	same
10	Texas	9-1-0	Dana X. Bible	10-1-0
11	USC	7-3-0	Jeff Cravath	7-4-0
12	Ohio St.	7-2-0	Carroll Widdoes	same
13	Duke	6-2-0	Eddie Cameron	same
14	Tennessee	8-1-0	John Barnhill	same
15	LSU	7-2-0	Bernie Moore	same
16	Holy Cross	8-1-0	John DeGrosa	8-2-0
17	Tulsa	8-2-0	Henry Frnka	8-3-0
18	Georgia	8-2-0	Wally Butts	same
19	Wake Forest	4-3-1	Peahead Walker	5-3-1
20	Columbia	8-1-0	Lou Little	same

Key Bowl Gaes

Rose–#2 Alabama over #11 USC, 34-14; **Sugar**– #5 Oklahoma A&M over #7 St. Mary's, 33-13; **Cotton**–#10 Texas over Missouri, 40-27; **Orange**–Miami-FL over #16 Holy Cross, 13-6.

1946

Final poll released Dec. 2. Top 20 regular season results after that: None.

		As of Dec. 2	Head Coach	After Bowls
1	Notre Dame	8-0-1	Frank Leahy	same
2	Army	9-0-1	Red Blaik	same
3	Georgia	10-0-0	Wally Butts	11-0-0
4	UCLA	10-0-0	Bert LaBrucherie	10-1-0
5	Illinois	7-2-0	Ray Eliot	8-2-0
6	Michigan	6-2-1	Fritz Crisler	same
7	Tennessee	9-1-0	Bob Neyland	9-2-0
8	LSU	9-1-0	Bernie Moore	9-1-1
9	North Carolina	8-1-1	Carl Snavely	8-2-1
10	Rice	8-2-0	Jess Neely	9-2-0
11	Georgia Tech	8-2-0	Bobby Dodd	9-2-0
12	Yale	7-1-1	Howard Odell	same
13	Penn	6-2-0	George Munger	same
14	Oklahoma	7-3-0	Jim Tatum	8-3-0
15	Texas	8-2-0	Dana X. Bible	same
16	Arkansas	6-3-1	John Barnhill	6-3-2
17	Tulsa	9-1-0	J.O. Brothers	same
18	N.C. State	8-2-0	Beattie Feathers	8-3-0
19	Delaware	9-0-0	Bill Murray	10-0-0
20	Indiana	6-3-0	Bo McMillan	same

Key Bowl Games

Sugar–#3 Georgia over #9 N. Carolina, 20-10; **Rose**– #5 Illinois over #4 UCLA, 45-14; **Orange**–#10 Rice over #7 Tennessee, 8-0; **Cotton**–#8 LSU tied #16 Arkansas, 0-0.

1947

Final poll released Dec. 8. Top 20 regular season results after that: None.

		As of Dec. 8	Head Coach	After Bowls
1	Notre Dame	9-0-0	Frank Leahy	same
2	Michigan	9-0-0	Fritz Crisler	10-0-0
3	SMU	9-0-1	Matty Bell	9-0-2
4	Penn St.	9-0-0	Bob Higgins	9-0-1
5	Texas	9-1-0	Blair Cherry	10-1-0
6	Alabama	8-2-0	Red Drew	8-3-0
7	Penn	7-0-1	George Munger	same
8	USC	7-1-1	Jeff Cravath	7-2-1
9	North Carolina	8-2-0	Carl Snavely	same
10	Georgia Tech	9-1-0	Bobby Dodd	10-1-0
11	Army	5-2-2	Red Blaik	same
12	Kansas	8-0-2	George Sauer	8-1-2
13	Mississippi	8-2-0	Johnny Vaught	9-2-0
14	William & Mary	9-1-0	Rube McCray	9-2-0
15	California	9-1-0	Pappy Waldorf	same
16	Oklahoma	7-2-1	Bud Wilkinson	same
17	N.C. State	5-3-1	Beattie Feathers	same
18	Rice	6-3-1	Jess Neely	same
19	Duke	4-3-2	Wallace Wade	same
20	Columbia	7-2-0	Lou Little	same

Key Bowl Games

Rose–#2 Michigan over #8 USC, 49-0; **Cotton**–#3 SMU tied #4 Penn St., 13-13; **Sugar**–#5 Texas over #6 Alabama, 27-7; **Orange**–#10 Georgia Tech over #12 Kansas, 20-14.

Note: An unprecedented Who's No. 1? poll was conducted by AP after the Rose Bowl game, pitting Notre Dame against Michigan. The Wolverines won the vote, 226-119, but AP ruled that the Irish would be the No. 1 team of record.

1948

Final poll released Nov. 29. Top 20 regular season results after that: **Dec. 3**–#12 Vanderbilt over Miami-FL, 33-6. **Dec. 4**–#2 Notre Dame tied USC, 14-14; #11 Clemson over The Citadel, 20-0.

		As of Nov. 29	Head Coach	After Bowls
1	Michigan	9-0-0	Bennie Oosterbaan	same
2	Notre Dame ..	9-0-0	Frank Leahy	9-0-1
3	North Carolina	9-0-1	Carl Snavely	9-1-1
4	California	10-0-0	Pappy Waldorf	10-1-0
5	Oklahoma	9-1-0	Bud Wilkinson	10-1-0
6	Army	8-0-1	Red Blaik	same
7	Northwestern .	7-2-0	Bob Voigts	8-2-0
8	Georgia	9-1-0	Wally Butts	9-2-0
9	Oregon	9-1-0	Jim Aiken	9-2-0
10	SMU	8-1-1	Matty Bell	9-1-1
11	Clemson	9-0-0	Frank Howard	11-0-0
12	Vanderbilt ...	7-2-1	Red Sanders	8-2-1
13	Tulane	9-1-0	Henry Frnka	same
14	Michigan St. ..	6-2-2	Biggie Munn	same
15	Mississippi ...	8-1-0	Johnny Vaught	same
16	Minnesota	7-2-0	Bernie Bierman	same
17	William & Mary	6-2-2	Rube McCray	7-2-2
18	Penn St.	7-1-1	Bob Higgins	same
19	Cornell	8-1-0	Lefty James	same
20	Wake Forest ..	6-3-0	Peahead Walker	6-4-0

Note: Big Nine no-repeat rule kept Michigan from Rose Bowl.

Key Bowl Games

Sugar–#5 Oklahoma over #3 North Carolina, 14-6; **Rose**–#7 Northwestern over #4 Cal, 20-14; **Orange**–Texas over #8 Georgia, 41-28; **Cotton**–#10 SMU over #9 Oregon, 21-13.

1949

Final poll released Nov. 28. Top 20 regular season results after that: **Dec. 2**–#14 Maryland over Miami-FL, 13-0. **Dec. 3**–#1 Notre Dame over SMU, 27-20; #10 Pacific over Hawaii, 75-0.

		As of Nov. 28	Head Coach	After Bowls
1	Notre Dame ..	9-0-0	Frank Leahy	10-0-0
2	Oklahoma	10-0-0	Bud Wilkinson	11-0-0
3	California	10-0-0	Pappy Waldorf	10-1-0
4	Army	9-0-0	Red Blaik	same
5	Rice	9-1-0	Jess Neely	10-1-0
6	Ohio St.	6-1-2	Wes Fesler	7-1-2
7	Michigan	6-2-1	Bennie Oosterbaan	same
8	Minnesota	7-2-0	Bernie Bierman	same
9	LSU	8-2-0	Gaynell Tinsley	8-3-0
10	Pacific	10-0-0	Larry Siemering	11-0-0
11	Kentucky	9-2-0	Bear Bryant	9-3-0
12	Cornell	8-1-0	Lefty James	same
13	Villanova	8-1-0	Jim Leonard	same
14	Maryland	7-1-0	Jim Tatum	9-1-0
15	Santa Clara ..	7-2-1	Len Casanova	8-2-1
16	North Carolina	7-3-0	Carl Snavely	7-4-0
17	Tennessee	7-2-1	Bob Neyland	same
18	Princeton	6-3-0	Charlie Caldwell	same
19	Michigan St. ..	6-3-0	Biggie Munn	same
20	Missouri	7-3-0	Don Faurot	7-4-0
	Baylor	8-2-0	Bob Woodruff	same

Key Bowl Games

Sugar–#2 Oklahoma over #9 LSU, 35-0; **Rose**–#6 Ohio St. over #3 Cal, 17-14; **Cotton**–#5 Rice over #16 North Carolina, 27-13; **Orange**–#15 Santa Clara over #11 Kentucky, 21-13.

1950

Final poll released Nov. 27. Top 20 regular season results after that: **Nov. 30**–#3 Texas over Texas A&M, 17-0. **Dec. 1**–#15 Miami-FL over Missouri, 27–9. **Dec. 2**–#1 Oklahoma over Okla. A&M, 41-14; Navy over #2 Army, 14-2; #4 Tennessee over Vanderbilt, 43-0; #16 Alabama over Auburn, 34-0; #19 Tulsa over Houston, 28-21; #20 Tulane tied LSU, 14-14. **Dec. 9**–#3 Texas over LSU, 21-6.

		As of Nov. 27	Head Coach	After Bowls
1	Oklahoma ...	9-0-0	Bud Wilkinson	10-1-0
2	Army	8-1-0	Red Blaik	same
3	Texas	7-1-0	Blair Cherry	9-2-0
4	Tennessee ...	9-1-0	Bob Neyland	11-1-0
5	California	9-0-1	Pappy Waldorf	9-1-1
6	Princeton	9-0-0	Charlie Caldwell	same
7	Kentucky	10-1-0	Bear Bryant	11-1-0
8	Michigan St. .	8-1-0	Biggie Munn	same
9	Michigan	5-3-1	Bennie Oosterbaan	6-3-1
10	Clemson	8-0-1	Frank Howard	9-0-1
11	Washington ..	8-2-0	Howard Odell	same
12	Wyoming	9-0-0	Bowden Wyatt	10-0-0
13	Illinois	7-2-0	Ray Eliot	same
14	Ohio St.	6-3-0	Wes Fesler	same
15	Miami-FL	8-0-1	Andy Gustafson	9-1-1
16	Alabama	8-2-0	Red Drew	9-2-0
17	Nebraska	6-2-1	Bill Glassford	same
18	Wash. & Lee ..	8-2-0	George Barclay	8-3-0
19	Tulsa	8-1-1	J.O. Brothers	9-1-1
20	Tulane	6-2-0	Henry Frnka	6-2-1

Key Bowl Games

Sugar–#7 Kentucky over #1 Oklahoma, 13-7; **Cotton**–#4 Tennessee over #3 Texas, 20-14; **Rose**–#9 Michigan over #5 Cal, 14-6; **Orange**–#10 Clemson over #15 Miami-FL, 15-14.

1951

Final poll released Dec. 3. Top 20 regular season results after that: None.

		As of Dec. 3	Head Coach	After Bowls
1	Tennessee	10-0-0	Bob Neyland	10-1-0
2	Michigan St.	9-0-0	Biggie Munn	same
3	Maryland	9-0-0	Jim Tatum	10-0-0
4	Illinois	8-0-1	Ray Eliot	9-0-1
5	Georgia Tech ...	10-0-1	Bobby Dodd	11-0-1
6	Princeton	9-0-0	Charlie Caldwell	same
7	Stanford	9-1-0	Chuck Taylor	9-2-0
8	Wisconsin	7-1-1	Ivy Williamson	same
9	Baylor	8-1-1	George Sauer	8-2-1
10	Oklahoma	8-2-0	Bud Wilkinson	same
11	TCU	6-4-0	Dutch Meyer	6-5-0
12	California	8-2-0	Pappy Waldorf	same
13	Virginia	8-1-0	Art Guepe	same
14	San Francisco ..	9-0-0	Joe Kuharich	same
15	Kentucky	7-4-0	Bear Bryant	8-4-0
16	Boston Univ. ...	6-4-0	Buff Donelli	same
17	UCLA	5-3-1	Red Sanders	same
18	Washington St. .	7-3-0	Forest Evashevski	same
19	Holy Cross	8-2-0	Eddie Anderson	same
	Clemson	7-2-0	Frank Howard	7-3-0

Key Bowl Games

Sugar–#3 Maryland over #1 Tennessee, 28-13; **Rose**–#4 Illinois over #7 Stanford, 40-7; **Orange**–#5 Georgia Tech over #9 Baylor, 17-14; **Cotton**–#15 Kentucky over #11 TCU, 20-7.

Associated Press Final Polls (Cont.)

1952

Final poll released Dec. 1. Top 20 regular season results after that: **Dec. 6**–#15 Florida over #20 Kentucky, 27-20.

		As of Dec. 1	Head Coach	After Bowls
1	Michigan St. ...	9-0-0	Biggie Munn	same
2	Georgia Tech .	11-0-0	Bobby Dodd	12-0-0
3	Notre Dame ..	7-2-1	Frank Leahy	same
4	Oklahoma	8-1-1	Bud Wilkinson	same
5	USC	9-1-0	Jess Hill	10-1-0
6	UCLA	8-1-0	Red Sanders	same
7	Mississippi ...	8-0-2	Johnny Vaught	8-1-2
8	Tennessee ...	8-1-1	Bob Neyland	8-2-1
9	Alabama	9-2-0	Red Drew	10-2-0
10	Texas	8-2-0	Ed Price	9-2-0
11	Wisconsin	6-2-1	Ivy Williamson	6-3-1
12	Tulsa	8-1-1	J.O. Brothers	8-2-1
13	Maryland	7-2-0	Jim Tatum	same
14	Syracuse	7-2-0	Ben Schwartzwalder	7-3-0
15	Florida	6-3-0	Bob Woodruff	8-3-0
16	Duke	8-2-0	Bill Murray	same
17	Ohio St.	6-3-0	Woody Hayes	same
18	Purdue	4-3-2	Stu Holcomb	same
19	Princeton	8-1-0	Charlie Caldwell	same
20	Kentucky	5-3-2	Bear Bryant	5-4-2

Note: Michigan St. would officially join Big Ten in 1953.

Key Bowl Games

Sugar–#2 Georgia Tech over #7 Ole Miss, 24-7; **Rose**–#5 USC over #11 Wisconsin, 7-0; **Cotton**–#10 Texas over #8 Tennessee, 16-0; **Orange**–#9 Alabama over #14 Syracuse, 61-6.

1953

Final poll released Nov. 30. Top 20 regular season results after that: **Dec. 5**–#2 Notre Dame over SMU, 40-14.

		As of Nov. 30	Head Coach	After Bowls
1	Maryland	10-0-0	Jim Tatum	10-1-0
2	Notre Dame ..	8-0-1	Frank Leahy	9-0-1
3	Michigan St. .	8-1-0	Biggie Munn	9-1-0
4	Oklahoma	8-1-1	Bud Wilkinson	9-1-1
5	UCLA	8-1-0	Red Sanders	8-2-0
6	Rice	8-2-0	Jess Neely	9-2-0
7	Illinois	7-1-1	Ray Eliot	same
8	Georgia Tech .	8-2-1	Bobby Dodd	9-2-1
9	Iowa	5-3-1	Forest Evashevski	same
10	West Virginia .	8-1-0	Art Lewis	8-2-0
11	Texas	7-3-0	Ed Price	same
12	Texas Tech	10-1-0	DeWitt Weaver	11-1-0
13	Alabama	6-2-3	Red Drew	6-3-3
14	Army	7-1-1	Red Blaik	same
15	Wisconsin	6-2-1	Ivy Williamson	same
16	Kentucky	7-2-1	Bear Bryant	same
17	Auburn	7-2-1	Shug Jordan	7-3-1
18	Duke	7-2-1	Bill Murray	same
19	Stanford	6-3-1	Chuck Taylor	same
20	Michigan	6-3-0	Bennie Oosterbaan	same

Key Bowl Games

Orange–#4 Oklahoma over #1 Maryland, 7-0; **Rose**–#3 Michigan St. over #5 UCLA, 28-20; **Cotton**–#6 Rice over #13 Alabama, 28-6; **Sugar**–#8 Georgia Tech over #10 West Virginia, 42-19.

1954

Final poll released Nov. 29. Top 20 regular season results after that: **Dec. 4**–#4 Notre Dame over SMU, 26-14.

		As of Nov. 29	Head Coach	After Bowls
1	Ohio St.	9-0-0	Woody Hayes	10-0-0
2	UCLA	9-0-0	Red Sanders	same
3	Oklahoma	10-0-0	Bud Wilkinson	same
4	Notre Dame ..	8-1-0	Terry Brennan	9-1-0
5	Navy	7-2-0	Eddie Erdelatz	8-2-0
6	Mississippi ...	9-1-0	Johnny Vaught	9-2-0
7	Army	7-2-0	Red Blaik	same
8	Maryland	7-2-1	Jim Tatum	same
9	Wisconsin	7-2-0	Ivy Williamson	same
10	Arkansas	8-2-0	Bowden Wyatt	8-3-0
11	Miami-FL	8-1-0	Andy Gustafson	same
12	West Virginia .	8-1-0	Art Lewis	same
13	Auburn	7-3-0	Shug Jordan	8-3-0
14	Duke	7-2-1	Bill Murray	8-2-1
15	Michigan	6-3-0	Bennie Oosterbaan	same
16	Virginia Tech .	8-0-1	Frank Moseley	same
17	USC	8-3-0	Jess Hill	8-4-0
18	Baylor	7-3-0	George Sauer	7-4-0
19	Rice	7-3-0	Jess Neely	same
20	Penn St.	7-2-0	Rip Engle	same

Note: PCC and Big Seven no-repeat rules kept UCLA and Oklahoma from Orange and Rose bowls, respectively.

Key Bowl Games

Rose–#1 Ohio St. over #17 USC, 20-7; **Sugar**–#5 Navy over #6 Ole Miss, 21-0; **Cotton**–Georgia Tech over #10 Arkansas, 14-6; **Orange**–#14 Duke over Nebraska, 34-7.

1955

Final poll released Nov. 28. Top 20 regular season results after that: None.

		As of Nov. 28	Head Coach	After Bowls
1	Oklahoma	10-0-0	Bud Wilkinson	11-0-0
2	Michigan St. ..	8-1-0	Duffy Daugherty	9-1-0
3	Maryland	10-0-0	Jim Tatum	10-1-0
4	UCLA	9-1-0	Red Sanders	9-2-0
5	Ohio St.	7-2-0	Woody Hayes	same
6	TCU	9-1-0	Abe Martin	9-2-0
7	Georgia Tech .	8-1-1	Bobby Dodd	9-1-1
8	Auburn	8-1-1	Shug Jordan	8-2-1
9	Notre Dame ..	8-2-0	Terry Brennan	same
10	Mississippi ...	9-1-0	Johnny Vaught	10-1-0
11	Pittsburgh ...	7-3-0	John Michelosen	7-4-0
12	Michigan	7-2-0	Bennie Oosterbaan	same
13	USC	6-4-0	Jess Hill	same
14	Miami-FL	6-3-0	Andy Gustafson	same
15	Miami-OH	9-0-0	Ara Parseghian	same
16	Stanford	6-3-1	Chuck Taylor	same
17	Texas A&M ...	7-2-1	Bear Bryant	same
18	Navy	6-2-1	Eddie Erdelatz	same
19	West Virginia .	8-2-0	Art Lewis	same
20	Army	6-3-0	Red Blaik	same

Note: Big Ten no-repeat rule kept Ohio St. from Rose Bowl.

Key Bowl Gaes

Orange–#1 Oklahoma over #3 Maryland, 20-6; **Rose**–#2 Michigan St. over #4 UCLA, 17-14; **Cotton**–#10 Ole Miss over #6 TCU, 14-13; **Sugar**–#7 Georgia Tech over #11 Pitt, 7-0; **Gator**–Vanderbilt over #8 Auburn, 25-13.

1956

Final poll released Dec. 3. Top 20 regular season results after that: **Dec. 8**–#13 Pitt over #6 Miami-FL, 14-7.

		As of Dec. 3	Head Coach	After Bowls
1	Oklahoma	10-0-0	Bud Wilkinson	same
2	Tennessee	10-0-0	Bowden Wyatt	10-1-0
3	Iowa	8-1-0	Forest Evashevski	9-1-0
4	Georgia Tech .	9-1-0	Bobby Dodd	10-1-0
5	Texas A&M ...	9-0-1	Bear Bryant	same
6	Miami-FL	8-0-1	Andy Gustafson	8-1-1
7	Michigan	7-2-0	Bennie Oosterbaan	same
8	Syracuse	7-1-0	Ben Schwartzwalder	7-2-0
9	Michigan St. ..	7-2-0	Duffy Daugherty	same
10	Oregon St. ...	7-2-1	Tommy Prothro	7-3-1
11	Baylor	8-2-0	Sam Boyd	9-2-0
12	Minnesota	6-1-2	Murray Warmath	same
13	Pittsburgh	6-2-1	John Michelosen	7-3-1
14	TCU	7-3-0	Abe Martin	8-3-0
15	Ohio St.	6-3-0	Woody Hayes	same
16	Navy	6-1-2	Eddie Erdelatz	same
17	G. Washington	7-1-1	Gene Sherman	8-1-1
18	USC	8-2-0	Jess Hill	same
19	Clemson	7-1-2	Frank Howard	7-2-2
20	Colorado	7-2-1	Dallas Ward	8-2-1

Note: Big Seven no-repeat rule kept Oklahoma from Orange Bowl and Texas A&M was on probation.

Key Bowl Games

Sugar–#11 Baylor over #2 Tennessee, 13-7; **Rose**– #3 Iowa over #10 Oregon St., 35-19; **Gator**–#4 Georgia Tech over #13 Pitt, 21-14; **Cotton**–#14 TCU over #8 Syracuse, 28-27; **Orange**–#20 Colorado over #19 Clemson, 27-21.

1957

Final poll released Dec. 2. Top 20 regular season results after that: **Dec. 7**–#10 Notre Dame over SMU, 54-21.

		As of Dec. 2	Head Coach	After Bowls
1	Auburn	10-0-0	Shug Jordan	same
2	Ohio St.	8-1-0	Woody Hayes	9-1-0
3	Michigan St. ...	8-1-0	Duffy Daugherty	same
4	Oklahoma	9-1-0	Bud Wilkinson	10-1-0
5	Navy	8-1-1	Eddie Erdelatz	9-1-1
6	Iowa	7-1-1	Forest Evashevski	same
7	Mississippi	8-1-1	Johnny Vaught	9-1-1
8	Rice	7-3-0	Jess Neely	7-4-0
9	Texas A&M ...	8-2-0	Bear Bryant	8-3-0
10	Notre Dame ...	6-3-0	Terry Brennan	7-3-0
11	Texas	6-3-1	Darrell Royal	6-4-1
12	Arizona St.	10-0-0	Dan Devine	same
13	Tennessee	7-3-0	Bowden Wyatt	8-3-0
14	Mississippi St. ..	6-2-1	Wade Walker	same
15	N.C. State	7-1-2	Earle Edwards	same
16	Duke	6-2-2	Bill Murray	6-3-2
17	Florida	6-2-1	Bob Woodruff	same
18	Army	7-2-0	Red Blaik	same
19	Wisconsin	6-3-0	Milt Bruhn	same
20	VMI	9-0-1	John McKenna	same

Note: Auburn on probation, ineligible for bowl game.

Key Bowl Games

Rose–#2 Ohio St. over Oregon, 10-7; **Orange**–#4 Oklahoma over #16 Duke, 48-21; **Cotton**–#5 Navy over #8 Rice, 20-7; **Sugar**–#7 Ole Miss over #11 Texas, 39-7; **Gator**–#13 Tennessee over #9 Texas A&M, 3-0.

1958

Final poll released Dec. 1. Top 20 regular season results after that: None.

		As of Dec. 1	Head Coach	After Bowls
1	LSU	10-0-0	Paul Dietzel	11-0-0
2	Iowa	7-1-1	Forest Evashevski	8-1-1
3	Army	8-0-1	Red Blaik	same
4	Auburn	9-0-1	Shug Jordan	same
5	Oklahoma	9-1-0	Bud Wilkinson	10-1-0
6	Air Force	9-0-1	Ben Martin	9-0-2
7	Wisconsin	7-1-1	Milt Bruhn	same
8	Ohio St.	6-1-2	Woody Hayes	same
9	Syracuse	8-1-0	Ben Schwartzwalder	8-2-0
10	TCU	8-2-0	Abe Martin	8-2-1
11	Mississippi	8-2-0	Johnny Vaught	9-2-0
12	Clemson	8-2-0	Frank Howard	8-3-0
13	Purdue	6-1-2	Jack Mollenkopf	same
14	Florida	6-3-1	Bob Woodruff	6-4-1
15	South Carolina	7-3-0	Warren Giese	same
16	California	7-3-0	Pete Elliott	7-4-0
17	Notre Dame ..	6-4-0	Terry Brennan	same
18	SMU	6-4-0	Bill Meek	same
19	Oklahoma St. .	7-3-0	Cliff Speegle	8-3-0
20	Rutgers	8-1-0	John Stiegman	same

Key Bowl Games

Sugar–#1 LSU over #12 Clemson, 7-0; **Rose**–#2 Iowa over #16 Cal, 38-12; **Orange**–#5 Oklahoma over #9 Syracuse, 21-6; **Cotton**–#6 Air Force tied #10 TCU, 0-0.

1959

Final poll released Dec. 7. Top 20 regular season results after that: None.

		As of Dec. 7	Head Coach	After Bowls
1	Syracuse	10-0-0	Ben Schwartzwalder	11-0-0
2	Mississippi	9-1-0	Johnny Vaught	10-1-0
3	LSU	9-1-0	Paul Dietzel	9-2-0
4	Texas	9-1-0	Darrell Royal	9-2-0
5	Georgia	9-1-0	Wally Butts	10-1-0
6	Wisconsin	7-2-0	Milt Bruhn	7-3-0
7	TCU	8-2-0	Abe Martin	8-3-0
8	Washington ...	9-1-0	Jim Owens	10-1-0
9	Arkansas	8-2-0	Frank Broyles	9-2-0
10	Alabama	7-1-2	Bear Bryant	7-2-2
11	Clemson	8-2-0	Frank Howard	9-2-0
12	PennSt.	8-2-0	Rip Engle	9-2-0
13	Illinois	5-3-1	Ray Eliot	same
14	USC	8-2-0	Don Clark	same
15	Oklahoma	7-3-0	Bud Wilkinson	same
16	Wyoming	9-1-0	Bob Devaney	same
17	Notre Dame ..	5-5-0	Joe Kuharich	same
18	Missouri	6-4-0	Dan Devine	6-5-0
19	Florida	5-4-1	Bob Woodruff	same
20	Pittsburgh	6-4-0	John Michelosen	same

Note: Big Seven no-repeat rule kept Oklahoma from Orange Bowl.

Key Bowl Games

Cotton–#1 Syracuse over #4 Texas, 23-14; **Sugar**–#2 Ole Miss over #3 LSU, 21-0; **Orange**–#5 Georgia over #18 Missouri, 14-0; **Rose**–#8 Washington over #6 Wisconsin, 44-8; **Bluebonnet**–#11 Clemson over #7 TCU, 23-7; **Gator**–#9 Arkansas over Georgia Tech, 14-7; **Liberty**–#12 Penn St. over #10 Alabama, 7-0.

Associated Press Final Polls (Cont.)

AP ranked only 10 teams from 1962-67.

1960

Final poll released Nov. 28. Top 20 regular season results after that: **Dec. 3**–UCLA over #10 Duke, 27-6.

		As of Nov. 28	Head Coach	After Bowls
1	Minnesota ...	8-1-0	Murray Warmath	8-2-0
2	Mississippi ..	9-0-1	Johnny Vaught	10-0-1
3	Iowa	8-1-0	Forest Evashevski	same
4	Navy	9-1-0	Wayne Hardin	9-2-0
5	Missouri	9-1-0	Dan Devine	10-1-0
6	Washington .	9-1-0	Jim Owens	10-1-0
7	Arkansas	8-2-0	Frank Broyles	8-3-0
8	Ohio St.	7-2-0	Woody Hayes	same
9	Alabama	8-1-1	Bear Bryant	8-1-2
10	Duke	7-2-0	Bill Murray	8-3-0
11	Kansas	7-2-1	Jack Mitchell	same
12	Baylor	8-2-0	John Bridgers	8-3-0
13	Auburn	8-2-0	Shug Jordan	same
14	Yale	9-0-0	Jordan Olivar	same
15	Michigan St. .	6-2-1	Duffy Daugherty	same
16	Penn St.	6-3-0	Rip Engle	7-3-0
17	New Mexico St.	10-0-0	Warren Woodson	11-0-0
18	Florida	8-2-0	Ray Graves	9-2-0
19	Syracuse	7-2-0	Ben Schwartzwalder	same
	Purdue	4-4-1	Jack Mollenkopf	same

Key Bowl Games

Rose–#6 Washington over #1 Minnesota, 17-7; **Sugar**–#2 Ole Miss over Rice, 14-6; **Orange**–#5 Missouri over #4 Navy, 21-14; **Cotton**–#10 Duke over #7 Arkansas, 7-6; **Bluebonnet**–#9 Alabama tied Texas, 3-3.

1961

Final poll released Dec. 4. Top 20 regular season results after that: None.

		As of Dec. 4	Head Coach	After Bowls
1	Alabama	10-0-0	Bear Bryant	11-0-0
2	Ohio St.	8-0-1	Woody Hayes	same
3	Texas	9-1-0	Darrell Royal	10-1-0
4	LSU	9-1-0	Paul Dietzel	10-1-0
5	Mississippi ...	9-1-0	Johnny Vaught	9-2-0
6	Minnesota	7-2-0	Murray Warmath	8-2-0
7	Colorado	9-1-0	Sonny Grandelius	9-2-0
8	Michigan St. ..	7-2-0	Duffy Daugherty	same
9	Arkansas	8-2-0	Frank Broyles	8-3-0
10	Utah St.	9-0-1	John Ralston	9-1-1
11	Missouri	7-2-1	Dan Devine	same
12	Purdue	6-3-0	Jack Mollenkopf	same
13	Georgia Tech .	7-3-0	Bobby Dodd	7-4-0
14	Syracuse	7-3-0	Ben Schwartzwalder	8-3-0
15	Rutgers	9-0-0	John Bateman	same
16	UCLA	7-3-0	Bill Barnes	7-4-0
17	Rice	7-3-0	Jess Neely	7-4-0
	Penn St.	7-3-0	Rip Engle	8-3-0
	Arizona	8-1-1	Jim LaRue	same
20	Duke	7-3-0	Bill Murray	same

Note: Ohio St. faculty council turned down Rose Bowl invitation citing concern with OSU's overemphasis on sports.

Key Bowl Games

Sugar–#1 Alabama over #9 Arkansas, 10-3; **Cotton**–#3 Texas over #5 Ole Miss, 12-7; **Orange**–#4 LSU over #7 Colorado, 25-7; **Rose**–#6 Minnesota over #16 UCLA, 21-3; **Gotham**–Baylor over #10 Utah St., 24-9.

1962

Final poll released Dec. 3. Top 10 regular season results after that: None.

		As of Dec. 3	Head Coach	After Bowls
1	USC	10-0-0	John McKay	11-0-0
2	Wisconsin ...	8-1-0	Milt Bruhn	8-2-0
3	Mississippi	9-0-0	Johnny Vaught	10-0-0
4	Texas	9-0-1	Darrell Royal	9-1-1
5	Alabama	9-1-0	Bear Bryant	10-1-0
6	Arkansas	9-1-0	Frank Broyles	9-2-0
7	LSU	8-1-1	Charlie McClendon	9-1-1
8	Oklahoma	8-2-0	Bud Wilkinson	8-3-0
9	Penn St.	9-1-0	Rip Engle	9-2-0
10	Minnesota	6-2-1	Murray Warmath	same

Key Bowl Games

Rose–#1 USC over #2 Wisconsin, 42-37; **Sugar**–#3 Ole Miss over #6 Arkansas, 17-13; **Cotton**–#7 LSU over #4 Texas, 13-0; **Orange**–#5 Alabama over #8 Oklahoma, 17-0; **Gator**–Florida over #9 Penn St.,17-7.

1963

Final poll released Dec. 9. Top 10 regular season results after that: **Dec.14**–#8 Alabama over Miami-FL, 17-12.

		As of Dec. 9	Head Coach	After Bowls
1	Texas	10-0-0	Darrell Royal	11-0-0
2	Navy	9-1-0	Wayne Hardin	9-2-0
3	Illinois	7-1-1	Pete Elliott	8-1-1
4	Pittsburgh	9-1-0	John Michelosen	same
5	Auburn	9-1-0	Shug Jordan	9-2-0
6	Nebraska	9-1-0	Bob Devaney	10-1-0
7	Mississippi	7-0-2	Johnny Vaught	7-1-2
8	Alabama	7-2-0	Bear Bryant	9-2-0
9	Michigan St.	6-2-1	Duffy Daugherty	same
10	Oklahoma	8-2-0	Bud Wilkinson	same

Key Bowl Games

Cotton–#1 Texas over #2 Navy, 28-6; **Rose**–#3 Illinois over Washington, 17-7; **Orange**–#6 Nebraska over #5 Auburn, 13-7; **Sugar**–#8 Alabama over #7 Ole Miss, 12-7.

1964

Final poll released Nov. 30. Top 10 regular season results after that: **Dec. 5**–Florida over #7 LSU, 20-6.

		As of Nov. 30	Head Coach	After Bowls
1	Alabama	10-0-0	Bear Bryant	10-1-0
2	Arkansas	10-0-0	Frank Broyles	11-0-0
3	Notre Dame .	9-1-0	Ara Parseghian	same
4	Michigan	8-1-0	Bump Elliott	9-1-0
5	Texas	9-1-0	Darrell Royal	10-1-0
6	Nebraska ...	9-1-0	Bob Devaney	9-2-0
7	LSU	7-1-1	Charlie McClendon	8-2-1
8	Oregon St. ...	8-2-0	Tommy Prothro	8-3-0
9	Ohio St.	7-2-0	Woody Hayes	same
10	USC	7-3-0	John McKay	same

Key Bowl Games

Orange–#5 Texas over #1 Alabama, 21-17; **Cotton**–#2 Arkansas over #6 Nebraska, 10-7; **Rose**– #4 Michigan over #8 Oregon St., 34-7; **Sugar**–#7 LSU over Syracuse, 13-10.

1965

Final poll taken after bowl games for the first time.

		After Bowls	Head Coach	Regular Season
1	Alabama	9-1-1	Bear Bryant	8-1-1
2	Michigan St. ..	10-1-0	Duffy Daugherty	10-0-0
3	Arkansas	10-1-0	Frank Broyles	10-0-0
4	UCLA	8-2-1	Tommy Prothro	7-1-1
5	Nebraska	10-1-0	Bob Devaney	10-0-0
6	Missouri	8-2-1	Dan Devine	7-2-1
7	Tennessee	8-1-2	Doug Dickey	6-1-2
8	LSU	8-3-0	Charlie McClendon	7-3-0
9	Notre Dame ..	7-2-1	Ara Parseghian	same
10	USC	7-2-1	John McKay	same

Key Bowl Games

Rankings below reflect final regular season poll, released Nov. 29. No bowls for then #8 USC or #9 Notre Dame. Rose–#5 UCLA over #1 Michigan St., 14-12; Cotton–LSU over #2 Arkansas, 14-7; Orange–#4 Alabama over #3 Nebraska, 39-28; Sugar–#6 Missouri over Florida, 20-18; Bluebonnet–#7 Tennessee over Tulsa, 27-6; Gator–Georgia Tech over #10 Texas Tech, 31-21.

1966

Final poll released Dec. 5, returning to pre-bowl status. Top 10 regular season results after that: None.

		As of Dec. 5	Head Coach	After Bowls
1	Notre Dame	9-0-1	Ara Parseghian	same
2	Michigan St.	9-0-1	Duffy Daugherty	same
3	Alabama	10-0-0	Bear Bryant	11-0-0
4	Georgia	9-1-0	Vince Dooley	10-1-0
5	UCLA	9-1-0	Tommy Prothro	same
6	Nebraska	9-1-0	Bob Devaney	9-2-0
7	Purdue	8-2-0	Jack Mollenkopf	9-2-0
8	Georgia Tech ...	9-1-0	Bobby Dodd	9-2-0
9	Miami-FL	7-2-1	Charlie Tate	8-2-1
10	SMU	9-1-0	Hayden Fry	8-3-0

Key Bowl Games

Sugar–#3 Alabama over #6 Nebraska, 34-7; Cotton–#4 Georgia over #10 SMU, 24-9; Rose–#7 Purdue over USC, 14-13; Orange–Florida over #8 Georgia Tech, 27-12; Liberty–#9 Miami-FL over Virginia Tech, 14-7.

1967

Final poll released Nov. 27. Top 10 regular season results after that: Dec. 2–#2 Tennessee over Vanderbilt, 41-14; #3 Oklahoma over Oklahoma St., 38-14; #8 Alabama over Auburn, 7-3.

		As of Nov. 27	Head Coach	After Bowls
1	USC	9-1-0	John McKay	10-1-0
2	Tennessee	8-1-0	Doug Dickey	9-2-0
3	Oklahoma	8-1-0	Chuck Fairbanks	10-1-0
4	Indiana	9-1-0	John Pont	9-2-0
5	Notre Dame ..	8-2-0	Ara Parseghian	same
6	Wyoming	10-0-0	Lloyd Eaton	10-1-0
7	Oregon St. ...	7-2-1	Dee Andros	same
8	Alabama	7-1-1	Bear Bryant	8-2-1
9	Purdue	8-2-0	Jack Mollenkopf	same
10	Penn St.	8-2-0	Joe Paterno	8-2-1

Key Bowl Games

Rose–#1 USC over #4 Indiana, 14-3; Orange–#3 Oklahoma over #2 Tennessee, 26-24; Sugar–LSU over #6 Wyoming, 20-13; Cotton–Texas A&M over #8 Alabama, 20-16; Gator–#10 Penn St. tied Florida St. 17-17.

1968

Final poll taken after bowl games for first time since close of 1965 season.

		After Bowls	Head Coach	Regular Season
1	Ohio St.	10-0-0	Woody Hayes	9-0-0
2	Penn St.	11-0-0	Joe Paterno	10-0-0
3	Texas	9-1-1	Darrell Royal	8-1-1
4	USC	9-1-1	John McKay	9-0-1
5	Notre Dame ..	7-2-1	Ara Parseghian	same
6	Arkansas	10-1-0	Frank Broyles	9-1-0
7	Kansas	9-2-0	Pepper Rodgers	9-1-0
8	Georgia	8-1-2	Vince Dooley	8-0-2
9	Missouri	8-3-0	Dan Devine	7-3-0
10	Purdue	8-2-0	Jack Mollenkopf	same
11	Oklahoma	7-4-0	Chuck Fairbanks	7-3-0
12	Michigan	8-2-0	Bump Elliott	same
13	Tennessee ...	8-2-1	Doug Dickey	8-1-1
14	SMU	8-3-0	Hayden Fry	7-3-0
15	Oregon St. ...	7-3-0	Dee Andros	same
16	Auburn	7-4-0	Shug Jordan	6-4-0
17	Alabama	8-3-0	Bear Bryant	8-2-0
18	Houston	6-2-2	Bill Yeoman	same
19	LSU	8-3-0	Charlie McClendon	7-3-0
20	Ohio Univ. ...	10-1-0	Bill Hess	10-0-0

Key Bowl Games

Rankings below reflect final regular season poll, released Dec. 2. No bowls for then #7 Notre Dame and #11 Purdue. Rose–#1 Ohio St. over #2 USC, 27-16; Orange–#3 Penn St. over #6 Kansas, 15-14; Sugar–#9 Arkansas over #4 Georgia, 16-2; Cotton–#5 Texas over #8 Tennessee, 36-13; Bluebonnet–#20 SMU over #10 Oklahoma, 28-27; Gator–#16 Missouri over #12 Alabama, 35-10.

1969

Final poll taken after bowl games.

		After Bowls	Head Coach	Regular Season
1	Texas	11-0-0	Darrell Royal	10-0-0
2	Penn St.	11-0-0	Joe Paterno	10-0-0
3	USC	10-0-1	John McKay	9-0-1
4	Ohio St.	8-1-0	Woody Hayes	same
5	Notre Dame ..	8-2-1	Ara Parseghian	8-1-1
6	Missouri	9-2-0	Dan Devine	9-1-0
7	Arkansas	9-2-0	Frank Broyles	9-1-0
8	Mississippi ...	8-3-0	Johnny Vaught	7-3-0
9	Michigan	8-3-0	Bo Schembechler	8-2-0
10	LSU	9-1-0	Charlie McClendon	same
11	Nebraska	9-2-0	Bob Devaney	8-2-0
12	Houston	9-2-0	Bill Yeoman	8-2-0
13	UCLA	8-1-1	Tommy Prothro	same
14	Florida	9-1-1	Ray Graves	8-1-1
15	Tennessee ...	9-2-0	Doug Dickey	9-1-0
16	Colorado	8-3-0	Eddie Crowder	7-3-0
17	West Virginia ..	10-1-0	Jim Carlen	9-1-0
18	Purdue	8-2-0	Jack Mollenkopf	same
19	Stanford	7-2-1	John Ralston	same
20	Auburn	8-3-0	Shug Jordan	8-2-0

Key Bowl Games

Rankings below reflect final regular season poll, released Dec. 8. No bowls for then #4 Ohio St., #8 LSU and #10 UCLA.

Cotton–#1 Texas over #9 Notre Dame, 21-17; Orange–#2 Penn St. over #6 Missouri, 10-3; Sugar–#13 Ole Miss over #3 Arkansas, 27-22; Rose–#5 USC over #7 Michigan, 10-3.

Associated Press Final Polls (Cont.)

1970

			After Bowls	Head Coach	Regular Season
1	Nebraska	...	11-0-1	Bob Devaney	10-0-1
2	Notre Dame	.	10-1-0	Ara Parseghian	9-0-1
3	Texas	....	10-1-0	Darrell Royal	10-0-0
4	Tennessee	.	11-1-0	Bill Battle	10-1-0
5	Ohio St.	.....	9-1-0	Woody Hayes	9-0-0
6	Arizona St.	.	11-0-0	Frank Kush	10-0-0
7	LSU		9-3-0	Charlie McClendon	9-2-0
8	Stanford	.....	9-3-0	John Ralston	8-3-0
9	Michigan	....	9-1-0	Bo Schembechler	same
10	Auburn	.....	9-2-0	Shug Jordan	8-2-0
11	Arkansas	....	9-2-0	Frank Broyles	same
12	Toledo	......	12-0-0	Frank Lauterbur	11-0-0
13	Georgia Tech		9-3-0	Bud Carson	8-3-0
14	Dartmouth		9-0-0	Bob Blackman	same
15	USC	....	6-4-1	John McKay	same
16	Air Force		9-3-0	Ben Martin	9-2-0
17	Tulane	......	8-4-0	Jim Pittman	7-4-0
18	Penn St.	.....	7-3-0	Joe Paterno	same
19	Houston		8-3-0	Bill Yeoman	same
20	Oklahoma	...	7-4-1	Chuck Fairbanks	7-4-0
	Mississippi	...	7-4-0	Johnny Vaught	7-3-0

Key Bowl Games

Rankings below reflect final regular season poll, released Dec. 7. No bowls for then #4 Arkansas and #7 Michigan.

Cotton—#6 Notre Dame over #1 Texas, 24-11; **Rose**—#12 Stanford over #2 Ohio St., 27-17; **Orange**—#3 Nebraska over #8 LSU, 17-12; **Sugar**— #5 Tennessee over #11 Air Force, 34-13; **Peach**—#9 Ariz. St. over N. Carolina, 48-26.

1971

			After Bowls	Head Coach	Regular Season
1	Nebraska	....	13-0-0	Bob Devaney	12-0-0
2	Oklahoma	....	11-1-0	Chuck Fairbanks	10-1-0
3	Colorado	....	10-2-0	Eddie Crowder	9-2-0
4	Alabama	....	11-1-0	Bear Bryant	11-0-0
5	Penn St.	......	11-1-0	Joe Paterno	10-1-0
6	Michigan	.....	11-1-0	Bo Schembechler	11-0-0
7	Georgia	.....	11-1-0	Vince Dooley	10-1-0
8	Arizona St.	...	11-1-0	Frank Kush	10-1-0
9	Tennessee	...	10-2-0	Bill Battle	9-2-0
10	Stanford	.....	9-3-0	John Ralston	8-3-0
11	LSU	....	9-3-0	Charlie McClendon	8-3-0
12	Auburn	.....	9-2-0	Shug Jordan	9-1-0
13	Notre Dame	..	8-2-0	Ara Parseghian	same
14	Toledo	......	12-0-0	John Murphy	11-0-0
15	Mississippi	...	10-2-0	Billy Kinard	9-2-0
16	Arkansas	.....	8-3-1	Frank Broyles	8-2-1
17	Houston	.....	9-3-0	Bill Yeoman	9-2-0
18	Texas	....	8-3-0	Darrell Royal	8-2-0
19	Washington	..	8-3-0	Jim Owens	same
20	USC	....	6-4-1	John McKay	same

Key Bowl Games

Rankings below reflect final regular season poll, released Dec. 6.

Orange—#1 Nebraska over #2 Alabama, 38-6; **Sugar**—#3 Oklahoma over #5 Auburn, 40-22; **Rose**—#16 Stanford over #4 Michigan, 13-12; **Gator**—#6 Georgia over N. Carolina, 7-3; **Bluebonnet**—#7 Colorado over #15 Houston, 29-17; **Fiesta**—#8 Ariz. St. over Florida St., 45-38; **Cotton**—#10 Penn St. over #12 Texas, 30-6.

1972

			After Bowls	Head Coach	Regular Season
1	USC	....	12-0-0	John McKay	11-0-0
2	Oklahoma	...	11-1-0	Chuck Fairbanks	10-1-0
3	Texas	....	10-1-0	Darrell Royal	9-1-0
4	Nebraska	...	9-2-1	Bob Devaney	8-2-1
5	Auburn	......	10-1-0	Shug Jordan	9-1-0
6	Michigan	...	10-1-0	Bo Schembechler	same
7	Alabama	....	10-2-0	Bear Bryant	10-1-0
8	Tennessee	...	10-2-0	Bill Battle	9-2-0
9	Ohio St.	.....	9-2-0	Woody Hayes	9-1-0
10	Penn St.	.....	10-2-0	Joe Paterno	10-1-0
11	LSU	....	9-2-1	Charlie McClendon	9-1-1
12	North Carolina		11-1-0	Bill Dooley	10-1-0
13	Arizona St.	.	10-2-0	Frank Kush	9-2-0
14	Notre Dame	.	8-3-0	Ara Parseghian	8-2-0
15	UCLA	....	8-3-0	Pepper Rodgers	same
16	Colorado	....	8-4-0	Eddie Crowder	8-3-0
17	N.C. State	..	8-3-1	Lou Holtz	7-3-1
18	Louisville	...	9-1-0	Lee Corso	same
19	Washington St.		7-4-0	Jim Sweeney	same
20	Georgia Tech	.	7-4-1	Bill Fulcher	6-4-1

Key Bowl Games

Rankings below reflect final regular season poll, released Dec. 4. No bowl for then #8 Michigan.

Rose—#1 USC over #3 Ohio St., 42-17; **Sugar**—#2 Oklahoma over #5 Penn St., 14-0; **Cotton**—#7 Texas over #4 Alabama, 17-13; **Orange**—#9 Nebraska over #12 Notre Dame, 40-6; **Gator**—#6 Auburn over #13 Colorado, 24-3; **Bluebonnet**—#11 Tennessee over #10 LSU, 24-17.

1973

			After Bowls	Head Coach	Regular Season
1	Notre Dame	.	11-0-0	Ara Parseghian	10-0-0
2	Ohio St.	.....	10-0-1	Woody Hayes	9-0-1
3	Oklahoma	...	10-0-1	Barry Switzer	same
4	Alabama	....	11-1-0	Bear Bryant	11-0-0
5	Penn St.	......	12-0-0	Joe Paterno	11-0-0
6	Michigan	....	10-0-1	Bo Schembechler	same
7	Nebraska	...	9-2-1	Tom Osborne	8-2-1
8	USC	....	9-2-1	John McKay	9-1-1
9	Arizona St.	...	11-1-0	Frank Kush	10-1-0
	Houston	......	11-1-0	Bill Yeoman	10-1-0
11	Texas Tech	....	11-1-0	Jim Carlen	10-1-0
12	UCLA	....	9-2-0	Pepper Rodgers	same
13	LSU	....	9-3-0	Charlie McClendon	9-2-0
14	Texas	....	8-3-0	Darrell Royal	8-2-0
15	Miami-OH	.....	11-0-0	Bill Mallory	10-0-0
16	N.C. State	....	9-3-0	Lou Holtz	8-3-0
17	Missouri	.....	8-4-0	Al Onofrio	7-4-0
18	Kansas	......	7-4-1	Don Fambrough	7-3-1
19	Tennessee	...	8-4-0	Bill Battle	8-3-0
20	Maryland	...	8-4-0	Jerry Claiborne	8-3-0
	Tulane	....	9-3-0	Bennie Ellender	9-2-0

Key Bowl Games

Rankings below reflect final regular season poll, released Dec. 3. No bowls for then #2 Oklahoma (probation), #5 Michigan and #9 UCLA.

Sugar—#3 Notre Dame over #1 Alabama, 24-23; **Rose**—#4 Ohio St. over #7 USC, 42-21; **Orange**—#6 Penn St. over #13 LSU, 16-9; **Cotton**—#12 Nebraska over #8 Texas, 19-3; **Fiesta**—#10 Ariz. St. over Pitt, 28-7; **Bluebonnet**—#14 Houston over #17 Tulane, 47-7.

1974

		After Bowls	Head Coach	Regular Season
1	Oklahoma	11-0-0	Barry Switzer	same
2	USC	10-1-1	John McKay	9-1-1
3	Michigan	10-1-0	Bo Schembechler	same
4	Ohio St.	10-2-0	Woody Hayes	10-1-0
5	Alabama	11-1-0	Bear Bryant	11-0-0
6	Notre Dame ...	10-2-0	Ara Parseghian	9-2-0
7	Penn St.	10-2-0	Joe Paterno	9-2-0
8	Auburn	10-2-0	Shug Jordan	9-2-0
9	Nebraska	9-3-0	Tom Osborne	8-3-0
10	Miami-OH	10-0-1	Dick Crum	9-0-1
11	N.C. State ...	9-2-1	Lou Holtz	9-2-0
12	Michigan St. ..	7-3-1	Denny Stolz	same
13	Maryland	8-4-0	Jerry Claiborne	8-3-0
14	Baylor	8-4-0	Grant Teaff	8-3-0
15	Florida	8-4-0	Doug Dickey	8-3-0
16	Texas A&M ...	8-3-0	Emory Ballard	same
17	Mississippi St.	9-3-0	Bob Tyler	8-3-0
	Texas	8-4-0	Darrell Royal	8-3-0
19	Houston	8-3-1	Bill Yeoman	8-3-0
20	Tennessee	7-3-2	Bill Battle	6-3-2

Key Bowl Games

Rankings below reflect final regular season poll, released Dec. 2. No bowls for #1 Oklahoma (probation) and then #4 Michigan.

Orange–#9 Notre Dame over #2 Alabama, 13-11; **Rose**–#5 USC over #3 Ohio St., 18-17; **Gator**–#6 Auburn over #11 Texas, 27-3; **Cotton**–#7 Penn St. over #12 Baylor, 41-20; **Sugar**–#8 Nebraska over #18 Florida, 13-10; **Liberty**–Tennessee over #10 Maryland, 7-3.

1975

		After Bowls	Head Coach	Regular Season
1	Oklahoma	11-1-0	Barry Switzer	10-1-0
2	Arizona St. ...	12-0-0	Frank Kush	11-0-0
3	Alabama	11-1-0	Bear Bryant	10-1-0
4	Ohio St.	11-1-0	Woody Hayes	11-0-0
5	UCLA	9-2-1	Dick Vermeil	8-2-1
6	Texas	10-2-0	Darrell Royal	9-2-0
7	Arkansas	10-2-0	Frank Broyles	9-2-0
8	Michigan	8-2-2	Bo Schembechler	8-1-2
9	Nebraska	10-2-0	Tom Osborne	10-1-0
10	Penn St.	9-3-0	Joe Paterno	9-2-0
11	Texas A&M ...	10-2-0	Emory Ballard	10-1-0
12	Miami-OH	11-1-0	Dick Crum	10-1-0
13	Maryland	9-2-1	Jerry Claiborne	8-2-1
14	California	8-3-0	Mike White	same
15	Pittsburgh	8-4-0	Johnny Majors	7-4-0
16	Colorado	9-3-0	Bill Mallory	9-2-0
17	USC	8-4-0	John McKay	7-4-0
18	Arizona	9-2-0	Jim Young	same
19	Georgia	9-3-0	Vince Dooley	9-2-0
20	West Virginia .	9-3-0	Bobby Bowden	8-3-0

Key Bowl Games

Rankings below reflect final regular season poll, released Dec. 1. Texas A&M was unbeaten and ranked 2nd in that poll, but lost to #18 Arkansas, 31-6, in its final regular season game on Dec. 6.

Rose–#11 UCLA over #1 Ohio St., 23-10; **Liberty**–#17 USC over #2 Texas A&M, 20-0; **Orange**–#3 Oklahoma over #5 Michigan, 14-6; **Sugar**–#4 Alabama over #8 Penn St., 13-6; **Fiesta**–#7 Ariz. St. over #6 Nebraska, 17-14; **Bluebonnet**–#9 Texas over #10 Colorado, 38-21; **Cotton**–#18 Arkansas over #12 Georgia, 31-10.

1976

		After Bowls	Head Coach	Regular Season
1	Pittsburgh	12-0-0	Johnny Majors	11-0-0
2	USC	11-1-0	John Robinson	10-1-0
3	Michigan	10-2-0	Bo Schembechler	10-1-0
4	Houston	10-2-0	Bill Yeoman	9-2-0
5	Oklahoma	9-2-1	Barry Switzer	8-2-1
6	Ohio St.	9-2-1	Woody Hayes	8-2-1
7	Texas A&M ...	10-2-0	Emory Bellard	9-2-0
8	Maryland	11-1-0	Jerry Claiborne	11-0-0
9	Nebraska	9-3-1	Tom Osborne	8-3-1
10	Georgia	10-2-0	Vince Dooley	10-1-0
11	Alabama	9-3-0	Bear Bryant	8-3-0
12	Notre Dame ..	9-3-0	Dan Devine	8-3-0
13	Texas Tech ...	10-2-0	Steve Sloan	10-1-0
14	Oklahoma St..	9-3-0	Jim Stanley	8-3-0
15	UCLA	9-2-1	Terry Donahue	9-1-1
16	Colorado	8-4-0	Bill Mallory	8-3-0
17	Rutgers	11-0-0	Frank Burns	same
18	Kentucky	8-4-0	Fran Curci	7-4-0
19	Iowa St.	8-3-0	Earle Bruce	same
20	Mississippi St.	9-2-0	Bob Tyler	same

Key Bowl Games

Rankings below reflect final regular season poll, released Nov. 29. No bowl for then #20 Miss. St. (probation).

Sugar–#1 Pitt over #5 Georgia, 27-3; **Rose**–#3 USC over #2 Michigan, 14-6; **Cotton**–#6 Houston over #4 Maryland, 30-21; **Liberty**–#16 Alabama over #7 UCLA, 36-6; **Fiesta**–#8 Oklahoma over Wyoming, 41-7; **Bluebonnet**–#13 Nebraska over #9 Texas Tech, 27-24; **Sun**–#10 Texas A&M over Florida, 37-14; **Orange**–#11 Ohio St. over #12 Colorado, 27-10.

1977

		After Bowls	Head Coach	Regular Season
1	Notre Dame ...	11-1-0	Dan Devine	10-1-0
2	Alabama	11-1-0	Bear Bryant	10-1-0
3	Arkansas	11-1-0	Lou Holtz	10-1-0
4	Texas	11-1-0	Fred Akers	11-0-0
5	Penn St.	11-1-0	Joe Paterno	10-1-0
6	Kentucky	10-1-0	Fran Curci	same
7	Oklahoma	10-2-0	Barry Switzer	10-1-0
8	Pittsburgh	9-2-1	Jackie Sherrill	8-2-1
9	Michigan	10-2-0	Bo Schembechler	10-1-0
10	Washington ...	8-4-0	Don James	7-4-0
11	Ohio St.	9-3-0	Woody Hayes	9-2-0
12	Nebraska	9-3-0	Tom Osborne	8-3-0
13	USC	8-4-0	John Robinson	7-4-0
14	Florida St.	10-2-0	Bobby Bowden	9-2-0
15	Stanford	9-3-0	Bill Walsh	8-3-0
16	San Diego St..	10-1-0	Claude Gilbert	same
17	North Carolina .	8-3-1	Bill Dooley	8-2-1
18	Arizona St.	9-3-0	Frank Kush	9-2-0
19	Clemson	8-3-1	Charley Pell	8-2-1
20	BYU	9-2-0	LaVell Edwards	same

Key Bowl Games

Rankings below reflect final regular season poll, released Nov. 28. No bowl for then #7 Kentucky (probation).

Cotton–#5 Notre Dame over #1 Texas, 38-10; **Orange**–#6 Arkansas over #2 Oklahoma, 31-6; **Sugar**–#3 Alabama over #9 Ohio St., 35-6; **Rose**–#13 Washington over #4 Michigan, 27-20; **Fiesta**–#8 Penn St. over #15 Ariz. St., 42-30; **Gator**–#10 Pitt over #11 Clemson, 34-3.

Associated Press Final Polls (Cont.)

1978

		After Bowls	Head Coach	Regular Season
1	Alabama	11-1-0	Bear Bryant	10-1-0
2	USC	12-1-0	John Robinson	11-1-0
3	Oklahoma ...	11-1-0	Barry Switzer	10-1-0
4	Penn St.	11-1-0	Joe Paterno	11-0-0
5	Michigan	10-2-0	Bo Schembechler	10-1-0
6	Clemson	11-1-0	Charley Pell	10-1-0
7	Notre Dame ..	9-3-0	Dan Devine	8-3-0
8	Nebraska	9-3-0	Tom Osborne	9-2-0
9	Texas	9-3-0	Fred Akers	8-3-0
10	Houston	9-3-0	Bill Yeoman	9-2-0
11	Arkansas	9-2-1	Lou Holtz	9-2-0
12	Michigan St. .	8-3-0	Darryl Rogers	same
13	Purdue	9-2-1	Jim Young	8-2-1
14	UCLA	8-3-1	Terry Donahue	8-3-0
15	Missouri	8-4-0	Warren Powers	7-4-0
16	Georgia	9-2-1	Vince Dooley	9-1-1
17	Stanford	8-4-0	Bill Walsh	7-4-0
18	N.C. State ...	9-3-0	Bo Rein	8-3-0
19	Texas A&M ..	8-4-0	Emory Bellard (4-2) & Tom Wilson (4-2)	7-4-0
20	Maryland	9-3-0	Jerry Claiborne	9-2-0

Key Bowl Games

Rankings below reflect final regular season poll, released Dec. 4. No bowl for then #12 Michigan St. (probation).

Sugar–#2 Alabama over #1 Penn St., 14-7; **Rose**–#3 USC over #5 Michigan, 17-10; **Orange**–#4 Oklahoma over #6 Nebraska, 31-24; **Gator**–#7 Clemson over #20 Ohio St., 17-15; **Fiesta**–#8 Arkansas tied #15 UCLA, 10-10; **Cotton**–#10 Notre Dame over #9 Houston, 35-34.

1979

		After Bowls	Head Coach	Regular Season
1	Alabama	12-0-0	Bear Bryant	11-0-0
2	USC	11-0-1	John Robinson	10-0-1
3	Oklahoma ...	11-1-0	Barry Switzer	10-1-0
4	Ohio St.	11-1-0	Earle Bruce	11-0-0
5	Houston	11-1-0	Bill Yeoman	10-1-0
6	Florida St.	11-1-0	Bobby Bowden	11-0-0
7	Pittsburgh	11-1-0	Jackie Sherrill	10-1-0
8	Arkansas	10-2-0	Lou Holtz	10-1-0
9	Nebraska	10-2-0	Tom Osborne	10-1-0
10	Purdue	10-2-0	Jim Young	9-2-0
11	Washington ..	9-3-0	Don James	8-3-0
12	Texas	9-3-0	Fred Akers	9-2-0
13	BYU	11-1-0	LaVell Edwards	11-0-0
14	Baylor	8-4-0	Grant Teaff	7-4-0
15	North Carolina	8-3-1	Dick Crum	7-3-1
16	Auburn	8-3-0	Doug Barfield	same
17	Temple	10-2-0	Wayne Hardin	9-2-0
18	Michigan	8-4-0	Bo Schembechler	8-3-0
19	Indiana	8-4-0	Lee Corso	7-4-0
20	Penn St.	8-4-0	Joe Paterno	7-4-0

Key Bowl Games

Rankings below reflect final regular season poll, released Dec. 3. No bowl for then #17 Auburn (probation).

Sugar–#2 Alabama over #6 Arkansas, 24-9; **Rose**–#3 USC over #1 Ohio St., 17-16; **Orange**–#5 Oklahoma over #4 Florida St., 24-7; **Sun**–#13 Washington over #11 Texas, 14-7; **Cotton**–#8 Houston over #7 Nebraska, 17-14; **Fiesta**–#10 Pitt over Arizona, 16-10.

1980

		After Bowls	Head Coach	Regular Season
1	Georgia	12-0-0	Vince Dooley	11-0-0
2	Pittsburgh ...	11-1-0	Jackie Sherrill	10-1-0
3	Oklahoma	10-2-0	Barry Switzer	9-2-0
4	Michigan	10-2-0	Bo Schembechler	9-2-0
5	Florida St.	10-2-0	Bobby Bowden	10-1-0
6	Alabama	10-2-0	Bear Bryant	9-2-0
7	Nebraska	10-2-0	Tom Osborne	9-2-0
8	Penn St.	10-2-0	Joe Paterno	9-2-0
9	Notre Dame ..	9-2-1	Dan Devine	9-1-1
10	North Carolina	11-1-0	Dick Crum	10-1-0
11	USC	8-2-1	John Robinson	same
12	BYU	12-1-0	LaVell Edwards	11-1-0
13	UCLA	9-2-0	Terry Donahue	9-2-0
14	Baylor	10-2-0	Grant Teaff	10-1-0
15	Ohio St.	9-3-0	Earle Bruce	9-2-0
16	Washington ..	9-3-0	Don James	9-2-0
17	Purdue	9-3-0	Jim Young	8-3-0
18	Miami-FL	9-3-0	H. Schnellenberger	8-3-0
19	Mississippi St.	9-3-0	Emory Bellard	9-2-0
20	SMU	8-4-0	Ron Meyer	8-3-0

Key Bowl Games

Rankings below reflect final regular season poll, released Dec. 8.

Sugar–#1 Georgia over #7 Notre Dame, 17-10; **Orange**–#4 Oklahoma over #2 Florida St., 18-17; **Gator**–#3 Pitt over #18 S. Carolina, 37-9; **Rose**–#5 Michigan over #16 Washington, 23-6; **Cotton**–#9 Alabama over #6 Baylor, 30-2; **Sun**–#8 Nebraska over #17 Miss. St., 31-17; **Fiesta**–#10 Penn St. over #11 Ohio St., 31-19; **Bluebonnet**–#13 N. Carolina over Texas, 16-7.

1981

		After Bowls	Head Coach	Regular Season
1	Clemson	12-0-0	Danny Ford	11-0-0
2	Texas	10-1-1	Fred Akers	9-1-1
3	Penn St.	10-2-0	Joe Paterno	9-2-0
4	Pittsburgh ...	11-1-0	Jackie Sherrill	10-1-0
5	SMU	10-1-0	Ron Meyer	same
6	Georgia	10-2-0	Vince Dooley	10-1-0
7	Alabama	9-2-1	Bear Bryant	9-1-1
8	Miami-FL	9-2-0	H. Schnellenberger	same
9	North Carolina	10-2-0	Dick Crum	9-2-0
10	Washington ..	10-2-0	Don James	9-2-0
11	Nebraska	9-3-0	Tom Osborne	9-2-0
12	Michigan	9-3-0	Bo Schembechler	8-3-0
13	BYU	11-2-0	LaVell Edwards	10-2-0
14	USC	9-3-0	John Robinson	9-2-0
15	Ohio St.	9-3-0	Earle Bruce	8-3-0
16	Arizona St. ..	9-2-0	Darryl Rogers	same
17	West Virginia .	9-3-0	Don Nehlen	8-3-0
18	Iowa	8-4-0	Hayden Fry	8-3-0
19	Missouri	8-4-0	Warren Powers	7-4-0
20	Oklahoma	7-4-1	Barry Switzer	6-4-1

Key Bowl Games

Rankings below reflect final regular season poll, released Nov. 30. No bowl for then #5 SMU (probation), #9 Miami-FL (probation), and #17 Ariz. St. (probation).

Orange–#1 Clemson over #4 Nebraska, 22-15; **Sugar**–#10 Pitt over #2 Georgia, 24-20; **Cotton**–#6 Texas over #3 Alabama, 14-12; **Fiesta**–#7 Penn St. over #8 USC, 26-10; **Gator**–#11 N. Carolina over Arkansas, 31-27; **Rose**–#12 Washington over #13 Iowa, 28-0.

1982

		After Bowls	Head Coach	Regular Season
1	Penn St.	11-1-0	Joe Paterno	10-1-0
2	SMU	11-0-1	Bobby Collins	10-0-1
3	Nebraska	12-1-0	Tom Osborne	11-1-0
4	Georgia	11-1-0	Vince Dooley	11-0-0
5	UCLA	10-1-1	Terry Donahue	9-1-1
6	Arizona St.	10-2-0	Darryl Rogers	9-2-0
7	Washington	10-2-0	Don James	9-2-0
8	Clemson	9-1-1	Danny Ford	same
9	Arkansas	9-2-1	Lou Holtz	8-2-1
10	Pittsburgh	9-3-0	Foge Fazio	9-2-0
11	LSU	8-3-1	Jerry Stovall	8-2-1
12	Ohio St.	9-3-0	Earle Bruce	8-3-0
13	Florida St.	9-3-0	Bobby Bowden	8-3-0
14	Auburn	9-3-0	Pat Dye	8-3-0
15	USC	8-3-0	John Robinson	same
16	Oklahoma	8-4-0	Barry Switzer	8-3-0
17	Texas	9-3-0	Fred Akers	9-2-0
18	North Carolina .	8-4-0	Dick Crum	7-4-0
19	West Virginia ...	9-3-0	Don Nehlen	9-2-0
20	Maryland	8-4-0	Bobby Ross	8-3-0

Key Bowl Games

Rankings below reflect final regular season poll, released Dec. 6. No bowl for then #7 Clemson (probation) and #15 USC (probation).

Sugar–#2 Penn St. over #1 Georgia, 27-23; **Orange**–#3 Nebraska over #13 LSU, 21-20; **Cotton**–#4 SMU over #6 Pitt, 7-3; **Rose**–#5 UCLA over #19 Michigan, 24-14; **Aloha**–#9 Washington over #16 Maryland, 21-20; **Fiesta**–#11 Ariz. St. over #12 Oklahoma, 32-21; **Bluebonnet**–#14 Arkansas over Florida, 28-24.

1983

		After Bowls	Head Coach	Regular Season
1	Miami-FL	11-1-0	H. Schnellenberger	10-1-0
2	Nebraska ...	12-1-0	Tom Osborne	12-0-0
3	Auburn	11-1-0	Pat Dye	10-1-0
4	Georgia	10-1-1	Vince Dooley	9-1-1
5	Texas	11-1-0	Fred Akers	11-0-0
6	Florida	9-2-1	Charley Pell	8-2-1
7	BYU	11-1-0	LaVell Edwards	10-1-0
8	Michigan	9-3-0	Bo Schembechler	9-2-0
9	Ohio St.	9-3-0	Earle Bruce	8-3-0
10	Illinois	10-2-0	Mike White	10-1-0
11	Clemson	9-1-1	Danny Ford	same
12	SMU	10-2-0	Bobby Collins	10-1-0
13	Air Force	10-2-0	Ken Hatfield	9-2-0
14	Iowa	9-3-0	Hayden Fry	9-2-0
15	Alabama	8-4-0	Ray Perkins	7-4-0
16	West Virginia	9-3-0	Don Nehlen	8-3-0
17	UCLA	7-4-1	Terry Donahue	6-4-1
18	Pittsburgh	8-3-1	Foge Fazio	8-2-1
19	Boston College	9-3-0	Jack Bicknell	9-2-0
20	East Carolina	8-3-0	Ed Emory	same

Key Bowl Games

Rankings below reflect final regular season poll, released Dec. 5. No bowl for then #12 Clemson (probation).

Orange–#5 Miami-FL over #1 Nebraska, 31-30; **Cotton**–#7 Georgia over #2 Texas, 10-9; **Sugar**– #3 Auburn over #8 Michigan, 9-7; **Rose**–UCLA over #4 Illinois, 45-9; **Holiday**–#9 BYU over Missouri, 21-17; **Gator**–#11 Florida over #10 Iowa, 14-6; **Fiesta**–#14 Ohio St. over #15 Pitt, 28-23.

1984

		After Bowls	Head Coach	Regular Season
1	BYU	13-0-0	LaVell Edwards	12-0-0
2	Washington ..	11-1-0	Don James	10-1-0
3	Florida	9-1-1	Charley Pell (0-1-1) & Galen Hall (9-0)	same
4	Nebraska	10-2-0	Tom Osborne	9-2-0
5	Boston College	10-2-0	Jack Bicknell	9-2-0
6	Oklahoma	9-2-1	Barry Switzer	9-1-1
7	Oklahoma St. .	10-2-0	Pat Jones	9-2-0
8	SMU	10-2-0	Bobby Collins	9-2-0
9	UCLA	9-3-0	Terry Donahue	8-3-0
10	USC	9-3-0	Ted Tollner	8-3-0
11	South Carolina	10-2-0	Joe Morrison	10-1-0
12	Maryland	9-3-0	Bobby Ross	8-3-0
13	Ohio St.	9-3-0	Earle Bruce	9-2-0
14	Auburn	9-4-0	Pat Dye	8-4-0
15	LSU	8-3-1	Bill Arnsparger	8-2-1
16	Iowa	8-4-1	Hayden Fry	7-4-1
17	Florida St. ...	7-3-2	Bobby Bowden	7-3-1
18	Miami-FL	8-5-0	Jimmy Johnson	8-4-0
19	Kentucky	9-3-0	Jerry Claiborne	8-3-0
20	Virginia	8-2-2	George Welsh	7-2-2

Key Bowl Games

Rankings below reflect final regular season poll, released Dec. 3. No bowl for then #3 Florida (probation). **Holiday**–#1 BYU over Michigan, 24-17;

Orange–#4 Washington over #2 Oklahoma, 28-17; **Sugar**–#5 Nebraska over #11 LSU, 28-10; **Rose**–#18 USC over #6 Ohio St., 20-17; **Gator**–#9 Okla. St. over #7 S. Carolina, 21-14; **Cotton**–#8 BC over Houston, 45-28; **Aloha**–#10 SMU over #17 Notre Dame, 27-20.

1985

		After Bowls	Head Coach	Regular Season
1	Oklahoma	11-1-0	Barry Switzer	10-1-0
2	Michigan	10-1-1	Bo Schembechler	9-1-1
3	Penn St.	11-1-0	Joe Paterno	11-0-0
4	Tennessee ...	9-1-2	Johnny Majors	8-1-2
5	Florida	9-1-1	Galen Hall	same
6	Texas A&M ...	10-2-0	Jackie Sherrill	9-2-0
7	UCLA	9-2-1	Terry Donahue	8-2-1
8	Air Force	12-1-0	Fisher DeBerry	11-1-0
9	Miami-FL	10-2-0	Jimmy Johnson	10-1-0
10	Iowa	10-2-0	Hayden Fry	10-1-0
11	Nebraska	9-3-0	Tom Osborne	9-2-0
12	Arkansas	10-2-0	Ken Hatfield	9-2-0
13	Alabama	9-2-1	Ray Perkins	8-2-1
14	Ohio St.	9-3-0	Earle Bruce	8-3-0
15	Florida St. ...	9-3-0	Bobby Bowden	8-3-0
16	BYU	11-3-0	LaVell Edwards	11-2-0
17	Baylor	9-3-0	Grant Teaff	8-3-0
18	Maryland	9-3-0	Bobby Ross	8-3-0
19	Georgia Tech ..	9-2-1	Bill Curry	8-2-1
20	LSU	9-2-1	Bill Arnsparger	9-1-1

Key Bowl Games

Rankings below reflect final regular season poll, released Dec. 9. No bowl for then #6 Florida (probation).

Orange–#3 Oklahoma over #1 Penn St., 25-10; **Sugar**–#8 Tennessee over #2 Miami-FL, 35-7; **Rose**–#13 UCLA over #4 Iowa, 45-28; **Fiesta**–#5 Michigan over #7 Nebraska, 27-23; **Bluebonnet**–#10 Air Force over Texas, 24-16; **Cotton**–#11 Texas A&M over #16 Auburn, 36-16.

Associated Press Final Polls (Cont.)

1986

		After Bowls	Head Coach	Regular Season
1	Penn St.	12-0-0	Joe Paterno	11-0-0
2	Miami-FL	11-1-0	Jimmy Johnson	11-0-0
3	Oklahoma	11-1-0	Barry Switzer	10-1-0
4	Arizona St.	10-1-1	John Cooper	9-1-1
5	Nebraska	10-2-0	Tom Osborne	9-2-0
6	Auburn	10-2-0	Pat Dye	9-2-0
7	Ohio St.	10-3-0	Earle Bruce	9-3-0
8	Michigan	11-2-0	Bo Schembechler	11-1-0
9	Alabama	10-3-0	Ray Perkins	9-3-0
10	LSU	9-3-0	Bill Arnsparger	9-2-0
11	Arizona	9-3-0	Larry Smith	8-3-0
12	Baylor	9-3-0	Grant Teaff	8-3-0
13	Texas A&M ...	9-3-0	Jackie Sherrill	9-2-0
14	UCLA	8-3-1	Terry Donahue	7-3-1
15	Arkansas	9-3-0	Ken Hatfield	9-2-0
16	Iowa	9-3-0	Hayden Fry	8-3-0
17	Clemson	8-2-2	Danny Ford	7-2-2
18	Washington ...	8-3-1	Don James	8-2-1
19	Boston College .	9-3-0	Jack Bicknell	8-3-0
20	Virginia Tech ..	9-2-1	Bill Dooley	8-2-1

Key Bowl Games

Rankings below reflect final regular season poll, released Dec. 1.

Fiesta—#2 Penn St. over #1 Miami-FL, 14-10; **Orange**—#3 Oklahoma over #9 Arkansas, 42-8; **Rose**— #7 Ariz. St. over #4 Michigan, 22-15; **Sugar**—#6 Nebraska over #5 LSU, 30-15; **Cotton**—#11 Ohio St. over #8 Texas A&M, 28-12; **Citrus**—#10 Auburn over USC, 16-7; **Sun**— #13 Alabama over #12 Washington, 28-6.

1987

		After Bowls	Head Coach	Regular Season
1	Miami-FL	12-0-0	Jimmy Johnson	11-0-0
2	Florida St.	11-1-0	Bobby Bowden	10-1-0
3	Oklahoma	11-1-0	Barry Switzer	11-0-0
4	Syracuse	11-0-1	Dick MacPherson	11-0-0
5	LSU	10-1-1	Mike Archer	9-1-1
6	Nebraska	10-2-0	Tom Osborne	10-1-0
7	Auburn	9-1-2	Pat Dye	9-1-1
8	Michigan St. ...	9-2-1	George Perles	8-2-1
9	UCLA	10-2-0	Terry Donahue	9-2-0
10	Texas A&M ...	10-2-0	Jackie Sherrill	9-2-0
11	Oklahoma St. ..	10-2-0	Pat Jones	9-2-0
12	Clemson	10-2-0	Danny Ford	9-2-0
13	Georgia	9-3-0	Vince Dooley	8-3-0
14	Tennessee	10-2-1	Johnny Majors	9-2-1
15	South Carolina .	8-4-0	Joe Morrison	8-3-0
16	Iowa	10-3-0	Hayden Fry	9-3-0
17	Notre Dame ...	8-4-0	Lou Holtz	8-3-0
18	USC	8-4-0	Larry Smith	8-3-0
19	Michigan	8-4-0	Bo Schembechler	7-4-0
20	Arizona St.	7-4-1	John Cooper	6-4-1

Key Bowl Games

Rankings below reflect final regular season poll, released Dec. 7.

Orange—#2 Miami-FL over #1 Oklahoma, 20-14; **Fiesta**—#3 Florida St. over #5 Nebraska, 31-28; **Sugar**—#4 Syracuse tied #6 Auburn, 16-16; **Gator**—#7 LSU over #9 S. Carolina, 30-13; **Rose**—#8 Mich. St. over #16 USC, 20-17; **Aloha**—#10 UCLA over Florida, 20-16; **Cotton**—#13 Texas A&M over #12 Notre Dame, 35-10.

1988

		After Bowls	Head Coach	Regular Season
1	Notre Dame ...	12-0-0	Lou Holtz	11-0-0
2	Miami-FL	11-1-0	Jimmy Johnson	10-1-0
3	Florida St.	11-1-0	Bobby Bowden	10-1-0
4	Michigan	9-2-1	Bo Schembechler	8-2-1
5	West Virginia ..	11-1-0	Don Nehlen	11-0-0
6	UCLA	10-2-0	Terry Donahue	9-2-0
7	USC	10-2-0	Larry Smith	10-1-0
8	Auburn	10-2-0	Pat Dye	10-1-0
9	Clemson	10-2-0	Danny Ford	9-2-0
10	Nebraska	11-2-0	Tom Osborne	11-1-0
11	Oklahoma St. ..	10-2-0	Pat Jones	9-2-0
12	Arkansas	10-2-0	Ken Hatfield	10-1-0
13	Syracuse	10-2-0	Dick MacPherson	9-2-0
14	Oklahoma	9-3-0	Barry Switzer	9-2-0
15	Georgia	9-3-0	Vince Dooley	8-3-0
16	Washington St.	9-3-0	Dennis Erickson	8-3-0
17	Alabama	9-3-0	Bill Curry	8-3-0
18	Houston	9-3-0	Jack Pardee	9-2-0
19	LSU	8-4-0	Mike Archer	8-3-0
20	Indiana	8-3-1	Bill Mallory	7-3-1

Key Bowl Games

Rankings below reflect final regular season poll, released Dec. 5.

Fiesta—#1 Notre Dame over #3 West Va., 34-21; **Orange**—#2 Miami-FL over #6 Nebraska, 23-3; **Sugar**—#4 Florida St. over #7 Auburn, 13-7; **Rose**—#11 Michigan over #5 USC, 22-14; **Cotton**—#9 UCLA over #8 Arkansas, 17-3; **Citrus**—#13 Clemson over #10 Oklahoma, 13-6.

1989

		After Bowls	Head Coach	Regular Season
1	Miami-FL ...	11-1-0	Dennis Erickson	10-1-0
2	Notre Dame	12-1-0	Lou Holtz	11-1-0
3	Florida St. ...	10-2-0	Bobby Bowden	9-2-0
4	Colorado ...	11-1-0	Bill McCartney	11-0-0
5	Tennessee ..	11-1-0	Johnny Majors	10-1-0
6	Auburn	10-2-0	Pat Dye	9-2-0
7	Michigan ...	10-2-0	Bo Schembechler	10-1-0
8	USC	9-2-1	Larry Smith	8-2-1
9	Alabama ...	10-2-0	Bill Curry	10-1-0
10	Illinois	10-2-0	John Mackovic	9-2-0
11	Nebraska ..	10-2-0	Tom Osborne	10-1-0
12	Clemson ...	10-2-0	Danny Ford	9-2-0
13	Arkansas ...	10-2-0	Ken Hatfield	10-1-0
14	Houston	9-2-0	Jack Pardee	same
15	Penn St. ...	8-3-1	Joe Paterno	7-3-1
16	Michigan St.	8-4-0	George Perles	7-4-0
17	Pittsburgh ..	8-3-1	Mike Gottfried (7-3-1) & Paul Hackett (1-0)	7-3-1
18	Virginia	10-3-0	George Welsh	10-2-0
19	Texas Tech ..	9-3-0	Spike Dykes	8-3-0
20	Texas A&M	8-4-0	R.C. Slocum	8-3-0

Key Bowl Games

Rankings below reflect final regular season poll, released Dec. 11. No bowl for then #13 Houston (probation).

Orange—#4 Notre Dame over #1 Colorado, 21-6; **Sugar**—#2 Miami-FL over #7 Alabama, 33-25; **Rose**— #12 USC over #3 Michigan, 17-10; **Fiesta**—#5 Florida St. over #6 Nebraska, 41-17; **Cotton**—#8 Tennessee over #10 Arkansas, 31-27; **Hall of Fame**—#9 Auburn over #21 Ohio St., 31-14; **Citrus**—#11 Illinois over #15 Virginia, 31-21.

1990

		After Bowls	Head Coach	Regular Season
1	Colorado	11-1-1	Bill McCartney	10-1-1
2	Georgia Tech ..	11-0-1	Bobby Ross	10-0-1
3	Miami-FL	10-2-0	Dennis Erickson	9-2-0
4	Florida St.	10-2-0	Bobby Bowden	9-2-0
5	Washington ..	10-2-0	Don James	9-2-0
6	Notre Dame ..	9-3-0	Lou Holtz	9-2-0
7	Michigan	9-3-0	Gary Moeller	8-3-0
8	Tennessee	9-2-2	Johnny Majors	8-2-2
9	Clemson	10-2-0	Ken Hatfield	9-2-0
10	Houston	10-1-0	John Jenkins	same
11	Penn St.	9-3-0	Joe Paterno	9-2-0
12	Texas	10-2-0	David McWilliams	10-1-0
13	Florida	9-2-0	Steve Spurrier	same
14	Louisville	10-1-1	H. Schnellenberger	9-1-1
15	Texas A&M ...	9-3-1	R.C. Slocum	8-3-1
16	Michigan St. ..	8-3-1	George Perles	7-3-1
17	Oklahoma	8-3-0	Gary Gibbs	same
18	Iowa	8-4-0	Hayden Fry	8-3-0
19	Auburn	8-3-1	Pat Dye	7-3-1
20	USC	8-4-1	Larry Smith	8-3-1

Key Bowl Games

Rankings below reflect final regular season poll, released Dec. 3. No bowl for then #9 Houston (probation), #11 Florida (probation) and #20 Oklahoma (probation).

Orange–#1 Colorado over #5 Notre Dame, 10-9; **Citrus**–#2 Ga. Tech over #19 Nebraska, 45-21; **Cotton**–#4 Miami-FL over #3 Texas, 46-3; **Blockbuster**–#6 Florida St. over #7 Penn St., 24-17; **Rose**–#8 Washington over #17 Iowa, 46-34; **Sugar**–#10 Tennessee over Virginia, 23-22; **Gator**–#12 Michigan over #15 Ole Miss, 35-3.

1992

		After Bowls	Head Coach	Regular Season
1	Alabama	13-0-0	Gene Stallings	12-0-0
2	Florida St. ...	11-1-0	Bobby Bowden	10-1-0
3	Miami-FL	11-1-0	Dennis Erickson	11-0-0
4	Notre Dame ..	10-1-1	Lou Holtz	9-1-1
5	Michigan	9-0-3	Gary Moeller	8-0-3
6	Syracuse	10-2-0	Paul Pasqualoni	9-2-0
7	Texas A&M ...	12-1-0	R.C. Slocum	12-0-0
8	Georgia	10-2-0	Ray Goff	9-2-0
9	Stanford	10-3-0	Bill Walsh	9-3-0
10	Florida	9-4-0	Steve Spurrier	8-4-0
11	Washington ..	9-3-0	Don James	9-2-0
12	Tennessee	9-3-0	Johnny Majors (5-3) & Phillip Fulmer (4-0)	8-3-0
13	Colorado	9-2-1	Bill McCartney	9-1-1
14	Nebraska	9-3-0	Tom Osborne	9-2-0
15	Washington St.	9-3-0	Mike Price	8-3-0
16	Mississippi ...	9-3-0	Billy Brewer	8-3-0
17	N.C. State	9-3-1	Dick Sheridan	9-2-1
18	Ohio St.	8-3-1	John Cooper	8-2-1
19	North Carolina	9-3-0	Mack Brown	8-3-0
20	Hawaii	11-2-0	Bob Wagner	10-2-0

Key Bowl Games

Rankings below reflect final regular season poll, taken Dec. 5.

Sugar–#2 Alabama over #1 Miami-FL, 34-13; **Orange**–#3 Florida St. over #11 Nebraska, 27-14; **Cotton**–#5 Notre Dame over #4 Texas A&M, 28-3; **Fiesta**–#6 Syracuse over #10 Colorado, 26-22; **Rose**–#7 Michigan over #9 Washington, 38-31; **Citrus**–#8 Georgia over #15 Ohio St., 21-14.

1991

		After Bowls	Head Coach	Regular Season
1	Miami-FL	12-0-0	Dennis Erickson	11-0-0
2	Washington ..	12-0-0	Don James	11-0-0
3	Penn St.	11-2-0	Joe Paterno	10-2-0
4	Florida St.	11-2-0	Bobby Bowden	10-2-0
5	Alabama	11-1-0	Gene Stallings	10-1-0
6	Michigan	10-2-0	Gary Moeller	10-1-0
7	Florida	10-2-0	Steve Spurrier	10-1-0
8	California	10-2-0	Bruce Snyder	9-2-0
9	East Carolina .	11-1-0	Bill Lewis	10-1-0
10	Iowa	10-1-1	Hayden Fry	10-1-0
11	Syracuse	10-2-0	Paul Pasqualoni	9-2-0
12	Texas A&M ...	10-2-0	R.C. Slocum	10-1-0
13	Notre Dame ..	10-3-0	Lou Holtz	9-3-0
14	Tennessee	9-3-0	Johnny Majors	9-2-0
15	Nebraska	9-2-1	Tom Osborne	9-1-1
16	Oklahoma	9-3-0	Gary Gibbs	8-3-0
17	Georgia	9-3-0	Ray Goff	8-3-0
18	Clemson	9-2-1	Ken Hatfield	9-1-1
19	UCLA	9-3-0	Terry Donahue	8-3-0
20	Colorado	8-3-1	Bill McCartney	8-2-1

Key Bowl Games

Rankings below reflect final regular season poll, taken Dec. 2.

Orange–#1 Miami-FL over #11 Nebraska, 22-0; **Rose**–#2 Washington over #4 Michigan, 34-14; **Sugar**–#18 Notre Dame over #3 Florida, 39-28; **Cotton**–#5 Florida St. over #9 Texas A&M, 10-2; **Fiesta**–#6 Penn St. over #10 Tennessee, 42-17; **Holiday**–#7 Iowa tied BYU, 13-13; **Blockbuster**–#8 Alabama over #15 Colorado, 30-25; **Citrus**–#14 California over #13 Clemson, 37-13; **Peach**–#12 East Carolina over #21 N.C. State, 37-34.

1993

		After Bowls	Head Coach	Regular Season
1	Florida St	12-1-0	Bobby Bowden	11-1-0
2	Notre Dame	11-1-0	Lou Holtz	10-1-0
3	Nebraska	11-1-0	Tom Osborne	11-0-0
4	Auburn	11-0-0	Terry Bowden	11-0-0
5	Florida	11-2-0	Steve Spurrier	10-2-0
6	Wisconsin	10-1-1	Barry Alvarez	9-1-1
7	West Virginia ...	11-1-0	Don Nehlen	11-0-0
8	Penn St	10-2-0	Joe Paterno	9-2-0
9	Texas A&M	10-2-0	R.C. Slocum	10-1-0
10	Arizona	10-2-0	Dick Tomey	9-2-0
11	Ohio St	10-1-1	John Cooper	9-1-1
12	Tennessee	9-2-1	Phillip Fulmer	9-1-1
13	Boston College ..	9-3-0	Tom Coughlin	8-3-0
14	Alabama	9-3-1	Gene Stallings	8-3-1
15	Miami-FL	9-3-0	Dennis Erickson	9-2-0
16	Colorado	8-3-1	Bill McCartney	7-3-1
17	Oklahoma	9-3-0	Gary Gibbs	8-3-0
18	UCLA	8-4-0	Terry Donahue	8-3-0
19	North Carolina .	10-3-0	Mack Brown	10-2-0
20	Kansas St	9-2-1	Bill Snyder	8-2-1

Key Bowl Games

Rankings below reflect final regular season poll, taken Dec. 5. No bowl for then #5 Auburn (probation).

Orange–#1 Florida St. over #2 Nebraska, 18-16; **Sugar**–#8 Florida over #3 West Virginia, 41-7; **Cotton**–#4 Notre Dame over #7 Texas A&M, 24-21; **Citrus**–#13 Penn St. over #6 Tennessee, 31-13; **Rose**–#9 Wisconsin over #14 UCLA, 21-16; **Fiesta**–#16 Arizona over #10 Miami-FL, 29-0; **Holiday**–#11 Ohio St. over BYU, 28-21; **Gator**–#18 Alabama over #12 North Carolina, 24-10; **Carquest**–#15 Boston College over Virginia, 31-13.

Associated Press Final Polls (Cont.)

1994

		After Bowls	Head Coach	Regular Season
1	Nebraska	13-0-0	Tom Osborne	12-0-0
2	Penn St	12-0-0	Joe Paterno	11-0-0
3	Colorado	11-1-0	Bill McCartney	10-1-0
4	Florida St	10-1-1	Bobby Bowden	9-1-1
5	Alabama	12-1-0	Gene Stallings	11-1-0
6	Miami-FL	10-2-0	Dennis Erickson	10-1-0
7	Florida	10-2-1	Steve Spurrier	10-1-1
8	Texas A&M	10-0-1	R.C. Slocum	same
9	Auburn	9-1-1	Terry Bowden	same
10	Utah	10-2-0	Ron McBride	9-2-0
11	Oregon	9-4-0	Rich Brooks	9-3-0
12	Michigan	8-4-0	Gary Moeller	7-4-0
13	USC	8-3-1	John Robinson	7-3-1
14	Ohio St	9-4-0	John Cooper	9-3-0
15	Virginia	9-3-0	George Welsh	8-3-0
16	Colorado St	10-2-0	Sonny Lubick	10-1-0
17	N.C. State	9-3-0	Mike O'Cain	8-3-0
18	BYU	10-3-0	LaVell Edwards	9-3-0
19	Kansas St	9-3-0	Bill Snyder	9-2-0
20	Arizona	8-4-0	Dick Tomey	8-3-0

Key Bowl Games

Rankings below reflect final regular season poll, taken Dec. 4. No bowls for then #8 Texas A&M (probation) and #9 Auburn (probation).

Orange– #1 Nebraska over #3 Miami-FL, 24-17; **Rose**– #2 Penn St. over #12 Oregon, 38-20; **Fiesta**– #4 Colorado over Notre Dame, 41-24; **Sugar**– #7 Florida St. over #5 Florida, 23-17; **Citrus**– #6 Alabama over #13 Ohio St., 24-17; **Freedom**– #14 Utah over #15 Arizona, 16-13.

1995

		After Bowls	Head Coach	Regular Season
1	Nebraska	12-0-0	Tom Osborne	11-0-0
2	Florida	12-1-0	Steve Spurrier	12-0-0
3	Tennessee	11-1-0	Phillip Fulmer	10-1-0
4	Florida St	10-2-0	Bobby Bowden	9-2-0
5	Colorado	10-2-0	Rick Neuheisel	9-2-0
6	Ohio St.	11-2-0	John Cooper	11-1-0
7	Kansas St.	10-2-0	Bill Snyder	9-2-0
8	Northwestern	10-2-0	Gary Barnett	10-1-0
9	Kansas	10-2-0	Glen Mason	9-2-0
10	Va. Tech	10-2-0	Frank Beamer	9-2-0
11	Notre Dame	9-3-0	Lou Holtz	9-2-0
12	USC	9-2-1	John Robinson	8-2-1
13	Penn St.	9-3-0	Joe Paterno	8-3-0
14	Texas	10-2-1	John Mackovic	10-1-1
15	Texas A&M	9-3-0	R.C. Slocum	8-3-0
16	Virginia	9-4-0	George Welsh	8-4-0
17	Michigan	9-4-0	Lloyd Carr	9-3-0
18	Oregon	9-3-0	Mike Bellotti	9-2-0
19	Syracuse	9-3-0	Paul Pasqualoni	8-3-0
20	Miami-FL	8-3-0	Butch Davis	same

Key Bowl Games

Rankings below reflect final regular season poll, taken Dec. 3. No bowl for then #22 Miami-FL (probation).

Fiesta– #1 Nebraska over #2 Florida, 62-24; **Rose**– #17 USC over #3 Northwestern, 41-32; **Citrus**– #4 (tie) Tennessee over #4 (tie) Ohio St., 20-14; **Orange**– #8 Florida St. over #6 Notre Dame, 31-26; **Cotton**– #7 Colorado over #12 Oregon, 38-6; **Sugar**– #13 Va. Tech over #9 Texas, 28-10; **Holiday**– #10 Kansas St. over Colo. St., 54-21; **Aloha**– #11 Kansas over UCLA, 51-30; **Alamo**– #19 Texas A&M over #14 Michigan, 22-20; **Outback**– #15 Penn St. over #16 Auburn, 43-14; **Peach**– #18 Virginia over Georgia, 34-27; **Gator**– Syracuse over #23 Clemson, 41-0.

1996

		After Bowls	Head Coach	Regular Season
1	Florida	12-1-0	Steve Spurrier	11-1-0
2	Ohio St.	11-1-0	John Cooper	10-1-0
3	Florida St	11-1-0	Bobby Bowden	11-0-0
4	Arizona St.	11-1-0	Bruce Snyder	11-0-0
5	BYU	14-1-0	LaVell Edwards	13-1-0
6	Nebraska	11-2-0	Tom Osborne	10-2-0
7	Penn St.	11-2-0	Joe Paterno	10-2-0
8	Colorado	10-2-0	Rick Neuheisel	9-2-0
9	Tennessee	10-2-0	Phillip Fulmer	9-2-0
10	North Carolina	10-2-0	Mack Brown	9-2-0
11	Alabama	10-3-0	Gene Stallings	9-3-0
12	LSU	10-2-0	Gerry DiNardo	9-2-0
13	Virginia Tech	10-2-0	Frank Beamer	10-1-0
14	Miami-FL	9-3-0	Butch Davis	8-3-0
15	Northwestern	9-3-0	Gary Barnett	9-2-0
16	Washington	9-3-0	Jim Lambright	9-2-0
17	Kansas St.	9-3-0	Bill Snyder	9-2-0
18	Iowa	9-3-0	Hayden Fry	8-3-0
19	Notre Dame	8-3-0	Lou Holtz	same
20	Michigan	8-4-0	Lloyd Carr	8-3-0

Key Bowl Games

Rankings below reflect final regular season poll, taken Dec. 8. No bowl for then #18 Notre Dame and #22 Wyoming.

Sugar– #3 Florida over #1 Florida St., 52-20; **Rose**– #4 Ohio St. over #2 Arizona St., 20-17; **Fiesta**– #7 Penn St. over #20 Texas, 38-15; **Cotton**– #5 BYU over #14 Kansas St., 19-15; **Citrus**– #9 Tennessee over #11 Northwestern, 48-28; **Orange**– #6 Nebraska over #10 Virginia Tech, 41-21; **Gator**– #12 North Carolina over #25 West Virginia, 20-13; **Outback**– #16 Alabama over #15 Michigan, 17-14. **Carquest**– #19 Miami over Virginia, 31-21.

All-Time AP Top 20

The composite AP Top 20 from the 1936 season through the 1996 season, based on the final rankings of each year. The final AP poll has been taken after the bowl games in 1965 and since 1968. Team point totals are based on 20 points for all 1st place finishes, 19 for each 2nd, etc. Also listed are the number of times each team has been named national champion by AP and times ranked in the final Top 10 and Top 20.

		Final AP			
		Pts	No.1	Top 10	Top 20
1	Notre Dame	626	8	34	44
2	Oklahoma	558	6	29	41
3	Alabama	551	6	30	41
4	Michigan	546	1	32	44
5	Ohio St	490	3	23	39
6	Nebraska	481	4	26	36
7	USC	414	3	20	36
8	Texas	400	2	19	31
9	Tennessee	387	1	19	33
10	Penn St	384	2	21	32
11	UCLA	293	0	14	27
12	Auburn	271	1	14	25
13	LSU	269	1	14	24
14	Miami-FL	264	4	13	21
15	Arkansas	259	0	13	23
16	Georgia	238	1	13	20
	Michigan St	238	1	12	19
18	Florida St	236	1	12	16
19	Texas A&M	205	1	11	20
20	Washington	199	0	10	17

Bowl Games

From Jan. 1, 1902 through Jan. 3, 1997. Corporate title sponsors and automatic berths updated through Aug. 15, 1997.

Rose Bowl

City: Pasadena, Calif. **Stadium:** Rose Bowl. **Capacity:** 102,083. **Playing surface:** Grass. **First game:** Jan. 1, 1902. **Playing sites:** Tournament Park (1902, 1916-22), Rose Bowl (1923-41 and since 1943) and Duke Stadium in Durham, N.C. (1942, due to wartime restrictions following Japan's attack at Pearl Harbor on Dec. 7, 1941).

Automatic berths: Pacific Coast Conference champion vs. opponent selected by PCC (1924-45 seasons); Big Ten champion vs. Pac-10 champion (since 1946 season).

Multiple wins: USC (20); Michigan (7); Ohio St. and Washington (6); Stanford and UCLA (5); Alabama (4); Illinois and Michigan St. (3); California and Iowa (2).

Year		Year		Year	
1902*	Michigan 49, Stanford 0	1943	Georgia 9, UCLA 0	1971	Stanford 27, Ohio St. 17
1916	Washington St. 14, Brown 0	1944	USC 29, Washington 0	1972	Stanford 13, Michigan 12
1917	Oregon 14, Penn 0	1945	USC 25, Tennessee 0	1973	USC 42, Ohio St. 17
1918	Mare Island 19, Camp Lewis 7	1946	Alabama 34, USC 14	1974	Ohio St. 42, USC 21
1919	Great Lakes 17, Mare Island 0	1947	Illinois 45, UCLA 14	1975	USC 18, Ohio St. 17
1920	Harvard 7, Oregon 6	1948	Michigan 49, USC 0	1976	UCLA 23, Ohio St. 10
1921	California 28, Ohio St. 0	1949	Northwestern 20, California 14	1977	USC 14, Michigan 6
1922	0-0, California vs Wash. & Jeff.	1950	Ohio St. 17, California 14	1978	Washington 27, Michigan 20
1923	USC 14, Penn St. 0	1951	Michigan 14, California 6	1979	USC 17, Michigan 10
1924	14-14, Navy vs Washington	1952	Illinois 40, Stanford 7	1980	USC 17, Ohio St. 16
1925	Notre Dame 27, Stanford 10	1953	USC 7, Wisconsin 0	1981	Michigan 23, Washington 6
1926	Alabama 20, Washington 19	1954	Michigan St. 28, UCLA 20	1982	Washington 28, Iowa 0
1927	7-7, Alabama vs Stanford	1955	Ohio St. 20, USC 7	1983	UCLA 24, Michigan 14
1928	Stanford 7, Pittsburgh 6	1956	Michigan St. 17, UCLA 14	1984	UCLA 45, Illinois 9
1929	Georgia Tech 8, California 7	1957	Iowa 35, Oregon St. 19	1985	USC 20, Ohio St. 17
1930	USC 47, Pittsburgh 14	1958	Ohio St. 10, Oregon 7	1986	UCLA 45, Iowa 28
1931	Alabama 24, Washington St. 0	1959	Iowa 38, California 12	1987	Arizona St. 22, Michigan 15
1932	USC 21, Tulane 12	1960	Washington 44, Wisconsin 8	1988	Michigan St. 20, USC 17
1933	USC 35, Pittsburgh 0	1961	Washington 17, Minnesota 7	1989	Michigan 22, USC 14
1934	Columbia 7, Stanford 0	1962	Minnesota 21, UCLA 3	1990	USC 17, Michigan 10
1935	Alabama 29, Stanford 13	1963	USC 42, Wisconsin 37	1991	Washington 46, Iowa 34
1936	Stanford 7, SMU 0	1964	Illinois 17, Washington 7	1992	Washington 34, Michigan 14
1937	Pittsburgh 21, Washington 0	1965	Michigan 34, Oregon St. 7	1993	Michigan 38, Washington 31
1938	California 13, Alabama 0	1966	UCLA 14, Michigan St. 12	1994	Wisconsin 21, UCLA 16
1939	USC 7, Duke 3	1967	Purdue 14, USC 13	1995	Penn St. 38, Oregon 20
1940	USC 14, Tennessee 0	1968	USC 14, Indiana 3	1996	USC 41, Northwestern 32
1941	Stanford 21, Nebraska 13	1969	Ohio St. 27, USC 16	1997	Ohio St. 20, Arizona St. 17
1942	Oregon St. 20, Duke 16	1970	USC 10, Michigan 3	*January game since 1902.	

Fiesta Bowl

City: Tempe, Ariz. **Stadium:** Sun Devil. **Capacity:** 73,656. **Playing surface:** Grass. **First game:** Dec. 27, 1971. **Playing site:** Sun Devil Stadium (since 1971). **Corporate title sponsors:** Sunkist Citrus Growers (1986-91), IBM OS/2 (1993-95) and Frito-Lay Tostitos chips (since 1996).

Automatic berths: Two of first five picks from 8-team Bowl Coalition pool (1992-94 seasons). Bowl Alliance matchups starting with 1995 season: #1 vs. #2 on Jan. 2, 1996; #3 vs. #5 on Jan. 1, 1997; and #4 vs. #6 on Dec. 31, 1997.

Multiple wins: Penn St. (6); Arizona St. (5); Florida St. (2).

Year		Year		Year	
1971†	Arizona St. 45, Florida St. 38	1980	Penn St. 31, Ohio St. 19	1990	Florida St. 41, Nebraska 17
1972	Arizona St. 49, Missouri 35	1982*	Penn St. 26, USC 10	1991	Louisville 34, Alabama 7
1973	Arizona St. 28, Pittsburgh 7	1983	Arizona St. 32, Oklahoma 21	1992	Penn St. 42, Tennessee 17
1974	Oklahoma St. 16, BYU 6	1984	Ohio St. 28, Pittsburgh 23	1993	Syracuse 26, Colorado 22
1975	Arizona St. 17, Nebraska 14	1985	UCLA 39, Miami-FL 37	1994	Arizona 29, Miami-FL 0
1976	Oklahoma 41, Wyoming 7	1986	Michigan 27, Nebraska 23	1995	Colorado 41, Notre Dame 24
1977	Penn St. 42, Arizona St. 30	1987	Penn St. 14, Miami-FL 10	1996	Nebraska 62, Florida 24
1978	10-10, Arkansas vs UCLA	1988	Florida St. 31, Nebraska 28	1997	Penn St. 38, Texas 15
1979	Pittsburgh 16, Arizona 10	1989	Notre Dame 34, West Va. 21		

†December game from 1971-80.   * January game since 1982.

Tiebreakers in Bowl Games

The NCAA tiebreaker system was approved for Division I-A bowl games beginning with the 1995 postseason. Unlike sudden-death overtime in the NFL, the NCAA tiebreaking procedure gives both teams a chance to score after regulation time has expired. Each team gets an offensive series beginning on the opponent's 25-yard line. A team's possession ends when it scores, turns the ball over or fails to convert a fourth-down play. This untimed procedure is repeated until the score is no longer tied at the end of an overtime period, which consists of one possession per team.

Bowl Games (Cont.)
Sugar Bowl

City: New Orleans, La. **Stadium:** Louisiana Superdome. **Capacity:** 77,446. **Playing surface:** AstroTurf. **First game:** Jan. 1, 1935. **Playing sites:** Tulane Stadium (1935-74) and Superdome (since 1975). **Corporate title sponsors:** USF&G Financial Services (1987-95) and Nokia cellular telephones of Finland (starting in 1995).

Automatic berths: SEC champion vs. at-large opponent (1976-91 seasons); SEC champion vs. one of first five picks from 8-team Bowl Coalition pool (1992-94 seasons). New Bowl Alliance matchups starting with 1995 season: #4 vs. #6 on Dec. 31, 1995; #1 vs. #2 on Jan. 2, 1997; and #3 vs. #5 on Jan. 1, 1998.

Multiple wins: Alabama (8); Mississippi (5); Georgia Tech, Oklahoma and Tennessee (4); LSU and Nebraska (3); Florida, Florida St., Georgia, Notre Dame, Pittsburgh, Santa Clara and TCU (2).

Year		Year		Year	
1935*	Tulane 20, Temple 14	1956	Georgia Tech 7, Pittsburgh 0	1977*	Pittsburgh 27, Georgia 3
1936	TCU 3, LSU 2	1957	Baylor 13, Tennessee 7	1978	Alabama 35, Ohio St. 6
1937	Santa Clara 21, LSU 14	1958	Mississippi 39, Texas 7	1979	Alabama 14, Penn St. 7
1938	Santa Clara 6, LSU 0	1959	LSU 7, Clemson 0		
1939	TCU 15, Carnegie Tech 7			1980	Alabama 24, Arkansas 9
		1960	Mississippi 21, LSU 0	1981	Georgia 17, Notre Dame 10
1940	Texas A&M 14, Tulane 13	1961	Mississippi 14, Rice 6	1982	Pittsburgh 24, Georgia 20
1941	Boston College 19, Tennessee 13	1962	Alabama 10, Arkansas 3	1983	Penn St. 27, Georgia 23
1942	Fordham 2, Missouri 0	1963	Mississippi 17, Arkansas 13	1984	Auburn 9, Michigan 7
1943	Tennessee 14, Tulsa 7	1964	Alabama 12, Mississippi 7	1985	Nebraska 28, LSU 10
1944	Georgia Tech 20, Tulsa 18	1965	LSU 13, Syracuse 10	1986	Tennessee 35, Miami-FL 7
1945	Duke 29, Alabama 26	1966	Missouri 20, Florida 18	1987	Nebraska 30, LSU 15
1946	Okla. A&M 33, St.Mary's 13	1967	Alabama 34, Nebraska 7	1988	16-16, Syracuse vs Auburn
1947	Georgia 20, N. Carolina 10	1968	LSU 20, Wyoming 13	1989	Florida St. 13, Auburn 7
1948	Texas 27, Alabama 7	1969	Arkansas 16, Georgia 2		
1949	Oklahoma 14, N. Carolina 6			1990	Miami-FL 33, Alabama 25
		1970	Mississippi 27, Arkansas 22	1991	Tennessee 23, Virginia 22
1950	Oklahoma 35, LSU 0	1971	Tennessee 34, Air Force 13	1992	Notre Dame 39, Florida 28
1951	Kentucky 13, Oklahoma 7	1972	Oklahoma 40, Auburn 22	1993	Alabama 34, Miami-FL 13
1952	Maryland 28, Tennessee 13	1972†	Oklahoma 14, Penn St. 0	1994	Florida 41, West Va. 7
1953	Georgia Tech 24, Mississippi 7	1973	Notre Dame 24, Alabama 23	1995	Florida St. 23, Florida 17
1954	Georgia Tech 42, West Va. 19	1974	Nebraska 13, Florida 10	1995†	Va. Tech 28, Texas 10
1955	Navy 21, Mississippi 0	1975	Alabama 13, Penn St. 6	1997	Florida 52, Florida St. 20

*January game from 1935-72 and since 1977 (except in 1995).   †Game played on Dec. 31 from 1972-75 and in 1995.

Orange Bowl

City: Miami, Fla. **Stadium:** Pro Player Stadium. **Capacity:** 74,916. **Playing surface:** Grass. **First game:** Jan. 1, 1935. **Playing sites:** Orange Bowl (since 1935); game moved to Pro Player Stadium Dec. 31, 1996. **Corporate title sponsor:** Federal Express (since 1989).

Automatic berths: Big 8 champion vs. at-large opponent (1953-63 seasons and 1975-91 seasons); Big 8 champion vs. one of first five picks from Bowl Coalition pool (1992-94 seasons). New Bowl Alliance matchups starting with 1995 season: #3 vs. #5 on Jan. 1, 1996; #4 vs. #6 on Dec. 31, 1996; and #1 vs. #2 on Jan. 2, 1998.

Multiple wins: Oklahoma (11); Nebraska (7); Miami-FL (5); Alabama (4); Florida State, Georgia Tech and Penn St. (3); Clemson, Colorado, Georgia, LSU, Notre Dame and Texas (2).

Year		Year		Year	
1935*	Bucknell 26, Miami-FL 0	1956	Oklahoma 20, Maryland 6	1977	Ohio St. 27, Colorado 10
1936	Catholic U. 20, Mississippi 19	1957	Colorado 27, Clemson 21	1978	Arkansas 31, Oklahoma 6
1937	Duquesne 13, Mississippi St. 12	1958	Oklahoma 48, Duke 21	1979	Oklahoma 31, Nebraska 24
1938	Auburn 6, Michigan St. 0	1959	Oklahoma 21, Syracuse 6		
1939	Tennessee 17, Oklahoma 0			1980	Oklahoma 24, Florida St. 7
		1960	Georgia 14, Missouri 0	1981	Oklahoma 18, Florida St. 17
1940	Georgia Tech 21, Missouri 7	1961	Missouri 21, Navy 14	1982	Clemson 22, Nebraska 15
1941	Mississippi St. 14, Georgetown 7	1962	LSU 25, Colorado 7	1983	Nebraska 21, LSU 20
1942	Georgia 40, TCU 26	1963	Alabama 17, Oklahoma 0	1984	Miami-FL 31, Nebraska 30
1943	Alabama 37, Boston College 21	1964	Nebraska 13, Auburn 7	1985	Washington 28, Oklahoma 17
1944	LSU 19, Texas A&M 14	1965†	Texas 21, Alabama 17	1986	Oklahoma 25, Penn St. 10
1945	Tulsa 26, Georgia Tech 12	1966	Alabama 39, Nebraska 28	1987	Oklahoma 42, Arkansas 8
1946	Miami-FL 13, Holy Cross 6	1967	Florida 27, Georgia Tech 12	1988	Miami-FL 20, Oklahoma 14
1947	Rice 8, Tennessee 0	1968	Oklahoma 26, Tennessee 24	1989	Miami-FL 23, Nebraska 3
1948	Georgia Tech 20, Kansas 14	1969	Penn St. 15, Kansas 14		
1949	Texas 41, Georgia 28			1990	Notre Dame 21, Colorado 6
		1970	Penn St. 10, Missouri 3	1991	Colorado 10, Notre Dame 9
1950	Santa Clara 21, Kentucky 13	1971	Nebraska 17, LSU 12	1992	Miami-FL 22, Nebraska 0
1951	Clemson 15, Miami-FL 14	1972	Nebraska 38, Alabama 6	1993	Florida St. 27, Nebraska 14
1952	Georgia Tech 17, Baylor 14	1973	Nebraska 40, Notre Dame 6	1994	Florida St. 18, Nebraska 16
1953	Alabama 61, Syracuse 6	1974	Penn St. 16, LSU 9	1995	Nebraska 24, Miami-FL 17
1954	Oklahoma 7, Maryland 0	1975	Notre Dame 13, Alabama 11	1996	Florida St. 31, Notre Dame 26
1955	Duke 34, Nebraska 7	1976	Oklahoma 14, Michigan 6	1996$	Nebraska 41, Virginia Tech 21

*January game 1935-1996. $December game in 1996.   †Night game since 1965.

Cotton Bowl

City: Dallas, Tex. **Stadium:** Cotton Bowl. **Capacity:** 68,252. **Playing surface:** Grass. **First game:** Jan 1, 1937. **Playing sites:** Fair Park Stadium (1937) and Cotton Bowl (since 1938). **Corporate title sponsor:** Mobil Corporation (1988-95).

Automatic berths: SWC champion vs. at-large opponent (1941-91 seasons); SWC champion vs. one of first five picks from 8-team Bowl Coalition pool (1992-1994 seasons). New Bowl Alliance matchup starting with 1995 season: first choice of WAC champion or second pick from Pac-10 vs. second pick from Big 12.

Multiple wins: Texas (9); Notre Dame (5); Texas A&M (4); Rice (3); Alabama, Arkansas, Georgia, Houston, LSU, Penn St., SMU, Tennessee and TCU (2).

Year		Year		Year	
1937*	TCU 16, Marquette 6	1958	Navy 20, Rice 7	1979	Notre Dame 35, Houston 34
1938	Rice 28, Colorado 14	1959	0-0, TCU vs Air Force		
1939	St. Mary's 20, Texas Tech 13			1980	Houston 17, Nebraska 14
		1960	Syracuse 23, Texas 14	1981	Alabama 30, Baylor 2
1940	Clemson 6, Boston College 3	1961	Duke 7, Arkansas 6	1982	Texas 14, Alabama 12
1941	Texas A&M 13, Fordham 12	1962	Texas 12, Mississippi 7	1983	SMU 7, Pittsburgh 3
1942	Alabama 29, Texas A&M 21	1963	LSU 13, Texas 0	1984	Georgia 10, Texas 9
1943	Texas 14, Georgia Tech 7	1964	Texas 28, Navy 6	1985	Boston College 45, Houston 28
1944	7-7, Texas vs Randolph Field	1965	Arkansas 10, Nebraska 7	1986	Texas A&M 36, Auburn 16
1945	Oklahoma A&M 34, TCU 0	1966	LSU 14, Arkansas 7	1987	Ohio St. 28, Texas A&M 12
1946	Texas 40, Missouri 27	1966†	Georgia 24, SMU 9	1988	Texas A&M 35, Notre Dame 10
1947	0-0, Arkansas vs LSU	1968*	Texas A&M 20, Alabama 16	1989	UCLA 17, Arkansas 3
1948	13-13, SMU vs Penn St.	1969	Texas 36, Tennessee 13		
1949	SMU 21, Oregon 13			1990	Tennessee 31, Arkansas 27
		1970	Texas 21, Notre Dame 17	1991	Miami-FL 46, Texas 3
1950	Rice 27, N. Carolina 13	1971	Notre Dame 24, Texas 11	1992	Florida St. 10, Texas A&M 2
1951	Tennessee 20, Texas 14	1972	Penn St. 30, Texas 6	1993	Notre Dame 28, Texas A&M 3
1952	Kentucky 20, TCU 7	1973	Texas 17, Alabama 13	1994	Notre Dame 24, Texas A&M 21
1953	Texas 16, Tennessee 0	1974	Nebraska 19, Texas 3	1995	USC 55, Texas Tech 14
1954	Rice 28, Alabama 6	1975	Penn St. 41, Baylor 20	1996	Colorado 38, Oregon 6
1955	Georgia Tech 14, Arkansas 6	1976	Arkansas 31, Georgia 10	1997	BYU 19, Kansas St. 15
1956	Mississippi 14, TCU 13	1977	Houston 30, Maryland 21		
1957	TCU 28, Syracuse 27	1978	Notre Dame 38, Texas 10		

*January game from 1937-66 and since 1968.   †Game played on Dec. 31, 1966.

Florida Citrus Bowl

City: Orlando, Fla. **Stadium:** Florida Citrus Bowl. **Capacity:** 70,188. **Playing surface:** Grass. **First game:** Jan. 1, 1947. **Name change:** Tangerine Bowl (1947-82) and Florida Citrus Bowl (since 1983). **Playing sites:** Tangerine Bowl (1947-72, 1974-82), Ben Hill Griffin Stadium in Gainesville (1973), Orlando Stadium (1983-85) and Florida Citrus Bowl (since 1986). The Tangerine Bowl, Orlando Stadium and Florida Citrus Bowl are all the same stadium. **Corporate title sponsors:** Florida Department of Cirtus (since 1983) and CompUSA (since 1992).

Automatic berths: Championship game of Atlantic Coast Regional Conference (1964-67 seasons); Mid-American Conference champion vs. Southern Conference champion (1968-75 seasons); ACC champion vs. at-large opponent (1987-91 seasons); second pick from SEC vs. second pick from Big 10 (1992-94 seasons). New Bowl Alliance matchup starting with 1995 season: second pick from SEC vs. second pick from Big 10.

Multiple wins: East Texas St., Miami-OH, Tennessee and Toledo (3); Auburn, Catawba, Clemson and East Carolina (2).

Year		Year		Year	
1947*	Catawba 31, Maryville 6	1963	Western Ky. 27, Coast Guard 0	1980	Florida 35, Maryland 20
1948	Catawba 7, Marshall 0	1964	E. Carolina 14, Massachusetts 13	1981	Missouri 19, Southern Miss. 17
1949	21-21, Murray St. vs Sul Ross St.	1965	E. Carolina 31, Maine 0	1982	Auburn 33, Boston College 26
		1966	Morgan St. 14, West Chester 6	1983	Tennessee 30, Maryland 23
1950	St. Vincent 7, Emory & Henry 6	1967	Tenn-Martin 25, West Chester 8	1984	17-17, Florida St. vs Georgia
1951	M. Harvey 35, Emory & Henry 14	1968	Richmond 49, Ohio U. 42	1985	Ohio St. 10, BYU 7
1952	Stetson 35, Arkansas St. 20	1969	Toledo 56, Davidson 33	1987*	Auburn 16, USC 7
1953	E. Texas St. 33, Tenn. Tech 0			1988	Clemson 35, Penn St. 10
1954	7-7, E. Texas St. vs Arkansas St.	1970	Toledo 40, Wm. & Mary 12	1989	Clemson 13, Oklahoma 6
1955	Neb.-Omaha 7, Eastern Ky. 6	1971	Toledo 28, Richmond 3		
1956	6-6, Juniata vs Missouri Valley	1972	Tampa 21, Kent St. 18	1990	Illinois 31, Virginia 21
1957	W. Texas St. 20, So. Miss. 13	1973	Miami-OH 16, Florida 7	1991	Georgia Tech 45, Nebraska 21
1958	E. Texas St. 10, So. Miss. 9	1974	Miami-OH 21, Georgia 10	1992	California 37, Clemson 13
1958†	E. Texas St. 26, Mo. Valley 7	1975	Miami-OH 20, S. Carolina 7	1993	Georgia 21, Ohio St. 14
		1976	Oklahoma 49, BYU 21	1994	Penn St. 31, Tennessee 13
1960*	Mid. Tenn. 21, Presbyterian 12	1977	Florida St. 40, Texas Tech 17	1995	Alabama 24, Ohio St. 17
1960†	Citadel 27, Tenn. Tech 0	1978	N.C. State 30, Pittsburgh 17	1996	Tennessee 20, Ohio St. 14
1961	Lamar 21, Middle Tenn. 14	1979	LSU 34, Wake Forest 10	1997	Tennessee 48, Northwestern 28
1962	Houston 49, Miami-OH 21				

*January game from 1947-58, in 1960 and since 1987.   †December game from 1958 and 1960-85.

Bowl Games (Cont.)

Gator Bowl

City: Jacksonville, Fla. **Stadium:** Alltel Stadium. **Capacity:** 73,000. **Playing surface:** Grass. **First game:** Jan. 1, 1946. **Playing sites:** Gator Bowl (1946-93), Ben Hill Griffin Stadium in Gainesville (1994) and New Gator Bowl (since 1995). Name was changed to Alltel Stadium in 1997. **Corporate title sponsors:** Mazda Motors of America, Inc. (1986-91), Outback Steakhouse, Inc. (1992-94) and Toyota Motor Co. (starting in 1995).

Automatic berths: Third pick from SEC vs. sixth pick from 8-team Bowl Coalition pool (1992-94 seasons). New Bowl Alliance matchup starting with 1995 season: second pick from ACC vs. second pick from Big East.

Multiple wins: Florida (6); Auburn, Clemson and North Carolina (4); Florida St. and Tennessee (3); Georgia, Georgia Tech, Maryland, Oklahoma, Pittsburgh, and Texas Tech (2).

Year		Year		Year	
1946*	Wake Forest 26, S. Carolina 14	1963	N. Carolina 35, Air Force 0	1981	N. Carolina 31, Arkansas 27
1947	Oklahoma 34, N.C. State 13	1965*	Florida St. 36, Oklahoma 19	1982	Florida St. 31, West Va. 12
1948	20-20, Maryland vs Georgia	1965†	Georgia Tech 31, Texas Tech 21	1983	Florida 14, Iowa 6
1949	Clemson 24, Missouri 23	1966	Tennessee 18, Syracuse 12	1984	Oklahoma St. 21, S. Carolina 14
1950	Maryland 20, Missouri 7	1967	17-17, Florida St. vs Penn St.	1985	Florida St. 34, Oklahoma St. 23
1951	Wyoming 20, Wash. & Lee 7	1968	Missouri 35, Alabama 10	1986	Clemson 27, Stanford 21
1952	Miami-FL 14, Clemson 0	1969	Florida 14, Tennessee 13	1987	LSU 30, S. Carolina 13
1953	Florida 14, Tulsa 13	1971*	Auburn 35, Mississippi 28	1989*	Georgia 34, Michigan St. 27
1954	Texas Tech 35, Auburn 13	1971†	Georgia 7, N. Carolina 3	1989†	Clemson 27, West Va. 7
1954†	Auburn 33, Baylor 13	1972	Auburn 24, Colorado 3	1991*	Michigan 35, Mississippi 3
1955	Vanderbilt 25, Auburn 13	1973	Texas Tech 28, Tennessee 19	1991†	Oklahoma 48, Virginia 14
1956	Georgia Tech 21, Pittsburgh 14	1974	Auburn 27, Texas 3	1992	Florida 27, N.C. State 10
1957	Tennessee 3, Texas A&M 0	1975	Maryland 13, Florida 0	1993	Alabama 24, N. Carolina 10
1958	Mississippi 7, Florida 3	1976	Notre Dame 20, Penn St. 9	1994	Tennessee 45, Va. Tech 23
1960*	Arkansas 14, Georgia Tech 7	1977	Pittsburgh 34, Clemson 3	1996*	Syracuse 41, Clemson 0
1960†	Florida 13, Baylor 12	1978	Clemson 17, Ohio St. 15	1997	N. Carolina 20, West Va. 13
1961	Penn St. 30, Georgia Tech 15	1979	N. Carolina 17, Michigan 15		
1962	Florida 17, Penn St. 7	1980	Pittsburgh 37, S. Carolina 9		

*January game from 1946-54, 1960, 1965, 1971, 1989, 1991 and since 1996.
†December game from 1954-58, 1960-63, 1965-69, 1971-87, 1989 and 1991-94.

Holiday Bowl

City: San Diego, Calif. **Stadium:** Qualcomm. **Capacity:** 71,000. **Playing surface:** Grass. **First game:** Dec. 22, 1978. **Playing sites:** San Diego/Jack Murphy Stadium (since 1978). Name was changed to Qualcomm Stadium in 1997. **Corporate title sponsors:** Sea World (1986-90), Thrifty Car Rental (1991-94) and Chrysler-Plymouth Division of Chrysler Corp. (starting in 1995).

Automatic berths: WAC champion vs. at-large opponent (1978-84, 1986-90 seasons); WAC champ vs. second pick from Big 10 (1991 season); WAC champ vs. third pick from Big 10 (1992-94 seasons). New Bowl Alliance matchup starting with 1995 season: second choice of WAC champion or second pick from Pac-10 vs. third pick from Big 12.

Multiple wins: BYU (4); Iowa and Ohio St. (2).

Year		Year		Year	
1978†	Navy 23, BYU 16	1985	Arkansas 18, Arizona St. 17	1992	Hawaii 27, Illinois 17
1979	Indiana 38, BYU 37	1986	Iowa 39, San Diego St. 38	1993	Ohio St. 28, BYU 21
1980	BYU 46, SMU 45	1987	Iowa 20, Wyoming 19	1994	Michigan 24, Colo. St. 14
1981	BYU 38, Washington St. 36	1988	Okla. St. 62, Wyoming 14	1995	Kansas St. 54, Colorado St. 21
1982	Ohio St. 47, BYU 17	1989	Penn St. 50, BYU 39	1996	Colorado 33, Washington 21
1983	BYU 21, Missouri 17	1990	Texas A&M 65, BYU 14		
1984	BYU 24, Michigan 17	1991	13-13, Iowa vs BYU		

†December game since 1978.

Bowl Matchups of Unbeaten Teams						
Date	**Bowl**	**Winner**	**Head Coach**	**Score**	**Loser**	**Head Coach**
1/1/21	Rose	California (8-0)	Andy Smith	28-0	Ohio St. (7-0)	John Wilce
1/2/22	Rose	Wash. & Jeff. (10-0)	Greasy Neale	0-0	California (9-0)	Andy Smith
1/1/27	Rose	Stanford (10-0)	Pop Warner	7-7	Alabama (9-0)	Wallace Wade
1/1/31	Rose	Alabama (9-0)	Wallace Wade	24-0	Washington St. (9-0)	Babe Hollingbery
1/2/39	Orange	Tennessee (10-0)	Bob Neyland	17-0	Oklahoma (10-0)	Tom Stidham
1/1/41	Sugar	Boston College (10-0)	Frank Leahy	19-13	Tennessee (10-0)	Bob Neyland
1/1/52	Sugar	Maryland (9-0)	Jim Tatum	28-13	Tennessee (10-0)	Bob Neyland
1/2/56	Orange	Oklahoma (10-0)	Bud Wilkinson	20-6	Maryland (10-0)	Jim Tatum
1/1/72	Orange	Nebraska (12-0)	Bob Devaney	38-6	Alabama (11-0)	Bear Bryant
12/31/73	Sugar	Notre Dame (10-0)	Ara Parseghian	24-23	Alabama (11-0)	Bear Bryant
1/2/87	Fiesta	Penn St. (11-0)	Joe Paterno	14-10	Miami-FL (11-0)	Jimmy Johnson
1/1/88	Orange	Miami-FL (11-0)	Jimmy Johnson	20-14	Oklahoma (11-0)	Barry Switzer
1/2/89	Fiesta	Notre Dame (11-0)	Lou Holtz	34-21	West Va. (11-0)	Don Nehlen
1/1/93	Sugar	Alabama (12-0)	Gene Stallings	34-13	Miami-FL (11-0)	Dennis Erickson
1/2/96	Fiesta	Nebraska (11-0)	Tom Osborne	62-24	Florida (12-0)	Steve Spurrier

Outback Bowl

City: Tampa, Fla. **Stadium:** Houlihan's Stadium. **Capacity:** 74,300. **Playing surface:** Grass. **First game:** Dec. 23, 1986. **Name change:** Hall of Fame Bowl (1986-95) and Outback Bowl (starting in 1995). **Playing site:** Tampa Stadium (since 1986). Name was changed to Houlihan's Stadium in 1996. **Corporate title sponsor:** Outback Steakhouse, Inc. (starting in 1995).

Automatic berths: Fourth pick from ACC vs. fourth pick from Big 10 (1993-94 seasons); New Bowl Alliance matchup starting with 1995 season: third pick from Big 10 vs. third pick from SEC.

Multiple wins: Michigan and Syracuse (2).

Year		Year		Year	
1986†	Boston College 27, Georgia 24	1991	Clemson 30, Illinois 0	1995	Wisconsin 34, Duke 20
1988*	Michigan 28, Alabama 24	1992	Syracuse 24, Ohio St. 17	1996	Penn St. 43, Auburn 14
1989	Syracuse 23, LSU 10	1993	Tennessee 38, Boston Col. 23	1997	Alabama 17, Michigan 14
1990	Auburn 31, Ohio St. 14	1994	Michigan 42, N.C. State 7		

†December game in 1986.   *January game since 1988.

Peach Bowl

City: Atlanta, Ga. **Stadium:** Georgia Dome. **Capacity:** 71,228. **Playing surface:** AstroTurf. **First game:** Dec. 30, 1968. **Playing sites:** Grant Field (1968-70), Atlanta-Fulton County Stadium (1971-92) and Georgia Dome (since 1993).

Automatic berths: Third pick from ACC vs. at-large opponent (1992 season); third pick from ACC vs. fourth pick from SEC (1993-94 seasons). Bowl Alliance matchup starting with 1995 season: third pick from ACC vs. fourth pick from SEC.

Multiple wins: N.C. State (4); West Virginia (3); LSU and Virginia (2).

Year		Year		Year	
1968†	LSU 31, Florida St. 27	1978	Purdue 41, Georgia Tech 21	1988†	N.C. State 28, Iowa 23
1969	West Va. 14, S. Carolina 3	1979	Baylor 24, Clemson 18	1989	Syracuse 19, Georgia 18
1970	Arizona St. 48, N. Carolina 26	1981*	Miami-FL 20, Va. Tech 10	1990	Auburn 27, Indiana 23
1971	Mississippi 41, Georgia Tech 18	1981†	West Va. 26, Florida 6	1992*	E. Carolina 37, N.C. State 34
1972	N.C. State 49, West Va. 13	1982	Iowa 28, Tennessee 22	1993	N. Carolina 21, Miss. St. 17
1973	Georgia 17, Maryland 16	1983	Florida St. 28, N. Carolina 3	1993†	Clemson 14, Kentucky 13
1974	6-6, Vanderbilt vs Texas Tech	1984	Virginia 27, Purdue 24	1995*	N.C. State 24, Miss. St. 24
1975	West Va. 13, N.C. State 10	1985	Army 31, Illinois 29	1995†	Virginia 34, Georgia 27
1976	Kentucky 21, N. Carolina 0	1986	Va. Tech 25, N.C. State 24	1996	LSU 10, Clemson 7
1977	N.C. State 24, Iowa St. 14	1988*	Tennessee 27, Indiana 22		

†December game from 1968-79, 1981-86, 1988-90, 1993 and since 1995.
*January game in 1981, 1988, 1992-93 and 1995.

Sun Bowl

City: El Paso, Tex. **Stadium:** Sun Bowl. **Capacity:** 52,000. **Playing surface:** AstroTurf. **First game:** Jan. 1, 1936. **Name changes:** Sun Bowl (1936-85), John Hancock Sun Bowl (1986-88), John Hancock Bowl (1989-93) and Sun Bowl (since 1994). **Playing sites:** Kidd Field (1936-62) and Sun Bowl (since 1963). **Corporate title sponsor:** John Hancock Financial Services (1986-93).

Automatic berths: Eighth pick from 8-team Boal Coalition pool vs. at-large opponent (1992); Seventh and eighth picks from 8-team Bowl Coalition pool (1993-94 seasons). New Bowl Alliance matchup starting with 1995 season: third pick from Pac-10 vs. fifth pick from Big-10.

Multiple wins: Texas Western/UTEP (5); Alabama and Wyoming (3); Nebraska, New Mexico St., North Carolina, Oklahoma, Pittsburgh, Southwestern-Texas, Stanford, Texas, West Texas St. and West Virginia (2).

Year		Year		Year	
1936*	14-14, Hardin-Simmons vs New Mexico St.	1955	Tex. Western 47, Florida St. 20	1975	Pittsburgh 33, Kansas 19
1937	Hardin-Simmons 34, Texas Mines 6	1956	Wyoming 21, Texas Tech 14	1977*	Texas A&M 37, Florida 14
		1957	Geo. Wash. 13, Tex. Western 0	1977†	Stanford 24, LSU 14
1938	West Va. 7, Texas Tech 6	1958	Louisville 34, Drake 0	1978	Texas 42, Maryland 0
1939	Utah 26, New Mexico 0	1958*	Wyoming 14, Hardin-Simmons 6	1979	Washington 14, Texas 7
1940	0-0, Catholic U. vs Arizona St.	1959	New Mexico St. 28, N. Texas 8	1980	Nebraska 31, Miss. St. 17
1941	W. Reserve 26, Arizona St. 13	1960	New Mexico St. 20, Utah St. 13	1981	Oklahoma 40, Houston 14
1942	Tulsa 6, Texas Tech 0			1982	N. Carolina 26, Texas 10
1943	Second Air Force 13, Hardin-Simmons 7	1961	Villanova 17, Wichita 9	1983	Alabama 28, SMU 7
1944	SW Texas 7, New Mexico 0	1962	West Texas 15, Ohio U. 14	1984	Maryland 28, Tennessee 27
1945	SW Texas 35, U. of Mexico 0	1963	Oregon 21, SMU 14	1985	13-13, Georgia vs Arizona
1946	New Mexico 34, Denver 24	1964	Georgia 7, Texas Tech 0	1986	Alabama 28, Washington 6
1947	Cincinnati 18, Va. Tech 6	1965	Texas Western 13, TCU 12	1987	Oklahoma St. 35, West Va. 33
1948	Miami-OH 13, Texas Tech 12	1966	Wyoming 28, Florida St. 20	1988	Alabama 29, Army 28
1949	West Va. 21, Texas Mines 12	1967	UTEP 14, Mississippi 7	1989	Pittsburgh 31, Texas A&M 28
1950	Tex. Western 33, Georgetown 20	1968	Auburn 34, Arizona 10	1990	Michigan St. 17, USC 16
1951	West Texas 14, Cincinnati 13	1969	Nebraska 45, Georgia 6	1991	UCLA 6, Illinois 3
1952	Texas Tech 25, Pacific 14	1970	Georgia Tech 17, Texas Tech 9	1992	Baylor 20, Arizona 15
1953	Pacific 26, Southern Miss. 7	1971	LSU 33, Iowa St. 15	1993	Oklahoma 41, Texas Tech 10
1954	Tex. Western 37, So. Miss. 14	1972	N. Carolina 32, Texas Tech 28	1994	Texas 35, N. Carolina 31
		1973	Missouri 34, Auburn 17	1995	Iowa 38, Washington 18
		1974	Miss. St. 26, N. Carolina 24	1996	Stanford 38, Michigan St. 0

*January game from 1936-58 and in 1977.   †December game from 1958-75 and since 1977.

Bowl Games (Cont.)
Alamo Bowl

City: San Antonio, Tex. **Stadium:** Alamodome. **Capacity:** 65,000. **Playing surface:** Turf. **First game:** Dec. 31, 1993. **Playing site:** Alamodome (since 1993). **Corporate title sponsor:** Builders Square (since 1993).
    Automatic berths: third pick from SWC vs. fourth pick from Pac-10 (1993-94 seasons). New Bowl Alliance matchup starting with 1995 season: fourth pick from Big 10 vs. fourth pick from Big 12.
    Multiple wins: None.

Year		Year		Year	
1993†	California 37, Iowa 3	1995	Texas A&M 22, Michigan 20	1996	Iowa 27, Texas Tech 0
1994	Washington St. 10, Baylor 3				

†December game since 1993.

Copper Bowl

City: Tucson, Ariz. **Stadium:** Arizona. **Capacity:** 57,803. **Playing surface:** Grass. **First game:** Dec. 31, 1989. **Playing site:** Arizona Stadium (since 1989). **Corporate title sponsors:** Domino's Pizza (1990-91) and Weiser Lock (since 1992).
    Automatic berths: third pick from WAC vs. at-large opponent (1992 season); third pick from WAC vs. fourth pick from Big Eight (1993-94 seasons). New Bowl Alliance matchup starting with 1995 season: second pick from WAC vs. sixth pick from Big 12.
    Multiple wins: None.

Year		Year		Year	
1989†	Arizona 17, N.C. State 10	1992	Washington St. 31, Utah 28	1995	Texas Tech 55, Air Force 41
1990	California 17, Wyoming 15	1993	Kansas St. 52, Wyoming 17	1996	Wisconsin 38, Utah 10
1991	Indiana 24, Baylor 0	1994	BYU 31, Oklahoma 6		

†December game since 1989.

Liberty Bowl

City: Memphis, Tenn. **Stadium:** Liberty Bowl Memorial. **Capacity:** 62,380. **Playing surface:** Grass. **First game:** Dec. 19, 1959. **Playing sites:** Municipal Stadium in Philadelphia (1959-63), Convention Hall in Atlantic City, N.J. (1964), Memphis Memorial Stadium (1965-75) and Liberty Bowl Memorial Stadium (since 1976). Memphis Memorial Stadium renamed Liberty Bowl Memorial in 1976. **Corporate title sponsor:** St. Jude's Hospital (since 1993).
    Automatic berths: Commander-in-Chief's Trophy winner (Army, Navy or Air Force) vs. at-large opponent (1989-92 seasons); none (1993 season); first pick from independent group of Cincinnati, East Carolina, Memphis, Southern Miss. and Tulane vs. at-large opponent (for the 1994 and '95 seasons). Starting with 1996 season, Conference USA champ or East Carolina vs. fourth pick from Big East.
    Multiple wins: Mississippi (4); Penn St. and Tennessee (3); Air Force, Alabama, N.C. State and Syracuse (2).

Year		Year		Year	
1959†	Penn St. 7, Alabama 0	1972	Georgia Tech 31, Iowa St. 30	1985	Baylor 21, LSU 7
1960	Penn St. 41, Oregon 12	1973	N.C. State 31, Kansas 18	1986	Tennessee 21, Minnesota 14
1961	Syracuse 15, Miami-FL 14	1974	Tennessee 7, Maryland 3	1987	Georgia 20, Arkansas 17
1962	Oregon St. 6, Villanova 0	1975	USC 20, Texas A&M 0	1988	Indiana 34, S. Carolina 10
1963	Mississippi St. 16, N.C. State 12	1976	Alabama 36, UCLA 6	1989	Mississippi 42, Air Force 29
1964	Utah 32, West Virginia 6	1977	Nebraska 21, N. Carolina 17	1990	Air Force 23, Ohio St. 11
1965	Mississippi 13, Auburn 7	1978	Missouri 20, LSU 15	1991	Air Force 38, Mississippi St. 15
1966	Miami-FL 14, Virginia Tech 7	1979	Penn St. 9, Tulane 6	1992	Mississippi 13, Air Force 0
1967	N.C. State 14, Georgia 7	1980	Purdue 28, Missouri 25	1993	Louisville 18, Michigan St. 7
1968	Mississippi 34, Virginia Tech 17	1981	Ohio St. 31, Navy 28	1994	Illinois 30, E. Carolina 0
1969	Colorado 47, Alabama 33	1982	Alabama 21, Illinois 15	1995	E. Carolina 19, Stanford 13
1970	Tulane 17, Colorado 3	1983	Notre Dame 19, Boston Col. 18	1996	Syracuse 30, Houston 17
1971	Tennessee 14, Arkansas 13	1984	Auburn 21, Arkansas 15		

†December game since 1959.

Carquest Bowl

City: Miami, Fla. **Stadium:** Pro Player Stadium. **Capacity:** 74,916. **Playing surface:** Grass. **First game:** Dec. 28, 1990. **Name change:** Blockbuster Bowl (1990-93) and Carquest Bowl (since 1994) **Playing site:** Joe Robbie Stadium (since 1990). Name was changed to Pro Player Stadium in 1996. **Corporate title sponsors:** Blockbuster Video (1990-93) and Carquest Auto Parts (since 1993).
    Automatic berths: Penn St. vs. seventh pick from 8-team Bowl Coalition pool (1992 season); third pick from Big East vs. fifth pick from SEC (1993-94 seasons). New Bowl Alliance matchup starting with 1995 season: third pick from Big East vs. fourth pick from ACC.

Year		Year		Year	
1990†	Florida St. 24, Penn St. 17	1994	Boston College 31, Virginia 13	1996†	Miami-FL 31, Virginia 21
1991	Alabama 30, Colorado 25	1995	S. Carolina 24, West Va. 21		
1993*	Stanford 24, Penn St. 3	1996	N. Carolina 20, Arkansas 10		

†December game from 1990-91 and since 1996.   *January game 1993-96.

Aloha Bowl

City: Honolulu, Hawaii. **Stadium:** Aloha. **Capacity:** 50,000. **Playing surface:** AstroTurf. **First game:** Dec. 25, 1982. **Playing site:** Aloha Stadium (since 1982). **Corporate title sponsor:** Jeep Eagle Division of Chrysler (since 1987).
    Automatic berths: second pick from WAC vs. third pick from Big Eight (1992-93 seasons); third pick from Big Eight vs. at-large opponent (1994 season) New Bowl Alliance matchup starting with 1995 season: fifth pick from Big 12 vs. fourth pick from Pac-10.
    Multiple wins: Kansas (2).

Year		Year		Year	
1982†	Washington 21, Maryland 20	1987	UCLA 20, Florida 16	1992	Kansas 23, BYU 20
1983	Penn St. 13, Washington 10	1988	Washington St. 24, Houston 22	1993	Colorado 41, Fresno St. 30
1984	SMU 27, Notre Dame 20	1989	Michigan St. 33, Hawaii 13	1994	Boston Col. 12, Kansas St. 7
1985	Alabama 24, USC 3	1990	Syracuse 28, Arizona 0	1995	Kansas 51, UCLA 30
1986	Arizona 30, N. Caroina 21	1991	Georgia Tech 18, Stanford 17	1996	Navy 42, California 38

†December game since 1982.

Las Vegas Bowl

City: Las Vegas, Nev. **Stadium:** Sam Boyd Stadium. **Capacity:** 40,000. **Playing surface:** AstroTurf. **First game:** Dec. 18, 1992. **Playing site:** Sam Boyd Stadium (since 1992).

Automatic berths: Mid-American champion vs. Big West champion (since 1992 season).

Note: the MAC and Big West champs have met in a bowl game since 1981, originally in Fresno at the California Bowl (1981-88, 1992) and California Raisin Bowl (1989-91). The results from 1981-91 are included below.

Multiple wins: Fresno St. (4); Bowling Green, San Jose St. and Toledo (2).

Year		Year		Year	
1981†	Toledo 27, San Jose St. 25	1987	E. Michigan 30, San Jose St. 27	1993	Utah St. 42, Ball St. 33
1982	Fresno St. 29, Bowling Green 28	1988	Fresno St. 35, W. Michigan 30	1994	UNLV 52, C. Michigan 24
1983	Northern Ill. 20, CS-Fullerton 13	1989	Fresno St. 27, Ball St. 6	1995	Toledo 40, Nevada 37 (OT)
1984	UNLV 30, Toledo 13	1990	San Jose St. 48, C. Michigan 24	1996	Nevada 18, Ball St. 15
1985	Fresno St. 51, Bowling Green 7	1991	Bowling Green 28, Fresno St. 21		
1986	San Jose St. 37, Miami-OH 7	1992	Bowling Green 35, Nevada 34		

†December game since 1981.
Note: Toledo later ruled winner of 1984 game by forfeit when UNLV was found to have used ineligible players.

Independence Bowl

City: Shreveport, La. **Stadium:** Independence. **Capacity:** 50,832. **Playing surface:** Grass. **First game:** Dec. 13, 1976. **Playing sites:** Independence Stadium (since 1976). **Corporate title sponsor:** Poulan/Weed Eater (since 1990).

Automatic berths: Beginning with 1995 season, fifth pick from SEC vs. at-large.

Multiple wins: Air Force and Southern Miss (2).

Year		Year		Year	
1976†	McNeese St. 20, Tulsa 16	1983	Air Force 9, Mississippi 3	1990	34-34, La. Tech vs Maryland
1977	La. Tech 24, Louisville 14	1984	Air Force 23, Va. Tech 7	1991	Georgia 24, Arkansas 15
1978	E. Carolina 35, La. Tech 13	1985	Minnesota 20, Clemson 13	1992	Wake Forest 39, Oregon 35
1979	Syracuse 31, McNeese St. 7	1986	Mississippi 20, Texas Tech 17	1993	Va. Tech 45, Indiana 20
1980	Southern Miss 16, McNeese St. 14	1987	Washington 24, Tulane 12	1994	Virginia 20, TCU 10
1981	Texas A&M 33, Oklahoma St. 16	1988	Southern Miss 38, UTEP 18	1995	LSU 45, Michigan St. 26
1982	Wisconsin 14, Kansas St. 3	1989	Oregon 27, Tulsa 24	1996	Auburn 32, Army 29

†December game since 1976.

The Bowl Alliance

Division I-A football remains the only NCAA sport on any level that does not have a sanctioned national champion. To that end, the Bowl Coalition was formed in 1992 in an attempt to keep the bowl system intact while forcing an annual championship game between the regular season's two top-ranked teams.

The Coalition, which lasted for three seasons, consolidated the resources of four major bowl games (the Cotton, Fiesta, Orange and Sugar), the champions of five major conferences (the ACC, Big East, Big Eight, Southeastern and Southwest) and the national following of independent Notre Dame. It worked two out of three years with No. 1 vs. No. 2 showdowns in the 1993 Sugar Bowl (#2 Alabama over #1 Miami-FL) and 1994 Orange Bowl (#1 Florida St. over #2 Nebraska). The 1995 Orange Bowl had to settle for No. 1 Nebraska beating No. 3 Miami-FL because #2 Penn St., the Big Ten champion, was obligated to play in the Rose Bowl.

The Bowl Alliance, which began a three-year run with the 1995 season, is an updated version of the Coalition. There will be a new Bowl Alliance—including the Rose Bowl—starting after the 1998 season that should guarantee a national championship (No. 1 vs. No. 2) game. The key difference in this new alliance, which is expected to run seven years (although only guaranteed for four), will be that it will include the Big 10 and the Pac-10 champions. Those teams, currently locked into playing the Rose Bowl, would be allowed to move to another bowl if needed to create a No. 1 vs. No. 2 game. The bowls (the Fiesta, Orange, and Sugar) which currently make up the Bowl Alliance must rebid to keep their spots in this new four-bowl alliance. The Rose Bowl, which is already guaranteed a spot in the new alliance, is expected to get the title game in 2002. Still yet to be determined under the new deal is whether the Bowl Alliance will continue to rely solely on the AP and USA Today/CNN polls to determine the teams playing in the title game.

The following is a breakdown of the current Bowl Alliance, set to run through the 1997 season.

Member conferences: ACC, Big East, Big 12, Big 10, Pac-10, SEC and independent Notre Dame. **Major bowls** (3): Fiesta, Orange and Sugar. **Major selection order:** 1995 season– FIESTA (No. 1 vs. No. 2), ORANGE (No. 3 vs. No. 5), SUGAR (No. 4 vs. No. 6); 1996 season– SUGAR (No. 1 vs. No. 2), FIESTA (No. 3 vs. No. 5), ORANGE (No. 4 vs. No. 6); 1997 season– ORANGE (No. 1 vs. No. 2), SUGAR (No. 3 vs. No. 5), FIESTA (No. 4 vs. No. 6). **Annual bowl dates:** Dec. 31 (No. 4 vs. No. 6); Jan. 1 (No. 3 vs. No. 5); and Jan. 2 (No. 1 vs. No. 2).

Pool of teams for six slots (ranked according to combined AP media and USA Today/CNN coaches' polls at the end of the regular season): ACC champion, Big East champ, Big 12 champ, SEC champ, and two at-large positions open to any Division I-A teams that meet one of the following requirements: a) had at least eight wins, b) is ranked in the Top 12 of the AP media or USA Today/CNN coaches' polls, or c) is ranked no lower in either poll than the lowest ranked conference champion.

Non-Alliance matchups: ALAMO (fourth pick from Big 12 vs. fourth pick from Big 10); ALOHA (fourth pick from Pac-10 vs. fifth pick from Big 12); CARQUEST (third pick from Big East vs. fourth pick from ACC); CITRUS (second pick from Big 10 vs. second pick from SEC); COPPER (second pick from WAC vs. sixth pick from the Big 12); COTTON (first choice of either WAC champ or second pick from Pac-10 vs. second pick from Big 12); OUTBACK (third pick from Big 10 vs. third pick from SEC); HOLIDAY (second choice of either WAC champ or second pick from Pac-10 vs. third pick from Big 12); INDEPENDENCE (fifth pick from SEC vs. at-large); LAS VEGAS (Big West champ vs. Mid-American champ); LIBERTY (Conference USA champ or East Carolina vs. fourth pick from Big East); PEACH (third pick from ACC vs. fourth pick from SEC); ROSE (Big 10 champ vs. Pac-10 champ); SUN (third pick from Pac-10 vs. fifth pick from Big 10); GATOR (second pick from Big East vs. second pick from ACC); MOTOR CITY (Mid American champ vs. at large).

All-Time Winningest Division I-A Teams

Schools classified as Division I-A for at least 10 years; through 1996 season (including bowl games).

Top 25 Winning Percentage

		Yrs	Gm	W	L	T	Pct	Bowls App	Bowls Record	1996 Season Bowl	1996 Season Record
1	Notre Dame	108	1010	746	222	42	.759	21	13-8-0	none	8-3-0
2	Michigan	117	1054	764	254	36	.742	28	13-15-0	lost Outback	8-4-0
3	Alabama	102	1009	713	253	43	.728	48	28-17-3	won Outback	10-3-0
4	Oklahoma	102	985	673	259	53	.710	32	20-11-1	none	3-8-0
5	Texas	104	1030	713	284	33	.708	37	17-18-2	lost Fiesta	8-5-0
6	Ohio St.	107	1015	690	272	53	.706	29	13-6-0	won Rose	11-1-0
7	Nebraska	107	1041	709	292	40	.700	35	17-18-0	won Orange	11-2-0
8	USC	104	972	653	265	54	.700	38	25-13-0	none	6-6-0
9	Penn St.	110	1043	706	296	41	.697	33	21-10-2	won Fiesta	11-2-0
10	Tennessee	100	1001	666	283	52	.691	37	21-16-0	won Citrus	10-2-0
11	Florida St.	50	544	347	180	17	.653	25	15-8-2	lost Sugar	11-1-0
12	Central Michigan	96	805	498	271	36	.641	5	3-2-0	none	5-6-0
13	Washington	107	956	585	321	50	.638	23	12-10-1	lost Holiday	9-3-0
14	Army	107	999	607	341	51	.633	4	2-2-0	lost Independence	10-2-0
15	Miami-OH	108	929	565	320	44	.632	7	5-2-0	none	6-5-0
16	LSU	103	979	594	338	47	.631	30	13-16-1	won Peach	10-2-0
17	Arizona St.	84	757	464	269	24	.629	16	9-6-1	lost Rose	11-1-0
18	Georgia	103	1009	606	349	54	.627	32	15-14-3	none	5-6-0
19	Auburn	104	974	583	344	47	.623	25	13-10-2	won Independence	8-4-0
20	Colorado	107	977	588	353	36	.620	21	9-12-0	won Holiday	10-2-0
21	Miami-FL	70	725	438	268	19	.617	22	11-11-0	won Carquest	9-3-0
22	Florida	90	901	525	336	40	.605	24	11-13-0	won Sugar	12-1-0
23	Bowling Green	78	716	407	257	52	.605	5	2-3-0	none	4-7-0
24	Michigan St.	100	927	538	345	44	.604	13	5-8-0	lost Sun	6-6-0
25	Texas A&M	102	992	574	370	48	.603	22	12-10-0	none	6-6-0

Note: Alabama was forced to forfeit 11 games in 1993 in which Antonio Langham played while ineligible.

Top 50 Victories

		Wins
1	Michigan	764
2	Notre Dame	746
3	Texas	713
	Alabama	713
5	Nebraska	709
6	Penn St	706
7	Ohio St	690
8	Oklahoma	673
9	Tennessee	666
10	USC	653
11	Syracuse	608
12	Army	607
13	Georgia	606
14	LSU	594
15	Colorado	588
16	Washington	585
17	Auburn	583

		Wins
18	West Virginia	577
19	Pittsburgh	576
20	Texas A&M	574
21	North Carolina	573
22	Arkansas	567
	Georgia Tech	567
24	Minnesota	565
	Miami-OH	565
26	Navy	563
27	Clemson	546
28	California	543
29	Rutgers	541
	Virginia Tech	541
31	Michigan St	538
32	Mississippi	529
33	Virginia	526
34	Florida	525

		Wins
35	Maryland	520
36	Missouri	518
37	Boston College	513
38	Vanderbilt	512
39	Illinois	510
40	Kentucky	498
	Central Michigan	498
	Utah	498
43	Kansas	497
	Stanford	497
	Wisconsin	497
46	Iowa	487
47	Baylor	486
48	Tulsa	485
49	Purdue	482
50	Arizona	478

Top 30 Bowl Appearances

		App	Record
1	Alabama	48	28-17-3
2	USC	38	25-13-0
3	Tennessee	37	21-16-0
	Texas	37	17-18-2
5	Nebraska	35	17-18-0
6	Penn St	33	21-10-2
7	Oklahoma	32	20-11-1
	Georgia	32	15-14-3
9	LSU	30	13-16-1
10	Ohio St	29	13-16-0
11	Arkansas	28	9-16-3
	Michigan	28	13-15-0

		App	Record
13	Georgia Tech	25	17-8-0
	Florida St	25	15-8-2
	Auburn	25	13-10-2
	Mississippi	25	14-11-0
17	Florida	24	11-13-0
18	Washington	23	12-10-1
19	Texas A&M	22	12-10-0
	Miami-FL	22	11-11-0
	Texas Tech	22	5-16-1
22	Notre Dame	21	13-8-0
	Clemson	21	12-9-0
	Colorado	21	9-12-0

		App	Record
	North Carolina	21	9-12-0
26	BYU	20	7-12-1
	UCLA	20	10-9-1
28	Missouri	19	8-11-0
29	Stanford	18	9-8-1
	Pittsburgh	18	8-10-0
	West Va.	18	8-10-0

Note: Alabama, Georgia, Georgia Tech, Notre Dame and Penn State are the only schools that have won all four of the traditional major bowl games– the Rose, Orange, Sugar and Cotton.

Major Conference Champions
Atlantic Coast Conference

Founded in 1953 when charter members all left Southern Conference to form ACC. **Charter members** (7): Clemson, Duke, Maryland, North Carolina, N.C. State, South Carolina and Wake Forest. **Admitted later** (3): Virginia in 1953 (began play in '54), Georgia Tech in 1979 (began play in '83); Florida St. in 1990 (began play in '92). **Withdrew later** (1): South Carolina in 1971 (became an independent after '70 season).

1997 playing membership (9): Clemson, Duke, Florida St., Georgia Tech, Maryland, North Carolina, N.C. State, Virginia and Wake Forest.

Multiple titles: Clemson (13); Maryland (8); Duke and N.C. State (7); Florida St. and North Carolina (5); Virginia (2).

Year		Year		Year		Year	
1953	Duke (4-0) & Maryland (3-0)	1964	N.C. State (5-2)	1977	North Carolina (5-0-1)	1989	Virginia (6-1) & Duke (6-1)
1954	Duke (4-0)	1965	Clemson (5-2) & N.C. State (5-2)	1978	Clemson (6-0)		
1955	Maryland (4-0) & Duke (4-0)	1966	Clemson (6-1)	1979	N.C. State (5-1)	1990	Georgia Tech (6-0-1)
1956	Clemson (4-0-1)	1967	Clemson (6-0)	1980	North Carolina (6-0)	1991	Clemson (6-0-1)
1957	N.C. State (5-0-1)	1968	N.C. State (6-1)	1981	Clemson (6-0)	1992	Florida St. (8-0)
1958	Clemson (5-1)	1969	South Carolina (6-0)	1982	Clemson (6-0)	1993	Florida St. (8-0)
1959	Clemson (6-1)			1983	Clemson (7-0) & Maryland (5-0)	1994	Florida St. (8-0)
1960	Duke (5-1)	1970	Wake Forest (5-1)	1984	Maryland (5-0)	1995	Virginia (7-1) & Florida St. (7-1)
1961	Duke (5-1)	1971	North Carolina (6-0)	1985	Maryland (6-0)		
1962	Duke (6-0)	1972	North Carolina (6-0)	1986	Clemson (5-1-1)	1996	Florida St. (8-0)
1963	North Carolina (6-1) & N.C. State (6-1)	1973	N.C. State (6-0)	1987	Clemson (6-1)		
		1974	Maryland (6-0)	1988	Clemson (6-1)		
		1975	Maryland (5-0)				
		1976	Maryland (5-0)				

Big East Conference

Founded in 1991 when charter members gave up independent football status to form Big East. **Charter members** (8): Boston College, Miami-FL, Pittsburgh, Rutgers, Syracuse, Temple, Virginia Tech and West Virginia. **Note:** Temple and Virginia Tech are Big East members in football only.

1997 playing membership (8): Boston College, Miami-FL, Pittsburgh, Rutgers, Syracuse, Temple, Virginia Tech and West Virginia.

Conference champion: Member schools needed two years to adjust their regular season schedules in order to begin round-robin conference play in 1993. In the meantime, the 1991 and '92 Big East titles went to the highest-ranked member in the final regular season USA Today/CNN coaches' poll.

Multiple titles: Miami-FL (5); Syracuse and Virginia Tech (2).

Year		Year		Year		Year	
1991	Miami-FL (2-0, #1) & Syracuse (5-0, #16)	1993	West Virginia (7-0)	1995	Virginia Tech (6-1) & Miami-FL (6-1)	1996	Virginia Tech (6-1), Miami-FL (6-1) & Syracuse (6-1)
1992	Miami-FL (4-0, #1)	1994	Miami-FL (7-0)				

Big Ten Conference

Originally founded in 1895 as the Intercollegiate Conference of Faculty Representatives, better known as the Western Conference. **Charter members** (7): Chicago, Illinois, Michigan, Minnesota, Northwestern, Purdue and Wisconsin. **Admitted later** (5): Indiana and Iowa in 1899; Ohio St. in 1912; Michigan St. in 1950 (began play in '53); Penn St. in 1990 (began play in '93). **Withdrew later** (2): Michigan in 1907 (rejoined in '17); Chicago in 1940 (dropped football after '39 season). **Note:** Iowa belonged to both the Western and Missouri Valley conferences from 1907-10.

Unofficially called the **Big Ten** from 1912 until Chicago's withdrawal in 1939, then the **Big Nine** from 1940 until Michigan St. began conference play in 1953. Formally named the **Big Ten** in 1984 and has kept the name even after adding Penn St. as its 11th member.

1997 playing membership (11): Illinois, Indiana, Iowa, Michigan, Michigan St., Minnesota, Northwestern, Ohio St., Penn St., Purdue, and Wisconsin.

Multiple titles: Michigan (37); Ohio St. (27); Minnesota (18); Illinois (14); Iowa and Wisconsin (9); Purdue and Northwestern (7); Chicago and Michigan St. (6); Indiana (2).

Year		Year		Year		Year	
1896	Wisconsin (2-0-1)	1904	Minnesota (3-0) & Michigan (2-0)	1912	Wisconsin (6-0)	1921	Iowa (5-0)
1897	Wisconsin (3-0)	1905	Chicago (7-0)	1913	Chicago (7-0)	1922	Iowa (5-0) & Michigan (4-0)
1898	Michigan (3-0)	1906	Wisconsin (3-0), Minnesota (2-0) & Michigan (1-0)	1914	Illinois (6-0)	1923	Illinois (5-0) & Michigan (4-0)
1899	Chicago (4-0)			1915	Minnesota (3-0-1) & Illinois (3-0-2)		
1900	Iowa (3-0-1) & Minnesota (3-0-1)	1907	Chicago (4-0)	1916	Ohio St. (4-0)	1924	Chicago (3-0-3)
1901	Michigan (4-0) & Wisconsin (2-0)	1908	Chicago (5-0)	1917	Ohio St. (4-0)	1925	Michigan (5-1)
		1909	Minnesota (3-0)	1918	Illinois (4-0), Michigan (2-0) & Purdue (1-0)	1926	Michigan (5-0) & Northwestern (5-0)
1902	Michigan (5-0)						
1903	Michigan (3-0-1), Minnesota (3-0-1) & Northwestern (1-0-2)	1910	Illinois (4-0) & Minnesota (2-0)	1919	Illinois (6-1)	1927	Illinois (5-0) & Minnesota (3-0-1)
		1911	Minnesota (3-0-1)	1920	Ohio St. (5-0)	1928	Illinois (4-1)

Major Conference Champions (Cont.)

Year		Year		Year		Year	
1929	Purdue (5-0)	1946	Illinois (6-1)	1966	Michigan St. (7-0)	1981	Iowa (6-2) & Ohio St. (6-2)
1930	Michigan (5-0) & Northwestern (5-0)	1947	Michigan (6-0)	1967	Indiana (6-1), Purdue (6-1) & Minnesota (6-1)	1982	Michigan (8-1)
1931	Purdue (5-1), Michigan (5-1) & Northwestern (5-1)	1948	Michigan (6-0)			1983	Illinois (9-0)
		1949	Ohio St. (4-1-1) & Michigan (4-1-1)	1968	Ohio St. (7-0)	1984	Ohio St. (7-2)
				1969	Ohio St. (6-1) & Michigan (6-1)	1985	Iowa (7-1)
1932	Michigan (6-0) & Purdue (5-0-1)	1950	Michigan (4-1-1)			1986	Michigan (7-1) & Ohio St. (7-1)
1933	Michigan (5-0-1) & Minnesota (2-0-4)	1951	Illinois (5-0-1)	1970	Ohio St. (7-0)		
1934	Minnesota (5-0)	1952	Wisconsin (4-1-1) & Purdue (4-1-1)	1971	Michigan (8-0)	1987	Michigan St. (7-0-1)
1935	Minnesota (5-0) & Ohio St. (5-0)	1953	Michigan St. (5-1) & Illinois (5-1)	1972	Ohio St. (7-1) & Michigan (7-1)	1988	Michigan (7-0-1)
1936	Northwestern (6-0)	1954	Ohio St. (7-0)	1973	Ohio St. (7-0-1) & Michigan (7-0-1)	1989	Michigan (8-0)
1937	Minnesota (5-0)	1955	Ohio St. (6-0)	1974	Ohio St. (7-1) & Michigan (7-1)	1990	Iowa (6-2), Michigan (6-2), Michigan St. (6-2) & Illinois (6-2)
1938	Minnesota (4-1)	1956	Iowa (5-1)	1975	Ohio St. (8-0)		
1939	Ohio St. (5-1)	1957	Ohio St. (7-0)	1976	Michigan (7-1) & Ohio St. (7-1)	1991	Michigan (8-0)
		1958	Iowa (5-1)	1977	Michigan (7-1) & Ohio St. (7-1)	1992	Michigan (6-0-2)
1940	Minnesota (6-0)	1959	Wisconsin (5-2)			1993	Wisconsin (6-1-1) & Ohio St. (6-1-1)
1941	Minnesota (5-0)	1960	Minnesota (5-1) & Iowa (5-1)	1978	Michigan (7-1) & Michigan St. (7-1)		
1942	Ohio St. (5-1)	1961	Ohio St. (6-0)	1979	Ohio St. (8-0)	1994	Penn St. (8-0)
1943	Purdue (6-0) & Michigan (6-0)	1962	Wisconsin (6-1)	1980	Michigan (8-0)	1995	Northwestern (8-0)
1944	Ohio St. (6-0)	1963	Illinois (5-1-1)			1996	Ohio St. (7-1) & Northwestern (7-1)
1945	Indiana (5-0-1)	1964	Michigan (6-1)				
		1965	Michigan St. (7-0)				

Big 12 Conference

Originally founded in 1907 as the Missouri Valley Intercollegiate Athletic Assn. **Charter members** (5): Iowa, Kansas, Missouri, Nebraska and Washington University of St. Louis. **Admitted later** (11): Drake and Iowa St. (then Ames College) in 1908; Kansas St. (then Kansas College of Applied Science and Agriculture) in 1913; Grinnell (Iowa) College in 1919; Oklahoma in 1920; Oklahoma A&M (now Oklahoma St.) in 1925; Colorado in 1947 (began play in '48); Baylor, Texas, Texas A&M and Texas Tech in 1994 (all four began play in '96).

Withdrew later (1): Iowa in 1911 (left for Big Ten after 1910 season); **Excluded later** (4): Drake, Grinnell, Oklahoma A&M and Washington-MO (left out when MVIAA cut membership to six teams in 1928.

Streamlined MVIAA unofficially called **Big Six** from 1928-47 with surviving members Iowa St., Kansas, Kansas St., Missouri, Nebraska and Oklahoma. Became the **Big Seven** after 1947 season when Colorado came over from the Skyline Conference, and then the **Big Eight** with the return of Oklahoma A&M in 1957. A&M, which resumed conference play in '60, became Oklahoma St. on July 10, 1957. The MVIAA was officially renamed the Big Eight in 1964 and became the **Big 12** after the 1995-96 academic year with the arrival of Baylor, Texas, Texas A&M and Texas Tech from the defunct Southwest Conference.

1997 playing membership (12): Baylor, Colorado, Iowa St., Kansas, Kansas St., Missouri, Nebraska, Oklahoma, Oklahoma St., Texas, Texas A&M and Texas Tech.

Multiple titles: Nebraska (42); Oklahoma (33); Missouri (12); Colorado and Kansas (5); Iowa St. and Oklahoma St. (2).

Year		Year		Year		Year	
1907	Iowa (1-0) & Nebraska (1-0)	1929	Nebraska (3-0-2)	1952	Oklahoma (5-0-1)	1976	Colorado (5-2), Oklahoma (5-2) & Okla. St. (5-2)
1908	Kansas (4-0)	1930	Kansas (4-1)	1953	Oklahoma (6-0)		
1909	Missouri (4-0-1)	1931	Nebraska (5-0)	1954	Oklahoma (6-0)	1977	Oklahoma (7-0)
		1932	Nebraska (5-0)	1955	Oklahoma (6-0)	1978	Nebraska (6-1) & Oklahoma (6-1)
1910	Nebraska (2-0)	1933	Nebraska (5-0)	1956	Oklahoma (6-0)		
1911	Iowa St. (2-0-1) & Nebraska (2-0-1)	1934	Kansas St. (5-0)	1957	Oklahoma (6-0)	1979	Oklahoma (7-0)
		1935	Nebraska (4-0-1)	1958	Oklahoma (6-0)		
1912	Iowa St. (2-0) & Nebraska (2-0)	1936	Nebraska (5-0)	1959	Oklahoma (5-1)	1980	Oklahoma (7-0)
1913	Missouri (4-0) & Nebraska (3-0)	1937	Nebraska (3-0-2)	1960	Missouri (7-0)	1981	Nebraska (7-0)
		1938	Oklahoma (5-0)	1961	Colorado (7-0)	1982	Nebraska (7-0)
1914	Nebraska (3-0)	1939	Missouri (5-0)	1962	Oklahoma (7-0)	1983	Nebraska (7-0)
1915	Nebraska (4-0)			1963	Nebraska (7-0)	1984	Oklahoma (6-1) & Nebraska (6-1)
1916	Nebraska (3-1)	1940	Nebraska (5-0)	1964	Nebraska (6-1)		
1917	Nebraska (2-0)	1941	Missouri (5-0)	1965	Nebraska (7-0)	1985	Oklahoma (7-0)
1918	Vacant (WW I)	1942	Missouri (4-0-1)	1966	Nebraska (6-1)	1986	Oklahoma (7-0)
1919	Missouri (4-0-1)	1943	Oklahoma (5-0)	1967	Oklahoma (7-0)	1987	Oklahoma (7-0)
		1944	Oklahoma (4-0-1)	1968	Kansas (6-1) & Oklahoma (6-1)	1988	Nebraska (7-0)
1920	Oklahoma (4-0-1)	1945	Missouri (5-0)			1989	Colorado (7-0)
1921	Nebraska (3-0)	1946	Oklahoma (4-1) & Kansas (4-1)	1969	Missouri (6-1) & Nebraska (6-1)		
1922	Nebraska (5-0)	1947	Kansas (4-0-1) & Oklahoma (4-0-1)			1990	Colorado (7-0)
1923	Nebraska (3-0-2) & Kansas (3-0-3)			1970	Nebraska (7-0)	1991	Nebraska (6-0-1) & Colorado (6-0-1)
1924	Missouri (5-1)	1948	Oklahoma (5-0)	1971	Nebraska (7-0)		
1925	Missouri (5-1)	1949	Oklahoma (5-0)	1972	Nebraska (5-1-1)*	1992	Nebraska (6-1)
1926	Okla. A&M (3-0-1)	1950	Oklahoma (6-0)	1973	Oklahoma (7-0)	1993	Nebraska (7-0)
1927	Missouri (5-1)	1951	Oklahoma (6-0)	1974	Oklahoma (7-0)	1994	Nebraska (7-0)
1928	Nebraska (4-0)			1975	Nebraska (6-1) & Oklahoma (6-1)	1995	Nebraska (7-0)
						1996	Nebraska (8-1)

*Oklahoma (6-1) forfeited title in 1972.

Big West Conference

Originally founded in 1969 as Pacific Coast Athletic Assn. **Charter members** (7): CS-Los Angeles, Fresno St., Long Beach St., Pacific, San Diego St., San Jose St. and UC-Santa Barbara. **Admitted later** (12): CS-Fullerton in 1974; Utah St. in 1977 (began play in '78); UNLV in 1982; New Mexico St. in 1983 (began play in '84); Nevada in 1991 (began play in '92); Arkansas St., Louisiana Tech, Northern Illinois and SW Louisiana in 1992 (all four began play in football only in '93); Boise St., Idaho and North Texas in 1994 (all three began play in '96). **Withdrew later** (13): CS-Los Angeles and UC-Santa Barbara in 1972 (both dropped football after '71 season); San Diego St. in 1975 (became an independent after '75 season); Fresno St. in 1991 (left for WAC after '91 season); Long Beach St. in 1991 (dropped football after '91 season); CS-Fullerton in 1992 (dropped football after '92 season); San Jose St. and UNLV in 1994 (left for WAC after '95 season); Pacific in 1995 (dropped football after '95 season); Arkansas St., Louisiana Tech, Northern Illinois and SW Louisiana in 1995 (all four returned to independent football status after '95 season). **Conference renamed** Big West in 1988.

   1997 playing membership (6): Boise St., Idaho, Nevada, New Mexico St., North Texas and Utah St.

   Multiple titles: San Jose St. (8); Fresno St. (6); San Diego St. (5); Nevada and Utah St. (4); Long Beach St. (3); CS-Fullerton and SW Louisiana (2).

Year	Year	Year	Year
1969 San Diego St. (6-0)	1977 Fresno St. (4-0)	1985 Fresno St. (7-0)	1993 Utah St. (5-1)
1970 Long Beach St. (5-1)	1978 San Jose St. (4-1)	1986 San Jose St. (7-0)	& SW La. (5-1)
& San Diego St. (5-1)	& Utah St. (4-1)	1987 San Jose St. (7-0)	1994 UNLV (5-1),
1971 Long Beach St. (5-1)	1979 Utah St. (4-0-1)*	1988 Fresno St. (7-0)	Nevada (5-1),
1972 San Diego St. (4-0)	1980 Long Beach St. (5-0)	1989 Fresno St. (7-0)	& SW La. (5-1)
1973 San Diego St. (3-0-1)	1981 San Jose St. (5-0)	1990 San Jose St. (7-0)	1995 Nevada (6-0)
1974 San Diego St. (4-0)	1982 Fresno St. (6-0)	1991 Fresno St. (6-1)	1996 Nevada (4-1)
1975 San Jose St. (5-0)	1983 CS-Fullerton (5-1)	& San Jose St. (6-1)	& Utah St. (4-1)
1976 San Jose St. (4-0)	1984 CS-Fullerton (6-1)†	1992 Nevada (5-1)	

*San Jose St. (4-0-1) forfeited share of title in 1979.   †UNLV (7-0) forfeited title in 1984.

Conference USA

Founded in 1994 by six independent football schools, who began play as a conference in 1996. **Charter members** (6): Cincinnati, Houston, Louisville, Memphis, Southern Mississippi and Tulane. **Admitted later** (2): Army and East Carolina in 1997; **1997 playing members** (8): Army, Cincinnati, East Carolina, Houston, Louisville, Memphis, Southern Mississippi and Tulane.

Year
1996 Southern Mississippi (4-1)
    & Houston (4-1)

Ivy League

First called the Ivy League in 1937 by sportswriter Caswell Adams of the *New York Herald Tribune*. Unofficial conference of 10 eastern teams was occasionally referred to as the Old 10 and included: Army, Brown, Columbia, Cornell, Dartmouth, Harvard, Navy, Pennsylvania, Princeton and Yale. Army and Navy were dropped from the group after 1940. **League formalized** in 1954 for play beginning in 1956. **Charter members** (8): Brown, Columbia, Cornell, Dartmouth, Harvard, Pennsylvania, Princeton, and Yale. League downgraded from Division I to Division I-AA after 1977 season. **Current playing membership:** the same.

   Multiple titles: Dartmouth (17); Yale (12); Penn (9); Harvard and Princeton (8); Cornell (3).

Year	Year	Year	Year
1956 Yale (7-0)	1968 Harvard (6-0-1)	1977 Yale (6-1)	1987 Harvard (6-1)
1957 Princeton (6-1)	& Yale (6-0-1)	1978 Dartmouth (6-1)	1988 Penn (6-1)
1958 Dartmouth (6-1)	1969 Dartmouth (6-1),	1979 Yale (6-1)	& Cornell (6-1)
1959 Penn (6-1)	Yale (6-1)	1980 Yale (6-1)	1989 Princeton (6-1)
1960 Yale (7-0)	& Princeton (6-1)	1981 Yale (6-1)	& Yale (6-1)
1961 Columbia (6-1)	1970 Dartmouth (7-0)	& Dartmouth (6-1)	1990 Cornell (6-1)
& Harvard (6-1)	1971 Cornell (6-1)	1982 Harvard (5-2),	& Dartmouth (6-1)
1962 Dartmouth (7-0)	& Dartmouth (6-1)	Penn (5-2)	1991 Dartmouth (6-0-1)
1963 Dartmouth (5-2)	1972 Dartmouth (5-1-1)	& Dartmouth (5-2)	1992 Dartmouth (6-1)
& Princeton (5-2)	1973 Dartmouth (6-1)	1983 Harvard (5-1-1)	& Princeton (6-1)
1964 Princeton (7-0)	1974 Harvard (6-1)	& Penn (5-1-1)	1993 Penn (7-0)
1965 Dartmouth (7-0)	& Yale (6-1)	1984 Penn (7-0)	1994 Penn (7-0)
1966 Dartmouth (6-1),	1975 Harvard (6-1)	1985 Penn (6-1)	1995 Princeton (5-1-1)
Harvard (6-1)	1976 Brown (6-1)	1986 Penn (7-0)	1996 Dartmouth (7-0)
& Princeton (6-1)	& Yale (6-1)		
1967 Yale (7-0)			

Major Conference Champions (Cont.)
Mid-American Conference

Founded in 1946. **Charter members** (6): Butler, Cincinnati, Miami-OH, Ohio University, Western Michigan and Western Reserve (Miami and WMU began play in '48). **Admitted later** (12): Kent St. (now Kent) and Toledo in 1951 (Toledo began play in '52); Bowling Green in 1952; Marshall in 1954; Central Michigan and Eastern Michigan in 1972 (CMU began play in '75 and EMU in '76); Ball St. and Northern Illinois in 1973 (both began play in '75); Akron in 1991 (began play in '92); Marshall and Northern Illinois in 1995 (both will resume play in '97); Buffalo in 1995 (will begin play in either '98 or '99). **Withdrew later** (5): Butler in 1950 (left for the Indiana Collegiate Conference); Cincinnati in 1953 (went independent); Western Reserve (now Case Western) in 1955 (left for President's Athletic Conference); Marshall in 1969 (went independent); Northern Illinois in 1986 (went independent).

1997 playing membership (10): Akron, Ball St., Bowling Green, Central Michigan, Eastern Michigan, Kent, Miami-OH, Ohio University, Toledo and Western Michigan.

Multiple titles: Miami-OH (13); Bowling Green (10); Toledo (8); Ball St. and Ohio University (5); Central Michigan and Cincinnati (4); Western Michigan (2).

Year		Year		Year		Year	
1947	Cincinnati (3-1)	1959	Bowling Green (6-0)	1971	Toledo (5-0)	1985	Bowling Green (9-0)
1948	Miami-OH (4-0)	1960	Ohio Univ. (6-0)	1972	Kent St. (4-1)	1986	Miami-OH (6-2)
1949	Cincinnati (4-0)	1961	Bowling Green (5-1)	1973	Miami-OH (5-0)	1987	Eastern Mich. (7-1)
		1962	Bowling Green (5-0-1)	1974	Miami-OH (5-0)	1988	Western Mich. (7-1)
1950	Miami-OH (4-0)	1963	Ohio Univ. (5-1)	1975	Miami-OH (6-0)	1989	Ball St. (6-1-1)
1951	Cincinnati (3-0)	1964	Bowling Green (5-1)	1976	Ball St. (4-1)		
1952	Cincinnati (3-0)	1965	Bowling Green (5-1)	1977	Miami-OH (5-0)	1990	Central Mich. (7-1)
1953	Ohio Univ. (5-0-1)		& Miami-OH (5-1)	1978	Ball St. (8-0)		& Toledo (7-1)
	& Miami-OH (3-0-1)	1966	Miami-OH (5-1)	1979	Central Mich. (8-0-1)	1991	Bowling Green (8-0)
1954	Miami-OH (4-0)		& Western Mich. (5-1)			1992	Bowling Green (8-0)
1955	Miami-OH (5-0)	1967	Toledo (5-1)	1980	Central Mich. (7-2)	1993	Ball St. (7-0-1)
1956	Bowling Green (5-0-1)		& Ohio Univ. (5-1)	1981	Toledo (8-1)	1994	Central Mich. (8-1)
	& Miami-OH (4-0-1)	1968	Ohio Univ. (6-0)	1982	Bowling Green (7-2)	1995	Toledo (7-0-1)
1957	Miami-OH (5-0)	1969	Toledo (5-0)	1983	Northern Ill. (8-1)	1996	Ball St. (7-1)
1958	Miami-OH (5-0)	1970	Toledo (5-0)	1984	Toledo (7-1-1)		

Pacific-10 Conference

Originally founded in 1915 as Pacific Coast Conference. **Charter members** (4): California, Oregon, Oregon St. and Washington. **Admitted later** (6): Washington St. in 1917; Stanford in 1918; Idaho and USC (Southern Cal) in 1922; Montana in 1924; UCLA in 1928. **Withdrew later** (1): Montana in 1950 (left for the Mountain States Conf.).

The **PCC** dissolved in 1959 and the **AAWU** (Athletic Assn. of Western Universities) was founded. **Charter members** (5): California, Stanford, UCLA, USC and Washington. **Admitted later** (5): Washington St. in 1962; Oregon and Oregon St. in 1964; Arizona and Arizona St. in 1978. **Conference renamed** Pacific-8 in 1968 and Pacific-10 in 1978.

1997 playing membership (10): Arizona, Arizona St., California, Oregon, Oregon St., Stanford, UCLA, USC, Washington and Washington St.

Multiple titles: USC (31); UCLA (15); Washington (14); California (13); Stanford (11); Oregon (5); Oregon St. (4); Arizona St. and Washington St. (2).

Year		Year		Year		Year	
1916	Washington (3-0-1)	1936	Washington (6-0-1)		& Oregon St. (6-2)	1978	USC (6-1)
1917	Washington St. (3-0)	1937	California (6-0-1)	1958	California (6-1)	1979	USC (6-0-1)
1918	California (3-0)	1938	USC (6-1)	1959	Washington (3-1),	1980	Washington (6-1)
1919	Oregon (2-1)		& California (6-1)		USC (3-1)	1981	Washington (6-2)
	& Washington (2-1)	1939	USC (5-0-2)		& UCLA (3-1)	1982	UCLA (5-1-1)
			& UCLA (5-0-3)			1983	UCLA (6-1-1)
1920	California (3-0)			1960	Washington (4-0)	1984	USC (7-1)
1921	California (5-0)	1940	Stanford (7-0)	1961	UCLA (3-1)	1985	UCLA (6-2)
1922	California (3-0)	1941	Oregon St. (7-2)	1962	USC (4-0)	1986	Arizona St. (5-1-1)
1923	California (5-0)	1942	UCLA (6-1)	1963	Washington (4-1)	1987	USC (7-1)
1924	Stanford (3-0-1)	1943	USC (4-0)	1964	Oregon St. (3-1)		& UCLA (7-1)
1925	Washington (5-0)	1944	USC (3-0-2)		& USC (3-1)	1988	USC (8-0)
1926	Stanford (4-0)	1945	USC (5-1)	1965	UCLA (4-0)	1989	USC (6-0-1)
1927	USC (4-0-1)	1946	UCLA (7-0)	1966	USC (4-1)		
	& Stanford (4-0-1)	1947	USC (6-0)	1967	USC (6-1)	1990	Washington (7-1)
1928	USC (4-0-1)	1948	California (6-0)	1968	USC (6-0)	1991	Washington (8-0)
1929	USC (6-1)		& Oregon (6-0)	1969	USC (6-0)	1992	Washington (6-2)
		1949	California (7-0)				& Stanford (6-2)
1930	Washington St. (6-0)			1970	Stanford (6-1)	1993	UCLA (6-2),
1931	USC (7-0)	1950	California (5-0-1)	1971	Stanford (6-1)		Arizona (6-2)
1932	USC (6-0)	1951	Stanford (6-1)	1972	USC (7-0)		& USC (6-2)
1933	Oregon (4-1)	1952	USC (6-0)	1973	USC (7-0)	1994	Oregon (7-1)
	& Stanford (4-1)	1953	UCLA (6-1)	1974	USC (6-0-1)	1995	USC (6-1-1)
1934	Stanford (5-0)	1954	UCLA (6-0)	1975	USC (6-1)		& Washington
1935	California (4-1),	1955	UCLA (6-0)		& California (6-1)		(6-1-1)
	Stanford (4-1)	1956	Oregon St. (6-1-1)	1976	USC (7-0)	1996	Arizona St. (8-0)
	& UCLA (4-1)	1957	Oregon (6-2)	1977	Washington (6-1)		

THROUGH THE YEARS 193

Southeastern Conference

Founded in 1933 when charter members all left Southern Conference to form SEC. **Charter members** (13): Alabama, Auburn, Florida, Georgia, Georgia Tech, Kentucky, LSU (Louisiana St.), Mississippi, Mississippi St., Sewanee, Tennessee, Tulane and Vanderbilt. **Admitted later** (2): Arkansas and South Carolina in 1990 (both began play in '92). **Withdrew later** (3): Sewanee in 1940; Georgia Tech in 1964; Tulane in 1966.

Current playing membership (12): Alabama, Arkansas, Auburn, Florida, Georgia, Kentucky, LSU, Mississippi, Mississippi St., South Carolina, Tennessee and Vanderbilt. **Note:** Conference title decided by championship game between Western and Eastern division winners since 1992.

Multiple titles: Alabama (20); Tennessee (11); Georgia (10); LSU (7); Mississippi (6); Auburn, Florida and Georgia Tech (5); Tulane (3); Kentucky (2).

Year		Year		Year		Year	
1933	Alabama (5-0-1)	1949	Tulane (5-1)		& Georgia (6-0)	1983	Auburn (6-0)
1934	Tulane (8-0)	1950	Kentucky (5-1)	1967	Tennessee (6-0)	1984	Florida (5-0-1)*
	& Alabama (7-0)	1951	Georgia Tech (7-0)	1968	Georgia (5-0-1)	1985	Florida (5-1)†
1935	LSU (5-0)		& Tennessee (5-0)	1969	Tennessee (5-1)		& Tennessee (5-1)
1936	LSU (6-0)	1952	Georgia Tech (6-0)	1970	LSU (5-0)	1986	LSU (5-1)
1937	Alabama (6-0)	1953	Alabama (4-0-3)	1971	Alabama (7-0)	1987	Auburn (5-0-1)
1938	Tennessee (7-0)	1954	Mississippi (5-1)	1972	Alabama (7-1)	1988	Auburn (6-1)
1939	Tennessee (6-0),	1955	Mississippi (5-1)	1973	Alabama (8-0)		& LSU (6-1)
	Georgia Tech (6-0)	1956	Tennessee (6-0)	1974	Alabama (6-0)	1989	Alabama (6-1),
	& Tulane (5-0)	1957	Auburn (7-0)	1975	Alabama (6-0)		Tennessee (6-1)
1940	Tennessee (5-0)	1958	LSU (6-0)	1976	Georgia (5-1)		& Auburn (6-1)
1941	Mississippi St. (4-0-1)	1959	Georgia (7-0)		& Kentucky (5-1)	1990	Florida (6-1)†
1942	Georgia (6-1)	1960	Mississippi (5-0-1)	1977	Alabama (7-0)		& Tennessee (5-1-1)
1943	Georgia Tech (3-0)	1961	Alabama (7-0)		& Kentucky (5-1)	1991	Florida (7-0)
1944	Georgia Tech (4-0)		& LSU (6-0)	1978	Alabama (6-0)	1992	Alabama (8-0)
1945	Alabama (6-0)	1962	Mississippi (6-0)	1979	Alabama (6-0)	1993	Florida (7-1)
1946	Georgia (5-0)	1963	Mississippi (5-0-1)	1980	Georgia (6-0)	1994	Florida (7-1)
	& Tennessee (5-0)	1964	Alabama (8-0)	1981	Georgia (6-0)	1995	Florida (8-0)
1947	Mississippi (6-1)	1965	Alabama (6-1-1)		& Alabama (6-0)	1996	Florida (9-0)
1948	Georgia (6-0)	1966	Alabama (6-0)	1982	Georgia (6-0)		

*Title vacated.   †On probation, ineligible for championship.

SEC Championship Game

Since expanding to 12 teams and splitting into two divisions in 1992, the SEC has staged a conference championship game between the two division winners on the first Saturday in December. The game has been played at Legion Field in Birmingham, Ala., (1992-93) and the Georgia Dome in Atlanta (since 1994).

Year		Year		Year	
1992	Alabama 28, Florida 21	1994	Florida 24, Alabama 23	1996	Florida 45, Alabama 30
1993	Florida 28, Alabama 23	1995	Florida 34, Arkansas 3		

Southwest Conference (1914–95)

Founded in 1914 as Southwest Intercollegiate Athletic Conference. **Charter members** (8): Arkansas, Baylor, Oklahoma, Oklahoma A&M (now Oklahoma St.), Rice, Southwestern, Texas and Texas A&M. **Admitted later** (5): SMU (Southern Methodist) in 1918; Phillips University in 1920; TCU (Texas Christian) in 1923; Texas Tech in 1956 (began play in '60); Houston in 1971 (began play in '76). **Withdrew later** (9): Southwestern in 1917 (went independent); Oklahoma in 1920 (left for Missouri Valley after '19 season); Phillips in 1921; Oklahoma A&M (now Oklahoma St.) in 1925 (left for Big Six); Arkansas in 1990 (left for SEC after '91 season); Baylor, Texas, Texas A&M and Texas Tech in 1994 (all four left for Big 12 after '95 season); Rice, SMU and TCU in 1994 (all three left for WAC after '95 season); Houston in 1994 (left for Conference USA after '95 season).

1997 playing membership: Conference folded on June 30, 1996.

Multiple titles: Texas (25); Texas A&M (17); Arkansas (13); SMU (9); TCU (9); Rice (7); Baylor (5); Houston (4); Texas Tech (2).

Year		Year		Year		Year	
1914	No champion	1937	Rice (4-1-1)	1958	TCU (5-1)	1976	Houston (7-1)
1915	Oklahoma (3-0)	1938	TCU (6-0)	1959	Texas (5-1), TCU (5-1)		& Texas Tech (7-1)
1916	No champion	1939	Texas A&M (6-0)		& Arkansas (5-1)	1977	Texas (8-0)
1917	Texas A&M (2-0)	1940	Texas A&M (5-1)	1960	Arkansas (6-1)	1978	Houston (7-1)
1918	No champion	1941	Texas A&M (5-1)	1961	Texas (6-1)	1979	Houston (7-1)
1919	Texas A&M (4-0)	1942	Texas (5-1)		& Arkansas (6-1)		& Arkansas (7-1)
1920	Texas (5-0)	1943	Texas (5-0)	1962	Texas (6-0)	1980	Baylor (8-0)
1921	Texas A&M (3-0-2)	1944	TCU (3-1-1)	1963	Texas (7-0)	1981	SMU (7-1)
1922	Baylor (5-0)	1945	Texas (5-1)	1964	Arkansas (7-0)	1982	SMU (7-0-1)
1923	SMU (5-0)	1946	Rice (5-1)	1965	Arkansas (7-0)	1983	Texas (8-0)
1924	Baylor (4-0-1)		& Arkansas (5-1)	1966	SMU (6-1)	1984	SMU (6-2)
1925	Texas A&M (4-1)	1947	SMU (5-0-1)	1967	Texas A&M (6-1)		& Houston (6-2)
1926	SMU (5-0)	1948	SMU (5-0-1)	1968	Arkansas (6-1)	1985	Texas A&M (7-1)
1927	Texas A&M (4-0-1)	1949	Rice (6-0)		& Texas (6-1)	1986	Texas A&M (7-1)
1928	Texas (5-1)	1950	Texas (6-0)	1969	Texas (7-0)	1987	Texas A&M (6-1)
1929	TCU (4-0-1)	1951	TCU (5-1)	1970	Texas (7-0)	1988	Arkansas (7-0)
1930	Texas (4-1)	1952	Texas (6-0)	1971	Texas (6-1)	1989	Arkansas (7-1)
1931	SMU (5-0-1)	1953	Texas (5-1)	1972	Texas (7-0)	1990	Texas (8-0)
1932	TCU (6-0)		& Texas (5-1)	1973	Texas (7-0)	1991	Texas A&M (8-0)
1933	Arkansas (4-1)*	1954	Arkansas (5-1)	1974	Baylor (6-1)	1992	Texas A&M (7-0)
1934	Rice (5-1)	1955	TCU (5-1)	1975	Arkansas (6-1),	1993	Texas A&M (7-0)
1935	SMU (6-0)	1956	Texas A&M (6-0)		Texas (6-1)	1994	Texas A&M (6-0-1)
1936	Arkansas (5-1)	1957	Rice (5-1)		& Texas A&M (6-1)	1995	Texas (7-0)

*Arkansas (4–1) forced to vacate 1933 title for use of ineligible player.

Major Conference Champions (Cont.)
Western Athletic Conference

Founded in 1962 when charter members left the Skyline and Border conferences to form the WAC. **Charter members** (6): Arizona and Arizona St. from Border; BYU (Brigham Young), New Mexico, Utah and Wyoming from Skyline. **Admitted later** (12): Colorado St. and UTEP (Texas-El Paso) in 1967 (both began play in '68); San Diego St. in 1978; Hawaii in 1979; Air Force in 1980; Fresno St. in 1991 (began play in '92); Rice, San Jose St., SMU (Southern Methodist), TCU (Texas Christian), Tulsa and UNLV (Nevada-Las Vegas) in 1994 (all began play in '96). **Withdrew later** (2): Arizona and Arizona St. in 1978 (left for Pac-10 after '77 season).

1997 playing membership (16): Air Force, BYU, Colorado St., Fresno St., Hawaii, New Mexico, Rice, San Diego St., San Jose St., SMU, TCU, Tulsa, UNLV, Utah, UTEP and Wyoming.

Multiple titles: BYU (19); Arizona St. and Wyoming (7); New Mexico (3); Air Force, Arizona, Colorado St., Fresno St. and Utah (2).

Year		Year		Year		Year	
1962	New Mexico (2-1-1)	1972	Arizona St. (5-1)	1981	BYU (7-1)	1992	Hawaii (6-2),
1963	New Mexico (3-1)	1973	Arizona St. (6-1)	1982	BYU (7-1)		BYU (6-2)
1964	Utah (3-1),		& Arizona (6-1)	1983	BYU (7-0)		& Fresno St. (6-2)
	New Mexico (3-1)	1974	BYU (6-0-1)	1984	BYU (8-0)	1993	BYU (6-2),
	& Arizona (3-1)	1975	Arizona St. (7-0)	1985	Air Force (7-1)		Fresno St. (6-2)
1965	BYU (4-1)	1976	BYU (6-1)		& BYU (7-1)		& Wyoming (6-2)
1966	Wyoming (5-0)		& Wyoming (6-1)	1986	San Diego St. (7-1)	1994	Colorado St. (7-1)
1967	Wyoming (5-0)	1977	Arizona St. (6-1)	1987	Wyoming (8-0)	1995	Colorado St. (6-2),
1968	Wyoming (6-1)		& BYU (6-1)	1988	Wyoming (8-0)		Air Force (6-2),
1969	Arizona St. (6-1)	1978	BYU (5-1)	1989	BYU (7-1)		BYU (6-2)
1970	Arizona St. (7-0)	1979	BYU (7-0)	1990	BYU (7-1)		& Utah (6-2)
1971	Arizona St. (7-0)	1980	BYU (6-1)	1991	BYU (7-0-1)	1996	BYU (9-0)

WAC Championship Game

In addition to expanding to 16 teams and splitting into two divisions in 1996, the WAC staged a conference championship game between the two division winners on Dec. 7 at Sam Boyd Stadium in Las Vegas.

Year	
1996	BYU 28, Wyoming 25 (OT)

Longest Division I Streaks

Winning Streaks
(Including bowl games)

No		Seasons	Spoiler	Score
47	Oklahoma	1953-57	Notre Dame	7-0
39	Washington	1908-14	Oregon St.	0-0
37	Yale	1890-93	Princeton	6-0
37	Yale	1887-89	Princeton	10-0
35	Toledo	1969-71	Tampa	21-0
34	Penn	1894-96	Lafayette	6-4
31	Oklahoma	1948-50	Kentucky	13-7*
31	Pittsburgh	1914-18	Cleve. Naval	10-9
31	Penn	1896-98	Harvard	10-0
30	Texas	1968-70	Notre Dame	24-11*
29	Miami-FL	1990-93	Alabama	34-13*
29	Michigan	1901-03	Minnesota	6-6
28	Alabama †	1991-93	Tennessee	17-17
28	Alabama	1978-80	Mississippi St.	6-3
28	Oklahoma	1973-75	Kansas	23-3
28	Michigan St.	1950-53	Purdue	6-0
27	Nebraska	1901-04	Colorado	6-0
26	Nebraska	1994-96	Arizona St.	19-0
26	Cornell	1921-24	Williams	14-7
26	Michigan	1903-05	Chicago	2-0
25	BYU	1983-85	UCLA	27-24
25	San Diego St.	1965-67	Utah St.	31-25
25	Michigan	1946-49	Army	21-7
25	Army	1944-46	Notre Dame	0-0
25	USC	1931-33	Oregon St.	0-0

*Note: Kentucky beat Oklahoma in 1951 Sugar Bowl and Notre Dame beat Texas in 1971 Cotton Bowl.

†Note: Alabama was forced to forfeit eight victories and one tie in 1993 by the NCAA Committee on Infractions.

Unbeaten Streaks
(Including bowl games)

No	W-T		Seasons	Spoiler	Score
63	59-4	Washington	1907-17	California	27-0
56	55-1	Michigan	1901-05	Chicago	2-0
50	46-4	California	1920-25	Olympic Club	15-0
48	47-1	Oklahoma	1953-57	N. Dame	7-0
48	47-1	Yale	1885-89	Princeton	10-0
47	42-5	Yale	1879-85	Princeton	6-5
44	42-2	Yale	1894-96	Princeton	24-6
42	39-3	Yale	1904-08	Harvard	4-0
39	37-2	N. Dame	1946-50	Purdue	28-14
37	36-1	Oklahoma	1972-75	Kansas	23-3
37	37-0	Yale	1890-93	Princeton	6-0
35	35-0	Toledo	1967-71	Tampa	21-0
35	34-1	Minnesota	1903-05	Wisconsin	16-12

Losing Streaks

No		Seasons	Victim	Score
68	Prairie View	1989-	current streak	
44	Columbia	1983-88	Princeton	16-14
34	Northwestern	1979-82	No. Illinois	31-6
28	Virginia	1958-61	Wm. & Mary	21-6
28	Kansas St	1944-48	Arkansas St.	37-6
27	Eastern Mich.	1980-82	Kent St.	9-7
27	New Mexico St.	1988-90	CS-Fullerton	43-9

Note: Virginia ended its losing streak in the opening game of the 1961 season.

Annual NCAA Division I-A Leaders

Note that Oklahoma A&M is now Oklahoma St. and Texas Mines is now UTEP.

Rushing

Individual championship decided on Rushing Yards (1937-69), and on Yards Per Game (since 1970).

Multiple winners: Troy Davis, Marshall Faulk, Art Luppino, Ed Marinaro, Rudy Mobley, Jim Pilot and O.J. Simpson (2).

Year		Car	Yards
1937	Byron (Whizzer) White, Colorado	181	1121
1938	Len Eshmont, Fordham	132	831
1939	John Polanski, Wake Forest	137	882
1940	Al Ghesquiere, Detroit	146	957
1941	Frank Sinkwich, Georgia	209	1103
1942	Rudy Mobley, Hardin-Simmons	187	1281
1943	Creighton Miller, Notre Dame	151	911
1944	Red Williams, Minnesota	136	911
1945	Bob Fenimore, Oklahoma A&M	142	1048
1946	Rudy Mobley, Hardin-Simmons	227	1262
1947	Wilton Davis, Hardin-Simmons	193	1173
1948	Fred Wendt, Texas Mines	184	1570
1949	John Dottley, Ole Miss	208	1312
1950	Wilford White, Arizona St	199	1502
1951	Ollie Matson, San Francisco	245	1566
1952	Howie Waugh, Tulsa	164	1372
1953	J.C. Caroline, Illinois	194	1256
1954	Art Luppino, Arizona	179	1359
1955	Art Luppino, Arizona	209	1313
1956	Jim Crawford, Wyoming	200	1104
1957	Leon Burton, Arizona St	117	1126
1958	Dick Bass, Pacific	205	1361
1959	Pervis Atkins, New Mexico St	130	971
1960	Bob Gaiters, New Mexico St	197	1338
1961	Jim Pilot, New Mexico St	191	1278
1962	Jim Pilot, New Mexico St	208	1247
1963	Dave Casinelli, Memphis St	219	1016
1964	Brian Piccolo, Wake Forest	252	1044
1965	Mike Garrett, USC	267	1440
1966	Ray McDonald, Idaho	259	1329
1967	O.J. Simpson, USC	266	1415

Year		Car	Yards
1968	O.J. Simpson, USC	355	1709
1969	Steve Owens, Oklahoma	358	1523

Year		Car	Yards	P/Gm
1970	Ed Marinaro, Cornell	285	1425	158.3
1971	Ed Marinaro, Cornell	356	1881	209.0
1972	Pete VanValkenburg, BYU	232	1386	138.6
1973	Mark Kellar, Northern Ill	291	1719	156.3
1974	Louie Giammona, Utah St.	329	1534	153.4
1975	Ricky Bell, USC	357	1875	170.5
1976	Tony Dorsett, Pittsburgh	338	1948	177.1
1977	Earl Campbell, Texas	267	1744	158.5
1978	Billy Sims, Oklahoma	231	1762	160.2
1979	Charles White, USC	293	1803	180.3
1980	George Rogers, S. Carolina	297	1781	161.9
1981	Marcus Allen, USC	403	2342	212.9
1982	Ernest Anderson, Okla. St.	353	1877	170.6
1983	Mike Rozier, Nebraska	275	2148	179.0
1984	Keith Byars, Ohio St.	313	1655	150.5
1985	Lorenzo White, Mich. St.	386	1908	173.5
1986	Paul Palmer, Temple	346	1866	169.6
1987	Ickey Woods, UNLV	259	1658	150.7
1988	Barry Sanders, Okla. St.	344	2628	238.9
1989	Anthony Thompson, Ind	358	1793	163.0
1990	Gerald Hudson, Okla. St.	279	1642	149.3
1991	Marshall Faulk, S. Diego St.	201	1429	158.8
1992	Marshall Faulk, S. Diego St.	265	1630	163.0
1993	LeShon Johnson, No. Ill.	327	1976	179.6
1994	Rashaan Salaam, Colorado	298	2055	186.8
1995	Troy Davis, Iowa St.	345	2010	182.7
1996	Troy Davis, Iowa St.	402	2185	198.6

All-Purpose Yardage

Multiple winners: Marcus Allen, Pervis Atkins, Ryan Benjamin, Troy Davis, Louie Giammona, Tom Harmon, Art Luppino, Napolean McCallum, O.J. Simpson, Charles White and Gary Wood (2).

Year		Yards	P/Gm
1937	Byron (Whizzer) White, Colorado	1970	246.3
1938	Parker Hall, Ole Miss	1420	129.1
1939	Tom Harmon, Michigan	1208	151.0
1940	Tom Harmon, Michigan	1312	164.0
1941	Bill Dudley, Virginia	1674	186.0
1942	Complete records not available		
1943	Stan Koslowski, Holy Cross	1411	176.4
1944	Red Williams, Minnesota	1467	163.0
1945	Bob Fenimore, Oklahoma A&M	1577	197.1
1946	Rudy Mobley, Hardin-Simmons	1765	176.5
1947	Wilton Davis, Hardin-Simmons	1798	179.8
1948	Lou Kusserow, Columbia	1737	193.0
1949	Johnny Papit, Virginia	1611	179.0
1950	Wilford White, Arizona St.	2065	206.5
1951	Ollie Matson, San Francisco	2037	226.3
1952	Billy Vessels, Oklahoma	1512	151.2
1953	J.C. Caroline, Illinois	1470	163.3
1954	Art Luppino, Arizona	2193	219.3
1955	Jim Swink, TCU	1702	170.2
	& Art Luppino, Arizona	1702	170.2
1956	Jack Hill, Utah St	1691	169.1
1957	Overton Curtis, Utah St	1608	160.8
1958	Dick Bass, Pacific	1878	187.8
1959	Pervis Atkins, New Mexico St	1800	180.0
1960	Pervis Atkins, New Mexico St	1613	161.3
1961	Jim Pilot, New Mexico St	1606	160.6
1962	Gary Wood, Cornell	1395	155.0
1963	Gary Wood, Cornell	1508	167.6
1964	Donny Anderson, Texas Tech	1710	171.0
1965	Floyd Little, Syracuse	1990	199.0

Year		Yards	P/Gm
1966	Frank Quayle, Virginia	1616	161.6
1967	O.J. Simpson, USC	1700	188.9
1968	O.J. Simpson, USC	1966	196.6
1969	Lynn Moore, Army	1795	179.5
1970	Don McCauley, North Carolina	2021	183.7
1971	Ed Marinaro, Cornell	1932	214.7
1972	Howard Stevens, Louisville	2132	213.2
1973	Willard Harrell, Pacific	1777	177.7
1974	Louie Giammona, Utah St	1984	198.4
1975	Louie Giammona, Utah St	2045	185.9
1976	Tony Dorsett, Pittsburgh	2021	183.7
1977	Earl Campbell, Texas	1855	168.6
1978	Charles White, USC	2096	174.7
1979	Charles White, USC	1941	194.1
1980	Marcus Allen, USC	1794	179.4
1981	Marcus Allen, USC	2559	232.6
1982	Carl Monroe, Utah	2036	185.1
1983	Napoleon McCallum, Navy	2385	216.8
1984	Keith Byars, Ohio St	2284	207.6
1985	Napoleon McCallum, Navy	2330	211.8
1986	Paul Palmer, Temple	2633	239.4
1987	Eric Wilkerson, Kent St	2074	188.6
1988	Barry Sanders, Oklahoma St.	3250	295.5
1989	Mike Pringle, CS-Fullerton	2690	244.6
1990	Glyn Milburn, Stanford	2222	202.0
1991	Ryan Benjamin, Pacific	2995	249.6
1992	Ryan Benjamin, Pacific	2597	236.1
1993	LeShon Johnson, Northern Ill.	2082	189.3
1994	Rashaan Salaam, Colorado	2349	213.5
1995	Troy Davis, Iowa St.	2466	224.2
1996	Troy Davis, Iowa St.	2364	214.9

Annual NCAA Division I-A Leaders (Cont.)
Total Offense

Individual championship decided on Total Yards (1937-69), and on Yards Per Game (since 1970).

Multiple winners: Johnny Bright, Bob Fenimore, Mike Maxwell and Jim McMahon (2).

Year		Plays	Yards
1937	Byron (Whizzer) White, Colorado	224	1596
1938	Davey O'Brien, TCU	291	1847
1939	Kenny Washington, UCLA	259	1370
1940	Johnny Knolla, Creighton	298	1420
1941	Bud Schwenk, Washington-MO	354	1928
1942	Frank Sinkwich, Georgia	341	2187
1943	Bob Hoernschemeyer, Indiana	355	1648
1944	Bob Fenimore, Oklahoma A&M	241	1758
1945	Bob Fenimore, Oklahoma A&M	203	1641
1946	Travis Bidwell, Auburn	339	1715
1947	Fred Enke, Arizona	329	1941
1948	Stan Heath, Nevada-Reno	233	1992
1949	Johnny Bright, Drake	275	1950
1950	Johnny Bright, Drake	320	2400
1951	Dick Kazmaier, Princeton	272	1827
1952	Ted Marchibroda, Detroit	305	1813
1953	Paul Larson, California	262	1572
1954	George Shaw, Oregon	276	1536
1955	George Welsh, Navy	203	1348
1956	John Brodie, Stanford	295	1642
1957	Bob Newman, Washington St	263	1444
1958	Dick Bass, Pacific	218	1440
1959	Dick Norman, Stanford	319	2018
1960	Billy Kilmer, UCLA	292	1889
1961	Dave Hoppmann, Iowa St	320	1638
1962	Terry Baker, Oregon St	318	2276
1963	George Mira, Miami-FL	394	2318
1964	Jerry Rhome, Tulsa	470	3128
1965	Bill Anderson, Tulsa	580	3343
1966	Virgil Carter, BYU	388	2545
1967	Sal Olivas, New Mexico St	368	2184

Year		Plays	Yards
1968	Greg Cook Cincinnati	507	3210
1969	Dennis Shaw, San Diego St	388	3197

Year		Plays	Yards	P/Gm
1970	Pat Sullivan, Auburn	333	2856	285.6
1971	Gary Huff, Florida St	386	2653	241.2
1972	Don Strock, Va. Tech	480	3170	288.2
1973	Jesse Freitas, San Diego St.	410	2901	263.7
1974	Steve Joachim, Temple	331	2227	222.7
1975	Gene Swick, Toledo	490	2706	246.0
1976	Tommy Kramer, Rice	562	3272	297.5
1977	Doug Williams, Gambling	377	3229	293.5
1978	Mike Ford, SMU	459	2957	268.8
1979	Marc Wilson, BYU	488	3580	325.5
1980	Jim McMahon, BYU	540	4627	385.6
1981	Jim McMahon, BYU	487	3458	345.8
1982	Todd Dillon, Long Beach St	585	3587	326.1
1983	Steve Young, BYU	531	4346	395.1
1984	Robbie Bosco, BYU	543	3932	327.7
1985	Jim Everett, Purdue	518	3589	326.3
1986	Mike Perez, San Jose St	425	2969	329.9
1987	Todd Santos, San Diego St.	562	3688	307.3
1988	Scott Mitchell, Utah	589	4299	390.8
1989	Andre Ware, Houston	628	4661	423.7
1990	David Klingler, Houston	704	5221	474.6
1991	Ty Detmer, BYU	478	4001	333.4
1992	Jimmy Klingler, Houston	544	3768	342.6
1993	Chris Vargas, Nevada	535	4332	393.8
1994	Mike Maxwell, Nevada	477	3498	318.0
1995	Mike Maxwell, Nevada	443	3623	402.6
1996	Josh Wallwork, Wyoming	525	4209	350.8

Passing

Individual championship decided on Completions (1937-69), on Completions Per Game (1970-78), and on Passing Efficiency rating points (since 1979).

Multiple winners: Elvis Grbac, Don Heinrich, Jim McMahon, Davey O'Brien and Don Trull (2).

Year		Cmp	Pct	TD	Yds
1937	Davey O'Brien, TCU	94	.402	–	969
1938	Davey O'Brien, TCU	93	.557	–	1457
1939	Kay Eakin, Arkansas	78	.404	–	962
1940	Billy Sewell, Wash. St	86	.494	–	1023
1941	Bud Schwenk, Wash.-MO	114	.487	–	1457
1942	Ray Evans, Kansas	101	.505	–	1117
1943	Johnny Cook, Georgia	73	.465	–	1007
1944	Paul Rickards, Pittsburgh	84	.472	–	997
1945	Al Dekdebrun, Cornell	90	.464	–	1227
1946	Travis Tidwell, Auburn	79	.500	5	943
1947	Charlie Conerly, Ole Miss	133	.571	18	1367
1948	Stan Heath, Nev-Reno	126	.568	22	2005
1949	Adrian Burk, Baylor	110	.576	14	1428
1950	Don Heinrich, Washington	134	.606	14	1846
1951	Don Klosterman, Loyola-CA	159	.505	9	1843
1952	Don Heinrich, Washington	137	.507	13	1647
1953	Bob Garrett, Stanford	118	.576	17	1637
1954	Paul Larson, California	125	.641	10	1537
1955	George Welsh, Navy	94	.627	8	1319
1956	John Brodie, Stanford	139	.579	12	1633
1957	Ken Ford, H-Simmons	115	.561	14	1254
1958	Buddy Humphrey, Baylor	112	.574	7	1316
1959	Dick Norman, Stanford	152	.578	11	1963
1960	Harold Stephens, H-Simm.	145	.566	3	1254
1961	Chon Gallegos, S. Jose St	117	.594	14	1480
1962	Don Trull, Baylor	125	.546	11	1627
1963	Don Trull, Baylor	174	.565	12	2157
1964	Jerry Rhome, Tulsa	224	.687	32	2870
1965	Bill Anderson, Tulsa	296	.582	30	3464
1966	John Eckman, Wichita St	195	.426	7	2339

Year		Cmp	Pct	TD	Yds
1967	Terry Stone, N. Mexico	160	.476	9	1946
1968	Chuck Hixson, SMU	265	.566	21	3103
1969	John Reaves, Florida	222	.561	24	2896

Year		Cmp	P/Gm	TD	Yds
1970	Sonny Sixkiller, Wash	186	18.6	15	2303
1971	Brian Sipe, S. Diego St.	196	17.8	17	2532
1972	Don Strock, Va. Tech	228	20.7	16	3243
1973	Jesse Freitas, S. Diego St.	227	20.6	21	2993
1974	Steve Bartkowski, Cal	182	16.5	12	2580
1975	Craig Penrose, S. Diego St.	198	18.0	15	2660
1976	Tommy Kramer, Rice	269	24.5	21	3317
1977	Guy Benjamin, Stanford	208	20.8	19	2521
1978	Steve Dils, Stanford	247	22.5	22	2943

Year		Cmp	TD	Yds	Rating
1979	Turk Schonert, Stanford	148	19	1922	163.0
1980	Jim McMahon, BYU	284	47	4571	176.9
1981	Jim McMahon, BYU	272	30	3555	155.0
1982	Tom Ramsey, UCLA	191	21	2824	153.5
1983	Steve Young, BYU	306	33	3902	168.5
1984	Doug Flutie, BC	233	27	3454	152.9
1985	Jim Harbaugh, Michigan	139	18	1913	163.7
1986	V. Testaverde, Miami-FL	175	26	2557	165.8
1987	Don McPherson, Syracuse	129	22	2341	164.3
1988	Timm Rosenbach, Wash. St.	199	23	2791	162.0
1989	Ty Detmer, BYU	265	32	4560	175.6
1990	Shawn Moore, Virginia	144	21	2262	160.7
1991	Elvis Grbac, Michigan	152	24	1955	169.0
1992	Elvis Grbac, Michigan	112	15	1465	154.2
1993	Trent Dilfer, Fresno St.	217	28	3276	173.1
1994	Kerry Collins, Penn St.	176	21	2679	172.9
1995	Danny Wuerffel, Florida	210	35	3266	178.4
1996	Steve Sarkisian, BYU	278	33	4027	173.6

Receptions

Championship decided on Passes Caught (1937-69), and on Catches Per Game (since 1970). Touchdown totals unavailable in 1939 and 1941-45.

Multiple winners: Neil Armstrong, Hugh Campell, Manny Hazard, Reid Mosely, Jason Phillips and Howard Twilley and Alex Van Dyke (2).

Year		No	TD	Yds
1937	Jim Benton, Arkansas	47	7	754
1938	Sam Boyd, Baylor	32	5	537
1939	Ken Kavanaugh, LSU	30	–	467
1940	Eddie Bryant, Virginia	30	2	222
1941	Hank Stanton, Arizona	50	–	820
1942	Bill Rogers, Texas A&M	39	–	432
1943	Neil Armstrong, Okla. A&M	39	–	317
1944	Reid Moseley, Georgia	32	–	506
1945	Reid Moseley, Georgia	31	–	662
1946	Neil Armstrong, Okla. A&M	32	1	479
1947	Barney Poole, Ole Miss	52	8	513
1948	Red O'Quinn, Wake Forest	39	7	605
1949	Art Weiner, N. Carolina	52	7	762
1950	Gordon Cooper, Denver	46	8	569
1951	Dewey McConnell, Wyoming	47	9	725
1952	Ed Brown, Fordham	57	6	774
1953	John Carson, Georgia	45	4	663
1954	Jim Hanifan, California	44	7	569
1955	Hank Burnine, Missouri	44	2	594
1956	Art Powell, San Jose St	40	5	583
1957	Stuart Vaughan, Utah	53	5	756
1958	Dave Hibbert, Arizona	61	4	606
1959	Chris Burford, Stanford	61	6	756
1960	Hugh Campbell, Wash. St	66	10	881
1961	Hugh Campbell, Wash. St	53	5	723
1962	Vern Burke, Oregon St	69	10	1007
1963	Lawrence Elkins, Baylor	70	8	873
1964	Howard Twilley, Tulsa	95	13	1178
1965	Howard Twilley, Tulsa	134	16	1779
1966	Glenn Meltzer, Wichita St	91	4	1115

Year		No	TD	Yds
1967	Bob Goodridge, Vanderbilt	79	6	1114
1968	Ron Sellers, Florida St	86	12	1496
1969	Jerry Hendren, Idaho	95	12	1452

Year		No	P/Gm	TD	Yds
1970	Mike Mikolayunas, Davidson	87	8.7	8	1128
1971	Tom Reynolds, San Diego St	67	6.7	7	1070
1972	Tom Forzani, Utah St	85	7.7	8	1169
1973	Jay Miller, BYU	100	9.1	8	1181
1974	D. McDonald, San Diego St	86	7.8	7	1157
1975	Bob Farnham, Brown	56	6.2	2	701
1976	Billy Ryckman, La. Tech	77	7.0	10	1382
1977	W. Tolleson, W. Carolina	73	6.6	7	1101
1978	Dave Petzke, Northern Ill	91	8.3	11	1217
1979	Rick Beasley, Appalach. St	74	6.7	12	1205
1980	Dave Young, Purdue	67	6.1	8	917
1981	Pete Harvey, N. Texas St	57	6.3	3	743
1982	Vincent White, Stanford	68	6.8	8	677
1983	Keith Edwards, Vanderbilt	97	8.8	8	909
1984	David Williams, Illinois	101	9.2	8	1278
1985	Rodney Carter, Purdue	98	8.9	4	1099
1986	Mark Templeton, L. Beach St	99	9.0	2	688
1987	Jason Phillips, Houston	99	9.0	3	875
1988	Jason Phillips, Houston	108	9.8	15	1444
1989	Manny Hazard, Houston	142	12.9	22	1689
1990	Manny Hazard, Houston	78	7.8	9	946
1991	Fred Gilbert, Houston	106	9.6	7	957
1992	Sherman Smith, Houston	103	9.4	6	923
1993	Chris Penn, Tulsa	105	9.6	12	1578
1994	Alex Van Dyke, Nevada	98	8.9	10	1246
1995	Alex Van Dyke, Nevada	129	11.7	16	1854
1996	Damond Wilkins, Nevada	114	10.4	4	1121

Scoring

Championship decided on Total Points (1937-69), and on Points Per Game (since 1970).

Multiple winners: Tom Harmon and Billy Sims (2).

Year		TD	XP	FG	Pts
1937	Byron (Whizzer) White, Colo	16	23	1	122
1938	Parker Hall, Ole Miss	11	7	0	73
1939	Tom Harmon, Michigan	14	15	1	102
1940	Tom Harmon, Michigan	16	18	1	117
1941	Bill Dudley, Virginia	18	23	1	134
1942	Bob Steuber, Missouri	18	13	0	121
1943	Steve Van Buren, LSU	14	14	0	98
1944	Glenn Davis, Army	20	0	0	120
1945	Doc Blanchard, Army	19	1	0	115
1946	Gene Roberts, Tenn-Chatt	18	9	0	117
1947	Lou Gambino, Maryland	16	0	0	96
1948	Fred Wendt, Texas Mines	20	32	0	152
1949	George Thomas, Oklahoma	19	3	0	117
1950	Bobby Reynolds, Nebraska	22	25	0	157
1951	Ollie Matson, San Francisco	21	0	0	126
1952	Jackie Parker, Miss. St.	16	24	0	120
1953	Earl Lindley, Utah St.	13	3	0	81
1954	Art Luppino, Arizona	24	22	0	166
1955	Jim Swink, TCU	20	5	0	125
1956	Clendon Thomas, Oklahoma	18	0	0	108
1957	Leon Burton, Ariz. St.	16	0	0	96
1958	Dick Bass, Pacific	18	8	0	116
1959	Pervis Atkins, N. Mexico St.	17	5	0	107
1960	Bob Gaiters, N. Mexico St.	23	7	0	145
1961	Jim Pilot, N. Mexico St.	21	12	0	138
1962	Jerry Logan, W. Texas St.	13	32	0	110
1963	Cosmo Iacavazzi, Princeton	14	0	0	84
	& Dave Casinelli, Memphis St.	14	0	0	84
1964	Brian Piccolo, Wake Forest	17	9	0	111

Year		TD	XP	FG	Pts
1965	Howard Twilley, Tulsa	16	31	0	127
1966	Ken Hebert, Houston	11	41	2	113
1967	Leroy Keyes, Purdue	19	0	0	114
1968	Jim O'Brien, Cincinnati	12	31	13	142
1969	Steve Owens, Oklahoma	23	0	0	138

Year		TD	XP	FG	Pts	P/Gm
1970	Brian Bream, Air Force	20	0	0	120	12.0
	& Gary Kosins, Dayton	18	0	0	108	12.0
1971	Ed Marinaro, Cornell	24	4	0	148	16.4
1972	Harold Henson, Ohio St	20	0	0	120	12.0
1973	Jim Jennings, Rutgers	21	2	0	128	11.6
1974	Bill Marek, Wisconsin	19	0	0	114	12.7
1975	Pete Johnson, Ohio St	25	0	0	150	13.6
1976	Tony Dorsett, Pitt	22	2	0	134	12.2
1977	Earl Campbell, Texas	19	0	0	114	10.4
1978	Billy Sims, Oklahoma	20	0	0	120	10.9
1979	Billy Sims, Oklahoma	22	0	0	132	12.0
1980	Sammy Winder, So. Miss	20	0	0	120	10.9
1981	Marcus Allen, USC	23	0	0	138	12.5
1982	Greg Allen, Fla. St	21	0	0	126	11.5
1983	Mike Rozier, Nebraska	29	0	0	174	14.5
1984	Keith Byars, Ohio St	24	0	0	144	13.1
1985	Bernard White, B. Green	19	0	0	114	10.4
1986	Steve Bartalo, Colo. St	19	0	0	114	10.4
1987	Paul Hewitt, S. Diego St.	24	0	0	144	12.0
1988	Barry Sanders, Okla.St.	39	0	0	234	21.3
1989	Anthony Thompson, Ind	25	4	0	154	14.0
1990	Stacey Robinson, No. Ill	19	6	0	120	10.9

Year		TD	XP	FG	Pts	P/Gm	Year		TD	XP	FG	Pts	P/Gm
1991	Marshall Faulk, S.D. St.	23	2	0	140	15.6	1994	Rashaan Salaam, Colo	24	0	0	144	13.1
1992	Garrison Hearst, Georgia	21	0	0	126	11.5	1995	Eddie George, Ohio St.	24	0	0	144	12.0
1993	Bam Morris, Texas Tech	22	2	0	134	12.2	1996	Corey Dillon, Washington	23	0	0	138	12.6

All-Time NCAA Division I-A Leaders

Through the 1996 regular season. The NCAA does not recognize active players among career Per Game leaders.

CAREER

Passing
(Minimum 500 Completions)

Passing Efficiency	Years	Rating
1 Danny Wuerffel, Florida	1993-96	163.6
2 Ty Detmer, BYU	1988-91	162.7
3 Steve Sarkisian, BYU	1995-96	162.0
4 Billy Blanton, S.D. St.	1993-96	157.1
5 Jim McMahon, BYU	1977-78, 80-81	156.9

Yards Gained	Years	Yards
1 Ty Detmer, BYU	1988-91	15,031
2 Todd Santos, San Diego St	1984-87	11,425
3 Eric Zeier, Georgia	1991-94	11,153
4 Alex Van Pelt, Pittsburgh	1989-92	10,913
5 Danny Wuerffel, Florida	1993-96	10,875

Completions	Years	No
1 Ty Detmer, BYU	1988-91	958
2 Todd Santos, San Diego St	1984-87	910
3 Brian McClure, Bowling Green	1982-85	900
4 Erik Wilhelm, Oregon St.	1985-88	870
5 Alex Van Pelt, Pittsburgh	1989-92	845

Rushing

Yards Gained	Years	Yards
1 Tony Dorsett, Pittsburgh	1973-76	6082
2 Charles White, USC	1976-79	5598
3 Herschel Walker, Georgia	1980-82	5259
4 Archie Griffin, Ohio St.	1972-75	5177
5 Darren Lewis, Texas A&M	1987-90	5012

Yards Per Game	Years	Yards	P/Gm
1 Ed Marinaro, Cornell	1969-71	4715	174.6
2 O.J. Simpson, USC	1967-68	3124	164.4
3 Herschel Walker, Georgia	1980-82	5259	159.4
4 LeShon Johnson, No. Ill.	1992-93	3314	150.6
5 Marshall Faulk, S. Diego St.	1991-93	4589	148.0

Receptions

Catches	Years	No
1 Aaron Turner, Pacific	1989-92	266
2 Chad Mackey, La. Tech	1993-96	264
3 Terance Mathis, New Mexico	1985-87, 89	263
4 Mark Templeton, Long Beach St	1983-86	262
5 Howard Twilley, Tulsa	1963-65	261

Catches Per Game	Years	No	P/Gm
1 Manny Hazard, Houston	1989-90	220	10.5
2 Alex Van Dyke, Nevada	1994-95	227	10.3
3 Howard Twilley, Tulsa	1963-65	261	10.0
4 Jason Phillips, Houston	1987-88	207	9.4
5 Bryan Reeves, Nevada	1991-93	234	7.6

Yards Gained	Years	No	Yards
1 Marcus Harris, Wyoming	1993-96	259	4518
2 Ryan Yarborough, Wyoming	1990-93	229	4357
3 Aaron Turner, Pacific	1989-92	266	4345
4 Terance Mathis, N. Mexico	1985-87, 89	263	4254
5 Chad Mackey, La. Tech	1993-96	264	3789

Total Offense

Yards Gained	Years	Yards
1 Ty Detmer, BYU	1988-91	14,665
2 Doug Flutie, Boston College	1981-84	11,317
3 Eric Zeier, Georgia	1991-94	10,841
4 Alex Van Pelt, Pittsburgh	1989-92	10,814
5 Stoney Case, New Mexico	1991-94	10,651

Yards Per Game	Years	Yards	P/Gm
1 Chris Vargas, Nevada	1992-93	6,417	320.9
2 Ty Detmer, BYU	1988-91	14,665	318.8
3 Mike Perez, San Jose St	1986-87	6,182	309.1
4 Josh Wallwork, Wyoming	1995-96	6,753	307.0
5 Doug Gaynor, L. Beach St	1984-85	6,710	305.0

All-Purpose Yardage

Yards Gained	Years	Yards
1 Napoleon McCallum, Navy	1981-85	7172
2 Darrin Nelson, Stanford	1977-78, 80-81	6885
3 Terance Mathis, N. Mexico	1985-87, 89	6691
4 Tony Dorsett, Pittsburgh	1973-76	6615
5 Paul Palmer, Temple	1983-86	6609

Yards Per Game	Years	Yards	P/Gm
1 Ryan Benjamin, Pacific	1990-92	5706	237.8
2 Sheldon Canley, S. Jose St.	1988-90	5146	205.8
3 Howard Stevens, Louisville	1971-72	3873	193.7
4 O.J. Simpson, USC	1967-68	3666	192.9
5 Ed Marinaro, Cornell	1969-71	4940	183.0

Miscellaneous

Interceptions	Years	No
1 Al Brosky, Illinois	1950-52	29
2 John Provost, Holy Cross	1972-74	27
Martin Bayless, Bowling Green	1980-83	27
4 Tom Curtis, Michigan	1967-69	25
Tony Thurman, Boston College	1981-84	25
Tracy Saul, Texas Tech.	1989-92	25

Punting Average*	Years	Avg
1 Todd Sauerbrun, West Va.	1991-94	46.3
2 Reggie Roby, Iowa	1979-82	45.6
3 Greg Montgomery, Mich. St	1985-87	45.4
4 Tom Tupa, Ohio St.	1984-87	45.2
5 Barry Helton, Colorado	1984-87	44.9

*At least 150 punts kicked.

Punt Return Average*	Years	Avg
1 Jack Mitchell, Oklahoma	1946-48	23.6
2 Gene Gibson, Cincinnati	1949-50	20.5
3 Eddie Macon, Pacific	1949-51	18.9
4 Jackie Robinson, UCLA	1939-40	18.8
Two tied at 17.7 each.		

*Minimum 1.2 punt returns per game and 30 career returns.

Kickoff Return Average*	Years	Avg
1 Anthony Davis, USC	1972-74	35.1
2 Overton Curtis, Utah St	1957-58	31.0
3 Fred Montgomery, New Mexico St.	1991-92	30.5
4 Allie Taylor, Utah St.	1966-68	29.3
5 Two tied at 28.8 each		

*Minimum 1.2 kickoff returns per game and 30 career returns.

Scoring
Non-kickers

Points		Years	TD	Xpt	FG	Pts
1	Anthony Thompson, Ind	1986-89	65	4	0	394
2	Marshall Faulk, S.D. St.	1991-93	62	4	0	376
3	Tony Dorsett, Pittsburgh	1973-76	59	2	0	356
4	Glenn Davis, Army	1943-46	59	0	0	354
5	Art Luppino, Arizona	1953-56	48	49	0	337

Points Per Game		Years	Pts	P/Gm
1	Marshall Faulk, S. Diego St.	1991-93	376	12.1
2	Ed Marinaro, Cornell	1969-71	318	11.8
3	Bill Burnett, Arkansas	1968-70	294	11.3
4	Steve Owens, Oklahoma	1967-69	336	11.2
5	Eddie Talboom, Wyoming	1948-50	303	10.8

Touchdowns Rushing		Years	No
1	Anthony Thompson, Indiana	1986-89	64
2	Marshall Faulk, S. Diego St.	1991-93	57
3	Steve Owens, Oklahoma	1967-69	56
4	Tony Dorsett, Pittsburgh	1973-76	55
5	Pete Johnson, Ohio St.	1973-76	51

Touchdowns Passing		Years	No
1	Ty Detmer, BYU	1988-91	121
2	Danny Wuerffel, Florida	1993-96	114
3	David Klingler, Houston	1988-91	91
4	Troy Kopp, Pacific	1989-92	87
5	Jim McMahon, BYU	1977-78, 80-81	84

Touchdown Catches		Years	No
1	Aaron Turner, Pacific	1989-92	43
2	Ryan Yarborough, Wyoming	1990-93	42
3	Clarkston Hines, Duke	1986-89	38
	Marcus Harris, Wyoming	1993-96	38
5	Terance Mathis, N. Mexico	1985-87, 89	36

Kickers

Points		Years	FG	XP	Pts
1	Roman Anderson, Hou	1988-91	70	213	423
2	Carlos Huerta, Mia-Fl	1988-91	73	178	397
3	Jason Elam, Hawaii	1988-89, 91-92	79	158	395
4	Derek Schmidt, Fla. St	1984-87	73	174	393
5	Luis Zendejas, Ariz. St	1981-84	78	134	368
6	Jeff Jaeger, Wash	1983-86	80	118	358
7	John Lee, UCLA	1982-85	79	116	353
	Max Zendejas, Arizona	1982-85	77	122	353
	Kevin Butler, Georgia	1981-84	77	122	353
10	Derek Mahoney, Fresno St	1990-93	45	216	351

Field Goals		Years	No
1	Jeff Jaeger, Washington	1983-86	80
2	John Lee, UCLA	1982-85	79
	Jason Elam, Hawaii	1988-89, 91-92	79
4	Philip Doyle, Alabama	1987-90	78
	Luis Zendejas, Arizona St	1981-84	78

SINGLE SEASON

Rushing

Yards Gained	Year	Gm	Car	Yards
Barry Sanders, Okla. St	1988	11	344	2628
Marcus Allen, USC	1981	11	403	2342
Troy Davis, Iowa St.	1996	11	402	2185
Mike Rozier, Nebraska	1983	12	275	2148

Yards Per Game	Year	Gm	Yards	P/Gm
Barry Sanders, Okla. St	1988	11	2628	238.9
Marcus Allen, USC	1981	11	2342	212.9
Ed Marinaro, Cornell	1971	9	1881	209.0
Troy Davis, Iowa St.	1996	11	2185	198.6

Total Offense

Yards Gained	Year	Gm	Plays	Yards
David Klingler, Houston	1990	11	704	5221
Ty Detmer, BYU	1990	12	635	5022
Andre Ware, Houston	1989	11	628	4661
Jim McMahon, BYU	1980	12	540	4627

Yards Per Game	Year	Gm	Yards	P/Gm
David Klingler, Houston	1990	11	5221	474.6
Andre Ware, Houston	1989	11	4661	423.7
Ty Detmer, BYU	1990	12	5022	418.5
Mike Maxwell, Nevada	1995	9	3623	402.6

All-Purpose Yardage

Yards Gained	Year	Yards
Barry Sanders, Okla. St	1988	3250
Ryan Benjamin, Pacific	1991	2995
Mike Pringle, CS-Fullerton	1989	2690
Paul Palmer, Temple	1986	2633

Yards Per Game	Year	Yards	P/Gm
Barry Sanders, Okla. St	1988	3250	295.5
Ryan Benjamin, Pacific	1991	2995	249.6
Byron (Whizzer) White, Colo	1937	1970	246.3
Mike Pringle, CS-Fullerton	1989	2690	244.6

Passing
(Minimum 15 Attempts Per Game)

Passing Efficiency	Year	Rating
Jim McMahon, BYU	1980	176.9
Ty Detmer, BYU	1989	175.6
Steve Sarkisian, BYU	1996	173.6
Trent Dilfer, Fresno St.	1993	173.1

Yards Gained	Year	Yards
Ty Detmer, BYU	1990	5188
David Klingler, Houston	1990	5140
Andre Ware, Houston	1989	4699
Jim McMahon, BYU	1980	4571

Completions	Year	Att	No
David Klingler, Houston	1990	643	374
Andre Ware, Houston	1989	578	365
Ty Detmer, BYU	1990	562	361
Robbie Bosco, BYU	1985	511	338

Receptions

Catches	Year	Gm	No
Manny Hazard, Houston	1989	11	142
Howard Twilley, Tulsa	1965	10	134
Alex Van Dyke, Nevada	1995	11	129
Damond Wilkins, Nevada	1996	11	114

Catches Per Game	Year	No	P/Gm
Howard Twilley, Tulsa	1965	134	13.4
Manny Hazard, Houston	1989	142	12.9
Alex Van Dyke, Nevada	1995	129	11.7
Damond Wilkins, Nevada	1996	114	10.4

Yards Gained	Year	No	Yards
Alex Van Dyke, Nevada	1995	129	1854
Howard Twilley, Tulsa	1965	134	1779
Manny Hazard, Houston	1989	142	1689
Marcus Harris, Wyoming	1996	109	1650

COLLEGE FOOTBALL

All-Time NCAA Division I-A Leaders (Cont.)
Scoring

Points	Year	TD	Xpt	FG	Pts
Barry Sanders, Okla. St	1988	39	0	0	234
Mike Rozier, Nebraska	1983	29	0	0	174
Lydell Mitchell, Penn St	1971	29	0	0	174
Art Luppino, Arizona	1954	24	22	0	166

Points Per Game	Year	Pts	P/Gm
Barry Sanders, Okla. St	1988	234	21.3
Bobby Reynolds, Nebraska	1950	157	17.4
Art Luppino, Arizona	1954	166	16.6
Ed Marinaro, Cornell	1971	148	16.4

Touchdowns Rushing	Year	No
Barry Sanders, Okla. St	1988	37
Mike Rozier, Nebraska	1983	29
Ed Marinaro, Cornell	1971	24
Anthony Thompson, Indiana	1988	24
Anthony Thompson, Indiana	1989	24
Rashaan Salaam, Colorado	1994	24

Touchdowns Passing	Year	No
David Klingler, Houston	1990	54
Jim McMahon, BYU	1980	47
Andre Ware, Houston	1989	46
Ty Detmer, BYU	1990	41

Touchdown Catches	Year	No
Manny Hazard, Houston	1989	22
Desmond Howard, Michigan	1991	19
Tom Reynolds, San Diego St	1969	18
Dennis Smith, Utah	1989	18
Aaron Turner, Pacific	1991	18

Field Goals	Year	No
John Lee, UCLA	1984	29
Paul Woodside, West Virginia	1982	28
Luis Zendejas, Arizona St	1983	28
Fuad Reveiz, Tennessee	1982	27
Three tied with 25 each.		

Miscellaneous

Interceptions	Year	No
Al Worley, Washington	1968	14
George Shaw, Oregon	1951	13
Eight tied with 12 each.		

Punting Average*	Year	Avg
Reggie Roby, Iowa	1981	49.8
Kirk Wilson, UCLA	1956	49.3
Todd Sauerbrun, West Virginia	1984	48.4
Zack Jordan, Colorado	1950	48.2
Ricky Anderson, Vanderbilt	1984	48.2

*Qualifiers for championship.

Punt Return Average*	Year	Avg
Bill Blackstock, Tennessee	1951	25.9
George Sims, Baylor	1948	25.0
Gene Derricotte, Michigan	1947	24.8

*At least 1.2 returns per game.

Kickoff Return Average*	Year	Avg
Paul Allen, BYU	1961	40.1
Tremain March, Miami-FL	1996	39.5
Leeland McElroy, Texas A&M	1993	39.3

*At least 1.2 kickoff returns per game.

SINGLE GAME
Rushing

Yards Gained	Opponent	Year	Yds
Tony Sands, Kansas	Missouri	1991	396
Marshall Faulk, San Diego St	Pacific	1991	386
Troy Davis, Iowa St.	Missouri	1996	378
Anthony Thompson, Indiana	Wisconsin	1989	377
Rueben Mayes, Wash. St	Oregon	1984	357

Passing

Yards Gained	Opponent	Year	Yds
David Klingler, Houston	Arizona St.	1990	716
Matt Vogler, TCU	Houston	1990	690
Scott Mitchell, Utah	Air Force	1988	631
Jeremy Leach, New Mexico	Utah	1989	622
Dave Wilson, Illinois	Ohio St.	1980	621

Completions	Opponent	Year	No
Rusty LaRue, Wake Forest	Duke	1995	55
David Klingler, Houston	SMU	1990	48
Jimmy Klingler, Houston	Rice	1992	46
Sandy Schwab, Northwestern	Michigan	1982	45

Total Offense

Yards Gained	Opponent	Year	Yds
David Klingler, Houston	Arizona St.	1990	732
Matt Vogler, TCU	Houston	1990	696
David Klingler, Houston	TCU	1990	625
Scott Mitchell, Utah	Air Force	1988	625
Jimmy Klingler, Houston	Rice	1992	612

Receptions

Catches	Opponent	Year	No
Randy Gatewood, UNLV	Idaho	1994	23
Jay Miller, BYU	New Mexico	1973	22
Rick Eber, Tulsa	Idaho St.	1967	20
Howard Twilley, Tulsa	Colo. St.	1965	19

Yards Gained	Opponent	Year	Yds
Randy Gatewood, UNLV	Idaho	1994	363
Chuck Hughes, UTEP*	N. Texas St.	1965	349
Rick Eber, Tulsa	Idaho St.	1967	322
Harry Wood, Tulsa	Idaho St.	1967	318

*UTEP was Texas Western in 1965.

Scoring

Points	Opponent	Year	Pts
Howard Griffith, Illinois	So. Ill.	1990	48
Marshall Faulk, S. Diego St	Pacific	1991	44
Jim Brown, Syracuse	Colgate	1956	43
Showboat Boykin, Ole Miss	Miss. St.	1951	42
Fred Wendt, UTEP*	N. Mex. St.	1948	42

*UTEP was Texas Mines in 1948.

Touchdowns Rushing	Opponent	Year	No
Howard Griffith, Illinois	So. Ill	1990	8
Showboat Boykin, Ole Miss	Miss. St.	1951	7

Note: Griffith's TD runs (5-51-7-41-5-18-5-3).

Touchdowns Passing	Opponent	Year	No
David Klingler, Houston	E. Wash.	1990	11
Dennis Shaw, S. Diego St	N. Mex. St.	1969	9

Note: Klingler's TD passes (5-48-29-7-3-7-40-8-7-8-51).

Touchdown Catches	Opponent	Year	No
Tim Delaney, S. Diego St	N. Mex. St.	1969	6

Note: Delaney's TD catches (2-22-34-31-30-9).

Field Goals	Opponent	Year	No
Dale Klein, Nebraska	Missouri	1985	7
Mike Prindle, W. Mich	Marshall	1984	7

Note: Klein's FGs (32-22-43-44-29-43-43); Prindle's FGs (32-44-42-23-48-41-27).

Extra Points (Kick)	Opponent	Year	No
Terry Leiweke, Houston	Tulsa	1968	13
Derek Mahoney, Fresno St	New Mexico	1991	13

Longest Plays (since 1941)

Rushing	Opponent	Year	Yds
Gale Sayers, Kansas	Nebraska	1963	99
Max Anderson, Ariz. St	Wyoming	1967	99
Ralph Thompson, W. Texas St	Wich. St.	1970	99
Kelsey Finch, Tennessee	Florida	1977	99
Eleven tied at 98 each.			

Passing	Opponent	Year	Yds
Fred Owens			
to Jack Ford, Portland	St. Mary's	1947	99
Bo Burris			
to Warren McVea, Houston	Wash. St.	1966	99
Colin Clapton			
to Eddie Jenkins, Holy Cross	Boston U.	1970	99
Terry Peel			
to Robert Ford, Houston	Syracuse	1970	99

Passing	Opponent	Year	Yds
Terry Peel			
to Robert Ford, Houston	S. Diego St.	1972	99
Cris Collinsworth			
to Derrick Gaffney, Florida	Rice	1977	99
Scott Ankrom			
to James Maness, TCU	Rice	1984	99
Gino Torretta			
to Horace Copeland, Miami-FL	Ark.	1991	99
John Paci to			
Thomas Lewis, Indiana	Penn St.	1993	99

Field Goals	Opponent	Year	Yds
Steve Little, Arkansas	Texas	1977	67
Russell Erxleben, Texas	Rice	1977	67
Joe Williams, Wichita St	So. Ill.	1978	67

Annual Awards
Heisman Trophy

Originally presented in 1935 as the DAC Trophy by the Downtown Athletic Club of New York City to the best college football player east of the Mississippi. In 1936, players across the country were eligible and the award was renamed the Heisman Trophy following the death of former college coach and DAC athletic director John W. Heisman.

Multiple winner: Archie Griffin (2).

Winners in junior year (12): Doc Blanchard (1945), Ty Detmer (1990); Archie Griffin (1974), Desmond Howard (1991), Vic Janowicz (1950), Rashaan Salaam (1994), Barry Sanders (1988), Billy Sims (1978), Roger Staubach (1963), Doak Walker (1948), Herschel Walker (1982), Andre Ware (1989).

Winners on AP national champions (9): Angelo Bertelli (Notre Dame, 1943); Doc Blanchard (Army, 1945); Tony Dorsett (Pittsburgh, 1976); Leon Hart (Notre Dame, 1949); Johnny Lujack (Notre Dame, 1947); Davey O'Brien (TCU, 1938); Bruce Smith (Minnesota, 1941); Charlie Ward (Florida St., 1993); Danny Wuerffel (Florida, 1996).

Year		Points
1935	**Jay Berwanger,** Chicago, HB	84
	2nd–Monk Meyer, Army, HB	29
	3rd–Bill Shakespeare, Notre Dame, HB	23
	4th–Pepper Constable, Princeton, FB	20
1936	**Larry Kelley,** Yale, E	219
	2nd–Sam Francis, Nebraska, FB	47
	3rd–Ray Buivid, Marquette, HB	43
	4th–Sammy Baugh, TCU, HB	39
1937	**Clint Frank,** Yale, HB	524
	2nd–Byron (Whizzer) White, Colo., HB	264
	3rd–Marshall Goldberg, Pitt, HB	211
	4th–Alex Wojciechowicz, Fordham, C	85
1938	**Davey O'Brien,** TCU, QB	519
	2nd–Marshall Goldberg, Pitt, HB	294
	3rd–Sid Luckman, Columbia, QB	154
	4th–Bob MacLeod, Dartmouth, HB	78
1939	**Nile Kinnick,** Iowa, HB	651
	2nd–Tom Harmon, Michigan, HB	405
	3rd–Paul Christman, Missouri, QB	391
	4th–George Cafego, Tennessee, HB	296
1940	**Tom Harmon,** Michigan, HB	1303
	2nd–John Kimbrough, Texas A&M, FB	841
	3rd–George Franck, Minnesota, HB	102
	4th–Frankie Albert, Stanford, QB	90
1941	**Bruce Smith,** Minnesota, HB	554
	2nd–Angelo Bertelli, N. Dame, QB	345
	3rd–Frankie Albert, Stanford, QB	336
	4th–Frank Sinkwich, Georgia, HB	249
1942	**Frank Sinkwich,** Georgia, TB	1059
	2nd–Paul Governali, Columbia, QB	218
	3rd–Clint Castleberry, Ga. Tech, HB	99
	4th–Mike Holovak, Boston College, FB	95
1943	**Angelo Bertelli,** Notre Dame, QB	648
	2nd–Bob Odell, Penn, HB	177
	3rd–Otto Graham, Northwestern, QB	140
	4th–Creighton Miller, Notre Dame, HB	134
1944	**Les Horvath,** Ohio St., TB-QB	412
	2nd–Glenn Davis, Army, HB	287
	3rd–Doc Blanchard, Army, FB	237
	4th–Don Whitmire, Navy, T	115

Year		Points
1945	**Doc Blanchard,** Army, FB	860
	2nd–Glenn Davis, Army, HB	638
	3rd–Bob Fenimore, Oklahoma A&M, HB	187
	4th–Herman Wedemeyer, St. Mary's, HB	152
1946	**Glenn Davis,** Army, HB	792
	2nd–Charlie Trippi, Georgia, HB	435
	3rd–Johnny Lujack, Notre Dame, QB	379
	4th–Doc Blanchard, Army, FB	267
1947	**Johnny Lujack,** Notre Dame, QB	742
	2nd–Bob Chappuis, Michigan, HB	555
	3rd–Doak Walker, SMU, HB	196
	4th–Charlie Conerly, Mississippi, QB	186
1948	**Doak Walker,** SMU, HB	778
	2nd–Charlie Justice, N. Carolina, HB	443
	3rd–Chuck Bednarik, Penn, C	336
	4th–Jackie Jensen, California, HB	143
1949	**Leon Hart,** Notre Dame, E	995
	2nd–Charlie Justice, N. Carolina, HB	272
	3rd–Doak Walker, SMU, HB	229
	4th–Arnold Galiffa, Army QB	196
1950	**Vic Janowicz,** Ohio St., HB	633
	2nd–Kyle Rote, SMU, HB	280
	3rd–Reds Bagnell, Penn, HB	231
	4th–Babe Parilli, Kentucky, QB	214
1951	**Dick Kazmaier,** Princeton, TB	1777
	2nd–Hank Lauricella, Tennessee, HB	424
	3rd–Babe Parilli, Kentucky, HB	344
	4th–Bill McColl, Stanford, E	313
1952	**Billy Vessels,** Oklahoma, HB	525
	2nd–Jack Scarbath, Maryland, QB	367
	3rd–Paul Giel, Minnesota, HB	329
	4th–Donn Moomaw, UCLA, C	257
1953	**Johnny Lattner,** Notre Dame, HB	1850
	2nd–Paul Giel, Minnesota, HB	1794
	3rd–Paul Cameron, UCLA, HB	444
	4th–Bernie Faloney, Maryland, QB	258
1954	**Alan Ameche,** Wisconsin, FB	1068
	2nd–Kurt Burris, Oklahoma, C	838
	3rd–Howard Cassady, Ohio St., HB	810
	4th–Ralph Guglielmi, Notre Dame, QB	691

Annual Awards (Cont.)

Year		
1955	**Howard Cassady,** Ohio St., HB	2219
	2nd–Jim Swink, TCU, HB	742
	3rd–George Welsh, Navy, QB	383
	4th–Earl Morrall, Michigan St., QB	323
1956	**Paul Hornung,** Notre Dame, QB	1066
	2nd–Johnny Majors, Tennessee, HB	994
	3rd–Tommy McDonald, Oklahoma, HB	973
	4th–Jerry Tubbs, Oklahoma, C	724
1957	**John David Crow,** Texas A&M, HB	1183
	2nd–Alex Karras, Iowa, T	693
	3rd–Walt Kowalczyk, Mich. St., HB	630
	4th–Lou Michaels, Kentucky, T	330
1958	**Pete Dawkins,** Army, HB	1394
	2nd–Randy Duncan, Iowa, QB	1021
	3rd–Billy Cannon, LSU, HB	975
	4th–Bob White, Ohio St., FB	365
1959	**Billy Cannon,** LSU, HB	1929
	2nd–Richie Lucas, Penn St., QB	613
	3rd–Don Meredith, SMU, QB	286
	4th–Bill Burrell, Illinois, G	196
1960	**Joe Bellino,** Navy, HB	1793
	2nd–Tom Brown, Minnesota, G	731
	3rd–Jake Gibbs, Mississippi, QB	453
	4th–Ed Dyas, Auburn, HB	319
1961	**Ernie Davis,** Syracuse, HB	824
	2nd–Bob Ferguson, Ohio St., HB	771
	3rd–Jimmy Saxton, Texas, HB	551
	4th–Sandy Stephens, Minnesota, QB	543
1962	**Terry Baker,** Oregon St., QB	707
	2nd–Jerry Stovall, LSU, HB	618
	3rd–Bobby Bell, Minnesota, T	429
	4th–Lee Roy Jordan, Alabama, C	321
1963	**Roger Staubach,** Navy, QB	1860
	2nd–Billy Lothridge, Ga. Tech, QB	504
	3rd–Sherman Lewis, Mich. St., HB	369
	4th–Don Trull, Baylor, QB	253
1964	**John Huarte,** Notre Dame, QB	1026
	2nd–Jerry Rhome, Tulsa, QB	952
	3rd–Dick Butkus, Illinois, C	505
	4th–Bob Timberlake, Michigan, QB	361
1965	**Mike Garrett,** USC, HB	926
	2nd–Howard Twilley, Tulsa, E	528
	3rd–Jim Grabowski, Illinois, FB	481
	4th–Donny Anderson, Texas Tech, HB	408
1966	**Steve Spurrier,** Florida, QB	1679
	2nd–Bob Griese, Purdue, QB	816
	3rd–Nick Eddy, Notre Dame, HB	456
	4th–Gary Beban, UCLA, QB	318
1967	**Gary Beban,** UCLA, QB	1968
	2nd–O.J. Simpson, USC, HB	1722
	3rd–Leroy Keyes, Purdue, HB	1366
	4th–Larry Csonka, Syracuse, FB	136
1968	**O.J. Simpson,** USC, HB	2853
	2nd–Leroy Keyes, Purdue, HB	1103
	3rd–Terry Hanratty, Notre Dame, QB	387
	4th–Ted Kwalick, Penn St., TE	254
1969	**Steve Owens,** Oklahoma, HB	1488
	2nd–Mike Phipps, Purdue, QB	1344
	3rd–Rex Kern, Ohio St., QB	856
	4th–Archie Manning, Mississippi, QB	582
1970	**Jim Plunkett,** Stanford, QB	2229
	2nd–Joe Theismann, Notre Dame, QB	1410
	3rd–Archie Manning, Mississippi, QB	849
	4th–Steve Worster, Texas, RB	398
1971	**Pat Sullivan,** Auburn, QB	1597
	2nd–Ed Marinaro, Cornell, RB	1445
	3rd–Greg Pruitt, Oklahoma, RB	586
	4th–Johnny Musso, Alabama, RB	365
1972	**Johnny Rodgers,** Nebraska, FL	1310
	2nd–Greg Pruitt, Oklahoma, RB	966
	3rd–Rich Glover, Nebraska, MG	652
	4th–Bert Jones, LSU, QB	351

Year		
1973	**John Cappelletti,** Penn St., RB	1057
	2nd–John Hicks, Ohio St., OT	524
	3rd–Roosevelt Leaks, Texas, RB	482
	4th–David Jaynes, Kansas, QB	394
1974	**Archie Griffin,** Ohio St., RB	1920
	2nd–Anthony Davis, USC, RB	819
	3rd–Joe Washington, Oklahoma, RB	661
	4th–Tom Clements, Notre Dame, QB	244
1975	**Archie Griffin,** Ohio St., RB	1800
	2nd–Chuck Muncie, California, RB	730
	3rd–Ricky Bell, USC, RB	708
	4th–Tony Dorsett, Pitt, RB	616
1976	**Tony Dorsett,** Pittsburgh, RB	2357
	2nd–Ricky Bell, USC, RB	1346
	3rd–Rob Lytle, Michigan, RB	413
	4th–Terry Miller, Oklahoma St., RB	197
1977	**Earl Campbell,** Texas, RB	1547
	2nd–Terry Miller, Oklahoma, RB	812
	3rd–Ken MacAfee, Notre Dame, TE	343
	4th–Doug Williams, Grambling, QB	266
1978	**Billy Sims,** Oklahoma, RB	827
	2nd–Chuck Fusina, Penn St., QB	750
	3rd–Rick Leach, Michigan, QB	435
	4th–Charles White, USC, RB	354
1979	**Charles White,** USC, RB	1695
	2nd–Billy Sims, Oklahoma, RB	773
	3rd–Marc Wilson, BYU, QB	589
	4th–Art Schlichter, Ohio St., QB	251
1980	**George Rogers,** South Carolina, RB	1128
	2nd–Hugh Green, Pittsburgh, DE	861
	3rd–Herschel Walker, Georgia, RB	683
	4th–Mark Herrmann, Purdue, QB	405
1981	**Marcus Allen,** USC, RB	1797
	2nd–Herschel Walker, Georgia, RB	1199
	3rd–Jim McMahon, BYU, QB	706
	4th–Dan Marino, Pitt, QB	256
1982	**Herschel Walker,** Georgia, RB	1926
	2nd–John Elway, Stanford, QB	1231
	3rd–Eric Dickerson, SMU, RB	465
	4th–Anthony Carter, Michigan, WR	142
1983	**Mike Rozier,** Nebraska, RB	1801
	2nd–Steve Young, BYU, QB	1172
	3rd–Doug Flutie, Boston College, QB	253
	4th–Turner Gill, Nebraska, QB	190
1984	**Doug Flutie,** Boston College, QB	2240
	2nd–Keith Byars, Ohio St., RB	1251
	3rd–Robbie Bosco, BYU, QB	443
	4th–Bernie Kosar, Miami-FL, QB	320
1985	**Bo Jackson,** Auburn, RB	1509
	2nd–Chuck Long, Iowa, QB	1464
	3rd–Robbie Bosco, BYU, QB	459
	4th–Lorenzo White, Michigan St., RB	391
1986	**Vinny Testaverde,** Miami-FL, QB	2213
	2nd–Paul Palmer, Temple, RB	672
	3rd–Jim Harbaugh, Michigan, QB	458
	4th–Brian Bosworth, Oklahoma, LB	395
1987	**Tim Brown,** Notre Dame, WR	1442
	2nd–Don McPherson, Syracuse, QB	831
	3rd–Gordie Lockbaum, Holy Cross, WR-DB	657
	4th–Lorenzo White, Michigan St., RB	632
1988	**Barry Sanders,** Oklahoma St., RB	1878
	2nd–Rodney Peete, USC, QB	912
	3rd–Troy Aikman, UCLA, QB	582
	4th–Steve Walsh, Miami-FL, QB	341
1989	**Andre Ware,** Houston, QB	1073
	2nd–Anthony Thompson, Ind., RB	1003
	3rd–Major Harris, West Va., QB	709
	4th–Tony Rice, Notre Dame, QB	523
1990	**Ty Detmer,** BYU, QB	1482
	2nd–Rocket Ismail, Notre Dame, FL	1177
	3rd–Eric Bieniemy, Colorado, RB	798
	4th–Shawn Moore, Virginia, QB	465

Year		
1991	**Desmond Howard,** Michigan, WR	2077
	2nd–Casey Weldon, Florida St., QB	503
	3rd–Ty Detmer, BYU, QB	445
	4th–Steve Emtman, Washington, DT	357
1992	**Gino Torretta,** Miami-FL, QB	1400
	2nd–Marshall Faulk, S. Diego St., RB	1080
	3rd–Garrison Hearst, Georgia, RB	982
	4th–Marvin Jones, Florida St., LB	392
1993	**Charlie Ward,** Florida St., QB	2310
	2nd–Heath Shuler, Tennessee, QB	688
	3rd–David Palmer, Alabama, RB	292
	4th–Marshall Faulk, S. Diego St., RB	250

Year		
1994	**Rashaan Salaam,** Colorado, RB	1743
	2nd–Ki-Jana Carter, Penn St., RB	901
	3rd–Steve McNair, Alcorn St., QB	655
	4th–Kerry Collins, Penn St., QB	639
1995	**Eddie George,** Ohio St., RB	1460
	2nd–Tommie Frazier, Nebraska, QB	1196
	3rd–Danny Wuerffel, Florida, QB	987
	4th–Darnell Autry, Northwestern, RB	535
1996	**Danny Wuerffel,** Florida, QB	1363
	2nd–Troy Davis, Iowa St., RB	1174
	3rd–Jake Plummer, Arizona St., QB	685
	4th–Orlando Pace, Ohio St., OT	599

Five Or More Heismans

Notre Dame (7)–Bertelli (1943), Brown (1987), Hart (1949), Hornung (1956), Huarte (1964), Lattner (1953) and Lujack (1947). **Ohio St.** (6)–Cassady (1955), George (1995), Griffin (1974-75), Horvath (1944) and Janowicz (1950).

Maxwell Award

First presented in 1937 by the Maxwell Memorial Football Club of Philadelphia, the award is named after Robert (Tiny) Maxwell, a Philadelphia native who was a standout lineman at the University of Chicago at the turn of the century. Like the Heisman, the Maxwell is given to the outstanding college player in the nation. Both awards have gone to the same player in the same season 32 times. Those players are preceded by (#). Glenn Davis of Army and Doak Walker of SMU won both but in different years.

Multiple winner: Johnny Lattner (2).

Year		Year		Year	
1937	#Clint Frank, Yale, HB	1958	#Pete Dawkins, Army, HB	1978	Chuck Fusina, Penn St., QB
1938	#Davey O'Brien, TCU, QB	1959	Rich Lucas, Penn St., QB	1979	#Charles White, USC, RB
1939	#Nile Kinnick, Iowa, HB				
1940	#Tom Harmon, Michigan, HB	1960	#Joe Bellino, Navy, HB	1980	Hugh Green, Pitt, DE
1941	Bill Dudley, Virginia, HB	1961	Bob Ferguson, Ohio St., HB	1981	#Marcus Allen, USC, RB
1942	Paul Governali, Columbia, QB	1962	#Terry Baker, Oregon St., QB	1982	#Herschel Walker, Georgia, RB
1943	Bob Odell, Penn, HB	1963	#Roger Staubach, Navy, QB	1983	#Mike Rozier, Nebraska, RB
1944	Glenn Davis, Army, HB	1964	Glenn Ressler, Penn St., G	1984	#Doug Flutie, Boston Col., QB
1945	#Doc Blanchard, Army, FB	1965	Tommy Nobis, Texas, LB	1985	Chuck Long, Iowa, QB
1946	Charley Trippi, Georgia, HB	1966	Jim Lynch, Notre Dame, LB	1986	#V. Testaverde, Miami-FL, QB
1947	Doak Walker, SMU, HB	1967	#Gary Beban, UCLA, QB	1987	Don McPherson, Syracuse, QB
1948	Chuck Bednarik, Penn, C	1968	#O.J. Simpson, USC, HB	1988	#Barry Sanders, Okla. St., RB
1949	#Leon Hart, Notre Dame, E	1969	Mike Reid, Penn St., DT	1989	Anthony Thompson, Indiana, RB
1950	Reds Bagnell, Penn, HB	1970	#Jim Plunkett, Stanford, QB	1990	#Ty Detmer, BYU, QB
1951	#Dick Kazmaier, Princeton, TB	1971	Ed Marinaro, Cornell, RB	1991	#Desmond Howard, Mich., WR
1952	Johnny Lattner, Notre Dame, HB	1972	Brad Van Pelt, Michigan St., DB	1992	#Gino Torretta, Miami-FL, QB
1953	#Johnny Lattner, N. Dame, HB	1973	#John Cappelletti, Penn St., RB	1993	#Charlie Ward, Florida St., QB
1954	Ron Beagle, Navy, E	1974	Steve Joachim, Temple, QB	1994	Kerry Collins, Penn St., QB
1955	#Howard Cassady, Ohio St., HB	1975	#Archie Griffin, Ohio St., RB	1995	#Eddie George, Ohio St., RB
1956	Tommy McDonald, Okla., HB	1976	#Tony Dorsett, Pitt, RB	1996	#Danny Wuerffel, Florida, QB
1957	Bob Reifsnyder, Navy, T	1977	Ross Browner, Notre Dame, DE		

Outland Trophy

First presented in 1946 by the Football Writers Association of America, honoring the nation's outstanding interior lineman. The award is named after its benefactor, Dr. John H. Outland (Kansas, Class of 1898). Players listed in bold type helped lead their team to a national championship (according to AP).

Multiple winner: Dave Rimington (2). **Winners in junior year:** Ross Browner (1976), Steve Emtman (1991), Orlando Pace (1996), and Rimington (1981).

Year		Year		Year	
1946	**George Connor**, N. Dame, T	1963	**Scott Appleton**, Texas, T	1980	Mark May, Pittsburgh, OT
1947	Joe Steffy, Army, G	1964	Steve DeLong, Tennessee, T	1981	Dave Rimington, Nebraska, C
1948	Bill Fischer, Notre Dame, G	1965	Tommy Nobis, Texas, G	1982	Dave Rimington, Nebraska, C
1949	Ed Bagdon, Michigan St., G	1966	Loyd Phillips, Arkansas, T	1983	Dean Steinkuhler, Nebraska, G
1950	Bob Gain, Kentucky, T	1967	**Ron Yary**, USC, T	1984	Bruce Smith, Virginia Tech, DT
1951	Jim Weatherall, Oklahoma, T	1968	Bill Stanfill, Georgia, T	1985	Mike Ruth, Boston College, NG
1952	Dick Modzelewski, Maryland, T	1969	Mike Reid, Penn St., DT	1986	Jason Buck, BYU, DT
1953	J.D. Roberts, Oklahoma, G			1987	Chad Hennings, Air Force, DT
1954	Bill Brooks, Arkansas, G	1970	Jim Stillwagon, Ohio St., MG	1988	Tracy Rocker, Auburn, DT
1955	Calvin Jones, Iowa, G	1971	**Larry Jacobson**, Neb., DT	1989	Mohammed Elewonibi, BYU, G
1956	Jim Parker, Ohio St., G	1972	Rich Glover, Nebraska, MG		
1957	Alex Karras, Iowa, T	1973	John Hicks, Ohio St., OT	1990	Russell Maryland, Miami-FL, NT
1958	Zeke Smith, Auburn, G	1974	Randy White, Maryland, DT	1991	Steve Emtman, Washington, DT
1959	Mike McGee, Duke, T	1975	**Lee Roy Selmon**, Okla., DT	1992	Will Shields, Nebraska, G
		1976	Ross Browner, Notre Dame, DE	1993	Rob Waldrop, Arizona, NG
1960	**Tom Brown**, Minnesota, G	1977	Brad Shearer, Texas, DT	1994	**Zach Wiegert**, Nebraska, OT
1961	Merlin Olsen, Utah St., T	1978	Greg Roberts, Oklahoma, G	1995	Jonathan Ogden, UCLA, OT
1962	Bobby Bell, Minnesota, T	1979	Jim Richter, N.C. State, C	1996	Orlando Pace, Ohio St., OT

Annual Awards (Cont.)
Butkus Award

First presented in 1985 by the Downtown Athletic Club of Orlando, Fla., to honor the nation's outstanding linebacker. The award is named after Dick Butkus, two-time consensus All-America at Illinois and six-time All-Pro with the Chicago Bears.
Multiple winner: Brian Bosworth (2).

Year		Year		Year	
1985	Brian Bosworth, Oklahoma	1989	Percy Snow, Michigan St.	1993	Trev Alberts, Nebraska
1986	Brian Bosworth, Oklahoma	1990	Alfred Williams, Colorado	1994	Dana Howard, Illinois
1987	Paul McGowan, Florida St.	1991	Erick Anderson, Michigan	1995	Kevin Hardy, Illinois
1988	Derrick Thomas, Alabama	1992	Marvin Jones, Florida St.	1996	Matt Russell, Colorado

Lombardi Award

First presented in 1970 by the Rotary Club of Houston, honoring the nation's best lineman. The award is named after pro football coach Vince Lombardi, who, as a guard, was a member of the famous Seven Blocks of Granite at Fordham in the 1930s. The Lombardi and Outland awards have gone to the same player in the same year ten times. Those players are preceded by (#). Ross Browner of Notre Dame won both, but in different years.
Multiple winner: Orlando Pace (2).

Year		Year		Year	
1970	#Jim Stillwagon, Ohio St., MG	1979	Brad Budde, USC, G	1988	#Tracy Rocker, Auburn, DT
1971	Walt Patulski, Notre Dame, DE	1980	Hugh Green, Pitt, DE	1989	Percy Snow, Michigan St., LB
1972	#Rich Glover, Nebraska, MG	1981	Kenneth Sims, Texas, DT	1990	Chris Zorich, Notre Dame, NT
1973	#John Hicks, Ohio St., OT	1982	#Dave Rimington, Neb., C	1991	#Steve Emtman, Wash., DT
1974	#Randy White, Maryland, DT	1983	#Dean Steinkuhler, Neb., G	1992	Marvin Jones, Florida St., LB
1975	#Lee Roy Selmon, Okla., DT	1984	Tony Degrate, Texas, DT	1993	Aaron Taylor, Notre Dame, OT
1976	Wilson Whitley, Houston, DT	1985	Tony Casillas, Oklahoma, NG	1994	Warren Sapp, Miami-FL, DT
1977	Ross Browner, Notre Dame, DE	1986	Cornelius Bennett, Alabama, LB	1995	Orlando Pace, Ohio St., OT
1978	Bruce Clark, Penn St., DT	1987	Chris Spielman, Ohio St., LB	1996	#Orlando Pace, Ohio St., OT

O'Brien Quarterback Award

First presented in 1977 as the O'Brien Memorial Trophy, the award went to the outstanding player in the Southwest. In 1981, however, the Davey O'Brien Educational and Charitable Trust of Ft. Worth renamed the prize the O'Brien National Quarterback Award and now honors the nation's best quarterback. The award is named after 1938 Heisman Trophy-winning QB Davey O'Brien of Texas Christian.
Multiple winners: Ty Detmer, Mike Singletary and Danny Wuerffel (2).

Memorial Trophy

Year		Year		Year	
1977	Earl Campbell, Texas, RB	1978	Billy Sims, Oklahoma, RB	1979	Mike Singletary, Baylor, LB
				1980	Mike Singletary, Baylor, LB

National QB Award

Year		Year		Year	
1981	Jim McMahon, BYU	1987	Don McPherson, Syracuse	1993	Charlie Ward, Florida St.
1982	Todd Blackledge, Penn St.	1988	Troy Aikman, UCLA	1994	Kerry Collins, Penn St.
1983	Steve Young, BYU	1989	Andre Ware, Houston	1995	Danny Wuerffel, Florida
1984	Doug Flutie, Boston College	1990	Ty Detmer, BYU	1996	Danny Wuerffel, Florida
1985	Chuck Long, Iowa	1991	Ty Detmer, BYU		
1986	Vinny Testaverde, Miami, FL	1992	Gino Torretta, Miami-FL		

Thorpe Award

First presented in 1986 by the Jim Thorpe Athletic Club of Oklahoma City to honor the nation's outstanding defensive back. The award is named after Jim Thorpe—Olympic champion, two-time consensus All-America HB at Carlisle.

Year		Year		Year	
1986	Thomas Everett, Baylor	1989	Mike Carrier, USC	1993	Antonio Langham, Alabama
1987	Bennie Blades, Miami-FL	1990	Darryl Lewis, Arizona	1994	Chris Hudson, Colorado
	& Rickey Dixon, Oklahoma	1991	Terrell Buckley, Florida St.	1995	Greg Myers, Colorado St.
1988	Deion Sanders, Florida St.	1992	Deon Figures, Colorado	1996	Lawrence Wright, Florida

Payton Award

First presented in 1987 by the Sports Network and Division I-AA sports information directors to honor the nation's outstanding Division I-AA player. The award is named after Walter Payton, the NFL's all-time leading rusher who was an All-America RB at Jackson St.

Year		Year		Year	
1987	Kenny Gamble, Colgate, RB	1991	Jamie Martin, Weber St., QB	1995	Dave Dickenson, Montana, QB
1988	Dave Meggett, Towson St., RB	1992	Michael Payton, Marshall, QB	1996	Archie Amerson, N. Arizona, RB
1989	John Friesz, Idaho, QB	1993	Doug Nussmeier, Idaho, QB		
1990	Walter Dean, Grambling, RB	1994	Steve McNair, Alcorn St., QB		

Hill Trophy

First presented in 1986 by the Harlon Hill Awards Committee in Florence, AL, to honor the nation's outstanding Division II player. The award is named after three-time NFL All-Pro Harlon Hill who played college ball at North Alabama.
Multiple winner: Johnny Bailey (3).

Year		Year		Year	
1986	Jeff Bentrim, N. Dakota St., QB	1990	Chris Simform, N. Dakota St. QB	1994	Chris Hatcher, Valdosta St., QB
1987	Johnny Bailey, Texas A&I, RB	1991	Ronnie West, Pittsburg St., WR	1995	Ronald McKinnon, N. Alabama, LB
1988	Johnny Bailey, Texas A&I, RB	1992	Ronald Moore, Pittsburg St., RB	1996	Jarrett Anderson, Truman St., RB
1989	Johnny Bailey, Texas A&I, RB	1993	Roger Graham, New Haven, RB		

All-Time Winningest Division I-A Coaches

Minimum of 10 years in Division I-A through 1996 season. Regular season and bowl games included. Coaches active in 1996 in **bold** type.

Top 25 Winning Percentage

		Yrs	W	L	T	Pct
1	Knute Rockne	13	105	12	5	**.881**
2	Frank Leahy	13	107	13	9	**.864**
3	George Woodruff	12	142	25	2	**.846**
4	Barry Switzer	16	157	29	4	**.837**
5	Percy Haughton	13	96	17	6	**.832**
6	**Tom Osborne**	24	242	49	3	**.829**
7	Bob Neyland	21	173	31	12	**.829**
8	Hurry Up Yost	29	196	36	12	**.828**
9	Bud Wilkinson	17	145	29	4	**.826**
10	Jock Sutherland	20	144	28	14	**.812**
11	Bob Devaney	16	136	30	7	**.806**
12	Frank Thomas	19	141	33	9	**.795**
13	**Joe Paterno**	31	289	74	3	**.794**
14	Henry Williams	23	141	34	12	**.786**
15	Gil Dobie	33	180	45	15	**.781**
16	Bear Bryant	38	323	85	17	**.780**
17	Fred Folsom	19	106	28	6	**.779**
18	Bo Schembechler	27	234	65	8	**.775**
19	**Steve Spurrier**	10	93	27	2	**.770**
20	Fritz Crisler	18	116	32	9	**.768**
21	Charley Moran	18	122	33	12	**.766**
22	Wallace Wade	24	171	49	10	**.765**
23	Frank Kush	22	176	54	1	**.764**
24	**Bobby Bowden**	31	270	82	4	**.764**
25	Dan McGugin	30	197	55	19	**.762**

Top 25 Victories

		Yrs	W	L	T	Pct
1	Bear Bryant	38	**323**	85	17	.780
2	Pop Warner	44	**319**	106	32	.733
3	Amos Alonzo Stagg	57	**314**	199	35	.605
4	**Joe Paterno**	31	**289**	74	3	.794
5	**Bobby Bowden**	31	**270**	82	4	.764
6	**Tom Osborne**	24	**242**	49	3	.829
7	Woody Hayes	33	**238**	72	10	.759
8	Bo Schembechler	27	**234**	65	8	.775
9	**LaVell Edwards**	25	**228**	81	3	.736
10	**Hayden Fry**	35	**222**	165	10	.572
11	**Lou Holtz**	27	**216**	95	7	.690
12	Jess Neely	40	**207**	176	19	.539
13	Warren Woodson	31	**203**	95	14	.673
14	Vince Dooley	25	**201**	77	10	.715
	Eddie Anderson	39	**201**	128	15	.606
16	**Jim Sweeney**	32	**200**	154	4	.564
17	Dana X. Bible	33	**198**	72	23	.715
18	Dan McGugin	30	**197**	55	19	.762
19	Hurry Up Yost	29	**196**	36	12	.828
20	Howard Jones	29	**194**	64	21	.733
21	Johnny Vaught	25	**190**	61	12	.745
22	John Heisman	36	**185**	70	17	.711
	Johnny Majors	29	**185**	137	10	.572
24	Darrell Royal	23	**184**	60	5	.749
25	Two tied at 180 wins each					

Note: Eddie Robinson of Division I-AA Grambling (1941-42, 1945–) is the all-time NCAA leader in coaching wins with a 405-157-15 record and .715 winning pct. over 54 seasons.

Where They Coached

Anderson–Loras (1922-24), DePaul (1925-31), Holy Cross (1933-38), Iowa (1939-42), Holy Cross (1950-64); **Bible**–Mississippi College (1913-15), LSU (1916), Texas A&M (1917, 1919-28), Nebraska (1929-36), Texas (1937-46); **Bowden**–Samford (1959-62), West Virginia (1970-75), Florida St. (1976–); **Bryant**–Maryland (1945), Kentucky (1946-53), Texas A&M (1954-57), Alabama (1958-82); **Crisler**–Minnesota (1930-31), Princeton (1932-37), Michigan (1938-47); **Devaney**–Wyoming (1957-61), Nebraska (1962-72); **V. Dooley**–Georgia (1964-88); **Edwards**–BYU (1972–); **Folsom**–Colorado (1895-99, 1901-02), Dartmouth (1903-06), Colorado (1908-15).

Fry–SMU (1962-72), North Texas (1973-78), Iowa (1979–); **Haughton**–Cornell (1899-1900), Harvard (1908-16), Columbia (1923-24); **Hayes**–Denison (1946-48), Miami-OH (1949-50), Ohio St. (1951-78); **Heisman**–Oberlin (1892), Akron (1893), Oberlin (1894), Auburn (1895-99), Clemson (1900-03), Georgia Tech (1904-19), Penn (1920-22), Washington & Jefferson (1923), Rice (1924-27); **Holtz**–William & Mary (1969-71), N.C. State (1972-75), Arkansas (1977-83), Minnesota (1984-85), Notre Dame (1986–); **Jones**–Syracuse (1908), Yale (1909), Ohio St. (1910), Yale (1913), Iowa (1916-23), Duke (1924), USC (1925-40); **Kush**–Arizona St. (1958-79); **Leahy**–Boston College (1939- 40), Notre Dame (1941-43, 1946-53); **Majors**–Iowa St. (1968-72), Pittsburgh (1973-76, 93–), Tennessee (1977-92); **McGugin**–Vanderbilt (1904-17, 1919-34); **Moran**–Texas A&M (1909-14), Centre (1919-23), Bucknell (1924-26), Catawba (1930-33).

Neely–Rhodes (1924-27), Clemson (1931-39), Rice (1940-66); **Neyland**–Tennessee (1926-34, 1936-40, 1946-52); **Osborne**–Nebraska (1973–); **Paterno**–Penn St. (1966–); **Rockne**–Notre Dame (1918-30); **Royal**–Mississippi St. (1954-55), Washington (1956), Texas (1957-76); **Schembechler**–Miami-OH (1963-68), Michigan (1969-89); **Spurrier**–Duke (1987-89), Florida (1990–); **Stagg**–Springfield College (1890-91), Chicago (1892-1932), Pacific (1933-46); **Sutherland**–Lafayette (1919-23), Pittsburgh (1924-38); **Sweeney**–Montana St. (1963-67), Washington St. (1968-75), Fresno St. (1976–); **Switzer**–Oklahoma (1973-88).

Thomas–Chattanooga (1925-28), Alabama (1931-42, 1944-46); **Vaught**–Mississippi (1947-70); **Wade**–Alabama (1923-30), Duke (1931-41, 1946-50); **Warner**–Georgia (1895-96), Cornell (1897-98), Carlisle (1899-1903), Cornell (1904-06), Carlisle (1907-13), Pittsburgh (1915-23), Stanford (1924-32), Temple (1933-38); **Wilkinson**–Oklahoma (1947-63); **Williams**–Army (1891), Minnesota (1900-21); **Woodruff**–Penn (1892-1901), Illinois (1903), Carlisle (1905); **Woodson**–Central Arkansas (1935-39), Hardin-Simmons (1941-42, 1946-51), Arizona (1952-56), New Mexico St. (1958-67), Trinity-TX (1972-73); **Yost**–Ohio Wesleyan (1897), Nebraska (1898), Kansas (1899), Stanford (1900), Michigan (1901-23, 1925-26).

All-Time Bowl Appearances

Coaches active in 1996 in **bold** type.

Active Coaches' Victories

(Minimum 5 years in Division I-A.)

		Overall		
		App	W	L	T

		App	W	L	T
1	Bear Bryant	29	15	12	2
2	**Joe Paterno**	27	18	8	1
3	**Tom Osborne**	24	11	13	0
4	**Bobby Bowden**	20	15	4	1
	Lou Holtz	20	10	8	2
	Vince Dooley	20	8	10	2
	LaVell Edwards	20	7	12	1
8	Johnny Vaught	18	10	8	0
9	Bo Schembechler	17	5	12	0
10	**Johnny Majors**	16	9	7	0
	Darrell Royal	16	8	7	1
	Hayden Fry	16	7	8	1
13	Don James	15	10	5	0
14	Bobby Dodd	13	9	4	0
	Terry Donahue	13	8	4	1
	Barry Switzer	13	8	5	0
	Charlie McClendon	13	7	6	0
18	Earle Bruce	12	7	5	0
	Woody Hayes	12	6	6	0
	Shug Jordan	12	5	7	0
	George Welsh	12	5	7	0

		Yrs	W	L	T	Pct
1	Joe Paterno, Penn St	31	289	74	3	.794
2	Bobby Bowden, Fla. St.	31	270	82	4	.764
3	Tom Osborne, Nebraska	24	242	49	3	.829
4	LaVell Edwards, BYU	25	228	81	3	.736
5	Hayden Fry, Iowa	35	222	165	10	.572
6	Don Nehlen, West Va	26	176	107	8	.619
7	George Welsh, Virginia	24	160	114	4	.583
8	John Cooper, Ohio St	20	157	70	6	.687
9	Jackie Sherrill, Miss. St	19	139	78	4	.638
10	Dick Tomey, Arizona	20	128	92	7	.579
11	Ken Hatfield, Rice	18	127	80	4	.611
12	Larry Smith, Missouri	20	121	102	7	.541
13	Danny Ford, Arkansas	16	118	52	5	.689
14	Dennis Franchione, N. Mex.	14	104	51	2	.669
15	Frank Beamer, Va. Tech	16	103	74	4	.580
16	John Robinson, USC	11	98	30	4	.758
	Fisher DeBerry, Air Force	13	98	60	1	.619
	Bruce Snyder, Arizona St.	17	98	86	6	.532
19	Steve Spurrier, Florida	10	93	27	2	.770
20	Mike Price, Wash. St.	16	89	91	0	.494

Note: Only four coaches— **Bill Alexander** of Georgia Tech (1920–44); **Bob Neyland** of Tennessee (1926–34, 36–40, 46–52); **Frank Thomas** of Alabama (1931–42, 44–46) and **Joe Paterno** of Penn State (1966–)— have taken teams to the Rose, Orange, Sugar and Cotton Bowls. Paterno has won all four, while Alexander and Thomas won three and Neyland two.

AFCA Coach of the Year

First presented in 1935 by the American Football Coaches Association. **Multiple winners:** Joe Paterno (4), Bear Bryant (3), John McKay and Darrell Royal (2).

Year

1935	Pappy Waldorf, Northwestern
1936	Dick Harlow, Harvard
1937	Hooks Mylin, Lafayette
1938	Bill Kern, Carnegie Tech
1939	Eddie Anderson, Iowa
1940	Clark Shaughnessy, Stanford
1941	Frank Leahy, Notre Dame
1942	Bill Alexander, Georgia Tech
1943	Amos Alonzo Stagg, Pacific
1944	Carroll Widdoes, Ohio St.
1945	Bo McMillin, Indiana
1946	Red Blaik, Army
1947	Fritz Crisler, Michigan
1948	Bennie Oosterbaan, Michigan
1949	Bud Wilkinson, Oklahoma
1950	Charlie Caldwell, Princeton
1951	Chuck Taylor, Stanford
1952	Biggie Munn, Michigan St.
1953	Jim Tatum, Maryland
1954	Red Sanders, UCLA
1955	Duffy Daugherty, Michigan St.
1956	Bowden Wyatt, Tennessee

1957	Woody Hayes, Ohio St.
1958	Paul Dietzel, LSU
1959	Ben Schwartzwalder, Syracuse
1960	Murray Warmath, Minnesota
1961	Bear Bryant, Alabama
1962	John McKay, USC
1963	Darrell Royal, Texas
1964	Frank Broyles, Arkansas & Ara Parseghian, N. Dame
1965	Tommy Prothro, UCLA
1966	Tom Cahill, Army
1967	John Pont, Indiana
1968	Joe Paterno, Penn St.
1969	Bo Schembechler, Michigan
1970	Charlie McClendon, LSU & Darrell Royal, Texas
1971	Bear Bryant, Alabama
1972	John McKay, USC
1973	Bear Bryant, Alabama
1974	Grant Teaff, Baylor
1975	Frank Kush, Arizona St.
1976	Johnny Majors, Pittsburgh

1977	Don James, Washington
1978	Joe Paterno, Penn St.
1979	Earle Bruce, Ohio St.
1980	Vince Dooley, Georgia
1981	Danny Ford, Clemson
1982	Joe Paterno, Penn St.
1983	Ken Hatfield, Air Force
1984	LaVell Edwards, BYU
1985	Fisher DeBerry, Air Force
1986	Joe Paterno, Penn St.
1987	Dick MacPherson, Syracuse
1988	Don Nehlen, West Virginia
1989	Bill McCartney, Colorado
1990	Bobby Ross, Georgia Tech
1991	Bill Lewis, East Carolina
1992	Gene Stallings, Alabama
1993	Barry Alvarez, Wisconsin
1994	Tom Osborne, Nebraska
1995	Gary Barnett, Northwestern
1996	Bruce Snyder, Arizona St.

FWAA Coach of the Year

First presented in 1957 by the Football Writers Association of America. The FWAA and AFCA awards have both gone to the same coach in the same season 27 times. Those double winners are preceded by (#).

Multiple winners: Woody Hayes and Joe Paterno (3); Lou Holtz, Johnny Majors and John McKay (2).

Year

1957	#Woody Hayes, Ohio St.
1958	#Paul Dietzel, LSU
1959	#Ben Schwartzwalder, Syracuse
1960	#Murray Warmath, Minnesota
1961	Darrell Royal, Texas
1962	#John McKay, USC
1963	#Darrell Royal, Texas
1964	#Ara Parseghian, Notre Dame
1965	Duffy Daugherty, Michigan St.
1966	#Tom Cahill, Army
1967	John Pont, Indiana
1968	Woody Hayes, Ohio St.
1969	#Bo Schembechler, Michigan
1970	Alex Agase, Northwestern

1971	Bob Devaney, Nebraska
1972	#John McKay, USC
1973	Johnny Majors, Pitt
1974	#Grant Teaff, Baylor
1975	Woody Hayes, Ohio St.
1976	#Johnny Majors, Pitt
1977	Lou Holtz, Arkansas
1978	#Joe Paterno, Penn St.
1979	#Earle Bruce, Ohio St.
1980	#Vince Dooley, Georgia
1981	#Danny Ford, Clemson
1982	#Joe Paterno, Penn St.
1983	Howard Schnellenberger, Miami-FL
1984	#LaVell Edwards, BYU

1985	#Fisher DeBerry, Air Force
1986	#Joe Paterno, Penn St.
1987	#Dick MacPherson, Syracuse
1988	Lou Holtz, Notre Dame
1989	#Bill McCartney, Colorado
1990	#Bobby Ross, Georgia Tech
1991	Don James, Washington
1992	#Gene Stallings, Alabama
1993	Terry Bowden, Auburn
1994	Rich Brooks, Oregon
1995	#Gary Barnett, Northwestern
1996	#Bruce Snyder, Arizona St.

All-Time NCAA Division I-AA Leaders
CAREER

Total Offense

Yards Gained	Years	Yards
1 Steve McNair, Alcorn St.	1991-94	16,823
2 Willie Totten, Miss. Valley	1982-85	13,007
3 Jamie Martin, Weber St.	1989-92	12,287
4 Doug Nussmeier, Idaho	1990-93	12,054
5 Neil Lomax, Portland St.	1978-80	11,647

Yards per Game	Years	Yards	P/Gm
1 Steve McNair, Alcorn St. ..	1991-94	16,823	400.5
2 Neil Lomax, Portland St. ..	1978-80	11,647	352.9
3 Dave Dickenson, Montana .	1992-95	11,523	329.2
4 Willie Totten, Miss. Valley .	1982-85	13,007	325.2
5 Tom Ehrhardt, Rhode Island ..	1984-85	6,492	309.1

Passing
(Minimum 500 Completions)

Passing Efficiency	Years	Rating
1 Shawn Knight, William & Mary	1991-94	170.8
2 Dave Dickenson, Montana	1992-95	166.3
3 Doug Nussmeier, Idaho	1990-93	154.4
4 Jay Johnson, Northern Iowa	1989-92	148.9
5 Michael Payton, Marshall	1989-92	148.2

Yards Gained	Years	Yards
1 Steve McNair, Alcorn St.	1991-94	14,496
2 Willie Totten, Miss. Valley	1982-85	12,711
3 Jamie Martin, Weber St.	1989-92	12,207
4 Neil Lomax, Portland St.	1978-80	11,550
5 Dave Dickenson, Montana	1992-95	11,080

Receiving

Catches	Years	No
1 Jerry Rice, Miss. Valley	1981-84	301
2 Kasey Dunn, Idaho	1988-91	268
3 Brian Forster, Rhode Island	1983-85,87	245
4 Mark Didio, Connecticut	1988-91	239
5 Rennie Benn, Lehigh	1982-85	237

Yards Gained	Years	No	Yards
1 Jerry Rice, Miss. Valley ..	1981-84	301	4693
2 Kasey Dunn, Idaho	1988-91	268	3847
3 Rennie Benn, Lehigh	1982-85	237	3662
4 David Rhodes, Central Fla.	1991-94	213	3618
5 Mark Didio, Connecticut	1988-91	239	3535

Rushing

Yards Gained	Years	Yards
1 Thomas Haskins, VMI	1993-96	5355
2 Frank Hawkins, Nevada	1977-80	5333
3 Kenny Gamble, Colgate	1984-87	5220
4 Markus Thomas, Eastern Ky.	1989-92	5149
5 Erik Marsh, Lafayette	1991-94	4834

Yards per Game	Years	Yards	P/Gm
1 Arnold Mickens, Butler	1994-95	3813	190.7
2 Tim Hall, Robert Morris	1994-95	2908	153.1
3 Archie Amerson, N. Ariz. ..	1995-96	3196	145.3
4 Keith Elias, Princeton	1991-93	4208	140.3
5 Mike Clark, Akron	1984-86	4257	133.0

Miscellaneous

Interceptions	Years	No
1 Dave Murphy, Holy Cross	1986-89	28
2 Cedric Walker, S.F. Austin	1990-93	25
3 Issiac Holt, Alcorn St.	1981-84	24
Bill McGovern, Holy Cross	1981-84	24
Darren Sharper, William & Mary	1993-96	24

Punting Average	Years	Avg
1 Pumpy Tudors, Tenn.-Chatt.	1989-91	44.4
2 Case de Brujin, Idaho St.	1978-81	43.7
3 Terry Belden, Northern Ariz.	1990-93	43.4
4 George Cimadevilla, East Tenn. St.	1983-86	43.0
5 Harold Alexander, Appalachian St.	1989-92	42.9

Punt Return Average*	Years	Avg
1 Willie Ware, Miss. Valley	1982-85	16.4
2 Buck Phillips, Western Ill.	1994-95	16.4
3 Tim Egerton, Delaware St.	1986-89	16.1
4 Mark Orlando, Towson St.	1991-94	15.7
5 John Armstrong, Richmond	1984-85	14.4

Kickoff Return Average*	Years	Avg
1 Troy Brown, Marshall	1991-92	29.7
2 Charles Swann, Indiana St.	1989-91	29.3
3 Craig Richardson, Eastern Wash.	1983-86	28.5
4 Kenyatta Sparks, Southern-BR	1992-95	28.2
5 Kerry Hayes, Western Caro.	1991-94	28.2

*(Minimum 1.2 returns per game)

Scoring
NON-KICKERS

Points	Years	TD	XP	Pts
1 Sherriden May, Idaho	1991-94	61	0	366
2 Charvez Foger, Nevada ...	1985-88	60	2	362
3 Kenny Gamble, Colgate ...	1984-87	57	0	342
4 Rene Ingoglia, U Mass	1992-95	55	2	332
5 Markus Thomas, Eastern Ky. .	1989-92	53	4	322

Touchdowns Passing	Years	No
1 Willie Totten, Miss. Valley	1982-85	139
2 Steve McNair, Alcorn St.	1991-94	119
3 Dave Dickenson, Montana	1992-95	96
4 Doug Nussmeier, Idaho	1990-93	91
5 Neil Lomax, Portland St.	1978-80	88

Touchdowns Rushing	Years	No
1 Kenny Gamble, Colgate	1984-87	55
2 Rene Ingoglia, Massachusetts	1992-95	54
3 Charvez Foger, Nevada	1985-88	52
4 Markus Thomas, Eastern Ky.	1989-92	51
5 Sherriden May, Idaho	1992-94	50
Paul Lewis, Boston Univ.	1982-84	50

Touchdown Catches	Years	No
1 Jerry Rice, Miss. Valley	1981-84	50
2 Rennie Benn, Lehigh	1982-85	44
3 Dedric Ward, N. Iowa	1993-96	41
4 Roy Banks, Eastern Ill.	1983-86	38
Mike Jones, Tennessee St.	1979-92	38

KICKERS

Points	Years	FG	XP	Pts
1 Marty Zendejas, Nevada .	1984-87	72	169	385
2 B. Mitchell, Marshall/N. Iowa	1987, 89-91	64	130	322
3 Thayne Doyle, Idaho ...	1988-91	49	160	307
4 Jose Larios, McNeese St. .	1992-95	57	133	304
5 Kirk Roach, W. Carolina .	1984-87	71	89	302

Field Goals	Years	No
1 Marty Zendejas, Nevada	1984-87	72
2 Kirk Roach, Western Carolina	1984-87	71
3 Tony Zendejas, Nevada	1981-83	70
4 B. Mitchell, Marshall/N. Iowa	1987,89-91	64
5 Todd Kurz, Illinois St.	1993-96	59

All-Time Winningest Division I-AA Teams
Includes records as a senior college only, minimum of 20 seasons of competition. Bowl and playoff games are included.
Top 25 Winning Percentage

		Yrs	Gm	W	L	T	Pct	I-AA Playoffs W-L-T
1	Yale	124	1122	783	284	55	.722	0-0-0
2	Grambling	54	577	405	157	15	.715	9-7-0
3	Florida A&M	64	641	444	179	18	.707	2-3-1
4	Tennessee St.	69	637	434	173	30	.705	8-2-1
5	Princeton	127	1074	724	300	50	.697	0-0-0
6	Harvard	122	1103	711	342	50	.667	1-0-0
7	Jackson St.	51	520	330	177	13	.647	1-10-1
8	Fordham	98	1093	677	363	53	.644	2-3-0
9	Dartmouth	115	990	612	332	46	.641	0-0-0
10	Eastern Ky.	73	722	443	252	27	.632	17-16-0
11	Pennsylvania	120	1175	716	417	42	.627	0-1-0
12	Southern-BR	75	722	438	259	25	.624	6-0-0
13	S. Carolina St.	69	633	380	226	27	.622	6-5-0
14	Dayton	89	840	504	310	26	.615	16-11-0
15	Hofstra	56	530	319	200	11	.612	2-8-0
16	Appalachian St.	67	698	412	257	29	.611	5-11-0
17	Ga. Southern	28	305	182	116	7	.608	22-4-0
18	McNeese St.	46	491	290	187	14	.605	8-8-0
19	Mid. Tenn. St.	80	767	449	290	28	.604	8-9-0
20	Alcorn St.	73	635	360	236	39	.598	1-4-0
21	Delaware	105	932	533	356	43	.595	20-12-0
22	N. Iowa	98	867	491	329	47	.593	8-10-0
23	Georgetown	85	715	407	277	31	.591	0-2-0
24	Western Ky.	78	733	417	285	31	.590	7-4-0
25	Butler	107	853	485	333	35	.589	0-3-0

Top 50 Victories

		Wins
1	Yale	783
2	Princeton	724
3	Penn	716
4	Harvard	711
5	Fordham	677
6	Dartmouth	612
7	Lafayette	578
8	Cornell	564
9	Delaware	533
10	Holy Cross	529
11	Lehigh	527
12	Dayton	504
13	Bucknell	494
14	Brown	492
15	N. Iowa	491
16	Colgate	489
17	Butler	485
18	Drake	467
19	Villanova	458
20	Furman	452
21	Mid. Tenn. St.	449
	William & Mary	449
23	Massachusetts	445
24	Florida A&M	444
25	Eastern Ky.	443
26	Southern-BR	438
27	Tennessee St.	434
28	Tenn-Chatt	426
	VMI	426
30	New Hampshire	421
31	Hampton	420
32	Western Ky.	417
33	Marshall	414
34	Northwestern St.	412
	Appalachian St.	412
36	Howard	409
37	Georgetown	407
	Maine	407
39	SW Texas St.	406
40	Grambling	405
41	Citadel	401
42	Richmond	398
43	Idaho St.	393
44	Western Ill.	391
45	Connecticut	389
46	Montana	386
47	S. Carolina St.	380
	Eastern Ill.	380
49	SW Missouri St.	378
	Murray St.	378

Top 30 Playoff Game Appearances

		Gm	Record
1	Delaware	33	20-13-0
	Eastern Ky.	33	17-16-0
3	Marshall	30	24-6-0
4	Jacksonville St.	29	19-10-0
5	Dayton	27	16-11-0
6	Ga. Southern	26	22-4-0
	Youngstown St.	26	22-4-0
8	Montana	19	11-8-0
9	Troy St.	18	13-5-0
	Furman	18	11-7-0
	N. Iowa	18	8-10-0
12	Boise St.	17	10-7-0
	Mid. Tenn. St	17	8-9-0
	Idaho	17	6-11-0
15	Grambling St.	16	9-7-0
	E. Illinois	16	8-8-0
	McNeese St.	16	8-8-0
	Appalachian St.	16	5-11-0
19	Tennessee St.	11	8-2-1
	S.F. Austin St.	11	7-4-0
	Western Ky.	11	7-4-0
	S. Carolina St.	11	6-5-0
	Wagner	11	6-5-0
	Jackson St.	11	1-11-0
25	Montana	10	7-1-2
	William & Mary	10	3-7-0
	Hofstra	10	2-8-0
28	Villanova	9	2-6-1
29	Bethune-Cookman	8	6-2-0
	Sam Houston St.	8	4-3-1
	Lehigh	8	4-4-0
	Boston Univ.	8	2-6-0

Active Division I-AA Coaches

Minimum of 5 years as a Division I-A and/or Division I-AA through 1996 season.

Top 5 Winning Percentage

		Yrs	W	L	T	Pct
1	Al Bagnoli, Pennsylvania	15	124	30	0	**.805**
2	Roy Kidd, Eastern Ky	33	272	99	8	**.728**
3	Tubby Raymond, Delaware ...	31	258	101	3	**.717**
4	Eddie Robinson Grambling ..	54	405	157	15	**.715**
5	Jim Tressel, Youngstown St. ..	11	95	44	2	**.681**

Top 5 Victories

		Yrs	W	L	T	Pct
1	Eddie Robinson, Grambling ..	54	**405**	157	15	.715
2	Roy Kidd, Eastern Ky	33	**272**	99	8	.728
3	Tubby Raymond, Delaware ..	31	**258**	101	3	.717
4	Ron Randleman, S. Hous. St. .	28	**170**	122	6	.581
5	Bill Bowes, New Hampshire ..	25	**166**	93	5	.638

Division I-AA Coach of the Year

First presented in 1983 by the American Football Coaches Association.

Multiple winners: Mark Duffner and Erk Russell (2).

Year	Year	Year
1983 Rey Dempsey, Southern Ill.	1988 Jimmy Satterfield, Furman	1993 Dan Allen, Boston Univ.
1984 Dave Arnold, Montana St.	1989 Erk Russell, Ga. Southern	1994 Jim Tressel, Youngstown St.
1985 Dick Sheridan, Furman	1990 Tim Stowers, Ga. Southern	1995 Don Read, Montana
1986 Erk Russell, Ga. Southern	1991 Mark Duffner, Holy Cross	1996 Ray Tellier, Columbia
1987 Mark Duffner, Holy Cross	1992 Charlie Taafe, Citadel	

NCAA PLAYOFFS

Division I-AA

Established in 1978 as a four-team playoff. Tournament field increased to eight teams in 1981, 12 teams in 1982 and 16 teams in 1986. Automatic berths have been awarded to champions of the Big Sky, Gateway, Ohio Valley, Southern, Southland and Yankee conferences since 1992.

Multiple winners: Georgia Southern (4); Youngstown St. (3); Eastern Kentucky and Marshall (2).

Year	Winner	Score	Loser	Year	Winner	Score	Loser
1978	Florida A&M	35-28	Massachusetts	1988	Furman, SC	17-12	Georgia Southern
1979	Eastern Kentucky	30-7	Lehigh, PA	1989	Georgia Southern	37-34	S.F. Austin St.
1980	Boise St., ID	31-29	Eastern Kentucky	1990	Georgia Southern	36-13	Nevada-Reno
1981	Idaho St.	34-23	Eastern Kentucky	1991	Youngstown St.	25-17	Marshall
1982	Eastern Kentucky	17-14	Delaware	1992	Marshall	31-28	Youngstown St.
1983	Southern Illinois	43-7	Western Carolina	1993	Youngstown St.	17-5	Marshall
1984	Montana St.	19-6	Louisiana Tech	1994	Youngstown St.	28-14	Boise St.
1985	Georgia Southern	44-42	Furman, SC	1995	Montana	22-20	Marshall
1986	Georgia Southern	48-21	Arkansas St.	1996	Marshall	49-29	Montana
1987	NE Louisiana	43-42	Marshall, WV				

Division II

Established in 1973 as an eight-team playoff. Tournament field increased to 16 teams in 1988. From 1964-72, eight qualifying NCAA College Division member institutions competed in four regional bowl games, but there was no tournament and no national championship until 1973.

Multiple winners: North Dakota St. (5); North Alabama (3); Southwest Texas St. and Troy St. (2).

Year	Winner	Score	Loser	Year	Winner	Score	Loser
1973	Louisiana Tech	34-0	Western Kentucky	1985	North Dakota St.	35-7	North Alabama
1974	Central Michigan	54-14	Delaware	1986	North Dakota St.	27-7	South Dakota
1975	Northern Michigan	16-14	Western Kentucky	1987	Troy St., AL	31-17	Portland St., OR
1976	Montana St.	24-13	Akron, OH	1988	North Dakota St.	35-21	Portland St., OR
1977	Lehigh, PA	33-0	Jacksonville St., AL	1989	Mississippi Col.	3-0	Jacksonville St., AL
1978	Eastern Illinois	10-9	Delaware	1990	North Dakota St.	51-11	Indiana, PA
1979	Delaware	38-21	Youngstown St., OH	1991	Pittsburg St., KS	23-6	Jacksonville St., AL
1980	Cal Poly-SLO	21-13	Eastern Illinois	1992	Jacksonville St., AL	17-13	Pittsburg St., KS
1981	SW Texas St.	42-13	North Dakota St.	1993	North Alabama	41-34	Indiana, PA
1982	SW Texas St.	34-9	UC-Davis	1994	North Alabama	16-10	Tex. A&M (Kings.)
1983	North Dakota St.	41-21	Central St., OH	1995	North Alabama	22-7	Pittsburg St., KS
1984	Troy St., AL	18-17	North Dakota St.	1996	Northern Colorado	23-14	Carson-Newman

Division III

Established in 1973 as a four-team playoff. Tournament field increased to eight teams in 1975 and 16 teams in 1985. From 1969-72, four qualifying NCAA College Division member institutions competed in two regional bowl games, but there was no tournament and no national championship until 1973.

Multiple winners: Augustana (4); Ithaca (3); Dayton, Mt. Union, Widener, WI-La Crosse and Wittenberg (2).

Year	Winner	Score	Loser	Year	Winner	Score	Loser
1973	Wittenberg, OH	41-0	Juniata, PA	1986	Augustana, IL	31-3	Salisbury St., MD
1974	Central, IA	10-8	Ithaca, NY	1987	Wagner, NY	19-3	Dayton, OH
1975	Wittenberg, OH	28-0	Ithaca, NY	1988	Ithaca, NY	39-24	Central, IA
1976	St. John's, MN	31-28	Towson St., MD	1989	Dayton, OH	17-7	Union, NY
1977	Widener, PA	39-36	Wabash, IN	1990	Allegheny, PA*	21-14	Lycoming, PA
1978	Baldwin-Wallace	24-10	Wittenberg, OH	1991	Ithaca, NY	34-20	Dayton, OH
1979	Ithaca, NY	14-10	Wittenberg, OH	1992	WI-La Crosse	16-12	Wash. & Jeff., PA
1980	Dayton, OH	63-0	Ithaca, NY	1993	Mt. Union, OH	34-24	Rowan, NJ
1981	Widener, PA	17-10	Dayton, OH	1994	Albion, MI	38-15	Wash. & Jeff., PA
1982	West Georgia	14-0	Augustana, IL	1995	WI-La Crosse	36-7	Rowan, NJ
1983	Augustana, IL	21-17	Union, NY	1996	Mt. Union, OH	56-24	Rowan, NJ
1984	Augustana, IL	21-12	Central, IA				
1985	Augustana, IL	20-7	Ithaca, NY	*Overtime			

NAIA PLAYOFFS

Division I

Established in 1956 as two-team playoff. Tournament field increased to four teams in 1958, eight teams in 1978 and 16 teams in 1987 before cutting back to eight teams in 1989. The title game has ended in a tie four times (1956, '64, '84 and '85).

Multiple winners: Texas A&I (7); Carson-Newman (5); Central Arkansas and Central St., OH (3); Abilene Christian, Central St.-OK, Elon, Pittsburg St. and St. John's-MN (2).

Year	Winner	Score	Loser	Year	Winner	Score	Loser
1956	Montana St.	0-0	St. Joseph's, IN	1977	Abilene Christian	24-7	SW Oklahoma
1957	Pittsburg St., KS	27-26	Hillsdale, MI	1978	Angelo St., TX	34-14	Elon, NC
1958	NE Oklahoma	19-13	Northern Arizona	1979	Texas A&I	20-14	Central St., OK
1959	Texas A&I	20-7	Lenoir-Rhyne, NC				
1960	Lenoir-Rhyne, NC	15-14	Humboldt St., CA	1980	Elon, NC	17-10	NE Oklahoma
1961	Pittsburg St., KS	12-7	Linfield, OR	1981	Elon, NC	3-0	Pittsburg St., KS
1962	Central St., OK	28-13	Lenoir-Rhyne, NC	1982	Central St., OK	14-11	Mesa, CO
1963	St. John's, MN	33-27	Prairie View, TX	1983	Car-Newman, TN	36-28	Mesa, CO
1964	Concordia, MN	7-7	Sam Houston, TX	1984	Car-Newman, TN	19-19	Central Arkansas
1965	St. John's, MN	33-0	Linfield, OR	1985	Hillsdale, MI	10-10	Central Arkansas
1966	Waynesburg, PA	42-21	WI-Whitewater	1986	Car-Newman, TN	17-0	Cameron, OK
1967	Fairmont St., WV	28-21	Eastern Wash.	1987	Cameron, OK	30-2	Car-Newman, TN
1968	Troy St., AL	43-35	Texas A&I	1988	Car-Newman, TN	56-21	Adams St., CO
1969	Texas A&I	32-7	Concordia, MN	1989	Car-Newman, TN	34-20	Emporia St., KS
1970	Texas A&I	48-7	Wofford, SC	1990	Central St., OH	38-16	Mesa, CO
1971	Livingston, AL	14-12	Arkansas Tech	1991	Central Arkansas	19-16	Central St., OH
1972	East Texas St.	21-18	Car-Newman, TN	1992	Central St., OH	19-16	Gardner-Webb, NC
1973	Abilene Christian	42-14	Elon, NC	1993	E. Central, OK	49-35	Glenville St., WV
1974	Texas A&I	34-23	Henderson St., AR	1994	N'eastern St., OK	13-12	Ark-Pine Bluff
1975	Texas A&I	37-0	Salem, WV	1995	Central St., OH	37-7	N'eastern St., OK
1976	Texas A&I	26-0	Central Arkansas	1996	SW Oklahoma St.	33-31	Montana Tech

Division II

Established in 1970 as four-team playoff. Tournament field increased to eight teams in 1978 and 16 teams in 1987. The title game has ended in a tie twice (1981 and '87).

Multiple winners: Westminster (6); Findlay, Linfield and Pacific Lutheran (3); Concordia-MN, Northwestern-IA and Texas Lutheran (2).

Year	Winner	Score	Loser	Year	Winner	Score	Loser
1970	Westminster, PA	21-16	Anderson, IN	1985	WI-La Crosse	24-7	Pacific Lutheran
1971	Calif. Lutheran	20-14	Westminster, PA	1986	Linfield, OR	17-0	Baker, KS
1972	Missouri Southern	21-14	Northwestern, IA	1987	Pacific Lutheran	16-16	WI-Stevens Pt.*
1973	Northwestern, IA	10-3	Glenville St., WV	1988	Westminster, PA	21-14	WI-La Crosse
1974	Texas Lutheran	42-0	Missouri Valley	1989	Westminster, PA	51-30	WI-La Crosse
1975	Texas Lutheran	34-8	Calif. Lutheran	1990	Peru St., NE	17-7	Westminster, PA
1976	Westminster, PA	20-13	Redlands, CA	1991	Georgetown-KY	28-20	Pacific Lutheran
1977	Westminster, PA	17-9	Calif. Lutheran	1992	Findlay, OH	26-13	Linfield, OR
1978	Concordia, MN	7-0	Findlay, OH	1993	Pacific Lutheran	50-20	Westminster, PA
1979	Findlay, OH	51-6	Northwestern, IA	1994	Westminster, PA	27-7	Pacific Lutheran
1980	Pacific Lutheran	38-10	Wilmington, OH	1995	Findlay, OH	21-21	Central Wash.
1981	Austin College, TX	24-24	Concordia, MN	1996	Sioux Falls, S.D.	47-25	W. Washington
1982	Linfield, OR	33-15	Wm. Jewell, MO				
1983	Northwestern, IA	25-21	Pacific Lutheran	*Wisconsin-Stevens Point forfeited its entire 1987 schedule due to its use of an ineligible player.			
1984	Linfield, OR	33-22	Northwestern, IA				

Pro Football

New England's **Mike McGruder** watches Green Bay's **Desmond Howard** break open a competitive Super Bowl XXXI by returning a third quarter kickoff 99 yards for a touchdown.

Wide World Photos

The Pack, Pack, Pack

is Back, Back, Back

by
Chris Berman

They call it Titletown, though there had been no NFL championship for 28 straight years.

But now the nom de guerre fits again. While the National Football League has changed in many ways since Bart Starr's Packers were walloping the Oakland Raiders in the second "AFL-NFL World Championship Game" (not yet called the Super Bowl), the fact that Green Bay is once more the home of football's best team is not that surprising. After all, the Pack's 35-21 triumph over the New England Patriots in Super Bowl XXXI was the franchise's NFL-best 12th title.

But ponder the changes since the late great Vince Lombardi was carried off the field following Green Bay's 33-14 win on January 14, 1968. Back then, the NFL and AFL merger had not yet taken place on the field and the younger league was home of the Boston Patriots. The Browns were an institution in Cleveland, the Rams were in Los Angeles, the Cardinals were in St. Louis and Shea Stadium was home to the J-E-T-S. Color, not

cable, television was a novelty to many, ESPN were just four-of-26 letters in the English alphabet and "surfing the net" was probably something they were doing at Venice Beach.

NFL franchises in Carolina and Jacksonville were nearly three decades from existence, but what a second season each enjoyed in '96. The Panthers shocked us by dethroning the 49ers in the NFC West, then put the defending Super Bowl champs out of their misery as midnight struck for the troubled Cowboys. The Jaguars slipped into the playoffs, but not only tripped up the Bills at Orchard Park (in what proved to be Jim Kelly's final game) but shocked the 13-3 Broncos at Mile High. A pair of second-year franchises in the conference title games? To quote the very quotable Lombardi: "What the hell is going on here?"

But back to the future. Just as they had done during their heydays in the 1960s, the '96 Pack spent the majority of the season dominating the opposition. They won their first three games by a combined score of 115-26, setting the tone for what would be THEIR

Chris Berman is the host of ESPN's *NFL Prime Time*.

Even though his season started off under the specter of his admission that he was addicted to a painkiller, **Brett Favre** looked past all distractions to win a second NFL MVP award and the Super Bowl.

year. They stumbled just three times during the regular season, most notably during back-to-back losses to the Chiefs and Cowboys when injuries to their wide receiving corps finally caught up with them. But they regained compusure on a Sunday night in St. Louis and never looked back. The Pack became the first team since the perfect '72 Miami Dolphins to not only lead the league in scoring but allow the fewest points as well. They handled the best the rest of the NFC had to offer in the playoffs in San Francisco (35-14) and Carolina (30-13), then wrestled with the Patriots until game MVP Desmond Howard put New England away with a record 99-yard kickoff return for a score in the waning minutes of the third quarter.

The heroes for this team were many, almost too numerous to men-tion. The leader was quarterback Brett Favre, overcoming personal adversity and establishing himself as the game's best signal-caller by setting a new conference record for touchdown passes (39) for the second consecutive year. Defensive end Reggie White got his long-awaited first championship of any kind and squashed all criticism of his supposedly-diminishing skills by recording a Super Bowl-record three sacks of Drew Bledsoe. And head coach Mike Holmgren showed he hadn't fallen far from the Bill Walsh tree, becoming the latest pupil of the Hall of Fame "Genius" to take a team to the pinnacle of success. The Pack was indeed back in 1996, and may continue to be for some time. In any case, it was a long time coming for the game's most legendary franchise. ∎

Chris Mortensen's Top Ten Highlights of the 1996 NFL season

10. Play of the Year: **Desmond Howard's 99–yard kickoff return** seals Green Bay's 35–21 victory in Super Bowl XXXI.

    Packer anxiety had begun to build as New England running back Curtis Martin had just scored on an 18–yard run to pull the Patriots close, 27–21. But with 3:27 left in the third quarter, Howard's return earned him MVP honors while breaking the spirit and the backs of the Patriots. Like previous Super Bowl MVP Larry Brown, Howard signed a free-agent contract with the Oakland Raiders.

9. **John Elway** and **Jim Kelly** both fall to the Jaguars in the playoffs; Kelly retires in Buffalo.

    The QB class of 1983, as great as it was with Elway, Kelly and Dan Marino, continued to fall short of the ultimate victory. One week after Jacksonville ended Kelly's run in Buffalo, the Jaguars stunned AFC-favorite Denver at Mile High Stadium.

8. **Barry Sanders** and **Thurman Thomas** become the NFL's first 1,000–yard rushers for eight straight seasons.

    Appreciate them for what they are: Two of the greatest NFL backs ever, who were teammates at Oklahoma State. Sanders is making a case for "best ever" comparisons by also becoming the first to amass three straight 1,500 yard seasons.

7. **The Great Purge**: 49ers and George Seifert head the list of 11 coaching changes.

    Pressure hit the NFL like it never had before. From Parcells in New England to Seifert, who had gotten to 100 wins faster than any coach in league history, the coaching carousel had never spun more out of control. When it stopped, Mike Ditka had taken over the Saints and the Rams convinced Dick Vermeil to end his 17–year coaching hiatus.

6. **Jimmy Johnson** replaces Don Shula in Miami.

    Two years after replacing a legend in Dallas, Johnson does the same in Miami. His 8–8 record was an improvement on the 1–15 he posted his first year with the Cowboys, though he did eventually win 2 Super Bowls.

5. Football returns to **Baltimore** but **Cleveland** rocks without the NFL.

    The scars from Bob Irsay's midnight run out of Baltimore in 1984 began to fade when the Ravens debuted in Memorial Stadium in 1996. But Baltimore's gain was Cleveland's loss as one of the NFL's great fan bases was deprived of football with the bittersweet promise that the game and the name (Browns) would return in 1999.

4. Drug scandals rock America's Team: **Michael Irvin** and **Leon Lett** take down the defending Super Bowl champion Dallas Cowboys.

    The Cowboys had a shot to become the first NFL team in history to win four Super Bowls in five years. But a felony cocaine conviction for Irvin led to an NFL suspension for the first five games and then Lett received a one-year suspension, costing the team one of the league's best defensive tackles.

3. **Bill Parcells** leads Patriots to Super Bowl but turncoat leaves for New York Jets.

In his fourth season, Parcells took the Patriots to the ultimate game, establishing his niche as one of the game's greatest coaches. But his relationship with Patriots owner Bob Kraft soured and an ugly public battle occurred during and after the Super Bowl. Parcells eventually bolted to the Jets — at a price of six draft picks over three years.

2. Expansion teams **Carolina** and **Jacksonville** reach NFC and AFC title games in only their second seasons.

An all-expansion Super Bowl? How did it almost happen? Neither organization wasted the generous allotment of available players (extra draft picks, free agency) that were put together by two outstanding coaches — Dom Capers in Carolina and Tom Coughlin in Jacksonville.

1. **Brett Favre** kicks painkiller habit; passes Packers to first Super Bowl title since 1968.

Favre, the NFL's reigning MVP, stunned the sports world when he announced that he had become addicted to painkillers. Doubts about his ability to recover were erased when he threw an NFC-record 39 TD passes and led the Packers over the Patriots in the Super Bowl. ■

THE NUMBERS

INSIDE

by
Pete McConville and Craig Wachs

SPEC —PACK—ULAR

The Packers recipe for their championship season was simple: dominate both sides of the ball.

	Packers	Opponents
Touchdowns	56	19*
Points	456	210
1st Downs Per Game	21.1	15.5
Net Yards Per Game	345.9	259.8

*NFL record low for 16-game season.

4,000 YARDS AND 50 CENTS WILL GET YOU...

No quarterback who has thrown for 4,000 yards during a season went on to win the NFL title that year. They haven't done so well in the conference titles games, either. And you thought Jay Schroeder had nothing in common with Steve Young.

	Passing Yards	Conference Title Game
Bledsoe '96	**4,086**	**Won**
Brunell '96	4,367	Lost
Favre '95	4,413	Lost
Young '93	4,023	Lost
Marino '92	4,116	Lost
Everett '89	4,310	Lost
Schroeder '86	4,109	Lost
Marino '85	4,137	Lost
Marino '84	5,084	**Won**
Fouts, '81	4,802	Lost
Fouts '80	4,715	Lost

Wide World Photos

Dallas Cowboy **Troy Aikman** and the Carolina Panthers' defense form a telling tableau for the 1996 NFL season; the old guard is down and the expansion teams are on the rise.

CINERGIZED!

In 1996, the most improved team in the league during the season was the Cincinnati Bengals. Mere pussycats under David Shula, they started out at 1-6. But Bruce Coslet turned them into tigers and finished the last nine games at a strong 7-2. Coslet's turnaround resulted in a modest 8-8 overall record but it was the team's best since 1990.

	Under Shula	Under Coslet
Record	1-6	7-2
PPG	18.3	27.1
Pt. Diff. PG	-4.6	+3.9
Total Off. PG	282.1	361.1
Turnover Diff.	-10	+9

Enter **SAND**man

Barry Sanders of the Detroit Lions is making a case as one of the best running backs in National Football League history. His latest, and perhaps most noteworthy, accomplishment is becoming the first back in league history to run for at least 1,500 yards in three straight seasons.

	Total Yards	100 Yard Games
1996	1,553	7
1995	1,500	7
1994	1,883	10

■

THE 1998

ESPN
INFORMATION PLEASE
SPORTS
ALMANAC

PRO FOOTBALL
S T A T I S T I C S

THE SEASON IN REVIEW
1996-1997
STANDINGS • PLAYOFFS • DRAFTS

SEC
B

PAGE
217

Final NFL Standings

Division champions (*) and Wild Card playoff qualifiers (†) are noted; division champions with two best records received first round byes. Number of seasons listed after each head coach refers to latest tenure with club through 1996 season.

American Football Conference

Eastern Division

	W	L	T	PF	PA	vs Div	vs AFC
*New England	11	5	0	418	313	6-2-0	9-3-0
†Buffalo	10	6	0	319	266	4-4-0	6-6-0
†Indianapolis	9	7	0	317	334	4-4-0	6-6-0
Miami	8	8	0	339	325	6-2-0	7-5-0
NY Jets	1	15	0	279	454	0-8-0	0-12-0

1996 Head coaches: NE—Bill Parcells (4th season); **Buf**—Marv Levy (11th); **Ind**—Lindy Infante (1st); **Mia**—Jimmy Johnson (1st); **NY**—Rich Kotite (2nd).
1995 Standings: 1. Buffalo (10-6); 2. Indianapolis (9-7); 3. Miami (9-7); 4. New England (6-10); 5. NY Jets (3-13).

Central Division

	W	L	T	PF	PA	vs Div	vs AFC
*Pittsburgh	10	6	0	344	257	4-4-0	8-4-0
†Jacksonville	9	7	0	325	335	5-3-0	7-5-0
Cincinnati	8	8	0	372	369	5-3-0	6-6-0
Houston	8	8	0	345	319	5-3-0	6-6-0
Baltimore	4	12	0	371	441	1-7-0	2-10-0

1996 Head coaches: Pit—Bill Cowher (5th season); **Jax**—Tom Coughlin (2nd); **Cin**—fired David Shula (5th, 1-6) on Oct. 21 and replaced him with off. coord. Bruce Coslet (7-2); **Hou**—Jeff Fisher (3rd); **Bal**—Ted Marchibroda (1st).
1995 Standings: 1. Pittsburgh (11-5); 2. Cincinnati (7-9); 3. Houston (7-9); 4. Cleveland (5-11); 5. Jacksonville (4-12).

Western Division

	W	L	T	PF	PA	vs Div	vs AFC
*Denver	13	3	0	391	275	6-2-0	10-2-0
Kansas City	9	7	0	297	300	4-4-0	5-7-0
San Diego	8	8	0	310	376	5-3-0	7-5-0
Oakland	7	9	0	340	293	3-5-0	6-6-0
Seattle	7	9	0	317	376	3-5-0	6-6-0

1996 Head coaches: Den—Mike Shanahan (2nd season); **KC**—Marty Schottenheimer (8th); **SD**—Bobby Ross (5th); **Oak**—Mike White (1st); **Sea**—Dennis Erickson (2nd).
1995 Standings: 1. Kansas City (13-3); 2. San Diego (9-7); 3. Denver (8-8); 4. Seattle (8-8); 5. Oakland (8-8).

National Football Conference

Eastern Division

	W	L	T	PF	PA	vs Div	vs NFC
*Dallas	10	6	0	286	250	5-3-0	8-4-0
†Philadelphia	10	6	0	363	341	5-3-0	8-4-0
Washington	9	7	0	364	312	4-4-0	6-6-0
Arizona	7	9	0	300	397	4-4-0	7-5-0
NY Giants	6	10	0	242	297	2-6-0	4-8-0

1996 Head coaches: Dal—Barry Switzer (3rd season); **Phi**—Ray Rhodes (2nd); **Wash**—Norv Turner (3rd); **Ariz**—Vince Tobin (1st); **NY**— Dan Reeves (4th).
1995 Standings: 1. Dallas (12-4); 2. Philadelphia (10-6); 3. Washington (6-10); 4. NY Giants (5-11); 5. Arizona (4-12).

Central Division

	W	L	T	PF	PA	vs Div	vs NFC
*Green Bay	13	3	0	456	210	7-1-0	10-2-0
†Minnesota	9	7	0	298	315	5-3-0	8-4-0
Chicago	7	9	0	283	305	3-5-0	5-7-0
Tampa Bay	6	10	0	221	293	2-6-0	4-8-0
Detroit	5	11	0	302	368	3-5-0	4-8-0

1996 Head coaches: GB—Mike Holmgren (5th season); **Min**—Dennis Green (5th); **Chi**—Dave Wannstedt (4th); **TB**—Tony Dungy (1st); **Det**— Wayne Fontes (9th).
1995 Standings: 1. Green Bay (11-5); 2. Detroit (10-6); 3. Chicago (9-7); 4. Minnesota (8-8); 5. Tampa Bay (7-9).

Western Division

	W	L	T	PF	PA	vs Div	vs NFC
*Carolina	12	4	0	367	218	7-1-0	9-3-0
†San Francisco	12	4	0	398	257	6-2-0	8-4-0
St. Louis	6	10	0	303	409	4-4-0	4-8-0
Atlanta	3	13	0	309	461	3-5-0	3-9-0
New Orleans	3	13	0	229	339	0-8-0	2-10-0

1996 Head coaches: Car—Dom Capers (2nd); **SF**—George Seifert (8th season) ; **St.L**—Rich Brooks (2nd); **Atl**—June Jones (3rd); **NO**— Jim Mora (11th, 2-6) was replaced on Oct. 21 by asst. Rick Venturi (1-7).
1995 Standings: 1. San Francisco (11-5); 2. Atlanta (9-7); 3. St. Louis (7-9); 4. Carolina (7-9); 5. New Orleans (7-9).

Playoff Tiebreakers

Division Championship—NFC: Carolina (12-4) qualified over San Francisco (12-4) by winning both regular season games; Dallas (10-6) over Philadelphia (10-6) with a better record (7-4 vs. 6-5) in games with common opponents.
Wild Card berths—AFC: Indianapolis (9-7) qualified over Kansas City (9-7) with a head-to-head victory; Jacksonville (9-7) over Kansas City with a better conference record. NFC: Minnesota (9-7) qualified over Washington (9-7) with a better conference record.

NFL Regular Season Individual Leaders
(* indicates rookies)

Passing Efficiency
(Minimum of 224 attempts)

AFC	Att	Cmp	Cmp Pct	Yds	Avg Gain	TD	Long	Int	Sack/Lost	Rating Points
John Elway, Den.	466	287	61.6	3328	7.14	26	51	14	26/194	89.2
Vinny Testaverde, Bal.	549	325	59.2	4177	7.61	33	86-td	19	34/270	88.7
Dan Marino, Mia.	373	221	59.2	2795	7.49	17	74-td	9	18/131	87.8
Mark Brunell, Jax.	557	353	63.4	4367	7.84	19	62	20	50/257	84.0
Drew Bledsoe, NE	623	373	59.9	4086	6.56	27	84-td	15	30/190	83.7
Jeff Hostetler, Oak.	402	242	60.2	2548	6.34	23	62-td	14	32/181	83.2
Jeff Blake, Cin.	549	308	56.1	3624	6.60	24	61-td	14	44/278	80.3
Chris Chandler, Hou.	320	184	57.5	2099	6.56	16	63-td	11	25/153	79.7
Stan Humphries, S.D.	416	232	55.8	2670	6.42	18	63-td	13	20/187	76.7
Jim Harbaugh, Ind.	405	232	57.3	2630	6.49	13	51	11	36/190	76.3
Jim Kelly, Buf.	379	222	58.6	2810	7.41	14	67-td	19	37/287	73.2
Mike Tomczak, Pit.	401	222	55.4	2767	6.90	15	70-td	17	16/105	71.8
Frank Reich, NYJ	331	175	52.9	2205	6.66	15	52-td	16	14/94	68.9
Steve Bono, K.C.	438	235	53.7	2572	5.87	12	69	13	22/161	68.0
Rick Mirer, Sea.	265	136	51.3	1546	5.83	5	60	12	22/84	56.6

NFC	Att	Cmp	Cmp Pct	Yds	Avg Gain	TD	Long	Int	Sack/Lost	Rating Points
Steve Young, SF	316	214	67.7	2410	7.63	14	52	6	34/160	97.2
Brett Favre, GB	543	325	59.9	3899	7.18	39	80-td	13	40/241	95.8
Brad Johnson, Min	311	195	62.7	2258	7.26	17	82-td	10	15/119	89.4
Ty Detmer, Phi	401	238	59.4	2911	7.26	15	42	13	27/171	80.8
Troy Aikman, Dal	465	296	63.7	3126	6.72	12	61	13	18/120	80.1
Kerry Collins, Car	364	204	56.0	2454	6.74	14	55	9	18/114	79.4
Gus Frerotte, Was	470	270	57.4	3453	7.35	12	52-td	11	22/134	79.3
Dave Krieg, Chi	377	226	59.9	2278	6.04	14	53-td	12	14/104	76.3
Kent Graham, Ariz	274	146	53.3	1624	5.93	12	69	7	19/120	75.1
Scott Mitchell, Det	437	253	57.9	2917	6.68	17	62-td	17	36/199	74.9
Bobby Hebert, Atl	489	295	60.3	3162	6.47	22	57	25	27/150	73.0
Tony Banks*, St.L	368	192	52.2	2544	6.91	15	77-td	15	48/306	71.0
Boomer Esiason, Ariz	339	190	56.0	2293	6.76	11	64-td	14	17/109	70.6
Jim Everett, NO	464	267	57.5	2797	6.03	12	51	16	19/154	69.4
Warren Moon, Min	247	134	54.3	1610	6.52	7	54-td	9	19/122	68.7

Receptions

AFC	No	Yds	Avg	Long	TD
Carl Pickens, Cin	100	1180	11.8	61-td	12
Terry Glenn*, NE	90	1132	12.6	37-td	6
Tim Brown, Oak	90	1104	12.3	42-td	9
Tony Martin, SD	85	1171	13.8	55	14
Keenan McCardell, Jax	85	1129	13.3	52	3
Wayne Chrebet, NYJ	84	909	10.8	44	3
Jimmy Smith, Jax	83	1244	15.0	62	7
Shannon Sharpe, Den	80	1062	13.3	51	10
Michael Jackson, Bal	76	1201	15.8	86-td	14
O.J. McDuffie, Mia	74	918	12.4	36	8
Andre Hastings, Pit	72	739	10.3	38	6
Andre Reed, Buf	66	1036	15.7	67-td	6
Marvin Harrison*, Ind	64	836	13.1	41	8
Keyshawn Johnson*, NYJ	63	844	13.4	50	8

NFC	No	Yds	Avg	Long	TD
Jerry Rice, SF	108	1254	11.6	39	8
Herman Moore, Det	106	1296	12.2	50-td	9
Larry Centers, Ariz	99	766	7.7	39	7
Cris Carter, Min	96	1163	12.1	43-td	10
Brett Perriman, Det	94	1021	10.9	44	5
Irving Fryar, Phi	88	1195	13.6	42	11
Isaac Bruce, St.L	84	1338	15.9	70	7
Curtis Conway, Chi	81	1049	13.0	58-td	7
Bert Emanuel, Atl	76	931	12.3	53	6
Jake Reed, Min	72	1320	18.3	82-td	7
Chris T. Jones, Phi.	70	859	12.3	38	5
Frank Sanders, Ariz	69	813	11.8	34	4
Terance Mathis, Atl	69	771	11.2	55	7
Mike Alstott*, TB	65	557	8.6	29	3

Rushing

AFC	Car	Yards	Avg	Long	TD
Terrell Davis, Den	345	1538	4.5	71-td	13
Jerome Bettis, Pit	320	1431	4.5	50-td	11
Eddie George*, Hou	335	1368	4.1	76	8
Adrian Murrell, NYJ	301	1249	4.1	78	6
Curtis Martin, NE	316	1152	3.6	57	14
Karim Abdul-Jabbar*, Mia	307	1116	3.6	29	11
Thurman Thomas, Buf	281	1033	3.7	36	8
Napoleon Kaufman, Oak	150	874	5.8	77	1
Chris Warren, Sea	203	855	4.2	51	5
Garrison Hearst, Cin	225	847	3.8	24	0
Marcus Allen, KC	206	830	4.0	35	9
Bam Morris, Bal	172	737	4.3	19	4
James Stewart, Jax	190	723	3.8	34	8
Leonard Russell, SD	219	713	3.3	21	7

NFC	Car	Yards	Avg	Long	TD
Barry Sanders, Det.	307	1553	5.1	54-td	11
Ricky Watters, Phi.	353	1411	4.0	56-td	13
Terry Allen, Was.	347	1353	3.9	49-td	21
Emmitt Smith, Dal.	327	1204	3.7	42	12
Anthony Johnson, Car.	300	1120	3.7	29	6
Jamal Anderson, Atl.	232	1055	4.5	32-td	5
Edgar Bennett, GB	222	899	4.0	23	2
Rodney Hampton, NYG	254	827	3.3	25	1
Raymont Harris, Chi.	194	748	3.9	23	4
Robert Smith, Min.	162	692	4.3	57	3
Leshon Johnson, Ariz	141	634	4.5	70-td	3
Lawrence Phillips*, St.L	193	632	3.3	38	4
Mario Bates, NO	164	584	3.6	33	4
Dorsey Levens, GB	121	566	4.7	24	5

Washington Redskins	San Francisco 49ers	Detroit Lions	Carolina Panthers
Terry Allen	**Jerry Rice**	**Barry Sanders**	**Kevin Greene**
Touchdowns	Receptions	Rushing	Sacks

All-Purpose Yardage

AFC	Rush	Rec	Ret	Total	NFC	Rush	Rec	Ret	Total
Terrell Davis, Den.	1538	310	0	1848	Brian Mitchell, Wash. ..	193	286	1516	1995
Dave Meggett, NE	122	292	1369	1783	Tyrone Hughes, NO	0	0	1943	1943
Andre Coleman, SD	0	486	1210	1696	Eric Metcalf, Atl.	8	599	1330	1937
Napoleon Kaufman, Oak..	874	143	548	1565	Glyn Milburn, Det.	0	0	1911	1911
Jerome Bettis, Pit.	1431	122	0	1553	Ricky Watters, Phi.	1411	444	0	1855
Eddie George*, Hou. ...	1368	182	0	1550	Eddie Kennison*, St.L. ..	0	924	877	1801
Eric Moulds*, Buf.	44	279	1205	1528	Barry Sanders, Det.	1553	147	0	1700
Curtis Martin, NE	1152	333	0	1485	Jamal Anderson, Atl. ...	1055	473	80	1608
Tim Brown, Oak.........	35	1104	296	1435	Terry Allen, Wash.	1353	194	0	1547
Mel Gray, Hou.	0	0	1429	1429	Leeland McElroy*, Ari. .	305	41	1148	1494
Vaughn Hebron, Den. ...	262	43	1099	1404	Emmitt Smith, Dal.	1204	249	0	1453
Aaron Bailey, Ind.	0	302	1041	1343	Desmond Howard, GB ..	0	95	1335	1430

Ret column includes all kickoff, punt, fumble and interception returns.

Scoring

Touchdowns

AFC	TD	Rush	Rec	Ret	Pts
Curtis Martin, NE	17	14	3	0	102
Terrell Davis, Den	15	13	2	0	90
Michael Jackson, Bal ...	14	0	14	0	84
Tony Martin, SD	14	0	14	0	84
Carl Pickens, Cin	12	0	12	0	72
K. Abdul-Jabbar*, Mia ..	11	11	0	0	66
Jerome Bettis, Pit	11	11	0	0	66
James Stewart, Jax	10	8	2	0	60
Shannon Sharpe, Den ..	10	0	10	0	60
Derrick Alexander, Bal ..	9	0	9	0	54
Marcus Allen, Kan	9	9	0	0	54
Ki-Jana Carter, Cin	9	8	1	0	54
Ben Coates, NE	9	0	9	0	54
Tim Brown, Oak	9	0	9	0	54

NFC	TD	Rush	Rec	Ret	Pts
Terry Allen, Wash	21	21	0	0	126
Emmitt Smith, Dal	15	12	3	0	90
Ricky Watters, Phi	13	13	0	0	78
Irving Fryar, Phi	11	0	11	0	66
Eddie Kennison*, St.l ..	11	0	9	2	66
Cris Carter, Min	10	0	10	0	60
Keith Jackson, GB	10	0	10	0	60
Dorsey Levens, GB	10	5	5	0	60
Barry Sanders, Det	10	10	0	0	60
Wesley Walls, Car	10	0	10	0	60
Larry Centers, Ariz	9	2	7	0	54
Antonio Freeman, GB ..	9	0	9	0	54
Jerry Rice, SF	9	1	8	0	54
Herman Moore, Det	8	0	8	0	48

Kickers

AFC	PAT	FG	Long	Pts
Cary Blanchard, Ind. ...	27/27	36/40	52	135
Al Del Greco, Hou.	35/35	32/38	56	131
Adam Vinatieri*, NE ...	39/42	27/35	50	120
John Carney, SD	31/31	29/36	53	118
Mike Hollis, Jax	27/27	30/36	53	117
Todd Peterson, Sea. ...	27/27	28/34	54	111
Doug Pelfrey, Cin.	41/41	23/28	49	110
Jason Elam, Den.	46/46	21/28	51	109
Cole Ford, Oak.	36/36	24/31	47	108
Norm Johnson, Pit.	37/37	23/30	49	106
Steve Christie, Buf. ...	33/33	24/29	48	105
Matt Stover, Bal.	34/35	19/25	50	91
Joe Nedney, Mia.	35/36	18/29	44	89
Pete Stoyanovich, KC ..	34/34	17/24	45	85
Nick Lowery, NYJ	26/27	17/24	46	77

NFC	PAT	FG	Long	Pts
John Kasay, Car.	34/35	37/45	53	145
Jeff Wilkins, SF	40/40	30/34	49	130
Chris Boniol, Dal.	24/25	32/36	52	120
Scott Blanton, Wash. ...	40/40	26/32	53	118
Gary Anderson, Phi. ...	40/40	25/29	46	115
Chris Jacke, GB	51/53	21/27	53	114
Morten Andersen, Atl. ..	31/31	22/29	54	97
Scott Sisson, Min.	30/30	22/29	44	96
Brad Daluiso, NYG	22/22	24/27	46	94
Michael Husted, TB	18/19	25/32	50	93
Chip Lohmiller, St.L	28/29	21/25	50	91
Doug Brien, NO	18/18	21/25	54	81
Jeff Jaeger, Chi.	23/23	19/23	49	80
Jason Hanson, Det.	36/36	12/17	51	72
Kevin Butler, Ariz	17/19	14/17	41	59

NFL Regular Season Individual Leaders (Cont.)

Interceptions

AFC	No	Yds	Long	TD
Tyrone Braxton, Den.	9	128	69-td	1
Ashley Ambrose, Cin.	8	63	31-td	1
Terrell Buckley, Mia.	6	164	91-td	1
Rod Woodson, Pit.	6	121	43-td	1
Mark Collins, KC	6	45	23	0

NFC	No	Yds	Long	TD
Keith Lyle, St.L	9	152	68	0
Eugene Robinson, GB	6	107	39	0
Marquez Pope, SF	6	98	55-td	1
Aeneas Williams, Ariz	6	89	65-td	1
Donnell Woolford, Chi.	6	37	28-td	1
Twelve tied with five each.				

Sacks

AFC	No
Michael McCrary, Sea.	13.5
Bruce Smith, Buf.	13.5
Chad Brown, Pit.	13.0
Michael Sinclair, Sea.	13.0
Derrick Thomas, KC	13.0
Alfred Williams, Den.	13.0

NFC	No
Kevin Greene, Car.	14.5
Lamar Lathon, Car.	13.5
William Fuller, Phi.	13.0
Roy Barker, SF	12.5
Simeon Rice*, Ariz.	12.5

Punting

AFC	No	Yds	Lg	Avg	In20
John Kidd, Mia.	78	3611	63	46.3	27
Chris Gardocki, Ind.	68	3105	61	45.7	23
Darren Bennett, SD	87	3967	66	45.6	23
Lee Johnson, Cin.	80	3630	67	45.4	16
Brian Hansen, NYJ	74	3311	69	44.7	13

NFC	No	Yds	Lg	Avg	In20
Matt Turk, Wash.	75	3386	63	45.1	25
Sean Landeta, St.L	78	3491	70	44.8	23
Todd Sauerbrun, Chi.	78	3491	72	44.8	15
Tommy Thompson, SF	73	3217	65	44.1	20
Jeff Feagles, Ariz	76	3328	68	43.8	23
Mark Royals, Det.	69	3020	60	43.8	11

Punt Returns
(Minimum of 20 returns)

AFC	No	FC	Yds	Avg	Long	TD
Darrien Gordon, SD	36	13	537	14.9	81-td	1
Rod Smith, Den.	23	15	283	12.3	36	0
Todd Kinchen, Den.	26	4	300	11.5	40	0
Dave Meggett, NE	52	9	588	11.3	60-td	1
Chris Hudson, Jax	32	12	348	10.9	60	0

NFC	No	FC	Yds	Avg	Long	TD
Desmond Howard, GB	58	16	875	15.1	92-td	3
Eddie Kennison*, St.L	29	16	423	14.6	78-td	2
Winslow Oliver*, Car.	52	17	598	11.5	84-td	1
Brian Mitchell, Wash.	23	16	258	11.2	71	0
Eric Metcalf, Atl.	27	9	296	11.0	39	0

Kickoff Returns
(Minimum of 20 returns)

AFC	No	Yds	Avg	Long	TD
Tamarick Vanover, KC	33	854	25.9	97-td	1
Mel Gray, Hou.	50	1224	24.5	88	0
Vaughn Hebron, Den.	45	1099	24.4	59	0
Irving Spikes, Mia.	28	681	24.3	59	0
Aaron Bailey, Ind.	43	1041	24.2	95-td	1

NFC	No	Yds	Avg	Long	TD
Michael Bates, Car.	33	998	30.2	93-td	1
Herschel Walker, Dal.	27	779	28.9	89	0
Tyrone Hughes, NO	70	1791	25.6	58	0
Glyn Milburn, Det.	64	1627	25.4	65	0
Derrick Witherspoon, Phi.	53	1271	24.0	97-td	2

Single Game Highs
(*) indicates overtime game.

Passing

AFC	Att/Cmp	Yds	TD
Mark Brunell, Jax. at NE (9/22)	23/39	432	3
V. Testaverde, Bal. vs. St. L (10/27)	31/51	429	3
Mark Brunell, Jax. at St.L (10/20)	37/52	421	0
Drew Bledsoe, NE vs. Mia. (11/3)	30/41	419	3
Drew Bledsoe, NE vs. Buf. (10/27)	32/45	373	1

NFC	Att/Cmp	Yds	TD
B. Esiason, Ariz. at Wash. (11/10)	35/59	522	3
Brett Favre, GB vs. SF (10/14)	28/61	395	1
Steve Young, SF vs. Car. (12/8)	27/41	393	3
B. Esiason, Ariz. vs. Phi. (11/24)	24/43	367	3
Kent Graham, Ariz. vs. St. L (9/29)	37/58	366	4

Rushing

AFC	Car	Yds	TD
Adrian Murrell, NYJ at Ariz. (10/27)	31	199	1
Terrell Davis, Den. vs. Bal. (10/20)	28	194	2
Curtis Martin, NE vs. Wash. (10/13)	17	164	2
Terrell Davis, Den. at NE (11/17)	32	154	3†
Eddie George, Hou. at Cin. (10/6)*	26	152	1
Karim Abdul-Jabbar, Mia. at NYJ (12/22)	30	152	1
†Davis had one TD catch and two TD rushes.			

NFC	Car	Yds	TD
Leshon Johnson, Ariz. at NO (9/22)	21	214	2
Barry Sanders, Det. at SF (12/23)	28	175	1
Ray Zellars, NO vs. Chi. (10/13)	20	174	1
Ricky Watters, Phi. vs. Mia. (10/20)	25	173	1
Barry Sanders, Det. at Min. (9/1)	24	163	0

Reception Yards

AFC	Ct	Yds	TD
Keenan McCardell, Jax. at St. L (10/20)	16	232	0
Derrick Alexander, Bal. vs. Pitt. (12/1)	7	198	1
Jeff Graham, NYJ at Ind. (11/17)	9	189	3
Carl Pickens, Cin. at Atl. (11/24)	11	176	3
Jimmy Smith, Jax. vs. Cin. (12/1)	7	162	0
Wayne Chrebet, NYJ at Jax. (10/13)	12	162	1

NFC	Ct	Yds	TD
Isaac Bruce, St.L at Bal. (10/27)	11	229	1
Eddie Kennison, St.L at Atl. (12/15)	5	226	2
Don Beebe, GB vs. SF (10/14)	11	220	1
Michael Irvin, Dal. at Ariz. (12/8)	8	198	1
Michael Irvin, Dal. at Mia. (10/27)	12	186	1

NFL Bests

Longest Field Goal
56 yds ....Al Del Greco, Hou. vs. SF (10/27)

Longest Run from Scrimmage
80 yds ....Kordell Stewart, Pit. at Car. (12/22), TD

Longest Pass Play
95 yds ..Todd Collins to Quinn Early, Buf. at Ind. (12/1), TD

Longest Interception Return
104 yds ....James Willis (14 yds) lateral to Troy Vincent
(90 yds), Phi. at Dal. (11/3), TD

Longest Punt Return
92 yds ....Desmond Howard, GB at Det. (12/15), TD

Longest Kickoff Return
97 yds ....by three players

NFL Regular Season Team Leaders

Offensive Downs

AFC	Tot	Rush	Pass	Pen	Made	Att	Pct	Made	Att	Pct
		First Downs				**3rd Downs**			**4th Downs**	
New England	339	103	206	30	84	228	36.8	19	34	55.9
Baltimore	338	108	208	22	88	201	43.8	4	10	40.0
Denver	336	134	180	22	112	229	48.9	6	11	54.5
Cincinnati	332	114	190	28	102	236	43.2	5	12	41.7
Jacksonville	325	90	208	27	87	208	41.8	5	8	62.5
NY Jets	319	94	191	34	95	232	40.9	9	22	40.9
Kansas City	312	111	168	33	77	221	34.8	8	17	47.1
Oakland	306	98	172	36	91	224	40.6	9	14	64.3
Pittsburgh	296	138	146	12	84	208	40.4	4	10	40.0
Buffalo	294	128	149	17	83	238	34.9	9	14	64.3
Miami	293	92	173	28	89	221	40.3	8	19	42.1
Indianapolis	288	89	172	27	81	215	37.7	5	12	41.7
Houston	287	110	157	20	79	206	38.3	7	11	63.6
San Diego	272	80	168	24	78	230	33.9	9	16	56.3
Seattle	268	94	147	27	64	212	30.2	7	17	41.2

NFC	Tot	Rush	Pass	Pen	Made	Att	Pct	Made	Att	Pct
		First Downs				**3rd Downs**			**4th Downs**	
Green Bay	338	118	197	23	97	219	44.3	5	11	45.5
Philadelphia	319	107	196	16	83	219	37.9	6	15	40.0
Detroit	317	105	180	32	73	190	38.4	9	20	45.0
San Francisco	315	108	188	19	76	216	35.2	12	19	63.2
Arizona	308	70	214	24	95	228	41.7	11	17	64.7
Washington	307	106	174	27	77	203	37.9	7	9	77.8
Chicago	300	104	176	20	78	231	33.8	20	28	71.4
Atlanta	293	67	203	23	79	200	39.5	4	10	40.0
Carolina	292	93	160	39	84	226	37.2	6	13	46.2
Dallas	286	105	163	18	89	213	41.8	4	8	50.0
Minnesota	284	75	186	23	101	240	42.1	3	5	60.0
Tampa Bay	260	90	152	18	89	225	39.6	9	24	37.5
St. Louis	255	93	141	21	84	224	37.5	9	19	47.4
NY Giants	248	82	145	21	61	220	27.7	9	20	45.0
New Orleans	232	77	135	20	65	207	31.4	6	19	31.6

Takeaways/Giveaways

AFC	Int	Fum	Tot	Int	Fum	Tot	Net Diff
	Takeaways			**Giveaways**			
Cincinnati	34	10	44	16	9	25	+19
Miami	20	16	36	11	13	24	+12
New England ..	23	11	34	15	12	27	+7
Pittsburgh	23	17	40	19	14	33	+7
San Diego	22	14	36	21	11	32	+4
Kansas City	17	10	27	14	10	24	+3
Seattle	14	18	32	17	12	29	+3
Denver	23	9	32	17	15	32	0
Indianapolis	13	10	23	11	13	24	-1
Jacksonville	13	14	27	20	10	30	-3
Houston	12	14	26	15	15	30	-4
Oakland	17	9	26	19	12	31	-5
Buffalo	14	14	28	24	13	37	-9
Baltimore	15	7	22	20	13	33	-11
NY Jets	11	15	26	30	16	46	-20

NFC	Int	Fum	Tot	Int	Fum	Tot	Net Diff
	Takeaways			**Giveaways**			
Green Bay	26	13	39	13	11	24	+15
Carolina	22	16	38	11	14	25	+13
Washington	21	9	30	11	7	18	+12
San Francisco ..	20	14	34	16	8	24	+10
Dallas	19	14	33	14	15	29	+4
Minnesota	22	13	35	19	13	32	+3
Chicago	17	11	28	18	9	27	+1
NY Giants	22	13	35	21	13	34	+1
Philadelphia	19	12	31	18	14	32	-1
St. Louis	26	13	39	23	21	44	-5
Tampa Bay	17	12	29	20	14	34	-5
Detroit	11	8	19	21	5	26	-7
Arizona	11	14	25	21	14	35	-10
New Orleans ...	12	10	22	17	20	37	-15
Atlanta	6	17	23	30	11	41	-18

Overall Club Rankings

Combined AFC and NFC rankings by yards gained on offense and yards given up on defense. Teams listed in alphabetical order with AFC teams in *italics*.

	Rush	Pass	Rank	Rush	Pass	Rank
	Offense			**Defense**		
Arizona	25	6	**12t**	21	21	**21**
Atlanta	27	7	**16**	26	27	**29**
Baltimore	14	2	**3**	23	30	**30**
Buffalo	8	17	**17**	14	8	**9**
Carolina	15	22	**23**	8	12	**10**
Chicago	16	19	**21**	11	14	**12**
Cincinnati	13	12	**10**	12	29	**25**
Dallas	18	20	**24**	10	2	**3**
Denver	1	13	**1**	1	10	**4**
Detroit	12	18	**20**	25	18	**20**
Green Bay ...	11	5	**5**	4	1	**1**
Houston	6	21	**18**	2	13	**6**
Indianapolis ...	28	16	**25**	18	23	**22**
Jacksonville ...	17	1	**2**	19	16	**16**
Kansas City ...	4	26	**22**	13	22	**18**
Miami	19	11	**14**	7	24	**17**
Minnesota	24	9	**11**	24	9	**15**
New England .	26	3	**7**	6	28	**19**
New Orleans ..	30	25	**29**	27	3	**14**
NY Giants	21	30	**30**	16	15	**14**
NY Jets	23	10	**12t**	29	19	**27**
Oakland	3	23	**8**	15	7	**8**
Philadelphia ..	9	4	**4**	9	6	**5**
Pittsburgh	2	27	**15**	3	5	**2**
St. Louis	20	28	**27**	20	26	**26**
San Diego	29	14	**26**	17	25	**23**
San Francisco .	10	8	**6**	5	11	**7**
Seattle	5	24	**19**	28	17	**24**
Tampa Bay	22	29	**28**	22	4	**11**
Washington ..	7	15	**9**	30	20	**28**

AFC Team by Team Statistics

Players with more than one team during the regular season are listed with club they ended season with; (*) indicates rookies.

Baltimore Ravens

Passing (5 Att)	Att	Cmp	Pct	Yds	TD	Rate
Vinny Testaverde ...	549	325	59.2	4177	33	88.7
Eric Zeier	21	10	47.6	97	1	57.0

Interceptions: Testaverde 19, Zeier.

Top Receivers	No	Yds	Avg	Long	TD
Michael Jackson ...	76	1201	15.8	86-td	14
Derrick Alexander ..	62	1099	17.7	64-td	9
Brian Kinchen	55	581	10.6	29	1
Floyd Turner	38	461	12.1	27-td	2
Earnest Byner	30	270	9.0	40	1
Bam Morris	25	242	9.7	52-td	1
Eric Green	15	150	10.0	23	1

Top Rushers	Car	Yds	Avg	Long	TD
Bam Morris	172	737	4.3	19	4
Earnest Byner	159	634	4.0	42	4
Vinny Testaverde ..	34	188	5.5	22	2
Carwell Gardner ..	26	108	4.2	19	0

Most Touchdowns	TD	Run	Rec	Ret	Pts
Michael Jackson	14	0	14	0	88
Derrick Alexander ..	9	0	9	0	56
Earnest Byner	5	4	1	0	30
Bam Morris	5	4	1	0	30
Vinny Testaverde ..	2	2	0	0	14
Floyd Turner	2	0	2	0	12

2-Pt. Conversions: Jackson 2, Alexander, Gardner, Testaverde.

Kicking	PAT/Att	FG/Att	Lg	Pts
Matt Stover	34/35	19/25	50	91

Punts (10 or more)	No	Yds	Long	Avg	In20
Greg Montgomery ..	68	2980	67	43.8	23

Most Interceptions		Most Sacks	
Antonio Langham ..	5	Mike Caldwell	4½
Eric Turner	5		

Buffalo Bills

Passing (5 Att)	Att	Cmp	Pct	Yds	TD	Rate
Jim Kelly	379	222	58.6	2810	14	73.2
Todd Collins	99	55	55.6	739	4	71.9
Alex Van Pelt	5	2	40.0	9	0	47.9

Interceptions: Kelly 19, Collins 5.

Top Receivers	No	Yds	Avg	Long	TD
Andre Reed	66	1036	15.7	67-td	6
Quinn Early	50	798	16.0	95-td	4
Lonnie Johnson	46	457	9.9	33	0
Thurman Thomas ...	26	254	9.8	69	0
Steve Tasker	21	372	17.7	62	3
Eric Moulds*	20	279	14.0	47	2
Tony Cline	19	117	6.2	15	1
Darick Holmes	16	102	6.4	20	1

Top Rushers	Car	Yds	Avg	Long	TD
Thurman Thomas ...	281	1033	3.7	36	8
Darick Holmes	189	571	3.0	37	4
Jim Kelly	19	66	3.5	22	2
Tim Tindale	14	49	3.5	15	0

Most Touchdowns	TD	Run	Rec	Ret	Pts
Thurman Thomas ...	8	8	0	0	48
Andre Reed	6	0	6	0	36
Darick Holmes	5	4	1	0	32
Quinn Early	4	0	4	0	26

2-Pt. Conversions: Early, Holmes.

Kicking	PAT/Att	FG/Att	Lg	Pts
Steve Christie	33/33	24/29	48	105

Punts (10 or more)	No	Yds	Long	Avg	In20
Chris Mohr	101	4194	80	41.5	27

Most Interceptions		Most Sacks	
Kurt Schulz	4	Bruce Smith	13½

Cincinnati Bengals

Passing (5 Att)	Att	Cmp	Pct	Yds	TD	Rate
Jeff Blake	549	308	56.1	3624	24	80.3
Erik Wilhelm	13	7	53.8	90	1	61.9

Interceptions: Blake 14, Wilhelm 2.

Top Receivers	No	Yds	Avg	Long	TD
Carl Pickens	100	1180	11.8	61-td	12
Darnay Scott	58	833	14.4	50-td	5
Tony McGee	38	446	11.7	22	4
David Dunn	32	509	15.9	40	1
Eric Bieniemy	32	272	8.5	42	0
Ki-Jana Carter	22	169	7.7	20	1

Top Rushers	Car	Yds	Avg	Long	TD
Garrison Hearst ...	225	847	3.8	24	0
Jeff Blake	72	317	4.4	18	2
Eric Bieniemy	56	269	4.8	33-td	2
Ki-Jana Carter	91	264	2.9	31-td	8
Jeff Cothran	15	44	2.9	9	1

Most Touchdowns	TD	Run	Rec	Ret	Pts
Carl Pickens	12	0	12	0	74
Ki-Jana Carter	9	8	1	0	54
Darnay Scott	5	0	5	0	30
Tony McGee	4	0	4	0	24

Three tied with two each.

2-Pt. Conversions: Hearst, Pickens.

Kicking	PAT/Att	FG/Att	Lg	Pts
Doug Pelfrey	41/41	23/28	49	110

Punts (10 or more)	No	Yds	Long	Avg	In20
Lee Johnson	80	3630	67	45.4	16

Most Interceptions		Most Sacks	
Ashley Ambrose ...	8	Dan Wilkinson	6½

Denver Broncos

Passing (5 Att)	Att	Cmp	Pct	Yds	TD	Rate
John Elway	466	287	61.6	3328	26	89.2
Bill Musgrave	52	31	59.6	276	0	57.9
Jeff Lewis*	17	9	52.9	58	0	35.9

Interceptions: Elway 14, Musgrave 2, Lewis.

Top Receivers	No	Yds	Avg	Long	TD
Shannon Sharpe ...	80	1062	13.3	51	10
Anthony Miller	56	735	13.1	46	3
Ed McCaffrey	48	553	11.5	39-td	7
Aaron Craver	39	297	7.6	39-td	1
Terrell Davis	36	310	8.6	23	2
Rod Smith	16	237	14.8	49-td	2
Mike Sherrard	16	186	11.6	25-td	1

Top Rushers	Car	Yds	Avg	Long	TD
Terrell Davis	345	1538	4.5	71-td	13
Vaughn Hebron	49	262	5.3	47	0
John Elway	50	249	5.0	22	4
Aaron Craver	59	232	3.9	28	2

Most Touchdowns	TD	Run	Rec	Ret	Pts
Terrell Davis	15	13	2	0	90
Shannon Sharpe	10	0	10	0	60
Ed McCaffrey	7	0	7	0	42
John Elway	4	4	0	0	24
Anthony Miller	4	1	3	0	24

2-Pt. Conversions: None.

Kicking	PAT/Att	FG/Att	Lg	Pts
Jason Elam	46/46	21/28	51	109

Punts (10 or more)	No	Yds	Long	Avg	In20
Tom Rouen	65	2714	57	41.8	16

Most Interceptions		Most Sacks	
Tyrone Braxton	9	Alfred Williams	13

Houston Oilers

Passing (5 Att)	Att	Cmp	Pct	Yds	TD	Rate
Chris Chandler	320	184	57.5	2099	16	79.7
Steve McNair	143	88	61.5	1197	6	90.6

Interceptions: Chandler 11, McNair 4.

Top Receivers	No	Yds	Avg	Long	TD
Frank Wycheck	53	511	9.6	29	6
Chris Sanders	48	882	18.4	83-td	4
Ronnie Harmon	42	488	11.6	43	2
Willie Davis	39	464	11.9	49	6
Derek Russell	34	421	12.4	29	2
Eddie George* ...	23	182	7.9	17	0

Top Rushers	Car	Yds	Avg	Long	TD
Eddie George*	335	1368	4.1	76	8
Steve McNair	31	169	5.5	24-td	2
Rodney Thomas ...	49	151	3.1	24-td	1
Ronnie Harmon	29	131	4.5	25	1
Chris Chandler	28	113	4.0	16	0

Most Touchdowns	TD	Run	Rec	Ret	Pts
Eddie George*	8	8	0	0	48
Willie Davis	6	0	6	0	36
Frank Wycheck	6	0	6	0	36
Chris Sanders	4	0	4	0	24
Ronnie Harmon	3	1	2	0	18

2-Pt. Conversions: None.

Kicking	PAT/Att	FG/Att	Lg	Pts
Al Del Greco	35/35	32/38	56	131

Punts (10 or more)	No	Yds	Long	Avg	In20
Reggie Roby	67	2973	68	44.4	25

Most Interceptions		Most Sacks	
Darryll Lewis	5	Anthony Cook	7½

Indianapolis Colts

Passing (5 Att)	Att	Cmp	Pct	Yds	TD	Rate
Jim Harbaugh	405	232	57.3	2630	13	76.3
Paul Justin	127	74	58.3	839	2	83.4
Kerwin Bell	5	5	100.0	75	1	158.3

Interceptions: Harbaugh 11.

Top Receivers	No	Yds	Avg	Long	TD
Marvin Harrison* ..	64	836	13.1	41	8
Marshall Faulk	56	428	7.6	30	0
Sean Dawkins	54	751	13.9	42	1
Ken Dilger	42	503	12.0	51	4
Lamont Warren	22	174	7.9	17	0
Aaron Bailey	18	302	16.8	40	0
Brian Stablein	18	192	10.7	30-td	1

Top Rushers	Car	Yds	Avg	Long	TD
Marshall Faulk	198	587	3.0	43	7
Lamont Warren	67	230	3.4	53	1
Jim Harbaugh	48	192	4.0	21	1
Cliff Groce	46	184	4.0	24	0
Zack Crockett	31	164	5.3	25	0
Vince Workman ...	24	70	2.9	11	0

Most Touchdowns	TD	Run	Rec	Ret	Pts
Marvin Harrison* ...	8	0	8	0	48
Marshall Faulk	7	7	0	0	42
Ken Dilger	4	0	4	0	24
Jason Belser	2	0	0	2	12

2-Pt. Conversions: None.

Kicking	PAT/Att	FG/Att	Lg	Pts
Cary Blanchard	27/27	36/40	52	135

Punts (10 or more)	No	Yds	Long	Avg	In20
Chris Gardocki	68	3105	61	45.7	23

Most Interceptions		Most Sacks	
Jason Belser	4	Richard Dent	6½

Jacksonville Jaguars

Passing (5 Att)	Att	Cmp	Pct	Yds	TD	Rate
Mark Brunell	557	353	63.4	4367	19	84.0

Interceptions: Brunell 20.

Top Receivers	No	Yds	Avg	Long	TD
Keenan McCardell .	85	1129	13.3	52	3
Jimmy Smith	83	1244	15.0	62	7
Pete Mitchell	52	575	11.1	30	1
Willie Jackson	33	486	14.7	58	3
James Stewart	30	177	5.9	21-td	2
Derek Brown	17	141	8.3	16	0

Released: Andre Rison on Nov. 18 (see Green Bay).

Top Rushers	Car	Yds	Avg	Long	TD
James Stewart	190	723	3.8	34	8
Natrone Means ...	152	507	3.3	35	2
Mark Brunell	80	396	5.0	33	3
Le'Shai Maston ...	8	22	2.8	7	0

Most Touchdowns	TD	Run	Rec	Ret	Pts
James Stewart	10	8	2	0	60
Jimmy Smith	7	0	7	0	42
Mark Brunnell	3	3	0	0	22
Keenan McCardell ..	3	0	3	0	22
Willie Jackson	3	0	3	0	20
Natrone Means	3	2	1	0	18

2-Pt. Conversions: Brunnell 2, McCardell 2, Jackson.

Kicking	PAT/Att	FG/Att	Lg	Pts
Mike Hollis	27/27	30/36	53	117

Punts (10 or more)	No	Yds	Long	Avg	In20
Bryan Barker	69	3016	62	43.7	16

Most Interceptions		Most Sacks	
Chris Hudson	2	Clyde Simmons	7½
Kevin Hardy*	2		
Dave Thomas	2		
Travis Davis	2		

Kansas City Chiefs

Passing (5 Att)	Att	Cmp	Pct	Yds	TD	Rate
Steve Bono	438	235	53.7	2572	12	68.0
Rich Gannon	90	54	60.0	491	6	92.4

Interceptions: Bono 13, Gannon.

Top Receivers	No	Yds	Avg	Long	TD
Kimble Anders	60	529	8.8	45	2
Chris Penn	49	628	12.8	22	5
Sean LaChapelle ...	27	422	15.6	69	2
Marcus Allen	27	270	10.0	59	0
Tamarick Vanover ..	21	241	11.5	24	1
Todd McNair	21	181	8.6	29	1

Top Rushers	Car	Yds	Avg	Long	TD
Marcus Allen	206	830	4.0	35	9
Greg Hill	135	645	4.8	28	4
Kimble Anders	54	201	3.7	15-td	0
Donnell Bennett	36	166	4.6	34	0
Rich Gannon	12	81	6.8	19	0

Most Touchdowns	TD	Run	Rec	Ret	Pts
Marcus Allen	9	9	0	0	54
Greg Hill	5	4	1	0	30
Chris Penn	5	0	5	0	30
Kimble Anders	4	2	2	0	24
Sean LaChapelle ...	2	0	2	0	12
Tamarick Vanover ..	2	0	1	1	12

2-Pt. Conversions: None.

Kicking	PAT/Att	FG/Att	Lg	Pts
Pete Stoyanovich ...	34/34	17/24	45	85

Punts (10 or more)	No	Yds	Long	Avg	In20
Louie Aguiar	88	3667	68	41.7	25

Most Interceptions		Most Sacks	
Mark Collins	6	Derrick Thomas	13

Miami Dolphins

Passing (5 Att)	Att	Cmp	Pct	Yds	TD	Rate
Dan Marino	373	221	59.2	2795	17	87.8
Craig Erickson	99	55	55.6	780	4	86.3
Bernie Kosar	32	24	75.0	208	1	102.1

Interceptions: Marino 9, Erickson 2.

Top Receivers	No	Yds	Avg	Long	TD
O.J. McDuffie	74	918	12.4	36	8
Fred Barnett	36	562	15.6	66	3
Stanley Pritchett*	33	354	10.7	74-td	0
Troy Drayton	28	331	11.8	51	0
ST.L	2	11	5.5	6	0
MIA	26	320	12.3	51	0
Karim Abdul-Jabbar* .	23	139	6.0	23	0
Randal Hill	21	409	19.5	61	4
Bernie Parmalee	21	189	9.0	17	0

Acquired: TE Drayton from St. Louis for T Billy Milner on Oct. 1.
Released: TE/RB Keith Byars on Oct. 1 (see New England).

Top Rushers	Car	Yds	Avg	Long	TD
Karim Abdul-Jabbar* .	307	1116	3.6	29	11
Irving Spikes	87	316	3.6	49	3
Bernie Parmalee	25	80	3.2	17	0

Most Touchdowns	TD	Run	Rec	Ret	Pts
Karim Abdul-Jabbar* .	11	11	0	0	66
O.J. McDuffie	8	0	8	0	48
Randal Hill	4	0	4	0	24
Irving Spikes	4	3	1	0	24
Fred Barnett	3	0	3	0	18

2-Pt. Conversions: Drayton.

Kicking	PAT/Att	FG/Att	Lg	Pts
Joe Nedney	35/36	18/29	44	89

Punts (10 or more)	No	Yds	Long	Avg	In20
John Kidd	78	3611	63	46.3	26

Most Interceptions		Most Sacks		
Terrell Buckley	6	Trace Armstrong ...		12

New England Patriots

Passing (5 Att)	Att	Cmp	Pct	Yds	TD	Rate
Drew Bledsoe	623	373	59.9	4086	27	83.7

Interceptions: Bledsoe 15.

Top Receivers	No	Yds	Avg	Long	TD
Terry Glenn*	90	1132	12.6	37-td	6
Ben Coates	62	682	11.0	84-td	9
Shawn Jefferson	50	771	15.4	42	4
Curtis Martin	46	333	7.2	41	3
Dave Meggett	33	292	8.8	26	0
Sam Gash	33	276	8.4	28	2
Keith Byars	32	289	9.0	27	2
MIA	5	40	8.0	16	0
NE	27	249	9.2	27	2

Signed: Byars on Oct. 15 (released by Miami, Oct. 1).

Top Rushers	Car	Yds	Avg	Long	TD
Curtis Martin	316	1152	3.6	57	14
Dave Meggett	40	122	3.1	12	0
Marrio Grier*	27	105	3.9	26	1

Most Touchdowns	TD	Run	Rec	Ret	Pts
Curtis Martin	17	14	3	0	104
Ben Coates	9	0	9	0	56
Terry Glenn*	6	0	6	0	36
Shawn Jefferson ...	4	0	4	0	24

Three tied with two each.

2-Pt. Conversions: Byars, Coates, Gash, Martin.

Kicking	PAT/Att	FG/Att	Lg	Pts
Adam Vinatieri* ...	39/42	27/35	50	120

Punts (10 or more)	No	Yds	Long	Avg	In20
Tom Tupa	63	2739	62	43.5	14

Most Interceptions		Most Sacks		
Willie Clay	4	Willie McGinest ...		9½

New York Jets

Passing (5 Att)	Att	Cmp	Pct	Yds	TD	Rate
Frank Reich	331	175	52.9	2205	15	68.9
Neil O'Donnell	188	110	58.5	1147	4	67.8
Glenn Foley	110	54	49.1	559	3	46.7

Interceptions: Reich 15, O'Donnell 7, Foley 7.

Top Receivers	No	Yds	Avg	Long	TD
Wayne Chrebet	84	909	10.8	44	3
Keyshawn Johnson* .	63	844	13.4	50	8
Jeff Graham	50	788	15.8	78-td	6
Richie Anderson	44	385	8.8	48	0
Webster Slaughter ..	32	434	13.6	53	2
Alex Van Dyke*	17	118	6.9	12	1
Adrian Murrell	17	81	4.8	30	1

Top Rushers	No	Yds	Avg	Long	TD
Adrian Murrell	301	1249	4.1	78	6
Richie Anderson ...	47	150	3.2	11	1
Reggie Cobb	25	85	3.4	9	1
Frank Reich	18	31	1.7	10	0

Most Touchdowns	TD	Run	Rec	Ret	Pts
Keyshawn Johnson* .	8	0	8	0	50
Adrian Murrell	7	6	1	0	42
Jeff Graham	6	0	6	0	36
Wayne Chrebet	3	0	3	0	18
Aaron Glenn	2	0	0	2	12
Webster Slaughter ..	2	0	2	0	12

2-Pt. Conversions: Kyle Brady, Johnson.

Kicking	PAT/Att	FG/Att	Lg	Pts
Nick Lowery	26/27	17/24	46	77

Punts (10 or more)	No	Yds	Long	Avg	In20
Brian Hansen	74	3311	69	44.7	13

Most Interceptions		Most Sacks		
Aaron Glenn	4	Hugh Douglas		8

Oakland Raiders

Passing (5 Att)	Att	Cmp	Pct	Yds	TD	Rate
Jeff Hostetler	402	242	60.2	2548	23	83.2
Billy Joe Hobert	104	57	54.8	667	4	67.3
David Klingler	24	10	41.7	87	0	51.9

Interceptions: Hostetler 14, Hobert 5.

Top Receivers	No	Yds	Avg	Long	TD
Tim Brown	90	1104	12.3	42-td	9
Daryl Hobbs	44	423	9.6	29	3
James Jett	43	601	14.0	58-td	4
Rickey Dudley*	34	386	11.4	62-td	4
Derrick Fenner	31	252	8.1	23-td	4
Napoleon Kaufman ..	22	143	6.5	19	1
Harvey Williams ...	22	143	6.5	20	0

Top Rushers	Car	Yds	Avg	Long	TD
Napoleon Kaufman .	150	874	5.8	77	1
Harvey Williams .	121	431	3.6	44	0
Joe Aska	62	326	5.3	38	1
Derrick Fenner	67	245	3.7	17	4
Jeff Hostetler	37	179	4.8	17	1

Most Touchdowns	TD	Run	Rec	Ret	Pts
Tim Brown	9	0	9	0	54
Derrick Fenner	8	4	4	0	48
Rickey Dudley*	4	0	4	0	24
James Jett	4	0	4	0	24
Daryl Hobbs	3	0	3	0	18
Napoleon Kaufman .	2	1	1	0	12

2-Pt. Conversions: None.

Kicking	PAT/Att	FG/Att	Lg	Pts
Cole Ford	36/36	24/31	47	108

Punts (10 or more)	No	Yds	Long	Avg	In20
Jeff Gossett	57	2264	64	39.7	19
Leo Araguz*	13	534	52	41.1	4

Most Interceptions		Most Sacks		
Terry McDaniel	5	Chester McGlockton .		8

Pittsburgh Steelers

Passing (5 Att)

Passing (5 Att)	Att	Cmp	Pct	Yds	TD	Rate
Mike Tomczak	401	222	55.4	2767	15	71.8
Kordell Stewart	30	11	36.7	100	0	18.8
Jim Miller	25	13	52.0	123	0	65.9

Interceptions: Tomczak 17, Stewart 2.

Top Receivers	No	Yds	Avg	Long	TD
Andre Hastings	72	739	10.3	38	6
Charles Johnson	60	1008	16.8	50-td	3
Jerome Bettis	22	122	5.5	16	0
Kordell Stewart	17	293	17.2	48	3
Erric Pegram	17	112	6.6	14	0
Yancey Thigpen	12	244	20.3	39	2
Mark Bruener	12	141	11.8	36	0

Top Rushers	Car	Yds	Avg	Long	TD
Jerome Bettis	320	1431	4.5	50-td	11
Erric Pegram	97	509	5.2	27	1
Kordell Stewart	39	171	4.4	80-td	5
Andre Hastings	4	71	17.8	37	0
Jon Witman*	17	69	4.1	15	0

Most Touchdowns	TD	Run	Rec	Ret	Pts
Jerome Bettis	11	11	0	0	66
Kordell Stewart	8	5	3	0	48
Andre Hastings	6	0	6	0	36
Charles Johnson	3	0	3	0	20

Four tied with two each.

2-Pt. Conversions: Bruener, C. Johnson.

Kicking	PAT/Att	FG/Att	Lg	Pts
Norm Johnson	37/37	23/30	49	106

Punts (10 or more)	No	Yds	Long	Avg	In20
Josh Miller	55	2256	61	41.0	18
Shayne Edge	17	675	48	39.7	7

Signed: Edge on Sept. 24. **Waived:** Edge on Oct. 25.

Most Interceptions		Most Sacks	
Rod Woodson	6	Chad Brown	13

San Diego Chargers

Passing (5 Att)	Att	Cmp	Pct	Yds	TD	Rate
Stan Humphries	416	232	55.8	2670	18	76.7
Sean Salisbury	161	82	50.9	984	5	59.6

Interceptions: Humphries 13, Salisbury 8.

Top Receivers	No	Yds	Avg	Long	TD
Tony Martin	85	1171	13.8	55	14
Terrell Fletcher	61	476	7.8	41	2
Charlie Jones*	41	524	12.8	63-td	4
Andre Coleman	36	486	13.5	50	2
Alfred Pupunu	24	271	11.3	41	1
Deems May	19	188	9.9	39	0

Top Rushers	No	Yds	Avg	Long	TD
Leonard Russell	219	713	3.3	21	7
Terrell Fletcher	77	282	3.7	19	0
Aaron Hayden	55	166	3.0	13	0
Freddie Bradley*	32	109	3.4	17	0
Stan Humphries	21	28	1.3	7	0

Most Touchdowns	TD	Run	Rec	Ret	Pts
Tony Martin	14	0	14	0	84
Leonard Russell	7	7	0	0	42
Charlie Jones*	4	0	4	0	24
Andre Coleman	2	0	2	0	12
Terrell Fletcher	2	0	2	0	12

2-Pt. Conversions: None.

Kicking	PAT/Att	FG/Att	Lg	Pts
John Carney	31/31	29/36	53	118

Punts (10 or more)	No	Yds	Long	Avg	In20
Darren Bennett	87	3967	66	45.6	23

Most Interceptions		Most Sacks	
Rodney Harrison	5	Junior Seau	7

Seattle Seahawks

Passing (5 Att)	Att	Cmp	Pct	Yds	TD	Rate
Rick Mirer	265	136	51.3	1546	5	56.6
John Friesz	211	120	56.9	1629	8	86.4
Gino Torretta	16	5	31.3	41	1	35.4

Interceptions: Mirer 12, Friesz 4, Torretta.

Top Receivers	No	Yds	Avg	Long	TD
Joey Galloway	57	987	17.3	65-td	7
Brian Blades	43	556	12.9	80-td	2
Chris Warren	40	273	6.8	33	0
Carlester Crumpler	26	258	9.9	26	0
Ricky Proehl	23	309	13.4	56	2
Mike Pritchard	21	328	15.6	44	1

Top Rushers	Car	Yds	Avg	Long	TD
Chris Warren	203	855	4.2	51	5
Lamar Smith	153	680	4.4	29	8
Rick Mirer	33	191	5.8	33	2
Joey Galloway	15	127	8.5	51	0

Most Touchdowns	TD	Run	Rec	Ret	Pts
Lamar Smith	8	8	0	0	54
Joey Galloway	8	0	7	1	48
Chris Warren	5	5	0	0	32
Brian Blades	2	0	2	0	12
Rick Mirer	2	2	0	0	12
Ricky Proehl	2	0	2	0	12

2-Pt. Conversions: Smith 3, Warren.

Kicking	PAT/Att	FG/Att	Lg	Pts
Todd Peterson	27/27	28/34	54	111

Punts (10 or more)	No	Yds	Long	Avg	In20
Rick Tuten	85	3746	66	44.1	21

Most Interceptions		Most Sacks	
Darryl Williams	5	Michael McCrary	13½

AFC Team Leaders

Offense

	Points		Yardage		
	For	Avg	Rush	Pass	Total	Avg
Denver	391	24.4	2362	3429	5791	361.9
Jacksonville	325	20.3	1650	4110	5760	360.0
Baltimore	371	23.2	1745	3978	5723	357.7
New England	418	26.1	1468	3901	5369	335.6
Oakland	340	21.3	2172	3080	5252	328.3
Cincinnati	372	23.3	1793	3432	5225	326.6
NY Jets	279	17.4	1565	3625	5190	324.4
Miami	339	21.2	1622	3543	5165	322.8
Pittsburgh	344	21.5	2299	2841	5140	321.3
Buffalo	319	19.9	1901	3218	5119	319.9
Houston	345	21.6	1950	3098	5048	315.5
Seattle	317	19.8	1997	3027	5024	314.0
Kansas City	297	18.6	2009	2890	4899	306.2
Indianapolis	317	19.8	1448	3296	4744	296.5
San Diego	310	19.4	1312	3358	4670	291.9

Defense

	Points		Yardage		
	Opp	Avg	Rush	Pass	Total	Avg
Pittsburgh	257	16.1	1415	2947	4362	272.6
Denver	275	17.2	1331	3139	4470	279.4
Houston	319	19.9	1385	3225	4610	288.1
Oakland	293	18.3	1676	3021	4697	293.6
Buffalo	266	16.6	1669	3068	4737	296.1
Jacksonville	335	20.9	1781	3314	5095	318.4
Miami	325	20.3	1536	3655	5191	324.4
Kansas City	300	18.8	1666	3538	5204	325.3
New England	313	19.6	1502	3803	5305	331.6
Indianapolis	334	20.9	1760	3643	5403	337.7
San Diego	376	23.5	1755	3666	5421	338.8
Seattle	376	23.5	2096	3341	5437	339.8
Cincinnati	369	23.1	1643	3826	5469	341.8
NY Jets	454	28.4	2200	3364	5564	347.8
Baltimore	441	27.6	1920	3969	5889	368.1

NFC Team by Team Statistics

Players with more than one team during the regular season are listed with club they ended season with; (*) indicates rookies.

Arizona Cardinals

Passing (5 Att)	Att	Cmp	Pct	Yds	TD	Rate
Boomer Esiason	339	190	56.0	2293	11	70.6
Kent Graham	274	146	53.3	1624	12	75.1

Interceptions: Esiason 14, Graham 7.

Top Receivers	No	Yds	Avg	Long	TD
Larry Centers	99	766	7.7	39	7
Frank Sanders	69	813	11.8	34	4
Rob Moore	58	1016	17.5	69	4
Anthony Edwards ..	29	311	10.7	31	1
Pat Carter	26	329	12.7	36	1
Marcus Dowdell ...	20	318	15.9	64-td	2
Leshon Johnson	15	176	11.7	35	1

Top Rushers	Car	Yds	Avg	Long	TD
Leshon Johnson	141	634	4.5	70-td	2
Larry Centers	116	425	3.7	24	2
Leeland McElroy* ..	89	305	3.4	32	1

Most Touchdowns	TD	Run	Rec	Ret	Pts
Larry Centers	9	2	7	0	54
Rob Moore	4	0	4	0	26
Leshon Johnson	4	3	1	0	24
Frank Sanders	4	0	4	0	24

Three tied with two each.

2-Pt. Conversions: Esiason, Moore.

Kicking	PAT/Att	FG/Att	Lg	Pts
Kevin Butler	17/19	14/17	41	59
Greg Davis	12/12	9/14	49	39

Signed: Butler on Nov. 5.

Punts (10 or more)	No	Yds	Long	Avg	In20
Jeff Feagles	76	3328	68	43.8	23

Most Interceptions		Most Sacks	
Aeneas Williams ...	6	Simeon Rice*	12½

Atlanta Falcons

Passing (5 Att)	Att	Cmp	Pct	Yds	TD	Rate
Bobby Hebert	489	295	60.3	3162	22	73.0
Jeff George	99	56	56.6	698	3	76.1
Browning Nagle ...	13	6	46.2	59	1	45.5

Interceptions: Hebert 25, George 3, Nagle 2.
Signed: Nagle on Sept. 24. **Waived:** George on Oct. 22.

Top Receivers	No	Yds	Avg	Long	TD
Bert Emanuel	76	931	12.3	53	6
Terance Mathis	69	771	11.2	55	7
Eric Metcalf	54	599	11.1	67	6
Jamal Anderson ...	49	473	9.7	34	1
J.J. Birden	30	319	10.6	57	2
Tyrone Brown	28	325	11.6	38	1
Roell Preston	21	208	9.9	17-td	1
Craig Heyward	16	168	10.5	25	0

Top Rushers	Car	Yds	Avg	Long	TD
Jamal Anderson ...	232	1055	4.5	32-td	5
Craig Heyward	72	321	4.5	34	3
Bobby Hebert	15	59	3.9	25	1

Most Touchdowns	TD	Run	Rec	Ret	Pts
Terance Mathis	7	0	7	0	44
Jamal Anderson ...	6	5	1	0	36
Bert Emanuel	6	0	6	0	36
Eric Metcalf	6	0	6	0	36
Craig Heyward	3	3	0	0	18

2-Pt. Conversions: Mathis.

Kicking	PAT/Att	FG/Att	Lg	Pts
Morten Andersen ..	31/31	22/29	54	97

Punts (10 or more)	No	Yds	Long	Avg	In20
Dan Stryzinski	75	3152	58	42.0	22

Most Interceptions		Most Sacks	
Brad Edwards	2	Clay Matthews	6½

Carolina Panthers

Passing (5 Att)	Att	Cmp	Pct	Yds	TD	Rate
Kerry Collins	364	204	56.0	2454	14	79.4
Steve Beuerlein ...	123	69	56.1	879	8	93.5

Interceptions: Collins 9, Beuerlein 2.

Top Receivers	No	Yds	Avg	Long	TD
Wesley Walls	61	713	11.7	40-td	10
Mark Carrier	58	808	13.9	39	6
Willie Green	46	614	13.3	50	3
Howard Griffith	27	223	8.3	21	1
Anthony Johnson ..	26	192	7.4	55	0
Mushin Muhammad* .	25	407	16.3	54-td	1
Winslow Oliver* ...	15	144	9.6	29	0

Top Rushers	Car	Yds	Avg	Long	TD
Anthony Johnson ..	300	1120	3.7	29	6
Tim Biakabutuka* ..	71	229	3.2	17	0
Winslow Oliver* ...	47	183	3.9	16	0
Raghib Ismail	8	80	10.0	35-td	1
Dino Philyaw	12	38	3.2	8	1
Kerry Collins	32	38	1.2	14	0

Most Touchdowns	TD	Run	Rec	Ret	Pts
Wesley Walls	10	0	10	0	60
Mark Carrier	6	0	6	0	36
Anthony Johnson ..	6	6	0	0	36
Willie Green	3	0	3	0	18
Howard Griffith	2	1	1	0	12

2-Pt. Conversions: Collins.

Kicking	PAT/Att	FG/Att	Lg	Pts
John Kasay	34/35	37/45	53	145

Punts (10 or more)	No	Yds	Long	Avg	In20
Rohn Stark	77	3128	60	40.6	21

Most Interceptions		Most Sacks	
Chad Cota	5	Kevin Greene	14½
Eric Davis	5		

Chicago Bears

Passing (5 Att)	Att	Cmp	Pct	Yds	TD	Rate
Dave Krieg	377	226	59.9	2278	14	76.3
Erik Kramer	150	73	48.7	781	3	54.3
Shane Matthews ...	17	13	76.5	158	1	124.1

Interceptions: Krieg 12, Kramer 6.

Top Receivers	No	Yds	Avg	Long	TD
Curtis Conway	81	1049	13.0	58-td	7
Michael Timpson ...	62	802	12.9	49	0
Tony Carter	41	233	5.7	29	0
Bobby Engram* ...	33	389	11.8	24	6
Raymont Harris ...	32	296	9.3	47	1
Ryan Wetnight	21	223	10.6	38	1

Top Rushers	Car	Yds	Avg	Long	TD
Raymont Harris ...	194	748	3.9	23	4
Rashaan Salaam ...	143	496	3.5	32	3
Robert Green	60	249	4.2	19	0

Most Touchdowns	TD	Run	Rec	Ret	Pts
Curtis Conway	7	0	7	0	42
Bobby Engram* ...	6	0	6	0	36
Raymont Harris ...	5	4	1	0	30
Rashaan Salaam ...	4	3	1	0	24

Nine tied with one each.

2-Pt. Conversions: None.

Kicking	PAT/Att	FG/Att	Lg	Pts
Jeff Jaeger	23/23	19/23	49	80

Waived: Carlos Huerta on Sept. 16 (see St. Louis Rams).
Signed: Jaeger on Sept. 17.

Punts (10 or more)	No	Yds	Long	Avg	In20
Todd Sauerbrun ...	78	3491	72	44.8	15

Most Interceptions		Most Sacks	
Donnell Woolford ..	6	Alonzo Spellman ...	8

Dallas Cowboys

Passing (5 Att)

	Att	Cmp	Pct	Yds	TD	Rate
Troy Aikman	465	296	63.7	3126	12	80.1
Wade Wilson	18	8	44.4	79	0	34.3

Interceptions: Aikman 13, Wilson.

Top Receivers

	No	Yds	Avg	Long	TD
Michael Irvin	64	962	15.0	61	2
Eric Bjornson	48	388	8.1	25	3
Emmitt Smith	47	249	5.3	21	3
Daryl Johnston	43	278	6.5	23	1
Deion Sanders	36	475	13.2	41	1
Kevin Williams	27	323	12.0	31	1
Kelvin Martin	25	380	15.2	60-td	1

Top Rushers

	Car	Yds	Avg	Long	TD
Emmitt Smith	327	1204	3.7	42	12
Sherman Williams	69	269	3.9	27	0
Herschel Walker	10	83	8.3	39-td	1
Daryl Johnston	22	48	2.2	7	0
Troy Aikman	35	42	1.2	10	1

Most Touchdowns

	TD	Run	Rec	Ret	Pts
Emmitt Smith	15	12	3	0	90
Eric Bjornson	3	0	3	0	20
Michael Irvin	2	0	2	0	14
Deion Sanders	2	0	1	1	12

2-Pt. Conversions: Bjornson, Irvin.

Kicking

	PAT/Att	FG/Att	Lg	Pts
Chris Boniol	24/25	32/36	52	120

Punts (10 or more)

	No	Yds	Long	Avg	In20
John Jett	74	3150	60	42.6	22

Most Interceptions

Kevin Smith	5
Darren Woodson	5

Most Sacks

Tony Tolbert	12

Detroit Lions

Passing (5 Att)

	Att	Cmp	Pct	Yds	TD	Rate
Scott Mitchell	437	253	57.9	2917	17	74.9
Don Majkowski	102	55	53.9	554	3	67.2

Interceptions: Mitchell 17, Majkowski 3, Barry Sanders.

Top Receivers

	No	Yds	Avg	Long	TD
Herman Moore	106	1296	12.2	50-td	9
Brett Perriman	94	1021	10.9	44	5
Johnnie Morton	55	714	13.0	62-td	6
Barry Sanders	24	147	6.1	28	0
Pete Metzelaars	17	146	8.6	20	0

Top Rushers

	Car	Yds	Avg	Long	TD
Barry Sanders	307	1553	5.1	54-td	11
Ron Rivers	19	86	4.5	26	0
Scott Mitchell	37	83	2.2	9	4
Don Majkowski	14	38	2.7	12	0

Most Touchdowns

	TD	Run	Rec	Ret	Pts
Barry Sanders	11	11	0	0	66
Herman Moore	9	0	9	0	56
Johnnie Morton	6	0	6	0	36
Brett Perriman	5	0	5	0	30
Scott Mitchell	4	4	0	0	24

2-Pt. Conversions: Moore.

Kicking

	PAT/Att	FG/Att	Lg	Pts
Jason Hanson	36/36	12/17	51	72

Punts (10 or more)

	No	Yds	Long	Avg	In20
Mark Royals	69	3020	60	43.8	11

Most Interceptions

Ryan McNeil	5

Most Sacks

Robert Porcher	10

Green Bay Packers

Passing (5 Att)

	Att	Cmp	Pct	Yds	TD	Rate
Brett Favre	543	325	59.9	3899	39	95.8

Interceptions: Favre 13.

Top Receivers

	No	Yds	Avg	Long	TD
Antonio Freeman	56	933	16.7	51-td	9
Andre Rison	47	593	12.6	61-td	3
JAX	34	458	13.5	61-td	2
GB	13	135	10.4	22-td	1
Keith Jackson	40	505	12.6	51-td	10
Don Beebe	39	699	17.9	80-td	4
Dorsey Levens	31	226	7.3	49	5
Edgar Bennett	31	176	5.7	25-td	1
Mark Chmura	28	370	13.2	29	0

Claimed: Rison on Nov. 19 (released by Jacksonville, Nov. 18).

Top Rushers

	Car	Yds	Avg	Long	TD
Edgar Bennett	222	899	4.0	23	2
Dorsey Levens	121	566	4.7	24	5
Brett Favre	49	136	2.8	23	2

Most Touchdowns

	TD	Run	Rec	Ret	Pts
Keith Jackson	10	0	10	0	60
Dorsey Levens	10	5	5	0	60
Antonio Freeman	9	0	9	0	54
Don Beebe	6	0	4	2	36
Robert Brooks	4	0	4	0	24

2-Pt. Conversions: Bennett 2.

Kicking

	PAT/Att	FG/Att	Lg	Pts
Chris Jacke	51/53	21/27	53	114

Punts (10 or more)

	No	Yds	Long	Avg	In20
Craig Hentrich	68	2886	65	42.4	28

Most Interceptions

Eugene Robinson	6

Most Sacks

Reggie White	8½

Minnesota Vikings

Passing (5 Att)

	Att	Cmp	Pct	Yds	TD	Rate
Brad Johnson	311	195	62.7	2258	17	89.4
Warren Moon	247	134	54.3	1610	7	68.7

Interceptions: Johnson 10, Moon 9.

Top Receivers

	No	Yds	Avg	Long	TD
Cris Carter	96	1163	12.1	43-td	10
Jake Reed	72	1320	18.3	82-td	7
Amp Lee	54	422	7.8	21	2
Qadry Ismail	22	351	16.0	54-td	3
Charles Evans	22	135	6.1	16	0

Top Rushers

	Car	Yds	Avg	Long	TD
Robert Smith	162	692	4.3	57	3
Leroy Hoard	125	492	3.9	25	3
BAL	15	61	4.1	10	0
CAR	5	11	2.2	5	0
MIN	105	420	4.0	25	3
Amp Lee	51	161	3.2	12	0
Scottie Graham	57	138	2.4	12	0

Signed: Hoard on Nov. 5 (released by Baltimore, Sept. 24 and Carolina, Oct. 21).

Most Touchdowns

	TD	Run	Rec	Ret	Pts
Cris Carter	10	0	10	0	60
Jake Reed	7	0	7	0	42
Leroy Hoard	3	3	0	0	18
Qadry Ismail	3	0	3	0	18
Robert Smith	3	3	0	0	18

2-Pt. Conversions: Jordan, Chris Walsh.

Kicking

	PAT/Att	FG/Att	Lg	Pts
Scott Sisson	30/30	22/29	44	96

Punts (10 or more)

	No	Yds	Long	Avg	In20
Mitch Berger	88	3616	63	41.1	26

Most Interceptions

Orlando Thomas	5

Most Sacks

John Randle	11½

New Orleans Saints

Passing (5 Att)

	Att	Cmp	Pct	Yds	TD	Rate
Jim Everett	464	267	57.5	2797	12	69.4
Doug Nussmeier ...	50	28	56.0	272	1	69.8

Interceptions: Everett 16, Nussmeier.

Top Receivers

	No	Yds	Avg	Long	TD
Torrance Small	50	558	11.2	41	2
Michael Haynes ...	44	786	17.9	51	4
Lorenzo Neal	31	194	6.3	23	1
Hendrick Lusk*	27	210	7.8	24	0
Ricky Whittle*	26	162	6.2	28	0
Haywood Jeffires ..	20	215	10.8	27-td	3

Top Rushers

	Car	Yds	Avg	Long	TD
Mario Bates	164	584	3.6	33	4
Ray Zellars	120	475	4.0	63	4
Lorenzo Neal	21	58	2.8	11	1
Ricky Whittle*	20	52	2.6	15	0

Most Touchdowns

	TD	Run	Rec	Ret	Pts
Michael Haynes	4	0	4	0	26
Mario Bates	4	4	0	0	24
Ray Zellars	4	4	0	0	24
Haywood Jeffires ...	3	0	3	0	18
Torrance Small	3	1	2	0	18
Lorenzo Neal	2	1	1	0	12

2-Pt. Conversions: Haynes, Klaus Wilmsmeyer.

Kicking

	PAT/Att	FG/Att	Lg	Pts
Doug Brien	18/18	21/25	54	81

Punts (10 or more)

	No	Yds	Long	Avg	In20
Klaus Wilmsmeyer .	87	3551	63	40.8	16

Most Interceptions

Greg Jackson	3
Anthony Newman ..	3

Most Sacks

Wayne Martin	11

New York Giants

Passing (5 Att)

	Att	Cmp	Pct	Yds	TD	Rate
Dave Brown	398	214	53.8	2412	12	61.3
Danny Kanell*	60	23	38.3	227	1	48.4

Interceptions: Brown 20, Kanell.

Top Receivers

	No	Yds	Avg	Long	TD
Chris Calloway	53	739	13.9	36	4
Thomas Lewis	53	694	13.1	34	4
Charles Way	32	328	10.3	37-td	1
Howard Cross	22	178	8.1	19	1
Lawrence Dawsey ..	18	233	12.9	28	0

Top Rushers

	Car	Yds	Avg	Long	TD
Rodney Hampton ..	254	827	3.3	25	1
Tyrone Wheatley ..	112	400	3.6	37	1
Dave Brown	50	170	3.4	18	0
Gary Downs	29	94	3.2	27	0
Charles Way	22	79	3.6	18	1

Signed: Downs on Oct. 31.

Most Touchdowns

	TD	Run	Rec	Ret	Pts
Chris Calloway	4	0	4	0	24
Thomas Lewis	4	0	4	0	24
Tyrone Wheatley ...	3	1	2	0	18
Aaron Pierce	2	1	1	0	12
Amani Toomer*	2	0	0	2	12
Charles Way	2	1	1	0	12

2-Pt. Conversions: None.

Kicking

	PAT/Att	FG/Att	Lg	Pts
Brad Daluiso	22/22	24/27	46	94

Punts (10 or more)

	No	Yds	Long	Avg	In20
Mike Horan	102	4289	63	42.0	32

Most Interceptions

Jason Sehorn	5

Most Sacks

Chad Bradtzke	5
Michael Strahan ...	5

Philadelphia Eagles

Passing (5 Att)

	Att	Cmp	Pct	Yds	TD	Rate
Ty Detmer	401	238	59.4	2911	15	80.8
Rodney Peete	134	80	59.7	992	3	74.6
Mark Rypien	13	10	76.9	76	1	116.2

Interceptions: Detmer 13, Peete 5.

Signed: Rypien on Oct. 3.

Top Receivers

	No	Yds	Avg	Long	TD
Irving Fryar	88	1195	13.6	42	11
Chris T. Jones	70	859	12.3	38	5
Ricky Watters	51	444	8.7	36	0
Kevin Turner	43	409	9.5	41	1
Mark Seay	19	260	13.7	35	0
Jason Dunn*	15	332	22.1	58	2

Top Rushers

	Car	Yds	Avg	Long	TD
Ricky Watters	353	1411	4.0	56-td	13
Charlie Garner	66	346	5.2	46	1
Ty Detmer	31	59	1.9	9	1
Kevin Turner	18	39	2.2	7	0

Most Touchdowns

	TD	Run	Rec	Ret	Pts
Ricky Watters	13	13	0	0	78
Irving Fryar	11	0	11	0	66
Chris T. Jones	5	0	5	0	30
Jason Dunn*	2	0	2	0	12
Derrick Witherspoon .	2	0	0	2	12

2-Pt. Conversions: None.

Kicking

	PAT/Att	FG/Att	Lg	Pts
Gary Anderson	40/40	25/29	46	115

Punts (10 or more)

	No	Yds	Long	Avg	In20
Tom Hutton	73	3107	60	42.6	17

Most Interceptions

Michael Zordich ...	4

Most Sacks

William Fuller	13

St. Louis Rams

Passing (5 Att)

	Att	Cmp	Pct	Yds	TD	Rate
Tony Banks*	368	192	52.2	2544	15	71.0
Steve Walsh	77	33	42.9	344	0	29.4
Jamie Martin	34	23	67.6	241	3	92.9

Interceptions: Banks 15, Walsh 5, Martin 2, Isaac Bruce.

Top Receivers

	No	Yds	Avg	Long	TD
Isaac Bruce	84	1338	15.9	70	7
Eddie Kennison* ...	54	924	17.1	77-td	9
Harold Green	37	246	6.6	19	1
Ernie Conwell*	15	164	10.9	26	0
Jermaine Ross	15	160	10.7	28	0
Aaron Laing	13	116	8.9	22	0

Top Rushers

	Car	Yds	Avg	Long	TD
Lawrence Phillips ...	193	632	3.3	38	4
Harold Green	127	523	4.1	35-td	4
Tony Banks*	61	212	3.5	22	0
Greg Robinson	32	134	4.2	24	1

Most Touchdowns

	TD	Run	Rec	Ret	PTS
Eddie Kennison*	11	0	9	2	66
Isaac Bruce	7	0	7	0	42
Harold Green	5	4	1	0	32
Lawrence Phillips	5	4	1	0	30
Anthony Parker	2	0	0	2	12

2-Pt. Conversions: Banks, Green.

Kicking

	PAT/Att	FG/Att	Lg	Pts
Chip Lohmiller	28/29	21/25	50	91
Carlos Huerta	5/5	4/7	42	17
CHI	3/3	4/7	42	15
ST.L	2/2	0/0	—	2

Signed: Huerta on Dec. 21 (waived by Chicago, Sept. 16).

Punts (10 or more)

	No	Yds	Long	Avg	In20
Sean Landeta	78	3491	70	44.8	23

Most Interceptions

Keith Lyle	9

Most Sacks

Kevin Carter	9½

San Francisco 49ers

Passing (5 Att)

	Att	Cmp	Pct	Yds	TD	Rate
Steve Young	316	214	67.7	2410	14	97.2
Elvis Grbac	197	122	61.9	1236	8	72.2
Jeff Brohm	34	21	61.8	189	1	86.5

Interceptions: Young, 6, Grbac 10.

Top Receivers

	No	Yds	Avg	Long	TD
Jerry Rice	108	1254	11.6	39	8
Terry Kirby	52	439	8.4	52	1
Terrell Owens*	35	520	14.9	46-td	4
Brent Jones	33	428	13.0	39	1
Tommy Vardell	28	179	6.4	22	0
Ted Popson	26	301	11.6	39-td	6
William Floyd	26	197	7.6	24	1
J.J. Stokes	18	249	13.8	40	0
Derek Loville	16	138	8.6	44-td	2

Top Rushers

	Car	Yds	Avg	Long	TD
Terry Kirby	134	559	4.2	31	3
Steve Young	52	310	6.0	33	4
Derek Loville	70	229	3.3	16	2
Tommy Vardell	58	192	3.3	17	2
William Floyd	47	186	4.0	12	2

Most Touchdowns

	TD	Run	Rec	Ret	Pts
Jerry Rice	9	1	8	0	54
Ted Popson	6	0	6	0	36
Steve Young	4	4	0	0	26
Terry Kirby	4	3	1	0	24
Derek Loville	4	2	2	0	24
Terrell Owens*	4	0	4	0	24

2-Pt. Conversions: Young.

Kicking

	PAT/Att	FG/Att	Lg	Pts
Jeff Wilkins	40/40	30/34	49	130

Punts (10 or more)

	No	Yds	Long	Avg	In20
Tommy Thompson	73	3217	65	44.1	20

Most Interceptions   **Most Sacks**
Marquez Pope 6   Roy Barker 12½

Tampa Bay Buccaneers

Passing (5 Att)

	Att	Cmp	Pct	Yds	TD	Rate
Trent Dilfer	482	267	55.4	2859	12	64.8
Casey Weldon	9	5	55.6	76	0	44.0

Interceptions: Dilfer 19, Weldon.

Top Receivers

	No	Yds	Avg	Long	TD
Mike Alstott*	65	557	8.6	29	3
Courtney Hawkins	46	544	11.8	45	1
Robb Thomas	33	427	12.9	31-td	2
Jackie Harris	30	349	11.6	36	1
Dave Moore	27	237	8.8	23	3
Karl Williams*	22	246	11.2	25	0
Alvin Harper	19	289	15.2	40-td	1
Jerry Ellison	18	208	11.6	42	0

Top Rushers

	Car	Yds	Avg	Long	TD
Errict Rhett	176	539	3.1	35	3
Mike Alstott*	96	377	3.9	39	3
Reggie Brooks	112	368	3.3	56	2

Most Touchdowns

	TD	Run	Rec	Ret	Pts
Mike Alstott*	6	3	3	0	36
Errict Rhett	4	3	1	0	24
Dave Moore	3	0	3	0	18
Reggie Brooks	2	2	0	0	12
Robb Thomas	2	0	2	0	12

2-Pt. Conversions: Harris.

Kicking

	PAT/Att	FG/Att	Lg	Pts
Michael Husted	18/19	25/32	50	93

Punts (10 or more)

	No	Yds	Long	Avg	In20
Tommy Barnhardt	70	3015	62	43.1	24

Most Interceptions   **Most Sacks**
Donnie Abraham* ... 5   Warren Sapp 9

Washington Redskins

Passing (5 Att)

	Att	Cmp	Pct	Yds	TD	Rate
Gus Frerotte	470	270	57.4	3453	12	79.3

Interceptions: Frerotte 11.

Top Receivers

	No	Yds	Avg	Long	TD
Henry Ellard	52	1014	19.5	51	2
Jamie Asher	42	481	11.5	34	4
Michael Westbrook	34	505	14.9	45	1
Brian Mitchell	32	286	8.9	20	0
Terry Allen	32	194	6.1	28	0
Leslie Shepherd	23	344	15.0	52-td	3
Marc Logan	23	269	11.7	26	0
Bill Brooks	17	224	13.2	31	0

Top Rushers

	Car	Yds	Avg	Long	TD
Terry Allen	347	1353	3.9	49-td	21
Brian Mitchell	39	193	4.9	32	0
Stephen Davis*	23	139	6.0	39-td	2
Marc Logan	20	111	5.6	36-td	2

Most Touchdowns

	TD	Run	Rec	Ret	Pts
Terry Allen	21	21	0	0	126
Leslie Shepherd	5	2	3	0	30
Jamie Asher	4	0	4	0	24

Four tied with two each.

2-Pt. Conversions: None.

Kicking

	PAT/Att	FG/Att	Lg	Pts
Scott Blanton	40/40	26/32	53	118

Punts (10 or more)

	No	Yds	Long	Avg	In20
Matt Turk	75	3386	63	45.1	25

Most Interceptions   **Most Sacks**
Tom Carter 5   Rich Owens 11

NFC Team Leaders
Offense

	Points		Yardage			
	For	Avg	Rush	Pass	Total	Avg
Philadelphia	363	22.7	1882	3745	5627	351.7
Green Bay	456	28.5	1838	3697	5535	345.9
San Francisco	398	24.9	1847	3659	5506	344.1
Washington	364	22.8	1910	3319	5229	326.8
Minnesota	298	18.6	1546	3658	5204	325.3
Arizona	300	18.8	1502	3688	5190	324.4
Atlanta	309	19.3	1461	3665	5126	320.4
Detroit	302	18.9	1810	3203	5013	313.3
Chicago	283	17.7	1720	3185	4905	306.6
Carolina	367	22.9	1729	3083	4812	300.8
Dallas	286	17.9	1641	3122	4763	297.7
St. Louis	303	18.9	1607	2765	4372	273.3
Tampa Bay	221	13.8	1589	2727	4316	269.8
New Orleans	229	14.3	1308	2898	4206	262.9
NY Giants	242	15.1	1603	2339	3942	246.4

Defense

	Points		Yardage			
	Opp	Avg	Rush	Pass	Total	Avg
Green Bay	210	13.1	1416	2740	4156	259.8
Dallas	250	15.6	1576	2806	4382	273.9
Philadelphia	341	21.3	1565	2979	4544	284.0
San Francisco	257	16.1	1497	3164	4661	291.3
Carolina	218	13.6	1562	3214	4776	298.5
Tampa Bay	293	18.3	1889	2925	4814	300.9
Chicago	305	19.1	1617	3267	4884	305.3
New Orleans	339	21.2	2076	2834	4910	306.9
NY Giants	297	18.6	1748	3299	5047	315.4
Minnesota	315	19.7	1966	3121	5087	317.9
Detroit	368	23.0	2007	3344	5351	334.4
Arizona	397	24.8	1862	3499	5361	335.1
St. Louis	409	25.6	1854	3675	5529	345.6
Washington	312	19.5	2275	3448	5723	357.7
Atlanta	461	28.8	2041	3745	5786	361.6

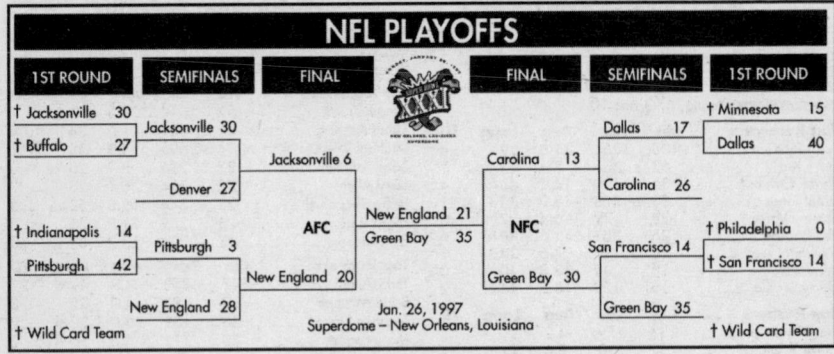

Game Summaries

Team records listed in parentheses indicate records before game.

WILD CARD ROUND

AFC

🏈 Jaguars, 30-27

Jacksonville (9-7)	10	7	3	10—	**30**
Buffalo (10-6)	14	3	3	7—	**27**

Date—Dec. 28 **Att**—70,213 **Time**—3:12

1st Quarter: BUF—Thurman Thomas 7-yd pass from Jim Kelly (Steve Christie kick), 3:30. JAX—Clyde Simmons 20-yd INT return (Mike Hollis kick), 8:34; BUF—Thomas 2-yd run (Christie kick), 12:34; JAX—Hollis 27-yd FG, 14:50.

2nd Quarter: JAX—Natrone Means 30-yd run (Hollis kick), 11:15; BUF—Christie 33-yd FG, 13:04.

3rd Quarter: BUF—Chrisite 47-yd FG, 4:40; JAX—Hollis 24-yd FG, 12:15.

4th Quarter: BUF—Jeff Burris 38-yd INT return (Christie kick), 0:43; JAX—Jimmy Smith 2-yd pass from Mark Brunell (Hollis kick), 6:20. JAX—Hollis 45-yd FG, 11:53.

🏈 Steelers, 42-14

Indianapolis (9-7)	0	14	0	0—	**14**
Pittsburgh (10-6)	10	3	8	21—	**42**

Date—Dec. 29 **Att**—58,078 **Time**—2:52

1st Quarter: PIT—Norm Johnson 29-yd FG, 6:41; PIT—Kordell Stewart 1-yd run (Johnson kick), 10:05

2nd Quarter: PIT—Johnson 50-yd FG, 0:10; IND—Eugene Daniel 59-yd INT return (Cary Blanchard kick), 10:25; IND—Aaron Bailey 9-yd pass from Jim Harbaugh (Blanchard kick), 14:29.

3rd Quarter: PIT—Jerome Bettis 1-yd run (Stewart pass to John Farquhar for 2-pt. conversion), 9:30.

4th Quarter: PIT—Bettis 1-yd run (Johnson kick), 0:39; PIT—Jon Witman 31-yd run (Johnson kick), 7:31; PIT—Stewart 3-yd run (Johnson kick), 11:50.

NFC

🏈 Cowboys, 40-15

Minnesota (9-7)	0	0	7	8—	**15**
Dallas (10-6)	7	23	7	3—	**40**

Date—Dec. 28 **Att**—64,682 **Time**—2:50

1st Quarter: DAL—Troy Aikman 2-yd run (Chris Boniol kick), 9:57.

2nd Quarter: DAL—Boniol 28-yd FG, 4:56; DAL—Emmitt Smith 37-yd run (Boniol kick), 5:24. DAL—George Teague 29-yd INT return (Boniol kick), 6:24; DAL—Boniol 31-yd FG, 9:41; DAL—Boniol 22-yd FG, 14:37.

3rd Quarter: MIN—Cris Carter 30-yd pass from Brad Johnson (Scott Sisson kick), 4:12; DAL—Smith 1-yd run (Boniol kick), 13:19.

4th Quarter: DAL—Boniol 25-yd FG, 5:31; MIN—Johnson 5-yd run (Johnson pass to Carter for 2-pt. conversion), 8:01.

🏈 49ers, 14-0

Philadelphia (10-6) ..	0	0	0	0—	**0**
San Francisco (12-4) .	0	7	7	0—	**14**

Date—Dec. 29 **Att**—56,460 **Time**—2:39

2nd Quarter: SF—Steve Young 9-yd run (Jeff Wilkins kick), 3:50.

3rd Quarter: SF—Jerry Rice 3-yd pass from Young (Wilkins kick), 10:13.

DIVISIONAL SEMIFINALS

AFC

● Jaguars, 30-27

Jacksonville (10-7) ...	0	13	7	10—	**30**
Denver (13-3)	12	0	0	15—	**27**

Date—Jan. 4   **Att**—75,678   **Time**—3:02

1st Quarter: DEN—Vaughn Hebron 1-yd run (kick blocked), 8:38; DEN—Shannon Sharpe 18-yd pass from John Elway (2-pt. conversion failed), 14:27.

2nd Quarter: JAX—Mike Hollis 46-yd FG, 3:45; JAX—Natrone Means 8-yd run (Hollis kick), 12:02; JAX—Hollis 42-yd FG, 14:50.

3rd Quarter: JAX—Keenan McCardell 31-yd pass from Mark Brunell (Hollis kick), 6:09.

4th Quarter: JAX—Hollis 22-yd FG, 4:09; DEN—Terrell Davis 2-yd run (Davis run for 2-pt. conversion), 7:23; JAX—Jimmy Smith 16-yd pass from Brunell (Hollis kick), 11:21; DEN—Ed McCaffrey 15-yd pass from Elway (Jason Elam kick), 13:10.

● Patriots, 28-3

Pittsburgh (11-6)	0	0	3	0—	**3**
New England (11-5) .	14	7	0	7—	**28**

Date—Jan. 5   **Att**—60,188   **Time**—2:48

1st Quarter: NE—Curtis Martin 2-yd run (Adam Vinatieri kick), 3:02; NE—Keith Byars 34-yd pass from Drew Bledsoe (Vinatieri kick), 7:05

2nd Quarter: NE—Martin 78-yd run (Vinatieri kick), 5:05.

3rd Quarter: PIT—Norm Johnson 29-yd FG, 11:10.

4th Quarter: NE—Martin 23-yd run (Vinatieri kick), 2:29.

NFC

● Packers, 35-14

San Francisco (13-4) .	0	7	7	0—	**14**
Green Bay (13-3)	14	7	7	7—	**35**

Date— Jan. 4   **Att**—60,787   **Time**—3:15

1st Quarter: GB—Desmond Howard 71-yd punt return (Chris Jacke kick), 2:15; GB—Andre Rison 4-yd pass from Brett Favre (Jacke kick), 8:44.

2nd Quarter: GB—Edgar Bennett 2-yd run (Jacke kick), 11:42; SF—Terry Kirby 8-yd pass from Elvis Grbac (Jeff Wilkins kick), 14:36.

3rd Quarter: SF—Grbac 2-yd run (Wilkins kick), 0:16; GB—Antonio Freeman fumble recovery in end zone (Jacke kick), 8:10.

4th Quarter: GB—Bennett 11-yd run (Jacke kick), 9:29.

● Panthers, 26-17

Dallas (11-6)	3	8	3	3—	**17**
Carolina (12-4)	7	10	3	6—	**26**

Date—Jan. 5   **Att**—72,808   **Time**—2:58

1st Quarter: DAL—Chris Boniol 22-yd FG, 6:33; CAR—Wesley Walls 1-yd pass from Kerry Collins (John Kasay kick), 9:32.

2nd Quarter: CAR—Willie Green 10-yd pass from Collins (Kasay kick), 2:11; DAL—Daryl Johnston 2-yd pass from Troy Aikman (2-pt. conversion failed), 10:41; DAL—Dallas recorded safety when a bad snap by Carolina on a punt went out of the end zone, 11:49; CAR—Kasay 24-yd FG, 14:57.

3rd Quarter: DAL—Boniol 21-yd FG, 4:53. CAR—Kasay 40-yd FG, 10:02.

4th Quarter: CAR—Kasay 40-yd FG, 3:19; Boniol 21-yd FG, 9:27; CAR—Kasay 32-yd FG, 13:12.

CONFERENCE CHAMPIONSHIPS

AFC

● Patriots, 20-6

Jacksonville (11-7) ...	0	3	3	0—	**6**
New England (12-5) .	7	6	0	7—	**20**

Date—Jan. 12   **Att**— 60,190   **Time**—3:11

1st Quarter: NE—Curtis Martin 1-yd run (Adam Vinatieri kick), 2:26.

2nd Quarter: JAX—Mike Hollis 32-yd FG, 4:27; NE—Vinatieri 29-yd FG, 7:37; NE—Vinatieri 20-yd FG, 15:00.

3rd Quarter: JAX—Hollis 28-yd FG, 12:23

4th Quarter: NE—Otis Smith 47-yd fumble return (Vinatieri kick), 12:36.

NFC

● Packers, 30-13

Carolina (13-4)	7	3	3	0—	**13**
Green Bay (14-3)	0	17	10	3—	**30**

Date—Jan. 12   **Att**— 60,216   **Time**— 3:04

1st Quarter: CAR—Howard Griffith 3-yd pass from Kerry Collins (John Kasay kick), 9:50.

2nd Quarter: GB—Dorsey Levens 29-yd pass from Brett Favre (Chris Jacke kick), 0:06; CAR—Kasay 22-yd FG, 6:20; GB—Antonio Freeman 6-yd pass from Favre (Jacke kick), 14:12; GB—Jacke 31-yd FG, 14:50.

3rd Quarter: GB—Jacke 32-yd FG, 6:44; CAR—Kasay 23-yd FG, 11:37; GB—Edgar Bennett 4-yd run (Jacke kick), 13:02.

4th Quarter: GB—Jacke 28-yd FG, 4:58.

Super Bowl XXXI

Sunday, Jan. 26 at the Superdome in New Orleans, Louisiana.

New England (13-5) .	14	0	7	0—	**21**
Green Bay (15-3) ..	10	17	8	0—	**35**

1st: GB—Andre Rison 54-yd pass from Brett Favre (Chris Jacke kick), 3:32. Drive: 55 yards in 2 plays. Key play: Desmond Howard 32-yd punt return. GB—Jacke 37-yd FG, 6:18. Drive: 9 yards in 4 plays. Key play: Doug Evans interception at NE 28. NE—Keith Byars 1-yd pass from Drew Bledsoe (Adam Vinatieri kick), 8:25. Drive: 79 yards in 6 plays. Key play: 26-yd pass interference penalty on Craig Newsome on 3rd-and-10 to GB 1. NE—Ben Coates 4-yd pass from Bledsoe (Vinatieri kick), 12:27. Drive: 57 yards in 4 plays. Key play: Bledsoe 44-yd pass to Terry Glenn to GB 4.

2nd: GB—Antonio Freeman 81-yd pass from Favre (Jacke kick), 0:56. Drive: 81 yards in 1 play. GB—Jacke 31-yd FG, 6:45. Drive: 33 yards in 8 plays. Key play: Howard 33-yd punt return to NE 47. GB—Favre 2-yd run (Jacke kick), 13:49. Drive: 74 yards in 9 plays. Key play: Mike Prior 5-yd interception return to GB 26.

3rd: NE—Curtis Martin 18-yd run (Vinatieri kick), 11:33. Drive: 53 yards in 7 plays. Key play: Bledsoe 13-yd pass to Coates on 3rd-and-5 to GB 35. GB—Howard 99-yd kickoff return (Favre pass to Mark Chmura for 2-pt conversion), 11:50.

Favorite: Packers by 14 **Attendance:** 72,301
Field: Artificial Turf   **Time:** 3:21
Start time: 5:25 CST   **TV Rating:** 43.3/65 share (Fox)

MVP—Desmond Howard, Green Bay, (4 kickoff returns for 154 yards and 1 TD.)

Officials: Gerald Austin (referee); Ron Botchan (umpire); Jeff Bergman (LJ); Tom Fincken (SJ); Earnie Frantz (HL); Scott Steenson (BJ); Phil Luckett (FJ).

Team Statistics

	Patriots	Packers
Touchdowns	3	4
Rushing	1	1
Passing	2	2
Returns	0	1
Field Goals made/attempted	0/0	2/3
Time of possession	25:45	34:15
First downs	16	16
Rushing	3	8
Passing	12	6
Penalties	1	2
3rd down efficiency	4/14	3/15
4th down efficiency	0/2	0/1
Total offense (net yards)	257	323
Plays	66	68
Average gain	3.9	4.8
Carries/yards	13/43	36/115
Yards per carry	3.3	3.2
Passing yards	214	208
Completions/attempts	25/48	14/27
Yards per pass	4.0	6.5
Times intercepted	4	0
Times sacked/yards lost	5/39	5/38
Return yardage	165	268
Punt returns/yards	5/30	7/90
Kickoff returns/yards	7/135	4/154
Interceptions/yards	0/0	4/24
Fumbles/lost	0/0	0/0
Penalties/yards	2/22	3/41
Punts/average	8/45.1	7/42.7
Punts blocked	0	0

Individual Statistics

New England Patriots

Passing	Att	Cmp	Pct.	Yds	TD	Int
Drew Bledsoe	48	25	52.1	253	2	4

Receiving	No	Yds	Avg	Long	TD
Ben Coates	6	67	11.2	19	1
Terry Glenn	4	62	15.5	44	0
Keith Byars	4	42	10.5	32	1
Shawn Jefferson	3	34	11.3	14	0
Curtis Martin	3	28	9.3	20	0
Dave Meggett	3	8	2.7	5	0
Vincent Brisby	2	12	6.0	7	0
TOTAL	25	253	10.1	44	2

Rushing	Car	Yds	Avg	Long	TD
Curtis Martin	11	42	3.8	18	1
Drew Bledsoe	1	1	1.0	1	0
Dave Meggett	1	0	0.0	0	0
TOTAL	13	43	3.3	18	1

Field Goals	20-29	30-39	40-49	50-59	Total
none					

Punting	No	Yds	Long	Avg	In 20	TB
Tom Tupa	8	361	53	45.1	3	0

Punt Returns	FC	Ret	Yds	Long	Avg	TD
Dave Meggett	2	2	30	20	15.0	0

Kickoff Returns	No	Yds	Long	Avg	TD
Dave Meggett	5	117	26	23.4	0
Hason Graham	1	18	18	18.0	0
TOTAL	6	135	26	22.5	0

Sacks		Most Tackles	
Tedy Bruschi	2	Chris Slade	11
Ferric Collons	1	Ted Johnson	10
Willie McGinest	1	Lawyer Milloy	8
Otis Smith	1		

Green Bay Packers

Passing	Att	Cmp	Pct.	Yds	TD	Int
Brett Favre	27	14	51.9	246	2	0

Receiving	No	Yds	Avg	Long	TD
Antonio Freeman	3	105	35.0	81	1
Dorsey Levens	3	23	7.7	14	0
Andre Rison	2	77	38.5	54	1
William Henderson	2	14	7.0	8	0
Mark Chmura	2	13	6.5	8	0
Keith Jackson	1	10	10.0	10	0
Edgar Bennett	1	4	4.0	4	0
TOTAL	14	246	17.6	81	2

Rushing	Car	Yds	Avg	Long	TD
Dorsey Levens	14	61	4.4	12	0
Edgar Bennett	17	40	2.4	10	0
Brett Favre	4	12	3.0	12	1
William Henderson	1	2	2.0	2	0
TOTAL	36	115	3.2	12	1

Field Goals	20-29	30-39	40-49	50-59	Total
Chris Jacke ...	0-0	2-2	0-1	0-0	2-3

Punting	No	Yds	Long	Avg	In 20	TB
Craig Hentrich	7	299	58	42.7	1	0

Punt Returns	FC	Ret	Yds	Long	Avg	TD
Desmond Howard	1	6	90	34	15.0	0

Kickoff Returns	No	Yds	Long	Avg	TD
Desmond Howard	4	154	99	38.5	1

Sacks		Most Tackles	
Reggie White	3	Eugene Robinson	9
LeRoy Butler	1	LeRoy Butler	7
Santana Dotson	1	Craig Newsome	6

Super Bowl Finalists' Playoff Statistics

New England (2-1)

Passing	Att	Cmp	Pct.	Yds	TD	Rating
Drew Bledsoe	105	59	56.2	595	3	54.3
Scott Zolak	2	1	50.0	3	0	56.3
TOTAL	107	60	56.1	598	3	54.2

Interceptions: Bledsoe 7.

Receiving	No	Yds	Avg	Long	TD
Terry Glenn	12	164	13.7	53	0
Keith Byars	12	111	9.3	34-td	2
Shawn Jefferson	10	143	14.3	38	0
Ben Coates	10	90	9.0	19	1
Curtis Martin	8	55	6.9	20	0
Dave Meggett	6	23	3.8	9	0
Vincent Brisby	2	12	6.0	7	0
TOTAL	60	598	10.0	53	3

Rushing	Car	Yds	Avg	Long	TD
Curtis Martin	49	267	5.4	78-td	5
Dave Meggett	6	27	4.5	14	0
Keith Byars	3	9	3.0	7	0
Marrio Grier	5	7	1.4	4	0
Drew Bledsoe	3	4	1.3	4	0
Scott Zolak	3	-4	-1.3	-1	0
TOTAL	69	310	4.5	78-td	5

Touchdowns	TD	Run	Rec	Ret	Pts
Curtis Martin	5	5	0	0	30
Keith Byars	2	0	2	0	12
Ben Coates	1	0	1	0	6
Otis Smith	1	0	0	1	6
TOTAL	9	5	3	1	54

Kicking	PAT/Att	FG/Att	Lg	Pts
Adam Vinatieri	9/9	2/3	29	15

Punts	No	Yds	Long	Avg	In20
Tom Tupa	21	904	53	43.0	8

Most Interceptions		Most Sacks	
Wille Clay	2	Tedy Bruschi	2
		Chris Slade	2

Green Bay (3-0)

Passing	Att	Cmp	Pct.	Yds	TD	Rating
Brett Favre	71	44	62.0	617	5	107.5

Interceptions: Favre.

Receiving	No	Yds	Avg	Long	TD
Dorsey Levens	10	156	15.6	66	1
Antonio Freeman	9	174	19.3	81-td	2
Andre Rison	7	143	20.4	54-td	2
Keith Jackson	5	44	8.8	19	0
Edgar Bennett	5	23	4.6	10	0
Mark Chmura	3	28	9.3	15	0
William Henderson	3	18	6.0	8	0
Don Beebe	2	31	15.5	29	0
TOTAL	44	617	14.0	81-td	5

Rushing	Car	Yds	Avg	Long	TD
Edgar Bennett	59	219	3.7	13	3
Dorsey Levens	39	195	5.0	35	0
Brett Favre	14	35	2.5	12	1
Willie Henderson	4	6	1.5	4	0
Jim McMahon	4	0	0.0	0	0
TOTAL	120	455	3.8	35	4

Touchdowns	TD	Run	Rec	Ret	Pts
Edgar Bennett	3	3	0	0	18
Antonio Freeman	3	0	2	1	18
Desmond Howard	2	0	0	2	12
Andre Rison	2	0	2	0	12
Brett Favre	1	1	0	0	6
Dorsey Levens	1	0	1	0	6
TOTAL	12	4	5	3	100

Kicking	PAT/Att	FG/Att	Lg	Pts
Chris Jacke	11/11	5/7	37	26

Punts	No	Yds	Long	Avg	In20
Craig Hentrich	15	630	63	42.0	4

Most Interceptions		Most Sacks	
Craig Newsome	3	Reggie White	3
Eugene Robinson	2		

Patriots' 1996 Schedule

Date	Regular Season (11-5)	Result	W-L
Sept. 1	at Miami (0-0)	L, 10-24	0-1
Sept. 8	at Buffalo (1-0)	L, 10-17	0-2
Sept. 15	Arizona (0-2)	W, 31-0	1-2
Sept. 22	Jacksonville (1-2)	W, 28-25 (OT)	2-2
Sept. 29	OPEN DATE	—	—
Oct. 6	at Baltimore (2-2)	W, 46-38	3-2
Oct. 13	Washington (4-1)	L, 22-27	3-3
Oct. 20	at Indianapolis (5-1)	W, 27-9	4-3
Oct. 27	Buffalo (5-2)	W, 28-25	5-3
Nov. 3	Miami (4-4)	W, 42-23	6-3
Nov. 10	at NY Jets (1-8)	W, 31-27	7-3
Nov. 17	Denver (9-1)	L, 8-34	7-4
Nov. 24	Indianapolis (6-6)	W, 27-13	8-4
Dec. 1	at San Diego (7-5)	W, 45-7	9-4
Dec. 8	NY Jets (1-12)	W, 34-10	10-4
Dec. 15	at Dallas (9-5)	L, 6-12	10-5
Dec. 21*	at NY Giants (6-9)	W, 23-22	11-5

Date	Playoffs (2-1)	Result	W-L
Dec. 28	Bye	—	—
Jan. 5	Pittsburgh (11-6)	W, 28-3	12-5
Jan. 12	Jacksonville (11-7)	W, 20-6	13-5
Jan. 26	Green Bay (15-3)	L, 21-35	13-6

* Saturday

Packers' 1996 Schedule

Date	Regular Season (13-3)	Result	W-L
Sept. 1	at Tampa Bay (0-0)	W, 34-3	1-0
Sept. 9*	Philadelphia (1-0)	W, 39-13	2-0
Sept. 15	San Diego (2-0)	W, 42-10	3-0
Sept. 22	at Minnesota (3-0)	L, 21-30	3-1
Sept. 29	at Seattle (1-3)	W, 31-10	4-1
Oct. 6	at Chicago (2-3)	W, 37-6	5-1
Oct. 14*	San Francisco (4-1)	W, 23-20	6-1
Oct. 20	OPEN DATE	—	—
Oct. 27	Tampa Bay (1-6)	W, 13-7	7-1
Nov. 3	Detroit (4-4)	W, 28-18	8-1
Nov. 10	at Kansas City (6-3)	L, 20-27	8-2
Nov. 18*	at Dallas (6-4)	L, 6-21	8-3
Nov. 24	at St. Louis (3-8)	W, 24-9	9-3
Dec. 1	Chicago (5-7)	W, 28-17	10-3
Dec. 8	Denver (12-1)	W, 41-6	11-3
Dec. 15	at Detroit (5-9)	W, 31-3	12-3
Dec. 22	Minnesota (9-6)	W, 38-10	13-3

Date	Playoffs (3-0)	Result	W-L
Dec. 28	Bye	—	—
Jan. 4	San Francisco (12-4)	W, 35-14	14-3
Jan. 12	Carolina (13-4)	W, 30-13	15-3
Jan. 26	New England (13-5)	W, 35-21	16-3

*Monday

NFL Pro Bowl

47th NFL Pro Bowl Game and 27th AFC-NFC contest (NFC leads series, 15-12). **Date:** Feb. 2 at Aloha Stadium in Honolulu. **Coaches:** Tom Coughlin, Jacksonville (AFC) and Dom Capers, Carolina (NFC). **Player of the Game:** QB Mark Brunell of Jacksonville, who was 12 for 22 for 236 yards and one touchdown.

AFC	0	3	7	13	3 —	**26**
NFC	9	0	6	8	0 —	**23**

1st: NFC—John Kasay 20-yd FG, 4:41. Drive: 63 yards in 9 plays. NFC—Randall McDaniel 5-yd pass from Brett Favre (Kasay kick failed), 11:16. Drive: 66 yards in 7 plays.

2nd: AFC—Cary Blanchard 28-yd FG, 14:33. Drive: 69 yards in 13 plays.

3rd: NFC—Barry Sanders 6-yd run (2-pt conversion failed), 6:09. Drive: 59 yards in 7 plays. AFC—Curtis Martin 3-yd run (Blanchard kick), 9:05. Drive: 71 yards in 6 plays.

4th: AFC—Ashley Ambrose 54-yd INT return (2-pt conversion failed). NFC—Cris Carter 53-yd pass from Gus Frerotte (Wesley Walls pass from Frerotte), 10:53. Drive: 78 yards to 4 plays. AFC— Tim Brown 80-yd pass from Mark Brunell (Blanchard kick), 14:16. Drive: 78 yards in 2 plays.

OT: AFC—Blanchard 37-yd FG, 8:16. Drive: 46 yards in 5 plays.

Attendance—50,031. **TV Rating**—9.1/15 share (ABC).

STARTING LINEUPS

As voted on by NFL players and coaches.

American Conference

Pos Offense	Pos Defense
WR Carl Pickens, Cin.	E Bruce Smith, Buf.
WR Tony Martin, SD	E Alfred Williams, Den.
TE Shannon Sharpe, Den.	T Chester McGlockton, Oak.
T Gary Zimmerman, Den.	T Cortez Kennedy, Sea.
T Bruce Armstrong, NE	LB Chad Brown, Pit.
G Will Shields, KC	LB Derrick Thomas, KC
G Bruce Matthews, Hou.	LB Junior Seau, SD
C Dermontti Dawson, Pit.	CB Dale Carter, KC
QB John Elway, Den.	CB Ashley Ambrose, Cin.
RB Terrell Davis, Den.	S Carnell Lake, Pit.
RB Jerome Bettis, Pit.	S Steve Atwater, Den.
K Cary Blanchard, Ind.	P Chris Gardocki, Ind.
KR Dave Meggett, NE	ST John Henry Mills, Hou.

Note: QB Elway, DE Smith, OT Zimmerman, S Atwater and CB Carter were injured and unable to play.

National Conference

Pos Offense	Pos Defense
WR Jerry Rice, SF	E Reggie White, GB
WR Herman Moore, Det.	E Tony Tolbert, Dal.
TE Wesley Walls, Car.	T John Randle, Min.
T William Roaf, NO	T Bryant Young, SF
T Erik Williams, Dal.	LB Kevin Greene, Car.
G Larry Allen, Dal.	LB Lamar Lathon, Car.
G Randall McDaniel, Min.	LB Sam Mills, Car.
C Kevin Glover, Det.	CB Deion Sanders, Dal.
QB Brett Favre, GB	CB Aeneas Williams, Ariz.
RB Terry Allen, Wash.	S Leroy Butler, GB
RB Barry Sanders, Det.	S Merton Hanks, SF
K John Kasay, Car.	P Matt Turk, Wash.
KR Michael Bates, Car.	ST Jim Schwantz, Dal.

Note: WR Rice and CB Sanders were injured and unable to play.

Reserves

Offense: WR—Tim Brown, Oak. and Keenan McCardell, Jax.; **TE**—Ben Coates, NE; **T**— Richmond Webb, Mia.; **G**—Ruben Brown, Buf.; **C**— Mark Stepnoski, Hou.; **QB**—Vinny Testaverde, Bal. and Drew Bledsoe, NE; **RB**—Curtis Martin, NE; **FB**— Kimble Anders, KC.

Defense: E—Michael Sinclair, Sea.; **T**—Michael Dean Perry, Den.; **LB**—Bryce Paup, Buf. and Levon Kirkland, Pit.; **CB**—Rod Woodson, Pit.; **S**—Blaine Bishop, Hou.

Replacements: OFFENSE—QB Mark Brunell, Jax. for Elway; OT Tony Boselli, Jax. for Zimmerman. DEFENSE—S Tyrone Braxton, Den. for Bishop; S Eric Turner, Bal. for Atwater; CB Terry McDaniel, Oak. for Carter; DE Willie McGinest, NE for Smith. NEED PLAYER—Bill Romanowski, Den., LB.

Reserves

Offense: WR—Cris Carter, Min. and Isaac Bruce, St. L; **TE**—Keith Jackson, GB; **T**— Lomas Brown, Ariz.; **G**—Nate Newton, Dal.; **C**—Ray Donaldson, Dal.; **QB**—Troy Aikman, Dal. and Steve Young, SF; **RB**—Ricky Watters, Phi. **FB**—Larry Centers, Ariz.

Defense: E—William Fuller, Phi.; **T**—Eric Swann, Ariz.; **LB**—Ken Harvey, Wash. and Hardy Nickerson, TB; **CB**—Eric Davis, Car.; **S**— Darren Woodson, Dal.

Replacements: OFFENSE—QB Gus Frerotte, Wash. for Aikman; QB Kerry Collins, Car. for Young; C Frank Winters for Donaldson; WR Irving Fryar, Phi. for Rice. DEFENSE—CB Darrell Green for Sanders. NEED PLAYER— William Thomas, Phi., LB.

Annual Awards

The NFL does not sanction any of the major postseason awards for player and coaches, but many are given out. Among the presenters for the 1996 regular season were AP, UPI, The Maxwell Football Club of Philadelphia, *The Sporting News* and the Pro Football Writers of America. Conference Most Valuable Player awards were also issued by the NFL Players Association.

Most Valuable Player

NFL	Brett Favre, Green Bay, QB .....AP, PFWA, Max, *TSN*
AFC	John Elway, Denver, QB ....NFLPA
NFC	Brett Favre ....NFLPA

Offensive Players of the Year

NFL	Brett Favre, Green Bay, QB ....PFWA
	Terrell Davis, Denver, RB ....AP
AFC	Terrell Davis ....UPI
NFC	Brett Favre ....UPI

Defensive Players of the Year

NFL	Bruce Smith, Buffalo, DE ....AP, PFWA
AFC	Bruce Smith ....UPI
NFC	Kevin Greene, Carolina, LB ....UPI

Rookies of the Year

NFL	Eddie George, Houston, RB ....*TSN* PFWA
AFC	Terry Glenn, New England, WR ....UPI
NFC	Simeon Rice, Arizona, DE ....UPI
Off	Eddie George ....AP
Def	Simeon Rice ....AP

Coaches of the Year

NFL	Dom Capers, Carolina ....AP, PFWA, Max, *TSN*
AFC	Tom Coughlin, Jacksonville ....UPI
NFC	Dom Capers ....UPI

1996 All-NFL Team

The 1996 All-NFL team combining the All-Pro selections of the Associated Press and the Pro Football Writers of America (PFWA). Holdovers from the 1995 All-NFL Team in **bold** type.

Offense

Pos		Selectors
WR—	**Jerry Rice**, San Francisco	AP, PFWA
WR—	**Herman Moore**, Detroit	AP
WR—	Carl Pickens, Cincinnati	PFWA
TE—	Shannon Sharpe, Denver	AP, PFWA
T—	Gary Zimmerman, Denver	AP, PFWA
T—	**William Roaf**, New Orleans	PFWA
T—	Erik Williams, Dallas	AP
G—	**Randall McDaniel**, Minnesota	AP, PFWA
G—	Larry Allen, Dallas	AP, PFWA
C—	**Dermontti Dawson**, Pittsburgh	AP, PFWA
QB—	**Brett Favre**, Green Bay	AP, PFWA
RB—	Terrell Davis, Denver	AP, PFWA
RB—	**Barry Sanders**, Detroit	PFWA
RB—	Jerome Bettis, Pittsburgh	AP

Defense

Pos		Selectors
DE—	**Bruce Smith**, Buffalo	AP, PFWA
DE—	Alfred Williams, Denver	AP, PFWA
DT—	**John Randle**, Minnesota	AP, PFWA
DT—	Bryant Young, San Francisco	AP, PFWA
LB—	Kevin Greene, Carolina	AP, PFWA
LB—	Chad Brown, Pittsburgh	AP, PFWA
LB—	Sam Mills, Carolina	AP, PFWA
LB—	**Junior Seau**, San Diego	AP
CB—	Deion Sanders, Dallas	AP, PFWA
CB—	**Aeneas Williams**, Arizona	PFWA
CB—	Ashley Ambrose, Cincinnati	AP
S—	**Darren Woodson**, Dallas	AP, PFWA
S—	LeRoy Butler, Green Bay	AP, PFWA

Specialists

Pos		Selectors
PK—	Cary Blanchard, Indianapolis	AP, PFWA
P—	Chris Gardocki, Indianapolis	AP, PFWA
P—	Matt Turk, Washington	AP

Pos		Selectors
KR—	Michael Bates, Carolina	AP, PFWA
PR—	Desmond Howard, Green Bay	PFWA
ST—	Jim Schwantz, Dallas	PFWA

1997 College Draft

First and second round selections at the 62nd annual NFL College Draft held April 19-20, 1997, in New York City. 16 underclassmen were among the first 60 players chosen and are listed in CAPITAL LETTERS.

First Round

No	Team		Pos
1	a-St. Louis	ORLANDO PACE, Ohio St.	OT
2	b-Oakland	DARRELL RUSSELL, USC	DT
3	c-Seattle	SHAWN SPRINGS, Ohio St.	CB
4	Baltimore	PETER BOULWARE, Florida St.	DE
5	Detroit	Bryant Westbrook, Texas	CB
6	d-Seattle	WALTER JONES, Florida St.	OT
7	NY Giants	IKE HILLIARD, Florida	WR
8	e-NY Jets	James Farrior, Virginia	LB
9	Arizona	Tom Knight, Iowa	CB
10	f-New Orleans	Chris Naeole, Colorado	OG
11	g-Atlanta	Michael Booker, Nebraska	CB
12	h-Tampa Bay	Warrick Dunn, Florida St.	RB
13	i-Kansas City	TONY GONZALEZ, California	TE
14	Cincinnati	Reinard Wilson, Florida St.	DE
15	Miami	YATIL GREEN, Miami-FL	WR
16	j-Tampa Bay	REIDEL ANTHONY, Florida	WR
17	Washington	KENARD LANG, Miami-FL	DE
18	k-Houston	Kenny Holmes, Miami-FL	DE
19	Indianapolis	Tarik Glenn, California	OG
20	Minnesota	DWAYNE RUDD, Alabama	LB
21	Jacksonville	Renaldo Wynn, Notre Dame	DE
22	l-Dallas	David LaFleur, LSU	TE
23	Buffalo	Antowain Smith, Houston	RB
24	Pittsburgh	Chad Scott, Maryland	CB
25	m-Philadelphia	John Harris, Virginia	DE
26	San Francisco	Jim Druckenmiller, Virginia Tech	QB
27	Carolina	Rae Carruth, Colorado	WR
28	Denver	TREVOR PRYCE, Clemson	DE
29	New England	CHRIS CANTY, Kansas St.	CB
30	Green Bay	Ross Verba, Iowa	OG

Second Round

No	Team		Pos
31	NY Jets	Rick Terry, N. Carolina	DT
32	Atlanta	Nathan Davis, Indiana	DT
33	New Orleans	Rob Kelly, Ohio St.	S
34	Baltimore	Jamie Sharper, Virginia	LB
35	Detroit	Juan Roque, Arizona St.	OG
36	NY Giants	Tiki Barber, Virginia	RB
37	Tampa Bay	Jerry Wunsch, Wisconsin	OT
38	n-Chicago	John Allred, USC	TE
39	o-New Orleans	Jared Tomich, Nebraska	DE
40	p-St. Louis	Dexter McCleon, Clemson	CB
41	q-Atlanta	BYRON HANSPARD, Texas Tech	RB
42	Arizona	Jake Plummer, Azizona St.	QB
43	Cincinnati	COREY DILLON, Washington	RB
44	Miami	Sam Madison, Louisville	CB
45	San Diego	Freddie Jones, N. Carolina	TE
46	Houston	Joey Kent, Tennessee	WR
47	Kansas City	Kevin Lockett, Kansas St.	WR
48	Indianapolis	Adam Meadows, Georgia	OT
49	Minnesota	Torrian Gray, Virginia Tech	S
50	Jacksonville	Mike Logan, W. Virginia	CB
51	Washington	Greg Jones, Colorado	LB
52	Buffalo	Marcellus Wiley, Columbia	DE
53	Pittsburgh	WILL BLACKWELL, San Diego St.	WR
54	r-Detroit	Kevin Abrams, Syracuse	CB
55	s-San Francisco	Marc Edwards, Notre Dame	RB
56	Carolina	Mike Minter, Nebraska	S
57	t-Philadelphia	James Darling, Washington St.	LB
58	u-Baltimore	Kim Herring, Penn St.	S
59	New England	Brandon Mitchell, Texas A&M	DE
60	Green Bay	Darren Sharper, William & Mary	DB

Acquired picks: a—from NY Jets; **b**— from New Orleans; **c**—from Atlanta; **d**—from St. Louis via NY Jets and Tampa Bay; **e**—from Tampa Bay; **f**—from New Orleans; **g**—from Chicago via Seattle; **h**—from Seattle; **i**—from Houston; **j**—from San Diego; **k**—from Kansas City; **l**—from Philadelphia; **m**—from Dallas.

Acquired picks: n—from St. Louis; **o**—from Oakland; **p**—from Chicago; **q**— from Seattle; **r**—from Dallas; **s**—from Philadelphia; **t**—from San Francisco; **u**—from Denver.

NFL Head Coaching Changes For 1997

As of March 1, 1997, eleven new head coaches were in place for the start of the '97 regular season.

AFC	Old Coach	Why Left?	New Coach	Hired	Old Job
Cincinnati	David Shula	Fired (Oct. 21)	Bruce Coslet	Oct. 21	Off. Coord., NFL Bengals
NY Jets	Rich Kotite	Fired (Dec. 20)	Bill Parcells	Feb. 10	Head Coach, NFL Patriots
Oakland	Mike White	Fired (Dec. 24)	Joe Bugel	Jan. 30	Off. Coord., NFL Raiders
San Diego	Bobby Ross	Resigned (Jan. 3)	Kevin Gilbride	Jan. 18	Off. Coord., NFL Jaguars
New England	Bill Parcells	Resigned (Jan. 31)	Pete Carroll	Feb. 3	Def. Coord., NFL 49ers

NFC	Old Coach	Why Left?	New Coach	Hired	Old Job
New Orleans	Jim Mora	Resigned (Oct. 21)	Mike Ditka	Jan. 28	NBC TV analyst
St. Louis	Rich Brooks	Fired (Dec. 22)	Dick Vermeil	Jan. 21	ABC TV analyst
NY Giants	Dan Reeves	Fired (Dec. 23)	Jim Fassel	Jan. 15	Off. Coord., NFL Cardinals
Atlanta	June Jones	Fired (Dec. 23)	Dan Reeves	Jan. 20	Head Coach, NFL Giants
Detroit	Wayne Fontes	Fired (Dec. 26)	Bobby Ross	Jan. 13	Head Coach, NFL Chargers
San Francisco	George Seifert	Fired (Jan. 15)	Steve Mariucci	Jan. 16	Head Coach, Univ. of Calif.

Note: Jim Mora was replaced by assistant Rick Venturi on an interim basis for the remainder of the 1996 season. Also, Bill Belichick was initially named interim head coach of the NY Jets (Feb. 4) until one week later when Bill Parcells took over the job.

Canadian Football League

Final 1996 Standings

Division champions (*) and other playoff qualifiers (†) are noted. Number of seasons listed after each head coach refers to latest tenure with club through 1996 season.

East Division

	W	L	T	Pts	PF	PA	Pct
*Toronto	15	3	0	30	556	359	.833
†Montreal	12	6	0	24	534	469	.667
†Hamilton	8	10	0	16	426	576	.444
Ottawa	3	15	0	6	353	524	.167

1996 Head Coaches: Tor—Don Matthews (1st); **Mon**—Bob Price (1st); **Ham**—Don Sutherin (3rd); **Ott**—replaced Jim Gilstrap (2nd, 0-2) with John Payne (3-13) on July 4.

1995 North Div. standings: 1. Calgary (15-3); 2. Edmonton (13-5); 3. B.C. Lions (10-8); 4. Hamilton (8-10); 5. Winnipeg (7-11); 6. Saskatchewan (6-12); 7. Toronto (4-14); Ottawa (3-15).

West Division

	W	L	T	Pts	PF	PA	Pct
*Calgary	13	5	0	26	608	365	.722
†Edmonton	11	7	0	22	459	354	.611
†Winnipeg	9	9	0	18	420	496	.500
Brit. Columbia	5	13	0	10	410	485	.278
Saskatchewan	5	13	0	10	360	498	.278

1996 Head Coaches: Calg—Wally Buono (7th season); **Edm**—Ron Lancaster (6th); **Win**—Cal Murphy (5th); **BC**—Joe Paopao (1st); **Sask**—Jim Daley (1st)

1995 South Div. standings: 1. Baltimore (15-3); 2. San Antonio (12-6); 3. Birmingham (10-8); 4. Memphis (9-9); 5. Shreveport (5-13).

All-CFL Team

The All-CFL team as selected by a Football Writers of Canada panel. Holdovers from the 1995 team are in **bold** type.

Pos Offense
WR Joe Rogers, Ott.
WR Eddie Brown, Edm.
T Fred Childress, Calg.
T Chris Perez, Tor.
G **Rocco Romano**, Calg.
G Leo Groenewegen, Edm.
C **Mike Kiselak**, Tor.
QB Doug Flutie, Tor.
FB Robert Drummond, Tor.
RB Robert Mimbs, Sask.
SB Mac Cody, Ham.
SB Darren Flutie, Edm.

Pos Defense
E Grant Carter, Mon.
E Malvin Hunter, Edm.
T Rob Waldrop, Tor.
T **Bennie Goods**, Edm.
LB Tracy Gravely, Mon.
LB **Willie Pless**, Edm.
LB K.D. Williams, Win.
CB Al Jordan, Calg.
CB Marvin Coleman, Calg.
HB **Glenn Rogers**, Edm.
HB Charles Gordon, Mon.
S Trent Brown, Edm.

Specialists
PK—Mark McLoughlin, Calg.
P—Paul Osbaldiston, Ham.
Special Teams—Jimmy Cunningham, Tor.

CFL Playoffs

Division Semifinals (Nov. 10)

East: at Montreal 22 .... Hamilton 11
West: at Edmonton 68 .... Winnipeg 7

Division Championships (Nov. 17)

East: at Toronto 43 .... Montreal 7
West: Edmonton 15 .... at Calgary 12

84th Grey Cup Championship

Nov. 24, 1996 at Ivor Wynne Stadium, Hamilton, Ont. (Att: 38,595)

Edmonton (13-7)	9	14	0	14— **37**
Toronto (16-3)	0	27	3	13— **43**

Most Outstanding Player: Doug Flutie, Toronto, QB (Passing— 22 for 35, 302 yds; 0 TD, 0 Int; Rushing—13 carries for 98 yds, 1 TD).

Most Outstanding Canadian: Mike Vanderjagt, Toronto, PK, (5/5 FG, 4/4 PAT).

Regular Season Individual Leaders

Passing Efficiency

(Minimum of 300 attempts)

	Att	Cmp	Cmp Pct	Yds	Avg Gain	Tds	TD Pct	Long	Int	Int Pct	Rating
Tracy Ham, Mon.	396	229	57.8	3313	14.5	28	7.1	62	10	2.5	98.2
Doug Flutie, Tor.	677	434	64.1	5720	13.2	29	4.3	97	17	2.5	94.5
Jeff Garcia, Calg.	537	315	58.7	4225	13.4	25	4.7	104	16	3.0	86.9
Damon Allen, B.C.	368	219	59.5	2772	12.7	13	3.5	64	10	2.7	83.5
David Archer, Ott	523	292	55.8	3977	13.6	23	4.4	90	17	3.3	81.4
Danny McManus, Edm.	582	310	53.3	4425	14.3	19	3.3	60	27	4.6	69.7

Rushing

	Car	Yds	Avg	Long	TD
Robert Mimbs, Sask.	292	1403	4.8	38	8
Eric L. Blount, Edm.	246	1091	4.4	55	4
Kelvin Anderson, Calg.	240	1068	4.5	49	10
Cory Philpot, BC	163	1024	6.3	77	1
Robert Drummond, Tor.	160	935	5.8	79	11
Mike Pringle, Mon.	127	825	6.5	65	5
Doug Flutie, Tor.	101	756	7.5	37	9
Jeff Garcia, Calg.	92	657	7.1	30	6
Tracy Ham, Mon.	74	604	8.2	57	4
Ronald Williams, B.C.	92	535	5.8	38	2
Norman Bradford, Mon.	77	465	6.0	34	6
Dave Dinnall, Ott.	54	449	8.3	69	4
Damon Allen, B.C.	52	400	7.7	31	2
Sean Millington, B.C.	74	381	5.1	26	7
M. Richardson, Win.	91	378	4.2	18	5

Receiving

	Rec	Yds	Avg	Long	TD
Mac Cody, Ham.	80	1426	17.8	74	11
Darren Flutie, Edm.	86	1362	15.8	42	6
Eddie Brown, Edm.	70	1325	18.9	46	7
Allen Pitts, Calg.	86	1309	15.2	41	11
Mike Clemons, Tor.	116	1268	10.9	52	4
Joseph Rogers, Ott.	79	1253	15.9	90	8
Jock Climie, Mon.	68	1209	17.8	62	9
Terry Vaughn, Calg.	74	1161	15.7	104	5
David Sapunjis, Calg.	82	1075	13.1	61	8
Robert Gordon, Ott.	70	1049	15.0	55	8
Paul Masotti, Tor.	73	1023	14.0	97	7
Mike Trevathan, B.C.	65	1006	15.5	52	10
Chris Armstrong, Mon.	63	979	15.5	45	7
Curtis Mayfield, Sask.	51	963	18.9	95	6
Jason Phillips, Ham.	64	928	14.5	55	6

Touchdowns

	TD	Rush	Rec	Ret	Pts
Robert Drummond, Tor.	17	11	6	0	102
Kelvin Anderson, Calg.	14	10	4	0	84
Allen Pitts, Calg.	11	0	11	0	66
Maclin Cody, Ham.	11	0	11	0	66
Mike Trevathan, B.C.	10	0	10	0	60
Sean Millington, B.C.	10	7	3	0	60
Doug Flutie, Tor.	9	9	0	0	54
Mike Clemons, Tor.	9	5	4	0	54
Jock Climie, Mon.	9	0	9	0	54
Tyrone Williams, Tor.	8	0	8	0	48
Tony Burse, Edm.	8	6	2	0	48

	TD	Rush	Rec	Ret	Pts
David Sapunjis, Calg.	8	0	8	0	48
Michael Soles, Mon.	8	0	8	0	48
Robert Gordon, Ott.	8	0	8	0	48
M. Richardson, Win.	8	5	3	0	48
Robert Mimbs, Sask.	8	8	0	0	48
Joseph Rogers, Ott.	8	0	8	0	48
Eddie Brown, Edm.	7	0	7	0	42
Mike Pringle, Mon.	7	5	2	0	42
Chris Armstrong, Mon.	7	0	7	0	42
Paul Masotti, Tor.	7	0	7	0	42

World Classic Bowl?

On April 9,1997, the CFL and the NFL announced a "formal association to help support the long-term growth of the game in Canada." As part of the agreement, the two leagues will look into playing an annual "World Classic Bowl" which would pit the previous season's World League of American Football (WLAF) champion against the CFL Grey Cup champion, starting in June of 1998. The WLAF serves as the NFL's spring league and 112 players from NFL clubs were allocated to the WLAF in 1997. The NFL and CFL will also discuss greater exchange of players between the two leagues.

Other Individual Leaders

Points (Kicking) ....220 Mark McLoughlin, Calg.
All-Purpose Yards ....2638 James Cunningham, Tor.
Receptions ....116 Mike Clemons, Tor.
Yards from Scrimmage .....1738 Robert Mimbs, Sask.
Interceptions ....8 Alfred Jordan, Calg.
Sacks ....15 Grant Carter, Mon.
& Angelo Snipers, Win.
Punting Average ....43.9 Paul Osbaldiston, Ham.

Most Outstanding Awards

Player ....Doug Flutie, Toronto, QB
Canadian ....Leroy Blugh, Edmonton, DE
Offensive Lineman ....Mike Kiselak, Toronto, C
Defensive Player ....Willie Pless, Edmonton, LB
Rookie ....Kelvin Anderson, Calgary, RB
Coach ....Ron Lancaster, Edmonton

World League of American Football

Final 1997 Standings

	W	L	T	Pct.	PF	PA
*Rhein	7	3	0	.700	206	146
Amsterdam	5	5	0	.500	156	160
Scotland	5	5	0	.500	134	154
*Barcelona	5	5	0	.500	236	209
Frankfurt	4	6	0	.400	147	142
London	4	6	0	.400	116	184

*Clinched World Bowl berth

1st Half Standings

	W	L	T	Pct.	PF	PA
*Barcelona	4	1	0	.800	122	89
Rhein	3	2	0	.600	93	72
Amsterdam	2	3	0	.400	91	89
Frankfurt	2	3	0	.400	53	53
Scotland	2	3	0	.400	50	65
London	2	3	0	.400	74	114

Note: The team that leads the standings after week 5 earns a bid and the right to host the World Bowl. The team which has the best overall record at the end of the season also qualifies for the World Bowl. If the host team also leads the standings after the second half of the season, the club with the second-best overall record qualifies for the World Bowl.

Regular Season Individual Leaders

Passing Efficiency

	Att	Cmp	Cmp Pct	Yds	Avg Gain	TD	TD Pct	Long	Int	Int Pct	Rating
Jon Kitna, Bar	317	171	53.9	2448	7.72	22	6.9	96-td	15	4.7	82.6
Dave Barr, Scot	164	98	59.8	1118	6.82	3	1.8	50-td	4	2.4	76.2
T.J. Rubley, Rhe	218	117	53.7	1473	6.76	12	5.5	73-td	9	4.1	76.1
Chad May, Fran	184	86	46.7	1016	5.52	4	2.2	47-td	3	1.6	64.5
Spence Fischer, Scot	148	78	52.7	839	5.67	1	0.7	46-td	6	4.1	55.0

Scoring

Touchdowns	TD	Rus	Rec	Ret	Pts
Sheddrick Wilson, Bar ..	9	0	9	0	54
Derrick Clark, Rhe	9	9	0	0	54
Tyree Davis, Bar	7	0	6	1	42
Bobby Phillips, Fran	6	6	0	0	36
Bill Schroeder, Rhe	6	0	6	0	36

Kicking	PAT	FG/FGA	Lg	Pts
Ralf Kleinmann, Fran	12/13	13/21	47	51
Manfred Burgsmuller, Rhe .	23/25	7/9	28	44
Jess Angoy, Bar	26/28	5/9	35	41
Oliver Quass, Ams	0/0	9/13	35	27
Kari Gronroos, Scot	2/2	8/10	35	26

Rushing

	Car	Yards	Avg	Long	TD
Siran Stacy, Sco	199	785	3.9	31	4
Bobby Phillips, Fran	144	760	5.3	65-td	6
Ontiwaun Carter, Rhe ..	120	587	4.9	50	2
Derrick Clark, Rhe	107	510	4.8	27	9
Terry Wilburn, Bar	107	429	4.0	24	1

Other Individual Leaders

Yards from Scrimmage	864	Siran Stacy, Sco.
Punting Average	45.1	Wayne Lammle, Sco.
Interceptions	6	Carlos Brooks, Bar.
Sacks	9	Malcolm Showell, Lon. & Herman Smith, Lon.
Punt Return Avg.	12.4	Vernon Turner, Fran.
Kickoff Return Avg.	26.3	Eric Smith, Sco.

Receptions

	No	Yds	Avg	Long	TD
Yo Murphy, Sco	47	559	11.9	50-td	2
Tyree Davis, Bar	43	738	17.2	55	6
Bill Schroeder, Rhe	43	702	16.3	73-td	6
Sheddrick Wilson, Bar ..	41	633	15.4	53	9
Bryce Burnett, Bar	35	357	10.2	36	2

Annual Awards

Offensive MVP	T.J. Rubley, Rhein, QB
Defensive MVP	Jason Simmons, Scotland, DE
Coach of the Year	Galen Hall, Rhein

All-World League Team

The All-World League Team as selected by members of the World League media.

Pos	Offense	Pos	Defense
QB	T.J. Rubley, Rhein	DE	Malcolm Showell, London
RB	Bobby Phillips, Frankfurt	DT	La'Roi Glover, Barcelona
RB	Siran Stacy, Scotland	DT	Troy Ridgley, Amsterdam
WR	Bill Schroeder, Rhein	DE	Jason Simmons, Scotland
WR	Sheddrick Wilson, Bar.	LB	Hillary Butler, Frankfurt
TE	Bryce Burnett, Bar.	LB	Richard Newbill, London
TE	Ethan Brooks, Rhein	LB	Shawn Banks, Frankfurt
G	Mike Sheldon, Rhein	CB	Jack Kellogg, Frankfurt
C	Bob Kronenberg, Rhein	S	Johnny Dixon, Frankfurt
G	Tom Robsock, Bar.	S	George Coghill, Scotland
T	Spence Folau, Rhein	CB	Cecil Doggette, Frankfurt

World Bowl '97

June 22, 1997 at Estadi Olimpic de Montjuic, Barcelona (Att: 31,100)

Rhein (7-3)	3	14	0	7—	**24**
Barcelona (5-5)	14	14	7	3—	**38**

MVP: Jon Kitna, Barcelona, QB (23 for 31, 401 yards and 2 TDs.)

Oh, Canada!
By Steve Lanthier

With so much disarray in Canadian Football right now, so much that the NFL had to send some cash north of the border, it seems like a good time to provide a reminder of the CFL's proud history.

Canadian football's roots can be traced back to 1861 when a group of students from the University of Toronto participated in the first documented football game in Canada. Then, in 1874, a group of students from McGill University took their version of football to the United States, meeting up with a team from Harvard University in a two-game series. It is generally accepted that both American and Canadian football evolved from these games.

The Grey Cup, symbolic of Canadian professional football supremacy, was donated in 1909 by Albert Henry George, the fourth Earl of Grey and Governor General of Canada. The first ever Grey Cup game was played that same year at Toronto Rosedale Field between the University of Toronto and the Parkdale Canoe Club. A crowd of 3,807 fans watched as the U of T captured the cup for the first time, defeating Parkdale by a 26-6 score.

In 1993 the League embarked on an aggressive penetration into the American market place. The Sacramento Gold Miners were added and played the first ever CFL regular season game on American soil on Saturday, July 17 when they hosted the Calgary Stampeders. In 1995, The Baltimore Stallions, now one of four US teams in the CFL, became the first ever American franchise to capture the Grey Cup as they defeated the Calgary Stampeders by a 37-20 margin.

However, following the '95 campaign, the Stallions transferred to Montreal while the rest of the American franchises withdrew. The return of football to Montreal meant a rebirth to the CFL in that city after a nine-year absence.

The 1996 CFL season found the League back to its customary grouping of nine Canadian teams. The Toronto Argonauts, piloted by Doug Flutie, dominated the regular season with a 15–3 record and a first place finish in the Eastern Division while the Calgary Stampeders topped the Western. Second place in the Eastern belonged to the newest franchise in the League, the Montreal Alouettes. The Als ended their season at 12–6. In the Western, the 2nd place Edmonton Eskimos finished with an impressive 11–7 record.

The 1996 playoff picture saw the Toronto Argonauts receive a berth in the Eastern Division Finals while the Montreal Alouettes defeated the Hamilton Tigercats 22-11 to advance. The Western Division win gave the Calgary Stampeders their berth into the Division Finals while the Semi-finals pitted the Edmonton Eskimos against the Winnipeg Blue Bombers. The Eskimos humiliated the Blue Bombers by a score of 68-7. The Eastern division finals saw the Toronto Argonauts predictably defeat the Montreal Alouettes by a score of 43-7. The Western division final had the Calgary Stampeders at home against Edmonton. In what proved to be a close and entertaining game the underdog Eskimos squeaked by the Stampeders 15-12.

On Sunday, November 24, 1996 at Ivor Wynne Stadium in Hamilton, Ontario, two CFL powerhouse teams met to contest for the Grey Cup. The Toronto Argonauts were the favorites after finishing the season with the best record in the CFL. The temperature hovered at the freezing mark and heavy snow covered the field. The first quarter belonged to the Eskimos as they led 9–0. The second quarter however saw Toronto QB quarterback Doug Flutie rally his squad for 27–23 lead at halftime. The third quarter saw only 3 points scored on a field goal by Toronto kicker Mike Vanderjact. The fourth quarter had both teams battling the snow storm and themselves for the lead. However, when the storm subsided so had the game, with the Toronto Argonauts victorious, 43-37. Both Flutie and Vanderjact were named game MVPs.

Steve Lanthier is the producer for ESPN's CFL coverage.

THE 1998

ESPN
INFORMATION PLEASE
SPORTS
ALMANAC

PRO FOOTBALL
S T A T I S T I C S

THROUGH THE YEARS
1869-1997
BOWLS • ALL-TIME LEADERS

SEC
B

PAGE
240

The Super Bowl

The first AFL-NFL World Championship Game, as it was originally called, was played seven months after the two leagues agreed to merge in June of 1966. It became the Super Bowl (complete with roman numerals) by the third game in 1969. The Super Bowl winner has been presented the Vince Lombardi Trophy since 1971. Lombardi, whose Green Bay teams won the first two title games, died in 1970. NFL champions (1966-69) and NFC champions (since 1970) are listed in CAPITAL letters.

Multiple winners: Dallas and San Francisco (5); Pittsburgh (4); Green Bay, Oakland-LA Raiders and Washington (3); Miami and NY Giants (2).

Bowl	Date	Winner	Head Coach	Score	Loser	Head Coach	Site
I	1/15/67	GREEN BAY	Vince Lombardi	35-10	Kansas City	Hank Stram	Los Angeles
II	1/14/68	GREEN BAY	Vince Lombardi	33-14	Oakland	John Rauch	Miami
III	1/12/69	NY Jets	Weeb Ewbank	16- 7	BALTIMORE	Don Shula	Miami
IV	1/11/70	Kansas City	Hank Stram	23- 7	MINNESOTA	Bud Grant	New Orleans
V	1/17/71	Baltimore	Don McCafferty	16-13	DALLAS	Tom Landry	Miami
VI	1/16/72	DALLAS	Tom Landry	24- 3	Miami	Don Shula	New Orleans
VII	1/14/73	Miami	Don Shula	14- 7	WASHINGTON	George Allen	Los Angeles
VIII	1/13/74	Miami	Don Shula	24- 7	MINNESOTA	Bud Grant	Houston
IX	1/12/75	Pittsburgh	Chuck Noll	16- 6	MINNESOTA	Bud Grant	New Orleans
X	1/18/76	Pittsburgh	Chuck Noll	21-17	DALLAS	Tom Landry	Miami
XI	1/ 9/77	Oakland	John Madden	32-14	MINNESOTA	Bud Grant	Pasadena
XII	1/15/78	DALLAS	Tom Landry	27-10	Denver	Red Miller	New Orleans
XIII	1/21/79	Pittsburgh	Chuck Noll	35-31	DALLAS	Tom Landry	Miami
XIV	1/20/80	Pittsburgh	Chuck Noll	31-19	LA RAMS	Ray Malavasi	Pasadena
XV	1/25/81	Oakland	Tom Flores	27-10	PHILADELPHIA	Dick Vermeil	New Orleans
XVI	1/24/82	SAN FRANCISCO	Bill Walsh	26-21	Cincinnati	Forrest Gregg	Pontiac, MI
XVII	1/30/83	WASHINGTON	Joe Gibbs	27-17	Miami	Don Shula	Pasadena
XVIII	1/22/84	LA Raiders	Tom Flores	38- 9	WASHINGTON	Joe Gibbs	Tampa
XIX	1/20/85	SAN FRANCISCO	Bill Walsh	38-16	Miami	Don Shula	Stanford
XX	1/26/86	CHICAGO	Mike Ditka	46-10	New England	Raymond Berry	New Orleans
XXI	1/25/87	NY GIANTS	Bill Parcells	39-20	Denver	Dan Reeves	Pasadena
XXII	1/31/88	WASHINGTON	Joe Gibbs	42-10	Denver	Dan Reeves	San Diego
XXIII	1/22/89	SAN FRANCISCO	Bill Walsh	20-16	Cincinnati	Sam Wyche	Miami
XXIV	1/28/90	SAN FRANCISCO	George Seifert	55-10	Denver	Dan Reeves	New Orleans
XXV	1/27/91	NY GIANTS	Bill Parcells	20-19	Buffalo	Marv Levy	Tampa
XXVI	1/26/92	WASHINGTON	Joe Gibbs	37-24	Buffalo	Marv Levy	Minneapolis
XXVII	1/31/93	DALLAS	Jimmy Johnson	52-17	Buffalo	Marv Levy	Pasadena
XXVIII	1/30/94	DALLAS	Jimmy Johnson	30-13	Buffalo	Marv Levy	Atlanta
XXIX	1/29/95	SAN FRANCISCO	George Seifert	49-26	San Diego	Bobby Ross	Miami
XXX	1/28/96	DALLAS	Barry Switzer	27-17	Pittsburgh	Bill Cowher	Tempe, AZ
XXXI	1/26/97	GREEN BAY	Mike Holmgren	35-21	New England	Bill Parcells	New Orleans

Pete Rozelle Award (MVP)

The Most Valuable Player in the Super Bowl. Currently selected by an 11-member panel made up of national pro football writers and broadcasters chosen by the NFL. Presented by *Sport* magazine from 1967-89 and by the NFL since 1990. Named after former NFL commissioner Pete Rozelle in 1990. Winner who did not play for Super Bowl champion is in **bold** type.

Multiple winners: Joe Montana (3); Terry Bradshaw and Bart Starr (2).

Bowl		Bowl		Bowl	
I	Bart Starr, Green Bay, QB	XII	Harvey Martin, Dallas, DE & Randy White, Dallas, DT	XXII	Doug Williams, Washington, QB
II	Bart Starr, Green Bay, QB			XXIII	Jerry Rice, San Francisco, WR
III	Joe Namath, NY Jets, QB	XIII	Terry Bradshaw, Pittsburgh, QB	XXIV	Joe Montana, San Francisco, QB
IV	Len Dawson, Kansas City, QB	XIV	Terry Bradshaw, Pittsburgh, QB	XXV	Ottis Anderson, NY Giants, RB
V	**Chuck Howley**, Dallas, LB	XV	Jim Plunkett, Oakland, QB	XXVI	Mark Rypien, Washington, QB
VI	Roger Staubach, Dallas, QB	XVI	Joe Montana, San Francisco, QB	XXVII	Troy Aikman, Dallas, QB
VII	Jake Scott, Miami, S	XVII	John Riggins, Washington, RB	XXVIII	Emmitt Smith, Dallas, RB
VIII	Larry Csonka, Miami, RB	XVIII	Marcus Allen, LA Raiders, RB	XXIX	Steve Young, San Francisco, QB
IX	Franco Harris, Pittsburgh, RB	XIX	Joe Montana, San Francisco, QB	XXX	Larry Brown, Dallas, CB
X	Lynn Swann, Pittsburgh, WR	XX	Richard Dent, Chicago, DE	XXXI	Desmond Howard, Green Bay, KR
XI	Fred Biletnikoff, Oakland, WR	XXI	Phil Simms, NY Giants, QB		

All-Time Super Bowl Leaders
Through Jan. 26, 1997; participants in Super Bowl XXXI in **bold** type.

CAREER
Passing Efficiency

Ratings based on performance standards established for completion percentage, average gain, touchdown percentage and interception percentage. Quarterbacks are allocated points according to how their statistics measure up to those standards. Minimum 25 passing attempts.

		Gm	Att	Cmp	Cmp%	Yards	Avg Gain	TD	TD%	Int	Int%	Rating
1	Phil Simms, NYG	1	25	22	88.0	268	10.72	3	12.0	0	0.0	150.9
2	Steve Young, SF	2	39	26	66.7	345	8.85	6	15.4	0	0.0	134.1
3	Doug Williams, Wash	1	29	18	62.1	340	11.72	4	13.8	1	3.4	128.1
4	Joe Montana, SF	4	122	83	68.0	1142	9.36	11	9.0	0	0.0	127.8
5	Jim Plunkett, Oak-LA	2	46	29	63.0	433	9.41	4	8.7	0	0.0	122.8
6	Terry Bradshaw, Pit	4	84	49	58.3	932	11.10	9	10.7	4	4.8	112.6
7	Troy Aikman, Dal	3	80	56	70.0	689	8.61	5	6.3	1	1.3	111.9
8	Roger Staubach, Dal	4	98	61	62.2	734	7.49	8	8.2	4	4.1	95.4
9	Ken Anderson, Cin	1	34	25	73.5	300	8.82	2	5.9	2	5.9	95.2
10	Bart Starr, GB	2	47	29	61.7	452	9.62	3	6.4	1	2.1	95.1

Passing Yards

		Gm	Att	Cmp	Pct	Yds
1	Joe Montana, SF	4	122	83	68.0	1142
2	Terry Bradshaw, Pit	4	84	49	58.3	932
3	Jim Kelly, Buf	4	145	81	55.9	829
4	Roger Staubach, Dal	4	98	61	62.2	734
5	Troy Aikman, Dal	3	80	56	70.0	689
6	John Elway, Den	3	101	46	45.5	669
7	Fran Tarkenton, Min	3	89	46	51.7	489
8	Bart Starr, GB	2	47	29	61.7	452
9	Jim Plunkett, Raiders	2	46	29	63.0	433
10	Joe Theismann, Wash	2	58	31	53.4	386
11	Len Dawson, KC	2	44	28	63.6	353
12	Steve Young, SF	2	26	39	66.7	345
13	Doug Williams, Wash	1	29	18	62.1	340
14	Dan Marino, Mia	1	50	29	58.0	318
15	Ken Anderson, Cin	1	34	25	73.5	300

Receptions

		Gm	No	Yds	Avg	TD
1	Jerry Rice, SF	3	28	512	18.3	7
2	Andre Reed, Buf	4	27	323	12.0	0
3	Roger Craig, SF	3	20	212	10.6	3
	Thurman Thomas, Buf	4	20	144	7.2	0
5	Jay Novacek, Dal	3	17	148	8.7	2
6	Lynn Swann, Pit	4	16	364	22.8	3
	Michael Irvin, Dal	3	16	256	16.0	2
8	Chuck Foreman, Min	3	15	139	9.3	0
9	Cliff Branch, Raiders	3	14	181	12.9	3
10	Don Beebe, Buf	3	12	171	14.3	2
	Preston Pearson, Bal-Pit-Dal	5	12	105	8.8	0
	Kenneth Davis, Buf	4	12	72	6.0	0
13	John Stallworth, Pit	4	11	268	24.4	3
	Dan Ross, Cin	1	11	104	9.5	2
15	Six tied with 10 catches each.					

Super Bowl Appearances

Through Super Bowl XXXI, 10 NFL teams have yet to play for the Vince Lombardi Trophy. In alphabetical order, they are: Arizona, Atlanta, Carolina, Cleveland Browns/Baltimore Ravens, Detroit, Houston, Jacksonville, New Orleans, Seattle and Tampa Bay. Of the 20 teams that have participated, Dallas has the most appearances (8) and, along with San Francisco, has the most titles (5).

App		W	L	Pct	PF	PA
8	Dallas	5	3	.625	221	132
5	San Francisco	5	0	1.000	188	89
5	Pittsburgh	4	1	.800	120	100
5	Washington	3	2	.600	122	103
5	Miami	2	3	.400	74	103
4	Oak/LA Raiders	3	1	.750	111	66
4	Buffalo	0	4	.000	73	139
4	Denver	0	4	.000	50	163
4	Minnesota	0	4	.000	34	95
3	Green Bay	3	0	1.000	103	45
2	NY Giants	2	0	1.000	59	39
2	Baltimore Colts	1	1	.500	23	29
2	Kansas City	1	1	.500	33	42
2	Cincinnati	0	2	.000	37	46
2	New England	0	2	.000	31	81
1	Chicago	1	0	1.000	46	10
1	NY Jets	1	0	1.000	16	7
1	LA Rams	0	1	.000	19	31
1	Philadelphia	0	1	.000	10	27
1	San Diego	0	1	.000	26	49

Rushing

		Gm	Car	Yds	Avg	TD
1	Franco Harris, Pit	4	101	354	3.5	4
2	Larry Csonka, Mia	3	57	297	5.2	2
3	Emmitt Smith, Dal	3	70	289	4.1	5
4	John Riggins, Wash	2	64	230	3.6	2
5	Timmy Smith, Wash	1	22	204	9.3	2
	Thurman Thomas, Buf	4	52	204	3.9	4
7	Roger Craig, SF	3	52	201	3.9	2
8	Marcus Allen, Raiders	1	20	191	9.5	2
9	Tony Dorsett, Dal	2	31	162	5.2	1
10	Mark van Eeghen, Raiders	2	37	153	4.1	0
11	Kenneth Davis, Buf	4	30	145	4.8	0
12	Rocky Bleier, Pit	4	44	144	3.3	0
13	Walt Garrison, Dal	2	26	139	5.3	0
14	Clarence Davis, Raiders	1	16	137	8.6	0
15	Duane Thomas, Dal	2	37	130	3.5	1

All-Purpose Yards

		Gm	Rush	Rec	Ret	Total
1	Jerry Rice, SF	3	15	512	0	527
2	Franco Harris, Pit	4	354	114	0	468
3	Roger Craig, SF	3	201	212	0	413
4	Lynn Swann, Pit	4	-7	364	34	391
5	Thurman Thomas, Buf	4	204	144	0	348
6	Emmitt Smith, Dal	3	289	56	0	345
7	Andre Reed, Buf	3	0	323	0	323
8	Larry Csonka, Mia	3	297	17	0	314
9	Fulton Walker, Mia	2	0	0	298	298
10	Ricky Sanders, Wash	2	-3	234	46	277

Scoring

Points

		Gm	TD	FG	PAT	Pts
1	Jerry Rice, SF	3	7	0	0	42
2	Emmitt Smith, Dal	3	5	0	0	30
3	Roger Craig, SF	3	4	0	0	24
	Franco Harris, Pit	4	4	0	0	24
	Thurman Thomas, Buf	4	4	0	0	24
6	Ray Wersching, SF	2	0	5	7	22
7	Don Chandler, GB	2	0	4	8	20
8	Cliff Branch, Raiders	3	3	0	0	18
	John Stallworth, Pit	4	3	0	0	18
	Lynn Swann, Pit	4	3	0	0	18
	Ricky Watters, SF	1	3	0	0	18
12	Chris Bahr, Raiders	2	0	3	8	17
13	Matt Bahr, Pit-NYG	2	0	3	6	15
	Mike Cofer, SF	2	0	2	9	15
	Uwe von Schamann, Mia .	2	0	4	3	15

Punting
(Minimum 10 Punts)

		Gm	No	Yds	Avg
1	Jerrel Wilson, KC	2	11	511	46.5
2	Ray Guy, Raiders	3	14	587	41.9
3	Larry Seiple, Mia	3	15	620	41.3
4	Mike Eischeid, Oak-Min	3	17	698	41.1
5	Danny White, Dal	2	10	406	40.6

Punt Returns
(Minimum 4 returns)

		Gm	No	Yds	Avg	TD
1	John Taylor, SF	3	6	94	15.7	0
2	**Desmond Howard**, GB	1	6	90	15.0	0
3	Neal Colzie, Oak	1	4	43	10.8	0
4	Dana McLemore, SF	1	5	51	10.2	0
5	Mike Fuller, Cin	1	4	35	8.8	0

Kickoff Returns
(Minimum 4 returns)

		Gm	No	Yds	Avg	TD
1	Fulton Walker, Mia	2	8	283	35.4	1
2	Andre Coleman, SD	1	8	242	30.3	1
3	Larry Anderson, Pit	2	8	207	25.9	0
4	**Desmond Howard**, GB ..	1	4	154	38.5	1
5	Darren Carrington, Den ..	1	6	146	24.3	1

Touchdowns

		Gm	Rush	Rec	Ret	TD
1	Jerry Rice, SF	3	0	7	0	7
2	Emmitt Smith, Dal	3	5	0	0	5
3	Roger Craig, SF	3	2	2	0	4
	Franco Harris, Pit	4	4	0	0	4
	Thurman Thomas, Buf	4	4	0	0	4
6	Cliff Branch, Raiders .	3	0	3	0	3
	John Stallworth, Pit ..	4	0	3	0	3
	Lynn Swann, Pit	4	0	3	0	3
	Ricky Watters, SF	1	1	2	0	3
10	Twenty-three tied with 2 TDs each:					

Marcus Allen, Raiders; Ottis Anderson, NYG; Pete Banaszak, Raiders; Don Beebe, Buf.; Gary Clark, Wash.; Larry Csonka, Mia.; John Elway, Den.; Michael Irvin, Dal.; Butch Johnson, Dal.; Jim Kiick, Mia.; Max McGee, GB; Jim McMahon, Chi.; Bill Miller, Raiders; Joe Montana, SF; Elijah Pitts, GB; Tom Rathman, SF; John Riggins, Wash.; Gerald Riggs, Wash.; Dan Ross, Cin.; Ricky Sanders, Wash.; Timmy Smith, Wash.; John Taylor, SF and Duane Thomas, Dal.

Interceptions

		Gm	No	Yds	TD
1	Larry Brown, Dal	2	3	77	0
	Chuck Howley, Dal	2	3	63	0
	Rod Martin, Raiders	2	3	44	0
4	Randy Beverly, NYJ	1	2	0	0
	Mel Blount, Pit	4	2	23	0
	Brad Edwards, Wash	1	2	56	0
	Thomas Everett, Dal	1	2	22	0
	Jake Scott, Mia	3	2	63	0
	Mike Wagner, Pit	3	2	45	0
	James Washington, Dal	2	2	25	0
	Barry Wilburn, Wash	1	2	11	0
	Eric Wright, SF	4	2	25	0

Sacks

		Gm	No
1	Charles Haley, SF-Dal	5	4
2	**Reggie White**, GB	1	3
	Leonard Marshall, NYG	2	3
	Danny Stubbs, SF	2	3
	Jeff Wright, Buf	4	3
6	Jim Jeffcoat, Dal	2	2½
	Dexter Manley, Wash	3	2½

Four or More Super Bowl Wins

Dallas Cowboys (5)

Year	Bowl	Head Coach	Quarterback	MVP	Opponent	Score	Site
1972	VI	Tom Landry	Roger Staubach	Staubach	Miami	24-3	New Orleans
1978	XII	Tom Landry	Roger Staubach	Harvey Martin & Randy White	Denver	27-10	New Orleans
1993	XXVII	Jimmy Johnson	Troy Aikman	Aikman	Buffalo	52-17	Pasadena
1994	XXVIII	Jimmy Johnson	Troy Aikman	Emmitt Smith	Buffalo	30-13	Atlanta
1996	XXX	Barry Switzer	Troy Aikman	Larry Brown	Pittsburgh	27-17	Tempe

San Francisco 49ers (5)

Year	Bowl	Head Coach	Quarterback	MVP	Opponent	Score	Site
1982	XVI	Bill Walsh	Joe Montana	Montana	Cincinnati	26-21	Pontiac
1985	XIX	Bill Walsh	Joe Montana	Montana	Miami	38-16	Stanford
1989	XXIII	Bill Walsh	Joe Montana	Jerry Rice	Cincinnati	20-16	Miami
1990	XXIV	George Seifert	Joe Montana	Montana	Denver	55-10	New Orleans
1995	XXIX	George Seifert	Steve Young	Young	San Diego	49-26	Miami

Pittsburgh Steelers (4)

Year	Bowl	Head Coach	Quarterback	MVP	Opponent	Score	Site
1975	IX	Chuck Noll	Terry Bradshaw	Franco Harris	Minnesota	16-6	New Orleans
1976	X	Chuck Noll	Terry Bradshaw	Lynn Swann	Dallas	21-17	Miami
1979	XIII	Chuck Noll	Terry Bradshaw	Bradshaw	Dallas	35-31	Miami
1980	XIV	Chuck Noll	Terry Bradshaw	Bradshaw	LA Rams	31-19	Pasadena

SINGLE GAME

Passing

Yards Gained

	Year	Att/Cmp	Yds
Joe Montana, SF vs Cin	1989	36/23	357
Doug Williams, Wash vs Den ...	1988	29/18	340
Joe Montana, SF vs Mia	1985	35/24	331
Steve Young, SF vs SD	1995	24/36	325
Terry Bradshaw, Pit vs Dal	1979	30/17	318
Dan Marino, Mia vs SF	1985	50/29	318
Terry Bradshaw, Pit vs Rams ...	1980	21/14	309
John Elway, Den vs NYG	1987	37/22	304
Ken Anderson, Cin vs SF	1982	34/25	300
Joe Montana, SF vs Den	1990	29/22	297

Touchdown Passes

	Year	TD	Int
Steve Young, SF vs SD	1995	6	0
Joe Montana, SF vs Den	1990	5	0
Terry Bradshaw, Pit vs Dal	1979	4	1
Doug Williams, Wash vs Den	1988	4	1
Troy Aikman, Dal vs Buf	1993	4	0
Roger Staubach, Dal vs Pit	1979	3	1
Jim Plunkett, Raiders vs Phi	1981	3	0
Joe Montana, SF vs Mia	1985	3	0
Phil Simms, NYG vs Den	1987	3	0

Rushing

Yards Gained

	Year	Car	Yds	TD
Timmy Smith, Wash vs Den	1988	22	204	2
Marcus Allen, Raiders vs Wash ...	1984	20	191	2
John Riggins, Wash vs Mia ...	1983	38	166	1
Franco Harris, Pit vs Min	1975	34	158	1
Larry Csonka, Mia vs Min	1974	33	145	2
Clarence Davis, Raiders vs Min.	1977	16	137	0
Thurman Thomas, Buf vs NYG .	1991	15	135	1
Emmitt Smith, Dal vs Buf	1994	30	132	2
Matt Snell, NYJ vs Bal	1969	30	121	1
Tom Matte, Bal vs NYJ	1969	11	116	0
Larry Csonka, Mia vs Wash ...	1973	15	112	1
Emmitt Smith, Dal vs Buf	1993	22	108	1
Ottis Anderson, NYG vs Buf ...	1991	21	102	1
Tony Dorsett, Dal vs Pit	1979	16	96	0
Duane Thomas, Dal vs Mia ...	1972	19	95	1

Scoring

Points

	Year	TD	FG	PAT	Pts
Roger Craig, SF vs Mia	1985	3	0	0	18
Jerry Rice, SF vs Den	1990	3	0	0	18
Jerry Rice, SF vs SD	1995	3	0	0	18
Ricky Watters, SF vs SD	1995	3	0	0	18
Don Chandler, GB vs Raiders .	1968	0	4	3	15

Touchdowns

	Year	TD	Rush	Rec
Roger Craig, SF vs Mia	1985	3	1	2
Jerry Rice, SF vs Den	1990	3	0	3
Jerry Rice, SF vs SD	1995	3	0	3
Ricky Watters, SF vs SD	1995	3	1	2
Max McGee, GB vs KC	1967	2	0	2
Elijah Pitts, GB vs KC	1967	2	2	0
Bill Miller, Raiders vs GB	1968	2	0	2
Larry Csonka, Mia vs Min	1974	2	2	0
Pete Banaszak, Raiders vs Min.	1977	2	2	0
John Stallworth, Pit vs Dal	1979	2	0	2
Franco Harris, Pit vs Rams ...	1980	2	2	0
Cliff Branch, Raiders vs Phi ...	1981	2	0	2
Dan Ross, Cin vs SF	1982	2	0	2
Marcus Allen, Raiders vs Wash.	1984	2	2	0
Jim McMahon, Chi vs NE	1986	2	2	0
Ricky Sanders, Wash vs Den ..	1988	2	0	2
Timmy Smith, Wash vs Den ...	1988	2	2	0
Tom Rathman, SF vs Den	1990	2	2	0
Gerald Riggs, Wash vs Buf ...	1992	2	2	0
Michael Irvin, Dal vs Buf	1993	2	0	2
Emmitt Smith, Dal vs Buf	1994	2	2	0
Emmitt Smith, Dal vs Pit	1996	2	2	0

Receptions

Catches

	Year	No	Yds	TD
Dan Ross, Cin vs SF	1982	11	104	2
Jerry Rice, SF vs Cin	1989	11	215	1
Tony Nathan, Mia vs SF	1985	10	83	0
Jerry Rice, SF vs SD	1995	10	149	3
Andre Hastings, Pit vs Dal	1996	10	98	0
Ricky Sanders, Wash vs Den ..	1988	9	193	2
George Sauer, NYJ vs Bal	1969	8	133	0
Roger Craig, SF vs Cin	1989	8	101	0
Andre Reed, Buf vs NYG	1991	8	62	0
Andre Reed, Buf vs Dal	1993	8	152	0
Ronnie Harmon, SD vs SF	1995	8	68	0
Ernie Mills, Pit vs Dal	1996	8	78	0

Yards Gained

	Year	No	Yds	TD
Jerry Rice, SF vs Cin	1989	11	215	1
Ricky Sanders, Wash vs Den ..	1988	9	193	2
Lynn Swann, Pit vs Dal	1976	4	161	1
Andre Reed, Buf vs Dal	1993	8	152	0
Jerry Rice, SF vs SD	1995	10	149	3
Jerry Rice, SF vs Den	1990	7	148	3
Max McGee, GB vs KC	1967	7	138	2
George Sauer, NYJ vs Bal	1969	8	133	0
Willie Gault, Chi vs NE	1986	4	129	0
Lynn Swann, Pit vs Dal	1979	7	124	1

All-Purpose Yards

Yards Gained

	Year	Run	Rec	Tot
Desmond Howard, GB vs NE	1997	0	0	*244
Andre Coleman, SD vs SF	1995	0	0	†242
Ricky Sanders, Wash vs Den ...	1988	193	-4	‡235
Jerry Rice, SF vs Cin	1989	5	215	220
Timmy Smith, Wash vs Den	1988	204	9	213
Marcus Allen, Raiders vs Wash	1984	191	18	209
Stephen Starring, NE vs Chi ...	1986	0	39	#192
Fulton Walker, Mia vs Wash ...	1983	0	0	$190
Thurman Thomas, Buf vs NYG .	1991	135	55	190
John Riggins, Wash vs Mia ...	1983	166	15	181
Roger Craig, SF vs Cin	1989	74	101	175

*Howard gained all his yards on four kickoff returns and six punt returns.
†Coleman gained all his yards on eight kickoff returns.
‡Sanders also returned three kickoffs for 48 yards.
#Starring also returned seven kickoffs for 153 yards.
$Walker gained all his yards on four kickoff returns.

Interceptions

	Year	No	Yds	TD
Rod Martin, Raiders vs Phi	1981	3	44	0

Six tied with two interceptions each.

Punting

(Minimum 4 punts)

	Year	No	Yds	Avg
Bryan Wagner, SD vs SF	1995	4	195	48.8
Jerrel Wilson, KC vs Min	1970	4	194	48.5
Jim Miller, SF vs Cin	1982	4	185	46.3

Punt Returns

(Minimum 3 returns)

	Year	No	Yds	Avg
John Taylor, SF vs Cin	1989	3	56	18.7
Desmond Howard, GB vs NE	1997	6	90	15.0
John Taylor, SF vs Den	1990	3	38	12.7
Kelvin Martin, Dal vs Buf	1993	3	35	11.7

Kickoff Returns

(Minimum 3 returns)

	Year	No	Yds	Avg
Fulton Walker, Mia vs Wash ...	1983	4	190	47.5
Desmond Howard, GB vs NE .	1997	4	154	38.5
Larry Anderson, Pit vs Rams ...	1980	5	162	32.4
Rick Upchurch, Den vs Dal	1978	3	94	31.3

Super Bowl Playoffs

The Super Bowl forced the NFL to set up pro football's first guaranteed multiple-game playoff format. Over the years, the NFL-AFL merger, the creation of two conferences comprised of three divisions each and the proliferation of Wild Card entries has seen the postseason field grow from four teams (1966), to six (1967-68), to eight (1969-77), to 10 (1978-81, 1983-89), to the present 12 (since 1990).

In 1968, there was a special playoff between Oakland and Kansas City who were both 12-2 and tied for first in the AFL's Western Division. In 1982, when a 57-day players' strike shortened the regular season to just nine games, playoff berths were extended to 16 teams (eight from each conference) and a 15-game tournament was played.

Note that in the following year-by-year summary, records of finalists include all games leading up to the Super Bowl; (*) indicates Wild Card teams.

1966 Season

AFL Playoffs

Championship . . . . .Kansas City 31, at Buffalo 7

NFL Playoffs

Championship . . . . .Green Bay 34, at Dallas 27

Super Bowl I
Jan. 15, 1967
Memorial Coliseum, Los Angeles
Favorite: Packers by 14   Attendance: 61,946

Kansas City (12-2-1)	0	10	0	0—**10**
Green Bay (13-2)	7	7	14	7—**35**

MVP: Green Bay QB Bart Starr (16 for 23, 250 yds, 2 TD, 1 Int)

1967 Season

AFL Playoffs

Championship . . . . .at Oakland 40, Houston 7

NFL Playoffs

Eastern Conference . . . . at Dallas 52, Cleveland 14
Western Conference . . . . at Green Bay 28, LA Rams 7
Championship . . . . at Green Bay 21, Dallas 17

Super Bowl II
Jan. 14, 1968
Orange Bowl, Miami
Favorite: Packers by 13½   Attendance: 75,546

Green Bay (11-4-1)	3	13	10	7—**33**
Oakland (14-1)	0	7	0	7—**14**

MVP: Green Bay QB Bart Starr (13 for 24, 202 yds, 1 TD)

1968 Season

AFL Playoffs

Western Div. Playoff . . . . . . .at Oakland 41, Kansas City 6
AFL Championship . . . . .at NY Jets 27, Oakland 23

NFL Playoffs

Eastern Conference . . . . .at Cleveland 31, Dallas 20
Western Conference . . . . . .at Baltimore 24, Minnesota 14
NFL Championship . . . . .Baltimore 34, at Cleveland 0

Super Bowl III
Jan. 12, 1969
Orange Bowl, Miami
Favorite: Colts by 18   Attendance: 75,389

NY Jets (12-3)	0	7	6	3—**16**
Baltimore (15-1)	0	0	0	7— **7**

MVP: NY Jets QB Joe Namath (17 for 28, 206 yds)

1969 Season

AFL Playoffs

Inter-Division . . . . *Kansas City 13, at NY Jets 6
                        at Oakland 56, *Houston 7
AFL Championship . . . . Kansas City 17, at Oakland 7

NFL Playoffs

Eastern Conference . . . . .Cleveland 38, at Dallas 14
Western Conference . . . . . . .at Minnesota 23, LA Rams 20
NFL Championship . . . . . .at Minnesota 27, Cleveland 7

Super Bowl IV
Jan. 11, 1970
Tulane Stadium, New Orleans
Favorite: Vikings by 12   Attendance: 80,562

Minnesota (14-2)	0	0	7	0— **7**
Kansas City (13-3)	3	13	7	0—**23**

MVP: KC QB Len Dawson (12 for 17, 142 yds, 1 TD, 1 Int)

1970 Season

AFC Playoffs

First Round . . . . .at Baltimore 17, Cincinnati 0
                       at Oakland 21,*Miami 14
Championship . . . . .at Baltimore 27, Oakland 17

NFC Playoffs

First Round . . . . .at Dallas 5, *Detroit 0
                       San Francisco 17, at Minnesota 14
Championship . . . . .Dallas 17, at San Francisco 10

Super Bowl V
Jan. 17, 1971
Orange Bowl, Miami
Favorite: Cowboys by 2½   Attendance: 79,204

Baltimore (13-2-1)	0	6	0	10—**16**
Dallas (12-4)	3	10	0	0— **13**

MVP: Dallas LB Chuck Howley (2 Interceptions for 22 yds)

1971 Season

AFC Playoffs

First Round . . . . .Miami 27, at Kansas City 24 (OT)
                       *Baltimore 20, at Cleveland 3
Championship . . . . .at Miami 21, Baltimore 0

NFC Playoffs

First Round . . . . .Dallas 20, at Minnesota 12
               at San Francisco 24,*Washington 20
Championship . . . . .at Dallas 14, San Francisco 3

Super Bowl VI
Jan. 16, 1972
Tulane Stadium, New Orleans
Favorite: Cowboys by 6   Attendance: 81,023

Dallas (13-3)	3	7	7	7—**24**
Miami (12-3-1)	0	3	0	0— **3**

MVP: Dallas QB Roger Staubach (12 for 19, 119 yds, 2 TD)

1972 Season

AFC Playoffs

First Round ....at Pittsburgh 13, Oakland 7
at Miami 20, *Cleveland 14
Championship ....Miami 21, at Pittsburgh 17

NFC Playoffs

First Round ....*Dallas 30, at San Francisco 28
at Washington 16, Green Bay 3
Championship ....at Washington 26, Dallas 3

Super Bowl VII
Jan. 14, 1973
Memorial Coliseum, Los Angeles
Favorite: Redskins by 1½   Attendance: 90,182

Miami (16-0)   7   7   0   0**—14**
Washington (13-3)   0   0   0   7**— 7**
MVP: Miami safety Jake Scott (2 Interceptions for 63 yds)

1973 Season

AFC Playoffs

First Round ....at Oakland 33, *Pittsburgh 14
at Miami 34, Cincinnati 16
Championship ....at Miami 27, Oakland 10

NFC Playoffs

First Round ....at Minnesota 27, *Washington 20
at Dallas 27, LA Rams 16
Championship ....Minnesota 27, at Dallas 10

Super Bowl VIII
Jan. 13, 1974
Rice Stadium, Houston
Favorite: Dolphins by 6½   Attendance: 71,882

Minnesota (14-2)   0   0   0   7**— 7**
Miami (12-4) 14   3   7   0**—24**
MVP: Miami FB Larry Csonka (33 carries, 145 yds, 2 TD)

1974 Season

AFC Playoffs

First Round ....at Oakland 28, Miami 26
at Pittsburgh 32, *Buffalo 14
Championship ....Pittsburgh 24, at Oakland 13

NFC Playoffs

First Round ....at Minnesota 30, St.Louis 14
at LA Rams 19, *Washington 10
Championship ....at Minnesota 14, LA Rams 10

Super Bowl IX
Jan. 12, 1975
Tulane Stadium, New Orleans
Favorite: Steelers by 3   Attendance: 80,997

Pittsburgh (12-3-1)   0   2   7   7**—16**
Minnesota (12-4)   0   0   0   6**— 6**
MVP: Pittsburgh RB Franco Harris (34 carries, 158 yds, 1 TD)

1975 Season

AFC Playoffs

First Round ....at Pittsburgh 28, Baltimore 10
at Oakland 31, *Cincinnati 28
Championship ....at Pittsburgh 16, Oakland 10

NFC Playoffs

First Round ....at LA Rams 35, St. Louis 23
*Dallas 17, at Minnesota 14
Championship ....Dallas 37, at LA Rams 7

Super Bowl X
Jan. 18, 1976
Orange Bowl, Miami
Favorite: Steelers by 6½   Attendance: 80,187

Dallas (12-4)   7   3   0   7**—17**
Pittsburgh (14-2)   0   7   0 14**—21**
MVP: Pittsburgh WR Lynn Swann (4 catches, 161 yds, 1 TD)

1976 Season

AFC Playoffs

First Round ....at Oakland 24, *New England 21
Pittsburgh 40, at Baltimore 14
Championship ....at Oakland 24, Pittsburgh 7

NFC Playoffs

First Round ....at Minnesota 35, *Washington 20
LA Rams 14, at Dallas 12
Championship ....at Minnesota 24, LA Rams 13

Super Bowl XI
Jan. 9, 1977
Rose Bowl, Pasadena
Favorite: Raiders by 4½   Attendance: 103,438

Oakland (15-1) ....   0 16   3 13**—32**
Minnesota (13-2-1)   0   0   7   7**—14**
MVP: Oakland WR Fred Biletnikoff (4 catches, 79 yds)

1977 Season

AFC Playoffs

First Round ....at Denver 34, Pittsburgh 21
*Oakland 37, at Baltimore 31 (OT)
Championship ....at Denver 20, Oakland 17

NFC Playoffs

First Round ....at Dallas 37, *Chicago 7
Minnesota 14, at LA Rams 7
Championship ....at Dallas 23, Minnesota 6

Super Bowl XII
Jan. 15, 1978
Louisiana Superdome, New Orleans
Favorite: Cowboys by 6   Attendance: 75,583

Dallas (14-2) 10   3   7   7**—27**
Denver (14-2)   0   0 10   0**—10**
MVPs: Dallas DE Harvey Martin and DT Randy White (Cowboys' defense forced 8 turnovers)

A Year Later
Super Bowl champions who did not qualify for the playoffs the following season.

Season		Record	Finish	Season		Record	Finish
1968	Green Bay	6-7-1	3rd in NFL Central	1982	San Francisco	3-6-0*	11th in overall NFC
1970	Kansas City	7-5-2	2nd in AFC West	1987	NY Giants	6-9-0*	5th in NFC East
1980	Pittsburgh	9-7-0	3rd in AFC Central	1988	Washington	7-9-0	3rd in NFC East
1981	Oakland	7-9-0	4th in AFC West	1991	NY Giants	8-8-0	4th in NFC East

* Seasons when player strikes interrupted schedule.

Super Bowl Playoffs (Cont.)

1978 Season

AFC Playoffs

First Round ....*Houston 17, at *Miami 9
Second Round ....Houston 31, at New England 14
                              at Pittsburgh 33, Denver 10
Championship ....at Pittsburgh 34, Houston 5

NFC Playoffs

First Round ....at *Atlanta 14, *Philadelphia 13
Second Round ....at Dallas 27, Atlanta 20
                              at LA Rams 34, Minnesota 10
Championship ....Dallas 28, at LA Rams 0

Super Bowl XIII
Jan. 21, 1979
Orange Bowl, Miami
Favorite: Steelers by 3½   Attendance: 79,484

Pittsburgh (16-2)	7	14	0	14—**35**
Dallas (14-4)	7	7	3	14—**31**

MVP: Pittsburgh QB Terry Bradshaw (17 for 30, 318 yds, 4 TD, 1 Int)

1979 Season

AFC Playoffs

First Round ....at *Houston 13, *Denver 7
Second Round ....Houston 17, at San Diego 14
                              at Pittsburgh 34, Miami 14
Championship ....at Pittsburgh 27, Houston 13

NFC Playoffs

First Round ....at *Philadelphia 27, *Chicago 17
Second Round ....at Tampa Bay 24, Philadelphia 17
                              LA Rams 21, at Dallas 19
Championship ....LA Rams 9, at Tampa Bay 0

Super Bowl XIV
Jan. 20, 1980
Rose Bowl, Pasadena
Favorite: Steelers by 10½   Attendance: 103,985

LA Rams (11-7)	7	6	6	0—**19**
Pittsburgh (14-4)	3	7	7	14—**31**

MVP: Pittsburgh QB Terry Bradshaw (14 for 21, 309 yds, 2 TD, 3 Int)

1980 Season

AFC Playoffs

First Round ....at *Oakland 27, *Houston 7
Second Round ....at San Diego 20, Buffalo 14
                              Oakland 14, at Cleveland 12
Championship ....Oakland 34, at San Diego 27

NFC Playoffs

First Round ....at *Dallas 34, *LA Rams 13
Second Round ....at Philadelphia 31, Minnesota 16
                              Dallas 30, at Atlanta 27
Championship ....at Philadelphia 20, Dallas 7

Super Bowl XV
Jan. 25, 1981
Louisiana Superdome, New Orleans
Favorite: Eagles by 3   Attendance: 76,135

Oakland (14-5)	14	0	10	3—**27**
Philadelphia (14-4)	0	3	0	7—**10**

MVP: Oakland QB Jim Plunkett (13 for 21, 261 yds, 3 TD)

1981 Season

AFC Playoffs

First Round ....*Buffalo 31, at *NY Jets 27
Second Round ....San Diego 41, at Miami 38 (OT)
                              at Cincinnati 28, Buffalo 21
Championship ....at Cincinnati 27, San Diego 7

NFC Playoffs

First Round ....*NY Giants 27, at *Philadelphia 21
Second Round ....at Dallas 38, Tampa Bay 0
                              at San Francisco 38, NY Giants 24
Championship ....at San Francisco 28, Dallas 27

Super Bowl XVI
Jan. 24, 1982
Pontiac Silverdome, Pontiac, Mich.
Favorite: Pick'em   Attendance: 81,270

San Francisco (15-3)	7	13	0	6—**26**
Cincinnati (14-4)	0	0	7	14—**21**

MVP: San Francisco QB Joe Montana (14 for 22, 157 yds, 1 TD; 6 carries, 18 yds, 1 TD)

1982 Season

A 57-day players' strike shortened the regular season from 16 games to nine. The playoff format was changed to a 16-team tournament open to the top eight teams in each conference.

AFC Playoffs

First Round ....at LA Raiders 27, Cleveland 10
                              at Miami 28, New England 13
                              NY Jets 44, at Cincinnati 17
                              San Diego 31, at Pittsburgh 28
Second Round ....Jets 17, at LA Raiders 14
                              at Miami 34, San Diego 13
Championship ....at Miami 14, NY Jets 0

NFC Playoffs

First Round ....at Washington 31, Detroit 7
                              at Dallas 30, Tampa Bay 17
                              at Green Bay 41, St. Louis 16
                              at Minnesota 30, Atlanta 24
Second Round ....at Washington 21, Minnesota 7
                              at Dallas 37, Green Bay 26
Championship ....at Washington 31, Dallas 17

Super Bowl XVII
Jan. 30, 1983
Rose Bowl, Pasadena
Favorite: Dolphins by 3   Attendance: 103,667

Miami (10-2)	7	10	0	0—**17**
Washington (11-1)	0	10	3	14—**27**

MVP: Washington RB John Riggins (38 carries, 166 yds, 1 TD; 1 catch, 15 yds)

Most Popular Playing Sites
Stadiums hosting more than one Super Bowl.

No		Years
5	Orange Bowl (Miami)	1968-69, 71, 76, 79
5	Rose Bowl (Pasadena)	1977, 80, 83, 87, 93
5	Superdome (N. Orleans)	1978, 81, 86, 90, 97
3	Tulane Stadium (N. Orleans)	1970, 72, 75
2	Joe Robbie Stadium (Miami)	1989, 95
2	LA Memorial Coliseum	1967, 73
2	Tampa Stadium	1984, 91

1983 Season

AFC Playoffs

First Round ....at *Seattle 31, *Denver 7
Second Round ....Seattle 27, at Miami 20
at LA Raiders 38, Pittsburgh 10
Championship ....at LA Raiders 30, Seattle 14

NFC Playoffs

First Round ....*LA Rams 24, at *Dallas 17
Second Round ....at San Francisco 24, Detroit 23
at Washington 51, LA Rams 7
Championship ......at Washington 24, San Francisco 21

Super Bowl XVIII
Jan. 22, 1984
Tampa Stadium, Tampa
Favorite: Redskins by 3   Attendance: 72,920

Washington (16-2)	....	0	3	6	0—**9**
LA Raiders (14-4)		7	14	14	3—**38**

MVP: LA Raiders RB Marcus Allen (20 carries, 191 yds, 2 TD; 2 catches, 18 yds)

1984 Season

AFC Playoffs

First Round ....at *Seattle 13, *LA Raiders 7
Second Round ....at Miami 31, Seattle 10
Pittsburgh 24, at Denver 17
Championship ....at Miami 45, Pittsburgh 28

NFC Playoffs

First Round ....*NY Giants 16, at *LA Rams 13
Second Round ....at San Francisco 21, NY Giants 10
Chicago 23, at Washington 19
Championship ....at San Francisco 23, Chicago 0

Super Bowl XIX
Jan. 20, 1985
Stanford Stadium, Stanford, Calif.
Favorite: 49ers by 3   Attendance: 84,059

Miami (16-2)	....	10	6	0	0—**16**
San Francisco (17-1)	....	7	21	10	0—**38**

MVP: San Francisco QB Joe Montana (24 for 35, 331 yds, 2 TD; 5 carries, 59 yards, 1 TD)

1985 Season

AFC Playoffs

First Round ....*New England 26, at *NY Jets 14
Second Round ....at Miami 24, Cleveland 21
New England 27, at LA Raiders 20
Championship ....New England 31, at Miami 14

NFC Playoffs

First Round ....at *NY Giants 17, *San Francisco 3
Second Round ....at LA Rams 20, Dallas 0
at Chicago 21, NY Giants 0
Championship ....at Chicago 24, LA Rams 0

Super Bowl XX
Jan. 26, 1986
Louisiana Superdome, New Orleans
Favorite: Bears by 10   Attendance: 73,818

Chicago Bears (17-1)	....	13	10	21	2—**46**
New England (14-5)	....	3	0	0	7—**10**

MVP: Chicago DE Richard Dent (Bears defense: 7 sacks, 6 turnovers, 1 safety and gave up just 123 total yards)

1986 Season

AFC Playoffs

First Round ....at *NY Jets 35, *Kansas City 15
Second Round ....at Cleveland 23, NY Jets 20 (OT)
at Denver 22, New England 17
Championship ....Denver 23, at Cleveland 20 (OT)

NFC Playoffs

First Round ....at *Washington 19, *LA Rams 7
Second Round ....Washington 27, at Chicago 13
at NY Giants 49, San Francisco 3
Championship ....at NY Giants 17, Washington 0

Super Bowl XXI
Jan. 25, 1987
Rose Bowl, Pasadena
Favorite: Giants by 9½   Attendance: 101,063

Denver (13-5)	....	10	0	0	10—**20**
NY Giants (16-2)	....	7	2	17	13—**39**

MVP: NY Giants QB Phil Simms (22 for 25, 268 yds, 3 TD; 3 carries, 25 yds)

1987 Season

A 24-day players' strike shortened the regular season to 15 games with replacement teams playing for three weeks.

AFC Playoffs

First Round ....at *Houston 23, *Seattle 20 (OT)
Second Round ....at Cleveland 38, Indianapolis 21
at Denver 34, Houston 10
Championship ....at Denver 38, Cleveland 33

NFC Playoffs

First Round ....*Minnesota 44, at *New Orleans 10
Second Round ....Minnesota 36, at San Francisco 24
Washington 21, at Chicago 17
Championship ....at Washington 17, Minnesota 10

Super Bowl XXII
Jan. 31, 1988
San Diego/Jack Murphy Stadium
Favorite: Broncos by 3½   Attendance: 73,302

Washington (13-4)	....	0	35	0	7—**42**
Denver (12-4-1)	....	10	0	0	0—**10**

MVP: Washington QB Doug Williams (18 for 29, 340 yds, 4 TD, 1 Int)

1988 Season

AFC Playoffs

First Round ....*Houston 24, at *Cleveland 23
Second Round ....at Buffalo 17, Houston 10
at Cincinnati 21, Seattle 13
Championship ....at Cincinnati 21, Buffalo 10

NFC Playoffs

First Round ....at *Minnesota 28, *LA Rams 17
Second Round ....at San Francisco 34, Minnesota 9
at Chicago 20, Philadelphia 12
Championship ....San Francisco 28, at Chicago 3

Super Bowl XXIII
Jan. 22, 1989
Joe Robbie Stadium, Miami
Favorite: 49ers by 7   Attendance: 75,129

Cincinnati (14-4)	....	0	3	10	3—**16**
San Francisco (12-6)	....	3	0	3	14—**20**

MVP: San Francisco WR Jerry Rice (11 catches, 215 yds, 1 TD; 1 carry, 5 yds)

Super Bowl Playoffs (Cont.)

1989 Season

AFC Playoffs

First Round ....*Pittsburgh 26, at *Houston 23
Second Round ....at Cleveland 34, Buffalo 30
                        at Denver 24, Pittsburgh 23
Championship ....at Denver 37, Cleveland 21

NFC Playoffs

First Round ....*LA Rams 21, at *Philadelphia 7
Second Round ....LA Rams 19, NY Giants 13 (OT)
                     at San Francisco 41, Minnesota 13
Championship ....at San Francisco 30, LA Rams 3

Super Bowl XXIV

Jan. 28, 1990
Louisiana Superdome, New Orleans
Favorite: 49ers by 12½   Attendance: 72,919

San Francisco (17-2)	....	13	14	14	14—**55**
Denver (13-6)	....	3	0	7	0—**10**

MVP: San Francisco QB Joe Montana (22 for 29, 297 yds, 5 TD, 0 Int)

1990 Season

AFC Playoffs

First Round ....at *Miami 17, *Kansas City 16
                       at Cincinnati 41, *Houston 14
Second Round ....at Buffalo 44, Miami 34
                       at LA Raiders 20, Cincinnati 10
Championship ....at Buffalo 51, LA Raiders 3

NFC Playoffs

First Round ....*Washington 20, at *Philadelphia 6
                      at Chicago 16, *New Orleans 6
Second Round ......at San Francisco 28, Washington 10
                      at NY Giants 31, Chicago 3
Championship ....NY Giants 15, at San Francisco 13

Super Bowl XXV

Jan. 27, 1991
Tampa Stadium, Tampa
Favorite: Bills by 7   Attendance: 73,813

Buffalo (15-4)	....	3	9	0	7—**19**
NY Giants (16-3)	....	3	7	7	3—**20**

MVP: NY Giants RB Ottis Anderson (21 carries, 102 yds, 1 TD; 1 catch, 7 yds)

1991 Season

AFC Playoffs

First Round ....at *Kansas City 10, *LA Raiders 6
                     at Houston 17, *NY Jets 10
Second Round ....at Denver 26, Houston 24
                     at Buffalo 37, Kansas City 14
Championship ....at Buffalo 10, Denver 7

NFC Playoffs

First Round ....*Atlanta 27, at New Orleans 20
                     *Dallas 17, at *Chicago 13
Second Round ....at Washington 24, Atlanta 7
                     at Detroit 38, Dallas 6
Championship ....at Washington 41, Detroit 10

Super Bowl XXVI

Jan. 26, 1992
Hubert Humphrey Metrodome, Minneapolis
Favorite: Redskins by 7   Attendance: 63,130

Washington (16-2)	....	0	17	14	6—**37**
Buffalo (15-3)	....	0	0	10	14—**24**

MVP: Washington QB Mark Rypien (18 for 33, 292 yds, 2 TD, 1 Int)

1992 Season

AFC Playoffs

First Round ....at *Buffalo 41, *Houston 38 (OT)
                   at San Diego 17, *Kansas City 0
Second Round ....Buffalo 24, at Pittsburgh 3
                   at Miami 31, San Diego 0
Championship ....Buffalo 29, at Miami 10

NFC Playoffs

First Round ....*Washington 24, at Minnesota 7
                   *Philadelphia 36, at *New Orleans 20
Second Round ......at San Francisco 20, Washington 13
                   at Dallas 34, Philadelphia 10
Championship ....Dallas 30, at San Francisco 20

Super Bowl XXVII

Jan. 31, 1993
Rose Bowl, Pasadena
Favorite: Cowboys by 7   Attendance: 98,374

Buffalo (14-5)	....	7	3	7	0—**17**
Dallas (15-3)	....	14	14	3	21—**52**

MVP: Dallas QB Troy Aikman (22 for 30, 273 yds, 4 TD, 0 Int)

1993 Season

AFC Playoffs

First Round ....at Kansas City 27, *Pittsburgh 24 (OT)
                  at *LA Raiders 42, *Denver 24
Second Round ....at Buffalo 29, LA Raiders 23
                   Kansas City 28, at Houston 20
Championship ....at Buffalo 30, Kansas City 13

NFC Playoffs

First Round ....Green Bay 28, at Detroit 24
                  at *NY Giants 17, *Minnesota 10
Second Round ....at San Francisco 44, NY Giants 3
                   at Dallas 27, Green Bay 17
Championship ....at Dallas 38, San Francisco 21

Super Bowl XXVIII

Jan. 30, 1994
Georgia Dome, Atlanta
Favorite: Cowboys by 10½   Attendance: 72,817

Dallas (15-4)	....	6	0	14	10—**30**
Buffalo (14-5)	....	3	10	0	0—**13**

MVP: Dallas RB Emmitt Smith (30 carries, 132 yds, 2 TDs; 4 catches, 26 yds)

1994 Season

AFC Playoffs

First Round ....at Miami 27, *Kansas City 17
                  at *Cleveland 20, *New England 13
Second Round ....at Pittsburgh 29, Cleveland 9
                  at San Diego 22, Miami 21
Championship ....San Diego 17, at Pittsburgh 13

NFC Playoffs

First Round ....at *Green Bay 16, *Detroit 12
                  *Chicago 25, at Minnesota 18
Second Round ....at San Francisco 44, Chicago 15
                  at Dallas 35, Green Bay 9
Championship ....at San Francisco 38, Dallas 28

Super Bowl XXIX

Jan. 29, 1995
Joe Robbie Stadium, Miami
Favorite: 49ers by 18   Attendance: 74,107

San Diego (13-5)	......	7	3	8	8—**26**
San Francisco (15-3)	......	14	14	14	7—**49**

MVP: San Francisco QB Steve Young (24 for 36, 325 yds, 6 TD, 0 Int.)

1995 Season

AFC Playoffs

First Round ....at Buffalo 37, *Miami 22
*Indianapolis 35, at *San Diego 20
Second Round ....at Pittsburgh 40, Buffalo 21
*Indianapolis 10, at Kansas City 7
Championship ....at Pittsburgh 20, *Indianapolis 16

NFC Playoffs

First Round ....at *Philadelphia 58, *Detroit 37
at Green Bay 37, *Atlanta 20
Second Round ....Green Bay 27, at San Francisco 17
at Dallas 30, *Philadelphia 11
Championship ....at Dallas 38, Green Bay 27

Super Bowl XXX
Jan. 28, 1996
Sun Devil Stadium, Tempe, Ariz.
Favorite: Cowboys by 13½   Attendance: 76,347

Dallas (14-4)	10	3	7	7—	**27**
Pittsburgh (13-5)	0	7	0	10—	**17**

MVP: Dallas CB Larry Brown (2 Interceptions for 77 yards.)

1996 Season

AFC Playoffs

First Round ....*Jacksonville 30, at *Buffalo 27
at Pittsburgh 42, *Indianapolis 14
Second Round ....*Jacksonville 30, at Denver 27
at New England 28, Pittsburgh 3
Championship ....at New England 20, *Jacksonville 6

NFC Playoffs

First Round ....at Dallas 40, *Minnesota 15
at *San Francisco 14, *Philadelphia 0
Second Round ......at Green Bay 35, *San Francisco 14
at Carolina 26, Dallas 14
Championship ....at Green Bay 30, Carolina 13

Super Bowl XXXI
Jan. 26, 1997
Louisiana Superdome, New Orleans
Favorite: Packers by 14   Attendance: 72,301

New England (13-5)	14	0	7	0—	**21**
Green Bay (15-3)	10	17	8	0—	**35**

MVP: Green Bay KR Desmond Howard (4 kickoff returns for 154 yards and 1 TD also 6 punt returns for 90 yards)

Before the Super Bowl

The first NFL champion was the Akron Pros in 1920, when the league was called the American Professional Football Association (APFA) and the title went to the team with the best regular season record. The APFA changed its name to the National Football League in 1922.

The first playoff game with the championship at stake came in 1932, when the Chicago Bears (6-1-6) and Portsmouth (Ohio) Spartans (6-1-4) ended the regular season tied for first place. The Bears won the subsequent playoff, 9-0. Due to a snowstorm and cold weather, the game was moved from Wrigley Field to an improvised 80-yard dirt field at Chicago Stadium, making it the first indoor title game as well.

The NFL Championship Game decided the league title until the NFL merged with the AFL and the first Super Bowl was played following the 1966 season.

NFL Champions, 1920-32

Winning player-coaches noted by position.
Multiple winners: Canton-Cleveland Bulldogs and Green Bay (3); Chicago Staleys/Bears (2).

Year	Champion	Head Coach
1920	Akron Pros	Fritz Pollard, HB & Elgie Tobin, QB
1921	Chicago Staleys	George Halas, E
1922	Canton Bulldogs	Guy Chamberlin, E
1923	Canton Bulldogs	Guy Chamberlin, E
1924	Cleveland Bulldogs	Guy Chamberlin, E
1925	Chicago Cardinals	Norm Barry
1926	Frankford Yellow Jackets	Guy Chamberlin, E
1927	New York Giants	Earl Potteiger, QB
1928	Providence Steam Roller	Jimmy Conzelman, HB
1929	Green Bay Packers	Curly Lambeau, QB
1930	Green Bay Packers	Curly Lambeau
1931	Green Bay Packers	Curly Lambeau
1932	Chicago Bears	Ralph Jones
	(Bears beat Portsmouth-OH in playoff, 9-0)	

Biggest Postseason Blowouts
(since the merger of the NFL and AFL in 1966)

Pts	Winner	Loser	Game	Date
49	at Oakland 56	Houston 7	1969 AFL Inter-Division Champ.	Dec. 21, 1969
48	at Buffalo 51	LA Raiders 3	1990 AFC Champ.	Jan. 20, 1991
46	at NY Giants 49	San Francisco 3	1986 NFC Champ.	Jan. 4, 1987
45	San Francisco 55	Denver 10	Super Bowl XXIV (Jan. 1990)	Jan. 28, 1990
44	at Washington 51	LA Rams 7	1983 NFC 2nd Rnd.	Jan. 1, 1984
41	at San Francisco 44	NY Giants 3	1993 NFC 2nd Rnd.	Jan. 15, 1994
38	at Dallas 52	Cleveland 14	1967 NFL East. Conf. Champ.	Dec. 24, 1967
38	at Dallas 38	Tampa Bay 0	1981 NFC 2nd Rnd.	Jan. 2, 1982
36	Chicago 46	New England 10	Super Bowl XX (Jan. 1986)	Jan. 26, 1986
35	at Oakland 41	Kansas City 6	1968 AFL West. Div. Champ.	Dec. 22, 1968
35	Dallas 52	Buffalo 17	Super Bowl XXVII (Jan. 1993)	Jan. 31, 1993
34	Minnesota 44	at New Orleans 10	1987 NFC 1st Rnd.	Jan. 3, 1988
34	Baltimore 34	at Cleveland 0	1968 NFL Champ.	Dec. 29, 1968
33	at Oakland 40	Houston 7	1967 AFL Champ.	Dec. 31, 1967
32	Washington 42	Denver 10	Super Bowl XXII (Jan. 1988)	Jan. 31, 1988
32	at Detroit 38	Dallas 6	1991 NFC 2nd Rnd.	Jan. 5, 1992
31	at Washington 41	Detroit 10	1991 NFC Champ.	Jan. 12, 1992
31	at Miami 31	San Diego 0	1992 AFC 2nd Rnd.	Jan. 10, 1993
30	Dallas 37	at LA Rams 7	1975 NFC Champ.	Jan. 4, 1976
30	at Dallas 37	Chicago 7	1977 NFC 1st Rnd	Dec. 26, 1977

NFL-NFC Championship Game

NFL Championship games from 1933-69 and NFC Championship games since the completion of the NFL-AFL merger following the 1969 season.

Multiple winners: Green Bay (9); Dallas (8); Chicago Bears and Washington (7); NY Giants and San Francisco (5); Cleveland Browns, Detroit, Minnesota, and Philadelphia (4); Baltimore (3); Cleveland-LA Rams (2).

Season	Winner	Head Coach	Score	Loser	Head Coach	Site
1933	Chicago Bears	George Halas	23-21	New York	Steve Owen	Chicago
1934	New York	Steve Owen	30-13	Chicago Bears	George Halas	New York
1935	Detroit	Potsy Clark	26-7	New York	Steve Owen	Detroit
1936	Green Bay	Curly Lambeau	21-6	Boston Redskins	Ray Flaherty	New York
1937	Washington Redskins	Ray Flaherty	28-21	Chicago Bears	George Halas	Chicago
1938	New York	Steve Owen	23-17	Green Bay	Curly Lambeau	New York
1939	Green Bay	Curly Lambeau	27-0	New York	Steve Owen	Milwaukee
1940	Chicago Bears	George Halas	73-0	Washington	Ray Flaherty	Washington
1941	Chicago Bears	George Halas	37-9	New York	Steve Owen	Chicago
1942	Washington	Ray Flaherty	14-6	Chicago Bears	Hunk Anderson & Luke Johnsos	Washington
1943	Chicago Bears	Hunk Anderson & Luke Johnsos	41-21	Washington	Arthur Bergman	Chicago
1944	Green Bay	Curly Lambeau	14-7	New York	Steve Owen	New York
1945	Cleveland Rams	Adam Walsh	15-14	Washington	Dudley DeGroot	Cleveland
1946	Chicago Bears	George Halas	24-14	New York	Steve Owen	New York
1947	Chicago Cardinals	Jimmy Conzelman	28-21	Philadelphia	Greasy Neale	Chicago
1948	Philadelphia	Greasy Neale	7-0	Chicago Cardinals	Jimmy Conzelman	Philadelphia
1949	Philadelphia	Greasy Neale	14-0	Los Angeles Rams	Clark Shaughnessy	Los Angeles
1950	Cleveland Browns	Paul Brown	30-28	Los Angeles	Joe Stydahar	Cleveland
1951	Los Angeles	Joe Stydahar	24-17	Cleveland	Paul Brown	Los Angeles
1952	Detroit	Buddy Parker	17-7	Cleveland	Paul Brown	Cleveland
1953	Detroit	Buddy Parker	17-16	Cleveland	Paul Brown	Detroit
1954	Cleveland	Paul Brown	56-10	Detroit	Buddy Parker	Cleveland
1955	Cleveland	Paul Brown	38-14	Los Angeles	Sid Gillman	Los Angeles
1956	New York	Jim Lee Howell	47-7	Chicago Bears	Paddy Driscoll	New York
1957	Detroit	George Wilson	59-14	Cleveland	Paul Brown	Detroit
1958	Baltimore	Weeb Ewbank	23-17*	New York	Jim Lee Howell	New York
1959	Baltimore	Weeb Ewbank	31-16	New York	Jim Lee Howell	Baltimore
1960	Philadelphia	Buck Shaw	17-13	Green Bay	Vince Lombardi	Philadelphia
1961	Green Bay	Vince Lombardi	37-0	New York	Allie Sherman	Green Bay
1962	Green Bay	Vince Lombardi	16-7	New York	Allie Sherman	New York
1963	Chicago	George Halas	14-10	New York	Allie Sherman	Chicago
1964	Cleveland	Blanton Collier	27-0	Baltimore	Don Shula	Cleveland
1965	Green Bay	Vince Lombardi	23-12	Cleveland	Blanton Collier	Green Bay
1966	Green Bay	Vince Lombardi	34-27	Dallas	Tom Landry	Dallas
1967	Green Bay	Vince Lombardi	21-17	Dallas	Tom Landry	Green Bay
1968	Baltimore	Don Shula	34-0	Cleveland	Blanton Collier	Cleveland
1969	Minnesota	Bud Grant	27-7	Cleveland	Blanton Collier	Minnesota
1970	Dallas	Tom Landry	17-10	San Francisco	Dick Nolan	San Francisco
1971	Dallas	Tom Landry	14-3	San Francisco	Dick Nolan	Dallas
1972	Washington	George Allen	26-3	Dallas	Tom Landry	Washington
1973	Minnesota	Bud Grant	27-10	Dallas	Tom Landry	Dallas
1974	Minnesota	Bud Grant	14-10	Los Angeles	Chuck Knox	Minnesota
1975	Dallas	Tom Landry	37-7	Los Angeles	Chuck Knox	Los Angeles
1976	Minnesota	Bud Grant	24-13	Los Angeles	Chuck Knox	Minnesota
1977	Dallas	Tom Landry	23-6	Minnesota	Bud Grant	Dallas
1978	Dallas	Tom Landry	28-0	Los Angeles	Ray Malavasi	Los Angeles
1979	Los Angeles	Ray Malavasi	9-0	Tampa Bay	John McKay	Tampa Bay
1980	Philadelphia	Dick Vermeil	20-7	Dallas	Tom Landry	Philadelphia
1981	San Francisco	Bill Walsh	28-27	Dallas	Tom Landry	San Francisco
1982	Washington	Joe Gibbs	31-17	Dallas	Tom Landry	Washington
1983	Washington	Joe Gibbs	24-21	San Francisco	Bill Walsh	Washington
1984	San Francisco	Bill Walsh	23-0	Chicago	Mike Ditka	San Francisco
1985	Chicago	Mike Ditka	24-0	Los Angeles	John Robinson	Chicago
1986	New York	Bill Parcells	17-0	Washington	Joe Gibbs	New York
1987	Washington	Joe Gibbs	17-10	Minnesota	Jerry Burns	Washington
1988	San Francisco	Bill Walsh	28-3	Chicago	Mike Ditka	Chicago
1989	San Francisco	George Seifert	30-3	Los Angeles	John Robinson	San Francisco
1990	New York	Bill Parcells	15-13	San Francisco	George Seifert	San Francisco
1991	Washington	Joe Gibbs	41-10	Detroit	Wayne Fontes	Washington
1992	Dallas	Jimmy Johnson	30-20	San Francisco	George Seifert	San Francisco
1993	Dallas	Jimmy Johnson	38-21	San Francisco	George Seifert	Dallas

Season	Winner	Head Coach	Score	Loser	Head Coach	Site
1994	San Francisco	George Seifert	38-28	Dallas	Barry Switzer	San Francisco
1995	Dallas	Barry Switzer	38-27	Green Bay	Mike Holmgren	Dallas
1996	Green Bay	Mike Holmgren	30-13	Carolina	Dom Capers	Green Bay

*Sudden death overtime

NFL-NFC Championship Game Appearances

App		W	L	Pct	PF	PA	App		W	L	Pct	PF	PA
16	Dallas Cowboys	8	8	.500	361	319	6	Minnesota	4	2	.667	108	80
16	NY Giants	5	11	.313	240	322	6	Detroit	4	2	.667	139	141
13	Chicago Bears	7	6	.538	286	245	5	Philadelphia	4	1	.800	79	48
12	Green Bay Packers	9	3	.750	280	167	4	Baltimore Colts	3	1	.750	88	60
12	Boston-Wash.Redskins ..	7	5	.583	222	255	2	Chicago Cardinals	1	1	.500	28	28
12	Cleveland-LA Rams ...	3	9	.250	123	270	1	Carolina	0	1	.000	13	30
11	San Francisco	6	5	.455	235	199	1	Tampa Bay	0	1	.000	0	9
11	Cleveland Browns	4	7	.364	224	253							

AFL-AFC Championship Game

AFL Championship games from 1960-69 and AFC Championship games since the completion of the NFL-AFL merger following the 1969 season.

Multiple winners: Buffalo (6); Miami and Pittsburgh (5); Denver, Oakland-LA Raiders (4); Dallas Texans-KC Chiefs (3); Cincinnati, Houston, New England and San Diego (2).

Season	Winner	Head Coach	Score	Loser	Head Coach	Site
1960	Houston	Lou Rymkus	24-16	LA Chargers	Sid Gillman	Houston
1961	Houston	Wally Lemm	10-3	SD Chargers	Sid Gillman	San Diego
1962	Dallas	Hank Stram	20-17*	Houston	Pop Ivy	Houston
1963	San Diego	Sid Gillman	51-10	Boston Patriots	Mike Holovak	San Diego
1964	Buffalo	Lou Saban	20-7	San Diego	Sid Gillman	Buffalo
1965	Buffalo	Lou Saban	23-0	San Diego	Sid Gillman	San Diego
1966	Kansas City	Hank Stram	31-7	Buffalo	Joel Collier	Buffalo
1967	Oakland	John Rauch	40-7	Houston	Wally Lemm	Oakland
1968	NY Jets	Webb Ewbank	27-23	Oakland	John Rauch	New York
1969	Kansas City	Hank Stram	17-7	Oakland	John Madden	Oakland
1970	Baltimore	Don McCafferty	27-17	Oakland	John Madden	Baltimore
1971	Miami	Don Shula	21-0	Baltimore	Don McCafferty	Miami
1972	Miami	Don Shula	21-17	Pittsburgh	Chuck Noll	Pittsburgh
1973	Miami	Don Shula	27-10	Oakland	John Madden	Miami
1974	Pittsburgh	Chuck Noll	24-13	Oakland	John Madden	Oakland
1975	Pittsburgh	Chuck Noll	16-10	Oakland	John Madden	Pittsburgh
1976	Oakland	John Madden	24-7	Pittsburgh	Chuck Noll	Oakland
1977	Denver	Red Miller	20-17	Oakland	John Madden	Denver
1978	Pittsburgh	Chuck Noll	34-5	Houston	Bum Phillips	Pittsburgh
1979	Pittsburgh	Chuck Noll	27-13	Houston	Bum Phillips	Pittsburgh
1980	Oakland	Tom Flores	34-27	San Diego	Don Coryell	San Diego
1981	Cincinnati	Forrest Gregg	27-7	San Diego	Don Coryell	Cincinnati
1982	Miami	Don Shula	14-0	NY Jets	Walt Michaels	Miami
1983	LA Raiders	Tom Flores	30-14	Seattle	Chuck Knox	Los Angeles
1984	Miami	Don Shula	45-28	Pittsburgh	Chuck Noll	Miami
1985	New England	Raymond Berry	31-14	Miami	Don Shula	Miami
1986	Denver	Dan Reeves	23-20*	Cleveland	Marty Schottenheimer	Cleveland
1987	Denver	Dan Reeves	38-33	Cleveland	Marty Schottenheimer	Denver
1988	Cincinnati	Sam Wyche	21-10	Buffalo	Marv Levy	Cincinnati
1989	Denver	Dan Reeves	37-21	Cleveland	Bud Carson	Denver
1990	Buffalo	Marv Levy	51-3	LA Raiders	Art Shell	Buffalo
1991	Buffalo	Marv Levy	10-7	Denver	Dan Reeves	Buffalo
1992	Buffalo	Marv Levy	29-10	Miami	Don Shula	Miami
1993	Buffalo	Marv Levy	30-13	Kansas City	Marty Schottenheimer	Buffalo
1994	San Diego	Bobby Ross	17-13	Pittsburgh	Bill Cowher	Pittsburgh
1995	Pittsburgh	Bill Cowher	20-16	Indianapolis	Ted Marchibroda	Pittsburgh
1996	New England	Bill Parcells	20-6	Jacksonville	Tom Coughlin	New England

*Sudden death overtime

AFL-AFC Championship Game Appearances

App		W	L	Pct	PF	PA	App		W	L	Pct	PF	PA
12	Oakland-LA Raiders ...	4	8	.333	228	264	3	Boston-NE Patriots	2	1	.750	61	71
9	Pittsburgh	5	4	.556	186	164	3	Baltimore-Indy Colts	1	2	.333	43	58
8	Buffalo	6	2	.750	180	92	3	Cleveland	0	3	.000	74	98
8	LA-San Diego Chargers	2	6	.250	128	161	2	Cincinnati	2	0	1.000	48	17
7	Miami	5	2	.714	152	115	2	NY Jets	1	1	.500	27	37
6	Houston	2	4	.333	76	140	1	Seattle	0	1	.000	14	30
5	Denver	4	1	.800	125	101	1	Jacksonville	0	1	.000	6	20
4	Dallas Texans/KC Chiefs	3	1	.750	81	61							

NFL Divisional Champions

The NFL adopted divisional play for the first time in 1967, splitting both conferences into two four-team divisions—the Capitol and Century divisions in the East and the Central and Coastal divisions in the West. Merger with the AFL in 1970 increased NFL membership to 26 teams and made it necessary for the league to realign. Two 13-team conferences—the AFC and NFC— were formed by moving established NFL clubs in Baltimore, Cleveland and Pittsburgh to the AFC and rearranging both conferences into Eastern, Central and Western divisions.

Division champions are listed below; teams that went on to win the Super Bowl are in **bold** type. Note that in 1980, Oakland won the Super Bowl as a wild card team; and in 1982, the players' strike shortened the regular season to nine games and eliminated divisional play for one season.

Multiple champions (since 1970): **AFC**–Pittsburgh (13); Miami (11); Oakland-LA Raiders (9); Denver (8); Buffalo (7); Cleveland (6); Baltimore-Indianapolis Colts, Cincinnati and San Diego (5); Kansas City and New England (3); Houston (2). **NFC**–San Francisco (15); Dallas (14); Minnesota (12); LA Rams (8); Chicago (6); Washington (5); Detroit, Green Bay and NY Giants (3); Philadelphia, St. Louis Cardinals and Tampa Bay (2).

American Football League

Season	East	West
1966	Buffalo	Kansas City

Season	East	West
1967	Houston	Oakland
1968	**NY Jets**	Oakland
1969	NY Jets	Oakland

National Football League

Season	East	West
1966	Dallas	**Green Bay**

Season	Capitol	Century	Central	Coastal
1967	Dallas	Cleveland	**Green Bay**	LA Rams
1968	Dallas	Cleveland	Minnesota	Baltimore
1969	Dallas	Cleveland	Minnesota	LA Rams

Note: Kansas City, an AFL Wild Card team, won the Super Bowl in 1969.

American Football Conference

Season	East	Central	West
1970	**Baltimore**	Cincinnati	Oakland
1971	Miami	Cleveland	Kansas City
1972	**Miami**	Pittsburgh	Oakland
1973	**Miami**	Cincinnati	Oakland
1974	Miami	**Pittsburgh**	Oakland
1975	Baltimore	**Pittsburgh**	Oakland
1976	Baltimore	Pittsburgh	**Oakland**
1977	Baltimore	Pittsburgh	Denver
1978	New England	**Pittsburgh**	Denver
1979	Miami	**Pittsburgh**	San Diego
1980	Buffalo	Cleveland	San Diego
1981	Miami	Cincinnati	San Diego
1982	—	—	—
1983	Miami	Pittsburgh	**LA Raiders**
1984	Miami	Pittsburgh	Denver
1985	Miami	Cleveland	LA Raiders
1986	New England	Cleveland	Denver
1987	Indianapolis	Cleveland	Denver
1988	Buffalo	Cincinnati	Seattle
1989	Buffalo	Cleveland	Denver
1990	Buffalo	Cincinnati	LA Raiders
1991	Buffalo	Houston	Denver
1992	Miami	Pittsburgh	San Diego
1993	Buffalo	Houston	Kansas City
1994	Miami	Pittsburgh	San Diego
1995	Buffalo	Pittsburgh	Kansas City
1996	New England	Pittsburgh	Denver

National Football Conference

Season	East	Central	West
1970	Dallas	Minnesota	San Francisco
1971	**Dallas**	Minnesota	San Francisco
1972	Washington	Green Bay	San Francisco
1973	Dallas	Minnesota	LA Rams
1974	St. Louis	Minnesota	LA Rams
1975	St. Louis	Minnesota	LA Rams
1976	Dallas	Minnesota	LA Rams
1977	**Dallas**	Minnesota	LA Rams
1978	Dallas	Minnesota	LA Rams
1979	Dallas	Tampa Bay	LA Rams
1980	Philadelphia	Minnesota	Atlanta
1981	Dallas	Tampa Bay	**San Francisco**
1982	—	—	—
1983	Washington	Detroit	San Francisco
1984	Washington	Chicago	**San Francisco**
1985	Dallas	**Chicago**	LA Rams
1986	**NY Giants**	Chicago	San Francisco
1987	**Washington**	Chicago	San Francisco
1988	Philadelphia	Chicago	**San Francisco**
1989	NY Giants	Minnesota	**San Francisco**
1990	**NY Giants**	Chicago	San Francisco
1991	**Washington**	Detroit	New Orleans
1992	**Dallas**	Minnesota	San Francisco
1993	**Dallas**	Detroit	San Francisco
1994	Dallas	Minnesota	**San Francisco**
1995	**Dallas**	Green Bay	San Francisco
1996	Dallas	**Green Bay**	Carolina

Note: Oakland, an AFC Wild Card team, won the Super Bowl in 1980.

Overall Postseason Games

The postseason records of all NFL teams, ranked by number of playoff games participated in from 1933 through the 1996 season.

Gm		W	L	Pct	PF	PA
51	Dallas Cowboys	32	19	.627	1254	932
36	Oakland-LA Raiders	21	15	.583	855	659
35	San Francisco 49ers	22	13	.629	888	667
35	Boston-Wash. Redskins	21	14	.600	738	625
33	Cleveland-LA Rams	13	20	.394	501	697
34	Pittsburgh Steelers	20	14	.588	773	677
32	New York Giants	14	18	.438	529	593
31	Miami Dolphins	17	14	.548	697	633
32	Minnesota Vikings	13	19	.406	568	686
30	Cleveland Browns	11	19	.367	596	702
28	Green Bay Packers	20	8	.714	677	480
28	Chicago Bears	14	14	.500	579	552
27	Buffalo Bills	14	13	.519	648	612
22	Houston Oilers	9	13	.409	371	533
20	Balt-Indianapolis Colts	10	10	.500	360	389

Gm		W	L	Pct	PF	PA
20	Denver Broncos	9	11	.450	407	532
20	Philadelphia Eagles	9	11	.450	356	369
18	Dallas Texans/KC Chiefs	8	10	.444	291	370
18	LA-San Diego Chargers	7	11	.389	332	428
15	Detroit Lions	7	8	.467	342	357
14	Boston-NE Patriots	6	8	.429	277	322
12	Cincinnati Bengals	5	7	.417	246	257
11	New York Jets	5	6	.455	216	200
7	Seattle Seahawks	3	4	.429	128	139
7	Atlanta Falcons	2	5	.286	139	181
5	Chi-St. L. Cardinals	1	4	.200	81	134
4	Tampa Bay Buccaneers	1	3	.250	41	94
4	New Orleans Saints	0	4	.000	56	123
3	Jacksonville Jaguars	2	1	.750	66	74
2	Carolina Panthers	1	1	.500	39	47

All-Time Postseason Leaders
Through Super Bowl XXXI, Jan. 26, 1997; participants in 1996 season playoffs in **bold** type.

CAREER

Passing Efficiency

Ratings based on performance standards established for completion percentage, average gain, touchdown percentage and interception percentage. Minimum 150 passing attempts.

		Gm	Cmp%	Yds	TD	Int	Rtg
1	Bart Starr	10	61.0	1753	15	3	104.8
2	**Troy Aikman** .	14	66.5	3372	22	13	96.0
3	Joe Montana ...	23	62.7	5772	45	21	95.6
4	**Brett Favre** ...	10	61.2	2430	18	7	94.7
4	Kenny Anderson .	6	66.3	1321	9	6	93.5
5	Joe Theismann ..	10	60.7	1782	11	7	91.4
6	**Steve Young** ..	18	62.3	2381	15	7	90.5
7	Warren Moon ...	10	64.3	2870	17	14	84.9
8	Ken Stabler	13	57.8	2641	19	13	84.2
9	Bernie Kosar ...	9	56.1	1943	16	10	83.3
10	Dan Marino	13	56.2	3600	29	17	83.2

Passing

Attempts

		Gm	Att
1	Joe Montana, S.F.-KC	23	734
2	**Jim Kelly**, Buffalo	17	545
3	Terry Bradshaw, Pittsburgh	19	456

Completions

		Gm	Cmp
1	Joe Montana, SF-KC	23	460
2	**Jim Kelly**, Buffalo	17	322
3	Terry Bradshaw, Pittsburgh	19	261

Yards Gained

		Gm	Yds
1	Joe Montana, SF-KC	23	5772
2	**Jim Kelly**, Buffalo	17	3863
3	Terry Bradshaw, Pittsburgh	19	3833
4	Dan Marino, Miami	13	3600

Games

Played

		Gm
1	D.D. Lewis, Dallas	27
2	Larry Cole, Dallas	26
3	Charlie Waters, Dallas	25

Coached

		Gm
1	Tom Landry, Dallas	36
	Don Shula, Baltimore-Miami	36
3	Chuck Noll, Pittsburgh	24

Rushing

Yards Gained

		Gm	Car	Yds	Avg
1	Franco Harris	19	400	1556	3.89
2	**Emmitt Smith**	15	318	1413	4.44
3	**Thurman Thomas**	19	327	1399	4.28
4	Tony Dorsett	17	302	1383	4.58
5	Marcus Allen	15	255	1310	5.14

Attempts

		Gm	Att
1	Franco Harris, Pittsburgh	19	400
2	**Thurman Thomas**, Buffalo	19	327
3	**Emmitt Smith**, Dallas	15	318
4	Tony Dorsett, Dallas	17	302

Receiving

Catches

		Gm	No	Yds	Avg
1	**Jerry Rice**, San Francisco ..	21	120	1788	14.9
2	**Michael Irvin**, Dallas	15	83	1283	15.5
3	**Andre Reed**, Buffalo	19	80	1169	14.6

Yards Gained

		Gm	Yds
1	**Jerry Rice**, San Francisco	21	1788
2	Cliff Branch, Oakland-LA	22	1289
3	**Michael Irvin**, Dallas	15	1283
4	**Andre Reed**, Buffalo	19	1169
5	Fred Biletnikoff, Oakland	19	1167

Average Gain

		Gm	Avg
1	Alvin Harper, Dallas	10	27.3
2	Willie Gault, Chicago-LA	12	23.7
3	Harold Jackson, LA-NE-Minn-Sea	14	22.8

Scoring

Points

		Gm	TD	FG	PAT	Pts
1	**Emmitt Smith**	15	20	0	0	120
	Thurman Thomas	19	20	0	0	120
3	George Blanda	19	0	22	49	115

Touchdowns

		Gm	Run	Rec	Ret	No
1	**Emmitt Smith**	15	18	2	0	20
	Thurman Thomas	19	15	5	0	20
3	**Jerry Rice**	21	0	18	0	18

Field Goals

		Gm	Att	FG	Pct
1	George Blanda	19	39	22	.564
2	Matt Bahr	14	25	21	.840
3	Toni Fritsch	14	28	20	.714

SINGLE GAME

Scoring

Points Scored

		Year	Pts
1	Ricky Watters, SF vs. NYG	1993	30
2	Pat Harder, Det. vs. LA	1952	19
	Paul Hornung, GB vs. NYG	1961	19

Field Goals

		Year	FG
1	Chuck Nelson, Min. vs. SF	1987	5
	Matt Bahr, NYG vs. SF	1990	5
	Steve Christie, Buf. vs. Mia	1992	5

Rushing

Yards Gained

		Year	Yds
1	Eric Dickerson, LA Rams vs. Dal.	1985	248
2	Keith Lincoln, SD vs. Bos.	1963	206
3	Timmy Smith, Wash. vs. Den.	1987	204

Most Attempts

		Year	Att
1	Ricky Bell, T.B. vs. Phi	1979	38
	John Riggins, Wash. vs. Mia.	1982	38
3	Lawrence McCutcheon, LA vs. St. L	1975	37
	John Riggins, Wash. vs. Minn.	1982	37

Passing

Attempts

		Year	Att
1	Steve Young, SF vs. GB	1995	65
2	Bernie Kosar, Cle. vs. NYJ	1986	64
	Dan Marino, Mia. vs. Buf.	1995	64

Completions

		Year	Cmp
1	Warren Moon, Hou. vs. Buf.	1992	36
2	Dan Fouts, SD vs. Mia.	1981	33
	Bernie Kosar, Cle. vs. NYJ	1986	33
	Dan Marino, Mia. vs. Buf.	1995	33

Yards Gained

		Year	Yds
1	Bernie Kosar, Cle. vs. NYJ	1986	489
2	Dan Fouts, SD vs. Mia.	1981	433
3	Dan Marino, Mia. vs. Buf.	1995	422

Receiving

Catches

		Year	Rec
1	Kellen Winslow, SD vs. Mia	1981	13
	Thurman Thomas, Buf. vs. Cle.	1989	13
	Shannon Sharpe, Den. vs. LA Raiders .	1993	13

Yards Gained

		Year	Yds
1	Anthony Carter, Min. vs. SF	1987	227
2	Jerry Rice, SF vs. Cin.	1988	215
3	Tom Fears, LA vs. Chi	1950	198

Champions of Leagues That No Longer Exist

No professional league in American sports has had to contend with more pretenders to the throne than the NFL. Seven times in as many decades a rival league has risen up to challenge the NFL and six of them went under in less than five seasons. Only the fourth American Football League (1960-69) succeeded, forcing the older league to sue for peace and a full partnership in 1966.

Of the six leagues that didn't make it, only the All-America Football Conference (1946-49) lives on—the Cleveland Browns and San Francisco 49ers joined the NFL after the AAFC folded in 1949. The champions of leagues past are listed below.

American Football League I

Year		Head Coach
1926	Philadelphia Quakers (7-2)	Bob Folwell

Note: Philadelphia was challenged to a postseason game by the 7th place New York Giants (8-4-1) of the NFL. The Giants won, 31-0, in a snowstorm.

American Football League II

Year		Head Coach
1936	Boston Shamrocks (8-3)	George Kenneally
1937	Los Angeles Bulldogs (8-0)	Gus Henderson

Note: Boston was scheduled to play 2nd place Cleveland (5-2-2) in the '36 championship game, but the Shamrock players refused to participate because they were owed pay for past games.

American Football League III

Year		Head Coach
1940	Columbus Bullies (8-1-1)	Phil Bucklew
1941	Columbus Bullies (5-1-2)	Phil Bucklew

All-America Football Conference

Year	Winner	Head Coach	Score	Loser	Head Coach	Site
1946	Cleveland Browns	Paul Brown	14-9	NY Yankees	Ray Flaherty	Cleveland
1947	Cleveland Browns	Paul Brown	14-3	NY Yankees	Ray Flaherty	New York
1948	Cleveland Browns	Paul Brown	49-7	Buffalo Bills	Red Dawson	Cleveland
1949	Cleveland Browns	Paul Brown	21-7	S.F. 49ers	Buck Shaw	Cleveland

World Football League

Year	Winner	Head Coach	Score	Loser	Head Coach	Site
1974	Birmingham Americans	Jack Gotta	22-21	Florida Blazers	Jack Pardee	Birmingham
1975	WFL folded Oct. 22.					

United States Football League

Year	Winner	Head Coach	Score	Loser	Head Coach	Site
1983	Michigan Panthers	Jim Stanley	24-22	Philadelphia Stars	Jim Mora	Denver
1984	Philadelphia Stars	Jim Mora	23-3	Arizona Wranglers	George Allen	Tampa
1985	Baltimore Stars	Jim Mora	28-24	Oakland Invaders	Charlie Sumner	E. Rutherford

Defunct Leagues

AFL I (1926): Boston Bulldogs, Brooklyn Horseman, Chicago Bulls, Cleveland Panthers, Los Angeles Wildcats, New York Yankees, Newark Bears, Philadelphia Quakers, Rock Island Independents.

AFL II (1936-37): Boston Shamrocks (1936-37); Brooklyn Tigers (1936); Cincinnati Bengals (1937); Cleveland Rams (1936); Los Angeles Bulldogs (1937); New York Yankees (1936-37); Pittsburgh Americans (1936-37); Rochester Tigers (1936-37).

AFL III (1940-41): Boston Bears (1940); Buffalo Indians (1940-41); Cincinnati Bengals (1940-41); Columbus Bullies (1940-41); Milwaukee Chiefs (1940-41); New York Yankees (1940) renamed Americans (1941).

AAFC (1946-49): Brooklyn Dodgers (1946-48) merged to become Brooklyn-New York Yankees (1949); Buffalo Bisons (1946) renamed Bills (1947-49); Chicago Rockets (1946-48) renamed Hornets (1949); Cleveland Browns (1946-49); Los Angeles Dons (1946-49); Miami Seahawks (1946) became Baltimore Colts (1947-49); New York Yankees (1946-48) merged to become Brooklyn-New York Yankees (1949); San Francisco 49ers (1946-49).

WFL (1974-75): Birmingham Americans (1974) renamed Vulcans (1975); Chicago Fire (1974) renamed Winds (1975); Detroit Wheels (1974); Florida Blazers (1974) became San Antonio Wings (1975); The Hawaiians (1974-75); Houston Texans (1974) became Shreveport (La.) Steamer (1974-75); Jacksonville Sharks (1974) renamed Express (1975); Memphis Southmen (1974) also known as Grizzlies (1975); New York Stars (1974) became Charlotte Hornets (1974-75); Philadelphia Bell (1974-75); Portland Storm (1974) renamed Thunder (1975); Southern California Sun (1974-75).

USFL (1983-85): Arizona Wranglers (1983-84) merged with Oklahoma to become Arizona Outlaws (1985); Birmingham Stallions (1983-85); Boston Breakers (1983) became New Orleans Breakers (1984) and then Portland Breakers (1985); Chicago Blitz (1983-84); Denver Gold (1983-85); Houston Gamblers (1984-85); Jacksonville Bulls (1984-85); Los Angeles Express (1983-85); Memphis Showboats (1984-85).

Michigan Panthers (1983-84) merged with Oakland (1985); New Jersey Generals (1983-85); Oakland Invaders (1983-85); Oklahoma Outlaws (1984) merged with Arizona to become Arizona Outlaws (1985); Philadelphia Stars (1983-84) became Baltimore Stars (1985); Pittsburgh Maulers (1984); San Antonio Gunslingers (1984-85); Tampa Bay Bandits (1983-85); Washington Federals (1983-84) became Orlando Renegades (1985).

NFL Pro Bowl

A postseason All-Star game between the new league champion and a team of professional all-stars was added to the NFL schedule in 1939. In the first game at Wrigley Field in Los Angeles, the NY Giants beat a team made up of players from NFL teams and two independent clubs in Los Angeles (the LA Bulldogs and Hollywood Stars). An all-NFL All-Star team provided the opposition over the next four seasons, but the game was cancelled in 1943.

The Pro Bowl was revived in 1951 as a contest between conference all-star teams: American vs National (1951-53), Eastern vs Western (1954-70), and AFC vs NFC (since 1971). The NFC leads the current series with the AFC, 15-12.

The MVP trophy was named the Dan McGuire Award in 1984 after the late SF 49ers publicist and *Honolulu Advertiser* sports columnist.

Year	Winner	Score	Loser
1939	NY Giants	13-10	All-Stars
1940	Green Bay	16-7	All-Stars
1940	Chicago Bears	28-14	All-Stars
1942	Chicago Bears	35-24	All-Stars
1942	All-Stars	17-14	Washington
1943-50		No game	

Year	Winner	MVP
1951	American, 28-27	Otto Graham, Cle., QB
1952	National, 30-13	Dan Towler, LA, HB
1953	National, 27-7	Don Doll, Det., DB
1954	East, 20-9	Chuck Bednarik, Phi., LB
1955	West, 26-19	Billy Wilson, SF, E
1956	East, 31-30	Ollie Matson, Cards, HB
1957	West, 19-10	Back—Bert Rechichar, Bal.
		Line—Ernie Stautner, Pit.
1958	West, 26-7	Back—Hugh McElhenny, SF
		Line—Gene Brito, Wash.
1959	East, 28-21	Back—Frank Gifford, NY
		Line—Doug Atkins, Chi.
1960	West, 38-21	Back—Johnny Unitas, Bal.
		Line—Big Daddy Lipscomb, Pit.
1961	West, 35-31	Back—Johnny Unitas, Bal.
		Line—Sam Huff, NY
1962	West, 31-30	Back—Jim Brown, Cle.
		Line—Henry Jordan, GB
1963	East, 30-20	Back—Jim Brown, Cle.
		Line—Big Daddy Lipscomb, Pit.
1964	West, 31-17	Back—Johnny Unitas, Bal.
		Line—Gino Marchetti, Bal.
1965	West, 34-14	Back—Fran Tarkenton, Min.
		Line—Terry Barr, Det.
1966	East, 36-7	Back—Jim Brown, Cle.
		Line—Dale Meinhart, St. L.
1967	East, 20-10	Back—Gale Sayers, Chi.
		Line—Floyd Peters, Phi.
1968	West, 38-20	Back—Gale Sayers, Chi.
		Line—Dave Robinson, GB

Year	Winner	MVP
1969	West, 10-7	Back—Roman Gabriel, LA
		Line—Merlin Olsen, LA
1970	West, 16-13	Back—Gale Sayers, Chi.
		Line—George Andrie, Dal.
1971	NFC, 27-6	Back—Mel Renfro, Dal.
		Line—Fred Carr, GB
1972	AFC, 26-13	Off—Jan Stenerud, KC
		Def—Willie Lanier, KC
1973	AFC, 33-28	O.J. Simpson, Buf., RB
1974	AFC, 15-13	Garo Yepremian, Mia., PK
1975	NFC, 17-10	James Harris, LA Rams, QB
1976	NFC, 23-20	Billy Johnson, Hou., KR
1977	AFC, 24-14	Mel Blount, Pit., CB
1978	NFC, 14-13	Walter Payton, Chi., RB
1979	NFC, 13-7	Ahmad Rashad, Min., WR
1980	NFC, 37-27	Chuck Muncie, NO, RB
1981	NFC, 21-7	Eddie Murray, Det., PK
1982	AFC, 16-13	Kellen Winslow, SD, WR
		& Lee Roy Selmon, TB, DE
1983	NFC, 20-19	Dan Fouts, SD, QB
		& John Jefferson, GB, WR
1984	NFC, 45-3	Joe Theismann, Wash., QB
1985	AFC, 22-14	Mark Gastineau, NYJ, DE
1986	NFC, 28-24	Phil Simms, NYG, QB
1987	AFC, 10-6	Reggie White, Phi., DE
1988	AFC, 15-6	Bruce Smith, Buf., DE
1989	NFC, 34-3	Randall Cunningham, Phi., QB
1990	NFC, 27-21	Jerry Gray, LA Rams, CB
1991	AFC, 23-21	Jim Kelly, Buf., QB
1992	NFC, 21-15	Michael Irvin, Dal., WR
1993	AFC, 23-20 (OT)	Steve Tasker, Buf., Sp. Teams
1994	NFC, 17-3	Andre Rison, Atl., WR
1995	AFC, 41-13	Marshall Faulk, Ind., RB
1996	NFC, 20-13	Jerry Rice, SF, WR
1997	AFC, 26-23 (OT)	Mark Brunell, Jax, QB

Playing sites: Wrigley Field in Los Angeles (1939); Gilmore Stadium in Los Angeles (both games); Polo Grounds in New York (Jan., 1942); Shibe Park in Philadelphia (Dec., 1942); Memorial Coliseum in Los Angeles (1951-72 and 1979); Texas Stadium in Irving, TX (1973); Arrowhead Stadium in Kansas City (1974); Orange Bowl in Miami (1975); Superdome in New Orleans (1976); Kingdome in Seattle (1977); Tampa Stadium in Tampa (1978) and Aloha Stadium in Honolulu (since 1980).

AFL All-Star Game

The AFL did not play an All-Star game after its first season in 1960 but did stage All-Star games from 1962-70. All-Star teams from the Eastern and Western divisions played each other every year except 1966 with the West winning the series, 6-2. In 1966, the league champion Buffalo Bills met an elite squad made up of the best players from the league's other eight clubs and lost, 30-19.

Year	Winner	MVP
1962	West, 47-27	Cotton Davidson, Oak., QB
1963	West, 21-14	Off—Curtis McClinton, Dal.
		Def—Earl Faison, SD
1964	West, 27-24	Off—Keith Lincoln, SD
		Def—Archie Matsos, Oak.
1965	West, 38-14	Off—Keith Lincoln, SD
		Def—Willie Brown, Den.
1966	All-Stars 30	Off—Joe Namath, NY
	Buffalo 19	Def—Frank Buncom, SD

Year	Winner	MVP
1967	East, 30-23	Off—Babe Parilli, Bos.
		Def—Verlon Biggs, NY
1968	East, 25-24	Off—Joe Namath, NY
		& Don Maynard, NY
		Def—Speedy Duncan, SD
1969	West, 38-25	Off—Len Dawson, KC
		Def—George Webster, Hou.
1970	West, 26-3	John Hadl, SD, QB

Playing sites: Balboa Stadium in San Diego (1962-64); Jeppesen Stadium in Houston (1965); Rice Stadium in Houston (1966); Oakland Coliseum (1967); Gator Bowl in Jacksonville (1968-69) and Astrodome in Houston (1970).

NFL Franchise Origins

Here is what the current 30 teams in the National Football League have to show for the years they have put in as members of the American Professional Football Association (APFA), the NFL, the All-America Football Conference (AAFC) and the American Football League (AFL). Years given for league titles indicate seasons championships were won.

American Football Conference

	First Season	League Titles	Franchise Stops
Buffalo Bills	1960 (AFL)	2 AFL (1964-65)	• Buffalo (1960-72) Orchard Park, NY (1973—)
Cincinnati Bengals	1968 (AFL)	None	• Cincinnati (1968—)
Baltimore Ravens	1996 (NFL)	None	• Baltimore (1996—)
Denver Broncos	1960 (AFL)	None	• Denver (1960—)
Indianapolis Colts	1953 (NFL)	3 NFL (1958-59,68) 1 Super Bowl (1970)	• Baltimore (1953-83) Indianapolis (1984—)
Jacksonville Jaguars	1995 (NFL)	None	• Jacksonville, FL (1995—)
Kansas City Chiefs	1960 (AFL)	3 AFL (1962,66,69) 1 Super Bowl (1969)	• Dallas (1960-62) Kansas City (1963—)
Miami Dolphins	1966 (AFL)	2 Super Bowls (1972-73)	• Miami (1966—)
New England Patriots	1960 (AFL)	None	• Boston (1960-70) Foxboro, MA (1971—)
New York Jets	1960 (AFL)	1 AFL (1968) 1 Super Bowl (1968)	• New York (1960-83) E. Rutherford, NJ (1984—)
Oakland Raiders	1960 (AFL)	1 AFL (1967) 3 Super Bowls (1976,80,83)	• Oakland (1960-81, 1995—) Los Angeles (1982-94)
Pittsburgh Steelers	1933 (NFL)	4 Super Bowls (1974-75,78-79)	• Pittsburgh (1933—)
San Diego Chargers	1960 (AFL)	1 AFL (1963)	• Los Angeles (1960) San Diego (1961—)
Seattle Seahawks	1976 (NFL)	None	• Seattle (1976—)
Tennessee Oilers	1960 (AFL)	2 AFL (1960-61)	• Houston (1960-96) Memphis (1997—)

National Football Conference

	First Season	League Titles	Franchise Stops
Arizona Cardinals	1920 (APFA)	2 NFL (1925,47)	• Chicago (1920-59) St. Louis (1960-87) Tempe, AZ (1988—)
Atlanta Falcons	1966 (NFL)	None	• Atlanta (1966—)
Carolina Panthers	1995 (NFL)	None	• Clemson, SC (1995) Charlotte, NC (1996)
Chicago Bears	1920 (APFA)	8 NFL (1921, 32-33,40-41,43, 46,63) 1 Super Bowl (1985)	• Decatur, IL (1920) Chicago (1921—)
Dallas Cowboys	1960 (NFL)	5 Super Bowls (1971,77,92-93,95)	• Dallas (1960-70) Irving, TX (1971—)
Detroit Lions	1930 (NFL)	4 NFL (1935,52-53,57)	• Portsmouth, OH (1930-33) Detroit (1934-74) Pontiac, MI (1975—)
Green Bay Packers	1921 (APFA)	11 NFL (1929-31,36,39,44, 61-62,65-67) 3 Super Bowls (1966-67,96)	• Green Bay (1921—)
Minnesota Vikings	1961 (NFL)	1 NFL (1969)	• Bloomington, MN (1961-81) Minneapolis, MN (1982—)
New Orleans Saints	1967 (NFL)	None	• New Orleans (1967—)
New York Giants	1925 (NFL)	4 NFL (1927,34,38,56) 2 Super Bowls (1986,90)	• New York (1925-73,75) New Haven, CT (1973-74) E. Rutherford, NJ (1976—)
Philadelphia Eagles	1933 (NFL)	3 NFL (1948-49,60)	• Philadelphia (1933—)
St. Louis Rams	1937 (NFL)	2 NFL (1945,51)	• Cleveland (1937-45) Los Angeles (1946-79) Anaheim (1980-94) St. Louis (1995—)
San Francisco 49ers	1946 (AAFC)	5 Super Bowls (1981,84,88-89,94)	• San Francisco (1946—)
Tampa Bay Buccaneers	1976 (NFL)	None	• Tampa, FL (1976—)
Washington Redskins	1932 (NFL)	2 NFL (1937, 42) 3 Super Bowls (1982, 87, 91)	• Boston (1932-36) Washington, DC (1937-96) Raljon, MD (1997—)

The Growth of the NFL

Of the 14 franchises that comprised the American Professional Football Association in 1920, only two remain—the Arizona Cardinals (then the Chicago Cardinals) and the Chicago Bears (originally the Decatur-IL Staleys). Green Bay joined the APFC in 1921 and the league changed its name to the NFL in 1922. Since then, 54 NFL clubs have come and gone, five rival leagues have expired and two other leagues have been swallowed up.

The NFL merged with the **All-America Football Conference** (1946-49) following the 1949 season and adopted three of its seven clubs—the Baltimore Colts, Cleveland Browns and San Francisco 49ers. The four remaining AAFC teams—the Brooklyn/NY Yankees, Buffalo Bills, Chicago Hornets and Los Angeles Dons—did not survive. After the 1950 season, the financially troubled Colts were sold back to the NFL. The league folded the team and added its players to the 1951 college draft pool. Since no AFL team actually played in Minneapolis, it is not considered the original home of the Oakland Raiders.

The formation of the **American Football League** (1960-69) was announced in 1959 with ownership lined up in eight cities—Boston, Buffalo, Dallas, Denver, Houston, Los Angeles, Minneapolis and New York. Set to begin play in the autumn of 1960, the AFL was stunned early that year when Minneapolis withdrew to accept an offer to join the NFL as an expansion team in 1961. The new league responded by choosing Oakland to replace Minneapolis and inherit the departed team's draft picks. Since no AFL team actually played in Minneapolis, it is not considered the original home of the Oakland Raiders.

In 1966, the NFL and AFL agreed to a merger that resulted in the first Super Bowl (originally called the AFL-NFL World Championship Game) following the '66 league playoffs. In 1970, the now 10-member AFL officially joined the NFL, forming a 26-team league made up of two conferences of three divisions each.

Expansion/Merger Timetable
For teams currently in NFL.

1921–Green Bay Packers; **1925**–New York Giants; **1930**–Portsmouth-OH Spartans (now Detroit Lions); **1932**–Boston Braves (now Washington Redskins); **1933**–Philadelphia Eagles and Pittsburgh Pirates (now Steelers); **1937**–Cleveland Rams (now St. Louis); **1950**–added AAFC's Cleveland Browns (now Baltimore Ravens) and San Francisco 49ers; **1953**–Baltimore Colts (now Indianapolis).

1960–Dallas Cowboys; **1961**–Minnesota Vikings; **1966**–Atlanta Falcons; **1967**–New Orleans Saints; **1970**–added AFL's Boston Patriots (now New England), Buffalo Bills, Cincinnati Bengals (1968 expansion team), Denver Broncos, Houston Oilers, Kansas City Chiefs, Miami Dolphins (1966 expansion team), New York Jets, Oakland Raiders and San Diego Chargers (the AFL-NFL merger divided the league into two 13-team conferences with old-line NFL clubs Baltimore, Cleveland and Pittsburgh moving to the AFC); **1976**–Seattle Seahawks and Tampa Bay Buccaneers (Seattle was originally in the NFC West and Tampa Bay in the AFC West, but were switched to their current divisions in 1977). **1995**–Carolina Panthers and Jacksonville Jaguars.

City and Nickname Changes

1921—Decatur Staleys move to Chicago; **1922**—Chicago Staleys renamed Bears; **1933**—Boston Braves renamed Redskins; **1937**—Boston Redskins move to Washington; **1934**—Portsmouth (Ohio) Spartans move to Detroit and become Lions; **1941**—Pittsburgh Pirates renamed Steelers; **1943**—Philadelphia and Pittsburgh merge for one season and become Phil-Pitt, or the Steagles; **1944**—Chicago Cardinals and Pittsburgh merge for one season and become Card-Pitt; **1946**—Cleveland Rams move to Los Angeles.

1960—Chicago Cardinals move to St. Louis; **1961**—Los Angeles Chargers (AFL) move to San Diego; **1963**—New York Titans (AFL) renamed Jets and Dallas Texans (AFL) move to Kansas City and become Chiefs; **1971**—Boston Patriots become New England Patriots; **1982**—Oakland Raiders move to Los Angeles; **1984**—Baltimore Colts move to Indianapolis; **1988**—St. Louis Cardinals move to Phoenix; **1994**—Phoenix Cardinals become Arizona Cardinals; **1995**—L.A. Rams move to St. Louis and L.A. Raiders move back to Oakland; **1996**—Cleveland Browns move to Baltimore and become Ravens. City of Cleveland retains rights to team name, colors and all memorobilia; **1997**—Houston Oilers move to Memphis and become Tennessee Oilers.

Defunct NFL Teams
Teams that once played in the APFA and NFL, but no longer exist.

Akron-OH–Pros (1920-25) and Indians (1926); **Baltimore**–Colts (1950); **Boston**–Bulldogs (1926) and Yanks (1944-48); **Brooklyn**–Lions (1926), Dodgers (1930-43) and Tigers (1944); **Buffalo**–All-Americans (1921-23), Bisons (1924-25), Rangers (1926), Bisons (1927,1929); **Canton-OH**–Bulldogs (1920-23,1925-26); **Chicago**–Tigers (1920); **Cincinnati**–Celts (1921) and Reds (1933-34); **Cleveland**–Tigers (1920), Indians (1921), Indians (1923), Bulldogs (1924-25,1927), Indians (1931) and Browns (1950-95); **Columbus-OH**–Panhandles (1920-22) and Tigers (1923-26); **Dallas**–Texans (1952); **Dayton-OH**–Triangles (1920-29).

Detroit–Heralds (1920-21), Panthers (1925-26) and Wolverines (1928); **Duluth-MN**–Kelleys (1923-25) and Eskimos (1926-27); **Evansville-IN**–Crimson Giants (1921-22); **Frankford-PA**–Yellow Jackets (1924-31); **Hammond-IN**–Pros (1920-26); **Hartford**–Blues (1926); **Kansas City**–Blues (1924) and Cowboys (1925-26); **Kenosha-WI**–Maroons (1924); **Los Angeles**–Buccaneers (1926); **Louisville**–Brecks (1921-23) and Colonels (1926); **Marion-OH**–Oorang Indians (1922-23); **Milwaukee**–Badgers (1922-26); **Minneapolis**–Marines (1922-24) and Red Jackets (1929-30); **Muncie-IN**–Flyers (1920-21).

New York–Giants (1921), Yankees (1927-28), Bulldogs (1949) and Yankees (1950-51); **Newark-NJ**–Tornadoes (1930); **Orange-NJ**–Tornadoes (1929); **Pottsville-PA**–Maroons (1925-28); **Providence-RI**–Steam Roller (1925-31); **Racine-WI**–Legion (1922-24) and Tornadoes (1926); **Rochester-NY**–Jeffersons (1920-25); **Rock Island-IL**–Independents (1920-26); **Staten Island-NY**–Stapletons (1929-32); **St. Louis**–All-Stars (1923) and Gunners (1934); **Toledo-OH**–Maroons (1922-23); **Tonawanda-NY**–Kardex (1921), also called Lumbermen; **Washington**–Senators (1921).

Annual NFL Leaders

Individual leaders in NFL (1932-69), NFC (since 1970), AFL (1960-69) and AFC (since 1970).

Passing

Since 1932, the NFL has used several formulas to determine passing leadership, from Total Yards alone (1932-37), to the current rating system—adopted in 1973—that takes Completions, Completion Pct., Yards Gained, TD Passes, Interceptions, Interception Pct. and other factors into account. The quarterbacks listed below all led the league according to the system in use at the time.

Multiple winners: Sammy Baugh (6); Joe Montana, Roger Staubach and Steve Young (5); Arnie Herber, Sonny Jurgensen, Bart Starr, and Norm Van Brocklin (3); Ed Danowski, Otto Graham, Cecil Isbell, Milt Plum and Bob Waterfield (2).

NFL-NFC

Year		Att	Cmp	Yds	TD	Year		Att	Cmp	Yds	TD
1932	Arnie Herber, GB	101	37	639	9	1964	Bart Starr, GB	272	163	2144	15
1933	Harry Newman, NY	136	53	973	11	1965	Rudy Bukich, Chi	312	176	2641	20
1934	Arnie Herber, GB	115	42	799	8	1966	Bart Starr, GB	251	156	2257	14
1935	Ed Danowski, NY	113	57	794	10	1967	Sonny Jurgensen, Wash	508	288	3747	31
1936	Arnie Herber, GB	173	77	1239	11	1968	Earl Morrall, Bal	317	182	2909	26
1937	Sammy Baugh, Wash	171	81	1127	8	1969	Sonny Jurgensen, Wash	442	274	3102	22
1938	Ed Danowski, NY	129	70	848	7	1970	John Brodie, SF	378	223	2941	24
1939	Parker Hall, Cle. Rams	208	106	1227	9	1971	Roger Staubach, Dal	211	126	1882	15
1940	Sammy Baugh, Wash	177	111	1367	12	1972	Norm Snead, NY	325	196	2307	17
1941	Cecil Isbell, GB	206	117	1479	15	1973	Roger Staubach, Dal	286	179	2428	23
1942	Cecil Isbell, GB	268	146	2021	24	1974	Sonny Jurgensen, Wash	167	107	1185	11
1943	Sammy Baugh, Wash	239	133	1754	23	1975	Fran Tarkenton, Min	425	273	2994	25
1944	Frank Filchock, Wash	147	84	1139	13	1976	James Harris, LA	158	91	1460	8
1945	Sammy Baugh, Wash	182	128	1669	11	1977	Roger Staubach, Dal	361	210	2620	18
	& Sid Luckman, Chi. Bears	217	117	1725	14	1978	Roger Staubach, Dal	413	231	3190	25
1946	Bob Waterfield, LA	251	127	1747	18	1979	Roger Staubach, Dal	461	267	3586	27
1947	Sammy Baugh, Wash	354	210	2938	25	1980	Ron Jaworski, Phi	451	257	3529	27
1948	Tommy Thompson, Phi	246	141	1965	25	1981	Joe Montana, SF	488	311	3565	19
1949	Sammy Baugh, Wash	255	145	1903	18	1982	Joe Theismann, Wash	252	161	2033	13
1950	Norm Van Brocklin, LA	233	127	2061	18	1983	Steve Bartkowski, Atl	432	274	3167	22
1951	Bob Waterfield, LA	176	88	1566	13	1984	Joe Montana, SF	432	279	3630	28
1952	Norm Van Brocklin, LA	205	113	1736	14	1985	Joe Montana, SF	494	303	3653	27
1953	Otto Graham, Cle	258	167	2722	11	1986	Tommy Kramer, Min	372	208	3000	24
1954	Norm Van Brocklin, LA	260	139	2637	13	1987	Joe Montana, SF	398	266	3054	31
1955	Otto Graham, Cle	185	98	1721	15	1988	Wade Wilson, Min	332	204	2746	15
1956	Ed Brown, Chi. Bears	168	96	1667	11	1989	Don Majkowski, GB	599	353	4318	27
1957	Tommy O'Connell, Cle	110	63	1229	9	1990	Joe Montana, SF	520	321	3944	26
1958	Eddie LeBaron, Wash	145	79	1365	11	1991	Steve Young, SF	279	180	2517	17
1959	Charlie Conerly, NY	194	113	1706	14	1992	Steve Young, SF	402	268	3465	25
1960	Milt Plum, Cle	250	151	2297	21	1993	Steve Young, SF	462	314	4023	29
1961	Milt Plum, Cle	302	177	2416	16	1994	Steve Young, SF	461	324	3969	35
1962	Bart Starr, GB	285	178	2438	12	1995	Brett Favre, GB	570	359	4413	38
1963	Y.A. Tittle, NY	367	221	3145	36	1996	Steve Young, SF	316	214	2410	14

Note: In 1945, Sammy Baugh and Sid Luckman tied with 8 points on an inverse rating system.

AFL-AFC

Multiple winners: Dan Marino (5); Ken Anderson and Len Dawson (4); John Elway, Bob Griese, Daryle Lamonica, Warren Moon and Ken Stabler (2).

Year		Att	Cmp	Yds	TD	Year		Att	Cmp	Yds	TD
1960	Jack Kemp, LA	406	211	3018	20	1979	Dan Fouts, SD	530	332	4082	24
1961	George Blanda, Hou	362	187	3330	36	1980	Brian Sipe, Cle	554	337	4132	30
1962	Len Dawson, Dal	310	189	2759	29	1981	Ken Anderson, Cin	479	300	3753	29
1963	Tobin Rote, SD	286	170	2510	20	1982	Ken Anderson, Cin	309	218	2495	12
1964	Len Dawson, KC	354	199	2879	30	1983	Dan Marino, Mia	296	173	2210	20
1965	John Hadl, SD	348	174	2798	20	1984	Dan Marino, Mia	564	362	5084	48
1966	Len Dawson, KC	284	159	2527	26	1985	Ken O'Brien, NY	488	297	3888	25
1967	Daryle Lamonica, Oak	425	220	3228	30	1986	Dan Marino, Mia	623	378	4746	44
1968	Len Dawson, KC	224	131	2109	17	1987	Bernie Kosar, Cle	389	241	3033	22
1969	Greg Cook, Cin	197	106	1854	15	1988	Boomer Esiason, Cin	388	223	3572	28
1970	Daryle Lamonica, Oak	356	179	2516	22	1989	Dan Marino, Mia	550	308	3997	24
1971	Bob Griese, Mia	263	145	2089	19	1990	Warren Moon, Hou	584	362	4689	33
1972	Earl Morrall, Mia	150	83	1360	11	1991	Jim Kelly, Buf	474	304	3844	33
1973	Ken Stabler, Oak	260	163	1997	14	1992	Warren Moon, Hou	346	224	2521	18
1974	Ken Anderson, Cin	328	213	2667	18	1993	John Elway, Den	551	348	4030	25
1975	Ken Anderson, Cin	377	228	3169	21	1994	Dan Marino, Mia	615	385	4453	30
1976	Ken Stabler, Oak	291	194	2737	27	1995	Jim Harbaugh, Ind	314	200	2575	17
1977	Bob Griese, Mia	307	180	2252	22	1996	John Elway, Den	466	287	3328	26
1978	Terry Bradshaw, Pit	368	207	2915	28						

Receptions

NFL-NFC

Multiple winners: Don Hutson (8); Raymond Berry, Tom Fears, Pete Pihos, Jerry Rice, Sterling Sharpe and Billy Wilson (3); Dwight Clark, Ahmad Rashad and Charley Taylor (2).

Year		No	Yds	Avg	TD	Year		No	Yds	Avg	TD
1932	Ray Flaherty, NY	21	350	16.7	3	1964	Johnny Morris, Chi. Bears	93	1200	12.9	10
1933	Shipwreck Kelly, Bklyn	22	246	11.2	3	1965	Dave Parks, SF	80	1344	16.8	12
1934	Joe Carter, Phi	16	238	14.9	4	1966	Charley Taylor, Wash	72	1119	15.5	12
	& Red Badgro, NY	16	206	12.9	1	1967	Charley Taylor, Wash	70	990	14.1	9
1935	Tod Goodwin, NY	26	432	16.6	4	1968	Clifton McNeil, SF	71	994	14.0	7
1936	Don Hutson, GB	34	536	15.8	8	1969	Dan Abramowicz, NO	73	1015	13.9	7
1937	Don Hutson, GB	41	552	13.5	7	1970	Dick Gordon, Chi	71	1026	14.5	13
1938	Gaynell Tinsley, Chi. Cards	41	516	12.6	1	1971	Bob Tucker, NY	59	791	13.4	4
1939	Don Hutson, GB	34	846	24.9	6	1972	Harold Jackson, Phi	62	1048	16.9	4
1940	Don Looney, Phi	58	707	12.2	4	1973	Harold Carmichael, Phi	67	1116	16.7	9
1941	Don Hutson, GB	58	739	12.7	10	1974	Charles Young, Phi	63	696	11.0	3
1942	Don Hutson, GB	74	1211	16.4	17	1975	Chuck Foreman, Min	73	691	9.5	9
1943	Don Hutson, GB	47	776	16.5	11	1976	Drew Pearson, Dal	58	806	13.9	6
1944	Don Hutson, GB	58	866	14.9	9	1977	Ahmad Rashad, Min	51	681	13.4	2
1945	Don Hutson, GB	47	834	17.7	9	1978	Rickey Young, Min	88	704	8.0	5
1946	Jim Benton, LA	63	981	15.6	6	1979	Ahmad Rashad, Min	80	1156	14.5	9
1947	Jim Keane, Chi. Bears	64	910	14.2	10	1980	Earl Cooper, SF	83	567	6.8	4
1948	Tom Fears, LA	51	698	13.7	4	1981	Dwight Clark, SF	85	1105	13.0	4
1949	Tom Fears, LA	77	1013	13.2	4	1982	Dwight Clark, SF	60	913	12.2	5
1950	Tom Fears, LA	84	1116	13.3	7	1983	Roy Green, St. L	78	1227	15.7	14
1951	Elroy Hirsch, LA	66	1495	22.7	17		Charlie Brown, Wash	78	1225	15.7	8
1952	Mac Speedie, Cle	62	911	14.7	5		& Earnest Gray, NY	78	1139	14.6	5
1953	Pete Pihos, Phi	63	1049	16.7	10	1984	Art Monk, Wash	106	1372	12.9	7
1954	Pete Pihos, Phi	60	872	14.5	10	1985	Roger Craig, SF	92	1016	11.0	6
	& Billy Wilson, SF	60	830	13.8	5	1986	Jerry Rice, SF	86	1570	18.3	15
1955	Pete Pihos, Phi	62	864	13.9	7	1987	J.T. Smith, St. L	91	1117	12.3	8
1956	Billy Wilson, SF	60	889	14.8	5	1988	Henry Ellard, LA	86	1414	16.4	10
1957	Billy Wilson, SF	52	757	14.6	6	1989	Sterling Sharpe, GB	90	1423	15.8	12
1958	Raymond Berry, Bal	56	794	14.2	9	1990	Jerry Rice, SF	100	1502	15.0	13
	& Pete Retzlaff, Phi	56	766	13.7	2	1991	Michael Irvin, Dal	93	1523	16.4	8
1959	Raymond Berry, Bal	66	959	14.5	14	1992	Sterling Sharpe, GB	108	1461	13.5	13
1960	Raymond Berry, Bal	74	1298	17.5	10	1993	Sterling Sharpe, GB	112	1274	11.4	11
1961	Red Phillips, LA	78	1092	14.0	5	1994	Cris Carter, Min	122	1256	10.3	7
1962	Bobby Mitchell, Wash	72	1384	19.2	11	1995	Herman Moore, Det	123	1686	13.7	14
1963	Bobby Joe Conrad, St. L	73	967	13.2	10	1996	Jerry Rice, SF	108	1254	11.6	8

AFL-AFC

Multiple winners: Lionel Taylor (5); Lance Alworth, Haywood Jeffires, Lydell Mitchell and Kellen Winslow (3); Fred Biletnikoff, Todd Christensen, Carl Pickens and Al Toon (2).

Year		No	Yds	Avg	TD	Year		No	Yds	Avg	TD
1960	Lionel Taylor, Den	92	1235	13.4	12	1979	Joe Washington, Bal	82	750	9.1	3
1961	Lionel Taylor, Den	100	1176	11.8	4	1980	Kellen Winslow, SD	89	1290	14.5	9
1962	Lionel Taylor, Den	77	908	11.8	4	1981	Kellen Winslow, SD	88	1075	12.2	10
1963	Lionel Taylor, Den	78	1101	14.1	10	1982	Kellen Winslow, SD	54	721	13.4	6
1964	Charley Hennigan, Hou	101	1546	15.3	8	1983	Todd Christensen, LA	92	1247	13.6	12
1965	Lionel Taylor, Den	85	1131	13.3	6	1984	Ozzie Newsome, Cle	89	1001	11.2	5
1966	Lance Alworth, SD	73	1383	18.9	13	1985	Lionel James, SD	86	1027	11.9	6
1967	George Sauer, NY	75	1189	15.9	6	1986	Todd Christensen, LA	95	1153	12.1	8
1968	Lance Alworth, SD	68	1312	19.3	10	1987	Al Toon, NY	68	976	14.4	5
1969	Lance Alworth, SD	64	1003	15.7	4	1988	Al Toon, NY	93	1067	11.5	5
1970	Marlin Briscoe, Buf	57	1036	18.2	8	1989	Andre Reed, Buf	88	1312	14.9	9
1971	Fred Biletnikoff, Oak	61	929	15.2	9	1990	Haywood Jeffires, Hou	74	1048	14.2	8
1972	Fred Biletnikoff, Oak	58	802	13.8	7		& Drew Hill, Hou	74	1019	13.8	5
1973	Fred Willis, Hou	57	371	6.5	1	1991	Haywood Jeffires, Hou	100	1181	11.8	7
1974	Lydell Mitchell, Bal	72	544	7.6	2	1992	Haywood Jeffires, Hou	90	913	10.1	9
1975	Reggie Rucker, Cle	60	770	12.8	3	1993	Reggie Langhorne, Ind	85	1038	12.2	3
	& Lydell Mitchell, Bal	60	544	9.1	4	1994	Ben Coates, NE	96	1174	12.2	7
1976	MacArthur Lane, KC	66	686	10.4	1	1995	Carl Pickens, Cin	99	1234	12.5	17
1977	Lydell Mitchell, Bal	71	620	8.7	4	1996	Carl Pickens, Cin	100	1180	11.8	12
1978	Steve Largent, Sea	71	1168	16.5	8						

Annual NFL Leaders (Cont.)
Rushing
NFL-NFC

Multiple winners: Jim Brown (8); Walter Payton (5); Barry Sanders, Emmitt Smith and Steve Van Buren (4); Eric Dickerson (3); Cliff Battles, John Brockington, Larry Brown, Bill Dudley, Leroy Kelly, Bill Paschal, Joe Perry, Gale Sayers and Whizzer White (2).

Year		Car	Yds	Avg	TD	Year		Car	Yds	Avg	TD
1932	Cliff Battles, Bos	148	576	3.9	3	1965	Jim Brown, Cle	289	1544	5.3	17
1933	Jim Musick, Bos	173	809	4.7	5	1966	Gale Sayers, Chi	229	1231	5.4	8
1934	Beattie Feathers, Chi. Bears	119	1004	8.4	8	1967	Leroy Kelly, Cle	235	1205	5.1	11
1935	Doug Russell, Chi. Cards	140	499	3.6	0	1968	Leroy Kelly, Cle	248	1239	5.0	16
1936	Tuffy Leemans, NY	206	830	4.0	2	1969	Gale Sayers, Chi	236	1032	4.4	8
1937	Cliff Battles, Wash	216	874	4.0	5	1970	Larry Brown, Wash	237	1125	4.7	5
1938	Whizzer White, Pit	152	567	3.7	4	1971	John Brockington, GB	216	1105	5.1	4
1939	Bill Osmanski, Chi. Bears	121	699	5.8	7	1972	Larry Brown, Wash	285	1216	4.3	8
1940	Whizzer White, Det	146	514	3.5	5	1973	John Brockington, GB	265	1144	4.3	3
1941	Pug Manders, Bklyn	111	486	4.4	5	1974	Lawrence McCutcheon, LA	236	1109	4.7	3
1942	Bill Dudley, Pit	162	696	4.3	5	1975	Jim Otis, St. L	269	1076	4.0	5
1943	Bill Paschal, NY	147	572	3.9	10	1976	Walter Payton, Chi	311	1390	4.5	13
1944	Bill Paschal, NY	196	737	3.8	9	1977	Walter Payton, Chi	339	1852	5.5	14
1945	Steve Van Buren, Phi	143	832	5.8	15	1978	Walter Payton, Chi	333	1395	4.2	11
1946	Bill Dudley, Pit	146	604	4.1	3	1979	Walter Payton, Chi	369	1610	4.4	14
1947	Steve Van Buren, Phi	217	1008	4.6	13	1980	Walter Payton, Chi	317	1460	4.6	6
1948	Steve Van Buren, Phi	201	945	4.7	10	1981	George Rogers, NO	378	1674	4.4	13
1949	Steve Van Buren, Phi	263	1146	4.4	11	1982	Tony Dorsett, Dal	177	745	4.2	5
1950	Marion Motley, Cle	140	810	5.8	3	1983	Eric Dickerson, LA	390	1808	4.6	18
1951	Eddie Price, NY Giants	271	971	3.6	7	1984	Eric Dickerson, LA	379	2105	5.6	14
1952	Dan Towler, LA	156	894	5.7	10	1985	Gerald Riggs, Atl	397	1719	4.3	10
1953	Joe Perry, SF	192	1018	5.3	10	1986	Eric Dickerson, LA	404	1821	4.5	11
1954	Joe Perry, SF	173	1049	6.1	8	1987	Charles White, LA	324	1374	4.2	11
1955	Alan Ameche, Bal	213	961	4.5	9	1988	Herschel Walker, Dal	361	1514	4.2	5
1956	Rick Casares, Chi. Bears	234	1126	4.8	12	1989	Barry Sanders, Det	280	1470	5.3	14
1957	Jim Brown, Cle	202	942	4.7	9	1990	Barry Sanders, Det	255	1304	5.1	13
1958	Jim Brown, Cle	257	1527	5.9	17	1991	Emmitt Smith, Dal	365	1563	4.3	12
1959	Jim Brown, Cle	290	1329	4.6	14	1992	Emmitt Smith, Dal	373	1713	4.6	18
1960	Jim Brown, Cle	215	1257	5.8	9	1993	Emmitt Smith, Dal	283	1486	5.3	9
1961	Jim Brown, Cle	305	1408	4.6	8	1994	Barry Sanders, Det	331	1883	5.7	7
1962	Jim Taylor, GB	272	1474	5.4	19	1995	Emmitt Smith, Dal	377	1773	4.7	25
1963	Jim Brown, Cle	291	1863	6.4	12	1996	Barry Sanders, Det	307	1553	5.1	11
1964	Jim Brown, Cle	280	1446	5.2	7						

Note: Jim Brown led the NFL in rushing eight of his nine years in the league. The one season he didn't win (1962) he finished fourth (996 yds) behind Jim Taylor, John Henry Johnson of Pittsburgh (1,141 yds) and Dick Bass of the LA Rams (1,033 yds).

AFL-AFC

Multiple winners: Earl Campbell and O.J. Simpson (4); Thurman Thomas (3); Cookie Gilchrist, Eric Dickerson, Floyd Little, Jim Nance and Curt Warner (2).

Year		Car	Yds	Avg	TD	Year		Car	Yds	Avg	TD
1960	Abner Haynes, Dal	157	875	5.6	9	1979	Earl Campbell, Hou	368	1697	4.6	19
1961	Billy Cannon, Hou	200	948	4.7	6	1980	Earl Campbell, Hou	373	1934	5.2	13
1962	Cookie Gilchrist, Buf	214	1096	5.1	13	1981	Earl Campbell, Hou	361	1376	3.8	10
1963	Clem Daniels, Oak	215	1099	5.1	3	1982	Freeman McNeil, NY	151	786	5.2	6
1964	Cookie Gilchrist, Buf	230	981	4.3	6	1983	Curt Warner, Sea	335	1449	4.3	13
1965	Paul Lowe, SD	222	1121	5.0	7	1984	Earnest Jackson, SD	296	1179	4.0	8
1966	Jim Nance, Bos	299	1458	4.9	11	1985	Marcus Allen, LA	380	1759	4.6	11
1967	Jim Nance, Bos	269	1216	4.5	7	1986	Curt Warner, Sea	319	1481	4.6	13
1968	Paul Robinson, Cin	238	1023	4.3	8	1987	Eric Dickerson, Ind	223	1011	4.5	5
1969	Dickie Post, SD	182	873	4.8	6	1988	Eric Dickerson, Ind	388	1659	4.3	14
1970	Floyd Little, Den	209	901	4.3	3	1989	Christian Okoye, KC	370	1480	4.0	12
1971	Floyd Little, Den	284	1133	4.0	6	1990	Thurman Thomas, Buf	271	1297	4.8	11
1972	O.J. Simpson, Buf	292	1251	4.3	6	1991	Thurman Thomas, Buf	288	1407	4.9	7
1973	O.J. Simpson, Buf	332	2003	6.0	12	1992	Barry Foster, Pit	390	1690	4.3	11
1974	Otis Armstrong, Den	263	1407	5.3	9	1993	Thurman Thomas, Buf	355	1315	3.7	6
1975	O.J. Simpson, Buf	329	1817	5.5	16	1994	Chris Warren, Sea	333	1545	4.6	9
1976	O.J. Simpson, Buf	290	1503	5.2	8	1995	Curtis Martin, NE	368	1487	4.0	14
1977	Mark van Eeghen, Oak	324	1273	3.9	7	1996	Terrell Davis, Den	345	1538	4.5	13
1978	Earl Campbell, Hou	302	1450	4.8	13						

Note: Eric Dickerson was traded to Indianapolis from the NFC's LA Rams during the 1987 season. In three games with the Rams, he carried the ball 60 times for 277 yds, a 4.6 avg and 1 TD. His official AFC statistics above came in nine games with the Colts.

Scoring

NFL-NFC

Multiple winners: Don Hutson (5); Dutch Clark, Pat Harder, Paul Hornung, Chip Lohmiller and Mark Moseley (3); Kevin Butler, Mike Cofer, Fred Cox, Jack Manders, Chester Marcol, Eddie Murray, Emmitt Smith, Gordy Soltau and Doak Walker (2).

Year		TD	FG	PAT	Pts	Year		TD	FG	PAT	Pts
1932	Dutch Clark, Portsmouth ..	6	3	10	55	1965	Gale Sayers, Chi	22	0	0	132
1933	Glenn Presnell, Portsmouth	6	6	10	64	1966	Bruce Gossett, LA	0	28	29	113
	& Ken Strong, NY	6	5	13	64	1967	Jim Bakken, St.L	0	27	36	117
1934	Jack Manders, Chi. Bears	3	10	31	79	1968	Leroy Kelly, Cle	20	0	0	120
1935	Dutch Clark, Det	6	1	16	55	1969	Fred Cox, Min	0	26	43	121
1936	Dutch Clark, Det	7	4	19	73	1970	Fred Cox, Min	0	30	35	125
1937	Jack Manders, Chi. Bears	5	8	15	69	1971	Curt Knight, Wash	0	29	27	114
1938	Clarke Hinkle, GB	7	3	7	58	1972	Chester Marcol, GB	0	33	29	128
1939	Andy Farkas, Wash	11	0	2	68	1973	David Ray, LA	0	30	40	130
1940	Don Hutson, GB	7	0	15	57	1974	Chester Marcol, GB	0	25	19	94
1941	Don Hutson, GB	12	1	20	95	1975	Chuck Foreman, Min	22	0	0	132
1942	Don Hutson, GB	17	1	33	138	1976	Mark Moseley, Wash	0	22	31	97
1943	Don Hutson, GB	12	3	26	117	1977	Walter Payton, Chi	16	0	0	96
1944	Don Hutson, GB	9	0	31	85	1978	Frank Corral, LA	0	29	31	118
1945	Steve Van Buren, Phi	18	0	2	110	1979	Mark Moseley, Wash	0	25	39	114
1946	Ted Fritsch, GB	10	9	13	100	1980	Eddie Murray, Det	0	27	35	116
1947	Pat Harder, Chi. Cards ...	7	7	39	102	1981	Rafael Septien, Dal	0	27	40	121
1948	Pat Harder, Chi. Cards ...	6	7	53	110		& Eddie Murray, Det	0	25	46	121
1949	Gene Roberts, NY Giants .	17	0	0	102	1982	Wendell Tyler, LA	13	0	0	78
	& Pat Harder, Chi. Cards	8	3	45	102	1983	Mark Moseley, Wash	0	33	62	161
1950	Doak Walker, Det	11	8	38	128	1984	Ray Wersching, SF	0	25	56	131
1951	Elroy Hirsch, LA	17	0	0	102	1985	Kevin Butler, Chi	0	31	51	144
1952	Gordy Soltau, SF	7	6	34	94	1986	Kevin Butler, Chi	0	28	36	120
1953	Gordy Soltau, SF	6	10	48	114	1987	Jerry Rice, SF	23	0	0	138
1954	Bobby Walston, Phi	11	4	36	114	1988	Mike Cofer, SF	0	27	40	121
1955	Doak Walker, Det	7	9	27	96	1989	Mike Cofer, SF	0	29	49	136
1956	Bobby Layne, Det	5	12	33	99	1990	Chip Lohmiller, Wash	0	30	41	131
1957	Sam Baker, Wash	1	14	29	77	1991	Chip Lohmiller, Wash	0	31	56	149
	& Lou Groza, Cle	0	15	32	77	1992	Chip Lohmiller, Wash	0	30	30	120
1958	Jim Brown, Cle	18	0	0	108		& Morten Andersen, NO .	0	29	33	120
1959	Paul Hornung, GB	7	7	31	94	1993	Jason Hanson, Det	0	34	28	130
1960	Paul Hornung, GB	15	15	41	176	1994	Emmitt Smith, Dal	22	0	0	132
1961	Paul Hornung, GB	10	15	41	146		& Fuad Reveiz, Min	0	34	30	132
1962	Jim Taylor, GB	19	0	0	114	1995	Emmitt Smith, Dal	25	0	0	150
1963	Don Chandler, NY	0	18	52	106	1996	John Kasay, Car.	0	37	34	145
1964	Lenny Moore, Bal	20	0	0	120						

AFL-AFC

Multiple winners: Gino Cappelletti (5); Gary Anderson (3); Jim Breech, Roy Gerela, Gene Mingo, Nick Lowery, John Smith, Pete Stoyanovich and Jim Turner (2).

Year		TD	FG	PAT	Pts	Year		TD	FG	PAT	Pts
1960	Gene Mingo, Den	6	18	33	123	1979	John Smith, NE	0	23	46	115
1961	Gino Cappelletti, Bos	8	17	48	147	1980	John Smith, NE	0	26	51	129
1962	Gene Mingo, Den	4	27	32	137	1981	Nick Lowery, KC	0	26	37	115
1963	Gino Cappelletti, Bos	2	22	35	113		& Jim Breech, Cin	0	22	49	115
1964	Gino Cappelletti, Bos	7	25	36	155	1982	Marcus Allen, LA	14	0	0	84
1965	Gino Cappelletti, Bos	9	17	27	132	1983	Gary Anderson, Pit	0	27	38	119
1966	Gino Cappelletti, Bos	6	16	35	119	1984	Gary Anderson, Pit	0	24	45	117
1967	George Blanda, Oak	0	20	56	116	1985	Gary Anderson, Pit	0	33	40	139
1968	Jim Turner, NY	0	34	43	145	1986	Tony Franklin, NE	0	32	44	140
1969	Jim Turner, NY	0	32	33	129	1987	Jim Breech, Cin	0	24	25	97
1970	Jan Stenerud, KC	0	30	26	116	1988	Scott Norwood, Buf	0	32	33	129
1971	Garo Yepremian, Mia	0	28	33	117	1989	David Treadwell, Den	0	27	39	120
1972	Bobby Howfield, NY	0	27	40	121	1990	Nick Lowery, KC	0	34	37	139
1973	Roy Gerela, Pit	0	29	36	123	1991	Pete Stoyanovich, Mia ...	0	31	28	121
1974	Roy Gerela, Pit	0	20	33	93	1992	Pete Stoyanovich, Mia ...	0	30	34	124
1975	O.J. Simpson, Buf	23	0	0	138	1993	Jeff Jaeger, LA	0	35	27	132
1976	Toni Linhart, Bal	0	20	49	109	1994	John Carney, SD	0	34	33	135
1977	Errol Mann, Oak	0	20	39	99	1995	Norm Johnson, Pit	0	34	39	141
1978	Pat Leahy, NY	0	22	41	107	1996	Cary Blanchard, Ind	0	36	27	135

All-Time NFL Leaders
Through 1996 regular season.

CAREER
Players active in 1996 in **bold** type.
Passing Efficiency

Ratings based on performance standards established for completion percentage, average gain, touchdown percentage and interception percentage. Quarterbacks are allocated points according to how their statistics measure up to those standards. Minimum 1500 passing attempts.

		Yrs	Att	Cmp	Cmp %	Yards	Avg Gain	TD	TD	Int	Int %	Rating
1	**Steve Young**	12	3192	2059	64.5	25,479	7.98	174	5.5	85	2.7	96.2
2	Joe Montana	15	5391	3409	63.2	40,551	7.52	273	5.1	139	2.6	92.3
3	**Brett Favre**	6	2693	1667	61.9	18,724	6.95	147	5.5	79	2.9	88.6
4	**Dan Marino**	14	6904	4134	59.9	51,636	7.48	369	5.3	209	3.0	88.3
5	**Jim Kelly**	11	4779	2874	60.1	35,467	7.42	237	5.0	175	3.7	84.4
6	Roger Staubach	11	2958	1685	57.0	22,700	7.67	153	5.2	109	3.7	83.4
7	**Troy Aikman**	8	3178	2000	62.9	22,733	7.15	110	3.5	98	3.1	83.0
8	Neil Lomax	8	3153	1817	57.6	22,771	7.22	136	4.3	90	2.9	82.7
9	Sonny Jurgensen	18	4262	2433	57.1	32,224	7.56	255	6.0	189	4.4	82.63
10	Len Dawson	19	3741	2136	57.1	28,711	7.67	239	6.4	183	4.9	82.56
11	Ken Anderson	16	4475	2654	59.3	32,838	7.34	197	4.4	160	3.6	81.86
12	**Bernie Kosar**	12	3365	1994	59.3	23,301	6.92	124	3.7	87	2.6	81.83
13	**Jeff Hostetler**	11	2194	1278	58.2	15,531	7.10	89	4.1	61	2.8	81.80
14	Danny White	13	2950	1761	59.7	21,959	7.44	155	5.3	132	4.5	81.7
15	**Dave Krieg**	17	5288	3092	58.5	37,946	7.18	261	4.9	199	3.8	81.5
16	**Warren Moon**	13	6000	3514	58.6	43,787	7.30	254	4.2	208	3.5	81.0
17	**Neil O'Donnell**	7	2059	1179	57.3	14,014	6.81	72	3.5	46	2.2	80.51
18	Bart Starr	16	3149	1808	57.4	24,718	7.85	152	4.8	138	4.4	80.47
19	Ken O'Brien	10	3602	2110	58.6	25,094	6.97	128	3.6	98	2.7	80.44
20	Fran Tarkenton	18	6467	3686	57.0	47,003	7.27	342	5.3	266	4.1	80.35
21	Dan Fouts	15	5604	3297	58.8	43,040	7.68	254	4.5	242	4.3	80.2
22	**Boomer Esiason**	13	5019	2851	56.8	36,442	7.26	234	4.7	182	3.6	80.1
23	Tony Eason	8	1564	911	58.2	11,142	7.12	61	3.9	51	3.3	79.7
24	**Mark Rypien**	9	2565	1442	56.2	18,146	7.07	115	4.5	86	3.4	79.4
25	**Jim Everett**	11	4848	2805	57.9	34,380	7.10	202	4.2	171	3.5	79.0

Note: The NFL does not recognize records from the All-American Football Conference (1946-49). If it did, **Otto Graham** would rank 5th (after Marino) with the following stats: 10 Yrs; 2,626 Att; 1,464 Comp; 55.8 Comp Pct; 23,584 Yards; 8.98 Avg Gain; 174 TD; 6.6 TD Pct; 135 Int; 5.1 Int Pct; and 86.6 Rating Pts.

Touchdown Passes

		No			No			No
1	**Dan Marino**	369	16	Terry Bradshaw	212	31	Steve Grogan	182
2	Fran Tarkenton	342		Y.A. Tittle	212	32	Ron Jaworski	179
3	Johnny Unitas	290	18	Jim Hart	209	33	Babe Parilli	178
4	Joe Montana	273	19	**Jim Everett**	202	34	**Steve Young**	174
5	**Dave Krieg**	261	20	Roman Gabriel	201	35	Charlie Conerly	173
6	Sonny Jurgensen	255	21	Phil Simms	199		Joe Namath	173
7	Dan Fouts	254	22	Ken Anderson	197		Norm Van Brocklin	173
	Warren Moon	254	23	Joe Ferguson	196	38	Charley Johnson	170
9	**John Elway**	251		Bobby Layne	196	39	Daryle Lamonica	164
10	John Hadl	244		Norm Snead	196		Jim Plunkett	164
11	Len Dawson	239	26	Ken Stabler	194	41	Earl Morrall	161
12	**Jim Kelly**	237	27	Steve DeBerg	193	42	Joe Theismann	160
13	George Blanda	236	28	Bob Griese	192	43	Tommy Kramer	159
14	**Boomer Esiason**	234	29	Sammy Baugh	187	44	**Vinny Testaverde**	157
15	John Brodie	214	30	Craig Morton	183	45	Steve Bartkowski	156

Note: The NFL does not recognize records from the All-American Football Conference (1946-49). If it did, **Y.A. Tittle** would rank 11th (after Hadl) with 242 TDs and **Otto Graham** would tie for 34th (after Parilli) with 174 TDs.

Passes Intercepted

		No			No			No
1	George Blanda	277	9	John Brodie	224	17	Steve Grogan	208
2	John Hadl	268	10	Ken Stabler	222		**Warren Moon**	208
3	Fran Tarkenton	266	11	Y.A. Tittle	221	19	Sammy Baugh	203
4	Norm Snead	253	12	Joe Namath	220		Steve DeBerg	203
	Johnny Unitas	253		Babe Parilli	220		**Dave Krieg**	199
6	Jim Hart	247	14	Terry Bradshaw	210	22	Jim Plunkett	198
7	Bobby Layne	243	15	Joe Ferguson	209	23	Tobin Rote	191
8	Dan Fouts	242		**Dan Marino**	209			

Passing Yards

		Yrs	Att	Comp	Pct	Yards
1	**Dan Marino** ..	14	6904	4134	59.9	51,636
2	Fran Tarkenton ...	18	6467	3686	57.0	47,003
3	**John Elway** ...	14	6392	3633	56.8	45,034
4	**Warren Moon** ..	13	6000	3514	58.6	43,787
5	Dan Fouts	15	5604	3297	58.8	43,040
6	Joe Montana	15	5391	3409	63.2	40,551
7	Johnny Unitas ...	18	5186	2830	54.6	40,239
8	**Dave Krieg** ...	17	5288	3092	58.5	37,946
9	**Boomer Esiason**	13	5019	2851	56.8	36,442
10	**Jim Kelly**	11	4779	2874	60.1	35,467
11	Jim Hart	19	5076	2593	51.1	34,665
12	**Jim Everett** ...	11	4848	2805	57.9	34,380
13	Steve DeBerg	16	4965	2844	57.3	33,872
14	John Hadl	16	4687	2363	50.4	33,503
15	Phil Simms	14	4647	2576	55.4	33,462
16	Ken Anderson ...	16	4475	2654	59.3	32,838
17	Sonny Jurgensen .	18	4262	2433	57.1	32,224
18	John Brodie	17	4491	2469	55.0	31,548
19	Norm Snead	15	4353	2276	52.3	30,797
20	Joe Ferguson	18	4519	2369	52.4	29,817
21	Roman Gabriel ..	16	4498	2366	52.6	29,444
22	Len Dawson	19	3741	2136	57.1	28,711
23	Y.A. Tittle	15	3817	2118	55.5	28,339
24	Ron Jaworski ...	16	4117	2187	53.1	28,190
25	Terry Bradshaw ..	14	3901	2025	51.9	27,989

Note: The NFL does not recognize records from the All-American Football Conference (1946-49). If it did, **Y.A. Tittle** would rank 16th (after Simms) with the following stats: 17 Yrs; 4,395 Att; 2,427 Comp; 55.2 Pct; and 33,070 Yards.

Receptions

		Yrs	No	Yards	Avg	TD
1	**Jerry Rice**	12	1050	16,377	15.6	154
2	**Art Monk**	16	940	12,721	13.5	68
3	Steve Largent	14	819	13,089	16.0	100
4	**Henry Ellard** ...	14	775	13,177	17.0	61
5	**Andre Reed**	12	766	10,884	14.2	75
6	James Lofton	16	764	14,004	18.3	75
7	Charlie Joiner	18	750	12,146	16.2	65
8	**Gary Clark**	11	699	10,856	15.5	65
9	**Cris Carter**	10	667	8,367	12.5	76
10	Ozzie Newsome ..	13	662	7,980	12.1	47
11	**Irving Fryar**	13	650	10,111	15.6	69
12	Charley Taylor ...	13	649	9,110	14.0	79
13	Drew Hill	15	634	9,831	15.5	60
14	Don Maynard	15	633	11,834	18.7	88
15	Raymond Berry ...	13	631	9,275	14.7	68
16	Sterling Sharpe ...	7	595	8,134	13.7	65
17	**Michael Irvin** ...	9	591	9,500	16.1	52
18	Harold Carmichael	14	590	8,985	15.2	79
19	Fred Biletnikoff ..	14	589	8,974	15.2	76
20	**Bill Brooks**	11	583	8,001	13.7	46
21	Mark Clayton	11	582	8,974	15.4	84
22	Harold Jackson ...	16	579	10,372	17.9	76
23	**Marcus Allen** ...	15	576	5,325	9.2	21
24	**Ernest Givins** ..	10	571	8,215	14.4	49
25	**Andre Rison**	8	569	7,747	13.6	66

Rushing

		Yrs	Car	Yards	Avg	TD
1	Walter Payton	13	3838	16,726	4.4	110
2	Eric Dickerson ...	11	2996	13,259	4.4	90
3	Tony Dorsett	12	2936	12,739	4.3	77
4	Jim Brown	9	2359	12,312	5.2	106
5	Franco Harris	13	2949	12,120	4.1	91
6	**Marcus Allen** ..	15	2898	11,738	4.1	112
7	**Barry Sanders** ..	8	2384	11,725	4.9	84
8	John Riggins	14	2916	11,352	3.9	104
9	O.J. Simpson	11	2404	11,236	4.7	61
10	**Thurman Thomas**	9	2566	10,762	4.2	62
11	Ottis Anderson ...	14	2562	10,273	4.0	81
12	**Emmitt Smith** ..	7	2334	10,160	4.4	108
13	Earl Campbell	8	2187	9,407	4.3	74
14	Jim Taylor	10	1941	8,597	4.4	83
15	Joe Perry	14	1737	8,378	4.8	53
16	**Herschel Walker**	11	1948	8,205	4.2	61
17	Roger Craig	11	1991	8,189	4.1	56
18	Gerald Riggs	10	1989	8,188	4.1	69
19	Larry Csonka	11	1891	8,081	4.3	64
20	Freeman McNeil ..	12	1798	8,074	4.5	38
21	James Brooks	12	1685	7,962	4.7	49
22	**Ernest Byner** ...	13	2011	7,948	4.0	56
23	Mike Pruitt	11	1844	7,378	4.0	51
24	Leroy Kelly	10	1727	7,274	4.2	74
25	George Rogers ...	7	1692	7,176	4.2	54

Note: The NFL does not recognize records from the All-American Football Conference (1946-49). If it did, **Joe Perry** would rank 13th (after Smith) with the following stats: 16 Yrs; 1,929 Att; 9,723 Yards; 5.0 Avg; and 71 TD.

All-Purpose Yards

		Rush	Rec	Ret	Total
1	Walter Payton	16,726	4,538	539	21,803
2	Tony Dorsett	12,739	3,554	33	16,326
3	**Marcus Allen** ...	11,738	5,325	-6	17,057
4	**Jerry Rice**	624	16,377	6	17,007
5	Herschel Walker ..	8,205	4,710	3,917	16,832
6	Jim Brown	12,312	2,499	648	15,459
7	Eric Dickerson ...	13,259	2,137	15	15,411
8	**Henry Ellard** ...	50	13.177	1,891	15,118
9	James Brooks	7,962	3,621	3,327	14,910
10	**Thurman Thomas**	10,762	3,876	0	14,638
11	Franco Harris	12,120	2,287	215	14,622
12	O.J. Simpson	11,236	2,142	990	14,368
13	James Lofton	246	14,004	27	14,277
14	**Barry Sanders** ..	11,725	2,327	118	14,170
15	Bobby Mitchell ...	2,735	7,954	3,389	14,078
16	John Riggins	11,352	2,090	-7	13,435
17	Steve Largent	83	13,089	224	13,396
18	Ottis Anderson ...	10,273	3,062	29	13,364
19	Drew Hill	19	9,831	3,487	13,337
20	Greg Pruitt	5,672	3,069	4,521	13,262
21	Roger Craig	8,189	4,911	43	13,143
22	Art Monk	332	12,721	10	13,063
23	**Earnest Byner** ..	7,948	4,477	631	13,056
24	Eric Metcalf	2,370	4,520	6,138	13,028
25	**Mel Gray**	99	164	12,662	12,925

Years played: Allen (15), Anderson (14), Brooks (13), J. Brown (9), Byner (13), Craig (11), Dickerson (11), Dorsett (12), Ellard (14), Gray (11), Harris (13), Hill (14), Largent (14), Lofton (16), Metcalf (8), Mitchell (11), Monk (16), Payton (13), Pruitt (12), Rice (12), Riggins (14), Sanders (8), Simpson (11), Thomas (9) and Walker (11).

All-Time NFL Leaders (Cont.)
Scoring

Points

		Yrs	TD	FG	PAT	Total
1	George Blanda ...	26	9	335	943	2002
2	Jan Stenerud	19	0	373	580	1699
3	**Nick Lowery**	18	0	383	562	1711
4	**Gary Anderson** .	15	0	356	488	1556
5	**Morten Andersen**	15	0	355	472	1537
6	Eddie Murray	16	0	325	498	1473
7	Pat Leahy	18	0	304	558	1470
8	**Norm Johnson** ...	15	0	300	522	1452
9	Jim Turner	16	1	304	521	1439
10	Matt Bahr	17	0	300	522	1422
11	Mark Moseley	16	0	300	482	1382
12	Jim Bakken	17	0	282	534	1380
13	Fred Cox	15	0	282	519	1365
14	Lou Groza	17	1	234	641	1349
15	Jim Breech	14	0	243	517	1246
16	Chris Bahr	14	0	241	490	1213
17	Gino Cappelletti	11	42	176	350	1130†
18	Ray Wersching ...	15	0	222	456	1122
19	**Kevin Butler**	12	0	257	404	1175
20	**Al Del Greco**	15	0	236	403	1111
21	Don Cockroft	13	0	216	432	1080
22	Garo Yepremian ..	14	0	210	444	1074
23	Bruce Gossett	11	0	219	374	1031
24	Jerry Rice	12	165	0	0	990
25	Sam Baker	15	2	179	428	977

† Cappelletti's total includes four 2-point conversions.

Note: The NFL does not recognize records from the All-American Football Conference (1946-49). If it did, **Lou Groza** would move up to 4th (after Lowery) with the following stats: 21 Yrs; 1 TD; 264 FG, 810 PAT; 1,608 Pts.

Touchdowns

		Yrs	Rush	Rec	Ret	Total
1	**Jerry Rice**	12	10	154	1	165
2	**Marcus Allen** ...	15	112	21	1	134
3	Jim Brown	9	106	20	0	126
4	Walter Payton ...	13	110	15	0	125
5	John Riggins	14	104	12	0	116
6	**Emmitt Smith** ...	7	108	7	0	115
7	Lenny Moore	12	63	48	2	113
8	Don Hutson	11	3	99	3	105
9	Steve Largent	14	1	100	0	101
	Franco Harris ...	13	91	9	0	100
11	Eric Dickerson ...	11	90	6	0	96
12	Jim Taylor	10	83	10	0	93
13	Tony Dorsett	12	77	13	1	91
	Bobby Mitchell ...	11	18	65	8	91
	Barry Sanders ..	8	84	7	0	91
16	Leroy Kelly	10	74	13	3	90
	Charley Taylor ...	13	11	79	0	90
18	Don Maynard	15	0	88	0	88
19	Lance Alworth ...	11	2	85	0	87
20	Ottis Anderson	14	81	5	0	86
	Paul Warfield	13	1	85	0	86
22	Mark Clayton	11	0	84	1	85
	Tommy McDonald .	12	0	84	1	85
24	Pete Johnson	8	76	6	0	82
	Art Powell	10	0	81	1	82
	Herschel Walker	11	61	19	2	82
	Thurman Thomas	9	62	20	0	82

Note: The NFL does not recognize records from the All-American Football Conference (1946-49). If it did, **Joe Perry** would rank 23rd (after Clayton and McDonald) with the following stats: 16 Yrs; 71 Rush; 12 Rec; 1 Ret; 84 TDs.

Interceptions

		Yrs	No	Yards	TD
1	Paul Krause	16	81	1185	3
2	Emlen Tunnell	14	79	1282	4
3	Dick (Night Train) Lane	14	68	1207	5
4	Ken Riley	15	65	596	5
5	Ronnie Lott	14	63	730	5

Sacks

		Yrs	No
1	**Reggie White**	12	163
2	**Bruce Smith**	12	141
3	Lawrence Taylor	12	132½
4	Rickey Jackson	15	128
5	Richard Dent	13	126½

Note: The NFL did not begin officially compiling sacks until 1982. Deacon Jones, who played with the Rams, Chargers and Redskins from 1961-74, is often credited with 173½ sacks. Jack Youngblood (150½) and Alan Page (148) would also make an unofficial top five. Also, Lawrence Taylor has 142 career sacks if you count his rookie year of 1981, the year before sacks became an official stat.

Safeties

		Yrs	No
1	Ted Hendricks	15	4
	Doug English	10	4
3	Fourteen players tied with three.		

Kickoff Returns
Minimum 75 returns.

		Yrs	No	Yards	Avg	TD
1	Gale Sayers	7	91	2781	30.6	6
2	Lynn Chandnois	7	92	2720	29.6	3
3	Abe Woodson	9	193	5538	28.7	5
4	Buddy Young	6	90	2514	27.9	2
5	Travis Williams	5	102	2801	27.5	6

Punting
Minimum 300 punts.

		Yrs	No	Yards	Avg
1	Sammy Baugh	16	338	15,245	45.1
2	Tommy Davis	11	511	22,833	44.7
3	Yale Lary	11	503	22,279	44.3
4	Horace Gillom	7	385	16,872	43.8
	Jerry Norton	11	358	15,671	43.8

Punt Returns
Minimum 75 returns.

		Yrs	No	Yards	Avg	TD
1	George McAfee	8	112	1431	12.8	2
	Jack Christiansen ...	8	85	1084	12.8	8
3	Claude Gibson	5	110	1381	12.6	4
4	Bill Dudley	9	124	1515	12.2	3
5	Rick Upchurch	9	248	3008	12.1	8

Long-Playing Records

Seasons

		No
1	George Blanda, QB-K	26
2	Earl Morrall, QB	21
3	Jim Marshall, DE	20
	Jackie Slater, OL	20

Games

		No
1	George Blanda, QB-K	340
2	Jim Marshall, DE	282
3	Jim Stenerud, K	263

Consecutive Games

		No
1	Jim Marshall, DE	282
2	Mick Tingelhoff, C	240
3	Jim Bakken, K	234

SINGLE SEASON
Passing

Yards Gained	Year	Att	Cmp	Pct	Yds
Dan Marino, Mia	1984	564	362	64.2	5084
Dan Fouts, SD	1981	609	360	59.1	4802
Dan Marino, Mia	1986	623	378	60.7	4746
Dan Fouts, SD	1980	589	348	59.1	4715
Warren Moon, Hou	1991	655	404	61.7	4690
Warren Moon, Hou	1990	584	362	62.0	4689
Neil Lomax, St.L	1984	560	345	61.6	4614
Drew Bledsoe, NE	1994	691	400	57.9	4555
Lynn Dicky, GB	1983	484	286	59.7	4458
Brett Favre, GB	1995	570	359	63.0	4413

Efficiency	Year	Att/Cmp	TD	Rtg
Steve Young, SF	1994	461/324	35	112.8
Joe Montana, SF	1989	386/271	26	112.4
Milt Plum, Cle	1960	250/151	21	110.4
Sammy Baugh, Wash	1945	182/128	11	109.9
Dan Marino, Mia	1984	564/362	48	108.9
Sid Luckman, Bears	1943	202/110	28	107.5
Steve Young, SF	1992	402/268	25	107.0
Bart Starr, GB	1966	251/156	14	105.0
Y.A. Tittle, NYG	1963	367/221	36	104.8
Roger Staubach, Dal	1971	211/126	15	104.8

Receptions

Catches	Year	No	Yds
Herman Moore, Det	1995	123	1686
Jerry Rice, SF	1995	122	1848
Cris Carter, Min	1995	122	1371
Cris Carter, Min	1994	122	1256
Isaac Bruce, St. L	1995	119	1781
Jerry Rice, SF	1994	112	1499
Sterling Sharpe, GB	1993	112	1274
Michael Irvin, Dal	1995	111	1603
Terance Mathis, Atl	1994	111	1342
Brett Perriman, Det	1995	108	1488
Sterling Sharpe, GB	1992	108	1461
Jerry Rice, SF	1996	108	1254

Rushing

Yards Gained	Year	Car	Yds	Avg
Eric Dickerson, LA Rams	1984	379	2105	5.6
O.J. Simpson, Buf	1973	332	2003	6.0
Earl Campbell, Hou	1980	373	1934	5.2
Barry Sanders, Det	1994	331	1883	5.7
Jim Brown, Cle	1963	291	1863	6.4
Walter Payton, Chi	1977	339	1852	5.5
Eric Dickerson, LA Rams	1986	404	1821	4.5
O.J. Simpson, Buf	1975	329	1817	5.5
Eric Dickerson, LA Rams	1983	390	1808	4.6
Emmitt Smith, Dal	1995	377	1773	4.7

Scoring
Points

	Year	TD	PAT	FG	Pts
Paul Hornung, GB	1960	15	41	15	176
Mark Moseley, Wash	1983	0	62	33	161
Gino Cappelletti, Bos	1964	7	38	25	155
Emmitt Smith, Dal	1995	25	0	0	150
Chip Lohmiller, Wash	1991	0	56	31	149
Gino Cappelletti, Bos	1961	8	48	17	147
Paul Hornung, GB	1961	10	41	15	146
Jim Turner, Jets	1968	0	43	34	145
John Kasay, Car.	1996	0	34	37	145
John Riggins, Wash	1983	24	0	0	144
Kevin Butler, Chi	1985	0	51	31	144
Tony Franklin, NE	1986	0	44	32	140

Touchdowns

	Year	Rush	Rec	Ret	Total
Emmitt Smith, Dal	1995	25	0	0	25
John Riggins, Wash	1983	24	0	0	24
O.J. Simpson, Buf	1975	16	7	0	23
Jerry Rice, SF	1987	1	22	0	23
Gale Sayers, Chi	1966	14	6	2	22
Chuck Foreman, Min	1975	13	9	0	22
Emmitt Smith, Dal	1994	21	1	0	22
Jim Brown, Cle	1965	17	4	0	21
Joe Morris, NY Giants	1985	21	0	0	21
Terry Allen, Wash	1996	21	0	0	21
Three tied with 20 each.					

Note: The NFL regular season schedule grew from 12 games (1947-60) to 14 (1961-77) to 16 (1978-present). The AFL regular season schedule was always 14 games (1960-69).

Touchdowns Passing

	Year	No
Dan Marino, Miami	1984	48
Dan Marino, Miami	1986	44
Brett Favre, Green Bay	1996	39
Brett Favre, Green Bay	1995	38
George Blanda, Houston	1961	36
Y.A. Tittle, NY Giants	1963	36
Steve Young, San Francisco	1994	35
Y.A. Tittle, NY Giants	1962	33
Dan Fouts, San Diego	1981	33
Warren Moon, Houston	1990	33
Jim Kelly, Buffalo	1991	33
Brett Favre, Green Bay	1994	33
Warren Moon, Minnesota	1995	33
Vinny Testaverde, Baltimore	1996	33

Touchdowns Rushing

	Year	No
Emmitt Smith, Dallas	1995	25
John Riggins, Washington	1983	24
Joe Morris, NY Giants	1985	21
Emmitt Smith, Dallas	1994	21
Terry Allen, Wash	1996	21
Jim Taylor, Green Bay	1962	19
Earl Campbell, Houston	1979	19
Chuck Muncie, San Diego	1981	19
Eric Dickerson, LA Rams	1983	18
George Rogers, Washington	1986	18
Emmitt Smith, Dallas	1992	18
Jim Brown, Cleveland	1958	17
Jim Brown, Cleveland	1965	17

Touchdowns Receiving

	Year	No
Jerry Rice, San Francisco	1987	22
Mark Clayton, Miami	1984	18
Sterling Sharpe, Green Bay	1994	18
Don Hutson, Green Bay	1942	17
Elroy (Crazylegs) Hirsch, LA Rams	1951	17
Bill Groman, Houston	1961	17
Jerry Rice, San Francisco	1989	17
Cris Carter, Minnesota	1995	17
Carl Pickens, Cincinnati	1995	17
Art Powell, Oakland	1963	16
Four tied with 15 each.		

Field Goals

	Year	Att	No
John Kasay, Carolina	1996	45	37
Cary Blanchard, Indianapolis	1996	40	36
Ali Haji-Sheikh, NY Giants	1983	42	35
Jeff Jaeger, LA Rams	1993	44	35
Nick Lowery, Kansas City	1990	37	34
Jim Turner, NY Jets	1968	46	34
Jason Hanson, Detroit	1993	43	34
John Carney, San Diego	1994	38	34
Fuad Reveiz, Minnesota	1994	39	34
Norm Johnson, Pittsburgh	1995	41	34
Three tied with 33 each.			

All-Time NFL Leaders (Cont.)

Interceptions

	Year	No
Dick (Night Train) Lane, Detroit	1952	14
Dan Sandifer, Washington	1948	13
Spec Sanders, NY Yanks	1950	13
Lester Hayes, Oakland	1980	13

Kickoff Returns

	Year	Avg
Travis Williams, Green Bay	1967	41.1
Gale Sayers, Chicago	1967	37.7
Ollie Matson, Chicago Cards	1958	35.5

Punting

Qualifiers	Year	Avg
Sammy Baugh, Washington	1940	51.4
Yale Lary, Detroit	1963	48.9
Sammy Baugh, Washington	1941	48.7

Punt Returns

	Year	Avg
Herb Rich, Baltimore	1950	23.0
Jack Christiansen, Detroit	1952	21.5
Dick Christy, NY Titans	1961	21.3
Bob Hayes, Dallas	1968	20.8

Sacks

	Year	No		Year	No
Mark Gastineau, NY Jets	1984	22	Chris Doleman, Minnesota	1989	21
Reggie White, Philadelphia	1987	21	Lawrence Taylor, NY Giants	1986	20½

Note: The NFL did not begin officially compiling sacks until 1982. Cincinnati's Coy Bacon is often, although not officially, credited with 26 sacks during the 1976 season.

SINGLE GAME

Passing

Yards Gained

	Date	Yds
Norm Van Brocklin, LA vs NY Yanks	9/28/51	554
Warren Moon, Hou at KC	12/16/90	527
Boomer Esiason, Ariz. at Wash.	11/10/96	522
Dan Marino, Mia vs NYJ	10/23/88	521
Phil Simms, NYG vs Cin	10/13/85	513

Completions

	Date	No
Drew Bledsoe, NE vs Min	11/13/94	45
Richard Todd, NYJ vs SF	9/21/80	42
Warren Moon, Hou vs Dal	11/10/91	41
Ken Anderson, Cin vs SD	12/20/82	40
Phil Simms, NYG vs Cin	10/13/85	40

Rushing

Yards Gained

	Date	Yds
Walter Payton, Chi vs Min	11/20/77	275
O.J. Simpson, Buf vs Det	11/25/76	273
O.J. Simpson, Buf vs NE	9/16/73	250
Willie Ellison, LA Rams vs NO	12/5/71	247
Cookie Gilchrist, Buf vs NYJ	12/8/63	243

Scoring

Points

	Date	Pts
Ernie Nevers, Chi. Cards vs Chi. Bears	11/28/29	40
Dub Jones, Cle vs Chi. Bears	11/25/51	36
Gale Sayers, Chi vs SF	12/12/65	36
Paul Hornung, GB vs Bal	10/8/61	33
Bob Shaw, Chi. Cards vs Bal	10/2/50	30
Jim Brown, Cle vs Bal	11/1/59	30
Abner Haynes, Dal. Texans vs Oak	11/26/61	30
Billy Cannon, Hou vs NY Titans	12/10/61	30
Cookie Gilchrist, Buf vs NY Jets	12/8/63	30
Kellen Winslow, SD vs Oak	11/22/81	30
Jerry Rice, SF at Atl	10/14/90	30

Note: Nevers celebrated Thanksgiving, 1929, by scoring all the Chicago Cardinals' points on six rushing TDs and four PATs. The Cards beat Red Grange and the Chicago Bears, 40-6.

Touchdowns Passing

	Date	No
Sid Luckman, Chi. Bears vs NYG	11/14/43	7
Adrian Burk, Phi vs Wash	10/17/54	7
George Blanda, Hou vs NY Titans	11/19/61	7
Y.A. Tittle, NYG vs Wash	10/28/62	7
Joe Kapp, Min vs Bal	9/28/69	7

Receptions

Catches

	Date	No
Tom Fears, LA vs GB	12/3/50	18
Clark Gaines, NYJ vs SF	9/21/80	17
Sonny Randle, St.L vs NYG	11/4/62	16
Keenan McCardle, Jax. at St.L.	10/20/96	16
Six tied with 15 each.		

Yards Gained

	Date	Yds
Flipper Anderson, LA Rams vs NO	11/26/89	336
Stephone Paige, KC vs SD	12/22/85	309
Jim Benton, Cle vs Det	11/22/45	303
Cloyce Box, Det vs Bal	12/3/50	302
Jerry Rice, SF at Det	9/25/95	289
John Taylor, SF vs LA Rams	12/11/89	286

All-Purpose Yards

	Date	Yds
Billy Cannon, Hou vs NY Titans	12/10/61	373
Lionel James, SD vs Raiders	11/10/85	345
Timmy Brown, Phi vs St.L	12/16/62	341
Gale Sayers, Chi vs Min	12/18/66	339
Gale Sayers, Chi vs SF	12/12/65	336

Touchdowns Receiving

	Date	No
Bob Shaw, Chi. Cards vs Bal	10/2/50	5
Kellen Winslow, SD vs Oak	11/22/81	5
Jerry Rice, SF at Atl	10/14/90	5

Touchdowns Rushing

	Date	No
Ernie Nevers, Chi. Cards vs Chi. Bears	11/28/29	6
Jim Brown, Cle vs Bal	11/1/59	5
Cookie Gilchrist, Buf vs NY Jets	12/8/63	5

Field Goals

	Date	No
Jim Bakken, St.L vs Pit	9/24/67	7
Chris Boniol, Dal vs GB	11/18/96	7
Rich Karlis, Min vs Rams	11/5/89	7
Eight players tied with 6 FGs.		

Note: Bakken was 7-for-9, Boniol and Karlis 7-for-7.

Extra Point Kicks

	Date	No
Pat Harder, Cards vs NYG	10/17/48	9
Bob Waterfield, LA vs Bal	10/22/50	9
Charlie Gogolak, Wash vs NYG	11/27/66	9

Longest Plays

Passing (all for TDs)	Date	Yds
Frank Filchock to Andy Farkas, Wash vs Pit	10/15/39	99
George Izo to Bobby Mitchell, Wash vs Cle	9/15/63	99
Karl Sweetan to Pat Studstill, Det vs Bal	10/16/66	99
Sonny Jurgensen to Gerry Allen, Wash vs Chi	9/15/68	99
Jim Plunkett to Cliff Branch, LA Raiders vs Wash	10/2/83	99
Ron Jaworski to Mike Quick, Phi vs Atl	11/10/85	99
Stan Humphries to Tony Martin, SD at Sea	9/18/94	99
Brett Favre to Robert Brooks, GB at Chi	9/11/95	99

Punt Returns (all for TDs)	Date	Yds
Robert Bailey, Rams at NO	10/23/94	103
Gil LeFebvre, Cin vs Bklyn	12/3/33	98
Charlie West, Min vs Wash	11/3/68	98
Dennis Morgan, Dal vs St.L	10/13/74	98

Punt Returns (all for TDs)	Date	Yds
Terance Mathis, NYJ vs Dal	11/4/90	98

Runs from Scrimmage (all for TDs)	Date	Yds
Tony Dorsett, Dal vs Min	1/3/83	99
Andy Uram, GB vs Chi. Cards	10/8/39	97
Bob Gage, Pit vs Bears	12/4/49	97

Field Goals	Date	Yds
Tom Dempsey, NO vs Det	11/8/70	63
Steve Cox, Cle vs Cin	10/21/84	60
Morten Andersen, NO vs Chi	10/27/91	60

Kickoff Returns (all for TDs)	Date	Yds
Al Carmichael, GB vs Chi. Bears	10/7/56	106
Noland Smith, KC vs Den	12/17/67	106
Roy Green, St.L vs Dal	10/21/79	106

Interception Returns (all for TDs)	Date	Yds
James Willis (14 yds) lateral to Troy Vincent (90 yds), Phi at Dal	11/3/96	104
Vencie Glenn, SD vs Den	11/29/87	103
Louis Oliver, Mia vs Buf	10/4/92	103

Six players tied with 102-yd returns.

Chicago College All-Star Game

On Aug. 31, 1934, a year after sponsoring Major League Baseball's first All-Star Game, *Chicago Tribune* sports editor Arch Ward presented the first Chicago College All-Star Game at Soldier Field. A crowd of 79,432 turned out to see an all-star team of graduated college seniors battle the 1933 NFL champion Chicago Bears to a scoreless tie. The preseason game was played at Soldier Field and pitted the college All-Stars against the defending NFL champions (1933–1966) or Super Bowl champions (1967–75) every year except 1935 until it was cancelled in 1977. The NFL champs won the series, 31-9-1.

Year		Year		Year	
1934	Chi. Bears 0, All-Stars 0	1949	Philadelphia 38, All-Stars 0	1964	Chi. Bears 28, All-Stars 17
1935	Chi. Bears 5, All-Stars 0	1950	All-Stars 17, Philadelphia 7	1965	Cleveland 24, All-Stars 16
1936	Detroit 7, All-Stars 0	1951	Cleveland 33, All-Stars 0	1966	Green Bay 38, All-Stars 0
1937	All-Stars 6, Green Bay 0	1952	LA Rams 10, All-Stars 7	1967	Green Bay 27, All-Stars 0
1938	All-Stars 28, Washington 16	1953	Detroit 24, All-Stars 10	1968	Green Bay 34, All-Stars 17
1939	NY Giants 9, All-Stars 0	1954	Detroit 31, All-Stars 6	1969	NY Jets 26, All-Stars 24
		1955	All-Stars 30, Cleveland 27		
1940	Green Bay 45, All-Stars 28	1956	Cleveland 26, All-Stars 0	1970	Kansas City 24, All-Stars 3
1941	Chi. Bears 37, All-Stars 13	1957	NY Giants 22, All-Stars 12	1971	Baltimore 24, All-Stars 17
1942	Chi. Bears 21, All-Stars 0	1958	All-Stars 35, Detroit 19	1972	Dallas 20, All-Stars 7
1943	All-Stars 27, Washington 7	1959	Baltimore 29, All-Stars 0	1973	Miami 14, All-Stars 3
1944	Chi. Bears 24, All-Stars 21			1974	No Game (NFLPA Strike)
1945	Green Bay 19, All-Stars 7	1960	Baltimore 32, All-Stars 7	1975	Pittsburgh 21, All-Stars 14
1946	All-Stars 16, LA Rams 0	1961	Philadelphia 28, All-Stars 14	1976	Pittsburgh 24, All-Stars 0*
1947	All-Stars 16, Chi. Bears 0	1962	Green Bay 42, All-Stars 20		
1948	Chi. Cards 28, All-Stars 0	1963	All-Stars 20, Green Bay 17		*Downpour flooded field, game called with 1:22 left in 3rd quarter.

Number One Draft Choices

In an effort to blunt the dominance of the Chicago Bears and New York Giants in the 1930s and distribute talent more evenly throughout the league, the NFL established the college draft in 1936. The first player chosen in the first draft was Jay Berwanger, who was also college football's Heisman Trophy winner. In all, 16 Heisman winners have also been the NFL's No.1 draft choice. They are noted in **bold** type. The American Football League (formed in 1960) held its own draft for six years before agreeing to merge with the NFL and select players in a common draft starting in 1967.

Year	Team		Year	Team	
1936	Philadelphia	**Jay Berwanger**, HB, Chicago	1954	Cleveland	Bobby Garrett, QB, Stanford
1937	Philadelphia	Sam Francis, FB, Nebraska	1955	Baltimore	George Shaw, QB, Oregon
1938	Cleveland Rams	Corbett Davis, FB, Indiana	1956	Pittsburgh	Gary Glick, DB, Colo. A&M
1939	Chicago Cards	Ki Aldrich, C, TCU	1957	Green Bay	**Paul Hornung**, QB, N. Dame
1940	Chicago Cards	George Cafego, HB, Tennessee	1958	Chicago Cards	King Hill, QB, Rice
1941	Chicago Bears	**Tom Harmon**, HB, Michigan	1959	Green Bay	Randy Duncan, QB, Iowa
1942	Pittsburgh	Bill Dudley, HB, Virginia	1960	NFL-LA Rams	**Billy Cannon**, HB, LSU
1943	Detroit	**Frank Sinkwich**, HB, Georgia		AFL-No choice	
1944	Boston Yanks	**Angelo Bertelli**, QB, N. Dame	1961	NFL-Minnesota	Tommy Mason, HB, Tulane
1945	Chicago Cards	Charley Trippi, HB, Georgia		AFL-Buffalo	Ken Rice, G, Auburn
1946	Boston Yanks	Frank Dancewicz, QB, N. Dame	1962	NFL-Washington	**Ernie Davis**, HB, Syracuse
1947	Chicago Bears	Bob Fenimore, HB, Okla. A&M		AFL-Oakland	Roman Gabriel, QB, N.C. State
1948	Washington	Harry Gilmer, QB, Alabama	1963	NFL-LA Rams	**Terry Baker**, QB, Oregon St.
1949	Philadelphia	Chuck Bednarik, C, Penn		AFL-Kan.City	Buck Buchanan, DT, Grambling
1950	Detroit	**Leon Hart**, E, Notre Dame	1964	NFL-San Fran	Dave Parks, E, Texas Tech
1951	NY Giants	Kyle Rote, HB, SMU		AFL-Boston	Jack Concannon, QB, Bos. Col.
1952	LA Rams	Bill Wade, QB, Vanderbilt	1965	NFL-NY Giants	Tucker Frederickson, HB, Auburn
1953	San Francisco	Harry Babcock, E, Georgia		AFL-Houston	Lawrence Elkins, E, Baylor

Year	Team		Year	Team	
1966	NFL–Atlanta	Tommy Nobis, LB, Texas	1982	New England	Kenneth Sims, DT, Texas
	AFL–Miami	Jim Grabowski, FB, Illinois	1983	Baltimore	John Elway, QB, Stanford
1967	Baltimore	Bubba Smith, DT, Michigan St.	1984	New England	Irving Fryar, WR, Nebraska
1968	Minnesota	Ron Yary, T, USC	1985	Buffalo	Bruce Smith, DE, Va. Tech
1969	Buffalo	**O.J. Simpson**, RB, USC	1986	Tampa Bay	**Bo Jackson**, RB, Auburn
1970	Pittsburgh	Terry Bradshaw, QB, La.Tech	1987	Tampa Bay	**V. Testaverde**, QB, Miami-FL
1971	New England	**Jim Plunkett**, QB, Stanford	1988	Atlanta	Aundray Bruce, LB, Auburn
1972	Buffalo	Walt Patulski, DE, Notre Dame	1989	Dallas	Troy Aikman, QB, UCLA
1973	Houston	John Matuszak, DE, Tampa	1990	Indianapolis	Jeff George, QB, Illinois
1974	Dallas	Ed (Too Tall) Jones, Tenn. St.	1991	Dallas	Russell Maryland, DL, Miami-FL
1975	Atlanta	Steve Bartkowski, QB, Calif.	1992	Indianapolis	Steve Emtman, DL, Washington
1976	Tampa Bay	Lee Roy Selmon, DE, Oklahoma	1993	New England	Drew Bledsoe, QB, Wash. St.
1977	Tampa Bay	Ricky Bell, RB, USC	1994	Cincinnati	Dan Wilkinson, DT, Ohio St.
1978	Houston	**Earl Campbell**, RB, Texas	1995	Cincinnati	Ki-Jana Carter, RB, Penn St.
1979	Buffalo	Tom Cousineau, LB, Ohio St.	1996	NY Jets	Keyshawn Johnson, WR, USC
1980	Detroit	**Billy Sims**, RB, Oklahoma	1997	St. Louis	Orlando Pace, OT, Ohio St.
1981	New Orleans	**George Rogers**, RB, S. Carolina			

All-Time Winningest NFL Coaches

NFL career victories through the 1996 season. Career, regular season and playoff records are noted along with NFL, AFL and Super Bowl titles won. Coaches active during 1996 season in **bold** type.

		Career				Regular Season				Playoffs			
		Yrs	W	L	T	Pct	W	L	T	Pct	W	L	Pct. League Titles
1	Don Shula	33	**347**	173	6	.665	328	156	6	.676	19	17	.528 2 Super Bowls and 1 NFL
2	George Halas	40	**324**	151	31	.671	318	148	31	.671	6	3	.667 5 NFL
3	Tom Landry	29	**270**	178	6	.601	250	162	6	.605	20	16	.556 2 Super Bowls
4	Curly Lambeau	33	**229**	134	22	.623	226	132	22	.624	3	2	.600 6 NFL
5	Chuck Noll	23	**209**	156	1	.572	193	148	1	.566	16	8	.667 4 Super Bowls
6	Chuck Knox	22	**193**	158	1	.550	186	147	1	.558	7	11	.389 —None—
7	Paul Brown	21	**170**	108	6	.609	166	100	6	.621	4	8	.333 3 NFL
8	Bud Grant	18	**168**	108	5	.607	158	96	5	.620	10	12	.455 1 NFL
9	Steve Owen	23	**153**	108	17	.581	151	100	17	.595	2	8	.200 2 NFL
10	**Dan Reeves**	16	**149**	113	1	.568	141	106	1	.571	8	7	.553 —None—
11	**Marv Levy**	16	**148**	110	0	.574	137	102	0	.573	11	8	.579 —None—
12	Joe Gibbs	12	**140**	65	0	.683	124	60	0	.674	16	5	.762 3 Super Bowls
13	Hank Stram	17	**136**	100	10	.573	131	97	10	.571	5	3	.625 1 Super Bowl and 3 AFL
14	Weeb Ewbank	20	**134**	130	7	.507	130	129	7	.502	4	1	.800 1 Super Bowl, 2 NFL, and 1 AFL
15	**M. Schottenheimer** .	13	**130**	83	1	.610	125	73	1	.631	5	10	.333 —None—
16	Sid Gillman	18	**123**	104	7	.541	122	99	7	.550	1	5	.167 1 AFL
17	**Bill Parcells**	11	**119**	86	1	.580	109	81	1	.573	10	5	.667 2 Super Bowls
18	George Allen	12	**118**	54	5	.681	116	47	5	.705	2	7	.222 —None—
19	Don Coryell	14	**114**	89	1	.561	111	83	1	.572	3	6	.333 —None—
20	John Madden	10	**112**	39	7	.731	103	32	7	.750	9	7	.563 1 Super Bowl
	Mike Ditka	11	**112**	68	0	.622	106	62	0	.631	6	6	.500 1 Super Bowl
22	**George Seifert**	8	**108**	35	0	.755	98	30	0	.766	10	5	.667 2 Super Bowls
23	Buddy Parker	15	**107**	76	9	.581	104	75	9	.577	3	1	.750 2 NFL
24	Vince Lombardi	10	**105**	35	6	.740	96	34	6	.728	9	1	.900 2 Super Bowls and 5 NFL
	Tom Flores	12	**105**	90	0	.538	97	87	0	.527	8	3	.727 2 Super Bowls

Notes: The NFL does not recognize records from the All-American Football Conference (1946-49). If it did, **Paul Brown** (52-4-3 in four AAFC seasons) would move up to 5th on the all-time list with the following career stats— 25 Yrs; 222 Wins; 112 Losses; 9 Ties; .660 Pct; 9-8 playoff record; and 4 AAFC titles.

The NFL also considers the Playoff Bowl or Runner-up Bowl (officially: the Bert Bell Benefit Bowl) as a post-season exhibition game. The Playoff Bowl was contested every year from 1960-69 in Miami between Eastern and Western Conference second place teams. While the games did not count, six of the coaches above went to the Playoff Bowl at least once and came away with the following records— Allen (2-0), Brown (0-1), Grant (0-1), Landry (1-2), Lombardi (1-1) and Shula (2-0).

Where They Coached

Allen—LA Rams (1966-70), Washington (1971-77); **Brown**—Cleveland (1950-62), Cincinnati (1968-75); **Coryell**—St.Louis (1973-77), San Diego (1978-86); **Ditka**—Chicago (1982-92), New Orleans (1997—); **Ewbank**— Baltimore (1954-62), NY Jets (1963-73); **Flores**—Oakland-LA Raiders (1979-87), Seattle (1992-94) **Gibbs**—Washington (1981-92); **Gillman**—LA Rams (1955-59), LA-San Diego Chargers (1960-69), Houston (1973-74).

Grant—Minnesota (1967-83,1985); **Halas**—Chicago Bears (1920-29,33-42,46-55,58-67); **Knox**— LA Rams (1973-77, 1992-94); Buffalo (1978-82), Seattle (1983-91); **Lambeau**— Green Bay (1921-49), Chicago Cards (1950-51), Washington (1952-53); **Landry**—Dallas (1960-88); **Levy**—Kansas City (1978-82), Buffalo (1986—); **Lombardi**— Green Bay (1959-67), Washington (1969); **Madden**—Oakland (1969-78).

Noll—Pittsburgh (1969-91); **Owen**—NY Giants (1931-53); **Parcells**— NY Giants (1983-90), New England (1993-97), NY Jets (1997—); **Parker**—Chicago Cards (1949), Detroit (1951-56), Pittsburgh (1957-64); **Reeves**— Denver (1981-92), NY Giants (1993-96), Atlanta (1997—); **Schottenheimer**— Cleveland (1984-88), Kansas City (1989—); **Seifert**—San Francisco (1989-96); **Shula**—Baltimore (1963-69), Miami (1970-95); **Stram**—Dallas-Kansas City (1960-74), New Orleans (1976-77).

Top Winning Percentages
Minimum of 85 NFL victories, including playoffs.

		Yrs	W	L	T	Pct
1	**George Seifert**	8	108	35	0	**.755**
2	Vince Lombardi	10	105	35	6	**.740**
3	John Madden	10	112	39	7	**.731**
4	Joe Gibbs	12	140	65	0	**.683**
5	George Allen	12	118	54	5	**.681**
6	George Halas	40	324	151	31	**.671**
7	Don Shula	33	347	173	6	**.665**
8	Curly Lambeau	33	229	134	22	**.623**
9	Mike Ditka	11	112	68	0	**.622**
10	Bill Walsh	10	102	63	1	**.617**
11	**M. Schottenheimer**	13	130	83	1	**.610**
12	Paul Brown	21	170	108	6	**.609**
13	Bud Grant	18	168	108	5	**.607**
14	Tom Landry	29	270	178	6	**.601**
15	Steve Owen	23	153	108	17	**.581**
16	Buddy Parker	15	107	76	9	**.581**
17	**Bill Parcells**	12	119	86	1	**.580**
18	**Marv Levy**	16	148	110	0	**.574**
19	Hank Stram	17	136	100	10	**.573**
20	Chuck Noll	23	209	156	1	**.572**
21	**Dan Reeves**	16	149	113	1	**.568**
22	Don Coryell	14	114	89	1	**.561**
23	Jimmy Conzelman	15	89	68	17	**.560**
24	Chuck Knox	22	193	158	1	**.550**
25	**Jim Mora**	11	93	78	0	**.544**

Note: If AAFC records are included, **Paul Brown** moves to 8th with a percentage of .660 (25 yrs, 222-112-9) and Buck Shaw would be 11th at .619 (8 yrs, 91-55-5).

Active Coaches' Victories
Through 1996 season, including playoffs.

		Yrs	W	L	T	Pct
1	Dan Reeves, Atlanta	16	**149**	113	0	.568
2	Marv Levy, Buffalo	16	**148**	110	0	.574
3	Marty Schottenheimer, KC ..	13	**130**	83	1	.610
4	Bill Parcells, NY Jets	12	**119**	86	1	.580
5	Mike Ditka, New Orleans ..	11	**112**	68	0	.622
6	Ted Marchibroda, Baltimore ..	10	**77**	83	0	.481
7	Jimmy Johnson, Miami	6	**59**	45	0	.567
8	Mike Holmgren, Green Bay .	5	**58**	32	0	.644
9	Bill Cowher, Pittsburgh	5	**57**	32	0	.640
	Dick Vermeil, St. Louis	7	**57**	51	0	.528
11	Bobby Ross, Detroit	5	**50**	36	0	.581
12	Dennis Green, Minnesota ...	4	**47**	37	0	.560
13	Barry Switzer, Dallas	3	**39**	16	0	.709
14	Dave Wannstedt, Chicago ..	4	**33**	33	0	.500
	Bruce Coslet, Cincinnati ...	5	**33**	41	0	.446
	Lindy Infante, Indianapolis ..	5	**33**	48	0	.407
17	Mike Shanahan, Denver	4	**29**	24	0	.547
18	Ray Rhodes, Philadelphia ..	2	**21**	14	0	.600
19	Dom Capers, Carolina	2	**20**	14	0	.588
	Joe Bugel, Oakland	4	**20**	44	0	.313
21	Norv Turner, Washington ...	3	**18**	30	0	.375
22	Jeff Fisher, Houston	3	**16**	22	0	.421
23	Dennis Erickson, Seattle	2	**15**	17	0	.469
	Tom Coughlin, Jacksonville .	2	**15**	20	0	.429
25	Vince Tobin, Arizona	1	**7**	9	0	.438
26	Tony Dungy, Tampa Bay	1	**6**	10	0	.375
	Pete Carroll, New England .	1	**6**	10	0	.375
28	Jim Fassel, NY Giants	0	**0**	0	0	.000
	Steve Mariucci, San Fran ...	0	**0**	0	0	.000
	Kevin Gilbride, San Diego ..	0	**0**	0	0	.000

Annual Awards

Most Valuable Player

Unlike other major pro team sports, the NFL does not sanction an MVP award. It gave out the Joe F. Carr Trophy (Carr was NFL president from 1921-39) for nine years but discontinued it in 1947. Since then, four principal MVP awards have been given out: UPI (1953-69), AP (since 1957), the Maxwell Club of Philadelphia's Bert Bell Trophy (since 1959) and the Pro Football Writers Assn. (since 1976). UPI switched to AFC and NFC Player of the Year awards in 1970.

Multiple winners (more than one season): Jim Brown (4); Johnny Unitas and Y.A. Tittle (3); Earl Campbell, Randall Cunningham, Brett Favre, Otto Graham, Don Hutson, Joe Montana, Walter Payton, Ken Stabler, Joe Theismann and Steve Young (2).

Year		Awards
1938	Mel Hein, NY Giants, C	Carr
1939	Parker Hall, Cleveland Rams, HB	Carr
1940	Ace Parker, Brooklyn, HB	Carr
1941	Don Hutson, Green Bay, E	Carr
1942	Don Hutson, Green Bay, E	Carr
1943	Sid Luckman, Chicago Bears, QB	Carr
1944	Frank Sinkwich, Detroit, HB	Carr
1945	Bob Waterfield, Cleveland Rams, QB	Carr
1946	Bill Dudley, Pittsburgh, HB	Carr
1947-52	No award	
1953	Otto Graham, Cleveland Browns, QB	UPI
1954	Joe Perry, San Francisco, FB	UPI
1955	Otto Graham, Cleveland, QB	UPI
1956	Frank Gifford, NY Giants, HB	UPI
1957	Y.A. Tittle, San Francisco, QB	UPI
	& Jim Brown, Cleveland, FB	AP
1958	Jim Brown, Cleveland, FB	UPI
	& Gino Marchetti, Baltimore, DE	AP
1959	Johnny Unitas, Baltimore, QB	UPI, Bell
	& Charley Conerly, NY Giants, QB	AP
1960	Norm Van Brocklin, Phi., QB	UPI, AP (tie),Bell
	& Joe Schmidt, Detroit, LB	AP (tie)
1961	Paul Hornung, Green Bay, HB	UPI, AP, Bell
1962	Y.A. Tittle, NY Giants, QB	UPI
	Jim Taylor, Green Bay, FB	AP
	& Andy Robustelli, NY Giants, DE	Bell
1963	Jim Brown, Cleveland, FB	UPI, Bell
	& Y.A. Tittle, NY Giants, QB	AP
1964	Johnny Unitas, Baltimore, QB	UPI, AP, Bell
1965	Jim Brown, Cleveland, FB	UPI, AP
	& Pete Retzlaff, Philadelphia, TE	Bell
1966	Bart Starr, Green Bay, QB	UPI, AP
	& Don Meredith, Dallas, QB	Bell
1967	Johnny Unitas, Baltimore, QB	UPI, AP, Bell
1968	Earl Morrall, Baltimore, QB	UPI, AP
	& Leroy Kelly, Cleveland, RB	Bell
1969	Roman Gabriel, LA Rams, QB	UPI, AP, Bell
1970	John Brodie, San Francisco, QB	AP
	& George Blanda, Oakland, QB-PK	Bell
1971	Alan Page, Minnesota, DT	AP
	& Roger Staubach, Dallas, QB	Bell
1972	Larry Brown, Washington, RB	AP, Bell
1973	O.J. Simpson, Buffalo, RB	AP, Bell
1974	Ken Stabler, Oakland, QB	AP
	& Merlin Olsen, LA Rams, DT	Bell
1975	Fran Tarkenton, Minnesota, QB	AP, Bell
1976	Bert Jones, Baltimore, QB	AP, PFWA
	& Ken Stabler, Oakland, QB	Bell
1977	Walter Payton, Chicago, RB	AP, PFWA
	& Bob Griese, Miami, QB	Bell
1978	Terry Bradshaw, Pittsburgh, QB	AP, Bell
	& Earl Campbell, Houston, RB	PFWA
1979	Earl Campbell, Houston, RB	AP, Bell, PFWA
1980	Brian Sipe, Cleveland, QB	AP, PFWA
	& Ron Jaworski, Philadelphia, QB	Bell

Annual Awards (Cont.)

Year	Awards	Year	Awards
1981	Ken Anderson, Cincinnati, QB ...AP, Bell, PFWA	1988	Boomer Esiason, Cincinnati, QB ......AP, PFWA
1982	Mark Moseley, Washington, PK ....AP		& Randall Cunningham, Phila, QB ....Bell
	Joe Theismann, Washington, QB ....Bell	1989	Joe Montana, San Francisco, QB .AP, Bell, PFWA
	& Dan Fouts, San Diego, QB ....PFWA	1990	Randall Cunningham, Phila., QB .....Bell, PFWA
1983	Joe Theismann, Washington, QB ....AP, PFWA		& Joe Montana, San Francisco, QB ....AP
	& John Riggins, Washington, RB ....Bell	1991	Thurman Thomas, Buffalo, RB ....AP, PFWA
1984	Dan Marino, Miami, QB ....AP, Bell, PFWA		& Barry Sanders, Detroit, RB ....Bell
1985	Marcus Allen, LA Raiders, RB ....AP, PFWA	1992	Steve Young, San Francisco, QB ..AP, Bell, PFWA
	& Walter Payton, Chicago, RB ....Bell	1993	Emmitt Smith, Dallas, RB ....AP, Bell, PFWA
1986	Lawrence Taylor, NY Giants, LB ..AP, Bell, PFWA	1994	Steve Young, San Francisco, QB ..AP, Bell, PFWA
1987	Jerry Rice, San Francisco, WR ....Bell, PFWA	1995	Brett Favre, Green Bay, QB ......AP, Bell, PFWA
	& John Elway, Denver, QB ....AP	1996	Brett Favre, Green Bay, QB ......AP, Bell, PFWA

NFC Player of the Year

Given out by UPI since 1970. Offensive and defensive players honored since 1983. Rookie winners are in **bold** type.

Multiple winners: Eric Dickerson, Reggie White and Mike Singletary (3); Brett Favre, Charles Haley, Walter Payton, Lawrence Taylor and Steve Young (2).

Year		Pos	Year		Pos
1970	John Brodie, San Francisco	QB	1987	Off–Jerry Rice, San Francisco	WR
1971	Alan Page, Minnesota	DT		Def–Reggie White, Philadelphia	DE
1972	Larry Brown, Washington	RB	1988	Off–Roger Craig, San Francisco	RB
1973	John Hadl, Los Angeles	QB		Def–Mike Singletary, Chicago	LB
1974	Jim Hart, St. Louis	QB	1989	Off–Joe Montana, San Francisco	QB
1975	Fran Tarkenton, Minnesota	QB		Def–Keith Millard, Minnesota	DT
1976	Chuck Foreman, Minnesota	RB	1990	Off–Randall Cunningham, Philadelphia	QB
1977	Walter Payton, Chicago	RB		Def–Charles Haley, San Francisco	LB
1978	Archie Manning, New Orleans	QB	1991	Off–Mark Rypien, Washington	QB
1979	Ottis Anderson, St. Louis	RB		Def–Reggie White, Philadelphia	DE
1980	Ron Jaworski, Philadelphia	QB	1992	Off–Steve Young, San Francisco	QB
1981	Tony Dorsett, Dallas	RB		Def–Chris Doleman, Minnesota	DE
1982	Mark Moseley, Washington	PK	1993	Off–Emmitt Smith, Dallas	RB
1983	Off–Eric Dickerson, Los Angeles	RB		Def–Eric Allen, Philadelphia	CB
	Def–Lawrence Taylor, New York	LB	1994	Off–Steve Young, San Francisco	QB
1984	Off–Eric Dickerson, Los Angeles	RB		Def–Charles Haley, Dallas	DE
	Def–Mike Singletary, Chicago	LB	1995	Off–Brett Favre, Green Bay	QB
1985	Off–Walter Payton, Chicago	RB		Def–Reggie White, Green Bay	DE
	Def–Mike Singletary, Chicago	LB	1996	Off–Brett Favre, Green Bay	QB
1986	Off–Eric Dickerson, Los Angeles	RB		Def–Kevin Greene, Carolina	LB
	Def–Lawrence Taylor, New York	LB			

AFL-AFC Player of the Year

Presented by UPI to the top player in the AFL (1960-69) and AFC (since 1970). Offensive and defensive players have been honored since 1983. Rookie winners are in **bold** type.

Multiple winners: Bruce Smith (4); O.J. Simpson (3); Cornelius Bennett, George Blanda, John Elway, Dan Fouts, Daryle Lamonica, Dan Marino and Curt Warner (2).

Year		Pos	Year		Pos
1960	**Abner Haynes**, Dallas Texans	HB	1984	Off–Dan Marino, Miami	QB
1961	George Blanda, Houston	QB		Def–Mark Gastineau, New York	DE
1962	Cookie Gilchrist, Buffalo	FB	1985	Off–Marcus Allen, Los Angeles	RB
1963	Lance Alworth, San Diego	FL		Def–Andre Tippett, New England	LB
1964	Gino Cappelletti, Boston	FL-PK	1986	Off–Curt Warner, Seattle	RB
1965	Paul Lowe, San Diego	HB		Def–Rulon Jones, Denver	DE
1966	Jim Nance, Boston	FB	1987	Off–John Elway, Denver	QB
1967	Daryle Lamonica, Oakland	QB		Def–Bruce Smith, Buffalo	DE
1968	Joe Namath, New York	QB	1988	Off–Boomer Esiason, Cincinnati	QB
1969	Daryle Lamonica, Oakland	QB		Def–Bruce Smith, Buffalo	DE
1970	George Blanda, Oakland	QB-PK		& Cornelius Bennett, Buffalo	LB
1971	Otis Taylor, Kansas City	WR	1989	Off–Christian Okoye, Kansas City	RB
1972	O.J. Simpson, Buffalo	RB		Def–Michael Dean Perry, Cleveland	NT
1973	O.J. Simpson, Buffalo	RB	1990	Off–Warren Moon, Houston	QB
1974	Ken Stabler, Oakland	QB		Def–Bruce Smith, Buffalo	DE
1975	O.J. Simpson, Buffalo	RB	1991	Off–Thurman Thomas, Buffalo	RB
1976	Bert Jones, Baltimore	QB		Def–Cornelius Bennett, Buffalo	LB
1977	Craig Morton, Denver	QB	1992	Off–Barry Foster, Pittsburgh	RB
1978	**Earl Campbell**, Houston	RB		Def–Junior Seau, San Diego	LB
1979	Dan Fouts, San Diego	QB	1993	Off–John Elway, Denver	QB
1980	Brian Sipe, Cleveland	QB		Def–Rod Woodson, Pittsburgh	CB
1981	Ken Anderson, Cincinnati	QB	1994	Off–Dan Marino, Miami	QB
1982	Dan Fouts, San Diego	QB		Def–Greg Lloyd, Pittsburgh	LB
1983	Off–**Curt Warner**, Seattle	RB	1995	Off–Jim Harbaugh, Indianapolis	QB
	Def–Rod Martin, Los Angeles	LB		Def–Bryce Paup, Buffalo	LB
			1996	Off–Terrell Davis, Denver	RB
				Def–Bruce Smith, Buffalo	DE

NFL-NFC Rookie of the Year

Presented by UPI to the top rookie in the NFL (1955-69) and NFC (since 1970). Players who were the overall first pick in the NFL draft are in **bold** type.

Year		Pos	Year		Pos	Year		Pos
1955	Alan Ameche, Bal	FB	1969	Calvin Hill, Dal	RB	1983	**Eric Dickerson**, LA	RB
1956	Lenny Moore, Bal	HB	1970	Bruce Taylor, SF	DB	1984	Paul McFadden, Phi	PK
1957	Jim Brown, Cle	FB	1971	John Brockington, GB	RB	1985	Jerry Rice, SF	WR
1958	Jimmy Orr, Pit	FL	1972	Chester Marcol, GB	PK	1986	Reuben Mayes, NO	RB
1959	Boyd Dowler, GB	FL	1973	Charle Young, Phi	TE	1987	Robert Awalt, St.L	TE
1960	Gail Cogdill, Det	FL	1974	John Hicks, NY	G	1988	Keith Jackson, Phi	TE
1961	Mike Ditka, Chi	TE	1975	Mike Thomas, Wash	RB	1989	Barry Sanders, Det	RB
1962	Ronnie Bull, Chi	FB	1976	Sammy White, Min	WR	1990	Mark Carrier, Chi	S
1963	Paul Flatley, Min	FL	1977	Tony Dorsett, Dal	RB	1991	Lawrence Dawsey, TB	WR
1964	Charley Taylor, Wash	HB	1978	Bubba Baker, Det	DE	1992	Robert Jones, Dal	LB
1965	Gale Sayers, Chi	HB	1979	**Ottis Anderson**, St.L	RB	1993	Jerome Bettis, LA	RB
1966	Johnny Roland, St.L	HB	1980	**Billy Sims**, Det	RB	1994	Bryant Young, SF	DT
1967	Mel Farr, Det	RB	1981	**George Rogers**, NO	RB	1995	Rashaan Salaam, Chi	RB
1968	Earl McCullough, Det	FL	1982	Jim McMahon, Chi	QB	1996	Simeon Rice, Ari.	DE

AFL-AFC Rookie of the Year

Presented by UPI to the top rookie in the AFL (1960-69) and AFC (since 1970). Players who were the overall first pick in the AFL or NFL draft are in **bold** type.

Year		Pos	Year		Pos	Year		Pos
1960	Abner Haynes, Dal	HB	1973	Boobie Clark, Cin	RB	1986	Leslie O'Neal, SD	DE
1961	Earl Faison, SD	DE	1974	Don Woods, SD	RB	1987	Shane Conlan, Buf	LB
1962	Curtis McClinton, Dal	FB	1975	Robert Brazile, Hou	LB	1988	John Stephens, NE	RB
1963	Billy Joe, Den	FB	1976	Mike Haynes, NE	DB	1989	Derrick Thomas, KC	LB
1964	Matt Snell, NY	FB	1977	A.J. Duhe, Mia	DE	1990	Richmond Webb, Mia	OT
1965	Joe Namath, NY	QB	1978	**Earl Campbell**, Hou	RB	1991	Mike Croel, Den	LB
1966	Bobby Burnett, Buf	HB	1979	Jerry Butler, Buf	WR	1992	Dale Carter, KC	CB
1967	George Webster, Hou	LB	1980	Joe Cribbs, Buf	RB	1993	Rick Mirer, Sea	QB
1968	Paul Robinson, Cin	RB	1981	Joe Delaney, KC	RB	1994	Marshall Faulk, Ind	RB
1969	Greg Cook, Cin	QB	1982	Marcus Allen, LA	RB	1995	Curtis Martin, NE	RB
1970	Dennis Shaw, Buf	QB	1983	Curt Warner, Sea	RB	1996	Terry Glenn, NE	WR
1971	**Jim Plunkett**, NE	QB	1984	Louis Lipps, Pit	WR			
1972	Franco Harris, Pit	RB	1985	Kevin Mack, Cle	RB			

NFL-NFC Coach of the Year

Presented by UPI to the top coach in the NFL (1955-69) and NFC (since 1970). Records indicate how much coach's team improved over one season.

Multiple winners: George Allen, Leeman Bennett, Mike Ditka, George Halas, Tom Landry, Jack Pardee, Allie Sherman, Don Shula and Bill Walsh (2).

Year		Improvement	Year		Improvement
1955	Joe Kuharich, Washington	3-9 to 8-4	1976	Jack Pardee, Chicago	4-10 to 7-7
1956	Buddy Parker, Detroit	3-9 to 9-3	1977	Leeman Bennett, Atlanta	4-10 to 7-7
1957	Paul Brown, Cleveland	5-7 to 9-2-1	1978	Dick Vermeil, Philadelphia	5-9 to 9-7
1958	Weeb Ewbank, Baltimore	7-5 to 9-3	1979	Jack Pardee, Washington	8-8 to 10-6
1959	Vince Lombardi, Green Bay	1-10-1 to 7-5	1980	Leeman Bennett, Atlanta	6-10 to 12-4
1960	Buck Shaw, Philadelphia	7-5 to 10-2	1981	Bill Walsh, San Francisco	6-10 to 13-3
1961	Allie Sherman, New York	6-4-2 to 10-3-1	1982	Joe Gibbs, Washington	8-8 to 8-1
1962	Allie Sherman, New York	10-3-1 to 12-2	1983	John Robinson, Los Angeles	2-7 to 9-7
1963	George Halas, Chicago	9-5 to 11-1-2	1984	Bill Walsh, San Francisco	10-6 to 15-1
1964	Don Shula, Baltimore	8-6 to 12-2	1985	Mike Ditka, Chicago	10-6 to 15-1
1965	George Halas, Chicago	5-9 to 9-5	1986	Bill Parcells, New York	10-6 to 14-2
1966	Tom Landry, Dallas	7-7 to 10-3-1	1987	Jim Mora, New Orleans	7-9 to 12-3
1967	George Allen, Los Angeles	8-6 to 11-1-2	1988	Mike Ditka, Chicago	11-4 to 12-4
1968	Don Shula, Baltimore	11-1-2 to 13-1	1989	Lindy Infante, Green Bay	4-12 to 10-6
1969	Bud Grant, Minnesota	8-6 to 12-2	1990	Jimmy Johnson, Dallas	1-15 to 7-9
1970	Alex Webster, New York	6-8 to 9-5	1991	Wayne Fontes, Detroit	6-10 to 12-4
1971	George Allen, Washington	6-8 to 9-4-1	1992	Dennis Green, Minnesota	8-8 to 11-5
1972	Dan Devine, Green Bay	4-8-2 to 10-4	1993	Dan Reeves, New York	6-10 to 11-5
1973	Chuck Knox, Los Angeles	6-7-1 to 12-2	1994	Dave Wannstedt, Chicago	7-9 to 9-7
1974	Don Coryell, St. Louis	4-9-1 to 10-4	1995	Ray Rhodes, Philadelphia	7-9 to 10-6
1975	Tom Landry, Dallas	8-6 to 10-4	1996	Dom Capers, Carolina	7-9 to 12-4

AFL-AFC Coach of the Year

Presented by UPI to the top coach in the AFL (1960-69) and AFC (since 1970). Records indicate how much coach's team improved over one season. The AFC began play in 1960.

Multiple winners: Chuck Knox, Marv Levy, Dan Reeves, Sam Rutigliano, Lou Saban, Marty Schottenheimer and Don Shula (2)

Year		Improvement	Year		Improvement
1960	Lou Rymkus, Houston	10-4	1979	Sam Rutigliano, Cleveland	8-8 to 9-7
1961	Wally Lemm, Houston	10-4 to 10-3-1	1980	Sam Rutigliano, Cleveland	9-7 to 11-5
1962	Jack Faulkner, Denver	3-11 to 7-7	1981	Forrest Gregg, Cincinnati	6-10 to 12-4
1963	Al Davis, Oakland	1-13 to 10-4	1982	Tom Flores, Los Angeles	7-9 to 8-1
1964	Lou Saban, Buffalo	7-6-1 to 12-2	1983	Chuck Knox, Seattle	4-5 to 9-7
1965	Lou Saban, Buffalo	12-2 to 10-3-1	1984	Chuck Knox, Seattle	9-7 to 12-4
1966	Mike Holovak, Boston	4-8-2 to 8-4-2	1985	Raymond Berry, New England	9-7 to 11-5
1967	John Rauch, Oakland	8-5-1 to 13-1	1986	Marty Schottenheimer, Cleveland	8-8 to 12-4
1968	Hank Stram, Kansas City	9-5 to 12-2	1987	Ron Meyer, Indianapolis	3-13 to 9-6
1969	Paul Brown, Cincinnati	3-11 to 4-9-1	1988	Marv Levy, Buffalo	7-8 to 12-4
1970	Don Shula, Miami	3-10-1 to 10-4	1989	Dan Reeves, Denver	8-8 to 11-5
1971	Don Shula, Miami	10-4 to 10-3-1	1990	Art Shell, Los Angeles	8-8 to 12-4
1972	Chuck Noll, Pittsburgh	6-8 to 11-3	1991	Dan Reeves, Denver	5-11 to 12-4
1973	John Ralston, Denver	5-9 to 7-5-2	1992	Bobby Ross, San Diego	4-12 to 11-5
1974	Sid Gillman, Houston	1-13 to 7-7	1993	Marv Levy, Buffalo	11-5 to 12-4
1975	Ted Marchibroda, Baltimore	2-12 to 10-4	1994	Bill Parcells, New England	5-11 to 10-6
1976	Chuck Fairbanks, New England	3-11 to 11-3	1995	Marty Schottenheimer, Kansas City	9-7 to 13-3
1977	Red Miller, Denver	9-5 to 12-2	1996	Tom Coughlin, Jacksonville	4-12 to 9-7
1978	Walt Michaels, New York	3-11 to 8-8			

CANADIAN FOOTBALL

The Grey Cup

Earl Grey, the Governor-General of Canada (1904-11) donated a trophy in 1909 for the Rugby Football Championship of Canada. The trophy, which later became known as the Grey Cup, was originally open to competition for teams registered with the Canada Rugby Union. Since 1954, the Cup has gone to the champion of the Canadian Football League (CFL).

Overall multiple winners: Toronto Argonauts (13); Edmonton Eskimos (11); Winnipeg Blue Bombers (9); Hamilton Tiger-Cats and Ottawa Rough Riders (7); Hamilton Tigers (5); Montreal Alouettes and University of Toronto (4); B.C. Lions, Calgary Stampeders and Queen's University (3); Ottawa Senators, Sarnia Imperials, Saskatchewan Roughriders and Toronto Balmy Beach (2).

CFL multiple winners (since 1954): Edmonton (11); Winnipeg (7); Hamilton (6); Ottawa (5); B.C. Lions, Montreal and Toronto (3); Calgary and Saskatchewan (2).

Year	Cup Final	Year	Cup Final
1909	Univ. of Toronto 26, Toronto Parkdale 6	1934	Sarnia Imperials 20, Regina Roughriders 12
1910	Univ. of Toronto 16, Hamilton Tigers 7	1935	Winnipeg 'Pegs 18, Hamilton Tigers 12
1911	Univ. of Toronto 14, Toronto Argonauts 7	1936	Sarnia Imperials 26, Ottawa Rough Riders 20
1912	Hamilton Alerts 11, Toronto Argonauts 4	1937	Toronto Argonauts 4, Winnipeg Blue Bombers 3
1913	Hamilton Tigers 44, Toronto Parkdale 2	1938	Toronto Argonauts 30, Winnipeg Blue Bombers 7
1914	Toronto Argonauts 14, Univ. of Toronto 2	1939	Winnipeg Blue Bombers 8, Ottawa Rough Riders 7
1915	Hamilton Tigers 13, Toronto Rowing 7	1940	Gm 1: Ottawa Rough Riders 8, Toronto B-Beach 2
1916-19	Not held (WWI)		Gm 2: Ottawa Rough Riders 12, Toronto B-Beach 5
1920	Univ. of Toronto 16, Toronto Argonauts 3	1941	Winnipeg Blue Bombers 18, Ottawa Rough Riders 16
1921	Toronto Argonauts 23, Edmonton Eskimos 0	1942	Toronto RACF 8, Winnipeg RACF 5
1922	Queens Univ. 13, Edmonton Elks 1	1943	Hamilton Wildcats 23, Winnipeg RACF 14
1923	Queens Univ. 54, Regina Roughriders 0	1944	Montreal HMCS 7, Hamilton Wildcats 6
1924	Queens Univ. 11, Toronto Balmy Beach 3	1945	Toronto Argonauts 35, Winnipeg Blue Bombers 0
1925	Ottawa Senators 24, Winnipeg Tigers 1	1946	Toronto Argonauts 28, Winnipeg Blue Bombers 6
1926	Ottawa Senators 10, Univ. of Toronto 7	1947	Toronto Argonauts 10, Winnipeg Blue Bombers 9
1927	Toronto Balmy Beach 9, Hamilton Tigers 6	1948	Calgary Stampeders 12, Ottawa Rough Riders 7
1928	Hamilton Tigers 30, Regina Roughriders 0	1949	Montreal Alouettes 28, Calgary Stampeders 15
1929	Hamilton Tigers 14, Regina Roughriders 3	1950	Toronto Argonauts 13, Winnipeg Blue Bombers 0
1930	Toronto Balmy Beach 11, Regina Roughriders 6	1951	Ottawa Rough Riders 21, Saskatch. Roughriders 14
1931	Montreal AAA 22, Regina Roughriders 0	1952	Toronto Argonauts 21, Edmonton Eskimos 11
1932	Hamilton Tigers 25, Regina Roughriders 6	1953	Hamilton Tiger-Cats 12, Winnipeg Blue Bombers 6
1933	Toronto Argonauts 4, Sarnia Imperials 3		

Year	Winner	Head Coach	Score	Loser	Head Coach	Site
1954	Edmonton	Frank (Pop) Ivy	26-25	Montreal	Doug Walker	Toronto
1955	Edmonton	Frank (Pop) Ivy	34-19	Montreal	Doug Walker	Vancouver
1956	Edmonton	Frank (Pop) Ivy	50-27	Montreal	Doug Walker	Toronto
1957	Hamilton	Jim Trimble	32-7	Winnipeg	Bud Grant	Toronto
1958	Winnipeg	Bud Grant	35-28	Hamilton	Jim Trimble	Vancouver
1959	Winnipeg	Bud Grant	21-7	Hamilton	Jim Trimble	Toronto
1960	Ottawa	Frank Clair	16-6	Edmonton	Eagle Keys	Vancouver

Year	Winner	Head Coach	Score	Loser	Head Coach	Site
1961	Winnipeg	Bud Grant	21-14 (OT)	Hamilton	Jim Trimble	Toronto
1962	Winnipeg	Bud Grant	28-27*	Hamilton	Jim Trimble	Toronto
1963	Hamilton	Ralph Sazio	21-10	B.C. Lions	Dave Skrien	Vancouver
1964	B.C. Lions	Dave Skrien	34-24	Hamilton	Ralph Sazio	Toronto
1965	Hamilton	Ralph Sazio	22-16	Winnipeg	Bud Grant	Toronto
1966	Saskatchewan	Eagle Keys	29-14	Ottawa	Frank Clair	Vancouver
1967	Hamilton	Ralph Sazio	24-1	Saskatchewan	Eagle Keys	Ottawa
1968	Ottawa	Frank Clair	24-21	Calgary	Jerry Williams	Toronto
1969	Ottawa	Frank Clair	29-11	Saskatchewan	Eagle Keys	Montreal
1970	Montreal	Sam Etcheverry	23-10	Calgary	Jim Duncan	Toronto
1971	Calgary	Jim Duncan	14-11	Toronto	Leo Cahill	Vancouver
1972	Hamilton	Jerry Williams	13-10	Saskatchewan	Dave Skrien	Hamilton
1973	Ottawa	Jack Gotta	22-18	Edmonton	Ray Jauch	Toronto
1974	Montreal	Marv Levy	20-7	Edmonton	Ray Jauch	Vancouver
1975	Edmonton	Ray Jauch	9-8	Montreal	Marv Levy	Calgary
1976	Ottawa	George Brancato	23-20	Saskatchewan	John Payne	Toronto
1977	Montreal	Marv Levy	41-6	Edmonton	Hugh Campbell	Montreal
1978	Edmonton	Hugh Campbell	20-13	Montreal	Joe Scannella	Toronto
1979	Edmonton	Hugh Campbell	17-9	Montreal	Joe Scannella	Montreal
1980	Edmonton	Hugh Campbell	48-10	Hamilton	John Payne	Toronto
1981	Edmonton	Hugh Campbell	26-23	Ottawa	George Brancato	Montreal
1982	Edmonton	Hugh Campbell	32-16	Toronto	Bob O'Billovich	Toronto
1983	Toronto	Bob O'Billovich	18-17	B.C. Lions	Don Matthews	Vancouver
1984	Winnipeg	Cal Murphy	47-17	Hamilton	Al Bruno	Edmonton
1985	B.C. Lions	Don Matthews	37-24	Hamilton	Al Bruno	Montreal
1986	Hamilton	Al Bruno	39-15	Edmonton	Jack Parker	Vancouver
1987	Edmonton	Joe Faragalli	38-36	Toronto	Bob O'Billovich	Vancouver
1988	Winnipeg	Mike Riley	22-21	B.C. Lions	Larry Donovan	Ottawa
1989	Saskatchewan	John Gregory	43-40	Hamilton	Al Bruno	Toronto
1990	Winnipeg	Mike Riley	50-11	Edmonton	Joe Faragalli	Vancouver
1991	Toronto	Adam Rita	36-21	Calgary	Wally Buono	Winnipeg
1992	Calgary	Wally Buono	24-10	Winnipeg	Urban Bowman	Toronto
1993	Edmonton	Ron Lancaster	33-23	Winnipeg	Cal Murphy	Calgary
1994	B.C. Lions	Dave Ritchie	26-23	Baltimore	Don Matthews	Vancouver
1995	Baltimore	Don Matthews	37-20	Calgary	Wally Buono	Regina
1996	Toronto	Don Matthews	43-37	Edmonton	Ron Lancaster	Hamilton

*Halted by fog in 4th quarter, final 9:29 played the following day.

CFL Most Outstanding Player

Regular season Player of the Year as selected by The Football Reporters of Canada since 1953.
Multiple winners: Doug Flutie (5); Russ Jackson and Jackie Parker (3); Dieter Brock, Ron Lancaster (2).

Year		Year		Year	
1953	Billy Vessels, Edmonton, RB	1968	Bill Symons, Toronto, RB	1983	Warren Moon, Edmonton, QB
1954	Sam Etcheverry, Montreal, QB	1969	Russ Jackson, Ottawa, QB	1984	Willard Reaves, Winnipeg, RB
1955	Pat Abbruzzi, Montreal, RB	1970	Ron Lancaster, Saskatch., QB	1985	Merv Fernandez, B.C. Lions, WR
1956	Hal Patterson, Montreal, E-DB	1971	Don Jonas, Winnipeg, QB	1986	James Murphy, Winnipeg, WR
1957	Jackie Parker, Edmonton, RB	1972	Garney Henley, Hamilton, WR	1987	Tom Clements, Winnipeg, QB
1958	Jackie Parker, Edmonton, RB	1973	Geo. McGowan, Edmonton, WR	1988	David Williams, B.C. Lions, WR
1959	Johnny Bright, Edmonton, RB	1974	Tom Wilkinson, Edmonton, QB	1989	Tracy Ham, Edmonton, QB
1960	Jackie Parker, Edmonton, RB	1975	Willie Burden, Calgary, RB	1990	Mike Clemons, Toronto, RB
1961	Bernie Faloney, Hamilton, QB	1976	Ron Lancaster, Saskatch., QB	1991	Doug Flutie, B.C. Lions, QB
1962	George Dixon, Montreal, RB	1977	Jimmy Edwards, Hamilton, RB	1992	Doug Flutie, Calgary, QB
1963	Russ Jackson, Ottawa, QB	1978	Tony Gabriel, Ottawa, TE	1993	Doug Flutie, Calgary, QB
1964	Lovell Coleman, Calgary, RB	1979	David Green, Montreal, QB	1994	Doug Flutie, Calgary, QB
1965	George Reed, Saskatchewan, RB	1980	Dieter Brock, Winnipeg, QB	1995	Mike Pringle, Baltimore, RB
1966	Russ Jackson, Ottawa, QB	1981	Dieter Brock, Winnipeg, QB	1996	Doug Flutie, Toronto, QB
1967	Peter Liske, Calgary, QB	1982	Condredge Holloway, Tor., QB		

CFL Most Outstanding Rookie

Regular season Rookie of the Year as selected by The Football Reporters of Canada since 1972.

Year		Year		Year	
1972	Chuck Ealey, Hamilton, QB	1981	Vince Goldsmith, Saskatch., LB	1990	Reggie Barnes, Ottawa, RB
1973	Johnny Rodgers, Montreal, WR	1982	Chris Issac, Ottawa, QB	1991	Jon Volpe, B.C. Lions, RB
1974	Sam Cvijanovich, Toronto, LB	1983	Johnny Shepherd, Hamilton, RB	1992	Mike Richardson, Winnipeg, RB
1975	Tom Clements, Ottawa, QB	1984	Dwaine Wilson, Montreal, RB	1993	Michael O'Shea, Hamilton, DT
1976	John Sciarra, B.C. Lions, QB	1985	Mike Gray, B.C. Lions, DT	1994	Matt Goodwin, Baltimore, DB
1977	Leon Bright, B.C. Lions, WR	1986	Harold Hallman, Calgary, DT	1995	Shalon Baker, Edmonton, WR
1978	Joe Poplawski, Winnipeg, WR	1987	Gill Fenerty, Toronto, RB	1996	Kelvin Anderson, Calgary, RB
1979	Brian Kelly, Edmonton, WR	1988	Orville Lee, Ottawa, RB		
1980	William Miller, Winnipeg, RB	1989	Stephen Jordan, Hamilton, DB		

CFL Most Outstanding Canadian

Regular season Canadian of the Year as selected by The Football Reporters of Canada since 1954.

Multiple winners: Tony Gabriel and Russ Jackson (4); Ray Elgaard (3); Paul Bennett, Rocky DiPietro, Terry Evanshen, Gerry James, Normie Kwong, Joe Poplawski, David Sapunjis and Jim Young (2).

Year		Year		Year	
1953	none selected	1968	Ken Nielsen, Winnipeg, FL	1983	Paul Bennett, Montreal, DB
1954	Gerry James, Winnipeg, RB	1969	Russ Jackson, Ottawa, QB	1984	Nick Arakgi, Montreal, TE
1955	Normie Kwong, Edmonton, RB	1970	Jim Young, B.C. Lions, WR	1985	Paul Bennett, Hamilton, DB
1956	Normie Kwong, Edmonton, RB	1971	Terry Evanshen, Montreal, WR	1986	Joe Poplawski, Winnipeg, SB
1957	Gerry James, Winnipeg, RB	1972	Jim Young, B.C. Lions, WR	1987	Scott Flagel, Winnipeg, S
1958	Ron Howell, Hamilton, FL	1973	Gerry Organ, Ottawa, K	1988	Ray Elgaard, Saskatchewan, SB
1959	Russ Jackson, Ottawa, QB	1974	Tony Gabriel, Hamilton, TE	1989	Rocky DiPietro, Hamilton, SB
1960	Ron Stewart, Ottawa, RB	1975	Jim Foley, Ottawa, WR	1990	Ray Elgaard, Saskatchewan, SB
1961	Tony Pajaczkowski, Calgary, DE	1976	Tony Gabriel, Ottawa, TE	1991	Blake Marshall, Edmonton, FB
1962	Harvey Wylie, Calgary, DB	1977	Tony Gabriel, Ottawa, TE	1992	Ray Elgaard, Saskatchewan, SB
1963	Russ Jackson, Ottawa, QB	1978	Tony Gabriel, Ottawa, TE	1993	David Sapunjis, Calgary, SB
1964	Tommy Grant, Hamilton, FL	1979	Dave Fennell, Edmonton, DT	1994	Gerald Wilcox, Winnipeg, SB
1965	Zeno Karcz, Hamilton, LB	1980	Gerry Dattilio, Montreal, QB	1995	David Sapunjis, Calgary, SB
1966	Russ Jackson, Ottawa, QB	1981	Joe Poplawski, Winnipeg, SB	1996	Leroy Blugh, Edmonton, DE
1967	Terry Evanshen, Calgary, WR	1982	Rocky DiPietro, Hamilton, SB		

CFL Coach of the Year

The Annis Stukus Trophy presented by the Edmonton Eskimo Alumni Association to the Coach of the Year as selected by The Football Reporters of Canada.

Multiple winners: Jack Gotta, and Don Matthews (3); Wally Buono, Ray Jauch, Cal Murphy, Bob O'Billovich and Mike Riley (2).

Year		Year		Year	
1961	Jim Trimble, Hamilton	1973	Jack Gotta, Ottawa	1985	Don Matthews, B.C. Lions
1962	Steve Owen, Saskatchewan	1974	Marv Levy, Montreal	1986	Al Bruno, Hamilton
1963	Dave Skrien, B.C. Lions	1975	George Brancato, Ottawa	1987	Bob O'Billovich, Toronto
1964	Ralph Sazio, Hamilton	1976	Bob Shaw, Hamilton	1988	Mike Riley, Winnipeg
1965	Bud Grant, Winnipeg	1977	Vic Rapp, B.C. Lions	1989	John Gregory, Sask.
1966	Frank Clair, Ottawa	1978	Jack Gotta, Calgary	1990	Mike Riley, Winnipeg
1967	Jerry Williams, Calgary	1979	Hugh Campbell, Edmonton	1991	Adam Rita, Toronto
1968	Eagle Keys, Saskatchewan	1980	Ray Jauch, Winnipeg	1992	Wally Buono, Calgary
1969	Frank Clair, Ottawa	1981	Joe Faragalli, Sask.	1993	Wally Buono, Calgary
1970	Ray Jauch, Edmonton	1982	Bob O'Billovich, Toronto	1994	Don Matthews, Baltimore
1971	Leo Cahill, Toronto	1983	Cal Murphy, Winnipeg	1995	Don Matthews, Baltimore
1972	Jack Gotta, Ottawa	1984	Cal Murphy, Winnipeg	1996	Ron Lancaster, Edmonton

All-Time CFL Leaders

Through the 1996 season. Players active in 1996 are in **bold** type.

CAREER

Passing Yards

	Yrs	Att	Cmp	Yards	Cmp %	Avg Gain	TD	Int	Rating
Ron Lancaster	19	6233	3384	50,535	54.3	14.9	333	396	72.4
Matt Dunigan	14	5476	3057	43,857	55.8	14.3	306	211	84.5
Tom Clements	12	4657	2807	39,041	60.3	13.9	252	214	86.1
Kent Austin	10	4700	2709	36,030	57.6	13.3	198	191	79.2
Doug Flutie	7	4181	2545	35,850	60.9	14.1	223	131	93.3
Dieter Brock	11	4535	2602	34,830	57.4	13.4	210	158	82.8
Damon Allen	12	4372	2289	33,558	52.4	14.7	194	163	77.0
Tom Burgess	10	4034	2118	30,308	52.5	14.3	190	191	73.1
Tracy Ham	9	3550	1871	29,048	52.7	15.5	208	123	85.2
Sam Etcheverry	7	2829	1630	25,582	57.6	15.7	183	163	85.3

Rushing

	Yrs	Car	Yards	Avg	TD
George Reed	13	3243	16,116	5.0	134
Johnny Bright	13	1969	10,909	5.5	69
Normie Kwong	13	1745	9,022	5.2	78
Leo Lewis	11	1351	8,861	6.5	48
Dave Thelen	9	1530	8,463	5.5	47

Receiving Yards

	Yrs	Ct	Yards	Avg	TD
Ray Elgaard	14	830	13,198	16.0	78
Brian Kelly	9	575	11,169	19.4	97
Tom Scott	11	649	10,837	16.7	88
Tommy Joe Coffey	14	650	10,320	15.9	63
Tony Gabriel	11	614	9,832	16.0	69

College Basketball

Arizona's **Miles Simon** savors the moment that his Wildcats defeated the Kentucky Wildcats, 84–79 in overtime, to win the 1997 NCAA Men's Basketball championship.

Wide World Photos

Penetrate and Pitch

Arizona's run to the championship was a great story. But was it great basketball?

by
Chris Fowler

A basketball floated through the airlock of the RCA Dome and landed softly in the net. Kentucky's second three-pointer in the final minute had forced overtime and not even the enormity of the place could muffle the delirium. In the too-often antiseptic atmosphere of Final Four games, all those decibels sounded delicious. Finally, an NCAA final worth savoring, a memory to be filed away forever alongside other classic moments.

Or was it?

Arizona's eventual triumph capped an unprecedented post-season joyride. The Wildcats conquered three top seeds, fabled programs Kansas, North Carolina and Kentucky. Just three days earlier, not a single member of the college hoops' media corps surveyed in a local paper had taken a walk on the Wildcats' side.

But as gritty as the 'Cats were, they weren't at all pretty. At least not in the way a beautifully played game used to be defined. All weekend the Dome became Indy's other "brickyard." Field goal percentages rarely topped forty, shots clanked and caromed everywhere, and at times only connoisseurs of long rebounds could bear to watch.

When another bunch of no-name Wildcats won their giant-killing place in history, they did it by missing only one shot in the second half. That Villanova-Georgetown final was 12 years ago—but it may as well have been fifty. Back then, the best high school prospects actually set foot on college courts—and stayed there long enough to develop personal rivalries and become promotable TV attractions, before becoming millionaires.

Chris Fowler has been the host of ESPN's college basketball coverage since 1989.

Arizona head coach **Lute Olson** holds the national championship trophy while his players celebrate their overtime victory over Kentucky on March 31, 1997 in Indianapolis.

So now, at the end of the millennium, college basketball is laid out on the examining table and the resident experts can't agree: Is the patient as robust as ever? Sick? Dying?

It's a complex diagnosis. In the hoops hotbeds, fan passion remains as pure as ever. Walk into Cameron when Carolina is in town and your two hours will be as entertaining and emotional as when Jordan, Worthy, Laettner or Hill thrilled. The front of the jerseys still read "Duke" and "North Carolina." Does it matter that the names on the back aren't as recognizable?

Yes, if you're a TV programmer. Stars sell. Networks don't promo the Lakers vs the Bulls. It's Michael against Shaq. You won't hear "Tune in to watch the PGA!" It's "Watch Tiger Woods go for another major!" But despite the numbing TV exposure, the only bankable college basketball figures are middle–aged men in sport coats. And coaches aren't captivating the casual, non-fanatics.

Neither are all of those missed shots. Show typical fans forty minutes of relentless pressing, turnovers and off-target threes and they'll probably label it "sloppy" no matter how close the final score.

College basketball is "penetrate and pitch." You win with quickness: slashing players who can beat defenders off the dribble and score, or send it to a shooter camped just beyond the arc.

There wasn't a single polished post player in the Final Four. Star centers who stick around, like Tim Duncan,

Clem Haskins (l) and **Tim Duncan** meet the press after being named AP Coach and Player of the Year respectively.

will be perhaps once-per-decade blessings. Champions aren't built around them anymore. And coaches who don't get it don't get too deep into the tournament.

It's a game for the "Young and the Raw." But that's not so bad, after all. The exuberance and fearlessness that Arizona embodied is inspiring. And maybe we can even learn to love ferocious pressing and thirty-five percent shooting.

So make your own diagnosis. At the end of the 20th century, men's college basketball is either evolving or decaying faster than any other American sport. ■

Dick Vitale's Highlights of the 1996–97 Men's College Basketball Season

10. **Coppin State, College of Charleston and Tennessee-Chattanooga**, despite having rela-

In 1997, the venerable **Dean Smith** of North Carolina moved ahead of the really venerable Adolph Rupp of Kentucky on the all-time win list of men's college basketball. Smith shocked the basketball world by announcing his retirement on October 9, 1997.

tively small programs, surprise the country by delivering big performances in the NCAA tourney.

9. Duke's **Mike Krzyzewski** delivers the nation's #1 recruiting class.

8. **Keith Van Horn** caps a brilliant career at Utah and retires as the all time leading scorer in the WAC.

7. Senior guard **Wes Flanigan** of Auburn, "Mr. Courage," beats cancer and plays all year.

6. Minnesota's **Clem Haskins** finally wins National Coach of the Year honors.

5. The **Kansas Jayhawks** put in a magnificent year, going 34–2 and making the Sweet Sixteen.

4. Coach **Don Haskins** of the University of Texas at El Paso is inducted in the basketball Hall of Fame.

3. **Tim Duncan** says no to the NBA and then wins all the awards as the #1 player in the country.

2. **Dean Smith** of the University of North Carolina surpasses Adolph Rupp of Kentucky as the all-time winningest coach in college basketball.

1. **Lute Olson and the Arizona Wildcats**, a #4 seed, win the NCAA title by becoming the first team to beat three #1 seeds (Kansas, North Carolina and Kentucky) on the way to the title. ∎

by
Michael Freer, Pete McConville and Craig Wachs

WHAT **MISMATCH**?

Arizona entered the national championship game a sizable underdog. A quick look at each team's numbers entering the game told a different story.

	Kentucky	Arizona
Points Per Game	83.2	83.8
Field Goal Pct.	47.2	45.5
3-Pt. FG Pct.	37.1	36.8
Rebounds Per Game	36.8	36.6
Turnovers Per Game	14.7	15.2

MARGIN OF **VICTORY**

Since the tournament was expanded to 64 teams, these national champions have had the smallest average margin of victory. While Arizona's margin of victory is second to Villanova's, this year's champs had the tougher road. None of Arizona's wins were by dou-

ble digits and two of its last three wins came in overtime.

	Avg. Margin of Victory	Double Digit Ws in Tourney
Villanova '85	5.0	1
Arizona '97	**5.3**	**0**
Kansas '88	7.8	2
Michigan '89	9.8	1

BIG **LEAST**

In 1997, Boston College won the Big East men's basketball tournament championship. Teams winning that title have not fared well in the NCAAs in recent years and the Eagles were no different.

Big East busts in the NCAAs (year)

	School	Result
1997	**Boston College**	**Out-2nd round**
1996	Connecticut	Out-3rd round
1995	Villanova	Out-1st round
1994	Providence	Out-1st round
1993	Seton Hall	Out-2nd round
1992	Syracuse	Out-2nd round

ISN'T THIS **ODD**?

1997 marked the fourth time this decade that Smith took his Tar Heels to the Final Four in an odd year. Even-year tournaments have not been nearly as nice. NC has never made it past the Sweet Sixteen in an even year in the 90's and lost in the second round in 1994 and 1996. Smith's tournament record in odd years this decade is a sparkling 18–2 but his even year record is a comparatively dusty 6–4. Maybe this even year tendency was part of what caused Smith to retire. Maybe not. So long, coach.

North Carolina in the Regional Finals in the 90's

	Result
1997	Defeated Louisville, 97-74
1995	Defeated Kentucky, 74-64
1993	Defeated Cincinnati, 75-68*
1991	Defeated Temple, 75-72

*Won National Championship ∎

COLLEGE BASKETBALL

S T A T I S T I C S

SEC
A

THE 1998

ESPN
INFORMATION PLEASE
SPORTS
ALMANAC

THE SEASON IN REVIEW

1996-1997

TOP 25 • NCAA'S • STANDINGS

PAGE
281

Final Regular Season AP Men's Top 25 Poll

Taken **before** start of NCAA tournament.

The sportswriters & broadcasters poll: first place votes in parentheses; records through Monday, March 10, 1997; total points (based on 25 for 1st, 24 for 2nd, etc.); record in NCAA tourney and team lost to; head coach (career years and record including 1997 postseason), and preseason ranking. Teams in **bold** type went on to reach NCAA Final Four.

		Mar. 10 Record	Points	NCAA Recap	Head Coach	Preseason Rank
1	Kansas (70)	32-1	1,750	2-1 (Arizona)	Roy Williams (9 yrs: 247-58)	2
2	Utah	26-3	1,578	3-1 (Kentucky)	Rick Majerus (13 yrs: 279-107)	6
3	**Minnesota**	27-3	1,571	4-1 (Kentucky)	Clem Haskins (17 yrs: 302-214)	22
4	**North Carolina**	24-6	1,566	4-1 (Arizona)	Dean Smith (36 yrs: 879-254)	8
5	**Kentucky**	30-4	1,559	5-1 (Arizona)	Rick Pitino (15 yrs: 352-124)	3
6	South Carolina	24-7	1,365	0-1 (Coppin St.)	Eddie Fogler (11 yrs: 204-36)	29
7	UCLA	21-7	1,343	3-1 (Minnesota)	Steve Lavin (1 yr: 24-8)	5
8	Duke	23-8	1,245	1-1 (Providence)	Mike Krzyzewski (22 yrs: 473-208)	10
9	Wake Forest	23-6	1,223	1-1 (Stanford)	Dave Odom (11 yrs: 204-121)	4
10	Cincinnati	25-7	1,014	1-1 (Iowa St.)	Bob Huggins (16 yrs: 360-143)	1
11	New Mexico	24-7	949	1-1 (Louisville)	Dave Bliss (22 yrs: 415-254)	17
12	St. Joseph's-PA	24-6	856	2-1 (Kentucky)	Phil Martelli (2 yrs: 45-20)	NR
13	Xavier-OH	22-5	765	1-1 (UCLA)	Skip Prosser (4 yrs: 76-39)	NR
14	Clemson	21-9	713	2-1 (Minnesota)	Rick Barnes (10 yrs: 184-120)	20
15	**Arizona**	19-9	654	6-0	Lute Olsen (24 yrs: 533-202)	19
16	Coll. of Charleston	28-2	599	1-1 (Arizona)	John Kresse (18 yrs: 441-112)	55
17	Georgia	24-8	524	0-1 (Tenn-Chattanooga)	Tubby Smith (6 yrs: 124-62)	NR
18	Iowa State	20-8	485	2-1 (UCLA)	Tim Floyd (11 yrs: 231-112)	11
19	Illinois	21-9	437	1-1 (Tenn-Chattanooga)	Lon Kruger (15 yrs: 259-195)	31
20	Villanova	23-9	387	1-1 (California)	Steve Lappas (9 yrs: 159-118)	7
21	Stanford	20-7	371	2-1 (Utah)	Mike Montgomery (19 yrs: 358-205)	18
22	Maryland	21-10	344	0-1 (Coll. of Charleston)	Gary Williams (19 yrs: 350-229)	NR
23	Boston College	21-8	255	1-1 (St. Joseph's)	Jim O'Brien (15 yrs: 235-217)	21
24	Colorado	21-9	244	1-1 (N. Carolina)	Ricardo Patton (2 yrs: 26-19)	NR
25	Louisville	23-8	226	3-1 (N. Carolina)	Denny Crum (26 yrs: 613-233)	28

Others receiving votes: 26. **Tulsa** (23-9) 128 pts; 27. **California** (21-8) and **Marquette** (22-8) 99; 29. **Iowa** (20-9) 89; 30. **Princeton** (23-3) 79; 31. **Indiana** (22-10) 55; 32. **NC-Charlotte** (21-8) 42; 33. **Wisconsin** (18-9) 35; 34. **Pacific** (22-5) 18; 36. **Mississippi** (19-8) 17; 37. **Purdue** (17-11) 13; 38. **Rhode Island** (20-9) 13; 39. **Georgetown** (19-9) 8; 40. **Texas Christian** (21-12) 7; 41. **N.C. State** (15-14) 6; 42. **South Alabama** (21-6) 5; 43. **Boston University** (25-4) and **St. Mary's-CA** (21-7) 4; 45. **Hawaii** (20-7) and **Illinois State** (24-5) 2; 47. **Long Island University** (21-8) and **Navy** (18-8) 1.

NCAA Men's Division I Tournament Seeds

	WEST		MIDWEST		SOUTHEAST		EAST
1	Kentucky (30-4)	1	Minnesota (27-3)	1	Kansas (32-1)	1	N. Carolina (24-6)
2	Utah (26-3)	2	UCLA (19-7)	2	Duke (23-8)	2	S. Carolina (24-7)
3	Wake Forest (23-6)	3	Cincinnati (25-7)	3	Georgia (24-8)	3	New Mexico (24-7)
4	St. Joseph's-PA (24-6)	4	Clemson (21-9)	4	Arizona (19-9)	4	Villanova (23-9)
5	Boston College (21-8)	5	Tulsa (23-9)	5	Maryland (21-10)	5	California (21-8)
6	Stanford (20-7)	6	Iowa St. (20-8)	6	Illinois (21-9)	6	Louisville (23-8)
7	NC-Charlotte (21-8)	7	Xavier-OH (22-5)	7	Marquette (22-8)	7	Wisconsin (18-9)
8	Iowa (21-9)	8	Mississippi (20-8)	8	Purdue (17-11)	8	Indiana (22-10)
9	Virginia (18-12)	9	Temple (19-10)	9	Rhode Island (20-9)	9	Colorado (21-9)
10	Georgetown (20-9)	10	Vanderbilt (19-11)	10	Providence (21-11)	10	Texas (16-11)
11	Oklahoma (19-10)	11	Illinois St. (24-5)	11	USC (17-10)	11	UMass (19-13)
12	Valparaiso (24-6)	12	Boston Univ. (25-4)	12	Coll. of Charleston (28-2)	12	Princeton (24-3)
13	Pacific (24-5)	13	Miami-OH (21-8)	13	S. Alabama (23-6)	13	Long Island U. (21-8)
14	St. Mary's-CA (23-7)	14	Butler (23-9)	14	Tenn.-Chattanooga (22-10)	14	Old Dominion (22-10)
15	Navy (20-8)	15	Charleston Southern (17-12)	15	Coppin St. (21-8)	15	Murray St. (20-9)
16	Montana (21-10)	16	S.W. Texas St. (16-12)	16	Jackson St. (14-15)	16	Fairfield (11-18)

1997 NCAA BASKETBALL MEN'S DIVISION I

EAST

FIRST ROUND (March 13-14)

- 1 N. Carolina 92
- 16 Fairfield 74
- 8 Indiana 62
- 9 Colorado 80
- 5 California 55
- 12 Princeton 52
- 4 Villanova 101
- 13 Long Island U. 91
- 6 Louisville 65
- 11 UMass 57
- 3 New Mexico 59
- 14 Old Dominion 55
- 7 Wisconsin 58
- 10 Texas 71
- 2 S. Carolina 65
- 15 Coppin St. 78

SECOND ROUND (March 15-16)

- N. Carolina 73 / Colorado 56
- California 75 / Villanova 68
- Louisville 64 / New Mexico 63
- Texas 82 / Coppin St. 81

REGIONALS (March 20-21) — SYRACUSE

- N. Carolina 63 / California 57
- Louisville 78 / Texas 63
- N. Carolina 97 / Louisville 74
- N. Carolina 58

SOUTHEAST

FIRST ROUND (March 13-14)

- 1 Kansas 78
- 16 Jackson St. 64
- 8 Purdue (OT) 83
- 9 Rhode Island 76
- 5 Maryland 66
- 12 Coll. of Charleston 75
- 4 Arizona 65
- 13 S. Alabama 57
- 6 Illinois 90
- 11 USC 77
- 3 Georgia 70
- 14 Tenn.-Chat. 73
- 7 Marquette 59
- 10 Providence 81
- 2 Duke 71
- 15 Murray St. 68

SECOND ROUND (March 15-16)

- Kansas 75 / Purdue 61
- Coll. of Charleston 69 / Arizona 73
- Illinois 63 / Tenn.-Chat. 75
- Providence 98 / Duke 87

REGIONALS (March 20-21) — BIRMINGHAM

- Kansas 82 / Arizona 85
- Tenn.-Chat. 65 / Providence 71
- Arizona 96 (OT) / Providence 92
- Arizona 66

MIDWEST

FIRST ROUND (March 13-14)

- 1 Minnesota 78
- 16 SW. Texas 46
- 8 Mississippi 40
- 9 Temple 62
- 5 Tulsa 82
- 12 Boston U. 52
- 4 Clemson 68
- 13 Miami OH 56
- 6 Iowa St. 69
- 11 Illinois St. 57
- 3 Cincinnati 86
- 14 Butler 69
- 7 Xavier 80
- 10 Vanderbilt 68
- 2 UCLA 109
- 15 Charleston So. 75

SECOND ROUND (March 15-16)

- Minnesota 90 (OT) / Temple 57
- Tulsa 59 / Clemson 84
- Iowa St. 67 / Cincinnati 66
- Xavier 83 / UCLA 96

REGIONALS (March 20-21) — SAN ANTONIO

- Minnesota 80 / Clemson 84
- Iowa St. 73 / UCLA 74 (OT)
- Minnesota 80 / UCLA 72
- Minnesota 69

WEST

FIRST ROUND (March 13-14)

- 1 Kentucky 92
- 16 Montana 54
- 8 Iowa 73
- 9 Virginia 60
- 5 Boston Coll. 73
- 12 Valparaiso 66
- 4 St. Joseph's 75
- 13 Pacific 65
- 6 Stanford 80
- 11 Oklahoma 67
- 3 Wake Forest 68
- 14 St. Mary's 46
- 7 NC Charlotte 79
- 10 Georgetown 67
- 2 Utah 75
- 15 Navy 61

SECOND ROUND (March 15-16)

- Kentucky 75 / Iowa 69
- Boston Coll. 77 / St. Joseph's 81 (OT)
- Stanford 72 / Wake Forest 66
- NC Charlotte 58 / Utah 77

REGIONALS (March 20-21) — SAN JOSE

- Kentucky 83 / St. Joseph's 68
- Stanford 77 / Utah 82 (OT)
- Kentucky 72 / Utah 59
- Kentucky 78

NATIONAL CHAMPIONSHIP

- Arizona 84
- Kentucky 79

FINAL FOUR
at the RCA Dome
in Indianapolis
•••
Semifinals: March 29
Finals: March 31

NCAA Men's Championship Game

59th NCAA Division I Championship Game. **Date:** Monday, March 31, at the RCA Dome. **Coaches:** Lute Olson of Arizona and Rick Pitino of Kentucky. **Favorite:** Kentucky by 7.

Attendance: 47,028; **Officials:** Tim Higgins, Ted Valentine, Tom O'Neil; **TV Rating:** 18.9/31 share (CBS).

Arizona 84

	Min	FG M-A	FT M-A	Pts	Reb O-T	A	PF
Bennett Davison .	29	3-9	3-3	9	4-7	0	2
Michael Dickerson .	24	1-8	2-2	5	2-4	0	0
A.J. Bramlett	27	1-3	1-1	3	3-6	1	5
Mike Bibby	38	5-12	6-6	19	2-9	4	1
Miles Simon	40	8-18	14-17	30	1-3	1	1
Jason Terry	33	2-6	2-2	8	0-2	5	1
Eugene Edgerson .	15	0-0	2-2	2	0-5	0	2
Donnell Harris ...	19	2-2	4-8	8	4-7	1	4
TOTALS	225	22-58	34-41	84	16-43	12	16

Three-point FG: 6–13 (Dickerson 1–3, Bibby 3–5, Simon 0–2, Terry 2–3); **Team Rebounds:** 2; **Blocked Shots:** 2 (Bramlett 2); **Turnovers:** 18 (Bibby 8, Simon 3, Davison 2, Dickerson 2, Edgerson 2, Bramlett); **Steals:** 7 (Bibby 3, Terry 3, Bramlett). **Percentages:** 2-Pt FG (.356), 3-Pt FG (.462), Total FG (.379), Free Throws (.829).

Kentucky 79

	Min	FG M-A	FT M-A	Pts	Reb O-T	A	PF
Ron Mercer	41	5-9	1-1	13	5-9	6	5
Scott Padgett	30	5-16	4-4	17	0-1	0	5
Jamaal Magloire ..	14	0-1	0-0	0	3-4	1	4
Wayne Turner ...	28	4-9	0-1	8	1-4	5	5
Anthony Epps ...	38	4-13	0-0	11	0-5	4	0
Allen Edwards ...	5	0-0	0-0	0	0-0	0	0
Jared Prickett	21	1-4	4-5	6	1-5	1	5
Nazr Mohammed ..	25	6-11	0-6	12	7-11	0	3
Cameron Mills ...	22	5-9	0-0	12	0-1	1	2
Stephen Masiello .	1	0-0	0-0	0	0-0	0	0
TOTALS	225	30-72	9-17	79	17-40	18	29

Three-point FG: 10–30 (Mercer 2–4, Padgett 3–12, Epps 3–8, Mills 2–6); **Team Rebounds:** none; **Blocked Shots:** 7 (Mohammed 3, Magloire 2, Turner, Prickett); **Turnovers:** 16 (Mercer 5, Padgett 3, Mohammed 2, Prickett 2, Turner 2, Edwards, Magloire); **Steals:** 9 (Epps 2, Padgett 2, Prickett 2, Mercer, Mills, Turner); **Percentages:** 2-Pt FG (.476), 3-Pt FG (.333), Total FG (.417), Free Throws (.529).

Arizona (Pacific-10)	....	33	41	10—	**84**
Kentucky (SEC)	....	32	42	5—	**79**

THE FINAL FOUR

RCA Dome in Indianapolis (Mar. 29-31).

Most Outstanding Player

Miles Simon, Arizona junior guard. SEMIFINAL—36 minutes, 24 points, 5 rebounds, 5 assists; FINAL—40 minutes, 30 points, 3 rebounds, 1 assist.

All-Tournament Team

Simon and guard Mike Bibby of Arizona, forwards Ron Mercer and Scott Padgett of Kentucky and guard Bobby Jackson of Minnesota.

Semifinal—Game One

Southeast Regional champ Arizona vs. East Regional champ North Carolina; Saturday, Mar. 29 (5:42 p.m. tipoff). **Coaches:** Lute Olson, Arizona and Dean Smith, North Carolina. **Favorite:** North Carolina by 5½.

Arizona (Pac-10)	....	34	32—	**66**
N. Carolina (ACC)	....	31	27—	**58**

High scorers— Miles Simon, Arizona (24) and Vince Carter, N. Carolina (21); **Att**— 47,028; **TV rating**— 9.9/23 share (CBS).

Semifinal—Game Two

Midwest Regional champion Minnesota vs. West Regional champion Kentucky; Saturday, Mar. 29 (8:07 p.m. tipoff). **Coaches:** Clem Haskins, Minnesota and Rick Pitino, Kentucky. **Favorite:** Kentucky by 6½.

Minnesota (Big Ten)	....	31	38—	**69**
Kentucky (SEC)	....	36	42—	**78**

High scorers— Bobby Jackson, Minnesota (23) and Ron Mercer, Kentucky (19); **Att**— 47,028; **TV rating**— 12.5/23 share (CBS).

Final USA Today/CNN Coaches Poll

Taken **after** NCAA Tournament.

Voted on by a panel of 30 Division I head coaches following the NCAA tournament: first place votes in parentheses with total points (based on 25 for 1st, 24 for 2nd, etc.). Schools on major probation are ineligible to be ranked.

		W-L	Pts	Before NCAAs W-L	Rank
1	Arizona (30)	25-9	750	19-9	13
2	Kentucky	35-5	719	30-4	4
3	Minnesota	31-4	675	27-3	3
4	North Carolina	28-7	653	24-6	5
5	Kansas	34-2	642	32-1	1
6	Utah	29-4	594	26-3	2
7	UCLA	24-8	551	21-7	7
8	Clemson	23-10	437	21-9	12
9	Wake Forest	24-7	432	23-6	9
10	Louisville	26-9	394	23-8	25
11	Duke	24-9	387	23-8	8
12	Stanford	22-8	365	20-7	21
13	Iowa St.	22-9	356	20-8	17
14	South Carolina	24-8	320	24-7	6
15	Providence	24-12	300	21-11	NR
16	Cincinnati	26-8	295	25-7	10
17	St. Joseph's-PA	26-7	283	24-6	15
18	California	25-9	242	23-8	NR
19	New Mexico	25-8	179	24-7	11
20	Texas	18-12	174	16-11	NR
21	Coll. of Charleston ..	29-3	167	28-2	18
22	Xavier-OH	23-6	142	22-5	14
23	Boston College	22-9	98	21-8	20
24	Michigan	23-11	92	18-11	NR
25	Colorado	22-10	81	21-9	23

Others receiving votes: 26. **Iowa** (22-10, 67 pts) and **Villanova** (24-10, 67); 28. **Tennessee-Chattanooga** (24-11, 60); 29. **Illinois** (22-10, 39); 30. **Georgia** (24-9, 38); 31. **Tulsa** (24-10, 35); 32. **Maryland** (21-11, 26); 33. **Purdue** (18-12, 21); 34. **Florida St.** (runner-up NIT, 20-12, 17); 35. **Marquette** (22-9, 12); 36. **Coppin St.** (22-9, 9); 37. **Rhode Island** (20-10, 7) and **Temple** (20-11, 7); 39. **Mississippi** (20-9, 5); 40. **Wisconsin** (18-10, 3); 41. **UNC-Charlotte** (22-9, 2), **Oklahoma** (19-11, 2) and **Princeton** (24-4, 2); 44. **Hawaii** (21-8, 1), **Illinois St.** (24-6, 1) and **Indiana** (22-11, 1).

NCAA Finalists' Tournament and Season Statistics

At least 10 games played during the overall season.

ARIZONA (25-9)

| | NCAA TOURNAMENT | | | | | OVERALL SEASON | | | | |
| | | | —Per Game— | | | | | | —Per Game— | | |
	Gm	FG%	TPts	Pts	Reb	Ast	Gm	FG%	TPts	Pts	Reb	Ast
Miles Simon	6	.462	132	22.0	4.0	3.2	23	.455	424	18.4	4.1	4.2
Mike Bibby	6	.456	108	18.0	4.8	3.3	34	.445	458	13.5	3.2	5.2
Michael Dickerson	6	.321	65	10.8	1.2	3.5	34	.412	642	18.9	4.5	1.5
A.J. Bramlett	6	.465	50	8.3	10.3	1.3	33	.529	266	8.1	6.9	0.6
Jason Terry	6	.394	46	7.7	1.7	2.8	34	.443	360	10.6	2.7	4.4
Bennett Davison	6	.444	40	6.7	6.8	1.0	34	.500	329	9.7	6.4	0.9
Donnell Harris	5	.556	17	3.4	4.2	0.5	33	.484	196	5.9	5.8	0.5
Eugene Edgerson	6	.333	11	1.8	3.2	0.2	33	.408	89	2.7	3.7	0.2
Jason Lee	0	—	—	—	—	—	19	.415	62	3.3	1.8	0.6
ARIZONA	6	.423	469	78.2	41.0	13.5	34	.453	2850	83.8	40.5	16.7
OPPONENTS	6	.406	437	72.8	41.7	15.7	34	.436	2491	73.3	38.2	15.8

Three-pointers: NCAA TOURNAMENT— Bibby (18-37), Simon (10-30), Terry (5-17), Dickerson (5-28), Team (38-112 for .339 pct.); OVERALL— Bibby (67-170), Dickerson (55-166), Simon (45-111), Terry (40-121), Lee (12-26), Stewart (2-2), Pastner (1-3), Bramlett (0-1), Team (222-600 for .370 pct.).

KENTUCKY (35-5)

| | NCAA TOURNAMENT | | | | | OVERALL SEASON | | | | |
| | | | —Per Game— | | | | | | —Per Game— | | |
	Gm	FG%	TPts	Pts	Reb	Ast	Gm	FG%	TPts	Pts	Reb	Ast
Ron Mercer	6	.492	98	16.3	5.3	2.2	40	.493	725	18.1	5.3	2.4
Wayne Turner	6	.455	76	12.7	3.0	4.5	40	.467	264	6.6	2.7	3.0
Cameron Mills	6	.615	71	11.8	1.7	1.0	31	.538	183	5.9	1.2	0.7
Scott Padgett	6	.407	66	11.0	4.2	1.5	32	.410	308	9.6	5.1	1.8
Anthony Epps	6	.275	54	9.0	4.2	5.3	40	.393	356	8.9	3.2	4.8
Jaren Prickett	6	.543	52	8.7	7.2	2.0	38	.550	300	7.9	5.9	2.1
Nazr Mohammed	6	.568	47	7.8	6.3	0.2	39	.510	309	7.9	5.8	0.3
Derek Anderson	1	.000	2	2.0	0.0	0.0	19	.491	337	17.7	4.1	3.5
Allen Edwards	4	.400	6	1.5	0.5	0.0	38	.424	328	8.6	3.2	2.9
Jamaal Magloire	6	.375	7	1.2	2.3	0.2	40	.490	195	4.9	4.4	0.4
Steve Masiello	2	.000	0	0.0	0.5	0.0	23	.240	20	0.9	0.4	0.2
KENTUCKY	6	.462	479	79.8	36.8	16.8	40	.471	3325	83.1	39.4	19.4
OPPONENTS	6	.395	403	67.2	37.5	11.2	40	.398	2512	62.8	34.2	12.1

Three-pointers: NCAA TOURNAMENT— Mills (17-27), Padgett (12-34), Epps (10-33), Mercer (6-19), Edwards (1-3), Prickett (0-2), Turner (0-2), Team (46-120 for .383 pct.); OVERALL— Epps (69-178), Mercer (49-141), Padgett (47-138), Mills (42-79), Anderson (38-94), Edwards (32-109), Prickett (5-12), Turner (4-15) Masiello (1-9), Mohammed (0-2), Team (287-777 for .369 pct.).

Arizona's Schedule

Reg. Season (19-9)

W	at N. Carolina .	83-72
W	N. Arizona	88-70
L	at N. Mexico	77-84
W	at Utah	69-61
W	Texas	83-78
W	Jackson St.	111-83
L	at Michigan	71-73
W	Robert Morris .	118-54
W	Pennsylvania ...	93-51
W	California	81-80
W	Stanford	76-75
W	at Arizona St. .	92-84
L	at USC	62-75
L	at UCLA (OT) ..	78-84
W	Oregon St.	99-48
W	Oregon	88-66
W	at Wash. St.	87-78
L	at Washington ..	88-92
W	Arizona St. ...	87-71
L	at Tulane	81-62
L	UCLA	64-66
W	USC	101-77
L	at Oregon	72-78
W	at Oregon St. ..	74-64
L	at Wash. St.	100-86
W	at Washington ..	103-82
L	at Stanford	80-81
L	at California ...	77-79

NCAA Tourney (6-0)

W	S. Alabama	65-57
W	College of Charleston .	73-69
W	Kansas	85-82
W	Providence (OT)	96-92
W	N. Carolina ...	66-58
W	Kentucky (OT) .	84-79

Kentucky's Schedule

Reg. Season (27-4)

L	Clemson (OT) .	71-79
W	at Syracuse ...	87-53
W	Alaska-Anchorage ..	104-72
W	College of Charleston ..	87-66
W	at Purdue	101-87
W	Indiana	99-65
W	Wright St.	90-62
W	Notre Dame ...	80-56
W	at GA Tech	88-59
W	UNC-Asheville .	105-51
W	at Ohio St.	81-65
W	at Louisville ...	74-54
W	Tennessee	74-40
W	Mississippi St..	90-61
W	Canisius	68-45
L	at Mississippi ..	69-73
W	at Georgia	86-65
W	Auburn	77-53
W	at Vanderbilt ..	58-46
W	at Arkansas ...	83-73
W	at Florida	92-65
W	Georgia	82-57
L	at S. Car. (OT) .	79-84
W	S. Carolina	82-55
W	Villanova	93-56
W	LSU	84-48
W	Florida	85-56
W	at Alabama ...	75-61
W	at Vanderbilt ..	82-79
W	at Tennessee ..	74-64
L	S. Carolina	66-72

SEC Tourney (3-0)

W	Auburn	92-50
W	Mississippi	88-70
W	Georgia	95-68

NCAA Tourney (5-1)

W	Montana	92-54
W	Iowa	75-69
W	St. Joseph's-PA .	83-68
W	Utah	72-59
W	Minnesota	78-69
L	Arizona (OT) ..	79-84

Final NCAA Men's Division I Standings

Conference records include regular season games only. Overall records include all postseason tournament games.

America East Conference

Team	Conference			Overall		
	W	L	Pct	W	L	Pct
*Boston University ...	17	1	.944	25	5	.833
†Drexel	16	2	.889	22	9	.710
Hartford	11	7	.611	17	11	.607
Hofstra	9	9	.500	12	15	.444
Delaware	8	10	.444	15	16	.484
Vermont	7	11	.389	14	13	.519
Northeastern	6	12	.333	7	20	.259
Maine	6	12	.333	11	20	.355
New Hampshire	5	13	.278	7	20	.259
Towson St.	5	13	.278	9	19	.321

Conf. Tourney Final: Boston University 68, Drexel 61.
*NCAA Tourney (0-1): Boston University (0-1).
†NIT (0-1): Drexel (0-1).

Atlantic Coast Conference

Team	Conference			Overall		
	W	L	Pct	W	L	Pct
*Duke	12	4	.750	24	9	.727
*Wake Forest	11	5	.688	24	7	.774
*North Carolina	11	5	.688	28	7	.800
*Clemson	9	7	.563	23	10	.697
*Maryland	9	7	.563	21	11	.656
*Virginia	7	9	.438	18	13	.581
†Florida St.	6	10	.375	20	12	.625
†N.C. State	4	12	.250	17	15	.531
Georgia Tech	3	13	.188	9	18	.333

Conf. Tourney Final: North Carolina 64, N.C. State 54.
*NCAA Tourney (8-6): N. Carolina (4-1), Clemson (2-1), Duke (1-1), Wake Forest (1-1), Maryland (0-1), Virginia (0-1).
†NIT (5-2): Florida St. (4-1, runners-up), N.C. State (1-1)

Atlantic 10 Conference

East	Conference			Overall		
	W	L	Pct	W	L	Pct
*St. Joseph's-PA	13	3	.813	26	7	.788
*Rhode Island	12	4	.750	20	10	.667
*Massachusetts	11	5	.688	19	14	.543
*Temple	10	6	.625	20	11	.645
St. Bonaventure	5	11	.313	14	14	.500
Fordham	1	15	.063	6	21	.222

West	Conference			Overall		
	W	L	Pct	W	L	Pct
*Xavier-OH	13	3	.813	23	6	.793
†Geo. Washington ...	8	8	.500	15	14	.517
Virginia Tech	7	9	.438	15	16	.484
Dayton	6	10	.375	13	14	.482
Duquesne	5	11	.313	9	18	.333
La Salle	5	11	.313	10	17	.370

Note: There are 12 teams in the Atlantic 10.
Conf. Tourney Final: St. Joseph's-PA 61, Rhode Island 56.
*NCAA Tourney (4-5): St. Joseph's-PA (2-1), Xavier (1-1), Temple (1-1), Massachusetts (0-1), Rhode Island (0-1).
†NIT Tourney (0-1): Geo. Washington (0-1).

Big East Conference

Big East 7	Conference			Overall		
	W	L	Pct	W	L	Pct
*Georgetown	11	7	.611	20	10	.667
*Providence	10	8	.556	24	12	.667
†Pittsburgh	10	8	.556	18	15	.545
†Syracuse	9	9	.500	19	13	.594
†Miami-FL	9	9	.500	16	13	.552
Rutgers	5	13	.278	11	16	.407
Seton Hall	5	13	.278	10	18	.357

Big East 6	Conference			Overall		
	W	L	Pct	W	L	Pct
*Villanova	12	6	.667	24	10	.706
*Boston College	12	6	.667	22	9	.710
†West Virginia	11	7	.611	21	10	.677
†Notre Dame	8	10	.444	16	14	.533
St. John's	8	10	.444	13	14	.481
†Connecticut	7	11	.389	18	15	.545

Conf. Tourney Final: Boston College 70, Villanova 58
*NCAA Tourney (5-4): Providence (3-1), Boston College (1-1), Villanova (1-1), Georgetown (0-1).
†NIT Tourney (9-6): Connecticut (4-1), Notre Dame (2-1), W. Virginia (2-1), Pittsburgh (1-1), Syracuse (0-1), Miami (0-1).

Big Sky Conference

Team	Conference			Overall		
	W	L	Pct	W	L	Pct
†Northern Arizona ...	14	2	.875	21	7	.750
*Montana	11	5	.688	21	11	.656
Montana St	10	6	.625	16	14	.533
Weber St	9	7	.563	15	13	.536
Idaho St	9	7	.563	14	13	.519
Cal St.-Northridge ..	8	8	.500	14	15	.483
Portland St.	6	10	.375	9	17	.346
Eastern Washington .	3	13	.188	7	19	.269
Cal St.-Sacramento ..	2	14	.125	3	23	.115

Conf. Tourney Final: Montana 82, Cal St.-Northridge 79
*NCAA Tourney (0-1): Montana (0-1).
†NIT Tourney (0-1): N. Arizona (0-1).

Big South Conference

Team	Conference			Overall		
	W	L	Pct	W	L	Pct
NC-Asheville	11	3	.785	18	10	.643
Liberty	11	3	.785	23	9	.719
Radford	8	6	.571	15	13	.536
*Charleston Southern .	7	7	.500	17	13	.567
Coastal Carolina ...	6	8	.428	11	16	.407
NC-Greensboro	6	8	.428	10	20	.333
Winthrop	5	9	.357	12	15	.444
MD-Balt. County	2	12	.142	5	22	.185

Conf. Tourney Final: Charleston Southern 64, Liberty 54
*NCAA Tourney (0-1): Charleston Southern (0-1).

Final NCAA Men's Division I Standings (Cont.)

Big Ten Conference

Team	Conference W	L	Pct	Overall W	L	Pct
*Minnesota	16	2	.889	31	4	.886
*Iowa	12	6	.667	22	10	.688
*Purdue	12	6	.667	18	12	.600
*Illinois	11	7	.611	22	10	.688
*Wisconsin	11	7	.611	18	10	.643
*Indiana	9	9	.500	22	11	.667
†Michigan	9	9	.500	24	11	.686
†Michigan St	9	9	.500	17	12	.586
Ohio St	5	13	.278	10	17	.370
Penn St	3	15	.167	10	17	.370
Northwestern	2	16	.111	7	22	.241

Note: There are 11 teams in the Big 10.

Conf. Tourney Final: Historically, the Big Ten has had no men's basketball tournament. However, the conference has announced it will stage a men's tournament beginning with the 1997-98 season.

*NCAA Tourney (7-6): Minnesota (4-1), Iowa (1-1), Purdue (1-1), Illinois (1-1), Wisconsin (0-1), Indiana (0-1).

†NIT Tourney (6-1): Michigan (5-0, NIT champions), Michigan St. (1-1).

Big 12 Conference

Team	Conference W	L	Pct	Overall W	L	Pct
*Kansas	15	1	.938	34	2	.944
*Colorado	11	5	.688	22	10	.688
*Texas	10	6	.625	18	12	.600
*Iowa St.	10	6	.625	22	9	.710
Texas Tech	10	6	.625	19	9	.679
*Oklahoma	9	7	.563	19	11	.633
†Nebraska	7	9	.438	18	15	.545
†Oklahoma St.	7	9	.438	17	15	.531
Baylor	6	10	.375	18	12	.600
Missouri	5	11	.312	16	17	.485
Texas A&M	3	13	.188	9	18	.333
Kansas St	3	13	.188	10	17	.370

Note: Texas Tech forfeited all 10 conference wins after discovering that two players (junior Gracen Averil and senior Deuce Jones) were ineligible.

Conf. Tourney Final: Kansas 87, Missouri 60

*NCAA Tourney (7-5): Kansas (2-1), Iowa St. (2-1), Texas (2-1), Colorado (1-1), Oklahoma (0-1).

†NIT Tourney (3-2): Nebraska (2-1), Oklahoma St. (1-1).

Big West Conference

Team	Conference W	L	Pct	Overall W	L	Pct
†Nevada	12	4	.750	21	10	.677
Utah St	12	4	.750	20	9	.690
New Mexico St	12	4	.750	19	9	.679
Boise St.	9	7	.563	14	13	.519
Idaho	5	11	.313	13	17	.433
North Texas	5	11	.313	10	16	.385

Team	Conference W	L	Pct	Overall W	L	Pct
*Pacific	12	4	.750	24	6	.800
Long Beach St	9	7	.563	13	14	.481
UC-Santa Barbara	7	9	.438	12	15	.444
Cal St.-Fullerton	6	10	.375	13	14	.481
Cal Poly-SLO	6	10	.375	14	16	.467
UC-Irvine	1	15	.063	1	25	.038

Conf. Tourney Final: Pacific 63, Nevada 55

*NCAA Tourney (0-1): Pacific (0-1).

†NIT Tourney (1-1): Nevada (1-1).

Colonial Athletic Association

Team	Conference W	L	Pct	Overall W	L	Pct
*Old Dominion	10	6	.625	22	11	.667
NC-Wilmington	10	6	.625	16	14	.533
East Carolina	9	7	.563	17	10	.629
Va. Commonwealth	9	7	.563	14	13	.518
William & Mary	8	8	.500	12	16	.428
James Madison	8	8	.500	16	13	.552
American	7	9	.437	11	16	.407
Richmond	7	9	.437	13	15	.464
George Mason	4	12	.250	10	17	.370

Conf. Tourney Final: Old Dominion 62, James Madison 58 (OT).

*NCAA Tourney (0-1): Old Dominion (0-1).

Conference USA

Red Division	Conference W	L	Pct	Overall W	L	Pct
†Tulane	11	3	.786	20	11	.645
†Ala-Birmingham	7	7	.500	18	14	.563
So. Mississippi	6	8	.429	12	15	.444
So. Florida	2	12	.143	8	19	.296

White Division	Conference W	L	Pct	Overall W	L	Pct
*NC-Charlotte	10	4	.714	22	9	.710
†Memphis	10	4	.714	16	15	.516
*Louisville	9	5	.643	26	9	.743
Houston	3	11	.214	11	16	.407

Blue Division	Conference W	L	Pct	Overall W	L	Pct
*Cincinnati	12	2	.857	26	8	.765
*Marquette	9	5	.643	22	9	.710
St. Louis	4	10	.286	11	18	.379
DePaul	1	13	.071	3	23	.130

Conf. Tourney Final: Marquette 60, NC-Charlotte 52.

*NCAA Tourney (5-4): Louisville (3-1), Cincinnati (1-1), NC-Charlotte (1-1), Marquette (0-1).

†NIT Tourney (0-3): Ala.-Birmingham (0-1), Memphis (0-1), Tulane (0-1).

Ivy League

Team	Conference W	L	Pct	Overall W	L	Pct
*Princeton	14	0	1.000	24	4	.857
Dartmouth	10	4	.714	18	8	.692
Harvard	10	4	.714	17	9	.654
Pennsylvania	8	6	.571	12	14	.462
Cornell	7	7	.500	15	11	.577
Yale	3	11	.214	10	16	.385
Brown	3	11	.214	4	22	.154
Columbia	1	13	.071	6	20	.231

Conf. Tourney Final: Ivy League has no tournament.

*NCAA Tourney (0-1): Princeton (0-1).

Metro Atlantic Conference

Team	Conference W	L	Pct	Overall W	L	Pct
†Iona	11	3	.786	22	8	.733
Canisius	10	4	.714	17	12	.586
Loyola-MD	10	4	.714	13	14	.481
St. Peter's	9	5	.643	13	15	.464
Niagara	5	9	.357	11	17	.393
Manhattan	5	9	.357	9	18	.333
Siena	4	10	.286	9	18	.333
*Fairfield	2	12	.143	11	19	.367

Conf. Tourney Final: Fairfield 78, Canisius 72.

*NCAA Tourney (0-1): Fairfield (0-1).

†NIT Tourney (0-1): Iona (0-1).

Mid-American Conference

Team	Conference			Overall		
	W	L	Pct	W	L	Pct
*Miami-OH	13	5	.722	21	9	.700
†Bowling Green	13	5	.722	22	10	.688
Ohio	12	6	.667	17	10	.630
Eastern Michigan ...	11	7	.611	22	10	.688
Ball St.	9	9	.500	16	13	.551
Western Michigan ..	9	9	.500	14	14	.500
Kent St.	7	11	.389	9	18	.333
Toledo	6	12	.333	13	14	.481
Akron	6	12	.333	8	18	.308
Central Michigan ...	4	14	.222	7	19	.369

Conf. Tourney Final: Miami-OH 96, Eastern Michigan 76.

*NCAA Tourney (0-1): Miami-OH (0-1).

†NIT Tourney (0-1): Bowling Green (0-1).

Mid-Continent Conference

Team	Conference			Overall		
	W	L	Pct	W	L	Pct
*Valparaiso	13	3	.813	24	7	.774
Buffalo	11	5	.688	17	11	.607
Western Illinois	11	5	.688	19	10	.655
Troy St.	10	6	.625	16	11	.593
Northeastern Illinois .	8	8	.500	16	12	.571
Missouri-KC	7	9	.438	10	17	.370
Youngstown St.	4	12	.250	9	18	.333
Chicago St.	4	12	.250	4	23	.148
Central Conn. St. ...	4	12	.250	8	19	.296

Note: Troy St. was not eligible for the conference postseason tournament.

Conf. Tourney Final: Valparaiso 63, Western Illinois 59.

*NCAA Tourney (0-1): Valparaiso (0-1).

Mid-Eastern Athletic Conference

Team	Conference			Overall		
	W	L	Pct	W	L	Pct
*Coppin St.	15	3	.833	22	9	.710
South Carolina St. ..	12	6	.667	14	14	.500
N. Carolina A&T ...	11	7	.611	15	13	.536
Bethune-Cookman ..	9	9	.500	12	16	.429
Florida A&M	8	10	.444	8	19	.296
Morgan St.	8	10	.444	9	18	.333
Delaware St.	7	11	.389	7	20	.259
Hampton	7	11	.389	8	19	.296
Howard	7	11	.389	7	20	.259
MD-Eastern Shore ..	6	12	.333	11	17	.393

Conf. Tourney Final: Coppin St. 81, N. Carolina A&T 74 (OT).

*NCAA Tourney (1-1): Coppin St. (1-1).

Midwestern Collegiate Conference

Team	Conference			Overall		
	W	L	Pct	W	L	Pct
*Butler	12	4	.750	23	10	.697
Detroit	11	5	.688	16	13	.551
Illinois-Chicago	11	5	.688	15	14	.517
WI-Green Bay	10	6	.625	14	14	.500
Loyola-IL	7	9	.438	12	15	.444
No. Illinois	6	10	.375	12	15	.444
Cleveland St	6	10	.375	9	19	.321
Wright St	5	11	.313	7	20	.259
WI-Milwaukee	4	12	.250	8	20	.296

Conf. Tourney Final: Butler 69, Illinois-Chicago 68.

*NCAA Tourney (0-1): Butler (0-1).

Missouri Valley Conference

Team	Conference			Overall		
	W	L	Pct	W	L	Pct
*Illinois St	14	4	.778	24	6	.800
†SW Missouri St.	12	6	.667	24	9	.727
†Bradley	12	6	.667	17	13	.567
Northern Iowa	11	7	.611	16	12	.571
Evansville	11	7	.611	17	14	.548
Creighton	10	8	.556	15	15	.500
Wichita St.	8	10	.444	14	13	.519
Indiana St.	6	12	.333	12	16	.429
Southern Illinois	6	12	.333	13	17	.433
Drake	0	18	.000	2	26	.071

Conf. Tourney Final: Illinois St. 75, SW Missouri St. 72.

*NCAA Tourney (0-1): Illinois St. (0-1).

†NIT Tourney (1-2): Bradley (1-1), SW Missouri St. (0-1).

Northeast Conference

Team	Conference			Overall		
	W	L	Pct	W	L	Pct
*LIU Brooklyn	15	3	.833	21	9	.700
Fairleigh Dickinson ..	13	5	.722	18	10	.643
Monmouth	12	6	.667	18	11	.621
Rider	10	8	.556	14	14	.500
Mt. St. Mary's	10	8	.556	14	13	.519
St. Francis-PA	9	9	.500	12	15	.444
St. Francis-NY	7	11	.389	13	15	.464
Wagner	7	11	.389	10	17	.370
Marist	4	14	.222	6	22	.214
Robert Morris	3	15	.167	4	23	.148

Conf. Tourney Final: LIU Brooklyn 72, Monmouth 67.

*NCAA Tourney (0-1): LIU Brooklyn (0-1).

Ohio Valley Conference

Team	Conference			Overall		
	W	L	Pct	W	L	Pct
*Murray St	12	6	.667	20	10	.667
Austin Peay	12	6	.667	17	14	.548
Middle Tenn. St	11	7	.611	19	12	.613
Tennessee Tech	10	8	.556	15	13	.536
Eastern Illinois	9	9	.500	12	15	.444
SE Missouri St	9	9	.500	12	18	.400
Tennessee-Martin	8	10	.444	11	16	.407
Tennessee St	7	11	.389	9	18	.333
Eastern Kentucky ...	6	12	.333	8	18	.308
Morehead St	6	12	.333	8	19	.296

Conf. Tourney Final: Murray St. 88, Austin Peay 85 (OT).

*NCAA Tourney (0-1): Murray St. (0-1).

Pacific-10 Conference

Team	Conference			Overall		
	W	L	Pct	W	L	Pct
*UCLA	15	3	.833	24	8	.750
*Stanford	12	6	.667	22	8	.733
*California	12	6	.667	23	9	.719
*USC	12	6	.667	17	11	.607
*Arizona	11	7	.611	23	9	.719
†Washington	10	8	.566	17	11	.607
†Oregon	8	10	.444	17	11	.607
Washington St	5	13	.278	13	17	.433
Oregon St	3	15	.167	7	20	.259
Arizona St	2	16	.111	10	20	.333

Conf. Tourney Final: Pac-10 has no tournament.

*NCAA Tourney (13-4): Arizona (6-0, NCAA champions), UCLA (3-1), Stanford (2-1), California (2-1), USC (0-1).

†NIT Tourney (0-2): Washington (0-1), Oregon (0-1).

COLLEGE BASKETBALL

Final NCAA Men's Division I Standings (Cont.)

Patriot League

Team	Conference W	L	Pct	Overall W	L	Pct
*Navy	10	2	.833	20	9	.690
Bucknell	9	3	.750	18	11	.621
Colgate	8	4	.667	12	16	.429
Holy Cross	5	7	.417	8	19	.296
Lafayette	5	7	.417	11	17	.393
Army	4	8	.333	10	16	.385
Lehigh	1	11	.083	1	26	.037

Conf. Tourney Final: Navy 76, Bucknell 75.
***NCAA Tourney (0-1):** Navy (0-1).

Southeastern Conference

Eastern Div.	Conference W	L	Pct	Overall W	L	Pct
*South Carolina	15	1	.938	24	8	.750
*Kentucky	13	3	.813	35	5	.875
*Georgia	10	6	.625	24	9	.727
*Vanderbilt	9	7	.563	19	12	.613
Florida	5	11	.313	13	17	.433
Tennessee	4	12	.250	11	16	.407

Western Div.	Conference W	L	Pct	Overall W	L	Pct
*Mississippi	11	5	.688	20	9	.690
†Arkansas	8	8	.500	18	14	.563
Alabama	6	10	.375	17	14	.548
Auburn	6	10	.375	16	15	.516
Mississippi St	6	10	.375	12	18	.400
LSU	3	13	.188	10	20	.333

Conf. Tourney Final: Kentucky 95, Georgia 68
***NCAA Tourney (5-5):** Kentucky (5-1), South Carolina (0-1), Georgia (0-1), Mississippi (0-1), Vanderbilt (0-1).
†**NIT Tourney (3-2):** Arkansas (3-2).

Southern Conference

North Div.	Conference W	L	Pct	Overall W	L	Pct
Marshall	10	4	.714	20	9	.690
Davidson	10	4	.714	18	10	.643
Appalachian St	8	6	.571	14	14	.500
Virginia Military	7	7	.500	12	16	.429
East Tennessee St	2	12	.143	7	20	.259

South Div.	Conference W	L	Pct	Overall W	L	Pct
*Tenn-Chattanooga	11	3	.786	24	11	.686
Western Carolina	7	7	.500	14	13	.518
The Citadel	6	8	.429	13	14	.481
Georgia Southern	5	9	.357	10	18	.357
Furman	4	10	.286	10	17	.370

Conf. Tourney Final: Tenn-Chattanooga 71, Marshall 70 (OT).
***NCAA Tourney (2-1):** Tenn-Chattanooga (2-1).

Southland Conference

Team	Conference W	L	Pct	Overall W	L	Pct
*SW Texas St.	10	6	.625	16	13	.552
NE Louisiana	10	6	.625	14	14	.500
McNeese St	10	6	.625	18	12	.600
Northwestern St	8	8	.500	13	15	.464
Stephen F. Austin	8	8	.500	12	15	.444
Texas-Arlington	8	8	.500	12	15	.444
Nicholls St	7	9	.438	10	16	.385
Sam Houston St	7	9	.438	8	18	.308
Texas-San Antonio	4	12	.250	9	17	.346

Conf. Tourney Final: SW Texas St. 74, NE Louisiana 54
***NCAA Tourney (0-1):** SW Texas St. (0-1).

Southwestern Athletic Conference

Team	Conference W	L	Pct	Overall W	L	Pct
Miss. Valley St	11	3	.786	19	10	.655
*Jackson St	9	5	.643	14	16	.467
Alcorn St	8	6	.571	11	17	.393
Prairie View A&M	7	7	.500	10	17	.370
Texas Southern	6	8	.429	12	16	.429
Southern	5	9	.357	10	17	.370
Grambling	5	9	.357	10	17	.370
Alabama St	5	9	.357	8	21	.276

Conf. Tourney Final: Jackson St. 81, Miss. Valley St. 74
***NCAA Tourney (0-1):** Jackson St. (0-1).

Sun Belt Conference

Team	Conference W	L	Pct	Overall W	L	Pct
*South Alabama	14	4	.778	23	7	.767
†New Orleans	14	4	.778	22	7	.759
Ark-Little Rock	11	7	.611	18	11	.621
Lamar	10	8	.556	15	12	.556
Louisiana Tech	10	8	.556	15	14	.517
Western Kentucky	9	9	.500	12	15	.444
SW Louisiana	9	9	.500	12	16	.429
Arkansas St	8	10	.444	15	12	.556
Jacksonville	4	14	.222	5	23	.179
Texas-Pan Am	1	17	.056	3	25	.107

Conf. Tourney Final: South Alabama 44, Louisiana Tech 43.
***NCAA Tourney (0-1):** South Alabama (0-1).
†**NIT Tourney (0-1):** New Orleans (0-1).

Trans America Athletic Conference

East	Conference W	L	Pct	Overall W	L	Pct
*Col. of Charleston	16	0	1.000	29	3	.906
Florida International	12	4	.750	16	13	.551
Florida Atlantic	11	5	.687	16	11	.592
Campbell	8	8	.500	11	16	.407
Stetson	5	11	.312	9	18	.333
Central Florida	4	12	.250	7	19	.269

West	Conference W	L	Pct	Overall W	L	Pct
Samford	11	5	.687	19	9	.678
Jacksonville St	9	7	.562	10	17	.370
SE Louisiana	7	9	.437	10	18	.357
Georgia St	6	10	.375	10	17	.370
Centenary	6	10	.375	9	18	.333
Mercer	1	15	.062	3	23	.115

Conf. Tourney Final: College of Charleston 83, Florida International 73.
***NCAA Tourney (1-1):** College of Charleston (1-1).

West Coast Conference

Team	Conference W	L	Pct	Overall W	L	Pct
Santa Clara	10	4	.714	16	11	.593
*St. Mary's-CA	10	4	.714	23	8	.742
San Francisco	9	5	.643	16	13	.552
San Diego	8	6	.571	17	11	.607
Gonzaga	8	6	.571	15	12	.556
Portland	4	10	.286	9	18	.333
Pepperdine	4	10	.286	6	21	.222
Loyola Marymount	3	11	.214	7	21	.250

Conf. Tourney Final: St. Mary's-CA 66, San Francisco 59.
***NCAA Tourney (0-1):** St. Mary's-CA (0-1).

Western Athletic Conference

	Conference			Overall		
Pacific	W	L	Pct	W	L	Pct
†Hawaii	12	4	.750	21	8	.724
†Fresno St	15	4	.750	20	12	.625
†UNLV	11	5	.688	22	10	.688
Colorado St	10	6	.625	20	9	.690
Wyoming	8	8	.500	12	16	.429
San Jose St.	5	11	.313	13	14	.481
San Diego St	4	12	.250	12	15	.444
Air Force	2	14	.125	7	19	.269

	Conference			Overall		
Mountain	W	L	Pct	W	L	Pct
*Utah	15	1	.938	29	4	.879
*Tulsa	12	4	.750	24	10	.706
*New Mexico	11	5	.688	25	8	.758
†TCU	7	9	.438	22	13	.629
SMU	7	9	.438	16	12	.571
UTEP	6	10	.375	13	13	.500
Rice	6	10	.375	12	15	.462
BYU	0	16	.000	1	25	.038

Conf. Tourney Final: Utah 89, TCU 68

*NCAA Tourney (5-3): Utah (3-1), New Mexico (1-1), Tulsa (1-1).

†NIT Tourney (4-4): UNLV (2-1), Hawaii (1-1), TCU (1-1), Fresno St. (0-1).

Division I Independents

	W	L	Pct
Oral Roberts	21	7	.750
Southern Utah	9	17	.346
Wofford	7	20	.259

Best in Show
Conferences with at least two wins in 1997 NCAA's; number of tournament teams in parentheses.

	W-L		W-L
Pac-10 (5)	13-4	Conference USA (4)	5-4
ACC (6)	8-6	Big East (4)	5-4
Big 12 (5)	7-5	SEC (5)	5-5
Big 10 (6)	7-6	Atlantic 10 (5)	4-5
WAC (3)	5-3	Southern (1)	2-1

Annual Awards

Player of the Year
Tim Duncan, Wake Forest . . . . AP, Naismith, Wooden, NABC, *TSN*, USBWA

Wooden Award Voting
Presented since 1977 by the Los Angeles Athletic Club and named after the former Purdue All-America and UCLA coach John Wooden. Voting done by 984-member panel of national media; candidates must have a cumulative college grade point average of 2.0 (out of 4.0).

		Cl	Pos	Pts
1	Tim Duncan, Wake Forest	Sr.	C	4764
2	Keith Van Horn, Utah	Sr.	F	4017
3	Raef LaFrentz, Kansas	Jr.	F	2870
4	Ron Mercer, Kentucky	So.	F	2840
5	Jacque Vaughn, Kansas	Sr.	G	1956
6	Brevin Knight, Stanford	Sr.	G	1787
7	Danny Fortson, Cincinnati	Jr.	F	1773
8	Antawn Jamison, North Carolina	So.	F	1552
9	Bobby Jackson, Minnesota	Sr.	G	1431
10	Charles O'Bannon, UCLA	Sr.	F	1030

Defensive Player of the Year
The Henry Iba Award, for defensive skills, sportsmanship and dedication; first presented by the Rotary Club of River Oaks in Houston in 1987 and named after the late Oklahoma St. and U.S. Olympic team coach. Voting done by NABC.

Tim Duncan, Wake Forest, C

Coaches of the Year
Clem Haskins, Minnesota . . . . AP, NABC, USBWA
Roy Williams, Kansas . . . . Naismith, *TSN*

Consensus All-America Team
The NCAA Division I players cited most frequently by the following All-America selectors: AP, U.S. Basketball Writers, National Assn. of Basketball Coaches and Wooden Award Committee. Holdover from the 1995-96 first team is in **bold** type; (*) indicates unanimous first team selection.

First Team
	Class	Hgt	Pos
Tim Duncan, Wake Forest*	Sr.	6-10	C
Keith Van Horn, Utah*	Sr.	6-10	F
Danny Fortson, Cincinnati*	Jr.	6-6	F
Ron Mercer, Kentucky*	So.	6-6	F
Raef LaFrentz, Kansas*	Jr.	6-11	F

Second Team
	Class	Hgt	Pos
Brevin Knight, Stanford	Sr.	5-10	G
Bobby Jackson, Minnesota	Sr.	6-6	G
Chauncey Billups, Colorado	So.	6-6	G
Jacque Vaughn, Kansas	Sr.	6-1	G
Antawn Jamison, N. Carolina	So.	6-8	F

Third Team
	Class	Hgt	Pos
Shea Seals, Tulsa	Sr.	6-5	G/F
Charles O'Bannon, UCLA	Sr.	6-5	F
Adonal Foyle, Colgate	Jr.	6-9	C
Andre Woolridge, Iowa	Sr.	6-0	G
Ed Gray, California	Sr.	6-3	G

Div. II and III Annual Awards
Awarded by the National Association of Basketball Coaches.

	Players of the Year
Div. II	Kebu Stewart, CS-Bakersfield
Div. III	Bryan Crabtree, Illinois-Wesleyan
	Coaches of the Year
Div. II	Pat Douglass, CS-Bakersfield
Div. III	Dennie Bridges, Illinois-Wesleyan
NAIA	Roger Kaiser, Life (Ga.)
JuCo	Terry Carroll, Indian Hills (Ia.) CC

NCAA Men's Division I Leaders

Includes games through NCAA and NIT tourneys.

INDIVIDUAL

Scoring

	Cl	Gm	FG%	3FG/Att	FT%	Reb	Ast	Stl	Blk	Pts	Avg	Hi
Charles Jones, LIU-Brooklyn	Jr.	30	.451	109/303	.634	180	139	70	7	903	30.1	46
Ed Gray, California	Sr.	26	.461	38/126	.790	105	56	44	6	644	24.8	48
Adonal Foyle, Colgate	Jr.	28	.565	1/7	.487	368	54	19	180	682	24.4	37
Raymond Tutt, UC-Santa Barbara	Jr.	27	.515	55/118	.800	190	43	43	9	649	24.0	37
Antonio Daniels, Bowling Green	Sr.	32	.547	45/104	.777	90	216	75	10	767	24.0	42
Donnie Carr, La Salle	Fr.	27	.350	99/289	.768	121	55	42	2	646	23.9	41
Olivier Saint Jean, San Jose St.	Jr.	26	.492	26/71	.730	229	28	39	19	619	23.8	37
James Cotton, Long Beach St	Jr.	27	.439	63/171	.833	134	24	36	9	634	23.5	31
Roderick Blakney, S.Carolina St.	Jr.	28	.428	61/101	.738	114	69	46	3	655	23.4	34
Cory Carr, Texas Tech	Jr.	28	.427	94/249	.792	128	82	25	4	646	23.1	34
Victor Page, Georgetown	So.	30	.378	76/204	.726	122	67	69	13	682	22.7	35
Randy Bolden, Texas Southern	Jr.	28	.367	80/247	.750	123	74	38	1	626	22.4	42
Kenderick Franklin, Nicholls St.	Jr.	26	.471	56/166	.783	160	64	22	38	574	22.1	40
Keith Van Horn, Utah	Sr.	32	.492	58/150	.904	303	45	22	37	705	22.0	41
Bonzi Wells, Ball St.	Jr.	29	.465	25/104	.691	230	127	73	30	637	22.0	46
Isaac Fontaine, Wash. St.	Sr.	30	.497	75/170	.785	119	76	38	10	657	21.9	33
Vincent Rainey, Murray St.	Sr.	30	.443	19/68	.774	247	56	49	14	656	21.9	33
Reggie Freeman, Texas	Sr.	30	.380	66/222	.369	228	125	55	14	654	21.8	45
Danny Fortson, Cincinnati	Jr.	33	.620	0/1	.772	299	36	19	15	703	21.3	34
Greg Smith, Delaware	Sr.	31	.609	0/3	.754	342	28	47	9	660	21.3	31

Rebounding

	Cl	Gm	No	Avg
Tim Duncan, Wake Forest	Sr.	31	457	14.7
Adonal Foyle, Colgate	Jr.	28	368	13.1
Lorenzo Coleman, Tennessee Tech	Sr.	28	333	11.9
Tony Battie, Texas Tech	Jr.	28	329	11.8
Muntrelle Dobbins, Arkansas-LR	Sr.	28	320	11.4
Eric Taylor, St. Francis-PA	Jr.	27	306	11.3
Kory Billups, Chicago St.	Sr.	27	304	11.3
Nate Huffman, Central Mich.	Sr.	26	287	11.0
Greg Smith, Delaware	Sr.	31	342	11.0
H L Coleman, Wyoming	Sr.	28	303	10.8
Jim Cruse, Indiana St.	Sr.	28	296	10.6
Antonio Smith, Michigan St.	So.	29	306	10.6
Bud Eley, Southeast Mo. St.	Jr.	30	310	10.3
Reginald Poole, SW Louisiana	Jr.	28	287	10.3
Tunji Awojobi, Boston Univ.	Sr.	27	275	10.2

Assists

	Cl	Gm	No	Avg
Kenny Mitchell, Dartmouth	Sr	26	203	7.8
Brevin Knight, Stanford	Sr	30	234	7.8
Kareem Gilbert, Tennessee St.	Jr	25	191	7.6
Jamar Smiley, Illinois St.	Jr	30	219	7.3
Chad Peckinpaugh, Eastern Ill.	So	27	196	7.3
Anthony Johnson, Charleston (SC)	Sr	32	229	7.2
Chad Townsend, Murray St.	Jr	30	212	7.1
Ed Cota, North Caro.	Fr	34	234	6.9
Ali Ton, Davidson	So	28	190	6.8
Antonio Daniels, Bowling Green	Sr	32	216	6.8
Admore White, Notre Dame	Sr	30	201	6.7
God Shammgod, Providence	So	36	239	6.6
Dominick Young, Fresno St.	Sr	32	211	6.6
Anthony Carter, Hawaii	Jr	29	191	6.6
Ed Norvell, Kent	So	27	174	6.4

Field Goal Percentage

Minimum 5 Field Goals made per game.

	Cl	Gm	FG	FGA	Pct
Todd MacCulloch, Wash	So.	28	163	241	67.6
Sean Scott, Central Conn. St.	Sr.	24	128	191	67.0
Rosell Ellis, McNeese St.	Sr.	30	213	319	66.8
Ed Sears, Ohio Univ.	Sr.	27	156	241	64.7
Lorenzo Coleman, Tenn. Tech	Sr.	28	198	307	64.5
Chianti Roberts, Okla St.	Sr.	32	178	285	62.5
Danny Fortson, Cincinnati	Jr.	33	243	392	62.0
Evan Eschmeyer, N'western	Jr.	29	147	240	61.3
Greg Smith, Delaware	Sr.	31	241	396	60.9
Tim Duncan, Wake Forest	Sr.	31	234	385	60.8

3-Pt Field Goal Percentage

Minimum 1.5 Three-Point FG made per game.

	Cl	Gm	FG	FGA	Pct
Kent McCausland, Iowa	So.	29	70	134	52.2
Bill Slack, Central Mich.	Sr.	26	49	96	51.0
Ross Land, N. Arizona	Fr.	28	64	126	50.8
Marcus Carreno, Florida Int'l	So.	28	52	104	50.0
Danny Sprinkle, Montana St.	So.	25	61	125	48.8
Patrick Lee, Va. Comm	Sr.	27	62	130	47.7
Corey Reed, Radford	Jr.	28	78	164	47.6
D J Bosse, Kent	Sr.	27	86	181	47.5
Louis Bullock, Michigan	Sr.	35	101	214	47.2
Andrew Mavis, N. Arizona	Jr.	28	82	174	47.1

Free Throw Percentage

Minimum 2.5 Free Throws made per game.

	Cl	Gm	FT	FTA	Pct
Aaron Zobrist, Bradley	Sr.	30	77	85	90.6
Keith Van Horn, Utah	Sr.	32	151	167	90.4
Jim Williamson, Loyola-CA	Jr.	28	110	122	90.2
Marcus Wilson, Evansville	So.	31	91	101	90.1
Trajan Langdon, Duke	So.	33	113	126	89.7
Austin Croshere, Providence	Sr.	36	182	205	88.8
Scott Gooden, Akron	Jr.	25	63	71	88.7
M J Nodilo, San Francisco	Jr.	29	85	96	88.5
Bryce Drew, Valparaiso	Jr.	31	131	149	87.9
Shawnta Rogers, G. Wash	So.	29	93	106	87.7

3-Pt Field Goals Per Game

	Cl	Gm	No	Avg
William Fourche, Southern U.	Sr.	27	122	4.5
Keith Veney, Marshall	Sr.	29	130	4.5
Troy Hudson, S. Illinois	Jr.	30	134	4.5
Dedric Willoughby, Iowa St.	Sr.	27	102	3.8
Tom Pipkins, Duquesne	Sr.	29	99	3.7
Donnie Carr, La Salle	Fr.	27	99	3.7
Charles Jones, LIU-Brooklyn	Jr.	30	109	3.6
Nate Erdmann, Oklahoma	Sr.	30	105	3.5
John Knox, Jacksonville	Jr.	28	98	3.5
Mark Heidersbach, NE Ill	Sr.	28	95	3.4

Wake Forest

Tim Duncan
Rebounding

Dartmouth

Kenny Mitchell
Assists

Colgate

Adonal Foyle
Blocked Shots

MD-Eastern Shore

Joel Hoover
Steals

Blocked Shots

	Cl	Gm	No	Avg
Adonal Foyle, Colgate	Jr.	28	180	6.4
Lorenzo Coleman, Tennessee Tech ..	Sr.	28	134	4.8
Richard Lugo, St. Francis (N.Y.)	Fr.	28	125	4.5
Jerome James, Florida A&M	Jr.	27	119	4.4
Kelvin Cato, Iowa St.	Sr.	28	118	4.2
Rodger Farrington, Arizona St.	Sr.	27	113	4.2
Keon Clark, UNLV	Jr.	29	112	3.9
Calvin Booth, Penn St.	So.	27	92	3.4
Erik Nelson, Vermont	Jr.	22	73	3.3
Tim Duncan, Wake Forest	Sr.	31	102	3.3

Steals

	CL	Gm	No	Avg
Joel Hoover, Md.East Shore	Fr.	28	90	3.2
Philip Huyler, Fla. Atlantic	Sr.	27	86	3.2
Kellii Taylor, Pittsburgh	Fr.	32	101	3.2
Moe Segar, St. Peter's	Sr.	28	87	3.1
Mustafa Barksdale, Monmouth	Sr.	27	81	3.0
Nate Langley, George Mason	Sr.	27	80	3.0
Mike Campbell, LIU-Brooklyn	Jr.	30	88	2.9
Jason Hart, Syracuse	Fr.	32	90	2.8
Shawnta Rogers, G. Washington ..	So.	29	81	2.8
Juan Sanchez, Temple	Fr.	31	86	2.8

Single Game Highs
Individual Points

No		Opponent	Date
51	Keith Veney, Marshall	Morehead St.	12/14
48	Ed Gray, California	Washington St.	2/22
46	Charles Jones, LIU-Brooklyn	St. Francis-PA	1/4
46	Bubba Wells, Austin Peay	Morehead St.	2/22
44	Jimmal Ball, Akron	Xavier-OH	12/21
44	Charles Jones, LIU-Brooklyn	Mt. St. Mary's	1/9
44	Mike Jones, TCU	Fresno St.	3/6
43	Vincent Rainey, Murray St.	Alcorn St.	12/5
43	Reggie Freeman, Texas	Fresno St.	12/14
43	Junior Broswell, App St.	Davidson	2/22
43	Bubba Wells, Austin Peay	Morehead St.	2/25

Team Points

No	Opponent		Date
143	Cal Poly-SLO	Cal Baptist (NAIA I)	12/3
138	S. F. Austin	Schreiner (NAIA I)	11/25
137	Arkansas	Troy St. (NCAA I)	12/10
134	Kansas	Niagara (NCAA I)	1/9
130	Morehead St.	Asbury (NAIA II)	11/30
130	NE Louisiana	Ark.-Monticello (NCAA II)	12/3
130	Winthrop	Johnson & Wales (NCAA III)	12/7

TEAM
Scoring Offense

	Gm	W-L	Pts	Avg
LIU-Brooklyn	30	21-9	2746	91.5
Kansas	36	34-2	3058	84.9
Arizona	34	25-9	2850	83.8
TCU	35	22-13	2931	83.7
Miss. Valley St........	29	19-10	2413	83.2
Xavier-OH	29	23-6	2413	83.2
Kentucky	40	35-5	3325	83.1
Fresno St.	32	20-12	2648	82.8
Bowling Green	32	22-10	2643	82.6
McNeese St.	30	18-12	2461	82.0
Morehead St.	27	8-19	2206	81.7
Cal Poly-SLO	30	14-16	2444	81.5
E. Michigan	32	22-10	2589	80.9
Stanford	30	22-8	2427	80.9
W. Virginia	31	21-10	2502	80.7

Scoring Defense

	Gm	W-L	Pts	Avg
Princeton	28	24-4	1496	53.4
Wisc.-Green Bay	28	14-14	1515	54.1
N.C. State	32	17-15	1749	54.7
Wisconsin	28	18-10	1548	55.3
S. Alabama	30	23-7	1699	56.6
Canisius	29	17-12	1649	56.9
Marquette	31	22-9	1791	57.8
Wake Forest	31	24-7	1807	58.3
Bradley	30	17-13	1789	59.6
Pacific	30	24-6	1800	60.0
Virginia Tech	31	15-16	1867	60.2
Iowa St.	31	22-9	1872	60.4
Temple	31	20-11	1880	60.6
Butler	33	23-10	2004	60.7
Connecticut	33	18-15	2010	60.9

Scoring Margin

	Off	Def	Mar
Kentucky	83.1	62.8	20.3
Kansas	84.9	66.1	18.8
Cincinnati	80.7	65.5	15.2
Minnesota	78.3	63.4	14.9
Duke	79.7	66.2	13.5
Pacific	72.9	60.0	12.9
Utah	74.4	61.7	12.8
Coll of Charleston	78.3	65.9	12.4
New Mexico	75.8	63.5	12.3
Stanford	80.9	69.0	11.9
Tenn-Chattanooga	76.6	65.2	11.4
Princeton	64.8	53.4	11.3
Xavier-OH	83.2	72.3	10.9
N. Carolina	77.4	66.7	10.7
Wake Forest	69.0	58.3	10.7

NCAA Men's Division I Leaders (Cont.)

Winning Percentage

	W	L	Pct
Kansas	34	2	.944
Coll. of Charleston	29	3	.906
Minnesota	31	4	.886
Utah	29	4	.879
Kentucky	35	5	.875
Princeton	24	4	.857
Boston Univ.	25	5	.833
North Carolina	28	7	.800
Illinois St.	24	6	.800
Pacific	24	6	.800
XavierOH	23	6	.793
St. Joseph's-PA	26	7	.788
Valparaiso	24	7	.774
Wake Forest	24	7	.774
South Alabama	23	7	.767

Field Goal Percentage

	FG	FGA	Pct
UCLA	932	1791	52.0
Northern Ariz.	763	1478	51.6
Princeton	631	1262	50.0
Cincinnati	962	1938	49.6
Utah	886	1785	49.6
Eastern Mich.	975	1970	49.5
Western Ill.	820	1657	49.5
McNeese St.	896	1821	49.2
Coll. of Charleston	937	1911	49.0
Houston	732	1499	48.8
Xavier-OH	838	1717	48.8
Kansas	1084	2222	48.8
Hawaii	821	1685	48.7
New Mexico St.	774	1589	48.7
Oral Roberts	775	1596	48.6

Field Goal Percentage Defense

	FG	FGA	Pct
Marquette	628	1735	36.2
Wake Forest	667	1832	36.4
WI-Green Bay	499	1368	36.5
Wisconsin	502	1329	37.8
Georgetown	659	1740	37.9
Miami-FL	632	1662	38.0
Utah	725	1896	38.2
Connecticut	707	1846	38.3
Tulsa	750	1953	38.4
South Ala.	595	1548	38.4
Minnesota	752	1952	38.5
Bradley	627	1621	38.7
Tennessee	557	1437	38.8
Old Dominion	771	1986	38.8
Liberty	697	1791	38.9

Rebound Margin

	Off	Def	Mar
Utah St.	37.4	26.6	10.9
Kansas	42.6	32.2	10.4
Iowa	38.5	28.7	9.8
North Carolina	41.6	32.2	9.4
Cincinnati	39.9	30.6	9.3
St. John's	42.8	34.3	8.5
S. Alabama	37.7	29.9	7.8
E. Carolina	38.5	30.8	7.7
Tenn.-Chattanooga	38.6	31.3	7.3
Navy	39.0	32.1	6.9
Miami-OH	37.1	30.2	6.9
Villanova	40.6	33.8	6.8
Xavier-OH	38.0	31.3	6.7
Ohio	37.6	31.0	6.6
Utah	37.9	31.4	6.5

Underclassmen in NBA Draft

Twenty five Division I players (19 juniors, five sophomores and one freshman), six junior college players, five Division II juniors, one NAIA player, one high school senior, one player from the Atlantic Basketball Association and one player from overseas forfeited the remainder of their college eligibility and declared for the 1997 NBA Draft which took place in Charlotte, N.C. on June 25.

Players are listed in alphabetical order; first round selections in **bold** type.

	Cl	Overall Drafted by Pick	
Gracen Averil, Texas Tech	Jr.	Not drafted	—
Tony Battie, Texas Tech	Jr.	Denver	5
Chauncey Billups, Colorado	So.	Boston	3
Carl Blanton, Southern	So.	Not drafted	—
Mark Blount, Pittsburgh	So.	Seattle	55
C.J. Bruton, Indian Hills (la.) CC	So.	Vancouver	53
Dan Buie, Washburn (Kan.)	Jr.	Not drafted	—
Keith Closs, C. Conn. St./ABA	—	Not drafted	—
James Cotton, Long Beach St.	Jr.	Denver	33
Tony Doyle, Columbia	Jr.	Not drafted	—
Ian Folmar, Slippery Rock	Jr.	Not drafted	—
Danny Fortson, Cincinnati	Jr.	Milwaukee	10
Adonal Foyle, Colgate	Jr.	Golden St.	8
Darryl Hardy, Winston-Salem	Jr.	Not drafted	—
Antjonne Holmes, C. Baptist JC	Jr.	Not drafted	—
Troy Hudson, S. Illinois	Jr.	Not drafted	—
Marc Jackson, Temple	Jr.	Golden St.	38
Stephen Jackson, Butler CC	Fr.	Phoenix	43
Ed Jenkins, Sullivan (Ky.)	Jr.	Not drafted	—
Marcus Johnson, Long Beach St.	Jr.	Not drafted	—
Damon Jones, Houston	Jr.	Not drafted	—
Nate Langley, George Mason	Jr.	Not drafted	—
Keith Love, Domican Univ.	Jr.	Not drafted	—
Gordon Malone, W. Virginia	Jr.	Minnesota	44
Amere May, Shaw	Fr.	Not drafted	—
Elgie McCoy, Kutztown	Jr.	Not drafted	—
Tracy McGrady, Mt. Zion (N.C.)	HS	Toronto	9
Ron Mercer, Kentucky	So.	Boston	6
Marco Milic, Slovenia	—	Philadelphia	34
Victor Page, Georgetown	So.	Not drafted	—
Shawn Ritzie, Norwalk CC	So.	Not drafted	—
Eddie Robinson, Brown Mackie JC	So.	Not drafted	—
Paul Rogers, Gonzaga	Jr.	LA Lakers	54
Bryon Ruffner, BYU	Jr.	Not drafted	—
Olivier Saint-Jean, San Jose St.	Jr.	Sacramento	11
Mark Sanford, Washington	Jr.	Miami	31
God Shammgod, Providence	So.	Washington	46
Maurice Taylor, Michigan	Jr.	LA Clippers	14
Tim Thomas, Villanova	Fr.	New Jersey	7
Mark Young, Kansas St.	Jr.	Not drafted	—

Note: Cory Carr of Texas Tech, Ronnie Fields of the Rockford Lightning (CBA), Demetri Papanikolaou of Greece, Larrell Redic of Utah St., Dawood Thomas of California (Pa.), Mirsad Turkcan of Turkey and Luca Victoriano of Argentina declared for the draft then withdrew their names before the June 18 deadline.

Other Men's 1997 Tournaments

NIT Tournament

The 60th annual National Invitation Tournament had a 32-team field. First three rounds played on home courts of higher seeded teams. Semifinal, Third Place and Championship games played March 25-27 at Madison Square Garden in New York City.

1st Round

at Connecticut 71 ....Iona 66
Florida St. 82 ....at Syracuse 67
at Michigan St. 65 ....George Washington 50
at West Virginia 98 ....Bowling Green 95
at Pittsburgh 82 ....New Orleans 63
at Notre Dame 74 ....Oral Roberts 58
at Bradley 66 ....Drexel 53
at Arkansas 101 ....N. Arizona 75
at Nebraksa 67 ....Washington 63
at TCU 85 ....Ala.-Birmingham 62
at N.C. State 77 ....SW Missouri St. 66
Nevada 97 ....at Fresno St. 86
at UNLV 66 ....Memphis 62
at Hawaii 71 ....Oregon 61
at Michigan 76 ....Miami-FL 63
at Oklahoma St. 79 ....Tulane 72

2nd Round

Florida St. 68 ....at Michigan St. 63
at West Virginia 76 ....................N.C. State 73
at Arkansas 76 ....Pittsburgh 71
at UNLV 89 ....OT ....Hawaii 80
at Notre Dame 82 ....TCU 72
at Connecticut 63 ....Bradley 47
at Michigan 75 ....Oklahoma St. 65
Nebraska 78 ....at Nevada 68

Quarterfinals

Florida St. 76 ....at West Virginia 71
at Arkansas 86 ....UNLV 73
Michigan 67 ....at Notre Dame 66
at Connecticut 76 ....Nebraska 67

Semifinals

Florida St. 71 ....Connecticut 65
Michigan 77 ....Arkansas 62

Third Place

Connecticut 74 ....Arkansas 64

Championship

Michigan 82 ....Florida St. 72

NCAA Division II

The eight regional winners of the 48-team field: NORTHEAST— S. Connecticut St. (28-3); EAST— Salem (W.Va.)-Teikyo (27-2); SOUTH ATLANTIC— Elizabeth City (N.C.) St. (22-6); SOUTH— Lynn, FL (27-2); SOUTH CENTRAL— Texas A&M Commerce (24-7); GREAT LAKES— Northern Kentucky (28-4); NORTH CENTRAL— South Dakota St. (25-4); WEST— Cal St.-Bakersfield (26-4).

The Elite Eight was played March 19-22, at the Commonwealth Convention Center in Louisville, Ky. There was no Third Place game.

Quarterfinals

Cal St.-Bakersfield 65 ....S. Connecticut St. 62
Salem-Teikyo 91 ....Elizabeth City St. 74
Lynn 78 ....South Dakota St. 72
Northern Kentucky 79 ....Texas A&M Commerce 67

Semifinals

Cal St.-Bakersfield 81 ....Salem-Teikyo 68
Northern Kentucky 79 ....Lynn 58

Championship

Cal St.-Bakersfield 57 ....N. Kentucky 56

NCAA Division III

Sixty-four teams played into the 32-team Division III field. The four sectional winners: NORTHEAST— Williams College (26-2); EAST— Alvernia College (26-4); MIDWEST— Illinois Wesleyan (27-2); WEST— Nebraska Wesleyan (24-5).

The Final Four was played March 21-22, at Salem Civic Center in Salem, Va.

Semifinals

Illinois Wesleyan 85 ....Alvernia 82
Nebraska Wesleyan 101 ....Williams 90

Third Place

Williams 78 ....Alvernia 77

Championship

Illinois Wesleyan 89 ....Nebraska Wesleyan 86

NAIA Division I

The quarterfinalists, in alphabetical order, after two rounds of the 32-team NAIA tournament: Birmingham-Southern, Ala. (28-6); Central Washington (18-13); Cumberland, Ky. (31-6); Hawaii-Pacific (26-4); Life, Ga. (35-1); McKendree, Ill. (28-9), Oklahoma Baptist (35-3), Point Park, Penn. (23-7).

All tournament games played, March 19-25, at the Mabee Center in Tulsa, Okla. There was no Third Place game.

Quarterfinals: Cumberland def. Central Washington, 89-68; Life def. Birmingham-Southern, 66-64; Point Park def. Hawaii Pacific, 88-84 (OT); Oklahoma Baptist def. McKendree, 82-73.

Semifinals: Life def. Cumberland, 69-52; Oklahoma Baptist def. Point Park, 93-75.

Championship: Life def. Oklahoma Baptist, 73-64.

NAIA Division II

The semifinalists, in alphabetical order, after three rounds of the 32-team NAIA tournament: Bethel, Ind. (33-5); Siena Heights, Mich. (30-6); Tabor, Kan. (24-9); William Jewell, Mo. (29-10).

All tournament games played, March 12-18, at Nampa, Idaho. There was no Third Place game.

Semifinals: Bethel def. William Jewell, 99-73; Siena Heights def. Tabor 89-80.

Championship: Bethel def. Siena Heights, 95-94.

Attitude, Belief and Chemistry

by Mimi Griffin

Tennessee as the *underdog*? You have to be kidding.

But that's exactly where the defending national champions found themselves at the start of the 1997 NCAA tournament. The Lady Vols were supposed to be in a rebuilding year. They were supposed to be decimated by the loss of not just one but two point guards during the regular season. They were supposed to be demoralized by ten regular season losses, the most suffered by any Lady Vol team since 1986.

Inexplicably, none of the above affected this team once the landscape changed to the sudden death format of the NCAA tournament. They wore that underdog label like a badge of honor and used it every time they needed to get fired up for their next opponent. Time and again, we heard the players talk about how no one believed in them. This was one Tennessee team that had the luxury of playing without the pressure of high expectations and they took advantage of it.

It's easy to point to Chamique Holdsclaw as the reason why Tennessee now has five national championships but let's look beyond the obvious. As they struggled through a brutal regular season schedule, it became clear that this team could not succeed if it continued to rely solely on Holdsclaw. The rest of the players had to contribute and they did. Abby Conklin regained her perimeter shooting touch. Fire and physical play returned to the games of Pashen Thompson and Tiffany Johnson. Kyra Elzy and Niya Butts began to contribute in ways that may have been silent but were deadly nonetheless. The outstanding defensive performances of these two players at the Final Four were memorable and big keys to the championship.

And, finally, you can't win a national championship without a point guard and Kellie Jolly was just what her team needed.

She was comfortable passing or scoring . . . whatever was needed at the moment. Her comfort and leadership at the point guard position allowed everyone else to excel. Jolly's quick return from major knee surgery and her seamless reintroduction to the team's play only added to the mystique of this team.

So, in the end, no one would say that this was one of Pat Summitt's most talented teams. But by the end of the year, it may have been one of her most cohesive. This team was more about attitude, belief and chemistry than it was about talent. It was a team that was fun to watch because *they* were having fun. And with the best recruiting class in the country arriving in Knoxville this fall, the trick will be to maintain the purity of purpose and team spirit that the Lady Vols exhibited during their championship run.

The attitude of this Tennessee team clearly epitomized the state of women's basketball this season. As the talent pool in women's basketball continues to spread and even out, attitude, chemistry and *health* will be the telling factors for success. From now on, the traditional powers will no longer be spotted ten points simply because of the name of the school on their jerseys. The accomplishments of programs like Notre Dame and Illinois during the 1997 tournament will have ramifications in the sport for years to come. They reached a high level of success without a roster full of high school All-Americans. They are programs with which the majority of schools trying to break into the big time can easily identify.

From start to finish, this was one of the most exciting collection of games in the NCAA women's tournament's sixteen year history. The first and second rounds, especially, provided several closer-than-expected outcomes. But even as parity continues to level the playing field, the sound of "Rocky Top" always seems to reverberate at the end. ∎

Mimi Griffin is ESPN's Women's NCAA Basketball Analyst.

Final Regular Season AP Women's Top 25 Poll

Taken **before** start of NCAA tournament.

The sportswriters & broadcasters poll: first place votes in parentheses; records through Monday, March 9, 1997; total points (based on 25 for 1st, 24 for 2nd, etc.); record in NCAA tourney and team lost to; head coach (career years and record including 1997 postseason), and preseason ranking. Teams in **bold** type went on to reach NCAA Final Four.

		Mar. 10 Record	Points	NCAA Recap	Head Coach	Preseason Rank
1	UConn (38)	30-0	1020	3-1 (Tennessee)	Geno Auriemma (12 yrs: 294-86)	5
2	**Old Dominion** (2)	29-1	980	5-1 (Tennessee)	Wendy Larry (13 yrs: 272-119)	7
3	Stanford (1)	30-1	951	4-1 (Old Dominion)	Tara VanDerveer (18 yrs: 437-115)	1
4	North Carolina	27-2	899	2-1 (G. Washington)	Sylvia Hatchell (22 yrs: 486-198)	23
5	Louisiana Tech	29-3	854	2-1 (Florida)	Leon Barmore (15 yrs: 428-67)	14
6	Georgia	22-5	765	3-1 (Stanford)	Andy Landers (22 yrs: 524-151)	3
7	Florida	21-8	752	3-1 (Old Dominion)	Carol Ross (7 yrs: 142-68)	21
8	Alabama	23-6	741	2-1 (Notre Dame)	Rick Moody (8 yrs: 175-71)	2
9	LSU	23-4	645	2-1 (Old Dominion)	Sue Gunter (27 yrs: 547-245)	29
10	**Tennessee**	23-10	638	6-0	Pat Summitt (23 yrs: 625-144)	4
11	Kansas	24-5	588	1-1 (Vanderbilt)	Marian Washington (24 yrs: 457-258)	12
12	Virginia	21-7	516	2-1 (Stanford)	Debbie Ryan (20 yrs: 462-155)	10
13	Auburn	21-9	506	1-1 (La. Tech)	Joe Ciampi (20 yrs: 471-140)	25
14	Texas	21-7	498	1-1 (Notre Dame)	Jody Conradt (28 yrs: 697-195)	19
15	**Notre Dame**	27-6	442	4-1 (Tennessee)	Muffet McGraw (15 yrs: 301-136)	20
16	Illinois	22-7	325	1-1 (UConn)	Theresa Grentz (23 yrs: 498-178)	39†
17	Texas Tech	19-8	304	1-1 (Stanford)	Marsha Sharp (15 yrs: 350-120)	11
18	Colorado	21-8	246	2-1 (Tennessee)	Ceal Barry (18 yrs: 372-181)	17
19	Stephen F. Austin	27-4	218	1-1 (Colorado)	Royce Chadwick (8 yrs: 157-85)	24
20	Vanderbilt	18-10	212	2-1 (Georgia)	Jim Foster (19 yrs: 396-172)	9
21	Clemson	19-10	200	0-1 (Marquette)	Jim Davis (11 yrs: 227-110)	26
22	George Washington	25-5	189	3-1 (Notre Dame)	Joe McKeown (11 yrs: 253-86)	28
23	Tulane	26-4	183	1-1 (G. Washington)	Lisa Stockton (6 yrs: 130-52)	43
24	Michigan St.	21-7	133	1-1 (N. Carolina)	Karen Langeland (21 yrs: 329-248)	37
25	W. Kentucky	22-8	112	0-1 (Arizona)	Paul Sanderford (15 yrs: 365-120)	8

Others receiving votes: 26. **Duke** (18-10, 74 pts); 27. **Iowa** (17-11, 60); 28. **St. Joseph's-PA** (25-4, 51); 29. **Oregon** (21-6, 32); 30. **Portland** (27-2, 22); 31. **Drake** (23-7, 15), **Kentucky** (8-19, 15) and **San Diego St.** (23-6, 15); 34. **Toledo** (27-3, 12); 35. **Arkansas** (18-10, 11), **N.C. State** (19-11, 11) and **USC** (19-8, 11); 38. **Purdue** (16-10, 10); 39. **Louisville** (20-8, 9) and **Marquette** (20-9, 9), 41. **San Francisco** (25-5, 8) and **Washington** (17-10, 8); 43. **Memphis** (22-6, 7); 44. **Utah** (24-5, 6); 43. **DePaul** (20-8, 5), 44. **Kansas St.** (19-11, 4), **Maryland** (18-9, 4) and **Nebraska** (19-9, 4); 47. **UC-Santa Barbara** (24-5, 2); 48. **Arizona** (22-7, 1), **E. Kentucky** (24-5, 1) and **Northwestern** (17-10, 1).

NCAA Women's Division I Tournament Seeds

	WEST		MIDWEST		MIDEAST		EAST
1	Stanford (30-1)	1	UConn (30-0)	1	Old Dominion (29-1)	1	N. Carolina (27-2)
2	Georgia (22-5)	2	Colorado (21-8)	2	La. Tech (29-3)	2	Alabama (23-6)
3	Kansas (24-5)	3	Tennessee (23-10)	3	Florida (21-8)	3	Texas (21-7)
4	Virginia (21-7)	4	Illinois (22-7)	4	LSU (23-4)	4	Tulane (26-4)
5	Utah (24-5)	5	Duke (18-10)	5	Clemson (19-10)	5	G. Washington (25-5)
6	Vanderbilt (18-10)	6	Oregon (21-6)	6	USC (19-8)	6	Notre Dame (27-6)
7	Arizona (22-7)	7	S.F. Austin (27-4)	7	Auburn (21-9)	7	St. Joseph's (25-4)
8	Texas Tech (19-8)	8	N.C. State (19-11)	8	Purdue (16-10)	8	Michigan St. (21-7)
9	Montana (25-3)	9	Iowa (17-11)	9	Maryland (18-9)	9	Portland (27-3)
10	W. Kentucky (22-8)	10	Toledo (27-3)	10	Louisville (20-8)	10	Kansas St. (19-11)
11	Washington (17-10)	11	San Diego St. (23-6)	11	San Francisco (25-5)	11	Memphis (22-6)
12	Iowa St. (17-11)	12	DePaul (20-8)	12	Marquette (20-9)	12	Northwestern (17-10)
13	Troy St. (23-6)	13	Drake (23-7)	13	Maine (22-7)	13	UC-Santa Barb. (24-5)
14	Detroit (23-6)	14	Grambling (24-5)	14	Florida Int'l. (21-8)	14	SW Texas St. (17-11)
15	E. Kentucky (24-5)	15	Marshall (18-11)	15	St. Peters (25-3)	15	St. Francis-PA (21-8)
16	Howard (21-5)	16	Lehigh (15-14)	16	Liberty (22-7)	16	Harvard (20-6)

1997 NCAA BASKETBALL WOMEN'S DIVISION I

EAST

FIRST ROUND — March 14-15
- 1 N. Carolina 78
- 16 Harvard 53
- 8 Michigan St. (OT) 75
- 9 Portland 70
- 5 G. Washington 61
- 12 Northwestern 46
- 4 Tulane 72
- 13 UC-Santa Bar. 69
- 6 Notre Dame 93
- 11 Memphis 62
- 3 Texas 66
- 14 SW Texas St 38
- 7 St. Joseph's 70
- 10 Kansas St 52
- 2 Alabama 94
- 15 St. Francis 50

SECOND ROUND — March 16-17
- N. Carolina 81 (OT)
- Michigan St. 75
- G. Wash. 81
- Tulane 67
- Notre Dame 86
- Texas 83
- St. Joseph's 52
- Alabama 61

REGIONALS — March 22
- N. Carolina 46
- G. Wash. 55
- Notre Dame 87
- Alabama 71

COLUMBIA, SC
- G. Wash. 52
- Notre Dame 62

Notre Dame 68

MIDEAST

FIRST ROUND
- 1 Old Dominion 102
- 16 Liberty 52
- 8 Purdue 74
- 9 Maryland 48
- 5 Clemson 66
- 12 Marquette 70
- 4 LSU 88
- 13 Maine 79
- 6 USC 68
- 11 San Francisco 55
- 3 Florida 92
- 14 Florida Int'l 68
- 7 Auburn 68
- 10 Louisville 65
- 2 LA Tech 94
- 15 St. Peters 50

SECOND ROUND — March 16-17
- Old Dominion 69
- Purdue 65
- Marquette 58
- LSU 71
- USC 78
- Florida 92
- Auburn 48
- LA Tech 74

REGIONALS — March 22
- Old Dominion 62
- LSU 49
- Florida 71
- LA Tech 57

WEST LAFAYETTE, IN
- Old Dominion 53
- Florida 51

Old Dominion 83 (OT)

MIDWEST

FIRST ROUND — March 14-15
- 1 UConn 103
- 16 Lehigh 35
- 8 N.C. St. 50
- 9 Iowa 56
- 5 Duke 70
- 12 DePaul 56
- 4 Illinois 79
- 13 Drake 62
- 6 Oregon 80
- 11 San Diego St. 68
- 3 Tennessee 91
- 14 Grambling 54
- 7 S.F. Austin 79
- 10 Toledo 66
- 2 Colorado 69
- 15 Marshall 49

SECOND ROUND
- UConn 72
- Iowa 53
- Duke 67
- Illinois 85
- Oregon 59
- Tennessee 76
- S.F. Austin 57
- Colorado 66

REGIONALS
- UConn 78
- Illinois 71
- Tennessee 75
- Colorado 67

IOWA CITY, IA
- UConn 81
- Tennessee 91

Tenn. 80

WEST

FIRST ROUND
- 1 Stanford 111
- 16 Howard 59
- 8 Texas Tech. 47
- 9 Montana 45
- 5 Utah 66
- 12 Iowa St. 57
- 4 Virginia 96
- 13 Troy St. 74
- 6 Vanderbilt 74
- 11 Washington 62
- 3 Kansas 81
- 14 Detroit 67
- 7 Arizona 76
- 10 W. Kentucky 54
- 2 Georgia 91
- 15 E. Kentucky 55

SECOND ROUND
- Stanford 67
- Texas Tech. 45
- Utah 46
- Virginia 65
- Vanderbilt 51
- Kansas 44
- Arizona 74
- Georgia 80

REGIONALS
- Stanford 91
- Virginia 69
- Vanderbilt 52
- Georgia 66

MISSOULA, MT
- Stanford 82
- Georgia 47

Stanford 82

NATIONAL CHAMPIONSHIP
- Old Dominion 59
- Tennessee 68

FINAL FOUR
at Riverfront Coliseum in Cincinnati.
•••
Semifinals: March 28; Finals: March 30

WOMEN'S FINAL FOUR

at Riverfront Coliseum in Cincinnati (March 28-30).

Semifinals

Old Dominion 83 . . . . OT . . . . Stanford 82
Tennessee 80 . . . . Notre Dame 66

Championship

Tennessee 68 . . . . Old Dominion 59
Final Records: Tennessee (29-10), Old Dominion (34-2), Notre Dame (31-7) and Stanford (34-2).
Most Outstanding Player: Chamique Holdsclaw, Tennessee sophomore forward. SEMIFINAL— 36 minutes, 31 points, 5 rebounds, 4 steals, 3 assists, 2 blocks; FINAL— 39 minutes, 24 points, 6 rebounds, 3 assists, 2 steals, 1 block.
All-Tournament Team: Holdsclaw and guard Kellie Jolly of Tennessee, guard Ticha Penicheiro, forward Clarisse Machanguana and center Nyree Roberts of Old Dominion.

NCAA Championship Game
Tennessee 68

	Min	FG M-A	FT M-A	Pts	Reb O-T	A	F
Tiffani Johnson	30	4-4	0-0	8	1-3	2	2
Chamique Holdsclaw	39	11-20	2-3	24	0-7	3	2
Pashen Thompson .	33	4-4	0-3	8	2-6	0	2
Kyra Elzy	22	1-3	0-1	2	0-3	1	2
Kellie Jolly	35	1-5	2-2	5	0-0	11	2
Niya Butts	8	4-7	0-0	8	0-2	0	0
Laurie Milligan . .	1	0-0	0-0	0	0-0	0	0
Misty Greene	9	0-1	1-2	1	0-1	0	0
Brynae Laxton	3	0-0	0-0	0	0-0	0	0
LaShonda Stephens	2	0-0	0-0	0	0-0	0	1
Abby Conklin	18	4-5	2-2	12	0-1	1	2
TOTALS	200	29-49	7-13	68	3-23	18	13

Three-point FG: 3–5 (Jolly 1–3, Conklin 2–2); **Team Rebounds:** 6; **Blocked Shots:** 2 (Johnson, Holdsclaw); **Turnovers:** 26 (Jolly 9, Holdsclaw 6, Conklin 3, Elzy 3, Butts 2, Greene, Johnson, Thompson); **Steals:** 12 (Jolly 5, Holdsclaw 2, Thompson 2, Butts, Conklin, Elzy). **Percentages:** 2-Pt FG (.591); 3-Pt FG (.600); Total FG (.592); Free Throws (.538).

Old Dominion 59

	Min	FG M-A	FT M-A	Pts	Reb O-T	A	F
Mery Andrade . .	28	2-7	0-0	4	0-0	1	5
C. Machanguana	38	7-13	2-2	16	4-10	4	5
Nyree Roberts . . .	40	6-8	1-2	13	4-9	0	2
Stacy Himes	15	0-1	0-0	0	0-0	1	0
Patricia Penicheiro	37	4-13	2-2	10	1-6	8	2
Amber Eller	15	2-4	0-0	5	2-3	0	0
Aubrey Eblin	11	3-11	2-4	11	1-1	1	0
Latoya Small	5	0-0	0-0	0	2-3	0	1
Natalie Diaz	10	0-5	0-0	0	0-0	1	0
Kelly Bradley	1	0-0	0-0	0	0-0	0	0
TOTALS	200	24-62	7-10	59	14-32	15	16

Three-point FG: 4–18 (Andrade 0–3, Penicheiro 0–1, Eller 1–2, Eblin 3–10, Diaz 0–2). **Team Rebounds:** 2 **Blocked Shots:** 1 (Machanguana) **Turnovers:** 26 (Penicheiro 11, Machanguana 5, Andrade 3, Roberts 3, Diaz, Eblin, Himes, Small); **Steals:** 16 (Penicheiro 8, Machanguana 3, Andrade, Diaz, Eblin, Eller, Himes). **Percentages:** 2-Pt FG (.455); 3-Pt FG (.222); Total FG (.387); Free Throws (.700).

Old Dominion (CAA) . . . . 22 37— **59**
Tennessee (SEC) . . . . 34 34— **68**

Technical Fouls: None. **Officials:** Dee Kantner, Violet Palmer, Yvette Mckinney. **Attendance:** 16,714. **TV Rating:** 4.0 (ESPN).

Final USA Today/CNN Coaches Poll

Taken **after** NCAA tournament.
Voted on by panel of 45 women's coaches and media following the NCAA tournament: first place votes in parentheses with final overall records.

		W-L			W-L
1	Tennessee (45) .	29-10	14 Virginia		23-8
2	Old Dominion .	34-2	15 Colorado		23-9
3	Stanford	34-2	16 Kansas		25-6
4	UConn	33-1	17 Vanderbilt		20-11
5	Notre Dame . .	31-7	18 Texas		22-8
6	Florida	24-9	19 Texas Tech		20-9
7	Georgia	25-6	20 Auburn		22-10
8	Louisiana Tech . .	31-4	21 Michigan St.		22-8
9	North Carolina . .	29-3	22 Stephen F. Austin		28-5
10	G. Washington . .	28-6	23 Purdue		17-11
11	Alabama	25-7	24 Tulane		27-5
12	LSU	25-5	25 Clemson		19-11
13	Illinois	24-8			

Annual Awards
Players of the Year

Kate Starbird, Stanford . . . . Naismith, USBWA, WBCA
Kara Wolters, UConn . . . . AP, Wade
Note: The Wade Trophy is awarded for academics and community service as well as player performance.

Coaches of the Year

Geno Auriemma, UConn . . . . AP, Naismith, WBCA
Wendy Larry, Old Dominion . . . . USBWA

Consensus All-America Team

The NCAA Division I players cited most frequently by the Associated Press, US Basketball Writers Assn., the Women's Basketball Coaches Assn. and the Women's Basketball News Service. Holdover from the 1995-96 All-America first team is in **bold** type; (*) indicates unanimous first team selection.

First Team

	Class	Hgt	Pos
Kate Starbird, Stanford*	Sr.	6-2	F
Chamique Holdsclaw, Tenn.*	So.	6-2	F
Kara Wolters, UConn*	Sr.	6-7	C
Ticha Penicheiro, Old Dominion*	Sr.	5-11	G
DeLisha Milton, Florida	Sr.	6-1	G

Second Team

	Class	Hgt	Pos
Tamecka Dixon, Kansas	Sr.	5-9	G
Tracy Reid, N. Carolina	Jr.	5-11	F
Tina Thompson, USC	Sr.	6-3	C
Nykesha Sales, UConn	Jr.	6-0	F
Clarisse Machanguana, ODU	Sr.	6-5	C

Other Women's Tournaments

NCAA Division II (Mar. 22 at Grand Forks, N.D.): Final— North Dakota def. Southern Indiana, 94-78.

NCAA Division III (Mar. 22 at New York, N.Y.): Final— NYU def. Wisconsin-Eau Claire, 72-70.

NAIA Division I (Mar. 25 at Jackson, Tenn.): Final— Southern Nazarene (Okla.) def. Union (Tenn.), 78-73.

NAIA Division II (Mar. 18 at Angola, Ind.): Final— NW Nazarene (Id.) def. Black Hills St. (S.D.), 64-46.

NCAA Women's Division I Leaders

Includes games through NCAA and NIT tourneys.

INDIVIDUAL

Scoring

	Cl	Gm	Pts	Avg
Cindy Blodgett, Maine	Jr.	30	810	27.0
Kim Williams, DePaul	Sr.	29	727	25.1
Sheila Danker, New Hampshire	Sr.	28	683	24.4
Amy Kieckbusch, Morehead St.	Jr.	28	670	23.9
Vita Redding, Brown	So.	26	618	23.8
Alicia Thompson, Texas Tech	Jr.	29	686	23.7
Korie Hlede, Duquesne	Jr.	28	634	22.6
Tina Thompson, USC	Sr.	29	653	22.5
Kisa Bradley, Oral Roberts	Sr.	26	580	22.3
Diane Seng, Tennessee Tech	Fr.	29	644	22.2
Becky Hammon, Colorado St.	So.	28	618	22.1
Samantha Tomlinson, Troy St.	So.	28	611	21.8
Elena Kisseleva, Liberty	Fr.	30	648	21.6
Allison Feaster, Harvard	Jr.	27	582	21.6
Kate Starbird, Stanford	Sr.	36	753	20.9
Tamecka Dixon, Kansas	Sr.	30	624	20.8
Tracy Reid, N. Carolina	Jr.	30	623	20.8
Chamique Holdsclaw, Tenn.	So.	39	803	20.6
Jamie Redd, Washington	So.	28	574	20.5
Katryna Gaither, Notre Dame	Sr.	38	776	20.4
Connie Swift, Tennessee St.	Sr.	27	550	20.4
Kim Knuth, Toledo	So.	31	631	20.4
Kisha Ford, Georgia Tech	Sr.	27	549	20.3
Emma Wilson, TCU	So.	23	467	20.3
Rosalyn Spann, Jackson St.	Jr.	28	565	20.2

Blocked Shots

	Cl	Gm	No	Avg
Amy Dorsett, Richmond	Sr.	27	110	4.1
Amy Lundquist, DePaul	Sr.	29	116	4.0
Angela Gorsica, Vanderbilt	Sr.	31	118	3.8
Delores Jones, NE Illinois	Jr.	27	100	3.7
Kisa Bradley, Oral Roberts	Sr.	26	94	3.6

Steals

	Cl	Gm	No	Avg
Kasia McClendon, Southern Ill.	Sr.	28	131	4.7
Jade Hyett, Washington St.	So.	27	125	4.6
Kim Williams, DePaul	Sr.	29	131	4.5
Ticha Penicheiro, Old Dominion	Sr.	36	161	4.5
Mimi LaMagna, Canisius	Sr.	27	114	4.2

Rebounding

	Cl	Gm	No	Avg
Etolia Mitchell, Georgia St.	Sr.	25	330	13.2
Angie Iverson, Minnesota	Jr.	28	344	12.3
Melanie Halker, Siena	So.	28	341	12.2
Mfon Udoka, DePaul	Jr.	28	339	12.1
Karen Johnson, Delaware St.	Sr.	28	327	11.7
Kathy Caldwell, New Hampshire	Sr.	28	321	11.5
Pam Durkin, Rider	Sr.	27	307	11.4
Amber Hall, Washington	So.	22	244	11.1
Angie Potthoff, Penn St.	Sr.	27	299	11.1
Dana Wynne, Seton Hall	Sr.	27	295	10.9
Jodi Wimmer, Weber St.	Sr.	28	301	10.8
Monica Logan, Md. Balt. County	So.	27	289	10.7
Allison Feaster, Harvard	Jr.	27	289	10.7
Stephanie Minor, Murray St.	Sr.	27	288	10.7
Janee Young, Fresno St.	Jr.	27	287	10.6
Tina Thompson, USC	Sr.	29	306	10.6
Kate Sanford, Charleston So.	Fr.	25	263	10.5
Pollyanna Johns, Michigan	Jr.	25	261	10.4
Michelle Maldonado, Penn	Jr.	26	271	10.4
Alicia Yapsuga, Lafayette	So.	29	299	10.3

Assists

	Cl	Gm	No	Avg
Tamika Matlock, Michigan St.	Sr.	30	229	7.6
Alli Bills, Utah	Jr.	28	213	7.6
Jade Hyett, Washington St.	So.	27	205	7.6
Ticha Penicheiro, Old Dominion	Sr.	36	271	7.5
Kelley Westhoff, Northern Iowa	Sr.	25	180	7.2
Gina Graziani, Miami-FL	Fr.	29	198	6.8
Katy Winski, Loyola-IL	Sr.	26	177	6.8
Tredena Robinson, Troy St.	So.	30	204	6.8
Heather Fiore, Canisius	Sr.	27	182	6.7
Nicki Taggart, Marquette	Jr.	31	206	6.6
Amber DeWall, Northwestern	Jr.	28	185	6.6
Krissy Holden, Indiana St.	Jr.	25	160	6.4
Amada Reese, Northern Ill.	So.	27	165	6.1
Lori Taylor, Vermont	Jr.	29	177	6.1
Deana Lansing, Portland	Sr.	30	181	6.0
Jamie Shadian, San Francisco	Sr.	31	187	6.0
Jenell Minor, Nicholls St.	So.	26	155	6.0
Catherine Jacob, Buffalo	So.	28	166	5.9
Shiakiea Carter, Grambling	Jr.	30	176	5.9
Skyla Sisco, Montana	Jr.	29	169	5.8

TEAM

Scoring Offense

	Gm	W-L	Pts	Avg
Old Dominion	36	34-2	3037	84.4
Stanford	36	34-2	3033	84.3
UC-Santa Barbara	30	24-6	2526	84.2
Connecticut	34	33-1	2850	83.8
Toledo	31	27-4	2592	83.6
Troy St.	30	23-7	2485	82.8
Illinois	32	24-8	2640	82.5
Youngstown St.	29	23-6	2370	81.7
Stephen F. Austin	33	28-5	2671	80.9
Grambling	30	24-6	2428	80.9

Scoring Defense

	Gm	W-L	Pts	Avg
San Diego St.	30	23-7	1559	52.0
Old Dominion	36	34-2	1887	52.4
San Francisco	31	25-6	1671	53.9
Montana	29	25-4	1566	54.0
Louisiana Tech	35	31-4	1928	55.1
George Washington	34	28-6	1887	55.5
St. Joseph's-PA	31	26-5	1737	56.0
Texas-San Antonio	27	14-13	1515	56.1
Maryland	28	18-10	1575	56.3
Colorado	32	23-9	1801	56.3

Scoring Margin

	Off	Def	Mar
Old Dominion	84.4	52.4	31.9
Connecticut	83.8	57.4	26.4
Louisiana Tech	80.5	55.1	25.4
Stanford	84.3	61.1	23.1
North Carolina	78.4	58.4	20.1
Grambling	80.9	61.4	19.5
George Washington	74.1	55.5	18.6
Maine	80.5	61.9	18.6
Alabama	78.4	61.1	17.4

High-Point Games

No		Opponent	Date
52	Cindy Blodgett, Maine	Towson St.	3/2
47	Alicia Thompson, Tex. Tech	Texas	2/5
46	Heather Fiore, Canisius	St. Peter's	1/19
45	Keisha Anderson, Wisc.	UC-Santa Barb.	11/30
42	Six tied.		

THE 1998

ESPN
INFORMATION PLEASE
SPORTS ALMANAC

COLLEGE BASKETBALL
S T A T I S T I C S

THROUGH THE YEARS
1901-1997
NCAA'S • ALL-TIME LEADERS

SEC
B

PAGE
299

National Champions

The Helms Foundation of Los Angeles, under the direction of founder Bill Schroeder, selected national college basketball champions from 1942-82 and researched retroactive picks from 1901-41. The first NIT tournament and then the NCAA tournament have settled the national championship since 1938, but there are four years (1939, '40, '44 and '54) where the Helms selections differ.

Multiple champions (1901-37): Chicago, Columbia and Wisconsin (3); Kansas, Minnesota, Notre Dame, Penn, Pittsburgh, Syracuse and Yale (2).

Multiple champions (since 1938): UCLA (11); Kentucky (6); Indiana (5); North Carolina (3); Cincinnati, Duke, Kansas, Louisville, N.C. State, Oklahoma A&M (now Oklahoma St.) and San Francisco (2).

Year		Record	Head Coach	Outstanding Player
1901	Yale	10-4	No coach	G.M. Clark, F
1902	Minnesota	11-0	Louis Cooke	W.C. Deering, F
1903	Yale	15-1	W.H. Murphy	R.B. Hyatt, F
1904	Columbia	17-1	No coach	Harry Fisher, F
1905	Columbia	19-1	No coach	Harry Fisher, F
1906	Dartmouth	16-2	No coach	George Grebenstein, F
1907	Chicago	22-2	Joseph Raycroft	John Schommer, C
1908	Chicago	21-2	Joseph Raycroft	John Schommer, C
1909	Chicago	12-0	Joseph Raycroft	John Schommer, C
1910	Columbia	11-1	Harry Fisher	Ted Kiendl, F
1911	St. John's-NY	14-0	Claude Allen	John Keenan, F/C
1912	Wisconsin	15-0	Doc Meanwell	Otto Stangel, F
1913	Navy	9-0	Louis Wenzell	Laurence Wild, F
1914	Wisconsin	15-0	Doc Meanwell	Gene Van Gent, C
1915	Illinois	16-0	Ralph Jones	Ray Woods, G
1916	Wisconsin	20-1	Doc Meanwell	George Levis, F
1917	Washington St	25-1	Doc Bohler	Roy Bohler, G
1918	Syracuse	16-1	Edmund Dollard	Joe Schwarzer, G
1919	Minnesota	13-0	Louis Cooke	Arnold Oss, F
1920	Penn	22-1	Lon Jourdet	George Sweeney, F
1921	Penn	21-2	Edward McNichol	Danny McNichol, G
1922	Kansas	16-2	Phog Allen	Paul Endacott, G
1923	Kansas	17-1	Phog Allen	Paul Endacott, G
1924	North Carolina	25-0	Bo Shepard	Jack Cobb, F
1925	Princeton	21-2	Al Wittmer	Art Loeb, G
1926	Syracuse	19-1	Lew Andreas	Vic Hanson, F
1927	Notre Dame	19-1	George Keogan	John Nyikos, C
1928	Pittsburgh	21-0	Doc Carlson	Chuck Hyatt, F
1929	Montana St.	36-2	Schubert Dyche	John (Cat) Thompson, F
1930	Pittsburgh	23-2	Doc Carlson	Chuck Hyatt, F
1931	Northwestern	16-1	Dutch Lonborg	Joe Reiff, C
1932	Purdue	17-1	Piggy Lambert	John Wooden, G
1933	Kentucky	20-3	Adolph Rupp	Forest Sale, F
1934	Wyoming	26-3	Willard Witte	Les Witte, G
1935	NYU	19-1	Howard Cann	Sid Gross, F
1936	Notre Dame	22-2-1	George Keogan	John Moir, F
1937	Stanford	25-2	John Bunn	Hank Luisetti, F

Year		Record	Winner	Head Coach	Outstanding Player
1938	Temple	23-2	NIT	James Usilton	Meyer Bloom, G
1939	Oregon	29-5	NCAA	Howard Hobson	Slim Wintermute, F
	& LIU-Brooklyn (Helms)	24-0	NIT	Clair Bee	Irv Torgoff, F
1940	Indiana	20-3	NCAA	Branch McCracken	Marv Huffman, G
	& USC (Helms)	20-3	*	Sam Barry	Ralph Vaughn, F
1941	Wisconsin	20-3	NCAA	Bud Foster	Gene Englund, F
1942	Stanford	27-4	NCAA	Everett Dean	Jim Pollard, F
1943	Wyoming	31-2	NCAA	Everett Shelton	Kenny Sailors, G
1944	Utah	21-4	NCAA	Vadal Peterson	Arnie Ferrin, F
	& Army (Helms)	15-0	**	Ed Kelleher	Dale Hall, F

National Champions (Cont.)

Year	Winner	Record	Winner	Head Coach	Outstanding Player
1945	Oklahoma A&M	27-4	NCAA	Hank Iba	Bob Kurland, C
1946	Oklahoma A&M	31-2	NCAA	Hank Iba	Bob Kurland, C
1947	Holy Cross	27-3	NCAA	Doggie Julian	George Kaftan, F
1948	Kentucky	36-3	NCAA	Adolph Rupp	Ralph Beard, G
1949	Kentucky	32-2	NCAA	Adolph Rupp	Alex Groza, C
1950	CCNY	24-5	NCAA & NIT	Nat Holman	Irwin Dambrot, G
1951	Kentucky	32-2	NCAA	Adolph Rupp	Bill Spivey, C
1952	Kansas	28-3	NCAA	Phog Allen	Clyde Lovellette, C
1953	Indiana	23-3	NCAA	Branch McCracken	Don Schlundt, C
1954	La Salle	26-4	NCAA	Ken Loeffler	Tom Gola, F
	& Kentucky (Helms)	25-0	***	Adolph Rupp	Cliff Hagan, G
1955	San Francisco	28-1	NCAA	Phil Woolpert	Bill Russell, C
1956	San Francisco	29-0	NCAA	Phil Woolpert	Bill Russell, C
1957	North Carolina	32-0	NCAA	Frank McGuire	Lennie Rosenbluth, F
1958	Kentucky	23-6	NCAA	Adolph Rupp	Vern Hatton, G
1959	California	25-4	NCAA	Pete Newell	Darrall Imhoff, C
1960	Ohio St	25-3	NCAA	Fred Taylor	Jerry Lucas, C
1961	Cincinnati	27-3	NCAA	Ed Jucker	Bob Wiesenhahn, F
1962	Cincinnati	29-2	NCAA	Ed Jucker	Paul Hogue, C
1963	Loyola-IL	29-2	NCAA	George Ireland	Jerry Harkness, F
1964	UCLA	30-0	NCAA	John Wooden	Walt Hazzard, G
1965	UCLA	28-2	NCAA	John Wooden	Gail Goodrich, G
1966	Texas Western	28-1	NCAA	Don Haskins	Bobby Joe Hill, G
1967	UCLA	30-0	NCAA	John Wooden	Lew Alcindor, C
1968	UCLA	29-1	NCAA	John Wooden	Lew Alcindor, C
1969	UCLA	29-1	NCAA	John Wooden	Lew Alcindor, C
1970	UCLA	28-2	NCAA	John Wooden	Sidney Wicks, F
1971	UCLA	29-1	NCAA	John Wooden	Sidney Wicks, F
1972	UCLA	30-0	NCAA	John Wooden	Bill Walton, C
1973	UCLA	30-0	NCAA	John Wooden	Bill Walton, C
1974	N.C. State	30-1	NCAA	Norm Sloan	David Thompson, F
1975	UCLA	28-3	NCAA	John Wooden	Dave Meyers, F
1976	Indiana	32-0	NCAA	Bob Knight	Scott May, F
1977	Marquette	25-7	NCAA	Al McGuire	Butch Lee, G
1978	Kentucky	30-2	NCAA	Joe B. Hall	Jack Givens, G
1979	Michigan St	26-6	NCAA	Jud Heathcote	Magic Johnson, G
1980	Louisville	33-3	NCAA	Denny Crum	Darrell Griffith, G
1981	Indiana	26-9	NCAA	Bob Knight	Isiah Thomas, G
1982	North Carolina	32-2	NCAA	Dean Smith	James Worthy, F
1983	N.C. State	26-10	NCAA	Jim Valvano	Sidney Lowe, G
1984	Georgetown	34-3	NCAA	John Thompson	Patrick Ewing, C
1985	Villanova	25-10	NCAA	Rollie Massimino	Ed Pinckney, C
1986	Louisville	32-7	NCAA	Denny Crum	Pervis Ellison, C
1987	Indiana	30-4	NCAA	Bob Knight	Steve Alford, G
1988	Kansas	27-11	NCAA	Larry Brown	Danny Manning, C
1989	Michigan	30-7	NCAA	Steve Fisher	Glen Rice, F
1990	UNLV	35-5	NCAA	Jerry Tarkanian	Larry Johnson, F
1991	Duke	32-7	NCAA	Mike Krzyzewski	Christian Laettner, F/C
1992	Duke	34-2	NCAA	Mike Krzyzewski	Christian Laettner, C
1993	North Carolina	34-4	NCAA	Dean Smith	Eric Montross, C
1994	Arkansas	31-3	NCAA	Nolan Richardson	Corliss Williamson, F
1995	UCLA	31-2	NCAA	Jim Harrick	Ed O'Bannon, F
1996	Kentucky	34-2	NCAA	Rick Pitino	Tony Delk, G
1997	Arizona	25-9	NCAA	Lute Olson	Miles Simon, G

*USC was beaten by Kansas in the West regional of the NCAA tournament.
**Army did not lift its policy against postseason play until accepting a bid to the 1961 NIT.
***Unbeaten Kentucky turned down a bid to the 1954 NCAA tournament after the NCAA declared seniors Cliff Hagan, Frank Ramsey and Lou Tsioropoulos ineligible for postseason play.

The Red Cross Benefit Games, 1943-45

For three seasons during World War II, the NCAA and NIT champions met in a benefit game at Madison Square Garden in New York to raise money for the Red Cross. The NCAA champs won all three games.

Year	Winner	Score	Loser
1943	Wyoming (NCAA)	52-47	St. John's (NIT)
1944	Utah (NCAA)	43-36	St. John's (NIT)
1945	Oklahoma A&M (NCAA)	52-44	DePaul (NIT)

NCAA Final Four

The NCAA basketball tournament began in 1939 under the sponsorship of the National Association of Basketball Coaches, but was taken over by the NCAA in 1940. From 1939-51, the winners of the Eastern and Western Regionals played for the national championship, while regional runners-up shared third place. The concept of a Final Four originated in 1952 when four teams qualified for the first national semifinals. Consolation games to determine overall third place were held between regional finalists from 1946-51 and then national semifinalists from 1952-81. Consolation games were discontinued in 1982.

Multiple champions: UCLA (11); Kentucky (6); Indiana (5); North Carolina (3); Cincinnati, Duke, Kansas, Louisville, N.C. State, Oklahoma A&M (now Oklahoma St.) and San Francisco (2).

Year	Champion	Runner-up	Score	Final Two	Third Place	
1939	Oregon	Ohio St.	46-33	@ Evanston, IL	Oklahoma	Villanova
1940	Indiana	Kansas	60-42	@ Kansas City	Duquesne	USC
1941	Wisconsin	Washington St.	39-34	@ Kansas City	Arkansas	Pittsburgh
1942	Stanford	Dartmouth	53-38	@ Kansas City	Colorado	Kentucky
1943	Wyoming	Georgetown	46-34	@ New York	DePaul	Texas
1944	Utah	Dartmouth	42-40 (OT)	@ New York	Iowa St.	Ohio St.
1945	Oklahoma A&M	NYU	49-45	@ New York	Arkansas	Ohio St.

Year	Champion	Runner-up	Score	Final Two	Third Place	Fourth Place
1946	Oklahoma A&M	North Carolina	43-40	@ New York	Ohio St.	California
1947	Holy Cross	Oklahoma	58-47	@ New York	Texas	CCNY
1948	Kentucky	Baylor	58-42	@ New York	Holy Cross	Kansas St.
1949	Kentucky	Oklahoma A&M	46-36	@ Seattle	Illinois	Oregon St.
1950	CCNY	Bradley	71-68	@ New York	N.C. State	Baylor
1951	Kentucky	Kansas St.	68-58	@ Minneapolis	Illinois	Oklahoma A&M

Year	Champion	Runner-up	Score	Third Place	Fourth Place	Final Four
1952	Kansas	St. John's	80-63	Illinois	Santa Clara	@ Seattle
1953	Indiana	Kansas	69-68	Washington	LSU	@ Kansas City
1954	La Salle	Bradley	92-76	Penn St.	USC	@ Kansas City
1955	San Francisco	La Salle	77-63	Colorado	Iowa	@ Kansas City
1956	San Francisco	Iowa	83-71	Temple	SMU	@ Evanston, IL
1957	North Carolina	Kansas	54-53 (3OT)	San Francisco	Michigan St.	@ Kansas City
1958	Kentucky	Seattle	84-72	Temple	Kansas St.	@ Louisville
1959	California	West Virginia	71-70	Cincinnati	Louisville	@ Louisville
1960	Ohio St.	California	75-55	Cincinnati	NYU	@ San Francisco
1961	Cincinnati	Ohio St.	70-65 (OT)	St. Joseph's-PA	Utah	@ Kansas City
1962	Cincinnati	Ohio St.	71-59	Wake Forest	UCLA	@ Louisville
1963	Loyola-IL	Cincinnati	60-58 (OT)	Duke	Oregon St.	@ Louisville
1964	UCLA	Duke	98-83	Michigan	Kansas St.	@ Kansas City
1965	UCLA	Michigan	91-80	Princeton	Wichita St.	@ Portland, OR
1966	Texas Western	Kentucky	72-65	Duke	Utah	@ College Park, MD
1967	UCLA	Dayton	79-64	Houston	North Carolina	@ Louisville
1968	UCLA	North Carolina	78-55	Ohio St.	Houston	@ Los Angeles
1969	UCLA	Purdue	92-72	Drake	North Carolina	@ Louisville
1970	UCLA	Jacksonville	80-69	New Mex. St.	St. Bonaventure	@ College Park, MD
1971	UCLA	Villanova	68-62	Western Ky.	Kansas	@ Houston
1972	UCLA	Florida St.	81-76	North Carolina	Louisville	@ Los Angeles
1973	UCLA	Memphis St.	87-66	Indiana	Providence	@ St. Louis
1974	N.C. State	Marquette	76-64	UCLA	Kansas	@ Greensboro, NC
1975	UCLA	Kentucky	92-85	Louisville	Syracuse	@ San Diego
1976	Indiana	Michigan	86-68	UCLA	Rutgers	@ Philadelphia
1977	Marquette	North Carolina	67-59	UNLV	NC-Charlotte	@ Atlanta
1978	Kentucky	Duke	94-88	Arkansas	Notre Dame	@ St. Louis
1979	Michigan St.	Indiana St.	75-64	DePaul	Penn	@ Salt Lake City
1980	Louisville	UCLA	59-54	Purdue	Iowa	@ Indianapolis
1981	Indiana	North Carolina	63-50	Virginia	LSU	@ Philadelphia

Year	Champion	Runner-up	Score	Third Place		Final Four
1982	North Carolina	Georgetown	63-62	Houston	Louisville	@ New Orleans
1983	N.C. State	Houston	54-52	Georgia	Louisville	@ Albuquerque
1984	Georgetown	Houston	84-75	Kentucky	Virginia	@ Seattle
1985	Villanova	Georgetown	66-64	Memphis St.	St. John's	@ Lexington
1986	Louisville	Duke	72-69	Kansas	LSU	@ Dallas
1987	Indiana	Syracuse	74-73	Providence	UNLV	@ New Orleans
1988	Kansas	Oklahoma	83-79	Arizona	Duke	@ Kansas City
1989	Michigan	Seton Hall	80-79 (OT)	Duke	Illinois	@ Seattle
1990	UNLV	Duke	103-73	Arkansas	Georgia Tech	@ Denver
1991	Duke	Kansas	72-65	North Carolina	UNLV	@ Indianapolis
1992	Duke	Michigan	71-51	Cincinnati	Indiana	@ Minneapolis
1993	North Carolina	Michigan	77-71	Kansas	Kentucky	@ New Orleans
1994	Arkansas	Duke	76-72	Arizona	Florida	@ Charlotte
1995	UCLA	Arkansas	89-78	North Carolina	Oklahoma St.	@ Seattle
1996	Kentucky	Syracuse	76-67	UMass	Mississippi St.	@ E. Rutherford, NJ
1997	Arizona	Kentucky	84-79 (OT)	Minnesota	North Carolina	@ Indianapolis

Note: Six teams have had their standing in the Final Four vacated for using ineligible players: 1961–St. Joseph's-PA (3rd place); 1971–Villanova (Runner-up) and Western Kentucky (3rd place); 1980–UCLA (Runner-up); 1985–Memphis St. (3rd place); 1996–UMass (3rd place).

Most Outstanding Player

A Most Outstanding Player has been selected every year of the NCAA tournament. Winners who did not play for the tournament champion are listed in **bold** type. The 1939 and 1951 winners are unofficial and not recognized by the NCAA. Statistics listed are for Final Four games only.

Multiple winners: Lew Alcindor (3); Alex Groza, Bob Kurland, Jerry Lucas and Bill Walton (2).

Year	Player	Gm	FGM	Pct	3PTM	3PTA	FTM	Pct	Reb	Ast	Blk	Stl	PPG
1939	**Jimmy Hull**, Ohio St.	—	—	—	—	—	—	—	—	—	—	—	—
1940	Marv Huffman, Indiana	2	7	—	—	—	4	—	—	—	—	—	9.0
1941	John Kotz, Wisconsin	2	8	—	—	—	6	—	—	—	—	—	11.0
1942	Howie Dallmar, Stanford	2	8	—	—	—	4	.667	—	—	—	—	10.0
1943	Kenny Sailors, Wyoming	2	10	—	—	—	8	.727	—	—	—	—	14.0
1944	Arnie Ferrin, Utah	2	11	—	—	—	6	—	—	—	—	—	14.0
1945	Bob Kurland, Okla. A&M	2	16	—	—	—	5	—	—	—	—	—	18.5
1946	Bob Kurland, Okla. A&M	2	21	—	—	—	10	.667	—	—	—	—	26.0
1947	George Kaftan, Holy Cross	2	18	—	—	—	12	.706	—	—	—	—	24.0
1948	Alex Groza, Kentucky	2	16	—	—	—	5	—	—	—	—	—	18.5
1949	Alex Groza, Kentucky	2	19	—	—	—	14	—	—	—	—	—	26.0
1950	Irwin Dambrot, CCNY	2	12	.429	—	—	4	.500	—	—	—	—	14.0
1951	Bill Spivey, Kentucky	—	—	—	—	—	—	—	—	—	—	—	—
1952	Clyde Lovellette, Kansas	2	24	—	—	—	18	—	—	—	—	—	33.0
1953	**B.H. Born**, Kansas	2	17	—	—	—	17	—	—	—	—	—	25.5
1954	Tom Gola, La Salle	2	12	—	—	—	14	—	—	—	—	—	19.0
1955	Bill Russell, San Francisco	2	19	—	—	—	9	—	—	—	—	—	23.5
1956	**Hal Lear**, Temple	2	32	—	—	—	16	—	—	—	—	—	40.0
1957	Wilt Chamberlain, Kansas	2	18	.514	—	—	19	.704	—	25	—	—	32.5
1958	**Elgin Baylor**, Seattle	2	18	.340	—	—	12	.750	—	41	—	—	24.0
1959	**Jerry West**, West Virginia	2	22	.667	—	—	22	.688	—	25	—	—	33.0
1960	Jerry Lucas, Ohio St.	2	16	.667	—	—	3	1.000	—	23	—	—	17.5
1961	**Jerry Lucas**, Ohio St.	2	20	.714	—	—	16	.941	—	25	—	—	28.0
1962	Paul Hogue, Cincinnati	2	23	.639	—	—	12	.632	—	38	—	—	29.0
1963	**Art Heyman**, Duke	2	18	.409	—	—	15	.682	—	19	—	—	25.5
1964	Walt Hazzard, UCLA	2	11	.550	—	—	8	.667	10	—	—	—	15.0
1965	**Bill Bradley**, Princeton	2	34	.630	—	—	19	.950	24	—	—	—	43.5
1966	**Jerry Chambers**, Utah	2	25	.532	—	—	20	.833	35	—	—	—	35.0
1967	Lew Alcindor, UCLA	2	14	.609	—	—	11	.458	38	—	—	—	19.5
1968	Lew Alcindor, UCLA	2	22	.629	—	—	9	.900	34	—	—	—	26.5
1969	Lew Alcindor, UCLA	2	23	.676	—	—	16	.640	41	—	—	—	31.0
1970	Sidney Wicks, UCLA	2	15	.714	—	—	9	.600	34	—	—	—	19.5
1971	**Howard Porter**, Villanova	2	20	.488	—	—	7	.778	24	—	—	—	23.5
1972	Bill Walton, UCLA	2	20	.690	—	—	17	.739	41	—	—	—	28.5
1973	Bill Walton, UCLA	2	28	.824	—	—	2	.400	30	—	—	—	29.0
1974	David Thompson, N.C. State	2	19	.514	—	—	11	.786	17	—	—	—	24.5
1975	Richard Washington, UCLA	2	23	.548	—	—	8	.727	20	—	—	—	27.0
1976	Kent Benson, Indiana	2	17	.500	—	—	7	.636	18	—	—	—	20.5
1977	Butch Lee, Marquette	2	11	.344	—	—	8	1.000	6	2	1	1	15.0
1978	Jack Givens, Kentucky	2	28	.651	—	—	8	.667	17	4	1	3	32.0
1979	Magic Johnson, Michigan St.	2	17	.680	—	—	19	.864	17	3	0	2	26.5
1980	Darrell Griffith, Louisville	2	23	.622	—	—	11	.688	7	15	0	2	28.5
1981	Isiah Thomas, Indiana	2	14	.560	—	—	9	.818	4	9	3	4	18.5
1982	James Worthy, N. Carolina	2	20	.741	—	—	2	.286	8	9	0	4	21.0
1983	**Akeem Olajuwon**, Houston	2	16	.552	—	—	9	.643	40	3	2	5	20.5
1984	Patrick Ewing, Georgetown	2	8	.571	—	—	2	1.000	18	1	15	1	9.0
1985	Ed Pinckney, Villanova	2	8	.571	—	—	12	.750	15	6	3	0	14.0
1986	Pervis Ellison, Louisville	2	15	.600	—	—	6	.750	24	2	3	1	18.0
1987	Keith Smart, Indiana	2	14	.636	0	1	7	.778	7	7	0	2	17.5
1988	Danny Manning, Kansas	2	25	.556	0	1	6	.667	17	4	8	9	28.0
1989	Glen Rice, Michigan	2	24	.490	7	16	4	1.000	16	1	0	3	29.5
1990	Anderson Hunt, UNLV	2	19	.613	9	16	2	.500	4	9	1	1	24.5
1991	Christian Laettner, Duke	2	12	.545	1	1	21	.913	17	2	1	2	23.0
1992	Bobby Hurley, Duke	2	10	.417	7	12	8	.800	3	11	0	3	17.5
1993	Donald Williams, N. Carolina	2	15	.652	10	14	10	1.000	4	1	0	2	25.0
1994	Corliss Williamson, Arkansas	2	21	.500	0	0	10	.714	21	8	3	4	26.0
1995	Ed O'Bannon, UCLA	2	16	.457	3	8	10	.769	25	3	1	7	22.5
1996	Tony Delk, Kentucky	2	15	.417	8	16	6	.546	9	2	3	2	22.0
1997	Miles Simon, Arizona	2	17	.459	3	10	17	.773	8	6	0	1	27.0

Final Four All-Decade Teams

To celebrate the 50th anniversary of the NCAA tournament in 1989, five All-Decade teams were selected by a blue ribbon panel of coaches and administrators. An All-Time Final Four team was also chosen. Selections were actually made prior to the 1988 tournament.

Selection panel: Vic Bubas, Denny Crum, Wayne Duke, Dave Gavitt, Joe B. Hall, Jud Heathcote, Hank Iba, Pete Newell, Dean Smith, John Thompson and John Wooden.

All-Time Team

	Years
Lew Alcindor, UCLA	1967-69
Larry Bird, Indiana St.	1979
Wilt Chamberlain, Kansas	1957
Magic Johnson, Mich. St	1979
Michael Jordan, N. Car.	1982

All-1950s

	Years
Elgin Baylor, Seattle	1958
Wilt Chamberlain, Kansas	1957
Tom Gola, La Salle	1954
K.C. Jones, San Francisco	1955
Clyde Lovellette, Kansas	1952
Oscar Robertson, Cinn.	1959-60
Guy Rodgers, Temple	1958
Lennie Rosenbluth, N. Car.	1957
Bill Russell, San Francisco	1955-56
Jerry West, West Virginia	1959

All-1970s

	Years
Kent Benson, Indiana	1976
Larry Bird, Indiana St	1979
Jack Givens, Kentucky	1978
Magic Johnson, Mich. St	1979
Marques Johnson, UCLA	1975-76
Scott May, Indiana	1976
David Thompson, N.C. State	1974
Bill Walton, UCLA	1972-74
Sidney Wicks, UCLA	1969-71
Keith Wilkes, UCLA	1972-74

All-1940s

	Years
Ralph Beard, Kentucky	1948-49
Howie Dallmar, Stanford	1942
Dwight Eddleman, Illinois	1949
Arnie Ferrin, Utah	1944
Alex Groza, Kentucky	1948-49
George Kaftan, Holy Cross	1947
Bob Kurland, Okla. A&M	1945-46
Jim Pollard, Stanford	1942
Kenny Sailors, Wyoming	1943
Gerry Tucker, Oklahoma	1947

All-1960s

	Years
Lew Alcindor, UCLA	1967-69
Bill Bradley, Princeton	1965
Gail Goodrich, UCLA	1964-65
John Havlicek, Ohio St	1961-62
Elvin Hayes, Houston	1967
Walt Hazzard, UCLA	1964
Jerry Lucas, Ohio St	1960-61
Jeff Mullins, Duke	1964
Cazzie Russell, Michigan	1965
Charlie Scott, N. Carolina	1968-69

All-1980s

	Years
Steve Alford, Indiana	1987
Johnny Dawkins, Duke	1986
Patrick Ewing, Georgetown	1982-84
Darrell Griffith, Louisville	1980
Michael Jordan, N. Carolina	1982
Rodney McCray, Louisville	1980
Akeem Olajuwon, Houston	1983-84
Ed Pinckney, Villanova	1985
Isiah Thomas, Indiana	1981
James Worthy, N. Carolina	1982

Note: Lew Alcindor later changed his name to Kareem Abdul-Jabbar; Keith Wilkes later changed his first name to Jamaal; and Akeem Olajuwon later changed the spelling of his first name to Hakeem.

Seeds at the Final Four

Seeds at the Final Four since the NCAA began seeding teams in 1979. Total refers to the combined sum of the four seeds. Teams that went on to win the national championship are in **bold** type.

Year	Seeds (Total)	Teams
1979	1,2,2,9 (14)	Indiana St., **Michigan St.**, DePaul, Pennsylvania
1980	2,5,6,8 (21)	**Louisville**, Iowa, Purdue, UCLA
1981	1,1,2,3 (7)	Virginia, LSU, N. Carolina, **Indiana**
1982	1,1,3,6 (11)	**N. Carolina**, Georgetown, Louisville, Houston
1983	1,1,4,6 (12)	Houston, Louisville, Georgia, **N.C. State**
1984	1,1,2,7 (11)	Kentucky, **Georgetown**, Houston, Virginia
1985	1,1,2,8 (12)	St. John's, Georgetown, Memphis, **Villanova**
1986	1,1,2,11 (15)	Duke, Kansas, **Louisville**, LSU
1987	1,1,2,6 (10)	UNLV, **Indiana**, Syracuse, Providence
1988	1,1,2,6 (10)	Arizona, Oklahoma, Duke, **Kansas**
1989	1,2,3,3 (9)	Illinois, Duke, Seton Hall, **Michigan**
1990	1,3,4,4 (12)	**UNLV**, Duke, Ga. Tech, Arkansas
1991	1,1,2,3 (7)	UNLV, N. Carolina, **Duke**, Kansas
1992	1,2,4,6 (13)	**Duke**, Indiana, Cincinnati, Michigan
1993	1,1,1,2 (5)	**N. Carolina**, Kentucky, Michigan, Kansas
1994	1,2,2,3 (8)	**Arkansas**, Arizona, Duke, Florida
1995	1,2,2,4 (9)	**UCLA**, Arkansas, N. Carolina, Okla. St.
1996	1,1,4,5 (11)	**Kentucky**, UMass, Syracuse, Miss. St.
1997	1,1,1,4 (7)	Kentucky, N. Carolina, Minnesota, **Arizona**

All Time Seeds Records

All-Time records of NCAA tournament seeds since tourney expanded to 64 teams in 1985. Note that 1st refers to championships. 2nd refers to runners-up and FF refers to Final Four appearances.

Seed	W	L	Pct.	1st	2nd	FF
1	226	68	.769	9	8	19
2	169	72	.701	4	5	10
3	107	74	.591	2	3	2
4	106	75	.586	1	1	7
5	86	77	.528	0	0	2
6	106	74	.589	2	1	3
7	66	76	.465	0	0	1
8	55	75	.423	1	1	0
9	46	77	.374	0	0	1
10	43	76	.361	0	0	0
11	32	72	.308	0	0	1
12	27	72	.273	0	0	0
13	11	52	.175	0	0	0
14	13	52	.200	0	0	0
15	3	52	.055	0	0	0
16	0	52	.000	0	0	0

Collegiate Commissioners Association Tournament

The Collegiate Commissioners Association staged an eight-team tournament for teams that didn't make the NCAA tournament in 1974 and '75.

Most Valuable Players: 1974–Kent Benson, Indiana; 1975–Bob Elliot, Arizona.

Year	Winner	Score	Loser	Site
1974	Indiana	85-60	USC	St. Louis
1975	Drake	83-76	Arizona	Louisville

NCAA Tournament Appearances

App		W-L	F4	Championships	App		W-L	F4	Championships
39	Kentucky	77-35	12	6 (1948-49,51,58,78,96)	19	Utah	25-22	3	1 (1944)
33	UCLA	74-25	15	11 (1964-65,67-73,75,95)	19	Connecticut	17-20	0	None
31	N. Carolina	72-31	13	3 (1957,82,93)	18	Ohio St.	31-17	8	1 (1960)
27	Louisville	48-29	7	2 (1980,86)	18	Houston	26-23	5	None
26	Indiana	50-21	7	5 (1940,53,76,81,87)	18	Illinois	22-19	4	None
26	Kansas	56-26	10	2 (1952,88)	18	BYU	11-21	0	None
24	Villanova	37-24	3	1 (1985)	17	N.C. State	27-16	3	2 (1974,83)
24	Notre Dame	25-28	1	None	17	Iowa	23-19	3	None
23	St. John's	23-25	2	None	17	West Virginia	11-17	1	None
23	Syracuse	35-24	3	None	16	Cincinnati	32-15	6	2 (1961-62)
22	Arkansas	37-22	6	1 (1994)	16	Arizona	23-15	3	1 (1997)
22	Kansas St.	27-26	4	None	16	Oklahoma	20-16	3	None
20	DePaul	20-23	2	None	16	Memphis	18-16	2	None
21	Duke	57-19	11	2 (1991-92)	16	Purdue	18-16	2	None
21	Georgetown	36-20	4	1 (1984)	16	Texas	16-19	2	None
21	Marquette	28-22	2	1 (1977)	16	Missouri	13-16	0	None
21	Temple	24-21	2	None	16	Oregon St.	12-19	2	None
20	Princeton	12-24	1	None	16	Pennsylvania	13-18	1	None
19	Michigan	40-18	6	1 (1989)	16	Western Ky.	15-17	1	None

Note: Although all NCAA tournament appearances are included above, the NCAA has officially voided the records of Villanova (4-1) and Western Ky. (4-1) in 1971, UCLA (5-1) in 1980, Oregon St. (2-3) from 1980-82, Memphis (9-5) from 1982-86, DePaul (6-4) from 1986-89, N.C. State (0-2) from 1987-88 and Kentucky (2-1) in 1988.

All-Time NCAA Division I Tournament Leaders

Through 1997; minimum of six games; **Last** column indicates final year played.

CAREER

Scoring

	Points	Yrs	Last	Gm	Pts
1	Christian Laettner, Duke	4	1992	23	407
2	Elvin Hayes, Houston	3	1968	13	358
3	Danny Manning, Kansas	4	1988	16	328
4	Oscar Robertson, Cincinnati	3	1960	10	324
5	Glen Rice, Michigan	4	1989	13	308
6	Lew Alcindor, UCLA	3	1969	12	304
7	Bill Bradley, Princeton	3	1965	9	303
8	Austin Carr, Notre Dame	3	1971	7	289
9	Juwan Howard, Michigan	3	1994	16	280
10	Calbert Cheaney, Indiana	4	1993	13	279

	Average	Yrs	Last	Pts	Avg
1	Austin Carr, Notre Dame	3	1971	289	41.3
2	Bill Bradley, Princeton	3	1965	303	33.7
3	Oscar Robertson, Cincinnati	3	1960	324	32.4
4	Jerry West, West Virginia	3	1960	275	30.6
5	Bob Pettit, LSU	2	1954	183	30.5
6	Dan Issel, Kentucky	3	1970	176	29.3
	Jim McDaniels, Western Ky	2	1971	176	29.3
8	Dwight Lamar, SW Louisiana	2	1973	175	29.2
9	Bo Kimble, Loyola-CA	3	1990	204	29.1
10	David Robinson, Navy	3	1987	200	28.6

Rebounds

	Total	Yrs	Last	Gm	No
1	Elvin Hayes, Houston	3	1968	13	222
2	Lew Alcindor, UCLA	3	1969	12	201
3	Jerry Lucas, Ohio St.	3	1962	12	197
4	Bill Walton, UCLA	3	1974	12	176
5	Christian Laettner, Duke	4	1992	23	169
6	Paul Hogue, Cincinnati	3	1962	12	160
7	Sam Lacey, New Mexico St.	3	1970	11	157
8	Derrick Coleman, Syracuse	4	1990	14	155
9	Akeem Olajuwon, Houston	3	1984	15	153
10	Patrick Ewing, Georgetown	4	1985	18	144

	Average	Yrs	Last	Reb	Avg
1	Johnny Green, Michigan St.	2	1959	118	19.7
2	Artis Gilmore, Jacksonville	2	1971	115	19.2
3	Paul Silas, Creighton	3	1964	111	18.5
4	Len Chappell, Wake Forest	2	1962	137	17.1
5	Elvin Hayes, Houston	3	1968	222	17.1
6	Lew Alcindor, UCLA	3	1969	201	16.8
7	Jerry Lucas, Ohio St.	3	1962	197	16.4
8	Bill Walton, UCLA	3	1974	176	14.7
9	Sam Lacey, New Mexico St.	3	1970	157	14.3
10	Bob Lanier, St. Bonaventure	3	1970	85	14.2

3-Pt Field Goals

	Total	Yrs	Last	Gm	No
1	Bobby Hurley, Duke	4	1993	20	42
2	Jeff Fryer, Loyola-CA	3	1990	7	38
3	Glen Rice, Michigan	4	1989	13	35
4	Anderson Hunt, UNLV	3	1991	15	34
5	Dennis Scott, Georgia Tech	3	1990	8	33

Assists

	Total	Yrs	Last	Gm	No
1	Bobby Hurley, Duke	4	1993	20	145
2	Sherman Douglas, Syracuse	4	1989	14	106
3	Greg Anthony, UNLV	3	1991	15	100
4	Mark Wade, UNLV	2	1987	8	93
	Rumeal Robinson, Michigan	3	1990	11	93

SINGLE TOURNAMENT

Scoring

	Points	Year	Gm	Pts
1	Glen Rice, Michigan	1989	6	184
2	Bill Bradley, Princeton	1965	5	177
3	Elvin Hayes, Houston	1968	5	167
4	Danny Manning, Kansas	1988	6	163
5	Hal Lear, Temple	1956	5	160
	Jerry West, West Virginia	1959	5	160

	Average	Year	Gm	Pts	Avg
1	Austin Carr, Notre Dame	1970	3	158	52.7
2	Austin Carr, Notre Dame	1971	3	125	41.7
3	Jerry Chambers, Utah	1966	4	143	35.8
	Bo Kimble, Loyola-CA	1990	4	143	35.8
5	Bill Bradley, Princeton	1965	5	177	35.4
6	Clyde Lovellette, Kansas	1952	4	141	35.3

Rebounds

	Total	Year	Gm	No	Avg
1	Elvin Hayes, Houston	1968	5	97	19.4
2	Artis Gilmore, Jacksonville	1970	5	93	18.6
3	Elgin Baylor, Seattle	1958	5	91	18.2
4	Sam Lacey, New Mexico St. ..	1970	5	90	18.0
5	Clarence Glover, Western Ky .	1971	5	89	17.8

Assists

	Total	Year	Gm	No	Avg
1	Mark Wade, UNLV	1987	5	61	12.2
2	Rumeal Robinson, Michigan ..	1989	6	56	9.3
3	Sherman Douglas, Syracuse ..	1987	6	49	8.2
4	Bobby Hurley, Duke	1992	6	47	7.8
5	Michael Jackson, Georgetown	1985	6	45	7.5

SINGLE GAME

Scoring

	Points	Year	Pts
1	Austin Carr, Notre Dame vs Ohio Univ ...	1970	61
2	Bill Bradley, Princeton vs Wichita St.	1965	58
3	Oscar Robertson, Cincinnati vs Arkansas .	1958	56
4	Austin Carr, Notre Dame vs Kentucky	1970	52
	Austin Carr, Notre Dame vs TCU	1971	52
6	David Robinson, Navy vs Michigan	1987	50
7	Elvin Hayes, Houston vs Loyola-IL	1968	49
8	Hal Lear, Temple vs SMU	1956	48
9	Austin Carr, Notre Dame vs Houston	1971	47
10	Dave Corzine, DePaul vs Louisville	1978	46
11	Bob Houbregs, Washington vs Seattle	1953	45
	Austin Carr, Notre Dame vs Iowa	1970	45
	Bo Kimble, Loyola-CA vs New Mexico St. .	1990	45
14	Seven players tied with 44 each.		

Rebounds

	Total	Year	No
1	Fred Cohen, Temple vs UConn	1956	34
2	Nate Thurmond, Bowl. Green vs Miss. St. .	1963	31
3	Jerry Lucas, Ohio St. vs Kentucky	1961	30
4	Toby Kimball, UConn vs St. Joseph's-PA ..	1965	29
5	Elvin Hayes, Houston vs Pacific	1966	28

Assists

	Total	Year	No
1	Mark Wade, UNLV vs Indiana	1987	18
2	Sam Crawford, N. Mexico St. vs Nebraska	1993	16
3	Kenny Patterson, DePaul vs Syracuse	1985	15
4	Keith Smart, Indiana vs Auburn	1987	15
5	Five players tied with 14 each.		

SINGLE FINAL FOUR GAME

Letters in the **Year** column indicate the following: C for Consolation Game, F for Final and S for Semifinal.

Scoring

	Points	Year	Pts
1	Bill Bradley, Princeton vs Wichita St	1965-C	58
2	Hal Lear, Temple vs SMU	1956-C	48
3	Bill Walton, UCLA vs Memphis St	1973-F	44
4	Bob Houbregs, Washington vs LSU	1953-C	42
	Jack Egan, St. Joseph's-PA vs Utah	1961-C	42*
	Gail Goodrich, UCLA vs Michigan	1965-C	42
7	Jack Givens, Kentucky vs Duke	1978-F	41
8	Oscar Robertson, Cincinnati vs L'ville	1959-C	39
	Al Wood, N. Carolina vs Virginia	1981-S	39
10	Jerry West, West Va. vs Louisville	1959-S	38
	Jerry Chambers, Utah vs Texas Western ..	1966-S	38
	Freddie Banks, UNLV vs Indiana	1987-S	38

* Four overtimes.

Rebounds

	Total	Year	No
1	Bill Russell, San Francisco vs Iowa	1956-F	27
2	Elvin Hayes, Houston vs UCLA	1967-S	24
3	Bill Russell, San Francisco vs SMU	1956-S	23
4	Four players tied with 22 each.		

Assists

	Total	Year	No
1	Mark Wade, UNLV vs Indiana	1987-S	18
2	Rumeal Robinson, Michigan vs Illinois ..	1989-S	12
3	Michael Jackson, G'town vs St. John's ..	1985-S	11
4	Milt Wagner, Louisville vs LSU	1986-S	11
5	Rumeal Robinson, Mich. vs Seton Hall ..	1989-F	11*

*Overtime.

Teams in both NCAA and NIT

Fourteen teams played in both the NCAA and NIT tournaments from 1940-52. Colorado (1940), Utah (1944), Kentucky (1949) and BYU (1951) won one of the titles, while CCNY won two in 1950, beating Bradley in both championship games.

Year		NIT	NCAA
1940	Colorado	**Won Final**	Lost 1st Rd
	Duquesne	Lost Final	Lost 2nd Rd
1944	Utah	Lost 1st Rd	**Won Final**
1949	Kentucky	Lost 2nd Rd	**Won Final**
1950	CCNY	**Won Final**	**Won Final**
	Bradley	Lost Final	Lost Final
1951	BYU	**Won Final**	Lost 2nd Rd
	St. John's	Lost 3rd Rd	Lost 2nd Rd
	N.C. State	Lost 2nd Rd	Lost 2nd Rd
	Arizona	Lost 2nd Rd	Lost 1st Rd
1952	St. John's	Lost Final	Lost 2nd Rd
	Dayton	Lost 1st Rd	Lost Final
	Duquesne	Lost 2nd Rd	Lost 2nd Rd
	Saint Louis	Lost 2nd Rd	Lost 2nd Rd

Most Popular Final Four Sites

The NCAA has staged its Men's Division I championship—the Final Two (1939-51) and Final Four (since 1952)—at 29 different arenas and indoor stadiums in 24 different cities. The following facilities have all hosted the event more than once. Note that the RCA Dome is scheduled to host the Final Four again in 2000.

No	Arena	Years
9	Municipal Auditorium (KC)	1940-42, 53-55, 57, 61, 64
7	Madison Sq. Garden (NYC)	1943-48, 50
6	Freedom Hall (Louisville)	1958-59, 62-63, 67, 69
3	Kingdome (Seattle)	1984, 89, 95
	Superdome (New Orleans)	1982, 87, 93
2	Cole Field House (College Park, Md.)	1966, 70
	Edmundson Pavilion (Seattle)	1949, 52
	LA Sports Arena	1968, 72
	RCA Dome (Indianapolis)	1991, 97
	St. Louis Arena	1973, 78
	Spectrum (Philadelphia)	1976, 81

NIT Championship

The National Invitation Tournament began under the sponsorship of the Metropolitan New York Basketball Writers Association in 1938. The NIT is now administered by the Metropolitan Intercollegiate Basketball Association. All championship games have been played at Madison Square Garden.

Multiple winners: St. John's (5); Bradley (4); BYU, Dayton, Kentucky, LIU-Brooklyn, Michigan, Providence, Temple, Virginia and Virginia Tech (2).

Year	Winner	Score	Loser	Year	Winner	Score	Loser
1938	Temple	60-36	Colorado	1968	Dayton	61-48	Kansas
1939	LIU-Brooklyn	44-32	Loyola-IL	1969	Temple	89-76	Boston Coll.
1940	Colorado	51-40	Duquesne	1970	Marquette	65-53	St. John's
1941	LIU-Brooklyn	56-42	Ohio Univ.	1971	North Carolina	84-66	Georgia Tech
1942	West Virginia	47-45	Western Ky.	1972	Maryland	100-69	Niagara
1943	St. John's	48-27	Toledo	1973	Virginia Tech	92-91 (OT)	Notre Dame
1944	St. John's	47-39	DePaul	1974	Purdue	97-81	Utah
1945	DePaul	71-54	Bowling Green	1975	Princeton	80-69	Providence
1946	Kentucky	46-45	Rhode Island	1976	Kentucky	71-67	NC-Charlotte
1947	Utah	49-45	Kentucky	1977	St. Bonaventure	94-91	Houston
1948	Saint Louis	65-52	NYU	1978	Texas	101-93	N.C. State
1949	San Francisco	48-47	Loyola-IL	1979	Indiana	53-52	Purdue
1950	CCNY	69-61	Bradley	1980	Virginia	58-55	Minnesota
1951	BYU	62-43	Dayton	1981	Tulsa	86-84 (OT)	Syracuse
1952	La Salle	75-64	Dayton	1982	Bradley	67-58	Purdue
1953	Seton Hall	58-46	St. John's	1983	Fresno St.	69-60	DePaul
1954	Holy Cross	71-62	Duquesne	1984	Michigan	83-63	Notre Dame
1955	Duquesne	70-58	Dayton	1985	UCLA	65-62	Indiana
1956	Louisville	93-80	Dayton	1986	Ohio St.	73-63	Wyoming
1957	Bradley	84-83	Memphis St.	1987	Southern Miss.	84-80	La Salle
1958	Xavier-OH	78-74 (OT)	Dayton	1988	Connecticut	72-67	Ohio St.
1959	St. John's	76-71 (OT)	Bradley	1989	St. John's	73-65	Saint Louis
1960	Bradley	88-72	Providence	1990	Vanderbilt	74-72	Saint Louis
1961	Providence	62-59	Saint Louis	1991	Stanford	78-72	Oklahoma
1962	Dayton	73-67	St. John's	1992	Virginia	81-76 (OT)	Notre Dame
1963	Providence	81-66	Canisius	1993	Minnesota	62-61	Georgetown
1964	Bradley	86-54	New Mexico	1994	Villanova	80-73	Vanderbilt
1965	St. John's	55-51	Villanova	1995	Virginia Tech	65-64 (OT)	Marquette
1966	BYU	97-84	NYU	1996	Nebraska	60-56	St. Joseph's
1967	Southern Illinois	71-56	Marquette	1997	Michigan	82-72	Florida St.

Most Valuable Player

A Most Valuable Player has been selected every year of the NIT tournament. Winners who did not play for the tournament champion are listed in **bold** type.

Multiple winners: None. However, Tom Gola is the only player to be named MVP in both the NIT (1952) and NCAA (1954) tournaments.

Year
1938 Don Shields, Temple
1939 **Bill Lloyd**, St. John's
1940 Bob Doll, Colorado
1941 **Frank Baumholtz**, Ohio U.
1942 Rudy Baric, West Virginia
1943 Harry Boykoff, St. John's
1944 Bill Kotsores, St. John's
1945 George Mikan, DePaul
1946 **Ernie Calverley**,Rhode Island
1947 Vern Gardner, Utah
1948 Ed Macauley, Saint Louis
1949 Don Lofgan, San Francisco
1950 Ed Warner, CCNY
1951 Roland Minson, BYU
1952 Tom Gola, La Salle
& Norm Grekin, La Salle
1953 Walter Dukes, Seton Hall
1954 Togo Palazzi, Holy Cross
1955 **Maurice Stokes**, St. Francis-PA
1956 Charlie Tyra, Louisville
1957 **Win Wilfong**, Memphis St.
1958 Hank Stein, Xavier-OH
1959 Tony Jackson, St. John's
1960 **Lenny Wilkens**, Providence
1961 Vin Ernst, Providence

Year
1962 Bill Chmielewski, Dayton
1963 Ray Flynn, Providence
1964 Lavern Tart, Bradley
1965 Ken McIntyre, St. John's
1966 **Bill Melchionni**, Villanova
1967 Walt Frazier, So. Illinois
1968 Don May, Dayton
1969 **Terry Driscoll**, Boston College
1970 Dean Meminger, Marquette
1971 Bill Chamberlain, N. Carolina
1972 Tom McMillen, Maryland
1973 **John Shumate**, Notre Dame
1974 **Mike Sojourner**, Utah
1975 **Ron Lee**, Oregon
1976 **Cedric Maxwell**, NC-Charlotte
1977 Greg Sanders, St. Bonaventure
1978 Ron Baxter, Texas
& Jim Krivacs, Texas
1979 Clarence Carter, Indiana
& Ray Tolbert, Indiana
1980 Ralph Sampson, Virginia
1981 Greg Stewart, Tulsa
1982 Mitchell Anderson, Bradley
1983 Ron Anderson, Fresno St.
1984 Tim McCormick, Michigan

Year
1985 Reggie Miller, UCLA
1986 Brad Sellers, Ohio St.
1987 Randolph Keys, So. Miss.
1988 Phil Gamble, Connecticut
1989 Jayson Williams, St. John's
1990 Scott Draud, Vanderbilt
1991 Adam Keefe, Stanford
1992 Bryant Stith, Virginia
1993 Voshon Lenard, Minnesota
1994 **Doremus Bennerman**, Siena
1995 Shawn Smith, Va. Tech
1996 Erick Strickland, Nebraska
1997 Robert Traylor, Michigan

All-Time NIT Team
As selected by a media panel.

Walt Frazier, S. Illinois
George Milkan, DePaul
Tom Gola, LaSalle
Maurice Stokes, St. Francis-PA
Ralph Beard, Kentucky

All-Time Winningest Division I Teams

Top 25 Winning Percentage

Division I schools with best winning percentages through 1996-97 season (including tournament games). Years in Division I only; minimum 20 years. NCAA tournament columns indicate years in tournament, record and number of championships.

		First Year	Yrs	Games	Won	Lost	Tied	Pct	NCAA Tourney Yrs	W-L	Titles
1	Kentucky	1903	94	2211	1685	525	1	.762	38	77-35	6
2	North Carolina	1911	87	2270	1675	595	0	.738	31	72-31	3
3	UNLV	1959	39	1105	811	294	0	.734	12	30-11	1
4	UCLA	1920	78	2002	1398	604	0	.698	33	77-26	11
5	Kansas	1899	99	2340	1630	710	0	.697	26	56-26	2
6	St. John's	1908	90	2228	1532	696	0	.688	23	23-25	0
7	Syracuse	1901	96	2134	1451	683	0	.680	23	35-24	0
8	Western Kentucky	1915	78	2006	1356	650	0	.676	16	15-17	0
9	Duke	1906	92	2265	1516	749	0	.669	21	57-19	2
10	Arkansas	1924	74	1930	1268	662	0	.657	22	37-22	1
11	Louisville	1912	83	2021	1325	696	0	.656	27	48-29	2
12	DePaul	1924	74	1803	1180	623	0	.654	20	20-23	0
13	Indiana	1901	97	2165	1410	755	0	.651	26	50-21	5
14	Notre Dame	1898	92	2177	1414	762	1	.650	24	25-28	0
15	Utah	1909	89	2074	1346	728	0	.649	19	25-22	1
16	Temple	1895	101	2278	1475	803	0	.647	21	24-21	0
17	Weber St.	1963	35	991	640	351	0	.646	11	5-12	0
18	Purdue	1897	99	2105	1355	750	0	.644	16	19-16	0
19	Illinois	1906	92	2057	1321	736	0	.642	18	22-19	0
20	Villanova	1921	77	1961	1256	705	0	.640	24	37-24	1
21	Penn	1897	97	2259	1437	820	2	.636	16	13-18	0
22	La Salle	1931	67	1715	1085	630	0	.633	11	11-10	1
23	Houston	1946	52	1443	912	531	0	.632	18	26-23	0
24	N.C. State	1913	85	2072	1309	763	0	.632	17	27-16	2
25	Illinois St.	1972	25	757	477	280	0	.630	4	2-4	0

Top 35 Victories

Division I schools with most victories through 1996-97 (including postseason tournaments). Minimum 20 years in Division I.

		Wins			Wins			Wins			Wins
1	Kentucky	1685	10	Notre Dame	1414	19	West Virginia	1325	28	Arkansas	1268
2	North Carolina	1675	11	Indiana	1410		Louisville	1325	29	Montana St.	1266
3	Kansas	1630	12	UCLA	1398	21	Illinois	1321	30	Ohio St	1256
4	St. John's	1532	13	Washington	1365	22	Fordham	1313		Villanova	1256
5	Duke	1516	14	Princeton	1359	23	N.C. State	1309	32	Alabama	1251
6	Temple	1475	15	Western Ky.	1356	24	Texas	1302	33	St. Joseph's	1249
7	Syracuse	1451	16	Purdue	1355	25	Wash. St.	1300	33	USC	1246
8	Oregon St.	1441	17	Utah	1346	26	Cincinnati	1283	35	Iowa	1245
9	Penn	1437	18	Bradley	1326	27	Arizona	1277			

Top 50 Single-Season Victories

Division I schools with most victories in a single season through 1996-97 (including postseason tournaments). NCAA champions in **bold** type.

		Year	Record			Year	Record			Year	Record
1	UNLV	1987	37-2	22	**N. Carolina**	1957	32-0		**Wyoming**	1943	31-2
	Duke	1986	37-3		**Indiana**	1976	32-0		**Okla. A&M**	1946	31-2
3	**Kentucky**	1948	36-3		**Kentucky**	1949	32-2		Seton Hall	1953	31-2
4	Massachusetts*	1996	35-2		**Kentucky**	1951	32-2		Houston	1968	31-2
	Georgetown	1985	35-3		**N. Carolina**	1982	32-2		Rutgers	1976	31-2
	Arizona	1988	35-3		Temple	1988	32-2		**UCLA**	1995	31-2
	Kansas	1986	35-4		Arkansas	1978	32-3		Houston	1983	31-3
	Oklahoma	1988	35-4		Bradley	1986	32-3		**Arkansas**	1994	31-3
	UNLV	1990	35-5		Connecticut*	1996	32-3		Memphis St	1985	31-4
	Kentucky	1997	35-5		Louisville	1983	32-4		St. John's	1985	31-4
11	UNLV	1991	34-1		Kentucky	1986	32-4		Indiana	1993	31-4
	Duke	1992	34-2		N. Carolina	1987	32-4		Minnesota	1997	31-4
	Kentucky	1996	34-2		Temple	1987	32-4		LSU	1981	31-5
	Kansas	1997	34-2		Bradley	1950	32-5		St. John's	1986	31-5
	Kentucky	1947	34-3		Marshall	1947	32-5		Illinois	1989	31-5
	Georgetown	1984	34-3		Houston	1984	32-5		Michigan	1993	31-5
	Arkansas	1991	34-4		Bradley	1951	32-6		Oklahoma	1985	31-6
	N. Carolina	1993	34-4		**Louisville**	1986	32-7		Connecticut	1990	31-6
19	Indiana St	1979	33-1		**Duke**	1991	32-7		Syracuse	1987	31-7
	Louisville	1980	33-3		Arkansas	1995	32-7		Seton Hall	1989	31-7
	UNLV	1986	33-5	42	Indiana	1975	31-1				

*NCAA later stripped UMass of its four 1996 tournament victories after learning that center Marcus Camby accepted gifts from an agent. UConn was stripped of its two 1996 tournament victories because two players illegally accepted plane tickets.

Associated Press Final Polls

The Associated Press introduced its weekly college basketball poll of sportswriters (later, sportswriters and broadcasters) during the 1948-49 season.

Since the NCAA Division I tournament has determined the national champion since 1939, the final AP poll ranks the nation's best teams through the regular season and conference tournaments.

Except for four seasons (see AP Post-Tournament Final Polls), the final AP poll has been released prior to the NCAA and NIT tournaments and has gone from a Top 10 (1949 and 1963-67) to a Top 20 (1950-62 and 1968-89) to a Top 25 (since 1990).

Tournament champions are in **bold** type.

1949

	Before Tourns	Head Coach	Final Record
1 **Kentucky**	29-1	Adolph Rupp	32-2
2 Oklahoma A&M	21-4	Hank Iba	23-5
3 Saint Louis	22-3	Eddie Hickey	22-4
4 Illinois	19-3	Harry Combes	21-4
5 Western Ky.	25-3	Ed Diddle	25-4
6 Minnesota	18-3	Ozzie Cowles	same
7 Bradley	25-6	Forddy Anderson	27-8
8 **San Francisco**	21-5	Pete Newell	25-5
9 Tulane	24-4	Cliff Wells	same
10 Bowling Green .	21-6	Harold Anderson	24-7

NCAA Final Four (at Edmundson Pavilion, Seattle): **Third Place**—Illinois 57, Oregon St. 53. **Championship** —Kentucky 46, Oklahoma A&M 36.

NIT Final Four (at Madison Square Garden): **Semifinals**—San Francisco 49, Bowling Green 39; Loyola-IL 55, Bradley 50. **Third Place**—Bowling Green 82, Bradley 77. **Championship**—San Francisco 48, Loyola-IL 47.

1950

	Before Tourns	Head Coach	Final Record
1 Bradley	28-3	Forddy Anderson	32-5
2 Ohio St.	21-3	Tippy Dye	22-4
3 Kentucky	25-4	Adolph Rupp	25-5
4 Holy Cross	27-2	Buster Sheary	27-4
5 N.C. State	25-5	Everett Case	27-6
6 Duquesne	22-5	Dudey Moore	23-6
7 UCLA	24-5	John Wooden	24-7
8 Western Ky. ...	24-5	Ed Diddle	25-6
9 St. John's	23-4	Frank McGuire	24-5
10 La Salle	20-3	Ken Loeffler	21-4
11 Villanova	25-4	Al Severance	same
12 San Francisco ..	19-6	Pete Newell	19-7
13 LIU-Brooklyn ..	20-4	Clair Bee	20-5
14 Kansas St.	17-7	Jack Gardner	same
15 Arizona	26-4	Fred Enke	26-5
16 Wisconsin	17-5	Bud Foster	same
17 San Jose St. ...	21-7	Walter McPherson	same
18 Washington St.	19-13	Jack Friel	same
19 Kansas	14-11	Phog Allen	same
20 Indiana	17-5	Branch McCracken	same

Note: Unranked **CCNY**, coached by Nat Holman, won both the NCAAs and NIT. The Beavers entered the postseason at 17-5 and had a final record of 24-5.

NCAA Final Four (at Madison Square Garden): **Third Place**—N. Carolina St. 53, Baylor 41. **Championship**— CCNY 71, Bradley 68.

NIT Final Four (at Madison Square Garden): **Semifinals**—Bradley 83, St. John's 72; CCNY 62, Duquesne 52. **Third Place**—St. John's 69, Duquesne 67 (OT). **Championship**—CCNY 69, Bradley 61.

1951

	Before Tourns	Head Coach	Final Record
1 **Kentucky**	28-2	Adolph Rupp	32-2
2 Oklahoma A&M	27-4	Hank Iba	29-6
3 Columbia	22-0	Lou Rossini	22-1
4 Kansas St.	22-3	Jack Gardner	25-4
5 Illinois	19-4	Harry Combes	22-5
6 Bradley	32-6	Forddy Anderson	same
7 Indiana	19-3	Branch McCracken	same
8 N.C. State	29-4	Everett Case	30-7
9 St. John's	22-3	Frank McGuire	26-5
10 Saint Louis	21-7	Eddie Hickey	22-8
11 **BYU**	22-8	Stan Watts	26-10
12 Arizona	24-4	Fred Enke	24-6
13 Dayton	24-4	Tom Blackburn	27-5
14 Toledo	23-8	Jerry Bush	same
15 Washington ...	22-5	Tippy Dye	24-6
16 Murray St.	21-6	Harlan Hodges	same
17 Cincinnati	18-3	John Wiethe	18-4
18 Siena	19-8	Dan Cunha	same
19 USC	21-6	Forrest Twogood	same
20 Villanova	25-6	Al Severance	25-7

NCAA Final Four (at Williams Arena, Minneapolis): **Third Place**—Illinois 61, Oklahoma St. 46. **Championship**—Kentucky 68, Kansas St. 58.

NIT Final Four (at Madison Sq. Garden): **Semifinals**—Dayton 69, St. John's 62 (OT); BYU 69, Seton Hall 59. **Third Place**—St. John's 70, Seton Hall 68 (2 OT). **Championship**—BYU 62, Dayton 43.

1952

	Before Tourns	Head Coach	Final Record
1 Kentucky	28-2	Adolph Rupp	29-3
2 Illinois	19-3	Harry Combes	22-4
3 Kansas St.	19-5	Jack Gardner	same
4 Duquesne	21-1	Dudey Moore	23-4
5 Saint Louis	22-6	Eddie Hickey	23-8
6 Washington ..	25-6	Tippy Dye	same
7 Iowa	19-3	Bucky O'Connor	same
8 **Kansas**	24-3	Phog Allen	28-3
9 West Virginia .	23-4	Red Brown	same
10 St. John's	22-3	Frank McGuire	25-5
11 Dayton	24-3	Tom Blackburn	28-5
12 Duke	24-6	Harold Bradley	same
13 Holy Cross	23-3	Buster Sheary	24-4
14 Seton Hall	25-2	Honey Russell	25-3
15 St. Bonaventure	19-5	Ed Melvin	21-6
16 Wyoming	27-6	Everett Shelton	28-7
17 Louisville	20-5	Peck Hickman	20-6
18 Seattle	29-7	Al Brightman	29-8
19 UCLA	19-10	John Wooden	19-12
20 SW Texas St. ..	30-1	Milton Jowers	same

Note: Unranked La Salle, coached by Ken Loeffler, won the NIT. The Explorers entered the postseason at 21-7 and had a final record of 25-7.

NCAA Final Four (at Edmundson Pavillion, Seattle): **Semifinals**—St. John's 61, Illinois 59; Kansas 74, Santa Clara 59. **Third Place**—Illinois 67, Santa Clara 64. **Championship**—Kansas 80, St. John's 63.

NIT Final Four (at Madison Sq. Garden): **Semifinals**—La Salle 59, Duquesne 46; Dayton 69, St. Bonaventure 62. **Third Place**—St. Bonaventure 48, Duquesne 34. **Championship**—La Salle 75, Dayton 64.

1953

	Before Tourns	Head Coach	Final Record
1 **Indiana**	18-3	Branch McCracken	23-3
2 La Salle	25-2	Ken Loeffler	25-3
3 **Seton Hall**	28-2	Honey Russell	31-2
4 Washington	27-2	Tippy Dye	30-3
5 LSU	22-1	Harry Rabenhorst	24-3
6 Kansas	16-5	Phog Allen	19-6
7 Oklahoma A&M	22-6	Hank Iba	23-7
Kansas St.	17-4	Jack Gardner	same
9 Western Ky.	25-5	Ed Diddle	25-6
10 Illinois	18-4	Harry Combes	same
11 Oklahoma City	18-4	Doyle Parrick	18-6
12 N.C. State	26-6	Everett Case	same
13 Notre Dame	17-4	John Jordan	19-5
14 Louisville	21-5	Peck Hickman	22-6
Seattle	27-3	Al Brightman	29-4
16 Miami-OH	17-5	Bill Rohr	17-6
17 Eastern Ky.	16-8	Paul McBrayer	16-9
18 Duquesne	18-7	Dudey Moore	21-8
Navy	16-4	Ben Carnevale	16-5
20 Holy Cross	18-5	Buster Sheary	20-6

NCAA Final Four (at Municipal Auditorium, Kansas City): **Semifinals**—Indiana 80, LSU 67; Kansas 79, Washington 53. **Third Place**—Washington 88, LSU 69. **Championship**—Indiana 69, Kansas 68.

NIT Final Four (at Madison Sq. Garden): **Semifinals**—Seton Hall 74, Manhattan 56; St. John's 64, Duquesne 55. **Third Place**—Duquesne 81, Manhattan 67. **Championship**—Seton Hall 58, St. John's 46.

1954

	Before Tourns	Head Coach	Final Record
1 Kentucky	25-0	Adolph Rupp	same*
2 Indiana	19-3	Branch McCracken	20-4
3 Duquesne	24-2	Dudey Moore	26-3
4 Western Ky.	28-1	Ed Diddle	29-3
5 Oklahoma A&M	23-4	Hank Iba	24-5
6 Notre Dame	20-2	John Jordan	22-3
7 Kansas	16-5	Phog Allen	same
8 **Holy Cross**	23-2	Buster Sheary	26-2
9 LSU	21-3	Harry Rabenhorst	21-5
10 **La Salle**	21-4	Ken Loeffler	26-4
11 Iowa	17-5	Bucky O'Connor	same
12 Duke	22-6	Harold Bradley	same
13 Colorado A&M	22-5	Bill Strannigan	22-7
14 Illinois	17-5	Harry Combes	same
15 Wichita	27-3	Ralph Miller	27-4
16 Seattle	26-1	Al Brightman	26-2
17 N.C. State	26-6	Everett Case	28-7
18 Dayton	24-6	Tom Blackburn	25-7
Minnesota	17-5	Ozzie Cowles	same
20 Oregon St.	19-10	Slats Gill	same
UCLA	18-7	John Wooden	same
USC	17-12	Forrest Twogood	19-14

*Kentucky turned down invitation to NCAA tournament after NCAA declared seniors Cliff Hagan, Frank Ramsey and Lou Tsioropoulos ineligible for postseason play.

NCAA Final Four (at Municipal Auditorium, Kansas City): **Semifinals**—La Salle 69, Penn St. 54; Bradley 74, USC 72. **Third Place**—Penn St. 70, USC 61. **Championship**—La Salle 92, Bradley 76.

NIT Final Four (at Madison Square Garden): **Semifinals**—Duquesne 66, Niagara 51; Holy Cross 75, Western Ky. 69. **Third Place**—Niagara 71, Western Ky. 65. **Championship**—Holy Cross 71, Duquesne 62.

1955

	Before Tourns	Head Coach	Final Record
1 **San Francisco**	23-1	Phil Woolpert	28-1
2 Kentucky	22-2	Adolph Rupp	23-3
3 La Salle	22-4	Ken Loeffler	26-5
4 N.C. State	28-4	Everett Case	same
5 Iowa	17-5	Bucky O'Connor	19-7
6 **Duquesne**	19-4	Dudey Moore	22-4
7 Utah	23-3	Jack Gardner	24-4
8 Marquette	22-2	Jack Nagle	24-3
9 Dayton	23-3	Tom Blackburn	25-4
10 Oregon St.	21-7	Slats Gill	22-8
11 Minnesota	15-7	Ozzie Cowles	same
12 Alabama	19-5	Johnny Dee	same
13 UCLA	21-5	John Wooden	same
14 G. Washington	24-6	Bill Reinhart	same
15 Colorado	16-5	Bebe Lee	19-6
16 Tulsa	20-6	Clarence Iba	21-7
17 Vanderbilt	16-6	Bob Polk	same
18 Illinois	17-5	Harry Combes	same
19 West Virginia	19-10	Fred Schaus	19-11
20 Saint Louis	19-7	Eddie Hickey	20-8

NCAA Final Four (at Municipal Auditorium, Kansas City): **Semifinals**—La Salle 76, Iowa 73; San Francisco 62, Colorado 50. **Third Place**—Colorado 75, Iowa 74. **Championship**—San Francisco 77, La Salle 63.

NIT Final Four (at Madison Square Garden): **Semifinals**—Dayton 79, St. Francis-PA 73 (OT); Duquesne 65, Cincinnati 51. **Third Place**—Cincinnati 96, St. Francis-PA 91 (OT). **Championship**—Duquesne 70, Dayton 58.

1956

	Before Tourns	Head Coach	Final Record
1 **San Francisco**	25-0	Phil Woolpert	29-0
2 N.C. State	24-3	Everett Case	24-4
3 Dayton	23-3	Tom Blackburn	25-4
4 Iowa	17-5	Bucky O'Connor	20-6
5 Alabama	21-3	Johnny Dee	same
6 **Louisville**	23-3	Peck Hickman	26-3
7 SMU	22-2	Doc Hayes	25-4
8 UCLA	21-5	John Wooden	22-6
9 Kentucky	19-5	Adolph Rupp	20-6
10 Illinois	18-4	Harry Combes	same
11 Oklahoma City	18-6	Abe Lemons	20-7
12 Vanderbilt	19-4	Bob Polk	same
13 North Carolina	18-5	Frank McGuire	same
14 Holy Cross	22-4	Roy Leenig	22-5
15 Temple	23-3	Harry Litwack	27-4
16 Wake Forest	19-9	Murray Greason	same
17 Duke	19-7	Harold Bradley	same
18 Utah	21-5	Jack Gardner	22-6
19 Oklahoma A&M	18-8	Hank Iba	18-9
20 West Virginia	21-8	Fred Schaus	21-9

NCAA Final Four (at McGaw Hall, Evanston, IL): **Semifinals**—Iowa 83, Temple 76; San Francisco 76, SMU 68. **Third Place**—Temple 90, SMU 81. **Championship**—San Francisco 83, Iowa 71.

NIT Final Four (at Madison Square Garden): **Semifinals**—Dayton 89, St. Francis-NY 58; Louisville 89, St. Joseph's-PA 79. **Third Place**—St. Joseph's-PA 93, St. Francis-NY 82. **Championship**—Louisville 93, Dayton 80.

Associated Press Final Polls (Cont.)

1957

		Before Tourns	Head Coach	Final Record
1	**N. Carolina** ..	27-0	Frank McGuire	32-0
2	Kansas	21-2	Dick Harp	24-3
3	Kentucky	22-4	Adolph Rupp	23-5
4	SMU	21-3	Doc Hayes	22-4
5	Seattle	24-2	John Castellani	24-3
6	Louisville	21-5	Peck Hickman	same
7	West Va.	25-4	Fred Schaus	25-5
8	Vanderbilt ...	17-5	Bob Polk	same
9	Oklahoma City	17-8	Abe Lemons	19-9
10	Saint Louis ...	19-7	Eddie Hickey	19-9
11	Michigan St. ..	14-8	Forddy Anderson	16-10
12	Memphis St. ..	21-5	Bob Vanatta	24-6
13	California	20-4	Pete Newell	21-5
14	UCLA	22-4	John Wooden	same
15	Mississippi St. .	17-8	Babe McCarthy	same
16	Idaho St.	24-2	John Grayson	25-4
17	Notre Dame ...	18-7	John Jordan	20-8
18	Wake Forest ...	19-9	Murray Greason	same
19	Canisius	20-5	Joe Curran	22-6
20	Oklahoma A&M	17-9	Hank Iba	same

Note: Unranked **Bradley**, coached by Chuck Osborn, won the NIT. The Braves entered the tourney at 19-7 and had a final record of 22-7.

NCAA Final Four (at Municipal Auditorium, Kansas City): **Semifinals**–North Carolina 74, Michigan St. 70 (3 OT); Kansas 80, San Francisco 56. **Third Place**–San Francisco 67, Michigan St. 60. **Championship**–North Carolina 54, Kansas 53 (3 OT).

NIT Final Four (at Madison Square Garden): **Semifinals**–Memphis St. 80, St. Bonaventure 78; Bradley 78, Temple 66. **Third Place**–Temple 67, St. Bonaventure 50. **Championship**–Bradley 84, Memphis St. 83.

1958

		Before Tourns	Head Coach	Final Record
1	West Virginia ..	26-1	Fred Schaus	26-2
2	Cincinnati	24-2	George Smith	25-3
3	Kansas St.	20-3	Tex Winter	22-5
4	San Francisco .	24-1	Phil Woolpert	25-2
5	Temple	24-2	Harry Litwack	27-3
6	Maryland	20-6	Bud Millikan	22-7
7	Kansas	18-5	Dick Harp	same
8	Notre Dame ...	22-4	John Jordan	24-5
9	**Kentucky**	19-6	Adolph Rupp	23-6
10	Duke	18-7	Harold Bradley	same
11	Dayton	23-3	Tom Blackburn	25-4
12	Indiana	12-10	Branch McCracken	13-11
13	North Carolina	19-7	Frank McGuire	same
14	Bradley	20-6	Chuck Orsborn	20-7
15	Mississippi St. .	20-5	Babe McCarthy	same
16	Auburn	16-6	Joel Eaves	same
17	Michigan St. ...	16-6	Forddy Anderson	same
18	Seattle	20-6	John Castellani	24-7
19	Oklahoma St. ..	19-7	Hank Iba	21-8
20	N.C. State	18-6	Everett Case	same

Note: Unranked **Xavier-OH**, coached by Jim McCafferty, won the NIT. The Musketeers entered the tourney at 15-11 and had a final record of 19-11.

NCAA Final Four (at Freedom Hall, Louisville): **Semifinals**–Kentucky 61, Temple 60; Seattle 73, Kansas St. 51. **Third Place**–Temple 67, Kansas St. 57. **Championship**–Kentucky 84, Seattle 72.

NIT Final Four (at Madison Square Garden): **Semifinals**–Dayton 80, St. John's 56; Xavier-OH 72, St. Bonaventure 53. **Third Place**–St. Bonaventure 84, St. John's 69. **Championship**–Xavier-OH 78, Dayton 74 (OT).

1959

		Before Tourns	Head Coach	Final Record
1	Kansas St.	24-1	Tex Winter	25-2
2	Kentucky	23-2	Adolph Rupp	24-3
3	Mississippi St. .	24-1	Babe McCarthy	same*
4	Bradley	23-3	Chuck Orsborn	25-4
5	Cincinnati	23-3	George Smith	26-4
6	N.C. State	22-4	Everett Case	same
7	Michigan St. ...	18-3	Forddy Anderson	19-4
8	Auburn	20-2	Joel Eaves	same
9	North Carolina	20-4	Frank McGuire	20-5
10	West Virginia ..	25-4	Fred Schaus	29-5
11	**California**	21-4	Pete Newell	25-4
12	Saint Louis	20-5	John Benington	20-6
13	Seattle	23-6	Vince Cazzetta	same
14	St. Joseph's-PA .	22-3	Jack Ramsay	22-5
15	St. Mary's-CA ..	18-5	Jim Weaver	19-6
16	TCU	19-5	Buster Brannon	20-6
17	Oklahoma City	20-6	Abe Lemons	20-7
18	Utah	21-5	Jack Gardner	21-7
19	St. Bonaventure	20-2	Eddie Donovan	20-3
20	Marquette	22-4	Eddie Hickey	23-6

*Mississippi St. turned down invitation to NCAA tournament because it was an integrated event.

Note: Unranked **St. John's**, coached by Joe Lapchick, won the NIT. The Redmen entered the tourney at 16-6 and had a final record of 20-6.

NCAA Final Four (at Freedom Hall, Louisville): **Semifinals**–West Virginia 94, Louisville 79; California 64, Cincinnati 58. **Third Place**–Cincinnati 98, Louisville 85. **Championship**–California 71, West Virginia 70.

NIT Final Four (at Madison Square Garden): **Semifinals**–Bradley 59, NYU 57; St. John's 76, Providence 55. **Third Place**–NYU 71, Providence 57. **Championship**–St. John's 76, Bradley 71 (OT).

1960

		Before Tourns	Head Coach	Final Record
1	Cincinnati	25-1	George Smith	28-2
2	California	24-1	Pete Newell	28-2
3	**Ohio St.**	21-3	Fred Taylor	25-3
4	**Bradley**	24-2	Chuck Orsborn	27-2
5	West Virginia ..	24-4	Fred Schaus	26-5
6	Utah	24-2	Jack Gardner	26-3
7	Indiana	20-4	Branch McCracken	same
8	Utah St.	22-4	Cecil Baker	24-5
9	St. Bonaventure	19-3	Eddie Donovan	21-5
10	Miami-FL	23-3	Bruce Hale	23-4
11	Auburn	19-3	Joel Eaves	same
12	NYU	19-4	Lou Rossini	22-5
13	Georgia Tech ..	21-5	Whack Hyder	22-6
14	Providence	21-4	Joe Mullaney	24-5
15	Saint Louis	19-7	John Benington	19-8
16	Holy Cross	20-5	Roy Leenig	20-6
17	Villanova	19-5	Al Severance	20-6
18	Duke	15-10	Vic Bubas	17-11
19	Wake Forest ...	21-7	Bones McKinney	same
20	St. John's	17-7	Joe Lapchick	17-8

NCAA Final Four (at the Cow Palace, San Fran.): **Semifinals**–Ohio St. 76, NYU 54; California 77, Cincinnati 69. **Third Place**–Cincinnati 95, NYU 71. **Championship**–Ohio St. 75, California 55.

NIT Final Four (at Madison Square Garden): **Semifinals**–Bradley 82, St. Bonaventure 71; Providence 68, Utah St. 62. **Third Place**–Utah St. 99, St. Bonaventure 93. **Championship**–Bradley 88, Providence 72.

1961

		Before Tourns	Head Coach	Final Record
1	Ohio St.	24-0	Fred Taylor	27-1
2	**Cincinnati**	23-3	Ed Jucker	27-3
3	St. Bonaventure	22-3	Eddie Donovan	24-4
4	Kansas St.	22-3	Tex Winter	23-4
5	North Carolina	19-4	Frank McGuire	same
6	Bradley	21-5	Chuck Orsborn	same
7	USC	20-6	Forrest Twogood	21-8
8	Iowa	18-6	S. Scheuerman	same
9	West Virginia ..	23-4	George King	same
10	Duke	22-6	Vic Bubas	same
11	Utah	21-6	Jack Gardner	23-8
12	Texas Tech	14-9	Polk Robison	15-10
13	Niagara	16-4	Taps Gallagher	16-5
14	Memphis St. ...	20-2	Bob Vanatta	20-3
15	Wake Forest ...	17-10	Bones McKinney	19-11
16	St. John's	20-4	Joe Lapchick	20-5
17	St. Joseph's-PA	22-4	Jack Ramsay	25-5
18	Drake	19-7	Maury John	same
19	Holy Cross	19-4	Roy Leenig	22-5
20	Kentucky	18-8	Adolph Rupp	19-9

Note: Unranked **Providence**, coached by Joe Mullaney, won the NIT. The Friars entered the tourney at 20-5 and had a final record of 24-5.

NCAA Final Four (at Municipal Auditorium, Kansas City): **Semifinals**–Ohio St. 95, St. Joseph's-PA 69; Cincinnati 82, Utah 67. **Third Place**–St. Joseph's-PA 127, Utah 120 (4 OT). **Championship**–Cincinnati 70, Ohio St. 65 (OT).

NIT Final Four (at Madison Square Garden) **Semifinals**–St. Louis 67, Dayton 60; Providence 90, Holy Cross 83 (OT). **Third Place**–Holy Cross 85, Dayton 67. **Championship**–Providence 62, St. Louis 59.

1962

		Before Tourns	Head Coach	Final Record
1	Ohio St.	23-1	Fred Taylor	26-2
2	**Cincinnati**	25-2	Ed Jucker	29-2
3	Kentucky	22-2	Adolph Rupp	23-3
4	Mississippi St. .	19-6	Babe McCarthy	same
5	Bradley	21-6	Chuck Orsborn	21-7
6	Kansas St.	22-3	Tex Winter	same
7	Utah	23-3	Jack Gardner	same
8	Bowling Green .	21-3	Harold Anderson	same
9	Colorado	18-6	Sox Walseth	19-7
10	Duke	20-5	Vic Bubas	same
11	Loyola-IL	21-3	George Ireland	23-4
12	St. John's	19-4	Joe Lapchick	21-5
13	Wake Forest ...	18-8	Bones McKinney	22-9
14	Oregon St.	22-4	Slats Gill	24-5
15	West Virginia ..	24-5	George King	24-6
16	Arizona St.	23-3	Ned Wulk	23-4
17	Duquesne	20-5	Red Manning	22-7
18	Utah St.	21-5	Ladell Andersen	22-7
19	UCLA	16-9	John Wooden	18-11
20	Villanova	19-6	Jack Kraft	21-7

Note: Unranked **Dayton**, coached by Tom Blackburn, won the NIT. The Flyers entered the tourney at 20-6 and had a final record of 24-6.

NCAA Final Four (at Freedom Hall, Louisville): **Semifinals**–Ohio St. 84, Wake Forest 68; Cincinnati 72, UCLA 70. **Third Place**–Wake Forest 82, UCLA 80. **Championship**–Cincinnati 71, Ohio St. 59.

NIT Final Four (at Madison Square Garden): **Semifinals**–Dayton 98, Loyola-IL 82; St. John's 76, Duquesne 65. **Third Place**–Loyola-IL 95, Duquesne 84. **Championship**–Dayton 73, St. John's 67.

1963

AP ranked only 10 teams from the 1962-63 season through 1967-68.

		Before Tourns	Head Coach	Final Record
1	Cincinnati	23-1	Ed Jucker	26-2
2	Duke	24-2	Vic Bubas	27-3
3	**Loyola-IL**	24-2	George Ireland	29-2
4	Arizona St.	24-2	Ned Wulk	26-3
5	Wichita	19-7	Ralph Miller	19-8
6	Mississippi St. .	21-5	Babe McCarthy	22-6
7	Ohio St.	20-4	Fred Taylor	same
8	Illinois	19-5	Harry Combes	20-6
9	NYU	17-3	Lou Rossini	18-5
10	Colorado	18-6	Sox Walseth	19-7

Note: Unranked **Providence**, coached by Joe Mullaney, won the NIT. The Friars entered the tourney at 21-4 and had a final record of 24-4.

NCAA Final Four (at Freedom Hall, Louisville): **Semifinals**–Loyola-IL 94, Duke 75; Cincinnati 80, Oregon St. 46. **Third Place**–Duke 85, Oregon St. 63. **Championship**–Loyola-IL 60, Cincinnati 58 (OT).

NIT Final Four (at Madison Square Garden): **Semifinals**–Providence 70, Marquette 64; Canisius 61, Villanova 46. **Third Place**–Marquette 66, Villanova 58. **Championship**–Providence 81, Canisius 66.

1964

AP ranked only 10 teams from the 1962-63 season through 1967-68.

		Before Tourns	Head Coach	Final Record
1	UCLA	26-0	John Wooden	30-0
2	Michigan	20-4	Dave Strack	23-5
3	Duke	23-4	Vic Bubas	26-5
4	Kentucky	21-4	Adolph Rupp	21-6
5	Wichita St. ...	22-5	Ralph Miller	23-6
6	Oregon St. ...	25-3	Slats Gill	25-4
7	Villanova	22-3	Jack Kraft	24-4
8	Loyola-IL	20-5	George Ireland	22-6
9	DePaul	21-3	Ray Meyer	21-4
10	Davidson	22-4	Lefty Driesell	same

Note: Unranked **Bradley**, coached by Chuck Orsborn, won the NIT. The Braves entered the tourney at 20-6 and finished with a record of 23-6.

NCAA Final Four (at Municipal Auditorium, Kansas City): **Semifinals**–Duke 91, Michigan 80; UCLA 90, Kansas St. 84. **Third Place**–Michigan 100, Kansas St. 90. **Championship**–UCLA 98, Duke 83.

NIT Final Four (12 at Madison Square Garden): **Semifinals**–New Mexico 72, NYU 65; Bradley 67, Army 52. **Third Place**–Army 60, NYU 59. **Championship**–Bradley 86, New Mexico 54.

Undefeated National Champions

The 1964 UCLA team is one of only seven NCAA champions to win the title with an undefeated record.

Year		W-L	Year		W-L
1956	San Francisco	29-0	1972	UCLA	30-0
1957	N. Carolina ..	32-0	1973	UCLA	30-0
1964	UCLA	30-0	1976	Indiana	32-0
1967	UCLA	30-0			

Associated Press Final Polls (Cont.)

1965

AP ranked only 10 teams from the 1962-63 season through 1967-68.

			Before Tourns	Head Coach	Final Record
1	Michigan	.....	21-3	Dave Strack	24-4
2	**UCLA**	....	24-2	John Wooden	28-2
3	St. Joseph's-PA	.	25-1	Jack Ramsay	26-3
4	Providence	....	22-1	Joe Mullaney	24-2
5	Vanderbilt	....	23-3	Roy Skinner	24-4
6	Davidson	......	24-2	Lefty Driesell	same
7	Minnesota	.....	19-5	John Kundla	same
8	Villanova	.....	21-4	Jack Kraft	23-5
9	BYU	....	21-5	Stan Watts	21-7
10	Duke	....	20-5	Vic Bubas	same

Note: Unranked **St. John's**, coached by Joe Lapchick, won the NIT. The Redmen entered the tourney at 17-8 and finished with a record of 21-8.

NCAA Final Four (at Memorial Coliseum, Portland, OR): **Semifinals**–Michigan 93, Princeton 76; UCLA 108, Wichita St. 89. **Third Place**–Princeton 118, Wichita St. 82. **Championship**–UCLA 91, Michigan 80.

NIT Final Four (at Madison Square Garden): **Semifinals**–Villanova 91, NYU 69; St. John's 67, Army 60. **Third Place**–Army 75, NYU 74. **Championship**–St.John's 55, Villanova 51.

1966

AP ranked only 10 teams from the 1962-63 season through 1967-68.

			Before Tourns	Head Coach	Final Record
1	Kentucky	......	24-1	Adolph Rupp	27-2
2	Duke		23-3	Vic Bubas	26-4
3	**Tex. Western**		23-1	Don Haskins	28-1
4	Kansas	......	22-3	Ted Owens	23-4
5	St. Joseph's-PA	.	22-4	Jack Ramsay	24-5
6	Loyola-IL	......	22-2	George Ireland	22-3
7	Cincinnati	.....	21-5	Tay Baker	21-7
8	Vanderbilt		22-4	Roy Skinner	same
9	Michigan	.....	17-7	Dave Strack	18-8
10	Western Ky.	...	23-2	Johnny Oldham	25-3

Note: Unranked **BYU**, coached by Stan Watts, won the NIT. The Cougars entered the tourney at 17-5 and had a final record of 20-5.

NCAA Final Four (at Cole Fieldhouse, College Park, MD): **Semifinals**–Kentucky 83, Duke 79; Texas Western 85, Utah 78. **Third Place**–Duke 79, Utah 77. **Championship**–Texas Western 72, Kentucky 65.

NIT Final Four (at Madison Square Garden): **Semifinals**–BYU 66, Army 60; NYU 69, Villanova 63. **Third Place**–Villanova 76, Army 65. **Championship**–BYU 97, NYU 84.

1967

AP ranked only 10 teams from the 1962-63 season through 1967-68.

			Before Tourns	Head Coach	Final Record
1	UCLA	....	26-0	John Wooden	30-0
2	Louisville	......	23-3	Peck Hickman	23-5
3	Kansas	......	22-3	Ted Owens	23-4
4	North Carolina		24-4	Dean Smith	26-6
5	Princeton	......	23-2	B. van Breda Kolff	25-3
6	Western Ky.	...	23-2	Johnny Oldham	23-3
7	Houston	....	23-3	Guy Lewis	27-4
8	Tennessee	.....	21-5	Ray Mears	21-7
9	Boston College	.	19-2	Bob Cousy	21-3
10	Texas Western	...	20-5	Don Haskins	22-6

Note: Unranked **Southern Illinois**, coached by Jack Hartman, won the NIT. The Salukis entered the tourney at 20-2 and had a final record of 24-2.

NCAA Final Four (at Freedom Hall, Louisville): **Semifinals**–Dayton 76, N. Carolina 62; UCLA 73, Houston 58. **Third Place**–Houston 84, N. Carolina 62. **Championship**–UCLA 79, Dayton 64.

NIT Final Four (at Madison Square Garden): **Semifinals**–Marquette 83, Marshall 78; Southern Ill. 79, Rutgers 70. **Third Place**–Rutgers 93, Marshall 76. **Championship**–Southern Ill. 71, Marquette 56.

1968

AP ranked only 10 teams from the 1962-63 season through 1967-68.

			Before Tourns	Head Coach	Final Record
1	Houston	....	28-0	Guy Lewis	31-2
2	**UCLA**	....	25-1	John Wooden	29-1
3	St. Bonaventure		22-0	Larry Weise	23-2
4	North Carolina		25-3	Dean Smith	28-4
5	Kentucky	......	21-4	Adolph Rupp	22-5
6	New Mexico	..	23-3	Bob King	23-5
7	Columbia	......	21-4	Jack Rohan	23-5
8	Davidson	......	22-4	Lefty Driesell	24-5
9	Louisville	......	20-6	John Dromo	21-7
10	Duke	....	21-5	Vic Bubas	22-6

Note: Unranked **Dayton**, coached by Don Donoher, won the NIT. The Flyers entered the tourney at 17-9 and had a final record of 21-9.

NCAA Final Four (at the Sports Arena, Los Angeles): **Semifinals**–N. Carolina 80, Ohio St. 66; UCLA 101, Houston 69. **Third Place**–Ohio St. 89, Houston 85. **Championship**–UCLA 78, N. Carolina 55.

NIT Final Four (at Madison Square Garden): **Semifinals**–Dayton 76, Notre Dame 74 (OT); Kansas 58, St. Peter's 46. **Third Place**–Notre Dame 81, St.Peter's 78. **Championship**–Dayton 61, Kansas 48.

Highest-Rated College Games on TV

The dozen highest-rated college basketball games seen on U.S. television have been NCAA tournament championship games, led by the 1979 Michigan State-Indiana State final that featured Magic Johnson and Larry Bird.

Listed below are the finalists (winning team first), date of game, TV network, and TV rating and audience share (according to Nielson Media Research).

		Date	Net	Rtg/Sh				Date	Net	Rtg/Sh
1	Michigan St.-Indiana St.	....	3/26/79	NBC	24.1/38	7	N. Carolina-Georgetown	...	3/29/82	CBS	21.6/31
2	Villanova-Georgetown	.....	4/1/85	CBS	23.3/33	8	UCLA-Kentucky	....	3/31/75	NBC	21.3/33
3	Duke-Michigan	....	4/6/92	CBS	22.7/35	9	Michigan-Seton Hall	......	4/3/89	CBS	21.3/33
4	N.C. State-Houston	......	4/4/83	CBS	22.3/32	10	Louisville-Duke	....	3/32/86	CBS	20.7/31
5	N. Carolina-Michigan	.....	4/5/93	CBS	22.2/34	11	Indiana-N. Carolina	....	3/30/81	NBC	20.7/29
6	Arkansas-Duke	....	4/4/94	CBS	21.6/33	12	UCLA-Memphis St.	......	3/26/73	NBC	20.5/32

1969

		Before Tourns	Head Coach	Final Record
1	**UCLA**	25-1	John Wooden	29-1
2	La Salle	23-1	Tom Gola	same*
3	Santa Clara ...	26-1	Dick Garibaldi	27-2
4	North Carolina	25-3	Dean Smith	27-5
5	Davidson	24-2	Lefty Driesell	26-3
6	Purdue	20-4	George King	23-5
7	Kentucky	22-4	Adolph Rupp	23-5
8	St. John's	22-4	Lou Carnesecca	23-6
9	Duquesne	19-4	Red Manning	21-5
10	Villanova	21-4	Jack Kraft	21-5
11	Drake	23-4	Maury John	26-5
12	New Mexico St.	23-3	Lou Henson	24-5
13	South Carolina	20-6	Frank McGuire	21-7
14	Marquette	22-4	Al McGuire	24-5
15	Louisville	20-5	John Dromo	21-6
16	Boston College .	21-3	Bob Cousy	24-4
17	Notre Dame ...	20-6	Johnny Dee	20-7
18	Colorado	20-6	Sox Walseth	21-7
19	Kansas	20-6	Ted Owens	20-7
20	Illinois	19-5	Harvey Schmidt	same

*On probation

Note: Unranked **Temple**, coached by Harry Litwack, won the NIT. The Owls entered the tourney at 18-8 and finished with a record of 22-8.

NCAA Final Four (at Freedom Hall, Louisville): **Semifinals**–Purdue 92, N. Carolina 65; UCLA 85, Drake 82. **Third Place**–Drake 104, N. Carolina 84. **Championship**–UCLA 92, Purdue 72.

NIT Final Four (at Madison Square Garden): **Semifinals**–Temple 63, Tennessee 58; Boston College 73, Army 61. **Third Place**–Tennessee 64, Army 52. **Championship**–Temple 89, Boston College 76.

1970

		Before Tourns	Head Coach	Final Record
1	Kentucky	25-1	Adolph Rupp	26-2
2	**UCLA**	24-2	John Wooden	28-2
3	St. Bonaventure	22-1	Larry Weise	25-3
4	Jacksonville ...	23-1	Joe Williams	27-2
5	New Mexico St.	23-2	Lou Henson	27-3
6	South Carolina .	25-3	Frank McGuire	25-3
7	Iowa	19-4	Ralph Miller	20-5
8	**Marquette** ...	22-3	Al McGuire	26-3
9	Notre Dame ...	20-6	Johnny Dee	21-8
10	N.C. State	22-6	Norm Sloan	23-7
11	Florida St.	23-3	Hugh Durham	23-3
12	Houston	24-3	Guy Lewis	25-5
13	Penn	25-1	Dick Harter	25-2
14	Drake	21-6	Maury John	22-7
15	Davidson	22-4	Terry Holland	22-5
16	Utah St.	20-6	Ladell Andersen	22-7
17	Niagara	21-5	Frank Layden	22-7
18	Western Ky. ...	22-2	John Oldham	22-3
19	Long Beach St. .	23-3	Jerry Tarkanian	24-5
20	USC	18-8	Bob Boyd	18-8

NCAA Final Four (at Cole Fieldhouse, College Park, MD): **Semifinals**–Jacksonville 91, St. Bonaventure 83; UCLA 93, New Mexico St. 77. **Third Place**–N. Mexico St. 79, St. Bonaventure 73. **Championship**–UCLA 80, Jacksonville 69.

NIT Final Four (at Madison Square Garden): **Semifinals**–St. John's 60, Army 59; Marquette 101, LSU 79. **Third Place**–Army 75, LSU 68. **Championship**–Marquette 65, St. John's 53.

1971

		Before Tourns	Head Coach	Final Record
1	**UCLA**	25-1	John Wooden	29-1
2	Marquette	26-0	Al McGuire	28-1
3	Penn	26-0	Dick Harter	28-1
4	Kansas	25-1	Ted Owens	27-3
5	USC	24-2	Bob Boyd	24-2
6	South Carolina .	23-4	Frank McGuire	23-6
7	Western Ky. ...	20-5	John Oldham	24-6
8	Kentucky	22-4	Adolph Rupp	22-6
9	Fordham	25-1	Digger Phelps	26-3
10	Ohio St.	19-5	Fred Taylor	20-6
11	Jacksonville	22-3	Tom Wasdin	22-4
12	Notre Dame ...	19-7	Johnny Dee	20-9
13	**N. Carolina** ..	22-6	Dean Smith	26-6
14	Houston	20-6	Guy Lewis	22-7
15	Duquesne	21-3	Red Manning	21-4
16	Long Beach St. .	21-4	Jerry Tarkanian	23-5
17	Tennessee	20-6	Ray Mears	21-7
18	Villanova	19-5	Jack Kraft	23-6
19	Drake	20-7	Maury John	21-8
20	BYU	18-9	Stan Watts	18-11

NCAA Final Four (at the Astrodome, Houston): **Semifinals**–Villanova 92, Western Ky. 89 (2 OT); UCLA 68, Kansas 60. **Third Place**–Western Ky. 77, Kansas 75. **Championship**–UCLA 68, Villanova 62.

NIT Final Four (at Madison Square Garden): **Semifinals**–N. Carolina 73, Duke 69; Ga.Tech 76, St. Bonaventure 71 (2 OT). **Third Place**–St. Bonaventure 92, Duke 88 (OT). **Championship**–N. Carolina 84, Ga.Tech 66.

1972

		Before Tourns	Head Coach	Final Record
1	**UCLA**	26-0	John Wooden	30-0
2	North Carolina	23-4	Dean Smith	26-5
3	Penn	23-2	Chuck Daly	25-3
4	Louisville	23-4	Denny Crum	26-5
5	Long Beach St. .	23-3	Jerry Tarkanian	25-4
6	South Carolina .	22-4	Frank McGuire	24-5
7	Marquette	24-2	Al McGuire	25-4
8	SW Louisiana ..	23-3	Beryl Shipley	25-4
9	BYU	21-4	Stan Watts	21-5
10	Florida St.	23-5	Hugh Durham	27-6
11	Minnesota	17-6	Bill Musselman	18-7
12	Marshall	23-3	Carl Tacy	23-4
13	Memphis St. ...	21-6	Gene Bartow	21-7
14	**Maryland**	23-5	Lefty Driesell	27-5
15	Villanova	19-6	Jack Kraft	20-8
16	Oral Roberts ..	25-1	Ken Trickey	26-2
17	Indiana	17-7	Bob Knight	17-8
18	Kentucky	20-6	Adolph Rupp	21-7
19	Ohio St.	18-6	Fred Taylor	same
20	Virginia	21-6	Bill Gibson	21-7

NCAA Final Four (at the Sports Arena, Los Angeles): **Semifinals**–Florida St. 79, N. Carolina 75; UCLA 96, Louisville 77. **Third Place**–N. Carolina 105, Louisville 91. **Championship**–UCLA 81, Florida St. 76.

NIT Final Four (at Madison Square Garden): **Semifinals**–Maryland 91, Jacksonville 77; Niagara 69, St. John's 67. **Third Place**–Jacksonville 83, St. John's 80. **Championship**–Maryland 100, Niagara 69.

Associated Press Final Polls (Cont.)

1973

		Before Tourns	Head Coach	Final Record
1	**UCLA**	26-0	John Wooden	30-0
2	N.C. State	27-0	Norm Sloan	same*
3	Long Beach St. .	24-2	Jerry Tarkanian	26-3
4	Providence	24-2	Dave Gavitt	27-4
5	Marquette	23-3	Al McGuire	25-4
6	Indiana	19-5	Bob Knight	22-6
7	SW Louisiana ...	23-2	Beryl Shipley	24-5
8	Maryland	22-6	Lefty Driesell	23-7
9	Kansas St.	22-4	Jack Hartman	23-5
10	Minnesota	20-4	Bill Musselman	21-5
11	North Carolina	22-7	Dean Smith	25-8
12	Memphis St. ...	21-5	Gene Bartow	24-6
13	Houston	23-3	Guy Lewis	23-4
14	Syracuse	22-4	Roy Danforth	24-5
15	Missouri	21-5	Norm Stewart	21-6
16	Arizona St.	18-7	Ned Wulk	19-9
17	Kentucky	19-7	Joe B. Hall	20-8
18	Penn	20-5	Chuck Daly	21-7
19	Austin Peay ...	21-5	Lake Kelly	22-7
20	San Francisco ..	22-4	Bob Gaillard	23-5

*N.C. State was ineligible for NCAA tournament for using improper methods to recruit David Thompson.
Note: Unranked **Virginia Tech**, coached by Don DeVoe, won the NIT. The Hokies entered the tourney at 18-5 and finished with a record of 22-5.
NCAA Final Four (at The Arena, St.Louis): **Semifinals**—Memphis St. 98, Providence 85; UCLA 70, Indiana 59. **Third Place**—Indiana 97, Providence 79. **Championship**—UCLA 87, Memphis St. 66.
NIT Final Four (at Madison Square Garden): **Semifinals**—Va. Tech 74, Alabama 73; Notre Dame 78, N. Carolina 71. **Third Place**—N. Carolina 88, Alabama 69. **Championship**—Va. Tech 92, Notre Dame 91 (OT).

1974

		Before Tourns	Head Coach	Final Record
1	**N.C. State** ...	26-1	Norm Sloan	30-1
2	UCLA	23-3	John Wooden	26-4
3	Notre Dame ...	24-2	Digger Phelps	26-3
4	Maryland	23-5	Lefty Driesell	same
5	Providence	26-3	Dave Gavitt	28-4
6	Vanderbilt	23-3	Roy Skinner	23-5
7	Marquette	22-4	Al McGuire	26-5
8	North Carolina	22-5	Dean Smith	22-6
9	Long Beach St. .	24-2	Lute Olson	same
10	**Indiana**	20-5	Bob Knight	23-5
11	Alabama	22-4	C.M. Newton	same
12	Michigan	21-4	Johnny Orr	22-5
13	Pittsburgh	23-3	Buzz Ridl	25-4
14	Kansas	21-5	Ted Owens	23-7
15	USC	22-4	Bob Boyd	24-5
16	Louisville	21-6	Denny Crum	21-7
17	New Mexico ..	21-6	Norm Ellenberger	22-7
18	South Carolina .	22-4	Frank McGuire	22-5
19	Creighton	22-6	Eddie Sutton	23-7
20	Dayton	19-7	Don Donoher	20-9

NCAA Final Four (at Greensboro, NC, Coliseum): **Semifinals**—N.C. State 80, UCLA 77 (2 OT); Marquette 64, Kansas 51. **Third Place**—UCLA 78, Kansas 61. **Championship**—N.C.State 76, Marquette 64.
NIT Final Four (at Madison Square Garden): **Semifinals**—Purdue 78, Jacksonville 63; Utah 117, Boston Col. 93. **Third Place**—Boston Col. 87, Jacksonville 77. **Championship**—Purdue 87, Utah 81.
CCA Final Four (at The Arena, St.Louis): Semifinals—Indiana 73, Toledo 72; USC 74, Bradley 73. Championship—Indiana 85, USC 60.

1975

		Before Tourns	Head Coach	Final Record
1	Indiana	29-0	Bob Knight	31-1
2	**UCLA**	23-3	John Wooden	28-3
3	Louisville	24-2	Denny Crum	28-3
4	Maryland	22-4	Lefty Driesell	24-5
5	Kentucky	22-4	Joe B. Hall	26-5
6	North Carolina	21-7	Dean Smith	23-8
7	Arizona St.	23-3	Ned Wulk	25-4
8	N.C.State	22-6	Norm Sloan	22-6
9	Notre Dame ...	18-8	Digger Phelps	19-10
10	Marquette	23-3	Al McGuire	23-4
11	Alabama	22-4	C.M. Newton	22-5
12	Cincinnati	21-5	Gale Catlett	23-6
13	Oregon St.	18-10	Ralph Miller	19-12
14	**Drake**	16-10	Bob Ortegel	19-10
15	Penn	23-4	Chuck Daly	23-5
16	UNLV	22-4	Jerry Tarkanian	24-5
17	Kansas St.	18-8	Jack Hartman	20-9
18	USC	18-7	Bob Boyd	18-8
19	Centenary	25-4	Larry Little	same
20	Syracuse	20-7	Roy Danforth	23-9

NCAA Final Four (at San Diego Sports Arena): **Semifinals**—Kentucky 95, Syracuse 79; UCLA 75, Louisville 74 (OT). **Third Place**—Louisville 96, Syracuse 88 (OT). **Championship**—UCLA 92, Kentucky 85.
NIT Championship (at Madison Sq. Garden): Princeton 80, Providence 69. No Top 20 teams played in NIT.
CCA Championship (at Freedom Hall, Louisville): Drake 83, Arizona 76. No.14 Drake and No.18 USC were only Top 20 teams in CCA.

1976

		Before Tourns	Head Coach	Final Record
1	**Indiana**	27-0	Bob Knight	32-0
2	Marquette	25-1	Al McGuire	27-2
3	UNLV	28-1	Jerry Tarkanian	29-2
4	Rutgers	28-0	Tom Young	31-2
5	UCLA	24-3	Gene Bartow	28-4
6	Alabama	22-4	C.M. Newton	23-5
7	Notre Dame ...	22-5	Digger Phelps	23-6
8	North Carolina	25-3	Dean Smith	25-4
9	Michigan	21-6	Johnny Orr	25-7
10	Western Mich. .	24-2	Eldon Miller	25-3
11	Maryland	22-6	Lefty Driesell	same
12	Cincinnati	25-5	Gale Catlett	25-6
13	Tennessee	21-5	Ray Mears	21-6
14	Missouri	24-4	Norm Stewart	26-5
15	Arizona	22-8	Fred Snowden	24-9
16	Texas Tech	24-5	Gerald Myers	25-6
17	DePaul	19-8	Ray Meyer	20-9
18	Virginia	18-11	Terry Holland	18-12
19	Centenary	22-5	Larry Little	same
20	Pepperdine	21-5	Gary Colson	22-6

NCAA Final Four (at the Spectrum, Phila.); Semifinals—Michigan 86, Rutgers 70; Indiana 65, UCLA 51. **Third Place**—UCLA 106, Rutgers 92. **Championship**—Indiana 86, Michigan 68.
NIT Championship (at Madison Square Garden): Kentucky 71, NC-Charlotte 67. No Top 20 teams played in NIT.

1977

		Before Tourns	Head Coach	Final Record
1	Michigan	24-3	Johnny Orr	26-4
2	UCLA	24-3	Gene Bartow	25-4
3	Kentucky	24-3	Joe B. Hall	26-4
4	UNLV	25-2	Jerry Tarkanian	29-3
5	North Carolina	24-4	Dean Smith	28-5
6	Syracuse	25-3	Jim Boeheim	26-4
7	**Marquette** ..	20-7	Al McGuire	25-7
8	San Francisco .	29-1	Bob Gaillard	29-2
9	Wake Forest ...	20-7	Carl Tacy	22-8
10	Notre Dame ...	21-6	Digger Phelps	22-7
11	Alabama	23-4	C.M. Newton	25-6
12	Detroit	24-3	Dick Vitale	25-4
13	Minnesota	24-3	Jim Dutcher	same*
14	Utah	22-6	Jerry Pimm	23-7
15	Tennessee	22-5	Ray Mears	22-6
16	Kansas St.	23-6	Jack Hartman	24-7
17	NC-Charlotte ..	25-3	Lee Rose	28-5
18	Arkansas	26-1	Eddie Sutton	26-2
19	Louisville	21-6	Denny Crum	21-7
20	VMI	25-3	Charlie Schmaus	26-4

*On probation

NCAA Final Four (at the Omni, Atlanta): **Semifinals–**Marquette 51, NC-Charlotte, 49; N. Carolina 84, UNLV 83. **Third Place–**UNLV 106, NC-Charlotte 94. **Championship–**Marquette 67, N. Carolina 59.

NIT Championship (at Madison Square Garden): St.Bonaventure 94, Houston 91. No.11 Alabama was only Top 20 team in NIT.

1978

		Before Tourns	Head Coach	Final Record
1	**Kentucky**	25-2	Joe B. Hall	30-2
2	UCLA	24-2	Gary Cunningham	25-3
3	DePaul	25-2	Ray Meyer	27-3
4	Michigan St. ...	23-4	Jud Heathcote	25-5
5	Arkansas	28-3	Eddie Sutton	32-3
6	Notre Dame ...	20-6	Digger Phelps	23-8
7	Duke	23-6	Bill Foster	27-7
8	Marquette	24-3	Hank Raymonds	24-4
9	Louisville	22-6	Denny Crum	23-7
10	Kansas	24-4	Ted Owens	24-5
11	San Francisco ..	22-5	Bob Gaillard	23-6
12	New Mexico ...	24-3	Norm Ellenberger	24-4
13	Indiana	20-7	Bob Knight	21-8
14	Utah	22-5	Jerry Pimm	23-6
15	Florida St.	23-5	Hugh Durham	23-6
16	North Carolina	23-7	Dean Smith	23-8
17	**Texas**	22-5	Abe Lemons	26-5
18	Detroit	24-3	Dave Gaines	25-4
19	Miami-OH	18-8	Darrell Hedric	19-9
20	Penn	19-7	Bob Weinhauer	20-8

NCAA Final Four (at the Checkerdome, St. Louis): **Semifinals–**Kentucky 64, Arkansas 59; Duke 90, Notre Dame 86. **Third Place–**Arkansas 71, Notre Dame 69. **Championship–**Kentucky 94, Duke 88.

NIT Championship (at Madison Square Garden): Texas 101, N.C.State 93. No. 17 Texas and No. 18 Detroit were only Top 20 teams in NIT.

1979

		Before Tourns	Head Coach	Final Record
1	Indiana St.	29-0	Bill Hodges	33-1
2	UCLA	23-4	Gary Cunningham	25-5
3	**Michigan St.** .	21-6	Jud Heathcote	26-6
4	Notre Dame ...	22-5	Digger Phelps	24-6
5	Arkansas	23-4	Eddie Sutton	25-5
6	DePaul	22-5	Ray Meyer	26-6
7	LSU	22-5	Dale Brown	23-6
8	Syracuse	25-3	Jim Boeheim	26-4
9	North Carolina	23-5	Dean Smith	23-6
10	Marquette	21-6	Hank Raymonds	22-7
11	Duke	22-7	Bill Foster	22-8
12	San Francisco ..	21-6	Dan Belluomini	22-7
13	Louisville	23-7	Denny Crum	24-8
14	Penn	21-5	Bob Weinhauer	25-7
15	Purdue	23-7	Lee Rose	27-8
16	Oklahoma	20-9	Dave Bliss	21-10
17	St. John's	18-10	Lou Carnesecca	21-11
18	Rutgers	21-8	Tom Young	22-9
19	Toledo	21-6	Bob Nichols	22-7
20	Iowa	20-7	Lute Olson	20-8

NCAA Final Four (at Special Events Center, Salt Lake City): **Semifinals–**Michigan St. 101, Penn 67; Indiana St. 76, DePaul 74. **Third Place** DePaul 96, Penn 93.**Championship–**Michigan St. 75, Indiana St. 64.

NIT Championship (at Madison Square Garden): Indiana 53, Purdue 52. No. 15 Purdue was only Top 20 team in NIT.

1980

		Before Tourns	Head Coach	Final Record
1	DePaul	26-1	Ray Meyer	26-2
2	**Louisville**	28-3	Denny Crum	33-3
3	LSU	24-5	Dale Brown	26-6
4	Kentucky	28-5	Joe B. Hall	29-6
5	Oregon St.	26-3	Ralph Miller	26-4
6	Syracuse	25-3	Jim Boeheim	26-4
7	Indiana	20-7	Bob Knight	21-8
8	Maryland	23-6	Lefty Driesell	24-7
9	Notre Dame ...	20-7	Digger Phelps	20-8
10	Ohio St.	24-5	Eldon Miller	21-8
11	Georgetown ...	24-5	John Thompson	26-6
12	BYU	24-4	Frank Arnold	24-5
13	St. John's	24-4	Lou Carnesecca	24-5
14	Duke	22-8	Bill Foster	24-9
15	North Carolina	21-7	Dean Smith	21-8
16	Missouri	23-5	Norm Stewart	25-6
17	Weber St.	26-2	Neil McCarthy	26-3
18	Arizona St.	21-6	Ned Wulk	22-7
19	Iona	28-4	Jim Valvano	29-5
20	Purdue	19-9	Lee Rose	23-10

NCAA Final Four (at Market Square Arena, Indianapolis): **Semifinals–**Louisville 80, Iowa 72; UCLA 67, Purdue 62; **Championship–**Louisville 59, UCLA 54.

NIT Championship (at Madison Square Garden): Virginia 58, Minnesota 55. No Top 20 teams played in NIT.

Associated Press Final Polls (Cont.)

1981

		Before Tourns	Head Coach	Final Record
1	DePaul	27-1	Ray Meyer	27-2
2	Oregon St.	26-1	Ralph Miller	26-2
3	Arizona St.	24-3	Ned Wulk	24-4
4	LSU	28-3	Dale Brown	31-5
5	Virginia	25-3	Terry Holland	29-4
6	North Carolina	25-7	Dean Smith	29-8
7	Notre Dame	22-5	Digger Phelps	23-6
8	Kentucky	22-5	Joe B. Hall	22-6
9	**Indiana**	21-9	Bob Knight	26-9
10	UCLA	20-6	Larry Brown	20-7
11	Wake Forest	22-6	Carl Tacy	22-7
12	Louisville	21-8	Denny Crum	21-9
13	Iowa	21-6	Lute Olson	21-7
14	Utah	24-4	Jerry Pimm	25-5
15	Tennessee	20-7	Don DeVoe	21-8
16	BYU	22-6	Frank Arnold	25-7
17	Wyoming	23-5	Jim Brandenburg	24-6
18	Maryland	20-9	Lefty Driesell	21-10
19	Illinois	20-7	Lou Henson	21-8
20	Arkansas	22-7	Eddie Sutton	24-8

NCAA Final Four (at the Spectrum, Phila.): **Semifinals**–N. Carolina 78, Virginia 65; Indiana 67, LSU 49. **Third Place**–Virginia 78, LSU 74. **Championship**–Indiana 63, N. Carolina 50.

NIT Championship (at Madison Square Garden): Tulsa 86, Syracuse 84. No Top 20 teams played in NIT.

1982

		Before Tourns	Head Coach	Final Record
1	**N. Carolina**	27-2	Dean Smith	32-2
2	DePaul	26-1	Ray Meyer	26-2
3	Virginia	29-3	Terry Holland	30-4
4	Oregon St.	23-4	Ralph Miller	25-5
5	Missouri	26-3	Norm Stewart	27-4
6	Georgetown	26-6	John Thompson	30-7
7	Minnesota	22-5	Jim Dutcher	23-6
8	Idaho	26-2	Don Monson	27-3
9	Memphis St.	23-4	Dana Kirk	24-5
10	Tulsa	24-5	Nolan Richardson	24-6
11	Fresno St.	26-2	Boyd Grant	27-3
12	Arkansas	23-5	Eddie Sutton	23-6
13	Alabama	23-6	Wimp Sanderson	24-7
14	West Virginia	26-3	Gale Catlett	27-4
15	Kentucky	22-7	Joe B. Hall	22-8
16	Iowa	20-7	Lute Olson	21-8
17	Ala-Birmingham	23-5	Gene Bartow	25-6
18	Wake Forest	20-8	Carl Tacy	21-9
19	UCLA	21-6	Larry Farmer	21-6
20	Louisville	20-9	Denny Crum	23-10

NCAA Final Four (at the Superdome, New Orleans): **Semifinals**–N. Carolina 68, Houston 63; Georgetown 50, Louisville 46. **Championship**–N. Carolina 63, Georgetown 62.

NIT Championship (at Madison Square Garden): Bradley 67, Purdue 58. No Top 20 teams played in NIT.

1983

		Before Tourns	Head Coach	Final Record
1	Houston	27-2	Guy Lewis	31-3
2	Louisville	29-3	Denny Crum	32-4
3	St. John's	27-4	Lou Carnesecca	28-5
4	Virginia	27-4	Terry Holland	29-5
5	Indiana	23-5	Bob Knight	24-6
6	UNLV	28-2	Jerry Tarkanian	28-3
7	UCLA	23-5	Larry Farmer	23-6
8	North Carolina	26-7	Dean Smith	28-8
9	Arkansas	25-3	Eddie Sutton	26-4
10	Missouri	26-7	Norm Stewart	26-8
11	Boston College	24-6	Gary Williams	25-7
12	Kentucky	22-7	Joe B. Hall	23-8
13	Villanova	22-7	Rollie Massimino	24-8
14	Wichita St.	25-3	Gene Smithson	same*
15	Tenn-Chatt.	26-3	Murray Arnold	26-4
16	**N.C. State**	20-10	Jim Valvano	26-10
17	Memphis St.	22-7	Dana Kirk	23-8
18	Georgia	21-9	Hugh Durham	24-10
19	Oklahoma St.	24-6	Paul Hansen	24-7
20	Georgetown	21-9	John Thompson	22-10

*On probation

NCAA Final Four (at The Pit, Albuquerque, NM): **Semifinals**–N.C. State 67, Georgia 60; Houston 94, Louisville 81. **Championship**–N.C. State 54, Houston 52.

NIT Championship (at Madison Square Garden): Fresno St. 69, DePaul 60. No Top 20 teams played in NIT.

1984

		Before Tourns	Head Coach	Final Record
1	North Carolina	27-2	Dean Smith	28-3
2	**Georgetown**	29-3	John Thompson	34-3
3	Kentucky	26-4	Joe B. Hall	29-5
4	DePaul	26-2	Ray Meyer	27-3
5	Houston	28-4	Guy Lewis	32-5
6	Illinois	24-4	Lou Henson	26-5
7	Oklahoma	29-4	Billy Tubbs	29-5
8	Arkansas	25-6	Eddie Sutton	25-7
9	UTEP	27-3	Don Haskins	27-4
10	Purdue	22-6	Gene Keady	22-7
11	Maryland	23-7	Lefty Driesell	24-8
12	Tulsa	27-3	Nolan Richardson	27-4
13	UNLV	27-5	Jerry Tarkanian	29-6
14	Duke	24-9	Mike Krzyzewski	24-10
15	Washington	22-6	Marv Harshman	24-7
16	Memphis St.	24-6	Dana Kirk	26-7
17	Oregon St.	22-6	Ralph Miller	22-7
18	Syracuse	22-8	Jim Boeheim	23-9
19	Wake Forest	21-8	Carl Tacy	23-9
20	Temple	25-4	John Chaney	26-5

NCAA Final Four (at the Kingdome, Seattle): **Semifinals**–Houston 49, Virginia 47 (OT); Georgetown 53, Kentucky 40. **Championship**–Georgetown 84, Houston 75.

NIT Championship (at Madison Square Garden): Michigan 83, Notre Dame 63. No Top 20 teams played in NIT.

1985

		Before Tourns	Head Coach	Final Record
1	Georgetown ...	30-2	John Thompson	35-3
2	Michigan	25-3	Bill Frieder	26-4
3	St. John's	27-3	Lou Carnesecca	31-4
4	Oklahoma	28-5	Billy Tubbs	31-6
5	Memphis St. ...	27-3	Dana Kirk	31-4
6	Georgia Tech ..	24-7	Bobby Cremins	27-8
7	North Carolina	24-8	Dean Smith	27-9
8	Louisiana Tech .	27-2	Andy Russo	29-3
9	UNLV	27-3	Jerry Tarkanian	28-4
10	Duke	22-7	Mike Krzyzewski	23-8
11	VCU	25-5	J.D. Barnett	26-6
12	Illinois	24-8	Lou Henson	26-9
13	Kansas	25-7	Larry Brown	26-8
14	Loyola-IL	25-5	Gene Sullivan	27-6
15	Syracuse	21-8	Jim Boeheim	22-9
16	N.C. State	20-9	Jim Valvano	23-10
17	Texas Tech	23-7	Gerald Myers	23-8
18	Tulsa	23-7	Nolan Richardson	23-8
19	Georgia	21-8	Hugh Durham	22-9
20	LSU	19-9	Dale Brown	19-10

Note: Unranked **Villanova**, coached by Rollie Massimino, won the NCAAs. The Wildcats entered the tourney at 19-10 and had a final record of 25-10.

NCAA Final Four (at Rupp Arena, Lexington, KY): **Semifinals**— Georgetown 77, St. John's 59; Villanova 52, Memphis St. 45. **Championship**—Villanova 66, Georgetown 64.

NIT Championship (at Madison Square Garden): UCLA 65, Indiana 62. No Top 20 teams played in NIT.

1986

		Before Tourns	Head Coach	Final Record
1	Duke	32-2	Mike Krzyzewski	37-3
2	Kansas	31-3	Larry Brown	35-4
3	Kentucky	29-3	Eddie Sutton	32-4
4	St. John's	30-4	Lou Carnesecca	31-5
5	Michigan	27-4	Bill Frieder	28-5
6	Georgia Tech ..	25-6	Bobby Cremins	27-7
7	**Louisville**	26-7	Denny Crum	32-7
8	North Carolina	26-5	Dean Smith	28-6
9	Syracuse	25-5	Jim Boeheim	26-6
10	Notre Dame ...	23-5	Digger Phelps	23-6
11	UNLV	31-4	Jerry Tarkanian	33-5
12	Memphis St. ...	27-5	Dana Kirk	28-6
13	Georgetown ...	23-7	John Thompson	24-8
14	Bradley	31-2	Dick Versace	32-3
15	Oklahoma	25-8	Billy Tubbs	26-9
16	Indiana	21-7	Bob Knight	21-8
17	Navy	27-4	Paul Evans	30-5
18	Michigan St. ...	21-7	Jud Heathcote	23-8
19	Illinois	21-9	Lou Henson	22-10
20	UTEP	27-5	Don Haskins	27-6

NCAA Final Four (at Reunion Arena, Dallas): **Semifinals**—Duke 71, Kansas 67; Louisville 88, LSU 77. **Championship**—Louisville 72, Duke 69.

NIT Championship (at Madison Square Garden): Ohio St. 73, Wyoming 63. No Top 20 teams played in NIT.

1987

		Before Tourns	Head Coach	Final Record
1	UNLV	33-1	Jerry Tarkanian	37-2
2	North Carolina	29-3	Dean Smith	32-4
3	**Indiana**	24-4	Bob Knight	30-4
4	Georgetown ...	26-4	John Thompson	29-5
5	DePaul	26-2	Joey Meyer	28-3
6	Iowa	27-4	Tom Davis	30-5
7	Purdue	24-4	Gene Keady	25-5
8	Temple	31-3	John Chaney	32-4
9	Alabama	26-4	Wimp Sanderson	28-5
10	Syracuse	26-6	Jim Boeheim	31-7
11	Illinois	23-7	Lou Henson	23-8
12	Pittsburgh	24-7	Paul Evans	25-8
13	Clemson	25-5	Cliff Ellis	25-6
14	Missouri	24-9	Norm Stewart	24-10
15	UCLA	24-6	Walt Hazzard	25-7
16	New Orleans ..	25-3	Benny Dees	26-4
17	Duke	22-8	Mike Krzyzewski	24-9
18	Notre Dame ...	22-7	Digger Phelps	24-8
19	TCU	23-6	Jim Killingsworth	24-7
20	Kansas	23-10	Larry Brown	25-11

NCAA Final Four (at the Superdome, New Orleans): **Semifinals**—Syracuse 77, Providence 63; Indiana 97, UNLV 93. **Championship**—Indiana 74, Syracuse 73.

NIT Championship (at Madison Square Garden): Southern Miss. 84, La Salle 80. No Top 20 teams played in NIT.

1988

		Before Tourns	Head Coach	Final Record
1	Temple	29-1	John Chaney	32-2
2	Arizona	31-2	Lute Olson	35-3
3	Purdue	27-3	Gene Keady	29-4
4	Oklahoma	30-3	Billy Tubbs	35-4
5	Duke	24-6	Mike Krzyzewski	28-7
6	Kentucky	25-5	Eddie Sutton	27-6
7	North Carolina	24-6	Dean Smith	27-7
8	Pittsburgh	23-6	Paul Evans	24-7
9	Syracuse	25-8	Jim Boeheim	26-9
10	Michigan	24-7	Bill Frieder	26-8
11	Bradley	26-4	Stan Albeck	26-5
12	UNLV	27-5	Jerry Tarkanian	28-6
13	Wyoming	26-5	Benny Dees	26-6
14	N.C. State	24-7	Jim Valvano	24-8
15	Loyola-CA	27-3	Paul Westhead	28-4
16	Illinois	22-9	Lou Henson	23-10
17	Iowa	22-9	Tom Davis	24-10
18	Xavier-OH	26-3	Pete Gillen	26-4
19	BYU	25-5	Ladell Andersen	26-6
20	Kansas St.	22-8	Lon Kruger	25-9

Note: Unranked **Kansas**, coached by Larry Brown, won the NCAAs. The Jayhawks entered the tourney at 21-11 and had a final record of 27-11.

NCAA Final Four (at Kemper Arena, Kansas City): **Semifinals**—Kansas 66, Duke 59; Oklahoma 86, Arizona 78. **Championship**—Kansas 83, Oklahoma 79.

NIT Championship (at Madison Square Garden): Connecticut 72, Ohio St. 67. No Top 20 teams played in NIT.

Associated Press Final Polls (Cont.)

1989

	Before Tourns	Head Coach	Final Record
1 Arizona	27-3	Lute Olson	29-4
2 Georgetown	26-4	John Thompson	29-5
3 Illinois	27-4	Lou Henson	31-5
4 Oklahoma	28-5	Billy Tubbs	30-6
5 North Carolina	27-7	Dean Smith	29-8
6 Missouri	27-7	Norm Stewart & Rich Daly	29-8
7 Syracuse	27-7	Jim Boeheim	30-8
8 Indiana	25-7	Bob Knight	27-8
9 Duke	24-7	Mike Krzyzewski	28-8
10 **Michigan**	24-7	Bill Frieder & Steve Fisher	30-7
11 Seton Hall	26-6	P.J. Carlesimo	31-7
12 Louisville	22-8	Denny Crum	24-9
13 Stanford	26-6	Mike Montgomery	26-7
14 Iowa	22-9	Tom Davis	23-10
15 UNLV	26-7	Jerry Tarkanian	29-8
16 Florida St.	22-7	Pat Kennedy	22-8
17 West Virginia	25-4	Gale Catlett	26-5
18 Ball State	28-2	Rick Majerus	29-3
19 N.C. State	20-8	Jim Valvano	22-9
20 Alabama	23-7	Wimp Sanderson	23-8

NCAA Final Four (at The Kingdome, Seattle): **Semifinals**–Seton Hall 95, Duke 78; Michigan 83, Illinois 81. **Championship**–Michigan 80, Seton Hall 79 (OT).

NIT Championship (at Madison Square Garden): St.John's 73, St. Louis 65. No Top 20 teams played in NIT.

1990

	Before Tourns	Head Coach	Final Record
1 Oklahoma	26-4	Billy Tubbs	27-5
2 **UNLV**	29-5	Jerry Tarkanian	35-5
3 Connecticut	28-5	Jim Calhoun	31-6
4 Michigan St.	26-5	Jud Heathcote	28-6
5 Kansas	29-4	Roy Williams	30-5
6 Syracuse	24-6	Jim Boeheim	26-7
7 Arkansas	26-4	Nolan Richardson	30-5
8 Georgetown	23-6	John Thompson	24-7
9 Georgia Tech	24-6	Bobby Cremins	28-7
10 Purdue	21-7	Gene Keady	22-8
11 Missouri	26-5	Norm Stewart	26-6
12 La Salle	29-1	Speedy Morris	30-2
13 Michigan	22-7	Steve Fisher	23-8
14 Arizona	24-6	Lute Olson	25-7
15 Duke	24-8	Mike Krzyzewski	29-9
16 Louisville	26-7	Denny Crum	27-8
17 Clemson	24-8	Cliff Ellis	26-9
18 Illinois	21-7	Lou Henson	21-8
19 LSU	22-8	Dale Brown	23-9
20 Minnesota	20-8	Clem Haskins	23-9
21 Loyola-CA	23-5	Paul Westhead	26-6
22 Oregon St.	22-6	Jim Anderson	22-7
23 Alabama	24-8	Wimp Sanderson	26-9
24 New Mexico St.	26-4	Neil McCarthy	26-5
25 Xavier-OH	26-4	Pete Gillen	28-5

NCAA Final Four (at McNichols Sports Arena, Denver): **Semifinals**–Duke 97, Arkansas 83; UNLV 90, Georgia Tech 81. **Championship**–UNLV 103, Duke 73.

NIT Championship (at Madison Square Garden): Vanderbilt 74, St.Louis 72. No Top 25 teams played in NIT.

1991

	Before Tourns	Head Coach	Final Record
1 UNLV	30-0	Jerry Tarkanian	34-1
2 Arkansas	31-3	Nolan Richardson	34-4
3 Indiana	27-4	Bob Knight	29-5
4 North Carolina	25-5	Dean Smith	29-6
5 Ohio St.	25-3	Randy Ayers	27-4
6 **Duke**	26-7	Mike Krzyzewski	32-7
7 Syracuse	26-5	Jim Boeheim	26-6
8 Arizona	26-6	Lute Olson	28-7
9 Kentucky	22-6	Rick Pitino	same*
10 Utah	28-3	Rick Majerus	30-4
11 Nebraska	26-7	Danny Nee	26-8
12 Kansas	22-7	Roy Williams	27-8
13 Seton Hall	22-8	P.J. Carlesimo	25-9
14 Oklahoma St.	22-7	Eddie Sutton	24-8
15 New Mexico St.	23-5	Neil McCarthy	23-6
16 UCLA	23-8	Jim Harrick	23-9
17 E.Tennessee St.	28-4	Alan LaForce	28-5
18 Princeton	24-2	Pete Carril	24-3
19 Alabama	21-9	Wimp Sanderson	23-10
20 St. John's	20-8	Lou Carnesecca	23-9
21 Mississippi St.	20-8	Richard Williams	20-9
22 LSU	20-9	Dale Brown	20-10
23 Texas	22-8	Tom Penders	23-9
24 DePaul	20-8	Joey Meyer	20-9
25 Southern Miss.	21-7	M.K. Turk	21-8

*On probation

NCAA Final Four (at the Hoosier Dome, Indianapolis): **Semifinals**–Kansas 79, North Carolina 73; Duke 79, UNLV 77. **Championship**–Duke 72, Kansas 65.

NIT Championship (at Madison Square Garden): Stanford 78, Oklahoma 72. No Top 25 teams played in NIT.

1992

	Before Tourns	Head Coach	Final Record
1 **Duke**	28-2	Mike Krzyzewski	34-2
2 Kansas	26-4	Roy Williams	27-5
3 Ohio St.	23-5	Randy Ayers	26-6
4 UCLA	25-4	Jim Harrick	28-5
5 Indiana	23-6	Bob Knight	27-7
6 Kentucky	26-6	Rick Pitino	29-7
7 UNLV	26-2	Jerry Tarkanian	same*
8 USC	23-5	George Raveling	24-6
9 Arkansas	25-7	Nolan Richardson	26-8
10 Arizona	24-6	Lute Olson	24-7
11 Oklahoma St.	26-7	Eddie Sutton	28-8
12 Cincinnati	25-4	Bob Huggins	29-5
13 Alabama	25-8	Wimp Sanderson	26-9
14 Michigan St.	21-7	Jud Heathcote	22-8
15 Michigan	20-8	Steve Fisher	25-9
16 Missouri	20-8	Norm Stewart	21-9
17 Massachusetts	28-4	John Calipari	30-5
18 North Carolina	21-9	Dean Smith	23-10
19 Seton Hall	21-8	P.J. Carlesimo	23-9
20 Florida St.	20-9	Pat Kennedy	22-10
21 Syracuse	21-9	Jim Boeheim	22-10
22 Georgetown	21-9	John Thompson	22-10
23 Oklahoma	21-8	Billy Tubbs	21-9
24 DePaul	20-8	Joey Meyer	20-9
25 LSU	20-9	Dale Brown	21-10

*On probation

NCAA Final Four (at the Metrodome, Minneapolis): **Semifinals**–Michigan 76, Cincinnati 72; Duke 81, Indiana 78. **Championship**–Duke 71, Michigan 51.

NIT Championship (at Madison Square Garden): Virginia 81, Notre Dame 76 (OT). No Top 25 teams played in NIT.

1993

	Before Tourns	Head Coach	Final Record
1 Indiana	28-3	Bob Knight	31-4
2 Kentucky	26-3	Rick Pitino	30-4
3 Michigan	26-4	Steve Fisher	31-5
4 N. Carolina	28-4	Dean Smith	34-4
5 Arizona	24-3	Lute Olson	24-4
6 Seton Hall	27-6	P.J. Carlesimo	28-7
7 Cincinnati	24-4	Bob Huggins	27-5
8 Vanderbilt	26-5	Eddie Fogler	28-6
9 Kansas	25-6	Roy Williams	29-7
10 Duke	23-7	Mike Krzyzewski	24-8
11 Florida St.	22-9	Pat Kennedy	25-10
12 Arkansas	20-8	Nolan Richardson	22-9
13 Iowa	22-8	Tom Davis	23-9
14 Massachusetts	23-6	John Calipari	24-7
15 Louisville	20-8	Denny Crum	22-9
16 Wake Forest	19-8	Dave Odom	21-9
17 New Orleans	26-3	Tim Floyd	26-4
18 Georgia Tech	19-10	Bobby Cremins	19-11
19 Utah	23-6	Rick Majerus	24-7
20 Western Ky.	24-5	Ralph Willard	26-6
21 New Mexico	24-6	Dave Bliss	24-7
22 Purdue	18-9	Gene Keady	18-10
23 Oklahoma St.	19-8	Eddie Sutton	20-9
24 New Mexico St.	25-7	Neil McCarthy	26-8
25 UNLV	21-7	Rollie Massimino	21-8

NCAA Final Four (at the Superdome, New Orleans): **Semifinals**–North Carolina 78, Kansas 68; Michigan 81, Kentucky 78 (OT). **Championship**–North Carolina 77, Michigan 71.

NIT Championship (at Madison Square Garden): Minnesota 62, Georgetown 61. No. 25 UNLV was the only Top 25 team that played in NIT.

1994

	Before Tourns	Head Coach	Final Record
1 North Carolina	27-6	Dean Smith	28-7
2 Arkansas	25-3	Nolan Richardson	31-3
3 Purdue	26-4	Gene Keady	29-5
4 Connecticut	27-4	Jim Calhoun	29-5
5 Missouri	25-3	Norm Stewart	28-4
6 Duke	23-5	Mike Krzyzewski	28-6
7 Kentucky	26-6	Rick Pitino	27-7
8 Massachusetts	27-6	John Calipari	28-7
9 Arizona	25-5	Lute Olson	29-6
10 Louisville	26-5	Denny Crum	28-6
11 Michigan	21-7	Steve Fisher	24-8
12 Temple	22-7	John Chaney	23-8
13 Kansas	25-7	Roy Williams	27-8
14 Florida	25-7	Lon Kruger	29-8
15 Syracuse	21-6	Jim Boeheim	23-7
16 California	22-7	Todd Bozeman	22-8
17 UCLA	21-6	Jim Harrick	21-7
18 Indiana	19-8	Bob Knight	21-9
19 Oklahoma St.	23-9	Eddie Sutton	24-10
20 Texas	25-7	Tom Penders	26-8
21 Marquette	22-8	Kevin O'Neill	24-9
22 Nebraska	20-9	Danny Nee	20-10
23 Minnesota	20-11	Clem Haskins	21-12
24 Saint Louis	23-5	Charlie Spoonhour	23-6
25 Cincinnati	22-9	Bob Huggins	22-10

NCAA Final Four (at the Charlotte Coliseum): **Semifinals**– Arkansas 91, Arizona 82; Duke 70, Florida 65. **Championship**– Arkansas 76, Duke 72.

NIT Championship (at Madison Square Garden): Villanova 80, Vanderbilt 73. No top 25 teams played in NIT.

1995

	Before Tourns	Head Coach	Final Record
1 UCLA	25-2	Jim Harrick	31-2
2 Kentucky	25-4	Rick Pitino	28-5
3 Wake Forest	24-5	Dave Odom	26-6
4 North Carolina	24-5	Dean Smith	28-6
5 Kansas	23-5	Roy Williams	25-6
6 Arkansas	27-6	Nolan Richardson	32-7
7 Massachusetts	26-4	John Calipari	26-5
8 Connecticut	25-4	Jim Calhoun	28-5
9 Villanova	25-7	Steve Lappas	25-8
10 Maryland	24-7	Gary Williams	26-8
11 Michigan St.	22-5	Jud Heathcote	22-6
12 Purdue	24-6	Gene Keady	25-7
13 Virginia	22-8	Jeff Jones	25-9
14 Oklahoma St.	23-9	Eddie Sutton	27-10
15 Arizona	23-7	Lute Olson	23-8
16 Arizona St.	22-8	Bill Frieder	24-9
17 Oklahoma	23-8	Kelvin Sampson	23-9
18 Mississippi St.	20-7	Richard Williams	22-8
19 Utah	27-5	Rick Majerus	28-6
20 Alabama	22-9	David Hobbs	23-11
21 Western Ky.	26-3	Matt Kilcullen	27-4
22 Georgetown	19-9	John Thompson	21-10
23 Missouri	19-8	Norm Stewart	20-9
24 Iowa St.	22-10	Tim Floyd	23-11
25 Syracuse	19-9	Jim Boeheim	20-10

NCAA Final Four (at the Kingdome, Seattle): **Semifinals**– UCLA 74, Oklahoma St. 61; Arkansas 75, North Carolina 68. **Championship**– UCLA 89, Arkansas 78.

NIT Championship (at Madison Square Garden): Virginia Tech 65, Marquette 64 (OT). No top 25 teams played in NIT.

1996

	Before Tourns	Head Coach	Final Record
1 Massachusetts	31-1	John Calipari	35-2
2 Kentucky	28-2	Rick Pitino	34-2
3 Connecticut	30-2	Jim Calhoun	32-3
4 Georgetown	26-7	John Thompson	29-8
5 Kansas	26-4	Roy Williams	29-5
6 Purdue	25-5	Gene Keady	26-6
7 Cincinnati	25-4	Bob Huggins	28-5
8 Texas Tech	28-1	James Dickey	30-2
9 Wake Forest	23-5	Dave Odom	26-6
10 Villanova	25-6	Steve Lappas	26-7
11 Arizona	24-6	Lute Olson	26-7
12 Utah	25-6	Rick Majerus	27-7
13 Georgia Tech	22-11	Bobby Cremins	24-12
14 UCLA	23-7	Jim Harrick	23-8
15 Syracuse	24-8	Jim Boeheim	29-9
16 Memphis	22-7	Larry Finch	22-8
17 Iowa St.	23-8	Tim Floyd	24-9
18 Penn St.	21-6	Jerry Dunn	21-7
19 Mississippi St.	22-7	Richard Williams	26-8
20 Marquette	22-7	Mike Deane	23-8
21 Iowa	22-8	Tom Davis	23-9
22 Virginia Tech	22-5	Bill Foster	23-6
23 New Mexico	27-4	Dave Bliss	28-5
24 Louisville	20-11	Denny Crum	22-12
25 North Carolina	20-10	Dean Smith	21-11

NCAA Final Four (at the Meadowlands, E. Rutherford, N.J.): **Semifinals**– Kentucky 81, Massachusetts 74; Syracuse 77, Mississippi St. 69. **Championship**– Kentucky 76, Syracuse 67.

NIT Championship (at Madison Square Garden): Nebraska 60, St. Joseph's 56. No top 25 teams played in NIT.

Associated Press Final Polls (Cont.)

1997

		Before Tourns	Head Coach	Final Record
1	Kansas	32-1	Roy Williams	34-2
2	Utah	26-3	Rick Majerus	29-4
3	Minnesota	27-3	Clem Haskins	31-4
4	North Carolina	24-6	Dean Smith	28-7
5	Kentucky	30-4	Rick Pitino	35-5
6	South Carolina	24-7	Eddie Fogler	24-8
7	UCLA	21-7	Steve Lavin	24-8
8	Duke	23-8	Mike Krzyzewski	24-9
9	Wake Forest	23-6	Dave Odom	24-7
10	Cincinnati	25-7	Bob Huggins	26-8
11	New Mexico	24-7	Dave Bliss	25-8
12	St. Joseph's	24-6	Phil Martelli	26-7
13	Xavier	22-5	Skip Prosser	23-6
14	Clemson	21-9	Rick Barnes	23-10
15	Arizona	19-9	Lute Olsen	25-9
16	Coll. of Charleston	28-2	John Kresse	29-3
17	Georgia	24-8	Tubby Smith	24-9
18	Iowa St.	20-8	Tim Floyd	22-9
19	Illinois	21-9	Lon Kruger	22-10
20	Villanova	23-9	Steve Lappas	24-10
21	Stanford	20-7	Mike Montgomery	22-8
22	Maryland	21-10	Gary Williams	21-11
23	Boston College	21-8	Jim O'Brien	22-9
24	Colorado	21-9	Ricardo Patton	22-10
25	Louisville	23-8	Denny Crum	26-9

NCAA Final Four (at the RCA Dome, Indianapolis): **Semifinals**– Kentucky 78, Minnesota 69; Arizona 66, North Carolina 58. **Championship**– Arizona 84, Kentucky 79 (OT).
NIT Championship (at Madison Square Garden): Michigan 82, Florida St. 72. No top 25 teams played in NIT.

All Time AP Top 20

The composite AP Top 20 from the 1948-49 season through 1996-97, based on the final regular season rankings of each year. The final AP poll has been taken before the NCAA and NIT tournaments each season since 1949 except in 1953 and '54 and again in 1974 and '75 when the final poll came out after the postseason. Team point totals are based on 20 points for all 1st place finishes, 19 for each 2nd, etc.). Also listed are the number of times ranked No. 1 by AP going into the tournaments, and times ranked in the pre-tournament Top 10 and Top 20.

		Pts	No.1	Top 10	Top 20
1	Kentucky	568	7	32	37
2	North Carolina	467	4	26	33
3	UCLA	435	7	22	32
4	Duke	317	2	18	27
5	Kansas	293	1	16	23
6	Indiana	290	4	16	22
7	Louisville	233	0	11	22
8	Cincinnati	197	2	9	14
9	Notre Dame	195	0	13	17
10	Michigan	191	2	10	14
11	N.C. State	176	1	9	16
12	UNLV	173	2	8	13
13	Marquette	166	0	11	15
14	Illinois	164	0	8	18
15	Arkansas	158	0	9	13
16	Syracuse	150	0	9	15
17	Ohio St	149	2	9	10
18	Kansas St	147	1	8	12
19	DePaul	141	2	8	10
20	Bradley	139	1	7	10
	Georgetown	139	1	7	10

AP Post-Tournament Final Polls

The final AP Top 20 poll has been released **after** the NCAA and NIT tournaments four times—in 1953 and '54 and again in 1974 and '75. Those four polls are listed below; teams that were not included in the last regular season polls are in *CAPITAL* letters.

1953

		Final Record
1	Indiana	23-3
2	Seton Hall	31-2
3	Kansas	19-6
4	Washington	30-3
5	LSU	24-3
6	La Salle	25-3
7	*ST. JOHN'S*	17-6
8	Okla. A&M	23-7
9	Duquesne	21-8
10	Notre Dame	19-5
11	Illinois	18-4
12	Kansas St.	17-4
13	Holy Cross	20-6
14	Seattle	29-4
15	*WAKE FOREST*	22-7
16	*SANTA CLARA*	20-7
17	Western Ky.	25-6
18	N.C. State	26-6
19	*DEPAUL*	19-9
20	*SW MISSOURI*	24-4

1954

		Final Record
1	Kentucky	25-0
2	La Salle	26-4
3	Holy Cross	26-2
4	Indiana	20-4
5	Duquesne	26-3
6	Notre Dame	22-3
7	*BRADLEY*	19-13
8	Western Ky.	29-3
9	*PENN ST.*	18-6
10	Okla. A&M	24-5
11	USC	19-14
12	*GEO. WASH.*	23-3
13	Iowa	17-5
14	LSU	21-5
15	Duke	22-6
16	*NIAGARA*	24-6
17	Seattle	26-2
18	Kansas	16-5
19	Illinois	17-5
20	*MARYLAND*	23-7

1974

		Final Record
1	N.C. State	30-1
2	UCLA	26-4
3	Marquette	26-5
4	Maryland	23-5
5	Notre Dame	26-3
6	Michigan	22-5
7	Kansas	23-7
8	Providence	28-4
9	Indiana	23-5
10	Long Beach St.	24-2
11	*PURDUE*	22-8
12	North Carolina	22-6
13	Vanderbilt	23-5
14	Alabama	22-4
15	*UTAH*	22-8
16	Pittsburgh	25-4
17	USC	24-5
18	*ORAL ROBERTS*	23-6
19	South Carolina	22-5
20	Dayton	20-9

1975

		Final Record
1	UCLA	28-3
2	Kentucky	26-5
3	Indiana	31-1
4	Louisville	28-3
5	Maryland	24-5
6	Syracuse	23-9
7	N.C. State	22-6
8	Arizona St.	25-4
9	North Carolina	23-8
10	Alabama	22-5
11	Marquette	23-4
12	*PRINCETON*	22-8
13	Cincinnati	23-6
14	Notre Dame	19-10
15	Kansas St.	20-9
16	Drake	19-10
17	UNLV	24-5
18	Oregon St.	19-12
19	*MICHIGAN*	19-8
20	Penn	23-5

Pre-Tournament Records

1953– St. John's (Al DeStefano, 14-5); Wake Forest (Murray Greason, 21-6); Santa Clara (Bob Feerick, 18-6); DePaul (Ray Meyer, 18-7); SW Missouri St. (Bob Vanatta, 19-4 before NAIA tourney). **1954**– Bradley (Forddy Anderson, 15-12); Penn St. (Elmer Gross, 14-5); George Washington (Bill Reinhart, 23-2); Niagara (Taps Gallagher, 22-5); Maryland (Bud Millikan, 23-7). **1974**– Purdue (Fred Schaus, 18-8); Utah (Bill Foster, 19-7); Oral Roberts (Ken Trickey, 21-5). **1975**– Princeton (Pete Carril, 18-8); Michigan (Johnny Orr, 19-7).

Division I Winning Streaks

Full Season
(Including tournaments)

No		Seasons	Broken by	Score
88	UCLA	1971-74	Notre Dame	71-70
60	San Francisco	1955-57	Illinois	62-33
47	UCLA	1966-68	Houston	71-69
45	UNLV	1990-91	Duke	79-77
44	Texas	1913-17	Rice	24-18
43	Seton Hall	1939-41	LIU-Bklyn	49-26
43	LIU-Brooklyn	1935-37	Stanford	45-31
41	UCLA	1968-69	USC	46-44
39	Marquette	1970-71	Ohio St.	60-59
37	Cincinnati	1962-63	Wichita St.	65-64
37	North Carolina	1957-58	West Virginia	75-64
36	N.C. State	1974-75	Wake Forest	83-78
35	Arkansas	1927-29	Texas	26-25

Regular Season
(Not including tournaments)

No		Seasons	Broken by	Score
76	UCLA	1971-74	Notre Dame	71-70
57	Indiana	1975-77	Toledo	59-57
56	Marquette	1970-72	Detroit	70-49
54	Kentucky	1952-55	Georgia Tech	59-58
51	San Francisco	1955-57	Illinois	62-33
48	Penn	1970-72	Temple	57-52
47	Ohio St	1960-62	Wisconsin	86-67
44	Texas	1913-17	Rice	24-18
43	UCLA	1966-68	Houston	71-69
43	LIU-Brooklyn	1935-37	Stanford	45-31
42	Seton Hall	1939-41	LIU-Bklyn	49-26

Home Court

No		Seasons	Broken By	Score
129	Kentucky	1943-55	Georgia Tech	59-58
99	St. Bonaventure	1948-61	Detroit	77-70
98	UCLA	1970-76	Oregon	65-45
86	Cincinnati	1957-64	Kansas	51-47
81	Arizona	1945-51	Kansas St.	76-57
81	Marquette	1967-73	Notre Dame	71-69
80	Lamar	1978-84	Louisiana Tech	68-65
75	Long Beach St.	1968-74	San Francisco	94-84
72	UNLV	1974-78	New Mexico	102-98
71	Arizona	1987-92	UCLA	89-87

Most Improved Teams
Since 1974

Team	Season	W-L	Previous W-L	Games Improved
N.C. A&T	1978	20-8	3-24	16.5
Murray St.	1980	23-8	4-22	16.5
Liberty	1992	22-7	5-23	16.5
North Texas	1976	22-4	6-20	16
Radford	1991	22-7	7-22	15
Tulsa	1981	26-7	8-19	15
Utah St.	1983	20-9	4-23	15
W. Michigan	1992	21-9	5-22	14.5
Tennessee St.	1993	19-10	4-24	14.5
Fresno St.	1978	21-6	7-20	14
James Madison	1987	20-10	5-23	14
Loyola-CA	1988	28-4	12-16	14
Cal Poly-SLO	1996	16-13	1-26	14

All-Time Highest Scoring Teams
SINGLE SEASON
Scoring Offense

Team	Season	Gm	Pts	Avg
Loyola-CA	1990	32	3918	122.4
Loyola-CA	1989	31	3486	112.5
UNLV	1976	31	3426	110.5
Loyola-CA	1988	32	3528	110.3
UNLV	1977	32	3426	107.1
Oral Roberts	1972	28	2943	105.1
Southern-BR	1991	28	2924	104.4
Loyola-CA	1991	31	3211	103.6
Oklahoma	1988	39	4012	102.9
Oklahoma	1989	36	3680	102.2

SINGLE GAME
Highest Scoring

	Score	Opponent	Date
Loyola-CA	186-140	US Int'l	1/5/91
Loyola-CA	181-150	US Int'l	1/31/89
Oklahoma	173-101	US Int'l	11/29/89
Oklahoma	172-112	Loyola-CA	12/15/90
Arkansas	166-101	US Int'l	12/9/89

Scoring Defense
Before 1965

Team	Season	Gm	Pts	Avg
Oklahoma St.	1948	31	1006	32.5
Oklahoma St.	1949	28	985	35.2
Oklahoma St.	1950	27	1059	39.2
Alabama	1948	27	1070	39.6
Creighton	1948	23	925	40.2

Since 1965

Team	Season	Gm	Pts	Avg
Fresno St.	1982	30	1412	47.1
Princeton	1992	28	1349	48.2
Princeton	1991	27	1320	48.9
N.C. State	1982	32	1570	49.1
Princeton	1982	26	1277	49.1

Scoring Margin

Team	Season	Off	Def	Mar
UCLA	1972	94.6	64.3	30.3
N.C. State	1948	75.3	47.2	28.1
Kentucky	1954	87.5	60.3	27.2
Kentucky	1952	82.3	55.4	26.9
UNLV	1991	97.7	71.0	26.7
UCLA	1968	93.4	67.2	26.2
UCLA	1967	89.6	63.7	25.9
Houston	1968	97.8	72.5	25.3
Kentucky	1948	69.0	44.4	24.6
Kentucky	1949	68.2	43.9	24.3

NCAA Champs with most losses

11	Kansas (27-11)	1988
10	Villanova (25-10)	1985
10	N.C. State (26-10)	1983
9	Arizona (25-9)	1997
9	Indiana (26-9)	1981

Annual NCAA Division I Leaders

Scoring

The NCAA did not begin keeping individual scoring records until the 1947-48 season. All averages include postseason games where applicable.

Multiple winners: Pete Maravich and Oscar Robertson (3); Darrell Floyd, Harry Kelly, Frank Selvy and Freeman Williams (2).

Year		Gm	Pts	Avg	Year		Gm	Pts	Avg
1948	Murray Wier, Iowa	19	399	21.0	1973	Bird Averitt, Pepperdine	25	848	33.9
1949	Tony Lavelli, Yale	30	671	22.4	1974	Larry Fogle, Canisius	25	835	33.4
1950	Paul Arizin, Villanova	29	735	25.3	1975	Bob McCurdy, Richmond	26	855	32.9
1951	Bill Mlkvy, Temple	25	731	29.2	1976	Marshall Rodgers, Texas-Pan Am	25	919	36.8
1952	Clyde Lovellette, Kansas	28	795	28.4	1977	Freeman Williams, Portland St.	26	1010	38.8
1953	Frank Selvy, Furman	25	738	29.5	1978	Freeman Williams, Portland St.	27	969	35.9
1954	Frank Selvy, Furman	29	1209	41.7	1979	Lawrence Butler, Idaho St	27	812	30.1
1955	Darrell Floyd, Furman	25	897	35.9	1980	Tony Murphy, Southern-BR	29	932	32.1
1956	Darrell Floyd, Furman	28	946	33.8	1981	Zam Fredrick, S. Carolina	27	781	28.9
1957	Grady Wallace, S. Carolina	29	906	31.2	1982	Harry Kelly, Texas Southern	29	862	29.7
1958	Oscar Robertson, Cincinnati	28	984	35.1	1983	Harry Kelly, Texas Southern	29	835	28.8
1959	Oscar Robertson, Cincinnati	30	978	32.6	1984	Joe Jakubick, Akron	27	814	30.1
1960	Oscar Robertson, Cincinnati	30	1011	33.7	1985	Xavier McDaniel, Wichita St	31	844	27.2
1961	Frank Burgess, Gonzaga	26	842	32.4	1986	Terrance Bailey, Wagner	29	854	29.4
1962	Billy McGill, Utah	26	1009	38.8	1987	Kevin Houston, Army	29	953	32.9
1963	Nick Werkman, Seton Hall	22	650	29.5	1988	Hersey Hawkins, Bradley	31	1125	36.3
1964	Howie Komives, Bowling Green	23	844	36.7	1989	Hank Gathers, Loyola-CA	31	1015	32.7
1965	Rick Barry, Miami-FL	26	973	37.4	1990	Bo Kimble, Loyola-CA	32	1131	35.3
1966	Dave Schellhase, Purdue	24	781	32.5	1991	Kevin Bradshaw, US Int'l	28	1054	37.6
1967	Jimmy Walker, Providence	28	851	30.4	1992	Brett Roberts, Morehead St	29	815	28.1
1968	Pete Maravich, LSU	26	1138	43.8	1993	Greg Guy, Texas-Pan Am	19	556	29.3
1969	Pete Maravich, LSU	26	1148	44.2	1994	Glenn Robinson, Purdue	34	1030	30.3
1970	Pete Maravich, LSU	31	1381	44.5	1995	Kurt Thomas, TCU	27	781	28.9
1971	Johnny Neumann, Ole Miss	23	923	40.1	1996	Kevin Granger, Texas Southern	24	648	27.0
1972	Dwight Lamar, SW La	29	1054	36.3	1997	Charles Jones, LIU-Brooklyn	30	903	30.1

Note: Seventeen underclassmen have won the title. **Sophomores** (4)–Robertson (1958), Maravich (1968), Neumann (1971) and Fogle (1974); **Juniors** (13)–Selvy (1953), Floyd (1955), Robertson (1959), Werkman (1963), Maravich (1969), Lamar (1972), Williams (1977), Kelly (1982), Bailey (1986), Gathers (1989), Guy (1993), Robinson (1994) and Jones (1997).

Rebounds

The NCAA did not begin keeping individual rebounding records until the 1950-51 season. From 1956-62, the championship was decided on highest percentage of recoveries out of all rebounds made by both teams in all games. All averages include postseason games where applicable.

Multiple winners: Artis Gilmore, Jerry Lucas, Xavier McDaniel, Kermit Washington and Leroy Wright (2).

Year		Gm	No	Avg	Year		Gm	No	Avg
1951	Ernie Beck, Penn	27	556	20.6	1975	John Irving, Hofstra	21	323	15.4
1952	Bill Hannon, Army	17	355	20.9	1976	Sam Pellom, Buffalo	26	420	16.2
1953	Ed Conlin, Fordham	26	612	23.5	1977	Glenn Moseley, Seton Hall	29	473	16.3
1954	Art Quimby, Connecticut	26	588	22.6	1978	Ken Williams, N. Texas	28	411	14.7
1955	Charlie Slack, Marshall	21	538	25.6	1979	Monti Davis, Tennessee St.	26	421	16.2
1956	Joe Holup, G. Washington	26	604	25.6	1980	Larry Smith, Alcorn State	26	392	15.1
1957	Elgin Baylor, Seattle	25	508	23.5	1981	Darryl Watson, Miss. Valley St.	27	379	14.0
1958	Alex Ellis, Niagara	25	536	26.2	1982	LaSalle Thompson, Texas	27	365	13.5
1959	Leroy Wright, Pacific	26	652	23.8	1983	Xavier McDaniel, Wichita St.	28	403	14.4
1960	Leroy Wright, Pacific	17	380	23.4	1984	Akeem Olajuwon, Houston	37	500	13.5
1961	Jerry Lucas, Ohio St.	27	470	19.8	1985	Xavier McDaniel, Wichita St.	31	460	14.8
1962	Jerry Lucas, Ohio St.	28	499	21.1	1986	David Robinson, Navy	35	455	13.0
1963	Paul Silas, Creighton	27	557	20.6	1987	Jerome Lane, Pittsburgh	33	444	13.5
1964	Bob Pelkington, Xavier-OH	26	567	21.8	1988	Kenny Miller, Loyola-IL	29	395	13.6
1965	Toby Kimball, Connecticut	23	483	21.0	1989	Hank Gathers, Loyola-CA	31	426	13.7
1966	Jim Ware, Oklahoma City	29	607	20.9	1990	Anthony Bonner, St. Louis	33	456	13.8
1967	Dick Cunningham, Murray St.	22	479	21.8	1991	Shaquille O'Neal, LSU	28	411	14.7
1968	Neal Walk, Florida	25	494	19.8	1992	Popeye Jones, Murray St.	30	431	14.4
1969	Spencer Haywood, Detroit	22	472	21.5	1993	Warren Kidd, Mid. Tenn. St.	26	386	14.8
1970	Artis Gilmore, Jacksonville	28	621	22.2	1994	Jerome Lambert, Baylor	24	355	14.8
1971	Artis Gilmore, Jacksonville	26	603	23.2	1995	Kurt Thomas, TCU	27	393	14.6
1972	Kermit Washington, American	23	455	19.8	1996	Marcus Mann, Miss. Valley St.	29	394	13.6
1973	Kermit Washington, American	22	439	20.0	1997	Tim Duncan, Wake Forest	31	457	14.7
1974	Marvin Barnes, Providence	32	597	18.7					

Note: Only three players have ever led the NCAA in scoring and rebounding in the same season: Xavier McDaniel of Wichita St. (1985), Hank Gathers of Loyola-Marymount (1989) and Kurt Thomas of TCU (1995).

Assists

The NCAA did not begin keeping individual assist records until the 1983-84 season. All averages include postseason games where applicable.

Multiple winner: Avery Johnson (2).

Year		Gm	No	Avg
1984	Craig Lathen, IL-Chicago	29	274	9.45
1985	Rob Weingard, Hofstra	24	228	9.50
1986	Mark Jackson, St. John's	36	328	9.11
1987	Avery Johnson, Southern-BR ...	31	333	10.74
1988	Avery Johnson, Southern-BR ...	30	399	13.30
1989	Glenn Williams, Holy Cross ...	28	278	9.93
1990	Todd Lehmann, Drexel	28	260	9.29
1991	Chris Corchiani, N.C. State ...	31	299	9.65
1992	Van Usher, Tennessee Tech ...	29	254	8.76
1993	Sam Crawford, N. Mexico St .	34	310	9.12
1994	Jason Kidd, California	30	272	9.06
1995	Nelson Haggerty, Baylor	28	284	10.14
1996	Raimonds Miglinieks, UC-Irvine	27	230	8.52
1997	Kenny Mitchell, Dartmouth	26	203	7.81

Blocked Shots

The NCAA did not begin keeping individual blocked shots records until the 1985-86 season. All averages include post-season games where applicable.

Multiple winner: Keith Closs and David Robinson (2).

Year		Gm	No	Avg
1986	David Robinson, Navy	35	207	5.91
1987	David Robinson, Navy	32	144	4.50
1988	Rodney Blake, St. Joe's-PA	29	116	4.00
1989	Alonzo Mourning, G'town	34	169	4.97
1990	Kenny Green, Rhode Island ...	26	124	4.77
1991	Shawn Bradley, BYU	34	177	5.21
1992	Shaquille O'Neal, LSU	30	157	5.23
1993	Theo Ratliff, Wyoming	28	124	4.43
1994	Grady Livingston, Howard	26	115	4.42
1995	Keith Closs, Cen. Conn. St. ...	26	139	5.35
1996	Keith Closs, Cen. Conn. St.	28	178	6.36
1997	Adonal Foyle, Colgate	28	180	6.43

All-Time NCAA Division I Individual Leaders

Through 1996-97; includes regular season and tournament games; **Last** column indicates final year played.

CAREER

Scoring

	Points	Yrs	Last	Gm	Pts
1	Pete Maravich, LSU	3	1970	83	3667
2	Freeman Williams, Port. St. ..	4	1978	106	3249
3	Lionel Simmons, La Salle	4	1990	131	3217
4	Alphonzo Ford, Miss. Val. St.	4	1993	109	3165
5	Harry Kelly, Texas-Southern .	4	1983	110	3066
6	Hersey Hawkins, Bradley ...	4	1988	125	3008
7	Oscar Robertson, Cincinnati .	3	1960	88	2973
8	Danny Manning, Kansas	4	1988	147	2951
9	Alfredrick Hughes, Loyola-IL ..	4	1985	120	2914
10	Elvin Hayes, Houston	3	1968	93	2884
11	Larry Bird, Indiana St.	3	1979	94	2850
12	Otis Birdsong, Houston	4	1977	116	2832
13	Kevin Bradshaw, US Int'l	4	1991	111	2804
14	Allan Houston, Tennessee ...	4	1993	128	2801
15	Hank Gathers, USC/Loyola-CA	4	1990	117	2723
16	Reggie Lewis, N'eastern	4	1987	122	2708
17	Daren Queenan, Lehigh	4	1988	118	2703
18	Byron Larkin, Xavier-OH	4	1988	121	2696
19	David Robinson, Navy	4	1987	127	2669
20	Wayman Tisdale, Oklahoma ..	3	1985	104	2661

	Average	Yrs	Last	Pts	Avg
1	Pete Maravich, LSU	3	1970	3667	44.2
2	Austin Carr, Notre Dame	3	1971	2560	34.6
3	Oscar Robertson, Cinn	3	1960	2973	33.8
4	Calvin Murphy, Niagara	3	1970	2548	33.1
5	Dwight Lamar, SW La	2	1973	1862	32.7
6	Frank Selvy, Furman	3	1954	2538	32.5
7	Rick Mount, Purdue	3	1970	2323	32.3
8	Darrell Floyd, Furman	3	1956	2281	32.1
9	Nick Werkman, Seton Hall ..	3	1964	2273	32.0
10	Willie Humes, Idaho St.	2	1971	1510	31.5
11	William Averitt, Pepperdine ..	2	1973	1541	31.4
12	Elgin Baylor, Idaho/Seattle ..	3	1958	2500	31.3
13	Elvin Hayes, Houston	3	1968	2884	31.0
14	Freeman Williams, Port. St. ..	4	1978	3249	30.7
15	Larry Bird, Indiana St.	3	1979	2850	30.3
16	Bill Bradley, Princeton	3	1965	2503	30.2
17	Rich Fuqua, Oral Roberts ...	2	1973	1617	29.9
18	Wilt Chamberlain, Kansas ...	2	1958	1433	29.9
19	Rick Barry, Miami-FL	3	1965	2298	29.8
20	Doug Collins, Illinois St.	3	1973	2240	29.1

	Field Goal Pct.	Yrs	Last	FG	FGA	Pct
1	Ricky Nedd, Appalach. St.	4	1994	412	597	.690
2	Stephen Scheffler, Purdue	4	1990	408	596	.685
3	Steve Johnson, Ore. St. .	4	1981	828	1222	.678
4	Murray Brown, Fla. St. .	4	1980	566	847	.668
5	Lee Campbell, SW Mo.St.	3	1990	411	618	.665
6	Warren Kidd, M.Tenn.St.	3	1993	496	747	.664
7	Joe Senser, West Chester	4	1979	476	719	.662
8	Kevin McGee, UC-Irvine	2	1982	552	841	.656
9	O. Phillips, Pepperdine ..	2	1983	404	618	.654
10	Bill Walton, UCLA	3	1974	747	1147	.651

Note: minimum 400 FGs made.

	Free Throw Pct.	Yrs	Last	FT	FTA	Pct
1	Greg Starrick, Ky/So.Ill	4	1972	341	375	.909
2	Jack Moore, Nebraska .	4	1982	446	495	.901
3	Steve Henson, Kansas St.	4	1990	361	401	.900
4	Steve Alford, Indiana ..	4	1987	535	596	.898
5	Bob Lloyd, Rutgers	3	1967	543	605	.898
6	Jim Barton, Dartmouth ..	4	1989	394	440	.895
7	Tommy Boyer, Arkansas	3	1963	315	353	.892
8	Rob Robbins, N. Mexico	4	1991	309	348	.888
9	Sean Miller, Pitt	4	1992	317	358	.885
10	Ron Perry, Holy Cross ..	4	1980	680	768	.885
	Joe Dykstra, Western Ill .	4	1983	587	663	.885

Note: minimum 300 FTs made.

	3-Pt Field Goals	Yrs	Last	Gm	3FG
1	Doug Day, Radford	4	1993	117	401
2	Ronnie Schmitz, Missouri-KC ..	4	1993	112	378
3	Mark Alberts, Akron	4	1993	107	375
4	Jeff Fryer, Loyola-CA	4	1990	112	363
5	Dennis Scott, Ga.Tech	3	1990	99	351

	3-Pt Field Goal Pct.	Yrs	Last	3FG	Att	Pct
1	Tony Bennett, Wisc-GB ..	4	1992	290	584	.497
2	Keith Jennings, E.Tenn.St.	4	1991	223	452	.493
3	Kirk Manns, Michigan St.	4	1990	212	446	.475
4	Tim Locum, Wisconsin ..	4	1991	227	481	.472
5	David Olson, Eastern Ill .	4	1992	262	562	.466

Note: minimum 200 3FGs made.

All-Time NCAA Division I Individual Leaders (Cont.)
Rebounds

	Total (before 1973)	Yrs	Last	Gm	No
1	Tom Gola, La Salle	4	1955	118	2201
2	Joe Holup, G. Washington	4	1956	104	2030
3	Charlie Slack, Marshall	4	1956	88	1916
4	Ed Conlin, Fordham	4	1955	102	1884
5	Dickie Hemric, Wake Forest	4	1955	104	1802
6	Paul Silas, Creighton	3	1964	81	1751
7	Art Quimby, Connecticut	4	1955	80	1716
8	Jerry Harper, Alabama	4	1956	93	1688
9	Jeff Cohen, Wm. & Mary	4	1961	103	1679
10	Steve Hamilton, Morehead St.	4	1958	102	1675

	Total (since 1973)	Yrs	Last	Gm	No
1	Derrick Coleman, Syracuse	4	1990	143	1537
2	Ralph Sampson, Virginia	4	1983	132	1511
3	Pete Padgett, Nevada-Reno	4	1976	104	1464
4	Lionel Simmons, La Salle	4	1990	131	1429
5	Anthony Bonner, St. Louis	4	1990	133	1424
6	Tyrone Hill, Xavier-OH	4	1990	126	1380
7	Popeye Jones, Murray St.	4	1992	123	1374
8	Michael Brooks, La Salle	4	1980	114	1372
9	Xavier McDaniel, Wichita St.	4	1985	117	1359
10	John Irving, Ariz./Hofstra	4	1977	103	1348

	Average (before 1973)	Yrs	Last	No	Avg
1	Artis Gilmore, Jacksonville	2	1971	1224	22.7
2	Charlie Slack, Marshall	4	1956	1916	21.8
3	Paul Silas, Creighton	3	1964	1751	21.6
4	Leroy Wright, Pacific	3	1960	1442	21.5
5	Art Quimby, Connecticut	4	1955	1716	21.5

Note: minimum 800 rebounds.

	Average (since 1973)	Yrs	Last	No	Avg
1	Glenn Mosley, Seton Hall	4	1977	1263	15.2
2	Bill Campion, Manhattan	3	1975	1070	14.2
3	Pete Padgett, Nevada-Reno	4	1976	1464	14.1
4	Bob Warner, Maine	4	1976	1304	13.6
5	Shaquille O'Neal, LSU	3	1992	1217	13.5

Note: minimum 650 rebounds.

Assists

	Total	Yrs	Last	Gm	No
1	Bobby Hurley, Duke	4	1993	140	1076
2	Chris Corchiani, N.C. State	4	1991	124	1038
3	Keith Jennings, E. Tenn. St.	4	1991	127	983
4	Sherman Douglas, Syracuse	4	1989	138	960
5	Tony Miller, Marquette	4	1995	123	956
6	Greg Anthony, Portland/UNLV	4	1991	138	950
7	Gary Payton, Oregon St.	4	1990	120	938
8	Orlando Smart, San Fran	4	1994	116	902
9	Andre LaFleur, N'eastern	4	1987	128	894
10	Jim Les, Bradley	4	1986	118	884

	Average	Yrs	Last	No	Avg
1	A. Johnson, Cameron/ Southern	3	1988	838	8.91
2	Sam Crawford, N. Mex. St.	2	1993	592	8.84
3	Mark Wade, Okla/UNLV	3	1987	693	8.77
4	Chris Corchiani, N.C.State	4	1991	1038	8.37
5	Taurence Chisholm, Delaware	4	1988	877	7.97
6	Van Usher, Tennessee Tech	3	1992	676	7.95
7	Anthony Manuel, Bradley	3	1989	855	7.92
8	Gary Payton, Oregon St.	4	1990	938	7.82
9	Orlando Smart, San Fran	4	1994	902	7.78
10	Tony Miller, Marquette	4	1995	956	7.77

Note: minimum 550 assists.

Blocked Shots

	Average	Yrs	Last	No	Avg
1	Keith Closs, Cen. Conn. St.	2	1996	317	5.87
2	Adonal Foyle, Colgate	3	1997	492	5.66
3	David Robinson, Navy	2	1987	351	5.24
4	Shaquille O'Neal, LSU	3	1992	412	4.58
5	Theo Ratliff, Wyoming	4	1995	425	3.83

Note: minimum 200 blocked shots.

Steals

	Average	Yrs	Last	No	Avg
1	Mookie Blaylock, Oklahoma	2	1989	281	3.80
2	Ronn McMahon, Eastern Wash	3	1990	225	3.52
3	Jason Kidd, California	2	1994	204	3.46
4	Eric Murdock, Providence	4	1991	376	3.21
5	Van Usher, Tennessee Tech	3	1992	270	3.18

Note: minimum 200 steals.

2000 Points/1000 Rebounds
For a combined total of 4000 or more.

		Gm	Pts	Reb	Total
1	Tom Gola, La Salle	118	2462	2201	4663
2	Lionel Simmons, La Salle	131	3217	1429	4646
3	Elvin Hayes, Houston	93	2884	1602	4486
4	Dickie Hemric, W.Forest	104	2587	1802	4389
5	Oscar Robertson, Cinn	88	2973	1338	4311
6	Joe Holup, G. Washington	104	2226	2030	4256

		Gm	Pts	Reb	Total
7	Harry Kelly, TX-Southern	110	3066	1085	4151
8	Danny Manning, Kansas	147	2951	1187	4138
9	Larry Bird, Indiana St.	94	2850	1247	4097
10	Elgin Baylor,Col.Idaho/ Seattle	80	2500	1559	4059
11	Michael Brooks, La Salle	114	2628	1372	4000

Years Played– Baylor (1956-58); **Bird** (1977-79); **Brooks** (1977-80); **Gola** (1952-55); **Hayes** (1966-68); **Hemric** (1952-55); **Holup** (1953-56); **Kelly** (1980-83); **Manning** (1985-88); **Robertson** (1958-60); **Simmons** (1987-90).

SINGLE SEASON
Scoring

	Points	Year	Gm	Pts
1	Pete Maravich, LSU	1970	31	1381
2	Elvin Hayes, Houston	1968	33	1214
3	Frank Selvy, Furman	1954	29	1209
4	Pete Maravich, LSU	1969	26	1148
5	Pete Maravich, LSU	1968	26	1138
6	Bo Kimble, Loyola-CA	1990	32	1131
7	Hersey Hawkins, Bradley	1988	31	1125
8	Austin Carr, Notre Dame	1970	29	1106
9	Austin Carr, Notre Dame	1971	29	1101
10	Otis Birdsong, Houston	1977	36	1090

	Average	Year	Gm	Pts	Avg
1	Pete Maravich, LSU	1970	31	1381	44.5
2	Pete Maravich, LSU	1969	26	1148	44.2
3	Pete Maravich, LSU	1968	26	1138	43.8
4	Frank Selvy, Furman	1954	29	1209	41.7
5	Johnny Neumann, Ole Miss	1971	23	923	40.1
6	Freeman Williams, Port. St.	1977	26	1010	38.8
7	Billy McGill, Utah	1962	26	1009	38.8
8	Calvin Murphy, Niagara	1968	24	916	38.2
9	Austin Carr, Notre Dame	1970	29	1106	38.1
10	Austin Carr, Notre Dame	1971	29	1101	38.0

Scoring

Field Goal Pct.

		Year	FG	FGA	Pct
1	Steve Johnson, Oregon St. ..	1981	235	315	.746
2	Dwayne Davis, Florida	1989	179	248	.722
3	Keith Walker, Utica	1985	154	216	.713
4	Steve Johnson, Oregon St. ..	1980	211	297	.710
5	Oliver Miller, Arkansas	1991	254	361	.704

Free Throw Pct.

		Year	FT	FTA	Pct
1	Craig Collins, Penn St.	1985	94	98	.959
2	Rod Foster, UCLA	1982	95	100	.950
3	Carlos Gibson, Marshall ...	1978	84	89	.944
4	Danny Basile, Marist	1994	84	89	.944
5	Jim Barton, Dartmouth	1986	65	69	.942

3-Pt Field Goal Pct.

		Year	3FG	Att	Pct
1	Glenn Tropf, Holy Cross	1988	52	82	.634
2	Sean Wightman, W.Mich	1992	48	76	.632
3	Keith Jennings, E.Tenn.St. ...	1991	84	142	.592
4	Dave Calloway, Monmouth .	1989	48	82	.585
5	Steve Kerr, Arizona	1988	114	199	.573

Assists

Average

		Year	Gm	No	Avg
1	Avery Johnson, Southern-BR .	1988	30	399	13.3
2	Anthony Manuel, Bradley ...	1988	31	373	12.0
3	Avery Johnson, Southern-BR .	1987	31	333	10.7
4	Mark Wade, UNLV	1987	38	406	10.7
5	Glenn Williams, Holy Cross .	1989	28	278	9.9

Rebounds

Average (before 1973)

		Year	Gm	No	Avg
1	Charlie Slack, Marshall	1955	21	538	25.6
2	Leroy Wright, Pacific	1959	26	652	25.1
3	Art Quimby, Connecticut ...	1955	25	611	24.4
4	Charlie Slack, Marshall	1956	22	520	23.6
5	Ed Conlin, Fordham	1953	26	612	23.5

Average (since 1973)

		Year	Gm	No	Avg
1	Kermit Washington, American	1973	25	511	20.4
2	Marvin Barnes, Providence .	1973	30	571	19.0
3	Marvin Barnes, Providence .	1974	32	597	18.7
4	Pete Padgett, Nevada	1973	26	462	17.8
5	Jim Bradley, Northern Ill	1973	24	426	17.8

Blocked Shots

Average

		Year	Gm	No	Avg
1	Adonal Foyle, Colgate	1997	28	180	6.42
2	Keith Closs, Cen. Conn. St. ..	1996	28	178	6.36
3	David Robinson, Navy	1986	35	207	5.91
4	Keith Closs, Cen. Conn. St. ..	1995	26	139	5.35
5	Shaquille O'Neal, LSU	1992	30	157	5.23

Steals

Average

		Year	Gm	No	Avg
1	Darron Brittman, Chicago St.	1986	28	139	4.96
2	Aldwin Ware, Florida A&M ..	1988	29	142	4.90
3	Ronn McMahon, East Wash .	1990	29	130	4.48
4	Pointer Williams, McNeese St.	1996	27	118	4.37
5	Jim Paguaga, St. Francis-NY ..	1986	28	120	4.29

SINGLE GAME

Scoring

Points vs Div. I Team

		Year	Pts
1	Kevin Bradshaw, US Int'l vs Loyola-CA ..	1991	72
2	Pete Maravich, LSU vs Alabama	1970	69
3	Calvin Murphy, Niagara vs Syracuse ...	1969	68
4	Jay Handlan, Wash. & Lee vs Furman .	1951	66
	Pete Maravich, LSU vs Tulane	1969	66
	Anthony Roberts, Oral Rbts vs N.C. A&T	1977	66
7	Anthony Roberts, Oral Rbts vs Ore ...	1977	65
	Scott Haffner, Evansville vs Dayton	1989	65
9	Pete Maravich, LSU vs Kentucky	1970	64
10	Johnny Neumann, Ole Miss vs LSU ...	1971	63
	Hersey Hawkins, Bradley vs Detroit	1988	63

Points vs Non-Div. I Team

		Year	Pts
1	Frank Selvy, Furman vs Newberry	1954	100
2	Paul Arizin, Villanova vs Phi. NAMC ...	1949	85
3	Freeman Williams, Port. St. vs Rocky Mt	1978	81
4	Bill Mlkvy, Temple vs Wilkes	1951	73
5	Freeman Williams, Port. St. vs So. Ore .	1977	71

Note: Bevo Francis of Division II Rio Grande (Ohio) scored an overall collegiate record 113 points against Hillsdale in 1954. He also scored 84 against Alliance and 82 against Bluffton that same season.

Assists

		Year	No
1	Tony Fairley, Baptist vs Armstrong St.	1987	22
	Avery Johnson, Southern-BR vs TX-South	1988	22
	Sherman Douglas, Syracuse vs Providence	1989	22
4	Mark Wade, UNLV vs Navy	1986	21
	Kelvin Scarborough, N. Mexico vs Hawaii	1987	21
	Anthony Manuel, Bradley vs UC-Irvine ...	1987	21
	Avery Johnson, Southern-BR vs Ala. St. .	1988	21

3-Pt Field Goals

		Year	No
1	Dave Jamerson, Ohio U. vs Charleston .	1989	14
	Askia Jones, Kansas St. vs Fresno St. ..	1994	14
3	Gary Bosserd, Niagara vs Siena	1987	12
	Darrin Fitzgerald, Butler vs Detroit	1987	12
	Al Dillard, Arkansas vs Delaware St.	1993	12
	Mitch Taylor, South-BR vs La. Christian	1995	12
	David McMahan, Winthrop vs C. Carolina	1996	12

Rebounds

Total (before 1973)

		Year	No
1	Bill Chambers, Wm. & Mary vs Virginia .	1953	51
2	Charlie Slack, Marshall vs M. Harvey ...	1954	43
3	Tom Heinsohn, Holy Cross vs BC	1955	42
4	Art Quimby, UConn vs BU	1955	40
5	Three players tied with 39 each.		

Total (since 1973)

		Year	No
1	David Vaughn, Oral Roberts vs Brandeis	1973	34
2	Robert Parish, Centenary vs So. Miss ...	1973	33
3	Durand Macklin, LSU vs Tulane	1976	32
	Jervaughn Scales, South-BR vs Grambling	1994	32
5	Jim Bradley, Northern Ill. vs WI-Milw ...	1973	31
	Calvin Natt, NE La. vs Ga. Southern ...	1976	31

Blocked Shots

		Year	No
1	David Robinson, Navy vs NC-Wilmington	1986	14
	Shawn Bradley, BYU vs Eastern Ky	1990	14
	Roy Rogers, Alabama vs Georgia	1996	14
4	Jim McIlvaine, Marquette vs No. Ill	1993	13
	Keith Closs, C. Conn. St. vs St. Fran-PA .	1994	13

Steals

		Year	No
1	Mookie Blaylock, Oklahoma vs Centenary	1987	13
	Mookie Blaylock, Oklahoma vs Loyola-CA	1988	13
3	Kenny Robertson, Cleve. St. vs Wagner ..	1988	12
	Terry Evans, Oklahoma vs Florida A&M ..	1993	12
5	Eight players tied with 11 each.		

Annual Awards

UPI picked the first national Division I Player of the Year in 1955. Since then, the U.S. Basketball Writers Assn. (1959), the Commonwealth Athletic Club of Kentucky's Adolph Rupp Trophy (1961), the Atlanta Tip-Off Club (1969), the National Assn. of Basketball Coaches (1975), and the LA Athletic Club's John Wooden Award (1977) have joined in.

Since 1977, the first year all six awards were given out, the same player has won all of them in the same season eight times: Marques Johnson in 1977, Larry Bird in 1979, Ralph Sampson in both 1982 and '83, Michael Jordan in 1984, David Robinson in 1987, Lionel Simmons in 1990, Calbert Cheaney in 1993 and Glenn Robinson in 1994.

United Press International

Voted on by a panel of UPI college basketball writers and first presented in 1955.

Multiple winners: Oscar Robertson, Ralph Sampson and Bill Walton (3); Lew Alcindor and Jerry Lucas (2).

Year		Year		Year	
1955	Tom Gola, La Salle	1970	Pete Maravich, LSU	1985	Chris Mullin, St. John's
1956	Bill Russell, San Francisco	1971	Austin Carr, Notre Dame	1986	Walter Berry, St. John's
1957	Chet Forte, Columbia	1972	Bill Walton, UCLA	1987	David Robinson, Navy
1958	Oscar Robertson, Cincinnati	1973	Bill Walton, UCLA	1988	Hersey Hawkins, Bradley
1959	Oscar Robertson, Cincinnati	1974	Bill Walton, UCLA	1989	Danny Ferry, Duke
1960	Oscar Robertson, Cincinnati	1975	David Thompson, N.C. State	1990	Lionel Simmons, La Salle
1961	Jerry Lucas, Ohio St.	1976	Scott May, Indiana	1991	Shaquille O'Neal, LSU
1962	Jerry Lucas, Ohio St.	1977	Marques Johnson, UCLA	1992	Jim Jackson, Ohio St.
1963	Art Heyman, Duke	1978	Butch Lee, Marquette	1993	Calbert Cheaney, Indiana
1964	Gary Bradds, Ohio St.	1979	Larry Bird, Indiana St.	1994	Glenn Robinson, Purdue
1965	Bill Bradley, Princeton	1980	Mark Aguirre, DePaul	1995	Joe Smith, Maryland
1966	Cazzie Russell, Michigan	1981	Ralph Sampson, Virginia	1996	Ray Allen, UConn
1967	Lew Alcindor, UCLA	1982	Ralph Sampson, Virginia	1997	no award
1968	Elvin Hayes, Houston	1983	Ralph Sampson, Virginia		
1969	Lew Alcindor, UCLA	1984	Michael Jordan, N. Carolina		

U.S. Basketball Writers Association

Voted on by the USBWA and first presented in 1959.

Multiple winners: Ralph Sampson and Bill Walton (3); Lew Alcindor, Jerry Lucas and Oscar Robertson (2).

Year		Year		Year	
1959	Oscar Robertson, Cincinnati	1972	Bill Walton, UCLA	1985	Chris Mullin, St. John's
1960	Oscar Robertson, Cincinnati	1973	Bill Walton, UCLA	1986	Walter Berry, St. John's
1961	Jerry Lucas, Ohio St.	1974	Bill Walton, UCLA	1987	David Robinson, Navy
1962	Jerry Lucas, Ohio St.	1975	David Thompson, N.C. State	1988	Hersey Hawkins, Bradley
1963	Art Heyman, Duke	1976	Adrian Dantley, Notre Dame	1989	Danny Ferry, Duke
1964	Walt Hazzard, UCLA	1977	Marques Johnson, UCLA	1990	Lionel Simmons, La Salle
1965	Bill Bradley, Princeton	1978	Phil Ford, North Carolina	1991	Larry Johnson, UNLV
1966	Cazzie Russell, Michigan	1979	Larry Bird, Indiana St.	1992	Christian Laettner, Duke
1967	Lew Alcindor, UCLA	1980	Mark Aguirre, DePaul	1993	Calbert Cheaney, Indiana
1968	Elvin Hayes, Houston	1981	Ralph Sampson, Virginia	1994	Glenn Robinson, Purdue
1969	Lew Alcindor, UCLA	1982	Ralph Sampson, Virginia	1995	Ed O'Bannon, UCLA
1970	Pete Maravich, LSU	1983	Ralph Sampson, Virginia	1996	Marcus Camby, UMass
1971	Sidney Wicks, UCLA	1984	Michael Jordan, N. Carolina	1997	Tim Duncan, Wake Forest

Rupp Trophy

Voted on by AP sportswriters and broadcasters and first presented in 1961 by the Commonwealth Athletic Club of Kentucky in the name of former University of Kentucky coach Adolph Rupp.

Multiple winners: Ralph Sampson (3); Lew Alcindor, Jerry Lucas, David Thompson and Bill Walton (2).

Year		Year		Year	
1961	Jerry Lucas, Ohio St.	1974	David Thompson, N.C. State	1987	David Robinson, Navy
1962	Jerry Lucas, Ohio St.	1975	David Thompson, N.C. State	1988	Hersey Hawkins, Bradley
1963	Art Heyman, Duke	1976	Scott May, Indiana	1989	Sean Elliott, Arizona
1964	Gary Bradds, Ohio St.	1977	Marques Johnson, UCLA	1990	Lionel Simmons, La Salle
1965	Bill Bradley, Princeton	1978	Butch Lee, Marquette	1991	Shaquille O'Neal, LSU
1966	Cazzie Russell, Michigan	1979	Larry Bird, Indiana St.	1992	Christian Laettner, Duke
1967	Lew Alcindor, UCLA	1980	Mark Aguirre, DePaul	1993	Calbert Cheaney, Indiana
1968	Elvin Hayes, Houston	1981	Ralph Sampson, Virginia	1994	Glenn Robinson, Purdue
1969	Lew Alcindor, UCLA	1982	Ralph Sampson, Virginia	1995	Joe Smith, Maryland
1970	Pete Maravich, LSU	1983	Ralph Sampson, Virginia	1996	Marcus Camby, UMass
1971	Austin Carr, Notre Dame	1984	Michael Jordan, N. Carolina	1997	Tim Duncan, Wake Forest
1972	Bill Walton, UCLA	1985	Patrick Ewing, Georgetown		
1973	Bill Walton, UCLA	1986	Walter Berry, St. John's		

Naismith Award

Voted on by a panel of coaches, sportswriters and broadcasters and first presented in 1969 by the Atlanta Tip-Off Club in 1969 in the name of the inventor of basketball, Dr. James Naismith.

Multiple winners: Ralph Sampson and Bill Walton (3).

Year	Year	Year
1969 Lew Alcindor, UCLA	1979 Larry Bird, Indiana St.	1989 Danny Ferry, Duke
1970 Pete Maravich, LSU	1980 Mark Aguirre, DePaul	1990 Lionel Simmons, La Salle
1971 Austin Carr, Notre Dame	1981 Ralph Sampson, Virginia	1991 Larry Johnson, UNLV
1972 Bill Walton, UCLA	1982 Ralph Sampson, Virginia	1992 Christian Laettner, Duke
1973 Bill Walton, UCLA	1983 Ralph Sampson, Virginia	1993 Calbert Cheaney, Indiana
1974 Bill Walton, UCLA	1984 Michael Jordan, N. Carolina	1994 Glenn Robinson, Purdue
1975 David Thompson, N.C. State	1985 Patrick Ewing, Georgetown	1995 Joe Smith, Maryland
1976 Scott May, Indiana	1986 Johnny Dawkins, Duke	1996 Marcus Camby, UMass
1977 Marques Johnson, UCLA	1987 David Robinson, Navy	1997 Tim Duncan, Wake Forest
1978 Butch Lee, Marquette	1988 Danny Manning, Kansas	

National Association of Basketball Coaches

Voted on by the National Assn. of Basketball Coaches and presented by the Eastman Kodak Co. from 1975-94.

Multiple winner: Ralph Sampson (2).

Year	Year	Year
1975 David Thompson, N.C. State	1983 Ralph Sampson, Virginia	1991 Larry Johnson, UNLV
1976 Scott May, Indiana	1984 Michael Jordan, N. Carolina	1992 Christian Laettner, Duke
1977 Marques Johnson, UCLA	1985 Patrick Ewing, Georgetown	1993 Calbert Cheaney, Indiana
1978 Phil Ford, North Carolina	1986 Walter Berry, St. John's	1994 Glenn Robinson, Purdue
1979 Larry Bird, Indiana St.	1987 David Robinson, Navy	1995 Shawn Respert, Mich. St.
1980 Michael Brooks, La Salle	1988 Danny Manning, Kansas	1996 Marcus Camby, UMass
1981 Danny Ainge, BYU	1989 Sean Elliott, Arizona	1997 Tim Duncan, Wake Forest
1982 Ralph Sampson, Virginia	1990 Lionel Simmons, La Salle	

Wooden Award

Voted on by a panel of coaches, sportswriters and broadcasters and first presented in 1977 by the Los Angeles Athletic Club in the name of former Purdue All-America and UCLA coach John Wooden. Unlike the other five Player of the Year awards, candidates for the Wooden must have a minimum grade point average of 2.00 (out of 4.00).

Multiple winner: Ralph Sampson (2).

Year	Year	Year
1977 Marques Johnson, UCLA	1984 Michael Jordan, N. Carolina	1991 Larry Johnson, UNLV
1978 Phil Ford, North Carolina	1985 Chris Mullin, St. John's	1992 Christian Laettner, Duke
1979 Larry Bird, Indiana St.	1986 Walter Berry St. John's	1993 Calbert Cheaney, Indiana
1980 Darrell Griffith, Louisville	1987 David Robinson, Navy	1994 Glenn Robinson, Purdue
1981 Danny Ainge, BYU	1988 Danny Manning, Kansas	1995 Ed O'Bannon, UCLA
1982 Ralph Sampson, Virginia	1989 Sean Elliott, Arizona	1996 Marcus Camby, UMass
1983 Ralph Sampson, Virginia	1990 Lionel Simmons, La Salle	1997 Tim Duncan, Wake Forest

Players of the Year and Top Draft Picks

Consensus college Players of the Year and first overall selections in NBA Draft since the abolition of the NBA's Territorial Draft in 1966. Top draft picks who become Rookie of the Year are in **bold** type; (*) indicates top draft pick chosen as junior and (**) indicates top draft pick chosen as sophomore.

Year	Player of the Year	Top Draft Pick	Year	Player of the Year	Top Draft Pick
1966	Cazzie Russell, Mich.	Cazzie Russell, NY	1983	Ralph Sampson, Va.	**Ralph Sampson**, Hou.
1967	Lew Alcindor, UCLA	Jimmy Walker, Det.	1984	Michael Jordan, N. Caro.	Akeem Olajuwon, Hou.
1968	Elvin Hayes, Houston	Elvin Hayes, SD	1985	Patrick Ewing, G'town	**Patrick Ewing**, NY
1969	Lew Alcindor, UCLA	**Lew Alcindor**, Milw.		& Chris Mullin, St. John's	
1970	Pete Maravich, LSU	Bob Lanier, Det.	1986	Walter Berry, St. John's	Brad Daugherty, Cle.
1971	Sidney Wicks, UCLA	Austin Carr, Cle.	1987	David Robinson, Navy	**David Robinson**, SA
1972	Bill Walton, UCLA	LaRue Martin, Port.	1988	Hersey Hawkins, Bradley	Danny Manning, LAC
1973	Bill Walton, UCLA	Doug Collins, Phi.		& Danny Manning, Kan.	
1974	Bill Walton, UCLA	Bill Walton, Port.	1989	Sean Elliott, Arizona	Pervis Ellison, Sac.
1975	David Thompson, N.C. St.	David Thompson, Atl.		& Danny Ferry, Duke	
1976	Scott May, Indiana	John Lucas, Hou.	1990	Lionel Simmons, La Salle	**Derrick Coleman**, NJ
1977	Marques Johnson, UCLA	Kent Benson, Ind.	1991	Shaquille O'Neal, LSU	**Larry Johnson**, Char.
1978	Butch Lee, Marquette	Mychal Thompson, Port.	1992	Christian Laettner, Duke	**Shaquille O'Neal**, Orl.*
	& Phil Ford, N. Caro.		1993	Calbert Cheaney, Ind.	**Chris Webber**, Orl.**
1979	Larry Bird, Indiana St.	Magic Johnson, LAL**	1994	Glenn Robinson, Purdue	Glenn Robinson, Mil**
1980	Mark Aguirre, DePaul	Joe Barry Carroll, G. St.	1995	Ed O'Bannon, UCLA	Joe Smith, G. St.**
1981	Ralph Sampson, Va.	Mark Aguirre, Dal.		& Joe Smith, Maryland	
	& Danny Ainge, BYU		1996	Marcus Camby, UMass	**Allen Iverson**, Phi.**
1982	Ralph Sampson, Va.	James Worthy, LAL*	1997	Tim Duncan, Wake Forest	Tim Duncan, SA

All-Time Winningest Division I Coaches

Minimum of 10 seasons as Division I head coach; regular season and tournament games included; coaches active during 1996-97 in **bold** type.

Top 30 Winning Percentage

		Yrs	W	L	Pct
1	Clair Bee	21	412	87	**.826**
2	Adolph Rupp	41	876	190	**.822**
3	**Jerry Tarkanian**	26	667	145	**.821**
4	John Wooden	29	664	162	**.804**
5	**Dean Smith**	36	879	254	**.776**
6	Harry Fisher	13	147	44	**.770**
7	Frank Keaney	27	387	117	**.768**
8	George Keogan	24	385	117	**.767**
9	Jack Ramsay	11	231	71	**.765**
10	Vic Bubas	10	213	67	**.761**
11	Chick Davies	21	314	106	**.748**
12	Ray Mears	21	399	135	**.747**
13	**Jim Boeheim**	21	502	172	**.745**
14	**Rick Pitino**	15	352	124	**.739**
15	Al McGuire	20	405	143	**.739**
16	**John Chaney**	25	560	198	**.739**
17	Everett Case	18	376	133	**.739**
18	Phog Allen	48	746	264	**.739**
19	**Nolan Richardson**	17	409	146	**.737**
20	Walter Meanwell	22	280	101	**.735**
21	**Bill Musselman**	12	232	85	**.732**
22	**Bob Knight**	32	700	258	**.731**
23	Lew Andreas	25	355	134	**.726**
24	**Denny Crum**	26	613	233	**.725**
25	Lou Carnesecca	24	526	200	**.725**
26	**John Thompson**	25	573	218	**.724**
27	**Lute Olson**	24	532	203	**.724**
28	Fred Schaus	12	251	96	**.723**
29	**Rick Majerus**	13	279	107	**.723**
30	Cam Henderson	35	630	243	**.722**

Top 30 Victories

		Yrs	W	L	Pct
1	**Dean Smith**	36	**879**	254	.776
2	Adolph Rupp	41	**876**	190	.822
3	Hank Iba	41	**767**	338	.694
4	Ed Diddle	42	**759**	302	.715
5	Phog Allen	48	**746**	264	.739
6	Ray Meyer	42	**724**	354	.672
7	**Bob Knight**	32	**700**	258	.731
8	**Norm Stewart**	36	**694**	351	.664
9	**Don Haskins**	36	**691**	327	.679
10	**Lefty Driesell**	35	**683**	335	.671
11	**Jerry Tarkanian**	26	**667**	145	.821
12	John Wooden	29	**664**	162	.804
13	Lou Henson	34	**663**	331	.667
14	Ralph Miller	38	**657**	382	.632
15	Marv Harshman	40	**654**	449	.593
16	Gene Bartow	34	**647**	353	.647
17	Cam Henderson	35	**630**	243	.722
18	Norm Sloan	37	**624**	393	.614
19	**Denny Crum**	26	**613**	233	.725
20	Slats Gill	36	**599**	392	.604
21	Abe Lemons	34	**597**	344	.634
22	Guy Lewis	30	**592**	279	.680
23	**Eddie Sutton**	27	**587**	234	.715
24	**John Thompson**	25	**573**	218	.725
25	Gary Colson	34	**563**	385	.594
26	**John Chaney**	25	**560**	198	.739
27	**Eldon Miller**	35	**558**	402	.581
28	Tony Hinkle	41	**557**	393	.586
29	Glenn Wilkes	36	**551**	436	.558
30	Frank McGuire	30	**549**	236	.699

Note: Clarence (Bighouse) Gaines of Division II Winston-Salem St. (1947-93) retired after the 1992-93 season to finish his 47-year career ranked No. 3 on the all-time NCAA list of all coaches regardless of division. His record is 828-446 with a .650 winning percentage.

Where They Coached

Allen–Baker (1906-08), Kansas (1908-09), Haskell (1909), Central Mo. St. (1913-19), Kansas (1920-56); **Andreas**–Syracuse (1925-43; 45-50); **Bartow**–Central Mo. St. (1962-64), Valparaiso (1965-70), Memphis St. (1971-74), Illinois (1975), UCLA (1976-77), UAB (1979–); **Bee**–Rider (1929-31), LIU-Brooklyn (1932-45, 46-51); **Boeheim**–Syracuse (1977–); **Bubas**–Duke (1960-69); **Carnesecca**–St. John's (1966-70, 74-92); **Case**–N.C. State (1947-64); **Chaney**–Cheyney St. (1973-82), Temple (1983–); **Colson**–Valdosta St. (1959-68), Pepperdine (1969-79), New Mexico (1981-88), Fresno St. (1991-95); **Crum**–Louisville (1972–); **Davies**–Duquesne (1925-43, 47-48); **Diddle**–Western Ky. (1923-64); **Driesell**–Davidson (1961-69), Maryland (1970-86), J. Madison (1989–97), Georgia St. (1997–); **Enke**–Louisville (1924-25), Arizona (1926-61); **Fisher**–Columbia (1907-16), Army (1922-23, 25).

Gill–Oregon St. (1929-64); **Harshman**–Pacific Lutheran (1946-58), Wash. St. (1959-71), Washington (1972-85); **Haskins**–UTEP (1962–); **Henderson**–Muskingum (1920-22), Davis & Elkins (1923-35), Marshall (1936-55); **Henson**–Hardin-Simmons (1963-66), N. Mexico St. (1967-75), Illinois (1976-96); **Hinkle**–Butler (1927-42, 46-70); **Iba**–NW Missouri St. (1930-33), Colorado (1934), Oklahoma St. (1935-70); **Keaney**–Rhode Island (1921-48); **Keogan**–St. Louis (1916), Allegheny (1919), Valparaiso (1920-21), Notre Dame (1924-43); **Knight**–Army (1966-71), Indiana (1972–).

Lapchick–St. John's (1937-47, 57-65); **Lemons**–Okla. City (1956-73), Pan American (1974-76), Texas (1977-82), Okla. City (1984-90); **Lewis**– Houston (1956-86); **Majerus**–Marquette (1984-86), Ball St. (1988-89), Utah (1991–); **A. McGuire**–Belmont Abbey (1958-64), Marquette (1965-77); **F. McGuire**–St. John's (1948-52), North Carolina (1953-61), South Carolina (1965-80); **Meanwell**–Wisconsin (1912-17, 21-34), Missouri (1918-20); **Mears**–Wittenberg (1957-62), Tennessee (1963-77); **Meyer**–DePaul (1943-84); **E. Miller**–Western Mich. (1970–75, Ohio St. (1976–85); Northern Iowa (1986–); **R. Miller**–Wichita St. (1952-64), Iowa (1965-70), Oregon St. (1971-89); **Musselman**–Ashland (1966-71), Minnesota (1972-75), S. Alabama (1996–); **Olson**–Long Beach St. (1974), Iowa (1975-83), Arizona (1984–), **Pitino**–Boston Univ. (1979-83), Providence (1986-87), Kentucky (1990-97).

Ramsay–St. Joseph's-PA (1956-66); **Richardson**–Tulsa (1981-85), Arkansas (1986–); **Rupp**–Kentucky (1931-72); **Schaus**–West Va. (1955-60), Purdue (1973-78); **Sloan**–Presbyterian (1952-55), Citadel (1957-60), Florida (1961-66), N.C. State (1967-80), Florida (1981-89); **Smith**–North Carolina (1962–); **Stewart**–No. Iowa (1962-67), Missouri (1968–); **Sutton**–Creighton (1970-74), Arkansas (1975-85), Kentucky (1986-89), Oklahoma St. (1991–); **Tarkanian**–Long Beach St. (1969-73), UNLV (1974-92), Fresno St. (1995–); **Thompson**–Georgetown (1973–); **Wilkes**–Stetson (1958-93); **Wooden**– Indiana St. (1947-48), UCLA (1949-75).

Most NCAA Tournaments

Through 1997; listed are number of appearances, overall tournament record, times reaching Final Four, and number of NCAA championships.

App		W-L	F4	Championships
27	**Dean Smith**	65-27	11	2 (1982, 93)
21	**Bob Knight**	40-18	5	3 (1976, 81, 87)
21	**Denny Crum**	42-21	6	2 (1980, 86)
20	Adolph Rupp	30-18	6	4 (1948-49, 51, 58)
20	**John Thompson**	34-19	3	1 (1984)
18	**Lute Olson**	28-18	4	1 (1997)
18	**Eddie Sutton**	27-18	2	None
18	Lou Henson	19-19	2	None
18	Lou Carnesecca	17-20	1	None
17	**Jim Boeheim**	27-17	2	None
16	John Wooden	47-10	12	10 (1964-65, 67-73, 75)
16	**Jerry Tarkanian**	37-16	4	1 (1990)
15	Digger Phelps	17-17	1	None
15	**Norm Stewart**	12-15	0	None
14	**Don Haskins**	14-13	1	1 (1966)
14	Guy Lewis	26-18	5	None
14	**Gene Keady**	11-14	0	None
13	**Mike Krzyzewski**	40-11	7	2 (1991-92)
13	**John Chaney**	16-13	0	0
13	Dale Brown	15-14	2	None
13	Ray Meyer	14-16	2	None

Active Coaches' Victories

Minimum five seasons in Division I.

		Yrs	W	L	Pct
1	Dean Smith, N. Carolina	36	**879**	254	.776
2	Jim Phelan, Mt. St. Mary's	43	**772**	413	.651
3	Bob Knight, Indiana	31	**700**	258	.731
4	Norm Stewart, Missouri	36	**694**	351	.664
5	Don Haskins, UTEP	36	**691**	327	.679
6	Lefty Driesell, Georgia St.	35	**683**	335	.671
7	Jerry Tarkanian, Fresno St.	26	**667**	145	.821
8	Denny Crum, Louisville	26	**613**	233	.725
9	Eddie Sutton, Okla. St.	27	**587**	234	.715
10	John Thompson, Georgetown	25	**573**	218	.724
11	John Chaney, Temple	25	**560**	198	.739
12	Eldon Miller, N. Iowa	35	**558**	402	.581
13	Lute Olson, Arizona	24	**532**	203	.724
14	Tom Davis, Iowa	26	**503**	269	.652
15	Jim Boeheim, Syracuse	21	**502**	172	.745
16	Billy Tubbs, TCU	23	**492**	241	.671
	Gale Catlett, West Va.	25	**492**	251	.662
18	Jim Calhoun, UConn	25	**488**	251	.660
19	Cal Luther, Tenn-Martin	36	**479**	424	.530
20	Mike Krzyzewski, Duke	22	**473**	208	.695

Annual Awards

UPI picked the first national Division I Coach of the Year in 1955. Since then, The U.S. Basketball Writers Assn. (1959), AP (1967), the National Assn. of Basketball Coaches (1969), and the Atlanta Tip-Off Club (1987) have joined in. Since 1987, the first year all five awards were given out, no coach has won all of them in the same season.

United Press International

Voted on by a panel of UPI college basketball writers and first presented in 1955.

Multiple winners: John Wooden (6); Bob Knight, Ray Meyer, Adolph Rupp, Norm Stewart, Fred Taylor and Phil Woolpert (2).

Year		Year		Year	
1955	Phil Woolpert, San Francisco	1970	John Wooden, UCLA	1985	Lou Carnesecca, St. John's
1956	Phil Woolpert, San Francisco	1971	Al McGuire, Marquette	1986	Mike Krzyzewski, Duke
1957	Frank McGuire, North Carolina	1972	John Wooden, UCLA	1987	John Thompson, Georgetown
1958	Tex Winter, Kansas St.	1973	John Wooden, UCLA	1988	John Chaney, Temple
1959	Adolph Rupp, Kentucky	1974	Digger Phelps, Notre Dame	1989	Bob Knight, Indiana
1960	Pete Newell, California	1975	Bob Knight, Indiana	1990	Jim Calhoun, Connecticut
1961	Fred Taylor, Ohio St.	1976	Tom Young, Rutgers	1991	Rick Majerus, Utah
1962	Fred Taylor, Ohio St.	1977	Bob Gaillard, San Francisco	1992	Perry Clark, Tulane
1963	Ed Jucker, Cincinnati	1978	Eddie Sutton, Arkansas	1993	Eddie Fogler, Vanderbilt
1964	John Wooden, UCLA	1979	Bill Hodges, Indiana St.	1994	Norm Stewart, Missouri
1965	Dave Strack, Michigan	1980	Ray Meyer, DePaul	1995	Leonard Hamilton, Miami-FL
1966	Adolph Rupp, Kentucky	1981	Ralph Miller, Oregon St.	1996	Gene Keady, Purdue
1967	John Wooden, UCLA	1982	Norm Stewart, Missouri	1997	no award
1968	Guy Lewis, Houston	1983	Jerry Tarkanian, UNLV		
1969	John Wooden, UCLA	1984	Ray Meyer, DePaul		

U.S. Basketball Writers Association

Voted on by the USBWA and first presented in 1959.

Multiple winners: John Wooden (5); Bob Knight (3); Lou Carnesecca, John Chaney, Gene Keady, Ray Meyer and Fred Taylor (2).

Year		Year		Year	
1959	Eddie Hickey, Marquette	1972	John Wooden, UCLA	1985	Lou Carnesecca, St. John's
		1973	John Wooden, UCLA	1986	Dick Versace, Bradley
1960	Pete Newell, California	1974	Norm Sloan, N.C. State	1987	John Chaney, Temple
1961	Fred Taylor, Ohio St.	1975	Bob Knight, Indiana	1988	John Chaney, Temple
1962	Fred Taylor, Ohio St.	1976	Bob Knight, Indiana	1989	Bob Knight, Indiana
1963	Ed Jucker, Cincinnati	1977	Eddie Sutton, Arkansas		
1964	John Wooden, UCLA	1978	Ray Meyer, DePaul	1990	Roy Williams, Kansas
1965	Butch van Breda Kolff, Princeton	1979	Dean Smith, North Carolina	1991	Randy Ayers, Ohio St.
1966	Adolph Rupp, Kentucky			1992	Perry Clark, Tulane
1967	John Wooden, UCLA	1980	Ray Meyer, DePaul	1993	Eddie Fogler, Vanderbilt
1968	Guy Lewis, Houston	1981	Ralph Miller, Oregon St.	1994	Charlie Spoonhour, St. Louis
1969	Maury John, Drake	1982	John Thompson, Georgetown	1995	Kelvin Sampson, Oklahoma
		1983	Lou Carnesecca, St. John's	1996	Gene Keady, Purdue
1970	John Wooden, UCLA	1984	Gene Keady, Purdue	1997	Clem Haskins, Minnesota
1971	Al McGuire, Marquette				

Annual Awards (Cont.)

Associated Press

Voted on by AP sportswriters and broadcasters and first presented in 1967.

Multiple winners: John Wooden (5); Bob Knight (3); Guy Lewis, Ray Meyer, Ralph Miller and Eddie Sutton (2).

Year		Year		Year	
1967	John Wooden, UCLA	1978	Eddie Sutton, Arkansas	1989	Bob Knight, Indiana
1968	Guy Lewis, Houston	1979	Bill Hodges, Indiana St.	1990	Jim Calhoun, Connecticut
1969	John Wooden, UCLA	1980	Ray Meyer, DePaul	1991	Randy Ayers, Ohio St.
1970	John Wooden, UCLA	1981	Ralph Miller, Oregon St.	1992	Roy Williams, Kansas
1971	Al McGuire, Marquette	1982	Ralph Miller, Oregon St.	1993	Eddie Fogler, Vanderbilt
1972	John Wooden, UCLA	1983	Guy Lewis, Houston	1994	Norm Stewart, Missouri
1973	John Wooden, UCLA	1984	Ray Meyer, DePaul	1995	Kelvin Sampson, Oklahoma
1974	Norm Sloan, N.C. State	1985	Bill Frieder, Michigan	1996	Gene Keady, Purdue
1975	Bob Knight, Indiana	1986	Eddie Sutton, Kentucky	1997	Clem Haskins, Minnesota
1976	Bob Knight, Indiana	1987	Tom Davis, Iowa		
1977	Bob Gaillard, San Francisco	1988	John Chaney, Temple		

National Association of Basketball Coaches

Voted on by NABC membership and first presented in 1969.

Multiple winner: John Wooden (3).

Year		Year		Year	
1969	John Wooden, UCLA	1979	Ray Meyer, DePaul	1989	P.J. Carlesimo, Seton Hall
1970	John Wooden, UCLA	1980	Lute Olson, Iowa	1990	Jud Heathcote, Michigan St.
1971	Jack Kraft, Villanova	1981	Ralph Miller, Oregon St.	1991	Mike Krzyzewski, Duke
1972	John Wooden, UCLA		& Jack Hartman, Kansas St.	1992	George Raveling, USC
1973	Gene Bartow, Memphis St.	1982	Don Monson, Idaho	1993	Eddie Fogler, Vanderbilt
1974	Al McGuire, Marquette	1983	Lou Carnesecca, St. John's	1994	Nolan Richardson, Arkansas
1975	Bob Knight, Indiana	1984	Marv Harshman, Washington		& Gene Keady, Purdue
1976	Johnny Orr, Michigan	1985	John Thompson, Georgetown	1995	Jim Harrick, UCLA
1977	Dean Smith, North Carolina	1986	Eddie Sutton, Kentucky	1996	John Calipari, UMass
1978	Bill Foster, Duke	1987	Rick Pitino, Providence	1997	Clem Haskins, Minnesota
	& Abe Lemons, Texas	1988	John Chaney, Temple		

Naismith Award

Voted on by a panel of coaches, sportswriters and broadcasters and first presented by the Atlanta Tip-Off Club in 1987 in the name of the inventor of basketball, Dr. James Naismith.

Multiple winner: Mike Krzyzewski (2).

Year		Year		Year	
1987	Bob Knight, Indiana	1991	Randy Ayers, Ohio St.	1995	Jim Harrick, UCLA
1988	Larry Brown, Kansas	1992	Mike Krzyzewski, Duke	1996	John Calipari, UMass
1989	Mike Krzyzewski, Duke	1993	Dean Smith, North Carolina	1997	Roy Williams, Kansas
1990	Bobby Cremins, Georgia Tech	1994	Nolan Richardson, Arkansas		

Other Men's Champions

The NCAA has sanctioned national championship tournaments for Divison II since 1957 and Division III since 1975. The NAIA sanctioned a single tournament from 1937-91, then split into two divisions in 1992.

NCAA Div. II Finals

Multiple winners: Kentucky Wesleyan (6); Evansville (5); CS-Bakersfield (3); North Alabama and Virginia Union (2).

Year	Winner	Score	Loser	Year	Winner	Score	Loser
1957	Wheaton, IL	89-65	Ky. Wesleyan	1978	Cheyney, PA	47-40	WI-Green Bay
1958	South Dakota	75-53	St. Michael's, VT	1979	North Alabama	64-50	WI-Green Bay
1959	Evansville, IN	83-67	SW Missouri St.	1980	Virginia Union	80-74	New York Tech
1960	Evansville, IN	90-69	Chapman, CA	1981	Florida Southern	73-68	Mt. St. Mary's, MD
1961	Wittenberg, OH	42-38	SE Missouri St.	1982	Dist. of Columbia	73-63	Florida Southern
1962	Mt. St. Mary's, MD	58-57*	CS-Sacramento	1983	Wright St., OH	92-73	Dist. of Columbia
1963	South Dakota St.	42-40	Wittenberg, OH	1984	Central Mo.St.	81-77	St. Augustine's,NC
1964	Evansville, IN	72-59	Akron, OH	1985	Jacksonville St.	74-73	South Dakota St.
1965	Evansville, IN	85-82*	Southern Illinois	1986	Sacred Heart, CT	93-87	SE Missouri St.
1966	Ky. Wesleyan	54-51	Southern Illinois	1987	Ky.Wesleyan	92-74	Gannon, PA
1967	Winston-Salem, NC	77-74	SW Missouri St.	1988	Lowell, MA	75-72	AK-Anchorage
1968	Ky. Wesleyan	63-52	Indiana St.	1989	N.C. Central	73-46	SE Missouri St.
1969	Ky. Wesleyan	75-71	SW Missouri St.	1990	Ky. Wesleyan	93-79	CS-Bakersfield
1970	Phila. Textile	76-65	Tennessee St.	1991	North Alabama	79-72	Bridgeport, CT
1971	Evansville, IN	97-82	Old Dominion, VA	1992	Virginia Union	100-75	Bridgeport, CT
1972	Roanoke, VA	84-72	Akron, OH	1993	CS-Bakersfield	85-72	Troy St., AL
1973	Ky. Wesleyan	78-76*	Tennessee St.	1994	CS-Bakersfield	92-86	Southern Ind.
1974	Morgan St., MD	67-52	SW Missouri St.	1995	Southern Indiana	71-63	CS-Riverside
1975	Old Dominion, VA	76-74	New Orleans	1996	Fort Hays St.	70-63	N. Kentucky
1976	Puget Sound, WA	83-74	Tennessee-Chatt.	1997	CS-Bakersfield	57-56	N. Kentucky
1977	Tennessee-Chatt.	71-62	Randolph-Macon		*Overtime		

NCAA Div. III Finals

Multiple winners: North Park (5); Potsdam St., Scranton, WI-Platteville and WI-Whitewater (2).

Year	Winner	Score	Loser	Year	Winner	Score	Loser
1975	LeMoyne-Owen, TN	57-54	Glassboro St., NJ	1987	North Park, IL	106-100	Clark, MA
1976	Scranton, PA	60-57	Wittenberg, OH	1988	Ohio Wesleyan	92-70	Scranton, PA
1977	Wittenberg, OH	79-66	Oneonta St., NY	1989	WI-Whitewater	94-86	Trenton St., NJ
1978	North Park, IL	69-57	Widener, PA	1990	Rochester, NY	43-42	DePauw, IN
1979	North Park, IL	66-62	Potsdam St., NY	1991	WI-Platteville	81-74	Franklin Marshall
1980	North Park, IL	83-76	Upsala, NJ	1992	Calvin, MI	62-49	Rochester, NY
1981	Potsdam St., NY	67-65*	Augustana, IL	1993	Ohio Northern	71-68	Augustana, IL
1982	Wabash, IN	83-62	Potsdam St., NY	1994	Lebanon Valley, PA	66-59*	NYU
1983	Scranton, PA	64-63	Wittenberg, OH	1995	WI-Platteville	69-55	Manchester, IN
1984	WI-Whitewater	103-86	Clark, MA	1996	Rowan, NJ	100-93	Hope, MI
1985	North Park, IL	72-71	Potsdam St., NY	1997	Illinois Wesleyan	89-86	Neb-Wesleyan
1986	Potsdam St., NY	76-73	LeMoyne-Owen, TN				

*Overtime

NAIA Finals, 1937-91

Multiple winners: Grand Canyon, Hamline, Kentucky St. and Tennessee St. (3); Central Missouri, Central St., Fort Hays St. and SW Missouri St. (2).

Year	Winner	Score	Loser	Year	Winner	Score	Loser
1937	Central Missouri	35-24	Morningside, IA	1965	Central St., OH	85-51	Oklahoma Baptist
1938	Central Missouri	45-30	Roanoke, VA	1966	Oklahoma Baptist	88-59	Georgia Southern
1939	Southwestern, KS	32-31	San Diego St.	1967	St.Benedict's, KS	71-65	Oklahoma Baptist
1940	Tarkio, MO	52-31	San Diego St.	1968	Central St., OH	51-48	Fairmont St., WV
1941	San Diego St.	36-32	Murray St., KY	1969	Eastern N. Mex	99-76	MD-Eastern Shore
1942	Hamline, MN	33-31	SE Oklahoma	1970	Kentucky St.	79-71	Central Wash.
1943	SE Missouri St.	34-32	NW Missouri St.	1971	Kentucky St.	102-82	Eastern Michigan
1944	Not held			1972	Kentucky St.	71-62	WI-Eau Claire
1945	Loyola-LA	49-36	Pepperdine, CA	1973	Guilford, NC	99-96	MD-Eastern Shore
1946	Southern Illinois	49-40	Indiana St.	1974	West Georgia	97-79	Alcorn St., MS
1947	Marshall, WV	73-59	Mankato St., MN	1975	Grand Canyon, AZ	65-54	M'western St., TX
1948	Louisville, KY	82-70	Indiana St.	1976	Coppin St., MD	96-91	Henderson St., AR
1949	Hamline, MN	57-46	Regis, CO	1977	Texas Southern	71-44	Campbell, NC
1950	Indiana St.	61-47	East Central, OK	1978	Grand Canyon, AZ	79-75	Kearney St., NE
1951	Hamline, MN	69-61	Millikin, IL	1979	Drury, MO	60-54	Henderson St., AR
1952	SW Missouri St.	73-64	Murray St., KY	1980	Cameron, OK	84-77	Alabama St.
1953	SW Missouri St.	79-71	Hamline, MN	1981	Beth. Nazarene, OK	86-85*	Al-Huntsville
1954	St.Benedict's, KS	62-56	Western Illinois	1982	SC-Spartanburg	51-38	Biola, CA
1955	East Texas St.	71-54	SE Oklahoma	1983	Charleston, SC	57-53	WV-Wesleyan
1956	McNeese St., LA	60-55	Texas Southern	1984	Fort Hays St., KS	48-46*	WI-Stevens Pt.
1957	Tennessee St.	92-73	SE Oklahoma	1985	Fort Hays St., KS	82-80*	Wayland Bapt., TX
1958	Tennessee St.	85-73	Western Illinois	1986	David Lipscomb, TN	67-54	AR-Monticello
1959	Tennessee St.	97-87	Pacific-Luth., WA	1987	Washburn, KS	79-77	West Virginia St.
1960	SW Texas St.	66-44	Westminster, PA	1988	Grand Canyon, AZ	88-86*	Auburn-Montg, AL
1961	Grambling, LA	95-75	Georgetown, KY	1989	St.Mary's, TX	61-58	East Central, OK
1962	Prairie View, TX	62-53	Westminster, PA	1990	Birm-Southern, AL	88-80	WI-Eau Claire
1963	Pan American, TX	73-62	Western Carolina	1991	Oklahoma City	77-74	Central Arkansas
1964	Rockhurst, MO	66-56	Pan American, TX				

*Overtime

NAIA Div. I Finals

NAIA split tournament into two divisions in 1992.
Multiple winner: Oklahoma City (3).

Year	Winner	Score	Loser
1992	Oklahoma City	82-73*	Central Arkansas
1993	Hawaii Pacific	88-83	Okla. Baptist
1994	Oklahoma City	99-81	Life, GA
1995	Birm-Southern	92-76	Pfeiffer, NC
1996	Oklahoma City	86-80	Georgetown, KY
1997	Life, GA	73-64	Okla. Baptist

*Overtime

NAIA Div. II Finals

NAIA split tournament into two divisions in 1992.
Multiple winner: Bethel, IN (2).

Year	Winner	Score	Loser
1992	Grace, IN	85-79*	Northwestern-IA
1993	Williamette, OR	63-56	Northern St., SD
1994	Eureka, IL	98-95*	Northern St., SD
1995	Bethel, IN	103-95*	NW Nazarene, ID
1996	Albertson, ID	81-72*	Whitworth, WA
1997	Bethel, IN	95-94	Siena Heights, MI

*Overtime

Player of the Year and NBA MVP

College basketball Players of the Year who have gone on to win the NBA's Most Valuable Player award.

Bill Russell COLLEGE–San Francisco (1956); PROS–Boston Celtics (1958, 1961, 1962, 1963 and 1965).

Oscar Robertson COLLEGE–Cincinnati (1958, 1959 and 1960); PROS–Cincinnati Royals (1964).

Kareem Abdul-Jabbar COLLEGE–UCLA (1967 and 1968); PROS–Milwaukee Bucks (1971, 1972 and 1974) and LA Lakers (1976, 1977 and 1980).

Bill Walton COLLEGE–UCLA (1972, 1973 and 1974); PROS–Portland Trail Blazers (1978).

Larry Bird COLLEGE–Indiana St. (1979); PROS–Boston Celtics (1984, 1985, and 1986).

Michael Jordan COLLEGE–North Carolina (1984); PROS–Chicago Bulls (1988, 1991, 1992 and 1996).

David Robinson COLLEGE–Navy (1987); PROS–San Antonio Spurs (1995).

WOMEN

NCAA Final Four

Replaced the Association of Intercollegiate Athletics for Women (AIAW) tournament in 1982 as the official playoff for the national championship.

Multiple winners: Tennessee (5); Louisiana Tech, Stanford and USC (2).

Year	Champion	Head Coach	Score	Runner-up	—Third Place—	
1982	Louisiana Tech	Sonya Hogg	76-62	Cheyney	Maryland	Tennessee
1983	USC	Linda Sharp	69-67	Louisiana Tech	Georgia	Old Dominion
1984	USC	Linda Sharp	72-61	Tennessee	Cheyney	Louisiana Tech
1985	Old Dominion	Marianne Stanley	70-65	Georgia	NE Louisiana	Western Ky.
1986	Texas	Jody Conradt	97-81	USC	Tennessee	Western Ky.
1987	Tennessee	Pat Summitt	67-44	Louisiana Tech	Long Beach St.	Texas
1988	Louisiana Tech	Leon Barmore	56-54	Auburn	Long Beach St.	Tennessee
1989	Tennessee	Pat Summitt	76-60	Auburn	Louisiana Tech	Maryland
1990	Stanford	Tara VanDerveer	88-81	Auburn	Louisiana Tech	Virginia
1991	Tennessee	Pat Summitt	70-67	Virginia	Connecticut	Stanford
1992	Stanford	Tara VanDerveer	78-62	Western Kentucky	SW Missouri St.	Virginia
1993	Texas Tech	Marsha Sharp	84-82	Ohio St.	Iowa	Vanderbilt
1994	North Carolina	Sylvia Hatchell	60-59	Louisiana Tech	Alabama	Purdue
1995	Connecticut	Geno Auriemma	70-64	Tennessee	Georgia	Stanford
1996	Tennessee	Pat Summitt	83-65	Georgia	Connecticut	Stanford
1997	Tennessee	Pat Summitt	68-59	Old Dominion	Stanford	Notre Dame

Final Four sites: 1982 (Norfolk, Va.), **1983** (Norfolk, Va.), **1984** (Los Angeles), **1985** (Austin), **1986** (Lexington), **1987** (Austin), **1988** (Tacoma), **1989** (Tacoma), **1990** (Knoxville), **1991** (New Orleans), **1992** (Los Angeles), **1993** (Atlanta), **1994** (Richmond), **1995** (Minneapolis), **1996** (Charlotte), **1997** (Cincinnati).

Most Outstanding Player

A Most Outstanding Player has been selected every year of the NCAA tournament. Winner who did not play for the tournament champion is listed in **bold,** type.

Multiple winner: Cheryl Miller (2).

Year		Year		Year	
1982	Janice Lawrence, La. Tech	1988	Erica Westbrooks, La. Tech	1994	Charlotte Smith, N. Carolina
1983	Cheryl Miller, USC	1989	Bridgette Gordon, Tennessee	1995	Rebecca Lobo, Connecticut
1984	Cheryl Miller, USC	1990	Jennifer Azzi, Stanford	1996	Michelle Marciniak, Tenn.
1985	Tracy Claxton, Old Dominion	1991	**Dawn Staley**, Virginia	1997	Chamique Holdsclaw, Tenn.
1986	Clarissa Davis, Texas	1992	Molly Goodenbour, Stanford		
1987	Tonya Edwards, Tennessee	1993	Sheryl Swoopes, Texas Tech		

All-Time NCAA Division I Tournament Leaders

Through 1996-97; minimum of six games; **Last** column indicates final year played.

CAREER

Scoring

	Points	Yrs	Last	Pts	Avg
1	Bridgette Gordon, Tenn	4	1989	388	21.6
2	Cheryl Miller, USC	4	1986	333	20.8
3	Janice Lawrence, La. Tech	3	1984	312	22.3
4	Penny Toler, L. Beach St	4	1989	291	22.4
5	Dawn Staley, Virginia	4	1992	274	18.3
6	Cindy Brown, L. Beach St	4	1987	263	21.9
7	Venus Lacy, La. Tech	3	1990	263	18.8
8	Clarissa Davis, Texas	3	1989	261	21.8
9	Janet Harris, Georgia	4	1985	254	19.5
10	Val Whiting, Stanford	4	1993	249	15.6

Rebounds

	Average	Yrs	Last	No	Avg
1	Cheryl Miller, USC	4	1986	170	10.6
2	Sheila Frost, Tennessee	4	1989	162	9.0
3	Val Whiting, Stanford	4	1993	161	10.1
4	Venus Lacy, La. Tech	3	1990	148	10.6
5	Bridgette Gordon, Tenn	4	1989	142	7.9
6	Kirsten Cummings, L. Beach St.	4	1985	136	10.5
7	Nora Lewis, La. Tech	3	1989	130	9.3
8	Pam McGee, USC	3	1984	127	9.8
9	Daedra Charles, Tenn	3	1991	125	9.6
	Paula McGee, USC	3	1984	125	9.6

SINGLE GAME

Scoring

		Year	Pts
1	Lorri Bauman, Drake vs Maryland	1982	50
2	Sheryl Swoopes, Texas Tech vs Ohio St ...	1993	47
3	Barbara Kennedy, Clemson vs Penn St ...	1982	43
4	LaTaunya Pollard, L. Beach St. vs Howard	1982	40
	Cindy Brown, L. Beach St. vs Ohio St ...	1987	40
6	Kerry Bascom, UConn vs Toledo	1991	39
	Portia Hill, S.F. Austin St. vs Arkansas ...	1990	39
	Delmonica DeHorney, Ark. vs Stanford ...	1990	39
9	LaTaunya Pollard, L. Beach St. vs USC ...	1983	37
	Teresa Edwards, Georgia vs Tennessee ..	1986	37

Rebounds

		Year	No
1	Cheryl Taylor, Tenn. Tech vs Georgia	1985	23
	Charlotte Smith, N. Car. vs La. Tech	1994	23
3	Daedra Charles, Tenn. vs SW Missouri ...	1991	22
4	Cherie Nelson, USC vs Western Ky	1987	21
5	Alison Lang, Oregon vs Missouri	1982	20
	Shelda Arceneaux, S.D. St. vs L. Beach St.	1984	20
	Tracy Claxton, ODU vs Georgia	1985	20
	Brigette Combs, West. Ky. vs West Va ...	1989	20
	Tandreia Green, West. Ky. vs West Va ...	1989	20
10	Six tied with 19 each.		

Associated Press Final Top 10 Polls

The Associated Press weekly women's college basketball poll was begun by Mel Greenberg of *The Philadelphia Inquirer* during the 1976-77 season. The Association of Intercollegiate Athletics for Women (AIAW) Tournament determined the Division I national champion for 1972-81. The NCAA began its women's Division I tournament in 1982. The final AP Polls were taken before the NCAA tournament. Eventual national champions are in **bold** type.

1977
1 **Delta St.**
2 Immaculata
3 St. Joseph's-PA
4 CS-Fullerton
5 Tennessee
6 Tennessee Tech
7 Wayland Baptist
8 Montclair St.
9 S.F. Austin St.
10 N.C. State

1978
1 Tennessee
2 Wayland Baptist
3 N.C. State
4 Montclair St.
5 **UCLA**
6 Maryland
7 Queens-NY
8 Valdosta St.
9 Delta St.
10 LSU

1979
1 **Old Dominion**
2 Louisiana Tech
3 Tennessee
4 Texas
5 S.F. Austin St.
6 UCLA
7 Rutgers
8 Maryland
9 Cheyney
10 Wayland Baptist

1980
1 **Old Dominion**
2 Tennessee
3 Louisiana Tech
4 South Carolina
5 S.F. Austin St.
6 Maryland
7 Texas
8 Rutgers
9 Long Beach St.
10 N.C. State

1981
1 **Louisiana Tech**
2 Tennessee
3 Old Dominion
4 USC
5 Cheyney
6 Long Beach St.
7 UCLA
8 Maryland
9 Rutgers
10 Kansas

1982
1 **Louisiana Tech**
2 Cheyney
3 Maryland
4 Tennessee
5 Texas
6 USC
7 Old Dominion
8 Rutgers
9 Long Beach St.
10 Penn St.

1983
1 **USC**
2 Louisiana Tech
3 Texas
4 Old Dominion
5 Cheyney
6 Long Beach St.
7 Maryland
8 Penn St.
9 Georgia
10 Tennessee

1984
1 Texas
2 Louisiana Tech
3 Georgia
4 Old Dominion
5 **USC**
6 Long Beach St.
7 Kansas St.
8 LSU
9 Cheyney
10 Mississippi

1985
1 Texas
2 NE Louisiana
3 Long Beach St.
4 Louisiana Tech
5 **Old Dominion**
6 Mississippi
7 Ohio St.
8 Georgia
9 Penn St.
10 Auburn

1986
1 **Texas**
2 Georgia
3 USC
4 Louisiana Tech
5 Western Ky.
6 Virginia
7 Auburn
8 Long Beach St.
9 LSU
10 Rutgers

1987
1 Texas
2 Auburn
3 Louisiana Tech
4 Long Beach St.
5 Rutgers
6 Georgia
7 **Tennessee**
8 Mississippi
9 Iowa
10 Ohio St.

1988
1 Tennessee
2 Iowa
3 Auburn
4 Texas
5 **Louisiana Tech**
6 Ohio St.
7 Long Beach St.
8 Rutgers
9 Maryland
10 Virginia

1989
1 **Tennessee**
2 Auburn
3 Louisiana Tech
4 Stanford
5 Maryland
6 Texas
7 Long Beach St.
8 Iowa
9 Colorado
10 Georgia

1990
1 **Louisiana Tech**
2 Stanford
3 Washington
4 Tennessee
5 UNLV
6 S.F. Austin St.
7 Georgia
8 Texas
9 Auburn
10 Iowa

1991
1 Penn St.
2 Virginia
3 Georgia
4 **Tennessee**
5 Purdue
6 Auburn
7 N.C. State
8 LSU
9 Arkansas
10 Western Ky.

1992
1 Virginia
2 Tennessee
3 **Stanford**
4 S.F. Austin St.
5 Mississippi
6 Miami-FL
7 Iowa
8 Maryland
9 Penn St.
10 SW Missouri St.

1993
1 Vanderbilt
2 Tennessee
3 Ohio St.
4 Iowa
5 **Texas Tech**
6 Stanford
7 Auburn
8 Penn St.
9 Virginia
10 Colorado

1994
1 Tennessee
2 Penn St.
3 Connecticut
4 **North Carolina**
5 Colorado
6 Louisiana Tech
7 USC
8 Purdue
9 Texas Tech
10 Virginia

1995
1 **Connecticut**
2 Colorado
3 Tennessee
4 Stanford
5 Texas Tech
6 Vanderbilt
7 Penn St.
8 Louisiana Tech
9 Western Ky.
10 Virginia

1996
1 Louisiana Tech
2 Connecticut
3 Stanford
4 **Tennessee**
5 Georgia
6 Old Dominion
7 Iowa
8 Penn St.
9 Texas Tech
10 Alabama

1997
1 Connecticut
2 Old Dominion
3 Stanford
4 North Carolina
5 Louisiana Tech
6 Georgia
7 Florida
8 Alabama
9 LSU
10 **Tennessee**

All-Time Winningest Division I Teams

Division I schools with best winning percentages and most victories through 1996-97 (including postseason tournaments). Although official NCAA women's basketball records didn't begin until the 1981-82 season, results from previous seasons are included below.

Top 10 Winning Percentage

		Yrs	W	L	Pct
1	Louisiana Tech	23	645	123	.840
2	Montana	19	458	109	.808
3	Texas	23	619	151	.804
4	Tennessee	29	693	171	.802
5	S. F. Austin St.	25	594	194	.754
6	Mount St. Mary's*	23	463	153	.752
7	Old Dominion	28	593	210	.738
8	Virginia	24	509	187	.731
9	Mississippi	23	516	193	.728
10	Auburn	26	525	197	.727

*Includes records prior to Division I.

Top 10 Victories

		Yrs	W	L	Pct
1	Tennessee	29	693	171	.802
2	Louisiana Tech	23	645	123	.840
3	Texas	23	619	151	.804
4	James Madison	72	616	328	.653
5	Long Beach St.	35	604	232	.726
6	S.F. Austin St.	24	594	194	.754
7	Old Dominion	28	593	210	.738
8	Tennessee Tech	27	584	244	.705
9	Ohio St.	32	543	236	.697
10	Auburn	26	525	197	.727

Annual NCAA Division I Leaders

All averages include postseason games

Scoring

Multiple winners: Cindy Blodgett, A. Congreaves (2).

Year		Gm	Pts	Avg
1982	Barbara Kennedy, Clemson	31	908	29.3
1983	LaTaunya Pollard, L. Beach St	31	907	29.3
1984	Deborah Temple, Delta St	28	873	31.2
1985	Anucha Browne, Northwestern	28	855	30.5
1986	Wanda Ford, Drake	30	919	30.6
1987	Tresa Spaulding, BYU	28	810	28.9
1988	LeChandra LeDay, Grambling	28	850	30.4
1989	Patricia Hoskins, Miss. Valley	27	908	33.6
1990	Kim Perrot, SW Louisiana	28	839	30.0
1991	Jan Jensen, Drake	30	888	29.6
1992	Andrea Congreaves, Mercer	28	925	33.0
1993	Andrea Congreaves, Mercer	26	805	31.0
1994	Kristy Ryan, CS-Sacramento	26	727	28.0
1995	Koko Lahanas, CS-Fullerton	29	778	26.8
1996	Cindy Blodgett, Maine	32	889	27.8
1997	Cindy Blodgett, Maine	30	810	27.0

Rebounds

Multiple winner: Patricia Hoskins (2).

Year		Gm	No	Avg
1982	Anne Donovan, Old Dominion	28	412	14.7
1983	Deborah Mitchell, Miss. Col	28	447	16.0
1984	Joy Kellog, Oklahoma City	23	373	16.2
1985	Rosina Pearson, Beth-Cookman	26	480	18.5
1986	Wanda Ford, Drake	30	506	16.9
1987	Patricia Hoskins, Miss. Valley	28	476	17.0
1988	Katie Beck, East Tenn. St.	25	441	17.6
1989	Patricia Hoskins, Miss. Valley	27	440	16.3
1990	Pam Hudson, Northwestern St	29	438	15.1
1991	Tarcha Hollis, Grambling	29	443	15.3
1992	Christy Greis, Evansville	28	383	13.7
1993	Ann Barry, Nevada	25	355	14.2
1994	DeShawne Blocker, E. Tenn. St.	26	450	17.3
1995	Tera Sheriff, Jackson St	29	401	13.8
1996	Dana Wynne, Seton Hall	29	372	12.8
1997	Etolia Mitchell, Georgia St.	25	330	13.2

Note: Wanda Ford (1986) and Patricia Hoskins (1989) each led the country in scoring and rebounds in the same year.

All-Time NCAA Division I Individual Leaders

Through 1996-97; includes regular season and tournament games; Official NCAA women's basketball records began with 1981-82 season. Players who competed earlier than that are not included below; **Last** column indicates final year played.

CAREER

Scoring

Average		Yrs	Last	Pts	Avg
1	Patricia Hoskins, Miss.Valley St.	4	1989	3122	28.4
2	Sandra Hodge, New Orleans	4	1984	2860	26.7
3	Lorri Bauman, Drake	4	1984	3115	26.0
4	Valorie Whiteside, Aplach St.	4	1988	2944	25.4
5	Joyce Walker, LSU	4	1984	2906	24.8
6	Tarcha Hollis, Grambling	4	1991	2058	24.2
7	Karen Pelphrey, Marshall	4	1986	2746	24.1
8	Erma Jones, Bethune-Cookman	3	1984	2095	24.1
9	Cheryl Miller, USC	4	1986	3018	23.6
10	Chris Starr, Nevada	4	1986	2356	23.3

Rebounds

Average		Yrs	Last	Reb	Avg
1	Wanda Ford, Drake	4	1986	1887	16.1
2	Patricia Hoskins, Miss.Valley St.	4	1989	1662	15.1
3	Tarcha Hollis, Grambling	4	1991	1185	13.9
4	Katie Beck, East Tenn. St.	4	1988	1404	13.4
5	Marilyn Stephens, Temple	4	1984	1519	13.0
6	Cheryl Taylor, Tenn. Tech	4	1987	1532	12.8
7	Olivia Bradley, West Virginia	4	1985	1484	12.7
8	Judy Mosley, Hawaii	4	1990	1441	12.6
9	Chana Perry,NE La./S. Diego St.	4	1989	1286	12.5
10	Three players tied at 12.2 each.				

SINGLE SEASON

Scoring

Average		Year	Gm	Pts	Avg
1	Patricia Hoskins, Miss.Valley St.	1989	27	908	33.6
2	Andrea Congreaves, Mercer	1992	28	925	33.0
3	Deborah Temple, Delta St.	1984	28	873	31.2
4	Andrea Congreaves, Mercer	1993	26	805	31.0
5	Wanda Ford, Drake	1986	30	919	30.6
6	Anucha Browne, Northwestern	1985	28	855	30.5
7	LeChandra LeDay, Grambling	1988	28	850	30.4
8	Kim Perrot, SW Louisiana	1990	28	839	30.0
9	Tina Hutchinson, San Diego St.	1984	30	898	29.9
10	Jan Jensen, Drake	1991	30	888	29.6

SINGLE GAME

Scoring

Average		Year	Pts
1	Cindy Brown, Long Beach St. vs San Jose St.	1987	60
2	Lorri Bauman, Drake vs SW Missouri St.	1984	58
	Kim Perrot, SW La. vs SE La	1990	58
4	Patricia Hoskins, Miss.Valley St. vs South-BR	1989	55
	Patricia Hoskins, Miss.Valley St. vs Ala. St.	1989	55
6	Wanda Ford, Drake vs SW Missouri St.	1986	54
7	Chris Starr, Nevada vs CS-Sacramento	1983	53
	Felisha Edwards, NE La. vs Southern Miss	1991	53
	Sheryl Swoopes, Texas Tech vs Texas	1993	53
10	Three players tied at 52 points each.		

Winningest Active Division I Coaches

Minimum of five seasons as Division I head coach; regular season and tournament games included.

Top 10 Winning Percentage

	Yrs	W	L	Pct
1 Leon Barmore, La. Tech	15	428	67	**.865**
2 Pat Summit, Tennessee	23	625	144	**.813**
3 Robin Selvig, Montana	19	458	109	**.808**
4 Bill Sheahan, Mt. St. Mary's	16	357	91	**.797**
5 Tara VanDerveer, Stanford	18	437	115	**.792**
6 Jody Conradt, Texas	28	697	198	**.779**
7 Sonja Hogg, Baylor	14	346	101	**.774**
8 Geno Auriemma, Connecticut	12	294	86	**.774**
9 Andy Landers, Georgia	18	442	130	**.773**
10 Joe Ciampi, Auburn	20	471	140	**.771**

Top 10 Victories

	Yrs	W	L	Pct
1 Jody Conradt, Texas	28	**697**	198	.779
2 Pat Summit, Tennessee	23	**625**	144	.813
3 Sue Gunter, LSU	27	**547**	245	.691
4 Vivian Stringer, Rutgers	25	**544**	167	.765
5 Kay Yow, N.C. State	26	**527**	214	.711
6 Theresa Grentz, Illinois	23	**498**	177	.738
7 Rene Portland, Penn St.	21	**480**	159	.751
8 Sylvia Hatchell, N. Carolina	22	**486**	198	.711
9 Joe Ciampi, Auburn	20	**471**	140	.771
10 Kay James, So. Miss.	25	**463**	214	.684

Annual Awards

The Broderick Award was first given out to the Women's Division I or Large School Player of the Year in 1977. Since then, the National Assn. for Girls and Women in Sports (1978), the Women's Basketball Coaches Assn. (1983) and the Atlanta Tip-Off Club (1983) and the Associated Press (1995) have joined in.

Since 1983, the first year as many as four awards were given out, the same player has won all of them in the same season twice: Cheryl Miller of USC in 1985 and Rebecca Lobo of Connecticut in 1995.

Associated Press

Voted on by AP sportswriters and broadcasters and first presented in 1995.

Year	Year	Year
1995 Rebecca Lobo, Connecticut	1996 Jennifer Rizzotti, Connecticut	1997 Kara Wolters, Connecticut

Broderick Award

Voted on by a national panel of women's collegiate athletic directors and first presented by the late Thomas Broderick, an athletic outfitter, in 1977. Honda has presented the award since 1987. Basketball Player of the Year is one of 10 nominated for Collegiate Woman Athlete of the Year; (*) indicates player also won Athlete of the Year.

Multiple winners: Nancy Lieberman, Cheryl Miller and Dawn Staley (2).

Year	Year	Year
1977 Lucy Harris, Delta St.*	1984 Cheryl Miller, USC*	1991 Dawn Staley, Virginia
1978 Anne Meyers, UCLA*	1985 Cheryl Miller, USC	1992 Dawn Staley, Virginia
1979 Nancy Lieberman, Old Dominion*	1986 Kamie Ethridge, Texas*	1993 Sheryl Swoopes, Texas Tech
1980 Nancy Lieberman, Old Dominion*	1987 Katrina McClain, Georgia	1994 Lisa Leslie, USC
1981 Lynette Woodward, Kansas	1988 Teresa Weatherspoon, La. Tech*	1995 Rebecca Lobo, Connecticut*
1982 Pam Kelly, La. Tech.	1989 Bridgette Gordon, Tennessee	1996 Jennifer Rizzotti, Connecticut
1983 Anne Donovan, Old Dominion	1990 Jennifer Azzi, Stanford	1997 TBA

Wade Trophy

Voted on by the National Assn. for Girls and Women in Sports (NAGWS) and awarded for academics and community service as well as player performance. First presented in 1978 in the name of former Delta St. coach Margaret Wade.

Multiple winner: Nancy Lieberman (2).

Year	Year	Year
1978 Carol Blazejowski, Montclair St.	1985 Cheryl Miller, USC	1992 Susan Robinson, Penn St.
1979 Nancy Lieberman, Old Dominion	1986 Kamie Ethridge, Texas	1993 Karen Jennings, Nebraska
1980 Nancy Lieberman, Old Dominion	1987 Shelly Pennefather, Villanova	1994 Carol Ann Shudlick, Minnesota
1981 Lynette Woodward, Kansas	1988 Teresa Weatherspoon, La. Tech	1995 Rebecca Lobo, Connecticut
1982 Pam Kelly, La. Tech	1989 Clarissa Davis, Texas	1996 Jennifer Rizzotti, Connecticut
1983 LaTaunya Pollard, L. Beach St.	1990 Jennifer Azzi, Stanford	1997 DeLisha Milton, Florida
1984 Janice Lawrence, La. Tech	1991 Daedra Charles, Tennessee	

Naismith Trophy

Voted on by a panel of coaches, sportwriters and broadcasters and first presented in 1983 by the Atlanta Tip-Off Club in the name of the inventor of basketball, Dr. James Naismith.

Multiple winners: Cheryl Miller (3); Clarissa Davis and Dawn Staley (2).

Year		Year		Year	
1983	Anne Donovan, Old Dominion	1988	Sue Wicks, Rutgers	1993	Sheryl Swoopes, Texas Tech
1984	Cheryl Miller, USC	1989	Clarissa Davis, Texas	1994	Lisa Leslie, USC
1985	Cheryl Miller, USC	1990	Jennifer Azzi, Stanford	1995	Rebecca Lobo, Connecticut
1986	Cheryl Miller, USC	1991	Dawn Staley, Virgina	1996	Saudia Roundtree, Georgia
1987	Clarissa Davis, Texas	1992	Dawn Staley, Virginia	1997	Kate Starbird, Stanford

Women's Basketball Coaches Association

Voted on by the WBCA and first presented by Champion athletic outfitters in 1983.

Multiple winners: Cheryl Miller and Dawn Staley (2).

Year		Year		Year	
1983	Anne Donovan, Old Dominion	1988	Michelle Edwards, Iowa	1993	Sheryl Swoopes, Texas Tech
1984	Janice Lawrence, La. Tech	1989	Clarissa Davis, Texas	1994	Lisa Leslie, USC
1985	Cheryl Miller, USC	1990	Venus Lacey, La. Tech	1995	Rebecca Lobo, Connecticut
1986	Cheryl Miller, USC	1991	Dawn Staley, Virgina	1996	Saudia Roundtree, Georgia
1987	Katrina McClain, Georgia	1992	Dawn Staley, Virginia	1997	Kate Starbird, Stanford

Coach of the Year Award

Voted on by the Women's Basketball Coaches Assn. and first presented by Converse athletic outfitters in 1983.

Multiple winners: Jody Conradt and Vivian Stringer (2).

Year		Year		Year	
1983	Pat Summitt, Tennessee	1988	Vivian Stringer, Iowa	1993	Vivian Stringer, Iowa
1984	Jody Conradt, Texas	1989	Tara VanDerveer, Stanford	1994	Marsha Sharp, Texas Tech
1985	Jim Foster, St. Joseph's-PA	1990	Kay Yow, N.C. State	1995	Gary Blair, Arkansas
1986	Jody Conradt, Texas	1991	Rene Portland, Penn St.	1996	Leon Barmore, La. Tech
1987	Theresa Grentz, Rutgers	1992	Ferne Labati, Miami-FL	1997	Geno Auriemma, Connecticut

Other Women's Champions

The NCAA has sanctioned national championship tournaments for Division II and Division III since 1982. The NAIA sanctioned a single tournament from 1981-91, then split in to two divisions in 1992.

NCAA Div. II Finals

Multiple winners: North Dakota St. (5); Cal Poly Pomona and Delta St. (3).

Year	Winner	Score	Loser
1982	Cal Poly Pomona	93-74	Tuskegee, AL
1983	Virginia Union	73-60	Cal Poly Pomona
1984	Central Mo.St.	80-73	Virginia Union
1985	Cal Poly Pomona	80-69	Central Mo.St.
1986	Cal Poly Pomona	70-63	North Dakota St.
1987	New Haven, CT	77-75	Cal Poly Pomona
1988	Hampton, VA	65-48	West Texas St.
1989	Delta St., MS	88-58	Cal Poly Pomona
1990	Delta St., MS	77-43	Bentley, MA
1991	North Dakota St.	81-74	SE Missouri St.
1992	Delta St., MS	65-63	North Dakota St.
1993	North Dakota St.	95-63	Delta St., MS
1994	North Dakota St.	89-56	CS-San Bernadino
1995	North Dakota St.	98-85	Portland St.
1996	North Dakota St.	105-78	Shippensburg, PA
1997	North Dakota	94-78	S. Indiana

NCAA Div. III Finals

Multiple winners: Capital and Elizabethtown (2).

Year	Winner	Score	Loser
1982	Elizabethtown, PA	67-66*	NC-Greensboro
1983	North Central, IL	83-71	Elizabethtown, PA
1984	Rust College, MS	51-49	Elizabethtown, PA
1985	Scranton, PA	68-59	New Rochelle, NY
1986	Salem St., MA	89-85	Bishop, TX
1987	WI-Stevens Pt.	81-74	Concordia, MN
1988	Concordia, MN	65-57	St. John Fisher, NY
1989	Elizabethtown, PA	66-65	CS-Stanislaus
1990	Hope, MI	65-63	St. John Fisher
1991	St. Thomas, MN	73-55	Muskingum, OH
1992	Alma, MI	79-75	Moravian, PA
1993	Central Iowa	71-63	Capital, OH
1994	Capital, OH	82-63	Washington, MO
1995	Capital, OH	59-55	WI-Oshkosh
1996	WI-Oshkosh	66-50	Mt. Union, OH
1997	NYU	72-70	WI-Eau Claire

*Overtime

NAIA Finals

Multiple winners: One tournament–SW Oklahoma (4); Div. I tourney–Southern Nazarene (4), Arkansas Tech (2); Div. II tourney–Northern St. and Western Oregon (2).

Year	Winner	Score	Loser
1981	Kentucky St.	73-67	Texas Southern
1982	SW Oklahoma	80-45	Mo. Southern
1983	SW Oklahoma	80-68	AL-Huntsville
1984	NC-Asheville	72-70*	Portland, OR
1985	SW Oklahoma	55-54	Saginaw Val., MI
1986	Francis Marion, SC	75-65	Wayland Baptist, TX
1987	SW Oklahoma	60-58	North Georgia
1988	Oklahoma City	113-95	Claflin, SC
1989	So. Nazarene, OK	98-96	Claflin, SC
1990	SW Oklahoma	82-75	AR-Monticello
1991	Ft. Hays St., KS	57-53	SW Oklahoma
1992	I– Arkansas Tech	84-68	Wayland Baptist, TX
	II– Northern St., SD	73-56	Tarleton St., TX
1993	I– Arkansas Tech	76-75	Union, TN
	II– No. Montana	71-68	Northern St., SD
1994	I– So. Nazarene	97-74	David Lipscomb, TN
	II– Northern St., SD	48-45	Western Oregon
1995	I– So. Nazarene	78-77	SE Oklahoma
	II– Western Oregon	75-67	NW Nazarene, ID
1996	I– So. Nazarene	80-79	SE Oklahoma
	II– Western Oregon	80-77	Huron, SD
1997	I– So. Nazarene	78-73	Union, TN
	II– NW Nazarene	64-46	Black Hills St., SD

*Overtime

AIAW Finals

The Association of Intercollegiate Athletics for Women Large College tournament determined the women's national champion for 10 years until supplanted by the NCAA.

In 1982, most Division I teams entered the first NCAA tournament rather than the last one staged by the AIAW.

Year	Winner	Score	Loser
1972	Immaculata, PA	52-48	West Chester, PA
1973	Immaculata, PA	59-52	Queens College, NY
1974	Immaculata, PA	68-53	Mississippi College
1975	Delta St., MS	90-81	Immaculata, PA
1976	Delta St., MS	69-64	Immaculata, PA
1977	Delta St., MS	68-55	LSU
1978	UCLA	90-74	Maryland
1979	Old Dominion	75-65	Louisiana Tech
1980	Old Dominion	68-53	Tennessee
1981	Louisiana Tech	79-59	Tennessee
1982	Rutgers	83-77	Texas

Pro Basketball

Michael Jordan again soared over the rest of the NBA in 1997, leading the Chicago Bulls to their fifth championship this decade.

Wide World Photos

Still the One

The Jackson-Jordan-Pippen edition of the Chicago Bulls is still one of the NBA's best ever.

by
David Aldridge

It's autumn in the reign of Michael Jordan, Scottie Pippen, Phil Jackson and the Chicago Bulls.

Yet their empire shone brightly and vastly over the NBA horizon in 1997. Their march to a fifth championship in seven seasons came despite their poor post-season play. There was no one in the East who could mount a strong challenge, though the Utah Jazz played six honorable games before losing in the finals.

Chicago's dominance was one of the few stable things in a season marked by big changes. True free agency led to a major talent shift, with Shaquille O'Neal leading dozens of players to different teams. Dikembe Mutombo took his shot blocking from Denver to Atlanta. Allan Houston's sharpshooting eye left Detroit for New York. Trades changed the addresses of Charles Barkley, Larry Johnson and Rod Strickland.

David Aldridge is ESPN's NBA analyst.

Yet the playoffs featured old standbys. Utah finally made the championship series after 11 years of Stockton to Malone had come up short. The Jazz delayed the rise of O'Neal and his Lakers, then knocked off the geriatric Houston Rockets—with thirty-somethings Barkley, Hakeem Olajuwon and Clyde Drexler leading the way—in the Western Conference Finals.

The Seattle Supersonics and New York Knicks, whom many thought would meet in the Finals, imploded along the way. Seattle's troubles with its leader, forward Shawn Kemp, plagued the Sonics all season, and Seattle lost in seven games to Houston in the second round. Kemp wanted his contract, now pedestrian at more than $3 million per season, re-done, especially after the Sonics spent $33 million for unspectacular center Jim McIlvaine. The Knicks blew a 3–1 lead against Miami in the Eastern Conference semi-finals after a brawl

From left to right, **Dennis Rodman, Michael Jordan, Scottie Pippen, Ron Harper** and coach **Phil Jackson** each hoist a Chicago Bulls NBA championship trophy. No word on how many more they will have to win before team owner Jerry Reinsdorf gets to hold one in public.

in game five led to suspensions at the worst possible time.

Elsewhere, young stars provided hope for their teams. Kevin Garnett and rookie guard Stephon Marbury led the Minnesota Timberwolves to their first playoff appearance. Chris Webber and Juwan Howard got the Washington Bullets (now the Washington Wizards) into the postseason for the first time in a decade. Philadelphia's Allen Iverson won Rookie of the Year honors, dazzling opponents with his ballhandling and scoring. The Portland Trailblazers, with Kenny Anderson, Rasheed Wallace and Isaiah Rider leading the way, came on strong in the second half of the season.

But until someone can beat them four times in seven games, the NBA night belongs to the Bulls. They overcame Dennis Rodman's antics during the regular season as well as injuries to Pippen and Bill Wennington in the playoffs. Jordan won his fifth Finals MVP award after beating the Jazz at the buzzer in Game One and then coming off his sickbed to score 38 points in the pivotal Game Five in Salt Lake City.

And with the score tied in waning seconds of Game Six, Jordan drew the Jazz to him, then found a wide-open Steve Kerr at the foul line. Kerr sank the series-winning shot and after Pippen stole Utah's inbounds pass, Chicago had won again.

The Running of the Bulls. One of the NBA's longest—and best— series. ∎

David Aldridge's Top Ten Highlights of the 1996 NBA Season

From *ESPN SportsZone* @espn.com

10. **Dumb words.** John Calipari calls the beat reporter for the Newark Star Ledger "a (bleeping) Mexican idiot"to another reporter. Meanwhile, in Miami, the Heat's

Utah Jazz' **John Stockton** (l) and **Karl Malone** (c) had plenty to celebrate in 1996–97, their best season together. The celebration above came after Stockton hit a three-pointer at the buzzer to win the Western Conference finals against the Phoenix Suns.

play-by-play man, David Halberstam, wonders aloud if Thomas Jefferson's slaves would have made good basketball players. Both are disciplined, in an unprecedented move, by commissioner David Stern.

9. **Slow Break.** The game slows down to a walk, led by the impenetrable Cavaliers. But it's not just Cleveland; trapping, rotating defenses and increasingly bad perimeter shooting drop scores into the 80s for weeks at a time.

8. **Jason's Lyric.** The Mavericks begin the dismantling of the Three Js by dealing Jason Kidd to the Phoenix Suns. They say Kidd doesn't practice long, doesn't play hard, doesn't shoot well and doesn't lead anyone anywhere. The Suns gleefully accept their new floor leader. Dallas takes Sam Cassell... then trades him to New Jersey two months later.

7. **Chuck in Paradise.** The rockets acquire Charles Barkley from Phoenix, starting Cassell on his merry way. Houston starts 21–2 with its geriatric threesome of Barkley, Hakeem Olajuwon and Clyde Drexler, but big minutes lead to big injuries for the Rocket Men. Still, Houston finishes a respectable third in the conference.

6. **A Big Bash.** Forty-seven of the 50 greatest players of all time assemble in Cleveland during All-Star Weekend. They fall over themselves getting one another's autographs. They are introduced at Gund Arena, and for one moment, there's no marketing, no commercials, just great basketball men of the game. If your pulse didn't run, you weren't human.

Shawn Kemp of the Seattle Supersonics was up against it for most of the 1996–97 season as contract problems and another underachieving performance by his team continues to preclude Kemp's entry into the league's truly elite.

5. **The Commish Speaks Up.** Stern's decision to disallow the Heat's contract with Juwan Howard, and to allow the Bullets to not only re-sign Howard but keep Tracy Murray and Lorenzo Williams without doing cap restructuring, saves the Washington franchise just in time for owner Abe Pollin to move into a brand new building next season.

4. **Shaq Attaqs.** Shaquille O'Neal signs with the Lakers for seven years and $121 million, confounding the Magic into searching for signs of tampering. None are found. O'Neal is free to pursue his on-court and off-court exploits in the same place. Meanwhile, the NBA salary structure goes to hell.

3. **Kick the Cameraman.** Dennis Rodman places one of his brand new Converse sneakers into the upper thigh of one Eugene Amos, a Minneapolis cameraman, in the third quarter of a Bulls-Timberwolves game. Amos sues, but settles. Rodman can't settle with the league, which suspends him for 11 games.

2. **Let's Make a Deal.** Don Nelson, general manager of the Dallas Mavericks for a week or so, trades nearly half of his team to the incredulous Nets and then rips into the departed players as "f***ing babies." New Jersey has cap flexibility and trade possibilities down the road. What Dallas gets out of it, only Nellie knows for sure.

1. **Revolution in a Hotel Room.** Penny Hardaway leads a coup in Orlando against coach Brian Hill. "It was handled badly," Dennis Scott said. "But Orlando is a new town to all of that, just eight years in the league. It's a player's league regardless of whether people want to admit it." ∎

THE NUMBERS

INSIDE

by

Paul Kinney, Craig Wachs and Kristen Micali

SAVING THE **BEST FOR LAST**

The Chicago Bulls own the best record in the NBA finals for teams that have played at least 20 games. Chicago's five NBA titles rank third on the all-time list behind the Celtics 16 and the Lakers' 11. The Lakers' record in the NBA finals is 66–75.

Best Winning Pct. in NBA Finals (20 game min.)

Bulls	20-9	.690
Celtics	70-46	.603
Warriors (Philadelphia/GoldenSt.)	17-14	.548
Pistons	15-13	.536
Rockets	12-11	.522

MIKE**VP**

The amazing Michael Jordan has five NBA Finals MVP awards to go with his five NBA championships. Here is how Jordan ranks with other major sports and their championship MVPs. The NHL is omitted because the Conn Smythe trophy covers the entire playoffs but several players have won that award twice (Bobby Orr, Wayne Gretzky, Patrick Roy, Mario Lemieux and Bernie Parent).

Championship MVPs

	Player	Times won
NBA	**Michael Jordan**	**5**
NFL	Joe Montana	3
MLB	Reggie Jackson	2
	Sandy Koufax	2
	Bob Gibson	2

THE NEARLY **GREAT**

Karl Malone and John Stockton of the Utah Jazz have played together for 12 years. Their winning percentage (.638) together is fourth all-time behind Jordan and Pippen (.739), Magic Johnson and Kareem Abdul-Jabbar (.739), and Larry Bird and Kevin McHale (.735). Those other duos have won at least three NBA titles together and that is where Malone and Stockton fall rather short. In fact, as this table shows, both men may pass Elgin Baylor on the all-time list of playing in the most playoff games without winning a title.

No Cigars

Player	Playoff games w/o title
Elgin Baylor	134
John Stockton	**127**
Charles Oakley	119
Caldwell Jones	119
Sam Perkins	118
Karl Malone	**117**

∎

PRO BASKETBALL
STATISTICS

THE 1998
INFORMATION PLEASE
SPORTS ALMANAC

THE SEASON IN REVIEW
1996-1997
STANDINGS • PLAYOFFS

SEC A

PAGE 343

Final NBA Standings

Division champions (*) and playoff qualifiers (†) are noted. Number of seasons listed after each head coach refers to current tenure with club.

Western Conference
Midwest Division

	W	L	Pct	GB	Per Game For	Per Game Opp
*Utah	64	18	.780	—	103.1	94.3
†Houston	57	25	.695	7	100.6	96.1
†Minnesota	40	42	.488	24	96.1	97.6
Dallas	24	58	.293	40	90.6	97.0
Denver	21	61	.256	43	97.8	104.1
San Antonio	20	62	.244	44	90.5	98.3
Vancouver	14	68	.171	50	89.2	99.4

Head Coaches: Utah— Jerry Sloan (9th season); **Hou**—Rudy Tomjanovich (6th); **Min**— Phil Saunders (2nd); **Dal**— Jim Cleamons (1st); **Den**— Bernie Bickerstaff (3rd, 4-9) resigned and replaced by Dick Motta on Nov. 26, 1996 (17-52); **SA**—Bob Hill (3-15) fired and replaced by GM Gregg Popovich (17-47) on Dec. 10, 1996; **Van**— Brian Winters (2nd, 8-35) fired and replaced by GM Stu Jackson on Jan. 24 (6-33).

1995-96 Standings: 1. San Antonio (59-23); 2. Utah (55-27); 3. Houston (48-34); 4. Denver (35-47); 5. Dallas (26-56); 6. Minnesota (26-56); 7. Vancouver (15-67).

Pacific Division

	W	L	Pct	GB	Per Game For	Per Game Opp
*Seattle	57	25	.695	—	100.9	93.2
†LA Lakers	56	26	.683	1	100.0	95.7
†Portland	49	33	.598	8	99.0	94.8
†Phoenix	40	42	.488	17	102.8	102.2
†LA Clippers	36	46	.439	21	97.2	99.5
Sacramento	34	48	.415	23	96.4	99.8
Golden St	30	52	.366	27	99.6	104.4

Head Coaches: Sea— George Karl (6th season); **LAL**— Del Harris (3rd); **Port**— P.J. Carlesimo (3rd); **Pho**— Cotton Fitzsimmons (2nd, 0-8) resigned and replaced by Danny Ainge (40-34) on Nov. 14, 1996; **LAC**— Bill Fitch (3rd); **Sac**— Garry St. Jean (5th, 28-39) fired and replaced by Eddie Jordan (6-9); **G.St.**— Rick Adelman (2nd).

1995-96 Standings: 1. Seattle (64-18); 2. LA Lakers (53-29); 3. Portland (44-38); 4. Phoenix (41-41); 5. Sacramento (39-43); 6. Golden St. (36-46); 7. LA Clippers (29-53).

Eastern Conference
Atlantic Division

	W	L	Pct	GB	Per Game For	Per Game Opp
*Miami	61	21	.744	—	94.8	89.3
†New York	57	25	.695	4	95.4	92.2
†Orlando	45	37	.549	16	94.1	94.5
†Washington	44	38	.537	17	99.4	97.7
New Jersey	26	56	.317	35	97.2	101.8
Philadelphia	22	60	.268	39	100.2	106.7
Boston	15	67	.183	46	100.6	107.9

Head Coaches: Mia— Pat Riley (2nd season); **NY**— Jeff Van Gundy (2nd); **Orl**— Brian Hill (4th, 24-25) fired and replaced by assistant Richie Adubato (21-12); **Wash**— Jim Lynam (3rd, 0-1) on Feb. 5 and then by Nuggets GM Bernie Bickerstaff (22-13) on Feb. 10; **NJ**— John Calipari (1st); **Phi**— Johnny Davis (1st); **Bos**— M.L. Carr (2nd).

1995-96 Standings: 1. Orlando (60-22); 2. New York (47-35); 3. Miami (42-40); 4. Washington (39-43) 5. Boston (33-49); 6. New Jersey (30-52); 7. Philadelphia (18-64).

Central Division

	W	L	Pct	GB	Per Game For	Per Game Opp
*Chicago	69	13	.841	—	103.1	92.3
†Atlanta	56	26	.683	13	94.8	89.4
†Charlotte	54	28	.659	15	98.9	97.0
†Detroit	54	28	.659	15	94.2	88.9
Cleveland	42	40	.512	27	87.5	85.6
Indiana	39	43	.476	30	95.4	94.4
Milwaukee	33	49	.402	36	95.3	97.2
Toronto	30	52	.366	39	95.5	98.6

Head Coaches: Chi— Phil Jackson (8th season); **Atl**— Lenny Wilkens (4th); **Char**— Dave Cowens (1st); **Det**— Doug Collins (2nd); **Cle**— Mike Fratello (4th); **Ind**— Larry Brown (4th); **Mil**—Chris Ford (1st); **Tor**— Darrell Walker (1st).

1995-96 Standings: 1. Chicago (72-10); 2. Indiana (52-30); 3. Cleveland (47-35); 4. Atlanta (46-36); 5. Detroit (46-36); 6. Charlotte (41-41); 7. Milwaukee (25-57); 8. Toronto (21-61).

Overall Conference Standings

Sixteen teams—eight from each conference—qualify for the NBA Playoffs; (*) indicates division champions.

Western Conference

		W	L	Home	Away	Div	Conf
1	Utah*	64	18	38-3	26-15	19-5	41-11
2	Seattle*	57	25	31-10	26-15	16-8	37-15
3	Houston	57	25	30-11	27-14	19-5	40-12
4	LA Lakers	56	26	31-10	25-16	18-6	37-15
5	Portland	49	33	29-12	20-21	15-9	36-16
6	Phoenix	40	42	25-16	15-26	13-11	27-25
7	Minnesota	40	42	25-16	15-26	16-8	28-24
8	LA Clippers	36	46	21-20	15-26	10-14	26-26
	Sacramento	34	48	22-19	12-29	8-16	23-29
	Golden St	30	52	18-23	12-29	4-20	19-33
	Dallas	24	58	14-27	10-31	9-15	16-36
	Denver	21	61	12-29	9-32	7-17	13-39
	San Antonio	20	62	12-29	8-33	8-16	12-40
	Vancouver	14	68	8-33	6-35	6-18	9-43

Eastern Conference

		W	L	Home	Away	Div	Conf
1	Chicago*	69	13	39-2	30-11	24-4	44-10
2	Miami*	61	21	29-12	32-9	16-8	40-14
3	New York	57	25	31-10	26-15	19-6	38-16
4	Atlanta	56	26	36-5	20-21	17-11	34-20
5	Charlotte	54	28	30-11	24-17	14-14	34-20
6	Detroit	54	28	30-11	24-17	17-11	34-20
7	Orlando	45	37	26-15	19-22	13-11	29-25
8	Washington	44	38	25-16	19-22	14-10	28-26
	Cleveland	42	40	25-16	17-24	13-15	26-28
	Indiana	39	43	21-20	18-23	11-17	22-32
	Milwaukee	33	49	20-21	13-28	10-18	22-32
	Toronto	30	52	18-23	12-29	6-22	16-38
	New Jersey	26	56	16-25	10-31	11-13	16-38
	Philadelphia	22	60	11-30	11-30	11-14	14-40
	Boston	15	67	11-30	4-37	1-23	8-46

1997 NBA All-Star Game

East, 132-120

47th NBA All-Star Game. **Date:** Feb. 9, at Gund Arena in Cleveland; **Coaches:** Doug Collins, Detroit (East) and Rudy Tomjanovich, Houston (West); **MVP:** Glen Rice, Charlotte (25 minutes, 26 points).

Starters chosen by fan vote, (for the eighth time in his career, Chicago's Michael Jordan was the leading vote-getter, receiving a record 2,451,136); bench chosen by conference coaches vote. **Team replacements:** EAST— Detroit guard Joe Dumars for Miami center Alonzo Mourning (tendinitis in right heel) and Washington forward Chris Webber for New York center Patrick Ewing (pulled groin muscle); WEST— Seattle forward Detlef Schrempf for Houston forward Charles Barkley (sprained right ankle), Dallas forward Chris Gatling for LA Lakers center Shaquille O'Neal (sprained right knee) and Minnesota forward Kevin Garnett for Houston guard Clyde Drexler (strained right hamstring).

Western Conference

Pos	Starters	Min	FG M-A	Pts	Reb	A
F	Shawn Kemp, Sea ...	19	4-7	10	4	1
F	Karl Malone, Utah ...	20	2-8	4	4	0
C	Hakeem Olajuwon, Hou ..	20	5-8	11	3	1
G	Gary Payton, Sea ...	28	7-15	17	1	10
G	John Stockton, Utah ..	20	5-6	12	0	5
Bench						
G	Mitch Richmond, Sac .	22	3-7	9	3	4
F	Tom Gugliotta, Min ...	19	3-7	9	8	3
G	Latrell Sprewell, GS ..	25	7-12	19	3	1
G	Eddie Jones, LAL	17	3-4	10	1	1
F	Kevin Garnett, Min ...	18	1-7	6	9	1
F	Chris Gatling, Dal	12	1-8	2	2	0
G	Detlef Schrempf, Sea .	20	5-8	11	4	2
	TOTALS	240	46-97	**120**	42	29

Three-Point FG: 9-21 (Kemp 1-2, Payton 1-5, Stockton 2-2, Richmond 3-4, Gugliotta 0-1, Sprewell 1-3, Jones 0-1, Schrempf 1-3); **Free Throws:** 19-28 (Kemp 1-2, Olajuwon 1-2, Payton 2-2, Gugliotta 3-4, Sprewell 4-6, Jones 4-7, Garnett 4-4, Schrempf 0-1); **Percentages:** FG (.474), Three-Pt. FG (.429), Free Throws (.679); **Turnovers:** 16 (Payton 4, Gugliotta 3, Jones 3, Kemp, Olajuwon, Richmond, Schrempf, Sprewell, Stockton); **Steals:** 11 (Gugliotta 2, Payton 2, Sprewell 2, Gatling, Jones, Kemp, Malone, Stockton); **Blocked Shots:** 6 (Jones 2, Garnett, Malone, Olajuwon, Schrempf); **Fouls:** 19 (Gugliotta 3, Schrempf 3, Garnett 2, Payton 2, Sprewell 2, Stockton 2, Gatling, Jones, Kemp, Olajuwon, Richmond); **Team Rebounds:** 11.

Eastern Conference

Pos	Starters	Min	FG M-A	Pts	Reb	A
F	Scottie Pippen, Chi ...	25	4-9	8	3	2
F	Grant Hill, Det	22	4-7	11	3	2
C	Dikembe Mutombo, Atl .	15	1-5	3	8	0
G	Michael Jordan, Chi ..	26	5-14	14	11	11
G	Anfernee Hardaway, Orl .	24	7-10	19	7	3
Bench						
F	Vin Baker, Mil	24	8-12	19	12	1
G	Terell Brandon, Cle ..	17	4-11	10	3	8
G	Tim Hardaway, Mia ..	14	4-10	10	3	2
G	Glen Rice, Cha	25	10-24	26	1	1
G	Joe Dumars, Det	10	1-4	3	1	1
F	Christian Laettner, Atl .	24	3-5	7	11	2
F	Chris Webber, Was ...	14	1-4	2	4	3
	TOTALS	240	52-115	**132**	67	36

Three-Point FG: 12-29 (Pippen 0-3, A. Hardaway 3-5, Brandon 2-4, T. Hardaway 2-6, Rice 4-7, Dumars 1-4); **Free Throws:** 16-22 (Hill 3-4. Mutombo 1-2, Jordan 4-7, A. Hardaway 2-2, Baker 3-4, Rice 2-2, Laettner 1-1); **Percentages:** FG (.452), Three-Pt. FG (.414), Free Throws (.727); **Turnovers:** 18 (Hill 3, Jordan 3, Webber 3, T. Hardaway 2, Laettner 2, Pippen 2, A. Hardaway, Mutombo, Rice); **Steals:** 12 (Brandon 2, A. Hardaway 2, Jordan 2, Rice 2, T. Hardaway, Hill, Laettner, Webber); **Blocked Shots:** 3 (Hill, Laettner, Mutombo); **Fouls:** 22 (Jordan 4, Laettner 4, Baker 2, Brandon 2, A. Hardaway 2, Hill 2, Rice 2, T. Hardaway); **Team Rebounds:** 9.

Halftime— West, 60-57; **Third Quarter—** East, 97-87; **Technical Fouls—** none; **Officials—** Hugh Evans, Bill Oakes, Ron Garretson; **Attendance—** 20,592; **Time—** 2:26; **Rating—** 11.2/19 share (NBC).

	1	2	3	4	F
West	34	26	27	33	—120
East	21	36	40	35	—132

NBA 3-point Shootout

Eight players are invited to compete in the annual three-point shooting contest held during All-Star weekend, since 1986. Each shooter has 60 seconds to shoot the 25 balls in five racks outside the three-point line. Each ball is worth one point, except the last ball in each rack, which is worth two. Highest scores advance. First prize: $20,000.

First Round	Pts	Semifinals	Pts
Walt Williams, Tor ...	18	Steve Kerr	22
Tim Legler, Wash. ..	17	Tim Legler	19
Glen Rice, Char	16		
Steve Kerr, Chi.	15	**Failed to advance**	
		Glen Rice	14
Failed to advance		Walt Williams	12
John Stockton, Utah ..	13		
Dale Ellis, Den	12	**Finals**	
Terry Mills, Cle	11	Steve Kerr	22
Sam Perkins, Sea	8	Tim Legler	18

NBA Slam Dunk Contest

Six players are invited to compete in the annual slam dunk contest held during All-Star weekend, since 1984. The players are selected based on "the creativity and artistry they have displayed in dunking over the course of the season." In the first round, each player has 90 seconds to attempt as many dunks as he chooses with a minimum of three. Points are awarded based on "creativity, artistry and athletic ability." Only the top three scores advance to the second and final round where each player gets two dunks each. First prize: $20,000.

First Round	Pts	Finals	Pts
Chris Carr, Min	44	Kobe Bryant	49
Michael Finley, Dal ..	39	Chris Carr	45
Kobe Bryant, LAL	37	Michael Finley	33
Failed to advance			
Ray Allen, Mil	35		
Bob Sura, Cle	35		
Darvin Ham, Den ...	30		

Indiana Pacers
Mark Jackson
Assists

Atlanta Hawks
Mookie Blaylock
Steals

Charlotte Hornets
Glen Rice
3–pt Shooting Pct.

Dallas Mavericks
Shawn Bradley
Blocked Shots

NBA Regular Season Individual Leaders

Scoring

	Gm	Min	FG	FG%	3pt/Att	FT	FT%	Reb	Ast	Stl	Blk	Pts	Avg	Hi
Michael Jordan, Chi	82	3106	920	.486	111/297	480	.833	482	352	140	44	2431	29.6	51
Karl Malone, Utah	82	2998	864	.550	0/13	521	.755	809	368	113	48	2249	27.4	41
Glen Rice, Char	79	3362	722	.477	207/440	464	.867	318	160	72	26	2115	26.8	48
Mitch Richmond, Sac	81	3125	717	.454	204/477	457	.861	319	338	118	24	2095	25.9	41
Latrell Sprewell, G.St.	80	3353	649	.449	147/415	493	.843	366	507	132	45	1938	24.2	46
Allen Iverson* Phi.	76	3045	625	.416	155/455	382	.702	312	567	157	24	1787	23.5	50
Hakeem Olajuwon, Hou	78	2852	727	.510	5/16	351	.787	716	236	117	173	1810	23.2	48
Patrick Ewing, NY	78	2887	655	.488	2/9	439	.754	834	156	69	189	1751	22.4	39
Kendall Gill, NJ	82	3199	644	.443	74/220	427	.797	499	326	154	46	1789	21.8	41
Gary Payton, Sea	82	3213	706	.476	119/380	254	.715	378	583	197	13	1785	21.8	32
Reggie Miller, Ind	81	2966	552	.444	229/536	418	.880	286	273	75	25	1751	21.6	40
Grant Hill, Det	80	3147	625	.496	10/33	450	.711	721	583	144	48	1710	21.4	38
Glenn Robinson, Mil	80	3114	669	.465	63/180	288	.791	502	248	103	68	1689	21.1	44
Vin Baker, Mil	78	3159	632	.505	15/54	358	.687	804	211	81	112	1637	21.0	36
Jerry Stackhouse, Phi	81	3166	533	.407	102/342	511	.766	338	253	93	63	1679	20.7	39
Tom Gugliotta, Min.	81	3131	592	.442	24/93	464	.820	702	335	130	89	1672	20.6	35
Tim Hardaway, Mia.	81	3136	575	.415	203/590	291	.799	277	695	151	9	1644	20.3	45
Scottie Pippen, Chi	82	3095	648	.474	156/424	204	.701	531	467	154	45	1656	20.2	47
Damon Stoudamire, Tor.	81	3311	564	.401	176/496	330	.823	330	709	123	13	1634	20.2	35
Kevin Johnson, Pho.	70	2658	441	.496	89/202	439	.852	253	653	102	12	1410	20.1	38
Steve Smith, Atl.	72	2818	491	.429	130/388	333	.847	238	305	62	23	1445	20.1	41
Chris Webber, Wash	72	2806	604	.518	60/151	177	.565	743	331	122	137	1445	20.1	34
Terrell Brandon, Cle	78	2868	575	.438	101/271	268	.902	301	490	138	30	1519	19.5	33
Juwan Howard, Wash	82	3324	638	.486	0/2	294	.756	652	311	93	23	1570	19.1	33
Shawn Kemp, Sea	81	2750	526	.510	12/33	452	.742	807	156	125	81	1516	18.7	34
Shareef Abdur-Rahim*, Van.	80	2802	550	.453	7/27	387	.746	555	175	79	79	1494	18.7	37
Joe Smith, G.St.	80	3086	587	.454	12/46	307	.814	679	125	74	86	1493	18.7	38

Rebounds

	Gm	Off	Def	Tot	Avg
Dennis Rodman, Chi	55	320	563	883	16.1
Dikembe Mutombo, Den	80	268	661	929	11.6
Anthony Mason, Char	73	186	643	829	11.4
Ervin Johnson, Den	82	231	682	913	11.1
Patrick Ewing, NY	78	175	659	834	10.7
Chris Webber, Wash	72	238	505	743	10.3
Vin Baker, Mil	78	267	537	804	10.3
Loy Vaught, LAC	82	222	595	817	10.0
Shawn Kemp, Sea	81	275	532	807	10.0
Tyrone Hill, Cle	74	259	477	736	9.9
Karl Malone, Utah	82	193	616	809	9.9
Charles Oakley, NY	80	246	535	781	9.8
Dale Davis, Ind	80	301	471	772	9.7
Michael Smith, Sac	81	257	512	769	9.5
Rony Seikaly, Orl	74	274	427	701	9.5

Assists

	Gm	Ast	Avg
Mark Jackson, Ind	82	935	11.4
John Stockton, Utah	82	860	10.5
Kevin Johnson, Pho	70	653	9.3
Jason Kidd, Pho	55	496	9.0
Rod Strickland, Port	82	727	8.9
Damon Stoudamire, Tor	81	709	8.8
Tim Hardaway, Mia	81	695	8.6
Nick Van Exel, LAL	79	672	8.5
Robert Pack, Dal	54	452	8.4
Stephon Marbury*, Min	67	522	7.8
Allen Iverson*, Phi	76	567	7.5
Grant Hill, Det	80	583	7.3
David Wesley, Bos	74	537	7.3
Mugsy Bogues, Char	65	469	7.2
Kenny Anderson, Port	82	584	7.1
Gary Payton, Sea	82	583	7.1

NBA Regular Season Individual Leaders (Cont.)

Field Goal Pct.

	Gm	FG	Att	Pct
Gheorghe Muresan, Wash ..	73	327	541	.604
Tyrone Hill, Cle	74	357	595	.600
Rasheed Wallace, Port	62	380	681	.558
Shaquille O'Neal, LAL	51	552	991	.557
Chris Mullin, G.St	79	438	792	.553
Karl Malone, Utah	82	864	1571	.550
John Stockton, Utah	82	416	759	.548
Dale Davis, Ind	80	370	688	.538
Danny Manning, Pho	77	426	795	.536
Gary Trent, Port	82	361	674	.536

Free Throw Pct.

	Gm	FT	Att	Pct
Mark Price, G.St	70	155	171	.906
Terrell Brandon, Cle	78	268	297	.902
Jeff Hornacek, Utah	82	293	326	.899
Ricky Pierce, Char	60	139	155	.897
Mario Elie, Hou	78	207	231	.896
Reggie Miller, Ind	81	418	475	.880
Malik Sealy, LAC	80	254	290	.876
Hersey Hawkins, Sea	82	258	295	.875
Darrick Martin, LAC	82	218	250	.872
Glen Rice, Char	79	464	535	.867
Joe Dumars, Det	79	222	256	.867

3-Point Field Goal Pct.

	Gm	3FG	Att	Pct
Glen Rice, Char	79	207	440	.470
Steve Kerr, Chi	82	110	237	.464
Kevin Johnson, Pho	70	89	202	.441
Joe Dumars, Det	79	166	384	.432
Mitch Richmond, Sac	81	204	477	.428
Reggie Miller, Ind	81	229	536	.427
Dell Curry, Char	68	126	296	.426
Terry Mills, Det	79	175	415	.422
Mario Elie, Hou	78	120	286	.420
Voshon Lenard, Mia	73	183	442	.414

High-Point Games

	Opp	Date	FG–FT–Pts
Michael Jordan, Chi	vs. NY	1/21	18-10—51
Michael Jordan, Chi	at Mia.	11/6	18-13—50
Allen Iverson, Phi	at Cle.	4/12	17-11—50
Hakeem Olajuwon, Hou .	vs. Den	1/30	24-0—48
Glen Rice, Char	vs. Bos.	3/6	18-7—48*
Scottie Pippen, Chi	vs. Den.	2/18	19-7—47
Latrell Sprewell, G.St.	vs. Dal.	1/21	16-8—46
Michael Jordan, Chi	vs. Cle.	12/28	13-19—45
Michael Jordan, Chi	at Sea.	2/2	19-5—45
Tim Hardaway, Mia.	at Wash.	3/7	13-13—45*

*Overtime.

Blocked Shots

	Gm	Blk	Avg
Shawn Bradley, Dal	73	248	3.40
Dikembe Mutombo, Atl	80	264	3.30
Shaquille O'Neal, LAL	51	147	2.88
Alonzo Mourning, Mia	66	189	2.86
Ervin Johnson, Den	82	227	2.77
Patrick Ewing, NY	78	189	2.42
Vlade Divac, Sac	81	180	2.22
Hakeem Olajuwon, Hou ..	78	173	2.22
Kevin Garnett, Min	77	163	2.12
Marcus Camby*, Tor	63	130	2.06

Steals

	Gm	Stl	Avg
Mookie Blaylock, Atl	78	212	2.72
Doug Christie, Tor	81	201	2.48
Gary Payton, Sea	82	197	2.40
Eddie Jones, LAL	80	189	2.36
Rick Fox, Bos	76	167	2.20
David Wesley, Bos	74	162	2.19
Allen Iverson*, Phi	76	157	2.07
John Stockton, Utah	82	166	2.02
Greg Anthony, Van	65	129	1.98
Kenny Anderson, Port	82	162	1.98

Rookie Leaders

Scoring	Gm	FG	FT	Pts	Avg
Allen Iverson, Phi	76	625	382	1787	23.5
Shareef Abdur-Rahim, Van	80	550	387	1494	18.7
Antoine Walker, Bos	82	576	231	1435	17.5
Kerry Kittles, NJ	82	507	175	1347	16.4
Stephon Marbury, Min	67	355	245	1057	15.8

Field Goal Pct.	Gm	FG	Att	Pct
Dean Garrett, Min	68	223	389	.573
Roy Rogers, Van	82	244	483	.505
Marcus Camby, Tor	63	375	778	.482
Lorenzen Wright, LAC	77	236	491	.481
Shareef Abdur-Rahim, Van ..	80	550	1214	.453

Rebounds	Gm	Off	Def	Tot	Avg
Antoine Walker, Bos	82	288	453	741	9.0
Dean Garrett, Min	68	149	346	495	7.3
Shareef Abdur-Rahim, Van ..	80	216	339	555	6.9
Marcus Camby, Tor	63	131	263	394	6.3
Lorenzen Wright, LAC	77	206	265	471	6.1

Assists	Gm	No	Avg
Stephon Marbury, Min	67	522	7.8
Allen Iverson, Phi	76	567	7.5
Matt Maloney, Hou	82	303	3.7
Antoine Walker, Bos	82	262	3.2
Kerry Kittles, NJ	82	249	3.0

Personal Fouls

Shawn Kemp, Sea	320
Charles Oakley, NY	305
Otis Thorpe, Det	298
Olden Polynice, Sac	298
Ervin Johnson, Den	288

Disqualifications

Shawn Kemp, Sea	11
Walt Williams, Tor	11
Sam Cassell, NJ	9
Antonio McDyess, Den	9
Alonzo Mourning, Mia	9

Turnovers

Allen Iverson*, Phi	337
Latrell Sprewell, G.St	322
Jerry Stackhouse, Phi	318
Tom Gugliotta, Min	293
Damon Stoudamire, Tor	288

Triple Doubles

Grant Hill, Det	13
Mark Jackson, Ind	4
Anthony Mason, Char	4
Clyde Drexler, Hou	3
Eight tied with two each.	

Minutes Played

Glen Rice, Char	3362
Latrell Sprewell, G.St	3353
Juwan Howard, Wash	3324
Damon Stoudamire, Tor	3311
Gary Payton, Sea	3213

Assist/Turnover Ratio

Mugsy Bogues, Char	4.34
Lee Mayberry, Van	3.66
Avery Johnson, SA	3.51
Jason Kidd, Pho	3.49
John Stockton, Utah	3.47

Team by Team Statistics

At least 16 games played, except for Cleveland, Dallas and Phoenix where the minimum is 30. Players who competed for more than one team during the regular season are listed with their final club; (*) indicates rookies.

Atlanta Hawks

	Gm	FG%	Tpts	PPG	RPG	APG
Steve Smith	72	.429	1445	20.1	3.3	4.2
Christian Laettner	82	.486	1486	18.1	8.8	2.7
Mookie Blaylock	78	.432	1354	17.4	5.3	5.9
Dikembe Mutombo	80	.527	1066	13.3	11.6	1.4
Tyrone Corbin	70	.422	666	9.5	4.2	1.8
Henry James	53	.408	356	6.7	1.5	0.4
Alan Henderson	30	.475	199	6.6	3.9	0.8
Willie Burton	24	.336	148	6.2	1.7	0.5
Eldridge Recasner	71	.423	405	5.7	1.6	1.3
Jon Barry	58	.407	285	4.9	1.7	2.0
Ken Norman	17	.287	64	3.8	2.3	0.7
Priest Lauderdale*	35	.551	111	3.2	1.2	0.3
Donnie Boyce	22	.333	55	2.5	0.7	0.6
Darrin Hancock	24	.457	42	1.8	0.8	0.5
MILW	9	.333	4	0.4	0.6	0.4
SA	1	.500	4	4.0	0.0	1.0
ATL	14	.481	34	2.4	0.9	0.5
Ivano Newbill	72	.440	100	1.4	2.8	0.3

Triple Doubles: none. **3-pt FG leader:** Blaylock (221).
Steals leader: Blaylock (212). **Blocks leader:** Mutombo (264).
Signed: F/G Hancock (Mar. 5).

Boston Celtics

	Gm	FG%	Tpts	PPG	RPG	APG
Antoine Walker*	82	.425	1435	17.5	9.0	3.2
David Wesley	74	.468	1240	16.8	3.6	7.3
Rick Fox	76	.456	1174	15.4	5.2	3.8
Eric Williams	72	.456	1078	15.0	4.6	1.8
Todd Day	81	.398	1178	14.5	4.1	1.4
Dino Radja	25	.440	349	14.0	8.4	1.9
Dana Barros	24	.435	300	12.5	2.0	3.4
Greg Minor	23	.480	220	9.6	3.5	1.5
Marty Conlon	74	.471	574	7.8	4.4	1.4
Dee Brown	21	.367	160	7.6	2.3	3.2
Frank Brickowski	17	.438	81	4.8	2.0	0.9
Michael Hawkins	29	.426	80	2.8	1.1	2.2
Brett Szabo*	70	.446	153	2.2	2.4	0.2
Steve Hamer*	35	.526	76	2.2	1.7	0.2
Alton Lister	53	.416	87	1.6	3.2	0.2

Triple Doubles: Walker (2). **3-pt FG leader:** Day (126).
Steals leader: Fox (167). **Blocks leader:** Walker (53).

Charlotte Hornets

	Gm	FG%	Tpts	PPG	APG	RPG
Glen Rice	79	.477	2115	26.8	2.0	4.0
Anthony Mason	73	.525	1186	16.2	5.7	11.4
Dell Curry	68	.459	1008	14.8	1.7	3.1
Vlade Divac	81	.494	1024	12.6	3.7	9.0
Ricky Pierce	60	.481	659	11.0	1.3	2.0
DEN	33	.462	335	10.2	0.9	1.6
CHAR	27	.502	324	12.0	1.8	2.5
Matt Geiger	49	.489	437	8.9	0.8	5.3
Muggsy Bogues	65	.460	522	8.0	7.2	2.2
Tony Delk*	61	.465	332	5.4	1.6	1.6
Tony Smith	19	.409	346	5.0	2.2	1.4
Donald Royal	62	.425	218	3.5	0.4	2.5
ORL	1	.400	12	12.0	1.0	1.0
G.St.	36	.385	136	3.8	0.4	2.6
CHAR	25	.525	70	2.8	0.4	1.6
Rafael Addison	41	.402	128	3.1	0.8	1.1
Malik Rose*	54	.477	160	3.0	0.6	3.0

Triple Doubles: Mason (4). **3-pt FG leader:** Rice (207).
Steals leader: Divac (103). **Blocks leader:** Divac (180).
Acquired: G Pierce from Denver for C George Zidek and G Anthony Goldwire (Feb. 20); F Royal from Golden St. for G Scott Burrell (Feb. 20).

Chicago Bulls

	Gm	FG%	Tpts	PPG	RPG	APG
Michael Jordan	82	.486	2431	29.6	5.9	4.3
Scottie Pippen	82	.474	1656	20.2	6.5	5.7
Toni Kukoc	57	.471	754	13.2	4.6	4.5
Luc Longley	59	.456	537	9.1	5.6	2.4
Steve Kerr	82	.533	662	8.1	1.6	2.1
Jason Caffey	75	.532	549	7.3	4.0	1.2
Ron Harper	76	.436	480	6.3	2.5	2.5
Dennis Rodman	55	.448	311	5.7	16.1	3.1
Randy Brown	72	.420	341	4.7	1.5	1.8
Bill Wennington	61	.498	280	4.6	2.1	0.7
Robert Parish	43	.490	161	3.7	2.1	0.5
Dickey Simpkins	48	.333	91	1.9	1.9	0.6
Jud Buechler	76	.367	139	1.8	1.7	0.8

Triple Doubles: Jordan. **3-pt FG leader:** Pippen (156).
Steals leader: Pippen (154). **Blocks leader:** Pippen (154).

Cleveland Cavaliers

	Gm	FG%	Tpts	PPG	RPG	APG
Terrell Brandon	78	.438	1519	19.5	3.9	6.3
Chris Mills	80	.453	1072	13.4	6.2	2.5
Tyrone Hill	74	.600	955	12.9	9.9	1.2
Bobby Phills	69	.428	866	12.6	3.6	3.4
Danny Ferry	82	.429	870	10.6	4.1	1.8
Bob Sura	82	.431	755	9.2	3.8	4.8
Vitaly Potapenko*	80	.440	465	5.8	2.7	0.5
Mark West	70	.556	227	3.2	2.7	0.3
Donny Marshall	56	.325	175	3.1	1.3	0.4
Antonio Lang	64	.420	171	2.7	2.0	0.5
Reggie Geary*	39	.379	57	1.5	0.4	0.9

Triple Doubles: none. **3-pt FG leader:** Ferry (114).
Steals leader: Brandon (138). **Blocks leader:** West (55).

Dallas Mavericks

	Gm	FG%	Tpts	PPG	RPG	APG
Michael Finley	83	.444	1249	15.0	4.5	2.7
PHO	27	.475	352	13.0	4.4	2.5
DAL	56	.432	897	16.0	4.5	2.8
Robert Pack	54	.392	771	14.3	2.7	8.4
NJ	34	.407	542	15.9	2.5	9.6
DAL	20	.361	229	11.5	3.0	6.4
Shawn Bradley	73	.449	961	13.2	8.4	0.7
NJ	40	.436	479	12.0	8.1	0.5
DAL	33	.461	482	14.6	5.5	8.7
Sasha Danilovic	56	.435	702	12.5	2.4	1.8
MIA	43	.442	486	11.3	2.4	1.8
DAL	13	.420	216	16.6	2.6	1.9
Derek Harper	75	.444	753	10.0	1.8	4.3
Khalid Reeves	63	.391	516	8.2	1.9	3.6
NJ	50	.393	414	8.3	1.3	1.8
DAL	13	.387	102	7.8	2.4	4.3
A.C. Green	83	.444	597	7.2	7.9	0.8
PHO	27	.477	153	5.7	5.1	0.6
DAL	56	.486	444	7.9	9.3	0.9
Samaki Walker*	43	.444	214	5.0	3.4	0.4
Martin Muursepp*	42	.412	156	3.7	1.6	0.5
MIA	10	.357	17	1.7	0.5	0.3
DAL	32	.419	139	4.3	1.9	0.5
Ed O'Bannon	64	.333	235	3.7	2.3	0.6
NJ	45	.367	189	4.2	2.5	0.6
DAL	19	.236	46	2.4	1.4	1.9
Greg Dreiling	40	.459	80	2.0	1.9	0.3

Triple Doubles: none. **3-pt FG leader:** Finley (101).
Steals leader: Pack (94). **Blocks leader:** Bradley (248).
Acquired: G Sam Cassell, F Finley, F Green and a 2nd round draft pick from Phoenix for G Jason Kidd, G Tony Dumas and C Loren Meyer (Dec. 26); F Kurt Thomas, G Danilovic and F Muursepp from Miami for F Jamal Mashburn (Feb. 14); C Bradley, F O'Bannon, G Pack and G Reeves from New Jersey for G Jim Jackson, G Sam Cassell, F Chris Gatling, F/G George McCloud and C Eric Montross (Feb. 17).

Denver Nuggets

	Gm	FG%	Tpts	PPG	RPG	APG
LaPhonso Ellis	55	.439	1203	21.9	7.0	2.4
Antonio McDyess .	74	.463	1352	18.3	7.3	1.4
Dale Ellis	82	.414	1361	16.6	3.6	2.0
Bryant Stith	52	.416	774	14.9	4.2	2.6
Ervin Johnson ...	82	.520	582	7.1	11.1	0.9
Sarunas Marciulionis .	17	.376	116	6.8	1.8	1.5
Brooks Thompson .	67	.399	445	6.6	1.4	2.7
UTAH	2	.000	0	0.0	0.0	0.5
DEN	65	.400	445	6.8	1.5	2.8
Anthony Goldwire ..	60	.397	387	6.5	1.4	3.7
CHAR	33	.403	190	5.8	1.2	2.8
DEN	27	.392	197	7.3	1.7	4.6
Kenny Smith	48	.423	300	6.3	0.9	2.4
DET	9	.400	23	2.6	0.6	1.1
ORL	6	.462	17	2.8	0.3	0.7
DEN	33	.422	260	7.9	1.1	3.1
Tom Hammonds	81	.480	506	6.2	5.0	0.8
Vincent Askew	43	.435	239	5.6	2.3	2.1
NJ	1	—	0	0.0	0.0	0.0
IND	41	.432	233	5.7	2.4	2.2
DEN	1	.667	6	6.0	0.0	0.0
Jerome Allen	76	.353	228	3.0	1.3	2.0
IND	51	.388	164	3.2	1.3	2.1
DEN	25	.284	64	2.6	1.3	1.7
George Zidek	52	.415	143	2.8	1.7	0.3
CHAR	36	.388	91	2.5	1.8	0.3
DEN	16	.485	52	3.3	1.4	0.3

Triple Doubles: Mark Jackson (2). **3-pt FG leader:** D. Ellis (192). **Steals leader:** Er. Johnson (65). **Blocks leader:** Er. Johnson (227).

Acquired: G Askew and G Eddie Johnson and two 2nd draft picks from Indiana for G Mark Jackson and C LaSalle Thompson (Feb. 20); G Allen from Indiana for G/F Darvin Ham (Feb. 20); C Zidek and G Goldwire from Charlotte for G Ricky Pierce (Feb. 20).

Signed: G Thompson (Nov. 21); G Smith (Jan. 24).

Note: Mark Jackson had two triple doubles with Denver, then two more with Indiana for a total of four for the season.

Detroit Pistons

	Gm	FG%	Tpts	PPG	RPG	APG
Grant Hill	80	.496	1710	21.4	9.0	7.3
Joe Dumars	79	.440	1158	14.7	2.4	4.0
Lindsey Hunter	82	.404	1166	14.2	2.8	1.9
Otis Thorpe	79	.532	1036	13.1	7.9	1.7
Terry Mills	79	.444	857	10.8	4.8	1.3
Theo Ratliff	76	.531	439	5.8	3.4	0.2
Aaron McKie	83	.411	433	5.2	2.7	1.9
PORT	41	.340	170	4.1	2.3	2.0
DET	42	.464	263	6.3	2.4	1.8
Grant Long	65	.447	326	5.0	3.4	0.6
Michael Curry	81	.448	318	3.9	1.5	0.5
Don Reid	47	.482	132	2.8	2.1	0.3
Rick Mahorn	22	.370	56	2.5	2.4	0.3
Litterial Green	45	.469	90	2.0	0.5	0.9
Randolph Childress .	23	.350	39	1.7	0.3	0.7
PORT	19	.333	29	1.5	0.3	0.8
DET	4	.400	10	2.5	0.3	0.5
Jerome Williams* .	33	.392	49	1.5	1.5	0.2

Triple Doubles: Hill (13). **3-pt FG leader:** Mills (175). **Steals leader:** Hill (144). **Blocks leader:** Ratliff (111).

Acquired: G McKie, G Childress and G Reggie Jordan from Portland for F/G Stacey Augmon (Jan. 24).

Golden St. Warriors

	Gm	FG%	Tpts	PPG	RPG	APG
Latrell Sprewell ...	80	.449	1938	24.2	4.6	6.3
Joe Smith	80	.454	1493	18.7	8.5	1.6
Chris Mullin	79	.553	1143	14.5	4.0	4.1
Mark Price	70	.447	793	11.3	2.6	4.9
B.J. Armstrong ...	49	.453	389	7.9	1.5	2.6
Donyell Marshall .	61	.413	444	7.3	4.5	0.9
Bimbo Coles	51	.389	311	6.1	2.3	2.9
Melvin Booker ...	21	.438	122	5.8	1.4	2.5
DEN	5	.500	5	1.0	0.2	0.6
G.St.	16	.436	117	7.3	1.8	3.1
Andrew DeClercq .	71	.520	375	5.3	4.2	0.5
Scott Burrell	57	.362	294	5.2	2.8	1.3
CHAR	28	.344	151	5.4	2.8	1.4
G.St.	29	.379	143	4.9	2.7	1.2
Felton Spencer ...	73	.489	372	5.1	5.7	0.3
ORL	1	1.000	4	4.0	6.0	1.0
G.St.	72	.486	368	5.1	5.7	0.3
Todd Fuller*	75	.429	304	4.1	3.3	0.3
Ray Owes*	57	.417	177	3.1	2.9	0.3
Lou Roe	17	.292	40	2.4	0.8	0.4

Triple Doubles: Mullin (2), Sprewell. **3-pt FG leader:** Sprewell (147).

Steals leader: Sprewell (132). **Blocks leader:** Smith (86).

Acquired: C Spencer, C Koncak and F Donald Royal from Orlando for C Rony Seikaly, F Clifford Rozier and a 2nd round draft pick (Nov. 2); G Burrell from Charlotte for F Donald Royal (Feb. 20).

Houston Rockets

	Gm	FG%	Tpts	PPG	RPG	APG
Hakeem Olajuwon .	78	.510	1810	23.2	9.2	3.0
Charles Barkley ...	53	.484	1016	19.2	13.5	4.7
Clyde Drexler	62	.442	1114	18.0	6.0	5.7
Mario Elie	78	.497	909	11.7	3.0	4.0
Kevin Willis	75	.481	842	11.2	7.5	0.9
Matt Maloney* ...	82	.441	767	9.4	2.0	3.7
Eddie Johnson ...	52	.442	424	8.2	2.7	1.0
IND	28	.434	147	5.3	1.4	0.6
HOU	24	.447	277	11.5	4.1	1.5
Sam Mack	52	.401	292	5.6	2.0	1.1
Brent Price	25	.419	126	5.0	1.2	2.6
Othella Harrington* ..	57	.549	273	4.8	3.5	0.3
Matt Bullard	71	.401	320	4.5	1.6	0.9
Randy Livingston* .	64	.437	251	3.9	1.5	2.4
Tracy Moore	27	.388	99	3.7	1.0	0.7
Sedale Threatt ...	21	.378	70	3.3	1.1	1.9

Triple Doubles: Drexler (3), Barkley, Olajuwon. **3-pt FG leader:** Maloney (154).

Steals leader: Drexler (119). **Blocks leader:** Olajuwon (173).

Signed: G Threatt (Mar. 1); G Johnson (Mar. 3).

Individual Single Game Highs
Most Field Goals Made
24 ....Hakeem Olajuwon, Hou vs Den (1/30)
Most Field Goals Attempted
40 ....Hakeem Olajuwon, Hou vs Den (1/30)
Most Assists
23 ....Nick Van Exel, LAL at Van (1/5)

Indiana Pacers

	Gm	FG%	Tpts	PPG	RPG	APG
Reggie Miller	81	.444	1751	21.6	3.5	3.4
Rik Smits	52	.486	887	17.1	6.9	1.3
Antonio Davis	82	.481	858	10.5	7.3	0.8
Dale Davis	80	.538	832	10.4	9.7	0.7
Travis Best	76	.442	754	9.9	2.2	4.2
Mark Jackson	82	.426	812	9.9	4.8	11.4
DEN	52	.425	541	10.4	5.2	12.3
IND	30	.427	271	9.0	4.1	9.8
Derrick McKey	50	.391	400	8.0	4.8	2.7
Jalen Rose	66	.456	482	7.3	1.8	2.3
Duane Ferrell	62	.472	394	6.4	2.3	1.1
Erick Dampier* . .	72	.390	370	5.1	4.1	0.6
Fred Hoiberg	47	.429	224	4.8	1.7	0.9
Darvin Ham*	36	.532	83	2.3	1.6	0.4
DEN	35	.525	80	2.3	1.6	0.4
IND	1	1.000	3	3.0	0.0	0.0
Brent Scott*	16	.471	19	1.2	0.6	0.2
LaSalle Thompson .	26	.158	10	0.4	1.3	0.1
DEN	17	.188	7	0.4	1.5	0.0
IND	9	.000	3	0.3	0.9	0.2

Triple Doubles: Jackson (2). **3-pt FG leader:** Miller (229).

Steals leader: Best (98). **Blocks leader:** A. Davis (84).

Acquired: G/F Vincent Askew from New Jersey for G/F Reggie Williams (Nov. 4); G Jackson and C Thompson from Denver for G Askew and G Johnson and two 2nd round draft picks (Feb. 20); G/F Ham from Denver for G Allen (Feb. 20).

Note: Mark Jackson had two triple doubles with Denver, then two more with Indiana for a total of four for the season.

Los Angeles Clippers

	Gm	FG%	Tpts	PPG	RPG	APG
Loy Vaught	82	.500	1220	14.9	10.0	1.3
Malik Sealy	80	.396	1079	13.5	3.0	2.1
Rodney Rogers . . .	81	.462	1072	13.2	5.1	2.7
Darrick Martin	82	.407	893	10.9	1.4	4.1
Stanley Roberts . .	18	.426	171	9.5	5.1	0.5
Charles Outlaw . . .	82	.609	625	7.6	5.5	1.9
Brent Barry	59	.409	442	7.5	1.9	2.6
Lamond Murray . .	74	.416	549	7.4	3.1	0.8
Lorenzen Wright* .	77	.481	561	7.3	6.1	0.6
Terry Dehere	73	.386	470	6.4	1.3	2.2
Eric Piatkowski . .	65	.450	388	6.0	1.6	0.8
Pooh Richardson . .	59	.381	330	5.6	1.7	2.9
Kevin Duckworth . .	26	.437	104	4.0	2.3	0.6
Rich Manning	26	.390	75	2.9	1.5	0.1
VAN	16	.375	44	2.8	1.4	0.1
LAC	10	.412	31	3.1	1.6	0.1

Triple Doubles: none. **3-pt FG leader:** Martin (91).

Steals leader: Sealy (124). **Blocks leader:** Outlaw (142).

Signed: C Manning (Apr. 1).

More Individual Single Game Highs
Most Rebounds
33 . . . . Charles Barkley, Hou at Pho (11/2)
Most Offensive Rebounds
15 . . . . Jayson Williams, NJ vs Minn (1/9)
Most Defensive Rebounds
25 . . . . Charles Barkley, Hou at Pho (11/2)

Los Angeles Lakers

	Gm	FG%	Tpts	PPG	RPG	APG
Shaquille O'Neal .	51	.557	1336	26.2	12.5	3.1
Eddie Jones	80	.438	1374	17.2	4.1	3.4
Nick Van Exel	79	.402	1206	15.3	2.9	8.5
Elden Campbell . .	77	.469	1148	14.9	8.0	1.6
George McCloud .	64	.412	658	10.3	2.8	1.7
DAL	41	.423	563	13.7	3.5	2.2
LAL	23	.354	95	4.1	1.6	0.7
Robert Horry	54	.436	423	7.8	4.4	2.2
PHO	32	.421	220	6.9	3.7	1.7
LAL	22	.455	203	9.2	5.4	2.5
Kobe Bryant*	71	.417	539	7.6	1.9	1.3
Jerome Kersey	70	.432	476	6.8	5.2	1.3
Byron Scott	79	.430	526	6.7	1.5	1.3
Travis Knight*	71	.509	342	4.8	4.5	0.5
Corie Blount	58	.514	241	4.2	4.8	0.6
Derek Fisher*	80	.397	309	3.9	1.2	1.5
Sean Rooks	69	.470	265	3.8	2.4	0.6

Triple Doubles: none. **3-pt FG leader:** Van Exel (177).

Steals leader: Jones (189). **Blocks leader:** O'Neal (147).

Acquired: F Horry and C Joe Kleine from Phoenix for F Cedric Ceballos and G Rumeal Robinson (Jan. 10); G/F McCloud from New Jersey for C Joe Kleine, a 1997 1st round and a conditional 2nd round draft pick.

Miami Heat

	Gm	FG%	Tpts	PPG	RPG	APG
Tim Hardaway . . .	81	.415	1644	20.3	3.4	8.6
Alonzo Mourning .	66	.534	1310	19.8	9.9	1.6
Voshon Lenard . . .	73	.459	897	12.3	3.0	2.2
Jamal Mashburn . .	69	.385	822	11.9	4.3	3.0
DAL	37	.372	394	10.6	3.1	2.5
MIA	32	.398	428	13.4	5.6	3.5
Dan Majerle	36	.406	390	10.8	4.5	3.2
Isaac Austin	82	.502	792	9.7	5.8	1.2
P.J. Brown	80	.457	761	9.5	8.4	1.2
Keith Askins	78	.433	384	4.9	3.5	1.0
John Crotty	48	.513	232	4.8	1.0	2.1
Gary Grant	28	.355	110	3.9	1.4	1.6
Willie Anderson . .	28	.453	83	3.0	1.5	1.2
Ed Pinckney	27	.535	66	2.4	2.4	0.2
Mark Strickland . . .	31	.417	62	2.0	1.2	0.0

Triple Doubles: none. **3-pt FG leader:** Hardaway (203).

Steals leader: Hardaway (151). **Blocks leader:** Mourning (189).

Acquired: F Mashburn from Dallas for F Kurt Thomas, G Sasha Danilovic and F Martin Muursepp (Feb. 14).

Signed: G Crotty (Jan. 6); G/F Anderson (Jan. 8).

Milwaukee Bucks

	Gm	FG%	Tpts	PPG	RPG	APG
Glenn Robinson . .	80	.465	1689	21.1	6.3	3.1
Vin Baker	78	.505	1637	21.0	10.3	2.7
Ray Allen*	82	.430	1102	13.4	4.0	2.6
Sherman Douglas .	79	.502	764	9.7	2.4	5.4
Johnny Newman . .	82	.450	715	8.7	2.3	1.4
Armon Gilliam	80	.471	691	8.6	6.2	0.7
Elliot Perry	82	.474	562	6.9	1.5	3.0
Andrew Lang	52	.464	274	5.3	5.3	0.5
Acie Earl	47	.372	188	4.0	2.0	0.4
TOR	38	.376	162	4.3	2.2	0.5
MILW	9	.348	26	2.9	1.2	0.2
Chucky Brown	70	.506	204	2.9	2.1	0.4
PHO	10	.500	34	3.4	1.6	0.4
MILW	60	.508	170	2.8	2.2	0.4
Joe Wolf	56	.449	95	1.7	2.0	0.4
David Wood	46	.526	57	1.2	0.6	0.3

Triple Doubles: none. **3-pt FG leader:** Allen (117).

Steals leader: Robinson (103). **Blocks leader:** Baker (112).

Acquired: F Brown from Phoenix for G/F Darrin Hancock and a conditional 2nd round draft pick (Dec. 4); C Earl from Toronto for G Shawn Respert (Feb. 20).

Minnesota Timberwolves

	Gm	FG%	Tpts	PPG	RPG	APG
Tom Gugliotta	81	.442	1672	20.6	8.7	4.1
Kevin Garnett	77	.499	1309	17.0	8.0	3.1
Stephon Marbury* .	67	.408	1057	15.8	2.7	7.8
Sam Mitchell	82	.446	766	9.3	4.0	1.0
James Robinson ...	69	.407	572	8.3	1.6	1.8
Dean Garrett*	68	.573	542	8.0	7.3	0.6
Doug West	68	.467	531	7.8	2.2	1.7
Terry Porter	82	.416	568	6.9	2.1	3.6
Chris Carr	55	.461	337	6.1	2.1	0.9
Stojko Vrankovic ..	53	.561	181	3.4	3.2	0.3
Cherokee Parks ...	76	.510	252	3.3	2.6	0.4
Reggie Jordan	19	.615	40	2.1	1.4	0.6
PORT	9	.500	20	2.2	2.6	1.2
MIN	10	.800	20	2.0	0.4	0.1
Shane Heal*	43	.268	75	1.7	0.4	0.8

Triple Doubles: none. **3-pt FG leader:** Marbury and Robinson (102).
Steals leader: Gugliotta (130). **Blocks leader:** Garnett (163).
Signed: G Jordan (Mar. 19).

New Jersey Nets

	Gm	FG%	Tpts	PPG	RPG	APG
Kendall Gill	82	.443	1789	21.8	6.1	4.0
Chris Gatling	47	.525	891	19.0	7.9	0.6
DAL	44	.533	840	19.1	7.9	0.6
NJ	3	.419	51	17.0	7.3	1.0
Kerry Kittles*	82	.426	1347	16.4	3.9	3.0
Jim Jackson	77	.431	1226	15.9	5.3	4.1
DAL	46	.442	714	15.5	4.9	3.4
NJ	31	.417	512	16.5	5.9	5.2
Sam Cassell	61	.430	967	15.9	3.0	5.0
PHO	22	.415	325	14.8	2.3	4.5
DAL	16	.424	197	12.3	3.1	3.6
NJ	23	.443	445	19.3	3.6	6.5
Jayson Williams ...	41	.409	550	13.4	13.5	1.2
Tony Massenburg ..	79	.485	568	7.2	6.5	0.3
Kevin Edwards ...	32	.377	190	5.9	1.3	1.8
Xavier McDaniel ..	62	.389	346	5.6	5.1	1.0
Lloyd Daniels	22	.303	98	4.5	2.0	1.2
SAC	5	.125	6	1.2	0.8	0.2
NJ	17	.330	92	5.4	2.3	1.5
Eric Montross	78	.456	339	4.3	6.6	0.8
DAL	47	.460	182	3.9	5.0	0.7
NJ	31	.451	157	5.1	9.1	0.9
Joe Kleine	59	.406	168	2.8	3.4	0.6
PHO	23	.400	78	3.4	3.5	0.5
LAL	8	.250	6	0.8	1.1	0.0
NJ	28	.427	84	3.0	4.1	0.8
Jack Haley	20	.351	40	2.0	1.6	0.3
Yinka Dare	41	.352	57	1.4	2.0	0.1

Triple Doubles: Jackson (2), Shawn Bradley (1). **3-pt FG leader:** Kittles (158).
Steals leader: Kittles (157). **Blocks leader:** Montross (73).
Acquired: G/F Williams for G/F Vincent Askew (Nov. 4); G Jackson, G Cassell, F Gatling, G/F George McCloud and C Montross from Dallas for C Shawn Bradley, F Ed O'Bannon, G Robert Pack and G Khalid Reeves (Feb. 17); C Kleine and a 1997 1st round and conditional 2nd round draft pick from the Los Angeles Lakers for F George McCloud (Feb. 20).
Signed: F Daniels (Dec. 21); F Haley (Jan. 30)

New York Knicks

	Gm	FG%	Tpts	PPG	RPG	APG
Patrick Ewing	78	.488	1751	22.4	10.7	2.0
Allen Houston ...	81	.423	1197	14.8	3.0	2.2
John Starks	77	.431	1061	13.8	2.7	2.8
Larry Johnson	76	.512	976	12.8	5.2	2.3
Charles Oakley ...	80	.488	864	10.8	9.8	2.8
Chris Childs	65	.414	605	9.3	2.9	6.1
Buck Walters	74	.537	465	6.3	5.4	0.7
Charlie Ward	79	.395	409	5.2	2.8	4.1
John Wallace* ...	68	.517	325	4.8	2.3	0.5
Herb Williams ...	21	.391	39	1.9	1.5	0.2
Walter McCarty* ..	35	.382	64	1.8	0.7	0.4
Scott Brooks	38	.487	57	1.5	0.5	0.8

Triple Doubles: Childs. **3-pt FG leader:** Starks (150).
Steals leader: Oakley (111). **Blocks leader:** Ewing (189).

Orlando Magic

	Gm	FG%	Tpts	PPG	RPG	APG
Anfernee Hardaway ..	59	.447	1210	20.5	4.5	5.6
Rony Seikaly	74	.507	1277	17.3	9.5	1.2
Horace Grant	67	.515	845	12.6	9.0	2.4
Dennis Scott	66	.398	823	12.5	3.1	2.1
Nick Anderson ...	63	.397	757	12.0	4.8	2.9
Gerald Wilkins ...	80	.426	848	10.6	2.2	2.2
Derek Strong	82	.447	699	8.5	6.3	0.9
Brian Shaw	77	.366	552	7.2	2.5	4.1
Darrell Armstrong ..	67	.383	411	6.1	1.1	2.6
Danny Schayes ...	45	.392	133	3.0	2.8	0.3
David Vaughn	35	.431	81	2.3	2.7	0.2
Amal McCaskill* ..	17	.313	28	1.6	1.3	0.4

Triple Doubles: none. **3-pt FG leader:** Scott (147).
Steals leader: Anderson (120). **Blocks leader:** Seikaly (107).
Acquired: C Seikaly, F Rozier and a future 2nd round draft pick from Golden St. for C Felton Spencer, C Jon Koncak, and F Donald Royal (Nov. 2).

Philadelphia 76ers

	Gm	FG%	Tpts	PPG	RPG	APG
Allen Iverson* ...	76	.416	1787	23.5	4.1	7.5
Jerry Stackhouse ..	81	.407	1679	20.7	4.2	3.1
Derrick Coleman ..	57	.435	1032	18.1	10.1	3.4
C. Weatherspoon ..	82	.491	1003	12.2	8.3	1.7
Don MacLean	37	.447	402	10.9	3.8	1.0
Mark Davis	75	.469	639	8.5	4.3	1.8
Rex Walters	59	.455	402	6.8	1.8	1.9
Scott Williams ...	62	.509	362	5.8	6.4	0.7
Lucious Harris ...	54	.381	293	5.4	1.3	0.9
Doug Overton ...	61	.426	217	3.6	1.1	1.7
Mark Hendrickson* ..	29	.416	85	2.9	3.2	0.1
Adrian Caldwell ..	45	.435	101	2.2	3.7	0.3
NJ	18	.286	29	1.6	3.1	0.3
PHI	27	.526	72	2.7	4.1	0.3
Michael Cage	82	.468	151	1.8	3.9	0.5
Mark Bradtke*	36	.431	59	1.6	1.9	0.2

Triple Doubles: none. **3-pt FG leader:** Iverson (155).
Steals leader: Iverson (157). **Blocks leader:** Weatherspoon (86).
Signed: F/C Caldwell (Jan. 15).

More Individual Single Game Highs

Most 3-point Field Goals Made

9 ....Steve Smith, Atl vs. Sea (3/14)

Most 3-point Field Goals Attempted

15 ....Steve Smith, Atl vs. Sea (3/14)
15 ......Walt Williams, Tor vs. Wash (12/5)
15 ....Nick Van Exel, LAL at Dal (3/4)

Most Free Throws Made

22 ....Latrell Sprewell, G.St. at LAC (3/10)

Most Free Throws Attempted

25 ....Latrell Sprewell, G.St. at LAC (3/10)

Most Blocked Shots

12 ....Vlade Divac, Char vs. NJ (2/12)

Most Steals

10 ....Clyde Drexler, Hou vs. Sac (11/1)

Phoenix Suns

	Gm	FG%	Tpts	PPG	RPG	APG
Kevin Johnson	70	.496	1410	20.1	3.6	9.3
Cedric Ceballos ..	50	.457	729	14.6	6.6	1.3
LAL	8	.410	86	10.8	6.6	1.9
PHO	42	.464	643	15.3	6.6	1.2
Rex Chapman	65	.443	898	13.8	2.8	2.8
Danny Manning ..	77	.536	1040	13.5	6.1	2.2
Wesley Person ...	80	.453	1080	13.5	3.7	1.5
Jason Kidd	55	.423	599	10.9	4.5	9.0
DAL	22	.369	217	9.9	4.1	9.1
PHO	33	.423	382	11.6	4.8	9.0
Mark Bryant	41	.553	380	9.3	5.2	1.1
John Williams	68	.490	541	8.0	8.3	1.5
Wayman Tisdale ..	53	.426	346	6.5	2.3	0.4
Loren Meyer	54	.443	266	4.9	2.7	0.4
DAL	19	.436	78	4.1	2.6	0.4
PHO	35	.446	188	5.4	2.7	0.3
Steve Nash*	65	.423	213	3.3	1.0	2.1

Triple Doubles: Johnson, Kidd (2). **3-pt FG leader:** Person (171).
Steals leader: Kidd (124). **Blocks leader:** Williams (88).
Acquired: G/F Hancock from Milwaukee for F Chucky Brown (Dec. 4); G Kidd, G Dumas and F Meyer from Dallas for G Sam Cassell, G Michael Finley, F A.C. Green and a 2nd round draft pick (Dec. 26); F Ceballos and G Rumeal Robinson from L.A. Lakers for F Robert Horry and C Joe Kleine (Jan. 10).

Portland Trailblazers

	Gm	FG%	Tpts	PPG	RPG	APG
Kenny Anderson ..	82	.427	1436	17.5	4.4	7.1
Isaiah Rider	76	.464	1223	16.1	4.0	2.6
Rasheed Wallace ..	62	.558	938	15.1	6.8	1.2
Clifford Robinson .	81	.426	1224	15.1	4.0	3.2
Arvydas Sabonis ..	69	.498	928	13.4	7.9	2.1
Gary Trent	82	.536	882	10.8	5.2	1.1
Stacey Augmon ...	60	.477	279	4.7	2.3	0.9
DET	20	.403	90	4.5	2.5	0.8
PORT	40	.517	189	4.7	2.2	1.0
Dontonio Wingfield .	47	.409	211	4.5	2.9	1.0
Jermaine O'Neal* ..	45	.451	185	4.1	2.8	0.2
Chris Dudley	81	.430	317	3.9	7.3	0.5
Marcus Brown* ...	21	.400	82	3.9	0.7	1.0
Rumeal Robinson ..	54	.402	176	3.3	0.9	1.4
LAL	15	.354	45	3.0	0.7	0.9
PHO	12	.471	36	3.0	0.6	0.7
PORT	27	.402	95	3.5	1.1	1.9
Mitchell Butler	49	.416	148	3.0	1.1	0.6

Triple Doubles: none. **3-pt FG leader:** Anderson (132).
Steals leader: Anderson (162). **Blocks leader:** Dudley (96).
Acquired: F/G Augmon from Detroit for G Aaron McKie, G Randolph Childress and G Reggie Jordan (Jan. 24).
Signed: G Robinson (Feb. 24).

Sacramento Kings

	Gm	FG%	Tpts	PPG	RPG	APG
Mitch Richmond ..	81	.454	2095	25.9	3.9	4.2
Mahmoud Abdul-Rauf .	75	.445	1031	13.7	1.6	2.5
Olden Polynice ..	82	.457	1025	12.5	9.4	2.2
Corliss Williamson .	79	.498	915	11.6	4.1	1.6
Billy Owens	66	.467	724	11.0	5.9	2.8
Brian Grant	24	.440	252	10.5	5.9	1.2
Tyus Edney	70	.384	485	6.9	1.6	3.2
Michael Smith ...	81	.539	532	6.6	9.5	2.4
Kevin Gamble	62	.430	307	5.0	1.7	1.2
Jeff Grayer	25	.458	91	3.6	1.5	1.0
Lionel Simmons ..	41	.331	139	3.4	2.5	1.4
Bobby Hurley	49	.368	143	2.9	0.8	3.0
Duane Causwell ..	46	.511	118	2.6	2.8	0.4
Kevin Salvadori* ..	23	.364	37	1.6	1.1	0.4

Triple Doubles: Richmond. **3-pt FG leader:** Richmond (204).
Steals leader: Richmond (118). **Blocks leader:** Polynice (80).

San Antonio Spurs

	Gm	FG%	Tpts	PPG	RPG	APG
Dominique Wilkins .	63	.417	1145	18.2	6.4	1.9
Sean Elliott	39	.422	582	14.9	4.9	3.2
Vernon Maxwell ..	72	.375	929	12.9	2.2	2.1
Vinnie Del Negro .	72	.467	886	12.3	2.9	3.2
Avery Johnson ...	76	.477	800	10.5	1.9	6.8
Monty Williams ...	65	.509	588	9.0	3.2	1.4
Will Perdue	65	.568	565	8.7	9.8	0.6
Carl Herrera	75	.433	597	8.0	4.5	0.7
Jason Alexander ..	80	.396	577	7.2	1.5	3.2
Charles Smith	19	.405	88	4.6	3.4	0.7
Greg Anderson ...	82	.496	322	3.9	5.5	0.4
Jamie Feick*	41	.357	151	3.7	5.2	0.6
CHAR	3	.500	5	1.7	1.0	0.0
SA	38	.353	146	3.8	5.6	0.7

Triple Doubles: none. **3-pt FG leader:** Maxwell (115).
Steals leader: Johnson (96). **Blocks leader:** Perdue (102).
Singed: F Feick (Jan. 28).

Seattle Supersonics

	Gm	FG%	Tpts	PPG	RPG	APG
Gary Payton	82	.476	1785	21.8	4.6	7.1
Shawn Kemp	81	.510	1516	18.7	10.0	1.9
Detlef Schrempf ...	61	.492	1022	16.8	6.5	4.4
Hersey Hawkins ..	82	.464	1139	13.9	3.9	3.0
Sam Perkins	81	.439	889	11.0	3.7	1.3
Terry Cummings ..	45	.486	370	8.2	4.1	0.9
Nate McMillan ...	37	.409	169	4.6	3.2	3.8
Larry Stewart	70	.444	300	4.3	2.4	0.7
Jim McIlvaine	82	.471	314	3.8	4.0	0.3
David Wingate ...	65	.416	236	3.6	1.1	1.2
Craig Ehlo	62	.351	214	3.5	1.8	1.1
Greg Graham	28	.363	93	3.3	0.5	0.4
Eric Snow	67	.451	199	3.0	1.0	2.4

Triple Doubles: Payton (2). **3-pt FG leader:** Hawkins (143).
Steals leader: Payton (197). **Blocks leader:** McIlvaine (164).
Signed: F Cummings (Jan. 13).

Toronto Raptors

	Gm	FG%	Tpts	PPG	RPG	APG
Damon Stoudamire .	81	.401	1634	20.2	4.1	8.8
Walt Williams ...	73	.427	1199	16.4	5.0	2.7
Marcus Camby* ..	63	.482	935	14.8	6.3	1.5
Doug Christie	81	.417	1176	14.5	5.3	3.9
Carlos Rogers ...	56	.525	551	9.8	5.4	0.7
Reggie Slater	26	.550	203	7.8	3.7	0.8
Popeye Jones	79	.480	616	7.8	8.6	1.1
Sharone Wright ...	60	.400	390	6.5	3.1	0.5
Hubert Davis	36	.402	181	5.0	1.1	0.9
Oliver Miller	61	.517	294	4.8	5.0	1.4
DAL	42	.494	180	4.3	5.5	1.4
TOR	19	.560	114	6.0	3.8	1.5
Clifford Rozier ...	42	.454	189	4.5	5.6	0.7
G.St.	1	.000	0	0.0	4.0	0.0
TOR	41	.457	189	4.6	5.7	0.8
Shawn Respert ...	41	.424	172	4.2	1.0	1.0
MILW	14	.316	20	1.4	0.5	0.6
TOR	27	.442	152	5.6	1.2	1.2
John Long	32	.393	129	4.0	1.3	0.7
Donald Whiteside .	27	.327	59	2.2	0.4	1.3

Triple Doubles: Stoudamire (2). **3-pt FG leader:** Stoudamire (176).
Steals leader: Christie (201). **Blocks leader:** Camby (130).
Acquired: G Respert from Milwaukee for C Acie Earl (Feb. 20).
Signed: G Long (Nov. 29); F Rozier (Jan. 23); F Slater (Jan. 25); C Miller (Feb. 13).

Utah Jazz

	Gm	FG%	Tpts	PPG	RPG	APG
Karl Malone	82	.550	2249	27.4	9.9	4.5
Jeff Hornacek	82	.482	1191	14.5	2.9	4.4
John Stockton	82	.548	1183	14.4	2.8	10.5
Bryon Russell	81	.479	873	10.8	4.1	1.5
Antoine Carr	82	.483	603	7.4	2.4	0.9
Greg Ostertag	77	.515	559	7.3	7.3	0.4
Shandon Anderson* ..	65	.462	386	5.9	2.8	0.8
Howard Eisley	82	.451	368	4.5	1.0	2.4
Chris Morris	73	.408	314	4.3	2.2	0.6
Adam Keefe	62	.513	235	3.8	3.5	0.5
Stephen Howard ..	49	.574	176	3.6	1.7	0.2
SA	7	.583	26	3.7	1.3	0.1
UTAH	42	.573	150	3.6	1.8	0.2
Greg Foster	79	.453	278	3.5	2.4	0.4

Triple Doubles: Malone. **3-pt FG leader:** Russell (108).
Steals leader: Stockton (166). **Blocks leader:** Ostertag (152).
Signed: F Howard (Jan. 15).

Vancouver Grizzlies

	Gm	FG%	Tpts	PPG	RPG	APG
Shareef Abdur-Rahim*	80	.453	1494	18.7	6.9	2.2
Bryant Reeves	75	.486	1213	16.2	8.1	2.1
Anthony Peeler ...	72	.398	1041	14.5	3.4	3.6
Greg Anthony	65	.393	616	9.5	2.8	6.3
George Lynch	41	.471	342	8.3	6.4	1.9
Blue Edwards	61	.397	478	7.8	3.1	1.9
Lawrence Moten ..	67	.388	447	6.7	1.8	1.9
Roy Rogers*	82	.505	543	6.6	4.7	0.6
Aaron Williams ...	33	.574	203	6.2	4.3	0.5
DEN	1	.600	6	6.0	5.0	0.0
VAN	32	.573	197	6.2	4.3	0.5
Lee Mayberry	80	.403	410	5.1	1.7	4.1
Chris Robinson* ..	41	.379	188	4.6	1.7	1.6
Pete Chilcutt	54	.436	182	3.4	2.9	0.9
Eric Mobley	28	.444	72	2.6	2.1	0.5
Eric Leckner	20	.424	34	1.7	1.8	0.3
CHAR	1	.000	0	0.0	1.0	1.0
VAN	19	.467	34	1.8	1.8	0.2

Triple Doubles: Abdur-Rahim. **3-pt FG leader:** Peeler (128).
Steals leader: Anthony (129). **Blocks leader:** Rogers (163).
Signed: F Williams (Jan. 29); C Leckner (Feb. 10).

Washington Bullets

	Gm	FG%	Tpts	PPG	RPG	APG
Chris Webber	72	.518	1445	20.1	10.3	4.6
Juwan Howard	82	.486	1570	19.1	8.0	3.8
Rod Strickland	82	.466	1410	17.2	4.1	8.9
Gheorghe Muresan	73	.604	777	10.6	6.6	0.4
Calbert Cheaney ..	79	.505	837	10.6	3.4	1.4
Tracy Murray	82	.425	817	10.0	3.1	1.0
Chris Whitney	82	.421	430	5.2	1.3	2.2
Jaren Jackson	75	.407	374	5.0	1.8	0.9
Harvey Grant	78	.411	316	4.1	3.3	0.9
Lorenzo Williams ..	19	.645	45	2.4	3.6	0.2
Ashraf Amaya	31	.300	40	1.3	1.7	0.1
Ben Wallace*	34	.348	38	1.1	1.7	0.1

Triple Doubles: Webber (2). **3-pt FG leader:** Murray
(106).
Steals leader: Strickland (143). **Blocks leader:** Webber (137).

NBA Regular Season Team Leaders

Offense

WEST	PPG	RPG	APG	FG%	3Pt%	FT%
Utah	103.1	40.2	26.8	.504	.370	.769
Phoenix	102.8	40.1	25.2	.469	.369	.761
Seattle	100.9	40.0	23.5	.467	.353	.752
Houston	100.6	42.6	24.5	.468	.365	.755
LA Lakers	100.0	42.8	22.5	.454	.367	.692
Golden St.	99.7	40.8	22.1	.456	.352	.778
Portland	99.0	43.3	20.9	.464	.358	.713
Denver	97.8	42.0	23.0	.439	.372	.761
LA Clippers ...	97.2	40.7	20.3	.446	.354	.731
Sacramento ...	96.4	41.5	21.9	.454	.391	.723
Minnesota	96.1	39.7	22.9	.456	.339	.751
Dallas	90.6	40.3	20.2	.436	.327	.717
San Antonio ..	90.5	39.4	20.3	.442	.320	.718
Vancouver	89.2	38.8	22.7	.437	.349	.709

EAST	PPG	RPG	APG	FG%	3Pt%	FT%
Chicago	103.2	45.1	26.1	.473	.373	.747
Boston	100.6	40.0	21.9	.440	.351	.750
Philadelphia ...	100.0	44.2	20.7	.438	.319	.725
Washington ...	99.3	41.8	23.4	.481	.331	.707
Charlotte	98.9	39.1	24.6	.471	.428	.777
New Jersey ...	97.2	46.2	21.0	.422	.353	.740
Toronto	95.5	41.3	20.9	.437	.363	.720
Indiana	95.3	41.7	21.3	.456	.381	.722
Milwaukee	95.3	39.2	19.6	.471	.352	.741
New York	95.3	42.6	22.0	.463	.364	.748
Atlanta	94.8	41.1	19.0	.446	.360	.763
Miami	94.8	41.0	21.2	.453	.364	.719
Detroit	94.2	38.4	19.0	.464	.388	.745
Orlando	94.1	40.1	20.6	.437	.341	.746
Cleveland	87.5	37.4	20.9	.453	.376	.723

Defense

WEST	PPG	RPG	APG	FG%	3Pt%	FT%
Seattle	93.2	39.9	21.4	.441	.373	.741
Utah	94.3	37.3	19.4	.438	.352	.750
Portland	94.8	38.4	20.8	.436	.357	.739
LA Lakers	95.7	42.4	22.9	.441	.347	.718
Houston	96.1	41.0	22.4	.443	.335	.729
Dallas	97.0	43.0	21.9	.458	.373	.751
Minnesota	97.6	41.9	21.8	.450	.362	.753
San Antonio ..	98.3	40.9	23.8	.471	.387	.738
Vancouver	99.4	44.3	24.1	.472	.365	.727
LA Clippers ...	99.5	42.7	20.2	.462	.357	.749
Sacramento ...	99.8	41.5	21.7	.462	.352	.737
Phoenix	102.2	42.8	24.2	.467	.368	.739
Denver	104.1	43.2	22.5	.467	.393	.750
Golden State ..	104.4	41.0	26.3	.475	.373	.750

EAST	PPG	RPG	APG	FG%	3Pt%	FT%
Cleveland	85.6	37.0	20.1	.441	.373	.742
Detroit	88.9	39.4	21.9	.444	.369	.737
Miami	89.3	40.5	18.4	.432	.363	.731
Atlanta	89.4	39.9	20.3	.435	.347	.737
New York	92.2	38.2	19.4	.425	.350	.743
Chicago	92.3	40.2	19.7	.436	.335	.737
Indiana	94.4	39.8	21.2	.440	.347	.753
Orlando	96.0	40.6	21.9	.460	.343	.732
Charlotte	97.0	40.6	21.7	.460	.357	.730
Milwaukee	97.2	39.4	22.2	.472	.342	.731
Washington ...	97.7	41.0	20.3	.454	.371	.749
Toronto	98.6	41.3	24.0	.465	.348	.724
New Jersey ...	101.8	43.0	23.4	.464	.372	.745
Philadelphia ...	106.7	44.4	25.2	.470	.365	.733
Boston	107.9	44.3	26.0	.503	.365	.720

NBA PLAYOFFS

FIRST ROUND	SEMI FINALS	FINALS		FINALS	SEMI FINALS	FIRST ROUND

Utah 3
L.A. Clippers 0
Utah 4
L.A. Lakers 3
Portland 1
L.A. Lakers 1
Utah 4
WESTERN CONFERENCE
Seattle 3
Phoenix 2
Seattle 3
Houston 2
Houston 3
Minnesota 0
Houston 4
Chicago 4
Utah 2

Chicago 3
Washington 0
Chicago 4
Atlanta 3
Detroit 2
Atlanta 1
Chicago 4
EASTERN CONFERENCE
Miami 3
Orlando 2
Miami 4
New York 3
Charlotte 0
New York 3
Miami 1

Series Summaries

WESTERN CONFERENCE

FIRST ROUND (Best of 5)

	W-L	Avg.	Leading Scorer
Utah	3-0	105.0	Malone (30.7)
LA Clippers	0-3	92.3	Vaught (15.0)

Date	Winner	Home Court
Apr. 24	Jazz, 106-86	at Utah
Apr. 26	Jazz, 105-99	at Utah
Apr. 28	Jazz, 104-92	at Los Angeles

	W-L	Avg.	Leading Scorer
Seattle	3-2	112.8	Payton (25.4)
Phoenix	2-3	100.2	Chapman (24.2)

Date	Winner	Home Court
Apr. 25	Suns, 106-101	at Seattle
Apr. 27	Supersonics, 122-78	at Seattle
Apr. 29	Suns, 110-103	at Phoenix
May 1	Supersonics, 122-115 OT	at Phoenix
May 3	Supersonics, 116-92	at Seattle

	W-L	Avg.	Leading Scorer
Houston	3-0	111.0	Barkley & Olajuwon (18.3)
Minnesota	0-3	99.7	Marbury (21.3)

Date	Winner	Home Court
Apr. 24	Rockets, 112-95	at Houston
Apr. 26	Rockets, 96-84	at Houston
Apr. 29	Rockets, 125-120	at Minnesota

	W-L	Avg.	Leading Scorer
LA Lakers	3-1	96.8	O'Neal (33.0)
Portland	1-3	89.8	Wallace (19.8)

Date	Winner	Home Court
Apr. 25	Lakers, 95-77	at Los Angeles
Apr. 27	Lakers, 107-93	at Los Angeles
Apr. 30	Trail Blazers, 98-90	at Portland
May 2	Lakers, 95-91	at Portland

SEMIFINALS (Best of 7)

	W-L	Avg.	Leading Scorer
Utah	4-1	97.6	Malone (28.6)
LA Lakers	1-4	94.0	O'Neal (22.0)

Date	Winner	Home Court
May 4	Jazz, 93-77	at Utah
May 6	Jazz, 103-101	at Utah
May 8	Lakers, 104-84	at Los Angeles
May 10	Jazz, 110-95	at Los Angeles
May 12	Jazz, 98-93 (OT)	at Utah

	W-L	Avg.	Leading Scorer
Houston	4-3	100.9	Olajuwon (21.7)
Seattle	3-4	99.6	Payton (22.6)

Date	Winner	Home Court
May 5	Rockets, 112-102	at Houston
May 7	Supersonics, 106-101	at Houston
May 9	Rockets, 97-93	at Seattle
May 11	Rockets, 110-96 (OT)	at Seattle
May 13	Supersonics, 100-94	at Houston
May 15	Supersonics, 99-96	at Seattle
May 17	Rockets, 96-91	at Houston

CHAMPIONSHIP (Best of 7)

	W-L	Avg.	Leading Scorer
Utah	4-2	100.2	Malone (23.5)
Houston	2-4	97.0	Olajuwon (27.2)

Date	Winner	Home Court
May 19	Jazz, 101-86	at Utah
May 21	Jazz, 104-92	at Utah
May 23	Rockets, 118-100	at Houston
May 25	Rockets, 95-92	at Houston
May 27	Jazz, 96-91	at Utah
May 29	Jazz, 103-100	at Houston

EASTERN CONFERENCE

FIRST ROUND (Best of 5)

	W-L	Avg.	Leading Scorer
Chicago	3-0	101.0	Jordan (37.3)
Washington	0-3	95.0	Strickland (19.7)

Date	Winner	Home Court
Apr. 25	Bulls, 98-86	at Chicago
Apr. 27	Bulls, 109-104	at Chicago
Apr. 30	Bulls, 96-95	at Washington

	W-L	Avg.	Leading Scorer
Miami	3-2	92.0	Mourning (18.2)
Orlando	2-3	84.2	Hardaway (31.0)

Date	Winner	Home Court
Apr. 24	Heat, 99-64	at Miami
Apr. 27	Heat, 104-87	at Miami
Apr. 29	Magic, 88-75	at Orlando
May 1	Magic, 99-91	at Orlando
May 4	Heat, 91-83	at Miami

	W-L	Avg.	Leading Scorer
New York	3-0	104.3	Ewing (20.3)
Charlotte	0-3	95.7	Rice (27.7)

Date	Winner	Home Court
Apr. 24	Knicks, 109-99	at New York
Apr. 26	Knicks, 100-93	at New York
Apr. 28	Knicks, 104-95	at Charlotte

	W-L	Avg.	Leading Scorer
Atlanta	3-2	87.6	Smith (20.2)
Detroit	2-3	85.6	Hill (23.6)

Date	Winner	Home Court
Apr. 25	Hawks, 89-75	at Atlanta
Apr. 27	Pistons, 93-80	at Atlanta
Apr. 29	Pistons, 99-91	at Detroit
May 2	Hawks, 94-82	at Detroit
May 4	Hawks, 84-79	at Atlanta

SEMIFINALS (Best of 7)

	W-L	Avg.	Leading Scorer
Chicago	4-1	98.2	Jordan (26.6)
Atlanta	1-4	90.4	Blaylock (20.6)

Date	Winner	Home Court
May 6	Bulls, 100-97	at Chicago
May 8	Hawks, 103-95	at Chicago
May 10	Bulls, 100-80	at Atlanta
May 11	Bulls, 89-80	at Atlanta
May 13	Bulls, 107-92	at Chicago

	W-L	Avg.	Leading Scorer
Miami	4-3	86.9	Hardaway (22.9)
New York	3-4	85.6	Ewing (23.7)

Date	Winner	Home Court
May 7	Knicks, 88-79	at Miami
May 9	Heat, 88-84	at Miami
May 11	Knicks, 77-73	at New York
May 12	Knicks, 89-76	at New York
May 14	Heat, 96-81	at Miami
May 16	Heat, 95-90	at New York
May 18	Heat, 101-90	at Miami

CHAMPIONSHIP (Best of 7)

	W-L	Avg.	Leading Scorer
Chicago	4-1	87.4	Jordan (30.2)
Miami	1-4	78.6	Hardaway (17.2)

Date	Winner	Home Court
May 20	Bulls, 84-77	at Chicago
May 22	Bulls, 75-68	at Chicago
May 24	Bulls, 98-74	at Miami
May 26	Heat, 87-80	at Miami
May 28	Bulls, 100-87	at Chicago

NBA FINALS (Best of 7)

	W-L	Avg.	Leading Scorer
Chicago	4-2	87.8	Jordan (32.3)
Utah	2-4	87.2	Malone (23.8)

Date	Winner	Home Court
June 1	Bulls, 84-82	at Chicago
June 4	Bulls, 97-85	at Chicago
June 6	Jazz, 104-93	at Utah
June 8	Jazz, 78-73	at Utah
June 11	Bulls, 90-88	at Utah
June 13	Bulls, 90-86	at Chicago

Most Valuable Player
Michael Jordan, Chicago, G
32.3 pts, 7.0 rebs, 6.0 assists.

Final Playoff Standings

(Ranked by victories)

	Gm	W	L	Pct	Per Game For	Opp
Chicago	19	15	4	.789	93.6	87.8
Utah	20	13	7	.650	97.5	92.8
Houston	16	9	7	.563	103.0	99.8
Miami	17	8	9	.471	85.8	85.7
New York	10	6	4	.600	95.0	91.3
Seattle	12	6	6	.500	106.2	100.6
LA Lakers	9	4	5	.444	95.4	93.7
Atlanta	10	4	6	.400	89.0	91.9
Phoenix	5	2	3	.400	100.2	112.8
Detroit	5	2	3	.400	85.6	87.6
Orlando	5	2	3	.400	84.2	92.0
Portland	4	1	3	.250	89.8	96.8
Minnesota	3	0	3	.000	99.7	111.0
Charlotte	3	0	3	.000	95.7	104.3
Washington	3	0	3	.000	95.0	101.0
LA Clippers	3	0	3	.000	92.3	105.0

Off-Season Coaching Changes

Team	Old Coach	Why left?	New Coach	Old Job
Boston	M.L. Carr	resigned (Apr. 30)	Rick Pitino	Head Coach, Kentucky
Denver	Dick Motta	fired (Apr. 21)	Bill Hanzlik	Asst., Hawks
Golden St.	Rick Adelman	fired (Apr. 28)	P.J. Carlesimo	Head Coach, Trailblazers
Indiana	Larry Brown	resigned (Apr. 30)	Larry Bird	Special Asst., Celtics
Orlando	Richie Adubato	Interim	Chuck Daly	Head Coach, Nets
Philadelphia	Johnny Davis	fired (Apr. 20)	Larry Brown	Head Coach, Pacers
Portland	P.J. Carlesimo	fired (May 8)	Mike Dunleavy	V.P. & G.M., Bucks

NBA Playoff Leaders

Scoring

	Gm	FG	FT	Pts	Avg
Michael Jordan, Chicago	19	227	123	590	31.1
Anfernee Hardaway, Orlando	5	52	40	155	31.0
Glen Rice, Charlotte	3	28	21	83	27.7
Shaquille O'Neal, LA Lakers	9	89	64	242	26.9
Karl Malone, Utah	20	187	144	519	26.0
Rex Chapman, Phoenix	5	41	17	121	24.2
Gary Payton, Seattle	12	105	50	285	23.8
Grant Hill, Detroit	5	45	28	118	23.6
Hakeem Olajuwon, Houston	16	147	76	370	23.1
Patrick Ewing, New York	9	88	27	203	22.6
Shawn Kemp, Seattle	12	85	87	259	21.6
Stephon Marbury, Minnesota	3	26	6	64	21.3
Rasheed Wallace, Portland	4	33	11	79	19.8
Rod Strickland, Washington	3	22	14	59	19.7
Allan Houston, New York	9	58	31	173	19.2
Scottie Pippen, Chicago	19	129	68	365	19.2
Steve Smith, Atlanta	10	55	61	189	18.9
Tim Hardaway, Miami	17	103	70	318	18.7
Juwan Howard, Washington	3	20	16	56	18.7

High Point Games

	Date	FG-FT—Pts
Michael Jordan, Chi vs Wash	4/27	22-10—55
Shaquille O'Neal, LAL vs Port.	4/25	17-12—46
Rex Chapman, Pho at Sea.	4/25	12-9—42
Anfernee Hardaway, Orl vs Mia	4/29	16-9—42
Karl Malone, Utah at LAL	5/10	12-18—42

Rebounds

	Gm	Off	Def	Tot	Avg
Shawn Kemp, Sea	12	52	96	148	12.3
Dikembe Mutombo, Atl	10	37	86	123	12.3
Charles Barkley, Hou.	16	64	128	192	12.0
Anthony Mason, Cha	3	8	28	36	12.0
Dean Garrett, Min	3	19	16	35	11.7

Assists

	Gm	No	Avg
Jason Kidd, Pho	5	49	9.8
John Stockton, Utah	20	191	9.6
Gary Payton, Sea	12	104	8.7
Rod Strickland, Wash	3	25	8.3
Stephon Marbury, Min	3	23	7.7

NBA Finalists' Composite Box Scores

Chicago Bulls (15-4)

	Overall Playoffs			Per Game			Finals vs. Utah			Per Game		
	Gm	FG%	TPts	Pts	Reb	Ast	Gm	FG%	TPts	Pts	Reb	Ast
Michael Jordan	19	.456	590	31.1	7.9	4.8	6	.456	194	32.3	7.0	6.0
Scottie Pippen	19	.417	365	19.2	6.8	3.8	6	.421	120	20.0	8.3	3.5
Toni Kukoc	19	.360	150	7.9	2.8	2.8	6	.405	48	8.0	3.2	2.7
Ron Harper	19	.400	142	7.5	4.3	3.0	6	.344	29	4.8	4.5	2.3
Luc Longley	19	.548	124	6.5	4.4	1.8	6	.606	41	6.8	3.8	1.2
Brian Williams	19	.481	116	6.1	3.7	0.6	6	.472	41	6.8	3.3	0.8
Steve Kerr	19	.429	95	5.0	0.9	1.1	6	.360	26	4.3	0.8	1.0
Dennis Rodman	19	.370	79	4.2	8.4	1.4	6	.250	14	2.3	7.7	1.5
Jason Caffey	17	.455	41	2.4	2.5	0.9	5	—	0	0.0	0.4	0.2
Jud Buechler	18	.419	33	1.8	1.3	0.3	6	.500	10	1.7	1.2	0.3
Randy Brown	17	.300	21	1.2	0.6	0.4	5	.200	4	0.8	0.2	0.2
Robert Parish	2	.143	2	1.0	2.0	0.0	—	—	—	—	—	—
BULLS	19	.432	1758	92.5	43.5	20.7	6	.432	527	87.8	40.3	19.7
OPPONENTS	19	.423	1653	87.0	38.7	16.4	6	.430	523	87.2	40.8	20.2

Three-pointers: PLAYOFFS—Pippen (39-for-113), Harper (21-61), Kukoc (19-53), Kerr (16-42), Jordan (13-67), Buechler (4-12), Rodman (4-16), Team (116-364 for .319 pct.); FINALS—Pippen (12-for-32), Kukoc (10-18), Jordan (8-25), Kerr (4-16), Harper (3-11), Buechler (1-4), Rodman (1-6), Team (39-112 for .348 pct.).

Utah Jazz (13-7)

	Overall Playoffs			Per Game			Finals vs. Chicago			Per Game		
	Gm	FG%	TPts	Pts	Reb	Ast	Gm	FG%	TPts	Pts	Reb	Ast
Karl Malone	20	.435	519	25.9	11.4	2.9	6	.443	143	23.8	10.3	3.5
John Stockton	20	.521	322	16.1	3.9	9.6	6	.500	90	15.0	4.0	8.8
Jeff Hornacek	20	.433	291	14.6	4.5	3.6	6	.379	72	12.0	3.5	2.2
Bryon Russell	20	.461	245	12.3	4.6	1.4	6	.390	68	11.3	5.8	0.7
Howard Eisley	20	.500	112	5.6	0.9	2.0	6	.500	32	5.3	0.7	2.5
Antoine Carr	20	.482	98	4.9	2.0	0.5	6	.409	18	3.0	1.7	0.8
Greg Ostertag	20	.410	94	4.7	6.8	0.3	6	.400	26	4.3	7.3	0.3
Shandon Anderson	18	.439	83	4.6	2.7	0.7	4	.316	17	4.3	1.8	0.5
Greg Foster	20	.389	84	4.2	2.8	0.6	6	.476	33	5.5	3.5	0.7
Chris Morris	20	.400	57	2.9	1.6	0.3	6	.471	21	3.5	1.7	0.2
Stephen Howard	5	.500	9	1.8	0.2	0.0	—	—	—	—	—	—
Adam Keefe	8	.333	8	1.0	2.0	0.3	4	.333	3	0.8	1.8	0.3
JAZZ	20	.452	1922	96.1	41.8	21.8	6	.430	523	87.2	40.8	20.2
OPPONENTS	20	.438	1856	92.8	38.0	19.3	6	.432	527	87.8	40.3	19.7

Three-pointers: PLAYOFFS—Russell (36-for-101), Stockton (19-50), Hornacek (19-53), Eisley (9-19), Morris (8-25), Anderson (5-12), Foster (2-8), Malone (1-2), Team (99-270 for .367 pct.); FINALS—Russell (15-for-34), Stockton (6-15), Hornacek (6-16), Morris (5-10), Eisley (1-2), Foster (1-3), Anderson (1-4), Team (35-85 for .412 pct.).

Annual Awards

Most Valuable Player

The Maurice Podoloff Trophy; voting by 115-member panel of local and national pro basketball writers and broadcasters. Each ballot has five entries; points awarded on 10-7-5-3-1 basis.

	1st	2nd	3rd	4th	5th	Pts
Karl Malone, Utah	.63	48	4	0	0	986
Michael Jordan, Chicago	.52	61	2	0	0	957
Grant Hill, Detroit	.0	3	54	23	16	376
Tim Hardaway, Miami	.0	1	17	43	17	238
Glen Rice, Charlotte	.0	1	13	13	23	134
Gary Payton, Seattle	.0	0	10	15	10	105
Hakeem Olajuwon, Hou.	.0	1	7	11	20	95
Patrick Ewing, New York	.0	0	5	5	17	57
Anthony Mason, Charlotte	.0	0	1	0	2	7
Shaquille O'Neal, LA Lakers	.0	0	0	2	1	7
Scottie Pippen, Chicago	.0	0	1	0	1	6
Alonzo Mourning, Miami	.0	0	1	0	0	5
Dikembe Mutombo, Atlanta	.0	0	0	1	1	4
Mitch Richmond, Sacramento	.0	0	0	1	1	4
John Stockton, Utah	.0	0	0	1	0	3
Charles Barkley, Phoenix	.0	0	0	0	2	2
Allen Iverson, Philadelphia	.0	0	0	0	1	1
Tom Gugliotta, Minnesota	.0	0	0	0	1	1
Kevin Johnson, Phoenix	.0	0	0	0	1	1
Steve Smith, Atlanta	.0	0	0	0	1	1

All-NBA Teams

Voting by a 115-member panel of local and national pro basketball writers and broadcasters. Each ballot has entries for three teams; points awarded on 5-3-1 basis. First Team repeaters from 1995-96 are in **bold** type.

Pos	First Team	1st	Pts
F	**Karl Malone**, Utah	115	575
F	Grant Hill, Detroit	76	483
C	Hakeem Olajuwon, Houston	89	514
G	**Michael Jordan**, Chicago	115	575
G	Tim Hardaway, Miami	62	435

Pos	Second Team	1st	Pts
F	Scottie Pippen, Chicago	19	337
F	Glen Rice, Charlotte	20	316
C	Patrick Ewing, New York	20	327
G	Gary Payton, Seattle	42	386
G	Mitch Richmond, Sacramento	1	198

Pos	Third Team	1st	Pts
F	Anthony Mason, Charlotte	0	110
F	Vin Baker, Milwaukee	0	61
C	Shaquille O'Neal, LA Lakers	3	72
G	John Stockton, Utah	6	142
G	Anfernee Hardaway, Orlando	2	62

All-Defensive Teams

Voting by NBA head coaches. Each ballot has entries for two teams; two points given for 1st team, one for 2nd. Coaches cannot vote for own players. First Team repeaters from 1995-96 are in **bold** type.

Pos	First Team	1st	Pts
F	**Scottie Pippen**, Chicago	26	53
F	Karl Malone, Utah	10	25
C	Dikembe Mutombo, Atlanta	23	50
G	**Gary Payton**, Seattle	21	49
G	**Michael Jordan**, Chicago	23	51

Pos	Second Team	1st	Pts
F	Anthony Mason, Charlotte	6	22
F	P.J. Brown, Miami	4	19
C	Hakeem Olajuwon, Houston	6	26
G	Mookie Blaylock, Atlanta	10	35
G	John Stockton, Utah	2	9

Coach of the Year

The Red Auerbach Trophy; voting by 115-member panel of local and national pro basketball writers and broadcasters. Each ballot has one entry.

	Votes	Improvement
Pat Riley, Miami	.69	42-40 to 61-21
Dave Cowens, Charlotte	.22	41-41 to 54-28
Jerry Sloan, Utah	.13	55-27 to 64-18
Danny Ainge, Phoenix	.5	41-41 to 40-42
Doug Collins, Detroit	.3	46-36 to 54-28
Bill Fitch, LA Clippers	.1	29-53 to 36-46

Rookie of the Year

The Eddie Gottlieb Trophy; voting by 115-member panel of local and national pro basketball writers and broadcasters. Each ballot has one entry.

	Pos	Votes
Allen Iverson, Philadelphia	.G	44
Stephon Marbury, Minnesota	.G	35
Shareef Abdur-Rahim, Vancouver	.F	25

All-Rookie Team

Voting by NBA's 29 head coaches, who cannot vote for players on their team. Each ballot has entries for two five-man teams, regardless of position; two points given for 1st team, one for 2nd. First team votes in parentheses.

First Team	College	Pts
Shareef Abdur-Rahim, Van. (28)	California	56
Allen Iverson, Philadelphia (27)	Georgetown	55
Stephon Marbury, Minnesota (27)	Georgia Tech	55
Marcus Camby, Toronto (22)	Massachusetts	49
Antoine Walker, Boston (22)	Kentucky	49

Second Team	College	Pts
Kerry Kittles, New Jersey (13)	Villanova	41
Ray Allen, Milwaukee (4)	Connecticut	31
Travis Knight, LA Lakers	Connecticut	18
Kobe Bryant, LA Lakers	none	15
Matt Maloney, Houston	Pennsylvania	13

IBM Award

Created prior to the 1983-84 season to honor the player who contributes most to his team's overall success and utilizes a computer evaluation of key offensive and defensive statistics to determine an overall leader. The formula is as follows: (Player pts.-FGA+REB+AST+STL+BLK-PF-TO+(team wins x 10) x 250)/(team pts.-FGA+REB+AST+STL+BLK-PF-TO).

	Pos	Pts
Grant Hill, Detroit	F	112.10
Karl Malone, Utah	F	97.42
Patrick Ewing, New York	C	97.00
Tim Hardaway, Miami	G	89.30
Mark Jackson, Indiana	G	86.80
Alonzo Mourning, Miami	C	85.69
Vin Baker, Milwaukee	F	84.66
Michael Jordan, Chicago	G	84.50

Other Awards

Defensive Player of the Year— Dikembe Mutombo, Atlanta; **Most Improved Player**— Isaac Austin, Miami; **Sixth Man Award**— John Starks, New York; **Kennedy PBWAA Citizenship Award**— P.J. Brown, Miami; **NBA Sportsmanship Award**— Terrell Brandon, Cleveland; **The Sporting News Executive of the Year**— Bob Bass, Charlotte.

1997 College Draft

First and second round picks at the 51st annual NBA College Draft held June 25, 1997 at Charlotte Coliseum. The order of the first 11 positions were determined by a Draft Lottery held May 18, in Secaucus, N.J. Toronto and Vancouver were not eligible to receive the first pick and Washington forfeited its 1997 first-round draft pick in connection with its signing of Juwan Howard. The Wizards would have had the 17th pick in the draft. Positions 12 through 28 reflect regular season records in reverse order. Underclassmen selected are noted in CAPITAL letters.

First Round

	Team		Pos
1	San Antonio	Tim Duncan, Wake Forest	C
2	a-Philadelphia	Keith Van Horn, Utah	F
3	Boston	CHAUNCEY BILLUPS, Colorado	G
4	Vancouver	Antonio Daniels, Bowling Green	G
5	Denver	TONY BATTIE, Texas Tech	C
6	b-Boston	RON MERCER, Kentucky	G/F
7	a-New Jersey	TIM THOMAS, Villanova	F
8	Golden St.	ADONAL FOYLE, Colgate	C
9	Toronto	TRACY McGRADY, Mt. Zion Acad. (HS)	F
10	c-Milwaukee	DANNY FORTSON, Cincinnati	F
11	Sacramento	OLIVIER SAINT-JEAN, San Jose St.	F
12	Indiana	Austin Croshere, Providence	F
13	Cleveland	Derek Anderson, Kentucky	G
14	LA Clippers	MAURICE TAYLOR, Michigan	F
15	d-Dallas	Kelvin Cato, Iowa St.	C
16	e-Cleveland	Brevin Knight, Stanford	G
17	Orlando	Johnny Taylor, Tenn-Chattanooga	F
18	Portland	Chris Anstey, SE Melbourne Magic	C
19	Detroit	Scot Pollard, Kansas	C
20	f-Minnesota	Paul Grant, Wisconsin	C
21	a-New Jersey	Anthony Parker, Bradley	G
22	Atlanta	Ed Gray, California	G
23	g-Seattle	Bobby Jackson, Minnesota	G
24	Houston	Rodrick Rhodes, USC	G/F
25	New York	John Thomas, Minnesota	F
26	Miami	Charles Smith, New Mexico	G
27	Utah	Jacque Vaughn, Kansas	G
28	Chicago	Keith Booth, Maryland	F

Second Round

	Team		Pos
30	h-Houston	Serge Zwikker, North Carolina	C
31	i-Miami	MARK SANFORD, Washington	F
32	j-Detroit	Charles O'Bannon, UCLA	F
33	Denver	JAMES COTTON, Long Beach St.	G
34	Philadelphia	Marko Milic, Smelt Olimpija	F
35	Dallas	Bubba Wells, Austin Peay	F
36	k-Philadelphia	Kebu Stewart, CS-Bakersfield	F
37	l-Philadelphia	James Collins, Florida St.	G
38	Golden St.	MARC JACKSON, Temple	C
39	Milwaukee	Jerald Honeycutt, Tulane	F
40	Sacramento	Anthony Johnson, Coll. of Charleston	G
41	m-Seattle	Ed Elisma, Georgia Tech	F
42	n-Denver	Jason Lawson, Villanova	C
43	Phoenix	STEPHEN JACKSON, Butler County CC	F
44	Minnesota	GORDON MALONE, West Virginia	F
45	Cleveland	Cedric Henderson, Memphis	F
46	Washington	GOD SHAMMGOD, Providence	G
47	n-Orlando	Eric Washington, Alabama	G
48	Portland	Alvin Williams, Villanova	G
49	o-Washington	Predrag Drobnjak, Partizan	C
50	p-Atlanta	Alain Digbeu, Villurbanne (France)	G
51	Atlanta	Chris Crawford, Marquette	F
52	LA Lakers	DeJuan Wheat, Louisville	G
53	q-Vancouver	CJ BRUTON, Indian Hills JC	G
54	r-LA Lakers	PAUL ROGERS, Gonzaga	C
55	Seattle	MARK BLOUNT, Pittsburgh	C
56	s-Boston	Ben Pepper, Newcastle Falcons (NBL)	C
57	Utah	Nate Erdmann, Oklahoma	G
58	Chicago	Roberto Duenas, FC Barcelona (Spain)	C

Acquired Picks

FIRST ROUND: a-Philadelphia traded the rights to F Keith Van Horn and F Don MacLean, F/C Michael Cage and G Lucious Harris to New Jersey for the rights to F Tim Thomas, G Anthony Parker (pick from LA Lakers), G Jim Jackson and C Eric Montross; b-from Dallas; c-Milwaukee traded F Johnny Newman, F/C Joe Wolf and the rights to F Danny Fortson to Denver for C Ervin Johnson; d-Dallas traded the rights to C Kelvin Cato (pick from Minnesota) to Portland for the rights to C Chris Anstey and an undisclosed amount of cash; e-from Phoenix; f- from Portland via Charlotte; g-Seattle traded the rights to G Bobby Jackson to Denver for the rights to G James Cotton and a 1998 second-round draft pick. SECOND ROUND: h-from Vancouver; i-from Boston; j-from San Antonio; k-from New Jersey; l-Philadelphia traded Collins (pick from Toronto) to LA Clippers for 1998 second-round pick; m-from LA Clippers; n-Denver traded Lawson (pick from Indiana) to Orlando for rights to G Eric Washington a 1999 second-round pick; o-from Charlotte; p-from Detroit; q-from Houston; r-from New York; s-from Miami.

1997 European Clubs Championship

The European Championship of Men's Clubs was played at the PalaEur in Rome, April 22-24, 1997. Also known as the European Final Four, the championship of what is known as EuroLeague Men debuted a new playing format this year. Now, the title is competed for by 24 clubs divided into four groups of six.

Final 16

Games played Mar. 6-13, 1997.
Pall. Olimpia Stefanel, Milan (ITA) def. Virtus Bologna Kinder (ITA) 2 games to 1.
Smelt Olimpija, Ljubljana (SLO) def. KK Cibona, Zagreb (CRO) 2 games to 1.
Panathinaikos, Athens (GRE) def. Limoges Geant (FRA) 2 games to 0.
Olympiakos B.C., Piraeus (GRE) def. Partizan-Inex, Belgrade (YUG) 2 games to 1.
Teamsystem Bologna (ITA) def. Caja San Fernando, Seville (SPA) 2 games to 0.
FC Barcelona (SPA) def. Alba Berlin (GER) 2 games to 0.
Efes Pilsen, Istanbul (TUR) def. Maccabi Elite, Tel Aviv (ISR) 2 games to 1.
ASVEL, Villerbanne (FRA) def. Estudiantes, Madrid (SPA) 2 games to 1.

Olympiakos BC 2	Panathinaikos 0
FC Barcelona 2	Teamsystem Bologna 1
Villurbanne 2	Efes Pilsen 1

Semifinals

Olympiakos BC 74	Smelt Olimpija 65
FC Barcelona 77	Villurbanne 70

Third Place

Smelt Olimpija 86 ... Villurbanne 79

Quarterfinals

Games played Mar. 27-Apr. 3, 1997.

Smelt Olimpija 2 ... Pall. Olimpia Stefanel 1

Championship Game

Olympiakos (GRE)	31	42—	**73**
FC Barcelona (SPA)	29	29—	**58**

Most Valuable Player

David Rivers, Olympiakos, guard

Continental Basketball Association
Final Standings

QW refers to quarters won. Teams get 3 points for a win, 1 point for each quarter won and ½ point for any quarters tied. Avg refers to average points per game played. (*) denotes playoff qualifiers.

American Conference

	W	L	QW	Pts	Home	Road
*Florida	38	18	137.5	251.5	21-7	17-11
*Grand Rapids .	32	24	124.5	220.5	19-9	13-15
*Quad City ...	27	29	110.0	191.0	16-12	11-17
*Rockford	28	28	105.0	189.0	19-9	9-19
Connecticut ..	21	35	107.5	170.5	15-13	6-22
Fort Wayne .	20	36	93.0	153.0	16-12	4-24

National Conference

	W	L	QW	Pts	Home	Road
*Sioux Falls ...	47	9	134.0	275.0	26-2	21-7
*Oklahoma City .	29	27	120.0	207.0	18-10	11-17
*Yakima	25	31	103.0	178.0	17-11	8-20
*Omaha	22	34	97.5	164.8	14-14	8-20
La Crosse ...	19	37	100.0	157.0	12-16	7-21

Playoffs
First two rounds are Best of 5

American Conference
First Round

Florida def. Rockford, 3 games to 0
Grand Rapids def. Quad City, 3 games to 2

Second Round

Florida def. Grand Rapids, 3 games to 2

National Conference
First Round

Omaha def. Sioux Falls, 3 games to 2
Oklahoma City def. Yakima, 3 games to 2

Second Round

Oklahoma City def. Omaha, 3 games to 1

Finals (Best of 7)
Oklahoma City wins series, 4 games to 2

	W-L	Avg	Leading Scorer
Oklahoma City	4-2	95.7	Bennett (18.3)
Florida	2-4	93.7	Robinson (17.0)

Date	Winner	Home Court
Apr. 15	Florida, 95-79	at Florida
Apr. 17	Oklahoma City, 99-97	at Florida
Apr. 19	Oklahoma City, 104-93	at Oklahoma City
Apr. 20	Florida, 103-96	at Oklahoma City
Apr. 22	Oklahoma City, 104-92	at Oklahoma City
Apr. 24	Oklahoma City, 92-82	at Florida

CBA Annual Awards

Most Valuable Player: Dexter Boney, Florida

Newcomer of the Year: Anthony Tucker, Florida

Rookies of the Year: Jason Sasser, Sioux Falls & Bernard Hopkins, Yakima

Defensive Player of the Year: Corey Beck, Sioux Falls

Coach of the Year: Mo McHone, Sioux Falls

Playoff MVP: Elmer Bennett, Oklahoma City

CBA Regular Season Individual Leaders

Scoring

	Gm	Pts	Avg
Gaylon Nickerson, Okla. City	41	923	22.5
Reggie Slater, La Crosse	30	671	22.4
Tony Harris, Sioux Falls	51	1126	22.1
Dexter Boney, Florida	41	890	21.7
Paul Graham, Omaha	56	1163	20.8

Blocks

	Gm	Blk	Avg
Jimmy Carruth, Ft. Wayne	50	190	3.8
Mike Bell, Sioux Falls	36	86	2.4
Kurt Portmann, Quad City	54	110	2.0
Michael McDonald, G. Rapids	56	99	1.8
Horacio Llamas, Sioux Falls	38	63	1.7

Rebounding

	Gm	Reb	Avg
Anthony Tucker, Florida	56	564	10.1
Stacey King, Sioux Falls	45	433	9.6
Kevin Holland, Yakima	54	496	9.2
Reggie Slater, La Crosse	30	269	9.0
Sylvester Gray, Yakima	31	267	8.6

Steals

	Gm	Stl	Avg
Michael Hawkins, Rockford	35	82	2.3
Stevin Smith, Sioux Falls	53	113	2.1
Dexter Boney, Florida	41	87	2.1
Terrence Rencher, Florida	54	113	2.1
Ruben Nembhard, Yakima	29	59	2.0

Assists

	Gm	Ast	Avg
Michael Hawkins, Rockford	35	325	9.3
Elmer Bennett, Okla. City	32	283	8.8
Chucky Atkins, La Crosse	50	375	7.5
Kelsey Weems, Omaha	51	357	7.0
Rick Brunson, Quad City	56	380	6.8

Field Goal Percentage

	FGM	FGA	FG%
Bernard Hopkins, Yakima	317	519	.611
Reggie Slater, La Crosse	258	423	.610
Tracey Ware, Florida	160	267	.599
Erik Martin, Omaha	184	310	.594
Justin Jennings, G. Rapids	103	174	.592

Women's Professional Basketball

American Basketball League

Final ABL Standings

Conference champions (*) and playoff qualifiers (†) are noted. GB refers to Games Behind leader.

Eastern Conference	W	L	Pct	GB
*Columbus	31	9	.775	—
†Richmond	21	19	.525	10
Atlanta	18	22	.450	13
New England	16	24	.400	15

Western Conference	W	L	Pct	GB
*Colorado	25	15	.625	—
†San Jose	18	22	.450	7
Seattle	17	23	.425	8
Portland	14	26	.350	11

ABL Playoffs
Semifinals

Date	Result
Feb. 23	at Richmond 80, Colorado 77
Feb. 25	Richmond 82, at Colorado 68
	Richmond wins series, 2-0

Date	Result
Feb. 23	Columbus 94, at San Jose 69
Feb. 25	at Columbus 81, San Jose 69
	Columbus wins series, 2-0

Finals (Best of 5)
Columbus wins series, 3 games to 2

	W-L	Avg	Leading Scorer
Columbus	3-2	78.2	Edwards (16.8)
Richmond	2-3	76.8	McWilliams (19.8)

Date	Winner	Home Court
Mar. 2	Columbus, 90-89	at Columbus
Mar. 4	Richmond, 75-62	at Columbus
Mar. 8	Richmond, 72-67	at Richmond
Mar. 9	Columbus, 95-84	at Richmond
Mar. 11	Columbus, 77-64	at Columbus

ABL Annual Awards

Most Valuable Player: Nikki McCray, Columbus
New Pro Award: Crystal Robinson, Colorado
Defensive Player of the Year: Debbie Black, Colo.
Coach of the Year: Brian Agler, Columbus

Women's National Basketball Association

Final WNBA Standings

Conference champions (*) and playoff qualifiers (†) are noted. GB refers to Games Behind leader.

Eastern Conference	W	L	Pct	GB
*Houston	18	10	.643	—
†New York	17	11	.607	1
†Charlotte	15	13	.536	3
Cleveland	15	13	.536	3

Western Conference	W	L	Pct	GB
*Phoenix	16	12	.571	—
Los Angeles	14	14	.500	2
Sacramento	10	18	.357	6
Utah	7	21	.250	9

WNBA Playoffs
Semifinals
Single-game elimination

Date	Result
Aug. 28	at Houston 70, Charlotte 54

(Leading Scorer: Cynthia Cooper, Hou., 31 pts.)

Date	Result
Aug. 28	New York 59, at Phoenix 41

(Leading Scorer: Rebecca Lobo, NY, 16 pts.)

Championship Game

Date	Result
Aug. 30	at Houston 65, New York 51

(Leading Scorer: Cynthia Cooper, Hou. 25 pts.)

All-WNBA First Team

Voting was done by a 37-member panel consisting of national and local media from the eight WNBA cities. Points were awarded on a 5-3 basis. Unanimous First-Team selection is in **bold**.

		Points
G	**Cynthia Cooper**, Houston	185
G	Ruthie Bolton-Holifield, Sac.	109
C	Lisa Leslie, Los Angeles	159
F	Eva Nemcova, Cleveland	129
F	Tina Thompson, Houston	137

WNBA Annual Awards

Most Valuable Player: Cynthia Cooper, Houston
Sportsmanship Award: Haixia Zheng, Los Angeles
Defensive Player of the Year: Teresa Weatherspoon, New York
Coach of the Year: Van Chancellor, Houston

THE 1998

PRO BASKETBALL
S T A T I S T I C S

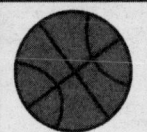

THROUGH THE YEARS
1947-1997
CHAMPIONS • NBA LEADERS

SEC
B

PAGE
360

The NBA Finals

Although the National Basketball Association traces its first championship back to the 1946-47 season, the league was then called the Basketball Association of America (BAA). It did not become the NBA until after the 1948-49 season when the BAA and the National Basketball League (NBL) agreed to merge.

In the chart below, the Eastern finalists (representing the NBA Eastern Division from 1947-70, and the NBA Eastern Conference since 1971) are listed in CAPITAL letters. Also, each NBA champion's wins and losses are noted in parentheses after the series score.

Multiple winners: Boston (16); Minneapolis-LA Lakers (11); Chicago Bulls (5); Phi-SF-Golden St. Warriors and Syracuse Nationals-Phi. 76ers (3); Detroit, Houston and New York (2).

Year	Winner	Head Coach	Series	Loser	Head Coach
1947	PHILADELPHIA WARRIORS	Eddie Gottlieb	4-1 (WWWLW)	Chicago Stags	Harold Olsen
1948	Baltimore Bullets	Buddy Jeannette	4-2 (LWWWLW)	PHILA. WARRIORS	Eddie Gottlieb
1949	Minneapolis Lakers	John Kundla	4-2 (WWWLLW)	WASH. CAPITOLS	Red Auerbach
1950	Minneapolis Lakers	John Kundla	4-2 (WLWWLW)	SYRACUSE	Al Cervi
1951	Rochester	Les Harrison	4-3 (WWWLLLW)	NEW YORK	Joe Lapchick
1952	Minneapolis Lakers	John Kundla	4-3 (WLWLWLW)	NEW YORK	Joe Lapchick
1953	Minneapolis Lakers	John Kundla	4-1 (WWWW)	NEW YORK	Joe Lapchick
1954	Minneapolis Lakers	John Kundla	4-3 (WLWLWLW)	SYRACUSE	Al Cervi
1955	SYRACUSE	Al Cervi	4-3 (WWLLLWW)	Ft. Wayne Pistons	Charley Eckman
1956	PHILADELPHIA WARRIORS	George Senesky	4-1 (WWWW)	Ft. Wayne Pistons	Charley Eckman
1957	BOSTON	Red Auerbach	4-3 (LWLWLWW)	St. Louis Hawks	Alex Hannum
1958	St. Louis Hawks	Alex Hannum	4-2 (WLWLWW)	BOSTON	Red Auerbach
1959	BOSTON	Red Auerbach	4-0	Mpls. Lakers	John Kundla
1960	BOSTON	Red Auerbach	4-3 (WLWLWLW)	St. Louis Hawks	Ed Macauley
1961	BOSTON	Red Auerbach	4-1 (WWLWW)	St. Louis Hawks	Paul Seymour
1962	BOSTON	Red Auerbach	4-3 (WLLWLWW)	LA Lakers	Fred Schaus
1963	BOSTON	Red Auerbach	4-2 (WWLWLW)	LA Lakers	Fred Schaus
1964	BOSTON	Red Auerbach	4-1 (WWLWW)	SF Warriors	Alex Hannum
1965	BOSTON	Red Auerbach	4-1 (WWLWW)	LA Lakers	Fred Schaus
1966	BOSTON	Red Auerbach	4-3 (WLWWLLW)	LA Lakers	Fred Schaus
1967	PHILADELPHIA 76ERS	Alex Hannum	4-2 (WWLWLW)	SF Warriors	Bill Sharman
1968	BOSTON	Bill Russell	4-2 (WLWLWW)	LA Lakers	B.van Breda Kolff
1969	BOSTON	Bill Russell	4-3 (LLWWLWW)	LA Lakers	B.van Breda Kolff
1970	NEW YORK	Red Holzman	4-3 (WLWLWLW)	LA Lakers	Joe Mullaney
1971	Milwaukee	Larry Costello	4-0	BALT. BULLETS	Gene Shue
1972	LA Lakers	Bill Sharman	4-1 (LWWWW)	NEW YORK	Red Holzman
1973	NEW YORK	Red Holzman	4-1 (LWWWW)	LA Lakers	Bill Sharman
1974	BOSTON	Tommy Heinsohn	4-3 (WLWLWLW)	Milwaukee	Larry Costello
1975	Golden St. Warriors	Al Attles	4-0	WASH. BULLETS	K.C. Jones
1976	BOSTON	Tommy Heinsohn	4-2 (WWLLWW)	Phoenix	John MacLeod
1977	Portland	Jack Ramsay	4-2 (LLWWWW)	PHILA. 76ERS	Gene Shue
1978	WASHINGTON BULLETS	Dick Motta	4-3 (LWLWLWW)	Seattle	Lenny Wilkens
1979	Seattle	Lenny Wilkens	4-1 (LWWWW)	WASH. BULLETS	Dick Motta
1980	LA Lakers	Paul Westhead	4-2 (WLWLWW)	PHILA. 76ERS	Billy Cunningham
1981	BOSTON	Bill Fitch	4-2 (WLWLWW)	Houston	Del Harris
1982	LA Lakers	Pat Riley	4-2 (WLWLWLW)	PHILA. 76ERS	Billy Cunningham
1983	PHILADELPHIA 76ERS	Billy Cunningham	4-0	LA Lakers	Pat Riley
1984	BOSTON	K.C. Jones	4-3 (LWWLWLW)	LA Lakers	Pat Riley
1985	LA Lakers	Pat Riley	4-2 (LWWLWW)	BOSTON	K.C. Jones
1986	BOSTON	K.C. Jones	4-2 (WWLWLW)	Houston	Bill Fitch
1987	LA Lakers	Pat Riley	4-2 (WWLWLW)	BOSTON	K.C. Jones
1988	LA Lakers	Pat Riley	4-3 (LWWLLWW)	DETROIT PISTONS	Chuck Daly
1989	DETROIT PISTONS	Chuck Daly	4-0	LA Lakers	Pat Riley
1990	DETROIT	Chuck Daly	4-1 (WLWWW)	Portland	Rick Adelman
1991	CHICAGO	Phil Jackson	4-1 (LWWWW)	LA Lakers	Mike Dunleavy
1992	CHICAGO	Phil Jackson	4-2 (WLWWLW)	Portland	Rick Adelman
1993	CHICAGO	Phil Jackson	4-2 (WWLWLW)	Phoenix	Paul Westphal

Year	Winner	Head Coach	Series	Loser	Head Coach
1994	Houston	Rudy Tomjanovich	4-3 (WLWLLWW)	NEW YORK	Pat Riley
1995	Houston	Rudy Tomjanovich	4-0	ORLANDO	Brian Hill
1996	CHICAGO	Phil Jackson	4-2 (WWWLLW)	Seattle	George Karl
1997	CHICAGO	Phil Jackson	4-2 (WWLLWW)	Utah	Jerry Sloan

Note: Four finalists were led by player-coaches: **1948**—Buddy Jeannette (guard) of Baltimore; **1950**—Al Cervi (guard) of Syracuse; **1968**—Bill Russell (center) of Boston; **1969**—Bill Russell (center) of Boston.

Most Valuable Player

Selected by an 11-member media panel. Winner who did not play for the NBA champion is in **bold** type.

Multiple winners: Michael Jordan (5); Magic Johnson (3); Kareem Abdul-Jabbar, Larry Bird, Hakeem Olajuwon and Willis Reed (2).

Year		Year		Year	
1969	**Jerry West**, LA Lakers, G	1979	Dennis Johnson, Seattle, G	1989	Joe Dumars, Detroit, G
1970	Willis Reed, New York, C	1980	Magic Johnson, LA Lakers, G/C	1990	Isiah Thomas, Detroit, G
1971	Lew Alcindor, Milwaukee, C	1981	Cedric Maxwell, Boston, F	1991	Michael Jordan, Chicago, G
1972	Wilt Chamberlain, LA Lakers, C	1982	Magic Johnson, LA Lakers, G	1992	Michael Jordan, Chicago, G
1973	Willis Reed, New York, C	1983	Moses Malone, Philadelphia, C	1993	Michael Jordan, Chicago, G
1974	John Havlicek, Boston, F	1984	Larry Bird, Boston, F	1994	Hakeem Olajuwon, Houston, C
1975	Rick Barry, Golden State, F	1985	K. Abdul-Jabbar, LA Lakers, C	1995	Hakeem Olajuwon, Houston, C
1976	Jo Jo White, Boston, G	1986	Larry Bird, Boston, F	1996	Michael Jordan, Chicago, G
1977	Bill Walton, Portland, C	1987	Magic Johnson, LA Lakers, G	1997	Michael Jordan, Chicago, G
1978	Wes Unseld, Washington, C	1988	James Worthy, LA Lakers, F		

Note: Lew Alcindor changed his name to Kareem Abdul-Jabbar after the 1970-71 season.

All-Time NBA Playoff Leaders

Through the 1997 playoffs.

CAREER

Years listed indicate number of playoff appearances. Players active in 1997 playoffs in **bold** type.

Points

		Yrs	Gm	Pts	Avg
1	Kareem Abdul-Jabbar	18	237	5762	24.3
2	**Michael Jordan**	12	158	5307	33.6
3	Jerry West	13	153	4457	29.1
4	Larry Bird	12	164	3897	23.8
5	John Havlicek	13	172	3776	22.0
6	Magic Johnson	13	190	3701	19.5
7	Elgin Baylor	12	134	3623	27.0
8	Wilt Chamberlain	13	160	3607	22.5
9	**Hakeem Olajuwon**	12	131	3572	27.3
10	Kevin McHale	13	169	3182	18.8
11	**Karl Malone**	12	117	3165	27.1
12	Dennis Johnson	13	180	3116	17.3
13	Julius Erving	11	141	3088	21.9
14	James Worthy	9	143	3022	21.1
15	Sam Jones	12	154	2909	18.9
16	**Clyde Drexler**	14	140	2888	20.6
17	**Scottie Pippen**	10	157	2864	18.2
18	**Robert Parish**	16	184	2820	15.3
19	**Charles Barkley**	11	115	2703	23.5
20	Bill Russell	13	165	2673	16.2

Scoring Average

Minimum of 25 games or 700 points.

		Yrs	Gm	Pts	Avg
1	**Michael Jordan**	12	158	5307	33.6
2	Jerry West	13	153	4457	29.1
3	**Hakeem Olajuwon**	12	131	3572	27.3
4	**Karl Malone**	12	117	3165	27.1
5	Elgin Baylor	12	134	3623	27.0
6	George Gervin	9	59	1592	27.0
7	Dominique Wilkins	9	55	1421	25.8
8	**Shaquille O'Neal**	4	45	1153	25.6
9	Bob Pettit	9	88	2240	25.5
10	Rick Barry	7	74	1833	24.8
11	Reggie Miller	7	49	1211	24.7
12	Bernard King	5	28	687	24.5
13	Alex English	10	68	1661	24.4
14	Kareem Abdul-Jabbar	18	237	5762	24.3
15	Paul Arizin	8	49	1186	24.2
16	David Robinson	6	53	1273	24.0
17	Larry Bird	12	164	3897	23.8
18	George Mikan	9	91	2141	23.5
19	**Charles Barkley**	11	115	2703	23.5
20	Bob Love	6	47	1076	22.9

Field Goals

		Yrs	FG	Att	Pct
1	Kareem Abdul-Jabbar	18	2356	4422	.533
2	**Michael Jordan**	12	1945	3971	.490
3	Jerry West	13	1622	3460	.469
4	Larry Bird	12	1458	3090	.472
5	John Havlicek	13	1451	3329	.436
6	**Hakeem Olajuwon**	11	1430	2672	.535
7	Wilt Chamberlain	13	1425	2728	.522
8	Elgin Baylor	12	1388	3161	.439
9	Magic Johnson	13	1291	2552	.506
10	James Worthy	9	1267	2329	.544

Free Throws

		Yrs	FT	Att	Pct
1	**Michael Jordan**	12	1282	1543	.831
2	Jerry West	13	1213	1507	.805
3	Kareem Abdul-Jabbar	18	1050	1419	.740
4	Magic Johnson	12	1040	1241	.838
5	Larry Bird	12	901	1012	.891
6	John Havlicek	13	874	1046	.836
7	**Karl Malone**	12	872	1204	.724
8	Elgin Baylor	12	847	1101	.769
9	Kevin McHale	13	766	972	.788
10	Wilt Chamberlain	13	757	1627	.465

Assists

		Yrs	Gm	No	Avg
1	Magic Johnson	13	190	2346	12.3
2	**John Stockton**	13	127	1366	10.8
3	Larry Bird	12	164	1062	6.5
4	Dennis Johnson	13	180	1006	5.6
5	Isiah Thomas	9	111	987	8.9

Appearances

	No		No
Kareem Abdul-Jabbar	18	John Havlicek	13
Robert Parish	16	Kevin McHale	13
Dolph Schayes	15	Dennis Johnson	13
Paul Silas	14	Magic Johnson	13
Wilt Chamberlain	13	Bill Russell	13
Maurice Cheeks	13	Chet Walker	13
Bob Cousy	13	Jerry West	13
Hal Greer	13		

Rebounds

		Yrs	Gm	No	Avg
1	Bill Russell	13	165	4104	24.9
2	Wilt Chamberlain	13	160	3913	24.5
3	Kareem Abdul-Jabbar	18	237	2481	10.5
4	Wes Unseld	12	119	1777	14.9
5	**Robert Parish**	16	184	1765	9.6

Games Played

	No		No
K. Abdul-Jabbar	237	Kevin McHale	169
Danny Ainge	193	Michael Cooper	168
Magic Johnson	190	Bill Russell	165
Robert Parish	184	Larry Bird	164
Byron Scott	183	Paul Silas	163
Dennis Johnson	180	Wilt Chamberlain	160
John Havlicek	170	**Michael Jordan**	158

SINGLE GAME

Points

	Date	FG-FT–Pts
Michael Jordan, Chi at Bos*	4/20/86	22-19–63
Elgin Baylor, LA at Bos	4/14/62	22-17–61
Wilt Chamberlain, Phi vs Syr	3/22/62	22-12–56
Michael Jordan, Chi at Mia	4/29/92	20-16–56
Charles Barkley, Pho vs G.St.	5/4/94	23-7–56
Rick Barry, SF vs Phi	4/18/67	22-11–55
Michael Jordan, Chi vs Cle	5/1/88	24-7–55
Michael Jordan, Chi vs Pho	4/16/93	21-13–55
Michael Jordan, Chi vs. Wash	4/27/97	22-10–55

*Double overtime.

Field Goals

	Date	FG	Att
Wilt Chamberlain, Phi vs Syr	3/14/60	24	42
John Havlicek, Bos vs Atl	4/1/73	24	36
Michael Jordan, Chi vs Cle	5/1/88	24	45

Eight tied with 22 each.

Miscellaneous

3-Pt Field Goals

	Date	No
Rex Chapman, Pho at Sea	4/25/97	9
Dan Majerle, Pho vs Sea	6/1/93	8

Eight tied with 7 each.

Assists

	Date	No
Magic Johnson, LA vs Pho	5/15/84	24
John Stockton, Utah at LA Lakers	5/17/88	24
Magic Johnson, LA Lakers at Port	5/3/85	23
John Stockton, Utah vs Port	4/25/96	23
Doc Rivers, Atl vs Bos	5/16/88	22

Four tied with 21 each.

Rebounds

	Date	No
Wilt Chamberlain, Phi vs Bos	4/5/67	41
Bill Russell, Bos vs Phi	3/23/58	40
Bill Russell, Bos vs St.L	3/29/60	40
Bill Russell, Bos vs LA*	4/18/62	40

Three tied with 39 each.

*Overtime.

NBA FINALS
Points

Series		Year	Pts
4-Gm	Hakeem Olajuwon, Hou vs Orl	1995	131
5-Gm	Jerry West, LA vs Bos	1965	169
6-Gm	Michael Jordan, Chi vs Pho	1993	246
7-Gm	Elgin Baylor, LA vs Bos	1962	284

Field Goals

Series		Year	No
4-Gm	Hakeem Olajuwon, Hou vs Orl	1995	56
5-Gm	Michael Jordan, Chi vs LAL	1991	63
6-Gm	Michael Jordan, Chi vs Pho	1993	101
7-Gm	Elgin Baylor, LA vs Bos	1962	101

Assists

Series		Year	No
4-Gm	Bob Cousy, Bos vs Mpls	1959	51
5-Gm	Magic Johnson, LAL vs Chi	1991	62
6-Gm	Magic Johnson, LAL vs Bos	1985	84
7-Gm	Magic Johnson, LA vs Bos	1984	95

Rebounds

Series		Year	No
4-Gm	Bill Russell, Bos vs Mpls	1959	118
5-Gm	Bill Russell, Bos vs St.L	1961	144
6-Gm	Wilt Chamberlain, Phi vs SF	1967	171
7-Gm	Bill Russell, Bos vs LA	1962	189

The National Basketball League

Formed in 1937 by three corporations-- General Electric and the Firestone and Goodyear rubber companies of Akron, Ohio-- who were interested in moving up from their midwestern industrial league origins and backing a fully professional league. The NBL started with 13 previously independent teams in 1937-38 and although GE, Firestone and Goodyear were gone by late 1942, ran 12 years before merging with the three-year-old Basketball Association of America in 1949 to form the NBA.

Multiple champions: Akron Firestone Non-Skids, Fort Wayne Zollner Pistons, Oshkosh All-Stars (2).

Year	Winner	Series	Loser	Year	Winner	Series	Loser
1938	Goodyear Wingfoots	2-1	Oshkosh All-Stars	1944	Ft. Wayne Pistons	3-0	Sheboygan Redskins
1939	Firestone Non-Skids	3-2	Oshkosh All-Stars	1945	Ft. Wayne Pistons	3-2	Sheboygan Redskins
1940	Firestone Non-Skids	3-2	Oshkosh All-Stars	1946	Rochester Royals	3-0	Sheboygan Redskins
1941	Oshkosh All-Stars	3-0	Sheboygan Redskins	1947	Chicago Gears	3-2	Rochester Royals
1942	Oshkosh All-Stars	2-1	Ft. Wayne Pistons	1948	Minneapolis Lakers	3-1	Rochester Royals
1943	Sheboygan Redskins	2-1	Ft. Wayne Pistons	1949	Anderson Packers	3-0	Oshkosh All-Stars

NBA All-Star Game

The NBA staged its first All-Star Game before 10,094 at Boston Garden on March 2, 1951. From that year on, the game has matched the best players in the East against the best in the West. Winning coaches are listed first. East leads series, 29-16.

Multiple MVP winners: Bob Pettit (4); Oscar Robertson (3); Bob Cousy, Julius Erving, Magic Johnson, Michael Jordan, Karl Malone and Isiah Thomas (2).

Year		Host	Coaches	Most Valuable Player
1951	East 111, West 94	Boston	Joe Lapchick, John Kundla	Ed Macauley, Boston
1952	East 108, West 91	Boston	Al Cervi, John Kundla	Paul Arizin, Philadelphia
1953	West 79, East 75	Ft. Wayne	John Kundla, Joe Lapchick	George Mikan, Minneapolis
1954	East 98, West 93 (OT)	New York	Joe Lapchick, John Kundla	Bob Cousy, Boston
1955	East 100, West 91	New York	Al Cervi, Charley Eckman	Bill Sharman, Boston
1956	West 108, East 94	Rochester	Charley Eckman, George Senesky	Bob Pettit, St. Louis
1957	East 109, West 97	Boston	Red Auerbach, Bobby Wanzer	Bob Cousy, Boston
1958	East 130, West 118	St. Louis	Red Auerbach, Alex Hannum	Bob Pettit, St. Louis
1959	West 124, East 108	Detroit	Ed Macauley, Red Auerbach	Bob Pettit, St. Louis & Elgin Baylor, Minneapolis
1960	East 125, West 115	Philadelphia	Red Auerbach, Ed Macauley	Wilt Chamberlain, Philadelphia
1961	West 153, East 131	Syracuse	Paul Seymour, Red Auerbach	Oscar Robertson, Cincinnati
1962	West 150, East 130	St. Louis	Fred Schaus, Red Auerbach	Bob Pettit, St. Louis
1963	East 115, West 108	Los Angeles	Red Auerbach, Fred Schaus	Bill Russell, Boston
1964	East 111, West 107	Boston	Red Auerbach, Fred Schaus	Oscar Robertson, Cincinnati
1965	East 124, West 123	St. Louis	Red Auerbach, Alex Hannum	Jerry Lucas, Cincinnati
1966	East 137, West 94	Cincinnati	Red Auerbach, Fred Schaus	Adrian Smith, Cincinnati
1967	West 135, East 120	San Francisco	Fred Schaus, Red Auerbach	Rick Barry, San Francisco
1968	East 144, West 124	New York	Alex Hannum, Bill Sharman	Hal Greer, Philadelphia
1969	East 123, West 112	Baltimore	Gene Shue, Richie Guerin	Oscar Robertson, Cincinnati
1970	East 142, West 135	Philadelphia	Red Holzman, Richie Guerin	Willis Reed, New York
1971	West 108, East 107	San Diego	Larry Costello, Red Holzman	Lenny Wilkens, Seattle
1972	West 112, East 110	Los Angeles	Bill Sharman, Tom Heinsohn	Jerry West, Los Angeles
1973	East 104, West 84	Chicago	Tom Heinsohn, Bill Sharman	Dave Cowens, Boston
1974	West 134, East 123	Seattle	Larry Costello, Tom Heinsohn	Bob Lanier, Detroit
1975	East 108, West 102	Phoenix	K.C. Jones, Al Attles	Walt Frazier, New York
1976	East 123, West 109	Philadelphia	Tom Heinsohn, Al Attles	Dave Bing, Washington
1977	West 125, East 124	Milwaukee	Larry Brown, Gene Shue	Julius Erving, Philadelphia
1978	East 133, West 125	Atlanta	Billy Cunningham, Jack Ramsay	Randy Smith, Buffalo
1979	West 134, East 129	Detroit	Lenny Wilkens, Dick Motta	David Thompson, Denver
1980	East 144, West 136 (OT)	Washington	Billy Cunningham, Lenny Wilkens	George Gervin, San Antonio
1981	East 123, West 120	Cleveland	Billy Cunningham, John MacLeod	Nate Archibald, Boston
1982	East 120, West 118	New Jersey	Bill Fitch, Pat Riley	Larry Bird, Boston
1983	East 132, West 123	Los Angeles	Billy Cunningham, Pat Riley	Julius Erving, Philadelphia
1984	East 154, West 145 (OT)	Denver	K.C. Jones, Frank Layden	Isiah Thomas, Detroit
1985	West 140, East 129	Indiana	Pat Riley, K.C. Jones	Ralph Sampson, Houston
1986	East 139, West 132	Dallas	K.C. Jones, Pat Riley	Isiah Thomas, Detroit
1987	West 154, East 149 (OT)	Seattle	Pat Riley, K.C. Jones	Tom Chambers, Seattle
1988	East 138, West 133	Chicago	Mike Fratello, Pat Riley	Michael Jordan, Chicago
1989	West 143, East 134	Houston	Pat Riley, Lenny Wilkens	Karl Malone, Utah
1990	East 130, West 113	Miami	Chuck Daly, Pat Riley	Magic Johnson, LA Lakers
1991	East 116, West 114	Charlotte	Chris Ford, Rick Adelman	Charles Barkley, Philadelphia
1992	West 153, East 113	Orlando	Don Nelson, Phil Jackson	Magic Johnson, LA Lakers
1993	West 135, East 132 (OT)	Salt Lake City	Paul Westphal, Pat Riley	Karl Malone, Utah & John Stockton, Utah
1994	East 127, West 118	Minneapolis	Lenny Wilkens, George Karl	Scottie Pippen, Chicago
1995	West 139, East 112	Phoenix	Paul Westphal, Brian Hill	Mitch Richmond, Sacramento
1996	East 129, West 118	San Antonio	Phil Jackson, George Karl	Michael Jordan, Chicago
1997	East 132, West 120	Cleveland	Doug Collins, Rudy Tomjanovich	Glen Rice, Charlotte

NBA Franchise Origins

Here is what the current 29 teams in the National Basketball Association have to show for the years they have put in as members of the National Basketball League (NBL), Basketball Association of America (BAA), the NBA, and the American Basketball Association (ABA). League titles are noted by year won.

Western Conference

	First Season		League Titles	Franchise Stops
Dallas Mavericks	1980-81	(NBA)	None	•Dallas (1980–)
Denver Nuggets	1967-68	(ABA)	None	•Denver (1967–)
Golden St. Warriors	1946-47	(BAA)	1 BAA (1947) 2 NBA (1956,75)	•Philadelphia (1946-62) San Francisco (1962-71) Oakland (1971–)
Houston Rockets	1967-68	(NBA)	2 NBA (1994,95)	•San Diego (1967-71) Houston (1971–)
Los Angeles Clippers	1970-71	(NBA)	None	•Buffalo (1970-78) San Diego (1978-84) Los Angeles (1984–)
Los Angeles Lakers	1947-48	(NBL)	1 NBL (1947) 1 BAA (1949) 10 NBA (1950,52-54,72, 80,82,85,87-88)	•Minneapolis (1947-60) Los Angeles (1960-67) Inglewood, CA (1967–)
Minnesota Timberwolves	1989-90	(NBA)	None	•Minneapolis (1989–)
Phoenix Suns	1968-69	(NBA)	None	•Phoenix (1968–)
Portland Trail Blazers	1970-71	(NBA)	1 NBA (1977)	•Portland (1970–)
Sacramento Kings	1945-46	(NBL)	1 NBL (1946) 1 NBA (1951)	•Rochester, NY (1945-58) Cincinnati (1958-72) KC-Omaha (1972-75) Kansas City (1975-85) Sacramento (1985–)
San Antonio Spurs	1967-68	(ABA)	None	•Dallas (1967-73) San Antonio (1973–)
Seattle SuperSonics	1967-68	(NBA)	1 NBA (1979)	•Seattle (1967–)
Utah Jazz	1974-75	(NBA)	None	•New Orleans (1974-79) Salt Lake City (1979–)
Vancouver Grizzlies	1995-96	(NBA)	None	•Vancouver (1995–)

Eastern Conference

	First Season		League Titles	Franchise Stops
Atlanta Hawks	1946-47	(NBL)	1 NBA (1958)	•Tri-Cities (1946-51) Milwaukee (1951-55) St. Louis (1955-68) Atlanta (1968–)
Boston Celtics	1946-47	(BAA)	16 NBA (1957,59-66,68-69 74,76,81,84,86)	•Boston (1946–)
Charlotte Hornets	1988-89	(NBA)	None	•Charlotte (1988–)
Chicago Bulls	1966-67	(NBA)	5 NBA (1991-93,96-97)	•Chicago (1966–)
Cleveland Cavaliers	1970-71	(NBA)	None	•Cleveland (1970-74) Richfield, OH (1974-94) Cleveland (1994–)
Detroit Pistons	1941-42	(NBL)	2 NBL (1944-45) 2 NBA (1989-90)	•Ft. Wayne, IN (1941-57) Detroit (1957-78) Pontiac, MI (1978-88) Auburn Hills, MI (1988–)
Indiana Pacers	1967-68	(ABA)	3 ABA (1970,72-73)	•Indianapolis (1967–)
Miami Heat	1988-89	(NBA)	None	•Miami (1988–)
Milwaukee Bucks	1968-69	(NBA)	1 NBA (1971)	•Milwaukee (1968–)
New Jersey Nets	1967-68	(ABA)	2 ABA (1974,76)	•Teaneck, NJ (1967-68) Commack, NY (1968-69) W. Hempstead, NY (1969-71) Uniondale, NY (1971-77) Piscataway, NJ (1977-81) E. Rutherford, NJ (1981–)
New York Knicks	1946-47	(BAA)	2 NBA (1970,73)	•New York (1946–)
Orlando Magic	1989-90	(NBA)	None	•Orlando, FL (1989–)
Philadelphia 76ers	1949-50	(NBA)	3 NBA (1955,67,83)	•Syracuse, NY (1949-63) Philadelphia (1963–)
Toronto Raptors	1995-96	(NBA)	None	•Toronto (1995–)
Washington Wizards	1961-62	(NBA)	1 NBA (1978)	•Chicago (1961-63) Baltimore (1963-73) Landover, MD (1973–)

Note: The Tri-Cities Blackhawks represented Moline and Rock Island, Ill., and Davenport, Iowa.

The Growth of the NBA

Of the 11 franchises that comprised the Basketball Association of America (BAA) at the start of the 1946-47 season, only three remain—the Boston Celtics, New York Knickerbockers and Golden State Warriors (originally Philadelphia Warriors).

Just before the start of the 1948-49 season, four teams from the more established **National Basketball League** (NBL)—the Ft. Wayne Pistons (now Detroit), Indianapolis Jets, Minneapolis Lakers (now Los Angeles) and Rochester Royals (now Sacramento Kings)—joined the BAA.

A year later, the six remaining NBL franchises—Anderson (Ind.), Denver, Sheboygan (Wisc.), the Syracuse Nationals (now Philadelphia 76ers), Tri-Cities Blackhawks (now Atlanta Hawks) and Waterloo (Iowa)—joined along with the new Indianapolis Olympians and the BAA became the 17-team **National Basketball Association**.

The NBA was down to 10 teams by the 1950-51 season and slipped to eight by 1954-55 with Boston, New York, Philadelphia and Syracuse in the Eastern Division, and Ft. Wayne, Milwaukee (formerly Tri-Cities), Minneapolis and Rochester in the West.

By 1960, five of those surviving eight teams had moved to other cities but by the end of the decade the NBA was a 14-team league. It also had a rival, the **American Basketball Association**, which began play in 1967 with a red, white and blue ball, a three-point line and 11 teams. After a nine-year run, the ABA merged four clubs—the Denver Nuggets, Indiana Pacers, New York Nets and San Antonio Spurs—with the NBA following the 1975-76 season. The NBA adopted the three-point play in 1979-80.

Expansion/Merger Timetable

For teams currently in NBA.

1948—Added NBL's Ft. Wayne Pistons (now Detroit), Minneapolis Lakers (now Los Angeles) and Rochester Royals (now Sacramento Kings); **1949**—Syracuse Nationals (now Philadelphia 76ers) and Tri-Cities Blackhawks (now Atlanta Hawks).

1961—Chicago Packers (now Washington Bullets); **1966**—Chicago Bulls; **1967**—San Diego Rockets (now Houston) and Seattle SuperSonics; **1968**—Milwaukee Bucks and Phoenix Suns.

1970—Buffalo Braves (now Los Angeles Clippers), Cleveland Cavaliers and Portland Trail Blazers; **1974**—New Orleans Jazz (now Utah); **1976**—added ABA's Denver Nuggets, Indiana Pacers, New York Nets (now New Jersey) and San Antonio Spurs.

1980—Dallas Mavericks; **1988**—Charlotte Hornets and Miami Heat; **1989**—Minnesota Timberwolves and Orlando Magic.

1995—Toronto Raptors and Vancouver Grizzlies.

City and Nickname Changes

1951—Tri-Cities Blackhawks, who divided home games between Moline and Rock Island, Ill., and Davenport, Iowa, move to Milwaukee and become the Hawks; **1955**—Milwaukee Hawks move to St. Louis; **1957**—Ft. Wayne Pistons move to Detroit, while Rochester Royals move to Cincinnati.

1960—Minneapolis Lakers move to Los Angeles; **1962**—Chicago Packers renamed Zephyrs, while Philadelphia Warriors move to San Francisco; **1963**—Chicago Zephyrs move to Baltimore and become Bullets, while Syracuse Nationals move to Philadelphia and become the 76ers; **1968**—St. Louis Hawks move to Atlanta.

1971—San Diego Rockets move to Houston, while San Francisco Warriors move to Oakland and become Golden State Warriors; **1972**—Cincinnati Royals move to Midwest, divide home games between Kansas City, Mo., and Omaha, Neb., and become Kings; **1973**—Baltimore Bullets move to Landover, Md., outside Washington and become Capital Bullets; **1974**—Capital Bullets renamed Washington Bullets; **1975**—KC-Omaha Kings settle in Kansas City; **1977**—New York Nets move from Uniondale, N.Y., to Piscataway, N.J. (later East Rutherford) and become New Jersey Nets; **1978**—Buffalo Braves move to San Diego and become Clippers; **1979**—New Orleans Jazz move to Salt Lake City and become Utah Jazz.

1984—San Diego Clippers move to Los Angeles; **1985**—Kansas City Kings move to Sacramento; **1997**—Washington Bullets become Washington Wizards.

Defunct NBA Teams

Teams that once played in the BAA and NBA, but no longer exist.

Anderson (Ind.)—Packers (1949-50); **Baltimore**—Bullets (1947-55); **Chicago**—Stags (1946-50); **Cleveland**—Rebels (1946-47); **Denver**—Nuggets (1949-50); **Detroit**—Falcons (1946-47); **Indianapolis**—Jets (1948-49) and Olympians (1949-53); **Pittsburgh**—Ironmen (1946-47); **Providence**—Steamrollers (1946-49); **St. Louis**—Bombers (1946-50); **Sheboygan (Wisc.)**—Redskins (1949-50); **Toronto**—Huskies (1946-47); **Washington**—Capitols (1946-51); **Waterloo (Iowa)**—Hawks (1949-50).

ABA Teams (1967-76)

Anaheim—Amigos (1967-68, moved to LA); **Baltimore**—Claws (1975, never played); **Carolina**—Cougars (1969-74, moved to St. Louis); **Dallas**—Chaparrals (1967-73, called Texas Chaparrals in 1970-71, moved to San Antonio); **Denver**—Rockets (1967-76, renamed Nuggets in 1974-76); **Miami**—Floridians (1968-72, called simply Floridians from 1970-72).

Houston—Mavericks (1967-69, moved to North Carolina); **Indiana**—Pacers (1967-76); **Kentucky**—Colonels (1967-76); **Los Angeles**—Stars (1968-70, moved to Utah); **Memphis**—Pros (1970-75, renamed Tams in 1972 and Sounds in 1974, moved to Baltimore); **Minnesota**—Muskies (1967-68, moved to Miami) and Pipers (1968-69, moved back to Pittsburgh); **New Jersey**—Americans (1967-68, moved to New York).

New Orleans—Buccaneers (1967-70, moved to Memphis); **New York**—Nets (1968-76); **Oakland**—Oaks (1967-69, moved to Washington); **Pittsburgh**—Pipers (1967-68, moved to Minnesota), Pipers (1969-72, renamed Condors in 1970); **St. Louis**—Spirits of St. Louis (1974-76); **San Antonio**—Spurs (1973-76); **San Diego**—Conquistadors (1972-75, renamed Sails in 1975); **Utah**—Stars (1970-75); **Virginia**—Squires (1970-76); **Washington**—Caps (1969-70, moved to Virginia).

Annual NBA Leaders

Scoring

Decided by total points from 1947-69, and per game average since 1970.

Multiple winners: Michael Jordan (9); Wilt Chamberlain (7); George Gervin (4); Neil Johnston, Bob McAdoo and George Mikan (3); Kareem Abdul-Jabbar, Paul Arizin, Adrian Dantley and Bob Pettit (2).

Year		Gm	Pts	Avg	Year		Gm	Pts	Avg
1947	Joe Fulks, Phi	60	1389	23.2	1973	Nate Archibald, KC-Omaha	80	2719	34.0
1948	Max Zaslofsky, Chi	48	1007	21.0	1974	Bob McAdoo, Buf	74	2261	30.6
1949	George Mikan, Mpls	60	1698	28.3	1975	Bob McAdoo, Buf	82	2831	34.5
					1976	Bob McAdoo, Buf	78	2427	31.1
1950	George Mikan, Mpls	68	1865	27.4	1977	Pete Maravich, NO	73	2273	31.1
1951	George Mikan, Mpls	68	1932	28.4	1978	George Gervin, SA	82	2232	27.2
1952	Paul Arizin, Phi	66	1674	25.4	1979	George Gervin, SA	80	2365	29.6
1953	Neil Johnston, Phi	70	1564	22.3					
1954	Neil Johnston, Phi	72	1759	24.4	1980	George Gervin, SA	78	2585	33.1
1955	Neil Johnston, Phi	72	1631	22.7	1981	Adrian Dantley, Utah	80	2452	30.7
1956	Bob Pettit, St.L	72	1849	25.7	1982	George Gervin, SA	79	2551	32.3
1957	Paul Arizin, Phi	71	1817	25.6	1983	Alex English, Den	82	2326	28.4
1958	George Yardley, Det	72	2001	27.8	1984	Adrian Dantley, Utah	79	2418	30.6
1959	Bob Pettit, St.L	72	2105	29.2	1985	Bernard King, NY	55	1809	32.9
					1986	Dominique Wilkins, Atl	78	2366	30.3
1960	Wilt Chamberlain, Phi	72	2707	37.6	1987	Michael Jordan, Chi	82	3041	37.1
1961	Wilt Chamberlain, Phi	79	3033	38.4	1988	Michael Jordan, Chi	82	2868	35.0
1962	Wilt Chamberlain, Phi	80	4029	50.4	1989	Michael Jordan, Chi	81	2633	32.5
1963	Wilt Chamberlain, SF	80	3586	44.8					
1964	Wilt Chamberlain, SF	80	2948	36.9	1990	Michael Jordan, Chi	82	2753	33.6
1965	Wilt Chamberlain, SF-Phi	73	2534	34.7	1991	Michael Jordan, Chi	82	2580	31.5
1966	Wilt Chamberlain, Phi	79	2649	33.5	1992	Michael Jordan, Chi	80	2404	30.1
1967	Rick Barry, SF	78	2775	35.6	1993	Michael Jordan, Chi	78	2541	32.6
1968	Dave Bing, Det	79	2142	27.1	1994	David Robinson, SA	80	2383	29.8
1969	Elvin Hayes, SD	82	2327	28.4	1995	Shaquille O'Neal, Orl	79	2315	29.3
					1996	Michael Jordan, Chi	82	2491	30.4
1970	Jerry West, LA	74	2309	31.2	1997	Michael Jordan, Chi	82	2431	29.7
1971	Lew Alcindor, Mil	82	2596	31.7					
1972	Kareem Abdul-Jabbar, Mil	81	2822	34.8					

Note: Lew Alcindor changed his name to Kareem Abdul-Jabbar after the 1970-71 season.

Rebounds

Decided by total rebounds from 1951-69 and per game average since 1970.

Multiple winners: Wilt Chamberlain (11); Moses Malone and Dennis Rodman (6); Bill Russell (4); Elvin Hayes and Hakeem Olajuwon (2).

Year		Gm	No	Avg	Year		Gm	No	Avg
1951	Dolph Schayes, Syr	66	1080	16.4	1974	Elvin Hayes, Cap*	81	1463	18.1
1952	Larry Foust, Ft. Wayne	66	880	13.3	1975	Wes Unseld, Wash	73	1077	14.8
	& Mel Hutchins, Mil	66	880	13.3	1976	Kareem Abdul-Jabbar, LA	82	1383	16.9
1953	George Mikan, Mpls	70	1007	14.4	1977	Bill Walton, Port	65	934	14.4
1954	Harry Gallatin, NY	72	1098	15.3	1978	Len Robinson, NO	82	1288	15.7
1955	Neil Johnston, Phi	72	1085	15.1	1979	Moses Malone, Hou	82	1444	17.6
1956	Bob Pettit, St.L	72	1164	16.2					
1957	Maurice Stokes, Roch	72	1256	17.4	1980	Swen Nater, SD	81	1216	15.0
1958	Bill Russell, Bos	69	1564	22.7	1981	Moses Malone, Hou	80	1180	14.8
1959	Bill Russell, Bos	70	1612	23.0	1982	Moses Malone, Hou	81	1188	14.7
					1983	Moses Malone, Phi	78	1194	15.3
1960	Wilt Chamberlain, Phi	72	1941	27.0	1984	Moses Malone, Phi	71	950	13.4
1961	Wilt Chamberlain, Phi	79	2149	27.2	1985	Moses Malone, Phi	79	1031	13.1
1962	Wilt Chamberlain, Phi	80	2052	25.7	1986	Bill Laimbeer, Det	82	1075	13.1
1963	Wilt Chamberlain, SF	80	1946	24.3	1987	Charles Barkley, Phi	68	994	14.6
1964	Bill Russell, Bos	78	1930	24.7	1988	Michael Cage, LA Clippers	72	938	13.0
1965	Bill Russell, Bos	78	1878	24.1	1989	Hakeem Olajuwon, Hou	82	1105	13.5
1966	Wilt Chamberlain, Phi	79	1943	24.6					
1967	Wilt Chamberlain, Phi	81	1957	24.2	1990	Hakeem Olajuwon, Hou	82	1149	14.0
1968	Wilt Chamberlain, Phi	82	1952	23.8	1991	David Robinson, SA	82	1063	13.0
1969	Wilt Chamberlain, LA	81	1712	21.1	1992	Dennis Rodman, Det	82	1530	18.7
					1993	Dennis Rodman, Det	62	1232	18.3
1970	Elvin Hayes, SD	82	1386	16.9	1994	Dennis Rodman, SA	79	1132	17.3
1971	Wilt Chamberlain, LA	82	1493	18.2	1995	Dennis Rodman, SA	49	823	16.8
1972	Wilt Chamberlain, LA	82	1572	19.2	1996	Dennis Rodman, Chi	64	952	14.9
1973	Wilt Chamberlain, LA	82	1526	18.6	1997	Dennis Rodman, Chi	55	883	16.1

*The Baltimore Bullets moved to Landover, MD in 1973-74 and became first the Capital Bullets, then the Washington Bullets in 1974-75.

Assists

Decided by total assists from 1952-69 and per game average since 1970.

Multiple winners: John Stockton (9); Bob Cousy (8); Oscar Robertson (6); Magic Johnson and Kevin Porter (4); Andy Phillip and Guy Rodgers (2).

Year		No	Year		No	Year		No
1947	Ernie Calverley, Prov	202	1964	Oscar Robertson, Cin	868	1981	Kevin Porter, Wash	9.1
1948	Howie Dallmar, Phi	120	1965	Oscar Robertson, Cin	861	1982	Johnny Moore, SA	9.6
1949	Bob Davies, Roch	321	1966	Oscar Robertson, Cin	847	1983	Magic Johnson, LA	10.5
1950	Dick McGuire, NY	386	1967	Guy Rodgers, Chi	908	1984	Magic Johnson, LA	13.1
1951	Andy Phillip, Phi	414	1968	Wilt Chamberlain, Phi	702	1985	Isiah Thomas, Det	13.9
1952	Andy Phillip, Phi	539	1969	Oscar Robertson, Cin	772	1986	Magic Johnson, Lakers	12.6
1953	Bob Cousy, Bos	547	1970	Lenny Wilkens, Sea	9.1	1987	Magic Johnson, Lakers	12.2
1954	Bob Cousy, Bos	518	1971	Norm Van Lier, Chi	10.1	1988	John Stockton, Utah	13.8
1955	Bob Cousy, Bos	557	1972	Jerry West, LA	9.7	1989	John Stockton, Utah	13.6
1956	Bob Cousy, Bos	642	1973	Nate Archibald, KC-O	11.4	1990	John Stockton, Utah	14.5
1957	Bob Cousy, Bos	478	1974	Ernie DiGregorio, Buf	8.2	1991	John Stockton, Utah	14.2
1958	Bob Cousy, Bos	463	1975	Kevin Porter, Wash	8.0	1992	John Stockton, Utah	13.7
1959	Bob Cousy, Bos	557	1976	Slick Watts, Sea	8.1	1993	John Stockton, Utah	12.0
1960	Bob Cousy, Bos	715	1977	Don Buse, Ind	8.5	1994	John Stockton, Utah	12.6
1961	Oscar Robertson, Cin	690	1978	Kevin Porter, Det-NJ	10.2	1995	John Stockton, Utah	12.3
1962	Oscar Robertson, Cin	899	1979	Kevin Porter, Det	13.4	1996	John Stockton, Utah	11.2
1963	Guy Rodgers, SF	825	1980	M.R. Richardson, NY	10.1	1997	Mark Jackson, Den-Ind	11.4

Field Goal Percentage

Multiple winners: Wilt Chamberlain (9); Artis Gilmore (4); Neil Johnston (3); Bob Feerick, Johnny Green, Alex Groza, Cedric Maxwell, Kevin McHale, Gheorghe Muresan, Ken Sears and Buck Williams (2).

Year		Pct	Year		Pct	Year		Pct
1947	Bob Feerick, Wash	.401	1964	Jerry Lucas, Cin	.527	1981	Artis Gilmore, Chi.	.670
1948	Bob Feerick, Wash	.340	1965	W. Chamberlain, SF-Phi	.510	1982	Artis Gilmore, Chi.	.652
1949	Arnie Risen, Roch	.423	1966	Wilt Chamberlain, Phi	.540	1983	Artis Gilmore, SA	.626
1950	Alex Groza, Indpls	.478	1967	Wilt Chamberlain, Phi	.683	1984	Artis Gilmore, SA	.631
1951	Alex Groza, Indpls	.470	1968	Wilt Chamberlain, Phi	.595	1985	James Donaldson, LAC	.637
1952	Paul Arizin, Phi	.448	1969	Wilt Chamberlain, LA	.583	1986	Steve Johnson, SA	.632
1953	Neil Johnston, Phi	.452	1970	Johnny Green, Cin	.559	1987	Kevin McHale, Bos	.604
1954	Ed Macauley, Bos	.486	1971	Johnny Green, Cin	.587	1988	Kevin McHale, Bos	.604
1955	Larry Foust, Ft.W	.487	1972	Wilt Chamberlain, LA	.649	1989	Dennis Rodman, Det.	.595
1956	Neil Johnston, Phi	.457	1973	Wilt Chamberlain, LA	.727	1990	Mark West, Pho.	.625
1957	Neil Johnston, Phi.	.447	1974	Bob McAdoo, Buf	.547	1991	Buck Williams, Port	.602
1958	Jack Twyman, Cin	.452	1975	Don Nelson, Bos	.539	1992	Buck Williams, Port	.604
1959	Ken Sears, NY	.490	1976	Wes Unseld, Wash	.561	1993	Cedric Ceballos, Pho	.576
1960	Ken Sears, NY	.477	1977	K. Abdul-Jabbar, LA	.579	1994	Shaquille O'Neal, Orl	.599
1961	Wilt Chamberlain, Phi	.509	1978	Bobby Jones, Den	.578	1995	Chris Gatling, G.St	.633
1962	Walt Bellamy, Chi	.519	1979	Cedric Maxwell, Bos	.584	1996	Gheorghe Muresan, Wash	.584
1963	Wilt Chamberlain, SF	.528	1980	Cedric Maxwell, Bos	.609	1997	Gheorghe Muresan, Wash	.604

Free Throw Percentage

Multiple winners: Bill Sharman (7); Rick Barry (6); Larry Bird (4); Mark Price and Dolph Schayes (3); Mahmoud Abdul-Rauf, Larry Costello, Ernie DiGregorio, Bob Feerick, Kyle Macy, Calvin Murphy, Oscar Robertson and Larry Siegfried (2).

Year		Pct	Year		Pct	Year		Pct
1947	Fred Scolari, Wash	.811	1964	Oscar Robertson, Cin	.853	1981	Calvin Murphy, Hou	.958
1948	Bob Feerick, Wash	.788	1965	Larry Costello, Phi	.877	1982	Kyle Macy, Pho	.899
1949	Bob Feerick, Wash	.859	1966	Larry Siegfried, Bos	.881	1983	Calvin Murphy, Hou	.920
1950	Max Zaslofsky, Chi	.843	1967	Adrian Smith, Cin	.903	1984	Larry Bird, Bos	.888
1951	Joe Fulks, Phi	.855	1968	Oscar Robertson, Cin	.873	1985	Kyle Macy, Pho	.907
1952	Bob Wanzer, Roch	.904	1969	Larry Siegfried, NY	.864	1986	Larry Bird, Bos	.896
1953	Bill Sharman, Bos	.850	1970	Flynn Robinson, Mil	.898	1987	Larry Bird, Bos	.910
1954	Bill Sharman, Bos	.844	1971	Chet Walker, Chi	.859	1988	Jack Sikma, Mil	.922
1955	Bill Sharman, Bos	.897	1972	Jack Marin, Bal	.894	1989	Magic Johnson, LAL	.911
1956	Bill Sharman, Bos	.867	1973	Rick Barry, G.St	.902	1990	Larry Bird, Bos	.930
1957	Bill Sharman, Bos	.905	1974	Ernie DiGregorio, Buf	.902	1991	Reggie Miller, Ind	.918
1958	Dolph Schayes, Syr	.904	1975	Rick Barry, G.St	.904	1992	Mark Price, Cle	.947
1959	Bill Sharman, Bos	.932	1976	Rick Barry, G.St	.923	1993	Mark Price, Cle	.948
1960	Dolph Schayes, Syr	.892	1977	Ernie DiGregorio, Buf	.945	1994	M. Abdul-Rauf, Den	.956
1961	Bill Sharman, Bos	.921	1978	Rick Barry, G.St	.924	1995	Spud Webb, Sac	.934
1962	Dolph Schayes, Syr	.896	1979	Rick Barry, Hou	.947	1996	M. Abdul-Rauf, Den	.930
1963	Larry Costello, Syr	.881	1980	Rick Barry, Hou	.935	1997	Mark Price, G.St.	.906

Blocked Shots

Decided by per game average since 1973-74 season.

Multiple winners: Kareem Abdul-Jabbar and Mark Eaton (4); George Johnson, Dikembe Mutombo and Hakeem Olajuwon (3); Manute Bol (2).

Year		Gm	No	Avg
1974	Elmore Smith, LA	81	393	4.85
1975	Kareem Abdul-Jabbar, Mil	65	212	3.26
1976	Kareem Abdul-Jabbar, LA	82	338	4.12
1977	Bill Walton, Port	65	211	3.25
1978	George Johnson, NJ	81	274	3.38
1979	Kareem Abdul-Jabbar, LA	80	316	3.95
1980	Kareem Abdul-Jabbar, LA	82	280	3.41
1981	George Johnson, SA	82	278	3.39
1982	George Johnson, SA	75	234	3.12
1983	Tree Rollins, Atl	80	343	4.29
1984	Mark Eaton, Utah	82	351	4.28
1985	Mark Eaton, Utah	82	456	5.56
1986	Manute Bol, Wash	80	397	4.96
1987	Mark Eaton, Utah	79	321	4.06
1988	Mark Eaton, Utah	82	304	3.71
1989	Manute Bol, G.St.	80	345	4.31
1990	Akeem Olajuwon, Hou	82	376	4.59
1991	Hakeem Olajuwon, Hou	56	221	3.95
1992	David Robinson, SA	68	305	4.49
1993	Hakeem Olajuwon, Hou	82	342	4.17
1994	Dikembe Mutombo, Den	82	336	4.10
1995	Dikembe Mutombo, Den	82	321	3.91
1996	Dikembe Mutombo, Den	74	332	4.49
1997	Shawn Bradley, Dal-NJ	73	248	3.40

Steals

Decided by per game average since 1973-74 season.

Multiple winners: Michael Jordan, Micheal Ray Richardson and Alvin Robertson (3); Magic Johnson and John Stockton (2).

Year		Gm	No	Avg
1974	Larry Steele, Port	81	217	2.68
1975	Rick Barry, G.St.	80	228	2.85
1976	Slick Watts, Sea	82	261	3.18
1977	Don Buse, Ind	81	281	3.47
1978	Ron Lee, Pho	82	225	2.74
1979	M.L. Carr, Det	80	197	2.46
1980	Micheal Ray Richardson, NY	82	265	3.23
1981	Magic Johnson, LA	37	127	3.43
1982	Magic Johnson, LA	78	208	2.67
1983	Micheal Ray Richardson, G. ST-NJ	64	182	2.84
1984	Rickey Green, Utah	81	215	2.65
1985	Micheal Ray Richardson, NJ	82	243	2.96
1986	Alvin Robertson, SA	82	301	3.67
1987	Alvin Robertson, SA	81	260	3.21
1988	Michael Jordan, Chi	82	259	3.16
1989	John Stockton, Utah	82	263	3.21
1990	Michael Jordan, Chi	82	227	2.77
1991	Alvin Robertson, SA	81	246	3.04
1992	John Stockton, Utah	82	244	2.98
1993	Michael Jordan, Chi	78	221	2.83
1994	Nate McMillan, Sea	73	216	2.96
1995	Scottie Pippen, Chi	79	232	2.94
1996	Gary Payton, Sea	81	231	2.85
1997	Mookie Blaylock, Atl	78	212	2.72

Note: Akeem Olajuwon changed the spelling of his first name to Hakeem during the 1990-91 season.

All-Time NBA Regular Season Leaders

Through the 1996-97 regular season.

CAREER

Players active in 1996-97 in **bold** type.

Points

		Yrs	Gm	Pts	Avg
1	Kareem Abdul-Jabbar	20	1560	38,387	24.6
2	Wilt Chamberlain	14	1045	31,419	30.1
3	Moses Malone	19	1329	27,409	20.6
4	Elvin Hayes	16	1303	27,313	21.0
5	**Michael Jordan**	12	848	26,920	31.7
6	Oscar Robertson	14	1040	26,710	25.7
7	**Dominique Wilkins**	14	1047	26,534	25.3
8	John Havlicek	16	1270	26,395	20.8
9	Alex English	15	1193	25,613	21.5
10	**Karl Malone**	12	980	25,592	26.1
11	Jerry West	14	932	25,192	27.0
12	**Hakeem Olajuwon**	13	978	23,650	24.2
13	**Robert Parish**	21	1611	23,334	14.5
14	Adrian Dantley	15	955	23,177	24.3
15	Elgin Baylor	14	846	23,149	27.4
16	**Charles Barkley**	13	943	21,816	23.1
17	Larry Bird	13	897	21,791	24.3
18	Hal Greer	15	1122	21,586	19.2
19	**Patrick Ewing**	12	913	21,539	23.6
20	Walt Bellamy	14	1043	20,941	20.1
21	**Clyde Drexler**	14	1016	20,908	20.6
22	Bob Pettit	11	792	20,880	26.4
23	George Gervin	10	791	20,708	26.2
24	Tom Chambers	15	1094	20,024	18.3
25	Bernard King	14	874	19,655	22.5
26	Walter Davis	15	1033	19,521	18.9
27	Dolph Schayes	16	1059	19,249	18.2
28	Bob Lanier	14	959	19,248	20.1
29	Gail Goodrich	14	1031	19,181	18.6
30	Reggie Theus	13	1026	19,015	18.5

Scoring Average

Minimum of 400 games or 10,000 points.

		Yrs	Gm	Pts	Avg
1	**Michael Jordan**	12	848	26,920	31.7
2	Wilt Chamberlain	14	1045	31,419	30.1
3	Elgin Baylor	14	846	23,149	27.4
4	Jerry West	14	932	25,192	27.0
5	Bob Pettit	11	792	20,880	26.4
6	George Gervin	10	791	20,708	26.2
7	**Karl Malone**	12	980	25,592	26.1
8	Oscar Robertson	14	1040	26,710	25.7
9	**David Robinson**	8	563	14,366	25.5
10	**Dominique Wilkins**	14	1047	26,454	25.3
11	Kareem Abdul-Jabbar	20	1560	38,387	24.6
12	Larry Bird	13	897	21,791	24.3
13	**Hakeem Olajuwon**	13	978	23,650	24.2
14	Adrian Dantley	15	955	23,177	24.3
15	Pete Maravich	10	658	15,948	24.2
16	**Patrick Ewing**	12	913	21,539	23.6
17	Rick Barry	10	794	18,395	23.2
18	**Charles Barkley**	13	943	21,816	23.1
19	**Mitch Richmond**	9	681	15,748	23.1
20	Paul Arizin	10	713	16,266	22.8
21	George Mikan	9	520	11,764	22.6
22	Bernard King	14	874	19,655	22.5
23	David Thompson	8	509	11,264	22.1
24	Bob McAdoo	14	852	18,787	22.1
25	Julius Erving	11	836	18,364	22.0
26	Alex English	15	1193	25,613	21.5
27	Elvin Hayes	16	1303	27,313	21.0
28	Billy Cunningham	9	654	13,626	20.8
29	John Havlicek	16	1270	26,395	20.8
30	**Glen Rice**	8	636	13,073	20.6

NBA-ABA Top 20
Points

All-Time combined regular season scoring leaders, including ABA service (1968-76). NBA players with ABA experience are listed in CAPITAL letters. Players active during 1996-97 are in **bold** type.

		Yrs	Pts	Avg
1	Kareem Abdul-Jabbar	20	38,387	24.6
2	Wilt Chamberlain	14	31,419	30.1
3	JULIUS ERVING	16	30,026	24.2
4	MOSES MALONE	21	29,580	20.3
5	DAN ISSEL	15	27,482	22.6
6	Elvin Hayes	16	27,313	21.0
7	**Michael Jordan**	12	26,920	31.7
8	Oscar Robertson	14	26,710	25.7
9	GEORGE GERVIN	14	26,595	25.1
10	**Dominique Wilkins**	14	26,534	25.3
11	John Havlicek	16	26,395	20.8
12	Alex English	15	25,613	21.5
13	**Karl Malone**	12	25,592	26.1
14	RICK BARRY	14	25,279	24.8
15	Jerry West	14	25,192	27.0
16	ARTIS GILMORE	17	24,941	18.8
17	**Hakeem Olajuwon**	13	23,650	24.2
18	**Robert Parish**	21	23,334	14.5
19	Adrian Dantley	15	23,177	24.3
20	Elgin Baylor	14	23,149	27.4

ABA Totals: BARRY (4 yrs, 226 gm, 6884 pts, 30.5 avg); ERVING (5 yrs, 407 gm, 11,662 pts, 28.7 avg); GERVIN (4 yrs, 269 gm, 5887 pts, 21.9 avg); GILMORE (5 yrs, 420 gm, 9362 pts, 22.3 avg); ISSEL (6 yrs, 500 gm, 12,823 pts, 25.6 avg); MALONE (2 yrs, 126 gm, 2171 pts, 17.2 avg).

Field Goals

		Yrs	FG	Att	Pct
1	Kareem Abdul-Jabbar	20	15,837	28,307	.559
2	Wilt Chamberlain	14	12,681	23,497	.540
3	Elvin Hayes	16	10,976	24,272	.452
4	Alex English	15	10,659	21,036	.507
5	John Havlicek	16	10,513	23,930	.439
6	**Michael Jordan**	12	10,077	19,793	.509
7	**Dominique Wilkins**	14	9,913	21,457	.462
8	**Robert Parish**	21	9,614	17,914	.537
9	**Karl Malone**	12	9,510	18,032	.527
10	Oscar Robertson	14	9,508	19,620	.485

Note: If field goals made in the ABA are included, consider these NBA-ABA totals: Julius Erving (11,818), Dan Issel (10,431), George Gervin (10,368), Moses Malone (10,277), Rick Barry (9,695) and Artis Gilmore (9,403).

Free Throws

		Yrs	FT	Att	Pct
1	Moses Malone	19	8531	11,090	.769
2	Oscar Robertson	14	7694	9,185	.838
3	Jerry West	14	7160	8,801	.814
4	Dolph Schayes	16	6979	8,273	.844
5	Adrian Dantley	15	6832	8,351	.818
6	Kareem Abdul-Jabbar	20	6712	9,304	.721
7	**Karl Malone**	12	6505	8,983	.724
8	**Michael Jordan**	12	6233	7394	.843
9	Bob Pettit	11	6182	8,119	.761
10	Wilt Chamberlain	14	6057	11,862	.511

Note: If free throws made in the ABA are included, consider these totals: Moses Malone (9,018), Dan Issel (6,591), Julius Erving (6,256) and Artis Gilmore (6,132).

Assists

		Yrs	Gm	No	Avg
1	**John Stockton**	13	1062	12,170	11.5
2	Magic Johnson	13	906	10,141	11.2
3	Oscar Robertson	14	1040	9,887	9.5
4	Isiah Thomas	13	979	9,061	9.3
5	Maurice Cheeks	15	1101	7,392	6.7
6	Lenny Wilkens	15	1077	7,211	6.7
7	Bob Cousy	14	924	6,955	7.5
8	Guy Rodgers	12	892	6,917	7.8
9	Nate Archibald	13	876	6,476	7.4
10	John Lucas	14	928	6,454	7.0

Rebounds

		Yrs	Gm	No	Avg
1	Wilt Chamberlain	14	1045	23,924	22.9
2	Bill Russell	13	963	21,620	22.5
3	Kareem Abdul-Jabbar	20	1560	17,440	11.2
4	Elvin Hayes	16	1303	16,279	12.5
5	Moses Malone	19	1329	16,212	12.2
6	**Robert Parish**	21	1611	14,715	9.1
7	Nate Thurmond	14	964	14,464	15.0
8	Walt Bellamy	14	1043	14,241	13.7
9	Wes Unseld	13	984	13,769	14.0
10	Jerry Lucas	11	829	12,942	15.6

Note: If rebounds accumulated in the ABA are included, consider the following totals: Moses Malone (17,834) and Artis Gilmore (16,330).

Steals

		Yrs	Gm	No
1	**John Stockton**	13	1062	2531
2	Maurice Cheeks	15	1101	2310
3	**Michael Jordan**	12	848	2165
4	Alvin Robertson	10	779	2112
5	**Clyde Drexler**	14	1016	2081

Note: Steals have only been an official stat since the 1973-74 season.

Blocked Shots

		Yrs	Gm	No
1	**Hakeem Olajuwon**	13	978	3363
2	Kareem Abdul-Jabbar	20	1560	3189
3	Mark Eaton	11	875	3064
4	Tree Rollins	18	1156	2542
5	**Patrick Ewing**	12	913	2516

Note: Blocked shots have only been an official stat since the 1973-74 season.

Games Played

		Yrs	Career	Gm
1	**Robert Parish**	21	1976-97	1611
2	Kareem Abdul-Jabbar	20	1970-89	1560
3	Moses Malone	19	1976-95	1329
4	Elvin Hayes	16	1969-84	1303
5	John Havlicek	16	1963-78	1270

Note: If ABA records are included, consider the following game totals: Moses Malone (1,455); Artis Gilmore (1,329); Caldwell Jones (1,299); Julius Erving (1,243); Dan Issel (1,218); Billy Paultz (1,124).

Personal Fouls

		Yrs	Gm	Fouls	DQ
1	Kareem Abdul-Jabbar	20	1560	4657	48
2	**Robert Parish**	21	1611	4443	86
3	Elvin Hayes	16	1303	4193	53
4	**Buck Williams**	16	1266	4174	57
5	James Edwards	19	1168	4042	96

Note: If ABA records are included, consider the following personal foul totals: Artis Gilmore (4,529) and Caldwell Jones (4,436).

SINGLE SEASON

Scoring Average

		Season	Avg
1	Wilt Chamberlain, Phi	1961-62	50.4
2	Wilt Chamberlain, SF	1962-63	44.8
3	Wilt Chamberlain, Phi	1960-61	38.4
4	Elgin Baylor, LA	1961-62	38.3
5	Wilt Chamberlain, Phi	1959-60	37.6
6	Michael Jordan, Chi	1986-87	37.1
7	Wilt Chamberlain, SF	1963-64	36.9
8	Rick Barry, SF	1966-67	35.6
9	Michael Jordan, Chi	1987-88	35.0
10	Elgin Baylor, LA	1960-61	34.8
	Kareem Abdul-Jabbar, Mil	1971-72	34.8

Field Goal Pct.

		Season	Pct
1	Wilt Chamberlain, LA	1972-73	.727
2	Wilt Chamberlain, SF	1966-67	.683
3	Artis Gilmore, Chi	1980-81	.670
4	Artis Gilmore, Chi	1981-82	.652
5	Wilt Chamberlain, LA	1971-72	.649

Free Throw Pct.

		Season	Pct
1	Calvin Murphy, Hou	1980-81	.958
2	Mahmond Abdul-Rauf, Den.	1993-94	.956
3	Mark Price, Cle	1992-93	.948
4	Mark Price, Cle	1991-92	.947
	Rick Barry, Hou	1978-79	.947

3-Pt Field Goal Pct.

		Season	Pct
1	Steve Kerr, Chi	1994-95	.524
2	Jon Sundvold, Mia	1988-89	.522
3	Tim Legler, Wash	1995-96	.522
4	Steve Kerr, Chi	1995-96	.515
5	Detlef Schrempf, Sea	1994-95	.514

Assists

		Season	Avg
1	John Stockton, Utah	1989-90	14.5
2	John Stockton, Utah	1990-91	14.2
3	Isiah Thomas, Det	1984-85	13.9
4	John Stockton, Utah	1987-88	13.8
5	John Stockton, Utah	1991-92	13.7
6	John Stockton, Utah	1988-89	13.6
7	Kevin Porter, Det	1978-79	13.4
8	Magic Johnson, LA Lakers	1983-84	13.1
9	Magic Johnson, LA Lakers	1988-89	12.8
10	Magic Johnson, LA Lakers	1984-85	12.6
	John Stockton, Utah	1993-94	12.6

Rebounds

		Season	Avg
1	Wilt Chamberlain, Phi	1960-61	27.2
2	Wilt Chamberlain, Phi	1959-60	27.0
3	Wilt Chamberlain, Phi	1961-62	25.7
4	Bill Russell, Bos	1963-64	24.7
5	Wilt Chamberlain, Phi	1965-66	24.6

Blocked Shots

		Season	Avg
1	Mark Eaton, Utah	1984-85	5.56
2	Manute Bol, Wash	1985-86	4.96
3	Elmore Smith, LA	1973-74	4.85
4	Mark Eaton, Utah	1985-86	4.61
5	Hakeem Olajuwon, Hou	1989-90	4.59

Steals

		Season	Avg
1	Alvin Robertson, SA	1985-86	3.67
2	Don Buse, Ind	1976-77	3.47
3	Magic Johnson, LA Lakers	1980-81	3.43
4	Micheal Ray Richardson, NY	1979-80	3.23
5	Alvin Robertson, SA	1986-87	3.21

SINGLE GAME

Points

	Date	FG-FT	Pts
Wilt Chamberlain, Phi vs NY	3/2/62	36-28-	100
Wilt Chamberlain, Phi vs LA***	12/8/61	31-16-	78
Wilt Chamberlain, Phi vs Chi	1/13/62	31-11-	73
Wilt Chamberlain, SF at NY	11/16/62	29-15-	73
David Thompson, Den at Det	4/9/78	28-17-	73
Wilt Chamberlain, SF at LA	11/3/62	29-14-	72
Elgin Baylor, LA at NY	11/15/60	28-15-	71
David Robinson, SA at LAC	4/24/94	26-18-	71
Wilt Chamberlain, Phi at Syr	3/10/63	27-16-	70
Michael Jordan, Chi at Cle*	3/28/90	23-21-	69
Wilt Chamberlain, Phi at Chi	12/16/67	30- 8-	68
Pete Maravich, NO vs NYK	2/25/77	26-16-	68
Wilt Chamberlain, Phi vs NY	3/9/61	27-13-	67
Wilt Chamberlain, Phi at St. L	2/17/62	26-15-	67
Wilt Chamberlain, Phi vs NY	2/25/62	25-17-	67
Wilt Chamberlain, SF vs LA	1/11/63	28-11-	67
Wilt Chamberlain, LA vs Pho	2/9/69	29- 8-	66
Wilt Chamberlain, Phi at Cin	2/13/62	24-17-	65
Wilt Chamberlain, Phi at St. L	2/27/62	25-15-	65
Wilt Chamberlain, Phi vs LA	2/7/66	28- 9-	65
Elgin Baylor, Mpls vs Bos	11/8/59	25-14-	64
Rick Barry, G.St. vs Port	3/26/74	30- 4-	64
Michael Jordan, Chi vs Orl	1/16/93	27- 9-	64

*Overtime
***Triple overtime.

Note: Wilt Chamberlain's 100-point game vs New York was played at Hershey, Pa.

Field Goals

	Date	FG	Att
Wilt Chamberlain, Phi vs NY	3/2/62	36	63
Wilt Chamberlain, Phi vs LA***	12/8/61	31	62
Wilt Chamberlain, Phi at Chi	12/16/67	30	40
Rick Barry, G.St. vs Port	2/26/74	30	45
Wilt Chamberlain made 29 four times.			

***Triple overtime.

Free Throws

	Date	FT	Att
Wilt Chamberlain, Phi vs NY	3/2/62	28	32
Adrian Dantley, Utah vs Hou	1/4/84	28	29
Adrian Dantley, Utah vs Den	11/25/83	27	31
Adrian Dantley, Utah vs Dal	10/31/80	26	29
Michael Jordan, Chi vs NJ	2/26/87	26	27

3-Pt Field Goals

	Date	No
Dennis Scott, Orl vs Atl	4/18/96	11
Brian Shaw, Mia at Mil	4/8/93	10
Joe Dumars, Det vs Min	11/8/94	10
George McCloud, Dal vs Pho	12/16/95	10*
Nine tied with 9 each		

* Overtime

Assists

	Date	No
Scott Skiles, Orl vs Den	12/30/90	30
Kevin Porter, NJ vs Hou	2/24/78	29
Bob Cousy, Bos vs Mpls	2/27/59	28
Guy Rodgers, SF vs St.L	3/14/63	28
John Stockton, Utah vs SA	1/15/91	28

Rebounds

	Date	No
Wilt Chamberlain, Phi vs Bos	11/24/60	55
Bill Russell, Bos vs Syr	2/5/60	51
Bill Russell, Bos vs Phi	11/16/57	49
Bill Russell, Bos vs Det	3/11/65	49
Wilt Chamberlain, Phi vs Syr	2/6/60	45
Wilt Chamberlain, Phi vs LA	1/21/61	45

Blocked Shots

	Date	No
Elmore Smith, LA vs Port	10/28/73	17
Manute Bol, Wash vs Atl	1/25/86	15
Manute Bol, Wash vs Ind	2/26/87	15
Shaquille O'Neal, Orl at NJ	11/20/93	15

Steals

	Date	No
Larry Kenon, San Antonio at KC	12/26/76	11

12 different players tied with 10 each, including Alvin Robertson who had 10 steals in a game four times.

All-Time Winningest NBA Coaches

Top 25 NBA career victories through the 1996-97 season. Career, regular season and playoff records are noted along with NBA titles won. Coaches active during 1996-97 season in **bold** type.

		Career			Regular Season			Playoffs			
		Yrs	W	L	Pct	W	L	Pct	W	L	Pct	NBA Titles
1	**Lenny Wilkens**	24	**1138**	952	.544	1070	876	.564	68	76	.472	1 (1979)
2	Red Auerbach	20	**1037**	548	.654	938	479	.662	99	69	.589	9 (1957, 59-66)
3	**Pat Riley**	15	**1002**	442	.694	859	360	.705	143	82	.636	4 (1982,85,87-88)
4	**Dick Motta**	25	**991**	1087	.477	935	1017	.479	56	70	.444	1 (1978)
5	**Bill Fitch**	24	**982**	1092	.473	927	1041	.471	55	54	.505	1 (1981)
6	Jack Ramsay	21	**908**	841	.519	864	783	.525	44	58	.431	1 (1977)
7	Don Nelson	19	**902**	690	.567	851	629	.575	51	61	.455	None
8	**Cotton Fitzsimmons**	21	**867**	824	.513	832	775	.518	35	49	.417	None
9	Gene Shue	22	**814**	908	.473	784	861	.477	30	47	.390	None
10	Red Holzman	18	**754**	652	.536	696	604	.535	58	48	.547	2 (1970, 73)
	John MacLeod	18	**754**	711	.515	707	657	.518	47	54	.465	None
12	**Larry Brown**	14	**665**	522	.560	624	480	.565	41	42	.494	None
13	Doug Moe	15	**661**	579	.533	628	529	.543	33	50	.398	None
14	Chuck Daly	12	**638**	427	.599	564	379	.598	74	48	.607	2 (1989-90)
15	**Jerry Sloan**	12	**629**	410	.605	577	359	.616	52	51	.505	None
16	K.C. Jones	10	**603**	309	.661	522	252	.674	81	57	.587	2 (1984,86)
17	Al Attles	14	**588**	548	.518	557	518	.518	31	30	.508	1 (1975)
18	**Phil Jackson**	8	**579**	208	.736	483	173	.736	96	35	.733	5 (1991-93,96-97)
19	**Mike Fratello**	12	**522**	433	.547	503	402	.558	19	31	.380	None
20	Billy Cunningham	8	**520**	235	.689	454	196	.698	66	39	.629	1 (1983)
	Del Harris	12	**520**	474	.523	489	430	.532	31	44	.413	None
22	Alex Hannum	12	**518**	446	.536	471	412	.533	47	34	.580	2 (1958, 67)
23	John Kundla	11	**485**	338	.589	423	302	.583	62	36	.633	5 (1949-50, 52-54)
24	**George Karl**	10	**483**	348	.581	442	305	.592	41	43	.488	None
25	Kevin Loughery	17	**480**	683	.413	474	662	.417	6	21	.222	None

Note: The NBA does not recognize records from the National Basketball League (1937-49), the American Basketball League (1961-62) or the American Basketball Assn. (1968-76), so the following NBL, ABL and ABA overall coaching records are not included above: NBL–**John Kundla** (51-19 and a title in 1 year). ABA– **Larry Brown** (249-129 in 4 yrs), **Alex Hannum** (194-164 and one title in 4 yrs), **K.C. Jones** (30-58 in 1 yr); **Kevin Loughery** (189-95 and one title in 3 yrs).

Where They Coached

Attles—Golden St. (1970-80,80-83); **Auerbach**—Washington (1946-49), Tri-Cities (1949-50), Boston (1950-66); **Brown**—Denver (1976-79), New Jersey (1981-83), San Antonio (1988-92), LA Clippers (1992-93), Indiana (1993-97), Philadelphia (1997–); **Cunningham**—Philadelphia (1977-85); **Daly**—Cleveland (1981-82), Detroit (1983-92), New Jersey (1992-94), Orlando (1997–); **Fitch**—Cleveland (1970-79), Boston (1979-83), Houston (1983-88), New Jersey (1989-92), LA Clippers (1994–); **Fitzsimmons**—Phoenix (1970-72), Atlanta (1972-76), Buffalo (1977-78), Kansas City (1978-84), San Antonio (1984-86), Phoenix (1988-92, 95-96); **Fratello**—Atlanta (1980-90), Cleveland (1993–).

Hannum—St. Louis (1957-58), Syracuse (1960-63), San Francisco (1963-66), Phila. 76ers (1966-68), Houston (1970-71); **Harris**—Houston (1979-83), Milwaukee (1987-92), LA Lakers (1994–); **Holzman**—Milwaukee-St. Louis Hawks (1954-57), NY Knicks (1968-77,78-82); **Jones**—Washington (1973-76), Boston (1983-88), Seattle (1990-92); **Karl**—Cleveland (1984-86); Golden St. (1986-88), Seattle (1991–); **Kundla**—Minneapolis (1948-57,58-59); **Loughery**—Philadelphia (1972-73), NY-NJ Nets (1976-81), Atlanta (1981-83), Chicago (1983-85), Washington (1985-88), Miami (1991-95); **MacLeod**—Phoenix (1973-87), Dallas (1987-89), NY Knicks (1990-91); **Moe**—San Antonio (1976-80), Denver (1981-90), Philadelphia (1992-93).

Motta—Chicago (1968-76), Washington (1976-80), Dallas (1980-87), Sacramento (1990-91), Dallas (1994-96), Denver (1997); **Nelson**—Milwaukee (1976-87), Golden St. (1988-95), New York (1995-96); **Ramsay**—Philadelphia (1968-72), Buffalo (1972-76), Portland (1976-86), Indiana (1986-89); **Riley**—LA Lakers (1981-90), New York (1991-95), Miami (1995–); **Shue**—Baltimore (1967-73), Philadelphia (1973-77), San Diego Clippers (1978-80), Washington (1980-86), LA Clippers (1987-89); **Sloan**—Chicago (1979-82), Utah (1988–); **Wilkens**—Seattle (1969-72), Portland (1974-76), Seattle (1977-85), Cleveland (1986-93), Atlanta (1993–).

Top Winning Percentages

Minimum of 350 victories, including playoffs; coaches active during 1996-97 season in **bold** type.

		Yrs	W	L	Pct
1	**Phil Jackson**	8	579	208	**.736**
2	**Pat Riley**	15	1002	442	**.694**
3	Billy Cunningham	8	520	235	**.689**
4	K.C. Jones	10	603	309	**.661**
5	Red Auerbach	20	1037	548	**.654**
6	Tommy Heinsohn	9	474	296	**.616**
7	**Jerry Sloan**	12	629	410	**.605**
8	Chuck Daly	12	638	427	**.599**
9	Larry Costello	10	467	323	**.591**
10	John Kundla	11	485	338	**.589**
11	**George Karl**	10	483	348	**.581**
12	**Rick Adelman**	8	393	285	**.580**
13	Bill Sharman	7	368	267	**.580**
14	Al Cervi	9	359	267	**.573**
15	Don Nelson	19	902	690	**.567**
16	Joe Lapchick	9	356	277	**.562**
17	**Larry Brown**	14	665	522	**.560**
18	**Mike Fratello**	12	522	433	**.547**
19	**Lenny Wilkens**	24	1138	952	**.544**
20	Bill Russell	8	375	317	**.542**
21	Alex Hannum	12	518	446	**.537**
22	Red Holzman	18	754	651	**.536**
23	Doug Moe	15	661	579	**.533**
24	**Del Harris**	12	520	474	**.523**
25	Richie Guerin	8	353	325	**.521**

Active Coaches' Victories

Through 1996-97 season, including playoffs.

		Yrs	W	L	Pct
1	Lenny Wilkens, Atlanta	24	**1138**	952	.544
2	Pat Riley, Miami	15	**1002**	442	.694
3	Bill Fitch, LA Clippers	24	**982**	1095	.473
4	Larry Brown, Philadelphia	14	**665**	522	.560
5	Chuck Daly, Orlando	12	**638**	427	.599
6	Jerry Sloan, Utah	12	**629**	410	.605
7	Phil Jackson, Chicago	8	**579**	208	.736
8	Mike Fratello, Cleveland	12	**522**	433	.547
9	Del Harris, LA Lakers	12	**520**	474	.523
10	George Karl, Seattle	10	**483**	348	.581
11	Rudy Tomjanovich, Houston	6	**329**	192	.631
12	Chris Ford, Milwaukee	6	**278**	253	.524
13	Bernie Bickerstaff, Wash.	8	**272**	286	.487
14	Doug Collins, Detroit	5	**252**	196	.562
15	Mike Dunleavy, Portland	6	**221**	294	.429
16	Brian Hill, Vancouver	4	**208**	122	.630
17	P.J. Carlesimo, Golden St.	3	**140**	118	.543
18	Rick Pitino, Boston	2	**96**	81	.542
19	Jeff Van Gundy, New York	2	**81**	43	.653
	Dave Cowens, Charlotte	2	**81**	82	.497
21	Phil Saunders, Minnesota	2	**60**	84	.417
22	Danny Ainge, Phoenix	1	**42**	36	.538
23	Darrell Walker, Toronto	1	**30**	52	.366
24	John Calipari, New Jersey	1	**26**	56	.317
25	Jim Cleamons, Dallas	1	**24**	58	.293
26	Gregg Popovich, San Antonio	1	**17**	47	.266
27	Eddie Jordan, Sacramento	1	**6**	9	.400
28	Larry Bird, Indiana	0	**0**	0	—
29	Bill Hanzlik, Denver	0	**0**	0	—

Annual Awards
Most Valuable Player

The Maurice Podoloff Trophy for regular season MVP. Named after the first commissioner (then president) of the NBA. Winners first selected by the NBA players (1956-80) then a national panel of pro basketball writers and broadcasters (since 1981). Winners' scoring averages are provided; (*) indicates led league.

Multiple winners: Kareem Abdul-Jabbar (6); Bill Russell (5); Wilt Chamberlain and Michael Jordan (4); Larry Bird, Magic Johnson and Moses Malone (3); Bob Pettit (2).

Year		Avg	Year		Avg
1956	Bob Pettit, St. Louis, F	25.7*	1978	Bill Walton, Portland, C	18.9
1957	Bob Cousy, Boston, G	20.6	1979	Moses Malone, Houston, C	24.8
1958	Bill Russell, Boston, C	16.6	1980	Kareem Abdul-Jabbar, LA, C	24.8
1959	Bob Pettit, St. Louis, F	29.2*	1981	Julius Erving, Philadelphia, F	24.6
1960	Wilt Chamberlain, Philadelphia, C	37.6*	1982	Moses Malone, Houston, C	31.1
1961	Bill Russell, Boston, C	16.9	1983	Moses Malone, Philadelphia, C	24.5
1962	Bill Russell, Boston, C	18.9	1984	Larry Bird, Boston, F	24.2
1963	Bill Russell, Boston, C	16.8	1985	Larry Bird, Boston, F	28.7
1964	Oscar Robertson, Cincinnati, G	31.4	1986	Larry Bird, Boston, F	25.8
1965	Bill Russell, Boston, C	14.1	1987	Magic Johnson, LA Lakers, G	23.9
1966	Wilt Chamberlain, Philadelphia, C	33.5*	1988	Michael Jordan, Chicago, G	35.0*
1967	Wilt Chamberlain, Philadelphia, C	24.1	1989	Magic Johnson, LA Lakers, G	22.5
1968	Wilt Chamberlain, Philadelphia, C	24.3	1990	Magic Johnson, LA Lakers, G	22.3
1969	Wes Unseld, Baltimore, C	13.8	1991	Michael Jordan, Chicago, G	31.5*
1970	Willis Reed, New York, C	21.7	1992	Michael Jordan, Chicago, G	30.1*
1971	Lew Alcindor, Milwaukee, C	31.7*	1993	Charles Barkley, Phoenix, F	25.6
1972	Kareem Abdul-Jabbar, Milwaukee, C	34.8*	1994	Hakeem Olajuwon, Houston, C	27.3
1973	Dave Cowens, Boston, C	20.5	1995	David Robinson, San Antonio, C	27.6
1974	Kareem Abdul-Jabbar, LA, C	27.0	1996	Michael Jordan, Chicago, G	30.4*
1975	Bob McAdoo, Buffalo, F	34.5*	1997	Karl Malone, Utah, F	27.4
1976	Kareem Abdul-Jabbar, LA, C	27.7			
1977	Kareem Abdul-Jabbar, LA, C	26.2			

Note: Lew Alcindor changed his name to Kareem Abdul-Jabbar after the 1970-71 season.

Rookie of the Year

The Eddie Gottlieb Trophy for outstanding rookie of the regular season. Named after the pro basketball pioneer and owner-coach of the first NBA champion Philadelphia Warriors. Winners selected by a national panel of pro basketball writers and broadcasters. Winners' scoring averages provided; (*) indicated led league; winners who were also named MVP are in **bold** type.

Year		Avg	Year		Avg
1953	Don Meineke, Ft. Wayne, F	10.8	1976	Alvan Adams, Phoenix, C	19.0
1954	Ray Felix, Baltimore, C	17.6	1977	Adrian Dantley, Buffalo, F	20.3
1955	Bob Pettit, Milwaukee Hawks, F	20.4	1978	Walter Davis, Phoenix, G	24.2
1956	Maurice Stokes, Rochester, F/C	16.8	1979	Phil Ford, Kansas City, G	15.9
1957	Tommy Heinsohn, Boston, F	16.2			
1958	Woody Sauldsberry, Philadelphia, F/C	12.8	1980	Larry Bird, Boston, F	21.3
1959	Elgin Baylor, Minneapolis, F	24.9	1981	Darrell Griffith, Utah, G	20.6
			1982	Buck Williams, New Jersey, F	15.5
1960	**Wilt Chamberlain**, Philadelphia, C	37.6*	1983	Terry Cummings, San Diego, F	23.7
1961	Oscar Robertson, Cincinnati, G	30.5	1984	Ralph Sampson, Houston, C	21.0
1962	Walt Bellamy, Chicago Packers, C	31.6	1985	Michael Jordan, Chicago, G	28.2
1963	Terry Dischinger, Chicago Zephyrs, F	25.5	1986	Patrick Ewing, New York, C	20.0
1964	Jerry Lucas, Cincinnati, F/C	17.7	1987	Chuck Person, Indiana, F	18.8
1965	Willis Reed, New York, C	19.5	1988	Mark Jackson, New York, G	13.6
1966	Rick Barry, San Francisco, F	25.7	1989	Mitch Richmond, Golden St., G	22.0
1967	Dave Bing, Detroit, G	20.0			
1968	Earl Monroe, Baltimore, G	24.3	1990	David Robinson, San Antonio, C	24.3
1969	**Wes Unseld**, Baltimore, C	13.8	1991	Derrick Coleman, New Jersey, F	18.4
			1992	Larry Johnson, Charlotte, F	19.2
1970	Lew Alcindor, Milwaukee Bucks, C	28.8	1993	Shaquille O'Neal, Orlando,C	23.4
1971	Dave Cowens, Boston, C	17.0	1994	Chris Webber, Golden St., F	17.5
	& Geoff Petrie, Portland, F	24.8	1995	Grant Hill, Detroit, F	19.9
1972	Sidney Wicks, Portland, F	24.5		& Jason Kidd, Dallas, G	11.7
1973	Bob McAdoo, Buffalo, C/F	18.0	1996	Damon Stoudamire, Toronto, G	19.0
1974	Ernie DiGregorio, Buffalo, G	15.2	1997	Allen Iverson, Philadelphia, G	23.5
1975	Keith Wilkes, Golden St., F	14.2			

Note: The Chicago Packers changed their name to the Zephyrs after 1961-62 season. Also, Lew Alcindor changed his name to Kareem Abdul-Jabbar after the 1970-71 season.

Sixth Man Award

Awarded to the Best Player Off the Bench for the regular season. Winners selected by a national panel of pro basketball writers and broadcasters.

Multiple winners: Kevin McHale, Ricky Pierce and Detlef Schrempf (2).

Year		Year		Year	
1983	Bobby Jones, Phi., F	1988	Roy Tarpley, Dal., F	1993	Cliff Robinson, Port., F
1984	Kevin McHale, Bos., F	1989	Eddie Johnson, Pho., F	1994	Dell Curry, Char., G
1985	Kevin McHale, Bos., F	1990	Ricky Pierce, Mil., G/F	1995	Anthony Mason, NY, F
1986	Bill Walton, Bos., F/C	1991	Detlef Schrempf, Ind., F	1996	Toni Kukoc, Chi., F
1987	Ricky Pierce, Mil., G/F	1992	Detlef Schrempf, Ind., F	1997	John Starks, NY, G

Number One Draft Choices

Overall first choices in the NBA draft since the abolition of the territorial draft in 1966. Players who became Rookie of the Year are in **bold** type. The draft lottery began in 1985.

Year		Overall 1st Pick	Year		Overall 1st Pick
1966	New York	Cazzie Russell, Michigan	1982	LA Lakers	James Worthy, N. Carolina
1967	Detroit	Jimmy Walker, Providence	1983	Houston	**Ralph Sampson**, Virginia
1968	San Diego	Elvin Hayes, Houston	1984	Houston	Akeem Olajuwon, Houston
1969	Milwaukee	**Lew Alcindor**, UCLA	1985	New York	**Patrick Ewing**, Georgetown
			1986	Cleveland	Brad Daugherty, N. Carolina
1970	Detroit	Bob Lanier, St. Bonaventure	1987	San Antonio	**David Robinson**, Navy
1971	Cleveland	Austin Carr, Notre Dame	1988	LA Clippers	Danny Manning, Kansas
1972	Portland	LaRue Martin, Loyola-Chicago	1989	Sacramento	Pervis Ellison, Louisville
1973	Philadelphia	Doug Collins, Illinois St.			
1974	Portland	Bill Walton, UCLA	1990	New Jersey	**Derrick Coleman**, Syracuse
1975	Atlanta	David Thompson, N.C. State	1991	Charlotte	**Larry Johnson**, UNLV
1976	Houston	John Lucas, Maryland	1992	Orlando	**Shaquille O'Neal**, LSU
1977	Milwaukee	Kent Benson, Indiana	1993	Orlando	**Chris Webber**, Michigan
1978	Portland	Mychal Thompson, Minnesota	1994	Milwaukee	Glenn Robinson, Purdue
1979	LA Lakers	Magic Johnson, Michigan St.	1995	Golden St.	Joe Smith, Maryland
1980	Golden St	Joe Barry Carroll, Purdue	1996	Philadelphia	**Allen Iverson**, Georgetown
1981	Dallas	Mark Aguirre, DePaul	1997	San Antonio	Tim Duncan, Wake Forest

Note: Lew Alcindor changed his name to Kareem Abdul-Jabbar after the 1970-71 season; Akeem Olajuwon changed his first name to Hakeem in 1991; In 1975 David Thompson signed with Denver of the ABA and did not play for Atlanta; David Robinson joined NBA for 1989-90 season after fulfilling military obligation.

Defensive Player of the Year

Awarded to the Best Defensive Player for the regular season. Winners selected by a national panel of pro basketball writers and broadcasters.

Multiple winners: Mark Eaton, Sidney Moncrief, Dikembe Mutombo, Hakeem Olajuwon and Dennis Rodman (2).

Year	Year	Year
1983 Sidney Moncrief, Mil., G	1988 Michael Jordan, Chi., G	1993 Hakeem Olajuwon, Hou., C
1984 Sidney Moncrief, Mil., G	1989 Mark Eaton, Utah, C	1994 Hakeem Olajuwon, Hou., C
1985 Mark Eaton, Utah, C	1990 Dennis Rodman, Det., F	1995 Dikembe Mutombo, Den., C
1986 Alvin Robertson, SA, G	1991 Dennis Rodman, Det., F	1996 Gary Payton, Sea., G
1987 Michael Cooper, LAL, F	1992 David Robinson, SA, C	1997 Dikembe Mutombo, Atl., C

Most Improved Player

Awarded to the Most Improved Player for the regular season. Winners selected by a national panel of pro basketball writers and broadcasters.

Year	Year	Year
1986 Alvin Robertson, SA, G	1990 Rony Seikaly, Mia., C	1994 Don MacLean, Wash., F
1987 Dale Ellis, Sea., G	1991 Scott Skiles, Orl., G	1995 Dana Barros, Phi., G
1988 Kevin Duckworth, Port., C	1992 Pervis Ellison, Wash., C	1996 Gheorghe Muresan, Wash., C
1989 Kevin Johnson, Pho., G	1993 Mahmoud Abdul-Rauf, Den., G	1997 Isaac Austin, Miami, C

Coach of the Year

The Red Auerbach Trophy for outstanding coach of the year. Renamed in 1967 for the former Boston coach who led the Celtics to nine NBA titles. Winners selected by a national panel of pro basketball writers and broadcasters. Previous season and winning season records are provided; (*) indicates division title.

Multiple winners: Don Nelson and Pat Riley (3); Bill Fitch, Cotton Fitzsimmons and Gene Shue (2).

Year		Improvement	Year		Improvement
1963	Harry Gallatin, St. L	29-51 to 48-32	1981	Jack McKinney, Ind	37-45 to 44-38
1964	Alex Hannum, SF	31-49 to 48-32*	1982	Gene Shue, Wash	39-43 to 43-39
1965	Red Auerbach, Bos	59-21* to 61-18*	1983	Don Nelson, Mil	55-27* to 51-31*
1966	Dolph Schayes, Phi	40-40 to 55-25*	1984	Frank Layden, Utah	30-52 to 45-37*
1967	Johnny Kerr, Chi	Expan. to 33-48	1985	Don Nelson, Mil	50-32* to 59-23*
1968	Richie Guerin, St. L	39-42 to 56-26*	1986	Mike Fratello, Atl	34-48 to 50-32
1969	Gene Shue, Balt	36-46 to 57-25*	1987	Mike Schuler, Port	40-42 to 49-33
1970	Red Holzman, NY	54-28 to 60-22*	1988	Doug Moe, Den	37-45 to 54-28*
1971	Dick Motta, Chi	39-43 to 51-31	1989	Cotton Fitzsimmons, Pho	28-54 to 55-27
1972	Bill Sharman, LA	48-34* to 69-13*	1990	Pat Riley, LA Lakers	57-25* to 63-19*
1973	Tommy Heinsohn, Bos	56-26* to 68-14*	1991	Don Chaney, Hou	41-41 to 52-30
1974	Ray Scott, Det	40-42 to 52-30	1992	Don Nelson, GS	44-38 to 55-27
1975	Phil Johnson, KC-Omaha	33-49 to 44-38	1993	Pat Riley, NY	51-31 to 60-22
1976	Bill Fitch, Cle	40-42 to 49-33*	1994	Lenny Wilkens, Atl	43-39 to 57-25*
1977	Tom Nissalke, Hou	40-42 to 49-33*	1995	Del Harris, LA Lakers	33-49 to 48-34
1978	Hubie Brown, Atl	31-51 to 41-41	1996	Phil Jackson, Chi	47-35 to 72-10*
1979	Cotton Fitzsimmons, KC	31-51 to 48-34*	1997	Pat Riley, Mia	42-40 to 61-21
1980	Bill Fitch, Bos	29-53 to 61-21*			

World Championships

The World Basketball Championships for men and women have been played regularly at four-year intervals (give or take a year) since 1970. The men's tournament began in 1950 and the women's in 1953. The Federation Internationale de Basketball Amateur (FIBA), which governs the World and Olympic tournaments, was founded in 1932. FIBA first allowed professional players from the NBA to participate in 1994.

Men

Multiple wins: Soviet Union, USA and Yugoslavia (3); Brazil (2).

Year	
1950	**Argentina**, United States, Chile
1954	**United States**, Brazil, Philippines
1959	**Brazil**, United States, Chile
1963	**Brazil**, Yugoslavia, Soviet Union
1967	**Soviet Union**, Yugoslavia, Brazil
1970	**Yugoslavia**, Brazil, Soviet Union
1974	**Soviet Union**, Yugoslavia, United States
1978	**Yugoslavia**, Soviet Union, Brazil
1982	**Soviet Union**, United States, Yugoslavia
1986	**United States**, Soviet Union, Yugoslavia
1990	**Yugoslavia**, Soviet Union, United States
1994	**United States**, Russia, Croatia
1998	at Athens (August)

Women

Multiple wins: Soviet Union (6); USA (5).

Year	
1953	**United States**, Chile, France
1957	**United States**, Soviet Union, Czechoslovakia
1959	**Soviet Union**, Bulgaria, Czechoslovakia
1964	**Soviet Union**, Czechoslovakia, Bulgaria
1967	**Soviet Union**, South Korea, Czechoslovakia
1971	**Soviet Union**, Czechoslovakia, Brazil
1975	**Soviet Union**, Japan, Czechoslovakia
1979	**United States**, South Korea, Canada
1983	**Soviet Union**, United States, China
1986	**United States**, Soviet Union, Canada
1990	**United States**, Yugoslavia, Cuba
1994	**Brazil**, China, United States
1998	at Berlin (July)

NBA Photos

50 Greatest Players

In October 1996, as part of its 50th anniversary celebration, the NBA named the 50 greatest players in league history. The voting was done by a league-approved panel of media, former players and coaches, current and former general managers and team executives. The players are listed alphabetically along with the dates of their professional careers and positions. Active players are in **bold** type.

Player	Pos	Player	Pos	Player	Pos
Kareem Abdul-Jabbar, 1969-89	C	George Gervin, 1972-86	G	Bob Pettit, 1954-65	F/C
Nate Archibald, 1970-84	G	Hal Greer, 1958-73	G	**Scottie Pippen**, 1987—	F
Paul Arizin, 1950-61	F/G	John Havlicek, 1962-78	F/G	Willis Reed, 1964-74	C
Charles Barkley, 1984—	F	Elvin Hayes, 1968-84	F/C	Oscar Robertson, 1960-74	G
Rick Barry, 1965-80	F	Magic Johnson, 1979-91, 95-96	G	**David Robinson**, 1989—	C
Elgin Baylor, 1958-72	F	Sam Jones, 1957-69	G	Bill Russell, 1956-69	C
Dave Bing, 1966-78	G	**Michael Jordan**, 1984-93, 94—	G	Dolph Schayes, 1948-64	F/C
Larry Bird, 1979-92	F	Jerry Lucas, 1963-74	F/C	Bill Sharman, 1950-61	G
Wilt Chamberlain, 1959-73	C	**Karl Malone**, 1985—	F	**John Stockton**, 1984—	G
Bob Cousy, 1950-70	G	Moses Malone, 1974-95	C	Isiah Thomas, 1981-94	G
Dave Cowens, 1970-80, 82-83	C	Pete Maravich, 1970-80	G	Nate Thurmond, 1963-77	C/F
Billy Cunningham, 1965-76	G	Kevin McHale, 1980-93	F	Wes Unseld, 1968-81	C/F
Dave DeBusschere, 1962-74	F	George Mikan, 1946-54, 55-56	C	Bill Walton, 1974-88	C
Clyde Drexler, 1983—	G	Earl Monroe, 1967-80	G	Jerry West, 1960-74	G
Julius Erving, 1971-87	F	**Hakeem Olajuwon**, 1984—	C	Lenny Wilkens, 1960-75	G
Patrick Ewing, 1985—	C	**Shaquille O'Neal**, 1992—	C	James Worthy, 1982-94	F
Walt Frazier, 1967-80	G	Robert Parish, 1976-1997	C		

Note: Rick Barry, Billy Cunningham, Julius Erving, George Gervin and Moses Malone all played part of their pro careers in the ABA.

10 Greatest Coaches

In December 1996, as part of its 50th anniversary celebration, the NBA named the 10 greatest coaches in league history. The voting was done by a league-approved panel of media. The coaches are listed alphabetically along with the dates of their professional coaching careers and overall records, including playoff games, and number of NBA titles won. Active coaches are in **bold** type.

Coach	W	L	Pct.	Titles
Red Auerbach, 1946-66	1037	548	.654	9
Chuck Daly, 1981-94, 97—	638	427	.599	2
Bill Fitch, 1970—	982	1095	.473	1
Red Holzman, 1953-82	754	652	.536	2
Phil Jackson, 1989—	579	208	.736	5
John Kundla, 1947-59	485	338	.589	5
Don Nelson, 1976-96	902	690	.567	0
Jack Ramsay, 1968-89	908	841	.519	1
Pat Riley, 1981—	1002	442	.694	4
Lenny Wilkens, 1969—	1138	952	.544	1
Totals	8425	6193	.576	30

American Basketball Association
ABA Finals

The American Basketball Assn. began play in 1967-68 as a 10-team rival of the 21-year-old NBA. The ABA, which introduced the three-point basket, a multi-colored ball and the All-Star Game Slam Dunk Contest, lasted nine seasons before folding following the 1975-76 season. Four ABA teams–Denver, Indiana, New York and San Antonio–survived to enter the NBA in 1976-77. The NBA also adopted the three-point basket (in 1979-80) and the All-Star Game Slam Dunk Contest. The older league, however, refused to take in the ABA ball.

Multiple winners: Indiana (3); New York (2).

Year	Winner	Head Coach	Series		Loser	Head Coach
1968	Pittsburgh Pipers	Vince Cazzetta	4-3	(WLLWLWW)	New Orleans Bucs	Babe McCarthy
1969	Oakland Oaks	Alex Hannum	4-1	(WLWWW)	Indiana Pacers	Bob Leonard
1970	Indiana Pacers	Bob Leonard	4-2	(WWLWLW)	Los Angeles Stars	Bill Sharman
1971	Utah Stars	Bill Sharman	4-3	(WWLLWLW)	Kentucky Colonels	Frank Ramsey
1972	Indiana Pacers	Bob Leonard	4-2	(WLWLWW)	New York Nets	Lou Carnesecca
1973	Indiana Pacers	Bob Leonard	4-3	(WLLWWLW)	Kentucky Colonels	Joe Mullaney
1974	New York Nets	Kevin Loughery	4-1	(WWWLW)	Utah Stars	Joe Mullaney
1975	Kentucky Colonels	Hubie Brown	4-1	(WWWLW)	Indiana Pacers	Bob Leonard
1976	New York Nets	Kevin Loughery	4-2	(WLWWLW)	Denver Nuggets	Larry Brown

Most Valuable Player

Winners' scoring averages provided; (*) indicates led league.

Multiple winners: Julius Erving (3); Mel Daniels (2).

Year		Avg
1968	Connie Hawkins, Pittsburgh, C	26.8*
1969	Mel Daniels, Indiana, C	24.0
1970	Spencer Haywood, Denver, C	30.0*
1971	Mel Daniels, Indiana, C	21.0
1972	Artis Gilmore, Kentucky, C	23.8
1973	Billy Cunningham, Carolina, F	24.1
1974	Julius Erving, New York, F	27.4*
1975	George McGinnis, Indiana, F	29.8*
	& Julius Erving, New York, F	27.9
1976	Julius Erving, New York, F	29.3*

Rookie of the Year

Winners' scoring averages provided; (*) indicates led league. Rookies who were also named Most Valuable Player are in **bold** type.

Year		Avg
1968	Mel Daniels, Minnesota, C	22.2
1969	Warren Armstrong, Oakland, G	21.5
1970	**Spencer Haywood**, Denver, C	30.0*
1971	Dan Issel, Kentucky, C	29.8*
	& Charlie Scott, Virginia, G	27.1
1972	**Artis Gilmore**, Kentucky, C	23.8
1973	Brian Taylor, New York, G	15.3
1974	Swen Nater, Virginia-SA, C	14.1
1975	Marvin Barnes, St. Louis, C	24.0
1976	David Thompson, Denver, F	26.0

Note: Warren Armstrong changed his name to Warren Jabali after the 1970-71 season.

Coach of the Year

Previous season and winning season records are provided; (*) indicates division title.

Multiple winner: Larry Brown (3).

Year		Improvement		
1968	Vince Cazetta, Pittsburgh			54-24*
1969	Alex Hannum, Oakland	22-56	to	60-18*
1970	Joe Belmont, Denver	44-34	to	51-33*
	& Bill Sharman, LA Stars	33-45	to	43-41
1971	Al Bianchi, Virginia	44-40	to	55-29*
1972	Tom Nissalke, Dallas	30-54	to	42-42
1973	Larry Brown, Carolina	35-49	to	57-27*
1974	Babe McCarthy, Kentucky	56-28	to	53-31
	& Joe Mullaney, Utah	55-29*	to	51-33*
1975	Larry Brown, Denver	37-47	to	65-19*
1976	Larry Brown, Denver	65-19*	to	60-24*

Scoring Leaders

Scoring championship decided by per game point average every season.

Multiple winner: Julius Erving (3).

Year		Gm	Avg	Pts
1968	Connie Hawkins, Pittsburgh	70	1875	26.8
1969	Rick Barry, Oakland	35	1190	34.0
1970	Spencer Haywood, Denver	84	2519	30.0
1971	Dan Issel, Kentucky	83	2480	29.8
1972	Charlie Scott, Virginia	73	2524	34.6
1973	Julius Erving, Virginia	71	2268	31.9
1974	Julius Erving, New York	84	2299	27.4
1975	George McGinnis, Indiana	79	2353	29.8
1976	Julius Erving, New York	84	2462	29.3

ABA All-Star Game

The ABA All-Star Game was an Eastern Division vs Western Division contest from 1968-75. League membership had dropped to seven teams by 1976, the ABA's last season, so the team in first place at the break (Denver) played an All-Star team made up from the other six clubs.

Series: East won 5, West 3 and Denver 1.

Year	Result	Host	Coaches	Most Valuable Player
1968	East 126, West 120	Indiana	Jim Pollard, Babe McCarthy	Larry Brown, New Orleans
1969	West 133, East 127	Louisville	Alex Hannum, Gene Rhodes	John Beasley, Dallas
1970	West 128, East 98	Indiana	Babe McCarthy, Bob Leonard	Spencer Haywood, Denver
1971	East 126, West 122	Carolina	Al Bianchi, Bill Sharman	Mel Daniels, Indiana
1972	East 142, West 115	Louisville	Joe Mullaney, Ladell Andersen	Dan Issel, Kentucky
1973	West 123, East 111	Utah	Ladell Andersen, Larry Brown	Warren Jabali, Denver
1974	East 128, West 112	Virginia	Babe McCarthy, Joe Mullaney	Artis Gilmore, Kentucky
1975	East 151, West 124	San Antonio	Kevin Loughery, Larry Brown	Freddie Lewis, St. Louis
1976	Denver 144, ABA 138	Denver	Larry Brown, Kevin Loughery	David Thompson, Denver

Hockey

Retiring Pittsburgh Penguins captain **Mario Lemieux** waves to the crowd after his last regular season game in Miami on April 11, 1997. ────

Wide World Photos

Red Wings of Victory

Detroit's first Stanley Cup since 1955 made Scotty Bowman the first coach to win the Cup with three different teams.

by
Steve Levy

Outside of three rough spots, the 1996–97 National Hockey League season could only be considered a success.

When a sport loses someone who is arguably its best player to an early retirement, the loss is incalculable. Hockey will feel the loss of Mario Lemieux for years to come. Never before had a player so effortlessly blended size, strength and grace. And in addition to his supreme talents, Lemieux was cordial and classy, a gentleman. I, for one, applaud the decision by the Hockey Hall of Fame to waive the traditional three year waiting period for Lemieux. Citing Mario's "outstanding pre-eminence and skill", the Hall inducted him only

months after his retirement.

Another minus was that the Stanley Cup Finals ended in a sweep for the third straight year. The last time we endured this trifecta was 1968–70. The St. Louis Blues were on the receiving end of the broom all three times. Their coach? Scotty Bowman.

In the 1997 NHL finals, however, Bowman, the winningest coach in league history, did the sweeping. Bowman led the Detroit Red Wings to their first title since 1955. The Wings were so much better than the Philadelphia Flyers that a sweep, while boring, was fitting. Against Detroit, Philadelphia couldn't do any of the things that had gotten them to the Finals. The Flyers couldn't score, defend or get anything close to NHL playoff-quality goaltending.

Steve Levy is the host of ESPN's *National Hockey Night.*

For the seventh time in his career, and with his third team, Detroit Red Wings coach **Scotty Bowman** hoists the Stanley Cup for a trip around the rink. Bowman also led the Montreal Canadiens (5) and Pittsburgh Penguins (1) to championships.

I believe that, outside of Philadelphia, the whole hockey world, including Russia, was rooting for the Red Wings and especially captain Steve Yzerman. For the organization, it was their first success in 42 years but for Stevie Y it meant, as he put it, "Now no one will be able to say, 'Yeah, but he never won a championship.'"

Sadly, in the midst of Cup victory parties, the city and the team fell silent. A limousine carrying players Viacheslav Fetisov, Vladimir Konstantinov and team masseur Sergei Mnatsakanov crashed into a tree while returning from a team dinner on June 13th. Fetisov was out of the hospital within a month but his friends remained comatose and in critical condition for much longer. The limousine driver, Richard Gnida, had traces of marijuana in his system and may have fallen asleep at the wheel. The team and city rallied around their fallen warriors with as much vigor as they had celebrated only days before.

Other thoughts from the season that was... Next season the Sabres will have a new GM and a new coach. You'd think they finished last instead of first... People will look back and sneer that the Mighty Ducks were swept in the second round of their first playoff appearance. But a closer look will reveal that three of their four losses came in overtime, with one single, one double and one triple overtime. And, of course, they lost to the eventual champions... The Rangers ended their Cup drought in 1994 and the Red Wings did the same this year. Next up on the clock is the Chicago Blackhawks who now have the distinction of going the longest time between Stanley Cup victories, thirty-six years and counting. Will Chris Chelios be hoisting the Cup around the United Center next June? ∎

Colorado Avalanche goaltender **Patrick Roy** is a lot worse for the wear after participating in the brawl of the year in a game against the Detroit Red Wings. Roy, one of the league's biggest stars, dislocated his shoulder and missed three games. The NHL needs to rethink its position on fighting.

Linda Cohn's Top Ten Highlights of the 1996–97 NHL season.

10. The amazing season of the **Buffalo Sabres**, who won their division despite not even making the playoffs last year and losing Pat LaFontaine early in the year, was a season-long surprise. Dominik Hasek became the first goalie to win the MVP trophy since Jacques Plante in 1962.

9. The **Dallas Stars** also won their division (and gave the Colorado Avalanche a run for the best record in the conference) after not making the playoffs last year.

8. Armed with new perspective, **Mario Lemieux** came back for one more run at the Stanley Cup and then retired. The game will

miss him. He literally saved NHL hockey in Pittsburgh. He retired with a two points per game average. Just imagine him healthy.

7. **Wayne Gretzky** teamed up with **Mark Messier** again, this time as New York Rangers. A not-past-his-prime Gretzky tied for the league lead in assists and was the Rangers' best player in the playoffs.

6. Due to the rivalry established in the 1996 playoffs, the first three meetings of the **Red Wings and Avalanche** during the regular season were filled with tension. And the fourth was downright ugly. There were 39 penalties called for 148 minutes, including 18 fighting majors, 10 roughing minors and 2

Mark Messier shook up the NHL when he left the New York Rangers and signed a free agent contract with the Vancouver Canucks. The Rangers also lost out when they signed Colorado's Joe Sakic to a prohibitive offer sheet only to have the Avalanche match it.

game misconducts. But no suspensions. And Patrick Roy missed ten days with an injured shoulder. He missed three games in which his team went 1–2 and gave up 11 goals. All of which begs the question: Does the sport really want to be one of the big four?

5. The **Anaheim Mighty Ducks** emerged as a legitimate, solid team. With Paul Kariya and Teemu Selanne up front and the talented Guy Hebert in goal, new coach Pierre Pagé will have a lot to build on.

4. The **Hartford Whalers** left Connecticut for North Carolina. Who is to blame here? Owner Peter Karmanos? The fans? Maybe no one thing or person is at fault but one thing is clear; you have to win

to be successful financially and the Whalers rarely won in 22 years in the mall.

3. Among the many odd coaching changes in the league, two stand out: **Ron Wilson** in Anaheim and **Don Hay** in Phoenix. Simply put, why were these men fired? Call me if you know.

2. The **Detroit Red Wings** win their first Stanley Cup since 1955. The Rangers ended a long drought recently as well and the key acquisition was Mark Messier. For the Wings, **Brendan Shanahan** provided the same intangibles that resulted in a championship.

1. Unfortunately, a **tragic car crash** muted the city's joy. Suddenly a Stanley Cup victory didn't mean

so much. A sign held up at a city-wide vigil said it best: "Please mend our broken Wings." ■

THE NUMBERS

INSIDE

by
Jim Samia

MARIO MAGNIFICENT

The remarkable Mario Lemieux finished his regular season career with 613 goals, 881 assists for 1,494 points in 745 games. He won six scoring titles. Lemieux also has the highest goals per game average in NHL history and is second only to Wayne Gretzky in several other key offensive numbers. A brilliant career.

Mario by the Numbers

	Number	All-time rank
Goals per game	.823	1st
Assists per game	1.83	2nd
Points per game	2.01	2nd
Hat Tricks	39	T-2nd
100 point seasons	10	2nd

WORST TO **FIRST**

In 1996–97, the Dallas Stars became only the seventh NHL team to go from last in their division to first the following season. This turnaround has only been accomplished three times since the league expanded in 1967. The 1994 Rangers and 1936 Red Wings also won the Cup in their year of reversed fortunes.

Top NHL Turnarounds	Worst	First
Stars	1995-96	1996-97
Rangers	1992-93	1993-94
Blackhawks	1968-69	1969-70
Red Wings	1934-35	1935-36
Bruins	1931-32	1932-33
Montreal Maroons	1928-29	1929-30
Hamilton	1923-24	1924-25

A NET FULL OF **HART**

For the first time in thirty-five years, and only the fifth time in league history, a goalie, Buffalo's Dominik Hasek, won the NHL's MVP award. The first netminder to take home the Hart trophy was the immortal Roy "Shrimpy" Worters. Shrimpy is the also the shortest goaltender in NHL history, skating in at 5' 3''.

MVP Winning Goaltenders	Year
Dominik Hasek, Buffalo	**1997**
Jacques Plante, Montreal	1962
Al Rollins, Toronto	1954
Chuck Rayner, NY Rangers	1950
Roy Worters, NY Americans	1929

FAST AS **HULL**

In 1996, Brett Hull became the fourth–fastest NHL player to score 500 goals and the twenty-fourth of all time. Hull put a huge gap between himself and the fifth fastest, Phil Esposito. This may be a bit *too* inside the numbers but both Hull and Esposito scored their 500th on December 22nd, 22 years apart. Joey Mullen and Dave Andreychuk also joined the 500 club last season.

Fastest to 500 Goals	Game Number
Wayne Gretzky	575
Mario Lemieux	605
Mike Bossy	647
Brett Hull	**693**
Phil Esposito	803
Jari Kurri	833
Bobby Hull	861

■

THE 1998 ESPN INFORMATION PLEASE SPORTS ALMANAC

HOCKEY STATISTICS

THE SEASON IN REVIEW
1996-1997
NHL • WORLD • U.S. COLLEGES

SEC A
PAGE 383

Final NHL Standings

Division champions (*) and playoff qualifiers (†) are noted. Number of seasons listed after each head coach refers to current tenure with club through 1996-97 season.

Western Conference

Central Division

	W	L	T	Pts	GF	GA	Dif
*Dallas	48	26	8	104	252	198	+54
†Detroit	38	26	18	94	253	197	+56
†Phoenix	38	37	7	83	240	243	-3
†St. Louis	36	35	11	83	236	239	-3
†Chicago	34	35	13	81	223	210	+13
Toronto	30	44	8	68	230	273	-43

Head Coaches: Dal— Ken Hitchcock (2nd season); **Det—** Scotty Bowman (4th); **Pho—** Don Hay (1st); **St.L—** fired Mike Keenan (3rd, 15-17-1) on Dec. 19 and replaced him with asst. Jimmy Roberts (3-3-3) and then Joel Quenneville (18-15-7) on Jan. 6; **Chi—** Craig Hartsburg (2nd); **Tor—** Mike Murphy (1st).

1995-96 Standings: 1. Detroit (62-13-7, 131 points); 2. Chicago (40-28-14, 94 pts); 3. Toronto (34-36-12, 80 pts); 4. St. Louis (32-34-16, 80 pts); 5. Winnipeg (36-40-6, 78 pts); 6. Dallas (26-42-14, 66 pts).

Note: Winnipeg moved to Phoenix before the 1996-97 season.

Pacific Division

	W	L	T	Pts	GF	GA	Dif
*Colorado	49	24	9	107	277	205	+72
†Anaheim	36	33	13	85	245	233	+12
†Edmonton	36	37	9	81	252	247	+5
Vancouver	35	40	7	77	257	273	-16
Calgary	32	41	9	73	214	239	-25
Los Angeles	28	43	11	67	214	268	-54
San Jose	27	47	8	62	211	278	-67

Head Coaches: Col— Marc Crawford (3rd season); **Ana—** Ron Wilson (4th); **Edm—** Ron Low (3rd); **Van—** Tom Renney (1st); **Cal—** Pierre Page (2nd); **LA—** Larry Robinson (2nd); **SJ—** Al Sims (2nd).

1995-96 Standings: 1. Colorado (47-25-10, 104 points); 2. Calgary (34-34-11, 79 pts); 3. Vancouver (32-35-15, 79 pts); 4. Anaheim (35-39-8, 78 pts); 5. Edmonton (30-44-8, 68 pts); 6. Los Angeles (24-40-18, 66 pts); 7. San Jose (20-55-7, 47 pts).

Eastern Conference

Northeast Division

	W	L	T	Pts	GF	GA	Dif
*Buffalo	40	30	12	92	237	208	+29
†Pittsburgh	38	36	8	84	285	280	+5
†Ottawa	31	36	15	77	226	234	-8
†Montreal	31	36	15	77	249	276	-27
Hartford	32	39	11	75	226	256	-30
Boston	26	47	9	61	234	300	-66

Head Coaches: Buf— Ted Nolan (2nd season); **Pit—** fired Eddie Johnston (4th, 31-26-5) on March 2 and replaced him with GM Craig Patrick (7-10-3); **Ott—** Jacques Martin (2nd); **Mon—** Mario Tremblay (2nd); **Hart—** Paul Maurice (2nd); **Bos—** Steve Kasper (2nd).

1995-96 Standings: 1. Pittsburgh (49-29-4, 102 points); 2. Boston (40-31-11, 91 pts); 3. Montreal (40-32-10, 90 pts); 4. Hartford (34-39-9, 77 pts); 5. Buffalo (33-42-7, 73 pts); 6. Ottawa (18-59-5, 41 pts).

Atlantic Division

	W	L	T	Pts	GF	GA	Dif
*New Jersey	45	23	14	104	231	182	+49
†Philadelphia	45	24	13	103	274	217	+57
†Florida	35	28	19	89	221	201	+20
†NY Rangers	38	34	10	86	258	231	+27
Washington	33	40	9	75	214	231	-17
Tampa Bay	32	40	10	74	217	247	-30
NY Islanders	29	41	12	70	240	250	-10

Head Coaches: Phi— Terry Murray (3rd season); **NYR—** Colin Campbell (3rd); **Fla—** Doug MacLean (3rd); **Wash—** Jim Schoenfeld (4th); **TB—** Terry Crisp (5th); **NJ—** Jacques Lemaire (4th); **NYI—** GM-coach Mike Milbury (2nd, 14-23-9) replaced himself with asst. Rick Bowness (15-18-3) on Jan. 24.

1995-96 Standings: 1. Philadelphia (45-24-13, 103 points); 2. NY Rangers (41-27-14, 96 pts); 3. Florida (41-31-10, 92 pts); 4. Washington (39-32-11, 89 pts); 5. Tampa Bay (38-32-12, 88 pts); 6. New Jersey (37-33-12, 86 pts); 7. NY Islanders (22-50-10, 54 pts).

Home & Away, Division, Conference Records

Sixteen teams— eight from each conference— qualify for the Stanley Cup Playoffs; (*) indicates division champions.

Western Conference

	Pts	Home	Away	Div	Conf
1 Colorado*	107	26-10-5	23-14-4	19-9-4	35-17-4
2 Dallas*	104	25-13-3	23-13-5	16-8-4	32-18-6
3 Detroit	94	20-12-9	18-14-9	9-11-8	21-20-15
4 Anaheim	85	22-13-6	13-21-7	13-12-7	24-22-10
5 Phoenix	83	15-19-7	23-18-0	15-10-3	29-24-3
6 St. Louis	83	17-20-4	19-15-7	11-12-5	27-23-6
7 Edmonton	81	21-16-4	15-21-5	12-16-4	21-28-7
8 Chicago	81	16-21-4	18-14-9	11-13-4	22-26-8
Vancouver	77	20-17-4	15-23-3	14-15-3	25-25-6
Calgary	73	21-18-2	11-23-7	15-14-3	22-29-5
Toronto	68	18-20-3	12-24-5	8-16-4	22-29-5
Los Angeles	67	18-16-7	10-27-4	12-16-4	19-29-8
San Jose	62	14-23-4	13-24-4	14-17-1	23-32-1

Eastern Conference

	Pts	Home	Away	Div	Conf
1 New Jersey*	104	23-9-9	22-14-5	14-12-6	29-16-11
2 Buffalo*	92	24-11-6	16-19-6	17-9-2	30-19-7
3 Philadelphia	103	23-12-6	22-12-7	14-14-4	29-19-8
4 Florida	89	21-12-8	14-16-11	13-10-9	23-20-13
5 NY Rangers	86	21-14-6	17-20-4	10-16-6	24-24-8
6 Pittsburgh	84	25-11-5	13-25-3	13-9-6	23-26-7
7 Ottawa	77	16-17-8	15-19-7	12-12-4	24-23-9
8 Montreal	77	17-17-7	14-19-8	8-13-7	18-26-12
Washington	75	19-17-5	14-23-4	14-14-4	23-25-8
Hartford	75	23-15-3	9-24-8	14-10-4	25-23-8
Tampa Bay	74	15-18-8	17-22-2	14-13-5	20-29-7
NY Islanders	70	19-18-4	10-23-8	14-14-4	22-27-7
Boston	61	14-20-7	12-27-2	8-19-1	19-32-5

1997 NHL All-Star Game

East, 11-7

47th NHL All-Star Game. **Date:** Jan. 18 at San Jose Arena in San Jose; **Coaches:** Doug MacLean, Florida (East) and Ken Hitchcock, Dallas (West); **MVP:** Mark Recchi, Montreal right wing (East) — three goals.

Starters were chosen by fan vote, reserves by a 5-man panel of league GMs. John LeClair was promoted to the Eastern Conference starting lineup in place of injured Pittsburgh RW Jaromir Jagr. Jagr's roster spot was filled by Adam Oates. Scott Lachance was added to the Eastern Conference reserves in place of injured NY Islanders RW Zigmund Palffy.

Tony Granato was promoted to the Western Conference starting lineup in place of injured Colorado C Joe Sakic. Teemu Selanne and Brendan Shanahan were added to the Western Conference in place of injured players Sakic and Colorado C Peter Forsberg. Dmitri Kristich, Keith Tkachuk and Guy Hebert were added to the Western Conference reserves in place of injured Los Angeles D Rob Blake, Dallas C Mike Modano and Detroit goalie Chris Osgood, respectively.

Dale Hawerchuk and Dale Hunter were added to the Eastern Conference lineup and Granato and Slava Fetisov to the Western Conference as special selections by NHL commissioner Gary Bettman.

Eastern Conference

	Starters	G	A	Pts	PM
LW	John LeClair, Philadelphia	2	1	3	0
RW	Dino Ciccarelli, Tampa Bay	0	1	1	0
C	Wayne Gretzky, NY Rangers	0	1	1	0
D	Ray Bourque, Boston	0	0	0	0
D	Brian Leetch, NY Rangers	0	0	0	0

	Reserves	G	A	Pts	PM
RW	Mark Recchi, Montreal	3	0	3	0
C	Mario Lemieux, Pittsburgh	2	1	3	0
C	Mark Messier, NY Rangers	1	2	3	0
C	Dale Hawerchuk, Philadelphia	2	0	2	0
RW	Daniel Alfredsson, Ottawa	0	2	2	0
RW	Peter Bondra, Washington	0	2	2	0
C	Eric Lindros, Philadelphia	0	2	2	0
C	Adam Oates, Boston	0	2	2	0
D	Scott Stevens, New Jersey	0	2	2	0
D	Robert Svehla, Florida	0	2	2	0
LW	Geoff Sanderson, Hartford	1	0	1	0
D	Paul Coffey, Philadelphia	0	1	1	2
D	Kevin Hatcher, Pittsburgh	0	1	1	2
C	Dale Hunter, Washington	0	0	0	0
D	Scott Lachance, NY Islanders	0	0	0	0
	TOTALS	11	20	31	4

Goaltenders	Mins	Shots	Saves	GA
John Vanbiesbrouck, Fla.	20:00	12	10	2
Martin Brodeur, NJ (W)	20:00	13	9	4
Dominik Hasek, Buf.	20:00	21	20	1
TOTALS	60:00	46	39	7

Western Conference

	Starters	G	A	Pts	PM
D	Sandis Ozolinsh, Colorado	0	3	3	0
LW	Paul Kariya, Anaheim	1	0	1	0
RW	Brett Hull, St. Louis	0	1	1	0
D	Chris Chelios, Chicago	0	0	0	0
C	Tony Granato, San Jose	0	0	0	0

	Reserves	G	A	Pts	PM
RW	Owen Nolan, San Jose	3	0	3	0
LW	Pavel Bure, Vancouver	2	1	3	0
RW	Tony Amonte, Chicago	0	2	2	0
LW	Brendan Shanahan, Detroit	1	0	1	0
D	Viacheslav Fetisov, Detroit	0	1	1	0
RW	Theoren Fleury, Calgary	0	1	1	0
RW	Teemu Selanne, Anaheim	0	1	1	0
C	Mats Sundin, Toronto	0	1	1	0
C	Jason Arnott, Edmonton	0	0	0	0
D	Derian Hatcher, Dallas	0	0	0	0
LW	Dmitri Khristich, Los Angeles	0	0	0	0
D	Al MacInnis, St. Louis	0	0	0	0
LW	Keith Tkachuk, Phoenix	0	0	0	0
D	Oleg Tverdovsky, Phoenix	0	0	0	0
C	Steve Yzerman, Detroit	0	0	0	0
	TOTALS	7	11	18	0

Goaltenders	Mins	Shots	Saves	GA
Patrick Roy, Colorado	20:00	15	11	4
Andy Moog, Dallas (L)	20:00	15	9	6
Guy Hebert, Anaheim	20:00	11	10	1
TOTALS	60:00	41	30	11

Score by Periods

	1	2	3	Final
Eastern	4	6	1	— 11
Western	2	4	1	—7

Power plays: Eastern — 0/0; Western — 1/2. **Officials:** Rob Schick (referee), Ron Asselfine, Bob Hodges and Leon Stickle (linesmen). **Attendance:** 17,422. **TV Rating:** 2.8/5 share (Fox).

Hat Tricks

Players scored three or more goals in one game a total of 74 times during the 1996-97 regular season. Brendan Shanahan of Detroit and Ray Sheppard of Florida led the way with three hat tricks each. (*) indicates rookie.

Five Goals	Date	Score
Sergei Fedorov, Det vs Wash	Dec. 26	Det, 5-4

Four Goals	Date	Score
Peter Bondra, Wash vs Col	Mar. 6	Wash, 6-3
Wendel Clark, Tor vs Edm	Nov. 9	Tor, 7-3
Martin Gelinas, Van vs Pho	Feb. 27	Van, 6-2
John LeClair, Phi vs Mon	Feb. 6	Phi, 9-5
Mario Lemieux, Pit vs Mon	Jan. 26	Pit, 5-2
Eric Lindros, Phi vs Tor	Mar. 19	Phi, 6-3
Jaroslav Svejkovsky*, Wash at Buf	Apr. 13	Wash, 8-3
Keith Tkachuk, Pho at Chi	Mar. 20	Pho, 4-2

Three Goals	Date	Score
Tony Amonte, Chi vs LA	Nov. 30	Chi, 5-3
Tony Amonte, Chi vs NYI	Mar. 16	Chi, 5-4

Three Goals	Date	Score
Peter Bondra, Wash at Ana	Dec. 13	Ana, 5-4
Dino Ciccarelli, TB vs Pit	Nov. 8	Tied, 5-5
Mariusz Czerkawski, Edm at Bos	Nov. 7	Edm, 6-0
Mariusz Czerkawski, Edm vs Tor	Feb. 11	Edm, 6-5
Vincent Damphousse, Mon vs Hart	Jan. 6	Mon, 5-4
Eric Daze, Chi at Dal	Apr. 13	Chi, 5-2
Theoren Fleury, Calg vs Col	Oct. 22	Calg, 5-1
Peter Forsberg, Col at Calg	Apr. 2	Col, 5-1
Mike Gartner, Pho at Bos	Oct. 7	Pho, 5-2
Martin Gelinas, Van at Det	Feb. 6	Van, 7-4
Tony Granato, SJ at LA	Oct. 6	SJ, 7-6
Tony Granato, SJ vs Col	Apr. 4	SJ, 7-6
Chris Gratton, TB at Tor	Oct. 12	TB, 7-4
Adam Graves, NYR at Ott	Mar. 14	NYR, 4-3

	Date	Score		Date	Score
Michal Grosek, Buf vs Van	Dec. 4	Van, 7-6	Owen Nolan, SJ at Chi	Oct. 27	SJ, 6-2
Bill Guerin, NJ at Buf	Dec. 31	Buf, 6-5	Ed Olczyk, LA vs Van	Jan. 7	LA, 6-2
Dale Hawerchuk, Phi vs Pit	Nov. 21	Phi, 7-3	Jeff O'Neill, Hart at Ana	Jan. 31	Ana, 6-3
Brett Hull, St.L vs LA	Dec. 22	St.L, 7-4	Zigmund Palffy, NYI vs Bos	Mar. 29	NYI, 8-2
Brett Hull, St.L vs Dal	Feb. 6	St.L, 6-4	Mark Recchi, Mon at Bos	Nov. 21	Mon, 6-2
Jaromir Jagr, Pit vs Ott	Nov. 2	Pit, 7-3	Dave Reid, Dal vs Det	Jan. 8	Dal, 6-3
Jaromir Jagr, Pit vs Bos	Nov. 30	Pit, 6-2	Brian Rolston, NJ vs TB	Nov. 16	NJ, 6-3
Joe Juneau, Wash vs Pit	Nov. 1	Wash, 4-2	Martin Rucinsky, Mon at Ana	Nov. 6	Mon, 6-5
Valeri Kamensky, Col at Det	Mar. 26	Det, 6-5	Joe Sakic, Col vs Pit	Mar. 14	Col, 6-3
Paul Kariya, Ana vs Buf	Jan. 10	Ana, 5-2	Miroslav Satan, Buf vs NYR	Apr. 4	Buf, 5-1
Paul Kariya, Ana at Pho	Jan 23	Pho, 6-3	Brian Savage, Mon vs Ana	Oct. 7	Tied, 6-6
Derek King, NYI at Hart	Jan. 24	NYI, 5-2	Teemu Selanne, Ana vs SJ	Nov. 1	Ana, 4-3
Trent Klatt, Phi at Bos	Mar. 1	Tied, 5-5	Brendan Shanahan, Det vs Tor	Nov. 27	Det, 5-2
Alexei Kovalev, NYR vs Pit	Oct. 15	NYR, 8-1	Brendan Shanahan, Det at Pit	Feb. 8	Det, 6-5
Eric Lacroix, Col vs Edm	Oct. 15	Col, 7-2	Brendan Shanahan, Det vs SJ	Feb. 12	Det, 7-1
John LeClair, Phi at Ott	Feb. 26	Phi, 5-2	Ray Sheppard, Fla vs Buf	Nov. 26	Fla, 4-3
Mario Lemieux, Pit at St.L	Dec. 19	Pit, 4-0	Ray Sheppard, Fla at NYR	Dec. 22	NYR, 7-3
Al MacInnis, St.L vs Dal	Dec. 11	Tied, 5-5	Ray Sheppard, Fla vs Van	Mar. 13	Fla, 5-4
Kent Manderville, Hart vs Bos	Mar. 12	Hart, 6-3	Ryan Smyth, Edm at Tor	Oct. 8	Edm, 4-2
Randy McKay, NJ vs Hart	Mar. 13	NJ, 6-0	Mats Sundin, Tor at Col	Dec. 21	Tor, 6-2
Jim McKenzie, Pho vs LA	Feb. 18	Pho, 6-1	German Titov, Calg at Pho	Dec. 22	Calg, 7-2
Mark Messier, NYR at Pho	Nov. 26	NYR, 3-1	Keith Tkachuk, Pho vs NJ	Nov. 28	Pho, 4-3
Mark Messier, NYR at NYI	Feb. 8	NYR, 5-2	Scott Young, Col vs Mon	Nov. 9	Col, 5-2
Alexander Mogilny, Van at St.L	Dec. 15	Van, 8-0	Alexei Zhamnov, Chi vs Calg	Apr. 11	Chi, 7-3
Rem Murray*, Edm at LA	Oct. 24	Edm, 8-2			

Game-Winning Goals in Overtime

A total of 214 games were tied after regulation during the 1996-97 regular season, with 70 being resolved in overtime. Teams play one five-minute overtime period during the regular season. (*) indicates rookie.

	Date	Time	Score		Date	Time	Score
Shawn Burr, TB at Pit	Oct. 5	1:37	TB, 4-3	Mats Lindgren*, Edm vs Hart	Jan. 12	2:27	Edm, 2-1
Viktor Kozlov, SJ at LA	Oct. 6	4:55	SJ, 7-6	Bill Houlder, TB vs Col	Jan. 21	2:02	TB, 3-2
Rod Brind'Amour, Phi vs LA	Oct. 10	0:33	Phi, 5-4	Robert Kron, Hart vs Fla	Jan. 22	4:46	Hart, 2-1
Rick Tocchet, Bos vs Van	Oct. 14	4:45	Bos, 5-4	Alexander Mogilny, Van at Chi	Jan. 22	1:24	Van, 4-3
Mike Gartner, Pho at Mon	Oct. 28	1:45	Pho, 5-4	Valeri Kamensky, Col at Pit	Jan. 23	3:55	Col, 4-3
Jeff Shantz, Chi at Dal	Nov. 1	1:48	Chi, 3-2	Kirk Muller, Tor at Chi	Jan. 24	2:07	Tor, 2-1
Jeremy Roenick, Pho at Calg	Nov. 1	4:08	Pho, 5-4	Jyrki Lumme, Van vs NYI	Jan. 30	1:30	Van, 2-1
Esa Tikkanen, Van at Edm	Nov. 1	0:42	Van, 5-4	Vyacheslav Kozlov, Det vs Dal	Feb. 2	1:20	Det, 4-3
Darren Turcotte, SJ vs Mon	Nov. 2	3:07	SJ, 4-3	Brendan Shanahan, Det at Pit	Feb. 8	2:01	Det, 6-5
Curtis Leschyshyn, Har vs Buf	Nov. 9	4:55	Hart, 4-3	Brian Savage, Mon vs Hart	Feb. 8	1:01	Mon, 3-2
Donald Audette, Buf vs Fla	Nov. 11	4:01	Buf, 5-4	Pat Verbeek, Dal at Pho	Feb. 8	3:50	Dal, 5-4
Saku Koivu, Mon vs Edm	Nov. 11	3:37	Mon, 3-2	Teemu Selanne, Ana at Edm	Feb. 8	0:45	Ana, 2-1
Scott Niedermayer, NJ vs Wash	Nov. 12	3:04	NJ, 3-2	Neal Broten, Dal vs LA	Feb. 9	4:16	Dal, 2-1
Bryan McCabe, NYI vs Van	Nov. 13	0:45	NYI, 5-4	Robert Reichel, Calg vs Edm	Feb. 13	2:20	Calg, 3-2
Adam Oates, Bos vs Pit	Nov. 14	1:05	Bos, 2-1	Steve Konowalchuk, Wash vs TB	Feb. 14	2:57	Wash, 5-4
German Titov, Calg at Chi	Nov. 14	4:55	Calg, 2-1	Mike Kennedy, Dal vs Det	Feb. 14	2:03	Dal, 4-3
Harry York*, St.L vs Pho	Nov. 21	0:57	St.L, 4-3	Claude Lapointe, NYI vs Fla	Feb. 15	2:46	NYI, 1-0
Chris Joseph, Van vs Chi	Nov. 21	3:51	Van, 5-4	Jay More, Pho vs Bos	Feb. 15	1:14	Pho, 5-4
Jody Hull, Fla at Dal	Nov. 22	4:55	Fla, 2-1	Claude Lemieux, Col vs Bos	Feb. 18	4:56	Col, 3-2
Michal Grosek, Buf at Bos	Nov. 23	2:39	Buf, 3-2	Mike Ricci, Col at Edm	Feb. 21	2:26	Col, 4-3
Keith Tkachuk, Pho vs NJ	Nov. 28	4:08	Pho, 4-3	Eric Lindros, Phi at Fla	Feb. 22	4:03	Phi, 4-3
Mike Sillinger, Van at Buf	Dec. 4	3:38	Van, 7-6	Rob Niedermayer, Fla at St.L	Feb. 27	3:50	Fla, 3-2
Darrin Shannon, Pho at NJ	Dec. 7	2:03	Pho, 4-3	Niklas Sundstrom, NYR vs SJ	Mar. 3	1:24	NYR, 5-4
Dixon Ward, Buf at Mon	Dec. 11	2:42	Buf, 3-2	Fredrik Olausson, Pit vs Phi	Mar. 8	0:19	Pit, 3-2
Mike Modano, Dal at Chi	Dec. 18	0:27	Dal, 3-2	Rob Zamuner, TB vs Calg	Mar. 9	2:20	TB, 2-1
Robert Kron, Hart vs TB	Dec. 21	2:11	Hart, 6-5	Michael Peca, Buf vs Phi	Mar. 11	0:42	Buf, 3-2
Luc Robitaille, NYR at Mon	Dec. 21	0:42	NYR, 3-2	Eric Lindros, Phi vs Edm	Mar. 13	4:16	Phi, 5-4
Ray Sheppard, Fla at NYI	Dec. 23	1:46	Fla, 4-3	Niklas Sundstrom, NYR at Ott	Mar. 14	1:24	NYR, 4-3
Sergei Fedorov, Det vs Wash	Dec. 26	2:39	Det, 5-4	Jeff Toms*, TB at Calg	Mar. 21	2:46	TB, 4-3
Steve Rucchin, Ana at Ott	Dec. 30	4:33	Ana, 4-3	Bryan Berard*, NYI at Buf	Mar. 26	1:00	NYI, 3-2
S. Konowalchuk, Wash vs Hart	Jan. 1	3:01	Wash, 3-2	Darren McCarty, Det vs Col	Mar. 26	0:39	Det, 6-5
Ted Donato, Bos at Hart	Jan. 2	2:21	Bos, 5-4	Larry Murphy, Det vs Buf	Mar. 28	3:10	Det, 2-1
Dave Gagner, Calg vs Tor	Jan. 7	4:00	Calg, 4-3	Steve Rucchin, Ana vs Det	Mar. 30	3:41	Ana, 1-0
Igor Larionov, Det at Pho	Jan. 9	0:58	Det, 5-4	Stephen Guolla*, SJ vs Col	Apr. 4	0:35	SJ, 7-6
Jason Dawe, Buf at Pho	Jan. 12	0:10	Buf, 3-2	Tomas Sandstrom, Det at Calg	Apr. 8	4:51	Det, 3-2

Pittsburgh Penguins
Mario Lemieux
Scoring

Phoenix Coyotes
Keith Tkachuk
Goals

New Jersey Devils
Martin Brodeur
Goals Against Avg.

Buffalo Sabres
Dominik Hasek
Save Pct.

NHL Regular Season Individual Leaders

(*) indicates rookie eligible for Calder Trophy.

Scoring

	Pos	Gm	G	A	Pts	+/-	PM	PP	SH	GW	GT	Shots	Pct
Mario Lemieux, Pittsburgh	C	76	50	72	**122**	27	65	15	2	7	1	327	15.3
Teemu Selanne, Anaheim	R	78	51	58	**109**	28	34	11	1	8	2	273	18.7
Paul Kariya, Anaheim	L	69	44	55	**99**	36	6	15	3	10	0	340	12.9
John LeClair, Philadelphia	L	82	50	47	**97**	44	58	10	0	5	2	324	15.4
Wayne Gretzky, NY Rangers	C	82	25	72	**97**	12	28	6	0	2	1	286	8.7
Jaromir Jagr, Pittsburgh	R	63	47	48	**95**	22	40	11	2	6	1	234	20.1
Mats Sundin, Toronto	C	82	41	53	**94**	6	59	7	4	8	1	281	14.6
Zigmund Palffy, NY Islanders	R	80	48	42	**90**	21	43	6	4	6	1	292	16.4
Ron Francis, Pittsburgh	C	81	27	63	**90**	7	20	10	1	2	0	183	14.8
Brendan Shanahan, Hart-Det ...	L	81	47	41	**88**	32	131	20	3	7	2	336	14
Keith Tkachuk, Phoenix	L	81	52	34	**86**	-1	228	9	2	7	1	296	17.6
Peter Forsberg, Colorado	C	65	28	58	**86**	31	73	5	4	4	0	188	14.9
Pierre Turgeon, Mon-St.L	C	78	26	59	**85**	8	14	5	0	7	1	216	12
Steve Yzerman, Detroit	C	81	22	63	**85**	22	78	8	0	3	0	232	9.5
Mark Messier, NY Rangers	C	71	36	48	**84**	12	88	7	5	9	1	227	15.9
Mike Modano, Dallas	C	80	35	48	**83**	43	42	9	5	9	2	291	12
Brett Hull, St. Louis	R	77	42	40	**82**	-9	10	12	2	6	2	302	13.9
Adam Oates, Bos-Wash	C	80	22	60	**82**	-5	14	3	2	5	0	160	13.8
Doug Gilmour, Tor-NJ	C	81	22	60	**82**	2	68	4	1	1	1	143	15.4
Doug Weight, Edmonton	C	80	21	61	**82**	1	80	4	0	2	0	235	8.9

Goals

Tkachuk, Pho	52
Selanne, Ana	51
Lemieux, Pit	50
LeClair, Phi	50
Palffy, NYI	48
Jagr, Pit	47
Shanahan, Hart-Det ..	47
Bondra, Wash	46
Kariya, Ana	44
Hull, St.L	42
Amonte, Chi	41
Sundin, Tor	41

Assists

Lemieux, Pit	72
Gretzky, NYR	72
Francis, Pit	63
Yzerman, Det	63
Weight, Edm	61
Oates, Bos-Wash	60
Gilmour, Tor-NJ	60
Turgeon, Mon-St.L ...	59
Forsberg, Col	58
Selanne, Ana	58
Leetch, NYR	58
Kariya, Ana	55
Stumpel, Bos	55

Defensemen Points

Leetch, NYR	78
Ozolinsh, Col	68
Lidstrom, Det	57
Tverdovsky, Pho	55
Hatcher, Pit	54
Mironov, Pit-Ana	52
Bourque, Bos	50
Chelios, Chi	48
Sydor, Dal	48
Berard*, NYI	48
Duchesne, Ott	47

Rookie Points

Iginla, Calg	50
Berard, NYI	48
Niinimaa, Phi	44
Campbell, St.L	43
Berezin, Tor	41
Langenbrunner, Dal ...	39
Sullivan, NJ-Tor	38
Hoglund, Calg	35
Grier, Edm	32
York, St.L	32
Pederson, NJ	32
Three tied with 31.	

Plus/Minus

LeClair, Phi	+44
Modano, Dal	+43
Konstantinov, Det ...	+38
Andreychuk, NJ	+38
Sydor, Dal	+37
Kariya, Ana	+36
Renberg, Phi	+36
Amonte, Chi	+35
Shanahan, Det	+32
Five tied at +31.	

Penalty Minutes

Odjick, Van	371
Probert, Chi	326
Laus, Fla	313
Ray, Buf	286
Domi, Tor	275
Barnaby, Buf	249
Brashear, Mon-Van ..	245
Daniels, Phi	237
Ciccone, Chi	233
Tkachuk, Pho	228

Power Play Goals

Shanahan, Hart-Det ..	20
Smyth, Edm	20
Kariya, Ana	15
Lemieux, Pit	15
Kovalenko, Edm	14
Jones, Wash-Col	14
Sheppard, Fla	13
Ozolinsh, Col	13
Gartner, Pho	13
Five tied with 12 each.	

Short-Handed Goals

Peca, Buf	6
Messier, NYR	5
Klatt, Phi	5
Modano, Dal	5
Eight tied with four each.	

Goaltending
(Minimum 25 games)

	Gm	Min	GAA	GA	Shots	Sv%	EN	SO	Record	G	A	Pts	PM
Martin Brodeur, New Jersey	67	3838	1.88	120	1633	.927	5	10	37-14-13	0	4	4	8
Andy Moog, Dallas	48	2738	2.15	98	1121	.913	0	3	28-13-5	0	1	1	12
Jeff Hackett, Chicago	41	2473	2.16	89	1212	.927	2	2	19-18-4	0	1	1	6
Dominik Hasek, Buffalo	67	4037	2.27	153	2177	.930	3	5	37-20-10	0	3	3	30
John Vanbiesbrouck, Florida	57	3347	2.29	128	1582	.919	3	2	27-19-10	0	2	2	8
Chris Osgood, Detroit	47	2769	2.30	106	1175	.910	3	6	23-13-9	0	2	2	6
Patrick Roy, Colorado	62	3698	2.32	143	1861	.923	3	7	38-15-7	0	1	1	15
Mark Fitzpatrick, Florida	30	1680	2.36	66	771	.914	4	0	8-9-9	0	1	1	13
Mike Vernon, Detroit	33	1952	2.43	79	782	.899	1	0	13-11-8	0	0	0	35
Garth Snow, Philadelphia	35	1884	2.52	79	816	.903	2	2	14-8-8	0	1	1	30
Mike Dunham*, New Jersey	26	1013	2.55	43	456	.906	1	2	8-7-1	0	0	0	2
Ron Hextall, Philadelphia	55	3094	2.56	132	1285	.897	5	4	31-16-5	0	0	0	43
Olaf Kolzig, Washington	29	1645	2.59	71	758	.906	6	2	8-15-4	0	0	0	4
Guy Hebert, Anaheim	67	3863	2.67	172	2133	.919	2	4	29-25-12	0	1	1	4
Mike Richter, NY Rangers	61	3598	2.68	161	1945	.917	9	4	33-22-6	0	0	0	4

Wins
Roy, Col	38
Brodeur, NJ	37
Hasek, Buf	37
Richter, NYR	33
Fuhr, St.L	33
Joseph, Edm	32
Hextall, Phi	31
Khabibulin, Pho	30
Hebert, Ana	29
Moog, Dal	28

Shutouts
Brodeur, NJ	10
Roy, Col	7
Khabibulin, Pho	7
Osgood, Det	6
Joseph, Edm	6
Hextall, Phi	5
Salo, NYI	5
Tabaracci, Calg-TB	5
Hasek, Buf	5
Five tied with four each.	

Save Pct.
Hasek, Buf	.930
Brodeur, NJ	.927
Hackett, Chi	.927
Roy, Col	.923
Hebert, Ana	.919
Vanbiesbrouck, Fla	.919
Richter, NYR	.917
Burke, Hart	.914
Fitzpatrick, Fla	.914
Lalime, Pit	.913
Moog, Dal	.913

Losses
Potvin, Tor	36
Khabibulin, Pho	33
Carey, Wash-Bos	31
Joseph, Edm	29
Tabaracci, Calg-TB	29
Fuhr, St.L	27
Salo, NYI	27
Hebert, Ana	25
Three tied with 24 each.	

Team Goaltending

WESTERN	GAA	Mins	GA	Shots	Sv%	EN	SO	EASTERN	GAA	Mins	GA	Shots	Sv%	EN	SO
Detroit	2.35	5031	197	2075	.905	4	7	New Jersey	2.18	4999	182	2160	.916	6	13
Dallas	2.39	4979	198	2078	.905	3	6	Florida	2.39	5041	201	2360	.915	7	2
Colorado	2.47	4980	205	2477	.917	6	8	Buffalo	2.49	5003	208	2728	.924	6	5
Chicago	2.52	5000	210	2415	.913	7	3	Philadelphia	2.61	4995	217	2107	.897	6	7
Anaheim	2.80	4994	233	2688	.913	6	6	Washington	2.78	4977	231	2163	.893	9	3
Calgary	2.87	4990	239	2337	.898	6	6	NY Rangers	2.79	4974	231	2588	.911	11	5
St. Louis	2.88	4980	239	2245	.894	6	3	Ottawa	2.81	5001	234	2117	.889	4	4
Phoenix	2.93	4974	243	2520	.904	8	8	Tampa Bay	2.97	4984	247	2365	.896	9	6
Edmonton	2.97	4982	247	2556	.903	6	7	NY Islanders	3.01	4988	250	2481	.899	8	5
Los Angeles	3.23	4985	268	2779	.904	9	4	Hartford	3.07	4996	256	2583	.901	7	4
Vancouver	3.29	4972	273	2477	.890	5	3	Montreal	3.31	5008	276	2780	.901	5	1
Toronto	3.30	4966	273	2823	.903	8	2	Pittsburgh	3.38	4969	280	2812	.900	11	5
San Jose	3.36	4970	278	2398	.884	9	1	Boston	3.61	4982	300	2431	.877	7	3

Power Play/Penalty Killing

Power play and penalty killing conversions. Power play: No— number of opportunities; GF— goals for; Pct— percentage. Penalty killing: No— number of times shorthanded; GA— goals against; Pct— percentage of penalties killed; SH— shorthanded goals for.

	Power Play			Penalty Killing					Power Play			Penalty Killing			
WESTERN	No	GF	Pct	No	GA	Pct	SH	EASTERN	No	GF	Pct	No	GA	Pct	SH
Colorado	403	83	20.6	339	42	87.6	14	NY Rangers	287	63	22.0	344	69	79.9	15
Phoenix	359	65	18.1	334	47	85.9	9	Pittsburgh	338	74	21.9	338	64	81.1	10
Edmonton	406	73	18.0	338	59	82.5	9	Hartford	321	58	18.1	332	51	84.6	12
Detroit	368	66	17.9	346	46	86.7	10	Ottawa	336	56	16.7	265	48	81.9	9
Calgary	361	61	16.9	345	58	83.2	11	Washington	322	51	15.8	354	54	84.7	8
Anaheim	333	56	16.8	336	62	81.5	9	Montreal	337	53	15.7	347	71	79.5	10
Vancouver	303	51	16.8	344	66	80.8	12	Boston	310	46	14.8	308	56	81.8	15
Toronto	309	48	15.5	328	59	82.0	11	Philadelphia	362	53	14.6	342	49	85.7	11
St. Louis	327	50	15.3	332	55	83.4	9	Florida	352	50	14.2	346	50	85.5	5
Chicago	304	45	14.8	374	59	84.2	5	NY Islanders	346	48	13.9	319	53	83.4	14
Dallas	314	46	14.6	308	51	83.4	11	New Jersey	288	40	13.9	235	28	88.1	4
San Jose	349	50	14.3	409	66	83.9	9	Tampa Bay	340	47	13.8	360	55	84.7	13
Los Angeles	338	46	13.6	352	45	87.2	5	Buffalo	326	43	13.2	364	59	83.8	16

Team by Team Statistics

High scorers and goaltenders with at least ten games played. Players who competed for more than one team during the regular season are listed with their final club; (*) indicates rookies eligible for Calder Trophy.

Mighty Ducks of Anaheim

Top Scorers	Gm	G	A	Pts	+/-	PM	PP
Teemu Selanne	78	51	58	109	28	34	11
Paul Kariya	69	44	55	99	36	6	15
Steve Rucchin	79	19	48	67	26	24	6
Dmitri Mironov	77	13	39	52	16	101	3
PIT	15	1	5	6	-4	24	0
ANA	62	12	34	46	20	77	3
Jari Kurri	82	13	22	35	-13	12	3
Brian Bellows	69	16	15	31	-15	22	8
TB	7	1	2	3	-4	0	0
ANA	62	15	13	28	-11	22	8
Kevin Todd	65	9	21	30	-7	44	0
Joe Sacco	77	12	17	29	1	35	1
J.J. Daigneault	66	5	23	28	0	58	0
PIT	53	3	14	17	-5	36	0
ANA	13	2	9	11	5	22	0
Darren Van Impe* ...	74	4	19	23	3	90	2
Jean-Francois Jomphe .	64	7	14	21	-9	53	0
Ted Drury	73	9	9	18	-9	54	1
Bobby Dollas	79	4	14	18	17	55	1
Warren Rychel	70	10	7	17	6	218	1
Sean Pronger*	39	7	7	14	6	20	1

Acquired: LW Bellows from TB for '97 sixth-round pick (Nov. 18); D Mironov and LW Shawn Antoski from Pit. for D Fredrik Olausson and C Alex Hicks (Nov. 19); D Daigneault from Pit. for LW Garry Valk (Feb. 21). **Claimed:** C Todd off waivers from Pit.

Goalies (10 Gm)	Gm	Min	GAA	Record	SV%
Guy Hebert	67	3863	2.67	29-25-12	.919
Mikhail Shtalenkov	24	1079	2.89	7-8-1	.904
ANAHEIM	82	4994	2.80	36-33-13	.913

Shutouts: Hebert (4), Shtalenkov (2). **Assists:** Hebert (1). **PM:** Hebert (4) and Shtalenkov (4) .

Boston Bruins

Top Scorers	Gm	G	A	Pts	+/-	PM	PP
Jozef Stumpel	78	21	55	76	-22	14	6
Ted Donato	67	25	26	51	-9	37	6
Ray Bourque	62	19	31	50	-11	18	8
Jason Allison	72	8	26	34	-6	34	2
WASH	53	5	17	22	-3	25	1
BOS	19	3	9	12	-3	9	1
Rob DiMaio	72	13	15	28	-21	82	0
Don Sweeney	82	3	23	26	-5	39	0
Steve Heinze	30	17	8	25	-8	27	4
Jean-Yves Roy	52	10	15	25	-8	22	2
Tim Sweeney	36	10	11	21	0	14	2
Landon Wilson*	49	8	12	20	-5	72	0
COL	9	1	2	3	1	23	0
BOS	40	7	10	17	-6	49	0
Anson Carter*	38	11	7	18	-7	9	2
WASH	19	3	2	5	0	7	1
BOS	19	8	5	13	-7	2	1
Sheldon Kennedy	56	8	10	18	-17	30	0
Barry Richter	50	5	13	18	-7	32	1
Brett Harkins	44	4	14	18	-3	8	3
Todd Elik	31	4	12	16	-12	16	1
Jeff Odgers	80	7	8	15	-15	197	1

Acquired: RW Wilson and D Anders Myrvold from Col. for '98 first-round pick (Nov. 22); G Carey, C Allison, C Carter, '97 third-round pick and a conditional '98 second-round pick from Wash. for C Adam Oates, RW Rick Tocchet and G Bill Ranford (Mar. 1).

Goalies (10 Gm)	Gm	Min	GAA	Record	SV%
Rob Tallas	28	1244	3.33	8-12-1	.882
Jim Carey	59	3279	3.09	22-31-3	.886
WASH	40	2293	2.75	17-18-3	.893
BOS	19	1004	3.82	5-13-0	.871
BOSTON	82	4982	3.61	26-47-9	.877

Shutouts: Carey and Tallas (1). **Assists:** none. **PM:** Carey (2).

Buffalo Sabres

Top Scorers	Gm	G	A	Pts	+/-	PM	PP
Derek Plante	82	27	26	53	14	24	5
Brian Holzinger	81	22	29	51	9	54	2
Donald Audette	73	28	22	50	-6	48	8
Michael Peca	79	20	29	49	26	80	5
Jason Dawe	81	22	26	48	14	32	4
Dixon Ward	79	13	32	45	17	36	1
Matthew Barnaby	68	19	24	43	16	249	2
Miroslav Satan	76	25	13	38	-3	26	7
EDM	64	17	11	28	-4	22	5
BUF	12	8	2	10	1	4	2
Garry Galley	71	4	34	38	10	102	1
Michal Grosek	82	15	21	36	25	71	5
Alexei Zhitnik	80	7	28	35	10	95	3
Randy Burridge	55	10	21	31	17	20	1
Richard Smehlik	62	11	19	30	19	43	2
Darryl Shannon	82	4	19	23	23	112	1
Mike Wilson	77	2	9	11	13	51	0
Rob Ray	82	7	3	10	3	286	0
Jay McKee*	43	1	9	10	3	35	0
Pat LaFontaine	13	2	6	8	-8	4	1
Bob Boughner	77	1	7	8	12	225	0

Acquired: LW Satan from Edm. for LW Barrie Moore and D Craig Millar (Mar. 18).

Goalies (10 Gms)	Gm	Min	GAA	Record	Sv%
Dominik Hasek	67	4037	2.27	37-20-10	.930
Steve Shields	13	789	2.97	3-8-2	.913
BUFFALO	82	5003	2.49	40-30-12	.924

Shutouts: Hasek (5). **Assists:** Hasek (3). **PM:** Hasek (30), Shields (4).

Calgary Flames

Top Scorers	Gm	G	A	Pts	+/-	PM	PP
Theoren Fleury	81	29	38	67	-12	104	9
Dave Gagner	82	27	33	60	2	48	9
German Titov	79	22	30	52	-12	36	12
Jarome Iginla*	82	21	29	50	-4	37	8
Marty McInnis	80	23	26	49	-8	22	5
NYI	70	20	22	42	-7	20	4
CALG	10	3	4	7	-1	2	1
Jonas Hoglund*	68	19	16	35	-4	12	3
Corey Millen	61	11	15	26	-19	32	1
Cory Stillman	58	6	20	26	-6	14	2
Aaron Gavey	57	8	11	19	-12	46	3
TB	16	1	2	3	-1	12	0
CALG	41	7	9	16	-11	34	3
Todd Hlushko	58	7	11	18	-2	49	0
Ronnie Stern	79	7	10	17	-4	157	0
Yves Racine	46	1	15	16	4	24	1
Tommy Albelin	72	4	11	15	-8	14	2
Todd Simpson*	82	1	13	14	-14	208	0
Ed Ward	40	5	8	13	-3	49	0
Mike Sullivan	67	5	6	11	-11	10	0
Glen Featherstone ...	54	3	8	11	-1	106	0
HART	41	2	5	7	0	87	0
CALG	13	1	3	4	-1	19	0

Acquired: C Gavey from TB for G Rick Tabaracci (Nov. 19); D Racine from SJ for future considerations (Dec. 25); D Featherstone, LW Hnat Domenichelli, '97 second-round pick and '98 third-round pick from Hart. for D Steve Chiasson and '97 third-round pick (Mar. 5); LW McInnis, G Tyrone Garner and '97 sixth-round pick from NYI for C Robert Reichel (Mar. 18).

Goalies (10 Gms)	Gm	Min	GAA	Record	SV%
Trevor Kidd	55	2979	2.84	21-23-6	.900
Dwayne Roloson	31	1618	2.89	9-14-3	.897
TOTAL	82	4990	2.87	32-41-9	.898

Shutouts: Kidd (4), Roloson (1). **Assists:** Kidd (2). **PM:** Kidd (16), Roloson (2).

Chicago Blackhawks

Top Scorers	Gm	G	A	Pts	+/-	PM	PP
Tony Amonte	81	41	36	77	35	64	9
Alexei Zhamnov	74	20	42	62	18	56	6
Chris Chelios	72	10	38	48	16	112	2
Eric Daze	71	22	19	41	-4	16	11
Murray Craven	75	8	27	35	0	12	2
Ulf Dahlen	73	14	19	33	-2	18	4
SJ	43	8	11	19	-11	8	3
CHI	30	6	8	14	9	10	1
Eric Weinrich	81	7	25	32	19	62	1
Ethan Moreau*	82	15	16	31	13	123	0
Kevin Miller	69	14	17	31	-10	41	5
Jeff Shantz	69	9	21	30	11	28	0
Gary Suter	82	7	21	28	-4	70	3
Denis Savard	64	9	18	27	-10	60	2
Sergei Krivokrasov ...	67	13	11	24	-1	42	2
James Black	64	12	11	23	6	20	0
Bob Probert	82	9	14	23	-3	326	1
Keith Carney	81	3	15	18	26	62	0
Michal Sykora	63	3	14	17	4	69	1
SJ	35	2	5	7	0	59	1
CHI	28	1	9	10	4	10	0
Brent Sutter	39	7	7	14	10	18	0
Jim Cummins	65	6	6	12	4	199	0

Acquired: G Terreri, RW Dahlen, D Sykora and a conditional '98 draft pick from SJ for G Ed Belfour (Jan. 25). **Signed:** free agent LW Basil McRae (Oct. 7).

Goalies (10 Gm)	Gm	Min	GAA	Record	SV%
Jeff Hackett	41	2473	2.16	19-18-4	.927
Chris Terreri	29	1628	2.73	10-11-5	.901
SJ	22	1200	2.75	6-10-3	.901
CHI	7	429	2.66	4-1-2	.901
CHICAGO	82	5000	2.52	34-35-13	.913

Shutouts: Hackett (2). **Assists:** Hackett (1). **PM:** Hackett (6).

Colorado Avalanche

Top Scorers	Gm	G	A	Pts	+/-	PM	PP
Peter Forsberg	65	28	58	86	31	73	5
Joe Sakic	65	22	52	74	-10	34	10
Sandis Ozolinsh	80	23	45	68	4	88	13
Valeri Kamensky	68	28	38	66	5	38	8
Adam Deadmarsh	78	33	27	60	8	136	10
Keith Jones	78	25	23	48	3	118	14
WASH	11	2	3	5	-2	13	1
COL	67	23	20	43	5	105	13
Scott Young	72	18	19	37	-5	14	7
Eric Lacroix	81	18	18	36	16	26	2
Mike Ricci	63	13	19	32	-3	59	5
Claude Lemieux	45	11	17	28	-4	43	5
Rene Corbet	76	12	15	27	14	67	1
Mike Keane	81	10	17	27	2	63	0
Stephane Yelle	79	9	17	26	1	38	0
Jon Klemm	80	9	15	24	12	37	1
Uwe Krupp	60	4	17	21	12	48	2
Adam Foote	78	2	19	21	16	135	0
Aaron Miller*	56	5	12	17	15	15	0
Alexei Gusarov	58	2	12	14	4	28	0
Sylvain Lefebvre	71	2	11	13	12	30	1
Brent Severyn	66	1	4	5	-6	193	0

Acquired: RW Jones, '98 first-round pick and '97 or '98 fourth-round pick from Wash. for LW Chris Simon and D Curtis Leschyshyn (Nov. 2).

Goalies (10 Gm)	Gm	Min	GAA	Record	SV%
Patrick Roy	62	3698	2.32	38-15-7	.923
Craig Billington	23	1200	2.65	11-8-2	.909
COLORADO	82	4980	2.47	49-24-9	.917

Shutouts: Roy (7), Billington (1). **Assists:** Billington (2), Roy (1). **PM:** Roy (15), Billington (2).

Dallas Stars

Top Scorers	Gm	G	A	Pts	+/-	PM	PP
Mike Modano	80	35	48	83	43	42	9
Pat Verbeek	81	17	36	53	3	128	5
Joe Nieuwendyk	66	30	21	51	-5	32	8
Darryl Sydor	82	8	40	48	37	51	2
Benoit Hogue	73	19	24	43	8	54	5
Jere Lehtinen	63	16	27	43	26	2	3
Sergei Zubov	78	13	30	43	19	24	1
Dave Reid	82	19	20	39	12	10	1
J. Langenbrunner* ...	76	13	26	39	-2	51	3
Greg Adams	50	21	15	36	27	2	5
Todd Harvey	71	9	22	31	19	142	1
Brent Gilchrist	67	10	20	30	6	24	2
Derian Hatcher	63	3	19	22	8	97	0
Guy Carbonneau	73	5	16	21	9	36	0
Neal Broten	42	8	12	20	-4	12	1
NJ	3	0	1	1	-1	0	0
LA	19	0	4	4	-9	0	0
DAL	20	8	7	15	6	12	1
Grant Ledyard	67	1	15	16	31	61	0
Craig Ludwig	77	2	11	13	17	62	0
Bob Bassen	46	5	7	12	5	41	0
Richard Matvichuk ...	57	5	7	12	1	87	0
Bill Huard	40	5	6	11	5	105	0
Grant Marshall	56	6	4	10	5	98	0

Claimed: C Broten off waivers from LA (Jan. 28).

Goalies (10 Gm)	Gm	Min	GAA	Record	SV%
Andy Moog	48	2738	2.15	28-13-5	.913
Arturs Irbe	35	1965	2.69	17-12-3	.893
DALLAS	82	4979	2.39	48-26-8	.905

Shutouts: Irbe (3), Moog (3). **Assists:** Irbe (2), Moog (1). **PM:** Moog (12), Irbe (8).

Detroit Red Wings

Top Scorers	Gm	G	A	Pts	+/-	PM	PP
Brendan Shanahan ...	81	47	41	88	32	131	20
HART	2	1	0	1	1	0	0
DET	79	46	41	87	31	131	20
Steve Yzerman	81	22	63	85	22	78	8
Sergei Fedorov	74	30	33	63	29	30	9
Nicklas Lidstrom	79	15	42	57	11	30	8
Igor Larionov	64	12	42	54	31	26	2
Darren McCarty	68	19	30	49	14	126	5
Vyacheslav Kozlov ...	75	23	22	45	21	46	3
Larry Murphy	81	9	36	45	3	20	5
TOR	69	7	32	39	1	20	4
DET	12	2	4	6	2	0	1
Tomas Sandstrom	74	18	24	42	6	69	1
PIT	40	9	15	24	4	33	1
DET	34	9	9	18	2	36	0
Vlad. Konstantinov ...	77	5	33	38	38	151	0
Martin Lapointe	78	16	17	33	-14	167	5
Viacheslav Fetisov ...	64	5	23	28	26	76	0
Kris Draper	76	8	5	13	-11	73	1
Doug Brown	49	6	7	13	-3	8	1
Bob Rouse	70	4	9	13	8	58	0
Mathieu Dandenault ..	65	3	9	12	-10	28	0
Jamie Pushor*	75	4	7	11	1	129	0

Acquired: LW Shanahan and D Brian Glynn from Hart. for C Keith Primeau, D Paul Coffey and '97 first-round pick (Oct. 9); RW Sandstrom from Pit. for C Greg Johnson (Jan. 27); D Murphy from Tor. for cash (Mar. 18).

Goalies (10 Gm)	Gm	Min	GAA	Record	Sv%
Chris Osgood	47	2769	2.30	23-13-9	.910
Mike Vernon	33	1952	2.43	13-11-8	.899
DETROIT	82	5031	2.35	38-26-18	.905

Shutouts: Osgood (6). **Assists:** Osgood (2). **PM:** Vernon (35), Osgood (6) .

Edmonton Oilers

Top Scorers

Top Scorers	Gm	G	A	PTS	+/-	PM	PP
Doug Weight	80	21	61	82	1	80	4
Ryan Smyth	82	39	22	61	-7	76	20
Andrei Kovalenko	74	32	27	59	-5	81	14
Jason Arnott	67	19	38	57	-21	92	10
Mariusz Czerkawski . .	76	26	21	47	0	16	4
Kelly Buchberger	81	8	30	38	4	159	0
Todd Marchant	79	14	19	33	11	44	0
Mike Grier*	79	15	17	32	7	45	4
Boris Mironov	55	6	26	32	2	85	2
Rem Murray*	82	11	20	31	9	16	1
Dean McAmmond	57	12	17	29	-15	28	4
Mats Lindgren*	69	11	14	25	-7	12	2
Daniel McGillis*	73	6	16	22	2	52	2
Drew Bannister*	65	4	14	18	-23	44	1
TB	64	4	13	17	-21	44	1
EDM	1	0	1	1	-2	0	0
Bryan Marchment	71	3	13	16	13	132	1
Petr Klima	33	2	12	14	-12	12	0
LA	8	0	4	4	-7	2	0
PIT	9	1	3	4	-4	4	0
EDM	16	1	5	6	-1	6	0
Kevin Lowe	64	1	13	14	-1	50	0
Luke Richardson	82	1	11	12	9	91	0

Acquired: D Bannister and '97 sixth-round pick from TB for D Jeff Norton. **Claimed:** LW Ralph Intranuovo off waivers from Tor. (Oct. 25). **Signed:** free agent LW Klima (Feb. 20).

Goalies (10 Gm)	Gm	Min	GAA	Record	Sv%
Bob Essensa	19	879	2.80	4-8-0	.899
Curtis Joseph	72	4089	2.93	32-29-9	.907
EDMONTON	82	4982	2.97	36-37-9	.903

Shutouts: Joseph (6), Essensa (1). **Assists:** Joseph (2). **PM:** Joseph (20), Essensa (4).

Florida Panthers

Top Scorers

Top Scorers	Gm	G	A	Pts	+/-	PM	PP
Ray Sheppard	68	29	31	60	4	4	13
Scott Mellanby	82	27	29	56	7	170	9
Robert Svehla	82	13	32	45	2	86	5
Kirk Muller	76	21	19	40	-25	89	10
TOR	66	20	17	37	-23	85	9
FLA	10	1	2	3	-24	4	1
Radek Dvorak	78	18	21	39	-2	30	2
Rob Niedermayer	60	14	24	38	4	54	3
Johan Garpenlov	53	11	25	36	10	47	1
Bill Lindsay	81	11	23	34	1	120	0
Dave Lowry	77	15	14	29	2	51	2
Martin Straka	55	7	22	29	9	12	2
Per Gustafsson	58	7	22	29	11	22	2
Tom Fitzgerald	71	10	14	24	7	64	0
Gord Murphy	80	8	15	23	3	51	2
Ed Jovanovski	61	7	16	23	-1	172	3
Brian Skrudland	51	5	13	18	4	48	0
Jody Hull	67	10	6	16	1	4	0
Mike Hough	69	8	6	14	12	48	0
David Nemirovsky* . . .	39	7	7	14	1	32	1
Terry Carkner	70	0	14	14	-4	96	0
Rhett Warrener	62	4	9	13	20	88	1
Paul Laus	77	0	12	12	13	313	0
Steve Washburn*	18	3	6	9	2	4	1
Chris Wells	47	2	6	8	5	42	0

Acquired: C Wells from Pit. for C Stu Barnes and D Jason Woolley (Nov. 19); C Muller from Tor. for C Jason Podollan (Mar. 18).

Goalies (10 Gm)	Gm	Min	GAA	Record	Sv%
John Vanbiesbrouck . .	57	3347	2.29	27-19-10	.919
Mark Fitzpatrick	30	1680	2.36	8-9-9	.914
FLORIDA	82	5041	2.39	35-28-19	.915

Shutouts: Vanbiesbrouck (2). **Assists:** Vanbiesbrouck (2), Fitzpatrick (1). **PM:** Fitzpatrick (13), Vanbiesbrouck (8).

Hartford Whalers

Top Scorers

Top Scorers	Gm	G	A	Pts	+/-	PM	PP
Geoff Sanderson	82	36	31	67	-9	29	12
Andrew Cassels	81	22	44	66	-16	46	8
Derek King	82	26	33	59	-6	22	6
NYI	70	23	30	53	-6	20	5
HART	12	3	3	6	0	2	1
Keith Primeau	75	26	25	51	-3	161	6
Kevin Dineen	78	19	29	48	-6	141	8
Nelson Emerson	66	9	29	38	-21	34	2
Steven Rice	78	21	14	35	-11	59	5
Glen Wesley	68	6	26	32	0	40	3
Jeff O'Neill	72	14	16	30	-24	40	2
Steve Chiasson	65	8	22	30	-21	39	4
CALG	47	5	11	16	-11	32	1
HART	18	3	11	14	-10	7	3
Sami Kapanen	45	13	12	25	6	2	3
Robert Kron	68	10	12	22	-18	10	2
Curtis Leschyshyn	77	4	18	22	-18	38	1
COL	11	0	5	5	1	6	0
WASH	2	0	0	0	2	0	0
HART	64	4	13	17	-19	30	1
Paul Ranheim	67	10	11	21	-13	18	0
Kevin Haller	62	2	11	13	-12	85	0
PHI	27	0	5	5	-1	37	0
HART	35	2	6	8	-11	48	0

Acquired: C Primeau, D Paul Coffey and '97 first-round pick from Det. for LW Brendan Shanahan and D Brian Glynn (Oct. 9); D Leschyshyn from Wash. for C Andrei Nikolishin (Nov. 9); D Haller and '97 first and seventh-round picks from Phi. for D Coffey and '97 third-round pick (Dec. 15); D Chiasson and '97 third-round pick from Calg. for D Glen Featherstone, LW Hnat Domenichelli, '97 second-round pick and '98 third-round pick (Mar. 5); LW King from NYI for '97 fifth-round pick (Mar. 18).

Goalies (10 Gm)	Gm	Min	GAA	Record	Sv%
Sean Burke	51	2985	2.69	22-22-6	.914
Jason Muzzatti	31	1591	3.43	9-13-5	.888
HARTFORD	82	4996	3.07	32-39-11	.901

Shutouts: Burke (4). **Assists:** Burke (2), Muzzatti (1). **PM:** Muzzatti (18) and Burke (14).

Los Angeles Kings

Top Scorers

Top Scorers	Gm	G	A	Pts	+/-	PM	PP
Dimitri Khristich	75	19	37	56	8	38	3
Ray Ferraro	81	25	21	46	-22	112	11
Vladimir Tsyplakov . . .	67	16	23	39	8	12	1
Kevin Stevens	69	14	20	34	-27	96	4
Vitali Yachmenev	65	10	22	32	-9	10	2
Rob Blake	62	8	23	31	-28	82	4
Glen Murray	77	16	14	30	-21	32	3
PIT	66	11	11	22	-19	24	3
LA	11	5	3	8	-2	8	0
Kai Nurminen	67	16	11	27	-3	22	4
Yanic Perreault	41	11	14	25	0	20	1
Philippe Boucher	60	7	18	25	0	25	2
Ian Laperriere	62	8	15	23	-25	102	0
Mattias Norstrom	80	1	21	22	-4	84	0
Brad Smyth*	52	9	8	17	-10	76	0
FLA	8	1	0	1	-3	2	0
LA	44	8	8	16	-7	74	0
Sean O'Donnell	55	5	12	17	-13	144	2
John Slaney	32	3	11	14	-10	4	1
Jeff Shevalier*	29	5	8	13	-13	-6	6	1

Acquired: RW Smyth from Fla. for '97 third-round pick (Nov. 28); RW Murray from Pit. for C Eddie Olczyk (Mar. 18).

Goalies (10 Gm)	Gm	Min	GAA	Record	Sv%
Byron Dafoe	40	2162	3.11	13-17-5	.905
Stephane Fiset	44	2482	3.19	13-24-5	.906
LOS ANGELES	82	4985	3.23	28-43-11	.904

Shutouts: Fiset (4). **Assists:** none. **PM:** Fiset (2).

Montreal Canadiens

Top Scorers

Top Scorers	Gm	G	A	Pts	+/-	PM	PP
Vincent Damphousse .	82	27	54	81	-6	82	7
Mark Recchi	82	34	46	80	-1	58	7
Brian Savage	81	23	37	60	-14	39	5
Saku Koivu	50	17	39	56	7	38	5
Martin Rucinsky	70	28	27	55	1	62	6
Stephane Richer	63	22	24	46	0	32	2
Valeri Bure	64	14	21	35	4	6	4
Vladimir Malakhov ...	65	10	20	30	3	43	5
Shayne Corson	58	8	16	24	-9	104	3
ST.L	11	2	1	3	-4	24	1
MON	47	6	15	21	-5	80	2
Benoit Brunet	39	10	13	23	6	14	2
Stephane Quintal ...	71	7	15	22	1	100	1
Dave Manson	75	4	18	22	-26	187	2
PHO	66	3	17	20	-25	164	2
MON	9	1	1	2	-1	23	0
Turner Stevenson ...	65	8	13	21	-14	97	1
Scott Thornton	73	10	10	20	-19	128	1
Darcy Tucker*	73	7	13	20	-5	110	1
Marc Bureau	43	6	9	15	4	16	1
David Wilkie*	61	6	9	15	-9	63	3
Patrice Brisebois ...	49	2	13	15	-7	24	0
Peter Popovic	78	1	13	14	9	32	0

Acquired: LW Corson, D Murray Baron and '97 fifth-round pick from St.L for C Pierre Turgeon, C Craig Conroy and D Rory Fitzpatrick (Oct. 29); D Manson from Pho. for D Baron and RW Chris Murray (Mar. 18).

Goalies (10 Gm)

Goalies (10 Gm)	Gm	Min	GAA	Record	Sv%
Jocelyn Thibault	61	3397	2.90	22-24-11	.910
Jose Theodore*	16	821	3.87	5-6-2	.896
Pat Jablonski	17	754	3.98	4-6-2	.886
MONTREAL	82	5008	3.31	31-36-15	.901

Shutouts: Thibault (1). **Assists:** none. **PM:** none.

New Jersey Devils

Top Scorers

Top Scorers	Gm	G	A	Pts	+/-	PM	PP
Doug Gilmour	81	22	60	82	2	68	4
TOR	61	15	45	60	-5	46	2
NJ	20	7	15	22	7	22	2
Bobby Holik	82	23	39	62	24	54	5
Dave Andreychuk ...	82	27	34	61	38	48	4
John MacLean	80	29	25	54	11	49	5
Bill Guerin	82	29	18	47	-2	95	7
Brian Rolston	81	18	27	45	6	20	2
Valeri Zelepukin ...	71	14	24	38	-10	36	3
Scott Niedermayer ...	81	5	30	35	-4	64	3
Steve Thomas	57	15	19	34	9	46	1
Denis Pederson*	70	12	20	32	7	62	3
Randy McKay	77	9	18	27	15	109	0
Scott Stevens	79	5	19	24	26	70	0
Dave Ellett	76	6	15	21	-6	40	1
TOR	56	4	10	14	-8	34	0
NJ	20	2	5	7	2	6	1
Shawn Chambers ...	73	4	17	21	17	19	1
Bob Carpenter	62	4	15	19	6	14	0
Peter Zezel	53	4	12	16	10	16	0
ST.L	35	4	9	13	6	12	0
NJ	18	0	3	3	4	4	0
Lyle Odelein	79	3	13	16	16	110	1
Jay Pandolfo*	46	6	8	14	-1	6	0

Acquired: C Zezel from St.L for D Chris McAlpine and '99 ninth-round pick (Feb. 11); C Gilmour and D Ellett from Tor. for D Jason Smith, C Steve Sullivan and D Alyn McCauley (Feb. 25).

Goalies (10 Gm)

Goalies (10 Gm)	Gm	Min	GAA	Record	Sv%
Martin Brodeur	67	3838	1.88	37-14-13	.927
Mike Dunham*	26	1013	2.55	8-7-1	.906
NEW JERSEY	82	4999	2.18	45-23-14	.916

Shutouts: Brodeur (10), Dunham (2). **Assists:** Brodeur (4). **PM:** Brodeur (8), Dunham (2).
Note: Brodeur and Dunham shared a shutout vs NYI on Nov. 9, 1996.

New York Islanders

Top Scorers

Top Scorers	Gm	G	A	Pts	+/-	PM	PP
Zigmund Palffy	80	48	42	90	21	43	6
Travis Green	79	23	41	64	-5	38	10
Robert Reichel	82	21	41	62	5	26	6
CALG	70	16	27	43	-2	22	6
NYI	12	5	14	19	7	4	0
Bryan Smolinski	64	28	28	56	8	25	9
Bryan Berard*	82	8	40	48	1	86	3
Niklas Andersson ...	74	12	31	43	4	57	1
Bryan McCabe	82	8	20	28	-2	165	2
Todd Bertuzzi	64	10	13	23	-3	68	3
Kenny Jonsson	81	3	18	21	10	24	1
Claude Lapointe	73	13	5	18	-11	49	0
Scott Lachance	81	3	11	14	-7	47	1
Derek Armstrong* ...	50	6	7	13	-8	33	0
Dan Plante	67	4	9	13	-6	75	0
Randy Wood	65	6	5	11	-7	61	0
Brent Hughes	51	7	3	10	-4	57	0
Doug Houda	70	2	8	10	1	99	0
Paul Kruse	62	6	2	8	-9	141	0
CALG	14	2	0	2	-4	30	0
NYI	48	4	2	6	-5	111	0

Acquired: RW Smolinski from Pit. for D Darius Kasparaitis and C Andreas Johansson (Nov. 17); LW Kruse from Calg. for '97 third-round pick (Nov. 27); C Reichel from Calg. for LW Marty McInnis, G Tyrone Garner and '97 sixth-round pick (Mar. 18).

Goalies (10 Gm)

Goalies (10 Gm)	Gm	Min	GAA	Record	Sv%
Tommy Salo	58	3208	2.82	20-27-8	.904
Eric Fichaud*	34	1759	3.10	9-14-4	.899
NY ISLANDERS	82	4988	3.01	29-41-12	.899

Shutouts: Salo (5). **Assists:** Salo (1). **PM:** Salo (4), Fichaud (2).

New York Rangers

Top Scorers

Top Scorers	Gm	G	A	Pts	+/-	PM	PP
Wayne Gretzky	82	25	72	97	12	28	6
Mark Messier	71	36	48	84	12	88	7
Brian Leetch	82	20	58	78	31	40	9
Adam Graves	82	33	28	61	10	66	10
Niklas Sundstrom ...	82	24	28	52	23	20	5
Luc Robitaille	69	24	24	48	16	48	5
Alexander Karpovtsev .	77	9	29	38	1	59	6
Alexei Kovalev	45	13	22	35	11	42	1
Russ Courtnall	61	11	24	35	1	26	2
VAN	47	9	19	28	4	24	1
NYR	14	2	5	7	-3	2	1
Esa Tikkanen	76	13	17	30	-9	72	4
VAN	62	12	15	27	-9	66	4
NYR	14	1	2	3	0	6	0
Bruce Driver	79	5	25	30	8	48	2
Patrick Flatley	68	10	12	22	6	26	0
Ulf Samuelsson	73	6	11	17	3	138	1
Bill Berg	67	8	6	14	2	37	0
Daniel Goneau*	41	10	3	13	-5	10	3
Jeff Beukeboom	80	3	9	12	22	167	0
Mike Eastwood	60	2	10	12	-1	14	0
PHO	33	1	3	4	-3	4	0
NYR	27	1	7	8	2	10	0
Vladimir Vorobiev* ...	16	5	5	10	4	6	2
Darren Langdon	60	3	6	9	-1	195	0

Acquired: C Eastwood and D Dallas Eakins from Pho. for D Jayson More (Feb. 6); RW Courtnall and LW Tikkanen from Van. for RW Brian Noonan and C Sergei Nemchinov (Mar. 8).

Goalies (10 Gm)

Goalies (10 Gm)	Gm	Min	GAA	Record	Sv%
Glenn Healy	23	1357	2.61	5-12-4	.907
Mike Richter	61	3598	2.68	33-22-6	.917
NY RANGERS	82	4974	2.79	38-34-10	.911

Shutouts: Richter (4), Healy (1). **Assists:** none. **PM:** Healy (4), Richter (4).

Ottawa Senators

Top Scorers	Gm	G	A	Pts	+/-	PM	PP
Alexei Yashin	82	35	40	75	-7	44	10
Daniel Alfredsson	76	24	47	71	5	30	11
Alexandre Daigle	82	26	25	51	-33	33	4
Steve Duchesne	78	19	28	47	-9	38	10
Randy Cunneyworth ..	76	12	24	36	-7	99	6
Andreas Dackell*	79	12	19	31	-6	8	2
Shawn McEachern ...	65	11	20	31	-5	18	0
Wade Redden*	82	6	24	30	1	41	2
Sergei Zholtok*	57	12	16	28	2	19	5
Tom Chorske	68	18	8	26	-1	16	1
Shaun Van Allen	80	11	14	25	-8	35	1
Bruce Gardiner*	67	11	10	21	4	49	0
Jason York	75	4	17	21	-8	67	1
Janne Laukkanen	76	3	18	21	-14	76	2
Denny Lambert	80	4	16	20	-4	217	0
Radek Bonk	53	5	13	18	-4	14	0
Lance Pitlick	66	5	5	10	2	91	0
Jason Zent*	22	3	3	6	5	9	0
Christer Olsson	30	2	4	6	-4	10	1
ST.L	5	0	1	1	1	0	0
OTT	25	2	3	5	-5	10	1
Denis Chasse	22	1	4	5	3	19	0
Frank Musil	57	0	5	5	6	58	0
Dave Hannan	34	2	2	4	-1	8	0

Acquired: D Olsson from St.L for RW Pavol Demitra (Nov. 27).

Goalies (10 Gm)	Gm	Min	GAA	Record	Sv%
Damian Rhodes	50	2934	2.72	14-20-14	.890
Ron Tugnutt	37	1991	2.80	17-15-1	.895
OTTAWA	82	5001	2.81	31-36-15	.889

Shutouts: Tugnutt (3), Rhodes (1). **Assists:** Rhodes (2), Tugnutt (1). **PM:** Rhodes (2).

Philadelphia Flyers

Top Scorers	Gm	G	A	Pts	+/-	PM	PP
John LeClair	82	50	47	97	44	58	10
Eric Lindros	52	32	47	79	31	136	9
Rod Brind'Amour	82	27	32	59	2	41	8
Mikael Renberg	77	22	37	59	36	65	1
Eric Desjardins	82	12	34	46	25	50	5
Trent Klatt	76	24	21	45	9	20	5
Janne Niinimaa*	77	4	40	44	12	58	1
Dale Hawerchuk	51	12	22	34	9	32	6
Paul Coffey	57	9	25	34	11	38	1
HART	20	3	5	8	0	18	1
PHI	37	6	20	26	11	20	0
Shjon Podein	82	14	18	32	7	41	0
Joel Otto	78	13	19	32	12	99	0
Chris Therien	71	2	22	24	26	64	0
Pat Falloon	52	11	12	23	-8	10	2
Dainius Zubrus*	68	8	13	21	3	22	1
Karl Dykhuis	62	4	15	19	7	35	2
John Druce	43	7	8	15	-5	12	1
Vaclav Prospal*	18	5	10	15	3	4	0
Petr Svoboda	67	2	12	14	10	94	1
Michel Petit	38	2	7	9	-11	71	0
EDM	18	2	4	6	-13	20	0
PHI	20	0	3	3	2	51	0
Daniel Lacroix	74	7	1	8	-1	163	1
Scott Daniels	56	5	3	8	2	237	0
Kjell Samuelsson	34	4	3	7	17	47	0

Acquired: D Coffey and '97 third-round pick from Hart. for D Kevin Haller and '97 first and seventh-round picks (Dec. 15). **Claimed:** D Petit off waivers from Edm. (Jan. 17).

Goalies (10 Gm)	Gm	Min	GAA	Record	Sv%
Garth Snow	35	1884	2.52	14-8-8	.903
Ron Hextall	55	3094	2.56	31-16-5	.897
PHILADELPHIA	82	4995	2.61	45-24-13	.897

Shutouts: Hextall (5), Snow (2). **Assists:** Snow (1). **PM:** Hextall (43), Snow (30).

Phoenix Coyotes

Top Scorers	Gm	G	A	Pts	+/-	PM	PP
Keith Tkachuk	81	52	34	86	-1	228	9
Jeremy Roenick	72	29	40	69	-7	115	10
Mike Gartner	82	32	31	63	-11	38	13
Oleg Tverdovsky	82	10	45	55	-5	30	3
Craig Janney	77	15	38	53	-1	26	5
Cliff Ronning	69	19	32	51	-9	26	8
Dallas Drake	63	17	19	36	-11	52	5
Teppo Numminen	82	2	25	27	-3	28	0
Darrin Shannon	82	11	13	24	4	41	1
Bob Corkum	80	9	11	20	-7	40	0
Mike Stapleton	55	4	11	15	-4	36	2
Deron Quint	27	3	11	14	-4	4	1
Kris King	81	3	11	14	-7	185	0
Gerald Diduck	67	2	12	14	-7	63	1
HART	56	1	10	11	-9	40	0
PHO	11	1	2	3	2	23	1
Norm MacIver	32	4	9	13	-11	24	1
Shane Doan	63	4	8	12	-3	49	0

Acquired: D More from NYR for C Mike Eastwood and D Dallas Eakins (Feb. 6); G Jablonski from Mon. for D Steve Cheredaryk (Mar. 18); D Diduck from Hart. for RW Chris Murray (Mar. 18).

Goalies (10 Gm)	Gm	Min	GAA	Record	Sv%
Nikolai Khabibulin ...	72	4091	2.83	30-33-6	.908
Darcy Wakaluk	16	782	2.99	8-3-1	.899
Pat Jablonski	19	813	3.84	4-7-2	.887
MON	17	754	3.98	4-6-2	.886
PHO	2	59	2.03	0-1-0	.917
PHOENIX	82	4974	2.93	38-37-7	.904

Shutouts: Khabibulin (7), Wakaluk (1). **Assists:** Khabibulin (3), Wakaluk (1). **PM:** Khabibulin (16), Wakaluk (4).

Pittsburgh Penguins

Top Scorers	Gm	G	A	Pts	+/-	PM	PP
Mario Lemieux	76	50	72	122	27	65	15
Jaromir Jagr	63	47	48	95	22	40	11
Ron Francis	81	27	63	90	7	20	12
Petr Nedved	74	33	38	71	-2	66	12
Ed Olczyk	79	25	30	55	-14	51	5
LA	67	21	23	44	-22	45	5
PIT	12	4	7	11	8	6	0
Kevin Hatcher	80	15	39	54	11	103	9
Stu Barnes	81	19	30	49	-23	26	5
FLA	19	2	8	10	-3	10	1
PIT	62	17	22	39	-20	16	4
Fredrik Olausson	71	9	29	38	16	32	3
ANA	20	2	9	11	-5	8	1
PIT	51	7	20	27	21	24	2
Jason Woolley	60	6	30	36	4	30	2
FLA	3	0	0	0	1	2	0
PIT	57	6	30	36	3	28	2
Greg Johnson	75	13	19	32	-18	26	1
DET	43	6	10	16	-5	12	0
PIT	32	7	9	16	-13	14	1
Alex Hicks	73	7	21	28	-5	90	0
ANA	18	2	6	8	1	14	0
PIT	55	5	15	20	-6	76	0
Darius Kasparaitis	75	2	21	23	17	100	0
NYI	18	0	5	5	-7	16	0
PIT	57	2	16	18	24	84	0

Acquired: D Kasparaitis and C Andreas Johansson from NYI for RW Bryan Smolinski (Nov. 17); D Olausson and C Hicks from Ana. for D Dmitri Mironov and LW Shawn Antoski (Nov. 19); C Barnes and D Woolley from Fla. for C Chris Wells (Nov. 19); C Johnson from Det. for RW Tomas Sandstrom (Jan. 27); C Olczyk from LA for RW Glen Murray (Mar. 18).

Goalies (10 Gm)	Gm	Min	GAA	Record	Sv%
Patrick Lalime*	39	2058	2.94	21-12-2	.913
Ken Wregget	46	2514	3.25	17-17-6	.902
PITTSBURGH	82	4969	3.38	38-36-8	.900

Shutouts: Lalime (3), Wregget (2). **Assists:** Wregget (1). **PM:** Wregget (6).

St. Louis Blues

Top Scorers	Gm	G	A	Pts	+/-	PM	PP
Pierre Turgeon	78	26	59	85	8	14	5
MON	9	1	10	11	4	2	0
ST.L	69	25	49	74	4	12	5
Brett Hull	77	42	40	82	-9	10	12
Geoff Courtnall	82	17	40	57	3	86	4
Joe Murphy	75	20	25	45	-1	69	4
Jim Campbell*	68	23	20	43	3	68	5
Al MacInnis	72	13	30	43	2	65	6
Stephane Matteau	74	16	20	36	11	50	1
Chris Pronger	79	11	24	35	15	143	4
Harry York*	74	14	18	32	1	24	3
Igor Kravchuk	82	4	24	28	7	35	1
Robert Petrovicky	44	7	12	19	2	10	0
Scott Pellerin	54	8	10	18	12	35	0
Craig Conroy	61	6	11	17	0	43	0
Ricard Persson	54	4	8	12	-2	45	1
NJ	1	0	0	0	0	0	0
ST.L	53	4	8	12	-2	45	1
Jamie Rivers*	15	2	5	7	-4	6	1
Craig MacTavish	50	2	5	7	-12	33	0
Mike Peluso	64	2	5	7	0	226	0
NJ	20	0	2	2	0	68	0
ST.L	44	2	3	5	0	158	0
Libor Zabransky*	34	1	5	6	-1	44	0

Acquired: C Turgeon, C Conroy and D Rory Fitzpatrick from Mon. for LW Shayne Corson, D Murray Baron and '97 fifth-round pick (Oct. 29); LW Peluso and D Persson from NJ for D Ken Sutton and '99 second-round pick (Nov. 26).

Goalies (10 Gm)	Gm	Min	GAA	Record	Sv%
Grant Fuhr	73	4261	2.72	33-27-11	.901
Jon Casey	15	707	3.39	3-8-0	.866
ST. LOUIS	82	4980	2.88	36-35-11	.894

Shutouts: Fuhr (3). **Assists:** Fuhr (2). **PM:** Fuhr (6).

San Jose Sharks

Top Scorers	Gm	G	A	Pts	+/-	PM	PP
Owen Nolan	72	31	32	63	-19	155	10
Jeff Friesen	82	28	34	62	-8	75	6
Bernie Nicholls	65	12	33	45	-21	63	2
Viktor Kozlov	78	16	25	41	-16	40	4
Tony Granato	76	25	15	40	-7	159	5
Darren Turcotte	65	16	21	37	-8	16	3
Andrei Nazarov	60	12	15	27	-4	222	1
Stephen Guolla*	43	13	8	21	-10	14	2
Todd Gill	79	0	21	21	-20	101	0
Greg Hawgood	63	6	12	18	-22	69	3
Marcus Ragnarsson	69	3	14	17	-18	63	2
Marty McSorley	57	4	12	16	-6	186	0
Doug Bodger	81	1	15	16	-14	64	0
Shean Donovan	73	9	6	15	-18	42	0
Al Iafrate	38	6	9	15	-10	91	3
Ron Sutter	78	5	7	12	-8	65	1
Bob Errey	66	4	8	12	-5	47	0
DET	36	1	2	3	-3	27	0
SJ	30	3	6	9	-2	20	0
Vlastimil Kroupa	35	2	6	8	-17	12	2
Mike Rathje	31	0	8	8	-1	21	0
Dody Wood	44	3	2	5	-3	193	0
Ville Peltonen	28	2	3	5	-8	0	1
Chris Tancill	25	4	0	4	-5	8	1
Tim Hunter	46	0	4	4	0	135	0

Acquired: G Belfour from Chi. for G Chris Terreri, RW Ulf Dahlen, D Michal Sykora and a conditional '98 draft pick. **Claimed:** LW Errey off waivers from Det. (Feb. 8).

Goalies (10 Gm)	Gm	Min	GAA	Record	Sv%
Ed Belfour	46	2723	2.89	14-24-6	.900
CHI	33	1966	2.69	11-15-6	.907
SJ	13	757	3.41	3-9-0	.884
Kelly Hrudey	48	2631	3.19	16-24-5	.889
SAN JOSE	82	4970	3.36	27-47-8	.884

Shutouts: Belfour (2). **Assists:** none. **PM:** Belfour (34).

Tampa Bay Lightning

Top Scorers	Gm	G	A	Pts	+/-	PM	PP
Chris Gratton	82	30	32	62	-28	201	9
Dino Ciccarelli	77	35	25	60	-11	116	12
John Cullen	70	18	37	55	-14	95	5
Rob Zamuner	82	17	33	50	3	56	0
Roman Hamrlik	79	12	28	40	-29	57	6
Shawn Burr	74	14	21	35	5	106	1
Alexander Selivanov	69	15	18	33	-3	61	3
Daymond Langkow*	79	15	13	28	1	35	3
Patrick Poulin	73	12	14	26	-16	56	2
Bill Houlder	79	4	21	25	16	30	0
Brian Bradley	35	7	17	24	2	16	1
Mikael Andersson	70	5	14	19	1	8	0
Jeff Norton	75	2	16	18	-7	58	0
EDM	62	2	11	13	-7	42	0
TB	13	0	5	5	0	16	0
Paul Ysebaert	39	5	12	17	1	4	2
Jason Wiemer	63	9	5	14	-13	134	2
David Shaw	57	1	10	11	1	72	0
Jeff Toms*	34	2	8	10	2	10	0
Cory Cross	72	4	5	9	6	95	0
Igor Ulanov	59	1	7	8	2	108	0
Rudy Poeschek	60	0	6	6	-3	120	0
Jamie Huscroft	52	0	5	5	-2	151	0
CALG	39	0	4	4	2	117	0
TB	13	0	1	1	-4	34	0

Acquired: G Tabaracci from Calg. for C Aaron Gavey (Nov. 19); D Huscroft from Calg. for G Tyler Moss (Mar. 18); D Norton from Edm. for D Drew Bannister (Mar. 18).

Goalies (10 Gm)	Gm	Min	GAA	Record	Sv%
Rick Tabaracci	62	3373	2.70	22-29-6	.903
CALG	7	361	2.33	2-4-0	.910
TB	55	3012	2.75	20-25-6	.902
Corey Schwab*	31	1462	3.04	11-12-1	.897
TAMPA BAY	82	4984	2.97	32-40-10	.896

Shutouts: Tabaracci (5), Schwab (1). **Assists:** Schwab (1), Tabaracci (1). **PM:** Tabaracci (12), Schwab (10).

Toronto Maple Leafs

Top Scorers	Gm	G	A	Pts	+/-	PM	PP
Mats Sundin	82	41	53	94	6	59	7
Wendel Clark	65	30	19	49	-2	75	6
Sergei Berezin*	73	25	16	41	-3	2	7
Steve Sullivan*	54	13	25	38	14	37	3
NJ	33	8	14	22	9	14	2
TOR	21	5	11	16	5	23	1
Todd Warriner	75	12	21	33	-3	41	2
Tie Domi	80	11	17	28	-17	275	2
Mike Craig	65	7	13	20	-20	62	1
Darby Hendrickson	64	11	6	17	-20	47	0
Jamie Baker	58	8	8	16	2	28	1
Dimitri Yushkevich	74	4	10	14	-24	56	1
Rob Zettler	48	2	12	14	8	51	0
Fredrik Modin*	76	6	7	13	-14	24	0
Mathieu Schneider	26	5	7	12	3	20	1
Jamie Macoun	73	1	10	11	-14	93	0
Brandon Convery*	39	2	8	10	-9	20	0
Zdenek Nedved*	23	3	5	8	4	6	0
Jason Smith	78	1	7	8	-12	54	0
NJ	57	1	2	3	-8	38	0
TOR	21	0	5	5	-4	16	0
David Cooper*	19	3	3	6	-3	16	2

Acquired: C Hendrickson from NYI for conditional '98 draft pick (Oct. 11); D Smith, C Sullivan and C Alyn McCauley from NJ for C Doug Gilmour and D Dave Ellett (Feb. 25).

Goalies (10 Gm)	Gm	Min	GAA	Record	Sv%
Felix Potvin	74	4271	3.15	27-36-7	.908
Marcel Cousineau*	13	566	3.29	3-5-1	.902
TORONTO	82	4966	3.30	30-44-8	.903

Shutouts: Cousineau (1). **Assists:** Potvin (3), Cousineau (1). **PM:** Potvin (19).
Note: Potvin and Cousineau shared a shutout vs St.L on Dec 3, 1996.

Vancouver Canucks

Top Scorers	Gm	G	A	Pts	+/-	PM	PP
Alexander Mogilny ...	76	31	42	73	9	18	7
Martin Gelinas	74	35	33	68	6	42	6
Pavel Bure	63	23	32	55	-14	40	4
Mike Ridley	75	20	32	52	0	42	3
Markus Naslund	78	21	20	41	-15	30	4
Trevor Linden	49	9	31	40	5	27	2
Mike Sillinger	78	17	20	37	-3	25	3
Jyrki Lumme	66	11	24	35	8	32	5
Brian Noonan	73	12	22	34	-3	34	3
ST.L	13	2	5	7	2	0	0
NYR	44	6	9	15	-7	28	3
VAN	16	4	8	12	2	6	0
David Roberts	58	10	17	27	11	51	1
Dave Babych	78	5	22	27	-2	38	2
Sergei Nemchinov ...	69	8	16	24	9	16	1
NYR	63	6	13	19	5	12	1
VAN	6	2	3	5	4	4	0
Lonny Bohonos*	36	11	11	22	-3	10	2
Adrian Aucoin	70	5	16	21	0	63	1
Bret Hedican	67	4	15	19	-3	51	2
Scott Walker	64	3	15	18	2	132	0
Steve Staios*	63	3	14	17	-24	91	0
BOS	54	3	8	11	-26	71	0
VAN	9	0	6	6	2	20	0
Chris Joseph	63	3	13	16	-21	62	2

Acquired: RW Noonan and C Nemchinov from NYR for RW Russ Courtnall and LW Esa Tikkanen (Mar. 8). **Claimed:** D Staios off waivers from Bos. (Mar. 18).

Goalies (10 Gm)	Gm	Min	GAA	Record	Sv%
Kirk McLean	44	2581	3.21	21-18-3	.889
Corey Hirsch	39	2127	3.27	12-20-4	.894
VANCOUVER	82	4972	3.29	35-40-7	.890

Shutouts: Hirsch (2). **Assists:** McLean (2), Hirsch (1). **PM:** Hirsch (6), McLean (2).

Washington Capitals

Top Scorers	Gm	G	A	Pts	+/-	PM	PP
Adam Oates	80	22	60	82	-5	14	3
BOS	63	18	52	70	-3	10	2
WASH	17	4	8	12	-2	4	1
Peter Bondra	77	46	31	77	7	72	10
Dale Hunter	82	14	32	46	-2	125	3
Steve Konowalchuk ..	78	17	25	42	-3	67	2
Joe Juneau	58	15	27	42	-11	8	9
Rick Tocchet	53	21	19	40	-3	98	4
BOS	40	16	14	30	-3	67	3
VAN	13	5	5	10	0	31	1
Phil Housley	77	11	29	40	-10	24	3
Sergei Gonchar	57	13	17	30	-11	36	3
Andrei Nikolishin ...	71	9	19	28	3	32	1
HART	12	2	5	7	-2	2	0
WASH	59	7	14	21	5	30	1
Kelly Miller	77	10	14	24	4	33	0
Sylvain Cote	57	6	18	24	11	28	2
Michal Pivonka	54	7	16	23	-15	22	2
Chris Simon	42	9	13	22	-1	165	3
Calle Johansson	65	6	11	17	-2	16	2
Todd Krygier	47	5	11	16	-10	37	1

Acquired: LW Simon and D Curtis Leschyschyn from Col. for RW Keith Jones, '98 first-round pick and '97 or '98 fourth-round pick (Nov. 2); C Nikolishin from Hart. for D Leschyschyn (Nov. 9); C Oates, RW Tocchet and D Leschyschyn from Bos. for G Jim Carey, C Jason Allison, C Anson Carter, '97 third-round pick and a conditional '98 second-round pick (Mar. 1).

Goalies (10 Gm)	Gm	Min	GAA	Record	Sv%
Olaf Kolzig	29	1645	2.59	8-15-4	.906
Bill Ranford	55	3156	3.25	20-23-10	.887
BOS	37	2147	3.49	12-16-8	.887
WASH	18	1009	2.74	8-7-2	.888
WASHINGTON	82	4977	2.78	33-40-9	.893

Shutouts: Kolzig (2), Ranford (2). **Assists:** Ranford (1). **PM:** Ranford (7), Kolzig (4).

1997 NHL Draft

First and second round selections at the 35th annual NHL Entry Draft held June 21, 1997, in Pittsburgh. The order of the first ten positions is determined by a draft lottery held May 11 in New York. Positions 11 through 26 reflect regular season records in reverse order. League and national affiliations are listed below.

First Round

Team		Pos
1 Boston .... Joe Thornton, Sault Ste. Marie		C
2 San Jose .... Patrick Marleau, Seattle		C
3 Los Angeles .... Olli Jokinen, IFK Helsinki		C
4 a-NY Islanders .... Roberto Luongo, Val d'Or		G
5 NY Islanders .... Eric Brewer, Prince George		D
6 Calgary .... Daniel Tkaczuk, Barrie		C
7 Tampa Bay .... Paul Mara, Sudbury		D
8 b-Boston ..... Sergei Samsonov, Detroit (IHL)		L
9 Washington .... Nick Boynton, Ottawa		D
10 Vancouver .... Brad Ference, Spokane		D
11 Montreal .... Jason Ward, Erie		C
12 Ottawa .... Marian Hossa, Dukla Trencin		R
13 Chicago .... Daniel Cleary, Belleville		L
14 Edmonton ...... Michael Riesen, Biel-Bienne		G
15 c-Los Angeles .... Matt Zultek, Ottawa		L
16 d-Chicago .... Ty Jones, Spokane		R
17 Pittsburgh .... Robert Dome, Long Beach		C
18 Anaheim ...... Mikael Holmqvist, Djurgarden		C
19 NY Rangers ..... Stefan Cherneski, Brandon		R
20 Florida .... Mike Brown, Red Deer		L
21 Buffalo .... Mika Noronen, Tappara		G
22 e-Carolina .... Nikos Tselios, Belleville		D
23 f-San Jose .... Scott Hannan, Kelowna		D
24 New Jersey ..... J.F. Damphousse, Moncton		G
25 Dallas .... Brenden Morrow, Portland		L
26 Colorado .... Kevin Grimes, Kingston		D

Second Round

Team		Pos
27 Boston .... Ben Clymer, Minnesota		D
28 g-Carolina ...... Brad DeFauw, North Dakota		L
29 Los Angeles ..... Scott Barney, Peterborough		C
30 h-Philadelphia ... Jean-Marc Pelletier, Cornell		G
31 NY Islanders .... Jeff Zehr, Windsor		L
32 Calgary .... Evan Lindsay, Prince Albert		G
33 Tampa Bay .... Kyle Kos, Red Deer		D
34 i-Vancouver ...... Ryan Bonni, Saskatoon		D
35 Washington ..... J.F. Fortin, Sherbrooke		D
36 Vancouver .... Harold Druken, Detroit (OHL)		C
37 Montreal ...... Gregor Baumgartner, Laval		C
38 j-New Jersey ... Stanislav Gron, Bratislava		C
39 Chicago .... Jeremy Reich, Seattle		C
40 St. Louis .... Tyler Rennette, North Bay		C
41 Edmonton .... Patrick Dovigi, Erie		G
42 k-Calgary .... John Tripp, Oshawa		R
43 Phoenix ..... Juha Gustafsson, Kieko Espoo		D
44 Pittsburgh ...... Brian Gaffaney, Northern Iowa		D
45 Anaheim ..... Maxim Balmochnykh, Lada Togliatti		L
46 NY Rangers .... Wes Jarvis, Kitchener		D
47 Florida .... Kristian Huselius, Farjestad		L
48 Buffalo .... Hendrik Tallinder, AIK		D
49 Detroit ...... Yuri Butsayev, Lada Togliatti		C
50 Philadelphia ..... Pat Kavanagh, Peterborough		R
51 l-Calgary ... Dmitri Kokorev, Moscow Dynamo		D
52 Dallas .... Roman Lyashenko, Yaroslavl		C
53 Colorado .... Graham Belak, Edmonton		D

Acquired picks: FIRST ROUND: **a**— from Toronto; **b**— from Carolina; **c**— from St. Louis; **d**— from Phoenix; **e**— from Detroit; **f**— from Philadelphia via Carolina; SECOND ROUND: **g**— from San Jose; **h**— from Toronto; **i**— from Carolina; **j**— from Ottawa; **k**— from St. Louis; **l**— from New Jersey via Carolina.

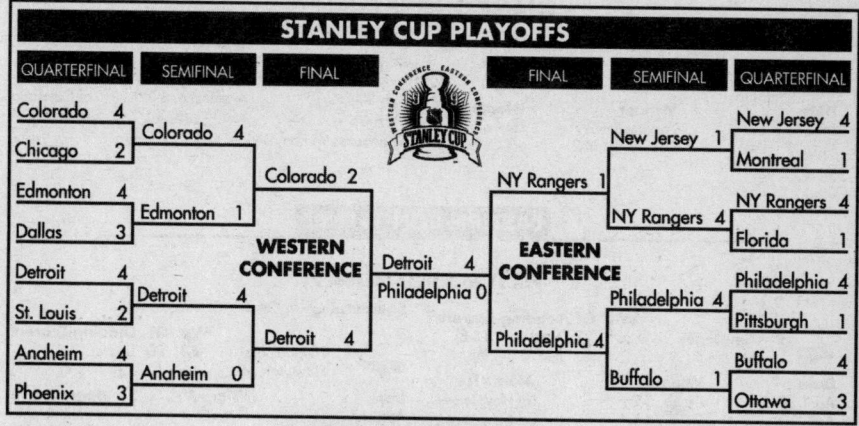

Series Summaries

WESTERN CONFERENCE

FIRST ROUND (Best of 7)

	W-L	GF	Leading Scorers
Colorado	4-2	28	Sakic (3-9-12)
Chicago	2-4	14	Amonte (4-2-6)

Date	Winner	Home Ice
April 16	Avalanche, 6-0	at Colorado
April 18	Avalanche, 3-1	at Colorado
April 20	Blackhawks, 4-3 (2OT)	at Chicago
April 22	Blackhawks, 6-3	at Chicago
April 24	Avalanche, 7-0	at Colorado
April 26	Avalanche, 6-3	at Chicago

Shutout: Roy, Colorado (2).

	W-L	GF	Leading Scorers
Detroit	4-2	13	Shanahan (3-3-6)
St. Louis	2-4	12	Hull (2-7-9)

Date	Winner	Home Ice
April 16	Blues, 2-0	at Detroit
April 18	Red Wings, 2-1	at Detroit
April 20	Red Wings, 3-2	at St. Louis
April 22	Blues, 4-0	at St. Louis
April 25	Red Wings, 5-2	at Detroit
April 27	Red Wings, 3-1	at St. Louis

Shutouts: Fuhr, St. Louis (2).

	W-L	GF	Leading Scorers
Edmonton	4-3	21	Weight (2-6-8)
Dallas	3-4	18	Modano (4-1-5)

Date	Winner	Home Ice
April 16	Stars, 5-3	at Dallas
April 18	Oilers, 4-0	at Dallas
April 20	Oilers, 4-3 (OT)	at Edmonton
April 22	Stars, 4-3	at Edmonton
April 25	Oilers, 1-0 (2OT)	at Dallas
April 27	Stars, 3-2	at Edmonton
April 29	Oilers, 4-3 (OT)	at Dallas

Shutout: Joseph, Edmonton (2).

	W-L	GF	Leading Scorers
Anaheim	4-3	17	Kariya (5-4-9)
Phoenix	3-4	17	Ronning (0-7-7)

Date	Winner	Home Ice
April 16	Mighty Ducks, 4-2	at Anaheim
April 18	Mighty Ducks, 4-2	at Anaheim
April 20	Coyotes, 4-1	at Phoenix
April 22	Coyotes, 2-0	at Phoenix
April 24	Coyotes, 5-2	at Anaheim
April 27	Mighty Ducks, 3-2	at Phoenix
April 29	Mighty Ducks, 3-0	at Anaheim

Shutouts: Khabibulin, Phoenix; Hebert, Anaheim.

SEMIFINALS (Best of 7)

	W-L	GF	Leading Scorers
Colorado	4-1	19	Kamensky (3-6-9)
Edmonton	1-4	11	Smyth (2-3-5)

Date	Winner	Home Ice
May 2	Avalanche, 5-1	at Colorado
May 4	Avalanche, 4-1	at Colorado
May 7	Oilers, 4-3	at Edmonton
May 9	Avalanche, 3-2 (OT)	at Edmonton
May 11	Avalanche, 4-3	at Colorado

	W-L	GF	Leading Scorers
Detroit	4-0	13	Fedorov (2-3-5)
Anaheim	0-4	8	Kariya (2-2-4)
			& Mironov (0-4-4)

Date	Winner	Home Ice
May 2	Red Wings, 2-1 (OT)	at Detroit
May 4	Red Wings, 3-2 (3OT)	at Detroit
May 6	Red Wings, 5-3	at Anaheim
May 8	Red Wings, 3-2 (2OT)	at Anaheim

CHAMPIONSHIP (Best of 7)

	W-L	GF	Leading Scorers
Detroit	4-2	16	Fedorov (3-4-7)
Colorado	4-2	12	Sakic (4-2-6)

Date	Winner	Home Ice
May 15	Avalanche, 2-1	at Colorado
May 17	Red Wings, 4-2	at Colorado
May 19	Red Wings, 2-1	at Detroit
May 22	Red Wings, 6-0	at Detroit
May 24	Avalanche, 6-0	at Colorado
May 26	Red Wings, 3-1	at Detroit

Shutouts: Vernon, Detroit; Roy, Colorado

EASTERN CONFERENCE

FIRST ROUND (Best of 7)

	W-L	GF	Leading Scorers
New Jersey	4-1	22	MacLean (3-5-8)
Montreal	1-4	11	Recchi (4-2-6)

Date	Winner	Home Ice
April 17	Devils, 5-2	at New Jersey
April 19	Devils, 4-1	at New Jersey
April 22	Devils, 6-4	at Montreal
April 24	Canadiens, 4-3 (3OT)	at Montreal
April 26	Devils, 4-0	at New Jersey

Shutout: Brodeur, New Jersey.

	W-L	GF	Leading Scorers
Buffalo	4-3	14	Holzinger (2-4-6)
Ottawa	3-4	13	Alfredsson (5-2-7)

Date	Winner	Home Ice
April 17	Sabres, 3-1	at Buffalo
April 19	Senators, 3-1	at Buffalo
April 21	Sabres, 3-2	at Ottawa
April 23	Senators, 1-0 (OT)	at Ottawa
April 25	Senators, 4-1	at Buffalo
April 27	Sabres, 3-0	at Ottawa
April 29	Sabres, 3-2 (OT)	at Buffalo

Shutout: Tugnutt, Ottawa; Shields, Buffalo.

	W-L	GF	Leading Scorers
Philadelphia	4-1	20	Lindros (3-6-9)
Pittsburgh	1-4	13	Jagr (4-4-8)

Date	Winner	Home Ice
April 17	Flyers, 5-1	at Philadelphia
April 19	Flyers, 3-2	at Philadelphia
April 21	Flyers, 5-3	at Pittsburgh
April 23	Penguins, 4-1	at Pittsburgh
April 26	Flyers, 6-3	at Philadelphia

	W-L	GF	Leading Scorers
NY Rangers	4-1	13	Gretzky (4-2-6)
Florida	1-4	10	Svehla (1-4-5) & Murphy (0-5-5)

Date	Winner	Home Ice
April 17	Panthers, 3-0	at Florida
April 20	Rangers, 3-0	at Florida
April 22	Rangers, 4-3 (OT)	at NY Rangers
April 23	Rangers, 3-2	at NY Rangers
April 25	Rangers, 3-2 (OT)	at Florida

Shutout: Vanbiesbrouck, Florida; Richter, New York.

SEMIFINALS (Best of 7)

	W-L	GF	Leading Scorers
NY Rangers	4-1	10	Gretzky (2-3-5)
New Jersey	1-4	5	Niedermayer & Rolston (1-1-2)

Date	Winner	Home Ice
May 2	Devils, 2-0	at New Jersey
May 4	Rangers, 2-0	at New Jersey
May 6	Rangers, 3-2	at NY Rangers
May 8	Rangers, 3-0	at NY Rangers
May 11	Rangers, 2-1 (OT)	at New Jersey

Shutout: Richter, NY Rangers (2); Brodeur, New Jersey.

	W-L	GF	Leading Scorers
Philadelphia	4-1	21	Brind'Amour (3-3-6) & Hawerchuk (2-4-6)
Buffalo	1-4	13	Plante (1-6-7)

Date	Winner	Home Ice
May 3	Flyers, 5-3	at Buffalo
May 5	Flyers, 2-1	at Buffalo
May 7	Flyers, 4-1	at Philadelphia
May 9	Sabres, 5-4 (OT)	at Philadelphia
May 11	Flyers, 6-3	at Buffalo

CHAMPIONSHIP (Best of 7)

	W-L	GF	Leading Scorers
Philadelphia	4-1	20	Lindros (5-4-9) & LeClair (2-7-9)
NY Rangers	1-4	13	Gretzky (4-5-9)

Date	Winner	Home Ice
May 16	Flyers, 3-1	at Philadelphia
May 18	Rangers, 5-4	at Philadelphia
May 20	Flyers, 6-3	at NY Rangers
May 23	Flyers, 3-2	at NY Rangers
May 25	Flyers, 4-2	at Philadelphia

STANLEY CUP FINAL (Best of 7)

	W-L	GF	Leading Scorers
Detroit	4-0	16	Fedorov (3-3-6)
Philadelphia	0-4	6	Brind'Amour (3-1-4)

Date	Winner	Home Ice
May 31	Red Wings, 4-2	at Philadelphia
June 3	Red Wings, 4-2	at Philadelphia
June 5	Red Wings, 6-1	at Detroit
June 7	Red Wings, 2-1	at Detroit

Conn Smythe Trophy (MVP)

Mike Vernon, Detroit, G

16-4, 1.76 GAA, .927 save pct.

Stanley Cup Final Box Scores

Game 1
Saturday, May 31, at Philadelphia

Detroit .... 2 1 1 — 4
Philadelphia .... 1 1 0 — 2
1st Period: DET— Maltby 4 (Draper) 6:38 (sh); PHI— Brind'Amour 11 (Lindros, Niinimaa) 7:37 (pp); DET— Kocur 1 (unassisted) 15:56.
2nd Period: DET— Fedorov 6 (Murphy, McCarty) 11:41; PHI— LeClair 8 (Renberg, Lindros) 17:11.
3rd Period: DET— Yzerman 5 (Murphy) 0:56.
Shots on Goal: Detroit— 8-12-10–30; Philadelphia— 10-9-9–28. **Power plays:** Detroit 0-5; Philadelphia 1-5. **Goalies:** Detroit, Vernon (28 shots, 26 saves); Philadelphia, Hextall (30 shots, 26 saves). **Attendance:** 20,291.

Game 2
Tuesday, June 3, at Philadelphia

Detroit .... 2 1 1 — 4
Philadelphia .... 2 0 0 — 2
1st Period: DET— Shanahan 7 (unassisted) 1:37; DET— Yzerman 6 (Murphy, Fetisov) 9:22 (pp); PHI— Brind'Amour 12 (Niinimaa) 17:42 (pp); PHI— Brind'Amour 13 (Niinimaa, LeClair) 18:51 (pp).
2nd Period: DET— Maltby 5 (Kocur) 2:39.
3rd Period: DET— Shanahan 8 (Lapointe, Fedorov) 9:56.
Shots on Goal: Detroit— 14-9-5–28; Philadelphia— 14-9-8–31. **Power plays:** Detroit 1-3; Philadelphia 2-4. **Goalies:** Detroit, Vernon (31 shots, 29 saves); Philadelphia, Hextall (28 shots, 24 saves). **Attendance:** 20,159.

Game 3
Thursday, June 5, at Detroit

Philadelphia .... 1 0 0 — 1
Detroit .... 3 2 1 — 6
1st Period: PHI— LeClair 9 (Desjardins, Brind'Amour) 7:03 (pp); DET— Yzerman 7 (Kozlov) 9:03 (pp); DET— Fedorov 7 (unassisted) 11:05; DET— Lapointe 3 (Brown, Fedorov) 19:00.
2nd Period: DET— Fedorov 8 (Kozlov, Shanahan) 3:12 (pp); DET— Shanahan 9 (McCarty, Fetisov) 19:17.
3rd Period: DET— Lapointe 4 (Fedorov, Vernon) 1:08 (pp).
Shots on Goal: Philadelphia— 8-7-7–22; Detroit— 10-12-7–29. **Power plays:** Philadelphia 1-7; Detroit 3-5. **Goalies:** Philadelphia, Hextall (29 shots, 23 saves); Detroit, Vernon (22 shots, 21 saves). **Attendance:** 19,983.

Game 4
Saturday, June 7, at Detroit

Philadelphia .... 0 0 1 — 1
Detroit .... 1 1 0 — 2
1st Period: DET— Lidstrom 2 (Maltby) 19:27.
2nd Period: DET— McCarty 3 (Sandstrom, Yzerman) 13:02.
3rd Period: PHI— Lindros 12 (Desjardins) 19:45.
Shots on Goal: Philadelphia— 8-12-7–27; Detroit— 9-10-9–28. **Power plays:** Philadelphia 0-3; Detroit 0-5. **Goalies:** Philadelphia, Hextall (28 shots, 26 saves); Detroit, Vernon (27 shots, 26 saves). **Attendance:** 19,983.

Stanley Cup Leaders

Scoring

	Gm	G	A	Pts	+/-	PM	PP
Eric Lindros, Phi	19	12	14	26	7	40	4
Joe Sakic, Col	17	8	17	25	5	14	3
Claude Lemieux, Col	17	13	10	23	7	32	4
Valeri Kamensky, Col	17	8	14	22	-1	16	5
Rod Brind'Amour, Phi	19	13	8	21	9	10	4
John LeClair, Phi	19	9	12	21	5	10	4
Wayne Gretzky, NYR	15	10	10	20	5	2	3
Sergei Fedorov, Det	20	8	12	20	5	12	3
Bren. Shanahan, Det	20	9	8	17	8	43	2
Peter Forsberg, Col	14	5	12	17	-6	10	3
Sandis Ozolinsh, Col	17	4	13	17	-1	24	2

Goals

Lemieux, Col	13
Brind'Amour, Phi	13
Lindros, Phi	12
Gretzky, NYR	10
Tikkanen, NYR	9
LeClair, Phi	9
Shanahan, Det	9

Power Play Goals

Kamensky, Col	5
Kariya, Ana	4
Lemieux, Col	4
Brind'Amour, Phi	4
LeClair, Phi	4
Lindros, Phi	4
Kozlov, Det	4

Plus/Minus

Murphy, Det	+16
Therien, Phi	+14
Lidstrom, Det	+12
Brind'Amour, Phi	+9
Desjardins, Phi	+9

Assists

Sakic, Col	17
Kamensky, Col	14
Lindros, Phi	14
Ozolinsh, Col	13
Forsberg, Col	12
LeClair, Phi	12
Niinimaa*, Phi	12
Fedorov, Det	12

Overtime Goals

Tikkanen, NYR	2
Fourteen tied with 1 each.	

Penalty Minutes

Foote, Col	62
Lapointe, Det	60
Rouse, Det	55
Shanahan, Det	43
Fetisov, Det	42
Probert, Chi	41
Lindros, Phi	40

Goaltending
(Minimum 420 minutes)

	Gm	Min	W-L	ShO	GAA
Martin Brodeur, NJ	10	659	5-5	2	1.73
Mike Vernon, Det	20	1229	16-4	1	1.76
Ron Tugnutt, Ott	7	425	3-4	1	1.98
Guy Hebert, Ana	9	534	4-4	1	2.02
Mike Richter, NYR	15	939	9-6	3	2.11
Nikolai Khabibulin, Pho	7	426	3-4	1	2.11
Patrick Roy, Col	17	1034	10-7	3	2.21

Wins

Vernon, Det	16-4
Roy, Col	10-7
Richter, NYR	9-6
Snow, Phi	8-4
Brodeur, NJ	5-5
Joseph, Edm	5-7

Save Pct.

Khabibulin, Pho	.932
Roy, Col	.932
Richter, NYR	.932
Hebert, Ana	.929
Brodeur, NJ	.929
Vernon, Det	.927

Final Stanley Cup Standings

				—Goals—		
	Gm	W	L	For	Opp	Dif
Detroit	20	16	4	58	38	+20
Philadelphia	19	12	7	67	55	+12
Colorado	17	10	7	59	41	+18
NY Rangers	15	9	6	36	35	+1
New Jersey	10	5	5	27	21	+6
Edmonton	12	5	7	32	37	-5
Buffalo	12	5	7	27	34	-7
Anaheim	11	4	7	25	30	-5
Phoenix	7	3	4	17	17	E
Ottawa	7	3	4	13	14	-1
Dallas	7	3	4	18	21	-3
St. Louis	6	2	4	12	13	-1
Chicago	6	2	4	14	28	-14
Florida	5	1	4	10	13	-3
Pittsburgh	5	1	4	13	20	-7
Montreal	5	1	4	11	22	-11

Finalists' Composite Box Scores

Detroit Red Wings (16–4)

Top Scorers	Pos	Overall Playoffs								Finals vs Philadelphia							
		Gm	G	A	Pts	+/-	PM	PP	S	GM	G	A	Pts	+/-	PM	PP	S
Sergei Fedorov	C	20	8	12	20	5	12	3	79	4	3	3	6	+2	2	1	16
Brendan Shanahan	L	20	9	8	17	8	43	2	82	4	3	1	4	+3	0	0	13
Vyacheslav Kozlov	L	20	8	5	13	3	14	4	58	4	0	2	2	+1	0	0	4
Steve Yzerman	C	20	7	6	13	3	4	3	65	4	3	1	4	+3	0	2	12
Igor Larionov	C	20	4	8	12	8	8	3	29	4	0	0	0	+3	4	0	1
Martin Lapointe	R	20	4	8	12	8	60	1	37	4	2	1	3	+3	6	1	7
Larry Murphy	D	20	2	9	11	16	8	1	51	4	0	3	3	+10	0	0	6
Nicklas Lidstrom	D	20	2	6	8	12	2	0	79	4	1	0	1	+6	0	0	14
Kirk Maltby	L	20	5	2	7	6	24	0	35	4	2	1	3	+2	2	0	8
Darren McCarty	R	20	3	4	7	1	34	0	34	4	1	2	3	+4	4	0	6
Doug Brown	R	14	3	3	6	4	2	0	23	4	0	1	1	+1	2	0	2
Kris Draper	C	20	2	4	6	5	12	0	30	4	0	1	1	+3	2	0	4
Joey Kocur	R	19	1	3	4	5	22	0	16	4	1	1	2	+3	2	0	6
Viacheslav Fetisov	D	20	0	4	4	2	42	0	27	4	0	2	2	0	10	0	5
Tomas Sandstrom	R	20	0	4	4	-3	24	0	36	4	0	1	1	+2	4	0	5
Vladimir Konstantinov	D	20	0	4	4	-1	29	0	29	4	0	0	0	-1	2	0	3
Jamie Pushor*	D	5	0	1	1	-1	5	0	3	0	0	0	0	0	0	0	0
Mike Vernon	G	20	0	1	1	0	12	0	0	4	0	1	1	0	0	0	0

Overtime goals— OVERALL (Kozlov, Lapointe, Shanahan); FINALS (none). **Shorthanded goals**— OVERALL (Draper, Maltby); FINALS (Maltby). **Power Play conversions**—OVERALL (17 for 117, 14.5%); FINALS (4 for 18, 22.2%).

Goaltending	Gm	Min	GAA	GA	SA	Sv%	W-L	Gm	Min	GAA	GA	SA	Sv%	W-L
Mike Vernon	20	1229	1.76	36	494	.927	16-4	4	240	1.50	6	108	.944	4-0
Chris Osgood	2	47	2.55	2	21	.905	0-0							
TOTAL	20	1280	1.78	38	515	.926	16-4	4	240	1.50	6	108	.944	4-0

Empty Net Goals— OVERALL (none); **Shutouts**— OVERALL (Vernon), FINALS (none); **Assists**— OVERALL (Vernon), FINALS (Vernon); **Penalty Minutes**— OVERALL (Vernon 12, Osgood 2), FINALS (none).

Philadelphia Flyers (12–7)

Top Scorers	Pos	Overall Playoffs								Finals vs Detroit							
		Gm	G	A	Pts	+/-	PM	PP	S	GM	G	A	Pts	+/-	PM	PP	S
Eric Lindros	C	19	12	14	26	7	40	4	71	4	1	2	3	-5	8	0	12
Rod Brind'Amour	L	19	13	8	21	9	10	4	65	4	3	1	4	0	3	0	10
John LeClair	L	19	9	12	21	5	10	4	79	4	2	1	3	-5	4	1	14
Janne Niinimaa*	D	19	1	12	13	3	16	1	56	4	0	3	3	-4	0	0	10
Mikael Renberg	R	18	5	6	11	1	4	2	35	4	0	1	1	-2	0	0	4
Eric Desjardins	D	19	2	8	10	9	12	0	49	4	0	2	2	-1	2	0	9
Dainius Zubrus*	R	19	5	4	9	3	12	1	28	4	0	0	0	-4	0	0	4
Paul Coffey	D	17	1	8	9	-3	6	0	37	4	0	2	2	-5	6	0	2
Trent Klatt	R	19	4	3	7	1	12	0	26	4	0	0	0	-3	6	0	2
Shjon Podein	L	19	4	3	7	4	16	0	52	4	0	0	0	-3	2	0	11
Dale Hawerchuk	C	17	2	5	7	-2	0	1	24	3	0	0	0	-3	0	0	2
Chris Therien	D	19	1	6	7	14	6	0	36	4	0	0	0	-2	0	0	5
Joel Otto	C	18	1	5	6	3	8	0	23	4	0	0	0	-3	0	0	4
Pat Falloon	R	14	3	1	4	-1	2	1	32	3	0	0	0	-1	2	0	4
Vaclav Prospal*	C	5	1	3	4	0	0	0	10	0	0	0	0	0	0	0	0
Petr Svoboda	D	16	1	2	3	4	16	0	9	1	0	0	0	0	2	0	3
Karl Dykhuis	D	18	0	3	3	1	2	0	15	3	0	0	0	-3	2	0	3
Garth Snow	G	12	0	2	2	0	11	0	0	1	0	0	0	0	0	0	0
Dan Kordic	L	12	1	0	1	1	22	0	3	3	0	0	0	0	0	0	0
John Druce	R	13	1	0	1	2	0	0	10	4	0	0	0	0	0	0	0
Daniel Lacroix	C	12	0	1	1	0	22	0	4	2	0	0	0	0	2	0	0

Overtime goals— OVERALL (none). **Shorthanded goals**— OVERALL (Brind'Amour 2, Druce 1); FINALS (none). **Power Play conversions**— OVERALL (18 for 94, 19.1%); FINALS (4 for 19, 21.1%).

Goaltending	Gm	Min	GAA	GA	SA	Sv%	W-L	Gm	Min	GAA	GA	SA	Sv%	W-L
Garth Snow	12	699	2.83	33	305	.892	8-4	1	60	4.00	4	28	.857	0-1
Ron Hextall	8	444	2.97	22	203	.892	4-3	3	180	4.00	12	87	.862	0-3
TOTAL	19	1146	2.88	55	508	.892	12-7	4	240	4.00	16	115	.861	0-4

Empty Net Goals— OVERALL (none); **Shutouts**— OVERALL (none); **Assists**— OVERALL (Snow 2), FINALS (none). **Penalty Minutes**— OVERALL (Snow 11), FINALS (none).

Annual Awards

Except for the Vezina Trophy and Adams Award, voting is done by a 54-member panel of the Pro Hockey Writers Assn., while full PHWA membership voted for Masterton Trophy. Vezina Trophy voted on by NHL general managers and Adams Award by NHL broadcasters. Points awarded on 10–7–5–3–1 basis except for the Vezina Trophy and the Adams Award which are awarded 5–3–1.

Hart Trophy
For Most Valuable Player

	Pos	1st	2nd	3rd	4th	5th	Pts
Dominik Hasek, Buf .	G	50	2	1	0	0—	519
Paul Kariya, Ana ...	L	3	21	9	4	5—	239
Mario Lemieux, Pit ..	C	1	11	12	10	4—	181
Martin Brodeur, NJ ..	G	0	7	6	11	3—	115
Teemu Selanne, Ana .	R	0	3	6	5	4—	70
John LeClair, Phi ...	L	0	4	5	2	7—	66

Calder Trophy
For Rookie of the Year

	Pos	1st	2nd	3rd	4th	5th	Pts
Bryan Berard, NYI ..	D	43	9	1	1	0—	501
Jarome Iginla, Calg .	R	8	36	7	1	2—	372
Jim Campbell, St.L ..	R	2	2	17	15	9—	173
Janne Niinimaa, Phi .	D	0	4	14	9	13—	138
Patrick Lalime, Pit ...	G	0	2	4	8	8—	66

Norris Trophy
For Best Defenseman

	1st	2nd	3rd	4th	5th	Pts
Brian Leetch, NYR	42	8	3	1	0—	494
Vlad. Konstantivov, Det	2	10	13	6	5—	178
Sandis Ozolinsh, Col	2	12	9	8	3—	176
Chris Chelios, Chi	0	7	18	9	6—	172
Scott Stevens, NJ	7	8	4	7	4—	171

Vezina Trophy
For Outstanding Goaltender

	1st	2nd	3rd	Pts
Dominik Hasek, Buf	22	3	1—	120
Martin Brodeur, NJ	3	18	4—	73
Patrick Roy, Col	1	3	11—	25
Guy Hebert, Ana	0	2	4—	10

Lady Byng Trophy
For Sportsmanship and Gentlemanly Play

	Pos	1st	2nd	3rd	4th	5th	Pts
Paul Kariya, Ana	L	43	7	2	1	0—	492
Teemu Selanne, Ana .	R	2	9	4	5	1—	119
Adam Oates, Wash ..	C	0	7	7	6	8—	110
Ron Francis, Pit	C	0	6	6	9	4—	103
Wayne Gretzky, NYR .	C	0	4	7	5	5—	83
Brett Hull, St.L	R	0	3	7	3	6—	71

Selke Trophy
For Best Defensive Forward

	Pos	1st	2nd	3rd	4th	5th	Pts
Michael Peca, Buf ..	C	20	4	6	8	2—	284
Peter Forsberg, Col ..	C	9	4	2	3	4—	141
Jere Lehtinen, Dal ...	R	1	9	6	4	3—	118
Mike Modano, Dal ..	C	3	6	4	2	1—	99
Joel Otto, Phi	C	2	3	4	8	9—	94
N. Sundstrom, NYR .	L	1	4	7	8	0—	91

Adams Award
For Coach of the Year

	1st	2nd	3rd	Pts
Ted Nolan, Buf	39	34	10—	307
Ken Hitchcock, Dal	38	32	14—	300
Jacques Martin, Ott	5	11	24—	82
Jacques Lemaire, NJ	2	5	11—	36
Marc Crawford, Col	2	3	11—	30
Ron Wilson, Ana	1	2	7—	18

Wide World Photos

Buffalo's **Dominik Hasek** takes home the Vezina and becomes the first goalie to win the Hart Trophy since 1962.

Other Awards

Lester B. Pearson Award (NHL Players Assn. MVP)— Dominik Hasek, Buffalo; **Jennings Trophy** (Goaltenders with a minimum of 25 games played for team with fewest goals against)— Martin Brodeur & Mike Dunham, New Jersey; **Masterton Trophy** (perseverance, sportsmanship,and dedication to hockey)— Tony Granato, San Jose; **King Clancy Trophy** (leadership and humanitarian contributions to community)— Trevor Linden, Vancouver; **Lester Patrick Trophy** (outstanding service to hockey)— Seymour Knox III, Bill Cleary and Pat LaFontaine.

All-NHL

Votings by Pro Hockey Writers' Association (PHWA). Holdovers from 1995–96 All-NHL first team in **bold** type.

First Team		1st	2nd	3rd	Pts
G	Dominik Hasek, Buf	40	12	1—	237
D	Brian Leetch, NYR	49	2	1—	252
D	Sandis Ozolinsh, Col	19	22	5—	166
C	**Mario Lemieux**, Pit	50	2	0—	256
R	Teemu Selanne, Ana	46	7	0—	251
L	**Paul Kariya**, Ana	36	14	3—	225

Second Team		1st	2nd	3rd	Pts
G	Martin Brodeur, NJ	13	35	4—	174
D	**Chris Chelios**, Chi	10	21	12—	125
D	Scott Stevens, NJ	12	12	6—	102
C	Wayne Gretzky, NYR	1	16	12—	65
R	**Jaromir Jagr**, Pit	6	41	5—	158
L	John LeClair, Phi	13	25	12—	152

All-Rookie Team
Voting by PHWA. Vote totals not released.

Pos		Pos	
G	Patrick Lalime, Pit.	F	Sergei Berezin, Tor.
D	Bryan Berard, NYI	F	Jim Campbell, St.L
D	Janne Niinimaa, Phi.	F	Jarome Iginla, Calg.

U.S. Division I College Hockey

Final regular season standings; overall records, including all postseason tournament games, in parentheses.

Central Collegiate Hockey Assn.

	W	L	T	Pts	GF	GA
*Michigan (35-4-4)	21	3	3	45	151	64
*Miami-OH (27-12-1)	19	7	1	39	112	79
*Michigan St. (23-13-4)	16	7	4	36	99	76
Lake Superior St. (19-14-5)	15	8	4	34	106	98
Bowling Green (17-16-5)	10	12	5	25	100	104
W. Michigan (14-18-5)	10	12	5	25	94	99
Ohio St. (12-25-2)	9	16	2	20	95	132
Alaska-Fairbanks (14-22-1)	8	18	1	17	92	126
Ferris St. (11-23-3)	7	18	2	16	83	121
Notre Dame (9-25-1)	6	20	1	13	73	106

Tiebreaker: Bowling Green was awarded fifth place over W. Michigan based on a 2-0-1 head-to-head record.
Conf. Tourney Final: Michigan 3, Michigan St. 1.
*NCAA Tourney (1-3): Michigan (1-1), Miami-OH (0-1), Michigan St. (0-1).

Eastern Collegiate Athletic Conf.

	W	L	T	Pts	GF	GA
*Clarkson (27-10-0)	17	5	0	34	94	54
*Cornell (21-9-5)	14	6	2	30	80	63
*Vermont (22-11-3)	13	6	3	29	67	60
Rensselaer (20-12-4)	12	7	3	27	83	71
Union (18-13-3)	11	8	3	25	63	54
Princeton (18-12-4)	11	8	3	25	70	59
Colgate (16-14-3)	10	9	3	23	79	79
Harvard (11-18-3)	9	11	2	20	64	67
St. Lawrence (10-20-5)	5	12	5	15	78	92
Yale (10-19-3)	6	14	2	14	61	82
Dartmouth (10-17-2)	5	15	2	12	75	100
Brown (7-19-3)	4	16	2	10	81	114

Conf. Tourney Final: Cornell 2, Clarkson 1.
*NCAA Tourney (1-3): Clarkson (0-1), Cornell (1-1), Vermont (0-1).

Hockey East Association

	W	L	T	Pts	GF	GA
*Boston University (26-9-6)	16	4	4	36	116	71
*New Hampshire (28-11-0)	18	6	0	36	130	76
Maine (24-10-1)	16	7	1	33	120	76
Providence (15-20-1)	12	11	1	25	101	88
Merrimack (15-19-2)	11	11	2	24	88	98
Boston College (15-19-4)	9	12	3	21	96	112
UMass-Lowell (15-21-2)	9	14	1	19	83	113
UMass-Amherst (12-23-0)	7	17	0	14	69	117
Northeastern (8-25-3)	3	19	2	8	66	118

Note: Maine was ruled ineligible for postseason play.
Conf. Tourney Final: Boston University 4, New Hampshire 2.
*NCAA Tourney (2-2): Boston University (2-1), New Hampshire (0-1).

Western Collegiate Hockey Assn.

	W	L	T	Pts	GF	GA
*North Dakota (31-10-2)	21	10	1	43	137	105
*Minnesota (28-13-1)	21	10	1	43	129	94
St. Cloud St. (23-13-4)	18	10	4	40	127	105
*Colorado College (25-15-4)	17	11	4	38	121	107
*Denver (24-13-4)	17	11	4	38	127	99
Minnesota-Duluth (18-16-4)	15	13	4	34	115	111
Wisconsin (15-21-2)	15	15	2	32	115	115
Northern Michigan (13-24-3)	9	21	2	20	78	127
Alaska-Anchorage (9-23-4)	7	21	4	18	75	109
Michigan Tech (8-27-4)	5	23	4	14	81	133

Conf. Tourney Final: North Dakota 4, Minnesota 3 (OT).
*NCAA Tourney (7-3): North Dakota (3-0), Minnesota (1-1), Colorado College (2-1), Denver (1-1).

USA Today/American Hockey Magazine Coaches Poll

Taken April 1, 1997 after NCAA Tournament. First place votes are in parentheses. Final Four teams are in **bold**.

		League	W	L	T	Pts
1	**North Dakota** (10)	WCHA	31	10	2	100
2	**Boston University**	HEA	26	9	6	90
3	**Michigan**	CCHA	35	4	4	80
4	Minnesota	WCHA	28	13	1	66
5	**Colorado College**	WCHA	25	15	4	64
6	Clarkson	ECAC	27	10	0	50
7	Denver	WCHA	24	13	4	40
8	New Hampshire	HEA	28	11	0	26
9	Cornell	ECAC	21	9	5	24
10	Michigan St.	CCHA	23	13	4	15

Also receiving votes: Miami-OH (3 pts), Vermont (2 pts).

Leading Scorers

Including postseason games.

	Cl	Gm	G	A	Pts	PPG
Brendan Morrison, Mich.	Sr.	42	30	55	85	**2.02**
Todd White, Clarkson	Sr.	37	38	36	74	**2.00**
Bill Muckalt, Michigan	Jr.	35	25	37	62	**1.77**
Jason Krog, UNH	So.	39	23	44	67	**1.72**
Martin St. Louis, Vermont	Sr.	36	24	36	60	**1.67**
Mike Harder, Colgate	Sr.	33	22	33	55	**1.67**
Eric Perrin, Vermont	Jr.	36	26	33	59	**1.64**
Mike Johnson, Bowl. Green	Sr.	37	27	32	59	**1.59**
Tom Nolan, UNH	Jr.	32	22	29	51	**1.59**
Eric Boguniecki, UNH	Jr.	36	26	31	57	**1.58**
Josh Oort, Canisius	Jr.	26	12	29	41	**1.58**
Eric Healey, Rensselaer	Jr.	36	30	26	56	**1.56**
Frank Fede, Army	Sr.	31	20	28	48	**1.55**
Jean-Francois Houle, Clarks.	Sr.	37	21	36	57	**1.54**
Andy Lundbohm, Army	So.	28	18	25	43	**1.54**
Curtis Fry, Bowl. Green	Sr.	36	19	36	55	**1.53**
Randy Robitaille, Miami-OH	So.	37	27	29	56	**1.51**
Chris Drury, BU	Jr.	41	38	24	62	**1.51**
Mark Mowers, UNH	Jr.	39	26	32	58	**1.49**
Jay Kasperek, Niagara	Fr.	27	20	20	40	**1.48**
Jason Botterill, Michigan	Sr.	41	36	24	60	**1.46**
John Madden, Michigan	Jr.	41	26	34	60	**1.46**
Mikko Sivonen, Niagara	Fr.	27	14	25	39	**1.44**
Steve Kariya, Maine	So.	34	18	30	48	**1.41**
Peter DeSantis, Niagara	Fr.	27	21	17	38	**1.41**

Leading Goaltenders

Including postseason games; minimum 15 games.

	Cl	Record	Sv%	GAA
Trevor Koenig, Union	Jr.	15-11-2	.931	2.03
Marty Turco, Michigan	Jr.	32-4-4	.894	2.29
Aaron Schweitzer, N. Dakota	Fr.	17-3-0	.908	2.31
Dan Murphy, Clarkson	Jr.	27-9-0	.917	2.33
Michel Larocque, BU	So.	16-4-4	.911	2.37
Jason Elliott, Cornell	Jr.	16-7-2	.909	2.73
Chad Alban, Michigan St.	Jr.	22-11-4	.894	2.74
Jim Mullin, Denver	Sr.	11-7-4	.900	2.75
Trevor Prior, Miami-OH	Jr.	16-10-1	.893	2.78
Tim Thomas, Vermont	Sr.	22-11-3	.914	2.81

The Fighting Sioux Will Do

by Jack Edwards

All year, it looked like Michigan.

The Wolverines were #1 in the nation for all but one week. The defending NCAA Champions were 35-3-4 going into their semi-final against Boston University. But then B.U. showed them how to win a tournament hockey game. With their forecheck buzzing, they discombobulated Michigan's attack from its source, keeping the Wolverines from moving the puck out of their own zone with ease. Michigan managed a measly 20 shots — a season low — and B.U. peppered-in 3 unanswered goals in the second period. See you later, Wolverines.

B.U. would lead North Dakota, 2-0, into the second period of the title game. The second one came off the stick of 1989 Little League World Series hero Chris Drury. That's about where B.U.'s game and a half long clinic, well, in Coach Jack Parker's words, "disintegrated."

Embellishing the Terriers' semi-final work, U.N.D. launched a five-goal middle-stanza blitz. David Hoogsteen tied it at 2, picking-off a clearing pass and scoring on the breakaway. Matt Henderson put the Fighting Sioux ahead 3-2. B.U. pulled even on Chris Kelleher's power-play goal. Then Henderson put North Dakota ahead for good at 4-3. The WCHA Champs won their sixth NCAA crown, their first in a decade, in this, the 50th NCAA hockey tournament. Parker said, "There's no question that the best team won the national championship."

Parker would later turn down a lucrative offer to coach the Boston Bruins, the second time Boston's Harry Sinden has taken a run at Parker. In 1997 at B.U., he simply added to an already legendary tradition. Parker is a teacher as well as a student. Rather than take huge money to toil in a league in which coaches-of-the-year regularly get fired within 12 months of winning their awards, he chose to stay on campus.

ESPN

Tom Mees

With a come-from-behind victory over the well-coached and tournament-savvy B.U. Terriers, chances are someone will come calling after Dean Blais at North Dakota, too.

It was, however, a bittersweet weekend for us at ESPN.

While the hockey was as scintillating as usual, the championship just wasn't the same without Tom Mees. "The Meeser" not only made the tournament a centerpiece of his annual play-by-play schedule, he also made sure that everyone around him shared in the passion. Tom's work – never trying to out-shout the action, always drawing us in while sharing and not dominating the telecast – used to be part of the fun of watching the tournament.

This was the the first NCAA hockey tourney since Tom died in August of 1996. No one would have been happier that Jack Parker chose to remain in the college game and no one would have been more appreciative of U.N.D. Still, his valuable contributions will echo throughout the college hockey family as long as we keep his memory alive. ∎

Jack Edwards is the co-anchor of ESPN's *Sunday SportsDay*.

NCAA Division I Tournament

Regional Seeds

West
1 **Michigan** (34-3-4)
2 **North Dakota** (28-10-2)
3 Miami-OH (27-11-1)
4 Minnesota (27-12-1)
5 Michigan St. (23-12-4)
6 Cornell (20-8-5)

East
1 Clarkson (27-9-0)
2 **Boston U.** (24-8-6)
3 Vermont (22-10-3)
4 New Hampshire (28-10-0)
5 **Colorado Col.** (23-14-4)
6 Denver (23-12-4)

West Regional

Held at Van Andel Arena in Grand Rapids, Mich., March 22-23. Single elimination, two second round winners advance to Final Four.

First Round

Cornell 4 .... Miami-OH 2
Minnesota 6 .... Michigan St. 3
(Byes: Michigan and North Dakota)

Second Round

North Dakota 6 .... Cornell 2
Michigan 7 .... Minnesota 4
(North Dakota and Michigan advance)

East Regional

Held at The Centrum in Worcester, Mass., March 21-22. Single elimination, two second round winners advance to Final Four.

First Round

Colorado College 3 .... New Hampshire 2
Denver 6 .... Vermont 3
(Byes: Clarkson and Boston University)

Second Round

Colorado College 5 .... Clarkson 4
Boston University 4 .... OT ....Denver 3
(Colorado College and Boston University advance)

Hobey Baker Award

For College Player of the Year. Presented since 1981 by the Decathlon Athletic Club of Bloomington, Minn. Voting done by 18-member panel of national media, coaches and pro scouts. Vote totals not released.

	Cl	Pos
Winner: Brendan Morrison, Michigan	Sr.	F
Runner-up: Chris Drury, BU	Jr.	F

Division I All-America

First team Titan Division I All-Americans as chosen by the American Hockey Coaches Association. Holdovers from 1995-96 All-America first teams are in **bold** type.

West Team

Pos		Yr	Hgt	Wgt
G	Marty Turco, Michigan	Jr.	5-11	160
D	Dan Boyle, Miami-OH	Jr.	5-10	170
D	**Mike Crowley**, Minnesota	Jr.	5-11	177
F	John Madden, Michigan	Sr.	5-11	170
F	**Brendan Morrison**, Michigan	Sr.	5-11	176
F	Randy Robitaille, Miami-OH	So.	5-11	180

East Team

Pos		Yr	Hgt	Wgt
G	Trevor Koenig, Union	Jr.	5-10	170
D	Jon Coleman, Boston U.	Sr.	6-2	197
D	Matt Pagnutti, Clarkson	Sr.	5-11	190
F	Chris Drury, Boston U.	Jr.	5-10	195
F	**Martin St. Louis**, Vermont	Sr.	5-9	170
F	Todd White, Clarkson	Sr.	5-10	181

THE FINAL FOUR

At the Bradley Center in Milwaukee, Wis., March 27 and March 29. Single elimination; no consolation game.

Semifinals

North Dakota 6 .... Colorado College 2
Boston University 3 .... Michigan 2

Championship

North Dakota 6 .... Boston University 4
Final records: North Dakota (31-10-2); Boston University (26-9-6); Colorado College (25-15-4); Michigan (35-4-4).
Outstanding Player: Matt Henderson, North Dakota junior forward; SEMIFINAL— 1 goal, 1 assist; FINAL— 2 goals, 1 assist.
All-Tournament Team: Henderson, forward Dave Hoogsteen, defenseman Curtis Murphy and goaltender Aaron Schweitzer of North Dakota; forward Chris Drury and defenseman Tom Poti of Boston University.

Championship Game

North Dakota, 6-4

Saturday, March 29, 1997, at the Bradley Center in Milwaukee, Wis.; Attendance: 17,537; TV Rating: 0.7/2 share (ESPN).

Boston University (HEA)	....	2	1	1	—	**4**
North Dakota (WCHA)	....	0	5	1	—	**6**

Scoring

1st Period: BU— Peter Donatelli (Tom Poti), 8:44; BU— Chris Drury (Poti, Albie O'Connell), 15:08 (pp).
2nd Period: ND— Curtis Murphy (Jay Panzer, Matt Henderson), 7:06; ND— David Hoogsteen (unassisted), 8:38; ND— Henderson (unassisted), 12:35 (sh); BU— Chris Kelleher (unassisted), 13:56 (pp); ND— Henderson (Adam Calder, Dane Litke), 15:49 (pp); ND— Hoogsteen (Murphy), 19:54.
3rd Period: BU— Jon Coleman (Kelleher, Mike Sylvia), 19:24; ND— Calder (unassisted), 19:47 (en).

Goaltenders

Saves: BU— Michel Larocque (29 shots/24 saves); ND— Aaron Schweitzer (29 shots/25 saves).

Other NCAA Tournaments

Division II

Two teams selected from limited national field. Championship decided in two games with mini-game (one 15-minute period), if necessary.

Final Two

March 14-15 in Bemidji, Minn.
Championship: GAME ONE— Bemidji St. (Minn.) 3, Alabama-Huntsville 2; GAME TWO— Bemidji St. 4, Alabama-Huntsville 2.
Final records: Bemidji St. (25-7-2), Alabama-Huntsville (20-8-0).

Division III

Final Four

March 21-22 in Middlebury, Vt.
Semifinals— Wis-Superior 2, Norwich 1 (2OT); Middlebury 2, St. John's (Minn.) 1. **Third Place**— St. John's 4, Norwich 3. **Championship**— Middlebury 3, Wis-Superior 2.
Final records: Middlebury (22-3-2); Wis-Superior (23-9-2); St. John's (26-6-1); Norwich (21-7-2).

MINOR LEAGUE HOCKEY

American Hockey League

Division champions (*) and playoff qualifiers (†) are noted. GF and GA refer to goals for and against. Losses in overtime are designated in parentheses and worth one point in the standings.

Northern Conference
Canadian Division

Team (Affiliate)	W	L	T	Pts	GF	GA
*St. John's (Tor.)	36	34(6)	10	88	265	264
†Saint John (Calg.)	28	39(3)	13	72	237	269
†Hamilton (Edm.)	28	43(4)	9	69	220	276
Fredericton (Mon.)	26	46(2)	8	62	234	283

Empire State Division

Team (Affiliate)	W	L	T	Pts	GF	GA
*Rochester (Buf.)	40	31(1)	9	90	298	257
†Adirondack (Det. & TB)	38	30(2)	12	90	258	249
†Albany (NJ)	38	33(5)	9	90	269	231
†Syracuse (Van.)	32	38	10	74	241	265
†Binghamton (NYR)	27	40(2)	13	69	245	300

Scoring Leaders

	G	A	Pts	PM
Peter White, Phi	44	61	105	28
Terry Yake, Roch	34	67	101	77
Brian Wiseman, S.J.'s	33	62	95	83
Vaclav Prospal, Phi	32	63	95	70
Patrik Juhlin, Phi	31	60	91	24

Goaltending Leaders

	GP	GAA	Sv%	Record
J.F. Labbe, Her	66	2.52	.914	34-22-9
Scott Langkow, Spring	33	2.64	.911	15-9-7
Dominic Roussel, Phi	36	2.66	.916	18-9-3

Southern Conference
New England Division

Team (Affiliate)	W	L	T	Pts	GF	GA
*Worcester (St.L & Ott.)	43	28(5)	9	100	256	234
†Springfield (Hart. & Pho.)	41	27(2)	12	96	268	229
†Portland (Wash.)	37	33(7)	10	91	279	264
†Providence (Bos.)	35	42(2)	3	75	262	289

Mid-Atlantic Division

Team (Affiliate)	W	L	T	Pts	GF	GA
*Philadelphia (Phi.)	49	21(3)	10	111	325	230
†Hershey (Col.)	43	27(5)	10	101	273	220
†Kentucky (SJ)	36	35	9	81	278	284
†Baltimore (Ana.)	30	40(3)	10	73	251	285
Carolina (Fla.)	28	48(5)	4	65	273	303

Calder Cup Finals

	W-L	GF	Leading Scorers
Hershey	4-1	19	Messier (2-5-7)
Hamilton	1-4	12	Three tied with 4 pts.

Date	Winner	Home Ice
June 4	Hershey, 4-2	at Hershey
June 7	Hershey, 6-5 (OT)	at Hershey
June 9	Hamilton, 2-1	at Hamilton
June 11	Hershey, 4-2	at Hamilton
June 13	Hershey, 4-1	at Hamilton

International Hockey League

Division champions (*) and playoff qualifiers (†) are noted. GF and GA refer to goals for and against. SOL refers to shootout losses and are worth one point in the standings.

Eastern Conference
Northeast Division

Team (Affiliate)	W	L	SOL	Pts	GF	GA
*Detroit (Indep.)	57	17	8	122	280	188
†Orlando (Indep.)	53	24	5	111	305	232
†Cincinnati (Indep.)	43	29	10	96	254	248
†Quebec (Indep.)	41	30	11	93	267	248
†Grand Rapids (Indep.)	40	29	13	93	244	246

Central Division

Team (Affiliate)	W	L	SOL	Pts	GF	GA
*Indianapolis (Chi.)	44	29	9	97	289	230
†Cleveland (Pit.)	40	32	10	90	286	280
†Michigan (Dal.)	31	44	7	69	208	272
Fort Wayne (Indep.)	28	47	7	63	223	318

Scoring Leaders

	G	A	Pts	PM
Rob Brown, Chi	37	80	117	98
Steve Maltais, Chi	60	54	114	62
Steve Larouche, Que	49	53	102	78
Michel Picard, GR	46	55	101	58
Patrice Lefebvre, LV	21	73	94	94

Goaltending Leaders

	GP	GAA	Sv%	Record
Jeff Reese, Det	32	1.87	.926	23-4-3
Rich Parent, Det	53	2.22	.920	31-13-4
Tom Draper, LB	39	2.30	.909	28-7-3

Western Conference
Midwest Division

Team (Affiliate)	W	L	SOL	Pts	GF	GA
*San Antonio (Indep.)	45	30	7	97	276	278
†Kansas City (Indep.)	38	29	15	91	271	270
†Chicago (Indep.)	40	36	6	86	273	283
†Milwaukee (Indep.)	38	36	8	84	253	298
Manitoba (Indep.)	32	40	10	74	262	300

Southwest Division

Team (Affiliate)	W	L	SOL	Pts	GF	GA
*Long Beach (Ana.)	54	19	9	117	309	247
†Houston (Indep.)	44	30	8	96	247	228
†Utah (NYI)	43	33	6	92	252	251
†Las Vegas (Indep.)	41	34	7	89	287	299
Phoenix (LA)	27	42	13	67	239	309

Turner Cup Finals

	W-L	GF	Leading Scorers
Detroit	4-2	16	Samsonov (5-1-6)
			& Ciavaglia (2-4-6)
Long Beach	2-4	10	Pittis (1-3-4)

Date	Winner	Home Ice
May 30	Detroit, 5-3	at Detroit
June 1	Long Beach, 3-0	at Detroit
June 9	Detroit, 5-1	at Long Beach
June 11	Detroit, 3-1	at Long Beach
June 13	Long Beach, 2-1 (OT)	at Long Beach
June 15	Detroit, 2-0	at Detroit

World Hockey Championships

MEN

The 50th World Hockey Championships, held in Helsinki and Turku, Finland from April 26 to May 14, 1997. Top three teams (*) in each group after preliminary round-robin advance to the medal round. Bottom three from each group play in the relegation round. Top two teams from the medal round advance to the best-of-three championship round.

Final Round Robin Standings

GROUP A	W-L-T	Pts	GF	GA
*Czech Republic	4-1-0	8	18	9
*Finland	4-1-0	8	25	9
*Russia	3-1-1	7	19	16
Slovakia	1-3-1	3	10	14
France	1-4-0	2	13	26
Germany	1-4-0	2	4	15

GROUP B	W-L-T	Pts	GF	GA
*Sweden	4-0-1	9	20	8
*Canada	3-1-1	7	23	11
*United States	3-2-0	6	14	15
Latvia	1-2-2	4	18	17
Italy	1-3-1	3	12	21
Norway	0-4-1	1	7	22

Medal Round

	W-L-T	Pts	GF	GA
Sweden	4-1-0	8	17	9
Canada	3-2-0	6	13	14
Russia	2-2-1	5	13	13
Czech Republic	2-3-0	4	13	11
Finland	2-3-0	4	12	12
United States	1-3-1	3	7	14

Relegation Round

	W-L-T	Pts	GF	GA
Latvia	4-1-0	8	29	14
Italy	3-1-1	7	23	13
Slovakia	3-2-0	6	15	13
France	2-3-0	4	12	23
Germany	2-3-0	4	8	17
Norway	0-3-1	1	8	14

Bronze Medal Game

Czech Republic 4 .... Russia 3

Championship (best of three)

Sweden 3 .... Canada 2
Canada 3 .... Sweden 1
Canada 2 .... Sweden 1

Leading Scorers

	Gm	G	A	Pts	PM
Vladimir Vujtek, Czech Repub.	8	7	7	14	31
Martin Prochazka, Czech Repub.	9	7	7	14	4
Michael Nylander, Sweden	11	6	5	11	6
Pavel Patera, Czech Repub.	9	3	8	11	4
Roger Dube, France	8	7	3	10	2
Olegs Znarkos, Latvia	8	3	7	10	6
Bruno Zarrillo, Italy	8	5	4	9	4
Gaetano Orlando, Italy	8	5	4	9	14
Harius Vitolins, Latvia	8	4	5	9	4
Travis Green, Canada	11	3	6	9	12

World All-Star Teams
(Selected by media)

First Team: G— Tommy Salo, Sweden; **D—** Teppo Numminen, Finland and Rob Blake, Canada; **F—** Michael Nylander, Sweden; Vladimir Vujtek, Czech Republic and Martin Prochazka, Czech Republic.

Second Team: G— Sean Burke, Canada; **D—** Mattius Ohlund, Sweden and Marcus Ragnarsson, Sweden; **F—** Saku Koivu, Finland; Alexander Korolyuk, Russia and Alexander Prokopiev, Russia.

WOMEN

The fourth sanctioned Women's World Championships, held in Kitchener, Ontario (Can.) from March 31 to April 6, 1997. With women's hockey being accepted as a full medal sport at the 1998 Winter Olympics, the world championships served as a qualifier with the top five teams joining host Japan at the 1998 games in Nagano. Top two teams (*) in each pool after preliminary round-robin advanced to the medal round. Remaining four teams played in the qualifying round for the final Olympic berth.

Final Round Robin Standings

POOL A	W-L-T	Pts	GF	GA
*Canada	3-0-0	6	22	2
*China	2-1-0	4	18	12
Russia	0-2-1	1	6	18
Switzerland	0-2-1	1	6	20

POOL B	W-L-T	Pts	GF	GA
*United States	2-0-1	5	20	3
*Finland	2-0-1	5	18	3
Sweden	0-2-1	1	2	17
Norway	0-2-1	1	2	19

Qualifying Round

Sweden 7 .... Switzerland 1
Russia 2 .... Norway 1

Medal Round

Canada 2 .... Finland 1
United States 6 .... China 0

Seventh Place: Switzerland 1 .... Norway 0
Fifth Place: Sweden 3 .... Russia 1
Bronze Medal: Finland 3 .... China 0
Gold Medal: Canada 4 ...... OT ...... United States 3

Leading Scorers

	Gm	G	A	Pts	PM
Riika Nieminen, Finland	5	5	5	10	0
Hayley Wickenheiser, Can.	5	4	5	9	12
Cammi Granato, USA	5	5	3	8	4
Tiia Reima, Finland	5	4	4	8	10
Cassie Campbell, Canada	5	2	6	8	4
Nancy Drolet, Canada	5	4	2	6	2
Shelley Looney, USA	5	4	2	6	2
Karyn Bye, USA	5	4	2	6	8
Laurie Baker, USA	5	4	2	6	8
Hongmzi Liu, China	5	3	3	6	2
Wei Guo, China	5	3	3	6	2
Lori Dupuis, Canada	5	2	4	6	8
Gretchen Ulion, USA	5	2	4	6	0
Sandra White, USA	5	1	5	6	2

All-Tournament Team

G— Patricia Sautter, Switzerland; **D—** Kelly O'Leary, USA; Cassie Campbell, Canada; **F—** Riika Nieminen, Finland; Hayley Wickenheiser, Canada; Cammi Granato, USA.

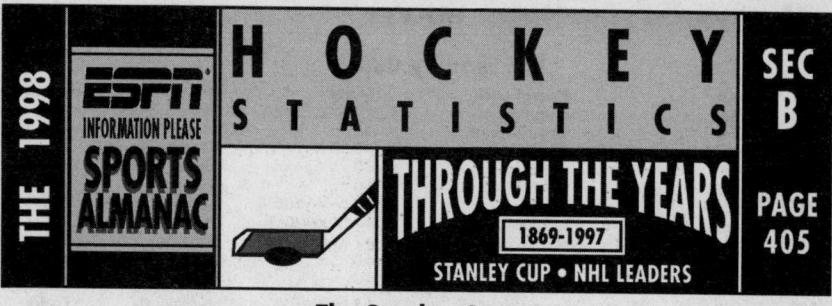

THE 1998

ESPN
INFORMATION PLEASE
SPORTS
ALMANAC

HOCKEY
STATISTICS

THROUGH THE YEARS
1869-1997
STANLEY CUP • NHL LEADERS

SEC
B

PAGE
405

The Stanley Cup

The Stanley Cup was originally donated to the Canadian Amateur Hockey Association by Sir Frederick Arthur Stanley, Lord Stanley of Preston and 16th Earl of Derby, who had become interested in the sport while Governor General of Canada from 1888 to 1893. Stanley wanted the trophy to be a challenge cup, contested for each year by the best amateur hockey teams in Canada.

In 1893, the Cup was presented without a challenge to the AHA champion Montreal Amateur Athletic Association team. Every year since, however, there has been a playoff. In 1914, Cup trustees limited the field challenging for the trophy to the champion of the eastern professional National Hockey Association (NHA, organized in 1910) and the western professional Pacific Coast Hockey Association (PCHA, organized in 1912).

The NHA disbanded in 1917 and the National Hockey League (NHL) was formed. From 1918 to 1926, the NHL and PCHA champions played for the Cup with the Western Canada Hockey League (WCHL) champion joining in a three-way challenge in 1923 and '24. The PCHA disbanded in 1924, while the WCHL became the Western Hockey League (WHL) for the 1925-26 season and folded the following year. The NHL playoffs have decided the winner of the Stanley Cup ever since.

Champions, 1893-1917

Multiple winners: Montreal Victorias and Montreal Wanderers (4); Montreal Amateur Athletic Association and Ottawa Silver Seven (3); Montreal Shamrocks, Ottawa Senators, Quebec Bulldogs and Winnipeg Victorias (2).

Year		Year		Year	
1893	Montreal AAA	1901	Winnipeg Victorias	1909	Ottawa Senators
1894	Montreal AAA	1902	Montreal AAA	1910	Montreal Wanderers
1895	Montreal Victorias	1903	Ottawa Silver Seven	1911	Ottawa Senators
1896	(Feb.) Winnipeg Victorias	1904	Ottawa Silver Seven	1912	Quebec Bulldogs
	(Dec.) Montreal Victorias	1905	Ottawa Silver Seven	1913	Quebec Bulldogs
1897	Montreal Victorias	1906	Montreal Wanderers	1914	Toronto Blueshirts (NHA)
1898	Montreal Victorias	1907	(Jan.) Kenora Thistles	1915	Vancouver Millionaires (PCHA)
1899	Montreal Shamrocks		(Mar.) Montreal Wanderers	1916	Montreal Canadiens (NHA)
1900	Montreal Shamrocks	1908	Montreal Wanderers	1917	Seattle Metropolitans (PCHA)

Champions Since 1918

Multiple winners: Montreal Canadiens (23); Toronto Arenas-St. Pats-Maple Leafs (13); Detroit Red Wings (8); Boston Bruins and Edmonton Oilers (5); NY Islanders, NY Rangers and Ottawa Senators (4); Chicago Blackhawks (3); Philadelphia Flyers, Pittsburgh Penguins and Montreal Maroons (2).

Year	Winner	Head Coach	Series	Loser	Head Coach
1918	Toronto Arenas	Dick Carroll	3-2 (WLWLW)	Vancouver (PCHA)	Frank Patrick
1919	No Decision*				
1920	Ottawa	Pete Green	3-2 (WWLLW)	Seattle (PCHA)	Pete Muldoon
1921	Ottawa	Pete Green	3-2 (LWWLW)	Vancouver (PCHA)	Frank Patrick
1922	Toronto St. Pats	Eddie Powers	3-2 (LWLWW)	Vancouver (PCHA)	Frank Patrick
1923	Ottawa	Pete Green	3-1 (WLWW)	Vancouver (PCHA)	Frank Patrick
			2-0	Edmonton (WCHL)	K.C. McKenzie
1924	Montreal	Leo Dandurand	2-0	Vancouver (PCHA)	Frank Patrick
			2-0	Calgary (WCHL)	Eddie Oatman
1925	Victoria (WCHL)	Lester Patrick	3-1 (WWLW)	Montreal	Leo Dandurand
1926	Montreal Maroons	Eddie Gerard	3-1 (WWLW)	Victoria (WHL)	Lester Patrick
1927	Ottawa	Dave Gill	2-0 (TWTW)	Boston	Art Ross
1928	NY Rangers	Lester Patrick	3-2 (LWLWW)	Montreal Maroons	Eddie Gerard
1929	Boston	Cy Denneny	2-0	NY Rangers	Lester Patrick
1930	Montreal	Cecil Hart	2-0	Boston	Art Ross
1931	Montreal	Cecil Hart	3-2 (WLLWW)	Chicago	Art Duncan
1932	Toronto	Dick Irvin	3-0	NY Rangers	Lester Patrick
1933	NY Rangers	Lester Patrick	3-1 (WWLW)	Toronto	Dick Irvin
1934	Chicago	Tommy Gorman	3-1 (WWLW)	Detroit	Jack Adams
1935	Montreal Maroons	Tommy Gorman	3-0	Toronto	Dick Irvin
1936	Detroit	Jack Adams	3-1 (WWLW)	Toronto	Dick Irvin
1937	Detroit	Jack Adams	3-2 (LWLWW)	NY Rangers	Lester Patrick
1938	Chicago	Bill Stewart	3-1 (WLWW)	Toronto	Dick Irvin
1939	Boston	Art Ross	4-1 (WLWWW)	Toronto	Dick Irvin

The Stanley Cup (Cont.)

Year	Winner	Head Coach	Series	Loser	Head Coach
1940	NY Rangers	Frank Boucher	4-2 (WWLLWW)	Toronto	Dick Irvin
1941	Boston	Cooney Weiland	4-0	Detroit	Jack Adams
1942	Toronto	Hap Day	4-3 (LLLWWWW)	Detroit	Jack Adams
1943	Detroit	Ebbie Goodfellow	4-0	Boston	Art Ross
1944	Montreal	Dick Irvin	4-0	Chicago	Paul Thompson
1945	Toronto	Hap Day	4-3 (WWWLLLW)	Detroit	Jack Adams
1946	Montreal	Dick Irvin	4-1 (WWWLW)	Boston	Dit Clapper
1947	Toronto	Hap Day	4-2 (LWWWLW)	Montreal	Dick Irvin
1948	Toronto	Hap Day	4-0	Detroit	Tommy Ivan
1949	Toronto	Hap Day	4-0	Detroit	Tommy Ivan
1950	Detroit	Tommy Ivan	4-3 (WLWLLWW)	NY Rangers	Lynn Patrick
1951	Toronto	Joe Primeau	4-1 (WLWWW)	Montreal	Dick Irvin
1952	Detroit	Tommy Ivan	4-0	Montreal	Dick Irvin
1953	Montreal	Dick Irvin	4-1 (WLWWW)	Boston	Lynn Patrick
1954	Detroit	Tommy Ivan	4-3 (WLWWLLW)	Montreal	Dick Irvin
1955	Detroit	Jimmy Skinner	4-3 (WWLWLLW)	Montreal	Dick Irvin
1956	Montreal	Toe Blake	4-1 (WWLWW)	Detroit	Jimmy Skinner
1957	Montreal	Toe Blake	4-1 (WWWLW)	Boston	Milt Schmidt
1958	Montreal	Toe Blake	4-2 (WWLWLW)	Boston	Milt Schmidt
1959	Montreal	Toe Blake	4-1 (WWLWW)	Toronto	Punch Imlach
1960	Montreal	Toe Blake	4-0	Toronto	Punch Imlach
1961	Chicago	Rudy Pilous	4-2 (WLWLWW)	Detroit	Sid Abel
1962	Toronto	Punch Imlach	4-2 (WWLLWW)	Chicago	Rudy Pilous
1963	Toronto	Punch Imlach	4-1 (WWLWW)	Detroit	Sid Abel
1964	Toronto	Punch Imlach	4-3 (WLLWLWW)	Detroit	Sid Abel
1965	Montreal	Toe Blake	4-3 (WWLWLWW)	Chicago	Billy Reay
1966	Montreal	Toe Blake	4-2 (LLWWWW)	Detroit	Sid Abel
1967	Toronto	Punch Imlach	4-2 (LWWLWW)	Montreal	Toe Blake
1968	Montreal	Toe Blake	4-0	St. Louis	Scotty Bowman
1969	Montreal	Claude Ruel	4-0	St. Louis	Scotty Bowman
1970	Boston	Harry Sinden	4-0	St. Louis	Scotty Bowman
1971	Montreal	Al MacNeil	4-3 (LLLWWLWW)	Chicago	Billy Reay
1972	Boston	Tom Johnson	4-2 (WWLWLW)	NY Rangers	Emile Francis
1973	Montreal	Scotty Bowman	4-2 (WWLWLW)	Chicago	Billy Reay
1974	Philadelphia	Fred Shero	4-2 (LWWWLW)	Boston	Bep Guidolin
1975	Philadelphia	Fred Shero	4-2 (WWLLWW)	Buffalo	Floyd Smith
1976	Montreal	Scotty Bowman	4-0	Philadelphia	Fred Shero
1977	Montreal	Scotty Bowman	4-0	Boston	Don Cherry
1978	Montreal	Scotty Bowman	4-2 (WWLWLW)	Boston	Don Cherry
1979	Montreal	Scotty Bowman	4-1 (LWWWW)	NY Rangers	Fred Shero
1980	NY Islanders	Al Arbour	4-2 (WLWWLW)	Philadelphia	Pat Quinn
1981	NY Islanders	Al Arbour	4-1 (WWWLW)	Minnesota	Glen Sonmor
1982	NY Islanders	Al Arbour	4-0	Vancouver	Roger Neilson
1983	NY Islanders	Al Arbour	4-0	Edmonton	Glen Sather
1984	Edmonton	Glen Sather	4-1 (WLWWW)	NY Islanders	Al Arbour
1985	Edmonton	Glen Sather	4-1 (LWWWW)	Philadelphia	Mike Keenan
1986	Montreal	Jean Perron	4-1 (LWWWW)	Calgary	Bob Johnson
1987	Edmonton	Glen Sather	4-3 (WWLWLLW)	Philadelphia	Mike Keenan
1988	Edmonton	Glen Sather	4-0	Boston	Terry O'Reilly
1989	Calgary	Terry Crisp	4-2 (WLLWWW)	Montreal	Pat Burns
1990	Edmonton	John Muckler	4-1 (WWLWW)	Boston	Mike Milbury
1991	Pittsburgh	Bob Johnson	4-2 (LWLWLW)	Minnesota	Bob Gainey
1992	Pittsburgh	Scotty Bowman	4-0	Chicago	Mike Keenan
1993	Montreal	Jacques Demers	4-1 (LWWWW)	Los Angeles	Barry Melrose
1994	NY Rangers	Mike Keenan	4-3 (LWWWLLW)	Vancouver	Pat Quinn
1995	New Jersey	Jacques Lemaire	4-0	Detroit	Scotty Bowman
1996	Colorado	Marc Crawford	4-0	Florida	Doug MacLean
1997	Detroit	Scotty Bowman	4-0	Philadelphia	Terry Murray

* The 1919 Finals were cancelled after five games due to an influenza epidemic with Montreal and Seattle (PCHA) tied at 2-2-1.

M.J. O'Brien Trophy

Donated by Canadian mining magnate M.J. O'Brien, whose son Ambrose founded the National Hockey Association in 1910. Originally presented to the NHA champion until the league's demise in 1917, the trophy then passed to the NHL champion through 1927. It was awarded to the NHL's Canadian Division winner from 1927-38 and the Stanley Cup runner-up from 1939-50 before being retired in 1950.

NHA winners included the Montreal Wanderers (1910), original Ottawa Senators (1911 and '15), Quebec Bulldogs (1912 and '13), Toronto Blueshirts (1914) and Montreal Canadiens (1916 and '17).

Conn Smythe Trophy

The Most Valuable Player of the Stanley Cup Playoffs, as selected by the Pro Hockey Writers Assn. Presented since 1965 by Maple Leaf Gardens Limited in the name of the former Toronto coach, Gm and owner, Conn Smythe. Winners who did not play for the Cup champion are in **bold** type.

Multiple winners: Wayne Gretzky, Mario Lemieux, Bobby Orr, Bernie Parent and Patrick Roy (2).

Year		Year		Year	
1965	Jean Beliveau, Mon., C	1976	**Reggie Leach**, Phi., RW	1987	**Ron Hextall**, Phi., G
1966	**Roger Crozier**, Det., G	1977	Guy Lafleur, Mon., RW	1988	Wayne Gretzky, Edm., C
1967	Dave Keon, Tor., C	1978	Larry Robinson, Mon., D	1989	Al MacInnis, Calg., D
1968	**Glenn Hall**, St.L., G	1979	Bob Gainey, Mon., LW	1990	Bill Ranford, Edm., G
1969	Serge Savard, Mon., D	1980	Bryan Trottier, NYI, C	1991	Mario Lemieux, Pit., C
1970	Bobby Orr, Bos., D	1981	Butch Goring, NYI, C	1992	Mario Lemieux, Pit., C
1971	Ken Dryden, Mon., G	1982	Mike Bossy, NYI, RW	1993	Patrick Roy, Mon., G
1972	Bobby Orr, Bos., D	1983	Billy Smith, NYI, G	1994	Brian Leetch, NYR, D
1973	Yvan Cournoyer, Mon., RW	1984	Mark Messier, Edm., LW	1995	Claude Lemieux, NJ, RW
1974	Bernie Parent, Phi., G	1985	Wayne Gretzky, Edm., C	1996	Joe Sakic, Col., C
1975	Bernie Parent, Phi., G	1986	Patrick Roy, Mon., G	1997	Mike Vernon, Det., G

Note: Ken Dryden (1971) and Patrick Roy (1986) are the only players to win as rookies.

All-Time Stanley Cup Playoff Leaders

CAREER

Stanley Cup Playoff leaders through 1997. Years listed indicate number of playoff appearances. Players active in 1997 in **bold** type; (DNP) indicates active player did not participate in 1997 playoffs.

Scoring

Points

		Yrs	Gm	G	A	Pts
1	**Wayne Gretzky**	16	208	122	260	382
2	**Mark Messier**	17	236	109	186	295
3	**Jari Kurri**	14	196	106	127	233
4	Glenn Anderson	15	225	93	121	214
5	**Paul Coffey**	15	189	59	136	195
6	Bryan Trottier	17	221	71	113	184
7	Jean Beliveau	17	162	79	97	176
8	**Denis Savard**	16	169	66	109	175
9	Denis Potvin	14	185	56	108	164
	Doug Gilmour	13	146	49	115	164
11	Mike Bossy	10	129	85	75	160
	Gordie Howe	20	157	68	92	160
	Bobby Smith	13	184	64	96	160
14	**Mario Lemieux**	7	89	70	85	155
15	Stan Mikita	18	155	59	91	150
16	Brian Propp	13	160	64	84	148
17	**Ray Bourque** (DNP)	17	162	34	112	146
18	Larry Robinson	20	227	28	116	144
19	Jacques Lemaire	11	145	61	78	139
20	Phil Esposito	15	130	61	76	137
21	Guy Lafleur	14	128	58	76	134
22	Steve Larmer	13	140	56	75	131
23	Bobby Hull	14	119	62	67	129
	Henri Richard	18	180	49	80	129
	Larry Murphy	16	168	32	97	129

Goals

		Yrs	Gm	G
1	**Wayne Gretzky**	16	208	122
2	**Mark Messier**	17	236	109
3	**Jari Kurri**	14	196	106
4	Glenn Anderson	15	225	93
5	Mike Bossy	10	129	85
6	Maurice Richard	15	133	82
7	Jean Beliveau	17	162	79
8	**Dino Ciccarelli** (DNP)	14	141	73
9	Bryan Trottier	17	221	71
10	**Mario Lemieux**	7	89	70
	Claude Lemieux	12	172	70
12	**Esa Tikkanen**	12	165	69
13	Gordie Howe	20	157	68
14	**Brett Hull**	12	98	66
	Denis Savard	16	169	66

Assists

		Yrs	Gm	A
1	**Wayne Gretzky**	16	208	260
2	**Mark Messier**	17	236	186
3	**Paul Coffey**	15	189	136
4	**Jari Kurri**	14	196	127
5	Glenn Anderson	15	225	121
6	Larry Robinson	20	227	116
7	**Doug Gilmour**	13	146	115
8	Bryan Trottier	17	221	113
9	**Ray Bourque** (DNP)	17	162	112
10	**Denis Savard**	16	169	109
11	Denis Potvin	14	185	108
12	Jean Beliveau	17	162	97
	Larry Murphy	16	168	97
14	Bobby Smith	13	184	96
15	Gordie Howe	20	157	92

Goaltending

Wins

		Gm	W-L	Pct	GAA
1	**Patrick Roy**	153	96-55	.636	2.37
2	Billy Smith	132	88-36	.710	2.73
3	Ken Dryden	112	80-32	.714	2.40
	Grant Fuhr	127	80-40	.667	3.00
5	**Mike Vernon**	123	73-45	.619	2.69
6	Jacques Plante	112	71-37	.657	2.17
7	**Andy Moog**	123	64-52	.552	3.04
8	Turk Broda	102	58-42	.580	1.98
9	Terry Sawchuk	106	54-48	.529	2.54
10	**Tom Barrasso** (DNP)	94	51-39	.567	3.11
11	Glenn Hall	115	49-65	.430	2.79
12	Gerry Cheevers	88	47-35	.573	2.69
	Ron Hextall	92	47-43	.522	3.04
14	Tony Esposito	99	45-53	.459	3.07
15	Gump Worsley	70	41-25	.621	2.82
	Mike Richter	76	41-33	.554	2.68

Shutouts

		Gm	GAA	No
1	Clint Benedict	48	1.80	15
	Jacques Plante	112	2.17	15
3	Turk Broda	102	1.98	13
4	Terry Sawchuk	106	2.54	12
5	**Patrick Roy**	153	2.37	11

All-Time Stanley Cup Playoff Leaders (Cont.)

Goals Against Average
Minimum of 50 games played

		Gm	Min	GA	GAA
1	George Hainsworth	52	3486	112	1.93
2	Turk Broda	101	6348	211	1.98
3	Jacques Plante	112	6651	241	2.17
4	**Patrick Roy**	153	9452	374	2.37
5	Ken Dryden	112	6846	274	2.40
6	Bernie Parent	71	4302	174	2.43
7	**Ed Belfour** (DNP)	68	3942	164	2.50
8	Harry Lumley	76	4759	199	2.51
9	Johnny Bower	74	4350	184	2.54
10	Terry Sawchuk	106	6311	267	2.54

Note: Clint Benedict had an average of 1.80 but played in only 48 games.

Games Played

		Yrs	Gm
1	**Patrick Roy**, Mon-Col	11	153
2	Billy Smith, NY Islanders	13	132
3	**Grant Fuhr**, Edm-Buf-St.L	12	127
4	**Andy Moog**, Edm-Bos-Dal	15	123
5	**Mike Vernon**, Calg-Det	11	123

Appearances in Cup Final

Standings of all teams that have reached the Stanley Cup championship round, since 1918.

App		Cups	Last Won
32	Montreal Canadiens	23*	1993
21	Toronto Maple Leafs	13†	1967
20	Detroit Red Wings	8	1997
17	Boston Bruins	5	1972
10	New York Rangers	4	1994
10	Chicago Blackhawks	3	1961
7	Philadelphia Flyers	2	1975
6	Edmonton Oilers	5	1990
5	New York Islanders	4	1983
5	Vancouver Millionaires (PCHA)	0	—
4	(original) Ottawa Senators	4	1927
3	Montreal Maroons	2	1935
2	St. Louis Blues	0	—
2	Pittsburgh Penguins	2	1992
2	Calgary Flames	1	1989
2	Victoria Cougars (WCHL-WHL)	1	1925
2	Minnesota North Stars	0	—
2	Seattle Metropolitans (PCHA)	0	—
2	Vancouver Canucks	0	—
1	Colorado Avalanche	1	1996
1	New Jersey Devils	1	1995
1	Buffalo Sabres	0	—
1	Calgary Tigers (WCHL)	0	—
1	Edmonton Eskimos (WCHL)	0	—
1	Florida Panthers	0	—
1	Los Angeles Kings	0	—

*Les Canadiens also won the Cup in 1916 for a total of 24. Also, their final with Seattle in 1919 was cancelled due to an influenza epidemic that claimed the life of the Habs' Joe Hall.

†Toronto has won the Cup under three nicknames—Arenas (1918), St. Pats (1922) and Maple Leafs (1932,42,45,47-49,51-62-64,67).

Teams now defunct (6): Calgary Tigers, Edmonton Eskimos, Montreal Maroons, (original) Ottawa Senators, Seattle, Vancouver Millionaires and Victoria. Edmonton (1923) and Calgary (1924) represented the WCHL and later the WHL, while Vancouver (1918,1921-24) and Seattle (1919-20) played out of the PCHA.

Miscellaneous

Championships

		Yrs	Cups
1	Henri Richard, Montreal	18	11
2	Yvan Cournoyer, Montreal	15	10
	Jean Beliveau, Montreal	17	10
4	Claude Provost, Montreal	14	9
5	Jacques Lemaire, Montreal	11	8
	Maurice Richard, Montreal	15	8
	Red Kelly, Detroit-Toronto	19	8

Years in Playoffs

		Yrs	Gm
1	Gordie Howe, Detroit-Hartford	20	157
	Larry Robinson, Montreal-Los Angeles	20	227
3	Red Kelly, Detroit-Toronto	19	164
4	Henri Richard, Montreal	18	180
5	Stan Mikita, Chicago	18	155

Games Played

		Yrs	Gm
1	**Mark Messier**, Edm-NY Rangers	17	236
2	Larry Robinson, Montreal-Los Angeles	20	227
3	Glenn Anderson, Edm-Tor-NYR-St.L	15	225
4	Bryan Trottier, NY Isles-Pittsburgh	17	221
5	**Kevin Lowe**, Edm-NYR-Edm	17	213

Penalty Minutes

		Yrs	Gm	Min
1	**Dale Hunter**, Que-Wash (DNP)	16	146	661
2	Chris Nilan, Mon-NYR-Bos-Mon	12	111	541
3	Willi Plett, Atl-Calg-Min-Bos	10	83	466
4	Dave Williams, Tor-Van-LA	12	83	455
	Claude Lemieux, Mon-NJ-Col	12	172	455

SINGLE SEASON

Scoring

Points

		Year	Gm	G	A	Pts
1	Wayne Gretzky, Edm	1985	18	17	30	47
2	Mario Lemieux, Pit	1991	23	16	28	44
3	Wayne Gretzky, Edm	1988	19	12	31	43
4	Wayne Gretzky, LA	1993	24	15	25	40
5	Wayne Gretzky, Edm	1983	16	12	26	38
6	Paul Coffey, Edm	1985	18	12	25	37
7	Mike Bossy, NYI	1981	18	17	18	35
	Wayne Gretzky, Edm	1984	19	13	22	35
	Doug Gilmour, Tor	1993	21	10	25	35
10	Mario Lemieux, Pit	1992	15	16	18	34
	Mark Messier, Edm	1988	19	11	23	34
	Mark Recchi, Pit	1991	24	10	24	34
	Wayne Gretzky, Edm	1987	21	5	29	34
	Brian Leetch, NYR	1994	23	11	23	34
	Joe Sakic, Col	1996	22	18	16	34

Goals

		Year	Gm	No
1	Reggie Leach, Philadelphia	1976	16	19
	Jari Kurri, Edmonton	1985	18	19
3	Joe Sakic, Colorado	1996	22	18
4	Newsy Lalonde, Montreal	1919	10	17
	Mike Bossy, NY Islanders	1981	18	17
	Wayne Gretzky, Edmonton	1985	18	17
	Steve Payne, Minnesota	1981	19	17
	Mike Bossy, NY Islanders	1982	19	17
	Mike Bossy, NY Islanders	1983	19	17
	Kevin Stevens, Pittsburgh	1991	24	17

Assists

		Year	Gm	No
1	Wayne Gretzky, Edmonton	1988	19	31
2	Wayne Gretzky, Edmonton	1985	18	30
3	Wayne Gretzky, Edmonton	1987	21	29
4	Mario Lemieux, Pittsburgh	1991	23	28
5	Wayne Gretzky, Edmonton	1983	16	26
6	Paul Coffey, Edmonton	1985	18	25
	Doug Gilmour, Toronto	1993	21	25
	Wayne Gretzky, Los Angeles	1993	24	25
9	Al MacInnis, Calgary	1989	22	24
	Mark Recchi, Pittsburgh	1991	24	24

Goaltending
Wins

		Year	Gm	Min	W-L
1	Grant Fuhr, Edm	1988	19	1136	16-2
	Mike Vernon, Det	1997	20	1229	16-4
	Patrick Roy, Mon	1993	20	1293	16-4
	Martin Brodeur, NJ	1995	20	1222	16-4
	Mike Vernon, Calg	1989	22	1381	16-5
	Tom Barrasso, Pit	1992	21	1233	16-5
	Bill Ranford, Edm	1990	22	1401	16-6
	Patrick Roy, Col	1996	22	1454	16-6
	Mike Richter, NYR	1994	23	1417	16-7
10	Six tied with 15 wins each.				

Shutouts

		Year	Gm	No
1	Clint Benedict, Mon. Maroons	1926	8	4
	Terry Sawchuk, Detroit	1952	8	4
	Clint Benedict, Mon. Maroons	1928	9	4
	Dave Kerr, NY Rangers	1937	9	4
	Frank McCool, Toronto	1945	13	4
	Ken Dryden, Montreal	1977	14	4
	Bernie Parent, Philadelphia	1975	17	4
	Mike Richter, NY Rangers	1994	23	4
	Kirk McLean, Vancouver	1994	24	4

Goals Against Average
(Minimum of eight games played.)

		Year	Gm	Min	GA	GAA
1	Terry Sawchuk, Det	1952	8	480	5	0.63
2	Clint Benedict, Mon-M	1928	9	555	8	0.89
3	Turk Broda, Tor	1951	9	509	9	1.06
4	Dave Kerr, NYR	1937	9	553	10	1.11
5	Jacques Plante, Mon	1960	8	489	11	1.35
6	Rogie Vachon, Mon	1969	8	507	12	1.42
7	Jacques Plante, St.L	1969	10	589	14	1.43
8	Frankie Brimsek, Bos	1939	12	863	18	1.50
9	Chuck Gardiner, Chi	1934	8	602	12	1.50
10	Ken Dryden, Mon	1977	14	849	22	1.55

Note: Average determined by games played through 1942-43 season and by minutes played since then.

SINGLE SERIES
Scoring
Points

	Year	Rd	G-A—Pts
Rick Middleton, Bos vs Buf	1983	DF	5-14—19
Wayne Gretzky, Edm vs Chi	1985	CF	4-14—18
Mario Lemieux, Pit vs Wash	1992	DSF	7-10—17
Barry Pederson, Bos vs Buf	1983	DF	7-9—16
Doug Gilmour, Tor vs SJ	1994	CSF	3-13—16
Jari Kurri, Edm vs Chi	1985	CF	12-3—15
Tim Kerr, Phi vs Pit	1989	DF	10-5—15
Mario Lemieux, Pit vs Bos	1991	CF	6-9—15
Wayne Gretzky, Edm vs LA	1987	DSF	2-13—15

Goals

	Year	Rd	No
Jari Kurri, Edm vs Chi	1985	CF	12
Newsy Lalonde, Mon vs Ott	1919	SF*	11
Tim Kerr, Phi vs Pit	1989	DF	10
Five tied with nine each.			

*NHL final prior to Stanley Cup series with Seattle.

Assists

	Year	Rd	No
Rick Middleton, Bos vs Buf	1983	DF	14
Wayne Gretzky, Edm vs Chi	1985	CF	14
Wayne Gretzky, Edm vs LA	1987	DSF	13
Doug Gilmour, Tor vs SJ	1994	CSF	13
Four tied with 11 each.			

SINGLE GAME
Scoring
Points

	Date	G	A	Pts
Patrik Sundstrom, NJ vs Wash	4/22/88	3	5	8
Mario Lemieux, Pit vs Phi	4/25/89	5	3	8
Wayne Gretzky, Edm at Calg	4/17/83	4	3	7
Wayne Gretzky, Edm at Win	4/25/85	3	4	7
Wayne Gretzky, Edm vs LA	4/9/87	1	6	7

Goals

	Date	No
Newsy Lalonde, Mon vs Ott	3/1/19	5
Maurice Richard, Mon vs Tor	3/23/44	5
Darryl Sittler, Tor vs Phi	4/22/76	5
Reggie Leach, Phi vs Bos	5/6/76	5
Mario Lemieux, Pit vs Phi	4/25/89	5

Assists

	Date	No
Mikko Leinonen, NYR vs Phi	4/8/82	6
Wayne Gretzky, Edm vs LA	4/9/87	6
Ten tied with five each.		

Ten Longest Playoff Overtime Games

The 10 longest overtime games in Stanley Cup history. Note the following Series initials: SF (semifinals), CQF (conference quarterfinal), DSF (division semifinal). QF (quarterfinal) and Final (Cup Final). Series winners are in **bold** type; (*) indicates deciding game of series.

		OTs	Elapsed Time	Goal Scorer	Date	Series	Location
1	**Detroit** 1, Montreal Maroons 0	6	116:30	Mud Bruneteau	3/24/36	SF, Gm 1	Montreal
2	**Toronto** 1, Boston 0	6	104:46	Ken Doraty	4/3/33	SF, Gm 5	Toronto
3	**Pittsburgh** 3 Washington 2	4	79:15	Petr Nedved	4/24/96	CQF, Gm 4	Washington
4	Toronto 3, **Detroit** 2	4	70:18	Jack McLean	3/23/43	SF, Gm 2	Detroit
5	**Montreal** 2, NY Rangers 1	4	68:52	Gus Rivers	3/28/30	SF, Gm 1	Montreal
6	**NY Islanders** 3, Washington 2	4	68:47	Pat LaFontaine	4/18/87	DSF, Gm 7*	Washington
7	Buffalo 1, **New Jersey** 0	4	65:43	Dave Hannan	4/27/94	QF, Gm 6	Buffalo
8	**Montreal** 3, Detroit 2	4	61:09	Maurice Richard	3/27/51	SF, Gm 1	Detroit
9	**NY Americans** 3, NY Rangers 2	4	60:40	Lorne Carr	3/27/38	QF, Gm 3*	New York
10	**NY Rangers** 4, Montreal 3	3	59:32	Fred Cook	3/26/32	SF, Gm 2	Montreal

NHL All-Star Game

Three benefit NHL All-Star games were staged in the 1930s for forward Ace Bailey and the families of Howie Morenz and Babe Siebert. Bailey, of Toronto, suffered a fractured skull on a career-ending check by Boston's Eddie Shore. Morenz, the Montreal Canadiens' legend, died of a heart attack at 35 after a severely broken leg ended his career. Siebert, who played with both Montreal teams, drowned at age 35.

The All-Star Game was revived at the start of the 1947-48 season as an annual exhibition match between the defending Stanley Cup champion and All-Stars from the league's other five teams. The format has changed several times since then. The game was moved to midseason in 1966-67 and became an East vs. West contest in 1968-69. The Eastern (East, 1968-1974; Wales, 1975-93) Conference leads the series 18-7-1.

Benefit Games

Date	Occasion		Host	Coaches
2/14/34	Ace Bailey Benefit	Toronto 7, All-Stars 3	Toronto	Dick Irvin, Lester Patrick
11/3/37	Howie Morenz Memorial	All-Stars 6, Montreals* 5	Montreal	Jack Adams, Ceil Hart
10/29/39	Babe Seibert Memorial	All-Stars 5, Canadiens 3	Montreal	Art Ross, Pit Lepine

*Combined squad of Montreal Canadiens and Montreal Maroons.

All-Star Games

Multiple MVP winners: Mario Lemieux (3); Wayne Gretzky, Bobby Hull and Frank Mahovolich (2).

Year		Host	Coaches	Most Valuable Player
1947	All-Stars 4, Toronto 3	Toronto	Dick Irvin, Hap Day	No award
1948	All-Stars 3, Toronto 1	Chicago	Tommy Ivan, Hap Day	No award
1949	All-Stars 3, Toronto 1	Toronto	Tommy Ivan, Hap Day	No award
1950	Detroit 7, All-Stars 1	Detroit	Tommy Ivan, Lynn Patrick	No award
1951	1st Team 2, 2nd Team 2	Toronto	Joe Primeau, Hap Day	No award
1952	1st Team 1, 2nd Team 1	Detroit	Tommy Ivan, Dick Irvin	No award
1953	All-Stars 3, Montreal 1	Montreal	Lynn Patrick, Dick Irvin	No award
1954	All-Stars 2, Detroit 2	Detroit	King Clancy, Jim Skinner	No award
1955	Detroit 3, All-Stars 1	Detroit	Jim Skinner, Dick Irvin	No award
1956	All-Stars 1, Montreal 1	Montreal	Jim Skinner, Toe Blake	No award
1957	All-Stars 5, Montreal 3	Montreal	Milt Schmidt, Toe Blake	No award
1958	Montreal 6, All-Stars 3	Montreal	Toe Blake, Milt Schmidt	No award
1959	Montreal 6, All-Stars 1	Montreal	Toe Blake, Punch Imlach	No award
1960	All-Stars 2, Montreal 1	Montreal	Punch Imlach, Toe Blake	No award
1961	All-Stars 3, Chicago 1	Chicago	Sid Abel, Rudy Pilous	No award
1962	Toronto 4, All-Stars 1	Toronto	Punch Imlach, Rudy Pilous	Eddie Shack, Tor., RW
1963	All-Stars 3, Toronto 3	Toronto	Sid Abel, Punch Imlach	Frank Mahovlich, Tor., LW
1964	All-Stars 3, Toronto 2	Toronto	Sid Abel, Punch Imlach	Jean Beliveau, Mon., C
1965	All-Stars 5, Montreal 2	Montreal	Billy Reay, Toe Blake	Gordie Howe, Det., RW
1966	No game (see below)			
1967	Montreal 3, All-Stars 0	Montreal	Toe Blake, Sid Abel	Henri Richard, Mon., C
1968	Toronto 4, All-Stars 3	Toronto	Punch Imlach, Toe Blake	Bruce Gamble, Tor., G
1969	West 3, East 3	Montreal	Scotty Bowman, Toe Blake	Frank Mahovlich, Det., LW
1970	East 4, West 1	St. Louis	Claude Ruel, Scotty Bowman	Bobby Hull, Chi., LW
1971	West 2, East 1	Boston	Scotty Bowman, Harry Sinden	Bobby Hull, Chi., LW
1972	East 3, West 2	Minnesota	Al MacNeil, Billy Reay	Bobby Orr, Bos., D
1973	East 5, West 4	NY Rangers	Tom Johnson, Billy Reay	Greg Polis, Pit., LW
1974	West 6, East 4	Chicago	Billy Reay, Scotty Bowman	Garry Unger, St.L., C
1975	Wales 7, Campbell 1	Montreal	Bep Guidolin, Fred Shero	Syl Apps Jr., Pit., C
1976	Wales 7, Campbell 5	Philadelphia	Floyd Smith, Fred Shero	Peter Mahovlich, Mon., C
1977	Wales 4, Campbell 3	Vancouver	Scotty Bowman, Fred Shero	Rick Martin, Buf., LW
1978	Wales 3, Campbell 2 (OT)	Buffalo	Scotty Bowman, Fred Shero	Billy Smith, NYI, G
1979	No game (see below)			
1980	Wales 6, Campbell 3	Detroit	Scotty Bowman, Al Arbour	Reggie Leach, Phi., RW
1981	Campbell 4, Wales 1	Los Angeles	Pat Quinn, Scotty Bowman	Mike Liut, St.L., G
1982	Wales 4, Campbell 2	Washington	Al Arbour, Glen Sonmor	Mike Bossy, NYI, RW
1983	Campbell 9, Wales 3	NY Islanders	Roger Neilson, Al Arbour	Wayne Gretzky, Edm., C
1984	Wales 7, Campbell 6	New Jersey	Al Arbour, Glen Sather	Don Maloney, NYR, LW
1985	Wales 6, Campbell 4	Calgary	Al Arbour, Glen Sather	Mario Lemieux, Pit., C
1986	Wales 4, Campbell 3 (OT)	Hartford	Mike Keenan, Glen Sather	Grant Fuhr, Edm., G
1987	No game (see below)			
1988	Wales 6, Campbell 5 (OT)	St. Louis	Mike Keenan, Glen Sather	Mario Lemieux, Pit., C
1989	Campbell 9, Wales 5	Edmonton	Glen Sather, Terry O'Reilly	Wayne Gretzky, LA, C
1990	Wales 12, Campbell 7	Pittsburgh	Pat Burns, Terry Crisp	Mario Lemieux, Pit., C
1991	Campbell 11, Wales 5	Chicago	John Muckler, Mike Milbury	Vincent Damphousse, Tor., LW
1992	Campbell 10, Wales 6	Philadelphia	Bob Gainey, Scotty Bowman	Brett Hull, St.L., RW
1993	Wales 16, Campbell 6	Montreal	Scotty Bowman, Mike Keenan	Mike Gartner, NYR, RW
1994	East 9, West 8	NY Rangers	Jacques Demers, Barry Melrose	Mike Richter, NYR, G
1995	No game (see below)			
1996	East 5, West 4	Boston	Doug MacLean, Scotty Bowman	Ray Bourque, Bos., D
1997	East 11, West 7	San Jose	Doug MacLean, Ken Hitchcock	Mark Recchi, Mon., RW

No All-Star Game: in 1966 (moved from start of season to mid-season); in 1979 (replaced by Challenge Cup series with USSR); in 1987 (replaced by Rendez-Vous '87 series with USSR); and in 1995 (cancelled when NHL lockout shortened season to 48 games).

NHL Franchise Origins

Here is what the current 26 teams in the National Hockey League have to show for the years they have put in as members of the NHL, the early National Hockey Association (NHA) and the more recent World Hockey Association (WHA). League titles and Stanley Cup championships are noted by year won. The Stanley Cup has automatically gone to the NHL champion since the 1926-27 season. Following the 1992-93 season, the NHL renamed the Clarence Campbell Conference the Western Conference, while the Prince of Wales Conference became the Eastern Conference.

Western Conference

	First Season	League Titles	Franchise Stops
Anaheim, Mighty Ducks of	1993-94 (NHL)	None	•Anaheim, CA (1993—)
Calgary Flames	1972-73 (NHL)	1 Cup (1989)	•Atlanta (1972-80) Calgary (1980—)
Chicago Blackhawks	1926-27 (NHL)	3 Cups (1934,38,61)	•Chicago (1926—)
Colorado Avalanche	1972-73 (WHA)	1 WHA (1977) 1 Cup (1996)	•Quebec City (1972-95) Denver (1995—)
Dallas Stars	1967-68 (NHL)	None	•Bloomington, MN (1967-93) Dallas (1993—)
Detroit Red Wings	1926-27 (NHL)	8 Cups (1936-37,43,50,52,54-55,97)	•Detroit (1926—)
Edmonton Oilers	1973-74 (WHA)	5 Cups (1984-85,87-88,90)	•Edmonton (1972—)
Los Angeles Kings	1967-68 (NHL)	None	•Inglewood, CA (1967—)
Phoenix Coyotes	1972-73 (WHA)	3 WHA (1976, 78-79)	•Winnipeg (1972-96) Phoenix (1996—)
St. Louis Blues	1967-68 (NHL)	None	•St. Louis (1967—)
San Jose Sharks	1991-92 (NHL)	None	•San Francisco (1991-93) San Jose (1993—)
Toronto Maple Leafs	1916-17 (NHA)	2 NHL (1918,22) 13 Cups (1918,22,32,42,45,47-49,51,62-64,67)	•Toronto (1916—)
Vancouver Canucks	1970-71 (NHL)	None	•Vancouver (1970—)

Eastern Conference

	First Season	League Titles	Franchise Stops
Boston Bruins	1924-25 (NHL)	5 Cups (1929,39,41,70,72)	•Boston (1924—)
Buffalo Sabres	1970-71 (NHL)	None	•Buffalo (1970—)
Carolina Hurricanes	1972-73 (WHA)	1 WHA (1973)	•Boston (1972-74) W. Springfield, MA (1974-75) Hartford, CT (1975-78) Springfield, MA (1978-80) Hartford (1980-97) Raleigh (1997—)
Florida Panthers	1993-94 (NHL)	None	•Miami (1993—)
Montreal Canadiens	1909-10 (NHA)	2 NHA (1916-17) 2 NHL (1924-25) 24 Cups (1916,24,30-31,44,46,53,56-60,65-66,68-69,71,73,76-79,86,93)	•Montreal (1909—)
New Jersey Devils	1974-75 (NHL)	1 Cup (1995)	•Kansas City (1974-76) Denver (1976-82) E. Rutherford, NJ (1982—)
New York Islanders	1972-73 (NHL)	4 Cups (1980-83)	•Uniondale, NY (1972—)
New York Rangers	1926-27 (NHL)	4 Cups (1928,33,40,94)	•New York (1926—)
Ottawa Senators	1992-93 (NHL)	None	•Ottawa (1992-1996) Kanata, Ont. (1996—)
Philadelphia Flyers	1967-68 (NHL)	2 Cups (1974-75)	•Philadelphia (1967—)
Pittsburgh Penguins	1967-68 (NHL)	2 Cups (1991-92)	•Pittsburgh (1967—)
Tampa Bay Lightning	1992-93 (NHL)	None	•Tampa, FL (1992-93) St. Petersburg, FL (1993-96) Tampa, FL (1996—)
Washington Capitals	1974-75 (NHL)	None	•Landover, MD (1974—)

Note: The Hartford Civic Center roof collapsed after a snowstorm in January 1978, forcing the Whalers (now known as the Carolina Hurricanes) to move their home games to Springfield, Mass., for two years.

The Growth of the NHL

Of the four franchises that comprised the National Hockey League (NHL) at the start of the 1917-18 season, only two remain—the Montreal Canadiens and the Toronto Maple Leafs (originally the Toronto Arenas). From 1919-26, eight new teams joined the league, but only four—the Boston Bruins, Chicago Blackhawks (originally Black Hawks), Detroit Red Wings (originally Cougars) and New York Rangers—survived.

It was 41 years before the NHL expanded again, doubling in size for the 1967-68 season with new teams in Los Angeles, Minnesota, Oakland, Philadelphia, Pittsburgh and St. Louis. The league had 16 clubs by the start of the 1972-73 season, but it also had a rival in the **World Hockey Association**, which debuted that year with 12 teams.

The NHL added two more teams in 1974 and merged the struggling Cleveland Barons (originally the Oakland Seals) and Minnesota North Stars in 1978, before absorbing four WHA clubs—the Edmonton Oilers, Hartford Whalers, Quebec Nordiques and Winnipeg Jets—in time for the 1979-80 season. Five expansion teams have joined the league so far in the 1990s, giving the NHL its current 26-team roster.

Expansion/Merger Timetable

For teams currently in NHL.

1919—Quebec Bulldogs finally take the ice after sitting out NHL's first two seasons; **1924**—Boston Bruins and Montreal Maroons; **1925**—New York Americans and Pittsburgh Pirates; **1926**—Chicago Black Hawks (now Blackhawks), Detroit Cougars (now Red Wings) and New York Rangers; **1932**—Ottawa Senators return after sitting out 1931-32 season.

1967—California Seals (later Cleveland Barons), Los Angeles Kings, Minnesota North Stars, Philadelphia Flyers, Pittsburgh Penguins and St. Louis Blues.

1970—Buffalo Sabres and Vancouver Canucks; **1972**—Atlanta Flames (now Calgary) and New York Islanders; **1974**—Kansas City Scouts (now New Jersey Devils) and Washington Capitals; **1978**—Cleveland Barons merge with Minnesota North Stars (now Dallas Stars) and team remains in Minnesota; **1979**—added WHA's Edmonton Oilers, Hartford Whalers, Quebec Nordiques (now Colorado Avalanche) and Winnipeg Jets (now Phoenix Coyotes).

1991—San Jose Sharks; **1992**—Ottawa Senators and Tampa Bay Lightning; **1993**—Mighty Ducks of Anaheim and Florida Panthers.

City and Nickname Changes

1919—Toronto Arenas renamed St. Pats; **1920**—Quebec moves to Hamilton and becomes Tigers (will fold in 1925); **1926**—Toronto St. Pats renamed Maple Leafs; **1929**—Detroit Cougars renamed Falcons.

1930—Pittsburgh Pirates move to Philadelphia and become Quakers (will fold in 1931); **1932**—Detroit Falcons renamed Red Wings; **1934**—Ottawa Senators move to St. Louis and become Eagles (will fold in 1935); **1941**—New York Americans renamed Brooklyn Americans (will fold in 1942).

1967—California Seals renamed Oakland Seals three months into first season; **1970**—Oakland Seals renamed California Golden Seals; **1975**—California Golden Seals renamed Seals; **1976**—California Seals move to Cleveland and become Barons, while Kansas City Scouts move to Denver and become Colorado Rockies; **1978**—Cleveland Barons merge with Minnesota North Stars and become Minnesota North Stars.

1980—Atlanta Flames move to Calgary; **1982**—Colorado Rockies move to East Rutherford, N.J., and become New Jersey Devils; **1986**—Chicago Black Hawks renamed Blackhawks; **1993**—Minnesota North Stars move to Dallas and become Stars. **1995**—Quebec Nordiques move to Denver and become Colorado Avalanche; **1996**—Winnipeg Jets move to Phoenix and become Coyotes; **1997**—Hartford Whalers move to Raleigh and become Carolina Hurricanes.

Defunct NHL Teams

Teams that once played in the NHL, but no longer exist.

Brooklyn—Americans (1941-42, formerly NY Americans from 1925-41); **Cleveland**—Barons (1976-78, originally California-Oakland Seals from 1967-76); **Hamilton (Ont.)**—Tigers (1920-25, originally Quebec Bulldogs from 1919-20); **Montreal**—Maroons (1924-38) and Wanderers (1917-18); **New York**—Americans (1925-42, later Brooklyn Americans for 1941-42); **Oakland**—Seals (1967-76, also known as California Seals and Golden Seals and later Cleveland Barons from 1976-78); **Ottawa**—Senators (1917-31 and 1932-34, later St. Louis Eagles for 1934-35); **Philadelphia**—Quakers (1930-31, originally Pittsburgh Pirates from 1925-30); **Pittsburgh**—Pirates (1925-30, later Philadelphia Quakers for 1930-31); **Quebec**—Bulldogs (1919-20, later Hamilton Tigers from 1920-25); **St. Louis**—Eagles (1934-35), originally Ottawa Senators (1917-31 and 1932-34).

WHA Teams (1972-79)

Baltimore—Blades (1975); **Birmingham**—Bulls (1976-78); **Calgary**—Cowboys (1975-77); **Chicago**—Cougars (1972-75); **Cincinnati**—Stingers (1975-79); **Cleveland**—Crusaders (1972-76, moved to Minnesota); **Denver**—Spurs (1975-76, moved to Ottawa); **Edmonton**—Oilers (1972-79, originally called Alberta Oilers in 1972-73); **Houston**—Aeros (1972-78); **Indianapolis**—Racers (1974-78).

Los Angeles—Sharks (1972-74, moved to Michigan); **Michigan**—Stags (1974-75, moved to Baltimore); **Minnesota**—Fighting Saints (1972-76) and New Fighting Saints (1976-77); **New England**—Whalers (1972-79, played in Boston from 1972-74, West Springfield, MA from 1974-75, Hartford from 1975-78 and Springfield, MA in 1979); **New Jersey**—Knights (1973-74, moved to San Diego); **New York**—Raiders (1972-73, renamed Golden Blades in 1973, moved to New Jersey).

Ottawa—Nationals (1972-73, moved to Toronto) and Civics (1976); **Philadelphia**—Blazers (1972-73, moved to Vancouver); **Phoenix**—Roadrunners (1974-77); **Quebec**—Nordiques (1972-79); **San Diego**—Mariners (1974-77); **Toronto**—Toros (1973-76, moved to Birmingham, AL); **Vancouver**—Blazers (1973-75, moved to Calgary); **Winnipeg**—Jets (1972-79).

Annual NHL Leaders

Art Ross Trophy (Scoring)

Given to the player who leads the league in points scored and named after the former Boston Bruins general manager-coach. First presented in 1947, names of prior leading scorers have been added retroactively. A tie for the scoring championship is broken three ways: 1. total goals; 2. fewest games played; 3. first goal scored.

Multiple Winners: Wayne Gretzky (10); Gordie Howe and Mario Lemieux (6); Phil Esposito (5); Stan Mikita (4); Guy Lafleur (3); Max Bentley, Charlie Conacher, Bill Cook, Babe Dye, Bernie Geoffrion, Bobby Hull, Elmer Lach, Newsy Lalonde, Joe Malone, Dickie Moore, Howie Morenz, Bobby Orr and Sweeney Schriner (2).

Year		Gm	G	A	Pts	Year		Gm	G	A	Pts
1918	Joe Malone, Mon	20	44	0	44	1958	Dickie Moore, Mon	70	36	48	84
1919	Newsy Lalonde, Mon	17	23	9	32	1959	Dickie Moore, Mon	70	41	55	96
1920	Joe Malone, Que	24	39	6	45	1960	Bobby Hull, Chi	70	39	42	81
1921	Newsy Lalonde, Mon	24	33	8	41	1961	Bernie Geoffrion, Mon	64	50	45	95
1922	Punch Broadbent, Ott	24	32	14	46	1962	Bobby Hull, Chi.	70	50	34	84
1923	Babe Dye, Tor	22	26	11	37	1963	Gordie Howe, Det	70	38	48	86
1924	Cy Denneny, Ott	21	22	1	23	1964	Stan Mikita, Chi	70	39	50	89
1925	Babe Dye, Tor	29	38	6	44	1965	Stan Mikita, Chi	70	28	59	87
1926	Nels Stewart, Maroons	36	34	8	42	1966	Bobby Hull, Chi	65	54	43	97
1927	Bill Cook, NYR	44	33	4	37	1967	Stan Mikita, Chi	70	35	62	97
1928	Howie Morenz, Mon	43	33	18	51	1968	Stan Mikita, Chi	72	40	47	87
1929	Ace Bailey, Tor	44	22	10	32	1969	Phil Esposito, Bos	74	49	77	126
1930	Cooney Weiland, Bos	44	43	30	73	1970	Bobby Orr, Bos	76	33	87	120
1931	Howie Morenz, Mon	39	28	23	51	1971	Phil Esposito, Bos	78	76	76	152
1932	Busher Jackson, Tor	48	28	25	53	1972	Phil Esposito, Bos	76	66	67	133
1933	Bill Cook, NYR	48	28	22	50	1973	Phil Esposito, Bos	78	55	75	130
1934	Charlie Conacher, Tor	42	32	20	52	1974	Phil Esposito, Bos	78	68	77	145
1935	Charlie Conacher, Tor	47	36	21	57	1975	Bobby Orr, Bos	80	46	89	135
1936	Sweeney Schriner, NYA	48	19	26	45	1976	Guy Lafleur, Mon	80	56	69	125
1937	Sweeney Schriner, NYA	48	21	25	46	1977	Guy Lafleur, Mon	80	56	80	136
1938	Gordie Drillon, Tor	48	26	26	52	1978	Guy Lafleur, Mon	79	60	72	132
1939	Toe Blake, Mon	48	24	23	47	1979	Bryan Trottier, NYI	76	47	87	134
1940	Milt Schmidt, Bos	48	22	30	52	1980	Marcel Dionne, LA	80	53	84	137
1941	Bill Cowley, Bos	46	17	45	62	1981	Wayne Gretzky, Edm	80	55	109	164
1942	Bryan Hextall, NYR	48	24	32	56	1982	Wayne Gretzky, Edm	80	92	120	212
1943	Doug Bentley, Chi	50	33	40	73	1983	Wayne Gretzky, Edm	80	71	125	196
1944	Herbie Cain, Bos	48	36	46	82	1984	Wayne Gretzky, Edm	74	87	118	205
1945	Elmer Lach, Mon	50	26	54	80	1985	Wayne Gretzky, Edm	80	73	135	208
1946	Max Bentley, Chi	47	31	30	61	1986	Wayne Gretzky, Edm	80	52	163	215
1947	Max Bentley, Chi	60	29	43	72	1987	Wayne Gretzky, Edm	79	62	121	183
1948	Elmer Lach, Mon	60	30	31	61	1988	Mario Lemieux, Pit	77	70	98	168
1949	Roy Conacher, Chi	60	26	42	68	1989	Mario Lemieux, Pit	76	85	114	199
1950	Ted Lindsay, Det	69	23	55	78	1990	Wayne Gretzky, LA	73	40	102	142
1951	Gordie Howe, Det	70	43	43	86	1991	Wayne Gretzky, LA	78	41	122	163
1952	Gordie Howe, Det	70	47	39	86	1992	Mario Lemieux, Pit.	64	44	87	131
1953	Gordie Howe, Det	70	49	46	95	1993	Mario Lemieux, Pit.	60	69	91	160
1954	Gordie Howe, Det	70	33	48	81	1994	Wayne Gretzky, LA	81	38	92	130
1955	Bernie Geoffrion, Mon	70	38	37	75	1995	Jaromir Jagr, Pit	48	32	38	70
1956	Jean Beliveau, Mon	70	47	41	88	1996	Mario Lemieux, Pit	70	69	92	161
1957	Gordie Howe, Det	70	44	45	89	1997	Mario Lemieux, Pit	76	50	72	122

Note: The three times players have tied for total points in one season the player with more goals has won the trophy. In 1961-62, Hull outscored Andy Bathgate of NY Rangers, 50 goals to 28. In 1979-80, Dionne outscored Wayne Gretzky of Edmonton, 53-51. In 1995, Jagr outscored Eric Lindros of Philadelphia, 32-29.

NHL 500-Goal Scorers

Of the 500-goal scorers listed below, three (Gartner, Bobby Hull and Lemieux) went on to score over 600, two (Dionne and Esposito) scored over 700, and two (Gretzky and Howe) have scored over 800. Players active in 1997 are in **bold** type.

	Date	Game#		Date	Game#
Maurice Richard, Mon vs Chi	10/19/57	863	Lanny McDonald, Calg vs NYI	3/21/89	1107
Gordie Howe, Det at NYR	3/14/62	1045	Bryan Trottier, NYI vs Calg	2/13/90	1104
Bobby Hull, Chi vs NYR	2/21/70	861	**Mike Gartner,** NYR vs Wash	10/14/91	936
Jean Beliveau, Mon vs Min	2/11/71	1101	Michel Goulet, Chi vs Calg	2/16/92	951
Frank Mahovlich, Mon vs Van	3/21/73	1105	**Jari Kurri,** LA vs Bos	10/17/92	833
Phil Esposito, Bos vs Det	12/22/74	803	**Dino Ciccarelli,** Det at LA	1/8/94	946
John Bucyk, Bos vs St.L	10/30/75	1370	**Mario Lemieux,** Pit at NYI	10/26/95	605
Stan Mikita, Chi vs Van	2/27/77	1221	**Mark Messier,** NYR vs Calg	11/6/95	1141
Marcel Dionne, LA at Wash	12/14/82	887	**Steve Yzerman,** Det vs Col	1/17/96	906
Guy Lafleur, Mon at NJ	12/20/83	918	**Dale Hawerchuk,** St.L at Tor	1/31/96	1103
Mike Bossy, NYI vs Bos	1/2/86	647	**Brett Hull,** St.L vs LA	12/22/96	693
Gilbert Perreault, Buf vs NJ	3/9/86	1159	**Joe Mullen,** Pit at Col	3/14/97	1052
Wayne Gretzky, Edm vs Van	11/22/86	575	**Dave Andreychuk,** NJ vs Wash	3/15/97	1070

Goals

Multiple Winners: Bobby Hull (7); Phil Esposito (6); Charlie Conacher, Wayne Gretzky, Gordie Howe and Maurice Richard (5); Bill Cooke, Babe Dye, Brett Hull and Mario Lemieux (3); Jean Beliveau, Doug Bentley, Mike Bossy, Bernie Geoffrion, Bryan Hextall, Joe Malone and Nels Stewart (2).

Year		No	Year		No	Year		No
1918	Joe Malone, Mon	44	1944	Doug Bentley, Chi	38	1972	Phil Esposito, Bos	66
1919	Odie Cleghorn, Mon	23	1945	Maurice Richard, Mon	50	1973	Phil Esposito, Bos	55
	& Newsy Lalonde, Mon	23	1946	Gaye Stewart, Tor	37	1974	Phil Esposito, Bos	68
1920	Joe Malone, Que	39	1947	Maurice Richard, Mon	45	1975	Phil Esposito, Bos	61
1921	Babe Dye, Ham-Tor	35	1948	Ted Lindsay, Det	33	1976	Reggie Leach, Phi	61
1922	Punch Broadbent, Ott	32	1949	Sid Abel, Det	28	1977	Steve Shutt, Mon	60
1923	Babe Dye, Tor	26	1950	Maurice Richard, Mon	43	1978	Guy Lafleur, Mon	60
1924	Cy Denneny, Ott	22	1951	Gordie Howe, Det	43	1979	Mike Bossy, NYI	69
1925	Babe Dye, Tor	38	1952	Gordie Howe, Det	47	1980	Danny Gare, Buf	56
1926	Nels Stewart, Maroons	34	1953	Gordie Howe, Det	49		Charlie Simmer, LA	56
1927	Bill Cook, NYR	.33	1954	Maurice Richard, Mon	37		& Blaine Stoughton, Hart	56
1928	Howie Morenz, Mon	33	1955	Bernie Geoffrion, Mon	38	1981	Mike Bossy, NYI	68
1929	Ace Bailey, Tor	22		& Maurice Richard, Mon	38	1982	Wayne Gretzky, Edm	92
1930	Cooney Weiland, Bos	43	1956	Jean Beliveau, Mon	47	1983	Wayne Gretzky, Edm	71
1931	Charlie Conacher, Tor	31	1957	Gordie Howe, Det	44	1984	Wayne Gretzky, Edm	87
1932	Charlie Conacher, Tor	34	1958	Dickie Moore, Mon	36	1985	Wayne Gretzky, Edm	73
	& Bill Cook, NYR	34	1959	Jean Beliveau, Mon	45	1986	Jari Kurri, Edm	68
1933	Bill Cook, NYR	28	1960	Bronco Horvath, Bos	39	1987	Wayne Gretzky, Edm	62
1934	Charlie Conacher, Tor	32		& Bobby Hull, Chi	39	1988	Mario Lemieux, Pit	70
1935	Charlie Conacher, Tor	36	1961	Bernie Geoffrion, Mon	50	1989	Mario Lemieux, Pit	85
1936	Charlie Conacher, Tor	23	1962	Bobby Hull, Chi	50	1990	Brett Hull, St.L	72
	& Bill Thoms, Tor	23	1963	Gordie Howe, Det	38	1991	Brett Hull, St.L	86
1937	Larry Aurie, Det	23	1964	Bobby Hull, Chi	43	1992	Brett Hull, St.L	70
	& Nels Stewart, Bos-NYA	23	1965	Norm Ullman, Tor	42	1993	Alexander Mogilny, Buf	76
1938	Gordie Drillon, Tor	26	1966	Bobby Hull, Chi	54		& Teemu Selanne, Win	76
1939	Roy Conacher, Bos	26	1967	Bobby Hull, Chi	52	1994	Pavel Bure, Van	60
1940	Bryan Hextall, NYR	24	1968	Bobby Hull, Chi	44	1995	Peter Bondra, Wash	34
1941	Bryan Hextall, NYR	26	1969	Bobby Hull, Chi	58	1996	Mario Lemieux, Pit	69
1942	Lynn Patrick, NYR	32	1970	Phil Esposito, Bos	43	1997	Keith Tkachuk, Pho	52
1943	Doug Bentley, Chi	33	1971	Phil Esposito, Bos	76			

Assists

Multiple Winners: Wayne Gretzky (15); Bobby Orr (5); Frank Boucher, Bill Cowley, Phil Esposito, Gordie Howe, Elmer Lach, Mario Lemieux, Stan Mikita and Joe Primeau (3); Syl Apps, Andy Bathgate, Jean Beliveau, Doug Bentley, Art Chapman, Bobby Clarke, Ron Francis, Ted Lindsay, Bert Olmstead, Henri Richard and Bryan Trottier (2).

Year		No	Year		No	Year		No
1918	No official records kept.		1945	Elmer Lach, Mon	54	1972	Bobby Orr, Bos	80
1919	Newsy Lalonde, Mon	9	1946	Elmer Lach, Mon	34	1973	Phil Esposito, Bos	75
1920	Corbett Denneny, Tor	12	1947	Billy Taylor, Det	46	1974	Bobby Orr, Bos	90
1921	Louis Berlinquette, Mon	9	1948	Doug Bentley, Chi	37	1975	Bobby Clarke, Phi	89
	Harry Cameron, Tor	9	1949	Doug Bentley, Chi	43		& Bobby Orr, Bos	89
	& Joe Matte, Ham	9	1950	Ted Lindsay, Det	55	1976	Bobby Clarke, Phi	89
1922	Punch Broadbent, Ott	14	1951	Gordie Howe, Det	43	1977	Guy Lafleur, Mon	80
	& Leo Reise, Ham	14		& Teeder Kennedy, Tor	43	1978	Bryan Trottier, NYI	77
1923	Ed Bouchard, Ham	12	1952	Elmer Lach, Mon	50	1979	Bryan Trottier, NYI	87
1924	King Clancy, Ott	8	1953	Gordie Howe, Det	46	1980	Wayne Gretzky, Edm	86
1925	Cy Denneny, Ott	15	1954	Gordie Howe, Det	48	1981	Wayne Gretzky, Edm	109
1926	Frank Nighbor, Ott	13	1955	Bert Olmstead, Mon	48	1982	Wayne Gretzky, Edm	120
1927	Dick Irvin, Chi	18	1956	Bert Olmstead, Mon	56	1983	Wayne Gretzky, Edm	125
1928	Howie Morenz, Mon	18	1957	Ted Lindsay, Det	55	1984	Wayne Gretzky, Edm	118
1929	Frank Boucher, NYR	16	1958	Henri Richard, Mon	52	1985	Wayne Gretzky, Edm	135
1930	Frank Boucher, NYR	36	1959	Dickie Moore, Mon	55	1986	Wayne Gretzky, Edm	163
1931	Joe Primeau, Tor	32	1960	Don McKenney, Bos	49	1987	Wayne Gretzky, Edm	121
1932	Joe Primeau, Tor	37	1961	Jean Beliveau, Mon	58	1988	Wayne Gretzky, Edm	109
1933	Frank Boucher, NYR	28	1962	Andy Bathgate, NYR	56	1989	Wayne Gretzky, LA	114
1934	Joe Primeau, Tor	32	1963	Henri Richard, Mon	50		& Mario Lemieux, Pit	114
1935	Art Chapman, NYA	34	1964	Andy Bathgate, NYR-Tor	58	1990	Wayne Gretzky, LA	102
1936	Art Chapman, NYA	28	1965	Stan Mikita, Chi	59	1991	Wayne Gretzky, LA	122
1937	Syl Apps, Tor	29	1966	Jean Beliveau, Mon	48	1992	Wayne Gretzky, LA	90
1938	Syl Apps, Tor	29		Stan Mikita, Chi	48	1993	Adam Oates, Bos	97
1939	Bill Cowley, Bos	34		& Bobby Rousseau, Mon	48	1994	Wayne Gretzky, LA	92
1940	Milt Schmidt, Bos	30	1967	Stan Mikita, Chi	62	1995	Ron Francis, Pit	48
1941	Bill Cowley, Bos	45	1968	Phil Esposito, Bos	49	1996	Ron Francis, Pit	92
1942	Phil Watson, NYR	37	1969	Phil Esposito, Bos	77		& Mario Lemieux, Pit	92
1943	Bill Cowley, Bos	45	1970	Bobby Orr, Bos	87	1997	Mario Lemieux, Pit	72
1944	Clint Smith, Chi	49	1971	Bobby Orr, Bos	102		& Wayne Gretzky, NYR	72

Goals Against Average

Average determined by games played through 1942-43 season and by minutes played since then. Minimum of 15 games from 1917-18 season through 1925-26; minimum of 25 games since 1926-27 season. Not to be confused with the Vezina Trophy. Goaltenders who posted the season's lowest goals against average, but did not win the Vezina are in **bold** type.

Multiple Winners: Jacques Plante (9); Clint Benedict and Bill Durnan (6); Johnny Bower, Ken Dryden and Tiny Thompson (4); Patrick Roy and Georges Vezina (3); Frankie Brimsek, Turk Broda, George Hainsworth, Harry Lumley, Bernie Parent, Pete Peeters and Terry Sawchuk (2).

Year		GAA	Year		GAA	Year		GAA
1918	Georges Vezina, Mon	3.82	1945	Bill Durnan, Mon	2.42	1972	Tony Esposito, Chi	1.77
1919	Clint Benedict, Ott	2.94	1946	Bill Durnan, Mon	2.60	1973	Ken Dryden, Mon	2.26
1920	Clint Benedict, Ott	2.67	1947	Bill Durnan, Mon	2.30	1974	Bernie Parent, Phi	1.89
1921	Clint Benedict, Ott	3.13	1948	Turk Broda, Tor	2.38	1975	Bernie Parent, Phi	2.03
1922	Clint Benedict, Ott	3.50	1949	Bill Durnan, Mon	2.10	1976	Ken Dryden, Mon	2.03
1923	Clint Benedict, Ott	2.25	1950	Bill Durnan, Mon	2.20	1977	Bunny Larocque, Mon	2.09
1924	Georges Vezina, Mon	2.00	1951	Al Rollins, Tor	1.77	1978	Ken Dryden, Mon	2.05
1925	Georges Vezina, Mon	1.87	1952	Terry Sawchuk, Det	1.90	1979	Ken Dryden, Mon	2.30
1926	Alex Connell, Ott	1.17	1953	Terry Sawchuk, Det	1.90	1980	Bob Sauve, Buf	2.36
1927	**Clint Benedict,** Mon-M	1.51	1954	Harry Lumley, Tor	1.86	1981	Richard Sevigny, Mon	2.40
1928	Geo. Hainsworth, Mon	1.09	1955	**Harry Lumley,** Tor	1.94	1982	**Denis Herron,** Mon	2.64
1929	Geo. Hainsworth, Mon	0.98	1956	Jacques Plante, Mon	1.86	1983	Pete Peeters, Bos	2.36
1930	Tiny Thompson, Bos	2.23	1957	Jacques Plante, Mon	2.02	1984	**Pat Riggin,** Wash	2.66
1931	Roy Worters, NYA	1.68	1958	Jacques Plante, Mon	2.11	1985	**Tom Barrasso,** Buf	2.66
1932	Chuck Gardiner, Chi	1.92	1959	Jacques Plante, Mon	2.16	1986	**Bob Froese,** Phi	2.55
1933	Tiny Thompson, Bos	1.83	1960	Jacques Plante, Mon	2.54	1987	**Brian Hayward,** Mon	2.81
1934	**Wilf Cude,** Det-Mon	1.57	1961	Johnny Bower, Tor	2.50	1988	**Pete Peeters,** Wash	2.78
1935	Lorne Chabot, Chi	1.83	1962	Jacques Plante, Mon	2.37	1989	Patrick Roy, Mon	2.47
1936	Tiny Thompson, Bos	1.71	1963	**Jacques Plante,** Mon	2.49	1990	**Mike Liut,** Hart-Wash	2.53
1937	Norm Smith, Det	2.13	1964	**Johnny Bower,** Tor	2.11	1991	Ed Belfour, Chi	2.47
1938	Tiny Thompson, Bos	1.85	1965	Johnny Bower, Tor	2.38	1992	Patrick Roy, Mon	2.36
1939	Frankie Brimsek, Bos	1.58	1966	**Johnny Bower,** Tor	2.25	1993	**Felix Potvin,** Tor	2.50
1940	Dave Kerr, NYR	1.60	1967	Glenn Hall, Chi	2.38	1994	Dominik Hasek, Buf	1.95
1941	Turk Broda, Tor	2.06	1968	Gump Worsley, Mon	1.98	1995	Dominik Hasek, Buf	2.11
1942	Frankie Brimsek, Bos	2.45	1969	**Jacques Plante,** St.L	1.96	1996	**Ron Hextall,** Phi	2.17
1943	John Mowers, Det	2.47	1970	**Ernie Wakely,** St.L	2.11	1997	**Martin Brodeur,** NJ	1.88
1944	Bill Durnan, Mon	2.18	1971	**Jacques Plante,** Tor	1.88			

Penalty Minutes

Multiple Winners: Red Horner (8); Gus Mortson and Dave Schultz (4); Bert Corbeau, Lou Fontinato and Tiger Williams (3); Billy Boucher, Carl Brewer, Red Dutton, Pat Egan, Bill Ezinicki, Joe Hall, Tim Hunter, Keith Magnuson, Chris Nilan and Jimmy Orlando (2).

Year		Min	Year		Min	Year		Min
1918	Joe Hall, Mon	60	1945	Pat Egan, Bos	86	1972	Bryan Watson, Pit	212
1919	Joe Hall, Mon	85	1946	Jack Stewart, Det	73	1973	Dave Schultz, Phi	259
1920	Cully Wilson, Tor	79	1947	Gus Mortson, Tor	133	1974	Dave Schultz, Phi	348
1921	Bert Corbeau, Mon	86	1948	Bill Barilko, Tor	147	1975	Dave Schultz, Phi	472
1922	Sprague Cleghorn, Mon	63	1949	Bill Ezinicki, Tor	145	1976	Steve Durbano, Pit-KC	370
1923	Billy Boucher, Mon	52	1950	Bill Ezinicki, Tor	144	1977	Tiger Williams, Tor	338
1924	Bert Corbeau, Tor	55	1951	Gus Mortson, Tor	142	1978	Dave Schultz, LA-Pit	405
1925	Billy Boucher, Mon	92	1952	Gus Kyle, Bos	127	1979	Tiger Williams, Tor	298
1926	Bert Corbeau, Tor	121	1953	Maurice Richard, Mon	112	1980	Jimmy Mann, Win	287
1927	Nels Stewart, Mon-M	133	1954	Gus Mortson, Chi	132	1981	Tiger Williams, Van	343
1928	Eddie Shore, Bos	165	1955	Fern Flaman, Bos	150	1982	Paul Baxter, Pit	409
1929	Red Dutton, Mon-M	139	1956	Lou Fontinato, NYR	202	1983	Randy Holt, Wash	275
1930	Joe Lamb, Ott	119	1957	Gus Mortson, Chi	147	1984	Chris Nilan, Mon	338
1931	Harvey Rockburn, Det	118	1958	Lou Fontinato, NYR	152	1985	Chris Nilan, Mon	358
1932	Red Dutton, NYA	107	1959	Ted Lindsay, Chi	184	1986	Joey Kocur, Det	377
1933	Red Horner, Tor	144	1960	Carl Brewer, Tor	150	1987	Tim Hunter, Calg	361
1934	Red Horner, Tor	146	1961	Pierre Pilote, Chi	165	1988	Bob Probert, Det	398
1935	Red Horner, Tor	125	1962	Lou Fontinato, Mon	167	1989	Tim Hunter, Calg	375
1936	Red Horner, Tor	167	1963	Howie Young, Det	273	1990	Basil McRae, Min	351
1937	Red Horner, Tor	124	1964	Vic Hadfield, NYR	151	1991	Rob Ray, Buf	350
1938	Red Horner, Tor	82	1965	Carl Brewer, Tor	177	1992	Mike Peluso, Chi	408
1939	Red Horner, Tor	85	1966	Reg Fleming, Bos-NYR	166	1993	Marty McSorley, LA	399
1940	Red Horner, Tor	87	1967	John Ferguson, Mon	177	1994	Tie Domi, Win	347
1941	Jimmy Orlando, Det	99	1968	Barclay Plager, St.L	153	1995	Enrico Ciccone, TB	225
1942	Pat Egan, NYA	124	1969	Forbes Kennedy, Phi-Tor	219	1996	Matthew Barnaby, Buf	335
1943	Jimmy Orlando, Det	99	1970	Keith Magnuson, Chi	213	1997	Gino Odjick, Van	371
1944	Mike McMahon, Mon	98	1971	Keith Magnuson, Chi	291			

All-Time NHL Regular Season Leaders
Through 1997 regular season.
CAREER
Players active during 1997 season in **bold** type.

Points

		Yrs	Gm	G	A	Pts
1	**Wayne Gretzky** ...	18	1335	862	1843	2705
2	Gordie Howe	26	1767	801	1049	1850
3	Marcel Dionne	18	1348	731	1040	1771
4	Phil Esposito	18	1282	717	873	1590
5	**Mark Messier**	18	1272	575	977	1552
6	**Mario Lemieux**	12	745	613	881	1494
7	Stan Mikita	22	1394	541	926	1467
8	**Paul Coffey**	17	1211	381	1063	1444
9	Bryan Trottier	18	1279	524	901	1425
10	**Dale Hawerchuk** ..	16	1188	518	891	1409
11	**Jari Kurri**	16	1181	596	780	1376
12	John Bucyk	23	1540	556	813	1369
13	**Ray Bourque**	18	1290	362	1001	1363
14	Guy Lafleur	17	1126	560	793	1353
15	**Ron Francis**	16	1166	403	944	1347
16	**Steve Yzerman**	14	1023	539	801	1340
17	**Denis Savard**	17	1196	473	865	1338
18	Gilbert Perreault	17	1191	512	814	1326
19	**Mike Gartner**	18	1372	696	612	1308
20	Alex Delvecchio	24	1549	456	825	1281
21	Jean Ratelle	21	1281	491	776	1267
22	Peter Stastny	15	977	450	789	1239
23	Norm Ullman	20	1410	490	739	1229
24	Jean Beliveau	20	1125	507	712	1219
25	Bobby Clarke	15	1144	358	852	1210
26	**Bernie Nicholls**	16	1057	469	710	1179
27	Bobby Hull	16	1063	610	560	1170
28	**Dino Ciccarelli**	17	1156	586	574	1160
29	Michel Goulet	15	1089	548	604	1152
30	Bernie Federko	14	1000	369	761	1130

Goals

		Yrs	Gm	No
1	**Wayne Gretzky**	18	1335	862
2	Gordie Howe	26	1767	801
3	Marcel Dionne	18	1348	731
4	Phil Esposito	18	1282	717
5	**Mike Gartner**	18	1372	696
6	**Mario Lemieux**	12	745	613
7	Bobby Hull	16	1063	610
8	**Jari Kurri**	16	1181	596
9	**Dino Ciccarelli**	17	1156	586
10	**Mark Messier**	18	1272	575
11	Mike Bossy	10	752	573
12	Guy Lafleur	17	1126	560
13	John Bucyk	23	1540	556
14	Michel Goulet	15	1089	548
15	Maurice Richard	18	978	544
16	Stan Mikita	22	1394	541
17	**Steve Yzerman**	14	1023	539
18	Frank Mahovlich	18	1181	533
19	**Brett Hull**	11	735	527
20	Bryan Trottier	18	1279	524
21	**Dale Hawerchuk**	16	1188	518
22	Gilbert Perreault	17	1191	512
23	Jean Beliveau	20	1125	507
24	**Dave Andreychuk**	15	1083	503
25	**Joe Mullen**	17	1062	502
26	Lanny McDonald	16	1111	500
27	Glenn Anderson	16	1128	498
28	Jean Ratelle	21	1281	491
29	Norm Ullman	20	1410	490
30	Darryl Sittler	15	1096	484

Assists

		Yrs	Gm	No
1	**Wayne Gretzky**	18	1335	1843
2	**Paul Coffey**	17	1211	1063
3	Gordie Howe	26	1767	1049
4	Marcel Dionne	18	1348	1040
5	**Ray Bourque**	18	1290	1001
6	**Mark Messier**	18	1272	977
7	**Ron Francis**	16	1166	944
8	Stan Mikita	22	1394	926
9	Bryan Trottier	18	1279	901
10	**Dale Hawerchuk**	16	1188	891
11	**Mario Lemieux**	12	745	881
12	Phil Esposito	18	1281	873
13	**Denis Savard**	17	1196	865
14	Bobby Clarke	15	1144	852
15	Alex Delvecchio	24	1549	825
16	Gilbert Perreault	17	1191	814
17	John Bucyk	23	1540	813
18	**Steve Yzerman**	14	1023	801
19	**Larry Murphy**	17	1313	797
20	Guy Lafleur	17	1126	793

Penalty Minutes

		Yrs	Gm	Min
1	Tiger Williams	14	962	3966
2	**Dale Hunter**	17	1263	3343
3	**Tim Hunter**	16	815	3146
4	**Marty McSorley**	14	832	3078
5	Chris Nilan	13	688	3043
6	**Bob Probert**	11	634	2653
7	Willi Plett	12	834	2572
8	**Rick Tocchet**	13	841	2469
9	**Basil McRae**	16	576	2457
10	Pat Verbeek	15	1065	2362
11	**Scott Stevens**	15	1120	2360
12	**Jay Wells**	18	1098	2359
13	**Joey Kocur**	13	718	2340

NHL-WHA Top 15

All-Time regular season scoring leaders, including games played in World Hockey Association (1972-79). NHL players with WHA experience are listed in CAPITAL letters. Players active during 1997 are in **bold** type.

Points

		Yrs	G	A	Pts
1	**WAYNE GRETZKY** ..	19	908	1907	2815
2	GORDIE HOWE	32	975	1383	2358
3	BOBBY HULL	23	913	895	1808
4	Marcel Dionne	18	731	1040	1771
5	Phil Esposito	18	717	873	1590
6	**MARK MESSIER**	19	576	987	1563
7	**Mario Lemieux**	12	613	881	1494
8	Stan Mikita	22	541	926	1467
9	**Paul Coffey**	17	381	1063	1444
10	Bryan Trottier	18	524	901	1425
11	**Dale Hawerchuk** ...	16	512	891	1409
12	**Jari Kurri**	16	596	780	1376
13	John Bucyk	23	556	813	1369
14	NORM ULLMAN	22	537	822	1359
15	Guy Lafleur	17	560	793	1353

WHA Totals: GRETZKY (1 yr, 80 gm, 46-64—110); HOWE (6 yrs, 419 gm, 174-334—508); HULL (7 yrs, 411 gm, 303-335—638); MESSIER (1 yr, 52 gm, 1-10—11); ULLMAN (2 yrs, 144 gm, 47-83—130).

Years Played

		Yrs	Career	Gm
1	Gordie Howe	26	1946-71, 79-80	1767
2	Alex Delvecchio	24	1950-74	1549
	Tim Horton	24	1949-50, 51-74	1446
4	John Bucyk	23	1955-78	1540
5	Stan Mikita	22	1958-80	1394
	Doug Mohns	22	1953-75	1390
	Dean Prentice	22	1952-74	1378
8	Harry Howell	21	1952-73	1411
	Ron Stewart	21	1952-73	1353
	Jean Ratelle	21	1960-81	1281
	Allan Stanley	21	1948-69	1244
	Eric Nesterenko	21	1951-72	1219
	Marcel Pronovost	21	1950-70	1206
	George Armstrong	21	1949-50, 51-71	1187
	Terry Sawchuk	21	1949-70	971
	Gump Worsley	21	1952-53, 54-74	862

Note: Combined NHL-WHA years played: Howe (32); Howell (24); Bobby Hull (23); Norm Ullman, Nesterenko, Frank Mahovlich and Dave Keon (22).

Games Played

		Yrs	Career	Gm
1	Gordie Howe	26	1946-71, 79-80	1767
2	Alex Delvecchio	24	1950-74	1549
3	John Bucyk	23	1955-78	1540
4	Tim Horton	24	1949-50, 51-74	1446
5	Harry Howell	21	1952-73	1411
6	Norm Ullman	20	1955-75	1410
7	Stan Mikita	22	1958-80	1394
8	Doug Mohns	22	1953-75	1390
9	Larry Robinson	20	1972-92	1384
10	Dean Prentice	22	1952-74	1378
11	**Mike Gartner**	18	1979—	1372
12	Ron Stewart	21	1952-73	1353
13	Marcel Dionne	18	1971-89	1348
14	**Wayne Gretzky**	18	1979—	1335
15	Red Kelly	20	1947-67	1316

Note: Combined NHL-WHA games played: Howe (2,186), Dave Keon (1,597), Howell (1,581), Ullman (1,554), Bobby Hull (1,474), Frank Mahovlich (1,418) and Gretzky (1,415).

Goaltending

Wins

		Yrs	Gm	W	L	T	Pct
1	Terry Sawchuk	21	971	**435**	337	188	.551
2	Jacques Plante	18	837	**434**	246	137	.615
3	Tony Esposito	16	886	**423**	307	151	.566
4	Glenn Hall	18	906	**407**	327	165	.544
5	Rogie Vachon	16	795	**355**	291	115	.542
6	**Andy Moog**	17	671	**354**	192	83	.629
7	**Grant Fuhr**	16	748	**353**	250	98	.573
8	**Patrick Roy**	12	652	**349**	205	74	.615
9	Gump Worsley	21	862	**335**	353	150	.489
10	Harry Lumley	16	804	**332**	324	143	.505
11	Billy Smith	18	680	**305**	233	105	.556
12	Turk Broda	12	629	**302**	224	101	.562
13	**Mike Vernon**	14	662	**301**	179	65	.612
14	**Tom Barrasso**	14	602	**295**	218	63	.567
15	Mike Liut	13	663	**293**	271	74	.517
16	Ed Giacomin	13	610	**289**	206	97	.570
17	**J. Vanbiesbrouck**	15	657	**288**	256	79	.526
18	Dan Bouchard	14	655	**286**	232	113	.543
19	Tiny Thompson	12	553	**284**	194	75	.581
20	Bernie Parent	13	608	**270**	197	121	.562
	Gilles Meloche	18	788	**270**	351	131	.446

Losses

		Yrs	Gm	W	L	T	Pct
1	Gump Worsley	21	862	335	**353**	150	.489
2	Gilles Meloche	18	788	270	**351**	131	.446
3	Terry Sawchuk	21	971	435	**337**	188	.551
4	Glenn Hall	18	906	407	**327**	165	.544
5	Harry Lumley	16	804	332	**324**	143	.505

Goals Against Average
Minimum of 300 games played.

Before 1950

		Gm	Min	GA	GAA
1	George Hainsworth	465	29,415	937	1.91
2	Alex Connell	416	26,030	837	2.01
3	Chuck Gardiner	316	19,687	664	2.02
4	Lorne Chabot	412	25,309	861	2.04
5	Tiny Thompson	552	34,174	1183	2.08

Since 1950

		Gm	Min	GA	GAA
1	Ken Dryden	397	23,352	870	2.24
2	Jacques Plante	837	49,633	1965	2.38
3	Glenn Hall	906	53,484	2239	2.51
4	Terry Sawchuk	971	57,205	2401	2.52
5	Johnny Bower	552	32,077	1347	2.52

Shutouts

		Yrs	Games	No
1	Terry Sawchuk	21	971	103
2	George Hainsworth	11	464	94
3	Glenn Hall	18	906	84
4	Jacques Plante	18	837	82
5	Alex Connell	12	417	81
	Tiny Thompson	12	553	81
7	Tony Esposito	16	886	76
8	Lorne Chabot	11	411	73
9	Harry Lumley	16	804	71
10	Roy Worters	12	484	66
11	Turk Broda	14	629	62
12	John Roach	14	492	58
13	Clint Benedict	13	362	57
14	Bernie Parent	13	608	55
15	Ed Giacomin	13	610	54

NHL-WHA Top 15

All-Time regular season wins leaders, including games played in World Hockey Association (1972-79). NHL goaltenders with WHA experience are listed in CAPITAL letters. Players active during 1997 are in **bold** type.

Wins

		Yrs	W	L	T	Pct
1	JACQUES PLANTE	19	449	260	138	.612
2	Terry Sawchuk	21	435	337	188	.551
3	Tony Esposito	16	423	307	151	.566
4	Glenn Hall	18	407	327	165	.544
5	Rogie Vachon	16	355	291	115	.542
6	**Andy Moog**	17	354	192	83	.629
7	**Grant Fuhr**	16	353	250	98	.573
8	**Patrick Roy**	12	349	205	74	.615
9	Gump Worsley	21	335	353	150	.489
10	Harry Lumley	16	332	324	143	.505
11	GERRY CHEEVERS	16	329	172	83	.634
12	MIKE LIUT	15	324	310	78	.510
13	Billy Smith	18	305	233	105	.556
14	BERNIE PARENT	14	303	225	121	.560
15	Turk Broda	12	302	224	101	.562

WHA Totals: CHEEVERS (4 yrs, 191 gm, 99-78-9); LIUT (2 yrs, 81 gm, 31-39-4); PARENT (1 yr, 63 gm, 33-28-0); PLANTE (1 yr, 31 gm, 15-14-1).

All-Time NHL Regular Season Leaders (Cont.)
SINGLE SEASON

Scoring
Points

		Season	G	A	Pts
1	Wayne Gretzky, Edm ...	1985-86	52	163	215
2	Wayne Gretzky, Edm ...	1981-82	92	120	212
3	Wayne Gretzky, Edm ...	1984-85	73	135	208
4	Wayne Gretzky, Edm ...	1983-84	87	118	205
5	Mario Lemieux, Pit	1988-89	85	114	199
6	Wayne Gretzky, Edm ...	1982-83	71	125	196
7	Wayne Gretzky, Edm ...	1986-87	62	121	183
8	Mario Lemieux, Pit	1987-88	70	98	168
9	Wayne Gretzky, LA	1988-89	54	114	168
10	Wayne Gretzky, Edm ...	1980-81	55	109	164
11	Wayne Gretzky, LA	1990-91	41	122	163
12	Mario Lemieux, Pit	1995-96	69	92	161
13	Mario Lemieux, Pit	1992-93	69	91	160
14	Steve Yzerman, Det	1988-89	65	90	155
15	Phil Esposito, Bos	1970-71	76	76	152
16	Bernie Nicholls, LA	1988-89	70	80	150
17	Jaromir Jagr, Pit	1995-96	62	87	149
	Wayne Gretzky, Edm ...	1987-88	40	109	149
19	Pat LaFontaine, Buf	1992-93	53	95	148
20	Mike Bossy, NYI	1981-82	64	83	147

WHA 150 points or more: 154—Marc Tardif, Que. (1977-78).

Goals

		Season	Gm	No
1	Wayne Gretzky, Edm	1981-82	80	92
2	Wayne Gretzky, Edm	1983-84	74	87
3	Brett Hull, St.L	1990-91	78	86
4	Mario Lemieux, Pit	1988-89	76	85
5	Alexander Mogilny, Buf	1992-93	77	76
	Phil Esposito, Bos	1970-71	78	76
	Teemu Selanne, Win	1992-93	84	76
8	Wayne Gretzky, Edm	1984-85	80	73
9	Brett Hull, St.L	1989-90	80	72
10	Jari Kurri, Edm	1984-85	73	71
	Wayne Gretzky, Edm	1982-83	80	71
12	Brett Hull, St.L	1991-92	73	70
	Mario Lemieux, Pit	1987-88	77	70
	Bernie Nicholls, LA	1988-89	79	70
15	Mario Lemieux, Pit	1992-93	60	69
	Mario Lemieux, Pit	1995-96	70	69
	Mike Bossy, NYI	1978-79	80	69
18	Phil Esposito, Bos	1973-74	78	68
	Jari Kurri, Edm	1985-86	78	68
	Mike Bossy, NYI	1980-81	79	68

WHA 70 goals or more: 77—Bobby Hull, Win. (1974-75); 75—Real Cloutier, Que. (1978-79); 71—Marc Tardif, Que. (1975-76); 70—Anders Hedberg, Win. (1976-77).

Assists

		Season	Gm	No
1	Wayne Gretzky, Edm	1985-86	80	163
2	Wayne Gretzky, Edm	1984-85	80	135
3	Wayne Gretzky, Edm	1982-83	80	125
4	Wayne Gretzky, LA	1990-91	78	122
5	Wayne Gretzky, Edm	1986-87	79	121
6	Wayne Gretzky, Edm	1981-82	80	120
7	Wayne Gretzky, Edm	1983-84	74	118
8	Mario Lemieux, Pit	1988-89	76	114
	Wayne Gretzky, LA	1988-89	78	114
10	Wayne Gretzky, Edm	1987-88	64	109
	Wayne Gretzky, Edm	1980-81	80	109
12	Wayne Gretzky, LA	1989-90	73	102
	Bobby Orr, Bos	1970-71	78	102
14	Mario Lemieux, Pit	1987-88	77	98
	Adam Oates, Bos	1992-93	84	97

WHA 95 assists or more: 106—Andre Lacroix, S.Diego (1974-75).

Goaltending
Wins

		Season	Record
1	Bernie Parent, Phi	1973-74	47-13-12
2	Bernie Parent, Phi	1974-75	44-14- 9
	Terry Sawchuk, Det	1950-51	44-13-13
	Terry Sawchuk, Det	1951-52	44-14-12
5	Tom Barrasso, Pit	1992-93	43-14- 5
	Ed Belfour, Chi	1990-91	43-19- 7
7	Jacques Plante, Mon	1955-56	42-12-10
	Jacques Plante, Mon	1961-62	42-14-14
	Ken Dryden, Mon	1975-76	42-10- 8
	Mike Richter, NYR	1993-94	42-12- 6

Most WHA wins in one season: 44—Richard Brodeur, Que. (1975-76).

Losses

		Season	Record
1	Gary Smith, Cal	1970-71	19-48- 4
2	Al Rollins, Chi	1953-54	12-47- 7
3	Peter Sidorkiewicz, Ott	1992-93	8-46- 3
4	Harry Lumley, Chi	1951-52	17-44- 9
5	Harry Lumley, Chi	1950-51	12-41-10
	Craig Billington, Ott	1993-94	11-41- 4

Most WHA losses in one season: 36—Don McLeod, Van. (1974-75) and Andy Brown, Ind. (1974-75).

Shutouts

		Season	Gm	No
1	George Hainsworth, Mon	1928-29	44	22
2	Alex Connell, Ottawa	1925-26	36	15
	Alex Connell, Ottawa	1927-28	44	15
	Hal Winkler, Bos	1927-28	44	15
	Tony Esposito, Chi	1969-70	63	15

Most WHA shutouts in one season: 5—Gerry Cheevers, Cle. (1972-73) and Joe Daly, Win. (1975-76).

Goals Against Average
Before 1950

		Season	Gm	GAA
1	George Hainsworth, Mon	1928-29	44	0.98
2	George Hainsworth, Mon	1927-28	44	1.09
3	Alex Connell, Ottawa	1925-26	36	1.17
4	Tiny Thompson, Bos	1928-29	44	1.18
5	Roy Worters, NY Americans ..	1928-29	38	1.21

Since 1950

		Season	Gm	GAA
1	Tony Esposito, Chi	1971-72	48	1.77
2	Al Rollins, Chi	1950-51	40	1.77
3	Harry Lumley, Tor	1953-54	69	1.86
4	Jacques Plante, Mon	1955-56	64	1.86
5	**Martin Brodeur**, NJ	1996-97	67	1.88

Penalty Minutes

		Season	PM
1	Dave Schultz, Phi	1974-75	472
2	Paul Baxter, Pit	1981-82	409
3	Mike Peluso, Chi	1991-92	408
4	Dave Schultz, LA-Pit	1977-78	405
5	Marty McSorley, LA	1992-93	399
6	Bob Probert, Det	1987-88	398
7	Basil McRae, Min	1987-88	382
8	Joey Kocur, Det	1985-86	377
9	Tim Hunter, Calg	1988-89	375
10	Gino Odjick, Van	1996-97	371

WHA 355 minutes or more: 365—Curt Brackenbury, Min-Que. (1975-76).

SINGLE GAME
Scoring

Points		Date	G-A—Pts
Darryl Sittler, Tor vs Bos.	....	2/7/76	6-4—10
Maurice Richard, Mon vs Det	......	12/28/44	5-3—8
Bert Olmstead, Mon vs Chi.	....	1/9/54	4-4—8
Tom Bladon, Phi vs Cle.	....	12/11/77	4-4—8
Bryan Trottier, NYI vs NYR	....	12/23/78	5-3—8
Peter Stastny, Que at Wash	....	2/22/81	4-4—8
Anton Stastny, Que at Wash	....	2/22/81	3-5—8
Wayne Gretzky, Edm vs NJ	....	11/19/83	3-5—8
Wayne Gretzky, Edm vs Min	....	1/4/84	4-4—8
Paul Coffey, Edm vs Det	....	3/14/86	2-6—8
Mario Lemieux, Pit vs St.L	....	10/15/88	2-6—8
Bernie Nicholls, LA vs Tor	....	12/1/88	2-6—8
Mario Lemieux, Pit vs NJ	....	12/31/88	5-3—8

Goals		Date	No
Joe Malone, Que vs Tor	....	1/31/20	7
Newsy Lalonde, Mon vs Tor	....	1/10/20	6
Joe Malone, Que vs Ott	....	3/10/20	6
Corb Denneny, Tor vs Ham	....	1/26/21	6
Cy Denneny, Ott vs Ham	....	3/7/21	6
Syd Howe, Det vs NYR	....	2/3/44	6
Red Berenson, St.L at Phi	....	11/7/68	6
Darryl Sittler, Tor vs Bos	....	2/7/76	6

Assists		Date	No
Billy Taylor, Det at Chi.	....	3/16/47	7
Wayne Gretzky, Edm vs Wash	....	2/15/80	7
Wayne Gretzky, Edm at Chi	....	12/11/85	7
Wayne Gretzky, Edm vs Que	....	2/14/86	7
24 players tied with 6 each.			

THE GREAT ONE: FOR THE RECORD

NY Rangers center Wayne Gretzky broke Gordie Howe's all-time NHL regular season goal-scoring record with his 802nd goal on Mar. 23, 1994. The record was the 60th league mark he has either tied or set outright. Gretzky will enter the 1997-98 regular season with 862 goals, 1,843 assists and 2,705 points—all league career records.

Year by Year Statistics

Season	Age	Club	Regular Season					Playoffs					Awards
			Gm	G	A	Pts	PM	Gm	G	A	Pts	PM	
1978-79	18	Indianapolis	8	3	3	6	0	—	—	—	—	—	
		Edmonton	72	43	61	104	19	13	10*	10	20*	2	WHA Top Rookie
1979-80	19	Edmonton	79	51	86*	137†	21	3	2	1	3	0	Hart, Byng
1980-81	20	Edmonton	80	55	109*	164*	28	9	7	14	21	4	Hart, Ross
1981-82	21	Edmonton	80	92*	120*	212*	26	5	5	7	12	8	Hart, Ross
1982-83	22	Edmonton	80	71*	125*	196*	59	16	12	26*	38*	4	Hart, Ross
1983-84	23	Edmonton	74	87*	118*	205*	39	19	13	22*	35*	12	Hart, Ross
1984-85	24	Edmonton	80	73*	135*	208*	52	18	17	30*	47*	4	Hart, Ross & Smythe
1985-86	25	Edmonton	80	52	163*	215*	46	10	8	11	19	2	Hart, Ross
1986-87	26	Edmonton	79	62*	121*	183*	28	21	5	29*	34*	6	Hart, Ross
1987-88	27	Edmonton	64	40	109*	149	24	19	12	31*	43*	16	Smythe
1988-89	28	Los Angeles	78	54	114†	168	26	11	5	17	22	0	Hart
1989-90	29	Los Angeles	73	40	102*	142*	42	7	3	7	10	0	Ross
1990-91	30	Los Angeles	78	41	122*	163*	16	12	4	11	15	2	Ross, Byng
1991-92	31	Los Angeles	74	31	90*	121	34	6	2	5	7	2	Byng
1992-93	32	Los Angeles	45	16	49	65	6	24	15*	25*	40*	4	—
1993-94	33	Los Angeles	81	38	92*	130*	20	—	—	—	—	—	Byng
1995	34	Los Angeles	48	11	37	48	6	—	—	—	—	—	—
1995-96	35	LA, St. Louis	80	23	79	102	34	13	2	14	16	0	—
1996-97	36	NY Rangers	82	25	72†	97	28	15	10	10	20	2	—
		WHA totals	80	46	64	110	19	13	10	10	20	2	
		NHL totals	1335	862	1843	2705	535	208	122	260	382	66	

*Led league; †Tied for league lead

Gretzky vs. Howe

The all-time records of Wayne Gretzky and Gordie Howe, pro hockey's two most prolific scorers. Below are their career records in the NHL, the WHA and the two leagues combined. Howe played with Detroit (1946-71) and Hartford (1979-80) in the NHL and with Houston (1973-77) and New England (1977-79) in the WHA.

NHL	Yrs	Regular Season					Playoffs					Stanley Cups
		Gm	G	A	Pts	PM	Yrs	Gm	G	A	Pts	PM
Wayne Gretzky	18	1335	862	1843	2705	535	16	208	122	260	382	66	4 (1984-85,87-88)
Gordie Howe	26	1767	801	1049	1850	1685	20	157	68	92	160	220	4 (1950,52,54-55)

WHA	Yrs	Regular Season					Playoffs					AVCO World Cups
		Gm	G	A	Pts	PM	Yrs	Gm	G	A	Pts	PM
Gordie Howe	6	419	174	334	508	399	6	78	28	43	71	115	2 (1974-75)
Wayne Gretzky	1	80	46	64	110	19	1	13	10	10	20	2	None

NHL/WHA	Yrs	Regular Season					Playoffs				
		Gm	G	A	Pts	PM	Yrs	Gm	G	A	Pts	PM
Wayne Gretzky	19	1415	908	1907	2815	554	17	221	132	270	402	68
Gordie Howe	32	2186	975	1383	2358	2084	26	235	96	135	231	335

All-Time Winningest NHL Coaches

Top 20 NHL career victories through the 1997 season. Career, regular season and playoff records are noted along with NHL titles won. Coaches active during 1997 season in **bold** type.

		Career				Regular Season				Playoffs			
	Yrs	W	L	T	Pct	W	L	T	Pct	W	L	T	Pct Stanley Cups
1 **Scotty Bowman** .	25	1191	565	263	.655	1013	460	263	.659	178	105	0	.629 7 (1973,76-79,92,97)
2 Al Arbour	22	902	662	246	.566	779	576	246	.563	123	86	0	.589 4 (1980-83)
3 Dick Irvin	26	790	609	248	.556	690	521	226	.559	100	88	2	.532 4 (1932,44,46,53)
4 Billy Reay	16	599	445	175	.563	542	385	175	.571	57	60	0	.487 None
5 Toe Blake	13	582	292	159	.640	500	255	159	.634	82	37	0	.689 8 (1956-60,65-66,68)
6 **Mike Keenan** ...	12	561	387	99	.583	470	318	99	.586	91	69	0	.569 1 (1994)
7 Glen Sather	11	553	305	110	.628	464	268	110	.616	89	37	0	.706 4 (1984-85,87-88)
8 Bryan Murray ...	12	501	381	115	.566	467	337	115	.571	34	44	0	.436 None
9 Punch Imlach ...	15	467	421	163	.522	423	373	163	.526	44	48	0	.478 4 (1962-64,67)
10 Jack Adams	21	465	442	162	.511	413	390	161	.512	52	52	1	.500 2 (1936-37)
11 Fred Shero	10	451	272	119	.606	390	225	119	.612	61	47	0	.565 2 (1974-75)
12 Emile Francis ...	13	433	326	112	.561	393	273	112	.577	40	53	0	.430 None
13 Jacques Demers ..	12	430	415	113	.508	375	372	113	.502	55	43	0	.561 1 (1993)
14 Roger Neilson	13	418	366	132	.528	381	326	132	.533	37	40	0	.481 None
15 Sid Abel	16	414	470	155	.473	382	426	155	.477	32	44	0	.421 None
16 Pat Quinn	12	410	335	102	.544	357	285	102	.548	53	50	0	.515 None
17 Bob Berry	11	395	377	121	.510	384	355	121	.517	11	22	0	.333 None
18 Art Ross	18	393	310	95	.552	361	277	90	.558	32	33	5	.493 1 (1939)
19 Michel Bergeron .	10	369	387	104	.490	338	350	104	.492	31	37	0	.456 None
20 Bob Pulford	11	364	348	130	.510	336	305	130	.520	28	43	0	.394 None

Note: The NHL does not recognize records from the World Hockey Association (1972-79), so the following WHA overall coaching records are not included above: **Demers** (155-164-44 in 4 yrs); **Sather** (103-97-1 in 3 yrs).

Where They Coached

Abel—Chicago (1952-54), Detroit (1957-68,69-70), St. Louis (1971-72), Kansas City (1975-76); **Adams**—Toronto (1922-23), Detroit (1927-47); **Arbour**—St. Louis (1970-73), NY Islanders (1973-86,88-94); **Bergeron**—Quebec (1980-87), NY Rangers (1987-89), Quebec (1989-90); **Berry**—Los Angeles (1978-81), Montreal (1981-84), Pittsburgh (1984-87), St. Louis (1992-94). **Blake**—Montreal (1955-68); **Bowman**—St. Louis (1967-71), Montreal (1971-79), Buffalo (1979-87), Pittsburgh (1991-93), Detroit (1993—).

Demers—Quebec (1979-80), St. Louis (1983-86), Detroit (1986-90), Montreal (1992-95); **Francis**—NY Rangers (1965-75), St. Louis (1976-77,81-83); **Imlach**—Toronto (1958-69), Buffalo (1970-72), Toronto (1979-81); **Irvin**—Chicago (1930-31,55-56), Toronto (1931-40), Montreal (1940-55); **Keenan**—Philadelphia (1984-88), Chicago (1988-92), NY Rangers (1993-94), St. Louis (1994-96); **Murray**—Washington (1982-90), Detroit (1990-93).

Neilson—Toronto (1977-79), Buffalo (1979-81), Vancouver (1982-83), Los Angeles (1984), NY Rangers (1989-93), Florida (1993-95); **Pulford**—Los Angeles (1972-77), Chicago (1977-79,81-82,85-87); **Quinn**—Philadelphia (1978-82), Los Angeles (1984-87), Vancouver (1990-94, 96); **Reay**—Toronto (1957-59), Chicago (1963-77); **Ross**—Montreal Wanderers (1917-18), Hamilton (1922-23), Boston (1924-28,29-34,36-39,41-45); **Sather**—Edmonton (1979-89, 93-94); **Shero**—Philadelphia (1971-78), NY Rangers (1978-81).

Top Winning Percentages

Minimum of 275 victories, including playoffs.

		Yrs	W	L	T	Pct.
1	**Scotty Bowman** ...	25	1191	565	263	**.655**
2	Toe Blake	13	582	292	159	**.640**
3	Glen Sather	11	553	305	110	**.628**
4	Fred Shero	10	451	272	119	**.606**
5	Don Cherry	6	281	177	77	**.597**
6	Tommy Ivan	9	324	205	111	**.593**
7	**Mike Keenan**	12	561	387	99	**.583**
8	**Terry Murray**	8	327	237	58	**.572**
9	Pat Burns	8	360	260	83	**.571**
10	Al Arbour	22	902	662	246	**.566**
11	Billy Reay	16	599	445	175	**.563**
12	Emile Francis	13	433	326	112	**.561**
13	Bryan Murray	12	501	381	115	**.560**
14	Hap Day	10	308	237	81	**.557**
15	Brian Sutter	7	300	233	66	**.556**
16	Dick Irvin	26	790	609	228	**.556**
17	Lester Patrick	13	312	242	115	**.552**
18	Art Ross	18	393	310	95	**.552**
19	Bob Johnson	6	275	223	58	**.547**
20	Pat Quinn	12	410	335	102	**.544**
21	Roger Neilson	13	418	366	132	**.528**
22	Punch Imlach	15	467	421	163	**.522**
23	**Terry Crisp**	8	308	279	76	**.522**
24	Jack Adams	21	465	442	162	**.511**
25	Bob Berry	11	395	377	121	**.510**

Active Coaches' Victories

Through 1997 season, including playoffs.

		Yrs	W	L	T	Pct.
1	Scotty Bowman, Det. ..	25	**1191**	565	263	.655
2	Pat Burns, Bos.	8	**360**	260	83	.571
3	Terry Crisp, TB	8	**308**	279	76	.522
4	Brian Sutter, Calg.	7	**300**	233	66	.556
5	Jacques Lemaire, NJ ...	4	**246**	166	58	.585
6	Pierre Page, Ana	7	**233**	274	69	.464
7	Jim Schoenfeld, Pho ...	4	**203**	203	54	.500
8	Marc Crawford, Col. ..	3	**154**	79	24	.646
9	Ron Wilson, Wash.	4	**124**	152	31	.454
10	Darryl Sutter, SJ	3	**121**	95	26	.554
11	Colin Campbell, NYR ..	2	**119**	102	27	.534
12	Jacques Martin, Ott. ...	4	**117**	144	42	.455
13	Rick Bowness, NYI	7	**106**	252	36	.315
14	Doug MacLean, Fla	2	**89**	73	29	.542
15	Craig Hartsburg, Chi. .	2	**82**	71	27	.531
16	Ron Low, Edm.	3	**76**	95	18	.450
17	Ken Hitchcock, Dal. ...	2	**66**	53	13	.549
	Kevin Constantine, Pit .	3	**66**	92	24	.429
19	Paul Maurice, Car.	2	**61**	72	19	.464
20	Larry Robinson, LA	2	**52**	83	29	.405
21	Mike Murphy, Tor.	3	**51**	85	16	.388
22	Tom Renney, Van	1	**35**	40	7	.470
23	Joel Quenneville, St.L. .	1	**20**	19	7	.511
24	Alain Vigneault, Mon. ..	0	**0**	0	0	.000
	Wayne Cashman, Phi ..	0	**0**	0	0	.000
	Lindy Ruff, Buf	0	**0**	0	0	.000

Annual Awards

Hart Memorial Trophy

Awarded to the player "adjudged to be the most valuable to his team" and named after Cecil Hart, the former manager-coach of the Montreal Canadiens. Winners selected by Pro Hockey Writers Assn. (PHWA). Winners' scoring statistics or goaltender W-L records and goals against average are provided; (*) indicates led or tied for league lead.

Multiple Winners: Wayne Gretzky (9); Gordie Howe (6); Eddie Shore (4); Bobby Clarke, Mario Lemieux, Howie Morenz and Bobby Orr (3); Jean Beliveau, Bill Cowley, Phil Esposito, Bobby Hull, Guy Lafleur, Mark Messier, Stan Mikita and Nels Stewart (2).

Year		G	A	Pts
1924	Frank Nighbor, Ottawa, C ...	10	3	13
1925	Billy Burch, Hamilton, C	20	4	24
1926	Nels Stewart, Maroons, C ...	34	8	42*
1927	Herb Gardiner, Mon., D	6	6	12
1928	Howie Morenz, Mon., C	33	18	51*
1929	Roy Worters, NYA, G	16-13-9;	1.21	
1930	Nels Stewart, Maroons, C ...	39	16	55
1931	Howie Morenz, Mon., C	28	23	51*
1932	Howie Morenz, Mon., C	24	25	49
1933	Eddie Shore, Bos., D	8	27	35
1934	Aurel Joliat, Mon., LW	22	15	37
1935	Eddie Shore, Bos., D	7	26	33
1936	Eddie Shore, Bos., D	3	16	19
1937	Babe Siebert, Mon., D	8	20	28
1938	Eddie Shore, Bos., D	3	14	17
1939	Toe Blake, Mon., LW	24	23	47*
1940	Ebbie Goodfellow, Det., D ...	11	17	28
1941	Bill Cowley, Bos., C	17	45	62*
1942	Tommy Anderson, NYA, D ...	12	29	41
1943	Bill Cowley, Bos., C	27	45	72
1944	Babe Pratt, Tor., D	17	40	57
1945	Elmer Lach, Mon., C	26	54	80*
1946	Max Bentley, Chi., C	31	30	61*
1947	Maurice Richard, Mon., RW .	45	26	71
1948	Buddy O'Connor, NYR, C ...	24	36	60
1949	Sid Abel, Det., C	28	26	54
1950	Chuck Rayner, NYR, G	28-30-11;	2.62	
1951	Milt Schmidt, Bos., C	22	39	61
1952	Gordie Howe, Det., RW	47	39	86*
1953	Gordie Howe, Det., RW	49	46	95*
1954	Al Rollins, Chi., G	12-47-7;	3.23	
1955	Ted Kennedy, Tor., C	10	42	52
1956	Jean Beliveau, Mon., C	47	41	88*
1957	Gordie Howe, Det., RW	44	45	89*
1958	Gordie Howe, Det., RW	33	44	77
1959	Andy Bathgate, NYR, RW ...	40	48	88
1960	Gordie Howe, Det., RW	28	45	73

Year		G	A	Pts
1961	Bernie Geoffrion, Mon., RW .	50	45	95*
1962	Jacques Plante, Mon., G	42-14-14;	2.37*	
1963	Gordie Howe, Det., RW	38	48	86*
1964	Jean Beliveau, Mon., C	28	50	78
1965	Bobby Hull, Chi., LW	39	32	71
1966	Bobby Hull, Chi., LW	54	43	97*
1967	Stan Mikita, Chi., C	35	62	97*
1968	Stan Mikita, Chi., C	40	47	87*
1969	Phil Esposito, Bos., C	49	77	126*
1970	Bobby Orr, Bos., D	33	87	120*
1971	Bobby Orr, Bos., D	37	102	139
1972	Bobby Orr, Bos., D	37	80	117
1973	Bobby Clarke, Phi., C	37	67	104
1974	Phil Esposito, Bos., C	68	77	145*
1975	Bobby Clarke, Phi., C	27	89	116
1976	Bobby Clarke, Phi., C	30	89	119
1977	Guy Lafleur, Mon., RW	56	80	136*
1978	Guy Lafleur, Mon., RW	60	72	132*
1979	Bryan Trottier, NYI., C	47	87	134*
1980	Wayne Gretzky, Edm., C ...	51	86	137*
1981	Wayne Gretzky, Edm., C ...	55	109	164*
1982	Wayne Gretzky, Edm., C ...	92	120	212*
1983	Wayne Gretzky, Edm., C ...	71	125	196*
1984	Wayne Gretzky, Edm., C ...	87	118	205*
1985	Wayne Gretzky, Edm., C ...	73	135	208*
1986	Wayne Gretzky, Edm., C ...	52	163	215*
1987	Wayne Gretzky, Edm., C ...	62	121	183*
1988	Mario Lemieux, Pit., C	70	98	168*
1989	Wayne Gretzky, LA, C	54	114	168
1990	Mark Messier, Edm., C	45	84	129
1991	Brett Hull, St. L., RW	86	45	131
1992	Mark Messier, NYR, C	35	72	107
1993	Mario Lemieux, Pit., C	69	91	160*
1994	Sergei Fedorov, Det., C	56	64	120
1995	Eric Lindros, Phi., C	29	41	70*
1996	Mario Lemieux, Pit., C	69	92	161*
1997	Dominik Hasek, Buf., G	37-20-10;	2.27	

Calder Memorial Trophy

Awarded to the most outstanding rookie of the year and named after Frank Calder, the late NHL president (1917-43). Since the 1990-91 season, all eligible candidates must not have attained their 26th birthday by Sept. 15 of their rookie year. Winners selected by PHWA. Winners' scoring statistics or goaltender W-L record & goals against average are provided.

Year		G	A	Pts
1933	Carl Voss, NYR-Det., C	8	15	23
1934	Russ Blinco, Maroons, C	14	9	23
1935	Sweeney Schriner, NYA, LW ...	18	22	40
1936	Mike Karakas, Chi., G	21-19-8;	1.92	
1937	Syl Apps, Tor., C	16	29	45
1938	Cully Dahlstrom, Chi., C	10	9	19
1939	Frankie Brimsek, Bos., G	33-9-1;	1.58	
1940	Kilby MacDonald, NYR, LW	15	13	28
1941	John Quilty, Mon., C	18	16	34
1942	Knobby Warwick, NYR, RW ...	16	17	33
1943	Gaye Stewart, Tor., LW	24	23	47
1944	Gus Bodnar, Tor., C	22	40	62
1945	Frank McCool, Tor., G	24-22-4;	3.22	
1946	Edgar Laprade, NYR, C	15	19	34
1947	Howie Meeker, Tor., RW	27	18	45
1948	Jim McFadden, Det., C	24	24	48

Year		G	A	Pts
1949	Pentti Lund, NYR, RW	14	16	30
1950	Jack Gelineau, Bos., G	22-30-15;	3.28	
1951	Terry Sawchuk, Det., G	44-13-13;	1.99	
1952	Bernie Geoffrion, Mon., RW ...	30	24	54
1953	Gump Worsley, NYR, G	13-29-8;	3.06	
1954	Camille Henry, NYR, LW	24	15	39
1955	Ed Litzenberger, Mon-Chi., RW ...	23	28	51
1956	Glenn Hall, Det., G	30-24-16;	2.11	
1957	Larry Regan, Bos., RW	14	19	33
1958	Frank Mahovlich, Tor., LW	20	16	36
1959	Ralph Backstrom, Mon., C	18	22	40
1960	Billy Hay, Chi., C	18	37	55
1961	Dave Keon, Tor., C	20	25	45
1962	Bobby Rousseau, Mon., RW ...	21	24	45
1963	Kent Douglas, Tor., D	7	15	22
1964	Jacques Laperriere, Mon., D ...	2	28	30

Annual Awards (Cont.)

Year		G	A	Pts	Year		G	A	Pts
1965	Roger Crozier, Det., G	40-23-7;		2.42	1982	Dale Hawerchuk, Win., C	45	58	103
1966	Brit Selby, Tor., LW	14	13	27	1983	Steve Larmer, Chi., RW	43	47	90
1967	Bobby Orr, Bos., D	13	28	41	1984	Tom Barrasso, Buf., G	26-12-3;		2.84
1968	Derek Sanderson, Bos., C	24	25	49	1985	Mario Lemieux, Pit., C	43	57	100
1969	Danny Grant, Min., LW	34	31	65	1986	Gary Suter, Calg., D	18	50	68
					1987	Luc Robitaille, LA, LW	45	39	84
1970	Tony Esposito, Chi., G	38-17-8;		2.17	1988	Joe Nieuwendyk, Calg., C	51	41	92
1971	Gilbert Perreault, Buf., C	38	34	72	1989	Brian Leetch, NYR, D	23	48	71
1972	Ken Dryden, Mon., G	39-8-15;		2.24					
1973	Steve Vickers, NYR, LW	30	23	53	1990	Sergei Makarov, Calg., RW	24	62	86
1974	Denis Potvin, NYI, D	17	37	54	1991	Ed Belfour, Chi., G	43-19-7;		2.47
1975	Eric Vail, Atl., LW	39	21	60	1992	Pavel Bure, Van., RW	34	26	60
1976	Bryan Trottier, NYI, C	32	63	95	1993	Teemu Selanne, Win., RW	76	56	132
1977	Willi Plett, Atl., RW	33	23	56	1994	Martin Brodeur, NJ, G	27-11-8;		2.40
1978	Mike Bossy, NYI, RW	53	38	91	1995	Peter Forsberg, Que., C	15	35	50
1979	Bobby Smith, Min., C	30	44	74	1996	Daniel Alfredsson, Ott., RW	26	35	61
					1997	Bryan Berard, NYI, D	8	40	48
1980	Ray Bourque, Bos., D	17	48	65					
1981	Peter Stastny, Que., C	39	70	109					

Vezina Trophy

From 1927-80, given to the principal goaltender(s) on the team allowing the fewest goals during the regular season. Trophy named after 1920's goalie Georges Vezina of the Montreal Canadiens, who died of tuberculosis in 1926. Since the 1980-81 season, the trophy has been awarded to the most outstanding goaltender of the year as selected by the league's general managers.

Multiple Winners: Jacques Plante (7, one of them shared); Bill Durnan (6); Ken Dryden (5, three shared); Bunny Larocque (4, all shared); Terry Sawchuk (4, one shared); Tiny Thompson (4); Tony Esposito (3, one shared); George Hainsworth (3); Dominik Hasek (3); Glenn Hall (3, two shared); Patrick Roy (3); Ed Belfour (2); Johnny Bower (2, one shared); Frankie Brimsek (2); Turk Broda (2); Chuck Gardiner (2); Charlie Hodge (2, one shared); Bernie Parent (2, one shared); Gump Worsley (2, both shared).

Year		Record	GAA	Year		Record	GAA
1927	George Hainsworth, Mon	28-14-2	1.52	1967	Glenn Hall, Chi	19-5-5	2.38
1928	George Hainsworth, Mon	26-11-7	1.09		& Denis Dejordy, Chi	22-12-7	2.46
1929	George Hainsworth, Mon	22-7-15	0.98	1968	Gump Worsley, Mon	19-9-8	1.98
					& Rogie Vachon, Mon	23-13-2	2.48
1930	Tiny Thompson, Bos	38-5-1	2.23	1969	Jacques Plante, St.L	18-12-6	1.96
1931	Roy Worters, NYA	18-16-10	1.68		& Glenn Hall, St.L	19-12-8	2.17
1932	Chuck Gardiner, Chi	18-19-11	1.92				
1933	Tiny Thompson, Bos	25-15-8	1.83	1970	Tony Esposito, Chi	38-17-8	2.17
1934	Chuck Gardiner, Chi	20-17-11	1.73	1971	Ed Giacomin, NYR	27-10-7	2.16
1935	Lorne Chabot, Chi	26-17-5	1.83		& Gilles Villemure, NYR	22-8-4	2.30
1936	Tiny Thompson, Bos	22-20-6	1.71	1972	Tony Esposito, Chi	31-10-6	1.77
1937	Norm Smith, Det	25-14-9	2.13		& Gary Smith, Chi	14-5-6	2.42
1938	Tiny Thompson, Bos	30-11-7	1.85	1973	Ken Dryden, Mon	33-7-13	2.26
1939	Frankie Brimsek, Bos	33-9-1	1.58	1974	(Tie) Bernie Parent, Phi	47-13-12	1.89
					Tony Esposito, Chi	34-14-21	2.04
1940	Dave Kerr, NYR	27-11-10	1.60	1975	Bernie Parent, Phi	44-14-10	2.03
1941	Turk Broda, Tor	28-14-6	2.06	1976	Ken Dryden, Mon	42-10-8	2.03
1942	Frankie Brimsek, Bos	24-17-6	2.45	1977	Ken Dryden, Mon	41-6-8	2.14
1943	John Mowers, Det	25-14-11	2.47		& Bunny Larocque, Mon	19-2-4	2.09
1944	Bill Durnan, Mon	38-5-7	2.18	1978	Ken Dryden, Mon	37-7-7	2.05
1945	Bill Durnan, Mon	38-8-4	2.42		& Bunny Larocque, Mon.	22-3-4	2.67
1946	Bill Durnan, Mon	24-11-5	2.60	1979	Ken Dryden, Mon	30-10-7	2.30
1947	Bill Durnan, Mon	34-16-10	2.30		& Bunny Larocque, Mon.	22-7-4	2.84
1948	Turk Broda, Tor	32-15-13	2.38				
1949	Bill Durnan, Mon	28-23-9	2.10	1980	Bob Sauve, Buf	20-8-4	2.36
					& Don Edwards, Buf.	27-9-12	2.57
1950	Bill Durnan, Mon	26-21-17	2.20	1981	Richard Sevigny, Mon	20-4-3	2.40
1951	Al Rollins, Tor	27-5-8	1.77		Denis Herron, Mon	6-9-6	3.50
1952	Terry Sawchuk, Det	44-14-12	1.90		& Bunny Larocque, Mon.	16-9-3	3.03
1953	Terry Sawchuk, Det	32-15-16	1.90	1982	Billy Smith, NYI	32-9-4	2.97
1954	Harry Lumley, Tor	32-24-13	1.86	1983	Pete Peeters, Bos	40-11-9	2.36
1955	Terry Sawchuk, Det	40-17-11	1.96	1984	Tom Barrasso, Buf	26-12-3	2.84
1956	Jacques Plante, Mon	42-12-10	1.86	1985	Pelle Lindbergh, Phi	40-17-7	3.02
1957	Jacques Plante, Mon	31-18-12	2.02	1986	John Vanbiesbrouck, NYR	31-21-5	3.32
1958	Jacques Plante, Mon	34-14-8	2.11	1987	Ron Hextall, Phi	37-21-6	3.00
1959	Jacques Plante, Mon	38-16-13	2.16	1988	Grant Fuhr, Edm	40-24-9	3.43
				1989	Patrick Roy, Mon	33-5-6	2.47
1960	Jacques Plante, Mon	40-17-12	2.54				
1961	Johnny Bower, Tor	33-15-10	2.50	1990	Patrick Roy, Mon	31-16-5	2.53
1962	Jacques Plante, Mon	42-14-14	2.37	1991	Ed Belfour, Chi	43-19-7	2.47
1963	Glenn Hall, Chi	30-20-16	2.55	1992	Patrick Roy, Mon.	36-22-8	2.36
1964	Charlie Hodge, Mon	33-18-11	2.26	1993	Ed Belfour, Chi	41-18-11	2.59
1965	Johnny Bower, Tor	13-13-8	2.38	1994	Dominik Hasek, Buf	30-20-6	1.95
	& Terry Sawchuk, Tor	17-13-6	2.56	1995	Dominik Hasek, Buf	19-14-7	2.11
1966	Gump Worsley, Mon	29-14-6	2.36	1996	Jim Carey, Wash	35-24-9	2.26
	& Charlie Hodge, Mon	12-7-2	2.58	1997	Dominik Hasek, Buf	37-20-10	2.27

Lady Byng Memorial Trophy

Awarded to the player "adjudged to have exhibited the best type of sportsmanship and gentlemanly conduct combined with a high standard of playing ability" and named after Lady Evelyn Byng, the wife of former Canadian Governor General (1921-26) Baron Byng of Vimy. Winners selected by PHWA.

Multiple winners: Frank Boucher (7); Wayne Gretzky and Red Kelly (4); Bobby Bauer, Mike Bossy and Alex Delvecchio (3); Johnny Bucyk, Marcel Dionne, Paul Kariya, Dave Keon, Stan Mikita, Joey Mullen, Frank Nighbor, Jean Ratelle, Clint Smith and Sid Smith (2).

Year		Year		Year	
1925	Frank Nighbor, Ott., C	1950	Edgar Laprade, NYR, C	1975	Marcel Dionne, Det., C
1926	Frank Nighbor, Ott., C	1951	Red Kelly, Det., D	1976	Jean Ratelle, NY-Bos., C
1927	Billy Burch, NYA, C	1952	Sid Smith, Tor., LW	1977	Marcel Dionne, LA, C
1928	Frank Boucher, NYR, C	1953	Red Kelly, Det., D	1978	Butch Goring, LA, C
1929	Frank Boucher, NYR, C	1954	Red Kelly, Det., D	1979	Bob MacMillan, Atl., RW
		1955	Sid Smith, Tor., LW		
1930	Frank Boucher, NYR, C	1956	Earl Reibel, Det., C	1980	Wayne Gretzky, Edm., C
1931	Frank Boucher, NYR, C	1957	Andy Hebenton, NYR, RW	1981	Rick Kehoe, Pit., RW
1932	Joe Primeau, Tor., C	1958	Camille Henry, NYR, LW	1982	Rick Middleton, Bos., RW
1933	Frank Boucher, NYR, C	1959	Alex Delvecchio, Det., LW	1983	Mike Bossy, NYI, RW
1934	Frank Boucher, NYR, C			1984	Mike Bossy, NYI, RW
1935	Frank Boucher, NYR, C	1960	Don McKenney, Bos., C	1985	Jari Kurri, Edm., RW
1936	Doc Romnes, Chi., F	1961	Red Kelly, Tor., D	1986	Mike Bossy, NYI, RW
1937	Marty Barry, Det., C	1962	Dave Keon, Tor., C	1987	Joey Mullen, Calg., RW
1938	Gordie Drillon, Tor., RW	1963	Dave Keon, Tor., C	1988	Mats Naslund, Mon., LW
1939	Clint Smith, NYR, C	1964	Ken Wharram, Chi., RW	1989	Joey Mullen, Calg., RW
		1965	Bobby Hull, Chi., LW		
1940	Bobby Bauer, Bos., RW	1966	Alex Delvecchio, Det., LW	1990	Brett Hull, St.L., RW
1941	Bobby Bauer, Bos., RW	1967	Stan Mikita, Chi., C	1991	Wayne Gretzky, LA, C
1942	Syl Apps, Tor., C	1968	Stan Mikita, Chi., C	1992	Wayne Gretzky, LA, C
1943	Max Bentley, Chi., C	1969	Alex Delvecchio, Det., LW	1993	Pierre Turgeon, NYI, C
1944	Clint Smith, Chi., C			1994	Wayne Gretzky, LA, C
1945	Bill Mosienko, Chi., RW	1970	Phil Goyette, St.L., C	1995	Ron Francis, Pit., C
1946	Toe Blake, Mon., LW	1971	Johnny Bucyk, Bos., LW	1996	Paul Kariya, Ana., LW
1947	Bobby Bauer, Bos., RW	1972	Jean Ratelle, NYR, C	1997	Paul Kariya, Ana., LW
1948	Buddy O'Connor, NYR, C	1973	Gilbert Perreault, Buf., C		
1949	Bill Quackenbush, Det., D	1974	Johnny Bucyk, Bos., LW		

Note: Bill Quackenbush and Red Kelly are the only defensemen to win the Lady Byng.

James Norris Memorial Trophy

Awarded to the most outstanding defenseman of the year and named after James Norris, the late Detroit Red Wings owner-president. Winners selected by PHWA.

Multiple winners: Bobby Orr (8); Doug Harvey (7); Ray Bourque (5); Chris Chelios, Paul Coffey, Pierre Pilote and Denis Potvin (3); Rod Langway, Brian Leetch and Larry Robinson (2).

Year		Year		Year	
1954	Red Kelly, Detroit	1969	Bobby Orr, Boston	1983	Rod Langway, Washington
1955	Doug Harvey, Montreal	1970	Bobby Orr, Boston	1984	Rod Langway, Washington
1956	Doug Harvey, Montreal	1971	Bobby Orr, Boston	1985	Paul Coffey, Edmonton
1957	Doug Harvey, Montreal	1972	Bobby Orr, Boston	1986	Paul Coffey, Edmonton
1958	Doug Harvey, Montreal	1973	Bobby Orr, Boston	1987	Ray Bourque, Boston
1959	Tom Johnson, Montreal	1974	Bobby Orr, Boston	1988	Ray Bourque, Boston
		1975	Bobby Orr, Boston	1989	Chris Chelios, Montreal
1960	Doug Harvey, Montreal	1976	Denis Potvin, NY Islanders		
1961	Doug Harvey, Montreal	1977	Larry Robinson, Montreal	1990	Ray Bourque, Boston
1962	Doug Harvey, NY Rangers	1978	Denis Potvin, NY Islanders	1991	Ray Bourque, Boston
1963	Pierre Pilote, Chicago	1979	Denis Potvin, NY Islanders	1992	Brian Leetch, NY Rangers
1964	Pierre Pilote, Chicago			1993	Chris Chelios, Chicago
1965	Pierre Pilote, Chicago	1980	Larry Robinson, Montreal	1994	Ray Bourque, Boston
1966	Jacques Laperriere, Montreal	1981	Randy Carlyle, Pittsburgh	1995	Paul Coffey, Detroit
1967	Harry Howell, NY Rangers	1982	Doug Wilson, Chicago	1996	Chris Chelios, Chicago
1968	Bobby Orr, Boston			1997	Brian Leetch, NY Rangers

Frank Selke Trophy

Awarded to the outstanding defensive forward of the year and named after the late Montreal Canadiens general manager. Winners selected by the PHWA.

Multiple winners: Bob Gainey (4); Guy Carbonneau (3); Sergei Fedorov (2).

Year		Year		Year	
1978	Bob Gainey, Mon., LW	1985	Craig Ramsay, Buf., LW	1992	Guy Carbonneau, Mon., C
1979	Bob Gainey, Mon., LW	1986	Troy Murray, Chi., C	1993	Doug Gilmour, Tor., C
		1987	Dave Poulin, Phi., C	1994	Sergei Fedorov, Det., C
1980	Bob Gainey, Mon., LW	1988	Guy Carbonneau, Mon., C	1995	Ron Francis, Pit., C
1981	Bob Gainey, Mon., LW	1989	Guy Carbonneau, Mon., C	1996	Sergei Fedorov, Det., C
1982	Steve Kasper, Bos., C			1997	Michael Peca, Buf., C
1983	Bobby Clarke, Phi., C	1990	Rick Meagher, St.L., C		
1984	Doug Jarvis, Wash., C	1991	Dirk Graham, Chi., RW		

Annual Awards (Cont.)

Jack Adams Award

Awarded to the coach "adjudged to have contributed the most to his team's success" and named after the late Detroit Red Wings coach and general manager. Winners selected by NHL Broadcasters' Assn.; (*) indicates division champion.
Multiple winners: Scotty Bowman, Pat Burns, Jacques Demers and Pat Quinn (2).

Year		Improvement			Year		Improvement		
1974	Fred Shero, Phi	37-30-11	to	50-16-12*	1986	Glen Sather, Edm	49-20-11*	to	56-17-7*
1975	Bob Pulford, LA	41-14-23	to	37-35-8	1987	Jacques Demers, Det	17-57-6	to	34-36-10
1976	Don Cherry, Bos	40-26-14	to	48-15-17*	1988	Jacques Demers, Det	34-36-10	to	41-28-11*
1977	Scotty Bowman, Mon	58-11-11*	to	60-8-12*	1989	Pat Burns, Mon	45-22-13	to	53-18-9*
1978	Bobby Kromm, Det	16-55-9	to	32-34-14	1990	Bob Murdoch, Win	26-42-12	to	37-32-11
1979	Al Arbour, NYI	48-17-15*	to	51-15-14*	1991	Brian Sutter, St.L	37-34-9	to	47-22-11
1980	Pat Quinn, Phi	40-25-15	to	48-12-20*	1992	Pat Quinn, Van	28-43-9	to	42-26-12*
1981	Red Berenson, St.L	34-34-12	to	45-18-17*	1993	Pat Burns, Tor	30-43-7	to	44-29-11
1982	Tom Watt, Win	9-57-14	to	33-33-14	1994	Jacques Lemaire, NJ	40-37-7	to	47-25-12
1983	Orval Tessier, Chi	30-38-12	to	47-23-10*	1995	Marc Crawford, Que	34-42-8	to	30-13-5*
1984	Bryan Murray, Wash	39-25-16	to	48-27-5	1996	Scotty Bowman, Det	33-11-4*	to	62-13-7*
1985	Mike Keenan, Phi	44-26-10	to	53-20-7*	1997	Ted Nolan, Buf	33-42-7	to	40-30-12*

Lester B. Pearson Award

Awarded to the season's most outstanding player and named after the former diplomat, Nobel Peace Prize winner and Canadian prime minister. Winners selected by the NHL Players Assn.
Multiple winners: Wayne Gretzky (5); Mario Lemieux (4); Guy Lafleur (3); Marcel Dionne, Phil Esposito and Mark Messier (2).

Year		Year		Year	
1971	Phil Esposito, Bos., C	1980	Marcel Dionne, LA, C	1989	Steve Yzerman, Det., C
1972	Jean Ratelle, NYR, C	1981	Mike Liut, St.L., G	1990	Mark Messier, Edm., C
1973	Bobby Clarke, Phi., C	1982	Wayne Gretzky, Edm., C	1991	Brett Hull, St.L., RW
1974	Phil Esposito, Bos., C	1983	Wayne Gretzky, Edm., C	1992	Mark Messier, NYR, C
1975	Bobby Orr, Bos., D	1984	Wayne Gretzky, Edm., C	1993	Mario Lemieux, Pit., C
1976	Guy Lafleur, Mon., RW	1985	Wayne Gretzky, Edm., C	1994	Sergei Fedorov, Det., C
1977	Guy Lafleur, Mon., RW	1986	Mario Lemieux, Pit., C	1995	Eric Lindros, Phi., C
1978	Guy Lafleur, Mon., RW	1987	Wayne Gretzky, Edm., C	1996	Mario Lemieux, Pit., C
1979	Marcel Dionne, LA, C	1988	Mario Lemieux, Pit., C	1997	Dominik Hasek, Buf., G

Bill Masterton Trophy

Awarded to the player who "best exemplifies the qualities of perseverance, sportsmanship and dedication to hockey" and named after the 29-year-old rookie center of the Minnesota North Stars who died of a head injury sustained in a 1968 NHL game. Presented by the PHWA.

Year		Year		Year	
1968	Claude Provost, Mon., RW	1978	Butch Goring, LA, C	1988	Bob Bourne, LA, C
1969	Ted Hampson, Oak., C	1979	Serge Savard, Mon., D	1989	Tim Kerr, Phi., C
1970	Pit Martin, Chi., C	1980	Al MacAdam, Min., RW	1990	Gord Kluzak, Bos., D
1971	Jean Ratelle, NYR, C	1981	Blake Dunlop, St.L., C	1991	Dave Taylor, LA, RW
1972	Bobby Clarke, Phi., C	1982	Chico Resch, Colo., C	1992	Mark Fitzpatrick, NYI, G
1973	Lowell MacDonald, Pit., RW	1983	Lanny McDonald, Calg., RW	1993	Mario Lemieux, Pit., C
1974	Henri Richard, Mon., C	1984	Brad Park, Det., D	1994	Cam Neely, Bos., RW
1975	Don Luce, Buf., C	1985	Anders Hedberg, NYR, RW	1995	Pat LaFontaine, Buf., C
1976	Rod Gilbert, NYR, RW	1986	Charlie Simmer, Bos., LW	1996	Gary Roberts, Calg., LW
1977	Ed Westfall, NYI, RW	1987	Doug Jarvis, Hart., C	1997	Tony Granato, SJ, LW

Number One Draft Choices

Overall first choices in the NHL Draft since the league staged its first universal amateur draft in 1969. Players are listed with team that selected them; those who became Rookie of the Year are in **bold** type.

Year		Year		Year	
1969	Rejean Houle, Mon., LW	1979	Rob Ramage, Colo., D	1989	Mats Sundin, Que., RW
1970	**Gilbert Perreault,** Buf., C	1980	**Doug Wickenheiser,** Mon., C	1990	Owen Nolan, Que., RW
1971	Guy Lafleur, Mon., RW	1981	**Dale Hawerchuk,** Win., C	1991	Eric Lindros, Que., C
1972	Billy Harris, NYI, RW	1982	Gord Kluzak, Bos., D	1992	Roman Hamrlik, TB, D
1973	**Denis Potvin,** NYI, D	1983	Brian Lawton, Min., C	1993	Alexandre Daigle, Ott., C
1974	Greg Joly, Wash., D	1984	**Mario Lemieux,** Pit., C	1994	Ed Jovanovski, Fla., C
1975	Mel Bridgman, Phi., C	1985	Wendel Clark, Tor., LW/D	1995	**Bryan Berard,** Ott., D
1976	Rick Green, Wash., D	1986	Joe Murphy, Det., C	1996	Chris Phillips, Ott., D
1977	Dale McCourt, Det., C	1987	Pierre Turgeon, Buf., C	1997	Joe Thornton, Bos., C
1978	**Bobby Smith,** Min., C	1988	Mike Modano, Min., C		

World Hockey Association
WHA Finals

The World Hockey Association began play in 1972-73 as a 12-team rival of the 56-year-old NHL. The WHA played for the AVCO World Trophy in its seven playoff finals (Avco Financial Services underwrote the playoffs).

Multiple winners: Winnipeg (3); Houston (2).

Year	Winner	Head Coach	Series	Loser	Head Coach
1973	New England Whalers	Jack Kelley	4-1 (WWLWW)	Winnipeg Jets	Bobby Hull
1974	Houston Aeros	Bill Dineen	4-0	Chicago Cougars	Pat Stapleton
1975	Houston Aeros	Bill Dineen	4-0	Quebec Nordiques	Jean-Guy Gendron
1976	Winnipeg Jets	Bobby Kromm	4-0	Houston Aeros	Bill Dineen
1977	Quebec Nordiques	Marc Boileau	4-3 (LWLWWLW)	Winnipeg Jets	Bobby Kromm
1978	Winnipeg Jets	Larry Hillman	4-0	NE Whalers	Harry Neale
1979	Winnipeg Jets	Larry Hillman	4-2 (WWLWLW)	Edmonton Oilers	Glen Sather

Playoff MVPs—1973—No award; **1974**—No award; **1975**—Ron Grahame, Houston, G; **1976**—Ulf Nilsson, Winnipeg, C; **1977**—Serg Bernier, Quebec, C; **1978**—Bobby Guindon, Winnipeg, C; **1979**—Rich Preston, Winnipeg, RW.

Most Valuable Player
(Gordie Howe Trophy, 1976-79)

Year		G	A	Pts
1973	Bobby Hull, Win., LW	51	52	103
1974	Gordie Howe, Hou., RW	31	69	100
1975	Bobby Hull, Win., LW	77	65	142
1976	Marc Tardif, Que., LW	71	77	148
1977	Robbie Ftorek, Pho., C	46	71	117
1978	Marc Tardif, Que., LW	65	89	154
1979	Dave Dryden, Edm., G	41-17-2; 2.89		

Scoring Leaders

Year		Gm	G	A	Pts
1973	Andre Lacroix, Phi	78	50	74	124
1974	Mike Walton, Min	78	57	60	117
1975	Andre Lacroix, S. Diego	78	41	106	147
1976	Marc Tardif, Que	81	71	77	148
1977	Real Cloutier, Que	76	66	75	141
1978	Marc Tardif, Que	78	65	89	154
1979	Real Cloutier, Que	77	75	54	129

Note: In 1979, 18 year-old Rookie of the Year Wayne Gretzky finished third in scoring (46-64—110).

Rookie of the Year

Year		G	A	Pts
1973	Terry Caffery, N. Eng., C	39	61	100
1974	Mark Howe, Hou., LW	38	41	79
1975	Anders Hedberg, Win., RW	53	47	100
1976	Mark Napier, Tor., RW	43	50	93
1977	George Lyle, N. Eng., LW	39	33	72
1978	Kent Nilsson, Win., C	42	65	107
1979	Wayne Gretzky, Ind.-Edm., C	46	64	110

Best Goaltender

Year		Record	GAA
1973	Gerry Cheevers, Cleveland	32-20-0	2.84
1974	Don McLeod, Houston	33-13-3	2.56
1975	Ron Grahame, Houston	33-10-0	3.03
1976	Michel Dion, Indianapolis	14-15-1	2.74
1977	Ron Grahame, Houston	27-10-2	2.74
1978	Al Smith, New England	30-20-3	3.22
1979	Dave Dryden, Edmonton	41-17-2	2.89

Best Defenseman

Year	
1973	J.C. Tremblay, Quebec
1974	Pat Stapleton, Chicago
1975	J.C. Tremblay, Quebec
1976	Paul Shmyr, Cleveland
1977	Ron Plumb, Cincinnati
1978	Lars-Erik Sjoberg, Winnipeg
1979	Rick Ley, New England

Coach of the Year

Year		Improvement		
1973	Jack Kelley, N. Eng			46-30-2*
1974	Billy Harris, Tor	35-39-4	to	41-33-4
1975	Sandy Hucul, Pho	Expan.	to	39-31-8
1976	Bobby Kromm, Win	38-35-5	to	52-27-2*
1977	Bill Dineen, Hou	53-27-0 *	to	50-24-6*
1978	Bill Dineen, Hou	50-24-6 *	to	42-34-4
1979	John Brophy, Birm	36-41-3	to	32-42-6
*Won Division.				

WHA All-Star Game

The WHA All-Star Game was an Eastern Division vs Western Division contest from 1973-75. In 1976, the league's five Canadian-based teams played the nine teams in the US. Over the final three seasons—East played West in 1977; AVCO Cup champion Quebec played a WHA All-Star team in 1978; and in 1979, a full WHA All-Star team played a three-game series with Moscow Dynamo of the Soviet Union.

Year	Result	Host	Coaches	Most Valuable Player
1973	East 6, West 2	Quebec	Jack Kelley, Bobby Hull	Wayne Carleton, Ottawa
1974	East 8, West 4	St. Paul, MN	Jack Kelley, Bobby Hull	Mike Walton, Minnesota
1975	West 6, East 4	Edmonton	Bill Dineen, Ron Ryan	Rejean Houle, Quebec
1976	Canada 6, USA 1	Cleveland	Jean-Guy Gendron, Bill Dineen	Can—Real Cloutier, Que. USA—Paul Shmyr, Cleve.
1977	East 4, West 2	Hartford	Jacques Demers, Bobby Kromm	East—L. Levasseur, Min. West—W. Lindstrom, Win.
1978	Quebec 5, WHA 4	Quebec	Marc Boileau, Bill Dineen	Quebec—Marc Tardif WHA—Mark Howe, NE
1979	WHA def. Moscow Dynamo 3 games to none (4-2, 4-2, 4-3)	Edmonton	Larry Hillman, P. Iburtovich	No awards

World Championship

The World Hockey Championship tournament has been played regularly since 1930. The International Ice Hockey Federation (IIHF), which governs both the World and Winter Olympic tournaments, considers the Olympic champions from 1920-68 to also be the World champions. However the IIHF has not recognized an Olympic champion as World champion since 1968. The IIHF has sanctioned separate World Championships in Olympic years three times–in 1972, 1976 and again in 1992. The World championship is officially vacant for the three Olympic years from 1980-88.

Multiple winners: Soviet Union/Russia (23); Canada (21); Czechoslovakia and Sweden (6); USA (2).

Year		Year		Year		Year	
1920	Canada	1950	Canada	1967	Soviet Union	1984	Not held
1924	Canada	1951	Canada	1968	Soviet Union	1985	Czechoslovakia
1928	Canada	1952	Canada	1969	Soviet Union	1986	Soviet Union
1930	Canada	1953	Sweden	1970	Soviet Union	1987	Sweden
1931	Canada	1954	Soviet Union	1971	Soviet Union	1988	Not held
1932	Canada	1955	Canada	1972	Czechoslovakia	1989	Soviet Union
1933	United States	1956	Soviet Union	1973	Soviet Union	1990	Soviet Union
1934	Canada	1957	Sweden	1974	Soviet Union	1991	Sweden
1935	Canada	1958	Canada	1975	Soviet Union	1992	Sweden
1936	Great Britain	1959	Canada	1976	Czechoslovakia	1993	Russia
1937	Canada	1960	United States	1977	Czechoslovakia	1994	Canada
1938	Canada	1961	Canada	1978	Soviet Union	1995	Finland
1939	Canada	1962	Sweden	1979	Soviet Union	1996	Czech Republic
1940-46	Not held	1963	Soviet Union	1980	Not held	1997	Canada
1947	Czechoslovakia	1964	Soviet Union	1981	Soviet Union		
1948	Canada	1965	Soviet Union	1982	Soviet Union		
1949	Czechoslovakia	1966	Soviet Union	1983	Soviet Union		

Canada vs. USSR Summits

The first competition between the Soviet National Team and the NHL took place Sept. 2-28, 1972. A team of NHL All-Stars emerged as the winner of the heralded 8-game series, but just barely—winning with a record of 4-3-1 after trailing 1-3-1.

Two years later a WHA All-Star team played the Soviet Nationals and could win only one game and tie three others in eight contests. Two other Canada vs USSR series took place during NHL All-Star breaks: the three-game Challenge Cup at New York in 1979, and the two-game Rendez-Vous &87 in Quebec City in 1987.

The NHL All-Stars played the USSR in a three-game Challenge Cup series in 1979.

1972 Team Canada vs. USSR
NHL All-Stars vs Soviet National Team.

Date	City	Result	Goaltenders
9/2	Montreal	USSR, 7-3	Tretiak/Dryden
9/4	Toronto	Canada, 4-1	Esposito/Tretiak
9/6	Winnipeg	Tie, 4-4	Tretiak/Esposito
9/8	Vancouver	USSR, 5-3	Tretiak/Dryden
9/22	Moscow	USSR, 5-4	Tretiak/Esposito
9/24	Moscow	Canada, 3-2	Dryden/Tretiak
9/26	Moscow	Canada, 4-3	Esposito/Tretiak
9/28	Moscow	Canada, 6-5	Dryden/Tretiak

Standings

	W	L	T	Pts	GF	GA
Team Canada (NHL) ...	4	3	1	9	32	32
Soviet Union	3	4	1	7	32	32

Leading Scorers

1. Phil Esposito, Canada, (7-6—13); **2.** Aleksandr Yakushev, USSR (7-4—11); **3.** Paul Henderson, Canada (7-2—9); **4.** Boris Shadrin, USSR (3-5—8); **5.** Valeri Kharlamov, USSR (3-4—7) and Vladimir Petrov, USSR (3-4—7); **7.** Bobby Clarke, Canada (2-4—6) and Yuri Liapkin, USSR (1-5—6).

1974 Team Canada vs. USSR
WHA All-Stars vs Soviet National Team.

Date	City	Result	Goaltenders
9/17	Quebec City	Tie, 3-3	Tretiak/Cheevers
9/19	Toronto	Canada, 4-1	Cheevers/Tretiak
9/21	Winnipeg	USSR, 8-5	Tretiak/McLeod
9/23	Vancouver	Tie, 5-5	Tretiak/Cheevers
10/1	Moscow	USSR, 3-2	Tretiak/Cheevers
10/3	Moscow	USSR, 5-2	Tretiak/Cheevers
10/5	Moscow	Tie, 4-4	Cheevers/Tretiak
10/6	Moscow	USSR, 3-2	Sidelinkov/Cheevers

Standings

	W	L	T	Pts	GF	GA
Soviet Union	4	1	3	11	32	27
Team Canada (WHA) ..	1	4	3	5	27	32

Leading Scorers

1. Bobby Hull, Canada (7-2—9); **2.** Aleksandr Yakushev, USSR (6-2—8), Ralph Backstrom, Canada (4-4—8) and Valeri Kharlamov, USSR (2-6—8); **5.** Gordie Howe, Canada (3-4—7), Andre Lacroix, Canada (1-6—7) and Vladimir Petrov, USSR (1-6-7).

1979 Challenge Cup Series
NHL All-Stars vs Soviet National Team

Date	City	Result	Goaltenders
2/8	New York	NHL, 4-2	K. Dryden/Tretiak
2/10	New York	USSR, 5-4	Tretiak/K. Dryden
2/11	New York	USSR, 6-0	Myshkin/Cheevers

Rendez-Vous '87
NHL All-Stars vs Soviet National Team

Date	City	Result	Goaltenders
2/11	Quebec	NHL, 4-3	Fuhr/Belosheykhin
2/13	Quebec	USSR, 5-3	Belosheykhin/Fuhr

The Canada Cup

After organizing the historic 8-game Team Canada-Soviet Union series of 1972, NHL Players Association executive director Alan Eagleson and the NHL created the Canada Cup in 1976. For the first time, the best players from the world's six major hockey powers—Canada, Czechoslovakia, Finland, Russia, Sweden and the USA competed together in one tournament.

1976
Round Robin Standings

	W	L	T	Pts	GF	GA
Canada	4	1	0	8	22	6
Czechoslovakia	3	1	1	7	19	9
Soviet Union	2	2	1	5	23	14
Sweden	2	2	1	5	16	18
United States	1	3	1	3	14	21
Finland	1	4	0	2	16	42

Finals (Best of 3)

Date	City	Score
9/13	Toronto	Canada 6, Czechoslovakia 0
9/15	Montreal	Canada 5, Czechoslovakia 4 (OT)

Note: Darryl Sittler scored the winning goal for Canada at 11:33 in overtime to clinch the Cup, 2 games to none.

Leading Scorers

1. Victor Hluktov, USSR (5-4—9), Bobby Orr, Canada (2-7—9) and Denis Potvin, Canada (1-8—9); **4.** Bobby Hull, Canada (5-3—8) and Milan Novy, Czechoslovakia (5-3—8).

Team MVPs

Canada—Rogie Vachon	Sweden—Borje Salming
Czech.—Milan Novy	USA—Robbie Ftorek
USSR—Alexandr Maltsev	Finland—Matti Hagman

Tournament MVP—Bobby Orr, Canada

1981
Round Robin Standings

	W	L	T	Pts	GF	GA
Canada	4	0	1	9	32	13
Soviet Union	3	1	1	7	20	13
Czechoslovakia	2	1	2	6	21	13
United States	2	2	1	5	17	19
Sweden	1	4	0	2	13	20
Finland	0	4	1	1	6	31

Semifinals

Date	City	Score
9/11	Ottawa	USSR 4, Czechoslovakia 1
9/11	Montreal	Canada 4, United States 1

Finals

Date	City	Score
9/13	Montreal	USSR 8, Canada 1

Leading Scorers

1. Wayne Gretzky, Canada (5-7—12); **2.** Mike Bossy, Canada (8-3—11), Bryan Trottier, Canada (3-8—11), Guy Lafleur, Canada (2-9—11), Alexei Kasatonov, USSR (1-10—11).

All-Star Team

Goal—Vladislav Tretiak, USSR; **Defense**—Arnold Kadlec, Czech. and Alexei Kasatonov, USSR; **Forwards**—Mike Bossy, Canada, Gil Perreault, Canada, and Sergei Shepelev, USSR. **Tournament MVP**—Tretiak.

1984
Round Robin Standings

	W	L	T	Pts	GF	GA
Soviet Union	5	0	0	10	22	7
United States	3	1	1	7	21	13
Sweden	3	2	0	6	15	16
Canada	2	2	1	5	23	18
West Germany	0	4	1	1	13	29
Czechoslovakia	0	4	1	1	10	21

Semifinals

Date	City	Score
9/12	Edmonton	Sweden 9, United States 2
9/15	Montreal	Canada 3, USSR 2 (OT)

Note: Mike Bossy scored the winning goal for Canada at 12:29 in overtime.

Finals (Best of 3)

Date	City	Score
9/16	Calgary	Canada 5, Sweden 2
9/18	Edmonton	Canada 6, Sweden 5

Leading Scorers

1. Wayne Gretzky, Canada (5-7—12); **2.** Michel Goulet, Canada (5-6—11), Kent Nilsson, Sweden (3-8—11), Paul Coffey, Canada (3-8—11); **5.** Hakan Loob, Sweden (6-4—10).

All-Star Team

Goal—Vladimir Myshkin, USSR; **Defense**—Paul Coffey, Canada and Rod Langway, USA; **Forwards**—Wayne Gretzky, Canada, John Tonelli, Canada, and Sergei Makarov, USSR. **Tournament MVP**—Tonelli.

1987
Round Robin Standings

	W	L	T	Pts	GF	GA
Canada	3	0	2	8	19	13
Soviet Union	3	1	1	7	22	13
Sweden	3	2	0	6	17	14
Czechoslovakia	2	2	1	5	12	15
United States	2	3	0	4	13	14
Finland	0	5	0	0	9	23

Semifinals

Date	City	Score
9/8	Hamilton	USSR 4, Sweden 2
9/9	Montreal	Canada 5, Czechoslovakia 3

Finals (Best of 3)

Date	City	Score
9/11	Montreal	USSR 6, Canada 5 (OT)
9/13	Hamilton	Canada 6, USSR 5 (2 OT)
9/15	Hamilton	Canada 6, USSR 5

Note: In Game 1, Alexander Semak of USSR scored at 5:33 in overtime. In Game 2, Mario Lemieux of Canada scored at 10:01 in the second overtime period. Lemieux also won Game 3 on a goal with 1:26 left in regulation time.

Leading Scorers

1. Wayne Gretzky, Canada (3-18—21); **2.** Mario Lemieux, Canada (11-7—18); **3.** Sergei Makarov, USSR (7-8—15); **4.** Vladimir Krutov, USSR (7-7—14); **5.** Viacheslav Bykov, USSR (2-7—9); **6.** Ray Bourque, Canada (2-6—8).

All-Star Team

Goal—Grant Fuhr, Canada; **Defense**—Ray Bourque, Canada and Viacheslav Fetisov, USSR; **Forwards**—Wayne Gretzky, Canada, Mario Lemieux, Canada, and Vladimir Krutov, USSR. **Tournament MVP**—Gretzky.

1991

Round Robin Standings

	W	L	T	Pts	GF	GA
Canada	3	0	2	8	21	11
United States	4	1	0	8	19	15
Finland	2	2	1	5	10	13
Sweden	2	3	0	4	13	17
Soviet Union	1	3	1	3	14	14
Czechoslovakia	1	4	0	2	11	18

Leading Scorers

1. Wayne Gretzky, Canada (4-8—12); **2.** Steve Larmer, Canada (6-5—11); **3.** Brett Hull, USA (2-7—9); **4.** Mike Modano, USA (2-7—9); **5.** Mark Messier, Canada (2-6—8).

Semifinals

Date	City	Score
9/11	Hamilton	United States 7, Finland 3
9/12	Toronto	Canada 4, Sweden 0

Finals (Best of 3)

Date	City	Score
9/14	Montreal	Canada 4, United States 1
9/16	Hamilton	Canada 4, United States 2

All-Star Team

Goal—Bill Ranford, Canada; **Defense**—Al MacInnis, Canada and Chris Chelios, USA; **Forwards**—Wayne Gretzky, Canada, Jeremy Roenick, USA and Mats Sundin, Sweden. **Tournament MVP**—Bill Ranford.

The World Cup

Formed jointly by the NHL and the NHL Players Association in cooperation with the International Ice Hockey Federation. The inaugural World Cup held games in nine different cities throughout North America and Europe, the most ever by a single international hockey tournament.

1996

Round Robin Standings

European Pool	W	L	T	Pts	GF	GA
Sweden	3	0	0	6	14	3
Finland	2	1	0	4	17	11
Germany	1	2	0	2	11	15
Czech Republic	0	3	0	0	4	17

North American Pool	W	L	T	Pts	GF	GA
United States	3	0	0	6	19	8
Canada	2	1	0	4	11	10
Russia	1	2	0	2	12	14
Slovakia	0	3	0	0	10	18

Semifinals

Date	City	Score
9/7	Philadelphia	Canada 3, Sweden 2 (OT)
9/8	Ottawa	United States 5, Russia 2

Finals (Best of 3)

Date	City	Score
9/10	Philadelphia	Canada 4, United States 3 (OT)
9/12	Montreal	United States 5, Canada 2
9/14	Montreal	United States 5, Canada 2

Leading Scorers

1. Brett Hull, USA (7-4—11); **2.** John LeClair, USA (6-4—10); **3.** Mats Sundin, Sweden (4-3—7); Wayne Gretzky, Canada (3-4—7); Doug Weight, USA (3-4—7); Paul Coffey, Canada (0-7—7); Brian Leetch, USA (0-7—7).

All-Tournament Team

Goal—Mike Richter, USA; **Defense**—Calle Johansson, Sweden and Chris Chelios, USA; **Forwards**—Brett Hull, USA; John LeClair, USA and Mats Sundin, Sweden. **Tournament MVP**—Mike Richter, USA.

U.S. DIVISION I COLLEGE HOCKEY

NCAA Final Four

The NCAA Division I hockey tournament began in 1948 and was played at the Broadmoor Ice Palace in Colorado Springs from 1948-57. Since 1958, the tournament has moved around the country, stopping for consecutive years only at Boston Garden from 1972-74. Consolation games to determine third place were played from 1949-89 and discontinued in 1990.

Multiple Winners: Michigan (8); North Dakota (6); Denver and Wisconsin (5); Boston University (4); Lake Superior St., Michigan Tech and Minnesota (3); Colorado College, Cornell, Michigan St. and RPI (2).

Year	Champion	Head Coach	Score	Runner-up	Third Place	
1948	Michigan	Vic Heyliger	8-4	Dartmouth	Colorado College and Boston College	

Year	Champion	Head Coach	Score	Runner-up	Third Place	Score	Fourth Place
1949	Boston College	Snooks Kelley	4-3	Dartmouth	Michigan	10-4	Colorado Col.
1950	Colorado College	Cheddy Thompson	13-4	Boston Univ.	Michigan	10-6	Boston Col.
1951	Michigan	Vic Heyliger	7-1	Brown	Boston U.	7-4	Colorado Col.
1952	Michigan	Vic Heyliger	4-1	Colorado Col.	Yale	4-1	St. Lawrence
1953	Michigan	Vic Heyliger	7-3	Minnesota	RPI	6-3	Boston Univ.
1954	RPI	Ned Harkness	5-4*	Minnesota	Michigan	7-2	Boston Col.
1955	Michigan	Vic Heyliger	5-3	Colorado Col.	Harvard	6-3	St. Lawrence
1956	Michigan	Vic Heyliger	7-5	Michigan Tech	St. Lawrence	6-2	Boston Col.
1957	Colorado College	Tom Bedecki	13-6	Michigan	Clarkson	2-1†	Harvard
1958	Denver	Murray Armstrong	6-2	North Dakota	Clarkson	5-1	Harvard
1959	North Dakota	Bob May	4-3*	Michigan St.	Boston Col.	7-6†	St. Lawrence
1960	Denver	Murray Armstrong	5-3	Michigan Tech	Boston Univ.	7-6	St. Lawrence
1961	Denver	Murray Armstrong	12-2	St. Lawrence	Minnesota	4-3	RPI
1962	Michigan Tech	John MacInnes	7-1	Clarkson	Michigan	5-1	St. Lawrence
1963	North Dakota	Barry Thorndycraft	6-5	Denver	Clarkson	5-3	Boston Col.
1964	Michigan	Allen Renfrew	6-3	Denver	RPI	2-1	Providence
1965	Michigan Tech	John MacInnes	8-2	Boston Col.	North Dakota	9-5	Brown
1966	Michigan St.	Amo Bessone	6-1	Clarkson	Denver	4-3	Boston Univ.
1967	Cornell	Ned Harkness	4-1	Boston Univ.	Michigan St.	6-1	North Dakota
1968	Denver	Murray Armstrong	4-0	North Dakota	Cornell	6-1	Boston Col.
1969	Denver	Murray Armstrong	4-3	Cornell	Harvard	6-5†	Michigan Tech

†Consolation game overtimes ended in 1st OT except in 1957, '59, and '69, which all ended in 2nd OT.

Year	Champion	Head Coach	Score	Runner-up	Third Place	Score	Fourth Place
1970	Cornell	Ned Harkness	6-4	Clarkson	Wisconsin	6-5	Michigan Tech
1971	Boston University	Jack Kelley	4-2	Minnesota	Denver	1-0	Harvard
1972	Boston University	Jack Kelley	4-0	Cornell	Wisconsin	5-2	Denver
1973	Wisconsin	Bob Johnson	4-2	Denver	Boston Col.	3-1	Cornell
1974	Minnesota	Herb Brooks	4-2	Michigan Tech	Boston Univ.	7-5	Harvard
1975	Michigan Tech	John MacInnes	6-1	Minnesota	Boston Univ.	10-5	Harvard
1976	Minnesota	Herb Brooks	6-4	Michigan Tech	Brown	8-7	Boston Univ.
1977	Wisconsin	Bob Johnson	6-5*	Michigan	Boston Univ.	6-5	N. Hampshire
1978	Boston University	Jack Parker	5-3	Boston Col.	Bowl. Green	4-3	Wisconsin
1979	Minnesota	Herb Brooks	4-3	North Dakota	Dartmouth	7-3	N. Hampshire
1980	North Dakota	Gino Gasparini	5-2	N. Michigan	Dartmouth	8-4	Cornell
1981	Wisconsin	Bob Johnson	6-3	Minnesota	Mich. Tech	5-2	N. Michigan
1982	North Dakota	Gino Gasparini	5-2	Wisconsin	Northeastern	10-4	N. Hampshire
1983	Wisconsin	Jeff Sauer	6-2	Harvard	Providence	4-3	Minnesota
1984	Bowling Green	Jerry York	5-4*	Minn-Duluth	North Dakota	6-5†	Michigan St.
1985	RPI	Mike Addesa	2-1	Providence	Minn-Duluth	7-6†	Boston Col.
1986	Michigan St.	Ron Mason	6-5	Harvard	Minnesota	6-4	Denver
1987	North Dakota	Gino Gasparini	5-3	Michigan St.	Minnesota	6-3	Harvard
1988	Lake Superior St.	Frank Anzalone	4-3*	St. Lawrence	Maine	5-2	Minnesota
1989	Harvard	Billy Cleary	4-3*	Minnesota	Michigan St.	7-4	Maine

Year	Champion	Head Coach	Score	Runner-up	Third Place		
1990	Wisconsin	Jeff Sauer	7-3	Colgate	Boston College and Boston University		
1991	Northern Michigan	Rick Comley	8-7*	Boston Univ.	Maine and Clarkson		
1992	Lake Superior St.	Jeff Jackson	5-3	Wisconsin	Michigan and Michigan St.		
1993	Maine	Shawn Walsh	5-4	Lake Superior St.	Boston University and Michigan		
1994	Lake Superior St.	Jeff Jackson	9-1	Boston Univ.	Harvard and Minnesota		
1995	Boston University	Jack Parker	6-2	Maine	Michigan and Minnesota		
1996	Michigan	Red Berenson	3-2*	Colorado Col.	Vermont and Boston University		
1997	North Dakota	Dean Blais	6-4	Boston Univ.	Colorado College and Michigan		

*Championship game overtime goals:1954—1:54; **1959**—4:22; **1977**—0: 23; **1984**—7:11 in 4th OT; **1988**—4:46; **1989**—4:16; **1991**—1:57 in 3rd OT; **1996**—3:35.

Note: Runners-up Denver (1973) and Wisconsin (1992) had participation voided by the NCAA for using ineligible players.

Most Outstanding Player

The Most Outstanding Players of each NCAA Div. I tournament since 1948. Winners of the award who did not play for the tournament champion are in **bold** type. In 1960, three players, none on the winning team, shared the award.

Multiple Winners: Lou Angotti and Marc Behrend (2).

Year		Year		Year	
1948	**Joe Riley,** Dartmouth, F	1964	Bob Gray, Michigan, G	1982	Phil Sykes, N. Dakota, F
1949	**Dick Desmond,** Dart., G	1965	Gary Milroy, Mich. Tech., F	1983	Marc Behrend, Wisc., G
1950	**Ralph Bevins,** Boston U., G	1966	Gaye Cooley, Mich. St., G	1984	Gary Kruzich, Bowl. Green, G
1951	**Ed Whiston,** Brown, G	1967	Walt Stanowski, Cornell, D	1985	**Chris Terreri,** Prov., G
1952	**Ken Kinsley,** Colo. Col., G	1968	Gerry Powers, Denver, G	1986	Mike Donnelly, Mich. St., F
1953	John Matchefts, Mich., F	1969	Keith Magnuson, Denver, D	1987	Tony Hrkac, N. Dakota, F
1954	Abbie Moore, RPI, F	1970	Dan Lodboa, Cornell, D	1988	Bruce Hoffort, Lk. Superior, G
1955	**Phil Hilton,** Colo. Col., D	1971	Dan Brady, Boston U., G	1989	Ted Donato, Harvard, F
1956	Lorne Howes, Mich., G	1972	Tim Regan, Boston, U., G	1990	Chris Tancill, Wisconsin, F
1957	Bob McCusker, Colo. Col., F	1973	Dean Talafous, Wisc., F	1991	Scott Beattie, No. Mich., F
1958	Murray Massier, Denver, F	1974	Brad Shelstad, Minn., G	1992	Paul Constantin, Lk. Superior, F
1959	Reg Morelli, N. Dakota, F	1975	Jim Warden, Mich. Tech, G	1993	Jim Montgomery, Maine, F
1960	**Lou Angotti,** Mich. Tech, F;	1976	Tom Vanelli, Minn., F	1994	Sean Tallaire, Lk. Superior, F
	Bob Marquis, Boston U., F;	1977	Julian Baretta, Wisc., G	1995	Chris O'Sullivan, Boston U., F
	& **Barry Urbanski,** BU, G	1978	Jack O'Callahan, Boston U., D	1996	Brendan Morrison, Michigan, F
1961	Bill Masterton, Denver, F	1979	Steve Janaszak, Minn., G	1997	Matt Henderson, N. Dakota, F
1962	Lou Angotti, Mich. Tech, F	1980	Doug Smail, N. Dakota, F		
1963	Al McLean, N. Dakota, F	1981	Marc Behrend, Wisc., G		

Hobey Baker Award

College hockey's Player of the Year award; voted on by a national panel of sportswriters, broadcasters, college coaches and pro scouts. First presented in 1981 by the Decathlon Athletic Club of Bloomington, Minn., in the name of the Princeton collegiate hockey and football star who was killed in World War I.

Year		Year		Year	
1981	Neal Broten, Minnesota, F	1987	Tony Hrkac, North Dakota, F	1993	Paul Kariya, Maine, F
1982	George McPhee, Bowl. Green, F	1988	Robb Stauber, Minnesota, G	1994	Chris Marinucci, Minn-Duluth, F
1983	Mark Fusco, Harvard, D	1989	Lane MacDonald, Harvard, F	1995	Brian Holzinger, Bowl. Green, F
1984	Tom Kurvers, Minn-Duluth, D	1990	Kip Miller, Michigan St., F	1996	Brian Bonin, Minnesota, F
1985	Bill Watson, Minn-Duluth, F	1991	Dave Emma, Boston College, F	1997	Brendan Morrison, Michigan, F
1986	Scott Fusco, Harvard, F	1992	Scott Pellerin, Maine, F		

U.S. Division I College Hockey (Cont.)

Coach of the Year

The Penrose Memorial Trophy, voted on by the American Hockey Coaches Association and first presented in 1951 in the name of Colorado gold and copper magnate Spencer T. Penrose. Penrose built the Broadmoor hotel and athletic complex in Colorado Springs, that originally hosted the NCAA hockey championship from 1948-57.

Multiple winners: Len Ceglarski and Charlie Holt (3); Rick Comley, Eddie Jeremiah, Snooks Kelly, John MacInnes, Jack Parker, Jack Riley and Cooney Weiland (2).

Year		Year		Year	
1951	Eddie Jeremiah, Dartmouth	1967	Eddie Jeremiah, Dartmouth	1984	Mike Sertich, Minn-Duluth
1952	Cheedy Thompson, Colo. Col.	1968	Ned Harkness, Cornell	1985	Len Ceglarski, BC
1953	John Mariucci, Minnesota	1969	Charlie Holt, New Hampshire	1986	Ralph Backstrom, Denver
1954	Vic Heyliger, Michigan	1970	John MacInnes, Michigan Tech	1987	Gino Gasparini, N. Dakota
1955	Cooney Weiland, Harvard	1971	Cooney Weiland, Harvard	1988	Frank Anzalone, Lk. Superior
1956	Bill Harrison, Clarkson	1972	Snooks Kelly, BC	1989	Joe March, St. Lawrence
1957	Jack Riley, Army	1973	Len Ceglarski, BC	1990	Terry Slater, Colgate
1958	Harry Cleverly, BU	1974	Charlie Holt, New Hampshire	1991	Rick Comley, No. Michigan
1959	Snooks Kelly, BC	1975	Jack Parker, BU	1992	Ron Mason, Michigan St.
1960	Jack Riley, Army	1976	John MacInnes, Michigan Tech	1993	George Gwozdecky, Miami-OH
1961	Murray Armstrong, Denver	1977	Jerry York, Clarkson	1994	Don Lucia, Colorado Col.
1962	Jack Kelley, Colby	1978	Jack Parker, BU	1995	Shawn Walsh, Maine
1963	Tony Frasca, Colorado Col.	1979	Charlie Holt, New Hampshire	1996	Bruce Crowder, UMass-Lowell
1964	Tom Eccleston, Providence	1980	Rick Comley, No. Michigan	1997	Dean Blais, N. Dakota
1965	Jim Fulllerton, Brown	1981	Bill O'Flarety, Clarkson		
1966	Amo Bessone, Michigan St.	1982	Fern Flaman, Northeastern		
	& Len Ceglarski, Clarkson	1983	Bill Cleary, Harvard		

Note: 1960 winner Jack Riley won the award for coaching the USA to its first hockey gold medal in the Winter Olympics at Squaw Valley.

All-Time Tournament Appearances

	App	Record		App	Record
Boston Univ.	23	32-27-0	New Hampshire	8	3-12-0
Minnesota	22	28-24-0	Maine	7	14-10-0
Michigan	20	30-14-0	Providence	7	9-12-0
Boston College	18	13-27-0	N. Michigan	6	8-7-0
Michigan St.	17	22-20-1	Dartmouth	5	4-5-0
Wisconsin	16	29-14-1	Minn.-Duluth	4	5-6-0
Harvard	16	14-24-1	Brown	4	2-5-0
Clarkson	15	12-18-0	Northeastern	3	3-3-1
North Dakota	14	25-11-0	UMass-Lowell	3	2-3-1
Denver	13	19-11-0	Ala-Anchorage	3	2-5-0
Colorado Coll.	12	10-13-0	Vermont	3	1-4-0
St. Lawrence	12	5-21-0	W. Michigan	3	0-4-0
Cornell	11	10-12-0	Miami-OH	2	0-2-0
Lake Superior St.	10	20-11-1	Colgate	1	3-1-0
Michigan Tech	10	13-9-0	Merrimack	1	2-2-0
Bowling Green	9	8-12-1	Yale	1	1-1-0
RPI	8	8-8-1	St. Cloud St.	1	0-2-0

Note: The NCAA voided tournament participation of Denver in 1973 and Wisconsin in 1992 for using ineligible players.

NCAA All-Time Team

To celebrate the 50th anniversary of the NCAA tournament in 1997, the NCAA announced its 50th Anniversary Team and introduced them during the 1997 championship game in Milwaukee. The team was chosen by current Division I coaches, coaches of teams that have participated in the NCAA tournament, and members of the Division I Hockey Committee. Players named to the team had to have played in at least one NCAA tournament game. Tournament years are listed below.

Forwards

Tony Amonte, Boston Univ., 1981, '83
Lou Angotti, Michigan Tech, 1960, '62
Red Berenson, Michigan, 1962
Bill Cleary, Harvard, 1955
Tony Hrkac, North Dakota, 1987
Paul Kariya, Maine, 1993
Bill Masterton, Denver, 1960, '61
John Matchetts, Michigan, 1951, '53
John Mayasich, Minnesota, 1953, '54
Jim Montgomery, Maine, 1990, '91, '92, '93
Tom Rendall, Michigan, 1955, '56, '57
Phil Sykes, North Dakota, 1979, '80, '82

Defensemen

Chris Chelios, Wisconsin, 1982, '83
Bruce Driver, Wisconsin, 1981, '82, '83
George Konik, Denver, 1960, '61
Dan Lodboa, Cornell, 1970
Keith Magnuson, Denver, 1968, '69
Jack O'Callahan, Boston Univ., 1976, '77, '78

Goaltenders

Marc Behrend, Wisconsin, 1981, '83
Ken Dryden, Cornell, 1967, '68, '69
Chris Terreri, Providence, 1983, '85

College Sports

Peyton Manning addresses a question at the press conference in which he announced that he would return to Tennessee for his senior season as the Vols' quarterback and the pre-season Heisman trophy favorite. ——————————

Wide World Photos

Voluntary Duty

Peyton Manning decided not to void his senior year at Tennessee and to make one more run at a national title

by
Chris Fowler

Tim Duncan had just finished dismantling Virginia when someone interrupted the Demon Deacons' locker room revelry to deliver a message. It seems some guy waiting in the hallway wanted to have a word with him. A guy named Peyton Manning.

Duncan figured it couldn't be "the" Peyton Manning but he was curious.

Sure enough, the soon-to-be NBA top pick found the future NFL first pick waiting for him. Manning was in Charlottesville visiting his girlfriend and wrestling with the biggest decision of his life, when he had a brainstorm. Why not ask the advice of a man who'd faced the same choice nine months earlier: instant riches or a final year of college?

Duncan told Manning he had no regrets about staying. A few months later, even after Wake's dream of win-

ning a national title was dead, Duncan still felt the same way. Manning listened to Duncan, and Michael Jordan, and ABC commentator Todd Blackledge and a bunch of other folks, too. Everybody seemed to have an opinion. Everybody, that is, except the one guy most people figured would be his closest advisor: his dad. Instead, Archie told Peyton, "You can't ask me what you should do. You decide."

In the end, Manning's heart told his head what to do. College football and college life were too much fun to pass up one final year. Spend five minutes with Manning and you begin to understand his decision. Nobody ever enjoyed the sport more.

On an August morning, three weeks before the 1997 opener, Peyton recreated the slow pre-game walk from the dormitory, down the hill to giant Neyland Stadium. With a childlike smile, he described the scene: the Vols in jackets and ties... slowly moving through a sea of orange... swarms of

Chris Fowler is the host of ESPN's *College GameDay*.

After wrestling with the decision himself, Wake Forest's **Tim Duncan** told Tennessee's quarterback Peyton Manning that he did not regret coming back to college for his senior season. Manning eventually decided to delay his NFL career for one more shot at a national title.

Wide World Photos

fans pushing close to shout encouragement. . . and the Tennessee band belting out "Rocky Top" just as the team approaches the gate. How could he pass up six more of these precious Saturdays?

Not that he didn't think about it. Peyton became an expert on signing bonuses, voidable years, and the intricacies of rookie mega-contracts. Often that day, he told me how close he came to turning pro, placing his thumb and index finger an inch apart. That's why the outpouring of love that accompanied his announcement makes him a bit uncomfortable. He wonders: Would the same deep passions have been channeled into hatred if he'd left early? Would Vols' supporters have quickly turned their backs on him the way they did to Heath Shuler after he passed on his final season? But with two words: "I'm staying," Manning became a Tennessee hero for life, some say surpassing even Davey Crockett.

I'm not sure if Davey stopped conversations and turned heads when he entered restaurants or golf pro shops, but Peyton sure does. In fact, it was at the golf course — or more specifically the driving range — where key elements of Manning's monumental decision were revealed. A friendly hitting session quickly turned into something else. Peyton had determined

Arizona State's quarterback **Jake Plummer** dives into the end zone in the Rose Bowl against Ohio State, the biggest play in the most exciting college football bowl game of 1997.

we'd have a long-drive contest and quickly decided on a format. Before I could politely decline the challenge of the 6-5, 225 pound twenty-one year old, Peyton had stepped to the ball and crushed a deep tee shot that sailed high and straight into the fading Tennessee twilight. Gone was the relaxed easy-going demeanor. His facial expression had suddenly changed. This was COMPETITION.

There was a reason for Manning's bravado. He'd scouted me, asking my producer about my golf weaknesses, learning that I was packing a driver that I'd just recently acquired and was less than comfortable with. Only after being assured that I'm a high handicapper and erratic off the tee did he issue his challenge. As usual, Peyton had cautiously covered all the angles

before making his move. That afternoon, I experienced first-hand exactly what All-American Pat Fitzgerald had described a few months earlier, still smarting from Manning's Citrus Bowl shredding of the Northwestern defense. Fitzgerald described the helpless feeling of lining up directly across the line from Manning, watching him probe for soft spots, staying one step ahead of the Cats' blitz calls, mentally intimidating opponents with his immense talents.

Back at the driving range, I understood how he felt. With one swing, Peyton had taken me out of my game, and my game is weak to being with. I was psyched out. For some reason, my pulse started racing. I knew I had to swing hard and connect perfectly to match his drive. Instead, my driver hit the ground and missed the ball completely! Now completely rattled, I smother-hooked my second drive, and popped up my third. After charitably ruling the contest a tie after four drives each — Manning stepped up for an "overtime" shot, clubbed it maybe 275 yards, flung his club to the ground, and raised his arms victoriously. End of contest.

In five minutes at the range, I'd witnessed Manning's cautiousness, his competitiveness, and his poise under pressure (OK, it didn't quite equal an afternoon at Florida's Swamp.) And about that post-victory taunting: it only lasted for a couple of seconds. Immediately, Manning reverted to the classy, completely gracious winner we've come to expect. Manning's decision was the right one not because of the wins, the records, and the awards that it may produce. But because he had listened to his heart.

That day, I left Tennessee believing what the state's residents have thought all along: the guy is too good to be true. ∎

Chris Fowler's Highs and Lows: College Sports '97

8. Steve Spurrier dancing to the "Macarena" at a post-Heisman ceremony dinner party. A mental picture I will never erase, try as I might.

7. Texas Tech revealing Byron Hanspard's grade point average to be 0.0. An embarassment for an alleged role model, his school, and the sport.

6. Ohio State fans loudly booing a shanked punt in the middle of the Buckeyes' brilliant thrashing of Penn State. To hear that sound was to understand the expectations in Columbus.

5. Alabama's much-maligned Freddie Kitchens quarterbacking a drive to beat Auburn on the night that Gene Stallings announced his retirement.

4. Dean Smith humbly and quickly exiting the floor after breaking Adolph Rupp's all-time victory record.

3. Peyton Manning says he'll stay for his senior season at Tennessee.

2. Kentucky hitting a pair of three-pointers against Arizona to force overtime in the best NCAA basketball final of the decade. The RCA dome crowd simply exploded.

1. Arizona State's Jake Plummer diving into the end zone for a go-ahead touchdown. Then Ohio State driving for the win in the best Rose Bowl that I have ever seen. ∎

THE NUMBERS

INSIDE

by
Pete McConville and Jeff Bennett

Wide World Photos

Tennessee Lady Volunteers **Chamique Holdsclaw (l) and Kellie Jolly** celebrate after defeating Old Dominion to win the 1997 NCAA women's college basketball tournament. Coach Pat Summitt's Lady Volunteers have won 5 national titles in the past 11 years.

THE **RATING** GAME

If there was any doubt that the women's NCAA basketball tournament is a strong and viable event, that doubt was erased on April 1st, the day the *important* numbers came out: the television ratings. The least impressive number posted by the championship game between Tennessee and Old Dominion was that it was the most-watched game in women's college basketball history. Consider these other landmarks.

- Watched by 2.85 million households.
- Most-watched game on ESPN since 1990.
- 3rd most-watched game in ESPN history.

Women's hoops is here to stay.

SUMMITT'S PEAK

Women's college basketball has no bigger star than Pat Summitt, the 23-year head coach of the Tennessee Lady Volunteers. In 1997, Tennessee became the first team to win a national title despite suffering ten losses and the Lady Vols were the first team to win back-to-back titles since USC in 1983–84. Here is how Summitt ranks with the top men's coaches at the 23-year mark of their careers.

Summitt vs men's coaching legends after 23 seasons			
	Wins	Titles	23rd season
Pat Summitt	**625**	**5**	**1996-97**
Dean Smith	524	1	1983-84
Adolph Rupp	497	3	1953-54
Bobby Knight	487	3	1987-88
John Wooden	449	5	1968-69

■

NCAA Division I Basketball Schools
1997-98 Season
Conferences and coaches as of Sept. 15, 1997.

Joining Mid-American in 1997-98 (2): MARSHALL from Southern and NORTHERN ILLINOIS from Midwestern.
Joining Metro Atlantic in 1997-98 (2): MARIST and RIDER from Northeast.
Joining Mid Continent in 1997-98 (2): ORAL ROBERTS and SOUTHERN UTAH from Independent.
Joining Northeast in 1997-98: CENTRAL CONNECTICUT ST. from Mid Continent.
Joining Southern in 1997-98 (2): NC-GREENSBORO from Big South and WOFFORD from Independent.
Joining Southland in 1997-98: SE LOUISIANA from Trans-America.
Joining Trans-America in 1997-98: TROY ST. from Mid Continent.
Joining Mid-American in 1998-99: BUFFALO from Mid Continent.
Joining Mid Continent in 1998-99: OAKLAND from Division II.
Joining Northeast in 1998-99: MD-BALTIMORE COUNTY from Big South.
Joining Southern in 1998-99: COLLEGE OF CHARLESTON from Trans-America.
Joining Southland in 1998-99: LAMAR from Sun Belt.
Joining Trans-America in 1998-99: JACKSONVILLE from Sun Belt.

	Nickname	Conference	Head Coach	Location	Colors
Air Force	Falcons	WAC	Reggie Minton	Colo. Springs, CO	Blue/Silver
Akron	Zips	Mid-American	Dan Hipsher	Akron, OH	Blue/Gold
Alabama	Crimson Tide	SEC-West	David Hobbs	Tuscaloosa, AL	Crimson/White
Alabama St.	Hornets	SWAC	Rob Spivery	Montgomery, AL	Black/Gold
Ala-Birmingham	Blazers	USA	Murry Bartow	Birmingham, AL	Green/Gold
Alcorn St.	Braves	SWAC	Davey Whitney	Lorman, MS	Purple/Gold
American	Eagles	Colonial	Art Perry	Washington, DC	Red/White/Blue
Appalachian St.	Mountaineers	Southern	Buzz Peterson	Boone, NC	Black/Gold
Arizona	Wildcats	Pac-10	Lute Olson	Tucson, AZ	Cardinal/Navy
Arizona St.	Sun Devils	Pac-10	Bill Frieder	Tempe, AZ	Maroon/Gold
Arkansas	Razorbacks	SEC-West	Nolan Richardson	Fayetteville, AR	Cardinal/White
Ark.-Little Rock	Trojans	Sun Belt	Wimp Sanderson	Little Rock, AR	Maroon/Silver/White
Ark.-Pine Bluff	Golden Lions	SWAC	Harold Blevins	Pine Bluff, AR	Black/Gold
Arkansas St.	Indians	Sun Belt	Dickey Nutt	State Univ., AR	Scarlet/Black
Army	Cadets, Black Knights	Patriot	Pat Harris	West Point, NY	Black/Gold/Gray
Auburn	Tigers	SEC-West	Cliff Ellis	Auburn, AL	Orange/Blue
Austin Peay St.	Governors	Ohio Valley	Dave Loos	Clarksville, TN	Red/White
Ball St.	Cardinals	Mid-American	Ray McCallum	Muncie, IN	Cardinal/White
Baylor	Bears	Big 12	Harry Miller	Waco, TX	Green/Gold
Bethune-Cookman	Wildcats	Mid-Eastern	Horace Broadnax	Daytona Beach, FL	Maroon/Gold
Boise St.	Broncos	Big West	Rod Jensen	Boise, ID	Orange/Blue
Boston College	Eagles	Big East	Al Skinner	Chestnut Hill, MA	Maroon/Gold
Boston University	Terriers	America East	Dennis Wolff	Boston, MA	Scarlet/White
Bowling Green	Falcons	Mid-American	Dan Dakich	Bowling Green, OH	Orange/Brown
Bradley	Braves	Mo. Valley	Jim Molinari	Peoria, IL	Red/White
BYU	Cougars	WAC	Steve Cleveland	Provo, UT	Royal Blue/White
Brown	Bears	Ivy	Frank Dobbs	Providence, RI	Brown/Cardinal/White
Bucknell	Bison	Patriot	Pat Flannery	Lewisburg, PA	Orange/Blue
Buffalo	Bulls	Mid-Continent	Tim Cohane	Buffalo, NY	Royal Blue/Red/White
Butler	Bulldogs	Midwestern	Barry Collier	Indianapolis, IN	Blue/White
California	Golden Bears	Pac-10	Ben Braun	Berkeley, CA	Blue/Gold
CS-Fullerton	Titans	Big West	Bob Hawking	Fullerton, CA	Blue/Orange/White
CS-Northridge	Matadors	Big Sky	Bobby Braswell	Northridge, CA	Red/White/Black
CS-Sacramento	Hornets	Big Sky	Tom Abatemarco	Sacramento, CA	Green/Gold
Cal Poly SLO	Mustangs	Big West	Jeff Schneider	San Luis Obispo, CA	Green/Gold
Campbell	Fighting Camels	Trans Am	Billy Lee	Buies Creek, NC	Orange/Black
Canisius	Golden Griffins	Metro Atlantic	Mike MacDonald	Buffalo, NY	Blue/Gold
Centenary	Gentlemen	Trans Am	Billy Kennedy	Shreveport, LA	Maroon/White
Central Conn. St.	Blue Devils	Northeast	Howie Dickenman	New Britain, CT	Blue/White

437

NCAA Division I Basketball Schools (Cont.)

	Nickname	Conference	Head Coach	Location	Colors
Central Florida	Golden Knights	Trans Am	Kirk Speraw	Orlando, FL	Black/Gold
Central Michigan	Chippewas	Mid-American	Jay Smith	Mt. Pleasant, MI	Maroon/Gold
Charleston So.	Buccaneers	Big South	Tom Conrad	Charleston, SC	Blue/Gold
Chicago St.	Cougars	Mid-Continent	Phil Gary	Chicago, IL	Green/White
Cincinnati	Bearcats	USA	Bob Huggins	Cincinnati, OH	Red/Black
The Citadel	Bulldogs	Southern	Pat Dennis	Charleston, SC	Blue/White
Clemson	Tigers	ACC	Rick Barnes	Clemson, SC	Purple/Orange
Cleveland St.	Vikings	Midwestern	Rollie Massimino	Cleveland, OH	Forest Green/White
Coastal Carolina	Chanticleers	Big South	Michael Hopkins	Myrtle Beach, SC	Green/Bronze/Black
Colgate	Red Raiders	Patriot	Jack Bruen	Hamilton, NY	Maroon/Gray/White
College of Charleston	Cougars	Trans Am	John Kresse	Charleston, SC	Maroon/White
Colorado	Buffaloes	Big 12	Ricardo Patton	Boulder, CO	Silver/Gold/Black
Colorado St.	Rams	WAC	Stew Morrill	Ft. Collins, CO	Green/Gold
Columbia	Lions	Ivy	Armond Hill	New York, NY	Lt. Blue/White
Connecticut	Huskies	Big East	Jim Calhoun	Storrs, CT	Blue/White
Coppin St.	Eagles	Mid-Eastern	Ron Mitchell	Baltimore, MD	Royal Blue/Gold
Cornell	Big Red	Ivy	Scott Thompson	Ithaca, NY	Carnelian Red/White
Creighton	Bluejays	Mo. Valley	Dana Altman	Omaha, NE	Blue/White
Dartmouth	Big Green	Ivy	Dave Faucher	Hanover, NH	Green/White
Davidson	Wildcats	Southern	Bob McKillop	Davidson, NC	Red/Black
Dayton	Flyers	Atlantic 10	Oliver Purnell	Dayton, OH	Red/Blue
DePaul	Blue Demons	USA	Pat Kennedy	Chicago, IL	Scarlet/Blue
Delaware	Blue Hens	America East	Mike Brey	Newark, DE	Blue/Gold
Delaware St.	Hornets	Mid-Eastern	James Dubose	Dover, DE	Red/Columbia Blue
Detroit Mercy	Titans	Midwestern	Perry Watson	Detroit, MI	Red/White/Blue
Drake	Bulldogs	Mo. Valley	Kurt Kanaskie	Des Moines, IA	Blue/White
Drexel	Dragons	America East	Bill Herrion	Philadelphia, PA	Navy Blue/Gold
Duke	Blue Devils	ACC	Mike Krzyzewski	Durham, NC	Royal Blue/White
Duquesne	Dukes	Atlantic 10	Scott Edgar	Pittsburgh, PA	Red/Blue
East Carolina	Pirates	Colonial	Joe Dooley	Greenville, NC	Purple/Gold
East Tenn. St.	Buccaneers	Southern	Ed DeChellis	Johnson City, TN	Blue/Gold
Eastern Illinois	Panthers	Ohio Valley	Rick Samuels	Charleston, IL	Blue/Gray
Eastern Kentucky	Colonels	Ohio Valley	Scott Perry	Richmond, KY	Maroon/White
Eastern Michigan	Eagles	Mid-American	Milton Barnes	Ypsilanti, MI	Green/White
Eastern Washington	Eagles	Big Sky	Steve Aggers	Cheney, WA	Red/White
Evansville	Aces	Mo. Valley	Jim Crews	Evansville, IN	Purple/White
Fairfield	Stags	Metro Atlantic	Paul Cormier	Fairfield, CT	Cardinal Red
Fairleigh Dickinson	Knights	Northeast	Tom Green	Teaneck, NJ	Blue/Black
Florida	Gators	SEC-East	Billy Donovan	Gainesville, FL	Orange/Blue
Florida A&M	Rattlers	Mid-Eastern	Mickey Clayton	Tallahassee, FL	Orange/Green
Florida Atlantic	Owls	Trans Am	Kevin Billerman	Boca Raton, FL	Blue/Gray
Florida Int'l	Golden Panthers	Trans Am	Shakey Rodriguez	Miami, FL	Blue/Yellow
Florida St.	Seminoles	ACC	Steve Robinson	Tallahassee, FL	Garnet/Gold
Fordham	Rams	Atlantic 10	Nick Macarchuk	Bronx, NY	Maroon/White
Fresno St.	Bulldogs	WAC	Jerry Tarkanian	Fresno, CA	Cardinal/Blue
Furman	Paladins	Southern	Larry Davis	Greenville, SC	Purple/White
George Mason	Patriots	Colonial	Jim Larranaga	Fairfax, VA	Green/Gold
George Washington	Colonials	Atlantic 10	Mike Jarvis	Washington, DC	Buff/Blue
Georgetown	Hoyas	Big East	John Thompson	Washington, DC	Blue/Gray
Georgia	Bulldogs, 'Dawgs	SEC-East	Ron Jirsa	Athens, GA	Red/Black
Georgia Southern	Eagles	Southern	Gregg Polinsky	Statesboro, GA	Blue/White
Georgia St.	Panthers	Trans Am	Lefty Driesell	Atlanta, GA	Royal Blue/Crimson
Georgia Tech	Yellow Jackets	ACC	Bobby Cremins	Atlanta, GA	Old Gold/White
Gonzaga	Bulldogs, Zags	West Coast	Dan Monson	Spokane, WA	Blue/White/Red
Grambling St.	Tigers	SWAC	Lacey Reynolds	Grambling, LA	Black/Gold
Hampton	Pirates	Mid-Eastern	Steve Merfeld	Hampton, VA	Royal Blue/White
Hartford	Hawks	America East	Paul Brazeau	W. Hartford, CT	Scarlet/White
Harvard	Crimson	Ivy	Frank Sullivan	Cambridge, MA	Crimson/Black/White
Hawaii	Rainbows	WAC	Riley Wallace	Honolulu, HI	Green/White
Hofstra	Flying Dutchmen	America East	Jay Wright	Hempstead, NY	Blue/White/Gold
Holy Cross	Crusaders	Patriot	Bill Raynor	Worcester, MA	Royal Purple
Houston	Cougars	USA	Alvin Brooks	Houston, TX	Scarlet/White
Howard	Bison	Mid-Eastern	Mike McLeese	Washington, DC	Blue/White/Red
Idaho	Vandals	Big West	David Farrar	Moscow, ID	Black/Gold
Idaho St.	Bengals	Big Sky	Herb Williams	Pocatello, ID	Orange/Black
Illinois	Fighting Illini	Big Ten	Lon Kruger	Champaign, IL	Orange/Blue
Illinois-Chicago	Flames	Midwestern	Jim Collins	Chicago, IL	Navy Blue/Red

	Nickname	Conference	Head Coach	Location	Colors
Illinois St.	Redbirds	Mo. Valley	Kevin Stallings	Normal, IL	Red/White
Indiana	Hoosiers	Big Ten	Bob Knight	Bloomington, IN	Cream/Crimson
Indiana St.	Sycamores	Mo. Valley	Royce Waltman	Terre Haute, IN	Royal Blue/White
Iona	Gaels	Metro Atlantic	Tim Welsh	New Rochelle, NY	Maroon/Gold
Iowa	Hawkeyes	Big Ten	Tom Davis	Iowa City, IA	Old Gold/Black
Iowa St.	Cyclones	Big 12	Tim Floyd	Ames, IA	Cardinal/Gold
Jackson St.	Tigers	SWAC	Andrew Stoglin	Jackson, MS	Blue/White
Jacksonville	Dolphins	Sun Belt	Hugh Durham	Jacksonville, FL	Green/White
Jacksonville St.	Gamecocks	Trans Am	Bill Jones	Jacksonville, AL	Red/White
James Madison	Dukes	Colonial	Sherman Dillard	Harrisonburg, VA	Purple/Gold
Kansas	Jayhawks	Big 12	Roy Williams	Lawrence, KS	Crimson/Blue
Kansas St.	Wildcats	Big 12	Tom Asbury	Manhattan, KS	Purple/White
Kent	Golden Flashes	Mid-American	Gary Waters	Kent, OH	Navy Blue/Gold
Kentucky	Wildcats	SEC-East	Tubby Smith	Lexington, KY	Blue/White
La Salle	Explorers	Atlantic 10	Speedy Morris	Philadelphia, PA	Blue/Gold
Lafayette	Leopards	Patriot	Fran O'Hanlon	Easton, PA	Maroon/White
Lamar	Cardinals	Sun Belt	Grey Giovanine	Beaumont, TX	Red/White
Lehigh	Mt. Hawks, Engineers	Patriot	Sal Mentesana	Bethlehem, PA	Brown/White
Liberty	Flames	Big South	Jeff Meyer	Lynchburg, VA	Red/White/Blue
Long Beach St.	49ers	Big West	Wayne Morgan	Long Beach, CA	Black/Gold
Long Island	Blackbirds	Northeast	Ray Haskins	Brooklyn, NY	Blue/White
LSU	Fighting Tigers	SEC-West	John Brady	Baton Rouge, LA	Purple/Gold
Louisiana Tech	Bulldogs	Sun Belt	Jim Wooldridge	Ruston, LA	Red/Blue
Louisville	Cardinals	USA	Denny Crum	Louisville, KY	Red/Black/White
Loyola-CA	Lions	West Coast	Charles Bradley	Los Angeles, CA	Crimson/Blue
Loyola-IL	Ramblers	Midwestern	Ken Burmeister	Chicago, IL	Maroon/Gold
Loyola-MD	Greyhounds	Metro Atlantic	Dino Gaudio	Baltimore, MD	Green/Gray
Maine	Black Bears	America East	John Giannini	Orono, ME	Blue/White
Manhattan	Jaspers	Metro Atlantic	John Leonard	Riverdale, NY	Kelly Green/White
Marist	Red Foxes	Metro Atlantic	Dave Magarity	Poughkeepsie, NY	Red/White
Marquette	Golden Eagles	USA	Mike Deane	Milwaukee, WI	Blue/Gold
Marshall	Thundering Herd	Mid American	Greg White	Huntington, WV	Green/White
Maryland	Terrapins, Terps	ACC	Gary Williams	College Park, MD	Red/White/Black/Gold
MD-Balt. County	Retrievers	Big South	Tom Sullivan	Baltimore, MD	Black/Gold/Red
MD-Eastern Shore	Hawks	Mid-Eastern	Lonnie Williams	Princess Anne, MD	Maroon/Gray
Massachusetts	Minutemen	Atlantic 10	James Bruiser Flint	Amherst, MA	Maroon/White
McNeese St.	Cowboys	Southland	Ron Everhart	Lake Charles, LA	Blue/Gold
Memphis	Tigers	USA	Tic Price	Memphis, TN	Blue/Gray
Mercer	Bears	Trans Am	Mark Slonaker	Macon, GA	Orange/Black
Miami-FL	Hurricanes	Big East	Leonard Hamilton	Coral Gables, FL	Orange/Green/White
Miami-OH	RedHawks	Mid-American	Charlie Coles	Oxford, OH	Red/White
Michigan	Wolverines	Big Ten	Steve Fisher	Ann Arbor, MI	Maize/Blue
Michigan St.	Spartans	Big Ten	Tom Izzo	East Lansing, MI	Green/White
Middle Tenn. St.	Blue Raiders	Ohio Valley	Randy Wiel	Murfreesboro, TN	Blue/White
Minnesota	Golden Gophers	Big Ten	Clem Haskins	Minneapolis, MN	Maroon/Gold
Mississippi	Ole Miss, Rebels	SEC-West	Rob Evans	Oxford, MS	Red/Blue
Mississippi St.	Bulldogs	SEC-West	Richard Williams	Starkville, MS	Maroon/White
Miss. Valley St.	Delta Devils	SWAC	Lafayette Stribling	Itta Bena, MS	Green/White
Missouri	Tigers	Big 12	Norm Stewart	Columbia, MO	Old Gold/Black
Missouri-KC	Kangaroos	Mid-Continent	Bob Sundvold	Kansas City, MO	Blue/Gold
Monmouth	Hawks	Northeast	Wayne Szoke	W. Long Branch, NJ	Royal Blue/White
Montana	Grizzlies	Big Sky	Blaine Taylor	Missoula, MT	Copper/Silver/Gold
Montana St.	Bobcats	Big Sky	Mick Durham	Bozeman, MT	Blue/Gold
Morehead St.	Eagles	Ohio Valley	Kyle Macy	Morehead, KY	Blue/Gold
Morgan St.	Bears	Mid-Eastern	Chris Fuller	Baltimore, MD	Blue/Orange
Mt. St. Mary's	Mountaineers	Northeast	Jim Phelan	Emmitsburg, MD	Blue/White
Murray St.	Racers	Ohio Valley	Mark Gottfried	Murray, KY	Blue/Gold
Navy	Midshipmen	Patriot	Don DeVoe	Annapolis, MD	Navy Blue/Gold
Nebraska	Cornhuskers	Big 12	Danny Nee	Lincoln, NE	Scarlet/Cream
Nevada	Wolf Pack	Big West	Pat Foster	Reno, NV	Silver/Blue
New Hampshire	Wildcats	America East	Jeff Jackson	Durham, NH	Blue/White
New Mexico	Lobos	WAC	Dave Bliss	Albuquerque, NM	Cherry/Silver
New Mexico St.	Aggies	Big West	Neil McCarthy	Las Cruces, NM	Crimson/White
New Orleans	Privateers	Sun Belt	Joey Stiebing	New Orleans, LA	Royal Blue/Silver
Niagara	Purple Eagles	Metro Atlantic	Jack Armstrong	Lewiston, NY	Purple/White/Gold
Nicholls St.	Colonels	Southland	Rickey Broussard	Thibodaux, LA	Red/Gray
North Carolina	Tar Heels	ACC	Dean Smith	Chapel Hill, NC	Carolina Blue/White
North Carolina A&T	Aggies	Mid-Eastern	Roy Thomas	Greensboro, NC	Blue/Gold
North Carolina St.	Wolfpack	ACC	Herb Sendek	Raleigh, NC	Red/White

NCAA Division I Basketball Schools (Cont.)

	Nickname	Conference	Head Coach	Location	Colors
NC-Asheville	Bulldogs	Big South	Eddie Biedenbach	Asheville, NC	Royal Blue/White
NC-Charlotte	49ers	USA	Melvin Watkins	Charlotte, NC	Green/White
NC-Greensboro	Spartans	Southern	Randy Peele	Greensboro, NC	Gold/White/Navy
NC-Wilmington	Seahawks	Colonial	Jerry Wainwright	Wilmington, NC	Green/Gold/Navy
North Texas	Eagles	Big West	Vic Trilli	Denton, TX	Green/White
NE Illinois	Golden Eagles	Mid-Continent	Rees Johnson	Chicago, IL	Navy Blue/Gold
NE Louisiana	Indians	Southland	Mike Vining	Monroe, LA	Maroon/Gold
Northeastern	Huskies	America East	Rudy Keeling	Boston, MA	Red/Black
Northern Arizona	Lumberjacks	Big Sky	Ben Howland	Flagstaff, AZ	Blue/Gold
Northern Illinois	Huskies	Mid American	Brian Hammel	De Kalb, IL	Cardinal/Black
Northern Iowa	Panthers	Mo. Valley	Eldon Miller	Cedar Falls, IA	Purple/Old Gold
Northwestern	Wildcats	Big Ten	Kevin O'Neill	Evanston, IL	Purple/White
Northwestern St.	Demons	Southland	J.D. Barnett	Natchitoches, LA	Burnt Orange/Purple
Notre Dame	Fighting Irish	Big East	John MacLeod	Notre Dame, IN	Gold/Blue
Ohio University	Bobcats	Mid-American	Larry Hunter	Athens, OH	Ohio Green/White
Ohio St.	Buckeyes	Big Ten	Jim O'Brien	Columbus, OH	Scarlet/Gray
Oklahoma	Sooners	Big 12	Kelvin Sampson	Norman, OK	Crimson/Cream
Oklahoma St.	Cowboys	Big 12	Eddie Sutton	Stillwater, OK	Orange/Black
Old Dominion	Monarchs	Colonial	Jeff Capel	Norfolk, VA	Slate Blue/Silver
Oral Roberts	Golden Eagles	Mid-Continent	Barry Hinson	Tulsa, OK	Navy Blue/White
Oregon	Ducks	Pac-10	Ernie Kent	Eugene, OR	Green/Yellow
Oregon St.	Beavers	Pac-10	Eddie Payne	Corvallis, OR	Orange/Black
Pacific	Tigers	Big West	Bob Thomason	Stockton, CA	Orange/Black
Pennsylvania	Quakers	Ivy	Fran Dunphy	Philadelphia, PA	Red/Blue
Penn St.	Nittany Lions	Big Ten	Jerry Dunn	University Park, PA	Blue/White
Pepperdine	Waves	West Coast	Lorenzo Romar	Malibu, CA	Blue/Orange
Pittsburgh	Panthers	Big East	Ralph Willard	Pittsburgh, PA	Gold/Blue
Portland	Pilots	West Coast	Rob Chavez	Portland, OR	Purple/White
Portland St.	Vikings	Big Sky	Ritchie Mckay	Portland, OR	Green/White
Prairie View A&M	Panthers	SWAC	Elwood Plummer	Prairie View, TX	Purple/Gold
Princeton	Tigers	Ivy	Bill Carmody	Princeton, NJ	Orange/Black
Providence	Friars	Big East	Pete Gillen	Providence, RI	Black/White
Purdue	Boilermakers	Big Ten	Gene Keady	W. Lafayette, IN	Old Gold/Black
Radford	Highlanders	Big South	Ron Bradley	Radford, VA	Blue/Red/Green
Rhode Island	Rams	Atlantic 10	Jim Harrick	Kingston, RI	Lt. Blue/White/Navy
Rice	Owls	WAC	Willis Wilson	Houston, TX	Blue/Gray
Richmond	Spiders	Colonial	John Beilein	Richmond, VA	Red/Blue
Rider	Broncs	Metro Atlantic	Don Harnum	Lawrenceville, NJ	Cranberry/White
Robert Morris	Colonials	Northeast	Jim Boone	Moon Township, PA	Blue/White
Rutgers	Scarlet Knights	Big East	Kevin Bannon	New Brunswick, NJ	Scarlet
St. Bonaventure	Bonnies	Atlantic 10	Jim Baron	St. Bonaventure, NY	Brown/White
St. Francis-NY	Terriers	Northeast	Ron Ganulin	Brooklyn, NY	Red/Blue
St. Francis-PA	Red Flash	Northeast	Tom McConnell	Loretto, PA	Red/White
St. John's	Red Storm	Big East	Fran Fraschilla	Jamaica, NY	Red/White
St. Joseph's-PA	Hawks	Atlantic 10	Phil Martelli	Philadelphia, PA	Crimson/Gray
Saint Louis	Billikens	USA	Charlie Spoonhour	St. Louis, MO	Blue/White
St. Mary's-CA	Gaels	West Coast	Dave Bollwinkel	Moraga, CA	Red/Blue
St. Peter's	Peacocks	Metro Atlantic	Rodger Blind	Jersey City, NJ	Blue/White
Sam Houston St.	Bearkats	Southland	Jerry Hopkins	Huntsville, TX	Orange/White
Samford	Bulldogs	Trans Am	Jimmy Tillette	Birmingham, AL	Red/Blue
San Diego	Toreros	West Coast	Brad Holland	San Diego, CA	Lt. Blue/Navy/White
San Diego St.	Aztecs	WAC	Fred Trenkle	San Diego, CA	Scarlet/Black
San Francisco	Dons	West Coast	Phil Mathews	San Francisco, CA	Green/Gold
San Jose St.	Spartans	WAC	Stan Morrison	San Jose, CA	Gold/White/Blue
Santa Clara	Broncos	West Coast	Dick Davey	Santa Clara, CA	Red/White
Seton Hall	Pirates	Big East	Tommy Amaker	South Orange, NJ	Blue/White
Siena	Saints	Metro Atlantic	Paul Hewitt	Loudonville, NY	Green/Gold
South Alabama	Jaguars	Sun Belt	Bill Musselman	Mobile, AL	Red/White/Blue
South Carolina	Gamecocks	SEC-East	Eddie Fogler	Columbia, SC	Garnet/Black
South Carolina St.	Bulldogs	Mid-Eastern	Cy Alexander	Orangeburg, SC	Garnet/Blue
South Florida	Bulls	USA	Seth Greenberg	Tampa, FL	Green/Gold
SE Louisiana	Lions	Southland	John Lyles	Hammond, LA	Green/Gold
SE Missouri St.	Indians	Ohio Valley	Gary Garner	Cape Girardeau, MO	Red/Black
Southern Illinois	Salukis	Mo. Valley	Rich Herrin	Carbondale, IL	Maroon/White
SMU	Mustangs	WAC	Mike Dement	Dallas, TX	Red/Blue
Southern Miss.	Golden Eagles	USA	James Green	Hattiesburg, MS	Black/Gold
Southern Utah	Thunderbirds	Mid Continent	Bill Evans	Cedar City, UT	Scarlet/White
Southern-BR	Jaguars	SWAC	Tommy Green	Baton Rouge, LA	Blue/Gold

	Nickname	Conference	Head Coach	Location	Colors
SW Missouri St.	Bears	Mo. Valley	Steve Alford	Springfield, MO	Maroon/White
SW Texas St.	Bobcats	Southland	Mike Miller	San Marcos, TX	Maroon/Gold
SW Louisiana	Ragin' Cajuns	Sun Belt	Jessie Evans	Lafayette, LA	Vermilion/White
Stanford	Cardinal	Pac-10	Mike Montgomery	Stanford, CA	Cardinal/White
S.F. Austin St.	Lumberjacks	Southland	Derek Allister	Nacogdoches, TX	Purple/White
Stetson	Hatters	Trans Am	Murray Arnold	DeLand, FL	Green/White
Syracuse	Orangemen	Big East	Jim Boeheim	Syracuse, NY	Orange
Temple	Owls	Atlantic 10	John Chaney	Philadelphia, PA	Cherry/White
Tennessee	Volunteers	SEC-East	Jerry Green	Knoxville, TN	Orange/White
Tenn-Chattanooga	Mocs	Southern	Henry Dickerson	Chattanooga, TN	Navy Blue/Gold
Tenn-Martin	Skyhawks	Ohio Valley	Cal Luther	Martin, TN	Orange/White/Blue
Tennessee St.	Tigers	Ohio Valley	Frankie Allen	Nashville, TN	Blue/White
Tennessee Tech	Golden Eagles	Ohio Valley	Frank Harrell	Cookeville, TN	Purple/Gold
Texas	Longhorns	Big 12	Tom Penders	Austin, TX	Burnt Orange/White
Texas A&M	Aggies	Big 12	Tony Barone	College Station, TX	Maroon/White
TCU	Horned Frogs	WAC	Billy Tubbs	Ft. Worth, TX	Purple/White
Texas Southern	Tigers	SWAC	Robert Moreland	Houston, TX	Maroon/Gray
Texas Tech	Red Raiders	Big 12	James Dickey	Lubbock, TX	Scarlet/Black
TX-Arlington	Mavericks	Southland	Eddie McCarter	Arlington, TX	Royal Blue/White
TX-Pan American	Broncs	Sun Belt	Delray Brooks	Edinburg, TX	Green/White
TX-San Antonio	Roadrunners	Southland	Tim Carter	San Antonio, TX	Orange/Navy/White
Toledo	Rockets	Mid-American	Stan Joplin	Toledo, OH	Blue/Gold
Towson	Tigers	America East	Mike Jaskulski	Towson, MD	Gold/White/Black
Troy St.	Trojans	Trans Am	Don Maestri	Troy, AL	Cardinal/Gray/Black
Tulane	Green Wave	USA	Perry Clark	New Orleans, LA	Olive Green/Sky Blue
Tulsa	Golden Hurricane	WAC	Bill Self	Tulsa, OK	Blue/Red/Gold
UC-Irvine	Anteaters	Big West	Pat Douglass	Irvine, CA	Blue/Gold
UCLA	Bruins	Pac-10	Steve Lavin	Los Angeles, CA	Blue/Gold
UC-Santa Barbara	Gauchos	Big West	Jerry Pimm	Santa Barbara, CA	Blue/Gold
UNLV	Runnin' Rebels	WAC	Billy Bayno	Las Vegas, NV	Scarlet/Gray
USC	Trojans	Pac-10	Henry Bibby	Los Angeles, CA	Cardinal/Gold
Utah	Utes	WAC	Rick Majerus	Salt Lake City, UT	Crimson/White
Utah St.	Aggies	Big West	Larry Eustachy	Logan, UT	Navy Blue/White
UTEP	Miners	WAC	Don Haskins	El Paso, TX	Orange/White/Blue
Valparaiso	Crusaders	Mid-Continent	Homer Drew	Valparaiso, IN	Brown/Gold
Vanderbilt	Commodores	SEC-East	Jan van Breda Kolff	Nashville, TN	Black/Gold
Vermont	Catamounts	Vermont	Tom Brennan	Burlington, VT	Green/Gold
Villanova	Wildcats	Big East	Steve Lappas	Villanova, PA	Blue/White
Virginia	Cavaliers	ACC	Jeff Jones	Charlottesville, VA	Orange/Blue
VCU	Rams	Colonial	Sonny Smith	Richmond, VA	Black/Gold
VMI	Keydets	Southern	Bart Bellairs	Lexington, VA	Red/White/Yellow
Virginia Tech	Hokies, Gobblers	Atlantic 10	Bob Hussey	Blacksburg, VA	Orange/Maroon
Wagner	Seahawks	Northeast	Tim Capstraw	Staten Island, NY	Green/White
Wake Forest	Demon Deacons	ACC	Dave Odom	Winston-Salem, NC	Old Gold/Black
Washington	Huskies	Pac-10	Bob Bender	Seattle, WA	Purple/Gold
Washington St.	Cougars	Pac-10	Kevin Eastman	Pullman, WA	Crimson/Gray
Weber St.	Wildcats	Big Sky	Ron Abegglen	Ogden, UT	Royal Purple/White
West Virginia	Mountaineers	Big East	Gale Catlett	Morgantown, WV	Old Gold/Blue
Western Carolina	Catamounts	Southern	Phil Hopkins	Cullowhee, NC	Purple/Gold
Western Illinois	Leathernecks	Mid-Continent	Jim Kerwin	Macomb, IL	Purple/Gold
Western Kentucky	Hilltoppers	Sun Belt	Matt Kilcullen	Bowling Green, KY	Red/White
Western Michigan	Broncos	Mid-American	Bob Donewald	Kalamazoo, MI	Brown/Gold
Wichita St.	Shockers	Mo. Valley	Randy Smithson	Wichita, KS	Yellow/Black
William & Mary	Tribe	Colonial	Charlie Woollum	Williamsburg, VA	Green/Gold/Silver
Winthrop	Eagles	Big South	Dan Kenney	Rock Hill, SC	Garnet/Gold
Wisconsin	Badgers	Big Ten	Dick Bennett	Madison, WI	Cardinal/White
WI-Green Bay	Phoenix	Midwestern	Mike Heideman	Green Bay, WI	Green/White/Red
WI-Milwaukee	Panthers	Midwestern	Ric Cobb	Milwaukee, WI	Black/Gold
Wofford	Terriers	Southern	Richard Johnson	Spartanburg, SC	Old Gold/Black
Wright St.	Raiders	Midwestern	Ed Schilling	Dayton, OH	Green/Gold
Wyoming	Cowboys	WAC	Larry Shyatt	Laramie, WY	Brown/Yellow
Xavier	Musketeers	Atlantic 10	Skip Prosser	Cincinnati, OH	Blue/White/Gray
Yale	Bulldogs, Elis	Ivy	Dick Kuchen	New Haven, CT	Yale Blue/White
Youngstown St.	Penguins	Mid-Continent	Dan Peters	Youngstown, OH	Red/White

NCAA Division I-A Football Schools

1997 Season

Conferences and coaches as of Sept. 15, 1997.

Joining Conference USA in 1997: EAST CAROLINA from Independent.
Joining Mid-American in 1997: MARSHALL from Div. I-AA Southern Conference and independent NORTHERN ILLINOIS.
Joining Conference USA in 1998: ARMY from Independent.
Joining Mid-American in 1998: BUFFALO from Div. I-AA Independent.
Joining Conference USA in 1999: ALABAMA–BIRMINGHAM from Independent.

	Nickname	Conference	Head Coach	Location	Colors
Air Force	Falcons	WAC-Pacific	Fisher DeBerry	Colo. Springs, CO	Blue/Silver
Akron	Zips	Mid-American	Lee Owens	Akron, OH	Blue/Gold
Alabama	Crimson Tide	SEC-West	Mike Dubose	Tuscaloosa, AL	Crimson/White
Alabama-Birm.	Blazers	Independent	Watson Brown	Birmingham, AL	Green/Gold/White
Arizona	Wildcats	Pac-10	Dick Tomey	Tucson, AZ	Cardinal/Navy
Arizona St.	Sun Devils	Pac-10	Bruce Snyder	Tempe, AZ	Maroon/Gold
Arkansas	Razorbacks	SEC-West	Danny Ford	Fayetteville, AR	Cardinal/White
Arkansas St.	Indians	Independent	Joe Hollis	State Univ., AR	Scarlet/Black
Army	Cadets, Black Knights	Independent	Bob Sutton	West Point, NY	Black/Gold/Gray
Auburn	Tigers	SEC-West	Terry Bowden	Auburn, AL	Orange/Blue
Ball St.	Cardinals	Mid-American	Bill Lynch	Muncie, IN	Cardinal/White
Baylor	Bears	Big 12	Dave Roberts	Waco, TX	Green/Gold
Boise St.	Broncos	Big West	Houston Nutt	Boise, ID	Orange/Blue
Boston College	Eagles	Big East	Tom O'Brien	Chestnut Hill, MA	Maroon/Gold
Bowling Green	Falcons	Mid-American	Gary Blackney	Bowling Green, OH	Orange/Brown
BYU	Cougars	WAC-Mountain	LaVell Edwards	Provo, UT	Royal Blue/White
California	Golden Bears	Pac-10	Tom Holmoe	Berkeley, CA	Blue/Gold
Central Florida	Golden Knights	Independent	Gene McDowell	Orlando, FL	Black/Gold
Central Michigan	Chippewas	Mid-American	Dick Flynn	Mt. Pleasant, MI	Maroon/Gold
Cincinnati	Bearcats	USA	Rick Minter	Cincinnati, OH	Red/Black
Clemson	Tigers	ACC	Tommy West	Clemson, SC	Purple/Orange
Colorado	Buffaloes	Big 12	Rick Neuheisel	Boulder, CO	Silver/Gold/Black
Colorado St.	Rams	WAC-Pacific	Sonny Lubick	Ft. Collins, CO	Green/Gold
Duke	Blue Devils	ACC	Fred Goldsmith	Durham, NC	Royal Blue/White
East Carolina	Pirates	USA	Steve Logan	Greenville, NC	Purple/Gold
Eastern Michigan	Eagles	Mid-American	Rick Rasnick	Ypsilanti, MI	Green/White
Florida	Gators	SEC-East	Steve Spurrier	Gainesville, FL	Orange/Blue
Florida St.	Seminoles	ACC	Bobby Bowden	Tallahassee, FL	Garnet/Gold
Fresno St.	Bulldogs	WAC-Pacific	Pat Hill	Fresno, CA	Cardinal/Blue
Georgia	Bulldogs, 'Dawgs	SEC-East	Jim Donnan	Athens, GA	Red/Black
Georgia Tech	Yellow Jackets	ACC	George O'Leary	Atlanta, GA	Old Gold/White
Hawaii	Rainbow Warriors	WAC-Pacific	Fred von Appen	Honolulu, HI	Green/White
Houston	Cougars	USA	Kim Helton	Houston, TX	Scarlet/White
Idaho	Vandals	Big West	Chris Tormey	Moscow, ID	Silver/Gold
Illinois	Fighting Illini	Big Ten	Ron Turner	Champaign, IL	Orange/Blue
Indiana	Hoosiers	Big Ten	Cam Cameron	Bloomington, IN	Cream/Crimson
Iowa	Hawkeyes	Big Ten	Hayden Fry	Iowa City, IA	Old Gold/Black
Iowa St.	Cyclones	Big 12	Dan McCarney	Ames, IA	Cardinal/Gold
Kansas	Jayhawks	Big 12	Terry Allen	Lawrence, KS	Crimson/Blue
Kansas St.	Wildcats	Big 12	Bill Snyder	Manhattan, KS	Purple/White
Kent	Golden Flashes	Mid-American	Jim Corrigall	Kent, OH	Navy Blue/Gold
Kentucky	Wildcats	SEC-East	Hal Mumme	Lexington, KY	Blue/White
LSU	Fighting Tigers	SEC-West	Gerry DiNardo	Baton Rouge, LA	Purple/Gold
Louisiana Tech	Bulldogs	Independent	Gary Crowtow	Ruston, LA	Red/Blue
Louisville	Cardinals	USA	Ron Cooper	Louisville, KY	Red/Black/White
Marshall	Thundering Herd	Mid-American	Bob Pruett	Huntington, WV	Green/White
Maryland	Terrapins, Terps	ACC	Ron Vanderlinden	College Park, MD	Red/White/Black/Gold
Memphis	Tigers	USA	Rip Scherer	Memphis, TN	Blue/Gray
Miami-FL	Hurricanes	Big East	Butch Davis	Coral Gables, FL	Orange/Green/White
Miami-OH	RedHawks	Mid-American	Randy Walker	Oxford, OH	Red/White
Michigan	Wolverines	Big Ten	Lloyd Carr	Ann Arbor, MI	Maize/Blue
Michigan St.	Spartans	Big Ten	Nick Saban	E. Lansing, MI	Green/White
Minnesota	Golden Gophers	Big Ten	Glen Mason	Minneapolis, MN	Maroon/Gold
Mississippi	Ole Miss, Rebels	SEC-West	Tommy Tuberville	Oxford, MS	Cardinal/Navy Blue
Mississippi St.	Bulldogs	SEC-West	Jackie Sherrill	Starkville, MS	Maroon/White
Missouri	Tigers	Big 12	Larry Smith	Columbia, MO	Old Gold/Black

	Nickname	Conference	Head Coach	Location	Colors
Navy	Midshipmen	Independent	Charlie Weatherbie	Annapolis, MD	Navy Blue/Gold
Nebraska	Cornhuskers	Big 12	Tom Osborne	Lincoln, NE	Scarlet/Cream
Nevada	Wolf Pack	Big West	Jeff Tisdel	Reno, NV	Silver/Blue
New Mexico	Lobos	WAC-Mountain	Dennis Franchione	Albuquerque, NM	Cherry/Silver
New Mexico St.	Aggies	Big West	Tony Samuel	Las Cruces, NM	Crimson/White
North Carolina	Tar Heels	ACC	Mack Brown	Chapel Hill, NC	Carolina Blue/White
North Carolina St.	Wolfpack	ACC	Mike O'Cain	Raleigh, NC	Red/White
North Texas	Eagles	Big West	Matt Simon	Denton, TX	Green/White
NE Louisiana	Indians	Independent	Ed Zaunbrecher	Monroe, LA	Maroon/Gold
Northern Illinois	Huskies	Mid-American	Joe Novak	De Kalb, IL	Cardinal/Black
Northwestern	Wildcats	Big Ten	Gary Barnett	Evanston, IL	Purple/White
Notre Dame	Fighting Irish	Independent	Bob Davie	Notre Dame, IN	Gold/Blue
Ohio University	Bobcats	Mid-American	Jim Grobe	Athens, OH	Ohio Green/White
Ohio St.	Buckeyes	Big Ten	John Cooper	Columbus, OH	Scarlet/Gray
Oklahoma	Sooners	Big 12	John Blake	Norman, OK	Crimson/Cream
Oklahoma St.	Cowboys	Big 12	Bob Simmons	Stillwater, OK	Orange/Black
Oregon	Ducks	Pac-10	Mike Bellotti	Eugene, OR	Green/Yellow
Oregon St.	Beavers	Pac-10	Mike Riley	Corvallis, OR	Orange/Black
Penn St.	Nittany Lions	Big Ten	Joe Paterno	University Park, PA	Blue/White
Pittsburgh	Panthers	Big East	Walt Harris	Pittsburgh, PA	Blue/Gold
Purdue	Boilermakers	Big Ten	Joe Tiller	W. Lafayette, IN	Old Gold/Black
Rice	Owls	WAC-Mountain	Ken Hatfield	Houston, TX	Blue/Gray
Rutgers	Scarlet Knights	Big East	Terry Shea	New Brunswick, NJ	Scarlet
San Diego St.	Aztecs	WAC-Pacific	Ted Tollner	San Diego, CA	Scarlet/Black
San Jose St.	Spartans	WAC-Pacific	Dave Baldwin	San Jose, CA	Gold/White/Blue
South Carolina	Gamecocks	SEC-East	Brad Scott	Columbia, SC	Garnet/Black
SMU	Mustangs	WAC-Mountain	Mike Cavan	Dallas, TX	Red/Blue
Southern Miss.	Golden Eagles	USA	Jeff Bower	Hattiesburg, MS	Black/Gold
SW Louisiana	Ragin' Cajuns	Independent	Nelson Stokley	Lafayette, LA	Vermilion/White
Stanford	Cardinal	Pac-10	Tyrone Willingham	Stanford, CA	Cardinal/White
Syracuse	Orangemen	Big East	Paul Pasqualoni	Syracuse, NY	Orange
Temple	Owls	Big East	Ron Dickerson	Philadelphia, PA	Cherry/White
Tennessee	Volunteers	SEC-East	Phillip Fulmer	Knoxville, TN	Orange/White
Texas	Longhorns	Big 12	John Mackovic	Austin, TX	Burnt Orange/White
Texas A&M	Aggies	Big 12	R.C. Slocum	College Station, TX	Maroon/White
TCU	Horned Frogs	WAC-Mountain	Pat Sullivan	Ft. Worth, TX	Purple/White
Texas Tech	Red Raiders	Big 12	Spike Dykes	Lubbock, TX	Scarlet/Black
Toledo	Rockets	Mid-American	Gary Pinkel	Toledo, OH	Blue/Gold
Tulane	Green Wave	USA	Tommy Bowden	New Orleans, LA	Olive Green/Sky Blue
Tulsa	Golden Hurricane	WAC-Mountain	Dave Rader	Tulsa, OK	Blue/Gold
UCLA	Bruins	Pac-10	Bob Toledo	Los Angeles, CA	Blue/Gold
UNLV	Runnin' Rebels	WAC-Pacific	Jeff Horton	Las Vegas, NV	Scarlet/Gray
USC	Trojans	Pac-10	John Robinson	Los Angeles, CA	Cardinal/Gold
Utah	Utes	WAC-Mountain	Ron McBride	Salt Lake City, UT	Crimson/White
Utah St.	Aggies	Big West	John L. Smith	Logan, UT	Navy Blue/White
UTEP	Miners	WAC-Mountain	Charlie Bailey	El Paso, TX	Orange/White/Blue
Vanderbilt	Commodores	SEC-East	Woody Widenhofer	Nashville, TN	Black/Gold
Virginia	Cavaliers	ACC	George Welsh	Charlottesville, VA	Orange/Blue
Virginia Tech	Hokies, Gobblers	Big East	Frank Beamer	Blacksburg, VA	Orange/Maroon
Wake Forest	Demon Deacons	ACC	Jim Caldwell	Winston-Salem, NC	Old Gold/Black
Washington	Huskies	Pac-10	Jim Lambright	Seattle, WA	Purple/Gold
Washington St.	Cougars	Pac-10	Mike Price	Pullman, WA	Crimson/Gray
West Virginia	Mountaineers	Big East	Don Nehlen	Morgantown, WV	Old Gold/Blue
Western Michigan	Broncos	Mid-American	Gary Darnell	Kalamazoo, MI	Brown/Gold
Wisconsin	Badgers	Big Ten	Barry Alvarez	Madison, WI	Cardinal/White
Wyoming	Cowboys	WAC-Pacific	Dana Dimel	Laramie, WY	Brown/Yellow

Native American Nicknames Down to 9

At the start of the 1997-98 academic year the number of Native American nickname variations stood at 9 in Division I basketball and football: INDIANS (3)– Arkansas St., Northeast Louisiana and Southeast Missouri St; BRAVES (2)– Alcorn St. and Bradley; CHIPPEWAS– Central Michigan; FIGHTING ILLINI– Illinois; SEMINOLES– Florida St.; and TRIBE– William & Mary.

NCAA Division I-AA Football Schools
1997 Season
Conferences and Coaches as of Sept. 15, 1997.

Changing conference name in 1997: Yankee becomes Atlantic 10.
Joining 1-AA in 1997: La Salle to independent.
Joining Gateway Conference in 1997: independent YOUNGSTOWN ST.
Joining Patriot League in 1997: independent TOWSON.
Joining Southern in 1997: independent WOFFORD
Becoming Independent in 1997: MOREHEAD ST. from Ohio Valley.
Beginning play in 1997: SOUTH FLORIDA to Independent.
Joining Southwestern Atheltic Conference in 1997: ARKANSAS–PINE BLUFF from NAIA Div. I.

	Nickname	Conference	Head Coach	Location	Colors
Alabama St.	Hornets	SWAC	Houston Markham	Montgomery, AL	Black/Gold
Alcorn St.	Braves	SWAC	Cardell Jones	Lorman, MS	Purple/Gold
Appalachian St.	Mountaineers	Southern	Jerry Moore	Boone, NC	Black/Gold
Ark.-Pine Bluff	Golden Lions	SWAC	Lee Hardman	Pine Bluff, AR	Black/Gold
Austin Peay St.	Governors	Independent	Bill Schmitz	Clarksville, TN	Red/White
Bethune-Cookman	Wildcats	Mid-Eastern	Alvin Wyatt	Daytona Beach, FL	Maroon/Gold
Boston University	Terriers	Atlantic 10	Tom Masella	Boston, MA	Scarlet/White
Brown	Bears	Ivy	Mark Whipple	Providence, RI	Brown/Red/White
Bucknell	Bison	Patriot	Tom Gadd	Lewisburg, PA	Orange/Blue
Buffalo	Bulls	Independent	Craig Cirbus	Buffalo, NY	Blue/White
Butler	Bulldogs	Pioneer	Ken LaRose	Indianapolis, IN	Blue/White
CS-Northridge	Matadors	Big Sky	Jim Fenwick	Northridge, CA	Red/Black/White
CS-Sacramento	Hornets	Big Sky	John Volek	Sacramento, CA	Green/Gold
Cal Poly SLO	Mustangs	Independent	Larry Welsh	San Luis Obispo, CA	Green/Gold
Canisius	Golden Griffins	Metro Atlantic	Chuck Williams	Buffalo, NY	Blue/Gold
Central Conn. St.	Blue Devils	Northeast	Sal Cintorino	New Britain, CT	Blue/White
Charleston So.	Buccaneers	Independent	David Dowd	Charleston, SC	Blue/Gold
The Citadel	Bulldogs	Southern	Don Powers	Charleston, SC	Blue/White
Colgate	Red Raiders	Patriot	Dick Biddle	Hamilton, NY	Maroon/White
Columbia	Lions	Ivy	Ray Tellier	New York, NY	Lt. Blue/White
Connecticut	Huskies	Atlantic 10	Skip Holtz	Storrs, CT	Blue/White
Cornell	Big Red	Ivy	Jim Hofher	Ithaca, NY	Red/White
Dartmouth	Big Green	Ivy	John Lyons	Hanover, NH	Green/White
Davidson	Wildcats	Independent	Tim Landis	Davidson, NC	Red/Black
Dayton	Flyers	Pioneer	Mike Kelly	Dayton, OH	Red/Blue
Delaware	Blue Hens	Atlantic 10	Tubby Raymond	Newark, DE	Blue/Gold
Delaware St.	Hornets	Mid-Eastern	John McKenzie	Dover, DE	Red/Blue
Drake	Bulldogs	Pioneer	Rob Ash	Des Moines, IA	Blue/White
Duquesne	Dukes	Metro Atlantic	Greg Gattuso	Pittsburgh, PA	Red/Blue
East Tenn. St.	Buccaneers	Southern	Paul Hamilton	Johnson City, TN	Blue/Gold
Eastern Illinois	Panthers	Gateway	Bob Spoo	Charleston, IL	Blue/Gray
Eastern Kentucky	Colonels	Ohio Valley	Roy Kidd	Richmond, KY	Maroon/White
Eastern Wash.	Eagles	Big Sky	Mike Kramer	Cheney, WA	Red/White
Evansville	Aces	Pioneer	Robin Cooper	Evansville, IN	Purple/White
Fairfield	Stags	Metro Atlantic	Kevin Kiesel	Fairfield, CT	Cardinal Red
Florida A&M	Rattlers	Mid-Eastern	Billy Joe	Tallahassee, FL	Orange/Green
Fordham	Rams	Patriot	Nick Quartaro	Bronx, NY	Maroon/White
Furman	Paladins	Southern	Bobby Johnson	Greenville, SC	Purple/White
Georgetown	Hoyas	Metro Atlantic	Bob Benson	Washington, DC	Blue/Gray
Georgia Southern	Eagles	Southern	Paul Johnson	Statesboro, GA	Blue/White
Grambling St.	Tigers	SWAC	Eddie Robinson	Grambling, LA	Black/Gold
Hampton	Pirates	Mid-Eastern	Joe Taylor	Hampton, VA	Royal Blue/White
Harvard	Crimson	Ivy	Tim Murphy	Cambridge, MA	Crimson/Black/White
Hofstra	Flying Dutchmen	Independent	Joe Gardi	Hempstead, NY	Gray/White/Gold
Holy Cross	Crusaders	Patriot	Dan Allen	Worcester, MA	Royal Purple
Howard	Bison	Mid-Eastern	Steve Wilson	Washington, DC	Blue/White
Idaho St.	Bengals	Big Sky	Tom Walsh	Pocatello, ID	Orange/Black
Illinois St.	Redbirds	Gateway	Todd Berry	Normal, IL	Red/White
Indiana St.	Sycamores	Gateway	Dennis Raetz	Terre Haute, IN	Royal Blue/White
Iona	Gaels	Metro Atlantic	Harold Crocker	New Rochelle, NY	Maroon/Gold
Jackson St.	Tigers	SWAC	James Carson	Jackson, MS	Blue/White
Jacksonville St.	Gamecocks	Southland	Mike Williams	Jacksonville, AL	Red/White
James Madison	Dukes	Atlantic 10	Alex Wood	Harrisonburg, VA	Purple/Gold

	Nickname	Conference	Head Coach	Location	Colors
Lafayette	Leopards	Patriot	Bill Russo	Easton, PA	Maroon/White
La Salle	Explorers	Independent	Bill Manlove	Philadelphia, PA	Blue/Gold
Lehigh	Engineers	Patriot	Kevin Higgins	Bethlehem, PA	Brown/White
Liberty	Flames	Independent	Sam Rutigliano	Lynchburg, VA	Red/White/Blue
Maine	Black Bears	Atlantic 10	Jack Cosgrove	Orono, ME	Blue/White
Marist	Red Foxes	Metro Atlantic	Jim Parady	Poughkeepsie, NY	Red/White
Massachusetts	Minutemen	Atlantic 10	Mike Hodges	Amherst, MA	Maroon/White
McNeese St.	Cowboys	Southland	Bobby Keasler	Lake Charles, LA	Blue/Gold
Middle Tenn. St.	Blue Raiders	Ohio Valley	Boots Donnelly	Murfreesboro, TN	Blue/White
Miss. Valley St.	Delta Devils	SWAC	Larry Dorsey	Itta Bena, MS	Green/White
Monmouth	Hawks	Northeast	Kevin Callahan	W. Long Branch, NJ	Royal Blue/White
Montana	Grizzlies	Big Sky	Mick Dennehy	Missoula, MT	Copper/Silver/Gold
Montana St.	Bobcats	Big Sky	Cliff Hysell	Bozeman, MT	Blue/Gold
Morehead St.	Eagles	Independent	Matt Ballard	Morehead, KY	Blue/Gold
Morgan St.	Bears	Mid-Eastern	Stump Mitchell	Baltimore, MD	Blue/Orange
Murray St.	Racers	Ohio Valley	Denver Johnson	Murray, KY	Blue/Gold
New Hampshire	Wildcats	Atlantic 10	Bill Bowes	Durham, NH	Blue/White
Nicholls St.	Colonels	Southland	Darren Barbier	Thibodaux, LA	Red/Gray
North Carolina A&T	Aggies	Mid-Eastern	Bill Hayes	Greensboro, NC	Blue/Gold
Northeastern	Huskies	Atlantic 10	Barry Gallup	Boston, MA	Red/Black
Northern Ariz.	Lumberjacks	Big Sky	Steve Axman	Flagstaff, AZ	Blue/Gold
Northern Iowa	Panthers	Gateway	Mike Dunbar	Cedar Falls, IA	Purple/Old Gold
Northwestern St.	Demons	Southland	Sam Goodwin	Natchitoches, LA	Purple/White
Pennsylvania	Quakers	Ivy	Al Bagnoli	Philadelphia, PA	Red/Blue
Portland St.	Vikings	Big Sky	Tim Walsh	Portland, OR	Green/White
Prairie View A&M	Panthers	SWAC	Gregory Johnson	Prairie View, TX	Purple/Gold
Princeton	Tigers	Ivy	Steve Tosches	Princeton, NJ	Orange/Black
Rhode Island	Rams	Atlantic 10	Floyd Keith	Kingston, RI	Lt. Blue/Navy/White
Richmond	Spiders	Atlantic 10	Jim Reid	Richmond, VA	Red/Blue
Robert Morris	Colonials	Independent	Joe Walton	Coraopolis, PA	Blue/White
St. Francis-PA	Red Flash	Independent	Pete Mayock	Loretto, PA	Red/White
St. John's-NY	Red Storm	Metro Atlantic	Bob Ricca	Jamaica, NY	Red/White
St. Mary's-CA	Gaels	Independent	Mike Rasmussen	Moraga, CA	Red/Blue
St. Peter's	Peacocks	Metro Atlantic	Mark Collins	Jersey City, NJ	Blue/White
Sam Houston St.	Bearkats	Southland	Ron Randleman	Huntsville, TX	Orange/White
Samford	Bulldogs	Independent	Pete Hurt	Birmingham, AL	Red/Blue
San Diego	Toreros	Pioneer	Kevin McGarry	San Diego, CA	Lt. Blue/Navy/White
Siena	Saints	Metro Atlantic	Ed Zaloom	Loudonville, NY	Green/Gold
South Carolina St.	Bulldogs	Mid-Eastern	Willie Jeffries	Orangeburg, SC	Garnet/Blue
South Florida	Bulls	Independent	Jim Leavitte	Tampa, FL	Gray/Gold
SE Missouri St.	Indians	Ohio Valley	John Mumford	Cape Girardeau, MO	Red/Black
Southern-BR	Jaguars	SWAC	Pete Richardson	Baton Rouge, LA	Blue/Gold
Southern Illinois	Salukis	Gateway	Jan Quarless	Cardondale, IL	Maroon/White
Southern Utah	Thunderbirds	Independent	C. Ray Gregory	Cedar City, UT	Scarlet/White
SW Missouri St.	Bears	Gateway	Del Miller	Springfield, MO	Maroon/White
SW Texas St.	Bobcats	Southland	Bob DeBesse	San Marcos, TX	Maroon/Gold
S.F. Austin St.	Lumberjacks	Southland	John Pearce	Nacogdoches, TX	Purple/White
Tenn-Chattanooga	Mocs	Southern	Buddy Green	Chattanooga, TN	Navy Blue/Gold
Tenn-Martin	Skyhawks	Ohio Valley	Jim Marshall	Martin, TN	Orange/White/Blue
Tennessee St.	Tigers	Ohio Valley	L.C. Cole	Nashville, TN	Blue/White
Tennessee Tech	Golden Eagles	Ohio Valley	Mike Hennigan	Cookeville, TN	Purple/Gold
Texas Southern	Tigers	SWAC	Bill Thomas	Houston, TX	Maroon/Gray
Towson	Tigers	Patriot	Gordy Combs	Towson, MD	Gold/White/Black
Troy St.	Trojans	Southland	Larry Blakeney	Troy, AL	Cardinal/Gray/Black
Valparaiso	Crusaders	Pioneer	Tom Horne	Valparaiso, IN	Brown/Gold
Villanova	Wildcats	Atlantic 10	Andy Talley	Villanova, PA	Blue/White
VMI	Keydets	Southern	Ted Cain	Lexington, VA	Red/White/Yellow
Wagner	Seahawks	Northeast	Walt Hameline	Staten Island, NY	Green/White
Weber St.	Wildcats	Big Sky	Dave Arslanian	Ogden, UT	Royal Purple/White
Western Carolina	Catamounts	Southern	Bill Bleil	Cullowhee, NC	Purple/Gold
Western Illinois	Leathernecks	Gateway	Randy Ball	Macomb, IL	Purple/Gold
Western Kentucky	Hilltoppers	Independent	Jack Harbaugh	Bowling Green, KY	Red/White
William & Mary	Tribe	Atlantic 10	Jimmye Laycock	Williamsburg, VA	Green/Gold
Wofford	Terriers	Southern	Mike Ayers	Spartanburg, SC	Old Gold/Black
Yale	Bulldogs, Elis	Ivy	Jack Siedlecki	New Haven, CT	Yale Blue/White
Youngstown St.	Penguins	Gateway	Jim Tressel	Youngstown, OH	Red/White

Notre Dame	Purdue	Kentucky	Rhode Island
Bob Davie	**Joe Tiller**	**Tubby Smith**	**Jim Harrick**
Notre Dame asst. to head	Wyoming to Purdue	Georgia to Kentucky	UCLA to Rhode Island

Coaching Changes

New head coaches were named at 24 Division 1-A and 20 Division 1-AA Football schools while 59 Division 1 Basketball schools changed head coaches after the 1996-97 season. Coaching changes listed below are as of Sept. 20, 1997.

Division I Basketball

	Old Coach	Record	Why Left?	New Coach	Old Job
American	Chris Knoche	11-16	Resigned	Art Perry	Coach, Delaware St.
Army	Dino Gaudio	10-16	to Loyola-MD*	Pat Harris	Women's coach, Army
Beth.-Cookman	Tony Sheals	12-16	to Towson**	Horace Broadnax	Coach, Valencia CC
Boston College	Jim O'Brien	22-9	to Ohio St.*	Al Skinner	Coach, Rhode Island
Bowling Green	Jim Larranga	22-10	to George Mason*	Dan Dakich	Asst., Indiana
BYU	Roger Reid	1-6	Fired#	Steve Cleveland	Coach, Fresno City
UC-Irvine	Rod Baker	1-25	Fired	Pat Douglass	Coach, CS-Bakersfield
Canisius	John Beilein	17-12	to Richmond*	Mike MacDonald	Asst., Canisius
CS-Sacramento	Don Newman	3-23	Resigned	Tom Abatemarco	Asst., Rutgers
Centenary	Tommy Vardeman	9-18	Resigned	Billy Kennedy	Assoc. head, California
Central Michigan	Leonard Drake	7-19	Fired	Jay Smith	Coach, Grand Valley St.
Chicago St.	Craig Hodges	0-6	Fired$	Phil Gary	Asst. Chicago St.
Delaware St.	Art Perry	7-20	to American*	James Dubose	Asst., Delaware St.
DePaul	Joey Meyer	3-23	Resigned	Pat Kennedy	Coach, Florida St.
Eastern Kentucky	Mike Calhoun	8-18	Resigned	Scott Perry	Asst., Michigan
Florida St.	Pat Kennedy	20-12	to DePaul*	Steve Robinson	Coach, Tulsa
Furman	Joe Cantafio	10-17	Resigned	Larry Davis	Asst., Minnesota
George Mason	Paul Westhead	10-17	Fired	Jim Larranaga	Coach, Bowling Green
Georgia	Tubby Smith	24-9	to Kentucky*	Ron Jirsa	Asst., Georgia
Georgia St.	Carter Wilson	10-17	Resigned	Lefty Driesell	Coach, James Madison
Gonzaga	Dan Fitzgerald	15-12	Resigned	Dan Monson	Assoc. head, Gonzaga
Hampton	Byrone Samuels	8-19	to Tennessee**	Steve Merfeld†	Asst., Hampton
Idaho	Kermit Davis	13-17	to LSU**	David Farrar	Assoc. head, Idaho
Indiana St.	Sherman Dillard	12-16	to James Madison*	Royce Waltman	Coach, Indianapolis
Jacksonville	George Scholz	0-6	Fired%	Hugh Durham	Former coach, Georgia
James Madison	Lefty Driesell	16-13	Fired	Sherman Dillard	Coach, Indiana St.
Kentucky	Rick Pitino	35-5	to NBA Celtics	Tubby Smith	Coach, Georgia
LSU	Dale Brown	10-20	Retired	John Brady	Coach, Samford
Loyola-CA	John Olive	7-21	Resigned	Charles Bradley	Coach, Metropolitan St.
Loyola-MD	Brian Ellerbe	13-14	Resigned	Dino Gaudio	Coach, Army
Memphis	Larry Finch	16-15	Resigned	Tic Price	Coach, New Orleans
Mercer	Bill Hodges	3-23	Retired	Mark Slonaker	Coach, Pensacola JC
Morehead St.	Dick Fick	8-19	Fired	Kyle Macy	Radio analyst
New Orleans	Tic Price	22-7	to Memphis*	Joey Steibing	Asst., New Orleans
North Texas	Tim Jankovich	10-16	Resigned	Vic Trilli	Asst., Texas
Northwestern	Ricky Byrdsong	7-22	Fired	Kevin O'Neill	Coach, Tennessee
Ohio St.	Randy Ayers	10-17	Fired	Jim O'Brien	Coach, Boston Coll.
Oral Roberts	Bill Self	21-7	to Tulsa*	Barry Hinson	Asst., Oral Roberts
Oregon	Jerry Green	17-11	to Tennessee*	Ernie Kent	Coach, St. Mary's
Rhode Island	Al Skinner	20-10	to Boston Coll.*	Jim Harrick	Former coach, UCLA
Richmond	Bill Dooley	13-15	Fired	John Beilein	Coach, Canisius
Rider	Kevin Bannon	14-14	to Rutgers*	Don Harnum	Asst., Rider
Rutgers	Bob Wenzel	11-16	Fired	Kevin Bannon	Coach, Rider
St. Mary's-CA	Ernie Kent	23-8	to Oregon*	Dave Bollwinkel	Asst., St. Mary's
Samford	John Brady	19-9	to LSU*	Jimmy Tillette	Asst., Samford
Seton Hall	George Blaney	10-18	Fired	Tommy Amaker	Asst., Duke

	Old Coach	Record	Why Left?	New Coach	Old Job
Siena	Bob Beyer	9-18	Fired	Paul Hewitt	Asst., Villanova
SE Missouri St.	Ron Shumate	12-18	Fired	Gary Garner	Coach, Fort Hays St.
Stetson	Randy Brown	9-18	Resigned	Murray Arnold	Coach, Okaloosa-Walton CC
SW Louisiana	Marty Fletcher	12-16	Resigned	Jessie Evans	Asst., Arizona
Tennessee	Kevin O'Neill	11-16	to Northwestern*	Jerry Green	Coach, Oregon
Tenn-Chattanooga ..	Mack McCarthy	24-11	Resigned	Henry Dickerson	Assoc. head., Tenn-Chat.
Texas-Pan Am	Mark Adams	3-25	Fired	Delray Brooks	Asst., Kentucky
Towson	Terry Truax	9-19	Fired	Mike Jaskulski	Asst., Miami-FL
Tulsa	Steve Robinson	24-10	to Florida St.*	Bill Self	Coach, Oral Roberts
UCLA	Jim Harrick	0-0	Fired@	Steve Lavin	Asst., UCLA
Virginia Tech	Bill Foster	15-16	Retired	Bobby Hussey	Asst., Virginia Tech
Wright St.	Ralph Underhill	0-0	Fired&	Ed Schilling	Asst., NBA Nets
Wyoming	Joby Wright	12-16	Resigned	Larry Shyatt	Assoc. head, Clemson

* as head coach
** as assistant coach
† on an interim basis
\# Reid was fired on Dec. 17, 1996 and replaced with assistant coach Tony Ingle (0-19) for the remainder of the season.
\$ Hodges was fired on December 13, 1996 and replaced with assistant coach Gary (4-17) for the remainder of the season. Gary was hired on a full-time basis after the conclusion of the season.
% Scholz was replaced by assistant coach Buster Harvey (5-17) on December 20, 1996. Scholz was officially fired on February 4, 1997.
& Underhill was fired on November 15, 1996, the day of the season opener, and replaced by assistant Jim Brown (7-20) for the remainder of the season.
@ Harrick was fired on November 6, 1996, two weeks prior to the season opener, and replaced by assistant Steve Lavin (24-8) on an interim and eventually permanent basis.

Division I-A Football

	Old Coach	Record	Why Left?	New Coach	Old Job
Alabama	Gene Stallings	10-3	Resigned	Mike Dubose	Def. coord., Alabama
Arkansas St.	John Bobo	4-7	Fired	Joe Hollis	Off. coord., Ohio St.
Baylor	Chuck Reedy	4-7	Fired	Dave Roberts	Off. coord., Notre Dame
Boise St.	Pokey Allen†	2-10	Resigned	Houston Nutt	Coach, Murray St.
Boston College	Dan Henning	5-7	Resigned	Tom O'Brien	Off. coord., Virginia
California	Steve Mariucci	6-6	to NFL 49ers*	Tom Holmoe	Def. coord., California
Fresno St.	Jim Sweeney	4-7	Retired	Pat Hill	Off. line coach, NFL Ravens
Illinois	Lou Tepper	2-9	Fired	Ron Turner	Off. coord., NFL Bears
Indiana	Bill Mallory	3-8	Fired	Cam Cameron	QB coach, NFL Redskins
Kansas	Glen Mason	4-7	to Minnesota*	Terry Allen	Coach, Northern Iowa
Kentucky	Bill Curry	4-7	Fired	Hal Mumme	Coach, Valdosta St.
Maryland	Mark Duffner	5-6	Fired	Ron Vanderlinden	Asst., Northwestern
Minnesota	Jim Wacker	4-7	Resigned	Glen Mason	Coach, Kansas
N. Mexico St.	Jim Hess	1-10	Resigned	Tony Samuel	Asst., Nebraska
Notre Dame	Lou Holtz	8-3	Resigned	Bob Davie	Asst., Notre Dame
Oregon St.	Jerry Pettibone	2-9	Resigned	Mike Riley	Off. coord., USC
Pittsburgh	Johnny Majors	4-7	Resigned	Walt Harris	QB coach, Ohio St.
Purdue	Jim Colletto	3-8	Resigned	Joe Tiller	Coach, Wyoming
San Jose St.	John Ralston	3-9	Retired	Dave Baldwin	Coach, CS-Northridge
SMU	Tom Rossley	5-6	Fired	Mike Cavan	Coach, E. Tenn. St.
Tulane	Buddy Teevens	2-9	Fired	Tommy Bowden	Off. coord., Auburn
Vanderbilt	Rod Dowhower	2-9	Resigned	Woody Widenhofer	Def. coord., Vanderbilt
Western Mich.	Al Molde	2-9	Fired	Gary Darnell	Def. coord., Texas
Wyoming	Joe Tiller	10-2	to Purdue*	Dana Dimel	Asst., Kansas St.

* As head coach
† Allen missed the first ten games of the season due to cancer but returned for the final two (1-1). He later resigned on Dec. 11. Assistant Tom Mason served as interim coach in his absence.

Division I-AA Football

	Old Coach	Record	Why Left?	New Coach	Old Job
Austin Peay	Roy Gregory	1-10	Reassigned	Bill Schmitz	Coach, Coast Guard
Bethune Cookman ..	Cy McClairen	2-9	Retired	Alvin Wyatt	Asst, Beth. Cookman
CS-Northridge ...	Dave Baldwin	7-4	to San Jose St.*	Jim Fenwick	Coach, LA Valley Coll.
Cal Poly SLO	Andre Patterson	5-6	to NFL Patriots**	Larry Welsh	Atascadero HS (Cal.)
Delaware St.	Bill Collick	3-8	Resigned to AD	John McKenzie	Off. coord., Fayetteville St.
E. Tenn. St.	Mike Cavan	10-3	to SMU*	Paul Hamilton	QB coach, Air Force
Georgia Southern ...	Frank Ellwood	4-7	Interim Basis	Paul Johnson	Off. coord., Navy
Idaho St.	Brian McNeely	4-7	Resigned	Thomas Walsh	CBS Radio analyst
Jacksonville St.	Bill Burgess	1-9	Fired	Mike Williams	Asst., Southern Miss.
La Salle%	—	—		Bill Manlove	Coach, Delaware Valley
Murray St.	Houston Nutt	11-2	to Boise St.*	Denver Johnson	Asst., Oklahoma
Northern Iowa	Terry Allen	12-2	to Kansas*	Mike Dunbar	Asst., Toledo

Coaching Changes (Cont.)

	Old Coach	Record	Why Left?	New Coach	Old Job
Prarie View A&M ...	Hensley Sapenter	0-10	Resigned	Gregory Johnson	Coach, Langston
Southern Illinois	Shawn Watson	5-6	Resigned	John Quarless	Off. coord., Wake Forest
Southern Utah	Rich Ellerson	3-7	Resigned	C. Ray Gregory	Asst., Georgia Southern
SW Texas St.	Jim Bob Helduser	5-6	Fired	Bob DeBesse	Off. coord., Minnesota
Tenn-Martin	Don McLeary	1-10	Fired	Jim Marshall	Off. line coach, Memphis
VMI	Bill Stewart	3-8	Resigned	Ted Cain	Off. coord., N.C. State
Western Carolina ...	Steve Hodgin	4-7	Fired	Bill Bleil	Off. coord., West. Car.
Yale	Carm Cozza	2-8	Retired	Jack Siedlecki	Coach, Amherst, MA

* As head coach
** As asst. coach
% LaSalle reinstated its football program for the 1997 season after a 56 year hiatus.

House Cleaning

There are five Division I member institutions who have new football and men's basketball head coaches for the 1997-98 season.

	Basketball			Football	
School	**Old Coach**	**New Coach**		**Old Coach**	**New Coach**
Boston College	Jim O'Brien	Al Skinner		Dan Henning	Tom O'Brien
Bethune Cookman	Tony Sheals	Horace Broadnax		Cy McClairen	Alvin Wyatt
Delaware St.	Art Perry	James Dubose		Bill Collick	John McKenzie
Kentucky	Rick Pitino	Tubby Smith		Bill Curry	Hal Mumme
Wyoming	Joby Wright	Larry Shyatt		Joe Tiller	Dana Dimel

NCAA Division I Schools on Probation

As of Sept. 1, 1997, there were 24 Division I member institutions serving NCAA probations.

School	Sport	Yrs	Penalty To End	School	Sport	Yrs	Penalty To End
Georgia Southern ..	M Basketball	2	11/11/97	Bethune-Cookman ..	Football	4	6/2/99
Alcorn St.	M/W Basketball	3	11/13/97	....	M/W Basketball	4	6/2/99
....	& Football	3	11/13/97	....	M Tennis	4	6/2/99
Morgan St	Football	3	2/3/98	....	& W Track	4	6/2/99
....	M/W Basketball	3	2/3/98	Michigan St.	Football	4	12/1/99
....	M/W X-Country	3	2/3/98	UCLA	Softball	3	2/1/00
....	M/W Tennis	3	2/3/98	Cal-Berkeley	M Basketball	3	6/1/00
....	M/W Track	3	2/3/98	Maine	M Ice Hockey	4	6/3/00
....	& Wrestling	3	2/3/98	....	Baseball	4	6/3/00
Arizona St.	M & W Track	2	6/2/98	....	Football	4	6/3/00
New Mexico St...	M Basketball	3	8/1/98	....	M/W Track and XC	4	6/3/00
Coastal Carolina ..	M Basketball	4	8/12/98	....	W Soccer	4	6/3/00
Louisville	M Basketball	2	9/21/98	....	Field Hockey	4	6/3/00
Montana St.	M Basketball	2	9/22/98	....	M Basketball	4	6/3/00
Mississippi	Football	4	9/30/98	....	& M Golf	4	6/3/00
Alabama St.	W Volleyball	3	9/30/98	Texas-Pan American ..	M Basketball	8	7/25/00
....	W Track	3	9/30/98	Weber St.	M Basketball	4	8/7/00
....	& M Basketball	3	9/30/98	Texas Southern	M/W Track and XC	5	8/11/01
Miami-FL	Football	3	11/10/98	....	Football	5	8/11/01
....	Baseball	3	11/10/98	....	Baseball	5	8/11/01
....	W Golf	3	11/10/98	....	M Tennis	5	8/11/01
....	& M Tennis	3	11/10/98	....	& M Golf	5	8/11/01
Texas A&M	Football	5	1/6/99	Texas-El Paso	M & W Basketball	5	5/1/02
Georgia	Football	2	1/31/99	....	Football	5	5/1/02
Kansas St.	W Basketball	3	5/31/99	....	& W Rifle	5	5/1/02
Grambling St.	Football	2	6/2/99				
....	& M&W Basketball	2	6/2/99				

Remaining postseason and TV sanctions

1997-98 postseason ban: Texas Southern men's and women's cross country; Cal-Berkeley men's basketball.
1997-98 television ban: none

1996-97 Directors' Cup

Officially, the Sears Directors' Cup and sponsored by the National Association of Collegiate Directors of Athletics. Introduced in 1993-94 to honor the nation's best overall NCAA Division I athletic department (combining men's and women's sports), winners in NCAA Division II and III and NAIA were named for the first time following the 1995-96 season.

Standings computed by NACDA with points awarded for each Div. I school's finish in 22 sports (9 core and two wild card sports for both men and women). Div. II schools are awarded points in 16 sports (6 core and two wild card sports for both men and women). Div III schools are awarded points in 18 sports (7 core and two wild card sports for both men and women). NAIA schools are awarded points in 16 sports (6 core and two wild card sports for both men and women). National champions in each sports get 64 points, runners-up get 63, etc., through tournament field. Division I-A football points based on final *USA Today*/CNN Coaches Top 25 poll. Listed below are team conferences (for Div. I only), combined Final Four finishes (1st thru 4th place) for men's and women's programs, overall points in **bold** type, and the previous year's ranking (for Div. I only).

Division I

		Conf	1-2-3-4	Pts	95-96 Rank			Conf	1-2-3-4	Pts	95-96 Rank
1	Stanford	Pac-10	6-2-2-2	**1084½**	1	14	Notre Dame	Indep.	0-2-1-0	**558½**	12
2	N. Carolina	ACC	2-0-2-0	**804**	6	15	Minnesota	Big Ten	0-0-2-0	**556½**	22
3	UCLA	Pac-10	2-2-2-1	**802**	2	16	BYU	WAC	0-0-1-0	**553**	NR
4	Nebraska	Big 12	0-0-1-0	**780½**	8	17	Tennessee	SEC	1-0-0-0	**531½**	13
5	Florida	SEC	1-1-1-0	**763**	3	18	Alabama	SEC	0-1-0-0	**529½**	NR
6	Arizona	Pac-10	2-0-1-1	**672½**	7	19	Auburn	SEC	1-1-0-0	**527**	14
7	Texas	Big 12	0-3-1-1	**671**	4	20	Penn St.	Big Ten	1-0-1-0	**520**	9
8	Ohio St.	Big Ten	0-1-0-2	**628**	17	21	Colorado	Big 12	0-0-1-1	**519½**	25
	USC	Pac-10	1-1-1-0	**628**	10	22	Virginia	ACC	0-0-0-1	**519**	19
10	LSU	SEC	3-0-0-0	**624**	16	23	Duke	ACC	0-0-2-0	**506½**	NR
11	Michigan	Big Ten	0-0-1-1	**610½**	5	24	Wisconsin	Big Ten	0-1-0-1	**505**	18
	Washington	Pac-10	1-0-1-0	**610½**	NR	25	California	Pac-10	1-0-0-0	**503½**	NR
13	Arizona St.	Pac-10	1-1-0-0	**571**	21						

Division II

		1-2-3-4	Pts			1-2-3-4	Pts
1	UC-Davis	0-0-4-0	**706**	14	Shippensburg, PA	0-0-0-0	**349**
2	Abilene Christian	3-1-0-0	**460½**	15	Oakland, MI	1-2-0-0	**334**
3	CS-Bakersfield	1-0-1-0	**435½**	16	Ashland, OH	0-0-0-0	**321½**
4	Central Oklahoma	0-1-1-0	**397**	17	Tampa	0-1-1-0	**320½**
5	Indianapolis	0-0-0-0	**390½**	18	Cal Poly Pomona	0-0-1-0	**317½**
6	Cent. Missouri St.	0-0-1-2	**390**	19	Nebraska Kearney	0-0-0-0	**312½**
7	South Dakota St.	1-0-0-1	**388½**		NW Missouri St.	0-0-0-0	**312½**
8	Lynn, FL	2-1-3-0	**376**	21	North Dakota	2-0-1-1	**310**
9	Western St., CO	0-1-0-1	**374½**	22	Edinboro, PA	0-0-0-0	**308½**
10	N. Colorado	1-0-0-0	**372**	23	Kennesaw St., GA	0-0-1-0	**308**
11	Bloomsburg, PA	1-0-0-0	**367**	24	Fort Hays St., KS	0-0-0-0	**298½**
12	North Dakota St.	0-0-0-0	**366**		Lewis, IL	0-1-2-1	**298½**
13	North Florida	0-1-1-0	**356½**				

Division III

		1-2-3-4	Pts			1-2-3-4	Pts
1	Williams, MA	0-1-2-0	**838½**	14	Gustavus Adolphus, MN	0-0-0-1	**376**
2	College of New Jersey	2-2-2-2	**755½**	15	Claremont-Mudd-Scripps, CA	0-0-0-0	**370**
3	UC-San Diego	1-1-1-0	**677**	16	Johns Hopkins, MD	0-0-1-0	**352½**
4	Emory, GA	0-0-1-0	**653**	17	Wisc.-Eau Claire	0-1-0-0	**341**
5	Wisc.-Oshkosh	2-0-1-2	**616½**	18	St. Thomas, MN	0-1-0-0	**340½**
6	Ithaca, NY	0-0-1-0	**598½**	19	Springfield, MA	0-0-0-0	**326**
7	Amherst, MA	0-0-1-0	**518½**	20	Kenyon, OH	3-1-0-0	**324**
8	Cortland St., NY	0-0-2-0	**465**	21	Mt. Union, OH	1-0-2-0	**323**
9	Rowan, NJ	0-1-0-0	**452**	22	Calvin, MI	0-0-0-1	**321½**
10	Wisc.-La Crosse	3-1-1-0	**438½**	23	Trinity, TX	0-1-0-0	**312½**
11	Wisc.-Stevens Point	0-0-1-1	**429**	24	Wooster, OH	0-1-0-0	**312**
12	Middlebury, VT	2-0-0-0	**410**	25	Salisbury St., MD	0-0-0-0	**300**
13	Binghamton, NY	0-0-0-0	**399**				

NAIA

		1-2-3-4	Pts			1-2-3-4	Pts
1	Simon Fraser, BC	3-2-0-0	588½	14	Life, GA	3-1-0-1	337
2	Pacific Lutheran, WA	0-0-2-1	496½	15	Western Washington	0-1-0-1	334½
3	Azusa Pacific, CA	0-0-1-1	486½	16	Concordia, NE	0-0-0-0	330½
4	Mobile, AL	2-2-1-0	446		Findlay, OH	0-0-1-1	330½
5	Willamette, OR	0-0-1-0	437½	18	Mary, ND	0-2-1-0	327
6	So. Nazarene, OK	1-0-1-1	412½	19	Taylor, IN	0-0-1-0	324½
7	Berry, GA	0-0-0-0	412	20	Hawaii Pacific	0-0-0-1	321
8	Nebraska Wesleyan	0-0-0-0	407½	21	Lindenwood, MO	0-0-0-0	317
9	Cumberland, KY	0-0-1-0	403½	22	Lindsey Wilson, KY	1-0-0-0	310½
10	Puget Sound, WA	1-2-0-0	390½	23	Northwestern, IA	0-0-0-0	300½
11	SW Oklahoma St.	1-0-3-0	373	24	Doane, NE	0-0-1-1	294
12	Oklahoma City	1-0-0-0	354½	25	Oklahoma Baptist	0-1-0-0	293
13	Westmont, CA	0-0-2-0	351½				

1996–97 NCAA Team Champions

Thirteen schools won two or more national championships during the 1996-97 academic year, led by Division I Stanford with six and four schools with three each.

Multiple winners: SIX— Stanford (Div. I men's cross country, women's cross country, women's volleyball, men's tennis, women's tennis and National division of men's volleyball). THREE— Abilene Christian (Div. II men's indoor track, women's indoor track and men's outdoor track); Kenyon, OH (Div III men's swimming & diving, women's swimming & diving and women's tennis); LSU (Div. I women's indoor track, baseball and women's outdoor track); Wisconsin LaCrosse (Div. III men's cross country, men's indoor track and men's outdoor track). TWO— Arizona (Div I softball and men's basketball); Arkansas (Div. I men's indoor track and men's outdoor track); College of New Jersey (Div. III field hockey and men's soccer); Lynn, FL (Combined Div. II and III women's golf and Div. II women's tennis); Middlebury, VT (Div. III ice hockey and women's lacrosse); North Carolina (Div. I field hockey and women's soccer); UCLA (National divisions of water polo and women's gymnastics); Wisconsin Oshkosh (Div. III women's cross country and women's outdoor track).

Overall titles in parentheses; (*) indicates defending champions.

FALL

Cross Country

Men

Div.	Winner		Runner-Up	Score
I	Stanford	(1)	Arkansas*	46-74
II	South Dakota St.	(5)	Lewis, IL	119-142
III	Wisc.-La Crosse	(1)	N. Central, IL	86-94

Women

Div.	Winner		Runner-Up	Score
I	Stanford	(1)	Villanova	101-106
II	Adams St., CO*	(5)	Western St., CO	35-94
III	Wisc.-Oshkosh	(4)	St. Thomas, MN	62-113

Field Hockey

Div.	Winner		Runner-Up	Score
I	North Carolina*	(3)	Princeton	3-0
II	Bloomsburg, PA	(3)	Lock Haven, PA*	1-0
III	Coll. of New Jersey	(8)	Hartwick	2-1

Football

Div.	Winner		Runner-Up	Score
I-A	Florida	(1)	Ohio St.	AP poll
I-AA	Marshall	(2)	Montana*	49-29
II	Northern Colo.	(1)	Carson-Newman, TN	23-14
III	Mt. Union, OH	(2)	Rowan, NJ	56-24

Note: There is no official Div. I-A playoff.

Soccer

Men

Div.	Winner		Runner-Up	Score
I	St. John's, NY	(1)	Florida Int'l.	4-1
II	Grand Canyon	(1)	Oakland, MI	3-1
III	Coll. of New Jersey	(1)	Kenyon, OH	2-1 (4OT)

Women

Div.	Winner		Runner-Up	Score
I	North Carolina	(13)	Notre Dame*	1-0 (OT)
II	Franklin Pierce, NH*	(3)	Lynn, FL	1-0
III	UC-San Diego*	(3)	Coll. of New Jersey	2-1

Volleyball

Women

Div.	Winner		Runner-Up	Score
I	Stanford	(3)	Hawaii	3 sets
II	Nebraska-Omaha	(1)	Tampa	5 sets
III	Washington, MO*	(7)	Juniata, PA	3 sets

Water Polo

Div.	Winner		Runner-Up	Score
National	UCLA*	(5)	USC	8-7

WINTER

Basketball

Men

Div.	Winner		Runner-Up	Score
I	Arizona	(1)	Kentucky*	84-79 (OT)
II	CS-Bakersfield	(3)	N. Kentucky	57-56
III	Ill-Wesleyan	(1)	Neb-Wesleyan	89-86

Women

Div.	Winner		Runner-Up	Score
I	Tennessee*	(5)	Old Dominion	68-59
II	North Dakota	(1)	Southern Indiana	94-78
III	New York U	(1)	Wisc-Eau Claire	72-70

Fencing

Div.	Winner		Runner-Up	Score
Combined	Penn St.*	(5)	Notre Dame	1530-1470

Gymnastics

Div.	Winner		Runner-Up	Margin
Men	California	(3)	Oklahoma	by 1.100
Women	UCLA	(1)	Arizona St.	by .300

Ice Hockey

Div.	Winner		Runner-Up	Score
I	North Dakota	(6)	Boston University	6-4
II	Bemidji St., MN	(5)	Alabama-Huntsville*	3-2,4-2†
III	Middlebury, VT*	(3)	Wisc-Superior	3-2

†Div. II championship is decided by a two-game series.

Rifle

Div.	Winner	Runner-Up	Score
Combined	....West Va.* (12)	Kentucky	6223-6175

Skiing

Div.	Winner	Runner-Up	Score
Combined	.......Utah* (9)	Vermont	686-646½

Swimming & Diving
Men

Div.	Winner	Runner-Up	Score
I	.............Auburn	(1) Stanford	496½-340
II	........Oakland, MI*	(5) Drury, MO	767-623
III	........Kenyon, OH*	(18) UC-San Diego	689½-336

Women

Div.	Winner	Runner-Up	Score
I	................USC	(1) Stanford*	406-395
II	.........Drury, MO	(1) Oakland, MI	690½-490
III	........Kenyan, OH*	(14) Williams, MA	572-377

Indoor Track
Men

Div.	Winner	Runner-Up	Score
I	...........Arkansas	(13) Auburn	59-27
II	...Abilene Christian*	(5) St. Augustine's	128-43
III	......Wisc-La Crosse	(7) Lincoln, PA*	44-41

Women

Div.	Winner	Runner-Up	Score
I	................LSU*	(8) (tie) Texas, Wisconsin	49-39
II	...Abilene Christian*	(9) St. Augustine's	76-61
III	......Chris. Newport	(5) CCNY	47-36

Wrestling

Div.	Winner	Runner-Up	Score
I	................Iowa*	(17) Oklahoma St.	170-113½
II	........San Fran. St.	(1) Neb-Omaha	95-81
III	.....Augsburg, MN	(4) Wartburg, IA*	122-80

SPRING
Baseball

Div.	Winner	Runner-Up	Score
I	.................LSU*	(4) Alabama	13-6
II	.........Cal St.-Chico	(1) Central Oklahoma	13-12
III	......Southern Maine	(2) Wooster, OH	15-1

Golf
Men

Div.	Winner	Runner-Up	Score
I	...........Pepperdine	(1) Wake Forest	1148-1151
II	........Columbus St.	(6) North Florida	1149-1153
III	......Methodist, NC*	(7) Greensboro, NC	1191-1226

Women

Div.	Winner	Runner-Up	Score
I	...........Arizona St.	(5) San Jose St.	1178-1180
II and III	........Lynn, FL	(1) Methodist*	1292-1318

Lacrosse
Men

Div.	Winner	Runner-Up	Score
I	...........Princeton*	(4) Maryland	19-7
II	........New York Tech	(1) Adelphi, NY	18-11
III	.......Nazareth, NY*	(3) Washington, MD	15-14 (OT)

Women

Div.	Winner	Runner-Up	Score
National	.....Maryland*	(5) Loyola, MD	8-7
III	......Middlebury, VT	(1) Coll. of New Jersey*	14-9

Rowing
Women

Div.	Winner	Runner-Up	Score
National	....Washington	(1)* Princeton	201-184

*The 1997 National Collegiate Women's Rowing Championships were the first to be sponsored by the NCAA. National championships had been held without NCAA sponsorship since 1979 with Washington winning seven titles.

Softball

Div.	Winner	Runner-Up	Score
I	.............Arizona*	(5) UCLA	10-2†
II	.......California, PA	(1) Wisc-Parkside	2-1
III	.......Simpson, IA	(1) Montclair St.	2-1

†Game was called after five innings due to the eight run "mercy rule."

Tennis

Note that both Div. II tournaments were team-only.

Men

Div.	Winner	Runner-Up	Score
I	.............Stanford*	(15) Georgia	4-0
II	...........Lander, SC*	(5) West Florida	5-1
III	.....Washington, MD	(2) Kalamazoo	4-2

Women

Div.	Winner	Runner-Up	Score
I	............Stanford	(9) Florida*	5-1
II	..............Lynn, FL	(1) Armstrong Atlantic*	5-4
III	..........Kenyon, OH	(3) Trinity, TX	6-3

Outdoor Track
Men

Div.	Winner	Runner-Up	Score
I	.............Arkansas*	(7) Texas	55-42½
II	.....Abilene Christian*	(9) Angelo St.	151-69
III	......Wisc-La Crosse	(5) Lincoln, PA*	69½-58⅓

Women

Div.	Winner	Runner-Up	Score
I	................LSU*	(11) Texas	63-62
II	......St. Augustine's	(1) Abilene Christian*	81-69
III	.....Wisc-Oshkosh	(5) Wisc-La Crosse	59-38¾

Volleyball
Men

Div.	Winner	Runner-Up	Score
National	.......Stanford	(1) UCLA*	5 sets

Ohio St.
Blaine Wilson
Gymnastics

Arizona
Amy Skieresz
Cross-country/Track

Iowa
Lincoln McIlravy
Wrestling

Denver
Roberta Pergher
Skiing

1996–97 Division I Individual Champions
Repeat champions in **bold** type.

FALL

Cross-country

Men (10,000 meters)	Time
1 **Godfrey Siamusiye**, Arkansas	29:49
2 Jonah Kiptarus, Nebraska	30:20
3 Cleophas Boor, Nebraska	30:24

Women (5,000 meters)	Time
1 Amy Skieresz, Arizona	17:04
2 Marie McMahon, Providence	17:20
3 Joanna Deeter, Notre Dame	17:24

WINTER

Fencing

Men

Event		Record
Foil	Cliff Bayer, Penn	20-3
Epee	Alden Clarke, Stanford	22-1
Sabre	Keeth Smart, St. John's	20-3

Women

Event		Record
Foil	Yelena Kalkina, Ohio St.	19-4
Epee	Magda Krol, Notre Dame	18-5

Gymnastics

Men

Event		Points
All-Around	**Blaine Wilson**, Ohio St.	58.625
Floor Exercise	Jeremy Killen, Oklahoma	9.825
Pommel Horse	**Drew Durbin**, Ohio St.	9.912
Rings	**Blaine Wilson**, Ohio St.	9.900
Vault	Blaine Wilson, Ohio St.	9.8125
Parallel Bars	Marshall Nelson, Nebraska	9.950
Horizontal Bar	Marshall Nelson, Nebraska	9.7875

Women

Event		Points
All-Around	Kim Arnold, Georgia	39.550
Vault	Susan Hines, Florida	9.8875
Uneven Bars	Jenni Beathard, Georgia	9.900
Balance Beam (tie)	**Summer Reid**, Utah	9.900
	& Elizabeth Reid, Arizona St.	9.900
Floor Exercise	Leah Brown, Georgia	9.950

Rifle
Combined
Smallbore

	Points
1 Marcos Scrivner, West Va.	1,176
2 Jeff Odor, Wyoming	1,172
3 Matt Aquaro, West Va.	1,170

Air Rifle

	Points
1 Marra Hastings, Murray St.	393
2 Daniel Pempel, Air Force	392
3 Kim Howe, West Va.	390

Skiing

Men

Event		Time
Slalom	Izidor Jerman, Alaska-Anch.	1:28.03
Giant Slalom	Brandon Dyksterhouse, Vermont	2:09.79
10-k Classical	Frode Lillefjell, Alaska-Anch.	30:45.9
20-k Freestyle	Thorodd Bakken, Vermont	56:05.4

Women

Event		Time
Slalom	**Roberta Pergher**, Denver	1:40.93
Giant Slalom	Christl Hager, Utah	2:14.39
5-k Classical	Doris Hausleitner, Alaska-Anch.	17:50
15-k Freestyle	Amy Crawford, Western St.	50:38.9

Wrestling

Wgt	Champion	Runner-Up
118	Jessie Whitmer, Iowa	Lindsey Durlacher, Illinois
126	Eric Guerrero, Okla. St.	Mike Mena, Iowa
134	Mark Ironside, Iowa	Steven Schmidt, Okla. St.
142	**Cary Kolat**, Lock Haven	Roger Chandler, Ind.
150	Lincoln McIlravy, Iowa	Chris Bono, Iowa St.
158	**Joe Williams**, Iowa	Tony Robie, Edinboro
167	Mark Branch, Okla. St.	Brandon Slay, Penn
177	Barry Weldon, Iowa St.	Mitch Clark, Ohio St.
190	Lee Fullhart, Iowa	John Kading, Oklahoma
Hvy	Kerry McCoy, Penn St.	Stephen Neal, CS-Bak.

SMU
Martina Moravcova
Swimming

Arkansas
Robert Howard
Track & Field

South Carolina
Dawn Ellerbe
Track & Field

Tennessee
Jeremy Linn
Swimming

Swimming & Diving
(*) indicates meet record

Men

Event (yards)		Time
50 free	Brett Hawke, Auburn	19.19
100 free	Lars Frolander, SMU	42.89
200 free	John Piersma, Michigan	1:34.88
500 free	John Piersma, Michigan	4:15.79
1650 free	Ryk Neethling, Arizona	14:43.44
100 back	Neil Walker, Texas	45.25*
200 back	Lenny Krayzelburg, USC	1:41.10
100 breast	**Jeremy Linn**, Tennessee	52.32*
200 breast	Jeremy Linn, Tennessee	1:55.27
100 butterfly	Lars Frolander, SMU	46.28
200 butterfly	Stephen Parry, Florida St.	1:44.28
200 IM	Kris Babylon, Georgia	1:45.19
400 IM	Tom Wilkens, Stanford	3:45.59
200 free relay	Auburn	1:17.54
400 free relay	**Auburn**	2:51.23
800 free relay	**Michigan**	6:23.51
200 medley relay	Auburn	1:25.40*
400 medley relay	Auburn	3:08.96

Diving		Points
1-meter	Rio Ramirez, Miami-FL	610.05
3-meter	Tyce Routson, Miami-FL	643.10
Platform	Tyce Routson, Miami-FL	811.80

Women

Event (yards)		Time
50 free	Catherine Fox, Stanford	22.00
100 free	Martina Moravcova, SMU	48.18
200 free	**Martina Moravcova**, SMU	1:43.08*
500 free	Lindsay Benko, USC	4:41.85
1650 free	Trina Jackson, Arizona	15:59.82
100 back	Catherine Fox, Stanford	53.23
200 back	**Lindsay Benko**, USC	1:54.42
100 breast	Gretchen Hegener, Minnesota	1:00.32
200 breast	**Kristine Quance**, USC	2:09.62
100 butterfly	Mimi Bowen, Auburn	52.05
200 butterfly	Lia Oberstar, SMU	1:56.76
200 IM	Martina Moravcova, SMU	1:55.81
400 IM	**Kristine Quance**, USC	4:06.54
200 free relay	**Arizona**	1:29.56
400 free relay	**Stanford**	3:16.72
800 free relay	SMU	7:09.92
200 medley relay	Auburn	1:39.57
400 medley relay	**SMU**	3:35.98

Diving		Points
1-meter	Vera Ilyina, Texas	455.90
3-meter	Vera Ilyina, Texas	587.80
Platform	Laura Wilkinson, Texas	606.10

Indoor Track
(*) indicates meet record

Men

Event		Time
55 meters	Bryan Howard, Auburn	6.19
200 meters	**Obadele Thompson**, UTEP	20.67
400 meters	Roxbert Martin, Oklahoma	45.69*
800 meters	David Krummenacker, Ga. Tech	1:47.49
Mile	**Julius Achon**, George Mason	3:59.85
3000 meters	Adam Goucher, Colorado	7:54.20
5000 meters	Mebrahtom Keflezighi, UCLA	13:52.72
55-m hurdles	Neil Gardner, Michigan	7.18
4x400-m relay	**Oklahoma**	3:04.25*
Distance medley relay	George Mason	9:32.27

Event		Hgt/Dist
High Jump	Eric Bishop, North Carolina	7-6
Pole Vault	Jason Hinkin, Long Beach St.	18-6½
Long Jump	Robert Howard, Arkansas	26-9¼
Triple Jump	**Robert Howard**, Arkansas	55-11
Shot Put	Aaron Ausmus, Tennessee	62-4
35-lb Throw	Sean McGehearty, BC	72-3

Women

Event		Time
55 meters	Sevatheda Fynes, Eastern Mich.	6.65
200 meters	Nanceen Perry, Texas	23.09
400 meters	LaTarsha Stroman, LSU	52.77
800 meters	Dawn Williams-Sewer, Ark.-LR	2:02.55
Mile	Becki Wells, Florida	4:33.04
3000 meters	Kristine Jost, Villanova	9:14.14
5000 meters	Amy Skieresz, Arizona	15:39.75*
55-m hurdles	Tiffany Lott, BYU	7.42
4x400-m relay	Rice	3:34.44
Distance medley relay	Georgetown	11:08.54*

Event		Hgt/Dist
High Jump	Amy Acuff, UCLA	6-3¼
Long Jump	Trecia Smith, Pittsburgh	21-10¼
Triple Jump	Suzette Lee, LSU	46-9*
Shot Put	Tressa Thompson, Nebraska	59-0*
20-lb Throw	**Dawn Ellerbe**, S. Carolina	71-8¾*

Spring

Golf

Men

			Total
1	Charles Warren, Clemson	71-68-73-67	—279*
2	Brad Elder, Texas	71-69-67-72	—279
3	Jason Gore, Pepperdine	65-72-71-72	—280
	Keith Nolan, E. Tenn. St.	71-66-69-74	—280

* Warren won on the first sudden death playoff hole.

Women

		Total
1	Heather Bowie, Texas	73-73-69-70—285
2	Marisa Baena, Arizona	72-73-73-69—287
	Janice Moodie, San Jose St.	68-74-74-71—287

Tennis

Men

Singles— Luke Smith (UNLV) def. George Bastl (USC), 6-4, 6-3.

Doubles— Tim Blenkiron & Luke Smith (UNLV) def. George Bastl & Kyle Spencer (USC), 6-4, 6-4.

Women

Singles— Lilia Osterloh (Stanford) def. M.C. White (Florida), 6-1, 6-1.

Doubles— Dawn Buth & Stephanie Nickitas (Florida) def. Marissa Catlin & Michelle Anderson (Georgia), 6-2, 3-6, 6-2.

Outdoor Track

(*) indicates meet record

Men

Event		Time
100 meters	Obadele Thompson, UTEP	10.13
200 meters	Obadele Thompson, UTEP	20.03
400 meters	Roxbert Martin, Oklahoma	44.77
800 meters	Bryan Woodward, Georgetown	1:46.45
1500 meters	Seneca Lassiter, Arkansas	3:40.22
5000 meters	Mebrahtom Keflezighi, UCLA	13:44.17
10,000 meters	Mebrahtom Keflezighi, UCLA	28:51.18
110-m hurdles	Reggie Torian, Wisconsin	13.39
400-m hurdles	Joey Woody, N. Iowa	48.59
3000-m steeple	Pascal Dobert, Wisconsin	8:31.68
4x100-m relay	Texas A&M	38.80
4x400-m relay	Oklahoma	3:01.25

Event		Hgt/Dist
High Jump	Ivan Wagner, Texas	7-6½
Pole Vault	Clark Humphreys, Auburn	18-4½
Long Jump	Robert Howard, Arkansas	26-11¼
Triple Jump	**Robert Howard**, Arkansas	55-6½
Shot Put	Adam Nelson, Dartmouth	64-4½
Discus	Jason Tunks, SMU	195-11
Javelin	Mats Nilsson, Alabama	245-9
Hammer	Bengt Johansson, USC	230-1
Decathlon	James Dunkleberger, Wisconsin	7924 pts

Women

Event		Time
100 meters	Sevatheda Fynes, Michigan St.	11.04
200 meters	Sevatheda Fynes, Michigan St.	22.61
400 meters	LaTarsha Stroman, LSU	50.60
800 meters	Dana Riley, Texas	2:02.89
1500 meters	Becki Wells, Florida	4:12.84
3000 meters	**Kathy Butler**, Wisconsin	9:01.23
5000 meters	Amy Skiersez, Arizona	15:46.76
10,000 meters	Amy Skiersez, Arizona	33:14.22
100-m hurdles	Astia Walker, LSU	12.85
400-m hurdles	Ryan Tolbert, Vanderbilt	54.54*
4x100-m relay	LSU	43.17
4x400-m relay	Texas	3:28.43

Event		Hgt/Dist
High Jump	Kajsa Bergqvist, SMU	6-4
Long Jump	Trecia Smith, Pittsburgh	21-10
Triple Jump	**Suzette Lee**, LSU	45-8
Shot Put	Tressa Thompson, Nebraska	60-8½*
Discus	Seilala Sua, UCLA	200-6
Javelin	**Windy Dean**, SMU	191-2
Hammer	**Dawn Ellerbe**, S. Carolina	207-4
Heptathlon	Tiffany Lott, BYU	6211 pts

Most Outstanding Players

Men

Baseball	Brandon Larson, LSU
Basketball	Miles Simon, Arizona
Cross-country	Godfrey Siamusiye, Arkansas*
Golf	Charles Warren, Clemson*
Gymnastics	Blaine Wilson, Ohio St.*
Ice Hockey	Matt Henderson, North Dakota
Lacrosse	Jon Hess, Princeton
Swimming & Diving	Neil Walker, Texas
Tennis	Luke Smith, UNLV*
Track: Indoor	Robert Howard, Arkansas
Outdoor	Robert Howard, Arkansas, Mebrahtom Keflezighi, UCLA & Obadele Thompson, UTEP
Volleyball	Mike Lambert, Stanford
Water Polo	Matt Swanson, UCLA
Wrestling	Lincoln McIlravy, Iowa

Women

Basketball	Chamique Holdsclaw, Tennessee
Cross-country	Amy Skiersez, Arizona*
Golf	Heather Bowie, Texas*
Gymnastics	Kim Arnold, Georgia*
Soccer: Offense	Debbie Keller, North Carolina
Soccer: Defense	Nel Fettig, North Carolina
Softball	Nancy Evans, Arizona
Swimming & Diving	Martina Moravcova, SMU
Tennis	Lilia Osterloh, Stanford*
Track: Indoor	Suzette Lee, LSU & Trecia Smith, Pitt
Track: Outdoor	Sevatheda Fynes, Michigan St., Amy Skiersez, Arizona & Astia Walker, LSU
Volleyball	Kerri Walsh, Stanford

(*) indicates won individual or all-around NCAA championship; There were no official Outstanding Players in field hockey, men's soccer, or the men's and women's combined sports of fencing, riflery and skiing. Outstanding players in indoor and outdoor track are the individuals earning the most points in the NCAA Championships.

1996-97 NAIA Team Champions

Total NAIA titles in parentheses.

FALL

Cross Country: MEN'S–Lubbock Christian, TX (7); WOMEN'S– Simon Fraser, BC (3). **Football:** MEN'S–Division I: SW Oklahoma St. (1) and Division II: Sioux Falls, SD (1). **Soccer:** MEN'S– Lindsey Wilson, KY (2); WOMEN'S– Simon Fraser, BC (1). **Volleyball:** WOMEN'S– BYU-Hawaii (7).

WINTER

Basketball: MEN'S– Division I: Life, GA (1) and Division II: Bethel, IN (2); WOMEN'S– Division I: Southern Nazarene, OK (5) and Division II: NW Nazarene (1). **Swimming & Diving:** MEN'S– Puget Sound, WA (3); WOMEN'S– Simon Fraser, BC (6). **Indoor Track:** MEN'S– Life, GA (1); WOMEN'S– Southern-New Orleans (2). **Wrestling:** MEN'S– Missouri Valley (2).

SPRING

Baseball: MEN'S– Brewton-Parker, GA (1); **Golf:** MEN'S– Mobile, AL (1); WOMEN'S– Tri-State, IN (1); **Softball:** WOMEN'S– Oklahoma City (4); **Tennis:** MEN'S– Mobile, AL (2); WOMEN'S– BYU-Hawaii (1); **Outdoor Track:** MEN'S– Life, GA (1); WOMEN'S– Southern-New Orleans (2).

Annual NCAA Division I Team Champions

Men's and Women's NCAA Division I team champions from Cross-country to Wrestling. Rowing is included, although the NCAA does not sanction championships on the men's side. 1997 was the first year of NCAA sanctioned women's rowing championships. Team champions in baseball, basketball, football, golf, ice hockey, soccer and tennis can be found in the appropriate chapters throughout the almanac. See pages 452-454 for list of 1996-97 individual champions.

CROSS-COUNTRY

Men

Stanford grabbed five of the top 15 individual spots to run away from defending champion Arkansas and win their first cross country team championship. The Cardinal finished with 46 points, 28 fewer than the 74 amassed by the Razorbacks. They were paced by Gregory Jimmerson who finished fourth, completing the 10,000-meter course in 30:38, 49 seconds behind individual champion Godfrey Siamusiye of Arkansas. *(Tucson, Ariz.; Nov. 25, 1996.)*

Multiple winners: Michigan St. and Arkansas (8); UTEP (7); Oregon and Villanova (4); Drake, Indiana, Penn St. and Wisconsin (3); Iowa St., San Jose St. and Western Michigan (2).

Year		Year		Year		Year		Year	
1938	Indiana	1949	Michigan St.	1961	Oregon St.	1973	Oregon	1985	Wisconsin
1939	Michigan St.	1950	Penn St.	1962	San Jose St.	1974	Oregon	1986	Arkansas
1940	Indiana	1951	Syracuse	1963	San Jose St.	1975	UTEP	1987	Arkansas
1941	Rhode Island	1952	Michigan St.	1964	Western Mich.	1976	UTEP	1988	Wisconsin
1942	Indiana	1953	Kansas	1965	Western Mich.	1977	Oregon	1989	Iowa St.
	& Penn St.	1954	Oklahoma St.	1966	Villanova	1978	UTEP	1990	Arkansas
1943	Not held	1955	Michigan St.	1967	Villanova	1979	UTEP	1991	Arkansas
1944	Drake	1956	Michigan St.	1968	Villanova	1980	UTEP	1992	Arkansas
1945	Drake	1957	Notre Dame	1969	UTEP	1981	UTEP	1993	Arkansas
1946	Drake	1958	Michigan St.	1970	Villanova	1982	Wisconsin	1994	Iowa St.
1947	Penn St.	1959	Michigan St.	1971	Oregon	1983	Vacated	1995	Arkansas
1948	Michigan St.	1960	Houston	1972	Tennessee	1984	Arkansas	1996	Stanford

Women

Stanford placed three runners in the top 17 and five in the top 55 to edge Villanova by just five points and take home their first women's cross country championship. Monal Chokshi was the top Cardinal finisher, finishing the 5,000-meter course in 17:58 for 10th place. Jessica Fry and Mary Cobb also garnered top 20 finishes, 16th and 17th respectively, to carry the Cardinal. Arizona sophomore Amy Skieresz, runner-up in the 1995 championships, won the individual crown in 17:04, 16 seconds faster than Providence's Marie McMahon. *(Tucson, Ariz.; Nov. 25, 1996.)*

Multiple winners: Villanova (6); Oregon, Virginia and Wisconsin (2).

Year		Year		Year		Year		Year	
1981	Virginia	1985	Wisconsin	1988	Kentucky	1991	Villanova	1994	Villanova
1982	Virginia	1986	Texas	1989	Villanova	1992	Villanova	1995	Providence
1983	Oregon	1987	Oregon	1990	Villanova	1993	Villanova	1996	Stanford
1984	Wisconsin								

FENCING

Men & Women

Penn St. held off a late Notre Dame rally to become the third school in history to win three consecutive fencing team titles. The well-balanced Nittany Lions accomplished the feat despite not having an individual title for the first time since 1990. They finished with 1,530 points, 60 more than the Irish who were runners-up for the second consecutive year. Penn St.'s best showing came in the men's sabre competition as Serge Lilov and Brian Walther each advanced to the medal round with Lilov being edged by St. John's' Keeth Smart in the championship. *(USAF Academy, Col.; Mar. 20-23, 1996.)*

Multiple winners: Penn St. (5); Columbia/Barnard (2). **Note:** Prior to 1990, men and women held separate championships. Men's multiple winners included: NYU (12); Columbia (11); Wayne St. (7); Navy, Notre Dame and Penn (3); Illinois (2). Women's multiple winners included: Wayne St. (3); Yale (2).

Year		Year		Year		Year		Year	
1990	Penn St.	1992	Columbia/	1993	Columbia/	1994	Notre Dame	1996	Penn St.
1991	Penn St.		Barnard		Barnard	1995	Penn St.	1997	Penn St.

FIELD HOCKEY

Women

North Carolina won its second consecutive title and third overall by blanking Princeton 3-0. The stellar Tar Heel defense made life easy for their goalkeeper Jana Withrow as they outshot the Tigers 28-4. Withrow recorded three saves for the shutout. Susannah Schott, Cindy Werley and Ashley Hanson scored for North Carolina, who finished the season with a 23-1 mark, a nice follow-up to their 24-0 season of a year ago. *(Chestnut Hill, Mass.; Nov. 24, 1996.)*

Multiple winners: Old Dominion (7); North Carolina (3); Connecticut and Maryland (2).

Year		Year		Year		Year		Year	
1981	Connecticut	1985	Connecticut	1988	Old Dominion	1991	Old Dominion	1994	J. Madison
1982	Old Dominion	1986	Iowa	1989	N. Carolina	1992	Old Dominion	1995	N. Carolina
1983	Old Dominion	1987	Maryland	1990	Old Dominion	1993	Maryland	1996	N. Carolina
1984	Old Dominion								

Annual NCAA Division I Team Champions (Cont.)

GYMNASTICS

Men

California scored a season-high 233.825 points behind the solid performances of senior Trent Wells to win their first title since 1975. Wells scored a 9.85 in the parallel bars, the floor exercise and the vault to lead the Bears to victory over Oklahoma (232.725) and host Iowa (231.800). Ohio State's Blaine Wilson claimed three individual events, including the all-around title as the Buckeyes finished fourth. *(Iowa City, Iowa; Apr. 17-19, 1997.)*

Multiple winners: Illinois and Penn St. (9); Nebraska (8); So. Illinois (4); California, Iowa St., Oklahoma and Stanford (3); Florida St., Michigan, Ohio St. and UCLA (2).

Year		Year		Year		Year		Year	
1938	Chicago	1955	Illinois	1967	So.Illinois	1977	Indiana St.	1989	Illinois
1939	Illinois	1956	Illinois	1968	California		& Oklahoma	1990	Nebraska
1940	Illinois	1957	Penn St.	1969	Iowa	1978	Oklahoma	1991	Oklahoma
		1958	Michigan St.		& Michigan (T)	1979	Nebraska	1992	Stanford
1941	Illinois		& Illinois	1970	Michigan	1980	Nebraska	1993	Stanford
1942	Illinois	1959	Penn St.		& Michigan (T)			1994	Nebraska
1943-47	Not held					1981	Nebraska	1995	Stanford
1948	Penn St.	1960	Penn St.	1971	Iowa St.	1982	Nebraska	1996	Ohio St.
1949	Temple	1961	Penn St.	1972	So. Illinois	1983	Nebraska	1997	California
1950	Illinois	1962	USC	1973	Iowa St.	1984	UCLA		
		1963	Michigan	1974	Iowa St.	1985	Ohio St.	(T) indicates won tram-	
1951	Florida St.	1964	So. Illinois	1975	California	1986	Arizona St.	poline competition	
1952	Florida St.	1965	Penn St.	1976	Penn St.	1987	UCLA	(1969-70).	
1953	Penn St.	1966	So.Illinois			1988	Nebraska		
1954	Penn St.								

Women

UCLA finally broke into the elite club of women's gymnastics champions as they edged runner-up Arizona St. 197.150–196.850. All previous NCAA titles had been won by either Utah, Alabama or Georgia but the Bruins were too well-rounded this year, scoring at least 49.200 points in three of the four events to capture the title. Leah Homma and Lena Degteva were UCLA's top performers, though third place Georgia laid claim to three individual titles. The Bulldogs' Kim Arnold won the overall title with 39.550 points, beating last year's champ Meredith Willard of Alabama (39.500). *(Gainesville, Fla.; Apr. 17-19, 1997.)*

Multiple Winners: Utah (9); Alabama and Georgia (3).

Year		Year		Year		Year		Year	
1982	Utah	1986	Utah	1989	Georgia	1992	Utah	1995	Utah
1983	Utah	1987	Georgia	1990	Utah	1993	Georgia	1996	Alabama
1984	Utah	1988	Alabama	1991	Alabama	1994	Utah	1997	UCLA
1985	Utah								

LACROSSE

Men

Princeton notched their second consecutive and fourth overall lacrosse championship with a 19-7 thrashing of host Maryland. The victory capped off a perfect season for the Tigers and extended their winning streak to 28 games, the third-longest in NCAA history. Princeton rolled to an 8-0 first-quarter lead led by junior attackman Jon Hess, who netted three goals and dished out five assists for the game. Goaltender Patrick Cairns stopped 17 Terrapin shots for the victory. *(College Park, Md.; May 24-26, 1997.)*

Multiple winners: Johns Hopkins (7); Syracuse (6); North Carolina and Princeton (4); Cornell (3); Maryland (2).

Year		Year		Year		Year		Year	
1971	Cornell	1977	Cornell	1983	Syracuse	1988	Syracuse	1993	Syracuse
1972	Virginia	1978	Johns Hopkins	1984	Johns Hopkins	1989	Syracuse	1994	Princeton
1973	Maryland	1979	Johns Hopkins	1985	Johns Hopkins	1990	Syracuse	1995	Syracuse
1974	Johns Hopkins	1980	Johns Hopkins	1986	North Carolina	1991	North Carolina	1996	Princeton
1975	Maryland	1981	North Carolina	1987	Johns Hopkins	1992	Princeton	1997	Princeton
1976	Cornell	1982	North Carolina						

Women

Sarah Forbes scored the game-winning goal with 4:02 left to give Maryland an 8-7 win over Loyola (Md.) for their third consecutive Division I Women's Lacrosse Championship. It was a nip-and-tuck affair all the way with the Terps jumping out to an early 4-1 lead only to have the Greyhounds score three unanswered goals to tie it up. The Greyhounds also fought back from a 7-5 deficit to tie the game, setting the stage for Forbes' heroics. Sascha Newmarch netted three goals in the contest for Maryland as did Loyola's Kerri Johnson. *(Bethlehem, Pa.; May 17-18, 1997.)*

Multiple winners: Maryland (5); Penn St., Temple and Virginia (2).

Year		Year		Year		Year		Year	
1982	Massachusetts	1986	Maryland	1989	Penn St.	1992	Maryland	1995	Maryland
1983	Delaware	1987	Penn St.	1990	Harvard	1993	Virginia	1996	Maryland
1984	Temple	1988	Temple	1991	Virginia	1994	Princeton	1997	Maryland
1985	N. Hampshire								

RIFLE

Men & Women

West Virginia continued its domination at the Men's and Women's Rifle Championships, sweeping both disciplines in the team competition to win their third consecutive title and 12th overall. The Mountaineers accumulated 4,675 points in the smallbore competition and 1,548 in the air rifle for a total of 6,223, 48 points more than runner-up Kentucky. Marcos Scrivener shot a 1,176 in the smallbore to take the individual title, West Virginia's first since 1993. Murray St.'s Marra Hastings took the air rifle crown with 393 points, squeeking by Daniel Pempel of Air Force (392). (*Murray, Ky, Mar. 6-8, 1997.*)

Multiple winners: West Virginia (12); Tennessee Tech (3); Murray St. (2).

Year		Year		Year		Year		Year	
1980	Tenn. Tech	1984	West Virginia	1988	West Virginia	1992	West Virginia	1995	West Virginia
1981	Tenn. Tech	1985	Murray St.	1989	West Virginia	1993	West Virginia	1996	West Virginia
1982	Tenn. Tech	1986	West Virginia	1990	West Virginia	1994	AK-Fairbanks	1997	West Virginia
1983	West Virginia	1987	Murray St.	1991	West Virginia				

ROWING

NCAA Championships
Women

Pre-race favorite Washington lived up to their billing, leading wire to wire to win the Varsity Eights en route to the overall title at the inaugural NCAA Women's Rowing Championships. The Huskies completed the 2000-meter Lake Natoma course in 6:31.8 to capture the featured race by more than five seconds over runner-up UMass. Washington finished runner-up to Brown in the Fours and to Princeton in the II Eights, giving it a total of 201 points for the overall title. Princeton took second place with 184 points while Brown finished third with 170. (*Sacramento, Calif.; May 30-June 1, 1997.*)

Year	Overall winner	Varsity Eights
1996	Washington	Washington

Intercollegiate Rowing Association Regatta
VARSITY EIGHTS
Men

After a runner-up finish in last year's event and a third place showing the year before, Washington finally took home the Challenge Cup by winning the 95th rowing of the IRA championships on Cooper River in Camden, N.J. Brown led the event at 850 meters but was overcome by the powerful Huskie squad, who took over and won in 5:51.02. The Bears finished in second with a time of 5:54.04 while California took third in 5:54.26. It was Washington's 11th IRA title but its first since 1970. (*Camden, N.J.; May 31, 1997.*)

The IRA was formed in 1895 by several northeastern colleges after Harvard and Yale quit the Rowing Association (established in 1871) to stage an annual race of their own. Since then the IRA Regatta has been contested over courses of varing lengths in Poughkeepsie, N.Y., Marietta, Ohio, Syracuse, N.Y. and Camden, N.J.

Distances: 4 miles (1895-97,1899-1916,1925-41); 3 miles (1898,1921-24,1947-49,1952-63,1965-67); 2 miles (1920,1950-51); 2000 meters (1964, since 1968).

Multiple winners: Cornell (24); Navy (13); Washington (11); California (10); Penn (9); Brown and Wisconsin (7); Syracuse (6); Columbia (4); Northeastern and Princeton (2).

Year		Year		Year		Year		Year	
1895	Columbia	1915	Cornell	1937	Washington			1981	Cornell
1896	Cornell	1916	Syracuse	1938	Navy	1961	California	1982	Cornell
1897	Cornell	1917-19	Not held	1939	California	1962	Cornell	1983	Brown
1898	Penn	1920	Syracuse	1940	Washington	1963	Cornell	1984	Navy
1899	Penn	1921	Navy			1964	California	1985	Princeton
1900	Penn	1922	Navy	1941	Washington	1965	Navy	1986	Brown
1901	Cornell	1923	Washington	1942-46	Not held	1966	Wisconsin	1987	Brown
1902	Cornell	1924	Washington	1947	Navy	1967	Penn	1988	Northeastern
1903	Cornell	1925	Navy	1948	Washington	1968	Penn	1989	Penn
1904	Syracuse	1926	Washington	1949	California	1969	Penn	1990	Wisconsin
1905	Cornell	1927	Columbia	1950	Washington	1970	Washington	1991	Northeastern
1906	Cornell	1928	California					1992	Dartmouth,
1907	Cornell	1929	Columbia	1951	Wisconsin	1971	Cornell		Navy & Penn†
1908	Syracuse	1930	Cornell	1952	Navy	1972	Penn	1993	Brown
1909	Cornell	1931	Navy	1953	Navy	1973	Wisconsin	1994	Brown
1910	Cornell	1932	California	1954	Navy*	1974	Wisconsin	1995	Brown
		1933	Not held	1955	Cornell	1975	Wisconsin	1996	Princeton
1911	Cornell	1934	California	1956	Cornell	1976	California	1997	Washington
1912	Cornell	1935	California	1957	Cornell	1977	Cornell		
1913	Syracuse	1936	Washington	1958	Cornell	1978	Syracuse		
1914	Columbia			1959	Wisconsin	1979	Brown		
				1960	California	1980	Navy		

*In 1954, Navy was disqualified because of an ineligible coxswain; no trophies were given.
†First dead heat in history of IRA Regatta.

Annual NCAA Division I Team Champions (Cont.)

The Harvard-Yale Regatta

Harvard bounced back from last year's loss to upset Yale in the 132nd Harvard/Yale Regatta for varsity eights on June 1, 1997. Yale jumped out to a half-boat-length lead after one mile and held their lead until the Crimson pulled even at the two and one-quarter mile mark. Harvard completed the four-mile course on the Thames River in New London, Conn. in 22:06.8, 3.5 seconds ahead of the Elis. The Harvard/Yale Regatta is the nation's oldest intercollegiate sporting event. Harvard holds a 80-52 series edge.

National Rowing Championships
VARSITY EIGHTS
Men

National championship raced annually from 1982-96 in Bantam, Ohio over a 2,000-meter course on Lake Harsha. Winner received the Herschede Cup. Regatta discontinued in 1997.

Multiple winners: Harvard (6); Brown (3); Wisconsin (2).

Year	Champion	Time	Runner-up	Time	Year	Champion	Time	Runner-up	Time
1982	Yale	5:50.8	Cornell	5:54.15	1990	Wisconsin	5:52.5	Harvard	5:56.84
1983	Harvard	5:59.6	Washington	6:00.0	1991	Penn	5:58.21	Northeastern	5:58.48
1984	Washington	5:51.1	Yale	5:55.6	1992	Harvard	5:33.97	Dartmouth	5:34.28
1985	Harvard	5:44.4	Princeton	5:44.87	1993	Brown	5:54.15	Penn	5:56.98
1986	Wisconsin	5:57.8	Brown	5:59.9	1994	Brown	5:24.52	Harvard	5:25.83
1987	Harvard	5:35.17	Brown	5:35.63	1995	Brown	5:23.40	Princeton	5:25.83
1988	Harvard	5:35.98	Northeastern	5:37.07	1996	Princeton	5:57.47	Penn	6:03.28
1989	Harvard	5:36.6	Washington	5:38.93	1997	discontinued			

Women

National championship held over various distances at 10 different venues from 1979-96. Distances— 1000 meters (1979-81); 1500 meters (1982-83); 1000 meters (1984); 1750 meters (1985); 2000 meters (1986-88, since 1991); 1852 meters (1989-90). Winner received the Ferguson Bowl. Regatta discontinued in 1997.

Multiple winners: Washington (7); Princeton (4); Boston University (2).

Year	Champion	Time	Runner-up	Time	Year	Champion	Time	Runner-up	Time
1979	Yale	3:06	California	3:08.6	1988	Washington	6:41.0	Yale	6:42.37
1980	California	3:05.4	Oregon St.	3:05.8	1989	Cornell	5:34.9	Wisconsin	5:37.5
1981	Washington	3:20.6	Yale	3:22.9	1991	Boston Univ.	7:03.2	Cornell	7:06.21
1982	Washington	4:56.4	Wisconsin	4:59.83	1992	Boston Univ.	6:28.79	Cornell	6:32.79
1983	Washington	4:57.5	Dartmouth	5:03.02	1993	Princeton	6:40.75	Washington	6:43.86
1984	Washington	3:29.48	Radcliffe	3:31.08	1994	Princeton	6:11.38	Yale	6:14.46
1985	Washington	5:28.4	Wisconsin	5:32.0	1995	Princeton	6:11.98	Washington	6:12.69
1986	Wisconsin	6:53.28	Radcliffe	6:53.34	1996	Brown	6:45.7	Princeton	6:49.3
1987	Washington	6:33.8	Yale	6:37.4	1997	discontinued			

SKIING
Men & Women

Utah defended its title and won its ninth overall NCAA Skiing Championship, amassing a total of 686 points. Ute Christl Hager won her third individual giant slalom championship, the first woman in NCAA history to do so. Host Vermont finished in second place with 646½ points, boosted by the men's giant slalom, where they claimed three of the top five spots. Roberta Perghier of Denver won the women's slalom title for the second consecutive year. (Stowe, Vermont; Mar. 5-8, 1997.)

Multiple winners: Denver (14); Colorado (13); Utah (9); Vermont (5); Dartmouth and Wyoming (2).

Year		Year		Year		Year		Year	
1954	Denver	1963	Denver	1972	Colorado	1980	Vermont	1989	Vermont
1955	Denver	1964	Denver	1973	Colorado	1981	Utah	1990	Vermont
1956	Denver	1965	Denver	1974	Colorado	1982	Colorado	1991	Colorado
1957	Denver	1966	Denver	1975	Colorado	1983	Utah	1992	Vermont
1958	Dartmouth	1967	Denver	1976	Colorado	1984	Utah	1993	Utah
1959	Colorado	1968	Wyoming		& Dartmouth	1985	Wyoming	1994	Vermont
1960	Colorado	1969	Denver	1977	Colorado	1986	Utah	1995	Colorado
1961	Denver	1970	Denver	1978	Colorado	1987	Utah	1996	Utah
1962	Denver	1971	Denver	1979	Colorado	1988	Utah	1997	Utah

SOFTBALL

Women

Arizona scored early and often as they crushed Pac-10 rival UCLA 10-2 in just five innings to win their second consecutive softball championship. The Wildcats rode the arm of ace pitcher and series MVP Nancy Evans, who recorded a 4-1 mark with a stellar 1.58 ERA during the World Series. First baseman Leah O'Brien provided the offensive clout, batting .600 with six RBI including two in the championship game. (Oklahoma City, Ok.; May 22-26, 1997.)

Multiple winners: UCLA (8); Arizona (5); Texas A&M (2).

Year	Year	Year	Year	Year
1982 UCLA	1986 CS-Fullerton	1989 UCLA	1992 UCLA	1995 UCLA*
1983 Texas A&M	1987 Texas A&M	1990 UCLA	1993 Arizona	1996 Arizona
1984 UCLA	1988 UCLA	1991 Colorado	1994 Arizona	1997 Arizona
1985 UCLA				

*Title was later vacated due to action by the NCAA Committee on Infractions.

SWIMMING & DIVING

Men

Auburn captured four of the five relay events to build an early lead and cruise to their first NCAA Swimming and Diving title. The Tigers, who finished in second in 1996, accumulated 496½ points overall to outdistance runner-up Stanford (340) and third place Georgia (297). Aside from the relay victories, Auburn also got a surprise from freshman Brett Hawke, who took the 50-yard freestyle in 19.19, just ahead of Texas' Neil Walker. SMU's Lars Frolander, Tennessee's Jeremy Linn, Miami-FL's Tyce Rouston and Michigan's John Piersma were the individual standouts with two wins apiece. Linn set a meet record (52.32) with his win in the 100-yard breaststroke. Other meet records set were Walker's time of 45.25 in the 100-yard backstroke and Auburn's 200-medley relay win in 1:25.40. Miami-FL swept the diving events behind Rouston's double win in the 3-meter and platform events. (Minneapolis, Minn.; Mar. 27-29, 1997.)

Multiple winners: Michigan and Ohio St. (11); USC (9); Stanford (7); Indiana and Texas (6); Yale (4); California and Florida (2).

1937 Michigan	1950 Ohio St.	1963 USC	1976 USC	1989 Texas
1938 Michigan	1951 Yale	1964 USC	1977 USC	1990 Texas
1939 Michigan	1952 Ohio St.	1965 USC	1978 Tennessee	1991 Texas
1940 Michigan	1953 Yale	1966 USC	1979 California	1992 Stanford
1941 Michigan	1954 Ohio St.	1967 Stanford	1980 California	1993 Stanford
1942 Yale	1955 Ohio St.	1968 Indiana	1981 Texas	1994 Stanford
1943 Ohio St.	1956 Ohio St.	1969 Indiana	1982 UCLA	1995 Michigan
1944 Yale	1957 Michigan	1970 Indiana	1983 Florida	1996 Texas
1945 Ohio St.	1958 Michigan	1971 Indiana	1984 Florida	1997 Auburn
1946 Ohio St.	1959 Michigan	1972 Indiana	1985 Stanford	
1947 Ohio St.	1960 USC	1973 Indiana	1986 Stanford	
1948 Michigan	1961 Michigan	1974 USC	1987 Stanford	
1949 Ohio St.	1962 Ohio St.	1975 USC	1988 Texas	

Women

USC won its first NCAA Swimming and Diving National Championship, dethroning five-time national champion Stanford. The Trojans scored 406 points, 11 ahead of the Cardinal and were led by double winners Lindsay Benko and Kristine Quance. Benko defended her titles in the 500-yard freestyle and 200-yard backstroke while Quance repeated in the 200-yard breaststroke and 400-yard individual medley. SMU's Martina Moravcova won the Swimmer of the Year award, garnering three victories including an NCAA and U.S. Open record of 1:43.08 in the 200-yard freestyle. Stanford's Catherine Fox and Texas diver Vera Ilyina were also double winners. (Indianapolis, Ind.; Mar. 20-22, 1997.)

Multiple winners: Stanford and Texas (7).

Year	Year	Year	Year	Year
1982 Florida	1986 Texas	1989 Stanford	1992 Stanford	1995 Stanford
1983 Stanford	1987 Texas	1990 Texas	1993 Stanford	1996 Stanford
1984 Texas	1988 Texas	1991 Texas	1994 Stanford	1997 USC
1985 Texas				

Wide World Photos

LSU sprinter **Astia Walker** uses whatever means necessary to beat out Miami's **Yolanda McCray** and the rest of the field to win the 100-meter hurdles finals in 12.85 seconds at the NCAA Outdoor Track and Field Championships, June 7 in Bloomington, Ind.

INDOOR TRACK

Men

Arkansas reclaimed its familiar position on top of the collegiate indoor track and field world by cruising to their 13th championship in the last 14 years. Third-place finishers in 1996, the Razorbacks destroyed the rest of the field, accumulating 59 points, 32 more than runner-up Auburn (27). Robert Howard paced Arkansas with two individual championships, defending his title in the triple jump with a 55-11 leap and adding the long jump victory (26-9¼) to his growing list of accomplishments. Oklahoma's Roxbert Martin was another individual standout, winning the 400-meters in a championships record-breaking 45.79. *(RCA Dome, Indianapolis, Ind.; March 7-8, 1997.)*

Multiple winners: Arkansas (13); UTEP (7); Kansas and Villanova (3); USC (2).

Year		Year		Year		Year		Year	
1965	Missouri	1972	USC	1979	Villanova	1986	Arkansas	1993	Arkansas
1966	Kansas	1973	Manhattan	1980	UTEP	1987	Arkansas	1994	Arkansas
1967	USC	1974	UTEP	1981	UTEP	1988	Arkansas	1995	Arkansas
1968	Villanova	1975	UTEP	1982	UTEP	1989	Arkansas	1996	George Mason
1969	Kansas	1976	UTEP	1983	SMU	1990	Arkansas	1997	Arkansas
1970	Kansas	1977	Washington St.	1984	Arkansas	1991	Arkansas		
1971	Villanova	1978	UTEP	1985	Arkansas	1992	Arkansas		

Women

Suzette Lee's record-breaking triple jump boosted LSU to its fifth consecutive indoor track championship and its eighth overall. Lee sailed 46 feet, 9 inches, breaking the previous championships mark of 45-9 set in 1990. LaTarsha Stroman claimed the 400-meter dash title for the Tigers as they compiled 49 points overall, ten more than runners-up Texas and Wisconsin. Arizona's Amy Skieresz (5,000-meters), Nebraska's Tressa Thompson (shot put), South Carolina's Dawn Ellerbe (20-lb wight throw) and the Georgetown distance medley relay team all set individual championships records. *(RCA Dome, Indianapolis, Ind.; March 7-8, 1997.)*

Multiple Winners: LSU (8); Texas (3); Nebraska (2).

Year		Year		Year		Year		Year	
1983	Nebraska	1986	Texas	1989	LSU	1992	Florida	1995	LSU
1984	Nebraska	1987	LSU	1990	Texas	1993	LSU	1996	LSU
1985	Florida St.	1988	Texas	1991	LSU	1994	LSU	1997	LSU

OUTDOOR TRACK

Men

Arkansas joined USC as the only team to win at least six consecutive outdoor track and field championships as they amassed 55 points behind the efforts of five individuals. Robert Howard, Seneca Lassiter, Phillip Price, Kevin White, and Ryan Wilson accounted for all of the Razorback's points with Howard's 20 leading the charge. Howard leaped 55-6½ in the triple jump to defend last year's title and added a win in the long jump with a mark of 26-11¼. Lassiter captured Arkansas' other individual title with a win in the 1,500-meter run (3:40.22). UTEP's Obadele Thompson (100 and 200-meters) and UCLA's Mebrahtom Keflezighi joined Howard as double winners. Texas finished runner-up to Arkansas with 42½ points while USC placed third with 34. (*Bloomington, Ind.; June 4-7, 1997.*)

Multiple winners: USC (26); UCLA (8); Arkansas (7); UTEP (6); Illinois and Oregon (5); Kansas, LSU and Stanford (3); SMU and Tennessee (2).

Year		Year		Year		Year		Year	
1921	Illinois	1937	USC	1952	USC	1968	USC	1982	UTEP
1922	California	1938	USC	1953	USC	1969	San Jose St.	1983	SMU
1923	Michigan	1939	USC	1954	USC	1970	BYU, Kansas	1984	Oregon
1924	Not held	1940	USC	1955	USC		& Oregon	1985	Arkansas
1925	Stanford*	1941	USC	1956	UCLA	1971	UCLA	1986	SMU
1926	USC*	1942	USC	1957	Villanova	1972	UCLA	1987	UCLA
1927	Illinois*	1943	USC	1958	USC	1973	UCLA	1988	UCLA
1928	Stanford	1944	Illinois	1959	Kansas	1974	Tennessee	1989	LSU
1929	Ohio St.	1945	Navy	1960	Kansas	1975	UTEP	1990	LSU
1930	USC	1946	Illinois	1961	USC	1976	USC	1991	Tennessee
1931	USC	1947	Illinois	1962	Oregon	1977	Arizona St.	1992	Arkansas
1932	Indiana	1948	Minnesota	1963	USC	1978	UCLA & UTEP	1993	Arkansas
1933	LSU	1949	USC	1964	Oregon	1979	UTEP	1994	Arkansas
1934	Stanford	1950	USC	1965	Oregon & USC	1980	UTEP	1995	Arkansas
1935	USC	1951	USC	1966	UCLA	1981	UTEP	1996	Arkansas
1936	USC			1967	USC			1997	Arkansas

(*) indicates unofficial championship.

Women

LSU compiled 43 points on the final day of competition to come from behind and edge Texas 63-62 to win their 11th consecutive outdoor track and field championship. Sprinters LaTarsha Stroman and Astia Walker sparked the Tigers with wins in the 400-meter run and 100-meter hurdles, respectively. The 4x100-meter relay squad repeated as champs with a 43.17 finish and Suzette Lee defended her triple jump title with a 45-8 mark to pace LSU. The Longhorns were runner-ups for the second consecutive year while UCLA claimed the third spot with 56 points. Michigan State's Sevatheda Fynes (100 and 200-m) and Arizona's Amy Skieresz (5,000 and 10,000-m) were both double winners while Wisconsin's Kathy Butler took the 3000-m to become only the second athlete to win three consecutive titles. (*Bloomington, Ind.; June 4-7, 1997.*)

Multiple winners: LSU (11); UCLA (2).

Year		Year		Year		Year		Year	
1982	UCLA	1986	Texas	1989	LSU	1992	LSU	1995	LSU
1983	UCLA	1987	LSU	1990	LSU	1993	LSU	1996	LSU
1984	Florida St.	1988	LSU	1991	LSU	1994	LSU	1997	LSU
1985	Oregon								

VOLLEYBALL

Men

Stanford won their first NCAA Men's Volleyball Championship by defeating perennial powerhouse and two-time defending champion UCLA in five dramatic games 15-7, 15-10, 9-15, 6-15, 15-13. The Cardinal jumped out to a comfortable 2-0 lead only to see the veteran Bruins squad roar back to tie things at two games apiece setting up a winner-take-all final game. Game five featured nine ties but Stanford eventually came out on top led by the kills of all-American Mike Lambert and the defense of Matt Fuerbringer and Mike Hoefer. The Cardinal's victory gave them a 27-4 mark for the season while UCLA finished at 27-3. (*Columbus, Ohio; May 3, 1997.*)

Multiple winners: UCLA (16); Pepperdine and USC (4).

Year		Year		Year		Year		Year	
1970	UCLA	1976	UCLA	1982	UCLA	1988	USC	1994	Penn St.
1971	UCLA	1977	USC	1983	UCLA	1989	UCLA	1995	UCLA
1972	UCLA	1978	Pepperdine	1984	UCLA	1990	USC	1996	UCLA
1973	San Diego St.	1979	UCLA	1985	Pepperdine	1991	Long Beach St.	1997	Stanford
1974	UCLA	1980	USC	1986	Pepperdine	1992	Pepperdine		
1975	UCLA	1981	UCLA	1987	UCLA	1993	UCLA		

Annual NCAA Division I Team Champions (Cont.)

Women

Stanford won its third women's volleyball title in the last five years, disposing Hawaii in three straight games 15-7, 15-3, 15-5. The Cardinal was led by freshman Kerri Walsh, who planted 17 kills in 32 attempts, and Kristin Folkl who pounded out 16 kills. Walsh was named tournament MVP for her efforts. In semifinal action, Stanford dethroned defending champ Nebraska 9-15, 15-7, 15-9, 15-8 while the Rainbows reached the final round by sweeping Florida 15-11, 15-8, 15-9. (Cleveland, Ohio, Dec. 21, 1996.)

Multiple winners: Hawaii, Stanford and UCLA (3); Long Beach St. and Pacific (2).

Year		Year		Year		Year		Year	
1981	USC	1985	Pacific	1988	Texas	1991	UCLA	1994	Stanford
1982	Hawaii	1986	Pacific	1989	Long Beach St.	1992	Stanford	1995	Nebraska
1983	Hawaii	1987	Hawaii	1990	UCLA	1993	Long Beach St.	1996	Stanford
1984	UCLA								

WATER POLO

Men

UCLA jumped out to a 6-3 first quarter lead and held on to squeak by USC and capture their second consecutive title at the NCAA Men's Water Polo Championship. Senior goaltender Matt Swanson stopped 14 Trojan shots to grab outstanding player honors, an award he shared last season with three others. Steve Covec netted two goals and Randy Wright added a two-point goal to lead the Bruins. (San Diego, Calif., Dec. 8, 1996.)

Multiple winners: California (11); Stanford (8); UCLA (5); UC-Irvine (3).

Year		Year		Year		Year		Year	
1969	UCLA	1975	California	1981	Stanford	1987	California	1993	Stanford
1970	UC-Irvine	1976	Stanford	1982	UC-Irvine	1988	California	1994	Stanford
1971	UCLA	1977	California	1983	California	1989	UC-Irvine	1995	UCLA
1972	UCLA	1978	Stanford	1984	California	1990	California	1996	UCLA
1973	California	1979	UC-S. Barbara	1985	Stanford	1991	California		
1974	California	1980	Stanford	1986	Stanford	1992	California		

WRESTLING

Men

Iowa boasted five individual champions en route to an events record 170 points to coast to their third consecutive team wrestling title. Pre-championships favorite Oklahoma St. was the closest team to the Hawkeyes with 113½ points while Minnesota (71) and Iowa St. (70) finished third and fourth, respectively. Jessie Whitmer, Mark Ironside, Lincoln McIlravy, Joe Williams and Lee Fullhart all captured individual titles for Iowa. McIlravy won the Most Outstanding Wrestler Award, beating Iowa State's Chris Bono in the 150-pound class. (Cedar Falls, Iowa; Mar. 20-22, 1997.)

Multiple winners: Oklahoma St. (30); Iowa (17); Iowa St. (8); Oklahoma (7).

Year		Year		Year		Year		Year	
1928	Okla. A&M*	1941	Okla. A&M	1957	Oklahoma	1971	Okla. St.	1985	Iowa
1929	Okla. A&M	1942	Okla. A&M	1958	Okla. St.	1972	Iowa St.	1986	Iowa
1930	Okla. A&M	1943-45	Not held	1959	Okla. St.	1973	Iowa St.	1987	Iowa St.
1931	Okla. A&M*	1946	Okla. A&M	1960	Oklahoma	1974	Oklahoma	1988	Arizona St.
1932	Indiana*	1947	Cornell Col.	1961	Oklahoma	1975	Iowa	1989	Okla. St.
1933	Okla. A&M* & Iowa St.*	1948	Okla. A&M	1962	Oklahoma	1976	Iowa	1990	Okla. St.
1934	Okla. A&M	1949	Okla. A&M	1963	Oklahoma	1977	Iowa St.	1991	Iowa
1935	Okla. A&M	1950	Northern Iowa	1964	Okla. St.	1978	Iowa	1992	Iowa
1936	Oklahoma	1951	Oklahoma	1965	Iowa St.	1979	Iowa	1993	Iowa
1937	Okla. A&M	1952	Oklahoma	1966	Okla. St.	1980	Iowa	1994	Okla. St.
1938	Okla. A&M	1953	Penn St.	1967	Michigan St.	1981	Iowa	1995	Iowa
1939	Okla. A&M	1954	Okla. A&M	1968	Okla. St.	1982	Iowa	1996	Iowa
1940	Okla. A&M	1955	Okla. A&M	1969	Iowa St.	1983	Iowa	1997	Iowa
		1956	Okla. A&M	1970	Iowa St.	1984	Iowa		

(*) indicates unofficial champions. Note: Oklahoma A&M became Oklahoma St. in 1958.

Halls of Fame & Awards

Green Bay Packers legend **Don Hutson** at his 1963 induction into the Pro Football Hall of Fame in Canton, Ohio. Hutson died in 1997 at age 84.

Wide World Photos

BASEBALL

National Baseball Hall of Fame & Museum

Established in 1935 by Major League Baseball to celebrate the game's 100th anniversary. **Address:** P.O. Box 590, Cooperstown, NY 13326. **Telephone:** (607) 547-7200.

Eligibility: Nominated players must have played at least part of 10 seasons in the Major Leagues and be retired for at least five but no more than 20 years. Voting done by Baseball Writers' Association of America. Certain nominated players not elected by the writers can become eligible via the Veterans' Committee 23 years after retirement. The Hall of Fame board of directors voted unanimously on Feb. 4, 1991, to exclude players on baseball's ineligible list from consideration. Pete Rose is the only living ex-player on that list.

Class of 1997 (4): BBWAA vote— pitcher **Phil Niekro**, Milwaukee-NL (1964-65), Atlanta (1966-83), New York-AL (1984-85), Cleveland (1986-87), Toronto (1987), Atlanta (1987). VETERAN'S COMMITTEE vote—second baseman **Nellie Fox**, Philadelphia (1947-49), Chicago-AL (1950-63), Houston (1964-65), manager **Tommy Lasorda**, Los Angeles (1976-96), negro leagues shortstop **Willie Wells**, .

1997 Top 10 vote-getters (473 BBWAA ballots cast, 355 needed to elect): 1. **Phil Niekro** (380); 2. **Don Sutton** (346); 3. **Tony Perez** (312); 4. **Ron Santo** (186); 5. **Jim Rice** (178); 6. **Steve Garvey** (167); 7. **Bruce Sutter** (130); 8. **Jim Kaat** (107), 9. **Joe Torre** (105), 10. **Tommy John** (97).

Elected first year on ballot (31): Hank Aaron, Ernie Banks, Johnny Bench, Lou Brock, Rod Carew, Steve Carlton, Ty Cobb, Bob Feller, Bob Gibson, Reggie Jackson, Walter Johnson, Al Kaline, Sandy Koufax, Mickey Mantle, Christy Mathewson, Willie Mays, Willie McCovey, Joe Morgan, Stan Musial, Jim Palmer, Brooks Robinson, Frank Robinson, Jackie Robinson, Babe Ruth, Mike Schmidt, Tom Seaver, Warren Spahn, Willie Stargell, Honus Wagner, Ted Williams and Carl Yastrzemski.

Members are listed with years of induction; (+) indicates deceased members.

Catchers

	Bench, Johnny	1989	+	Cochrane, Mickey	1947	+	Hartnett, Gabby	1955
	Berra, Yogi	1972	+	Dickey, Bill	1954	+	Lombardi, Ernie	1986
+	Bresnahan, Roger	1945	+	Ewing, Buck	1939	+	Schalk, Ray	1955
+	Campanella, Roy	1969	+	Ferrell, Rick	1984			

1st Basemen

+	Anson, Cap	1939	+	Connor, Roger	1976		Killebrew, Harmon	1984
+	Beckley, Jake	1971	+	Foxx, Jimmie	1951		McCovey, Willie	1986
+	Bottomley, Jim	1974	+	Gehrig, Lou	1939	+	Mize, Johnny	1981
+	Brouthers, Dan	1945	+	Greenberg, Hank	1956	+	Sisler, George	1939
+	Chance, Frank	1946	+	Kelly, George	1973	+	Terry, Bill	1954

2nd Basemen

	Carew, Rod	1991	+	Frisch, Frankie	1947	+	Lazzeri, Tony	1991
+	Collins, Eddie	1939	+	Gehringer, Charley	1949		Morgan, Joe	1990
	Doerr, Bobby	1986	+	Herman, Billy	1975	+	Robinson, Jackie	1962
+	Evers, Johnny	1946	+	Hornsby, Rogers	1942		Schoendienst, Red	1989
	Fox, Nellie	1997	+	Lajoie, Nap	1937			

Shortstops

	Aparicio, Luis	1984	+	Jackson, Travis	1982	+	Tinker, Joe	1946
+	Appling, Luke	1964	+	Jennings, Hugh	1945	+	Vaughan, Arky	1985
+	Bancroft, Dave	1971	+	Maranville, Rabbit	1954	+	Wagner, Honus	1936
	Banks, Ernie	1977		Reese, Pee Wee	1984	+	Wallace, Bobby	1953
	Boudreau, Lou	1970		Rizzuto, Phil	1994	+	Ward, Monte	1964
+	Cronin, Joe	1956	+	Sewell, Joe	1977			

3rd Basemen

+	Baker, Frank	1955	+	Lindstrom, Fred	1976		Schmidt, Mike	1995
+	Collins, Jimmy	1945		Mathews, Eddie	1978	+	Traynor, Pie	1948
	Kell, George	1983		Robinson, Brooks	1983			

Left Fielders

	Brock, Lou	1985	+	Kelley, Joe	1971	+	Simmons, Al	1953
+	Burkett, Jesse	1946		Kiner, Ralph	1975		Stargell, Willie	1988
+	Clarke, Fred	1945	+	Manush, Heinie	1964	+	Wheat, Zack	1959
+	Delahanty, Ed	1945	+	Medwick, Joe	1968		Williams, Billy	1987
+	Goslin, Goose	1968		Musial, Stan	1969		Williams, Ted	1966
+	Hafey, Chick	1971	+	O'Rourke, Jim	1945		Yastrzemski, Carl	1989

Center Fielders

+	Ashburn, Richie	1995		DiMaggio, Joe	1955	+	Roush, Edd	1962
+	Averill, Earl	1975	+	Duffy, Hugh	1945		Snider, Duke	1980
+	Carey, Max	1961	+	Hamilton, Billy	1961	+	Speaker, Tris	1937
+	Cobb, Ty	1936	+	Mantle, Mickey	1974	+	Waner, Lloyd	1967
+	Combs, Earle	1970		Mays, Willie	1979	+	Wilson, Hack	1979

Right Fielders

Aaron, Hank 1982	Jackson, Reggie 1993	+ Rice, Sam 1963
+ Clemente, Roberto 1973	Kaline, Al 1980	Robinson, Frank 1982
+ Crawford, Sam 1957	+ Keeler, Willie 1939	+ Ruth, Babe 1936
+ Cuyler, Kiki 1968	+ Kelly, King 1945	Slaughter, Enos 1985
+ Flick, Elmer 1963	+ Klein, Chuck 1980	+ Thompson, Sam 1974
+ Heilmann, Harry 1952	+ McCarthy, Tommy 1946	+ Waner, Paul 1952
+ Hooper, Harry 1971	+ Ott, Mel 1951	+ Youngs, Ross 1972

Pitchers

+ Alexander, Grover 1938	+ Haines, Jess 1970	+ Pennock, Herb 1948
+ Bender, Chief 1953	+ Hoyt, Waite 1969	Perry, Gaylord 1991
+ Brown, Mordecai 1949	+ Hubbell, Carl 1947	+ Plank, Eddie 1946
Bunning, Jim 1996	Hunter, Catfish 1987	+ Radbourne, Old Hoss 1939
Carlton, Steve 1994	Jenkins, Ferguson 1991	+ Rixey, Eppa 1963
+ Chesbro, Jack 1946	+ Johnson, Walter 1936	Roberts, Robin 1976
+ Clarkson, John 1963	+ Joss, Addie 1978	+ Ruffing, Red 1967
+ Coveleski, Stan 1969	+ Keefe, Tim 1964	+ Rusie, Amos 1977
+ Dean, Dizzy 1953	Koufax, Sandy 1972	Seaver, Tom 1992
+ Drysdale, Don 1984	Lemon, Bob 1976	Spahn, Warren 1973
+ Faber, Red 1964	+ Lyons, Ted 1955	+ Vance, Dazzy 1955
Feller, Bob 1962	Marichal, Juan 1983	+ Waddell, Rube 1946
Fingers, Rollie 1992	+ Marquard, Rube 1971	+ Walsh, Ed 1946
Ford, Whitey 1974	+ Mathewson, Christy 1936	+ Welch, Mickey 1973
+ Galvin, Pud 1965	+ McGinnity, Joe 1946	Wilhelm, Hoyt 1985
Gibson, Bob 1981	Niekro, Phil 1997	+ Willis, Vic 1995
+ Gomez, Lefty 1972	Newhouser, Hal 1992	Wynn, Early 1972
+ Grimes, Burleigh 1964	+ Nichols, Kid 1949	+ Young, Cy 1937
+ Grove, Lefty 1947	Palmer, Jim 1990	

Managers

+ Alston, Walter 1983	Lasorda, Tommy 1997	+ McKechnie, Bill 1962
+ Durocher, Leo 1994	Lopez, Al 1977	+ Robinson, Wilbert 1945
+ Hanlon, Ned 1996	+ Mack, Connie 1937	+ Stengel, Casey 1966
+ Harris, Bucky 1975	+ McCarthy, Joe 1957	+ Stengel, Casey 1966
+ Huggins, Miller 1964	+ McGraw, John 1937	Weaver, Earl 1996

Umpires

+ Barlick, Al 1989	+ Evans, Billy 1973	+ McGowan, Bill 1992
+ Conlan, Jocko 1974	+ Hubbard, Cal 1976	
+ Connolly, Tom 1953	+ Klem, Bill 1953	

From Negro Leagues

+ Bell, Cool Papa (OF) 1974	+ Foster, Rube (P-Mgr) 1981	Leonard, Buck (1B) 1972
+ Charleston, Oscar (1B-OF) ...1976	+ Foster, Willie (P) 1996	+ Lloyd, Pop (SS) 1977
+ Dandridge, Ray (3B) 1987	+ Gibson, Josh (C) 1972	+ Paige, Satchel (P) 1971
+ Day, Leon (P-OF-2B) 1995	Irvin, Monte (OF) 1973	+ Wells, Willie (SS) 1997
+ Dihigo, Martin (P-OF) 1977	+ Johnson, Judy (3B) 1975	

Pioneers and Executives

+ Barrow, Ed 1953	+ Giles, Warren 1979	+ Spalding, Al 1939
+ Bulkeley, Morgan 1937	+ Griffith, Clark 1946	+ Veeck, Bill 1991
+ Cartwright, Alexander 1938	+ Harridge, Will 1972	+ Weiss, George 1971
+ Chadwick, Henry 1938	+ Hulbert, William 1995	+ Wright, George 1937
+ Chandler, Happy 1982	+ Johnson, Ban 1937	+ Wright, Harry 1953
+ Comiskey, Charles 1939	+ Landis, Kenesaw 1944	+ Yawkey, Tom 1980
+ Cummings, Candy 1939	+ MacPhail, Larry 1978	
+ Frick, Ford 1970	+ Rickey, Branch 1967	

Ford Frick Award

First presented in 1978 by Hall of Fame for meritorious contributions by baseball broadcasters. Named in honor of the late newspaper reporter, broadcaster, National League president and commissioner, the Frick Award does not constitute induction into the Hall of Fame.

Year	Year	Year
1978 Mel Allen & Red Barber	1985 Buck Canel	1992 Milo Hamilton
1979 Bob Elson	1986 Bob Prince	1993 Chuck Thompson
1980 Russ Hodges	1987 Jack Buck	1994 Bob Murphy
1981 Ernie Harwell	1988 Lindsey Nelson	1995 Bob Wolff
1982 Vin Scully	1989 Harry Caray	1996 Herb Carneal
1983 Jack Brickhouse	1990 Byrum Saam	1997 Jimmy Dudley
1984 Curt Gowdy	1991 Joe Garagiola	

Baseball (Cont.)

J.G. Taylor Spink Award

First presented in 1962 by the Baseball Writers' Association of America for meritorious contributions by members of the BBWAA. Named in honor of the late publisher of *The Sporting News*, the Spink Award does not constitute induction into the Hall of Fame. Winners are honored in the year following their selection.

Year		Year		Year	
1962	J.G. Taylor Spink	1974	John Carmichael & James Isaminger	1986	Jack Lang
1963	Ring Lardner			1987	Jim Murray
1964	Hugh Fullerton	1975	Tom Meany & Shirley Povich	1988	Bob Hunter & Ray Kelly
1965	Charley Dryden	1976	Harold Kaese & Red Smith	1989	Jerome Holtzman
1966	Grantland Rice	1977	Gordon Cobbledick & Edgar Munzel	1990	Phil Collier
1967	Damon Runyon			1991	Ritter Collett
1968	H.G. Salsinger	1978	Tim Murnane & Dick Young	1992	Leonard Koppett & Buzz Saidt
1969	Sid Mercer	1979	Bob Broeg & Tommy Holmes		
1970	Heywood C. Broun	1980	Joe Reichler & Milt Richman	1993	John Wendell Smith
1971	Frank Graham	1981	Bob Addie & Allen Lewis	1994	No award
1972	Dan Daniel, Fred Lieb & J. Roy Stockton	1982	Si Burick	1995	Joseph Durso
		1983	Ken Smith	1996	Charley Feeney
1973	Warren Brown, John Drebinger & John F. Kieran	1984	Joe McGuff		
		1985	Earl Lawson		

Major League Baseball's All-Time Team—Then and Now

The Baseball Writers Association of America originally selected an all-time team as part of major league baseball's 100th anniversary, announcing the outcome of its vote on July 21, 1969. Vote totals were not released. Recently, another vote was released when a panel of 36 BWAA members picked an all-time team for the Classic Sports Network just before the 1997 All-Star game. This time around vote totals were given, the single outfield category was divided into three (left, center and right) and two recently popularized positions—the designated hitter and relief pitcher—were added. In the most recent vote two points were awarded for first-place votes and one point for second place. Point totals follow the names with the number of first-place votes in parentheses. All-time team members are listed in **bold** type

1969 Vote

C	**Mickey Cochrane**, Bill Dickey, Roy Campanella	OF	**Babe Ruth, Ty Cobb, Joe DiMaggio**, Ted Williams, Tris Speaker, Willie Mays
1B	**Lou Gehrig**, George Sisler, Stan Musial,	RHP	**Walter Johnson**, Christy Mathewson, Cy Young
2B	**Rogers Hornsby**, Charley Gehringer, Eddie Collins	LHP	**Lefty Grove**, Sandy Koufax, Carl Hubbell
SS	**Honus Wagner**, Joe Cronin, Ernie Banks	Mgr.	**John McGraw**, Casey Stengel, Joe McCarthy
3B	**Pie Traynor**, Brooks Robinson, Jackie Robinson		

1969 Vote All-Time Outstanding Player: **Ruth**, Cobb, Wagner, DiMaggio

1997 Vote

C **Johnny Bench** (24) 52; Yogi Berra (4) 22; Roy Campanella (4) 17; Mickey Cochrane (1) 5; Bill Dickey (1) 4; Gabby Hartnett (1) 3; Carlton Fisk 2.

1B **Lou Gehrig** (31) 66½; Jimmie Foxx (3) 19; George Sisler (2) 8; Willie McCovey 6; Hank Greenberg 2½; Stan Musial, Eddie Murray, Mark McGwire and Frank Thomas 1.

2B **Rogers Hornsby** (17) 44; Joe Morgan (6) 23; Jackie Robinson (6) 15; Charley Gehringer (4) and Napolean Lajoie (3) 11; Eddie Collins (1) 3; Rod Carew 2; Ryne Sandberg 1.

SS **Honus Wagner** (23) 55; Cal Ripken Jr. (6) 24; Ozzie Smith (5) 16; Ernie Banks (1) 8; Lou Boudreau and Luke Appling 1.

3B **Mike Schmidt** (21) 50; Brooks Robinson (13) 37; Eddie Mathews (5) George Brett (1) 8; Pie Traynor 3; Pete Rose (1) 2; Frank Baker, Al Rosen and Wade Boggs 1.

LF **Ted Williams** (32) 68; Stan Musial (4) 36; Pete Rose, Ralph Kiner, Rickey Henderson and Barry Bonds 1.

CF **Willie Mays** (25) 57; Ty Cobb (7) 22; Joe DiMaggio (3) 17; Mickey Mantle (1) 10; Tris Speaker 2.

RF **Babe Ruth** (31) 67; Hank Aaron (5) 36; Frank Robinson 2; Al Kaline, Roberto Clemente and Tony Gwynn 1.

DH **Paul Molitor** (22) 48; Harold Baines (3) 12; Don Baylor (1) 10; Edgar Martinez (2) 9; Ty Cobb (2) 6; Hal McRae (1) 5; Mickey Mantle (1) and Dave Parker (1) 3; Joe DiMaggio (1) 2; Lee May, Frank Robinson and Tony Oliva 1.

RHP **Walter Johnson** (9) 30, Cy Young (12) 25; Christy Mathewson (5) 18; Bob Feller (4) 10; Bob Gibson (2) 9; Nolan Ryan (2) 7; Tom Seaver (1) 3; Greg Maddux (1), Grover Cleveland Alexander and Juan Marichal 2.

LHP **Sandy Koufax** (11) 32; Warren Spahn (11) 28; Lefty Grove (8) 25; Steve Carlton (4) 12; Carl Hubbell (6) Whitey Ford (1) 3; Eddie Plank (1) 2.

RP **Dennis Eckersley** (16) 40; Rollie Fingers (9) 29; Lee Smith (4) 13; Hoyt Wilhelm (3) 10; Rich Gossage (3) 9; Bruce Sutter (1) 6, Dan Quisenberry 1.

Mgr. **Casey Stengel** (6) 22, Joe McCarthy (6) 18; Connie Mack (7) 17; John McGraw (6) 14; Sparky Anderson (3) 11; Leo Durocher (2) 6; Dick Williams (1) 4; Billy Martin (1) 3; Al Lopez (1), Ned Hanlon (1), Whitey Herzog (1), Earl Weaver and Bobby Cox 2; Tony LaRussa 1.

BASKETBALL

Naismith Memorial Basketball Hall of Fame

Established in 1949 by the National Association of Basketball Coaches in memory of the sport's inventor, Dr. James Naismith. Original Hall opened in 1968 and current Hall in 1985. **Address:** 1150 West Columbus Avenue, Springfield, MA 01105. **Telephone:** (413) 781-6500.

Eligibility: Nominated players and referees must be retired for five years, coaches must have coached 25 years or be retired for five, and contributors must have already completed their noteworthy service to the game. Voting done by 24-member honors committee made up of media representatives, Hall of Fame members and trustees. Any nominee not elected after five years becomes eligible for consideration by the Veterans' Committee after a five-year wait.

Class of 1997 (7): PLAYERS—center **Joan Crawford**, AAU, (Clarendon, Texas, 1955-57; Nashville Business College 1957-69); forward **Denise Curry**, college (UCLA, 1978-81), 1984 Olympic team; forward **Alex English**, NBA (Milwaukee 1976-78; Indiana 1978-80; Denver 1980-90; Dallas 1990-91); forward **Bailey Howell**, NBA (Detroit 1959-64; Baltimore 1964-66; Boston 1966-70; Philadelphia 1970-71). COACHES—**Pete Carril**, college (Lehigh 1967; Princeton 1968-96); Antonio Diaz-Miguel, Spanish national team (1965-92); **Don Haskins**, college (UTEP 1962-present).

1997 finalists (nominated but not elected): PLAYERS—Dennis Johnson, Gus Johnson, Sidney Moncrief, Arnie Risen, Jo Jo White, Jamaal Wilkes. COACHES—Alex Hannum, Jim Phelan, Jerry Tarkanian, John Thompson, Tex Winter and Ubiratan Ceriera Maciel. CONTRIBUTOR—Lee Williams.

Note: John Wooden is the only member to be honored as both a player and a coach.

Members are listed with years of induction; (+) indicates deceased members.

Men

Abdul-Jabbar, Kareem 1995	Gola, Tom 1975	Mikkelsen, Vern 1995
Archibald, Nate 1991	Goodrich, Gail 1996	Monroe, Earl 1990
Arizin, Paul 1977	Greer, Hal 1981	Murphy, Calvin 1993
+ Barlow, Thomas (Babe) 1980	+ Gruenig, Robert 1963	+ Murphy, Charles (Stretch) 1960
Barry, Rick 1987	Hagan, Cliff 1977	+ Page, Harlan (Pat) 1962
Baylor, Elgin 1976	+ Hanson, Victor 1960	Pettit, Bob 1970
+ Beckman, John 1972	Havlicek, John 1983	Phillip, Andy 1961
Bellamy, Walt 1993	Hawkins, Connie 1992	+ Pollard, Jim 1977
Belov, Sergei 1992	Hayes, Elvin 1990	Ramsey, Frank 1981
Bing, Dave 1990	Heinsohn, Tom 1986	Reed, Willis 1981
+ Borgmann, Benny 1961	+ Holman, Nat 1964	Robertson, Oscar 1979
Bradley, Bill 1982	Houbregs, Bob 1987	+ Roosma, John 1961
+ Brennan, Joe 1974	Howell, Bailey 1997	Russell, Bill 1974
Cervi, Al 1984	+ Hyatt, Chuck 1959	+ Russell, John (Honey) 1964
Chamberlain, Wilt 1978	Issel, Dan 1993	Schayes, Dolph 1972
+ Cooper, Charles (Tarzan) 1976	Jeannette, Buddy 1994	+ Schmidt, Ernest J 1973
+ Cosic, Kresimir 1996	+ Johnson, Bill (Skinny) 1976	+ Schommer, John 1959
Cousy, Bob 1970	+ Johnston, Neil 1990	+ Sedran, Barney 1962
Cowens, Dave 1991	Jones, K.C 1989	Sharman, Bill 1975
Cunningham, Billy 1986	Jones, Sam 1983	+ Steinmetz, Christian 1961
+ Davies, Bob 1969	+ Krause, Edward (Moose) 1975	Thompson, David 1996
+ DeBernardi, Forrest 1961	Kurland, Bob 1961	+ Thompson, John (Cat) 1962
DeBusschere, Dave 1982	Lanier, Bob 1992	Thurmond, Nate 1984
+ Dehnert, Dutch 1968	+ Lapchick, Joe 1966	Twyman, Jack 1982
+ Endacott, Paul 1971	Lovellette, Clyde 1988	Unseld, Wes 1988
English, Alex 1997	Lucas, Jerry 1979	+ Vandivier, Robert (Fuzzy) 1974
Erving, Julius (Dr. J) 1993	Luisetti, Hank 1959	+ Wachter, Ed 1961
Foster, Bud 1964	Macauley, Ed 1960	Walton, Bill 1993
Frazier, Walt 1987	+ Maravich, Pete 1987	Wanzer, Bobby 1987
+ Friedman, Marty 1971	Martin, Slater 1981	West, Jerry 1979
+ Fulks, Joe 1977	+ McCracken, Branch 1960	Wilkens, Lenny 1989
Gale, Laddie 1976	+ McCracken, Jack 1962	Wooden, John 1960
Gallatin, Harry 1991	+ McDermott, Bobby 1988	Yardley, George 1996
Gates, William (Pop) 1989	McGuire, Dick 1993	
Gervin, George 1996	Mikan, George 1959	

Women

Blazejowski, Carol 1994	Harris, Lucy 1992	Semenova, Juliana 1993
Crawford, Joan 1997	Lieberman-Cline, Nancy 1996	White, Nera 1992
Curry, Denise 1997	Meyers, Ann 1993	
Donovan, Anne 1995	Miller, Cheryl 1995	

Teams

Buffalo Germans 1961	New York Renaissance 1963	Original Celtics 1959
First Team 1959		

Referees

+ Enright, Jim 1978	+ Leith, Lloyd 1982	+ Shirley, J. Dallas 1979
+ Hepbron, George 1960	+ Mihalik, Red 1986	+ Strom, Earl 1995
+ Hoyt, George 1961	Nucatola, John 1977	Tobey, Dave 1961
+ Kennedy, Pat 1959	+ Quigley, Ernest (Quig) 1961	+ Walsh, David 1961

Basketball (Cont.)

Coaches

+ Allen, Forrest (Phog) 1959
+ Anderson, Harold (Andy) 1984
  Auerbach, Red 1968
+ Barry, Sam 1978
+ Blood, Ernest (Prof) 1960
+ Cann, Howard 1967
+ Carlson, Henry (Doc) 1959
  Carnesecca, Lou 1992
  Carnevale, Ben 1969
  Carril, Pete 1997
+ Case, Everett 1981
  Crum, Denny 1994
  Daly, Chuck 1994
+ Dean, Everett 1966
  Diaz-Miguel, Antonio 1997
+ Diddle, Ed 1971
+ Drake, Bruce 1972
  Gaines, Clarence (Bighouse) .1981

  Gardner, Jack 1983
  Gill, Amory (Slats) 1967
  Gomelsky, Aleksandr 1995
  Harshman, Marv 1984
  Haskins, Don 1997
+ Hickey, Eddie 1978
+ Hobson, Howard (Hobby) ...1965
  Holzman, Red 1986
+ Iba, Hank 1968
+ Julian, Alvin (Doggie) 1967
+ Keaney, Frank 1960
+ Keogan, George 1961
  Knight, Bob 1991
  Kundla, John 1995
+ Lambert, Ward (Piggy) 1960
  Litwack, Harry 1975
+ Loeffler, Ken 1964
+ Lonborg, Dutch 1972

+ McCutchan, Arad 1980
  McGuire, Al 1992
+ McGuire, Frank 1976
+ Meanwell, Walter (Doc) 1959
  Meyer, Ray 1978
  Miller, Ralph 1988
  Ramsay, Jack 1992
  Rubini, Cesare 1994
+ Rupp, Adolph 1968
+ Sachs, Leonard 1961
+ Shelton, Everett 1979
  Smith, Dean 1982
  Taylor, Fred 1985
+ Wade, Margaret 1984
  Watts, Stan 1985
  Wooden, John 1972
+ Woolpert, Phil 1992

Contributors

+ Abbott, Senda Berenson 1984
+ Bee, Clair 1967
+ Brown, Walter A 1965
+ Bunn, John 1964
+ Douglas, Bob 1971
+ Duer, Al 1981
  Fagen, Clifford B 1983
+ Fisher, Harry 1973
+ Fleisher, Larry 1991
+ Gottlieb, Eddie 1971
+ Gulick, Luther 1959
  Harrison, Les 1979
+ Hepp, Ferenc 1980
+ Hickox, Ed 1959
+ Hinkle, Tony 1965

+ Irish, Ned 1964
+ Jones, R. William 1964
+ Kennedy, Walter 1980
+ Liston, Emil (Liz) 1974
  McLendon, John 1978
+ Mokray, Bill 1965
+ Morgan, Ralph 1959
+ Morgenweck, Frank (Pop) ..1962
+ Naismith, James 1959
  Newell, Pete 1978
+ O'Brien, John J. (Jack) 1961
+ O'Brien, Larry 1991
+ Olsen, Harold G 1959
+ Podoloff, Maurice 1973
+ Porter, Henry (H.V.) 1960

+ Reid, William A 1963
+ Ripley, Elmer 1972
+ St. John, Lynn W 1962
+ Saperstein, Abe 1970
+ Schabinger, Arthur 1961
+ Stagg, Amos Alonzo 1959
  Stankovic, Boris 1991
+ Steitz, Ed 1983
+ Taylor, Chuck 1968
+ Teague, Bertha 1984
+ Tower, Oswald 1959
+ Trester, Arthur (A.L.) 1961
+ Wells, Cliff 1971
+ Wilke, Lou 1982

Curt Gowdy Award

First presented in 1990 by the Hall of Fame Board of Trustees for meritorious contributions by the media. Named in honor of the former NBC sportscaster, the Gowdy Award does not constitute induction into the Hall of Fame.

Year	Year	Year
1990 Curt Gowdy & Dick Herbert	1993 Leonard Lewin & Johnny Most	1995 Dick Enberg & Bob Hammel
1991 Dave Dorr & Marty Glickman	1994 Leonard Koppett	1996 Billy Packer & Bob Hentzen
1992 Sam Goldaper & Chick Hearn	& Cawood Ledford	1997 Marv Albert & Bob Ryan

BOWLING

National Bowling Hall of Fame & Museum

The National Bowling Hall is one museum with separate wings for honorees of the American Bowling Congress (ABC), Professional Bowlers' Association (PBA) and Women's International Bowling Congress (WIBC). The museum does not include the new Ladies Pro Bowlers Tour Hall of Fame, which is located in Las Vegas. **Address:** 111 Stadium Plaza, St. Louis, MO 63102. **Telephone:** (314) 231-6340.

Professional Bowlers Association

Established in 1975. **Eligibility:** Nominees must be PBA members and at least 35 years old. Voting done by 50-member panel that includes writers who have covered bowling for at least 12 years.
   Class of 1997 (3): PERFORMANCE—**Dave Ferraro** and **Amleto Monacelli**. VETERANS—**Ernie Schlegel**.
   Members are listed with years of induction; (+) indicates deceased members.

Performance

+ Allen, Bill 1983
  Anthony, Earl 1986
  Aulby, Mike 1996
  Berardi, Joe 1990
  Bluth, Ray 1975
  Buckley, Roy 1992
  Burton, Nelson Jr 1979
  Carter, Don 1975
  Colwell, Paul 1991

  Cook, Steve 1993
  Davis, Dave 1978
  Dickinson, Gary 1988
  Durbin, Mike 1984
+ Fazio, Buzz 1976
  Ferraro, Dave 1997
  Godman, Jim 1987
  Hardwick, Billy 1977
  Holman, Marshall 1990

  Hudson, Tommy 1989
  Husted, Dave 1996
  Johnson, Don 1977
  Laub, Larry 1985
  Monacelli, Amleto 1997
  Ozio, David 1995
  Pappas, George 1986
  Petraglia, John 1982
  Ritger, Dick 1978

Roth, Mark 1987
Salvino, Carmen 1975
Smith, Harry 1975
Soutar, Dave 1979

Stefanich, Jim 1980
Voss, Brian 1994
Webb, Wayne 1993
Weber, Dick 1975

+ Welu, Billy 1975
Williams, Walter Ray Jr. 1995
Zahn, Wayne 1981

Veterans

Allison, Glenn 1984
Asher, Barry 1988
Foremsky, Skee 1992
Guenther, Johnny 1986

+ Joseph, Joe 1985
Limongello, Mike 1994
Marzich, Andy 1990
McCune, Don 1991

McGrath, Mike 1988
Schlegel, Ernie 1997
+ St. John, Jim 1989
Strampe, Bob 1987

Meritorious Service

+ Antenora, Joe 1993
Archibald, John 1989
Clemens, Chuck 1994
Elias, Eddie 1976
Esposito, Frank 1975
Evans, Dick 1986
Firestone, Raymond 1987
Fisher, E.A. (Bud) 1984

+ Frantz, Lou 1978
Golden, Harry 1983
Hoffman, Ted Jr 1985
Jowdy, John 1988
Kelley, Lee 1989
Lichstein, Larry 1996
+ Nagy, Steve 1977
Pezzano, Chuck 1975

Reichert, Jack 1992
+ Richards, Joe 1976
Schenkel, Chris 1976
Stitzlein, Lorraine 1980
Thompson, Al 1991
Zeller, Roger 1995

American Bowling Congress

Established in 1941 and open to professional and amateur bowlers. **Eligibility:** Nominated bowlers must have competed in at least 20 years of ABC tournaments. Voting done by 170-member panel made up of ABC officials, Hall of Fame members and media representatives.

Class of 1997 (5): PERFORMANCE— **Ernie Schlegel**. PIONEERS— **Bill Rhodman, Fuzzy Shimada** and **Louis Stein**. MERITORIOUS SERVICE— **Frank Esposito**.

Members are listed with years of induction; (+) indicates deceased members.

Performance

Allison, Glenn 1979
Anthony, Earl 1986
+ Asplund, Harold 1978
Baer, Gordy 1987
Beach, Bill 1991
Benkovic, Frank 1958
Berlin, Mike 1994
+ Billick, George 1982
+ Blouin, Jimmy 1953
Bluth, Ray 1973
+ Bodis, Joe 1941
+ Bomar, Buddy 1966
+ Brandt, Allie 1960
+ Brosius, Eddie 1976
+ Bujack, Fred 1967
Bunetta, Bill 1968
Burton, Nelson Jr 1981
+ Burton, Nelson Sr 1964
+ Campi, Lou 1968
+ Carlson, Adolph 1941
Carter, Don 1970
+ Caruana, Frank 1977
+ Cassio, Marty 1972
+ Castellano, Graz 1976
+ Clause, Frank 1980
Cohn, Alfred 1985
+ Crimmins, Johnny 1962
Davis, Dave 1990
+ Daw, Charlie 1941
+ Day, Ned 1952
Dickinson, Gary 1992
+ Easter, Sarge 1963
Ellis, Don 1981
+ Falcaro, Joe 1968
+ Faragalli, Lindy 1968
Fazio, Buzz 1963
Fehr, Steve 1993
+ Gersonde, Russ 1968
Gibson, Therm 1965
Godman, Jim 1987
Goike, Robert 1996

Golembiewski, Billy 1979
Griffo, Greg 1995
Guenther, Johnny 1988
Hardwick, Billy 1985
Hart, Bob 1994
Hennessey, Tom 1976
Hoover, Dick 1974
Horn, Bud 1992
Howard, George 1986
Jackson, Eddie 1988
Johnson, Don 1982
Johnson, Earl 1987
+ Joseph, Joe 1969
+ Jouglard, Lee 1979
+ Kartheiser, Frank 1967
+ Kawolics, Ed 1968
+ Kissoff, Joe 1976
+ Klares, John 1982
+ Knox, Billy 1954
+ Koster, John 1941
+ Krems, Eddie 1973
Kristof, Joe 1968
+ Krumske, Paul 1968
+ Lange, Herb 1941
+ Lauman, Hank 1976
Lillard, Bill 1972
Lindemann, Tony 1979
+ Lindsey, Mort 1941
+ Lippe, Harry 1989
Lubanski, Ed 1971
Lucci, Vince Sr 1978
+ Marino, Hank 1941
+ Martino, John 1969
Marzich, Andy 1993
McGrath, Mike 1993
+ McMahon, Junie 1967
+ Mercurio, Skang 1967
+ Meyers, Norm 1984
+ Nagy, Steve 1963
Norris, Joe 1954
O'Donnell, Chuck 1968

Pappas, George 1989
+ Patterson, Pat 1974
Ritger, Dick 1984
+ Rogoznica, Andy 1993
Salvino, Carmen 1979
Schissler, Les 1991
Schlegel, Ernie 1997
Schroeder, Jim 1990
+ Schwoegler, Connie 1968
Semiz, Teata 1991
+ Sielaff, Lou 1968
+ Sinke, Joe 1977
Sixty, Billy 1961
Smith, Harry 1978
+ Smith, Jimmy 1941
Soutar, Dave 1985
+ Sparando, Tony 1968
+ Spinella, Barney 1968
+ Steers, Harry 1941
Stefanich, Jim 1983
+ Stein, Otto Jr 1971
Stoudt, Bud 1991
Strampe, Bob 1977
+ Thoma, Sykes 1971
Toft, Rod 1991
Tountas, Pete 1989
Tucker, Bill 1988
Tuttle, Tommy 1995
+ Varipapa, Andy 1957
+ Ward, Walter 1959
Weber, Dick 1970
+ Welu, Billy 1975
+ Wilman, Joe 1951
+ Wolf, Phil 1961
Wonders, Rich 1990
+ Young, George 1959
Zahn, Wayne 1980
Zikes, Les 1983
+ Zunker, Gil 1941

Bowling (Cont.)

Pioneers

+ Allen, Lafayette Jr.	1994	Hirashima, Hirohito	1995	Shimada, Fuzzy	1997
+ Carow, Rev. Charles	1995	+ Karpf, Samuel	1993	Stein, Louis	1997
+ Celestine, Sydney	1993	+ Pasdeloup, Frank	1993	+ Thompson, William V.	...1993
+ Curtis, Thomas	1993	Rhodman, Bill	1997	+ Timm, Dr. Henry	1993
de Freitas, Eric	1994	+ Satow, Masao	1994		
Hall, William Sr.	1994	+ Schutte, Louis	1993		

Meritorious Service

+ Allen, Harold	1966	Franklin, Bill	1992	Pezzano, Chuck	1982
Archibald, John	1996	+ Hagerty, Jack	1963	Picchietti, Remo	1993
+ Baker, Frank	1975	+ Hattstrom, H.A. (Doc)	1980	Pluckhahn, Bruce	1989
+ Baumgarten, Elmer	1963	+ Hermann, Cone	1968	+ Raymer, Milt	1972
+ Bellisimo, Lou	1986	+ Howley, Pete	1941	+ Reed, Elmer	1978
+ Bensinger, Bob	1969	+ Kennedy, Bob	1981	Rudo, Milt	1984
+ Chase, LeRoy	1972	+ Langtry, Abe	1963	Schenkel, Chris	1988
+ Coker, John	1980	+ Levine, Sam	1971	+ Sweeney, Dennis	1974
+ Collier, Chuck	1963	+ Luby, David	1969	Tessman, Roger	1994
+ Cruchon, Steve	1983	Luby, MortJr..	1988	+ Thum, Joe	1980
+ Ditzen, Walt	1973	+ Luby, Mort Sr.	1974	Weinstein, Sam	1970
+ Doehrman, Bill	1968	Matzelle, Al	1995	+ Whitney, Eli	1975
Elias, Eddie	1985	+ McCullough, Howard	1971	Wolf, Fred	1976
Esposito, Frank	1997	+ Patterson, Morehead	1985		
Evans, Dick	1992	+ Petersen, Louie	1963		

Women's International Bowling Congress

Established in 1953. Eligibility: Performance nominees must have won at least one WIBC Championship Tournament title, a WIBC Queens tournament title or an international competition title and have bowled in at least 15 national WIBC Championship Tournaments (unless injury or illness cut career short).

Class of 1997 (2): PERFORMANCE—**Carol Miller** and **Nikki Gianulias**.

Members are listed with years of induction; (+) indicates deceased members.

Performance

Abel, Joy	1984	+ Harman, Janet	1985	Norton, Virginia	....,.....1988
Adamek, Donna	1996	+ Hartrick, Stella	1972	Notaro, Phyllis	1979
Ann, Patty	1995	+ Hatch, Grayce	1953	Ortner, Bev	1972
Bolt, Mae	1978	Havlish, Jean	1987	+ Powers, Connie	1973
Bouvia, Gloria	1987	+ Hoffman, Martha	1979	Rickard, Robbie	1994
Boxberger, Loa	1984	Holm, Joan	1974	+ Robinson, Leona	1969
Buckner, Pam	1990	+ Humphreys, Birdie	1979	Romeo, Robin	1995
+ Burling, Catherine	1958	Ignizio, Mildred	1975	+ Rump, Anita	1962
+ Burns, Nina	1977	Jacobson, D.D	1981	+ Ruschmeyer, Addie	1961
Cantaline, Anita	1979	+ Jaeger, Emma	1953	+ Ryan, Esther	1963
Carter, LaVerne	1977	Kelly, Annese	1985	+ Sablatnik, Ethel	1979
Carter, Paula	1994	+ Knechtges, Doris	1983	+ Schulte, Myrtle	1965
Coburn, Doris	1976	Kuczynski, Betty	1981	+ Shablis, Helen	1977
Costello, Pat	1986	Ladewig, Marion	1964	Sill, Aleta	1996
Costello, Patty	1989	Martin, Sylvia Wene	1966	+ Simon, Violet (Billy)	1960
Dryer, Pat	1978	Martorella, Millie	1975	+ Small, Tess	1971
Duval, Helen	1970	+ Matthews, Merle	1974	+ Smith, Grace	1968
Fellmeth, Catherine	1970	+ McCutcheon, Floretta	1956	Soutar, Judy	1976
Fothergill, Dotty	1980	Merrick, Marge	1980	+ Stockdale, Louise	1953
+ Fritz, Deane	1966	+ Mikiel, Val	1979	Toepfer, Elvira	1976
Garms, Shirley	1971	Miller, Carol	1997	+ Twyford, Sally	1964
Gianulias, Nikki	1997	+ Miller, Dorothy	1954	+ Warmbier, Marie	1953
Gloor, Olga	1976	Mivelaz, Betty	1991	Wilkinson, Dorothy	1990
Graham, Linda	1992	Mohacsi, Mary	1994	+ Winandy, Cecelia	1975
Graham, Mary Lou	1989	Morris, Betty	1983	Zimmerman, Donna	1982
+ Greenwald, Goldie	1953	Nichols, Lorrie	1989		
Grinfelds, Vesma	1991	Norman, Edie Jo	1993		

Meritorious Service

Baetz, Helen	1977	+ Chapman, Emily	1957	+ Hochstadter, Bee	1967
+ Baker, Helen	1989	+ Crowe, Alberta	1982	+ Kay, Nora	1964
+ Banker, Gladys	1994	+ Dornblaser, Gertrude	1979	+ Kelly, Ellen	1979
+ Bayley, Clover	1992	Duffy, Agnes	1987	Kelone, Theresa	1978
+ Berger, Winifred	1976	Finke, Gertrude	1990	+ Knepprath, Jeannette	1963
+ Bohlen, Philena	1955	+ Fisk, Rae	1983	+ Lasher, Iolia	1967
Borschuk, Lo	1988	+ Haas, Dorothy	1977	Marrs, Mabel	1979
+ Botkin, Freda	1986	+ Higley, Margaret	1969	+ McBride, Bertha	1968

+ Menne, Catherine 1979
  Mitchell, Flora 1996
+ Mraz, Jo 1959
  O'Connor, Billie 1992
+ Phaler, Emma 1965
+ Porter, Cora 1986
+ Quin, Zoe 1979

+ Rishling, Gertrude 1972
  Simone, Anne 1991
  Sloan, Catherine 1985
+ Speck, Berdie 1966
  Spitalnick, Mildred 1994
+ Spring, Alma 1979
+ Switzer, Pearl 1973

  Todd, Trudy 1993
+ Veatch, Georgia 1974
+ White, Mildred 1975
+ Wood, Ann 1970

Ladies Pro Bowlers Tour

Established in 1995 by the Ladies Pro Bowlers Tour. **Address:** Sam's Town Hotel, Gambling Hall and Bowling Center, 5111 Boulder Highway, Las Vegas, NV 89122. **Telephone:** (815) 332-5756.

Eligibility: Nominees in performance category must have at least five titles from organizations including All-Star, World Invitational, LPBT, WPBA, PWBA, TPA and LPBA. Voting done by 10-member committee of bowling writers appointed by LPBT president John Falzone.

Class of 1997 (7): PERFORMANCE—**Cindy Colburn-Carroll**, **Pat Costello** and **Vesma Grinfelds**. PIONEERS—**Judy Soutar** and **Loa Boxberger**. BUILDERS—**Pearl Keller** and **John Sommer Jr.**

Members are listed with year of induction; (+) indicates deceased member.

Performance

Adamek, Donna 1995
Colburn-Carroll, Cindy 1997
Costello, Pat 1997
Costello, Patty 1995
Fothergill, Dotty 1995

Gianulias, Nikki 1996
Grinfelds, Vesma 1997
Ladewig, Marion 1995
Martorella, Millie 1995
Morris, Betty 1995

Nichols, Lorrie 1996
Romeo, Robin 1996
Wagner, Lisa 1996

Pioneers

Boxberger, Loa 1997
Carter, LaVerne 1995
Coburn, Doris 1996

Duval, Helen 1995
Garms, Shirley 1995

Soutar, Judy 1997
Zimmerman, Donna 1996

Builders

Buhler, Janet 1996
Keller, Pearl 1997

Robinson, Jeanette 1996
Sommer Jr., John 1997

+ Veatch, Georgia 1995

BOXING

International Boxing Hall of Fame

Established in 1989 and opened in 1990. **Address:** 1 Hall of Fame Drive, Canastota, NY 13032. **Telephone:** (315) 697-7095.

Eligibility: All nominees must be retired for five years. Voting done by 142-member panel made up of Boxing Writers' Association members and world-wide boxing historians.

Class of 1997 (13): MODERN ERA—**Sugar Ray Leonard** (middleweight), **Luis Rodriguez** (welterweight), **Jose Torres** (lt. heavyweight), **Chalky Wright** (featherweight). OLD TIMERS—**Pete Herman** (bantamweight), **Joe Jeannette** (heavyweight), **Freddie Miller** (featherweight), **Freddie Welsh** (lightweight). PIONEERS—**Tom Molineaux** (heavyweight) and **Dutch Sam** (lightweight). NON-PARTICIPANTS— **Richard K. Fox** (journalist), **Joe Humphreys** (ring announcer) and **Don King** (promoter).

Members are listed with year of induction; (+) indicates deceased member.

Modern Era

Ali, Muhammad 1990
Arguello, Alexis 1992
+ Armstrong, Henry 1990
Basilio, Carmen 1990
Benitez, Wilfredo 1996
Benvenuti, Nino 1992
+ Berg, Jackie (Kid) 1994
Brown, Joe 1996
+ Burley, Charley 1992
+ Cerdan, Marcel 1991
+ Charles, Ezzard 1990
+ Conn, Billy 1990
+ Elorde, Gabriel (Flash) 1993
Foster, Bob 1990
Frazier, Joe 1990
Fullmer, Gene 1991
Gavilan, Kid 1990
Giardello, Joey 1993
Gomez, Wilfredo 1995
+ Graham, Billy 1992

+ Graziano, Rocky 1991
Griffith, Emile 1990
Hagler, Marvelous Marvin ..1993
Harado, Masahiko (Fighting) ...1995
Jack, Beau 1991
Jofre, Eder 1992
Johnson, Harold 1993
LaMotta, Jake 1990
Leonard, Sugar Ray 1997
+ Liston, Sonny 1991
+ Louis, Joe 1990
+ Marciano, Rocky 1990
Maxim, Joey 1994
Montgomery, Bob 1995
+ Monzon, Carlos 1990
Moore, Archie 1990
Napoles, Jose 1990
Norton, Ken 1992
Olivares, Ruben 1991
Ortiz, Carlos 1991

Ortiz, Manuel 1996
Patterson, Floyd 1991
Pep, Willie 1990
+ Perez, Pasqual 1995
Pryor, Aaron 1996
+ Robinson, Sugar Ray 1990
+ Rodriguez, Luis 1997
Saddler, Sandy 1990
+ Sanchez, Salvadore 1991
Schmeling, Max 1992
Spinks, Michael 1994
+ Tiger, Dick 1991
Torres, Jose 1997
+ Walcott, Jersey Joe 1990
+ Williams, Ike 1990
+ Wright, Chalky 1997
+ Zale, Tony 1991
Zarate, Carlos 1994
+ Zivic, Fritzie 1993

Boxing (Cont.)

Old-Timers

Ambers, Lou 1992	+ Gans, Joe 1990	+ McFarland, Packey 1992
+ Attell, Abe 1990	+ Gibbons, Mike 1992	+ McGovern, Terry 1990
+ Baer, Max 1995	+ Gibbons, Tommy 1993	McLarnin, Jimmy 1991
+ Britton, Jack 1990	+ Greb, Harry 1990	+ Miller, Freddie 1997
+ Brown, Panama Al 1992	+ Griffo, Young 1991	+ Nelson, Battling 1992
+ Burns, Tommy 1996	+ Herman, Pete 1997	+ O'Brien, Philadelphia Jack .1994
+ Canzoneri, Tony 1990	+ Jackson, Peter 1990	+ Rosenbloom, Maxie 1993
+ Carpentier, Georges 1991	+ Jeanette, Joe 1997	+ Ross, Barney 1990
+ Chocolate, Kid 1991	+ Jeffries, James J 1990	+ Ryan, Tommy 1991
+ Corbett, James J. 1990	+ Johnson, Jack 1990	+ Sharkey, Jack 1994
+ Darcy, Les 1993	+ Ketchel, Stanley 1990	+ Stribling, Young 1996
+ Delaney, Jack 1996	+ Kilbane, Johnny 1995	+ Tunney, Gene 1990
+ Dempsey, Jack 1990	+ LaBarba, Fidel 1996	+ Villa, Pancho 1994
+ Dempsey, Jack (Nonpareil) .1992	+ Langford, Sam 1990	+ Walcott, Joe 1991
+ Dillon, Jack 1995	+ Leonard, Benny 1990	+ Walker, Mickey 1990
+ Dixon, George 1990	+ Lewis, John Henry 1994	+ Welsh, Freddie 1997
+ Driscoll, Jem 1990	+ Lewis, Ted (Kid) 1992	+ Wilde, Jimmy 1990
+ Dundee, Johnny 1991	+ Loughran, Tommy 1991	+ Williams, Kid 1996
+ Fitzsimmons, Bob 1990	+ McAuliffe, Jack 1995	+ Wills, Harry 1992
+ Flowers, Theodore (Tiger) ..1993	+ McCoy, Charles (Kid) 1991	

Pioneers

+ Belcher, Jem 1992	+ Johnson, Tom 1995	+ Pearce, Henry 1993
+ Brain, Ben 1994	+ King, Tom 1992	+ Sam, Dutch 1997
+ Broughton, Jack 1990	+ Langham, Nat 1992	+ Sayers, Tom 1990
+ Burke, James (Deaf) 1992	+ Mace, Jem 1990	Spring, Tom 1992
+ Cribb, Tom 1991	+ Mendoza, Daniel 1990	+ Sullivan, John L 1990
+ Duffy, Paddy 1994	+ Molineaux, Tom 1997	+ Thompson, William 1991
+ Figg, James 1992	+ Morrisey, John 1996	+ Ward, Jem 1995
+ Jackson, Gentleman John ...1992		

Non-Participants

+ Andrews, Thomas S 1992	+ Fleischer, Nat 1990	Mercante, Arthur 1995
+ Arcel, Ray 1991	+ Fox, Richard K. 1997	+ Muldoon, William 1996
+ Blackburn, Jack 1992	Futch, Eddie 1994	Odd, Gilbert 1995
Brenner, Teddy 1993	+ Goldman, Charley 1992	+ Parker, Dan 1996
+ Chambers, John Graham ...1990	+ Goldstein, Ruby 1994	+ Parnassus, George 1991
Clancy, Gil 1993	+ Humphreys, Joe 1997	+ Queensberry, Marquis of ..1990
+ Coffroth, James W. 1991	+ Jacobs, Jimmy 1993	+ Rickard, Tex 1990
+ D'Amato, Cus. 1995	+ Jacobs, Mike 1990	+ Siler, George 1995
+ Donovan, Arthur 1993	+ Kearns, Jack (Doc) 1990	+ Solomons, Jack 1995
Dundee, Angelo 1992	King, Don 1997	Steward, Emanuel 1996
Dundee, Chris 1994	+ Liebling, A.J 1992	+ Taub, Sam 1994
Dunphy, Don 1993	+ Lonsdale, Lord 1990	+ Walker, James J. (Jimmy) ...1992
+ Egan, Pierce 1991	Markson, Harry 1992	

Old *Ring* Hall Members Not in Int'l. Boxing Hall

Nat Fleischer, the late founder and editor-in-chief of *The Ring*, established his magazine's Boxing Hall of Fame in 1954, but it was abandoned after the 1987 inductions. One hundred and five members of the old *Ring* Hall have been elected to the International Hall since 1989. The 54 boxers and one sportswriter who have yet to be elected to the International Hall are listed below with their year of induction into the *Ring* Hall.

Modern Group

+ Apostoli, Fred 1978	+ Garcia, Ceferino 1977	+ Petrolle, Billy 1962
+ Braddock, James J 1964	+ Jenkins, Lew 1976	+ Shirai, Yoshio 1977
+ Escobar, Sixto 1975	+ Lesnevich, Gus 1973	+ Tendler, Lew 1961

Old-Timers

+ Berlenbach, Paul 1971	+ Jeffra, Harry 1982	+ Ortiz, Manuel 1985
+ Britt, Jimmy 1976	+ Kid, The Dixie 1975	+ Papke, Billy 1972
+ Chaney, George (K.O.) 1974	+ Klaus, Frank 1974	+ Ritchie, Willie 1962
+ Choynski, Joe 1959	+ Lavigne, George (Kid) 1959	+ Root, Jack 1961
+ Corbett, Young II 1965	+ Levinsky, Battling 1966	+ Sharkey, Tom 1959
+ Coulon, Johnny 1965	+ Lynch, Benny 1986	+ Smith, Jeff 1969
+ Fields, Jackie 1977	+ Maher, Peter 1978	+ Taylor, Bud 1986
+ Genaro, Frankie 1973	+ McVey, Sam 1986	+ Willard, Jess 1977
+ Houck, Leo 1969	+ Mitchell, Charley 1957	+ Wolgast, Ad 1958

Pioneers

+ Aaron, Barney (Young) 1967	+ Collyer, Sam 1964	+ Gully, John 1959
+ Chambers, Arthur 1954	+ Donnelly, Dan 1960	+ Heenan, John C 1954
+ Chandler, Tom 1972	+ Donovan, Prof. Mike 1970	+ Hyer, Jacob 1968
+ Clark, Nobby 1971	+ Goss, Joe 1969	+ Hyer, Tom 1954

+ Jackling, Thomas 1985	+ Price, Ned 1962	**Non-Participant**
+ Kilrain, Jack 1965	+ Richmond, Bill 1956	+ Daniel, Dan (sportswriter) ...1977
+ Molineaux, Tom 1958	+ Ryan, Paddy 1973	

FOOTBALL

College Football Hall of Fame

Established in 1955 by the National Football Foundation. **Address:** 111 South St. Joseph St., South Bend, IN 46601. **Telephone:** (219) 235-9999.

Eligibility: Nominated players must be out of college 10 years and a first team All-America pick by a major selector during their careers; coaches must be retired three years. Voting done by 12-member panel of athletic directors, conference and bowl officials and media representatives. 1996 was the first year representatives from NCAA Div. I-AA, II, and III, and the NAIA are eligible for induction.

Class of 1997 (28): LARGE COLLEGE—G **Ray Beck**, Georgia Tech (1948-51); QB **Randy Duncan**, Iowa (1956-58); CB **Dave Elmendorf**, Texas A&M (1968-70); FB **Charlie Flowers**, Mississippi (1957-59); LB **Rick Hunley**, Arizona (1981-83); C/LB **Alex Kroll**, Rutgers (1960-61); TE **Ken McAfee**, Notre Dame (1974-77); T **Bob Reifsnyder**, Navy (1956-58); C **Dave Rimington**, Nebraska (1979-82); E **Dave Robinson**, Penn St. (1960-62); RB **George Rogers**, South Carolina (1978-80); QB **Danny White**, Arizona St. (1971-73). COACHES—**Wally Butts**, Georgia (1939-60); **Don James**, Kent St. (1971-74) and Washington (1975-92); **Bowden Wyatt**, Wyoming (1947-52), Arkansas (1953-54) and Tennessee (1955-62). SMALL COLLEGE— DB **Joe Cichy**, N. Dakota St. (1968-70); RB **Joe Delaney**, Northwestern St. (1977-80); DE **Fred Dryer**, San Diego St. (1967-68); RB **Joe Dudek**, Plymouth St. (1982-85); E **William Grinnell**, Tufts (1932-34); RB **Frank Hawkins**, Nevada (1977-80); DT **Pierce Holt**, Angelo St. (1984-87); DT **Gary Johnson**, Grambling St. (1971-74); QB **Ken O'Brien**, UC-Davis (1980-82); DB **Bruce Taylor**, Boston University (1967-69); DT **Lynn Thomsen**, Austana (1983-86). COACHES—**Jim Butterfield**, Ithaca (1967-93); **Paul Hoernemann**, Heidelberg-OH (1946-59).

Note: Bobby Dodd and **Amos Alonzo Stagg** are the only members to be honored as both players and coaches.

Players are listed with final year they played in college and coaches are listed with year of induction; (+) indicates deceased members.

Players

+ Abell, Earl-Colgate 1915	Below, Marty-Wisconsin 1923	Cappelletti, John-Penn St 1973
Agase, Alex-Purdue/Ill 1946	+ Benbrook, Al-Michigan 1910	+ Carideo, Frank-N.Dame ...1930
+ Agganis, Harry-Boston U ...1952	+ Berry, Charlie-Lafayette 1924	+ Carney, Charles-Illinois 1921
Albert, Frank-Stanford 1941	Bertelli, Angelo-N.Dame 1943	Caroline, J.C.-Illinois 1954
+ Aldrich, Ki-TCU 1938	Berwanger, Jay-Chicago 1935	Carpenter, Bill-Army 1959
+ Aldrich, Malcolm-Yale 1921	+ Bettencourt, L.-St.Mary's 1927	+ Carpenter, Hunter-Va.Tech ...1905
+ Alexander, Joe-Syracuse 1920	Biletnikoff, Fred-Fla.St. 1964	Carroll, Chas.-Washington ...1928
Alworth, Lance-Arkansas 1961	Blanchard, Doc-Army 1946	Casanova, Tommy-LSU 1971
+ Ameche, Alan-Wisconsin 1954	+ Blozis, Al-Georgetown 1942	+ Casey, Edward-Harvard 1919
+ Ames, Knowlton-Princeton ...1889	Bock, Ed-Iowa St 1938	Cassady, Howard-Ohio St· ...1955
Amling, Warren-Ohio St 1946	Bomar, Lynn-Vanderbilt 1924	+ Chamberlin, Guy-Neb. 1915
Anderson, Dick-Colorado ...1967	+ Bomeisler, Bo-Yale 1913	Chapman, Sam-California 1938
Anderson, Donny-Tex.Tech ...1966	+ Booth, Albie-Yale 1931	Chappuis, Bob-Michigan 1947
+ Anderson, Hunk-N.Dame 1921	+ Borries, Fred-Navy 1934	+ Christman, Paul-Missouri 1940
Atkins, Doug-Tennessee 1952	+ Bosley, Bruce-West Va 1955	+ Clark, Dutch-Colo. Col. 1929
Babich, Bob-Miami-OH 1968	Bosseler, Don-Miami,FL 1956	Cleary, Paul-USC 1947
+ Bacon, Everett-Wesleyan 1912	Bottari, Vic-California 1938	+ Clevenger, Zora-Indiana 1903
+ Bagnell, Reds-Penn 1950	+ Boynton, Ben-Williams 1920	Cloud, Jack-Wm. & Mary 1948
+ Baker, Hobey-Princeton 1913	+ Brewer, Charles-Harvard 1895	+ Cochran, Gary-Princeton 1897
+ Baker, John-USC 1931	+ Bright, Johnny-Drake 1951	+ Cody, Josh-Vanderbilt 1919
+ Baker, Moon-N'western 1926	Brodie, John-Stanford 1956	Coleman, Don-Mich.St 1951
Baker, Terry-Oregon St 1962	+ Brooke, George-Penn 1895	+ Conerly, Charlie-Miss 1947
+ Ballin, Harold-Princeton 1914	Brown, Bob-Nebraska 1963	Connor, George-HC/ND 1947
+ Banker, Bill-Tulane 1929	Brown, Geo-Navy/S.Diego St .1947	+ Corbin, William-Yale 1888
Banonis, Vince-Detroit 1941	+ Brown, Gordon-Yale 1900	Corbus, William-Stanford 1933
+ Barnes, Stan-California 1921	Brown, Jim-Syracuse 1956	+ Cowan, Hector-Princeton 1889
+ Barrett, Charles-Cornell 1915	+ Brown, John, Jr.-Navy 1913	+ Coy, Edward (Tad)-Yale 1909
+ Baston, Bert-Minnesota 1916	+ Brown, Johnny Mack-Ala 1925	+ Crawford, Fred-Duke 1933
+ Battles, Cliff-WV Wesleyan ...1931	Brown, Tay-USC 1932	Crow, John David-Tex.A&M .1957
Baugh, Sammy-TCU 1936	+ Bunker, Paul-Army 1902	+ Crowley, Jim-Notre Dame ...1924
Baughan, Maxie-Ga.Tech 1959	Burford, Chris-Stanford 1959	Csonka, Larry-Syracuse 1967
+ Bausch, James-Kansas 1930	Burton, Ron-N'western 1959	Cutter, Slade-Navy 1934
Beagle, Ron-Navy 1955	Butkus, Dick-Illinois 1964	+ Czarobski, Ziggie-N.Dame ..1947
Beban, Gary-UCLA 1967	+ Butler, Robert-Wisconsin 1912	Dale, Carroll-Va.Tech 1959
Bechtol, Hub-Texas 1946	Cafego, George-Tenn 1939	+ Dalrymple, Gerald-Tulane ...1931
Beck, Ray-Ga. Tech 1951	+ Cagle, Red-SWLa/Army 1929	+ Dalton, John-Navy 1911
+ Beckett, John-Oregon 1916	+ Cain, John-Alabama 1932	+ Daly, Chas.-Harvard/Army ..1902
Bednarik, Chuck-Penn 1948	Cameron, Ed-Wash.& Lee ...1924	+ Daniell, Averell-Pitt 1936
Behm, Forrest-Nebraska 1940	+ Campbell, David-Harvard ...1901	+ Daniell, James-Ohio St 1941
Bell, Bobby-Minnesota 1962	Campbell, Earl-Texas 1977	+ Davies, Tom-Pittsburgh 1921
Bellino, Joe-Navy 1960	+ Cannon, Jack-N.Dame 1929	+ Davis, Ernie-Syracuse 1961

College Football Hall of Fame (Cont.)

Davis, Glenn-Army 1946
Davis, Robert-Ga.Tech 1947
Dawkins, Pete-Army 1958
DeLong, Steve-Tennessee 1964
+ DeRogatis, Al-Duke 1948
+ DesJardien, Paul-Chicago ..1914
+ Devine, Aubrey-Iowa 1921
+ DeWitt, John-Princeton 1903
Dial, Buddy-Rice 1958
Ditka, Mike-Pittsburgh 1960
Dobbs, Glenn-Tulsa 1942
+ Dodd, Bobby-Tennessee 1930
Donan, Holland-Princeton ...1950
+ Donchess, Joseph-Pitt 1929
Dorsett, Tony-Pitt 1976
+ Dougherty, Nathan-Tenn ...1909
Drahos, Nick-Cornell 1940
+ Driscoll, Paddy-N'western ..1917
+ Drury, Morley-USC 1927
Dudley, Bill-Virginia 1941
Duncan, Randy-Iowa 1958
Easley, Kenny-UCLA 1980
+ Eckersall, Walter-Chicago ...1906
+ Edwards, Turk-Wash.St 1931
+ Edwards, Wm.-Princeton 1899
+ Eichenlaub, Ray-N.Dame ...1914
Eisenhauer, Steve-Navy 1953
Elkins, Larry-Baylor 1964
Elliott, Bump-Mich/Purdue ..1947
Elliott, Pete-Michigan 1948
Elmendorf, Dave-Tex. A&M ..1970
Evans, Ray-Kansas 1947
+ Exendine, Albert-Carlisle 1907
Falaschi, Nello-S.Clara 1936
Fears, Tom-S.Clara/UCLA ...1947
+ Feathers, Beattie-Tenn 1933
Fenimore, Bob-Okla.St 1946
+ Fenton, Doc-LSU 1909
Ferguson, Bob-Ohio St. 1961
Ferraro, John-USC 1944
Fesler, Wes-Ohio St 1930
+ Fincher, Bill-Ga.Tech 1920
Fischer, Bill-Notre Dame 1948
+ Fish, Hamilton-Harvard 1909
+ Fisher, Robert-Harvard 1911
+ Flowers, Allen-Ga.Tech 1920
Flowers, Charlie-Ole Miss. ...1959
+ Fortmann Danny-Colgate ...1935
Francis, Sam-Nebraska 1936
Franco, Ed-Fordham 1937
+ Frank, Clint-Yale 1937
Franz, Rodney-California 1949
Frederickson, Tucker-Auburn .1964
+ Friedman, Benny-Michigan ..1926
Gabriel, Roman-N.C. State ..1961
Gain, Bob-Kentucky 1950
+ Galiffa, Arnold-Army 1949
Gallarneau, Hugh-Stanford ..1940
+ Garbisch, Edgar-W.& J./Army ..1924
Garrett, Mike-USC 1965
+ Gelbert, Charles-Penn 1896
+ Geyer, Forest-Oklahoma 1915
Gibbs, Jake-Miss 1960
Giel, Paul-Minnesota 1953
Gifford, Frank-USC 1951
+ Gilbert, Walter-Auburn 1936
Gilmer, Harry-Alabama 1947
+ Gipp, George-N.Dame 1920

+ Gladchuk, Chet-Boston Col ..1940
Glass, Bill-Baylor 1956
Glover, Rich-Nebraska 1972
Goldberg, Marshall-Pitt 1938
Goodreault, Gene-BC 1940
+ Gordon, Walter-Calif 1918
+ Governali, Paul-Columbia ...1942
Grabowski, Jim-Illinois 1965
Graham, Otto-N'western 1943
+ Grange, Red-Illinois 1925
+ Grayson, Bobby-Stanford ...1935
Green, Hugh-Pitt 1980
+ Green, Jack-Tulane/Army ...1945
+ Greene, Joe-N.Texas St 1968
Griese, Bob-Purdue 1966
Griffin, Archie-Ohio St 1975
Groom, Jerry-Notre Dame ...1950
+ Gulick, Merle-Toledo/Hobart ..1929
+ Guyon, Joe-Ga.Tech 1918
Hadl, John-Kansas 1961
+ Hale, Edwin-Miss.College ...1921
Hall, Parker-Miss 1938
+ Ham, Jack-Penn St 1970
+ Hamilton, Bob-Stanford 1935
+ Hamilton, Tom-Navy 1926
+ Hanson, Vic-Syracuse 1926
+ Harder, Pat-Wisconsin 1942
+ Hardwick, Tack-Harvard 1914
+ Hare, T.Truxton-Penn 1900
+ Harley, Chick-Ohio St 1919
+ Harmon, Tom-Michigan 1940
+ Harpster, Howard-Carnegie ..1928
+ Hart, Edward-Princeton 1911
+ Hart, Leon-Notre Dame 1949
Hartman, Bill-Georgia 1937
+ Hazel, Homer-Rutgers 1924
+ Hazeltine, Matt-Calif 1954
+ Healey, Ed.-Dartmouth 1916
+ Heffelfinger, Pudge-Yale 1891
+ Hein, Mel-Washington St 1930
+ Heinrich, Don-Washington ...1952
Hendricks, Ted-Miami,FL 1968
+ Henry, Pete-Wash&Jeff 1919
+ Herschberger, C.-Chicago ...1898
+ Herwig, Robert-Calif 1937
+ Heston, Willie-Michigan 1904
+ Hickman, Herman-Tenn 1931
+ Hickok, William-Yale 1894
Hill, Dan-Duke 1938
+ Hillebrand, Art-Princeton 1899
+ Hinkey, Frank-Yale 1894
+ Hinkle, Carl-Vanderbilt 1937
+ Hinkle, Clarke-Bucknell 1931
Hirsch, Elroy-Wisc./Mich 1943
+ Hitchcock, James-Auburn ...1932
Hoffmann, Frank-N.Dame ...1931
+ Hogan, James J.-Yale 1904
+ Holland, Brud-Cornell 1938
+ Holleder, Don-Army 1955
+ Hollenback, Bill-Penn 1908
+ Holovak, Mike-Boston Col ...1942
Holub, E.J.-Texas Tech 1960
Hornung, Paul-N.Dame 1956
+ Horrell, Edwin-California 1924
+ Horvath, Les-Ohio St 1944
+ Howe, Arthur-Yale 1911
+ Howell, Dixie-Alabama 1934
+ Hubbard, Cal-Centenary 1926
+ Hubbard, John-Amherst 1906
+ Hubert, Pooley-Ala. 1925
Huff, Sam-West Virginia 1955
Humble, Weldon-Rice 1946

Hunley, Ricky-Arizona 1983
+ Hunt, Joe-Texas A&M 1927
Huntington, Ellery-Colgate ..1914
+ Hutson, Don-Alabama 1934
+ Ingram, Jonas-Navy 1906
+ Isbell, Cecil-Purdue 1937
+ Jablonsky, J.-Army/Wash ...1933
+ Janowicz, Vic-Ohio St 1951
+ Jenkins, Darold-Missouri 1941
+ Jensen, Jackie-California 1948
+ Joesting, Herbert-Minn 1927
Johnson, Bob-Tennessee 1967
+ Johnson, Jimmie-Carlisle/N'western .1903
Johnson, Ron-Michigan 1968
+ Jones, Calvin-Iowa 1955
+ Jones, Gomer-Ohio St 1935
Jordan, Lee Roy-Alabama ...1962
+ Juhan, Frank-U.of South 1910
Justice, Charlie-N.Car 1949
+ Kaer, Mort-USC 1926
Karras, Alex-Iowa 1957
Kavanaugh, Ken-LSU 1939
+ Kaw, Edgar-Cornell 1922
Kazmaier, Dick-Princeton ...1951
+ Keck, James-Princeton 1921
Kelley, Larry-Yale 1936
+ Kelly, Wild Bill-Montana 1926
Kenna, Doug-Army 1944
+ Kerr, George-Boston Col 1941
+ Ketcham, Henry-Yale 1913
Keyes, Leroy-Purdue 1968
+ Killinger, Glenn-Penn St 1921
+ Kilpatrick, John-Yale 1910
Kimbrough, John-Tex A&M ..1940
+ Kinard, Frank-Mississippi 1937
+ King, Phillip-Princeton 1893
+ Kinnick, Nile-Iowa 1939
+ Kipke, Harry-Michigan 1923
+ Kitzmiller, John-Oregon 1930
+ Koch, Barton-Baylor 1931
+ Koppisch, Walt-Columbia ...1924
Kramer, Ron-Michigan 1956
+ Kroll, Alex-Rutgers 1961
Krueger, Charlie-Tex. A&M ..1957
Kutner, Malcolm-Texas 1941
+ Kwalick, Ted-Penn St 1968
+ Lach, Steve-Duke 1941
Lane, Myles-Dartmouth 1927
Lattner, Johnny-N.Dame 1953
Lauricella, Hank-Tenn 1952
+ Lautenschlaeger, Les-Tulane ..1925
+ Layden, Elmer-N.Dame 1924
+ Layne, Bobby-Texas 1947
+ Lea, Langdon-Princeton 1895
LeBaron, Eddie-Pacific 1949
+ Leech, James-VMI 1920
+ Lester, Darrell-TCU 1935
Lilly, Bob-TCU 1960
Little, Floyd-Syracuse 1966
+ Lio, Augie-Georgetown 1940
+ Locke, Gordon-Iowa 1922
+ Lourie, Don-Princeton 1921
Lucas, Richie-Penn St 1959
Luckman, Sid-Columbia 1938
Lujack, Johnny-N.Dame 1947
+ Lund, Pug-Minnesota 1934
Lynch, Jim-Notre Dame 1966
+ Macomber, Bart-Illinois 1915
MacLeod, Robert-Dart. 1938
Maegle, Dick-Rice 1954
+ Mahan, Eddie-Harvard 1915
Majors, John-Tennessee 1956

College Football Hall of Fame (Cont.)

Small College

Players

Brasdshaw, Terry-La. Tech 1969
+ Buchanan, Buck-Grambling ..1962
Cichy, Joe-N.Dakota St. 1970
+ Delaney, Joe-N'western St. ...1980
Den Herder, Vern-Central IA .1970
Dryer, Fred-S. Diego St. 1968
Dudek, Joe-Plymouth St. 1985

Grinnell, William-Tufts 1934
Hawkins, Frank-Nevada 1980
Holt, Pierce-Angelo St. 1987
Johnson, Billy-Widener, PA ..1973
Johnson, Gary-Grambling St. ..1974
Lomax, Neil-Portland St. 1980
McGriff, Tyrone-Jackson St. ..1974

Montgomery, Wilbert-Ab. Christ 1976
O'Brien, Ken-UC–Davis 1982
Payton, Walter-Jackson St. ...1974
Reasons, Gary-N'western St. .1983
Taylor, Bruce-Boston U. 1969
Thomsen, Lynn-Augustana 1986
Youngblood, Jim-Tenn. Tech ..1972

Coaches

+ Burry, Harold 1996
Butterfield, Jim 1997

+ Hoernemann, Paul 1997
Sherman, Edgar 1996

+ Steinke, Gilbert 1996
+ Tressel, Lee 1996

Pro Football Hall of Fame

Established in 1963 by National Football League to commemorate the sport's professional origins. **Address:** 2121 George Halas Drive NW, Canton, OH 44708. **Telephone:** (330) 456-8207.

Eligibility: Nominated players must be retired five years, coaches must be retired, and contributors can still be active. Voting done by 36-member panel made up of media representatives from all 30 NFL cities, one PFWA representative and five selectors-at-large.

Class of 1997 (4): PLAYERS—CB **Mike Haynes**, New England (1976-82) and Oakland (1983-89); C **Mike Webster**, Pittsburgh (1974-88) and Kansas City (1989-90). COACH— **Don Shula**, Baltimore (1963-69) and Miami (1970-95). CONTRIBUTOR— **Wellington Mara** (1937–present)

Quarterbacks

Baugh, Sammy 1963
Blanda, George (also PK) ...1981
Bradshaw, Terry 1989
+ Clark, Dutch 1963
+ Conzelman, Jimmy 1964
Dawson, Len 1987
+ Driscoll, Paddy 1965
Fouts, Dan 1993

Graham, Otto 1965
Griese, Bob 1990
+ Herber, Arnie 1966
Jurgensen, Sonny 1983
+ Layne, Bobby 1967
Luckman, Sid 1965
Namath, Joe 1985
Parker, Clarence (Ace) 1972

Starr, Bart 1977
Staubach, Roger 1985
Tarkenton, Fran 1986
Tittle, Y.A 1971
Unitas, Johnny 1979
+ Van Brocklin, Norm 1971
+ Waterfield, Bob 1965

Running Backs

+ Battles, Cliff 1968
Brown, Jim 1971
Campbell, Earl 1991
Canadeo, Tony 1974
Csonka, Larry 1987
Dorsett, Tony 1994
Dudley, Bill 1966
Gifford, Frank 1977
+ Grange, Red 1963
+ Guyon, Joe 1966
Harris, Franco 1990
+ Hinkle, Clarke 1964

Hornung, Paul 1986
Johnson, John Henry 1987
Kelly, Leroy 1994
+ Leemans, Tuffy 1978
Matson, Ollie 1972
McAfee, George 1966
McElhenny, Hugh 1970
+ McNally, Johnny (Blood) 1963
Moore, Lenny 1975
Motley, Marion 1968
+ Nagurski, Bronko 1963
+ Nevers, Ernie 1963

Payton, Walter 1993
Perry, Joe 1969
Riggins, John 1992
Sayers, Gale 1977
Simpson, O.J 1985
+ Strong, Ken 1967
Taylor, Jim 1976
+ Thorpe, Jim 1963
Trippi, Charley 1968
Van Buren, Steve 1965
Walker, Doak 1986

Ends & Wide Receivers

Alworth, Lance 1978
Badgro, Red 1981
Berry, Raymond 1973
Biletnikoff, Fred 1988
+ Chamberlin, Guy 1965
Ditka, Mike 1988
Fears, Tom 1970
+ Hewitt, Bill 1971

Hirsch, Elroy (Crazylegs) 1968
+ Hutson, Don 1963
Joiner, Charlie 1996
Largent, Steve 1995
Lavelli, Dante 1975
Mackey, John 1992
Maynard, Don 1987

+ Millner, Wayne 1968
Mitchell, Bobby 1983
Pihos, Pete 1970
Smith, Jackie 1994
Taylor, Charley 1984
Warfield, Paul 1983
Winslow, Kellen 1995

Linemen (pre-World War II)

+ Edwards, Turk (T) 1969
+ Fortmann, Dan (G) 1985
+ Healey, Ed (T) 1964
+ Hein, Mel (C) 1963
+ Henry, Pete (T) 1963

+ Hubbard, Cal (T) 1963
+ Kiesling, Walt (G) 1966
+ Kinard, Bruiser (T) 1971
+ Lyman, Link (T) 1964
+ Michalske, Mike (G) 1964

Musso, George (T-G) 1982
+ Stydahar, Joe (T) 1967
+ Trafton, George (C) 1964
Turner, Bulldog (C) 1966
+ Wojciechowicz, Alex (C) ...1968

Offensive Linemen

Bednarik, Chuck (C-LB) 1967
Brown, Roosevelt (T) 1975
Dierdorf, Dan (T) 1996
Gatski, Frank (C) 1985
Gregg, Forrest (T-G) 1977
Groza, Lou (T-PK) 1974
Hannah, John (G) 1991

Jones, Stan (T-G-DT) 1991
Langer, Jim (C) 1987
Little, Larry (G) 1993
McCormack, Mike (T) 1984
Mix, Ron (T-G) 1979
Otto, Jim (C) 1980
Parker, Jim (G) 1973

Ringo, Jim (C) 1981
St. Clair, Bob (T) 1990
Shell, Art (T) 1989
Upshaw, Gene (G) 1987
Webster, Mike (C) 1997

Pro Football Hall of Fame (Cont.)

Defensive Linemen

Atkins, Doug 1982	Jones, Deacon 1980	Robustelli, Andy 1971
+ Buchanan, Buck 1990	+ Jordan, Henry 1995	Selmon, Lee Roy 1995
Creekmur, Lou 1996	Lilly, Bob 1980	Stautner, Ernie 1969
Davis, Willie 1981	Marchetti, Gino 1972	Weinmeister, Arnie 1984
Donovan, Art 1968	Nomellini, Leo 1969	White, Randy 1994
+ Ford, Len 1976	Olsen, Merlin 1982	Willis, Bill 1977
Greene, Joe 1987	Page, Alan 1988	

Linebackers

Bell, Bobby 1983	Ham, Jack 1988	Lanier, Willie 1986
Butkus, Dick 1979	Hendricks, Ted 1990	Nitschke, Ray 1978
Connor, George (DT-OT) 1975	Huff, Sam 1982	Schmidt, Joe 1973
+ George, Bill 1974	Lambert, Jack 1990	

Defensive Backs

Adderley, Herb 1980	Haynes, Mike 1997	Renfro, Mel 1996
Barney, Lem 1992	Houston, Ken 1986	+ Tunnell, Emlen 1967
Blount, Mel 1989	Johnson, Jimmy 1994	Wilson, Larry 1978
Brown, Willie 1984	Lane, Dick (Night Train) 1974	Wood, Willie 1989
+ Christiansen, Jack 1970	Lary, Yale 1979	

Placekicker

Stenerud, Jan 1991

Coaches

+ Brown, Paul 1967	Grant, Bud 1994	+ Neale, Earle (Greasy) 1969
Ewbank, Weeb 1978	+ Halas, George 1963	Noll, Chuck 1993
+ Flaherty, Ray 1976	+ Lambeau, Curly 1963	+ Owen, Steve 1966
Gibbs, Joe 1996	Landry, Tom 1990	Shula, Don 1997
Gillman, Sid 1983	+ Lombardi, Vince 1971	Walsh, Bill 1993

Contributors

+ Bell, Bert 1963	+ Halas, George 1963	+ Ray, Hugh (Shorty) 1966
+ Bidwill, Charles 1967	Hunt, Lamar 1972	+ Reeves, Dan 1967
+ Carr, Joe 1963	+ Mara, Tim 1963	+ Rooney, Art 1964
Davis, Al 1992	Mara, Wellington 1997	+ Rozelle, Pete 1985
+ Finks, Jim 1995	+ Marshall, George 1963	Schramm, Tex 1991

Dick McCann Award

First presented in 1969 by the Pro Football Writers of America for long and distinguished reporting on pro football. Named in honor of the first director of the Hall, the McCann Award does not constitute induction into the Hall of Fame.

Year		Year		Year	
1969	George Strickler	1979	Pat Livingston	1989	Vito Stellino
1970	Arthur Daley	1980	Chuck Heaton	1990	Will McDonough
1971	Joe King	1981	Norm Miller	1991	Dick Connor
1972	Lewis Atchison	1982	Cameron Snyder	1992	Frank Luska
1973	Dave Brady	1983	Hugh Brown	1993	Ira Miller
1974	Bob Oates	1984	Larry Felser	1994	Don Pierson
1975	John Steadman	1985	Cooper Rollow	1995	Ray Didinger
1976	Jack Hand	1986	Bill Wallace	1996	Paul Zimmerman
1977	Art Daley	1987	Jerry Magee	1997	Bob Roesler
1978	Murray Olderman	1988	Gordon Forbes		

Pete Rozelle Award

First presented in 1989 by the Hall of Fame for exceptional longtime contributions to radio and TV in pro football. Named in honor of the former NFL commissioner, who was also a publicist and GM for the LA Rams, the Rozelle Award does not constitute induction into the Hall of Fame.

Year		Year		Year	
1989	Bill McPhail	1992	Chris Schenkel	1995	Frank Gifford
1990	Lindsey Nelson	1993	Curt Gowdy	1996	Jack Buck
1991	Ed Sabol	1994	Pat Summerall	1997	Charlie Jones

NFL's 75th Anniversary All-Time Team

Selected by a 15-member panel of former players, NFL and Pro Football Hall of Fame officials and media representatives and released Sept. 1, 1994.

Offense

Wide Receivers (4): Lance Alworth, Raymond Berry, Don Hutson and Jerry Rice

Tight Ends (2): Mike Ditka and Kellen Winslow

Tackles (3): Roosevelt Brown, Forrest Gregg and Anthony Munoz

Guards (3): John Hannah, Jim Parker and Gene Upshaw

Centers (2): Mel Hein and Mike Webster

Quarterbacks (4): Sammy Baugh, Otto Graham, Joe Montana and Johnny Unitas

Running Backs (6): Jim Brown, Marion Motley, Bronko Nagurski, Walter Payton, O.J. Simpson and Steve Van Buren

Defense

Ends (3): Deacon Jones, Gino Marchetti and Reggie White

Tackles (3): Joe Greene, Bob Lilly and Merlin Olsen

Linebackers (7): Dick Butkus, Jack Ham, Ted Hendricks, Jack Lambert, Willie Lanier, Ray Nitschke and Lawrence Taylor

Cornerbacks (4): Mel Blount, Mike Haynes, Dick (Night Train) Lane and Rod Woodson

Safties (3): Ken Houston, Ronnie Lott and Larry Wilson

Specialists

Placekicker: Jan Stenerud
Punter: Ray Guy

Kick Returner: Gale Sayers
Punt Returner: Billy (White Shoes) Johnson

Canadian Football Hall of Fame

Established in 1963. Current Hall opened in 1972. **Address:** 58 Jackson Street West, Hamilton, Ontario, L8P 1L4. **Telephone:** (905) 528-7566.

Eligibility: Nominated players must be retired three years, but coaches and builders can still be active. Voting done by 15-member panel of Canadian pro and amateur football officials.

Class of 1997 (5): PLAYERS—DE **Junior Ah You**, Montreal (1972-81); SB **Rocky DiPietro**, Hamilton (1978-91); RB **Bill Symons**, British Columbia (1966), Toronto (1967-73); C **Al Wilson**, British Columbia (1972-86). BUILDER—**Bruce Coulter**, Bishops Univ. AD (1961-90).

Members are listed with year of induction; (+) indicates deceased members.

Players

	Name	Year		Name	Year		Name	Year
	Ah You, Junior	1997		Fieldgate, Norm	1979	+	McCance, Ches	1976
	Atchison, Ron	1978		Fleming, Willie	1982	+	McGill, Frank	1965
	Bailey, Byron	1975		Gabriel, Tony	1985		McQuarters, Ed	1988
	Baker, Bill	1994		Gaines, Gene	1994		Miles, Rollie	1980
	Barrow, John	1976	+	Gall, Hugh	1963	+	Molson, Percy	1963
+	Batstone, Harry	1963		Golab, Tony	1964		Morris, Frank	1983
+	Beach, Ormond	1963		Grant, Tom	1995	+	Morris, Ted	1964
	Benecick, Al	1996		Gray, Herbert	1983		Mosca, Angelo	1987
	Box, Ab	1965		Griffing, Dean	1965	+	Nelson, Roger	1986
+	Breen, Joe	1963	+	Hanson, Fritz	1963		Neumann, Peter	1979
+	Bright, Johnny	1970		Harris, Wayne	1976		O'Quinn, John (Red)	1981
	Brown, Tom	1984		Harrison, Herm	1993		Pajaczkowski, Tony	1988
	Brock, Dieter	1995		Helton, John	1986		Parker, Jackie	1971
	Campbell, Jerry (Soupy)	1996		Henley, Garney	1979		Patterson, Hal	1971
	Casey, Tom	1964		Hinton, Tom	1991		Perry, Gordon	1970
	Charlton, Ken	1992	+	Huffman, Dick	1987	+	Perry, Norm	1963
	Clarke, Bill	1996	+	Isbister, Bob Sr	1965		Ploen, Ken	1975
	Clements, Tom	1994		Jackson, Russ	1973	+	Quilty, S.P. (Silver)	1966
	Coffey, Tommy Joe	1977	+	Jacobs, Jack	1963	+	Rebholz, Russ	1963
+	Conacher, Lionel	1963	+	James, Eddie (Dynamite)	1963		Reed, George	1979
	Copeland, Royal	1988		James, Gerry	1981	+	Reeve, Ted	1963
	Corrigall, Jim	1990	+	Kabat, Greg	1966		Rigney, Frank	1985
+	Cox, Ernest	1963		Kapp, Joe	1984	+	Rodden, Mike	1964
+	Craig, Ross	1964		Keeling, Jerry	1989		Rowe, Paul	1964
+	Cronin, Carl	1967		Kelly, Brian	1991		Ruby, Martin	1974
+	Cutler, Wes	1968		Kelly, Ellison	1992	+	Russel, Jeff	1963
	Dalla Riva, Peter	1993		Kepley, Dan	1996	+	Scott, Vince	1982
	DiPietro, Rocky	1997		Krol, Joe	1963		Shatto, Dick	1975
+	Dixon, George	1974		Kwong, Normie	1969	+	Simpson, Ben	1963
+	Eliowitz, Abe	1969		Lancaster, Ron	1982		Simpson, Bob	1976
+	Emerson, Eddie	1963	+	Lawson, Smirle	1963	+	Sprague, David	1963
	Etcheverry, Sam	1969	+	Leadlay, Frank (Pep)	1963		Stevenson, Art	1969
	Evanshen, Terry	1984	+	Lear, Les	1974		Stewart, Ron	1977
	Faloney, Bernie	1974		Lewis, Leo	1973	+	Stirling, Hugh (Bummer)	1966
+	Fear, A.H. (Cap)	1967		Lunsford, Earl	1983		Sutherin, Don	1992
	Fennell, Dave	1990		Luster, Marv	1990		Symons, Bill	1997
+	Ferraro, John	1966		Luzzi, Don	1986		Thelen, Dave	1989

Canadian Football Hall of Fame (Cont.)

+ Timmis, Brian 1963
Tinsley, Bud 1982
+ Tommy, Andy 1989

+ Back, Leonard 1971
+ Bailey, Harold 1965
+ Ballard, Harold 1987
+ Berger, Sam 1993
+ Brook, Tom 1975
+ Brown, D. Wes 1963
+ Chipman, Arthur 1969
Clair, Frank 1981
+ Cooper, Ralph 1992
Coulter, Bruce 1997
+ Crighton, Hec 1986
+ Currie, Andrew 1974
+ Davies, Dr. Andrew 1969
+ DeGruchy, John 1963
Dojack, Paul 1978
+ Duggan, Eck 1981
+ DuMoulin, Seppi 1963
+ Foulds, Willliam 1963
Fulton, Greg 1995

+ Trawick, Herb 1975
+ Tubman, Joe 1968
Tucker, Whit 1993
Urness, Ted 1989
Vaughan, Kaye 1978
Wagner, Virgil 1980
+ Welch, Hawley (Huck) 1964

Builders

Gaudaur, J.G. (Jake) 1984
Gibson, Frank 1996
Grant, Bud 1983
+ Grey, Lord Earl 1963
+ Griffith, Dr. Harry 1963
+ Halter, Sydney 1966
+ Hannibal, Frank 1963
+ Hayman, Lew 1975
+ Hughes, W.P. (Billy) 1974
Keys, Eagle 1990
Kimball, Norman 1991
+ Kramer, R.A. (Bob) 1987
+ Lieberman, M.I. (Moe) 1973
+ McBrien, Harry 1978
+ McCaffrey, Jimmy 1967
+ McCann, Dave 1966
McNaughton, Don 1994
+ McPherson, Don 1983

Wilkinson, Tom 1987
Wilson, Al 1997
Wylie, Harvey 1980
Young, Jim 1991
+ Zock, Bill 1985

+ Metras, Johnny 1980
+ Montgomery, Ken 1970
+ Newton, Jack 1964
+ Preston, Ken 1990
+ Ritchie, Alvin 1963
+ Ryan, Joe B. 1968
Sazio, Ralph 1988
+ Shaughnessy, Frank (Shag) ..1963
+ Shouldice, W.T. (Hap) 1977
+ Simpson, Jimmie 1986
+ Slocomb, Karl 1989
+ Spring, Harry 1976
Stukus, Annis 1974
+ Taylor, N.J. (Piffles) 1963
+ Tindall, Frank 1985
+ Warner, Clair 1965
+ Warwick, Bert 1964
+ Wilson, Seymour 1984

GOLF

A new Golf Museum and Hall of Fame is expected to open in Spring 1998 at World Golf Village. Groundbreaking was August 1996 at St. Johns County, Fla., between Jacksonville and St. Augustine. The new hall will incorporate the inactive PGA/World Golf Hall of Fame (formerly run by the PGA of America) and the active LPGA Hall as well as provide a role for the USGA and the Royal and Ancient Golf Club of St. Andrews. The building will feature more than 70 exhibits and and a 300–seat IMAX theater. Questions concerning the new Golf Hall of Fame and Museum should be directed to the PGA Tour at (904) 273-3350.

Eligibility: Professionals will have three avenues into the WGHF. A PGA Tour player qualifies for the ballot if he has at least 10 victories in approved tournaments, or at least two victories among The Players Championship, Masters, U.S. Open, British Open and PGA Championship, is at least 40 years old and has been a member of the Tour for 10 years. Any player qualifying for the LPGA Hall automatically qualifies for the WGHF. For players not eligible for either the PGA Tour or the LPGA Hall of Fame, a body of over 300 international golf writers and historians will vote each year.

PGA/World Golf Hall of Fame

Established in 1974, but inactive since 1993. Will become part of the PGA Tour's new Golf Museum and Hall of Fame in 1998. Members are listed with year of induction; (+) indicates deceased members.

Men

+ Anderson, Willie 1975
+ Armour, Tommy 1976
+ Ball, John, Jr 1977
+ Barnes, Jim 1989
+ Boros, Julius 1982
+ Braid, James 1976
Casper, Billy 1978
Cooper, Lighthorse Harry ..1992
+ Cotton, Thomas 1980
+ Demaret, Jimmy 1983
DeVicenzo, Roberto 1989
+ Evans, Chick 1975
Floyd, Ray 1989
+ Guldahl, Ralph 1981

+ Hagen, Walter 1974
+ Hilton, Harold 1978
+ Hogan, Ben 1974
Irwin, Hale 1992
+ Jones, Bobby 1974
+ Little, Lawson 1980
Littler, Gene 1990
+ Locke, Bobby 1977
Middlecoff, Cary 1986
+ Morris, Tom, Jr 1975
+ Morris, Tom, Sr 1976
Nelson, Byron 1974
Nicklaus, Jack 1974
+ Ouimet, Francis 1974

Palmer, Arnold 1974
Player, Gary 1974
Runyan, Paul 1990
Sarazen, Gene 1974
+ Smith, Horton 1990
Snead, Sam 1974
+ Taylor, John H 1975
Thomson, Peter 1988
+ Travers, Jerry 1976
Travis, Walter 1979
Trevino, Lee 1981
+ Vardon, Harry 1974
Watson, Tom 1988

Women

Berg, Patty 1974
Carner, JoAnne 1985
+ Howe, Dorothy C.H 1978
Lopez, Nancy 1989

Rawls, Betsy 1987
Suggs, Louise 1979
+ Vare, Glenna Collett 1975
+ Wethered, Joyce 1975

Whitworth, Kathy 1982
Wright, Mickey 1976
+ Zaharias, Babe Didrikson ...1974

Contributors

Campbell, William 1990
+ Corcoran, Fred 1975
+ Crosby, Bing 1978
+ Dey, Joe 1975

+ Graffis, Herb 1977
+ Harlow, Robert 1988
Hope, Bob 1983
Jones, Robert Trent 1987

+ Roberts, Clifford 1978
Rodriguez, Chi Chi 1992
+ Ross, Donald 1977
+ Tufts, Richard 1992

Old PGA Hall Members Not in PGA/World Hall

The original PGA Hall of Fame was established in 1940 by the PGA of America, but abandoned after the 1982 inductions in favor of the PGA/World Hall of Fame.. Twenty-seven members of the old PGA Hall have been elected to the PGA/World Hall since then. Players yet to make the cut are listed below with year of induction into old PGA Hall.

+	Brady, Mike	1960	Ford, Doug	1975	+ McLeod, Fred	1960
+	Burke, Billy	1966	+ Ghezzi, Vic	1965	+ Picard, Henry	1961
	Burke, Jack Jr	1975	+ Harbert, Chick	1968	+ Revolta, Johnny	1963
+	Cruickshank, Bobby	1967	Harper, Chandler	1969	+ Shute, Denny	1957
+	Diegel, Leo	1955	+ Harrison, Dutch	1962	+ Smith, Alex	1940
+	Dudley, Ed	1964	+ Hutchison, Jock Sr	1959	+ Smith, Macdonald	1954
+	Dutra, Olin	1962	+ McDermott, John	1940	+ Wood, Craig	1956
+	Farroll, Johnny	1961	+ Mangrum, Lloyd	1964		

LPGA Hall of Fame

Established in 1967 by the LPGA to replace the old Women's Golf Hall of Fame (founded in 1950). Originally located in Augusta, GA (1967-77), the Hall has been moved to Pinehurst, NC (1977-83), Sugar Land, TX (1983-89) and Daytona, FL (since 1990). Will become part of the PGA Tour's new Golf Museum and Hall of Fame in 1998. **Address:** LPGA Headquarters, 100 International Golf Drive, Daytona, FL 32124. **Telephone:** (904) 274-6200.

Eligibility: Nominees must have played 10 years on the LPGA tour and won 30 official events, including two major championships; 35 official events and one major; or 40 official events and no majors.

Latest inductee: **Betsy King** (30 wins, 5 majors) became the 14th player to gain entry by capturing the ShopRite Classic in Somers Point, N.J. on June 25, 1995. **Leading candidates** (through Sept. 15, 1996): Amy Alcott (29 wins, 5 majors) and Beth Daniel (32 wins, 1 major).

Members are listed with year of induction; (+) indicates deceased members.

Players

Berg, Patty	1951	Lopez, Nancy	1987	Wright, Mickey	1964
Bradley, Pat	1991	Mann, Carol	1977	+ Zaharias, Babe Didrikson	1951
Carner, JoAnne	1982	Rawls, Betsy	1960		
Haynie, Sandra	1977	Sheehan, Patty	1993	**Contributor**	
Jameson, Betty	1951	Suggs, Louise	1951		
King, Betsy	1995	Whitworth, Kathy	1975	+ Shore, Dinah	1994

HOCKEY

Hockey Hall of Fame

Established in 1945 by the National Hockey League and opened in 1961. **Address:** BCE Place, 30 Yonge Street, Toronto, Ontario, M5E 1X8. **Telephone:** (416) 360-7735.

Eligibility: Nominated players and referees must be retired three years. Voting done by 15-member panel made up of pro and amateur hockey personalities and media representatives. A 15-member Veterans Committee selects older players.

Class of 1997 (3): PLAYERS—center **Mario Lemieux**, Pittsburgh (1984-94, 95-97); center **Bryan Trottier**, New York Islanders (1975-90), Pittsburgh (1990-94). BUILDER—**Glen Sather** (NHL coach from 1979-89, 93-94).

Members are listed with year of induction; (+) indicates deceased members.

Forwards

	Abel, Sid	1969	+ Cowley, Bill	1968	Howe, Gordie	1972
+	Adams, Jack	1959	+ Crawford, Rusty	1962	+ Howe, Syd	1965
	Apps, Syl	1961	+ Darragh, Jack	1962	Hull, Bobby	1983
	Armstrong, George	1975	+ Davidson, Scotty	1950	+ Hyland, Harry	1962
+	Bailey, Ace	1975	Day, Hap	1961	+ Irvin, Dick	1958
+	Bain, Dan	1945	Delvecchio, Alex	1977	+ Jackson, Busher	1971
+	Baker, Hobey	1945	+ Denneny, Cy	1959	+ Joliat, Aurel	1947
	Barber, Bill	1990	Dionne, Marcel	1992	+ Keats, Duke	1958
+	Barry, Marty	1965	+ Drillon, Gordie	1975	Kennedy, Ted (Teeder)	1966
	Bathgate, Andy	1978	+ Drinkwater, Graham	1950	Keon, Dave	1986
+	Bauer, Bobby	1996	Dumart, Woody	1992	Lach, Elmer	1966
+	Beliveau, Jean	1972	+ Dunderdale, Tommy	1974	Lafleur, Guy	1988
+	Bentley, Doug	1964	Dye, Babe	1970	+ Lalonde, Newsy	1950
+	Bentley, Max	1966	Esposito, Phil	1984	Laprade, Edgar	1993
+	Blake, Toe	1966	+ Farrell, Arthur	1965	Lemaire, Jacques	1984
	Bossy, Mike	1991	+ Foyston, Frank	1958	Lemieux, Mario	1997
+	Boucher, Frank	1958	+ Frederickson, Frank	1958	+ Lewis, Herbie	1989
+	Bowie, Dubbie	1945	Gainey, Bob	1992	Lindsay, Ted	1966
+	Broadbent, Punch	1962	+ Gardner, Jimmy	1962	+ MacKay, Mickey	1952
	Bucyk, John (Chief)	1981	Geoffrion, Bernie	1972	Mahovlich, Frank	1981
+	Burch, Billy	1974	+ Gerard, Eddie	1945	+ Malone, Joe	1950
	Clarke, Bobby	1987	Gilbert, Rod	1982	+ Marshall, Jack	1965
+	Colville, Neil	1967	+ Gilmour, Billy	1962	+ Maxwell, Fred	1962
+	Conacher, Charlie	1961	+ Griffis, Si	1950	McDonald, Lanny	1992
+	Cook, Bill	1952	Hay, George	1958	+ McGee, Frank	1945
+	Cook, Bun	1995	+ Hextall, Bryan	1969	+ McGimsie, Billy	1962
	Cournoyer, Yvan	1982	+ Hooper, Tom	1962	Mikita, Stan	1983

Hockey Hall of Fame (Cont.)

Moore, Dickie 1974
+ Morenz, Howie 1945
+ Mosienko, Bill 1965
+ Nighbor, Frank 1947
+ Noble, Reg 1962
+ O'Connor, Buddy 1988
+ Oliver, Harry 1967
Olmstead, Bert 1985
+ Patrick, Lynn 1980
Perreault, Gilbert 1990
+ Phillips, Tom 1945
+ Primeau, Joe 1963
Pulford, Bob 1991

+ Benedict, Clint 1965
Bower, Johnny 1976
Brimsek, Frankie 1966
+ Broda, Turk 1967
Cheevers, Gerry 1985
+ Connell, Alex 1958
Dryden, Ken 1983
+ Durnan, Bill 1964
Esposito, Tony 1988
+ Gardiner, Chuck 1945

Boivin, Leo 1986
+ Boon, Dickie 1952
Bouchard, Butch 1966
+ Boucher, George 1960
+ Cameron, Harry 1962
+ Clancy, King 1958
+ Clapper, Dit 1947
+ Cleghorn, Sprague 1958
+ Conacher, Lionel 1994
Coulter, Art 1974
+ Dutton, Red 1958
Flaman, Fernie 1990
Gadsby, Bill 1970
+ Gardiner, Herb 1958
+ Goheen, F.X. (Moose) 1952
+ Goodfellow, Ebbie 1963
+ Grant, Mike 1950
+ Green, Wilf (Shorty) 1962

Armstrong, Neil 1991
Ashley, John 1981
Chadwick, Bill 1964
D'Amico, John 1993
+ Elliott, Chaucer 1961

+ Adams, Charles 1960
+ Adams, Weston W. Sr 1972
+ Ahearn, Frank 1962
+ Ahearne, J.F. (Bunny) 1977
+ Allan, Sir Montagu 1945
Allen, Keith 1992
Arbour, Al 1996
Ballard, Harold 1977
+ Bauer, Fr. David 1989
+ Bickell, J.P 1978
Bowman, Scotty 1991
+ Brown, George 1961
+ Brown, Walter 1962

+ Rankin, Frank 1961
Ratelle, Jean 1985
Richard, Henri 1979
Richard, Maurice (Rocket) 1961
+ Richardson, George 1950
+ Roberts, Gordie 1971
+ Russel, Blair 1965
+ Russell, Ernie 1965
+ Ruttan, Jack 1962
+ Scanlan, Fred 1965
Schmidt, Milt 1961
+ Schriner, Sweeney 1962
+ Seibert, Oliver 1961
Shutt, Steve 1993
+ Siebert, Babe 1964
Sittler, Darryl 1989
+ Smith, Alf 1962

Goaltenders

Giacomin, Eddie 1987
+ Hainsworth, George 1961
Hall, Glenn 1975
+ Hern, Riley 1962
+ Holmes, Hap 1972
+ Hutton, J.B. (Bouse) 1962
+ Lehman, Hughie 1958
+ LeSueur, Percy 1961
Lumley, Harry 1980
+ Moran, Paddy 1958

Defensemen

+ Hall, Joe 1961
+ Harvey, Doug 1973
Horner, Red 1965
+ Horton, Tim 1977
Howell, Harry 1979
+ Johnson, Ching 1958
+ Johnson, Ernie 1952
Johnson, Tom 1970
Kelly, Red 1969
Laperriere, Jacques 1987
Lapointe, Guy 1993
+ Laviolette, Jack 1962
+ Mantha, Sylvio 1960
+ McNamara, George 1958
Orr, Bobby 1979
Park, Brad 1988
+ Patrick, Lester 1947
Pilote, Pierre 1975

Referees & Linesmen

+ Hayes, George 1988
+ Hewitson, Bobby 1963
+ Ion, Mickey 1961
Pavelich, Matt 1987

Builders

+ Buckland, Frank 1975
Butterfield, Jack 1980
+ Calder, Frank 1945
+ Campbell, Angus 1964
+ Campbell, Clarence 1966
+ Cattarinich, Joseph 1977
+ Dandurand, Leo 1963
Dilio, Frank 1964
+ Dudley, George 1958
+ Dunn, James 1968
Eagleson, Alan 1989
Francis, Emile 1982
+ Gibson, Jack 1976

Smith, Clint 1991
+ Smith, Hooley 1972
+ Smith, Tommy 1973
+ Stanley, Barney 1962
+ Stewart, Nels 1962
+ Stuart, Bruce 1961
+ Taylor, Fred (Cyclone) 1947
+ Trihey, Harry 1950
Trottier, Bryan 1997
Ullman, Norm 1982
+ Walker, Jack 1960
+ Walsh, Marty 1962
Watson, Harry 1994
+ Watson, Harry (Moose) 1962
+ Weiland, Cooney 1971
+ Westwick, Harry (Rat) 1962
+ Whitcroft, Fred 1962

Parent, Bernie 1984
+ Plante, Jacques 1978
Rayner, Chuck 1973
+ Sawchuk, Terry 1971
Smith, Billy 1993
+ Thompson, Tiny 1959
Tretiak, Vladislav 1989
+ Vezina, Georges 1945
Worsley, Gump 1980
+ Worters, Roy 1969

+ Pitre, Didier 1962
Potvin, Denis 1991
+ Pratt, Babe 1966
Pronovost, Marcel 1978
+ Pulford, Harvey 1945
Quackenbush, Bill 1976
Reardon, Kenny 1966
Robinson, Larry 1995
+ Ross, Art 1945
Salming, Borje 1996
Savard, Serge 1986
Seibert, Earl 1963
+ Shore, Eddie 1947
+ Simpson, Joe 1962
Stanley, Allan 1981
+ Stewart, Jack 1964
+ Stuart, Hod 1945
+ Wilson, Gordon (Phat) 1962

+ Rodden, Mike 1962
+ Smeaton, J. Cooper 1961
Storey, Red 1967
Udvari, Frank 1973

+ Gorman, Tommy 1963
+ Griffiths, Frank A. 1993
+ Hanley, Bill 1986
+ Hay, Charles 1984
+ Hendy, Jim 1968
+ Hewitt, Foster 1965
+ Hewitt, W.A 1945
+ Hume, Fred 1962
+ Imlach, Punch 1984
Ivan, Tommy 1964
+ Jennings, Bill 1975
+ Johnson, Bob 1992
+ Juckes, Gordon 1979

+ Kilpatrick, John 1960
+ Knox, Seymour III 1993
+ Leader, Al 1969
  LeBel, Bob 1970
+ Lockhart, Tom 1965
+ Loicq, Paul 1961
+ Mariucci, John 1985
  Mathers, Frank 1992
+ McLaughlin, Frederic 1963
+ Milford, Jake 1984
  Molson, Hartland 1973
+ Nelson, Francis 1945
+ Norris, Bruce 1969
+ Norris, James D 1962
+ Norris, James Sr 1958
+ Northey, William 1945

+ O'Brien, J.A 1962
  O'Neill, Brian 1994
  Page, Fred 1993
+ Patrick, Frank 1958
+ Pickard, Allan 1958
+ Pilous, Rudy 1985
  Poile, Bud 1990
  Pollock, Sam 1978
+ Raymond, Donat 1958
+ Robertson, John Ross 1945
+ Robinson, Claude 1945
+ Ross, Philip 1976
  Sather, Glen 1997
  Sebetzki, Gunther 1995
+ Selke, Frank 1960

  Sinden, Harry 1983
+ Smith, Frank 1962
+ Smythe, Conn 1958
  Snider, Ed 1988
+ Stanley, Lord of Preston ..1945
+ Sutherland, James 1945
+ Tarasov, Anatoli 1974
  Torrey, Bill 1995
+ Turner, Lloyd 1958
+ Tutt, William Thayer 1978
  Voss, Carl 1974
+ Waghorne, Fred 1961
+ Wirtz, Arthur 1971
  Wirtz, Bill 1976
  Ziegler, John 1987

Elmer Ferguson Award

First presented in 1984 by the Professional Hockey Writers' Association for meritorious contributions by members of the PHWA. Named in honor of the late Montreal newspaper reporter, the Ferguson Award does not constitute induction into the Hall of Fame and is not necessarily an annual presentation.

1984– Jacques Beauchamp, Jim Burchard, Red Burnett, Dink Carroll, Jim Coleman, Ted Damata, Marcel Desjardins, Jack Dulmage, Milt Dunnell, Elmer Ferguson, Tom Fitzgerald, Trent Frayne, Al Laney, Joe Nichols, Basil O'Meara, Jim Vipond and Lewis Walter

1985– Charlie Barton, Red Fisher, George Gross, Zotique L'Esperance, Charles Mayer & Andy O'Brien

1986– Dick Johnston, Leo Monahan & Tim Moriarty

1987– Bill Brennan, Rex MacLeod, Ben Olan & Fran Rosa

1988– Jim Proudfoot & Scott Young
1989– Claude Larochelle & Frank Orr
1990– Bertrand Raymond
1991– Hugh Delano
1992– No award
1993– Al Strachan
1994– No award
1995– Jake Gatecliff
1996– No award
1997– Ken McKenzie

Foster Hewitt Award

First presented in 1984 by the NHL Broadcasters' Association for meritorious contributions by members of the NHLBA. Named in honor of Canada's legendary "Voice of Hockey," the Hewitt Award does not constitute induction into the Hall of Fame and is not necessarily an annual presentation.

1985– Budd Lynch & Doug Smith
1986– Wes McKnight & Lloyd Pettit
1987– Bob Wilson
1988– Dick Irvin
1989– Dan Kelly

1990– Jiggs McDonald
1991– Bruce Martyn
1992– Jim Robson
1993– Al Shaver

1994– Ted Darling
1995– Brian McFarlane
1996– Bob Cole
1997–Gene Hart

U.S. Hockey Hall of Fame

Established in 1968 by the Eveleth (Minn.) Civic Association Project H Committee and opened in 1973. **Address:** 801 Hat Trick Ave., P.O. Box 657, Eveleth, MN 55734. **Telephone:** (218) 744-5167.

Eligibility: Nominated players and referees must be American-born and retired five years; coaches must be American-born and must have coached predominantly American teams. Voting done by 12-member panel made up of Hall of Fame members and U.S. hockey officials.

Class of 1997 (3): PLAYERS—**William D. Nyrop, Timothy Sheehy**. COACH—**Charles E. Holt Jr.**

Members are listed with year of induction; (+) indicates deceased members.

Players

+ Abel, Clarence (Taffy) 1973
+ Baker, Hobey 1973
  Bartholome, Earl 1977
+ Bessone, Peter 1978
  Blake, Bob 1985
  Boucha, Henry 1995
  Brimsek, Frankie 1973
  Cavanaugh, Joe 1994
+ Chaisson, Ray 1974
  Chase, John 1973
  Christian, Bill 1984
  Christian, Roger 1989
  Cleary, Bill 1976
  Cleary, Bob 1981
+ Conroy, Tony 1975
  Dahlstrom, Carl (Cully) ...1973
+ DesJardins, Vic 1974
+ Desmond, Richard 1988
+ Dill, Bob 1979
  Everett, Doug 1974

  Ftorek, Robbie 1991
+ Garrison, John 1974
  Garrity, Jack 1986
+ Goheen, Frank (Moose) 1973
  Grant, Wally 1994
+ Harding, Austie 1975
  Iglehart, Stewart 1975
  Ikola, Willard 1990
  Johnson, Virgil 1974
+ Karakas, Mike 1973
  Kirrane, Jack 1987
+ Lane, Myles 1973
  Langevin, Dave 1993
  Larson, Reed 1996
+ Linder, Joe 1975
+ LoPresti, Sam 1973
+ Mariucci, John 1973
  Matchefts, John 1991
  Mayasich, John 1976

  McCartan, Jack 1983
  Moe, Bill 1974
  Morrow, Ken 1995
+ Moseley, Fred 1975
+ Murray, Hugh (Muzz) Sr 1987
+ Nelson, Hub 1978
+ Nyrop, William D. 1997
  Olson, Eddie 1977
+ Owen, George 1973
+ Palmer, Winthrop 1973
  Paradise, Bob 1989
  Purpur, Clifford (Fido) ...1974
  Riley, Bill 1977
+ Romnes, Elwin (Doc) 1973
  Rondeau, Dick 1985
  Sheehy, Timothy 1997
+ Williams, Tom 1981
+ Winters, Frank (Coddy) 1973
+ Yackel, Ken 1986

Hockey Hall of Fame (Cont.)

Coaches

+ Almquist, Oscar 1983	Harkness, Ned 1994	+ Kelly, John (Snooks) 1974
Bessone, Amo 1992	Heyliger, Vic 1974	Pleban, Connie 1990
Brooks, Herb 1990	Holt Jr., Charles E. 1997	Riley, Jack 1979
Ceglarski, Len 1992	Ikola, Willard 1990	+ Ross, Larry 1988
+ Fullerton, James 1992	+ Jeremiah, Eddie 1973	+ Thompson, Cliff 1973
Gambucci, Sergio 1996	Johnson, Bob 1991	+ Stewart, Bill 1982
+ Gordon, Malcolm 1973	Kelley, Jack 1993	+ Winsor, Ralph 1973

Referee

Chadwick, Bill 1974

Contributor

Schulz, Charles M. 1993

Administrators

+ Brown, George 1973	+ Jennings, Bill 1981	Ridder, Bob 1976
+ Brown, Walter 1973	+ Kahler, Nick 1980	Trumble, Hal 1970
Bush, Walter 1980	+ Lockhart, Tom 1973	+ Tutt, Thayer 1973
Clark, Don 1978	Marvin, Cal 1982	Wirtz, Bill 1967
Claypool, Jim 1995	Patrick, Craig 1996	+ Wright, Lyle 1973
+ Gibson, J.L. (Doc) 1973		

Members of Both Hockey and U.S. Hockey Halls of Fame

(as of Sept. 9, 1997)

Players	**Coach**		**Builders**
Hobey Baker	Bob Johnson	George Brown	Tom Lockhart
Frankie Brimsek	**Referee**	Walter Brown	Thayer Tutt
Frank (Moose) Goheen	Bill Chadwick	Doc Gibson	Bill Wirtz
John Mariucci		Bill Jennings	

HORSE RACING

National Horse Racing Hall of Fame

Established in 1950 by the Saratoga Springs Racing Association and opened in 1955. **Address:** National Museum of Racing and Hall of Fame, 191 Union Ave., Saratoga Springs, NY 12866. **Telephone:** (518) 584-0400.

Eligibility: Nominated horses must be retired five years; jockeys must be active at least 15 years; trainers must be active at least 25 years. Voting done by 100-member panel of horse racing media.

Class of 1997 (6): JOCKEY—**Gary Stevens**. TRAINERS—**Philip G. Johnson** and **Michael G. Walsh**. HORSES—**Easy Goer, Bold 'n Determined** and **Granville**.

Members are listed with year of induction; (+) indicates deceased members.

Jockeys

+ Adams, Frank (Dooley)* 1970	+ Garner, Andrew (Mack) 1969	+ Parke, Ivan 1978
+ Adams, John 1965	+ Garrison, Snapper 1955	+ Patrick, Gil 1970
+ Aitcheson, Joe Jr.* 1978	Griffin, Henry 1956	Pincay, Laffit Jr. 1975
Arcaro, Eddie 1958	+ Guerin, Eric 1972	+ Purdy, Sam 1970
Atkinson, Ted 1957	Hartack, Bill 1959	+ Reiff, John 1956
Baeza, Braulio 1976	Hawley, Sandy 1992	+ Robertson, Alfred 1971
Bailey, Jerry 1995	+ Johnson, Albert 1971	Rotz, John L. 1983
+ Barbee, George 1996	+ Knapp, Willie 1969	+ Sande, Earl 1955
+ Bassett, Carroll* 1972	+ Kummer, Clarence 1972	+ Schilling, Carroll 1970
+ Blum, Walter 1987	+ Kurtsinger, Charley 1967	Shoemaker, Bill 1958
+ Bostwick, George H.* 1968	+ Loftus, Johnny 1959	+ Simms, Willie 1977
+ Boulmetis, Sam 1973	+ Longden, Johnny 1958	+ Sloan, Todhunter 1955
+ Brooks, Steve 1963	Maher, Danny 1955	+ Smithwick, A. Patrick* 1973
Brumfield, Don 1996	+ McAtee, Linus 1956	Stevens, Gary 1997
+ Burns, Tommy 1983	McCarron, Chris 1989	+ Stout, James 1968
+ Butwell, Jimmy 1984	+ McCreary, Conn 1974	+ Taral, Fred 1955
Cauthen, Steve 1994	+ McKinney, Rigan 1968	+ Tuckman, Bayard Jr.* 1973
+ Coltiletti, Frank 1970	+ McLaughlin, James 1955	Turcotte, Ron 1979
Cordero, Angel Jr. 1988	+ Miller, Walter 1955	+ Turner, Nash 1955
+ Crawford, Robert (Specs)* ..1973	+ Murphy, Isaac 1955	Ussery, Robert 1980
Day, Pat 1991	+ Neves, Ralph 1960	Velasquez, Jorge 1990
Delahoussaye, Eddie 1993	+ Notter, Joe 1963	+ Woolfe, George 1955
+ Ensor, Lavelle (Buddy) 1962	+ O'Connor, Winnie 1956	+ Workman, Raymond 1956
+ Fator, Laverne 1955	+ Odom, George 1955	Ycaza, Manuel 1977
Fishback, Jerry* 1992	+ O'Neill, Frank 1956	*Steeplechase jockey

Trainers

+ Barrera, Laz 1979
+ Bedwell, H. Guy 1971
+ Brown, Edward D. 1984
  Burch, Elliot 1980
+ Burch, Preston M. 1963
+ Burch, W.P. 1955
+ Burlew, Fred 1973
+ Byers, J.D. (Dilly) 1967
+ Childs, Frank E. 1968
  Cocks, W. Burling 1985
  Conway, James P. 1996
  Croll, Jimmy 1994
+ Duke, William 1956
+ Feustel, Louis 1964
+ Fitzsimmons, J. (Sunny Jim) ..1958
  Frankel, Bobby 1995
+ Gaver, John M. 1966
+ Healey, Thomas 1955
+ Hildreth, Samuel 1955
+ Hirsch, Max 1959
+ Hirsch, W.J. (Buddy) 1982
+ Hitchcock, Thomas Sr. 1973
+ Hughes, Hollie 1973

+ Hyland, John 1956
+ Jacobs, Hirsch 1958
  Jerkens, H. Allen 1975
  Johnson, Philip 1997
+ Johnson, William R. 1986
  Jolley, LeRoy 1987
+ Jones, Ben A. 1958
  Jones, H.A. (Jimmy) 1959
+ Joyner, Andrew 1955
  Kelly, Tom 1993
  Laurin, Lucien 1977
+ Lewis, J. Howard 1969
+ Luro, Horatio 1980
+ Madden, John 1983
+ Maloney, Jim 1989
  Martin, Frank (Pancho) 1981
  McAnally, Ron 1990
+ McDaniel, Henry 1956
+ Miller, MacKenzie 1987
+ Molter, William, Jr. 1960
+ Mulholland, Winbert 1967
+ Neloy, Eddie 1983
  Nerud, John 1972

+ Parke, Burley 1986
+ Penna, Angel Sr. 1988
+ Pincus, Jacob 1988
+ Rogers, John 1955
+ Rowe, James Sr. 1955
  Schulhofer, Scotty 1992
  Sheppard, Jonathan 1990
+ Smith, Robert A. 1976
+ Smithwick, Mike 1976
  Stephens, Woody 1976
+ Thompson, H.J. 1969
+ Trotsek, Harry 1984
  Van Berg, Jack 1985
+ Van Berg, Marion 1970
+ Veitch, Sylvester 1977
+ Walden, Robert 1970
  Walsh, Michael 1997
+ Ward, Sherrill 1978
  Whiteley, Frank Jr. 1978
  Whittingham, Charlie 1974
  Winfrey, W.C. (Bill) 1971

Horses

Year foaled in parentheses.

+ Ack Ack (1966) 1986
  Affectionately (1960) 1989
+ Affirmed (1975) 1980
  All-Along (1979) 1990
+ Alsab (1939) 1976
+ Alydar (1975) 1989
  Alysheba (1984) 1993
+ American Eclipse (1814) ...1970
+ Armed (1941) 1963
  Artful (1902) 1956
+ Arts and Letters (1966) 1994
+ Assault (1943) 1964
+ Battleship (1927) 1969
+ Bed O'Roses (1947) 1976
+ Beldame (1901) 1956
+ Ben Brush (1893) 1955
+ Bewitch (1945) 1977
+ Bimelech (1937) 1990
+ Black Gold (1919) 1989
+ Black Helen (1932) 1991
+ Blue Larkspur (1926) 1957
  Bold 'n Determined (1977) ..1997
+ Bold Ruler (1954) 1973
+ Bon Nouvel (1960) 1976
+ Boston (1833) 1955
+ Broomstick (1901) 1956
+ Buckpasser (1963) 1970
+ Busher (1942) 1964
+ Bushranger (1930) 1967
+ Cafe Prince (1970) 1985
+ Carry Back (1958) 1975
+ Cavalcade (1931) 1993
+ Challendon (1936) 1977
+ Chris Evert (1971) 1988
+ Cicada (1959) 1967
+ Citation (1945) 1959
+ Colin (1905) 1956
+ Commando (1898) 1956
+ Count Fleet (1940) 1961
+ Crusader (1923) 1995
+ Dahlia (1971) 1981
+ Damascus (1964) 1974
+ Dark Mirage (1965) 1974
+ Davona Dale (1976) 1985

+ Desert Vixen (1970) 1979
+ Devil Diver (1939) 1980
+ Discovery (1931) 1969
+ Domino (1891) 1955
+ Dr. Fager (1964) 1971
+ Easy Goer (1986) 1997
+ Eight 30 (1936) 1994
+ Elkridge (1938) 1966
+ Emperor of Norfolk (1885) ..1988
+ Equipoise (1928) 1957
+ Exterminator (1915) 1957
+ Fairmount (1921) 1985
+ Fair Play (1905) 1956
+ Firenze (1885) 1981
  Flatterer (1979) 1994
  Foolish Pleasure (1972) 1995
+ Forego (1971) 1979
+ Gallant Bloom (1966) 1977
+ Gallant Fox (1927) 1957
+ Gallant Man (1954) 1987
+ Gallorette (1942) 1962
+ Gamely (1964) 1980
  Genuine Risk (1977) 1986
+ Go For Wand (1987) 1996
+ Good and Plenty (1900) 1956
+ Granville (1933) 1997
+ Grey Lag (1918) 1957
+ Hamburg (1895) 1986
+ Hanover (1884) 1955
+ Henry of Navarre (1891) ...1985
+ Hill Prince (1947) 1991
+ Hindoo (1878) 1955
+ Imp (1894) 1965
+ Jay Trump (1957) 1971
  John Henry (1975) 1990
+ Johnstown (1936) 1992
+ Jolly Roger (1922) 1965
+ Kingston (1884) 1955
+ Kelso (1957) 1967
+ Kentucky (1861) 1983
  Lady's Secret (1982) 1992
  La Prevoyante (1970) 1995
+ L'Escargot (1963) 1977
+ Lexington (1850) 1955
+ Longfellow (1867) 1971

+ Luke Blackburn (1877) 1956
+ Majestic Prince (1966) 1988
+ Man o' War (1917) 1957
+ Miss Woodford (1880) 1967
+ Myrtlewood (1933) 1979
+ Nashua (1952) 1965
+ Native Dancer (1950) 1963
+ Native Diver (1959) 1978
+ Northern Dancer (1961) 1976
+ Neji (1950) 1966
+ Oedipus (1941) 1978
+ Old Rosebud (1911) 1968
+ Omaha (1932) 1965
+ Pan Zareta (1910) 1972
+ Parole (1873) 1984
  Personal Ensign (1984) 1993
+ Peter Pan (1904) 1956
  Princess Rooney (1980) 1991
+ Real Delight (1949) 1987
+ Regret (1912) 1957
+ Reigh Count (1925) 1978
+ Roamer (1911) 1981
+ Roseben (1901) 1956
+ Round Table (1954) 1972
+ Ruffian (1972) 1976
+ Ruthless (1864) 1975
+ Salvator (1886) 1955
+ Sarazen (1921) 1957
+ Seabiscuit (1933) 1958
+ Searching (1952) 1978
  Seattle Slew (1974) 1981
+ Secretariat (1970) 1974
+ Shuvee (1966) 1975
+ Silver Spoon (1956) 1978
+ Sir Archy (1805) 1955
+ Sir Barton (1916) 1957
  Slew o'Gold (1980) 1992
+ Sun Beau (1925) 1996
  Sunday Silence (1986) 1996
+ Stymie (1941) 1975
+ Susan's Girl (1969) 1976
+ Swaps (1952) 1966
+ Sword Dancer (1956) 1977
+ Sysonby (1902) 1956
+ Ta Wee (1966) 1994

Horse Racing (Cont.)

+ Tim Tam (1955)	1985
+ Tom Fool (1949)	1960

+ Top Flight (1929)	1966
+ Tosmah (1961)	1984
+ Twenty Grand (1928)	1957
+ Twilight Tear (1941)	1963
+ War Admiral (1934)	1958

+ Whirlaway (1938)	1959
+ Whisk Broom II (1907)	1979
Zaccio (1976)	1990
+ Zev (1920)	1983

Exemplars of Racing

+ Hanes, John W	1982
+ Jeffords, Walter M	1973

Mellon, Paul	1989

Widener, George D	1971

Harness Racing Living Hall of Fame

Established by the U.S. Harness Writers Association (USHWA) in 1958. **Address:** Trotting Horse Museum, 240 Main Street, P.O. Box 590, Goshen, NY 10924; **Telephone:** (914) 294-6330.

Eligibility: Open to all harness racing drivers, trainers and executives. Voting done by USHWA membership. There are 73 members of the Living Hall of Fame, but only the 37 drivers and trainer-drivers are listed below.

Class of 1997 (5): BREEDER—**George Segal**. EXECUTIVE—**Dominic Freinzi**. JOURNALIST— **Bowman Brown Jr.** HORSES— **Niatross** and **Super Bowl**.

Members are listed with years of induction; (+) indicates deceased members.

Trainer-Drivers

Abbatiello, Carmine	1986	Farrington, Bob	1980	O'Donnell, Bill	1991
Abbatiello, Tony	1995	Filion, Herve	1976	Patterson, John Sir	1994
Ackerman, Doug	1995	+ Garnsey, Glen	1983	+ Pownall, Harry	1971
+ Avery, Earle	1975	Galbraith, Clint	1990	Riegle, Gene	1992
+ Baldwin, Ralph	1972	Gilmour, Buddy	1990	+ Russell, Sanders	1971
Beissinger, Howard	1975	Harner, Levi	1986	+ Shively, Bion	1968
Bostwick, Dunbar	1989	+ Haughton, Billy	1969	Sholty, George	1985
+ Cameron, Del	1975	+ Hodgins, Clint	1973	Simpson, John Sr	1972
Campbell, John	1991	Insko, Del	1981	+ Smart, Curly	1970
+ Chapman, John	1980	Kopas, Jack	1996	Waples, Keith	1987
Cruise, Jimmy	1987	Lachance, Michel	1996	Waples, Ron	1994
Dancer, Stanley	1970	Miller, Del	1969		
+ Ervin, Frank	1969	+ O'Brien, Joe	1971		

MEDIA

National Sportscasters and Sportswriters Hall of Fame

Established in 1959 by the National Sportscasters and Sportswriters Association. **Mailing Address:** P.O. Box 559, Salisbury, NC 28144. A permanent museum is scheduled to open in early 1998. **Telephone:** (704) 633-4275.

Eligibility: Nominees must be active for at least 25 years. Voting done by NSSA membership and other media representatives.

Class of 1997 (2): sportswriter **Bob Broeg** and sportscaster **Chick Hearn**.

Members are listed with year of induction; (+) indicates deceased members.

Sportscasters

+ Allen, Mel	1972	Glickman, Marty	1992	McKay, Jim	1987
+ Barber, Walter (Red)	1973	Gowdy, Curt	1981	+ McNamee, Graham	1964
Brickhouse, Jack	1983	Harwell, Ernie	1989	+ Nelson, Lindsey	1979
Buck, Jack	1990	Hearn, Chick	1997	+ Prince, Bob	1986
Caray, Harry	1989	+ Hodges, Russ	1975	Schenkel, Chris	1981
+ Cosell, Howard	1993	+ Hoyt, Waite	1987	Scott, Ray	1982
+ Dean, Dizzy	1976	+ Husing, Ted	1963	Scully, Vin	1991
Dunphy, Don	1986	Jackson, Keith	1995	+ Stern, Bill	1974
Elson, Bob	1995	+ McCarthy, Clem	1970	Summerall, Pat	1994
Enberg, Dick	1996				

Sportswriters

Anderson, Dave	1990	+ Graham, Frank Sr.	1995	Povich, Shirley	1984
Bisher, Furman	1989	+ Grimsley, Will	1987	+ Rice, Grantland	1962
Broeg, Bob	1997	Heinz, W.C.	1987	+ Runyon, Damon	1964
Burick, Si	1985	Jenkins, Dan	1996	Russell, Fred	1988
+ Cannon, Jimmy	1986	+ Kieran, John	1971	Sherrod, Blackie	1991
+ Carmichael, John P.	1994	+ Lardner, Ring	1967	+ Smith, Walter (Red)	1977
Connor, Dick	1992	+ Murphy, Jack	1988	+ Spink, J.G. Taylor	1969
+ Considine, Bob	1980	Murray, Jim	1978	+ Ward, Arch	1973
+ Daley, Arthur	1976	Olderman, Murray	1993	+ Woodward, Stanley	1974
Durslag, Mel	1995	+ Parker, Dan	1975		
Gould, Alan	1990	Pope, Edwin	1994		

American Sportscasters Hall of Fame

Established in 1984 by the American Sportscasters Association. Address: 5 Beekman Street, Suite 814, New York, NY 10038. A permanent museum site is in the planning stages. Telephone: (212) 227-8080.

Eligibility: nominations made by selection committee of previous winners, voting by ASA membership.

Class of 1996: Chris Schenkel.

Members are listed with year of induction; (+) indicates deceased members.

+ Allen, Mel 1985	Glickman, Marty 1993	McKay, Jim 1987
+ Barber, Walter (Red) 1984	Gowdy, Curt 1985	+ McNamee, Graham 1984
Brickhouse, Jack 1985	Harwell, Ernie 1991	+ Nelson, Lindsey 1986
Buck, Jack 1990	Hearn, Chick 1995	Schenkel, Chris 1997
Caray, Harry 1989	+ Husing, Ted 1984	Scully, Vin 1992
+ Cosell, Howard 1993	Jackson, Keith 1994	+ Stern, Bill 1984
Dunphy, Don 1984	+ McCarthy, Clem 1987	

MOTOR SPORTS

Motorsports Hall of Fame of America

Established in 1989. **Mailing Address:** P.O. Box 194, Novi, MI 48376. **Telephone:** (810) 349-7223.

Eligibility: Nominees must be retired at least three years or engaged in their area of motor sports for at least 20 years. Areas include: open wheel, stock car, dragster, sports car, motorcycle, off road, power boat, air racing and land speed records.

Class of 1997 (9): DRIVERS—**Betty Cook** (power boats), **Bill "Grumpy" Jenkins** (dragsters), **Lee Petty** (stock cars), **Peter Revson** (sports cars), **Johnny Rutherford** (open wheel), **Malcolm Smith** (motorcycles). CONTRIBUTORS—**Henry Ford**, **Mauri Rose** and **A.J. Watson**.

Members are listed with year of induction; (+) indicates deceased members.

Drivers

Allison, Bobby 1992	Glidden, Bob 1994	+ Oldfield, Barney 1989
Andretti, Mario 1990	Gurney, Dan 1991	Parks, Wally 1993
Arfons, Art 1991	Hanauer, Chip 1995	Pearson, David 1993
+ Baker, Cannonball 1989	Hill, Phil 1989	+ Petrali, Joe 1992
Bettenhausen, Tony 1997	+ Holbert, Al 1993	Petty, Lee 1996
Breedlove, Craig 1993	+ Horn, Ted 1993	Petty, Richard 1989
+ Campbell, Sir Malcolm 1994	Jarrett, Ned 1997	Prudhomme, Don 1991
Cantrell, Bill 1992	Jenkins, Bill (Grumpy) 1996	+ Revson, Peter 1996
+ Chenoweth, Dean 1991	Johnson, Junior 1991	+ Roberts, Fireball 1995
Chrisman, Art 1997	Jones, Parnelli 1992	Roberts, Kenny 1990
+ Clark, Jim 1990	Kalitta, Connie 1992	Rutherford, Johnny 1996
+ Cook, Betty 1996	Leonard, Joe 1991	+ Shaw, Wilbur 1991
Cunningham, Briggs 1997	+ McLaren, Bruce 1995	Smith, Malcolm 1996
Davis, Jim 1997	Mann, Dick 1993	+ Thompson, Mickey 1990
DeCoster, Roger 1994	Mays, Rex 1995	Unser, Al 1991
+ DePalma, Ralph 1992	+ Meyer, Louis 1993	Unser, Bobby 1994
+ DePaolo, Peter 1995	Muldowney, Shirley 1990	+ Vukovich, Bill Sr 1992
+ Donahue, Mark 1990	+ Muncy, Bill 1989	Ward, Rodger 1995
Foyt, A.J 1989	Musson, Ron 1993	+ Wood, Gar 1990
Garlits, Don 1989	Nordskog, Bob 1997	Yarborough, Cale 1994

Pilots

+ Cochran, Jacqueline 1993	+ Earhart, Amelia 1992	Greenmayer, Darryl 1997
+ Curtiss, Glenn 1990	+ Falck, Bill 1994	+ Turner, Roscoe 1991
+ Doolittle, Jimmy 1989		

Contributors

+ Agajanian, J.C 1992	Economacki, Chris 1994	Penske, Roger 1995
Bignotti, George 1993	+ Ford, Henry 1996	+ Rickenbacker, Eddie 1994
+ Black, Keith 1995	+ France, Bill Sr. 1990	+ Rose, Mauri 1996
Chapman, Colin 1997	Hall, Jim 1994	Shelby, Carroll 1992
+ Chevrolet, Louis 1995	+ Hulman, Tony 1991	Watson, A.J. 1996
Duesenberg, Fred 1997	Little, Bernie 1994	

Motor Sports (Cont.)
International Motorsports Hall of Fame

Established in 1990 by the International Motorsports Hall of Fame Commission. **Mailing Address:** P.O. Box 1018, Talladega, AL 35160. **Telephone:** (205) 362-5002.

Eligibility: Nominees must be retired from their specialty in motorsports for five years. Voting done by 150-member panel made up of the world-wide auto racing media.

Class of 1996 (6): **Richie Evans, Donald Haley, Bobby Isaac, Ferdinand Porsche, Johnny Rutherford** and **John Surtees.**

Members are listed with year of induction; (+) indicates deceased members.

Drivers

Allison, Bobby 1993	Hill, Phil 1991	Petty, Lee 1990
+ Ascari, Alberto 1992	+ Holbert, Al 1993	+ Roberts, Fireball 1990
Baker, Buck 1990	+ Isaac, Bobby 1996	Roberts, Kenny 1992
+ Bettenhausen, Tony 1991	Jarrett, Ned 1991	Rose, Mauri 1994
Brabham, Jack 1990	Johnson, Junior 1990	Rutherford, Johnny 1996
+ Campbell, Sir Malcolm 1990	Jones, Parnelli 1990	+ Shaw, Wilbur 1991
+ Clark, Jim 1990	Lauda, Niki 1993	Stewart, Jackie 1990
+ DePalma, Ralph 1991	Lorenzen, Fred 1991	Surtees, John 1996
+ Donahue, Mark 1990	+ Lund, Tiny 1994	Thomas, Herb 1994
+ Evans, Richie 1996	+ Mays, Rex 1993	+ Turner, Curtis 1992
+ Fangio, Juan Manuel 1990	+ McLaren, Bruce 1991	Unser, Bobby 1990
Flock, Tim 1991	+ Meyer, Louis 1992	+ Vukovich, Bill 1991
+ Gregg, Peter 1992	Moss, Stirling 1990	Ward Rodger 1992
Gurney, Dan 1990	+ Oldfield, Barney 1990	+ Weatherly, Joe 1994
+ Haley, Donald 1996	Parsons, Benny 1994	Yarborough, Cale 1993
+ Hill, Graham 1990	Pearson, David 1993	

Contributors

Bignotti, George 1993	Granatelli, Andy 1992	+ Rickenbacker, Eddie 1992
+ Chapman, Colin 1994	+ Hulman, Tony 1990	Shelby, Carroll 1991
+ Chevrolet, Louis 1992	Marcum, John 1994	+ Thompson, Mickey 1990
+ Ferrari, Enzo 1994	Moody, Ralph 1994	Yunick, Smokey 1990
+ Ford, Henry 1993	Parks, Wally 1992	
+ France, Bill Sr 1990	+ Porsche, Ferdinand 1996	

OLYMPICS

U.S. Olympic Hall of Fame

Established in 1983 by the United States Olympic Committee. **Mailing Address:** U.S. Olympic Committee, 1750 East Boulder Street, Colorado Springs, CO 80909. Plans for a permanent museum site have been suspended due to lack of funding. **Telephone:** (719) 578-4529.

Eligibility: Nominated athletes must be five years removed from active competition. Voting done by National Sportscasters and Sportswriters Association, Hall of Fame members and the USOC board members of directors.

Voting for membership in the Hall was suspended in 1993.

Members are listed with year of induction; (+) indicates deceased members.

Teams

1956 Basketball Dick Boushka, Carl Cain, Chuck Darling, Bill Evans, Gib Ford, Burdy Haldorson, Bill Hougland, Bob Jeangerard, K.C. Jones, Bill Russell, Ron Tomsic, +Jim Walsh and coach +Gerald Tucker.

1960 Basketball Jay Arnette, Walt Bellamy, Bob Boozer, Terry Dischinger, Burdy Haldorson, Darrall Imhoff, Allen Kelley, +Lester Lane, Jerry Lucas, Oscar Robertson, Adrian Smith, Jerry West and coach Pete Newell.

1964 Basketball Jim Barnes, Bill Bradley, Larry Brown, Joe Caldwell, Mel Counts, Richard Davies, Walt Hazzard, Luke Jackson, John McCaffrey, Jeff Mullins, Jerry Shipp, George Wilson and coach +Hank Iba.

1960 Ice Hockey Billy Christian, Roger Christian, Billy Cleary, Bob Cleary, Gene Grazia, Paul Johnson, Jack Kirrane, John Mayasich, Jack McCartan, Bob McKay, Dick Meredith, Weldon Olson, Ed Owen, Rod Paavola, Larry Palmer, Dick Rodenheiser, +Tom Williams and coach Jack Riley.

1980 Ice Hockey Bill Baker, Neal Broten, Dave Christian, Steve Christoff, Jim Craig, Mike Eruzione, John Harrington, Steve Janaszak, Mark Johnson, Ken Morrow, Rob McClanahan, Jack O'Callahan, Mark Pavelich, Mike Ramsey, Buzz Schneider, Dave Silk, Eric Strobel, Bob Suter, Phil Verchota, Mark Wells and coach Herb Brooks.

The Olympic Order

Established in 1974 by the International Olympic Committee (IOC) to honor athletes, officials and media members who have made remarkable contributions to the Olympic movement. The IOC's Council of the Olympic Order is presided over by the IOC president and active IOC members are not eligible for consideration. Through 1996, only three American officials have received the Order's highest commendation—the gold medal:

Avery Brundage, president of USOC (1928-53) and IOC (1952-72), was given the award posthumously in 1975.
Peter Ueberroth, president of Los Angeles Olympic Organizing Committee, was given the award in 1984.
Billy Payne, president of the Atlanta Committee for the Olympic Games, was given the award in 1996.

Alpine Skiing

Mahre, Phil 1992

Bobsled

+ Eagan, Eddie (see Boxing) ..1983

Boxing

Clay, Cassius* 1983
+ Eagan, Eddie (see Bobsled) .1983
Foreman, George 1990
Frazier, Joe 1989
Leonard, Sugar Ray 1985
Patterson, Floyd 1987
*Clay changed name to Muhammad Ali in 1964.

Cycling

Carpenter-Phinney, Connie ..1992

Diving

King, Miki 1992
Lee, Sammy 1990
Louganis, Greg 1985
McCormick, Pat 1985

Figure Skating

Albright, Tenley 1988
Button, Dick 1983
Fleming, Peggy 1983
Hamill, Dorothy 1991
Hamilton, Scott 1990

Gymnastics

Conner, Bart 1991
Retton, Mary Lou 1985
Vidmar, Peter 1991

Rowing

+ Kelly, Jack Sr. 1990

Speed Skating

Heiden, Eric 1983

Swimming

Babashoff, Shirley 1987
Caulkins, Tracy 1990
+ Daniels, Charles 1988
de Varona, Donna 1987
+ Kahanamoku, Duke 1984
+ Madison, Helene 1992
Meyer, Debbie 1986
Naber, John 1984
Schollander, Don 1983
Spitz, Mark 1983
+ Weissmuller, Johnny 1983

Track & Field

Beamon, Bob 1983
Boston, Ralph 1985
+ Calhoun, Lee 1991
Campbell, Milt 1992
Davenport, Willie 1991
Davis, Glenn 1986
+ Didrikson, Babe 1983
Dillard, Harrison 1983
Evans, Lee 1989
+ Ewry, Ray 1983
Fosbury, Dick 1992
Jenner, Bruce 1986
Johnson, Rafer 1983
+ Kraenzlein, Alvin 1985
Lewis, Carl 1985

Mathias, Bob 1983
Mills, Billy 1984
Morrow, Bobby 1989
Moses, Edwin 1985
O'Brien, Parry 1984
Oerter, Al 1983
+ Owens, Jesse 1983
+ Paddock, Charley 1991
Richards, Bob 1983
+ Rudolph, Wilma 1983
+ Sheppard, Mel 1989
Shorter, Frank 1984
+ Thorpe, Jim 1983
Toomey, Bill 1984
Tyus, Wyomia 1985
Whitfield, Mal 1988
+ Wykoff, Frank 1984

Weight Lifting

+ Davis, John 1989
Kono, Tommy 1990

Wrestling

Gable, Dan 1985

Contributors

Arledge, Roone 1989
+ Brundage, Avery 1983
+ Bushnell, Asa 1990
Hull, Col. Don 1992
+ Iba, Hank 1985
+ Kane, Robert 1986
+ Kelly, Jack Jr. 1992
McKay, Jim 1988
Miller, Don 1984
Simon, William 1991
Walker, LeRoy 1987

SOCCER

National Soccer Hall of Fame

Established in 1950 by the Philadelphia Oldtimers Association. First exhibit unveiled in Oneonta, NY in 1982. Moved into present building in 1987. New Hall of Fame planned at Wright National Soccer Campus in Oneonta. **Address:** 5-11 Ford Avenue, Oneonta, NY 13820. **Telephone:** (607) 432-3351.

Eligibility: Nominated players must have represented the U.S. in international competition and be retired five years; other categories include Meritorious Service and Special Commendation.

Nominations made by state organizations and a veterans' committee. Voting done by nine-member committee made up of Hall of Famers, U.S. Soccer officials and members of the national media.

Class of 1997 (5): PLAYERS—**Alexandre Ely**, **Johnny Moore** and **James Roe**. CONTRIBUTORS—**Phil Woosnam** and **Walter Chyzowych**.

Members are listed with home state and year of induction; (+) indicates deceased members.

Members

Abronzino, Umberto (CA) ...1971
Aimi, Milton (TX) 1991
+ Alonso, Julie (NY) 1972
+ Andersen, William (NY) 1956
+ Armstrong, James (NY) 1952
+ Auld, Andrew (RI) 1986
Bahr, Walter (PA) 1976
Barr, George (NY) 1983
+ Barriskill, Joe (NY) 1953
+ Beardsworth, Fred (MA) 1965
Berling, Clay (CA) 1995
Bernabei, Ray (PA) 1978
Best, John O. (CA) 1982
+ Bookie, Michael (PA) 1986
+ Booth, Joseph (CT) 1952
Borghi, Frank (MO) 1976
Boulos, Frenchy (NY) 1980
+ Boxer, Matt (CA) 1961
Bradley, Gordon (Eng) 1996

+ Briggs, Lawrence E. (MA) ..1978
+ Brittan, Harold (PA) 1951
+ Brock, John (MA) 1950
+ Brown, Andrew M. (OH) 1950
+ Brown, David (NJ) 1951
Brown, George (NJ) 1995
Brown, James (NY) 1986
+ Cahill, Thomas W (NY) 1950
+ Carenza, Joe (MO) 1982
+ Caraffi, Ralph (OH) 1959
Chacurian, Chico (CT) 1992
+ Chesney, Stan (NY) 1966
Chyzowych, Walter (PA) 1997
+ Coll, John (NY) 1986
+ Collins, George M. (MA) ...1951
+ Colombo, Charlie (MO) 1976
+ Commander, Colin (OH) 1967
+ Cordery, Ted (CA) 1975
+ Craddock, Robert (PA) 1959
+ Craggs, Edmund (WA) 1969

Craggs, George (WA) 1981
+ Cummings, Wilfred R. (IL) ..1953
+ Delach, Joseph (PA) 1973
DeLuca, Enzo (NY) 1979
+ Dick, Walter (CA) 1989
Diorio, Nick (PA) 1974
+ Donaghy, Edward J. (NY) ...1951
+ Donelli, Buff (PA) 1954
+ Donnelly, George (NY) 1989
+ Douglas, Jimmy (NJ) 1954
+ Dresmich, John W. (PA) 1968
+ Duff, Duncan (CA) 1972
+ Dugan, Thomas (NJ) 1951
+ Dunn, James (MO) 1974
Edwards, Gene (WI) 1985
Ely, Alexander (PA) 1997
+ Epperlein, Rudy (NJ) 1951
+ Fairfield, Harry (PA) 1951
Feibusch, Ernst (CA) 1984
+ Ferguson, John (PA) 1950

National Soccer Hall of Fame (Cont.)

+ Fernley, John A. (MA) 1951
+ Ferro, Charles (NY) 1958
+ Fishwick, George E. (IL) 1974
+ Flamhaft, Jack (NY) 1964
+ Fleming, Harry G. (PA) 1967
+ Florie, Thomas (NJ) 1986
+ Foulds, Pal (MA) 1953
+ Foulds, Sam (MA) 1969
+ Fowler, Dan (NY) 1970
+ Fowler, Peg (NY) 1979
  Fricker, Werner (PA) 1992
+ Fryer, William J. (NJ) 1951
+ Gaetjens, Joe (NY) 1976
+ Gallagher, James (NY) 1986
+ Garcia, Pete (MO) 1964
+ Gentle, James (PA) 1986
  Getzinger, Rudy (IL) 1991
+ Giesler, Walter (MO) 1962
  Glover, Teddy (NY) 1965
+ Gonsalves, Billy (MA) 1950
  Gormley, Bob (PA) 1989
+ Gould, David L. (PA) 1953
+ Govier, Sheldon (IL) 1950
  Greer, Don (CA) 1985
  Gryzik, Joe (IL) 1973
+ Guelker, Bob (MO) 1980
  Guennel, Joe (CO) 1980
  Harker, Al (PA) 1979
+ Healy, George (MI) 1951
  Heilpern, Herb (NY) 1988
+ Hemmings, William (IL) 1961
+ Hudson, Maurice (CA) 1966
  Hunt, Lamar (TX) 1982
  Hynes, John (NY) 1977
+ Iglehart, Alfredda (MD) 1951
+ Japp, John (PA) 1953
+ Jeffrey, William (PA) 1951
  Jewell, Frank (FA) 1996
+ Johnson, Jack (IL) 1952
  Kabanica, Mike (WI) 1987
  Kehoe, Bob (MO) 1990
  Kelly, Frank (NJ) 1994
+ Kempton, George (WA) 1950
  Keough, Harry (MO) 1976
+ Klein, Paul (NJ) 1953
  Kleinaitis, Al (IN) 1995
+ Koszma, Oscar (CA) 1964
  Kracher, Frank (IL) 1983
  Kraft, Granny (MD) 1984
+ Kraus, Harry (NY) 1963

  Kropfelder, Nicholas 1996
+ Kunter, Rudy (NY) 1963
+ Lamm, Kurt (NY) 1979
  Lang, Millard (MD) 1950
  Larson, Bert (CT) 1988
  Leonard, Abbot (Eng) 1996
+ Lewis, H. Edgar (PA) 1950
  Lombardo, Joe (NY) 1984
  Long, Denny (MO) 1993
+ MacEwan, John J. (MI) 1953
+ Maca, Joe (NY) 1976
+ Magnozzi, Enzo (NY) 1978
+ Maher, Jack (IL) 1970
+ Manning, Dr. Randolf (NY) ..1950
+ Marre, John (MO) 1953
  McBride, Pat (MO) 1994
+ McClay, Allan (MA) 1971
+ McGhee, Bart (NY) 1986
+ McGrath, Frank (MA) 1978
+ McGuire, Jimmy (NY) 1951
+ McGuire, John (NY) 1951
+ McIlveney, Eddie (PA) 1976
  McLaughlin, Bennie (PA) 1977
+ McSkimming, Dent (MO) 1951
  Merovich, Pete (PA) 1971
+ Mieth, Werner (NY) 1974
+ Millar, Robert (NY) 1950
  Miller, Al (OH) 1995
+ Miller, Milton (NY) 1971
+ Mills, Jimmy (PA) 1954
  Monson, Lloyd (NY) 1994
  Moore, James F. (MO) 1971
  Moore, Johnny (CA) 1997
+ Moorehouse, George (NY) ..1986
+ Morrison, Robert (PA) 1951
+ Morrissette, Bill (MA) 1967
  Nanoski, Jukey (PA) 1993
+ Netto, Fred (IL) 1958
  Newman, Ron (CA) 1992
+ Niotis, D.J. (IL) 1963
+ O'Brien, Shamus (NY) 1990
  Olaff, Gene (NJ) 1971
+ Oliver, Arnie (MA) 1968
  Oliver, Len (PA) 1996
+ Palmer, William (PA) 1952
  Pariani, Gino (MO) 1976
+ Patenaude, Bert (MA) 1971
+ Pearson, Eddie (GA) 1990
+ Peel, Peter (IL) 1951
  Pelé (Brazil) 1993
  Peters, Wally (NJ) 1967
  Phillipson, Don (CO) 1987
+ Piscopo, Giorgio (NY) 1978
+ Pomeroy, Edgar (CA) 1955

+ Ramsden, Arnold (TX) 1957
+ Ratican, Harry (MO) 1950
  Reese, Doc (MD) 1957
+ Renzulli, Pete (NY) 1951
  Ringsdorf, Gene (MD) 1979
  Roe, James (MO) 1997
  Roth, Werner (NY) 1989
+ Rottenberg, Jack (NJ) 1971
  Roy, Willy (IL) 1989
+ Ryan, Hun (PA) 1958
+ Sager, Tom (PA) 1968
  Saunders, Harry (NY) 1981
  Schaller, Willy (IL) 1995
  Schellscheidt, Mannie (NJ) ..1990
  Schillinger, Emil (PA) 1960
+ Schroeder, Elmer (PA) 1951
+ Scwarcz, Erno (NY) 1951
+ Shields, Fred (PA) 1968
+ Single, Erwin (NY) 1981
+ Slone, Philip (NY) 1986
+ Smith, Alfred (PA) 1951
+ Souza, Ed (MA) 1976
  Souza, Clarkie (MA) 1976
+ Spalding, Dick (PA) 1951
+ Stark, Archie (NJ) 1950
+ Steelink, Nicolaas (CA) 1971
+ Steur, August (NY) 1969
+ Stewart, Douglas (PA) 1950
+ Stone, Robert T. (CO) 1971
+ Swords, Thomas (MA) 1976
+ Tintle, Joseph (NJ) 1952
+ Tracey, Ralph (MO) 1986
+ Triner, Joseph (IL) 1951
+ Vaughan, Frank (MO) 1986
+ Walder, Jimmy (PA) 1971
+ Wallace, Frank (MO) 1976
+ Washauer, Adolph (CA) 1977
+ Webb, Tom (WA) 1987
+ Weir, Alex (NY) 1975
+ Weston, Victor (WA) 1956
+ Wilson, Peter (NJ) 1950
+ Wood, Alex (MI) 1986
+ Woods, John W. (IL) 1952
  Woosnam, Phil (GA) 1997
  Yeagley, Jerry (IN) 1989
+ Young, John (CA) 1958
+ Zampini, Dan (PA) 1963
  Zerhusen, Al (CA) 1978

Hall of Champions to Open in 1998

The $50 million **International Soccer Hall of Champions** is set to open in the spring of 1998 in Paris. The 93,000-square foot complex will be located at Disneyland Paris and honor the world's greatest soccer players and teams. The Hall, organized by FIFA (world soccer's governing body) and International Sports and Entertainment Concepts Incorporated of Atlanta, will induct a maximum of five players annually along with the greatest teams of all-time. A life-sized bronze statue will be at the center of each player's individual shrine. There will be a special inaugural induction of 10 players in January of 1998 who will be voted in by a panel of experts. The criteria for enshrinement includes the following: the player's career must have lasted at least 10 years and they must have been retired from competitive soccer for at least five years.

SWIMMING

International Swimming Hall of Fame

Established in 1965 by the U.S. College Coaches' Swim Forum. **Address:** One Hall of Fame Drive, Ft. Lauderdale, FL 33316. **Telephone:** (954) 462-6536.

Categories for induction are: swimming, diving, water polo, synchronized swimming, coaching, pioneers and contributors. Of the 481 members, 266 are from the United States. Contributors are not included in the following list. Only U.S. men, women and coaches listed below.

Members are listed with year of induction; (+) indicates deceased members.

U.S. Men

+ Anderson, Miller 1967	Hencken, John 1988	+ Ris, Wally 1966
Barrowman, Mike 1997	Hickcox, Charles 1976	Robie, Carl 1976
Biondi, Matt 1997	Higgins, John 1971	Roper, Gail 1997
+ Boggs, Phil 1985	Holiday, Harry 1991	Ross, Clarence 1988
Brack, Walter 1997	Irwin, Juno Stover 1980	+ Ross, Norman 1967
Breen, George 1975	Jastremski, Chet 1977	Roth, Dick 1987
+ Browning, Skippy 1975	+ Kahanamoku, Duke 1965	+ Ruddy, Joe 1986
Bruner, Mike 1988	+ Kealoha, Warren 1968	Russell, Doug 1985
Burton, Mike 1977	Kiefer, Adolph 1965	Saari, Roy 1976
+ Cann, Tedford 1967	Kinsella, John 1986	+ Schaeffer, E. Carroll 1968
Carey, Rick 1993	+ Kojac, George 1968	Scholes, Clarke 1980
Clark, Earl 1972	Konno, Ford 1972	Schollander, Don 1965
Clark, Steve 1966	+ Kruger, Stubby 1986	Shaw, Tim 1989
Cleveland, Dick 1991	Kuehn, Louis 1988	+ Sheldon, George 1989
Clotworthy, Robert 1980	+ Langer, Ludy 1988	+ Skelton, Robert 1988
+ Crabbe, Buster 1965	Larson, Lance 1980	Smith, Bill 1966
+ Daniels, Charlie 1965	Lee, Dr. Sammy 1968	+ Smith, Dutch 1979
Degener, Dick 1971	+ LeMoyne, Harry 1988	+ Smith, Jimmy 1992
DeMont, Rick 1990	Louganis, Greg 1993	Smith, R. Jackson 1983
Dempsey, Frank 1996	Lundquist, Steve 1990	Spitz, Mark 1977
+ Desjardins, Pete 1966	Mann, Thompson 1984	Stack, Allen 1979
Edgar, David 1996	McCormick, Pat 1965	Stickles, Ted 1995
+ Faricy, John 1990	+ McDermott, Turk 1969	Stock, Tom 1989
+ Farrell, Jeff 1968	+ McGillivray, Perry 1981	+ Swendsen, Clyde 1991
+ Fick, Peter 1978	McKenzie, Don 1989	Tobian, Gary 1978
+ Flanagan, Ralph 1978	McKinney, Frank 1975	Troy, Mike 1971
Ford, Alan 1966	McLane, Jimmy 1970	Vande Weghe, Albert 1990
Furniss, Bruce 1987	+ Medica, Jack 1966	Vassallo, Jesse 1997
Gaines, Rowdy 1995	Montgomery, Jim 1986	+ Verdeur, Joe 1966
Garton, Tim 1997	Mullikan, Bill 1984	Vogel, Matt 1996
Glancy, Harrison 1990	Naber, John 1982	+ Vollmer, Hal 1990
+ Goodwin, Budd 1971	Nakama, Keo 1975	Wayne, Marshall 1981
Graef, Jed 1988	+ O'Connor, Wally 1966	Webster, Bob 1970
Haines, George 1977	Oyakawa, Yoshi 1979	+ Weissmuller, Johnny 1965
Hall, Gary 1981	+ Patnik, Al 1969	+ White, Al 1965
+ Harlan, Bruce 1973	Phillips, William Berge 1997	Wrightson, Bernie 1984
+ Hebner, Harry 1968	+ Riley, Mickey 1977	Yorzyk, Bill 1971

U.S. Women

Anderson, Terry 1986	Curtis, Ann 1966	Josephson, Sarah 1997
Atwood, Sue 1992	Daniel, Ellie 1997	Kane, Marion 1981
Babashoff, Shirley 1982	de Varona, Donna 1969	+ Kaufman, Beth 1967
Ball, Catie 1976	Dean, Penny 1996	Kight, Lenore 1981
+ Bauer, Sybil 1967	Dorfner, Olga 1970	King, Micki 1978
Bean, Dawn Pawson 1996	Draves, Vickie 1969	Kolb, Claudia 1975
Belote, Melissa 1983	Duenkel, Ginny 1985	+ Lackie, Ethel 1969
Bleibtrey, Ethelda 1967	Ederle, Gertrude 1965	Linehan, Kim 1997
+ Boyle, Charlotte 1988	Ellis, Kathy 1991	Lord-Landon, Alice 1993
Burke, Lynne 1978	Ferguson, Cathy 1978	+ Madison, Helene 1966
Bush, Lesley 1986	Finneran, Sharon 1985	Mann, Shelly 1966
Callen, Gloria 1984	+ Galligan, Claire 1970	McGrath, Margo 1989
Caretto, Patty 1987	+ Garatti-Seville, Eleanor 1992	McKim, Josephine 1991
Carr, Cathy 1988	Gestring, Marjorie 1976	Meagher, Mary T. 1993
Caulkins, Tracy 1990	Gossick, Sue 1988	+ Meany, Helen 1971
+ Chadwick, Florence 1970	+ Guest, Irene 1990	Meyer, Debbie 1977
Chandler, Jennifer 1987	Hall, Kaye 1979	Mitchell, Michele 1995
Cohen, Tiffany 1996	Henne, Jan 1979	Moe, Karen 1992
+ Coleman, Georgia 1966	Holm, Eleanor 1966	Morris, Pam 1965
Cone, Carin 1984	Hunt-Newman, Virginia 1993	Neilson, Sandra 1986
Costie, Candy 1995	Johnson, Gail 1983	Neyer, Megan 1997
Crlenkovich, Helen 1981	Josephson, Karen 1997	+ Norelius, Martha 1967

Swimming (Cont.)

Olsen, Zoe-Ann 1989
O'Rourke, Heidi 1980
+ Osipowich, Albina 1986
Pedersen, Susan 1995
Pinkston, Betty Becker ...1967
Pope, Paula Jean Meyers ...1979
Potter, Cynthia 1987
+ Poynton, Dorothy 1968
+ Rawls, Katherine 1965

+ Armbruster, Dave 1966
+ Bachrach, Bill 1966
Billingsley, Hobie 1983
+ Brandsten, Ernst 1966
+ Brauninger, Stan 1972
+ Cady, Fred 1969
+ Center, George (Dad) 1991
Chavoor, Sherman 1977
+ Cody, Jack 1970
Counsilman, Dr. James 1976
+ Curtis, Katherine 1979
Daland, Peter 1977
+ Daughters, Ray 1971
Draves, Lyle 1989

Redmond, Carol 1989
Riggin, Aileen 1967
Ross, Anne 1984
Rothammer, Keena 1991
Ruiz-Conforto, Tracie 1993
Ruuska, Sylvia 1976
Schuler, Carolyn 1989
Seller, Peg 1988
+ Smith, Caroline 1988
Stouder, Sharon 1972
+ Toner, Vee 1995

U.S. Coaches

Gambril, Don 1983
Haines, George 1977
Handley, L. de B. 1967
Hannula, Dick 1987
Kimball, Dick 1985
+ Kiphuth, Bob 1965
Mann, Matt II 1965
+ McCormick, Glen 1995
Moriarty, Phil 1980
Mowerson, Robert 1986
Muir, Bob 1989
+ Neuschafer, Al 1967
Nitzkowski, Monte 1991
O'Brien, Ron 1988

+ Vilen, Kay 1978
Von Saltza, Chris 1966
Oho Wahle 1996
+ Wainwright, Helen 1972
+ Watson, Lillian (Pokey) 1984
Wehselau, Mariechen 1989
Welshons, Kim 1988
Wichman, Sharon 1991
Williams, Esther 1966
+ Woodbridge, Margaret ...1989

+ Papenguth, Richard 1986
+ Peppe, Mike 1966
+ Pinkston, Clarence 1966
+ Robinson, Tom 1965
Sakamoto, Soichi 1966
+ Sava, Charlie 1970
+ Schlueter, Walt 1978
Schubert, Mark 1997
Smith, Dick 1979
Stager, Gus 1982
Thornton, Nort 1995
Tinkham, Stan 1989

TENNIS

International Tennis Hall of Fame

Originally the National Tennis Hall of Fame. Established in 1953 by James Van Alen and sanctioned by the U.S. Tennis Association in 1954. Renamed the International Tennis Hall of Fame in 1976. **Address:** 194 Bellevue Ave., Newport, RI 02840. **Telephone:** (401) 849-3990.

Eligibility: Nominated players must be five years removed from being a "significant factor" in competitive tennis. Voting done by members of the international tennis media.

Class of 1997 (3): PLAYERS— **Bunny Austin** and **Lesley Turner Bowrey**. CONTRIBUTOR— **Maj. Walter Clopton Wingfield.**

Members are listed with year of induction; (+) indicates deceased members.

Men

+ Adee, George 1964
+ Alexander, Fred 1961
+ Allison, Wilmer 1963
+ Alonso, Manuel 1977
+ Ashe, Arthur 1985
+ Behr, Karl 1969
Borg, Bjorn 1987
+ Borotra, Jean 1976
Bromwich, John 1984
+ Brookes, Norman 1977
+ Brugnon, Jacques 1976
Budge, Don 1964
+ Campbell, Oliver 1955
+ Chace, Malcolm 1961
+ Clark, Clarence 1983
+ Clark, Joseph 1955
+ Clothier, William 1956
+ Cochet, Henri 1976
Cooper, Ashley 1991
+ Crawford, Jack 1979
+ Doeg, John 1962
+ Doherty, Lawrence 1980
+ Doherty, Reginald 1980
Drobny, Jaroslav 1983
+ Dwight, James 1955
Emerson, Roy 1982
+ Etchebaster, Pierre 1978
Falkenburg, Bob 1974
Fraser, Neale 1984
+ Garland, Chuck 1969
+ Gonzales, Pancho 1968

+ Grant, Bryan (Bitsy) 1972
+ Griffin, Clarence 1970
+ Hackett, Harold 1961
Hewitt, Bob 1992
+ Hoad, Lew 1980
+ Hovey, Fred 1974
+ Hunt, Joe 1966
+ Hunter, Frank 1961
+ Johnston, Bill 1958
+ Jones, Perry 1970
Kodes, Jan 1990
Kramer, Jack 1968
+ Lacoste, Rene 1976
+ Larned, William 1956
Larsen, Art 1969
Laver, Rod 1981
+ Lott, George 1964
Mako, Gene 1973
+ McKinley, Chuck 1986
+ McLoughlin, Maurice 1957
McMillan, Frew 1992
+ McNeill, Don 1965
Mulloy, Gardnar 1972
+ Murray, Lindley 1958
+ Myrick, Julian 1963
Nastase, Ilie 1991
Newcombe, John 1986
+ Nielsen, Arthur 1971
Olmedo, Alex 1987
+ Osuna, Rafael 1979
Parker, Frank 1966

+ Patterson, Gerald 1989
Patty, Budge 1977
+ Perry, Fred 1975
+ Pettitt, Tom 1982
Pietrangeli, Nicola 1986
+ Quist, Adrian 1984
Ralston, Dennis 1987
+ Renshaw, Ernest 1983
+ Renshaw, William 1983
+ Richards, Vincent 1961
+ Riggs, Bobby 1967
Roche, Tony 1986
Rosewall, Ken 1980
Santana, Manuel 1984
Savitt, Dick 1976
Schroeder, Ted 1966
+ Sears, Richard 1955
Sedgman, Frank 1979
Segura, Pancho 1984
Seixas, Vic 1971
+ Shields, Frank 1964
+ Slocum, Henry 1955
Smith, Stan 1987
Stolle, Fred 1985
Talbert, Bill 1967
+ Tilden, Bill 1959
Trabert, Tony 1970
Van Ryn, John 1963
Vilas, Guillermo 1991
+ Vines, Ellsworth 1962
+ von Cramm, Gottfried ...1977

+ Ward, Holcombe 1956
+ Washburn, Watson 1965
+ Whitman, Malcolm 1955

+ Wilding, Anthony 1978
+ Williams, Richard 2nd 1957
  Wood, Sidney 1964

+ Wrenn, Robert 1955
+ Wright, Beals 1956

Women

  Fry Irvin, Shirley 1970
  Gibson, Althea 1971
  Goolagong Cawley, Evonne .1988
+ Hansell, Ellen 1965
  Hard, Darlene 1973
  Hart, Doris 1969
  Haydon Jones, Ann 1985
  Heldman, Gladys 1979
+ Hotchkiss Wightman, Hazel .1957
+ Jacobs, Helen Hull 1962
  King, Billie Jean 1987
+ Lenglen, Suzanne 1978
  Mandlikova, Hana 1994
+ Marble, Alice 1964
  McKane Godfree, Kitty 1978
+ Moore, Elisabeth 1971

+ Atkinson, Juliette 1974
  Austin, Bunny 1997
  Austin, Tracy 1992
+ Barger-Wallach, Maud 1958
  Betz Addie, Pauline 1965
+ Bjurstedt Mallory, Molla ...1958
  Bowrey, Lesley Turner 1997
  Brough Clapp, Louise 1967
+ Browne, Mary 1957
  Bueno, Maria 1978
+ Cahill, Mabel 1976
  Casals, Rosie 1996
+ Connolly Brinker, Maureen ..1968
+ Dod, Charlotte (Lottie) 1983
+ Douglass Chambers, Dorothy ..1981
  Evert, Chris 1995

  Mortimer Barrett, Angela 1993
+ Nuthall Shoemaker, Betty ...1977
  Osborne duPont, Margaret ..1967
+ Palfrey Danzig, Sarah 1963
+ Roosevelt, Ellen 1975
+ Round Little, Dorothy 1986
+ Ryan, Elizabeth 1972
+ Sears, Eleanora 1968
  Smith Court, Margaret 1979
+ Sutton Bundy, May 1956
+ Townsend Toulmin, Bertha ..1974
  Wade, Virginia 1989
+ Wagner, Marie 1969
  Wills Moody Roark, Helen ..1959

Contributors

+ Baker, Lawrence Sr 1975
  Chatrier, Philippe 1992
  Collins, Bud 1994
  Cullman, Joseph F. 3rd 1990
+ Danzig, Allison 1968
+ Davis, Dwight 1956
+ Gray, David 1985

+ Gustaf, V (King of Sweden) .1980
+ Hester, W.E. (Slew) 1981
+ Hopman, Harry 1978
  Hunt, Lamar 1993
+ Laney, Al 1979
  Martin, Alastair 1973
  Martin, William McC 1982

  Maskell, Dan 1996
+ Outerbridge, Mary 1981
+ Pell, Theodore 1966
+ Tingay, Lance 1982
+ Tinling, Ted 1986
+ Van Alen, James 1965
+ Wingfield, Walter Clopton ...1997

TRACK & FIELD

National Track & Field Hall of Fame

Established in 1974 by the The Athletics Congress (now USA Track & Field). Originally located in Charleston, WV, the Hall moved to Indianapolis in 1983 and reopened at the Hoosier Dome in 1986. **Address:** One RCA Dome, Indianapolis, IN 46225. **Telephone:** (317) 261-0500.

Eligibility: Nominated athletes must be retired three years and coaches must have coached at least 20 years, if retired, or 35 years, if still coaching. Voting done by 800-member panel made up of Hall of Fame and USA Track & Field officials, Hall of Fame members, current U.S. champions and members of the Track & Field Writers of America.

Class of 1996 (7): MEN— **Don Bragg, Dr. Dallas Long, Joe McCluskey, Earle Meadows** and **Dr. Walter Tewksbury;** COACHES—**Cleve Abbott** and **Vern Wolfe.**

Members are listed with year of induction; (+) indicates deceased members.

Men

+ Albritton, Dave 1980
  Ashenfelter, Horace 1975
+ Bausch, James 1979
  Beamon, Bob 1977
  Beatty, Jim 1990
  Bell, Greg 1988
+ Boeckmann, Dee 1976
  Boston, Ralph 1974
  Bragg, Don 1996
+ Calhoun, Lee 1974
  Campbell, Milt 1989
+ Clark, Ellery 1991
  Connolly, Harold 1984
  Courtney, Tom 1978
+ Cunningham, Glenn 1974
+ Curtis, William 1979
  Davenport, Willie 1982
  Davis, Glenn 1974
  Davis, Harold 1974
  Dillard, Harrison 1974
  Dumas, Charley 1990
  Evans, Lee 1983
+ Ewell, Barney 1986
+ Ewry, Ray 1974
+ Flanagan, John 1975
  Fosbury, Dick 1981
+ Gordien, Fortune 1979
  Greene, Charlie 1992

+ Hahn, Archie 1983
+ Hardin, Glenn 1978
  Hayes, Bob 1976
  Held, Bud 1987
  Hines, Jim 1979
+ Houser, Bud 1979
+ Hubbard, DeHart 1979
  Jenkins, Charlie 1992
  Jenner, Bruce 1980
+ Johnson, Cornelius 1994
  Johnson, Rafer 1974
  Jones, Hayes 1976
  Kelley, John 1980
  Kiviat, Abel 1985
+ Kraenzlein, Alvin 1974
  Laird, Ron 1986
+ Lash, Don 1995
  Liquori, Marty 1995
  Long, Dr. Dallas 1996
  Mathias, Bob 1974
  Matson, Randy 1984
  McCluskey, Joe 1996
+ Meadows, Earle 1996
+ Meredith, Ted 1982
+ Metcalfe, Ralph 1975
  Milburn, Rod 1993
  Mills, Billy 1976
  Moore, Tom 1988

  Morrow, Bobby 1975
+ Mortensen, Jess 1992
  Moses, Edwin 1994
+ Myers, Lawrence 1974
  O'Brien, Parry 1974
  Oerter, Al 1974
+ Osborn, Harold 1974
  Owens, Jesse 1974
+ Paddock, Charley 1976
  Patton, Mel 1985
+ Peacock, Eulace 1987
+ Prefontaine, Steve 1976
+ Ray, Joie 1976
+ Rice, Greg 1977
  Richards, Bob 1975
+ Rose, Ralph 1976
  Ryun, Jim 1980
+ Scholz, Jackson 1977
  Schul, Bob 1991
  Seagren, Bob 1986
+ Sheppard, Mel 1976
+ Sheridan, Martin 1988
  Shorter, Frank 1989
  Sime, Dave 1981
+ Simpson, Robert 1974
  Smith, Tommie 1978
+ Stanfield, Andy 1977
  Steers, Les 1974

Track & Field (Cont.)

+ Tewksbury, Dr. Walter 1996
  Thomas, John 1985
+ Thomson, Earl 1977
+ Thorpe, Jim 1975
+ Tolan, Eddie 1982

  Brisco, Valerie 1995
  Coachman, Alice 1975
+ Copeland, Lillian 1994
+ Didrikson, Babe 1974
  Faggs, Mae 1976
  Ferrell, Barbara 1988
  Griffith Joyner, Florence 1995
+ Hall Adams, Evelyne 1988

+ Abbott, Cleve 1996
+ Baskin, Weems 1982
+ Beard, Percy 1981
  Bell, Sam 1992
  Botts, Tom 1983
  Bowerman, Bill 1981
  Bush, Jim 1987
+ Cromwell, Dean 1974
+ Doherty, Ken 1976
  Easton, Bill 1975
+ Elliott, Jumbo 1981
+ Giegengack, Bob 1978

+ Abramson, Jesse 1981
  Andersen, Roxanne 1991
+ Bakjian, Andy 1986
+ Brundage, Avery 1974

  Toomey, Bill 1975
+ Towns, Forrest (Spec) 1976
  Warmerdam, Cornelius 1974
  Whitfield, Mal 1974
  Wilkins, Mac 1993
+ Williams, Archie 1992
  Wohlhuter, Rick 1990

Women

  Heritage, Doris Brown 1990
+ Jackson, Nell 1989
  Manning, Madeline 1984
  McDaniel, Mildred 1983
  McGuire, Edith 1979
  Ritter, Louise 1995
  Robinson, Betty 1977
+ Rudolph, Wilma 1974

Coaches

+ Hamilton, Brutus 1974
+ Haydon, Ted 1975
+ Hayes, Billy 1976
+ Haylett, Ward 1979
+ Higgins, Ralph 1982
+ Hillman, Harry 1976
+ Hurt, Edward 1975
+ Hutsell, Wilbur 1977
+ Jones, Thomas 1977
  Jordan, Payton 1982
+ Littlefield, Clyde 1981
+ Moakley, Jack 1988

Contributors

+ Ferris, Dan 1974
+ Griffith, John 1979
+ Lebow, Fred 1994
+ Nelson, Bert 1991

  Woodruff, John 1978
  Wottle, Dave 1982
+ Wykoff, Frank 1977
  Young, George 1981

+ Schmidt, Kate 1994
  Shiley Newhouse, Jean 1993
+ Stephens, Helen 1975
  Tyus, Wyomia 1980
+ Walsh, Stella 1975
  Watson, Martha 1987
  White, Willye 1981

+ Murphy, Michael 1974
  Rosen, Mel 1995
+ Snyder, Larry 1978
  Temple, Ed 1989
+ Templeton, Dink 1976
  Walker, LeRoy 1983
+ Wilt, Fred 1981
+ Winter, Bud 1985
  Wolfe, Vern 1996
  Wright, Stan 1993
+ Yancy, Joseph 1984

  Nelson, Cordner 1988
+ Sullivan, James 1977

VOLLEYBALL

Volleyball Hall of Fame

Established in 1985. **Address:** P.O. Box 1895, 444 Dwight St., Holyoke, MA 01041. **Telephone:** (413) 536-0926.

Eligibility: Nominees must have contributed at least seven years of outstanding service to volleyball within his/her respective category. Nominees in the player or official category must be retired for five years. A nominee may appear on the ballot a maximum of seven times at which point he/she can be nominated in the Veterans category an unlimited number of times. Voting is done by a panel of no more than 30 individuals from the greater volleyball community.

Class of 1997: (3): MEN—**Pedro "Pete" Velasco**; LEADER—**Albert Monaco, Jr.** COACH—**Andy Banachowski**, UCLA Women's coach (1968–).

Members are listed with year of induction; (+) indicates deceased members.

Men

  Bright, Mike 1993
  Engen, Rolf 1991
+ Haine, Thomas 1991
  O'Hara, Michael 1989
  Rundle, Larry 1994
  Selznick, Eugene 1988
  Stanley, Jon 1992
  Velasco, Pedro "Pete" 1997
  Von Hagen, Ron 1992

Women

  Bright, Patti 1996
  Dowdell, Patty 1994
  Gregory, Kathy 1989
  Green, Debbie 1995
+ Hyman, Flo 1988
  Peppler, Mary Jo 1990
  Ward, Jane 1988

Coaches

  Banachowski, Andy 1997
  Beal, Douglas 1989
  Coleman, Dr. James 1992
  DeGroot, Col. Edward 1990
  Dunphy, Marv 1994
  Scates, Al 1993
  Selinger, Arie 1995
  Shondell, Donald 1996
+ Wilson, Harry 1988

Leaders

+ Fisher, Dr. George J. 1991
  Friermood, Dr. Harold T. 1986
+ Gibson, Leonard 1988
+ Koch, John 1994
+ Lindsey, Robert L. 1995
  Monaco, Jr., Albert 1997
+ Morgan, Dr. William G. 1985

Officials

  Davies, Glen 1989
+ Fish, Alton 1990
  Ignacio, Catalino 1991
  Kennedy, Merton H. 1992
  Miller, C.L. (Bobb) 1995

WOMEN

International Women's Sports Hall of Fame

Established in 1980 by the Women's Sports Foundation. **Address:** Women's Sports Foundation, Eisenhower Park, East Meadow, NY 11554. **Telephone:** (516) 542-4700.

Eligibility: Nominees' achievements and commitment to the development of women's sports must be internationally recognized. Athletes are elected in two categories—Pioneer (before 1960) and Contemporary (since 1960). Members are divided below by sport for the sake of easy reference; (*) indicates member inducted in Pioneer category. Coaching nominees must have coached at least 10 years.

Class of 1996 (3): PIONEER—**Florence Chadwick** (distance swimming) and sprinter **Aeriwentha Mae Faggs Star** (track & field). COACHES—**Diana Holum** (speed skating and cycling).

Members are listed with year of induction; (+) indicates deceased members.

Alpine Skiing

Cranz, Christl* 1991
Lawrence, Andrea Mead* ...1983
Moser-Pröll, Annemarie 1982

Auto Racing

Guthrie, Janet 1980

Aviation

+ Coleman, Bessie* 1992
+ Earhart, Amelia* 1980
+ Marvingt, Marie* 1987

Badminton

Hashman, Judy Devlin* 1995

Baseball

Stone, Toni* 1993

Basketball

Meyers, Ann 1985
Miller, Cheryl 1991

Bowling

Ladewig, Marion* 1984

Cycling

Carpenter Phinney, Connie ..1990

Diving

King, Micki 1983
McCormick, Pat* 1984
Riggin, Aileen* 1988

Equestrian

Hartel, Lis 1994

Fencing

Schacherer-Elek, Ilona* 1989

Figure Skating

Albright, Tenley* 1983
+ Blanchard, Theresa Weld* ..1989
Fleming, Peggy 1981
Heiss Jenkins, Carol* 1992
+ Henie, Sonja* 1982
Protopopov, Ludmila 1992
Rodnina, Irena 1988

Golf

Berg, Patty* 1980
Carner, JoAnne 1987
Hicks, Betty* 1995
Mann, Carol 1982
Rawls, Betsy* 1986
Suggs, Louise* 1987
+ Vare, Glenna Collett* 1981
Whitworth, Kathy 1984
Wright, Mickey 1981

Golf/Track & Field

+ Zaharias, Babe Didrikson* ..1980

Gymnastics

Caslavska, Vera 1991
Comaneci, Nadia 1990
Korbut, Olga 1982
Latynina, Larissa* 1985
Retton, Mary Lou 1993
Tourischeva, Lyudmila 1987

Shooting

Murdock, Margaret 1988

Softball

Joyce, Joan 1989

Speed Skating

+ Klein Outland, Kit* 1993
Young, Sheila 1981

Swimming

Caulkins, Tracy 1986
+ Chadwick, Florence* 1996
Curtis Cuneo, Ann* 1985
de Varona, Donna 1983
Ederle, Gertrude* 1980
Fraser, Dawn 1985
Holm, Eleanor* 1980
Meagher, Mary T. 1993
Meyer-Reyes, Debbie 1987

Tennis

+ Connolly, Maureen* 1987
+ Dod, Charlotte (Lottie)* 1986
Evert, Chris 1981
Gibson, Althea* 1980

Goolagong Cawley, Evonne .1989
+ Hotchkiss Wightman, Hazel* ..1986
King, Billie Jean 1980
+ Lenglen, Suzanne* 1984
Navratilova, Martina 1984
+ Sears, Eleanora* 1984
Smith Court, Margaret 1986

Track & Field

Blankers-Koen, Fanny* 1982
Cheng, Chi 1994
Coachman Davis, Alice* ...1991
Faggs Star, Aeriwentha
Mae* 1996
Manning Mims, Madeline ...1987
+ Rudolph, Wilma 1980
+ Stephens, Helen* 1983
Szewinska, Irena 1992
Tyus, Wyomia 1981
Waitz, Grete 1995
White, Willye 1988

Volleyball

+ Hyman, Flo 1986

Water Skiing

McGuire, Willa Worthington* ..1990

Orienteering

Kringstad, Annichen 1995

Coaches

Applebee, Constance 1991
Backus, Sharron 1993
Conradt, Judy 1995
Grossfeld, Muriel 1991
Holum, Diana 1996
Jacket, Barbara 1995
+ Jackson, Nell 1990
Kanakogi, Rusty 1994
Summitt, Pat Head 1990
+ Wade, Margaret 1992

Women's Global Challenge

The Women's Sports Foundation has announced the creation of the "Women's Global Challenge" to feature the best amateur and professional female athletes and to be held every two years beginning in 1999. The inaugural event will be held over a five day period from April 28 through May 2, 1999 at a site that is yet to be determined and will consist of eight sports—basketball, beach volleyball, diving, figure skating, gymnastics, soccer, swimming and track & field. The top ten athletes in each individual sport and the top four to eight teams in each sport will be invited to compete. The inaugural "Challenge" will be broadcast by CBS and will be syndicated to an estimated 100 countries.

Wide World Photos

Jackie Robinson's **#42** was a familiar sight in major league ballparks this year. As part of the 50th anniversary celebration of the integration of baseball, Robinson's number was retired by every team in the majors. Above, his number hangs next to Tom Seaver's #41 at Shea Stadium in New York.

RETIRED NUMBERS

Major League Baseball

The New York Yankees have retired the most uniform numbers (14) in the Major Leagues; followed the Brooklyn/Los Angeles Dodgers (9), the Pittsburgh Pirates and St. Louis Cardinals (8), the Chicago White Sox (7) and the New York/San Francisco Giants (6). **Nolan Ryan** has had his number retired by three teams—#34 by Texas and Houston and #30 by California. Four players and a manager have had their numbers retired by two teams: **Hank Aaron**—#44 by the Boston/Milwaukee/Atlanta Braves and the Milwaukee Brewers; **Rod Carew**—#29 by Minnesota and California; **Rollie Fingers**—#34 by Milwaukee and Oakland; **Frank Robinson**—#20 by Cincinnati and Baltimore; and **Casey Stengel**—#37 by the New York Yankees and New York Mets.

Numbers retired in 1997 (8): MLB—#42 worn by second baseman **Jackie Robinson**. The number was retired as part of the celebration marking the 50th anniversary of major league baseball's racial integration. Those players currently wearing #42 will be allowed to continue but the number will not be given out in the future; CHICAGO—#72 worn by catcher Carlton Fisk (1981-93 with White Sox); DETROIT—#16 worn by pitcher **Hal Newhouser** (1939-53 with Tigers); LOS ANGELES—#2 worn by manager **Tommy Lasorda** (1976-96 with Dodgers); MINNESOTA—#34 worn by outfielder **Kirby Puckett** (1984-96 with Twins); MONTREAL—#10 worn by outfielder **Andre Dawson** (1976-86 with Expos); NEW YORK—#23 worn by first baseman **Don Mattingly** (1982-95 with Yankees); SAN DIEGO—#35 **Randy Jones** (1973-80 with Padres).

American League

Two AL teams—the Seattle Mariners and Toronto Blue Jays—have not retired any numbers. The Blue Jays have a "level of excellence" which includes Dave Steib (#11) and George Bell (#37). Both numbers are currently being used, however.

Anaheim Angels

26 Gene Autry
29 Rod Carew
30 Nolan Ryan
50 Jimmie Reese
72 Carlton Fisk

Baltimore Orioles

4 Earl Weaver
5 Brooks Robinson
20 Frank Robinson
22 Jim Palmer
33 Eddie Murray

Boston Red Sox

1 Bobby Doerr
4 Joe Cronin
8 Carl Yastrzemski
9 Ted Williams

Chicago White Sox

2 Nellie Fox
3 Harold Baines
4 Luke Appling
9 Minnie Minoso
11 Luis Aparicio
16 Ted Lyons
19 Billy Pierce
72 Carlton Fisk

Cleveland Indians

3 Earl Averill
5 Lou Boudreau
14 Larry Doby
18 Mel Harder
19 Bob Feller

Detroit Tigers

2 Charley Gehringer
5 Hank Greenberg
6 Al Kaline
16 Hal Newhouser

Kansas City Royals

5 George Brett
10 Dick Howser
20 Frank White

Milwaukee Brewers

19 Robin Yount
34 Rollie Fingers
44 Hank Aaron

Minnesota Twins

3 Harmon Killebrew
6 Tony Oliva
14 Kent Hrbek
29 Rod Carew
34 Kirby Puckett

New York Yankees

1 Billy Martin
3 Babe Ruth
4 Lou Gehrig
5 Joe DiMaggio
7 Mickey Mantle
8 Yogi Berra & Bill Dickey
9 Roger Maris
10 Phil Rizzuto
15 Thurman Munson
16 Whitey Ford
23 Don Mattingly
32 Elston Howard
37 Casey Stengel
44 Reggie Jackson

Oakland Athletics

27 Catfish Hunter
34 Rollie Fingers

Texas Rangers

34 Nolan Ryan

National League

San Francisco has honored former NY Giants Christy Mathewson and John McGraw even though they played before numbers were worn.

Atlanta Braves

3 Dale Murphy
21 Warren Spahn
35 Phil Niekro
41 Eddie Mathews
44 Hank Aaron

Chicago Cubs

14 Ernie Banks
26 Billy Williams

Cincinnati Reds

1 Fred Hutchinson
5 Johnny Bench

Houston Astros

25 Jose Cruz
32 Jim Umbricht
33 Mike Scott
34 Nolan Ryan
40 Don Wilson

Los Angeles Dodgers

1 Pee Wee Reese
2 Tommy Lasorda
4 Duke Snider
19 Jim Gilliam
24 Walter Alston
32 Sandy Koufax
39 Roy Campanella
42 Jackie Robinson
53 Don Drysdale

Montreal Expos

8 Gary Carter
10 Rusty Staub
   & Andre Dawson

New York Mets

14 Gil Hodges
37 Casey Stengel
41 Tom Seaver

Philadelphia Phillies

1 Richie Ashburn
20 Mike Schmidt
32 Steve Carlton
36 Robin Roberts

Pittsburgh Pirates

1 Billy Meyer
4 Ralph Kiner
8 Willie Stargell
9 Bill Mazeroski
20 Pie Traynor
21 Roberto Clemente
33 Honus Wagner
40 Danny Murtaugh

St. Louis Cardinals

1 Ozzie Smith
2 Red Schoendienst
6 Stan Musial
14 Ken Boyer
17 Dizzy Dean
20 Lou Brock
45 Bob Gibson
85 August (Gussie) Busch

San Diego Padres

6 Steve Garvey
35 Randy Jones

San Francisco Giants

3 Bill Terry
4 Mel Ott
11 Carl Hubbell
24 Willie Mays
27 Juan Marichal
44 Willie McCovey

National Basketball Association

Boston has retired the most numbers (19) in the NBA; followed by Portland (8); the Los Angeles Lakers, New York Knicks and the KC/Sacramento Kings have (7); Milwaukee and the Rochester/Cincinnati Royals have (6); Cleveland, Detroit and the Syracuse Nats/Philadelphia 76ers (5). Six players have had their numbers retired by two teams: **Kareem Abdul-Jabbar**—#33 by LA Lakers and Milwaukee; **Wilt Chamberlain**—#13 by the Los Angeles Lakers and Philadelphia; **Julius Erving**—#6 by Philadelphia and #32 by New Jersey; **Bob Lanier**—#16 by Detroit and Milwaukee; **Oscar Robertson**—#1 by Milwaukee and #14 by Sacramento; and **Nate Thurmond**—#42 by Cleveland and Golden State.

Numbers retired in 1997 (2): CLEVELAND—#43 worn by center Brad Daugherty (1986-96 with Cavaliers); LOS ANGELES LAKERS—#25 worn by guard Gail Goodrich (1955-76 with Lakers).

Eastern Conference

Three Eastern teams—the Miami Heat, Orlando Magic, and Toronto Raptors—have not retired any numbers.

Boston Celtics

1 Walter A. Brown
2 Red Auerbach
3 Dennis Johnson
6 Bill Russell
10 Jo Jo White
14 Bob Cousy
15 Tom Heinsohn
16 Tom (Satch) Sanders
17 John Havlicek
18 Dave Cowens
19 Don Nelson
21 Bill Sharman
22 Ed Macauley
23 Frank Ramsey
24 Sam Jones
25 K.C. Jones
32 Kevin McHale
33 Larry Bird
35 Reggie Lewis
Loscy Jim Loscutoff
Radio mic Johnny Most

Atlanta Hawks

9 Bob Pettit
23 Lou Hudson

Charlotte Hornets

6 Fans ("Sixth Man")

Chicago Bulls

4 Jerry Sloan
10 Bob Love
23 Michael Jordan

Cleveland Cavaliers

7 Bingo Smith
22 Larry Nance
34 Austin Carr
42 Nate Thurmond
43 Brad Daugherty

Detroit Pistons

11 Isiah Thomas
15 Vinnie Johnson
16 Bob Lanier
21 Dave Bing
40 Bill Laimbeer

Indiana Pacers

30 George McGinnis
34 Mel Daniels
35 Roger Brown

Milwaukee Bucks

1 Oscar Robertson
2 Junior Bridgeman
4 Sidney Moncrief
14 Jon McGlocklin
16 Bob Lanier
32 Brian Winters
33 Kareem Abdul-Jabbar

New York Knicks

10 Walt Frazier
12 Dick Barnett
15 Dick McGuire
   & Earl Monroe
19 Willis Reed
22 Dave DeBusschere
24 Bill Bradley
613 Red Holzman

New Jersey Nets

3 Drazen Petrovic
4 Wendell Ladner
23 John Williamson
25 Bill Melchionni
32 Julius Erving

Philadelphia 76ers

6 Julius Erving
10 Maurice Cheeks
13 Wilt Chamberlain
15 Hal Greer
24 Bobby Jones
32 Billy Cunningham
P.A. mic Dave Zinkoff

Washington Wizards

11 Elvin Hayes
25 Gus Johnson
41 Wes Unseld

Western Conference

Three Western teams—the Los Angeles Clippers, Minnesota Timberwolves, and Vancouver Grizzlies—have not retired any numbers.

Dallas Mavericks

15 Brad Davis

Denver Nuggets

2 Alex English
33 David Thompson
40 Byron Beck
44 Dan Issel

Golden St. Warriors

14 Tom Meschery
16 Al Attles
24 Rick Barry
42 Nate Thurmond

Houston Rockets

23 Calvin Murphy
45 Rudy Tomjanovich

Los Angeles Lakers

13 Wilt Chamberlain
22 Elgin Baylor
25 Gail Goodrich
32 Magic Johnson
33 Kareem Abdul-Jabbar
42 James Worthy
44 Jerry West

Phoenix Suns

5 Dick Van Arsdale
6 Walter Davis
33 Alvan Adams
42 Connie Hawkins
44 Paul Westphal

Retired Numbers (Cont.)

Portland Trail Blazers
1 Larry Weinberg
13 Dave Twardzik
15 Larry Steele
20 Maurice Lucas
32 Bill Walton
36 Lloyd Neal
45 Geoff Petrie
77 Jack Ramsay

Sacramento Kings
1 Nate Archibald
6 Fans ("Sixth Man")
11 Bob Davies
12 Maurice Stokes
14 Oscar Robertson
27 Jack Twyman
44 Sam Lacey

San Antonio Spurs
13 James Silas
44 George Gervin

Seattle SuperSonics
19 Lenny Wilkens
32 Fred Brown
43 Jack Sikma
Radio Mic Bob Blackburn

Utah Jazz
1 Frank Layden
7 Pete Maravich
35 Darrell Griffith
53 Mark Eaton

National Football League

The Chicago Bears have retired the most uniform numbers (13) in the NFL; followed by the New York Giants (9); the Dallas Texans/Kansas City Chiefs (8); the Baltimore-Indianapolis Colts, the Boston-New England Patriots and San Francisco (7); Detroit (6); Cleveland and Philadelphia (5). No player has ever had his number retired by more than one NFL team.

Numbers retired in 1997 (1): ST. LOUIS—#78 worn by offensive tackle **Jackie Slater** (1976-95 with Rams).

AFC

Five AFC teams—the Baltimore Ravens, Buffalo Bills, Oakland Raiders, Pittsburgh Steelers and Jacksonville Jaguars—have not retired any numbers. The Cleveland Browns have retired five numbers— #14 Otto Graham, #32 Jim Brown, #45 Ernie Davis, #46 Don Fleming and #76 Lou Groza.

Cincinnati Bengals
54 Bob Johnson

Denver Broncos
18 Frank Tripucka
44 Floyd Little

Tennessee Oilers
34 Earl Campbell
43 Jim Norton
63 Mike Munchak
65 Elvin Bethea

Indianapolis Colts
19 Johnny Unitas
22 Buddy Young
24 Lenny Moore
70 Art Donovan
77 Jim Parker
82 Raymond Berry
89 Gino Marchetti

Kansas City Chiefs
3 Jan Stenerud
16 Len Dawson
28 Abner Haynes
33 Stone Johnson
36 Mack Lee Hill
63 Willie Lanier
78 Bobby Bell
86 Buck Buchanan

Miami Dolphins
12 Bob Griese

New England Patriots
14 Steve Grogan
20 Gino Cappelletti
40 Mike Haynes
57 Steve Nelson
73 John Hannah
79 Jim Hunt
89 Bob Dee

New York Jets
12 Joe Namath
13 Don Maynard

San Diego Chargers
14 Dan Fouts

Seattle Seahawks
12 Fans ("12th Man")
80 Steve Largent

NFC

Atlanta, Dallas and the Carolina Panthers are the only NFC teams that haven't officially retired any numbers. The Falcons haven't issued uniforms #10 (Steve Bartkowski), #31 (William Andrews) and #60 (Tommy Nobis) since those players retired; while the Cowboys have a "Ring of Honor" at Texas Stadium that includes nine players and one coach—Tony Dorsett, Chuck Howley, Lee Roy Jordan, Tom Landry, Bob Lilly, Don Meredith, Don Perkins, Mel Renfro, Roger Staubach and Randy White.

Arizona Cardinals
8 Larry Wilson
77 Stan Mauldin
88 J.V. Cain
99 Marshall Goldberg

Chicago Bears
3 Bronko Nagurski
5 George McAfee
7 George Halas
28 Willie Galimore
34 Walter Payton
40 Gale Sayers
41 Brian Piccolo
42 Sid Luckman
51 Dick Butkus
56 Bill Hewitt
61 Bill George
66 Bulldog Turner
77 Red Grange

Detroit Lions
7 Dutch Clark
22 Bobby Layne
37 Doak Walker
56 Joe Schmidt
85 Chuck Hughes
88 Charlie Sanders

Green Bay Packers
3 Tony Canadeo
14 Don Hutson
15 Bart Starr
66 Ray Nitschke

Minnesota Vikings
10 Fran Tarkenton
88 Alan Page

New Orleans Saints
31 Jim Taylor
81 Doug Atkins

New York Giants
1 Ray Flaherty
7 Mel Hein
11 Phil Simms
14 Y.A. Tittle
32 Al Blozis
40 Joe Morrison
42 Charlie Conerly
50 Ken Strong
56 Lawrence Taylor

Philadelphia Eagles
15 Steve Van Buren
40 Tom Brookshier
44 Pete Retzlaff
60 Chuck Bednarik
70 Al Wistert
99 Jerome Brown

St. Louis Rams
7 Bob Waterfield
74 Merlin Olsen
78 Jackie Slater

San Francisco 49ers
12 John Brodie
34 Joe Perry
37 Jimmy Johnson
39 Hugh McElhenny
70 Charlie Krueger
73 Leo Nomellini
87 Dwight Clark

Tampa Bay Bucs
63 Lee Roy Selmon

Wash. Redskins
33 Sammy Baugh

National Hockey League

The Boston Bruins and Montreal Canadiens have retired the most uniform numbers (7) in the NHL; followed by Detroit (6); the N.Y. Islanders (5); Buffalo, Chicago, St. Louis and Philadelphia (4); and the Boston-New England-Hartford Whalers, Los Angeles Kings and Quebec Nordiques-Colorado Avalanche (3). Two players have had their numbers retired by two teams: Gordie Howe—#9 by Detroit and Hartford; and Bobby Hull—#9 by Chicago and Winnipeg.

Numbers retired in 1997 (1): ISLANDERS—#9 worn by forward Clark Gillies (1974-86 with Islanders);

Eastern Conference

Four Eastern teams—the Carolina Hurricanes, New Jersey Devils, Tampa Bay Lightning and Florida Panthers—have not retired a number. The Hartford Whalers had retired three numbers: #2 Rick Ley, #9 Gordie Howe and #19 John McKenzie.

Boston Bruins

2 Eddie Shore
3 Lionel Hitchman
4 Bobby Orr
4 Dit Clapper
7 Phil Esposito
9 John Bucyk
15 Milt Schmidt

Buffalo Sabres

2 Tim Horton
7 Rick Martin
11 Gilbert Perreault
14 Rene Robert

Montreal Canadiens

1 Jacques Plante
2 Doug Harvey
4 Jean Beliveau
7 Howie Morenz
9 Maurice Richard
10 Guy Lafleur
16 Henri Richard

New York Islanders

5 Denis Potvin
9 Clark Gillies
22 Mike Bossy
23 Bob Nystrom
31 Billy Smith

New York Rangers

1 Eddie Giacomin
7 Rod Gilbert

Ottawa Senators

8 Frank Finnigan

Philadelphia Flyers

1 Bernie Parent
4 Barry Ashbee
7 Bill Barber
16 Bobby Clarke

Pittsburgh Penguins

21 Michel Briere

Washington Capitals

7 Yvon Labre

Western Conference

Three Western teams—the Colorado Avalance, San Jose Sharks and Mighty Ducks of Anaheim—have not retired a number. Note, the Quebec Nordiques retired the numbers of J.C. Tremblay (3), Marc Tardiff (8), and Michel Goulet (16) but these numbers have been worn since the team moved to Colorado.

Calgary Flames

9 Lanny McDonald

Chicago Blackhawks

1 Glenn Hall
9 Bobby Hull
21 Stan Mikita
35 Tony Esposito

Dallas Stars

8 Bill Goldsworthy
19 Bill Masterton

Detroit Red Wings

1 Terry Sawchuk
6 Larry Aurie
7 Ted Lindsay
9 Gordie Howe
10 Alex Delvecchio
12 Sid Abel

Edmonton Oilers

3 Al Hamilton

Los Angeles Kings

16 Marcel Dionne
18 Dave Taylor
30 Rogie Vachon

Phoenix Coyotes

9 Bobby Hull
25 Thomas Steen

St. Louis Blues

3 Bob Gassoff
8 Barclay Plager
11 Brian Sutter
24 Bernie Federko

Toronto Maple Leafs

5 Bill Barilko
6 Ace Bailey

Vancouver Canucks

12 Stan Smyl

AWARDS

Associated Press Athletes of the Year

Selected annually by AP newspaper sports editors since 1931.

Male

Michael Johnson, who became the first man to win gold medals in both the 200 and 400-meter runs at one Olympics, was named the top male athlete of 1996 by Associated Press sports editors. Johnson completed the unprecedented double by running a 19.32 in the 200-meter dash, shattering the existing world record.

The Top 10 vote-getters (first place votes in parentheses): 1. **Michael Johnson**, track (76), 300 points; 2. **Tiger Woods**, golf (87), 200 pts; 3. **Evander Holyfield**, boxing (14), 116 pts; 4. **Michael Jordan**, basketball (15), 111 pts; 5. **Brett Favre**, football (6), 41 pts; 6. **Cigar**, horse racing (7) 39; 7. **Alex Rodriguez**, baseball (2), 27 pts; 8. **Brett Butler**, baseball (4), 24 pts; 9. **John Smoltz**, baseball, 16 pts; 10. **Danny Wuerffel**, football (2), 15 pts.

Multiple winners: Michael Jordan (3); Don Budge, Sandy Koufax, Carl Lewis, Joe Montana and Byron Nelson (2).

Year		Year		Year	
1931	**Pepper Martin**, baseball	1945	**Byron Nelson**, golf	1958	**Herb Elliott**, track
1932	**Gene Sarazen**, golf	1946	**Glenn Davis**, college football	1959	**Ingemar Johansson**, boxing
1933	**Carl Hubbell**, baseball	1947	**Johnny Lujack**, college football	1960	**Rafer Johnson**, track
1934	**Dizzy Dean**, baseball	1948	**Lou Boudreau**, baseball	1961	**Roger Maris**, baseball
1935	**Joe Louis**, boxing	1949	**Leon Hart**, college football	1962	**Maury Wills**, baseball
1936	**Jesse Owens**, track	1950	**Jim Konstanty**, baseball	1963	**Sandy Koufax**, baseball
1937	**Don Budge**, tennis	1951	**Dick Kazmaier**, college football	1964	**Don Schollander**, swimming
1938	**Don Budge**, tennis	1952	**Bob Mathias**, track	1965	**Sandy Koufax**, baseball
1939	**Nile Kinnick**, college football	1953	**Ben Hogan**, golf	1966	**Frank Robinson**, baseball
1940	**Tom Harmon**, college football	1954	**Willie Mays**, baseball	1967	**Carl Yastrzemski**, baseball
1941	**Joe DiMaggio**, baseball	1955	**Hopalong Cassady**, col. football	1968	**Denny McLain**, baseball
1942	**Frank Sinkwich**, college football	1956	**Mickey Mantle**, baseball	1969	**Tom Seaver**, baseball
1943	**Gunder Haegg**, track	1957	**Ted Williams**, baseball	1970	**George Blanda**, pro football
1944	**Byron Nelson**, golf			1971	**Lee Trevino**, golf

Awards (Cont.)

Year		Year		Year	
1972	**Mark Spitz**, swimming	1979	**Willie Stargell**, baseball	1989	**Joe Montana**, pro football
1973	**O.J. Simpson**, pro football	1980	**U.S. Olympic hockey team**	1990	**Joe Montana**, pro football
1974	**Muhammad Ali**, boxing	1981	**John McEnroe**, tennis	1991	**Michael Jordan**, pro basketball
1975	**Fred Lynn**, baseball	1982	**Wayne Gretzky**, hockey	1992	**Michael Jordan**, pro basketball
1976	**Bruce Jenner**, track	1983	**Carl Lewis**, track	1993	**Michael Jordan**, pro basketball
1977	**Steve Cauthen**, horse racing	1984	**Carl Lewis**, track	1994	**George Foreman**, boxing
1978	**Ron Guidry**, baseball	1985	**Dwight Gooden**, baseball	1995	**Cal Ripken Jr.**, baseball
		1986	**Larry Bird**, pro basketball	1996	**Michael Johnson**, track
		1987	**Ben Johnson**, track		
		1988	**Orel Hershiser**, baseball		

Female

Olympic swimmer Amy Van Dyken, who became the first American woman in history to win 4 gold medals in a single Olympic Games, was named the top female athlete of 1996 by Associated Press sports editors. Van Dyken won gold in the 50-meter freestyle, 100-meter butterfly, 4x100 freestyle relay and 4x100 medley relays in Atlanta.

The Top 10 vote-getters (first place votes in parentheses): 1. **Amy Van Dyken**, swimming (45), 191 points; 2. **Kerri Strug**, gymnastics (34), 159 pts; 3. **Steffi Graf**, tennis (27), 142 pts; 4. **Dot Richardson**, softball (11), 74 pts; 5. **Mia Hamm**, socccer (5), 50 pts; 6. **Lisa Leslie**, basketball (4), 41 pts; 7. **Karrie Webb**, golf (3), 36 pts; 8. **Annika Sorenstam**, golf (2), 29 pts; 9. **Picabo Street**, skiing (3), 28 pts; 10. **Gail Devers**, track (4), 25 pts.

Multiple winners: Babe Didrikson Zaharias (6); Chris Evert (4); Patty Berg and Maureen Connolly (3); Tracy Austin, Althea Gibson, Billie Jean King, Nancy Lopez, Alice Marble, Martina Navratilova, Wilma Rudolph, Monica Seles, Kathy Whitworth and Mickey Wright (2).

Year		Year		Year	
1931	**Helene Madison**, swimming	1953	**Maureen Connolly**, tennis	1975	**Chris Evert**, tennis
1932	**Babe Didrikson**, track	1954	**Babe Didrikson Zaharias**, golf	1976	**Nadia Comaneci**, gymnastics
1933	**Helen Jacobs**, tennis	1955	**Patty Berg**, golf	1977	**Chris Evert**, tennis
1934	**Virginia Van Wie**, golf	1956	**Pat McCormick**, diving	1978	**Nancy Lopez**, golf
1935	**Helen Wills Moody**, tennis	1957	**Althea Gibson**, tennis	1979	**Tracy Austin**, tennis
1936	**Helen Stephens**, track	1958	**Althea Gibson**, tennis	1980	**Chris Evert Lloyd**, tennis
1937	**Katherine Rawls**, swimming	1959	**Maria Bueno**, tennis	1981	**Tracy Austin**, tennis
1938	**Patty Berg**, golf	1960	**Wilma Rudolph**, track	1982	**Mary Decker Tabb**, track
1939	**Alice Marble**, tennis	1961	**Wilma Rudolph**, track	1983	**Martina Navratilova**, tennis
1940	**Alice Marble**, tennis	1962	**Dawn Fraser**, swimming	1984	**Mary Lou Retton**, gymnastics
1941	**Betty Hicks Newell**, golf	1963	**Mickey Wright**, golf	1985	**Nancy Lopez**, golf
1942	**Gloria Callen**, swimming	1964	**Mickey Wright**, golf	1986	**Martina Navratilova**, tennis
1943	**Patty Berg**, golf	1965	**Kathy Whitworth**, golf	1987	**Jackie Joyner-Kersee**, track
1944	**Ann Curtis**, swimming	1966	**Kathy Whitworth**, golf	1988	**Florence Griffith Joyner**, track
1945	**Babe Didrikson Zaharias**, golf	1967	**Billie Jean King**, tennis	1989	**Steffi Graf**, tennis
1946	**Babe Didrikson Zaharias**, golf	1968	**Peggy Fleming**, skating	1990	**Beth Daniel**, golf
1947	**Babe Didrikson Zaharias**, golf	1969	**Debbie Meyer**, swimming	1991	**Monica Seles**, tennis
1948	**Fanny Blankers-Koen**, track	1970	**Chi Cheng**, track	1992	**Monica Seles**, tennis
1949	**Marlene Bauer**, golf	1971	**Evonne Goolagong**, tennis	1993	**Sheryl Swoopes**, basketball
1950	**Babe Didrikson Zaharias**, golf	1972	**Olga Korbut**, gymnastics	1994	**Bonnie Blair**, speed skating
1951	**Maureen Connolly**, tennis	1973	**Billie Jean King**, tennis	1995	**Rebecca Lobo**, col. basketball
1952	**Maureen Connolly**, tennis	1974	**Chris Evert**, tennis	1996	**Amy Van Dyken**, swimming

UPI International Athletes of the Year

Selected annually by United Press International's European newspaper sports editors since 1974.

Male

Multiple winners: Sebastian Coe, Alberto Juantorena and Carl Lewis (2).

Year		Year		Year	
1974	**Muhammad Ali**, boxing	1982	**Daley Thompson**, track	1990	**Stefan Edberg**, tennis
1975	**Joao Oliveira**, track	1983	**Carl Lewis**, track	1991	**Sergei Bubka**, track
1976	**Alberto Juantorena**, track	1984	**Carl Lewis**, track	1992	**Kevin Young**, track
1977	**Alberto Juantorena**, track	1985	**Steve Cram**, track	1993	**Miguel Indurain**, cycling
1978	**Henry Rono**, track	1986	**Diego Maradona**, soccer	1994	**Johan Olav Koss**, speed skating
1979	**Sebastian Coe**, track	1987	**Ben Johnson**, track	1995	**Jonathan Edwards**, track
1980	**Eric Heiden**, speed skating	1988	**Matt Biondi**, swimming	1996	no award
1981	**Sebastian Coe**, track	1989	**Boris Becker**, tennis		

Female

Multiple winners: Nadia Comaneci, Steffi Graf, Marita Koch and Monica Seles (2).

Year		Year		Year	
1974	**Irena Szewinska**, track	1980	**Hanni Wenzel**, alpine skiing	1986	**Heike Drechsler**, track
1975	**Nadia Comaneci**, gymnastics	1981	**Chris Evert Lloyd**, tennis	1987	**Steffi Graf**, tennis
1976	**Nadia Comaneci**, gymnastics	1982	**Marita Koch**, track	1988	**Florence Griffith Joyner**, track
1977	**Rosie Ackermann**, track	1983	**Jarmila Kratochvilova**, track	1989	**Steffi Graf**, tennis
1978	**Tracy Caulkins**, swimming	1984	**Martina Navratilova**, tennis	1990	**Merlene Ottey**, track
1979	**Marita Koch**, track	1985	**Mary Decker Slaney**, track	1991	**Monica Seles**, tennis

Year		Year		Year	
1992	**Monica Seles**, tennis	1994	**Le Jingyi**, swimming	1996	no award
1993	**Wang Junxia**, track	1995	**Gwen Torrence**, track		

Jesse Owens International Trophy

Presented annually by the International Amateur Athletic Association since 1981 and selected by a worldwide panel of electors. The Jesse Owens International Trophy is named after the late American Olympic champion, who won four gold medals at the 1936 Summer Games in Berlin.

Year		Year		Year	
1981	**Eric Heiden**, speed skating	1987	**Greg Louganis**, diving	1994	**Wang Junxia**, track
1982	**Sebastian Coe**, track	1988	**Ben Johnson**, track	1995	**Johan Olva Koss**, speed skating
1983	**Mary Decker**, track	1990	**Roger Kingdom**, track	1996	**Michael Johnson**, track
1984	**Edwin Moses**, track	1991	**Greg LeMond**, cycling	1997	**Michael Johnson**, track
1985	**Carl Lewis**, track	1992	**Mike Powell**, track		
1986	**Said Aouita**, track	1993	**Vitaly Scherbo**, gymnastics		

James E. Sullivan Memorial Award

Presented annually by the Amateur Athletic Union since 1930. The Sullivan Award is named after the former AAU president and given to the athlete who, "by his or her performance, example and influence as an amateur, has done the most during the year to advance the cause of sportsmanship." An athlete cannot win the award more than once.

The 1996 winner was sprinter **Michael Johnson**, the gold medalist in both the 200 and 400 meter races at the Summer Olympics in Atlanta. Johnson, a Sullivan Award finalist in 1995, became the first man to ever complete this rare feat. The other nine finalists are listed alphabetically: **Gail Devers** (track), **Teresa Edwards** (college basketball), **Shannon Miller** (gymnastics), **Dan O'Brien** (track), **Dot Richardson** (softball), **Amy Van Dyken** (swimming), **Michelle Kwan** (figure skating), **Tiger Woods** (golf) and **Danny Wuerffel** (college football). Vote totals were not released.

Year		Year		Year	
1930	**Bobby Jones**, golf	1952	**Horace Ashenfelter**, track	1975	**Tim Shaw**, swimming
1931	**Barney Berlinger**, track	1953	**Sammy Lee**, diving	1976	**Bruce Jenner**, track
1932	**Jim Bausch**, track	1954	**Mal Whitfield**, track	1977	**John Naber**, swimming
1933	**Glenn Cunningham**, track	1955	**Harrison Dillard**, track	1978	**Tracy Caulkins**, swimming
1934	**Bill Bonthron**, track	1956	**Pat McCormick**, diving	1979	**Kurt Thomas**, gymnastics
1935	**Lawson Little**, golf	1957	**Bobby Morrow**, track	1980	**Eric Heiden**, speed skating
1936	**Glenn Morris**, track	1958	**Glenn Davis**, track	1981	**Carl Lewis**, track
1937	**Don Budge**, tennis	1959	**Parry O'Brien**, track	1982	**Mary Decker**, track
1938	**Don Lash**, track	1960	**Rafer Johnson**, track	1983	**Edwin Moses**, track
1939	**Joe Burk**, rowing	1961	**Wilma Rudolph**, track	1984	**Greg Louganis**, diving
1940	**Greg Rice**, track	1963	**John Pennel**, track	1985	**Joan B. Samuelson**, track
1941	**Leslie MacMitchell**, track	1964	**Don Schollander**, swimming	1986	**Jackie Joyner-Kersee**, track
1942	**Cornelius Warmerdam**, track	1965	**Bill Bradley**, basketball	1987	**Jim Abbott**, baseball
1943	**Gilbert Dodds**, track	1966	**Jim Ryun**, track	1988	**Florence Griffith Joyner**, track
1944	**Ann Curtis**, swimming	1967	**Randy Matson**, track	1989	**Janet Evans**, swimming
1945	**Doc Blanchard**, football	1968	**Debbie Meyer**, swimming	1990	**John Smith**, wrestling
1946	**Arnold Tucker**, football	1969	**Bill Toomey**, track	1991	**Mike Powell**, track
1947	**John B. Kelly, Jr.**, rowing	1970	**John Kinsella**, swimming	1992	**Bonnie Blair**, speed skating
1948	**Bob Mathias**, track	1971	**Mark Spitz**, swimming	1993	**Charlie Ward**, football
1949	**Dick Button**, skating	1972	**Frank Shorter**, track	1994	**Dan Jansen**, speed skating
1950	**Fred Wilt**, track	1973	**Bill Walton**, basketball	1995	**Bruce Baumgartner**, wrestling
1951	**Bob Richards**, track	1974	**Rich Wohlhuter**, track	1996	**Michael Johnson**, track

USOC Sportsman & Sportswoman of the Year

To the outstanding overall male and female athletes from within the U.S. Olympic Committee member organizations. Winners are chosen from nominees of the national governing bodies for Olympic and Pan American Games and affiliated organizations. Voting is done by members of the national media, USOC board of directors and Athletes' Advisory Council.

Sportsman

Multiple winners: Eric Heiden and Michael Johnson (3); Matt Biondi and Greg Louganis (2).

Year		Year		Year	
1974	**Jim Bolding**, track	1982	**Greg Louganis**, diving	1990	**John Smith**, wrestling
1975	**Clint Jackson**, boxing	1983	**Rick McKinney**, archery	1991	**Carl Lewis**, track
1976	**John Naber**, swimming	1984	**Edwin Moses**, track	1992	**Pablo Morales**, swimming
1977	**Eric Heiden**, speed skating	1985	**Willie Banks**, track	1993	**Michael Johnson**, track
1978	**Bruce Davidson**, equestrian	1986	**Matt Biondi**, swimming	1994	**Dan Jansen**, speed skating
1979	**Eric Heiden**, speed skating	1987	**Greg Louganis**, diving	1995	**Michael Johnson**, track
1980	**Eric Heiden**, speed skating	1988	**Matt Biondi**, swimming	1996	**Michael Johnson**, track
1981	**Scott Hamilton**, fig. skating	1989	**Roger Kingdom**, track		

Sportswoman

Multiple winners: Bonnie Blair, Tracy Caulkins, Jackie Joyner-Kersee and Sheila Young Ochowicz (2).

Year		Year		Year	
1974	**Shirley Babashoff**, swimming	1977	**Linda Fratianne**, fig. skating	1980	**Beth Heiden**, speed skating
1975	**Kathy Heddy**, swimming	1978	**Tracy Caulkins**, swimming	1981	**Sheila Ochowicz**, speed skating & cycling
1976	**Sheila Young**, speedskating	1979	**Sippy Woodhead**, swimming		

Awards (Cont.)

Year		
1982	**Melanie Smith**, equestrian	
1983	**Tamara McKinney**, skiing	
1984	**Tracy Caulkins**, swimming	
1985	**Mary Decker Slaney**, track	

Year		
1986	**Jackie Joyner-Kersee**, track	
1987	**Jackie Joyner-Kersee**, track	
1988	**Florence Griffith Joyner**, track	
1989	**Janet Evans**, swimming	
1990	**Lynn Jennings**, track	
1991	**Kim Zmeskal**, gymnastics	
1992	**Bonnie Blair**, speed skating	

Year		
1993	**Gail Devers**, track	
1994	**Bonnie Blair**, speed skating	
1995	**Picabo Street**, skiing	
1996	**Amy Van Dyken**, swimming	

Honda Broderick Cup

To the outstanding collegiate woman athlete of the year in NCAA competition. Winner is chosen from nominees in each of the NCAA's 10 competitive sports. Final voting is done by member athletic directors. Award is named after founder and sportswear manufacturer Thomas Broderick.

Multiple winner: Tracy Caulkins (2).

Year		
1977	**Lucy Harris**, Delta St	basketball
1978	**Ann Meyers**, UCLA	basketball
1979	**Nancy Lieberman**, Old Dominion	basketball
1980	**Julie Shea**, N.C. State	track & field
1981	**Jill Sterkel**, Texas	swimming
1982	**Tracy Caulkins**, Florida	swimming
1983	**Deitre Collins**, Hawaii	volleyball
1984	**Tracy Caulkins**, Florida	swimming
	& Cheryl Miller, USC	basketball
1985	**Jackie Joyner**, UCLA	track & field
1986	**Kamie Ethridge**, Texas	basketball

Year		
1987	**Mary T. Meagher**, California	swimming
1988	**Teresa Weatherspoon**, La. Tech	basketball
1989	**Vicki Huber**, Villanova	track
1990	**Suzy Favor**, Wisconsin	track
1991	**Dawn Staley**, Virginia	basketball
1992	**Missy Marlowe**, Utah	gymnastics
1993	**Lisa Fernandez**, UCLA	softball
1994	**Mia Hamm**, North Carolina	soccer
1995	**Rebecca Lobo**, UConn	basketball
1996	**Jennifer Rizzotti**, UConn	basketball

Flo Hyman Award

Presented annually since 1987 by the Women's Sports Foundation for "exemplifying dignity, spirit and commitment to excellence" and named in honor of the late captain of the 1984 U.S. Women's Volleyball team. Voting by WSF members.

Year		
1987	**Martina Navratilova**, tennis	
1988	**Jackie Joyner-Kersee**, track	
1989	**Evelyn Ashford**, track	
1990	**Chris Evert**, tennis	

Year		
1991	**Diana Golden**, skiing	
1992	**Nancy Lopez**, golf	
1993	**Lynette Woodward**, basketball	
1994	**Patty Sheehan**, golf	

Year		
1995	**Mary Lou Retton**, gymnastics	
1996	**Donna de Varona**, swimming	
1997	**Billie Jean King**, tennis	

ESPY Awards

The ESPY Awards, which represent the convergence of the sports and entertainment communities, were created by ESPN in 1993 and are given for Excellence in Sports Performance in more than 30 categories. ESPYs are awarded by a panel of sports executives, journalists and retired athletes. Note that not all categories are listed below.

Breakthrough Athlete of the Year

1993	Gary Sheffield, San Diego Padres
1994	Mike Piazza, Los Angeles Dodgers
1995	Jeff Bagwell, Houston Astros
1996	Hideo Nomo, Los Angeles Dodgers
1997	Tiger Woods, golf

Outstanding Female Athlete of the Year

1993	Monica Seles, tennis
1994	Julie Krone, jockey
1995	Bonnie Blair, speed skater
1996	Rebecca Lobo, women's hoops
1997	Amy Van Dyken, Olympic swimmer

Coach/Manager of the Year

1993	Jimmy Johnson, Dallas Cowboys
1994	Jimmy Johnson, Dallas Cowboys
1995	George Siefert, San Francisco 49ers
1996	Gary Barnett, Northwestern
1997	Joe Torre, New York Yankees

Outstanding Male Athlete of the Year

1993	Michael Jordan, Chicago Bulls
1994	Barry Bonds, San Francisco Giants
1995	Steve Young, San Francisco 49ers
1996	Cal Ripken, Baltimore Orioles
1997	Michael Johnson, Olympic sprinter

Comeback Athlete of the Year

1993	Dave Winfield, Toronto Blue Jays
1994	Mario Lemieux, Pittsburgh Penguins
1995	Dan Marino, Miami Dolphins
1996	Michael Jordan, Chicago Bulls
1997	Evander Holyfield, boxer

Outstanding Performance Under Pressure

1993	Christian Laettner, Duke
1994	Joe Carter, Toronto Blue Jays
1995	Mark Messier, New York Rangers
1996	Martin Broduer, New Jersey Devils
1997	Kerri Strug, Olympic gymnast

Time Man of the Year

Since Charles Lindbergh was named *Time* magazine's first Man of the Year for 1927, two individuals with significant sports credentials have won the honor.

Year	
1984	**Peter Ueberroth**, president of the Los Angeles Olympic Organizing Committee.
1991	**Ted Turner**, owner-president of Turner Broadcasting System, founder of CNN cable news network, owner of the Atlanta Braves (NL) and Atlanta Hawks (NBA), and former winning America's Cup skipper.

Outstanding Team

1993 Dallas Cowboys
1994 Toronto Blue Jays
1995 New York Rangers
1996 UConn women's hoops
1997 New York Yankees

Outstanding Baseball Performer of the Year

1993 Dennis Eckersley, Oakland A's
1994 Barry Bonds, San Francisco Giants
1995 Jeff Bagwell, Houston Astros
1996 Greg Maddux, Atlanta Braves
1997 Ken Caminiti, San Diego Padres

Outstanding Pro Football Performer of the Year

1993 Emmitt Smith, Dallas Cowboys
1994 Emmitt Smith, Dallas Cowboys
1995 Barry Sanders, Detroit Lions
1996 Brett Favre, Green Bay Packers
1997 Brett Favre, Green Bay Packers

Outstanding Pro Basketball Performer of the Year

1993 Michael Jordan, Chicago Bulls
1994 Charles Barkley, Phoenix Suns
1995 Hakeem Olajuwon, Houston Rockets
1996 Hakeem Olajuwon, Houston Rockets
1997 Michael Jordan, Chicago Bulls

Outstanding Pro Hockey Performer of the Year

1993 Mario Lemieux, Pittsburgh Penguins
1994 Mario Lemieux, Pittsburgh Penguins
1995 Mark Messier, New York Rangers
1996 Eric Lindros, Philadelphia Flyers
1997 Joe Sakic, Colorado Avalanche

Outstanding College Football Performer of the Year

1993 Garrison Hearst, Georgia
1994 Charlie Ward, Florida State
1995 Rashaan Salaam, Colorado
1996 Eddie George, Ohio State
1997 Danny Wuerffel, Florida

Outstanding College Basketball Performer of the Year

1993 Christian Laettner, Duke
1994 Bobby Hurley, Duke
1995 Grant Hill, Duke
1996 Ed O'Bannon, UCLA
1997 Tim Duncan, Wake Forest

Outstanding Women's College Hoops Performer of the Year

1993 Dawn Staley, Virginia
1994 Sheryl Swoopes, Texas Tech
1995 Charlotte Smith, North Carolina
1996 Rebecca Lobo, Connecticut
1997 Saudia Roundtree, Georgia

Outstanding Men's Tennis Performer of the Year

1993 Jim Courier
1994 Pete Sampras
1995 Pete Sampras
1996 Pete Sampras
1997 Pete Sampras

Outstanding Women's Tennis Performer of the Year

1993 Monica Seles
1994 Steffi Graf
1995 Aranxta Sanchez-Vicario
1996 Steffi Graf
1997 Steffi Graf

Outstanding Men's Golf Performer of the Year

1993 Fred Couples
1994 Nick Price
1995 Nick Price
1996 Corey Pavin
1997 Tom Lehman

Outstanding Women's Golf Performer of the Year

1993 Dottie Monroe
1994 Betsy King
1995 Laura Davies
1996 Annika Sorenstam
1997 Karrie Webb

Outstanding Jockey of the Year

1994 Mike Smith
1995 Chris McCarron
1996 Jerry Bailey
1997 Jerry Bailey

Outstanding Bowling Performer of the Year

1995 Norm Duke
1996 Mike Aulby
1997 Bob Learn Jr.

Outstanding Auto Racing Performer of the Year

1993 Nigel Mansell
1994 Nigel Mansell
1995 Al Unser Jr.
1996 Jeff Gordon
1997 Jimmy Vasser

Outstanding Men's Track Performer of the Year

1993 Kevin Young
1994 Michael Johnson
1995 Dennis Mitchell
1996 Michael Johnson
1997 Michael Johnson

Outstanding Women's Track Performer of the Year

1993 Evelyn Ashford
1994 Gail Devers
1995 Gwen Torrence
1996 Kim Batten
1997 Marie-Jose Perec

Outstanding Boxing Performer of the Year

1993 Riddick Bowe
1994 Evander Holyfield
1995 George Foreman
1996 Roy Jones Jr.
1997 Evander Holyfield

Game of the Year

1996 AFC Championship between Colts and Steelers
1997 Ohio State edges Arizona State in the Rose Bowl

Awards (Cont.)
Arthur Ashe Award for Courage

Presented since 1993 on the annual ESPN "Espys" telecast. Given to a member of the sports community who has exemplified the same courage, spirit and determination to help others despite personal hardship that characterized Arthur Ashe, the late tennis champion and humanitarian. Voting done by select 26-member committee of media and sports personalities.

Year	Year	Year
1993 **Jim Valvano**, basketball	1995 **Howard Cosell**, TV & radio	1996 **Loretta Clairborne**, special
1994 **Steve Palermo**, baseball		olympics
		1997 **Muhammad Ali**, boxing

The Hickok Belt

Officially known as the S. Rae Hickok Professional Athlete of the Year Award and presented by the Kickik Manufacturing Co. of Arlington, Texas, from 1950-76. The trophy was a large belt of gold, diamonds and other jewels, reportedly worth $30,000 in 1976, the last year it was handed out. Voting was done by 270 newspaper sports editors from around the country.

Multiple winner: Sandy Koufax (2).

Year	Year	Year
1950 **Phil Rizzuto**, baseball	1960 **Arnold Palmer**, golf	1970 **Brooks Robinson**, baseball
1951 **Allie Reynolds**, baseball	1961 **Roger Maris**, baseball	1971 **Lee Trevino**, golf
1952 **Rocky Marciano**, boxing	1962 **Maury Wills**, baseball	1972 **Steve Carlton**, baseball
1953 **Ben Hogan**, golf	1963 **Sandy Koufax**, baseball	1973 **O.J. Simpson**, football
1954 **Willie Mays**, baseball	1964 **Jim Brown**, football	1974 **Muhammad Ali**, boxing
1955 **Otto Graham**, football	1965 **Sandy Koufax**, baseball	1975 **Pete Rose**, baseball
1956 **Mickey Mantle**, baseball	1966 **Frank Robinson**, baseball	1976 **Ken Stabler**, football
1957 **Carmen Basilio**, boxing	1967 **Carl Yastrzemski**, baseball	1977 Discontinued
1958 **Bob Turley**, baseball	1968 **Joe Namath**, football	
1959 **Ingemar Johansson**, boxing	1969 **Tom Seaver**, baseball	

ABC's "Wide World of Sports" Athlete of the Year

Selected annually by the producers of ABC Sports since 1962.

Multiple winner: Greg Lemond (2).

Year	Year	Year
1962 **Jim Beatty**, track	1974 **Muhammad Ali**, boxing	1986 **Debi Thomas**, figure skating
1963 **Valery Brumel**, track	1975 **Jack Nicklaus**, golf	1987 **Dennis Conner**, yachting
1964 **Don Schollander**, swimming	1976 **Nadia Comaneci**, gymnastics	1988 **Greg Louganis**, diving
1965 **Jim Clark**, auto racing	1977 **Steve Cauthen**, horse racing	1989 **Greg Lemond**, cycling
1966 **Jim Ryun**, track	1978 **Ron Guidry**, baseball	1990 **Greg Lemond**, cycling
1967 **Peggy Fleming**, figure skating	1979 **Willie Stargell**, baseball	1991 **Carl Lewis**, track
1968 **Bill Toomey**, track	1980 **U.S. Olympic hockey team**	& **Kim Zmeskal**, gymnastics
1969 **Mario Andretti**, auto racing	1981 **Sugar Ray Leonard**, boxing	1992 **Bonnie Blair**, speed skating
1970 **Willis Reed**, basketball	1982 **Wayne Gretzky**, hockey	1993 **Evander Holyfield**, boxing
1971 **Lee Trevino**, golf	1983 **Australia II**, yachting	1994 **Al Unser Jr.**, auto racing
1972 **Olga Korbut**, gymnastics	1984 **Edwin Moses**, track	1995 **Miguel Induráin**, cycling
1973 **O.J. Simpson**, football	1985 **Pete Rose**, baseball	1996 **Michael Johnson**, track
& **Jackie Stewart**, auto racing		

The Sporting News Sportsman of the Year

Selected annually by the editors of The Sporting News since 1968. 'Man of the Year' changed to 'Sportsman' of the Year in 1993.

Year	Year	Year
1968 **Denny McLain**, baseball	1978 **Ron Guidry**, baseball	1988 **Jackie Joyner-Kersee**, track
1969 **Tom Seaver**, baseball	1979 **Willie Stargell**, baseball	1989 **Joe Montana**, football
1970 **John Wooden**, basketball	1980 **George Brett**, baseball	1990 **Nolan Ryan**, baseball
1971 **Lee Trevino**, golf	1981 **Wayne Gretzky**, hockey	1991 **Michael Jordan**, basketball
1972 **Charles O. Finley**, baseball	1982 **Whitey Herzog**, baseball	1992 **Mike Krzyzewski**, col. bask.
1973 **O.J. Simpson**, pro football	1983 **Bowie Kuhn**, baseball	1993 **Cito Gaston**
1974 **Lou Brock**, baseball	1984 **Peter Ueberroth**, LA Olympics	& **Pat Gillick**, baseball
1975 **Archie Griffin**, football	1985 **Pete Rose**, baseball	1994 **Emmitt Smith**, pro football
1976 **Larry O'Brien**, basketball	1986 **Larry Bird**, pro basketball	1995 **Cal Ripken Jr.**, baseball
1977 **Steve Cauthen**, horse racing	1987 No award	1996 **Joe Torre**, baseball

Presidential Medal of Freedom

Since President John F. Kennedy established the Medal of Freedom as America's highest civilian honor in 1963, only nine sports figures have won the award. Note that (*) indicates the presentation was made posthumously.

Year	President	Year	President
1963 **Bob Kiphuth**, swimming	Kennedy	1986 **Earl (Red) Blaik**, football	Reagan
1976 **Jesse Owens**, track & field	Ford	1991 **Ted Williams**, baseball	Bush
1977 **Joe DiMaggio**, baseball	Ford	1992 **Richard Petty**, auto racing	Bush
1983 **Paul (Bear) Bryant***, football	Reagan	1993 **Arthur Ashe***, tennis	Clinton
1984 **Jackie Robinson***, baseball	Reagan		

TROPHY CASE

From the first organized track meet at Olympia in 776 B.C., to the Atlanta Summer Olympics over 2,700 years later, championships have been officially recognized with prizes that are symbolically rich and eagerly pursued. Here are 15 of the most coveted trophies in America.

America's Cup

First presented by England's Royal Yacht Squadron to the winner of an invitational race around the Isle of Wight on Aug. 22, 1851. . . originally called the Hundred Guinea Cup. . . renamed after the U.S. boat America, winner of the first race. . . made of sterling silver and designed by London jewelers R. & G. Garrard. . . measures 2 feet, 3 inches high and weighs 16 lbs. . . originally cost 100 guineas ($500), now valued at $250,000 . . . bell-shaped base added in 1958. . . challenged for every three to four years. . . trophy held by yacht club sponsoring winning boat...Cup was badly damaged when a Maori protester repeatedly smashed it with a sledgehammer on March 14, 1997. It was sent back to the original maker and fully restored.

Vince Lombardi Trophy

First presented at the AFL-NFL World Championship Game (now Super Bowl) on Jan. 15, 1967. . . originally called the World Championship Game Trophy . . . renamed in 1971 in honor of former Green Bay Packers GM-coach and two-time Super Bowl winner Vince Lombardi, who died in 1970 as coach of Washington . . . made of sterling silver and designed by Tiffany & Co. of New York . . . measures 21 inches high and weighs 7 lbs (football depicted is regulation size). . . valued at $12,500. . . competed for annually. . . winning team keeps trophy.

Olympic Gold Medal

First presented by International Olympic Committee in 1908 (until then winners received silver medals). . . second and third place finishers also got medals of silver and bronze for first time in 1908. . . each medal must be at least 2.4 inches in diameter and 0.12 inches thick. . . the gold medal is actually made of silver, but must be gilded with at least 6 grams (0.21 ounces) of pure gold. . . the medals for the 1996 Atlanta Games were designed by Malcolm Grear Designers and produced by Reed & Barton of Taunton, Mass...604 gold, 604 silver and 630 bronze medals were made. . . competed for every two years as Winter and Summer Games alternate. . . winners keep medals.

Stanley Cup

Donated by Lord Stanley of Preston, the Governor General of Canada and first presented in 1893. . . original cup was made of sterling silver by an unknown London silversmith and measured 7 inches high with an 11½-inch diameter. . . in order to accommodate all the rosters of winning teams, the cup now measures 35½ inches high with a base 54 inches around and weighs 32 lbs. . . originally bought for 10 guineas ($48.67), it is now insured for $75,000. . . actual cup retired to Hall of Fame and replaced in 1970. . . presented to NHL playoff champion since 1918. . . trophy loaned to winning team for one year.

World Cup

First presented by the Federation Internationale de Football Association (FIFA). . . originally called the World Cup Trophy. . . renamed the Jules Rimet Cup (after the then FIFA president) in 1946, but retired by Brazil after that country's third title in 1970. . . new World Cup trophy created in 1974. . . designed by Italian sculptor Silvio Gazzaniga and made of solid 18 carat gold with two malachite rings inlaid at the base. . . measures 14.2 inches high and weighs 11 lbs. . . insured for $200,000 (U.S.). . . competed for every four years. . . winning team gets gold-plated replica.

Commissioner's Trophy

First presented by the Commissioner of baseball to the winner of the 1967 World Series. . . also known as the World Championship Trophy. . . made of brass and gold plate with an ebony base and a baseball in the center made of pewter with a silver finish. . . designed by Balfour & Co. of Attleboro, Mass. . . 28 pennants represent 14 AL and 14 NL teams . . . measures 30 inches high and 36 inches around at the base and weighs 30 lbs. . . valued at $15,000. . . competed for annually. . . winning team keeps trophy.

Larry O'Brien Trophy

First presented in 1978 to winner of NBA Finals. . . originally called the Walter A. Brown Trophy after the league pioneer and Boston Celtics owner (an earlier NBA championship bowl was also named after Brown). . . renamed in 1984 in honor of outgoing commissioner O'Brien, who served from 1975-84 . . . made of sterling silver with 24 carat gold overlay and designed by Tiffany & Co. of New York. . . measures 2 feet high and weighs 14½ lbs (basketball depicted is regulation size). . . valued at $13,500. . . competed for annually. . . winning team keeps trophy.

Heisman Trophy

First presented in 1935 to the best college football player east of the Mississippi by the Downtown Athletic Club of New York. . . players across the entire country eligible since 1936. . . originally called the DAC Trophy. . . renamed in 1936 following the death of DAC athletic director and former college coach John W. Heisman. . . made of bronze and designed by New York sculptor Frank Eliscu, it measures 13½ in. high, 6½ in. wide and 14 in. long at the base and weighs 25 lbs. . . valued at $2,000 . . . voting done by national media and former Heisman winners. . . awarded annually. . . winner keeps trophy.

James E. Sullivan Memorial Award

First presented by the Amateur Athletic Union (AAU) in 1930 as a gold medal and given to the nation's outstanding amateur athlete. . . trophy given since 1933. . . named after the amateur sports movement pioneer, who was a founder and past president of AAU and the director of the 1904 Olympic Games in St. Louis. . . made of bronze with a marble base, it measures 17½ in. high and 11 in. wide at the base and weighs 13½ lbs. . . valued at $2,500. . . voting done by AAU and USOC officials, former winners and selected media. . . awarded annually. . . winner keeps trophy.

Ryder Cup

Donated in 1927 by English seed merchant Samuel Ryder, who offered the gold cup for a biennial match between teams of golfing pros from Great Britain and the United States. . . the format changed in 1977 to include the best players on the European PGA Tour. . . . made of 14 carat gold on a wood base and designed by Mappin and Webb of London. . . the golfer depicted on the top of the trophy is Ryder's friend and teaching pro Abe Mitchell. . . . the cup measures 16 in. high and weighs 4 lbs. . . insured for $50,000 . . . competed for every two years at alternating British and U.S. sites . . . the cup is held by the PGA headquarters of the winning side.

Davis Cup

Donated by American college student and U.S. doubles champion Dwight F. Davis in 1900 and presented by the International Tennis Federation (ITF) to the winner of the annual 16-team men's competition. . . officially called the International Lawn Tennis Challenge Trophy. . . made of sterling silver and designed by Shreve, Crump and Low of Boston, the cup has a matching tray (added in 1921) and a very heavy two-tiered base containing rosters of past winning teams. . . it stands 34½ in. high and 108 in. around at the base and weighs 400 lbs. . . insured for $150,000. . . competed for annually. . . trophy loaned to winning country for one year.

Borg-Warner Trophy

First presented by the Borg-Warner Automotive Co. of Chicago in 1936 to the winner of the Indianapolis 500. . . replaced the Wheeler-Schebler Trophy which went to the 400-mile leader from 1911-32. . . made of sterling silver with bas-relief sculptured heads of each winning driver and a gold bas-relief head of Tony Hulman, the owner of the Indy Speedway from 1945-77 . . . designed by Robert J. Hill and made by Gorham, Inc. of Rhode Island . . . measures 51½ in. high and weighs over 80 lbs. . . new base added in 1988 and the entire trophy restored in 1991. . . competed for annually. . . insured for $1 million. . . trophy stays at Speedway Hall of Fame. . . winner gets a 14-in. high replica valued at $30,000.

NCAA Championship Trophy

First presented in 1952 by the NCAA to all 1st, 2nd and 3rd place teams in sports with sanctioned tournaments. . . 1st place teams receive gold-plated awards, 2nd place award is silver-plated and 3rd is bronze. . . replaced silver cup given to championship teams from 1939-1951. . . made of walnut, the trophy stands 24¾ in. high, 14⅛ in. wide and 4½ in. deep at the base and weighs 15 lbs . . . designed by Medallic Art Co. of Danbury, Conn. and made by House of Usher of Kansas City since 1990. . . valued at $500. . . competed for annually. . . winning teams keep trophies.

World Championship Belt

First presented in 1921 by the World Boxing Association, one of the three organizations (the World Boxing Council and International Boxing Federation are the others) generally accepted as sanctioning legitimate world championship fights. . . belt weighs 8 lbs. and is made of hand tanned leather. . . the outsized buckle measures 10½ in. high and 8 in. wide with 24 carat gold plate and contains crystal and semi-precious stones . . . side panels of polished brass are for engraving title bout results . . . currently made by Phil Valentino Originals of Jersey City, N.J.. . . champions keep belts even if they lose their title.

World Championship Ring

Rings decorated with gems and engraving date back to ancient Egypt where the wealthy wore heavy gold and silver rings to indicate social status. . . championship rings in sports serve much the same purpose, indicating the wearer is a champion. . . the Dallas Cowboys' ring for winning Superbowl XXX on Jan. 28, 1996 was designed by Diamond Cutters International of Houston. . . each ring is made of 14-carat yellow gold, weighs 48–51 penny weights and features five trimmed marquis diamonds interlocking in the shape of the Cowboys' star logo as well as five more marquis diamonds (for the team's five Super Bowl wins) on a bed of 51 smaller diamonds. . . rings were appraised at over $30,000 each.

Who's Who

1997 marked the 50th anniversary of **Jackie Robinson**'s breaking of the color barrier in major league baseball. Robinson is shown in this 1951 photo at home with his wife, **Rachel.**

Archive Photos

Sports Personalities

Eight hundred and twenty-seven entries dating back to the turn of the century. Pages updated through Sept. 20, 1997.

Hank Aaron (b. Feb. 5, 1934): Baseball OF; led NL in HRs and RBI 4 times each and batting twice with Milwaukee and Atlanta Braves; MVP in 1957; played in 24 All-Star Games, all-time leader in HRs (755) and RBI (2,297), 3rd in hits (3,771); executive with Braves and TBS, Inc.

Jim Abbott (b. Sept. 19, 1967): Baseball LHP; born without a right hand; All-America hurler at Michigan; won Sullivan Award in 1987; threw 4-0 no-hitter for NY Yankees vs. Cleveland (Sept. 4, 1993).

Kareem Abdul-Jabbar (b. Lew Alcindor, Apr. 16, 1947): Basketball C; led UCLA to 3 NCAA titles (1967-69); tourney MVP 3 times; Player of Year twice; led Milwaukee (1) and LA Lakers (5) to 6 NBA titles; playoff MVP twice (1971,85), regular season MVP 6 times (1971-72,74,76-77,80); retired in 1989 after 20 seasons as all-time leader in over 20 categories.

Andre Agassi (b. Apr. 29, 1970): Tennis; former No. 1 men's player in the world with 31 career tournament wins and 3 grand slam titles; won Wimbledon in 1992, U.S. Open as unseeded entry in '94 and Australian Open in 1996; helped U.S. win 2 Davis Cup finals (1990,92).

Troy Aikman (b. Nov. 21, 1966): Football QB; consensus All-America at UCLA (1988); 1st overall pick in 1989 NFL Draft (by Dallas); led Cowboys to 2 straight Super Bowl titles (1992 and '93 seasons); MVP in Super Bowl XXVII.

Tenley Albright (b. July 18, 1935): Figure skater; 2-time world champion (1953,55); won Olympic silver (1952) and gold (1956) medals; became a surgeon.

Grover Cleveland (Pete) Alexander (b. Feb. 26, 1887, d. Nov. 4, 1950): Baseball RHP; won 20 or more games 9 times; 373 career wins and 90 shutouts.

Muhammad Ali (b. Cassius Clay, Jan. 17, 1942): Boxer; 1960 Olympic light heavyweight champion; only 3-time world heavyweight champ (1964-67, 1974-78,1978-79); defeated Sonny Liston (1964), George Foreman (1974) and Leon Spinks (1978) for title; fought Joe Frazier in 3 memorable bouts (1971-75), winning twice; adopted Black Muslim faith in 1964 and changed name; stripped of title in 1967 after conviction for refusing induction into U.S. Army; verdict reversed by Supreme Court in 1971; career record of 56-5 with 37 KOs and 19 successful title defenses; lit the flaming cauldron to signal the beginning of the 1996 Summer Olympics in Atlanta.

Forrest (Phog) Allen (b. Nov. 18, 1885, d. Sept. 16, 1974): Basketball; college coach 48 years; directed Kansas to NCAA title (1952); 5th on all-time list with 746 career wins.

Bobby Allison (b. Dec. 3, 1937): Auto racer; 3-time winner of Daytona 500 (1978,82,88); NASCAR national champ in 1983; father of Davey.

Davey Allison (b. Feb. 25, 1961, d. July 13, 1993): Auto racer; stock car Rookie of Year (1987); winner of 19 NASCAR races including 1992 Daytona 500; killed at age 32 in helicopter accident at Talladega Superspeedway; son of Bobby.

Roberto Alomar (b. Feb. 5, 1968): Baseball; member of two World Series champions as a Toronto Blue Jay; a switch-hitter who combines speed, power and batting average with fielding skills that have earned him six Gold Gloves; seven-time All-Star; MVP of 1992 ALCS; became known well beyond baseball for spitting in the face of umpire John Hirschbeck during final weekend of 1996 season; the muddled and weak reaction (five-game suspension with pay to be served in 1997) by major league baseball underscored the vacuum that exists in the leadership of the game.

Walter Alston (b. Dec. 1, 1911, d. Oct. 1, 1984): Baseball; managed Brooklyn-LA Dodgers 23 years, won 7 pennants and 4 World Series (1955,59,63,65); retired after 1976 season with 2,060 wins (2,040 regular season and 20 postseason).

Sparky Anderson (b. Feb. 22, 1934): Baseball; only manager to win World Series in each league— Cincinnati in NL (1975-76) and Detroit in AL (1984); 3rd-ranked skipper on all-time career list with 2,168 wins (2,134 regular season and 34 postseason).

Willie Anderson (b. May 1878, d. Oct. 25, 1910): Scottish golfer; became an American citizen and won 4 U.S. Open titles, including an unmatched 3 straight from 1903-05; also won four Western Opens from 1902-09.

Mario Andretti (b. Feb. 28, 1940): Auto racer; 4-time USAC-CART national champion (1965-66,69,84); only driver to win Daytona 500 (1967), Indy 500 (1969) and Formula One world title (1978); Indy 500 Rookie of Year (1965); retired following 1994 racing season ranked 1st in poles (67) and starts (407) and 2nd in wins (52) on all-time IndyCar list; father of Michael and Jeff, uncle of John.

Michael Andretti (b. Oct. 5, 1962): Auto racer; 1991 CART national champion with single-season record 8 wins; Indy 500 Rookie of Year (1984); left Indy-Car circuit for ill-fated Formula One try in 1993; returned to IndyCar in '94; son of Mario.

Earl Anthony (b. Apr. 27, 1938): Bowler; 6-time PBA Bowler of Year; 41 career titles; first to earn $100,000 in 1 season (1975); first to earn $1 million in career. Came out of retirement in '96.

Said Aouita (b. Nov. 2, 1959): Moroccan runner; won gold (5000m) and bronze (800m) in 1984 Olympics; won 5000m at 1987 World Championships; formerly held 2 world records recognized by IAAF— 2000m and 5000m.

Luis Aparicio (b. Apr. 29, 1934): Baseball SS; all-time leader in most games, assists, chances and double plays by shortstop; led AL in stolen bases 9 times (1956-64); 506 career steals.

Al Arbour (b. Nov. 1, 1932): Hockey; coached NY Islanders to 4 straight Stanley Cup titles (1980-83); retired after 1993-94 season 2nd on all-time career list with 902 wins (779 regular season and 123 postseason); elected to Hockey Hall of Fame in 1996.

Eddie Arcaro (b. Feb. 19, 1916): Jockey; 2-time Triple Crown winner (Whirlaway in 1941, Citation in '48); from 1938-52, he won Kentucky Derby 5 times, Preakness and Belmont 6 times each.

Roone Arledge (b. July 8, 1931): Sports TV innovator of live events, anthology shows, Olympic coverage and "Monday Night Football"; ran ABC Sports from 1968-86; has run ABC News since 1977.

Henry Armstrong (b. Dec. 12, 1912, d. Oct. 22, 1988): Boxer; held feather-, light- and welterweight titles simultaneously in 1938; pro record 145-20-9 with 98 KOs.

Arthur Ashe (b. July 10, 1943, d. Feb. 6, 1993): Tennis; first black man to win U.S. Championship (1968) and Wimbledon (1975); 1st U.S. player to earn $100,000 in 1 year (1970); won Davis Cup as player (1968-70) and captain (1981-82); wrote black sports history, Hard Road to Glory; announced in 1992 that he was infected with AIDS virus from a blood transfusion during 1983 heart surgery; died Feb. 6, 1993 at age 49; in 1997, the new home for the U.S. Open was named Arthur Ashe Stadium.

Evelyn Ashford (b. Apr. 15, 1957): Track & Field; winner of 4 Olympic gold medals— 100m in 1984, and 4x100m in 1984, '88 and '92; also won silver medal in 100m in '88; member of 5 U.S. Olympic teams (1976-92).

Red Auerbach (b. Sept. 20, 1917): Basketball; 2nd winningest coach (regular season and playoffs) in NBA history; won 1,037 times in 20 years; as coach-GM, led Boston to 9 NBA titles, including 8 in a row (1959-66); also coached defunct Washington Capitols (1946-49); NBA Coach of the Year award named after him; retired as Celtics coach in 1966 and as GM in '84; club president from 1970 to 1997.

Tracy Austin (b. Dec. 12, 1962): Tennis; youngest player to win U.S. Open (age 16 in 1979); won 2nd U.S. Open in '81; named AP Female Athlete of Year twice before she was 20; recurring neck and back injuries shortened career after 1983; youngest player ever inducted into Tennis Hall of Fame (age 29 in 1992).

Paul Azinger (b. Jan. 6, 1960): Golf; PGA Player of Year in 1987; 11 career wins, including '93 PGA Championship; missed 1st 7 months of '94 season overcoming lymphoma (a form of cancer) in right shoulder blade.

Donovan Bailey (b. Dec. 16, 1967): Track; Jamaican-born Canadian sprinter who is currently the world's fastest human; world record holder for the 100m (9.84) set in gold medal-winning performance at 1996 Olympics; set indoor record in 50M (5.56) in 1996; member of Canadian 4x100 relay that won gold in 1996 Olympics.

Oksana Baiul (b. Feb. 26, 1977): Ukrainian figure skater; 1993 world champion at age 15; edged Nancy Kerrigan by a 5-4 judges' vote for 1994 Olympic gold medal.

Hobey Baker (b. Jan. 15, 1892, d. Dec 21, 1918): Football and hockey star at Princeton (1911-14); member of college football and pro hockey halls of fame; college hockey Player of Year award named after him; killed in WWI plane crash.

Seve Ballesteros (b. Apr. 9, 1957): Spanish golfer; has won British Open 3 times (1979,84,88) and Masters twice (1980,83); 3-time European Golfer of Year (1986,88,91); has led Europe to 3 Ryder Cup titles (1985,87,89); 72 world-wide victories; captain of 1997 European Ryder Cup team.

Ernie Banks (b. Jan. 31, 1931): Baseball SS-1B; led NL in home runs and RBI twice each; 2-time MVP (1958-59) with Chicago Cubs; 512 career HRs.

Roger Bannister (b. Mar. 23, 1929): British runner; first to run mile in less than 4 minutes (3:59.4 on May 6, 1954).

Walter (Red) Barber (b. Feb. 17, 1908, d. Oct. 22, 1992): Radio-TV; renowned baseball play-by-play broadcaster for Cincinnati, Brooklyn and N.Y. Yankees from 1934-66; won Peabody Award for radio commentary in 1991.

Charles Barkley (b. Feb. 20, 1963): Basketball F; 5-time All-NBA 1st team with Philadelphia and Phoenix; traded to Suns for 3 players (June 17, 1992); U.S. Olympic Dream Team member in '92; NBA regular season MVP in 1993. Traded to Houston Rockets in 1996.

Rick Barry (b. Mar. 28, 1944): Basketball F; only player to lead both NBA and ABA in scoring; 5-time All-NBA 1st team; playoff MVP with Golden St. in 1975.

Sammy Baugh (b. Mar. 17, 1914): Football QB-DB-P; led Washington to NFL titles in 1937 (his rookie year) and '42; led league in passing 6 times, punting 4 times and interceptions once.

Elgin Baylor (b. Sept. 16, 1934): Basketball F; MVP of NCAA tournament in 1958; led Minneapolis-LA Lakers to 8 NBA Finals; 10-time All-NBA 1st team (1959-65,67-69).

Bob Beamon (b. Aug. 29, 1946): Track & Field; won 1968 Olympic gold medal in long jump with world record (29-ft, 2 1/2 in.) that shattered old mark by nearly 2 feet; record finally broken by 2 inches in 1991 by Mike Powell.

Franz Beckenbauer (b. Sept. 11, 1945): Soccer; captain of West German World Cup champions in 1974 then coached West Germany to World Cup title in 1990; invented sweeper position; played in U.S. for NY Cosmos (1977-80,83).

Boris Becker (b. Nov. 22, 1967): German tennis player; 3-time Wimbledon champ (1985-86,89); youngest male (17) to win Wimbledon; led country to 1st Davis Cup win in 1988; has also won U.S. (1989) and Australian (1991,96) Opens; announced his retirement after being eliminated by Pete Sampras at 1997 Wimbledon.

Chuck Bednarik (b. May 1, 1925): Football C-LB; 2-time All-America at Penn and 7-time All-Pro with NFL Philadelphia Eagles as both center (1950) and linebacker (1951-56); missed only 3 games in 14 seasons; led Eagles to 1960 NFL title as a 35-year-old two-way player.

Clair Bee (b. Mar. 2, 1896, d. May 20, 1983): Basketball coach who led LIU to 2 undefeated seasons (1936,39) and 2 NIT titles (1939,41); his teams won 95 percent of their games between 1931-51, including 43 in a row from 1935-37; coached NBA Baltimore Bullets from 1952-54, but was only 34-116; contributions to game include 1-3-1 zone defense, 3-second rule and NBA 24-second clock; also authored sports manuals and fictional Chip Hilton sports books for kids.

Jean Beliveau (b. Aug. 31, 1931): Hockey C; led Montreal to 10 Stanley Cups in 17 playoffs; playoff MVP (1965); 2-time regular season MVP (1956,64).

Bert Bell (b. Feb. 25, 1895, d. Oct. 11, 1959): Football; team owner and 2nd NFL commissioner (1946-59); proposed college draft in 1935 and instituted TV blackout rule.

Albert Belle (b. August 25, 1966): Baseball OF; tremendous hitter and stupendous troublemaker; in strike–shortened 1995 season, became first player in major league history to hit 50 home runs and 50 doubles in the same season; all-time Cleveland Indians home run leader with 242; five-time All-Star; three-time AL RBI leader; in 1996, was fined $50,000 for a profanity-laced tirade he aimed at NBC's Hannah Storm during 1895 World Series; also in 1996, was suspended for a brutal hit on Milwaukee's Fernando Vina, although the suspension was reduced from five to three to two games; suspended in 1994 for ten games for using a corked bat.

Deane Beman (b. Apr. 22, 1938): Golf; 1st commissioner of PGA Tour (1974-94); introduced "stadium golf"; as player, won U.S. Amateur twice and British Amateur once.

Johnny Bench (b. Dec. 7, 1947): Baseball C; led NL in HRs twice and RBI 3 times; 2-time regular season MVP (1970,72) with Cincinnati, World Series MVP in 1976; 389 career HRs.

Patty Berg (b. Feb. 13, 1918): Golfer; 57 career pro wins including 15 Majors; 3-time AP Female Athlete of Year (1938,43,55).

Chris Berman (b. May 10, 1955): Radio-TV; 5-time Sportscaster of Year known for his nicknames and jovial studio anchoring on ESPN; play-by-play man only year Brown University football team won Ivy League (1976); began doing weekly highlights on "Monday Night Football" in 1996.

Yogi Berra (b. May 12, 1925): Baseball C; played on 10 World Series winners with NY Yankees; holds several WS records — games played (75), at bats (259) and hits (71); 3-time AL MVP (1951,54-55); managed both Yankees (1964) and NY Mets (1973) to pennants.

Jay Berwanger (b. Mar. 19, 1914): Football HB; University of Chicago star; won 1st Heisman Trophy in 1935.

Gary Bettman (b. June 2, 1952): Hockey; former NBA executive, who was named first commissioner of NHL on Dec. 11, 1992; took office on Feb. 1, 1993.

Abebe Bikila (b. Aug. 7, 1932, d. Oct. 25, 1973): Ethiopian runner; 1st to win consecutive Olympic marathons (1960,64).

Matt Biondi (b. Oct. 8, 1965): Swimmer; won 7 medals in 1988 Olympics, including 5 gold (2 individual, 3 relay); has won a total of 11 medals (8 gold, 2 silver and a bronze) in 3 Olympics (1984,88,92).

Larry Bird (b. Dec. 7, 1956): Basketball F; college Player of Year (1979) at Indiana St.; 1980 NBA Rookie of Year; 9-time All-NBA 1st team; 3-time regular season MVP (1984-86); led Boston to 3 NBA titles (1981,84, 86); 2-time playoff MVP (1984,86); U.S. Olympic Dream Team member in '92; in 1997, named coach of Indiana Pacers.

The Black Sox: Eight Chicago White Sox players who were banned from baseball for life in 1921 for allegedly throwing the 1919 World Series— RHP Eddie Cicotte (1884-1969), OF Happy Felsch (1891-1964), 1B Chick Gandil (1887-1970), OF Shoeless Joe Jackson (1889-1951), INF Fred McMullin (1891-1952), SS Swede Risberg (1894-1975), 3B-SS Buck Weaver (1890-1956), and LHP Lefty Williams (1893-1959).

Earl (Red) Blaik (b. Feb. 15, 1897, d. May 6, 1989): Football; coached Army to consecutive national titles in 1944-45; 166 career wins and 3 Heisman winners (Blanchard, Davis, Dawkins).

Bonnie Blair (b. Mar. 18, 1964): Speedskater; only American woman to win 5 Olympic gold medals in Winter or Summer Games; won 500-meters in 1988, then 500m and 1,000m in both 1992 and '94; added 1,000m bronze in 1988; Sullivan Award winner (1992); retired on 31st birthday as reigning world sprint champ.

Hector (Toe) Blake (b. Aug. 21, 1912, d. May 17, 1995): Hockey LW; led Montreal to 2 Stanley Cups as a player and 8 more as coach; regular season MVP in 1939.

Felix (Doc) Blanchard (b. Dec. 11, 1924): Football FB; 3-time All-America; led Army to national titles in 1944-45; Glenn Davis' running mate; won Heisman Trophy and Sullivan Award in 1945.

George Blanda (b. Sept. 17, 1927): Football QB-PK; NFL's all-time leading scorer (2,002 points); led Houston to 2 AFL titles (1960-61); played 26 pro seasons; retired at 48.

Fanny Blankers-Koen (b. Apr. 26, 1918): Dutch sprinter; 30-year-old mother of two, who won 4 gold medals (100m, 200m, 800m hurdles and 4x100m relay) at 1948 Olympics.

Drew Bledsoe (b. Feb. 14, 1972): Football QB; 1st overall pick in 1993 NFL draft (by New England); holds NFL single-season record for most passes attempted (691) and single-game records for most passes completed (45), attempted (70); entered 1996 season as highest-paid player in NFL ($42 million over 7 years).

Wade Boggs (b. June 15, 1958): Baseball 3B; 5 AL batting titles (1983,85-88) with Boston Red Sox; 11-time All-Star; two Gold Gloves; signed with New York Yankees in 1992; member of 1996 World Series champion Yankees.

Barry Bonds (b. July 24, 1964): Baseball OF; 3-time NL MVP, twice with Pittsburgh (1990,92) and once with San Francisco (1993); NL's HR and RBI leader in 1993; became only second player to hit 40 homers and steal 40 bases in same season in 1996; son of Bobby.

Bjorn Borg (b. June 6, 1956): Swedish tennis player; 2-time Player of Year (1979-80); won 6 French Opens and 5 straight Wimbledons (1976-80); led Sweden to 1st Davis Cup win in 1975; retired in 1983 at age 26; attempted unsuccessful comeback in 1991.

Mike Bossy (b. Jan. 22, 1957): Hockey RW; led NY Isles to 4 Stanley Cups; playoff MVP in 1982; scored 50 goals or more 9 straight years; 573 career goals.

Ralph Boston (b. May 9, 1939): Track & Field; medaled in 3 consecutive Olympic long jumps— gold (1960), silver (1964), bronze (1968).

Ray Bourque (b. Dec. 28, 1960): Hockey D; 11-time all-NHL 1st team, has won Norris Trophy 5 times (1987-88,1990-91,94) with Boston. '96 All-Star Game MVP.

Bobby Bowden (b. Nov. 8, 1929): Football; coached Florida St. to a national title in 1993; over 270 career wins, including a 15-4-1 bowl record in 31 years as coach at Samford, West Va. and FSU; father of Terry.

Terry Bowden (b. Feb. 24, 1956): Football; led Auburn to 11-0 record in his first season as Division I-A head coach in 1993; NCAA probation earned under previous staff prevented bowl appearance; son of Bobby.

Riddick Bowe (b. Aug. 10, 1967): Boxing; won world heavyweight title with unanimous decision over champion Evander Holyfield on Nov. 13, 1992; lost title to Holyfield on majority decision Nov. 6, 1993; in 1996, was fined $250,000 because members of his entourage caused a riot at Madison Square Garden after opponent Andrew Golota was disqualified for repeated low blows; joined the Marines for a few days in 1997 and then quit.

Scotty Bowman (b. Sept. 18, 1933): Hockey coach; all-time winningest NHL coach in both regular season and playoffs over 25 seasons; led Montreal to 5 Stanley Cups (1973,76-79) and Pittsburgh to another (1992) and Detroit to yet another (1997).

Jack Brabham (b. Apr. 2, 1926): Australian auto racer; 3-time Formula One champion (1959-60,66); 14 career wins.

Bill Bradley (b. July 28, 1943): Basketball F; 3-time All-America at Princeton; Player of Year and NCAA tourney MVP in 1965; captain of gold medal-winning 1964 U.S. Olympic team; Sullivan Award winner (1965); led NY Knicks to 2 NBA titles (1970,73); U.S. Senator (D, N.J.) since 1979, but announced in 1995 he would not seek re-election in '96.

Pat Bradley (b. Mar. 24, 1951): Golfer; 2-time LPGA Player of Year (1986,91); has won all four majors on LPGA tour, including 3 du Maurier Classics; inducted into the LPGA Hall of Fame on Jan. 18, 1992; entered 1995 as all-time LPGA money leader and 13th in wins (30).

Terry Bradshaw (b. Sept. 2, 1948): Football QB; led Pittsburgh to 4 Super Bowl titles (1975-76,79-80); 2-time Super Bowl MVP (1979-80).

George Brett (b. May 15, 1953): Baseball 3B-1B; AL batting champion in 3 different decades (1976,80,90); MVP in 1980; led KC to World Series title in 1985; retired after 1993 season with 3,154 hits and .305 career average.

Valerie Brisco-Hooks (b. July 6, 1960): Track & Field; won three gold medals at the 1984 Olympics (200 meters, 400 meters and 4x100 relay); first athlete to ever win the 200 and 400 in the same Olympic (note: the 1984 games were boycotted by the Soviet bloc); first American woman to break 50 seconds in the 400 meter run.

Lou Brock (b. June 18, 1939): Baseball OF; former all-time stolen base leader (938); led NL in steals 8 times; led St. Louis to 2 World Series titles (1964,67); had 3,023 career hits.

Herb Brooks (b. Aug. 5, 1937): Hockey; former U.S. Olympic player (1964,68) who coached 1980 team to gold medal; coached Minnesota to 3 NCAA titles (1974,76,78); also coached NY Rangers, Minnesota and New Jersey in NHL.

Jim Brown (b. Feb. 17, 1936): Football FB; All-America at Syracuse (1956) and NFL Rookie of Year (1957); led NFL in rushing 8 times; 8-time All-Pro (1957-61,63-65); 3-time MVP (1958,63,65) with Cleveland; ran for 12,312 yards and scored 756 points in just 9 seasons.

Larry Brown (b. Sept. 14, 1940): Basketball; played in ACC, AAU, 1964 Olympics and ABA; 3-time assist leader (1968-70) and 3-time Coach of Year (1973,75-76) in ABA; coached ABA's Carolina and Denver and NBA's Denver, N. J., San Antonio, LA Clippers, Indiana and Phila.; also coached UCLA to Final Four (1980) and Kansas to NCAA title (1988).

Mordecai (Three-Finger) Brown (b. Oct. 18, 1876, d. Feb. 14, 1948): Baseball; nickname derived from loss of three fingers in a childhood accident; injury gave him a particularly nasty curve ball; won the decisive game of the the 1907 World Series as a Chicago Cub; in 1908, first pitcher to record 4 consecutive shutouts and his overall record was 29-9; career record of 239-130 with lifetime E.R.A. of 2.06; member of Baseball Hall of Fame.

Paul Brown (b. Sept. 7, 1908, d. Aug. 5, 1991): Football innovator; coached Ohio St. to national title in 1942; in pros, directed Cleveland Browns to 4 straight AAFC titles (1946-49) and 3 NFL titles (1950,54-55); formed Cincinnati Bengals as head coach and part-owner in 1968 (reached playoffs in '70).

Sergi Bruguera (b. Jan. 16, 1971): Spanish tennis player; won consecutive French Opens in 1993 and '94; entered 1996 as decade's winningest clay court player.

Valery Brumel (b. Apr. 14, 1942): Soviet high jumper; dominated event from 1961-64; broke world record 5 times; won silver medal in 1960 Olympics and gold in 1964; highest jump was 7-5.

Avery Brundage (b. Sept. 28, 1887, d. May 5, 1975): Amateur sports czar for over 40 years as president of AAU (1928-35), U.S. Olympic Committee (1929-53) and International Olympic Committee (1952-72).

Paul (Bear) Bryant (b. Sept. 11, 1913, d. Jan. 26, 1983): Football; coached at 4 colleges over 38 years; directed Alabama to 5 national titles (1961,64-65,78-79); 323 career wins; 15 bowl wins including 8 Sugar Bowls.

Sergey Bubka (b. Dec. 4, 1963): Ukrainian pole vaulter; 1st man to clear 20 feet both indoors and out (1991); holder of indoor (20-2) and outdoor (20-13/4) world records as of Sept. 10, 1995; 6-time world champion (1983,87,91,93,95,97); won Olympic gold medal in 1988, but failed to clear any height in 1992 Games.

Buck Buchanan (b. Sept. 10, 1940, d. July 16, 1992): Football; played both ways in college at Grambling; first player chosen in the first AFL draft by the Dallas Texans who later became the Kansas City Chiefs; missed one game in a 13-year pro career; played in six AFL All-Star games and two Pro Bowls at defensive tackle; defensive star of the Chiefs team that won Super Bowl IV; later coached for the New Orleans Saints and Cleveland Browns; member of Pro Football Hall of Fame.

Don Budge (b. June 13, 1915): Tennis; in 1938 became 1st player to win the Grand Slam— the French, Wimbledon, U.S. and Australian titles in 1 year; led U.S. to 2 Davis Cups (1937-38); turned pro in late '38.

Maria Bueno (b. Oct. 11, 1939): Brazilian tennis player; won 4 U.S. Championships (1959,63-64,66) and 3 Wimbledons (1959-60,64).

Leroy Burrell (b. Feb. 21, 1967): Track & Field; set former world record of 9.85 in 100 meters, July 6, 1994; previously held record (9.90) in 1991; member of 4 world record-breaking 4 x 100m relay teams.

George Bush (b. June 12, 1924): 41st President of U.S. (1989-93) and avid sportsman; played 1B on 1947 and '48 Yale baseball teams that placed 2nd in College World Series; captain of 1948 team.

Susan Butcher (b. Dec. 26, 1956): Sled Dog racer; 4-time winner of Iditarod Trail race (1986-88,90).

Dick Butkus (b. Dec. 9, 1942): Football LB; 2-time All-America at Illinois (1963-64); All-Pro 7 of 9 NFL seasons with Chicago Bears.

Dick Button (b. July 18, 1929): Figure skater; 5-time world champion (1948-52); 2-time Olympic champ (1948,52); Sullivan Award winner (1949); won Emmy Award as Best Analyst for 1980-81 TV season.

Walter Byers (b. Mar. 13, 1922): College athletics; 1st executive director of NCAA, serving from 1951-88.

Frank Calder (b. Nov. 17, 1877, d. Feb. 4, 1943): Hockey; 1st NHL president (1917-43); guided league through its formative years; NHL's Rookie of the Year award named after him.

Lee Calhoun (b. Feb. 23, 1933, d. June 22, 1989): Track & Field; won consecutive Olympic gold medals in the 110m hurdles (1956,60).

Walter Camp (b. Apr. 7, 1859, d. Mar. 14, 1925): Football coach and innovator; established scrimmage line, center snap, downs, 11 players per side; elected 1st All-America team (1889).

Roy Campanella (b. Nov. 19, 1921, d. June 26, 1993): Baseball C; 3-time NL MVP (1951,53,55); led Brooklyn to 5 pennants and 1st World Series title (1955); career cut short when 1958 car accident left him paralyzed.

Clarence Campbell (b. July 9, 1905, d. June 24, 1984): Hockey; 3rd NHL president (1946-77), league tripled in size from 6 to 18 teams during his tenure.

Earl Campbell (b. Mar. 29, 1955): Football RB; won Heisman Trophy in 1977; led NFL in rushing 3 times; 3-time All-Pro; 2-time MVP (1978-79) at Houston.

John Campbell (b. Apr. 8, 1955): Harness racing; 4-time winner of Hambletonian (1987,88,90,95); 3-time Driver of Year; first driver to go over $100 million in career winnings; entered 1996 with 7,019 career wins.

Milt Campbell (b. Dec. 9, 1933): Track & Field; won silver medal in 1952 Olympic decathlon and gold medal in '56.

Jimmy Cannon (b. 1910, d. Dec. 5, 1973): Tough, opinionated New York sportswriter and essayist who viewed sports as an extension of show business; protégé of Damon Runyon; covered World War II for *Stars & Stripes*.

Tony Canzoneri (b. Nov. 6, 1908, d. Dec. 9, 1959): Boxer; 2-time world lightweight champion (1930-33,35-36); pro record 141-24-10 with 44 KOs.

Jennifer Capriati (b. Mar. 29, 1976): Tennis; youngest Grand Slam semifinalist ever (age 14 in 1990 French Open); also youngest to win a match at Wimbledon (1990); upset Steffi Graf to win gold medal at 1992 Olympics; left tour in '94 due to personal problems including an arrest for marijuana possession.

Harry Caray (b. Mar. 1, 1917): Radio-TV; baseball play-by-play broadcaster for St. Louis Cardinals, Oakland, Chicago White Sox and Cubs since 1945; father of sportscaster Skip and grandfather of sportscaster Chip.

Rod Carew (b. Oct. 1, 1945): Baseball 2B-1B; led AL in batting 7 times (1969,72-75,77-78) with Minnesota; MVP in 1977; had 3,053 career hits.

Steve Carlton (b. Dec. 22, 1944): Baseball LHP; won 20 or more games 6 times; 4-time Cy Young winner (1972,77,80,82) with Philadelphia; 329 career wins.

JoAnne Carner (b. Apr. 4, 1939): Golfer; 5-time U.S. Amateur champion; 2-time U.S. Open champ; 3-time LPGA Player of Year (1974,81-82); 7th in career wins (42).

Cris Carter (b. Nov. 25, 1965): Football; wide receiver for the Minnesota Vikings; twice caught 122 passes in a season (1994, '95), the first time establishing an NFL record for catches in a season that was beaten by the Detroit Lions' Herman Moore the next year.

Don Carter (b. July 29, 1926): Bowler; 6-time Bowler of Year (1953-54,57-58,60-61); voted Greatest of All-Time in 1970.

Joe Carter (b. Mar. 7, 1960): Baseball OF; 3-time All-America at Wichita St. (1979-81); won 1993 World Series for Toronto with 3-run HR in bottom of the 9th of Game 6.

Alexander Cartwright (b. Apr. 17, 1820, d. July 12, 1892): Baseball; engineer and draftsman who spread gospel of baseball from New York City to California gold fields; widely regarded as the father of modern game; his guidelines included setting 3 strikes for an out and 3 outs for each half inning.

Billy Casper (b. June 4, 1931): Golfer; 2-time PGA Player of Year (1966,70); has won U.S. Open (1959,66), Masters (1970), U.S. Senior Open (1983); compiled 51 PGA wins and 9 on Senior Tour.

Tracy Caulkins (b. Jan. 11, 1963): Swimmer; won 3 gold medals (2 individual) at 1984 Olympics; set 5 world records and won 48 U.S. national titles from 1978-84; Sullivan Award winner (1978); 2-time Honda Broderick Cup winner (1982,84).

Evonne Goolagong Cawley (b. July 31, 1951): Australian tennis player; won Australian Open 4 times, Wimbledon twice (1971,79), French once.

Florence Chadwick (b. Nov. 9, 1917, d. Mar. 15, 1995): Dominant distance swimmer of 1950's; set English Channel records from France to England (1950) and England to France (1951 and '55).

Wilt Chamberlain (b. Aug. 21, 1936): Basketball C; consensus All-America in 1957 and '58 at Kansas; Final Four MVP in 1957; led NBA in scoring 7 times and rebounding 11 times; 7-time All-NBA first team; 4-time MVP (1960,66-68) in Philadelphia; scored 100 points vs. NY Knicks in Hershey, Pa., Mar. 2, 1962; led Philadelphia 76ers (1967) and LA Lakers (1972) to NBA titles; playoff MVP in 1972.

A.B. (Happy) Chandler (b. July 14, 1898, d. June 15, 1991): Baseball; former Kentucky governor and U.S. Senator who succeeded Judge Landis as commissioner in 1945; backed Branch Rickey's move in 1947 to make Jackie Robinson 1st black player in major leagues; deemed too pro-player and ousted by owners in 1951.

Julio Cesar Chavez (b. July 12, 1962): Mexican boxer; world jr. welterweight champ; also held titles as jr. lightweight (1984-87) and lightweight (1987-89); fought Pernell Whitaker to controversial draw for welterweight title on Sept. 10, 1993; career record of 97-1-1 record with 79 KOs; 90-bout unbeaten streak ended Jan. 29, 1994 when Frankie Randall won title on split decision; Chavez won title back four months later.

Linford Christie (b. Apr. 2, 1960): British sprinter; won 100-meter gold medals at both 1992 Olympics (9.96) and '93 World Championships (9.87); set indoor world record in 200-meters (20.25) on Feb. 19, 1995 in Lievin, France.

Jim Clark (b. Mar. 14, 1936, d. Apr. 7, 1968): Scottish auto racer; 2-time Formula One world champion (1963,65); won Indy 500 in 1965; killed in car crash.

Bobby Clarke (b. Aug. 13, 1949): Hockey C; led Philadelphia Flyers to consecutive Stanley Cups in 1974-75; 3-time regular season MVP (1973,75-76); currently Flyers general manager.

Ron Clarke (b. Feb. 21, 1937): Australian runner; from 1963-70 set 17 world records in races from 2 miles to 20,000 meters; never won Olympic gold medal.

Roger Clemens (b. Aug. 4, 1962): Baseball RHP; twice fanned MLB record 20 batters in 9-inning game (April 29, 1986 and Sept. 18, 1996); 3 Cy Young Awards (1986-87,91) with Boston; AL MVP in 1986; signed free agent contract with Toronto Blue Jays in December of 1996.

Roberto Clemente (b. Aug. 18, 1934, d. Dec. 31, 1972): Baseball OF; hit .300 or better 13 times with Pittsburgh; led NL in batting 4 times; World Series MVP in 1971; regular season MVP in 1966; had 3,000 career hits; killed in plane crash.

Ty Cobb (b. Dec. 18, 1886, d. July 17, 1961): Baseball OF; all-time highest career batting average (.367); hit .400 or better 3 times; led AL in batting 12 times and stolen bases 6 times with Detroit; MVP in 1911; had 4,191 career hits and 892 steals.

Mickey Cochrane (b. Apr. 6, 1903, d. June 28, 1962): Baseball C; led Philadelphia A's (1929-30) and Detroit (1935) to 3 World Series titles; 2-time AL MVP (1928,34).

Sebastian Coe (b. Sept. 29, 1956): British runner; won gold medal in 1500m and silver medal in 800m at both 1980 and '84 Olympics; long time world record holder in 800m and 1000m; elected to Parliament as Conservative in 1992.

Paul Coffey (b. June 1, 1961): Hockey D; holds NHL record for goals, assists and points by a defenseman; member of four Stanley Cup championship teams at Edmonton (1984-85,87) and Pittsburgh (1991).

Eddie Collins (b. May 2, 1887, d. Mar. 25, 1951): Baseball 2B; led Philadelphia A's (1910-11) and Chicago White Sox (1917) to 3 World Series titles; AL MVP in 1914; had 3,311 career hits and 743 stolen bases.

Nadia Comaneci (b. Nov. 12, 1961): Romanian gymnast; 1st to record perfect 10 in Olympics; won 3 individual gold medals at 1976 Olympics and 2 more in '80.

Lionel Conacher (b. May 24, 1901, d. May 26, 1954): Canada's greatest all-around athlete; NHL hockey (2 Stanley Cups), CFL football (1 Grey Cup), minor league baseball, soccer, lacrosse, track, amateur boxing champion; also member of Parliament (1949-54).

Gene Conley (b. Nov. 10, 1930): Baseball and Basketball; played for World Series and NBA champions with Milwaukee Braves (1957) and Boston Celtics (1959-61); winning pitcher in 1954 All-Star Game; won 91 games in 11 seasons.

Billy Conn (b. Oct. 8, 1917, d. May 29, 1993): Boxer; Pittsburgh native and world light heavyweight champion from 1939-41; nearly upset heavyweight champ Joe Louis in 1941 title bout, but was knocked out in 13th round; pro record 63-11-1 with 14 KOs.

Dennis Conner (b. Sept. 16, 1942): Sailing; 3-time America's Cup-winning skipper aboard *Freedom* (1980), *Stars & Stripes* (1987) and the *Stars & Stripes* catamaran (1988); only American skipper to lose Cup, first in 1983 when *Australia II* beat *Liberty* and again in '95 when New Zealand's *Black* Magic swept Conner and his *Stars & Stripes* crew aboard the borrowed *Young America*.

Maureen Connolly (b. Sept. 17, 1934, d. June 21, 1969): Tennis; in 1953 1st woman to win Grand Slam (at age 19); riding accident ended her career in '54; won both Wimbledon and U.S. titles 3 times (1951-53); 3-time AP Female Athlete of Year (1951-53).

Jimmy Connors (b. Sept. 2, 1952): Tennis; No.1 player in world 5 times (1974-78); won 5 U.S. Opens, 2 Wimbledons and 1 Australian; rose from No. 936 at the close of 1990 to U.S. Open semifinals in 1991 at age 39; NCAA singles champ (1971); all-time leader in pro singles titles (109) and matches won at U.S. Open (98) and Wimbledon (84).

Jack Kent Cooke (b. Oct. 25, 1912, d. April 6, 1997): Football; sole owner of NFL Washington Redskins from 1985-97; teams have won 2 Super Bowls (1987,91); also owned NBA Lakers and NHL Kings in LA; built LA Forum for $12 million in 1967.

Cynthia Cooper (b. April 14, 1963): Women's basketball G; won two NCAA basketball titles at USC in 1983-84; far and away the best player in the inaugural season of the WNBA; unanimous MVP selection for regular season and championship series; led Houston Comets over New York Liberty in title game with 25 points, 4 rebounds and 4 assists; played in Europe between college and WNBA, winning various scoring titles, shooting contests and MVP awards.

Angel Cordero Jr. (b. Nov. 8, 1942): Jockey; third on all-time list with 7,057 wins in 38,646 starts; won Kentucky Derby 3 times (1974,76,85), Preakness twice and Belmont once; 2-time Eclipse Award winner (1982-83); resumed career on Oct. 1, 1995 after retiring in 1992.

Howard Cosell (b. Mar. 25, 1920, d. Apr. 23, 1995): Radio-TV; former ABC commentator on *Monday Night Football* and *Wide World of Sports*, who energized TV sports journalism with abrasive "tell it like it is" style.

Bob Costas (b. Mar. 22, 1952): Radio-TV; NBC anchor for NBA, NFL and Summer Olympics as well as baseball play-by-play man; 6-time Emmy winner and Sportscaster of Year.

James (Doc) Counsilman (b. Dec. 28, 1920): Swimming; coached Indiana men's swim team to 6 NCAA championships (1968-73); coached the 1964 and '76 U.S. men's Olympic teams that won a combined 21 of 24 gold medals; in 1979 became oldest person (59) to swim English Channel; retired in 1990 with dual meet record of 287-36-1.

Fred Couples (b. Oct. 3, 1959): Golfer; 2-time PGA Tour Player of the Year (1991,92); 12 Tour victories, including 1992 Masters.

Jim Courier (b. Aug. 17, 1970): Tennis; No. 1 player in world in 1992, has won two Australian Opens (1992-93) and two French (1991-92); played on 1992 Davis Cup winner; Nick Bollettieri Academy classmate of Andre Agassi.

Margaret Smith Court (b. July 16, 1942): Australian tennis player; won Grand Slam in both singles (1970) and mixed doubles (1963 with Ken Fletcher); 26 Grand Slam singles titles— 11 Australian, 7 U.S., 5 French and 3 Wimbledon.

Bob Cousy (b. Aug. 9, 1928): Basketball G; led NBA in assists 8 times; 10-time All-NBA 1st team (1952-61); MVP in 1957; led Boston to 6 NBA titles (1957,59-63).

Buster Crabbe (b. Feb. 7, 1910, d. Apr. 23, 1983): Swimmer; 2-time Olympic freestyle medalist with bronze in 1928 (1500m) and gold in '32 (400m); became movie star and King of Serials as Flash Gordon and Buck Rogers.

Ben Crenshaw (b. Jan. 11, 1952): Golfer; co-NCAA champion with Tom Kite in 1972; battled Graves' disease in mid-1980's; 19 career Tour victories; won Masters for second time on April 9, 1995 and dedicated it to 90-year-old mentor Harvey Penick, who had died on April 2.

Joe Cronin (b. Oct. 12, 1906, d. Sept. 7, 1984): Baseball SS; hit over .300 and drove in over 100 runs 8 times each; MVP in 1930; player-manager in Washington and Boston (1933-47); AL president (1959-73).

Ann Curtis (b. Mar. 6, 1926): Swimming; won 2 gold medals and 1 silver in 1948 Olympics; set 4 world and 18 U.S. records during career; 1st woman and swimmer to win Sullivan Award (1944).

Betty Cuthbert (b. Apr. 20, 1938): Australian runner; won gold medals in 100 and 200 meters and 4x100m relay at 1956 Olympics; also won 400m gold at 1964 Olympics.

Chuck Daly (b. July 20, 1930): Basketball; coached Detroit to two NBA titles (1989-90) before leaving in 1992 to coach New Jersey; retired after 1993-94 season with 638 career wins (including playoffs) in 12 years; coached NBA "Dream Team" to gold medal in 1992 Olympics; unretired in 1997 to coach Orlando Magic.

John Daly (b. Apr. 28, 1966): Golfer; surprise winner of 1991 PGA Championship as unknown 25-year-old; battled through personal troubles in 1994 to return in '95 and win 2nd major at British Open, beating Italy's Costantino Rocca in 4-hole playoff.

Stanley Dancer (b. July 25, 1927): Harness racing; winner of 4 Hambletonians; trainer-driver of Triple Crown winners in Trotting (Nevele Pride in 1968 and Super Bowl in '72) and Pacing (Most Happy Fella in 1970); entered 1995 with 3,780 career wins.

Tamas Darnyi (b. June 3, 1967): Hungarian swimmer; 2-time double gold medal winner in 200m and 400m individual medley at 1988 and '92 Olympics; also won both events in 1986 and '91 world championships; set world records in both at '91 worlds; 1st swimmer to break 2 minutes in 200m IM (1:59:36).

Al Davis (b. July 4, 1929): Football; GM-coach of Oakland 1963-66; helped force AFL-NFL merger as AFL commissioner (April-July 1966); returned to Oakland as managing general partner and directed club to 3 Super Bowl wins (1977,81,84); defied fellow NFL owners and moved Raiders to LA in 1982; turned down owners' 1995 offer to build him a new stadium in LA and moved back to Oakland instead.

Dwight Davis (b. July 5, 1879, d. Nov. 28, 1945): Tennis; donor of Davis Cup; played for winning U.S. team in 1st two Cup finals (1900,02); won U.S. and Wimbledon doubles titles in 1901; Secretary of War (1925-29) under Coolidge.

Glenn Davis (b. Dec. 26, 1924): Football HB; 3-time All-America; led Army to national titles in 1944-45; Doc Blanchard's running mate; won Heisman Trophy in 1946.

John Davis (b. Jan. 12, 1921, d. July 13, 1984): Weightlifting; 6-time world champion; 2-time Olympic super-heavyweight champ (1948,52); undefeated from 1938-53.

Dizzy Dean (b. Jan. 16 1911, d. July 17, 1974): Baseball RHP; led NL in strikeouts and complete games 4 times; last NL pitcher to win 30 games (30-7 in 1934); MVP in 1934 with St. Louis; 150 career wins.

Dave DeBusschere (b. Oct. 16, 1940): Basketball F; 3-time All-America at Detroit; youngest coach in NBA history (24 in 1964); player-coach of Detroit Pistons (1964-67); played in 8 All-Star games; won 2 NBA titles as player with NY Knicks; ABA commissioner (1975-76); also pitched 2 seasons for Chicago White Sox (1962-63) with 3-4 record.

Pierre de Coubertin (b. Jan. 1, 1863, d. Sept. 2, 1937): French educator; father of the Modern Olympic Games; IOC president from 1896-1925.

Anita DeFrantz (b. Oct. 4, 1952): Olympics; attorney who is one of 2 American delegates to the International Olympic Committee (James Easton is the other); first woman to represent U.S. on IOC; member of USOC Executive Committee; member of bronze medal U.S. women's eight-oared shell at Montreal in 1976.

Cedric Dempsey (b. Apr. 14, 1932): College sports; named to succeed Dick Schultz as NCAA executive director on Nov. 5, 1993; served as athletic director at Pacific (1967-79), San Diego St. (1979), Houston (1979-82) and Arizona (1983-93).

Jack Dempsey (b. June 24, 1895, d. May 31, 1983): Boxer; world heavyweight champion from 1919-26; lost title to Gene Tunney, then lost "Long Count" rematch in 1927 when he floored Tunney in 7th round but failed to retreat to neutral corner; pro record 62-6-10 with 49 KOs.

Bob Devaney (b. April 13, 1915, d. May 9, 1997): Football; head coach at Wyoming from 1957-1961; from 1962 to 1972 built Nebraska into a college football power; won two consecutive national championships in 1970-'71; won eight Big Eight Conference titles; overall record of 136-30-11; later served as Nebraska's athletic director; College Football Hall of Fame.

Donna de Varona (b. Apr. 26, 1947): Swimming; won gold medals in 400 IM and 400 freestyle relay at 1964 Olympics; set 18 world records during career; co-founder of Women's Sports Foundation in 1974.

Gail Devers (b. Nov. 19, 1966): Track & Field; fastest-ever woman sprinter-hurdler; overcame thyroid disorder (Graves' disease) that sidelined her in 1989-90 and nearly resulted in having both feet amputated; won Olympic gold medal in 100 meters in 1992 and '96; 3-time world champion in 100 meters (1993) and 100-meter hurdles (1993,95).

Klaus Dibiasi (b. Oct. 6, 1947): Italian diver; won 3 consecutive Olympic gold medals in platform event (1968,72,76).

Eric Dickerson (b. Sept. 2, 1960): Football RB; led NFL in rushing 4 times (1983-84,86,88); ran for single-season record 2,105 yards in 1984; NFC Rookie of Year in 1983; All-Pro 5 times; traded from LA Rams to Indianapolis (Oct. 31, 1987) in 3-team, 10-player deal (including draft picks) that also involved Buffalo; 2nd on all-time career rushing list with 13,259 yards in 11 seasons.

Harrison Dillard (b. July 8, 1923): Track & Field; only man to win Olympic gold medals in both sprints (100m in 1948) and hurdles (110m in 1952).

Joe DiMaggio (b. Nov. 25, 1914): Baseball OF; hit safely in 56 straight games (1941); led AL in batting, HRs and RBI twice each; 3-time MVP (1939,41,47); hit .325 with 361 HRs over 13 seasons; led NY Yankees to 10 World Series titles.

Mike Ditka (b. Oct. 18, 1939): Football; All-America at Pitt (1960); NFL Rookie of Year (1961); 5-time Pro Bowl tight end for Chicago Bears; also played for Philadelphia and Dallas in 12-year career; returned to Chicago as head coach in 1982; won Super Bowl XX; compiled 112-68-0 record in 11 seasons with Bears; left Bears in 1992 and worked as a broadcaster at NBC for four years; named head coach of New Orleans Saints in 1997.

Charlotte (Lottie) Dod (b. Sept. 24, 1871, d. June 27, 1960): British athlete; was 5-time Wimbledon singles champion (1887-88,91-93); youngest player ever to win Wimbledon (15 in 1887); archery silver medalist at 1908 Olympics; member of national field hockey team in 1899; British Amateur golf champ in 1904.

Tony Dorsett (b. Apr. 7, 1954): Football RB; won Heisman Trophy leading Pitt to national title in 1976; all-time NCAA Div. I-A rushing leader with 6,082 yards; led Dallas to Super Bowl title as NFC Rookie of Year (1977); NFC Player of Year (1981); ranks 3rd on all-time NFL list with 12,739 yards gained in 12 years; holds NFL record for run from scrimmage (99 yards vs. Min. in 1983).

James (Buster) Douglas (b. Apr. 7, 1960): Boxing; 50-1 shot who knocked out undefeated Mike Tyson in 10th round on Feb. 10, 1990 to win heavyweight title in Tokyo; 10 months later, lost only title defense to Evander Holyfield by KO in 3rd round.

The Dream Team Head coach Chuck Daly's "Best Ever" 12-man NBA All-Star squad that headlined the 1992 Summer Olympics in Barcelona and easily won the basketball gold medal; co-captained by Larry Bird and Magic Johnson, with veterans Charles Barkley, Clyde Drexler, Patrick Ewing, Michael Jordan, Karl Malone, Chris Mullin, Scottie Pippen, David Robinson, John Stockton and rookie Christian Laettner.

Dream Team II Head coach Don Nelson's 12-man NBA All-Star squad that cruised to gold medal at 1994 World Basketball Championships in Toronto— Derrick Coleman, Joe Dumars, Kevin Johnson, Larry Johnson, Shawn Kemp, Dan Majerle, Reggie Miller, Alonzo Mourning, Shaquille O'Neal, Mark Price, Steve Smith and Dominique Wilkins.

Dream Team III Head coach Lenny Wilkens' 10-man NBA All-Star squad that represented the U.S. at the 1996 Summer Olympics in Atlanta— Anfernee Hardaway, Grant Hill, Karl Malone, Reggie Miller, Hakeem Olajuwon, Shaquille O'Neal, Gary Payton, Scottie Pippen, Mitch Richmond, David Robinson, Glenn Robinson and John Stockton.

Heike Drechsler (b. Dec. 16, 1964): German long jumper and sprinter; East German before reunification in 1991; set world long jump record (24-2 1/4) in 1988; won long jump gold medals at 1992 Olympics and 1983 and '93 World Championships; won silver medal in long jump and bronze medals in both 100- and 200-meter sprints at 1988 Olympics.

Ken Dryden (b. Aug. 8, 1947): Hockey G; led Montreal to 6 Stanley Cup titles; playoff MVP as rookie in 1971; won or shared 5 Vezina Trophies; 2.24 career GAA; currently Pres. and G.M. of Toronto Maple Leafs.

Don Drysdale (b. July 23, 1936, d. July 3, 1993): Baseball RHP; led NL in strikeouts 3 times and games started 4 straight years; pitched and won record 6 shutouts in a row in 1968; Cy Young Award winner in 1962; won 209 games and hit 29 HRs in 14 years.

Charley Dumas (b. Feb. 12, 1937): U.S. high jumper; first man to clear 7 feet (7-0 1/2) on June 29, 1956; won gold medal at 1956 Olympics.

Margaret Osborne du Pont (b. Mar. 4, 1918): Tennis; won 5 French, 7 Wimbledon and an unprecedented 24 U.S. national titles in singles, doubles and mixed doubles from 1941-62.

Roberto Duran (b. June 16, 1951): Panamanian boxer; one of only 4 fighters to hold 4 different world titles— lightweight (1972-79), welterweight (1980), junior middleweight (1983) and middleweight (1989-90); lost famous "No Mas" welterweight title bout when he quit in 8th round against Sugar Ray Leonard (1980); pro record stood at 94-11 and 65 KOs after 12-round loss to Vinny Pazienza on Jan. 14, 1995.

Leo Durocher (b. July 27, 1905, d. Oct. 7, 1991): Baseball; managed in NL 24 years; won 2,015 games, including postseason; 3 pennants with Brooklyn (1941) and NY Giants (1951,54); won World Series in 1954.

Eddie Eagan (b. Apr. 26, 1898, d. June 14, 1967): Only athlete to win gold medals in both Summer and Winter Olympics (Boxing in 1920, Bobsled in 1932).

Alan Eagleson (b. Apr. 24, 1933): Hockey; Toronto lawyer, agent and 1st executive director of NHL Players Assn. (1967-90); midwifed Team Canada vs. Soviet series (1972) and Canada Cup; charged with racketeering and defrauding NHLPA in 32-count indictment handed down by U.S. grand jury on Mar. 3, 1994.

Dale Earnhardt (b. Apr. 29, 1952): Auto racer; 7-time NASCAR national champion (1980,86-87,90-91, 93-94); Rookie of Year in 1979; all-time NASCAR money leader with over $28 million won and 3rd on career wins list with 70; in 21 years, has never won Daytona 500.

James Easton (b. July 26, 1935): Olympics; archer and sporting goods manufacturer (Easton softball bats); one of 2 American delegates to the International Olympic Committee; president of International Archery Federation (FITA); member of LA Olympic Organizing Committee in 1984.

Dick Ebersol (b. July 28, 1947): Radio-TV; protégé of ABC Sports czar Roone Arledge; key NBC exec in launching of *Saturday Night Live* in 1975; became president of NBC Sports in 1989, won U.S. TV rights to both 2000 Summer and 2002 Winter Olympics with unprecedented combined bid of $1.27 billion in August 1995.

Stefan Edberg (b. Jan. 19, 1966): Swedish tennis player; 2-time No. 1 player (1990-91); 2-time winner of Australian Open (1985,87), Wimbledon (1988,90) and U.S. Open (1991-92); has never won French.

Gertrude Ederle (b. Oct. 23, 1906): Swimmer; 1st woman to swim English Channel, breaking men's record by 2 hours in 1926; won 3 medals in 1924 Olympics.

Krisztina Egerszegi (b. Aug. 16, 1974): Hungarian swimmer; 3-time gold medal winner (100m and 200m backstroke and 400m IM) in 1992 Olympics; also won a gold (200m back) and silver (100m back) in 1988 Games; youngest (age 14) ever to win swimming gold. Won fifth gold medal (200m back) at '96 Games.

Bill Elliott (b. Oct. 8, 1955): Auto racer; 2-time winner of Daytona 500 (1985,87); NASCAR national champ in 1988; entered 1996 with 40 NASCAR wins.

Herb Elliott (b. Feb. 25, 1938): Australian runner; undefeated from 1958-60; ran 17 sub-4:00 miles; 3 world records; won gold medal in 1500 meters at 1960 Olympics; retired at age 22.

John Elway (b. June 28, 1960): Football QB; Consensus All American at Stanford; first overall pick in the fabled quarterback draft of 1983; famous for his last-minute, game-winning scoring drives, most notably in the 1986 AFC Championship game against the Cleveland Browns (98 yards in 15 plays to tie game at end of regulation, then 60 yards in 9 plays to set up winning field goal); led Broncos to three Super Bowl losses; 1987 NFL MVP; four-time Pro Bowl selection; first QB to receive a pass in the Super Bowl (1987); one of only two QBs in league history (Marino) to throw for over 3,000 yards in ten seasons; dangerous runner, with over 30 rushing TDs in his career and more than 3,000 rushing yards.

Roy Emerson (b. Nov. 3, 1936): Australian tennis player; won 12 Majors in singles— 6 Australian, 2 French, 2 Wimbledon and 2 U.S. from 1961-67.

Kornelia Ender (b. Oct. 25, 1958): East German swimmer; 1st woman to win 4 gold medals at one Olympics (1976), all in world-record time.

Julius Erving (b. Feb. 22, 1950): Basketball F; in ABA (1972-76)— 3-time MVP, 2-time playoff MVP, led NY Nets to 2 titles (1974-76); in NBA (1977-87)— 5-time All-NBA 1st team, MVP in 1981, led Philadelphia 76ers to title in 1983.

Phil Esposito (b. Feb. 20, 1942): Hockey C; 1st NHL player to score 100 points in a season (126 in 1969); 6-time All-NHL 1st team with Boston, 2-time MVP (1969,74); 5-time scoring champ; star of 1972 Canada-Soviet series; president-GM of NHL's Tampa Bay Lightning.

Janet Evans (b. Aug. 28, 1971): Swimmer; won 3 individual gold medals (400m & 800m freestyle, 400m IM) at 1988 Olympics; 1989 Sullivan Award winner; entered 1995 as world record-holder in 400m, 800m and 1500m freestyles; won 1 gold (800m) and 1 silver (400m) at 1992 Olympics.

Lee Evans (b. Feb. 25, 1947): Track & Field; dominant quarter-miler in world from 1966-72; world record in 400m at 1968 Olympics stood 20 years.

Chris Evert (b. Dec. 21, 1954): Tennis; No.1 player in world 5 times (1975-77,80-81); won at least 1 Grand Slam singles title every year from 1974-86; 18 Majors in all— 7 French, 6 U.S., 3 Wimbledon and 2 Australian; retired after 1989 season.

Weeb Ewbank (b. May 6, 1907): Football; only coach to win NFL and AFL titles; led Baltimore to 2 NFL titles (1958-59) and NY Jets to Super Bowl III win.

Patrick Ewing (b. Aug. 5, 1962): Basketball C; 3-time All-America; led Georgetown to 3 NCAA Finals and 1984 title; tourney MVP in '84; NBA Rookie of Year with New York in '86; All-NBA in 1990; led U.S. Olympic team to gold medals in 1984 and '92.

Ray Ewry (b. Oct. 14, 1873, d. Sept. 29, 1937): Track & Field; won 10 gold medals over 4 consecutive Olympics (1900,04,06,08); all events he won (Standing HJ, LJ and TJ) were discontinued in 1912.

Nick Faldo (b. July 18, 1957): British golfer; 3-time winner of British Open (1987,90,92) and Masters (1989, 90, 96); 3-time European Golfer of Year (1989-90,92); PGA Player of Year in 1990.

Juan Manuel Fangio (b. June 24, 1911, d. July 17, 1995): Argentine auto racer; 5-time Formula One world champion (1951,54-57); 24 career wins, retired in 1958.

Brett Favre (b. Oct. 10, 1969): Football QB; Selected in the second round (33rd overall) by the Atlanta Falcons in the 1991 NFL draft; traded to Green Bay Packers in 1992; league MVP in 1995 and '96; four-time Pro Bowl QB; 100th TD pass came in his 62nd game, third fastest in league history; 39 TD passes in 1996 season broke his own NFC record of 38 set in 1995; led Packers to NFC title game in 1996 and to Super Bowl victory in 1997.

Sergei Fedorov (b. Dec. 13, 1969): Hockey C; first Russian to win NHL Hart Trophy as 1993-94 regular season MVP; 3-time All-Star with Detroit.

Donald Fehr (b. July 18, 1948): Baseball labor leader; protégé of Marvin Miller; executive director and general counsel of Major League Players Assn. since 1983; led players in 1994 "salary cap" strike that lasted eight months and resulted in first cancellation of World Series since 1904.

Bob Feller (b. Nov. 3, 1918): Baseball RHP; led AL in strikeouts 7 times and wins 6 times with Cleveland; threw 3 no-hitters and 12 one-hitters; 266 career wins.

Tom Ferguson (b. Dec. 20, 1950): Rodeo; 6-time All-Around champion (1974-79); 1st cowboy to win $100,000 in one season (1978); 1st to win $1 million in career (1986).

Cecil Fielder (b. Sept. 21, 1963): Baseball 1B; returned from one season with Hanshin Tigers in Japan to hit 51 HRs for Detroit Tigers in 1990; led MLB in RBI 3 straight years (1990-92); AL MVP runner-up in 1990 and '91. Traded to New York Yankees for pennant drive in 1996.

Herve Filion (b. Feb. 1, 1940): Harness racing; 10-time Driver of Year; entered 1996 season as all-time leader in races won with 14,783 in 35 years.

Rollie Fingers (b. Aug. 25, 1946): Baseball RHP; relief ace with 341 career saves; won AL MVP and Cy Young awards in 1981 with Milwaukee; World Series MVP in 1974 with Oakland.

Charles O. Finley (b. Feb. 22, 1918, d. Feb, 19, 1997): Baseball owner; moved KC A's to Oakland in 1968; won 3 straight World Series from 1972-74; also owned teams in NHL and ABA.

Bobby Fischer (b. Mar. 9, 1943): Chess; at 15, became youngest international grandmaster in chess history; only American to hold world championship (1972-75); was stripped of title in 1975 after refusing to defend against Anatoly Karpov and became recluse; re-emerged to defeat old foe and former world champion Boris Spassky in 1992.

Carlton Fisk (b. Dec. 26, 1947): Baseball C; set all-time major league record at age 45 for games caught (2,226); also all-time HR leader for catchers (376); AL Rookie of Year (1972) and 10-time All-Star; hit epic, 12th-inning Game 6 homer for Boston Red Sox in 1975 World Series.

Emerson Fittipaldi (b. Dec. 12, 1946): Brazilian auto racer; 2-time Formula One world champion (1972,74); 2-time winner of Indy 500 (1989,93); won overall IndyCar title in 1989.

Bob Fitzsimmons (b. May 26, 1863, d. Oct. 22, 1917): British boxer; held three world titles— middleweight (1881-97), heavyweight (1897-99) and light heavyweight (1903-05); pro record 40-11 with 32 KOs.

James (Sunny Jim) Fitzsimmons (b. July 23, 1874, d. Mar. 11, 1966): Horse racing; trained horses that won over 2,275 races, including 2 Triple Crown winners— Gallant Fox in 1930 and Omaha in '35.

Jim Fixx (b. Apr. 23, 1932, d. July 20, 1984): Running; author who popularized the sport of running; his 1977 bestseller The Complete Book of Running, is credited with helping start America's fitness revolution; died of a heart attack while running.

Larry Fleisher (b. Sept. 26, 1930, d. May 4, 1989): Basketball; led NBA players union from 1961-89; increased average yearly salary from $9,400 in 1967 to $600,000 without a strike.

Peggy Fleming (b. July 27, 1948): Figure skating; 3-time world champion (1966-68); won Olympic gold medal in 1968.

Curt Flood (b. Jan. 18, 1938, d. Jan. 20, 1997): Baseball OF; played 15 years (1956-69,71) mainly with St. Louis; hit over .300 6 times with 7 gold gloves; refused trade to Phillies in 1969; lost challenge to baseball's reserve clause in Supreme Court in 1972 (see Peter Seitz).

Ray Floyd (b. Sept. 14, 1942): Golfer; entered 1995 with 22 PGA victories in 4 decades; joined Senior PGA Tour in 1992; has won Masters (1976), U.S. Open (1986), PGA twice (1969,82) and PGA Seniors Championship (1995); only player to ever win on PGA and Senior tours in same year (1992); member of 8 Ryder Cup teams and captain in 1989.

Doug Flutie (b. Oct. 23, 1962): Football QB; won Heisman Trophy with Boston College (1984); has played in USFL, NFL and CFL since then; 5-time CFL MVP with B.C. Lions (1991), Calgary (1992-94)and Toronto in '96; led Calgary to Grey Cup title in '92and Toronto in '96; missed 2nd half of 1995 season with injured right elbow; moved to the Toronto Argonauts in 1996.

Gerald Ford (b. July 14, 1913): 38th President of the U.S.; lettered as center on undefeated Michigan football teams in 1932 and '33; MVP on 1934 squad.

Whitey Ford (b. Oct. 21, 1928): Baseball LHP; all-time leader in World Series wins (10); led AL in wins 3 times; won both Cy Young and World Series MVP in 1961 with NY Yankees.

George Foreman (b. Jan. 10, 1949): Boxer; Olympic heavyweight champ (1968); world heavyweight champ (1973-74 and 94-95); lost title to Muhammad Ali (KO-8th) in '74; recaptured it on Nov. 5, 1994 at age 45 with a 10-round KO of WBA/IBF champ Michael Moorer, becoming the oldest man to win heavyweight crown; named AP Male Athlete of Year 20 years after losing title to Ali; stripped of WBA title on Mar. 4, 1995 after declining to fight No. 1 contender; successfully defended title at age 46 against 26-year-old Axel Schultz of Germany in controversial majority decision on Apr. 22; gave up IBF title in June after refusing rematch with Schultz.

Dick Fosbury (b. Mar. 6, 1947): Track & Field; revolutionized high jump with back-first "Fosbury Flop"; won gold medal at 1968 Olympics.

Greg Foster (b. Aug. 4, 1958): Track & Field; 3-time winner of World Championship gold medal in 110-meter hurdles (1983,87,91); best Olympic performance a silver in 1984; world indoor champion in 1991; made world Top 10 rankings 15 years (a record for running events).

The Four Horsemen Senior backfield that led Notre Dame to national collegiate football championship in 1924; put together as sophomores by Irish coach Knute Rockne; immortalized by sportswriter Grantland Rice, whose report of the Oct. 19, 1924, Notre Dame-Army game began: "Outlined against a blue, gray October sky the Four Horsemen rode again. . . "; HB Jim Crowley (b. Sept. 10, 1902, d. Jan. 15, 1986), FB Elmer Layden (b. May 4, 1903, d. June 30, 1973), HB Don Miller (b. May 30, 1902, d. July 28, 1979) and QB Harry Stuhldreher (b. Oct. 14, 1901, d. Jan. 26, 1965).

The Four Musketeers French quartet that dominated men's tennis in 1920s and '30s, winning 8 straight French singles titles (1925-32), 6 Wimbledons in a row (1924-29) and 6 consecutive Davis Cups (1927-32)— Jean Borotra (b. Aug. 13, 1898, d. July 17, 1994), Jacques Brugnon (b. May 11, 1895, d. Mar. 20, 1978), Henri Cochet (b. Dec. 14, 1901, d. Apr. 1, 1987), Rene Lacoste (b. July 2, 1905, d. Oct. 13, 1996).

Jimmie Foxx (b. Oct. 22, 1907, d. July 21, 1967): Baseball 1B; led AL in HRs 4 times and batting twice; won Triple Crown in 1933; 3-time MVP (1932-33,38) with Philadelphia and Boston; hit 30 HRs or more 12 years in a row; 534 career HRs.

A.J. Foyt (b. Jan. 16, 1935): Auto racer; 7-time USAC-CART national champion (1960-61,63-64,67,75,79); 4-time Indy 500 winner (1961,64,67,77); only driver in history to win Indy 500, Daytona 500 (1972) and 24 Hours of LeMans (1967 with Dan Gurney); retired in 1993 as all-time IndyCar wins leader with 67.

Bill France Sr. (b. Sept. 26, 1909, d. June 7, 1992): Stock car pioneer and promoter; founded NASCAR in 1948; guided race circuit through formative years; built both Daytona (Fla.) Int'l Speedway and Talladega (Ala.) Superspeedway.

Dawn Fraser (b. Sept. 4, 1937): Australian swimmer; won gold medals in 100m freestyle at 3 consecutive Olympics (1956,60,64).

Joe Frazier (b. Jan. 12, 1944): Boxer; 1964 Olympic heavyweight champion; world heavyweight champ (1970-73); fought Muhammad Ali 3 times and won once; pro record 32-4-1 with 27 KOs.

Ford Frick (b. Dec. 19, 1894, d. Apr. 8, 1978): Baseball; sportswriter and radio announcer who served as NL president (1934-51) and commissioner (1951-65); convinced record-keepers to list Roger Maris' and Babe Ruth's season records separately; major leagues moved to west coast and expanded from 16 to 20 teams during his tenure.

Frankie Frisch (b. Sept. 9, 1898, d. Mar. 12, 1973): Baseball 2B; played on 8 NL pennant winners in 19 years with NY and St. Louis; hit .300 or better 11 years in a row (1921-31); MVP in 1931; player-manager from 1933-37.

Dan Gable (b. Oct. 25, 1948): Wrestling; career college wrestling record of 118-1 at Iowa St., where he was a 2-time NCAA champ (1968,69) and tourney MVP in 1969 (137 lbs); won gold medal (149 lbs) at 1972 Olympics; coached U.S. freestyle team in 1988; coached Iowa to 9 straight NCAA titles (1978-86) and has added five more since 1991.

Eddie Gaedel (b. June 8, 1925, d. June 18, 1961): Baseball pinch hitter; St. Louis Browns' midget whose career lasted one at bat (he walked) on Aug 19, 1951.

Clarence (Bighouse) Gaines (b. May 21, 1924): Basketball; retired as coach of Div. II Winston-Salem after 1992-93 season with 828-446 record in 47 years; ranks 3rd on all-time NCAA list behind Adolph Rupp (876) and Dean Smith (830).

Alonzo (Jake) Gaither (b. Apr. 11, 1903, d. Feb. 18, 1994): Football; head coach at Florida A&M for 25 years; led Rattlers to 6 national black college titles; retired after 1969 season with record of 203-36-4 and a winning percentage of .844; coined phrase, "I like my boys agile, mobile and hostile."

Cito Gaston (b. Mar. 17, 1944): Baseball; managed Toronto to consecutive World Series titles (1992-93); first black manager to win Series; shared *The Sporting News* 1993 Man of Year award with Blue Jays GM Pat Gillick.

Lou Gehrig (b. June 19, 1903, d. June 2, 1941): Baseball 1B; played in 2,130 consecutive games from 1923-39 a major league record until Cal Ripken Jr. surpassed it in 1995; led AL in RBI 5 times and HRs 3 times; drove in 100 runs or more 13 years in a row; 2-time MVP (1927,36); hit .340 with 493 HRs over 17 seasons; led NY Yankees to 7 World Series titles; died at age 37 of Amyotrophic lateral sclerosis (ALS), a rare and incurable disease of the nervous system better known as Lou Gehrig's disease.

Charley Gehringer (b. May 11, 1903, d. Jan. 21, 1993): Baseball 2B; hit .300 or better 13 times; AL batting champion and MVP with Detroit in 1937.

A. Bartlett Giamatti (b. Apr. 14, 1938, d. Sept. 1, 1989): Scholar and 7th commissioner of baseball; banned Pete Rose for life for betting on Major League games and associating with known gamblers and drug dealers; also served as president of Yale (1978-86) and National League (1986-89).

Joe Gibbs (b. Nov. 25, 1940): Football; coached Washington to 140 victories and 3 Super Bowl titles in 12 seasons before retiring on Mar. 5, 1993; owner of NASCAR racing team that won 1993 Daytona 500.

Althea Gibson (b. Aug. 25, 1927): Tennis; won both Wimbledon and U.S. championships in 1957 and '58; 1st black to play in either tourney and 1st to win each title.

Bob Gibson (b. Nov. 9, 1935): Baseball RHP; won 20 or more games 5 times; won 2 NL Cy Young Awards (1968,70); MVP in 1968; led St. Louis to 2 World Series titles; Series MVP twice (1964,67); 251 career wins.

Josh Gibson (b. Dec. 21, 1911, d. Jan. 20, 1947): Baseball C; the "Babe Ruth of the Negro Leagues"; Satchel Paige's battery mate with Pittsburgh Crawfords. The Negro Leagues did not keep accurate records but Gibson hit 84 homeruns in one season and his Baseball Hall of Fame plaque says he hit "almost 800" homeruns in his seventeen-year career.

Kirk Gibson (b. May 28, 1957): Baseball OF; All-America flanker at Michigan St. in 1978; chose baseball career and was AL playoff MVP with Detroit in 1984 and NL regular season MVP with Los Angeles in 1988.

Frank Gifford (b. Aug. 16, 1930): Football HB; 4-time All-Pro (1955-57,59); NFL MVP in 1956; led NY Giants to 3 NFL title games; TV sportscaster since 1958, beginning career while still a player.

Sid Gillman (b. Oct. 26, 1911): Football innovator; only coach in both College and Pro Football halls of fame; led college teams at Miami-OH and Cincinnati to combined 81-19-2 record from 1944-54; coached LA Rams (1955-59) in NFL, then led LA-San Diego Chargers to 5 Western titles and 1 league championship in first six years of AFL.

George Gipp (b. Feb. 18, 1895, d. Dec. 14, 1920): Football FB; died of throat infection 2 weeks before he made All-America (Notre Dame's 1st); rushed for 2,341 yards, scored 156 points and averaged 38 yards a punt in 4 years (1917-20).

Marc Girardelli (b. July 18, 1963): Luxembourg Alpine skier; Austrian native who refused to join Austrian Ski Federation because he wanted to be coached by his father; won unprecedented 5th overall World Cup title in 1993; winless at Olympics, although he won 2 silver medals in 1992.

Tom Glavine (b. Mar 26, 1996): Baseball; Atlanta Braves' left-handed pitcher led the majors in wins from 1991-'95 with 91; won NL Cy Young award in 1991 with 20 wins and a 2.55 E.R.A.; named to four All-Star teams and was the NL starter twice; member of 1995 World Series champion Braves and won Series MVP award; pitched the first complete game shutout at Coors Field on June 16, 1995.

Tom Gola (b. Jan. 13, 1933): Basketball F; 4-time All-America and 1955 Player of Year at La Salle; MVP in 1952 NIT and '54 NCAA tournaments, leading Pioneers to both titles; won NBA title as rookie with Philadelphia Warriors in 1956; 4-time NBA All-Star.

Marshall Goldberg (b. Oct. 24, 1917): Football HB; 2-time consensus All-America at Pittsburgh (1937-38); led Pitt to national championship in 1937; played with NFL champion Chicago Cardinals 10 years later.

Lefty Gomez (b. Nov. 26, 1908, d. Feb. 17, 1989): Baseball LHP; 4-time 20-game winner with NY Yankees; holds World Series record for most wins (6) without a defeat; pitched on 5 world championship clubs in 1930s.

Pancho Gonzales (b. May 9, 1928, d. July 3, 1995): Tennis; won consecutive U.S. Championships in 1947-48 before turning pro at 21; dominated pro tour from 1950-61; in 1969 at age 41, played longest Wimbledon match ever (5:12), beating Charlie Pasarell 22-24,1-6,16-14,6-3,11-9.

Bob Goodenow (b. Oct. 29, 1952): Hockey; succeeded Alan Eagleson as executive director of NHL Players Assn. in 1990; led players out on 10-day strike (Apr. 1-10) in 1992 and during 103-day owners' lockout in 1994-95.

Jeff Gordon (b. Aug. 4, 1971): Auto racer; NASCAR Rookie of Year (1993); won inaugural Brickyard 400 in 1994; 1995 Winston Cup champion with 7 wins and 8 poles; in 1997, at 25 became youngest winner of the Daytona 500; in 1997, became the second winner of the Winston Million, a $1 million dollar bonus prize, for winning the Daytona 500, the Coca Cola 600 and the Southern 500; also first driver to win the Southern 500 three times in a row.

Dr. Harold Gores (b. Sept. 20, 1909, d. May 28, 1993): Educator and first president of Education Facilities Laboratories in New York; in 1964 hired Monsanto Co. to produce a synthetic turf that kids could play on in city schoolyards; resulting ChemGrass proved too expensive for playground use, but it was just what the Houston Astros were looking for in 1966 to cover the floor of the Astrodome where grass refused to grow; and AstroTurf was born.

Shane Gould (b. Nov. 23, 1956): Australian swimmer; set world records in 5 different freestyle events between July 1971 and Jan. 1972; won 3 gold medals, a silver and bronze in 1972 Olympics then retired at age 16.

Alf Goullet (b. Apr. 5, 1891, d. Mar. 11, 1995): Cycling; Australian who gained fame and fortune early in century as premier performer on U.S. 6-day bike race circuit; won 8 annual races at Madison Square Garden with 6 different partners from 1913-23.

Curt Gowdy (b. July 31, 1919): Radio-TV; former radio voice of NY Yankees and then Boston Red Sox from 1949-66; TV play-by-play man for AFL, NFL and major league baseball; has broadcast World Series, All-Star Games, Rose Bowls, Super Bowls, Olympics and NCAA Final Fours for all 3 networks; hosted "The American Sportsman."

Steffi Graf (b. June 14, 1969): German tennis player; won Grand Slam and Olympic gold medal in 1988 at age 19; won three of four majors in 1993, '95 and '96; has won 21 Grand Slam titles— 7 at Wimbledon, 4 Australian, 2 French, and 2 U.S. Opens.

Otto Graham (b. Dec. 6, 1921): Football QB and basketball All-America at Northwestern; in pro ball, led Cleveland Browns to 7 league titles in 10 years, winning 4 AAFC championships (1946-49) and 3 NFL (1950,54-55); 5-time All-Pro; 2-time NFL MVP (1953,55).

Red Grange (b. June 13, 1903, d. Jan. 28, 1991): Football HB; 3-time All-America at Illinois who brought 1st huge crowds to pro football when he signed with Chicago Bears in 1925; formed 1st AFL with manager-promoter C.C. Pyle in 1926, but league folded and he returned to NFL.

Bud Grant (b. May 20, 1927): Football and Basketball; only coach to win 100 games in both CFL and NFL and only member of both CFL and U.S. Pro Football halls of fame; led Winnipeg to 4 Grey Cup titles (1958-59,61-62) in 6 appearances, but his Minnesota Vikings lost all 4 Super Bowl attempts in 1970's; all-time rank of 3rd in CFL wins (122) and 8th in NFL wins (168); also All-Big Ten at Minnesota in both football and basketball in late 1940's; a 3-time CFL All-Star offensive end; also member of 1950 NBA champion Minneapolis Lakers.

Rocky Graziano (b. June 7, 1922, d. May 22, 1990): Boxer; world middleweight champion (1946-47); fought Tony Zale for title 3 times in 21 months, losing twice; pro record 67-10-6 with 52 KOs; movie "Somebody Up There Likes Me" based on his life.

Hank Greenberg (b. Jan. 1, 1911, d. Sept. 4, 1986): Baseball 1B; led AL in HRs and RBI 4 times each; 2-time MVP (1935,40) with Detroit; 331 career HRs.

Joe Greene (b. Sept. 24, 1946): Football DT; 5-time All-Pro (1972-74,77,79); led Pittsburgh to 4 Super Bowl titles in 1970s.

Bud Greenspan (b. Sept. 18, 1926): Filmmaker specializing in the Olympic Games; has won Emmy awards for 22-part "The Olympiad" (1976-77) and historical vignettes for ABC-TV's coverage of 1980 Winter Games; won 1994 Emmy award for edited special on Lillehammer Winter Olympics.

Wayne Gretzky (b. Jan. 26, 1961): Hockey C; 10-time NHL scoring champion; 9-time regular season MVP (1979-87,89) and 9-time All-NHL first team; has scored 200 points or more in a season 4 times; led Edmonton to 4 Stanley Cups (1984-85,87-88); 2-time play-off MVP (1985,88); traded to LA Kings (Aug. 9, 1988); broke Gordie Howe's all-time NHL goal scoring record of 801 on Mar. 23, 1994; all-time NHL leader in point, goals and assists; also all-time Stanley Cup leader in points, goals and assists; spent the end of the 1996 season with the St; Louis Blues and then signed a free agent contract with the New York Rangers.

Bob Griese (b. Feb. 3, 1945): Football QB; 2-time All-Pro (1971,77); led Miami to undefeated season (17-0) in 1972 and consecutive Super Bowl titles (1973-74).

Ken Griffey Jr. (b. Nov. 21, 1969): Baseball OF; overall 1st pick of 1987 Draft by Seattle; 7-time Gold Glove winner; 7–time All-Star; in 1997, set major league record for home runs in April with 13; in many categories, is among the youngest ever to reach certain plateaus, like 200 home runs and 1,000 hits; in 1996, hit 49 home runs and knocked in 140 despite missing 20 games with wrist injury; Mariners all-time leader in home runs and RBIs; MVP of 1992 All-Star game at age 23; hit home runs in 8 consecutive games in 1993; son of Ken Sr.and on August 31, 1990 they became the first father-son combination to appear in the same major league lineup.

Archie Griffin (b. Aug. 21, 1954): Football RB; only college player to win two Heisman Trophies (1974-75); rushed for 5,177 yards in career at Ohio St.

Emile Griffith (b. Feb. 3, 1938): Boxer; world welterweight champion (1961,62-63,63-65); world middleweight champ (1966-67,67-68); pro record 85-24-2 with 23 KOs.

Dick Groat (b. Nov. 4, 1930): Basketball and Baseball SS; 2-time basketball All-America at Duke and college Player of Year in 1951; won NL MVP award as shortstop with Pittsburgh in 1960; won World Series with Pirates (1960) and St. Louis (1964).

Lefty Grove (b. Mar. 6, 1900, d. May 22, 1975): Baseball LHP; won 20 or more games 8 times; led AL in ERA 9 times and strikeouts 7 times; 31-4 record and MVP in 1931 with Philadelphia; 300 career wins.

Lou Groza (b. Jan. 25, 1924): Football T-PK; 6-time All-Pro; played in 13 championship games for Cleveland from 1946-67; kicked winning field goal in 1950 NFL title game; 1,608 career points (1,349 in NFL).

Janet Guthrie (b. Mar. 7, 1938): Auto racer; in 1977, became 1st woman to race in Indianapolis 500; placed 9th at Indy in 1978.

Tony Gwynn (b. May 9, 1960): Baseball OF; 7-time NL batting champion (1984,87-89,94-96) at San Diego; was hitting .394 on Aug. 12, 1994 when players' strike began.

Harvey Haddix (b. Sept. 18, 1925, d. Jan. 9, 1994): Baseball LHP; pitched 12 perfect innings for Pittsburgh, but lost to Milwaukee in the 13th, 1-0 (May 26, 1959).

Walter Hagen (b. Dec. 21, 1892, d. Oct. 5, 1969): Pro golf pioneer; won 2 U.S. Opens (1914,19), 4 British Opens (1922,24,28-29), 5 PGA Championships (1921,24-27) and 5 Western Opens; retired with 40 PGA wins; 6-time U.S. Ryder Cup captain.

Marvin Hagler (b. May 23, 1954): Boxer; world middleweight champion 1980-87; enjoyed his nickname "Marvelous Marvin" so much he would have his name legally changed; pro record 62-3-2 with 52 KOs.

George Halas (b. Feb. 2, 1895, d. Oct. 31, 1983): Football pioneer; MVP in 1919 Rose Bowl; player-coach-owner of Chicago Bears from 1920-83; signed Red Grange in 1925; coached Bears for 40 seasons and won 7 NFL titles (1932-33,40-41,43,46,63); 2nd on all-time career list with 324 wins.

Dorothy Hamill (b. July 26, 1956): Figure skater; won Olympic gold medal and world championship in 1976; Ice Capades headliner from 1977-84; bought financially-strapped Ice Capades in 1993.

Scott Hamilton (b. Aug. 28, 1958): Figure skater; 4-time world champion (1981-84); won gold medal at 1984 Olympics.

Tonya Harding (b. Nov. 12, 1970): Figure skater; 1991 U.S. women's champion; involved in bizarre plot hatched by ex-husband Jeff Gillooly to injure rival Nancy Kerrigan on Jan. 6, 1994 and keep her off Olympic team; won '94 U.S. women's title in Kerrigan's absence; denied any role in assault and used USOC when her berth on Olympic team was threatened; finished 8th at Lillehammer (Kerrigan recovered and won silver medal); pleaded guilty on Mar. 16 to conspiracy to hinder investigation; stripped of 1994 title by U.S. Figure Skating Assn.

Tom Harmon (b. Sept. 28, 1919, d. Mar. 17, 1990): Football HB; 2-time All-America at Michigan; won Heisman Trophy in 1940; played with AFL NY Americans in 1941 and NFL LA Rams (1946-47); World War II fighter pilot who won Silver Star and Purple Heart; became radio-TV commentator.

Franco Harris (b. Mar. 7, 1950): Football RB; ran for over 1,000 yards a season 8 times; rushed for 12,120 yards in 13 years; led Pittsburgh to 4 Super Bowl titles.

Leon Hart (b. Nov. 2, 1928): Football E; only player to win 3 national championships in college and 3 more in the NFL; won his titles at Notre Dame (1946-47,49) and with Detroit Lions (1952-53,57); 3-time All-America and last lineman to win Heisman Trophy (1949); All-Pro on both offense and defense in 1951.

Bill Hartack (b. Dec. 9, 1932): Jockey; won Kentucky Derby 5 times (1957,60,62,64,69), Preakness 3 times (1956,64,69), but the Belmont only once (1960).

Doug Harvey (b. Dec. 19, 1924, d. Dec. 26, 1989): Hockey D; 10-time All-NHL 1st team; won Norris Trophy 7 times (1955-58,60-62); led Montreal to 6 Stanley Cups.

Dominik Hasek (b. Jan. 29, 1965): Czech hockey G; 3-time Vezina Trophy winner with Buffalo (1994,95,97); led NHL with a 1.95 GAA in 1993-94—the first sub-2.00 GAA since Bernie Parent in 1974; in 1997, became first goalie since Jacques Plante in 1962 to win league MVP award.

Billy Haughton (b. Nov. 2, 1923, d. July 15, 1986): Harness racing; 4-time winner of Hambletonian; trainer-driver of one Pacing Triple Crown winner (1968); 4,910 career wins.

João Havelange (b. May 8, 1916): Soccer; Brazilian-born president of Federation Internationale de Football Assoc. (FIFA) since 1974; also member of International Olympic Committee.

John Havlicek (b. Apr. 8, 1940): Basketball; played in 3 NCAA Finals at Ohio St. (1960-62); led Boston to 8 NBA titles (1963-66,68-69,74,76); playoff MVP in 1974; 4-time All-NBA 1st team.

Bob Hayes (b. Dec. 20, 1942): Track & Field and Football; won gold medal in 100m at 1964 Olympics; All-Pro SE for Dallas in 1966; convicted of drug trafficking in 1979 and served 18 months of a 5-year sentence.

Woody Hayes (b. Feb. 14, 1913, d. Mar. 12, 1987): Football; coached Ohio St. to 3 national titles (1954,57,68) and 4 Rose Bowl victories; 238 career wins in 28 seasons at Denison, Miami-OH and OSU.

Thomas Hearns (b. Oct. 18, 1958): Boxer; has held recognized world titles as welterweight, light middleweight, middleweight and light heavyweight; four career losses have come against Sugar Ray Leonard, Marvin Hagler and twice to Iran Barkley; entered 1995 with pro record of 53-4-1 and 42 KOs.

Eric Heiden (b. June 14, 1958): Speedskater; 3-time overall world champion (1977-79); won all 5 men's gold medals at 1980 Olympics, setting new records in each; Sullivan Award winner (1980).

Mel Hein (b. Aug. 22, 1909, d. Jan. 31, 1992): Football C; NFL All-Pro 8 straight years (1933-40); MVP in 1938 with NY Giants; didn't miss a game in 15 seasons.

John W. Heisman (b. Oct. 23, 1869, d. Oct. 3, 1936): Football; coached at 9 colleges from 1892-1927; won 185 games; Director of Athletics at Downtown Athletic Club in NYC (1928-36); DAC named Heisman Trophy after him.

Carol Heiss (b. Jan. 20, 1940): Figure skater; 5-time world champion (1956-60); won Olympic silver medal in 1956 and gold in '60; married 1956 men's gold medalist Hayes Jenkins.

Rickey Henderson (b. Dec. 25, 1958): Baseball OF; AL playoff MVP (1989) and AL regular season MVP (1990); set single-season base stealing record of 130 in 1982; has led AL in steals a record 11 times; broke Lou Brock's all-time record of 938 on May 1; all-time leader in steals and HRs as leadoff batter.

Sonja Henie (b. Apr. 8, 1912, d. Oct. 12, 1969): Norwegian figure skater; 10-time world champion (1927-36); won 3 consecutive Olympic gold medals (1928,32,36); became movie star.

Foster Hewitt (b. Nov. 21, 1902, d. Apr. 21, 1985): Radio-TV; Canada's premier hockey play-by-play broadcaster from 1923-81; coined phrase, "He shoots, he scores!"

Graham Hill (b. Feb. 15, 1929, d. Nov. 29, 1975): British auto racer; 2-time Formula One world champion (1962,68); won Indy 500 in 1966; killed in plane crash; father of fellow driver Damon.

Phil Hill (b. Apr. 20, 1927): Auto racer; first U.S. driver to win Formula One championship (1961); 3 career wins (1958-64).

Max Hirsch (b. July 30, 1880, d. Apr. 3, 1969): Horse racing; trained 1,933 winners from 1908-68; won Triple Crown with Assault in 1946.

Tommy Hitchcock (b. Feb. 11, 1900, d. Apr. 19, 1944): Polo; world class player at 20; achieved 10-goal rating 18 times from 1922-40.

Lew Hoad (b. Nov. 23, 1934, d. July 3, 1994): Australian tennis player; 2-time Wimbledon winner (1956-57); won Australian, French and Wimbledon titles in 1956, but missed capturing Grand Slam at Forest Hills when beaten by Ken Rosewall in 4-set final.

Ben Hogan (b. Aug. 13, 1912, d. July 25, 1997): Golfer; 4-time PGA Player of Year; one of only four players to win all four Grand Slam titles (others are Nicklaus, Player and Sarazen); won 4 U.S. Opens, 2 Masters, 2 PGAs and 1 British Open between 1946-53; only player to win three majors in one year when he won Masters, U.S. Open and British Open in 1953; nearly killed in Feb. 13, 1949 car accident, but came back to win U.S. Open in '50; third on all-time list with 63 career wins.

Eleanor Holm (b. Dec. 6, 1913): Swimmer; won gold medal in 100m backstroke at 1932 Olympics; thrown off '36 U.S. team for drinking champagne in public and shooting craps on boat to Germany.

Nat Holman (b. Oct. 18, 1896, d. Feb. 12, 1995): Basketball pioneer; played pro with Original Celtics (1920-28); coached CCNY to both NCAA and NIT titles in 1950 (a year later, several of his players were caught up in a point-shaving scandal); 423 career wins.

Larry Holmes (b. Nov. 3, 1949): Boxer; heavyweight champion (WBC or IBF) from 1978-85; successfully defended title 20 times before losing to Michael Spinks; returned from first retirement in 1988 and was KO'd in 4th by then champ Mike Tyson; launched second comeback in 1991; fought and lost title bids against Evander Holyfield in '92 and Oliver McCall on Apr. 8, 1995; fought McCall at age 45 years and 5 months; entered 1996 with pro record of 62-5 and 40 KOs.

Lou Holtz (b. Jan. 6, 1937): Football; coached Notre Dame to national title in 1988; 2-time Coach of Year (1977,88) retired aftwer 1996 season with 216–95–7 record in 27 seasons with 5 schools— Wm. & Mary (3 years), N.C. State (4), Arkansas (7), Minnesota (2) and ND (11); also coached NFL NY Jets for 13 games (3-10) in 1976.

Evander Holyfield (b. Oct. 19, 1962): Boxer; missed shot at Olympic gold medal in 1984 when he lost controversial light heavyweight semifinal after knocking his opponent out (referee ruled it was a late hit); knocked out Buster Douglas in 3rd round to become world heavyweight champion on Oct. 25, 1990; 2 of first 4 title defenses included decisions over 42-year-old ex-champs George Foreman and Larry Holmes; lost title to Riddick Bowe by unanimous decision on Nov. 13, 1992; beat Bowe by majority decision to reclaim title on Nov. 6, 1993; lost title again to Michael Moorer by majority decision on Apr. 22, 1994; after retiring in '94 due to an apparent heart defect, he returned to the ring in 1995 with a cleaner bill of health; defeated Mike Tyson in November of 1996 to win WBA crown; in the 1997 re-match, Tyson was disqualified for twice biting Holyfield's ear.

Red Holzman (b. Aug. 10, 1920): Basketball; played for NBL and NBA champions at Rochester (1946,51); coached NY Knicks to 2 NBA titles (1970,73); Coach of Year (1970); ranks 10th on all-time NBA list with 754 wins (including playoffs).

Rogers Hornsby (b. Apr. 27, 1896, d. Jan. 5, 1963): Baseball 2B; hit .400 three times, including .424 in 1924; led NL in batting 7 times; 2-time MVP (1925,29) with St. Louis; career average of .358 over 23 years is all-time highest in NL.

Paul Hornung (b. Dec. 23, 1935): Football HB-PK; only Heisman Trophy winner to play for losing team (2-8 Notre Dame in 1956); 3-time NFL scoring leader (1959-61) at Green Bay; 176 points in 1960, an all-time record; MVP in 1961; suspended by NFL for 1963 season for betting on his own team.

Gordie Howe (b. Mar. 31, 1928): Hockey RW; played 32 seasons in NHL and WHA from 1946-80; led NHL in scoring 6 times; all-NHL 1st team 12 times; MVP 6 times in NHL (1952-53,57-58,60,63) with Detroit and once in WHA (1974) with Houston; ranks 2nd on all-time NHL list in goals (801) and points (1,850) to Wayne Gretzky; played with sons Mark and Marty at Houston (1973-77) and New England-Hartford (1977-80).

Cal Hubbard (b. Oct. 31, 1900, d. Oct. 19, 1977): Member of college football, pro football and baseball halls of fame; 9 years in NFL; 4-time All-Pro at end and tackle; AL umpire for 15 years (1936-51).

Carl Hubbell (b. June 22, 1903, d. Nov. 21, 1988): Baseball LHP; led NL in wins and ERA 3 times each; 2-time MVP (1933,36) with NY Giants; fanned Ruth, Gehrig, Foxx, Simmons and Cronin in succession in 1934 All-Star Game; 253 career wins.

Sam Huff (b. Oct. 4, 1934): Football LB; glamorized NFL's middle linebacker position with NY Giants from 1956-63; subject of "The Violent World of Sam Huff" TV special in 1961; helped lead club to 6 division titles and a world championship (1956).

Miller Huggins (b. Mar. 27, 1879, d. Sept. 25, 1929): Baseball; managed NY Yankees from 1918 until his death late in '29 season; led Yanks to 6 pennants and 3 World Series titles from 1921-28.

H. Wayne Huizenga (b. Dec. 29, 1937): Owner; vice chairman of Viacom Inc. and chairman of Blockbuster Entertainment Group; co-founded Waste Management Inc., the world's largest waste collection and disposal company in 1971; majority owner of baseball's Florida Marlins and 100-percent owner of NFL Miami Dolphins, NHL Florida Panthers and Pro Player Park, where Marlins and Dolphins play.

Bobby Hull (b. Jan. 3, 1939): Hockey LW; led NHL in scoring 3 times; 2-time MVP (1965-66) with Chicago; All-NHL first team 10 times; jumped to WHA in 1972, 2-time MVP there (1973,75) with Winnipeg; scored 913 goals in both leagues; father of Brett.

Brett Hull (b. Aug. 9, 1964): Hockey RW; named NHL MVP in 1991 with St. Louis; holds single season RW scoring record with 86 goals; he and father Bobby have both won Hart (MVP), Lady Byng (sportsmanship) and All-Star Game MVP trophies.

Jim (Catfish) Hunter (b. Apr. 8, 1946): Baseball RHP; won 20 games or more 5 times (1971-75); played on 5 World Series winners with Oakland and NY Yankees; threw perfect game in 1968; won Cy Young Award in '74.

Ibrahim Hussein (b. June 3, 1958): Kenyan distance runner; 3-time winner of Boston Marathon (1988,91-92) and 1st African runner to win in Boston; won New York Marathon in 1987.

Don Hutson (b. Jan. 31, 1913, d. June 24, 1997): Football E-PK; led NFL in receptions 8 times and interceptions once; 9-time All-Pro (1936,38-45) for Green Bay; 99 career TD catches.

Flo Hyman (b. July 31, 1954, d. Jan. 24, 1986): Volleyball; 3-time All-America spiker at Houston and captain of 1984 U.S. Women's Olympic team; died of heart attack caused by Marfan Syndrome during a match in Japan in 1986; Women's Sports Foundation's Hyman Award for excellence and dedication named after her.

Hank Iba (b. Aug. 6, 1904, d. Jan. 15, 1993): Basketball; coached Oklahoma A&M to 2 straight NCAA titles (1945-46); 767 career wins in 41 years; coached U.S. Olympic team to 2 gold medals (1964,68), but lost to Soviets in controversial '72 final.

Mike Ilitch (b. July 20, 1929): Baseball and Hockey owner; chairman of Little Caesar's, the international pizza chain; bought Detroit Red Wings of NHL for $8 million in 1982 and AL Detroit Tigers for $85 million in 1992.

Punch Imlach (b. Mar. 15, 1918, d. Dec. 1, 1987): Hockey; directed Toronto to 4 Stanley Cups (1962-64,67) in 11 seasons as GM-coach.

Miguel Induráin (b. July 16, 1964): Spanish cyclist; won a record 5th straight Tour de France in 1995, joining legends Jacques Anquetil and Bernard Hinault of France and Eddy Merckx of Belgium as the only 5 time winners; won gold in time trial at '96 Olympics; retired in 1997.

Hale Irwin (b. June 3, 1945): Golfer; oldest player ever to win U.S. Open (45 in 1990); NCAA champion in 1967; 20 PGA victories, including 3 U.S. Opens (1974,79,90); 5-time Ryder Cup team member.

Bo Jackson (b. Nov. 30, 1962): Baseball OF and Football RB; won Heisman Trophy in 1985 and MVP of baseball All-Star Game in 1989; starter for both baseball's KC Royals and NFL's LA Raiders in 1988 and '89; severely injured left hip Jan. 13, 1991, in NFL playoffs; waived by Royals but signed by Chicago White Sox in 1991; missed entire 1992 season recovering from hip surgery; played for White Sox in 1993 and California in '94 before retiring.

Joe Jackson (b. July 16, 1889, d. Dec. 5, 1951): Baseball OF; hit .300 or better 11 times; nicknamed "Shoeless Joe"; career average of .356 (see Black Sox).

Phil Jackson (b. Sept. 17, 1945): Basketball; NBA champion as reserve forward with New York in 1973 (injured when Knicks won in '70); coached Chicago to three straight NBA titles (1991-93) and two more in 1996–97; coach of the year in 1996 and 97; all-time leader in winning percentage for NBA coaches with 500 or more wins.

Reggie Jackson (b. May 18, 1946): Baseball OF; led AL in HRs 4 times; MVP in 1973; played on 5 World Series winners with Oakland, NY Yankees; 1977 Series MVP with 5 HRs; 563 career HRs; all-time strikeout leader (2,597).

Dr. Robert Jackson (b. Aug. 6, 1932): Surgeon; revolutionized sports medicine by popularizing the use of othroscopic surgery to treat injuries; learned technique from Japanese physician that allowed athletes to return quickly from potentially career-ending injuries.

Helen Jacobs (b. Aug. 6, 1908): Tennis; 4-time winner of U.S. Championship (1932-35); Wimbledon winner in 1936; lost 4 Wimbledon finals to arch-rival Helen Wills Moody.

Dan Jansen (b. June 17, 1965): Speedskater; 1993 world record-holder in 500m; fell in 500m and 1,000m in 1988 Olympics at Calgary after learning of death of sister Jane; placed 4th in 500m and didn't attempt 1,000m 4 years later in Albertville; fell in 500m at '94 Games in Lillehammer, but finally won an Olympic medal with world record (1:12.43) effort in 1,000m, then took victory lap with baby daughter Jane in his arms; won 1994 Sullivan Award.

James J. Jeffries (b. Apr. 15, 1875, d. Mar. 3, 1953): Boxer; world heavyweight champion (1899-1905); retired undefeated but came back to fight Jack Johnson in 1910 and lost (KO,15th).

David Jenkins (b. June 29, 1936): Figure skater; brother of Hayes; 3-time world champion (1957-59); won gold medal at 1960 Olympics.

Hayes Jenkins (b. Mar. 23, 1933): Figure skater; 4-time world champion (1953-56); won gold medal at 1956 Olympics; married 1960 women's gold medalist Carol Heiss.

Bruce Jenner (b. Oct. 28, 1949): Track & Field; won gold medal in 1976 Olympic decathlon.

Jackie Jensen (b. Mar. 9, 1927, d. July 14, 1982): Football RB and Baseball OF; consensus All-America at California in 1948; American League MVP with Boston Red Sox in 1958.

Ben Johnson (b. Dec. 30, 1961): Canadian sprinter; set 100m world record (9.83) at 1987 World Championships; won 100m at 1988 Olympics, but flunked drug test and forfeited gold medal; 1987 world record revoked in '89 for admitted steroid use; returned drug-free in 1991, but performed poorly; banned for life by IAAF in 1993 for testing positive after a meet in Montreal.

Bob Johnson (b. Mar. 4, 1931, d. Nov. 26, 1991): Hockey; coached Pittsburgh Penguins to 1st Stanley Cup title in 1991; led Wisconsin to 3 NCAA titles (1973,77,81) in 15 years; also coached 1976 U.S. Olympic team and NHL Calgary (1982-87).

Earvin (Magic) Johnson (b. Aug. 14, 1959): Basketball G; led Michigan St. to NCAA title in 1979 and was tourney MVP; All-NBA 1st team 9 times; 3-time MVP (1987,89-90); led LA Lakers to 5 NBA titles; 3-time playoff MVP (1980, 82, 87); 2nd all-time in NBA assists with 9,921; retired on Nov. 7, 1991 after announcing he was HIV-positive; returned to score 25 points in 1992 NBA All-Star game; U.S. Olympic Dream Team member in '92; announced NBA comeback then retired again before start of 1992-93 season; named head coach of Lakers on Mar. 23, 1994, but finished season at 5-11 and quit; later named minority owner of team.

Jack Johnson (b. Mar. 31, 1878, d. June 10, 1946): Boxer; controversial heavyweight champion (1908-15) and 1st black to hold title; defeated Tommy Burns for crown at age 30; fled to Europe in 1913 after Mann Act conviction; lost title to Jess Willard in Havana, but claimed to have taken a dive; pro record 78-8-12 with 45 KOs.

Jimmy Johnson (b. July 16, 1943): Football; All-SWC defensive lineman on Arkansas' 1964 national championship team; coached Miami-FL to national title in 1987; college record of 81-34-3 in 10 years; hired by old friend and new Dallas owner Jerry Jones to succeed Tom Landry in February 1989; went 1-15 in '89, then led Cowboys to consecutive Super Bowl victories in 1992 and '93 seasons; quit on Mar. 29, 1994 after feuding with Jones; became TV analyst; replaced Don Shula as Miami Dolphins head coach in 1996.

Judy Johnson (b. Oct. 26, 1899, d. June 13, 1989): Baseball; one of the great stars of the Negro Leagues; a great fielding third baseman who regularly batted over .300; when baseball integrated Johnson's playing days were over but he coached and scouted for the Philadelphia Athletics, Boston Braves and Philadelphia Phillies; member of Baseball Hall of Fame.

Junior Johnson (b. 1930): Auto Racing; won the second Daytona 500 in 1960; also won 13 NASCAR races in 1965 including the Rebel 300 at Darlington; retired from racing to become a highly successful car owner; his first driver was Bobby Allison.

Michael Johnson (b. Sep 13, 1967): Track & Field; had won 55 straight 400 meter finals going into the 1996 Olympic final which he won in an OR 43.49 seconds; in 1996, became the first man to win gold in 200 and 400 meter races in the same Olympics.

Rafer Johnson (b. Aug. 18, 1934): Track & Field; won silver medal in 1956 Olympic decathlon and gold medal in 1960.

Randy Johnson (b. Sept. 10, 1963): Baseball LHP; commanding, 6'10" flamethrower; threw no-hitter on June 2, 1990; in 1993, struck out 308 batters; led AL in strikeouts from 1992 to '95, led majors in '93 and '94; pitched two perfect innings in 1993 All-Star game including memorable strikeout of a cowering John Kruk; similar antics occurred in 1997 All-Star game at-bat of Larry Walker; won AL Cy Young award in 1995 with 18 wins and league leading ERA of 2.48.

Walter Johnson (b. Nov. 6, 1887, d. Dec. 10, 1946): Baseball RHP; won 20 games or more 10 straight years; led AL in ERA 5 times, wins 6 times and strikeouts 12 times; twice MVP (1913, 24) with Washington; all-time leader in shutouts (110) and 2nd in wins (416).

Ben A. Jones (b. Dec. 31, 1882, d. June 13, 1961): Horse racing; Calumet Farm trainer (1939-47); saddled 6 Kentucky Derby champions and 2 Triple Crown winners—Whirlaway in 1941 and Citation in '48.

Bobby Jones (b. Mar. 17, 1902, d. Dec. 18, 1971): Won U.S. and British Opens plus U.S. and British Amateurs in 1930 to become golf's only Grand Slam winner ever; from 1922-30, won 4 U.S. Opens, 5 U.S. Amateurs, 3 British Opens, and played in 6 Walker Cups; founded Masters tournament in 1934.

Deacon Jones (b. Dec. 9, 1938): Football DE; 5-time All-Pro (1965-69) with LA Rams; unofficial all-time NFL sack leader with 172 in 14 years.

Jerry Jones (b. Oct. 13, 1942): Football; owner-GM of Dallas Cowboys; maverick who bought declining team (3-13) and Texas Stadium for $140 million in 1989; hired old friend Jimmy Johnson to replace legendary Tom Landry as coach; their partnership led Cowboys to Super Bowl titles in 1992 and '93 seasons; when feud developed in 1994, Jones let Johnson go and hired Barry Switzer; defied NFL Properties by signing separate sponsorship deals with Pepsi and Nike in 1995, causing NFL to file a $300 million lawsuit against him on Sept. 19.

Roy Jones Jr. (b. Jan. 16, 1969): Boxing; robbed of gold medal at 1988 Summer Olympics due to an error in scoring; still voted Outstanding Boxer of the Games; won IBF middleweight crown by beating Bernard Hopkins in 1993; moved up to super middleweight and won IBF title from James Toney on Nov. 18, 1994; pro record of 34-0 with 29 KOs.

Michael Jordan (b. Feb. 17, 1963): Basketball G; College Player of Year with North Carolina in 1984; led NBA in scoring 7 years in a row (1987-93) and also in 1996, 1997; 9-time All-NBA 1st team; 4-time regular season MVP (1988,91-92,96,) and 5-time MVP of NBA Finals (1991-93,96,97); only 3-time AP Male Athlete of Year; led U.S. Olympic team to gold medals in 1984 and '92; stunned sports world when he retired at age 30 on Oct. 6, 1993; signed as OF with Chicago White Sox and spent summer of '94 in Double A with Birmingham; barely hit his weight with .204 average; made one of the most anticipated comebacks in sports history when he returned to the Bulls lineup on Mar. 19, 1995 and shot 7-for-28; lost first playoff series since 1990 when Bulls were eliminated by Orlando in second round; led Bulls to 5 NBA titles (1991–93, 96, 97); in 1997, as part of the league's 50th anniversary celebration, named as one of the NBA's 50 Greatest Players. Duh.

Florence Griffith Joyner (b. Dec. 21, 1959): Track & Field; set world records in 100 and 200 meters in 1988; won 3 gold medals at '88 Olympics (100m, 200m, 4x100m relay); Sullivan Award winner (1988); retired in 1989; designed NBA Indiana Pacers uniforms (1990); named as co-chairperson of President's Council on Physical Fitness and Sports in 1993.

Jackie Joyner-Kersee (b. Mar. 3, 1962): Track & Field; 2-time world champion in both long jump (1987,91) and heptathlon (1987,93); won heptathlon gold medals at 1988 and '92 Olympics and LJ gold at '88 Games; has also won Olympic silver (1984) in heptathlon and bronze (1992) in LJ; Sullivan Award winner (1986); only woman to receive The Sporting News Man of Year award.

Alberto Juantorena (b. Nov. 21, 1950): Cuban runner; won both 400m and 800m gold medals at 1976 Olympics.

Sonny Jurgensen (b. Aug. 23, 1934): Football QB; played 18 seasons with Philadelphia and Washington; led NFL in passing twice (1967,69); All-Pro in 1961; 255 career TD passes.

Duke Kahanamoku (b. Aug. 24, 1890, d. Jan. 22, 1968): Swimmer; won 3 gold medals and 2 silver over 3 Olympics (1912,20,24); also surfing pioneer.

Al Kaline (b. Dec. 19, 1934): Baseball; youngest player (at age 20) to win batting title (led AL with .340 in 1955); had 3,007 hits, 399 HRs in 22 years with Detroit.

Anatoly Karpov (b. May 23, 1951): Chess; Russian world champion from 1975-85; regained International Chess Federation (FIDE) version of championship in 1993 when countryman Garry Kasparov was stripped of title after forming new Professional Chess Association.

Garry Kasparov (b. Apr. 13, 1963): Chess; Azerbaijani who became youngest player (22 years, 210 days) ever to win world championship as Russian in 1985; defeated countryman Anatoly Karpov for title; split with International Chess Federation (FIDE) to form Professional Chess Association (PCA) in 1993; stripped of FIDE title in '93 but successfully defended PCA title against Briton Nigel Short; beat IBM supercomputer "Deep Blue" 4 games to 2 in 1996 much-publicized match in New York; lost rematch to computer in 1997.

Ewing Kauffman (b. Sept. 21, 1916, d. Aug. 1, 1993): Baseball; pharmaceutical billionaire and long-time owner of Kansas City Royals; Royals Stadium renamed for Kauffman on July 2, 1993, one month before his death.

Mike Keenan (b. Oct. 21, 1949): Hockey; coach who finally led NY Rangers to Stanley Cup title in 1994 after 54 unsuccessful years; quit a month later in pay dispute and signed with St. Louis as coach-GM; entered 1995-96 season with 507 wins (including playoffs); also reached Cup finals with Philadelphia (1987) and Chicago (1992); coached Team Canada to Canada Cup wins in 1987 and '91.

Kipchoge (Kip) Keino (b. Jan. 17, 1940): Kenyan runner; young policeman who beat USA's Jim Ryun to win 1,500m gold medal at 1968 Olympics; won again in steeplechase at 1972 Summer Games; his success spawned long line of international distance champions from Kenya.

Johnny Kelley (b. Sept. 6, 1907): Distance runner; ran in his 61st and final Boston Marathon at age 84 in 1992, finishing in 5:58:36; won Boston twice (1935,45) and was 2nd 4 times.

Leroy Kelly (b. May 20, 1942): Football; replaced Jim Brown in the Cleveland Brown's backfield; in 1967, Kelly led the NFL in rushing yards (1,205), rushing average (5.1 per carry) and rushing touchdowns (11); in 1968, he led the league again in yards (1,269) and touchdowns (16); played in six Pro Bowls; retired with 7,274 yards and 74 touchdowns; member of Pro Football Hall of Fame.

Jim Kelly (b. Feb. 14, 1960): Football QB; led Buffalo to four consecutive Super Bowl appearances, and is only QB to lose four times; named to AFC Pro Bowl team 5 times.

Walter Kennedy (b. June 8, 1912, d. June 26, 1977): Basketball; 2nd NBA commissioner (1963-75), league doubled in size to 18 teams during his term of office.

Nancy Kerrigan (b. Oct. 13, 1969): Figure skating; 1993 U.S. women's champion and Olympic medalist in 1992 (bronze) and '94 (silver); victim of Jan. 6, 1994 assault at U.S. nationals in Detroit when Shane Stant clubbed her in right knee with metal baton after a practice session; conspiracy hatched by Jeff Gillooly, ex-husband of rival Tonya Harding; although unable to compete in nationals, she quickly recovered and was granted berth on Olympic team; finished 2nd in Lillehammer to Oksana Baiul of Ukraine by a 5-4 judges' vote.

Billy Kidd (b. Apr. 13, 1943): Skiing; the first great Amercian male Alpine skier; first American male to win an Olympic medal when he won a silver in the slalom and a bronze in the Alpine combined in 1964; competed respectably with the great Jean-Claude Killy; won the world Alpine combined event in 1970 which was the first world championship for an American male.

Harmon Killebrew (b. June 29, 1936): Baseball 3B-1B; led AL in HRs 6 times and RBI 3 times; MVP in 1969 with Minnesota; 573 career HRs.

Jean-Claude Killy (b. Aug. 30, 1943): French alpine skier; 2-time World Cup champion (1967-68); won 3 gold medals at 1968 Olympics in Grenoble, co-president of 1992 Winter Games in Albertville.

Ralph Kiner (b. Oct. 27, 1922): Baseball OF; led NL in home runs 7 straight years (1946-52) with Pittsburgh; 369 career HRs.

Betsy King (b. Aug. 13, 1955): Golfer; 2-time LPGA Player of Year (1984,89), who entered 1995 as Tour's all-time money winner with $4,892,873; 2-time winner of both U.S. Open (1989,90) and Dinah Shore (1987,90); became only 14th player to qualify for LPGA Hall of Fame on June 25, 1995 when she won the Shop-Rite Classic for her 30th career victory since 1977.

Billie Jean King (b. Nov. 22, 1943): Tennis; women's rights pioneer; Wimbledon singles champ 6 times; U.S. champ 4 times; first woman athlete to earn $100,000 in one year (1971); beat 55-year-old Bobby Riggs 6-4, 6-3, 6-3, to win $100,000 in 1973.

Don King (b. Aug. 20, 1931): Boxing promoter; controlled heavyweight title from 1978-90 while Larry Holmes and Mike Tyson were champions; 1st major promotion was Muhammad Ali's comeback fight in 1970; former numbers operator who served 4 years for manslaughter (1967-70); acquitted of tax evasion and fraud in 1985; indicted July 14, 1994 for allegedly bilking Lloyd's of London out of $350,000 on a false insurance claim involving a training injury to Julio Cesar Chavez in June 1991; regained control of heavyweight title in 1994 with wins by Oliver McCall (WBC) and Bruce Seldon (WBA); resumed role as Tyson's promoter after ex-champion's release from prison on Mar. 25, 1995.

Karch Kiraly (b. Nov. 3, 1960): Volleyball; USA's preeminent volleyball player; led UCLA to three NCAA championships (1979, '81, '82); played on US national teams that won Olympic gold medals in 1984 and '88, world championships in '82 and '86; won the inaugural gold medal for Olympic beach volleyball with Kent Steffes in 1996.

Tom Kite (b. Dec. 9, 1949): Golfer; entered 1996 as 2nd on all-time PGA Tour money list with over $9.6 million; finally won 1st major with victory in 1992 U.S. Open at Pebble Beach; co-NCAA champion with Ben Crenshaw (1972); PGA Rookie of Year (1973); PGA Player of Year (1989); captain of 1997 US Ryder Cup team

Gene Klein (b. Jan. 29, 1921, d. Mar. 12, 1990): Horseman; won 3 Eclipse awards as top owner (1985-87); filly Winning Colors won 1988 Kentucky Derby; also owned San Diego Chargers football team (1966-84).

Bob Knight (b. Oct. 25, 1940): Basketball; has coached Indiana to 3 NCAA titles (1976,81,87); 3-time Coach of Year (1975-76, 89); coached 1984 U.S. Olympic team to gold medal.

Phil Knight (b. Feb. 24, 1938): Founder and chairman of Nike, Inc., the $4 billion shoe and fitness company founded in 1972 and based in Beaverton, Ore.; stable of endorsees includes Michael Jordan, Andre Agassi and Tiger Woods; named "The Most Powerful Man in Sports" by The Sporting News in 1992.

Bill Koch (b. June 7, 1955): Cross-country skiing; first highly-accomplished American male in his sport; first American male to win a cross-country Olympic medal when he took home a silver in the 30-kilometer race in 1976; in 1982, he was the first American male to win the Nordic World Cup.

Olga Korbut (b. May 16, 1955): Soviet gymnast; 3 gold medals at 1972 Olympics; first to perform back somersault on balance beam.

Johann Olav Koss (b. Oct. 29, 1968): Norwegian speedskater; won three gold medals at 1994 Olympics in Lillehammer with world records in the 1,500m, 5,000m and 10,000m; also won 1,500m gold and 10,000m silver in 1992 Games; retired shortly after Olympics.

Sandy Koufax (b. Dec. 30, 1935): Baseball LHP; led NL in strikeouts 4 times and ERA 5 straight years; won 3 Cy Young Awards (1963,65,66) with LA Dodgers; MVP in 1963; 2-time World Series MVP (1963, 65); threw perfect game against Chicago Cubs (1-0, Sept. 9, 1965) and had 3 other no-hitters in 1962, '63 and '64.

Alvin Kraenzlein (b. Dec. 12, 1876, d. Jan. 6, 1928): Track & Field; won 4 individual gold medals in 1900 Olympics (60m, long jump, 110m and 200m hurdles).

Jack Kramer (b. Aug. 1, 1921): Tennis; Wimbledon singles champ 1947; U.S. champ 1946-47; promoter and Open pioneer.

Ingrid Kristiansen (b. Mar. 21, 1956): Norwegian runner; 2-time Boston Marathon winner (1986,89); won New York City Marathon in 1989; entered 1997 as world record holder in the marathon.

Julie Krone (b. July 24, 1963): Jockey; only woman to ride winning horse in a Triple Crown race when she captured Belmont Stakes aboard Colonial Affair in 1993; entered 1996 as all-time winningest female jockey with 3,016 wins.

Mike Krzyzewski (b. Feb. 13, 1947): Basketball; has coached Duke to 7 Final Four appearances in last 10 years; won consecutive NCAA titles in 1991 and '92; missed most of 1994-95 season with a back injury and stress-related exhaustion; 22-year record of 473–208.

Alan Kulwicki (b. Dec. 14, 1954, d. Apr. 1, 1993): Auto racer; 1992 NASCAR national champion; 1st college grad and Northerner to win title; NASCAR Rookie of Year in 1986; famous for driving car backwards on victory lap; killed at age 38 in plane crash near Bristol, Tenn.

Marion Ladewig (b. Oct. 30, 1914): Bowler; named Woman Bowler of the Year 9 times (1950-54,57-59,63).

Guy Lafleur (b. Sept. 20, 1951): Hockey RW; led NHL in scoring 3 times (1975-78); 2-time MVP (1977-78); played for 5 Stanley Cup winners in Montreal; playoff MVP in 1977; returned to NHL as player in 1988 after election to Hall of Fame; retired again in 1991.

Napoleon (Nap) Lajoie (b. Sept. 5, 1874, d. Feb. 7, 1959): Baseball 2B; led AL in batting 3 times (1901,03-04); batted .422 in 1901; hit .338 for career with 3,244 hits.

Jack Lambert (b. July 8, 1952): Football LB; 6-time All-Pro (1975-76,79-82); led Pittsburgh to 4 Super Bowl wins.

Kenesaw Mountain Landis (b. Nov. 20, 1866, d. Nov. 25, 1944): U.S. District Court judge who became first baseball commissioner (1920-44); banned Black Sox for life.

Tom Landry (b. Sept. 11, 1924): Football; All-Pro DB for NY Giants (1954); coached Dallas for 29 years (1960-88); won 2 Super Bowls (1972,78); 3rd on NFL all-time list with 270 wins.

Steve Largent (b. Sept. 28, 1954): Football WR; retired in 1989 after 14 years in Seattle with then NFL records in passes caught (819) and TD passes caught (100); elected to U.S. House of Representatives (R, Okla.) in 1994 and Pro Football Hall of fame in '95.

Don Larsen (b. Aug. 7, 1929): Baseball RHP; NY Yankees hurler who pitched the only perfect game in World Series history— a 2-0 victory over Brooklyn in Game 5 of the 1956 Series (Oct. 8); Series MVP that year; had career record of 81-91 in 14 seasons with 6 clubs.

Tommy Lasorda (b. Sept. 22, 1927): Baseball; managed LA Dodgers to 2 World Series titles (1981,88) in 4 appearances; retired during 1996 season with 1,599 regular-season wins in 21 years; member of Baseball Hall of Fame

Larissa Latynina (b. Dec. 27, 1934): Soviet gymnast; won total of 18 medals, (9 gold) in 3 Olympics (1956,60,64).

Nikki Lauda (b. Feb. 22, 1949): Austrian auto racer; 3-time world Formula One champion (1975,77,84); 25 career wins from 1971-85.

Rod Laver (b. Aug. 9, 1938): Australian tennis player; only player to win Grand Slam twice (1962,69); Wimbledon champion 4 times; 1st to earn $1 million in prize money.

Andrea Mead Lawrence (b. Apr. 19, 1932): Alpine skier; won 2 gold medals at 1952 Olympics.

Bobby Layne (b. Dec. 19, 1926, d. Dec. 1, 1986): Football QB; college star at Texas; master of 2-minute offense; led Detroit to 4 divisional titles and 3 NFL championships in 1950's.

Frank Leahy (b. Aug. 27, 1908, d. June 21, 1973): Football; coached Notre Dame to four national titles (1943,46-47,49); career record of 107-13-9 for a winning pct. of .864.

Brian Leetch (b. Mar. 3, 1968): Hockey D; NHL Rookie of Year in 1989; won Norris Trophy as top defenseman in 1992; Conn Smythe Trophy winner as playoffs' MVP in 1994 when he helped lead NY Rangers to 1st Stanley Cup title in 54 years.

Jacques Lemaire (b. Sept. 7, 1945): Hockey C; member of 8 Stanley Cup champions in Montreal; scored 366 goals in 12 seasons; coached Canadiens from 1983-85; directed New Jersey Devils to surprising 4-game sweep of Detroit to win 1995 Stanley Cup.

Claude Lemieux (b. July 16, 1965): Hockey RW; pivotal member of Stanley Cup championship teams in Montreal (1986) and New Jersey (1995); playoff MVP with Devils in '95 and Colorado in 96; no relation to Mario.

Mario Lemieux (b. Oct. 5, 1965): Hockey C; 5-time NHL scoring leader (1988-89,92-93,96); Rookie of Year (1985); 4-time All-NHL 1st team (1988-89,93,96); 3-time regular season MVP (1988,93,96); 3-time All-Star Game MVP; led Pittsburgh to consecutive Stanley Cup titles (1991 and '92) and was playoff MVP both years; won 1993 scoring title despite missing 24 games to undergo radiation treatments for Hodgkin's disease; missed 62 games during 1993-94 season mostly due to back injuries; sat out 1994-95 season due to fatigue; returned in 1995-96 to lead the league in scoring and win the MVP trophy; retired after 1997 season in which he led the league in scoring.

Greg LeMond (b. June 26, 1961): Cyclist; 3-time Tour de France winner (1986,89-90); only non-European to win the event; retired in Dec. 1994 after being diagnosed with a rare muscular disease known as mitochondrial myopathy.

Ivan Lendl (b. Mar. 7, 1960): Czech tennis player; No.1 player in world 4 times (1985-87,89); has won both French and U.S. Opens 3 times and Australian twice; owns 94 career tournament wins.

Suzanne Lenglen (b. May 24, 1899, d. July 4, 1938): French tennis player; dominated women's tennis from 1919-26; won both Wimbledon and French singles titles 6 times.

Sugar Ray Leonard (b. May 17, 1956): Boxer; light welterweight Olympic champ (1976); won world welterweight title 1979 and four other titles; retired after losing to Terry Norris on Feb. 9, 1991, with record of 36-2-1 and 25 KOs; misguided comeback in 1997 resulted in resounding defeat by Hector Camacho.

Marv Levy (b. Aug. 3, 1928): Football; coached Buffalo to four consecutive Super Bowls, but is one of two coaches who are 0-4 (Bud Grant is the other); won 50 games and two CFL Grey Cups with Montreal (1974,77).

Carl Lewis (b. July 1, 1961): Track & Field; won 4 Olympic gold medals in 1984 (100m, 200m, 4x100m, LJ), 2 more in '88 (100m, LJ), 2 more in '92 (4x100m, LJ) and 1 more in '96 for a career total of 9; has record 8 World Championship titles and 9 medals in all; Sullivan Award winner (1981); entered 1996 with 71 long jumps over 28 feet.

Nancy Lieberman-Cline (b. July 1, 1958): Basketball; 3-time All-America and 2-time Player of Year (1979-80); led Old Dominion to consecutive AIAW titles in 1979 and '80; played in defunct WPBL and WABA and became 1st woman to play in men's pro league (USBL) in 1986; played in the inaugural season of the WNBA in 1997 for the Phoenix Mercury.

Eric Lindros (b. Feb. 28, 1973): Hockey C; No. 1 pick in 1991 NHL draft by the Nordiques; sat out 1991-92 season rather than play in Quebec; traded to Philadelphia in 1992 for 6 players, 2 No. 1 picks and $15 million; elected Flyers captain at age 22; won Hart Trophy as league MVP in 1995.

Sonny Liston (b. May 8, 1932, d. Dec. 30, 1970): Boxer; heavyweight champion (1962-64), who knocked out Floyd Patterson twice in the first round, then lost title to Muhammad Ali (then Cassius Clay) in 1964; pro record of 50-4 with 39 KOs.

Rebecca Lobo (b. Oct. 6, 1973): Basketball F; women's college basketball Player of the Year in 1995; led Connecticut to undefeated season (35-0) and national title; member of 1996 U.S. Olympic team; premier player for the New York Liberty in WNBA; led Liberty to league's first championship game in 1997 but lost to Houston Comets.

Vince Lombardi (b. June 11, 1913, d. Sept. 3, 1970): Football; coached Green Bay to 5 NFL titles; won first 2 Super Bowls ever played (1967-68); died as NFL's all-time winningest coach with percentage of .740 (105-35-6); Super Bowl trophy named in his honor.

Johnny Longden (b. Feb. 14, 1907): Jockey; first to win 6,000 races; rode Count Fleet to Triple Crown in 1943.

Nancy Lopez (b. Jan. 6, 1957): Golfer; 4-time LPGA Player of the Year (1978-79,85,88); Rookie of Year (1977); 3-time winner of LPGA Championship; reached Hall of Fame by age 30 with 35 victories; entered 1995 with 47 career wins.

Donna Lopiano (b. Sept. 11, 1946): Former basketball and softball star who was women's athletic director at Texas for 18 years before leaving to become executive director of Women's Sports Foundation in 1992.

Greg Louganis (b. Jan. 29, 1960): U.S. diver; won platform and springboard gold medals at both 1984 and '88 Olympics; revealed on Feb. 22, 1995 that he has AIDS.

Joe Louis (b. May 13, 1914, d. Apr. 12, 1981): Boxer; world heavyweight champion from June 22, 1937 to Mar. 1, 1949; his reign of 11 years, 8 months longest in division history; successfully defended title 25 times; retired in 1949, but returned to lose title shots against successors Ezzard Charles in 1950 and Rocky Marciano in '51; pro record of 63-3 with 49 KOs.

Sid Luckman (b. Nov. 21, 1916): Football QB; 6-time All-Pro; led Chicago Bears to 4 NFL titles (1940-41,43,46); MVP in 1943.

Hank Luisetti (b. June 16, 1916): Basketball F; 3-time All-America at Stanford (1935-38); revolutionized game with one-handed shot.

Johnny Lujack (b. Jan. 4, 1925): Football QB; led Notre Dame to three national titles (1943,46-47); won Heisman Trophy in 1947.

Darrell Wayne Lukas (b. Sept. 2, 1935): Horse racing; 4-time Eclipse Award-winning trainer who saddled Horses of Year Lady's Secret in 1988 and Criminal Type in 1990; first trainer to earn over $100 million in purses; led nation in earnings 11 times from 1983-94; Grindstone's Kentucky Derby win in 1996 gave him six Triple Crown wins in a row; also won 1996 Belmont Stakes with Editor's Note; has now won Preakness four times and Kentucky Derby and Belmont three times.

Gen. Douglas MacArthur (b. Jan. 26, 1880, d. Apr. 5, 1964): Controversial U.S. general of World War II and Korea; president of U.S. Olympic Committee (1927-28); college football devotee, National Football Foundation MacArthur Bowl (for No.1 team) named after him.

Connie Mack (b. Dec. 22, 1862, d. Feb. 8, 1956): Baseball owner; managed Philadelphia A's until he was 87 (1901-50); all-time major league wins leader with 3,755, including postseason; won 9 AL pennants and 5 World Series (1910-11,13,29-30); also finished last 18 times.

Andy MacPhail (b. Apr. 5, 1953): Baseball; Chicago Cubs president, who was GM of 2 World Series champions in Minnesota (1987,91); won first title at age 34; son of Lee, grandson of Larry.

Larry MacPhail (b. Feb. 3, 1890, d. Oct. 1, 1975): Baseball executive and innovator; introduced major leagues to night games at Cincinnati (May 24, 1935); won pennant in Brooklyn (1941) and World Series with NY Yankees (1947); father of Lee.

Lee MacPhail (b. Oct. 25, 1917): Baseball; AL president (1974-83); president of owners' Player Relations Committee (1984-85); also GM of Baltimore (1959-65) and NY Yankees (1967-74); son of Larry and father of Andy.

John Madden (b. Apr. 10, 1936): Football and Radio-TV; won 112 games and a Super Bowl (1976 season) as coach of Oakland Raiders; has won 10 Emmy Awards since 1982 as NFL analyst with CBS and Fox; signed 4-year, $32 million deal with Fox in 1994—a richer contract than any NFL player.

Greg Maddux (b. Apr. 14, 1966): Baseball RHP; won unprecedented 4 straight NL Cy Young Awards with Cubs (1992) and Atlanta (1993-95); has led NL in ERA three times (1993-95).

Larry Mahan (b. Nov. 21, 1943): Rodeo; 6-time All-Around world champion (1966-70,73).

Phil Mahre (b. May 10, 1957): Alpine skier; 3-time World Cup overall champ (1981-83); finished 1-2 with twin brother Steve in 1984 Olympic slalom.

Karl Malone (b. July 24, 1963): Basketball F; 9-time All-NBA 1st team (1989-97) with Utah; member of the 1992 and '96 Olympic Dream Teams; league MVP in 1997.

Moses Malone (b. Mar. 23, 1955): Basketball C; signed with Utah of ABA at age 19; has led NBA in rebounding 6 times; 4-time All-NBA 1st team; 3-time NBA MVP (1979,82-83); playoff MVP with Philadelphia in 1983; played in 21st pro season in 1994-95.

Nigel Mansell (b. Aug. 8, 1953): British auto racer; won 1992 Formula One driving championship with record 9 victories and 14 poles; quit Grand Prix circuit to race Indy cars in 1993; 1st rookie to win IndyCar title; 3rd driver to win IndyCar and F1 titles; returned to F1 after 1994 IndyCar season and won '94 Australian Grand Prix; left F1 again on May 23, 1995 with 31 wins and 32 poles in 15 years.

Mickey Mantle (b. Oct. 20, 1931, d. Aug. 13, 1995): Baseball OF; named after Hall of Fame catcher Mickey Cochrane; led AL in home runs 4 times; won Triple Crown in 1956; hit 52 HRs in 1956 and 54 in '61; 3-time MVP (1956-57,62); hit 536 career HRs; played in 12 World Series with NY Yankees and won 7 times; all-time Series leader in HRs (18), RBI (40), runs (42) and strikeouts (54); underwent liver transplant on June 8, 1995 and died of cancer two months later.

Diego Maradona (b. Oct. 30, 1960): Soccer F; captain and MVP of 1986 World Cup champion Argentina; also led national team to 1990 World Cup final; consensus Player of Decade in 1980's; led Napoli to 2 Italian League titles (1987,90) and UEFA Cup (1989); tested positive for cocaine and suspended 15 months by FIFA in 1991; returned to World Cup as Argentine captain in 1994, but was kicked out of tournament after two games when doping test found 5 banned substances in his urine.

Pete Maravich (b. June 27, 1947, d. Jan. 5, 1988): Basketball; NCAA scoring leader 3 times (1968-70); averaged 44.2 points a game over career; Player of Year in 1970; NBA scoring champ in '77 with New Orleans.

Alice Marble (b. Sept. 28, 1913, d. Dec. 13, 1990): Tennis; 4-time U.S. champion (1936,38-40); won Wimbledon in 1939; swept U.S. singles, doubles and mixed doubles from 1938-40.

Gino Marchetti (b. Jan. 2, 1927): Football DE; 8-time NFL All-Pro (1957-64) with Baltimore Colts.

Rocky Marciano (b. Sept. 1, 1923, d. Aug. 31, 1969): Boxer; heavyweight champion (1952-56); retired undefeated; pro record of 49-0 with 43 KOs; killed in plane crash.

Juan Marichal (b. Oct. 20, 1938): Baseball RHP; won 21 or more games 6 times for S.F. Giants from 1963-69; ended 16-year career with 243 wins.

Dan Marino (b. Sept. 15, 1961): Football QB; 4-time leading passer in AFC (1983-84,86,89); set NFL single-season records for TD passes (48) and passing yards (5,084) with Miami in 1984; all-time leader in career TD passes, passing yards, attempts and completions.

Roger Maris (b. Sept. 10, 1934, d. Dec. 14, 1985): Baseball OF; broke Babe Ruth's single-season HR record with 61 in 1961; 2-time AL MVP (1960-61) with NY Yankees.

Billy Martin (b. May 16, 1928, d. Dec. 25, 1989): Baseball; 5-time manager of NY Yankees; won 2 pennants and 1 World Series (1977); also managed Minnesota, Detroit, Texas and Oakland; played 2B on 4 Yankee world champions in 1950's.

Eddie Mathews (b. Oct. 13, 1931): Baseball 3B; led NL in HRs twice (1953,59); hit 30 or more home runs 9 straight years; 512 career HRs.

Christy Mathewson (b. Aug. 12, 1880, d. Oct. 7, 1925): Baseball RHP; won 22 or more games 12 straight years (1903-14); 373 career wins; pitched 3 shutouts in 1905 World Series.

Bob Mathias (b. Nov. 17, 1930): Track & Field; youngest winner of decathlon with gold medal in 1948 Olympics at age 17; first to repeat as decathlon champ in 1952; Sullivan Award winner (1948); 4-term member of U.S. Congress (R, Calif.) from 1967-74.

Ollie Matson (b. May 1, 1930): Football HB; All-America at San Francisco (1951); bronze medal winner in 400m at 1952 Olympics; 4-time All-Pro for NFL Chicago Cardinals (1954-57); traded to LA Rams for 9 players in 1959; accounted for 12,884 all-purpose yards and scored 73 TDs in 14 seasons.

Willie Mays (b. May 6, 1931): Baseball OF; nicknamed the "Say Hey Kid"; led NL in HRs and stolen bases 4 times each; 2-time MVP (1954,65) with NY-SF Giants; Hall of Famer who played in 24 All-Star Games; 660 HRs and 3,283 hits in career.

Bill Mazeroski (b. Sept. 5, 1936): Baseball 2B; career .260 hitter who won the 1960 World Series for Pittsburgh with a lead-off HR in the bottom of the 9th inning of Game 7; the pitcher was Ralph Terry of the NY Yankees, the count was 1-0 and the score was tied 9-9; also a sure-fielder, Maz won 8 gold gloves in 17 seasons.

Joe McCarthy (b. Apr. 21, 1887, d. Jan. 13, 1978): Baseball; first manager to win pennants in both leagues (Chicago Cubs in 1929 and New York Yankees in 1932); greatest success came with Yankees when he won seven pennants and six World Series championships from 1936 to 1943; first manager to win four World Series in a row (1936-'39); finished his career with the Boston Red Sox (1948-'50); lifetime record of 2,125-1,333; member of Baseball Hall of Fame.

Mark McCormack (b. Nov. 6, 1930): Founder and CEO of International Management Group (IMG), the sports management conglomerate who represent, among others, Joe Montana, Wayne Gretzky, Arnold Palmer, Andre Agassi and Pete Sampras.

Pat McCormick (b. May 12, 1930): U.S. diver; won women's platform and springboard gold medals in both 1952 and '56 Olympics.

Willie McCovey (b. Jan. 10, 1938): Baseball 1B; led NL in HRs 3 times and RBI twice; MVP in 1969 with SF; 521 career HRs; indicted for tax evasion in July 1995.

John McEnroe (b. Feb. 16, 1959): Tennis; No.1 player in the world 4 times (1981-84); 4-time U.S. Open singles champ (1979-81,84); 3-time Wimbledon champ (1981,83-84); has played on 5 Davis Cup winners (1978-79,81-82,92); won NCAA singles title (1978); finished career with 77 championships in singles, 77 more in doubles (including 9 Grand Slam titles), and American Davis Cup records for years played (13) and singles matches won (41).

John McGraw (b. Apr. 7, 1873, d. Feb. 25, 1934): Baseball; managed NY Giants to 9 NL pennants between 1905-24; won World Series 3 times in 1905 and 1921-22; 2nd on all-time career list with 2,810 wins in 33 seasons (2,784 regular season and 26 postseason).

Frank McGuire (b. Nov. 8, 1916, d. Oct. 11, 1994): Basketball; winner of 731 games as high school, college and pro coach; only coach to win 100 games at 3 colleges— St. John's (103), North Carolina (164) and South Carolina (283); won 550 games in 30 college seasons; 1957 UNC team went 32-0 and beat Kansas 54-53 in triple OT to win NCAA title; coached NBA Philadelphia Warriors to 49-31 record in 1961-62 season, but refused to move with team to San Francisco.

Jim McKay (b. Sept. 24, 1921): Radio-TV; host and commentator of ABC's Olympic coverage and "Wide World of Sports" show since 1961; 12-time Emmy winner; also given Peabody Award in 1988 and Life Achievement Emmy in 1990; became part owner of Baltimore Orioles in 1993.

John McKay (b. July 5, 1923): Football; coached USC to 3 national titles (1962,67,72); won Rose Bowl 5 times; reached NFL playoffs 3 times with Tampa Bay.

Tamara McKinney (b. Oct. 16, 1962): Skiing; only American woman to win overall Alpine World Cup championship (1983); won World Cup slalom (1984) and giant slalom titles twice (1981,83).

Denny McLain (b. Mar. 29, 1944): Baseball RHP; last pitcher to win 30 games (1968); 2-time Cy Young winner (1968-69) with Detroit; convicted of racketeering, extortion and drug possession in 1985, served 29 months of 25-year jail term, sentence overturned when court ruled he had not received a fair trial.

Rick Mears (b. Dec. 3, 1951): Auto racer; 3-time CART national champ (1979,81-82); 4-time winner of Indianapolis 500 (1979,84,88,91) and only driver to win 6 Indy 500 poles; Indy 500 Rookie of Year (1978); retired after 1992 season with 29 IndyCar wins and 40 poles.

Mark Messier (b. Jan. 18, 1961): Hockey C; 2-time Hart Trophy winner as MVP with Edmonton (1990) and NY Rangers (1992); captain of Rangers team that finally won 1st Stanley Cup since 1940; ranks 2nd (behind Gretzky) in all-time playoff points and assists; signed free agent contract with Vancouver Canucks in 1997.

Debbie Meyer (b. Aug. 14, 1952): Swimmer; 1st swimmer to win 3 individual gold medals at one Olympics (1968).

George Mikan (b. June 18, 1924): Basketball C; 3-time All-America (1944-46); led DePaul to NIT title (1945); led Minneapolis Lakers to 5 NBA titles in 6 years (1949-54); first commissioner of ABA (1967-69).

Stan Mikita (b. May 20, 1940): Hockey C; led NHL in scoring 4 times; won both MVP and Lady Byng awards in 1967 and '68 with Chicago.

Cheryl Miller (b. Jan. 3, 1964): Basketball; 3-time college Player of Year (1984-86); led USC to NCAA title and U.S. to Olympic gold medal in 1984; coached USC to 44-14 record in 2 seasons before quitting to join Turner Sports as NBA reporter; coached Phoenix Mercury in first season of WNBA.

Del Miller (b. July 5, 1913): Harness racing; driver, trainer, owner, breeder, seller and track owner; drove to 2,441 wins from 1939-90.

Marvin Miller (b. Apr. 14, 1917): Baseball labor leader; executive director of Players' Assn. from 1966-82; increased average salary from $19,000 to over $240,000; led 13-day strike in 1972 and 50-day walkout in '81.

Shannon Miller (b. Mar. 10, 1977): Gymnast; won 5 medals in 1992 Olympics and 2 golds in '96 Games; All-Around women's world champion in 1993 and '94.

Billy Mills (b. June 30, 1938): Track & Field; upset winner of 10,000m gold medal at 1964 Olympics.

Bora Milutinovic (b. Sept. 7, 1944): Soccer; Serbian who coached United States national team from 1991-95, but was fired on Apr. 14, 1995 when he refused to accept additional duties as director of player development; hired 4 months later to revive Mexican national team; known as a miracle worker, he led Mexico, Costa Rica and the U.S. into the 2nd round of the last three World Cups.

Tommy Moe (b. Feb. 17, 1970): Alpine skier; won Downhill and placed 2nd in Super-G at 1994 Winter Olympics; 1st U.S. man to win 2 Olympic alpine medals in one year.

Paul Molitor (b. Aug. 22, 1956): Baseball DH-1B; All-America SS at Minnesota in 1976; signed as free agent by Toronto on Dec. 7, 1992, after 15 years with Milwaukee; led Blue Jays to 2nd straight World Series title as MVP (1993); has hit .418 in 2 Series appearances (1982,93); holds World Series record with five hits in one game; got career hit 3,000 with a triple on Sept. 16, 1996.

Joe Montana (b. June 11, 1956): Football QB; led Notre Dame to national title in 1977; led San Francisco to 4 Super Bowl titles in 1980s; only 3-time Super Bowl MVP; 2-time NFL MVP (1989-90); has led NFL in passing 5 times; missed all of 1991 season and nearly all of '92 after elbow surgery; traded to Kansas City in 1993; ranked 2nd in all-time passing efficiency (92.3), 4th in TD passes (273) and yards passing (40,551); announced retirement in San Francisco on Apr. 18, 1995.

Helen Wills Moody (b. Oct. 6, 1905): Tennis; won 8 Wimbledon singles titles, 7 U.S. and 4 French from 1923-38.

Warren Moon (b. Nov. 18, 1956): Football QB; MVP of 1978 Rose Bowl with Washington; MVP of CFL with Edmonton in 1983; led Eskimos to 5 consecutive Grey Cup titles (1978-82) and was playoff MVP twice (1980,82); joined Houston of NFL in 1984; led NFL in attempts, completions and yards in 1990 and '91; picked for 8 Pro Bowls; traded to Minnesota in 1994; signed with Seattle Seahawks in 1997.

Archie Moore (b. Dec. 13, 1913): Boxer; world light-heavyweight champion (1952-60); pro record 199-26-8 with 145 KOs.

Herman Moore (b. Oct. 20, 1969): Football; wide receiver for the Detroit Lions; caught an NFL-record 123 passes in 1995.

Michael Moorer (b. Nov. 12, 1967): Boxer; became 1st left-hander to win heavyweight title when he scored majority decision over Evander Holyfield on Apr. 22, 1994; lost title to George Foreman on 10th round KO Nov. 5, 1994; pro record of 37-1 with 30 KOs.

Noureddine Morceli (b. Feb. 28, 1970): Algerian runner; 3-time world champion at 1,500 meters (1991,93, 95); set world records at mile (3:44.39) in 1993, at 3,000m (7:25.11) in '94 and at 1,500m (3:27.37) in 1995.

Howie Morenz (b. June 21, 1902, d. Mar. 8, 1937): Hockey C; 3-time NHL MVP (1928,31-32); led Montreal Canadiens to 3 Stanley Cups; voted Outstanding Player of the Half-Century in 1950.

Joe Morgan (b. Sept. 19, 1943): Baseball 2B; led NL in walks 4 times; regular-season MVP both years he led Cincinnati to World Series titles (1975-76); 3rd behind Babe Ruth and Ted Williams in career walks with 1,865.

Bobby Morrow (b. Oct. 15, 1935): Track & Field; won 3 gold medals at 1956 Olympics (100m, 200m and 4x400m relay).

Willie Mosconi (b. June 27, 1913, d. Sept. 12, 1993): Pocket Billiards; 14-time world champion from 1941-57.

Annemarie Moser-Pröll (b. Mar. 27, 1953): Austrian alpine skier; won World Cup overall title 6 times (1971-75,79); all-time women's World Cup leader in career wins with 61; won Downhill in 1980 Olympics.

Edwin Moses (b. Aug. 31, 1955): Track & Field; won 400m hurdles at 1976 and '84 Olympics, bronze medal in '88; also winner of 122 consecutive races from 1977-87.

Stirling Moss (b. Sept. 17, 1929): Auto racer; won 194 of 466 career races and 16 Formula One events, but was never world champion.

Marion Motley (b. June 5, 1920): Football FB; all-time leading AAFC rusher; rushed for over 4,700 yards and 31 TDs for Cleveland Browns (1946-53).

Dale Murphy (b. Mar. 12, 1956): Baseball OF; led NL in RBI 3 times and HRs twice; 2-time MVP (1982-83) with Atlanta; also played with Philadelphia and Colorado; retired May 27, 1993, with 398 HRs.

Jack Murphy (b. Feb. 5, 1923, d. Sept. 24, 1980): Sports editor and columnist of *The San Diego Union* from 1951-80; instrumental in bringing AFL Chargers south from LA in 1961, landing Padres as NL expansion team in '69; and lobbying for 54,000-seat San Diego stadium that would later bear his name.

Eddie Murray (b. Feb. 24, 1956): Baseball 1B-DH; AL Rookie of Year in 1977; became 20th player in history, but only 2nd switch hitter (after Pete Rose) to get 3,000 hits; belted 500th homer off Detroit's Felipe Lira on Sept. 6, 1996.

Jim Murray (b. Dec. 29, 1919): Sports columnist for *LA Times* since 1961; 14-time Sportswriter of the Year; won Pulitzer Prize for commentary in 1990.

Ty Murray (b. Oct. 11, 1969): Rodeo cowboy; 6-time All-Around world champion (1989-94); Rookie of Year in 1988; youngest (age 20) to win All-Around title; set single season earnings mark with $297,896 in 1993; missed most of 1995 season with knee injury.

Stan Musial (b. Nov. 21, 1920): Baseball OF-1B; led NL in batting 7 times; 3-time MVP (1943,46,48) with St. Louis; played in 24 All-Star Games; had 3,630 career hits and .331 average.

John Naber (b. Jan. 20, 1956): Swimmer; won 4 gold medals and a silver in 1976 Olympics.

Bronko Nagurski (b. Nov. 3, 1908, d. Jan. 7, 1990): Football FB-T; All-America at Minnesota (1929); All-Pro with Chicago Bears (1932-34); charter member of college and pro halls of fame.

James Naismith (b. Nov. 6, 1861, d. Nov. 28, 1939): Canadian physical education instructor who invented basketball in 1891 at the YMCA Training School (now Springfield College) in Springfield, Mass.

Joe Namath (b. May 31, 1943): Football QB; signed for unheard-of $400,000 as rookie with AFL's NY Jets in 1965; 2-time All-AFL (1968-69) and All-NFL (1972); led Jets to Super Bowl title as MVP in '69.

Ilie Nastase (b. July 19, 1946): Romanian tennis player; No.1 in the world twice (1972-73); won U.S. (1972) and French (1973) Opens.

Martina Navratilova (b. Oct. 18, 1956): Tennis player; No.1 player in the world 7 times (1978-79,82-86); won her record 9th Wimbledon singles title in 1990; also won 4 U.S. Opens, 3 Australian and 2 French; in all, won 18 Grand Slam singles titles and 38 Grand Slam doubles titles; all-time leader among men and women in singles titles (167) and money won ($20.3 million) over 21 years; retired from singles play after 1994 season with No. 8 ranking and appearance in 12th Wimbledon final.

Cosmas Ndeti (b. Nov. 24, 1971): Kenyan distance runner; winner of three consecutive Boston Marathons (1993-95), set course record of 2:07:15 in 1994.

Earle (Greasy) Neale (b. Nov. 5, 1891, d. Nov. 2, 1973): Baseball and Football; hit .357 for Cincinnati in 1919 World Series; also played with pre-NFL Canton Bulldogs; later coached Philadelphia Eagles to 2 NFL titles (1948-49).

Primo Nebiolo (b. July 14, 1923): Italian president of International Amateur Athletic Federation (IAAF) since 1981; also an at-large member of International Olympic Committee; regarded as dictatorial, but credited with elevating track & field to world class financial status.

Byron Nelson (b. Feb. 4, 1912): Golfer; 2-time winner of both Masters (1937,42) and PGA (1940,45); also U.S. Open champion in 1939; won 19 tournaments in 1945, including 11 in a row; also set all-time PGA stroke average with 68.33 strokes per round over 120 rounds in '45.

Lindsey Nelson (b. May 25, 1919, d. June 10, 1995): Radio-TV; all-purpose play-by-play broadcaster for CBS, NBC and others; 4-time Sportscaster of the Year (1959-62); voice of Cotton Bowl for 25 years and NY Mets from 1962-78; given Life Achievement Emmy Award in 1991.

Ernie Nevers (b. July 11, 1903, d. May 3, 1976): Football FB; earned 11 letters in four sports at Stanford; played pro football, baseball and basketball; scored 40 points for Chicago Cardinals in one NFL game (1929).

Paula Newby-Fraser (b. June 2, 1962): Zimbabwean triathlete; 8-time winner of Ironman Triathlon in Hawaii; established women's record of 8:55:28 in 1992.

John Newcombe (b. May 23, 1944): Australian tennis player; No.1 player in world 3 times (1967,70-71); won Wimbledon 3 times and U.S. and Australian championships twice each.

Pete Newell (b. Aug. 31, 1915): Basketball; coached at University of San Francisco, Michigan State and the University of California; first coach to win NIT (San Francisco -1949), NCAA (California - 1959) and Olympic gold medal (1960); later served as the general manager of the San Diego Rockets and Los Angeles Lakers in the NBA; member of Basketball Hall of Fame.

Bob Neyland (b. Feb. 17, 1892, d. Mar. 28, 1962): Football; 3-time coach at Tennessee; had 173-31-12 record in 21 years; won national title in 1951; Vols' stadium named for him; also Army general who won Distinguished Service Cross as supply officer in World War II.

Jack Nicklaus (b. Jan. 21, 1940): Golfer; all-time leader in major tournament wins with 20— including 6 Masters, 5 PGAs, 4 U.S. Opens and 3 British Opens; oldest player to win Masters (46 in 1986); PGA Player of Year 5 times (1967,72-73,75-76); named Golfer of Century by PGA in 1988; 6-time Ryder Cup player and 2-time captain (1983,87); won NCAA title (1961) and 2 U.S. Amateurs (1959,61); entered 1995 with 70 PGA Tour wins (2nd to Sam Snead's 81); 3rd win in Tradition in '95 gave him 7 majors in 6 years on Seniors Tour.

Chuck Noll (b. Jan. 5, 1932): Football; coached Pittsburgh to 4 Super Bowl titles (1975-76,79-80); retired after 1991 season ranked 5th on all-time list with 209 wins (including playoffs) in 23 years.

Greg Norman (b. Feb. 10, 1955): Australian golfer; PGA Tour's all-time money winner ($10.4 million), passing Tom Kite on Aug. 27, 1995; 72 tournament wins worldwide; 2-time British Open winner (1986,93); lost Masters by a stroke in both 1986 (to Jack Nicklaus) and '87 (to Larry Mize in sudden death).

James D. Norris (b. Nov. 6, 1906, d. Feb. 25, 1966): Boxing promoter and NHL owner; president of International Boxing Club from 1949 until U.S. Supreme Court ordered its break-up (for anti-trust violations) in 1958; only NHL owner to win Stanley Cups in two cities' Detroit (1936-37,43) and Chicago (1961).

Paavo Nurmi (b. June 13, 1897, d. Oct. 2, 1973): Finnish runner; won 9 gold medals (6 individual) in 1920, '24 and '28 Olympics; from 1921-31 broke 23 world outdoor records in events ranging from 1,500 to 20,000 meters.

Dan O'Brien (b. July 18, 1966): Track & Field; set world record in decathlon (8,891 pts) on Sept. 4-5, 1992, after failing to qualify for event at U.S. Olympic Trials; three-time gold medalist at World Championships (1991,93,95).

Larry O'Brien (b. July 7, 1917, d. Sept. 27, 1990): Basketball; former U.S. Postmaster General and 3rd NBA commissioner (1975-84); league absorbed 4 ABA teams and created salary cap during his term in office.

Parry O'Brien (b. Jan. 28, 1932): Track & Field; in 4 consecutive Olympics, won two gold medals, a silver and placed 4th in the shot put (1952-64).

Al Oerter (b. Sept. 19, 1936): Track & Field; his 4 discus gold medals in consecutive Olympics from 1956-68 is an unmatched Olympic record.

Sadaharu Oh (b. May 20, 1940): Baseball 1B; led Japan League in HRs 15 times; 9-time MVP for Tokyo Giants; hit 868 HRs in 22 years.

Hakeem Olajuwon (b. Jan. 21, 1963): Basketball C; Nigerian native who was consensus All-America in 1984 and Final Four MVP in 1983 for Houston; overall 1st pick by Houston Rockets in 1984 NBA draft; led Rockets to back-to-back NBA titles (1994,95); regular season MVP ('94) and playoff MVP ('94,'95); 6-time All-NBA 1st team (1987-89,93-95). Member of Dream Team III.

José Maria Olazábal (b. Feb. 5, 1966): Spanish golfer; Has 14 worldwide victories; won only major at '94 Masters.

Barney Oldfield (b. Jan. 29, 1878, d. Oct. 4, 1946): Auto racing pioneer; drove cars built by Henry Ford; first man to drive car a mile per minute (1903).

Walter O'Malley (b. Oct. 9, 1903, d. Aug. 9, 1979): Baseball owner; moved Brooklyn Dodgers to Los Angeles after 1957 season; won 4 World Series (1955,59,63,65).

Shaquille O'Neal (b. Mar. 6, 1972): Basketball C; 2-time All-America at LSU (1991-92); overall 1st pick (as a junior) by Orlando in 1992 NBA draft; Rookie of Year in 1993; led NBA in scoring in 1995; member of Dream Teams II and III. Signed with LA Lakers in 1996.

Bobby Orr (b. Mar. 20, 1948): Hockey D; 8-time Norris Trophy winner as best defenseman; led NHL in scoring twice and assists 5 times; All-NHL 1st team 8 times; regular season MVP 3 times (1970-72); playoff MVP twice (1970,72) with Boston.

Tom Osborne (b. Feb. 23, 1937): Football; entered 1996 season with record of 231-47-3 in 23 seasons as coach at Nebraska; his win percentage of .827 is best of any active coach in Division I-A; finally won national championship in 1994; won 2nd national title in '95.

Mel Ott (b. Mar. 2, 1909, d. Nov. 21, 1958): Baseball OF; joined NY Giants at age 16; led NL in HRs 6 times; had 511 HRs and 1,860 RBI in 22 years.

Kristin Otto (b. Feb. 7, 1966): East German swimmer; 1st woman to win 6 gold medals (4 individual) at one Olympics (1988).

Francis Ouimet (b. May 8, 1893, d. Sept. 3, 1967): Golfer; won 1913 U.S. Open as 20-year-old amateur playing on Brookline, Mass. course where he used to caddie; won U.S. Amateur twice; 8-time Walker Cup player.

Steve Owen (b. Apr. 21, 1898, d. May 17, 1964): Football; All-Pro guard (1927); coached NY Giants for 23 years (1931-53); won 153 career games and 2 NFL titles (1934,38).

Jesse Owens (b. Sept. 12, 1913, d. Mar. 31, 1980): Track & Field; broke 5 world records in one afternoon at Big Ten Championships (May 25, 1935); a year later, he won 4 gold medals (100m, 200m, 4x100m relay and long jump) at Berlin Summer Olympics.

Alan Page (b. Aug. 7, 1945): Football DE; consensus All-America at Notre Dame in 1966 and member of two national championship teams; 6-time NFL All-Pro and 1971 Player of Year with Minnesota Vikings; also a lawyer who was elected to Minnesota Supreme Court in 1992.

Satchel Paige (b. July 7, 1906, d. June 6, 1982): Baseball RHP; pitched 55 career no-hitters over 20 seasons in Negro Leagues; entered Major Leagues with Cleveland in 1948 at age 42; had 28-31 record in 5 years; returned to AL at age 59 to start 1 game for Kansas City in 1965; went 3 innings, gave up a hit and got a strikeout.

Arnold Palmer (b. Sept. 10, 1929): Golfer; winner of 4 Masters, 2 British Opens and a U.S. Open; 2-time PGA Player of Year (1960,62); 1st player to earn over $1 million in career (1968); annual PGA Tour money leader award named after him; 60 wins on PGA Tour and 10 more on Senior Tour.

Jim Palmer (b. Oct. 15, 1945): Baseball RHP; 3-time Cy Young Award winner (1973,75-76); won 20 or more games 8 times with Baltimore; 1991 comeback attempt at age 45 scrubbed in spring training.

Bill Parcells (b. Aug. 22, 1941): Football; coached NY Giants to 2 Super Bowl titles (1986,90); retired after 1990 season then returned in '93 as coach of New England; led Patriots to Super Bowl loss in 1997; left Patriots in 1997 and signed to coach the New York Jets.

Jack Pardee (b. Apr. 19, 1936): Football; All-America linebacker at Texas A&M; 2-time All-Pro with LA Rams (1963) and Washington (1971); 2-time NFL Coach of Year (1976,79) and winner of 87 games in 11 seasons; only man hired as head coach in NFL, WFL, USFL and CFL; also coached at University of Houston.

Bernie Parent (b. Apr. 3, 1945): Hockey G; led Philadelphia Flyers to 2 Stanley Cups as playoff MVP (1974,75); 2-time Vezina Trophy winner; posted 55 career shutouts and 2.55 GAA in 13 seasons.

Joe Paterno (b. Dec. 21, 1926): Football; has coached Penn State to 2 national titles (1982,86) and 18-8-1 bowl record in 31 years; also had three unbeaten teams that didn't finish No. 1; Coach of Year 4 times (1968,78,82,86); leads all active Div. I-A coaches in career wins (including bowls).

Craig Patrick (b. May 20, 1946): Hockey; 3rd generation Patrick to have name inscribed on Stanley Cup; GM of 2-time Stanley Cup champion Pittsburgh Penguins (1991-92); also captain of 1969 NCAA champion at Denver; assistant coach-GM of 1980 gold medal-winning U.S. Olympic team; scored 72 goals in 8 NHL seasons and won 69 games in 3 years as coach; grandson of Lester.

Lester Patrick (b. Dec. 30, 1883, d. June 1, 1960): Hockey; pro hockey pioneer as player, coach and general manager for 43 years; led NY Rangers to Stanley Cups as coach (1928,33) and GM (1940); grandfather of Craig.

Floyd Patterson (b. Jan. 4, 1935): Boxer; Olympic middleweight champ in 1952; world heavyweight champion (1956-59,60-62); 1st to regain heavyweight crown; fought Ingemar Johansson 3 times in 22 months from 1959-61 and won last two; pro record 55-8-1 with 40 KOs; jr. lightweight champion Tracy Harris Patterson is his adopted son.

Walter Payton (b. July 25, 1954): Football RB; NFL's all-time leading rusher with 16,726 yards; scored 109 career TDs; All-Pro 7 times with Chicago; MVP in 1977; led Bears to Super Bowl title in Jan. 1986.

Pelé (b. Oct. 23, 1940): Brazilian soccer F; given name— Edson Arantes do Nascimento; led Brazil to 3 World Cup titles (1958,62,70); came to U.S. in 1975 to play for NY Cosmos in NASL; scored 1,281 goals in 22 years; currently Brazil's minister of sport.

Roger Penske (b. Feb. 20, 1937): Auto racing; national sports car driving champion (1964); established racing team in 1961; co-founder of Championship Auto Racing Teams (CART); Penske Racing entered 1995 with a record 91 IndyCar victories, including 10 Indianapolis 500s and 9 IndyCar points titles; shocked racing world by failing to qualify car for 1995 Indy 500.

Willie Pep (b. Sept. 19, 1922): Boxer; 2-time world featherweight champion (1942-48,49-50); pro record 230-11-1 with 65 KOs.

Marie-Jose Perec (b. 1968): Track & Field; French sprinter who became 2nd woman to win the 200m and 400m events in the same Olympics (1996); her time in the 400 (48.25) set an Olympic record; Valerie Brisco-Hooks did it in the boycotted 1984 games; also won the 400M in 1992 games.

Fred Perry (b. May 18, 1909, d. Feb. 2, 1995): British tennis player; 3-time Wimbledon champ (1934-36); fist player to win all four Grand Slam singles titles, though not simultaneously; last native to win All-England men's title.

Gaylord Perry (b. Sept. 15, 1938): Baseball RHP; only pitcher to win a Cy Young Award in both leagues; retired in 1983 with 314 wins and 3,534 strikeouts over 22 years and with 8 teams; brother Jim won 215 games for family total of 529.

Bob Pettit (b. Dec. 12, 1932): Basketball F; All-NBA 1st team 10 times (1955-64); 2-time MVP (1956,59) with St. Louis Hawks; first player to score 20,000 points.

Richard Petty (b. July 2, 1937): Auto racer; 7-time winner of Daytona 500; 7-time NASCAR national champ (1964,67,71-72,74-75,79); first stock car driver to win $1 million in career; all-time NASCAR leader in races won (200), poles (127) and wins in a single season (27 in 1967); retired after 1992 season; son of Lee (54 career wins) and father of Kyle (7 career wins).

Laffit Pincay Jr. (b. Dec. 29, 1946): Jockey; 5-time Eclipse Award winner (1971,73-74,79,85); winner of 3 Belmonts and 1 Kentucky Derby (aboard Swale in 1984); entered 1995 with 8,217 career wins, trailing only Bill Shoemaker's 8,833.

Scottie Pippen (b. Sept. 25, 1965): Basketball; Chicago Bulls forward has started on five NBA championships (1991,92,93, 96, 97); All-NBA first team in '94, '95.

Nelson Piquet (b. Aug. 17, 1952): Brazilian auto racer; 3-time Formula One world champion (1981,83, 87); left circuit in 1991 with 23 career wins.

Rick Pitino (b. Sept. 18, 1952): Basketball; won 1996 NCAA championship in his seventh year at Kentucky; previously coached the New York Knicks in the NBA (96-81 overall); Providence College (42-23) and Boston University (46-24); in 1997, named coach and general manager of the Boston Celtics.

Jacques Plante (b. Jan. 17, 1929, d. Feb. 27, 1986): Hockey G; led Montreal to 6 Stanley Cups (1953,56-60); won 7 Vezina Trophies; MVP in 1962; first goalie to regularly wear a mask; posted 82 shutouts with 2.38 GAA.

Gary Player (b. Nov. 1, 1936): South African golfer; 3-time winner of Masters and British Open; only player in 20th century to win British Open in three different decades (1959,68,74); one of only four players to win all four Grand Slam titles (others are Hogan, Nicklaus and Sarazen); has also won 2 PGAs, a U.S. Open and 2 U.S. Senior Opens; entered 1995 with 21 wins on PGA Tour and 17 more on Senior Tour.

Jim Plunkett (b. Dec. 5, 1947): Football QB; Heisman Trophy winner in 1970; AFL Rookie of the Year in 1971; led Oakland-LA Raiders to Super Bowl wins in 1981 and '84; MVP in '81.

Maurice Podoloff (b. Aug. 18, 1890, d. Nov. 24, 1985): Basketball; engineered merger of Basketball Assn. of America and National Basketball League into NBA in 1949; NBA commissioner (1949-63); league MVP trophy named after him.

Fritz Pollard (b. Jan. 27, 1894, d. May 11, 1986): Football; 1st black All-America RB (1916 at Brown); 1st black to play in Rose Bowl; 7-year NFL pro (1920-26); 1st black NFL coach, at Milwaukee and Hammond, Ind.

Sam Pollock (b. Dec. 15, 1925): Hockey GM; managed NHL Montreal Canadiens to 9 Stanley Cups in 14 years (1965-78).

Denis Potvin (b. Oct. 29, 1953): Hockey D; won Norris Trophy 3 times (1976,78-79); 5-time All-NHL 1st-team; led NY Islanders to 4 Stanley Cups.

Mike Powell (b. Nov. 10, 1963): Track & Field; broke Bob Beamon's 23-year-old long jump world record by 2 inches with leap of 29-ft., 41/2 in. at the 1991 World Championships; Sullivan Award winner (1991); won long jump silver medals in 1988 and '92 Olympics; repeated as world champ in 1993.

Steve Prefontaine (b. Jan. 25, 1951, d. June 1, 1975): Track & Field; All-America distance runner at Oregon; first athlete to win same event at NCAA championships 4 straight years (5,000 meters from 1970-73); finished 4th in 5,000 at 1972 Munich Olympics; first athlete to endorse Nike running shoes; killed in a one-car accident.

Nick Price (b. Jan. 28, 1957): Zimbabwean golfer; PGA Tour Player of Year in 1993 and '94; became 1st player since Nick Faldo in 1990 to win 2 Grand Slam titles in same year when he took British Open and PGA Championship in 1994; also won PGA in '92.

Alain Prost (b. Feb. 24, 1955): French auto racer; 4-time Formula One world champion (1985-86,89,93); sat out 1992 then returned to win 4th title in 1993; retired after '93 season as all-time F1 wins leader with 51.

Kirby Puckett (b. Mar. 14, 1961): Baseball OF; led Minnesota Twins to World Series titles in 1987 and '91; retired in 1996 with a batting title (1989), 2,304 hits and a .318 career average in 12 seasons.

C.C. Pyle (b. 1882, d. Feb. 3, 1939): Promoter; known as "Cash and Carry"; hyped Red Grange's pro football debut by arranging 1925 barnstorming tour with Chicago Bears; had Grange bolt NFL for new AFL in 1926 (AFL folded in '27); also staged 2 Transcontinental Races (1928-29), known as "Bunion Derbies."

Bobby Rahal (b. Jan. 10, 1953): Auto racer; 3-time PPG Cup champ (1986,87,92); entered 1995 with 24 career IndyCar wins, including 1986 Indy 500.

Jack Ramsay (b. Feb. 21, 1925): Basketball; coach who won 239 college games with St. Joseph's-PA in 11 seasons and 906 NBA games (including playoffs) with 4 teams over 21 years; placed 3rd in 1961 Final Four; led Portland to NBA title in 1977.

Bill Rassmussen (b. Oct. 15, 1932): Radio-TV; unemployed radio broadcaster who founded ESPN, the nation's first 24-hour all-sports cable-TV network, in 1978; bought out by Getty Oil in 1981.

Willis Reed (b. June 25, 1942): Basketball C; led NY Knicks to NBA titles in 1970 and '73, playoff MVP both years; regular season MVP 1970.

Mary Lou Retton (b. Jan. 24, 1968): Gymnast; won gold medal in women's All-Around at the 1984 Olympics, also won 2 silvers and 2 bronzes.

Butch Reynolds (b. June 8, 1964): Track & Field; set current world record in 400 meters (43.29) in 1988; banned for 2 1/2 years for allegedly failing drug test in 1990; sued IAAF and won $27.4 million judgment in 1992, but award was voided in '94; won silver medal in 400 meters and gold as member of U.S. 4x400-meter relay team at both 1993 and '95 World Championships.

Grantland Rice (b. Nov. 1, 1880, d. July 13, 1954): First celebrated American sportswriter; chronicled the Golden Age of Sport in 1920s; immortalized Notre Dame's "Four Horsemen."

Jerry Rice (b. Oct. 13, 1962): Football WR; 2-time Div. I-AA All-America at Mississippi Valley St. (1983-84); 7-time All-Pro; regular season MVP in 1987 and Super Bowl MVP in 1989 with San Francisco; NFL all-time leader in touchdowns and receptions.

Henri Richard (b. Feb. 29, 1936): Hockey C; leap year baby who played on more Stanley Cup championship teams (11) than anybody else; at 5-foot-7, known as the "Pocket Rocket"; brother of Maurice.

Maurice Richard (b. Aug. 4, 1921): Hockey RW; the "Rocket"; 8-time NHL 1st team All-Star; MVP in 1947; 1st to score 50 goals in one season (1945); 544 career goals; played on 8 Stanley Cup winners in Montreal.

Bob Richards (b. Feb. 2, 1926): Track & Field; pole vaulter, ordained minister and original *Wheaties* pitchman, who won gold medals at 1952 and '56 Olympics; remains only 2-time Olympic pole vault champ.

Nolan Richardson (b. Dec. 27, 1941): Basketball; coached Arkansas to consecutive NCAA finals, beating Duke in 1994 and losing to UCLA in '95.

Tex Rickard (b. Jan. 2, 1870, d. Jan. 6, 1929): Promoter who handled boxing's first $1 million gate (Dempsey vs. Carpentier in 1921); built Madison Square Garden in 1925; founded NY Rangers as Garden tenant in 1926 and named NHL team after himself (Tex's Rangers); also built Boston Garden in 1928.

Eddie Rickenbacker (b. Oct. 8, 1890, d. July 23, 1973): Mechanic and auto racer; became America's top flying ace (22 kills) in World War I; owned Indianapolis Speedway (1927-45) and ran Eastern Air Lines (1938-59).

Branch Rickey (b. Dec. 20, 1881, d. Dec. 9, 1965): Baseball innovator; revolutionized game with creation of modern farm system while general manager of St. Louis Cardinals (1917-42); integrated Major Leagues in 1947 as president-GM of Brooklyn Dodgers when he brought up Jackie Robinson (whom he had signed on Oct. 23, 1945); later GM of Pittsburgh Pirates.

Leni Riefenstahl (b. Aug. 22, 1902): German filmmaker of 1930's; directed classic sports documentary "Olympia" on 1936 Berlin Summer Olympics; infamous, however, for also making 1934 Hitler propaganda film "Triumph of the Will."

Roy Riegels (b. Apr. 4, 1908, d. Mar. 26, 1993): Football; California center who picked up fumble in 2nd quarter of 1929 Rose Bowl and raced 70 yards in the wrong direction to set up a 2-point safety in 8-7 loss to Georgia Tech.

Bobby Riggs (b. Feb. 25, 1918, d. Oct. 25, 1995): Tennis; won Wimbledon once (1939) and U.S. title twice (1939,41); legendary hustler who made his biggest score in 1973 as 55-year-old male chauvinist challenging the best women players; beat No. 1 Margaret Smith Court 6-2, 6-1, but was thrashed by No. 2 Billie Jean King, 6-4, 6-3, 6-3 in nationally-televised "Battle of the Sexes" on Sept. 20, before 30,492 at the Astrodome.

Pat Riley (b. Mar. 20, 1945): Basketball; coached LA Lakers to 4 of their 5 NBA titles in 1980s (1982,85,87-88); coached New York from 1991-95; 2-time Coach of Year (1990,93) and all-time NBA leader in playoff wins (137); quit Knicks after 1994-95 season with year left on contract; signed with Miami Heat on Sept. 2 as coach, team president and part-owner after Knicks agreed to drop tampering charges in exchange for $1 million and a conditional first round draft pick.

Cal Ripken Jr. (b. Aug. 24, 1960): Baseball SS; broke Lou Gehrig's major league Iron Man record of 2,130 consecutive games played on Sept. 6, 1995; record streak began on May 30, 1982; 2-time AL MVP (1983,91) for Baltimore; AL Rookie of Year (1982); AL starting SS in All-Star Game since 1984; holds record for career home runs by a shortstop.

Joe Robbie (b. July 7, 1916, d. Jan. 7, 1990): Football; original owner of Miami Dolphins (1966-90); won 2 Super Bowls (1972-73); built $115-million Robbie Stadium with private funds in 1987.

Oscar Robertson (b. Nov. 24, 1938): Basketball G; 3-time college Player of Year (1958-60) at Cincinnati; led 1960 U.S. Olympic team to gold medal; NBA Rookie of Year (1961); 9-time All-NBA 1st team; MVP in 1964 with Cincinnati Royals; NBA champion in 1971 with Milwaukee Bucks; 3rd in career assists with 9,887.

Paul Robeson (b. Apr. 8, 1898, d. Jan. 23, 1976): Black 4-sport star and 2-time football All-America (1917-18) at Rutgers; 3-year NFL pro; also scholar, lawyer, singer, actor and political activist; long-tainted by Communist sympathies, he was finally inducted into College Football Hall of Fame in 1995.

Brooks Robinson (b. May 18, 1937): Baseball 3B; led AL in fielding 12 times from 1960-72 with Baltimore; regular season MVP in 1964; World Series MVP in 1970.

David Robinson (b. Aug. 6, 1965): Basketball C; college Player of Year at Navy in 1987; overall 1st pick by San Antonio in 1987 NBA draft; served in military from 1987-89; NBA Rookie of Year in 1990 and regular season MVP in '95; 2-time All-NBA 1st team (1991,92); led NBA in scoring in 1994; member of 1988, '92 and '96 U.S. Olympic teams.

Eddie Robinson (b. Feb. 13, 1919): Football; head coach at Div. I-AA Grambling State for 54 years; winningest coach in college history; has led Tigers to 8 national black college titles.

Frank Robinson (b. Aug. 31, 1935): Baseball OF; won MVP in NL (1961) and AL (1966); Triple Crown winner and World Series MVP in 1966 with Baltimore; 1st black manager in Major Leagues with Cleveland in 1975; also managed in SF and Baltimore.

Jackie Robinson (b. Jan. 31, 1919, d. Oct. 24, 1972): Baseball 1B-2B-3B; 4-sport athlete at UCLA; hit .387 with K.C. Monarchs of Negro Leagues in 1945; signed by Brooklyn Dodgers on Oct. 23, 1945 and broke Major League baseball's color line in 1947; Rookie of Year in 1947 and NL's MVP in '49; hit .311 over 10 seasons.

Sugar Ray Robinson (b. May 3, 1921, d. Apr. 12, 1989): Boxer; world welterweight champion (1946-51); 5-time middleweight champ; retired at age 45 after 25 years in the ring; pro record 174-19-6 with 109 KOs.

Knute Rockne (b. Mar. 4, 1888, d. Mar. 31, 1931): Football; coached Notre Dame to 3 consensus national titles (1924,29,30), all-time winningest college coach (.881) with record of 105-12-5 over 13 seasons; killed in plane crash.

Bill Rodgers (b. Dec. 23, 1947): Distance runner; won Boston and New York City marathons 4 times each from 1975-80.

Dennis Rodman (b. May 13, 1961): Basketball F; ferocious rebounder and tenacious defender; also known for dyeing his hair various colors and for getting suspended regularly; in 1997, he was suspended for 11 games for kicking a courtside cameraman in the groin; led the NBA in rebounding six years in a row, 1991–97; member of 4 NBA champion teams, Detroit Pistons (1989, 90) and Chicago Bulls (1996, 97); 2 time All Star (1990, 92), 2 time defensive player of the year (1990–91)and six time member of the NBA All-Defensive team (1989–93,96).

Irina Rodnina (b. Sept. 12, 1949): Soviet figure skater; won 10 world championships and 3 Olympic gold medals in pairs competition from 1971-80.

Alex Rodriguez (b. July 27, 1975): Baseball SS; highly-touted prospect exploded on the scene in 1996 with a .358 batting average (led league), 36 home runs, 123 RBIs and 15 stolen bases.

Diann Roffe-Steinrotter (b. Mar. 24, 1967): Alpine skier; 2-time Olympic medalist in Super-G; won silver at Albertville in 1992, then gold at Lillehammer in '94.

Art Rooney (b. Jan. 27, 1901, d. Aug. 25, 1988): Race track legend and pro football pioneer; bought Pittsburgh Steelers franchise in 1933 for $2,500; finally won NFL title with 1st of 4 Super Bowls in 1974 season.

Theodore Roosevelt (b. Oct. 27, 1858, d. Jan. 6, 1919): 26th President of the U.S.; physical fitness buff who boxed as undergraduate at Harvard; credited with presidential assist in forming of Intercollegiate Athletic Assn. (now NCAA) in 1905-06.

Mauri Rose (b. May 26, 1906, d. Jan. 1, 1981): Auto racer; 3-time winner of Indy 500 (1941,47-48).

Murray Rose (b. Jan. 6, 1939): Australian swimmer; won 3 gold medals at 1956 Olympics; added a gold, silver and bronze in 1960.

Pete Rose (b. Apr. 14, 1941): Baseball OF-IF; all-time hits leader with 4,256; led NL in batting 3 times; regular-season MVP in 1973; World Series MVP in 1975; had 44-game hitting streak in '78; managed Cincinnati (1984-89); banned for life in 1989 for conduct detrimental to baseball; convicted of tax evasion in 1990 and sentenced to 5 months in prison; released Jan. 7, 1991.

Ken Rosewall (b. Nov. 2, 1934): Tennis; won French and Australian singles titles at age 18; U.S. champ twice, but never won Wimbledon.

Mark Roth (b. Apr. 10, 1951): Bowler; 4-time PBA Player of Year (1977-79,84); entered 1995 with 33 tournament wins; victory in Apr. 15, 1995 Foresters Open was first in 7 year; U.S. Open champ in 1984.

Alan Rothenberg (b. Apr. 10, 1939): Soccer; president of U.S. Soccer since 1990; surprised European skeptics by directing hugely successful 1994 World Cup tournament; successfully got oft-delayed outdoor Major League Soccer off ground in 1996.

Patrick Roy (b. Oct. 5, 1965): Hockey G; led Montreal to 2 Stanley Cup titles; playoff MVP as rookie in 1986 and again in '93; has won Vezina Trophy 3 times (1989-90,92). Won 3rd Stanley Cup with Colorado ('96).

Pete Rozelle (b. Mar. 1, 1926, d. December 6, 1996): Football; NFL Commissioner from 1960-89; presided over growth of league from 12 to 28 teams, merger with AFL, creation of Super Bowl and advent of huge TV rights fees.

Wilma Rudolph (b. June 23, 1940, d. Nov. 12, 1994): Track & Field; won 3 gold medals (100m, 200m and 4x400m relay) at 1960 Olympics; also won relay silver in '56 Games; 2-time AP Athlete of Year (1960-61) and Sullivan Award winner in 1961.

Damon Runyon (b. Oct. 4, 1884, d. Dec. 10, 1946): Kansas native who gained fame as New York journalist, sports columnist and short-story writer; best known for 1932 story collection, "Guys and Dolls."

Adolph Rupp (b. Sept. 2, 1901, d. Dec. 10, 1977): Basketball; all-time Div. I college wins leader with 876; coached Kentucky to 4 NCAA championships (1948-49,51,58) and an NIT title (1946).

Bill Russell (b. Feb. 12, 1934): Basketball C; won titles in college, Olympics and pros; 5-time NBA MVP; led Boston to 11 titles from 1957-69; also became first big league black head coach in 1966.

Babe Ruth (b. Feb. 6, 1895, d. Aug. 16, 1948): Baseball LHP-OF; 2-time 20-game winner with Boston Red Sox (1916-17); had a 94-46 regular season record with a 2.28 ERA, while he was 3-0 in the World Series with an ERA of 0.87; sold to NY Yankees for $100,000 in 1920; AL MVP in 1923; led AL in slugging average 13 times, HRs 12 times, RBI 6 times and batting once (.378 in 1924); hit 60 HRs in 1927 and 50 or more 3 other times; ended career with Boston Braves in 1935 with 714 HRs, 2,211 RBI and a batting average of .342; remains all-time leader in times walked (2,056) and slugging average (.690).

Johnny Rutherford (b. Mar. 12, 1938): Auto racer; 3-time winner of Indy 500 (1974,76,80); CART national champion in 1980.

Nolan Ryan (b. Jan. 31, 1947): Baseball RHP; author of record 7 no-hitters against Kansas City and Detroit (1973), Minnesota (1974), Baltimore (1975), LA Dodgers (1981), Oakland A's (1990) and Toronto (1991 at age 44); 2-time 20-game winner (1973-74); 2-time NL leader in ERA (1981,87); led AL in strikeouts 9 times and NL twice in 27 years; retired after 1993 season with 324 wins, 292 losses and all-time leader for strikeouts (5,714) and walks (2,795); never won Cy Young Award.

Samuel Ryder (b. Mar. 24, 1858, d. Jan. 2, 1936): Golf; English seed merchant who donated the Ryder Cup in 1927 for competition between pro golfers from Great Britain and the U.S.; made his fortune by coming up with idea of selling seeds to public in small packages.

Toni Sailer (b. Nov. 17, 1935): Austrian skier; 1st to win 3 alpine gold medals in Winter Olympics— taking downhill, slalom and giant slalom events in 1956.

Juan Antonio Samaranch (b. July 17, 1920): Native of Barcelona, Spain; president of International Olympic Committee since 1980; reelected in 1996 after IOC's move in '95 to bump membership age limit to 80.

Pete Sampras (b. Aug. 12, 1971): Tennis; No.1 player in world in 1993 and '94; overtaken briefly as No. 1 in 1995 by Andre Agassi but later regained the top ranking that year; youngest ever U.S. Open men's champion (19 years, 28 days) in 1990; has won 8 majors, Australian Open (1994, 97), Wimbledon (1993,94,95,97) and U.S. Open (1995, 96); won 5-set doubles match with John McEnroe to help win 1992 Davis Cup final.

Joan Benoit Samuelson (b. May 16, 1957): Distance runner; has won Boston Marathon twice (1979,83); won first women's Olympic marathon in 1984 Games at Los Angeles; Sullivan Award recipient in 1985.

Arantxa Sanchez Vicario (b. Dec. 18, 1971): Spanish tennis player; entered 1996 season with 22 tour victories, including 1989 French Open; won both French and U.S. Opens in 1994 and was finalist in three of four Slam finals in '95; teamed with Conchita Martinez to win 3 of 4 Federation Cups from 1991-94.

Earl Sande (b. Nov. 13, 1898, d. Aug. 19, 1968): Jockey; rode Gallant Fox to Triple Crown in 1930; won 5 Belmonts and 3 Kentucky Derbys.

Barry Sanders (b. July 16, 1968): Football RB; won 1988 Heisman Trophy as junior at Oklahoma St.; all-time NCAA single season leader in rushing (2,628 yards), scoring (234 points) and TDs (39); 2-time NFL rushing leader with Detroit (1990,94); NFC Rookie of Year (1988); 2-time NFL Player of Year (1991,94); NFC MVP (1994).

Deion Sanders (b. Aug. 9, 1967): Baseball OF and Football DB-KR-WR; 2-time All-America at Florida St. in football (1987-88); 4-time NFL All-Pro with Atlanta and San Francisco (1991-94); led Major Leagues in triples (14) with Atlanta in 1992 and hit .533 in World Series the same year; signed with San Francisco 49ers as free agent in 1994 and helped Niners win Super Bowl XXIX; only athlete to play in both World Series and Super Bowl; traded from Cincinnati to S.F. Giants on July 21, 1995 and signed a 7-year, $35 million deal with Dallas Cowboys on Sept. 9 of that year; returned to the Cincinnati Reds in 1997.

Abe Saperstein (b. July 4, 1901, d. Mar. 15, 1966): Basketball; founded all-black, Harlem Globetrotters barnstorming team in 1927; coached sharpshooting comedians to 1940 world pro title in Chicago and established troupe as game's foremost goodwill ambassadors; also served as 1st commissioner of American Basketball League (1961-62).

Gene Sarazen (b. Feb. 27, 1902): Golfer; one of only four players to win all four Grand Slam titles (others are Hogan, Nicklaus and Player); won Masters, British Open, 2 U.S. Opens and 3 PGA titles between 1922-35; invented sand wedge in 1930.

Glen Sather (b. Sept. 2, 1943): Hockey; GM-coach of 4 Stanley Cup winners in Edmonton (1984-85,87-88) and GM-only for another in 1990; ranks 6th on all-time NHL list with 553 wins (including playoffs); entered Hockey Hall of Fame in 1997.

Terry Sawchuk (b. Dec. 28, 1929, d. May 31, 1970): Hockey G; recorded 103 shutouts in 21 NHL seasons; 4-time Vezina Trophy winner; played on 4 Stanley Cup winners at Detroit and Toronto; posted career 2.52 GAA.

Gale Sayers (b. May 30, 1943): Football HB; 2-time All-America at Kansas; NFL Rookie of Year (1965) and 5-time All-Pro with Chicago; scored then-record 22 TDs in rookie year.

Chris Schenkel (b. Aug. 21, 1923): Radio-TV; 4-time Sportscaster of Year; easy-going baritone who has covered basketball, bowling, football, golf and the Olympics for ABC and CBS; host of ABC's Pro Bowlers Tour for 33 years; received lifetime achievement Emmy Award in 1993.

Vitaly Scherbo (b. Jan. 13, 1972): Russian gymnast; winner of unprecedented 6 gold medals in gymnastics, including men's All-Around, for Unified Team in 1992 Olympics; won 3 bronze in '96 Games.

Mike Schmidt (b. Sept. 27, 1949): Baseball 3B; led NL in HRs 8 times; 3-time MVP (1980,81,86) with Philadelphia; 548 career HRs and 10 gold gloves; inducted into Hall of Fame in 1995.

Don Schollander (b. Apr. 30, 1946): Swimming; won 4 gold medals at 1964 Olympics, plus one gold and one silver in 1968; won Sullivan Award in 1964.

Dick Schultz (b. Sept. 5, 1929): Reform-minded executive director of NCAA from 1988-93; announced resignation on May 11, 1993, in wake of special investigator's report citing Univ. of Virginia with improper student-athlete loan program during Schultz's tenure as athletic director (1981-87); named executive director of the USOC on June 23, 1995.

Michael Schumacher (b. Jan. 3, 1969): Auto racer; entered 1996 with 19 career Formula One wins; world champion in 1994 and '95.

Bob Seagren (b. Oct. 17, 1946): Track & Field; won gold medal in pole vault at 1968 Olympics; broke world outdoor record 5 times.

Tom Seaver (b. Nov. 17, 1944): Baseball RHP; won 3 Cy Young Awards (1969,73,75); had 311 wins, 3,640 strikeouts and 2.86 ERA over 20 years.

George Seifert (b. Jan. 22, 1940): Football; coached San Francisco to a record 17 wins in his 1st season as head coach in 1989; guided 49ers to Super Bowl-winning seasons in 1989 and '94; entered 1996 season as NFL's winningest coach ever with 95-30 record and .760 winning pct.

Peter Seitz (b. May 17, 1905, d. Oct. 17, 1983): Baseball arbitrator; ruled on Dec. 23, 1975 that players who perform for one season without a signed contract can become free agents; decision ushered in big money era for players.

Monica Seles (b. Dec. 2, 1973): Yugoslav tennis player; No.1 in the world in 1991 and '92 after winning Australian, French and U.S. Opens both years; 4-time winner of Australian and 3-time winner of French; youngest to win Grand Slam title this century when she won French at age 16 in 1990; winner of 30 singles titles in just 5 years before she was stabbed in the back by Steffi Graf fan Gunter Parche on Apr. 30, 1993 during match in Hamburg, Germany; spent remainder of 1993, all of '94 and most of '95 recovering; returned to WTA Tour with win at the Canadian Open on Aug. 20, 1995; reached U.S. Open final before losing to Graf in 3 sets; comeback complete with 1996 Australian Open win.

Bud Selig (b. July 30, 1934): Baseball; Milwaukee car dealer who bought AL Seattle Pilots for $10.8 million in 1970 and moved team to Midwest; chairman of owners' executive council and de facto commissioner since he and colleagues forced Fay Vincent to resign on Sept. 7, 1992; presided over 232-day players' strike that resulted in cancellation of World Series for first time since 1904 and delayed opening of 1995 season until Apr. 25.

Frank Selke (b. May 7, 1893, d. July 3, 1985): Hockey; GM of 6 Stanley Cup champions in Montreal (1953,56-60); the annual NHL trophy for best defensive forward bears his name.

Ayrton Senna (b. Mar. 21, 1960, d. May 1, 1994): Brazilian auto racer; 3-time Formula One champion (1988,90-91); entered 1994 season as all-time F1 leader in poles (62) and 2nd in wins (41); killed in crash at Imola, Italy during '94 San Marino Grand Prix.

Wilbur Shaw (b. Oct. 13, 1902, d. Oct. 30, 1954): Auto racer; 3-time winner and 3-time runner-up of Indy 500 from 1933-1940.

Patty Sheehan (b. Oct. 27, 1956): Golfer; LPGA Player of Year in 1983; clinched entry into LPGA Hall of Fame with 30th career win in 1993; entered 1995 season with 3 LPGA titles (1983-84,93) and 2 U.S. Opens (1992, 94).

Bill Shoemaker (b. Aug. 19, 1931): Jockey; all-time career wins leader with 8,833; 3-time Eclipse Award winner as Jockey (1981) and special award recipient (1976,81); won Belmont 5 times, Kentucky Derby 4 times and Preakness twice; oldest jockey to win Kentucky Derby (age 54, aboard Ferdinand in 1986); retired in 1990 to become trainer; paralyzed in 1991 auto accident but continues to train horses.

Eddie Shore (b. Nov. 25, 1902, d. Mar. 16, 1985): Hockey D; only NHL defenseman to win Hart Trophy as MVP 4 times (1933,35-36,38); led Boston Bruins to Stanley Cup titles in 1929 and '39; had 105 goals and 1,047 penalty minutes in 14 seasons.

Frank Shorter (b. Oct. 31, 1947): Track & Field; won gold medal in marathon at 1972 Olympics, 1st American to win in 64 years.

Don Shula (b. Jan. 4, 1930): Football; one of only two NFL coaches with 300 wins (George Halas is the other); has taken 6 teams to Super Bowls and won twice with Miami (1973-74); 4-time Coach of Year, twice with Baltimore (1964,68) and twice with Miami (1970-71); retired after 1995 season with NFL-record 347 career wins (including playoffs) and a winning percentage of .670; father of former Cincinnati head coach David.

Al Simmons (b. May 22, 1902, d. May 26, 1956): Baseball OF; led AL in batting twice (1930-31) and knocked in 100 runs or more 11 straight years (1924-34).

O.J. Simpson (b. July 9, 1947): Football RB; won Heisman Trophy in 1968 at USC; ran for 2,003 yards in NFL in 1973; All-Pro 5 times; MVP in 1973; rushed for 11,236 career yards; TV analyst and actor after career ended; arrested June 17, 1994 as suspect in double murder of ex-wife Nicole Brown Simpson and her friend Ronald Goldman; acquitted on Oct. 3, 1995 by a Los Angeles jury.

George Sisler (b. Mar. 24, 1893, d. Mar. 26, 1973): Baseball 1B; hit over .400 twice (1920,22); 257 hits in 1920 still a major league record.

Mary Decker Slaney (b. Aug. 4, 1958): U.S. middle distance runner; has held 7 separate American track & field records from the 800 to 10,000 meters; won both 1,500 and 3,000 meters at 1983 World Championships in Helsinki, but no Olympic medals.

Raisa Smetanina (b. Feb. 29, 1952): Russian Nordic skier; all-time Winter Olympics medalist with 10 cross-country medals (4 gold, 5 silver and a bronze) in 5 appearances (1976,80,84,88,92) for USSR and Unified Team.

Billy Smith (b. Dec. 12, 1950): Hockey G; led NY Islanders to 4 consecutive Stanley Cups (1980-83); won Vezina Trophy in 1982; Stanley Cup MVP in 1983.

Dean Smith (b. Feb. 28, 1931): Basketball; has coached North Carolina to 25 NCAA tournaments in 34 years, reaching Final Four 10 times and winning championship twice (1982,93); coached U.S. Olympic team to gold medal in 1976; number one on all-time Div. I victory list.

Emmitt Smith (b. May 15, 1969): Football RB; consensus All-America (1989) at Florida; 3-time NFL rushing leader (1991-93); 3-time All-Pro (1992-94); regular season and Super Bowl MVP in 1993; played on three Super Bowl champions (1992, '93 and '96 seasons).

John Smith (b. Aug. 9, 1965): Wrestler; 2-time NCAA champion for Oklahoma St. at 134 lbs (1987-88) and Most Outstanding Wrestler of '88 championships; 3-time world champion; gold medal winner at 1988 and '92 Olympics at 137 lbs; only wrestler ever to win Sullivan Award (1990); coached Oklahoma St. to 1994 NCAA title and brother Pat was Most Outstanding Wrestler.

Lee Smith (b. Dec. 4, 1957): Baseball RHP; 3-time NL saves leader (1983,91-92); retired in 1997 as all-time saves leader with 478 and an ERA of 3.03; eleven seasons with 30 or more saves and 4 times saved over 40.

Michelle Smith (b. Apr. 7, 1969): Swimming; Irish-woman who won three gold medals at the 1996 Olympics; accused of using performance-enhancing drugs but passed all tests.

Ozzie Smith (b. Dec. 26, 1954): Baseball SS; won 13 straight gold gloves (1980-92); played in 12 straight All-Star Games (1981-92); MVP of 1985 NL playoffs; entered 1996 season with all-time assist record for shortstops with 8,213.

Walter (Red) Smith (b. Sept. 25, 1905, d. Jan. 15, 1982): Sportswriter for newspapers in Philadelphia and New York from 1936-82; won Pulitzer Prize for commentary in 1976.

Conn Smythe (b. Feb. 1, 1895, d. Nov. 18, 1980): Hockey pioneer; built Maple Leaf Gardens in 1931; managed Toronto to 7 Stanley Cups before retiring in 1961.

Sam Snead (b. May 27, 1912): Golfer; won both Masters and PGA 3 times and British Open once; runner-up in U.S. Open 4 times; PGA Player of Year in 1949; oldest player (52 years, 10 months) to win PGA event with Greater Greensboro Open title in 1965; all-time PGA Tour career victory leader with 81.

Peter Snell (b. Dec. 17, 1938): Track & Field; New Zealander who won gold medal in 800m at 1960 Olympics, then won both the 800m and 1,500m in 1964 Games.

Annika Sorenstam (b. Oct. 9, 1970): Golf; Swedish golfer won the 1995 U.S. Women's Open as her first LPGA victory; won the event again in 1996; College Player of the Year and NCAA champion in 1991.

Javier Sotomayor (b. Oct. 13, 1967): Cuban high jumper; first man to clear 8 feet (8-0) on July 29, 1989; won gold medal at 1992 Olympics with jump of only 7-ft, 8-in.; broke world record with leap of 8-01/2 in 1993.

Warren Spahn (b. Apr. 23, 1921): Baseball LHP; led NL in wins 8 times; won 20 or more games 13 times; Cy Young winner in 1957; most career wins (363) by a left-hander.

Tris Speaker (b. Apr. 4, 1888, d. Dec. 8, 1958): Baseball OF; all-time leader in outfield assists (449) and doubles (793); had .344 career batting average and 3,515 hits.

J.G. Taylor Spink (b. Nov. 6, 1888, d. Dec. 7, 1962): Publisher of The Sporting News from 1914-62; Baseball Writers' Assn. annual meritorious service award named after him.

Mark Spitz (b. Feb. 10, 1950): Swimmer; set 23 world and 35 U.S. records; won all-time record 7 gold medals (4 individual, 3 relay) in 1972 Olympics; also won 4 medals (2 gold, a silver and a bronze) in 1968 Games for a total of 11; comeback attempt at age 41 foundered in 1991.

Amos Alonzo Stagg (b. Aug. 16, 1862, d. Mar. 17, 1965): Football innovator; coached at U. of Chicago for 41 seasons and College of the Pacific for 14 more; won 314 games; elected to both college football and basketball halls of fame.

Willie Stargell (b. Mar. 6, 1940): Baseball OF-1B; led NL in home runs twice (1971,73); 475 career HRs; regular-season and World Series MVP in 1979.

Bart Starr (b. Jan. 9, 1934): Football QB; led Green Bay to 5 NFL titles and 2 Super Bowl wins from 1961-67; regular season MVP in 1966; MVP of Super Bowls I and II.

Roger Staubach (b. Feb. 5, 1942): Football QB; Heisman Trophy winner as Navy junior in 1963; led Dallas to 2 Super Bowl titles (1972,78) and was Super Bowl MVP in 1972; 5-time leading passer in NFC (1971,73,77-79).

George Steinbrenner (b. July 4, 1930): Baseball; principal owner of NY Yankees since 1973; teams have won 4 pennants and 2 World Series (1977-78); has changed managers 21 times and GMs 10 times in 23 years; ordered by baseball commissioner Fay Vincent in 1990 to surrender control of club for dealings with small-time gambler; reinstated on Mar. 1, 1993; also serves as one of 3 VPs of U.S. Olympic Committee.

Casey Stengel (b. July 30, 1890, d. Sept. 29, 1975): Baseball; player for 14 years and manager for 25; outfielder and lifetime .284 hitter with 5 clubs (1912-25); guided NY Yankees to 10 AL pennants and 7 World Series titles from 1949-60; 1st NY Mets skipper from 1962-65.

Ingemar Stenmark (b. Mar. 18, 1956): Swedish alpine skier; 3-time World Cup overall champ (1976-78); posted 86 World Cup wins in 16 years; won 2 gold medals at 1980 Olympics.

Helen Stephens (b. Feb. 3, 1918, d. Jan. 17, 1994): Track & Field; set 3 world records in 100-yard dash and 4 more in 100 meters in 1935-36; won gold medals in 100 meters and 4x100-meter relay in 1936 Olympics; retired in 1937.

Woody Stephens (b. Sept. 1, 1913): Horse racing; trainer who saddled an unprecedented 5 straight winners in Belmont Stakes (1982-86); also had two Kentucky Derby winners (1974,84); trained 1982 Horse of Year Conquistador Cielo; won Eclipse award as nation's top trainer in 1983.

David Stern (b. Sept. 22, 1942): Basketball; marketing expert and NBA commissioner since 1984; took office the year Michael Jordan turned pro; has presided over stunning artistic and financial success of NBA both nationally and internationally, best demonstrated by reception of the Dream Team at 1992 Olympics; league has grown from 23 teams to 29 during his watch; received unprecedented 5-year, $27.5 million contract extension in 1990; in 1996, imposed owners' lockout on July 1 when league and players failed to agree on new contract; ended lockout on Sept.18 when players voted down bid to decertify their union .

Teófilo Stevenson (b. Mar. 29, 1952): Cuban boxer; won 3 consecutive gold medals as Olympic heavyweight (1972,76,80); did not turn pro.

Jackie Stewart (b. June 11, 1939): Auto racer; won 27 Formula One races and 3 world driving titles from 1965-73.

John Stockton (b. Mar 26, 1962): Basketball; entering the 1996-97 season the point guard for the Utah Jazz is the all-time NBA leader in every major assist category, including most in a season (1,164), highest average in a season (14.4 per game) and most overall (11,310); also holds the NBA records for career steals (2,365); All-NBA team in '94 and '95; member of 1992 and '96 US Olympic basketball Dream Team; 8-time All-Star.

Curtis Strange (b. Jan. 30, 1955): Golfer; won consecutive U.S. Open titles (1988-89); 3-time leading money winner on PGA Tour (1985,87-88); first PGA player to win $1 million in one year (1988).

Picabo Street (b. Apr. 3, 1971): Skiing; won silver in women's downhill at 1994 Winter Olympics; her '95 World Cup downhill series title first-ever by U.S. women.

Kerri Strug (b. Nov. 19, 1977): Gymnastics; delivered the most dramatic moment of the 1996 summer Olympics when she completed a vault after spraining her ankle on the previous attempt; the heroic second vault assured the first all-around gold medal for a US Women's gymnastics team after poor vaulting by her teammates had put the medal in doubt; a poor performance by the Russian team on the beam later clinched the gold medal for the USA but Strug did not know that when she decided to make the second vault; second vault score was 9.712; the injury prevented her from participating in any individual events.

Louise Suggs (b. Sept. 7, 1923): Golfer; won 11 Majors and 50 LPGA events overall from 1949-62.

James E. Sullivan (b. Nov. 18, 1862, d. Sept. 16, 1914): Track & Field; pioneer who founded Amateur Athletic Union (AAU) in 1888; director of St. Louis Olympic Games in 1904; AAU's annual Sullivan Award for performance and sportsmanship named after him.

John L. Sullivan (b. Oct. 15, 1858, d. Feb. 2, 1918): Boxer; world heavyweight champion (1882-92); last of bare-knuckle champions.

Pat Summitt (b. June 14, 1952): Basketball; women's basketball coach at Tennessee (1974—); 2nd all-time in career victories to Jody Conradt of Texas; coached 1984 US women's basketball team to its first Olympic gold medal; has coached Lady Vols to 5 national championships (1987,89,91, 96, 97)).

Barry Switzer (b. Oct. 5, 1937): Football; coached Oklahoma to 3 national titles (1974-75,85); 4th on all-time winningest list with 157-29-4 record and .837 win percentage; resigned in 1989 after OU was slapped with 3-year NCAA probation and 5 players were brought up on criminal charges; hired as Dallas Cowboys head coach on Mar. 30, 1994 and led Dallas to a victory in Super Bowl XXX on Jan. 28, 1996.

Paul Tagliabue (b. Nov. 24, 1940): Football; NFL attorney who was elected league's 4th commissioner in 1989; ushered in salary cap in 1994; league expanded by 2 teams in 1995 for 1st time since '76; brought $300 million suit against Dallas owner Jerry Jones on Sept. 18, 1995 for Jones' rogue sponsorship deals with Pepsi and Nike.

Anatoli Tarasov (b. 1918, d. June 23, 1995): Hockey; coached Soviet Union to 9 straight world championships and 3 Olympic gold medals (1964,68,72).

Jerry Tarkanian (b. Aug. 30, 1930): Basketball; all-time winningest college coach with .837 winning pct.; had record of 625-122 in 24 years at Long Beach St. and UNLV; led UNLV to 4 Final Fours and one national title (1990); fought 16-year battle with NCAA over purity of UNLV program; quit as coach after going 26-2 in 1991-92; fired after 20 games (9-11) as coach of NBA San Antonio Spurs in 1992; left retirement on April 5, 1995 to coach his alma mater, Fresno St.

Fran Tarkenton (b. Feb. 3, 1940): Football QB; 2-time NFL All-Pro (1973,75); Player of Year (1975); threw for 47,003 yards and 342 TDs (both NFL records) in 18 seasons with Minnesota and NY Giants.

Chuck Taylor (b. June 24, 1901, d. June 23, 1969): Converse traveling salesman whose name came to grace the classic, high-top canvas basketball sneakers known as "Chucks"; over 500 million pairs have been sold since 1917; he also ran clinics worldwide and edited Converse Basketball Yearbook from 1922-68.

Lawrence Taylor (b. Feb. 4, 1959): Football LB; All-America at North Carolina (1980); only defensive player in NFL history to be consensus Player of Year (1986); led NY Giants to Super Bowl titles in 1986 and '90 seasons; played in a record 10 Pro Bowls (1981-90); retired after 1993 season with 1321/2 sacks.

Gustavo Thoeni (b. Feb. 28, 1951): Italian alpine skier; 4-time World Cup overall champion (1971-73,75); won giant slalom at 1972 Olympics.

Frank Thomas (b. May 27, 1968): Baseball 1B; All-America at Auburn in 1989; 2-time AL MVP with Chicago (1993,94); six time All Star; fourth player in major league history to hit .300, hit at least 20 home runs and have over 100 walks, RBIs and runs scored in three straight seasons, the others being Jimmie Foxx, Lou Gehrig and Ted Williams; has hit 40 home runs 3 times (1993, 95, 96) and has seven consecutive seasons with at least 100 RBIs (1991–97)

Isiah Thomas (b. Apr. 30, 1961): Basketball; led Indiana to NCAA title as sophomore and tourney MVP in 1981; consensus All-America guard in '81; led Detroit to 2 NBA titles in 1989 and '90; NBA Finals MVP in 1990; 3-time All-NBA 1st team (1984-86); retired in 1994 at age 33 after tearing right Achilles tendon; GM of expansion Toronto Raptors.

Thurman Thomas (b. May 16, 1966): Football RB; 3-time AFC rushing leader (1990-91,93); 2-time All-Pro (1990-91); NFL Player of Year (1991); led Buffalo to 4 straight Super Bowls (1991-94).

Daley Thompson (b. July 30, 1958): British Track & Field; won consecutive gold medals in decathlon at 1980 and '84 Olympics.

John Thompson (b. Sept. 2, 1941): Basketball; has coached centers Patrick Ewing, Alonzo Mourning and Dikembe Mutombo at Georgetown; reached NCAA tourney final 3 out of 4 years with Ewing, winning title in 1984; also led Hoyas to 6 Big East tourney titles; coached 1988 U.S. Olympic team to bronze medal.

Bobby Thomson (b. Oct. 25, 1923): Baseball OF; career .270 hitter who won the 1951 NL pennant for the NY Giants with a 1-out, 3-run HR in the bottom of the 9th inning of Game 3 of a best-of-3 playoff with Brooklyn; the pitcher was Ralph Branca, the count was 0-1 and the Dodgers were ahead 4-2; the Giants had trailed Brooklyn by 13 games on Aug. 11th.

Jim Thorpe (b. May 28, 1888, d. May 28, 1953): 2-time All-America in football; won both pentathlon and decathlon at 1912 Olympics; stripped of medals a month later for playing semi-pro baseball prior to Games; medals restored in 1982; played major league baseball (1913-19) and pro football (1920-26,28); chosen "Athlete of the Half Century" by AP in 1950.

Bill Tilden (b. Feb. 10, 1893, d. June 5, 1953): Tennis; won 7 U.S. and 3 Wimbledon titles in 1920's; led U.S. to 7 straight Davis Cup victories (1920-26).

Tinker to Evers to Chance Chicago Cubs double play combination from 1903-08; immortalized in poem by New York sportswriter Franklin P. Adams—SS Joe Tinker (1880-1948), 2B Johnny Evers (1883-1947) and 1B Frank Chance (1877-1924); all 3 managed the Cubs and made the Hall of Fame.

Y.A. Tittle (b. Oct. 24, 1926): Football QB; played 17 years in AFC and NFL; All-Pro 4 times; league MVP with San Francisco (1957) and NY Giants (1962); passed for 28,339 career yards.

Alberto Tomba (b. Dec. 19, 1966): Italian alpine skier; all-time Olympic alpine medalist with 5 (3 gold, 2 silver); became 1st alpine skier to win gold medals in 2 consecutive Winter Games when he won the slalom and giant slalom in 1988 then repeated in the GS in '92; also won silvers in slalom in 1992 and '94; won 1st overall World Cup championship along with slalom and giant slalom titles in 1995.

Vladislav Tretiak (b. Apr. 25, 1952): Hockey G; led USSR to Olympic gold medals in 1972 and '76; starred for Soviets against Team Canada in 1972, and again in 2,Canada Cups (1976,81).

Lee Trevino (b. Dec. 1, 1939): Golfer; 2-time winner of 3 Majors— U.S. Open (1968,71), British Open (1971-72) and PGA (1974,84); Player of Year once on PGA Tour (1971) and 3 times with Seniors (1990,92,94); 27 PGA Tour wins and 26 on Senior Tour.

Bryan Trottier (b. July 17, 1956): Hockey C; led NY Islanders to 4 straight Stanley Cups (1980-83); Rookie of Year (1976); scoring champion (134 points) and regular season MVP in 1979; playoff MVP (1980); added 5th and 6th Cups with Pittsburgh in 1991 and '92; entered Hockey Hall of Fame in 1997.

Gene Tunney (b. May 25, 1897, d. Nov. 7, 1978): Boxer; world heavyweight champion from 1926-28; beat 31-year-old champ Jack Dempsey in unanimous 10 round decision in 1926; beat him again in famous "long count" rematch in '27; quit while still champion in 1928 with 65-1-1 record and 47 KOs.

Ted Turner (b. Nov. 19, 1938): Sportsman and TV mogul; skippered *Courageous* to America's Cup win in 1977; owner of both Atlanta Braves and Hawks; owner of superstation WTBS, and cable stations CNN and TNT; founder of Goodwill Games; 1991 **Time** Man of Year.

Mike Tyson (b. June 30, 1966): Boxer; youngest (age 19) to win heavyweight title (WBC in 1986); undisputed champ from 1987 until upset loss to 50-1 shot Buster Douglas on Feb. 10, 1990, in Tokyo; found guilty on Feb. 10, 1992, of raping 18-year-old Miss Black America contestant Desiree Washington in Indianapolis on July 19, 1991; sentenced to 6-year prison term; released May 9, 1995 after serving 3 years; reclaimed WBC and WBA belts with wins over Frank Bruno and Bruce Seldon in 1996; lost WBA title to Evander Holyfield in 1996; brought his career to a halt when he bit Holyfield twice in the ear during their WBA championship fight in 1997; see career fight record in Boxing chapter.

Wyomia Tyus (b. Aug. 29, 1945): Track & Field; 1st woman to win consecutive Olympic gold medals in 100m (1964-68).

Peter Ueberroth (b. Sept. 2, 1937): Organizer of 1984 Summer Olympics in LA; 1984 **Time** Man of Year; baseball commissioner from 1984-89; headed Rebuild Los Angeles for one year after 1992 riots.

Johnny Unitas (b. May 7, 1933): Football QB; led Baltimore Colts to 2 NFL titles (1958-59) and a Super Bowl win (1971); All-Pro 5 times; 3-time MVP (1959,64,67); passed for 40,239 career yards and 290 TDs.

Al Unser Jr. (b. Apr. 19, 1962): Auto racer; 2-time CART-IndyCar national champion (1990,94); captured Indy 500 for 2nd time in 3 years in '94, giving Unser family 9 overall titles at the Brickyard; 31 IndyCar wins in 16 years; son of Al and nephew of Bobby.

Al Unser Sr. (b. May 29, 1939): Auto racer; 3-time USAC-CART national champion (1970,83,85); 4-time winner of Indy 500 (1970-71,78,87); retired in 1994 ranked 3rd on all-time IndyCar list with 39 wins; younger brother of Bobby and father of Little Al.

Bobby Unser (b. Feb. 20, 1934): Auto racer; 2-time USAC-CART national champion (1968,74); 3-time winner of Indy 500 (1968,75,81); retired after 1981 season; ranks 4th on all-time IndyCar list with 35 wins.

Gene Upshaw (b. Aug. 15, 1945): Football G; 2-time All-AFL and 3-time All-NFL selection with Oakland; helped lead Raiders to 2 Super Bowl titles in 1976 and '80 seasons; executive director of NFL Players Assn. since 1987; agreed to application of salary cap in 1994.

Norm Van Brocklin (b. Mar. 15, 1926, d. May 2, 1983): Football QB-P; led NFL in passing 3 times and punting twice; led LA Rams (1951) and Philadelphia (1960) to NFL titles; MVP in 1960.

Amy Van Dyken (b. Feb. 17, 1973): Swimming; first American woman to win four gold medals in one Olympics (1996); won the individual 50M freestyle, 100M butterfly, and was on the US team for the 4X100 freestyle and 4X50 medley; known for clapping, spitting and growling on the platform just before the start of a race.

Johnny Vander Meer (b. Nov. 2, 1914, d. Oct. 6, 1997): Baseball LHP; only major leaguer to pitch consecutive no-hitters (June 11 & 15, 1938).

Harold S. Vanderbilt (b. July 6, 1884, d. July 4, 1970): Sportsman; successfully defended America's Cup 3 times (1930, 34,37); also invented contract bridge in 1926.

Glenna Collett Vare (b. June 20, 1903, d. Feb. 10, 1989): Golfer; won record 6 U.S. Women's Amateur titles from 1922-35;"the female Bobby Jones."

Andy Varipapa (b. Mar. 31, 1891, d. Aug. 25, 1984): Bowler; trick-shot artist; won consecutive All-Star match game titles (1947-48) at age 53.

Mo Vaughn (b. Dec. 15, 1967): Baseball; slugging first baseman for Boston Red Sox; led team to 1995 Eastern Division title and named American League MVP with 39 homeruns, 126 RBIs, .300 batting average and 11 stolen bases; two time All-Star.

Bill Veeck (b. Feb. 9, 1914, d. Jan. 2, 1986): Maverick baseball executive; owned AL teams in Cleveland, St. Louis and Chicago from 1946-80; introduced ballpark giveaways, exploding scoreboards, Wrigley Field's ivy-covered walls and midget Eddie Gaedel; won World Series with Indians (1948) and pennant with White Sox (1959).

Jacques Villeneuve (b. Apr. 9, 1971): Canadian auto racer; Indianapolis 500 runner-up and IndyCar Rookie of Year in 1994; won 500 and IndyCar driving championship in 1995; announced plans to jump to Formula One racing in 1996.

Fay Vincent (b. May 29, 1938): Baseball; became 8th commissioner after death of A. Bartlett Giamatti in 1989; presided over World Series earthquake, owners' lockout and banishment of NY Yankees owner George Steinbrenner in his first year on the job; contentious relationship with owners resulted in his resignation on Sept. 7, 1992, four days after 18-9 "no confidence" vote; office has been vacant since.

Lasse Viren (b. July 22, 1949): Finnish runner; won gold medals at 5,000 and 10,00 meters in 1972 Munich Olympics; repeated 5,000/10,000 double in 1976 Games but added a 5th place in the marathon.

Lanny Wadkins (b. Dec. 5, 1949): Golfer; member of 8 Ryder Cup teams and captain of 1995 team; 21PGA Tour wins.

Honus Wagner (b. Feb. 24, 1874, d. Dec. 6, 1955): Baseball SS; hit .300 for 17 consecutive seasons (1897-1913) with Pittsburgh; led NL in batting 8 times; ended career with 3,418 career hits, a .327 average and 722 stolen bases.

Lisa Wagner (b. May 19, 1961): Bowler; 3-time LPBT Player of Year (1983,88,93); 1980's Bowler of Decade; first woman to earn $100,000 in a season; entered 1996 season with a record 29 pro titles.

Grete Waitz (b. Oct. 1, 1953): Norwegian runner; 9-time winner of New York City Marathon from 1978-88; won silver medal at 1984 Olympics.

Doak Walker (b. Jan. 1, 1927): Football HB; won Heisman Trophy as SMU junior in 1948; led Detroit to 2 NFL titles (1952-53); All-Pro 4 times in 6 years.

Herschel Walker (b. Mar. 3, 1962): Football RB; led Georgia to national title as freshman in 1980; won Heisman in 1982 then jumped to USFL in '83; signed by Dallas after USFL folded; led NFL in rushing in 1988; traded to Minnesota in 1989 for 5 players and 6 draft picks; has since played for Philadelphia and NY Giants and again with Dallas.

Bill Walsh (b. Nov. 30, 1931): Football; coached San Francisco to 3 Super Bowl titles (1982,85,89); retired after 1989 Super Bowl with 102 wins in 10 seasons; returned to college coaching in 1992 for his second stint at Stanford; retired again after 1994 season; entering 1995 NFL season, six former Walsh assistants were head coaches.

Bill Walton (b. Nov. 5, 1952): Basketball C; 3-time college Player of Year (1972-74); led UCLA to 2 national titles (1972-73); led Portland to NBA title as MVP in 1977; regular season MVP in 1978.

Arch Ward (b. Dec. 27, 1896, d. July 9, 1955): Promoter and sports editor of **Chicago Tribune** from 1930-55; founder of baseball All-Star Game (1933), Chicago College All-Star Football Game (1934) and the All-America Football Conference (1946-49).

Charlie Ward (b. Oct. 12, 1970): Football QB and Basketball G; led Florida St. to national football championship in 1993; 1st Heisman Trophy winner to play for national champs since Tony Dorsett in 1976, won Sullivan Award same year; 3-year starter for FSU basketball team; not taken in NFL Draft; 1st round pick (26th overall) of NY Knicks in 1994 NBA draft.

Glenn (Pop) Warner (b. Apr. 5, 1871, d. Sept. 7, 1954): Football innovator; coached at 7 colleges over 49 years; 319 career wins 2nd only to Bear Bryant's 323 in Div. I-A; produced 47 All-Americas, including Jim Thorpe and Ernie Nevers.

Tom Watson (b. Sept. 4, 1949): Golfer; 6-time PGA Player of the Year (1977-80,82,84); has won 5 British Opens, 2 Masters and a U.S. Open; 4-time Ryder Cup member and captain of 1993 team; 33 PGA tour wins.

Dick Weber (b. Dec. 23, 1929): Bowler; 3-time PBA Bowler of the Year (1961,63,65); won 30 PBA titles in 4 decades.

Johnny Weissmuller (b. June 2, 1904, d. Jan. 20 1984): Swimmer; won 3 gold medals at 1924 Olympics and 2 more at 1928 Games; became Hollywood's most famous Tarzan.

Jerry West (b. May 28, 1938): Basketball G; 2-time All-America and NCAA tourney MVP (1959) at West Virginia; led 1960 U.S. Olympic team to gold medal; 10-time All-NBA 1st-team; NBA finals MVP (1969); led LA Lakers to NBA title once as player (1972) and 5 times as GM in 1980's; his silhouette serves as the NBA's logo.

Pernell Whitaker (b. Jan. 2, 1964): Boxer; won Olympic gold medal as lightweight in 1984; has won 4 world championships as lightweight, jr. welterweight, welterweight and jr. middleweight; outfought but failed to beat Julio Cesar Chavez when Sept. 10, 1993 welterweight title defense ended in controversial draw; pro record of 40-1-1 and 16 KOs.

Bill White (b. Jan. 28, 1934): Baseball; NL president and highest ranking black executive in sports from 1989-94; as 1st baseman, won 7 gold gloves and hit .286 with 202 HRs in 13 seasons.

Byron (Whizzer) White (b. June 8, 1917): Football; All-America HB at Colorado (1935-37); signed with Pittsburgh in 1938 for the then largest contract in pro history ($15,800); took Rhodes scholarship in 1939; returned to NFL in 1940 to lead league in rushing and retired in 1941; named to U.S. Supreme Court by President Kennedy in 1962 and stepped down in 1993.

Reggie White (b. Dec. 19, 1961): Football DE; consensus All-America in 1983 at Tennessee; 7-time All-NFL (1986-92) with Philadelphia; signed as free agent with Green Bay in 1993 for $17 million over 4 years; all-time NFL leader in sacks; played key role in Packers 1997 Super Bowl victory.

Kathy Whitworth (b. Sept. 27, 1939): Golf; 7-time LPGA Player of the Year (1966-69,71-73); won 6 Majors; 88 tour wins, most on LPGA or PGA tour.

Hazel Hotchkiss Wightman (b. Dec. 20, 1886, d. Dec. 5, 1974): Tennis; won 16 U.S. national titles; 4-time U.S. Women's champion (1909-11,19); donor of Wightman Cup.

Hoyt Wilhelm (b. July 26, 1923): Baseball RHP; Knuckleballer who is all-time leader in games pitched (1,070), games finished (651) and games won in relief (124); had career ERA of 2.52 and 227 saves; 1st relief pitcher inducted into Hall of Fame (1985); threw no-hitter vs. NY Yankees (1958); also hit lone HR of career in first major league at bat (1952).

Lenny Wilkens (b. Oct. 28, 1937): Basketball; passed Red Auerbach as NBA's all-time winningest regular-season coach with his 939th victory on Jan. 6, 1995; 1,070 regular-season wins and 1,138 wins including playoffs; MVP of 1960 NIT as Providence guard; played 15 years in NBA, including 4 as player-coach; MVP of 1971 All-Star Game; coached Seattle to NBA title in 1979; Coach of Year in 1994 with Atlanta.

Dominique Wilkins (b. Jan. 12, 1960): Basketball F; last player to lead NBA in scoring (1986) before Michael Jordan's reign; All-NBA 1st team in 1986; elder statesman of Dream Team II.

Bud Wilkinson (b. Apr. 23, 1916, d. Feb. 9, 1994): Football; played on 1936 national championship team at Minnesota; coached Oklahoma to 3 national titles (1950,55,56); won 4 Orange and 2 Sugar Bowls; teams had winning streaks of 47 (1953-57) and 31 (1948-50); retired after 1963 season with 145-29-4 record in 17 years; also coached St. Louis of NFL to 9-20 record in 1978-79.

Ted Williams (b. Aug. 30, 1918): Baseball OF; led AL in batting 6 times, and HRs and RBI 4 times each; won Triple Crown twice (1942,47); 2-time MVP (1946,49); last player to bat .400 when he hit .406 in 1941; Marine Corps combat pilot who missed three full seasons during World War II (1943-45) and most of two others (1952-53) during Korean War; hit .344 lifetime with 521 HRs in 19 years with Boston Red Sox.

Walter Ray Williams Jr. (b. Oct. 6, 1959): Bowling and Horseshoes; 3-time PBA Bowler of Year (1986,93,96); won 6 World Horseshoe Pitching titles.

Hack Wilson (b. Apr. 26, 1900, d. Nov. 23, 1948): Baseball; as a Chicago Cub, he produced one of baseball's most outstanding seasons in 1930 with 56 homeruns, .356 batting average, 105 walks and, most amazingly, a major league record 190 RBIs that still stands; finished with 1,461 hits, 244 homeruns, 1,062 RBIs; member of Baseball Hall of Fame.

Dave Winfield (b. Oct. 3, 1951): Baseball OF-DH; selected in 4 major sports league drafts in 1973— NFL, NBA, ABA, and MLB; chose baseball and has played in 12 All-Star Games over 20-year career; at age 41, helped lead Toronto to World Series title in 1992; reached 3,000 hits in 1993.

Katarina Witt (b. Dec. 3, 1965): East German figure skater; 4-time world champion (1984-85,87-88); won consecutive Olympic gold medals (1984,88).

John Wooden (b. Oct. 14, 1910): Basketball; college Player of Year at Purdue in 1932; coached UCLA to 10 national titles (1964-65,67-73,75); only member of Basketball Hall of Fame inducted as both player and coach; Bruins won first title since Wooden era in 1995.

Tiger Woods (b. Dec. 30, 1975): Golfer; became youngest player (age 18) and first black to win U.S. Amateur in 1994, won it again in '95 and '96; turned pro in Sept. of '96 and won the fifth event he entered, the Las Vegas Invitational; in his first full year on the tour, he won six of the 25 events he entered and broke the single season money record; won 1997 Masters by a record 18 under par and 13 stroke margin of victory, the latter being a record for all majors.

Mickey Wright (b. Feb. 14, 1935): Golfer; won 3 of 4 Majors (LPGA, U.S. Open, Titleholders) in 1961; 4-time winner of both U.S. Open and LPGA titles; 82 career wins including 13 Majors.

Early Wynn (b. Jan. 6, 1920): Baseball RHP; won 20 games 5 times; Cy Young winner in 1959; 300 career wins in 23 years.

Kristi Yamaguchi (b. July 12, 1971): Figure Skating; finished second in the 1991 American nationals but won the world title that year; dominated the sport in 1992 by winning the national, world and Olympic titles and then turned professional.

Cale Yarborough (b. Mar. 27, 1940): Auto racer; 3-time NASCAR national champion (1976-78); 4-time winner of Daytona 500 (1968,77,83-84); ranks 4th on NASCAR all-time list with 83 wins.

Carl Yastrzemski (b. Aug. 22, 1939): Baseball OF; led AL in batting 3 times; won Triple Crown and MVP in 1967; had 3,419 hits and 452 HRs in 23 years with Boston; member of Baseball Hall of Fame.

Cy Young (b. Mar. 29, 1867, d. Nov. 4, 1955): Baseball RHP; all-time leader in wins (511), losses (315), complete games (750) and innings pitched (7,355); had career 2.63 ERA in 22 years (1890-1911); 30-game winner 5 times and 20-game winner 10 other times; threw 3 no-hitters and perfect game (1904); AL and NL pitching awards named after him.

Sheila Young (b. Oct. 14, 1950): Speed skater and cyclist; 1st U.S. athlete to win 3 medals at Winter Olympics (1976); won speed skating overall and sprint cycling world titles in 1976.

Steve Young (b. Oct. 11, 1961): Football QB; consensus All-America at BYU (1983); NFL Player of Year (1992) with S.F. 49ers; only QB to lead NFL in passer rating 4 straight years (1991-94); rating of 112.8 in 1994 was highest ever; threw playoff-record 6 TD passes in MVP performance against San Diego in Super Bowl XXIX; holds NFL career records for highest passer rating (96.8) and completion percentage (63.6).

Robin Yount (b. Sept. 16, 1955): Baseball SS-OF; AL MVP at 2 positions— as SS in 1982 and OF in '89; retired after 1993 season with 3,142 hits, 251 HRs and a major league record 123 sacrifice flies after 20 seasons with Milwaukee Brewers.

Mario Zagalo (b. Aug. 9, 1931): Soccer; Brazilian forward who is one of only two men (Franz Beckenbauer is the other) to serve as both captain (1962) and coach (1970) of World Cup champion.

Babe Didrikson Zaharias (b. June 26, 1914, d. Sept. 27, 1956): All-around athlete who was chosen AP Female Athlete of Year 6 times from 1932-54; won 2 gold medals (javelin and 80-meter hurdles) and a silver (high jump) at 1932 Olympics; took up golf in 1935 and went on to win 55 pro and amateur events; won 10 majors, including 3 U.S. Opens (1948,50,54); helped found LPGA in 1949; chosen female "Athlete of the Half Century" by AP in 1950.

Tony Zale (b. May 29, 1913, d. March 20, 1997): Boxer; 2-time world middleweight champion (1941-47,48); fought Rocky Graziano for title 3 times in 21 months in 1947-48, winning twice; pro record 67-18-2 with 44 KOs.

Frank Zamboni (b. Jan. 16, 1901, d. July 27, 1988): Mechanic, ice salesman and skating rink owner in Paramount, Calif.; invented 1st ice-resurfacing machine in 1949; over 4,000 sold in more than 33 countries since then.

Emil Zatopek (b. Sept. 19, 1922): Czech distance runner; winner of 1948 Olympic gold medal at 10,000 meters; 4 years later, won unprecedented Olympic triple crown (5,000 meters, 10,000 meters and marathon) at 1952 Games in Helsinki.

John Ziegler (b. Feb. 9, 1934): Hockey; NHL president from 1977-92; negotiated settlement with rival WHA in 1979 that led to inviting four WHA teams (Edmonton, Hartford, Quebec and Winnipeg) to join NHL; stepped down June 12, 1992, 2 months after settling 10-day players' strike.

Kim Zmeskal (b. Feb 6, 1976): Gymnastics; Won three U.S. all-around championships in a row (1990-'92); first American gymnast to win the all-around competition in the world championships (1991); only athlete to win two golds in the 1992 world championships (balance beam and floor exercise).

Pirmin Zurbriggen (b. Feb. 4, 1963): Swiss alpine skier; 4-time World Cup overall champ (1984,87-88,90) and 3-time runner-up; 40 World Cup wins in 10 years; won gold and bronze medals at 1988 Olympics.

Ballparks & Arenas

Hartford Whalers owner **Peter Karmanos** was just taking care of business when he moved his NHL team to North Carolina. But his action reverberated painfully in the neighborhoods where his players had made homes and friends. ——————————————————————

Wide World Photos

Hurricane in Hartford

When the Whalers left town, one neighborhood was damaged beyond repair.

by
Karl Ravech

The first time my wife and I actually met Glen and Barb Wesley was sometime in the beginning of September, 1994. Glen had recently been traded by the Boston Bruins to the Hartford Whalers. The Wesleys were looking for a place to live. When we first saw them they were standing in the road, talking to the builder of the home they were about to purchase. Just two doors down from ours.

Diane and I walked down the street and within minutes of exchanging small talk, you could tell that they were special people. In my 32 years on earth, I have yet to come across a person who immediately made you feel more comfortable than Barb. That feeling was not fleeting and it has only gotten stronger as time has passed.

Karl Ravech has been an ESPN anchor and reporter since 1993.

Our scrapbook of memories grew as quickly as our firstborn. True friendships are like that. As much as you'd like time to slow down, you're having too much fun to really want it to stop. So you just relax and enjoy yourself.

There was my 30th birthday party, the birth of my own son, then the birth of their second child. There was game one of Glen's Whalers career. All the guys from our street piled into my house to watch it on television. Wes scored the winning goal against the Rangers. It seemed like a pretty good omen.

I could tell you a lot about the Wesleys. Barb and Glen redefined hospitality. Their parties weren't of the chip and dip variety. Instead it was enough Chinese food to feed 300 when only 30 were invited. And we had many parties. The Wesley's gifts were always thoughtful and generous though

Wide World Photos

In today's sporting world, teams move around easily as their owners seek more money. While callous businessmen pusue the almighty dollar, families like that of Hartford Whaler **Glen Wesley (c)** pay the real price.

not because of the size of their bank account, rather the size of their hearts.

Our hearts began to break when word came out that the Whalers were considering moving. It was as if our closely knit neighborhood had been invaded by a giant cat whose claws were tearing away at the very fabric which held us together. We read the papers and asked ourselves the questions, though we really didn't want to hear the answers. It was almost as if that silence was a way of avoiding the truth.

Then one day it was announced the Whalers were going to leave. The city of Hartford protested. The mayor vowed to lie down in front of any moving vans. In our small world, tears were shed. Not because a professional sports team was leaving but because in less than 3 years, our neighborhood had become a family. Now the family was being ripped apart, for reasons beyond our control. And it hurt.

It is my job to report the facts and to leave emotion out of each story. But the move of the Whalers from Hartford, and the Wesleys from our neighborhood, has opened my eyes a little bit. I am a little more sympathetic to the sad reality that Cleveland Browns fans and Baltimore Colts fans and Los Angeles Rams fans and Brooklyn Dodgers fans and so many others have experienced. For every one hundred fans losing a team there are nearly as many friends and extended family members who are losing friends.

Sports has always been and always will be a diversion. I've learned to live with the ups and downs. And, now, to have a part of me die with them as well. ∎

As the old parks give way to the new facilities, scenes like the August 2 demolition of **Fulton County Stadium** in Atlanta will play out well into the next millennium. We will skip the gratuitous mention of how certain owners might be chained to their seats for these events.

Karl Ravech's Top Ten List of Ballparks and Arenas In the News

10. **Greensboro** — The Greensboro Coliseum is now home to the new Carolina Hurricanes of the NHL. Most involved with the team expect a near-disastrous first two seasons before they move to a new facility being built in Raleigh. Let's hope the team survives that long.

9. **Atlanta** — The New Turner Field is everything that Camden Yards and the Ballpark at Arlington and Coors Field is, except that it hosts the best team in the Major Leagues.

8. **Milwaukee** — Bud Selig's dream is slowly coming true. The team has surprised on the field yet fan reaction has been like a beer taste test—and it isn't going down well. Miller Field, with a retractable roof, is set to open in 2000. But Bud may not care. He could be baseball's commissioner by then.

7. **Boston** — A new Fenway Park? A new home for the Patriots? Like everything in Boston, politics is involved. Combine the slow-motion wheel that sports turns on with the nearly impossible task of accomplishing anything concrete in Beantown and you begin to see that the Red Sox won't be moving any time before 2000. The Patriots almost left for Rhode Island and won't get a new home but rather a touchup on the old one.

6. **Arizona** — Jerry Colangelo just keeps winning. Even his Arena Football team won a title. Shortly his new baby will be born and it will be playing in, to say the least, a state of the art facility. Bring your baseball glove and your bathing suit. There will be a pool just outside of center field.

5. **Pennsylvania** — The Phillies and Eagles call Veteran's Stadium home. The Pirates and Steelers get their mail at Three Rivers Stadium. Guess what? They all want

Wide World Photos

Professional sports team owners around the country could learn from the New England Patriots' **Robert Kraft** (r), shown here with Boston mayor **Thomas Menino**. By not playing his political cards correctly, Kraft lost out on his first–choice location for a new stadium on Boston's waterfront and almost ended up in Rhode Island. Latest plans call for renovating the current stadium in Foxborough.

new addresses and they all want the state of Pennsylvania to help them. Guess what else? It isn't going to happen.

4. **New York** — George Steinbrenner points to traffic troubles and the fact that the area around Yankee Stadium has a bad reputation as major reasons for wanting to bug out of the Bronx. Heck, his own car got stuck in the private lot. Word is that Steinbrenner is interested in buying the New York Islanders. Maybe he moves the Yankees to Long Island.

3. **Seattle** — Right now they are pouring a foundation for a retractable roof, natural grass stadium that air will flow through even when the roof is closed. Think umbrella. Considering what taxpayers are forking over for this building, let's hope nobody gets wet. First pitch is scheduled for 1999.

2. **Chicago** — In the new Comiskey, we have proof that newer is not necessarily better. Like everything in real estate, it's location, location, location. Fans will flock to Wrigley Field to watch little league baseball. But Albert Belle and Frank Thomas play in front of an average home crowd of 24,307, about 4,000 fewer than Mark Grace and Sammy Sosa.

1. **Anaheim** — The Angels collapsed on the field in 1995. Some fans are concerned that their facility will do the same. Said one visitor, "It looks like hell." Have patience, people. First of all, Anaheim Stadium is now Edison Field thanks to a reported $50 million sponsorship deal with Edison International, a Southern California utility company. By 1998, the ballpark will be baseball-only and Mickey may even greet you at the door. ■

by

Matthew Ipsan, Craig Wachs, Steve Rutkowski, Jeff Bennett and Paul Kinney

NASH**VILLAINS**

The city of Nashville, Tennessee has long sought a professional sports franchise. With the arrival of the Tennessee (formerly Houston) Oilers, the city got its wish even though the Oilers will call Memphis home through 1998. Over the years, however, the city has displayed a cold, cold, heart in its pursuit of existing teams.

Franchises Courted	Decision
Houston Oilers	**W**
Hartford Whalers	L
New Jersey Devils	L
Los Angeles Clippers	L
Minnesota Timberwolves	L
San Antonio Spurs	L

Now a word from our sponsors

In the last five years, the number of commercially-sponsored sports arenas has risen dramatically. Since these operations rarely make money, captains of industry are actually doing a good deed when they slap their names on playing fields, hockey rinks and stadiums.

Growth of Sponsored Homes	1992	1997
National Football League	1	8
Major League Baseball	0	5
National Basketball Association	5	12
National Hockey League	1	11

NEW STADIUMS **NUMBERS**

Through September 3, 1997, the top four baseball teams in attendance and percentage of capacity were teams that play in stadiums that were built this decade. Six of the seven new stadiums draw over 70% with only the White Sox drawing under the major league average.

	Avg.	Cap.	Pct.
Jacobs Field	42,484	43,863	96.9
Coors Field	48,134	50,200	95.9
Oriole Park	46,209	48,262	95.7
Turner Field	42,549	43,863	84.2
Ballpark at Arlington	37,765	49,166	76.8
Pro Player Stadium	29,652	41,855	70.8
New Comiskey	24,297	44,321	54.8*

*MLB Avg. 58.5

RIGHT ON **TRACK**

The emergence of auto racing as the number one spectator sport in the country has resulted in the construction of several new venues. Since 1996, the following superspeedways have delighted racing fans and increased the local demand for ear plugs.

New Superspeedways

Track	Length	Location	First Race
California Speedway	2 mi	Fontana, Calif	June 21, 1997
Pikes Peak Int. Raceway	1 mi	Fountain, Col	June 8, 1997
Gateway Int. Raceway	1.2 mi	Madison, Il	May 24, 1997
Texas Motor Speedway	1.5 mi	Ft. Worth, Tex	April 5, 1997
Las Vegas Motor Speedway	1.5 mi	Las Vegas, Nev	September 18, 1996
Walt Disney World Speedway	1 mi	Orlando, Fla	January 1, 1996

■

BALLPARKS & ARENAS
COMING ATTRACTIONS

1997

BASEBALL

Atlanta (NL): Turner Field opened on April 4, 1997 with a 5-4 Braves win over the Chicago Cubs in front of a crowd of 45,044. Stadium was converted to 49,714-seat baseball-only ballpark from the 85,000-seat Centennial Olympic Stadium, originally built for 1996 Summer Games; Located across from the site of the recently demolished Atlanta-Fulton County Stadium; open air, grass field; includes approximately 59 luxury suites; estimated cost $230 million to build Olympic stadium and convert to smaller ballpark.

NBA BASKETBALL

Golden St. (West): Complete reconstruction of Oakland Coliseum, using the existing walls, began immediately after the 1995-96 season. The new-and-improved arena, which will likely be renamed, will seat 19,200; will include 72 luxury suites; estimated cost: $121 million; Warriors' home opener scheduled for November 8, 1997. Warriors played their home games for the 1996-97 season at San Jose Arena.

Washington (East): Construction of MCI Center (MCI is title sponsor) near completion. To be located above the Gallery Place Metro Station near National Mall; will seat 21,500 for basketball and 20,000 for NHL Capitals; will include 110 luxury suites; estimated cost: $175 million. Wizards home opener scheduled for November 1, 1997 against the Miami Heat.

NFL FOOTBALL

Washington (NFC): Construction of Jack Kent Cooke Stadium is near completion. Located on site six miles east of RFK Stadium in Landover, Md.; will seat 78,600 for football; open air, grass field; will include 280 luxury suites; estimated cost: $165 million. Redskins' home opener scheduled for September 1997.

NHL HOCKEY

Washington (East): Construction of MCI Center (MCI is title sponsor) near completion. To be located above the Gallery Place Metro Station near National Mall; will seat 20,000 for hockey and 21,500 for NBA Wizards; will include 110 luxury suites; estimated cost: $175 million. Capitals' home opener scheduled for October 3, 1997 against the Buffalo Sabres.

1998

BASEBALL

Arizona (expansion team): Construction of Bank One Ballpark (Bank One is title sponsor) underway. To be located one block from America West Arena and feature a retractable roof; will seat 48,500; grass field; will include 69 luxury suites and six larger party suites; estimated cost: $350 million. Diamondbacks' major league home opener scheduled for April 1998.

Tampa Bay (expansion team): Plans call for renovating Tropicana Field, formerly known as the Thunder Dome and the Florida Suncoast Dome when it opened in 1990. Located in St. Petersburg at the corner of 16th St. and 1st Ave. South; will seat 48,000 for baseball; indoor, artificial turf field; will include 66 luxury suites; estimated cost: $50 million. Devil Rays' major league home opener scheduled for April 1998.

NBA BASKETBALL

Miami (East): Groundbreaking for the as-yet-unnamed arena tentatively scheduled for late 1997/early 1998. To be located on the FEC tract next to Bayside on the Miami waterfront. Estimated cost: $165 million. Earliest Heat home opener would be late 1998.

NFL FOOTBALL

Baltimore (AFC): Construction of as-yet-unnamed stadium underway. The open-air grass field stadium will be located next to Camden Yards and cost an estimated $200 million. It will seat 68,400 and include 108 luxury suites; Earliest Ravens' home opener would be September 1998.

Tampa Bay (NFC): Construction of Tampa Community Stadium underway. The open-air, grass-field stadium will be located in West Tampa across the street from Houlihan's Stadium. It will seat 65,000 and include 120 luxury suites; to be part of larger complex and include the team's training facility as well; estimated cost: $220 million. Opening date set for September 20, 1998.

NHL HOCKEY

Florida (East): Groundbreaking for Broward County Civic Arena started in November 1996. To be located in Sunrise, Fla., west of Ft. Lauderdale; will seat between 19,000 and 20,000 for hockey; include 62 luxury suites and four larger party suites; estimated cost: $212 million. Earliest Panthers' home opener would be September 1998.

1999

BASEBALL

Cincinnati (NL): New ballpark in planning stages. Would be part of $540 million downtown project including separate football stadium for NFL Bengals. Earliest groundbreaking would be late 1997 possibly near Cinergy Field; would seat 47,000 for baseball; open air, grass field; to include 65 luxury suites; estimated cost: $203 million. Earliest opening would be spring 1999.

Detroit (AL): New ballpark in planning stages. Groundbreaking set for August 1997. To be located near a new stadium for the Detroit Lions in downtown Detroit's Foxtown Theater district. The baseball-only park would seat approximately 42,000 and have 80 luxury suites. Estimated cost: $260 million. Earliest opening would be spring 1999.

Seattle (AL): New ballpark in planning stages. To be located two blocks south of Kingdome; seating capacity of 45,000 for baseball only; retractable-roof, grass field; would include 70 luxury suites; estimated cost: $320 million. Earliest Mariners' home opener would be April 1999.

NBA BASKETBALL

Atlanta (East): New arena to house both the Hawks and Atlanta's NHL expansion team. To be located on site of old Omni which was demolished on July 27, 1997. The as-yet-unnamed building will seat at least 20,000 and contain more than 100 luxury suites; estimated cost $215 million; Hawks' home opener scheduled for October 1999. In the meantime, Hawks will split home games between the Georgia Dome and Georgia Tech's Alexander Memorial Coliseum.

Denver (West): Groundbreaking for Pepsi Center (Pepsi-Cola is title sponsor) tentatively scheduled for early 1998. To be built by team owner Ascent Entertainment, along with a television studio on downtown site adjacent to the new Elitch

Gardens theme park; will seat 19,100 for basketball and 17,700 for NHL Avalanche; will include 95 luxury suites; estimated cost: $165 million. Nuggets' home opener planned for November 1999.

Indiana (East): Construction for new 19,000-seat arena underway. The as-yet-unnamed building will be located in downtown Indianapolis between Pennsylvania and Delaware streets. Estimated cost: $175 million. The arena would contain at least 66 luxury suites and serve as home to the Pacers and IHL's Indianapolis Ice. Earliest Pacers' home opener would be October 1999.

Los Angeles (West): New arena to house both the Lakers and NHL Kings in planning stages. Groundbreaking tentatively scheduled for September 1997. The site for the new 20,000-seat complex has been narrowed down to downtown Los Angeles. The project is targeted for completion in September 1999.

Toronto (East): Construction of Air Canada Center (Air Canada is title sponsor) underway. To be located on site of Old Canada Post Building at corner of Bay Street and Lake Shore Road; will seat 22,500 for basketball and 21,325 for hockey (the NHL Maple Leafs will not be tenants); will include 124 luxury suites; estimated cost: $172 million (US). Raptors' home opener scheduled for February 1999.

NFL FOOTBALL

Chicago (NFC): New stadium in planning stages. To be located next to the existing McCormick Place Exposition Center. The proposed multi-purpose domed stadium would seat approximately 75,000 and cost an estimated $465 million. Earliest opening would be fall of 1999.

Cleveland (expansion team): Construction of new stadium for resurrected Browns underway. The 70,000-seat open-air stadium will be located on the old site of Cleveland Stadium and include 124 luxury suites. Grand opening set for August 21, 1999.

Nashville (AFC): Construction for new stadium to house the relocated Tennessee Oilers underway. The natural grass, open-air stadium will seat 67,000 and have 144 luxury suites. To be located in the East Bank area of downtown Nashville. Estimated cost: $292 million. Earliest opening would be summer of 1999.

NHL HOCKEY

Atlanta (expansion team): New arena to house both the NHL expansion team and NBA's Hawks. To be located on site of old Omni which was demolished on July 27, 1997. The as-yet-unnamed building will seat at least 20,000 and contain more than 100 luxury suites; estimated cost $215 million; Home opener scheduled for Novmeber 1999.

Colorado (West): Groundbreaking for Pepsi Center (Pepsi-Cola is title sponsor) tentatively scheduled for early 1998. To be built by team owner Ascent Entertainment, along with a television studio in downtown Denver, adjacent to the new Elitch Gardens theme park; will seat 17,700 for hockey and 19,100 for NBA Nuggets; will include 95 luxury suites; estimated cost: $165 million. Avalanche home opener planned for October 1999.

Los Angeles (West): New arena to house both the Kings and NBA Lakers in planning stages. Ground-breaking tentatively scheduled for September 1997. The site for the new 20,000-seat complex has been narrowed down to downtown Los Angeles. The project is targeted for completion in September 1999.

2000

BASEBALL

Houston (NL): Groundbreaking for the Ballpark at Union Station on the east side of downtown Houston was scheduled for Nov. 9, 1997. The natural grass ballpark will feature a retractable roof which can open and close in 20 minutes; will seat 42,000 and have over 60 luxury suites; left field

will be connected to Union train station which will also house the Astros administrative offices, retail stores and a cafe; estimated cost between $200-230 million. Grand opening slated for opening day 2000.

Milwaukee (AL): Groundbreaking for Miller Park (Miller Brewing Co. is the title sponsor) on a site adjacent to the existing County Stadium took place Nov. 9, 1996. The retractable-roof stadium will have natural grass and seat approximately 45,000; estimated cost: $250 million. Brewers' home opener scheduled for April 2000.

San Francisco (NL): Groundbreaking for a Pacific Bell Park (Pacific Bell is the title sponsor) set for late 1997; to be located on the waterfront at China Basin; the open-air baseball-only park will seat 42,000 including 63 luxury suites; estimated cost: $262 million. Giant's home opener scheduled for April 2000.

NFL FOOTBALL

Cincinnati (AFC): Paul Brown Stadium in planning stages. Would be part of $540 million downtown project including separate baseball park for NL Reds. Earliest groundbreaking would be March 1998 near Cinergy Field; would seat 66,965 for football; open air, grass field; would include 104 luxury suites; estimated cost: $170 million. Earliest Bengals' home opener would be September 2000.

Pittsburgh (AFC): Two plans in place for new Steelers stadium. Team will either completely renovate Three Rivers at an estimated cost of $122 million or start construction on brand-new facility. New open-air, grass-field stadium would seat between 62-64,000 and contain 120 luxury suites. To be located 300 yards west of Three Rivers Stadium as part of city's large new construction project, including convention center and new ballpark for MLB's Pirates. Estimated cost for new football stadium: $200 million. Earliest opening would be September 2000.

San Francisco (NFC): Groundbreaking for as-yet-unnamed stadium set for fall of 1998. To be part of larger complex including shopping mall and parking garage. Estimated cost: $525 million. The open-air, grass stadium would seat 75,000 and include 200 luxury suites. To be located in same area as 3Com Park. Earliest opening would be September 2000.

2001

BASEBALL

Pittsburgh (NL): New ballpark in planning stages. To be located on a site between Three Rivers Stadium and the Sixth Street bridge. The as-yet-unnamed baseball-only park would seat approximately 37,000. Earliest Pirates' home opener would be April 2001.

2002

NFL FOOTBALL

Seattle (AFC): Groundbreaking for as-yet-unnamed stadium set for 1998 or as soon as Kingdome is demolished. Stadium and exhibition center are to be located on old site of Kingdome; would seat 72,000 and include 116 luxury suites and 10,000 club seats; open-air, grass-field would cost an estimated $425 million. Earliest Seahawks home opener would be September 2002.

2004

NFL FOOTBALL

Detroit (NFC): New stadium in planning stages. To be located near a new stadium for AL Tigers in downtown Detroit's Foxtown Theater district. The domed stadium will seat between 65,000-72,000 for football; estimated cost: $225 million. The Lions would move to the as-yet-unnamed stadium after the lease with the Pontiac Silverdome expires in 2004.

Home, Sweet Home

The home fields, home courts and home ice of the AL, NL, NBA, NFL, CFL, NHL, NCAA Division I-A college football and Division I basketball. Also included are Formula One, IndyCar, Indy Racing League and NASCAR auto racing tracks plus other miscellaneous sites.

Attendance figures for the 1996 NFL regular season and the 1996-97 NBA and NHL regular seasons are provided. See Baseball chapter for 1997 AL and NL attendance figures.

MAJOR LEAGUE BASEBALL

American League

				Outfield Fences				
		Built	Capacity	LF	LCF	CF	RCF	RF	Field
Anaheim Angels	Anaheim Stadium	1966	**64,593**	333	386	404	386	333	Grass
Baltimore Orioles	Oriole Park at Camden Yards	1992	**48,262**	333	410	400	373	318	Grass
Boston Red Sox	Fenway Park	1912	**33,871**	315	379	390	380	302	Grass
Chicago White Sox	Comiskey Park	1991	**44,321**	347	375	400	375	347	Grass
Cleveland Indians	Jacobs Field	1994	**43,863**	325	370	405	375	325	Grass
Detroit Tigers	Tiger Stadium	1912	**46,945**	340	365	440	375	325	Grass
Kansas City Royals	Kauffman Stadium	1973	**40,625**	330	375	400	375	330	Grass
Milwaukee Brewers	County Stadium	1953	**53,192**	315	392	402	392	315	Grass
Minnesota Twins	Hubert H. Humphrey Metrodome	1982	**48,678**	343	385	408	367	327	Turf
New York Yankees	Yankee Stadium	1923	**57,545**	318	399	408	385	314	Grass
Oakland Athletics	Oakland-Alameda County Coliseum	1966	**43,662**	330	367	400	367	330	Grass
Seattle Mariners	The Kingdome	1976	**59,856**	331	389	405	380	312	Turf
Texas Rangers	The Ballpark in Arlington	1994	**49,166**	332	390	400	381	325	Grass
Toronto Blue Jays	SkyDome	1989	**50,516**	328	375	400	375	328	Turf

National League

				Outfield Fences				
		Built	Capacity	LF	LCF	CF	RCF	RF	Field
Atlanta Braves	Turner Field	1996	**49,714**	335	385	401	385	330	Grass
Chicago Cubs	Wrigley Field	1914	**38,884**	355	368	400	368	353	Grass
Cincinnati Reds	Cinergy Field	1970	**52,952**	330	375	404	375	330	Turf
Colorado Rockies	Coors Field	1995	**50,200**	347	390	415	375	350	Grass
Florida Marlins	Pro Player Stadium	1987	**41,855**	330	385	434	385	345	Grass
Houston Astros	The Astrodome	1965	**54,370**	325	375	400	375	325	Turf
Los Angeles Dodgers	Dodger Stadium	1962	**56,000**	330	385	395	385	330	Grass
Montreal Expos	Olympic Stadium	1976	**46,500**	325	375	404	375	325	Turf
New York Mets	Shea Stadium	1964	**55,775**	338	371	410	371	338	Grass
Philadelphia Phillies	Veterans Stadium	1971	**62,363**	330	371	408	371	330	Turf
Pittsburgh Pirates	Three Rivers Stadium	1970	**47,972**	335	375	400	375	335	Turf
St. Louis Cardinals	Busch Stadium	1966	**49,676**	330	375	402	372	330	Grass
San Diego Padres	Qualcomm Stadium	1967	**59,690**	327	370	405	370	327	Grass
San Francisco Giants	3Com Park	1960	**62,000**	335	365	400	365	328	Grass

1998 Expansion Teams

				Outfield Fences				
		Built	Capacity	LF	LCF	CF	RCF	RF	Field
Arizona Diamondbacks	Bank One Ballpark	1998	**48,500**	328	376	402	376	335	Grass
Tampa Bay Devil Rays	Tropicana Field	1990	**48,000**	335	385	410	385	335	Turf

Rank by Capacity

AL		NL	
Anaheim	64,593	Philadelphia	62,363
Seattle	59,856	San Francisco	62,000
New York	57,545	San Diego	59,690
Milwaukee	53,192	Los Angeles	56,000
Toronto	50,516	New York	55,775
Texas	49,166	Houston	54,370
Minnesota	48,678	Cincinnati	52,952
Baltimore	48,262	Colorado	50,200
Detroit	46,945	Atlanta	49,714
Chicago	44,321	St. Louis	49,676
Cleveland	43,863	Pittsburgh	47,972
Oakland	43,662	Montreal	46,500
Kansas City	40,625	Florida	41,855
Boston	33,871	Chicago	38,884

Rank by Age

AL		NL	
Boston	1912	Chicago	1914
Detroit	1912	San Francisco	1960
New York	1923	Los Angeles	1962
Milwaukee	1953	New York	1964
Anaheim	1966	Houston	1965
Oakland	1966	St. Louis	1966
Kansas City	1973	San Diego	1967
Seattle	1976	Cincinnati	1970
Minnesota	1982	Pittsburgh	1970
Toronto	1989	Philadelphia	1971
Chicago	1991	Montreal	1976
Baltimore	1992	Florida	1987
Cleveland	1994	Colorado	1995
Texas	1994	Atlanta	1996

Note: New York's Yankee Stadium (AL) was rebuilt in 1976.

Major League Baseball (Cont.)

Home Fields

Listed below are the principal home fields used through the years by current American and National League teams. The NL became a major league in 1876, the AL in 1901.

The capacity figures in the right-hand column indicate the largest seating capacity of the ballpark while the club played there. Capacity figures before 1915 (and the introduction of concrete grandstands) are sketchy at best and have been left blank.

American League

Anaheim Angels

1961	Wrigley Field (Los Angeles)	20,457
1962-65	Dodger Stadium	56,000
1966–	Anaheim Stadium	64,593
	(1966 capacity-43,250)	

Baltimore Orioles

1901	Lloyd Street Grounds	–
1902-53	Sportsman's Park II (St. Louis)	30,500
1954-91	Memorial Stadium (Baltimore)	53,371
1992–	Camden Yards	48,262

Boston Red Sox

1901-11	Huntington Ave. Grounds	–
1912–	Fenway Park	33,871
	(1934 capacity-27,000)	

Chicago White Sox

1901-10	Southside Park	–
1910-90	Comiskey Park I	43,931
1991–	Comiskey Park II	44,321

Cleveland Indians

1901-09	League Park I	–
1910-46	League Park II	21,414
1932-93	Cleveland Stadium	74,483
1994–	Jacobs Field	43,863

Detroit Tigers

1901-11	Bennett Park	–
1912–	Tiger Stadium	46,945
	(1912 capacity-23,000)	

Kansas City Royals

1969-72	Municipal Stadium	35,020
1973–	Kauffman Stadium	40,625
	(1973 capacity-40,762)	

Milwaukee Brewers

1969	Sick's Stadium (Seattle)	25,420
1970–	County Stadium (Milwaukee)	53,192
	(1970 capacity-46,62)	

Minnesota Twins

1901-02	American League Park (Wash., DC)	....
1903-60	Griffith Stadium	27,410
1960-81	Metropolitan Stadium	
	(Bloomington, MN)	45,919
1982–	HHH Metrodome (Minneapolis)	48,678
	(1982 capacity-54,000)	

New York Yankees

1901-02	Oriole Park (Baltimore)	
1903-12	Hilltop Park (New York)	
1913-22	Polo Grounds II	38,000
1923-73	Yankee Stadium I	67,224
1974-75	Shea Stadium	55,101
1976–	Yankee Stadium II	57,545
	(1976 capacity-57,145)	

Oakland Athletics

1901-08	Columbia Park (Philadelphia)	–
1909-54	Shibe Park	33,608
1955-67	Municipal Stadium (Kansas City)	35,020
1968–	Oakland Alameda County Coliseum	43,662
	(1968 capacity-48,621)	

Seattle Mariners

1977–	The Kingdome	59,856
	(1977 capacity-59,438)	

Texas Rangers

1961	Griffith Stadium (Washington, DC)	27,410
1962-71	RFK Stadium	45,016
1972-93	Arlington Stadium (Texas)	43,521
1994–	The Ballpark in Arlington	49,166

Toronto Blue Jays

1977-89	Exhibition Stadium	43,737
1989–	SkyDome	50,516
	(1989 capacity-49,500)	

Ballpark Name Changes: CHICAGO—**Comiskey Park I** originally White Sox Park (1910-12), then Comiskey Park in 1913, then White Sox Park again in 1962, then Comiskey Park again in 1976; CLEVELAND—**League Park** renamed Dunn Field in 1920, then League Park again in 1928; Cleveland Stadium originally Municipal Stadium (1932-74); DETROIT—**Tiger Stadium** originally Navin Field (1912-37), then Briggs Stadium (1938-60); KANSAS CITY—**Kauffman Stadium** originally Royals Stadium (1973–93); LOS ANGELES—**Dodger Stadium** referred to as Chavez Revine by AL while Angels played there (1962–65); PHILADELPHIA—**Shibe Park** renamed Connie Mack Stadium in 1953; ST. LOUIS—**Sportsman's Park** renamed Busch Stadium in 1953; WASHINGTON—**Griffith Stadium** originally National Park (1892–1920), **RFK Stadium** originally D.C. Stadium (1961–68).

National League

Atlanta Braves

1876-94	South End Grounds I (Boston)	–
1894-1914	South End Grounds II	
1915-52	Braves Field	40,000
1953-65	County Stadium (Milwaukee)	43,394
1966-96	Atlanta-Fulton County Stadium	52,769
	(1966 capacity-50,000)	
1997–	Turner Field	49,714

Chicago Cubs

1876-77	State Street Grounds	–
1878-84	Lakefront Park	–
1885-91	West Side Park	–
1891-93	Brotherhood Park	–
1893-1915	West Side Grounds	–
1916–	Wrigley Field	38,884
	(1916 capacity-16,000)	

Cincinnati Reds

1876-79	Avenue Grounds	–
1880	Bank Street Grounds	–
1890-1901	Redland Field I	–
1902-11	Palace of the Fans	–
1912-70	Crosley Field	29,603
1970–	Cinergy Field	52,952
	(1970 capacity-52,000)	

Colorado Rockies

1993-94	Mile High Stadium (Denver)	76,100
1995–	Coors Field	50,200

Florida Marlins

1993–	Pro Player Stadium (Miami)	41,855

Houston Astros

1962-64	Colt Stadium	32,601
1965–	The Astrodome	54,370
	(1965 capacity-45,011)	

Los Angeles Dodgers

1890	Washington Park I (Brooklyn)	–
1891-97	Eastern Park	–
1898-1912	Washington Park II	–
1913-56	Ebbets Field	31,497
1957	Ebbets Field	31,497
	& Roosevelt Stadium (Jersey City)	24,167
1958-61	Memorial Coliseum (Los Angeles)	93,600
1962–	Dodger Stadium	56,000

Montreal Expos

1969-76	Jarry Park	28,000
1977–	Olympic Stadium	46,500
	(1977 capacity-58,500)	

New York Mets

1962-63	Polo Grounds	55,987
1964–	Shea Stadium	55,775
	(1964 capacity-55,101)	

Philadelphia Phillies

1883-86	Recreation Park	–
1887-94	Huntingdon Ave.Grounds	–
1895-1938	Baker Bowl	18,800
1938-70	Shibe Park	33,608
1971–	Veterans Stadium	62,363
	(1971 capacity-56,371)	

Pittsburgh Pirates

1887-90	Recreation Park	–
1891-1909	Exposition Park	–
1909-70	Forbes Field	35,000
1970–	Three Rivers Stadium	47,972
	(1970 capacity-50,235)	

St. Louis Cardinals

1876-77	Sportsman's Park I	–
1885-86	Vandeventer Lot	–
1892-1920	Robison Field	18,000
1920-66	Sportsman's Park II	30,500
1966–	Busch Stadium	49,676
	(1966 capacity-50,126)	

San Diego Padres

1969–	Qualcomm Stadium	59,690
	(1969 capacity-47,634)	

San Francisco Giants

1876	Union Grounds (Brooklyn)	–
1883-88	Polo Grounds I (New York)	–
1889-90	Manhattan Field	–
1891-1957	Polo Grounds II	55,987
1958-59	Seals Stadium (San Francisco)	22,900
1960–	3Com Park	62,000
	(1960 capacity-42,553)	

Ballpark Name Changes: ATLANTA—**Atlanta-Fulton County Stadium** originally Atlanta Stadium (1966-1974), **Turner Field** originally Centennial Olympic Stadium (1996); CHICAGO—**Wrigley Field** originally Weeghman Park (1914-17), then Cubs Park (1918-25); CINCINNATI—**Redland Field** originally League Park (1890-93), **Crosley Field** originally Redland Field II (1912-33) and **Cinergy Field** originally Riverfront Stadium (1970-96); FLORIDA—**Pro Player Stadium** originally Joe Robbie Stadium (1987-96); HOUSTON—**Astrodome** originally Harris County Domed Stadium before it opened in 1965; PHILADELPHIA—**Shibe Park** renamed Connie Mack Stadium in 1953; ST. LOUIS—**Robison Field** originally Vandeventer Lot, then League Park, then Cardinal Park all before becoming Robison Field in 1901, **Sportsman's Park** renamed Busch Stadium in 1953, and **Busch Stadium** originally Busch Memorial Stadium (1966-82); SAN DIEGO—**Qualcomm Stadium** originally San Diego Stadium (1967-81) and San Diego/Jack Murphy Stadium (1982–96); SAN FRANCISCO—**3Com Park** originally Candlestick Park (1960–95).

NATIONAL BASKETBALL ASSOCIATION

Western Conference

		Location	Built	Capacity
Dallas Mavericks	**Reunion Arena**	Dallas, Texas	1980	**18,042**
Denver Nuggets	**McNichols Arena**	Denver, Colo.	1975	**17,171**
Golden State Warriors	**New Oakland Coliseum**	Oakland, Calif.	1997	**19,200**
Houston Rockets	**The Summit**	Houston, Texas	1975	**16,285**
Los Angeles Clippers	**Los Angeles Sports Arena**	Los Angeles, Calif.	1959	**16,021**
	& Arrowhead Pond	Anaheim, Calif.	1993	**18,211**
Los Angeles Lakers	**Great Western Forum**	Inglewood, Calif.	1967	**17,505**
Minnesota Timberwolves	**Target Center**	Minneapolis, Minn.	1990	**19,006**
Phoenix Suns	**America West Arena**	Phoenix, Ariz.	1992	**19,023**
Portland Trail Blazers	**Rose Garden**	Portland, Ore.	1995	**21,538**
Sacramento Kings	**ARCO Arena**	Sacramento, Calif.	1988	**17,317**
San Antonio Spurs	**Alamodome**	San Antonio, Texas	1993	**25,557**
Seattle SuperSonics	**Key Arena at Seattle Center**	Seattle, Wash.	1962	**17,100**
Utah Jazz	**Delta Center**	Salt Lake City, Utah	1991	**19,911**
Vancouver Grizzlies	**General Motors Place**	Vancouver, B.C.	1995	**19,193**

Notes: Seattle's Key Arena was originally the Seattle Coliseum before being rebuilt in 1995; San Antonio's Alamodome seating is expandable to hold 32,500; and the Los Angeles Clippers are scheduled to play eight of 41 regular season home games at the Arrowhead Pond in Anaheim in 1997-98.

National Basketball Association (Cont.)

Eastern Conference

		Location	Built	Capacity
Atlanta Hawks	**Georgia Dome**	Atlanta, Ga.	1992	**21,570**
	& Alexander Memorial Coliseum	Atlanta, Ga.	1956	**9,300**
Boston Celtics	**FleetCenter**	Boston, Mass.	1995	**18,624**
Charlotte Hornets	**Charlotte Coliseum**	Charlotte, N.C.	1988	**24,042**
Chicago Bulls	**United Center**	Chicago, Ill.	1994	**21,711**
Cleveland Cavaliers	**Gund Arena**	Cleveland, Ohio	1994	**20,562**
Detroit Pistons	**The Palace of Auburn Hills**	Auburn Hills, Mich.	1988	**21,454**
Indiana Pacers	**Market Square Arena**	Indianapolis, Ind.	1974	**16,530**
Miami Heat	**Miami Arena**	Miami, Fla.	1988	**15,200**
Milwaukee Bucks	**Bradley Center**	Milwaukee, Wisc.	1988	**18,600**
New Jersey Nets	**Continental Airlines Arena**	E. Rutherford, N.J.	1981	**20,049**
New York Knicks	**Madison Square Garden**	New York, N.Y.	1968	**19,763**
Orlando Magic	**Orlando Arena**	Orlando, Fla.	1989	**17,248**
Philadelphia 76ers	**CoreStates Center**	Philadelphia, Pa.	1996	**20,444**
Toronto Raptors	**SkyDome**	Toronto, Ont.	1989	**22,911**
Washington Wizards	**MCI Center**	Washington, DC	1997	**21,500**

Note: Atlanta is scheduled to play 13 regular season games at Georgia Tech's Alexander Memorial Coliseum.

Rank by Capacity

West		East	
San Antonio	25,557	Charlotte	24,042
Portland	21,538	Toronto	22,911
Utah	19,911	Chicago	21,711
Golden St.	19,200	Atlanta	21,570
Vancouver	19,193	Washington	21,500
Phoenix	19,023	Detroit	21,454
Minnesota	19,006	Cleveland	20,562
Dallas	18,042	Philadelphia	20,444
LA Lakers	17,505	New Jersey	20,049
Sacramento	17,317	New York	19,763
Denver	17,171	Boston	18,624
Seattle	17,100	Milwaukee	18,600
Houston	16,285	Orlando	17,248
LA Clippers	16,021	Indiana	16,530
		Miami	15,200

Note: Alamodome seating is expandable to 32,500 and Georgia Dome seating is expandable to 34,821.

Rank by Age

West		East	
LA Clippers	1959	New York	1968
Seattle	1962	Atlanta	1972
LA Lakers	1967	Indiana	1974
Denver	1975	New Jersey	1981
Houston	1975	Charlotte	1988
Dallas	1980	Detroit	1988
Sacramento	1988	Miami	1988
Minnesota	1990	Milwaukee	1988
Utah	1991	Orlando	1989
Phoenix	1992	Toronto	1989
San Antonio	1993	Chicago	1994
Portland	1995	Cleveland	1994
Vancouver	1995	Boston	1995
Golden St.	1997	Philadelphia	1996
		Washington	1997

Note: The Seattle Coliseum was rebuilt and renamed Key Arena in 1995.

1996-97 NBA Attendance

Official overall attendance in the NBA for the 1996-97 season was 20,304,629 for an average per game crowd of 17,077 over 1,189 games. Teams in each conference are ranked by attendance over 41 home games based on total tickets distributed; sellouts are listed in S/O column. Numbers in parentheses indicate rank in 1995-96.

Western Conference

	Attendance	S/O	Average
1 Portland (1)	852,799	9	20,800
2 Utah (2)	811,439	36	19,791
3 Phoenix (4)	779,943	41	19,023
4 Sacramento (5)	709,997	41	17,317
5 San Antonio (3)	706,641	10	17,235
6 Seattle (7)	699,952	41	17,072
7 Minnesota (13)	697,727	6	17,018
8 LA Lakers (11)	697,159	22	17,004
9 Vancouver (6)	679,422	6	16,571
10 Houston (10)	667,685	41	16,285
11 Golden St. (12)	621,844	2	15,167
12 Dallas (8)	619,178	6	15,102
13 Denver (9)	461,408	1	11,254
14 LA Clippers (14)	400,637	7	9,772
TOTAL	9,405,831	269	16,386

Note: LA Clippers played 35 games at LA Sports Arena (six sellouts and 8,836 avg.) and six at The Arrowhead Pond in Anaheim (one sellout and 15,231 avg.)

Eastern Conference

	Attendance	S/O	Average
1 Charlotte (1)	985,722	41	24,042
2 Chicago (2)	978,455	41	23,865
3 Detroit (6)	820,585	29	20,014
4 New York (4)	810,283	41	19,763
5 Toronto (3)	748,927	5	18,267
6 Orlando (8)	726,597	36	17,722
7 Washington (9)	700,646	29	17,089
8 Cleveland (7)	692,684	3	16,895
9 New Jersey (12)	670,628	9	16,357
10 Boston (5)	664,022	6	16,196
11 Indiana (10)	636,735	12	15,530
12 Milwaukee (11)	636,083	3	15,514
13 Philadelphia (15)	626,478	5	15,280
14 Miami (13)	615,160	21	15,004
15 Atlanta (14)	585,793	16	14,288
TOTAL	10,898,798	297	17,722

Note: Washington played 37 games at USAir Arena (28 sellouts and 13,681 avg.) and four at Baltimore Arena (1 sellout, 11,616 avg.); Toronto played 37 games at Skydome (5 sellouts and 18,551 avg.), three at Maple Leaf Gardens (0 sellouts, 15,301 avg.) and one at Copps Coliseum (0 sellouts and 16,630 avg.).

Home Courts

Listed below are the principal home courts used through the years by current NBA teams. The largest capacity of each arena is noted in the right-hand column. ABA arenas (1972-76) are included for Denver, Indiana, New Jersey and San Antonio.

Western Conference

Dallas Mavericks

1980– Reunion Arena 18,042

Denver Nuggets

1967-75 Auditorium Arena 6,841
1975– McNichols Sports Arena 17,171
       (1975 capacity-16,700)

Golden State Warriors

1946-52 Philadelphia Arena 7,777
1952-62 Convention Hall (Philadelphia) 9,200
       & Philadelphia Arena 7,777
1962-64 Cow Palace (San Francisco) 13,862
1964-66 Civic Auditorium 7,500
       & (USF Memorial Gym) 6,000
1966-67 Cow Palace, Civic Auditorium
       & Oakland Coliseum Arena 15,000
1967-71 Cow Palace 14,500
1971-96 Oakland Coliseum Arena 15,025
       (1971 capacity-12,905)
1996-97 San Jose Arena 18,500
1997– New Oakland Coliseum 19,200

Houston Rockets

1967-71 San DiegoSports Arena 14,000
1971-72 Hofheinz Pavilion (Houston) 10,218
1972-73 Hofheinz Pavilion 10,218
       & HemisFair Arena (San Antonio) 10,446
1973-75 Hofheinz Pavilion 10,218
1975– The Summit 16,285
       (1975 capacity-15,600)

Los Angeles Clippers

1970-78 Memorial Auditorium (Buffalo) 17,300
1978-84 San Diego Sports Arena 12,167
1985-94 Los Angeles Sports Arena 16,005
1994– Los Angeles Sports Arena 16,021
       & Arrowhead Pond 18,211

Los Angeles Lakers

1948-60 Minneapolis Auditorium 10,000
1960-67 Los Angeles Arena 14,781
1967– Great Western Forum (Inglewood, CA) . 17,505
       (1967 capacity-17,086)

Minnesota Timberwolves

1989-90 Hubert H. Humphrey Metrodome 23,000
1990– Target Center 19,006

Phoenix Suns

1968-92 Arizona Veterans' Memorial Coliseum .. 14,487
1992– America West Arena 19,023

Portland Trail Blazers

1970-95 Memorial Coliseum 12,888
1995– Rose Garden 21,538

Sacramento Kings

1948-55 Edgarton Park Arena (Rochester, NY) .. 5,000
1955-58 Rochester War Memorial 10,000
1958-72 Cincinnati Gardens 11,438
1972-74 Municipal Auditorium (Kansas City) 9,929
       & Omaha (NE) Civic Auditorium 9,136
1974-78 Kemper Arena (Kansas City) 16,785
       & Omaha Civic Auditorium 9,136
1978-85 Kemper Arena 16,785
1985-88 ARCO Arena I 10,333
1988– ARCO Arena II 17,317
       (1988 capacity-16,517)

San Antonio Spurs

1967-70 Memorial Auditorium (Dallas) 8,088
       & Moody Coliseum (Dallas) 8,500
1970-71 Moody Coliseum 8,500
       Tarrant Convention Center (Ft. Worth) .. 13,500
       & Municipal Coliseum (Lubbock) 10,400
1971-73 Moody Coliseum 9,500
       & Memorial Auditorium 8,088
1973-93 HemisFair Arena (San Antonio) 16,057
1993– The Alamodome 25,557

Seattle SuperSonics

1967-78 Seattle Center Coliseum 14,098
1978-85 Kingdome 40,192
1985-94 Seattle Center Coliseum 14,252
1994-95 Tacoma Dome 19,000
1995– Key Arena at Seattle Center 17,100

Utah Jazz

1974-75 Municipal Auditorium 7,853
       & Louisiana Superdome 47,284
1975-79 Superdome 47,284
1979-83 Salt Palace (Salt Lake City) 12,519
1983-84 Salt Palace 12,519
       & Thomas & Mack Center (Las Vegas) .. 18,500
1985-91 Salt Palace 12,616
1991– Delta Center 19,911

Vancouver Grizzlies

1995– General Motors Place 19,193

Eastern Conference

Atlanta Hawks

1949-51 Wheaton Field House (Moline, IL) 6,000
1951-55 Milwaukee Arena 11,000
1955-68 Kiel Auditorium (St. Louis) 10,000
1968-72 Alexander Mem. Coliseum (Atlanta) 7,166
1972-96 The Omni 16,378
1997– Georgia Dome 21,570
       & Alexander Mem. Coliseum 9,300

Boston Celtics

1946-95 Boston Garden 14,890
1995– FleetCenter 18,624
Note: From 1975-95 the Celtics played some regular season games at the Hartford Civic Center (15,418).

Charlotte Hornets

1988– Charlotte Coliseum 24,042
       (1988 capacity-23,500)

Chicago Bulls

1966-67 Chicago Amphitheater 11,002
1967-94 Chicago Stadium 18,676
1994– United Center 21,711

Cleveland Cavaliers

1970-74 Cleveland Arena 11,000
1974-94 The Coliseum (Richfield, OH) 20,273
1994– Gund Arena 20,562

National Basketball Association (Cont.)

Detroit Pistons

1948-52	North Side H.S. Gym (Ft. Wayne, IN) ..	3,800
1952-57	Memorial Coliseum (Ft. Wayne)	9,306
1957-61	Olympia Stadium (Detroit)	14,000
1961-78	Cobo Arena	11,147
1978-88	Silverdome (Pontiac, MI)	22,366
1988–	The Palace of Auburn Hills	21,454

Indiana Pacers

1967-74	State Fairgrounds (Indianapolis)	9,479
1974–	Market Square Arena	16,530
	(1974 capacity-17,287)	

Miami Heat

1988–	Miami Arena	15,200

Milwaukee Bucks

1968-88	Milwaukee Arena (The Mecca)	11,052
1988–	Bradley Center	18,600

New Jersey Nets

1967-68	Teaneck (NJ) Armory	3,500
1968-69	Long Island Arena (Commack, NY)	6,500
1969-71	Island Garden (W. Hempstead, NY) ...	5,200
1971-77	Nassau Coliseum (Uniondale, NY)	15,500
1977-81	Rutgers Ath. Center (Piscataway, NJ) ...	9,050
1981–	Continental Airlines Arena (E. Rutherford,NJ)	20,049

New York Knicks

1946-68	Madison Sq. Garden III (50th St.)	18,496
1968–	Madison Sq. Garden IV (33rd St.)	19,763
	(1968 capacity-19,694)	

Orlando Magic

1989–	Orlando Arena	17,248

Philadelphia 76ers

1949-51	State Fair Coliseum (Syracuse, NY)	7,500
1951-63	Onondaga County (NY) War Memorial ...	8,000
1963-67	Convention Hall (Philadelphia)	12,000
	& Philadelphia Arena	7,777
1967-96	CoreStates Spectrum	18,136
1996—	CoreStates Center	20,444

Toronto Raptors

1995–	SkyDome	22,911

Washington Wizards

1961-62	Chicago Amphitheater	11,000
1962-63	Chicago Coliseum	7,100
1963-73	Baltimore Civic Center	12,289
1973-97	USAir Arena (Landover, MD)	18,756
1997—	MCI Center	21,500

Note: From 1988-96 the Wizards (then Bullets) played four regular season games at Baltimore Arena (12,756).

Building Name Changes: New Jersey– **Continental Airlines Arena** originally Byrne Meadowlands Arena (1981-96); PHILADELPHIA– **CoreStates Spectrum** originally The Spectrum (1967-94); WASHINGTON–**USAir Arena** originally Capital Centre (1973-93).

NATIONAL FOOTBALL LEAGUE

American Football Conference

		Location	Built	Capacity	Field
Baltimore Ravens	**Memorial Stadium**	Baltimore, Md.	1954	**65,000**	Grass*
Buffalo Bills	**Rich Stadium**	Orchard Park, N.Y.	1973	**80,024**	Turf
Cincinnati Bengals	**Cinergy Field**	Cincinnati, Ohio	1970	**60,389**	Turf
Denver Broncos	**Mile High Stadium**	Denver, Colo.	1948	**76,273**	Grass
Indianapolis Colts	**RCA Dome**	Indianapolis, Ind.	1984	**60,273**	Turf
Jacksonville Jaguars	**Alltel Stadium**	Jacksonville, Fla.	1995	**73,000**	Grass
Kansas City Chiefs	**Arrowhead Stadium**	Kansas City, Mo.	1972	**79,409**	Grass
Miami Dolphins	**Pro Player Stadium**	Miami, Fla.	1987	**74,916**	Grass
New England Patriots	**Foxboro Stadium**	Foxboro, Mass.	1971	**60,292**	Grass
New York Jets	**Giants Stadium**	E. Rutherford, N.J.	1976	**77,716**	Turf
Oakland Raiders	**Oakland-Alameda County Coliseum**	Oakland, Calif.	1966	**62,500**	Grass
Pittsburgh Steelers	**Three Rivers Stadium**	Pittsburgh, Pa.	1970	**59,600**	Turf
San Diego Chargers	**Qualcomm Stadium**	San Diego, Calif.	1967	**71,000**	Grass
Seattle Seahawks	**Kingdome**	Seattle, Wash.	1976	**66,400**	Turf
Tennessee Oilers	**Liberty Bowl**	Memphis, Tenn.	1965	**62,380**	Grass

National Football Conference

		Location	Built	Capacity	Field
Arizona Cardinals	**Sun Devil Stadium**	Tempe, Ariz.	1958	**73,273**	Grass
Atlanta Falcons	**Georgia Dome**	Atlanta, Ga.	1992	**71,228**	Turf
Carolina Panthers	**Ericsson Stadium**	Charlotte, N.C.	1996	**73,248**	Grass
Chicago Bears	**Soldier Field**	Chicago, Ill.	1924	**66,944**	Grass
Dallas Cowboys	**Texas Stadium**	Irving, Texas	1971	**65,921**	Turf
Detroit Lions	**Pontiac Silverdome**	Pontiac, Mich.	1975	**80,368**	Turf
Green Bay Packers	**Lambeau Field**	Green Bay, Wisc.	1957	**60,790**	Grass
Minnesota Vikings	**Hubert H. Humphrey Metrodome**	Minneapolis, Minn.	1982	**64,000**	Turf
New Orleans Saints	**Louisiana Superdome**	New Orleans, La.	1975	**69,420**	Turf
New York Giants	**Giants Stadium**	E. Rutherford, N.J.	1976	**78,148**	Turf
Philadelphia Eagles	**Veterans Stadium**	Philadelphia, Pa.	1971	**65,352**	Turf
St. Louis Rams	**Trans World Dome**	St. Louis, Mo.	1995	**66,000**	Turf
San Francisco 49ers	**3Com Park**	San Francisco, Calif.	1960	**70,207**	Grass
Tampa Bay Buccaneers ...	**Houlihan's Stadium**	Tampa, Fla.	1967	**74,300**	Grass
Washington Redskins	**Jack Kent Cooke Stadium**	Landover, MD	1997	**78,600**	Grass

*The field at Memorial Stadium is Sportsgrass, a combination of natural grass turf with a below-the-surface system of synthetic elements to provide a more stable and durable playing surface. The grass is grown in a base of sand and is rooted through artificial grass blades and inserted into a woven backing.

Rank by Capacity

AFC		NFC	
Buffalo	80,024	Detroit	80,365
Kansas City	79,409	Washington	78,600
NY Jets	77,716	NY Giants	78,148
Denver	76,273	Tampa Bay	74,300
Miami	74,916	Arizona	73,273
Jacksonville	73,000	Carolina	73,248
San Diego	71,000	Atlanta	71,228
Seattle	66,400	San Francisco	70,207
Baltimore	65,000	New Orleans	69,420
Oakland	62,500	Chicago	66,944
Tennessee	62,380	St. Louis	66,000
Cincinnati	60,389	Dallas	65,921
New England	60,292	Philadelphia	65,352
Indianapolis	60,273	Minnesota	64,000
Pittsburgh	59,600	Green Bay	60,790

Rank by Age

AFC		NFC	
Denver	1948	Chicago	1924
Baltimore	1954	Green Bay	1957
Tennessee	1965	Arizona	1958
Oakland	1966	San Francisco	1960
San Diego	1967	Tampa Bay	1967
Cincinnati	1970	Dallas	1971
Pittsburgh	1970	Philadelphia	1971
New England	1971	New Orleans	1975
Kansas City	1972	Detroit	1975
Buffalo	1973	NY Giants	1976
NY Jets	1976	Minnesota	1982
Seattle	1976	Atlanta	1992
Indianapolis	1984	St. Louis	1995
Miami	1987	Carolina	1996
Jacksonville	1995	Washington	1997

1996 NFL Attendance

Official overall paid attendance in the NFL for the 1996 season was 14,612,417 for an average per game crowd of 60,885 over 240 games. Cumulative announced (day of game) attendance figures listed by *The Sporting News* in its 1997 Pro Football Guide show an overall NFL attendance of 13,695,748 for an average per game crowd of 57,066. Teams in each conference are ranked by attendance over eight home games, according to *TSN* figures. Rank column indicates rank in entire league. Numbers in parentheses indicate conference rank in 1995.

AFC

		Attendance	Rank	Average
1	Kansas City (1)	610,617	1	76,327
2	Buffalo (5)	598,321	2	74,790
3	Denver (2)	589,296	3	73,662
4	Miami (3)	545,518	6	68,190
5	Jacksonville (4)	533,533	7	66,692
6	Baltimore (6)	471,665	14	58,958
7	New England (8)	468,301	15	58,538
8	Pittsburgh (9)	466,944	16	58,368
9	San Diego (7)	460,355	17	57,544
10	Indianapolis (11)	438,026	20	54,753
11	Oakland (12)	398,915	22	49,864
12	NY Jets (10)	397,816	23	49,727
13	Cincinnati (13)	382,324	24	47,791
14	Seattle (14)	357,570	25	44,696
15	Houston (15)	254,600	30	31,825
	TOTAL	6,973,801	—	58,115

NFC

		Attendance	Rank	Average
1	Carolina (11)	553,382	4	69,173
2	NY Giants (2)	552,870	5	69,109
3	Philadelphia (5)	514,003	8	64,250
4	Dallas (4)	513,794	9	64,224
5	San Francisco (3)	502,534	10	62,817
6	Detroit (1)	491,948	11	61,494
7	St. Louis (6)	484,896	12	60,612
8	Green Bay (7)	482,988	13	60,374
9	Chicago (8)	456,348	18	57,044
10	Minnesota (10)	449,940	19	56,243
11	Washington (13)	427,750	21	53,469
12	Atlanta (12)	335,638	26	41,955
13	Tampa Bay (9)	333,350	27	41,669
14	Arizona (15)	320,508	28	40,064
15	New Orleans (14)	301,998	29	37,750
	TOTAL	6,721,947	—	56,016

Home Fields

Listed below are the principal home fields used through the years by current NFL teams. The largest capacity of each stadium is noted in the right-hand column. All-America Football Conference stadiums (1946-49) are included for Cleveland and San Francisco.

AFC

Baltimore Ravens

1946-95	Cleveland Stadium	78,512
	(1946 capacity-85,703)	
1996–	Memorial Stadium (Baltimore)	65,000

Buffalo Bills

1960-72	War Memorial Stadium	45,748
1973–	Rich Stadium (Orchard Park, NY)	80,024
	(1973 capacity-80,020)	

Cincinnati Bengals

1968-69	Nippert Stadium (Univ. of Cincinnati)	26,500
1970–	Cinergy Field	60,389
	(1970 capacity-56,200)	

Denver Broncos

1960–	Mile High Stadium	76,273
	(1960 capacity-34,000)	

Indianapolis Colts

1953-83	Memorial Stadium (Baltimore)	60,020
1984–	RCA Dome (Indianapolis)	60,273
	(1984 capacity-60,127)	

Jacksonville Jaguars

1995–	Alltel Stadium	73,000

Kansas City Chiefs

1960-62	Cotton Bowl (Dallas)	72,000
1963-71	Municipal Stadium (Kansas City)	47,000
1972–	Arrowhead Stadium	79,409
	(1972 capacity-78,097)	

Miami Dolphins

1966-86	Orange Bowl	75,206
1987–	Pro Player Stadium	74,916
	(1987 capacity-75,500)	

National Football League (Cont.)

New England Patriots

1960-62	Nickerson Field (Boston Univ.)	17,369
1963-68	Fenway Park	33,379
1969	Alumni Stadium (Boston College)	26,000
1970	Harvard Stadium	37,300
1971–	Foxboro Stadium	60,292
	(1971 capacity-61,114)	

New York Jets

1960-63	Polo Grounds	55,987
1964-83	Shea Stadium	60,372
1984–	Giants Stadium (E. Rutherford, NJ)	77,716

Oakland Raiders

1960	Kesar Stadium (San Francisco)	59,636
1961	Candlestick Park	42,500
1962-65	Frank Youell Field (Oakland)	20,000
1966-81	Oakland-Alameda County Coliseum	54,587
1982-94	Memorial Coliseum (Los Angeles)	67,800
1995–	Oakland-Alameda County Coliseum	54,500

Pittsburgh Steelers

1933-57	Forbes Field	35,000
1958-63	Forbes Field	35,000
	& Pitt Stadium	54,500
1964-69	Pitt Stadium	54,500
1970–	Three Rivers Stadium	59,600
	(1970 capacity-49,000)	

San Diego Chargers

1960	Memorial Coliseum (Los Angeles)	92,604
1961-66	Balboa Stadium (San Diego)	34,000
1967–	Qualcomm Stadium	71,000
	(1967 capacity-54,000)	

Seattle Seahawks

1976-94	Kingdome	66,000
1994	Kingdome	66,400
	& Husky Stadium	72,500
1995–	Kingdome	66,400

Tennessee Oilers

1960-64	Jeppesen Stadium	23,500
1965-67	Rice Stadium (Rice Univ.)	70,000
1968-96	Astrodome	59,969
1997–	Liberty Bowl	62,380

Ballpark Name Changes: Baltimore—**Cleveland Stadium** originally Municipal Stadium (1932-74); CINCINNATI—**Cinergy Field** originally Riverfront Stadium (1970-96); DENVER—**Mile High Stadium** originally Bears Stadium (1948-66); INDIANAPOLIS—**RCA Dome** originally Hoosier Dome (1984-94); Jacksonville—**Alltel Stadium** originally Jacksonville Municipal Stadium (1995-97); MIAMI—**Pro Player Stadium** originally Joe Robbie Stadium (1987-96); NEW ENGLAND—**Foxboro Stadium** originally Schaefer Stadium (1971-82), then Sullivan Stadium (1983-89); SAN DIEGO—**Qualcomm Stadium** originally San Diego Stadium (1967-81) then San Diego/Jack Murphy Stadium (1981-96).

NFC

Arizona Cardinals

1920-21	Normal Field (Chicago)	7,500
1922-25	Comiskey Park	28,000
1926-28	Normal Field	7,500
1929-59	Comiskey Park	52,000
1960-65	Busch Stadium (St. Louis)	34,000
1966-87	Busch Memorial Stadium	54,392
1988–	Sun Devil Stadium (Tempe, AZ)	73,273

Atlanta Falcons

1966-91	Atlanta-Fulton County Stadium	59,643
1992–	Georgia Dome	71,228

Carolina Panthers

1995	Memorial Stadium (Clemson, SC)	81,473
1996–	Ericsson Stadium	73,248

Chicago Bears

1920	Staley Field (Decatur, IL)	–
1921-70	Wrigley Field (Chicago)	37,741
1971–	Soldier Field	66,944
	(1971 capacity-55,049)	

Dallas Cowboys

1960-70	Cotton Bowl	72,132
1971–	Texas Stadium (Irving, TX)	65,921
	(1971 capacity-65,101)	

Detroit Lions

1930-33	Spartan Stadium (Portsmouth, OH)	8,200
1934-37	Univ. of Detroit Stadium	25,000
1938-74	Tiger Stadium	54,468
1975–	Pontiac Silverdome	80,368
	(1975 capacity-80,638)	

Green Bay Packers

1921-22	Hagemeister Brewery Park	–
1923-24	Bellevue Park	–
1925-56	City Stadium I	24,800
1957–	Lambeau Field	60,790
	(1957 capacity-32,150)	

Note: The Packers played games in Milwaukee from 1933-94: at Borchert Field, State Fair Park and Marquette Stadium (1933-52), and County Stadium (1953-94).

Minnesota Vikings

1961-81	Metropolitan Stadium (Bloomington)	48,446
1982–	HHH Metrodome (Minneapolis)	64,000
	(1982 capacity-62,220)	

New Orleans Saints

1967-74	Tulane Stadium	80,997
1975–	Louisiana Superdome	69,420
	(1975 capacity-74,472)	

New York Giants

1925-55	Polo Grounds II	55,200
1956-73	Yankee Stadium I	63,800
1973-74	Yale Bowl (New Haven, CT)	70,896
1975	Shea Stadium	60,372
1976–	Giants Stadium (E. Rutherford, NJ)	78,148
	(1976 capacity-76,800)	

Philadelphia Eagles

1933-35	Baker Bowl	18,800
1936-39	Municipal Stadium	73,702
1940	Shibe Park	33,608
1941	Municipal Stadium	73,702
1942	Shibe Park	33,608
1943	Forbes Field (Pittsburgh)	34,528
1944-57	Shibe Park	33,608
1958-70	Franklin Field (Univ. of Penn.)	60,546
1971–	Veterans Stadium	65,352
	(1971 capacity-65,000)	

San Francisco 49ers

1946-70	Kezar Stadium	59,636
1971–	3Com Park	70,207
	(1971 capacity-61,246)	

St. Louis Rams

1937-42	Municipal Stadium (Cleveland)	85,703
1945	Suspended operations for one year.	
1944-45	Municipal Stadium	85,703
1946-79	Memorial Coliseum (Los Angeles)	92,604
1980-94	Anaheim Stadium	69,008
1995–	Trans World Dome	66,000

Tampa Bay Buccaneers

1976–	Houlihan's Stadium	74,300
	(1976 capacity-71,951)	

Washington Redskins

1932	Braves Field (Boston)	40,000
1933-36	Fenway Park	27,000
1937-60	Griffith Stadium (Washington, DC)	35,000
1961-97	RFK Stadium	56,454
1997—	Jack Kent Cooke Stadium	78,600

Ballpark Name Changes: ATLANTA—**Atlanta-Fulton County Stadium** originally Atlanta Stadium (1966-74); CHICAGO— **Wrigley Field** originally Cubs Park (1916-25), also, Comiskey Park originally White Sox Park (1910-12); DETROIT— **Tiger Stadium** originally Navin Field (1912-37), then Briggs Stadium (1938-60), also, **Pontiac Silverdome** originally Pontiac Metropolitan Stadium (1975); GREEN BAY—**Lambeau Field** originally City Stadium II (1957-64); PHILADELPHIA— **Shibe Park** renamed Connie Mack Stadium in 1953; ST. LOUIS—**Busch Memorial Stadium** renamed Busch Stadium in 1983; SAN FRANCISCO—**3Com Park** originally Candlestick Park (1960-94); TAMPA BAY—**Houlihan's Stadium** originally Tampa Stadium (1976-96); WASHINGTON—**RFK Stadium** originally D.C. Stadium (1961-68).

NATIONAL HOCKEY LEAGUE

Western Conference

		Location	Built	Capacity
Anaheim, Mighty Ducks of	**Arrowhead Pond**	Anaheim, Calif.	1993	**17,174**
Calgary Flames	**Canadian Airlines Saddledome**	Calgary, Alb.	1983	**18,882**
Chicago Blackhawks	**United Center**	Chicago, Ill.	1994	**20,500**
Colorado Avalanche	**McNichols Arena**	Denver, Colo.	1975	**16,061**
Dallas Stars	**Reunion Arena**	Dallas, Texas	1980	**16,924**
Detroit Red Wings	**Joe Louis Arena**	Detroit, Mich.	1979	**19,275**
Edmonton Oilers	**Edmonton Coliseum**	Edmonton, Alb.	1974	**17,099**
Los Angeles Kings	**Great Western Forum**	Inglewood, Calif.	1967	**16,005**
Phoenix Coyotes	**America West**	Phoenix, Ariz.	1992	**16,210**
St. Louis Blues	**Kiel Center**	St. Louis, Mo.	1994	**19,260**
San Jose Sharks	**San Jose Arena**	San Jose, Calif.	1993	**17,442**
Toronto Maple Leafs	**Maple Leaf Gardens**	Toronto, Ont.	1931	**15,726**
Vancouver Canucks	**General Motors Place**	Vancouver, B.C.	1995	**18,422**

Eastern Conference

		Location	Built	Capacity
Boston Bruins	**FleetCenter**	Boston, Mass.	1995	**17,565**
Buffalo Sabres	**Marine Midland Arena**	Buffalo, N.Y.	1996	**18,595**
Carolina Hurricanes	**Greensboro Coliseum**	Greensboro, N.C.	1959	**21,500**
Florida Panthers	**Miami Arena**	Miami, Fla.	1988	**14,703**
Montreal Canadiens	**Molson Centre**	Montreal, Que.	1996	**21,273**
New Jersey Devils	**Continental Airlines Arena**	E. Rutherford, N.J.	1981	**19,040**
New York Islanders	**Nassau Veterans' Mem. Coliseum**	Uniondale, N.Y.	1972	**16,297**
New York Rangers	**Madison Square Garden**	New York, N.Y.	1968	**18,200**
Ottawa Senators	**Corel Centre**	Kanata, Ont.	1996	**18,500**
Philadelphia Flyers	**CoreStates Center**	Philadelphia, Pa.	1996	**19,511**
Pittsburgh Penguins	**Civic Arena**	Pittsburgh, Pa.	1961	**17,355**
Tampa Bay Lightning	**Ice Palace**	Tampa Bay, Fla.	1996	**19,500**
Washington Capitals	**MCI Center**	Washington, D.C.	1997	**20,000**

Note: When Buffalo closed Memorial Auditorium and moved into the new Marine Midland Arena in 1996 all the ice surfaces in the NHL became the same size (200 x 85 feet).

Rank by Capacity

Western		Eastern	
Chicago	20,500	Carolina	21,500
Detroit	19,275	Montreal	21,273
St. Louis	19,260	Washington	20,000
Calgary	18,882	Philadelphia	19,511
Vancouver	18,422	Tampa Bay	19,500
San Jose	17,442	New Jersey	19,040
Anaheim	17,174	Buffalo	18,595
Edmonton	17,099	Ottawa	18,500
Dallas	16,924	NY Rangers	18,200
Phoenix	16,210	Boston	17,565
Colorado	16,061	Pittsburgh	17,355
Los Angeles	16,005	NY Islanders	16,297
Toronto	15,726	Florida	14,703

Rank by Age

Western		Eastern	
Toronto	1931	Carolina	1959
Los Angeles	1967	Pittsburgh	1961
Edmonton	1974	NY Rangers	1968
Colorado	1975	NY Islanders	1972
Detroit	1979	New Jersey	1981
Dallas	1980	Florida	1988
Calgary	1983	Boston	1995
Phoenix	1992	Montreal	1996
Anaheim	1993	Ottawa	1996
San Jose	1993	Buffalo	1996
Chicago	1994	Philadelphia	1996
St. Louis	1994	Tampa Bay	1996
Vancouver	1995	Washington	1997

National Hockey League (Cont.)

1996-97 NHL Attendance

Official overall paid attendance for the 1996-97 season according to the NHL accounting office was 17,640,529 (paid tickets) for an average per game crowd of 16,548 over 1,066 games. This amounts to a 3.5% increase over 1995-96 totals. Teams in each conference are ranked by attendance over 41 home games. There were no neutral site games. Number of sellouts are listed in S/O column. Numbers in parentheses indicate rank in 1995-96. Note that Phoenix moved from Winnipeg before the 1996-97 season.

	Western Conference	Attendance	S/O	Average		Eastern Conference	Attendance	S/O	Average
1	Detroit (2)	819,007	41	19,976	1	Montreal (2)	861,072	26	21,002
2	Chicago (1)	795,265	14	19,397	2	Philadelphia (5)	791,853	15	19,313
3	San Jose (6)	714,328	37	17,423	3	NY Rangers (3)	745,714	40	18,188
4	Vancouver (5)	710,136	14	17,320	4	Tampa Bay (1)	715,158	10	17,443
5	Calgary (4)	700,643	7	17,089	5	Buffalo (9)	693,379	18	16,912
6	Anaheim (7)	696,047	29	16,977	6	Pittsburgh (6)	684,342	8	16,691
7	St. Louis (3)	689,079	8	16,807	7	New Jersey (7)	672,318	10	16,398
8	Colorado (8)	658,491	41	16,061	8	Washington (8)	646,234	19	15,762
9	Edmonton (12)	657,786	12	16,044	9	Boston (4)	637,575	7	15,551
10	Dallas (10)	655,878	9	15,997	10	Ottawa (11)	630,469	7	15,377
11	Toronto (9)	643,862	33	15,704	11	Florida (10)	602,823	41	14,703
12	Phoenix (13)	639,745	18	15,604	12	Hartford (12)	560,878	7	13,680
13	Los Angeles (11)	504,190	4	12,297	13	NY Islanders (13)	512,279	10	12,495
	TOTAL	8,885,457	267	16,671		TOTAL	8,755,072	218	16,426

Home Ice

Listed below are the principal home buildings used through the years by current NHL teams. The largest capacity of each arena is noted in the right hand column. World Hockey Association arenas (1972-76) are included for Edmonton, Hartford (now Carolina), Quebec (now Colorado) and Winnipeg (now Phoenix).

Western Conference

Anaheim, Mighty Ducks of

1993–	Arrowhead Pond	17,174

Calgary Flames

1972-80	The Omni (Atlanta)	15,278
1980-83	Calgary Corral	7,424
1983–	Canadian Airlines Saddledome	18,882
	(1983 capacity-16,674)	

Chicago Blackhawks

1926-29	Chicago Coliseum	5,000
1929-94	Chicago Stadium	17,317
1994–	United Center	20,500

Colorado Avalanche

1972-95	Le Colisee de Quebec	15,399
1995–	McNichols Arena (Denver)	16,061

Dallas Stars

1967-93	Met Center (Bloomington, MN)	15,174
1993–	Reunion Arena (Dallas)	16,924

Detroit Red Wings

1926-27	Border Cities Arena (Windsor, Ont.)	3,200
1927-79	Olympia Stadium (Detroit)	16,700
1979–	Joe Louis Arena	19,275

Edmonton Oilers

1972-74	Edmonton Gardens	7,200
1974–	Edmonton Coliseum	17,099
	(1974 capacity-15,513)	

Los Angeles Kings

1967–	Great Western Forum (Inglewood)	16,005
	(1967 capacity-15,651)	

Note: The Kings played 17 games at Long Beach Sports Arena and LA Sports Arena at the start of the 1967-68 season.

Phoenix Coyotes

1972-96	Winnipeg Arena	15,393
	(1972 capacity-10,177)	
1996—	America West (Phoenix)	16,210

St. Louis Blues

1967-94	St. Louis Arena	17,188
1994–	Kiel Center	19,260

San Jose Sharks

1991-93	Cow Palace (Daly City, CA)	11,100
1993–	San Jose Arena	17,442

Toronto Maple Leafs

1917-31	Mutual Street Arena	8,000
1931–	Maple Leaf Gardens	15,726
	(1931 capacity-13,542)	

Vancouver Canucks

1970-95	Pacific Coliseum	16,150
1995–	General Motors Place	18,422

Building Name Changes: CALGARY—**Canadian Airlines Saddledome** originally Olympic Saddledome (1983-1995); DALLAS—**Met Center** in Minneapolis originally Metropolitan Sports Center (1967-82); EDMONTON—**Edmonton Coliseum** originally Northlands Coliseum (1974-94); LOS ANGELES—**Great Western Forum** originally The Forum (1967-88); ST. LOUIS—**St. Louis Arena** renamed The Checkerdome in 1977, then St. Louis Arena again in 1982.

Eastern Conference

Boston Bruins

1924-28	Boston Arena	6,200
1928-95	Boston Garden	14,448
1995–	FleetCenter	17,565

Buffalo Sabres

1970-96	Memorial Auditorium (The Aud) (1970 capacity-10,429)	16,284
1996–	Marine Midland Arena	18,595

Carolina Hurricanes

1972-73	Boston Garden	14,442
1973-74	Boston Garden (regular season)	14,442
	West Springfield (MA) Big E (playoffs)	5,513
1974-75	West Springfield Big E	5,513
	& Hartford (CT) Civic Center	10,507
1975-77	Hartford Civic Center	10,507
1977-78	Hartford Civic Center	10,507
	& Springfield (MA) Civic Center	7,725
1978-79	Springfield Civic Center	7,725
1979-80	Springfield Civic Center	7,725
	& Hartford Civic Center II	14,250
1980-97	Hartford Civic Center II	15,635
1997–	Greensboro Coliseum	21,500

Note: The Hartford Civic Center roof caved in January 1978, forcing the Whalers to move their home games to Springfield, MA for two years.

Florida Panthers

1993–	Miami Arena	14,703

Montreal Canadiens

1910-20	Jubilee Arena	3,200
1913-18	Montreal Arena (Westmount)	6,000
1918-26	Mount Royal Arena	6,750
1926-68	Montreal Forum I	15,500
1968-96	Montreal Forum II	17,959
1996–	Molson Centre	21,273

New Jersey Devils

1974-76	Kemper Arena (Kansas City)	16,300
1976-82	McNichols Arena (Denver)	15,900
1982–	Continental Airlines Arena (1982 capacity-19,023)	19,040

New York Islanders

1972–	Nassau Veterans' Mem. Coliseum (1972 capacity-14,500)	16,297

New York Rangers

1925-68	Madison Square Garden III	15,925
1968–	Madison Square Garden IV (1968 capacity-17,250)	18,200

Ottawa Senators

1992-95	Ottawa Civic Center	10,755
1996–	Corel Centre (Kanata)	18,500

Philadelphia Flyers

1967-96	CoreStates Spectrum (1967 capacity-14,558)	17,380
1996–	CoreStates Center	19,511

Pittsburgh Penguins

1967–	Civic Arena (1967 capacity-12,508)	17,355

Tampa Bay Lightning

1992-93	Expo Hall (Tampa)	10,500
1993–96	ThunderDome (St. Petersburg)	26,000
1996–	Ice Palace	19,500

Washington Capitals

1974-97	USAir Arena (Landover, MD)	18,130
1997–	MCI Center	20,000

Building Name Changes: NEW JERSEY—**Continental Airlines Arena** originally Meadowlands Arena (1982-96); PHILADELPHIA—**CoreStates Spectrum** originally The Spectrum (1967-94); WASHINGTON—**USAir Arena** originally Capital Centre (1974-93).

AUTO RACING

Formula One, NASCAR Winston Cup, IndyCar and Indy Racing League (IRL) racing circuits. Qualifying records accurate as of Sept. 1, 1997. Capacity figures for NASCAR, IndyCar and IRL tracks are approximate and pertain to grandstand seating only. Standing room and hillside terrain seating featured at most road courses are not included.

CART

	Location	Miles	Qual.mph record	Set by	Seats
Belle Isle Park	Detroit, Mich.	2.1**	108.649	Nigel Mansell (1994)	18,000
Burke Lakefront Airport	Cleveland, Ohio	2.37**	147.512	Gil de Ferran (1995)	36,000
California Speedway	Fontana, Calif.	2.0	—	First race in 1997	69,000
Exhibition Place	Toronto, Ont.	1.78**	110.396	Jacques Villeneuve (1995)	60,000
Laguna Seca Raceway	Monterey, Calif.	2.21*	113.768	Paul Tracy (1994)	8,000
Long Beach	Long Beach, Calif.	1.59**	109.639	Gil de Ferran (1996)	45,000
Homestead Motorsports Complex	Homestead, Fla.	1.5	198.590	Paul Tracy (1996)	50,000
Houston Grand Prix	Houston, Tex.	1.68**	—	First race in 1998	TBA
Michigan International Speedway	Brooklyn, Mich.	2.0	234.275	Mario Andretti (1993)	70,000
Mid-Ohio Sports Car Course	Lexington, Ohio	2.25*	122.649	Bryan Herta (1997)	6,000
The Milwaukee Mile	West Allis, Wisc.	1.0	176.058	Paul Tracy (1996)	36,800
Nazareth Speedway	Nazareth, Pa.	1.0	190.737	Paul Tracy (1996)	35,000
Pacific Place	Vancouver, B.C.	1.65**	110.293	Scott Goodyear (1993)	65,000
Portland International Raceway	Portland, Ore.	1.95	117.614	Jacques Villeneuve (1995)	27,000
Piquet Int'l Raceway	Rio de Janeiro, Brazil	1.6	167.084	Alex Zanardi (1996)	80,000
Road America	Elkhart Lake, Wisc.	4.0*	142.206	Jacques Villeneuve (1995)	10,000
Surfers Paradise	Gold Coast, Australia	2.804	106.053	Nigel Mansell (1994)	55,000
Twin Ring Motegi	Motegi, Japan	1.5	—	First race in 1998	TBA

Road courses (not ovals). **Temporary street circuits.

Auto Racing (Cont.)
Indy Racing League

Founded by Indianapolis Motor Speedway president Tony George, the Indy Racing League competes with CART and fielded eight races, anchored by the Indianapolis 500, in 1997.

	Location	Miles	Qual.mph Record	Set by	Seats
Charlotte Motor Speedway	Concord, N.C.	1.5	217.164	Tony Stewart (1997)	140,000
Indianapolis Motor Speedway	Indianapolis, Ind.	2.5	232.618	Arie Luyendyk (1996)	265,000
Las Vegas Motor Speedway	Las Vegas, Nev.	1.5	226.491	Arie Luyendyk (1996)	107,000
New Hampshire Intl. Speedway	Loudon, N.H.	1.06	177.436	Andre Ribeiro (1995)	72,000
Phoenix International Raceway	Phoenix, Ariz.	1.0	181.952	Bryan Herta (1995)	50,000
Pikes Peak Intl. Raceway	Fountain, Colo.	1.0	176.117	Scott Sharp (1997)	42,787
Texas Intl. Raceway	Fort Worth, Tex.	1.5	216.494	Tony Stewart (1997)	150,061
Walt Disney World Speedway	Orlando, Fla.	1.1	181.388	Buddy Lazier (1996)	55,000

NASCAR

	Location	Miles	Qual.mph Record	Set By	Seats
Atlanta Motor Speedway	Hampton, Ga.	1.522	186.507	Robby Gordon (1997)	78,000
Bristol International Raceway	Bristol, Tenn.	0.533	125.093	Mark Martin (1995)	65,000
Charlotte Motor Speedway	Concord, N.C.	1.5	185.759	Ward Burton (1994)	140,000
Darlington International Raceway	Darlington, N.C.	1.37	173.797	Ward Burton (1996)	55,000
Daytona International Speedway	Daytona Beach, Fla.	2.5	210.364	Bill Elliott (1987)	97,900
Dover Downs International Speedway	Dover, Del.	1.0	154.785	Jeff Gordon (1996)	55,000
Indianapolis Motor Speedway	Indianapolis, Ind.	2.5	177.736	Ernie Irvan (1997)	265,000
Martinsville Speedway	Martinsville, Va.	0.526	94.129	Ted Musgrave (1994)	56,000
Michigan International Speedway	Brooklyn, Mich.	2.0	186.611	Jeff Gordon (1995)	70,000
New Hampshire Int'l Speedway	Loudon, N.H.	1.058	129.423	Ken Schrader (1997)	60,000
North Carolina Motor Speedway	Rockingham, N.C.	1.017	157.885	Mark Martin (1997)	55,000
Phoenix International Raceway	Phoenix, Ariz.	1.0	130.020	Bill Elliott (1995)	50,000
Pocono International Raceway	Long Pond, Pa.	2.5	169.725	Jeff Gordon (1996)	77,000
Richmond International Raceway	Richmond, Va.	0.75	124.757	Jeff Gordon (1995)	71,350
Sears Point International Raceway	Sonoma, Calif.	2.52*	92.807	Mark Martin (1997)	42,500
Talladega Superspeedway	Talladega, Ala.	2.66	212.809	Bill Elliott (1987)	85,000
Texas Motor Speedway	Ft. Worth, Tex.	1.5	—		150,061
Watkins Glen	Watkins Glen, N.Y.	2.45*	120.733	Dale Earnhardt (1996)	35,000

*Road courses (not ovals).
Notes: Richmond sells reserved seats only (no infield) for Winston Cup races. What would have been the first NASCAR Winston Cup qualifying rounds at Texas Motor Speedway were rained out in 1997.

Formula One

Race track capacity figures unavailable.

Grand Prix		Miles	Qual.mph Record	Set by
Argentine	**Oscar A. Galvez** (Buenos Aires)	2.645	112.722	Jacques Villeneuve (1997)
Austrian	**A1-Ring** (Austria)	2.683	—	New circuit
Australian	**Albert Park** (Melbourne)	3.274	132.731	Jacques Villeneuve (1997)
Belgian	**Spa-Francorchamps**	4.333	141.123	Nigel Mansell (1992)
Brazilian	**Interlagos** (Sao Paulo)	2.687	127.799	Nigel Mansell (1992)
British	**Silverstone** (Towcester)	3.247	148.043	Nigel Mansell (1992)
Canadian	**Circuit Gilles Villeneuve** (Montreal)	2.747	126.630	Michael Schumacher (1997)
European	**Nürburgring** (Nürburg/Eifel, Germany)	2.822	131.219	Teo Fabi (1985)
French	**Magny Cours** (Nevers)	2.641	128.709	Nigel Mansell (1992)
German	**Hockenheimring** (Hockenheim)	4.235	156.722	Nigel Mansell (1991)
Hungarian	**Hungaroring** (Budapest)	2.465	117.602	Riccardo Patrese (1992)
Italian	**Autodromo di Nazionale, Monza** (Milan)	3.604	159.951	Ayrton Senna (1991)
Japanese	**Suzuka** (Nagoya)	3.641	138.515	Gerhard Berger (1991)
Monaco	**Monte Carlo**	2.068	96.286	Heinz-Harald Frentzen (1997)
Pacific	**T1 Circuit Aida** (Japan)	2.301	117.970	Ayrton Senna (1994)
Portuguese	**Autodromo do Estoril**	2.703	133.224	Nigel Mansell (1992)
San Marino	**Ferrari Circuit** (Imola, Italy)	3.040	138.265	Ayrton Senna (1994)
Spanish	**Catalunya** (Barcelona)	2.937	138.205	Jacques Villeneuve (1997)

SOCCER

World's Premier Soccer Stadiums
(Listed by city)

Stadium	Location	Seats	Stadium	Location	Seats
Olimpiako	Athens, Greece	74,160	Olympiastadion	Munich, Germany	74,000
Eden Park	Auckland, New Zealand	48,000	San Paolo	Naples, Italy	72,810
Nou Camp	Barcelona, Spain	115,000	Parc des Princes	Paris, France	49,700
Olympiastadion	Berlin, Germany	76,234	Rose Bowl	Pasadena, Calif.	102,083
Népstadion	Budapest, Hungary	72,000	Spartakiadni Stadion	Prague, Czech Republic	250,000
Monumental	Buenos Aires, Argentina	77,000	Rungnado	Pyongyang, N. Korea	150,000
D.A. Nasser	Cairo, Egypt	100,000	Maracana	Rio de Janeiro, Brazil	165,000
Westfalenstadion	Dortmund, Germany	42,800	King Fahd II	Riyadh, Saudi Arabia	75,000
Lansdowne Road	Dublin, Ireland	51,000	Olimpico	Rome, Italy	82,922
Hampden Park	Glasgow, Scotland	50,000	Stade de France	Saint-Denis, France	80,000
Ellis Park	Johannesburg, S. Africa	62,000	Nacional	Santiago, Chile	75,000
Republikansky	Kiev, Ukraine	100,000	Morumbi	Sao Paulo, Brazil	120,000
Estadio da Luz	Lisbon, Portugal	130,000	Olympic Stadium	Seoul, S. Korea	100,000
Wembley	London, England	80,000	Olympic Stadium	Sydney, Australia	120,000
Santiago Bernabeu	Madrid, Spain	110,000	Olympic Stadium	Tokyo, Japan	62,000
Azteca	Mexico City, Mexico	114,000	Delle Alpi	Turin, Italy	71,012
Guiseppe Meazza	Milan, Italy	83,107	Prater	Vienna, Austria	62,958
Centenario	Montevideo, Uruguay	76,609	Dziesieiolecia	Warsaw, Poland	100,000
Luzhniki Stadion	Moscow, Russia	100,000			

France '98 World Cup Stadiums

The 16th World Cup of Soccer will be held across France June 10 to July 12, 1998. Listed below are the stadiums which will host the 64 World Cup matches. Note that many of the stadiums have undergone extensive renovations in anticipation of the World Cup and their seating capacities are reflected below. The Cup final will be held July 12 at the newly-built Stade de France in St. Denis, a suburb of Paris.

Stadium	Location	Built	Seats	Stadium	Location	Built	Seats
Stade de France	Paris/St. Denis	1998	80,000	Lescure Park	Bordeaux	1934	36,500
Velodrome	Marseilles	1937	60,000	Geoffroy Guichard	St. Etienne	1931	35,924
Parc des Princes	Paris	1972	49,700	Mosson	Montpellier	1987	35,500
Beaujoire	Nantes	1984	40,000	Felix-Bollaert	Lens	1934	35,050
Municipal	Toulouse	1950	37,638	Gerland	Lyon	1920	32,000

Major League Soccer

Major League Soccer added two expansion teams (Chicago and Miami) for its third season. The 12-team MLS is the only U.S. Division I professional outdoor league sanctioned by FIFA and U.S. Soccer. Note that all capacity figures are approximate given the adjustments of football stadium seating to soccer.

Western Conference

	Stadium	Built	Seats	Field
Chicago (expansion)	Soldier Field	1924	TBA	Grass
Colorado Rapids	Mile High	1948	30,000	Grass
Dallas Burn	Cotton Bowl	1935	25,704	Grass
Kansas City Wizards	Arrowhead	1972	20,269	Grass
L.A. Galaxy	Rose Bowl	1922	65,000	Grass
San Jose Clash	Spartan	1933	26,000	Grass

Eastern Conference

	Stadium	Built	Seats	Field
Columbus Crew	Ohio Stadium	1922	25,134	Grass
N.Y./N.J. Metro Stars	Giants	1976	32,000	Both
N.E. Revolution	Foxboro	1971	24,871	Grass
Miami Fusion	Orange Bowl	1935	TBA	Grass
Tampa Bay Mutiny	Houlihan's	1967	16,000	Grass
Washington D.C. United	RFK	1961	23,865	Grass

MISCELLANEOUS

Minor League Baseball

AAA Ballparks
American Association

Western		Built	Seats	Field
Iowa (Cubs)	Sec Taylor Stadium	1992	11,000	Grass
New Orleans (Astros)	Zephyr Field	1997	10,000	Grass
Omaha (Royals)	Rosenblatt Stadium	1948	22,000	Turf
Oklahoma City	All Sports Stadium	1961	12,000	Grass
Eastern		**Built**	**Seats**	**Field**
Buffalo (Indians)	Northamericare Park	1988	21,050	Grass
Indianapolis (Reds)	Victory Field	1996	15,500	Grass
Louisville (Cardinals)	Cardinal Stadium	1957	33,500	Turf
Nashville (White Sox)	Herschel Greer Stadium	1978	16,000	Grass

Miscellaneous (Cont.)

International League

Western		Built	Seats	Field
Charlotte (Marlins)	**Knights Castle**	1990	10,002	Grass
Columbus (Yankees)	**Cooper Stadium**	1932	15,000	Turf
Norfolk (Mets)	**Harbor Park**	1993	12,059	Grass
Richmond (Braves)	**The Diamond**	1985	12,134	Grass
Toledo (Tigers)	**Ned Skeldon Stadium**	1965	10,025	Grass
Eastern		**Built**	**Seats**	**Field**
Ottawa (Expos)	**JetForm Park**	1993	10,332	Grass
Pawtucket (Red Sox)	**McCoy Stadium**	1942	7,002	Grass
Rochester (Orioles)	**Frontier Field**	1997	10,600	Grass
Scranton/Wilkes-Barre (Phillies)	**Lackawanna County Stadium**	1989	10,400	Turf
Syracuse (Blue Jays)	**P&C Stadium**	1997	11,200	Turf

Pacific Coast League

Northern		Built	Seats	Field
Calgary (Pirates)	**Burns Stadium**	1966	8,000	Grass
Edmonton (Athletics)	**Telus Field**	1995	9,200	Grass
Salt Lake (Twins)	**FranklinQuest Field**	1993	15,500	Grass
Tacoma (Mariners)	**Cheney Stadium**	1960	9,600	Grass
Vancouver (Angels)	**Nat Bailey Stadium**	1951	6,500	Grass
Southern		**Built**	**Seats**	**Field**
Albuquerque (Dodgers)	**Albuquerque Sports Stadium**	1969	10,510	Grass
Colorado Springs (Rockies)	**Sky Fox Stadium**	1988	9,000	Grass
Las Vegas (Padres)	**Cashman Field**	1982	9,334	Grass
Phoenix (Giants)	**Scottsdale Stadium**	1992	10,000	Grass
Tucson (Brewers)	**HiCorbett Field**	1937	8,000	Grass

Japanese Baseball Leagues
Central League

		Location	Seats
Chunichi Dragons	**Nagoya Stadium**	Nagoya	35,000
	& Nagoya Dome	Nagoya	40,500
Hanshin Tigers	**Koshien Stadium**	Nisinomiya	58,000
Hiroshima Carp	**Hiroshima Shimin Stadium**	Hiroshima	32,920
Yakult Swallows	**Jingu Stadium**	Tokyo	48,785
Yokohama BayStars	**Yokohama Stadium**	Yokohama	30,000
Yomiuri Giants	**Tokyo Dome**	Tokyo	56,000

Pacific League

		Location	Seats
Chiba Lotte Marines	**Chiba Marine Stadium**	Chiba	30,000
Fukuoka Daiei Hawks	**Fukuoka Dome**	Fukuoka	48,000
Kintetsu Buffaloes	**Fujidera Stadium**	Osaka	32,000
	& Osaka City Dome	Osaka	55,000
Nippon Ham Fighters	**Tokyo Dome**	Tokyo	56,000
Orix Blue Wave	**Kobe Green**	Kobe	35,000
Seibu Lions	**Seibu Stadium**	Tokorozawa	37,008

Women's Professional Basketball
American Basketball League

		Location	Built	Seats
Atlanta Glory	**Morehouse Olympic Arena**	Atlanta, Ga.	1996	5,700
Colorado Xplosion	**Denver Coliseum**	Denver, Colo.	1953	9,300
	& McNichols Arena	Denver, Colo.	1975	14,500
Columbus Quest	**Batelle Hall**	Columbus, Ohio	1980	6,313
Long Beach StingRays	**The Pyramid**	Long Beach, Calif.	1994	4,000
New England Blizzard	**Hartford Civic Center**	Hartford, Conn.	1975	15,418
	& Springfield Civic Center	Springfield, Mass.	1972	8,715
Philadelphia Rage	**The Palestra**	Philadelphia, Pa.	1927	8,700
	& The Apollo	Philadelphia, Pa.	1997	10,000
Portland Power	**Memorial Coliseum**	Portland, Ore.	1960	10,934
San Jose Lasers	**San Jose Event Center**	San Jose, Calif.	1989	4,550
Seattle Reign	**Mercer Arena**	Seattle, Wash.	1929	4,623

Women's National Basketball Association

The WNBA teams play in the same arenas as the NBA teams in their respective cities. However, the capacities of the venues are "down-sized" for most games. The new, smaller capacity for WNBA games is listed below.

		Location	Built	Seats
Charlotte Sting	Charlotte Coliseum	Charlotte, NC	1988	8,333
Cleveland Rockers	Gund Arena	Cleveland, Ohio	1994	10,647
Houston Comets	The Summit	Houston, Tex.	1975	6,812
Los Angeles Sparks	Great Western Forum	Inglewood, Calif.	1967	7,850
New York Liberty	Madison Square Garden	New York, N.Y.	1968	9,822
Phoenix Mercury	America West Arena	Phoenix, Ariz.	1992	8,394
Sacramento Monarchs	ARCO Arena	Sacramento, Calif.	1988	7,619
Utah Starzz	Delta Center	Salt Lake City, Utah	1991	8,915

Canadian Football League

East Division

		Location	Built	Seats	Field
Hamilton Tiger-Cats	Ivor Wynne Stadium	Hamilton, Ont.	1932	29,133	Turf
Montreal Alouettes	Olympic Stadium	Montreal, Que.	1976	35,000	Turf
Toronto Argonauts	SkyDome	Toronto, Ont.	1989	54,282	Turf
Winnipeg Blue Bombers	Winnipeg Stadium	Winnipeg, Man.	1953	33,675	Turf

West Division

		Location	Built	Seats	Field
British Columbia Lions	B.C. Place	Vancouver, B.C.	1983	42,800	Turf
Calgary Stampeders	McMahon Stadium	Calgary, Alb.	1960	37,317	Turf
Edmonton Eskimos	Commonwealth Stadium	Edmonton, Alb.	1978	60,000	Grass
Saskatchewan Roughriders	Taylor Field	Regina, Sask.	1948	27,637	Turf

World League of American Football

		Location	Seats
Amsterdam Admirals	Amsterdam Arena	Amsterdam, The Netherlands	51,000
Barcelona Dragons	Estadi Olimpic de Monthuic	Barcelona, Spain	54,000
Frankfurt Galaxy	Waldstadion	Frankfurt, Germany	57,000
London Monarchs	Stamford Bridge	Chelsea, England	28,000
Rhein Fire	Rheinstadion	Dusseldorf, Germany	57,000
Scottish Claymores	Murrayfield Stadium	Edinburgh, Scotland	67,000

Arena Football League

American Conference

		Location	Built	Seats
Anaheim Piranhas	Arrowhead Pond	Anaheim, Calif.	1993	17,194
Arizona Rattlers	America West Arena	Phoenix, Ariz.	1992	16,923
Iowa Barnstormers	Veterans Auditorium	Des Moines, Iowa	1955	11,250
Milwaukee Mustangs	Bradley Center	Milwaukee, Wisc.	1988	17,819
Portland Forest Dragons	Rose Garden	Portland, Ore.	1995	18,000
Texas Terror	The Summit	Houston, Texas	1975	15,050
San Jose SaberCats	San Jose Arena	San Jose, Calif.	1990	16,929

National Conference

		Location	Built	Seats
Albany Firebirds	Pepsi Arena	Albany, NY	1990	13,652
Florida Bobcats	W. Palm Beach Auditorium	W. Palm Beach, Fla.	1966	4,700
Nashville Kats	Nashville Arena	Nashville, Tenn.	1996	16,200
New Jersey Red Dogs	Continental Airlines Arena	E. Rutherford, N.J.	1981	17,500
N.Y. Cityhawks	Madison Square Garden	New York, N.Y.	1968	18,900
Orlando Predators	Orlando Arena	Orlando, Fla.	1989	16,613
Tampa Bay Storm	Ice Palace	Tampa Bay, Fla.	1996	20,282

Horse Racing

Triple Crown race tracks

Race	Racetrack	Seats	Infield
Kentucky Derby	Churchill Downs	48,500	100,000
Preakness	Pimlico Race Course	40,000	60,000
Belmont Stakes	Belmont Park	32,491	50,000

Record crowds: Kentucky Derby– 163,628 (1974); Preakness– 98,896 (1989); Belmont– 82,694 (1971).

Tennis

Grand Slam center courts

Event	Main Stadium	Seats
Australian Open	Flanders Park	15,000
French Open	Stade Roland Garros	16,500
Wimbledon	Centre Court	13,118
U.S. Open	Arthur Ashe Stadium	23,000

COLLEGE BASKETBALL
The 50 Largest Arenas
The 50 largest arenas in Division I for the 1997–98 NCAA regular season. Note that (*) indicates part-time home court.

#		Seats	Home Team		#		Seats	Home Team
1	Carrier Dome	33,000	Syracuse		25	Allen Field House	16,300	Kansas
2	Thompson-Boling Arena	24,535	Tennessee		26	Hartford Civic Center	16,294	UConn*
3	Rupp Arena	24,000	Kentucky		27	Erwin Center	16,175	Texas
4	Greensboro Coliseum	23,100	NC-Greensboro		28	LA Sports Arena	15,509	USC
5	Marriott Center	22,700	BYU		29	Miami Arena	15,508	Miami
6	Dean Smith Center	21,572	N. Carolina		30	Carver-Hawkeye Arena	15,500	Iowa
7	MCI Center	21,500	Georgetown*			Pepsi Arena	15,500	Siena*
8	The Rose Garden	21,401	Portland St.		32	Memorial Gymnasium	15,311	Vanderbilt
9	The Pyramid	20,142	Memphis		33	Breslin Events Center	15,138	Michigan St.
10	Continental Airlines Arena	20,029	Seton Hall*		34	Coleman Coliseum	15,043	Alabama
11	Kiel Center	20,000	Saint Louis		35	Arena-Auditorium	15,028	Wyoming
12	Marine Midland Arena	19,500	Canisius* &		36	Bryce Jordan Center	15,000	Penn St.
			Niagara*			Huntsman Center	15,000	Utah
13	Bud Walton Arena	19,200	Arkansas		38	Cole Fieldhouse	14,500	Maryland
14	Madison Square Garden	18,876	St. John's*		39	McKale Center	14,459	Arizona
15	Freedom Hall	18,865	Louisville		40	Joel Memorial Coliseum	14,407	Wake Forest
16	Bradley Center	18,592	Marquette		41	Williams Arena	14,300	Minnesota
17	Thomas & Mack Center	18,500	UNLV		42	University Activity Center	14,287	Arizona St.
18	CoreStates Spectrum	18,060	Villanova* &		43	Devaney Sports Center	14,200	Nebraska
			La Salle		44	Maravich Assembly Center	14,164	LSU
19	University Arena (The Pit)	18,018	New Mexico		45	Mackey Arena	14,123	Purdue
20	Assembly Hall	17,507	Indiana		46	Hilton Coliseum	14,020	Iowa St.
21	Rosemont Horizon	17,500	DePaul*		47	WVU Coliseum	14,000	West Va.
22	Pittsburgh Civic Arena	16,725	Pittsburgh*		48	Henry Goodman Arena	13,610	Cleveland St.
23	Kohle Center	16,500	Wisconsin		49	Crisler Arena	13,562	Michigan
24	Assembly Hall	16,450	Illinois		50	U. of Dayton Arena	13,511	Dayton

Division I Conference Home Courts
NCAA Division I conferences for the 1996-97 season. Teams with home games in more than one arena are noted.

America East

	Home Floor	Seats
Boston University	Case Center	2,500
Delaware	Bob Carpenter Center	5,058
Drexel	Phys. Education Center	2,300
Hartford	The Sports Center	4,475
Hofstra	Physical Fitness Center	3,500
Maine	Alfond Arena	5,668
New Hampshire	Whittemore Center	6,500
Northeastern	Cabot Gym	2,000
Towson St	Towson Center	5,000
Vermont	Patrick Gym	3,200

Atlantic Coast

	Home Floor	Seats
Clemson	Littlejohn Coliseum	11,020
Duke	Cameron Indoor Stadium	9,314
Florida St	Leon County Civic Center	12,500
Georgia Tech	Alexander Mem. Coliseum	10,000
Maryland	Cole Field House	14,500
North Carolina	Dean Smith Center	21,572
N.C. State	Reynolds Coliseum	12,400
Virginia	University Hall	8,457
Wake Forest	Joel Mem. Coliseum	14,407

Atlantic 10

	Home Floor	Seats
Dayton	U. of Dayton Arena	13,511
Duquesne	Palumbo Center	6,200
Fordham	Rose Hill Gym	3,470
G. Washington	Smith Center	5,000
La Salle	CoreStates Spectrum	18,060
Massachusetts	Mullins Center	9,493
Rhode Island	Keaney Gymnasium	4,000
	& Providence Civic Center	12,993
St. Bonaventure	Reilly Center	6,000
St. Joseph's-PA	Alumni Mem. Fieldhouse	3,200
Temple	Apollo Center	10,000
Virginia Tech	Cassell Coliseum	10,052
Xavier-OH	Cincinnati Gardens	10,100

Note: There are 12 schools in the Atlantic 10.

Big East

Big East 7	Home Floor	Seats
Georgetown	MCI Center	21,500
Miami-FL	Miami Arena	15,508
Pittsburgh	Fitzgerald Field House	6,798
	& Pittsburgh Civic Arena	16,725
Providence	Providence Civic Center	12,993
Rutgers	Brown Athletic Center	8,500
Seton Hall	Continental Airlines Arena	20,029
Syracuse	Carrier Dome	33,000

Big East 6	Home Floor	Seats
Boston College	Conte Forum	8,606
Connecticut	Gampel Pavilion	10,249
	& Hartford Civic Center	16,294
Notre Dame	Joyce Center	11,418
St. John's	Alumni Hall	6,008
Villanova	duPont Pavilion	6,500
	& CoreStates Spectrum	18,060
West Virginia	WVU Coliseum	14,000

Biggest Not Fullest
While Syracuse continues to have the largest basketball arena in the nation, it finished behind Kentucky for the second straight year in attendance rankings. After 11 consecutive years at the top, Syracuse lost the attendance title to Kentucky in 1996, the same year the Orangemen lost to the Wildcats in the Final Four championship game. Kentucky was runner-up to Arizona in the national championship picture in 1997 but second to none in nightly crowd size. Kentucky averaged 23,804 fans over 13 home games during the 1996–97 season.

Big Sky

	Home Floor	Seats
CS-Northridge	The Matadome	3,000
CS-Sacramento	Memorial Auditorium	2,603
Eastern Wash	Reese Court	5,000
Idaho St	Holt Arena	8,721
Montana	Dahlberg Arena	8,950
Montana St	Alterowitz Gym	3,500
Northern Ariz	Walkup Skydome	7,000
Portland St.	Rose Garden	21,401
Weber St	Dee Events Center	12,000

Big South

	Home Floor	Seats
Charleston So	CSU Fieldhouse	1,000
	& Charleston Coliseum	13,000
Coastal Carolina	Kimbel Gymnasium	1,800
	& Myrtle Beach Con. Center	5,000
Liberty	Vines Center	9,000
MD-Balt.County	UMBC Fieldhouse	4,024
NC-Asheville	Justice Center	2,000
	& Asheville Civic Center	6,800
Radford	Dedmon Center	5,000
Winthrop	Winthrop Coliseum	6,100

Big Ten

	Home Floor	Seats
Illinois	Assembly Hall	16,450
Indiana	Assembly Hall	17,507
Iowa	Carver-Hawkeye Arena	15,500
Michigan	Crisler Arena	13,562
Michigan St	Breslin Events Center	15,138
Minnesota	Williams Arena	14,300
Northwestern	Welsh-Ryan Arena	8,117
Ohio St	St. John Arena	13,276
Penn St	Bryce Jordan Center	15,000
Purdue	Mackey Arena	14,123
Wisconsin	Wisconsin Field House	11,500
	& Kohle Center	16,500

Note: There are 11 schools in the Big Ten.

Big 12

North	Home Floor	Seats
Colorado	Coors Events Center	11,198
Iowa St	Hilton Coliseum	14,020
Kansas	Allen Fieldhouse	16,300
Kansas St	Bramlage Coliseum	13,500
Missouri	Hearnes Center	13,300
Nebraska	Devaney Sports Center	14,200

South	Home Floor	Seats
Baylor	Ferrell Center	10,084
Oklahoma	Lloyd Noble Center	11,100
Oklahoma St	Gallagher-Iba Arena	6,381
Texas	Erwin Center	16,175
Texas A&M	G. Rollie White Coliseum	7,500
Texas Tech	Lubbock Muni. Coliseum	8,174

Note: The Big Eight became the Big 12 in 1996-97 with the addition of Baylor, Texas, Texas A&M and Texas Tech from the SWC which folded after the 1995-96 school year.

Big West

	Home Floor	Seats
Boise St.	BSU Pavilion	12,380
Cal Poly SLO	Mott Gym	3,500
CS-Fullerton	Titan Gym	4,000
Idaho	Kibbie Dome	10,000
Long Beach St	The Pyramid	5,000
Nevada	Lawlor Events Center	11,200
New Mexico St	Pan American Center	13,071
North Texas	The Super Pit	10,032
Pacific	Spanos Center	6,150
UC-Irvine	Bren Events Center	5,000
UC-Santa Barbara	The Thunderdome	6,000
Utah St	The Smith Spectrum	10,270

Colonial

	Home Floor	Seats
American	Bender Arena	5,000
East Carolina	Minges Coliseum	7,500
George Mason	Patriot Center	10,000
James Madison	JMU Convocation Center	7,612
NC-Wilmington	Trask Coliseum	6,100
Old Dominion	Norfolk Scope	10,239
Richmond	Robins Center	9,171
VCU	Richmond Coliseum	12,500
Wm. & Mary	William & Mary Hall	10,000

Conference USA

	Home Floor	Seats
Ala-Birmingham	Bartow Arena	8,500
Cincinnati	Shoemaker Center	13,176
DePaul	Rosemont Horizon	17,500
Houston	Hofheinz Pavilion	10,245
Louisville	Freedom Hall	18,865
Marquette	Bradley Center	18,592
Memphis	The Pyramid	20,142
NC-Charlotte	Halton Arena	9,200
Saint Louis	Kiel Center	20,000
South Florida	Sun Dome	10,411
Southern Miss	Green Coliseum	8,095
Tulane	Fogelman Arena	3,600

Ivy League

	Home Floor	Seats
Brown	Pizzitola Sports Center	2,800
Columbia	Levien Gymnasium	3,408
Cornell	Newman Arena	4,750
Dartmouth	Berry Sports Center	2,200
Harvard	Briggs Athletic Center	2,195
Penn	The Palestra	8,700
Princeton	Jadwin Gymnasium	7,500
Yale	Lee Amphitheater	3,100

Metro Atlantic

	Home Floor	Seats
Canisius	Marine Midland Arena	19,500
	& Koessler Athletic Center	1,800
Fairfield	Alumni Hall	2,479
Iona	Mulcahy Center	3,200
Loyola-MD	Reitz Arena	3,000
Manhattan	Draddy Gymnasium	3,000
Marist	McCann Center	3,944
Niagara	Marine Midland Arena	19,500
	& Gallagher Center	3,200
Rider	Alumni Gymnasium	1,650
St. Peter's	Yanitelli Center	3,200
Siena	Pepsi Arena	15,500

College Basketball (Cont.)

Mid American

	Home Floor	Seats
Akron	JAR Arena	5,948
Ball St	University Arena	11,500
Bowling Green	Anderson Arena	5,000
Central Mich	Rose Arena	6,000
Eastern Mich	Bowen Field House	4,800
Kent	MAC Center	6,327
Marshall	Henderson Center	10,250
Miami-OH	Millett Hall	9,200
Northern Illinois	Chick Evans Field House	6,044
Ohio Univ	The Convo	13,000
Toledo	Savage Hall	9,000
Western Mich	University Arena	5,800

Mid-Continent

	Home Floor	Seats
Buffalo	Alumni Arena	8,500
Chicago St	Dickens Athletic Center	2,500
Missouri-K.C	Municipal Auditorium	11,126
NE Illinois	Phys. Ed. Complex	2,000
Oral Roberts	Mabee Center	10,575
Southern Utah	Centrum	5,300
Valparaiso	Athletics-Recreation Center	4,500
Western Ill	Western Hall	5,139
Youngstown St	Beeghly Center	8,000

Mid-Eastern Athletic

	Home Floor	Seats
Bethune-Cookman	Moore Gym	3,000
Coppin St	Coppin Center	3,000
Delaware St	Memorial Hall	3,000
Florida A&M	Gaither Gym	3,350
Hampton	Hampton Convocation Center	7,200
Howard	Burr Gym	3,000
MD-East.Shore	Tawes Gym	1,200
Morgan St	Baltimore City CC	2,000
N. Carolina A&T	Corbett Sports Center	7,500
S. Carolina St	SHM Center	3,200

Midwestern

	Home Floor	Seats
Butler	Hinkle Fieldhouse	10,400
Cleveland St	Goodman Arena	13,610
Detroit Mercy	Calihan Hall	8,837
IL-Chicago	UIC Pavilion	8,000
Loyola-IL	Gentile Center	5,200
WI-Green Bay	Brown County Arena	5,600
WI-Milwaukee	Wisconsin Center	11,052
Wright St	Nutter Center	10,632

Missouri Valley

	Home Floor	Seats
Bradley	Carver Arena	10,825
Butler	Hinkle Fieldhouse	11,043
Creighton	Omaha Civic Auditorium	9,000
Drake	Knapp Center	7,002
Evansville	Roberts Stadium	12,300
Illinois St	Redbird Arena	10,200
Indiana St	Hulman Center	10,200
Northern Iowa	UNI-Dome	10,000
Southern Ill	SIU Arena	10,014
SW Missouri St	Hammons Student Center	8,858
Wichita St	Levitt Arena	10,545

Northeast

	Home Floor	Seats
Central Conn. St.	Detrick Gym	4,500
Farleigh Dickinson	Rothman Center	5,000
LIU-Brooklyn	Schwartz Athletic Center	1,700
Monmouth	Boylan Gym	2,500
Mt. St. Mary's	Knott Arena	3,500
Robert Morris	Sewall Center	3,056
St. Francis-NY	Phys. Ed. Center	1,400
St. Francis-PA	DeGol Arena	3,500
Wagner	College of State Island	1,400

Ohio Valley

	Home Floor	Seats
Austin Peay	Dunn Center	9,000
Eastern Illinois	Lantz Gym	6,200
Eastern Ky	McBrayer Arena	6,500
Middle Tenn. St	Murphy Center	11,520
Morehead St	Johnson Arena	6,500
Murray St	Racer Arena	5,550
SE Missouri St	Show Me Center	7,000
Tennessee-Martin	Skyhawk Arena	6,700
Tennessee St	Gentry Complex	10,500
Tennessee Tech	Eblen Center	10,152

Pacific-10

	Home Floor	Seats
Arizona	McKale Center	14,459
Arizona St	Univ. Activity Center	14,287
California	Oakland Coliseum	19,200
Oregon	McArthur Court	10,063
Oregon St	Gill Coliseum	10,400
Stanford	Maples Pavilion	7,500
UCLA	Pauley Pavilion	12,819
USC	LA Sports Arena	15,509
Washington	Hec Edmundson Pavilion	7,900
Washington. St	Friel Court	12,058

Patriot League

	Home Floor	Seats
Army	Christl Arena	5,043
Bucknell	Davis Gym	2,500
Colgate	Cotterell Court	3,000
Holy Cross	Hart Recreation Center	3,600
Lafayette	Kirby Field House	3,500
Lehigh	Stabler Arena	5,600
Navy	Alumni Hall	5,710

Southeastern

Eastern	Home Floor	Seats
Florida	O'Connell Center	12,000
Georgia	Stegeman Coliseum	10,512
Kentucky	Rupp Arena	24,000
South Carolina	McGuire Arena	12,401
Tennessee	Thompson-Boling Arena	24,535
Vanderbilt	Memorial Gymnasium	15,311
Western	**Home Floor**	**Seats**
Alabama	Coleman Coliseum	15,043
Arkansas	Bud Walton Arena	19,200
Auburn	Eaves-Memorial Coliseum	10,108
LSU	Maravich Assembly Center	14,164
Mississippi	Tad Smith Coliseum	8,135
Mississippi St	Humphrey Coliseum	10,000

Southern

Home Floor	Seats
Appalachian St .... Varsity Gymnasium	8,000
The Citadel .... McAlister Field House	6,000
Davidson .... Belk Arena	6,000
E. Tenn. St .... Memorial Center	12,000
Furman .... Timmons Arena	5,000
Ga. Southern ...... Hanner Fieldhouse	5,500
NC-Greensboro ... Fleming Gymnasium	2,320
& Greensboro Coliseum	23,100
Tenn-Chatt .... UTC Arena	11,218
VMI .... Cameron Hall	5,029
W. Carolina ...... Ramsey Center	7,826
Wofford .... Johnson Arena	3,500

Southland

Home Floor	Seats
McNeese St .... Burton Coliseum	8,000
Nicholls St .... Stopher Gym	3,800
NE Louisiana ...... Ewing Coliseum	8,000
Northwestern St .... Prather Coliseum	3,900
Sam Houston St .... Johnson Coliseum	6,172
SE Louisiana ...... University Center	7,500
SW Texas St ...... Strahan Coliseum	7,200
S.F. Austin St ..... W.R. Johnson Coliseum	7,203
TX-Arlington ...... Texas Hall	4,200
TX-San Antonio .... Convocation Center	5,100

Southwestern

Home Floor	Seats
Alabama St .... Joe Reed Acadome	7,000
Alcorn St .... Whitney Complex	7,000
Grambling St. ..... Memorial Gym	4,500
Jackson St .... Williams Center	8,000
Miss.Valley .... Harrison Athletic Complex	6,000
Prairie View .... The Baby Dome	6,600
Southern-BR ...... Clark Activity Center	7,500
TX Southern ...... Health & P.E. Building	7,500

Sun Belt

Home Floor	Seats
Ark-Little Rock .... Barton Coliseum	8,303
Arkansas St ...... Convocation Center	10,563
Jacksonville .... Jacksonville Coliseum	9,150
Lamar .... Montagne Center	10,080
Louisiana Tech .... Thomas Assembly Center	8,000
New Orleans ...... Lakefront Arena	10,000
South Alabama .... Jaguar Gym	3,138
SW Louisiana ..... The Cajundome	12,800
Texas-Pan Am .... UTPA Field House	5,000
Western Ky .... E.A. Diddle Arena	11,300

Trans America

Home Floor	Seats
Campbell .... Carter Gym	945
Centenary .... Gold Dome	3,000
Central Fla .... UCF Arena	5,100
Charleston .... Kresse Arena	3,052
Fla. Atlantic ...... FAU Gym	5,000
Florida Int'l ...... Golden Panther Arena	5,000
Georgia St .... GSU Sports Arena	4,200
Jacksonville St. .... Mathews Coliseum	5,500
Mercer .... Macon Coliseum	8,500
Samford .... Seibert Hall	4,000
Stetson .... Edmunds Center	5,000
Troy St .... Sartain Hall	3,500

West Coast

Home Floor	Seats
Gonzaga .... Martin Centre	4,000
Loyola-CA .... Gersten Pavilion	4,156
Pepperdine .... Firestone Fieldhouse	3,104
Portland .... Chiles Center	5,000
St. Mary's-CA ..... McKeon Pavilion	3,500
San Diego .... USD Sports Center	2,500
San Francisco ..... War Memorial Gym	5,300
Santa Clara .... Toso Pavilion	5,000

Western Athletic

Mountain	Home Floor	Seats
BYU	Marriott Center	22,700
New Mexico	University Arena (The Pit)	18,018
Rice	Autry Court	5,000
SMU	Moody Coliseum	8,998
TCU	Daniel-Meyer Coliseum	7,166
Tulsa	Tulsa Conv. Center	8,564
Utah	Huntsman Center	15,000
UTEP	Special Events Center	12,222

Pacific	Home Floor	Seats
Air Force	Clune Arena	6,002
Colorado St	Moby Arena	9,000
Fresno St	Selland Arena	10,132
Hawaii	Special Events Arena	10,225
San Diego St	Aztec Bowl Arena	12,000
San Jose St.	The Events Center	5,000
UNLV	Thomas & Mack Center	18,500
Wyoming	Arena-Auditorium	15,028

Future NCAA Final Four Sites

Men

Year	Arena	Seats	Location
1998	Alamodome	40,000	San Antonio
1999	ThunderDome	32,351	St. Petersburg
2000	RCA Dome	47,100	Indianapolis
2001	Metrodome	50,000	Minneapolis
2002	Georgia Dome	40,000	Atlanta

Women

Year	Arena	Seats	Location
1998	Kemper Arena	16,668	Kansas City
1999	San Jose Arena	17,500	San Jose
2000	CoreStates Spectrum ...	16,975	Philadelphia
2001	Kiel Center	20,000	St. Louis
2002	Alamodome	26,000	San Antonio

COLLEGE FOOTBALL

The 40 Largest I-A Stadiums

The 40 largest stadiums in NCAA Division I-A college football heading into the 1997 season. Note that (*) indicates stadium not on campus.

		Location	Seats	Home Team	Conference	Built	Field
1	Neyland Stadium	Knoxville, Tenn.	102,544	Tennessee	SEC-East	1921	Grass
2	Michigan Stadium	Ann Arbor, Mich.	102,501	Michigan	Big Ten	1927	Grass
3	Rose Bowl*	Pasadena, Calif.	102,083	UCLA	Pac-10	1922	Grass
4	Beaver Stadium	University Park, Pa.	93,967	Penn St.	Big Ten	1960	Grass
5	LA Memorial Coliseum*	Los Angeles, Calif.	92,000	USC	Pac-10	1923	Grass
6	Ohio Stadium	Columbus, Ohio	89,800	Ohio St.	Big Ten	1922	Grass
7	Sanford Stadium	Athens, Ga.	86,117	Georgia	SEC-East	1929	Grass
8	Stanford Stadium	Stanford, Calif.	85,500	Stanford	Pac-10	1921	Grass
9	Jordan-Hare Stadium	Auburn, Ala.	85,214	Auburn	SEC-West	1939	Grass
10	Legion Field*	Birmingham, Ala.	83,000	Alabama/UAB	SEC-West/Indy	1927	Grass
	Florida Field	Gainesville, Fla.	83,000	Florida	SEC-East	1929	Grass
12	Memorial Stadium	Clemson, S.C.	81,473	Clemson	ACC	1942	Grass
13	Notre Dame Stadium	Notre Dame, Ind.	80,900	Notre Dame	Independent	1930	Grass
14	Williams-Brice Stadium	Columbia, S.C.	80,250	South Carolina	SEC-East	1934	Grass
15	Doak Campbell Stadium	Tallahasse, Fla.	80,000	Florida St.	ACC	1950	Grass
16	Tiger Stadium	Baton Rouge, La.	79,940	LSU	SEC-West	1924	Grass
17	Camp Randall Stadium	Madison, Wisc.	77,745	Wisconsin	Big Ten	1917	Turf
18	Memorial Stadium	Austin, Tex.	75,512	Texas	Big 12-South	1924	Grass
19	Oklahoma Memorial Field	Norman, Okla.	75,004	Oklahoma	Big 12-South	1924	Grass
20	Memorial Stadium	Berkeley, Calif.	74,909	California	Pac-10	1923	Grass
21	Husky Stadium	Seattle, Wash.	74,000	Washington	Pac-10	1920	Turf
22	Sun Devil Stadium	Tempe, Ariz.	73,656	Arizona St.	Pac-10	1959	Grass
23	Orange Bowl*	Miami, Fla.	72,319	Miami-FL	Big East	1935	Grass
24	Memorial Stadium	Lincoln, Neb.	72,700	Nebraska	Big 12-North	1923	Turf
25	Spartan Stadium	East Lansing, Mich.	72,027	Michigan St.	Big Ten	1957	Turf
26	Qualcom Stadium*	San Diego, Calif.	71,000	San Diego St.	WAC-Pac.	1967	Grass
27	Memorial Stadium	Champaign, Ill.	70,904	Illinois	Big Ten	1923	Turf
28	Kinnick Stadium	Iowa City, Iowa	70,397	Iowa	Big Ten	1929	Grass
29	Kyle Field	College Station, Tex.	70,210	Texas A&M	Big 12-South	1925	Grass
30	Citrus Bowl*	Orlando, Fla.	70,188	Central Florida	Independent	1936	Grass
31	Bryant-Denny Stadium	Tuscaloosa, Ala.	70,123	Alabama	SEC-West	1929	Grass
32	Rice Stadium	Houston, Tex.	70,000	Rice	WAC-Mtn.	1950	Turf
33	Cotton Bowl*	Dallas, Tex.	68,252	SMU	WAC-Mtn.	1932	Grass
34	Ross-Ade Stadium	W. Lafayette, Ind.	67,861	Purdue	Big Ten	1924	Grass
35	Veterans Stadium*	Philadelphia, Pa.	66,592	Temple	Big East	1971	Turf
36	Cougar Stadium	Provo, Utah	65,000	BYU	WAC-Mtn.	1964	Grass
37	Superdome*	New Orleans, La.	64,992	Tulane	USA	1975	Turf
38	HHH Metrodome*	Minneapolis, Minn.	63,699	Minnesota	Big Ten	1982	Turf
39	Mountaineer Field	Morgantown, W. Va.	63,500	West Virginia	Big East	1980	Turf
40	Liberty Bowl*	Memphis, Tenn.	62,380	Memphis	Conf. USA	1965	Grass

Note: Kentucky is undertaking a $24 million expansion and renovation of Commonwealth Stadium (which currently seats 57,800) that will increase capacity to between 63,000 and 66,000 prior to the 1998 season.

1997 Conference Home Fields

NCAA Division I-A conference by conference listing includes member teams heading into the 1997 season. Note that (*) indicates stadium is not on campus.

Atlantic Coast

	Stadium	Built	Seats	Field
Clemson	Memorial	1942	81,473	Grass
Duke	Wallace Wade	1929	33,941	Grass
Florida St	Doak Campbell	1950	80,000	Grass
Ga. Tech	Dodd	1913	46,000	Grass
Maryland	Byrd	1950	48,055	Grass
N. Carolina	Kenan Memorial	1927	52,000	Grass
N.C. State	Carter-Finley	1966	52,000†	Grass
Virginia	Harrison Field	1931	40,000	Grass
Wake Forest	Groves	1968	31,500	Grass

† Grass bank holds additional 10,000.

Big East

	Stadium	Built	Seats	Field
Boston Col	Alumni	1957	44,500	Turf
Miami-FL	Orange Bowl*	1935	72,319	Grass
Pittsburgh	Pitt	1925	56,150	Turf
Rutgers	Rutgers	1994	42,000	Grass
Syracuse	Carrier Dome	1980	50,000	Turf
Temple	Veterans*	1971	66,592	Turf
Va. Tech	Lane	1965	51,000	Grass
West Va	Mountaineer Field	1980	63,500	Turf

University of Notre Dame

The Fighting Irish will play before a significantly larger home crowd this year at **Notre Dame Stadium.** The University recently completed a two-year, $50 million renovation of the stadium that added 20,000 seats and a new press box to the 66-year-old facility.

Big Ten

	Stadium	Built	Seats	Field
Illinois	Memorial	1923	70,904	Turf
Indiana	Memorial	1960	52,354	Turf
Iowa	Kinnick	1929	70,397	Grass
Michigan	Michigan	1927	102,501	Grass
Michigan St	Spartan	1957	72,027	Turf
Minnesota	Metrodome*	1982	63,699	Turf
Northwestern	Ryan Field	1926	49,256	Grass
Ohio St	Ohio	1922	89,800	Grass
Penn St	Beaver	1960	93,967	Grass
Purdue	Ross-Ade	1924	67,861	Grass
Wisconsin	Camp Randall	1917	77,745	Turf

Big 12

With the breakup of the Southwest Conference on June 30, 1996, the Big Eight became the Big 12 with the addition of Baylor, Texas, Texas A&M and Texas Tech from the SWC.

NORTH	Stadium	Built	Seats	Field
Colorado	Folsom Field	1924	51,808	Turf
Iowa St	Trice Field	1975	43,000	Grass
Kansas	Memorial	1921	50,250	Turf
Kansas St.	KSU	1968	42,000	Turf
Missouri	Faurot Field	1926	62,000	Grass
Nebraska	Memorial	1923	72,700	Turf

SOUTH	Stadium	Built	Seats	Field
Baylor	Floyd Casey	1950	50,000	Turf
Oklahoma	Memorial	1924	75,004	Grass
Oklahoma St	Lewis Field	1920	50,614	Turf
Texas	Royal Mem.	1924	75,512	Grass
Texas A&M	Kyle Field	1925	70,210	Grass
Texas Tech	Jones	1947	50,500	Turf

Note: The annual Oklahoma-Texas game has been played at the Cotton Bowl (capacity 68,252) in Dallas since 1937.

Big West

	Stadium	Built	Seats	Field
Boise St	Bronco	1970	30,000	Turf
Idaho	Kibbie Dome	1975	16,500	Turf
Nevada	Mackay	1967	31,545	Grass
New Mexico St	Aggie Mem.	1978	30,343	Grass
North Texas	Fouts Field	1952	30,500	Turf
Utah St	Romney	1968	30,257	Grass

Conference USA

	Stadium	Built	Seats	Field
Houston	Astrodome*	1965	60,000	Turf
	& Robertson	1942	22,000	Grass
Cincinnati	Nippert	1924	35,000	Turf
E. Carolina	Dowdy-Ficklen	1963	43,000	Grass
Louisville	Cardinal*	1956	35,500	Turf
Memphis	Liberty Bowl*	1965	62,380	Grass
Southern Miss	Roberts	1976	33,000	Grass
Tulane	Superdome*	1975	64,992	Turf

I-A Independents

	Stadium	Built	Seats	Field
Alabama-Birm.	Legion	1927	83,000	Grass
Army	Michie	1924	39,929	Turf
Arkansas St	Indian	1974	33,410	Grass
C. Florida	Citrus Bowl	1936	70,188	Grass
Louisiana Tech	Joe Aillet	1968	30,600	Grass
Navy	Navy-Marine Corps Memorial	1959	30,000	Grass
NE Louisiana	Malone	1978	30,427	Grass
Notre Dame	Notre Dame	1930	80,900	Grass
SW Louisiana	Cajun Field	1971	31,000	Grass

Mid-American

	Stadium	Built	Seats	Field
Akron	Rubber Bowl*	1940	35,202	Turf
Ball St	Ball State	1967	16,319	Grass
Bowling Green	Doyt Perry	1966	30,599	Grass
Central Mich	Kelly/Shorts	1972	20,086	Turf
Eastern Mich	Rynearson	1969	30,200	Turf
Kent	Dix	1969	30,520	Turf
Marshall	Marshall	1991	30,000	Turf
Miami-OH	Fred Yager	1983	30,000	Grass
Northern Ill	Huskie	1965	31,000	Turf
Ohio Univ	Peden	1929	20,000	Grass
Toledo	Glass Bowl	1937	26,248	Turf
Western Mich	Waldo	1939	30,200	Grass

Pacific-10

	Stadium	Built	Seats	Field
Arizona	Arizona	1928	57,803	Grass
Arizona St	Sun Devil	1959	73,656	Grass
California	Memorial	1923	74,909	Grass
Oregon	Autzen	1967	35,362	Turf
Oregon St	Parker	1953	35,547	Grass
Stanford	Stanford	1921	85,500	Grass
UCLA	Rose Bowl*	1922	102,083	Grass
USC	LA Coliseum*	1923	92,000	Grass
Washington	Husky	1920	74,000	Turf
Washington St	Martin	1972	37,600	Turf

Southeastern

EASTERN	Stadium	Built	Seats	Field
Florida	Florida Field	1929	83,000	Grass
Georgia	Sanford	1929	86,117	Grass
Kentucky	Commonwealth	1973	57,800	Grass
S. Carolina	Williams-Brice	1934	80,250	Grass
Tennessee	Neyland	1921	102,544	Grass
Vanderbilt	Vanderbilt	1922	41,000	Turf

WESTERN	Stadium	Built	Seats	Field
Alabama	Bryant-Denny	1929	70,123	Grass
	& Legion Field*	1927	83,000	Grass
Arkansas	Razorback	1938	51,000	Grass
	& War Memorial*	1948	53,727	Grass
Auburn	Jordan-Hare	1939	85,214	Grass
LSU	Tiger	1924	79,940	Grass
Mississippi	Vaught-Hem'way	1941	42,577	Grass
Miss. St	Scott Field	1915	40,656	Grass

Notes: EAST— Kentucky is expanding Commonwealth Stadium to increase capacity to between 63,000 and 66,000 prior to the 1998 season; Vanderbilt Stadium was rebuilt in 1981. WEST— at Alabama, Bryant-Denny Stadium is in Tuscaloosa and Legion Field is in Birmingham.

SEC Championship Game

The first two SEC Championship Games were played at Legion Field in Birmingham, Ala., in 1992 and 1993. The game was moved to Atlanta's 71,230-seat Georgia Dome in 1994.

Western Athletic

Mountain	Stadium	Built	Seats	Field
BYU	Cougar	1964	65,000	Grass
New Mexico	University	1960	31,218	Grass
Rice	Rice	1950	70,000	Turf
SMU	Cotton Bowl*	1932	68,252	Grass
TCU	Amon Carter	1929	46,000	Grass
Tulsa	Skelly	1930	40,385	Turf
Utah	Rice	1927	32,500	Grass
UTEP	Sun Bowl*	1963	52,000	Turf

Pacific	Stadium	Built	Seats	Field
Air Force	Falcon	1962	52,480	Grass
Colorado St	Hughes	1968	30,000	Grass
Fresno St	Bulldog	1980	41,031	Grass
Hawaii	Aloha*	1975	50,000	Turf
San Diego St	Qualcom*	1967	71,000	Grass
San Jose St	Spartan	1933	31,218	Grass
UNLV	Sam Boyd*	1971	40,000	Turf
Wyoming	War Memorial	1950	33,500	Grass

WAC Championship Game

The first WAC championship game between division winners took place on Dec. 7, 1996 at Sam Boyd Stadium in Las Vegas.

Bowl Games

Listed alphabetically and updated as of Sept. 1, 1997. The Bowl Alliance, which went into effect with the 1995 season, calls for the national championship game (No. 1-ranked alliance team vs. No. 2 alliance team) to rotate between the Fiesta Bowl (Jan. 2, 1996), Sugar Bowl (Jan. 2, 1997) and Orange Bowl (Jan. 2, 1998). See page 187.

	Stadium	Built	Seats	Field
Alamo	Alamodome	1993	65,000	Turf
Aloha	Aloha	1975	50,000	Turf
Carquest	Pro Player	1987	74,916	Grass
Copper	Arizona	1928	57,803	Grass
Cotton	Cotton	1930	68,252	Grass
Fiesta	Sun Devil	1959	73,656	Grass
Fla. Citrus	Fla. Citrus Bowl	1936	70,188	Grass
Gator	Alltel	1995	73,000	Grass
Holiday	Qualcomm	1967	71,000	Grass
Independence	Independence	1936	50,832	Grass

	Stadium	Built	Seats	Field
Las Vegas	Sam Boyd	1971	40,000	Turf
Liberty	Liberty Bowl	1965	62,380	Grass
Motor City	Pontiac Silverdome	1975	80,368	Turf
Orange	Pro Player	1987	74,916	Grass
Outback	Houlihan's	1967	74,300	Grass
Peach	Georgia Dome	1992	71,228	Turf
Rose	Rose Bowl	1922	102,083	Grass
Sugar	Superdome	1975	77,446	Turf
Sun	Sun Bowl	1963	52,000	Turf

Playing Sites

Alamo— San Antonio; **Aloha**— Honolulu; **Carquest**— Miami; **Copper**— Tucson; **Cotton**— Dallas; **Fiesta**— Tempe; **Florida Citrus**— Orlando; **Gator**— Jacksonville; **Holiday**— San Diego; **Independence**— Shreveport; **Las Vegas**— Las Vegas; **Liberty**— Memphis; **Motor City**— Pontiac; **Orange**— Miami; **Outback**— Tampa; **Peach**— Atlanta; **Rose**— Pasadena; **Sugar**— New Orleans; **Sun**— El Paso.

Business

When **Tiger Woods**, shown during a practice round before the 1997 Ryder Cup, wasn't tearing up a golf course in 1997, he was tearing up the business world. Even his poor performance in the Ryder Cup didn't affect his appeal to sponsors.

Wide World Photos

Tiger, Tiger Burning Bright

In 1997, corporate America strengthened its investment in sporting America.

by
John Helyar

The twin towers of sports business in 1997 were star power and media power. Tiger Woods became a golfing conglomerate. Michael Jordan became a Nike division. Rupert Murdoch became a baseball owner. Networks scrimmaged fiercely for the right to bestow billions on the National Football League.

Corporate America rewarded the sports world for a year absent labor strife and franchise shifts by showering it with money. Corporate sponsorships alone rose 8.5 percent, according to the Chicago-based newsletter IEG Sponsorship Report. "Corporations have discovered they can use these relationships with sports as a platform for lots of communications with customers," said IEG vice presi-

dent Jim Andrews.

Some of the deals were huge but conventional, like General Motors' 12-year $900 million Olympic sponsorship, which will kick in particularly strong for the 2002 Salt Lake City winter games. Some of the deals were far smaller but hugely altered the sports lexicon. Joe Robbie Stadium, in Miami, became Pro Player Stadium and Jack Murphy Stadium, in San Diego, morphed into Qualcomm Stadium.

What corporate titans particularly clamored to invest in was sports titans. Michael Jordan remained the endorsement king, raking in an estimated $40 million in 1997. That stature was only enhanced by a deal with Nike to head his own footwear and apparel line. But Tiger Woods was coming up fast on the outside, parlaying his Masters green jacket into lucrative deals with such blue-chip

---

John Helyar has covered the sports business for seven years and is the author of *Lords of the Realm: The Real History of Baseball.*

The crowds drawn by golfing sensation **Tiger Woods** not only caught the attention of sports companies like Nike but also less obvious sponsors like American Express and Rolex.

companies as American Express and Rolex. Altogether, his endorsements are valued at an estimated $100 million over five years. Credit Woods too, with helping the PGA Tour double its TV money, in a new four-year deal with networks valued at $650 million.

The TV companies were in a spendthrift mood all over sports. Murdoch's News Corp. agreed to buy the Los Angeles Dodgers for a record $350 million, ensuring baseball aplenty for its Fox SportsNet. The Walt Disney Co. spent a reported $175 million to buy the Classic Sports Network which created a franchise by re-airing vintage events. CBS launched a $100 million investment into cyberspace, for a stake in Sportsline USA, the online service. Two TV deals projected to close by year end were expected to particularly mark 1997. The National Basketball Association was expected to make NBC pay dearly to retain its TV rights. The NFL was expected to make EVERYBODY in its five-network confab dig deep to retain their TV rights and fend off a hungry CBS, itching to get back into the NFL game.

What happened at The Tiffany Network, hurt badly by losing the NFL to Fox in 1993, is an object lesson which helps spur spending. "Sports is being seen as a strategic asset that reflects on the values and qualities of a network," says Neal Pilson, former president of CBS Sports. "To maintain your position with Wall Street, the advertisers and the public, you just have to have the special events like

There aren't a lot of words that **Bud Selig** brings new meaning to, but "interim" is one of them. In 1997, Selig marked his fifth year as interim baseball commissioner.

the Olympics or Super Bowl or World Series." ∎

John Helyar's Top Ten 1997 Sports Business Highlights

10. **Major League Baseball** played its first interleague games and celebrated the fifth anniversary of Bud Selig as interim commissioner.

9. **General Motors** made a 12–year, $900 million sponsorship deal with the United States Olympic Committee.

8. **The Indy Racing League (IRL) and Championship Auto Racing Teams (CART)** stayed at war and, for the second year, diminished the luster of the Indianapolis 500.

7. **Rupert Murdoch's News Corp.** agreed to pay $350 million for the Los Angeles Dodgers, a record sum for a sports franchise.

6. **The National Hockey League** approved expansion teams in Atlanta, Minneapolis-St. Paul, Nashville and Columbus, OH.

5. **The WNBA** debuted, adding another women's pro basketball league and, for the first time, bringing sponsors and TV coverage to the game.

4. **Voters in San Francisco and Seattle** narrowly approved new football stadiums, keeping the NFL's stadium-referendum wins going.

3. Even **Michael Jordan**'s new $36 million contract with the Chicago Bulls couldn't match his estimated $40 million in endorsement earnings.

2. **Tiger Woods** racked up a win in The Masters and endorsement riches.

1. **NASCAR** continued its zooming growth, opening up spectacular new tracks in California and Texas. ■

THE NUMBERS

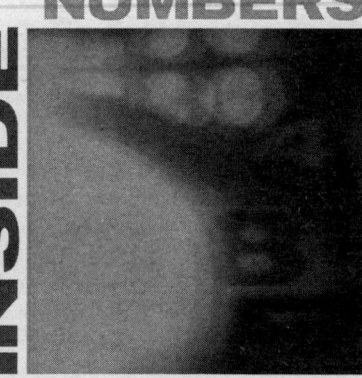

INSIDE

by
Craig Wachs and Kristen Micali

BULL MARKET

What did you do on your summer vacation? In 1997, the following athletes, one from each of the major sports, signed ridiculously huge contracts. This is a small point but, in light of this kind of money being thrown around, isn't it slightly annoying that the teams also have to feed these guys on game days? Like Greg Maddux can't buy his own lunch at this point. Just as a gesture, a sign that they actually know that they work in a fantasy land, it would be nice if the per diems from all major sports were given to a fund for older players, without whom today's stars. . . . . naah, it'll never happen.

Enough Already

	Contract value	Length
Michael Jordan	$36 million	1 year
Greg Maddux	$57.5 million	5 years
Steve Young	$45 million	6 years*
Joe Sakic	$21 million	3 years

*Obviously, Young will not play six more years but it's the thought that counts.

BULL MARKET II

Let's make this clear. There is no better athlete in the world than Michael Jordan. He shoots, he scores, he wins. He genuinely seems to be a nice guy. Most important, he induces ticket buying. And sneaker buying. He made a nice movie, too. He does it all. That being said, he makes an absurd amount of money. Absurd. The following chart offers a little perspective on what Mike made in the 1996–97 season as a basketball player, albeit the world's best. You don't want to see the chart for school teachers, cops and firemen.

An inside look at Michael Jordan's 1997 NBA compensation

Bi-weekly check	$634,615
Per game	$402,439
Per Minute	$8,384
USA median salary*	$31,200

* Ages 25-54

Bull Market III

We don't mean to pick on Michael Jordan. He deserves to be the highest paid athlete in the world. And Jerry

Michael Jordan made a bold move towards his post-basketball life when he announced the formation of his own footwear and apparel company, "Jordan," a joint venture with Nike.

Reinsdorf would not pay him more than he can afford. But there is something in these numbers that is not right.

Michael Jordan makes as much as........

	Salary
165 President Clintons	$200,000
12.2 Scottie Pippens	$2.7 million
10 Brian Jordans	$3.3 million
1.3 Arnold Schwarzeneggers	$25 million for *Batman IV*

CARAYING ON

There are a few baseball broadcasters who simply are no less than the "voice" of their teams. It seems like they witnessed, and described, every great moment in the team's history.

So, with some help from the Baseball Hall of Fame library, we determined which broadcasters have been on the longest streaks with the same teams. Caray, Scully and Buck have worked continuously with these teams but both Harwell and Thompson took some minor breaks since their debuts. In any event, Holy Cow!

Iron Men of the baseball broadcast booth

	First year	Years
Harry Caray - Cubs	1945	52
Ernie Harwell - Tigers	1948	49
Vin Scully - Dodgers	1950	47
Chuck Thompson - Orioles	1953	39
Jack Buck - Cardinals	1954	43

■

1996-97 Top Rated TV Sports Events

Final 1996-97 network television ratings for nationally-telecast sports events, according to Nielsen Media Research. Covers period from Oct. 1, 1996 through Aug. 17, 1997. Events are listed with ratings points and audience share; each ratings point represents 959,000 households and shares indicate percentage of TV sets in use.

Multiple entries: SPORTS—NFL Football (22); Major League Baseball (16); NBA Basketball (12); Figure Skating (8); NCAA Basketball (5); College Football bowl games (3). NETWORKS—NBC (28); FOX (23); ABC and CBS (9).

		Date	Net	Rtg/Sh
1	**Super Bowl XXXI** (Patriots vs. Packers)	1/26/97	FOX	43.3/65
2	**NFC Championship Game** (Panthers at Packers)	1/12/97	FOX	30.1/58
3	**AFC Championship Game** (Jaguars at Patriots)	1/12/97	NBC	28.5/47
4	**NFC Playoff Game** (Cowboys at Panthers)	1/5/97	FOX	27.6/49
5	**AFC Playoff Game** (Steelers at Patriots)	1/5/97	NBC	21.2/46
6	**NBA Finals-Game 5** (Bulls at Jazz)	6/11/97	NBC	20.1/35
7	**MLB World Series-Game 5** (Yankees at Braves)	10/24/96	FOX	20.0/32
8	**AFC Playoff Game** (Jaguars at Broncos)	1/4/97	NBC	19.6/40
9	**MLB World Series-Game 6** (Braves at Yankees)	10/26/96	FOX	19.1/34
10	**NCAA Men's Basketball Championship Game** (Arizona vs Kentucky)	3/31/97	CBS	18.9/31
11	**NFC Wildcard Playoff Game** (Eagles at 49ers)	12/29/96	FOX	18.8/38
12	**NBA Finals-Game 6** (Jazz at Bulls)	6/13/97	NBC	18.5/35
13	**NFC Playoff Game** (49ers at Packers)	1/4/97	FOX	18.1/45
14	**MLB World Series-Game 4** (Yankees at Braves)	10/23/96	FOX	17.9/32
	Sugar Bowl (Florida vs Florida St.)	1/2/97	ABC	17.9/29
16	**MLB World Series-Game 3** (Yankees at Braves)	10/22/96	FOX	17.5/28
17	**AFC Wildcard Playoff Game** (Colts at Steelers)	12/29/96	NBC	17.4/41
18	**NBA Finals-Game 4** (Bulls at Jazz)	6/8/97	NBC	16.9/30
	NFC Playoff Game (Vikings at Cowboys)	12/28/96	ABC	16.7/38
20	**NFL Thanksgiving Day Game** (Redskins at Cowboys)	11/28/96	FOX	16.6/45
21	**NFL Thanksgiving Day Game** (Chiefs at Lions)	11/28/96	NBC	16.6/44
22	**Rose Bowl** (Ohio St. vs. Ariz. St.)	1/1/97	ABC	16.5/29
23	**NFL Regular Season Early Game** (Various teams)	10/13/96	FOX	16.2/33
24	**NBA Finals-Game 1** (Jazz at Bulls)	6/1/97	NBC	15.8/27
25	**MLB World Series-Game 1** (Braves at Yankees)	10/20/96	FOX	15.7/25
26	**Monday Night Football** (Steelers at Chiefs)	10/7/96	ABC	15.6/26
27	**NBA Finals-Game 2** (Jazz at Bulls)	6/4/97	NBC	15.1/27
28	**NFL Regular Season Late Game** (Various teams)	10/6/96	NBC	14.3/29
29	**NBA Finals-Game 3** (Bulls at Jazz)	6/6/97	NBC	14.2/27
30	**Masters Golf Tournament-Final Round** (Tiger Woods leads)	4/13/97	CBS	14.1/31

Wide World Photos

Rabid **Green Bay Packer fans**, often known as "Cheeseheads," helped make Super Bowl XXXI one of the most-watched Super Bowl games ever.

1996-97 Top Rated TV Sports Events (Cont.)

	Date	Net	Rtg/Sh
31 **MLB World Series-Game 2**			
(Braves at Yankees) 10/21/96	FOX	14.0/23
32 **AFC Playoff Game**			
(Jaguars at Bills) 12/28/96	ABC	13.5/37
NBA Eastern Conference Finals-Game 5			
(Heat at Bulls) 5/28/97	NBC	13.5/24
34 **NBA Western Conference Finals-Game 6**			
(Jazz at Rockets) 5/29/97	NBC	13.0/23
35 **NCAA Men's Basketball National Semifinal**			
(Minn. vs Kentucky) 3/29/97	CBS	12.5/23
36 **MLB NLCS-Game 6**			
(Cardinals at Braves) 10/16/96	FOX	11.9/19
37 **MLB 1997 All-Star Game**			
(Cleveland, Ohio) 7/8/97	FOX	11.8/21
38 **NFL Regular Season Early Game**			
(Various teams) 10/6/96	FOX	11.7/29
39 **MLB NLCS-Game 7**			
(Cardinals at Braves) 10/17/96	FOX	11.2/18
NBA All-Star Game			
(Cleveland, Ohio) 2/9/97	NBC	11.2/19
41 **NFL Regular Season Early Game**			
(Various teams) 10/13/97	NBC	11.0/27
42 **NBA Western Conference Finals-Game 5**			
(Rockets at Jazz) 5/27/97	NBC	10.9/19
43 **MLB ALCS-Game 3**			
(Yankees at Orioles) 10/11/96	NBC	10.0/19
Fiesta Bowl			
(Penn. St. vs Texas) 1/1/97	CBS	10.0/17
45 **NCAA Men's Basketball National Semifinal**			
(N. Carolina vs Arizona) 3/29/97	CBS	9.9/23
46 **NBA Eastern Conference Finals-Game 4**			
(Bulls at Heat) 5/26/97	NBC	9.8/25
47 **NFL Regular Season Late Game**			
(Various teams) 12/14/96	NBC	9.6/26
48 **MLB NLCS-Game 4**			
(Braves at Cardinals) 10/13/96	FOX	9.5/15
49 **Battle of the Sexes on Ice**			
(Figure Skating) 3/12/97	FOX	9.4/16

	Date	Net	Rtg/Sh
50 **World Figure Skating Championships**			
(Day 2) 3/22/97	ABC	9.2/17
World Professional Figure Skating Championships			
(Day 1) 1/24/97	NBC	9.2/16
52 **NFL Pro Bowl**			
(Honolulu, Hawaii) 2/2/97	ABC	9.1/15
Gold Championship			
(Figure Skating) 11/23/96	NBC	9.1/16
54 **NCAA Men's Basketball Tournament**			
(Providence vs Arizona) ..3/23/97	CBS	9.0/20
55 **NCAA Men's Basketball Tournament**			
(Various teams) 3/16/97	CBS	8.9/19
Ultimate Four competition			
(Figure Skating) 3/29/97	NBC	8.9/16
Ice Wars 2: USA vs the World			
(Figure Skating) 11/29/96	CBS	8.9/16
MLB ALCS-Game 5			
(Yankees at Orioles) 10/13/96	NBC	8.9/20
59 **MLB NLCS-Game 1**			
(Cardinals at Braves) 10/9/96	FOX	8.8/15
60 **MLB NLCS-Game 2**			
(Cardinals at Braves) 10/10/96	FOX	8.8/14
61 **MLB ALCS-Game 4**			
(Yankees at Orioles) 10/12/96	NBC	8.8/18
62 **NASCAR Winston Cup Daytona 500**			
................2/16/97	CBS	8.6/23
World Professional Figure Skating Championships			
(Day 2) 1/25/97	NBC	8.6/15
64 **MLB AL Div. Series-Game 1**			
(Rangers at Yankees) 10/1/96	NBC	8.5/15
65 **NBA Playoffs**			
(Various teams) 4/27/97	NBC	8.4/18
66 **NFL Regular Season Late Game**			
(Various teams) 3/20/97	FOX	8.3/20
World Figure Skating Championships			
(Day 1) 10/22/96	ABC	8.3/14
68 **NFL Regular Season Early Game**			
(Eagles at Jets) 12/14/96	FOX	8.2/26
69 **Evander Holyfield vs. Mike Tyson II Rebroadcast**			
(Tyson disqualified) 8/14/97	ABC	8.2/15

All-Time Pay Per View Events

According to SET Database, Multichannel News, boxing has dominated the USA's all-time most-purchased pay-per-view events. The 1997 Mike Tyson-Evander Holyfield rematch in which Tyson was disqualified for biting Holyfield's ears, was the most-watched pay-per-view event in history. Mike Tyson has appeared in seven of the fights, Evander Holyfield in five.

Top 10 Pay-Per-View Events

		Year	Buys
1	Tyson-Holyfield II	1997	1,960,000
2	Tyson-Holyfield I	1996	1,590,000
3	Tyson-McNeeley	1995	1,580,000
4	Tyson-Bruno	1996	1,390,000
5	Holyfield-Foreman	1991	1,360,000
6	Tyson-Ruddock II	1991	1,228,000
7	Holyfield-Douglas	1990	1,059,000
8	Tyson-Seldon	1996	1,003,000
9	Tyson-Ruddock I	1991	957,000
10	Holyfield-Bowe I	1992	929,000
11	Chavez-Whitaker	1993	902,000
12	Wrestlemania	1988	880,000

Wide World Photos

All-Time Top-Rated TV Programs

NFL Football dominates television's All-Time Top-Rated 50 Programs with 20 Super Bowls and the 1981 NFC Championship Game making the list. Rankings based on surveys taken from July 1960 through August 1997; include only sponsored programs seen on individual networks; and programs under 30 minutes scheduled duration are excluded. Programs are listed with ratings points, audience share and number of households watching, according to Nielsen Media Research.

Multiple entries: The Super Bowl (20); "Roots" (7); "The Beverly Hillbillies" and "The Thorn Birds" (3); "The Bob Hope Christmas Show," "The Ed Sullivan Show," "Gone With The Wind" and 1994 Winter Olympics (2).

	Program	Episode/Game	Net	Date	Rating	Share	Households
1	M*A*S*H (series)	Final episode	CBS	2/28/83	60.2	77	50,150,000
2	Dallas (series)	"Who Shot J.R.?"	CBS	11/21/80	53.3	76	41,470,000
3	Roots (mini-series)	Part 8	ABC	1/30/77	51.1	71	36,380,000
4	**Super Bowl XVI**	49ers 26, Bengals 21	CBS	1/24/82	49.1	73	40,020,000
5	**Super Bowl XVII**	Redskins 27, Dolphins 17	NBC	1/30/83	48.6	69	40,480,000
6	XVII Winter Olympics	Women's Figure Skating	CBS	2/23/94	48.5	64	45,690,000
7	**Super Bowl XX**	Bears 46, Patriots 10	NBC	1/26/86	48.3	70	41,490,000
8	Gone With the Wind (movie)	Part 1	NBC	11/7/76	47.7	65	33,960,000
9	Gone with the Wind (movie)	Part 2	NBC	11/8/76	47.4	64	33,750,000
10	**Super Bowl XII**	Cowboys 27, Broncos 10	CBS	1/15/78	47.2	67	34,410,000
11	**Super Bowl XIII**	Steelers 35, Cowboys 31	NBC	1/21/79	47.1	74	35,090,000
12	Bob Hope Special	Christmas Show	NBC	1/15/70	46.6	64	27,260,000
13	**Super Bowl XVIII**	Raiders 38, Redskins 9	CBS	1/22/84	46.4	71	38,800,000
	Super Bowl XIX	49ers 38, Dolphins 16	ABC	1/20/85	46.4	63	39,390,000
15	**Super Bowl XIV**	Steelers 31, Rams 19	NBC	1/20/80	46.3	67	35,330,000
16	**Super Bowl XXX**	Cowboys 27, Steelers 17	NBC	1/28/96	46.0	68	44,114,400
	ABC Theater (special)	"The Day After"	ABC	11/20/83	46.0	62	38,550,000
18	Roots (mini-series)	Part 6	ABC	1/28/77	45.9	66	32,680,000
	The Fugitive (series)	Final episode	ABC	8/29/67	45.9	72	25,700,000
20	**Super Bowl XXI**	Giants 39, Broncos 20	CBS	1/25/87	45.8	66	40,030,000
21	Roots (mini-series)	Part 5	ABC	1/27/77	45.7	71	32,540,000
22	**Super Bowl XXVIII**	Cowboys 30, Bills 13	NBC	1/29/94	45.5	66	42,860,000
	Cheers	Final episode	NBC	5/20/93	45.5	64	42,360,500
24	The Ed Sullivan Show	Beatles' 1st appearance	CBS	2/9/64	45.3	60	23,240,000
25	**Super Bowl XXVII**	Cowboys 52, Bills 17	NBC	1/31/93	45.1	66	41,988,100
26	Bob Hope Special	Christmas Show	NBC	1/14/71	45.0	61	27,050,000
27	Roots (mini-series)	Part 3	ABC	1/25/77	44.8	68	31,900,000
28	**Super Bowl XI**	Raiders 32, Vikings 14	NBC	1/9/77	44.4	73	31,610,000
	Super Bowl XV	Raiders 27, Eagles 10	NBC	1/25/81	44.4	63	34,540,000
30	**Super Bowl VI**	Cowboys 24, Dolphins 3	CBS	1/16/72	44.2	74	27,450,000
31	XVII Winter Olympics	Women's Figure Skating	CBS	2/25/94	44.1	64	41,540,000
	Roots (mini-series)	Part 2	ABC	1/24/77	44.1	62	31,400,000
33	The Beverly Hillbillies	Regular episode	CBS	1/8/64	44.0	65	22,570,000
34	Roots (mini-series)	Part 4	ABC	1/26/77	43.8	66	31,190,000
	The Ed Sullivan Show	Beatles' 2nd appearance	CBS	2/16/64	43.8	60	22,445,000
36	**Super Bowl XXIII**	49ers 20, Bengals 16	NBC	1/22/89	43.5	68	39,320,000
37	The Academy Awards	John Wayne wins Oscar	ABC	4/7/70	43.4	78	25,390,000
38	**Super Bowl XXXI**	Packers 35, Patriots 21	FOX	1/26/97	43.3	65	42,000,000
39	The Thorn Birds (mini-series)	Part 3	ABC	3/29/83	43.2	62	35,990,000
40	The Thorn Birds (mini-series)	Part 4	ABC	3/30/83	43.1	62	35,900,000
41	**NFC Championship Game**	49ers 28, Cowboys 27	CBS	1/10/82	42.9	62	34,940,000
42	The Beverly Hillbillies	Regular episode	CBS	1/15/64	42.8	62	21,960,000
43	**Super Bowl VII**	Dolphins 14, Redskins 7	NBC	1/14/73	42.7	72	27,670,000
44	The Thorn Birds (mini-series)	Part 2	ABC	3/28/83	42.5	59	35,400,000
45	**Super Bowl IX**	Steelers 16, Vikings 6	NBC	1/12/75	42.4	72	29,040,000
	The Beverly Hillbillies	Regular episode	CBS	2/26/64	42.4	60	21,750,000
47	**Super Bowl X**	Steelers 21, Cowboys 17	CBS	1/18/76	42.3	78	29,440,000
	ABC Sunday Night Movie	"Airport"	ABC	11/11/73	42.3	63	28,000,000
	ABC Sunday Night Movie	"Love Story"	ABC	10/1/72	42.3	62	27,410,000
	Cinderella	Musical special	CBS	2/22/65	42.3	59	22,250,000
	Roots (mini-series)	Part 7	ABC	1/29/77	42.3	65	30,120,000

All-Time Top-Rated Cable TV Sports Events

All-time cable television for sports events, according to ESPN and Turner Sports research. Covers period from Sept. 1, 1980 through Sept. 1, 1997.

NFL Telecasts

		Date	Net	Rtg
1	Chicago at Minnesota	12/6/87	ESPN	17.6
2	Detroit at Miami	12/25/94	ESPN	15.1
3	Chicago at Minnesota	12/3/89	ESPN	14.7
4	Cleveland at San Fran	11/29/87	ESPN	14.2
5	Pittsburgh at Houston	12/30/90	ESPN	13.8

Non-NFL Telecasts

		Date	Net	Rtg
1	NBA: Detroit-Boston	6/1/88	TBS	8.8
2	NBA: Chicago-Detroit	5/31/89	TBS	8.2
3	NBA: Detroit-Boston	5/26/88	TBS	8.1
4	NCAA: G'town-St. John's	2/27/85	ESPN	8.0
5	NBA: Chicago-Orlando	5/10/95	TNT	7.9

The Rights Stuff

The roster of major 1997-98 television rights on network and cable TV as of Sept. 20, 1997.

ABC

Auto Racing—1998 Indianapolis 500 and four other Indy Racing League races; NASCAR Brickyard 400.

College Basketball—1998 regular season games.

College Football—Big Ten, Big 12, Pac-10 and WAC regular season for 1997; Big 12, SEC and WAC Championship Games; Aloha, Citrus, Rose and Sugar bowls for 1997 seasons.

Cycling—weekend coverage of the 1998 Tour de France

Figure Skating—1998 World, U.S. and European Championships.

NFL Football—ABC Monday Night Football; two 1997 season Wild Card playoff games; 1998 Pro Bowl.

Golf—1998 British Open; British Senior Open; LPGA Dinah Shore; PGA, LPGA and Seniors Skins games.

Horse Racing—1998 Kentucky Derby; Preakness; Belmont Stakes.

Little League Baseball—1998 Little League World Series

Soccer—1997 MLS championship game.

CBS

Auto Racing—Daytona 500 through 2001, three other NASCAR Winston Cup races and NASCAR truck series.

College Basketball—1997-98 Big East, Big 12 and SEC regular season games and Big 12 and SEC conference tournaments; NCAA Men's tournament and Final Four through 2002.

College Football—Fiesta, Orange, Cotton and Sun bowls for 1997 seasons; Big East and SEC regular season games in 1997; 1997 Army-Navy game.

Golf—1998 PGA Tour; Masters; PGA Championship, LPGA Championship.

Olympics—1998 Winter Games at Nagano.

Tennis—1998 U.S. Open.

ESPN (and ESPN2)

Auto Racing—1998 IndyCar and NASCAR.

Major League Baseball—1998 regular season.

College Basketball—Men's 1997-98 regular season and conference tournaments and pre- and postseason NIT; Women's 1997-98 regular season and NCAA tournament and Final Four.

Bowling—1998 PBA and LPBT tours.

Boxing—ESPN Championship series.

Cycling—weekday coverage of the 1998 Tour de France.

College Football—ACC, Big East, Big 10, SEC and WAC regular season for '97 season; Heisman Trophy Show; Alamo, Copper, Haka, Heritage, Holiday, Independence, Liberty, Outback and Peach Bowls.

NFL Football—Sunday Night Football (2nd half of 1997 season); 1998 College Draft.

Golf—1998 U.S. Open and British Open (early rounds); PGA, Senior and LPGA tour events.

NHL Hockey—selected regular season and Stanley Cup playoff games through 1997-98 season.

College Hockey—1998 NCAA Final Four.

Soccer—1998 Major League Soccer regular season and playoffs; U.S. National Team games.

Tennis—1997-98 Davis Cup, Grand Slam Cup and Fed Cup; 1998 ATP Tour and Australian Open.

FOX

Figure Skating—1998 Skate International Champions Series

NFL Football—NFC regular season and playoffs through 1997 season; 1997 Super Bowl.

NHL Hockey—1998 and '99 All-Star Games and selected regular season and Stanley Cup Playoff games.

Major League Baseball—1998 and 2000 World Series, 1999 All-Star Game as well as selected playoff and regular season games through 2000.

NBC

Major League Baseball—selected playoff games through the year 2000.

NBA Basketball—regular season and playoffs, NBA finals and All-Star Games through the 1997-98 season.

College Football—Notre Dame home games through 2000.

NFL Football—AFC regular season and playoffs through 1997 season; 1998 Super Bowl.

Golf—PGA Tour through 2002; Ryder Cup and PGA Seniors through 2005; Presidents Cup through 2006; U.S. Open, U.S. Women's Open and U.S. Senior Open through 1999.

Horse Racing—The Breeders' Cup through 2000.

Olympics—2000 Summer Games in Sydney; 2002 Winter Games in Salt Lake City, 2004 Summer Games; 2006 Winter Games; 2008 Summer Games.

Tennis—1998 French Open and Wimbledon through 1999.

Turner (TBS and TNT)

Auto Racing—1998 select races from NASCAR circuit on TBS.

Major League Baseball—1998 Atlanta Braves regular season on TBS.

NBA Basketball—1997-98 regular season and playoffs on TBS and TNT; NBA Draft on TNT.

Golf—PGA Championship (early rounds, partial 3rd and 4th), Grand Slam of Golf, Senior Slam of Golf and Sarazen World Open on TBS.

Olympics—50 hours of 1998 Winter Olympics in Nagano on TNT.

Olympics TV Rights

On Dec. 12, 1995 the IOC announced that NBC had successfully bid a record $2.3 billion for the exclusive U.S. television rights to the 2004 and 2008 Summer Games and the 2006 Winter Games.

Year	Games	Location	Rights Fee	TV Net	TV Hrs
1960	Winter	Squaw Valley	$ 50,000	CBS	15
	Summer	Rome	394,000	CBS	20
1964	Winter	Innsbruck	$597,000	ABC	17¼
	Summer	Tokyo	1.5 mil.	NBC	14
1968	Winter	Grenoble	$2.5 mil.	ABC	27
	Summer	Mexico City	4.5 mil.	ABC	43¾
1972	Winter	Sapporo	$6.4 mil.	NBC	37
	Summer	Munich	7.5 mil.	ABC	62¾
1976	Winter	Innsbruck	$10 mil.	ABC	43½
	Summer	Montreal	25 mil.	ABC	76½
1980	Winter	Lake Placid	$15.5 mil.	ABC	53¼
	Summer	Moscow	87 mil.	NBC	150*
1984	Winter	Sarajevo	$91.5 mil.	ABC	63
	Summer	Los Angeles	225 mil.	ABC	180
1988	Winter	Calgary	$309 mil.	ABC	94½
	Summer	Seoul	300 mil.	NBC	179½
1992	Winter	Albertville	$243 mil.	CBS	116
	Summer	Barcelona	401 mil.	NBC	161
1994	Winter	Lillehammer	$300 mil.	CBS	120
1996	Summer	Atlanta	456 mil.	NBC	168
1998	Winter	Nagano	$375 mil.	CBS	128
2000	Summer	Sydney	$715 mil.	NBC	TBD
2002	Winter	Salt Lake City	$555 mil.	NBC	TBD
2004	Summer	Athens	$793 mil.	NBC	TBD
2006	Winter	TBD	$613 mil.	NBC	TBD
2008	Summer	TBD	$894 mil.	NBC	TBD

*NBC planned 150 hours of coverage for the 1980 Summer Olympics, but since the U.S. boycotted the Games, NBC did not cover them and did not pay the rights fee.

What Major League Franchises Are Worth

The estimated total market value of the 113 major league baseball, basketball, football and hockey franchises operating in the U.S. and Canada in 1996-97. Figures according to *Financial World* magazine's sixth annual survey, released in their June 17, 1997 issue. Franchise values are estimates of what a team would have been worth if put up for sale in early 1997. Values are based on gate receipts, radio and TV revenues, stadium/arena income (luxury suites, concessions, parking, etc.), operating income, player salaries and other expenses. Figures are in millions of dollars.

Avg. franchise values: NFL ($205 million); **NBA** ($148 million), **Baseball** ($134 million) and **NHL** ($90 million).

BASEBALL

	Value				
1996	1995	1994	1993	1992	1991
NY Yankees .$241	$209	$185	$166	$160	$200
Baltimore 207	168	164	129	130	140
Atlanta 199	163	120	96	88	83
Colorado 184	138	117	110	—	—
LA Dodgers ...178	147	143	138	135	180
Cleveland 175	125	103	100	81	77
Texas 174	140	157	132	106	123
Boston 172	143	143	141	136	160
Chicago-NL ...165	143	135	120	101	132
Toronto 155	152	146	150	150	160
Chicago-AL ...149	144	152	133	123	140
NY Mets 144	133	134	147	145	170
St. Louis 134	112	110	105	98	132
San Francisco .128	122	102	93	103	99
Florida 123	98	92	81	—	—
Oakland 115	97	101	114	124	115
Houston 114	97	92	85	87	95
Philadelphia ..112	103	96	96	96	115
Detroit 110	106	83	89	97	85
Seattle 107	92	76	80	86	79
Cincinnati 95	99	84	86	103	98
Anaheim 93	90	88	93	105	103
Milwaukee 92	71	75	96	86	77
Kansas City ...88	80	96	94	111	117
San Diego 86	67	74	85	103	96
Montreal 77	68	76	75	86	75
Minnesota 77	74	80	83	95	83
Pittsburgh 71	62	70	79	95	87

NFL

	Value				
1996	1995	1994	1993	1992	1991
Dallas $320	$272	$238	$190	$165	$146
St. Louis 243	193	153	148	128	126
Miami 242	214	186	161	145	150
Carolina 240	133	—	—	—	—
Jacksonville ...239	145	—	—	—	—
Baltimore 235	201	163	165	133	125
San Francisco .218	196	186	167	139	134
NY Giants 211	183	168	176	146	150
Oakland 210	162	145	146	124	128
Philadelphia ..209	192	182	172	149	146
Kansas City ...204	188	172	153	130	123
Chicago 204	184	161	160	136	139
Washington ...200	184	151	158	123	117
Buffalo 200	188	172	164	138	125
New Orleans .199	184	171	154	130	123
New England .197	165	151	142	102	103
Tennessee 193	159	158	157	132	128
Atlanta 191	167	156	148	125	120
San Diego 191	169	153	142	119	115
Cincinnati 188	171	137	142	128	115
Tampa Bay ...187	164	151	142	118	113
Green Bay 186	166	154	141	116	115
NY Jets 186	153	149	142	119	117
Minnesota 186	167	154	147	123	120
Arizona 184	166	155	146	125	120
Denver 182	164	150	147	119	114
Detroit 181	150	141	138	118	110
Pittsburgh 173	154	144	143	120	121
Seattle 171	154	152	148	137	130
Indianapolis ...170	145	134	141	122	121

NBA

	Value				
1996	1995	1994	1993	1992	1991
New York ...$250	$205	$173	$136	$87	$83
Phoenix 220	191	156	108	71	80
Chicago 214	178	166	149	102	100
LA Lakers 211	171	169	168	155	150
Detroit 202	186	180	154	132	120
Cleveland 180	151	133	118	81	81
Portland 179	137	132	122	84	78
Utah 163	142	127	98	72	52
Orlando 156	121	101	84	60	62
San Antonio ..156	126	110	100	65	63
Boston 155	134	127	117	91	110
Houston 154	116	95	84	58	61
Toronto 138	—	—	—	—	—
New Jersey ...137	108	92	79	54	54
Seattle 137	129	119	96	51	45
Charlotte 136	113	110	104	77	74
Sacramento ...131	114	108	84	66	63
Golden St 130	114	93	85	62	63
Washington ...129	113	96	78	53	46
Vancouver 127	—	—	—	—	—
Minnesota 123	110	99	92	65	62
Miami 118	97	88	76	58	60
Denver 116	102	88	69	50	46
Indiana 114	94	77	67	45	43
Philadelphia ..113	93	81	83	59	63
Atlanta 111	96	84	72	54	57
Dallas 104	89	81	79	56	60
Milwaukee 103	103	92	77	54	56
LA Clippers ...95	88	87	83	54	54

NHL

	Value				
1996	1995	1994	1993	1992	1991
Chicago $151	$122	$102	$80	$67	$61
NY Rangers ...147	118	108	81	76	62
Detroit 146	126	124	104	87	70
Boston 130	111	106	88	79	67
Philadelphia ..128	102	86	69	58	51
Toronto 105	96	90	77	63	54
Anaheim 104	99	108	—	—	—
San Jose 104	77	66	52	43	—
Pittsburgh 96	76	75	62	53	41
St. Louis 95	74	69	59	52	39
Montreal 95	86	86	82	73	62
Vancouver 91	91	87	69	61	45
Washington ...85	70	59	47	45	40
Los Angeles ..83	78	81	85	71	60
Colorado 81	47	49	43	48	45
New Jersey ...79	58	54	51	47	41
NY Islanders ..74	60	53	53	55	53
Buffalo 74	65	60	55	44	39
Calgary 72	54	50	50	52	55
Ottawa 67	56	56	50	—	—
Florida 67	45	47	—	—	—
Tampa Bay ...64	48	55	39	—	—
Dallas 63	53	50	46	42	34
Edmonton 52	42	42	46	51	55
Hartford* 48	40	43	46	48	49
Phoenix 43	34	35	35	35	30

*The Whalers were moved to Greensboro, NC and renamed the Carolina Hurricanes in 1997.

Teams Bought in 1997

Three major league clubs acquired new majority owners or significant minority owners from Nov. 1, 1996 through Sept. 30, 1997.

NBA Basketball

New York Knicks: Cablevision Systems Corp. acquired a majority stake in Madison Square Garden Properties from business partner ITT Corp on June 17, 1997. MSG Properites include the Madison Square Garden complex, the NBA's Knicks and the NHL's Rangers as well as the MSG television network . Under the agreement, Cablevision's Rainbow Programming subsidiary increased its equity interest in the MSG properties from 50 percent to 89.8 percent. ITT received $500 million and maintains an 10.2 percent interest in the properties. Cablevision and ITT orginally teamed up in 1995 to buy MSG Properties for $1 billion.

NFL Football

Seattle Seahawks: Paul Allen, the billionaire co-founder of Microsoft, exercised his option to buy the Seahawks from owner Ken Behring for $200 million on June 30, 1997. Allen, who also owns the NBA's Portland Trailblazers, decided to go through with the deal after the passage of Referendum 48, the ballot issue that asked Washington voters to replace the Kingdome with a $425 million open-air stadium and exhibition hall. The measure was approved by a 51-49 percent margin. Ken Behring and Ken Hofmann originally bought the Seahawks from the Nordstrom family on Aug. 30, 1988.

NHL Hockey

New York Rangers: Cablevision Systems Corp. acquired a majority stake in Madison Square Garden Properties from business partner ITT Corp on June 17, 1997. MSG Properites include the Madison Square Garden complex, the NHL's Rangers and the NBA's Knicks as well as the MSG television network . Under the agreement, Cablevision's Rainbow Programming subsidiary increased its equity interest in the MSG properties from 50 percent to 89.8 percent. ITT received $500 million and maintains an 10.2 percent interest in the properties. Cablevision and ITT originally teamed up in 1995 to buy MSG Properties for $1 billion.

The 1996 *Forbes* Top 40

The 40 highest-paid athletes of 1996 (including salary, winnings, endorsements, etc.), according to the Dec. 16, 1996 issue of *Forbes* magazine. Nationality, birth date, and each athlete's rank on the 1995 list are also given. Age refers to athlete's age as of Dec. 31, 1996.

		Sport	Salary/ Winnings	Other Income	Total	Nat	Birthdate	Age	1995 Rank
1	Mike Tyson	Boxing	$75.0	$ 0.0	**$75.0**	USA	June 30, 1966	30	2
2	Michael Jordan	Basketball	12.6	40.0	**52.6**	USA	Feb. 17, 1963	33	1
3	Michael Schumacher	Auto Racing	25.0	8.0	**33.0**	GBR	Jan. 3, 1969	27	9
4	Shaquille O'Neal	Basketball	7.4	17.0	**24.4**	USA	Mar. 6, 1972	24	5
5	Emmitt Smith	Football	13.0	3.5	**16.5**	USA	May 15, 1969	27	NR
6	Evander Holyfield	Boxing	15.0	0.5	**15.5**	USA	Oct. 19, 1962	34	14
7	Andre Agassi	Tennis	2.2	13.0	**15.2**	USA	Apr. 29, 1970	26	7
8	Arnold Palmer	Golf	0.1	15.0	**15.1**	USA	Sept. 10, 1929	67	11
9	Dennis Rodman	Basketball	3.9	9.0	**12.9**	USA	May 13, 1961	33	NR
10	Patrick Ewing	Basketball	10.9	1.5	**12.4**	USA	Aug. 5, 1962	34	19
11	Cal Ripken Jr.	Baseball	6.0	6.0	**12.0**	USA	Aug. 24, 1960	36	16
12	Roy Jones Jr.	Boxing	12.0	0.0	**12.0**	USA	Jan. 16, 1969	26	NR
13	Dan Marino	Football	9.2	2.5	**11.7**	USA	Sept. 15, 1961	35	40
14	Wayne Gretzky	Hockey	6.0	5.5	**11.5**	CAN	Jan. 26, 1961	35	10
15	Riddick Bowe	Boxing	11.5	0.0	**11.5**	USA	Aug. 10, 1967	29	4
16	Pete Sampras	Tennis	3.3	8.0	**11.3**	USA	Aug. 12, 1971	25	15
17	Oscar De La Hoya	Boxing	10.8	0.5	**11.3**	USA	Feb. 4, 1973	23	NR
18	Grant Hill	Basketball	4.3	6.5	**10.8**	USA	Oct. 5, 1972	24	24
19	Ken Griffey Jr.	Baseball	8.0	2.8	**10.8**	USA	Nov. 21, 1969	27	23
20	Dale Earnhardt	Auto Racing	2.5	8.0	**10.5**	USA	Apr. 29, 1952	44	20
21	David Robinson	Basketball	7.4	2.0	**9.4**	USA	Aug. 6, 1965	31	18
22	Hakeem Olajuwon	Basketball	6.8	2.5	**9.3**	NGR	Jan. 21, 1963	33	27
23	Clyde Drexler	Basketball	8.9	0.3	**9.2**	USA	June 22, 1962	35	NR
24	Michael Chang	Tennis	2.5	6.5	**9.0**	USA	Feb. 22, 1972	24	28
25	Julio Cesar Chavez	Boxing	9.0	0.0	**9.0**	MEX	July 12, 1962	34	NR
26	Tiger Woods	Golf	0.8	8.0	**8.8**	USA	Dec. 30, 1975	20	NR
27	John Elway	Football	6.8	2.0	**8.8**	USA	June 28, 1960	36	NR
28	Neil O'Donnell	Football	8.5	0.3	**8.8**	USA	July 3, 1966	30	NR
29	Steve Young	Football	4.5	4.0	**8.5**	USA	Oct. 11, 1961	35	35
30	Frank Thomas	Baseball	7.2	1.2	**8.4**	USA	Mar. 27, 1968	28	25
31	Mario Lemieux	Hockey	7.5	0.8	**8.3**	CAN	Oct. 5, 1965	31	NR
32	Barry Bonds	Baseball	8.0	0.3	**8.3**	USA	July 24, 1964	32	29
33	Jack Nicklaus	Golf	0.4	7.8	**8.2**	USA	Jan. 20, 1940	56	8
34	Damon Hill	Auto Racing	7.5	0.7	**8.2**	GBR	Sept. 17, 1960	36	NR
35	Troy Aikman	Football	4.9	3.2	**8.1**	USA	Nov. 21, 1966	30	NR
36	George Foreman	Boxing	3.0	5.0	**8.0**	USA	Jan 10, 1949	47	6
37	Charles Barkley	Basketball	4.5	3.5	**8.0**	USA	Feb. 20, 1963	33	32
38	Greg Norman	Golf	0.9	7.0	**7.9**	AUS	Feb. 10, 1955	41	17
39	Cecil Fielder	Baseball	7.4	0.2	**7.6**	USA	Sept. 21, 1963	33	39
40	Gerhard Berger	Auto Racing	7.0	0.5	**7.5**	AUT	Aug. 27, 1959	37	13

AWARDS

The Peabody Award

Presented annually since 1940 for outstanding achievement in radio and television broadcasting. Only 13 Peabodys have been given for sports programming. Named after Georgia banker and philanthropist George Foster Peabody, the awards are administered by the Henry W. Grady College of Journalism and Mass Communication at the University of Georgia. Documentary filmmaker Bud Greenspan won a Personal Peabody award in 1996 for his series of Olympic films.

Television

Year
1960 **CBS** for coverage of 1960 Winter and Summer Olympic Games
1966 ABC's **"Wide World of Sports"** (for Outstanding Achievement in Promotion of International Understanding).
1968 **ABC Sports** coverage of both the 1968 Winter and Summer Olympic Games.
1972 **ABC Sports** coverage of the 1972 Summer Olympics in Munich.
1973 **Joe Garagiola** of NBC Sports (for "The Baseball World of Joe Garagiola").
1976 **ABC Sports** coverage of both the 1976 Winter and Summer Olympic Games.
1984 **Roone Arledge**, president of ABC News & Sports (for significant contributions to news and sports programming).
1986 **WFAA-TV**, Dallas for its investigation of the Southern Methodist University football program.
1988 **Jim McKay** of ABC Sports (for pioneering efforts and career accomplishments in the world of TV sports).
1991 **CBS Sports** coverage of the 1991 Masters golf tournament
    & **HBO Sports** and Black Canyon Productions for the baseball special "When It Was A Game."
1995 **Kartemquin Educational Films** and **KTCA-TV** in St. Paul, MN, presented on PBS for "Hoop Dreams" & Turner Original Productions for the baseball special "Hank Aaron: Chasing the Dream."

Radio

Year
1974 **WSB** radio in Atlanta for "Henry Aaron: A Man with a Mission."
1991 **Red Barber** of National Public Radio (for his six decades as a broadcaster and his 10 years as a commentator on NPR's "Morning Edition").

National Emmy Awards

Sports Programming

Presented by the Academy of Television Arts and Sciences since 1948. Eligibility period covered the calendar year from 1948-57 and since 1988.

Multiple major award winners: ABC "Wide World of Sports" (19); ABC Olympics coverage (9); NFL Films Football coverage (8); ABC "Monday Night Football" (7); CBS NFL Football coverage (6); CBS NCAA Basketball coverage and CBS "NFL Today", ESPN "Outside the Lines" series (5); ESPN "SportsCenter" and NBC Olympics coverage (4); ABC "The American Sportsman," ABC Indianapolis 500 coverage and ESPN "GameDay" (3); ABC Kentucky Derby coverage, ABC "Sportsbeat," Bud Greenspan Olympic specials, CBS Olympics coverage, CBS Golf coverage, ESPN Speedworld, HBO Real Sports with Bryant Gumbel, MTV Sports series and NBC World Series coverage (2).

1949
Coverage—"Wrestling" (KTLA, Los Angeles)

1950
Program—"Rams Football" (KNBH-TV, Los Angeles)

1954
Program—"Gillette Cavalcade of Sports" (NBC)

1965-66
Programs—"Wide World of Sports" (ABC), "Shell's Wonderful World of Golf" (NBC) and "CBS Golf Classic" (CBS)

1966-67
Program—"Wide World of Sports" (ABC)

1967-68
Program—"Wide World of Sports" (ABC)

1968-69
Program—"1968 Summer Olympics" (ABC)

1969-70
Programs—"NFL Football" (CBS) and "Wide World of Sports" (ABC)

1970-71
Program—"Wide World of Sports" (ABC)

1971-72
Program—"Wide World of Sports" (ABC)

1972-73
News Special—"Coverage of Munich Olympic Tragedy" (ABC)
Sports Programs—"1972 Summer Olympics" (ABC) and "Wide World of Sports" (ABC)

1973-74
Program—"Wide World of Sports" (ABC)

1974-75
Non-Edited Program—"Jimmy Connors vs. Rod Laver Tennis Challenge" (CBS)
Edited Program—"Wide World of Sports" (ABC)

1975-76
Live Special—"1975 World Series: Cincinnati vs. Boston" (NBC)
Live Series—"NFL Monday Night Football" (ABC)
Edited Specials—"1976 Winter Olympics" (ABC)and "Triumph and Tragedy: The Olympic Experience" (ABC)
Edited Series—"Wide World of Sports" (ABC)

1976-77
Live Special—"1976 Summer Olympics" (ABC)
Live Series—"The NFL Today/NFL Football" (CBS)
Edited Special—"1976 Summer Olympics Preview" (ABC)
Edited Series—"The Olympiad" (PBS)

1977-78
Live Special—"Muhammad Ali vs. Leon Spinks Heavyweight Championship Fight" (CBS)
Live Series—"The NFL Today/NFL Football" (CBS)
Edited Special—"The Impossible Dream: Ballooning Across the Atlantic" (CBS)
Edited Series—"The Way It Was" (PBS)

National Emmy Awards (Cont.)

1978-79

Live Special—"Super Bowl XIII: Pittsburgh vs Dallas" (NBC)
Live Series—"NFL Monday Night Football" (ABC)
Edited Special—"Spirit of '78: The Flight of Double Eagle II" (ABC)
Edited Series—"The American Sportsman" (ABC)

1979-80

Live Special—"1980 Winter Olympics" (ABC)
Live Series—"NCAA College Football" (ABC)
Edited Special—"Gossamer Albatross: Flight of Imagination" (CBS)
Edited Series—"NFL Game of the Week" (NFL Films)

1980-81

Live Special—"1981 Kentucky Derby" (ABC)
Live Series—"PGA Golf Tour" (CBS)
Edited Special—"Wide World of Sports 20th Anniversary Show" (ABC)
Edited Series—"The American Sportsman" (ABC)

1981-82

Live Special—"1982 NCAA Basketball Final: North Carolina vs Georgetown" (CBS)
Live Series—"NFL Football" (CBS)
Edited Special—"1982 Indianapolis 500" (ABC)
Edited Seris—"Wide World of Sports" (ABC)

1982-83

Live Special—"1982 World Series: St. Louis vs Milwaukee" (NBC)
Live Series—"NFL Football" (CBS)
Edited Special—"Wimbledon '83" (NBC)
Edited Series—"Wide World of Sports" (ABC)
Journalism—"ABC Sportsbeat" (ABC)

1983-84

No awards given

1984-85

Live Special—"1984 Summer Olympics" (ABC)
Live Series—No award given
Edited Special—"Road to the Super Bowl '85" (NFL Films)
Edited Series—"The American Sportsman" (ABC)
Journalism—"ABC Sportsbeat" (ABC), "CBS Sports Sunday" (CBS), Dick Schaap features (ABC) and 1984 Summer Olympic features (ABC)

1985-86

No awards given

1986-87

Live Special—"1987 Daytona 500" (CBS)
Live Series—"NFL Football" (CBS)
Edited Special—"Wide World of Sports 25th Anniversary Special" (ABC)
Edited Series—"Wide World of Sports" (ABC)

1987-88

Live Special—"1987 Kentucky Derby" (ABC)
Live Series—"NFL Monday Night Football" (ABC)
Edited Special—"Paris-Roubaix Bike Race" (CBS)
Edited Series—"Wide World of Sports" (ABC)

1988

Live Special —"1988 Summer Olympics" (NBC)
Live Series—"1988 NCAA Basketball" (CBS)
Edited Special—"Road to the Super Bowl '88" (NFL Films)
Edited Series—"Wide World of Sports" (ABC)
Studio Show—"NFL GameDay" (ESPN)
Journalism—1988 Summer Olympic reporting (NBC)

1989

Live Special—"1989 Indianapolis 500" (ABC)
Live Series—"NFL Monday Night Football" (ABC)
Edited Special—"Trans-Antarctical The International Expedition" (ABC)
Edited Series—"This is the NFL" (NFL Films)
Studio Show—"NFL Today" (CBS)
Journalism—1989 World Series Game 3 earthquake coverage (ABC)

1990

Live Special—"1990 Indianapolis 500" (ABC)
Live Series—"1990 NCAA Basketball Tournament" (CBS)
Edited Special—"Road to Super Bowl XXIV" (NFL Films)
Edited Series—"Wide World of Sports" (ABC)
Studio Show—"SportsCenter" (ESPN)
Journalism—"Outside the Lines: The Autograph Game" (ESPN)

1991

Live Special—"1991 NBA Finals: Chicago vs LA Lakers" (NBC)
Live Series—"1991 NCAA Basketball Tournament" (CBS)
Edited Special—"Wide World of Sports 30th Anniversary Special" (ABC)
Edited Series—"This is the NFL" (NFL Films)
Studio Show—"NFL GameDay" (ESPN) and "NFL Live" (NBC)
Journalism—"Outside the Lines: Steroids–Whatever It Takes" (ESPN)

1992

Live Special—"1992 Breeders' Cup" (NBC)
Live Series—"1992 NCAA Basketball Tournament" (CBS)
Edited Special—"1992 Summer Olympics" (NBC)
Edited Series—"MTV Sports" (MTV)
Studio Show—"The NFL Today" (CBS)
Journalism—"Outside the Lines: Portraits in Black and White" (ESPN)

1993

Live Special—"1993 World Series" (CBS)
Live Series—"Monday Night Football" (ABC)
Edited Special—"Road to the Super Bowl" (NFL Films)
Edited Series—"This is the NFL" (NFL Films)
Studio Show—"The NFL Today" (CBS)
Journalism (TIE)—"Outside the Lines: Mitch Ivey Feature" (ESPN) and "SportsCenter: University of Houston Football" (ESPN).
Feature—"Arthur Ashe: His Life, His Legacy" (NBC).

1994

Live Special —"NHL Stanley Cup Finals" (ESPN)
Live Series —"Monday Night Football" (ABC)
Edited Special —"Lillehammer '94: 16 Days of Glory" (Disney/Cappy Productions)
Edited Series —"MTV Sports" (MTV)
Studio Show —"NFL GameDay" (ESPN)
Journalism —"1994 Winter Olympic Games: Mossad feature" (CBS)
Feature (TIE) —"Heroes of Telemark" on Winter Olympic Games (CBS); and "SportsCenter: Vanderbilt running back Brad Gaines" (ESPN).

"Baseball" Wins Prime Time Emmy

Ken Burns's miniseries "Baseball" won the 1994 Emmy Award for Outstanding Informational Series. The nine-part documentary aired from Sept. 18-28, 1994 and ran more than 18 hours, drawing the largest audience in PBS history.

1995

Live Special —"Cal Ripken 2131" (ESPN)

Live Series — "ESPN Speedworld" (ESPN)

Edited Special (quick turn-around) —"Outside the Lines: Playball– Opening Day in America" (ESPN)

Edited Special (long turn-around) —"Lillehammer, an Olympic Diary" (CBS)

Edited Series —"NFL Films Presents" (NFL Films)

Studio Show (TIE) —"NFL GameDay" (ESPN) and "Fox NFL Sunday"(Fox)

Journalism —"Real Sports with Bryant Gumbel: Broken Promises" (HBO)

Feature (TIE) —"SportsCenter: Jerry Quarry" (ESPN) and "Real Sports with Bryant Gumbel: Coach" (HBO).

1996

Live Special —"1996 World Series" (Fox)

Live Series —"ESPN Speedworld" (ESPN)

Edited Special —"Football America" (TNT/NFL Films)

Edited Series —"NFL Films Presents" (NFL Films)

Live Event Turnaround —"The Centennial Olympic Games" (NBC)

Studio Show —"SportsCenter" (ESPN)

Journalism —"Outside the Lines: AIDS in Sports" (ESPN)

Feature —"Real Sports with Bryant Gumbel: 1966 Texas Western NCAA Champs" (HBO).

Sportscasters of the Year
National Emmy Awards

An Emmy Award for Sportscasters was first introduced in 1968 and given for Outstanding Host/Commentator for the 1967-68 TV season. Two awards, one for Outstanding Host or Play-by-Play and the other for Outstanding Analyst, were first presented in 1981 for the 1980-81 season. Three awards, for Outstanding Studio Host, Play-by-Play and Analyst, have been given since the 1993 season

Multiple winners: John Madden (11); Jim McKay (9); Bob Costas (8); Dick Enberg (4); Al Michaels (3); Keith Jackson (2). Note that Jim McKay has won a total of 12 Emmy awards: eight for Host/Commentator, one for Host/Play-by-Play, two for Sports Writing, and one for News Commentary.

Season	Host/Commentator	Season	Host/Play-by-Play	Season	Analyst
1967-68	Jim McKay, ABC	1980-81	Dick Enberg, NBC	1980-81	Dick Button, ABC
1968-69	No award	1981-82	Jim McKay, ABC	1981-82	John Madden, CBS
1969-70	No award	1982-83	Dick Enberg, NBC	1982-83	John Madden, CBS
1970-71	Jim McKay, ABC	1983-84	No award	1983-84	No award
	& Don Meredith, ABC	1984-85	George Michael, NBC	1984-85	No award
1971-72	No award	1985-86	No award	1985-86	No award
1972-73	Jim McKay, ABC	1986-87	Al Michaels, ABC	1986-87	John Madden, CBS
1973-74	Jim McKay, ABC	1987-88	Bob Costas, NBC	1987-88	John Madden, CBS
1974-75	Jim McKay, ABC	1988	Bob Costas, NBC	1988	John Madden, CBS
1975-76	Jim McKay, ABC	1989	Al Michaels, ABC	1989	John Madden, CBS
1976-77	Frank Gifford, ABC	1990	Dick Enberg, NBC	1990	John Madden, CBS
1977-78	Jack Whitaker, CBS	1991	Bob Costas, NBC	1991	John Madden, CBS
1978-79	Jim McKay, ABC	1992	Bob Costas, NBC	1992	John Madden, CBS
1979-80	Jim McKay, ABC				

Year	Studio Host	Year	Play-by-Play	Year	Analyst
1993	Bob Costas, NBC	1993	Dick Enberg, NBC	1993	Billy Packer, CBS
1994	Bob Costas, NBC	1994	Keith Jackson, ABC	1994	John Madden, Fox
1995	Bob Costas, NBC	1995	Al Michaels, ABC	1995	John Madden, Fox
1996	Bob Costas, NBC	1996	Keith Jackson, ABC	1996	Howie Long, Fox

Life Achievement Emmy Award

For outstanding work as an exemplary television sportscaster over many years.

Year		Year		Year		Year	
1989	Jim McKay	1991	Curt Gowdy	1993	Pat Summerall	1995	Vin Scully
1990	Lindsey Nelson	1992	Chris Schenkel	1994	Howard Cosell	1996	Frank Gifford

National Sportscasters and Sportswriters Assn. Award

Sportscaster of the Year presented annually since 1959 by the National Sportscasters and Sportswriters Association, based in Salisbury, N.C. Voting is done by NSSA members and selected national media.

Multiple winners: Bob Costas (6); Chris Berman and Keith Jackson (5); Lindsey Nelson and Chris Schenkel (4); Dick Enberg, Al Michaels and Vin Scully (3); Curt Gowdy and Ray Scott (2).

Year		Year		Year		Year	
1959	Lindsey Nelson	1969	Curt Gowdy	1979	Dick Enberg	1988	Bob Costas
1960	Lindsey Nelson	1970	Chris Schenkel	1980	Dick Enberg	1989	Chris Berman
1961	Lindsey Nelson	1971	Ray Scott		& Al Michaels	1990	Chris Berman
1962	Lindsey Nelson	1972	Keith Jackson	1981	Dick Enberg	1991	Bob Costas
1963	Chris Schenkel	1973	Keith Jackson	1982	Vin Scully	1992	Bob Costas
1964	Chris Schenkel	1974	Keith Jackson	1983	Al Michaels	1993	Chris Berman
1965	Vin Scully	1975	Keith Jackson	1984	John Madden	1994	Chris Berman
1966	Curt Gowdy	1976	Keith Jackson	1985	Bob Costas	1995	Bob Costas
1967	Chris Schenkel	1977	Pat Summerall	1986	Al Michaels	1996	Chris Berman
1968	Ray Scott	1978	Vin Scully	1987	Bob Costas		

American Sportscasters Association Award

Sportscaster of the Year presented annually from 1984-94, with the exception of 1988, by the New York-based American Sportscasters Association. Two awards presented starting in 1995 to honor top play-by-play personality and studio host. Voting done by ASA members and officials. All four-time winners become ineligible for additional awards.

Multiple winners: Bob Costas and Dick Enberg (4); Chris Berman (2).

Sportscaster of the Year

Year		Year	
1984	Dick Enberg	1990	Dick Enberg
1985	Vin Scully	1991	Bob Costas
1986	Dick Enberg	1992	Bob Costas
1987	Dick Enberg	1993	Bob Costas
1988	No award	1994	Pat Summerall
1989	Bob Costas		

Play-by-Play

Year	
1995	Al Michaels
1996	Marv Albert

Studio Host

Year	
1995	Chris Berman
1996	Chris Berman

The Pulitzer Prize

The Pulitzer Prizes for journalism, letters and music have been presented annually since 1917 in the name of Joseph Pulitzer (1847-1911), the publisher of the *New York World*. Prizes are awarded by the president of Columbia University on the recommendation of a board of review. Fifteen Pulitzers have been awarded for newspaper sports reporting, sports commentary and sports photography.

News Coverage

1935 **Bill Taylor,** *NY Herald Tribune*, for his reporting on the 1934 America's Cup yacht races.

Special Citation

1952 **Max Kase**, *NY Journal-American*, for his reporting on the 1951 college basketball point-shaving scandal.

Meritorious Public Service

1954 *Newsday* (Garden City, N.Y.) for its expose of New York State's race track scandals and labor racketeering.

General Reporting

1956 **Arthur Daley,** *NY Times*, for his 1955 columns.

Investigative Reporting

1981 **Clark Hallas** & **Robert Lowe, (Tucson)** *Arizona Daily Star*, for their 1980 investigation of the University of Arizona athletic department.

Specialized Reporting

1985 **Randall Savage** & **Jackie Crosby,***Macon* (Ga.) *Telegraph and News, for their 1984 investigation of athletics and academics at the University of Georgia and Georgia Tech.*

Feature Writing

1996 **Lisa Pollak**, *Baltimore Sun*, for her story "The Umpire's Son" about baseball umpire John Hirschbeck and his son.

Commentary

1976 **Red Smith**, *NY Times*, for his 1975 columns.
1981 **Dave Anderson,** *NY Times*, for his 1980 columns.
1990 **Jim Murray**, *LA Times*, for his 1989 columns.

Photography

1949 **Nat Fein,** *NY Herald Tribune*, for his photo, "Babe Ruth Bows Out."

1952 **John Robinson** & **Don Ultang,** *Des Moines* (Iowa) *Register and Tribune, for their sequence of six pictures of the 1951 Drake-Oklahoma A&M football game, in which Drake's Johnny Bright had his jaw broken.*

1985 **The Photography Staff** of the *Orange County* (Calif.) *Register, for their coverage of the 1984 Summer Olympics in Los Angeles.*

1993 **William Snyder** & **Ken Geiger,** *The Dallas Morning News, for their coverage of the 1992 Summer Olympics in Barcelona, Spain.*

Sportswriter of the Year
NSSA Award

Presented annually since 1959 by the National Sportscasters and Sportswriters Association, based in Salisbury, N.C. Voting is done by NSSA members and selected national media.

Multiple winners: Jim Murray (14); Frank Deford (6); Rick Reilly and Red Smith (5); Will Grimsley (4); Peter Gammons (3).

Year		Year		Year	
1959	Red Smith, *NY Herald-Tribune*	1972	Jim Murray, *LA Times*	1985	Frank Deford, *Sports Ill.*
1960	Red Smith, *NY Herald-Tribune*	1973	Jim Murray, *LA Times*	1986	Frank Deford, *Sports Ill.*
1961	Red Smith, *NY Herald-Tribune*	1974	Jim Murray, *LA Times*	1987	Frank Deford, *Sports Ill.*
1962	Red Smith, *NY Herald-Tribune*	1975	Jim Murray, *LA Times*	1988	Frank Deford, *Sports Ill.*
1963	Arthur Daley, *NY Times*	1976	Jim Murray, *LA Times*	1989	Peter Gammons, *Sports Ill.*
1964	Jim Murray, *LA Times*	1977	Jim Murray, *LA Times*	1990	Peter Gammons, *Boston Globe*
1965	Red Smith, *NY Herald-Tribune*	1978	Will Grimsley, AP	1991	Rick Reilly, *Sports Ill.*
1966	Jim Murray, *LA Times*	1979	Jim Murray, *LA Times*	1992	Rick Reilly, *Sports Ill.*
1967	Jim Murray, *LA Times*	1980	Will Grimsley, AP	1993	Peter Gammons, *Boston Globe*
1968	Jim Murray, *LA Times*	1981	Will Grimsley, AP	1994	Rick Reilly, *Sports Ill.*
1969	Jim Murray, *LA Times*	1982	Frank Deford, *Sports Ill.*	1995	Rick Reilly, *Sports Ill.*
1970	Jim Murray, *LA Times*	1983	Will Grimsley, AP	1996	Rick Reilly, *Sports Ill.*
1971	Jim Murray, *LA Times*	1984	Frank Deford, *Sports Ill.*		

Best Newspaper Sports Sections of 1996

Winners of the Annual Associated Press Sports Editors contest for best daily and Sunday sports sections. Awards are divided into three different categories, based on circulation figures. Selections are made by a committee of APSE members.

Circulation Over 175,000

Top 10 Daily		Top 10 Sunday	
Atlanta Journal and Constitution	Detroit Free Press	Atlanta Journal and Constitution	Miami Herald
Boston Globe	Los Angeles Times	Boston Globe	New York Daily News
Chicago Sun-Times	Miami Herald	Chicago Tribune	New York Times
Chicago Tribune	Philadelphia Inquirer	Dallas Morning News	Philadelphia Inquirer
Dallas Morning News	Washington Post	Los Angeles Times	Washington Post

Circulation 50,000-175,000

Top 10 Daily		Top 10 Sunday	
Akron Beacon Journal	Munster (Ind.) Times	Akron Beacon Journal	Raleigh News and Observer
Daily Herald (Arlington Hgts., Ill.)	Raleigh News and Observer	Asbury Park Press	The Record (Hackensack, N.J.)
Asbury Park Press	San Francisco Examiner	Augusta (Ga.) Chronicle	San Francisco Examiner
The State (Columbia, S.C.)	The News Tribune (Tacoma, Wash.)	The State(Columbia, S.C)	The News Tribune (Tacoma, Wash.)
Fresno Bee	Vancouver (B.C.) Province	Lexington (Ky.) Herald-Leader	Wichita Eagle

Circulation Under 50,000

Top 10 Daily		Top 10 Sunday	
Aurora (Ill.) Beacon News	The Post-Star (Glens Falls, N.Y.)	Anniston (Ala.) Star	Myrtle Beach (S.C.) Sun News
The Sun Herald (Biloxi, Miss.)	La Crosse (Wis.) Tribune	Athens Daily News/Banner-Herald	Northwest Herald (Crystal Lake, Ill.)
Bremerton (Wash.) Sun	Journal and Courier (Lafayette, Ind.)	The Post Star (Glens Falls, N.Y.)	Palm Springs Desert Sun
Decatur (Ga.) Daily	Marin Independent Journal (Novata, Calif.)	Grand Forks (N.D.) Herald	Poughkeepsie (N.Y.) Journal
Gaston (N.C.) Gazette	Northwest Herald (Crystal Lake, Ill.)	The Daily Times-Call (Longmont, Colo.)	York (Pa.) Sunday News

Best Sportswriting of 1996

Winners of the Annual Associated Press Sports Editors Contest for best sportswriting in 1996. Eventual winners were chosen from five finalists in each writing division. Selections are made by a committee of APSE members. Note the investigative writing division included all three circulation categories.

Circulation over 175,000

Column:	Mitch Albom, Detroit Free Press	**Feature:**	Mitch Albom, Detroit Free Press
Enterprise:	Bob Glauber, Mark Herrmann, Greg Logan, Ivan Maisel, Shaun Powell, Manny Topol, John Valenti and Jeff Williams, Newsday	**Game Story:**	Joan Ryan, San Francisco Chronicle
		News story:	Greg Sandoval and Maryann Hudson, Los Angeles Times

Circulation 50,000-175,000

Column:	Terry Pluto, Akron Beacon Journal	**Feature:**	Mike Berardino, Augusta (Ga.) Chronicle
Enterprise:	Patricia Alex, Ken Davidoff, Raphael Hermoso, Steve Hirsch, Bill Pennington and Greg Schutta, The Record (Hackensack, N.J.)	**Game Story:**	Bill Shaikin, Riverside Press-Enterprise
		News story:	Dave Zink, Riverside Press-Enterprise

Circulation under 50,000

Column:	Eric Gongola, New Bedford (Mass.) Standard-Times	**Game Story:**	Bill Plunkett, Palm Springs Desert Sun
Enterprise:	Jim Carty, Bridgewater (N.J.) Courier-News	**News story:**	Mike Brohard, Daily Reporter-Herald (Loveland, Colo.)
Feature:	Darren Samuelsohn, Columbia Missourian		

All Categories

Investigative:	Desmond Conner, Ken Davis, Greg Garber, Mark Pazniokas, Lynne Tuohy and Thomas D. Williams, Hartford Courant

Directory of Organizations

Listing of the major sports organizations, teams and media addresses and officials as of Sept. 30, 1997.

AUTO RACING

CART
(Championship Auto Racing Teams, Inc.)
755 W. Big Beaver Rd., Suite 800, Troy, MI 48084
(248) 362-8800
President-CEO . . . . Andrew Craig
Director of Publicity . . . . Mike Zizzo

IRL
(Indy Racing League)
4565 West 16th St., Indianapolis, ID 46222
(317) 484-6526
Exec. Director & CEO . . . . Leo Mehl
Commissioner . . . . Tom Binford
Director of Public Relations . . . . Tony Trolano

FIA— Formula One
(Federation Internationale de L'Automobile)
8 Bis Rue Boissy D'anglas 75008 Paris, France
TEL: 011-33-1-4312-4455
President . . . . Max Mosley
Secretary General . . . . Pierre de Coninck
Director of Public Relations . . . . Francesco Longanesi

NASCAR
(National Assn. for Stock Car Auto Racing)
P.O. Box 2875, Daytona beach, FL 32120
(904) 253-0611
President . . . . Bill France Jr.
Director of Communications-Worldwide . . . . . . John Griffin

NHRA
(National Hot Rod Association)
2035 Financial Way, Glendora, CA 91741
(818) 914-4761
President . . . . Dallas Gardner
Director of Communications . . . . Jim Trace

MAJOR LEAGUE BASEBALL

Office of the Commissioner
350 Park Ave., 17th Floor, New York, NY 10022
(212) 339-7800
Commissioner . . . . vacant
(Fay Vincent resigned Sept. 7, 1992)
Chairman, Executive Council . . . . Bud Selig
President-COO . . . . Paul Beeston
General Counsel . . . . Thomas Ostertag
Executive Dir. of Public Relatons . . . . Rich Levin

Player Relations Committee
350 Park Ave., New York, NY 10022
(212) 339-7400
Chief Labor Negotiator . . . . Randy Levine
Associate Counsels . . . . John Westhoff
& Louis Melendez

Major League Baseball Players Association
12 East 49th St., 24th Floor, New York, NY 10017
(212) 826-0808
Exec. Director & General Counsel . . . . Donald Fehr
Special Assistant . . . . Mark Belanger

AL

American League Office
350 Park Ave., New York, NY 10022
(212) 339-7600
President . . . . Gene Budig
V.P., Admin. & Media Affairs . . . . Phyllis Merhige

Anaheim Angels
P. O. Box 2000, Anaheim, CA 92803
(714) 940-2000
Chairman . . . . Gene Autry
Minority Owner . . . . Walt Disney Co.
President & CEO . . . . Tony Tavares
V.P. & General Manager . . . . Bill Bavasi
Director of Communications . . . . Bill Robertson

Baltimore Orioles
333 West Camden St., Baltimore, MD 21201
(410) 685-9800
CEO . . . . Peter Angelos
Vice Chairman, Business & Finance . . . . Joseph Foss
General Manager . . . . Pat Gillick
Director of Public Relations . . . . John Maroon

Boston Red Sox
Fenway Park, 4 Yawkey Way, Boston, MA 02215
(617) 267-9440
General Partner . . . . Jean R. Yawkey Trust
President-CEO . . . . John Harrington
Exec. V.P. & General Manager . . . . Dan Duquette
V.P., Public Relations . . . . Dick Bresciani

Chicago White Sox
Comiskey Park, 333 W. 35th St., Chicago, IL 60616
(312) 674-1000
Chairman . . . . Jerry Reinsdorf
Vice Chairman . . . . Eddie Einhorn
Senior V.P. & General Manager . . . . Ron Schueler
Director of Public Relations . . . . Scott Reifert

Cleveland Indians
Jacobs Field, 2401 Ontario St., Cleveland, OH 44115
(216) 420-4200
Owner-Chairman-CEO . . . . Richard Jacobs
Exec. V.P. & General Manager . . . . John Hart
V.P., Public Relations . . . . Bob DiBiasio

Detroit Tigers
Tiger Stadium, 2121 Trumbull Ave., Detroit, MI 48216
(313) 962-4000
Owner-Chairman . . . . Mike Ilitch
Owner-Secretary-Treasurer . . . . Marian Ilitch
President-CEO . . . . John McHale Jr.
General Manager-VP . . . . Randy Smith
Director, Public Relations . . . . Tyler Barnes

Kansas City Royals
P.O. Box 419969, Kansas City, MO 64141
(816) 921-2200
Owner . . . . Ewing Kauffman Irrevocable Trust
Chairman-CEO . . . . David Glass
Exec. V.P. & General Manager . . . . Herk Robinson
Director of Media Relations . . . . Steve Fink

Milwaukee Brewers
County Stadium, P.O. Box 3099, Milwaukee, WI 53201
(414) 933-4114
President-CEO . . . . Bud Selig
Senior V.P., Baseball Operations . . . . Sal Bando
V.P. & General Counsel . . . . Wendy Selig-Prieb
Director of Media Relations . . . . Jon Greenberg

Minnesota Twins
Hubert H. Humphrey Metrodome
501 Chicago Ave. South, Minneapolis, MN 55415
(612) 375-1366
Owner . . . . Carl Pohlad
President . . . . Jerry Bell
V.P. & General Manager . . . . Terry Ryan
Manager of Media Relations . . . . Sean Harlin

New York Yankees
Yankee Stadium, Bronx, NY 10451
(718) 293-4300
Principal Owner ....George Steinbrenner
General Partners .... Hal Steinbrenner & Joe Molloy
V.P. & General Manager ....Bob Watson
Dir. of Media Relations/Publicity ....Rick Cerrone

Oakland Athletics
Oakland-Alameda County Coliseum
Oakland, CA 94621
(510) 638-4900
Co-Owners ....Steve Schott and Ken Hofmann
President & General Manager ....Sandy Alderson
Director of Baseball Information ....Mike Selleck

Seattle Mariners
P.O. Box 4100, Seattle, WA 98104
(206) 628-3555
Chairman-CEO ....John Ellis
President-COO ....Chuck Armstrong
V.P., Baseball Operations ....Woody Woodward
Director of Public Relations ....Dave Aust

Tampa Bay Devil Rays
Tropicana Field, One Tropicana Dr., St. Petersburg, FL 33705
(813) 825-3137
Managing General Partner ....Vincent Naimoli
General Manager ....Chuck Lamar
VP Public Relations ....Rick Vaughn

Texas Rangers
1000 Ballpark Way, Arlington, TX 76011
(817) 273-5222
General Partners ....Rusty Rose and Tom Schieffer
V.P., General Manager ....Doug Melvin
V.P., Public Relations ....John Blake

Toronto Blue Jays
SkyDome, One Blue Jays Way, Suite 3200
Toronto, Ontario M5V 1J1
(416) 341-1000
Chairman ....Sam Pollock
President-CEO ....TBA
Exec. V.P. & General Manager ....Gord Ash
Director of Public Relations ....Howie Starkman

NL

National League Office
350 Park Ave., New York, NY 10022
(212) 339-7700
President & Treasurer ....Leonard Coleman
Exec. Dir. of Public Relations ....Ricky Clemons

Arizona Diamondbacks
P.O. Box 2095, Phoenix, AZ 85001
(602) 514-8500
Chief Executive Officer ....Jerry Colangelo
President ....Rich Dozer
V.P. & General Manager ....Joe Garagiola Jr.
Media Relations Mgr. ....Bob Crawford

Atlanta Braves
P.O. Box 4064, Atlanta, GA 30302
(404) 522-7630
Owner ....Ted Turner
President ....Stan Kasten
Exec. V.P. & General Manager ....John Schuerholz
Director of Public Relations ....Jim Schultz

Chicago Cubs
1060 West Addison St., Chicago, IL 60613
(773) 404-2827
Owner ....The Tribune Company
President-CEO ....Andy MacPhail
General Manager ....Ed Lynch
Director of Media Relations ....Sharon Pannozzo

Cincinnati Reds
100 Cinergy Field, Cincinnati, OH 45202
(513) 421-4510
General Partner-President-CEO ....Marge Schott
General Manager ....Jim Bowden
Director of Media Relations ....Rob Butcher

Colorado Rockies
Coors Field, 2001 Blake St., Denver, CO 80205
(303) 292-0200
Chairman-President-CEO ....Jerry McMorris
Senior V.P. & General Manager ....Bob Gebhard
Director of Public Relations ....Mike Swanson

Florida Marlins
2267 N.W. 199th St., Miami, FL 33056
(305) 626-7400
Owner ....Wayne Huizenga
Exec. V.P. & General Manager ....Dave Dombrowski
Director of Media Relations ....Ron Colangelo

Houston Astros
The Astrodome, P.O. Box 288, Houston, TX 77001
(713) 799-9500
Chairman-CEO ....Drayton McLane Jr.
President ....Tal Smith
General Manager ....Gerry Hunsicker
Director of Media Relations ....Rob Matwick

Los Angeles Dodgers
1000 Elysian Park Ave., Los Angeles, CA 90012
(213) 224-1500
President ....Peter O'Malley
Exec. V.P. & General Manager ....Fred Claire
Director of Publicity ....Derrick Hall

Montreal Expos
P.O. Box 500, Station M, Montreal, Quebec H1V 3P2
(514) 253-3434
General Partner-President ....Claude Brochu
V.P., Baseball Operations ....Bill Stoneman
Director of Media Relations ....Peter Loyello

New York Mets
123-01 Roosevelt Ave., Flushing, NY 11368
(718) 507-6387
Chairman ....Nelson Doubleday
President-CEO ....Fred Wilpon
General Manager ....Steve Phillips
Director of Media Relations ....Jay Horwitz

Philadelphia Phillies
P.O. Box 7575, Philadelphia, PA 19101
(215) 463-6000
Managing General Partner ....Bill Giles
Senior V.P. & General Manager ....Lee Thomas
Manager, Media Relations ....Gene Dias

Pittsburgh Pirates
P.O. Box 7000, Pittsburgh, PA 15212
(412) 323-5000
Managing General Partner ....Kevin McClatchy
COO ....Richard Freeman
Senior V.P. & General Manager ....Cam Bonifay
Director of Media Relations ....Jim Trdinich

St. Louis Cardinals
250 Stadium Plaza, St. Louis, MO 63102
(314) 421-3060
Owner ....Frederick O. Hanser
President ....Mark Lamping
V.P. & General Manager ....Walt Jocketty
Director of Public Relations ....Brian Bartow

San Diego Padres
P.O. Box 2000, San Diego, CA 92112
(619) 283-4494
Chairman ....John Moores
President-CEO ....Larry Lucchino
V.P., Baseball Operations & G.M ....Kevin Towers
Director of Media Relations ....Glenn Geffner

San Francisco Giants
3Com Park at Candlestick Point, San Francisco, CA 94124
(415) 468-3700
Managing General Partner ....Peter Magowan
Senior V.P. & General Manager ....Brian Fabean
V.P. of Communications ....Bob Rose

PRO BASKETBALL

NBA

League Office
Olympic Tower, 645 Fifth Ave., New York, NY 10022
(212) 407-8000
Commissioner ....David Stern
Deputy Commissioner ....Russell Granik
V.P., Public Relations ....Brian McIntyre
Director of Media Relations ....Chris Rienza

NBA Players Association
1700 Broadway, Suite 1400, New York, NY 10019
(212) 333-7510
Exec. Dir. & Gen. Counsel ....Bill Hunter
President ....Buck Williams

Atlanta Hawks
One CNN Center, South Tower, Suite 405
Atlanta, GA 30303
(404) 827-3800
Owner ....Ted Turner
President ....Stan Kasten
General Manager ....Pete Babcock
Director of Media Relations ....Arthur Triche

Boston Celtics
151 Merrimac St., 4th Floor, Boston, MA 02114
(617) 523-6050
Chairman ....Paul Gaston
President & Head Coach ....Rick Pitino
General Manager ....Chris Wallace
Director of Public Relations ....Jeff Twiss

Charlotte Hornets
100 Hive Drive, Charlotte, NC 28217
(704) 357-0252
Owner ....George Shinn
V.P., Basketball Operations ....Bob Bass
Director of Media Relations ....Harold Kaufman

Chicago Bulls
United Center, 1901 West Madison St.
Chicago, IL 60612
(312) 455-4000
Chairman ....Jerry Reinsdorf
V.P., Basketball Operations ....Jerry Krause
Director of Media Services ....Tim Hallam

Cleveland Cavaliers
One Centre Court, Cleveland, OH 44115
(216) 420-2000
Owner-Chairman ....Gordon Gund
Owner-Vice Chairman ....George Gund III
President & General Manager ....Wayne Embry
Director of Media Relations ....Bob Zink

Dallas Mavericks
Reunion Arena, 777 Sports St., Dallas, TX 75207
(972) 988-0117
Owners   Ross Perot Jr., David McDavid & Frank Zaccanelli
General Manager ....Don Nelson
VP Communications ....Kevin Sullivan

Denver Nuggets
1635 Clay St., Denver, CO 80204
(303) 893-6700
Owner ....Ascent Ent. Group
General Manager ....Allan Bristow
Director of Media Services ....Tommy Sheppard

Detroit Pistons
The Palace of Auburn Hills
Two Championship Dr., Auburn Hills, MI 48326
(248) 377-0100
Managing Partner ....William Davidson
President ....Tom Wilson
V.P. of Player Personnel ....Rick Sund
V.P. of Public Relations ....Matt Dobek

Golden State Warriors
1221 Broadway, 20th floor, Oakland, CA 94612
(510) 986-2200
Owner-CEO ....Chris Cohan
General Manager ....Garry St. Jean
Director of Media Relations ....Eric McDowell

Houston Rockets
2 Greenway Plaza, Suite 400, Houston, TX 77046
(713) 627-3865
Owner ....Les Alexander
Sr. Exec. V.P. of Basketball Affairs ....Robert Barr
Director of Public Relations ....Tim Frank

Indiana Pacers
300 East Market St., Indianapolis, IN 46204
(317) 263-2100
Owners ....Melvin Simon & Herb Simon
President & General Manager ....Donnie Walsh
Director of Media Relations ....David Benner

Los Angeles Clippers
L.A. Sports Arena
3939 S. Figueroa St., Los Angeles, CA 90037
(213) 748-8000
Owner-Chairman ....Donald Sterling
V.P., Basketball Operations ....Elgin Baylor
Director of Communications ....Jill Wiggins

Los Angeles Lakers
Great Western Forum
3900 W. Manchester Blvd., Inglewood, CA 90305
(310) 419-3100
Owner ....Jerry Buss
Exec. V.P., Basketball Operations ....Jerry West
General Manager ....Mitch Kupchak
Director of Public Relations ....John Black

Miami Heat
Suntrust International Bldg, 1 SE 3rd Ave., Suite 2300, Miami, FL 33131
(305) 577-4328
Managing General Partner ....Micky Arison
President-Head Coach ....Pat Riley
General Manager ....Randy Pfund
Director of Media Relations ....Tim Donovan

Milwaukee Bucks
Bradley Center, 1001 N. Fourth St., Milwaukee, WI 53203
(414) 227-0500
President ....Sen. Herb Kohl (D., Wisc.)
General Manager ....Bob Weinhauer
Director of Publicity ....Bill King II

Minnesota Timberwolves
Target Center, 600 First Ave. North, Minneapolis, MN 55403
(612) 673-1600
Owner . . . . .Glen Taylor
President . . . . .Rob Moor
V.P., Basketball Operations . . . . .Kevin McHale
Dir. of Public Relations/Communications . . . . . . .Kent Wipf

New Jersey Nets
405 Murray Hill Pkwy., East Rutherford, NJ 07073
(201) 935-8888
President . . . . .Henry Taub
COO . . . . .Michael Rowe
Exec. V.P. of Bask. Ops . . . . .John Calipari
Director of Public Relations . . . . John Mertz

New York Knickerbockers
Madison Square Garden
2 Penn Plaza, 14th Floor, New York, NY 10121
(212) 465-6471
Owner . . . . .ITT Corp./Cablevision Systems Inc.
President (MSG) . . . . .Dave Checketts
Pres. (Knicks) & General Manager . . . . . . .Ernie Grunfeld
Director of Public Relations . . . . .Chris Weiller

Orlando Magic
Orlando Arena, 1 Magic Place, Orlando, FL 32801
(407) 649-3200
Owner . . . . .Rich DeVos
President . . . . .Bob Vander Weide
V.P., Basketball Ops. & GM . . . . .John Gabriel
Dir. of Publicity/Media Relations . . . . .Alex Martins

Philadelphia 76ers
CoreStates Center
Broad St. and Pattison Ave., Philadelphia, PA 19148
(215) 339-7600
Owner-President . . . . .Pat Croce
V.P., Basketball Adm. . . . . .Billy King
Personnel Director . . . . .Kevin O'Connor
Director of Public Relations . . . . Jody Silverman

Phoenix Suns
P.O. Box 1369, Phoenix, AZ 85001
(602) 379-7900
President-CEO . . . . Jerry Colangelo
V.P., Administration-G.M. . . . . .Bryan Colangelo
V.P., Dir. of Player Personnel . . . . .Dick Van Arsdale
Media Relations Director . . . . Julie Fie

Portland Trail Blazers
One Center Court, Suite 200, Portland, OR 97227
(503) 234-9291
Owner-Chairman . . . . .Paul Allen
President & General Manager . . . . .Bob Whitsitt
Director of Communications . . . . John Christensen

Sacramento Kings
One Sports Parkway, Sacramento, CA 95834
(916) 928-0000
Managing General Partner . . . . Jim Thomas
President . . . . .Rick Benner
V.P., Basketball Operations . . . . .Geoff Petrie
Director of Media Relations . . . . .Travis Stanley

San Antonio Spurs
Alamodome, 100 Montana St., San Antonio, TX 78203
(210) 554-7700
Chairman . . . . .Peter Holt
GM and Head Coach . . . . .Gregg Popovich
Director of Media Relations . . . . .Tom James

Seattle SuperSonics
190 Queen Anne Ave. N., Suite 200, Seattle, WA 98109
(206) 281-5800
Owner-Chairman . . . . .Barry Ackerley
President & General Manager . . . . .Wally Walker
Director of Media Relations . . . . .Cheri White

Toronto Raptors
20 Bay St., Suite 1702, Toronto, Ontario M5J 2N8
(416) 214-2255
President . . . . .Richard Peddie
Exec. V.P. Basketball Operations . . . . .Isiah Thomas
Comms. Mgr. . . . . .Rick Kaplan

Utah Jazz
Delta Center, 301 West South Temple
Salt Lake City, UT 84101
(801) 325-2500
Owner . . . . .Larry Miller
General Manager . . . . .Tim Howells
President . . . . .Frank Layden
Director of Media Relations . . . . .Kim Turner

Vancouver Grizzlies
General Motors Place, 800 Griffiths Way
Vancouver, B.C. V6B 6G1
(604) 899-4666
Owner . . . . .Orca Bay Sports Ent.
CEO . . . . .Arthur Griffiths
President & GM . . . . .Stu Jackson
Director of Media Relations . . . . .Steve Frost

Washington Wizards
One Harry S. Truman Dr., Landover, MD 20785
(301) 773-2255
Chairman . . . . .Abe Pollin
President . . . . .Susan O'Malley
Executive V.P. & GM .Wes Unseld
Director of Public Relations . . . . .Maureen Lewis

Other Men's Pro Leagues

Continental Basketball Assocation
400 North 5th St., Suite 1425, Phoenix, AZ 85004
(602) 254-6677
Commissioner . . . . .Steve Patterson
V.P. of Basketball Operations . . . . .Mark Munhall
V.P. of Communications .Brett Meister
   Member teams (12): Connecticut Pride, Florida
BeachDogs, Ft. Wayne (IN) Fury, Grand Rapids Hoops,
Idaho Stampede, LaCrosse Bobcats, Oklahoma City Cav-
alry, Omaha Racers, Quad City (IL) Thunder, Rockford (IL)
Lightning, Sioux Falls (SD) Skyforce, and Yakima (WA) Sun
Kings.

Women's Pro Leagues

ABL

American Basketball League
1900 Embarcadero Road, Suite 110
Palo Alto, CA 94303
(415) 856-3225
ABL Co-Founders .Steve Hams, Anne Cribbs & Gary Cavalli
V.P. of Basketball Operations . . . . .Tracey Williams
Director of Media Relations . . . . .Dean Jutilla

Atlanta Glory
2100 Powers Ferry Road., Suite 400
Atlanta, GA 30339-5144
(770) 541-9017
General Manager . . . . .D.J. Mackovets
Head Coach/Player . . . . .Teresa Edwards
Director of Media Relations . . . . .Nelson Holmberg

Colorado Xplosion
800 Grant St., Suite 410
Denver, CO 80203
(303) 832-2225
General Manager . . . . .Lark Birdsong
Head Coach . . . . .Sheryl Estes
Director of Media Relations . . . . .Tim Simmons

Columbus Quest
7451 State Route 161
Dublin, OH 43016
(614) 873-6555
General Manager/Head Coach ....Brian Agler
Director of Media Relations ....Jim Day

Long Beach StingRays
One World Trade Center, Suite 202
Long Beach, CA 90831
(562) 951-7297
General Manager ....Bill McGillis
Head Coach ....Maura McHugh
Director of Media Relations ....Linda Reid

New England Blizzard
179 Allyn St., Suite 403
Hartford, CT 06103
(860) 522-4667
General Manager ....Pam Batalis
Head Coach ..............................K.C. Jones
Director of Media Relations ....Steve Raczynski

Philadelphia Rage
143 Chestnut St., 4th Floor
Philadelphia, PA 19148
(908) 462-6272
General Manager ....Cathy Andruzzi
Head Coach ....Lisa Boyer
Director of Media Relations ....TBA

Portland Power
439 North Broadway
Portland, OR 97227
(503) 249-1130
General Manager ....Linda Weston
Head Coach ....Lin Dunn
Director of Media Relations ....Kevin Toon

San Jose Lasers
1530 Parkmoor Ave., Suite A
San Jose, CA 95128
(408) 271-1500
General Manager ....Christine Forter
Head Coach/Asst. GM ....Angela Beck
Director of Media Relations ....Shana Daum

Seattle Reign
400 Mercer St., Suite 408
Seattle, WA 98109
(206) 285-5225
General Manager ....Jim Weyermann
Head Coach ....Jacquie Hullah
Director of Media Relations ....Cindy Fester

WNBA

Women's National Basketball Association
645 5th Ave., New York, NY 10022
(212) 688-9622
President ....Val Ackerman
Director of Communications ....Alice McGillian

Charlotte Sting
2709 Water Ridge Parkway, Suite 400
Charlotte, NC 28217
(704) 424-9622
General Manager ....Mary Meadors
Head Coach ....Mary Meadors
Director of Media Relations ....Cheryl Harden

Cleveland Rockers
Gund Arena, 1 Center Court
Cleveland, OH 44115
(216) 263-7625
General Manager ....Wayne Embry
Head Coach ....Linda Hill-MacDonald
Director of Media Relations ....Lori Montgomery

Houston Comets
Two Greenway Plaza, Suite 400
Houston, TX 77046
(713) 627-9622
General Manager ....Carroll Dawson
Head Coach ....Van Chancellor
Director of Media Relations ....Tom Savage

Los Angeles Sparks
Great Western Forum, 3900 W. Manchester Blvd.
Inglewood, CA 90306
(310) 412-5000
General Manager ....Rhonda Windham
Head Coach ....Julie Rousseau
Director of Media Relations ....Raymond Ridder

New York Liberty
Two Penn Plaza
New York, NY 10121
(212) 564-9622
General Manager ....Carol Blazejowski
Head Coach ....Nancy Darsch
Director of Media Relations ....Maureen Coyle

Phoenix Mercury
America West Arena, 201 E. Jefferson
Phoenix, AZ 85004
(602) 514-8333
General Manager ....Cheryl Miller
Head Coach ....Cheryl Miller
Director of Media Relations ....Erica Calhoun

Sacramento Monarchs
ARCO Arena, One Sports Pkwy.
Sacramento, CA 95834
(916) 928-0000
General Manager ....Jerry Reynolds
Head Coach ....Heidi VanDerveer
Director of Media Relations ....Andrea Lepore

Utah Starzz
Delta Center, 301 West South Temple
Salt Lake City, UT 84101
(801) 355-3865
General Manager ....Tim Howells
Head Coach ....Denise Taylor
Director of Media Relations ....Patti Balli

BOWLING

ABC
(American Bowling Congress)
5301 South 76th St., Greendale, WI 53129
(414) 421-6400
Executive Director ....TBA
Asst. Exec. Director ....Roger Dalkin

BPAA
(Bowling Proprietors' Assn. of America)
P.O. Box 5802, Arlington, TX 76005
(817) 649-5105
Chief Exec. Officer ....Don A. Harris
President ....Charlie Brehob
Director of Public Relations ....Cary Richmond

LPBT
(Ladies Professional Bowlers Tour)
7171 Cherryvale Blvd., Rockford, IL 61112
(815) 332-5756
President ....John Falzone
Media Director ....Dan Howe

PBA
(Professional Bowlers Association)
1720 Merriman Road, P.O. Box 5118, Akron, OH 44334
(330) 836-5568
Commissioner ....Mark Gerberich
Public Relations Director ....Dave Schroeder

WIBC
(Women's International Bowling Congress, Inc.)
5301 South 76th St., Greendale, WI 53129
(414) 421-9000
President ....Joyce Deitch
Public Relations Manager ....Rory Gillespie

BOXING

IBF
(International Boxing Federation)
134 Evergreen Place, 9th Floor,
East Orange, NJ 07018
(201) 414-0300
President ....Robert (Bob) Lee
Executive Secretary ....Marian Muhammad
Champs. & Ratings Chairman ....Doug Beavers
  P.O. Box 7577, Portsmouth, VA 23707
  (804) 399-6608

WBA
(World Boxing Association)
P.O. Box 377, Maracay 2110–A
Venezuela
TEL: 011-58-44-63-1584
President ....Gilberto Mendoza
General Counsel/U.S. Spokesman ....Jimmy Binns
  1735 Market St., 39th Floor, Phila., PA 19103
  (215) 557-8000
Ratings Chairman ....Bolivar Icaza
  P.O. Box 1833, Panama 1, Rep. de Panama
  TEL: 011-507-63-5167

WBC
(World Boxing Council)
Genova 33-503, Col. Juarez,
MEXICO, 06600, D.F., Mexico
TEL: 011-525-533-3787
President ....Jose Sulaiman
Ratings Chairman ....Frank Quill
Press Information/U.S. Spokesman ....John Brister
  411 Ballentine St., Bay St. Louis, MS 39520
  (601) 467-3304

WBO
(World Boxing Organization)
1st Federal Bldg., 1056 Ave Munoz Revera,
Suite 714, P.R. 00927
(787) 756-6740
President ....Francisco Valcarcel
Championship Chairman ....John Montano
  Phoenix, Arizona
  (602) 542-1417
Ratings Chairman ....Louis Perez
  San Juan, P.R.
  (809) 258-0340

Don King Productions, Inc.
501 Fairway Dr., Deerfield Beach, FL 33441
(954) 418-5800
President ....Don King
Director of Public Relations ....Mike Marley

Top Rank
3900 Paradise Road, Suite 227, Las Vegas, NV 89109
(702) 732-2717
Chairman ....Bob Arum
Director of Marketing ....Michael Malitz

Golden Gloves Assn. of America, Inc.
8801 Princess Jeanne N.E., Albuquerque, NM 87112
(505) 298-8042
Executive Director ....Stan Gallup
President ....Chick Paris

COLLEGE SPORTS

CCA
(Collegiate Commissioners Association)
800 South Broadway, Suite 400, Walnut Creek, CA 94596
(510) 932-4411
President ....Jim Delany (Big Ten)
Exec. V.P. ....Mike Gilleran (West Coast Conf.)
Secretary-Treasurer ....David Price

NAIA
(National Assn. of Intercollegiate Athletics)
6120 South Yale, Suite 1450, Tulsa, OK 74136
(918) 494-8828
President-CEO ....Steve Baker
Public Relations Contact ....Kevin Henry

NCAA
(National Collegiate Athletic Association)
6201 College Blvd., Overland Park, KS 66211
(913) 339-1906
Chief Operating Officer ....Daniel Boggan Jr.
Executive Director ....Cedric Dempsey
Asst. Exec. Dir. for Enforcement ....David Berst
Director of Communications ....Wallace I. Renfro

WSF
(Women's Sports Foundation)
Eisenhower Park, East Meadow, NY 11554
(516) 542-4700
Executive Director ....Donna Lopiano
Public Relations Director ....Rachel Zuk

Major NCAA Conferences

See pages 437-445 for basketball coaches, football
coaches, nicknames and colors of all Division I basketball
schools and Division I-A and I-AA football schools.

ATLANTIC COAST CONFERENCE
P.O. Drawer ACC
Greensboro, NC 27417
(910) 854-8787   Founded: 1953
Commissioner ....John Swofford
Director of Media Relations ....Brian Morrison
1997-98 members: BASKETBALL & FOOTBALL (9)—
Clemson, Duke, Florida St., Georgia Tech, Maryland,
North Carolina, North Carolina St., Virginia and Wake
Forest.

Clemson University
Clemson, SC 29633   Founded: 1889
SID: (864) 656-2114   Enrollment: 16,327
President ....Deno Curris
Athletic Director ....Bobby Robinson
Sports Information Director ....Tim Baurret

Duke University
Durham, NC 27708   Founded: 1838
SID: (919) 684-2633   Enrollment: 6,085
President ....Nannerl Keohane
Athletic Director ....Tom Butters
Sports Information Director ....Mike Cragg

Florida State University
Tallahassee, FL 32316   Founded: 1857
SID: (904) 644-1403   Enrollment: 30,200
President ....Talbot (Sandy) D'Alemberte
Athletic Director ....Dave Hart Jr.
Sports Information Director ....Rob Wilson

592 BUSINESS

Georgia Tech
Atlanta, GA 30332
SID: (404) 894-5445
President ....Wayne Clough
Athletic Director ....Dave Braine
Sports Information Director ....Mike Finn

Founded: 1885
Enrollment: 13,000

University of Maryland
College Park, MD 20741
SID: (301) 314-7064
President ....William E. Kirwan
Athletic Director ....Deborah Yow
Sports Information Director ....Charles Walsh

Founded: 1807
Enrollment: 30,600

University of North Carolina
Chapel Hill, NC 27514
SID: (919) 962-2123
Chancellor ....Michael K. Hooker
Athletic Director ....Dick Baddour
Sports Information Director ....Rick Brewer

Founded: 1789
Enrollment: 24,439

North Carolina State University
Raleigh, NC 27695
SID: (919) 515-2102
Chancellor ....Larry Monteith
Athletic Director ....Les Robinson
Sports Information Director ....Joan vonThron

Founded: 1887
Enrollment: 27,169

University of Virginia
Charlottesville, VA 22903
SID: (804) 982-5500
President ....John T. Casteen III
Athletic Director ....Terry Holland
Sports Information Director ....Rich Murray

Founded: 1819
Enrollment: 18,398

Wake Forest University
Winston-Salem, NC 27109
SID: (910) 759-5640
President ....Thomas K. Hearn Jr.
Athletic Director ....Ron Wellman
Sports Information Director ....John Justus

Founded: 1834
Enrollment: 3,620

✱

BIG EAST CONFERENCE
56 Exchange Terrace
Providence, RI 02903
(401) 272-9108
Commissioner ....Mike Tranghese
Assoc. Commissioner/P.R ....John Paquette
1997-98 members: BASKETBALL (13)— Boston College, Connecticut, Georgetown, Miami-FL, Notre Dame, Pittsburgh, Providence, Rutgers, St. John's, Seton Hall, Syracuse, Villanova and West Virginia; FOOTBALL (8)— Boston College, Miami-FL, Pittsburgh, Rutgers, Syracuse, Temple, Virginia Tech and West Virginia.

Founded: 1979

Boston College
Chestnut Hill, MA 02167
SID: (617) 552-3004
President ....Rev. William P. Leahy, S.J.
Athletic Director ....TBA
Sports Information Director ....Reid Oslin

Founded: 1863
Enrollment: 8,958

University of Connecticut
Storrs, CT 06269
SID: (860) 486-3531
President ....Harry J. Hartley
Athletic Director ....Lew Perkins
Sports Information Director ....Tim Tolokan

Founded: 1881
Enrollment: 13,629

Georgetown University
Washington, DC 20057
SID: (202) 687-2492
President ....Rev. Leo J. O'Donovan, SJ
Athletic Director ....Joseph C. Lang
Sports Information Director ....Bill Shapland

Founded: 1789
Enrollment: 6,173

University of Miami
Coral Gables, FL 33124
SID: (305) 284-3244
President ....Edward T. Foote II
Athletic Director ....Paul Dee
Sports Information Director ....Bob Burda

Founded: 1926
Enrollment: 13,842

University of Notre Dame
Notre Dame, IN 46556
SID: (219) 631-7516
President ....Rev. Edward (Monk) Malloy
Athletic Director ....Michael Wadsworth
Sports Information Director ....John Heisler

Founded: 1842
Enrollment: 10,126

University of Pittsburgh
Pittsburgh, PA 15213
SID: (412) 648-8240
Chancellor ....Mark A. Nordenberg
Athletic Director ....Steve Pederson
Sports Information Director ....Ron Wahl

Founded: 1787
Enrollment: 32,187

Providence College
Providence, RI 02918
SID: (401) 865-2272
President ....Philip A. Smith, OP
Athletic Director ....John Marinatto
Sports Information Director ....Tim Connor

Founded: 1917
Enrollment: 3,596

Rutgers University
New Brunswick, NJ 08903
SID: (908) 445-4200
President ....Francis L. Lawrence
Athletic Director ....Fred Gruninger
Sports Information Director ....Pete Kowalski

Founded: 1766
Enrollment: 34,000

St. John's University
Jamaica, NY 11439
SID: (718) 990-6367
President ....Rev. Donald J. Harrington, CM
Athletic Director ....Edward J. Manetta Jr.
Sports Information Director ....Dominic Scianna

Founded: 1870
Enrollment: 17,250

Seton Hall University
South Orange, NJ 07079
SID: (201) 761-9493
Chancellor ....Rev. Thomas R. Peterson, OP
Athletic Director ....Sue Regan
Sports Information Director ....John Wooding

Founded: 1856
Enrollment: 10,538

Syracuse University
Syracuse, NY 13244
SID: (315) 443-2608
Chancellor ....Kenneth Shaw
Athletic Director ....Jake Crouthamel
Sports Information Director ....Sue Cornelius-Edson

Founded: 1870
Enrollment: 10,200

Temple University
Philadelphia, PA 19122
SID: (215) 204-7445
President ....Peter J. Liacouras
Athletic Director ....David O'Brien
Sports Information Director ....Scott Cathcart

Founded: 1884
Enrollment: 31,000

Villanova University
Villanova, PA 19085
SID: (610) 519-4120
President ....Rev. Edmund J. Dobbin, OSA
Athletic Director ....Gene DeFilippo
Sports Information Director ....Karen Frascona

Founded: 1842
Enrollment: 5,995

Virginia Tech
Blacksburg, VA 24061
SID: (540) 231-6796
President ....Paul Torgersen
Interim Athletic Director ....Sharon McCloskey
Sports Information Director ....Dave Smith

Founded: 1872
Enrollment: 23,674

West Virginia University
Morgantown, WV 26507   Founded: 1867
SID: (304) 293-2821   Enrollment: 23,000
President ....David Hardesty
Athletic Director ....Ed Pastilong
Sports Information Director ....Shelly Poe

✳

BIG 12 CONFERENCE
2201 Stemmons Fwy., 28th Floor, Dallas, TX 75207
(214) 742-1212   Founded: 1996
Commissioner ....Steve Hatchell
Service Bureau Director ....Bo Carter
  1997-98 members: BASKETBALL & FOOTBALL (12)—
Baylor, Colorado, Iowa St., Kansas, Kansas St., Missouri,
Nebraska, Oklahoma, Oklahoma St., Texas, Texas A&M
and Texas Tech.

Baylor University
Waco, TX 76711   Founded: 1845
SID: (817) 755-2743   Enrollment: 12,500
President ....Robert B. Sloan
Athletic Director ....Tom Stanton
Sports Information Director ....Maxey Parrish

University of Colorado
Boulder, CO 80309   Founded: 1876
SID: (303) 492-5626   Enrollment: 25,000
President ....Dr. John Buechner
Interim Athletic Director ....Dick Tharp
Sports Information Director ....Dave Plati

Iowa State University
Ames, IA 50011   Founded: 1858
SID: (515) 294-3372   Enrollment: 25,000
President ....Martin Jischke
Athletic Director ....Eugene Smith
Sports Information Director ....Tom Kroeschell

University of Kansas
Lawrence, KS 66045   Founded: 1866
SID: (913) 864-3417   Enrollment: 25,200
Chancellor ....Robert Hemenway
Athletic Director ....Bob Frederick
Sports Information Director ....Dean Buchan

Kansas State University
Manhattan, KS 66502   Founded: 1863
SID: (913) 532-6735   Enrollment: 20,400
President ....Jon Wefald
Athletic Director ....Max Urick
Sports Information Director ....Kent Brown

University of Missouri
Columbia, MO 65205   Founded: 1839
SID: (573) 882-3241   Enrollment: 22,483
Interim Chancellor ....Richard Wallace
Athletic Director ....Joe Castiglione
Sports Information Director ....Bob Brendel

University of Nebraska
Lincoln, NE 68588   Founded: 1869
SID: (402) 472-2263   Enrollment: 25,000
Chancellor ....Dr. James Moeser
Athletic Director ....Bill Byrne
Sports Information Director ....Chris Anderson

University of Oklahoma
Norman, OK 73019   Founded: 1890
SID: (405) 325-8231   Enrollment: 25,000
President ....David Boren
Athletic Director ....Steve Owens
Sports Information Director ....Mike Prusinski

Oklahoma State University
Stillwater, OK 74078   Founded: 1890
SID: (405) 744-5749   Enrollment: 18,500
President ....James Halligan
Athletic Director ....Terry Don Phillips
Sports Information Director ....Steve Buzzard

University of Texas
Austin, TX 78713   Founded: 1883
SID: (512) 471-7437   Enrollment: 47,719
Interim President ....Peter Flawn
Athletic Director ....De Loss Dodds
Sports Information Director ....Dave Saba

Texas A&M University
College Station, TX 77843   Founded: 1876
SID: (409) 845-5725   Enrollment: 43,031
President ....Ray Bowen
Athletic Director ....Wally Groff
Sports Information Director ....Alan Cannon

Texas Tech University
Lubbock, TX 79409   Founded: 1923
SID: (806) 742-2770   Enrollment: 25,000
President ....John Montford
Athletic Director ....Gerald Myers
Sports Information Director ....Richard Kilwein

✳

BIG TEN CONFERENCE
1500 West Higgins Road
Park Ridge, IL 60068-6300
(847) 696-1010   Founded: 1895
Commissioner ....Jim Delany
Dir. of Information Services ....Dennis LaBissonier
  1997-98 members: BASKETBALL & FOOTBALL (11)—
Illinois, Indiana, Iowa, Michigan, Michigan St., Minnesota,
Northwestern, Ohio St., Penn St., Purdue and Wisconsin.

University of Illinois
Champaign, IL 61820   Founded: 1867
SID: (217) 333-1390   Enrollment: 36,000
President ....James J. Stukel
Athletic Director ....Ron Guenther
Dir. of Communications ....Dave Johnson

Indiana University
Bloomington, IN 47405   Founded: 1820
SID: (812) 855-9399   Enrollment: 36,000
President ....Myles Brand
Athletic Director ....Clarence Doninger
Sports Information Director ....Kit Klingelhoffer

University of Iowa
Iowa City, IA 52242   Founded: 1847
SID: (319) 335-9411   Enrollment: 27,597
President ....Mary Sue Coleman
Athletic Director ....Bob Bowlsby
Sports Information Director ....Phil Haddy

University of Michigan
Ann Arbor, MI 48109   Founded: 1817
SID: (313) 763-1381   Enrollment: 36,617
President ....Lee Bollinger
Athletic Director ....Tom Goss
Sports Information Director ....Bruce Madej

Michigan State University
East Lansing, MI 48824   Founded: 1855
SID: (517) 355-2271   Enrollment: 41,545
President ....Peter McPherson
Athletic Director ....Merritt J. Norvell Jr.
Sports Information Director ....John Lewandowski

594 BUSINESS

University of Minnesota
Minneapolis, MN 55455 — Founded: 1851
SID: (612) 625-4090 — Enrollment: 38,000
President ....Mark Yudof
Athletic Director ....Dr. Mark Dienhart
Sports Information Director ....Marc Ryan

Northwestern University
Evanston, IL 60208 — Founded: 1851
SID: (847) 491-7503 — Enrollment: 7,400
President ....Henry S. Bienen
Athletic Director ....Rick Taylor
Sports Information Director ....Brad Hurlbut

Ohio State University
Columbus, OH 43210 — Founded: 1870
SID: (614) 292-6861 — Enrollment: 49,542
President ....E. Gordon Gee
Athletic Director ....Andy Geiger
Sports Information Director ....Steve Snapp

Penn State University
University Park, PA 16802 — Founded: 1855
SID: (814) 865-1757 — Enrollment: 38,200
President ....Graham Spanier
Athletic Director ....Tim Curley
Sports Information Director ....Jeff Nelson

Purdue University
West Lafayette, IN 47907 — Founded: 1869
SID: (317) 494-3202 — Enrollment: 35,156
President ....Steven C. Beering
Athletic Director ....Morgan Burke
Sports Information Director ....Mark Adams

University of Wisconsin
Madison, WI 53711 — Founded: 1848
SID: (608) 262-1811 — Enrollment: 40,300
Chancellor ....David Ward
Athletic Director ....Pat Richter
Sports Information Director ....Steve Malchow

✳

BIG WEST CONFERENCE
2 Corporate Park, Suite 206
Irvine, CA 92606
(714) 261-2525 — Founded: 1969
Commissioner ....Dennis Farrell
Director of Information ....Dennis Bickmeier
1997-98 members: BASKETBALL (12)— Boise St.,
CS-Fullerton, Cal Poly-SLO, Idaho, Long Beach St., Nevada,
New Mexico St., North Texas, Pacific, UC-Irvine, UC-Santa
Barbara, Utah St.; FOOTBALL (6)— Boise St., Idaho,
Nevada, New Mexico St., North Texas, Utah St.

Boise State
Boise, ID 83725 — Founded: 1932
SID: (208) 385-1515 — Enrollment: 15,060
President ....Charles P. Ruch
Athletic Director ....Gene Bleymaier
Sports Information Director ....Max Corbet

Cal State-Fullerton
Fullerton, CA 92834 — Founded: 1957
SID: (714) 278-3970 — Enrollment: 24,000
President ....Milton A. Gordon
Athletic Director ....John Easterbrook
Sports Information Director ....Mel Franks

Cal Poly SLO
San Luis Obispo, CA 93407 — Founded: 1901
SID: (805) 756-6531 — Enrollment: 17,000
President ....Dr. Warren J. Baker
Athletic Director ....John McCutcheon
Sports Information Director ....Jason Sullivan

University of Idaho
Moscow, ID 83844 — Founded: 1889
SID: (208) 885-0211 — Enrollment: 13,000
President ....Bob Hoover
Athletic Director ....Oval Jaynes
Sports Information Director ....Beck Pavll

Long Beach State
Long Beach, CA 90840 — Founded: 1949
SID: (562) 985-8569 — Enrollment: 27,431
President ....Robert Maxson
Athletic Director ....Bill Shumard
Sports Information Director ....Steve Janisch

University of Nevada
Reno, NV 89557 — Founded: 1874
SID: (702) 784-4600 — Enrollment: 12,500
President ....Joe Crowley
Athletic Director ....Chris Ault
Sports Information Director ....Paul Stuart

New Mexico State University
Las Cruces, NM 88003 — Founded: 1888
SID: (505) 646-3929 — Enrollment: 15,165
President ....Michael Orenduff
Athletic Director ....Jim Paul
Sports Information Director ....Steve Shutt

University of North Texas
Denton, TX 76203 — Founded: 1890
SID: (817) 565-2664 — Enrollment: 26,400
President ....Dr. Alfred F. Hurley
Athletic Director ....Craig Helwig
Sports Information Director ....Sean Johnson

University of the Pacific
Stockton, CA 95211 — Founded: 1851
SID: (209) 946-2479 — Enrollment: 6,000
President ....Donald DeRosa
Athletic Director ....Michael McNeely
Sports Information Director ....Mike Millerick

University of California, Irvine
Irvine, CA 92697 — Founded: 1962
SID: (714) 824-5814 — Enrollment: 17,889
Chancellor ....Laurel Wilkening
Athletic Director ....Dan Guerrero
Sports Information Director ....Bob Olson

University of California, Santa Barbara
Santa Barbara, CA 93106 — Founded: 1944
SID: (805) 893-3428 — Enrollment: 18,200
Chancellor ....Henry Yang
Athletic Director ....Gary Cunningham
Sports Information Director ....Bill Mahoney

Utah State University
Logan, UT 84322 — Founded: 1888
SID: (801) 797-1361 — Enrollment: 19,861
President ....George Emert
Athletic Director ....Chuck Bell
Sports Information Director ....Mike Strauss

✳

CONFERENCE USA
35 East Wacker Drive, Suite 650, Chicago, IL 60601
(312) 553-0483 — Founded: 1995
Commissioner ....Mike L. Slive
Director of Creative Services ....Erika Amstadt
1997-98 members: BASKETBALL (12)— Alabama-
Birmingham, Cincinnati, DePaul, Houston, Louisville, Mar-
quette, Memphis, NC-Charlotte, Saint Louis, South Florida,
Southern Miss and Tulane; FOOTBALL (7)— Cincinnati, East
Carolina, Houston, Louisville, Memphis, Southern Miss and
Tulane.
New in 1998-99: FOOTBALL (1)— Army

DIRECTORY

595

University of Alabama-Birmingham
Birmingham, AL 35294
SID: (205) 934-0722
President ....W. Ann Reynolds
Athletic Director ....Gene Bartow
Sports Information Director ....Grant Shingleton
Founded: 1969
Enrollment: 16,156

University of Cincinnati
Cincinnati, OH 45221
SID: (513) 556-5191
President ....Joseph A. Steger
Athletic Director ....Gerald O'Dell
Sports Information Director ....Tom Hathaway
Founded: 1819
Enrollment: 36,000

DePaul University
Chicago, IL 60614
SID: (773) 325-7525
President ....Rev. John P. Minogue
Athletic Director ....Bill Bradshaw
Sports Information Director ....John Lanctot
Founded: 1898
Enrollment: 17,133

East Carolina University
Greenville, NC 27858
SID: (919) 328-4522
Chancellor ....Richard Eakin
Athletic Director ....Mike Hamrick
Sports Information Director ....Norm Reilly
Founded: 1907
Enrollment: 18,000

University of Houston
Houston, TX 77204
SID: (713) 743-9404
President ....Arthur Smith
Athletic Director ....Chet Gladchuk
Sports Information Director ....Donna Turner
Founded: 1927
Enrollment: 30,757

University of Louisville
Louisville, KY 40292
SID: (502) 852-6581
President ....John W. Shumaker
Athletic Director ....Bill Olsen
Sports Information Director ....Kenny Klein
Founded: 1798
Enrollment: 22,000

Marquette University
Milwaukee, WI 53233
SID: (414) 288-7447
President ....Rev. Robert A. Wild S.J.
Athletic Director ....Bill Cords
Sports Information Director ....Kathleen Hohl
Founded: 1881
Enrollment: 10,750

Memphis University
Memphis, TN 38152
SID: (901) 678-2337
President ....V. Lane Rawlins
Athletic Director .........................R.C. Johnson
Sports Information Director ....Bob Winn
Founded: 1912
Enrollment: 21,500

University of North Carolina-Charlotte
Charlotte, NC 28223
SID: (704) 547-4937
Chancellor ....J. H. Woodward
Athletic Director ....Judy Rose
Sports Information Director ....Tom Whitestone
Founded: 1946
Enrollment: 15,895

Saint Louis University
St. Louis, MO 63103
SID: (314) 977-2524
President ....Rev. Lawrence Biondi
Athletic Director ....Doug Woolard
Sport Information Director ....Doug McIlhagga
Founded: 1818
Enrollment: 11,000

University of South Florida
Tampa, FL 33620
SID: (813) 974-4086
President ....Betty Castor
Atheltic Director ....Paul Griffin
Sports Information Director ....John Gerdes
Founded: 1956
Enrollment: 37,000

University of Southern Mississippi
Hattiesburg, MS 39406
SID: (601) 266-4503
President ....Horace W. Fleming Jr.
Athletic Director ....Bill McLellan
Sports Information Director ....Regiel Napier
Founded: 1910
Enrollment: 14,000

Tulane University
New Orleans, LA 70118
SID: (504) 865-5506
President ....Eamon M. Kelly
Athletic Director ....Sandy Barbour
Sports Information Director ....Lenny Vangilder
Founded: 1834
Enrollment: 10,800

✳

MID-AMERICAN CONFERENCE
Four SeaGate, Suite 102, Toledo, OH 43604
(419) 249-7177
Commissioner ....Jerry Ippoliti
Director of Communications ....Tom Lessig
Founded: 1946

1997-98 members: BASKETBALL & FOOTBALL (12)—
Akron, Ball St., Bowling Green, Central Michigan, Eastern
Michigan, Kent, Marshall, Miami-OH, Northern Illinois,
Ohio University, Toledo and Western Michigan.

University of Akron
Akron, OH 44325
SID: (330) 972-7468
President ....Marion Ruebel
Athletic Director ....Mike Bobinski
Sports Information Director ....Jeff Brewer
Founded: 1870
Enrollment: 25,098

Ball State University
Muncie, IN 47306
SID: (317) 285-8242
President ....John Worthen
Athletic Director ....Andrea Seger
Sports Information Director ....Joe Hernandez
Founded: 1918
Enrollment: 19,115

Bowling Green State University
Bowling Green, OH 43403
SID: (419) 372-7075
President ....Sidney Ribeau
Athletic Director ....Ron Zwierlein
Sports Information Director ....Steve Barr
Founded: 1910
Enrollment: 17,000

Central Michigan University
Mt. Pleasant, MI 48859
SID: (517) 774-3277
President ....Leonard Plachta
Athletic Director ....Herb Deromedi
Sports Information Director ....Fred Stabley Jr.
Founded: 1892
Enrollment: 16,435

Eastern Michigan University
Ypsilanti, MI 48197
SID: (313) 487-0317
President ....William Shelton
Athletic Director ....Tim Weiser
Sports Information Director ....Jim Streeter
Founded: 1849
Enrollment: 24,000

Kent State University
Kent, OH 44242
SID: (330) 672-2110
President ....Carol Cartwright
Athletic Director ....Laing Kennedy
Sports Information Director ....Dale Gallagher
Founded: 1910
Enrollment: 29,862

Marshall University
Huntington, WV 25715
SID: (304) 696-4660
President ....J. Wade Gilley
Athletic Director ....Lance West
Sports Information Director ....Clark Haptonstall
Founded: 1837
Enrollment: 13,000

Miami University
Oxford, OH 45056
Founded: 1809
SID: (513) 529-4327
Enrollment: 16,000
President ....James C. Garland
Athletic Director ....Eric Hyman
Sports Information Director ....John Estes

Northen Illinois University
DeKalb, IL 60115
Founded: 1895
SID: (815) 753-1706
Enrollment: 21,609
President .... John LaTourette
Athletic Director ....Cary Groth
Sports Information Director ....Michael Korcek

Ohio University
Athens, OH 45701
Founded: 1804
SID: (614) 593-1298
Enrollment: 19,000
President ....Robert Glidden
Athletic Director ....Tom Boeh
Sports Information Director ....George Mauzy

University of Toledo
Toledo, OH 43606
Founded: 1872
SID: (419) 530-3790
Enrollment: 21,692
President ....Frank E. Horton
Athletic Director ....Pete Liske
Sports Information Director ....Rod Brandt

Western Michigan University
Kalamazoo, MI 49008
Founded: 1903
SID: (616) 387-4138
Enrollment: 26,537
President ....Diether Haenicke
Athletic Director ....Jim Weaver
Sports Information Director ....John Beatty

✳

PACIFIC-10 CONFERENCE
800 South Broadway, Suite 400
Walnut Creek, CA 94596
(510) 932-4411
Founded: 1915
Commissioner ....Thomas Hansen
Asst. Commissioner, Public Relations ....Jim Muldoon
1997-98 members: BASKETBALL & FOOTBALL (10)—
Arizona, Arizona St., California, Oregon, Oregon St.,
Stanford, UCLA, USC, Washington and Washington St.

University of Arizona
Tucson, AZ 85721
Founded: 1885
SID: (520) 621-4163
Enrollment: 35,306
President ....Peter Likins
Athletic Director ....Jim Livengood
Sports Information Director ....Tom Duddleston

Arizona State University
Tempe, AZ 85287
Founded: 1885
SID: (602) 965-6592
Enrollment: 42,600
President ....Lattie F. Coor
Athletic Director ....Kevin White
Sports Information Director ....Mark Brand

University of California
Berkeley, CA 94720
Founded: 1868
SID: (510) 642-5363
Enrollment: 30,000
Chancellor ....Robert Berdahl
Athletic Director ....John Kasser
Sports Information Director ....Kevin Reneau

University of Oregon
Eugene, OR 97401
Founded: 1876
SID: (541) 346-5488
Enrollment: 16,600
President ....David Frohnmeyer
Athletic Director ....Bill Moos
Co-Sports Information Directors ....Jamie Klund
& Dave Williford

Oregon State University
Corvallis, OR 97331
Founded: 1868
SID: (541) 737-3720
Enrollment: 14,500
President ....Paul G. Risser
Athletic Director ....TBA
Sports Information Director ....Hal Cowan

Stanford University
Stanford, CA 94305
Founded: 1891
SID: (415) 723-4418
Enrollment: 13,075
President ....Gerhard Casper
Athletic Director ....Ted Leyland
Sports Information Director ....Gary Migdol

UCLA— Univ. of California, Los Angeles
Los Angeles, CA 90024
Founded: 1919
SID: (310) 206-6831
Enrollment: 34,000
Chancellor ....Albert Carnesale
Athletic Director ....Pete Dalis
Sports Information Director ....Marc Dellins

USC— Univ. of Southern California
Los Angeles, CA 90089
Founded: 1880
SID: (213) 740-8480
Enrollment: 27,970
President ....Steven Sample
Athletic Director ....Mike Garrett
Sports Information Director ....Tim Tessalone

University of Washington
Seattle, WA 98195
Founded: 1861
SID: (206) 543-2230
Enrollment: 25,000
President ....Richard McCormick
Athletic Director ....Barbara Hedges
Sports Information Director ....Jim Daves

Washington State University
Pullman, WA 99164
Founded: 1890
SID: (509) 335-0270
Enrollment: 19,500
President ....Samuel Smith
Athletic Director ....Rick Dickson
Sports Information Director ....Rod Commons

✳

SOUTHEASTERN CONFERENCE
2201 Civic Center Blvd.
Birmingham, AL 35203
(205) 458-3010
Founded: 1933
Commissioner ....Roy Kramer
Director of Communications ....Charles Bloom
1997-98 members: BASKETBALL & FOOTBALL (12)—
Alabama, Arkansas, Auburn, Florida, Georgia, Kentucky,
LSU, Mississippi, Mississippi St., South Carolina, Tennessee
and Vanderbilt.

University of Alabama
Tuscaloosa, AL 35487
Founded: 1831
SID: (205) 348-6084
Enrollment: 19,400
President ....Dr. Andrew Sorensen
Athletic Director ....Robert Bockrath
Sports Information Director ....Larry White

University of Arkansas
Fayetteville, AR 72701
Founded: 1871
SID: (501) 575-2751
Enrollment: 14,700
Chancellor ....John White
Athletic Director ....Frank Broyles
Sports Information Director ....Rick Schaeffer

Auburn University
Auburn, AL 36831
Founded: 1856
SID: (334) 844-9800
Enrollment: 22,122
President ....William V. Muse
Athletic Director ....David Housel
Sports Information Director ....Kent Partridge

University of Florida
Gainesville, FL 32604
SID: (904) 375-4683 ext. 6100
Founded: 1853
Enrollment: 40,000
President ....John Lombardi
Athletic Director ....Jeremy Foley
Sports Information Director ....John Humenik

University of Georgia
Athens, GA 30603
SID: (706) 542-1621
Founded: 1785
Enrollment: 28,383
President ....Michael F. Adams
Athletic Director ....Vince Dooley
Sports Information Director ....Claude Felton

University of Kentucky
Lexington, KY 40506
SID: (606) 257-3838
Founded: 1865
Enrollment: 24,200
President ....Charles T. Wethington Jr.
Athletic Director ........................C.M. Newton
Sports Information Director ....Rena Vicini

LSU— Louisiana State University
Baton Rouge, LA 70894
SID: (504) 388-8226
Founded: 1860
Enrollment: 26,851
Chancellor ....William L. Jenkins
Athletic Director ....Joe Dean
Sports Information Director ....Herb Vincent

University of Mississippi
U. of M., MS 38677
SID: (601) 232-7522
Founded: 1848
Enrollment: 12,542
Chancellor ....Dr. Robert C. Khayat
Athletic Director ....Pete Boone
Sports Information Director ....Langston Rogers

Mississippi State University
Starkville, MS 39762
SID: (601) 325-2703
Founded: 1878
Enrollment: 13,557
President ....Donald Zacharias
Athletic Director ....Larry Templeton
Sports Information Director ....Mike Nemeth

University of South Carolina
Columbia, SC 29208
SID: (803) 777-5204
Founded: 1801
Enrollment: 26,700
President ....John Palms
Athletic Director ....Mike McGee
Sports Information Director ....Kerry Tharp

University of Tennessee
Knoxville, TN 37916
SID: (423) 974-1212
Founded: 1794
Enrollment: 25,489
President ....Joe Johnson
Athletic Director ....Doug Dickie
Sports Information Director ....Bud Ford

Vanderbilt University
Nashville, TN 37212
SID: (615) 322-4121
Founded: 1873
Enrollment: 5,600
Chancellor ....Joe B. Wyatt
Athletic Director ....Todd Turner
Sports Information Director ....Rod Williamson

✱

WESTERN ATHLETIC CONFERENCE
9250 East Costilla Ave., Suite 300
Englewood, CO 80112
(303) 799-9221
Commissioner ....Karl Benson
Directors of Communications .....Dave Chaffin & Lisa Vad
Founded: 1962
1997-98 members: BASKETBALL & FOOTBALL (16)—
Air Force, BYU, Colorado St., Fresno St., Hawaii, New
Mexico, Rice, San Diego St., San Jose St., SMU, TCU,
Tulsa, UNLV, Utah, UTEP and Wyoming.

U.S. Air Force Academy
US Academy, CO 80840
SID: (719) 333-2313
Founded: 1959
Enrollment: 4,100
Superintendent ....Lt. Gen. Tad Oelstrom
Athletic Director ....Col. Randall W. Spetman
Sports Information Director ....Dave Kellogg

Brigham Young University
Provo, UT 84602
SID: (801) 378-4911
Founded: 1875
Enrollment: 27,000
President ....Merril J. Bateman
Athletic Director ....Rondo Fehlberg
Sports Information Director ....Ralph Zobell

Colorado State University
Fort Collins, CO 80523
SID: (970) 491-5067
Founded: 1870
Enrollment: 21,600
President ....Albert Yates
Athletic Director ....Tom Jurich
Sports Information Director ....Gary Ozzello

Fresno State University
Fresno, CA 93740
SID: (209) 278-2509
Founded: 1911
Enrollment: 18,900
President ....John D. Welty
Athletic Director ....Al Bohl
Sports Information Director ....Dave Haglund

University of Hawaii
Honolulu, HI 96822
SID: (808) 956-7523
Founded: 1907
Enrollment: 19,062
President ....Kenneth Mortimer
Athletic Director ....Hugh Yoshida
Interim Sports Information Director ....Lois Manin

University of New Mexico
Albuquerque, NM 87131
SID: (505) 277-2026
Founded: 1889
Enrollment: 22,890
President ....Richard Peck
Athletic Director ....Rudy Davalos
Sports Information Director ....Greg Remington

Rice University
Houston, TX 77005
SID: (713) 527-4077
Founded: 1912
Enrollment: 2,600
President ....Malcolm Gillis
Athletic Director ....Bobby May
Sports Information Director ....Bill Cousins

San Diego State University
San Diego, CA 92182
SID: (619) 594-5547
Founded: 1897
Enrollment: 29,000
President ....Stephen L. Weber
Athletic Director ....Rick Bay
Sports Information Director ....John Rosenthal

San Jose State University
San Jose, CA 95192
SID: (408) 924-1217
Founded: 1857
Enrollment: 27,000
President ....Robert Caret
Athletic Director ....Tom Brennan
Sports Information Director ....Lawrence Fan

SMU— Southern Methodist University
Dallas, TX 75275
SID: (214) 768-2883
Founded: 1911
Enrollment: 9,464
President ....R. Gerald Turner
Athletic Director ....Jim Copeland
Sports Information Director ....Jon Jackson

TCU— Texas Christian University
Fort Worth, TX 76129
SID: (817) 921-7969
Founded: 1873
Enrollment: 6,986
Chancellor ....William Tucker
Athletic Director ....Frank Windegger
Sports Information Director ....Glen Stone

University of Tulsa

Tulsa, OK 74104
Founded: 1894
SID: (918) 631-2395
Enrollment: 4,300
President ....Dr. Bob Lawless
Athletic Director ....Judy MacLeod
Sports Information Director ....Don Tomkalski

University of Utah

Salt Lake City, UT 84112
Founded: 1850
SID: (801) 581-3510
Enrollment: 27,100
Interim President ....Jerilyn McIntyre
Athletic Director ....Chris Hill
Sports Information Director ....Liz Able

UNLV— University of Nevada, Las Vegas

Las Vegas, NV 89154
Founded: 1957
SID: (702) 895-3207
Enrollment: 20,200
President ....Carol Harter
Athletic Director ....Charles Cavognaro
Sports Information Director ....Jim Gemma

UTEP— University of Texas at El Paso

El Paso, TX 79968
Founded: 1914
SID: (915) 747-5330
Enrollment: 15,389
President ....Diana Natalicio
Athletic Director ....John Thompson
Sports Information Director ....Gary Richter

University of Wyoming

Laramie, WY 82071
Founded: 1886
SID: (307) 766-2256
Enrollment: 11,200
President ....Philip Dubois
Athletic Director ....Lee Moon
Sports Information Director ....Kevin McKinney

✳

MAJOR INDEPENDENTS
Division I-A football independents in 1997.

University of Alabama-Birmingham

Birmingham, AL 35294
Founded: 1969
SID: (205) 934-0722
Enrollment: 16,165
President ....W. Ann Reynolds
Athletic Director ....Gene Bartow
Sports Information Director ....Grant Shingleton

Arkansas State University

State University, AR 72467
Founded: 1909
SID: (501) 972-2541
Enrollment: 9,818
President ....Les Wyatt
Athletic Director ....Barry Dowd
Sports Information Director ....Gina Bowman

Army— U.S. Military Academy

West Point, NY 10996
Founded: 1802
SID: (914) 938-3303
Enrollment: 4,000
Superintendent ....Lt. Gen. Daniel W. Christman
Athletic Director ....Al Vanderbush
Sports Information Director ....Bob Beretta

University of Central Florida

Orlando, FL 32816
Founded: 1963
SID: (407) 823-2256
Enrollment: 28,000
President ....Dr. John C. Hitt
Athletic Director ....Steve Sloan
Sports Information Director ....John Marini

East Carolina University

Greenville, NC 27858
Founded: 1907
SID: (919) 328-4522
Enrollment: 17,500
Chancellor ....Richard R. Eakin
Athletic Director ....Mike Hamrick
Sports Information Director ....Norm Reilly

Louisiana Tech University

Ruston, LA 71272
Founded: 1894
SID: (318) 257-3144
Enrollment: 9,667
President ....Dan Reneau
Athletic Director ....Jim Oakes
Sports Information Director ....Byron Avery

Navy— U.S. Naval Academy

Annapolis, MD 21402
Founded: 1845
SID: (410) 268-6226
Enrollment: 4,100
Superintendent ....Adm. Charles R. Larson
Athletic Director ....Jack Lengyel
Sports Information Director ....Scott Strasemeier

Northeast Louisiana University

Monroe, LA 71209
Founded: 1931
SID: (318) 342-5460
Enrollment: 11,107
President ....Lawson Swearingen, Jr.
Athletic Director ....Richard Giannini
Sports Information Director ....Robby Edwards

Northern Illinois University

DeKalb, IL 60115
Founded: 1895
SID: (815) 753-1706
Enrollment: 21,609
President ....John E. LaTourette
Athletic Director ....Cary Groth
Sports Information Director ....Mike Korcek

University of Notre Dame

Notre Dame, IN 46556
Founded: 1842
SID: (219) 631-7516
Enrollment: 10,126
President ....Rev. Edward (Monk) Malloy
Athletic Director ....Michael Wadsworth
Sports Information Director ....John Heisler

University of Southwestern Louisiana

Lafayette, LA 70506
Founded: 1898
SID: (318) 482-6331
Enrollment: 17,000
President ....Ray Authement
Athletic Director ....Nelson Schexnayder
Sports Information Director ....Dan McDonald

✳

OTHER MAJOR DIVISION I CONFERENCES
Conferences that play either Division I basketball or Division I-AA football, or both.

America East
(formerly North Atlantic Conference)
10 High St., Suite 860
Boston, MA 02110
(617) 695-6369
Founded: 1979
Commissioner ....Chris Monasch
Director of Communications ....Matt Bourque
1997-98 members: BASKETBALL (10)— Boston University, Delaware, Drexel, Hartford, Hofstra, Maine, New Hampshire, Northeastern, Towson and Vermont.

Female Athletic Directors

As of Sept. 1, 1997, there were 19 female athletic directors at the nation's 305 NCAA Div. I schools. Here they are (in alphabetical order): Eve Atkinson, Lafayette; Sandy Barbour, Tulane; Judith Davidson, CS-Sacramento; Vivian L. Fuller, NE Illinois; Cary Groth, N. Illinois; Barbara Hedges, Washington; Judy Macleod, Tulsa; Sharon McCloskey (interim), Virginia Tech; Marilyn McNeil, Monmouth; Patricia Meiser-McKnett, Hartford; Mary Pankowski (interim), Florida Int'l; Judith Ray, New Hampshire; Sue Regan, Seton Hall; Judy Rose, NC-Charlotte; Andrea Seger, Ball St.; Helen Smiley, W. Illinois; Suzanne Tyler, Maine; Carrol Williams, Santa Clara; Deborah Yow, Maryland.

DIRECTORY 599

Atlantic 10 Conference
2 Penn Center Plaza, Suite 1410
Philadelphia, PA 19102   Founded: 1976
(215) 751-0500   A-10 Football founded 1997.
Commissioner ....Linda Bruno
Director of Communications ....Ray Cella
  1997-98 members: BASKETBALL (12)— Dayton, Duquesne, Fordham, George Washington, La Salle, Massachusetts, Rhode Island, St. Bonaventure, St. Joseph's-PA, Temple, Virginia Tech and Xavier-OH. FOOTBALL (12)— Boston University, Connecticut, Delaware, James Madison, Maine, Massachusetts, New Hampshire, Northeastern, Rhode Island, Richmond, Villanova and William & Mary.

Big Sky Conference
P.O. Box 1459
Ogden, UT 84402
(801) 392-1978, ext. 2   Founded: 1963
Commissioner ....Douglas Fullerton
Director of Information ....Ron Loghry
  1997-98 members: BASKETBALL & FOOTBALL (9)— Cal St. Northridge, Cal. St. Sacramento, Eastern Washington, Idaho St., Montana, Montana St., Northern Arizona, Portland St. and Weber St.

Big South Conference
Winthop Colisem
Rock Hill, SC 29733
(803) 817-6340   Founded: 1983
Commissioner ....Kyle Kallander
Director of Media Relations ....Shannon Fritts
  1997-98 members: BASKETBALL (7)— Charleston Southern, Coastal Carolina, Liberty, MD-Baltimore County, NC-Asheville, Radford, and Winthrop.

Colonial Athletic Association
8625 Patterson Ave.
Richmond, VA 23229
(804) 754-1616   Founded: 1985
Commissioner ....Tom Yeager
Sports Information Director ....Steve Vehorn
  1997-98 members: BASKETBALL (9)— American, East Carolina, George Mason, James Madison, NC-Wilmington, Old Dominion, Richmond, Virginia Commonwealth and William & Mary.

Gateway Football Conference
1000 Union Station, Suite 333
St. Louis, MO 63103
(314) 421-2268   Founded: 1985
Commissioner ....Patty Viverito
Asst. Commissioner, Information ....Mike Kern
  1997 members (7): Illinois St., Indiana St., Northern Iowa, Southern Illinois, SW Missouri St., Western Illinois and Youngstown St..

Ivy League
120 Alexander Street
Princeton, NJ 08544
(609) 258-6426   Founded: 1954
Executive Director ....Jeffrey Orleans
Director of Information ....Chuck Yrigoyen
  1997-98 members: BASKETBALL & FOOTBALL (8)— Brown, Columbia, Cornell, Dartmouth, Harvard, Pennsylvania, Princeton and Yale.

Metro Atlantic Athletic Conference
1090 Amboy Avenue
Edison, NJ 08837
(908) 225-0202   Founded: 1980
Commissioner ....Richard Ensor
Director of Media Relations ....Mike Scala
  1997-98 members: BASKETBALL (10)— Canisius, Fairfield, Iona, Loyola-MD, Manhattan, Marist, Niagara, Rider, St. Peter's and Siena. FOOTBALL (9)— Canisius, Duquesne, Fairfield, Georgetown, Iona, Marist, St. John's, St. Peter's and Siena.

Mid-Continent Conference
40 Shuman Blvd., Suite 118
Naperville, IL 60563
(630) 416-7560   Founded: 1982
Commissioner ....Jon Steinbrecher
Director of Media Relations ....Mark Simpson
  1997-98 members: BASKETBALL (9)— Buffalo, Chicago St., Missouri/K.C., Oral Robert, NE Illinois, Southern Utah, Valparaiso, Western Illinois, Youngstown St.

Mid-Eastern Athletic Conference
102 North Elm St. SE Building, Suite 401
Greensboro, NC 27401
(910) 275-9961   Founded: 1970
Commissioner ....Charles S. Harris
Director of Media Relations ....Larry Barber
  1997-98 members: BASKETBALL (10)— Bethune-Cookman, Coppin St., Delaware St., Florida A&M, Hampton, Howard, MD-Eastern Shore, Morgan St., North Carolina A&T and South Carolina St.; FOOTBALL (8)— all but Coppin St. and MD-Eastern Shore.

Midwestern Collegiate Conference
201 South Capitol Ave., Suite 500
Indianapolis, IN 46225
(317) 237-5622   Founded: 1979
Commissioner ....John LeCrone
Director of Communications ....Terry Powers
  1997-98 members: BASKETBALL (8)— Butler, Cleveland St., Detroit Mercy, Illinois-Chicago, Loyola-IL, Wisconsin- Green Bay, Wisconsin-Milwaukee and Wright St.

Missouri Valley Conference
1000 St. Louis Union Station, Suite 105
St. Louis, MO 63103
(314) 421-0339   Founded: 1907
Commissioner ....Doug Elgin
Asst. Commissioner ....Jack Watkins
  1997-98 members: BASKETBALL (10)— Bradley, Creighton, Drake, Evansville, Illinois St., Indiana St., Northern Iowa, Southern Illinois, SW Missouri St., and Wichita St.

Northeast Conference
220 Old New Brunswick Rd.
Piscataway, NJ 08854
(908) 562-0877   Founded: 1981
Commissioner ....John Lamarino
Asst. Commissioner, Media Relations .....Denise Gormley
  1997-98 members: BASKETBALL (9)— Cent. Conn. St., Fairleigh Dickinson, LIU-Brooklyn, Monmouth, Mount St. Mary's, Robert Morris, St. Francis-NY, St. Francis-PA and Wagner. FOOTBALL (5)—Cent. Conn. St., Monnouth, Robert Morris, St. Francis (PA) and Wagner.

Ohio Valley Conference
278 Franklin Road, Suite 103
Brentwood, TN 37027
(615) 371-1698   Founded: 1948
Commissioner ....Dan Beebe
Director of Information ....Rob Washburn
  1997-98 members: BASKETBALL & FOOTBALL (10)— Austin Peay St., Eastern Illinois, Eastern Kentucky, Middle Tennessee St., Morehead St., Murray St., SE Missouri St., Tennessee-Martin, Tennessee St. and Tennessee Tech.

Division I Hockey Conferences
The four Division I hockey conferences are the Eastern Collegiate Athletic Conference (ECAC) in Centerville, Mass., (508) 771-5060; the Central Collegiate Hockey Assn. (CCHA) in Ann Arbor, Mich. (313) 764-2590; Hockey East in Lawrence, Mass., (508) 687-8535 and the Western Collegiate Hockey Assn. in Madison, Wisc. (608) 829-0100.

Patriot League
3897 Adler Place, Building C, Suite 310
Bethlehem, PA 18017
(610) 691-2414   Founded: 1984
Executive Director ....Constance Hurlbut
Director of Information ....Todd Newcomb
    1997-98 members: BASKETBALL (7)— Army, Bucknell, Colgate, Holy Cross, Lafayette, Lehigh and Navy; FOOTBALL (7)— Bucknell, Colgate, Fordham, Holy Cross, Lafayette, Lehigh and Towson.

Pioneer Football League
1000 St. Louis Union Station, Suite 105
St. Louis, MO 63103
(314) 421-0339   Founded: 1993
Commissioner ....Patty Viverito
Media Relations ....Cindy Kern
    1997 members: FOOTBALL (6): Butler, Dayton, Drake, Evansville, San Diego and Valparaiso.

Southern Conference
1 West Pack Square, Suite 1508
Asheville, NC 28801
(704) 255-7872   Founded: 1921
Commissioner ....Wright Waters
Asst. Commissioner, Media Relations ....Heather Czeczok
    1997-98 members: BASKETBALL (11)— Appalachian St., The Citadel, Davidson, East Tennessee St., Furman, Georgia Southern, NC-Greensboro, Tennessee-Chattanooga, VMI, Western Carolina and Wofford; FOOTBALL (9)—all except Davidson and NC-Greensboro.

Southland Conference
8150 North Central Expressway, Suite 930
Dallas, TX 75206
(214) 750-7522   Founded: 1963
Commissioner ....Greg Sankey
Director of Media Relations ....Tommy Newsome
    1997-98 members: BASKETBALL (10)— McNeese St., Nicholls St., North Texas, NE Louisiana, Northwestern St., Sam Houston St., SE Louisiana, Southwest Texas St., Stephen F. Austin St., Texas-Arlington and Texas-San Antonio; FOOTBALL (8)— Jacksonville St., McNeese St., Nicholls St., Northwestern St., Sam Houston St., Southwest Texas St., Stephen F. Austin St. and Troy St.

Southwestern Athletic Conference
1500 Sugar Bowl Drive, Superdome
New Orleans, LA 70112
(504) 523-7574   Founded: 1920
Commissioner ....James Frank
Director of Publicity ....Lonza Hardy Jr.
    1997-98 members: BASKETBALL & FOOTBALL (8)— Alabama St., Alcorn St., Grambling St., Jackson St., Mississippi Valley St., Prairie View A&M, Southern-Baton Rouge and Texas Southern.

Sun Belt Conference
One Galleria Boulevard, Suite 2115
Metairie, LA 70001
(504) 834-6600   Founded: 1976
Commissioner ....Craig Thompson
Director of Media Services ....Dayna Wells
    1997-98 members: BASKETBALL (10)— Arkansas-Little Rock, Arkansas St., Jacksonville, Lamar, Louisiana Tech, New Orleans, South Alabama, SW Louisiana, Texas-Pan American and Western Kentucky.

And Then There Were Two

    With the Yankee Conference being absorbed by the Atlantic 10 in 1997, only two football-only conferences remain: The Gateway Football Conference and the Pioneer Football Conference.

Trans America Athletic Conference
The Commons, 3370 Vineville Ave., Suite 108-B,
Macon, GA 31204
(912) 474-3394   Founded: 1978
Commissioner ....Bill Bibb
Director of Information ....Tom Snyder
    1997-98 members: BASKETBALL (12)— Campbell, Centenary, Central Florida, College of Charleston, Florida Atlantic, Florida International, Georgia St., Jacksonville St., Mercer, Samford, SE Louisiana and Stetson.

West Coast Conference
400 Oyster Point Blvd., Suite 221
South San Francisco, CA 94080
(415) 873-8622   Founded: 1952
Commissioner ....Michael Gilleran
Director of Information ....Don Ott
    1997-98 members: BASKETBALL (8)— Gonzaga, Loyola Marymount, Pepperdine, Portland, St. Mary's, San Diego, San Francisco and Santa Clara.

PRO FOOTBALL

National Football League

League Office
280 Park Ave., New York, NY 10017
(212) 450-2000
Commissioner ....Paul Tagliabue
President ....Neil Austrian
Exec. V.P. & League Counsel ....Jeff Pash
Director of Information, AFC ....Leslie Hammond
Director of Information, NFC ....Reggie Roberts

NFL Management Council
280 Park Ave., New York, NY 10017
(212) 450-2000
Chairman ....Harold Henderson
V.P. & General Counsel ....Dennis Curran

NFL Players Association
2021 L Street NW, Suite 600, Washington, DC 20036
(202) 463-2200
Executive Director ....Gene Upshaw
Asst. Exec. Director ....Doug Allen
General Counsel ....Richard Berthelsen
Director of Public Relations ....Frank Woschitz

AFC

Baltimore Ravens
11001 Owings Mills Blvd.
Owings Mills, MD 21117
(410) 654-6200
Owner-President ....Art Modell
Exec. V.P., Legal & Administration ....Jim Bailey
V.P., Assistant to President ....David Modell
V.P., Public Relations ....Kevin Byrne

Buffalo Bills
One Bills Drive, Orchard Park, NY 14127
(716) 648-1800
Owner-President ....Ralph Wilson
Exec. V.P. & General Manager ....John Butler
V.P. & Head Coach ....Marv Levy
Director of Media Relations ....Scott Berchtold

Cincinnati Bengals
200 Riverfront Stadium, Cincinnati, OH 45202
(513) 621-3550
Chairman ....Austin Knowlton
President & General Manager ....Mike Brown
Public Relations Director ....Jack Brennan

Denver Broncos
13655 Broncos Parkway, Englewood, CO 80112
(303) 649-9000
Owner-President-CEO ....Pat Bowlen
General Manager ....John Beake
Director of Media Relations ....Jim Saccomano

Indianapolis Colts
P.O. Box 535000, 7001 W 56th St., Indianapolis, IN 46253
(317) 297-2658
Owner-President-CEO-GM ....Jim Irsay
V.P., Football Operations ....Bill Tobin
Director of Public Relations ....Craig Kelley

Jacksonville Jaguars
One Stadium Place, Jacksonville, FL 32202
(904) 633-6000
Chairman-CEO-President ....Wayne Weaver
Sr. V.P., Football Operations ....Michael Huyghue
Exec. Director of Communications ....Dan Edwards

Kansas City Chiefs
1528 Commerce Bank Building
1000 Walnut St., Kansas City, MO 64106
(816) 924-9300
Owner-Founder ....Lamar Hunt
Chairman ....Jack Steadman
President-CEO-General Manager ....Carl Peterson
Director of Public Relations ....Bob Moore

Miami Dolphins
7500 SW 30th St., Davie, FL 33314
(954) 452-7000
Owner-Chairman ....Wayne Huizenga
President & COO ....Eddie Jones
Director of Media Relations ....Harvey Greene

New England Patriots
Foxboro Stadium, Route 1, Foxboro, MA 02035
(508) 543-8200
Owner-President-CEO & General Manager .....Bob Kraft
Dir. of Player Personnel ....Bobby Grier
Director of Public Relations ....Don Lowery

New York Jets
1000 Fulton Ave., Hempstead, NY 11550
(516) 560-8100
Owner-Chairman ....Leon Hess
President ....Steve Gutman
General Manager & Head Coach ....Bill Parcells
Director of Public Relations ....Frank Ramos

Oakland Raiders
1220 Harborbay Parkway, Alameda, CA 94502
(510) 864-5000
Managing General Partner ....Al Davis
Executive Assistant ....Al LoCasale
Publications Director ....Mike Taylor

Pittsburgh Steelers
300 Stadium Circle, Pittsburgh, PA 15212
(412) 323-0300
Owner-President ....Dan Rooney
Vice Presidents ....John McGinley & Art Rooney Jr.
Media Relations Coordinator ....Rob Boulware

San Diego Chargers
Jack Murphy Stadium, Box 609609
San Diego, CA 92108
(619) 874-4500
Owner-Chairman ....Alex Spanos
President -Vice Chairman ....Dean Spanos
General Manager ....Bobby Beathard
Director of Public Relations ....Bill Johnston

Seattle Seahawks
11220 NE 53rd Street, Kirkland, WA 98033
(206) 827-9777
Owner ....Paul Allen
President ....Bob Whitsitt
Public Relations Director ....Dave Neubert

Tennessee Oilers
P.O. Box 198497, Nashville, TN 37219
(713) 881-3500
Owner-President ...................K.S. (Bud) Adams Jr.
Exec. V.P. & General Manager ....Floyd Reese
Director of Media Services ....Dave Pearson

NFC

Arizona Cardinals
P.O. Box 888, Phoenix, AZ 85001
(602) 379-0101
Owner-President ....Bill Bidwill
Assistants to the President .....Bob Ferguson, Joe Wooley
Public Relations Director ....Paul Jensen

Atlanta Falcons
One Falcon Place, Suwanee, GA 30024
(770) 945-1111
Owner-Chairman ....Rankin Smith Sr.
President ....Taylor Smith
V.P., Player Personnel ....Ken Herock
Director of Public Relations ....Charlie Taylor

Carolina Panthers
800 South Mint St., Charlotte, NC 28202-1502
(704) 358-7000
Founder-Owner ....Jerry Richardson
President ....Mark Richardson
General Manager ....Bill Polian
Director of Communications ....Charlie Dayton

Chicago Bears
Halas Hall, 250 N. Washington, Lake Forest, IL 60045
(847) 295-6600
Owner-Chairman ....Edward McCaskey
President-CEO ....Mike McCaskey
V.P., Football Operations ....Ted Phillips
Director of Public Relations ....Bryan Harlan

Dallas Cowboys
Cowboys Center
One Cowboys Parkway, Irving, TX 75063
(972) 556-9900
Owner-President-GM ....Jerry Jones
Public Relations Director ....Rich Dalrymple

Detroit Lions
Pontiac Silverdome
1200 Featherstone Rd., Pontiac, MI 48342
(810) 335-4131
Owner-President ....William Clay Ford
Executive V.P. & COO ....Chuck Schmidt
Director of Media Relations ....Mike Murray

Green Bay Packers
1265 Lombardi Ave., P.O. Box 10628, Green Bay, WI 54307
(414) 496-5700
President-CEO ....Bob Harlan
Exec. V.P. & General Manager ....Ron Wolf
Exec. Dir. of Public Relations ....Lee Remmel

Minnesota Vikings
9520 Viking Drive, Eden Prairie, MN 55344
(612) 828-6500
Owner-Chairman ....John Skoglund
President-CEO ....Roger Headrick
V.P., Team Operations ....Jeff Diamond
Director of Public Relations ....David Pelletier

New Orleans Saints
5800 Airline Highway, Metairie, LA 70003
(504) 733-0255
Owner-President ....Tom Benson
Exec. VP & General Manager ....Bill Kuharich
V.P. & Head Coach ....Mike Dikta
Director of Media Relations ....Greg Bensel

New York Giants
Giants Stadium, East Rutherford, NJ 07073
(201) 935-8111
President/co-CEO ....Wellington Mara
Chairman/co-CEO ....Preston Robert Tisch
Sr. V.P. & General Manager ....George Young
Director of Public Relations ....Pat Hanlon

Philadelphia Eagles
Veterans Stadium, Broad St. & Pattison Ave.
Philadelphia, PA 19148
(215) 463-2500
Owner ....Jeff Lurie
Director of Football Administration ....Dick Daniels
Director of Public Relations ....Ron Howard

St. Louis Rams
One Rams Way, St. Louis, MO 63045
(314) 982-7267
Owner-Chairman ....Georgia Frontiere
President ....John Shaw
V.P., Football Operations ....Lynn Stiles
Director of Public Relations ....Rick Smith

San Francisco 49ers
4949 Centennial Blvd., Santa Clara, CA 95054
(408) 562-4949
Owner ....Edward DeBartolo Jr.
President ....Carmen Policy
V.P., Football Operations ....Dwight Clark
Director of Public Relations ....Rodney Knox

Tampa Bay Buccaneers
1 Buccaneer Place, Tampa, FL 33607
(813) 870-2700
Owner-President ....Malcolm Glazer
General Manager ....Rich McKay
Director of Public Relations ....Reggie Roberts

Washington Redskins
Redskin Park, P.O. Box.17247, Washington D.C. 20041
(703) 478-8900
Owner-President ....John Kent Cooke
General Manager ....Charley Casserly
Director of Public Relations ....Mike McCall

Canadian Football League

League Office
CFL Building, 110 Eglinton Avenue West, 5th Floor
Toronto, Ontario M4R 1A3
(416) 322-9650
Chairman .... John Tory
V.P., Football Operations ....Ed Chalupka
Manager of Communications ....Jim Neish

CFL Players Association
467 Speers Rd., Unit 5, Oakville, Ontario L6K 3S4
(905) 844-7852
President ....Dan Ferrone
Legal Counsel ....Ed Molstad

British Columbia Lions
10605 135th St., Surrey, B.C. V3T 4C8
(604) 930-5466
Owner ....David Braylay
President & CEO ....Glen Ringdal
Dir. of Media/Public Relations ....Jim Dorash

Calgary Stampeders
McMahon Stadium, 1817 Crowchild Trail, NW
Calgary, Alberta T2M 4R6
(403) 289-0205
Owner-President ....Sig Gutsche
General Manager & Head Coach ....Wally Buono
Media Relations Coordinator ....Ron Rooke

Edmonton Eskimos
9023 111th Ave., Edmonton, Alberta T5B 0C3
(403) 448-1525
Owner ....Community-owned
President ....Ken Bailey
General Manager ....Hugh Campbell
Asst. General Manager of Adm. ....Allan Watt

Hamilton Tiger-Cats
75 Balsam Ave., Hamilton, Ontario L8L 8C1
(905) 947-2418
Chairman ....David M. Macdonald
General Manager ....Neil Lumsden
Communications Director ....Norm Miller

Montreal Alouettes
4545 Avenue Pierre-De Coubertin
P.O. Box 65, Station M
Montreal, Quebec H1V 3L6
(514) 254-2400
Owner ....Robert Welenhall
President & CEO ....Larry Smith
Dir. of Football Ops/GM ....Jim Popp
Dir. of Media/Public Relations ....Christian Hassen

Saskatchewan Roughriders
2940 — 10th Avenue, P.O. Box 1277
Regina, Saskatchewan S4P 3B8
(306) 569-2323
Owner ....Community-owned
President ....Fred Wagman
CEO & General Manager ....Alan Ford
Media Coordinator ....Tony Playter

Toronto Argonauts
SkyDome Gate 3, Suite 1300, P.O. Box 2005, Station B
Toronto, Ontario M5T 3H8
(416) 341-5151
Owners ....Labatt Brewing Co.
CEO ....Paul Beesten
President ....Bob Nicholson
General Manager & Head Coach ....Don Matthews
V.P., Business Ops. ....Dave Watkins

Winnipeg Blue Bombers
1465 Maroons Road, Winnipeg, Manitoba R3G 0L6
(204) 784-2583
Owner ....Community-owned
President ....Lynn Bishop
Dir. Football Operations & Head Coach ......Cal Murphy
Manager of Media Relations ................J.D. Boyd

WLAF

World League of American Football
26-A Albemarle St.
London, England W1X 3FA
TEL: 011-44-171-355-1995
President ....Oliver Luck
Public Relations Contact ....Alastair MacPhail
    Member teams (6): Amsterdam Admirals, Barcelona
Dragons, Frankfurt Galaxy, London Monarchs, Rhein Fire
(Dusseldorf), Scottish Claymores (Edinburgh).

Arena Football League
75 E Wacker, Suite 400
Chicago, IL 60601
(312) 332-5510
Commissioner ....C. David Baker
Director, Media Services ....David Cooper
   Member teams (15): American Conference— Anaheim Piranhas, Arizona Rattlers, Iowa Barnstormers, Milwaukee Mustangs, Portland (OR) Forest Dragons, San Jose Sabrecats and Texas Terror. National Conference— Albany (NY) Firebirds, Florida Bob Cats, Nashville Kats, New Jersey Red Dogs, New York Cityhawks, Orlando Predators and Tampa Bay Storm. Expansion— Miami

GOLF

LPGA Tour
(Ladies' Professional Golf Association)
100 International Golf Drive
Daytona Beach, FL 32114
(904) 274-6200
Commissioner .... Jim Ritts
Deputy Commissioner ....Jim Webb
Director of Communications ....Elaine Scott

PGA of America
100 Avenue of the Champions
Palm Beach Gardens, FL 33418
(407) 624-8400
President ....Ken Lindsay
CEO ....Jim Awtrey
Director of Communications ....Terry McSweeney

PGA European Tour
Wentworth Drive, Virginia Water
Surrey, England GU25 4LX
TEL: 011-44-1344-842881
Executive Director ....Ken Schofield
Director of Communications ....Mitchell Platts

PGA Tour
112 TPC Blvd., Ponte Vedra, FL 32082
(904) 285-3700
Commissioner ....Tim Finchem
Director of Information ....Dave Lancer

Royal & Ancient Golf Club of St. Andrews
St. Andrews, Fife, Scotland KY16 9JD
TEL: 011-44-1334-472112
Secretary ....Michael Bonallack
Deputy Secretary ....George Wilson

USGA
(United States Golf Association)
P.O. Box 708, Liberty Corner Road, Far Hills, NJ 07931
(908) 234-2300
President ....Judy Bell
Executive Director ....David Fay
Director of Communications ....Marty Parkes

PRO HOCKEY

NHL

National Hockey League
Commissioner ....Gary Bettman
Senior V.P., Hockey Operations ....Brian Burke
Senior V.P., COO ....Stephen Solomon
V.P., Public Relations ....Arthur Pincus

League Offices

Montreal
1800 McGill College Ave., Suite 2600
Montreal, Quebec H3A 3J6
(514) 288-9220

New York
251 Sixth Ave., 47th Floor
New York, NY 10020
(212) 789-2000

Toronto
75 International Blvd., Suite 300
Rexdale, Ontario M9W 6L9
(416) 798-0809

NHL Players' Association
777 Bay St., Suite 2400, P.O. Box 121
Toronto, Ontario M5G 2C8
(416) 408-4040
Executive Director ....Bob Goodenow
Associate Counsel ....Ian Pulver,
                      J.P. Barry and Jeff Citron

Anaheim, Mighty Ducks of
Arrowhead Pond of Anaheim, P.O. Box 61077
Anaheim, CA 92806
(714) 704-2700
Owner ....Walt Disney Co.
President & Governor ....Tony Tavares
General Manager ....Jack Ferreira
Director of Public Relations ....Bill Robertson

Boston Bruins
1 FleetCenter, Suite 250, Boston, MA 02114
(617) 624-1909
Owner ....Jeremy Jacobs
President & General Manager ....Harry Sinden
Director of Media Relations ....Heidi Holland

Buffalo Sabres
Marine Midland Arena, 1 Seymour H. Knox III Plaza,
Buffalo, NY 14203-3096
(716) 855-4100
President-CEO ....Larry Quinn
General Manager ....Darcy Regrier
Director of Public Relations ....John Isherwood

Calgary Flames
Canadian Airlines Saddledome, P.O. Box 1540 Station M
Calgary, Alberta T2P 3B9
(403) 777-2177
Owners ......Harley Hotchkiss, Grant A. Bartlett, Murray
Edwards, Ronald V. Joyce, Alvin G. Libin, Allan P. Markin,
                      J.R. McCaig, Byron and Daryl Seamen
President & CEO ....Ron Bremner
V.P. & General Manager ....Al Coates
Asst., Director of Public Relations ....Kathy Geick

Carolina Hurricanes
5000 Aerial Center Pkwy., Suite 100
Morrisville, NC 27560
(919) 467-7825
Owner-CEO ....Peter Karmanos Jr.
General Partner ....Thomas Thewes
President & General Manager ....Jim Rutherford
Director of Public Relations ....Chris Brown

Chicago Blackhawks
United Center, 1901 West Madison St.
Chicago, IL 60612
(312) 455-7000
Owner-President ....William Wirtz
General Manager ....Bob Murray
V.P. of Public Relations ....Jim DeMaria

Colorado Avalanche
1635 Clay St., Denver, CO 80204
(303) 893-6700
Owner ....Ascent Entertainment
President ....Charlie Lyons
Exec. V.P., Hockey Operations & GM. ......Pierre Lacroix
Director of Media Relations ....Jean Martineau

Dallas Stars
211 Cowboys Parkway, Irving, TX 75063
(972) 868-2890
Owner ....Thomas O. Hicks
General Manager ....Bob Gainey
Director of Public Relations ....Larry Kelly

Detroit Red Wings
Joe Louis Arena, 600 Civic Center Drive
Detroit, MI 48226
(313) 396-7544
Owner/President ....Mike Ilitch
Owner/Secretary-Treasurer ....Marian Ilitch
General Manager ....Ken Holland
Dir. of Player Personnel & Head Coach ....Scotty Bowman
Public Relations Coordinators ..Karen Davis & Tony Lasher

Edmonton Oilers
11230 110th St., 2nd Flr.
Edmonton, Alberta, T56 368
(403) 474-8561
Owner ....Peter Pocklington
President & General Manager ....Glen Sather
Exec. V.P. & Assistant GM ....Bruce MacGregor
Director of Public Relations ....Bill Tuele

Florida Panthers
100 North East Third Ave., 2nd Floor
Fort Lauderdale, FL 33301
(954) 768-1900
Owner ....Wayne Huizenga
President ....Bill Torrey
General Manager ....Bryan Murray
Dir. of Public & Media Relations ....Mike Hanson

Los Angeles Kings
Great Western Forum, 3900 West Manchester Blvd.
Inglewood, CA 90305
(310) 419-3160
Majority Owners ....Philip Anschutz and Ed Roski
President ....Tim Leiweke
General Manager ....Dave Taylor
Director of Public Relations ....Mike Altieri

Montreal Canadiens
Molson Centre, 1260 Gauchetière St. West
Montreal, Quebec H3B 5E8
(514) 932-2582
Owner ....Molson Companies, Ltd.
Chairman-President ....Ronald Corey
General Manager ....Rejean Houle
Director of Communications ....Don Beauchamp

New Jersey Devils
Continental Airlines Arena
P.O. Box 504, East Rutherford, NJ 07073
(201) 935-6050
Chairman ....John McMullen
President & General Manager ....Lou Lamoriello
Director of Public Relations ....Michael Gilbert

New York Islanders
Nassau Veterans' Memorial Coliseum
Uniondale, NY 11553
(516) 794-4100
Owner ....John Pickett
V.P. & General Manager ....Mike Milbury
Director of Media Relations ....Ginger Killian

New York Rangers
2 Penn Plaza, 14th Floor, New York, NY 10121
(212) 465-6486
Owner ....Cablevision Systems Inc.
President (MSG) ....Dave Checketts
President & General Manager ....Neil Smith
Director of Communications ....John Rosasco

Ottawa Senators
1000 Palladium Dr., Kanata, Ontario, K2V 1A5
(613) 721-0115
Chairman & Gov. ....Rod Bryden
President & CEO ....Roy Mlaker
General Manager ....Pierre Gauthier
Director of Media Relations ....Phil Legault

Philadelphia Flyers
1 CoreStates Complex, Philadelphia, PA 19148
(215) 465-4500
Chairman ....Ed Snider
President & General Manager ....Bob Clarke
V.P. of Public Relations ....Mark Piazza

Phoenix Coyotes
1 Renaissance Square, 2 North Central, Suite 1930
Phoenix, AZ 85004
(602) 379-2800
Owners ....Richard Burke & Steven Gluckstern
COO ....Shawn Hunter
General Manager ....Bobby Smith
Director of Media Relations ....Richard Nairn

Pittsburgh Penguins
Civic Arena, Pittsburgh, PA 15219
(412) 642-1800
Owners ....Roger Marino & Howard Baldwin
Exec. V.P. & General Manager ....Craig Patrick
V.P., Communications ....Thomas McMillan

St. Louis Blues
Kiel Center, 1401 Clark Ave., St. Louis, MO 63103
(314) 622-2500
President-CEO ....Mark Sauer
General Manager ....Larry Pleau
Director of Public Relations ....Jeff Trammel

San Jose Sharks
525 West Santa Clara St., San Jose, CA 95113
(408) 287-7070
Owner-Chairman ....George Gund III
Co-Owner ....Gordon Gund
President-CEO ....Greg Jamison
Exec. V.P.& Dir. of Hockey Operations ....Dean Lombardi
Director of Media Relations ....Ken Arnold

Tampa Bay Lightning
401 Channelside Drive, Tampa, FL 33602
(813) 229-2658
Owners ....Lightning Partners, Inc.
General Manager ....Phil Esposito
Director of Hockey Development & Scouting .Tony Esposito
V.P., Communications ....Gerry Helper

Toronto Maple Leafs
Maple Leaf Gardens
60 Carlton Street, Toronto, Ontario M5B 1L1
(416) 977-1641
Chairman-CEO ....Steve Stavro
President-GM ....Ken Dryden
Assoc. GM ....Mike Smith
Media Relations Coordinator ....Pat Park

Vancouver Canucks
General Motors Place, 800 Griffiths Way
Vancouver, B.C. V6B 6G1
(604) 899-4600
Owner-Vice Chairman ....John McCaw Jr.
Vice Chairman & Alt. Governor ....Arthur Griffiths
President & General Manager ....Pat Quinn
Dir. of Public & Media Relations ....Steve Tambellini

Washington Capitals
USAir Arena, Landover, MD 20785
(301) 386-7000
Chairman ....Abe Pollin
President ,...............................Dick Patrick
V.P. & General Manager ....George McPhee
V.P. of Communications ....Matt Williams

American Hockey League
425 Union St., W. Springfield, MA 01089
(413) 781-2030
President ....David Andrews
Sr. V.P. of Operations ....Gordon Anziano

International Hockey League
1577 N. Woodward Ave., Suite 212 Bloomfield Hills, MI 48304
(810) 258-0580
Commissioner ....Robert P. Uter
V.P., Public Relations ....Tim Bryant

IIHF

International Ice Hockey Federation
Parkring 11
CH-8002 Zurich, Switzerland
TEL: 011-411-289-8600
President ....Rene Fasel
General Secretary ....Jan-Ake Edvinsson
PR/Marketing Mgr. ....Kimmo Leinonen

HORSE RACING

Breeders' Cup Limited
2525 Harrodsburg Road, Suite 500
Lexington, KY 40504
(606) 223-5444
President ...........................D.G. Van Clief, Sr.
Executive Director ..................D.G. Van Clief, Jr.
Director of Communications ....Dan Metzger

National Museum of Racing and Hall of Fame
191 Union Ave., Saratoga Springs, NY 12866
(518) 584-0400
Executive Director ....Peter Hammell
Assistant Director ....Catherine Maguire

The Jockeys' Guild
250 West Main Street, Suite 1820, Lexington, KY 40507
(606) 259-3211
President ....Gary Stevens
National Manager ....John Giovanni

TRA
(Thoroughbred Racing Associations of N. America, Inc.)
420 Fair Hill Drive, Suite 1, Elkton, MD 21921
(410) 392-9200
President ....Clifford C. Goodrich
Executive V.P ....Chris Scherf
Director of Services ....Conrad Sobkowiak

TRC
(Thoroughbred Racing Communications)
40 East 52nd Street, New York, NY 10022
(212) 371-5910
Executive Director ....Tom Merritt
Director of Media Relations ....Bob Curran

USTA
(United States Trotting Association)
750 Michigan Ave., Columbus, OH 43215
(614) 224-2291
President ....Corwin Nixon
Executive V.P ....Fred Noe
Director of Public Relations ....John Pawlak

MEDIA

PERIODICALS

Sports Illustrated
Time & Life Bldg., Rockefeller Center
New York, NY 10020
(212) 522-1212
Publisher ....David Long
Managing Editor ....William Colson
Executive Editor ....Peter Carry

The Sporting News
10176 Corporate Square Dr., Suite 200
St. Louis, MO 63132
(314) 997-7111
Editor .... John Rawlings

USA Today
1000 Wilson Blvd., Arlington, VA 22229
(703) 276-3400
Owner ....Gannett Co.
President-Publisher ....Tom Curley
Managing Editor/Sports ....Monte Lorell

WIRE SERVICES

Associated Press
50 Rockefeller Plaza, New York, NY 10020
(212) 621-1630
Sports Editor ....Terry Taylor
Deputy Sports Editor ....Brian Friedman

United Press International
1500 H Street, Washington, DC 20005
(202) 898-8000
Sports Editor ....Ian Love

The Sports Network
95 James Way, Suite 107 & 109
Southampton, PA 18966
(215) 942-7890
President ....Mickey Charles
Director of Operations ....Phil Sokol
Managing Editor ....Bill Shearer

Sportsticker
600 Plaza Two, Harborside Financial Ctr., Jersey City, NJ 07311
(201) 309-1200
Vice President & General Manager ....Rick Alessandri
Managing Editor ....Doug Mittler

TV NETWORKS

ABC Sports
47 West 66th St., 13th Floor, New York, NY 10023
(212) 456-4867
President ....Steve Bornstein
Senior V.P., Production ....Steve Anderson
Director of Information ....Mark Mandel

CBC Sports
P.O. Box 500, Station A 5H 100
Toronto, Ontario M5W 1E6
(416) 205-6523
Head of Sports ....Alan Clark
Sr. Executive Producer ....Joe Darling
Publicist ....Susan Proctor

Classic Sports Network
300 Park Ave. South, 6th Floor, New York, NY 10010
(212) 529-8000
President ....Steve Greenberg
Executive Producer ....Douglas Warshaw
V.P. Marketing ....Bert Gould

CBS Sports

51 West 52nd St., 25th Floor, New York, NY 10019
(212) 975-5230
President ....Sean McManus
Senior V.P., Production ....Terry Ewert
Senior V.P., Programming ....Tony Petitti
Director of Public Relations ....Leslie Ann Wade

ESPN

ESPN Plaza, Bristol, CT 06010
(860) 585-2000
President-CEO ....Steve Bornstein
Sr. V.P., Programming ....John Wildhack
Sr. V.P. & Executive Editor ....John Walsh
Managing Editor, ESPN2 ....Vince Doria
Director of Communications ....Mike Soltys

FOX Sports

5746 Sunset Blvd., Los Angeles, CA 90028
(212) 556-2472
President ....David Hill
Exec. Producer ....Ed Goren
V.P., Media Relations (NYC) ....Vince Wladika

The Golf Channel

7580 Commerce Center Drive, Orlando, FL 32819
(407) 363-4653
President-CEO ....Joe Gibbs
V.P., Production ....Mike Whelan
Director of Public Relations ....Debra Sweeney

HBO Sports

1100 Ave. of the Americas, New York, NY 10036
(212) 512-1987
President-CEO ....Seth Abraham
V.P., Executive Producer ....Ross Greenburg
Sr. V.P., Programming ....Lou DiBella
Director of Publicity ....Ray Stallone

MTV Sports

1633 Broadway, 32nd Floor, New York, NY 10024
(212) 846-4684
Executive Producer ....Patrick Byrnes
Publicity Contact ....Sheryl Jones

NBC Sports

30 Rockefeller Plaza, New York, NY 10112
(212) 664-2160
President ....Dick Ebersol
Executive Producer ....Tommy Roy
Director of Public Relations ....Ed Markey

Prime SportsChannel Networks

3 Crossways Park West
Woodbury, NY 11797
(516) 921-3764
CEO ....James Dolan
COO ....Josh Sapan
V.P., Programming ....Michael Lardner
Communications Manager ....Rich Burg

TSN-The Sports Network

2225 Shepherd Ave. East, Suite 100
Willowdale, Ontario, M2J-5C2
(416) 494-1212
President & General Manager ....Rick Brace
Public Relations Manager ....Rosemary Pitfield

Turner Sports

One CNN Center, 13th Floor, Atlanta, GA 30303
(404) 827-1735
President ....Dr. Harvey Schiller
Vice President ....Mike Pearl
Sr. V.P., Programming ....Kevin O'Malley
V.P. of Public Relations ....Greg Hughes

Univision (Spanish)

9405 NW 41st St., Miami, FL 33178
(305) 471-4008
Sports Director ....Jorge Hidalgo
Publicity Coordinator ....Rosalyn Sariol

USA Network

1230 Ave. of the Americas, New York, NY 10020
(212) 408-9100
V.P., Production in Sports ....Gordon Beck
V.P., Sports Programming ....Wayne Becker
Dir. of Media Relations ....David Schwarz

OLYMPICS

IOC
(International Olympic Committee)

Chateau de Vidy, CH-1007 Lausanne, Switzerland
TEL: 011-41-21-621-6111
President ....Juan Antonio Samaranch
Director General ....Francois Carrard
Secretary General ....Francoise Zweifel
Coordinator, Public Information ....Fekrou Kidane
Director of Information ....Michele Verdier

1998 WINTER GAMES
Nagano Olympic Organizing Committee

KT Building, 3109-63 Kawaishinden
Nagano City 380, Japan
TEL: 011-81-26-225-1998
Time difference: 13 hours ahead of New York (EDT)
President ....M. Eishiro Saito
Director General ....M. Makoto Kobayashi
Head of Media ....Koh Yamaguchi
(XVIIIth Olympic Winter Games, Feb. 7-22)

2000 SUMMER GAMES
Sydney Olympic Organizing Committee

GPO Box 2000, Sydney NSW 2001
TEL: 011-61-29-297-2000
Time difference: 14 hours ahead of New York (EDT)
CEO ....Sandy Hollway
Director General ....Bob Elphinston
Director of Information ....Ian Dose
(Games of XXVIIth Olympiad, Sept. 15-Oct. 1)

2002 WINTER GAMES
Salt Lake Olympic Organizing Committee

257 East, 200 South, Suite 600
Salt Lake City, UT 84111
(801) 322-2002
Chairman ....Frank Joklik
President & CEO ....Frank Joklik, Interim
Sr. Vice Presidents ....Dave Johnson, Gordon Crabtree
Dir. of Public Information ....Mike Korologos
(XIXth Olympic Winter Games, Feb. 9-24)

COA
(Canadian Olympic Association)

2380 Avenue Pierre Dupuy, Montreal, Quebec H3C-3R4
(514) 861-3371
CEO-General Secretary ....Carol Anne Letheren
President ....Bill Warren
IOC members ....Carol Anne Letheren & Richard Pound
Manager of Media Relations ....Lorraine Lafreniere (613)
748-5647

USOC
(United States Olympic Committee)

One Olympic Plaza, Colorado Springs, CO 80909
(719) 632-5551
President ....Bill Hybl
Director ....Dick Schultz
IOC members ..Anita DeFrantz, James Easton & George Killian
Director of Public/Media Relations ....Mike Moran

1998 GOODWILL GAMES

Goodwill Games, Inc.
One CNN Center, P.O. Box 105366
Atlanta, GA 30348
(404) 827-3400
President ....Michael Plant
Managing Director ....Scott Hallenbeck
V.P., Communications ....Don Smith
Project Director ....Stephen Chriss
   (4th Goodwill Games, July 19-Aug. 2)

1999 PAN AMERICAN GAMES

**Pan American Games Society
(Winnipeg 1999, Inc.)**
500 Shaftesbury Blvd., Winninpeg, Manitoba R3P 0M1
(204) 985-1999
President-CEO ....Don MacKenzie
Media Contact ....Ernie Nairn
   (XIIIth Pan American Games, July 24-Aug. 8)

U.S. OLYMPICS TRAINING CENTERS

Colorado Springs Training Center
One Olympic Plaza, Colorado Springs, CO 80909
(719) 578-4500 ext. 5500
Dir. of U.S. Training Centers ....John Smyth
Director ....Patrice Milkovich

Lake Placid Training Center
421 Old Military Road, Lake Placid, NY 12946
(518) 523-2600
Director ....Jack Favro

San Diego Training Center
1750 Wueste Rd., Chula Vista, CA 91915
(619) 656-1500
Director ....Benita Fitzgerald

U.S. OLYMPIC ORGANIZATIONS

National Archery Association
One Olympic Plaza, Colorado Springs, CO 80909
(719) 578-4576
President ....Jane Johnson
Executive Director ....Robert C. Balink
Media Contact ....Bill Kellick

U.S. Badminton Association
One Olympic Plaza, Colorado Springs, CO 80909
(719) 578-4808
President ....Diane Cornell
Executive Director ....Terry Madden
Communications Director ....Mark Whitney

USA Baseball
2160 Greenwood Avenue, Trenton, NJ 08609
(609) 586-2381
President ....Mark Marquess
Executive Director & CEO ....Daniel F. O'Brien
Dir. of Media Relations ....George Doig

USA Basketball
5465 Mark Dabling Blvd., Colorado Springs, CO 80918
(719) 590-4800
President ....Russell Granik
Executive Director ....Warren Brown
Director of Public Relations ....Craig Miller

U.S. Biathlon Association
P.O. Box 297
Burlington, VT 05402
(802) 862-0338 or (802) 862-0360
President ....Maj. Gen. Donald E. Edwards, Ret.
Exec. Director ....Stephen Sands
Director of Summer Biathlon ....Jerry Kokesh

U.S. Bobsled and Skeleton Federation
P.O. Box 828, 421 Old Military Road
Lake Placid, NY 12946
(518) 523-1842
President ....Jim Morris
Executive Director ....Matt Roy

USA Boxing
One Olympic Plaza, Colorado Springs, CO 80909
(719) 578-4506
President ....Gary Tony
Executive Director ....Chris Campbell
Communications Director ....Stephen Ross

U.S. Canoe and Kayak Team
Pan American Plaza, Suite 610
201 South Capitol Avenue, Indianapolis, IN 46225
(317) 237-5690
Chairman ....Helen Collins
Executive Director ....Terry Kent
Communications Manager ....Lisa Fish

USA Cycling
One Olympic Plaza, Colorado Springs, CO 80909
(719) 578-4581
President ....Mike Plant
Executive Director & CEO ....Lisa Voight
Managing Director ....Evan Call
Director of Communications ....Cheryl Kvasnicka

United States Diving, Inc.
Pan American Plaza, Suite 430,
201 South Capitol Avenue, Indianapolis, IN 46225
(317) 237-5252
President ....Steve McFarland
Executive Director ....Todd Smith
Director of Communications ....Dave Shatkowski

U.S. Equestrian Team
Pottersville Road, Gladstone, NJ 07934
(908) 234-1251
President .................................D.D. Matz
Executive Director ....Bob Standish
Director of Public Relations ....Marty Bauman
                                       (508) 698-6810

U.S. Fencing Association
One Olympic Plaza, Colorado Springs, CO 80909
(719) 578-4511
President ....Donald Alperstien
Executive Director ....Michael Massik
Media Relations Coord. ....Coleen Walker-Mar

U.S. Field Hockey Assocation
One Olympic Plaza, Colorado Springs, CO 80909
(719) 578-4567
President ....Jenepher Shillingford
Executive Director ....Jane Betts
Director of Media/Public Relations .....Kathleen Callahan

U.S. Figure Skating Association
20 First Street, Colorado Springs, CO 80906
(719) 635-5200
President ....Morry Stillwell
Executive Director ....Jerry Lace
Communications Coordinator ....Heather Linhart

USA Gymnastics
Pan American Plaza, Suite 300
201 South Capitol Avenue, Indianapolis, IN 46225
(317) 237-5050
President-Exec. Director ....Kathy Scanlan
Director of Public Relations ....Luan Peszek

USA Hockey
4965 North 30th St., Colorado Springs, CO 80919
(719) 599-5500
President ....Walter Bush
Executive Director ....Dave Ogrean
Dir. of Public Relations & Media ....Darryl Seibel

United States Judo, Inc.
One Olympic Plaza, Suite 202
Colorado Springs, CO 80909
(719) 574-8754
President ....Yosh Uchida
Media Contact ....Chris Cordes

U.S. Luge Association
P.O. Box 651, Lake Placid, NY 12946
(518) 523-2071
President ....Dwight Bell
Executive Director ....Ron Rossi
Public Relations Specialist ....Sandy Caligiore
Communications Manager ....Dmitry Feld

U.S. Modern Pentathlon Association
530 McCullough, Suite 248, San Antonio, TX 78215
(210) 246-3000
President ....Dr. Risto Hurme
Executive Director ....Dean Billick

U.S. Rowing
Pan American Plaza, Suite 400
201 South Capitol Avenue, Indianapolis, IN 46225
(317) 237-5656
President ....Dave Vogel
Executive Director ....Frank Coyle
Media Contact ....Maureen Merhoff

U.S. Sailing Association
P.O. Box 1260, 15 Maritime Drive
Portsmouth, RI 02871
(401) 683-0800
President ....Dave Irish
Executive Director ....Terry D. Harper
Media Contact ....Barby MacGowan
                                          (401) 849-0220

U.S. Shooting Team
One Olympic Plaza, Colorado Springs, CO 80909
(719) 578-4670
Executive Director ....Robert Jusnick
Public Relations Director ....Valerie Larabee

U.S. Ski & Snowboard Assoc.
P.O. Box 100, 1500 Kearns Blvd., Park City, UT 84060
(801) 649-9090
Chairman ....Nick Badami
CEO ....Bill Marolt
V.P. of Public Relations ....Tom Kelly

U.S. Soccer Federation
U.S. Soccer House
1801-1811 South Prairie Ave., Chicago, IL 60616
(312) 808-1300
President ....Alan Rothenberg
Executive Director ....Hank Steinbrecher
Director of Communications ....Jim Trecker

Amateur Softball Association
2801 N.E. 50th Street, Oklahoma City, OK 73111
(405) 424-5266
President ....Bill Humphrey
Executive Director ....Don Porter
Director of Communications ....Ron Babb

U.S. Speedskating
P.O. Box 16157, Rocky River, OH 44116
(216) 899-0128
President ....Bill Cushman
Executive Director ....Katie Marquard
Media Relations Director ....Wendy Day

U.S. Swimming, Inc.
One Olympic Plaza, Colorado Springs, CO 80909
(719) 578-4578
President ....Carol Zaleski
Executive Director ....Chuck Weilgus
Director of Communications ....Charlie Snyder

U.S. Synchronized Swimming, Inc.
Pan American Plaza, Suite 901
201 South Capitol Avenue, Indianapolis, IN 46225
(317) 237-5700
President ....Laurette Longmire
Executive Director ....Debbie Hesse
Communications Coordinator ....Brian Eaton

USA Table Tennis
One Olympic Plaza, Colorado Springs, CO 80909
(719) 578-4583
President ....Terry Timmins
Executive Director ....Paul Montville
Communications Director ....Seth Pederson

U.S. Taekwondo Union
One Olympic Plaza, Suite 405
Colorado Springs, CO 80909
(719) 578-4632
President ....Feng Lee
Executive Director ....Michael Weintraub

USA Team Handball
One Olympic Plaza, Colorado Springs, CO 80909
(719) 578-4582
President ....Dennis Berkholtz
Executive Director ....Maureen Stone

U.S. Tennis Association
70 West Red Oak Lane, White Plains, NY 10604
(914) 696-7000
President ....Harry Marmion
Executive Director ....Richard D. Fermin
Dir. of Communications ....Page Dahl Crosland

USA Track and Field
P.O. Box 120, Indianapolis, IN 46206
(317) 261-0500
President ....Larry Ellis
CEO ....Craig Masback
Press Information Director ....Pete Cava

USA Triathlon
3595 East Fountain Blvd., Suite F-1
Colorado Springs, CO 80910
(719) 597-9090
Executive Director ....Steve Locke
Media Contact and Deputy Director ....Tim Yount

USA Volleyball
3595 East Fountain Blvd., Suite I-2
Colorado Springs, CO 80910
(719) 637-8300
President ....Rebecca Howard
Director of Communications ....Lorene Graves

United States Water Polo
1685 W. Uintah St.
Colorado Springs, CO 80904
(719) 634-0699
President ....Brett Bernard
Executive Director ....Bruce Wigo
Dir. of Media/Public Relations ....Kyle Utsumi

USA Weightlifting
One Olympic Plaza, Colorado Springs, CO 80909
(719) 578-4508
President ....Brian Derwin
Executive Director ....George Greenway
Communications Director ....Anthony Bartokowski

USA Wrestling
6155 Lehman Drive, Colorado Springs, CO 80918
(719) 598-8181
President .... Larry Sciacchetano
Executive Director .... Jim Scherr
Dir. of Communications .... Gary Abbott

AFFILIATED ORGANIZATIONS

USA Curling
1100 Center Point Drive, Box 866
Stevens Point, WI 54481
(715) 344-1199
President .... Tom Brooke
Executive Director .... David Garber
Media Contact .... Rick Patzke

U.S. Orienteering Federation
P.O. Box 1444, Forest Park, GA 30051
(404) 363-2110
President .... Rick Worner
Executive Director .... Robin Shannonhouse
Media Contact .... Jon Nash

USA Roller Skating
P.O. Box 6579, Lincoln, NE 68506
(402) 483-7551
President .... Betty Ann Danna
Executive Director .... George Pickard
Information Director .... Andy Sealey

United States Raquetball Association
1685 West Uintah, Colorado Springs, CO 80904
(719) 635-5396
President .... Van Dubolsky
Executive Director .... Luke Saint Onge
Communications Director .... Linda Mojer

American Water Ski Association
799 Overlook Drive, S.E., Winter Haven, FL 33884
(941) 324-4341
President .... Andrea Plough
Executive Director .... Duke Waldrop
Director of Communications .... Don Cullimore

U.S. Windsurfing
P.O. Box 978
Hood River, OR 97031
(541) 386-8708
President .... Bill Collins
Executive Director .... Holly Macpherson

SOCCER

FIFA
(Federation Internationale de Football Assn.)
P.O. Box 85, 8030 Zurich, Switzerland
TEL: 011-41-1-384-9595
President .... Joao Havelange
General Secretary .... Joseph Blatter
Director of Communications .... Keith Cooper

MLS

Major League Soccer
110 E. 42nd Street, Suite 1502
New York, NY 10017
(212) 450-1200
Chairman .... Alan I. Rothenburg
Commissioner .... Douglas G. Logan
Director of Communications .... Dan Courtemanche

Colorado Rapids
555 17th Street, Suite 3350
Denver, CO 80202
(303) 299-1570
Investor/Operator .... Philip F. Anschutz
President .... Robert Sanderman
General Manager .... Dan Counch
Director of Public Relations .... Ben Grossman

Columbus Crew
77 E. Nationwide Blvd.
Columbus, OH 43215
(614) 221-2739
Investor/Operator .... Lamar Hunt and Family
General Manager .... Jamey Rootes
Director of Public Relations .... Adam Low

Dallas Burn
2602 McKinney, Suite 200
Dallas, TX 75204
(214) 979-0303
Investor/Operator .... League-owned
President/GM .... Billy Hicks
Director of Media Relations .... Chris Ward

Kansas City Wizards
706 Broadway St., Suite 100
Kansas City, MO 64105
(816) 472-4625
Investor/Operator .... Lamar Hunt and Family
General Manager .... Tim Latta
Director of Media Relations .... Chris Taylor

Los Angeles Galaxy
1640 So. Sepulveda Blvd., Suite 114
Los Angeles, CA 90025
(310) 445-1260
Investor/Operator .... LA Soccer Partners
Chairman .... Mark Rapaport
General Manager .... Danny Villanueva Jr.
Director of Media Relations .... Ron Acosta

New England Revolution
Foxboro Stadium, Route 1
Foxboro, MA 02035
(508) 543-0350
Investor/Operator .... Robert Kraft and Family
General Manager .... Brian O'Donovan
Director of Public Relations .... Derek Aframe

New York/New Jersey MetroStars
One Harmon Plaza, 8th Floor
Seacausus, NJ 07094
(201) 583-7000
Investor/Operator ...... John Kluge and Stuart Subotnick
Vice President/GM .... Charlie Stillitano
Director of Media Relations .... Jeff Bradley

San Jose Clash
1265 El Camino Real, 2nd Floor
Santa Clara, CA 95050
(408) 241-9922
Investor/Operator .... League-owned
President/GM .... Peter Bridgwater
Director of Media Relations .... Rick La Plante

Tampa Bay Mutiny
1408 N. Westshore Blvd., Suite 1004
Tampa, FL 33607
(813) 288-0096
Investor/Operator .... League-owned
President/GM .... Nick Sakiewicz
Director of Media Relations .... Jim Henderson

Washington D.C. United
13832 Redskin Drive
Herndon, VA 20171
(703) 478-6600
Owner ....Washington Soccer, L.P.
President/GM ....Kevin Payne
Director of Media Relations ....Rick Lawes

1998 WORLD CUP

French Organizing Committee
90 Avenue des Champs Elysees
F-75008 Paris, France   Time difference: five hours
TEL: 011-33-1-44-95-1998   ahead of New York (EDT)
Co-Presidents ....Fernand Sastre and Michel Platini
General Director ....Jacques Lambert
Dir. of Press & Communications ....Alain Leiblang
   (16th World Cup, June 10-July 12)

CONCACAF
(Confederation of North, Central American & Caribbean Association Football)
725 Fifth Ave., 17th Floor, New York, NY 10022
(212) 308-0044
President ....Jack Austin Warner
General Secretary ....Chuck Blazer

U.S. Soccer
(United States Soccer Federation)
Soccer House, 1801-1811 South Prairie Ave.
Chicago, IL 60616
(312) 808-1300
President ....Alan Rothenberg
Exec. Director/Sec. General ....Hank Steinbrecher
Director of Communications ....Jim Trecker

CISL
(Continental Indoor Soccer League)
16027 Ventura Blvd., Suite 605, Encino, CA 91436
(818) 906-7627
Commissioner ....Ron Weinstein
League Counsel ....Dan Grigsby
Director of Media Relations ....Tim Sullivan
   Member teams (11): Eastern Division— Dallas Sidekicks, Detroit Safari, Houston Hotshots, Indiana Twisters, Monterrey La Raza, Washington Warthogs. Western Division— Anaheim Splash, Arizona Sandsharks, Portland Pride, Sacramento Knights, Seattle SeaDogs.

NPSL
(National Professional Soccer League)
115 Dewalt Avenue, NW, Canton, OH 44702
(330) 455-4625
Commissioner ....Steve M. Paxos
Director of Operations ....Paul Luchowski
Director of Media Relations ....Chuck Murr
   Member teams (15): American Conference— Baltimore Spirit, Cincinnati Silverbacks, Cleveland Crunch, Columbus Invaders, Harrisburg Heat, Philadelphia Kixx and Tamp Bay Terror. National Conference—Buffalo Blizzard, Detroit Rockers, Edmonton Drillers, Kansas City Attack, Milwaukee Wave, St. Louis Ambush, Toronto Shooting Stars and Wichita Wings.

USISL
(United Systems of Independent Soccer Leagues)
14497 N. Dale Mabry Hwy., Tampa, FL 33618
(813) 963-3909
Commissioner ....Francisco Marcos
Administrative Manager ....Beverly Wright
Director of Public Relations ....Mike Agnew

SWIMMING

FINA
(Federation Internationale de Natation Amateur)
9 ave de Beaumont, 1012 Lausanne, Switzerland
011-4121-312-6602
President ....Mustapha Larfaoui
General Secretary ....Gunnar Werner

Organizing Committee of the VIII Swimming World Championships
Sports House P.O. Box 1998, Wembley-Perth, Western Australia
011-619-284-1998
Chairman ....Tom Hoad
Executive Director ....Alan Melchert

TENNIS

ATP Tour
(Association of Tennis Professionals)
200 ATP Tour Blvd., Ponte Vedra Beach, FL 32082
(904) 285-8000
Chief Executive Officer ....Mark Miles
V.P., Communications ....Pete Alfano

ITF
(International Tennis Federation)
Palliser Rd., Barons Court
London, England W14 9EN
TEL: 011-44-171-381-8060
President ....Brian Tobin
Media Administrator ....Ian Barnes

World TeamTennis
445 North Wells, Suite 404, Chicago, IL 60610
(312) 245-5300
Chief Executive Officer ....Billie Jean King
Executive Director ....Ilana Kloss
Communications Director ....Tracey Donnelly

USTA
(United States Tennis Association)
70 West Red Oak Lane, White Plains, NY 10604
(914) 696-7000
President ....Lester Snyder
Executive Director ....Richard D. Fermin
Dir. of Communications ....Page Dahl Crosland

WTA Tour
(Women's Tennis Association)
1266 East Main St. 4th Floor, Stamford, CT 06902
(203) 978-1740
Executive Director & CEO ....Anne Person Worcester
Communications Director ....Joe Favorito

TRACK & FIELD

IAAF
(International Ameteur Athletics Federation)
17 Rue Princesse Florestine
BP 359, MC-98007, Monaco Cedex
TEL: 011-377-10-88-88
President ....Primo Nebiolo
General Secretary ....Istvan Gyulai
Director of Information ....Giorgio Reinei

AAU
(Amateur Athletic Union)
6751 Forum Dr., Suite 200 Orlando, FL 32821
(407) 363-6170
President ....Bobby Dodd
Communications Director ....Erin Habersack

USA Track & Field
P.O. Box 120
Indianapolis, IN 46206
(317) 261-0500
Executive Director ....Ollan Cassell
Director of Information ....Pete Cava

YACHTING

1999-2000 America's Cup

New Zealand Defense Committee
(Royal New Zealand Yacht Squadron)
P.O. Box 1927, Auckland, New Zealand
TEL: 011-64-9-357-6712
   Time difference: 16 hours ahead of New York (EDT)
Exec. Director & Contact ....Alan Sefton
   (Next America's Cup defense scheduled to begin in Oct. 1999 and run through Feb. 2000, off the coast of Auckland.)

MISCELLANEOUS

All-American Soap Box Derby
P.O. Box 7233, Akron, OH 44306
(330) 733-8723
President .....................................F.A. Wahl
Chairman of the Board ....John Piscitelli
Executive Director ....Anthony DeLuca
Public Relations Director ....Bob Troyer

American Armwrestling Association
P.O. Box 79, Scranton, PA 18504
(717) 342-4984
Executive Director ....Bob O'Leary

American Athletic Association for the Deaf
3607 Washington Blvd., Suite 4, Ogden, UT 84403
(801) 546-2982 then (801) 393-8710
Executive Director ....Shirley H. Platt
President/CEO ....Dr. Lawrence R. Fleischer
Publicity Director ....Jack Levesque

American Powerboating Association
P.O. Box 377, Eastpointe, MI 48021
(810) 733-9700
President ....Fred Hauenstein Jr.
Executive Director ....Gloria Urbin

Association of Surfing Professionals
P.O. Box 309, Huntington Beach, CA 92648
(714) 851-2774
President ....George Stokes
Executive Director ....Graham Stapelberg

Association of Volleyball Professionals
15260 Ventura Blvd., Suite 2250, Sherman Oaks, CA 91403
(310) 577-0775
Executive Director ....Jerry Solomon
COO ....Lon Monk
Sr. V.P. Tour Operations ....Jon Stevenson

BASS, Inc.
(Bass Anglers Sportsmen Society)
5845 Carmichael Road, Mongomery, AL 36117
(334) 272-9530
CEO ....Helen Sevier
Publicity Director ....Ann Lewis

Center for the Study of Sport in Society
360 Huntington Ave., Boston, MA 02115
(617) 373-4025
Director ....Richard E. Lapchick
Associate Director ....Art Taylor

Disabled Sports USA
451 Hungerford Dr., Suite 100, Rockville, MD 20850
(301) 217-8960 or for hearing impaired (301) 217-8963
Executive Director ....Kirk M. Bauer
President ....Doug Sato
Publicity Director ....Ed Harrison

Iditarod Trail Committee
P.O. Box 870800, Wasilla, AK 99687
(907) 376-5155
Executive Director ....Stan Hooley
Race Director ....Joanne Potts

International Game Fish Association
1301 East Atlantic Blvd., Pompano Beach, FL 33060
(954) 941-3474
Chairman ....George Matthews
President ....Mike Leach
Editor ....Ray Crawford

International Motor Sports Association
3502 Henderson Blvd., Tampa, FL 33609
(813) 877-4672
President ....Jack Long
Communications Director ....Ed Nicholls

Little League Baseball Incorporated
P.O. Box 3485, Williamsport, PA 17701
(717) 326-1921
CEO-President ....Steven Keener
Director of Communications ....Dennis Sullivan

National Assn. for Girls and Women in Sport
1900 Association Drive, Reston, VA 20191
(703) 476-3452
Executive Director ....Diana Everett
President ....Donna Pastore

National Lacrosse League
2310 West 75th St., Prairie Village, KS 66208
(913) 384-8960
Chairman-CEO ....Chris Fritz
President ....Russ Cline
Director of Public Relations ....Mary Havel
   Member teams (8): Baltimore; Buffalo; Hamilton, ONT; New England; Philadelphia; Rochester, NY; Syracuse, NY; and Long Island, NY.

National Rifle Assocation
11250 Waples Mill Road, Fairfax, VA 22030
(703) 267-1000
Executive VP ....Wayne LaPierre
Public Affairs Director ....Bill Powers

National Sports Foundation
P.O. Box 888886, Atlanta, GA 30356
(770) 698-8600
Executive Director ....Ed Harris

NORBA
(National Off-Road Bicycle Association)
1 Olympic Plaza, Colorado Springs, CO 80909
(719) 578-4717
Sr. Managing Director ....Philip M. Milburn
Managing Director ....Brian Stickel

Professional Billiards Tour Association
4412 Commercial Way, Spring Hill, FL 34606
(352) 596-7868
Commissioner ....Don Mackey

Professional Rodeo Cowboys Association
101 Pro Rodeo Drive, Colorado Springs, CO 80919
(719) 593-8840
Commissioner ....Lewis Cryer
Director of Public Relations ....Steve Fleming

Roller Hockey International
13070 Fawn Hill Dr., Grass Valley, CA 95945
(714) 385-1769
Commissioner ....Ralph Backstrom
COO ....David B. McLane
CEO ....Larry King
Public Relations Director ....Nancy King

Special Olympics
1325 G St. NW Suite 500
Washington, DC 20005
(202) 628-3630
Founder ....Eunice Kennedy Shriver
COB ....Sargent Shriver
COO ....Kim Elliott
Media Relations Manager ....Mike Janes

U.S. Association for Blind Athletes
33 N. Institute St., Colorado Springs, CO 80903
(719) 630-0422
Executive Director ....Charlie Huebner
Asst. Exec. Director ....Mark Lucas

USA Bowling
5301 South 76th St., Greendale, WI 53129
(414) 421-9008
President ....Max Skelton
Executive Director ....Gerald Koenig
Director of Marketing/P.R. ....Christine Krebs

U.S. Chess Federation
3054 N.W.S. Route 9W, New Windsor, NY 12553
(914) 562-8350
President ....Mike Cavallo

U.S. Polo Association
4059 Iron Works Pike, Lexington, KY 40511
(606) 255-0593
Executive Director ....George Alexander Jr.

U.S. Pro Beach Volleyball
P.O. Box 57, Huntington Beach, CA 92648
(714) 536-4900
President ....Gary Pope

USA Rugby
3595 East Fountain Blvd., Colorado Springs, CO 80910
(719) 637-1022
President ....Gene Roberts
Executive V.P. ....Tony Skillbeck

Wheelchair Sports USA
3595 East Fountain Blvd., Suite L-1,
Colorado Springs, CO 80910
(719) 574-1150
Chairman ....Paul DePace
Executive Director ....Patricia Shepherd

Commissioners and Presidents
Chief Executives of Established Major Sports Organizations since 1876

Major League Baseball

Commissioner	Tenure
Kenesaw Mountain Landis*	1920-44
Albert (Happy) Chandler	1945-51
Ford Frick	1951-65
William Eckert	1965-68
Bowie Kuhn	1969-84
Peter Ueberroth	1984-89
A. Bartlett Giamatti*	1989
Fay Vincent	1989-92
Bud Selig†	1992—

*Died in office.
†Chairman of Executive Committee.

National League

President	Tenure
Morgan G. Bulkeley	1876
William A. Hulbert*	1877-82
A.G. Mills	1883-84
Nicholas Young	1885-1902
Henry Pulliam*	1903-09
Thomas J. Lynch	1910-13
John K. Tener	1914-18
John A. Heydler	1918-34
Ford Frick	1935-51
Warren Giles	1951-69
Charles (Chub) Feeney	1970-86
A. Bartlett Giamatti	1987-89
Bill White	1989-94
Leonard Coleman	1994—

*Died in office.

American League

President	Tenure
Bancroft (Ban) Johnson	1901-27
Ernest Barnard*	1927-31
William Harridge	1931-59
Joe Cronin	1959-73
Lee McPhail	1974-83
Bobby Brown	1984-94
Gene Budig	1994—

*Died in office.

NBA

Commissioner	Tenure
Maurice Podoloff	1949-63
Walter Kennedy	1963-75
Larry O'Brien	1975-84
David Stern	1984—

NFL

President	Tenure
Jim Thorpe	1920
Joe Carr	1921-39
Carl Storck	1939-41

Commissioner	Tenure
Elmer Layden	1941-46
Bert Bell*	1946-59
Austin Gunsel	1959-60
Pete Rozelle	1960-89
Paul Tagliabue	1989—

*Died in office.

NHL

President	Tenure
Frank Calder*	1917-43
Red Dutton	1943-46
Clarence Campbell	1946-77
John Ziegler	1977-92
Gil Stein	1992-93

Commissioner	Tenure
Gary Bettman	1993—

*Died in office.

NCAA

Executive Director	Tenure
Walter Byers	1951-88
Dick Schultz	1988-93
Cedric Dempsey	1993—

IOC

President	Tenure
Demetrius Vikelas, Greece	1894-96
Baron Pierre de Coubertin, France	1896-1925
Count Henri de Baillet-Latour, Belgium	1925-42
Vacant	1942-46
J. Sigfried Edstrom, Sweden	1946-52
Avery Brundage, USA	1952-72
Lord Michael Killanin, Ireland	1972-80
Juan Antonio Samaranch, Spain	1980—

Olympics

Ireland's Michelle Smith won 3 gold medals and a bronze at the 1996 Summer Games in Atlanta, but many have questioned just how she was able to perform at such a high level.

World Wide Photos

Modern Olympic Games

The original Olympic Games were celebrated as a religious festival from 776 B.C. until 393 A.D., when Roman emperor Theodosius I banned all pagan festivals (the Olympics celebrated the Greek god Zeus). On June 23, 1894, French educator Baron Pierre de Coubertin, speaking at the Sorbonne in Paris to a gathering of international sports leaders, proposed that the ancient games be revived on an international scale. The idea was enthusiastically received and the Modern Olympics were born. The first Olympics were held two years later in Athens, where 311 athletes from 14 nations competed in the ancient Panathenaic stadium to large and enthusiastic crowds. Americans captured nine out of 12 track and field events, but Greece won the most medals with 47.

The Summer Olympics

Year	No	Location	Dates	Nations	Most medals	USA Medals
1896	I	Athens, GRE	Apr. 6-15	14	Greece (10-19-18—47)	11- 6- 2— 19 (2nd)
1900	II	Paris, FRA	May 20-Oct. 28	26	France (26-37-32—95)	18-14-15— 47 (2nd)
1904	III	St. Louis, USA.	July 1-Nov. 23	13	USA (78-84-82—244)	78-84-82—244 (1st)
1906-a		Athens, GRE	Apr. 22-May 2	20	France (15-9-16—40)	12- 6- 6— 24 (3rd)
1908	IV	London, GBR	Apr. 27-Oct. 31	22	Britain (54-46-38—138)	23-12-12— 47 (2nd)
1912	V	Stockholm, SWE ..	May 5-July 22	28	Sweden (23-24-17—64)	25-18-20— 63 (2nd)
1916	VI	Berlin, GER	Cancelled (WWI)			
1920	VII	Antwerp, BEL	Apr. 20-Sept. 12	29	USA (41-27-27—95)	41-27-27— 95 (1st)
1924	VIII	Paris, FRA	May 4-July 27	44	USA (45-27-27—99)	45-27-27— 99 (1st)
1928	IX	Amsterdam, NET ...	May 17-Aug. 12	46	USA (22-18-16—56)	22-18-16— 56 (1st)
1932	X	Los Angeles, USA. .	July 30-Aug. 14	37	USA (41-32-30—103)	41-32-30—103 (1st)
1936	XI	Berlin, GER	Aug. 1-16	49	Germany (33-26-30-89)	24-20-12— 56 (2nd)
1940-b	XII	Tokyo, JPN	Cancelled (WWII)			
1944	XIII	London, GBR	Cancelled (WWII)			
1948	XIV	London, GBR	July 29-Aug. 14	59	USA (38-27-19—84)	38-27-19— 84 (1st)
1952-cd	XV	Helsinki, FIN	July 19-Aug. 3	69	USA (40-19-17—76)	40-19-17— 76 (1st)
1956-e	XVI	Melbourne, AUS ..	Nov. 22-Dec .8	72	USSR (37-29-32—98)	32-25-17— 74 (2nd)
1960	XVII	Rome, ITA	Aug. 25-Sept. 11	83	USSR (43-29-31—103)	34-21-16— 71 (2nd)
1964	XVIII	Tokyo, JPN	Oct. 10-24	93	USSR (30-31-35—96)	36-26-28— 90 (2nd)
1968-f	XIX	Mexico City, MEX ..	Oct. 12-27	113	USA (45-28-34—107)	45-28-34—107 (1st)
1972	XX	Munich, W. GER ..	Aug. 26-Sept. 10	122	USSR (50-27-22—99)	33-31-30— 94 (2nd)
1976-g	XXI	Montreal, CAN ...	July 17-Aug. 1	88	USSR (49-41-35—125)	34-35-25— 94 (3rd)
1980-h	XXII	Moscow, USSR ...	July 19-Aug. 3	81	USSR (80-69-46—195)	Boycotted Games
1984-i	XXIII	Los Angeles, USA. .	July 28-Aug. 12	140	USA (83-61-30—174)	83-61-30—174 (1st)
1988	XXIV	Seoul, S. KOR	Sept. 17-Oct. 2	160	USSR (55-31-46—132)	36-31-27— 94 (3rd)
1992-j	XXV	Barcelona, SPA ...	July 25-Aug. 9	172	UT (45-38-29—112)	37-34-37—108 (2nd)
1996	XXVI	Atlanta, USA	July 20-Aug. 4	197	USA (44-32-25—101)	44-32-25—101 (1st)
2000	XXVII	Sydney, AUS	Sept. 16-Oct. 1			
2004	XXVII	Athens, GRE	TBA			

a—The 1906 Intercalated Games in Athens are considered unofficial by the IOC because they did not take place in the four-year cycle established in 1896. However, most record books include these interim games with the others.

b—The 1940 Summer Games are originally scheduled for Tokyo, but Japan resigns as host after the outbreak of the Sino-Japanese war in 1937. Helsinki is the next choice, but the IOC cancels the Games after Russian troops invade Finland in 1939.

c—Germany and Japan are allowed to rejoin Olympic community for first Summer Games since 1936. Though a divided country, the Germans send a joint East-West team.

d—The Soviet Union (USSR) participates in its first Olympics, Winter or Summer, since the Russian revolution in 1917 and takes home the second most medals (22-30-19—71).

e—Due to Australian quarantine laws, the equestrian events for the 1956 Games are held in Stockholm, June 10-17.

f—East Germany and West Germany send separate teams for the first time and will continue to do so through 1988.

g—The 1976 Games are boycotted by 32 nations, most of them from black Africa, because the IOC will not ban New Zealand. Earlier that year, a rugby team from New Zealand had toured racially-segregated South Africa.

h—The 1980 Games are boycotted by 64 nations, led by the USA, to protest the Russian invasion of Afghanistan on Dec. 27, 1979.

i—The 1984 Games are boycotted by 14 Eastern Bloc nations, led by the USSR, to protest America's overcommercialization of the Games, inadequate security and an anti-Soviet attitude by the U.S. government. Most believe, however, the communist walkout is simply revenge for 1980.

j—Germany sends a single team after East and West German reunification in 1990 and the USSR competes as the Unified Team after the breakup of the Soviet Union in 1991.

1896

Athens

The ruins of ancient Olympia were excavated by the German archaeologist Ernst Curtius from 1875-81.

Among the remains uncovered was the ancient stadium where the original Olympic Games were celebrated from 776 B.C. to 393 A.D., when Roman emperor Theodosius I banned all pagan festivals.

Athletics played an important role in the religious festivals of the ancient Greeks, who believed competitive sports pleased the spirits of the dead. The festivals honoring gods like Zeus were undertaken by many Greek tribes and cities and usually held every four years.

During the first 13 Olympiads (an Olympiad is an interval of four years between celebrations of the Olympic Games), the only contested event was a footrace of 200 yards (180 meters). Longer races were gradually introduced and by 708 B.C., field events like the discus and javelin throws and the long jump were part of the program. Wrestling and boxing followed and in 640 B.C., four-horse chariot races became a fixture at the Games.

During the so-called Golden Age of Greece, which most historians maintain lasted from 477 to 431 B.C., Olympia was considered holy ground. Victorious athletes gave public thanks to the gods and were revered as heroes. Three-time winners had statues erected in their likeness and received various gifts and honors, including exemption from taxation.

Eventually, however, winning and the rewards that went with victory corrupted the original purpose of the Ancient Games. Idealistic amateurs gave way to skilled foreign athletes, who were granted the citizenship needed to compete and were paid handsomely by rich Greek gamblers.

There is evidence to suggest that the Games continued until the temples of Olympia were physically demolished in 426 A.D. by a Roman army sent by Theodosius II. Over the next 15 centuries, earthquakes and floods buried the site, until its discovery in 1875.

On June 23, 1894, French educator Baron Pierre de Coubertin, speaking at the Sorbonne in Paris to a gathering of international sports leaders from nine nations— including the United States and Russia— proposed that the ancient Games be revived on an international scale. The idea was enthusiastically received and the Modern Olympics, as we know them, were born.

The first Olympiad was celebrated two years later in Athens, where an estimated 245 athletes (all men) from 14 nations competed in the ancient Panathenaic stadium before large and enthusiastic crowds.

Americans won nine of the 12 track and field events, but Greece won the most medals with 47. The highlight was the victory by native peasant Spiridon Louis in the first marathon race, which was run over the same course covered by the Greek hero Pheidippides after the battle of Marathon in 490 B.C.

Top 10 Standings

National medal standings are not recognized by the IOC. The unofficial point totals are based on 3 points for a gold medal, 2 for a silver and 1 for a bronze.

		Gold	Silver	Bronze	Total	Pts
1	Greece	10	19	18	47	86
2	USA	11	6	2	19	47
3	Germany	7	5	3	15	34
4	France	5	4	2	11	25
5	Great Britain	3	3	1	7	16
6	Denmark	1	2	4	7	11
	Hungary	2	1	3	6	11
8	Austria	2	0	3	5	9
9	Switzerland	1	2	0	3	7
10	Australia	2	0	0	2	6

Leading Medal Winners

Number of individual medals won on the left; gold, silver and bronze breakdown to the right.

No		Sport	G-S-B
6	Hermann Weingärtner, GER	Gymnastics	3-2-1
4	Karl Schuman, GER	Gymnastics & Wrestling	4-0-0
4	Alfred Flatow, GER	Gymnastics	3-1-0
4	Bob Garrett, USA	Track/Field	2-1-1
4	Viggo Jensen, DEN	Shooting & Weightlifting	1-2-1
3	Paul Masson, FRA	Cycling	3-0-0
3	Teddy Flack, AUS	Track/Field & Tennis	2-0-1
3	Jules Zutter, SWI	Gymnastics	1-2-0
3	James Connolly, USA	Track/Field	1-1-1
3	Leon Flameng, FRA	Cycling	1-1-1
3	Adolf Schmal, AUT	Cycling	1-0-2
3	Efstathios Choraphas, GRE	Swimming	0-1-2
3	Holger Nielsen, DEN	Shooting	0-1-2

Track & Field

Event		Time
100m	Tom Burke, USA	12.0
400m	Tom Burke, USA	54.2
800m	Teddy Flack, AUS	2:11.0
1500m	Teddy Flack, AUS	4:33.2
Marathon	Spiridon Louis, GRE	2:58:50
110m H	Tom Curtis, USA	17.6

Event		Mark
High Jump	Ellery Clark, USA	5-11¼
Pole Vault	William Hoyt, USA	10-10
Long Jump	Ellery Clark, USA	20-10
Triple Jump	James Connolly, USA	44-11¾
Shot Put	Bob Garrett, USA	36-9¾
Discus	Bob Garrett, USA	95-7½

Swimming

Event		Time
100m Free	Alfréd Hajós, HUN	1:22.2
500m Free	Paul Neumann, AUT	8:12.6
1200m Free	Alfréd Hajós, HUN	18:22.2
Other		Time
Sailors' 100m Free	Ioannis Malokinis, GRE	2:20.4

Team Sports

None

Also Contested

Cycling, Fencing, Gymnastics, Shooting, Tennis, Weightlifting and Greco-Roman Wrestling.

1900

Paris

The success of the revived Olympics moved Greece to declare itself the rightful host of all future Games, but de Coubertin and the International Olympic Committee were determined to move the athletic feast around. In France, however, the Games were overshadowed by the brand new Eiffel Tower and all but ignored by the organizers of the 1900 Paris Exposition.

Despite their sideshow status, the Games attracted 1,330 athletes from 22 nations and enjoyed more publicity, if not bigger crowds, than in Athens.

University of Pennsylvania roommates Alvin Kraenzlein, Irving Baxter and John Tewksbury and Purdue grad Ray Ewry dominated the 23 track and field events, winning 11 and taking five seconds and a third. Kraenzlein remains the only track and fielder to win four individual titles in one year. Women were invited to compete for the first time and Britain's Charlotte Cooper won the singles and mixed doubles in tennis.

No gold medals were given out in Paris. Winners received silver medals with bronze for second place.

Top 10 Standings

National team medal standings are not recognized by the IOC. The unofficial point totals are based on 3 points for a gold medal, 2 for a silver and 1 for a bronze.

		Gold	Silver	Bronze	Total	Pts
1	France	26	37	32	95	184
2	USA	18	14	15	47	97
3	Great Britain	16	6	8	30	68
4	Belgium	6	5	5	16	33
5	Switzerland	6	1	1	8	21
6	Germany	3	2	2	7	15
7	Denmark	1	3	2	6	11
	Hungary	1	3	2	6	11
9	Australia	2	0	4	6	10
	Holland	1	2	3	6	10

Leading Medal Winners

Number of individual medals won on the left; gold, silver and bronze breakdown to the right.

MEN

No		Sport	G-S-B
5	Irving Baxter, USA	Track/Field	2-3-0
5	John W. Tewksbury, USA	Track/Field	2-2-1
4	Alvin Kraenzlein, USA	Track/Field	4-0-0
4	Konrad Stäheli, SWI	Shooting	3-0-1
4	Achille Paroche, FRA	Shooting	1-2-1
4	Stan Rowley, AUS	Track/Field	1-0-3
4	Ole Östmo, NOR	Shooting	0-2-2
3	Ray Ewry, USA	Track/Field	3-0-0
3	Charles Bennett, AUS	Track/Field	2-1-0
3	Emil Kellenberger, SWI	Shooting	2-1-0
3	Laurie Doherty, GBR	Tennis	2-0-1

No		Sport	G-S-B
3	Reggie Doherty, GBR	Tennis	2-0-1
3	E. Michelet, FRA	Yachting	1-0-2
3	F. Michelet, FRA	Yachting	1-0-2
3	Anders Nielsen, DEN	Shooting	0-3-0
3	Zoltán Halmay, HUN	Swimming	0-2-1
3	Léon Moreaux, FRA	Shooting	0-2-1

WOMEN

No		Sport	G-S-B
2	Charlotte Cooper, GBR	Tennis	2-0-0
2	Marion Jones, USA	Tennis	0-0-2

Track & Field

Event		Time	
60m	Alvin Kraenzlein, USA	7.0	WR
100m	Frank Jarvis, USA	11.0	OR
200m	John W. Tewksbury, USA	22.2	
400m	Maxey Long, USA	49.4	OR
800m	Alfred Tysoe, GBR	2:01.2	
1500m	Charles Bennett, GBR	4:06.2	WR
Marathon	Michel Théato, FRA	2:59:45	
110m H	Alvin Kraenzlein, USA	15.4	OR
200m H	Alvin Kraenzlein, USA	25.4	
400m H	John W. Tewksbury, USA	57.6	
3000m Steeple	George Orton, CAN	7:34.4	
4000m Steeple	John Rimmer, GBR	12:58.4	
5000m Team	GBR (Charles Bennett, John Rimmer, Sidney Robinson, Alfred Tysoe, Stanley Rowley)	26 pts	

Event		Mark	
High Jump	Irving Baxter, USA	6- 2¾	OR
Pole Vault	Irving Baxter, USA	10-10	
Long Jump	Alvin Kraenzlein, USA	23- 6¾	OR
Triple Jump	Meyer Prinstein, USA	47- 5¾	OR
Shot Put	Richard Sheldon, USA	46- 3	OR
Discus	Rudolf Bauer, HUN	118- 3	OR
Hammer	John Flanagan, USA	163- 1	

Standing		Mark	
High Jump	Ray Ewry, USA	5- 5	WR
Long Jump	Ray Ewry, USA	10- 6¼	
Triple Jump	Ray Ewry, USA	34- 8½	

Swimming

Event		Time
220yd Free	Frederick Lane, AUS	2:25.2
1000m Free	John Jarvis, GBR	13:40.2
4000m Free	John Jarvis, GBR	58:24.0
200m Back	Ernst Hoppenberg, GER	2:47.0
200m Team	GER (Ernst Hoppenberg, Max Hainle, Max Schone, Julius Frey, Herbert von Petersdorff)	32 pts

Team Sports

Sport	Champion
Cricket	Great Britain
Polo	Great Britain/USA
Rugby	France
Soccer	Great Britain
Tug-of-War	Sweden/Norway
Water Polo	Great Britain

Note: In Polo, Foxhunters Hurlingham defeated Club Rugby in a contest of teams made up of British and American players. A combined 6-man team of Swedes and Norwegians won the Tug-of-War.

Also Contested

Archery, Croquet, Cycling, Equestrian, Fencing, Golf, Gymnastics, Rowing, Shooting, Tennis and Yachting.

1904

St. Louis

Originally scheduled for Chicago, the Games were moved to St. Louis and held in conjunction with the centennial celebration of the Louisiana Purchase.

The program included more sports than in Paris, but with only 11 nations sending athletes, the first Olympics to be staged in the United States had a decidedly All-American flavor—over 500 of the 681 competitors were Americans. Little wonder the home team won 80 percent of the medals.

The rout was nearly total in track and field where the U.S.–led by triple-winners Ray Ewry, Archie Hahn, Jim Lightbody and Harry Hillman–took 23 of 25 gold medals and swept 20 events.

The marathon, which was run over dusty roads in brutally hot weather, was the most bizarre event of the Games. Thomas Hicks of the U.S. won, but only after his handlers fed him painkillers during the race. And an impostor nearly stole the victory when Fred Lorz, who dropped out after nine miles, was seen trotting back to the finish line to retrieve his clothes. Amused that officials thought he had won the race, Lorz played along until he was found out shortly after the medal ceremony. Banned for life by the AAU, Lorz was reinstated a year later and won the 1905 Boston Marathon.

Top 10 Standings

National medal standings are not recognized by the IOC. The unofficial point totals are based on 3 points for a gold medal, 2 for a silver and 1 for a bronze.

		Gold	Silver	Bronze	Total	Pts
1	USA	78	84	82	244	484
2	Germany	4	4	4	12	24
3	Canada	4	1	1	6	15
4	Hungary	2	1	1	4	9
	Cuba	3	0	0	3	9
6	Austria	1	1	1	3	6
	Britian/Ireland	1	1	1	3	6
8	Greece	1	0	1	2	4
	Switzerland	1	0	1	2	4
10	Cuba/USA	1	0	0	1	3

Leading Medal Winners

Number of individual medals won on the left; gold, silver and bronze breakdown to the right.

MEN

No		Sport	G-S-B
6	Anton Heida, USA	Gymnastics	5-1-0
6	George Eyser, USA	Gymnastics	3-2-1
6	Burton Downing, USA	Cycling	2-3-1
5	Marcus Hurley, USA	Cycling	4-0-1
5	Charles Daniels, USA	Swimming	3-1-1
5	Albertson Van Zo Post, USA	Fencing	2-1-2
5	William Merz, USA	Gymnastics	0-1-4
4	Jim Lightbody, USA	Track/Field	3-1-0
4	Francis Gailey, USA	Swimming	0-3-1
4	Teddy Billington, USA	Cycling	0-1-3
4	Frank Kungler, USA	Weightlifting, Wrestling & Tug of War	0-1-3
3	Ray Ewry, USA	Track/Field	3-0-0
3	Ramón Fonst, CUB	Fencing	3-0-0
3	Archie Hahn, USA	Track/Field	3-0-0
3	Harry Hillman, USA	Track/Field	3-0-0
3	Julius Lenhart, AUT	Gymnastics	2-1-0
3	George Bryant, USA	Archery	2-0-1
3	Emil Rausch, GER	Swimming	2-0-1
3	Robert Williams, USA	Archery	1-2-0
3	Ralph Rose, USA	Track/Field	1-1-1
3	William Thompson, USA	Archery	1-0-2
3	Charles Tatham, USA	Fencing	0-2-1
3	William Hogenson, USA	Track/Field	0-1-2
3	Emil Voigt, USA	Gymnastics	0-1-2

WOMEN

No		Sport	G-S-B
2	Lida Howell, USA	Archery	2-0-0
2	Emma Cooke, USA	Archery	0-2-0
2	Jessie Pollack, USA	Archery	0-0-2

Track & Field

Event		Time	
60m	Archie Hahn, USA	7.0	=WR
100m	Archie Hahn, USA	11.0	
200m	Archie Hahn, USA	21.6	OR
400m	Harry Hillman, USA	49.2	OR
800m	Jim Lightbody, USA	1:56.0	OR
1500m	Jim Lightbody, USA	4:05.4	WR
Marathon	Thomas Hicks, USA	3:28:53	
110m H	Frederick Schule, USA	16.0	
200m H	Harry Hillman, USA	24.6	OR
400m H	Harry Hillman, USA	53.0	
3000m Steeple	Jim Lightbody, USA	7:39.6	
4-mile Team	New York AC (Arthur Newton, George Underwood, Paul Pilgrim, Howard Valentine, David Munson)	27 pts	

Event		Mark	
High Jump	Sam Jones, USA	5-11	
Pole Vault	Charles Dvorak, USA	11-5¾	
Long Jump	Meyer Prinstein, USA	24-1	OR
Triple Jump	Meyer Prinstein, USA	47-1	
Shot Put	Ralph Rose, USA	48-7	WR
56-lb Throw	Étienne Desmarteau, CAN	34-4	
Discus	Martin Sheridan, USA	128-10½	OR
Hammer	John Flanagan, USA	168-1	OR
Triathlon	Max Emmerich, USA	35.7 pts	
Decathlon	Tom Kiely, IRL	6036 pts	

Note: Sheridan won Discus throw-off after tying with Rose for 1st.

Standing		Mark	
High Jump	Ray Ewry, USA	5-3	
Long Jump	Ray Ewry, USA	11-4⅞	WR
Triple Jump	Ray Ewry, USA	34-7¼	

1904 (Cont.)
Swimming

Event		Time
50yd Free	Zoltán Halmay, HUN	.28.0
100yd Free	Zoltán Halmay, HUN	1:02.8
220yd Free	Charles Daniels, USA	2:44.2
440yd Free	Charles Daniels, USA	6:16.2
880yd Free	Emil Rausch, GER	13:11.4
Mile Free	Emil Rausch, GER	27:18.2
100yd Back	Walter Brack, GER	1:16.8
400yd Brst	Georg Zacharias, GER	7:23.6
4x50yd Free	USA (Joe Ruddy, Leo Goodwin, Louis Handle, Charles Daniels) 2:04.6	

Note: Halmay won 50-Free in swim-off with Scott Leary of USA.

Diving		Points
Platform	George Sheldon, USA	12.66
Plunge		**Mark**
for Distance	William Dickey, USA	62-6

Team Sports

Sport	Champion
Lacrosse	Canada (Shamrock-Winnipeg)
Soccer	Canada (Galt Football Club)
Tug-of-War	USA (Milwaukee AC)
Water Polo	USA (New York AC)

Also Contested
Archery, Boxing, Cycling, Fencing, Golf, Gymnastics, Roque (Croquet), Rowing, Tennis, Weightlifting and Freestyle Wrestling.

1906
Athens

After disappointing receptions in Paris and St. Louis, the Olympic movement returned to Athens for the Intercalated Games of 1906.

The mutual desire of Greece and Baron de Coubertin to recapture the spirit of the 1896 Games led to an understanding that the Greeks would host an interim games every four years between Olympics.

Nearly 900 athletes from 20 countries came to Athens, including, for the first time, an official American team picked by the USOC.

As usual, the U.S. dominated track and field, taking 11 of 21 events, including double wins by Martin Sheridan (shot put and freestyle discus) and Ray Ewry (standing high and long jumps) and Paul Pilgrim (400 and 800 meters). The previously unknown Pilgrim had been an 11th-hour addition to the team.

Verner Jarvinen, the first Finn to compete in the Olympics, won the Greek-style discus throw and placed second in the freestyle discus. He returned home a national hero and inspired Finland to become a future Olympic power.

The Intercalated Games were cancelled due to political unrest in 1910 and never reappeared. Medals won are considered unofficial by the IOC.

Top 10 Standings
National medal standings are not recognized by the IOC. The unofficial point totals are based on 3 points for a gold medal, 2 for a silver and 1 for a bronze.

	Gold	Silver	Bronze	Total	Pts
1 France	15	9	16	40	79
2 Greece	8	13	12	33	62
3 USA	12	6	6	24	54
4 Great Britain	8	11	5	24	51
5 Italy	7	6	3	16	36
6 Switzerland	5	6	4	15	31
7 Germany	4	6	5	15	29
8 Sweden	2	5	7	14	23
9 Hungary	2	5	3	10	19
10 Austria	3	3	2	8	17
Norway	4	2	1	7	17

Leading Medal Winners
Number of individual medals won on the left; gold, silver and bronze breakdown to the right.

MEN

No		Sport	G-S-B
6	Louis Richardet, SWI	Shooting	4-2-0
5	Martin Sheridan, USA	Track/Field	2-3-0
5	Konrad Stäheli, SWI	Shooting	2-2-1
5	Léon Moreaux, FRA	Shooting	2-1-2
5	Jean Reich, SWI	Shooting	1-1-3
4	Gudbrand Skatteboe, NOR	Shooting	3-1-0
4	Gustav Casmir, GER	Fencing	2-2-0
4	Eric Lemming, SWE	Track/Field & Tug of War	1-0-3
3	Francesco Verri, ITA	Cycling	3-0-0
3	Enrico Bruna, ITA	Rowing	3-0-0
3	Georgio Cesana, ITA	Rowing	3-0-0
3	Max Decugis, FRA	Tennis	3-0-0
3	Emilio Fontanella, ITA	Rowing	3-0-0
3	Georges Dillon-Cavanaugh, FRA	Fencing	2-1-0
3	Henry Taylor, GBR	Swimming	1-1-1
3	Fernand Vast, FRA	Cycling	1-0-2
3	Raoul de Boigne, FRA	Shooting	0-1-2
3	John Jarvis, GBR	Swimming	0-1-2

WOMEN

No		Sport	G-S-B
2	Sophia Marinou, GRE	Tennis	0-2-0

Track & Field

Event		Time
100m	Archie Hahn, USA	11.2
400m	Paul Pilgrim, USA	53.2
800m	Paul Pilgrim, USA	2:01.5
1500m	Jim Lightbody, USA	4:12.0
5 Miles	Henry Hawtrey, GBR	26:11.8
Marathon	Billy Sherring, CAN	2:51:23.6
110m H	Robert Leavitt, USA	16.2
500m Walk	George Bonhag, USA	7:12.6
3000m Walk	György Sztantics, HUN	15:13.2

Event		Mark
High Jump	Con Leahy, GBR/IRL	5-10
Pole Vault	Fernand Gonder, FRA	11-5¾
Long Jump	Meyer Prinstein, USA	23-7½
Triple Jump	Peter O'Connor, GBR/IRL	46-2¼
Shot Put	Martin Sheridan, USA	40-5¼
Stone Throw	Nicolaos Georgantas, GRE	65-4½
Discus	Martin Sheridan, USA	136-0
Greek Discus	Verner Järvinen, FIN	115-4½
Freestyle Javelin	Eric Lemming, SWE	176-10　　**WR**
Pentathlon	Hjalmar Mellander, SWE	24 pts

Notes: Weight in Stone Throw was 14.08 lbs; spinning not allowed in Greek-style Discus.

Standing		Mark
High Jump	Ray Ewry, USA	5- 1¼
Long Jump	Ray Ewry, USA	10-10

Swimming

Event		Time
100m Free	Charles Daniels, USA	1:13.4
400m Free	Otto Scheff, AUT	6:23.8
Mile Free	Henry Taylor, GBR	28:28.0
4x250m Free	HUN (József Ónody, Henrik Hajós, Geza Kiss, Zoltán Halmay)	16:52.4

Diving		Points
Platform	Gottlob Walz, GER	156.0

Team Sports

Sport	Champion
Soccer	Denmark
Tug-of-War	Germany

Also Contested

Canoeing, Cycling, Fencing, Gymnastics, Rowing, Shooting, Tennis, Weightlifting and Greco-Roman Wrestling.

1908

London

The fourth Olympic Games were certainly the wettest and probably the most contentious in history.

Held at a new 68,000-seat stadium in the Shepherds Bush section of London, the 1908 Games were played out under continually rainy skies and suffered from endless arguments between British officials and many of the other countries involved—especially the United States.

"The Battle of Shepherds Bush" began almost immediately, when the U.S. delegation noticed that there was no American flag among the national flags decorating the stadium for the opening ceremonies. U.S. flag bearer and discus champion Martin Sheridan responded by refusing to dip the Stars and Stripes when he passed King Edward VII's box in the parade of athletes. "This flag dips to no earthly king," Sheridan said. And it hasn't since.

The Americans, at least, got to march with their flag. Finland, then ruled by Russia, could not. Informed they would have to use a Russian flag, the furious Finns elected to march with no flag at all.

Once again the marathon proved to be the Games' most memorable event. Laid out over a 26-mile, 365-yard course that stretched from Windsor Castle to the royal box at Shepherds Bush, the race ended in controversy when leader Dorando Pietri of Italy staggered into the packed stadium, took a wrong turn, collapsed, was helped up by doctors, wobbled and fell three more times before

being half-carried across the finish line by race officials. Caught up in the drama of Pietri's agony, the cheering crowd hardly noticed that he was declared the winner just as second place runner, Johnny Hayes of the U.S., entered the stadium.

Pietri was later disqualified in favor of Hayes, but only after British and U.S. officials argued for an hour and fights had broken out in the stands.

Top 10 Standings

National medal standings are not recognized by the IOC. The unofficial point totals are based on 3 points for a gold medal, 2 for a silver and 1 for a bronze.

		Gold	Silver	Bronze	Total	Pts
1	Great Britain	54	46	38	138	292
2	USA	23	12	12	47	105
3	Sweden	8	6	11	25	47
4	France	5	5	9	19	34
5	Canada	3	3	10	16	25
6	Germany	3	5	5	13	24
7	Hungary	3	4	2	9	19
8	Norway	2	3	3	8	15
	Belgium	1	5	2	8	15
10	Italy	2	2	0	4	10

Leading Medal Winners

Number of individual medals won on the left; gold, silver and bronze breakdown to the right.

MEN

No		Sport	G-S-B
3	Mel Sheppard, USA	Track/Field	3-0-0
3	Henry Taylor, GBR	Swimming	3-0-0
3	Benjamin Jones, GBR	Cycling	2-1-0
3	Martin Sheridan, USA	Track/Field	2-0-1
3	Oscar Swahn, SWE	Shooting	2-0-1
3	Josiah Ritchie, GBR	Tennis	1-1-1
3	Ted Ranken, GBR	Shooting	0-3-0

WOMEN

No		Sport	G-S-B
2	Madge Syers, GBR	Figure Skating	1-0-1

Note: Figure Skating was part of the Summer Olympics in 1908 and '20.

Track & Field

Event		Time	
100m	Reggie Walker, SAF	10.8	=OR
200m	Bobby Kerr, CAN	22.6	
400m	Wyndham Halswelle, GBR	50.0	
800m	Mel Sheppard, USA	1:52.8	WR
1500m	Mel Sheppard, USA	4:03.4	OR
5 Miles	Emil Voigt, GBR	25:11.2	
Marathon	Johnny Hayes, USA	2:55:18.4	OR
110m H	Forrest Smithson, USA	15.0	WR
400m H	Charley Bacon, USA	55.0	WR
3200m Steeple	Arthur Russell, GBR	10:47.8	
3500m Walk	George Larner, GBR	14:55.0	
10-mi Walk	George Larner, GBR	1:15:57.4	
Medley Relay	USA (William Hamilton, Nathaniel Cartmell, John Taylor, Mel Sheppard)	3:29.4	
3-mile Relay	GBR (Joseph Deakin, Archie Robertson, Wilfred Coales)	6 pts	

Note: Medley Relay made up of two 200m runs, a 400m and an 800m.

1908 (Cont.)

Event		Mark	
High Jump	Harry Porter, USA	6-3	OR
Pole Vault	Edward Cooke, USA	12-2	OR
Long Jump	Frank Irons, USA	24-6½	OR
Triple Jump	Timothy Ahearne, GBR/IRL	48-11½	OR
Shot Put	Ralph Rose, USA	46-7½	
Discus	Martin Sheridan, USA	134-2	OR
Greek Discus	Martin Sheridan, USA	128-4	OR
Hammer	John Flanagan, USA	170-4	OR
Javelin	Eric Lemming, SWE	179-10	WR
Freestyle Javelin	Eric Lemming, SWE	178-7½	

Note: Spinning not allowed in Greek-style Discus.

Standing		Mark
High Jump	Ray Ewry, USA	5-2
Long Jump	Ray Ewry, USA	10-11¼

Swimming
MEN

Event		Time	
100m Free	Charles Daniels, USA	1:05.6	WR
400m Free	Henry Taylor, GBR	5:36.8	
1500m Free	Henry Taylor, GBR	22:48.4	WR
100m Back	Arno Bieberstein, GER	1:24.6	WR
200m Brst	Frederick Holman, GBR	3:09.2	WR
4x200m Free	GBR (John Derbyshire, Paul Radmilovic, William Foster, Henry Taylor)	10:55.6	WR

Diving		Points
Platform	Hjalmar Johansson, SWE	83.75
Spring	Albert Zürner, GER	85.5

Team Sports

Sport	Champion
Field Hockey	Great Britain (England)
Lacrosse	Canada
Polo	Great Britain (Roehampton)
Rugby	Australia
Soccer	Great Britain
Tug-of-War	Great Britain (City Police)
Water Polo	Great Britain

Also Contested

Archery, Boxing, Cycling, Fencing, Figure Skating, Gymnastics, Jeu de Paume (court tennis), Racquets, Rowing, Shooting, Tennis, Freestyle Wrestling, Greco-Roman Wrestling and Yachting.

1912

Stockholm

The belligerence of 1908 was replaced with benevolence four years later, as Sweden provided a well-organized and pleasant haven for the troubled Games.

And then there were Jim Thorpe and Hannes Kolehmainen.

Thorpe, a 24-year-old American Indian who was a two-time consensus All-America football player at Carlisle (Pa.) Institute, won the two most demanding events in track and field—the pentathlon and decathlon. And he did it with ease. "You sir," said the Swedes' King Gustav V at the medal ceremony, "are the greatest athlete in the world." To which Thorpe is said to have replied, "Thanks, King."

Kolehmainen, a 22-year-old Finnish vegetarian, ran away with three distance events being run for the first time—the 5,000- and 10,000-meter races and the 12,000-meter cross-country run. He also picked up a silver medal in the 12,000-meter team race.

Ralph Craig of the U.S. was the only other winner of two individual track gold medals, taking both the 100- and 200-meter runs. The 100 final had seven false starts, one with Craig sprinting the entire distance before being called back.

Although Thorpe returned to the U.S. a hero, a year later it was learned that he had played semi-pro baseball for $25 a week in 1910. The IOC, with the full support of the American Olympic Committee, stripped him of his medals and erased his records.

The medals and records were returned in 1982—30 years after Thorpe's death.

Top 10 Standings

National medal standings are not recognized by the IOC. The unofficial point totals are based on 3 points for a gold medal, 2 for a silver and 1 for a bronze.

		Gold	Silver	Bronze	Total	Pts
1	Sweden	23	24	17	64	134
2	USA	25	18	20	63	131
3	Great Britain	10	15	16	41	76
4	Finland	9	8	9	26	52
5	Germany	5	13	7	25	48
6	France	7	4	3	14	32
7	Denmark	1	6	5	12	20
8	Norway	3	2	5	10	18
9	Canada	3	2	3	8	16
	Hungary	3	2	3	8	16
	South Africa	4	2	0	6	16

Leading Medal Winners

Number of individual medals won on the left; gold, silver and bronze breakdown to the right.

MEN

No		Sport	G-S-B
6	Louis Richardet, SWI	Shooting	4-2-0
5	Wilhelm Carlberg, SWE	Shooting	3-2-0
4	Hannes Kolehmainen, FIN	Track/Field	3-1-0
4	Eric Carlberg, SWE	Shooting	2-2-0
4	Johan von Holst, SWE	Shooting	2-1-1
4	Carl Osburn, USA	Shooting	1-2-1
3	Alfred Lane, USA	Shooting	3-0-0
3	Åke Lundeberg, SWE	Shooting	2-1-0
3	Frederick Hird, USA	Shooting	2-0-1
3	Jean Cariou, FRA	Equestrian	1-1-1
3	Charles Dixon, GBR	Tennis	1-1-1
3	Harold Hardwick, AUS	Swimming	1-0-2
3	Jack Hatfield, GBR	Swimming	0-2-1
3	Charles Stewart, GBR	Shooting	0-0-3

WOMEN

No		Sport	G-S-B
2	Edith Hannam, GBR	Tennis	2-0-0
2	Jennie Fletcher, GBR	Swimming	1-0-1
2	Sigrid Fick, SWE	Tennis	0-1-1

Track & Field

Event		Time	
100m	Ralph Craig, USA	10.8	=OR
200m	Ralph Craig, USA	21.7	
400m	Charlie Reidpath, USA	48.2	OR
800m	Ted Meredith, USA	1:51.9	WR
1500m	Arnold Jackson, GBR	3:56.8	OR
5000m	Hannes Kolehmainen, FIN	14:36.6	WR
10,000m	Hannes Kolehmainen, FIN	31:20.8	
X-country (12,000m)	Hannes Kolehmainen, FIN	45:11.6	
Marathon	Kenneth McArthur, SAF	2:36:54.8	
110m H	Frederick Kelly, USA	15.1	
10k Walk	George Goulding, CAN	46:28.4	
4x100m	GBR (David Jacobs, Harold Macintosh, Victor d'Arcy, William Applegarth)	42.4	OR
4x400m	USA (Mel Sheppard, Edward Lindberg, Ted Meredith, Charlie Reidpath)	3:16.6	WR
3000m Team	USA (Tel Berna, Norman Taber, George Bonhag)	9 pts	
X-country (12,000m)	SWE (Hjalmar Andersson, John Eke, Josef Ternström)	10 pts	

Event		Mark	
High Jump	Alma Richards, USA	6-4	OR
Pole Vault	Harry Babcock, USA	12-11½	OR
Long Jump	Albert Gutterson, USA	24-11¼	OR
Triple Jump	Gustaf Lindblom, SWE	48-5¼	
Shot Put	Babe McDonald, USA	50-4	OR
Discus	Armas Taipale, FIN	148-3	OR
Hammer	Matt McGrath, USA	179-7	OR
Javelin	Eric Lemming, SWE	198-11	WR
Pentathlon	Jim Thorpe, USA	7 pts	
Decathlon	Jim Thorpe, USA	8412 pts	WR

Event		Mark
High Jump	Platt Adams, USA	5-4¼
Long Jump	Constantin Tsiklitiras, GRE	11-0¾

Both Hands		Mark
Shot Put	Ralph Rose, USA	90-10½
Discus	Armas Taipale, FIN	271-10
Javelin	Juho Saaristo, FIN	359-0

Swimming
MEN

Event		Time	
100m Free	Duke Kahanamoku, USA	1:03.4	
400m Free	George Hodgson, CAN	5:24.4	
1500m Free	George Hodgson, CAN	22:00.0	WR
100m Back	Harry Hebner, USA	1:21.2	
200m Brst	Walter Bathe, GER	3:01.8	OR
400m Brst	Walter Bathe, GER	6:29.6	OR
4x200m Free	AUS (Cecil Healy, Malcolm Champion, Leslie Boardman, Harold Hardwick)	10:11.6	WR

Diving		Points
Spring	Paul Günther, GER	79.23
Platform	Erik Adlerz, SWE	73.94
Plain High	Erik Adlerz, SWE	40.0

WOMEN

Event		Time	
100m Free	Fanny Durack, AUS	1:22.2	
4x100m Free	GBR (Bella Moore, Jennie Fletcher, Annie Speirs, Irene Steer)	5:52.8	WR

Diving		Points
Platform	Greta Johansson, SWE	39.9

Team Sports

Sports	Champion
Soccer	Great Britain
Tug-of-War	Sweden
Water Polo	Great Britain

Also Contested

Cycling, Equestrian, Fencing, Gymnastics, Modern Pentathlon, Rowing, Shooting, Tennis, Greco-Roman Wrestling and Yachting.

1920

Antwerp

The Olympic quadrennial, scheduled for Berlin in 1916, was interrupted by World War I—the so-called "War to End All Wars," which had involved 28 countries and killed nearly 10 million troops in four years.

The four-year cycle of Olympiads–Berlin would have been the sixth–is still counted, however, even though the Games were not played.

Less than two years after the armistice, the Olympics resumed in Belgium, a symbolic and austere choice considering it had been occupied for four years by enemy forces. Still, 29 countries (one more than participated in the war) sent a record 2,600 athletes to the Games. Germany and Austria, the defeated enemy of Belgium and the Allies, were not invited.

The United States turned in the best overall team performance, winning 41 gold medals, but the talk of the Games was 23-year-old distance runner Paavo Nurmi of Finland. Nurmi won the 10,000-meter run and 8,000-meter cross-country, took a third gold in the team cross-country and silver in the 5,000-meter run. In all, Finland won nine track and field gold medals to break the U.S. dominance in the sport.

Elsewhere, Albert Hill of Britain made his Olympic debut at age 36 and won both the 800- and 1,500-meter runs. World record holder Charley Paddock of the U.S. won the 100 meters, but was upset in the 200 by teammate Allan Woodring, who was a last-minute addition to the team. And in swimming, the U.S. won 11 of 15 events, led by triple gold medalists Norman Ross and Ethelda Bleibtrey, defending men's 100-meter freestyle champion Duke Kahanamoku and 14-year-old springboard diving champion Aileen Riggin.

The Antwerp Games were also noteworthy for the introduction of the Olympic oath–uttered for the first time by Belgium fencer Victor Bion–and the Olympic flag, with its five multicolored, intersecting rings.

1920 (Cont.)

Top 10 Standings

National medal standings are not recognized by the IOC. The unofficial point totals are based on 3 points for a gold medal, 2 for a silver and 1 for a bronze.

	Gold	Silver	Bronze	Total	Pts
1 USA	41	27	27	95	204
2 Sweden	19	20	25	64	122
3 Great Britain	14	15	13	42	85
4 France	9	19	13	41	78
5 Finland	15	10	9	34	74
Belgium	13	11	11	35	72
7 Norway	13	9	9	31	66
8 Italy	13	5	5	23	54
9 Denmark	3	9	1	13	28
10 Holland	4	2	5	11	21

Leading Medal Winners

Number of individual medals won on the left; gold, silver and bronze breakdown to the right.

MEN

No		Sport	G-S-B
7	Willis Lee, USA	Shooting	5-1-1
7	Lloyd Spooner, USA	Shooting	4-1-2
6	Hubert van Innis, BEL	Archery	4-2-0
6	Carl Osburn, USA	Shooting	4-1-1
5	Nedo Nadi, ITA	Fencing	5-0-0
5	Otto Olsen, NOR	Shooting	3-2-0
5	Larry Nuesslein, USA	Shooting	2-1-2
5	Julien Brulé, FRA	Archery	1-3-1
4	Dennis Fenton, USA	Shooting	3-0-1
4	Aldo Nadi, ITA	Fencing	3-1-0
4	Paavo Nurmi, FIN	Track/Field	3-1-0
4	Harold Natvig, NOR	Shooting	2-1-1
4	Östen Östensen, NOR	Shooting	0-2-2
4	Erik Backman, SWE	Track/Field	0-1-3
4	Fritz Kuchen, SWI	Shooting	0-0-4
3	Norman Ross, USA	Swimming	3-0-0
3	Albert Hill, GBR	Track/Field	2-1-0
3	Morris Kirksey, USA	Track/Field & Rugby	2-1-0
3	Charley Paddock, USA	Track/Field	2-1-0
3	Bevil Rudd, SAF	Track/Field	1-0-2
3	Ettore Caffaratti, ITA	Equestrian	0-1-2

Fourteen shooters tied with 3 each.

WOMEN

No		Sport	G-S-B
3	Ethelda Bleibtrey, USA	Swimming	3-0-0
3	Suzanne Lenglen, FRA	Tennis	2-0-1
3	Kitty McKane, GBR	Tennis	1-1-1
3	Frances Schroth, USA	Swimming	1-0-2
2	Irene Guest, USA	Swimming	1-1-0
2	Margaret Woodbridge, USA	Swimming	1-1-0
2	Dorothy Holman, GBR	Tennis	0-2-0

Track & Field

Event		Time	
200m	Allen Woodring, USA	22.0	
400m	Bevil Rudd, SAF	49.6	
800m	Albert Hill, GBR	1:53.4	
1500m	Albert Hill, GBR	4:01.8	
5000m	Joseph Guillemot, FRA	14:55.6	
10,000m	Paavo Nurmi, FIN	31:45.8	
X-country (8000m)	Paavo Nurmi, FIN	27:15.0	
Marathon	Hannes Kolehmainen, FIN	2:32:35.8	WB
110m H	Earl Thomson, CAN	14.8	WR
400m H	Frank Loomis, USA	54.0	WR
3000m Steeple	Percy Hodge, GBR	10:00.4	OR

Event		Time	
3k Walk	Ugo Frigerio, ITA	13:14.2	OR
10k Walk	Ugo Frigerio, ITA	48:06.2	
4x100m	USA (Charley Paddock, Jackson Scholz, Loren Murchison, Morris Kirksey)	42.2	WR
4x400m	GBR (Cecil Griffiths, Robert Lindsay, John Ainsworth-Davis, Guy Butler)	3:22.2	
3000m Team	USA (Horace Brown, Arlie Schardt, Ivan Dresser)	10 pts	
X-country (8000m)	FIN (Paavo Nurmi, Heikki Liimatainen, Teudor Koskenniemi)	10 pts	

Event		Mark	
High Jump	Richmond Landon, USA	6-4	=OR
Pole Vault	Frank Foss, USA	13-5	WR
Long Jump	William Petersson, SWE	23-5½	
Triple Jump	Vilho Tuulos, FIN	47-7	
Shot Put	Ville Pörhölä, FIN	48-7¼	
56-lb Throw	Babe McDonald, USA	36-11½	OR
Discus	Elmer Niklander, FIN	146-7	
Hammer	Pat Ryan, USA	173-5	
Javelin	Jonni Myyrä, FIN	215-10	OR
Pentathlon	Eero Lehtonen, FIN	14 pts	
Decathlon	Helge Lövland, NOR	6803 pts	

Swimming

MEN

Event		Time	
100m Free	Duke Kahanamoku, USA	1:01.4	
400m Free	Norman Ross, USA	5:26.8	
1500m Free	Norman Ross, USA	22:23.2	
100m Back	Warren Kealoha, USA	1:15.2	
200m Brst	Håkan Malmroth, SWE	3:04.4	
400m Brst	Håkan Malmroth, SWE	6:31.8	
4x200m Free	USA (Perry McGillivray, Pua Kealoha, Norman Ross, Duke Kahanamoku)	10:04.4	WR

Diving		Points
Plain High	Arvid Wallman, SWE	183.5
Platform	Clarence Pinkston, USA	100.67
Spring	Louis Kuehn, USA	675.4

WOMEN

Event		Time	
100m Free	Ethelda Bleibtrey, USA	1:13.6	WR
300m Free	Ethelda Bleibtrey, USA	4:34.0	WR
4x100m Free	USA (Margaret Woodbridge, Frances Schroth, Irene Guest, Ethelda Bleibtrey)	5:11.6	WR

Diving		Points
Platform	Stefani Fryland-Clausen, DEN	34.6
Spring	Aileen Riggin, USA	539.9

Team Sports

Sport	Champion
Field Hockey	Great Britain
Ice Hockey	Canada
Polo	Great Britain
Soccer	Belgium
Rugby	United States
Tug-of-War	Great Britain
Water Polo	Great Britain/Ireland

Also Contested

Archery, Boxing, Cycling, Equestrian, Fencing, Figure Skating, Gymnastics, Modern Pentathlon, Rowing, Shooting, Tennis, Weightlifting, Freestyle Wrestling, Greco-Roman Wrestling and Yachting.

1924

Paris

Paavo Nurmi may have been the talk of Antwerp in 1920, but he was the sensation of Paris four years later.

It wasn't just that the "Flying Finn" won five gold medals, it was the way he did it. Running with a stopwatch on his wrist, Peerless Paavo captured the 1,500 and 5,000-meter finals within an hour of each other and set Olympic records in both. Two days later, he blew away the field in the 10,000-meter cross-country run where the heat and an unusually difficult course combined to knock out 23 of 38 starters (Finland also won the team gold in the event). And finally, the next day he led the Finns to victory in the 3,000-meter team race. His performance overshadowed the four gold medals of teammate Ville Ritola.

The gold medals won by British runners Harold Abrahams in the 100 meters and Eric Liddell in the 400 were chronicled in the 1981 Academy Award-winning film Chariots of Fire. The movie, however, was not based on fact. Liddell, a devout Christian, knew months in advance that the preliminary for the 100 (his best event) was on a Sunday, so he had plenty of time to change plans and train for the 400. Also, he and Abrahams never competed against each other in real life.

Speaking of the movies, Johnny Weissmuller of the U.S. won three swimming gold medals in the 100- and 400-meter freestyles and water polo. He would later become Hollywood's most famous Tarzan.

Top 10 Standings

National medal standings are not recognized by the IOC. The unofficial point totals are based on 3 points for a gold medal, 2 for a silver and 1 for a bronze.

		Gold	Silver	Bronze	Total	Pts
1	USA	45	27	27	99	216
2	France	13	15	10	38	79
3	Finland	14	13	10	37	78
4	Great Britain	9	13	12	34	65
5	Sweden	4	13	12	29	50
6	Switzerland	7	8	10	25	47
7	Italy	8	3	5	16	35
8	Belgium	3	7	3	13	26
9	Norway	5	2	3	10	22
10	Holland	4	1	5	10	19

Leading Medal Winners

Number of individual medals won on the left; gold, silver and bronze breakdown to the right.

MEN

No		Sport	G-S-B
6	Ville Ritola, FIN	Track/Field	4-2-0
5	Paavo Nurmi, FIN	Track/Field	5-0-0
5	Roger Ducret, FRA	Fencing	3-2-0

No		Sport	G-S-B
4	Johnny Weissmuller, USA	Swimming Water Polo	3-0-1
3	Ole Lilloe-Olsen, NOR	Shooting	2-1-0
3	Vincent Richards, USA	Tennis	2-1-0
3	Albert Séquin, FRA	Gymnastics	1-2-0
3	Boy Charlton, AUS	Swimming	1-1-1
3	August Güttinger, SWI	Gymnastics	1-0-2
3	Robert Prazák, CZE	Gymnastics	0-3-0
3	Arne Borg, SWE	Swimming	0-2-1
3	Jean Gutweniger, SWI	Gymnastics	0-2-1
3	Henri Hoevenaers, BEL	Cycling	0-2-1

WOMEN

No		Sport	G-S-B
3	Gertrude Ederle, USA	Swimming	1-0-2
2	Ethel Lackie, USA	Swimming	2-0-0
2	Hazel Wightman, USA	Tennis	2-0-0
2	Helen Wills, USA	Tennis	2-0-0
2	Betty Becker, USA	Diving	1-1-0
2	Mariechen Wehselau, USA	Swimming	1-1-0
2	Kitty McKane, GBR	Tennis	0-1-1
2	Aileen Riggin, USA	Swimming & Diving	0-1-1

Track & Field

Event		Time	
100m	Harold Abrahams, GBR	10.6	=OR
200m	Jackson Scholz, USA	21.6	
400m	Eric Liddell, GBR	47.6	OR
800m	Douglas Lowe, GBR	1:52.4	
1500m	Paavo Nurmi, FIN	3:53.6	OR
5000m	Paavo Nurmi, FIN	14:31.2	OR
10,000m	Ville Ritola, FIN	30:23.2	WR
X-country (10,000m)	Paavo Nurmi, FIN	32:54.8	
Marathon	Albin Stenroos, FIN	2:41:22.6	
110m H	Daniel Kinsey, USA	15.0	
400m H	Morgan Taylor, USA	52.6	
3000m Steeple	Ville Ritola, FIN	9:33.6	OR
10k Walk	Ugo Frigerio, ITA	47:49.0	
4x100m	USA (Francis Hussey, Louis Clarke, Loren Murchison, Alfred Leconey)	41.0	=WR
4x400M	USA (C.S. Cochrane, Alan Helffrich, J.O. MacDonald, William Stevenson)	3:16.0	WR
3000m Team	FIN (Paavo Nurmi, Ville Ritola, Elias Katz)	8 pts	
X-country (10,000m)	FIN (Paavo Nurmi, Ville Ritola, Hekki Liimatainen)	11 pts	

Event		Mark	
High Jump	Harold Osborn, USA	6- 6	OR
Pole Vault	Lee Barnes, USA	12-11½	
Long Jump	De Hart Hubbard, USA	24- 5	
Triple Jump	Nick Winter, AUS	50-11¼	WR
Shot Put	Bud Houser, USA	49- 2¼	
Discus	Bud Houser, USA	151- 4	OR
Hammer	Fred Tootell, USA	174-10	
Javelin	Jonni Myyrä, FIN	206- 7	
Pentathlon	Eero Lehtonen, FIN	14 pts	
Decathlon	Harold Osborn, USA	7711 pts	WR

Swimming

MEN

Event		Time	
100m Free	Johnny Weissmuller, USA	59.0	OR
400m Free	Johnny Weissmuller, USA	5:04.2	OR
1500m Free	Boy Charlton, AUS	20:06.6	WR
100m Back	Warren Kealoha, USA	1:13.2	OR
200m Brst	Robert Skelton, USA	2:56.6	

1924 (Cont.)

Event		Time
4x200m Free	USA (Wallace O'Connor, Harry Glancy, Ralph Breyer, Johnny Weissmuller)	.......9:53.4 **WR**

Diving		Points
Plain High	Richmond Eve, AUS	.......160.0
Platform	Albert White, USA	.......97.46
Spring	Albert White, USA	.......696.4

WOMEN

Event		Time
100m Free	Ethel Lackie, USA	.........1:12.4
400m Free	Martha Norelius, USA	......6:02.2 **OR**
100m Back	Sybil Bauer, USA	.......1:23.2 **OR**
200m Brst	Lucy Morton, GBR	.......3:33.2 **OR**
4x100m Free	USA (Gertrude Ederle, Euphrasia Donnelly, Ethel Lackie, Mariechen Wehselau)	......4:58.8 **WR**

Diving		Points
Platform	Caroline Smith, USA	.............33.2
Spring	Elizabeth Becker, USA	..........474.5

Team Sports

Sport	Champion
Polo	.........Argentina
Rugby	......United States
Soccer	..........Uruguay
Water Polo	.........France

Also Contested

Boxing, Cycling, Equestrian, Fencing, Gymnastics, Modern Pentathlon, Rowing, Shooting, Tennis, Weightlifting, Freestyle Wrestling, Greco-Roman Wrestling and Yachting.

1928

Amsterdam

"We are here to represent the greatest country on earth. We did not come here to lose gracefully. We came here to win—and win decisively."

So ordered American Olympic Committee president Gen. Douglas MacArthur before the start of the 1928 Games and his athletes delivered, easily winning the unofficial national standings for the third Olympiad in a row.

The U.S. men won eight gold medals in track and field, but were victorious in only one individual running race (Ray Barbuti in the 400 meters). In the sprints, Canada's Percy Williams became the first non-American to win both the 100 and 200. Finland claimed four running titles, including Paavo Nurmi's victory in the 10,000 meters—his ninth overall gold medal in three Olympic Games. Teammate and arch-rival Ville Ritola placed second in the 10,000 and outran Nurmi in the 5,000.

These Games marked Germany's return to the Olympic fold after serving a 10-year probation for its "aggressiveness" in World War I. It was also the first Olympics that women were allowed to participate in track and field (despite objections from Pope Pius IX). And in swimming, the U.S. got double gold performances from Martha Norelius, Albina Osipowich and Johnny Weissmuller, and diver Pete Desjardins.

Top 10 Standings

National medal standings are not recognized by the IOC. The unofficial point totals are based on 3 points for a gold medal, 2 for a silver and 1 for a bronze.

		Gold	Silver	Bronze	Total	Pts
1	USA	22	18	16	56	118
2	Germany	10	7	14	31	58
3	Finland	8	8	9	25	49
4	Sweden	7	6	12	25	45
5	France	6	10	5	21	43
6	Holland	6	9	4	19	40
7	Italy	7	5	7	19	38
8	Great Britain	3	10	7	20	36
9	Switzerland	7	4	4	15	33
10	Canada	4	4	7	15	27

Leading Medal Winners

Number of individual medals won on the left; gold, silver and bronze breakdown to the right.

MEN

No			Sport	G-S-B
4	Georges Miez, SWI	....	Gymnastics	3-1-0
4	Hermann Hänggi, SWI	....	Gymnastics	2-1-1
3	Lucien Gaudin, FRA	....	Fencing	2-1-0
3	Eugen Mack, SWI	....	Gymnastics	2-0-1
3	Paavo Nurmi, FIN	....	Track/Field	1-2-0
3	Ladislav Vácha, CZE	....	Gymnastics	1-2-0
3	Leon Stukelj, YUG	....	Gymnastics	1-0-2
3	Emanuel Löffler, CZE	....	Gymnastics	0-2-1

WOMEN

No			Sport	G-S-B
3	Joyce Cooper, GBR	....	Swimming	0-1-2
2	Martha Norelius, USA	....	Swimming	2-0-0
2	Albina Osipowich, USA	....	Swimming	2-0-0
2	Maria Braun, HOL	....	Swimming	1-1-0
2	Eleanor Garatti, USA	....	Swimming	1-1-0
2	Betty Robinson, USA	....	Track/Field	1-1-0
2	Fanny Rosenfeld, CAN	....	Track/Field	1-1-0
2	Ethel Smith, CAN	....	Track/Field	1-0-1
2	Ellen King, GBR	....	Swimming	0-2-0
2	Georgia Coleman, USA	....	Diving	0-1-1

Track & Field
MEN

Event		Time
100m	Percy Williams, CAN	.........10.8
200m	Percy Williams, CAN	.........21.8
400m	Ray Barbuti, USA	...........47.8
800m	Douglas Lowe, GBR	.......1:51.8 **OR**
1500m	Harri Larva, FIN	.........3:53.2 **OR**
5000m	Ville Ritola, FIN	...........14:38.0
10,000m	Paavo Nurmi, FIN	.........30:18.8 **OR**
Marathon	Mohamed El Ouafi, FRA	.2:32:57.0
110m H	Syd Atkinson, SAF	...........14.8
400m H	David Burghley, GBR	.........53.4 **OR**
3000m Steeple	Toivo Loukola, FIN	.........9:21.8 **WR**
4x100m	USA (Frank Wykoff, Jimmy Quinn, Charley Borah, Hank Russell)	..41.0 **WR**
4x400m	USA (George Baird, Bud Spencer, Fred Alderman, Ray Barbuti)	.............3:14.2 **WR**

Event		Mark	
High Jump	Bob King, USA	6-4½	
Pole Vault	Sabin Carr, USA	13-9¼	OR
Long Jump	Ed Hamm, USA	25- 4½	OR
Triple Jump	Mikio Oda, JPN	49-11	
Shot Put	Johnny Kuck, USA	52-0¾	WR
Discus	Bud Houser, USA	155- 3	OR
Hammer	Pat O'Callaghan, IRL	168-7	
Javelin	Erik Lundkvist, SWE	218- 6	OR
Decathlon	Paavo Yrjölä, FIN	8053 pts	WR

WOMEN

Event		Time	
100m	Betty Robinson, USA	12.2	=WR
800m	Lina Radke, GER	2:16.8	WR
4x100m	CAN (Fanny Rosenfeld, Ethel Smith, Florence Bell, Myrtle Cook)	48.4	WR

Event		Mark	
High Jump	Ethel Catherwood, CAN	5- 2½	
Discus	Halina Konopacka, POL	129-11¾	WR

Swimming

MEN

Event		Time	
100m Free	Johnny Weissmuller, USA	58.6	OR
400m Free	Alberto Zorilla, ARG	5:01.6	OR
1500m Free	Arne Borg, SWE	19:51.8	OR
100m Back	George Kojac, USA	1:08.2	WR
200m Brst	Yoshiyuki Tsuruta, JPN	2:48.8	OR

Event		Time	
4x200m Free	USA (Austin Clapp, Walter Laufer, Gorge Kojac, Johnny Weissmuller)	9:36.2	WR

Diving		Points
Platform	Pete Desjardins, USA	98.74
Spring	Pete Desjardins, USA	185.04

WOMEN

Event		Time	
100m Free	Albina Osipowich, USA	1:11.0	OR
400m Free	Martha Norelius, USA	5:42.8	WR
100m Back	Maria Braun, HOL	1:22.0	
200m Brst	Hilde Schrader, GER	3:12.6	
4x100m Free	USA (Adelaide Lambert, Eleanor Garatti, Albina Osipowich, Martha Norelius)	4:47.6	WR

Diving		Points
Platform	Elizabeth Becker Pinkston, USA	31.6
Spring	Helen Meany, USA	78.62

Team Sports

Sport	Champion
Field Hockey	India
Soccer	Uruguay
Water Polo	Germany

Also Contested

Boxing, Cycling, Equestrian, Fencing, Gymnastics, Modern Pentathlon, Rowing, Weightlifting, Freestyle Wrestling, Greco-Roman Wrestling and Yachting.

1932

Los Angeles

Despite a world-wide economic depression and predictions that the 1932 Summer Olympics were doomed to failure, 37 countries sent over 1,300 athletes to southern California and the Games were a huge success.

Energized by perfect weather and the buoyant atmosphere of the first Olympic Village, the competition was fierce. Sixteen world and Olympic records fell in men's track and field alone.

In women's track, 18-year-old Babe Didrikson, who had set world records in the 80-meter hurdles, javelin and high jump at the AAU Olympic Trials three weeks before, came to L.A. and announced, "I am out to beat everybody in sight." She almost did, too–winning the hurdles and javelin, but taking second in the high jump (despite tying teammate Jean Shiley for first) when her jumping style was ruled illegal.

Didrikson's heroics, along with American Eddie Tolan's double in the 100 and 200 meters and Italian Luigi Beccali's upset victory in the 1,500, were among the Games' highlights, but they didn't quite make up for the absence of Finland's famed distance runner Paavo Nurmi.

Just before the Games, the IOC said that Nurmi would not be allowed to participate in his fourth Olympics because he had received excessive expense money on a trip to Germany in 1929. The ruling came as no surprise in the track world where it was said, "Nurmi has the lowest heartbeat and the highest asking price of any athlete in the world."

The Japanese men and American women dominated in swimming, each winning five of six events. Helene Madison of the U.S. won two races and anchored the winning relay team.

Top 10 Standings

National medal standings are not recognized by the IOC. The unofficial point totals are based on 3 points for a gold medal, 2 for a silver and 1 for a bronze.

	Gold	Silver	Bronze	Total	Pts
1 USA	41	32	30	103	217
2 Italy	12	12	12	36	72
3 Sweden	9	5	9	23	46
4 France	10	5	4	19	44
5 Finland	5	8	12	25	43
6 Germany	3	12	5	20	38
7 Japan	7	7	4	18	39
8 Great Britain	4	7	5	16	31
Hungary	6	4	5	15	31
10 Canada	2	5	8	15	24

Leading Medal Winners

Number of individual medals won on the left; gold, silver and bronze breakdown to the right.

MEN

No		Sport	G-S-B
4	István Pelle, HUN	Gymnastics	2-2-0
4	Giulio Gaudini, ITA	Fencing	0-3-1
4	Heikki Savolainen, FIN	Gymnastics	0-1-3
3	Romeo Neri, ITA	Gymnastics	3-0-0
3	Alex Wilson, CAN	Track/Field	0-1-2
3	Philip Edwards, CAN	Track/Field	0-0-3

1932 (Cont.)

WOMEN

No		Sport	G-S-B
3	Helene Madison, USA	Swimming	3-0-0
3	Babe Didrikson, USA	Track/Field	2-1-0
2	Georgia Coleman, USA	Diving	1-1-0
2	Eleanor Garatti, USA	Swimming	1-0-1
2	Willy den Ouden, HOL	Swimming	0-2-0
2	Valerie Davies, GBR	Swimming	0-0-2

Track & Field

MEN

Event		Time	
100m	Eddie Tolan, USA	10.3	OR
200m	Eddie Tolan, USA	21.2	OR
400m	Bill Carr, USA	46.2	WR
800m	Tommy Hampson, GBR	1:49.7	OR
1500m	Luigi Beccali, ITA	3:51.2	OR
5000m	Lauri Lehtinen, FIN	14:30.0	OR
10,000m	Janusz Kusocinski, POL	30:11.4	OR
Marathon	Juan Carlos Zabala, ARG	2:31:36.0	OR
110m H	George Saling, USA	14.6	
400m H	Bob Tisdall, IRL	51.7	
3000m Steeple	Volmari Iso-Hollo, FIN	10:33.4	
50k Walk	Thomas Green, GBR	4:50:10	
4x100m	USA (Bob Kiesel, Emmett Toppino, Hector Dyer, Frank Wykoff)	40.0	WR
4x400m	USA (Ivan Fuqua, Edgar Ablowich, Karl Warner, Bill Carr)	3:08.2	WR

Note: Due to a lap count error, the 3000-meter steeplechase actually went 3460 meters, or one lap too many.

Event		Mark	
High Jump	Duncan McNaughton, CAN	.6- 5½	
Pole Vault	Bill Miller, USA	14- 1¾	OR
Long Jump	Edward Gordon, USA	25- 0¾	
Triple Jump	Chuhei Nambu, JPN	51- 7	WR
Shot Put	Leo Sexton, USA	52- 6	OR
Discus	John Anderson, USA	162- 4	OR
Hammer	Pat O'Callaghan, IRL	176-11	
Javelin	Matti Järvinen, FIN	238- 6	OR
Decathlon	Jim Bausch, USA	8462 pts	WR

WOMEN

Event		Time	
100m	Stella Walsh, POL	11.9	=WR
80m H	Babe Didrikson, USA	11.7	WR
4x100m	USA (Mary Carew, Evelyn Furtsch, Annette Rogers, Wilhelmina Von Bremen)	46.9	WR

Event		Mark	
High Jump	Jean Shiley, USA	.5- 5¼	WR
Discus	Lillian Copeland, USA	133- 2	OR
Javelin	Babe Didrikson, USA	143- 4	OR

Swimming

MEN

Event		Time	
100m Free	Yasuji Miyazaki, JPN	58.2	
400m Free	Buster Crabbe, USA	4:48.4	OR
1500m Free	Kusuo Kitamura, JPN	19:12.4	OR
100m Back	Masaji Kiyokawa, JPN	1:08.6	
200m Brst	Yoshiyuki Tsuruta, JPN	2:45.4	
4x200m Free	JPN (Yasuji Miyazaki, Masonori Yusa, Takashi Yokoyama, Hisakichi Toyoda)	8:58.4	WR

Diving		Points
Platform	Harold Smith, USA	124.80
Spring	Michael Galitzen, USA	161.38

WOMEN

Event		Time	
100m Free	Helene Madison, USA	1:06.8	OR
400m Free	Helene Madison, USA	5:28.5	WR
100m Back	Eleanor Holm, USA	1:19.4	
200m Brst	Clare Dennis, AUS	3:06.3	OR
4x100m Free	USA (Josephine McKim, Helen Johns, Eleanor Saville-Garatti, Helene Madison)	4:38.0	WR

Diving		Points
Platform	Dorothy Poynton, USA	40.26
Spring	Georgia Coleman, USA	87.52

Team Sports

Sport	Champion
Field Hockey	India
Water Polo	Hungary

Also Contested

Boxing, Cycling, Equestrian, Fencing, Gymnastics, Modern Pentathlon, Rowing, Shooting, Weightlifting, Freestyle Wrestling, Greco-Roman Wrestling and Yachting.

1936

Berlin

At the Big Ten track and field championships of 1935, Ohio State's Jesse Owens equaled or set world records in four events: the 100 and 220-yard dashes, 200-yard low hurdles and the long jump. He was also credited with world marks in the 200-meter run and 200-meter hurdles. That's six world records in one afternoon, and he did it all in 45 minutes!

The following year, he swept the 100 and 200 meters and long jump at the Olympic Trials and headed for Germany favored to win all three.

In Berlin, dictator Adolf Hitler and his Nazi followers felt sure that the Olympics would be the ideal venue to demonstrate Germany's oft-stated racial superiority. He directed that $25 million be spent on the finest facilities, the cleanest streets and the temporary withdrawal of all outward signs of the state-run anti-Jewish campaign. By the time over 4,000 athletes from 49 countries arrived for the Games, the stage was set.

Then Jesse Owens, a black sharecropper's son from Alabama, stole the show—winning his three individual events and adding a fourth gold medal in the 400-meter relay. The fact that four other American blacks also won did little to please Herr Hitler, but the applause from the German crowds, especially for Owens, was thunderous. As it was for New Zealander Jack Lovelock's thrilling win over Glenn Cunningham and defending champ Luigi Beccali in the 1,500 meters.

Germany won only five combined gold medals in men's and women's track and field, but saved face for the "master race" in the overall medal count with an 89-56 margin over the United States.

The top female performers in Berlin were 17-year-old Dutch swimmer Rie Mastenbroek, who won three gold medals, and 18-year-old American runner Helen Stephens, who captured the 100 meters and anchored the winning 4x100-meter relay team.

Basketball also made its debut as a medal sport and was played outdoors. The U.S. men easily won the first gold medal championship game with a 19-8 victory over Canada, in the rain.

Top 10 Standings

National medal standings are not recognized by the IOC. The unofficial point totals are based on 3 points for a gold medal, 2 for a silver and 1 for a bronze.

		Gold	Silver	Bronze	Total	Pts
1	Germany	33	26	30	89	181
2	USA	24	20	12	56	124
3	Italy	8	9	5	22	47
4	Finland	7	6	6	19	39
	France	7	6	6	19	39
6	Sweden	6	5	9	20	37
	Hungary	10	1	5	16	37
8	Japan	6	4	8	18	34
9	Holland	6	4	7	17	33
10	Great Britain	4	7	3	14	29

Leading Medal Winners

Number of individual medals won on the left; gold, silver and bronze breakdown to the right.

MEN

No		Sport	G-S-B
6	Konrad Frey, GER	Gymnastics	3-1-2
5	Alfred Schwarzmann, GER	Gymnastics	3-0-2
5	Eugen Mack, SWI	Gymnastics	0-4-1
4	Jesse Owens, USA	Track/Field	4-0-0
3	Robert Charpentier, FRA	Cycling	3-0-0
3	Guy Lapébie, FRA	Cycling	2-1-0
3	Jack Medica, USA	Swimming	1-2-0
3	Matthias Volz, GER	Gymnastics	1-0-2

WOMEN

No		Sport	G-S-B
4	Rie Mastenbroek, HOL	Swimming	3-1-0
2	Helen Stephens, USA	Track/Field	2-0-0
2	Dorothy Poynton Hill, USA	Diving	1-0-1
2	Gisela Arendt, GER	Swimming	0-1-1

Track & Field
MEN

Event		Time	
100m	Jesse Owens, USA	10.3	
200m	Jesse Owens, USA	20.7	OR
400m	Archie Williams, USA	46.5	
800m	John Woodruff, USA	1:52.9	
1500m	Jack Lovelock, NZE	3:47.8	WR
5000m	Gunnar Höckert, FIN	14:22.2	OR
10,000m	Ilmari Salminen, FIN	30:15.4	
Marathon	Sohn Kee-chung, JPN	2:29:19.2	OR
110m H	Forrest Towns, USA	14.2	
400m H	Glenn Hardin, USA	52.4	
3000m Steeple	Volmari Iso-Hollo, FIN	9:03.8	WR
50k walk	Harold Whitlock, GBR	4:30:41.4	OR

Note: Marathon winner Sohn was a Korean, but was forced to run for Japan which occupied his country.

Event		Time	
4x100m	USA (Jesse Owens, Ralph Metcalfe, Foy Draper, Frank Wykoff)	39.8	WR
4x400m	GBR (Frederick Wolff, Godfrey Rampling, William Roberts, A.G. Brown)	3:09.0	

Event		Mark	
High Jump	Cornelius Johnson, USA	6-8	OR
Pole Vault	Earle Meadows, USA	14-3¼	OR
Long Jump	Jesse Owens, USA	26-5½	OR
Triple Jump	Naoto Tajima, JPN	52-6	WR
Shot Put	Hans Woellke, GER	53-1¾	OR
Discus	Ken Carpenter, USA	165-7	OR
Hammer	Karl Hein, GER	185-4	OR
Javelin	Gerhard Stöck, GER	235-8	
Decathlon	Glenn Morris, USA	7900 pts	WR

WOMEN

Event		Time	
100m	Helen Stephens, USA	11.5 w	
80m H	Trebisonda Valla, ITA	11.7	
4x100m	USA (Harriet Bland, Annette Rogers, Betty Robinson, Helen Stephens)	46.9	

w indicates wind-aided.

Event		Mark	
High Jump	Ibolya Csák, HUN	5-3	
Discus	Gisela Mauermayer, GER	156-3	OR
Javelin	Tilly Fleischer, GER	148-3	OR

Swimming
MEN

Event		Time	
100m Free	Ferenc Csík, HUN	57.6	
400m Free	Jack Medica, USA	4:44.5	OR
1500m Free	Noboru Terada, JPN	19:13.7	
100m Back	Adolf Kiefer, USA	1:05.9	OR
200m Brst	Tetsuo Hamuro, JPN	2:41.5	OR
4x200m Free	JPN (Masanori Yusa, Shigeo Sugiura, Masaharu Taguchi, Shigeo Arai)	8:51.5	WR

Diving		Points
Platform	Marshall Wayne, USA	113.58
Spring	Richard Degener, USA	163.57

WOMEN

Event		Time	
100m Free	Rie Mastenbroek, HOL	1:05.9	OR
400m Free	Rie Mastenbroek, HOL	5:26.4	OR
100m Back	Nida Senff, HOL	1:18.9	
200m Brst	Hideko Maehata, JPN	3:03.6	
4x100m Free	HOL (Johanna Selbach, Catherina Wagner, Willemijntje den Ouden, Rie Mastenbroek)	4:36.0	OR

Diving		Points
Platform	Dorothy Poynton Hill, USA	33.93
Spring	Marjorie Gestring, USA	89.27

Team Sports

Sport	Champion
Basketball	United States
Field Hockey	India
Handball	Germany
Polo	Argentina
Soccer	Italy
Water Polo	Hungary

Note: In Water Polo, both Hungary and Germany finished with records of 8-0-1. The Hungarians were awarded the gold medal on total goals (57-56).

Also Contested

Boxing, Canoeing, Cycling, Equestrian, Fencing, Gymnastics, Modern Pentathlon, Rowing, Shooting, Weightlifting, Freestyle Wrestling, Greco-Roman Wrestling and Yachting.

1948

London

The Summer Olympics were scheduled for Tokyo in 1940, but by mid 1938, Japan was at war with China and withdrew as host. The IOC immediately transferred the Games to Helsinki and the Finns eagerly began preparations only to be invaded by Russia in 1939.

By then, of course, Germany had marched into Poland and World War II was on. The Japanese attacked Pearl Harbor two years later, and the bombs didn't stop falling until 1945. Against this backdrop of global conflict, the Olympic Games were cancelled again in 1940 and '44. Many of the participants in the 1936 Games died in the war.

Eager to come back after two dormant Olympiads, the IOC offered the 1948 Games to London. Much of the British capital had been reduced to rubble in the blitz, but the offer was accepted and the Games went on—successfully, without frills, and without invitations extended to Germany and Japan. The Soviet Union was invited, but chose not to show.

The United States reclaimed its place at the top of the overall medal standings, but the primary individual stars were a 30-year-old Dutch mother of two and a 17-year-old kid from California.

Fanny Blankers-Koen duplicated Jesse Owens' track and field grand slam of 12 years before by winning the 100-meter run and 200-meter run, the 80-meter hurdles, and anchoring the women's 400-meter relay.

And Bob Mathias, just two months after graduating from Tulare High School, won the gold medal in the decathlon, an event he had taken up for the first time during the summer.

Top 10 Standings

National medal standings are not recognized by the IOC. The unofficial point totals are based on 3 points for a gold medal, 2 for a silver and 1 for a bronze.

	Gold	Silver	Bronze	Total	Pts
1 USA	38	27	19	84	187
2 Sweden	16	11	17	44	87
3 Italy	8	12	9	29	57
4 France	10	6	13	29	55
5 Hungary	10	5	12	27	52
6 Great Britain	3	14	6	23	43
Finland	8	7	5	20	43
8 Switzerland	5	10	5	20	40
9 Denmark	5	7	8	20	37
10 Holland	5	2	9	16	28
Turkey	6	4	2	12	28

Leading Medal Winners

Number of individual medals won on the left; gold, silver and bronze breakdown to the right.

MEN

No		Sport	G-S-B
5	Veikko Huhtanen, FIN	Gymnastics	3-1-1
4	Paavo Aaltonen, FIN	Gymnastics	3-0-1
3	Jimmy McLane, USA	Swimming	2-1-0
3	Humberto Mariles, MEX	Equestrian	2-0-1
3	Mal Whitfield, USA	Track/Field	2-0-1
3	Barney Ewell, USA	Track/Field	1-2-0
3	Michael Reusch, SWI	Gymnastics	1-2-0
3	Josef Stalder, SWI	Gymnastics	1-1-1
3	Ferenc Pataki, HUN	Gymnastics	1-0-2
3	Walter Lehmann, SWI	Gymnastics	0-3-0
3	Edoardo Mangiarotti, ITA	Fencing	0-2-1
3	János Mogyorósi, HUN	Gymnastics	0-1-2

WOMEN

No		Sport	G-S-B
4	Fanny Blankers-Koen, HOL	Track/Field	4-0-0
3	Ann Curtis, USA	Swimming	2-1-0
3	Micheline Ostermeyer, FRA	Track/Field	2-0-1
3	Karen-Margrete Harup, DEN	Swimming	1-2-0
3	Shirley Strickland, AUS	Track/Field	0-1-2

Track & Field

MEN

Event		Time	
100m	Harrison Dillard, USA	10.3	=OR
200m	Mel Patton, USA	21.1	
400m	Arthur Wint, JAM	46.2	
800m	Mal Whitfield, USA	1:49.2	OR
1500m	Henri Eriksson, SWE	3:49.8	
5000m	Gaston Reiff, BEL	14:17.6	OR
10,000m	Emil Zátopek, CZE	29:59.6	OR
Marathon	Delfo Cabrera, ARG	2:34:51.6	
110m H	Bill Porter, USA	13.9	OR
400m H	Roy Cochran, USA	51.1	OR
3000m Steeple	Thore Sjöstrand, SWE	9:04.6	
10k Walk	John Mikaelsson, SWE	45:13.2	
50k Walk	John Ljunggren, SWE	4:41:52	
4x100m	USA (Barney Ewell, Lorenzo Wright, Harrison Dillard, Mel Patton)	40.6	
4x400m	USA (Art Harnden, Cliff Bourland, Roy Cochran, Mal Whitfield)	3:10.4	

Event		Mark	
High Jump	John Winter, AUS	6-6	
Pole Vault	Guinn Smith, USA	14-1¼	
Long Jump	Willie Steele, USA	25-8	
Triple Jump	Arne Åhman, SWE	50-6¼	
Shot Put	Wilbur Thompson, USA	56-2	OR
Discus	Adolfo Consolini, ITA	173-2	OR
Hammer	Imre Németh, HUN	183-11	
Javelin	Tapio Rautavaara, FIN	228-10	
Decathlon	Bob Mathias, USA	7139 pts	

WOMEN

Event		Time	
100m	Fanny Blankers-Koen, HOL	11.9	
200m	Fanny Blankers-Koen, HOL	24.4	
80m H	Fanny Blankers-Koen, HOL	11.2	OR
4x100m	HOL (Xenia Stad-de Jong, Jeanette Witziers-Timmer, Gerda van der Kade-Koudijs, Fanny Blankers-Koen)	47.5	

Event		Mark	
High Jump	Alice Coachman, USA	.......5- 6	**OR**
Long Jump	Olga Gyarmati, HUN	.......18- 8¼	
Shot Put	Micheline Ostermeyer, FRA	.45- 1½	
Discus	Micheline Ostermeyer, FRA	....137- 6	
Javelin	Herma Bauma, AUT	......149- 6	

Note: Coachman and Dorothy Odam of Britain tied for 1st place, but Coachman was awarded gold medal for making height on first try.

Swimming
MEN

Event		Time	
100m Free	Wally Ris, USA	...............57.3	**OR**
400m Free	Bill Smith, USA	...........4:41.0	**OR**
1500m Free	Jimmy McLane, USA	......19:18.5	
100m Back	Allen Stack, USA	...........1:06.4	
200m Brst	Joe Verdeur, USA	..........2:39.3	**OR**
4x200m Free	USA (Wally Ris, Jimmy McLane, Wally Wolf, Bill Smith)	..... 8:46.0	**WR**

Diving		Points
Platform	Sammy Lee, USA	...........130.05
Spring	Bruce Harlan, USA	........163.64

WOMEN

Event		Time	
100m Free	Greta Andersen, DEN	....1:06.3	
400m Free	Ann Curtis, USA	.......5:17.8	**OR**
100m Back	Karen M. Harup, DEN	......1:14.4	**OR**
200m Brst	Nel van Vliet, HOL	.........2:57.2	
4x100m Free	USA (Marie Corridon, Thelma Kalama, Brenda Helser, Ann Curtis)	................4:29.2	**OR**

Diving		Points
Platform	Vicki Draves, USA	.........68.87
Spring	Vicki Draves, USA	.........108.74

Team Sports

Sport	Champion
Basketball	....................................United States
Field Hockey	......................................India
Soccer	....Sweden
Water Polo	....Italy

Also Contested

Boxing, Canoeing, Cycling, Equestrian, Fencing, Gymnastics, Modern Pentathlon, Rowing, Shooting, Weightlifting, Freestyle Wrestling, Greco-Roman Wrestling and Yachting.

1952

Helsinki

The Soviet Union returned to the Olympic fold in 1952 after a 40-year absence, a period of time that included a revolution and two world wars. Ironically, the Soviets chose to make their comeback in Finland, a country they had invaded twice during World War II.

This time it was the United States that was surprised by the Russians, and the USA had to scramble on the last day of competition to hold off the USSR's assault on first place in the overall standings. It was the beginning of an all-consuming 36-year Cold War rivalry.

Despite the Soviets' impressive debut, it was a Communist from another Iron Curtain country who turned in the most memorable individual performance of the Games. Emil Zátopek of Czechoslovakia, the 10,000-meter champion in London, not only repeated at 10,000 meters, but also won at 5,000 and in the marathon–an event he had never run before. He also set Olympic records in each race and topped it off by watching his wife Dana Zátopková win the women's javelin.

Zátopek's unique triple was wildly applauded by the distance-minded Finns, but their greatest outburst came in the opening ceremonies when legendary countryman Paavo Nurmi, now 56, ran into the stadium with the Olympic torch and handed it off to another native legend Hannes Kolehmainen, now 62, who lit the flame to start the Games.

Also, Harrison Dillard of the U.S. won the 110-meter hurdles. In 1948, Dillard, the world's best hurdler, failed to qualify for the hurdles and won the 100-meter dash instead.

Top 10 Standings

National medal standings are not recognized by the IOC. The unofficial point totals are based on 3 points for a gold medal, 2 for a silver and 1 for a bronze.

	Gold	Silver	Bronze	Total	Pts
1 USA	40	19	17	76	175
2 USSR	21	30	18	69	141
3 Hungary	16	10	16	42	84
4 Sweden	12	13	10	35	72
5 Italy	8	9	4	21	46
6 Finland	6	3	13	22	37
7 France	6	6	6	18	36
8 Germany	0	7	17	24	31
9 Czechoslovakia ...	7	3	3	13	30
10 Australia	6	2	3	11	25

Leading Medal Winners

Number of individual medals won on the left; gold, silver and bronze breakdown to the right.

MEN

No		Sport	G-S-B
6	Viktor Chukarin, USSR	..........Gymnastics	4-2-0
4	Edoardo Mangiarotti, ITA	..........Fencing	2-2-0
4	Grant Shaginyan, USSR	........Gymnastics	2-2-0
4	Josef Stalder, SWI	.............Gymnastics	0-2-2
3	Emil Zátopek, CZE	..............Track/Field	3-0-0
3	Ford Konno, USA	...............Swimming	2-1-0
3	Herb McKenley, JAM	..........Track/Field	1-2-0
3	Hans Eugster, SWI	.............Gymnastics	1-1-1

WOMEN

No		Sport	G-S-B
7	Maria Gorokhovskaya, USSR	....Gymnastics	2-5-0
6	Margit Korondi, HUN	............Gymnastics	1-1-4
4	Nina Bocharova, USSR	........Gymnastics	2-2-0
4	Á gnes Keleti, HUN	.............Gymnastics	1-1-2
3	Yekaterina Kalinchuk, USSR	....Gymnastics	2-1-0
3	Éva Novák, HUN	...............Swimming	1-2-0
3	Galina Minaicheva, USSR	......Gymnastics	1-1-1
3	Aleksandra Chudina, USSR	......Track/Field	0-2-1

1952 (Cont.)

Track & Field
MEN

Event		Time	
100m	Lindy Remigino, USA	10.4	
200m	Andy Stanfield, USA	20.7	
400m	George Rhoden, JAM	45.9	OR
800m	Mal Whitfield, USA	1:49.2	=OR
1500m	Josy Barthel, LUX	3:45.1	OR
5000m	Emil Zátopek, CZE	14:06.6	OR
10,000m	Emil Zátopek, CZE	29:17.0	OR
Marathon	Emil Zátopek, CZE	2:23:03.2	OR
110m H	Harrison Dillard, USA	13.7	OR
400m H	Charley Moore, USA	50.8	OR
3000m Steeple	Horace Ashenfelter, USA	8:45.4	WR
10k Walk	John Mikaelsson, SWE	45:02.8	OR
50k Walk	Giuseppe Dordoni, ITA	4:28:07.8	OR
4x100m	USA (Dean Smith, Harrison Dillard, Lindy Remigino,Andy Stanfield)	40.1	
4x400m	JAM (Arthur Wint, Leslie Laing, Herb McKenley, George Rhoden)	3:03.9	WR

Event		Mark	
High Jump	Walt Davis, USA	6- 8½	OR
Pole Vault	Bob Richards, USA	14-11	OR
Long Jump	Jerome Biffle, USA	24-10	
Triple Jump	Adhemar da Silva, BRA	53- 2¾	WR
Shot Put	Parry O'Brien, USA	57- 1½	OR
Discus	Sim Iness, USA	180- 6	OR
Hammer	József Csermák, HUN	197-11	WR
Javelin	Cy Young, USA	242- 1	OR
Decathlon	Bob Mathias, USA	7887 pts	WR

WOMEN

Event		Time	
100m	Marjorie Jackson, AUS	11.5	WR
200m	Marjorie Jackson, AUS	23.7	
80m H	Shirley Strickland, AUS	10.9	WR
4x100m	USA (Mae Faggs, Barbara Jones, Janet Moreau, Catherine Hardy)	45.9	WR

Event		Mark	
High Jump	Esther Brand, SAF	5- 5¾	
Long Jump	Yvette Williams, NZE	20- 5¾	OR
Shot Put	Galina Zybina, USSR	50- 1¾	WR
Discus	Nina Romaschkova, USSR	168- 8	OR
Javelin	Dana Zátopková, CZE	165- 7	

Swimming
MEN

Event		Time	
100m Free	Clarke Scholes, USA	57.4	
400m Free	Jean Boiteux, FRA	4:30.7	OR
1500m Free	Ford Konno, USA	18:30.3	OR
100m Back	Yoshi Oyakawa, USA	1:05.4	OR
200m Brst	John Davies, AUS	2:34.4	OR
4x200m Free	USA (Wayne Moore, Bill Woolsey, Ford Konno, Jimmy McLane)	8:31.1	OR

Diving		Points
Platform	Sammy Lee, USA	156.28
Spring	Skippy Browning, USA	205.29

WOMEN

Event		Time	
100m Free	Katalin Szöke, HUN	1:06.8	
400m Free	Valéria Gyenge, HUN	5:12.1	OR
100m Back	Joan Harrison, SAF	1:14.3	
200m Brst	Éva Szekely, HUN	2:51.7	OR
4x100m Free	HUN (Ilona Novák, Judit Temes, Eva Novák, Katalin Szöke)	4:24.4	WR

Diving		Points
Platform	Pat McCormick, USA	79.37
Spring	Pat McCormick, USA	147.30

Team Sports

Sport	Champion
Basketball	United States
Field Hockey	India
Soccer	Hungary
Water Polo	Hungary

Also Contested

Boxing, Canoeing, Cycling, Equestrian, Fencing, Gymnastics, Modern Pentathlon, Rowing, Shooting, Weightlifting, Freestyle Wrestling, Greco-Roman Wrestling and Yachting.

1956

Melbourne

Armed conflicts in Egypt and Hungary threatened to disrupt the 1956 Games, which were scheduled to begin on Nov. 22 (during the summer Down Under).

In July, Egypt seized the Suez Canal from British and French control. In October, Britain and France invaded Egypt in an attempt to retake the canal. Then in November, Russian tanks rolled into Hungary to crush an anti-Communist revolt.

The only direct bearing these events had in Melbourne came when the Soviet water polo team met the Hungarians in the semifinals. Hungary won 4-0, but the match turned ugly after a Hungarian player was pulled bleeding from the pool with a deep gash over his eye from a Russian head butt. A brawl quickly ensued involving both players and spectators and the police had to step in to prevent a riot.

Otherwise, the Soviets outmedaled the U.S. for the first time, cleaning up in gymnastics and winning their first track and field titles when Vladimir Kuts ran off with the 5,000 and 10,000 meters.

The American men won 15 track and field titles, including three golds for sprinter Bobby Morrow and Al Oerter's first victory in the discus.

Harold Connolly of the U.S. won the hammer throw and the heart of the women's discus champion, Olga Fikotová of Czechoslovakia. Their romance captured the imagination of the world and three months after the Games they were married.

Emil Zátopek, the Czech hero of Helsinki, returned to defend his marathon title and came in sixth. Winner Alain Mimoun, of France, had finished second to Zátopek three times in previous Olympics.

Top 10 Standings

National medal standings are not recognized by the IOC. The unofficial point totals are based on 3 points for a gold medal, 2 for a silver and 1 for a bronze.

		Gold	Silver	Bronze	Total	Pts
1	USSR	37	29	32	98	201
2	USA	32	25	17	74	163
3	Australia	13	8	14	35	69
4	Hungary	9	10	7	26	54
5	Germany	6	13	7	26	51
6	Italy	8	8	9	25	49
7	Great Britain	6	7	11	24	43
8	Sweden	8	5	6	19	40
9	Japan	4	10	5	19	37
10	Romania	5	3	5	13	26
	France	4	4	6	14	26

Leading Medal Winners

Number of individual medals won on the left; gold, silver and bronze breakdown to the right.

MEN

No		Sport	G-S-B
5	Viktor Chukarin, USSR	Gymnastics	3-1-1
5	Takashi Ono, JPN	Gymnastics	1-3-1
4	Valentin Muratov, USSR	Gymnastics	3-1-0
4	Yuriy Titov, USSR	Gymnastics	1-1-2
4	Masao Takemoto, JPN	Gymnastics	0-1-3
3	Bobby Morrow, USA	Track/Field	3-0-0
3	Murray Rose, AUS	Swimming	3-0-0
3	Edoardo Mangiarotti, ITA	Fencing	2-0-1
3	Thane Baker, USA	Track/Field	1-1-1
3	Masami Kubota, JPN	Gymnastics	0-2-1
3	George Breen, USA	Swimming	0-1-2

WOMEN

No		Sport	G-S-B
6	Agnes Keleti, HUN	Gymnastics	4-2-0
6	Larissa Latynina, USSR	Gymnastics	4-1-1
4	Tamara Manina, USSR	Gymnastics	1-2-1
4	Sofiya Muratova, USSR	Gymnastics	1-0-3
3	Betty Cuthbert, AUS	Track/Field	3-0-0
3	Lorraine Crapp, AUS	Swimming	2-1-0
3	Dawn Fraser, AUS	Swimming	2-1-0
3	Olga Tass, HUN	Gymnastics	1-1-1

Track & Field

MEN

Event		Time	
100m	Bobby Morrow, USA	10.5	
200m	Bobby Morrow, USA	20.6	OR
400m	Charley Jenkins, USA	46.7	
800m	Tom Courtney, USA	1:47.7	OR
1500m	Ron Delany, IRL	3:41.2	OR
5000m	Vladimir Kuts, USSR	13:39.6	OR
10,000m	Vladimir Kuts, USSR	28:45.6	OR
Marathon	Alain Mimoun, FRA	2:25:00.0	
110m H	Lee Calhoun, USA	13.5	OR
400m H	Glenn Davis, USA	50.1	=OR
3000m Steeple	Chris Brasher, GBR	8:41.2	OR
20k Walk	Leonid Spirin, USSR	1:31:27.4	
50k Walk	Norman Read, NZE	4:30:42.8	
4x100m	USA (Ira Murchison, Leamon King, Thane Baker, Bobby Morrow)	39.5	WR
4x400m	USA (Lou Jones, Jesse Mashburn, Charlie Jenkins, Tom Courtney)	3:04.8	

Event		Mark	
High Jump	Charley Dumas, USA	6-11½	OR
Pole Vault	Bob Richards, USA	14-11½	OR
Long Jump	Greg Bell, USA	25-8¼	
Triple Jump	Adhemar da Silva, BRA	53-7¾	OR
Shot Put	Parry O'Brien, USA	60-11¼	OR
Discus	Al Oerter, USA	184-11	OR
Hammer	Harold Connolly, USA	207-3	OR
Javelin	Egil Danielson, NOR	281-2	WR
Decathlon	Milt Campbell, USA	7937 pts	OR

WOMEN

Event		Time	
100m	Betty Cuthbert, AUS	11.5	
200m	Betty Cuthbert, AUS	23.4	=OR
80m H	Shirley Strickland, AUS	10.7	OR
4x100m	AUS (Shirley Strickland, Norma Croker, Fleur Mellor, Betty Cuthbert)	44.5	WR

Event		Mark	
High Jump	Mildred McDaniel, USA	5-9¼	WR
Long Jump	Elzbieta Krzesinska, POL	20-10	=WR
Shot Put	Tamara Tyshkevich, USSR	54-5	OR
Discus	Olga Fikotová, CZE	176-1	OR
Javelin	Inese Jaunzeme, USSR	176-8	

Swimming

MEN

Event		Time	
100m Free	Jon Henricks, AUS	55.4	OR
400m Free	Murray Rose, AUS	4:27.3	OR
1500m Free	Murray Rose, AUS	17:58.9	
100m Back	David Theile, AUS	1:02.2	OR
200m Brst	Masaru Furukawa, JPN	2:34.7	OR
200m Fly	Bill Yorzyk, USA	2:19.3	OR
4x200m Free	AUS (Kevin O'Halloran, John Devitt, Murray Rose, Jon Henricks)	8:23.6	WR

Diving		Points
Platform	Joaquin Capilla, MEX	152.44
Spring	Bob Clotworthy, USA	159.56

WOMEN

Event		Time	
100m Free	Dawn Fraser, AUS	1:02.0	WR
400m Free	Lorraine Crapp, AUS	4:54.6	OR
100m Back	Judy Grinham, GBR	1:12.9	OR
200m Brst	Ursula Happe, GER	2:53.1	OR
100m Fly	Shelly Mann, USA	1:11.0	OR
4x100m Free	AUS (Dawn Fraser, Faith Leech, Sandra Morgan, Lorraine Crapp)	4:17.1	WR

Diving		Points
Platform	Pat McCormick, USA	84.85
Spring	Pat McCormick, USA	142.36

Team Sports

Sport	Champion
Basketball	United States
Field Hockey	India
Soccer	Soviet Union
Water Polo	Hungary

Also Contested

Boxing, Canoeing, Cycling, Equestrian, Fencing, Gymnastics, Modern Pentathlon, Rowing, Shooting, Weightlifting, Freestyle Wrestling, Greco-Roman Wrestling and Yachting.
Note: Equestrian events were held in Stockholm, Sweden, June 10-17, due to Australian quarantine laws.

1960

Rome

Free of political entanglements, save the ruling that Nationalist China had to compete as Formosa, the 1960 Games attracted a record 5,348 athletes from 83 countries. More importantly, it was the first Summer Games covered by U.S. television. CBS bought the rights for $394,000.

Rome was a coming-out party for 18-year-old Louisville boxer Cassius Clay. The brash but engaging Clay, who would later change his name to Muhammad Ali and hold the world heavyweight title three times, won the Olympic light heavyweight crown, pummeling Polish opponent Zbigniew Pietryskowsky in the final. Clay was so proud of his gold medal he didn't take it off for two days.

Sprinter Wilma Rudolph and swimmer Chris von Saltza each won three gold medals for the U.S. Rudolph, who was one of 19 children and who couldn't walk without braces until she was 11, struck gold at 100 and 200 meters and anchored the winning 400-meter relay team. Von Saltza won the 400-meter freestyle, placed second in the 100-free and anchored the winning 400-free and medley relays.

The U.S. men won nine track and field titles, including repeat gold medals for Lee Calhoun, Glenn Davis and Al Oerter. Rafer Johnson and C.K. Yang of Formosa, college teammates at UCLA, finished 1-2 in the decathlon.

Among the other stars in Rome were barefoot Ethiopian marathoner Abebe Bikila, Australia's Herb Elliott in the 1,500 meters, Russian gymnasts Boris Shakhlin and Larissa Latynina.

Finally, the greatest amateur basketball team ever assembled represented the U.S. and won easily. The 12-man roster included Oscar Robertson, Jerry West, Jerry Lucas, Walt Bellamy and Terry Dischinger-four of whom would become NBA Rookies of the Year from 1961-64.

Top 10 Standings

National medal standings are not recognized by the IOC. The unofficial point totals are based on 3 points for a gold medal, 2 for a silver and 1 for a bronze.

		Gold	Silver	Bronze	Total	Pts
1	USSR	43	29	31	103	218
2	USA	34	21	16	71	160
3	Germany	12	19	11	42	85
4	Italy	13	10	13	36	72
5	Australia	8	8	6	22	46
6	Hungary	6	8	7	21	41
7	Poland	4	6	11	21	35
8	Japan	4	7	7	18	33
9	Great Britain	2	6	12	20	30
10	Turkey	7	2	0	9	25

Leading Medal Winners

Number of individual medals won on the left; gold, silver and bronze breakdown to the right.

MEN

No		Sport	G-S-B
7	Boris Shakhlin, USSR	Gymnastics	4-2-1
6	Takashi Ono, JPN	Gymnastics	3-1-2
3	Murray Rose, AUS	Swimming	1-1-1
3	John Konraads, AUS	Swimming	1-0-2
3	Yuri Titov, USSR	Gymnastics	0-2-1

WOMEN

No		Sport	G-S-B
6	Larissa Latynina, USSR	Gymnastics	3-2-1
4	Chris von Saltza, USA	Swimming	3-1-0
4	Polina Astakhova, USSR	Gymnastics	2-1-1
4	Sofia Muratova, USSR	Gymnastics	1-2-1
3	Wilma Rudolph, USA	Track/Field	3-0-0
3	Dawn Fraser, AUS	Swimming	1-2-0
3	Tamara Lyukhina, USSR	Gymnastics	1-0-2

Track & Field

MEN

Event		Time	
100m	Armin Hary, GER	10.2	OR
200m	Livio Berruti, ITA	:20.5	=WR
400m	Otis Davis, USA	44.9	WR
800m	Peter Snell, NZE	1:46.3	OR
1500m	Herb Elliott, AUS	3:35.6	WR
5000m	Murray Halberg, NZE	13:43.4	
10,000m	Pyotr Bolotnikov, USSR	28:32.2	OR
Marathon	Abebe Bikila, ETH	2:15:16.2	WB
110m H	Lee Calhoun, USA	13.8	
400m H	Glenn Davis, USA	49.3	=OR
3000m Steeple	Zdzislaw Krzyszkowiak, POL	8:34.2	OR
20k Walk	Vladimir Golubnichiy, USSR	1:34:07.2	
50k Walk	Don Thompson, GBR	4:25:30.0	OR
4x100m	GER (Bernd Cullmann, Armin Hary, Walter Mahlendorf, Martin Lauer)	39.5	=WR
4x400m	USA (Jack Yerman, Earl Young, Glenn Davis, Otis Davis)	3:02.2	WR

Event		Mark	
High Jump	Robert Shavlakadze, USSR	7- 1	OR
Pole Vault	Don Bragg, USA	15- 5	OR
Long Jump	Ralph Boston, USA	26- 7¾	OR
Triple Jump	Józef Schmidt, POL	55- 2	
Shot Put	Bill Nieder, USA	64- 6¾	OR
Discus	Al Oerter, USA	194- 2	OR
Hammer	Vasily Rudenkov, USSR	220- 2	OR
Javelin	Viktor Tsibulenko, USSR	277- 8	
Decathlon	Rafer Johnson, USA	8392 pts	OR

WOMEN

Event		Time	
100m	Wilma Rudolph, USA	11.0w	
200m	Wilma Rudolph, USA	24.0	
800m	Lyudmila Shevtsova, USSR	2:04.3	=WR
80m H	Irina Press, USSR	10.8	
4x100m	USA (Martha Hudson, Lucinda Williams, Barbara Jones, Wilma Rudolph)	44.5	

w indicates wind-aided.

Event		Mark	
High Jump	Iolanda Balas, ROM	6- 0¾	OR
Long Jump	Vyera Krepkina, USSR	20-10¾	OR
Shot Put	Tamara Press, USSR	56-10	OR
Discus	Nina R. Ponomaryeva, USSR	180- 9	OR
Javelin	Elvira Ozolina, USSR	183- 8	OR

Boxing

Weight Class	Champion
Flyweight (112 lbs)	Gyula Török, HUN
Bantamweight (119)	Oleg Grigoryev, USSR
Featherweight (125)	Francesco Musso, ITA
Lightweight (132)	Kazimierz Pazdzior, POL
Lt. Welterweight (139)	Bohumil Nemecek, CZE
Welterweight (148)	Nino Benvenuti, ITA
Lt. Middleweight (156)	Skeeter McClure, USA
Middleweight (165)	Eddie Crook, USA
Lt. Heavyweight (178)	Cassius Clay, USA
Heavyweight (178+)	Franco De Piccoli, ITA

Gymnastics
MEN

Individual		Points
All-Around	Boris Shakhlin, USSR	115.95
Floor	Nobuyuki Aihara, JPN	19.45
Horiz.Bar	Takashi Ono, JPN	19.60
Paral.Bars	Boris Shakhlin, USSR	19.40
Rings	Albert Azaryan, USSR	19.725
Side Horse	Boris Shakhlin, USSR	
	Eugen Ekman, FIN	19.375
Vault	Boris Shakhlin, USSR	
	Takashi Ono, JPN	19.35

Team		Points
All-Around	JPN (Ono, Tsurumi, Aihara, Endo, Takemoto, Mitsukuri)	575.20

WOMEN

Individual		Points
All-Around	Larissa Latynina, USSR	77.031
Bal.Beam	Eva Bosáková, CZE	19.283
Floor	Larissa Latynina, USSR	19.583
Uneven Bars	Polina Astakhova, USSR	19.616
Vault	Margarita Nikolayeva, USSR	19.316

Team		Points
All-Around	USSR (Latynina, Muratova, Astakhova, Nikolayeva, Ivanova, Lyukhina)	382.320

Swimming
MEN

Event		Time	
100m Free	John Devitt, AUS	55.2	OR
400m Free	Murray Rose, AUS	4:18.3	OR
1500m Free	John Konrads, AUS	17:19.6	OR
100m Back	David Theile, AUS	1:09.9	OR
200m Brst	Bill Mulliken, USA	2:37.4	
200m Fly	Mike Troy, USA	2:12.8	WR
4x200m Free	USA (George Harrison, Dick Blick, Mike Troy, Jeff Farrell)	8:10.2	WR
4x100m Mdly	USA (Frank McKinney, Paul Hait, Lance Larson, Jeff Farrell)	4:05.4	WR

Diving		Points
Platform	Bob Webster, USA	165.56
Spring	Gary Tobian, USA	170.00

WOMEN

Event		Time	
100m Free	Dawn Fraser, AUS	1:01.2	OR
400m Free	Chris von Saltza, USA	4:50.6	OR
100m Back	Lynn Burke, USA	1:09.3	OR
200m Brst	Anita Lonsbrough, GBR	2:49.5	WR
100m Fly	Carolyn Schuler, USA	1:09.5	OR
4x100m Free	USA (Joan Spillane, Shirley Stobs, Carolyn Wood, Chris von Saltza)	4:08.9	WR
4x100m Mdly	USA (Lynn Burke, Patty Kempner, Carolyn Schuler, Chris von Saltza)	4:41.1	WR

Diving

Diving		Points
Platform	Ingrid Krämer, GER	91.28
Spring	Ingrid Krämer, GER	155.81

Team Sports

Men	Champion
Basketball	United States
Field Hockey	Pakistan
Soccer	Yugoslavia
Water Polo	Italy

Also Contested

Canoeing, Cycling, Equestrian, Fencing, Modern Pentathlon, Rowing, Shooting, Weightlifting, Freestyle Wrestling, Greco-Roman Wrestling and Yachting.

1964

Tokyo

Twenty-six years after Japan's wartime government forced the Japanese Olympic Committee to resign as hosts of the 1940 Summer Games, Tokyo welcomed the world to the first Asian Olympics. The new Japan spared no expense–a staggering $3 billion was spent to rebuild the city–and was rewarded with a record-breaking fortnight.

Twelve world and six Olympic records fell in swimming, with Americans accounting for 13. Eighteen-year-old Don Schollander led the way, winning two individual and two relay gold medals to become the first swimmer to win four events in one Games. Sharon Stouder collected three golds and a silver for the U.S. women, but the most remarkable performance of all belonged to Australian Dawn Fraser, who won the 100-meter freestyle for the third straight Olympics.

In track and field, Al Oerter of the U.S. won the discus for the third straight time. His record toss was one of 25 world and Olympic marks broken. Another fell when Billy Mills of the U.S. electrified the Games by coming from behind for an upset win in the 10,000 meters. New Zealander Peter Snell, the defending 800-meter champion, won both the 800 and 1,500 (last done in 1920).

Sprinter Bob Hayes of the U.S. equaled the world record of 10 seconds flat in the 100 meters, but stunned the crowd with a sub-9 second, come-from-behind anchor leg to lead the U.S. to set a new world record in the 4 x 100 meters.

Abebe Bikila of Ethiopia became the first runner to win consecutive marathons. The remarkable Betty Cuthbert of Australia, who won three sprint gold medals in Melbourne, came back eight years later at age 26 to win the 400. And Russian gymnast Larissa Latynina won six medals for the second Olympics in a row.

1964 (Cont.)

Top 10 Standings

National medal standings are not recognized by the IOC. The unofficial point totals are based on 3 points for a gold medal, 2 for a silver and 1 for a bronze.

		Gold	Silver	Bronze	Total	Pts
1	USA	36	26	28	90	188
2	USSR	30	31	35	96	187
3	Germany	10	22	18	50	92
4	Japan	16	5	8	29	66
5	Italy	10	10	7	27	57
6	Hungary	10	7	5	22	49
7	Poland	7	6	10	23	43
8	Great Britain	4	12	2	18	38
9	Australia	6	2	10	18	32
10	Czechoslovakia	5	6	3	14	30

Leading Medal Winners

Number of individual medals won on the left; gold, silver and bronze breakdown to the right.

MEN

No			Sport	G-S-B
4	Don Schollander, USA		Swimming	4-0-0
4	Yukio Endo, JPN		Gymnastics	3-1-0
4	Shuji Tsurumi, JPN		Gymnastics	1-3-0
4	Boris Shakhlin, USSR		Gymnastics	1-2-1
4	Viktor Lisitsky, USSR		Gymnastics	0-4-0
4	Hans-Joachim Klein, GER		Swimming	0-3-1
3	Steve Clark, USA		Swimming	3-0-0
3	Franco Menichelli, ITA		Gymnastics	1-1-1
3	Frank Wiegard, GER		Swimming	0-3-0

WOMEN

No			Sport	G-S-B
6	Larissa Latynina, USSR		Gymnastics	2-2-2
4	Vera Cáslavská, CZE		Gymnastics	3-1-0
4	Polina Astakhova, USSR		Gymnastics	2-1-1
4	Sharon Stouder, USA		Swimming	3-1-0
4	Kathy Ellis, USA		Swimming	2-0-2
4	Irena Kirszenstein, POL		Track/Field	1-2-0
3	Ada Kok, HOL		Swimming	1-2-0
3	Edith Maguire, USA		Track/Field	1-2-0
3	Mary Rand, GBR		Track/Field	1-1-1

Track & Field

MEN

Event		Time	
100m	Bob Hayes, USA	10.0	=WR
200m	Henry Carr, USA	20.3	OR
400m	Mike Larrabee, USA	45.1	
800m	Peter Snell, NZE	1:45.1	OR
1500m	Peter Snell, NZE	3:38.1	
5000m	Bob Schul, USA	13:48.8	
10,000m	Billy Mills, USA	28:24.4	OR
Marathon	Abebe Bikila, ETH	2:12:11.2	WB
110m H	Hayes Jones, USA	13.6	
400m H	Rex Cawley, USA	49.6	
3000m Steeple	Gaston Roelants, BEL	8:30.8	OR
20k Walk	Ken Matthews, GBR	1:29:34.0	OR
50k Walk	Abdon Pamich, ITA	4:11:12.4	OR
4x100m	USA (Paul Drayton, Gerald Ashworth, Richard Stebbins, Bob Hayes)	39.0	WR
4x400m	USA (Ollan Cassell, Mike Larrabee, Ulis Williams, Henry Carr)	3:00.7	WR

Event		Mark	
High Jump	Valery Brumel	7- 1¾	OR
Pole Vault	Fred Hansen, USA	16- 8¾	OR
Long Jump	Lynn Davies, GBR	26- 5¾	
Triple Jump	Józef Schmidt, POL	55- 3½	OR
Shot Put	Dallas Long, USA	66- 8½	OR
Discus	Al Oerter, USA	200- 1	OR
Hammer	Romuald Klim, USSR	228-10	OR
Javelin	Pauli Nevala, FIN	271- 2	
Decathlon	Willi Holdorf, GER	7887 pts	

WOMEN

Event		Time	
100m	Wyomia Tyus, USA	11.4	
200m	Edith McGuire, USA	23.0	OR
400m	Betty Cuthbert, AUS	52.0	OR
800m	Ann Packer, GBR	2:01.1	OR
80m H	Karin Balzer, GER	10.5w	
4x100m	POL (Teresa Ciepla, Irena Kirszenstein, Halina Górecka, Ewa Klobukowska)	43.6	

w indicates wind-aided.

Event		Mark	
High Jump	Iolanda Balas, ROM	6- 2¾	OR
Long Jump	Mary Rand GBR	22- 2¼	WR
Shot Put	Tamara Press, USSR	59- 6¼	OR
Discus	Tamara Press, USSR	187-10	OR
Javelin	Mihaela Penes, ROM	198- 7	
Pentathlon	Irina Press, USSR	5246 pts	WR

Boxing

Weight Class	Champion
Flyweight (112 lbs)	Fernando Atzori, ITA
Bantamweight (119)	Takao Sakurai, JPN
Featherweight (125)	Stanislav Stepashkin, USSR
Lightweight (132)	Józef Grudzien, POL
Lt. Welterweight (139)	Jerzy Kulej, POL
Welterweight (148)	Marian Kasprzyk, POL
Lt. Middleweight (156)	Boris Lagutin, USSR
Middleweight (165)	Valery Popenchenko, USSR
Lt. Heavyweight (178)	Cosimo Pinto, ITA
Heavyweight (178+)	Joe Frazier, USA

Gymnastics

MEN

Individual		Points
All-Around	Yukio Endo, JPN	115.95
Floor	Franco Menichelli, ITA	19.45
Horiz.Bar	Boris Shakhlin, USSR	19.625
Paral.Bars	Yukio Endo, JPN	19.675
Rings	Takuji Haytta, JPN	19.475
Side Horse	Miroslav Cerar, YUG	19.525
Vault	Haruhiro Yamashita, JPN	19.60

Team		Points
All-Around	JPN (Endo, Tsurumi, Yamashita, Hayata, Mitsukuri, Ono)	577.95

WOMEN

Individual		Points
All-Around	Vera Cáslavská, CZE	77.564
Bal.Beam	Vera Cáslavská, CZE	19.449
Floor	Larissa Latynina, USSR	19.599
Uneven Bars	Polina Astakhova, USSR	19.332
Vault	Vera Cáslavská, CZE	19.483

Team		Points
All-Around	USSR (Latynina, Astakhova, Volchetskaya, Zamotailova, Manina, Gromova)	280.890

Swimming

MEN

Event		Time	
100m Free	Don Schollander, USA	.53.4	**OR**
400m Free	Don Schollander, USA	4:12.2	**WR**
1500m Free	Robert Windle, AUS	17:01.7	**OR**
200m Back	Jed Graef, USA	2:10.3	**WR**
200m Brst	Ian O'Brien, AUS	2:27.8	**WR**
200m Fly	Kevin Berry, AUS	2:06.6	**WR**
400m I.M.	Dick Roth, USA	4:45.4	**WR**
4x100m Free	USA (Steve Clark, Mike Austin, Gary Ilman, Don Schollander)	3:32.3	**WR**
4x200m Free	USA (Steve Clark, Roy Saari, Gary Ilman, Don Schollander)	7:52.1	**WR**
4x100m Mdly	USA (Thompson Mann, Bill Craig, Fred Schmidt, Steve Clark)	3:58.4	**WR**

Diving		Points
Platform	Bob Webster, USA	148.58
Spring	Ken Sitzberger, USA	159.90

WOMEN

Event		Time	
100m Free	Dawn Fraser, AUS	.59.5	**OR**
400m Free	Ginny Duenkel, USA	4:43.3	**OR**
100m Back	Cathy Ferguson, USA	1:07.7	**WR**
200m Brst	G. Prozumenshikova, USSR	2:46.4	**OR**
100m Fly	Sharon Stouder, USA	1:04.7	**WR**
400m Mdly	Donna de Varona, USA	5:18.7	**OR**
4x100m Free	USA (Sharon Stouder, Donna de Varona, Pokey Watson, Kathy Ellis)	4:03.8	**WR**
4x100m Mdly	USA (Cathy Ferguson, Cynthia Goyette, Sharon Stouder, Kathy Ellis)	4:33.9	**WR**

Diving		Points
Platform	Lesley Bush, USA	99.80
Spring	Ingrid Engel-Krämer, GER	145.00

Team Sports

Men	Champion
Basketball	United States
Field Hockey	India
Soccer	Hungary
Volleyball	Soviet Union
Water Polo	Hungary

Women	Champion
Volleyball	Japan

Also Contested

Canoeing, Cycling, Equestrian, Fencing, Judo, Modern Pentathlon, Rowing, Shooting, Weightlifting, Freestyle Wrestling, Greco-Roman Wrestling and Yachting.

1968

Mexico City

The Games of the Nineteenth Olympiad were the highest and most controversial ever held.

Staged at 7,349 feet above sea level where the thin air was a major concern to many competing countries, the Mexico City Olympics were another chapter in a year buffeted by the Vietnam War, the assassinations of Martin Luther King and Robert Kennedy, the Democratic Convention in Chicago, and the Russian invasion of Czechoslovakia.

Ten days before the Olympics were scheduled to open on Oct. 12, over 30 Mexico City university students were killed by army troops when a campus protest turned into a riot. Still, the Games began on time and were free of discord until black Americans Tommie Smith and John Carlos, who finished 1-3 in the 200-meter run, bowed their heads and gave the Black Power salute during the national anthem as a protest against racism in the U.S.

They were immediately thrown off the team by the USOC.

The thin air helped shatter records in every men's and women's race up to 1,500 meters and played a role in U.S. long jumper Bob Beamon's incredible gold medal leap of 29-feet, 2½ inches –beating the existing world mark by nearly two feet.

Other outstanding American performances included Al Oerter's record fourth consecutive discus title, Debbie Meyer's three individual swimming gold medals, the innovative Dick Fosbury winning the high jump with his backwards "flop," and Wyomia Tyus becoming the first woman to win back-to-back golds in the 100 meters.

Top 10 Standings

National medal standings are not recognized by the IOC. The unofficial point totals are based on 3 points for a gold medal, 2 for a silver and 1 for a bronze.

	Gold	Silver	Bronze	Total	Pts
1 USA	45	28	34	107	225
2 USSR	29	32	30	91	181
3 Hungary	10	10	12	32	62
4 Japan	11	7	7	25	54
5 E. Germany	9	9	7	25	52
6 W. Germany	5	10	10	25	45
7 Australia	5	7	5	17	34
8 France	7	3	5	15	32
9 Poland	5	2	11	18	30
10 Czechoslovakia	7	2	4	13	29
Romania	4	6	5	15	29

Leading Medal Winners

Number of individual medals won on the left; gold, silver and bronze breakdown to the right.

MEN

No		Sport	G-S-B
7	Mikhail Voronin, USSR	Gymnastics	2-4-1
6	Akinori Nakayama, JPN	Gymnastics	4-1-1
4	Charles Hickcox, USA	Swimming	3-1-0
4	Sawao Kato, JPN	Gymnastics	3-0-1
4	Mark Spitz, USA	Swimming	2-1-1
4	Mike Wenden, AUS	Swimming	2-1-1
3	Roland Matthes, E. Ger	Swimming	2-1-0
3	Ken Walsh, USA	Swimming	2-1-0
3	Pierre Trentin, FRA	Cycling	2-0-1
3	Vladimir Kosinski, USSR	Swimming	0-2-1
3	Leonid Ilyichev, USSR	Swimming	0-1-2

1968 (Cont.)
WOMEN

No		Sport	G-S-B
6	Vera Cáslavská, CZE	Gymnastics	4-2-0
4	Sue Pedersen, USA	Swimming	2-2-0
4	Natalya Kuchinskaya, USSR	Gymnastics	2-0-2
4	Jan Henne, USA	Swimming	2-1-1
4	Zinaida Voronina, USSR	Gymnastics	1-1-2
3	Debbie Meyer, USA	Swimming	3-0-0
3	Kaye Hall, USA	Swimming	2-0-1
3	Larissa Petrik, USSR	Gymnastics	2-0-1
3	Ellie Daniel, USA	Swimming	1-1-1
3	Linda Gustavson, USA	Swimming	1-1-1
3	Elaine Tanner, CAN	Swimming	0-2-1

Track & Field
MEN

Event		Time	
100m	Jim Hines, USA	9.95	WR
200m	Tommie Smith, USA	19.83	WR
400m	Lee Evans, USA	43.86	WR
800m	Ralph Doubell, AUS	1:44.3	=WR
1500m	Kip Keino, KEN	3:34.9	OR
5000m	Mohamed Gammoudi, TUN	14:05.0	
10,000m	Naftali Temu, KEN	29:27.4	
Marathon	Mamo Wolde, ETH	2:20:26.4	
110m H	Willie Davenport, USA	13.3	OR
400m H	David Hemery, GBR	48.12	WR
3000m Steeple	Amos Biwott, KEN	8:51.0	
20k Walk	Vladimir Golubnichiy, USSR	1:33:58.4	
50k Walk	Christoph Höhne, E. Ger	4:20:13.6	
4x100m	USA (Charlie Greene, Mel Pender, Ronnie Ray Smith, Jim Hines)	38.2	WR
4x400m	USA (Vince Matthews, Ron Freeman, Larry James, Lee Evans)	2:56.16	WR

Event		Mark	
High Jump	Dick Fosbury, USA	7-4¼	OR
Pole Vault	Bob Seagren, USA	17-8½	OR
Long Jump	Bob Beamon, USA	29-2½	WR
Triple Jump	Viktor Saneyev, USSR	57-0¾	WR
Shot Put	Randy Matson, USA	67-4¾	
Discus	Al Oerter, USA	212-6	OR
Hammer	Gyula Zsivótzky, HUN	240-8	OR
Javelin	Janis Lusis, USSR	295-7	OR
Decathlon	Bill Toomey, USA	8193 pts	OR

WOMEN

Event		Time	
100m	Wyomia Tyus, USA	11.0	WR
200m	Irena K. Szewinska, POL	22.5	WR
400m	Colette Besson, FRA	52.0	=OR
800m	Madeline Manning, USA	2:00.9	OR
80m H	Maureen Caird, AUS	10.3	OR
4x100m	USA (Barbara Ferrell, Margaret Bailes, Mildrette Netter, Wyomia Tyus)	42.8	WR

Event		Mark	
High Jump	Miloslava Rezková, CZE	5-11½	
Long Jum	Viorica Viscopoleanu, ROM	22-4½	WR
Shot Put	Margitta Gummel, E. Ger	64-4	WR
Discus	Lia Manoliu, ROM	191-2	OR
Javelin	Angéla Németh, HUN	198-0	
Pentathlon	Ingrid Becker, GER	5098 pts	

Boxing

Weight Class	Champion
Lt. Flyweight (106 lbs)	Francisco Rodriquez, VEN
Flyweight (112)	Ricardo Delgado, MEX
Bantamweight (119)	Valery Sokolov, USSR
Featherweight (125)	Antonio Roldan, MEX
Lightweight (132)	Ron Harris, USA
Lt. Welterweight (139)	Jerzy Kulej, POL
Welterweight (148)	Manfred Wolke, E. Ger
Lt. Middleweight (156)	Boris Lagutin, USSR
Middleweight (165)	Chris Finnegan, GBR
Lt. Heavyweight (178)	Dan Poznjak, USSR
Heavyweight (178+)	George Foreman, USA

Gymnastics
MEN

Individual		Points
All-Around	Sawao Kato, JPN	115.9
Floor	Sawao Kato, JPN	19.475
Horiz.Bar	Akinori Nakayama, JPN Mikhail Voronin, USSR	19.55
Paral.Bars	Akinori Nakayama, JPN	19.475
Rings	Akinori Nakayama, JPN	19.45
Side Horse	Miroslav Cerar, YUG	19.325
Vault	Mikhail Voronin, USSR	19.00

Team		Points
All-Around	JPN (Kato, Nakayama, Kenmotsu, Kato, Endo, Tsukahara)	575.90

WOMEN

Individual		Points
All-Around	Vera Cáslavská, CZE	78.25
Bal.Beam	Natayla Kuchinskaya, USSR	19.65
Floor	Vera Cáslavská, CZE Larissa Petrik, USSR	19.675
Uneven Bars	Vera Cáslavská, CZE	19.65
Vault	Vera Cáslavská, CZE	19.775

Team		Points
All-Around	USSR (Voronina, Kuchinskaya, Petrik, Karasseva, Tourischeva, Burda)	382.85

Swimming
MEN

Event		Time	
100m Free	Mike Wenden, AUS	52.2	WR
200m Free	Mike Wenden, AUS	1:55.2	OR
400m Free	Mike Burton, USA	4:09.0	OR
1500m Free	Mike Burton, USA	16:38.9	OR
100m Back	Roland Matthes, E. Ger	58.7	OR
200m Back	Roland Matthes, E. Ger	2:09.6	OR
100m Brst	Don McKenzie, USA	1:07.7	OR
200m Brst	Felipe Muñoz, MEX	2:28.7	
100m Fly	Doug Russell, USA	55.9	OR
200m Fly	Carl Robie, USA	2:08.7	
200m I.M.	Charles Hickcox, USA	2:12.0	OR
400m I.M.	Charles Hickcox, USA	4:48.4	
4x100m Free	USA (Zack Zorn, Steve Rerych, Mark Spitz, Ken Walsh)	3:31.7	WR
4x200m Free	USA (John Nelson, Steve Rerych, Mark Spitz, Don Schollander)	7:52.33	
4x100m Mdly	USA (Charles Hickcox, Don McKenzie, Doug Russell, Ken Walsh)	3:54.9	WR

Diving		Points
Platform	Klaus Dibiasi, ITA	164.18
Spring	Bernie Wrightson, USA	170.15

WOMEN

Event		Time	
100m Free	Jan Henne, USA	1:00.0	
200m Free	Debbie Meyer, USA	2:10.5	OR
400m Free	Debbie Meyer, USA	4:31.8	OR
800m Free	Debbie Meyer, USA	9:24.0	OR
100m Back	Kaye Hall, USA	1:06.2	WR
200m Back	Pokey Watson, USA	2:24.8	OR
100m Brst	Djurdjica Bjedov, YUG	1:15.8	OR
200m Brst	Sharon Wichman, USA	2:44.4	OR

Event		Time	
100m Fly	Lyn McClements, AUS	1:05.5	
200m Fly	Ada Kok, HOL	2:24.7	**OR**
200m I.M.	Claudia Kolb, USA	2:24.7	**OR**
400m I.M.	Claudia Kolb, USA	5:08.5	**OR**
4x100m Free	USA (Jane Barkman, Linda Gustavson, Sue Pedersen, Jan Henne)	4:02.5	**OR**
4x100m Mdly	USA (Kaye Hall, Catie Ball, Ellie Daniel, Sue Pedersen)	4:28.3	**OR**

Diving		Points
Platform	Milena Duchková, CZE	109.59
Spring	Sue Gossick, USA	150.77

Team Sports

Men	Champion
Basketball	United States
Field Hockey	Pakistan
Soccer	Hungary
Volleyball	Soviet Union
Water Polo	Yugoslavia

Women	Champion
Volleyball	Soviet Union

Also Contested

Canoeing, Cycling, Equestrian, Fencing, Modern Pentathlon, Rowing, Shooting, Weightlifting, Freestyle Wrestling, Greco-Roman Wrestling and Yachting.

1972

Munich

On Sept. 5, with six days left in the Games, eight Arab commandos slipped into the Olympic Village, killed two Israeli team members and seized nine others as hostages. Later that night, all nine were killed in a shootout between the terrorists and West German police at a military airport.

The tragedy stunned the world and stopped the XXth Olympiad in its tracks. But after suspending competition for 24 hours and holding a memorial service attended by 80,000 at the main stadium, 84-year-old outgoing IOC president Avery Brundage and his committee ordered the Games to continue.

They went on without 22-year-old swimmer Mark Spitz, who had set an Olympic gold medal record by winning four individual and three relay events, all in world record times. Spitz, an American Jew, was an inviting target for further terrorism and agreed with West German officials when they advised him to leave the country.

The pall that fell over Munich quieted an otherwise boisterous Games that saw American swimmer Rick DeMont stripped of a gold medal for taking asthma medication and track medalists Vince Matthews and Wayne Collett of the U.S. banned for life for fooling around on the victory stand during the American national anthem.

The United States also lost an Olympic basketball game for the first time ever (they were 62-0) when the Russians were given three chances to convert a last-second inbound pass and finally won, 51-50. The U.S. refused the silver medal.

Munich was also where 17-year-old Soviet gymnast Olga Korbut and 16-year-old swimmer Shane Gould of Australia won three gold medals each and Britain's 33-year-old Mary Peters won the pentathlon.

Top 10 Standings

National medal standings are not recognized by the IOC. The unofficial point totals are based on 3 points for a gold medal, 2 for a silver and 1 for a bronze.

		Gold	Silver	Bronze	Total	Pts
1	USSR	50	27	22	99	226
2	USA	33	31	30	94	191
3	E. Germany	20	23	23	66	129
4	W. Germany	13	11	16	40	77
5	Japan	13	8	8	29	63
6	Hungary	6	13	16	35	60
7	Bulgaria	6	10	5	21	43
8	Australia	8	7	2	17	40
	Poland	7	5	9	21	40
10	Italy	5	3	10	18	31
	Great Britain	4	5	9	18	31

Leading Medal Winners

Number of individual medals won on the left; gold, silver and bronze breakdown to the right.

MEN

No		Sport	G-S-B
7	Mark Spitz, USA	Swimming	7-0-0
5	Sawao Kato, JPN	Gymnastics	3-2-0
4	Jerry Heidenreich, USA	Swimming	2-1-1
4	Roland Matthes, E. Ger	Swimming	2-1-1
4	Akinori Nakayama, JPN	Gymnastics	2-1-1
4	Shigeru Kasamatsu, JPN	Gymnastics	1-1-2
4	Eizo Kenmotsu, JPN	Gymnastics	1-1-2
3	Valery Borsov, USSR	Track/Field	2-1-0
3	Mitsuo Tsukahara, JPN	Gymnastics	2-0-1
3	Steve Genter, USA	Swimming	1-2-0
3	Viktor Klimenko, USSR	Gymnastics	1-2-0
3	Mike Stamm, USA	Swimming	1-2-0
3	Vladimir Bure, USSR	Swimming	0-1-2

WOMEN

No		Sport	G-S-B
5	Shane Gould, AUS	Swimming	3-1-1
5	Karin Janz, E. Ger	Gymnastics	2-2-1
4	Olga Korbut, USSR	Gymnastics	3-1-0
4	Lyudmila Tourischeva, USSR	Gymnastics	2-1-1
4	Tamara Lazakovitch, USSR	Gymnastics	1-1-2

Track & Field

MEN

Event		Time	
100m	Valery Borzov, USSR	10.14	
200m	Valery Borzov, USSR	20.00	
400m	Vince Matthews, USA	44.66	
800m	Dave Wottle, USA	1:45.9	
1500m	Pekka Vasala, FIN	3:36.3	
5000m	Lasse Viren, FIN	13:26.4	**OR**
10,000m	Lasse Viren, FIN	27:38.4	**WR**
Marathon	Frank Shorter, USA	2:12:19.8	
110m H	Rod Milburn, USA	13.24	**=WR**
400m H	John Akii-Bua, UGA	47.82	**WR**
3000m Steeple	Kip Keino, KEN	8:23.6	**OR**

1972 (Cont.)

Event		Time	
20k Walk	Peter Frenkel, E. Ger	1:26:42.4	OR
50k Walk	Bernd Kannenberg, W. Ger	3:56:11.6	OR
4x100m	USA (Larry Black, Robert Taylor, Gerald Tinker, Eddie Hart)	38.19	=WR
4x400m	KEN (Charles Asati, Hezaklah Nyamau, Robert Ouko, Julius Sang)	2:59.8	

Event		Mark	
High Jump	Yuri Tarmak, USSR	7- 3¾	
Pole Vault	Wolfgang Nordwig, E. Ger	18- 0½	OR
Long Jump	Randy Williams, USA	27- 0½	
Triple Jump	Viktor Saneyev, USSR	56-11¼	
Shot Put	Wladyslaw Komar, POL	69- 6	OR
Discus	Ludvik Danek, CZE	211- 3	
Hammer	Anatoly Bondarchuk, USSR	247- 8	OR
Javelin	Klaus Wolfermann, W. Ger	296-10	OR
Decathlon	Nikolai Avilov, USSR	8454 pts	WR

WOMEN

Event		Time	
100m	Renate Stecher, E. Ger	11.07	
200m	Renate Stecher, E. Ger	22.40	=WR
400m	Monika Zehrt, E. Ger	51.08	OR
800m	Hildegard Falck, W. Ger	1:58.55	WR
1500m	Lyudmila Bragina, USSR	4:01.4	WR
100m H	Annelie Ehrhardt, E. Ger	12.59	WR
4x100m	W. Ger. (Christiane Krause, Ingrid Mickler, Annegret Richter, Heidemarie Rosendahl)	42.81	=WR
4x400m	E. Ger. (Dägmar Käsling, Rita Kühne, Helga Seidler, Monika Zehrt)	3:23.0	WR

Event		Mark	
High Jump	Ulrike Meyfarth, W. Ger	6- 3½	=WR
Long Jump	Heidemarie Rosendahl, W. Ger	22- 3	
Shot Put	Nadezhda Chizhova, USSR	69- 0	WR
Discus	Faina Melnik, USSR	218- 7	OR
Javelin	Ruth Fuchs, E. Ger	209- 7	OR
Pentathlon	Mary Peters, GBR	4801 pts	WR

Boxing

Weight Class	Champion
Lt. Flyweight (106 lbs)	György Gedó, HUN
Flyweight (112)	Georgi Kostadinov, BUL
Bantamweight (119)	Orlando Martinez, CUB
Featherweight (125)	Boris Kousnetsov, USSR
Lightweight (132)	Jan Szczepanski, POL
Lt. Welterweight (139)	Ray Seales, USA
Welterweight (148)	Emilio Correa, CUB
Lt. Middleweight (156)	Dieter Kottysch, W. Ger
Middleweight (165)	Vyacheslav Lemechev, USSR
Lt. Heavyweight (178)	Mate Parlov, YUG
Heavyweight (178+)	Teófilo Stevenson, CUB

Gymnastics
MEN

Individual		Points
All-Around	Sawao Kato, JPN	114.650
Floor	Nikolai Andrianov, USSR	19.175
Horiz.Bar	Mitsuo Tsukahara, JPN	19.725
Paral.Bars	Sawao Kato, JPN	19.475
Rings	Akinori Nakayama, JPN	19.35
Side Horse	Viktor Klimenko, USSR	19.125
Vault	Klaus Köste, E. Ger	18.85

Team		Points
All-Around	JPN (Kato, Kenmotsu, Kasamatsu, Nakayama, Tsukahara, Okamura)	571.25

WOMEN

Individual		Points
All-Around	Lyudmila Tourischeva, USSR	77.025
Bal.Beam	Olga Korbut, USSR	19.40
Floor	Olga Korbut, USSR	19.575
Uneven Bars	Karin Janz, E. Ger	19.675
Vault	Karin Janz, E. Ger	19.525

Team		Points
All-Around	USSR (Tourischeva, Korbut, Lazakovitch, Burda, Saadi, Koshel)	380.50

Swimming
MEN

Event		Time	
100m Free	Mark Spitz, USA	51.22	WR
200m Free	Mark Spitz, USA	1:52.78	WR
400m Free	Brad Cooper, USA	4:00.27	OR
1500m Free	Mike Burton, USA	15:52.58	WR
100m Back	Roland Matthes, E. Ger	56.58	OR
200m Back	Roland Matthes, E. Ger	2:02.82	=WR
100m Brst	Nobutaka Taguchi, JPN	1:04.94	WR
200m Brst	John Hencken, USA	2:21.55	WR
100m Fly	Mark Spitz, USA	54.27	WR
200m Fly	Mark Spitz, USA	2:00.70	WR
200m I.M.	Gunnar Larsson, SWE	2:07.17	WR
400m I.M.	Gunnar Larsson, SWE	4:31.98	OR
4x100m Free	USA (Dave Edgar, John Murphy, Jerry Heidenreich, Mark Spitz)	3:26.42	WR
4x200m Free	USA (John Kinsella, Fred Tyler, Steve Genter, Mark Spitz)	7:35.78	WR
4x100m Mdly	USA (Mike Stamm, Tom Bruce, Mark Spitz, Jerry Heidenreich)	3:48.16	WR

Diving		Points
Platform	Klaus Dibiasi, ITA	504.12
Spring	Vladimir Vasin, USSR	594.09

WOMEN

Event		Time	
100m Free	Sandra Neilson, USA	58.59	OR
200m Free	Shane Gould, AUS	2:03.56	WR
400m Free	Shane Gould, AUS	4:19.44	WR
800m Free	Keena Rothhammer, USA	8:53.68	WR
100m Back	Melissa Belote, USA	1:05.78	OR
200m Back	Melissa Belote, USA	2:19.19	WR
100m Brst	Cathy Carr, USA	1:13.58	WR
200m Brst	Beverly Whitfield, AUS	2:41.71	WR
100m Fly	Mayumi Aoki, JPN	1:03.34	WR
200m Fly	Karen Moe, USA	2:15.57	WR
200m I.M.	Shane Gould, AUS	2:23.07	WR
400m I.M.	Gail Neall, AUS	5:02.97	WR
4x100m Free	USA (Sandra Neilson, Jennifer Kemp, Jane Barkman, Shirley Babashoff)	3:55.19	WR
4x100m Mdly	USA (Melissa Belote, Cathy Carr, Deena Deardurff, Sandra Neilson)	4:20.75	WR

Diving		Points
Platform	Ulrika Knape, SWE	390.00
Spring	Micki King, USA	450.03

Team Sports

Men	Champion
Basketball	Soviet Union
Field Hockey	West Germany
Handball	Yugoslavia
Soccer	Poland
Volleyball	Japan
Water Polo	Soviet Union

Women	Champion
Volleyball	Soviet Union

Also Contested

Archery, Canoeing, Cycling, Equestrian, Fencing, Judo, Modern Pentathlon, Rowing, Shooting, Weightlifting, Freestyle Wrestling, Greco-Roman Wrestling and Yachting.

1976

CANADA
1976

Montreal

In 1970, when Montreal was named to host the Summer Olympics '76, organizers estimated it would cost $310 million to stage the Games. However, due to political corruption, mismanagement, labor disputes, inflation and a $100 million outlay for security to prevent another Munich, the final bill came to more than $1.5 billion.

Then, right before the Games were scheduled to open in July, 32 nations, most of them from black Africa, walked out when the IOC refused to ban New Zealand because its national rugby team was touring racially-segregated South Africa. Taiwan also withdrew when Communist China pressured trading partner Canada to deny the Taiwanese the right to compete as the Republic of China.

When the Games finally got started they were quickly stolen by 14-year-old Romanian gymnast Nadia Comaneci, who scored seven perfect 10s on her way to three gold medals.

East Germany's Kornelia Ender did Comaneci one better, winning four times as the GDR captured 11 of 13 events in women's swimming. John Naber (4 gold) and the U.S. men did the East German women one better when they won 12 of 13 in swimming.

In track and field, Cuba's Alberto Juantorena won the 400- and 800-meter runs, and Finland's Lasse Viren took the 5,000 and 10,000. Viren missed a third gold when he placed fifth in the marathon.

Four Americans who became household names during the Games were decathlon winner Bruce Jenner and three future world boxing champions—Ray Leonard and the Spinks brothers, Michael and Leon.

Top 10 Standings

National medal standings are not recognized by the IOC. The unofficial point totals are based on 3 points for a gold medal, 2 for a silver and 1 for a bronze.

	Gold	Silver	Bronze	Total	Pts
1 USSR	49	41	35	125	264
2 USA	34	35	25	94	197
3 E. Germany	40	25	25	90	195
4 W. Germany	10	12	17	39	71
5 Japan	9	6	10	25	49
6 Poland	7	6	13	26	46
7 Romania	4	9	14	27	44
8 Bulgaria	6	9	7	22	43
9 Cuba	6	4	3	13	29
10 Hungary	4	5	13	22	35

Leading Medal Winners

Number of individual medals won on the left; gold, silver and bronze breakdown to the right.

MEN

No		Sport	G-S-B
7	Nikolai Andrianov, USSR	Gymnastics	4-2-1
5	John Naber, USA	Swimming	4-1-0
5	Mitsuo Tsukahara, JPN	Gymnastics	2-1-2
4	Jim Montgomery, USA	Swimming	3-0-1
3	John Hencken, USA	Swimming	2-1-0
3	Sawao Kato, JPN	Gymnastics	2-1-0
3	Eizo Kenmotsu, JPN	Gymnastics	1-2-0
3	Rüdiger Helm, E. Ger	Canoeing	1-0-2

WOMEN

No		Sport	G-S-B
5	Kornelia Ender, E. Ger	Swimming	4-1-0
5	Nadia Comaneci, ROM	Gymnastics	3-1-1
5	Shirley Babashoff, USA	Swimming	1-4-0
4	Nelli Kim, USSR	Gymnastics	3-1-0
4	Andrea Pollack, E. Ger	Swimming	2-2-0
4	Lyudmila Tourischeva, USSR	Gymnastics	1-2-1
3	Ulrike Richter, E. Ger	Swimming	3-0-0
3	Annagret Richter, W. Ger	Track/Field	1-2-0
3	Renate Stecher, E. Ger	Track/Field	1-1-1
3	Teodora Ungureanu, ROM	Gymnastics	0-2-1

Track & Field

MEN

Event		Time	
100m	Hasely Crawford, TRI	10.06	
200m	Donald Quarrie, JAM	20.23	
400m	Alberto Juantorena, CUB	44.26	
800m	Alberto Juantorena, CUB	1:43.50	WR
1500m	John Walker, NZE	3:39.17	
5000m	Lasse Viren, FIN	13:24.76	
10,000m	Lasse Viren, FIN	27:40.38	
Marathon	Waldemar Cierpinski, E. Ger	2:09:55	OR
110m H	Guy Drut, FRA	13.30	
400m H	Edwin Moses, USA	47.64	WR
3000m Steeple	Anders Gärdeud, SWE	8:08.2	WR
20k Walk	Daniel Bautista, MEX	1:24:40.6	OR
4x100m	USA (Harvey Glance, Johnny Jones, Millard Hampton, Steve Riddick)	38.33	
4x400m	USA (Herman Frazier, Benjamin Brown, Fred Newhouse, Maxie Parks)	2:58.65	

Event		Mark	
High Jump	Jacek Wszola, POL	7- 4½	OR
Pole Vault	Tadeusz Slusarski, POL	18- 0½	=OR
Long Jump	Arnie Robinson, USA	27- 4¾	
Triple Jump	Viktor Saneyev, USSR	56- 8¾	
Shot Put	Udo Beyer, E. Ger	69- 0¾	
Discus	Mac Wilkins, USA	221- 5	
Hammer	Yuri Sedykh, USSR	254- 4	OR
Javelin	Miklos Nèmeth, HUN	310- 4	WR
Decathlon	Bruce Jenner, USA	8617 pts	WR

WOMEN

Event		Time	
100m	Annegret Richter, W. Ger	11.08	
200m	Bärbel Eckert, E. Ger	22.37	OR
400m	Irena K. Szewinska, POL	49.29	WR
800m	Tatyana Kazankina, USSR	1:54.94	WR
1500m	Tatyana Kazankina, USSR	4:05.48	
100m H	Johanna Schaller, E. Ger	12.77	

1976 (Cont.)

Event		Time	
4x100m	E. Ger. (Marlies Oelsner, Renate Stecher, Carla Bodendorf, Barbel Eckert)	42.55	OR
4x400m	E. Ger. (Doris Maletzki, Brigitte Rohde, Ellen Streidt, Christina Brehmer)	3:19.23	WR

Event		Mark	
High Jump	Rosemarie Ackermann, E. Ger	.6- 4	OR
Long Jump	Angela Voigt, E. Ger	22- 0¾	
Shot Put	Ivanka Hristova, BUL	69- 5¼	OR
Discus	Evelin Schlaak, E. Ger	226- 4	OR
Javelin	Ruth Fuchs, E. Ger	216- 4	OR
Pentathlon	Siegrun Siegl, E. Ger	4745 pts	

Boxing

Weight Class	Champion
Lt. Flyweight (106 lbs)	Jorge Hernandez, CUB
Flyweight (112)	Leo Randolph, USA
Bantamweight (119)	Gu Yong-Ju, N. Kor
Featherweight (125)	Angel Herrera, CUB
Lightweight (132)	Howard Davis, USA
Lt. Welterweight (139)	Ray Leonard, USA
Welterweight (148)	Jochen Bachfeld, E. Ger
Lt. Middleweight (156)	Jerzy Rybicki, POL
Middleweight (165)	Michael Spinks, USA
Lt. Heavyweight (178)	Leon Spinks, USA
Heavyweight (178+)	Teófilo Stevenson, CUB

Gymnastics
MEN

Individual		Points
All-Around	Nikolai Andrianov, USSR	116.65
Floor	Nikolai Andrianov, USSR	19.45
Horiz.Bar	Mitsuo Tsukahara, JPN	19.675
Paral.Bars	Sawao Kato, JPN	19.675
Rings	Nikolai Andrianov, USSR	19.65
Side Horse	Zoltan Magyar, HUN	19.70
Vault	Nikolai Andrianov, USSR	19.45

Team		Points
All-Around	JPN (Kato, Tsukahara, Kajiyama, Kenmotsu, Igarashi, Fujimoto)	576.85

WOMEN

Individual		Points
All-Around	Nadia Comaneci, ROM	79.275
Bal.Beam	Nadia Comaneci, ROM	19.95
Floor	Nelli Kim, USSR	19.85
Uneven Bars	Nadia Comaneci, ROM	20.00
Vault	Nelli Kim, USSR	19.80

Team		Points
All-Around	USSR (Kim, Touriseva, Korbut, Saadi, Filatova, Grozdova)	466.00

Swimming
MEN

Event		Time	
100m Free	Jim Montgomery, USA	49.99	WR
200m Free	Bruce Furniss, USA	1:50.29	WR
400m Free	Brian Goodell, USA	3:51.93	WR
1500m Free	Brian Goodell, USA	15:02.40	WR
100m Back	John Naber, USA	55.49	WR
200m Back	John Naber, USA	1:59.19	WR
100m Brst	John Hencken, USA	1:03.11	WR
200m Brst	David Wilkie, GBR	2:15.11	WR
100m Fly	Matt Vogel, USA	54.35	
200m Fly	Mike Bruner, USA	1:59.23	WR
400m I.M.	Rod Strachan, USA	4:23.68	WR
4x200m Free	USA (Mike Bruner, Bruce Furniss, John Naber, Jim Montgomery)	7:23.22	WR

Event		Time	
4x100m Mdly	USA (John Naber, John Hencken, Matt Vogel, Jim Montgomery)	3:42.22	WR

Diving		Points
Platform	Klaus Dibiasi, ITA	600.51
Spring	Phil Boggs, USA	619.05

WOMEN

Event		Time	
100m Free	Kornelia Ender, E. Ger	55.65	WR
200m Free	Kornelia Ender, E. Ger	1:59.26	WR
400m Free	Petra Thümer, E. Ger	4:09.89	WR
800m Free	Petra Thümer, E. Ger	8:37.14	WR
100m Back	Ulrike Richter, E. Ger	1:01.83	OR
200m Back	Ulrike Richter, E. Ger	2:13.43	OR
100m Brst	Hannelore Anke, E. Ger	1:11.16	
200m Brst	Marina Koshevaia, USSR	2:33.35	WR
100m Fly	Kornelia Ender, E. Ger	1:00.13	WR
200m Fly	Andrea Pollack, E. Ger	2:11.41	OR
400m I.M.	Ulrike Tauber, E. Ger	4:42.77	WR
4x100m Free	USA (Kim Peyton, Wendy Boglioli, Jill Sterkel, Shirley Babashoff)	3:44.82	WR
4x100m Mdly	GDR (Ulrike Richter, Hannelore Anke, Andrea Pollack, Kornelia Ender)	4:07.95	WR

Diving		Points
Platform	Elena Vaytsekhovskaya, USSR	406.59
Spring	Jennifer Chandler, USA	506.19

Team Sports

Men	Champion
Basketball	United States
Field Hockey	New Zealand
Handball	Soviet Union
Soccer	East Germany
Volleyball	Poland
Water Polo	Hungary

Women	Champion
Basketball	Soviet Union
Handball	Soviet Union
Volleyball	Japan

Also Contested

Archery, Canoeing, Cycling, Equestrian, Fencing, Judo, Modern Pentathlon, Rowing, Shooting, Weightlifting, Freestyle Wrestling, Greco-Roman Wrestling and Yachting.

OLYMPIAD 80
MOSCOU MOSCOW МОСКВА

1980

Moscow

Four years after 32 nations walked out of the Montreal Games, twice that many chose to stay away from Moscow—many in support of an American-led boycott to protest the December, 1979, Russian invasion of Afghanistan.

Unable to persuade the IOC to cancel or move the Summer Games, U.S. President Jimmy Carter pressured the USOC to officially withdraw in April. Many western governments, like West Germany and Japan, followed suit and withheld their athletes.

But others, like Britain and France, while supporting the boycott, allowed their Olympic committees to participate if they wished.

The first Games to be held in a Communist country opened in July with 81 nations in attendance and were dominated by the USSR and East Germany. They were also plagued by charges of rigged judging and poor sportsmanship by Moscow fans who, without the Americans around, booed the Poles and East Germans unmercifully.

Otherwise, Soviet gymnast Aleksandr Dityatin became the first athlete to win eight medals in one year; the belle of Montreal, Nadia Comaneci of Romania, returned to win two more gold medals; and Cuban heavyweight Teofilo Stevenson became the first boxer to win three golds in the same weight division.

In track and field, Miruts Yifter of Ethiopia won at 5,000 and 10,000 meters, but the most thrilling moment of the Games came in the last lap of the 1,500 meters where Sebastian Coe of Great Britain outran countryman Steve Ovett and Jurgen Straub of East Germany for the gold.

Top 10 Standings

National medal standings are not recognized by the IOC. The unofficial point totals are based on 3 points for a gold medal, 2 for a silver and 1 for a bronze.

		Gold	Silver	Bronze	Total	Pts
1	USSR	80	69	46	195	424
2	E. Germany	47	37	42	126	257
3	Bulgaria	8	16	17	41	73
4	Hungary	7	10	15	32	56
5	Poland	3	14	15	32	52
6	Cuba	8	7	5	20	43
	Romania	6	6	13	25	43
8	Great Britain	5	7	9	21	38
9	Italy	8	3	4	15	34
10	France	6	5	3	14	31

Leading Medal Winners

Number of individual medals won on the left; gold, silver and bronze breakdown to the right.

MEN

No		Sport	G-S-B
8	Aleksandr Dityatin, USSR	Gymnastics	3-4-1
5	Nikolai Andrianov, USSR	Gymnastics	2-2-1
4	Roland Brückner, E. Ger	Gymnastics	1-1-2
3	Vladimir Parfenovich, USSR	Canoeing	3-0-0
3	Vladimir Salnikov, USSR	Swimming	3-0-0
3	Sergei Kopliakov, USSR	Swimming	2-1-0
3	Aleksandr Tkachyov, USSR	Gymnastics	2-1-0
3	Andrei Krylov, USSR	Swimming	1-2-0
3	Arsen Miskarov, USSR	Swimming	0-2-1

WOMEN

No		Sport	G-S-B
5	Ines Diers, E. Ger	Swimming	2-2-1
4	Caren Metschuck, E. Ger	Swimming	3-1-0
4	Nadia Comaneci, ROM	Gymnastics	2-2-0
4	Natalya Shaposhnikova, USSR	Gymnastics	2-0-2
4	Maxi Gnauck, E. Ger	Gymnastics	1-1-2
3	Barbara Krause, E. Ger	Swimming	3-0-0
3	Rica Reinisch, E. Ger	Swimming	3-0-0
3	Yelena Davydova, USSR	Gymnastics	2-1-0
3	Steffi Kraker, E. Ger	Gymnastics	0-1-2
3	Melita Ruhn, ROM	Gymnastics	0-1-2

Track & Field

MEN

Event		Time	
100m	Allan Wells, GBR	10.25	
200m	Pietro Mennea, ITA	20.19	
400m	Viktor Markin, USSR	44.60	
800m	Steve Ovett, GBR	1:45.4	
1500m	Sebastian Coe, GBR	3:38.4	
5000m	Miruts Yifter, ETH	13:21.0	
10,000m	Miruts Yifter, ETH	27:42.7	
Marathon	Waldemar Cierpinski, E. Ger	2:11:03	
110m H	Thomas Munkelt, E. Ger	13.39	
400m H	Volker Beck, E. Ger	48.70	
3000m Steeple	Bronislaw Malinowski, POL	8:09.7	
20k Walk	Maurizio Damilano, ITA	1:23:35.5	OR
50k Walk	Hartwig Gauder, E. Ger	3:49:24.0	
4x100m	USSR (Vladimir Muravyov, Nikolai Sidorov, Aleksandr Aksinin, Andrei Prokofiev)	38.26	
4x400m	USSR (Remigius Valiulis, Mikhail Linge, Nikolai Chernetsky, Viktor Markin)	3:01.1	

Event		Mark	
High Jump	Gerd Wessig, E. Ger	7- 8¾	WR
Pole Vault	Wladyslaw Kozakiewicz, POL	18-11½	WR
Long Jump	Lutz Dombrowski, E. Ger	28- 0¼	
Triple Jump	Jaak Uudmäe, USSR	56-11¼	
Shot Put	Vladimir Kiselyov, USSR	70- 0½	OR
Discus	Viktor Rashchupkin, USSR	218- 8	
Hammer	Yuri Sedykh, USSR	268- 4	WR
Javelin	Dainis Kla, USSR	299- 2	
Decathlon	Daley Thompson, GBR	8495 pts	

WOMEN

Event		Time	
100m	Lyudmila Kondratyeva, USSR	11.06	
200m	Bärbel E. Wöckel, E. Ger	22.03	OR
400m	Marita Koch, E. Ger	48.88	OR
800m	Nadezhda Olizarenko, USSR	1:53.42	WR
1500m	Tatyana Kazankina, USSR	3:56.6	OR
100m H	Vera Komisova, USSR	12.56	OR
4x100m	E. Ger. (Romy Müller, Bärbel E. Wöckel, Ingrid Auerswald, Marlies O. Göhr)	41.60	WR
4x400m	USSR (Tatyana Prorochenko, Tatyana Goistschik, Nina Zyuskova, Irina Nazarova)	3:20.2	

Event		Mark	
High Jump	Sara Simeoni, ITA	6- 5½	OR
Long Jump	Tatiana Kolpakova, USSR	23- 2	OR
Shot Put	Ilona Slupianke, E. Ger	73- 6¼	
Discus	Evelin S. Jahl, E. Ger	229- 6	OR
Javelin	Maria Colon, CUB	224- 5	OR
Pentathlon	Nadezhda Tkachenko, USSR	5083 pts	WR

Boxing

Weight Class	Champion
Lt. Flyweight (106 lbs)	Shamil Sabyrov, USSR
Flyweight (112)	Peter Lessov, BUL
Bantamweight (119)	Juan Hernandez, CUB
Featherweight (125)	Rudi Fink, E. Ger
Lightweight (132)	Angel Herrera, CUB
Lt. Welterweight (139)	Patrizio Oliva, ITA
Welterweight (148)	Andres Aldama, CUB
Lt. Middleweight (156)	Armando Martinez, CUB
Middleweight (165)	Jose Gomez, CUB
Lt. Heavyweight (178)	Slobodan Kacar, YUG
Heavyweight (178+)	Teofilo Stevenson, CUB

1980 (Cont.)
Gymnastics
MEN

Individual		Points
All-Around	Aleksandr Dityatin, USSR	118.65
Floor	Roland Brückner, E. Ger	19.75
Horiz.Bar	Stoyan Deltchev, BUL	19.825
Paral.Bars	Aleksandr Tkachyov, USSR	19.775
Rings	Aleksandr Dityatin, USSR	19.875
Side Horse	Zoltán Magyar, HUN	19.925
Vault	Nikolai Andrianov, USSR	19.825

Team		Points
All-Around	USSR (Dityatin, Andrianov, Azaryan, Tkachyov, Makuts, Markelov)	598.60

WOMEN

Individual		Points
All-Around	Yelena Davydova, USSR	79.15
Bal.Beam	Nadia Comaneci, ROM	19.80
Floor	Nadia Comaneci, ROM & Nelli Kim, USSR	19.875
Uneven Bars	Maxi Gnauk, E. Ger	19.875
Vault	Natalya Shaposhnikova, USSR	19.725

Team		Points
All-Around	USSR (Shaposhnikova, Davydova, Kim, Filatova, Zakharova, Naimushina)	394.90

Swimming
MEN

Event		Time	
100m Free	Jörg Woithe, E. Ger	50.40	
200m Free	Sergei Kopliakov, USSR	1:49.91	OR
400m Free	Vladimir Salnikov, USSR	3:51.31	OR
1500m Free	Vladimir Salnikov, USSR	14:58.27	WR
100m Back	Bengt Baron, SWE	56.33	
200m Back	Sándor Wladár, HUN	2:01.93	
100m Brst	Duncan Goodhew, GBR	1:03.44	
200m Brst	Robertas Zhulpa, USSR	2:15.85	
100m Fly	Pär Arvidsson, SWE	54.92	
200m Fly	Sergei Fesenko, USSR	1:59.76	
400m I.M.	Aleksandr Sidorenko, USSR	4:22.89	OR
4x200m Free	USSR (Sergei Kopliakov, Vladimir, Salnikov, Ivar Stukolkin, Andrei Krylov)	7:23.50	
4x100m Mdly	AUS (Mark Kerry, Peter Evans, Mark Tonelli, Neil Brooks)	3:45.70	

Diving		Points
Platform	Falk Hoffmann, E. Ger	835.650
Spring	Aleksandr Portnov, USSR	905.025

WOMEN

Event		Time	
100m Free	Barbara Krause, E. Ger	54.79	WR
200m Free	Barbara Krause, E. Ger	1:58.33	OR
400m Free	Ines Diers, E. Ger	4:08.76	OR
800m Free	Michelle Ford, AUS	8:28.90	OR
100m Back	Rica Reinisch, E. Ger	1:00.86	WR
200m Back	Rica Reinisch, E. Ger	2:11.77	WR
100m Brst	Ute Geweniger, E. Ger	1:10.22	
200m Brst	Lina Kaciusyté, USSR	2:29.54	OR
100m Fly	Caren Metschuck, E. Ger	1:00.42	
200m Fly	Ines Geissler, E. Ger	2:10.44	OR
400m I.M.	Petra Schneider, E. Ger	4:36.29	WR
4x100m Free	E. Ger. (Barbara Krause, Caren Metschuck, Ines Diers, Sarina Hülsenbeck)	3:42.71	WR
4x100m Mdly	E. Ger. (Rica Reinisch, Ute Geweniger, Andrea Pollack, Caren Metschuck)	4:06.67	WR

Diving		Points
Platform	Martina Jäschke, E. Ger	596.25
Spring	Irina Kalinina, USSR	725.91

Team Sports

Men	Champion
Basketball	Yugoslavia
Field Hockey	India
Handball	East Germany
Soccer	Czechoslovakia
Volleyball	Soviet Union
Water Polo	Soviet Union
Women	**Champion**
Basketball	Soviet Union
Field Hockey	Zimbabwe
Handball	Soviet Union
Volleyball	Soviet Union

Also Contested
Archery, Canoeing, Cycling, Equestrian, Fencing, Judo, Modern Pentathlon, Rowing, Shooting, Weightlifting, Freestyle Wrestling, Greco-Roman Wrestling and Yachting.

1984

Los Angeles

For the third consecutive Olympiad, a boycott prevented all member nations from attending the Summer Games. This time, the Soviet Union and 13 Communist allies stayed home in an obvious payback for the West's snub of Moscow in 1980. Romania was the only Warsaw Pact country to come to L.A.

While a record 141 nations did show up, the level of competition was hardly what it might have been had the Soviets and East Germans made the trip. As a result, the United States won a record 83 gold medals in the most lopsided Summer Games since St. Louis 80 years before.

The American gold rush was led by 23-year-old Carl Lewis, who duplicated Jesse Owens' 1936 track and field grand slam by winning the 100 and 200 meters and the long jump, and anchoring the 400-meter relay. Teammate Valerie Brisco-Hooks won three times, taking the 200, 400 and 1,600 relay.

Sebastian Coe of Britain became the first repeat winner of the 1,500 meters since Jim Lightbody of the U.S. in 1906. Other repeaters were Briton Daley Thompson in the decathlon and U.S. hurdler Edwin Moses, who won in 1976 but was not allowed to defend his title in '80.

Romanian gymnast Ecaterina Szabó matched Lewis' four gold medals and added a silver, but the darling of the Games was little (4-foot-8¾), 16-year-old Mary Lou Retton, who won the women's All-Around with a pair of 10s in her last two events.

The L.A. Olympics were the first privately financed Games ever and made an unheard of profit of $215 million. Time magazine was so impressed it made Organizing president Peter Ueberroth its Man of the Year.

Top 10 Standings

National medal standings are not recognized by the IOC. The unofficial point totals are based on 3 points for a gold medal, 2 for a silver and 1 for a bronze.

		Gold	Silver	Bronze	Total	Pts
1	USA	83	61	30	174	401
2	W. Germany	17	19	23	59	112
3	Romania	20	16	17	53	109
4	Canada	10	18	16	44	82
5	China	15	8	9	32	70
6	Italy	14	6	12	32	66
7	Japan	10	8	14	32	60
8	Great Britain	5	11	21	37	58
9	France	5	7	16	28	45
10	Australia	4	8	12	24	40

Leading Medal Winners

Number of individual medals won on the left; gold, silver and bronze breakdown to the right.

MEN

No		Sport	G-S-B
6	Li Ning, CHN	Gymnastics	3-2-1
5	Koji Gushiken, JPN	Gymnastics	2-1-2
4	Carl Lewis, USA	Track/Field	4-0-0
4	Mike Heath, USA	Swimming	3-1-0
4	Michael Gross, W. Ger	Swimming	2-2-0
4	Mitch Gaylord, USA	Gymnastics	1-1-2
3	Rick Carey, USA	Swimming	3-0-0
3	Ian Ferguson, NZE	Canoeing	3-0-0
3	Rowdy Gaines, USA	Swimming	3-0-0
3	Peter Vidmar, USA	Gymnastics	2-1-0
3	Victor Davis, CAN	Swimming	1-2-0
3	Pablo Morales, USA	Swimming	1-2-0
3	Lou Yun, CHN	Gymnastics	1-2-0
3	Shinji Morisue, JPN	Gymnastics	1-1-1
3	Lars-Erik Moberg, SWE	Canoeing	0-3-0
3	Mark Stockwell, AUS	Swimming	0-2-1

WOMEN

No		Sport	G-S-B
5	Ecaterina Szabó, ROM	Gymnastics	4-1-0
5	Mary Lou Retton, USA	Gymnastics	1-2-2
4	Nancy Hogshead, USA	Swimming	3-1-0
3	Valerie Brisco-Hooks, USA	Track/Field	3-0-0
3	Tracy Caulkins, USA	Swimming	3-0-0
3	Mary T. Meagher, USA	Swimming	3-0-0
3	Agneta Andersson, SWE	Canoeing	2-1-0
3	Chandra Cheeseborough, USA	Track/Field	2-1-0
3	Simona Pauca, ROM	Gymnastics	2-0-1
3	Julie McNamara, USA	Gymnastics	1-2-0
3	Anne Ottenbrite, CAN	Swimming	1-1-1
3	Karin Seick, W. Ger	Swimming	0-1-2
3	Annemarie Verstappen, HOL	Swimming	0-1-2

Track & Field

MEN

Event		Time	
100m	Carl Lewis, USA	9.99	
200m	Carl Lewis, USA	19.80	OR
400m	Alonzo Babers, USA	44.27	
800m	Joaquim Cruz, BRA	1:43.00	OR
1500m	Sebastian Coe, GBR	3:32.53	OR
5000m	Said Aouita, MOR	13:05.59	OR
10,000m	Alberto Cova, ITA	27:47.54	
Marathon	Carlos Lopes, POR	2:09:21	OR
110m H	Roger Kingdom, USA	13.20	OR
400m H	Edwin Moses, USA	47.75	
3000m			
Steeple	Julius Korir, KEN	8:11.80	
20k Walk	Ernesto Canto, MEX	1:23:13.0	OR
50k Walk	Raúl González, MEX	3:47:26.0	OR
4x100m	USA (Sam Graddy, Ron Brown, Calvin Smith, Carl Lewis)	37.83	WR

Event		Time	
4x400m	USA (Sunder Nix, Ray Armstead, Alonzo Babers, Antonio McKay)	2:57.91	

Event		Mark	
High Jump	Dietmar Mögenburg, W. Ger	7- 8½	
Pole Vault	Pierre Quinon, FRA	18-10¼	
Long Jump	Carl Lewis, USA	28- 0¼	
Triple Jump	Al Joyner, USA	56- 7½	
Shot Put	Alessandro Andrei, ITA	69- 9	
Discus	Rolf Danneberg, W. Ger	218- 6	
Hammer	Juha Tiainen, FIN	256- 2	
Javelin	Arto Härkönen, FIN	284- 8	
Decathlon	Daley Thompson, GBR	8798 pts	=WR

WOMEN

Event		Time	
100m	Evelyn Ashford, USA	10.97	OR
200m	Valerie Brisco-Hooks, USA	21.81	OR
400m	Valerie Brisco-Hooks, USA	48.83	OR
800m	Doina Melinte, ROM	1:57.60	
1500m	Gabriella Dorio, ITA	4:03.25	
3000m	Maricica Puica, ROM	8:35.96	OR
Marathon	Joan Benoit, USA	2:24.52	
100m H	Benita Fitzgerald-Brown, USA	12.84	
400m H	Nawal El Moutawakel, MOR	54.61	OR
4x100m	USA (Alice Brown, Jeanette Bolden, Chandra Cheeseborough, Evelyn Ashford)	41.65	
4x400m	USA (Lillie Leatherwood, Sherri Howard, Valerie Brisco-Hooks, Chandra Cheeseborough)	3:18.29	OR

Event		Mark	
High Jump	Ulrike Meyfarth, W. Ger	6- 7½	OR
Long Jump	Anisoara Stanciu, ROM	22-10	
Shot Put	Claudia Losch, W. Ger	67- 2¼	
Discus	Ria Stalman, HOL	214- 5	
Javelin	Tessa Sanderson, GBR	228- 2	OR
Heptathlon	Glynis Nunn, AUS	6390 pts	OR

Boxing

Weight Class	Champion
Lt. Flyweight (106 lbs)	Paul Gonzales, USA
Flyweight (112)	Steve McCrory, USA
Bantamweight (119)	Maurizio Stecca, ITA
Featherweight (125)	Meldrick Taylor, USA
Lightweight (132)	Pernell Whitaker, USA
Lt. Welterweight (139)	Jerry Page, USA
Welterweight (148)	Mark Breland, USA
Lt. Middleweight (156)	Frank Tate, USA
Middleweight (165)	Shin Joon-Sup, S. Kor
Lt. Heavyweight (178)	Anton Josipovic, YUG
Heavyweight (200)	Henry Tillman, USA
Super Heavyweight (200+)	Tyrell Biggs, USA

Gymnastics

MEN

Individual		Points
All-Around	Koji Gushiken, JPN	118.7
Floor	Li Ning, CHN	19.925
Horiz.Bar	Shinji Morisue, JPN	20.00
Paral.Bars	Bart Conner, USA	19.95
Rings	Koji Gushiken, JPN	
	Li Ning, CHN	19.85
Side Horse	Li Ning, CHN	
	Peter Vidmar, USA	19.95
Vault	Lou Yun, CHN	19.95

Team		Points
All-Around	USA (Peter Vidmar, Bart Conner, Mitch Gaylord, Tim Daggett, James Hartung, Scott Johnson)	591.40

1984 (Cont.)

WOMEN

Individual		Points
All-Around	Mary Lou Retton, USA	79.175
Bal.Beam	Simona Pauco, ROM	
	Ecaterina Szabó, ROM	19.80
Floor	Ecaterina Szabó, ROM	19.975
Uneven Bars	Julie McNamara, USA	
	Ma Yanhong, CHN	19.95
Vault	Ecaterina Szabó, ROM	19.875

Team		Points
All-Around	ROM (Szabó, Cutina, Pauca, Grigoras, Stanulet, Agache)	392 .02

Rhythmic		Points
All-Around	Lori Fung, CAN	57.950

Swimming
MEN

Event		Time	
100m Free	Rowdy Gaines, USA	49.80	OR
200m Free	Michael Gross, W. Ger	1:47.44	WR
400m Free	George DiCarlo, USA	3:51.23	OR
1500m Free	Mike O'Brien, USA	15:05.20	
100m Back	Rick Carey, USA	55.79	
200m Back	Rick Carey, USA	2:00.23	
100m Brst	Steve Lundquist, USA	1:01.65	WR
200m Brst	Victor Davis, CAN	2:13.34	WR
100m Fly	Michael Gross, W. Ger	53.08	WR
200m Fly	Jon Sieben, AUS	1:57.04	WR
200m I.M.	Alex Baumann, CAN	2:01.42	WR
400m I.M.	Alex Baumann, CAN	4:17.41	WR
4x100m Free	USA (Chris Cavanaugh, Mike Heath, Matt Biondi, Rowdy Gaines)	3:19.03	WR
4x200m Free	USA (Mike Heath, David Larson, Jeff Float, Bruce Hayes)	7:15.69	WR
4x100m Mdly	USA (Rick Carey, Steve Lundquist, Pablo Morales, Rowdy Gaines)	3:39.30	WR

Diving		Points
Platform	Greg Louganis, USA	710.91
Spring	Greg Louganis, USA	754.41

WOMEN

Event		Time	
100m Free	Nancy Hogshead, USA	55.92	
200m Free	Mary Wayte, USA	1:59.23	
400m Free	Tiffany Cohen, USA	4:07.10	OR
800m Free	Tiffany Cohen, USA	8:24.95	OR
100m Back	Theresa Andrews, USA	1:02.55	
200m Back	Jolanda de Rover, HOL	2:12.38	
100m Brst	Petra van Staveren, HOL	1:09.88	OR
200m Brst	Anne Ottenbrite, CAN	2:30.38	
100m Fly	Mary T. Meagher, USA	59.26	
200m Fly	Mary T. Meagher, USA	2:06.90	OR
200m I.M.	Tracy Caulkins, USA	2:12.64	OR
400m I.M.	Tracy Caulkins, USA	4:39.24	
4x100m Free	USA (Jenna Johnson, Carrie Steinseifer, Dara Torres, Nancy Hogshead)	3:43.43	
4x100m Mdly	USA (Theresa Andrews, Tracy Caulkins, Mary T. Meagher, Nancy Hogshead)	4:08.34	

Diving		Points
Platform	Zhou Jihong, CHN	435.51
Spring	Sylvie Bernier, CAN	530.70

Team Sports

Men	Champion
Basketball	United States
Field Hockey	Pakistan

Men	Champion
Handball	Yugoslavia
Soccer	France
Volleyball	United States
Water Polo	Yugoslavia

Women	Champion
Basketball	United States
Field Hockey	Holland
Handball	Yugoslavia
Volleyball	China

Also Contested

Archery, Canoeing, Cycling, Equestrian, Fencing, Judo, Modern Pentathlon, Rowing, Shooting, Synchronized Swimming, Weightlifting, Freestyle Wrestling, Greco-Roman Wrestling and Yachting.

1988

Seoul

For the first time since Munich in 1972, there was no organized boycott of the Summer Olympics. Cuba and Ethiopia stayed away in support of North Korea (the IOC turned down the North Koreans' demand to co-host the Games, so they refused to participate), but that was about it.

More countries (160) sent more athletes (9,627) to South Korea than to any previous Olympics. There were also more security personnel (100,000) than ever before given Seoul's proximity (30 miles) to the North and the possibility of student demonstrations for reunification.

Ten days into the Games, Canadian Ben Johnson beat defending champion Carl Lewis in the 100-meter dash with a world record time of 9.79. The next day, however, Johnson was stripped of his gold medal and sent packing by the IOC when his post-race drug test indicated steroid use.

Lewis, who finished second in the 100, was named the winner. He also repeated in the long jump, but was second in the 200 and did not run the 400 relay. Teammate Florence Griffith Joyner claimed four medals—gold in the 100, 200 and 400-meter relay, and silver in the 1,600 relay. Her sister-in-law Jackie Joyner-Kersee won the long jump and heptathlon.

The most gold medals were won by swimmers—Kristin Otto of East Germany (6) and American Matt Biondi (5). Otherwise, Steffi Graf added an Olympic gold medal to her Grand Slam sweep in tennis, Greg Louganis won both men's diving events for the second straight time, and the U.S. men's basketball team had to settle for third place after losing to the gold medal-winning Soviets, 82-76, in the semifinals.

Top 10 Standings

National medal standings are not recognized by the IOC. The unofficial point totals are based on 3 points for a gold medal, 2 for a silver and 1 for a bronze.

	Gold	Silver	Bronze	Total	Pts
1 USSR	55	31	46	132	273
2 E. Germany	37	35	30	102	211
3 USA	36	31	27	94	197
4 W. Germany	11	14	15	40	76
5 Bulgaria	10	12	13	35	67
South Korea	12	10	11	33	67
7 Hungary	11	6	6	23	51
8 China	5	11	12	28	49
Romania	7	11	6	24	49
10 Great Britain	5	10	9	24	44

Leading Medal Winners

Number of individual medals won on the left; gold, silver and bronze breakdown to the right.

MEN

No		Sport	G-S-B
7	Matt Biondi, USA	Swimming	5-1-1
5	Vladimir Artemov, USSR	Gymnastics	4-1-0
4	Dmitri Bilozerchev, USSR	Gymnastics	3-0-1
4	Valeri Lyukin, USSR	Gymnastics	2-2-0
3	Chris Jacobs, USA	Swimming	2-1-0
3	Carl Lewis, USA	Track/Field	2-1-0
3	Holger Behrendt, E. Ger	Gymnastics	1-1-1
3	Uwe Dassler, E. Ger	Swimming	1-1-1
3	Paul McDonald, NZE	Canoeing	1-1-1
3	Igor Polianski, USSR	Swimming	1-0-2
3	Gennadi Prigoda, USSR	Swimming	0-1-2
3	Sven Tippelt, E. Ger	Gymnastics	0-1-2

WOMEN

No		Sport	G-S-B
6	Kristin Otto, E. Ger	Swimming	6-0-0
6	Daniela Silivas, ROM	Gymnastics	3-2-1
4	Florence Griffith Joyner, USA	Track/Field	3-1-0
4	Svetlana Boguinskaya, USSR	Gymnastics	2-1-1
4	Elena Shushunova, USSR	Gymnastics	2-1-1
3	Janet Evans, USA	Swimming	3-0-0
3	Silke Hörner, E. Ger	Swimming	2-0-1
3	Daniela Hunger, E. Ger	Swimming	2-0-1
3	Katrin Meissner, E. Ger	Swimming	2-0-1
3	Birgit Schmidt, E. Ger	Canoeing	2-1-0
3	Birte Weigang, E. Ger	Swimming	1-2-0
3	Vania Guecheva, BUL	Canoeing	1-1-1
3	Gabriela Potorac, ROM	Gymnastics	0-2-1
3	Heike Drechsler, E. Ger	Track/Field	0-1-2

Track & Field
MEN

Event		Time	
100m	Carl Lewis, USA	9.92	OR
200m	Joe DeLoach, USA	19.75	OR
400m	Steve Lewis, USA	43.87	
800m	Paul Ereng, KEN	1:43.45	
1500m	Peter Rono, KEN	3:35.96	
5000m	John Ngugi, KEN	13:11.70	
10,000m	Brahim Boutaib, MOR	27:21.46	OR
Marathon	Gelindo Bordin, ITA	2:10:32	
110m H	Roger Kingdom, USA	12.98	OR
400m H	Andre Phillips, USA	47.19	OR
3000m Steeple	Julius Kariuki, KEN	8:05.51	OR
20k Walk	Jozef Pribilinec, CZE	1:19:57	OR
50k Walk	Viacheslav Ivanenko, USSR	3:38:29	OR
4x100m	USSR (Victor Bryzgine, Vladimir Krylov, Vladimir Mouraviev, Vitaly Savine)	38.19	

Event		Time	
4x400m	USA (Danny Everett, Steve Lewis, Kevin Robinzine, Butch Reynolds)	2:56.16	=WR

Event		Mark	
High Jump	Guennadi Avdeenko, USSR	7- 9¾	OR
Pole Vault	Sergey Bubka, USSR	19- 4¼	OR
Long Jump	Carl Lewis, USA	28- 7¼	
Triple Jump	Hristo Markov, BUL	57- 9¼	OR
Shot Put	Ulf Timmermann, E. Ger	73- 8¾	OR
Discus	Jürgen Schult, E. Ger	225- 9	OR
Hammer	Sergey Litvinov, USSR	278- 2	OR
Javelin	Tapio Korjus, FIN	276- 6	
Decathlon	Christian Schenk, E. Ger	8488 pts	

WOMEN

Event		Time	
100m	Florence Griffith Joyner, USA	10.54	OR
200m	Florence Griffith Joyner, USA	21.34	WR
400m	Olga Bryzgina, USSR	48.65	OR
800m	Sigrun Wodars, E. Ger	1:56.10	
1500m	Paula Ivan, ROM	3:53.96	OR
3000m	Tatiana Samolenko, USSR	8:26.53	OR
10,000m	Olga Bondarenko, USSR	31:05.21	OR
Marathon	Rosa Mota, POR	2:25:40	
100m H	Yordanka Donkova, BUL	12.38	OR
400m H	Debra Flintoff-King, AUS	53.17	OR
4x100m	USA (Alice Brown, Sheila Echols, Florence Griffith Joyner, Evelyn Ashford)	41.98	
4x400m	USSR (Tatyana Ledovskaia, Olga Nazarova, Maria Piniguina, Olga Bryzgina)	3:15.18	WR

Event		Mark	
High Jump	Louise Ritter, USA	6- 8	OR
Long Jump	Jackie Joyner-Kersee, USA	24- 3¼	OR
Shot Put	Natalya Lisovskaya, USSR	72-11¼	
Discus	Martina Hellmann, E. Ger	237- 2½	OR
Javelin	Petra Felke, E. Ger	245- 0	OR
Heptathlon	Jackie Joyner-Kersee, USA	7291 pts	WR

Boxing

Weight Class	Champion
Lt. Flyweight (106 lbs)	Ivailo Hristov, BUL
Flyweight (112)	Kim Kwang-Sun, S. Kor
Bantamweight (119)	Kennedy McKinney, USA
Featherweight (125)	Giovanni Parisi, ITA
Lightweight (132)	Andreas Zuelow, E. Ger
Lt. Welterweight (139)	Vyacheslav Yanovsky, USSR
Welterweight (148)	Robert Wangila, KEN
Lt. Middleweight (156)	Park Si-Hun, S. Kor
Middleweight (165)	Henry Maske, E. Ger
Lt. Heavyweight (178)	Andrew Maynard, USA
Heavyweight (200)	Ray Mercer, USA
Super Heavyweight (200+)	Lennox Lewis, CAN

Gymnastics
MEN

Individual		Points
All-Around	Vladimir Artemov, USSR	119.125
Floor	Sergey Kharkov, USSR	19.925
Horiz.Bar	Vladimir Artemov, USSR Valeri Lyukin, USSR	19.900
Paral.Bars	Vladimir Artemov, USSR	19.925
Rings	Dmitri Bilozerchev, USSR Holger Behrendt, E. Ger	19.925
Side Horse	Dmitri Bilozerchev, USSR, Lyubomir Geraskov, BUL Zsolt Borkai, HUN	19.950
Vault	Lou Yun, CHN	19.875

Team		Points
All-Around	USSR (Artemov, Bilozerchev, Kharkov, Lyukin, Gogoladze, Nouvikov)	593.350

1988 (Cont.)
WOMEN

Individual		Points
All-Around	Yelena Shushunova, USSR	79.662
Bal.Beam	Daniela Silivas, ROM	19.924
Floor	Daniela Silivas, ROM	19.937
Uneven Bars	Daniela Silivas, ROM	20.000
Vault	Svetlana Boguinskaya, USSR	19.905
Team		**Points**
All-Around	USSR (Shushunova, Boguinskaya, Baitova, Chevtchenko, Strajeva, Lachtchenova)	395.475
Rhythmic		**Points**
All-Around	Marina Lobatch, USSR	60.0

Swimming
MEN

Event		Time	
50m Free	Matt Biondi, USA	22.14	WR
100m Free	Matt Biondi, USA	48.63	OR
200m Free	Duncan Armstrong, AUS	1:47.25	WR
400m Free	Uwe Dassler, E. Ger	3:46.95	WR
1500m Free	Vladimir Salnikov, USSR	15:00.04	
100m Back	Daichi Suzuki, JPN	55.05	
200m Back	Igor Polianski, USSR	1:59.37	
100m Brst	Adrian Moorhouse, GBR	1:02.04	
200m Brst	József Szabó, HUN	2:13.52	
100m Fly	Anthony Nesty, SUR	53.00	OR
200m Fly	Michael Gross, W. Ger	1:56.94	OR
200m I.M.	Tamás Darnyi, HUN	2:00.17	WR
400m I.M.	Tamás Darnyi, HUN	4:14.75	WR
4x100mFree	USA (Chris Jacobs, Troy Dalbey, Tom Jager, Matt Biondi)	3:16.53	WR
4x200m Free	USA (Troy Dalbey, Matt Cetlinski, Doug Gjertsen, Matt Biondi)	7:12.51	WR
Event		**Time**	
4x100m Med	USA (David Berkoff, Rich Schroeder, Matt Biondi, Chris Jacobs)	3:36.93	WR
Diving		**Points**	
Platform	Greg Louganis, USA	638.61	
Spring	Greg Louganis, USA	730.80	

WOMEN

Event		Time	
50m Free	Kristin Otto, E. Ger	25.49	OR
100m Free	Kristin Otto, E. Ger	54.93	
200m Free	Heike Freidrich, E. Ger	1:57.65	OR
400m Free	Janet Evans, USA	4:03.85	WR
800m Free	Janet Evans, USA	8:20.20	OR
100m Back	Kristin Otto, E. Ger	1:00.89	
200m Back	Krisztina Egerszegi, HUN	2:09.29	OR
100m Brst	Tania Dangalakova, BUL	1:07.95	OR
200m Brst	Silke Hörner, E. Ger	2:26.71	WR
100m Fly	Kristin Otto, E. Ger	59.00	OR
200m Fly	Kathleen Nord, E. Ger	2:09.51	
200m I.M.	Daniela Hunger, E. Ger	2:12.59	OR
400m I.M.	Janet Evans, USA	4:37.76	
4x100m Free	E. Ger. (Kristin Otto, Katrin Meissner, Daniela Hunger, Manuela Stellmach)	3:40.63	OR
4x100m Med	E. Ger. (Kristin Otto, Silke Horner, Birte Weigang, Katrin Meissner)	4:03.74	OR
Diving		**Points**	
Platform	Xu Yanmei, CHN	445.20	
Spring	Gao Min, CHN	580.23	

Tennis
MEN

Singles: Miloslav Mecir, CZE, def. Tim Mayotte, USA, 3-6,6-2,6-4,6-2

Doubles: Ken Flach & Robert Seguso, USA, def. Emilio Sanchez & Sergio Casal, SPA, 6-3,6-4,6-7,6-7,9-7

WOMEN

Singles: Steffi Graf, W. Ger, def. Gabriela Sabatini, ARG, 6-3,6-3

Doubles: Pam Shriver and Zina Garrison, USA, def. Jana Novotna and Helena Sukova, CZE, 4-6,6-2,10-8

Team Sports

Men	Champion
Basketball	Soviet Union
Field Hockey	Great Britain
Handball	Soviet Union
Soccer	Soviet Union
Volleyball	United States
Water Polo	Yugoslavia
Women	**Champion**
Basketball	United States
Field Hockey	Australia
Handball	South Korea
Volleyball	Soviet Union

Also Contested

Archery, Canoeing, Cycling, Equestrian, Fencing, Judo, Modern Pentathlon, Shooting, Synchronized Swimming, Table Tennis, Weightlifting, Freestyle Wrestling, Greco-Roman Wrestling and Yachting.

1992

Barcelona

The year IOC president Juan Antonio Samaranch brought the Olympics to his native Spain marked the first renewal of the Summer Games since the fall of communism in Eastern Europe and the reunification of Germany in 1990.

A record 10,563 athletes from 172 nations gathered without a single country boycotting the Games. Both Cuba and North Korea returned after 12 years and South Africa was welcomed back after 32, following the national government's denunciation of apartheid racial policies.

While Germany competed under one flag and ideology for the first time since 1936, 12 nations from the former Soviet Union joined forces one last time as the Unified Team.

This was also the year the IOC threw open the gates to professional athletes after 96 years of high-minded opposition. Basketball was the chief beneficiary as America's popular "Dream Team" of NBA All-Stars easily won the gold.

Carl Lewis earned his seventh and eighth career gold medals with a third consecutive Olympic win in the long jump, and an anchor-leg performance on the American 400-meter relay team that helped establish a world record. Gail Devers of the U.S., whose feet had nearly been amputated by doctors in 1990 as a result of radiation treatment for Graves' disease, won the women's 100 meters.

Other track and field athletes stumbled, however. After Olympic favorite and world champion Dan O'Brien failed to even make the U.S. team, Dave Johnson, the new favorite, settled for the bronze. Ukrainian pole vaulter Sergey Bubka, who had dominated the sport for the past decade was the heavy favorite but failed to clear any height.

China's Fu Mingxia, 13, won the women's platform diving gold, becoming the second-youngest person to win an individual gold medal. In gymnastics, Vitaly Scherbo of Belarus, competing for the Unified Team, won six golds. Cuba made their Olympic return rewarding, capturing seven boxing golds as well as the gold in baseball.

Top 10 Standings

National medal standings are not recognized by the IOC. The unofficial point totals are based on 3 points for a gold medal, 2 for a silver and 1 for a bronze.

		Gold	Silver	Bronze	Total	Pts
1	Unified Team	45	38	29	112	240
2	United States	37	34	37	108	216
3	Germany	33	21	28	82	169
4	China	16	22	16	54	108
5	Cuba	14	6	11	31	65
6	Hungary	11	12	7	30	64
7	South Korea	12	5	12	29	58
8	Spain	13	7	2	22	55
9	France	8	5	16	29	50
	Australia	7	9	11	27	50

Leading Medal Winners

Number of individual medals won on the left; gold, silver and bronze breakdown to the right.

MEN

No		Sport	G-S-B
6	Vitaly Scherbo, UT	Gymnastics	6-0-0
5	Grigory Misiutin, UT	Gymnastics	1-4-0
4	Aleksandr Popov, UT	Swimming	2-2-0
3	Yevgeny Sadovyi, UT	Swimming	3-0-0
3	Matt Biondi, USA	Swimming	2-1-0
3	Jon Olsen, USA	Swimming	2-0-1
3	Mel Stewart, USA	Swimming	2-0-1
3	Vladimir Pychnenko, UT	Swimming	1-2-0
3	Li Xiaoshuang, CHN	Gymnastics	1-1-1
3	Li Jing, CHN	Gymnastics	0-3-0
3	Anders Holmertz, SWE	Swimming	0-2-1
3	Andreas Wecker, GER	Gymnastics	0-1-2

WOMEN

No		Sports	G-S-B
5	Shannon Miller, USA	Gymnastics	0-2-3
4	Tatiana Gutsu, UT	Gymnastics	2-1-1
4	Lavinia Milosovici, ROM	Gymnastics	2-1-1
4	Summer Sanders, USA	Swimming	2-1-1
4	Franziska van Almsick, GER	Swimming	0-2-2
3	Krisztina Egerszegi, HUN	Swimming	3-0-0
3	Nicole Haislett, USA	Swimming	3-0-0
3	Crissy Ahmann-Leighton, USA	Swimming	2-1-0
3	Jenny Thompson, USA	Swimming	2-1-0
3	Gwen Torrence, USA	Track/Field	2-1-0
3	Tatyana Lysenko, UT	Gymnastics	2-0-1
3	Lin Li, CHN	Swimming	1-2-0
3	Dagmar Hase, GER	Swimming	1-2-0
3	Zhuang Yong, CHN	Swimming	1-2-0
3	Rita Koban, HUN	Kayaking	1-1-1
3	Anita Hall, USA	Swimming	1-1-1
3	Daniela Hunger, GER	Swimming	0-1-2

Track & Field

MEN

Event		Time
100m	Linford Christie, GBR	9.96

Event		Time	
200m	Mike Marsh, USA	20.01	
400m	Quincy Watts, USA	43.50	OR
800m	William Tanui, KEN	1:43.66	
1500m	Fermin Cacho, SPA	3:40.12	
5000m	Dieter Baumann, GER	13:12.52	
10,000m	Khalid Skah, MOR	27:46.70	
Marathon	Hwang Young-Cho, S. Kor	2:13.23	
110m H	Mark McKoy, CAN	13.12	
400m H	Kevin Young, USA	46.78	WR
3000m Steeple	Matthew Birir, KEN	8:08.84	
20k Walk	Daniel Plaza Montero, SPA	1:21:45	
50k Walk	Andrei Perlov, UT	3:50:13	
4x100m	USA (Mike Marsh, Leroy Burrell, Dennis Mitchell, Carl Lewis)	37.40	WR
4x400m	USA (Andrew Valmon, Quincy Watts, Michael Johnson, Steve Lewis)	2:55.74	WR

Event		Mark	
High Jump	Javier Sotomayor, CUB	7-8	
Pole Vault	Maksim Tarasov, UT	19-0¼	
Long Jump	Carl Lewis, USA	28-5½	
Triple Jump	Mike Conley, USA	59-7½w	
Shot Put	Michael Stulce, USA	71-2½	
Discus	Romas Ubartas, LIT	213-8	
Hammer	Andrei Abduvaliyev, UT	270-9	
Javelin	Jan Zelezny, CZE	294-2	OR
Decathlon	Robert Zmelik, CZE	8611 pts	

w indicates wind-aided.

WOMEN

Event		Time
100m	Gail Devers, USA	10.82
200m	Gwen Torrence, USA	21.81
400m	Marie-Jose Perec, FRA	48.83
800m	Ellen van Langen, HOL	1:55.54
1500m	Hassiba Boulmerka, ALG	3:55.30
3000m	Elena Romanova, UT	8:46.04
10,000m	Derartu Tulu, ETH	31:06.02
Marathon	Valentina Yegorova, UT	2:32:41
100m H	Paraskevi Patoulidou, GRE	12.64
400m H	Sally Gunnell, GBR	53.23
10K Walk	Chen Yueling, CHN	44.32
4x100m	USA (Evelyn Ashford, Esther Jones, Carlette Guidry-White, Gwen Torrence)	42.11
4x400m	UT (Yelena Ruzina, Lyudmila Dzhigalova, Olga Nazarova, Olga Bryzgina)	3:20.20

Event		Mark
High Jump	Heike Henkel, GER	6-7½
Long Jump	Heike Drechsler, GER	23-5¼
Shot Put	Svetlana Krivaleva, UT	69-1¼
Discus	Maritza Marten, CUB	229-10
Javelin	Silke Renk, GER	224-2
Heptathlon	Jackie Joyner-Kersee, USA	7044 pts

Boxing

Weight Class	Champion
Lt. Flyweight (106 lbs)	Rogelio Marcelo, CUB
Flyweight (112)	Su Choi-Chol, N. Kor
Bantamweight (119)	Joel Casamayor, CUB
Featherweight (125)	Andreas Tews, GER
Lightweight (132)	Oscar De La Hoya, USA
Lt. Welterweight (139)	Hector Vinent, CUB
Welterweight (147)	Michael Carruth, IRE
Lt. Middleweight (156)	Juan Lemus, CUB
Middleweight (165)	Ariel Hernandez, CUB
Lt. Heavyweight (178)	Torsten May, GER
Heavyweight (201)	Felix Savon, CUB
Super Heavyweight (200+)	Roberto Balado, CUB

1992 (Cont.)
Gymnastics
MEN

Individual		Points
All-Around	Vitaly Scherbo, UT	59.025
Floor	Li Xiaosahuang, CHN	9.925
Horiz.Bar	Trent Dimas, USA	9.875
Paral.Bars	Vitaly Scherbo, UT	9.900
Rings	Vitaly Scherbo, UT	9.937
Side Horse	Vitaly Scherbo, UT	
	Pae Gil-Su, N. Kor	9.925
Vault	Vitaly Scherbo, UT	9.856

Team		Points
All Around	UT (Scherbo, Belenki, Misiutin, Korobchinski, Voropayev, Sharipov)	585.450

WOMEN

Individual		Points
All-Around	Tatiana Gutsu, UT	39.737
Bal.Beam	Tatiana Lyssenko, UT	9.975
Floor	Lavinia Milosovici, ROM	10.000
Uneven Bars	Lu Li, CHN	10.000
Vault	Henrietta Onodi, HUN	
	& Lavinia Milosovici, ROM	9.925

Team		Points
All Around	UT (Boginskaya, Lyssenko, Galiyeva, Goutsou, Grudneva, Chusovitina)	395.666

Rythmic		Points
All Around	Aleksandra Timoshenko, UT	59.037

Swimming
MEN

Event		Time	
50m Free	Aleksandr Popov, UT	21.91	OR
100m Free	Aleksandr Popov, UT	49.02	
200m Free	Yevgeny Sadovyi, UT	1:46.70	OR
400m Free	Yevgeny Sadovyi, UT	3:45.00	WR
1500m Free	Kieren Perkins, AUS	14:43.48	WR
100m Back	Mark Tewksbury, CAN	53.98	OR
200m Back	Martin Lopez-Zubero, SPA	1:58.47	OR
100m Brst	Nelson Diebel, USA	1:01.50	OR
200m Brst	Mike Barrowman, USA	2:10.16	WR
100m Fly	Pablo Morales, USA	53.32	
200m Fly	Mel Stewart, USA	1:56.26	OR
200m I.M.	Tamas Darnyi, HUN	2:00.76	
400m I.M.	Tamas Darnyi, HUN	4:14.23	OR
4x100m Free	USA (Joe Hudepohl, Matt Biondi, Tom Jager, Jon Olsen)	3:16.74	
4x200m Free	UT (Dmitri Lepikov, Vladimir Yevgeny Sadovyi)	7:11.95	WR

Diving		Points
Platform	Sun Shuwei, CHN	677.31
Spring	Mark Lenzi, USA	676.53

WOMEN

Event		Time	
50m Free	Yang Wenyi, CHN	24.79	WR
100m Free	Zhuang Yong, CHN	54.64	OR
200m Free	Nicole Haislett, USA	1:57.90	
400m Free	Dagmar Hase, GER	4:07.18	
800m Free	Janet Evans, USA	8:25.52	
100m Back	Krisztina Egerszegi, HUN	1:00.68	OR
200m Back	Krisztina Egerszegi, HUN	2:07.06	OR
100m Brst	Yelena Rudkovskaya, UT	1:08.00	
200m Brst	Kyoko Iwasaki, JPN	2:26.65	OR
100m Fly	Qian Hong, CHN	58.62	OR
200m Fly	Summer Sanders, USA	2:08.67	
200m I.M.	Lin Li, CHN	2:11.65	WR
400m I.M.	Krisztina Egerszegi, HUN	4:36.54	
4x100m Free	USA (Nicole Haislett, Dara Torres, Angel Martino, Jenny Thompson)	3:39.46	WR

Event		Time	
4x100m Med	USA (Lea Loveless, Anita Nall, Crissy Ahmann-Leighton, Jenny Thompson)	4:02.54	WR

Diving		Points
Platform	Fu Mingxia, CHN	461.43
Spring	Gao Min, CHN	572.40

Tennis
MEN

Singles: Marc Rosset, SWI, def. Jordi Arrese, SPA, 7-6,6-4,3-6,4-6,8-6.

Doubles: Boris Becker and Michael Stich, GER, def. Wayne Ferreira and Piet Norval, SAF, 7-6,4-6,7-6,6-3.

WOMEN

Singles: Jennifer Capriati, USA, def. Steffi Graf, GER, 3-6,6-3,6-4.

Doubles: Gigi Fernandez and Mary Joe Fernandez, USA, def. Conchita Martinez and Arantxa Sanchez Vicario, SPA, 7-5,2-6,6-2.

Team Sports

Men	Champion
Baseball	Cuba
Basketball	United States
Field Hockey	Germany
Handball	Unified Team
Soccer	Spain
Volleyball	Brazil
Water Polo	Italy

Women	Champion
Basketball	Unified Team
Field Hockey	Spain
Handball	South Korea
Volleyball	Cuba

Also Contested

Archery, Badminton, Canoeing, Cycling, Equestrian, Fencing, Judo, Modern Pentathlon, Shooting, Table Tennis, Weightlifting, Freestyle Wrestling, Greco-Roman Wrestling and Yachting.

1996
Atlanta

The Atlanta games were certainly the largest (a record 197 nations competed), most logistically complicated Olympics to date and perhaps the most hyped and overcommercialized as well. Despite all the troubles that organizers faced from computer scoring snafus and transportation problems to a horrific terrorist attack, these Olympics had some of the best stories ever.

The Games began so joyously with Muhammad Ali, the world's best-known sports figure now stricken by illness, igniting the Olympic cauldron. Sadly, just eight days later horror was the prevailing mood after a terrorist's bomb ripped apart a peaceful Friday evening in Centennial Olympic Park. In the explosion, one women was killed, 111 were injured and the entire world was reminded of the terror and tragedy of Munich in 1972.

As they did in '72, the games would go on. In track and field, Michael Johnson delivered on his much-anticipated, yet still startling, double in the 200 and 400 meters. One thing that many didn't foresee is that he would be matched by France's Marie-Jose Perec, who converted her own 200-400 double, albeit with much less attention. Carl Lewis pulled out one last bit of magic to win the long jump for the ninth gold medal of his amazing Olympic career. Donovan Bailey set a world record in the 100 and led Canada to a win over a faltering U.S. team in the 4x100 relay.

The U.S. women's gymnastics squad took the team gold after Kerri Strug hobbled up and completed her final gutsy vault in the games most compelling moment. Swimmer Amy Van Dyken became the first American woman to win four golds in a single games. Ireland's Michelle Smith won three golds (and a bronze) of her own but her victories were somewhat tainted by controversy surrounding unproven charges of drug use.

The USA faired well in team sports also. The men's basketball "Dream Team" was back and, predictably, stomped the competition on their way back to the winner's podium. Also the U.S. women won gold at the Olympic debut of two sports: softball and soccer.

Top 10 Standings

National medal standings are not recognized by the IOC. The unofficial point totals are based on 3 points for a gold medal, 2 for a silver and 1 for a bronze.

	Gold	Silver	Bronze	Total	Points
1 United States ..	44	32	25	101	221
2 Russia	26	21	16	63	136
3 Germany	20	18	27	65	123
4 China	16	22	12	50	104
5 France	15	7	15	37	74
6 Italy	13	10	12	35	71
7 Australia	9	9	23	41	68
8 South Korea ...	7	15	5	27	56
9 Cuba	9	8	8	25	51
10 Ukraine	9	2	12	23	43

Leading Medal Winners

Number of individual medals won on the left; gold, silver and bronze breakdown to the right.

MEN

No		Sport	G-S-B
6	Alexei Nemov, RUS	Gymnastics	2-1-3
4	Gary Hall Jr., USA	Swimming	2-2-0
4	Aleksandr Popov, RUS	Swimming	2-2-0
3	Josh Davis, USA	Swimming	3-0-0
3	Denis Pankratov, RUS	Swimming	2-1-0
3	Daniel Kowalski, AUS	Swimming	0-1-2
3	Vitaly Scherbo, BEL	Gymnastics	0-0-3

WOMEN

No		Sport	G-S-B
4	Amy Van Dyken, USA	Swimming	4-0-0
4	Michelle Smith, IRE	Swimming	3-0-1
4	Angel Martino, USA	Swimming	2-0-2
4	Simona Amanar, ROM	Gymnastics	1-1-2
4	Dagmar Hase, GER	Swimming	0-3-1
4	Gina Gogean, ROM	Gymnastics	0-1-3

No		Sport	G-S-B
3	Jenny Thompson, USA	Swimming	3-0-0
3	Lilia Podkopayeva, UKR	Gymnastics	2-1-0
3	Amanda Beard, USA	Swimming	1-2-0
3	Le Jingyi, CHN	Swimming	1-2-0
3	Wendy Hedgepeth, USA	Swimming	1-2-0
3	Susan O'Neill, AUS	Swimming	1-1-1
3	Merlene Ottey, JAM	Track & Field	0-2-1
3	Franziska van Almsick, GER	Swimming	0-2-1
3	Sandra Volker, GER	Swimming	0-1-2

Track & Field
MEN

Event		Time	
100m	Donovan Bailey, CAN	9.84	WR
200m	Michael Johnson, USA	19.32	WR
400m	Michael Johnson, USA	43.49	OR
800m	Vebjoern Rodal, NOR	1:42.58	OR
1500m	Noureddine Morceli, ALG ..	3:35.78	
5000m	Venuste Niyongabo, BUR ..	13:07.96	
10,000m	Haile Gebrselassie, ETH ..	27:07.34	OR
Marathon	Josia Thugwane, S. Afr ..	2:12:36	
110m H	Allen Johnson, USA	12.95	OR
400m H	Derrick Adkins, USA	47.54	
3000m			
Steeple	Joseph Keter, KEN	8:07.12	
20k Walk	Jefferson Perez, ECU	1:20:07	
50k Walk	Robert Korzeniowski, POL ..	3:43:30	
4x100m	Canada (Donovan Bailey, Robert Esmie, Glenroy Gilbert, Bruny Surin, Carlton Chambers)	37.69	
4x400m	USA (Anthuan Maybank, Derek Mills, LaMont Smith, Alvin Harrison, Jason Rouser)	2:55.99	

Event		Mark	
High Jump	Charles Austin, USA	7-10	OR
Pole Vault	Jean Galfione, FRA	19-5¼	OR
Long Jump	Carl Lewis, USA	27-10 ¾	
Triple Jump	Kenny Harrison, USA	59-4¼	OR
Shot Put	Randy Barnes, USA	70-11¼	
Discus	Lars Riedel, GER	227-8	
Hammer	Balazs Kiss, HUN	266-6	
Javelin	Jan Zelezny, CZE	289-3	
Decathlon	Dan O'Brien, USA	8824 pts	

WOMEN

Event		Time	
100m	Gail Devers, USA	10.94	
200m	Marie-Jose Perec, FRA	22.12	
400m	Marie-Jose Perec, FRA	48.25	OR
800m	Svetlana Masterkova, RUS ..	1:57.73	
1500m	Svetlana Masterkova, RUS ..	4:00.83	
5000m	Wang Junxia, CHN	14:59.88	
10,000m	Fernanda Ribeiro, POR ..	31:01.63	OR
Marathon	Fatuma Roba, ETH	2:26:05	
100m H	Ludmila Engquist, SWE ..	12.58	
400m H	Deon Hemmings, JAM	52.82	OR
10K Walk	Yelena Ninikolayeva, RUS ...	41:49	
4x100m	USA (Chryste Gaines, Gail Devers, Inger Miller, Gwen Torrence)	.41.95	
4x400m	USA (Rochelle Stevens, Maicel Malone, Kim Graham, Jearl Miles, Linetta Wilson)	3:20.91	

Event		Mark	
High Jump	Stefka Kostadinova, BUL ...	6-8¾	
Long Jump	Chioma Ajunwa, NGR	23-4½	
Triple Jump	Inessa Kravets, UKR	50-3½	
Shot Put	Astrid Kumbernuss, GER ...	67-5½	
Discus	Ilke Wyludda, GER	228-6	
Javelin	Heli Rantanen, FIN	222-11	
Heptathlon	Ghada Shouaa, SYR	6780 pts	

1996 (Cont.)

Boxing

Weight Class	Champion
Lt. Flyweight (106 lbs)	Daniel Petrov Bojilov, BUL
Flyweight (112)	Maikro Romero, CUB
Bantamweight (119)	Istvan Kovacs, HUN
Featherweight (125)	Somluck Kamsing, THA
Lightweight (132)	Hocine Soltani, ALG
Lt. Welterweight (139)	Hector Vinent, CUB
Welterweight (147)	Oleg Saitov, RUS
Lt. Middleweight (156)	David Reid, USA
Middleweight (165)	Ariel Hernandez, CUB
Lt. Heavyweight (178)	Vasilii Jirov, KAZ
Heavyweight (201)	Felix Savon, CUB
Super Heavyweight (200+)	Vladimir Klichko, UKR

Gymnastics

MEN

Individual		Points
All-Around	Li Xiaosahuang, CHN	58.423
Floor	Ioannis Melissanidis, GRE	9.850
Horiz.Bar	Andreas Wecker, GER	9.850
Paral.Bars	Cuba	9.837
Rings	Yuri Chechi, ITA	9.887
Side Horse	Li Donghua, SWI	9.875
Vault	Alexei Nemov, RUS	9.787

Team		Points
All Around	Russia	576.778

WOMEN

Individual		Points
All-Around	Lilia Podkopayeva, UKR	39.255
Bal.Beam	Shannon Miller, USA	9.862
Floor	Lilia Podkopayeva, UKR	9.887
Uneven Bars	Svetlana Chorkina, RUS	9.850
Vault	Simona Amanar, ROM	9.775

Team		Points
All Around	USA (Borden, Chow, Dawes, Miller, Moceanu, Phelps and Strug)	389.225

Rythmic		Points
All Around	Ekaterina Serebryanskaya, UKR	39.683
Team	Spain	38.933

Swimming

MEN

Event		Time
50m Free	Aleksandr Popov, RUS	22.13
100m Free	Aleksandr Popov, UT	48.74
200m Free	Danyon Loader, NZE	1:47.63
400m Free	Danyon Loader, NZE	3:47.97
1500m Free	Kieren Perkins, AUS	14:56.40
100m Back	Jeff Rouse, USA	54.10
200m Back	Brad Bridgewater, USA	1:58.54
100m Brst	Fred Deburghgraeve, BEL	1:00.60
200m Brst	Norbert, Rozsa, HUN	2:12.57
100m Fly	Denis Pankratov, RUS	52.27
200m Fly	Denis Pankratov, RUS	1:56.51
200m I.M.	Attila Czene, HUN	1:59.51
400m I.M.	Tom Dolan, USA	4:14.90
4x100m Free	USA (Jon Olsen, Josh Davis, Bradley Schumacher, Gary Hall Jr.)	3:15.41
4x200m Free	USA (Josh Davis, Joe Hudepohl, Ryan Berube, Bradley Schumacher)	7:14.84
4x100m Med.	USA (Jeff Rouse, Mark Henderson, Gary Hall Jr., Jeremy Linn)	3:34.84

Diving		Points
Platform	Dmitri Saoutine, RUS	692.34
Spring	Xiong Ni, CHN	701.46

WOMEN

Event		Time
50m Free	Amy Van Dyken, USA	24.87
100m Free	Le Jingyi, CHN	54.50
200m Free	Claudia Poll, COS	1:58.16
400m Free	Michelle Smith, IRE	4:07.25
800m Free	Brooke Bennett, USA	8:27.89
100m Back	Beth Botsford, USA	1:01.19
200m Back	Krisztina Egerszegi, HUN	2:07.83
100m Brst	Penny Heyns, S. Afr.	1:07.73
200m Brst	Penny Heyns, S. Afr.	2:25.41
100m Fly	Amy Van Dyken, USA	59.13
200m Fly	Susan O'Neill, AUS	2:07.76
200m I.M.	Michelle Smith, IRE	2:13.93
400m I.M.	Michelle Smith, IRE	4:39.18
4x100m Free	USA (Angel Martino, Amy Van Dyken, Catherine Fox, Jenny Thompson)	3:39.29
4x200m Free	USA (Jenny Thompson, Sheila Taorima, Trina Jackson, Christina Teuscher)	7:59.87
4x100m Med	USA (Angel Martino, Amy Van Dyken, Amanda Beard, Beth Botsford)	4:02.88

Diving		Points
Platform	Fu Mingxia, CHN	521.58
Spring	Fu Mingxia, CHN	547.68

Tennis

MEN

Singles: Andre Agassi, USA, def. Sergi Bruguera, SPA, 6-2, 6-3, 6-1.

Doubles: Todd Woodbridge and Mark Woodforde, AUS, def. Neil Broad and Tim Henman, GBR 6-4, 6-4, 6-2.

WOMEN

Singles: Lindsay Davenport, USA, def. Arantxa Sanchez Vicario, SPA, 7-6 (8-6), 6-2.

Doubles: Gigi Fernandez and Mary Joe Fernandez, USA, def. Jana Novotna and Helena Sukova, CZE, 7-6 (8-6), 6-4.

Team Sports

Men	Champion
Baseball	Cuba
Basketball	United States
Field Hockey	Netherlands
Handball	Croatia
Soccer	Nigeria
Volleyball	Netherlands
Water Polo	Spain

Women	Champion
Basketball	United States
Field Hockey	Australia
Handball	Denmark
Soccer	United States
Softball	United States
Volleyball	Cuba

Also Contested

Archery, Badminton, Beach Volleyball, Canoeing, Cycling, Equestrian, Fencing, Judo, Modern Pentathlon, Mountain Biking, Shooting, Table Tennis, Weightlifting, Freestyle Wrestling, Greco-Roman Wrestling and Yachting.

New Events for 2000

Taekwondo and Triathlon will make their Summer Olympic debuts in Sydney. The triathlon will consist of 1.5-kilometer swim, 40-kilometer cycle and 10-kilometer run, while taekwondo will be contested in four separate weights classes for both men and women. Other changes set to occur include reductions in the number of weight classes in boxing, weightlifting and wrestling.

Event-by-Event

Gold medal winners from 1896-1996 in the following events: Baseball, Basketball, Boxing, Diving, Field Hockey, Gymnastics, Soccer, Swimming, Tennis, and Track & Field.

BASEBALL

Multiple gold medals: Cuba (2).

Year			Year		
1992	**Cuba**, Taiwan, Japan		1996	**Cuba**, Japan, United States	

BASKETBALL

MEN

Multiple gold medals: USA (11); USSR (2).

Year			Year		
1936	**United States**, Canada, Mexico		1972	**Soviet Union**, United States, Cuba	
1948	**United States**, France, Brazil		1976	**United States**, Yugoslavia, Soviet Union	
1952	**United States**, Soviet Union, Uruguay		1980	**Yugoslavia**, Italy, Soviet Union	
1956	**United States**, Soviet Union, Uruguay		1984	**United States**, Spain, Yugoslavia	
1960	**United States**, Soviet Union, Brazil		1988	**Soviet Union**, Yugoslavia, United States	
1964	**United States**, Soviet Union, Brazil		1992	**United States**, Croatia, Lithuania	
1968	**United States**, Yugoslavia, Soviet Union		1996	**United States**, Yugoslavia, Lithuania	

U.S. Medal-Winning Men's Basketball Teams

1936 (gold medal): Sam Balter, Ralph Bishop, Joe Fortenberry, Tex Gibbons, Francis Johnson, Carl Knowles, Frank Lubin, Art Mollner, Don Piper, Jack Ragland, Carl Shy, Willard Schmidt, Duane Swanson and William Wheatley. Coach—Jim Needles; Assistant—Gene Johnson. Final: USA over Canada, 19-8.

1948 (gold medal): Cliff Barker, Don Barksdale, Ralph Beard, Louis Beck, Vince Boryla, Gordon Carpenter, Alex Groza, Wallace Jones, Bob Kurland, Ray Lumpp, R.C. Pitts, Jesse Renick, Robert (Jackie) Robinson and Ken Rollins. Coach—Omar Browning; Assistant—Adolph Rupp. Final: USA over France, 65-21.

1952 (gold medal): Ron Bontemps, Mark Freiberger, Wayne Glasgow, Charlie Hoag, Bill Hougland, John Keller, Dean Kelley, Bob Kenney, Bob Kurland, Bill Lienhard, Clyde Lovellette, Frank McCabe, Dan Pippin and Howie Williams. Coach—Warren Womble; Assistant—Forrest (Phog) Allen. Final: USA over USSR, 36-25.

1956 (gold medal): Dick Boushka, Carl Cain, Chuck Darling, Bill Evans, Gib Ford, Burdy Haldorson, Bill Hougland, Bob Jeangerard, K.C. Jones, Bill Russell, Ron Tomsic, Jim Walsh. Coach—Gerald Tucker; Assistant—Bruce Drake. Final: USA over USSR, 89-55.

1960 (gold medal): Jay Arnette, Walt Bellamy, Bob Boozer, Terry Dischinger, Jerry Lucas, Oscar Robertson, Adrian Smith, Burdy Haldorson, Darrall Imhoff, Allen Kelley, Lester Lane and Jerry West. Coach—Pete Newell; Assistant—Warren Womble. Final round: USA defeated USSR (81-57), Italy (112-81) and Brazil (90-63) in round robin.

1964 (gold medal): Jim (Bad News) Barnes, Bill Bradley, Larry Brown, Joe Caldwell, Mel Counts, Dick Davies, Walt Hazzard, Lucius Jackson, Pete McCaffrey, Jeff Mullins, Jerry Shipp and George Wilson. Coach—Hank Iba; Assistant—Henry Vaughn. Final: USA over USSR, 73-59.

1968 (gold medal): Mike Barrett, John Clawson, Don Dee, Cal Fowler, Spencer Haywood, Bill Hosket, Jim King, Glynn Saulters, Charlie Scott, Mike Silliman, Ken Spain, and JoJo White. Coach—Hank Iba; Assistant—Henry Vaughn. USA over Yugoslavia, 65-50.

1972 (silver medal refused): Mike Bantom, Jim Brewer, Tom Burleson, Doug Collins, Kenny Davis, Jim Forbes, Tom Henderson, Bobby Jones, Dwight Jones, Kevin Joyce, Tom McMillen and Ed Ratleff. Coach—Hank Iba; Assistants— John Bach and Don Haskins. Final: USSR over USA, 51-50.

1976 (gold medal): Tate Armstrong, Quinn Buckner, Kenny Carr, Adrian Dantley, Walter Davis, Phil Ford, Ernie Grunfeld, Phil Hubbard, Mitch Kupchak, Tommy LaGarde, Scott May and Steve Sheppard. Coach—Dean Smith; Assistants—Bill Guthridge and John Thompson. Final: USA over Yugoslavia, 95-74.

1980 (no medal): USA boycotted Moscow Games. Final: Yugoslavia over Italy, 86-77.

1984 (gold medal): Steve Alford, Patrick Ewing, Vern Fleming, Michael Jordan; Joe Kleine, Jon Koncak, Chris Mullin, Sam Perkins, Alvin Robertson, Wayman Tisdale, Jeff Turner and Leon Wood. Coach—Bobby Knight; Assistants— Don Donoher and George Raveling. Final: USA over Spain, 96-65.

1988 (bronze medal): Stacey Augmon, Willie Anderson, Bimbo Coles, Jeff Grayer, Hersey Hawkins, Dan Majerle, Danny Manning, Mitch Richmond, J.R. Reid, David Robinson, Charles D. Smith and Charles E. Smith. Coach—John Thompson; Assistants—George Raveling and Mary Fenlon. Final: USSR over USA, 76-63.

1992 (gold medal): Charles Barkley, Larry Bird, Clyde Drexler, Patrick Ewing, Magic Johnson, Michael Jordan, Christian Laettner, Karl Malone, Chris Mullin, Scottie Pippen, David Robinson and John Stockton. Coach—Chuck Daly; Assistants—Lenny Wilkens, Mike Krzyzewski and P.J. Carlesimo. Final: USA over Croatia, 117-85.

1996 (gold medal): Charles Barkley, Anfernee Hardaway, Grant Hill, Karl Malone, Reggie Miller, Hakeem Olajuwon, Shaquille O'Neal, Gary Payton, Scottie Pippen, David Robinson and John Stockton. Coach—Lenny Wilkens; Assistants—Bobby Cremins, Clem Haskins and Jerry Sloan. Final: USA over Yugoslavia, 95-69.

WOMEN

Multiple gold medals: USSR/UT (3); USA (2).

Year			Year		
1976	**Soviet Union**, United States, Bulgaria		1988	**United States**, Yugoslavia, Soviet Union	
1980	**Soviet Union**, Bulgaria, Yugoslavia		1992	**Unified Team**, China, United States	
1984	**United States**, South Korea, China		1996	**United States**, Brazil, Australia	

U.S. Gold Medal-Winning Women's Basketball Teams

1984: Cathy Boswell, Denise Curry, Anne Donovan, Teresa Edwards, Lea Henry, Janice Lawrence, Pamela McGee, Carol Menken-Schaudt, Cheryl Miller, Kim Mulkey, Cindy Noble, Lynette Woodard. Coach—Pat Summitt; Assistant—Kay Yow. Final: USA over South Korea, 85-55.

Basketball (Cont.)

1988: Cindy Brown, Vicky Bullett, Cynthia Cooper, Anne Donovan, Teresa Edwards, Kamie Ethridge, Jennifer Gillom, Bridgette Gordon, Andrea Lloyd, Katrina McClain, Suzie McConnell, Teresa Weatherspoon. Coach–Kay Yow; Assistants–Sylvia Hatchell and Susan Yow. Final: USA over Yugoslavia, 77-70.

1996: Jennifer Azzi, Ruthie Bolton, Teresa Edwards, Venus Lacy, Lisa Leslie, Rebecca Lobo, Katrina McClain, Nikki McCray, Carla McGee, Dawn Staley, Katy Steding and Sheryl Swoopes. Coach—Tara VanDerveer; Assistants–Ceal Barry, Nancy Darsch and Marian Washington. Final: USA over Brazil, 111–87.

BOXING

Multiple gold medals: László Papp and Teófilo Stevenson (3); Ariel Hernandez, Angel Herrera, Oliver Kirk, Jerzy Kulej, Boris Lagutin, Harry Mallin, Felix Savon and Hector Vinent (2). All fighters won titles in consecutive Olympics, except Kirk, who won both the bantamweight and featherweight titles in 1904 (he only had to fight once in each division).

Light Flyweight (106 lbs)

Year	Final Match	Year	Final Match
1968 Francisco Rodriguez, VEN	Decision, 3-2	1984 Paul Gonzales, USA	Default
1972 György Gedó, HUN	Decision, 5-0	1988 Ivailo Hristov, BUL	Decision, 5-0
1976 Jorge Hernandez, CUB	Decision, 4-1	1992 Rogelio Marcelo, CUB	Decision, 24-10
1980 Shamil Sabyrov, USSR	Decision, 3-2	1996 Daniel Petrov Bojilov, BUL	Decision, 19-6

Flyweight (112 lbs)

Year	Final Match	Year	Final Match
1904 George Finnegan, USA	Stopped, 1st	1964 Fernando Atzori, ITA	Decision, 4-1
1920 Frank Di Gennara, USA	Decision	1968 Ricardo Delgado, MEX	Decision, 5-0
1924 Fidel LaBarba, USA	Decision	1972 Georgi Kostadinov, BUL	Decision, 5-0
1928 Antal Kocsis, HUN	Decision	1976 Leo Randolph, USA	Decision, 3-2
1932 István Énekes, HUN	Decision	1980 Peter Lessov, BUL	Stopped, 2nd
1936 Willi Kaiser, GER	Decision	1984 Steve McCrory, USA	Decision, 4-1
1948 Pascual Perez, ARG	Decision	1988 Kim Kwang-Sun, S. Kor	Decision, 4-1
1952 Nate Brooks, USA	Decision, 3-0	1992 Su Choi-Chol, N. Kor	Decision, 12-2
1956 Terence Spinks, GBR	Decision	1996 Maikro Romero, CUB	Decision, 12-11
1960 Gyula Török, HUN	Decision, 3-2		

Bantamweight (119 lbs)

Year	Final Match	Year	Final Match
1904 Oliver Kirk, USA	Stopped, 3rd	1960 Oleg Grigoryev, USSR	Decision
1908 Henry Thomas, GBR	Decision	1964 Takao Sakurai, JPN	Stopped, 2nd
1920 Clarence Walker, SAF	Decision	1968 Valery Sokolov, USSR	Stopped, 2nd
1924 William Smith, SAF	Decision	1972 Orlando Martinez, CUB	Decision, 5-0
1928 Vittorio Tamagnini, ITA	Decision	1976 Gu Yong-Ju, N. Kor	Decision, 5-0
1932 Horace Gwynne, CAN	Decision	1980 Juan Hernandez, CUB	Decision, 5-0
1936 Ulderico Sergo, ITA	Decision	1984 Maurizio Stecca, ITA	Decision, 4-1
1948 Tibor Csik, HUN	Decision	1988 Kennedy McKinney, USA	Decision, 5-0
1952 Pentti Hämäläinen, FIN	Decision, 2-1	1992 Joel Casamayor, CUB	Decision, 14-8
1956 Wolfgang Behrendt, GER	Decision	1996 Istvan Kovacs, HUN	Decision, 14-7

Featherweight (125 lbs)

Year	Final Match	Year	Final Match
1904 Oliver Kirk, USA	Decision	1960 Francesco Musso, ITA	Decision, 4-1
1908 Richard Gunn, GBR	Decision	1964 Stanislav Stepashkin, USSR	Decision, 3-2
1920 Paul Fritsch, FRA	Decision	1968 Antonio Roldan, MEX	Won on Disq.
1924 John Fields, USA	Decision	1972 Boris Kousnetsov, USSR	Decision, 3-2
1928 Lambertus van Klaveren, HOL	Decision	1976 Angel Herrera, CUB	KO, 2nd
1932 Carmelo Robledo, ARG	Decision	1980 Rudi Fink, E. Ger	Decision, 4-1
1936 Oscar Casanovas, ARG	Decision	1984 Meldrick Taylor, USA	Decision, 5-0
1948 Ernesto Formenti, ITA	Decision	1988 Giovanni Parisi, ITA	Stopped, 1st
1952 Jan Zachara, CZE	Decision, 2-1	1992 Andreas Tews, GER	Decision, 16-7
1956 Vladimir Safronov, USSR	Decision	1996 Somluck Kamsing, THA	Decision, 8-5

Lightweight (132 lbs)

Year	Final Match	Year	Final Match
1904 Harry Spanger, USA	Decision	1960 Kazimierz Pazdzior, POL	Decision, 4-1
1908 Frederick Grace, GBR	Decision	1964 Józef Grudzien, POL	Decision
1920 Samuel Mosberg, USA	Decision	1968 Ronnie Harris, USA	Decision, 5-0
1924 Hans Nielsen, DEN	Decision	1972 Jan Szczepanski, POL	Decision, 5-0
1928 Carlo Orlandi, ITA	Decision	1976 Howard Davis, USA	Decision, 5-0
1932 Lawrence Stevens, SAF	Decision	1980 Angel Herrera, CUB	Stopped, 3rd
1936 Imre Harangi, HUN	Decision	1984 Pernell Whitaker, USA	Foe quit, 2nd
1948 Gerald Dreyer, SAF	Decision	1988 Andreas Zuelow, E. Ger	Decision, 5-0
1952 Aureliano Bolognesi, ITA	Decision, 2-1	1992 Oscar De La Hoya, USA	Decision, 7-2
1956 Richard McTaggart, GBR	Decision	1996 Hocine Soltani, ALG	Tiebreak, 3-3

Light Welterweight (139 lbs)

Year		Final Match	Year		Final Match
1952	Charles Adkins, USA	Decision, 2-1	1976	Ray Leonard, USA	Decision, 5-0
1956	Vladimir Yengibaryan, USSR	Decision	1980	Patrizio Oliva, ITA	Decision, 4-1
1960	Bohumil Nemecek, CZE	Decision, 5-0	1984	Jerry Page, USA	Decision, 5-0
1964	Jerzy Kulej, POL	Decision, 5-0	1988	Vyacheslav Yanovsky, USSR	Decision, 5-0
1968	Jerzy Kulej, POL	Decision, 3-2	1992	Hector Vinent, CUB	Decision, 11-1
1972	Ray Seales, USA	Decision, 3-2	1996	Hector Vinent, CUB	Decision, 20-13

Welterweight (147 lbs)

Year		Final Match	Year		Final Match
1904	Albert Young, USA	Decision	1964	Marian Kasprzyk, POL	Decision, 4-1
1920	Bert Schneider, CAN	Decision	1968	Manfred Wolke, E. Ger	Decision, 4-1
1924	Jean Delarge, BEL	Decision	1972	Emilio Correa, CUB	Decision, 5-0
1928	Edward Morgan, NZE	Decision	1976	Jochen Bachfeld, E. Ger	Decision, 3-2
1932	Edward Flynn, USA	Decision	1980	Andrés Aldama, CUB	Decision, 4-1
1936	Sten Suvio, FIN	Decision	1984	Mark Breland, USA	Decision, 5-0
1948	Julius Torma, CZE	Decision	1988	Robert Wangila, KEN	KO, 2nd
1952	Zygmunt Chychla, POL	Decision, 3-0	1992	Michael Carruth, IRE	Decision, 13-10
1956	Nicolae Linca, ROM	Decision, 3-2	1996	Oleg Saitov, RUS	Decision, 14-9
1960	Nino Benvenuti, ITA	Decision, 4-1			

Light Middleweight (156 lbs)

Year		Final Match	Year		Final Match
1952	László Papp, HUN	Decision, 3-0	1976	Jerzy Rybicki, POL	Decision, 5-0
1956	László Papp, HUN	Decision	1980	Armando Martinez, CUB	Decision, 4-1
1960	Skeeter McClure, USA	Decision, 4-1	1984	Frank Tate, USA	Decision, 5-0
1964	Boris Lagutin, USSR	Decision, 4-1	1988	Park Si-Hun, S. Kor	Decision, 3-2
1968	Boris Lagutin, USSR	Decision, 5-0	1992	Juan Lemus, CUB	Decision, 6-1
1972	Dieter Kottysch, W.Ger	Decision, 3-2	1996	David Reid, USA	KO, 3rd

Middleweight (165 lbs)

Year		Final Match	Year		Final Match
1904	Charles Mayer, USA	Stopped, 3rd	1960	Eddie Crook, USA	Decision, 3-2
1908	John Douglas, GBR	Decision	1964	Valery Popenchenko, USSR	Stopped, 1st
1920	Harry Mallin, GBR	Decision	1968	Christopher Finnegan, GBR	Decision, 3-2
1924	Harry Mallin, GBR	Decision	1972	Vyacheslav Lemechev, USSR	KO, 1st
1928	Piero Toscani, ITA	Decision	1976	Michael Spinks, USA	Stopped, 3rd
1932	Carmen Barth, USA	Decision	1980	José Gomez, CUB	Decision, 4-1
1936	Jean Despeaux, FRA	Decision	1984	Shin Joon-Sup, S. Kor	Decision, 3-2
1948	László Papp, HUN	Decision	1988	Henry Maske, E. Ger	Decision, 5-0
1952	Floyd Patterson, USA	KO, 1st	1992	Ariel Hernandez, CUB	Decision, 12-7
1956	Gennady Schatkov, USSR	KO, 1st	1996	Ariel Hernandez, CUB	Decision, 11-3

Light Heavyweight (178 lbs)

Year		Final Match	Year		Final Match
1920	Eddie Eagan, USA	Decision	1964	Cosimo Pinto, ITA	Decision, 3-2
1924	Harry Mitchell, GBR	Decision	1968	Dan Poznjak, USSR	Default
1928	Victor Avendaño, ARG	Decision	1972	Mate Parlov, YUG	Stopped, 2nd
1932	David Carstens, SAF	Decision	1976	Leon Spinks, USA	Stopped, 3rd
1936	Roger Michelot, FRA	Decision	1980	Slobodan Kacar, YUG	Decision, 4-1
1948	George Hunter, SAF	Decision	1984	Anton Josipovic, YUG	Default
1952	Norvel Lee, USA	Decision, 3-0	1988	Andrew Maynard, USA	Decision, 5-0
1956	Jim Boyd, USA	Decision	1992	Torsten May, GER	Decision, 8-3
1960	Cassius Clay, USA	Decision, 5-0	1996	Vasilii Jirov, KAZ	Decision, 17-4

Note: Cassius Clay changed his name to Muhammad Ali after winning the world heavyweight championship in 1964.

Heavyweight (201 lbs)

Year		Final Match	Year		Final Match
1984	Henry Tillman, USA	Decision, 5-0	1992	Felix Savon, CUB	Decision, 14-1
1988	Ray Mercer, USA	KO, 1st	1996	Felix Savon, CUB	Decision, 20-2

Super Heavyweight (Unlimited)

Year		Final Match	Year		Final Match
1904	Samuel Berger, USA	Decision	1960	Franco De Piccoli, ITA	KO, 1st
1908	Albert Oldham, GBR	KO, 1st	1964	Joe Frazier, USA	Decision, 3-2
1920	Ronald Rawson, GBR	Decision	1968	George Foreman, USA	Stopped, 2nd
1924	Otto von Porat, NOR	Decision	1972	Teófilo Stevenson, CUB	Default
1928	Arturo Rodriguez Jurado, ARG	Stopped, 1st	1976	Teófilo Stevenson, CUB	KO, 3rd
1932	Santiago Lovell, ARG	Decision	1980	Teófilo Stevenson, CUB	Decision, 4-1
1936	Herbert Runge, GER	Decision	1984	Tyrell Biggs, USA	Decision, 4-1
1948	Rafael Iglesias, ARG	KO, 2nd	1988	Lennox Lewis, CAN	Stopped, 2nd
1952	Ed Sanders, USA	Won on Disq.*	1992	Roberto Balado, CUB	Decision, 13-2
1956	Pete Rademacher, USA	Stopped, 1st	1996	Vladimir Klichko, UKR	Decision, 7-3

* Sanders' opponent, Ingemar Johansson was disqualified in 2nd round for not trying.

DIVING

MEN

Multiple gold medals: Greg Louganis (4); Klaus Dibiasi (3); Pete Desjardins, Sammy Lee, Bob Webster and Albert White (2).

Springboard

Year		Points	Year		Points
1908	Albert Zürner, GER	85.5	1960	Gary Tobian, USA	170.00
1912	Paul Günther, GER	79.23	1964	Ken Sitzberger, USA	159.90
1920	Louis Kuehn, USA	675.4	1968	Bernie Wrightson, USA	170.15
1924	Albert White, USA	696.4	1972	Vladimir Vasin, USSR	594.09
1928	Pete Desjardins, USA	185.04	1976	Phil Boggs, USA	619.05
1932	Michael Galitzen, USA	161.38	1980	Aleksandr Portnov, USSR	905.03
1936	Richard Degener, USA	163.57	1984	Greg Louganis, USA	754.41
1948	Bruce Harlan, USA	163.64	1988	Greg Louganis, USA	730.80
1952	David Browning, USA	205.29	1992	Mark Lenzi, USA	676.53
1956	Bob Clotworthy, USA	159.56	1996	Ni Xiong, CHN	701.46

Platform

Year		Points	Year		Points
1904	George Sheldon, USA	12.66	1956	Joaquin Capilla, MEX	152.44
1906	Gottlob Walz, GER	156.0	1960	Bob Webster, USA	165.56
1908	Hjalmar Johansson, SWE	83.75	1964	Bob Webster, USA	148.58
1912	Erik Adlerz, SWE	73.94	1968	Klaus Dibiasi, ITA	164.18
1920	Clarence Pinkston, USA	100.67	1972	Klaus Dibiasi, ITA	504.12
1924	Albert White, USA	97.46	1976	Klaus Dibiasi, ITA	600.51
1928	Pete Desjardins, USA	98.74	1980	Falk Hoffmann, E. Ger	835.65
1932	Harold Smith, USA	124.80	1984	Greg Louganis, USA	710.91
1936	Marshall Wayne, USA	113.58	1988	Greg Louganis, USA	638.61
1948	Sammy Lee, USA	130.05	1992	Sun Shuwei, CHN	677.31
1952	Sammy Lee, USA	156.28	1996	Dmitri Saoutine, RUS	692.34

WOMEN

Multiple gold medals: Pat McCormick (4); Ingrid Engel-Krämer and Fu Mingxia (3); Vicki Draves, Dorothy Poynton Hill, Gao Min (2).

Springboard

Year		Points	Year		Points
1920	Aileen Riggin, USA	539.9	1964	Ingrid Engel-Kräamer, GER	145.00
1924	Elizabeth Becker, USA	474.5	1968	Sue Gossick, USA	150.77
1928	Helen Meany, USA	78.62	1972	Micki King, USA	450.03
1932	Georgia Coleman, USA	87.52	1976	Jennifer Chandler, USA	506.19
1936	Marjorie Gestring, USA	89.27	1980	Irina Kalinina, USSR	725.91
1948	Vicki Draves, USA	108.74	1984	Sylvie Bernier, CAN	530.70
1952	Pat McCormick, USA	147.30	1988	Gao Min, CHN	580.23
1956	Pat McCormick, USA	142.36	1992	Gao Min, CHN	572.40
1960	Ingrid Krämer, GER	155.81	1996	Fu Mingxia, CHN	547.68

Platform

Year		Points	Year		Points
1912	Greta Johansson, SWE	39.9	1964	Lesley Bush, USA	99.80
1920	Stefani Fryland-Clausen, DEN	34.6	1968	Milena Duchková, CZE	109.59
1924	Caroline Smith, USA	33.2	1972	Ulrika Knape, SWE	390.00
1928	Elizabeth Becker Pinkston, USA	31.6	1976	Elena Vaytsekhovskaya, USSR	406.59
1932	Dorothy Poynton, USA	40.26	1980	Martina Jäschke, E. Ger	596.25
1936	Dorothy Poynton Hill, USA	33.93	1984	Zhou Jihong, CHN	435.51
1948	Vicki Draves, USA	68.87	1988	Xu Yanmei, CHN	445.20
1952	Pat McCormick, USA	79.37	1992	Fu Mingxia, CHN	461.43
1956	Pat McCormick, USA	84.85	1996	Fu Mingxia, CHN	521.58
1960	Ingrid Krämer, GER	91.28			

FIELD HOCKEY

MEN

Multiple gold medals: India (8); Great Britain and Pakistan (3); West Germany/Germany (2).

Year		Year	
1908	**Great Britain**, Ireland, Scotland	1964	**India**, Pakistan, Australia
1920	**Great Britain**, Denmark, Belgium	1968	**Pakistan**, Australia, India
1928	**India**, Netherlands, Germany	1972	**West Germany**, Pakistan, India
1932	**India**, Japan, United States	1976	**New Zealand**, Australia, Pakistan
1936	**India**, Germany, Netherlands	1980	**India**, Spain, Soviet Union
1948	**India**, Great Britain, Netherlands	1984	**Pakistan**, West Germany, Great Britain
1952	**India**, Netherlands, Great Britain	1988	**Great Britain**, West Germany, Netherlands
1956	**India**, Pakistan, Germany	1992	**Germany**, Australia, Pakistan
1960	**Pakistan**, India, Spain	1996	**Netherlands**, Spain, Australia

WOMEN

Multiple gold medals: Australia (2).

Year		Year	
1980	**Zimbabwe**, Czechoslovakia, Soviet Union	1992	**Spain**, Germany, Great Britain
1984	**Netherlands**, West Germany, United States	1996	**Australia**, South Korea, Netherlands
1988	**Australia**, South Korea, Netherlands		

GYMNASTICS

MEN

At least 4 gold medals (including team events): Sawao Kato (8); Nikolai Andrianov, Viktor Chukarin and Boris Shakhlin (7); Akinori Nakayama and Vitaly Scherbo (6); Yukio Endo, Anton Heida, Mitsuo Tsukahara and Takashi Ono (5); Vladimir Artemov, Georges Miez and Valentin Muratov (4).

All-Around

Year		Points	Year		Points
1900	Gustave Sandras, FRA	302.0	1956	Viktor Chukarin, USSR	114.25
1904	Julius Lenhart, AUT	69.80	1960	Boris Shakhlin, USSR	115.95
1906	Pierre Payssé, FRA	97.0	1964	Yukio Endo, JPN	115.95
1908	Alberto Braglia, ITA	317.0	1968	Sawao Kato, JPN	115.9
1912	Alberto Braglia, ITA	135.0	1972	Sawao Kato, JPN	114.650
1920	Giorgio Zampori, ITA	88.35	1976	Nikolai Andrianov, USSR	116.65
1924	Leon Stukelj, YUG	110.340	1980	Aleksandr Dityatin, USSR	118.65
1928	Georges Miez, SWI	247.500	1984	Koji Gushiken, JPN	118.7
1932	Romeo Neri, ITA	140.625	1988	Vladimir Artemov, USSR	119.125
1936	Alfred Schwarzmann, GER	113.100	1992	Vitaly Scherbo, UT	59.025
1948	Veikko Huhtanen, FIN	229.7	1996	Li Xiaoshuang, CHN	58.423
1952	Viktor Chukarin, USSR	115.7			

Horizontal Bar

Year		Points	Year		Points
1896	Hermann Weingärtner, GER	–	1964	Boris Shakhlin, USSR	19.625
1904	(TIE) Anton Heida, USA	40.0	1968	(TIE) Akinori Nakayama, JPN	19.55
	& Edward Hennig, USA	40.0		& Mikhail Voronin, USSR	19.55
1924	Leon Stukelj, YUG	19.73	1972	Mitsuo Tsukahara, JPN	19.725
1928	Georges Miez, SWI	19.17	1976	Mitsuo Tsukahara, JPN	19.675
1932	Dallas Bixler, USA	18.33	1980	Stoyan Deltchev, BUL	19.825
1936	Aleksanteri Saarvala, FIN	19.367	1984	Shinji Morisue, JPN	20.00
1948	Josef Stalder, SWI	19.85	1988	(TIE) Vladimir Artemov, USSR	19.900
1952	Jack Günthard, SWI	19.55		& Valeri Lyukin, USSR	19.900
1956	Takashi Ono, JPN	19.60	1992	Trent Dimas, USA	9.875
1960	Takashi Ono, JPN	19.60	1996	Andreas Wecker, GER	9.850

Parallel Bars

Year		Points	Year		Points
1896	Alfred Flatow, GER	–	1964	Yukio Endo, JPN	19.675
1904	George Eyser, USA	44.0	1968	Akinori Nakayama, JPN	19.475
1924	August Güttinger, SWI	21.63	1972	Sawao Kato, JPN	19.475
1928	Ladislav Vácha, CZE	18.83	1976	Sawao Kato, JPN	19.675
1932	Romeo Neri, ITA	18.97	1980	Aleksandr Tkachyov, USSR	19.775
1936	Konrad Frey, GER	19.067	1984	Bart Conner, USA	19.95
1948	Michael Reusch, SWI	19.75	1988	Vladimir Artemov, USSR	19.925
1952	Hans Eugster, SWI	19.65	1992	Vitaly Scherbo, UT	9.900
1956	Viktor Chukarin, USSR	19.20	1996	Rustam Sharipov, UKR	9.837
1960	Boris Shakhlin, USSR	19.40			

Vault

Year		Points	Year		Points
1896	Karl Schumann, GER	–	1960	(TIE) Takashi Ono, JPN	19.35
1904	(TIE) George Eyser, USA	36.0		& Boris Shakhlin, USSR	19.35
	&Anton Heida, USA	36.0	1964	Haruhiro Yamashita, JPN	19.60
1924	Frank Kriz, USA	9.98	1968	Mikhail Voronin, USSR	19.00
1928	Eugen Mack, SWI	9.58	1972	Klaus Köste, E. Ger	18.85
1932	Savino Guglielmetti, ITA	18.03	1976	Nikolai Andrianov, USSR	19.45
1936	Alfred Schwarzmann, GER	19.20	1980	Nikolai Andrianov, USSR	19.825
1948	Paavo Aaltonen, FIN	19.55	1984	Lou Yun, CHN	19.95
1952	Viktor Chukarin, USSR	19.20	1988	Lou Yun, CHN	19.875
1956	(TIE) Helmut Bantz, GER	18.85	1992	Vitaly Scherbo, UT	9.856
	&Valentin Muratov, USSR	18.85	1996	Alexei Nemov, RUS	9.787

Pommel Horse

Year		Points	Year		Points
1896	Louis Zutter, SWI	–	1924	Josef Wilhelm, SWI	21.23
1904	Anton Heida, USA	42	1928	Hermann Hänggi, SWI	19.75

Gymnastics (Cont.)

Year		Points
1932	Istvän Pelle, HUN	19.07
1936	Konrad Frey, GER	19.333
1948	(TIE) Paavo Aaltonen, FIN	19.35
	Veikko Huhtanen, FIN	19.35
	& Heikki Savolainen, FIN	19.35
1952	Viktor Chukarin, USSR	19.50
1956	Boris Shakhlin, USSR	19.25
1960	(TIE) Eugen Ekman, FIN	19.375
	& Boris Shakhlin, USSR	19.375
1964	Miroslav Cerar, YUG	19.525
1968	Miroslav Cerar, YUG	19.325

Year		Points
1972	Viktor Klimenko, SOV	19.125
1976	Zoltán Magyar, HUN	19.70
1980	Zoltán Magyar, HUN	19.925
1984	(TIE) Li Ning, CHN	19.95
	& Peter Vidmar, USA	19.95
1988	(TIE) Dmitri Bilozerchev, USSR	19.95
	& Zsolt Borkai, HUN	19.95
	Lyubomir Geraskov, BUL	19.95
1992	(TIE) Pae Gil-Su, N. Kor	9.925
	& Vitaly Scherbo, UT	9.925
1996	Li Donghua, SWI	9.875

Rings

Year		Points
1896	Ioannis Mitropoulos, GRE	–
1904	Hermann Glass, USA	45
1924	Francesco Martino, ITA	21.553
1928	Leon Stukelj, YUG	19.25
1932	George Gulack, USA	18.97
1936	Alois Hudec, CZE	19.433
1948	Karl Frei, SWI	19.80
1952	Grant Shaginyan, USSR	19.75
1956	Albert Azaryan, USSR	19.35
1960	Albert Azaryan, USSR	19.725
1964	Takuji Haytta, JPN	19.475

Year		Points
1968	Akinori Nakayama, JPN	19.45
1972	Akinori Nakayama, JPN	19.35
1976	Nikolai Andrianov, USSR	19.65
1980	Aleksandr Dityatin, USSR	19.875
1984	(TIE) Koji Gushiken, JPN	19.85
	& Li Ning, CHN	19.85
1988	(TIE) Holger Behrendt, E. Ger	19.925
	& Dmitri Bilozerchev, USSR	19.925
1992	Vitaly Scherbo, UT	9.937
1996	Yuri Chechi, ITA	9.887

Floor Exercise

Year		Points
1932	Istvan Pelle, HUN	9.60
1936	Georges Miez, SWI	18.666
1948	Ferenc Pataki, HUN	19.35
1952	William Thoresson, SWE	19.25
1956	Valentin Muratov, USSR	19.20
1960	Nobuyuki Aihara, JPN	19.45
1964	Franco Menichelli, ITA	19.45
1968	Sawao Kato, JPN	19.475

Year		Points
1972	Nikolai Andrianov, USSR	19.175
1976	Nikolai Andrianov, USSR	19.45
1980	Roland Brückner, E. Ger	19.75
1984	Li Ning, CHN	19.925
1988	Sergei Kharkov, USSR	19.925
1992	Li Xiaosahuang, CHN	9.925
1996	Ioannis Melissanidis, GRE	9.850

Team Combined Exercises

Year		Points
1904	United States	374.43
1906	Norway	19.00
1908	Sweden	438
1912	Italy	265.75
1920	Italy	359.855
1924	Italy	839.058
1928	Switzerland	1718.625
1932	Italy	541.850
1936	Germany	657.430
1948	Finland	1358.30
1952	Soviet Union	574.40

Year		Points
1956	Soviet Union	568.25
1960	Japan	575.20
1964	Japan	577.95
1968	Japan	575.90
1972	Japan	571.25
1976	Japan	576.85
1980	Soviet Union	598.60
1984	United States	591.40
1988	Soviet Union	593.35
1992	Unified Team	585.45
1996	Russia	576.778

WOMEN

At least 4 gold medals (including team events): Larissa Latynina (9); Vera Cáslavská (7); Polina Astakhova, Nadia Comaneci, Agnes Keleti and Nelli Kim (5); Olga Korbut, Ecaterina Szabó and Lyudmila Tourischeva (4).

All-Around

Year		Points
1952	Maria Gorokhovskaya, USSR	76.78
1956	Larissa Latynina, USSR	74.933
1960	Larissa Latynina, USSR	77.031
1964	Vera Cáslavská, CZE	77.564
1968	Vera Cáslavská, CZE	78.25
1972	Lyudmila Tourischeva, USSR	77.025

Year		Points
1976	Nadia Comaneci, ROM	79.275
1980	Yelena Davydova, USSR	79.15
1984	Mary Lou Retton, USA	79.175
1988	Yelena Shushunova, USSR	79.662
1992	Tatiana Gutsu, UT	39.737
1996	Lilia Podkopayeva, UKR	39.255

Vault

Year		Points
1952	Yekaterina Kalinchuk, USSR	19.20
1956	Larissa Latynina, USSR	18.833
1960	Margarita Nikolayeva, USSR	19.316

Year		Points
1964	Vera Cáslavská, CZE	19.483
1968	Vera Cáslavská, CZE	19.775
1972	Karin Janz, E. Ger	19.525

Year	Points	Year	Points
1976 Nelli Kim, USSR	19.80	1992 (TIE) Henrietta Onodi, HUN	9.925
1980 Natalia Shaposhnikova, USSR	19.725	& Lavinia Milosovici, ROM	9.925
1984 Ecaterina Szabó, ROM	19.875	1996 Simona Amanar, ROM	9.775
1988 Svetlana Boginskaya, USSR	19.905		

Uneven Bars

Year	Points	Year	Points
1952 Margit Korondi, HUN	19.40	1980 Maxi Gnauck, E. Ger	19.875
1956 Agnes Keleti, HUN	18.966	1984 (TIE) Julianne McNamora, USA	19.95
1960 Polina Astakhova, USSR	19.616	& Ma Yanhong, CHN	19.95
1964 Polina Astakhova, USSR	19.332	1988 Daniela Silivas, ROM	20.00
1968 Vera Cáslavská, CZE	19.65	1992 Lu Li, CHN	10.00
1972 Karin Janz, E. Ger	19.675	1996 Svetlana Chorkina, RUS	9.850
1976 Nadia Comaneci, ROM	20.00		

Balance Beam

Year	Points	Year	Points
1952 Nina Bocharova, USSR	19.22	1980 Nadia Comaneci, ROM	19.80
1956 Agnes Keleti, HUN	18.80	1984 (TIE) Simona Pauca, ROM	19.80
1960 Eva Bosakova, CZE	19.283	& Ecaterina Szabó, ROM	19.80
1964 Vera Cáslavská, CZE	19.449	1988 Daniela Silivas, ROM	19.924
1968 Natalya Kuchinskaya, USSR	19.65	1992 Tatiana Lyssenko, UT	9.975
1972 Olga Korbut, USSR	19.40	1996 Shannon Miller, USA	9.862
1976 Nadia Comaneci, ROM	19.95		

Floor Exercise

Year	Points	Year	Points
1952 Agnes Keleti, HUN	19.36	1976 Nelli Kim, USSR	19.85
1956 (TIE) Agnes Keleti, HUN	18.733	1980 (TIE) Nadia Comaneci, ROM	19.875
& Larissa Latynina, USSR	18.733	& Nelli Kim, USSR	19.875
1960 Larissa Latynina, USSR	19.583	1984 Ecaterina Szabó, ROM	19.975
1964 Larissa Latynina, USSR	19.599	1988 Daniela Silivas, ROM	19.937
1968 (TIE) Vera Cáslavská, CZE	19.675	1992 Lavinia Milosovici, ROM	10.000
& Larissa Petrik, USSR	19.675	1996 Lilia Podkopayeva, UKR	9.887
1972 Olga Korbut, USSR	19.575		

Team Combined Exercises

Year	Points	Year	Points
1928 Holland	316.75	1972 Soviet Union	380.50
1936 Germany	506.50	1976 Soviet Union	466.00
1948 Czechoslovakia	445.45	1980 Soviet Union	394.90
1952 Soviet Union	527.03	1984 Romania	392.02
1956 Soviet Union	444.800	1988 Soviet Union	395.475
1960 Soviet Union	382.320	1992 Unified Team	395.666
1964 Soviet Union	280.890	1996 United States	389.225
1968 Soviet Union	382.85		

SOCCER

MEN

Multiple gold medals: Great Britain and Hungary (3); Uruguay and USSR (2).

Year		Year	
1900	**Great Britain**, France, Belgium	1956	**Soviet Union**, Yugoslavia, Bulgaria
1904	**Canada**, USA I, USA II	1960	**Yugoslavia**, Denmark, Hungary
1906	**Denmark**, Smyrna (Int'l entry), Greece	1964	**Hungary**, Czechoslovakia, Germany
1908	**Great Britain**, Denmark, Netherlands	1968	**Hungary**, Bulgaria, Japan
1912	**Great Britain**, Denmark, Netherlands	1972	**Poland**, Hungary, East Germany & Soviet Union
1920	**Belgium**, Spain, Netherlands	1976	**East Germany**, Poland, Soviet Union
1924	**Uruguay**, Switzerland, Sweden	1980	**Czechoslovakia**, East Germany, Soviet Union
1928	**Uruguay**, Argentina, Italy	1984	**France**, Brazil, Yugoslavia
1936	**Italy**, Austria, Norway	1988	**Soviet Union**, Brazil, West Germany
1948	**Sweden**, Yugoslavia, Denmark	1992	**Spain**, Poland, Ghana
1952	**Hungary**, Yugoslavia, Sweden	1996	**Nigeria**, Argentina, Brazil

WOMEN

Year	
1996	**United States**, China, Norway

SWIMMING

World and Olympic records below that appear to be broken or equaled by winning times in subsequent years, but are not so indicated, were all broken in preliminary heats leading up to the finals. Some events were not held at every Olympics.

MEN

At least 4 gold medals (including relays): Mark Spitz (9); Matt Biondi (8); Charles Daniels, Tom Jager, Don Schollander, and Johnny Weissmuller (5); Tamás Darnyi, Roland Matthes, John Naber, Aleksandr Popov, Murray Rose, Vladimir Salnikov and Henry Taylor (4).

50-meter Freestyle

Year		Time		Year		Time	
1904	Zoltán Halmay, HUN (50 yds)	.28.0		1992	Aleksandr Popov, UT	.21.91	OR
1906-84	Not held			1996	Aleksandr Popov, RUS	.22.13	
1988	Matt Biondi, USA	.22.14	WR				

100-meter Freestyle

Year		Time		Year		Time	
1896	Alfréd Hajós, HUN	1:22.2	OR	1956	Jon Henricks, AUS	55.4	OR
1904	Zoltán Halmay, HUN (100 yds)	1:02.8		1960	John Devitt, AUS	55.2	OR
1906	Charles Daniels, USA	1:13.4		1964	Don Schollander, USA	53.4	OR
1908	Charles Daniels, USA	1:05.6	WR	1968	Michael Wenden, AUS	52.2	WR
1912	Duke Kahanamoku, USA	1:03.4		1972	Mark Spitz, USA	51.22	WR
1920	Duke Kahanamoku, USA	1:00.4	WR	1976	Jim Montgomery, USA	49.99	WR
1924	Johnny Weissmuller, USA	59.0	OR	1980	Jorg Woithe, E. Ger	50.40	
1928	Johnny Weissmuller, USA	58.6	OR	1984	Rowdy Gaines, USA	49.80	OR
1932	Yasuji Miyazaki, JPN	58.2		1988	Matt Biondi, USA	48.63	OR
1936	Ferenc Csik, HUN	57.6		1992	Aleksandr Popov, UT	49.02	
1948	Wally Ris, USA	57.3	OR	1996	Aleksandr Popov, RUS	48.74	
1952	Clarke Scholes, USA	57.4					

200-meter Freestyle

Year		Time		Year		Time	
1900	Frederick Lane, AUS (220 yds)	2:25.2	OR	1980	Sergei Kopliakov, USSR	1:49.81	OR
1904	Charles Daniels, USA (220 yds)	2:44.2		1984	Michael Gross, W. Ger	1:47.44	WR
1968	Michael Wenden, AUS	1:55.2	OR	1988	Duncan Armstrong, AUS	1:47.25	WR
1972	Mark Spitz, USA	1:52.78	WR	1992	Yevgeny Sadovyi, UT	1:46.70	OR
1976	Bruce Furniss, USA	1:50.29	WR	1996	Danyon Loader, NZE	1:47.63	

400-meter Freestyle

Year		Time		Year		Time	
1896	Paul Neumann, AUT (550m)	8:12.6		1956	Murray Rose, AUS	4:27.3	OR
1904	Charles Daniels, USA (440 yds)	6:16.2		1960	Murray Rose, AUS	4:18.3	OR
1906	Otto Scheff, AUT	6:23.8		1964	Don Schollander, USA	4:12.2	WR
1908	Henry Taylor, GBR	5:36.8		1968	Mike Burton, USA	4:09.0	
1912	George Hodgson, CAN	5:24.4		1972	Bradford Cooper, AUS*	4:00.27	OR
1920	Norman Ross, USA	5:26.8		1976	Brian Goodell, USA	3:51.93	WR
1924	Johnny Weissmuller, USA	5:04.2	OR	1980	Vladimir Salnikov, USSR	3:51.31	
1928	Alberto Zorilla, ARG	5:01.6	OR	1984	George DiCarlo, USA	3:51.23	OR
1932	Buster Crabbe, USA	4:48.4	OR	1988	Uwe Dassler, E. Ger	3:46.95	WR
1936	Jack Medica, USA	4:44.5	OR	1992	Yevgeny Sadovyi, UT	3:45.00	WR
1948	Bill Smith, USA	4:41.0	OR	1996	Danyon Loader, NZE	3:47.97	
1952	Jean Boiteux, FRA	4:30.7	OR				

*Australian Cooper finished second to Rick DeMont of the U.S., who was disqualified when he flunked the post-race drug test (his asthma medication was on the IOC's banned list).

1500-meter Freestyle

Year		Time		Year		Time	
1896	Alfréd Hajós, HUN (1200m)	18:22.2	OR	1952	Ford Konno, USA	18:30.3	OR
1900	John Arthur Jarvis, GBR (1000m)	13:40.2		1956	Murray Rose, AUS	17:58.9	
1904	Emil Rausch, GER (1 mile)	27:18.2		1960	Jon Konrads, AUS	17:19.6	OR
1906	Henry Taylor, GBR (1 mile)	28:28.0		1964	Robert Windle, AUS	17:01.7	OR
1908	Henry Taylor, GBR	22:48.4	WR	1968	Mike Burton, USA	16:38.9	OR
1912	George Hodgson, CAN	22:00.0	WR	1972	Mike Burton, USA	15:52.58	WR
1920	Norman Ross, USA	22:23.2		1976	Brian Goodell, USA	15:02.40	WR
1924	Andrew (Boy) Charlton, AUS	20:06.6	WR	1980	Vladimir Salnikov, USSR	14:58.27	WR
1928	Arne Borge, SWE	19:51.8	OR	1984	Mike O'Brien, USA	15:05.20	
1932	Kusuo Kitamura, JPN	19:12.4	OR	1988	Vladimir Salnikov, USSR	15:00.40	
1936	Noboru Terada, JPN	19:13.7		1992	Kieren Perkins, AUS	14:43.48	WR
1948	James McLane, USA	19:18.5		1996	Kieren Perkins, AUS	14:56.40	

100-meter Backstroke

Year		Time		Year		Time	
1904	Walter Brack, GER (100 yds)	1:16.8		1956	David Theile, AUS	1:02.2	OR
1908	Arno Bieberstein, GER	1:24.6	WR	1960	David Theile, AUS	1:01.9	OR
1912	Harry Hebner, USA	1:21.2		1968	Roland Matthes, E. Ger	58.7	OR
1920	Warren Kealoha, USA	1:15.2		1972	Roland Matthes, E. Ger	56.58	OR
1924	Warren Kealoha, USA	1:13.2	OR	1976	John Naber, USA	55.49	WR
1928	George Kojac, USA	1:08.2	WR	1980	Bengt Baron, SWE	56.33	
1932	Masaji Kiyokawa, JPN	1:08.6		1984	Rick Carey, USA	55.79	
1936	Adolf Kiefer, USA	1:05.9	OR	1988	Daichi Suzuki, JPN	55.05	
1948	Allen Stack, USA	1:06.4		1992	Mark Tewksbury, CAN	53.98	OR
1952	Yoshinobu Oyakawa, USA	1:05.4	OR	1996	Jeff Rouse, USA	54.10	

200-meter Backstroke

Year		Time		Year		Time	
1900	Ernst Hoppenberg, GER	2:47.0		1980	Sándor Wládár, HUN	2:01.93	
1964	Jed Graef, USA	2:10.3	WR	1984	Rick Carey, USA	2:00.23	
1968	Roland Matthes, E. Ger	2:09.6	OR	1988	Igor Poliansky, USSR	1:59.37	
1972	Roland Matthes, E. Ger	2:02.82	=WR	1992	Martin Lopez-Zubero, SPA	1:58.47	OR
1976	John Naber, USA	1:59.19	WR	1996	Brad Bridgewater, USA	1:58.54	

100-meter Breaststroke

Year		Time		Year		Time	
1968	Don McKenzie, USA	1:07.7	OR	1984	Steve Lundquist, USA	1:01.65	WR
1972	Nobutaka Taguchi, JPN	1:04.94	WR	1988	Adrian Moorhouse, GBR	1:02.04	
1976	John Hencken, USA	1:03.11	WR	1992	Nelson Diebel, USA	1:01.50	
1980	Duncan Goodhew, GBR	1:03.44		1996	Fred deBurghgraeve, BEL	1:00.60	

200-meter Breaststroke

Year		Time		Year		Time	
1908	Frederick Holman, GBR	3:09.2	WR	1960	Bill Mulliken, USA	2:37.4	
1912	Walter Bathe, GER	3:01.8	OR	1964	Ian O'Brien, AUS	2:27.8	WR
1920	Hakan Malmroth, SWE	3:04.4		1968	Felipe Muñoz, MEX	2:28.7	
1924	Robert Skelton, USA	2:56.6		1972	John Hencken, USA	2:21.55	WR
1928	Yoshiyuki Tsuruta, JPN	2:48.8	OR	1976	David Wilkie, GBR	2:15.11	WR
1932	Yoshiyuki Tsuruta, JPN	2:45.4		1980	Robertas Zhulpa, USSR	2:15.85	
1936	Tetsuo Hamuro, JPN	2:41.5	OR	1984	Victor Davis, CAN	2:13.34	WR
1948	Joseph Verdeur, USA	2:39.3	OR	1988	József Szabó, HUN	2:13.52	
1952	John Davies, AUS	2:34.4	OR	1992	Mike Barrowman, USA	2:10.16	WR
1956	Masaru Furukawa, JPN	2:34.7*	OR	1996	Norbert Rozsa, HUN	2:12.57	

*In 1956, the butterfly stroke and breaststroke were separated into two different events.

100-meter Butterfly

Year		Time		Year		Time	
1968	Doug Russell, USA	55.9	OR	1984	Michael Gross, W. Ger	53.08	WR
1972	Mark Spitz, USA	54.27	WR	1988	Anthony Nesty, SUR	53.0	OR
1976	Matt Vogel, USA	54.35		1992	Pablo Morales, USA	53.32	
1980	Pär Arvidsson, SWE	54.92		1996	Dennis Pankratov, RUS	52.27	

200-meter Butterfly

Year		Time		Year		Time	
1956	Bill Yorzyk, USA	2:19.3	OR	1980	Sergei Fesenko, USSR	1:59.76	
1960	Mike Troy, U	2:12.8	WR	1984	Jon Sieben, AUS	1:57.04	WR
1964	Kevin Berry, AUS	2:06.6	WR	1988	Michael Gross, W. Ger	1:56.94	OR
1968	Carl Robie, USA	2:08.7		1992	Melvin Stewart, USA	1:56.26	OR
1972	Mark Spitz, USA	2:00.70	WR	1996	Dennis Pankratov, RUS	1:56.51	
1976	Mike Bruner, USA	1:59.23	WR				

200-meter Individual Medley

Year		Time		Year		Time	
1968	Charles Hickcox, USA	2:12.0	OR	1988	Tamás Darnyi, HUN	2:00.17	WR
1972	Gunnar Larsson, SWE	2:07.17	WR	1992	Tamás Darnyi, HUN	2:00.76	
1984	Alex Baumann, CAN	2:01.42	WR	1996	Attila Czene, HUN	1:59.91	

400-meter Individual Medley

Year		Time		Year		Time	
1964	Richard Roth, USA	4:45.4	WR	1984	Alex Baumann, CAN	4:17.41	WR
1968	Charles Hickcox, USA	4:48.4		1988	Tamás Darnyi, HUN	4:14.75	WR
1972	Gunnar Larsson, SWE	4:31.98	OR	1992	Tamás Darnyi, HUN	4:14.23	OR
1976	Rod Strachan, USA	4:23.68	WR	1996	Tom Dolan, USA	4:14.90	
1980	Aleksandr Sidorenko, USSR	4:22.89	OR				

Swimming (Cont.)

4x100-meter Freestyle Relay

Year		Time		Year		Time	
1964	United States	3:32.2	WR	1984	United States	3:19.03	WR
1968	United States	3:31.7	WR	1988	United States	3:16.53	WR
1972	United States	3:26.42	WR	1992	United States	3:16.74	
1976-80 Not held				1996	United States	3:15.41	

4x200-meter Freestyle Relay

Year		Time		Year		Time	
1906	Hungary (x250m)	16:52.4		1960	United States	8:10.2	WR
1908	Great Britain	10:55.6	WR	1964	United States	7:52.1	WR
1912	Australia/New Zealand	10:11.6	WR	1968	United States	7:52.33	
1920	United States	10:04.4	WR	1972	United States	7:35.78	WR
1924	United States	9:53.4	WR	1976	United States	7:23.22	WR
1928	United States	9:36.2	WR	1980	Soviet Union	7:23.50	
1932	Japan	8:58.4	WR	1984	United States	7:15.69	WR
1936	Japan	8:51.5	WR	1988	United States	7:12.51	WR
1948	United States	8:46.0	WR	1992	Unified Team	7:11.95	WR
1952	United States	8:31.1	OR	1996	United States	7:14.84	
1956	Australia	8:23.6	WR				

4x100-meter Medley Relay

Year		Time		Year		Time	
1960	United States	4:05.4	WR	1980	Australia	3:45.70	
1964	United States	3:58.4	WR	1984	United States	3:39.30	WR
1968	United States	3:54.9	WR	1988	United States	3:36.93	WR
1972	United States	3:48.16	WR	1992	United States	3:36.93	=WR
1976	United States	3:42.22	WR	1996	United States	3:34.84	

WOMEN

At least 4 gold medals (including relays): Kristin Otto (6); Krisztina Egerszegi and Jenny Thompson (5), Kornelia Ender, Janet Evans, Dawn Fraser and Amy Van Dyken (4).

50-meter Freestyle

Year		Time		Year		Time	
1988	Kristin Otto, E. Ger	25.49	OR	1996	Amy Van Dyken, USA	24.87	
1992	Yang Wenyi, CHN	24.79	WR				

100-meter Freestyle

Year		Time		Year		Time	
1912	Fanny Durack, AUS	1:22.2		1964	Dawn Fraser, AUS	59.5	OR
1920	Ethelda Bleibtrey, USA	1:13.6	WR	1968	Jan Henne, USA	1:00.0	
1924	Ethel Lackie, USA	1:12.4		1972	Sandra Neilson, USA	58.59	OR
1928	Albina Osipowich, USA	1:11.0	OR	1976	Kornelia Ender, E. Ger	55.65	WR
1932	Helene Madison, USA	1:06.8	OR	1980	Barbara Krause, E. Ger	54.79	WR
1936	Rie Mastenbroek, HOL	1:05.9	WR	1984	(TIE) Nancy Hogshead, USA	55.92	
1948	Greta Andersen, DEN	1:06.3			Carrie Steinseifer, USA	55.92	
1952	Katalin Szöke, HUN	1:06.8		1988	Kristin Otto, E. Ger	54.93	
1956	Dawn Fraser, AUS	1:02.0	WR	1992	Zhuang Yong, CHN	54.65	OR
1960	Dawn Fraser, AUS	1:01.2	OR	1996	Le Jingyi, CHN	54.50	

200-meter Freestyle

Year		Time		Year		Time	
1968	Debbie Meyer, USA	2:10.5	OR	1984	Mary Wayte, USA	1:59.23	
1972	Shane Gould, AUS	2:03.56	OR	1988	Heike Friedrich, E. Ger	1:57.65	OR
1976	Kornelia Ender, E. Ger	1:59.26	WR	1992	Nicole Haislett, USA	1:57.90	
1980	Barbara Krause, E. Ger	1:58.33	OR	1996	Claudia Poll, COS	1:58.16	

400-meter Freestyle

Year		Time		Year		Time	
1920	Ethelda Bleibtrey, USA (300m)	4:34.0	WR	1964	Ginny Duenkel, USA	4:43.3	OR
1924	Martha Norelius, USA	6:02.2	OR	1968	Debbie Meyer, USA	4:31.8	OR
1928	Martha Norelius, USA	5:42.8	WR	1972	Shane Gould, AUS	4:19.44	WR
1932	Helene Madison, USA	5:28.5	WR	1976	Petra Thümer, E. Ger	4:09.89	WR
1936	Rie Mastenbroek, HOL	5:26.4	OR	1980	Ines Diers, E. Ger	4:08.76	OR
1948	Ann Curtis, USA	5:17.8	OR	1984	Tiffany Cohen, USA	4:07.10	OR
1952	Valéria Gyenge, HUN	5:12.1	OR	1988	Janet Evans, USA	4:03.85	WR
1956	Lorraine Crapp, AUS	4:54.6	OR	1992	Dagmar Hase, GER	4:07.18	
1960	Chris von Saltza, USA	4:50.6	OR	1996	Michelle Smith, IRE	4:07.25	

800-meter Freestyle

Year		Time		Year		Time	
1968	Debbie Meyer, USA	9:24.0	OR	1984	Tiffany Cohen, USA	8:24.95	OR
1972	Keena Rothhammer, USA	8:53.68	WR	1988	Janet Evans, USA	8:20.20	OR
1976	Petra Thümer, E. Ger	8:37.14	WR	1992	Janet Evans, USA	8:25.52	
1980	Michelle Ford, AUS	8:28.90	OR	1996	Brooke Bennett, USA	8:27.89	

100-meter Backstroke

Year		Time		Year		Time	
1924	Sybil Bauer, USA	1:23.2	OR	1968	Kaye Hall, USA	1:06.2	WR
1928	Maria Braun, HOL	1:22.0		1972	Melissa Belote, USA	1:05.78	OR
1932	Eleanor Holm, USA	1:19.4		1976	Ulrike Richter, E. Ger	1:01.83	OR
1936	Dina Senff, HOL	1:18.9		1980	Rica Reinisch, E. Ger	1:00.86	WR
1948	Karen-Margrete Harup, DEN	1:14.4	OR	1984	Theresa Andrews, USA	1:02.55	
1952	Joan Harrison, SAF	1:14.3		1988	Kristin Otto, E. Ger	1:00.89	
1956	Judy Grinham, GBR	1:12.9	OR	1992	Krisztina Egerszegi, HUN	1:00.68	OR
1960	Lynn Burke, USA	1:09.3	OR	1996	Beth Botsford, USA	1:01.19	
1964	Cathy Ferguson, USA	1:07.7	WR				

200-meter Backstroke

Year		Time		Year		Time	
1968	Pokey Watson, USA	2:24.8	OR	1984	Jolanda de Rover, NET	2:12.38	
1972	Melissa Belote, USA	2:19.19	WR	1988	Krisztina Egerszegi, HUN	2:09.29	OR
1976	Ulrike Richter, E. Ger	2:13.43	OR	1992	Krisztina Egerszegi, HUN	2:07.06	OR
1980	Rica Reinisch, E. Ger	2:11.77	WR	1996	Krisztina Egerszegi, HUN	2:07.83	

100-meter Breaststroke

Year		Time		Year		Time	
1968	Djurdjica Bjedov, YUG	1:15.8	OR	1984	Petra van Staveren, NET	1:09.88	OR
1972	Cathy Carr, USA	1:13.58	WR	1988	Tania Dangalakova, BUL	1:07.95	OR
1976	Hannelore Anke, E. Ger	1:11.16		1992	Yelena Rudkovskaya, UT	1:08.00	
1980	Ute Geweniger, E. Ger	1:10.22		1996	Penny Heyns, S. Afr.	1:07.73	

200-meter Breaststroke

Year		Time		Year		Time	
1924	Lucy Morton, GBR	3:33.2	OR	1968	Sharon Wichman, USA	2:44.4	OR
1928	Hilde Schrader, GER	3:12.6		1972	Beverley Whitfield, AUS	2:41.71	OR
1932	Clare Dennis, AUS	3:06.3	OR	1976	Marina Koshevaya, USSR	2:33.35	WR
1936	Hideko Maehata, JPN	3:03.6		1980	Lina Kaciusyte, USSR	2:29.54	OR
1948	Petronella van Vliet, NET	2:57.2		1984	Anne Ottenbrite, CAN	2:30.38	
1952	Éva Székely, HUN	2:51.7	OR	1988	Silke Hörner, E. Ger	2:26.71	WR
1956	Ursula Happe, GER	2:53.1	OR	1992	Kyoko Iwasaki, JPN	2:26.65	OR
1960	Anita Lonsbrough, GBR	2:49.5	WR	1996	Penny Heyns, S. Afr.	2:25.41	
1964	Galina Prozumenshikova, USSR	2:46.4	OR				

100-meter Butterfly

Year		Time		Year		Time	
1956	Shelly Mann, USA	1:11.0	OR	1980	Caren Metschuck, E. Ger	1:00.42	
1960	Carolyn Schuler, USA	1:09.5	OR	1984	Mary T. Meagher, USA	59.26	
1964	Sharon Stouder, USA	1:04.7	WR	1988	Kristin Otto, E. Ger	59.00	OR
1968	Lynn McClements, AUS	1:05.5		1992	Qian Hong, CHN	58.62	OR
1972	Mayumi Aoki, JPN	1:03.34	WR	1996	Amy Van Dyken, USA	59.13	
1976	Kornelia Ender, E. Ger	1:00.13	=WR				

200-meter Butterfly

Year		Time		Year		Time	
1968	Ada Kok, NET	2:24.7	OR	1984	Mary T. Meagher, USA	2:06.90	OR
1972	Karen Moe, USA	2:15.57	WR	1988	Kathleen Nord, E. Ger	2:09.51	
1976	Andrea Pollack, E. Ger	2:11.41	OR	1992	Summer Sanders, USA	2:08.67	
1980	Ines Geissler, E. Ger	2:10.44	OR	1996	Susan O'Neill, AUS	2:07.76	

200-meter Individual Medley

Year		Time		Year		Time	
1968	Claudia Kolb, USA	2:24.7	OR	1988	Daniela Hunger, E. Ger	2:12.59	OR
1972	Shane Gould, AUS	2:23.07	WR	1992	Lin Li, CHN	2:11.65	WR
1984	Tracy Caulkins, USA	2:12.64	OR	1996	Michelle Smith, IRE	2:13.93	

400-meter Individual Medley

Year		Time		Year		Time	
1964	Donna de Varona, USA	5:18.7	OR	1984	Tracy Caulkins, USA	4:39.24	
1968	Claudia Kolb, USA	5:08.5	OR	1988	Janet Evans, USA	4:37.76	
1972	Gail Neall, AUS	5:02.97	WR	1992	Krisztina Egerszegi, HUN	4:36.54	
1976	Ulrike Tauber, E. Ger	4:42.77	WR	1996	Michelle Smith, IRE	4:39.18	
1980	Petra Schneider, E. Ger	4:36.29	WR				

Swimming (Cont.)

4x100-meter Freestyle Relay

Year		Time		Year		Time	
1912	Great Britain	5:52.8	WR	1964	United States	4:03.8	WR
1920	United States	5:11.6	WR	1968	United States	4:02.5	OR
1924	United States	4:58.8	WR	1972	United States	3:55.19	WR
1928	United States	4:47.6	WR	1976	United States	3:44.82	WR
1932	United States	4:38.0	WR	1980	East Germany	3:42.71	WR
1936	Netherlands	4:36.0	OR	1984	United States	3:43.43	
1948	United States	4:29.2	WR	1988	East Germany	3:40.63	OR
1952	Hungary	4:24.4	WR	1992	United States	3:39.46	WR
1956	Australia	4:17.1	WR	1996	United States	3:39.29	
1960	United States	4:08.9	WR				

4x200-meter Freestyle Relay

Year		Time
1996	United States	7:59.87

4x100-meter Medley Relay

Year		Time		Year		Time	
1960	United States	4:41.1	WR	1980	East Germany	4:06.67	WR
1964	United States	4:33.9	WR	1984	United States	4:08.34	
1968	United States	4:28.3	OR	1988	East Germany	4:03.74	OR
1972	United States	4:20.75	WR	1992	United States	4:02.54	WR
1976	East Germany	4:07.95	WR	1996	United States	4:02.88	

TENNIS

MEN

Multiple gold medals (including doubles): John Boland, Max Decugis, Laurie Doherty, Reggie Doherty, Arthur Gore, Andre Grobert, Vincent Richards, Charles Winslow and Beals Wright (2).

Singles

Year			Year		
1896	John Boland	Great Britain/Ireland	1920	Louis Raymond	South Africa
1900	Laurie Doherty,	Great Britain	1924	Vincent Richards	United States
1904	Beals Wright	United States	1928-84	Not held	
1906	Max Decugis	France	1988	Miloslav Mecir	Czechoslovakia
1908	Josiah Ritchie	Great Britain	1992	Marc Rosset	Switzerland
	(Indoor) Arthur Gore	Great Britain	1996	Andre Agassi	United States
1912	Charles Winslow	South Africa			
	(Indoor) André Gobert	France			

Doubles

Year		Year	
1896	John Boland, IRE & Fritz Traun, GER	1920	Noel Turnbull & Max Woosnam, GBR
1900	Laurie and Reggie Doherty, GBR	1924	Vincent Richards & Frank Hunter, USA
1904	Edgar Leonard & Beals Wright, USA	1928-84	Not held
1906	Max Decugis & Maurice Germot, FRA	1988	Ken Flach & Robert Seguso, USA
1908	George Hillyard & Reggie Doherty, GBR	1992	Boris Becker & Michael Stich, GER
	(Indoor) Arthur Gore & Herbert Barrett, GBR	1996	Todd Woodbridge & Mark Woodforde, AUS
1912	Charles Winslow & Harold Kitson, S. Afr.		
	(Indoor) Andre Gobert & Maurice Germot, FRA		

WOMEN

Multiple gold medals (including doubles): Helen Wills (2).

Singles

Year			Year		
1900	Charlotte Cooper	Great Britain	1920	Suzanne Lenglen	France
1906	Esmee Simiriotou	Greece	1924	Helen Wills	United States
1908	Dorothea Chambers	Great Britain	1928-84	Not held	
	(Indoor) Gwen Eastlake-Smith	Great Britain	1988	Steffi Graf	West Germany
1912	Marguerite Broquedis	France	1992	Jennifer Capriati	United States
	(Indoor) Edith Hannam	Great Britain	1996	Lindsay Davenport	United States

Doubles

Year		Year	
1920	Winifred McNair & Kitty McKane, GBR	1988	Pam Shriver & Zina Garrison, USA
1924	Hazel Wightman & Helen Wills, USA	1992	Gigi Fernandez & Mary Joe Fernandez, USA
1928-84	Not held	1996	Gigi Fernandez & Mary Joe Fernandez, USA

TRACK & FIELD

World and Olympic records below that appear to be broken or equaled by winning times, heights and distances in subsequent years, but are not so indicated, were all broken in preliminary races and field events leading up to the finals.

MEN

At least 5 gold medals (including relays and discontinued events): Ray Ewry (10); Carl Lewis and Paavo Nurmi (9); Ville Ritola and Martin Sheridan (5). Note that all of Ewry's gold medals came before 1912, in the Standing High Jump, Standing Long Jump and Standing Triple Jump.

100 meters

Year		Time		Year		Time	
1896	Tom Burke, USA	12.0		1952	Lindy Remigino, USA	10.4	
1900	Frank Jarvis, USA	11.0		1956	Bobby Morrow, USA	10.5	
1904	Archie Hahn, USA	11.0		1960	Armin Hary, GER	10.2	OR
1906	Archie Hahn, USA	11.2		1964	Bob Hayes, USA	10.0	=WR
1908	Reggie Walker, S. Afr.	10.8	=OR	1968	Jim Hines, USA	9.95	WR
1912	Ralph Craig, USA	10.8		1972	Valery Borzov, USSR	10.14	
1920	Charley Paddock, USA	10.8		1976	Hasely Crawford, TRI	10.06	
1924	Harold Abrahams, GBR	10.6	=OR	1980	Allan Wells, GBR	10.25	
1928	Percy Williams, CAN	10.8		1984	Carl Lewis, USA	9.99	
1932	Eddie Tolan, USA	10.3	OR	1988	Carl Lewis, USA*	9.92	WR
1936	Jesse Owens, USA	10.3w		1992	Linford Christie, GBR	9.96	
1948	Harrison Dillard, USA	10.3	=OR	1996	Donovan Bailey, USA	9.84	WR

*Lewis finished second to Ben Johnson of Canada, who set a world record of 9.79 seconds. A day later, Johnson was stripped of his gold medal and his record when he tested positive for steroid use in a post-race drug test.

200 meters

Year		Time		Year		Time	
1900	John Walter Tewksbury, USA	22.2		1956	Bobby Morrow, USA	20.6	OR
1904	Archie Hahn, USA	21.6	OR	1960	Livio Berruti, ITA	20.5	=WR
1908	Bobby Kerr, CAN	22.6		1964	Henry Carr, USA	20.3	OR
1912	Ralph Craig, USA	21.7		1968	Tommie Smith, USA	19.83	WR
1920	Allen Woodring, USA	22.0		1972	Valery Borzov, USSR	20.00	
1924	Jackson Scholz, USA	21.6		1976	Donald Quarrie, JAM	20.23	
1928	Percy Williams, CAN	21.8		1980	Pietro Mennea, ITA	20.19	
1932	Eddie Tolan, USA	21.2	OR	1984	Carl Lewis, USA	19.80	OR
1936	Jesse Owens, USA	20.7	OR	1988	Joe DeLoach, USA	19.75	OR
1948	Mel Patton, USA	21.1		1992	Mike Marsh, USA	20.01	
1952	Andy Stanfield, USA	20.7		1996	Michael Johnson, USA	19.32	WR

400 meters

Year		Time		Year		Time	
1896	Tom Burke, USA	54.2		1952	George Rhoden, JAM	45.9	OR
1900	Maxey Long, USA	49.4	OR	1956	Charley Jenkins, USA	46.7	
1904	Harry Hillman, USA	49.2	OR	1960	Otis Davis, USA	44.9	WR
1906	Paul Pilgrim, USA	53.2		1964	Mike Larrabee, USA	45.1	
1908	Wyndham Halswelle, GBR	50.0		1968	Lee Evans, USA	43.86	WR
1912	Charlie Reidpath, USA	48.2	OR	1972	Vince Matthews, USA	44.66	
1920	Bevil Rudd, S. Afr.	49.6		1976	Alberto Juantorena, CUB	44.26	
1924	Eric Liddell, GBR	47.6	OR	1980	Viktor Markin, USSR	44.60	
1928	Ray Barbuti, USA	47.8		1984	Alonzo Babers, USA	44.27	
1932	Bill Carr, USA	46.2	WR	1988	Steve Lewis, USA	43.87	
1936	Archie Williams, USA	46.5		1992	Quincy Watts, USA	43.50	OR
1948	Arthur Wint, JAM	46.2		1996	Michael Johnson, USA	43.49	OR

800 meters

Year		Time		Year		Time	
1896	Teddy Flack, AUS	2:11.0		1952	Mal Whitfield, USA	1:49.2	=OR
1900	Alfred Tysoe, GBR	2:01.2		1956	Tom Courtney, USA	1:47.7	OR
1904	Jim Lightbody, USA	1:56.0	OR	1960	Peter Snell, NZE	1:46.3	OR
1906	Paul Pilgrim, USA	2:01.5		1964	Peter Snell, NZE	1:45.1	OR
1908	Mel Sheppard, USA	1:52.8	WR	1968	Ralph Doubell, AUS	1:44.3	=WR
1912	Ted Meredith, USA	1:51.9	WR	1972	Dave Wottle, USA	1:45.9	
1920	Albert Hill, GBR	1:53.4		1976	Alberto Juantorena, CUB	1:43.50	WR
1924	Douglas Lowe, GBR	1:52.4		1980	Steve Ovett, GBR	1:45.4	
1928	Douglas Lowe, GBR	1:51.8	OR	1984	Joaquim Cruz, BRA	1:43.00	OR
1932	Tommy Hampson, GBR	1:49.7	WR	1988	Paul Ereng, KEN	1:43.45	
1936	John Woodruff, USA	1:52.9		1992	William Tanui, KEN	1:43.66	
1948	Mal Whitfield, USA	1:49.2	OR	1996	Vebjoern Rodal, NOR	1:42.58	OR

1500 meters

Year		Time		Year		Time	
1896	Teddy Flack, AUS	4:33.2		1904	Jim Lightbody, USA	4:05.4	WR
1900	Charles Bennett, GBR	4:06.2	WR	1906	Jim Lightbody, USA	4:12.0	

Track & Field (Cont.)

Year		Time	
1908	Mel Sheppard, USA	4:03.4	OR
1912	Arnold Jackson, GBR	3:56.8	OR
1920	Albert Hill, GBR	4:01.8	
1924	Paavo Nurmi, FIN	3:53.6	OR
1928	Harry Larva, FIN	3:53.2	OR
1932	Luigi Beccali, ITA	3:51.2	OR
1936	John Lovelock, NZE	3:47.8	WR
1948	Henry Eriksson, SWE	3:49.8	
1952	Josy Barthel, LUX	3:45.1	OR

Year		Time	
1956	Ron Delany, IRL	3:41.2	OR
1960	Herb Elliott, AUS	3:35.6	WR
1964	Peter Snell, NZE	3:38.1	
1968	Kip Keino, KEN	3:34.9	OR
1972	Pekka Vasala, FIN	3:36.3	
1976	John Walker, NZE	3:39.17	
1980	Sebastian Coe, GBR	3:38.4	
1984	Sebastian Coe, GBR	3:32.53	OR
1988	Peter Rono, KEN	3:35.96	
1992	Fermin Cacho, SPA	3:40.12	
1996	Noureddine Morceli, ALG	3:35.78	

5000 meters

Year		Time	
1912	Hannes Kolehmainen, FIN	14:36.6	WR
1920	Joseph Guillemot, FRA	14:55.6	
1924	Paavo Nurmi, FIN	14:31.2	OR
1928	Ville Ritola, FIN	14:38.0	
1932	Lauri Lehtinen, FIN	14:30.0	OR
1936	Gunnar Höckert, FIN	14:22.2	OR
1948	Gaston Reiff, BEL	14:17.6	OR
1952	Emil Zátopek, CZE	14:06.6	OR
1956	Vladimir Kuts, USSR	13:39.6	OR
1960	Murray Halberg, NZE	13:43.4	

Year		Time	
1964	Bob Schul, USA	13:48.8	
1968	Mohamed Gammoudi, TUN	14:05.0	
1972	Lasse Viren, FIN	13:26.4	
1976	Lasse Viren, FIN	13:24.76	
1980	Miruts Yifter, ETH	13:21.0	
1984	Said Aouita, MOR	13:05.59	OR
1988	John Ngugi, KEN	13:11.70	
1992	Dieter Baumann, GER	13:12.52	
1996	Venuste Niyongabo, BUR	13:07.96	

10,000 meters

Year		Time	
1912	Hannes Kolehmainen, FIN	31:20.8	
1920	Paavo Nurmi, FIN	31:45.8	
1924	Ville Ritola, FIN	30:23.2	WR
1928	Paavo Nurmi, FIN	30:18.8	OR
1932	Janusz Kusocinski, POL	30:11.4	OR
1936	Ilmari Salminen, FIN	30:15.4	
1948	Emil Zátopek, CZE	29:59.6	OR
1952	Emil Zátopek, CZE	29:17.0	OR
1956	Vladimir Kuts, USSR	28:45.6	OR
1960	Pyotr Bolotnikov, USSR	28:32.2	OR

Year		Time	
1964	Billy Mills, USA	28:24.4	OR
1968	Naftali Temu, KEN	29:27.4	
1972	Lasse Viren, FIN	27:38.4	WR
1976	Lasse Viren, FIN	27:40.38	
1980	Miruts Yifter, ETH	27:42.7	
1984	Alberto Cova, ITA	27:47.54	
1988	Brahim Boutaib, MOR	27:21.46	OR
1992	Khalid Skah, MOR	27:46.70	
1996	Haile Gebrselassie, ETH	27:07.34	OR

Marathon

Year		Time	
1896	Spiridon Louis, GRE	2:58:50	
1900	Michel Théato, FRA	2:59:45	
1904	Thomas Hicks, USA	3:28:53	
1906	Billy Sherring, CAN	2:51:23.6	
1908	Johnny Hayes, USA*	2:55:18.4	OR
1912	Kenneth McArthur, S. Afr.	2:36:54.8	
1920	Hannes Kolehmainen, FIN	2:32:35.8	WB
1924	Albin Stenroos, FIN	2:41:22.6	
1928	Boughèra El Ouafi, FRA	2:32:57.0	
1932	Juan Carlos Zabala, ARG	2:31:36.0	OR
1936	Sohn Kee-Chung, JPN†	2:29:19.2	OR
1948	Delfo Cabrera, ARG	2:34:51.6	

Year		Time	
1952	Emil Zátopek, CZE	2:23:03.2	OR
1956	Alain Mimoun, FRA	2:25:00.0	
1960	Abebe Bikila, ETH	2:15:16.2	WB
1964	Abebe Bikila, ETH	2:12:11.2	WB
1968	Mamo Wolde, ETH	2:20:26.4	
1972	Frank Shorter, USA	2:12:19.8	
1976	Waldemar Cierpinski, E. Ger	2:09:55.0	OR
1980	Waldemar Cierpinski, E. Ger	2:11:03.0	
1984	Carlos Lopes, POR	2:09:21.0	OR
1988	Gelindo Bordin, ITA	2:10:32	
1992	Hwang Young-Cho, S. Kor	2:13:23	
1996	Josia Thugwane, S. Afr.	2:12:36	

*Dorando Pietri of Italy placed first, but was disqualified for being helped across the finish line.
† Sohn was a Korean, but he was forced to compete under the name Kitei Son by Japan, which occupied Korea at the time.
Note: Marathon distances–40,000 meters (1896,1904); 40,260 meters (1900); 41,860 meters (1906); 42,195 meters (1908 and since 1924); 40,200 meters (1912); 42,750 meters (1920). Current distance of 42,195 meters measures 26 miles, 385 yards.

110-meter Hurdles

Year		Time	
1896	Tom Curtis, USA	17.6	
1900	Alvin Kraenzlein, USA	15.4	OR
1904	Frederick Schule, USA	16.0	
1906	Robert Leavitt, USA	16.2	
1908	Forrest Smithson, USA	15.0	WR
1912	Frederick Kelly, USA	15.1	
1920	Earl Thomson, CAN	14.8	WR
1924	Daniel Kinsey, USA	15.0	
1928	Syd Atkinson, S. Afr.	14.8	
1932	George Saling, USA	14.6	
1936	Forrest (Spec) Towns, USA	14.2	
1948	William Porter, USA	13.9	OR

Year		Time	
1952	Harrison Dillard, USA	13.7	OR
1956	Lee Calhoun, USA	13.5	OR
1960	Lee Calhoun, USA	13.8	
1964	Hayes Jones, USA	13.6	
1968	Willie Davenport, USA	13.3	OR
1972	Rod Milburn, USA	13.24	=WR
1976	Guy Drut, FRA	13.30	
1980	Thomas Munkelt, E. Ger	13.39	
1984	Roger Kingdom, USA	13.20	OR
1988	Roger Kingdom, USA	12.98	OR
1992	Mark McKoy, CAN	13.12	
1996	Allen Johnson, USA	12.95	OR

400-meter Hurdles

Year		Time		Year		Time	
1900	John Walter Tewksbury, USA	57.6		1960	Glenn Davis, USA	49.3	OR
1904	Harry Hillman, USA	53.0		1964	Rex Cawley, USA	49.6	
1908	Charley Bacon, USA	55.0	WR	1968	David Hemery, GBR	48.12	WR
1920	Frank Loomis, USA	54.0	WR	1972	John Akii-Bua, UGA	47.82	WR
1924	Morgan Taylor, USA	52.6		1976	Edwin Moses, USA	47.64	WR
1928	David Burghley, GBR	53.4	OR	1980	Volker Beck, E. Ger	48.70	
1932	Bob Tisdall, IRE	51.7		1984	Edwin Moses, USA	47.75	
1936	Glenn Hardin, USA	52.4		1988	Andre Phillips, USA	47.19	OR
1948	Roy Cochran, USA	51.1	OR	1992	Kevin Young, USA	46.78	WR
1952	Charley Moore, USA	50.8	OR	1996	Derrick Adkins, USA	47.54	
1956	Glenn Davis, USA	50.1	=OR				

3000-meter Steeplechase

Year		Time		Year		Time	
1900	George Orton, CAN	7:34.4		1960	Zdzislaw Krzyszkowiak, POL	8:34.2	OR
1904	Jim Lightbody, USA	7:39.6		1964	Gaston Roelants, BEL	8:30.8	OR
1908	Arthur Russell, GBR	10:47.8		1968	Amos Biwott, KEN	8:51.0	
1920	Percy Hodge, GBR	10:00.4	OR	1972	Kip Keino, KEN	8:23.6	OR
1924	Ville Ritola, FIN	9:33.6	OR	1976	Anders Gärderud, SWE	8:08.2	WR
1928	Toivo Loukola, FIN	9:21.8	WR	1980	Bronislaw Malinowski, POL	8:09.7	
1932	Volmari Iso-Hollo, FIN	10:33.4*		1984	Julius Korir, KEN	8:11.80	
1936	Volmari Iso-Hollo, FIN	9:03.8	WR	1988	Julius Kariuki, KEN	8:05.51	OR
1948	Thore Sjöstrand, SWE	9:04.6		1992	Matthew Birir, KEN	8:08.84	
1952	Horace Ashenfelter, USA	8:45.4	WR	1996	Joseph Keter, KEN	8:07.12	
1956	Chris Brasher, GBR	8:41.2	OR				

*Iso-Hollo ran one extra lap due to lap counter's mistake.
Note: Other steeplechase distances– 2500 meters (1900); 2590 meters (1904); 3200 meters (1908) and 3460 meters (1932).

4x100-meter Relay

Year		Time		Year		Time	
1912	Great Britain	42.4		1964	United States	39.0	WR
1920	United States	42.2	WR	1968	United States	38.23	WR
1924	United States	41.0	=WR	1972	United States	38.19	WR
1928	United States	41.0	=WR	1976	United States	38.33	
1932	United States	40.0	WR	1980	Soviet Union	38.26	
1936	United States	39.8	WR	1984	United States	37.83	WR
1948	United States	40.6		1988	Soviet Union	38.19	
1952	United States	40.1		1992	United States	37.40	WR
1956	United States	39.5	WR	1996	Canada	37.69	
1960	Germany	39.5	=WR				

4x400-meter Relay

Year		Time		Year		Time	
1908	United States	3:29.4		1960	United States	3:02.2	WR
1912	United States	3:16.6	WR	1964	United States	3:00.7	WR
1920	Great Britain	3:22.2		1968	United States	2:56.16	WR
1924	United States	3:16.0	WR	1972	Kenya	2:59.8	
1928	United States	3:14.2	WR	1976	United States	2:58.65	
1932	United States	3:08.2	WR	1980	Soviet Union	3:01.1	
1936	Great Britain	3:09.0		1984	United States	2:57.91	
1948	United States	3:10.4		1988	United States	2:56.16	=WR
1952	Jamaica	3:03.9	WR	1992	United States	2:55.74	WR
1956	United States	3:04.8		1996	United States	2:55.99	

20-kilometer Walk

Year		Time		Year		Time	
1956	Leonid Spirin, USSR	1:31:27.4		1980	Maurizio Damilano, ITA	1:23:35.5	OR
1960	Vladimir Golubnichiy, USSR	1:34:07.2		1984	Ernesto Canto, MEX	1:23:13	OR
1964	Ken Matthews, GBR	1:29:34.0	OR	1988	Jozef Pribilinec, CZE	1:19:57	OR
1968	Vladimir Golubnichiy, USSR	1:33:58.4		1992	Daniel Plaza Montero, SPA	1:21:45	
1972	Peter Frenkel, E. Ger	1:26:42.4	OR	1996	Jefferson Perez, ECU	1:20:07	
1976	Daniel Bautista, MEX	1:24:40.6	OR				

50-kilometer Walk

Year		Time		Year		Time	
1932	Thomas Green, GBR	4:50:10		1972	Bernd Kannenberg, W. Ger	3:56:11.6	OR
1936	Harold Whitlock, GBR	4:30:41.4	OR	1976	Not held		
1948	John Ljunggren, SWE	4:41:52		1980	Hartwig Gauder, E. Ger	3:49:24.0	OR
1952	Giuseppe Dordoni, ITA	4:28:07.8	OR	1984	Raul Gonzalez, MEX	3:47:26	OR
1956	Norman Read, NZE	4:30:42.8		1988	Vyacheslav Ivanenko, USSR	3:38:29	OR
1960	Don Thompson, GBR	4:25:30.0	OR	1992	Andrei Perlov, UT	3:50:13	
1964	Abdon Pamich, ITA	4:11:12.4	OR	1996	Robert Korzeniowski, POL	3:43:30	
1968	Christoph Höhne, E. Ger	4:20:13.6					

Track & Field (Cont.)

High Jump

Year		Height		Year		Height	
1896	Ellery Clark, USA	5-11¼		1952	Walt Davis, USA	6- 8½	OR
1900	Irving Baxter, USA	6- 2¾	OR	1956	Charley Dumas, USA	6-11½	OR
1904	Sam Jones, USA	5-11		1960	Robert Shavlakadze, USSR	7- 1	OR
1906	Cornelius Leahy, GBR/IRE	5-10		1964	Valery Brumel, USSR	7- 1¾	OR
1908	Harry Porter, USA	6- 3	OR	1968	Dick Fosbury, USA	7- 4¼	OR
1912	Alma Richards, USA	6- 4	OR	1972	Yuri Tarmak, USSR	7- 3¾	
1920	Richmond Landon, USA	6- 4	=OR	1976	Jacek Wszola, POL	7- 4½	OR
1924	Harold Osborn, USA	6- 6	OR	1980	Gerd Wessig, E. Ger	7- 8¾	WR
1928	Bob King, USA	6- 4½		1984	Dietmar Mögenburg, W. Ger	7- 8½	
1932	Duncan McNaughton, CAN	6- 5½		1988	Gennady Avdeyenko, USSR	7- 9¾	OR
1936	Cornelius Johnson, USA	6- 8	OR	1992	Javier Sotomayor, CUB	7- 8	
1948	John Winter, AUS	6- 6		1996	Charles Austin, USA	7-10	OR

Pole Vault

Year		Height		Year		Height	
1896	William Hoyt, USA	10-10		1952	Bob Richards, USA	14-11	OR
1900	Irving Baxter, USA	10-10		1956	Bob Richards, USA	14-11½	OR
1904	Charles Dvorak, USA	11- 5¾		1960	Don Bragg, USA	15- 5	OR
1906	Fernand Gonder, FRA	11- 5¾		1964	Fred Hansen, USA	16- 8¾	OR
1908	(TIE) Edward Cooke, USA	12- 2		1968	Bob Seagren, USA	17- 8½	OR
	Alfred Gilbert, USA	12- 2	OR	1972	Wolfgang Nordwig, E. Ger	18- 0½	OR
1912	Harry Babcock, USA	12-11½	OR	1976	Tadeusz Slusarski, POL	18- 0½	=OR
1920	Frank Foss, USA	13- 5	WR	1980	Wladyslaw Kozakiewicz, POL	18-11½	WR
1924	Lee Barnes, USA	12-11½		1984	Pierre Quinon, FRA	18-10¼	
1928	Sabin Carr, USA	13- 9¼	OR	1988	Sergey Bubka, USSR	19- 4¼	OR
1932	Bill Miller, USA	14- 1¾	OR	1992	Maksim Tarasov, UT	19- 0¼	
1936	Earle Meadows, USA	14- 3¼	OR	1996	Jean Galfione, FRA	19-5¼	
1948	Guinn Smith, USA	14- 1¼					

Long Jump

Year		Distance		Year		Distance	
1896	Ellery Clark, USA	20-10		1952	Jerome Biffle, USA	24-10	
1900	Alvin Kraenzlein, USA	23- 6¾	OR	1956	Greg Bell, USA	25- 8¼	
1904	Meyer Prinstein, USA	24- 1	OR	1960	Ralph Boston, USA	26- 7¾	OR
1906	Meyer Prinstein, USA	23- 7½		1964	Lynn Davies, GBR	26- 5¾	
1908	Frank Irons, USA	24- 6½	OR	1968	Bob Beamon, USA	29- 2½	WR
1912	Albert Gutterson, USA	24-11¼	OR	1972	Randy Williams, USA	27- 0½	
1920	William Petersson, SWE	23- 5½		1976	Arnie Robinson, USA	27- 4¾	
1924	De Hart Hubbard, USA	24- 5		1980	Lutz Dombrowski, E. Ger	28- 0¼	
1928	Ed Hamm, USA	25- 4½	OR	1984	Carl Lewis, USA	28- 0¼	
1932	Ed Gordon, USA	25- 0¾		1988	Carl Lewis, USA	28- 7¼	
1936	Jesse Owens, USA	26- 5½	OR	1992	Carl Lewis, USA	28- 5½	
1948	Willie Steele, USA	25- 8		1996	Carl Lewis, USA	27-10¾	

Triple Jump

Year		Distance		Year		Distance	
1896	James Connolly, USA	44-11¾		1952	Adhemar da Silva, BRA	53- 2¾	WR
1900	Meyer Prinstein, USA	47- 5¾	OR	1956	Adhemar da Silva, BRA	53- 7¾	OR
1904	Meyer Prinstein, USA	47- 1		1960	Józef Schmidt, POL	55- 2	
1906	Peter O'Connor, GBR/IRE	46- 2¼		1964	Józef Schmidt, POL	55- 3½	OR
1908	Timothy Ahearne, GBR/IRE	48-11¼	OR	1968	Viktor Saneyev, USSR	57- 0¾	WR
1912	Gustaf Lindblom, SWE	48- 5¼		1972	Viktor Saneyev, USSR	56-11¼	
1920	Vilho Tuulos, FIN	47- 7		1976	Viktor Saneyev, USSR	56- 8¾	
1924	Nick Winter, AUS	50-11¼	WR	1980	Jaak Uudmäe, USSR	56-11¼	
1928	Mikio Oda, JPN	49-11		1984	Al Joyner, USA	56- 7½	
1932	Chuhei Nambu, JPN	51- 7	WR	1988	Khristo Markov, BUL	57- 9¼	OR
1936	Naoto Tajima, JPN	52- 6	WR	1992	Mike Conley, USA	57-10¼	OR
1948	Arne Ahman, SWE	50- 6¼		1996	Kenny Harrison, USA	59-4¼	OR

Shot Put

Year		Distance		Year		Distance	
1896	Bob Garrett, USA	36- 9¾		1928	John Kuck, USA	52- 0¾	WR
1900	Richard Sheldon, USA	46- 3¼	OR	1932	Leo Sexton, USA	52- 6	OR
1904	Ralph Rose, USA	48- 7	WR	1936	Hans Woellke, GER	53- 1¾	OR
1906	Martin Sheridan, USA	40- 5¼		1948	Wilbur Thompson, USA	56- 2	OR
1908	Ralph Rose, USA	46- 7½		1952	Parry O'Brien, USA	57- 1½	OR
1912	Patrick McDonald, USA	50- 4	OR	1956	Parry O'Brien, USA	60-11¼	OR
1920	Ville Pörhölä, FIN	48- 7¼		1960	Bill Nieder, USA	64- 6¾	OR
1924	Bud Houser, USA	49- 2¼		1964	Dallas Long, USA	66- 8½	OR

Year		Distance		Year		Distance	
1968	Randy Matson, USA	67- 4¾		1984	Alessandro Andrei, ITA	69- 9	
1972	Wladyslaw Komar, POL	69- 6	OR	1988	Ulf Timmermann, E. Ger	73- 8¾	OR
1976	Udo Beyer, E. Ger	69- 0¾		1992	Mike Stulce, USA	71- 2½	
1980	Vladimir Kiselyov, USSR	70- 0½	OR	1996	Randy Barnes, USA	70-11¼	

Discus Throw

Year		Distance		Year		Distance	
1896	Bob Garrett, USA	95- 7½		1952	Sim Iness, USA	180- 6	OR
1900	Rudolf Bauer, HUN	118- 3	OR	1956	Al Oerter, USA	184-11	OR
1904	Martin Sheridan, USA	128-10½	OR	1960	Al Oerter, USA	194- 2	OR
1906	Martin Sheridan, USA	136- 0		1964	Al Oerter, USA	200- 1	OR
1908	Martin Sheridan, USA	134- 2	OR	1968	Al Oerter, USA	212- 6	OR
1912	Armas Taipale, FIN	148- 3	OR	1972	Ludvik Danek, CZE	211- 3	
1920	Elmer Niklander, FIN	146- 7		1976	Mac Wilkins, USA	221- 5	
1924	Bud Houser, USA	151- 4	OR	1980	Viktor Rashchupkin, USSR	218- 8	
1928	Bud Houser, USA	155- 3	OR	1984	Rolf Danneberg, W. Ger	218- 6	
1932	John Anderson, USA	162- 4	OR	1988	Jürgen Schult, E. Ger	225- 9	OR
1936	Ken Carpenter, USA	165- 7	OR	1992	Romas Ubartas, LIT	213- 8	
1948	Adolfo Consolini, ITA	173- 2	OR	1996	Lars Riedel, GER	227-8	

Hammer Throw

Year		Distance		Year		Distance	
1900	John Flanagan, USA	163- 1		1956	Harold Connolly, USA	207- 3	OR
1904	John Flanagan, USA	168- 1	OR	1960	Vasily Rudenkov, USSR	220- 2	OR
1908	John Flanagan, USA	170- 4	OR	1964	Romuald Klim, USSR	228-10	OR
1912	Matt McGrath, USA	179- 7	OR	1968	Gyula Zsivótzky, HUN	240- 8	OR
1920	Pat Ryan, USA	173- 5		1972	Anatoly Bondarchuk, USSR	247- 8	OR
1924	Fred Tootell, USA	174-10		1976	Yuri Sedykh, USSR	254- 4	OR
1928	Pat O'Callaghan, IRE	168- 7		1980	Yuri Sedykh, USSR	268- 4	WR
1932	Pat O'Callaghan, IRE	176-11		1984	Juha Tiainen, FIN	256- 2	
1936	Karl Hein, GER	185- 4	OR	1988	Sergey Litvinov, USSR	278- 2	OR
1948	Imre Németh, HUN	183-11		1992	Andrei Abduvaliyev, UT	270- 9	
1952	József Csérmák, HUN	197-11	WR	1996	Balazs Kiss, HUN	266-6	

Javelin Throw

Year		Distance		Year		Distance	
1908	Eric Lemming, SWE	179-10	WR	1960	Viktor Tsibulenko, USSR	277- 8	
1912	Eric Lemming, SWE	198-11	WR	1964	Pauli Nevala, FIN	271- 2	
1920	Jonni Myyrä, FIN	215-10	OR	1968	Jänis Lüsis, USSR	295- 7	OR
1924	Jonni Myyrä, FIN	206- 7		1972	Klaus Wolfermann, W. Ger	296-10	OR
1928	Erik Lundkvist, SWE	218- 6	OR	1976	Miklos Németh, HUN	310- 4	WR
1932	Matti Järvinen, FIN	238- 6	OR	1980	Dainis Kla, USSR	299- 2	
1936	Gerhard Stöck, GER	235- 8		1984	Arto Härkönen, FIN	284- 8	
1948	Kai Tapio Rautavaara, FIN	228-10		1988	Tapio Korjus, FIN	276- 6	
1952	Cy Young, USA	242- 1	OR	1992	Jan Zelezny, CZE	294- 2*	OR
1956	Egil Danielson, NOR	281- 2	WR	1996	Jan Zelezny, CZE	289-3	

*In 1986 the balance point of the javelin was modified and new records have been kept since.

Decathlon

Year		Points		Year		Points	
1904	Thomas Kiely, IRL	6036		1960	Rafer Johnson, USA	8392	OR
1906-08 Not held				1964	Willi Holdorf, GER	7887	
1912	Jim Thrope, USA	8412	WR	1968	Bill Toomey, USA	8193	OR
1920	Helge Lövland, NOR	6803		1972	Nikolai Avilov, USSR	8454	WR
1924	Harold Osborn, USA	7711	WR	1976	Bruce Jenner, USA	8617	WR
1928	Paavo Yrjölä, FIN	8053	WR	1980	Daley Thompson, GBR	8495	
1932	Jim Bausch, USA	8462	WR	1984	Daley Thompson, GBR	8798	=WR
1936	Glenn Morris, USA	7900	WR	1988	Christian Schenk, E. Ger	8488	
1948	Bob Mathias, USA	7139		1992	Robert Zmelik, CZE	8611	
1952	Bob Mathias, USA	7887	WR	1996	Dan O'Brien, USA	8824	
1956	Milt Campbell, USA	7937	OR				

WOMEN

At least 4 gold medals (including relays): Evelyn Ashford, Fanny Blankers-Koen, Betty Cuthbert and Bärbel Eckert Wöckel (4).

100 meters

Year		Time		Year		Time	
1928	Betty Robinson, USA	12.2	=WR	1952	Marjorie Jackson, AUS	11.5	=WR
1932	Stella Walsh, POL*	11.9	=WR	1956	Betty Cuthbert, AUS	11.5	
1936	Helen Stephens, USA	11.5w		1960	Wilma Rudolph, USA	11.0w	
1948	Fanny Blankers-Koen, HOL	11.9		1964	Wyomia Tyus, USA	11.4	

Track & Field (Cont.)

Year		Time	
1968	Wyomia Tyus, USA	11.08	WR
1972	Renate Stecher, E. Ger	11.07	
1976	Annegret Richter, W. Ger	11.08	

Year		Time	
1980	Lyudmila Kondratyeva, USSR	11.06	
1984	Evelyn Ashford, USA	10.97	OR
1988	Florence Griffith Joyner, USA	10.54w	
1992	Gail Devers, USA	10.82	OR
1996	Gail Devers, USA	10.94	

*An autopsy performed after Walsh's death in 1980 revealed that she was a man.
w indicates wind-aided.

200 meters

Year		Time	
1948	Fanny Blankers-Koen, HOL	24.4	
1952	Marjorie Jackson, AUS	23.7	OR
1956	Betty Cuthbert, AUS	23.4	=OR
1960	Wilma Rudolph, USA	24.0	
1964	Edith McGuire, USA	23.0	OR
1968	Irena Szewinska, POL	22.5	WR
1972	Renate Stecher, E. Ger	22.40	=WR

Year		Time	
1976	Bärbel Eckert, E. Ger	22.37	OR
1980	Bärbel Eckert Wockel, E. Ger	22.03	OR
1984	Valerie Brisco-Hooks, USA	21.81	OR
1988	Florence Griffith Joyner, USA	21.34	WR
1992	Gwen Torrence, USA	21.81	
1996	Marie-Jose Perec, FRA	22.12	

400 meters

Year		Time	
1964	Betty Cuthbert, AUS	52.0	
1968	Colette Besson, FRA	52.03	=OR
1972	Monika Zehrt, E. Ger	51.08	OR
1976	Irena Szewinska, POL	49.29	WR
1980	Marita Koch, E. Ger	48.88	OR

Year		Time	
1984	Valerie Brisco-Hooks, USA	48.83	OR
1988	Olga Bryzgina, USSR	48.65	OR
1992	Marie-Jose Perec, FRA	48.83	
1996	Marie-Jose Perec, FRA	48.25	OR

800 meters

Year		Time	
1928	Lina Radke, GER	2:16.8	WR
1932-56	Not held		
1960	Lyudmila Shevtsova, USSR	2:04.3	=WR
1964	Ann Packer, GBR	2:01.1	OR
1968	Madeline Manning, USA	2:00.9	OR
1972	Hildegard Falck, W. Ger	1:58.55	OR

Year		Time	
1976	Tatyana Kazankina, USSR	1:54.94	WR
1980	Nadezhda Olizarenko, USSR	1:53.42	WR
1984	Doina Melinte, ROM	1:57.60	
1988	Sigrun Wodars, E. Ger	1:56.10	
1992	Ellen van Langen, HOL	1:55.54	
1996	Svetlana Masterkova, RUS	1:57.73	

1500 meters

Year		Time	
1972	Lyudmila Bragina, USSR	4:01.4	WR
1976	Tatyana Kazankina, USSR	4:05.48	
1980	Tatyana Kazankina, USSR	3:56.6	OR
1984	Gabriella Dorio, ITA	4:03.25	

Year		Time	
1988	Paula Ivan, ROM	3:53.96	OR
1992	Hassiba Boulmerka, ALG	3:55.30	
1996	Svetlana Masterkova, RUS	4:00.83	

5000 meters

Year		Time	
1984	Maricica Puica, ROM	8:35.96	
1988	Tatyana Samolenko, USSR	8:26.53	OR
1992	Elena Romanova, UT	8:46.04	

Year		Time
1996	Wang Junxia, CHN	14:59.88

Note: Event held over 3000 meters from 1984-92.

10,000 meters

Year		Time	
1988	Olga Bondarenko, USSR	31:05.21	OR
1992	Derartu Tulu, ETH	31:06.02	

Year		Time	
1996	Fernanda Ribeiro, POR	31:01.63	OR

Marathon

Year		Time
1984	Joan Benoit, USA	2:24:52
1988	Rosa Mota, POR	2:25:40

Year		Time
1992	Valentina Yegorova, UT	2:32:41
1996	Fatuma Roba, ETH	2:26:05

100-meter Hurdles

Year		Time	
1932	Babe Didrikson, USA	11.7	WR
1936	Trebisonda Valla, ITA	11.7	
1948	Fanny Blankers-Koen, HOL	11.2	OR
1952	Shirley Strickland, AUS	10.9	WR
1956	Shirley Strickland, AUS	10.7	OR
1960	Irina Press, USSR	10.8	
1964	Karin Balzer, GER	10.5w	
1968	Maureen Caird, AUS	10.3	OR
1972	Annelie Ehrhardt, E. Ger	12.59	WR

Year		Time	
1976	Johanna Schaller, E. Ger	12.77	
1980	Vera Komisova, USSR	12.56	OR
1984	Benita Fitzgerald-Brown, USA	12.84	
1988	Yordanka Donkova, BUL	12.38	OR
1992	Paraskevi Patoulidou, GRE	12.64	
1996	Ludmila Enquist, SWE	12.58	

w indicates wind-aided.

Note: Event held over 80 meters from 1932-68.

400-meter Hurdles

Year		Time	
1984	Nawal El Moutawakel, MOR	54.61	OR
1988	Debra Flintoff-King, AUS	53.17	OR

Year		Time	
1992	Sally Gunnell, GBR	53.23	
1996	Deon Hemmings, JAM	52.82	OR

4x100-meter Relay

Year		Time		Year		Time	
1928	Canada	48.4	WR	1968	United States	42.87	WR
1932	United States	46.9	WR	1972	West Germany	42.81	WR
1936	United States	46.9		1976	East Germany	42.55	OR
1948	Holland	47.5		1980	East Germany	41.60	WR
1952	United States	45.9	WR	1984	United States	41.65	
1956	Australia	44.5	WR	1988	United States	41.98	
1960	United States	44.5		1992	United States	42.11	
1964	Poland	43.6		1996	United States	41.95	

4x400-meter Relay

Year		Time		Year		Time	
1972	East Germany	3:23.0	WR	1988	Soviet Union	3:15.18	WR
1976	East Germany	3:19.23	WR	1992	Unified Team	3:20.20	
1980	Soviet Union	3:20.2		1996	United States	3:20.91	
1984	United States	3:18.29	OR				

10-kilometer Walk

Year		Time	Year		Time
1992	Chen Yueling, CHN	44:32	1996	Yelena Ninikolayeva, RUS	41:49

High Jump

Year		Height		Year		Height	
1928	Ethel Catherwood, CAN	5- 2½		1968	Miloslava Rezkova, CZE	5-11½	
1932	Jean Shiley, USA	5- 5¼	WR	1972	Ulrike Meyfarth, W. Ger	6- 3½	=WR
1936	Ibolya Csák, HUN	5- 3		1976	Rosemarie Ackermann, E. Ger	6- 4	OR
1948	Alice Coachman, USA	5- 6		1980	Sara Simeoni, ITA	6- 5½	OR
1952	Esther Brand, SAF	5- 5¾		1984	Ulrike Meyfarth, W. Ger	6- 7½	OR
1956	Mildred McDaniel, USA	5- 9¼	WR .	1988	Louise Ritter, USA	6- 8	OR
1960	Iolanda Balas, ROM	6- 0¾	OR	1992	Heike Henkel, GER	6- 7½	
1964	Iolanda Balas, ROM	6- 2¾	OR	1996	Stefka Kostadinova, BUL	6-8¾	

Long Jump

Year		Distance		Year		Distance	
1948	Olga Gyarmati, HUN	18- 8¼		1976	Angela Voigt, E. Ger	22- 0¾	
1952	Yvette Williams, NZE	20- 5¾	OR	1980	Tatyana Kolpakova, USSR	23- 2	OR
1956	Elzbieta Krzesinska, POL	20-10	=WR	1984	Anisoara Cusmir-Stanciu, ROM	22-10	
1960	Vyera Krepkina, USSR	20-10¾	OR	1988	Jackie Joyner-Kersee, USA	24- 3¼	OR
1964	Mary Rand, GBR	22- 2¼	WR	1992	Heike Drechsler, GER	23- 5¼	
1968	Viorica Viscopoleanu, ROM	22- 4½	WR	1996	Chioma Ajunwa, NGR	23-4½	
1972	Heidemarie Rosendahl, W. Ger	22- 3					

Triple Jump

Year		Distance
1996	Inessa Kravets, UKR	50-3½

Shot Put

Year		Distance		Year		Distance	
1948	Micheline Ostermeyer, FRA	45- 1½		1976	Ivanka Hristova, BUL	69- 5¼	OR
1952	Galina Zybina, USSR	50- 1¾	WR	1980	Ilona Slupianek, E. Ger	73- 6¼	OR
1956	Tamara Tyshkevich, USSR	54- 5	OR	1984	Claudia Losch, W. Ger	67- 2¼	
1960	Tamara Press, USSR	56-10	OR	1988	Natalia Lisovskaya, USSR	72-11¾	
1964	Tamara Press, USSR	59- 6¼	OR	1992	Svetlana Krivaleva, UT	69- 1¼	
1968	Margitta Gummel, E. Ger	64- 4	WR	1996	Astrid Kumbernuss, GER	67-5½	
1972	Nadezhda Chizhova, USSR	69- 0	WR				

Discus Throw

Year		Distance		Year		Distance	
1928	Halina Konopacka, POL	129-11¾	WR	1968	Lia Manoliu, ROM	191- 2	OR
1932	Lillian Copeland, USA	133- 2	OR	1972	Faina Melnik, USSR	218- 7	OR
1936	Gisela Mauermayer, GER	156- 3	OR	1976	Evelin Schlaak, E. Ger	226- 4	OR
1948	Micheline Ostermeyer, FRA	137- 6		1980	Evelin Schlaak Jahl, E. Ger	229- 6	OR
1952	Nina Romaschkova, USSR	168- 8	OR	1984	Ria Stalman, HOL	214- 5	
1956	Olga Fikotová, CZE	176- 1	OR	1988	Martina Hellmann, E. Ger	237- 2½	OR
1960	Nina Ponomaryeva, USSR	180- 9	OR	1992	Maritza Marten, CUB	229-10	
1964	Tamara Press, USSR	187-10	OR	1996	Ilke Wyludda, GER	228-6	

Javelin Throw

Year		Distance		Year		Distance	
1932	Babe Didrikson, USA	143- 4		1960	Elvira Ozolina, USSR	183- 8	OR
1936	Tilly Fleischer, GER	148- 3	OR	1964	Mihaela Penes, ROM	198- 7	OR
1948	Herma Bauma, AUT	149- 6	OR	1968	Angéla Németh, HUN	198- 0	
1952	Dana Zátopková, CZE	165- 7	OR	1972	Ruth Fuchs, E. Ger	209- 7	OR
1956	Ineze Jaunzeme, USSR	176- 8	OR	1976	Ruth Fuchs, E. Ger	216- 4	OR

Track & Field (Cont.)

Year		Distance	
1980	Maria Colon Rueñes, CUB	224- 5	**OR**
1984	Tessa Sanderson, GBR	228- 2	**OR**

Year		Distance	
1988	Petra Felke, E. Ger	245- 0	**OR**
1992	Silke Renk, GER	224- 2	
1996	Heli Rantanen, FIN	222-11	

Heptathlon

Year		Points	
1964	Irina Press, USSR	5246	**WR**
1968	Ingrid Becker, W. Ger	5098	
1972	Mary Peters, GBR	4801	**WR**
1976	Siegrun Siegl, E. Ger	4745	
1980	Nadezhda Tkachenko, USSR	5083	**WR**

Year		Points	
1984	Glynis Nunn, AUS	6390	**OR**
1988	Jackie Joyner-Kersee, USA	7291	**WR**
1992	Jackie Joyner-Kersee, USA	7044	
1996	Ghada Shouaa, SYR	6780	

Note: Seven-event Heptathlon replaced five-event Pentathlon in 1984.

All-Time Leading Medal Winners – Single Games

Athletes who have won the most medals in a single Summer Olympics through Atlanta in 1996. Note that totals include individual, relay and team medals. U.S. athletes are in **bold** type.

MEN

No		Sport	G-S-B
8	Aleksandr Dityatin, USSR (1980)	Gym	3-4-1
7	**Mark Spitz** , USA (1976)	Swim	7-0-0
7	**Willis Lee** , USA (1920)	Shoot	5-1-1
7	**Matt Biondi** , USA (1988)	Swim	5-1-1
7	Boris Shakhlin, USSR (1960)	Gym	4-2-1
7	**Lloyd Spooner** , USA (1920)	Shoot	4-1-2
7	Mikhail Voronin, USSR (1968)	Gym	2-4-1
7	Nikolai Andrianov, USSR (1976)	Gym	2-4-1
6	Vitaly Scherbo, UT (1992)	Gym	6-0-0
6	Li Ning, CHN (1984)	Gym	3-2-1
6	Akinori Nakayama, JPN (1968)	Gym	4-1-1
6	Takashi Ono, JPN (1960)	Gym	3-1-2
6	Viktor Chukarin, USSR (1956)	Gym	4-2-0
6	Konrad Frey, GER (1936)	Gym	3-1-2
6	Ville Ritola, FIN (1924)	Track	4-2-0
6	Hubert Van Innis, BEL (1920)	Arch	4-2-0
6	**Carl Osburn** , USA (1920)	Shoot	4-1-1
6	Louis Richardet, SWI (1906)	Shoot	3-3-0
6	**Anton Heida** , USA (1904)	Gym	5-1-0
6	**George Eyser** , USA (1904)	Gym	3-2-1
6	**Burton Downing** , USA (1904)	Cycle	2-3-1
6	Alexei Nemov, RUS (1996)	Gym	2-1-3

WOMEN

No		Sport	G-S-B
7	Maria Gorokhovskaya, USSR (1952)	Gym	2-5-0
6	Kristin Otto, E. Ger (1988)	Swim	6-0-0
6	Agnes Keleti, HUN (1956)	Gym	4-2-0
6	Vera Cáslavská, CZE (1968)	Gym	4-2-0
6	Larisa Latynina, USSR (1956)	Gym	4-1-1
6	Larisa Latynina, USSR (1960)	Gym	3-2-1
6	Daniela Silivas, ROM (1988)	Gym	3-2-1
6	Larisa Latynina, USSR (1964)	Gym	2-2-2
6	Margit Korondi, HUN, (1956)	Gym	1-1-4
6	Kornelia Ender, E. Ger (1976)	Swim	4-1-0
6	Ecaterina Szabó, ROM (1984)	Gym	4-1-0
5	Shane Gould, AUS (1972)	Swim	3-1-1
5	Nadia Comaneci, ROM (1976)	Gym	3-1-1
5	Karin Janz, E. Ger (1972)	Gym	2-2-1
5	Ines Diers, E. Ger (1980)	Swim	2-2-1
5	**Shirley Babashoff**, USA (1976)	Swim	1-4-0
5	**Mary Lou Retton**, USA (1984)	Gym	1-2-2
5	**Shannon Miller**, USA (1992)	Gym	0-2-3

All-Time Leading Medal Winners – Career

All Nations

Most Overall Medals

MEN

No		Sport	G-S-B
15	Nikolai Andrianov, USSR	Gymnastics	7-5-3
13	Boris Shakhlin, USSR	Gymnastics	7-4-2
13	Edoardo Mangiarotti, ITA	Fencing	6-5-2
13	Takashi Ono, JPN	Gymnastics	5-4-4
12	Paavo Nurmi, FIN	Track/Field	9-3-0
12	Sawao Kato, JPN	Gymnastics	8-3-1
11	**Mark Spitz**, USA	Swimming	9-1-1
11*	**Matt Biondi**, USA	Swimming	8-2-1
11	Viktor Chukarin, USSR	Gymnastics	7-3-1
11	**Carl Osburn**, USA	Shooting	5-4-2

No		Sport	G-S-B
10	**Ray Ewry**, USA	Track/Field	10-0-0
10	**Carl Lewis**, USA	Track/Field	9-1-0
10	Aladár Gerevich, HUN	Fencing	7-1-2
10	Akinori Nakayama, JPN	Gymnastics	6-2-2
10	Aleksandr Dityatin, USSR	Gymnastics	3-6-1
9	Vitaly Scherbo, BLR	Gymnastics	6-0-3
9	**Martin Sheridan**, USA	Track/Field	5-3-1
9	Zoltán Halmay, HUN	Swimming	3-5-1
9	Giulio Gaudini, ITA	Fencing	3-4-2
9	Mikhail Voronin, USSR	Gymnastics	2-6-1
9	Heikki Savolainen, FIN	Gymnastics	2-1-6
9	Yuri Titov, USSR	Gymnastics	1-5-3

* Includes gold medal as preliminary member of 1st-place relay team.
Note: Medals won by Ewry (2-0-0), Sheridan (2-3-0) and Halmay (1-1-0) at the 1906 Intercalated games are not officially recognized by the IOC.

Games Participated In

Andrianov (1972,76,80); **Biondi** (1984,88,92); **Chukarin** (1952,56); **Dityatin** (1976,80); **Ewry** (1900,04,06,08); **Gerevich** (1932,36,48,52,56,60); **Gaudini** (1928,32,36); **Halmay** (1900,04,06,08); **Kato** (1968,72,76); **Lewis** (1984,88,92,96); **Mangiarotti** (1936,48,52,56,60); **Nakayama** (1968,72); **Nurmi** (1920,24,28); **Ono** (1952,56,60,64); **Osburn** (1912,20, 24); **Savolainen** (1928,32,36,48,52); **Scherbo** (1992,96); **Shakhlin** (1956,60,64); **Sheridan** (1904,06,08); **Spitz** (1968,72); **Titov** (1956,60,64); **Voronin** (1968,72).

WOMEN

No		Sport	G-S-B
18	Larissa Latynina, USSR ....Gymnastics		9-5-4
11	Vera Cáslavská, CZE ....Gymnastics		7-4-0
10	Agnes Keleti, HUN ....Gymnastics		5-3-2
10	Polina Astaknova, USSR ....Gymnastics		5-2-3
9	Nadia Comaneci, ROM ....Gymnastics		5-3-1
9	Lyudmila Touristcheva, USSR ......Gymnastics		4-3-2
8	Kornelia Ender, E. Ger ....Swimming		4-4-0
8	Dawn Fraser, AUS ....Swimming		4-4-0
8	**Shirley Babashoff**, USA ....Swimming		2-6-0
8	Sofia Muratova, USSR ....Gymnastics		2-2-4
7	Krisztina Egerszegi, HUN ....Swimming		5-1-1
7	Irena Kirszenstein Szewinska, POL .Track/Field		3-2-2
7	Shirley Strickland, AUS ....Track/Field		3-1-3
7	Maria Gorokhovskaya, USSR ....Gymnastics		2-5-0
7	Ildikó Ságiné-Uilaki-Rejtö, HUN ......Fencing		2-3-2
7	**Shannon Miller**, USA ....Gymnastics		2-2-3
7	Merlene Ottey, JAM ....Track/Field		0-2-5

Games Participated In

Astaknova (1956,60,64); **Babashoff** (1972,76); **Cáslavská** (1960,64,68); **Comaneci** (1976,80); **Egerszegi** (1988,92,96) **Ender** (1972,76); **Fraser** (1956,60,64); **Gorokhovskaya** (1952); **Keleti** (1952,56); **Latynina** (1956,60,64); **Miller** (1992,96); **Muratova** (1956,60); **Ottey** (1980,84,88,92,96) **Sdáginé-Uilaki-Rejtä** (1960,64,68,72,76); **Strickland** (1948,52,56); **Szewinska** (1964,68,72,76,80); **Tourischeva** (1968, 72,76).

Most Individual Medals
Not including team competition.

		Sport	G-S-B
Men:	12-Nikolai Andrianov, USSR ...Gym		6-3-3
Women:	14-Larissa Latynina, USSR ...Gym		7-4-3

Most Gold Medals
MEN

No		Sport	G-S-B
10	**Ray Ewry**, USA ....Track/Field		10-0-0
9	Paavo Nurmi, FIN ....Track/Field		9-3-0
9	**Mark Spitz**, USA ....Swimming		9-1-1
9	**Carl Lewis**, USA ....Track/Field		9-1-0
8	Sawao Kato, JPN ....Gymnastics		8-3-1
8*	**Matt Biondi**, USA ....Swimming		8-2-1
7	Nikolai Andrianov, USSR ....Gymnastics		7-5-3
7	Boris Shakhlin, USSR ....Gymnastics		7-4-2
7	Viktor Chukarin, USSR ....Gymnastics		7-3-1
7	Aladar Gerevich, HUN ....Fencing		7-1-2

* Includes gold medal as preliminary member of 1st-place relay team.

WOMEN

No		Sport	G-S-B
9	Larissa Latynina, USSR ....Gymnastics		9-5-4
7	Vera Cáslavská, CZE ....Gymnastics		7-4-0
6	Kristin Otto, E. Ger ....Swimming		6-0-0
5	Agnes Keleti, HUN ....Gymnastics		5-3-2
5	Nadia Comaneci, ROM ....Gymnastics		5-3-1
5	Polina Astaknova, USSR ....Gymnastics		5-2-3
5	Krisztina Egerszegi, HUN ....Swimming		5-1-1
5	**Jenny Thompson**, USA ....Swimming		5-1-0
4	Kornelia Ender, E. Ger ....Swimming		4-4-0
4	Dawn Fraser, AUS ....Swimming		4-4-0
4	Lyudmila Touristcheva, USSR ......Gymnastics		4-3-2
4	**Evelyn Ashford**, USA ....Track/Field		4-1-0
4	**Janet Evans**, USA ....Swimming		4-1-0
4	Fanny Blankers-Koen, NET ....Track/Field		4-0-0
4	Betty Cuthbert, AUS ....Track/Field		4-0-0
4	**Pat McCormick**, USA ....Diving		4-0-0
4	**Amy Van Dyken**, USA ....Swimming		4-0-0
4	Bärbel Eckert Wäckel, E. Ger. ....Track/Field		4-0-0

Most Silver Medals
MEN

No		Sport	G-S-B
6	Alexandr Dityatin, USSR ....Gymnastics		3-6-1
6	Mikhail Voronin, USSR ....Gymnastics		2-6-1
5	Nikolai Andrianov, USSR ....Gymnastics		7-5-3
5	Edoardo Mangiarotti, ITA ....Fencing		6-5-2
5	Zoltán Halmay, HUN ....Swimming		3-5-1
5	Gustavo Marzi, ITA ....Fencing		2-5-0
5	Yuri Titov, USSR ....Gymnastics		1-5-3
5	Viktor Lisitsky, USSR ....Gymnastics		0-5-0

WOMEN

No		Sport	G-S-B
6	**Shirley Babashoff**, USA ....Swimming		2-6-0
5	Larissa Latynina, USSR ....Gymnastics		9-5-4
5	Maria Gorokhovskaya, USSR ....Gymnastics		2-5-0
4	Vera Cáslavská, CZE ....Gymnastics		7-4-0
4	Kornelia Ender, E. Ger ....Swimming		4-4-0
4	Dawn Fraser, AUS ....Swimming		4-4-0
4	Erica Zuchold, E. Ger ....Gymnastics		0-4-1

Most Bronze Medals
MEN

No		Sport	G-S-B
6	Heikki Savolainen, FIN ....Gymnastics		2-1-6
5	Daniel Revenu, FRA ....Fencing		1-0-5
5	Philip Edwards, CAN ....Track/Field		0-0-5
5	Adrianus Jong, NET ....Fencing		0-0-5

WOMEN

No		Sport	G-S-B
5	Merlene Ottey, JAM ....Track/Field		0-2-5
4	Larissa Latynina, USSR ....Gymnastics		9-5-4
4	Sofia Muratova, USSR ....Gymnastics		2-2-4

All-Time Leading USA Medal Winners
Most Overall Medals
MEN

No		Sport	G-S-B
11	Mark Spitz ....Swimming		9-1-1
11*	Matt Biondi ....Swimming		8-2-1
11	Carl Osburn ....Shooting		5-4-2
10	Ray Ewry ....Track/Field		10-0-0
10	Carl Lewis ....Track/Field		9-1-0
9	Martin Sheridan ....Track/Field		5-3-1
8	Charles Daniels ....Swimming		5-1-2
7†	Tom Jager ....Swimming		5-1-1
7	Willis Lee ....Shooting		5-1-1

No		Sport	G-S-B
7	Lloyd Spooner ....Shooting		4-1-2
6	Anton Heida ....Gymnastics		5-1-0
6	Don Schollander ....Swimming		5-1-0
6	Johnny Weissmuller ....Swim/Water Polo		5-0-1
6	Alfred Lane ....Shooting		5-0-1
6	Jim Lightbody ....Track/Field		4-2-0
6	George Eyser ....Gymnastics		3-2-1
6	Michael Plumb ....Equestrian		2-4-0
6	Burton Downing ....Cycling		2-3-1
6	Bob Garrett ....Track/Field		2-2-2

*Includes gold medal as prelim. member of 1st-place relay team.
†Includes 3 gold medals as prelim. member of 1st-place relay teams.
Note: Medals won by Ewry (2–0–0) and Sheridan (2–3–0) at the 1906 Intercalated games are not officially recognized by the IOC.

Most Overall Medals (Cont.)

Games Participated In

Biondi (1984,88,92); **Daniels** (1904,06,08); **Downing** (1904); **Ewry** (1900,04,06,08); **Eyser** (1904); **Garrett** (1896,1900); **Heida** (1904); **Jager** (1984,88,92); **Lane** (1912,20); **Lee** (1920); **Lewis** (1984,88,92,96); **Lightbody** (1904,06); **Osburn** (1912,20,24); **Plumb** (1960, 64,68,72,76,84); **Schollander** (1964, 68); **Sheridan** (1904,06,08); **Spitz** (1968,72); **Spooner** (1920); **Weissmuller** (1924,28).

WOMEN

No		Sport	G-S-B
8	Shirley Babashoff	Swimming	2-6-0
7	Shannon Miller	Gymnastics	2-2-3
6	Jenny Thompson	Swimming	5-1-0
5	Evelyn Ashford	Track/Field	4-1-0
5	Janet Evans	Swimming	4-1-0
5*	Mary T. Meagher	Swimming	3-1-1
5	Florence Griffith Joyner	Track/Field	3-2-0
5	Jackie Joyner-Kersee	Track/Field	3-1-1
5	Mary Lou Retton	Gymnastics	1-2-2
4	Pat McCormick	Diving	4-0-0
4	Amy Van Dyken	Swimming	4-0-0
4	Valerie Brisco-Hooks	Track/Field	3-1-0

Most Gold Medals

MEN

No		Sport	G-S-B
10	Raymond Ewry	Track/Field	10-0-0
9	Mark Spitz	Swimming	9-1-1
9	Carl Lewis	Track/Field	9-1-0
8*	Matt Biondi	Swimming	8-2-1
5	Carl Osburn	Shooting	5-4-2
5	Martin Sheridan	Track/Field	5-3-1
5	Charles Daniels	Swimming	5-1-2
5†	Tom Jager	Swimming	5-1-1
5	Willis Lee	Shooting	5-1-1
5	Anton Heida	Gymnastics	5-1-0
5	Don Schollander	Swimming	5-1-0
5	Johnny Weissmuller	Swim/Water Polo	5-0-1
5	Alfred Lane	Shooting	5-0-1
5	Morris Fisher	Shooting	5-0-0
4	Jim Lightbody	Track/Field	4-2-0
4	Lloyd Spooner	Shooting	4-1-2
4	Greg Louganis	Diving	4-1-0
4	John Naber	Swimming	4-1-0
4	Meyer Prinstein	Track/Field	4-1-0
4	Mel Sheppard	Track/Field	4-1-0
4	Marcus Hurley	Cycling	4-0-1
4	Harrison Dillard	Track/Field	4-0-0
4	Archie Hahn	Track/Field	4-0-0
4	Alvin Kraenzlein	Track/Field	4-0-0
4	Al Oerter	Track/Field	4-0-0
4	Jesse Owens	Track/Field	4-0-0

*Includes gold medal as prelim. member of 1st-place relay team.

†Includes 3 gold medals as prelim. member of 1st-place relay teams.

WOMEN

No		Sport	G-S-B
5	Jenny Thompson	Swimming	5-1-0
4	Evelyn Ashford	Track/Field	4-1-0
4	Janet Evans	Swimming	4-1-0
4	Pat McCormick	Diving	4-0-0

No		Sport	G-S-B
4	Nancy Hogshead	Swimming	3-1-0
4	Sharon Stouder	Swimming	3-1-0
4	Wyomia Tyus	Track/Field	3-1-0
4	Wilma Rudolph	Track/Field	3-0-1
4	Chris von Saltza	Swimming	3-1-0
4	Sue Pederson	Swimming	2-2-0
4	Jan Henne	Swimming	2-1-1
4	Dorothy Poynton Hill	Diving	2-1-1
4*	Summer Sanders	Swimming	2-1-1
4*	Dara Torres	Swimming	2-1-1
4	Kathy Ellis	Swimming	2-0-2
4	Georgia Coleman	Diving	1-2-1

*Includes silver medal as prelim. member of 2nd-place relay team.

Games Participated In

Ashford (1976,84,88,92); **Babashoff** (1972,76); **Brisco-Hooks** (1984,88); **Coleman** (1928,32); **Ellis** (1964); **Evans** (1988,92); **Griffith Joyner** (1984,88); **Henne** (1968); **Hogshead** (1984); **Joyner-Kersee** (1984,88,92); **McCormick** (1952,56); **Meagher** (1984,88); **Miller** (1992, 96); **Pederson** (1968); **Poynton Hill** (1928,32,36); **Retton** (1984); **Rudolph** (1956,60); **Sanders** (1992); **Stouder** (1964); **Thompson** (1988,92,96); **Torres** (1984,88,92); **Tyus** (1964,68); **Van Dyken** (1996); **von Saltza** (1960).

No		Sport	G-S-B
4	Amy Van Dyken	Swimming	4-0-0
3	Florence Griffith Joyner	Track/Field	3-2-0
3	Jackie Joyner-Kersee	Track/Field	3-1-1
3*	Mary T. Meagher	Swimming	3-1-1
3	Valerie Brisco-Hooks	Track/Field	3-1-0
3	Nancy Hogshead	Swimming	3-1-0
3	Sharon Stouder	Swimming	3-1-0
3	Wyomia Tyus	Track/Field	3-1-0
3	Chris von Saltza	Swimming	3-1-0
3	Wilma Rudolph	Track/Field	3-0-1
3	Melissa Belote	Swimming	3-0-0
3	Ethelda Bleibtrey	Swimming	3-0-0
3	Tracy Caulkins	Swimming	3-0-0
3*	Nicole Haislett	Swimming	3-0-0
3	Helen Madison	Swimming	3-0-0
3	Debbie Meyer	Swimming	3-0-0
3	Sandra Neilson	Swimming	3-0-0
3	Martha Norelius	Swimming	3-0-0
3*	Carrie Steinseifer	Swimming	3-0-0

*Includes gold medal as prelim. member of 1st-place relay team.

Most Silver Medals
MEN

No		Sport	G-S-B
4	Carl Osburn	Shooting	5-4-2
4	Michael Plumb	Equestrian	2-4-0
3	Martin Sheridan	Track/Field	5-3-1
3	Burton Downing	Cycling	2-3-1
3	Irving Baxter	Track/Field	2-3-0
3	Earl Thomson	Equestrian	2-3-0

WOMEN

No		Sport	G-S-B
6	Shirley Babashoff	Swimming	2-6-0

All-Time Medal Standings, 1896-1996

All-time Summer Games medal standings, according to *The Golden Book of the Olympic Games*. Medal counts include the 1906 Intercalated Games which are not recognized by the IOC.

#	Country	G	S	B	Total	#	Country	G	S	B	Total
1	**United States**	832	634	553	2019	71	Peru	1	3	0	4
2	USSR (1952-88)	395	319	296	1010		Bahamas	1	1	2	4
3	Great Britain	169	223	218	610		Lithuania	1	0	3	4
4	France	175	179	206	560		Namibia	0	4	0	4
5	Sweden	132	151	174	457		Lebanon	0	2	2	4
6	Italy	166	135	144	445		Slovenia	0	2	2	4
	East Germany (1956-88)	159	150	136	445		Ghana	0	1	3	4
8	Hungary	142	129	155	426		Luxembourg	2	1	0	3
9	Germany (1896-36,92–)	124	121	134	379		Slovakia	1	1	1	3
10	West Germany (1952-88)	77	104	120	301		Israel	0	1	2	3
11	Finland	99	80	113	292		Malaysia	0	1	2	3
	Australia	86	85	121	292	82	Armenia	1	1	0	2
13	Japan	92	8p	97	278		Costa Rica	1	1	0	2
14	Romania	63	77	99	239		Syria	1	1	0	2
15	Poland	50	67	110	227		Japan/Korea	1	0	1	2
16	Canada	48	78	90	216		Surinam	1	0	1	2
17	Netherlands	49	58	81	188		Tanzania	0	2	0	2
18	Bulgaria	43	76	63	182		Cameroon	0	1	1	2
19	Switzerland	46	69	59	174		Great Britain/USA	0	1	1	2
20	China	52	63	49	164		Haiti	0	1	1	2
21	Denmark	38	60	57	155		Iceland	0	1	1	2
22	Czechoslovakia (1924-92)	49	49	44	142		Moldova	0	1	1	2
23	Belgium	37	49	49	135		Russia/Estonia	0	1	1	2
24	South Korea	38	42	46	126		United Arab Republic	0	1	1	2
25	Norway	45	41	38	124		Uzbekistan	0	1	1	2
26	Greece	28	42	43	113		Zambia	0	1	1	2
27	Unified Team (1992)	45	38	29	112		The Antilles	0	0	2	2
28	Cuba	44	33	31	108		Georgia	0	0	2	2
29	Yugoslavia (1924-88, 96—)	27	31	32	90		Panama	0	0	2	2
30	Austria	18	31	34	83	100	Australia/New Zealand	1	0	0	1
31	New Zealand	29	12	29	70		Burundi	1	0	0	1
32	Russia	26	24	18	68		Cuba/USA	1	0	0	1
33	Spain	22	25	17	64		Denmark/Sweden	1	0	0	1
34	Turkey	30	16	13	59		Ecuador	1	0	0	1
35	South Africa	19	18	21	58		Gr. Britain/Ireland/Germany	1	0	0	1
36	Brazil	12	13	29	54		Gr. Britain/Ireland/USA	1	0	0	1
37	Argentina	13	21	16	50		Hong Kong	1	0	0	1
38	Kenya	14	17	16	47		Ireland/USA	1	0	0	1
39	Mexico	9	13	19	41		Zimbabwe	1	0	0	1
40	Iran	5	13	18	36		Azerbaijan	0	1	0	1
41	Jamaica	5	16	9	30		Belgium/Greece	0	1	0	1
42	North Korea	8	6	12	26		Ceylon	0	1	0	1
43	Estonia	7	6	10	23		France/USA	0	1	0	1
44	Great Britain/Ireland	6	11	3	20		France/Gr. Britain/Ireland	0	1	0	1
45	Ireland	8	5	6	19		Ivory Coast	0	1	0	1
46	Ethiopia	8	1	7	16		Netherlands Antilles	0	1	0	1
	Egypt	6	5	5	16		Senegal	0	1	0	1
48	India	8	3	4	15		Singapore	0	1	0	1
	Portugal	3	4	8	15		Smyrna	0	1	0	1
50	Nigeria	2	5	7	14		Tonga	0	1	0	1
	Mongolia	0	5	9	14		Virgin Islands	0	1	0	1
52	Czech Republic	4	3	4	11		Australia/Great Britain	0	0	1	1
	Morocco	4	2	5	11		Bermuda	0	0	1	1
54	Indonesia	3	4	3	10		Bohemia/Great Britain	0	0	1	1
	Pakistan	3	3	4	10		Djibouti	0	0	1	1
56	Uruguay	2	1	6	9		Dominican Republic	0	0	1	1
	Trinidad & Tobago	1	2	6	9		France/Great Britain	0	0	1	1
	Philippines	0	2	7	9		Guyana	0	0	1	1
59	Venezuela	1	2	5	8		Iraq	0	0	1	1
	Chile	0	6	2	8		Mexico/Spain	0	0	1	1
61	Algeria	3	0	4	7		Mozambique	0	0	1	1
	Latvia	0	5	2	7		Niger	0	0	1	1
63	Uganda	1	3	2	6		Qatar	0	0	1	1
	Tunisia	1	2	3	6		Scotland	0	0	1	1
	Thailand	1	1	4	6		Thessalonika	0	0	1	1
	Colombia	0	2	4	6		Wales	0	0	1	1
	Bohemia	0	1	5	6						
	Puerto Rico	0	1	5	6						
69	Croatia	1	2	2	5						
	Chinese Taipei	0	3	2	5						

Combined totals:	G	S	B	Total
USSR/UT/Russia	466	381	343	1190
Germany/E. Ger/W. Ger	360	375	390	1125

Notes: Athletes from the USSR participated in the Summer Games from 1952-88, returned as the Unified Team in 1992 after the breakup of the Soviet Union (in 1991) and then competed for the independent republics of Belarus, Kazakhstan, Russia, Ukraine, Uzbekistan and three others in the 1994 Winter Games. Yugoslavia divided into Croatia and Bosnia-Herzegovina in 1991, while Czechoslovakia split into Slovenia and the Czech Republic the same year.

THE 1998

ESPN INFORMATION PLEASE SPORTS ALMANAC

OLYMPICS STATISTICS

THROUGH THE YEARS
1924-1994
WINTER OLYMPICS

SEC B
PAGE 674

The Winter Olympics

The move toward a winter version of the Olympics began in 1908 when figure skating made an appearance at the Summer Games in London. Ten-time world champion Ulrich Salchow of Sweden, who originated the backwards, one revolution jump that bears his name, and Madge Syers of Britain were the first singles champions. Germans Anna Hubler and Heinrich Berger won the pairs competition.

Organizers of the 1916 Summer Games in Berlin planned to introduce a "Skiing Olympia," featuring nordic events in the Black Forest, but the Games were cancelled after the outbreak of World War I in 1914.

The Games resumed in 1920 at Antwerp, Belgium, where figure skating returned and ice hockey was added as a medal event. Sweden's Gillis Grafstrom and Magda Julin took individual honors, while Ludovika and Walter Jakobsson were the top pair. In hockey, Canada won the gold medal with the United States second and Czechoslovakia third.

Despite the objections of Modern Olympics' founder Baron Pierre de Coubertin and the resistance of the Scandinavian countries, which had staged their own Nordic championships every four or five years from 1901-26 in Sweden, the International Olympic Committee sanctioned an "International Winter Sports Week" at Chamonix, France, in 1924. The 11-day event, which included nordic skiing, speed skating, figure skating, ice hockey and bobsledding, was a huge success and was retroactively called the First Olympic Winter Games.

Seventy years after those first cold weather Games, the 17th edition of the Winter Olympics took place in Lillehammer, Norway, in 1994. The event ended the four-year Olympic cycle of staging both Winter and Summer Games in the same year and began a new schedule that calls for the two Games to alternate every two years.

Year	No	Location	Dates	Nations	Most medals	USA Medals
1924	I	Chamonix, FRA	Jan. 25-Feb. 4	16	Norway (4-7-6–17)	1-2-1– 4 (3rd)
1928	II	St. Moritz, SWI	Feb. 11-19	25	Norway (6-4-5–15)	2-2-2– 6 (2nd)
1932	III	Lake Placid, USA	Feb. 4-15	17	USA (6-4-2–12)	6-4-2–12 (1st)
1936	IV	Garmisch-Partenkirchen, GER .	Feb. 6-16	28	Norway (7-5-3–15)	1-0-3– 4 (T-5th)
1940-a	–	Sapporo, JPN	Cancelled (WWII)			
1944	–	Cortina d'Ampezzo, ITA	Cancelled (WWII)			
1948	V	St. Moritz, SWI	Jan. 30-Feb. 8	28	Norway (4-3-3–10), Sweden (4-3-3–10) & Switzerland (3-4-3–10)	3-4-2– 9 (4th)
1952-b	VI	Oslo, NOR	Feb. 14-25	30	Norway (7-3-6–16)	4-6-1–11 (2nd)
1956-c	VII	Cortina d'Ampezzo, ITA	Jan. 26-Feb. 5	32	USSR (7-3-6–16)	2-3-2– 7 (T-4th)
1960	VIII	Squaw Valley, USA	Feb. 18-28	30	USSR (7-5-9–21)	3-4-3–10 (2nd)
1964	IX	Innsbruck, AUT	Jan. 29-Feb. 9	36	USSR (11-8-6–25)	1-2-3– 6 (7th)
1968-d	X	Grenoble, FRA	Feb. 6-18	37	Norway (6-6-2–14)	1-5-1– 7 (T-7th)
1972	XI	Sapporo, JPN	Feb. 3-13	35	USSR (8-5-3–16)	3-2-3– 8 (6th)
1976-e	XII	Innsbruck, AUT	Feb. 4-15	37	USSR (13-6-8–27)	3-3-4–10 (T-3rd)
1980	XIII	Lake Placid, USA	Feb. 14-23	37	E. Germany (9-7-7–23)	6-4-2–12 (3rd)
1984	XIV	Sarajevo, YUG	Feb. 7-19	49	USSR (6-10-9–25)	4-4-0– 8 (T-5th)
1988	XV	Calgary, CAN	Feb. 13-28	57	USSR (11-9-9–29)	2-1-3– 6 (T-8th)
1992-f	XVI	Albertville, FRA	Feb. 8-23	63	Germany (10-10-6–26)	5-4-2–11 (6th)
1994-g	XVII	Lillehammer, NOR	Feb. 12-27	67	Norway (10-11-5–26)	6-5-2–13 (T-5th)
1998	XVIII	Nagano, JPN	Feb. 7-22			
2002	XIX	Salt Lake City, USA	Feb. 9-24			

a–The 1940 Winter Games are originally scheduled for Sapporo, but Japan resigns as host in 1937 when the Sino-Japanese war breaks out. St. Moritz is the next choice, but the Swiss feel that ski instructors should not be considered professionals and the IOC withdraws its offer. Finally, Garmisch-Partenkirchen is asked to serve again as host, but the Germans invade Poland in 1939 and the Games are eventually cancelled.

b–Germany and Japan are allowed to rejoin the Olympic community for the first time since World War II. Though a divided country, the Germans send a joint East-West team.

c–The Soviet Union (USSR) participates in its first Winter Olympics and takes home the most medals, including the gold medal in ice hockey.

d–East Germany and West Germany officially send separate teams for the first time and will continue to do so through 1988.

e–The IOC grants the 1976 Winter Games to Denver in May 1970, but in 1972 Colorado voters reject a $5 million bond issue to finance the undertaking. Denver immediately withdraws as host and the IOC selects Innsbruck, the site of the 1964 Games, to take over.

f–Germany sends a single team after East and West German reunification in 1990 and the USSR competes as the Unified Team after the breakup of the Soviet Union in 1991.

g–The IOC moves the Winter Games' four-year cycle ahead two years in order to separate them from the Summer Games and alternate Olympics every two years.

Event-by-Event

Gold medal winners from 1924-94 in the following events: Alpine Skiing, Biathlon, Bobsled, Cross-country Skiing, Figure Skating, Ice Hockey, Luge, Nordic Combined, Ski Jumping and Speed Skating.

ALPINE SKIING

MEN

Multiple gold medals: Jean-Claude Killy, Toni Sailer and Alberto Tomba (3); Henri Oreiller, Ingemar Stenmark and Markus Wasmeier (2).

Downhill

Year		Time	Year		Time
1948	Henri Oreiller, FRA	2:55.0	1976	Franz Klammer AUT	1:45.73
1952	Zeno Colò, ITA	2:30.8	1980	Leonhard Stock, AUS	1:45.50
1956	Toni Sailer, AUT	2:52.2	1984	Bill Johnson, USA	1:45.59
1960	Jean Vuarnet, FRA	2:06.0	1988	Pirmin Zurbriggen, SWI	1:59.63
1964	Egon Zimmermann, AUT	2:18.16	1992	Patrick Ortlieb, AUT	1:50.37
1968	Jean-Claude Killy, FRA	1:59.85	1994	Tommy Moe, USA	1:45.75
1972	Bernhard Russi, SWI	1:51.43			

Slalom

Year		Time	Year		Time
1948	Edi Reinalter, SWI	2:10.3	1976	Piero Gros, ITA	2:03.29
1952	Othmar Schneider, AUT	2:00.0	1980	Ingemar Stenmark, SWE	1:44.26
1956	Toni Sailer, AUT	3:14.7	1984	Phil Mahre, USA	1:39.41
1960	Ernst Hinterseer, AUT	2:08.9	1988	Alberto Tomba, ITA	1:39.47
1964	Pepi Stiegler, AUT	2:11.13	1992	Finn Christian Jagge, NOR	1:44.39
1968	Jean-Claude Killy, FRA	1:39.73	1994	Thomas Stangassinger, AUT	2:02.02
1972	Francisco Ochoa, SPA	1:49.27			

Giant Slalom

Year		Time	Year		Time
1952	Stein Eriksen, NOR	2:25.0	1976	Heini Hemmi, SWI	3:26.97
1956	Toni Sailer, AUS	3:00.1	1980	Ingemar Stenmark, SWE	2:40.74
1960	Roger Staub, SWI	1:48.3	1984	Max Julen, SWI	2:41.18
1964	Francois Bonlieu, FRA	1:46.71	1988	Alberto Tomba, ITA	2:06.37
1968	Jean-Claude Killy, FRA	3:29.28	1992	Alberto Tomba, ITA	2:06.98
1972	Gustav Thöni, ITA	3:09.62	1994	Markus Wasmeier, GER	2:52.46

Super Giant Slalom

Year		Time	Year		Time
1988	Frank Piccard, FRA	1:39.66	1994	Markus Wasmeier, GER	1:32.53
1992	Kjetil Andre Aamodt, NOR	1:13.04			

Alpine Combined

Year		Points	Year		Points
1936	Franz Pfnür, GER	99.25	1992	Josef Polig, ITA	14.58
1948	Henri Oreiller, FRA	3.27	Year		Time
1952-84 Not held			1994	Lasse Kjus, NOR	3:17.53
1988	Hubert Strolz, AUT	36.55			

WOMEN

Multiple gold medals: Vreni Schneider (3); Deborah Compagnoni, Marielle Goitschel, Trude Jochum-Beiser, Petra Kronberger, Andrea Mead Lawrence, Rosi Mittermaier, Marie-Theres Nadig, Hanni Wenzel and Pernilla Wiberg (2).

Downhill

Year		Time	Year		Time
1948	Hedy Schlunegger, SWI	2:28.3	1976	Rosi Mittermaier, W. Ger	1:46.16
1952	Trude Jochum-Beiser, AUT	1:47.1	1980	Annemarie Moser-Pröll, AUT	1:37.52
1956	Madeleine Berthod, SWI	1:40.7	1984	Michela Figini, SWI	1:13.36
1960	Heidi Biebl, GER	1:37.6	1988	Marina Kiehl, W. Ger	1:25.86
1964	Christl Haas, AUT	1:55.39	1992	Kerrin Lee-Gartner, CAN	1:52.55
1968	Olga Pall, AUT	1:40.87	1994	Katja Seizinger, GER	1:35.93
1972	Marie-Theres Nadig, SWI	1:36.68			

Slalom

Year		Time	Year		Time
1948	Gretchen Fraser, USA	1:57.2	1976	Rosi Mittermaier, W. Ger	1:30.54
1952	Andrea Mead Lawrence, USA	2:10.6	1980	Hanni Wenzel, LIE	1:25.09
1956	Renée Colliard, SWI	1:52.3	1984	Paoletta Magoni, ITA	1:36.47
1960	Anne Heggtveit, CAN	1:49.6	1988	Vreni Schneider, SWI	1:36.69
1964	Christine Goitschel, FRA	1:29.86	1992	Petra Kronberger, AUT	1:32.68
1968	Marielle Goitschel, FRA	1:25.86	1994	Vreni Schneider, SWI	1:56.01
1972	Barbara Cochran, USA	1:31.24			

Alpine Skiing (Cont.)

Giant Slalom

Year		Time	Year		Time
1952	Andrea Mead Lawrence, USA	2:06.8	1976	Kathy Kreiner, CAN	1:29.13
1956	Ossi Reichert, GER	1:56.5	1980	Hanni Wenzel, LIE	2:41.66
1960	Yvonne Rügg, SWI	1:39.9	1984	Debbie Armstrong, USA	2:20.98
1964	Marielle Goitschel, FRA	1:52.24	1988	Vreni Schneider, SWI	2:06.49
1968	Nancy Greene, CAN	1:51.97	1992	Pernilla Wiberg, SWE	2:12.74
1972	Marie-Theres Nadig, SWI	1:29.90	1994	Deborah Compagnoni, ITA	2:30.97

Super Giant Slalom

Year		Time	Year		Time
1988	Sigrid Wolf, AUT	1:19.03	1994	Diann Roffe-Steinrotter, USA	1:22.15
1992	Deborah Compagnoni, ITA	1:21.22			

Alpine Combined

Year		Points	Year		Points
1936	Christl Cranz, GER	97.06	1992	Petra Kronberger, AUT	2.55
1948	Trude Beiser, AUT	6.58	**Year**		**Time**
1952-84 Not held			1994	Pernilla Wiberg, SWE	3:05.16
1988	Anita Wachter, AUT	29.25			

BIATHLON

MEN

Multiple gold medals (including relays): Aleksandr Tikhonov (4); Mark Kirchner (3); Anatoly Alyabyev, Ivan Biakov, Sergei Chepikov, Viktor Mamatov, Frank-Peter Roetsch, Magnar Solberg and Dmitri Vasilyev (2).

10 kilometers

Year		Time	Year		Time
1980	Frank Ullrich, E. Ger	32:10.69	1992	Mark Kirchner, GER	26:02.3
1984	Erik Kvalfoss, NOR	30:53.8	1994	Sergei Chepikov, RUS	28:07.0
1988	Frank-Peter Roetsch, E. Ger	25:08.1			

20 kilometers

Year		Time	Year		Time
1960	Klas Lestander, SWE	1:33:21.6	1980	Anatoly Alyabyev, USSR	1:08:16.31
1964	Vladimir Melanin, USSR	1:20:26.8	1984	Peter Angerer, W. Ger	1:11:52.7
1968	Magnar Solberg, NOR	1:13:45.9	1988	Frank-Peter Roetsch, E. Ger	56:33.3
1972	Magnar Solberg, NOR	1:15:55.50	1992	Yevgeny Redkine, UT	57:34.4
1976	Nikolai Kruglov, USSR	1:14:12.26	1994	Sergei Tarasov, RUS	57:25.3

4x7.5-kilometer Relay

Year		Time	Year		Time	Year		Time
1968	Soviet Union	2:13:02.4	1980	Soviet Union	1:34:03.27	1992	Germany	1:24:43.5
1972	Soviet Union	1:51:44.92	1984	Soviet Union	1:38:51.7	1994	Germany	1:30:22.1
1976	Soviet Union	1:57:55.64	1988	Soviet Union	1:22:30.0			

WOMEN

Multiple gold medals (including relays): Myriam Bedard and Anfisa Reztsova (2). Note that Reztsova won a third gold medal in 1988 in the Cross-country 4x5-kilometer Relay.

7.5 kilometers

Year		Time	Year		Time
1992	Anfisa Reztsova, UT	24:29.2	1994	Myriam Bedard, CAN	26:08.8

15 kilometers

Year		Time	Year		Time
1992	Antje Misersky, GER	51:47.2	1994	Myriam Bedard, CAN	52:06.6

4x7.5 kilometer Relay

Year		Time	Year		Time
1992	France	1:15:55.6	1994	Russia	1:47:19.5

Note: Event featured three skiers per team in 1992.

Youngest and Oldest Gold Medalists in an Individual Event

Youngest: MEN– Toni Nieminen, Finland, Large Hill Ski Jumping, 1992 (16 years, 261 days); WOMEN–Sonja Henie, Norway, Figure Skating, 1928 (15 years, 315 days).
Oldest: MEN– Magnar Solberg, NOR, 20-km Biathlon, 1972 (35 years, 4 days); WOMEN– Christina Baas-Kaiser, Holland, 3,000m Speed Skating, 1972 (33 years, 268 days).

BOBSLED

Multiple gold medals: DRIVERS–Meinhard Nehmer (3); Billy Fiske, Wolfgang Hoppe, Eugenio Monti, Andreas Ostler and Gustav Weder (2). CREW–Bernard Germeshausen (3); Donat Acklin, Luciano De Paolis, Cliff Gray, Lorenz Nieberl and Dietmar Schauerhammer (2).

Two-Man

Year		Time	Year		Time
1932	United States (Hubert Stevens)	8:14.74	1972	West Germany (Wolfgang Zimmerer)	4:57.07
1936	United States (Ivan Brown)	5:29.29	1976	East Germany (Meinhard Nehmer)	3:44.42
1948	Switzerland (Felix Endrich)	5:29.2	1980	Switzerland (Erich Schärer)	4:09.36
1952	Germany (Andreas Ostler)	5:24.54	1984	East Germany (Wolfgang Hoppe)	3:25.56
1956	Italy (Lamberto Dalla Costa)	5:30.14	1988	Soviet Union (Janis Kipurs)	3:54.19
1960	Not held		1992	Switzerland I (Gustav Weder)	4:03.26
1964	Great Britain (Anthony Nash)	4:21.90	1994	Switzerland I (Gustav Weder)	3:30.81
1968	Italy (Eugenio Monti)	4:41.54			

Four-Man

Year		Time	Year		Time
1924	Switzerland (Eduard Scherrer)	5:45.54	1968	Italy (Eugenio Monti)	2:17.39
1928	United States (Billy Fiske)	3:20.5	1972	Switzerland (Jean Wicki)	4:43.07
1932	United States (Billy Fiske)	7:53.68	1976	East Germany (Meinhard Nehmer)	3:40.43
1936	Switzerland (Pierre Musy)	5:19.85	1980	East Germany (Meinhard Nehmer)	3:59.92
1948	United States (Francis Tyler)	5:20.1	1984	East Germany (Wolfgang Hoppe)	3:20.22
1952	Germany (Andreas Ostler)	5:07.84	1988	Switzerland (Ekkehard Fasser)	3:47.51
1956	Switzerland (Franz Kapus)	5:10.44	1992	Austria I (Ingo Appelt)	3:53.90
1960	Not held		1994	Germany II (Harald Czudaj)	3:27.78
1964	Canada (Vic Emery)	4:14.46			

Note: Five-man sleds were used in 1928.

CROSS-COUNTRY SKIING

There have been two significant changes in men's and women's Cross-country racing since the end of the 1984 Winter Games in Sarajevo. First, the classical and freestyle (i.e., skating) techniques were designated for specific events beginning in 1988, and the Pursuit race was introduced in 1992.

MEN

Multiple gold medals (including relays): Bjorn Dählie (5); Sixten Jernberg, Gunde Svan, Thomas Wassberg and Nikolai Zimyatov (4); Veikko Hakulinen, Eero Mäntyranta and Vegard Ulvang (3); Hallgeir Brenden, Harald Grönningen, Thorlief Haug, Jan Ottoson, Pál Tyldum and Vyacheslav Vedenine (2).
Multiple gold medals (including Nordic Combined): Johan Gröttumsbråten and Thorlief Haug (3).

10-kilometer Classical

Year		Time	Year		Time
1924-88	Not held		1994	Bjorn Dählie, NOR	24:20.1
1992	Vegard Ulvang, NOR	27:36.0			

15-kilometer Freestyle Pursuit

A 15-km Freestyle race in which the starting order is determined by order of finish in the 10-km Classical race. Time given is combined time of both events.

Year		Time	Year		Time
1924-88	Not held		1994	Bjorn Dählie, NOR	1:00.08.8
1992	Bjorn Dählie, NOR	1:05:37.9			

15-kilometer Classical (Discont.)

Discontinued in 1992 and replaced by 15-km Freestyle Pursuit. Event was held over 18 kilometers from 1924-52.

Year		Time	Year		Time
1924	Thorleif Haug, NOR	1:14:31.0	1964	Eero Mäntyranta, FIN	50:54.1
1928	Johan Gröttumsbråten, NOR	1:37:01.0	1968	Harald Grönningen, NOR	47:54.2
1932	Sven Utterström, SWE	1:23:07.0	1972	Sven-Ake Lundback, SWE	45:28.24
1936	Erik-August Larsson, SWE	1:14:38.0	1976	Nikolai Bazhukov, USSR	43:58.47
1948	Martin Lundström, SWE	1:13:50.0	1980	Thomas Wassberg, SWE	41:57.63
1952	Hallgeir Brenden, NOR	1:01:34.0	1984	Gunde Svan, SWE	41:25.6
1956	Hallgeir Brenden, NOR	49:39.0	1988	Mikhail Devyatyarov, USSR	41:18.9
1960	Hakon Brusveen NOR	51:55.5			

30-kilometer Freestyle

Year		Time	Year		Time
1924-52	Not held		1976	Sergei Saveliev, USSR	1:30:29.38
1956	Veikko Hakulinen, FIN	1:44:06.0	1980	Nikolai Zimyatov, USSR	1:27:02.80
1960	Sixten Jernberg, SWE	1:51:03.9	1984	Nikolai Zimyatov, USSR	1:28:56.3
1964	Eero Mäntyranta, FIN	1:30:50.7	1988	Alexi Prokurorov, USSR	1:24:26.3
1968	Franco Nones, ITA	1:35:39.2	1992	Vegard Ulvang, NOR	1:22:27.8
1972	Vyacheslav Vedenine, USSR	1:36:31.15	1994	Thomas Alsgaard, NOR	1:12:26.4

Cross-Country Skiing (Cont.)

50-kilometer Classical

Year		Time	Year		Time
1924	Thorleif Haug, NOR	3:44:32.0	1968	Ole Ellefsaeter, NOR	2:28:45.8
1928	Per Erik Hedlund, SWE	4:52:03.0	1972	Päl Tyldum, NOR	2:43:14.75
1932	Veli Saarinen, FIN	4:28:00.0	1976	Ivar Formo, NOR	2:37:30.05
1936	Elis Wiklund, SWE	3:30:11.0	1980	Nikolai Zimyatov, USSR	2:27:24.60
1948	Nils Karlsson, SWE	3:47:48.0	1984	Thomas Wassberg, SWE	2:15:55.8
1952	Veikko Hakulinen, FIN	3:33:33.0	1988	Gunde Svan, SWE	2:04:30.9
1956	Sixten Jernberg, SWE	2:50:27.0	1992	Bjorn Dählie, NOR	2:03:41.5
1960	Kalevi Hämäläinen, FIN	2:59:06.3	1994	Vladimir Smirnov, KAZ	2:07:20.3
1964	Sixten Jernberg, SWE	2:43:52.6			

4x10-kilometer Mixed Relay
Two Classical and two Freestyle legs.

Year		Time	Year		Time	Year		Time
1936	Finland	2:41:33.0	1964	Sweden	2:18:34.6	1984	Sweden	1:55:06.3
1948	Sweden	2:32:08.0	1968	Norway	2:08:33.5	1988	Sweden	1:43:58.6
1952	Finland	2:20:16.0	1972	Soviet Union	2:04:47.94	1992	Norway	1:39:26.0
1956	Soviet Union	2:15:30.0	1976	Finland	2:07:59.72	1994	Italy	1:41:15.0
1960	Finland	2:18:45.6	1980	Soviet Union	1:57:03.46			

WOMEN

Multiple gold medals (including relays): Lyubov Egorova (6); Galina Kulakova and Raisa Smetanina (4); Claudia Boyarskikh and Marja-Liisa Hämäläinen (3); Manuela Di Centa, Toini Gustafsson, Larisa Lazutina, Barbara Petzold and Elena Valbe (2).

Multiple gold medals (including relays and Biathlon): Anfisa Reztsova (2).

5-kilometer Classical

Year		Time	Year		Time
1952-60	Not held		1980	Raisa Smetanina, USSR	15:06.92
1964	Claudia Boyarskikh, USSR	17:50.5	1984	Marja-Liisa Hämäläinen, FIN	17:04.0
1968	Toini Gustafsson, SWE	16:45.2	1988	Marjo Matikainen, FIN	15:04.0
1972	Galina Kulakova, USSR	17:00.50	1992	Marjut Lukkarinen, FIN	14:13.8
1976	Helena Takalo, FIN	15:48.69	1994	Lyubov Egorova, RUS	14:08.8

10-kilometer Freestyle Pursuit
A 10-km Freestyle race in which the starting order is determined by order of finish in the 5-km Classical race. Time given is combined time of both events.

Year		Time	Year		Time
1952-88	Not held		1994	Lyubov Egorova, RUS	41:38.1
1992	Lyubov Egorova, UT	40:07.7			

10-kilometer Classical (Discont.)
Discontinued in 1992 and replaced by 10-km Freestyle Pursuit. Event was held over 18 kilometers from 1924-52.

Year		Time	Year		Time
1952	Lydia Wideman, FIN	41:40.0	1972	Galina Kulakova, USSR	34:17.82
1956	Lyubov Kosyreva, USSR	38:11.0	1976	Raisa Smetanina, USSR	30:13.41
1960	Maria Gusakova, USSR	39:46.6	1980	Barbara Petzold, E. Ger	30:31.54
1964	Claudia Boyarskikh, USSR	40:24.3	1984	Marja-Liisa Hämäläinen, FIN	31:44.2
1968	Toini Gustafsson, SWE	36:46.5	1988	Vida Venciene, USSR	30:08.3

15-kilometer Freestyle

Year		Time	Year		Time
1952-88	Not held		1994	Manuela Di Centa, ITA	39:44.5
1992	Lyubov Egorova, UT	42:20.8			

30-kilometer Classical
Event was held over 20 kilometers from 1984-88.

Year		Time	Year		Time
1984	Marja-Liisa Hämäläinen, FIN	1:01:45.0	1992	Stefania Belmondo, ITA	1:22:30.1
1988	Tamara Tikhonova, USSR	55:53.6	1994	Manuela Di Centa, ITA	1:25:41.6

4x5-kilometer Mixed Relay
Two Classical and two Freestyle legs. Event featured three skiers per team from 1956-72.

Year		Time	Year		Time	Year		Time
1956	Finland	1:09:01.0	1972	Soviet Union	48:46.15	1988	Soviet Union	59:51.1
1960	Sweden	1:04:21.4	1976	Soviet Union	1:07:49.75	1992	Unified Team	59:34.8
1964	Soviet Union	59:20.2	1980	East Germany	1:02:11.10	1994	Russia	57:12.5
1968	Norway	57:30.0	1984	Norway	1:06:49.7			

FIGURE SKATING

MEN

Multiple gold medals: Gillis Grafström (3); Dick Button and Karl Schäfer (2).

Year		Year		Year	
1908	Ulrich Salchow .... SWE	1948	Dick Button .... USA	1976	John Curry .... GBR
1912	Not held	1952	Dick Button .... USA	1980	Robin Cousins .... GBR
1920	Gillis Grafström .... SWE	1956	Hayes Alan Jenkins ..... USA	1984	Scott Hamilton .... USA
1924	Gillis Grafström .... SWE	1960	David Jenkins .... USA	1988	Brian Boitano .... USA
1928	Gillis Grafström .... SWE	1964	Manfred Schnelldorfer ... GER	1992	Victor Petrenko .... UT
1932	Karl Schäfer .... AUT	1968	Wolfgang Schwarz ...... AUT	1994	Alexei Urmanov .... RUS
1936	Karl Schäfer .... AUT	1972	Ondrej Nepela .... CZE		

WOMEN

Multiple gold medals: Sonja Henie (3); Katarina Witt (2).

Year		Year		Year	
1908	Madge Syers .... GBR	1948	Barbara Ann Scott ..... CAN	1976	Dorothy Hamill .... USA
1912	Not held	1952	Jeanette Altwegg .... GBR	1980	Anett Pötzsch .... E. Ger
1920	Magda Julin-Mauroy .... SWE	1956	Tenley Albright .... USA	1984	Katarina Witt .... E. Ger
1924	Herma Planck-Szabó .... AUT	1960	Carol Heiss .... USA	1988	Katarina Witt .... E. Ger
1928	Sonja Henie .... NOR	1964	Sjoukje Dijkstra .... HOL	1992	Kristi Yamaguchi .... USA
1932	Sonja Henie .... NOR	1968	Peggy Fleming .... USA	1994	Oksana Baiul .... UKR
1936	Sonja Henie .... NOR	1972	Beatrix Schuba .... AUT		

PAIRS

Multiple gold medals: MEN–Pierre Brunet, Sergei Grinkov, Oleg Protopopov and Aleksandr Zaitsev (2). WOMEN–Irina Rodnina (3); Ludmila Belousova, Ekaterina Gordeeva and Andree Joly Brunet (2).

Year		Year	
1908	Anna Hübler & Heinrich Burger .... Germany	1960	Barbara Wagner & Robert Paul .... Canada
1912	Not held	1964	Ludmila Belousova & Oleg Protopopov ...... USSR
1920	Ludovika & Walter Jakobsson .... Finland	1968	Ludmila Belousova & Oleg Protopopov ...... USSR
1924	Helene Engelmann & Alfred Berger .... Austria	1972	Irina Rodnina & Aleksei Ulanov .... USSR
1928	Andrée Joly & Pierre Brunet .... France	1976	Irina Rodnina & Aleksandr Zaitsev .... USSR
1932	Andrée & Pierre Brunet .... France	1980	Irina Rodnina & Aleksandr Zaitsev .... USSR
1936	Maxi Herber & Ernst Baier .... Germany	1984	Elena Valova & Oleg Vasiliev .... USSR
1948	Micheline Lannoy & Pierre Baugniet ...... Belgium	1988	Ekaterina Gordeeva & Sergei Grinkov ...... USSR
1952	Ria & Paul Falk .... Germany	1992	Natalya Mishkutienok & Arthur Dmitriev .... UT
1956	Elisabeth Schwartz & Kurt Oppelt .... Austria	1994	Ekaterina Gordeeva & Sergei Grinkov ...... RUS

Ice Dancing

Year		Year	
1976	Lyudmila Pakhomova & Aleksandr Gorshkov . USSR	1988	Natalia Bestemianova & Andrei Bukin ...... USSR
1980	Natalia Linichuk & Gennady Karponosov .... USSR	1992	Marina Klimova & Sergei Ponomarenko .... UT
1984	Jayne Torvill & Christopher Dean .... Great Britain	1994	Oksana Gritschuk & Yevgeny Platov .... RUS

ICE HOCKEY

Multiple gold medals: Soviet Union/Unified Team (8); Canada (6); United States (2).

Year		Year	
1920	**Canada**, United States Czechoslovakia	1964	**Soviet Union**, Sweden, Czechoslovakia
1924	**Canada**, United States, Great Britain	1968	**Soviet Union**, Czechoslovakia, Canada
1928	**Canada**, Sweden, Switzerland	1972	**Soviet Union**, United States, Czechoslovakia
1932	**Canada**, United States, Germany	1976	**Soviet Union**, Czechoslovakia, West Germany
1936	**Great Britain**, Canada, United States	1980	**United States**, Soviet Union, Sweden
1948	**Canada**, Czechoslovakia, Switzerland	1984	**Soviet Union**, Czechoslovakia, Sweden
1952	**Canada**, United States, Sweden	1988	**Soviet Union**, Finland, Sweden
1956	**Soviet Union**, United States, Canada	1992	**Unified Team**, Canada, Czechoslovakia
1960	**United States**, Canada, Soviet Union	1994	**Sweden**, Canada, Finland

U.S. Gold Medal Hockey Teams

1960

Forwards: Billy Christian, Roger Christian, Billy Cleary, Gene Grazia, Paul Johnson, Bob McVey, Dick Meredith, Weldy Olson, Dick Rodenheiser and Tom Williams. **Defensemen:** Bob Cleary, Jack Kirrane (captain), John Mayasich, Bob Owen and Rod Paavola. **Goaltenders:** Jack McCartan and Larry Palmer. **Coach:** Jack Riley.

1980

Forwards: Neal Broten, Steve Christoff, Mike Eruzione (captain), John Harrington, Mark Johnson, Rob McClanahan, Mark Pavelich, Buzz Schneider, Dave Silk, Eric Strobel, Phil Verchota and Mark Wells. **Defensemen:** Bill Baker, Dave Christian, Ken Morrow, Jack O'Callahan, Mike Ramsey and Bob Suter. **Goaltenders:** Jim Craig and Steve Janaszak. **Coach:** Herb Brooks.

LUGE

MEN

Multiple gold medals: (including doubles): Norbert Hahn, Georg Hackl, Paul Hildgartner, Thomas Kohler and Hans Rinn (2).

Singles

Year		Time	Year		Time
1964	Thomas Köhler, GER	3:26.77	1984	Paul Hildgartner, ITA	3:04.258
1968	Manfred Schmid, AUT	2:52.48	1988	Jens Müller, E. Ger	3:05.548
1972	Wolfgang Scheidel, E. Ger	3:27.58	1992	Georg Hackl, GER	3:02.363
1976	Dettlef Günther, E. Ger	3:27.688	1994	Georg Hackl, GER	3:21.571
1980	Bernhard Glass, E. Ger	2:54.796			

Doubles

Year		Time	Year		Time	Year		Time
1964	Austria	1:41.62	1976	East Germany	1:25.604	1992	Germany	1:32.053
1968	East Germany	1:35.85	1980	East Germany	1:19.331	1994	Italy	1:36.720
1972	(TIE) East Germany	1:28.35	1984	West Germany	1:23.620			
	& Italy	1:28.35	1988	East Germany	1:31.940			

WOMEN

Multiple gold medals: Steffi Martin Walter (2).

Singles

Year		Time	Year		Time
1964	Ortrun Enderlein, GER	3:24.67	1984	Steffi Martin, E. Ger	2:46.570
1968	Erica Lechner, ITA	2:28.66	1988	Steffi Martin Walter, E. Ger	3:03.973
1972	Anna-Maria Müller, E. Ger	2:59.18	1992	Doris Neuner, AUT	3:06.696
1976	Margit Schumann, E. Ger	2:50.621	1994	Gerda Weissensteiner, ITA	3:15.517
1980	Vera Zozulya, USSR	2:36.537			

NORDIC COMBINED

Multiple gold medals: Ulrich Wehling (3); Johan Gröttumsbråten (2).

Individual

Year		Points	Year		Points
1924	Thorleif Haug, NOR	18.906	1968	Franz Keller, W. Ger	449.04
1928	Johan Gröttumsbråten, NOR	17.833	1972	Ulrich Wehling, E. Ger	413.340
1932	Johan Gröttumsbråten, NOR	446.00	1976	Ulrich Wehling, E. Ger	423.39
1936	Oddbjörn Hagen, NOR	430.3	1980	Ulrich Wehling, E. Ger	432.200
1948	Heikki Hasu, FIN	448.80	1984	Tom Sandberg, NOR	422.595
1952	Simon Slattvik, NOR	451.621	1988	Hippolyt Kempf, SWI	432.230
1956	Sverre Stenersen, NOR	455.000	1992	Fabrice Guy, FRA	426.470
1960	Georg Thoma, GER	457.952	1994	Fred Borre Lundberg, NOR	457.970
1964	Tormod Knutsen, NOR	469.28			

Team

Year		Points	Year		Points
1924-84	Not held		1992	Japan	1247.180
1988	West Germany	792.08	1994	Japan	1368.860

SKI JUMPING

Multiple gold medals (including team jumping): Matti Nykänen (4); Jens Weissflog (3); Birger Ruud and Toni Nieminen (2).

Normal Hill–70 Meters

Year		Points	Year		Points
1924-60	Not held		1980	Anton Innauer, AUT	266.3
1964	Veikko Kankkonen, FIN	229.9	1984	Jens Weissflog, E. Ger	215.2
1968	Jiri Raska, CZE	216.5	1988	Matti Nykänen, FIN	229.1
1972	Yukio Kasaya, JPN	244.2	1992	Ernst Vettori, AUT	222.8
1976	Hans-Georg Aschenbach, E. Ger	252.0	1994	Espen Bredesen, NOR	282.0

Large Hill–90 Meters

Year		Points	Year		Points
1924	Jacob Tullin Thams, NOR	18.960	1968	Vladimir Beloussov, USSR	231.3
1928	Alf Andersen, NOR	19.208	1972	Wojciech Fortuna, POL	219.9
1932	Birger Ruud, NOR	228.1	1976	Karl Schäabl, AUT	234.8
1936	Birger Ruud, NOR	232.0	1980	Jouko Törmänen, FIN	271.0
1948	Petter Hugsted, NOR	228.1	1984	Matti Nykänen, FIN	231.2
1952	Arnfinn Bergmann, NOR	226.0	1988	Matti Nykänen, FIN	224.0
1956	Antti Hyvärinen, FIN	227.0	1992	Toni Nieminen, FIN	239.5
1960	Helmut Recknagel, GER	227.2	1994	Jens Weissflog, GER	274.5
1964	Toralf Engan, NOR	230.7			

Note: Jump held at various lengths from 1924-56; at 80 meters from 1960-64; at 90 meters from 1968-88; and at 120 meters in 1992.

Team Large Hill

Year		Points	Year		Points
1924-84	Not held		1992	Finland	644.4
1988	Finland	634.4	1994	Germany	970.1

SPEED SKATING

MEN

Multiple gold medals: Eric Heiden and Clas Thunberg (5); Ivar Ballangrud, Yevgeny Grishin and Johann Olav Koss (4); Hjalmar Andersen, Tomas Gustafson, Irving Jaffee and Ard Schenk (3); Gaétan Boucher, Knut Johannesen, Erhard Keller, Uwe-Jens Mey and Jack Shea (2). Note that Thunberg's total includes the All-Around, which was contested for the only time in 1924.

500 meters

Year		Time		Year		Time	
1924	Charles Jewtraw, USA	44.0		1964	Terry McDermott, USA	40.1	OR
1928	(TIE) Bernt Evensen, NOR	43.4	OR	1968	Erhard Keller, W. Ger	40.3	
	& Clas Thunberg, FIN	43.4	OR	1972	Erhard Keller, W. Ger	39.44	OR
1932	Jack Shea, USA	43.4	=OR	1976	Yevgeny Kulikov, USSR	39.17	OR
1936	Ivar Ballangrud, NOR	43.4	=OR	1980	Eric Heiden, USA	38.03	OR
1948	Finn Helgesen, NOR	43.1	OR	1984	Sergei Fokichev, USSR	38.19	
1952	Ken Henry, USA	43.2		1988	Uwe-Jens Mey, E. Ger	36.45	WR
1956	Yevgeny Grishin, USSR	40.2	=WR	1992	Uwe-Jens Mey, GER	37.14	
1960	Yevgeny Grishin, USSR	40.2	=WR	1994	Aleksandr Golubev, RUS	36.33	OR

1000 meters

Year		Time		Year		Time	
1924-72	Not held			1988	Nikolai Gulyaev, USSR	1:13.03	OR
1976	Peter Mueller, USA	1:19.32		1992	Olaf Zinke, GER	1:14.85	
1980	Eric Heiden, USA	1:15.18	OR	1994	Dan Jansen, USA	1:12.43	WR
1984	Gaétan Boucher, CAN	1:15.80					

1500 meters

Year		Time		Year		Time	
1924	Clas Thunberg, FIN	2:20.8		1964	Ants Antson, USSR	2:10.3	
1928	Clas Thunberg, FIN	2:21.1		1968	Kees Verkerk, NET	2:03.4	OR
1932	Jack Shea, USA	2:57.5		1972	Ard Schenk, NET	2:02.96	OR
1936	Charles Mathisen, NOR	2:19.2	OR	1976	Jan Egil Storholt, NOR	1:59.38	OR
1948	Sverre Farstad, NOR	2:17.6	OR	1980	Eric Heiden, USA	1:55.44	OR
1952	Hjalmar Andersen, NOR	2:20.4		1984	Gaétan Boucher, CAN	1:58.36	
1956	(TIE)Yevgeny Grishin, USSR	2:08.6	WR	1988	Andre Hoffman, E. Ger	1:52.06	WR
	& Yuri Mikhailov, USSR	2:08.6	WR	1992	Johann Olav Koss, NOR	1:54.81	
1960	(TIE) Roald Aas, NOR	2:10.4		1994	Johann Olav Koss, NOR	1:51.29	WR
	& Yevgeny Grishin, USSR	2:10.4					

5000 meters

Year		Time		Year		Time	
1924	Clas Thunberg, FIN	8:39.0		1968	Fred Anton Maier, NOR	7:22.4	WR
1928	Ivar Ballangrud, NOR	8:50.5		1972	Ard Schenk, NET	7:23.61	
1932	Irving Jaffee, USA	9:40.8		1976	Sten Stensen, NOR	7:24.48	
1936	Ivar Ballangrud, NOR	8:19.6	OR	1980	Eric Heiden, USA	7:02.29	OR
1948	Reidar Liaklev, NOR	8:29.4		1984	Tomas Gustafson, SWE	7:12.28	
1952	Hjalmar Andersen, NOR	8:10.6	OR	1988	Tomas Gustafson, SWE	6:44.63	WR
1956	Boris Shilkov, USSR	7:48.7	OR	1992	Geir Karlstad, NOR	6:59.97	
1960	Viktor Kosichkin, USSR	7:51.3		1994	Johann Olav Koss, NOR	6:34.96	WR
1964	Knut Johannesen, NOR	7:38.4	OR				

Speed Skating (Cont.)

10,000 meters

Year		Time		Year		Time	
1924	Julius Skutnabb, FIN	18:04.8		1968	Johnny Höglin, SWE	15:23.6	**OR**
1928	Irving Jaffee, USA*	18:36.5		1972	Ard Schenk, NET	15:01.35	**OR**
1932	Irving Jaffee, USA	19:13.6		1976	Piet Kleine, NET	14:50.59	**OR**
1936	Ivar Ballangrud, NOR	17:24.3	**OR**	1980	Eric Heiden, USA	14:28.13	**WR**
1948	Ake Seyffarth, SWE	17:26.3		1984	Igor Malkov, USSR	14:39.90	
1952	Hjalmar Andersen, NOR	16:45.8	**OR**	1988	Tomas Gustafson, SWE	13:48.20	**WR**
1956	Sigvard Ericsson, SWE	16:35.9	**OR**	1992	Bart Veldkamp, NET	14:12.12	
1960	Knut Johannesen, NOR	15:46.6	**WR**	1994	Johann Olav Koss, NOR	13:30.55	**WR**
1964	Jonny Nilsson, SWE	15:50.1					

*Unofficial, according to the IOC. Jaffee recorded the fastest time, but the event was called off in progress due to thawing ice.

WOMEN

Multiple gold medals: Lydia Skoblikova (6); Bonnie Blair (5); Karin Enke and Yvonne van Gennip (3); Tatiana Averina, Gunda Niemann and Christa Rothenburger (2).

500 meters

Year		Time		Year		Time	
1960	Helga Haase, GER	45.9		1980	Karin Enke, E. Ger	41.78	**OR**
1964	Lydia Skoblikova, USSR	45.0	**OR**	1984	Christa Rothenburger, E. Ger	41.02	**OR**
1968	Lyudmila Titova, USSR	46.1		1988	Bonnie Blair, USA	39.10	**WR**
1972	Anne Henning, USA	43.33	**OR**	1992	Bonnie Blair, USA	40.33	
1976	Sheila Young, USA	42.76	**OR**	1994	Bonnie Blair, USA	39.25	

1000 meters

Year		Time		Year		Time	
1960	Klara Guseva, USSR	1:34.1		1980	Natalia Petruseva, USSR	1:24.10	**OR**
1964	Lydia Skoblikova, USSR	1:33.2	**OR**	1984	Karin Enke, E. Ger	1:21.61	**OR**
1968	Carolina Geijssen, NET	1:32.6	**OR**	1988	Christa Rothenburger, E. Ger	1:17.65	**WR**
1972	Monika Pflug, W. Ger	1:31.40	**OR**	1992	Bonnie Blair, USA	1:21.90	
1976	Tatiana Averina, USSR	1:28.43	**OR**	1994	Bonnie Blair, USA	1:18.74	

1500 meters

Year		Time		Year		Time	
1960	Lydia Skoblikova, USSR	2:25.2	**WR**	1980	Annie Borckink, NET	2:10.95	**OR**
1964	Lydia Skoblikova, USSR	2:22.6	**OR**	1984	Karin Enke, E. Ger	2:03.42	**WR**
1968	Kaija Mustonen, FIN	2:22.4	**OR**	1988	Yvonne van Gennip, NET	2:00.68	**OR**
1972	Dianne Holum, USA	2:20.85	**OR**	1992	Jacqueline Börner, GER	2:05.87	
1976	Galina Stepanskaya, USSR	2:16.58	**OR**	1994	Emese Hunyady, AUT	2:02.19	

3000 meters

Year		Time		Year		Time	
1960	Lydia Skoblikova, USSR	5:14.3		1980	Bjorg Eva Jensen, NOR	4:32.13	**OR**
1964	Lydia Skoblikova, USSR	5:14.9		1984	Andrea Schöne, E. Ger	4:24.79	**OR**
1968	Johanna Schut, NET	4:56.2	**OR**	1988	Yvonne van Gennip, NET	4:11.94	**WR**
1972	Christina Baas-Kaiser, NET	4:52.14	**OR**	1992	Gunda Niemann, GER	4:19.90	
1976	Tatiana Averina, USSR	4:45.19	**OR**	1994	Svetlana Bazhanova, RUS	4:17.43	

5000 meters

Year		Time		Year		Time	
1960-84	Not held			1992	Gunda Niemann, GER	7:31.57	
1988	Yvonne van Gennip, NET	7:14.13	**WR**	1994	Claudia Pechstein, GER	7:14.37	

Athletes with Winter and Summer Medals

Only three athletes have won medals in both the Winter and Summer Olympics:

Eddie Eagan, USA– Light Heavyweight Boxing gold (1920) and Four-man Bobsled gold (1932).

Jacob Tullin Thams, Norway– Ski Jumping gold (1924) and 8-meter Yachting silver (1936).

Christa Luding-Rothenburger, East Germany– Speed Skating gold at 500 meters (1984) and 1,000m (1988), silver at 500m (1988) and bronze at 500m (1992) and Match Sprint Cycling silver (1988). Luding-Rothenburger is the only athlete to ever win medals in both Winter and Summer Games in the same year.

All-Time Leading Medal Winners

MEN

No		Sport	G-S-B
9	Sixten Jernberg, SWE	Cross-country	4-3-2
8	Bjorn Dählie, NOR	Cross-country	5-3-0
7	Clas Thunberg, FIN	Speed Skating	5-1-1
7	Ivar Ballangrud, NOR	Speed Skating	4-2-1
7	Veikko Hakulinen, FIN	Cross-country	3-3-1
7	Eero Mäntyranta, FIN	Cross-country	3-2-2
7	Bogdan Musiol, E. Ger/GER	Bobsled	1-5-1
6	Gunde Svan, SWE	Cross-country	4-1-1
6	Vegard Ulvang, NOR	Cross-country	3-2-1
6	Johan Gröttumsbråten, NOR	Nordic	3-1-2
6	Wolfgang Hoppe, E. Ger/GER	Bobsled	2-3-1
6	Eugenio Monti, ITA	Bobsled	2-2-2
6	Roald Larsen, NOR	Speed Skating	0-2-4
6	**Eric Heiden**, USA	Speed Skating	5-0-0
5	Yevgeny Grishin, USSR	Speed Skating	4-1-0
5	Johann Olav Koss, NOR	Speed Skating	4-1-0
5	Matti Nykänen, FIN	Ski Jumping	4-1-0
5	Aleksandr Tikhonov, USSR	Biathlon	4-1-0
5	Nikolai Zimyatov, USSR	Cross-country	4-1-0
5	Alberto Tomba, ITA	Alpine	3-2-0
5	Harald Grönningen, NOR	Cross-country	2-3-0
5	Pål Tyldum, NOR	Cross-country	2-3-0
5	Knut Johannesen, NOR	Speed Skating	2-2-1
5	Vladimir Smirnov, USSR/UT/KAZ	X-country	1-4-0
5	Kjetil André Aamodt, NOR	Alpine	1-2-2

No		Sport	G-S-B
5	Peter Angerer, W. Ger/GER	Biathlon	1-2-2
5	Juha Mieto, FIN	Cross-country	1-2-2
5	Fritz Feierabend, SWI	Bobsled	0-3-2

WOMEN

No		Sport	G-S-B
10	Raisa Smetanina, USSR/UT	Cross-country	4-5-1
9	Lyubov Egorova, UT/RUS	Cross-country	6-3-0
8	Galina Kulakova, USSR	Cross-country	4-2-2
8	Karin (Enke) Kania, E. Ger	Speed Skating	3-4-1
7	Marja-Liisa (Hämäläinen) Kirvesniemi, FIN	Cross-country	3-0-4
7	Andrea (Mitscherlich, Schöne) Ehrig, E. Ger	Speed Skating	1-5-1
6	Lydia Skoblikova, USSR	Speed Skating	6-0-0
6	**Bonnie Blair**, USA	Speed Skating	5-0-1
6	Manuela Di Centa, ITA	Cross-country	2-2-2
6	Elena Valbe, UT/RUS	Cross-country	2-0-4
5	Anfisa Reztsova, USSR/UT	CC/Biathlon	3-1-1
5	Vreni Schneider, SWI	Alpine	3-1-1
5	Gunda Neimann, GER	Speed Skating	2-2-1
5	Helena Takalo, FIN	Cross-country	1-3-1
5	Stefania Belmondo, ITA	Cross-country	1-1-3
5	Alevtina Kolchina, USSR	Cross-country	1-1-3

Games Medaled In

MEN– **Aamodt** (1992,94); **Angerer** (1980,84,88); **Ballangrud** (1928,32,36); **Dählie** (1992,94); **Feierabend** (1936,48,52); **Grishin** (1956,60,64); **Gröttumsbråten** (1924,28,32); **Grönningen** (1960,64,68); **Hakulinen** (1952,56,60); **Heiden** (1980); **Hoppe** (1984,88,92,94); **Jernberg** (1956,60,64); **Johannesen** (1992,94). **Larsen** (1924,28); **Mäntyranta** (1960,64,68); **Mieto** (1976,80,84); **Monti** (1956,60,64,68); **Musiol** (1980,84,88,92); **Nykänen** (1984,88); **Smirnov** (1988,92,94); **Svan** (1984,88); **Thunberg** (1924,28); **Tikhonov** (1968,72,76,80); **Tomba** (1988,92,94); **Tyldum** (1968,72,76); **Ulvang** (1988,92,94); **Zimyatov** (1980,84).

WOMEN– **Belmondo** (1992,94); **Blair** (1988,92,94); **Di Centa** (1992,94); **Egorova** (1992,94); **Ehrig** (1976,80,84,88); **Kania** (1980,84,88); **Kirvesniemi** (1984,88,94); **Kolchina** (1956,64,68); **Kulakova** (1968,72,76,80); **Niemann** (1992-94); **Reztsova** (1988,92,94); **Schneider** (1988,92,94); **Skoblikova** (1960,64); **Smetanina** (1976,80,84,88,92); **Takalo** (1972,76,80); **Valbe** (1992,94).

Most Gold Medals

MEN

No		Sport	G-S-B
5	Bjorn Dählie, NOR	Cross-country	5-3-0
5	Clas Thunberg, FIN	Speed Skating	5-1-1
5	**Eric Heiden, USA**	Speed Skating	5-0-0
4	Sixten Jernberg, SWE	Cross-country	4-3-2
4	Ivar Ballangrud, NOR	Speed Skating	4-2-1
4	Gunde Svan, SWE	Cross-country	4-1-1
4	Yevgeny Grishin, USSR	Speed Skating	4-1-0
4	Johann Olav Koss, NOR	Speed Skating	4-1-0
4	Matti Nykänen, FIN	Ski Jumping	4-1-0
4	Aleksandr Tikhonov, USSR	Biathlon	4-1-0
4	Nikolai Zimyatov, USSR	Cross-country	4-1-0
4	Thomas Wassberg, SWE	Cross-country	4-0-0
3	Veikko Hakulinen, FIN	Cross-country	3-3-1
3	Eero Mäntyranta, FIN	Cross-country	3-2-2
3	Vegard Ulvang, NOR	Cross-country	3-2-1
3	Alberto Tomba, ITA	Alpine	3-2-0
3	Johan Gröttumsbråten, NOR	Nordic	3-1-2
3	Bernhard Germeshausen, E. Ger	Bobsled	3-1-0
3	Gillis Grafström, SWE	Figure Skating	3-1-0
3	Tomas Gustafson, SWE	Speed Skating	3-1-0
3	Vladislav Tretiak, USSR	Ice Hockey	3-1-0
3	Jens Weissflog, E. Ger/GER	Ski Jumping	3-1-0
3	Meinhard Nehmer, E. Ger	Bobsled	3-0-1
3	Hjalmar Andersen, NOR	Speed Skating	3-0-0
3	Vitaly Davydov, USSR	Ice Hockey	3-0-0
3	Anatoly Firsov, USSR	Ice Hockey	3-0-0

No		Sport	G-S-B
3	Thorleif Haug, NOR	Cross-country	3-0-0
3	**Irving Jaffee, USA**	Speed Skating	3-0-0
3	Andrei Khomoutov, USSR/UT	Ice Hockey	3-0-0
3	Jean-Claude Killy, FRA	Alpine	3-0-0
3	Viktor Kuzkin, USSR	Ice Hockey	3-0-0
3	Aleksandr Ragulin, USSR	Ice Hockey	3-0-0
3	Toni Sailer, AUT	Alpine	3-0-0
3	Ard Schenk, NET	Speed Skating	3-0-0
3	Ulrich Wehling, E. Ger	Ski Jumping	3-0-0

WOMEN

No		Sport	G-S-B
6	Lyubov Egorova, UT/RUS	Cross-country	6-3-0
6	Lydia Skoblikova, USSR	Speed Skating	6-0-0
5	**Bonnie Blair, USA**	Speed Skating	5-0-1
4	Raisa Smetanina, USSR/UT	Cross-country	4-5-1
4	Galina Kulakova, USSR	Cross-country	4-2-2
3	Karin (Enke) Kania, E. GER	Speed Skating	3-4-1
3	Anfisa Reztsova, USSR/UT	CC/Biathlon	3-1-1
3	Vreni Schneider, SWI	Alpine	3-1-1
3	Marja-Liisa (Hämäläinen) Kirvesniemi, FIN	Cross-country	3-0-4
3	Claudia Boyarskikh, USSR	Cross-country	3-0-0
3	Sonja Henie, NOR	Figure Skating	3-0-0
3	Irina Rodnina, USSR	Figure Skating	3-0-0
3	Yvonne van Gennip, NET	Speed Skating	3-0-0

Speed Skating (Cont.)

All-Time Leading USA Medalists

MEN

No		Sport	G-S-B	No		Sport	G-S-B
5	Eric Heiden	Speed Skating	5-0-0	2	Terry McDermott	Speed Skating	1-1-0
3*	Irving Jaffee	Speed Skating	3-0-0	2	Dick Meredith	Ice Hockey	1-1-0
3	Pat Martin	Bobsled	1-2-0	2	Tommy Moe	Alpine	1-1-0
3	John Heaton	Bobsled/Cresta	0-2-1	2	Weldy Olson	Ice Hockey	1-1-0
2	Dick Button	Figure Skating	2-0-0	2	Dick Rodenheiser	Ice Hockey	1-1-0
2†	Eddie Eagan	Boxing/Bobsled	2-0-0	2	David Jenkins	Figure Skating	1-1-0
2	Billy Fiske	Bobsled	2-0-0	2	Stan Benham	Bobsled	0-2-0
2	Cliff Gray	Bobsled	2-0-0	2	Herb Drury	Ice Hockey	0-2-0
2	Jack Shea	Speed Skating	2-0-0	2	Eric Flaim	Sp. Skate/ST Sp. Skate	0-2-0
2	Billy Cleary	Ice Hockey	1-1-0	2	Frank Synott	Ice Hockey	0-2-0
2	Jennison Heaton	Bobsled/Cresta	1-1-0	2	John Garrison	Ice Hockey	0-1-1
2	John Mayasich	Ice Hockey	1-1-0				

*Jaffee is generally given credit for a third gold medal in the 10,000-meter Speed Skating race of 1928. He had the fastest time before the race was cancelled due to thawing ice. The IOC considers the race unofficial.

†Eagan won the Light Heavyweight boxing title at the 1920 Summer Games in Antwerp and the four-man Bobsled at the 1932 Winter Games in Lake Placid. He is the only athlete ever to win gold medals in both the Winter and Summer Olympics.

WOMEN

No		Sport	G-S-B	No		Sport	G-S-B
6	Bonnie Blair	Speed Skating	5-0-1	2	Gretchen Fraser	Alpine	1-1-0
4	Cathy Turner	ST Sp. Skating	2-1-1	2	Carol Heiss	Figure Skating	1-1-0
4	Dianne Holum	Speed Skating	1-2-1	2	Diann Roffe-Steinrotter	Alpine	1-1-0
3	Sheila Young	Speed Skating	1-1-1	2	Anne Henning	Speed Skating	1-0-1
3	Leah Poulos Mueller	Speed Skating	0-3-0	2	Penny Pitou	Alpine	0-2-0
3	Beatrix Loughran	Figure Skating	0-2-1	2	Nancy Kerrigan	Figure Skating	0-1-1
3	Amy Peterson	ST Sp. Skating	0-2-1	2	Jean Saubert	Alpine	0-1-1
2	Andrea Mead Lawrence	Alpine	2-0-0	2	Nikki Ziegelmeyer	ST Sp. Skating	0-1-1
2	Tenley Albright	Figure Skating	1-1-0				

Notes: The Cresta run is undertaken on a heavy sled ridden head first in the prone position and has only been held at St. Moritz in 1928 and '48. Also, the term ST Sp. Skating refers to Short Track (or pack) Speed Skating.

All-Time Medal Standings, 1924-94

All-time Winter Games medal standings, according to *The Golden Book of the Olympic Games* and updated through 1994. Medal counts include figure skating medals (1908 and '20) and hockey medals (1920) awarded at the Summer Games. National medal standings for the Winter and Summer Games are not recognized by the IOC.

		G	S	B	Total			G	S	B	Total
1	Norway	73	77	64	214	22	China	0	4	2	6
2	Soviet Union (1956-88)	78	57	59	194	23	Hungary	0	2	4	6
3	**United States**	53	56	37	146	24	Belgium	1	1	2	4
4	Austria	36	48	44	128		Poland	1	1	2	4
5	East Germany (1956-88)	43	39	36	118		Yugoslavia (1924-88)	0	3	1	4
6	Finland	36	45	42	123		Kazakhstan (1994-)	1	2	0	3
7	Sweden	39	26	34	99	28	Spain	1	0	1	2
8	Switzerland	27	29	29	85		Ukraine (1994-)	1	0	1	2
9	Italy	25	21	21	67		Belarus (1994-)	0	2	0	2
10	Germany (1928-36,92-)	23	21	17	61		Luxembourg	0	2	0	2
11	Canada	19	20	25	64	32	Slovenia (1992-)	0	0	3	3
12	West Germany (1952-88)	18	20	19	57		North Korea	0	1	1	2
13	France	16	16	21	53		Uzbekistan (1994-)	1	0	0	1
14	Netherlands	14	19	17	50	35	New Zealand	0	1	0	1
15	Russia (1994-)	12	8	4	24	36	Australia	0	0	1	1
16	Unified Team (1992)	9	6	8	23		Bulgaria	0	0	1	1
17	Great Britain	7	4	12	23		Romania	0	0	1	1
18	Czechoslovakia (1924-92)	2	8	16	26						
19	Japan	3	8	8	19		**Combined totals**	**G**	**S**	**B**	**Total**
20	South Korea	6	2	2	10		USSR/UT/Russia	99	71	71	241
21	Liechtenstein	2	2	5	9		Germany/E. Ger/W. Ger	84	80	72	236

Notes: Athletes from the USSR participated in the Winter Games from 1956-88, returned as the Unified Team in 1992 after the breakup of the Soviet Union (in 1991) and then competed for the independent republics of Belarus, Kazakhstan, Russia, Ukraine, Uzbekistan and three others in 1994. Yugoslavia divided into Croatia and Bosnia-Herzegovina in 1991, while Czechoslovakia split into Slovenia and the Czech Republic the same year.

Germany was barred from the Olympics in 1924 and 1948 as an aggressor nation in both World Wars I and II. Divided into East and West Germany after WWII, both countries competed under one flag from 1952-64, then as separate teams from 1968-88. Germany was reunified in 1990.

International Sports

In 1997, fourteen-year old **Tara Lipinski** of the United States won both the US and World Figure Skating Championships. ————————

Wide World Photos

It Takes Two

In 1997, both Wilson Kipketers made a name for themselves.

by
Jack Edwards

"Who's your favorite track and field athlete?"

"Wilson Kipketer," you say.

"Which one?" I ask.

"What?" you exclaim.

"Well, there's Wilson Boit Kipketer," I elucidate.

"Umm, yeah, that sounds right."

"He's the one who set the world steeplechase record. Or are you thinking of the Danish emigre, also named Wilson Kipketer? He not only ran five consecutive sub 1:43 800–meter races but then he broke the longest standing record in track, held by Sebastian Coe, when he won the world title with a 1:41.25 in Athens. That one?"

"Yeah. That's the guy."

Despite the great year delivered by the Kipketers, they may have a hard time keeping up with Jones. Marion Jones, who was a guard at North Carolina, emerged as the world's pre-eminent female sprinter in the summer of 1997. Although she had the second-slowest reaction time out of the blocks in the 100–meter final, she blazed to victory at the Worlds, winning in 10.83 seconds. She nipped Jamaican legend Merlene Ottey in Monte Carlo, winning the 200 there in 21.92. The WNBA can fantasize all it wants about Jones but roundball will have to wait. Jones is at the beginning of what could be a long and dominant run on the world's track and field stage.

Not to be forgotten in this 1997 roundup, is the "other" Johnson, Allen. Johnson exploded to gold in the 110 hurdles in Athens, continuing the supremacy that he established in Atlanta in 1996. The only problem with Allen Johnson may be in his timing. Not his time of 12.93 but the fact that his Olympic glory came the same night that *Michael* Johnson took over the stadium in Hot 'Lanta.

Off the beaten track, there was Germany's Jan Ullrich, pedaling to prominence. Ullrich is just 23 years old—his cardiovascular engine has not even reached its peak—and he won the

---

Jack Edwards is the co-anchor of ESPN's *Sunday SportsDay.*

In a great year for Kipketers, **Wilson Boit Kipketer** (l) beats fellow Kenyans **Bernard Barmasi** (c) and **Moses Kiptanui** (r) in the 3,000 meters steeplechase at the World Track and Field Championships in Athens on August 6, 1997. A week later Kipketer set a new world record for this event with a time of 7:59.08.

1997 Tour de France by the biggest margin the race has seen since 1984: a fat nine minutes and nine seconds over Richard Virenque. Five-time champion Miguel Indurain, who retired on New Year's Day, was older than Ullrich when he began his dynasty. So was Bernard Hinault who also won the Tour five times. The reason why Ullrich may dominate in the coming years: he took the lead in the Pyrenees and then expanded it during one of the most punishing "climbing tours" of all time.

Speaking of climbing, American skiers did precious little when it came to the awards podium in the Winter of 1997. Sweden's Pernilla Wiberg won the season World Cup by a whopping 536 points (whopping because skiers get 100 points for winning a race, down to one for finishing 30th). Two-time defending downhill champion Picabo Street never saw the 1997 side of the season. Street blew out a knee (for the second time in her career) in December at Vail. She intends to come back for the Olympic season. It'll be a wire-to-wire shot.

Tommy Moe should know. Moe won gold at the Men's downill in Lillehammer but suffered a torn anterior cruciate ligament on the same course a year later. Moe was just

For a sport in dire need of some publicity, the most anticipated track and field showdown of the year was a letdown. **Donovan Bailey (r)** beat **Michael Johnson (l)** in a 150 meter race in which Johnson pulled up lame just past the turn.

approaching top form in January of 1997 when a freak accident occurred at the (mandatory) post-race party at the Londoner in Kitzbuhl. Moe was tending bar and sliced a tendon in his hand. Looking forward to the 98 season, Moe said he was feeling healthy for the first time in years.

Is there anything healthy about competing in luge? The doubles event looks like a couple of mating insects; strangely joined and seemingly out of control, they veer ever downward. Americans Gordy Sheer and Chris Thorpe won the first season championship by a U.S. team in 1997. After getting buried in 12th in Albertville and rising to fifth in Lillehammer, they are aiming for gold in Nagano.

Gold, of course, is expected from American figure skaters. It's just that it wasn't expected quite yet from Tara Lipinski, who won the United States championship when Michelle Kwan stumbled. . . then followed it up with a World Championship. At 14, she became the youngest champion ever to win at the Worlds. A one-two sweep in Nagano for Kwan and Lipinski?

Let's wait to see if there's a plot involving a bludgeon first. ∎

Jack Edwards' Top Ten Highlights of the Year in International Sports

10. U.S. luge doubles team of **Gordy Sheer and Chris Thorpe** win the first season championship by an American team.

9. American skier **Picabo Street,** two-time defending Women's Downhill world champion, has a season-ending injury.

8. Kenyan **Wilson Kipketer** breaks track's oldest standing record. Kipketer's time in the 800 meters

In 1997, Sweden's **Pernilla Wiberg** was the best female skier on, and occasionally off, earth. Here she is winning the World Cup Downhill race in Vail, Colo. on March 12.

of 1 minute 41:24 seconds bested the 1 minute 41:73 seconds posted by Sebastian Coe in 1981.

7. American sprinter **Marion Jones** is victorious in the 100 meter World Championship race. Jones also ran the second leg of the gold medal-winning American team in the 4x100 meter race.

6. **Luc Alphand** of France wins the Men's Alpine World Cup and then retires.

5. Sweden's **Pernilla Wiberg** dominates the Women's Alpine World Cup, winning by 536 points.

4. **Jan Ullrich** of Germany wins the Tour de France bike race.

3. Fourteen year-old American **Tara Lipinski** becomes the youngest skater to win the World Figure Skating Championship.

2. World class cyclist **Miguel Indurain** of Spain hangs up his bike. Indurain won the grueling Tour de France five times in a row from 1991 to 1995.

1. American track and field star **Carl Lewis** retires from competition after a stellar international career that included 9 Olympic Gold medals and 8 IAAF World Championship gold medals. ∎

THE NUMBERS

INSIDE

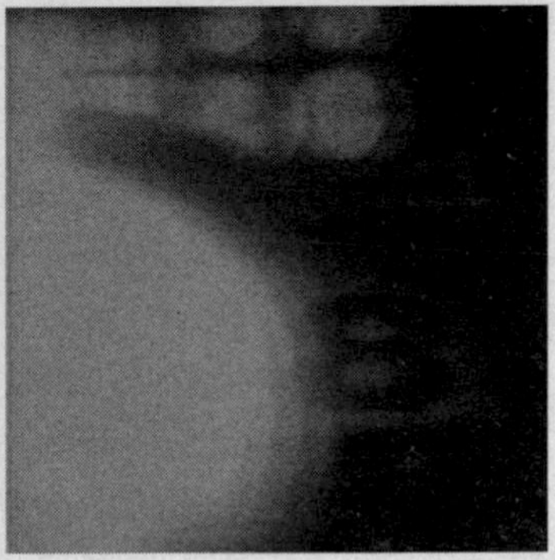

by
Stu Hothem

OH VERY **YOUNG**

Tara Lipinski's triumph in the World Figure Skating Championship at 14 years and nine months seemed such a '90s thing. In the old days, we didn't exploit kids who were barely teenagers for fun and profit. Well, as it turns out, Lipinski broke the record of 14 years and 10 months set by Sonia Henie in . . . 1927! If Henie went on the talk show circuit, she'd have been on the couch next to Babe Ruth and Bill Tilden! Note that from 1928 to 1993, the female World Figure Skating Champion was at least 16.

Youngest Female World Figure Skating Champions

	Age	Year Won
Tara Lipinski, USA	**14 yrs, 9 mos**	**1997**
Sonja Henie, Norway	14 yrs, 10 mos	1927
Oksana Baiul, Ukraine	15 yrs, 3 mos	1993
Michelle Kwan, USA	15 yrs, 8 mos	1996
Sonja Henie, Norway	15 yrs, 10 mos	1928

KEEPING UP WITH **JONES**

Several interesting things happened in the 100 meter races at the World Championships in Athens in 1997. For the first time, an American won both of them, Marion Jones and Maurice Greene. Later in the season, Marion Jones had the third fastest 100m by a woman in history on August 22, 1997 at the Van Damme Memorial Grand Prix in Brussels. Oddly enough, 13 years earlier to the day, Evelyn Ashford also ran that distance at 10.76.

Fastest Women in the 100m

	Time	Year	Age
Florence Griffith-Joyner, USA	10.40	1988	28
Merlene Ottey, Jamaica	10.74	1996	36
Marion Jones	**10.76**	**1997**	**21**
Evelyn Ashford	10.76	1984	27
Irina Privalova, Russia	10.77	1994	25

PINNING IT DOWN

In 1997, Bruce Baumgartner didn't wrestle on the mat as often as he did off it. As he flirted with retirement, Baumgartner accepted an interim athletic director's job at Edinboro University where he has coached for many years. Should he retire, it would be significant because Bruce Baumgartner is the most-decorated wrestler in history. Baumgartner has won nine World Championship medals (three gold, three silver and three bronze) and four Olympic medals (two gold, one silver, one bronze). In addition to being a 15–time U.S. Nationals Champion, he was a finalist for the Sullivan Award as best U.S. amateur athlete four times and finally won it in 1995. Whatever he decides, he has already achieved one of the most distinguished amateur careers in any sport.

Most Wrestling Medals

	Country	Medals
B. Baumgartner	USA	13
V. Jordanov	Bul	12
A. Medved	USSR	12
M. Khardatsev	Rus.	11
A. Karelin	Rus.	10
W. Dietrich	Ger.	10

■

THE 1998

INT'L SPORTS
STATISTICS

THE SEASON IN REVIEW
1996-1997
CHAMPIONS • RECORDS

SEC A

PAGE 691

TRACK & FIELD

1997 IAAF World Championships

The 6th IAAF World Championships in Athletics at Athens, Greece (Aug. 3-10). Note that (WR) indicates a world record, (AR) an American record and (CR) a championship meet record.

Final Medal Standings

Unofficial point totals based on three points for every gold medal, two for each silver and one for each bronze.

		G	S	B	Total	Pts			G	S	B	Total	Pts
1	**United States**	7	3	8	18	35		Japan	1	0	1	2	4
2	Germany	5	1	4	10	21		Mexico	1	0	1	2	4
3	Cuba	4	1	1	6	15	24	Denmark	1	0	0	1	3
	Kenya	3	2	2	7	15		Ethiopia	1	0	0	1	3
	Ukraine	2	4	1	7	15		New Zealand	1	0	0	1	3
6	Russia	1	4	3	8	14		Sweeden	1	0	0	1	3
7	Great Britain & N.I.	0	5	1	6	11		Trinidad & Tobago	1	0	0	1	3
8	Spain	1	3	1	5	10		Greece	0	1	1	2	3
	Jamaica	0	3	4	7	10		Lithuania	0	1	1	2	3
10	Morocco	2	1	1	4	9	31	Bulgaria	0	1	0	1	2
11	Portugal	1	2	1	4	8		Finland	0	1	0	1	2
12	Australia	1	1	2	4	7		Namibia	0	1	0	1	2
13	Czech Republic	2	0	0	2	6		Nigeria	0	1	0	1	2
	Norway	2	0	0	2	6		Sri Lanka	0	1	0	1	2
	Italy	1	1	1	3	6		Uganda	0	1	0	1	2
	Romania	1	1	1	3	6	37	Bahamas	0	0	1	1	1
	Belarus	0	2	2	4	6		Brazil	0	0	1	1	1
18	Canada	1	1	0	2	5		Mozambique	0	0	1	1	1
	Poland	1	1	0	2	5		Slovak Republic	0	0	1	1	1
	South Africa	1	1	0	2	5		Switzerland	0	0	1	1	1
21	France	1	0	1	2	4		Totals	44	45	43	132	265

MEN

Two medals: Donovan Bailey, CAN (1-1-0); Tyree Washington, USA (1-0-1).

100 meters
		Time
1	Maurice Greene, USA	9.86 =CR
2	Donovan Bailey, CAN	9.91
3	Tim Montgomery, USA	9.94

Other Top 8 USA: 8th— Michael Marsh (10.29).

200 meters
		Time
1	Ato Boldon, TRI	20.04
2	Frank Fredericks, NAB	20.23
3	Claudinei Da Silva, BRA	20.26

Top 8 USA: 7th— Jon Drummond (20.44).

400 meters
		Time
1	Michael Johnson, USA	44.12
2	Davis Kamoga, UGA	44.37
3	Tyree Washington, USA	44.39

Other Top 8 USA: 5th— Jerome Young (44.51); 7th— Antonio Pettigrew (44.58).

800 meters
		Time
1	Wilson Kipketer, DEN	1:43.38
2	Norberto Tellez, CUB	1:44.00
3	Rich Kenah, USA	1:44.25

Other Top 8 USA: 8th— Mark Everett (1:49.02).

1500 meters
		Time
1	Hicham El Guerrouj, MOR	3:35.83
2	Fermin Cacho, SPA	3:36.63
3	Reyes Estevez, SPA	3:37.26

5000 meters
		Time
1	Daniel Komen, KEN	13:07.38
2	Khalid Boulami, MOR	13:09.34
3	Thomas Nyariki, KEN	13:11.09

Top 10 USA: 6th— Bob Kennedy (13:19.45).

10,000 meters

		Time
1	Haile Gebrselassie, ETH	27:24.58
2	Paul Tergat, KEN	27:25.62
3	Salah Hissou, MOR	27:28.67

Marathon

		Time
1	Abel Anton, SPA	2:13:16
2	Martin Fiz, SPA	2:13:21
3	Steve Moneghetti, AUS	2:14:16

Best USA: 13th— Douglas Scudamore (2:18.41).

4x100-meter Relay

		Time
1	Canada	37.86
2	Nigeria	38.07
3	Great Britain & N.I.	38.14

CAN— Robert Esmie, Glenroy Gilbert, Bruny Surin, Donovan Bailey; **NGR**— O. Ezinwa, Adeniken, Obikwelu, D. Ezinwa; **GBR&NI**— Braithwaite, Campbell, Walker, Golding.

4x400-meter Relay

		Time
1	United States	2:56.47
2	Great Britain & N.I.	2:56.65
3	Jamaica	2:56.75

USA— Jerome Young, Antonio Pettigrew, Chris Jones, Tyree Washington; **GBR&NI**— Thomas, Black, Baulch, Richardson; **JAM**— McDonald, Haughton, McFarlane, Clarke.

110-meter Hurdles

		Time
1	Allen Johnson, USA	12.93
2	Colin Jackson, GBR	13.05
3	Igor Kovac, SVK	13.18

Other Top 8 USA: 6th— Terry Reese (13.30); 7th— Mark Crear (13.55).

400-meter Hurdles

		Time
1	Stephane Diagana, FRA	47.70
2	Llewellyn Herbert, RUS	47.86
3	Bryan Bronson, USA	47.88

3000-meter Steeplechase

		Time
1	Wilson Boit Kipketer, KEN	8:05.84
2	Moses Kiptanui, KEN	8:06.04
	Bernard Barmasai, KEN	8:06.04

Top 10 USA: 6th— Mark Croghan (8:14.09).

20-kilometer Walk

		Time
1	Daniel Garcia, MEX	1:21:43
2	Mikhail Shchennikov, RUS	1:21:53
3	Mikhail Khmelnitskiy, BLR	1:22:01

Best USA: 34th— Curt Clausen (1:32.05).

50-kilometer Walk

		Time
1	Robert Korzeniowski, POL	3:44:46
2	Jesus Angel Garcia, SPA	3:44:59
3	Miguel Rodriguez, MEX	3:48:30

High Jump

		Height
1	Javier Sotomayor, CUB	7- 9¼
2	Artur Partyka, POL	7- 8½
3	Tim Forsyth, AUS	7- 8½

Pole Vault

		Height
1	Sergey Bubka, UKR	19- 8½ CR
2	Maksim Tarasov, RUS	19- 6½
3	Dean Starkey, USA	19- 4¾

Other Top 10 USA: 6th— Pat Manson (18-8¼)

Long Jump

		Distance
1	Ivan Pedroso, CUB	27-7½
2	Erick Walder, USA	27-6
3	Kiril Sosunov, RUS	26-10

Other Top 10 USA: 8th— Kevin Dilworth (25-10¼)

Triple Jump

		Distance
1	Yoelvis Quesada, CUB	58-6¾
2	Jonathan Edwards, GBR	58-0½
3	Eliecer Urrutia, CUB	57-10½

Top 10 USA: 9th— Kenny Harrison (55–11¼).

Shot Put

		Distance
1	John Godina, USA	70-4¼
2	Oliver-Sven Buder, GER	69-8¼
3	C.J. Hunter, USA	66-8¼

Other Top 8 USA: 7th— Kevin Toth (65-8¼).

Note: Ukraine's **Aleksandr Bagach** was the original gold medalist in the shot put but was stripped of his medal after testing positive for the stimulant ephedrine.

Discus

		Distance
1	Lars Riedel, GER	224-10
2	Virgilijus Alekna, LIT	218-10
3	Jurgen Schult, GER	217-0

Top 10 USA: 5th— John Godina (214–7); 7th— Adam Setliff (208–2).

Hammer Throw

		Distance
1	Heinz Weis, GER	268-4
2	Andrey Skvaruk, UKR	267-3
3	Vasiliy Sidorenko, RUS	264-11

Javelin

		Distance
1	Marius Corbett, RSA	290-0
2	Steve Backley, GBR	284-9
3	Kostas Gatsioudis, GRE	284-3

Decathlon

		Points
1	Tomas Dvorak, CZE	8837 CR
2	Eduard Hamalainen, FIN	8730
3	Frank Busemann, GER	8652

Top 10 USA: 4th— Steve Fritz (8,463 pts).

WOMEN

Two medals: Marion Jones, USA (2-0-0); Zhanna Pintusevich, UKR (1-0-1); Kim Batten, USA (0-1-1); Deon Hemmings, JAM (0-1-1); Jearl Miles, USA (0-1-1); Fernanda Ribeiro, POR (0-1-1); Sandie Richards, JAM (0-1-1).

100 meters

		Time
1	Marion Jones, USA	10.83
2	Zhanna Pintusevich, UKR	10.85
3	Savatheda Fynes, BAH	11.03

Other Top 8 USA: 5th— Inger Miller (11.18); 8th— Chryste Gaines (11.32).

200 meters

		Time
1	Zhanna Pintusevich, UKR	22.32
2	Susanthika Jayasinghe, SRI	22.39
3	Merlene Ottey, JAM	22.40

Top 8 USA 5th— Inger Miller (22.52).

400 meters

		Time
1	Cathy Freeman, AUS	49.77
2	Sandie Richards, JAM	49.79
3	Jearl Miles, USA	49.90

800 meters

		Time
1	Ana Fidelia Quirot, CUB	1:57.14
2	Yelena Afansyeva, RUS	1:57.56
3	Maria Mutola, MOZ	1:57.59

Top 10 USA: 7th— Joetta Clark (2:02.05).

1500 meters

		Time
1	Carla Sacramento, POR	4:04.24
2	Regina Jacobs, USA	4:04.63
3	Anita Weyermann, SUI	4:04.70

5000 meters

		Time
1	Gabriela Szabo, ROM	14:57.68
2	Roberta Brunet, ITA	14:58.29
3	Fernanda Ribeiro, POR	14:58.85

Top 8 USA: 7th— Libbie Hickman (15:11.15).

10,000 meters

		Time
1	Sally Barsosio, KEN	31:32.92
2	Fernanda Ribeiro, POR	31:39.15
3	Masako Chiba, JPN	31:41.93

Best USA: 13th— Annette Peters (32:43.38).

Marathon

		Time
1	Hiromi Suzuki, JPN	2:29:48
2	Manuela Machado, POR	2:31:12
3	Lidia Simon, ROM	2:31:55

Best USA: 25th— Cheryl Collins (2:43.42).

4x100-meter Relay

		Time
1	United States	41.47 **CR**
2	Jamaica	42.10
3	France	42.21

USA— Chryste Gaines, Marion Jones, Inger Miller, Gail Devers; **JAM**— McDonald, Frazer, Cuthbert, Grant; **FRA**— Girard, Arron, Combe, Felix.

4x400-meter Relay

		Time
1	Germany	3:20.92
2	United States	3:21.03
3	Jamaica	3:21.30

GER— Anke Feller, Uta Rohlander, Anja Rucker, Grit Breuer; **USA**— Malone-Wallace, Graham, Batten, Miles; **JAM**— Turner, Graham, Hemmings, Richards.

100-meter Hurdles

		Time
1	Ludmila Engquist, SWE	12.50
2	Svetla Dimitrova, BUL	12.58
3	Michelle Freeman, JAM	12.61

400-meter Hurdles

		Time
1	Nezha Bidouane, MOR	52.97
2	Deon Hemmings, JAM	53.09
3	Kim Batten, USA	53.52

Other Top 8 USA: 6th— Tonja Buford-Bailey (54.77).

10-kilometer Walk

		Time
1	Anna Rita Sidoti, ITA	42:55
2	Olga Kardopoltseva, BLR	43:30
3	Valentina Tsybulskaya, BLR	43:49

Note: Russia's **Olimpiada Ivanova** was the original silver medalist in the 10-k walk but was stripped of her medal after testing positive for steroids.

High Jump

		Height
1	Hanne Haugland, NOR	6-6¼
2	Olga Kaliturina, RUS	6-5
3	Inga Babakova, UKR	6-5

Long Jump

		Distance
1	Lyudmila Galkina, RUS	23-1¾
2	Niki Xanthou, GRE	22-9¼
3	Fiona May, ITA	22-8

Top 10 USA: 5th— Jackie Joyner-Kersee (22-3½); 10th— Marion Jones (21-9).

Triple Jump

		Distance
1	Sarka Kasparkova, CZE	49-10½
2	Rodica Mateescu, ROM	49-9
3	Yelena Govorova, UKR	48-1¾

Top 12 USA: 11th— Cynthea Rhodes (45-3).

Shot Put

		Distance
1	Astrid Kumbernuss, GER	67-11½
2	Vita Pavlysh, UKR	67-9½
3	Stephanie Storp, GER	63-0¾

Top 12 USA: 5th— Connie Price-Smith (62-4); 11th— Valeyta Althouse (55-6¼); 12th— Tressa Thompson (54-1).

Discus

		Distance
1	Beatrice Faumuina, NZL	219-3
2	Ellina Zvereva, BLR	216-2
3	Natalya Sadova, RUS	213-8

Javelin

		Distance
1	Trine Hattestad, NOR	225-8
2	Joanna Stone, AUS	225-2
3	Tanja Damaske, GER	220-2

Heptathlon

		Points
1	Sabine Braun, GER	6739
2	Denise Lewis, GBR	6654
3	Remigia Nazaroviene, LIT	6566

Top 10 USA: 7th— DeDe Nathan (6298); 10th— Kelly Blair (6253).

World Outdoor Records Set in 1997

World outdoor records set or equaled between Oct. 1, 1996 and Sept. 1, 1997; (p) indicates record is pending ratification by the IAAF.

MEN

Event	Name	Record	Old Mark	Former Holder
800 meters	**Wilson Kipketer**, DEN	1:41.73	1:41.73	Sebastian Coe, GBR (1981)
800 meters	**Wilson Kipketer**, DEN	1:41.24	1:41.73	Sebastian Coe, GBR (1981) & Wilson Kipketer (1997)
800 meters	**Wilson Kipketer**, DEN	1:41.11	1:41.24	Wilson Kipketer (1997)
3000 steeplechase	**Wilson Boit Kipketer**, KEN	7:59.08	7:59.18	Moses Kiptanui, KEN (1995)
3000 steeplechase	**Bernard Barmasai**, KEN	7:55.72	7:59.08	Wilson Boit Kipketer, KEN (1997)
5000 meters	**Haile Gebrselassie**, ETH	12:41.86	12:44.39	Haile Gebrselassie, ETH (1995)
5000 meters	**Daniel Komen**, KEN	12:39.74	12:41.86	Haile Gebrselassie, ETH (1997)
10,000 meters	**Haile Gebrselassie**, ETH	26:31.32	26:38.08	Salah Hissou, MOR (1996)
10,000 meters	**Paul Tergat**, KEN	26:27.85	26:31.32	Haile Gebrselassie, ETH (1997)

WOMEN

Event	Name	Record	Old Mark	Former Holder
Pole Vault	**Emma George**, AUS	14-11	14-7 ½	Emma George, AUS (1996)
Hammer Throw	**Mihaela Melinte**, ROM	228-3	227-11	Olga Kuzenkova, RUS (1996)
Hammer Throw	**Olga Kuzenkova**, RUS	232-3	228-3	Mihaela Melinte, ROM (1996)
Hammer Throw	**Olga Kuzenkova**, RUS	233-8	232-3	Olga Kuzenkova, RUS (1997)
Hammer Throw	**Olga Kuzenkova**, RUS	239-10	233-8	Olga Kuzenkova, RUS (1997)

1997 IAAF Mobil Grand Prix Final

The final meeting of the International Amateur Athletic Federation's Outdoor Grand Prix season, which includes the world's 16 leading outdoor invitational meets. Athletes earn points throughout the season with the leading point winners invited to the Grand Prix Final. The 1997 final was held Sept. 13, 1997 in Fukuoka, Japan.

MEN

Event		Time	Event		Time
200m	Frank Fredericks, NAM	19.81	400m Hurdles	Samuel Matete, ZAM	48.01
800m	Wilson Kipketer, DEN	1:42.98			**Hgt/Distance**
Mile	Robert Anderson, DEN	4:04.53	Long Jump	Ivan Pedroso, CUB	28-0
5000m	Khalid Boulami, MAR	13:09.40	Pole Vault	Sergey Bubka, UKR	19-10¼
3000m Steeple	Joseph Keter, KEN	8:21.75	Discus	Lars Riedel, GER	223-0
110m Hurdles	Mark Crear, USA	13.03	Javelin	Jan Zelezny, CZE	293-11

WOMEN

Event		Time	Event		Time
200m	Marion Jones, USA	21.84	400m Hurdles	Kim Batten, USA	53.45
800m	Ana Fidelia Quirot, CUB	1:56.53			**Hgt/Distance**
Mile	Carla Sacramento, POR	4:40.25	High Jump	Inga Babakova, UKR	6-7½
5000m	Sally Barsosio, KEN	15:13.46	Triple Jump	Ashia Hansen, GBR	48-8½
100m Hurdles	Michelle Freeman, JAM	12.40	Shot Put	Astrid Kumbernuss, GER	68-8¾

Final Top 10 Standings

Overall Men's and Women's winners receive $200,000 (US) each; all ties broken by complex Grand Prix scoring system.

MEN

1. Wilson Kipketer, DEN (114 pts); 2. Lar Riedel, GER (99); 3. Mark Crear, USA (95); 4. Hicham El Guerrouj, MAR (93); 5. Moses Kiptanui, KEN (88); 6. Daniel Komen, KEN (86); 7. Jan Zelezny, CZE (85); 8. James Beckford, JAM (85); 9. Boris Henry, GER (82); 10. Maksim Tarasov, RUS (79).

WOMEN

1. Astrid Kumbernuss, GER (99 pts); 2. Deon Hemmings, JAM (93); 3. Kim Batten, USA (91); 4. Inga Babakova, UKR (90); 5. Sarka Kasparkova, CZE (87); 6. Ashia Hansen, GBR (79); 7. Ana Fidelia Quirot, CUB (79); 8. Maria Mutola, MOZ (73); 9. Yelena Afanasyeva, RUS (72); 10. Tatyana Tereshchuk, UKR (70).

World, Olympic and American Records

As of Sept. 1, 1997

World outdoor records officially recognized by the International Amateur Athletics Federation (IAAF); (p) indicates record is pending ratification by the IAAF.

MEN
Running

Event		Time		Date Set	Location
100 meters:	**World**	9.84p	**Donovan Bailey**, Canada	July 27, 1996	Atlanta
	Olympic	9.84	Bailey (same as World)	—	—
	American	9.85	Leroy Burrell	July 6, 1994	Lausanne, SWI
200 meters:	**World**	19.32p	**Michael Johnson**, USA	Aug. 1, 1996	Atlanta
	Olympic	19.32	Johnson (same as World)	—	—
	American	19.32	Johnson (same as World)	—	—
400 meters:	**World**	43.29	**Butch Reynolds,** USA	Aug. 17, 1988	Zurich
	Olympic	43.49	Michael Johnson, USA	July 29, 1996	Atlanta
	American	43.29	Reynolds (same as World)	—	—
800 meters:	**World**	1:41.11p	**Wilson Kipketer**, Denmark	Aug. 24, 1997	Cologne
	Olympic	1:42.58	Vebjoern Rodal, Norway	July 31, 1996	Atlanta
	American	1:42.60	Johnny Gray	Aug. 28, 1985	Koblenz, W. Ger.
1000 meters:	**World**	2:12.18	**Sebastian Coe,** Great Britain	July 11, 1981	Oslo
	Olympic		Not an event	—	—
	American	2:13.9	Rick Wohlhuter	July 30, 1974	Oslo
1500 meters:	**World**	3:27.37	**Noureddine Morceli**, Algeria	July 12, 1995	Nice, FRA
	Olympic	3:32.53	Sebastian Coe, Great Britain	Aug. 11, 1984	Los Angeles
	American	3:29.77	Sydney Maree	Aug. 25, 1985	Cologne
Mile:	**World**	3:44.39	**Noureddine Morceli,** Algeria	Sept. 5, 1993	Rieti, ITA
	Olympic		Not an event	—	—
	American	3:47.69	Steve Scott	July 7, 1982	Oslo
2000 meters:	**World**	4:47.88	**Noureddine Morceli**, Algeria	July 3, 1995	Paris
	Olympic		Not an event	—	—
	American	4:52.44	Jim Spivey	Sept. 15, 1987	Lausanne
3000 meters:	**World**	7:20.67	**Daniel Komen**, Kenya	Sept. 1, 1996	Riete, ITA
	Olympic		Not an event	—	—
	American	7:31.69	Bob Kennedy	Aug. 23, 1996	Brussels
5000 meters:	**World**	12:39.74	**Daniel Komen**, Kenya	Aug. 22, 1997	Brussels
	Olympic	13:05.59	Said Aouita, Morocco	Aug. 11, 1984	Los Angeles
	American	12:58.21	Bob Kennedy	Aug. 14, 1996	Zurich
10,000 meters:	**World**	26:27.85	**Paul Tergat**, Kenya	Aug. 22, 1997	Brussels
	Olympic	27:07.34	Haile Gebrselassie, Ethiopia	July 29, 1996	Atlanta
	American	27:20.56	Mark Nenow	Sept. 5, 1986	Brussels
20,000 meters:	**World**	56:55.6	**Arturo Barrios,** Mexico	Mar. 30, 1991	La Fleche, FRA
	Olympic		Not an event	—	—
	American	58:15.0	Bill Rodgers	Aug. 9, 1977	Boston
Marathon:	**World**	2:06:50	**Belayneh Densimo**, Ethiopia	Apr. 17, 1988	Rotterdam
	Olympic	2:09:21	Carlos Lopes, Portugal	Aug. 12, 1984	Los Angeles
	American	2:10:04	Pat Petersen	Apr. 23, 1989	London
			& Jerry Lawson	Oct. 20, 1996	Chicago
		2:08:52*	Alberto Salazar	Apr. 19, 1982	Boston

Note: The Mile run is 1,609.344 meters and the Marathon is 42,194.988 meters (26 miles, 385 yards).

*Former American record no longer officially recognized.

Walking

Event		Time		Date Set	Location
20 km:	**World**	1:17:25.5	**Bernardo Segura**, Mexico	May 7, 1994	Fana, NOR
	Olympic	1:19:57	Jozef Pribilinec, Czechoslovakia	Sept. 23, 1988	Seoul
	American	1:24:26.9	Allen James	May 7, 1994	Fana, NOR
50 km:	**World**	3:40:57.9	**Thierry Toutain**, France	Sept. 29, 1996	Hericourt, FRA
	Olympic	3:38:29	Vyacheslav Ivanenko, USSR	Sept. 30, 1988	Seoul
	American	3:59:41.2	Herm Nelson	June 9, 1996	Seattle

Hurdles

Event		Time		Date Set	Location
110 meters:	**World**	12.91	**Colin Jackson,** Great Britain	Aug. 20, 1993	Stuttgart
	Olympic	12.95	Allen Johnson, USA	July 29, 1996	Atlanta
	American	12.92	Roger Kingdom	Aug. 16, 1989	Zurich
		12.92	Allen Johnson	June 23, 1996	Atlanta
400 meters:	**World**	46.78	**Kevin Young**, USA	Aug. 6, 1992	Barcelona
	Olympic	46.78	Young (same as World)	—	—
	American	46.78	Young (same as World)	—	—

Note: The hurdles at 110 meters are 3 feet, 6 inches high and the hurdles at 400 meters are 3 feet. There are 10 hurdles in both races.

World, Olympic and American Records (Cont.)

Steeplechase

Event		Time		Date Set	Location
3000 meters:	**World**	7:55.72p	**Bernard Barmasai**, Kenya	Aug. 24, 1997	Cologne
	Olympic	8:05.51	Julius Kariuki, Kenya	Sept. 30, 1988	Seoul
	American	8:09.17	Henry Marsh	Aug. 28, 1985	Koblenz

Note: A steeplechase course consists of 28 hurdles (3 feet high) and seven water jumps (12 feet long).

Relays

Event		Time		Date Set	Location
4 x 100m:	**World**	37.40	**USA** (Marsh, Burrell, Mitchell, C. Lewis)	Aug. 8, 1992	Barcelona
		37.40	**USA** (Drummond, Cason, Mitchell, Burrell)	Aug. 21, 1993	Stuttgart
	Olympic	37.40	USA (same as World)	—	—
	American	37.40	USA (same as World)	—	—
4 x 200m:	**World**	1:18.68	**USA** (Marsh, Burrell, Heard, C. Lewis)	Apr. 17, 1994	Walnut, Calif.
	Olympic		Not an event	—	—
	American	1:18.68	USA (same as World)	—	—
4 x 400m:	**World**	2:54.29	**USA** (Valmon, Watts, Reynolds, Johnson)	Aug. 22, 1993	Stuttgart
	Olympic	2:55.74	USA (Valmon, Watts, Johnson, S. Lewis)	Aug. 8, 1992	Barcelona
	American	2:54.29	USA (same as World)	—	—
4 x 800m:	**World**	7:03.89	**Great Britain** (Elliott, Cook, Cram, Coe)	Aug. 30, 1982	London
	Olympic		Not an event	—	—
	American	7:06.5	SMTC (J. Robinson, Mack, E. Jones, Gray)	Apr. 26, 1986	Walnut, Calif.
4 x 1500m:	**World**	14:38.8	**West Germany** (Wessinghage, Hudak, Lederer, Fleschen)	Aug. 17, 1977	Cologne
	Olympic		Not an event	—	—
	American	14:46.3	USA (Aldredge, Clifford, Harbour, Duits)	June 24, 1979	Bourges, FRA

Field Events

Event		Mark		Date Set	Location
High Jump:	**World**	8-0½	**Javier Sotomayor,** Cuba	July 27, 1993	Salamanca, SPA
	Olympic	7- 10	Charles Austin, USA	July 28, 1996	Atlanta
	American	7-10½	Charles Austin	Aug. 7, 1991	Zurich
Pole Vault:	**World**	20-1¾	**Sergey Bubka,** Ukraine	July 31, 1994	Sestriere, ITA
	Olympic	19-5¼	Jean Galfione, France	Aug. 2, 1996	Atlanta
		19-5¼	Igor Trandenkov, Russia	Aug. 2, 1996	Atlanta
		19-5¼	Andrei Tiwontschik, Germany	Aug. 2, 1996	Atlanta
	American	19-7½	Lawrence Johnson	May 25, 1996	Knoxville, Tenn.
Long Jump:	**World**	29-4¾*	**Ivan Pedroso,** Cuba	July 29, 1995	Sestriere, ITA
		29-4½	**Mike Powell,** USA	Aug. 30, 1991	Tokyo
	Olympic	29-2½	Bob Beamon, USA	Oct. 18, 1968	Mexico City
	American	29-4½	Powell (same as World)	—	—
Triple Jump:	**World**	60- 0¼	**Jonathan Edwards,** GBR	Aug. 7, 1995	Göteborg
	Olympic	59-4¼	Kenny Harrison, USA	July 27, 1996	Atlanta
	American	59-4¼	Kenny Harrison (same as Olympic)	—	—
Shot Put:	**World**	75-10¼	**Randy Barnes,** USA	May 20, 1990	Los Angeles
	Olympic	73- 8¾	Ulf Timmermann, East Germany	Sept. 23, 1988	Seoul
	American	75-10¼	Barnes (same as World)	—	—
Discus:	**World**	243- 0	**Jurgen Schult,** East Germany	June 6, 1986	Neubrandenburg
	Olympic	227- 8	Lare Reidel, Germany	July 31, 1996	Atlanta
	American	237-4	Ben Plucknett	July 7, 1981	Stockholm
Javelin:	**World**	323- 1p	**Jan Zelezny,** Czech Republic	May 25, 1996	Jena, GER
	Olympic	294-2	Jan Zelezny, Czechoslovakia	Aug. 8, 1992	Barcelona
	American	284-10	Tom Pukstys	Aug. 25, 1996	Sheffield, ENG
Hammer:	**World**	284- 7	**Yuri Sedykh,** USSR	Aug. 30, 1986	Stuttgart
	Olympic	278- 2	Sergey Litvinov, USSR	Sept. 26, 1988	Seoul
	American	270- 9	Lance Deal	Sept. 7, 1996	Milan

Note: The international weights for men— **Shot** (16 lbs); **Discus** (4 lbs/6.55 oz); **Javelin** (minimum 1 lb/124¼ oz.); **Hammer** (16 lbs).

*Apparent world record disallowed because of interference with wind gauge at altitude.

Decathlon

Event		Points		Date Set	Location
Ten Events:	**World**	8891	**Dan O'Brien,** USA	Sept. 4-5, 1992	Talence, FRA
	Olympic	8847	Daley Thompson, Great Britain	Aug. 8-9, 1984	Los Angeles
	American	8891	O'Brien (same as World)	—	—

Note: O'Brien's WR times and distances, in order over two days— **100m** (10.43); **LJ** (26- 6¼); **Shot** (54- 9¼); **HJ** (6- 9½); **400m** (48.51); **110m H** (13.98); **Discus** (159- 4); **PV** (16- 4¾); **Jav** (205-4); **1500m** (4:42.10).

WOMEN
Running

Event		Time		Date Set	Location
100 meters:	**World**	10.49	**Florence Griffith Joyner,** USA	July 16, 1988	Indianapolis
	Olympic	10.62	Florence Griffith Joyner, USA	Sept. 24, 1988	Seoul
	American	10.49	Griffith Joyner (same as World)	—	—
200 meters:	**World**	21.34	**Florence Griffith Joyner,** USA	Sept. 29, 1988	Seoul
	Olympic	21.34	Griffith Joyner (same as World)	—	—
	American	21.34	Griffith Joyner (same as World)	—	—
400 meters:	**World**	47.60	**Marita Koch,** East Germany	Oct. 6, 1985	Canberra, AUS
	Olympic	48.65	Olga Bryzgina, USSR	Sept. 26, 1988	Seoul
	American	48.83	Valerie Brisco	Aug. 6, 1984	Los Angeles
800 meters:	**World**	1:53.28	**Jarmila Kratochvilova,** Czech.	July 26, 1983	Munich
	Olympic	1:53.42	Nadezhda Olizarenko, USSR	July 27, 1980	Moscow
	American	1:56.78	Jearl Miles-Clark	Aug. 22, 1997	Brussels
1000 meters:	**World**	2:28.98	**Svetlana Masterkova,** Russia	Aug. 23, 1996	Brussels
	Olympic		Not an event	—	—
	American	2:33.93	Suzy Hamilton	June 4, 1995	Eugene, Ore.
1500 meters:	**World**	3:50.46	**Qu Yunxia,** China	Sept. 11, 1993	Beijing
	Olympic	3:53.96	Paula Ivan, Romania	Oct. 1, 1988	Seoul
	American	3:57.12	Mary Decker	July 26, 1983	Stockholm
Mile:	**World**	4:12.56	**Svetlana Masterkova,** Russia	Aug. 14, 1996	Zurich
	Olympic		Not an event	—	—
	American	4:16.71	Mary Decker Slaney	Aug. 21, 1985	Zurich
2000 meters:	**World**	5:25.36	**Sonia O'Sullivan,** Ireland	July 8, 1994	Edinburgh
	Olympic		Not an event	—	—
	American	5:32.7	Mary Decker	Aug. 3, 1984	Eugene
3000 meters:	**World**	8:06.11	**Wang Junxia,** China	Sept. 13, 1993	Beijing
	Olympic	8:26.53	Tatyana Samolenko, USSR	Sept. 25, 1988	Seoul
	American	8:25.83	Mary Decker Slaney	Sept. 7, 1985	Rome
5000 meters:	**World**	14:36.45p	**Fernanda Ribiero,** Portugal	July 22, 1995	Hechtel, BEL
	Olympic		Not an event	—	—
	American	14:56.04	Amy Rudolph	July 8, 1996	Stockholm
10,000 meters:	**World**	29:31.78	**Wang Junxia,** China	Sept. 8, 1993	Beijing
	Olympic	31:05.21	Olga Bondarenko, USSR	Sept. 30, 1988	Seoul
	American	31:19.89	Lynn Jennings	Aug. 7, 1992	Barcelona
Marathon:	**World**	2:21:06	**Ingrid Kristiansen,** Norway	Apr. 21, 1985	London
	Olympic	2:24:52	Joan Benoit, USA	Aug. 5, 1984	Los Angeles
	American	2:21:21	Joan Benoit Samuelson	Oct. 20, 1985	Chicago

Note: The Mile run is 1,609.344 meters and the Marathon is 42,194.988 meters (26 miles, 385 yards).

Relays

Event		Time		Date Set	Location
4 x 100m:	**World**	41.37	**East Germany** (Gladisch, Rieger, Auerswald, Gohr);	Oct. 6, 1985	Canberra, AUS
	Olympic	41.60	East Germany (Muller, Wockel, Auerswald, Gohr)	Aug. 1, 1980	Moscow
	American	41.47	USA (Gaines, Jones, Miller, Devers)	Aug. 9, 1997	Athens
4 x 200m:	**World**	1:28.15	**East Germany** (Gohr, Muller, Wockel, Koch)	Aug. 9, 1980	Jena, E. Ger.
	Olympic		Not an event	—	—
	American	1:32.30	Univ. of Texas (Howard, Backus, Brown, Perry)	Apr. 5, 1997	Austin, Tex
4 x 400m:	**World**	3:15.17	**USSR** (Ledovskaya, Nazarova, Pinigina, Bryzgina)	Oct. 1, 1988	Seoul
	Olympic	3:15.17	USSR (same as World)	—	—
	American	3:15.51	USA (Howard, Dixon, Brisco, Griffith Joyner)	Oct. 1, 1988	Seoul

Hurdles

Event		Time		Date Set	Location
100 meters:	**World**	12.21	**Yordanka Donkova,** Bulgaria	Aug. 20, 1988	Stara Zagora, BUL
	Olympic	12.38	Yordanka Donkova, Bulgaria	Sept. 30, 1988	Seoul
	American	12.46	Gail Devers	Aug. 20, 1993	Stuttgart
400 meters:	**World**	52.61p	**Kim Batten,** USA	Aug. 11, 1995	Göteborg
	Olympic	53.17	Debra Flintoff-King, Australia	Sept. 28, 1988	Seoul
	American	52.61p	Batten (same as World)	—	—

Note: The hurdles at 110 meters are 3 feet, 6 inches high and the hurdles at 400 meters are 3 feet. There are 10 hurdles in both races.

World, Olympic and American Records (Cont.)

Walking

Event		Time		Date Set	Location
5 km:	**World**	..........20:13.26	**Kerry Saxby-Junna**, Australia	Feb. 25, 1996	Hobart, AUS
	Olympic	....	Not an event	—	—
	American	.........21:28.17	Teresa Vaill	Apr. 24, 1993	Philadelphia
10 km:	**World**	..........41:37.9	**Gao Hongmiao,** China	Apr. 7, 1994	Beijing
	Olympic	.........44:32	Chen Yueling, China	Aug. 3, 1992	Barcelona
	American	.........44:17p	Michelle Rohl	Aug. 7, 1995	Göteborg

Field Events

Event		Mark		Date Set	Location
High Jump:	**World**	............6-10¼	**Stefka Kostadinova**, Bulgaria	Aug. 30, 1987	Rome
	Olympic	6-8	Louise Ritter, USA	Sept. 30, 1988	Seoul
	American	6-8	Louise Ritter	July 8, 1988	Austin
		6-8	Ritter (see Olympic)	—	—
Pole Vault:	**World**	14-11	**Emma George**, Australia	Feb. 20, 1997	Melbourne
	Olympic	....	Not an event	—	—
	American	13-10	Stacy Dragila	Apr. 12, 1997	Eugene, Ore.
Long Jump:	**World**	.........24-8¼	**Galina Chistyakova**, USSR	June 11, 1988	Leningrad
	Olympic	.........24-3¼	Jackie Joyner-Kersee, USA	Sept. 29, 1988	Seoul
	American	24-7	Jackie Joyner-Kersee	May 22, 1994	New York
Triple Jump:	**World**	..........50-0¼p	**Inessa Kravets**, Ukraine	Aug. 8, 1995	Göteborg
	Olympic	....	Event as of 1996	—	—
	American	.........47-3½	Sheila Hudson	July 8, 1996	Stockholm
Shot Put:	**World**	74-3	**Natalya Lisovskaya**, USSR	June 7, 1987	Moscow
	Olympic	.........73-6¼	Ilona Slupianek, E. Germany	July 24, 1980	Moscow
	American	.........66-2½	Ramona Pagel	June 25, 1988	San Diego
Discus:	**World**	252-0	**Gabriele Reinsch**, E. Germany	July 9, 1988	Neubrandenburg
	Olympic	.........237-2½	Martina Hellmann, E. Germany	Sept. 29, 1988	Seoul
	American	216-10	Carol Cady	May 31, 1986	San Jose
Javelin:	**World**	262-5	**Petra Felke**, E. Germany	Sept. 9, 1988	Potsdam, E. Ger.
	Olympic	245-0	Petra Felke, E. Germany	Sept. 26, 1988	Seoul
	American	227-5	Kate Schmidt	Sept. 10, 1977	Furth, W. Ger.
Hammer:	**World**	239-10	**Olga Kuzenkova**, Russia	June 22, 1997	Munich
	Olympic	....	Not an event	—	—
	American	209-2	Dawn Ellerbe	June 1, 1996	Eugene, Ore.

Note: The international weights for women— **Shot** (8 lbs/13 oz); **Discus** (2 lbs/3.27 oz); **Javelin** (minimum 1 lb/5.16 oz); **Hammer** (16 lbs).

Heptathlon

		Points		Date Set	Location
Seven Events:	**World**	7291	**Jackie Joyner-Kersee,** USA	Sept. 23-24, 1988	Seoul
	Olympic	7291	Joyner-Kersee (same as World)	—	—
	American	7291	Joyner-Kersee (same as World)	—	—

Note: Joyner-Kersee's WR times and distances, in order over two days— **100m H** (12.69); **HJ** (61¼); **Shot** (51-10); **200m** (22.56); **LJ** (2310¼); **Jav** (149-10); **800m** (2:08.51).

World Indoor Records Set in 1997
World indoor records set or equaled between Oct. 1, 1996 and Sept. 20, 1997.

MEN

Event		Record	Old Mark	Former Holder
800 meters	**Wilson Kipketer**, DEN	1:43.96	1:44.84	Paul Ereng, KEN (1989)
800 meters	**Wilson Kipketer**, DEN	1:42.67	1:43.96	Wilson Kipketer, DEN (1997)
1500 meters	**Hicham El Guerrouj**, MOR	3:31.17	3:34.16	Noureddine Morceli, ALG (1991)
Mile	**Hicham El Guerrouj**, MOR	3:48.45	3:49.78	Eamonn Coghlan, IRE (1983)
5000 meters	**Haile Gebrselassie**, ETH	12:59.04	13:10.98	Haile Gebrselassie, ETH (1996)
Triple Jump	**Aliecer Urrutia**, CUB	58-6	58-3¾	Leonid Voloshin, RUS (1994)

WOMEN

Event		Record	Old Mark	Former Holder
Pole Vault	**Emma George**, AUS	14-5¼	14-0½	Sun Caiyun, CHN (1996)
Pole Vault	**Stacy Dragila**, USA	14-5¼	14-5¼	Emma George, AUS (1997)
4x400 Relay	**Russia**	3:26.84	3:27.22	Germany (1991)

1997 IAAF World Indoor Championships

The 6th IAAF World Indoor Championships at Paris, France (Mar. 7-9). Note that (WR) indicated world record.

Final Medal Standings

The unofficial point totals are based on three points for every gold, two for each silver and one for each bronze.

		G	S	B	Total	Pts			G	S	B	Total	Pts
1	United States	6	3	7	16	31	11	Czech Republic	1	0	2	3	5
2	Russia	3	1	4	8	15	12	France	0	0	3	3	3
3	Jamaica	1	5	0	6	13		Kenya	0	1	1	2	3
4	Cuba	3	1	0	4	11		Bulgaria	1	0	0	1	3
5	Germany	1	3	1	5	10		Denmark	1	0	0	1	3
	Ukraine	2	2	0	4	10		Ethiopia	1	0	0	1	3
7	Nigeria	1	2	1	4	8		Italy	1	0	0	1	3
	Greece	2	1	0	3	8		Kazakhstan	1	0	0	1	3
9	Morocco	1	1	1	3	6		Mozambique	1	0	0	1	3
	Great Britain	0	3	0	3	6		Romania	1	0	0	1	3

One silver medal (2pts): Australia, Bahamas, Belarus, Estonia and Ireland. **One bronze medal** (1 pt): Bermuda, China, Iceland, Japan, Norway, Poland, Portugal and Yugoslavia.

MEN

Event		Time	
60m	Haralambros Papadias, GRE	6.50	
200m	Kevin Little, USA	20.40	
400m	Sunday Bada, NGR	45.51	
800m	Wilson Kipketer, DEN	1:42.67	**WR**
1500m	Hicham El Guerrouj, MOR	3:35.31	
3000m	Haile Gebrselassie, ETH	7:34.71	
60m H	Anier Garcia, CUB	7.48	
4x400m	USA (Rouser, Everett, Maye, Minor)	3:04.93	

Event		Hgt/Dist
High Jump	Charles Austin, USA	7-8½
Pole Vault	Igor Potapovich, KAZ	19-4¼
Long Jump	Ivan Pedroso, CUB	27-11
Triple Jump	Joel Garcia, CUB	56-9¼
Shot Put	Yuriy Belonog, UKR	68-11¾
Heptathlon	Robert Zmelik, CZE	6228 pts

Other USA medalists: 800m— Rich Kenah (3rd, 1:46.16); **60m H—**Anthony Dees (3rd, 7.50); **Pole Vault—** Lawrence Johnson (2nd, 19-2¼); **Long Jump—** Joe Greene (3rd, 27-7¼); **Shot Put—** John Godina (3rd, 68-5¾).

WOMEN

Event		Time	
60m	Gail Devers, USA	7.06	
200m	Ekaterini Koffa, GRE	22.76	
400m	Jearl Miles-Clark, USA	50.96	
800m	Maria Mutola, MOZ	1:58.96	
1500m	Yekaterina Podkopayeva, RUS	4:05.19	
3000m	Gabriela Szabo, ROM	8:45.75	
60m H	Michelle Freeman, JAM	7.82	
4x400m	Russia (Chebykina, Goncharenko, Kotlyarova, Alekseyeva)	3:26.84	**WR**

Event		Hgt/Dist	
High Jump	Stefka Kostadinova, BUL	6-7½	
Pole Vault	Stacy Dragila, USA	14-5¼	**=WR**
Long Jump	Fiona May, ITA	22-6¼	
Triple Jump	Inna Lasovskaya, RUS	49-3	
Shot Put	Vita Pavlysh, UKR	65-7½	
Pentathlon	Sabine Braun, GER	4780 pts	

Other USA medalists: 800m— Joetta Clark (3rd, 1:59.82); **1500m—**Mary Slaney (2nd, 4:05.22); **60m H—**Cheryl Dickey (Tied 3rd, 7.84); **4x400m relay—** Porter, Kaiser-Brown, Howard, Miles-Clark (2nd, 3:27.66 AR); **Pentathlon—** Kym Carter (3rd, 4627 pts).

World and American Indoor Records

As of Sept. 20, 1997

World indoor records officially recognized by the International Amateur Athletics Federation (IAAF); (p) indicates record is pending ratification by the IAAF.

MEN
Running

Event		Time		Date Set	Location
50 meters:	**World**	5.56p	**Donovan Bailey,** Canada	Feb. 9, 1996	Reno, NV
	American	5.61	James Sanford, USA	Feb. 20, 1981	San Diego
60 meters:	**World**	6.41	**Andre Cason,** USA	Feb. 14, 1992	Madrid
	American	6.41	Cason (same as World)	–	–
200 meters:	**World**	19.92	**Frankie Fredericks,** Namibia	Feb. 18, 1996	Lievin, FRA
	American	20.40	Jeff Williams	Feb. 18, 1996	Lievin, FRA
			& Kevin Little	Mar. 8, 1997	Paris
400 meters:	**World**	44.63p	**Michael Johnson,** USA	Mar. 4, 1995	Atlanta
	American	44.63p	Johnson (same as World)	–	–
800 meters:	**World**	1:42.67	**Wilson Kipketer,** Kenya	Mar. 9, 1997	Paris
	American	1:45.00	Johnny Gray	Mar. 8, 1992	Sindelfingen, GER
1000 meters:	**World**	2:15.26	**Noureddine Morceli,** Algeria	Feb. 22, 1992	Birmingham, ENG
	American	2:18.19	Ocky Clark	Feb. 12, 1989	Stuttgart
1500 meters:	**World**	3:31.17	**Hicham El Guerrouj,** Morocco	Feb. 2, 1997	Stuttgart
	American	3:38.12	Jeff Atkinson	Mar. 5, 1989	Budapest
Mile:	**World**	3:48.45	**Hicham El Guerrouj,** Morocco	Feb. 12, 1997	Ghent, BEL
	American	3:51.8	Steve Scott	Feb. 20, 1981	San Diego
3000 meters:	World	7:30.72	**Haile Gebrselassie,** Ethiopa	Feb. 4, 1996	Stuttgart
	American	7:39.94	Steve Scott	Feb. 10, 1989	E. Rutherford, N.J.
5000 meters:	**World**	12:59.04	**Haile Gebrselassie,** Ethiopa	Feb. 20, 1997	Stockholm
	American	13:20.55	Doug Padilla	Feb. 12, 1982	New York

Note: The Mile run is 1,609.344 meters.

Hurdles

Event		Time		Date Set	Location
50 meters:	**World**	.6.25	**Mark McKoy,** Canada	Mar. 5, 1986	Kobe, JPN
	American	.6.35	Greg Foster	Jan. 27, 1985	Rosemont, Ill.
		.6.35	Greg Foster	Jan. 31, 1987	Ottawa
60 meters:	**World**	.7.30	**Colin Jackson**, Britain	Mar. 6, 1994	Sindelfingen, GER
	American	.7.36	Greg Foster	Jan. 16, 1987	Los Angeles

Note: The hurdles for both distances are 3 feet, 6 inches high. There are four hurdles in the 50 meters and five in the 60.

Relays

Event		Time		Date Set	Location
4x200 meters:	**World**	1:22.11	**Great Britain**	Mar. 3, 1991	Glasgow
	American	1:22.71	National Team	Mar. 3, 1991	Glasgow
4x400 meters:	**World**	3:03.05	**Germany**	Mar. 10, 1991	Seville
	American	3:03.24	National Team	Mar. 10, 1991	Seville

Field Events

Events		Time		Date Set	Location
High Jump:	**World**	.7-11¼	**Javier Sotomayor,** Cuba	Mar. 4, 1989	Budapest
	American	.7-10½	Hollis Conway	Mar. 10, 1991	Seville
Pole Vault:	**World**	.20-2	**Sergey Bubka,** Ukraine	Feb. 21, 1993	Donyetsk, UKR
	American	.19-3¾	Billy Olson	Jan. 25, 1986	Albuquerque
Long Jump:	**World**	.28-10¼	**Carl Lewis**, USA	Jan. 27, 1984	New York
	American	.28-10¼	Lewis (same as World)	—	—
Triple Jump:	**World**	.58-6	**Aliecer Urrutia,** Cuba	Mar. 1, 1997	Sindelfingen, GER
	American	.58-3¼	Mike Conley	Feb. 27, 1987	New York
Shot Put:	**World**	.74-4¼	**Randy Barnes**, USA	Jan. 20, 1989	Los Angeles
	American	.74-4¼	Barnes (same as World)	—	—

Note: The international shot put weight for men is 16 lbs.

Heptathlon

		Points		Date Set	Location
Seven Events:	**World**	6476	**Dan O'Brien,** USA	Mar. 13-14, 1993	Toronto
	American	6476	O'Brien (same as World)	—	—

Note: O'Brien's WR times and distances, in order over two days— **60m** (6.67); **LJ** (25-8¾); **SP** (52-6¾); **HJ** (6-11¾); **60m H** (7.85); **PV** (17-0¾); **1000m** (2:57.96).

WOMEN

Running

Event		Time		Date Set	Location
50 meters:	**World**	.5.96p	**Irina Privalova,** Russia	Feb. 9, 1995	Madrid
	American	.6.02	Gwen Torrence	Feb. 9, 1996	Reno, NV
60 meters:	**World**	.6.92	**Irina Privalova,** Russia	Feb. 11, 1993	Madrid
		.6.92	**Irina Privalova,** Russia	Feb. 9, 1995	Madrid
	American	.6.95	Gail Devers	Mar. 12, 1993	Toronto
200 meters:	**World**	.21.87	**Merlene Ottey,** Jamaica	Feb. 13, 1993	Lievin, FRA
	American	.22.33	Gwen Torrence	Mar. 2, 1996	Atlanta
400 meters:	**World**	.49.59	**Jarmila Kratochvilova,** Czech.	Mar. 7, 1982	Milan
	American	.50.64	Diane Dixon	Mar. 10, 1991	Seville
800 meters:	**World**	.1:56.40	**Christine Wachtel,** E. Germany	Feb. 13, 1988	Vienna
	American	.1:58.9	Mary Decker	Feb. 22, 1980	San Diego
1000 meters:	**World**	.2:31.23	**Maria Mutola,** Mozambique	Feb. 25, 1996	Stockholm
	American	.2:37.6	Mary Decker Slaney	Jan. 21, 1989	Portland
1500 meters:	**World**	.4:00.27	**Doina Melinte,** Romania	Feb. 9, 1990	E. Rutherford, N.J.
	American	.4:00.8	Mary Decker	Feb. 8, 1980	New York
Mile:	**World**	.4:17.13	**Doina Melinte,** Romania	Feb. 9, 1990	E. Rutherford, N.J.
	American	.4:20.5	Mary Decker	Feb. 19, 1982	San Diego
3000 meters:	**World**	.8:33.82	**Elly van Hulst,** Holland	Mar. 4, 1989	Budapest
	American	.8:40.45	Lynn Jennings	Feb. 23, 1990	New York
5000 meters:	**World**	.15:03.17	**Liz McGolgan,** Great Britain	Feb. 22, 1992	Birmingham, ENG
	American	.15:22.64	Lynn Jennings	Jan. 7, 1990	Hanover, N.H.

Note: The Mile run is 1,609.344 meters.

Hurdles

Event		Time		Date Set	Location
50 meters:	**World**	.6.58	**Cornelia Oschkenat,** E. Ger.	Feb. 20, 1988	East Berlin
	American	.6.67	Jackie Joyner-Kersee	Feb. 10, 1995	Reno, Nev.
60 meters:	**World**	.7.69	**Lyudmila Narozhilenko,** USSR	Feb. 4, 1990	Chelyabinsk, USSR
	American	.7.81	Jackie Joyner-Kersee	Feb. 5, 1989	Fairfax, Va.

Note: The hurdles for both distances are 2 feet, 9 inches high. There are four hurdles in the 50 meters and five in the 60.

Walking

Event		Time		Date Set	Location
3000 meters:	World	11:44.00	Alina Ivanova, Russia	Feb. 7, 1992	Moscow
	American	12:20.79	Debbi Lawrence	Mar. 12, 1993	Toronto

Relays

Event		Time		Date Set	Location
4x200 meters:	World	1:32.55	West Germany	Feb. 20, 1988	Dortmund, W. Ger.
	American	1:33.24	National Team	Feb. 12, 1994	Glasgow
4x400 meters:	World	3:26.84	Russia	Mar. 9, 1997	Paris
	American	3:27.66	National Team	Mar. 9, 1997	Paris
4x800 meters:	World	8:18.71	Russia	Feb. 4, 1994	Moscow
	American	8:25.5	Villanova	Feb. 7, 1987	Gainesville, Fla.

Field Events

Event		Mark		Date Set	Location
High Jump:	World	6- 9½	Heike Henkel, Germany	Feb. 9, 1992	Karlsruhe, GER
	American	6-6¾	Coleen Sommer	Feb. 13, 1982	Ottawa
Pole Vault:	World	14-5¼	Emma George, Australia	Dec. 10, 1996	Melbourne
			& Stacy Dragila, USA	& Mar. 9, 1997	& Paris
	American	13-6¼	Melissa Price	Feb. 17, 1996	Fresno, Calif.
Long Jump:	World	24- 2¼	Heike Drechsler, E. Germany	Feb. 13, 1988	Vienna
	American	23- 4¾	Jackie Joyner-Kersee	Mar. 5, 1992	Atlanta
Triple Jump:	World	49- 3¾p	Yolanda Chen, Russia	Mar. 11, 1995	Barcelona
	American	46- 8¼	Sheila Hudson-Strudwick	Mar. 4, 1995	Atlanta
Shot Put:	World	73-10	Helena Fibingerova, Czech.	Feb. 19, 1977	Jablonec, CZE
	American	65- 0¾	Ramona Pagel	Feb. 20, 1987	Inglewood, Calif.

Note: The international shotput weight for women is 8 lbs. and 13 oz.

Pentathlon

Event		Points		Date Set	Location
Five Events:	World	4991	Irina Byelova, Russia	Feb. 14-15, 1993	Berlin
	American	4632	Kym Carter	Mar. 10, 1995	Barcelona

Note: Byelova's WR times and distances, in order over two days– **60m H** (8.22); **HJ** (6-4); **SP** (43- 5¾); **LJ** (21-1¾); **800m** (2:10.26).

SWIMMING

World, Olympic and American Records
As of Sept. 1, 1997

World long course records officially recognized by the Federation Internationale de Natation Amateur (FINA). Note that (ph) indicates preliminary heat; (r) relay lead-off split; and (s) indicates split time.

MEN
Freestyle

Distance		Time		Date Set	Location
50 meters:	World	21.81	Tom Jager, USA	Mar. 24, 1990	Nashville
	Olympic	21.91	Aleksandr Popov, Unified Team	July 30, 1992	Barcelona
	American	21.81	Jager (same as World)	—	—
100 meters:	World	48.21	Aleksandr Popov, Russia	June 18, 1994	Monte Carlo
	Olympic	48.63	Matt Biondi, USA	Sept.22, 1988	Seoul
	American	48.42	Matt Biondi	Aug. 10, 1988	Austin, Tex.
200 meters:	World	1:46.69	Giorgio Lamberti, Italy	Aug. 15, 1989	Bonn, W. Ger.
	Olympic	1:46.70	Yevgeny Sadovyi, Unified Team	July 26, 1992	Barcelona
	American	1:47.72ph	Matt Biondi	Aug. 8, 1988	Austin, Tex.
400 meters:	World	3:43.80	Kieren Perkins, Australia	Sept. 9, 1994	Rome
	Olympic	3:45.00	Yevgeny Sadovyi, Unified Team	July 29, 1992	Barcelona
	American	3:48.06	Matt Cetlinski	Aug. 11, 1988	Austin, Tex.
800 meters:	World	7:46.00s	Kieren Perkins, Australia	Aug. 24, 1994	Victoria, CAN
	Olympic		Not an event	—	—
	American	7:52.45	Sean Killion	July 27, 1987	Clovis, Calif.
1500 meters:	World	14:41.66	Kieren Perkins, Australia	Aug. 24, 1994	Victoria, CAN
	Olympic	14:43.48	Kieren Perkins, Australia	July 31, 1992	Barcelona
	American	15:01.51	George DiCarlo	June 30, 1984	Indianapolis

Backstroke

Distance		Time		Date Set	Location
100 meters:	World	53.86r	Jeff Rouse, USA	July 31, 1992	Barcelona
	Olympic	53.98	Mark Tewksbury, Canada	July 30, 1992	Barcelona
	American	53.86r	Rouse (same as World)	—	—
200 meters:	World	1:56.57	Martin Zubero, Spain	Nov. 23, 1991	Tuscaloosa, Ala.
	Olympic	1:58.47	Martin Zubero, Spain	July 28, 1992	Barcelona
	American	1:58.04	Lenny Krayzelburg	Aug. 1, 1997	Nashville

Breaststroke

Distance		Time		Date Set	Location
100 meters:	**World**	1:00.60p	**Fred deBurghgraeve,** Belgium	July 20, 1996	Atlanta
	Olympic	1:00.60	deBurghgraeve, BEL (same as World)	—	—
	American	1:00.77	Jeremy Linn, USA	July 20, 1996	Atlanta
200 meters:	**World**	2:10.16	**Mike Barrowman,** USA	July 29, 1992	Barcelona
	Olympic	2:10.16	Barrowman (same as World)	—	—
	American	2:10.16	Barrowman (same as World)	—	—

Butterfly

Distance		Time		Date Set	Location
100 meters:	**World**	52.27	**Denis Pankratov,** Russia	July 24, 1996	Atlanta
	Olympic	52.27	Pankratov, Russia (same as World)	—	—
	American	52.84	Pablo Morales	June 23, 1986	Orlando
200 meters:	**World**	1:55.22	**Denis Pankratov,** Russia	June 14, 1995	Canet, FRA
	Olympic	1:56.26	Melvin Stewart, USA	July 30, 1992	Barcelona
	American	1:55.69	Melvin Stewart	Jan. 12, 1991	Perth, Aus

Individual Medley

Distance		Time		Date Set	Location
200 meters:	**World**	1:58.16	**Jani Sievinen,** Finland	Sept. 11, 1994	Rome
	Olympic	1:59.91	Atilla Czene, Hungary	July 25, 1996	Atlanta
	American	2:00.11	David Wharton	Aug. 20, 1989	Tokyo
400 meters:	**World**	4:12.30	**Tom Dolan,** USA	Sept. 6, 1994	Rome
	Olympic	4:14.23	Tamas Darnyi, Hungary	July 27, 1992	Barcelona
	American	4:12.30	Dolan (same as World)	—	—

Relays

Distance		Time		Date Set	Location
4x100m medley:	**World**	3:34.84	**USA** (Rouse, Linn, Henderson, Hall Jr.)	July 26, 1996	Atlanta
	Olympic	3:34.84	USA (same as World)	—	—
	American	3:34.84	USA (same as World)	—	—
4x100m free:	**World**	3:15.11	**USA** (Fox, Hudepohl, Olsen, Hall)	Aug. 12, 1995	Atlanta
	Olympic	3:15.41	USA (Olsen, Davis, Schumacher, Hall Jr.)	July 23, 1996	Atlanta
	American	3:15.11	USA (same as World)	—	—
4x200m free:	**World**	7:11.95	**Unified Team** (Lepikov, Pychnenko, Taianovitch, Sadovyi)	July 27, 1992	Barcelona
	Olympic	7:11.95	Unified Team (same as World)	—	—
	American	7:12.51	USA (Dalbey, Cetlinski, Gjertsen, Biondi)	Sept. 21, 1988	Seoul

WOMEN

Freestyle

Distance		Time		Date Set	Location
50 meters:	**World**	24.51	**Le Jingyi,** China	Sept. 11, 1994	Rome
	Olympic	24.79	Yang Wenyi, China	July 31, 1992	Barcelona
	American	24.87	Amy Van Dyken	July 26, 1996	Atlanta
100 meters:	**World**	54.01	**Le Jingyi,** China	Sept. 5, 1994	Rome
	Olympic	54.65	Zhaung Yong, China	July 26, 1992	Barcelona
	American	54.48	Jenny Thompson	Mar. 1, 1992	Indianapolis
200 meters:	**World**	1:56.78	**Franziska Van Almsick,** Ger.	Sept. 6, 1994	Rome
	Olympic	1:57.65	Heike Friedrich, E. Germany	Sept. 21, 1988	Seoul
	American	1:57.90	Nicole Haislett	July 27, 1992	Barcelona
400 meters:	**World**	4:03.85	**Janet Evans,** USA	Sept. 22, 1988	Seoul
	Olympic	4:03.85	Evans (same as World)	—	—
	American	4:03.85	Evans (same as World)	—	—
800 meters:	**World**	8:16.22	**Janet Evans,** USA	Aug. 20, 1989	Tokyo
	Olympic	8:20.20	Janet Evans, USA	Sept. 24, 1988	Seoul
	American	8:16.22	Evans (same as World)	—	—
1500 meters:	**World**	15:52.10	**Janet Evans,** USA	Mar. 26, 1988	Orlando
	Olympic	Not an event	—	—	—
	American	15:52.10	Evans (same as World)	—	—

Backstroke

Distance		Time		Date Set	Location
100 meters:	**World**	1:00.16	**He Cihong,** China	Sept. 10, 1994	Rome
	Olympic	1:00.68	Krisztina Egerszegi, Hungary	July 28, 1992	Barcelona
	American	1:00.82r	Lea Loveless	July 30, 1992	Barcelona
200 meters:	**World**	2:06.62	**Krisztina Egerszegi,** Hungary	Aug. 25, 1991	Athens
	Olympic	2:07.06	Krisztina Egerszegi, Hungary	July 31, 1992	Barcelona
	American	2:08.60	Betsy Mitchell	June 27, 1986	Orlando

Breaststroke

Distance		Time		Date Set	Location
100 meters:	**World**	1:07.02p	**Penny Heyns**, South Africa	July 21, 1996	Atlanta
	Olympic	1:07.02p	Penny Heyns (same as World)	—	—
	American	1:08.09	Amanda Beard	July 21, 1996	Atlanta
200 meters:	**World**	2:24.76	**Rebecca Brown**, Australia	Mar. 16, 1994	Queensland, AUS
	Olympic	2:26.65	Kyoko Iwasaki, Japan	July 27, 1992	Barcelona
	American	2:25.35	Anita Nall	Mar. 2, 1992	Indianapolis

Butterfly

Distance		Time		Date Set	Location
100 meters:	**World**	57.93	**Mary T. Meagher,** USA	Aug. 16, 1981	Brown Deer, Wisc.
	Olympic	58.62	Qian Hong, China	July 29, 1992	Barcelona
	American	57.93	Meagher (same as World)	—	—
200 meters:	**World**	2:05.96	**Mary T. Meagher,** USA	Aug. 13, 1981	Brown Deer, Wisc.
	Olympic	2:06.90	Mary T. Meagher, USA	Aug. 4, 1984	Los Angeles
	American	2:05.96	Meagher (same as World)	—	—

Individual Medley

Distance		Time		Date Set	Location
200 meters:	**World**	2:11.65	**Lin Li,** China	July 30, 1992	Barcelona
	Olympic	2:11.65	Li (same as World)	—	—
	American	2:11.91	Summer Sanders	July 28, 1992	Barcelona
400 meters:	**World**	4:36.10	**Petra Schneider**, E. Germany	Aug. 1, 1982	Guayaquil, ECU
	Olympic	4:36.29	Petra Schneider, E. Germany	July 26, 1980	Moscow
	American	4:37.58	Summer Sanders	July 30, 1992	Barcelona

Relays

Distance		Time		Date Set	Location
4x100m free:	**World**	3:37.91	**China** (Jingyi, S.Ying, L. Ying, Lu)	Sept. 7, 1994	Rome
	Olympic	3:39.29	USA (Martino, Van Dyken, Fox, Thompson)	July 22, 1996	Atlanta
	American	3:39.29	USA (same as Olympic)	—	—
4x200m free:	**World**	7:55.47	**E. Germany** (Stellmach, Strauss, Mohring, Friedrich)	Aug. 18, 1987	Strasbourg, FRA
	Olympic	7:59.87	USA (Jackson, Teuscher, Taormina, Thompson)	July 25, 1996	Atlanta
	American	7:59.87	USA (same as Olympic)	—	—
4x100m med.:	**World**	4:01.67	**China** (Cihong, Guohong, Limin, Jingyi)	Sept. 10, 1994	Rome
	Olympic	4:02.54	USA (Loveless, Nall, Ahmann-Leighton, Thompson)	July 30, 1992	Barcelona
	American	4:02.54	USA (same as Olympic)	—	—

Pan Pacific Championships

at Fukuoka, Japan, Aug. 10-13, 1997

Men

Event		Time	
50m free	Ricardo Busquets, PUR & William Pilczuk, USA	22.42	
100m free	Michael Klim, AUS	49.46	
200m free	Michael Klim, AUS	1:47.60	CR
400m free	Grant Hackett, AUS	3:47.27	CR
800m free	Grant Hackett, AUS	7:50.30	
1500m free	Grant Hackett, AUS	15:13.25	
100m back	Lenny Krayzelburg, USA	54.43	
200m back	Lenny Krayzelburg, USA	1:57.87	
100m breast	Kurt Grote, USA	1:01.22	CR
200m breast	Kurt Grote, USA	2:14.05	
100m fly	Neil Walker, USA	52.76	CR
200m fly	Ugur Taner, USA	1:57.35	CR
200m I.M.	Matthew Dunn, AUS	2:01.14	
400m I.M.	Matthew Dunn, AUS	4:16.11	

Relays

Event		Time	
400m free	USA (Scott Tucker, Brad Schumacher, Jon Olsen, Neil Walker)	3:18.18	
800m free	USA (Chad Carvin, Tom Malchow, Ugur Taner, Josh Davis)	7:13.99	CR
400m med.	USA (Lenny Krayzelburg, Kurt Grote, Nate Dusing, Neil Walker)	3:36.93	CR

WOMEN

Event		Time	
50m free	Le Jingyi, CHN	25.24	
100m free	Jenny Thompson, USA	54.82	CR
200m free	Claudia Poll, COS	1:57.48	CR
400m free	Grant Hackett, AUS	3:47.27	CR
800m free	Brooke Bennett, USA	8:26.36	
1500m free	Brooke Bennett, USA	16:10.24	
100m back	Mai Nakamura, JPN	1:01.13	
200m back	Mai Nakamura, JPN	2:11.40	
100m breast	Samantha Riley, AUS	1:07.81	CR
200m breast	Samantha Riley, AUS	2:25.34	
100m fly	Jenny Thompson, USA	59.00	CR
200m fly	Susan O'Neill, AUS	2:08.59	
200m I.M.	Kristine Quance, USA	2:13.79	
400m I.M.	Kristine Quance, USA	4:39.61	

Relays

Event		Time
400m free	USA (Catherine Fox, Melanie Valerio, Nicole DeMan, Jenny Thompson)	3:43.77
800m free	USA (Lindsay Benko, Ashley Whitney, Jamie Cail, Jenny Thompson)	8:07.82
400m med.	USA (Lea Loveless-Maurer, Kristy Kowal, Richelle Fox, Jenny Thompson)	4:04.27

WINTER SPORTS

Alpine Skiing

1997 World Championships
at Sestreire, Italy (Feb. 3-15)

MEN

Slalom
1 Tom Stiansen, NOR 1:51.70
2 Sebastien Amiez, FRA 1:51.75
3 Alberto Tomba, ITA 1:52.14

Giant Slalom
1 Michael Von Gruenigen, SWI 2:48.23
2 Lasse Kjus, NOR 2:49.35
3 Andreas Schifferer, AUT 2:49.68

Super G
1 Atle Skaardal, NOR 1:29.58
2 Lasse Kjus, NOR 1:29.89
3 Guenther Mader, AUT 1:30.01

Downhill
1 Bruno Kernen II, SWI 1:51.11
2 Lasse Kjus, NOR ....Thomas Kjus, 1:51.18
3 Kristian Ghedina, ITA 1:51.46

Combined
1 Kjetil Aamodt, NOR 3:10.40
2 Bruno Kernen II, SWI 3:10.68
3 Mario Reiter, AUT 3:11.89

WOMEN

Slalom
1 Deborah Compagnoni, ITA 1:43.99
2 Lara Magoni, ITA 1:45.15
3 Karin Roten, SWI 1:45.48

Giant Slalom
1 Deborah Compagnoni, ITA 2:39.19
2 Karin Roten, SWI 2:39.99
3 Leila Piccard, FRA 2:40.86

Super G
1 Isolde Kostner, ITA 1:23.50
2 Katja Seizinger, GER 1:23.58
3 Hilde Gerg, GER 1:23.54

Downhill
1 Hilary Lindh, USA 1:41.18
2 Heidi Zurbriggen, SWI 1:41.24
3 Pernilla Wiberg, SWE 1:41.44

Combined
1 Renate Goetschl, AUT 3:03.38
2 Katja Seizinger, GER 3:03.42
3 Hilde Gerge, GER 3:03.45

World Cup Champions

MEN

Overall ....Luc Alphand, FRA
Downhill ....Luc Alphand, FRA
Slalom ....Thomas Sykora, AUT
Giant Slalom ....Michael von Gruenigen, SWI
Super G ....Hans Knaus, AUT
Nation's Cup ....Austria

WOMEN

Overall ....Pernilla Wiberg, SWE
Downhill ....Katja Seizinger, GER
Slalom ....Pernilla Wiberg, SWE
Giant Slalom ....Katja Seizinger, GER
Super G ....Hilde Gerg, GER
Nation's Cup ....Germany

Top Five Standings — MEN

Overall 1. Luc Alphand, FRA (637 pts); 2. Michael von Gruenigen, SWI (606); 3. Kjetil Andre Aamodt, NOR (605); 4. Kristian Ghedina, ITA (584); 5. Thomas Sykora, AUT (582). *Best USA*— Matthew Grosjean (39th, 131 pts).

Downhill 1. Luc Alphand, FRA (605 pts); 2. Kristian Ghedina, ITA (534); 3. Werner Franz, AUT (438); 4. Fritz Strobl, AUT (399); 5. Atle Skaardal, NOR (386). *Best USA*— Kyle Rasmussen (25th, 65 pts).

Slalom 1. Thomas Sykora, AUT (480 pts); 2. Thomas Stangassinger, AUT (280); 3. Sebastien Amiez, FRA (208); 4. Tom Stiansen, NOR (178); 5. Kjetil Andre Aamodt, NOR (152). *Best USA*— Matt Grosjean (14th, 95 pts).

Giant Slalom 1. Michael von Gruenigen, SWI (460 pts); 2. Kjetil Andre Aamodt, NOR (301); 3. Hans Knaus, AUT (280); 4. Steve Locher, SWI (276); 5. Fredrik Nyberg, SWE (252).

Super G 1. Hans Knaus, AUT (100 pts); 2. Gunther Mader, AUT (80); 3. Steve Locher, SWI (60); 4. Patrick Ortlieb, AUT (50); 5. Christian Mayer, AUT (45). *Best USA*— Daron Rhalves (11th, 24 pts).

Top Five Standings — WOMEN

Overall 1. Pernilla Wiberg, SWE (612 pts); 2. Katja Seizinger, GER (494); 3. Hilde Gerg, GER (415); 4. Deborah Compagnoni, ITA (300); 5. Claudia Riegler, MZL (289). *Best USA*— Megan Gerety (27th, 88 pts).

Downhill 1. Katja Seizinger, GER (180 pts); 2. Renate Goetschl, AUT (132); 3. Carole Montillet, FRA (86); 4. Pernilla Wiberg, SWE (75); 5. Heidi Zurbriggen, SWI (69). *Best USA*— Megan Gerety (10th, 56 pts).

Slalom 1. Pernilla Wiberg, SWE (310 pts); 2. Claudia Riegler, MZL (289); 3. Deborah Compagnoni, ITA (220); 4. Patricia Chauvet, FRA (206); 5. Urska Hrovat, SLO (157).

Giant Slalom 1. Katja Seizinger, GER (160); 2. Sabina Panzanini, ITA (100); 3. Hilde Gerg, GER (86); 4. Deborah Compagnoni, ITA & Anita Wachter, AUT (80).

Super G 1. Hilde Gerg, GER (230 pts); 2. Pernilla Wiberg, SWE (209); 3. Katja Seizinger, GER (154); 4. Warwara Zelenskaja (132); 5. Isolde Kostner, ITA & Svetlana Gladishiva (125). *Best USA*— Megen Gerety (22nd, 32 pts).

Combined Nation's Cup 1. Austria (7509 pts); 2. Italy (4211); 3. Switzerland (3867) 4. France (3109); 5. Germany (2958); 6. Norway (2136); 7. Sweden (2126); 8. Slovenia (1337); 9. United States (686); 10. Canada (560).

Freestyle Skiing

1997 World Championships
at Nagano, Japan (Feb. 4-9)

MEN

Combined
1 Darcy Downs, CAN 30.00
2 Toben Sutherland, CAN 27.60
3 Oleg Kouleshov, BLR 24.00

Acro
1 Fabrice Becker, FRA 26.90
2 Ian Edmondson, USA 26.40
3 Heini Baumgartner, SWI 25.40

Moguls
1 Jean-Luc Brassard, CAN 27.52
2 Stephane Rochon, CAN 26.00
3 Jesper Ronnback, SWE 25.43

Aerials
1 Nicolas Fontaine, CAN 254.98
2 Eric Bergoust, USA 245.63
3 Andy Capicik, CAN 235.39

WOMEN

Acro
1 Oksana Kushenko, RUS 25.80
2 Asa Magnusson, SWE 25.25
3 Annika Johansson, SWE 25.25

Moguls
1 Candice Gilg, FRA 24.84
2 Donna Weinbrecht, USA 24.60
3 Tatjana Mittermayer, GER 24.20

Aerials
1 Kirstie Marshall, AUS 197.92
2 Michele Rohrbach, SWI 177.84
3 Veronica Brenner, CAN 176.79

World Cup Champions

MEN

Overall ....Darcy Downs, CAN
Aerials ....Nicolas Fontaine, CAN
Moguls ....Jean-Luc Brassard, CAN
Dual Moguls ....Thony Hemery, FRA
Acroski ....Fabrice Becker, FRA

WOMEN

Overall ....Stacey Blumer, USA
Aerials ....Veronica Brenner, CAN
Moguls ....Tatjana Mittermayer, GER
Dual Moguls ....Candice Gilg, FRA
Acroski ....Elena Batalova, RUS

Nordic Skiing

1997 World Championships
at Trondheim, Norway (Feb. 21-Mar. 2)

MEN

10-km classical ....Bjorn Daehlie, NOR
50-km classical ....Mika Myllyla, FIN
15-km pursuit ....Bjorn Daehlie, NOR
30-km freestyle ....Alexey Prokurorov, RUS
4x10-km relay ....Norway

WOMEN

5-km classical ....Elena Valbe, RUS
30-km classical ....Elena Valbe, RUS
10-km pursuit ....Elena Valbe, RUS
15-km freestyle ....Elena Valbe, RUS
4x5-km relay ....Russia

Ski Jumping

Large Hill (120 meters) .... Masahiko Harada, JPN
Normal Hill (90 meters) .... Janne Ahonen, FIN
Team (120 meters) ....Finland

Nordic Combined
90-meter jump/15-km cross-country ski

Individual ....Kenji Ogiwara, JPN
Team ....Norway

Snowboarding

1997 World Championships
at Innichen/San Candido, Italy (Jan. 21-26)

MEN

Halfpipe	**Pts**
1 Fabien Rohrer, SWI	38.10
2 Markus Hurme, FIN	37.70
3 Roge Hjelmstadstuen, NOR	40.20

Giant Slalom	**Time**
1 Thomas Prugger, ITA	2:12.86
2 Mike Jacoby, USA	2:13.75
3 Ian Price, USA	2:13.94

Slalom
1 Bernd Kroschweski, GER 1:09.39
2 Dieter Moherndl, GER 1:09.44
3 Anton Pogue, USA 1:09.79

Parallel Slalom
1 Mike Jacoby, USA ....—
2 Elmar Messner, ITA ....—
3 Bernd Kroschweski, GER ....—

Snowboard Cross
1 Helmut Pramstaller, AUT ....—
2 Klaus Sammer, AUT ....—
3 Jacob Bergstedt, SWE ....—

Snowboarding (Cont.)
WOMEN

Halfpipe	Pts
1 Anita Schwaller, SWI	24.90
2 Christel Thoresen, NOR	23.80
3 Sabine Wehr-Hassler, GER	24.00

Giant Slalom	Time
1 Sondra Van Ert, USA	2:26.04
2 Karine Ruby, FRA	2:27.31
3 Margherita Parini, ITA	2:28.99

Slalom	
1 Heidi Renoth, GER	1:12.78
2 Dag Mair Unter Der Eggen, ITA	1:13.14
3 Dorothee Fournier, FRA	1:14.16

Parallel Slalom	
1 Dag Mair Unter Der Eggen, ITA	—
2 Karine Ruby, FRA	—
3 Marie Birkle, SWE	—

Snowboard Cross	
1 Karine Ruby, FRA	—
2 Manuela Riegler, AUT	—
3 Maria Pichler, AUT	—

World Cup Final Standings

MEN

Overall	Pts
1 Harald Walder, AUT	1090.75
2 Peter Pechhacker, AUT	897.00
3 Anton Pogue, USA	819.50

Halfpipe	Pts
1 Jonas Gunnarson, SWE	3770
2 Dan Smith, USA	3680
3 Trevor Andrew, CAN	2980

Slalom	Pts
1 Karl Frenademez, ITA	5450
2 Harald Walder, AUT	5190
3 Anton Pogue, USA	4060

Giant Slalom	Pts
1 Peter Pechhacker, AUT	6020
2 Harald Walder, AUT	4420
3 Ross Rebagliati, CAN	4280

Snowboard Cross	Pts
1 Elmar Messner, ITA	2990
2 Alex Voyat, ITA	2790
3 Richard Richardsson, SWE	1790

WOMEN

Overall	Pts
1 Karine Ruby, FRA	1637.50
2 Sondra Van Ert, USA	1080.00
3 Manuela Riegler, AUT	1005.75

Halfpipe	Pts
1 Tara Teigen, CAN	3350
2 Sabrina Sadeghi, USA	2620
3 Maelle Ricker, CAN	2470

Slalom	Pts
1 Karine Ruby, FRA	6700
2 Heidi Renoth, GER	5360
3 Marion Posch, ITA	4650

Giant Slalom	Pts
1 Karine Ruby, FRA	6590
2 Margherita Parini, ITA	5420
3 Sondra Van Ert, USA	5320

Snowboard Cross	Pts
1 Karine Ruby, FRA	4000
2 Manuel Riegler, AUT	2910
3 Sondra Van Ert, USA	2740

Speed Skating
World Cup Champions
MEN

500 meters	Hiroyasu Shimizu, JPN
1000 meters	Manabu Horii, JPN
1500 meters	Rintje Ritsma, NET
5000 meters	Rintje Ritsma, NET

WOMEN

500 meters	Ruihong Xue, CHN
1000 meters	Franziska Schenk, GER
1500 meters	Gunda Niemann, GER
3000 meters	Tonny de Jong, NET

1997 World Championships
at Nagano, Japan (Feb. 14-16)
MEN

500 meters	Kyou-Hyuk Lee, ROK
1500 meters	Ids Postma, NET
5000 meters	Bart Veldkamp, NET
10,000 meters	Bart Veldkamp, NET
All-Around	Ids Postma, NET

WOMEN

500 meters	Annamarie Thomas, NET
1500 meters	Gunda Niemann, GER
3000 meters	Gunda Niemann, GER
5000 meters	Gunda Niemann, GER
All-Around	Gunda Niemann, GER

Figure Skating
World Championships
at Lausanne, Switzerland (Mar. 16–23)

Men's — 1. Elivs Stojko, Canada; 2. Todd Eldredge, USA; 3. Alexei Yagudin, Russia

Women's — 1. Tara Lipinski, USA; 2. Michelle Kwan, USA; 3. Vanessa Gusmeroli, France

Pairs — 1. Mandy Wotzel & Ingo Steuer, Germany; 2. Marina Eltsova & Andrey Bushkov, Russia; 3. Oksana Kasakova & Arthur Dmitriev, Russia

Ice Dance — 1. Oksana Gritschuk & Evgeny Platov, Russia; 2. Anjelika Krylova & Oleg Ovsiannikov, Russia; 3. Shae-Lynn Bourne & Victor Kraatz, Canada

U.S. Championships
at Nashville, Tenn. (Feb. 6-15)

Men's	Todd Eldredge, Chatham, Mass.
Women's	Tara Lipinski, Sugarland, Texas
Pairs	Kyoko Ina, Guttenburg, N.Y. & Jason Dungjen, Goshin, N.Y.
Ice Dance	Elizabeth Punsalan, Sheffield Lake, Ohio & Jerod Swallow, Northville, Mich.

European Championships
at Paris (Jan. 20-26)

Men's	Alexei Urmanov, Russia
Women's	Irina Slutskaya, Russia
Pairs	Marina Eltsova & Artur Dmitriev, Russia
Ice Dance	Oksana Grishuk & Yevgeny Platov, Russia

SUMMER SPORTS

Cross-country
IAAF World Championships
at Turin, Italy (Mar. 23)

MEN 7.65 miles ....1. Paul Tergat, KEN 35:11
2. Salah Hissou, MOR 35:13
3. Tom Nyariki, KEN 35:20
Best USA— Scott Larson, 51st
37:14

WOMEN 4.1 miles ....1. Derartu Tulu, ETH 20:53
2. Paula Radcliffe, GBR 20:55
3. Gete Wami, ETH 21:00
Best USA— Amy Rudolph, 26th
22:00

Cycling

Tour de France

The 84th Tour de France (July 5-27) ran 21 stages plus a prologue, covering 2,455 miles starting in Normandy, passing through the Swiss Alps and finishing on the Avenue des Champs-Elysees in Paris.

Jan Ullrich, nicknamed "the Terminator" by his home country's press, became the first German winner in the Tour's history. He finished with a time of 100 hours, 30 minutes and 35 seconds for an average speed of 24.38 mph, making it the fastest Tour on record. Ullrich's time was 9 minutes, 9 seconds ahead of second-place Richard Virenque of France. It was the largest margin of victory since France's Laurent Fignon beat his countryman Bernard Hinault by 10:32 in 1984.

The 23-year-old German became the eighth youngest winner ever and earned $360,000. Ullrich captured the leader's yellow jersey in the 10th stage of the race, during the race's second day in the Pyrenees mountain range in the south of France. He never relinquished it, excelling in the Tour's two individual time trials and putting more and more time between himself and Virenque. Last year in his first ever Tour de France, Ullrich placed second to Telekom teammate Bjarne Riis and claimed the "best young rider" award for the top rider under 25.

		Team	Behind
1	Jan Ullrich, GER ....Telekom		—
2	Richard Virenque, FRA ....Festina		9:09
3	Marco Pantani, ITA ....Mercantone Uno		14:03
4	Abraham Olano, SPA ....Mapei		15:15
5	Fernando Escartin, SPA ....Kelme		20:32
6	Francesco Casagrande, ITA ....Saeco		22:47

		Team	Behind
7	Bjarne Riis, DEN ....Telekom		26:34
8	Jose-Maria Jimenez, SPA ....Banesto		31:17
9	Laurent Dufaux, SWI ....Festina		31:55
10	Roberto Conti, ITA ....Mercatone Uno		32:26

Best USA: 17th— Bobby Julich, Glenwood Spring, Colo., Cofidis, 1:01:10 behind.

Other Worldwide Champions
1997 UCI (Union Cycliste Internationale) Elite Results
MEN

Mediterranean Tour (FRA) ....Emmanuel Magnien, FRA
Ruta del Sol (SPA) ....Erik Zable, GER
Tour of Valencia (SPA) ...... Juan Carlos Dominguez, SPA
Het Volk (BEL) ....Peter Van Petegem, BEL
Paris-Nice (FRA) ....Laurent Jalabert, FRA
Tirreno-Adriatico (ITA) ....Roberto Petito, ITA
Criterium International (FRA) ...Marcelino Garcia Alonso, SPA
Tour of the Basque Country (SPA) ....Alex Zulle, SWI
Ghent-Wevelgen (BEL) ....Philippe Gaumont, FRA

Fleche Wallone (BEL) ....Laurent Jalabert, FRA
Tour de Romandie (SWI) ....Pavel Tonkov, RUS
Giro d'Italia (ITA) ....Ivan Gotti, ITA
GP du Midi Libre (FRA) ....Alberto Elli, ITA
Dauphine Libere (FRA) ....Udo Bolts, GER
Tour of Switzerland (SWI) ......Christophe Agnolutto, FRA
Tour of Catalonia (SPA) ....Fernando Escartin, SPA
World Time Trial ....ends Oct. 3
World Pro Road Race ....ends Oct. 6

WOMEN

Thrift Drug USPRO Champ. (USA) .....Karen Kurreck, USA
CoreStates Liberty Classic (USA) .....Edita Pucinskaite, LIT
H-P International (USA) ....Rasa Polikeviciute, LIT

Tour Cycliste Feminin (FRA) .... Fabiana Luperini, ITA
Giro d'Italia Femminile (ITA) .... Fabiana Luperini, ITA

Mountain Biking
1997 World Championships
at Chateau d'Oex, Switzerland (Sept. 12-21).
MEN

Cross Country (51.2 km)	Time
1 Hubert Pallhuber, ITA 2:42:26
2 Henrik Djernis, DEN ....at 1:04
3 Luca Bramati, ITA ....at 1:36

Downhill (4.15 km)	Time
1 Nicholas Vouilloz, FRA 6:22.62
2 John Tomac, USA 6:28.81
3 Cedric Gracia, FRA 6:28.84

Other Top Americans — Cross Country: 23rd-David Wiens (at 12:58); Downhill: 7th-Myles Rockwell (6:33.47)

Mountain Biking (Cont.)

WOMEN

Cross Country (33.1 km)	Time	Downhill (4.15 km)	Time
1 Paola Pezzo, ITA	1:59.42	1 Anne-Caroline Chausson, FRA	6:59.92
2 Nadia de Negri, ITA	at 3:40	2 Marielle Saner, SWI	7:19.55
3 Margarita Fullana, SPA	at 4:12	3 Katja Repo, FIN	7:22.84

Top Americans — Cross Country: 7th— Alison Dunlap (at 7:23); Downhill: 4th—Elke Brutsaert (7:26.97).

1997 UCI World Cup Champions

MEN

Cross Country	Pts
1 Miguel Martinez, FRA	638
2 Christophe Duponey, FRA	632
3 Cadel Evans, AUS	600

Downhill	Pts
1 Carrado Herin, ITA	277
2 Jurgen Beneke, GER	265
3 Tomas Misser, SPA	233

WOMEN

Cross Country	Pts
1 Paolo Pezzo, ITA	525
2 Alison Syder, CAN	482
3 Chantal Daucourt, SWI	433

Downhill	Pts
1 Missy Giove, USA	190
2 Anne-Caroline Chausson, FRA	190
3 Leigh Donovan, USA	152

Note: Giove won the tie-breaker with Chausson because she beat her in the World Cup final Aug. 17 at Kaprun, Austria.

Marathons

Boston Marathon

101st edition of the Boston Marathon, held Monday, April 21, 1997 and run, as always, from Hopkinton through Ashland, Framingham, Natick, Wellesley, Newton and Brookline to Boston, Mass. Lameck Aguta of Kenya broke away from the lead pack in the 25th mile and won in a time of two hours, 10 minutes and 34 seconds. Ethiopia's Fatuma Roba ended Uta Pippig's three-year reign as the women's champion with a move also late in the race. It was Roba's first Boston and the first time an African woman won the race. Franz Nietlispach of Swiitzerland won the men's wheelchair division (1:28:14) and Australia's Louise Sauvage (1:54:28) held off American Jean Driscoll's bid for an eighth straight victory in the women's wheelchair division. Driscoll caught a wheel in the trolley tracks while running just inches behind Savauge and fell over. Driscoll would finish in second place about seven minutes behind Savauge. Winners in the men's and women's divisions earned $75,000. **Distance:** 26.2 miles.

MEN

		Time
1	Lameck Aguta, KEN	2:10:34
2	Joseph Kamau, KEN	2:10:46
3	Dionicio Ceron, MEX	2:10:59
4	German Silva, MEX	2:11:21
5	Moses Tanui, KEN	2:11:38
6	Jimmy Muindi, KEN	2:12:49
7	Andre Ramos, BRZ	2:13:10
8	Jose Luis Molina, CRC	2:13:34
9	Bekele Tesfaye, ETH	2:14:02
10	Nelson Ndereva, KEN	2:14:12

Note: Best USA: 18th— Daniel Gonzalez, Rancho Santa Marguerita, Calif., 2:18:30.

WOMEN

		Time
1	Fatuma Roba, ETH	2:26:23
2	Elana Meyer, S. Afr	2:27:09
3	Colleen de Reuck, S. Afr	2:28:03
4	Uta Pippig, GER	2:28:51
5	Derartu Tulu, ETH	2:30:28
6	Junko Asari, JPN	2:31:12
7	Alla Jiliaeva, RUS	2:31:55
8	Sonia Maccioni, ITA	2:31:59
9	Kim Jones, USA	2:32:52
10	Debbie Kilpatrick, USA	2:36:04

Other 1997 Winners

Los Angeles

			Time
Mar. 2	Men	El-Maati Chaham, MOR	2:14:16
	Women	Lornah Kiplagat, KEN	2:33:50

London

			Time
Apr. 13	Men	Antonio Pinto, POR	2:07:55
	Women	Joyce Chepchumba, KEN	2:26:51

Rotterdam

			Time
Apr. 20	Men	Domingos Castro, POR	2:07:51
	Women	Tegla Laroupe, KEN	2:22:07

Late 1996

New York City

			Time
Nov. 3	Men	Giacomo Leone, ITA	2:09:54
	Women	Anuta Catuna, ROM	2:28:18

Fukuoka

			Time
Dec. 1	Men	Lee Bong-Ju, KOR	2:10:48
	(No women's division)		

INT'L SPORTS

S T A T I S T I C S

THROUGH THE YEARS

1896-1997

WINNERS • RECORDS

THE 1998

ESPN INFORMATION PLEASE SPORTS ALMANAC

SEC B

PAGE 709

TRACK & FIELD

IAAF World Championships

While the Summer Olympics have served as the unofficial world outdoor championships for track and field throughout the century, a separate World Championship meet was started in 1983 by the International Amateur Athletic Federation (IAAF). The meet was held every four years from 1983-91, but began an every-other-year cycle in 1993. World Championship sites include Helsinki (1983), Rome (1987), Tokyo (1991), Stuttgart (1993), Göteborg, Sweden (1995), Athens (1997) and Seville (1999). Note that (WR) indicates world record and (CR) indicates championship meet record.

MEN

Multiple gold medals (including relays): Carl Lewis (8); Michael Johnson (7); Sergey Bubka (6); Calvin Smith and Lars Riedel (4); Donovan Bailey, Greg Foster, Haile Gebrselassie, Werner Gunthor, Moses Kiptanui, Noureddine Morceli, Dan O'Brien and Butch Reynolds (3); Andrey Abduvaliyev, Leroy Burrell, Andre Cason, Maurizio Damilano, John Godina, Allen Johnson, Wilson Kipketer, Ismael Kirui, Billy Konchellah, Sergey Litvinov, Dennis Mitchell, Edwin Moses, Ivan Pedroso, Mike Powell, Javier Sotmayor and Jan Zelezny (2).

100 meters

Year		Time	
1983	Carl Lewis, USA	10.07	
1987	Carl Lewis, USA	9.93	
1991	Carl Lewis, USA	9.86	**WR**
1993	Linford Christie, GBR	9.87	
1995	Donovan Bailey, CAN	9.97	
1997	Maurice Greene, USA	9.86	**=CR**

Note: Ben Johnson was the original winner in 1987, but was stripped of his title and world record time (9.83) following his 1989 admission of drug taking.

200 meters

Year		Time	
1983	Calvin Smith, USA	20.14	
1987	Calvin Smith, USA	20.16	
1991	Michael Johnson, USA	20.01	
1993	Frank Fredericks, NAM	19.85	
1995	Michael Johnson, USA	19.79	**CR**
1997	Ato Boldon, USA	20.04	

400 meters

Year		Time	
1983	Bert Cameron, JAM	45.05	
1987	Thomas Schonlebe, E.Ger	44.33	
1991	Antonio Pettigrew, USA	44.57	
1993	Michael Johnson, USA	43.65	
1995	Michael Johnson, USA	43.39	**CR**
1997	Michael Johnson, USA	44.12	

800 meters

Year		Time	
1983	Willi Wülbeck, W.Ger	1:43.65	
1987	Billy Konchellah, KEN	1:43.06	**CR**
1991	Billy Konchellah, KEN	1:43.99	
1993	Paul Ruto, KEN	1:44.71	
1995	Wilson Kipketer, DEN	1:45.08	
1997	Wilson Kipketer, DEN	1:43.38	

1500 meters

Year		Time	
1983	Steve Cram, GBR	3:41.59	
1987	Abdi Bile, SOM	3:36.80	
1991	Noureddine Morceli, ALG	3:32.84	**CR**
1993	Noureddine Morceli, ALG	3:34.24	
1995	Noureddine Morceli, ALG	3:33.73	
1997	Hicham El Guerrouj, MAR	3:35.83	

5000 meters

Year		Time	
1983	Eammon Coghlan, IRE	13:28.53	
1987	Said Aouita, MOR	13:26.44	
1991	Yobes Ondieki, KEN	13:14.45	
1993	Ismael Kirui, KEN	13:02.75	**CR**
1995	Ismael Kirui, KEN	13:16.77	
1997	Daniel Komen, KEN	13:07.38	

10,000 meters

Year		Time	
1983	Alberto Cova, ITA	28:01.04	
1987	Paul Kipkoech, KEN	27:38.63	
1991	Moses Tanui, KEN	27:38.74	
1993	Haile Gebrselassie, ETH	27:46.02	
1995	Haile Gebrselassie, ETH	27:12.95	**CR**
1997	Haile Gebrselassie, ETH	27:24.58	

Marathon

Year		Time	
1983	Rob de Castella, AUS	2:10:03	**CR**
1987	Douglas Wakiihuri, KEN	2:11:48	
1991	Hiromi Taniguchi, JPN	2:14:57	
1993	Mark Plaatjes, USA	2:13:57	
1995	Martin Fiz, SPA	2:11:41	
1997	Abel Anton, SPA	2:13:16	

110-meter Hurdles

Year		Time	
1983	Greg Foster, USA	13.42	
1987	Greg Foster, USA	13.21	
1991	Greg Foster, USA	13.06	
1993	Colin Jackson, GBR	12.91	**WR**
1995	Allen Johnson, USA	13.00	
1997	Allen Johnson, USA	12.93	

Track & Field (Cont.)

400-meter Hurdles

Year		Time	
1983	Edwin Moses, USA	47.50	
1987	Edwin Moses, USA	47.46	
1991	Samuel Matete, ZAM	47.64	
1993	Kevin Young, USA	47.18	CR
1995	Derrick Adkins, USA	47.98	
1997	Stephane Diagana, FRA	47.70	

3000-meter Steeplechase

Year		Time	
1983	Patriz Ilg, W. Ger	8:15.06	
1987	Francesco Panetta, ITA	8:08.57	
1991	Moses Kiptanui, KEN	8:12.59	
1993	Moses Kiptanui, KEN	8:06.36	
1995	Moses Kiptanui, KEN	8:04.16	CR
1997	Wilson B. Kipketer, KEN	8:05.84	

4x100-meter Relay

Year		Time	
1983	United States	37.86	WR
1987	United States	37.90	
1991	United States	37.50	WR
1993	United States	37.48	CR
1995	Canada	38.31	
1997	Canada	37.86	

4x400-meter Relay

Year		Time	
1983	Soviet Union	3:00.79	
1987	United States	2:57.29	
1991	Great Britain	2:57.53	
1993	United States	2:54.29	WR
1995	United States	2:57.32	
1997	United States	2:56.47	

20-kilometer Walk

Year		Time	
1983	Ernesto Canto, MEX	1:20.49	
1987	Maurizio Damilano, ITA	1:20.45	
1991	Maurizio Damilano, ITA	1:19.37	CR
1993	Valentin Massana, SPA	1:22.31	
1995	Michele Didoni, ITA	1:19.59	
1997	Daniel Garcia, MEX	1:21:43	

50-kilometer Walk

Year		Time	
1983	Ronald Weigel, E. Ger	3:43:08	
1987	Hartwig Gauder, E. Ger	3:40:53	CR
1991	Aleksandr Potashov, USSR	3:53:09	
1993	Jesus Angel Garcia, SPA	3:41:41	
1995	Valentin Kononen, FIN	3:43.42	
1997	Robert Korzeniowski, POL	3:44:46	

High Jump

Year		Height	
1983	Gennedy Avdeyenko, USSR	7- 7¼	
1987	Patrik Sjoberg, SWE	7- 9¾	
1991	Charles Austin, USA	7- 9¾	
1993	Javier Sotomayor, CUB	7-10½	CR
1995	Troy Kemp, BAH	7- 9¼	
1997	Javier Sotomayor, CUB	7- 9¼	

Pole Vault

Year		Height	
1983	Sergey Bubka, USSR	18- 8¼	
1987	Sergey Bubka, USSR	19- 2¼	
1991	Sergey Bubka, USSR	19- 6¼	CR
1993	Sergey Bubka, UKR	19- 8¼	
1995	Sergey Bubka, UKR	19- 5	
1997	Sergey Bubka, UKR	19- 8½	CR

Long Jump

Year		Distance	
1983	Carl Lewis, USA	28- 0¾	
1987	Carl Lewis, USA	28- 0¼	
1991	Mike Powell, USA	29- 4½	WR
1993	Mike Powell, USA	28- 2¼	
1995	Ivan Pedroso, CUB	28- 6½	
1997	Ivan Pedroso, CUB	27- 7½	

Triple Jump

Year		Distance	
1983	Zdzislaw Hoffmann, POL	57- 2	
1987	Khristo Markov, BUL	58- 9	
1991	Kenny Harrison, USA	58- 4	
1993	Mike Conley, USA	58- 7¼	
1995	Jonathan Edwards, GBR	60- 0¼	WR
1997	Yoelvis Quesada, CUB	58- 6¾	

Shot Put

Year		Distance	
1983	Edward Sarul, POL	70- 2¼	
1987	Werner Günthör, SWI	72-11¼	CR
1991	Werner Günthör, SWI	71- 1¼	
1993	Werner Günthör, SWI	72- 1	
1995	John Godina, USA	70- 5¼	
1997	John Godina, USA	70- 4¼	

Discus

Year		Distance	
1983	Imrich Bugar, CZE	222- 2	
1987	Jurgen Schult, E. Ger	225- 6	
1991	Lars Riedel, GER	217- 2	
1993	Lars Riedel, GER	222- 2	
1995	Lars Riedel, GER	225- 7	CR
1997	Lars Riedel, GER	224- 10	

Hammer Throw

Year		Distance	
1983	Sergey Litvinov, USSR	271- 3	
1987	Sergey Litvinov, USSR	272- 6	CR
1991	Yuri Sedykh, USSR	268- 0	
1993	Andrey Abduvaliyev, TAJ	267-10	
1995	Andrey Abduvaliyev, TAJ	267- 7	
1997	Heinz Weis, GER	268-4	

Javelin

Year		Distance	
1983	Detlef Michel, E. Ger	293- 7	
1987	Seppo Raty, FIN	274- 1	
1991	Kimmo Kinnunen, FIN	297-11	CR
1993	Jan Zelezny, CZE	282- 1	
1995	Jan Zelezny, CZE	293-11	
1997	Marius Corbett, S. Afr.	290-0	

Decathlon

Year		Points	
1983	Daley Thompson, GBR	8714	
1987	Torsten Voss, E. Ger	8680	
1991	Dan O'Brien, USA	8812	
1993	Dan O'Brien, USA	8817	CR
1995	Dan O'Brien, USA	8695	
1997	Tomas Dvorak, CZE	8837	CR

WOMEN

Multiple gold medals (including relays): Gail Devers and Jackie Joyner-Kersee (4); Tatyana Samolenko Dorovskikh, Silke Gladisch, Marita Koch, Jearl Miles, Merlene Ottey and Gwen Torrence (3); Hassiba Boulmerka, Sabine Braun, Olga Bryzgina, Mary Decker, Heike Daute Drechsler, Chryste Gaines, Trine Hattestad, Martina Optiz Hellmann, Marion Jones, Stefka Kostadinova, Katrin Krabbe, Jarmila Kratochvilova, Astrid Kumbernuss, Marie-José Pérec, Ana Quirot and Huang Zhihong (2).

100 meters

Year		Time	
1983	Marlies Gohr, E. Ger	10.97	
1987	Silke Gladisch, E. Ger	10.90	
1991	Katrin Krabbe, GER	10.99	
1993	Gail Devers, USA	10.81	**CR**
1995	Gwen Torrence, USA	10.85	
1997	Marion Jones, USA	10.83	

200 meters

Year		Time	
1983	Marita Koch, E. Ger	22.13	
1987	Silke Gladisch, E. Ger	21.74	**CR**
1991	Katrin Krabbe, GER	22.09	
1993	Merlene Ottey, JAM	21.98	
1995	Merlene Ottey, JAM	22.12	
1997	Zhanna Pintusevich, UKR	22.32	

400 meters

Year		Time	
1983	Jarmila Kratochvilova, CZE	47.99	**WR**
1987	Olga Bryzgina, USSR	49.38	
1991	Marie-José Pérec, FRA	49.13	
1993	Jearl Miles, USA	49.82	
1995	Marie-José Pérec, FRA	49.28	
1997	Cathy Freeman, AUS	49.77	

800 meters

Year		Time	
1983	Jarmila Kratochvilova, CZE	1:54.68	**CR**
1987	Sigrun Wodars, E. Ger	1:55.26	
1991	Lilia Nurutdinova, USSR	1:57.50	
1993	Maria Mutola, MOZ	1:55.43	
1995	Ana Quirot, CUB	1:56.11	
1997	Ana Quirot, CUB	1:57.14	

1500 meters

Year		Time	
1983	Mary Decker, USA	4:00.90	
1987	Tatiana Samolenko, USSR	3:58.56	**CR**
1991	Hassiba Boulmerka, ALG	4:02.21	
1993	Liu Dong, CHN	4:00.50	
1995	Hassiba Boulmerka, ALG	4:02.42	
1997	Carla Sacramento, POR	4:04.24	

5000 meters

Held as 3000-meter race from 1983-93

Year		Time	
1983	Mary Decker, USA	8:34.62	
1987	Tatyana Samolenko, USSR	8:38.73	
1991	T. Samolenko Dorovskikh, USSR	8:35.82	
1993	Qu Yunxia, CHN	8:28.71	**CR**
1995	Sonia O'Sullivan, IRE	14:46.47	**CR**
1997	Gabriela Szabo, ROM	14:57.68	

10,000 meters

Year		Time	
1983	Not held		
1987	Ingrid Kristiansen, NOR	31:05.85	
1991	Liz McColgan, GBR	31:14.31	
1993	Wang Junxia, CHN	30:49.30	**CR**
1995	Fernanda Ribeiro, POR	31:04.99	
1997	Sally Barsosio, KEN	31:32.92	

Marathon

Year		Time	
1983	Grete Waitz, NOR	2:28:09	
1987	Rose Mota, POR	2:25:17	**CR**
1991	Wanda Panfil, POL	2:29:53	
1993	Junko Asari, JPN	2:30:03	
1995	Manuela Machado, POR	2:25:39	
1997	Hiromi Suzuki, JPN	2:29:48	

100-meter Hurdles

Year		Time	
1983	Bettine Jahn, E. Ger	12.35^w	
1987	Ginka Zagorcheva, BUL	12.34	**CR**
1991	Lyudmila Narozhilenko, USSR	12.59	
1993	Gail Devers, USA	12.46	
1995	Gail Devers, USA	12.68	
1997	Ludmila Engquist, SWE	12.50	

^{w} indicates wind-aided.

400-meter Hurdles

Year		Time	
1983	Yekaterina Fesenko, USSR	54.14	
1987	Sabine Busch, E. Ger	53.62	
1991	Tatiana Ledovskaya, USSR	53.11	
1993	Sally Gunnell, GBR	52.74	**WR**
1995	Kim Batten, USA	52.61	**WR**
1997	Nezha Bidouane, MOR	52.97	

4x100-meter Relay

Year		Time	
1983	East Germany	41.76	
1987	United States	41.58	
1991	Jamaica	41.94	
1993	Russia	41.49	**CR**
1995	United States	42.12	
1997	United States	41.47	**CR**

4x400-meter Relay

Year		Time	
1983	East Germany	3:19.73	
1987	East Germany	3:18.63	
1991	Soviet Union	3:18.43	
1993	United States	3:16.71	**CR**
1995	United States	3:22.39	
1997	Germany	3:20.92	

10-kilometer Walk

Year		Time	
1983	Not held		
1987	Irina Strakhova, USSR	44:12	
1991	Alina Ivanova, USSR	42:57	
1993	Sari Essayah, FIN	42:59	
1995	Irina Stankina, RUS	42:13	**CR**
1997	Anna Sidoti, ITA	42:55	

High Jump

Year		Height	
1983	Tamara Bykova, USSR	6-7	
1987	Stefka Kostadinova, BUL	6-10¼	**WR**
1991	Heike Henkel, GER	6- 8¾	
1993	Ioamnet Quintero, CUB	6- 6¼	
1995	Stefka Kostadinova, BUL	6-7	
1997	Hanne Haugland, NOR	6- 6¼	

Track & Field (Cont.)

Long Jump

Year		Distance
1983	Heike Daute, E. Ger	23-10¼ʷ
1987	Jackie Joyner-Kersee, USA	24- 1¾ **CR**
1991	Jackie Joyner-Kersee, USA	24- 0¼
1993	Heike Drechsler, GER	23- 4
1995	Fiona May, ITA	22-10¾ʷ
1997	Lyudmila Galkina, RUS	23- 1¾

ʷ indicates wind-aided.

Triple Jump

Year		Distance
1983	Not held	
1987	Not held	
1991	Not held	
1993	Ana Biryukova, RUS	46- 6¼ **WR**
1995	Inessa Kravets, UKR	50-10¾ **WR**
1997	Sarka Kasparkova, CZE	49-10½

Shot Put

Year		Distance
1983	Helena Fibingerova, CZE	69- 0
1987	Natalia Lisovskaya, USSR	69- 8 **CR**
1991	Huang Zhihong, CHN	68- 4
1993	Huang Zhihong, CHN	67- 6
1995	Astrid Kumbernuss, GER	69- 7½
1997	Astrid Kumbernuss, GER	67- 11½

Discus

Year		Distance
1983	Martina Opitz, E. Ger	226- 2
1987	Martina Opitz Hellmann, E. Ger	235- 0 **CR**
1991	Tsvetanka Khristova, BUL	233- 0
1993	Olga Burova, RUS	221- 1
1995	Ellina Zvereva, BLR	225- 2
1997	Beatrice Faumuina, NZL	219-3

Javelin

Year		Distance
1983	Tiina Lillak, FIN	232- 4
1987	Fatima Whitbread, GBR	251- 5 **CR**
1991	Xu Demei, CHN	225- 8
1993	Trine Hattestad, NOR	227- 0
1995	Natalya Shikolenko, BLR	221- 8
1997	Trine Hattestad, NOR	225- 8

Heptathlon

Year		Points
1983	Ramona Neubert, E. Ger	6770
1987	Jackie Joyner-Kersee, USA	7128 **CR**
1991	Sabine Braun, GER	6672
1993	Jackie Joyner-Kersee, USA	6837
1995	Ghada Shouaa, SYR	6651
1997	Sabine Braun, GER	6739

Marathons

Boston

America's oldest regularly contested foot race, the Boston Marathon is held on Patriots' Day every April. It has been run at four different distances: 24 miles, 1232 yards (1897-1923); 26 miles, 209 yards (1924-26); 26 miles, 385 yards (1927-52); 25 miles, 958 yards (1953-56); and 26 miles, 385 yards (since 1957).

MEN

Multiple winners: Clarence DeMar (7); Gerard Cote and Bill Rodgers (4); Ibrahim Hussein, Cosmas Ndeti and Leslie Pawson (3); Tarzan Brown, Jim Caffrey, John A. Kelley, John Miles, Eino Oksanen, Toshihiko Seko, Geoff Smith and Aurele Vandendriessche (2).

Year		Time
1897	John McDermott, New York	2:55:10
1898	Ronald McDonald, Massachusetts	2:42:00
1899	Lawrence Brignolia, Massachusetts	2:54:38
1900	Jim Caffrey, Canada	2:39:44
1901	Jim Caffrey, Canada	2:29:23
1902	Sam Mellor, New York	2:43:12
1903	J.C. Lorden, Massachusetts	2:41:29
1904	Mike Spring, New York	2:38:04
1905	Fred Lorz, New York	2:38:25
1906	Tim Ford, Massachusetts	2:45:45
1907	Tom Longboat, Canada	2:24:24
1908	Tom Morrissey, New York	2:25:43
1909	Henri Renaud, New Hampshire	2:53:36
1910	Fred Cameron, Nova Scotia	2:28:52
1911	Clarence DeMar, Massachusetts	2:21:39
1912	Mike Ryan, Illinois	2:21:18
1913	Fritz Carlson, Minnesota	2:25:14
1914	James Duffy, Canada	2:25:01
1915	Edouard Fabre, Canada	2:31:41
1916	Arthur Roth, Massachusetts	2:27:16
1917	Bill Kennedy, New York	2:28:37
1918	World War relay race	
1919	Carl Linder, Massachusetts	2:29:13
1920	Peter Trivoulidas, New York	2:29:31
1921	Frank Zuna, New Jersey	2:18:57
1922	Clarence DeMar, Massachusetts	2:18:10
1923	Clarence DeMar, Massachusetts	2:23:37
1924	Clarence DeMar, Massachusetts	2:29:40
1925	Charles Mellor, Illinois	2:33:00
1926	John Miles, Nova Scotia	2:25:40

Year		Time
1927	Clarence DeMar, Massachusetts	2:40:22
1928	Clarence DeMar, Massachusetts	2:37:07
1929	John Miles, Nova Scotia	2:33:08
1930	Clarence DeMar, Massachusetts	2:34:48
1931	James Henigan, Massachusetts	2:46:45
1932	Paul deBruyn, Germany	2:33:36
1933	Leslie Pawson, Rhode Island	2:31:01
1934	Dave Komonen, Canada	2:32:53
1935	John A. Kelley, Massachusetts	2:32:07
1936	Ellison (Tarzan) Brown, Rhode Island	2:33:40
1937	Walter Young, Canada	2:33:20
1938	Leslie Pawson, Rhode Island	2:35:34
1939	Ellison (Tarzan) Brown, Rhode Island	2:28:51
1940	Gerard Cote, Canada	2:28:28
1941	Leslie Pawson, Rhode Island	2:30:38
1942	Joe Smith, Massachusetts	2:26:51
1943	Gerard Cote, Canada	2:28:25
1944	Gerard Cote, Canada	2:31:50
1945	John A. Kelley, Massachusetts	2:30:40
1946	Stylianos Kyriakides, Greece	2:29:27
1947	Yun Bok Suh, Korea	2:25:39
1948	Gerard Cote, Canada	2:31:02
1949	Karle Leandersson, Sweden	2:31:50
1950	Kee Yonh Ham, Korea	2:32:39
1951	Shigeki Tanaka, Japan	2:27:45
1952	Doroteo Flores, Guatemala	2:31:53
1953	Keizo Yamada, Japan	2:18:51
1954	Veiko Karvonen, Finland	2:20:39
1955	Hideo Hamamura, Japan	2:18:22
1956	Antti Viskari, Finland	2:14:14

Year		Time	Year		Time
1957	John J. Kelley, Connecticut	2:20:05	1979	Bill Rodgers, Massachusetts	2:09:27
1958	Franjo Mihalic, Yugoslavia	2:25:54			
1959	Eino Oksanen, Finland	2:22:42	1980	Bill Rodgers, Massachusetts	2:12:11
			1981	Toshihiko Seko, Japan	2:09:26
1960	Paavo Kotila, Finland	2:20:54	1982	Alberto Salazar, Oregon	2:08:52
1961	Eino Oksanen, Finland	2:23:39	1983	Greg Meyer, New Jersey	2:09:00
1962	Eino Oksanen, Finland	2:23:48	1984	Geoff Smith, England	2:10:34
1963	Aurele Vandendriessche, Belgium	2:18:58	1985	Geoff Smith, England	2:14:05
1964	Aurele Vandendriessche, Belgium	2:19:59	1986	Rob de Castella, Australia	2:07:51
1965	Morio Shigematsu, Japan	2:16:33	1987	Toshihiko Seko, Japan	2:11:50
1966	Kenji Kimihara, Japan	2:17:11	1988	Ibrahim Hussein, Kenya	2:08:43
1967	David McKenzie, New Zealand	2:15:45	1989	Abebe Mekonnen, Ethiopia	2:09:06
1968	Amby Burfoot, Connecticut	2:22:17			
1969	Yoshiaki Unetani, Japan	2:13:49	1990	Gelindo Bordin, Italy	2:08:19
			1991	Ibrahim Hussein, Kenya	2:11:06
1970	Ron Hill, England	2:10:30	1992	Ibrahim Hussein, Kenya	2:08:14
1971	Alvaro Mejia, Colombia	2:18:45	1993	Cosmas Ndeti, Kenya	2:09:33
1972	Olavi Suomalainen, Finland	2:15:39	1994	Cosmas Ndeti, Kenya	2:07:15*
1973	Jon Anderson, Oregon	2:16:03	1995	Cosmas Ndeti, Kenya	2:09:22
1974	Neil Cusack, Ireland	2:13:39	1996	Moses Tanui, Kenya	2:09:16
1975	Bill Rodgers, Massachusetts	2:09:55	1997	Lameck Aguta, Kenya	2:10:34
1976	Jack Fultz, Pennsylvania	2:20:19	*Course record.		
1977	Jerome Drayton, Canada	2:14:46			
1978	Bill Rodgers, Massachusetts	2:10:13			

WOMEN

Multiple winners: Rosa Mota and Uta Pippig (3); Joan Benoit, Miki Gorman, Ingrid Kristiansen and Olga Markova (2).

Year		Time	Year		Time
1972	Nina Kuscsik, New York	3:08:58	1986	Ingrid Kristiansen, Norway	2:24:55
1973	Jacqueline Hansen, California	3:05:59	1987	Rosa Mota, Portugal	2:25:21
1974	Miki Gorman, California	2:47:11	1988	Rosa Mota, Portugal	2:24:30
1975	Liane Winter, West Germany	2:42:24	1989	Ingrid Kristiansen, Norway	2:24:33
1976	Kim Merritt, Wisconsin	2:47:10			
1977	Miki Gorman, California	2:48:33	1990	Rosa Mota, Portugal	2:25:23
1978	Gayle Barron, Georgia	2:44:52	1991	Wanda Panfil, Poland	2:24:18
1979	Joan Benoit, Maine	2:35:15	1992	Olga Markova, CIS	2:23:43
			1993	Olga Markova, Russia	2:25:27
1980	Jacqueline Gareau, Canada	2:34:28	1994	Uta Pippig, Germany	2:21:45*
1981	Allison Roe, New Zealand	2:26:46	1995	Uta Pippig, Germany	2:25:11
1982	Charlotte Teske, West Germany	2:29:33	1996	Uta Pippig, Germany	2:27:12
1983	Joan Benoit, Maine	2:22:43	1997	Fatuma Roba, Ethiopia	2:26:23
1984	Lorraine Moller, New Zealand	2:29:28	*Course record.		
1985	Lisa Larsen Weidenbach, Mass	2:34:06			

New York City

Started in 1970, the New York City Marathon is run in the fall, usually on the first Sunday in November. The route winds through all of the city's five boroughs and finishes in Central Park.

MEN

Multiple winners: Bill Rodgers (4); Alberto Salazar (3); Tom Fleming, Orlando Pizzolato and German Silva (2).

Year		Time	Year		Time
1970	Gary Muhrcke, USA	2:31:38	1984	Orlando Pizzolato, Italy	2:14:53
1971	Norman Higgins, USA	2:22:54	1985	Orlando Pizzolato, Italy	2:11:34
1972	Sheldon Karlin, USA	2:27:52	1986	Gianni Poli, Italy	2:11:06
1973	Tom Fleming, USA	2:21:54	1987	Ibrahim Hussein, Kenya	2:11:01
1974	Norbert Sander, USA	2:26:30	1988	Steve Jones, Wales	2:08:20
1975	Tom Fleming, USA	2:19:27	1989	Juma Ikangaa, Tanzania	2:08:01*
1976	Bill Rodgers, USA	2:10:09			
1977	Bill Rodgers, USA	2:11:28	1990	Douglas Wakiihuri, Kenya	2:12:39
1978	Bill Rodgers, USA	2:12:12	1991	Salvador Garcia, Mexico	2:09:28
1979	Bill Rodgers, USA	2:11:42	1992	Willie Mtolo, South Africa	2:09:29
			1993	Andres Espinosa, Mexico	2:10:04
1980	Alberto Salazar, USA	2:09:41	1994	German Silva, Mexico	2:11:21
1981	Alberto Salazar, USA	2:08:13	1995	German Silva, Mexico	2:11:00
1982	Alberto Salazar, USA	2:09:29	1996	Giacomo Leone, Italy	2:09:54
1983	Rod Dixon, New Zealand	2:08:59	*Course record.		

Track & Field (Cont.)

WOMEN

Multiple winners: Grete Waitz (9); Miki Gorman, Nina Kuscsik and Tegla Laroupe (2).

Year		Time	Year		Time
1970	No Finisher		1984	Grete Waitz, Norway	2:29:30
1971	Beth Bonner, USA	2:55:22	1985	Grete Waitz, Norway	2:28:34
1972	Nina Kuscsik, USA	3:08:41	1986	Grete Waitz, Norway	2:28:06
1973	Nina Kuscsik, USA	2:57:07	1987	Priscilla Welch, Britain	2:30:17
1974	Katherine Switzer, USA	3:07:29	1988	Grete Waitz, Norway	2:28:07
1975	Kim Merritt, USA	2:46:14	1989	Ingrid Kristiansen, Norway	2:25:30
1976	Miki Gorman, USA	2:39:11			
1977	Miki Gorman, USA	2:43:10	1990	Wanda Panfil, Poland	2:30:45
1978	Grete Waitz, Norway	2:32:30	1991	Liz McColgan, Scotland	2:27:23
1979	Grete Waitz, Norway	2:27:33	1992	Lisa Ondieki, Australia	2:24:40*
			1993	Uta Pippig, Germany	2:26:24
1980	Grete Waitz, Norway	2:25:41	1994	Tegla Laroupe, Kenya	2:27:37
1981	Allison Roe, New Zealand	2:25:29	1995	Tegla Laroupe, Kenya	2:28:06
1982	Grete Waitz, Norway	2:27:14	1996	Anuta Catuna, ROM	2:28:18
1983	Grete Waitz, Norway	2:27:00			

*Course record.

Annual Awards

Track & Field News Athletes of the Year

Voted on by an international panel of track and field experts and presented since 1959 for men and 1974 for women.

MEN

Multiple winners: Carl Lewis (3); Sergey Bubka, Sebastian Coe, Michael Johnson, Alberto Juantorena, Noureddine Morceli, Jim Ryun and Peter Snell (2).

Year		Event	Year		Event
1959	Martin Lauer, W. Germany	110H/Decathlon	1978	Henry Rono, Kenya	5000/10,000/Steeplechase
			1979	Sebastian Coe, Great Britain	800/1500
1960	Rafer Johnson, USA	Decathlon	1980	Edwin Moses, USA	400 Hurdles
1961	Ralph Boston, USA	Long Jump/110 Hurdles	1981	Sebastian Coe, Great Britain	800/1500
1962	Peter Snell, New Zealand	800/1500	1982	Carl Lewis, USA	100/200/Long Jump
1963	C.K. Yang, Taiwan	Decathlon/Pole Vault	1983	Carl Lewis, USA	100/200/Long Jump
1964	Peter Snell, New Zealand	800/1500	1984	Carl Lewis, USA	100/200/Long Jump
1965	Ron Clarke, Australia	5000/10,000	1985	Said Aouita, Morocco	1500/5000
1966	Jim Ryun, USA	800/1500	1986	Yuri Sedykh, USSR	Hammer Throw
1967	Jim Ryun, USA	1500	1987	Ben Johnson, Canada	100
1968	Bob Beamon, USA	Long Jump	1988	Sergey Bubka, USSR	Pole Vault
1969	Bill Toomey, USA	Decathlon	1989	Roger Kingdom, USA	110 Hurdles
1970	Randy Matson, USA	Shot Put	1990	Michael Johnson, USA	200/400
1971	Rod Milburn, USA	110 Hurdles	1991	Sergey Bubka, USSR	Pole Vault
1972	Lasse Viren, Finland	5000/10,000	1992	Kevin Young, USA	400 Hurdles
1973	Ben Jipcho, Kenya	1500/5000/Steeplechase	1993	Noureddine Morceli, Algeria	Mile/1500/3000
1974	Rick Wohlhuter, USA	800/1500	1994	Noureddine Morceli, Algeria	Mile/1500/3000
1975	John Walker, New Zealand	800/1500	1995	Haile Gebrselassie, Ethopia	5000/10,000
1976	Alberto Juantorena, Cuba	400/800	1996	Michael Johnson, USA	200/400
1977	Alberto Juantorena, Cuba	400/800			

WOMEN

Multiple winners: Marita Koch (4); Jackie Joyner-Kersee (3); Evelyn Ashford (2).

Year		Event	Year		Event
1974	Irena Szewinska, Poland	100/200/400	1986	Jackie Joyner-Kersee, USA	Heptathlon/Long Jump
1975	Faina Melnik, USSR	Shot Put/Discus	1987	Jackie Joyner-Kersee, USA	100H/Heptathlon/LJ
1976	Tatiana Kazankina, USSR	800/1500	1988	Florence Griffith Joyner, USA	100/200
1977	Rosemarie Ackermann, E. Germany	High Jump	1989	Ana Quirot, Cuba	400/800
1978	Marita Koch, E. Germany	100/200/400			
1979	Marita Koch, E. Germany	100/200/400	1990	Merlene Ottey, Jamaica	100/200
			1991	Heike Henkel, Germany	High Jump
1980	Ilona Briesenick, E. Germany	Shot Put	1992	Heike Drechsler, Germany	Long Jump
1981	Evelyn Ashford, USA	100/200	1993	Wang Junxia, China	1500/3000/10,000
1982	Marita Koch, E. Germany	100/200/400	1994	Jackie Joyner-Kersee, USA	100H/Heptathlon/LJ
1983	Jarmila Kratochvilova, Czech	200/400/800	1995	Sonia O'Sullivan, Ireland	1500/3000/5000
1984	Evelyn Ashford, USA	100	1996	Svetlana Masterkova, Russia	800/1500
1985	Marita Koch, E. Germany	100/200/400			

SWIMMING & DIVING

FINA World Championships

While the Summer Olympics have served as the unofficial world championships for swimming and diving throughout the century, a separate World Championship meet was started in 1973 by the International Amateur Swimming Federation (FINA). The meet was held three times between 1973-78, then every four years since then. Sites have included Belgrade (1973); Cali, COL (1975); West Berlin (1978); Guayaquil, ECU (1982); Madrid (1986); Perth (1991) and Rome (1994). The next world championships will take place Jan. 8-18, 1998 in Perth.

MEN

Most gold medals (including relays): Jim Montgomery (7); Matt Biondi (6); Rowdy Gaines (5); Joe Bottom, Tamas Darnyi, Michael Gross, Tom Jager, David McCagg, Vladimir Salnikov and Tim Shaw (4); Billy Forrester, Andras Hargitay, Roland Matthes, John Murphy, Jeff Rouse, Norbert Rozsa and David Wilkie (3).

50-meter Freestyle

Year		Time	
1973-82	Not held		
1986	Tom Jager, USA	22.49	
1991	Tom Jager, USA	22.16	CR
1994	Aleksandr Popov, RUS	22.17	

100-meter Freestyle

Year		Time	
1973	Jim Montgomery, USA	51.70	
1975	Tim Shaw, USA	51.25	
1978	David McCagg, USA	50.24	
1982	Jorg Woithe, E. Ger	50.18	
1986	Matt Biondi, USA	48.94	CR
1991	Matt Biondi, USA	49.18	
1994	Aleksandr Popov, RUS	49.12	

200-meter Freestyle

Year		Time	
1973	Jim Montgomery, USA	1:53.02	
1975	Tim Shaw, USA	1:52.04	
1978	Billy Forrester, USA	1:51.02	
1982	Michael Gross, W. Ger	1:49.84	
1986	Michael Gross, W. Ger	1:47.92	
1991	Giorgio Lamberti, ITA	1:47.27	
1994	Antti Kasvio, FIN	1:47.32	CR

400-meter Freestyle

Year		Time	
1973	Rick DeMont, USA	3:58.18	
1975	Tim Shaw, USA	3:54.88	
1978	Vladimir Salnikov, USSR	3:51.94	
1982	Vladimir Salnikov, USSR	3:51.30	
1986	Rainer Henkel, W. Ger	3:50.05	
1991	Jorg Hoffman, GER	3:48.04	
1994	Kieren Perkins, AUS	3:43.80	WR

1500-meter Freestyle

Year		Time	
1973	Stephen Holland, AUS	15:31.85	
1975	Tim Shaw, USA	15:28.92	
1978	Vladimir Salnikov, USSR	15:03.99	
1982	Vladimir Salnikov, USSR	15:01.77	
1986	Rainer Henkel, W. Ger	15:05.31	
1991	Jorg Hoffman, GER	14:50.36	WR
1994	Kieren Perkins, AUS	14:50.52	

100-meter Backstroke

Year		Time	
1973	Roland Matthes, E. Ger	57.47	
1975	Roland Matthes, E. Ger	58.15	
1978	Bob Jackson, USA	56.36	
1982	Dirk Richter, E. Ger	55.95	
1986	Igor Polianski, USSR	55.58	
1991	Jeff Rouse, USA	55.23	
1994	Martin Lopez-Zubero, SPA	55.17	CR

200-meter Backstroke

Year		Time	
1973	Roland Matthes, E. Ger	2:01.87	
1975	Zoltan Varraszto, HUN	2:05.05	
1978	Jesse Vassallo, USA	2:02.16	
1982	Rick Carey, USA	2:00.82	
1986	Igor Polianski, USSR	1:58.78	CR
1991	Martin Zubero, SPA	1:59.52	
1994	Vladimir Selkov, RUS	1:57.42	

100-meter Breaststroke

Year		Time	
1973	John Hencken, USA	1:04.02	
1975	David Wilkie, GBR	1:04.26	
1978	Walter Kusch, W. Ger	1:03.56	
1982	Steve Lundquist, USA	1:02.75	
1986	Victor Davis, CAN	1:02.71	
1991	Norbert Rozsa, HUN	1:01.45	WR
1994	Norbert Rozsa, HUN	1:01.24	

200-meter Breaststroke

Year		Time	
1973	David Wilkie, GBR	2:19.28	
1975	David Wilkie, GBR	2:18.23	
1978	Nick Nevid, USA	2:18.37	
1982	Victor Davis, CAN	2:14.77	WR
1986	Jozsef Szabo, HUN	2:14.27	
1991	Mike Barrowman, USA	2:11.23	WR
1994	Norbert Rozsa, HUN	2:12.81	

100-meter Butterfly

Year		Time	
1973	Bruce Robertson, CAN	55.69	
1975	Greg Jagenburg, USA	55.63	
1978	Joe Bottom, USA	54.30	
1982	Matt Gribble, USA	53.88	
1986	Pablo Morales, USA	53.54	
1991	Anthony Nesty, SUR	53.29	CR
1994	Rafal Szukala, POL	53.51	

200-meter Butterfly

Year		Time	
1973	Robin Backhaus, USA	2:03.32	
1975	Billy Forrester, USA	2:01.95	
1978	Mike Bruner, USA	1:59.38	
1982	Michael Gross, W. Ger	1:58.85	
1986	Michael Gross, W. Ger	1:56.53	
1991	Melvin Stewart, USA	1:55.69	WR
1994	Denis Pankratov, RUS	1:56.54	

200-meter Individual Medley

Year		Time	
1973	Gunnar Larsson, SWE	2:08.36	
1975	Andras Hargitay, HUN	2:07.72	
1978	Graham Smith, CAN	2:03.65	WR
1982	Alexander Sidorenko, USSR	2:03.30	
1986	Tamás Darnyi, HUN	2:01.57	
1991	Tamás Darnyi, HUN	1:59.36	WR
1994	Janis Sievinen, FIN	1:58.16	WR

Swimming & Diving (Cont.)

400-meter Individual Medley

Year		Time	
1973	Andras Hargitay, HUN	4:31.11	
1975	Andras Hargitay, HUN	4:32.57	
1978	Jesse Vassallo, USA	4:20.05	WR
1982	Ricardo Prado, BRA	4:19.78	WR
1986	Tamás Darnyi, HUN	4:18.98	
1991	Tamás Darnyi, HUN	4:12.36	WR
1994	Tom Dolan, USA	4:12.30	WR

4 x 100-meter Freestyle Relay

Year		Time	
1973	United States	3:27.18	
1975	United States	3:24.85	
1978	United States	3:19.74	
1982	United States	3:19.26	WR
1986	United States	3:19.98	
1991	United States	3:17.15	
1994	United States	3:16.90	CR

4 x 200-meter Freestyle Relay

Year		Time	
1973	United States	7:33.22	WR
1975	West Germany	7:39.44	
1978	United States	7:20.82	
1982	United States	7:21.09	
1986	East Germany	7:15.91	
1991	Germany	7:13.50	CR
1994	Sweden	7:17.34	

4 x 100-meter Medley Relay

Year		Time	
1973	United States	3:49.49	
1975	United States	3:49.00	
1978	United States	3:44.63	
1982	United States	3:40.84	WR
1986	United States	3:41.25	
1991	United States	3:39.66	
1994	United States	3:37.74	CR

WOMEN

Most gold medals (including relays): Kornelia Ender (8); Kristin Otto (7); Tracy Caulkins, Heike Friedrich, Le Jingyi, Rosemarie Kother and Ulrike Richter (4); Hannalore Anke, Lu Bin, He Cihong, Janet Evans, Nicole Haislett, Lui Limin, Birgit Meineke, Joan Pennington, Manuela Stellmach, Renate Vogel and Cynthia Woodhead (3).

50-meter Freestyle

Year		Time	
1973-82	Not held		
1986	Tamara Costache, ROM	25.28	WR
1991	Zhuang Yong, CHN	25.47	
1994	Le Jingyi, CHN	24.51	WR

100-meter Freestyle

Year		Time	
1973	Kornelia Ender, E. Ger	57.54	
1975	Kornelia Ender, E. Ger	56.50	
1978	Barbara Krause, E. Ger	55.68	
1982	Birgit Meineke, E. Ger	55.79	
1986	Kristin Otto, E. Ger	55.05	
1991	Nicole Haislett, USA	55.17	
1994	Le Jingyi, CHN	54.01	WR

200-meter Freestyle

Year		Time	
1973	Keena Rothhammer, USA	2:04.99	
1975	Shirley Babashoff, USA	2:02.50	
1978	Cynthia Woodhead, USA	1:58.53	WR
1982	Annemarie Verstappen, HOL	1:59.53	
1986	Heike Friedrich, E. Ger	1:58.26	
1991	Hayley Lewis, AUS	2:00.48	
1994	Franziska Van Almsick, GER	1:56.78	WR

400-meter Freestyle

Year		Time	
1973	Heather Greenwood, USA	4:20.28	
1975	Shirley Babashoff, USA	4:22.70	
1978	Tracey Wickham, AUS	4:06.28	WR
1982	Carmela Schmidt, E. Ger	4:08.98	
1986	Heike Friedrich, E. Ger	4:07.45	
1991	Janet Evans, USA	4:08.63	
1994	Yang Aihua, CHN	4:09.64	

800-meter Freestyle

Year		Time	
1973	Novella Calligaris, ITA	8:52.97	
1975	Jenny Turrall, AUS	8:44.75	
1978	Tracey Wickham, AUS	8:25.94	
1982	Kim Linehan, USA	8:27.48	
1986	Astrid Strauss, E. Ger	8:28.24	
1991	Janet Evans, USA	8:24.05	CR
1994	Janet Evans, USA	8:29.85	

100-meter Backstroke

Year		Time	
1973	Ulrike Richter, E. Ger	1:05.42	
1975	Ulrike Richter, E. Ger	1:03.30	
1978	Linda Jezek, USA	1:02.55	
1982	Kristin Otto, E. Ger	1:01.30	
1986	Betsy Mitchell, USA	1:01.74	
1991	Krisztina Egerszegi, HUN	1:01.78	
1994	He Cihong, CHN	1:00.57	WR

200-meter Backstroke

Year		Time	
1973	Melissa Belote, USA	2:20.52	
1975	Birgit Treiber, E. Ger	2:15.46	WR
1978	Linda Jezek, USA	2:11.93	WR
1982	Cornelia Sirch, E. Ger	2:09.91	WR
1986	Cornelia Sirch, E. Ger	2:11.37	
1991	Krisztina Egerszegi, HUN	2:09.15	
1994	He Cihong, CHN	2:07.40	CR

100-meter Breaststroke

Year		Time	
1973	Renate Vogel, E. Ger	1:13.74	
1975	Hannalore Anke, E. Ger	1:12.72	
1978	Julia Bogdanova, USSR	1:10.31	WR
1982	Ute Geweniger, E. Ger	1:09.14	
1986	Sylvia Gerasch, E. Ger	1:08.11	WR
1991	Linley Frame, AUS	1:08.81	
1994	Samantha Riley, AUS	1:07.69	WR

200-meter Breaststroke

Year		Time	
1973	Renate Vogel, E. Ger	2:40.01	
1975	Hannalore Anke, E. Ger	2:37.25	
1978	Lina Kachushite, USSR	2:31.42	WR
1982	Svetlana Varganova, USSR	2:28.82	
1986	Silke Hoerner, E. Ger	2:27.40	WR
1991	Elena Volkova, USSR	2:29.53	
1994	Samantha Riley, AUS	2:26.87	CR

100-meter Butterfly

Year		Time	
1973	Kornelia Ender, E. Ger	1:02.53	
1975	Kornelia Ender, E. Ger	1:01.24	WR
1978	Joan Pennington, USA	1:00.20	
1982	Mary T. Meagher, USA	59.41	
1986	Kornelai Gressler, E. Ger	59.51	
1991	Qian Hong, CHN	59.68	
1994	Liu Limin, CHN	58.98	CR

200-meter Butterfly

Year		Time	
1973	Rosemarie Kother, E. Ger	2:13.76	
1975	Rosemarie Kother, E. Ger	2:15.92	
1978	Tracy Caulkins, USA	2:09.78	WR
1982	Ines Geissler, E. Ger	2:08.66	
1986	Mary T. Meagher, USA	2:08.41	
1991	Summer Sanders, USA	2:09.24	
1994	Liu Limin, CHN	2:07.25	CR

200-meter Individual Medley

Year		Time	
1973	Andre Huebner, E. Ger	2:20.51	
1975	Kathy Heddy, USA	2:19.80	
1978	Tracy Caulkins, USA	2:19.80	WR
1982	Petra Schneider, E. Ger	2:11.79	CR
1986	Kristin Otto, E. Ger	2:15.56	
1991	Lin Li, CHN	2:13.40	
1994	Lu Bin, CHN	2:12.34	

400-meter Individual Medley

Year		Time	
1973	Gudrun Wegner, E. Ger	4:57.71	
1975	Ulrike Tauber, E. Ger	4:52.76	
1978	Tracy Caulkins, USA	4:40.83	WR
1982	Petra Schneider, E. Ger	4:36.10	WR
1986	Kathleen Nord, E. Ger	4:43.75	
1991	Lin Li, CHN	4:41.45	
1994	Dai Guohong, CHN	4:39.14	

4 x 100-meter Freestyle Relay

Year		Time	
1973	East Germany	3:52.45	
1975	East Germany	3:49.37	
1978	United States	3:43.43	WR
1982	East Germany	3:43.97	
1986	East Germany	3:40.57	
1991	United States	3:43.26	
1994	China	3:37.91	WR

4 x 200-meter Freestyle Relay

Year		Time	
1973-82 Not held			
1986	East Germany	7:59.33	WR
1991	Germany	8:02.56	
1994	China	7:57.96	CR

4 x 100-meter Medley Relay

Year		Time	
1973	East Germany	4:16.84	
1975	East Germany	4:14.74	
1978	United States	4:08.21	
1982	East Germany	4:05.8	WR
1986	East Germany	4:04.82	
1991	United States	4:06.51	
1994	China	4:01.67	CR

Diving

Multiple Gold Medals: MEN– Greg Louganis (5); Phil Boggs (3); Klaus Dibiasi (2). WOMEN– Irina Kalinina and Gao Min (3); Fu Mingxia (2).

MEN
1-meter Springboard

Year		Pts
1991	Edwin Jongejans, HOL	588.51
1994	Evan Stewart, ZIM	382.14

3-meter Springboard

Year		Pts
1973	Phil Boggs, USA	618.57
1975	Phil Boggs, USA	597.12
1978	Phil Boggs, USA	913.95
1982	Greg Louganis, USA	752.67
1986	Greg Louganis, USA	750.06
1991	Kent Ferguson, USA	650.25
1994	Yu Zhuocheng, CHN	655.44

Platform

Year		Pts
1973	Klaus Dibiasi, ITA	559.53
1975	Klaus Dibiasi, ITA	547.98
1978	Greg Louganis, USA	844.11
1982	Greg Louganis, USA	634.26
1986	Greg Louganis, USA	668.58
1991	Sun Shuwei, CHN	626.79
1994	Dmitri Sautin, RUS	634.71

WOMEN
1-meter Springboard

Year		Pts
1991	Gao Min, CHN	478.26
1994	Chen Lixia, CHN	279.30

3-meter Springboard

Year		Pts
1973	Christa Koehler, E. Ger	442.17
1975	Irina Kalinina, USSR	489.81
1978	Irina Kalinina, USSR	691.43
1982	Megan Neyer, USA	501.03
1986	Gao Min, CHN	582.90
1991	Gao Min, CHN	539.01
1994	Tan Shuping, CHN	548.49

Platform

Year		Pts
1973	Ulrike Knape, SWE	406.77
1975	Janet Ely, USA	403.89
1978	Irina Kalinina, USSR	412.71
1982	Wendy Wyland, USA	438.79
1986	Chen Lin, CHN	449.67
1991	Fu Mingxia, CHN	426.51
1994	Fu Mingxia, CHN	434.04

ALPINE SKIING

World Cup Overall Champions

World Cup Overall Champions (downhill and slalom events combined) since the tour was organized in 1967.

MEN

Multiple winners: Marc Girardelli (5), Gustavo Thoeni and Pirmin Zurbriggen (4); Phil Mahre, and Ingemar Stenmark (3); Jean-Claude Killy and Karl Schranz (2).

Year		Year		Year	
1967	Jean-Claude Killy, France	1978	Ingemar Stenmark, Sweden	1989	Marc Girardelli, Luxembourg
1968	Jean Claude Killy, France	1979	Peter Luescher, Switzerland	1990	Pirmin Zurbriggen, Switzerland
1969	Karl Schranz, Austria	1980	Andreas Wenzel, Liechtenstein	1991	Marc Girardelli, Luxembourg
1970	Karl Schranz, Austria	1981	Phil Mahre, USA	1992	Paul Accola, Switzerland
1971	Gustavo Thoeni, Italy	1982	Phil Mahre, USA	1993	Marc Girardelli, Luxembourg
1972	Gustavo Thoeni, Italy	1983	Phil Mahre, USA	1994	Kjetil Andre Aamodt, Norway
1973	Gustavo Thoeni, Italy	1984	Pirmin Zurbriggen, Switzerland	1995	Alberto Tomba, Italy
1974	Piero Gros, Italy	1985	Marc Girardelli, Luxembourg	1996	Lasse Kjus, Norway
1975	Gustavo Thoeni, Italy	1986	Marc Girardelli, Luxembourg	1997	Luc Alphand, France
1976	Ingemar Stenmark, Sweden	1987	Pirmin Zurbriggen, Switzerland		
1977	Ingemar Stenmark, Sweden	1988	Pirmin Zurbriggen, Switzerland		

WOMEN

Multiple winners: Annemarie Moser-Proell (6); Petra Kronberger and Vreni Schneider (3); Michela Figini, Nancy Greene, Erika Hess, Maria Walliser and Hanni Wenzel (2).

Year		Year		Year	
1967	Nancy Greene, Canada	1978	Hanni Wenzel, Liechtenstein	1989	Vreni Schneider, Switzerland
1968	Nancy Greene, Canada	1979	Annemarie Moser-Pröll, Austria	1990	Petra Kronberger, Austria
1969	Gertrud Gabi, Austria	1980	Hanni Wenzel, Liechtenstein	1991	Petra Kronberger, Austria
1970	Michele Jacot, France	1981	Marie-Theres Nadig, Switzerland	1992	Petra Kronberger, Austria
1971	Annemarie Pröll, Austria	1982	Erika Hess, Switzerland	1993	Anita Wachter, Austria
1972	Annemarie Pröll, Austria	1983	Tamara McKinney, USA	1994	Vreni Schneider, Switzerland
1973	Annemarie Pröll, Austria	1984	Erika Hess, Switzerland	1995	Vreni Schneider, Switzerland
1974	Annemarie Pröll, Austria	1985	Michela Figini, Switzerland	1996	Katja Seizinger, Germany
1975	Annemarie Moser-Pröll, Austria	1986	Maria Walliser, Switzerland	1997	Pernilla Wiberg, Sweden
1976	Rosi Mittermaier, W. Germany	1987	Maria Walliser, Switzerland		
1977	Lise-Marie Morerod, Switzerland	1988	Michela Figini, Switzerland		

TOUR DE FRANCE

The world's premier cycling event, the Tour de France is staged throughout the country (sometimes passing through neighboring countries) over four weeks. The 1946 Tour, however, the first after World War II, was only a five-day race.

Multiple winners: Jacques Anquetil, Bernard Hinault, Miguel Induráin and Eddy Merckx (5); Louison Bobet, Greg LeMond and Phillippe Thys (3); Gino Bartali Ottavio Bottecchia; Fausto Coppi, Laurent Fignon, Nicholas Frantz, Firmin Lambot, André Leducq, Sylvere Maes, Antonin Magne, Lucien Petit-Breton and Bernard Thevenet (2).

Year		Year		Year	
1903	Maurice Garin, France	1936	Sylvere Maes, Belgium	1970	Eddy Merckx, Belgium
1904	Henri Cornet, France	1937	Roger Lapebie, France	1971	Eddy Merckx, Belgium
1905	Louis Trousselier, France	1938	Gino Bartali, Italy	1972	Eddy Merckx, Belgium
1906	René Pottier, France	1939	Sylvere Maes, Belgium	1973	Luis Ocana, Spain
1907	Lucien Petit-Breton, France	1940-45	Not held	1974	Eddy Merckx, Belgium
1908	Lucien Petit-Breton, France	1946	Jean Lazarides, France	1975	Bernard Thevenet, France
1909	Francois Faber, Luxembourg	1947	Jean Robic, France	1976	Lucien van Impe, Belgium
		1948	Gino Bartali, Italy	1977	Bernard Thevenet, France
1910	Octave Lapize, France	1949	Fausto Coppi, Italy	1978	Bernard Hinault, France
1911	Gustave Garrigou, France			1979	Bernard Hinault, France
1912	Odile Defraye, France	1950	Ferdinand Kubler, Switzerland		
1913	Philippe Thys, Belgium	1951	Hugo Koblet, Switzerland	1980	Joop Zoetemelk, Holland
1914	Philippe Thys, Belgium	1952	Fausto Coppi, Italy	1981	Bernard Hinault, France
1915-18	Not held	1953	Louison Bobet, France	1982	Bernard Hinault, France
1919	Firmin Lambot, Belgium	1954	Louison Bobet, France	1983	Laurent Fignon, France
		1955	Louison Bobet, France	1984	Laurent Fignon, France
1920	Philippe Thys, Belgium	1956	Roger Walkowiak, France	1985	Bernard Hinault, France
1921	Léon Scieur, Belgium	1957	Jacques Anquetil, France	1986	Greg LeMond, USA
1922	Firmin Lambot, Belgium	1958	Charly Gaul, Luxembourg	1987	Stephen Roche, Ireland
1923	Henri Pelissier, France	1959	Federico Bahamontes, Spain	1988	Pedro Delgado, Spain
1924	Ottavio Bottecchia, Italy			1989	Greg LeMond, USA
1925	Ottavio Bottecchia, Italy	1960	Gastone Nencini, Italy		
1926	Lucien Buysse, Belgium	1961	Jacques Anquetil, France	1990	Greg LeMond, USA
1927	Nicholas Frantz, Luxembourg	1962	Jacques Anquetil, France	1991	Miguel Induráin, Spain
1928	Nicholas Frantz, Luxembourg	1963	Jacques Anquetil, France	1992	Miguel Induráin, Spain
1929	Maurice Dewaele, Belgium	1964	Jacques Anquetil, France	1993	Miguel Induráin, Spain
		1965	Felice Gimondi, Italy	1994	Miguel Induráin, Spain
1930	André Leducq, France	1966	Lucien Aimar, France	1995	Miguel Induráin, Spain
1931	Antonin Magne, France	1967	Roger Pingeon, France	1996	Bjarne Riis, Denmark
1932	André Leducq, France	1968	Jan Janssen, Holland	1997	Jan Ullrich, Germany
1933	Georges Speicher, France	1969	Eddy Merckx, Belgium		
1934	Antonin Magne, France				
1935	Romain Maes, Belgium				

FIGURE SKATING

World Champions

Skaters who won World and Olympic championships in the same year are listed in **bold** type.

MEN

Multiple winners: Ulrich Salchow (10); Karl Schafer (7); Dick Button (5); Willy Bockl, Kurt Browning, Scott Hamilton and Hayes Jenkins (4); Emmerich Danzer, Gillis Grafstrom, Gustav Hugel, David Jenkins, Fritz Kachler, Ondrej Nepela and Elvis Stojko (3); Brian Boitano, Gilbert Fuchs, Jan Hoffmann, Felix Kaspar, Vladimir Kovalev and Tim Wood (2).

Year		Year		Year	
1896	Gilbert Fuchs, Germany	1932	**Karl Schafer**, Austria	1968	Emmerich Danzer, Austria
1897	Gustav Hugel, Austria	1933	Karl Schafer, Austria	1969	Tim Wood, USA
1898	Henning Grenander, Sweden	1934	Karl Schafer, Austria		
1899	Gustav Hugel, Austria	1935	Karl Schafer, Austria	1970	Tim Wood, USA
		1936	**Karl Schafer**, Austria	1971	Ondrej Nepela, Czechoslovakia
1900	Gustav Hugel, Austria	1937	Felix Kaspar, Austria	1972	**Ondrej Nepela**, Czechoslovakia
1901	Ulrich Salchow, Sweden	1938	Felix Kaspar, Austria	1973	Ondrej Nepela, Czechoslovakia
1902	Ulrich Salchow, Sweden	1939	Graham Sharp, Britain	1974	Jan Hoffmann, E. Germany
1903	Ulrich Salchow, Sweden	1940-46 Not held		1975	Sergie Volkov, USSR
1904	Ulrich Salchow, Sweden	1947	Hans Gerschwiler, Switzerland	1976	**John Curry**, Britain
1905	Ulrich Salchow, Sweden	1948	**Dick Button**, USA	1977	Vladimir Kovalev, USSR
1906	Gilbert Fuchs, Germany	1949	Dick Button, USA	1978	Charles Tickner, USA
1907	Ulrich Salchow, Sweden			1979	Vladimir Kovalev, USSR
1908	**Ulrich Salchow**, Sweden	1950	Dick Button, USA		
1909	Ulrich Salchow, Sweden	1951	Dick Button, USA	1980	Jan Hoffmann, E. Germany
		1952	**Dick Button**, USA	1981	Scott Hamilton, USA
1910	Ulrich Salchow, Sweden	1953	Hayes Jenkins, USA	1982	Scott Hamilton, USA
1911	Ulrich Salchow, Sweden	1954	Hayes Jenkins, USA	1983	Scott Hamilton, USA
1912	Fritz Kachler, Austria	1955	Hayes Jenkins, USA	1984	**Scott Hamilton**, USA
1913	Fritz Kachler, Austria	1956	**Hayes Jenkins**, USA	1985	Alexander Fadeev, USSR
1914	Gosta Sandhal, Sweden	1957	David Jenkins, USA	1986	Brian Boitano, USA
1915-21 Not held		1958	David Jenkins, USA	1987	Brian Orser, Canada
1922	Gillis Grafstrom, Sweden	1959	David Jenkins, USA	1988	**Brian Boitano**, USA
1923	Fritz Kachler, Austria			1989	Kurt Browning, Canada
1924	**Gillis Grafstrom,** Sweden	1960	Alan Giletti, France		
1925	Willy Bockl, Austria	1961	Not held	1990	Kurt Browning, Canada
1926	Willy Bockl, Austria	1962	Donald Jackson, Canada	1991	Kurt Browning, Canada
1927	Willy Bockl, Austria	1963	Donald McPherson, Canada	1992	**Viktor Petrenko**, CIS
1928	Willy Bockl, Austria	1964	**Manfred Schnelldorfer**, W. Ger	1993	Kurt Browning, Canada
1929	Gillis Grafstrom, Sweden	1965	Alain Calmat, France	1994	Elvis Stojko, Canada
		1966	Emmerich Danzer, Austria	1995	Elvis Stojko, Canada
1930	Karl Schafer, Austria	1967	Emmerich Danzer, Austria	1996	Todd Eldredge, USA
1931	Karl Schafer, Austria			1997	Elvis Stojko, Canada

WOMEN

Multiple winners: Sonja Henie (10); Carol Heiss and Herma Planck Szabo (5); Lily Kronberger and Katarina Witt (4); Sjoukje Dijkstra, Peggy Fleming, Meray Horvath (3); Tenley Albright, Linda Fratianne, Anett Poetzsch, Beatrix Schuba, Barbara Ann Scott, Gabriele Seyfert, Megan Taylor, Alena Vrzanova, and Kristi Yamaguchi (2).

Year		Year		Year	
1906	Madge Syers, Britain	1935	Sonja Henie, Norway	1964	**Sjoukje Dijkstra**, Holland
1907	Madge Syers, Britian	1936	**Sonja Henie**, Norway	1965	Petra Burka, Canada
1908	Lily Kronberger, Hungary	1937	Cecilia Colledge, Britain	1966	Peggy Fleming, USA
1909	Lily Kronberger, Hungary	1938	Megan Taylor, Britain	1967	Peggy Fleming, USA
		1939	Megan Taylor, Britain	1968	**Peggy Fleming**, USA
1910	Lily Kronberger, Hungary	1940-46 Not held		1969	Gabriele Seyfert, E. Germany
1911	Lily Kronberger, Hungary	1947	Barbara Ann Scott, Canada		
1912	Meray Horvath, Hungary	1948	**Barbara Ann Scott**, Canada	1970	Gabriele Seyfert, E. Germany
1913	Meray Horvath, Hungary	1949	Alena Vrzanova, Czechoslovakia	1971	Beatrix Schuba, Austria
1914	Meray Horvath, Hungary			1972	**Beatrix Schuba**, Austria
1915-21 Not held		1950	Alena Vrzanova, Czechoslovakia	1973	Karen Magnussen, Canada
1922	Herma Planck-Szabo, Austria	1951	Jeannette Altwegg, Britain	1974	Christine Errath, E. Germany
1923	Herma Planck-Szabo, Austria	1952	Jacqueline Du Bief, France	1975	Dianne DeLeeuw, Holland
1924	**Herma Planck-Szabo**, Austria	1953	Tenley Albright, USA	1976	**Dorothy Hamill**, USA
1925	Herma Planck-Szabo, Austria	1954	Gundi Busch, W. Germany	1977	Linda Fratianne, USA
1926	Herma Planck-Szabo, Austria	1955	Tenley Albright, USA	1978	Anett Poetzsch, E. Germany
1927	Sonja Henie, Norway	1956	Carol Heiss, USA	1979	Linda Fratianne, USA
1928	**Sonja Henie**, Norway	1957	Carol Heiss, USA		
1929	Sonja Henie, Norway	1958	Carol Heiss, USA	1980	**Anett Poetzsch**, E. Germany
		1959	Carol Heiss, USA	1981	Denise Biellmann, Switzerland
1930	Sonja Henie, Norway			1982	Elaine Zayak, USA
1931	Sonja Henie, Norway	1960	**Carol Heiss**, USA	1983	Rosalyn Sumners, USA
1932	**Sonja Henie**, Norway	1961	Not held	1984	**Katarina Witt**, E. Germany
1933	Sonja Henie, Norway	1962	Sjoukje Dijkstra, Holland	1985	Katarina Witt, E. Germany
1934	Sonja Henie, Norway	1963	Sjoukje Dijkstra, Holland	1986	Debi Thomas, USA

Figure Skating (Cont.)

Year		Year		Year	
1987	Katarina Witt, E. Germany	1991	Kristi Yamaguchi, USA	1995	Lu Chen, China
1988	**Katarina Witt**, E. Germany	1992	**Kristi Yamaguchi**, USA	1996	Michelle Kwan, USA
1989	Midori Ito, Japan	1993	Oksana Baiul, Ukraine	1997	Tara Lipinski, USA
1990	Jill Trenary, USA	1994	Yuka Sato, Japan		

U.S. Champions

Skaters who won U.S., World and Olympic championships in same year are in **bold** type.

MEN

Multiple winners: Dick Button and Roger Turner (7); Sherwin Badger and Robin Lee (5); Brian Boitano, Todd Eldredge, Scott Hamilton, David Jenkins, Hayes Jenkins and Charles Tickner (4); Gordon McKellen, Nathaniel Niles and Tim Wood (3); Scott Allen, Christopher Bowman, Scott Davis, Eugene Turner and Gary Visconti (2).

Year		Year		Year		Year	
1914	Norman Scott	1937	Robin Lee	1959	David Jenkins	1980	Charles Tickner
1915-17	Not held	1938	Robin Lee	1960	David Jenkins	1981	Scott Hamilton
1918	Nathaniel Niles	1939	Robin Lee	1961	Bradley Lord	1982	Scott Hamilton
1919	Not held	1940	Eugene Turner	1962	Monty Hoyt	1983	Scott Hamilton
1920	Sherwin Badger	1941	Eugene Turner	1963	Thomas Litz	1984	**Scott Hamilton**
1921	Sherwin Badger	1942	Robert Specht	1964	Scott Allen	1985	Brian Boitano
1922	Sherwin Badger	1943	Arthur Vaughn	1965	Gary Visconti	1986	Brian Boitano
1923	Sherwin Badger	1944-45	Not held	1966	Scott Allen	1987	Brian Boitano
1924	Sherwin Badger	1946	Dick Button	1967	Gary Visconti	1988	**Brian Boitano**
1925	Nathaniel Niles	1947	Dick Button	1968	Tim Wood	1989	Christopher Bowman
1926	Chris Christenson	1948	**Dick Button**	1969	Tim Wood		
1927	Nathaniel Niles	1949	Dick Button	1970	Tim Wood	1990	Todd Eldredge
1928	Roger Turner	1950	Dick Button	1971	John (Misha) Petkevich	1991	Todd Eldredge
1929	Roger Turner	1951	Dick Button	1972	Ken Shelley	1992	Christopher Bowman
1930	Roger Turner	1952	**Dick Button**	1973	Gordon McKellen	1993	Scott Davis
1931	Roger Turner	1953	Hayes Jenkins	1974	Gordon McKellen	1994	Scott Davis
1932	Roger Turner	1954	Hayes Jenkins	1975	Gordon McKellen	1995	Todd Eldredge
1933	Roger Turner	1955	Hayes Jenkins	1976	Terry Kubicka	1996	Rudy Galindo
1934	Roger Turner	1956	**Hayes Jenkins**	1977	Charles Tickner	1997	Todd Eldredge
1935	Robin Lee	1957	David Jenkins	1978	Charles Tickner		
1936	Robin Lee	1958	David Jenkins	1979	Charles Tickner		

WOMEN

Multiple winners: Maribel Vinson (9); Theresa Weld Blanchard and Gretchen Merrill (6); Tenley Albright, Peggy Fleming, and Janet Lynn (5); Linda Fratianne and Carol Heiss (4); Dorothy Hamill, Beatrix Loughran, Rosalyn Summers, Joan Tozzer and Jill Trenary (3); Yvonne Sherman and Debi Thomas (2).

Year		Year		Year		Year	
1914	Theresa Weld	1937	Maribel Vinson	1958	Carol Heiss	1979	Linda Fratianne
1915-17	Not held	1938	Joan Tozzer	1959	Carol Heiss	1980	Linda Fratianne
1918	Rosemary Beresford	1939	Joan Tozzer	1960	**Carol Heiss**	1981	Elaine Zayak
1919	Not held	1940	Joan Tozzer	1961	Laurence Owen	1982	Rosalyn Sumners
1920	Theresa Weld	1941	Jane Vaughn	1962	Barbara Pursley	1983	Rosalyn Sumners
1921	Theresa Blanchard	1942	Jane Sullivan	1963	Lorraine Hanlon	1984	Rosalyn Sumners
1922	Theresa Blanchard	1943	Gretchen Merrill	1964	Peggy Fleming	1985	Tiffany Chin
1923	Theresa Blanchard	1944	Gretchen Merrill	1965	Peggy Fleming	1986	Debi Thomas
1924	Theresa Blanchard	1945	Gretchen Merrill	1966	Peggy Fleming	1987	Jill Trenary
1925	Beatrix Loughran	1946	Gretchen Merrill	1967	Peggy Fleming	1988	Debi Thomas
1926	Beatrix Loughran	1947	Gretchen Merrill	1968	**Peggy Fleming**	1989	Jill Trenary
1927	Beatrix Loughran	1948	Gretchen Merrill	1969	Janet Lynn		
1928	Maribel Vinson	1949	Yvonne Sherman	1970	Janet Lynn	1990	Jill Trenary
1929	Maribel Vinson	1950	Yvonne Sherman	1971	Janet Lynn	1991	Tonya Harding
1930	Maribel Vinson	1951	Sonya Klopfer	1972	Janet Lynn	1992	**Kristi Yamaguchi**
1931	Maribel Vinson	1952	Tenley Albright	1973	Janet Lynn	1993	Nancy Kerrigan
1932	Maribel Vinson	1953	Tenley Albright	1974	Dorothy Hamill	1994	vacated*
1933	Maribel Vinson	1954	Tenley Albright	1975	Dorothy Hamill	1995	Nicole Bobek
1934	Suzanne Davis	1955	Tenley Albright	1976	**Dorothy Hamill**	1996	Michelle Kwan
1935	Maribel Vinson	1956	Tenley Albright	1977	Linda Fratianne	1997	Tara Lipinski
1936	Maribel Vinson	1957	Carol Heiss	1978	Linda Fratianne		

* Tonya Harding was stripped of the 1994 women's title and banned from membership in the U.S. Figure Skating Assn. for life on June 30, 1994 for violating the USFSA Code of Ethics after she pleaded guilty to a charge of conspiracy to hinder the prosecution related to the Jan. 6, 1994 attack on Nancy Kerrigan.

Soccer

The fancy footwork of American goal scorers like **Eric Wynalda** may be the key to the long term success of Major League Soccer.

Wide World Photos

The Goal's the Thing

The success of the MLS may depend on developing more Americans who can score.

by
Jack Edwards

Eric Cantona beat the devil in a memorable television commercial for Nike. Booted a flaming soccer ball right through Satan's gut, a fitting finish for the assault convict/ brilliant striker who announced his retirement at the end of the English Premier League season. Cantona is probably best-known in the U.S. for his altercation with a fan which resulted in a conviction and an eight-month ban. That, and the TV ad. He should be known more for his incredible thrusts which made crowds rise every time he got the ball on his foot. If this were 20 years ago, we could have anticipated Cantona showing up soon on the New York Cosmos.

But all the aging foreign superstars in the world (and it had most of 'em) wouldn't have made the old North American Soccer League work. And what ultimately will make or break Major League Soccer is not another host of international scorers, though they certainly will help. What the MLS desperately needs is a supply of *American* finishers. Home-grown guys who make the back of the net billow. The league sorely needs to develop the descendants of Kyle Rote Jr., who led the NASL in scoring in 1973.

Guys like Eric Wynalda who scored the first goal in MLS history. And guys with a flair for the dramatic like Wynalda, who scored that historic goal just moments before the league's first game was about to go-down as a 0-0 yawner, to be settled in a shootout.

With that flair comes a certain attitude, however. Goal-scorers are unabashedly cocky. "You have to be arrogant," the U.S. National Team's Eric Wynalda told ESPN.

Jack Edwards is the co-anchor of ESPN's *Sunday SportsDay*.

Eric Cantona of Manchester United tries a bicycle kick against Dortmund in the UEFA Champions League semifinal match on April 23, 1997. Cantona, an exciting crowd-pleasing player, retired after the season.

American defenseman, and one of the few native breakout stars in the MLS, Alexi Lalas had a slightly different take: "They are a pain in the ass. And you sort of have to deal with them because they score goals."

U.S.-born Roy Lassiter scored 27 of 'em in MLS's inaugural season, to lead the league. He subscribes to the theory that great goal-scorers cannot be made -- they must be born. "That kind of instinct is within," he said. But why are there so few pure scorers within U.S. borders? Says Lassiter, "At the college level, there were a lot of them, but I think they faded away."

Wynalda has another take: "I believe it's a little kink in our system. I believe it's a flaw in the American mentality toward this game. Too many coaches in this country are trying to create players who are good at everything or who are average at everything -- the 'well-rounded player.'"

Consider Pele, who, even after 15 years as the best player on Earth, STILL wouldn't use his left foot unless he had to. If such a youth coach had demanded that Pele "round out" his game, would he ever have been so great? Says Wynalda, "I didn't want to fall into that trap. I was always a

United States forward **Jovan Kirovski** hugs teammate **Roy Lassiter** after Lassiter scored the only US goal of the game in a 1–1 tie with El Salvador in a World Cup qualifying match on June 29, 1997.

player who concentrated on getting good at one thing, getting great at one thing, knowing that would take me to the next level. My little problem was defense. I stayed away from it, because that's not my job. My job is to be a good goal-scorer. That's it."

Such arrogance. What a pain.

Still, pass the ibuprofen and lift a toast. Here's hoping there are more of Wynalda's rare kind on the way. Because at the start of 1997, the United States National Team was ranked in the top 20 worldwide but the October 15th poll had our boys at a distressing 35th. Not exactly the kind of movement you would like to see with the World Cup just around the corner.

For proof of the importance of goal-scoring maybe U.S. coach Steve Sampson, and other American coaches at all levels, should study what the American women are doing. The U.S. Women's National Team is a dominant force internationally. Not coincidentally, the U.S. women have no trouble putting the ball in the net ■

Jack Edwards' Top Ten Highlights of the Year in Soccer

10. **U.S. progresses** toward qualifying for 1998 World Cup Finals with a solid performance against a strong Mexican team in a 2–2 tie in April and 1–0 win over Costa Rica in September. Despite these strong showings, the U.S. has not clinched a berth in the Cup Finals due to a series of poor showings against lesser teams. They will need a strong performance in the final three qualifying matches to ensure that they will be playing

Flashy American defenseman **Alexi Lalas** is good for American soccer but the sport's long-term success will depend on the emergence of flashy American goal scorers.

with the big boys in France the summer of 1998.

9. **Carlos Valderrama** of the Tampa Bay Mutiny is selected as the Most Valuable Player in the inaugural season of Major League Soccer. The Mutiny won the Eastern Conference and Valderrama finished second in the league in assists and also won the MVP award in the first MLS All-Star Game.

8. **American Roy Lassiter** of the D.C. United wins the MLS scoring title with a league-leading 27 goals and four assists for a total of 58 points. Preki of Kansas City is second with 18 goals and 13 assists.

7. **Japanese league officials** are "worried" that attendance has sunk to 10,611 per game. As cohosts with South Korea of the 2002 World Cup, Japan doesn't need the sport's popularity to wane, though everyone knows that the J-league is not quite the draw that the championship of the most popular sport in the world is.

6. **Schalke 04** beats heavily favored Inter Milan 4–1 for the UEFA Cup in front of 82, 000 fans. After the second leg, each team had scored a 1–0 victory so the UEFA Cup was decided on penalty kicks. Schalke coach Huub Stevens used a computer printout to predict where the Inter Milan players

would shoot as they only scored on one of the four kicks.

5. **Juventus** runneth over as Italian champions, winning their 24th league title as they celebrated their 100th birthday in 1997. This victory marks the seventh major trophy the team has won in the past three years. Since 1994, the team known as the "old lady" has won two league titles, a European Cup, the Italian Super Cup, the Intercontinental and European Super Cups, and the Italian Cup.

4. **Chelsea** ends a 27–year drought by defeating Middlesborough 2–0 to win the FA Cup. Roberto Di Matteo's strike from 25 yards out proved to the game winner just 25 seconds into the match.

3. **Borussia Dortmund** wins the Champions League. In the biggest triumph in team history, Dortmund defeated Juventus 3–1. Substitute Lars Ricken, 20, scored one of the most exciting goals in European Cup final history just 16 seconds after entering the game. Ricken streaked down the right flank and beat goalkeeper Angelo Peruzzi from 25 yards out on his first touch.

2. **Eric Cantona** retires. The 30–year old Frenchman and Manchester United star announced he was leaving the game after five seasons with the club. Cantona was never short on talent but will probably be more remembered for his furious temper. He once earned an eight month suspension for an ugly "Kung-Fu" kick on a fan. Cantona's legacy, though, is that

of a gifted player with a colorful 13–year career.

1. **D.C. United** wins the first MLS Championsip and D.C.'s Mario Etcheverry is chosen as the MVP of the championship game, the MLS Cup '96. ∎

THE **NUMBERS**

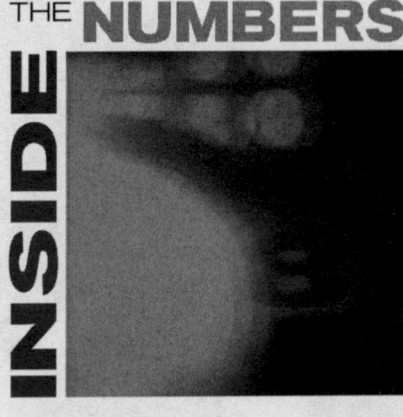

by
Andrew Villa

UNITED THEY STAND

In 1996, the D.C. United didn't finish badly, as they came in second in the Eastern Conference and went on to win the first MLS Cup. Perhaps even more impressive, though, has been their defense of the Cup. In 1997, they led the league in points scored and road record, tied Kansas CIty for the lead in wins and led the Eastern Conference in conference record. They also scored a league-record 70 goals, eight more than last year.

Second Time Around

	1996	1997
Wins	16	21*
Points	46	55*
Conference Record	9-7	12-4
Road Record	5-11	110-6*

* Led MLS.

∎

726

THE 1998 | ESPN INFORMATION PLEASE SPORTS ALMANAC

S O C C E R
S T A T I S T I C S

THE SEASON IN REVIEW
1996-1997
WORLD • EUROPE • AMERICA

SEC **A**

PAGE 727

FIFA Top 50 World Rankings

FIFA announced a new monthly world ranking system on Aug. 13, 1993 designed to "provide a constant international comparison of national team performances." The rankings are based on a mathematical formula that weighs strength of schedule, importance of matches and goals scored for and against. Games considered include World Cup qualifying and final rounds, Continental championship qualifying and final rounds, and friendly matches. At the end of the year, FIFA designates a Team of the Year. Teams of the Year so far have been Germany (1993) and Brazil (1994, '95, '96).

1996

		Points	1995 Rank				Points	1995 Rank				Points	1995 Rank
1	Brazil	68.38	1	18	USA	54.78	19	35	Greece	46.15	34
2	Germany	64.46	2	19	South Africa	54.32	40	36	Ireland	46.08	28
3	France	61.37	8	20	Zambia	53.76	25	37	Saudi Arabia	46.00	54
4	Colombia	61.34	15	21	Japan	53.35	31	38	Paraguay	45.69	64
5	Czech Republic	61.11	14	22	Argentina	52.72	7	39	Bolivia	45.05	53
6	Denmark	60.67	9	23	Tunisia	51.94	22	40	Canada	44.89	65
7	Russia	60.51	5	24	Croatia	51.29	41	41	Trinidad & Tobago	44.72	57
8	Spain	60.21	4	25	Ghana	50.93	29				
9	Netherlands	59.59	6	26	Chile	50.46	36	42	Belgium	44.49	24
10	Italy	58.68	3	27	Morocco	50.31	38	43	Uruguay	44.08	32
11	Mexico	56.92	12	28	Egypt	49.76	23	44	South Korea	44.05	46
12	England	56.42	21	29	Scotland	48.71	26	45	Honduras	43.87	49
13	Portugal	56.13	16	30	Slovakia	48.57	35	46	Gabon	43.80	67
14	Norway	55.71	10	31	Turkey	47.94	30	47	Switzerland	43.54	18
15	Bulgaria	55.64	17	32	Jamaica	47.83	56	48	Lithuania	43.30	43
16	Romania	55.57	11	33	Ecuador	46.81	55	49	Algeria	43.03	48
17	Sweden	55.50	13	34	Austria	46.33	39	50	Australia	42.99	51

1997 (as of Oct. 15)

		Points	1996 Rank				Points	1996 Rank				Points	1996 Rank
1	Brazil	72.15	1	18	Bulgaria	56.76	15	35	USA	52.40	18
2	Spain	65.20	8	19	Zambia	56.07	20	36	Yugoslavia	52.31	55
3	Germany	63.03	2	20	Japan	56.00	21	37	Saudi Arabia	51.39	37
4	Czech Republic	61.97	5	21	Portugal	55.45	13	38	Peru	51.34	54
5	Romania	61.87	16	22	Bolivia	55.27	39	39	Turkey	51.32	31
6	Denmark	60.85	6	23	Austria	55.11	34	40	Jamaica	50.64	32
7	England	60.66	12	24	Tunisia	55.07	23	41	Greece	50.40	35
8	Netherlands	60.59	9	25	Scotland	54.38	29	42	Lithuania	48.12	48
9	Russia	60.01	7	26	South Africa	53.75	19	43	Ireland	47.33	36
10	Mexico	59.94	11	27	Chile	53.62	26	44	Cameroon	47.22	56
11	Colombia	59.51	4	28	Paraguay	53.55	38	45	Poland	47.20	53
12	Norway	59.45	14	29	Croatia	53.39	24	46	Ivory Coast	46.51	51
13	Argentina	58.09	22	30	Slovakia	53.11	30	47	Kuwait	46.43	62
14	France	57.88	3	31	Ecuador	53.03	33	48	Belgium	46.08	42
15	Morocco	57.65	27	32	Egypt	52.55	28	49	Iran	45.91	83
16	Italy	57.56	10	33	Australia	52.53	50	50	Ghana	45.72	25
17	Sweden	57.18	17	34	South Korea	52.49	44				

Countdown to World Cup France '98

Date	Activity	Date	Activity
Nov. 16, 1997	End of preliminary competition	June 10, 1998	Final 32-team tournament begins in France
Nov. 30, 1997	Completion of any necessary playoffs		
Dec. 4, 1997	Draw for final competition held in Marseilles	July 12, 1998	Championship game at Stade de France in Paris

1996 Indoor World Championships

The 3rd Futsal Indoor Five-a-Side World Championship held Nov. 24-Dec 8, 1996 in Spain. Note that (*) indicates teams advancing to second stage.

First Stage Results

Group A	Gm	W	L	T	GF	GA	Pts
*Spain	3	3	0	0	18	3	9
*Ukraine	3	2	1	0	22	9	6
Egypt	3	1	2	0	13	19	3
Australia	3	0	3	0	4	26	0

RESULTS: **Nov. 24**– Spain 7, Egypt 2; Ukraine 11, Australia 2. **Nov. 26**– Egypt 8, Australia 2; Spain 4, Ukraine 1. **Nov. 28**– Ukraine 10, Egypt 3; Spain 7, Australia 0.

Group B	Gm	W	L	T	GF	GA	Pts
*Netherlands	3	2	0	1	13	6	7
*Russia	3	1	0	2	15	5	5
Argentina	3	1	1	1	7	9	4
China	3	0	3	0	3	18	0

RESULTS: **Nov. 25**– Argentina 2, China 1; Russia 2, Netherlands 2. **Nov. 27**– Argentina 2, Russia 2; Netherlands 5, China 1. **Nov. 28**– Russia 11, China 1; Netherlands 6, Argentina 3.

Group C	Gm	W	L	T	GF	GA	Pts
*Italy	3	2	0	1	16	5	7
*Uruguay	3	2	0	1	7	3	7
United States	3	1	2	0	12	7	3
Malaysia	3	0	3	0	4	24	0

RESULTS: **Nov. 24**– Uruguay 1, United States 0; Italy 10, Malaysia 1. **Nov. 26**– Italy 4, United States 2; Uruguay 4, Malaysia 1. **Nov. 28**– Italy 2, Uruguay 2; United States 10, Malaysia 2.

Group D	Gm	W	L	T	GF	GA	Pts
*Brazil	3	3	0	0	31	5	9
*Belgium	3	2	1	0	13	10	6
Iran	3	1	2	0	12	14	3
Cuba	3	0	3	0	4	31	0

RESULTS: **Nov. 25**– Iran 7, Cuba 1; Brazil 5, Belgium 2. **Nov. 27**– Belgium 5, Iran 2; Brazil 18, Cuba 0. **Nov. 28**– Brazil 8, Iran 3; Belgium 6, Cuba 3.

Second Stage Results

Note that (*) indicates teams advancing to semifinals.

Group E	Gm	W	L	T	GF	GA	Pts
*Spain	3	3	0	0	8	2	9
*Russia	3	2	1	0	9	4	6
Italy	3	1	2	0	5	8	3
Belgium	3	0	3	0	4	12	0

RESULTS: **Dec. 1**– Italy 4, Belgium 1; Spain 2, Russia 0. **Dec. 2**– Russia 3, Italy 0; Spain 2, Belgium 1. **Dec. 4**– Russia 6, Belgium 2; Spain 4, Italy 1.

Group F	Gm	W	L	T	GF	GA	Pts
*Brazil	3	2	0	1	12	5	7
*Ukraine	3	1	0	2	11	9	5
Uruguay	3	1	2	0	10	14	3
Netherlands	3	0	2	1	9	14	1

RESULTS: **Nov. 30**– Netherlands 4, Ukraine 4; Brazil 4, Uruguay 2. **Dec. 1**– Uruguay 5, Netherlands 4; Ukraine 2, Brazil 2. **Dec. 3**– Ukraine 5, Uruguay 3; Brazil 5, Netherlands 1.

Semifinals

Dec. 6	Brazil 6	Russia 2
Dec. 6	Spain 4	Ukraine 1

Third-Place Game

Dec. 8	Russia 3	Ukraine 2

Final

Dec. 8, 1996 at Palau Sant Jordi in Barcelona.
Attendance:15,500 (capacity crowd)

Brazil 6 ....Spain 4

1997 Copa America

Regarded as the Championship of South America since its inception in 1916, the Copa America began extending invitations to Central and North American teams in 1993. Mexico and Costa Rica participated in 1997. Held June 11-29 in Bolivia. Note that (*) indicates team advancing to quarterfinals.

First Round

Group A	Gm	W	L	T	GF	GA	Pts
*Ecuador	3	2	0	1	4	1	7
*Argentina	3	1	0	2	3	1	5
*Paraguay	3	1	1	1	2	3	4
Chile	3	0	3	0	1	5	0

RESULTS: **June 11**– Paraguay 2, Chile 0; Argentina 1, Ecuador 0. **June 14**– Argentina 2, Chile 0; Ecuador 2, Paraguay 0. **June 17**– Ecuador 2, Chile 1; Argentina 1, Paraguay 1.

Group B	Gm	W	L	T	GF	GA	Pts
*Bolivia	3	3	0	0	4	0	9
*Peru	3	2	1	0	3	2	6
Uruguay	3	1	2	0	2	2	3
Venezuela	3	0	3	0	0	5	0

RESULTS: **June 12**– Peru 1, Uruguay 0; Bolivia 1, Venezuela 0. **June 15**– Bolivia 2, Peru 0; Uruguay 2, Venezuela 0. **June 18**– Peru 2, Venezuela 0; Bolivia 1, Uruguay 0.

Group C	Gm	W	L	T	GF	GA	Pts
*Brazil	3	3	0	0	10	2	9
*Mexico	3	1	1	1	5	5	4
*Colombia	3	1	2	0	5	5	3
Costa Rica	3	0	2	1	2	10	1

RESULTS: **June 13**– Mexico 2, Colombia 1; Brazil 5, Costa Rica 0. **June 16**– Colombia 4, Costa Rica 1; Brazil 3, Mexico 2. **June 19**– Mexico 1, Costa Rica 1; Brazil 2, Colombia 0.

Quarterfinals

June 21	Sucre (9,000)	Peru 2, Argentina 1
June 21	La Paz (25,000)	Bolivia 2, Colombia 1
June 22	Santa Cruz (35,000)	Brazil 2, Paraguay 0
June 22	Cochabamba (7,000)	Mexico 1, Ecuador 1*

*Mexico wins shootout, 4-3.

Semifinals

June 25	La Paz (46,000)	Bolivia 3, Mexico 1
June 26	Santa Cruz (20,000)	Brazil 7, Peru 0

Third Place

June 28	Oruro (8,000)	Mexico 1, Peru 0

Final

June 29	La Paz (46,000)	Brazil 3, Bolivia 1

Leading Goal Scorers

6 goals— Luis Hernandez, Mexico. **5 goals**— Ronaldo, Brazil. **3 goals**— Marcelo Gallardo, Argentina; Romario, Brazil; Leonardo, Brazil; Erwin Sanchez, Bolivia.

1997 World Youth Championships

Held June 16-July 5 in Malaysia for Under-20 national teams.

First Round

Group A	Gm	W	L	T	GF	GA	Pts
*Uruguay	3	2	0	1	6	1	7
*Morocco	3	1	0	2	4	2	5
*Belgium	3	1	1	1	4	4	4
Malaysia	3	0	3	0	2	9	0

RESULTS: **June 16**– Morocco 3, Malaysia 1. **June 17**– Uruguay 3, Belgium 0. **June 19**– Uruguay 3, Malaysia 1; Morocco 1, Belgium 1. **June 22**– Belgium 3, Malaysia 0; Uruguay 0, Morocco 0.

Group B	Gm	W	L	T	GF	GA	Pts
*Brazil	3	3	0	0	15	3	9
*France	3	2	1	0	8	7	6
South Africa	3	0	2	1	2	6	1
South Korea	3	0	2	1	5	14	1

RESULTS: **June 17**– South Africa 0, South Korea 0; Brazil 3, France 0. **June 19**– France 4, South Korea 2; Brazil 2, South Africa 0. **June 21**– Brazil 10, South Korea 3; France 4, South Africa 2.

Group C	Gm	W	L	T	GF	GA	Pts
*Ghana	3	2	0	1	4	2	7
*Ireland	3	1	1	1	4	4	4
*United States	2	1	2	0	2	3	3
China	3	0	1	2	2	3	2

RESULTS: **June 17**– Ghana 2, Ireland 1; United States 1, China 0. **June 19**– Ghana 1, China 1; Ireland 2, United States 1. **June 22**– Ghana 1, United States 0; Ireland 2, China 1.

Group D	Gm	W	L	T	GF	GA	Pts
*Spain	3	3	0	0	8	2	9
*Japan	3	1	1	1	10	7	4
Paraguay	3	0	1	2	5	6	2
Costa Rica	3	0	1	2	2	11	1

RESULTS: **June 18**– Spain 2, Japan 1; Costa Rica 1, Paraguay 1. **June 20**– Japan 6, Costa Rica 2; Spain 2, Paraguay 1. **June 23**– Japan 3, Paraguay 3; Spain 4, Costa Rica 0.

Group E	Gm	W	L	T	GF	GA	Pts
*Australia	3	2	0	1	5	3	7
*Argentina	3	2	1	0	8	5	6
*Canada	3	1	1	1	3	3	4
Hungary	3	0	3	0	1	6	0

RESULTS: **June 18**– Argentina 3, Hungary 0; Australia 0, Canada 0. **June 20**– Australia 1, Hungary 0; Argentina 2, Canada 1. **June 23**– Australia 4, Argentina 3; Canada 2, Hungary 1.

Group F	Gm	W	L	T	GF	GA	Pts
*England	3	3	0	0	8	1	9
*Mexico	3	1	1	1	6	2	4
*UAE	3	1	2	0	2	10	3
Iory Coast	3	0	2	1	2	5	1

RESULTS: **June 18**– Mexico 5, UAE 0; England 2, Ivory Coast 1. **June 20**– Mexico 1, Ivory Coast 1; England 5, UAE 0. **June 23**– England 1, Mexico 0; UAE 2, Ivory Coast 0.

Second Round

June 25	Kuching (8,267)	Brazil 10, Belgium 0
June 25	Shah Alam (2,500)	Uruguay 3, USA 0
June 25	Kuching (10,101)	France 1, Mexico 0
June 26	Shah Alam (3,000)	Ireland 2, Morocco 1 (OT)
June 26	Kangar (8,000)	Japan 1, Australia 0
June 26	Johor Bahru (17,000)	Argentina 2, England 1
June 26	Kuantan (10,000)	Spain 2, Canada 0
June 26	Alor Setar (17,000)	Ghana 3, UAE 0

Quarterfinals

June 29	Shah Alam (9,000)	Ireland 1, Spain 0
June 29	Kuching (34,896)	Argentina 2, Brazil 0
June 29	Johor Bahru (18,700)	Ghana 2, Japan 1 (OT)
June 29	Shah Alam (9,000)	Uruguay 1, France 1*

*Uruguay wins shootout, 7-6.

Semifinals

July 2	Kuching (14,976)	Argentina 1, Ireland 0
July 2	Shah Alam (15,000)	Uruguay 3, Ghana 2 (OT)

Third Place

July 5	Shah Alam (28,000)	Ireland 2, Ghana 1

Final

July 5	Shah Alam (62,000)	Argentina 2, Uruguay 1

Award Winners

Golden Shoe (Top Goal-Scorers) — Goals

Adailton, Brazil 10
David Treaeguet, France 5
Alex, Brazil 4

Golden Ball (Best Player)

1 ....Nicholas Olivera, Uruguay
2 ....Marcelo Danubio Zalayeta, Uruguay
3 ....Pablo Aimar, Argentina

1997 Under-17 World Championship

Held Sept. 4-21 in Egypt for Under-17 national teams. Note that (*) indicates teams advancing to quaterfinals.

First Round

Group A	Gm	W	L	T	GF	GA	Pts
*Germany	3	2	0	1	5	1	7
*Egypt	3	1	0	2	5	4	5
Chile	3	1	1	1	7	4	4
Thailand	3	0	3	0	4	12	0

RESULTS: **Sept. 4**– Egypt 3, Thailand 2; Germany 1, Chile 0. **Sept. 7**– Egypt 1, Chile 1; Germany 3, Thailand 0. **Sept. 10**–Egypt 1, Germany; Chile 6, Thailand 2.

Group B	Gm	W	L	T	GF	GA	Pts
*Spain	3	3	0	0	17	2	9
*Mali	3	2	1	0	7	2	6
Mexico	3	1	2	0	8	6	3
New Zealand	3	0	3	0	0	22	0

RESULTS: **Sept. 6**–Mali 4, New Zealand 0; Spain 3, Mexico 2. **Sept. 8**– Spain 1, Mali 0; Mexico 5, New Zealand 0. **Sept. 11**– Spain 13, New Zealand 0; Mali 3, Mexico 1.

1997 Under-17 World Championship (Cont.)

Group C	Gm	W	L	T	GF	GA	Pts
*Brazil	3	3	0	0	13	1	9
*Oman	3	2	1	0	8	4	6
United States	3	1	2	0	4	7	3
Austria	3	0	3	0	1	14	0

RESULTS: **Sept. 6**– Oman 4, United States 0; Brazil 7, Austria 0. **Sept. 8**– Brazil 3, United States 0; Oman 3, Austria 1. **Sept. 11**– United States 4, Austria 0; Brazil 3, Oman 1.

Group D	Gm	W	L	T	GF	GA	Pts
*Ghana	3	2	0	1	7	1	7
*Argentina	3	2	0	1	3	0	7
Bahrain	3	1	2	0	4	8	3
Costa Rica	3	0	3	0	1	6	0

RESULTS: **Sept. 5**– Bahrain 3, Costa Rica 1; Argentina 1, Ghana 0. **Sept. 7**– Ghana 5, Bahrain 1; Argentina 1, Costa Rica 0. **Sept. 10**– Argentina 2, Bahrain 0; Ghana 2, Costa Rica 0.

Quarterfinals

Sept. 14 Alexandria (20,000) . . . . . .Brazil 2, Argentina 0
Sept. 14 Cairo (7,000) . . . . .Germany 0, Mali 0*
Sept. 15 Port Said (15,000) . . . . .Ghana 4, Oman 1
Sept. 15 Ismailya (13,500) . . . . .Spain 2, Egypt 1
*Gemany wins shootout, 4-3.

Semifinals

Sept. 18 Cairo (4,000) . . . . .Ghana 2, Spain 1
Sept. 18 Ismailya (8,500) . . . . .Brazil 4, Germany 0

Third Place

Sept. 21 Cairo (8,000) . . . . .Spain 2, Gemay 1

Final

Sept. 21 Cairo (35,000) . . . . .Brazil 2, Ghana 1

U.S. National Team

1997 Schedule and Results

Through Oct. 15, 1997. World Cup Qualifiers are in **bold** type. All other matches are international friendlies.

Date	Result	USA Goals	Site	Crowd
Jan. 17	Peru (U.S. Cup) . . . . .L, 0-1	—	San Diego, Calif.	35,232
Jan. 19	Mexico (U.S. Cup) . . . . .L, 0-2	—	Pasadena, Calif.	31,725
Jan. 22	Denmark (U.S. Cup) . . . . . . .L, 1-4	Joe Max-Moore	Pasadena, Calif.	17,342
Jan. 29	China .L, 1-2	Eric Wynalda	Kunming, China	40,000
Feb. 1	China .T, 1-1	Alexi Lalas	Guangzhou, China	35,000
Mar. 2	**Jamaica** . . . . .T, 0-0	—	Kingston, Jamaica	35,764
Mar. 16	**Canada** . . . . .W, 3-2	Wynalda, Eddie Pope, Ernie Stewart	Palo Alto, Calif.	28,896
Mar. 23	**Costa Rica** . . . . .L, 2-3	Wynalda, Roy Lassiter	San Jose, Calif.	23,000
Apr. 20	**Mexico** . . . . .T, 2-2	Pope, own goal	Foxboro, Mass.	57,877
June 4	Paraguay . . . . .T, 0-0	—	St. Louis, Mo.	7,016
June 17	Israel .W, 2-1	Lalas, Jovan Kirovski	Jacksonville, Fla.	8,436
June 29	**El Salvador** . . . . .T, 1-1	Lassiter	San Salvador	32,000
Aug. 7	Ecuador . . . . .L, 0-1	—	Baltimore, Md.	13,629
Sept. 7	**Costa Rica** . . . . .W, 1-0	Tab Ramos	Portland, Ore.	22,396
Oct. 3	**Jamaica** . . . . .T, 1-1	Wynalda	Washington, D.C.	51,528

Remaining World Cup Qualifying games: Nov. 2 at Mexico, Nov. 9 at Canada, Nov. 16 vs. El Salvador.
Overall record: 3-6-6. **US Cup '97 record:** 0-3-0. **Team scoring:** Goals for– 14; Goals against– 19.

1997 U.S. National Team Statistics

Individual records for entire season through Oct. 3, 1997. Note that the column labeled "Career C/G" refers to career caps and goals.

Forwards	GP	GS	Mins	G	A	Pts	Career C/G
Jovan Kirovski	6	4	374	1	0	2	24/4
Roy Lassiter	11	5	570	2	0	4	21/4
Brian McBride	6	5	453	0	0	0	14/2
Joe-Max Moore	3	3	270	1	0	2	56/16
Preki	6	2	283	0	0	0	10/1
Ernie Stewart	6	6	524	1	0	2	41/5
David Wagner	5	4	256	0	1	1	6/0
Dante Washington	1	0	26	0	0	0	6/2
Roy Wegerle	1	1	73	0	0	0	27/3
Eric Wynalda	9	9	810	4	2	10	88/31

Defenders	GP	GS	Mins	G	A	Pts	Career C/G
Jeff Agoos	12	11	1024	0	1	1	74/3
Marcelo Balboa	6	6	720	0	1	1	121/12
Mike Burns	11	8	779	0	1	1	59/0
Dan Calichman	3	2	154	0	0	0	3/0
Ted Chronopolous	1	0	18	0	0	0	1/0
Ramiro Corrales	2	1	120	0	0	0	3/0
Thomas Dooley	7	7	617	0	0	0	69/7
Robin Fraser	1	1	90	0	0	0	16/0
Alexi Lalas	12	11	1015	2	0	4	89/8
Steve Pittman	1	1	60	0	0	0	3/0
Eddie Pope	7	7	593	2	0	4	12/2

Defenders	GP	GS	Mins	G	A	Pts	Career C/G
Mark Sanbal	1	1	90	0	0	0	11/1
Greg Vanney	1	1	90	0	0	0	2/0
Martin Vasquez	4	4	271	0	0	0	5/0
Peter Vermes	1	0	16	0	0	0	71/11

Midfielders	GP	GS	Mins	G	A	Pts	Career C/G
Dario Brose	1	1	45	0	0	0	4/1
Mark Chung	1	1	59	0	0	0	23/2
Chad Deering	1	1	45	0	0	0	5/0
John Harkes	8	8	890	0	2	2	81/6
Frankie Hejduk	3	1	97	0	0	0	8/1
Chris Henderson	1	0	31	0	0	0	74/2
Cobi Jones	11	8	685	0	0	0	93/8
Miles Joseph	1	1	45	0	0	0	3/0
Jason Kreis	5	2	235	0	0	0	7/0
Brian Maisonneuve	2	1	111	0	0	0	2/0
Michael Mason	5	1	138	0	1	1	5/0
Steve Ralston	4	3	181	0	0	0	4/0
Tab Ramos	3	3	270	1	0	2	77/6
Claudio Reyna	10	9	774	0	0	0	52/4
Tony Sanneh	3	2	225	0	2	2	3/0
Mike Sorber	6	6	506	0	0	0	65/2

Goalkeepers	GP	GS	Mins	Record	SO	Career Caps	Goalkeepers	GP	GS	Mins	Record	SO	Career Caps
Mark Dodd	3	2	225	0-1-1	0	15	Kasey Keller	6	6	540	2-1-3	3	25
Brad Friedel	7	7	556	1-4-2	1	50	Juergen Sommer	1	0	27	0-0-0	0	6

Yellow cards: Cobi Jones and Ernie Stewart (3), John Harkes, Alexi Lalas, Claudio Reyna and Tony Sanneh (2), Jeff Agoos, Marcelo Balboa, Mike Burns, Jovan Kirovski, Mark Sanbal, Eric Wynalda. **Red cards:** Lalas.
Head coach: Steve Sampson; **Assistant coach:** Clive Charles; **Goal coach:** Milutin Soskic; **General Manager:** Tom King; **Captain:** John Harkes.

U.S. Cup '97

Fourth U.S. Cup hosted by the United States, Jan. 17-22, 1997. Match results listed with city and attendance.

Round Robin Standings

	Gm	W	L	T	GF	GA	Pts
Mexico	3	2	0	1	5	1	7
Denmark	3	2	1	0	7	4	6
Peru	3	1	1	1	2	2	4
United States	3	0	3	0	1	7	0

Match Results

Jan 17 San Diego (35,232) Peru 1, United States 0
Jan. 17 San Diego (35,232) Mexico 3, Denmark 1
Jan. 19 Pasadena (31,725) Denmark 2, Peru 1
Jan. 19 Pasadena (31,725) Mexico 2, United States 0
Jan. 22 Pasadena (17,342) Denmark 4, United States 1
Jan. 22 Pasadena (17,342) Mexico 0, Peru 0

U.S. Women's National Team
1997 Schedule and Results

Date	Result	USA Goals	Site	Crowd
Feb. 20	Australia ...... W, 4-0	Parlow, Venturini, Fotopolous, Mia Hamm	Melbourne	1,500
Mar. 3	Australia ...... W, 3-1	Baumgardt, Kristine Lilly, Chastain	New South Wales	3,228
Mar. 5	Australia ...... W, 3-0	Chastain, Julie Foudy, Tiffeny Milbrett	Canberra	4,031
Apr. 24	France ...... W, 4-2	Confer, Venturini, Shannon MacMillan, Lilly	Greensboro, N.C.	3,376
Apr. 27	France ...... W, 2-1	Venturini (2)	Tampa, Fla.	1,803
May 2	South Korea .. W, 7-0	Hamm (2), MacMillan (2), Milbrett (2), Christie Pearce	Milwaukee, Wisc.	5,530
May 4	South Korea ..... W, 6-1	Lilly, Hamm (2), Keller, Baumgart, own goal	St. Charles, Ill.	4,147
May 10	England ...... W, 5-0	MacMillan, Hamm (3), Foudy	San Jose, Calif.	17,358
May 11	England ...... W, 6-0	Hamm, Parlow (2), Milbrett, Lilly, Keller	Portland, Ore.	5,039
May 31	Canada ...... W, 4-0	Milbrett, Hamm (3)	New Britain, Conn.	6,562
June 6	Australia ...... W, 9-1	Milbrett, Parlow (2), Hamm (2), Pearce, Lilly, Venturini, Keller	Ambler, Pa.	4,826
June 8	Italy .... W, 2-0	Parlow, Hamm	Washington, D.C.	11,208
Oct. 9	Germany .... L, 1-3	Lilly	Duisburg, Germany	7,050
Oct. 12	Germany ...... W, 3-0	Hamm (2), Milbrett	Salzgitter, Germany	4,906

Overall record: 13-1-0.
Team Scoring: Goals For— 59; Goals against— 9.

1997 U.S. Women's National Team Statistics

Individual records for entire season through Oct. 12, 1997. Note that the column labeled "Career C/G" refers to career caps and goals.

Forwards	GP	GS	Mins	G	A	Pts	Career C/G
Danielle Fotopolous	3	0	55	1	1	3	5/4
Mia Hamm	12	12	946	17	4	38	132/80
Debbie Keller	12	4	553	3	4	10	21/4
Tiffeny Milbrett	13	13	1088	7	13	27	78/32
Cindy Parlow	8	5	409	6	0	12	28/14

Defenders	GP	GS	Mins	G	A	Pts	Career C/G
Brandi Chastain	9	2	459	2	1	5	10/2
Lorrie Fair	9	8	737	0	0	0	20/0
Ronnie Fair	2	0	41	0	1	1	2/0
Jen Grubb	2	0	90	0	0	0	11/1
Holly Manthei	2	2	180	0	1	1	21/0
Christie Pearce	14	13	1117	2	1	5	14/2
Tammy Pearman	4	0	174	0	0	0	8/1
Thori Staples	7	4	345	0	0	0	50/0
Jill Stewart	1	0	7	0	0	0	1/0
Sarah Whalen	5	5	419	0	0	0	5/0

Midfielders	GP	GS	Mins	G	A	Pts	Career C/G
Justi Baumgardt	9	2	459	2	1	5	10/2
Robin Confer	4	3	222	1	0	2	5/1
Kerry Connors	4	2	193	0	0	0	4/0

Midfielders	GP	GS	Mins	G	A	Pts	Career C/G
Amanda Cromwell	6	0	149	0	0	0	47/1
Cindy Daws	2	0	55	0	0	0	2/0
Michelle Demko	1	0	13	0	0	0	1/0
Kristi DeVert	1	0	30	0	0	0	1/0
Julie Foudy	14	14	1138	2	2	6	110/19
Michelle French	1	0	37	0	0	0	1/0
Kristine Lilly	14	14	1229	6	7	19	135/52
Shannon MacMillan	7	7	630	4	6	14	35/13
Tiffany Roberts	2	2	123	0	0	0	57/6
Laurie Schwoy	3	1	154	0	0	0	3/0
Tisha Venturini	13	13	777	5	3	13	84/31

Goalkeepers	GP	GS	Mins	Record	SO	Career Caps
Tracy Ducar	9	0	385	4-0-0	1	11
Jen Mead	1	0	37	0-0-0	0	4
Jaime Pagliarulo	1	0	16	0-0-0	0	1
Briana Scurry	14	14	822	9-1-0	7	58

Yellow Cards: Cindy Parlow and Tisha Venturini (2), Debbie Keller, Tiffany Milbrett, Thori Staples. **Red Cards:** none.
Head coach: Tony DiCiccio; **Assistant coaches:** Lauren Gregg and April Heinrichs; **Co-Captain:** Julie Foudy and Carla Overbeck.

World Cup '98 Qualifying

Qualifying records through Oct. 16, 1997 for 32-team FIFA World Cup to be held in France, June 10-July 12, 1998. Defending champion Brazil and host country France receive automatic bids.

Note that (*) indicates team has qualified for France '98.

Africa

Each group winner qualifies for France '98.

Group 1	Gm	W	L	T	GF	GA	Pts
*Nigeria	6	4	1	1	10	4	13
Guinea	6	4	2	0	10	5	12
Kenya	6	3	2	1	11	12	10
Burkina Faso	6	0	6	0	7	17	0

Group 2	Gm	W	L	T	GF	GA	Pts
*Tunisia	6	5	0	1	10	1	16
Egypt	6	3	2	1	15	5	10
Liberia	6	1	4	1	2	10	4
Namibia	6	1	4	1	6	17	4

Group 3	Gm	W	L	T	GF	GA	Pts
*South Africa	6	4	1	1	7	3	13
Congo	6	3	2	1	5	5	10
Zambia	6	2	2	2	7	6	8
Congo	6	0	4	2	4	9	2

Group 4	Gm	W	L	T	GF	GA	Pts
*Cameroon	6	4	0	2	10	4	14
Angola	6	2	0	4	7	4	10
Zimbabwe	6	1	4	1	6	7	4
Togo	6	1	4	1	6	14	4

Group 5	Gm	W	L	T	GF	GA	Pts
*Morocco	6	5	0	1	14	2	16
Sierra Leone	5	2	2	1	4	6	7
Ghana	6	1	2	3	7	7	6
Gabon	5	0	4	1	1	11	1

Remaining Games: Oct. 26– Gabon vs. Sierra Leone.

Asia

At least three but no more than four teams from the Asian Football Confederation will qualify for France '98. Group winners automatically qualify then the two second place teams will play on neutral ground on Nov. 16, 1997. The winner qualifies, the loser must then play Oceania Group winner Australia in a home-and-home series on Nov. 22 and 29, 1997 for a bid.

Group 1	Gm	W	L	T	GF	GA	Pts
Iran	4	2	0	2	9	4	8
Saudi Arabia	4	2	1	1	4	3	7
China	4	2	1	1	6	6	7
Kuwait	4	1	2	1	5	5	4
Qatar	4	0	3	1	1	7	1

Remaining Games: Oct. 17– Iran vs. China; Kuwait vs. Saudi Arabia. Oct. 24– Kuwait vs. Qatar; Saudi Arabia vs. Iran. Oct 31– China vs. Qatar; Iran vs. Kuwait. Nov. 6– Saudi Arabia vs. China. Nov. 7– Qatar vs. Iran . Nov 12– China vs. Kuwait; Qatar vs. Saudi Arabia..

Group 2	Gm	W	L	T	GF	GA	Pts
South Korea	5	4	0	1	11	3	13
UAE	4	2	1	1	7	5	7
Japan	5	1	1	3	9	7	6
Kazakhstan	5	0	2	3	3	10	3
Uzbekistan	5	0	3	2	8	13	2

Remaining Games: Oct. 18– Uzbekistan vs. S. Korea; Kazakhstan vs. UAE. Oct. 25– Uzbekistan vs. Kazakhstan. Oct 26– Japan vs. UAE. Nov. 1– S. Korea vs. Japan. Nov. 2– UAE vs. Uzbekistan. Nov 8– Japan vs. Kazakhstan. Nov. 9– UAE vs. S. Korea.

CONCACAF

The top three teams from the final round of the Confederation of North, Central and Carribean American Football qualify for France. '98.

Final Round	Gm	W	L	T	GF	GA	Pts
Mexico	7	4	0	3	20	4	15
Jamaica	8	3	2	3	5	10	12
United States	7	2	1	4	10	7	10
El Salvador	8	2	3	3	7	10	9
Costa Rica	8	2	4	2	7	8	8
Canada	8	1	4	3	4	14	6

Remaining Games: Nov. 2– Mexico vs. United States. Nov. 9– Canada vs. United States; El Salvador vs. Jamaica; Mexico vs. Costa Rica. Nov. 16– Jamaica vs. Mexico; Costa Rica vs. Canada; United States vs. El Salvador.

Europe

Each group winner from the final round of UEFA, the second place team with the most points, plus France as the host country automatically qualify for France. '98. The remaining eight second-place teams in each group earn spots in the playoff for the four remaining UEFA bids. See below for play-off schedule.

Group 1	Gm	W	L	T	GF	GA	Pts
*Denmark	8	5	1	2	14	6	17
Croatia	8	4	1	3	17	12	15
Greece	8	4	2	2	11	4	14
Bosnia-Herzegovina	8	3	5	0	9	14	9
Slovenia	8	0	7	1	5	20	1

Group 2	Gm	W	L	T	GF	GA	Pts
*England	8	6	1	1	15	2	19
Italy	8	5	0	3	11	1	18
Poland	8	3	4	1	10	12	10
Georgia	8	3	4	1	7	9	10
Moldova	8	0	8	0	2	21	0

Group 3	Gm	W	L	T	GF	GA	Pts
*Norway	8	6	0	2	21	2	20
Hungary	8	3	2	3	10	8	12
Finland	8	3	3	2	11	12	11
Switzerland	8	3	4	1	11	12	10
Azerbaijan	8	1	7	0	3	22	3

Group 4	Gm	W	L	T	GF	GA	Pts
*Austria	10	8	1	1	17	4	25
*Scotland	10	7	1	2	15	3	23
Sweden	10	7	3	0	16	9	21
Latvia	10	3	6	1	10	14	10
Estonia	10	1	8	1	4	16	4
Belarus	10	1	8	1	5	21	4

Note: Scotland qualifies ahead of Yugoslavia even though both teams finished in second place with 23 points in their respective groups because Scotland earned more of its points against the first, third and fourth placed teams in its division.

Group 5	Gm	W	L	T	GF	GA	Pts
*Bulgaria	8	6	2	0	18	9	18
ussia	8	5	1	2	19	5	17
Israel	8	4	3	1	9	7	13
Cyprus	8	3	4	1	10	15	10
Luxembourg	8	0	8	0	2	22	0

Group 6	Gm	W	L	T	GF	GA	Pts
*Spain	10	8	0	2	26	6	26
Yugoslavia	10	7	1	2	29	7	23
Czech Republic	10	5	4	1	16	6	16
Slovakia	10	5	4	1	18	14	16
Faroe Islands	10	2	8	0	10	31	6
Malta	10	0	10	0	2	37	0

Group 7	Gm	W	L	T	GF	GA	Pts
*Netherlands	8	6	1	1	26	4	19
Belgium	8	6	2	0	20	11	18
Turkey	8	4	2	2	21	9	14
Wales	8	2	5	1	20	25	7
San Marino	8	0	8	0	0	42	0

Group 8	Gm	W	L	T	GF	GA	Pts
*Romania	10	9	0	1	37	4	28
Ireland	10	5	2	3	22	8	18
Lithuania	10	5	3	2	11	8	17
Macedonia	10	4	5	1	22	18	13
Iceland	10	2	5	3	11	16	9
Liechtenstein	10	0	10	0	3	52	0

Group 9	Gm	W	L	T	GF	GA	Pts
*Germany	10	6	0	4	23	9	22
Ukraine	10	6	2	2	10	6	20
Portugal	10	5	1	4	12	4	19
Armenia	10	1	4	5	8	17	8
Northern Ireland	10	1	5	4	6	10	7
Albania	10	1	8	1	7	20	4

Playoff Games: Oct. 29– Russia vs. Italy; Hungary vs. Yugoslavia; Ireland vs. Belgium; Croatia vs. Ukraine. Nov. 15– Ukraine vs. Croatia; Yugoslavia vs. Hungary; Belgium vs. Ireland; Italy vs. Russia.

South America

The top four teams from the final round of CONMEBOL plus defending champions Brazil qualify for France '98.

Final Round	Gm	W	L	T	GF	GA	Pts
*Argentina	15	8	2	5	22	12	29
*Paraguay	15	9	4	2	21	13	29

Final Round	Gm	W	L	T	GF	GA	Pts
*Colombia	15	8	4	3	22	14	27
Chile	15	6	5	4	29	18	22
Peru	15	6	5	4	18	20	22
Ecuador	15	6	6	3	19	16	21
Uruguay	15	5	7	3	13	18	18
Bolivia	15	4	6	5	18	18	17
Venezuela	16	0	13	3	8	41	3

Remaining Games: Nov. 16– Argentina vs. Colombia; Chile vs. Bolivia; Peru vs. Paraguay; Uruguay vs. Ecuador.

Oceania

The winner from each group play each other in a home-and-home series to decide whom shall meet the fourth place Asian team in another home-and-home series Nov. 22 and 29, 1997. The winner of that series qualifies for France '98.

Group 1	Gm	W	L	T	GF	GA	Pts
Australia	4	4	0	0	26	2	12
Solomon Islands	4	1	2	1	7	21	4
Tahiti	4	0	3	1	2	12	1

Group 2	Gm	W	L	T	GF	GA	Pts
New Zealand	4	3	0	1	13	1	9
Fiji	4	2	2	0	4	7	6
Papua New Guinea	4	1	3	0	2	11	3

Third Round

The winner qualifies to play against the fourth-place Asian team. Home team listed first.

June 28   New Zealand 0 ....Australia 3
July 5   Australia 2 ....New Zealand 0
         Australia wins on aggregate, 5-0

Club Team Competition

1996 Toyota Cup

Formerly the Intercontinental Cup; a year-end match for the World Club Championship between the European Cup and Copa Libertadores winners. Played Nov. 26, 1996, before 60,000 at Tokyo's National Stadium.

Final

Juventus (Italy) 1 ....River Plate (Argentina) 0
Scoring: Juventus—Alessandro Del Piero, 82nd minute.

SOUTH AMERICA

1997 Liberatadores Cup

Contested by the league champions of South America's football union. Two-leg Semifinals and two-leg Final; home teams listed first. Winner Cruziero of Brazil plays European Cup champion Borussia Dortmund of Germany in 1997 Toyota Cup in Tokyo this November.

   Final Four: Colo Colo (Chile), Cruziero (Brazil), Racing Club (Argentina) and Sporting Cristal (Peru).

Semifinals

Racing Club (ARG) vs. Sporting Cristal (PER)

July 23   Buenos Aires (40,000) .Racing Club 3, Cristal 2
July 30   Lima (45,000) ....Cristal 4, Racing Club 1
      Sporting Cristal wins on aggregate, 6-4

Cruziero (BRA) vs. Colo Colo (CHI)

July 23   Belo Horizonte (30,000) ...Cruziero 1, Colo Colo 0
July 30   Santiago (35,000) .....Colo Colo 3, Cruziero 2
      Aggregate 3-3, Cruziero wins 5-4 on aggregate after shootout

Final

Aug. 6   Lima (45,000) ....Cristal 0, Cruziero 0
Aug. 13   Belo Horizonte (95,472) ...Cruziero 1, Cristal 0
      Cruziero wins on aggregate, 1-0

Club Team Competition (Cont.)

EUROPE

There are three European club competitions sanctioned by the Union of European Football Associations (UEFA). The **European Cup** (officially, the Champions' Cup) is a knockout contest between national league champions of UEFA member countries; the **Cup Winners' Cup** is between winners of domestic cup competitions (note that a double winner– league and cup titles– would play for the European Cup and be replaced in the Cup Winners' Cup by the team it defeated in the domestic cup final); and the **UEFA Cup** is between the so-called "best of the rest," usually the national league runners-up. Note that home teams are listed first.

1996-97 European Cup

Champions League: Six-game double round-robin in four 4-team groups (Sept. ?-Dec. ?, 1996); top two teams in each group advance to quarterfinal round. Winner Borussia Dortmund of Germany plays Libertadores Cup champion Cruzeiro of Brazil in the 1997 Toyota Cup this November in Tokyo.

Round Robin Standings

Group A	W	L	T	GF	GA	Pts
*Auxerre (FRA)	4	2	0	8	7	12
*Ajax Amsterdam (NET)	4	2	0	8	4	12
Grasshoppers Zurich (SWI)	3	3	0	8	5	9
Glasgow Rangers (SCO)	1	5	0	5	13	3

Group B	W	L	T	GF	GA	Pts
*Atletico Madrid	4	1	1	13	5	13
*Borussia Dortmund	4	1	1	14	8	13
Steaua Bucharest	1	4	1	5	15	4
Widzew Lodz	1	4	1	6	10	4

Group C	W	L	T	GF	GA	Pts
*Juventus (ITA)	5	0	1	11	1	16
*Manchester Utd. (ENG)	3	3	0	6	3	9
Fenerbache (TUR)	2	3	1	3	6	7
Rapid Vienna (AUT)	0	4	2	2	12	2

Group D	W	L	T	GF	GA	Pts
*FC Porto (POR)	5	0	1	12	4	16
*Rosenborg (NOR)	3	3	0	7	11	9
AC Milan (ITA)	2	3	1	13	11	7
IFK Göteborg (SWE)	1	5	0	8	12	3

Quarterfinals

Two legs, total goals; home team listed first.

Borussia Dortmund vs. Auxerre

Mar. 5 –Borussia Dortmund 3 ....Auxerre 1
Mar. 19 –Auxerre 0 ....Borussia Dortmund 1
Borussia Dortmund wins on aggregate, 4-1

Ajax Amsterdam vs. Atletico Madrid

Mar. 5 –Ajax Amsterdam 1 ....Atletico Madrd 1
Mar. 19 –Atletico Madrid 2 .....Ajax Amsterdam 3 (OT)
Ajax Amsterdam wins on aggregate, 4-3

Manchester United vs. FC Porto

Mar. 5 –Manchester United 4 ....FC Porto 0
Mar. 19 –Porto 0 ....Manchester United 0
Manchester United wins on aggregate, 4-0

Juventus vs. Rosenborg

Mar. 5 –Rosenborg 1 ....Juventus 1
Mar. 19 –Juventus 2 ....Rosenborg 0
Juventus wins on aggregate, 3-1

Semifinals

Two legs, total goals; home team listed first.

Borussia Dortmund vs. Manchester United

Apr. 9 –Borussia Dortmund 1 .....Manchester United 0
Apr. 23 –Manchester United 0 .....Borussia Dortmund 1
Borussia Dortmund wins on aggregate, 2-0

Juventus vs. Ajax Amsterdam

Apr. 9 –Ajax Amsterdam 1 ....Juventus 2
Apr. 23 –Juventus 4 ....Ajax Amsterdam 1
Juventus wins on aggregate, 6-2

Final

May 28 at Munich, Germany; Att– 55,000

Borussia Dortmund 3 ....Juventus 1

Goals: Borussia Dortmund– Karlheinz Riedle, 29th minute, 34th; Lars Ricken, 71st. Juventus– Alessandro Del Piero, 64th.

1997 Cup Winners' Cup

Two-leg Semifinals one-game Final; home team listed first.
Final Four: Barcelona (Spain), Fiorentina (Italy), Liverpool (England), Paris-St. Germain (France).

Semifinals

Barcelona vs. Fiorentina

Apr. 8 –Fiorentina 1 ....Barcelona 1
Apr. 24 –Barcelona 2 ....Fiorentina 0
Barcelona wins on aggregate, 3-1

Paris-St. Germain vs. Liverpool

Apr. 8 –Paris-St. Germain 3 ....Liverpool 0
Apr. 24 –Liverpool 2 ....Paris-St. Germain 0
Paris-SG wins on aggregate, 3-2

Final

May 14 at Rotterdam, Netherlands
Att– 52,000

Barcelona 1 ....Paris-St. Germain 0

Goal: Barcelona– Ronaldo (pen.) 37th minute.

1997 UEFA Cup

Two-leg Semifinals, two-game Final; home team listed first.
Final Four: AS Monaco (France), Internazionale of Milan (Italy), Schalke '04 (Germany), Tenerife (Spain).

Semifinals

Inter Milan vs. AS Monaco

Apr. 9   –Inter Milan 3 ....AS Monaco 1
Apr. 22 –AS Monaco 1 ....Inter Milan 0
        Inter Milan wins on aggregate, 3-2

Tenerife vs. Schalke '04

Apr. 9   –Tenerife 1 ....Schalke 0
Apr. 22 –Schalke 2 ....Tenerife 0
        Schalke wins on aggregate, 2-1

Final

May 7 (58,264)   –Schalke 1 ....Inter Milan 0
Goals: Schalke– Marc Wilmots, 70th minute.

May 21 (81,675) –Inter Milan 1 ....Schalke 0
        Aggregate, 1-1. Schalke wins on shootout, 4-1.

Goals: Inter Milan– Ivan Zamorano, 84th minute.

Shootout: Schalke– Ingo Anderbruegge (goal), Olaf Thon (goal), Martin Max (goal), Marc Wilmots (goal); Inter– Ivan Zamorano (saved), Djorkaeff (goal), Aaron Winter (wide).

Major League Soccer

1997 Final Regular Season Standings

Conference champions (*) and playoff qualifiers (†) are noted. SOW refers to shootout wins. Teams receive three points for a win and one point for a shootout win. SOW are included in W (win) column. The GF and GA columns refer to Goals For and Goals Against in regulation play. Number of seasons listed after each head coach refers to current tenure with club through the 1997 season.

Eastern Conference

Team	W	L	Pts	GF	GA	SOW
* D.C. United	21	11	55	70	53	4
† Tampa Bay	17	15	45	55	60	3
† Columbus	15	17	39	42	41	3
† New England	15	17	37	40	53	4
NY/NJ	13	19	35	43	53	2

Head Coaches: DC– Bruce Arena (2nd season); TB– John Kowalski (1st); Clb– Tom Fitzgerald (1st); NE– Tom Rongen (1st); NY/NJ– Carlos Alberto Parreira (1st).

Western Conference

Team	W	L	Pts	GF	GA	SOW
* Kansas City	21	11	49	57	51	7
† Los Angeles	16	16	44	55	44	2
† Dallas	16	16	42	55	49	3
† Colorado	14	18	38	50	59	2
San Jose	12	20	30	55	59	3

Head Coaches: KC– Ron Newman (2nd season); LA– fired Lothar Osiander (2nd, 3-9) on June 10 and replaced him with asst. Octavio Zambrano (13-7); Dal– David Dir (2nd); Colo– Glenn Myernick (1st); SJ– fired Laurie Calloway (2nd, 5-10) on June 23 and replaced him with Brian Quinn (7-10).

Leading Scorers

Points

	Gm	G	A	Pts
Preki, KC	27	12	17	41
Jaime Moreno, D.C.	20	16	8	40
Raul Diaz Arce, D.C.	22	15	6	36
Ronald Cerritos, SJ	22	12	10	34
Giovanni Savarese, NY/NJ .	29	14	4	32
Dante Washington, Dal	30	12	6	30
Lawrence Lozzano, SJ	29	10	10	30
Damian, Dal	19	11	7	29
Mark Chung, KC	32	10	8	28
Chris Henderson, Colo	30	7	14	28
Antony De Avila, NY/NJ	23	9	9	27
Welton, LA	29	11	4	26
Carlos Valderrama, TB	20	3	19	25
Mauricio Cienfuegos, LA	22	6	12	24
Nine tied with 22 pts. each.				

Goals

	Gm	No
Jaime Moreno, DC	20	16
Raul Diaz Arce, DC	22	15
Giovanni Savarese, NY/NJ	29	14
Ronald Cerritos, SJ	22	12
Preki, KC	27	12
Dante Washington, Dal	30	12
Damian, Dal	19	11
Welton, LA	29	11
Roy Lassiter, TB	24	10
Lawrence Lozzano, SJ	29	10
Mark Chung, KC	32	10
Jeff Baicher, SJ	32	10

Assists

	Gm	No
Carlos Valderrama, TB	20	19
Preki, KC	27	17
Chris Henderson, Colo	30	14
Eddie Lewis, SJ	29	13
Mauricio Cienfuegos, LA	22	12
Steve Ralston, TB	29	12
Eric Wynalda, SJ	14	11
Marco Etcheverry, DC	20	11
Adrian Paz, Colo	25	11
Tony Sanneh, DC	29	11
Robert Warzycha, Clb	31	11

MLS Attendance

Number in parentheses indicates last year's rank.

		Gm	Total	Avg.
1	New England (3)	16	342,762	21,423
2	Los Angeles (1)	16	330,010	20,626
3	N.Y./N.J.(2)	16	270,388	16,899
4	Wash. D.C. (7)	16	267,271	16,704
5	Columbus (4)	16	240,680	15,043
6	San Jose (5)	16	217,546	13,597
7	Colorado (10)	16	188,893	11,806
8	Tampa Bay (9)	16	181,323	11,333
9	Dallas (6)	16	154,845	9,678
10	Kansas City (8)	16	144,935	9,058
	TOTAL	160	2,338,653	14,616

Major League Soccer (Cont.)

Leading Goaltenders
Goals Against Avg.
(minimum 1395 mins)

	Gm	Min	Shts	Svs	GAA	W-L
Brad Friedel, Clb ..	29	2609	168	131	1.21	14-15
Walter Zenga, NE	22	1980	110	79	1.27	15-7
Jorge Campos, LA	19	1584	85	60	1.31	12-5
M. Hahnemann, Colo ..	25	2157	144	111	1.54	13-11
Mike Ammann, KC ..	29	2597	157	110	1.56	21-8
Mark Dodd, Dal .	30	2700	240	183	1.60	14-16
Tony Meola, NY/NJ ...	30	2683	207	147	1.61	12-18
David Kramer, LA-SJ ...	21	1832	115	84	1.62	7-14
David Salzwedel, SJ ...	20	1678	115	71	1.88	7-11
Mark Dougherty, TB ...	25	2143	150	108	1.89	15-8

Saves

	Gm	No
Mark Dodd, Dal	30	183
Tony Meola, NY/NJ	30	147
Brad Friedel, Col	29	131
Marcus Hahnemann, Clb	25	111
Mike Ammann, KC	29	110
Mark Dougherty, TB	25	108
David Kramer, LA-SJ	21	84
Walter Zenga, NE	22	79
Dave Salzwedel, SJ	20	71
Jorge Campos, LA	19	60

MLS All-Star Game
East, 5-4

Date: Wednesday, July 9, 1997 at Giants Stadium in E. Rutherford, NJ.; **Attendance:** 24,816; **Coaches:** Ron Newman, Kansas City (West) and Bruce Arena, D.C. (East); **MVP:** Carlos Valderrama, Tampa Bay midfielder (East) — one goal, two assists.

	1	2	Final
West	2	2	— 4
East	0	5	— 5

Scoring
1st Half: West— Dante Washington (Preki, Diego Sonora) 11; West— Jorge Campos (Preki, Damian) 44.

2nd Half: East— Carlos Valderrama (Giuseppe Galderisi, Robert Warzycha) 50; East— Galderisi (Richie Williams, Valderrama) 64; East— Warzycha (Brian McBride, Steve Ralston) 67; East— Williams (Valderrama) 70; West— Vitalis Takawira (Ronald Cerritos, Mauricio Cienfuegos) 80; West— Mo Johnston (Cobi Jones) 86; East— McBride (Galderisi) 88.

Goaltenders
Saves: West— Mark Dodd 5, Jorge Campos 6; East— Walter Zenga 3, Tony Meola 3.

Shutouts

	Gm	No		Gm	No
Brad Friedel, Clb	29	8	Mike Ammann, KC	29	5
Marcus Hahnemann, Colo	25	6	Tony Meola, NY/NJ	30	5
Walter Zenga, NE	22	5			

Miscellaneous Leaders

Shootout Goals

	Gm	No
Mark Chung, KC	32	7
Iamd Baba, NE	29	6
Preki, KC	27	5
Pete Marino, Clb	28	5
Four tied with four each.		

Shots

	Gm	No
Robert Warzycha, Clb	31	92
Preki, KC	27	83
Harut Karapetyan, LA	30	76
Jeff Baicher, SJ	32	74
Alberto Naveda, NE	29	71

Shots on Goal

	Gm	No
Jaime Moreno, D.C.	20	48
Preki, KC	27	48
Raul Diaz Arce, D.C.	22	47
Dante Washington, Dal	30	42
Two tied with 39 each.		

Shot Percentage

	Gm	SOG	Shts	Pct
Gerell Elliott, Dal	28	34	45	75.6
Jaime Moreno, D.C.	20	48	66	72.7
Pete Marino, Clb	28	28	40	70.0
Raul Diaz Arce, D.C. ...	22	47	68	69.1
Vitalis Takawira, KC	28	32	47	68.1

Fouls Committed

	Gm	No
Matt McKeon, KC	31	75
Cle Kooiman, TB	27	68
Alberto Naveda, NE	29	66
Alexi Lalas, NE	30	63
Chris Armas, LA	28	58

Fouls Suffered

	Gm	No
Roberto Donadoni, NY/NJ	32	94
Cobi Jones, LA	26	74
Alberto Naveda, NE	29	74
Robert Warzycha, Clb	31	72
Giuseppe Galderisi, NE	23	70

Cautions

	Gm	No
Frankie Hejduk, TB	23	9
Mo Johnston, KC	29	9
Matt McKeon, KC	31	9
Five tied with eight each.		

Ejections

	Gm	No
Branco, NY/NJ	11	3
Damian, Dal	19	2
Frankie Hejduk, TB	23	2
Cle Kooiman, TB	27	2
Ted Chronopoulos, NE	30	2

1996 MLS Recap

1996 Regular Season Standings

Conference champions (*) and playoff qualifiers (†) are noted. SOW refers to shootout wins. Teams receive three points for a win and one point for a shootout win. SOW are included in W (win) column. The GF and GA columns refer to Goals For and Goals Against in regulation play.

Eastern Conference

Team	W	L	Pts	GF	GA	SOW
*Tampa Bay	20	12	58	66	51	1
†D.C. United	16	16	46	62	56	1
†NY/NJ	15	17	39	45	47	3
†Columbus	15	17	37	59	60	4
New England	15	17	33	43	56	6

Western Conference

Team	W	L	Pts	GF	GA	SOW
*Los Angeles	19	13	49	59	49	4
†Dallas	17	15	41	50	48	5
†Kansas City	17	15	41	61	63	5
†San Jose	15	17	39	50	50	3
Colorado	11	21	29	44	59	2

Annual Awards

MVP: Carlos Valderrama, Tampa Bay
Coach of the Year: Thomas Rongen, Tampa Bay
Goalkeeper of the Year: Mark Dodd, Dallas
Tough Defender: John Doyle, San Jose
Rookie of the Year: Steve Ralston, Tampa Bay
Goal of the Year: Eric Wynalda (S.J. vs. D.C., April 6)

MLS Cup '96

Oct. 20 at Foxboro Stadium, Foxboro, Mass.
Attendance: 34,643
D.C. United, 3-2 (OT)

Los Angeles Galaxy	. . . .	1 1 0— **2**
D.C. United	. . . .	0 2 1— **3**

First Half—L.A., Eduardo Hurtado (Mauricio Cienfuegos) 5th minute.

Second Half—L.A., Chis Armas (unassisted), 56th; D.C., Tony Sanneh (Marco Etcheverry), 73rd; D.C., Shawn Medved (unassisted), 82nd.

Overtime— D.C., Eddie Pope (Etcheverry), 94th.

MVP: Marco Etcheverry, D.C. United

All MLS Team

G— Mark Dodd, Dallas
D— Robin Fraser, L.A.
D— John Doyle, S.J.
M— Leonel Alvarez, Dallas
M— C. Valderrama, T.B.
M— Preki, Kansas City
M— M. Cienfuegos, L.A.
M— M. Etcheverry, D.C.
M— R. Donadoni, NY/NJ
F— Eduardo Hurtado, L.A.
F— Roy Lassiter, D.C.

Playoffs

Quarterfinals (Best of 3)

WESTERN

Kansas City Wizards vs. Colorado Rapids

Date	Result	Site
Oct. 4	Rapids, 3-0	at Kansas City
Oct. 8	Rapids, 3-2	at Colorado

Colorado wins series, 2-0.

Los Angeles Galaxy vs. Dallas Burn

Date	Result	Site
Oct. 5	Burn, 0-0*	at Los Angeles
Oct. 8	Burn, 3-0	at Dallas

*Burn wins in a shootout, 2-0.
Dallas wins series, 2-0.

EASTERN

New England Revolution vs. D.C. United

Date	Result	Site
Oct. 5	United, 4-1	at D.C.
Oct. 8	United, 1-1*	at New England

*United wins in a shootout, 4-3.
Washington, D.C. wins series, 2-0.

Tampa Bay Mutiny vs. Columbus Crew

Date	Result	Site
Oct. 5	Crew, 2-1	at Tampa Bay
Oct. 8	Crew, 2-0	at Columbus

Columbus wins series, 2-0.

Semifinals (Best of 3)

Dallas Burn vs. Colorado Rapids

Date	Result	Site
Oct. 12	Rapids, 1-0	at Dallas
Oct. 15	Rapids, 2-1	at Colorado

Colorado wins series, 2-0.

D.C. United vs. Columbus Crew

Date	Result	Site
Oct. 12	United, 3-2	at D.C.
Oct. 15	United, 1-0	at Columbus

Washington, D.C. wins series, 2-0.

MLS Cup '97

Sunday, Oct. 26 at RFK Stadium, Washington, D.C.
D.C. United vs. Colorado Rapids
(See Updates chapter for results.)

MLS Expansion

Major League Soccer will be expanded to 12 teams for the 1998 season with the addition of franchises in Miami and Chicago. The Miami Fusion will join the Eastern Conference and play their home games in the Orange Bowl while the Chicago Fire will be part of the Western Conference and play their home games at Soldier Field.

Team-by-Team Statistics

Players who played with more than one club during the season are listed with final team.

Eastern Conference

Columbus Crew

Top Scorers	Pos	Gm	Min	G	A	Pts
Pete Marino	F	28	1239	8	4	20
Brian McBride	F	13	1069	6	6	18
Robert Warzycha ..	M	31	2720	3	11	17
A.J. Wood	M	29	1833	5	4	14
Brian Maisonneuve .	M	32	2734	3	7	13
Thomas Dooley ...	D	15	1309	4	1	9
Jorge Salcedo	M	28	2240	1	6	8
Doctor Khumalo ...	M	18	1318	2	4	8
Marcelo Carrera ..	F	20	1226	3	2	8

Top Goalies	Gm	Min	W-L	Shts	Svs	GAA
Brad Friedel	29	2609	14-15	168	131	1.21
David Winner	4	271	1-2	17	11	2.00

D.C. United

Top Scorers	Pos	Gm	Min	G	A	Pts
Jaime Moreno	F	20	1725	16	8	40
Raul Diaz Arce	F	22	1789	15	6	36
Tony Sanneh	M	29	2271	5	11	21
John Harkes	M	25	2067	5	9	19
Marco Etcheverry ..	M	20	1696	3	11	17
Roy Wegerle	F	31	1932	5	4	14
Richie Williams	M	30	2604	2	9	13
John Maessner	M	32	2012	2	9	13
Ben Iroha	M	21	1389	4	5	13

Top Goalies	Gm	Min	W-L	Shts	Svs	GAA
Mark Simpson	7	629	4-2	35	26	1.00
Scott Garlick	14	1170	9-5	82	57	1.69
Tom Presthus	7	630	3-2	40	32	1.86

New York/New Jersey MetroStars

Top Scorers	Pos	Gm	Min	G	A	Pts
Giovanni Savarese .	F	29	2069	14	4	32
Antony De Avila ...	F	23	1915	9	9	27
Roberto Donadoni ..	M	32	2696	3	9	15
Miles Joseph	F	29	1771	2	10	14
Mike Sorber	M	22	1888	4	0	8
Shaun Bartlett	F	23	1431	3	2	8
Tab Ramos	M	13	955	2	4	8

Top Goalies	Gm	Min	W-L	Shts	Svs	GAA
Tony Meola	30	2683	12-18	207	147	1.61
Zach Thornton	3	197	1-1	19	12	2.28

New England Revolution

Top Scorers	Pos	Gm	Min	G	A	Pts
Alberto Naveda ...	M	29	2391	7	7	21
Imad Baba	M	29	2389	7	5	19
Giuseppe Galderisi ...	F	23	1722	5	8	18
Ivan McKinley	M	26	1982	5	4	14
Joe-Max Moore	F	13	986	4	2	10
John Kerr	M	19	1136	2	5	9
Alexi Lalas	D	30	2607	2	3	7

Top Goalies	Gm	Min	W-L	Shts	Svs	GAA
Walter Zenga	22	1980	15-7	110	79	1.27
Scott Coufal	4	360	0-4	28	17	2.25
Jeff Causey	12	991	4-8	85	56	2.45

Tampa Bay Mutiny

Top Scorers	Pos	Gm	Min	G	A	Pts
Carlos Valderrama .	M	20	1740	3	19	25
Steve Ralston	M	29	2491	5	12	22
Roy Lassiter	F	24	1879	10	2	22
Gilmar	F	16	1272	8	6	22
Chiquinho Conde ..	F	25	2153	6	7	19
Alan Prampin	F	24	1215	7	3	17
Martin Vasquez	M	28	2475	4	3	11

Top Goalies	Gm	Min	W-L	Shts	Svs	GAA
Scott Budnick	9	737	2-6	45	35	1.83
Mark Dougherty ...	25	2143	15-8	150	108	1.89

Western Conference

Colorado Rapids

Top Scorers	Pos	Gm	Min	G	A	Pts
Chris Henderson ...	M	30	2501	7	14	28
Paul Bravo	M	30	2443	8	6	22
Adrian Paz	M	25	2064	4	11	19
Peter Vermes	D	26	2207	6	4	16
David Patino	M	23	1733	5	6	16
Wolde Harris	F	27	1486	5	5	15
Steve Trittschuh	D	29	2566	5	1	11
Ross Paule	M	19	863	2	3	7

Top Goalies	Gm	Min	W-L	Shts	Svs	GAA
Marcus Hahnemann ...	25	2157	13-11	144	111	1.54
Paul Grafer	9	723	1-7	55	38	2.74

Dallas Burn

Top Scorers	Pos	Gm	Min	G	A	Pts
Dante Washington .	F	30	2161	12	6	30
Damian	F	19	1475	11	7	29
Jason Kreis	M	32	2204	8	6	22
Gerell Elliott	M	28	1503	7	5	19
Alain Sutter	M	21	1800	2	8	12
Mark Santel	D	31	2471	2	6	10
Jorge Rodriguez ...	D	24	1872	4	1	9
Daniel Peinado	M	25	1869	2	4	8

Top Goalies	Gm	Min	W-L	Shts	Svs	GAA
Garth Lagerwey ...	2	180	2-0	18	13	0.50
Mark Dodd	30	2700	14-16	240	183	1.60

Kansas City Wizards

Top Scorers	Pos	Gm	Min	G	A	Pts
Preki	M	27	2330	12	17	41
Mark Chung	M	32	2871	10	8	28
Mo Johnston	F	29	2564	6	10	22
Vitalis Takawira	F	28	2153	8	6	22
Frank Klopas	M	27	1964	5	7	17
Paul Wright	M	30	1647	5	4	14
Matt McKeon	D	31	2736	4	1	9

Top Goalies	Gm	Min	W-L	Shts	Svs	GAA
Mike Ammann	29	2597	21-8	157	110	1.56
Chris Snitko	5	283	0-3	17	11	1.91

Los Angeles Galaxy

Top Scorers	Pos	Gm	Min	G	A	Pts
Welton	F	29	1324	11	4	26
Mauricio Cienfuegos .	M	22	1980	6	12	24
Cobi Jones	M	26	2227	7	8	22
Harut Karapetyan ..	F	30	1763	8	4	20
Eduardo Hurtado ..	F	22	1767	8	3	19
Marin Machon	D	30	2435	4	7	15
Chris Armas	M	28	2306	3	4	10
Danny Pena	D	27	2229	2	3	7

Top Goalies	Gm	Min	W-L	Shts	Svs	GAA
Jorge Campos	19	1584	12-5	85	60	1.31
Kevin Hartman	8	484	2-4	24	14	1.49

San Jose Clash

Top Scorers	Pos	Gm	Min	G	A	Pts
Ronald Cerritos	M	22	1845	12	10	34
Lawrence Lozzano .	F	29	2095	10	10	30
Jeff Baicher	F	32	2027	10	2	22
Eric Wynalda	F	14	927	5	11	21
Eddie Lewis	F	29	2227	2	13	17
Shawn Medved	M	31	1594	4	4	12
Chris Sullivan	M	24	1023	2	6	10
Dominic Kinnear ...	M	28	1939	2	4	8
Troy Dayak	D	21	1817	3	2	8

Top Goalies	Gm	Min	W-L	Shts	Svs	GAA
David Kramer	21	1832	7-14	115	84	1.62
Dave Salzwedel ...	20	1678	7-11	115	71	1.88
Tom Liner	2	180	0-2	19	14	2.00

Other U.S. Pro Leagues

Division champions (*) and playoff qualifiers (†) are noted.

NPSL Final Standings (Indoor)

Division champions Harrisburg, Cleveland, Buffalo and St. Louis drew first-round byes.

American Conference

East Division	W	L	Pct.	GB	GF	GA
* Harrisburg Heat	22	18	.550	—	523	457
† Baltimore Spirit	20	20	.500	2	506	494
† Philadelphia Kixx	17	23	.425	5	451	593
† Tampa Bay Terror	15	25	.375	7	503	541

Central Division	W	L	Pct.	GB	GF	GA
* Cleveland Crunch	29	11	.725	—	772	550
† Cincinnati Silverbacks	21	19	.525	8	570	517
Columbus Invaders	5	35	.125	24	479	895

National Conference

North Division	W	L	Pct.	GB	GF	GA
* Buffalo Blizzard	21	19	.525	—	545	469
† Edmonton Drillers	21	19	.525	—	538	475
Detroit Rockers	20	20	.500	1	563	532
Toronto Shooting Stars	6	34	.150	15	416	685

Midwest Division	W	L	Pct	GB	GF	GA
* St. Louis Ambush	27	13	.675	—	637	545
† Kansas City Attack	26	14	.650	1	525	472
† Milwaukee Wave	26	14	.650	1	605	500
† Wichita Wings	24	16	.600	3	589	497

Playoffs

American Conference

First Round (Best of 3): Cincinnati def. Tampa Bay (2-1); Baltimore def. Philadelphia (2-0).

Semifinals (Best of 3): Cleveland def. Baltimore (2-1); Harrisburg def. Cincinnati (2-0).

Finals (Best of 5): Cleveland def. Harrisburg (3-1).

National Conference

First Round (Best of 3): Edmonton def. Milwaukee (2-0); Kansas City def. Wichita (2-1).

Semifinals (Best of 3): St. Louis def. Edmonton (2-1); Kansas City def. Buffalo (2-0).

Finals (Best of 5): Kansas City def. St. Louis (3-1).

Championship (Best of 7)

	W-L	GF	GA
Kansas City	4-0	72	53
Cleveland	0-4	53	72

Date	Result	Site
Apr. 30	Attack, 18-14	at Cleveland
May 4	Attack, 25-19	at Cleveland
May 9	Attack, 14-8	at Kansas City
May 11	Attack, 15-12	at Kansas City

A-League Final Standings (Outdoor)

Eastern Conference

Northeast Division	W	L	Pts	GF	GA
* Montreal Impact	21	7	61	58	19
† Long Island Rough Riders	16	12	42	44	36
† Rochester Raging Rhinos	14	14	42	56	47
† Toronto Lynx	14	14	38	44	43
Connecticut Wolves	12	16	28	31	45
Worcester Wildfire	7	21	19	26	61

Atlantic Division	W	L	Pts	GF	GA
* Hershey Wildcats	19	9	55	56	33
† Carolina Dynamo	18	10	50	63	33
† Richmond Kickers	15	13	45	41	35
† Charleston Battery	12	16	32	39	50
Raleigh Flyers	12	16	28	34	52
Jacksonville Cyclones	5	23	13	28	73

Western Conference

Central Division	W	L	Pts	GF	GA
* New Orleans R. Gamblers	16	12	42	45	42
† Nashville Metros	17	11	37	42	34
† Milwaukee Rampage	14	14	36	33	36
† Orlando Sundogs	12	16	36	39	40
Minnesota Thunder	13	15	35	22	30
Atlanta Ruckus	12	16	27	39	48

Pacific Division	W	L	Pts	GF	GA
* California Jaguars	18	10	52	48	34
† Seattle Sounders	18	10	50	42	19
† Colorado Foxes	16	12	46	55	49
† Vancouver 86ers	16	12	46	50	29
Orange County Zodiac	11	17	31	35	62
El Paso Patriots	8	20	18	30	50

Playoffs

Semifinals (Best of 3)

Eastern Conference

Carolina vs. Long Island

Carolina wins series, 2-0

Western Conference

Milwaukee vs. Vancouver

Milwaukee wins series, 2-1

Final

Sept. 27 at Milwaukee

Milwaukee 2* ....Carolina 1

*Rampage win in a shootout, 3-0.

CISL Final Standings (Indoor)

Division champions (*) and playoff qualifiers (†) are noted.

Eastern Division

	W	L	Pct.	GB	GF	GA
* Monterrey La Raza	20	8	.714	—	190	166
† Indianapolis Twisters	17	11	.607	3	194	177
† Houston Hotshots	17	11	.607	3	199	157
† Dallas Sidekicks	13	15	.464	7	165	160
Washington Warthogs	12	16	.429	8	170	178
Detroit Safari	3	25	.107	17	134	217

Western Division

	W	L	Pct.	GB	GF	GA
* Seattle SeaDogs	21	7	.750	—	170	128
† Anaheim Splash	16	12	.571	5	165	134
† Sacramento Knights	14	14	.500	7	146	148
† Portland Pride	13	15	.464	8	144	158
Arizona Sandsharks	8	20	.286	13	135	189

Playoffs

Division Semifinals (Best of 3): Monterrey over Dallas (2-1); Houston over Indiana (2-1); Seattle over Portland (2-0); Sacramento over Anaheim (2-0).

Division Finals (Best of 3): Houston over Monterrey (2-1); Seattle over Sacramento (2-0).

Finals (Best of 3)
Houston Hotshots vs. Seattle SeaDogs
began Oct. 18 (see Updates).

Colleges

MEN

1996 Final *Soccer America* Top 20

Final 1996 regular season poll including games through Nov. 18. Conducted by the national weekly *Soccer America* and released in the Dec. 2nd issue. Listing includes records through conference playoffs as well as NCAA tournament record and team lost to. Teams in **bold** type went on to reach NCAA Final Four. All tournament games decided by penalty kicks are considered ties.

		Nov.18 Record	NCAA Recap
1	UCLA	16-3-0	0-1 (CS-Fullerton)
2	Washington	14-2-1	1-1 (Fresno St.)
3	Virginia	16-2-3	0-1 (George Mason)
4	Indiana	13-2-3	2-1 (Florida Int'l)
5	William & Mary	18-2-1	2-1 (St. John's)
6	SMU	14-4-1	0-1 (Creighton)
7	UNC-Greensboro	21-1-0	0-1 (Notre Dame)
8	**St. John's**	17-2-2	5-0
9	**Florida Int'l**	13-4-2	4-1 (St. John's)
10	Bowling Green	17-3-1	1-1 (Indiana)
11	South Florida	17-3-0	0-1 (Florida Int'l)
12	Maryland	13-5-3	1-1 (William & Mary)
13	Fresno St.	15-4-1	2-1 (Creighton)
14	Harvard	15-1-0	1-1 (Hartford)
15	George Mason	13-5-3	1-1 (St. John's)
16	Furman	16-4-1	did not play
17	Notre Dame	13-6-2	1-1 (UNC-Charlotte)
18	Air Force	14-3-3	did not play
19	Evansville	18-4-0	0-1 (Indiana)
20	Connecticut	15-3-3	did not play

NCAA Division I Tournament

First Round (Nov. 23-24)

at Washington 2	OT	Santa Clara 1
at Fresno St. 2		California 1
CS-Fullerton 2		UCLA 1
Creighton 3		at SMU 0
George Mason 1		at Virginia 0
at St. John's 5		Fordham 1
at Maryland 2	OT	James Madison 1
at William & Mary 3		Army 1
Notre Dame 1		at NC-Greensboro 0
at NC-Charlotte 3		Col. of Charleston 1
at Harvard 3		Boston University 2
Hartford 3	OT	at Rhode Island 2
at Bowling Green 4		Detroit Mercy 0
at Indiana 4		Evansville 1
at Rutgers 2	OT	Cornell 1
at Florida Int'l 6		S. Florida 1

Second Round (Dec. 1)

Fresno St. 2		at Washington 1
Creighton 0		at CS-Fullerton 0
(Creighton advances on PK's)		
at St. John's 2		George Mason 1
William & Mary 3		at Maryland 0
at NC-Charlotte 1		Notre Dame 0
Hartford 3	OT	at Harvard 2
at Indiana 2		Bowling Green 0
Florida Int'l 2		at Rutgers 0

Quarterfinals (Dec. 8)

Creighton 2		at Fresno St. 0
St. John's 2	OT	at William & Mary 1
at NC-Charlotte		Hartford 0
at Florida Int'l 1		Indiana 0

> **FINAL FOUR**
> at Richmond, VA (Dec. 13 and 15)
> **Semifinals**
> St. John's 2 .... Creighton 1
> Florida Int'l 4 .... N.C.-Charlotte 0
> **Championship**
> St. John's 4 .... Florida Int'l 1
> **Scoring:** SJ—Jesse Van Saun (26th minute), Wojciech Krakowiak (28th), Ben Hickey (67th), Medufia Kulego (88th); FIU—Ignace Moleka (63rd).
> **Attendance:** 20,874
> **Final Records:** St. John's (22-2-2); Florida Int'l (17-5-1); Creighton (17-5-2); N.C.-Charlotte (16-4-0).

WOMEN

1996 Final *Soccer America* Top 20

Final 1996 regular season poll including games through Nov. 11. Conducted by the national weekly *Soccer America* and released in the Nov. 25th issue. Listing includes records through conference playoffs as well as NCAA tournament record and team lost to. Teams in **bold** type went on to reach NCAA Final Four. All tournament games decided by penalty kicks are considered ties.

		Nov.11 Record	NCAA Recap
1	**Notre Dame**	20-1-0	4-1 (N. Carolina)
2	**North Carolina**	20-1-0	5-0
3	**Portland**	16-0-2	3-1 (Notre Dame)
4	Connecticut	20-2-0	2-1 (Santa Clara)
5	Nebraska	21-0-0	2-1 (Portland)
6	Texas A&M	19-3-0	0-1 (San Diego)
7	Harvard	15-1-0	0-1 (Massachusetts)
8	**Santa Clara**	15-3-2	3-1 (N. Carolina)
9	Florida	20-2-0	2-1 (N.Carolina)
10	Virginia	12-6-2	0-1 (Duke)
11	Clemson	15-6-1	0-1 (Wake Forest)
12	William & Mary	14-8-0	0-1 (N. Carolina)
13	Maryland	17-4-2	2-1 (Notre Dame)
14	Wisconsin	14-4-4	1-1 (Notre Dame)
15	NC-Greensboro	16-5-1	0-1 (James Madison)
16	George Mason	14-6-2	0-1 (Penn St.)
17	Indiana	11-10-0	0-1 (Notre Dame)
18	Wake Forest	13-7-0	1-1 (Florida)
19	California	13-3-2	did not play
20	Duke	9-9-3	1-1 (Nebraska)

NCAA Division I Tournament

First Round (Nov. 16-17)

at North Carolina 5		William & Mary 0
James Madison 3		at NC-Greensboro 1
Wake Forest 2		Clemson 1
at Florida 7		N.C. State 3
at Santa Clara 3		Stanford 2
Penn St. 2		at George Mason 0
Massachusetts 2	3 OT	at Harvard 1
at Connecticut 1		Dartmouth 0
at Portland 1		Washington 0
Vanderbilt 2	3 OT	at Kentucky 1
at Duke 1		Virginia 0
at Nebraska 3	2 OT	Minnesota 0
San Diego 5		at Texas A&M 3
at Maryland 2		George Washington 0
at Wisconsin 1		Northwestern 0
at Notre Dame 8		Indiana 1

Second Round (Nov. 23-24)

at North Carolina 5 .... James Madison 0
at Florida 5 ....Wake Forest 0
at Santa Clara 3 ....Penn St. 1
at Connecticut 2 ....Massachusetts 0
at Portland 3 ....2 OT ....Vanderbilt 1
at Nebraska 3 ....Duke 0
at Maryland 1 ....San Diego 0
at Notre Dame 5 ....Wisconsin 0

Quarterfinals (Nov. 30-Dec. 1)

at North Carolina 9 ....Florida 0
Santa Clara 1 ....at Connecticut 0
at Portland 1 ....Nebraska 0
at Notre Dame 2 ....Maryland 0

1996 Annual Awards

Men's Players of the Year

Hermann Trophy ....Mike Fisher, Virginia, MF
MAC Award ....Mike Fisher
Soccer America ....Johnny Torres, Creighton, F

Women's Player of the Year

Hermann Trophy ....Cindy Daws, Notre Dame, MF
MAC Award ....Cindy Daws
Soccer America ....Debbie Keller, N. Carolina, F

NSCAA Coaches of the Year

Division I: Men's ....Dave Masur, St. John's
                  Women's ....John Walker, Nebraska

Division I All-America Teams

MEN

The combined 1996 first team All-America selections of the National Soccer Coaches Assn. of America (NSCAA) and the 11 *Soccer America* MVPs. Holdovers from the combined 1995 All-America team are in **bold** type.

GOALKEEPERS— John Busch, NC-Charlotte, Jr.; Scott Coufal, Indiana, Sr.

DEFENDERS— Tahj Jakins, UCLA, Sr.; Pete Santora, Furman, Jr.; John Stratton, Air Force, Sr.; Kevin Daly, St. John's, Jr.

MIDFIELDERS— **Mike Fisher**, Virginia, Sr.; Steve Klein, Bowling Green, Sr.; Mike Mekelburg, S. Florida, Sr.; Ricardo Joseph, St. John's, Sr.; Alen Kozic, Florida International, Soph.

FORWARDS— Tony Kuhn, Vanderbilt, Jr.; Ignace Moleka, Florida International, Jr.; Johnny Torres, Creighton, Jr.; **Andrew Williams**, Rhode Island, Jr.; Siggi Eyjolfsson, NC-Greensboro, Soph.; Waughn Hughes, William & Mary, Sr.

WOMEN

The combined 1996 first team All-America selections of the National Soccer Coaches Assn. of America (NSCAA) and the 11 *Soccer America* MVPs. Holdovers from the combined 1995 All-America team are in **bold** type.

GOALKEEPER— Jen Renola, Notre Dame, Sr.

DEFENDERS— Erin Taylor, Maryland, Sr.; **Sara Whalen**, Connecticut, Jr.; **Staci Wilson**, North Carolina, Jr.; Nel Fettig, North Carolina, Jr.

MIDFIELDERS—**Emily Stauffer**, Harvard, Jr.; Justi Baumgardt, Portland, Jr.; Cindy Daws, Notre Dame, Sr.; Jennifer Lalor, Santa Clara, Sr.; Tiffany Roberts, North Carolina, Soph.; Kari Uppinghouse, Nebraska, Jr.

FORWARDS— Bryn Blalack, Texas A&M, Jr.; Kerry Connors, Connecticut, Sr.; Danielle Fotopoulos, Florida, Jr.; **Debbie Keller**, North Carolina, Sr; **Cindy Parlow**, North Carolina, Soph.

FINAL FOUR
at Santa Clara, Calif.. (Dec. 6 and 8)
Semifinals

Notre Dame 3 ....Portland 2
North Carolina 2 ....Santa Clara 1

Championship

North Carolina 1 ......2 OT ....Notre Dame 0
Scoring: NC— Debbie Keller (Rakel Karvelsson, Tiffany Roberts) at 110:56.
Attendance: 8,800.
Final records: North Carolina (25-1); Notre Dame (24-2); Portland (19-1-2); Santa Clara (18-4-2).
Most Outstanding Players: OFFENSE— Debbie Keller, North Carolina, F; DEFENSE— Nel Fettig, North Carolina, D.

Small College Final Fours

MEN
NCAA Division II
at Phoenix, Ariz. (Dec. 6 and 8)
Att: 1,649

Semifinals: Grand Canyon (Ariz.) def. Lynn (Fla.), 1-0; Oakland (Mich.) def. S. Connecticut, 1-0.

Championship: Grand Canyon def. Oakland, 3-1. Final records: Grand Canyon (12-4-5) and Oakland (15-6-2).

NCAA Division III
at Gambier, Ohio. (Nov. 30 and Dec. 1)
Semifinals: Kenyon (Ohio) def. Chicago, 3-2; College of New Jersey def. Ithaca (N.Y.), 4-4, College of New Jersey wins shootout.

Championship: College of New Jersey def. Kenyon, 2-1, 4 OT. Final records: College of New Jersey (17-5-1) and Kenyon (18-3-1).

NAIA
at Birmingham, Ala. (Nov. 30)
Semifinals: Lindsey Wilson (Ky.) def. Illinois-Springfield, 3-1; Birmingham Southern def. Rockhurst, 3-2.

Championship: Lindsey Wilson def. Birmingham Southern 5-0. Final records: Lindsey Wilson (23-4-1) and Birmingham Southern (17-6-2).

WOMEN
NCAA Division II
at Boca Raton, Fla. (Nov. 22 and 24)
Semifinals: Franklin Pierce (N.H.) def. St. Joseph's (Ind.), 2-0; Lynn (Fla.) def. Regis (Colo.), 2-1.

Championship: Franklin Pierce def. Lynn 1-0. Final records: Franklin Pierce (18-1-0) and Lynn (20-1-0).

NCAA Division III
at Amherst, Mass. (Nov. 16-17)
Semifinals: UC-San Diego def. Amherst (Mass.), 2-1; College of New Jersey def. Chicago, 1-0.

Championship: UC-San Diego def. College of New Jersey, 2-1. Final records: UC-San Diego (21-1-0) and College of New Jersey (19-2-2).

NAIA
at San Antonio (Nov. 29-30)
Semifinals: Simon Fraser def. Southen Nazarene (Okla.), 2-1; Mobile def. Brewton-Parker, 1-0.

Championship: Simor Fraser def. Mobile, 3-2 (OT). Final records: Simon Fraser (19-3-1) and Mobile (20-4-1).

Who are these guys?

by Jack Edwards

The Confederacy is long gone.

But the capital of college soccer, Richmond, Virginia—now seemingly, and deservedly, the perennial tournament site— was the gathering place for rebels in December of 1996.

The NCAA tournament had broken wildly from the gate. Powerhouses from the University of Virginia and UCLA both lost in the first round: UVA to George Mason, 1-0, and UCLA to Cal State Fullerton, 2-1. The NCAA Tournament 3-seed, UNC-Greensboro, also went down in the first round. Indiana also lost, to Florida International, 1-0 in the third.

So hear the rebel yell: "WHO ARE THESE GUYS?" St. John's, Creighton, Florida International, and UNC-Charlotte had been a collective 1-13 in previous NCAA tournament experiences (all short ones). None, obviously, ever had been to a Final Four, much less had any climbed to the pinnacle of college soccer. North Carolina-Charlotte had an All-American goalkeeper in Jon Busch. FIU's Tyronne Marshall shocked him with a goal for the ages in the semi's, a bicycle kick early in the second half. FIU exploded for a 4-0 win. Creighton hadn't allowed a goal, going into its semi-final match against St. John's. The Red Storm popped that balloon on Wojtek Krakowiak's goal in the 27th minute, then won it on Jesse Van Saun's 1-1 tiebreaker in the 64th.

So there they were: St. John's (0-4 all-time in NCAA tournament play before 1996) and FIU (0-2). Florida International had outscored its tournament opponents, 13-1, and it had beaten St. John's, 2-0, in October. But in mid-December, the Red Storm hit Richmond. FIU's wreckage was found in the wake of the destruction. Ben Hickey, from the wing, crossed to Jimmy Buscemi. Buscemi made a rare chest pass to Van Saun, who whipped a side-volley.

That's a shot that's hard even to get on goal. Van Saun put it in the back of the net. One minute later, Krakowiak fired a one-timer from the six-yard box. FIU got within 2-1 early in the second half, but St. John's Hickey finished a pinball play, the second header off a Van Saun corner, and it was 3-1. In celebration time, Medufia Kulego headed-home the final tally. St. John's had its first NCAA title in any sport.

The 4-1 blowout marked the most goals in an NCAA Final since 1980, the biggest margin of victory since 1975. The semi's drew 20,269...the finals, 20,874. The tournament returns to Richmond for 1997 and '98. Every rebel team in the country now knows it can be there, too.

In women's soccer, there has been anything but a changing of the guard. North Carolina has won all but two of the NCAA women's soccer tournaments since they started in 1982, losing only to George Mason in 1985 and to Notre Dame, in triple overtime, in 1995. So, since it wasn't a year ending in five, the 1996 women's college soccer champion was North Carolina, their 13th national title.

The Tar Heels defeated Notre Dame in an overtime thriller, 1-0. The winning goal was scored by Debbie Keller, who was voted the national player of the year in 1995 and '96. Coach Anson Dorrance explained Keller's wonderful career to *College Soccer Weekly* by saying, "Debbie Keller is a total genius. She scored goals in our system because of her discipline and the fact that she is one of the smartest players to ever play at Carolina. A player of her caliber can never be fully replaced in our program."

With all due respect to Keller and Dorrance, which is plenty, the women's soccer program at Carolina will probably find *somebody* to keep the dynasty going.

Jack Edwards is the co-anchor of ESPN's *Sunday SportsDay* and played Division I soccer at the University of New Hampshire.

SOCCER STATISTICS

THROUGH THE YEARS
1900-1997
WORLD • U.S. • COLLEGE

THE 1998 SPORTS ALMANAC

INFORMATION PLEASE

SEC B

PAGE 743

The World Cup

The Federation Internationale de Football Association (FIFA) began the World Cup championship tournament in 1930 with a 13-team field in Uruguay. Sixty-four years later, 138 countries competed in qualifying rounds to fill 24 berths in the 1994 World Cup finals. FIFA has increased the World Cup '98 tournament field from 24 to 32 teams, including automatic berths for defending champion Brazil and host France. The other 30 slots are allotted by region: Europe (14), Africa (5), South America (4), CONCACAF (3), Asia (3), and the one remaining position to the winner of a playoff between the fourth place team in Asia and the champion of Oceania.

The United States hosted the World Cup for the first time in '94 and American crowds shattered tournament attendance records (see Year-by-Year Comparisons). Tournaments have now been played three times in North America (Mexico 2 and U.S.), four times in South America (Argentina, Chile, Brazil and Uruguay) and eight times in Europe (Italy 2, England, France, Spain, Sweden, Switzerland and West Germany).

Brazil retired the first World Cup (called the Jules Rimet Trophy after FIFA's first president) in 1970 after winning it for the third time. The new trophy, first presented in 1974, is known as simply the World Cup.

Multiple winners: Brazil (4); Italy and West Germany (3); Argentina and Uruguay (2).

Year	Champion	Manager	Score	Runner-up	Host Country	Third Place
1930	Uruguay	Alberto Suppici	4-2	Argentina	Uruguay	No game
1934	Italy	Vittório Pozzo	2-1*	Czechoslovakia	Italy	Germany 3, Austria 2
1938	Italy	Vittório Pozzo	4-2	Hungary	France	Brazil 4, Sweden 2
1942-46 Not held						
1950	Uruguay	Juan Lopez	2-1	Brazil	Brazil	No game
1954	West Germany	Sepp Herberger	3-2	Hungary	Switzerland	Austria 3, Uruguay 1
1958	Brazil	Vicente Feola	5-2	Sweden	Sweden	France 6, W. Ger. 3
1962	Brazil	Aimoré Moreira	3-1	Czechoslovakia	Chile	Chile 1, Yugoslavia 0
1966	England	Alf Ramsey	4-2*	W. Germany	England	Portugal 2, USSR 1
1970	Brazil	Mario Zagalo	4-1	Italy	Mexico	W. Ger. 1, Uruguay 0
1974	West Germany	Helmut Schoen	2-1	Holland	W. Germany	Poland 1, Brazil 0
1978	Argentina	Cesar Menotti	3-1*	Holland	Argentina	Brazil 2, Italy 1
1982	Italy	Enzo Bearzot	3-1	W. Germany	Spain	Poland 3, France 2
1986	Argentina	Carlos Bilardo	3-2	W. Germany	Mexico	France 4, Belgium 2*
1990	West Germany	Franz Beckenbauer	1-0	Argentina	Italy	Italy 2, England 1
1994	Brazil	Carlos Parreira	0-0†	Italy	USA	Sweden 4, Bulgaria 0
1998	at France (June 10-July 12)					
2002	at Japan/South Korea					

*Winning goals scored in overtime (no sudden death); †Brazil defeated Italy in shootout (3-2) after scoreless overtime period (30 minutes).

All-Time World Cup Leaders

Career Goals

World Cup scoring leaders through 1994. Years listed are years played in World Cup.

	No
Gerd Müller, West Germany (1970, 74)	14
Just Fontaine, France (1958)	13
Pelé, Brazil (1958, 62, 66, 70)	12
Sandor Kocsis, Hungary (1954)	11
Helmut Rahn, West Germany (1954, 58)	11
Teofilo Cubillas; Peru (1970, 78)	10
Gregorz Lato, Poland (1974, 78, 82)	10
Gary Lineker, England (1986, 90)	10

Most Valuable Player

Officially, the Golden Ball Award, the Most Valuable Player of the World Cup tournament has been selected since 1982 by a panel of international soccer journalists.

Year		Year	
1982	Paolo Rossi, Italy	1990	Toto Schillaci, Italy
1986	Diego Maradona, Arg.	1994	Romario, Brazil

Single Tournament Goals

World Cup tournament scoring leaders through 1994.

Year		Gm	No
1930	Guillermo Stabile, Argentina	4	8
1934	Angelo Schiavio, Italy	3	4
	Oldrich Nejedly, Czechoslovakia	4	4
	& Edmund Conen, Germany	4	4
1938	Leônidas, Brazil	3	8
1950	Ademir, Brazil	6	7
1954	Sandor Kocsis, Hungary	5	11
1958	Just Fontaine, France	6	13
1962	Drazen Jerkovic, Yugoslavia	6	5
1966	Eusébio, Portugal	6	9
1970	Gerd Müller, West Germany	6	10
1974	Grzegorz Lato, Poland	7	7
1978	Mario Kempes, Argentina	7	6
1982	Paolo Rossi, Italy	7	6
1986	Gary Lineker, England	5	6
1990	Toto Schillaci, Italy	7	6
1994	Oleg Salenko, Russia	3	6
	Hristo Stoichkov, Bulgaria	7	6

All-Time World Cup Ranking Table

Since the first World Cup in 1930, Brazil is the only country to play in all 15 final tournaments and win the championship four times. The FIFA All-Time Table below ranks all nations that have ever qualified for a World Cup final tournament by points earned through 1994. Victories, which earned two points from 1930-90, were awarded three points starting in 1994. Note that Germany's appearances include 10 made by West Germany from 1954-90. Participants in the 1994 World Cup final are in **bold** type.

		App	Gm	W	L	T	Pts	GF	GA			App	Gm	W	L	T	Pts	GF	GA
1	**Brazil**	15	73	49	11	13	**111**	159	68		Denmark	1	4	3	1	0	**6**	10	6
2	**Germany**	13	73	42	15	16	**100**	154	97		East Germany	1	6	2	2	2	**6**	5	5
3	**Italy**	13	61	35	12	14	**84**	97	59	34	**Morocco**	3	10	1	6	3	**5**	7	13
4	**Argentina**	11	52	26	17	9	**61**	90	65		Algeria	2	6	2	3	1	**5**	6	10
5	England	9	41	18	11	12	**48**	55	38		Wales	1	5	1	1	3	**5**	4	4
6	**Spain**	9	37	15	13	9	**39**	53	44	37	Costa Rica	1	4	2	2	0	**4**	4	6
7	Uruguay	9	37	15	14	8	**38**	61	52		**Nigeria**	1	4	2	2	0	**4**	7	4
	Russia	8	34	16	12	6	**38**	60	40		**Saudi Arabia**	1	4	2	2	0	**4**	5	6
9	**Sweden**	9	38	14	15	9	**37**	66	60	40	**South Korea**	4	11	0	8	3	**3**	9	34
10	France	9	34	15	14	5	**35**	71	56		Norway	2	4	1	2	1	**3**	2	3
	Yugoslavia	8	33	14	12	7	**35**	55	42		Cuba	1	3	1	1	1	**3**	5	12
12	Hungary	9	32	15	14	3	**33**	87	57		North Korea	1	4	1	2	1	**3**	5	9
13	Poland	5	25	13	7	5	**31**	39	29		Tunisia	1	3	1	1	1	**3**	3	2
14	**Holland**	6	25	11	8	6	**28**	43	29	45	Egypt	2	4	0	2	2	**2**	3	6
15	Czech Rep.	8	30	11	14	5	**27**	44	45		Honduras	1	3	0	1	2	**2**	2	3
16	Austria	6	26	12	12	2	**26**	40	43		Israel	1	3	0	1	2	**2**	1	3
17	**Mexico**	10	33	7	18	8	**22**	31	68		Turkey	1	3	1	2	0	**2**	10	11
	Belgium	9	29	9	16	4	**22**	37	53	49	**Bolivia**	3	6	0	5	1	**1**	1	20
19	Chile	6	21	7	11	3	**17**	26	32		Australia	1	3	0	2	1	**1**	0	5
20	**Romania**	6	17	6	7	4	**16**	26	29		Iran	1	3	0	2	1	**1**	2	8
21	**Switzerland**	7	22	6	13	3	**15**	33	51		Kuwait	1	3	0	2	1	**1**	2	6
22	Scotland	7	20	4	10	6	**14**	23	35	53	El Salvador	2	6	0	6	0	**0**	1	22
23	**Bulgaria**	6	23	3	13	7	**13**	21	46		Canada	1	3	0	3	0	**0**	0	5
24	Portugal	2	9	6	3	0	**12**	19	12		East Indies	1	1	0	1	0	**0**	0	6
25	Peru	4	15	4	8	3	**11**	19	31		**Greece**	1	3	0	3	0	**0**	0	10
	No. Ireland	3	13	3	5	5	**11**	13	23		Haiti	1	3	0	3	0	**0**	2	14
27	Paraguay	4	11	3	4	4	**10**	16	25		Iraq	1	3	0	3	0	**0**	1	4
	Cameroon	3	11	3	4	4	**10**	11	21		New Zealand	1	3	0	3	0	**0**	2	12
29	**USA**	5	14	4	9	1	**9**	17	33		UAE	1	3	0	3	0	**0**	2	11
30	Ireland	2	9	1	3	5	**7**	4	7		Zaire	1	3	0	3	0	**0**	0	14
31	**Colombia**	3	10	2	6	2	**6**	13	20										

The United States in the World Cup

While the United States has fielded a national team every year of the World Cup, only four of those teams have been able to make it past the preliminary competition and qualify for the final World Cup tournament. The 1994 national team automatically qualified because the U.S. served as host of the event for the first time. The U.S. has played in three of the first four World Cups (1930, '34 and '50) and each of the last two (1990, '94). The Americans have a record of 4-9-1 in 14 World Cup matches, with two victories in 1930, a 1-0 upset of England in 1950, and a 2-1 shocker over Colombia in 1994.

1930

1st Round Matches

United States 3 ....Belgium 0
United States 3 ....Paraguay 0

Semifinals

Argentina 6 ....United States 1
U.S. Scoring—Bert Patenaude (3), Bart McGhee (2), James Brown, Thomas Florie.

1934

1st Round Match

Italy 7 ....United States 1
U.S. Scoring—Buff Donelli (who later became a noted college and NFL football coach).

1950

1st Round Matches

Spain 3 ....United States 1
United States 1 ....England 0
Chile 5 ....United States 2
U.S. Scoring—Joe Gaetjens, Joe Maca, John Souza, Frank Wallace.

1990

1st Round Matches

Czechoslovakia 5 ....United States 1
Italy 1 ....United States 0
Austria 2 ....United States 1
U.S. Scoring—Paul Caligiuri, Bruce Murray.

1994

1st Round Matches

United States 1 ....Switzerland 1
United States 2 ....Colombia 1
Romania 1 ....United States 0

Round of 16

Brazil 1 ....United States 0
Overall U.S. Scoring— Eric Wynalda, Ernie Stewart, own goal (Colombia defender Andres Escobar).

World Cup Finals

Current World Cup champion Brazil and finalist Italy each appeared in their fifth Cup championship game in 1994 and played to the first scoreless overtime draw in the history of the Cup final. The match was also the first decided by a shootout (Brazil winning, 3-2). West Germany (now Germany) has played in the most Cup finals with six. Note that a four-team round robin determined the 1950 championship–the deciding game turned out to be the last one of the tournament between Uruguay and Brazil.

1930

Uruguay 4, Argentina 2
(at Montevideo, Uruguay)

		1	2–T
July 30	Uruguay (4-0)	1	3–4
	Argentina (4-1)	2	0–2

Goals: Uruguay–Pablo Dorado (12th minute), Pedro Cea (54th), Santos Iriarte (68th), Castro (89th); Argentina–Carlos Peucelle (20th), Guillermo Stabile (37th).

Uruguay–Ballesteros, Nasazzi, Mascheroni, Andrade, Fernandez, Gestido, Dorado, Scarone, Castro, Cea, Iriarte.

Argentina–Botasso, Della Torre, Paternoster, J. Evaristo, Monti, Suarez, Peucelle, Varallo, Stabile, Ferreira, M. Evaristo.

Attendance: 90,000. **Referee:** Langenus (Belgium).

1934

Italy 2, Czechoslovakia 1 (OT)
(at Rome)

		1	2	OT–T
June 10	Italy (4-0-1)	0	1	1–2
	Czechoslovakia (3-1)	0	1	0–1

Goals: Italy–Raimondo Orsi (80th minute), Angelo Schiavio (95th); Czechoslovakia–Puc (70th).

Italy–Combi, Monzeglio, Allemandi, Ferraris IV, Monti, Bertolini, Guaita, Meazza, Schiavio, Ferrari, Orsi.

Czechoslovakia–Planicka, Zenisek, Ctyroky, Kostalek, Cambal, Krcil, Junek, Svoboda, Sobotka, Nejedly, Puc.

Attendance: 55,000. **Referee:** Eklind (Sweden).

1938

Italy 4, Hungary 2
(at Paris)

		1	2–T
June 19	Italy (4-0)	3	1–4
	Hungary (3-1)	1	1–2

Goals: Italy–Gino Colaussi (5th minute), Silvio Piola (16th), Colassi (35th), Piola (82nd); Hungary–Titkos (7th), Georges Sarosi (70th).

Italy–Olivieri, Foni, Rava, Serantoni, Andreolo, Locatelli, Biavati, Meazza, Piola, Ferrari, Colaussi.

Hungary–Szabo, Polgar, Biro, Szalay, Szucs, Lazar, Sas, Vincze, G. Sarosi, Szengeller, Titkos.

Attendance: 65,000. **Referee:** Capdeville (France).

1950

Uruguay 2, Brazil 1
(at Rio de Janeiro)

		1	2–T
July 16	Uruguay (3-0-1)	0	2–2
	Brazil (4-1-1)	0	1–1

Goals: Uruguay–Juan Schiaffino (66th minute), Chico Ghiggia (79th); Brazil–Friaca (47th).

Uruguay–Maspoli, M. Gonzales, Tejera, Gambetta, Varela, Andrade, Ghiggia, Perez, Miguez, Schiaffino, Moran.

Brazil–Barbosa, Augusto, Juvenal, Bauer, Danilo, Bigode, Friaça, Zizinho, Ademir, Jair, Chico.

Attendance: 199,854. **Referee:** Reader (England).

1954

West Germany 3, Hungary 2
(at Berne, Switzerland)

		1	2–T
July 4	West Germany (4-1)	2	1–3
	Hungary (4-1)	2	0–2

Goals: West Germany–Max Morlock (10th minute), Helmut Rahn (18th), Rahn (84th); Hungary–Ferenc Puskas (4th), Zoltan Czibor (9th).

West Germany–Turek, Posipal, Liebrich, Kohlmeyer, Eckel, Mai, Rahn, Morlock, O. Walter, F. Walter, Schaefer.

Hungary–Grosics, Buzansky, Lorant, Lantos, Bozsik, Zakarias, Czibor, Kocsis, Hidegkuti, Puskas, J. Toth.

Attendance: 60,000. **Referee:** Ling (England).

1958

Brazil 5, Sweden 2
(at Stockholm)

		1	2–T
June 29	Brazil (5-0-1)	2	3–5
	Sweden (4-1-1)	1	1–2

Goals: Brazil–Vava (9th minute), Vava (32nd), Pelé (55th), Mario Zagalo (68th), Pelé (90th); Sweden–Nils Liedholm (3rd), Agne Simonsson (80th).

Brazil–Gilmar, D. Santos, N. Santos, Zito, Bellini, Orlando, Garrincha, Didi, Vava, Pelé, Zagalo.

Sweden–Svensson, Bergmark, Axbom, Boerjesson, Gustavsson, Parling, Hamrin, Gren, Simonsson, Liedholm, Skoglund.

Attendance: 49,737. **Referee:** Guigue (France).

1962

Brazil 3, Czechoslovakia 1
(at Santiago, Chile)

		1	2–T
June 17	Brazil (5-0-1)	1	2–3
	Czechoslovakia (3-2-1)	1	0–1

Goals: Brazil–Amarildo (17th minute), Zito (68th), Vava (77th); Czechoslovakia–Josef Masopust (15th).

Brazil–Gilmar, D. Santos, N. Santos, Zito, Mauro, Zozimo, Garrincha, Didi, Vava, Amarildo, Zagalo.

Czechoslovakia–Schroiff, Tichy, Novak, Pluskal, Popluhar, Masopust, Pospichal, Scherer, Kvasniak, Kadraba, Jelinek.

Attendance: 68,679. **Referee:** Latishev (USSR).

1966

England 4, West Germany 2 (OT)
(at London)

		1	2	OT–T
July 30	England (5-0-1)	1	1	2–4
	West Germany (4-1)	1	1	0–2

Goals: England–Geoff Hurst (18th minute), Martin Peters (78th), Hurst (101st), Hurst (120th); West Germany–Helmut Haller (12th), Wolfgang Weber (90th).

England–Banks, Cohen, Wilson, Stiles, J. Charlton, Moore, Ball, Hurst, B. Charlton, Hunt, Peters.

West Germany–Tilkowski, Hottges, Schnellinger, Beckenbauer, Schulz, Weber, Haller, Seeler, Held, Overath, Emmerich.

Attendance: 93,802. **Referee:** Dienst (Switzerland).

World Cup Finals (Cont.)

1970
Brazil 4, Italy 1
(at Mexico City)

	1	2–T
June 21 Brazil (6-0)	1	3–4
Italy (3-1-2)	1	0–1

Goals: Brazil–Pelé (18th minute), Gerson (65th), Jairzinho (70th), Carlos Alberto (86th); Italy–Roberto Boninsegna (37th).
Brazil–Felix, C. Alberto, Everaldo, Clodoaldo, Brito, Piazza, Jairzinho, Gerson, Tostão, Pelé, Rivelino.
Italy–Albertosi, Burgnich, Facchetti, Bertini (Juliano, 73rd), Rosato, Cera, Domenghini, Mazzola, Boninsegna (Rivera, 84th), De Sisti, Riva.
Attendance: 107,412. **Referee:** Glockner (E. Germany).

1974
West Germany 2, Holland 1
(at Munich)

	1	2–T
July 7 West Germany (6-1)	2	0–2
Holland (5-1-1)	1	0–1

Goals: West Germany–Paul Breitner (25th minute, penalty kick), Gerd Müller (43rd); Holland–Johan Neeskens (1st, penalty kick).
West Germany–Maier, Beckenbauer, Vogts, Breitner, Schwarzenbeck, Overath, Bonhof, Hoeness, Grabowski, Muller, Holzenbein.
Holland–Jongbled, Suurbier, Rijsbergen (De Jong, 58th), Krol, Haan, Jansen, Van Hanegem, Neeskens, Rep, Cruyff, Rensenbrink (R. Van de Kerkhof, 46th).
Attendance: 77,833. **Referee:** Taylor (England).

1978
Argentina 3, Holland 1 (OT)
(at Buenos Aires)

	1	2	OT–T
June 25 Argentina (5-1-1)	1	0	2–3
Holland (3-2-2)	0	1	0–1

Goals: Argentina–Mario Kempes (37th minute), Kempes (104th), Daniel Bertoni (114th); Holland–Dirk Nanninga (81st).
Argentina–Fillol, Olguin, L. Galvan, Passarella, Tarantini, Ardiles (Larrosa, 65th), Gallego, Kempes, Luque, Bertoni, Ortiz (Houseman, 77th).
Holland–Jongbled, Jansen (Suurbier, 72nd), Brandts, Krol, Poortvliet, Haan, Neeskens, W. Van de Kerkhof, R. Van de Kerkhof, Rep (Nanninga, 58th), Rensenbrink.
Attendance: 77,260. **Referee:** Gonella (Italy).

1982
Italy 3, West Germany 1
(at Madrid)

	1	2–T
July 11 Italy (4-0-3)	0	3–3
West Germany (4-2-1)	0	1–1

Goals: Italy–Paolo Rossi (57th minute), Marco Tardelli (68th), Alessandro Altobelli (81st); West Germany–Paul Breitner (83rd).
Italy–Zoff, Scirea, Gentile, Cabrini, Collovati, Bergomi, Tardelli, Oriali, Conti, Rossi, Graziani (Altobelli, 8th, and Causio, 89th).
West Germany–Schumacher, Stielike, Kaltz, Briegel, K.H. Forster, B. Forster, Breitner, Dremmler (Hrubesch, 61st), Littbarski, Fischer, Rummenigge (Muller, 69th).
Attendance: 90,080. **Referee:** Coelho (Brazil).

1986
Argentina 3, West Germany 2
(at Mexico City)

	1	2–T
June 29 Argentina (6-0-1)	1	2–3
West Germany (4-2-1)	0	2–2

Goals: Argentina–Jose Brown (22nd minute), Jorge Valdano (55th), Jorge Burruchaga (83rd); West Germany–Karl-Heinz Rummenigge (73rd), Rudi Voller (81st).
Argentina–Pumpido, Cuciuffo, Olarticoechea, Ruggeri, Brown, Batista, Burruchaga (Trobbiani, 89th), Giusti, Enrique, Maradona, Valdano.
West Germany–Schumacher, Jakobs, B. Forster, Berthold, Briegel, Eder, Brehme, Matthaus, Rummenigge, Magath (Hoeness, 61st), Allofs (Voller, 46th).
Attendance: 114,590. **Referee:** Filho (Brazil).

1990
West Germany 1, Argentina 0
(at Rome)

	1	2–T
July 8 West Germany (6-0-1)	0	1–1
Argentina (4-2-1)	0	0–0

Goals: West Germany–Andreas Brehme (85th minute, penalty kick).
West Germany–Illgner, Berthold (Reuter, 73rd), Kohler, Augenthaler, Buchwald, Brehme, Haessler, Matthaus, Littbarski, Klinsmann, Voller.
Argentina: Goycoechea, Ruggeri (Monzon, 46th), Simon, Serrizuela, Lorenzo, Basualdo, Troglio, Burruchaga (Calderon, 53rd), Sensini, Dezotti, Maradona.
Attendance: 73,603. **Referee:** Codesal (Mexico).

1994
Brazil 0, Italy 0 (SO)
(at Pasadena, Calif.)

	1	2	OT– T
July 17 Brazil (6-0-1)	0	0	0–0*
Italy (4-2-1)	0	0	0–0

*Brazil wins shootout, 3-2.
Shootout (five shots each, alternating): ITA– Baresi (miss, 0-0); BRA– Santos (blocked, 0-0): ITA– Albertini (goal, 1-0); BRA–Romario (goal, 1-1); ITA– Evani (goal, 2-1); BRA–Branco (goal, 2-2); ITA– Massaro (blocked, 2-2); BRA–Dunga (goal, 2-3); ITA–R. Baggio (miss, 2-3).
Brazil–Taffarel, Jorginho (Cafu, 21st minute), Branco, Aldair, Santos, Mazinho, Silva, Dunga, Zinho (Viola, 106th), Bebeto, Romario.
Italy– Pagliuca, Mussi (Apolloni, 35th minute), Baresi, Benarrivo, Maldini, Albertini, D. Baggio (Evani, 95th), Berti, Donadoni, R. Baggio, Massaro.
Attendance: 94,194. **Referee:** Puhl (Hungary).

World Cup Shootouts
Introduced in 1982; winning sides in **bold** type.

Year	Round		Final	SO
1982	Semi	**W. Germany** vs. France	3-3	(5-4)
1986	Quarter	**Belgium** vs. Spain	1-1	(5-4)
	Quarter	**France** vs. Brazil	1-1	(4-3)
	Quarter	**W. Germany** vs. Mexico	0-0	(4-1)
1990	Second	**Ireland** vs Romania	0-0	(5-4)
	Quarter	**Argentina** vs Yugoslavia	0-0	(3-2)
	Semi	**Argentina** vs Italy	1-1	(4-3)
	Semi	**W. Germany** vs England	1-1	(4-3)
1994	Second	**Bulgaria** vs Mexico	1-1	(3-1)
	Quarter	**Sweden** vs Romania	2-2	(5-4)
	Final	**Brazil** vs Italy	0-0	(3-2)

Year-by-Year Comparisons

How the 15 World Cup tournaments have compared in nations qualifying, matches played, players participating, goals scored, average goals per game, overall attendance and attendance per game.

Year	Host	Continent	Nations	Matches	Players	Scored	Goals Per Game	Attendance Overall	Per Game
1930	Uruguay	So. America	13	18	189	70	3.8	434,500	24,138
1934	Italy	Europe	16	17	208	70	4.1	395,000	23,235
1938	France	Europe	15	18	210	84	4.7	483,000	26,833
1942-46	Not held								
1950	Brazil	So. America	13	22	192	88	4.0	1,337,000	60,772
1954	Switzerland	Europe	16	26	233	140	5.3	943,000	36,270
1958	Sweden	Europe	16	35	241	126	3.6	868,000	24,800
1962	Chile	So. America	16	32	252	89	2.8	776,000	24,250
1966	England	Europe	16	32	254	89	2.8	1,614,677	50,458
1970	Mexico	No. America	16	32	270	95	3.0	1,673,975	52,311
1974	West Germany	Europe	16	38	264	97	2.6	1,774,022	46,684
1978	Argentina	So. America	16	38	277	102	2.7	1,610,215	42,374
1982	Spain	Europe	24	52	396	146	2.8	1,856,277	33,967
1986	Mexico	No. America	24	52	414	132	2.5	2,402,951	46,211
1990	Italy	Europe	24	52	413	115	2.2	2,517,348	48,411
1994	United States	No. America	24	52	437	140	2.7	3,567,415	68,102
1998	France	Europe	32	–	–	–	–	–	–

OTHER WORLDWIDE COMPETITION

The Olympic Games

Held every four years since 1896, except during World War I (1916) and World War II (1940-44). Soccer was not a medal sport in 1896 at Athens or in 1932 at Los Angeles. By agreement between FIFA and the IOC, Olympic soccer competition is currently limited to players 23 years old and under.

Multiple winners: England and Hungary (3); Soviet Union and Uruguay (2).

MEN

Year		Year	
1900	**England**, France, Belgium	1956	**Soviet Union,** Yugoslavia, Bulgaria
1904	**Canada,** USA I, USA II	1960	**Yugoslavia,** Denmark, Hungary
1906	**Denmark,** Smyrna (Int'l entry), Greece	1964	**Hungary,** Czechoslovakia, East Germany
1908	**England,** Denmark, Holland	1968	**Hungary,** Bulgaria, Japan
1912	**England,** Denmark, Holland	1972	**Poland,** Hungary, East Germany
1920	**Belgium,** Spain, Holland	1976	**East Germany,** Poland, Soviet Union
1924	**Uruguay,** Switzerland, Sweden	1980	**Czechoslovakia,** East Germany, Soviet Union
1928	**Uruguay,** Argentina, Italy	1984	**France,** Brazil, Yugoslavia
1936	**Italy,** Austria, Norway	1988	**Soviet Union,** Brazil, West Germany
1948	**Sweden,** Yugoslavia, Denmark	1992	**Spain,** Poland, Ghana
1952	**Hungary,** Yugoslavia, Sweden	1996	**Nigeria,** Argentina, Brazil

WOMEN

Year	
1996	**USA,** China, Norway

The Under-20 World Cup

Held every two years since 1977. Officially, The World Youth Championship for the FIFA/Coca-Cola Cup.

Multiple winners: Argentina and Brazil (3); Portugal (2).

Year		Year	
1977	Soviet Union	1989	Portugal
1979	Argentina	1991	Portugal
1981	West Germany	1993	Brazil
1983	Brazil	1995	Argentina
1985	Brazil	1997	Argentina
1987	Yugoslavia	1999	(at South America)

The Under-17 World Cup

Held every two years since 1985. Officially, The U-17 World Tournament for the FIFA/JVC Cup.

Multiple winners: Ghana and Nigeria (2).

Year		Year	
1985	Nigeria	1993	Nigeria
1987	Soviet Union	1995	Ghana
1989	Saudi Arabia	1997	Brazil
1991	Ghana	1999	(at New Zealand)

Indoor World Championship

First held in 1989. FIFA's only Five-a-Side tournament.

Multiple winners: Brazil (3).

Year		Year	
1989	Brazil	1996	Brazil
1992	Brazil		

Women's World Cup

First held in 1991. Officially, the FIFA Women's World Championship.

Year		Year	
1991	United States	1999	(at United States)
1995	Norway		

Intercontinental Cup

First held in 1992. Contested by the Continental champions of Africa, Asia, Europe, North America and South America.

Year		Year	
1992	Argentina	1995	Denmark

CONTINENTAL COMPETITION

European Championship

Held every four years since 1960. Officially, the European Football Championship. Winners receive the Henri Delaunay trophy, named for the frenchman who first proposed the idea of a European Soccer Championship in 1927. The first one would not be played until five years after his death in 1955.

Multiple winner: West Germany (2).

Year		Year		Year		Year	
1960	Soviet Union	1972	West Germany	1984	France	1996	Germany
1964	Spain	1976	Czechoslovakia	1988	Holland		
1968	Italy	1980	West Germany	1992	Denmark		

Copa America

Held irregularly since 1916. Unofficially, the Championship of South America.

Multiple winners: Argentina and Uruguay (14); Brazil (5); Paraguay and Peru (2).

Year		Year		Year		Year	
1916	Uruguay	1927	Argentina	1949	Brazil	1979	Paraguay
1917	Uruguay	1929	Argentina	1953	Paraguay	1983	Uruguay
1919	Brazil	1935	Uruguay	1955	Argentina	1987	Uruguay
1920	Uruguay	1937	Argentina	1956	Uruguay	1989	Brazil
1921	Argentina	1939	Peru	1957	Argentina	1991	Argentina
1922	Brazil	1941	Argentina	1958	Argentina	1993	Argentina
1923	Uruguay	1942	Uruguay	1959	Uruguay	1995	Uruguay
1924	Uruguay	1945	Argentina	1963	Bolivia	1997	Brazil
1925	Argentina	1946	Argentina	1967	Uruguay		
1926	Uruguay	1947	Argentina	1975	Peru		

African Nations' Cup

Contested since 1957 and held every two years since 1968.

Multiple winners: Ghana (4); Congo/Zaire and Egypt (3); Cameroon and Nigeria (2).

Year		Year		Year		Year	
1957	Egypt	1968	Zaire	1978	Ghana	1988	Cameroon
1959	Egypt	1970	Sudan	1980	Nigeria	1990	Algeria
1962	Ethiopia	1972	Congo	1982	Ghana	1992	Ivory Coast
1963	Ghana	1974	Zaire	1984	Cameroon	1994	Nigeria
1965	Ghana	1976	Morocco	1986	Egypt	1996	South Africa

CONCACAF Gold Cup

The Confederation of North, Central American and Caribbean Football Championship. Contested irregularly from 1963-81 and revived as CONCACAF Gold Cup in 1991.

Multiple winners: Mexico (5); Costa Rica (2).

Year		Year		Year		Year	
1963	Costa Rica	1969	Costa Rica	1977	Mexico	1993	Mexico
1965	Mexico	1971	Mexico	1981	Honduras	1996	Mexico
1967	Guatemala	1973	Haiti	1991	United States		

CLUB COMPETITION

Toyota Cup

Also known as the World Club Championship. Contested annually in December between the winners of the European Cup and South America's Copa Libertadores. Four European Cup winners refused to participate in the championship match in the 1970s and were replaced each time by the European Cup runner-up: Panathinaikos (Greece) for Ajax Amsterdam (Holland) in 1971; Juventus (Italy) for Ajax in 1973; Atlético Madrid (Spain) for Bayern Munich (West Germany) in 1974; and Malmo (Sweden) for Nottingham Forest (England) in 1979. Another European Cup winner, Marseille of France, was prohibited by the Union of European Football Associations (UEFA) from playing for the 1993 Toyota Cup because of its involvement in the match-rigging scandal.

Best-of-three game format from 1960-68, then a two-game/total goals format from 1969-79. Toyota became Cup sponsor in 1980, changed the format to a one-game championship and moved it to Toyko.

Multiple winners: AC Milan, Nacional and Penarol (3); Ajax Amsterdam, Independiente, Inter-Milan, Juventus, Santos and Sao Paulo (2).

Year		Year		Year	
1960	Real Madrid (Spain)	1973	Independiente (Argentina)	1986	River Plate (Argentina)
1961	Peñarol (Uruguay)	1974	Atlético Madrid (Spain)	1987	FC Porto (Portugal)
1962	Santos (Brazil)	1975	Not held	1988	Nacional (Uruguay)
1963	Santos (Brazil)	1976	Bayern Munich(W. Germany)	1989	AC Milan (Italy)
1964	Inter-Milan (Italy)	1977	Boca Juniors (Argentina)	1990	AC Milan (Italy)
1965	Inter-Milan (Italy)	1978	Not held	1991	Red Star (Yugoslavia)
1966	Penarol (Uruguay)	1979	Olimpia (Paraguay)	1992	Sao Paulo (Brazil)
1967	Racing Club (Argentina)	1980	Nacional (Uruguay)	1993	Sao Paulo (Brazil)
1968	Estudiantes (Argentina)	1981	Flamengo (Brazil)	1994	Velez Sarsfield (Argentina)
1969	AC Milan (Italy)	1982	Peñarol (Uruguay)	1995	Ajax Amsterdam (Holland)
1970	Feyenoord (Holland)	1983	Gremio (Brazil)	1996	Juventus (Italy)
1971	Nacional (Uruguay)	1984	Independiente (Argentina)		
1972	Ajax Amsterdam (Holland)	1985	Juventus (Italy)		

European Cup

Contested annually since the 1955-56 season by the league champions of the member countries of the Union of European Football Associations (UEFA).

Multiple winners: Real Madrid (6); AC Milan (5); Ajax Amsterdam and Liverpool (4); Bayern Munich (3); Benfica, Inter-Milan, Juventus and Nottingham Forest (2).

Year		Year		Year	
1956	Real Madrid (Spain)	1970	Feyenoord (Holland)	1984	Liverpool (England)
1957	Real Madrid (Spain)	1971	Ajax Amsterdam (Holland)	1985	Juventus (Italy)
1958	Real Madrid (Spain)	1972	Ajax Amsterdam (Holland)	1986	Steaua Bucharest (Romania)
1959	Real Madrid (Spain)	1973	Ajax Amsterdam (Holland)	1987	FC Porto (Portugal)
1960	Real Madrid (Spain)	1974	Bayern Munich (W. Germany)	1988	PSV Eindhoven (Holland)
1961	Benfica (Portugal)	1975	Bayern Munich (W. Germany)	1989	AC Milan (Italy)
1962	Benfica (Portugal)	1976	Bayern Munich (W. Germany)	1990	AC Milan (Italy)
1963	AC Milan (Italy)	1977	Liverpool (England)	1991	Red Star Belgrade (Yugo.)
1964	Inter-Milan (Italy)	1978	Liverpool (England)	1992	Barcelona (Spain)
1965	Inter-Milan (Italy)	1979	Nottingham Forest (England)	1993	Marseille (France)*
1966	Real Madrid (Spain)	1980	Nottingham Forest (England)	1994	AC Milan (Italy)
1967	Glasgow Celtic (Scotland)	1981	Liverpool (England)	1995	Ajax Amsterdam (Holland)
1968	Manchester United (England)	1982	Aston Villa (England)	1996	Juventus (Italy)
1969	AC Milan (Italy)	1983	SV Hamburg (W. Germany)	1997	Borussia Dortmund (Germany)

*title vacated

European Cup Winner's Cup

Contested annually since the 1960-61 season by the cup winners of the member countries of the Union of European Football Associations (UEFA).

Multiple winners: Barcelona (4); AC Milan, RSC Anderlecht and Dinamo Kiev (2).

Year		Year		Year	
1961	Fiorentina (Italy)	1974	FC Magdeburg (E. Germany)	1987	Ajax Amsterdam (Holland)
1962	Atletico Madrid (Spain)	1975	Dinamo Kiev (USSR)	1988	Mechelen (Belgium)
1963	Tottenham Hotspur (England)	1976	RSC Anderlecht (Belgium)	1989	Barcelona (Spain)
1964	Sporting Lisbon (Portugal)	1977	SV Hamburg (W. Germany)	1990	Sampdoria (Italy)
1965	West Ham United (England)	1978	RSC Anderlecht (Belgium)	1991	Manchester United (England)
1966	Borussia Dortmund (W.Germany)	1979	Barcelona (Spain)	1992	Werder Bremen (Germany)
1967	Bayern Munich (W. Germany)	1980	Valencia (Spain)	1993	Parma (Italy)
1968	AC Milan (Italy)	1981	Dinamo Tbilisi (USSR)	1994	Arsenal (England)
1969	Slovan Bratislava (Czech.)	1982	Barcelona (Spain)	1995	Real Zaragoza (Spain)
1970	Manchester City (England)	1983	Aberdeen (Scotland)	1996	Paris St. Germain (France)
1971	Chelsea (England)	1984	Juventus (Italy)	1997	Barcelona (Spain)
1972	Glasgow Rangers (Scotland)	1985	Everton (England)		
1973	AC Milan (Italy)	1986	Dinamo Kiev (USSR)		

UEFA Cup

Contested annually since the 1957-58 season by teams other than league champions and cup winners of the Union of European Football Associations (UEFA). Teams selected by UEFA based on each country's previous performance in the tournament. Teams from England were banned from UEFA Cup play from 1985-90 for the criminal behavior of their supporters.

Multiple winners: Barcelona and Juventus (3); Borussia Mönchengladbach, IFK Göteborg, Leeds United, Liverpool, Real Madrid, Tottenham Hotspur and Valencia (2).

Year		Year		Year	
1958	Barcelona (Spain)	1973	Liverpool (England)	1986	Real Madrid (Spain)
1959	Not held	1974	Feyenoord (Holland)	1987	IFK Göteborg (Sweden)
1960	Barcelona (Spain)	1975	Borussia Mönchengladbach (W. Germany)	1988	Bayer Leverkusen (W. Germany)
1961	AS Roma (Italy)			1989	Napoli (Italy)
1962	Valencia (Spain)	1976	Liverpool (England)	1990	Juventus (Italy)
1963	Valencia (Spain)	1977	Juventus (Italy)	1991	Inter-Milan (Italy)
1964	Real Zaragoza (Spain)	1978	PSV Eindhoven (Holland)	1992	Ajax Amsterdam (Holland)
1965	Ferencvaros (Hungary)	1979	Borussia Mönchengladbach (W. Germany)	1993	Juventus (Italy)
1966	Barcelona (Spain)			1994	Inter-Milan (Italy)
1967	Dinamo Zagreb (Yugoslavia)	1980	Eintracht Frankfurt (W. Germany)	1995	Parma (Italy)
1968	Leeds United (England)	1981	Ipswich Town (England)	1996	Bayern Munich (Germany)
1969	Newcastle United (England)	1982	IFK Göteborg (Sweden)	1997	Schalke 04 (Germany)
1970	Arsenal (England)	1983	RSC Anderlecht (Belgium)		
1971	Leeds United (England)	1984	Tottenham Hotspur (England)		
1972	Tottenham Hotspur (England)	1985	Real Madrid (Spain)		

Copa Libertadores

Contested annually since the 1955-56 season by the league champions of South America's football union.

Multiple winners: Independiente (7); Peñarol (5); Estudiantes and Nacional-Uruguay (3); Boca Juniors, Cruzeiro, Gremio, Olimpia, River Plate, Santos and São Paulo (2).

Year		Year		Year	
1960	Peñarol (Uruguay)	1973	Independiente (Argentina)	1986	River Plate (Argentina)
1961	Peñarol (Uruguay)	1974	Independiente (Argentina)	1987	Peñarol (Uruguay)
1962	Santos (Brazil)	1975	Independiente (Argentina)	1988	Nacional (Uruguay)
1963	Santos (Brazil)	1976	Cruzeiro (Brazil)	1989	Nacional Medellin (Colombia)
1964	Independiente (Argentina)	1977	Boca Juniors (Argentina)		
1965	Independiente (Argentina)	1978	Boca Juniors (Argentina)	1990	Olimpia (Paraguay)
1966	Peñarol (Uruguay)	1979	Olimpia (Paraguay)	1991	Colo Colo (Chile)
1967	Racing Club (Argentina)			1992	São Paulo (Brazil)
1968	Estudiantes de la Plata (Argentina)	1980	Nacional (Uruguay)	1993	São Paulo (Brazil)
1969	Estudiantes de la Plata (Argentina)	1981	Flamengo (Brazil)	1994	Velez Sarsfield (Argentina)
		1982	Peñarol (Uruguay)	1995	Gremio (Brazil)
1970	Estudiantes de la Plata (Argentina)	1983	Gremio (Brazil)	1996	River Plate (Argentina)
1971	Nacional (Uruguay)	1984	Independiente (Argentina)	1997	Cruzeiro (Brazil)
1972	Independiente (Argentina)	1985	Argentinos Jrs. (Argentina)		

Annual Awards

World Player of the Year

Presented by FIFA, the European Sports Magazine Association (ESM) and Adidas, the sports equipment manufacturer, since 1991. Winners are selected by national team coaches from around the world.

Year		Nat'l Team	Year		Nat'l Team
1991	Lothar Matthäus, Inter-Milan	Germany	1994	Romario, Barcelona	Brazil
1992	Marco Van Basten, AC Milan	Holland	1995	George Weah, AC Milan	Liberia
1993	Roberto Baggio, Juventus	Italy	1996	Ronaldo, Barcelona	Brazil

European Player of the Year

Officially, the "Ballon d'Or" and presented by *France Football* magazine since 1956. Candidates are limited to European players in European leagues and winners are selected by a panel of 49 European soccer journalists.

Multiple winners: Johan Cruyff, Michel Platini and Marco Van Basten (3); Franz Beckenbauer, Alfredo di Stéfano, Kevin Keegan and Karl-Heinz Rummenigge (2).

Year		Nat'l Team	Year		Nat'l Team
1956	Stanley Matthews, Blackpool	England	1977	Allan Simonsen, B. Mönchengladbach	Denmark
1957	Alfredo di Stéfano, Real Madrid	Arg./Spain	1978	Kevin Keegan, SV Hamburg	England
1958	Raymond Kopa, Real Madrid	France	1979	Kevin Keegan, SV Hamburg	England
1959	Alfredo di Stéfano, Real Madrid	Arg./Spain	1980	K.H. Rummenigge, Bayern Munich	W. Ger.
1960	Luis Suarez, Barcelona	Spain	1981	K.H. Rummenigge, Bayern Munich	W. Ger.
1961	Enrique Sivori, Juventus	Arg./Italy	1982	Paolo Rossi, Juventus	Italy
1962	Josef Masopust, Dukla Prague	Czech.	1983	Michel Platini, Juventus	France
1963	Lev Yashin, Dinamo Moscow	Soviet Union	1984	Michel Platini, Juventus	France
1964	Denis Law, Manchester United	Scotland	1985	Michel Platini, Juventus	France
1965	Eusébio, Benfica	Portugal	1986	Igor Belanov, Dinamo Kiev	Soviet Union
1966	Bobby Charlton, Manchester United	England	1987	Ruud Gullit, AC Milan	Holland
1967	Florian Albert, Ferencvaros	Hungary	1988	Marco Van Basten, AC Milan	Holland
1968	George Best, Manchester United	No. Ireland	1989	Marco Van Basten, AC Milan	Holland
1969	Gianni Rivera, AC Milan	Italy	1990	Lothar Matthäus, Inter-Milan	W. Ger.
1970	Gerd Müller, Bayern Munich	W. Ger.	1991	Jean-Pierre Papin, Marseille	France
1971	Johan Cruyff, Ajax Amsterdam	Holland	1992	Marco Van Basten, AC Milan	Holland
1972	Franz Beckenbauer, Bayern Munich	W. Ger.	1993	Roberto Baggio, Juventus	Italy
1973	Johan Cruyff, Barcelona	Holland	1994	Hristo Stoitchkov, Barcelona	Bulgaria
1974	Johan Cruyff, Barcelona	Holland	1995	George Weah, AC Milan	Liberia
1975	Oleg Blokhin, Dinamo Kiev	Soviet Union	1996	Matthias Sammer, Bor. Dortmund	Germany
1976	Franz Beckenbauer, Bayern Munich	W. Ger.			

South American Player of the Year

Presented by El Pais of Uruguay since 1971. Candidates are limited to South American players in South American leagues and winners are selected by a panel of 80 Latin American sports editors.

Multiple winners: Elias Figueroa and Zico (3); Enzo Francescoli, Diego Maradona and Carlos Valderrama (2).

Year		Nat'l Team	Year		Nat'l Team
1971	Tostao, Cruzeiro	Brazil	1978	Mario Kempes, Valencia	Argentina
1972	Teofilo Cubillas, Alianza Lima	Peru	1979	Diego Maradona, Argentinos Juniors	Argentina
1973	Pelé, Santos	Brazil	1980	Diego Maradona, Boca Juniors	Argentina
1974	Elias Figueroa, Internacional	Chile	1981	Zico, Flamengo	Brazil
1975	Elias Figueroa, Internacional	Chile	1982	Zico, Flamengo	Brazil
1976	Elias Figueroa, Internacional	Chile	1983	Socrates, Corinthians	Brazil
1977	Zico, Flamengo	Brazil	1984	Enzo Francescoli, River Plate	Uruguay

Year		Nat'l Team	Year		Nat'l Team
1985	Julio Cesar Romero, Fluminense	Paraguay	1991	Oscar Ruggeri, Velez Sarsfield	Argentina
1986	Antonio Alzamendi, River Plate	Uruguay	1992	Rai, Sao Paulo	Brazil
1987	Carlos Valderrama, Deportivo Cali	Colombia	1993	Carlos Valderrama, Atl. Junior	Colombia
1988	Ruben Paz, Racing Buenos Aires	Uruguay	1994	Cafu, Sao Paulo	Brazil
1989	Bebeto, Vasco da Gama	Brazil	1995	Enzo Francescoli, River Plate	Uruguay
1990	Raul Amarilla, Olimpia	Paraguay	1996	Jose Luis Chilavert, Velez Sarsfield	Paraguay

African Player of the Year

Officially, the African "Ballon d'Or" and presented by *France Football* magazine since 1970. All African players are eligible for the award and winners are selected by a panel of 52 African soccer journalists.

Multiple winners: Abedi Pelé and George Weah (3); Roger Milla and Thomas N'Kono (2).

Year		Year		Year	
1970	Salif Keita, Mali	1979	Thomas N'Kono, Cameroon	1988	Kalusha Bwalya, Zambia
1971	Ibrahim Sunday, Ghana	1980	Jean Manga Onguene, Cameroon	1989	George Weah, Liberia
1972	Cherif Souleymane, Guinea	1981	Lakhdar Belloumi, Algeria	1990	Roger Milla, Cameroon
1973	Tshimimu Bwanga, Zaire	1982	Thomas N'Kono, Cameroon	1991	Abedi Pelé, Ghana
1974	Paul Moukila, Congo	1983	Mahmoud Al-Khatib, Egypt	1992	Abedi Pelé, Ghana
1975	Ahmed Faras, Morocco	1984	Theophile Abega, Cameroon	1993	Abedi Pelé, Ghana
1976	Roger Milla, Cameroon	1985	Mohamed Timoumi, Morocco	1994	George Weah, Liberia
1977	Dhiab Tarak, Tunisia	1986	Badou Zaki, Morocco	1995	George Weah, Liberia
1978	Abdul Razak, Ghana	1987	Rabah Madjer, Algeria	1996	George Weah, Liberia

U.S. Player of the Year

Presented by Honda and the Spanish-speaking radio show "Futbol de Primera" since 1991. Candidates are limited to American players who have played at least five games in the APSL or with the U.S. National Team and winners are selected by a panel of U.S. soccer journalists.

Multiple winner: Eric Wynalda (2).

Year		Year		Year		Year	
1991	Hugo Perez	1993	Thomas Dooley	1995	Alexi Lalas	1996	Eric Wynalda
1992	Eric Wynalda	1994	Marcelo Balboa				

U.S. PRO LEAGUES

OUTDOOR

National Professional Soccer League (1967)

Not sanctioned by FIFA, the international soccer federation. The NPSL recruited individual players to fill the rosters of its 10 teams. The league lasted only one season.

	Playoff Final			Regular Season			
Year	Winner	Score(s)	Loser	Leading Scorer	G	A	Pts
1967	Oakland Clippers	0-1, 4-1	Baltimore Bays	Yanko Daucik, Toronto	20	8	48

United Soccer Association (1967)

Sanctioned by FIFA. Originally called the North American Soccer League, it became the USA to avoid being confused with the National Professional Soccer League (see above). Instead of recruiting individual players, the USA imported 12 entire teams from Europe to represent its 12 franchises. It, too, only lasted a season. The league champion Los Angeles Wolves were actually Wolverhampton of England and the runner-up Washington Whips were Aberdeen of Scotland.

	Playoff Final			Regular Season			
Year	Winner	Score	Loser	Leading Scorer	G	A	Pts
1967	Los Angeles Wolves	6-5 (OT)	Washington Whips	Roberto Boninsegna, Chicago	10	1	21

North American Soccer League (1968-84)

The NPSL and USA merged to form the NASL in 1968 and the new league lasted until 1985. The NASL championship was known as the Soccer Bowl from 1975-84. One game decided the NASL title every year but five. There were no playoffs in 1969; a two-game/aggregate goals format was used in 1968 and '70; and a best-of-three games format was used in 1971 and '84; (*) indicates overtime and (†) indicates game decided by shootout.

Multiple winners: NY Cosmos (5); Chicago (2).

	Playoff Final			Regular Season			
Year	Winner	Score(s)	Loser	Leading Scorer	G	A	Pts
1968	Atlanta Chiefs	0-0,3-0	San Diego Toros	John Kowalik, Chicago	30	9	69
1969	Kansas City Spurs	No game	Atlanta Chiefs	Kaiser Motaung, Atlanta	16	4	36
1970	Rochester Lancers	3-0,1-3	Washington Darts	Kirk Apostolidis, Dallas	16	3	35
1971	Dallas Tornado	1-2*,4-1,2-0	Atlanta Chiefs	Carlos Metidieri, Rochester	19	8	46
1972	New York Cosmos	2-1	St. Louis Stars	Randy Horton, New York	9	4	22
1973	Philadelphia Atoms	2-0	Dallas Tornado	Kyle Rote, Jr. Dallas	10	10	30
1974	Los Angeles Aztecs	3-3†	Miami Toros	Paul Child, San Jose	15	6	36
1975	Tampa Bay Rowdies	2-0	Portland Timbers	Steve David, Miami	23	6	52
1976	Toronto Metros	3-0	Minnesota Kicks	Giorgio Chinaglia, New York	19	11	49
1977	New York Cosmos	2-1	Seattle Sounders	Steve David, Los Angeles	26	6	58

Note: In 1969, Kansas City won the NASL regular season championship with 110 points to 109 for Atlanta. There were no playoffs.

North American Soccer League (Cont.)

	Playoff Final			Regular Season			
Year	Winner	Score(s)	Loser	Leading Scorer	G	A	Pts
1978	New York Cosmos	3-1	Tampa Bay Rowdies	Giorgio Chinaglia, New York	34	11	79
1979	Vancouver Whitecaps	2-1	Tampa Bay Rowdies	Oscar Fabbiani, Tampa Bay	25	8	58
1980	New York Cosmos	3-0	Ft. Laud. Strikers	Giorgio Chinaglia, New York	32	13	77
1981	Chicago Sting	0-0†	New York Cosmos	Giorgio Chinaglia, New York	29	16	74
1982	New York Cosmos	1-0	Seattle Sounders	Giorgio Chinaglia, New York	20	15	55
1983	Tulsa Roughnecks	2-0	Toronto Blizzard	Roberto Cabanas, New York	25	16	66
1984	Chicago Sting	2-1,3-2	Toronto Blizzard	Steve Zungul, Golden Bay	20	10	50

Regular Season MVP

Regular season Most Valuable Player as designated by the NASL.

Multiple winner: Carlos Metidieri (2).

Year		Year		Year	
1967	Rueben Navarro, Phila (NPSL)	1973	Warren Archibald, Miami	1979	Johan Cruyff, Los Angeles
1968	John Kowalik, Chicago	1974	Peter Silvester, Baltimore	1980	Roger Davies, Seattle
1969	Cirilio Fernandez, KC	1975	Steve David, Miami	1981	Giorgio Chinaglia, New York
1970	Carlos Metidieri, Rochester	1976	Pelé, New York	1982	Peter Ward, Seattle
1971	Carlos Metidieri, Rochester	1977	Franz Beckenbauer, New York	1983	Roberto Cabanas, New York
1972	Randy Horton, New York	1978	Mike Flanagan, New England	1984	Steve Zungul, Golden Bay

A-League (American Professional Soccer League)

The American Professional Soccer League was formed in 1990 with the merger of the Western Soccer League and the New American Soccer League. The APSL was officially sanctioned as an outdoor pro league in 1992 and changed its name to the A-League in 1995.

Multiple winners: Colorado and Seattle (2).

Year		Year		Year		Year	
1990	Maryland Bays	1992	Colorado Foxes	1994	Montreal Impact	1996	Seattle Sounders
1991	SF Bay Blackhawks	1993	Colorado Foxes	1995	Seattle Sounders	1997	Milwaukee Rampage

INDOOR
Major Soccer League (1978-92)

Originally the Major Indoor Soccer League from 1978-79 season through 1989-90. The MISL championship was decided by one game in 1980 and 1981; a best-of-three games series in 1979, best-of-five games in 1982 and 1983; and best-of-seven games since 1984. The MSL folded after the 1991-92 season.

Multiple winners: San Diego (8); New York (4).

	Playoff Final			Regular Season			
Year	Winner	Series	Loser	Leading Scorer	G	A	Pts
1979	New York Arrows	2-0 (WW)	Philadelphia	Fred Grgurev, Philadelphia	46	28	74
1980	New York Arrows	7-4 (1 game)	Houston	Steve Zungul, New York	90	46	136
1981	New York Arrows	6-5 (1 game)	St. Louis	Steve Zungul, New York	108	44	152
1982	New York Arrows	3-2 (LWWLW)	St. Louis	Steve Zungul, New York	103	60	163
1983	San Diego Sockers	3-2 (WWLLW)	Baltimore	Steve Zungul, NY/Golden Bay	75	47	122
1984	Baltimore Blast	4-1 (LWWWW)	St. Louis	Stan Stamenkovic, Baltimore	34	63	97
1985	San Diego Sockers	4-1 (WWLWW)	Baltimore	Steve Zungul, San Diego	68	68	136
1986	San Diego Sockers	4-3 (WLLLWWW)	Minnesota	Steve Zungul, Tacoma	55	60	115
1987	Dallas Sidekicks	4-3 (LLWWLWW)	Tacoma	Tatu, Dallas	73	38	111
1988	San Diego Sockers	4-0	Cleveland	Eric Rasmussen, Wichita	55	57	112
1989	San Diego Sockers	4-3 (LWWWLLW)	Baltimore	Preki, Tacoma	51	53	104
1990	San Diego Sockers	4-2 (LWWWLW)	Baltimore	Tatu, Dallas	64	49	113
1991	San Diego Sockers	4-2 (WLWLWW)	Cleveland	Tatu, Dallas	78	66	144
1992	San Diego Sockers	4-2 (WWWLLW)	Dallas	Zoran Karic, Cleveland	39	63	102

Playoff MVPs

MSL playoff Most Valuable Players, selected by a panel of soccer media covering the playoffs.

Multiple winners: Zungul (4); Quinn (2).

Year		Year	
1979	Shep Messing, NY	1986	Brian Quinn, SC
1980	Steve Zungul, NY	1987	Tatu, Dallas
1981	Steve Zungul, NY	1988	Hugo Perez, SD
1982	Steve Zungul, NY	1989	Victor Nogueira, SD
1983	Juli Veee, SD	1990	Brian Quinn, SD
1984	Scott Manning, Bal.	1991	Ben Collins, SD
1985	Steve Zungul, SD	1992	Thompson Usiyan, SD

Regular Season MVPs

MSL regular season Most Valuable Players, selected by a panel of soccer media from every city in the league.

Multiple winner: Zungul (6); Nogueira and Tatu (2).

Year		Year	
1979	Steve Zungul, NY	1986	Steve Zungul, SD/Tac.
1980	Steve Zungul, NY	1987	Tatu, Dallas
1981	Steve Zungul, NY	1988	Erik Rasmussen, Wich.
1982	Steve Zungul, NY & Stan Terlecki, Pit.	1989	Preki, Tacoma
		1990	Tatu, Dallas
1983	Alan Mayer, SD	1991	Victor Nogueira, SD
1984	Stan Stamenkovic, Bal.	1992	Victor Nogueira, SD
1985	Steve Zungul, SD		

NASL Indoor Champions (1980-84)

The North American Soccer League started an indoor league in the fall of 1979. The indoor NASL, which featured many of the same teams and players who played in the outdoor NASL, crowned champions from 1980-82 before suspending play. It was revived for the 1983-84 indoor season but folded for good in 1984.

Multiple winners: San Diego (2).

Year		Year		Year		Year	
1980	Memphis Rogues	1982	San Diego Sockers	1983	Play suspended	1984	San Diego Sockers
1981	Edmonton Drillers						

National Professional Soccer League

The winter indoor NPSL began as the American Indoor Soccer Association in 1984-85, then changed its name in 1989-90.

Multiple winner: Canton (5); Cleveland and Kansas City (2).

Year		Year		Year		Year	
1985	Canton (OH) Invaders	1989	Canton Invaders	1993	Kansas City Attack	1997	Kansas City Attack
1986	Canton Invaders	1990	Canton Invaders	1994	Cleveland Crunch		
1987	Louisville Thunder	1991	Chicago Power	1995	St. Louis Ambush		
1988	Canton Invaders	1992	Detroit Rockers	1996	Cleveland Crunch		

Continental Indoor Soccer League

The summer indoor CISL played its first season in 1993.

Multiple winners: Monterrey (2).

Year		Year		Year		Year	
1993	Dallas Sidekicks	1994	Las Vegas Dustdevils	1995	Monterrey La Raza	1996	Monterrey La Raza

U.S. COLLEGES

NCAA Men's Division I Champions

NCAA Division I champions since the first title was contested in 1959. The championship has been shared three times—in 1967, 1968 and 1989. There was a playoff for third place from 1974-81.

Multiple winners: Saint Louis (10); San Francisco and Virginia (5); Indiana (3); Clemson, Howard, and Michigan St. (2).

Year	Winner	Head Coach	Score	Runner-up	Host/Site	Semifinalists
1959	Saint Louis	Bob Guelker	5-2	Bridgeport	UConn	West Chester, CCNY
1960	Saint Louis	Bob Guelker	3-2	Maryland	Brooklyn	West Chester, UConn
1961	West Chester	Mel Lorback	2-0	Saint Louis	Saint Louis	Bridgeport, Rutgers
1962	Saint Louis	Bob Guelker	4-3	Maryland	Saint Louis	Mich. St., Springfield
1963	Saint Louis	Bob Guelker	3-0	Navy	Rutgers	Army, Maryland
1964	Navy	F.H. Warner	1-0	Michigan St.	Brown	Army, Saint Louis
1965	Saint Louis	Bob Guelker	1-0	Michigan St.	Saint Louis	Army, Navy
1966	San Francisco	Steve Negoesco	5-2	LIU-Brooklyn	California	Army, Mich. St.
1967-a	Michigan St. & Saint Louis	Gene Kenney, Harry Keough	0-0	–	Saint Louis	LIU-Bklyn, Navy
1968-b	Michigan St. & Maryland	Gene Kenney, Doyle Royal	2-2 (2 OT)	–	Ga. Tech	Brown, San Jose St.
1969	Saint Louis	Harry Keough	4-0	San Francisco	San Jose St.	Harvard, Maryland
1970	Saint Louis	Harry Keough	1-0	UCLA	SIU-Ed'sville	Hartwick, Howard
1971-c	Howard	Lincoln Phillips	3-2	Saint Louis	Miami	Harvard, San Fran.
1972	Saint Louis	Harry Keough	4-2	UCLA	Miami	Cornell, Howard
1973	Saint Louis	Harry Keough	2-1 (OT)	UCLA	Miami	Brown, Clemson

Year	Winner	Head Coach	Score	Runner-up	Host/Site	Third Place
1974	Howard	Lincoln Phillips	2-1 (4OT)	Saint Louis	Saint Louis	Hartwick 3, UCLA 1
1975	San Francisco	Steve Negoesco	4-0	SIU-Ed'sville	SIU-Ed'sville	Brown 2, Howard 0
1976	San Francisco	Steve Negoesco	1-0	Indiana	Penn	Hartwick 4, Clemson 3
1977	Hartwick	Jim Lennox	2-1	San Francisco	California	SIU-Ed'sville 3, Brown 2
1978-d	San Francisco	Steve Negoesco	4-3 (OT)	Indiana	Tampa	Clemson 6, Phi. Textile 2
1979	SIU-Ed'sville	Bob Guelker	3-2	Clemson	Tampa	Penn St. 2, Columbia 1
1980	San Francisco	Steve Negoesco	4-3 (OT)	Indiana	Tampa	Ala. A&M 2, Hartwick 0
1981	Connecticut	Joe Morrone	2-1 (OT)	Alabama A&M	Stanford	East. Ill. 4, Phi. Textile 2

Year	Winner	Head Coach	Score	Runner-up	Host/Site	Semifinalists
1982	Indiana	Jerry Yeagley	2-1 (8 OT)	Duke	Ft. Lauderdale	UConn, SIU-Ed'sville
1983	Indiana	Jerry Yeagley	1-0 (2 OT)	Columbia	Ft. Lauderdale	UConn, Virginia
1984	Clemson	I.M. Ibrahim	2-1	Indiana	Seattle	Hartwick, UCLA
1985	UCLA	Sigi Schmid	1-0 (8 OT)	American	Seattle	Evansville, Hartwick
1986	Duke	John Rennie	1-0	Akron	Tacoma	Fresno St., Harvard
1987	Clemson	I.M. Ibrahim	2-0	San Diego St.	Clemson	Harvard, N. Carolina
1988	Indiana	Jerry Yeagley	1-0	Howard	Indiana	Portland, S. Carolina
1989-e	Santa Clara & Virginia	Steve Sampson, Bruce Arena	1-1 (2 OT)	–	Rutgers	Indiana, Rutgers
1990-f	UCLA	Sigi Schmid	0-0 (PKs)	Rutgers	South Fla.	Evansville, N.C. State
1991-g	Virginia	Bruce Arena	0-0 (PKs)	Santa Clara	Tampa	Indiana, Saint Louis
1992	Virginia	Bruce Arena	2-0	San Diego	Davidson	Davidson, Duke

NCAA Men's Division I Champions (Cont.)

Year	Winner	Head Coach	Score	Runner-up	Host/Site	Semifinalists
1993	Virginia	Bruce Arena	2-0	South Carolina	Davidson	CS-Fullerton, Princeton
1994	Virginia	Bruce Arena	1-0	Indiana	Davidson	Rutgers, UCLA
1995	Wisconsin	Jim Launder	2-0	Duke	Richmond	Portland, Virginia
1996	St. John's	Dave Masur	4-1	Fla. International	Richmond	Creighton, NC-Charlotte

a–game declared a draw due to inclement weather after regulation time; b–game declared a draw after two overtimes; c–Howard vacated title for using ineligible player; d–San Francisco vacated title for using ineligible player; e–game declared a draw due to inclement weather after two overtimes. f–UCLA wins on penalty kicks (4-3) after four overtimes; g–Virginia wins on penalty kicks (3-1) after four overtimes.

Women's NCAA Division I Champions

NCAA Division I women's champions since the first tournament was contested in 1982.

Multiple winner: North Carolina (13).

Year	Winner	Score	Runner-up	Year	Winner	Score	Runner-up
1982	North Carolina	2-0	Central Florida	1990	North Carolina	6-0	Connecticut
1983	North Carolina	4-0	George Mason	1991	North Carolina	3-1	Wisconsin
1984	North Carolina	2-0	Connecticut	1992	North Carolina	9-1	Duke
1985	George Mason	2-0	North Carolina	1993	North Carolina	6-0	George Mason
1986	North Carolina	2-0	Colorado College	1994	North Carolina	5-0	Notre Dame
1987	North Carolina	1-0	Massachusetts	1995	Notre Dame	1-0 (3OT)	Portland
1988	North Carolina	4-1	N.C. State	1996	North Carolina	1-0 (2OT)	Notre Dame
1989	North Carolina	2-0	Colorado College				

Annual Awards
MEN
Hermann Trophy

College Player of the Year. Voted on by Division I college coaches and selected sportswriters and first presented in 1967 in the name of Robert Hermann, one of the founders of the North American Soccer League.

Multiple winners: Mike Fisher, Mike Seerey, Ken Snow and Al Trost (2).

Year		Year		Year	
1967	Dov Markus, LIU	1977	Billy Gazonas, Hartwick	1987	Bruce Murray, Clemson
1968	Manuel Hernandez, San Jose St.	1978	Angelo DiBernardo, Indiana	1988	Ken Snow, Indiana
1969	Al Trost, Saint Louis	1979	Jim Stamatis, Penn St.	1989	Tony Meola, Virginia
1970	Al Trost, Saint Louis	1980	Joe Morrone, Jr. UConn	1990	Ken Snow, Indiana
1971	Mike Seerey, Saint Louis	1981	Armando Betancourt, Indiana	1991	Alexi Lalas, Rutgers
1972	Mike Seerey, Saint Louis	1982	Joe Ulrich, Duke	1992	Brad Friedel, UCLA
1973	Dan Counce, Saint Louis	1983	Mike Jeffries, Duke	1993	Claudio Reyna, Virginia
1974	Farrukh Quraishi, Oneonta St.	1984	Amr Aly, Columbia	1994	Brian Maisonneuve, Indiana
1975	Steve Ralbovsky, Brown	1985	Tom Kain, Duke	1995	Mike Fisher, Virginia
1976	Glenn Myernick, Hartwick	1986	John Kerr, Duke	1996	Mike Fisher, Virginia

Missouri Athletic Club Award

College Player of the Year. Voted on by men's team coaches around the country from Division I to junior college level and first presented in 1986 by the Missouri Athletic Club of St. Louis.

Multiple winner: Claudio Reyna and Ken Snow (2).

Year		Year		Year	
1986	John Kerr, Duke	1990	Ken Snow, Indiana	1994	Todd Yeagley, Indiana
1987	John Harkes, Virginia	1991	Alexi Lalas, Rutgers	1995	Matt McKeon, St. Louis
1988	Ken Snow, Indiana	1992	Claudio Reyna, Virginia	1996	Mike Fisher, Virginia
1989	Tony Meola, Virginia	1993	Claudio Reyna, Virginia		

WOMEN
Hermann Trophy

Women's College Player of the year. Voted on by Division I college coaches and selected sportswriters and first presented in 1988 in the name of Robert Hermann, one of the founders of the North American Soccer League.

Multiple winner: Mia Hamm (2).

Year		Year		Year	
1988	Michelle Akers, Central Fla.	1991	Kristine Lilly, N. Carolina	1994	Tisha Venturini, N. Carolina
1989	Shannon Higgins, N. Carolina	1992	Mia Hamm, N. Carolina	1995	Shannon McMillan, Portland
1990	April Kater, Massachusetts	1993	Mia Hamm, N. Carolina	1996	Cindy Daws, Notre Dame

Missouri Athletic Club Award

Women's College Player of the Year. Voted on by women's team coaches around the country from Division I to junior college level and first presented in 1991 by the Missouri Athletic Club of St. Louis.

Multiple winner: Mia Hamm (2).

Year		Year		Year	
1991	Kristine Lilly, N. Carolina	1993	Mia Hamm, N. Carolina	1995	Shannon McMillan, Portland
1992	Mia Hamm, N. Carolina	1994	Tisha Venturini, N. Carolina	1996	Cindy Daws, Notre Dame

Bowling

Jeremy Sonnenfeld poses shortly after bowling the first sanctioned 900 series in history. Sonnenfeld, a University of Nebraska sophomore, bowled three perfect games on February 2 in Lincoln. ──────────

Wide World Photos

Perfect Games

Collegian Jeremy Sonnenfeld grabbed the bowling headlines with the first sanctioned 900 series in history.

by
Mike Durbin

On February 2, 1997, University of Nebraska sophomore Jeremy Sonnenfeld had as good a day as you can have in a bowling alley. The 20–year old Sonnenfeld bowled three consecutive 300 games over six lanes in the Junior Husker Tournament at Sun Valley Lanes in Lincoln, Neb. Sonnenfeld had rolled four previous 300 games and had a previous series high of 826. The previous three game mark was held by three different bowlers at 899. Two other bowlers had ripped off three 300 games in a row but those games did not count as 900 series because they were rolled in separate squads during tournament play.

So, on February 8 in a special ceremony in Huntsville, Alabama, American Bowling Congress president Walt Roberson presented the first-ever 900 series award to Sonnenfeld, a native of Sioux Falls, South Dakota. Sonnen-

feld, a collegiate all-American bowler, has set a new standard for everyone. Unlike other college athletes, there was no controversy over whether or not Sonnenfeld would leave school early and turn pro.

The Winter Pro Bowlers Tour started with a minor oddity and a major inconvenience. The first telecast, the Brunswick World Tournament of Champions featured five lefthanders (the oddity) and was delayed for over 30 minutes by a supply truck that damaged power lines at the bowling center (the inconvenience). John Gant proved to be the most patient, emerging the winner in a steady performance topping Parker Bohn 238 to 224 and Mike Aulby in the title match, 208-187.

A major story on the national tour continues to be the race for PBA Player of the Year. Pete Weber, in a quest to become #1, finished first twice, compiled an average of 222.65, and totaled $158,184 in winnings.

Mike Durbin is an analyst for ESPN's bowling coverage and a bowler on the Sr. PBA Tour.

Walter Ray Williams Jr. reached a big milestone in 1997 when he went over $2 million in career earnings.

Impossible to top? Walter Ray Williams Jr. and Parker Bohn don't seem to think so. Walter Ray has accomplished the almost unbelievable, winning three tournaments, averaging just under Weber at 221.90, finishing with $162,914 and becoming the first player to win $2 million in career earnings. Parker Bohn leads in money with $166,320, is third in average with 220.38 and has also won two titles. As of this writing, with seven tournaments to go, Player of the the Year could be any of the three.

The last telecast on the Winter Tour PBT was an emotion-filled ending yet also a hopeful beginning. In a storybook finale, Walter Ray Williams and Pete Weber met head to head in a match which could well be a deciding factor in the PBA National Player of the Year contest. Walter Ray won by getting the first two strikes in the 10th frame to edge Pete 206-196. The ending was emotional, not just for the players involved but for the whole bowling world. It was the last time in a 36–year history of telecasts that the Winter Tour would be shown on ABC; but it would prove to be an exciting beginning for the PBA who wasted no time in linking new agreements with CBS and ESPN.

The story on the Senior Tour to date has been Gary Dickinson, Larry Laub and Earl Anthony. These three players have dominated with Laub and Dickinson winning three titles each, and Anthony coming out of retirement to win two. With three tournaments

PBA Tour

Pete Weber, son of bowling legend Dick Weber, had a great year in his own right in 1997 nabbing two wins and over $150,000 in prize money.

remaining any of these three could be Senior Player of the Year.

On the Sam's Town Ladies Professional Bowling Tour, Wendy Macpherson was easily the most outstanding player of 1997. Macpherson set a new single-season earnings mark with over $130,000 in prize money. The previous record was set in 1994 when Aleta Sill won $126,325.

At press time, Macpherson had won four tournaments, bowled two 300 games and led the tour with an average score of 215.65. Other bowlers having solid years were Carol Gianotti-Block who won over $94,000 and Liz Johnson who won three tournaments. ∎

Mike Durbin's Top Ten Highlights from the year in Bowling

10. In a move that saddened all bowling and Chris Schenkel fans, **ABC stops telecasting Pro Bowlers Tour** after 36 years.

9. The PBA bounced right back and announced **new multi-year television contracts with CBS and ESPN.**

8. Five lefties featured on telecast at Brunswick World Tournament of Champions.

7. In a pleasant business development, Showboat debuted an umbrella **sponsorship of PBA Senior Tour.**

6. In a personal triumph that everyone enjoyed, **Pete Weber re-emerged as a force on the National Tour.**

5. Fans had plenty to debate as they watched the **battle between Pete Weber, Walter Ray Williams Jr. and Parker Bohn for PBA National Player of the Year.**

4. On the Senior Tour, **Gary Dickinson had an outstanding year**, winning the ABC Sr. Masters, 2 other Sr. titles and going over $100,000 in 1997 earnings.

3. In another intense competition for supremacy, **Dickinson, Larry Laub and Earl Anthony fought it out for Sr. Player of the Year**.

2. 1997 was just another good year for **Walter Ray Williams Jr.** as he **went over $2 million in career earnings**.

1. Perfection comes to bowling as **Jeremy Sonnenfeld shoots the first American Bowling Congress 900 series.** ∎

THE NUMBERS

by
Steve Rutkowski

Top Ten Averages

In a very tight race for scoring leader, only five pins separated the top ten scorers on the PBA tour. Dave Husted competed in the fewest tournaments (11) while Steve Jaros entered all 20 of the events played through the Spring/Summer Tour.

1997 Pin Averages*

	Average	Games
Pete Weber	222.65	648
Walter Ray Williams Jr.	221.90	701
Parker Bohn III	220.38	634
Dave Husted	218.98	340
Brian Voss	218.98	647
Amleto Monacelli	218.87	637
Norm Duke	218.32	599
Ricky Ward	218.11	439
Steve Jaros	218.00	759
Mike Aulby	217.38	392

*Through Spring/Summer Tour

Top Ten Senior Averages

While not as tight as the regular tour, the Senior PBA Tour featued a close scoring average race as well. George Pappas played in only 9 tourneys through the end of August while Dickinson, Pete Couture, Laub, John Hricsina and Gene Stus entered all 13 events.

Bowling got a huge boost when the greatest bowler of all-time, **Earl Anthony**, came out of retirement and joined the PBA Senior Tour. It was more than a lark as Anthony won two events and competed for Bowler of the Year. Welcome back, big guy.

round now and then.

	Average	Games
Gary Dickinson	225.77	538
Earl Anthony	224.62	374
Pete Couture	223.77	559
Larry Laub	223.10	532
George Pappas	222.99	337
John Hricsina	221.81	521
Dale Eagle	220.89	464
Gene Stus	220.55	493
Avery LeBlanc	220.38	412
John Handegard	219.49	415

*Through end of August

	Earnings	Titles
Gary Dickinson	$100,740	3
Larry Laub	$53,685	3
John Hricsina	$46,765	1
Earl Anthony	$42,120	2
Pete Couture	$39,600	1
Gene Stus	$31,530	0
Roger Tramp	$31,285	0
Johnny Petraglia	$31,000	0
John Handegard	$27,590	1
Avery Leblanc	$24,585	0

*Through end of August.

Senior Tour Money Winners

It isn't like the Senior PGA Tour but the top senior bowlers can buy a

THE 1998 ESPN INFORMATION PLEASE SPORTS ALMANAC

BOWLING STATISTICS

SEC A

THE SEASON IN REVIEW
1996-1997
PBA • SENIORS • LPBT

PAGE 761

Tournament Results

Winners of stepladder finals in all PBA, Seniors and LPBT tournaments from Oct. 30, 1996, through Sept. 11, 1997; major tournaments in **bold** type. Note that (*) indicates winner was top seeded player entering championship round; and (a) indicates amateur. See Updates Chapter for later results.

PBA
Late 1996 Fall Tour

Final	Event	Winner	Earnings	Score	Runner-up
Oct. 30	Touring Pro-Senior Doubles	Eric Forkel/ Gene Stus	$22,000	231-201	Jason Couch/ Larry Laub
Nov. 6	Greater Harrisburg Open	W.R. Williams Jr.	16,000	214-202	Bob Learn Jr.
Nov. 12	Bayer-Brunswick TPC	Mike Aulby*	40,000	268-259	Parker Bohn III
Dec. 15	Merit Mixed Doubles Champ.	Mark Williams/ Aleta Sill	40,000	14,510 - 14,195†	Pete Weber/ Anne Marie Duggan

† Scoring in the Merit Mixed Doubles is based on total pins. In the "Merit Showdown", PBA's Walter Ray Williams defeated LPBT's Wendy Macpherson, 765-732 to win the $30,000 prize.

1997 Winter/Spring Tour

Final	Event	Winner	Earnings	Score	Runner-up
Jan. 24	**Tournament of Champions**	John Gant	$60,000#	208-187	Mike Aulby
Feb. 1	Columbia 300	W.R. Williams Jr.*	22,000	233-200	Andy Neuer
Feb. 8	Tucson Open	Pete Weber*	16,000	208-191	Brian Himmler
Feb. 15	Brentwood Classic	John Mazza*	16,000	227-156	Parker Bohn III
Feb. 22	Northwest Classic	Brian Voss*	18,000	219-185	Norm Duke
Feb. 28	Oregon Open	Jim Johnson Jr.*	18,000	232-197	Pete Weber
March 8	AC-Delco Classic	Parker Bohn III	48,000	238-234	Jason Couch
March 15	Showboat Invitational	Parker Bohn III	35,000	206-204	W.R. Williams Jr.
March 22	Peoria Open	Wayne Webb	18,000	268-203	Steve Jaros
March 29	**PBA National Championship**	Rick Steelsmith	30,000	218-190	Brian Voss
April 5	Flagship Open	Tim Criss*	18,000	242-208	Mike Shady
April 12	Bud Light Championship	Wayne Webb*	37,000	181-173	Amleto Monacelli
April 19	Comfort Inn Classic	Pete Weber	50,000†	257-208	Parker Bohn Jr.
April 26	Greater Sebring Open	Tim Criss	18,000	236-225	Steve Jaros
May 3	**ABC Masters**	Jason Queen	50,700	248-194	Eric Forkel
May 10	Johnny Petraglia Open	W.R. Williams Jr.	30,000	237-184	Amleto Monacelli
May 17	IOF Foresters Open	Norm Duke	40,000%	279-203	Bob Learn Jr.
May 31	Harrisburg Open	Tom Baker	18,000	200-166	W.R. Williams Jr.
June 7	Greater Detroit Open	Ricky Ward	18,000	240-188	Pete Weber
June 14	Wichita Open	Brian Voss	18,000	226-201	Parker Bohn III
June 21	St. Clair Classic	W.R. Williams Jr.*	18,000	206-196	Pete Weber

Note: The American Bowling Congress Masters tournament is not a PBA Tour event.

Does not include Bayliner boat package received as a bonus.

† In the "Winning Never Gets Old"; Challenge match, Weber defeated PBA Senior Tour representative Dale Eagle 256-246, for a bonus of $25,000.

% Does not include $10,000 bonus Learn received for defeating Canadian champion Marc Doi, 277-205.

1996-97 Bowlers Journal International All-American Teams

The 59th annual All-American First and Second teams as selected by the editors of Bowlers Journal International.

MEN		WOMEN	
First Team	**Second Team**	**First Team**	**Second Team**
Walter Ray Williams Jr. (capt.)	Mike Aulby	Wendy Macpherson (capt.)	Leanne Barrette
Parker Bohn III	Norm Duke	Kim Adler	Cheryl Daniels
Tim Criss	Steve Jaros	Marianne DiRupo	Carol Norman
Brian Voss	Wayne Webb	Carol Gianotti-Block	Aleta Sill
Pete Weber	Mark Williams	Liz Johnson	Sandra Jo Shiery-Odom

SENIOR PBA
1997 Spring/Summer Tour

Final	Event	Winner	Earnings	Score	Runner-up
March 13	Greater Albany Senior Open	Earl Anthony	$9,000	248-243	Avery LeBlanc
March 20	Vermont Senior Open	Larry Laub	8,000	212-180	Avery LeBlanc
March 27	PBA Senior South Bend Open	John Handegard*	10,000	219-215	Teata Semiz
April 3	Senior Jackson Open	Larry Laub*	8,000	205-182	Ron Winger
April 10	Showboat/Citgo Tournament of Champs.	George Pappas*	10,000	236-207	Gary Dickinson
July 3	Northwest Senior Classic	Gary Dickinson	8,000	247-202	Earl Anthony
July 11	Seattle Senior Open	Gary Dickinson*	8,000	276-235	Gene Stus
July 17	Tri-Cities Senior Open	Earl Anthony	8,000	235-223	Gary Mage
July 24	PBA Boise Senior Open	Gary Mage	8,000	225-194	Pete Couture
Aug. 2	Showboat Senior Invitational	John Hricsina*	20,000	220-206	Don Johnson
Aug. 16	**ABC/PBA Senior Masters**	Gary Dickinson	60,000	238-236	Johhny Petraglia
Aug. 21	Glass City Senior Open	Pete Couture	9,000	255-202	Dave Soutar
Aug. 29	**PBA Senior Championship**	Larry Laub	16,000	226-226†	John Hricsina

† After tying at 226, Laub defeated Hricsina, 60-50 in a two-frame rolloff to decide the championship.

LPBT
Late 1996 Fall Tour

Final	Event	Winner	Earnings	Score	Runner-up
Oct. 31	Lady Ebonite Classic	Kim Adler	$11,000	202-182	Wendy Macpherson
Nov. 7	**Hammer Players Championship**	Kim Adler	16,000	216-190	Carol Norman
Nov. 17	**Sam's Town Invitational**	Carol Gianotti-Block	17,000	222-215	Leanne Barrette
Dec. 15	Merit Mixed Doubles Champ.	Mark Williams/	40,000	14,510 -	Pete Weber/
		Aleta Sill		14,195†	Anne Marie Duggan

† Scoring in the Merit Mixed Doubles is based on total pins. In the "Merit Showdown", PBA's Walter Ray Williams defeated LPBT's Wendy Macpherson, 765-732 to win the $30,000 prize.

1997 Winter/Spring Tour

Final	Event	Winner	Earnings	Score	Runner-up
Feb. 6	Clabber Girl Open	Lisa Bishop	$10,000	224-204	Carol Norman
Feb. 13	Lubbock Open	Wendy Macpherson	9,000	205-204	Carol Gianotti-Block
Mar. 20	Texas Border Shoot-Out	Liz Johnson	9,000	234-181	Carol Norman
May 8	Storm Doubles	Wendy Macpherson/	14,500	245-204	Anne Marie Duggan/
		Darris Street*			Stacy Rider
May 17	**WIBC Queen's**	Sandra Jo Odom*	23,302	209-185	Audrey Mullan
May 22	Omaha Open	Leanne Barrette	9,000	238-162	Wendy Macpherson

1997 Summer/Fall Tour
(Through September 11)

Final	Event	Winner	Earnings	Score	Runner-up
June 19	Tunica Mid South Classic	Kim Adler	$9,000	244-170	Marianne DiRupo
June 26	Music City Country Classic	Liz Johnson*	9,000	235-191	Dede Davidson
July 3	Blue Ribbon Classic	Liz Johnson	9,000	235-187	Nikki Gianulias
July 10	Southern Virginia Open	Michelle Feldman	9,000	300-183	Carolyn Dorin-Ballard
July 17	**AMF Gold Cup**	Aleta Sill	25,000	221-179	Carol Gianotti-Block
July 24	Berkeley Invitational	Anne Marie Duggan	9,000	234-215	Carolyn Dorin-Ballard
Aug. 21	Hammer Players Champs.	Marianne DiRupo	16,000	227-181	Wendy Macpherson
Aug. 28	Lady Ebonite Open	Nikki Gianulias	10,000	245-232	Marianne DiRupo
Sept. 4	Long Island Open	Carol Gianotti-Block*	11,000	228-191	Sandra Jo Odom
Sept. 11	Columbia 300 Delaware Open	Wendy Macpherson	11,000	225-192	Carol Gianotti-Block

Note: The Women's International Bowling Congress Queens tournament is not an LPBT Tour event.

1997 Fall Tour Schedules
PBA
Events: Ebonite Challenge – Windsor Locks, CT (Oct. 4-8); Ebonite Challenge – Rochester, NY (Oct. 11-15); Mobil One Classic (Oct. 18-22); Ebonite Challenge – Indianapolis, IN (Oct. 25-29); Ebonite Challenge – Chesapeake, VA (Nov. 1-5); Bayer/Brunswick Touring Players Championship (Nov. 8-12).

SENIOR PBA
Events: St. Petersburg/Clearwater Senior Open (Sept. 14-18); Naples Senior Open (Sept. 21-25); PBA Senior World Open (Nov. 1-8).

LPBT
Events: Baltimore Eastern Open (Sept. 13-18); Three Rivers Open (Sept. 20-25); Triton Open (Sept. 28-Oct. 2); **Sam's Town Invitational** (Nov. 15-22).

Tour Leaders

Official standings for 1996 and unofficial standings (through Sept. 11) for 1997. Note that (TB) indicates Tournaments Bowled; (CR) Championship Rounds as Stepladder Finalist; and (1st) Titles Won.

Final 1996 — PBA — Top 10 Money Winners

		TB	CR	1st	Earnings
1	W.R. Williams Jr.	26	10	5	$241,330
2	Bob Learn Jr.	27	7	1	236,232
3	Steve Wilson	27	2	2	132,140
4	Dave D'Entremont	28	3	1	117,874
5	Mike Aulby	22	2	2	115,225
6	Parker Bohn III	27	9	0	109,217
7	Danny Wiseman	27	5	0	107,217
8	David Traber	29	2	1	105,382
9	Tom Baker	27	2	1	102,327
10	Dave Husted	13	3	1	94,595

1997 (through Sept. 11) — PBA — Top 10 Money Winners

		TB	CR	1st	Earnings
1	Parker Bohn III	18	6	2	$166,320
2	W.R. Williams Jr.	18	11	3	162,914
3	Pete Weber	16	10	2	158,184
4	Brian Voss	18	6	2	102,625
5	Norm Duke	15	4	1	87,420
6	Wayne Webb	19	4	2	83,950
7	John Gant	12	1	1	83,700
8	Tim Criss	19	6	2	80,380
9	Amleto Monacelli	16	2	0	79,605
10	Steve Jaros	20	5	0	75,474

Top 10 Averages — Final 1996

		TB	Games	Avg
1	W.R. Williams Jr.	26	1,020	225.37
2	Norm Duke	22	721	222.28
3	Parker Bohn III	27	875	222.07
4	Bob Learn Jr.	27	886	222.05
5	Pete Weber	24	670	222.01
6	Brian Voss	23	729	221.83
7	Eric Forkel	28	690	221.15
8	Danny Wiseman	27	837	220.73
9	Steve Wilson	27	732	220.69
10	David Traber	29	904	220.50

Top 10 Averages — 1997

		TB	Games	Avg
1	Pete Weber	16	648	222.65
2	W.R. Williams Jr.	18	701	221.90
3	Parker Bohn III	18	634	220.38
4	Dave Husted	11	340	218.98
5	Brian Voss	18	647	218.98
6	Amleto Monacelli	16	637	218.87
7	Norm Duke	15	599	218.32
8	Ricky Ward	15	439	218.11
9	Steve Jaros	20	759	218.00
10	Mike Aulby	14	392	217.38

SENIOR PBA — Top 5 Money Winners — Final 1996

		TB	CR	1st	Earnings
1	Dave Davis	6	1	1	$63,815
2	Earl Anthony	8	5	1	35,810
3	Dale Eagle	10	3	1	33,730
4	Gary Dickinson	11	3	2	32,650
5	Teata Semiz	12	4	0	32,002

SENIOR PBA — Top 5 Money Winners — 1997

		TB	CR	1st	Earnings
1	Gary Dickinson	13	7	3	$100,740
2	Larry Laub	13	5	3	53,685
3	John Hricsina	13	4	1	46,765
4	Earl Anthony	10	5	2	42,120
5	Pete Couture	13	7	1	39,600

Top 5 Averages — Final 1996

		TB	Games	Avg
1	Earl Anthony	8	306	226.95
2	John Handegard	12	476	223.98
3	Teata Semiz	12	456	223.66
4	Dale Eagle	10	366	221.51
5	Gary Dickinson	11	400	221.34

Top 5 Averages — 1997

		TB	Games	Avg
1	Gary Dickinson	13	538	225.77
2	Earl Anthony	10	374	224.62
3	Pete Couture	13	559	223.77
4	Larry Laub	13	532	223.10
5	George Pappas	9	337	222.99

LPBT — Top 10 Money Winners — Final 1996

		TB	CR	1st	Earnings
1	Wendy Macpherson	22	7	3	$107,230
2	Kim Adler	22	7	2	99,130
3	Aleta Sill	21	6	2	83,600
4	Lisa Wagner	19	6	1	83,140
5	Liz Johnson	19	5	2	78,532
6	Anne Marie Duggan	21	7	0	76,740
7	Marianne DiRupo	21	6	0	73,363
8	Carol Norman	22	4	0	69,581
9	Tammy Turner	13	5	2	66,255
10	Sandra Jo Shiery	22	5	1	65,323

Note: Earnings include WIBC Queens.

LPBT — Top 10 Money Winners — 1997

		TB	CR	1st	Earnings
1	Wendy Macpherson	16	10	3	$117,125
2	Carol Gianotti-Block	16	8	1	93,300
3	Liz Johnson	15	6	3	79,150
4	Marianne DiRupo	16	7	1	79,025
5	Carolyn Dorin-Ballard	16	6	0	60,125
6	Nikki Gianulias	16	3	1	54,178
7	Sandra Jo Odom	14	2	1	53,852
8	Leanne Barrette	16	4	1	53,225
9	Anne Marie Duggan	15	4	1	46,825
10	Aleta Sill	14	2	1	44,250

Top 5 Averages — Final 1996

		TB	Games	Avg
1	Tammy Turner	13	485	215.23
2	Wendy Macpherson	22	788	214.81
3	Carolyn Dorin-Ballard	22	729	214.24
4	Aleta Sill	21	682	213.64
5	Kim Adler	22	735	213.61

Top 5 Averages — 1997

		TB	Games	Avg
1	Wendy Macpherson	16	712	215.13
2	Marianne DiRupo	16	658	213.81
3	Carol Gianotti-Block	16	647	212.70
4	Nikki Gianulias	16	686	212.47
5	Liz Johnson	15	642	212.05

BOWLING STATISTICS

SEC B

THE 1998

ESPN INFORMATION PLEASE SPORTS ALMANAC

THROUGH THE YEARS 1942-1997

CHAMPIONS • AWARDS

PAGE 764

Major Championships
MEN

BPAA U.S. Open

Started in 1941 by the Bowling Proprietors' Association of America, 18 years before the founding of the Professional Bowlers Association. Originally the BPAA All-Star Tournament, it became the U.S. Open in 1971. There were two BPAA All-Star tournaments in 1955, in January and December.

Multiple winners: Don Carter and Dick Weber (4); Dave Husted (3); Del Ballard, Jr., Marshall Holman, Junie McMahon, Connie Schwoegler, Andy Varipapa and Pete Weber (2)

Year		Year		Year		Year	
1942	John Crimmons	1956	Bill Lillard	1970	Bobby Cooper	1984	Mark Roth
1943	Connie Schwoegler	1957	Don Carter	1971	Mike Limongello	1985	Marshall Holman
1944	Ned Day	1958	Don Carter	1972	Don Johnson	1986	Steve Cook
1945	Buddy Bomar	1959	Billy Welu	1973	Mike McGrath	1987	Del Ballard Jr.
1946	Joe Wilman	1960	Harry Smith	1974	Larry Laub	1988	Pete Weber
1947	Andy Varipapa	1961	Bill Tucker	1975	Steve Neff	1989	Mike Aulby
1948	Andy Varipapa	1962	Dick Weber	1976	Paul Moser		
1949	Connie Schwoegler	1963	Dick Weber	1977	Johnny Petraglia	1990	Ron Palombi Jr.
		1964	Bob Strampe	1978	Nelson Burton Jr.	1991	Pete Weber
1950	Junie McMahon	1965	Dick Weber	1979	Joe Berardi	1992	Robert Lawrence
1951	Dick Hoover	1966	Dick Weber			1993	Del Ballard Jr.
1952	Junie McMahon	1967	Les Schissler	1980	Steve Martin	1994	Justin Hromek
1953	Don Carter	1968	Jim Stefanich	1981	Marshall Holman	1995	Dave Husted
1954	Don Carter	1969	Billy Hardwick	1982	Dave Husted	1996	Dave Husted
1955	Steve Nagy			1983	Gary Dickinson		

PBA National Championship

The Professional Bowlers Association was formed in 1958 and its first national championship tournament was held in Memphis in 1960. The tournament has been held in Toledo, Ohio, since 1981.

Multiple winners: Earl Anthony (6); Mike Aulby, Dave Davis, Mike McGrath and Wayne Zahn (2).

Year		Year		Year		Year	
1960	Don Carter	1970	Mike McGrath	1980	Johnny Petraglia	1990	Jim Pencak
1961	Dave Soutar	1971	Mike Limongello	1981	Earl Anthony	1991	Mike Miller
1962	Carmen Salvino	1972	Johnny Guenther	1982	Earl Anthony	1992	Eric Forkel
1963	Billy Hardwick	1973	Earl Anthony	1983	Earl Anthony	1993	Ron Palombi Jr.
1964	Bob Strampe	1974	Earl Anthony	1984	Bob Chamberlain	1994	David Traber
1965	Dave Davis	1975	Earl Anthony	1985	Mike Aulby	1995	Scott Alexander
1966	Wayne Zahn	1976	Paul Colwell	1986	Tom Crites	1996	Butch Soper
1967	Dave Davis	1977	Tommy Hudson	1987	Randy Pedersen	1997	Rick Steelsmith
1968	Wayne Zahn	1978	Warren Nelson	1988	Brian Voss		
1969	Mike McGrath	1979	Mike Aulby	1989	Pete Weber		

Brunswick World Tournament of Champions

Originally the Firestone Tournament of Champions (1965-93), the tournament has also been sponsored by General Tire (1994) and Brunswick Corp. (since 1995). Held annually in Akron, Ohio from 1965-94, the T of C was moved to suburban Chicago in 1995.

Multiple winners: Mike Durbin (3); Earl Anthony, Jim Godman, Marshall Holman and Mark Williams (2).

Year		Year		Year		Year	
1965	Billy Hardwick	1974	Earl Anthony	1983	Joe Berardi	1992	Marc McDowell
1966	Wayne Zahn	1975	Dave Davis	1984	Mike Durbin	1993	George Branham III
1967	Jim Stefanich	1976	Marshall Holman	1985	Mark Williams	1994	Norm Duke
1968	Dave Davis	1977	Mike Berlin	1986	Marshall Holman	1995	Mike Aulby
1969	Jim Godman	1978	Earl Anthony	1987	Pete Weber	1996	Dave D'Entremont
1970	Don Johnson	1979	George Pappas	1988	Mark Williams	1997	John Gant
1971	Johnny Petraglia	1980	Wayne Webb	1989	Del Ballard Jr.		
1972	Mike Durbin	1981	Steve Cook				
1973	Jim Godman	1982	Mike Durbin	1990	Dave Ferraro		
				1991	David Ozio		

ABC Masters Tournament

Sponsored by the American Bowling Congress. The Masters is not a PBA event, but is considered one of the four major tournaments on the men's tour and is open to qualified pros and amateurs.

Multiple winners: Earl Anthony, Mike Aulby, Billy Golembiewski, Dick Hoover and Billy Welu (2).

Year		Year		Year		Year	
1951	Lee Jouglard	1963	Harry Smith	1975	Eddie Ressler	1987	Rick Steelsmith
1952	Willard Taylor	1964	Billy Welu	1976	Nelson Burton Jr.	1988	Del Ballard Jr.
1953	Rudy Habetler	1965	Billy Welu	1977	Earl Anthony	1989	Mike Aulby
1954	Red Elkins	1966	Bob Strampe	1978	Frank Ellenburg		
1955	Buzz Fazio	1967	Lou Scalia	1979	Doug Myers	1990	Chris Warren
1956	Dick Hoover	1968	Pete Tountas			1991	Doug Kent
1957	Dick Hoover	1969	Jim Chestney	1980	Neil Burton	1992	Ken Johnson
1958	Tom Hennessey			1981	Randy Lightfoot	1993	Norm Duke
1959	Ray Bluth	1970	Don Glover	1982	Joe Berardi	1994	Steve Fehr
		1971	Jim Godman	1983	Mike Lastowski	1995	Mike Aulby
1960	Billy Golembiewski	1972	Bill Beach	1984	Earl Anthony	1996	Ernie Schlegel
1961	Don Carter	1973	Dave Soutar	1985	Steve Wunderlich	1997	Jason Queen
1962	Billy Golembiewski	1974	Paul Colwell	1986	Mark Fahy		

WOMEN
BPAA U.S. Open

Started by the Bowling Proprietors' Association of America in 1949, 11 years before the founding of the Professional Women's Bowling Association. Originally the BPAA Women's All-Star Tournament, it became the U.S. Open in 1971. There were two BPAA All-Star tournaments in 1955, in January and December. Note that (a) indicates amateur.

Multiple winners: Marion Ladewig (8); Donna Adamek, Paula Sperber Carter, Pat Costello, Dotty Fothergill, Dana Miller-Mackie and Sylvia Wene (2).

Year		Year		Year		Year	
1949	Marion Ladewig	1960	Sylvia Wene	1973	Millie Martorella	1985	Pat Mercatanti
1950	Marion Ladewig	1961	Phyllis Notaro	1974	Pat Costello	1986	Wendy Macpherson
1951	Marion Ladewig	1962	Shirley Garms	1975	Paula Sperber Carter	1987	Carol Norman
1952	Marion Ladewig	1963	Marion Ladewig	1976	Patty Costello	1988	Lisa Wagner
1953	Not held	1964	LaVerne Carter	1977	Betty Morris	1989	Robin Romeo
1954	Marion Ladewig	1965	Ann Slattery	1978	Donna Adamek		
1955	Sylvia Wene	1966	Joy Abel	1979	Diana Silva	1990	Dana Miller-Mackie
1955	Anita Cantaline	1967	Gloria Simon			1991	Anne Marie Duggan
1956	Marion Ladewig	1968	Dotty Fothergill	1980	Pat Costello	1992	Tish Johnson
1957	Not held	1969	Dotty Fothergill	1981	Donna Adamek	1993	Dede Davidson
1958	Merle Matthews	1970	Mary Baker	1982	Shinobu Saitoh	1994	Aleta Sill
1959	Marion Ladewig	1971	a-Paula Sperber	1983	Dana Miller	1995	Cheryl Daniels
		1972	a-Lorrie Koch	1984	Karen Ellingsworth	1996	Liz Johnson

WIBC Queens

Sponsored by the Women's International Bowling Congress, the Queens is a double elimination, match play tournament. It is not an LPBT event, but is open to qualified pros and amateurs. Note that (a) indicates amateur.

Multiple winners: Millie Martorella (3); Donna Adamek, Dotty Fothergill, Aleta Sill and Katsuko Sugimoto (2).

Year		Year		Year		Year	
1961	Janet Harman	1971	Millie Martorella	1980	Donna Adamek	1989	Carol Gianotti
1962	Dorothy Wilkinson	1972	Dotty Fothergill	1981	Katsuko Sugimoto	1990	a-Patty Ann
1963	Irene Monterosso	1973	Dotty Fothergill	1982	Katsuko Sugimoto	1991	Dede Davidson
1964	D.D. Jacobson	1974	Judy Soutar	1983	Aleta Sill	1992	Cindy Coburn-Carroll
1965	Betty Kuczynski	1975	Cindy Powell	1984	Kazue Inahashi	1993	Jan Schmidt
1966	Judy Lee	1976	Pam Rutherford	1985	Aleta Sill	1994	Anne Marie Duggan
1967	Millie Martorella	1977	Dana Stewart	1986	Cora Fiebig	1995	Sandra Postma
1968	Phyllis Massey	1978	Loa Boxberger	1987	Cathy Almeida	1996	Lisa Wagner
1969	Ann Feigel	1979	Donna Adamek	1988	Wendy Macpherson	1997	Sandra Jo Odom
1970	Millie Martorella						

Sam's Town Invitational

Originally held in Milwaukee as the Pabst Tournament of Champions, but discontinued after one year (1981). The event was revived in 1984, moved to Las Vegas and renamed the Sam's Town Tournament of Champions. Since then it has been known as the LPBT Tournament of Champions (1985), the Sam's Town National Pro/Am (1986-88) and the Sam's Town Invitational (since 1989).

Multiple winners: Tish Johnson (3); Aleta Sill (2).

Year		Year		Year		Year	
1981	Cindy Coburn	1986	Aleta Sill	1991	Lorrie Nichols	1994	Tish Johnson
1982-83	Not held	1987	Debbie Bennett	1992	Tish Johnson	1995	Michelle Mullen
1984	Aleta Sill	1988	Donna Adamek	1993	Robin Romeo	1996	Carol Gianotti-Block
1985	Patty Costello	1989	Tish Johnson				

Major Championships (Cont.)

WOMEN

WPBA National Championship (1960-1980)

The Women's Professional Bowling Association National Championship tournament was discontinued when the WPBA broke up in 1981. The WPBA changed its name from the Professional Women Bowlers Association (PWBA) in 1978.

Multiple winners: Patty Costello (3); Dotty Fothergill (2).

Year		Year		Year		Year		Year	
1960	Marion Ladewig	1965	Helen Duval	1969	Dotty Fothergill	1973	Betty Morris	1977	Vesma Grinfelds
1961	Shirley Garms	1966	Judy Lee	1970	Bobbe North	1974	Pat Costello	1978	Toni Gillard
1962	Stephanie Balogh	1967	Betty Mivelaz	1971	Patty Costello	1975	Pam Buckner	1979	Cindy Coburn
1963	Janet Harman	1968	Dotty Fothergill	1972	Patty Costello	1976	Patty Costello	1980	Donna Adamek
1964	Betty Kuczynski								

Annual Leaders
Average
PBA Tour

The George Young Memorial Award, named after the late ABC Hall of Fame bowler. Based on at least 16 national PBA tournaments from 1959-78, and at least 400 games of tour competition since 1979.

Multiple winners: Mark Roth (6); Earl Anthony (5); Marshall Holman (3); Norm Duke, Billy Hardwick, Don Johnson, Walter Ray Williams Jr. and Wayne Zahn (2).

Year		Avg	Year		Avg	Year		Avg
1962	Don Carter	212.84	1974	Earl Anthony	219.34	1986	John Gant	214.38
1963	Bill Hardwick	210.35	1975	Earl Anthony	219.06	1987	Marshall Holman	216.80
1964	Ray Bluth	210.51	1976	Mark Roth	215.97	1988	Mark Roth	218.04
1965	Dick Weber	211.90	1977	Mark Roth	218.17	1989	Pete Weber	215.43
1966	Wayne Zahn	208.63	1978	Mark Roth	219.83			
1967	Wayne Zahn	212.14	1979	Mark Roth	221.66	1990	Amleto Monacelli	218.16
1968	Jim Stefanich	211.90				1991	Norm Duke	218.21
1969	Billy Hardwick	212.96	1980	Earl Anthony	218.54	1992	Dave Ferraro	219.70
			1981	Mark Roth	216.70	1993	Walter R. Williams Jr.	222.98
1970	Nelson Burton Jr.	214.91	1982	Marshall Holman	216.15	1994	Norm Duke	222.83
1971	Don Johnson	213.98	1983	Earl Anthony	216.65	1995	Mike Aulby	225.49
1972	Don Johnson	215.29	1984	Marshall Holman	213.91	1996	Walter R. Williams Jr.	225.37
1973	Earl Anthony	215.80	1985	Mark Baker	213.72			

LPBT Tour

Based on at least 282 games of tour competition.

Multiple winners: Leanne Barrette, Nikki Gianulias and Lisa Rathgeber Wagner (3); Anne Marie Duggan and Aleta Sill (2).

Year		Avg	Year		Avg	Year		Avg
1981	Nikki Gianulias	213.71	1987	Wendy Macpherson	211.11	1992	Leanne Barrette	211.36
1982	Nikki Gianulias	210.63	1988	Lisa Wagner	213.02	1993	Tish Johnson	215.39
1983	Lisa Rathgeber	208.50	1989	Lisa Wagner	211.87	1994	Anne Marie Duggan	213.47
1984	Aleta Sill	210.68	1990	Leanne Barrette	211.53	1995	Anne Marie Duggan	215.79
1985	Aleta Sill	211.10	1991	Leanne Barrette	211.48	1996	Tammy Turner	215.23
1986	Nikki Gianulias	213.89						

Money Won
PBA Tour

Multiple winners: Earl Anthony (6); Dick Weber and Mark Roth (4); Mike Aulby and Walter Ray Williams Jr. (3); Don Carter (2).

Year		Earnings	Year		Earnings	Year		Earnings
1959	Dick Weber	$ 7,672	1972	Don Johnson	56,648	1985	Mike Aulby	201,200
1960	Don Carter	22,525	1973	Don McCune	69,000	1986	W.R. Williams Jr	145,550
1961	Dick Weber	26,280	1974	Earl Anthony	99,585	1987	Pete Weber	179,516
1962	Don Carter	49,972	1975	Earl Anthony	107,585	1988	Brian Voss	225,485
1963	Dick Weber	46,333	1976	Earl Anthony	110,833	1989	Mike Aulby	298,237
1964	Bob Strampe	33,592	1977	Mark Roth	105,583			
1965	Dick Weber	47,675	1978	Mark Roth	134,500	1990	Amleto Monacelli	204,775
1966	Wayne Zahn	54,720	1979	Mark Roth	124,517	1991	David Ozio	225,585
1967	Dave Davis	54,165				1992	Marc McDowell	176,215
1968	Jim Stefanich	67,375	1980	Wayne Webb	116,700	1993	W.R. Williams Jr	296,370
1969	Billy Hardwick	64,160	1981	Earl Anthony	164,735	1994	Norm Duke	273,753
			1982	Earl Anthony	134,760	1995	Mike Aulby	219,792
1970	Mike McGrath	52,049	1983	Earl Anthony	135,605	1996	W.R. Williams Jr.	241,330
1971	Johnny Petraglia	85,065	1984	Mark Roth	158,712			

WPBA and LPBT Tours

WPBA leaders through 1980; LPBT leaders since 1981.

Multiple winners: Aleta Sill (5); Donna Adamek (4); Patty Costello, Tish Johnson and Betty Morris (3); Dotty Fothergill and Aleta Sill (2)

Year		Earnings	Year		Earnings	Year		Earnings
1965	Betty Kuczynski	$ 3,792	1976	Patty Costello	39,585	1987	Betty Morris	63,735
1966	Joy Abel	5,795	1977	Betty Morris	23,802	1988	Lisa Wagner	105,500
1967	Shirley Garms	4,920	1978	Donna Adamek	31,000	1989	Robin Romeo	113,750
1968	Dotty Fothergill	16,170	1979	Donna Adamek	26,280			
1969	Dotty Fothergill	9,220	1980	Donna Adamek	31,907	1990	Tish Johnson	94,420
1970	Patty Costello	9,317	1981	Donna Adamek	41,270	1991	Leanne Barrette	87,618
1971	Vesma Grinfelds	4,925	1982	Nikki Gianulias	45,875	1992	Tish Johnson	96,872
1972	Patty Costello	11,350	1983	Aleta Sill	42,525	1993	Aleta Sill	57,995
1973	Judy Cook	11,200	1984	Aleta Sill	81,452	1994	Aleta Sill	126,325
1974	Betty Morris	30,037	1985	Aleta Sill	52,655	1995	Tish Johnson	123,440
1975	Judy Soutar	20,395	1986	Aleta Sill	36,962	1996	Wendy Macpherson	107,230

All-Time Leaders

All-time leading money winners on the PBA and LPBT tours, through 1996. PBA figures date back to 1959, while LPBT figures include Women's Pro Bowlers Association (WPBA) earnings through 1980. National tour titles are also listed.

Money Won

PBA Top 20

		Titles	Earnings
1	Walter Ray Williams Jr.	21	$1,832,159
2	Pete Weber	21	1,827,031
3	Mike Aulby	25	1,772,130
4	Marshall Holman	22	1,683,625
5	Mark Roth	34	1,486,148
6	Brian Voss	16	1,485,525
7	Amleto Monacelli	16	1,466,676
8	Dave Husted	13	1,441,666
9	Earl Anthony	41	1,397,741
10	Parker Bohn III	11	1,189,948
11	David Ozio	11	1,189,534
12	Wayne Webb	18	1,187,376
13	Norm Duke	11	1,144,561
14	Del Ballard Jr.	12	1,061,145
15	Gary Dickinson	8	1,060,671
16	Dave Ferraro	9	1,034,176
17	Mark Williams	7	1,017,297
18	Tom Baker	8	955,970
19	Dick Weber	26	914,548
20	Ernie Schlegel	6	872,467

WPBA-LPBT Top 12

		Titles	Earnings
1	Aleta Sill	27	$821,462
2	Tish Johnson	21	786,256
3	Lisa Wagner	30	701,183
4	Robin Romeo Mossonite	16	617,330
5	Anne Marie Duggan	13	607,516
6	Leanne Barrette	16	557,758
7	Cheryl Daniels	10	532,444
8	Nikki Gianulias	18	522,735
9	Wendy Macpherson	9	503,354
10	Donna Adamek	19	473,984
11	Lorrie Nichols	15	472,686
12	Cindy Coburn-Carroll	15	455,941

Senior PBA Top 5

		Titles	Earnings
1	John Handegard	12	$357,906
2	Gene Stus	7	283,210
3	Teata Semiz	7	278,540
4	John Hricsina	5	251,982
5	Dick Weber	6	215,669

Annual Awards

MEN

BWAA Bowler of the Year

Winners selected by Bowling Writers Association of America.

Multiple winners: Earl Anthony and Don Carter (6); Mark Roth (4); Mike Aulby, Dick Weber and Walter Ray Williams Jr. (3); Buddy Bomar, Ned Day, Billy Hardwick, Don Johnson, and Steve Nagy (2).

Year		Year		Year		Year	
1942	Johnny Crimmins	1956	Bill Lillard	1970	Nelson Burton Jr.	1984	Mark Roth
1943	Ned Day	1957	Don Carter	1971	Don Johnson	1985	Mike Aulby
1944	Ned Day	1958	Don Carter	1972	Don Johnson	1986	Walter Ray Williams Jr.
1945	Buddy Bomar	1959	Ed Lubanski	1973	Don McCune	1987	Marshall Holman
1946	Joe Wilman	1960	Don Carter	1974	Earl Anthony	1988	Brian Voss
1947	Buddy Bomar	1961	Dick Weber	1975	Earl Anthony	1989	Mike Aulby
1948	Andy Varipapa	1962	Don Carter	1976	Earl Anthony		
1949	Connie Schwoegler	1963	Dick Weber	1977	Mark Roth	1990	Amleto Monacelli
1950	Junie McMahon	1964	Billy Hardwick	1978	Mark Roth	1991	David Ozio
1951	Lee Jouglard	1965	Dick Weber	1979	Mark Roth	1992	Marc McDowell
1952	Steve Nagy	1966	Wayne Zahn	1980	Wayne Webb	1993	Walter Ray Williams Jr.
1953	Don Carter	1967	Dave Davis	1981	Earl Anthony	1994	Norm Duke
1954	Don Carter	1968	Jim Stefanich	1982	Earl Anthony	1995	Mike Aulby
1955	Steve Nagy	1969	Billy Hardwick	1983	Earl Anthony	1996	Walter Ray Williams Jr.

Annual Awards (Cont.)

PBA Player of the Year

Winners selected by members of Professional Bowlers Association. The PBA Player of the Year has differed from the BWAA Bowler of the Year four times—in 1963, '64, '89 and '92.

Multiple winners: Earl Anthony (6); Mark Roth (4); Walter Ray Williams Jr. (3); Mike Aulby, Billy Hardwick, Don Johnson and Amleto Monacelli (2).

Year		Year		Year		Year	
1963	Billy Hardwick	1972	Don Johnson	1981	Earl Anthony	1990	Amleto Monacelli
1964	Bob Strampe	1973	Don McCune	1982	Earl Anthony	1991	David Ozio
1965	Dick Weber	1974	Earl Anthony	1983	Earl Anthony	1992	Dave Ferraro
1966	Wayne Zahn	1975	Earl Anthony	1984	Mark Roth	1993	Walter Ray Williams Jr.
1967	Dave Davis	1976	Earl Anthony	1985	Mike Aulby	1994	Norm Duke
1968	Jim Stefanich	1977	Mark Roth	1986	Walter Ray Williams Jr.	1995	Mike Aulby
1969	Billy Hardwick	1978	Mark Roth	1987	Marshall Holman	1996	Walter Ray Williams Jr.
1970	Nelson Burton Jr.	1979	Mark Roth	1988	Brian Voss		
1971	Don Johnson	1980	Wayne Webb	1989	Amleto Monacelli		

PBA Rookie of the Year

Winners selected by members of Professional Bowlers Association.

Year		Year		Year		Year	
1964	Jerry McCoy	1973	Steve Neff	1981	Mark Fahy	1989	Steve Hoskins
1965	Jim Godman	1974	Cliff McNealy	1982	Mike Steinbach	1990	Brad Kiszewski
1966	Bobby Cooper	1975	Guy Rowbury	1983	Toby Contreras	1991	Ricky Ward
1967	Mike Durbin	1976	Mike Berlin	1984	John Gant	1992	Jason Couch
1968	Bob McGregor	1977	Steve Martin	1985	Tom Crites	1993	Mark Scroggins
1969	Larry Lichstein	1978	Joseph Groskind	1986	Marc McDowell	1994	Tony Ament
1970	Denny Krick	1979	Mike Aulby	1987	Ryan Shafer	1995	Billy Myers Jr.
1971	Tye Critchlow	1980	Pete Weber	1988	Rick Steelsmith	1996	C.K. Moore
1972	Tommy Hudson						

WOMEN
BWAA Bowler of the Year

Winners selected by Bowling Writers Association of America.

Multiple winners: Marion Ladewig (9); Donna Adamek and Lisa Rathgeber Wagner (4); Tish Johnson and Betty Morris (3); Patty Costello, Dotty Fothergill, Shirley Garms, Val Mikiel, Aleta Sill, Judy Soutar and Sylvia Wene (2).

Year		Year		Year		Year	
1948	Val Mikiel	1961	Shirley Garms	1973	Judy Soutar	1985	Aleta Sill
1949	Val Mikiel	1962	Shirley Garms	1974	Betty Morris	1986	Lisa Wagner
1950	Marion Ladewig	1963	Marion Ladewig	1975	Judy Soutar	1987	Betty Morris
1951	Marion Ladewig	1964	LaVerne Carter	1976	Patty Costello	1988	Lisa Wagner
1952	Marion Ladewig	1965	Betty Kuczynski	1977	Betty Morris	1989	Robin Romeo
1953	Marion Ladewig	1966	Joy Abel	1978	Donna Adamek	1990	Tish Johnson
1954	Marion Ladewig	1967	Millie Martorella	1979	Donna Adamek	1991	Leanne Barrette
1955	Sylvia Wene	1968	Dotty Fothergill	1980	Donna Adamek	1992	Tish Johnson
1956	Anita Cantaline	1969	Dotty Fothergill	1981	Donna Adamek	1993	Lisa Wagner
1957	Marion Ladewig	1970	Mary Baker	1982	Nikki Gianulias	1994	Anne Marie Duggan
1958	Marion Ladewig	1971	Paula Sperber	1983	Lisa Rathgeber	1995	Tish Johnson
1959	Marion Ladewig	1972	Patty Costello	1984	Aleta Sill	1996	Wendy Macpherson
1960	Sylvia Wene						

LPBT Player of the Year

Winners selected by members of Ladies Professional Bowlers Tour. The LPBT Player of the Year has differed from the BWAA Bowler of the Year three times—in 1985, '86 and '90.

Multiple winners: Lisa Rathgeber Wagner (3); Leanne Barrette and Tish Johnson (2).

Year		Year		Year		Year	
1983	Lisa Rathgeber	1987	Betty Morris	1991	Leanne Barrette	1994	Anne Marie Duggan
1984	Aleta Sill	1988	Lisa Wagner	1992	Tish Johnson	1995	Tish Johnson
1985	Patty Costello	1989	Robin Romeo	1993	Lisa Wagner	1996	Wendy Macpherson
1986	Jeanne Maiden	1990	Leanne Barrette				

WPBA and LPBT Rookie of the Year

Winners selected by members of Women's Professional Bowlers Association (1978-80) and the Ladies Professional Bowlers Tour (since 1981).

Year		Year		Year		Year	
1978	Toni Gillard	1983	Anne Marie Pike	1988	Mary Martha Cerniglia	1993	Kathy Zielke
1979	Nikki Gianulias	1984	Paula Vidad	1989	Kim Terrell	1994	Tammy Turner
1980	Lisa Rathgeber	1985	Dede Davidson	1990	Debbie McMullen	1995	Krissy Stewart
1981	Cindy Mason	1986	Wendy Macpherson	1991	Kim Kahrman	1996	Liz Johnson
1982	Carol Norman	1987	Paula Drake	1992	Marianne DiRupo		

Horse Racing

Jockey **Gary Stevens** stands cheering in the saddle after riding **Silver Charm** to victory in the 1997 Kentucky Derby on May 3.

Wide World Photos

Silver and Gold

Silver Charm and Touch Gold battled it out in one of the best triple crown campaigns in two decades.

by
Hank Goldberg

If the racing establishment was anxious about a follow-up to Cigar's year, it did not have to wait long. 1997 presented as exciting a triple crown campaign as the industry has enjoyed since the classic Affirmed-Alydar duels.

The three-year-old story began to unfold at Gulfstream when Pulpit, unraced as a two-year-old, dominated the stakes schedule early in the Florida meet. Then, in the Florida Derby, the late running Captain Bodgit outran the favored Claiborne colt to the top of the stretch to score in the mile and one eighth event.

Meanwhile, on the West Coast, Hello, Free House, and Silver Charm were slugging it out, and while Free House captured the Santa Anita Derby, Silver Charm hinted that he was special by surviving some blistering splits to come back only to lose that race by a bob.

Hank Goldberg is an analyst for ESPN's horse racing coverage.

On to Kentucky and the Derby where Silver Charm lasted by a head over Captain Bodgit who ducked in less than a furlong from the finish line, a step that might have cost him the race. So, former quarter horse trainer Bob Baffert collected his first Derby after losing a photo in 1996 with Cavonnier. Silver Charm's jockey, Gary Stevens, celebrated the announcement that he was to be inducted into the Hall of Fame by riding his first of four $1 million stakes winner.

Silver Charm also won the Preakness, the second leg of the triple crown, although Touch Gold, a fresh entrant to the three-year-old picture, aroused attention by falling to his knees to the point of scraping his noggin on the Pimlico surface at the break, yet came on fourth behind Free House and Captain Bodgit. He also grabbed a quarter in the process, making his presence in the Belmont uncertain. An injury to his left front leg

Silver Charm (r) with **Gary Stevens** riding edges out **Captain Bodgit**, with **Alex Solis** aboard, to win the 123rd Kentucky Derby on May 3, 1997. Later in the year, Captain Bodgit was retired due to an injury after the Preakness.

forced Captain Bodgit into retirement.

But Silver Charm shipped into New York in the best of health as he attempted to be the first since 1979 to sweep the triple. Trainer David Hofmans, however, did a great job of keeping Touch Gold together. Thanks to a heady ride by Chris McCarron, their horse was able to deny Silver Charm by running him down in the last fifty yards, although throughout the stretch run, it appeared that we had a triple crown winner.

The Baffert-Hofmans combination snapped the D. Wayne Lukas-Nick Zito dominance of the classics for three-year-olds. Between them, they had taken the last eight, including six straight by Lukas. D. Wayne did produce on the distaff side with Sharp Cat, who won major stakes on both coasts including the Acorn. Lukas' Blushing K.D. took the Kentucky Oaks. And by the summer's end, there was no question that Gentlemen was the best of the male handicap division.

Gentlemen, another Stevens mount trained by Richard Mandella and owned by R. D. Hubbard, won, among others, the Pimlico Special, Hollywood Gold Cup and Pacific Classic at Del Mar. Lukas also scored with Marlin in the Arlington Million on the turf, adding to successes in the San Juan Capistrano, and the Sunset Handicap.

On the business side, the year saw the opening of Lone Star in the Dallas-Fort Worth area and Colonial Downs near Richmond, Virginia. However, in a downer of an announcement for the game, Arlington International Racecourse informed the Illinois Racing Board that it has withdrawn its application for all 1998 racing dates. ∎

Silver Charm (c) beats out **Captain Bodgit** (l) and **Free House** (r) to win the 1997 Preakness at Pimlico on May 17, 1997. The win gave Silver Charm the first two thirds of horse racing's triple crown.

Hank Goldberg's Highlights of the Year in Horse Racing

In the milestone department, riders **Laffit Pincay** and **Pat Day** rode their 8,500th and 7,000th career winners, respectively.

Horse of the Year in 1974, '75 and '76, **Forego**, passed away in August. He was 27.

The 1996 Eclipse Award winners were:

Two-Year-Old Colt or Gelding: Boston Harbor.

Two-Year-Old Filly: Storm Song.

Three-Year-Old Colt or Gelding: Skip Away.

Three-Year-Old Filly: Yank's Music

Older Horse, Colt, or Gelding: Cigar.

Older Filly or Male: Jewel Princess.

Male Turf Horse: Singspiel.

Female Turf Horse: Wandesta.

Sprinter: Lit de Justice.

Steeplechase Horse: Correggio.

Horse of the Year: Cigar. ■

Touch Gold, with **Chris McCarron** up, grabs the 1997 Belmont Stakes on June 7 and spoils the hopes of Silver Charm to win the Triple Crown.

THE NUMBERS

INSIDE

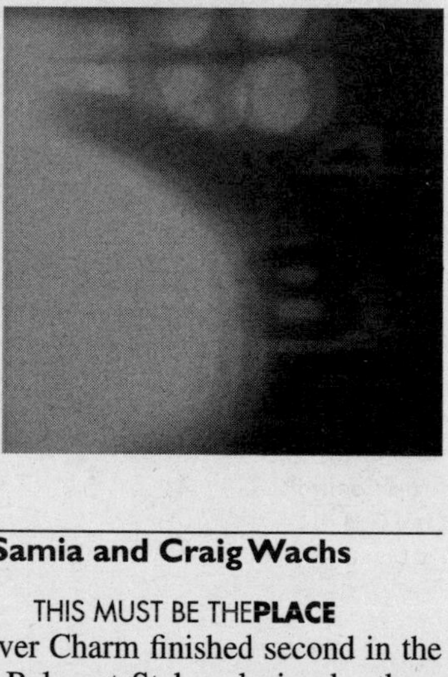

by
Jim Samia and Craig Wachs

THIS MUST BE THE**PLACE**

Silver Charm finished second in the 1997 Belmont Stakes, losing by three quarters of a length. Close calls are his thing. In nine career starts, Silver Charm has five wins and four seconds. And after losing his first career race by four lengths, he has not lost by more than a length.

Silver Charm: Length of Losses

Race	Length	Winner
97 Belmont Stakes	3/4 length	Touch Gold
97 Santa Anita Derby	Head	Free House
97 San Felipe	3/4 length	Free House
96 Maiden	4 lengths	Deeds Not Words

ONEDERFUL

The Michael Johnson vs Donovan Bailey 150 meter race of 1997 was only the latest in a long line of one on one exhibitions. Horse racing had one of the more memorable ones in 1975 when Foolish Pleasure raced Ruffian

773

Jockey **Gary Stevens** poses with the famed roses and **Silver Charm** in the winner's circle at the 1997 Kentucky Derby.

before a television audience of 18 million. Foolish Pleasure had won the 1975 Kentucky Derby and finished second in the Preakness and Belmont Stakes. But Ruffian, the two-year-old filly of the year in 1974, led by half a length before she broke down. Sadly, she was destroyed after the race.

One on One Exhibitions

Participants / Results	Year
Donovan Bailey def. Michael Johnson	1997
Jimmy Connors def. Martina Navratilova	1992
K. Abdul-Jabbar def. Julius Erving	1992
Foolish Pleasure def. Ruffian	**1975**
Billie Jean King def. Bobby Riggs	1973

TALL IN THE SADDLE

On August 25, 1997 Pat Day became the fifth jockey to win 7,000 races in his career. Day has led the nation in races won six times and he set the record for winners in one day when he won with eight of nine mounts on September 14, 1989 at Arlington International. He won the Eclipse Award as the nation's outstanding jockey in 1984, '86, '87 and '91. Day was inducted into the Racing Hall of Fame in 1991.

7,000 Wins
(as of Aug. 25, 1997)

	Wins
Bill Shoemaker	8,833
Laffit Pincay	8,541
Angel Cordero	7,372
Dave Gall	7,122
Pat Day	7,000

■

THE 1998

ESPN
INFORMATION PLEASE
SPORTS
ALMANAC

HORSE RACING
S T A T I S T I C S

SEC
A

THE SEASON IN REVIEW
1996-1997
THOROUGHBRED • HARNESS

PAGE
775

Thoroughbred Racing
Major Stakes Races

Winners of major stakes races from Nov. 3, 1996 through Sept. 21, 1997; (T) indicates turf race course; (F) indicates furlongs.
See Updates for later results.

LATE 1996

Date	Race	Track	Miles	Winner	Jockey	Purse
Nov. 3	Yellow Ribbon Stakes	Santa Anita	1¼ (T)	Donna Viola	Gary Stevens	$600,000
Nov. 16	Hawthorne Gold Cup	Hawthorne	1¼	Come On Flip	Chris Emigh	300,000
Nov. 24	Japan Cup	Tokyo Racecourse	1½ (T)	Singspiel	Frankie Dettori	3,029,629
Dec. 1	Matriarch Stakes	Hollywood	1¼ (T)	Wandesta	Corey Nakatani	700,000
Dec. 1	Hollywood Derby	Hollywood	1⅛ (T)	Marlin	John Velazquez	500,000
Dec. 15	Hollywood Turf Cup	Hollywood	1½ (T)	Running Flame	Chris McCarron	500,000
Dec. 15	Hollywood Futurity	Hollywood	1¹⁄₁₆	Swiss Yodeler	Alex Solis	580,850

1997 (through Sept. 21)

Date	Race	Track	Miles	Winner	Jockey	Purse
Jan. 5	Spectacular Bid B.C. Stakes*	Gulfstream	6 F	Confide	Mike Smith	$75,000
Jan. 18	Holy Bull Stakes*	Gulfstream	1¹⁄₁₆	Arthur L.	John Velazquez	100,000
Jan. 18	Golden Gate Derby	Golden Gate	1¹⁄₁₆	Pacificbounty	Kent Desormeaux	200,000
Feb. 2	Hutcheson Stakes*	Gulfstream	7 F	Frisk Me Now	Eddie King	100,000
Feb. 2	Charles H. Strub Stakes	Santa Anita	1¼	Victory Speech	Jerry Bailey	500,000
Feb. 8	Donn Handicap	Gulfstream	1⅛	Formal Gold	Joe Bravo	300,000
Feb. 8	San Vicente Stakes*	Santa Anita	7 F	Silver Charm	Chris McCarron	106,400
Feb. 22	Fountain of Youth Stakes*	Gulfstream	1¹⁄₁₆	Pulpit	Shane Sellers	200,000
Feb. 23	Rampart Handicap	Gulfstream	1¹⁄₁₆	Chip	Joe Bravo	200,000
Mar. 1	Southwest Stakes*	Oaklawn	1	Smoke Glacken	Craig Perret	100,000
Mar. 1	Gulfstream Park Handi.	Gulfstream	1¼	Mt. Sassafras	Jerry Bailey	500,000
Mar. 2	Santa Anita Handicap	Santa Anita	1¼	Siphon (BRZ)	David Flores	1,000,000
Mar. 2	San Rafael Stakes*	Santa Anita	1	Funontherun	Goncalino Almeida	201,800
Mar. 8	El Camino Real Derby*	Bay Meadows	1¹⁄₁₆	Pacificbounty	Kent Desormeaux	200,000
Mar. 9	Santa Anita Oaks	Santa Anita	1¹⁄₁₆	Sharp Cat	Corey Nakatani	208,800
Mar. 9	Santa Margarita Handicap	Santa Anita	1⅛	Jewel Princess	Corey Nakatani	300,000
Mar. 15	Florida Derby*	Gulfstream	1⅛	Captain Bodgit	Alex Solis	500,000
Mar. 15	Swale Stakes*	Gulfstream	7 F	Confide	Mike Smith	75,000
Mar. 16	Louisiana Derby*	Fairgrounds	1¹⁄₁₆	Crypto Star	Pat Day	400,000
Mar. 16	San Felipe Stakes*	Santa Anita	1¹⁄₁₆	Free House	David Flores	252,400
Mar. 22	Rebel Stakes*	Oaklawn	1¹⁄₁₆	Phantom On Tour	Larry Melancon	125,000
Mar. 23	Tampa Bay Derby*	Tampa Bay	1¹⁄₁₆	Zede	Jerry Bailey	150,000
Mar. 23	San Luis Rey Stakes*	Santa Anita	1½ (T)	Marlin	Chris McCarron	266,600
Mar. 29	Dubai Classic	Nad al-Sheba	1¼	Singspiel (IRE)	Jerry Bailey	4,000,000
Mar. 29	Jim Beam Stakes*	Turfway	1⅛	Concerto	Carlos Marquez Jr.	600,000
Mar. 29	Gotham Stakes*	Aqueduct	1	Smokin Mel	John Velazquez	200,000
Apr. 5	Santa Anita Derby*	Santa Anita	1⅛	Free House	Kent Desormeaux	750,000
Apr. 5	Flamingo Stakes	Hialeah	1⅛	Frisk Me Now	Eddie King Jr.	200,000
Apr. 5	Ashland Stakes	Keeneland	1¹⁄₁₆	Glitter Woman	Mike Smith	543,750
Apr. 5	Oaklawn Handicap	Oaklawn	1⅛	Atticus	Shane Sellers	750,000
Apr. 9	Lafayette Stakes*	Keeneland	7 F	Trafalgar	Jerry Bailey	108,800
Apr. 11	Apple Blossom Handicap	Oaklawn	1¹⁄₁₆	Halo America	Calvin Borel	500,000
Apr. 12	Blue Grass Stakes*	Keeneland	1⅛	Pulpit	Shane Sellers	700,000
Apr. 12	Arkansas Derby*	Oaklawn	1⅛	Crypto Star	Pat Day	500,000
Apr. 12	Wood Memorial*	Aqueduct	1⅛	Captain Bodgit	Alex Solis	500,000
Apr. 13	Bay Shore Stakes*	Aqueduct	7 F	Hawks Landing	Richard Migliore	112,000
Apr. 19	Federico Tesio Stakes*	Pimlico	1⅛	Concerto	Carlos Marquez Jr.	155,500
Apr. 19	California Derby	Golden Gate	9F (T)	I'm A Jewel	Agapito Delgadillo	200,000
Apr. 20	San Juan Capistrano	Santa Anita	1¾ (T)	Marlin	Eddie Delahoussaye	400,000
Apr. 20	Lexington Stakes*	Keeneland	1¹⁄₁₆	Touch Gold	Gary Stevens	175,000

Thoroughbred Racing (Cont.)
1997 (through Sept. 21)

Date	Race	Track	Miles	Winner	Jockey	Purse
Apr. 20	Lone Star Derby*	Lone Star	1 1/16	Anet	David Flores	$250,000
Apr. 26	Derby Trial*	Churchill Downs	1	Richter Scale	Shane Sellers	100,000
May 2	Kentucky Oaks	Churchill Downs	1 1/8	Blushing K.D.	Lonnie Meche	584,700
May 3	**Kentucky Derby***	Churchill Downs	1 1/4	Silver Charm	Gary Stevens	1,000,000
May 3	Withers Stakes*	Belmont	1	Statesmanship	Herb McCauley	100,000
May 10	Pimlico Special	Pimlico	1 3/16	Gentlemen	Gary Stevens	600,000
May 10	Illinois Derby*	Sportsman's Park	1 1/8	Wild Rush	Kent Desormeaux	500,000
May 11	2,000 Guineas Stakes	Longchamp	1	Daylami	Gerald Mosse	200,000
May 16	Black-Eyed Susan Stakes	Pimlico	1 1/8	Salt It	Carlos Marquez Jr.	200,000
May 17	**Preakness Stakes***	Pimlico	1 3/16	Silver Charm	Gary Stevens	751,000
May 18	Peter Pan Stakes*	Belmont	1 1/8	Banker's Gold	Eddie Maple	150,000
May 26	Metropolitan Mile	Belmont	1	Langfuhr	Jorge Chavez	400,000
May 26	Hollywood Turf Handicap	Hollywood Park	1 1/4 (T)	Rainbow Dancer	Alex Solis	400,000
May 31	Massachusetts Handicap	Suffolk Downs	1 1/8	Skip Away	Shane Sellers	300,000
May 31	Acorn Stakes	Belmont	1	Sharp Cat	Gary Stevens	150,000
June 1	Californian Stakes	Hollywood Park	1 1/8	River Keen	Kent Desormeaux	250,000
June 7	Riva Ridge Stakes*	Belmont	7 F	Smoke Glacken	Craig Perret	100,000
June 7	Vodafone English Derby	Epsom Downs	1 1/2 (T)	Benny the Dip	Willie Ryan	1,297,975
June 7	**Belmont Stakes***	Belmont	1 1/2	Touch Gold	Chris McCarron	721,000
June 15	Shoemaker BC Mile	Hollywood	1 (T)	Pinfloron	David Flores	569,000
June 15	Affirmed Handicap*	Hollywood Park	1 1/16	Deputy Commander	Corey Nakatani	100,000
June 21	Leonard Richards Stakes*	Delaware	1 1/16	Leestown	J. Velez Jr.	150,000
June 21	Mother Goose Stakes	Belmont	1 1/8	Ajina	Mike Smith	200,000
June 22	Ohio Derby*	Thistledown	1 1/8	Frisk Me Now	Eddie King Jr.	300,000
June 28	Jersey Shore BC*	Monmouth	7 F	Smoke Glacken	Craig Perret	75,000
June 28	Caesars Int'l Handicap	Atlantic City	1 3/16 (T)	Influent	Jean-Luc Samyn	500,000
June 29	Hollywood Gold Cup	Hollywood Park	1 1/4	Gentlemen	Gary Stevens	1,000,000
June 29	Irish Derby	Curragh	1 1/2 (T)	Desert King	Christy Roche	£700,000
June 29	Beverly Hills Handicap	Hollywood Park	1 1/4 (T)	Windsharp	Corey Nakatani	300,000
June 29	Queen's Plate	Woodbine	1 1/4	Awesome Again	Mike Smith	425,800
July 4	Suburban Handicap	Belmont	1 1/4	Skip Away	Shane Sellers	550,000
July 5	Dwyer Stakes*	Belmont	1 1/16	Behrens	Jerry Bailey	150,000
July 5	Round Table Stakes*	Arlington	1 1/8	Rojo Dinero	Mark Guidry	100,000
July 6	Hollywood Oaks	Hollywood Park	1 1/8	Sharp Cat	Alex Solis	200,000
July 19	Frank J. DeFrancis Memorial	Laurel Park	6F	Smoke Glacken	Craig Perret	300,000
July 19	Coaching Club Am. Oaks	Belmont	1 1/4	Ajina	Mike Smith	250,000
July 20	Swaps Stakes*	Hollywood Park	1 1/8	Free House	Kent Desormeaux	500,000
July 20	Vanity Handicap	Hollywood	1 1/8	Twice the Vice	Kent Desormeaux	400,000
July 26	K. George VI and Q. Elizabeth Diamond Stakes	Ascot	1 1/2 (T)	Swain (IRE)	John Reid	776,300
July 27	Go for Wand Handicap	Saratoga	1 1/8	Hidden Lake	Richard Migliore	250,000
Aug. 2	Whitney Handicap	Saratoga	1 1/8	Will's Way	Jerry Bailey	350,000
Aug. 3	Haskell Invitational*	Monmouth	1 1/8	Touch Gold	Chris McCarron	1,240,000
Aug. 3	Jim Dandy Stakes*	Saratoga	1 1/8	Awesome Again	Mike Smith	250,000
Aug. 9	Pacific Classic	Del Mar	1 1/4	Gentlemen	Gary Stevens	1,000,000
Aug. 10	Remington Park Derby*	Remington	1 1/16	Wild Rush	Gary Stevens	300,000
Aug. 16	Alabama Stakes	Saratoga	1 1/4	Runup the Colors	Jerry Bailey	250,000
Aug. 22	John A. Morris Handicap	Saratoga	1 1/4	Clear Mandate	Mike Smith	350,000
Aug. 23	Travers Stakes*	Saratoga	1 1/4	Deputy Commander	Chris McCarron	750,000
Aug. 23	Philip H. Iselin Handicap	Monmouth	1 1/16	Formal Gold	Kent Desormeaux	340,000
Aug. 24	Saratoga Cup Handicap	Saratoga	1 1/4	Cairo Express	Jean-Luc Samyn	300,000
Aug. 24	Arlington Million	Arlington	1 1/4 (T)	Marlin	Gary Stevens	1,000,000
Aug. 24	Beverly D. Stakes	Arlington	1 3/16 (T)	Memories of Silver	Jerry Bailey	500,000
Aug. 24	Secretariat Stakes	Arlington	1 1/4 (T)	Honor Glide	Garrett Gomez	400,000
Sept. 13	Kentucky Cup Classic	Turfway	1 1/8	Semoran	Kent Desormeaux	380,000
Sept. 13	Turfway Breeders' Cup	Turfway	1 1/16	Feasibility Study	Mike Smith	253,100
Sept. 20	Buick Pegasus Handicap	Meadowlands	1 1/8	Behrens	Jerry Bailey	1,000,000
Sept. 20	Woodbine Mile	Woodbine	1	Geri	Chris Antley	500,000
Sept. 20	Woodward Stakes	Belmont	1 1/8	Formal Gold	Kent Desormeaux	500,000
Sept. 20	Ruffian Handicap	Belmont	1 1/16	Tomisue's Delight	Jerry Bailey	250,000
Sept. 21	Man o' War Stakes	Belmont	1 3/8 (T)	Influent	Jerry Bailey	400,000

* VISA 3-yo Championship Series race (see following tables).

Final VISA 3-year old Series Standings

The VISA Championship Series consists of 44 stakes races to determine the VISA Three-Year-Old Champion. Points are awarded to the first, second and third-place finishers as follows: Triple Crown races are scored 15-10-7; Grade I races are scored 10-7-5; Grade II races 7-5-3; and Grade III and ungraded 5-3-1. Top 20 horses, jockeys and trainers are listed below.

Horses

	Pts			Pts			Pts			Pts
1 Silver Charm	.57	7 Pulpit	.21	13 Phantom On Tour	.13	19 Banker's Gold	.10
2 Free House	.56	Smoke Glacken	.21	14 Awesome Again	.12	Glitman	.10
3 Captain Bodgit	.38	9 Deputy Commander	.20	Concerto	.12	Smokin Mel	.10
4 Touch Gold	.32	10 Confide	.15	Crypto Star	.12	Zede	.10
5 Anet	.22	Wild Rush	.15	17 Hello (IRE)	.11		
Frisk Me Now	.22	12 Behrens	.14	Trafalgar	.11		

Jockeys

	Pts			Pts			Pts			Pts
1 Gary Stevens	.75	6 Jerry Bailey	.36	11 Pat Day	.20	16 Eddie Maple	.10
2 Chris McCarron	.57	7 Craig Perret	.31	Corey Nakatani	.20	Herb McCauley	.10
3 Kent Desormeaux	.54	Shane Sellers	.31	13 Larry Melancon	.13	Richard Migliore	.10
4 Mike Smith	.43	9 David Flores	.24	John Velazquez	.13	19 Gary Boulanger	.8
5 Alex Solis	.42	10 Eddie King Jr.	.22	15 C.H. Marquez, Jr.	.12	20 Goncalino Almeida	.7

Trainers

	Pts			Pts			Pts			Pts
1 Bob Baffert	.85	7 Robert Durso	.22	13 Ben Perkins, Sr.	.16	18 Ron McAnally	.11
2 Paco Gonzalez	.56	8 Henry Carroll	.21	14 H. Allen Jerkens	.13	19 John DeStefano	.10
3 David Hofmans	.44	9 Wallace Dollase	.20	Lynn Whiting	.13	John Kimmel	.10
4 Gary Capuano	.38	10 Nick Zito	.19	16 Wayne Catalano	.12	Bill Mott	.10
5 D. Wayne Lukas	.28	11 H. James Bond	.17	John Tammaro III	.12		
6 Frank Brothers	.24	Richard Mandella	.17				

The 1997 Triple Crown

Thoroughbred racing's Triple Crown for 3-year-olds consists of the Kentucky Derby, Preakness Stakes and Belmont Stakes run over six weeks on May 3, May 17 and June 7, respectively.

123rd KENTUCKY DERBY

Grade I for three-year olds; 8th race at Churchill Downs in Louisville. **Date**— May 3, 1997; **Distance**— 1 1/4 miles;

Stakes Purse— $1,000,000 ($700,000 to winner; $170,000 for 2nd; $85,000 for 3rd; $45,000 for 4th); **Track**— Cloudy and Fast; **Off**— 5:34 p.m. EDT; **Favorite**— Captain Bodgit (3-1 odds).

Winner— Silver Charm; **Field**— 13 horses; **Time**— 2:02 2/5; **Start**— Good; **Won**— Driving; **Sire**— Silver Buck (Buckpasser); **Dam**— Bonnie's Poker (Poker); **Record** (going into race)— 6 starts, 3 wins, 3 seconds; **Last start**— 2nd in Santa Anita Derby (Apr. 5); **Breeder**— Mary Lou Wootton (Fla.).

Order of Finish	Jockey	PP	1/4	1/2	3/4	Mile	Stretch	Finish	To $1
Silver Charm	Gary Stevens	5	6-1	4-1	3-hd	3-1	1-hd	1-hd	4.00
Captain Bodgit	Alex Solis	4	9-1/2	7-hd	6-hd	5-1/2	3-2	2-3 1/2	3.10
Free House	David Flores	13	1-hd	2-1	2-1 1/2	1-hd	2-1 1/2	3-3	10.60
Pulpit	Shane Sellers	7	2-1/2	1-1/2	1-hd	2-1/2	4-1 1/2	4-no	5.70
Crypto Star	Pat Day	1	12-5	12-8	12-5	10-hd	6-hd	5-nk	4.80
Phantom On Tour	Jerry Bailey	2	7-1/2	5-1 1/2	5-2 1/2	4-1 1/2	5-2	6-nk	19.50
Jack Flash	Craig Perret	9	11-hd	11-1/2	10-hd	7-hd	7-1/2	7-1	20.90
Hello (Ire)	Mike Smith	8	10-2 1/2	10-2	9-1 1/2	8-1	8-3	8-5 1/2	9.60
Concerto	Carlos Marquez Jr.	3	3-hd	3-1/2	4-hd	6-2 1/2	9-3	9-1 1/2	10.80
Celtic Warrior	Francisco Torres	6	13	13	13	12-1	10-1 1/2	10-1/2	37.10
Crimson Classic	Robby Albarado	12	4-1/2	6-hd	7-1 1/2	9-hd	11-5	11-9	80.10
Shammy Davis	Willie Martinez	10	5-hd	8-1	11-1/2	13	13	12-nk	20.90
Deeds Not Words	Corey Nakatani	11	8-2	9-1	8-1/2	11-3	12-1	13	32.40

Times 23 2/5; 47 2/5; 1:12 1/5; 1:37 1/5; 2:02 2/5.

$2 Mutual Prices— #6 Silver Charm ($10.00, $4.80, $4.20); #5 Captain Bodgit ($4.80, $3.80); #12 Free House ($5.80). **Exacta**— (6-5) for $31.00; **Trifecta**— (6-5-12) for $205.40; **Superfecta**— (6-5-12-8) for $350.00; **Pick Six**— (7-7-10-7-1-6) five correct for $742.20; **Scratched**— none. **Overweights**— none. **Attendance**— 141,981; **TV Rating**— 7.1/19 share (ABC).

Trainers & Owners (by finish): **1**— Bob Baffert & Robert and Beverly Lewis; **2**— Gary Capuano & Team Valor; **3**— Paco Gonzalez & John A. Toffan and Trudy McCaffery; **4**— Frank Brothers & Claiborne Farm (Ky.); **5**— Wayne Catalano & Darrell and Evelyn Yates; **6**— Lynn Whiting & W. Cal Partee; **7**— Nick Zito & Dogwood Stable; **8**— Ron McAnally & Al and Sandee Kirkwood; **9**— John Tammaro III & Kinsman Stable (George Steinbrenner); **10**— Danny Hutt & Robert Quackenbush, William Schaffrick and Danny Hut; **11**— Forrest Kaelin & John Clay; **12**— Nick Zito & Rick Porter; **13**— D. Wayne Lukas & Michael Tabor and Mrs. John Magnier.

122nd PREAKNESS STAKES

Grade I for three-year olds; 10th race at Pimlico in Baltimore. **Date**— May 17, 1997; **Distance**— 1³/₁₆ miles; **Stakes Purse**— $751,000 ($488,150 to winner; $150,200 for 2nd; $75,100 for 3rd; $37,550 for 4th); **Track**— Fast; **Off**— 5:34 p.m. EDT; **Favorites**— Captain Bodgit and Free House (2-1).

Winner— Silver Charm; **Field**— 10 horses; **Time**— 1:54²/₅; **Start**— Good for all but Touch Gold; **Won**— Driving; **Sire**— Silver Buck (Buck Passer); **Dam**— Bonnie's Poker (Poker); **Record** (going into race)— 7 starts, 4 wins, 3 second; **Last start**— Won the Kentucky Derby (May 3); **Breeder**— Mary Lou Wootton (Fla.)

Order of Finish	Jockey	PP	1/4	1/2	3/4	Stretch	Finish	To $1
Silver Charm	Gary Stevens	7	4-1	3-½	2-1½	2-½	1-hd	3.10
Free House	Kent Desormeaux	4	2-1	2-1½	1-1½	1-1	2-hd	2.40
Captain Bodgit	Alex Solis	9	9-½	9-2	8-4	4-4	3-1¼	2.10
Touch Gold	Chris McCarron	5	10	7-hd	5-2	2-1½	4-7¼	4.60
Frisk Me Now	Eddie King	8	6-2½	6-1	6-1	6-6	5-1¼	29.60
Concerto	Mike Smith	6	5-2	5-2	3-½	5-2	6-11	9.00
Hoxie	Jose Santos	3	7-2	8-2½	9-5	8-10	7-2¾	68.10*
Wild Tempest	Joe Bravo	2	3-½	4-1	4-hd	7-1	8-14	61.30
Cryp Too	C.C. Lopez	10	1-2½	1-hd	7-½	10	9-hd	54.30
Jack At The Bank	Herb McCauley	1	8-½	10	10	9-4	10	68.10*

Times— 22⅘; 46⅘; 1:10²/₅; 1:35²/₅; 1:54²/₅.
$2 Mutual Prices— #6 Silver Charm ($8.20, $4.00, $2.60); #3 Free House ($3.60, $2.60); #8 Captain Bodgit ($2.40).
Exacta— (6-3) for $22.40; **Trifecta**— (6-3-8) for $38.20; **Pick Six**— none; **Scratched**— none. **Overweights**— none.
Attendance— 88,594; **TV Rating**— 4.9/14 share (ABC).
Trainers & Owners (by finish): 1— Bob Baffert & Robert and Beverly Lewis; 2— Paco Gonzalez & John A. Toffan and Trudy McCaffery; 3— Gary Capuano & Team Valor; 4— David Hofmans & Frank Stronach and Stonerside Stable; 5— Robert J. Durso & Carol C. Dender; 6— John Tammaro III & Kinsman Stable; 7— Alfredo Callejas & Robert Perez; 8— Nick Zito & William J. Condren; 9— Allen Borosh & Lauri Hegarty; 10— Alfredo Callejas & Robert Perez.

129th BELMONT STAKES

Grade I for three-year olds; 9th race at Belmont Park in Elmont, N.Y. **Date**— June 7, 1997; **Distance**— 1½ miles; **Stakes Purse**— $721,000 ($432,600 to winner; $144,200 for 2nd; $79,310 for 3rd; $43,260 for 4th; $21,630 for fifth); **Track**— Fast; **Off**— 5:31 p.m. EDT; **Favorite**— Silver Charm (6-5).

Winner— Touch Gold; **Field**— 7 horses; **Time**— 2:28⁴/₅; **Start**— Good; **Won**— Driving; **Sire**— Deputy Minister (Vice Regent); **Dam**— Passing Mood (Buckpasser); **Record** (going into race): 7 starts, 3 wins, 2 second, 1 third; **Last Start**— 4th in Preakness Stakes (May 17); **Breeder**— Hill N' Dale Farm & Holtsinger Inc. (Ky.)

Order of Finish	Jockey	PP	1/4	1/2	1-Mile	1 1/4-M	Stretch	Finish	To $1
a-Touch Gold	Chris McCarron	1	1-1	1-1	4-4	3-½	3-8	1-¾	2.65
Silver Charm	Gary Stevens	2	3-1½	3-½	2-1½	1-hd	1-½	2-1	1.05
Free House	Kent Desormeaux	6	5-½	4-2½	3-½	2-1	2-1	3-14	4.40
Crypto Star	Pat Day	3	7	7	7	6-10	4-½	4-11½	4.20
Irish Silence	John Velazquez	7	4-hd	5-2	5-6	5-1½	5-11½	5-9	34.25
a-Wild Rush	Jerry Bailey	4	2-1½	2-½	1-½	4-4	6-20	6-18	2.65
Mr. Energizer	Manuel Ortega	5	6-9	6-6	6-½	7	7	7	45.00

Times— 23⅗; 49¹/₅; 1:13⅘; 1:38⅘; 2:04; 2:28⅘.
a- coupled.
$2 Mutual Prices— #1 Touch Gold ($7.30, $3.30, $2.60); #2 Silver Charm ($3.00, $2.40); #5 Free House ($2.70).
Exacta— (1-2) for $13.60; **Trifecta**— (1-2-5) for $23.80; **Pick Six**—none; **Scratched**— None. **Overweights**— None.
Attendance— 70,682; **TV Rating**— 5.3/16 share (ABC)
Trainers & Owners (by finish): 1— David Hofmans & Frank Stronach and Stonerside Stable; 2— Bob Baffert & Robert and Beverly Lewis; 3— Paco Gonzalez & John A. Toffan and Trudy McCaffery; 4— Wayne Catalano & Darrell and Evelyn Yates; 5— Leo O'Brien & Austin Delaney; 6— Richard Mandella & Frank H. Stronach; 7— Alfredo Callejas & Robert Perez.

TRC National Thoroughbred Poll
(Sept. 23, 1997)

Poll conducted by Thoroughbred Racing Communications, Inc. and covering races through Sept. 21, 1997. Voting is done by 28 sports and Thoroughbred media representatives. Horses receive 10 points for a first place finish, nine for second, etc. First place votes are in parentheses.

		Pts	Age	Sex	'96 Record Sts-1-2-3	Owner	Trainer
1	Gentlemen (9)	191	5	Horse	6—4-0-1	E. Andrea & R.D. Hubbard	Richard Mandella
2	Formal Gold (6)	176	4	Colt	9—4-2-1	John Murphy Sr.	William Perry
3	Silver Charm (6)	144	3	Colt	6—3-3-0	Robert & Beverly Lewis	Bob Baffert
4	Touch Gold	131	3	Colt	6—4-0-0	F. Stronach/Stonerside	David Hofmans
5	Marlin	117	4	Colt	9—4-0-2	Michael Tabor	D. Wayne Lukas
6	Siphon	95	6	Horse	5—2-3-0	Rio Claro Thoroghbreds	Richard Mandella
7	Free House	65	3	Colt	9—3-2-3	J. Toffan & T. McCaffery	Paco Gonzalez
8	Skip Away	59	4	Colt	9—2-5-2	Carolyn Hine	Sonny Hine
9	Will's Way	32	4	Colt	5—2-1-2	W.L. Clifton Jr./Rudlein	H. James Bond
10	Behrens	29	3	Colt	6—4-1-0	W.L. Clifton Jr./Rudlein	H. James Bond

Others receiving votes: 11. Hidden Lake (28 points); **12.** Influent (22); **13.** Favorite Trick (19); **14.** Sandpit (11); **15.** Geri, Twice the Vice and Memories of Silver (6); **18.** Anet, Tomisue's Delight and Windsharp (4); **21.** Blushing K.D. and Beautiful Pleasure (2); **23.** Honor Glide and Smoke Glacken (1).

1996-97 Money Leaders

Official Top 10 standings for 1996 and unofficial Top 10 standings for 1997, through September 21.

Final 1996   **1997** (through Sept. 21)

HORSES	Age	Sts	1-2-3	Earnings	HORSES	Age	Sts	1-2-3	Earnings
Cigar	6	8	5-2-1	$4,910,000	Gentlemen	5	6	4-0-1	$2,125,300
Skip Away	3	12	6-2-2	2,699,280	Siphon	6	5	2-3-0	1,961,000
Alphabet Soup	5	7	4-1-1	2,536,450	Silver Charm	3	6	3-3-0	1,598,750
Boston Harbor	2	7	6-1-0	1,928,605	Touch Gold	3	6	4-0-0	1,522,313
Louis Quatorze	3	12	4-3-1	1,854,908	Marlin	4	9	4-0-2	1,503,600
Editor's Note	3	12	2-2-2	1,258,360	Free House	3	9	3-2-3	1,336,910
Mecke	4	14	5-1-2	1,223,230	Skip Away	4	9	2-5-2	1,201,000
Grindstone	3	4	2-2-0	1,201,000	Formal Gold	4	9	4-2-1	1,198,500
Serena's Song	4	16	5-7-2	1,161,133	Sandpit	8	6	1-2-2	1,094,000
Jewel Princess	4	9	5-3-1	1,150,800	Anet	3	9	4-4-0	1,007,200

JOCKEYS	Mts	1st	Earnings	JOCKEYS	Mts	1st	Earnings
Jerry Bailey	1187	298	$19,465,376	Jerry Bailey	969	232	$14,232,630
Chris McCarron	802	187	14,440,968	Gary Stevens	698	151	12,350,224
Corey Nakatani	1059	228	13,803,433	Shane Sellers	1119	222	10,055,565
Pat Day	1339	272	13,486,096	Pat Day	950	193	9,580,805
Gary Stevens	809	164	12,715,314	Alex Solis	1071	195	9,279,509
Mike Smith	1410	253	12,437,079	Mike Smith	989	176	8,648,402
Shane Sellers	1328	287	12,080,380	Chris McCarron	484	100	8,367,132
Alex Solis	1455	273	11,493,848	Kent Desormeaux	747	122	7,797,460
Jorge Chavez	1468	246	9,827,859	Corey Nakatani	576	114	7,110,246
John Velazquez	1358	212	9,163,843	Jorge Chavez	1064	193	6,575,660

TRAINERS	Sts	1st	Earnings	TRAINERS	Sts	1st	Earnings
D. Wayne Lukas	1006	192	$15,966,344	Richard Mandella	264	46	$8,234,759
Bill Mott	747	177	14,103,723	D. Wayne Lukas	678	143	7,872,658
Richard Mandella	362	82	8,087,813	Bob Baffert	327	88	7,038,580
Nick Zito	398	62	5,758,267	Bill Mott	466	100	5,500,426
Ron McAnally	434	79	5,549,283	David Hofmans	204	44	3,948,489
David Hofmans	237	58	5,514,529	Jerry Hollendorfer	676	158	3,805,419
Bobby Frankel	324	58	4,977,349	John Kimmel	328	80	3,631,577
Bob Baffert	338	76	4,449,529	W. Elliott Walden	370	80	3,102,485
Jerry Hollendorfer	874	197	4,248,328	Wallace Dollase	130	34	3,057,550
Shug McGaughey	278	59	4,103,998	Bobby Barnett	450	81	2,757,111

Harness Racing

1996–97 Major Stakes Races

Winners of major stakes races from Nov. 1, 1996 through Sept. 18, 1997; all paces and trots cover one mile; (BC) indicates year-end Breeders' Crown series. See Updates for later results.

LATE 1996

Date	Race	Raceway	Winner	Time	Driver	Purse
Nov. 1	Three Diamonds Pace	Garden St.	Michelle's Jackpot	1:54⅘	Luc Ouellette	$452,600
Nov. 8	Valley Victory	Garden St.	Allison Hollow	1:58⅖	Peter Wrenn	347,800
Nov. 15	Windy City Pace	Maywood	Oye Vay	1:54⅕	Doug Brown	350,000
Nov. 15	Governer's Cup	Garden St.	The Big Dog	1:51⅗	Joe Anderson	612,600

1997 (through Sept. 19)

Date	Race	Raceway	Winner	Time	Driver	Purse
June 6	New Jersey Classic	Meadowlands	Arturo	1:51⅖	Luc Ouellette	$500,000
June 14	North America Cup	Woodbine	Gothic Dream	1:50⅘	John Campbell	1,000,000
July 4	Yonkers Trot	Yonkers	Lord Stormont	1:58⅘	Doug Brown	291,948
July 11	Meadowlands Pace	Meadowlands	Dream Away	1:50⅖	Ron Pierce	1,000,000
July 12	Del Miller Memorial	Meadowlands	No Nonsense Woman	1:55	Jim Doherty	320,000
July 19	Budweiser Beacon Course	Meadowlands	Malabar Man	1:55⅗	Mal Burroughs	416,000
July 26	Art Rooney Pace	Yonkers	Western Dreamer	1:53⅖	Mike Lachance	303,083
Aug. 2	BC Open Pace	Meadowlands	Armbro Operative	1:50⅗	Mike Lachance	300,000
Aug. 2	BC Open Trot	Meadowlands	Wesgate Crown	1:52⅘	John Campbell	500,000
Aug. 2	BC Mare Pace	Meadowlands	Extreme Velocity	1:50⅗	John Campbell	287,500
Aug. 2	Adios Final	Ladbroke	Legacy Of Power	1:52⅕	Dan Ross	490,624
Aug. 6	Sweetheart Pace	Meadowlands	Closer Hanover	1:52⅖	Jack Moiseyev	604,800
Aug. 7	Peter Haughton Memorial	Meadowlands	Harry's Bar	1:58⅕	Berndt Lindstedt	408,000
Aug. 7	Merrie Annabelle Final	Meadowlands	Feel The Motion	1:57⅘	John Campbell	390,200
Aug. 8	Woodrow Wilson Pace	Meadowlands	Real Artist	1:52	John Campbell	765,750
Aug. 9	**Hambletonian**	Meadowlands	Malabar Man	1:55	Mal Burroughs	1,000,000
Aug. 9	Hambletonian Oaks	Meadowlands	Must Be Victory	1:53⅖	Berndt Lindstedt	500,000
Aug. 22	Cane Pace	Yonkers	Western Dreamer	1:53⅖	Mike Lachance	318,141

Harness Racing (Cont.)

Date	Race	Raceway	Winner	Time	Driver	Purse
Aug. 22	Hoosier Cup	Hoosier Park	Perfect Art	1:51	George Brennan	$500,000
Aug. 30	Metro Stakes	Woodbine	Rustler Hanover	1:52⅗	Paul MacDonnel	601,400
Aug. 30	World Trotting Derby	Du Quoin	Lord Stormont	2:00⅖	Doug Brown	565,000
Sept. 18	**Little Brown Jug**	Delaware	Western Dreamer	1:51⅕	Mike Lachance	605,210

1996-97 Money Leaders

Official Top 10 standings for 1996 and unofficial Top 10 standings for 1997 through Sept. 21.

Final 1996

HORSES	Age	Sts	1-2-3	Earnings
Continentalvictory	3tf	12	9-0-1	$1,178,360
Hot Lead	3pg	20	11-6-1	987,687
Stout	3pc	26	10-8-3	985,752
Mystical Maddy	3pf	21	19-1-0	945,250
His Mattjesty	2tc	18	9-7-0	804,022
Koochie	2tf	18	15-1-2	698,937
Running Sea	3tc	17	8-3-2	686,338
Moni Maker	3tf	20	19-1-0	675,574
Arizona Jack	3pc	17	4-3-0	661,273
Riyadh	6ph	30	17-8-0	648,830

DRIVERS	Mts	1st	Earnings
Mike Lachance	1930	285	$8,408,231
John Campbell	1573	301	8,180,991
Jack Moiseyev	2360	384	6,345,477
Doug Brown	1922	345	5,539,627
Tony Morgan	3782	853	5,201,715
Luc Ouellette	2418	620	4,957,981
George Brennan	2615	405	4,737,145
Howard Parker	2642	405	4,548,166
Steve Condren	1529	220	4,405,652
Cat Manzi	2907	463	4,168,091

1997 (through Sept. 21)

HORSES	Age	Sts	1-2-3	Earnings
Malabar Man	3tc	12	9-3-0	$1,116,972
Western Dreamer	3pg	23	11-7-2	1,060,657
Gothic Dream	3pc	12	5-1-1	771,624
Village Jasper	3pc	25	13-5-2	749,545
Dream Away	3pc	15	6-3-1	677,123
Lord Stormont	3tg	19	17-1-0	655,935
Arturo	3pc	19	3-6-6	604,413
Armbro Plato	3tg	18	9-3-2	533,281
No Nonsense Woman ..	3tf	13	10-3-0	516,638
Clover Hanover	2pf	8	7-1-0	489,472

DRIVERS	Mts	1st	Earnings
John Campbell	1390	224	$7,295,795
Mike Lachance	1766	286	6,770,847
Jack Moiseyev	1807	250	4,573,583
Ronald Pierce	1368	175	4,113,064
Luc Ouellette	1759	316	4,021,052
Tony Morgan	2595	591	3,987,898
George Brennan	2210	349	3,960,406
Doug Brown	1352	245	3,487,922
Cat Manzi	2384	334	3,429,456
Howard Parker	1905	283	3,283,222

Hambletonian Society/Breeders Crown Standardbred Poll

Poll is conducted by Harness Racing Communications as of Sept. 22, 1997 and based on the votes of harness racing media representatives. Horses receive 10 points for a first place finish, nine for second, etc. Number in parentheses indicates first place votes. (p-pacer, t-trotter, h-horse, f-filly, m-mare, c-colt, g-gelding).

		Pts	Age/Gait/Sex	'96 Sts—1-2-3	Earnings
1	Malabar Man (18)	325	3tc	12—9-3-0	$1,116,972
2	Lord Stormont (13)	305	3tg	19—7-1-0	655,935
3	Western Dreamer (4)	264	3pg	23—11-7-2	1,060,657
4	No Nonsense Woman	204	3tf	13—10-3-0	516,638
5	Steinam's Place	200	3pf	13—8-2-0	402,199
6	Sanabelle Island	176	3pf	11—9-0-2	233,941
7	Moni Maker	115	4tm	7—4-2-0	336,250
8	Wesgate Crown	69	6th	5—3-0-2	337,300
9	Hi Ho Silverheels	67	6ph	11—7-3-1	313,250
10	Riyadh	47	7ph	14—7-1-3	195,950

Others receiving votes: 11. Dream Away (42 points); **12.** Gee Gee Digger (39); **13.** Mystical Maddy (18); **14.** Tune Town and Must Be Victory (12); **16.** Real Artist (7); **17.** Clover Hanover and Armbro Operative (6); **19.** The Wiz (4); **20.** Village Connection and T Cody (3); **22.** Hot Lead (1).

Steeplechase Racing

1996-97 Major Stakes Races

Winners of major steeplechase races from Oct. 26, 1996 through Aug. 21, 1997; See Updates for later results.

LATE 1996

Date	Race	Location	Miles	Winner	Jockey	Purse
Oct. 26	Grand National	Far Hills, N.J.	2⅝	Correggio	Arch Kingsley	$150,000
Nov. 17	Colonial Cup	Camden, S.C.	2¾	Correggio	Jeff Teter	100,000

1997

Date	Race	Location	Miles	Winner	Jockey	Purse
April 5	Atlanta Cup	Kingston, Ga.	2⅜	Mario	Arch Kingsley	$100,000
April 26	Maryland Hunt Cup	Glyndon, Md.	4 (T)	Buck Jakes	Anne Moran	50,000
May 3	Virginia Gold Cup	The Plains, Va.	4 (T)	Saluter	Jack Fisher	40,000
May 10	Iroquois	Nashville, Tn.	3	Correggio	Arch Kingsley	100,000
Aug. 21	N.Y. Turf Writers	Saratoga, N.Y.	2⅜	Bisbalense	Arch Kingsley	107,700

THE 1998 ESPN INFORMATION PLEASE SPORTS ALMANAC

HORSE RACING S T A T I S T I C S

SEC **B**

THROUGH THE YEARS

1867-1997

THOROUGHBRED • HARNESS

PAGE **781**

Thoroughbred Racing

The Triple Crown

The term "Triple Crown" was coined by sportswriter Charles Hatton while covering the 1930 victories of Gallant Fox in the Kentucky Derby, Preakness Stakes and Belmont Stakes. Before then, only Sir Barton (1919) had won all three races in the same year. Since then, nine horses have won the Triple Crown. Two trainers, James (Sunny Jim) Fitzsimmons and Ben A. Jones, have saddled two Triple Crown champions, while Eddie Arcaro is the only jockey to ride two champions.

Year		Jockey	Trainer	Owner	Sire/Dam
1919	**Sir Barton**	Johnny Loftus	H. Guy Bedwell	J.K.L. Ross	Star Shoot/Lady Sterling
1930	**Gallant Fox**	Earl Sande	J.E. Fitzsimmons	Belair Stud	Sir Gallahad III/Marguerite
1935	**Omaha**	Willie Saunders	J.E. Fitzsimmons	Belair Stud	Gallant Fox/Flambino
1937	**War Admiral**	Charley Kurtsinger	George Conway	Samuel Riddle	Man o' War/Brushup
1941	**Whirlaway**	Eddie Arcaro	Ben A. Jones	Calumet Farm	Blenheim II/Dustwhirl
1943	**Count Fleet**	Johnny Longden	Don Cameron	Mrs. J.D. Hertz	Reigh Count/Quickly
1946	**Assault**	Warren Mehrtens	Max Hirsch	King Ranch	Bold Venture/Igual
1948	**Citation**	Eddie Arcaro	Ben A. Jones	Calumet Farm	Bull Lea/Hydroplane II
1973	**Secretariat**	Ron Turcotte	Lucien Laurin	Meadow Stable	Bold Ruler/Somethingroyal
1977	**Seattle Slew**	Jean Cruguet	Billy Turner	Karen Taylor	Bold Reasoning/My Charmer
1978	**Affirmed**	Steve Cauthen	Laz Barrera	Harbor View Farm	Exclusive Native/Won't Tell You

Note: Gallant Fox (1930) is the only Triple Crown winner to sire another Triple Crown winner, Omaha (1935). Wm. Woodward Sr., owner of Belair Stud, was breeder-owner of both horses and both were trained by Sunny Jim Fitzsimmons.

Triple Crown Near Misses

Forty-two horses have won two legs of the Triple Crown. Of those, thirteen won the Kentucky Derby (KD) and Preakness Stakes (PS) only to be beaten in the Belmont Stakes (BS). Two others, Burgoo King (1932) and Bold Venture (1936), each won the Derby and Preakness but were forced out of the Belmont with the same injury—a bowed tendon—that effectively ended their racing careers. In 1978, Alydar finished second to Affirmed in all three races, the only time that has happened. Note that the Preakness preceded the Kentucky Derby in 1922, '23 and '31; (*) indicates won on disqualification.

Year		KD	PS	BS	Year		KD	PS	BS
1877	**Cloverbrook**	DNS	won	won	1961	**Carry Back**	won	won	7th
1878	**Duke of Magenta**	DNS	won	won	1963	**Chateaugay**	won	2nd	won
1880	**Grenada**	DNS	won	won	1964	**Northern Dancer**	won	won	3rd
1881	**Saunterer**	DNS	won	won	1966	**Kauai King**	won	won	4th
1895	**Belmar**	DNS	won	won	1967	**Damascus**	3rd	won	won
					1968	**Forward Pass**	won*	won	2nd
1920	**Man o'War**	DNS	won	won	1969	**Majestic Prince**	won	won	2nd
1922	**Pillory**	DNS	won	won					
1923	**Zev**	won	12th	won	1971	**Canonero II**	won	won	4th
					1972	**Riva Ridge**	won	4th	won
1931	**Twenty Grand**	won	2nd	won	1974	**Little Current**	5th	won	won
1932	**Burgoo King**	won	won	DNS	1976	**Bold Forbes**	won	3rd	won
1936	**Bold Venture**	won	won	DNS	1979	**Spectacular Bid**	won	won	3rd
1939	**Johnstown**	won	5th	won					
1940	**Bimelech**	2nd	won	won	1981	**Pleasant Colony**	won	won	3rd
1942	**Shut Out**	won	5th	won	1984	**Swale**	won	7th	won
1944	**Pensive**	won	won	2nd	1987	**Alysheba**	won	won	4th
1949	**Capot**	2nd	won	won	1988	**Risen Star**	3rd	won	won
					1989	**Sunday Silence**	won	won	2nd
1950	**Middleground**	won	2nd	won					
1953	**Native Dancer**	2nd	won	won	1991	**Hansel**	10th	won	won
1955	**Nashua**	2nd	won	won	1994	**Tabasco Cat**	6th	won	won
1956	**Needles**	won	2nd	won	1995	**Thunder Gulch**	won	3rd	won
1958	**Tim Tam**	won	won	2nd	1997	**Silver Charm**	won	won	2nd

The Triple Crown Challenge (1987-93)

Seeking to make the Triple Crown more than just a media event and to insure that owners would not be attracted to more lucrative races, officials at Churchill Downs, the Maryland Jockey Club and the New York Racing Association created Triple Crown Productions in 1985 and announced that a $1 million bonus would be given to the horse that performs best in the Kentucky Derby, Preakness Stakes and Belmont Stakes. Furthermore, a bonus of $5 million would be presented to any horse winning all three races.

Revised in 1991, the rules stated that the winning horse must: 1. finish all three races; 2. earn points by finishing first, second, third or fourth in at least one of the three races; and 3. earn the highest number of points based on the following system—10 points to win, five to place, three to show and one to finish fourth. In the event of a tie, the $1 million is distributed equally among the top point-getters. From 1987-90, the system was five points to win, three to place and one to show. The Triple Crown Challenge was discontinued in 1994.

Year		KD	PS	BS	Pts	Year		KD	PS	BS	Pts
1987	1 **Bet Twice**	2nd	2nd	1st —	11	1991	1 **Hansel**	10th	1st	1st —	20
	2 Alysheba	1st	1st	4th —	10		2 Strike the Gold	1st	6th	2nd —	15
	3 Cryptoclearance ..	4th	3rd	2nd —	4		3 Mane Minister	3rd	3rd	3rd —	9
1988	1 **Risen Star**	3rd	1st	1st —	11	1992	1 **Pine Bluff**	5th	1st	3rd —	13
	2 Winning Colors ...	1st	3rd	6th —	6		2 Casual Lies	2nd	3rd	5th —	8
	3 Brian's Time	6th	2nd	3rd —	4		(No other horses ran all three races.)					
1989	1 **Sunday Silence** ..	1st	1st	2nd —	13	1993	1 **Sea Hero**	1st	5th	7th —	10
	2 Easy Goer	2nd	2nd	1st —	11		2 Wild Gale	3rd	8th	3rd —	6
	3 Hawkster	5th	5th	5th —	0		(No other horses ran all three races.)					
1990	1 **Unbridled**	1st	2nd	4th —	8						
	2 Summer Squall	2nd	1st	DNR —	8						
	3 Go and Go	DNR	DNR	1st —	5						
	(Unbridled was only horse to run all three races.)										

Kentucky Derby

For three-year-olds. Held the first Saturday in May at Churchill Downs in Louisville, Ky. Inaugurated in 1875. Originally run at 1½ miles (1875-95), shortened to present 1¼ miles in 1896.

Trainers with most wins: Ben Jones (6); Dick Thompson (4); Sunny Jim Fitzsimmons, Max Hirsch and D. Wayne Lukas (3).

Jockeys with most wins: Eddie Arcaro and Bill Hartack (5); Bill Shoemaker (4); Angel Cordero Jr., Issac Murphy, Earl Sande and Gary Stevens (3).

Winning fillies: Regret (1915), Genuine Risk (1980) and Winning Colors (1988).

Year		Time	Jockey	Trainer	2nd place	3rd place
1875	**Aristides**	2:37¾	Oliver Lewis	Ansel Anderson	Volcano	Verdigris
1876	**Vagrant**	2:38¼	Bobby Swim	James Williams	Creedmore	Harry Hill
1877	**Baden-Baden**	2:38	Billy Walker	Ed Brown	Leonard	King William
1878	**Day Star**	2:37¼	Jimmy Carter	Lee Paul	Himyar	Leveler
1879	**Lord Murphy**	2:37	Charlie Shauer	George Rice	Falsetto	Strathmore
1880	**Fonso**	2:37½	George Lewis	Tice Hutsell	Kimball	Bancroft
1881	**Hindoo**	2:40	Jim McLaughlin	James Rowe Sr.	Lelex	Alfambra
1882	**Apollo**	2:40¼	Babe Hurd	Green Morris	Runnymede	Bengal
1883	**Leonatus**	2:43	Billy Donohue	John McGinty	Drake Carter	Lord Raglan
1884	**Buchanan**	2:40¼	Isaac Murphy	William Bird	Loftin	Audrain
1885	**Joe Cotton**	2:37¼	Babe Henderson	Alex Perry	Bersan	Ten Booker
1886	**Ben Ali**	2:36½	Paul Duffy	Jim Murphy	Blue Wing	Free Knight
1887	**Montrose**	2:39¼	Isaac Lewis	John McGinty	Jim Gore	Jacobin
1888	**MacBeth II**	2:38¼	George Covington	John Campbell	Gallifet	White
1889	**Spokane**	2:34½	Thomas Kiley	John Rodegap	Proctor Knott	Once Again
1890	**Riley**	2:45	Isaac Murphy	Edward Corrigan	Bill Letcher	Robespierre
1891	**Kingman**	2:52¼	Isaac Murphy	Dud Allen	Balgowan	High Tariff
1892	**Azra**	2:41½	Lonnie Clayton	John Morris	Huron	Phil Dwyer
1893	**Lookout**	2:39¼	Eddie Kunze	Wm. McDaniel	Plutus	Boundless
1894	**Chant**	2:41	Frank Goodale	Eugene Leigh	Pearl Song	Sigurd
1895	**Halma**	2:37½	Soup Perkins	Byron McClelland	Basso	Laureate
1896	**Ben Brush**	2:07¾	Willie Simms	Hardy Campbell	Ben Eder	Semper Ego
1897	**Typhoon II**	2:12½	Buttons Garner	J.C. Cahn	Ornament	Dr. Catlett
1898	**Plaudit**	2:09	Willie Simms	John E. Madden	Lieber Karl	Isabey
1899	**Manuel**	2:12	Fred Taral	Robert Walden	Corsini	Mazo
1900	**Lieut. Gibson**	2:06¼	Jimmy Boland	Charles Hughes	Florizar	Thrive
1901	**His Eminence**	2:07¾	Jimmy Winkfield	F.B. Van Meter	Sannazarro	Driscoll
1902	**Alan-a-Dale**	2:08¾	Jimmy Winkfield	T.C. McDowell	Inventor	The Rival
1903	**Judge Himes**	2:09	Hal Booker	J.P. Mayberry	Early	Bourbon
1904	**Elwood**	2:08½	Shorty Prior	C.E. Durnell	Ed Tierney	Brancas
1905	**Agile**	2:10¾	Jack Martin	Robert Tucker	Ram's Horn	Layson
1906	**Sir Huon**	2:08⅘	Roscoe Troxler	Pete Coyne	Lady Navarre	James Reddick
1907	**Pink Star**	2:12⅗	Andy Minder	W.H. Fizer	Zal	Ovelando
1908	**Stone Street**	2:15⅕	Arthur Pickens	J.W. Hall	Sir Cleges	Dunvegan

Year		Time	Jockey	Trainer	2nd place	3rd place
1909	**Wintergreen**	2:08⅕	Vincent Powers	Charles Mack	Miami	Dr. Barkley
1910	**Donau**	2:06⅖	Fred Herbert	George Ham	Joe Morris	Fighting Bob
1911	**Meridian**	2:05	George Archibald	Albert Ewing	Governor Gray	Colston
1912	**Worth**	2:09⅖	C.H. Shilling	Frank Taylor	Duval	Flamma
1913	**Donerail**	2:04⅘	Roscoe Goose	Thomas Hayes	Ten Point	Gowell
1914	**Old Rosebud**	2:03⅖	John McCabe	F.D. Weir	Hodge	Bronzewing
1915	**Regret**	2:05⅖	Joe Notter	James Rowe Sr.	Pebbles	Sharpshooter
1916	**George Smith**	2:04	Johnny Loftus	Hollie Hughes	Star Hawk	Franklin
1917	**Omar Khayyam**	2:04⅗	Charles Borel	C.T. Patterson	Ticket	Midway
1918	**Exterminator**	2:10⅘	William Knapp	Henry McDaniel	Escoba	Viva America
1919	**SIR BARTON**	2:09⅘	Johnny Loftus	H. Guy Bedwell	Billy Kelly	Under Fire
1920	**Paul Jones**	2:09	Ted Rice	Billy Garth	Upset	On Watch
1921	**Behave Yourself**	2:04⅕	Charles Thompson	Dick Thompson	Black Servant	Prudery
1922	**Morvich**	2:04⅗	Albert Johnson	Fred Burlew	Bet Mosie	John Finn
1923	**Zev**	2:05⅖	Earl Sande	David Leary	Martingale	Vigil
1924	**Black Gold**	2:05⅕	John Mooney	Hanly Webb	Chilhowee	Beau Butler
1925	**Flying Ebony**	2:07⅗	Earl Sande	William Duke	Captain Hal	Son of John
1926	**Bubbling Over**	2:03⅘	Albert Johnson	Dick Thompson	Bagenbaggage	Rock Man
1927	**Whiskery**	2:06	Linus McAtee	Fred Hopkins	Osmand	Jock
1928	**Reigh Count**	2:10⅖	Chick Lang	Bert Michell	Misstep	Toro
1929	**Clyde Van Dusen**	2:10⅘	Linus McAtee	Clyde Van Dusen	Naishapur	Panchio
1930	**GALLANT FOX**	2:07⅗	Earl Sande	Jim Fitzsimmons	Gallant Knight	Ned O.
1931	**Twenty Grand**	2:01⅘	Charley Kurtsinger	James Rowe Jr.	Sweep All	Mate
1932	**Burgoo King**	2:05⅕	Eugene James	Dick Thompson	Economic	Stepenfetchit
1933	**Brokers Tip**	2:06⅘	Don Meade	Dick Thompson	Head Play	Charley O.
1934	**Cavalcade**	2:04	Mack Garner	Bob Smith	Discovery	Agrarian
1935	**OMAHA**	2:05	Willie Saunders	Jim Fitzsimmons	Roman Soldier	Whiskolo
1936	**Bold Venture**	2:03⅗	Ira Hanford	Max Hirsch	Brevity	Indian Broom
1937	**WAR ADMIRAL**	2:03⅕	Charley Kurtsinger	George Conway	Pompoon	Reaping Reward
1938	**Lawrin**	2:04⅘	Eddie Arcaro	Ben Jones	Dauber	Can't Wait
1939	**Johnstown**	2:03⅖	James Stout	Jim Fitzsimmons	Challedon	Heather Broom
1940	**Gallahadion**	2:05	Carroll Bierman	Roy Waldron	Bimelech	Dit
1941	**WHIRLAWAY**	2:01⅖	Eddie Arcaro	Ben Jones	Staretor	Market Wise
1942	**Shut Out**	2:04⅖	Wayne Wright	John Gaver	Alsab	Valdina Orphan
1943	**COUNT FLEET**	2:04	Johnny Longden	Don Cameron	Blue Swords	Slide Rule
1944	**Pensive**	2:04⅕	Conn McCreary	Ben Jones	Broadcloth	Stir Up
1945	**Hoop Jr**	2:07	Eddie Arcaro	Ivan Parke	Pot O'Luck	Darby Dieppe
1946	**ASSAULT**	2:06⅗	Warren Mehrtens	Max Hirsch	Spy Song	Hampden
1947	**Jet Pilot**	2:06⅘	Eric Guerin	Tom Smith	Phalanx	Faultless
1948	**CITATION**	2:05⅖	Eddie Arcaro	Ben Jones	Coaltown	My Request
1949	**Ponder**	2:04⅕	Steve Brooks	Ben Jones	Capot	Palestinian
1950	**Middleground**	2:01⅗	William Boland	Max Hirsch	Hill Prince	Mr. Trouble
1951	**Count Turf**	2:02⅗	Conn McCreary	Sol Rutchick	Royal Mustang	Ruhe
1952	**Hill Gail**	2:01⅗	Eddie Arcaro	Ben Jones	Sub Fleet	Blue Man
1953	**Dark Star**	2:02	Hank Moreno	Eddie Hayward	Native Dancer	Invigorator
1954	**Determine**	2:03	Raymond York	Willie Molter	Hasty Road	Hasseyampa
1955	**Swaps**	2:01⅘	Bill Shoemaker	Mesh Tenney	Nashua	Summer Tan
1956	**Needles**	2:03⅖	David Erb	Hugh Fontaine	Fabius	Come On Red
1957	**Iron Liege**	2:02⅕	Bill Hartack	Jimmy Jones	Gallant Man	Round Table
1958	**Tim Tam**	2:05	Ismael Valenzuela	Jimmy Jones	Lincoln Road	Noureddin
1959	**Tomy Lee**	2:02⅕	Bill Shoemaker	Frank Childs	Sword Dancer	First Landing
1960	**Venetian Way**	2:02⅖	Bill Hartack	Victor Sovinski	Bally Ache	Victoria Park
1961	**Carry Back**	2:04	John Sellers	Jack Price	Crozier	Bass Clef
1962	**Decidedly**	2:00⅖	Bill Hartack	Horatio Luro	Roman Line	Ridan
1963	**Chateaugay**	2:01⅘	Braulio Baeza	James Conway	Never Bend	Candy Spots
1964	**Northern Dancer**	2:00	Bill Hartack	Horatio Luro	Hill Rise	The Scoundrel
1965	**Lucky Debonair**	2:01⅕	Bill Shoemaker	Frank Catrone	Dapper Dan	Tom Rolfe
1966	**Kauai King**	2:02	Don Brumfield	Henry Forrest	Advocator	Blue Skyer
1967	**Proud Clarion**	2:00⅗	Bobby Ussery	Loyd Gentry	Barbs Delight	Damascus
1968	**Forward Pass***	—	Ismael Valenzuela	Henry Forrest	Francie's Hat	T.V. Commercial
1969	**Majestic Prince**	2:01⅘	Bill Hartack	Johnny Longden	Arts and Letters	Dike
1970	**Dust Commander**	2:03⅖	Mike Manganello	Don Combs	My Dad George	High Echelon
1971	**Canonero II**	2:03⅕	Gustavo Avila	Juan Arias	Jim French	Bold Reason
1972	**Riva Ridge**	2:01⅘	Ron Turcotte	Lucien Laurin	No Le Hace	Hold Your Peace
1973	**SECRETARIAT**	1:59⅖	Ron Turcotte	Lucien Laurin	Sham	Our Native
1974	**Cannonade**	2:04	Angel Cordero Jr.	Woody Stephens	Hudson County	Agitate
1975	**Foolish Pleasure**	2:02	Jacinto Vasquez	LeRoy Jolley	Avatar	Diabolo
1976	**Bold Forbes**	2:01⅗	Angel Cordero Jr.	Laz Barrera	Honest Pleasure	Elocutionist

Kentucky Derby (Cont.)

Year		Time	Jockey	Trainer	2nd place	3rd place
1977	**SEATTLE SLEW**	2:02⅕	Jean Cruguet	Billy Turner	Run Dusty Run	Sanhedrin
1978	**AFFIRMED**	2:01⅕	Steve Cauthen	Laz Barrera	Alydar	Believe It
1979	**Spectacular Bid**	2:02⅖	Ron Franklin	Bud Delp	General Assembly	Golden Act
1980	**Genuine Risk**	2:02	Jacinto Vasquez	LeRoy Jolley	Rumbo	Jaklin Klugman
1981	**Pleasant Colony**	2:02	Jorge Velasquez	John Campo	Woodchopper	Partez
1982	**Gato Del Sol**	2:02⅖	E. Delahoussaye	Eddie Gregson	Laser Light	Reinvested
1983	**Sunny's Halo**	2:02⅕	E. Delahoussaye	David Cross Jr.	Desert Wine	Caveat
1984	**Swale**	2:02⅖	Laffit Pincay Jr.	Woody Stephens	Coax Me Chad	At The Threshold
1985	**Spend A Buck**	2:00⅕	Angel Cordero Jr.	Cam Gambolati	Stephan's Odyssey	Chief's Crown
1986	**Ferdinand**	2:02⅘	Bill Shoemaker	Chas. Whittingham	Bold Arrangement	Broad Brush
1987	**Alysheba**	2:03⅖	Chris McCarron	Jack Van Berg	Bet Twice	Avies Copy
1988	**Winning Colors**	2:02⅕	Gary Stevens	D. Wayne Lukas	Forty Niner	Risen Star
1989	**Sunday Silence**	2:05	Pat Valenzuela	Chas. Whittingham	Easy Goer	Awe Inspiring
1990	**Unbridled**	2:02	Craig Perret	Carl Nafzger	Summer Squall	Pleasant Tap
1991	**Strike the Gold**	2:03	Chris Antley	Nick Zito	Best Pal	Mane Minister
1992	**Lil E. Tee**	2:03	Pat Day	Lynn Whiting	Casual Lies	Dance Floor
1993	**Sea Hero**	2:02⅖	Jerry Bailey	Mack Miller	Prairie Bayou	Wild Gale
1994	**Go For Gin**	2:03⅗	Chris McCarron	Nick Zito	Strodes Creek	Blumin Affair
1995	**Thunder Gulch**	2:01⅕	Gary Stevens	D. Wayne Lukas	Tejano Run	Timber Country
1996	**Grindstone**	2:01	Jerry Bailey	D. Wayne Lukas	Cavonnier	Prince of Thieves
1997	**Silver Charm**	2:02⅖	Gary Stevens	Bob Baffert	Captain Bodgit	Free House

*Dancer's Image finished first (in 2:02½), but was disqualified after traces of prohibited medication were found in his system.

Preakness Stakes

For three-year-olds. Held two weeks after the Kentucky Derby at Pimlico Race Course in Baltimore, Md. Inaugurated 1873. Originally run at 1½ miles (1873-88), then at 1¼ miles (1889), 1½ miles (1890), 1 1/16 miles (1894-1900), 1 mile & 70 yards (1901-07), 1 1/16 miles (1908), 1 mile (1909-1910), 1⅛ miles (1911-24), and the present 1 3/16 miles since 1925

Trainers with most wins: Robert W. Walden (7); T.J. Healey (5); Sunny Jim Fitzsimmons, Jimmy Jones and D. Wayne Lukas (4); and J. Whalen (3).

Jockeys with most wins: Eddie Arcaro (6); Pat Day (5); G. Barbee, Bill Hartack and Lloyd Hughes (3).

Winning fillies: Flocarline (1903), Whimsical (1906), Rhine Maiden (1915) and Nellie Morse (1924).

Year		Time	Jockey	Trainer	2nd place	3rd place
1873	**Survivor**	2:43	G. Barbee	A.D. Pryor	John Boulger	Artist
1874	**Culpepper**	2:56½	W. Donohue	H. Gaffney	King Amadeus	Scratch
1875	**Tom Ochiltree**	2:43½	L. Hughes	R.W. Walden	Viator	Bay Final
1876	**Shirley**	2:44¾	G. Barbee	W. Brown	Rappahannock	Compliment
1877	**Cloverbrook**	2:45½	C. Holloway	J. Walden	Bombast	Lucifer
1878	**Duke of Magenta**	2:41¾	C. Holloway	R.W. Walden	Bayard	Albert
1879	**Harold**	2:40½	L. Hughes	R.W. Walden	Jericho	Rochester
1880	**Grenada**	2:40½	L. Hughes	R.W. Walden	Oden	Emily F.
1881	**Saunterer**	2:40½	T. Costello	R.W. Walden	Compensation	Baltic
1882	**Vanguard**	2:44½	T. Costello	R.W. Walden	Heck	Col. Watson
1883	**Jacobus**	2:42½	G. Barbee	R. Dwyer	Parnell	(2-horse race)
1884	**Knight of Ellerslie**	2:39½	S. Fisher	T.B. Doswell	Welcher	(2-horse race)
1885	**Tecumseh**	2:49	Jim McLaughlin	C. Littlefield	Wickham	John C.
1886	**The Bard**	2:45	S. Fisher	J. Huggins	Eurus	Elkwood
1887	**Dunboyne**	2:39½	W. Donohue	W. Jennings	Mahoney	Raymond
1888	**Refund**	2:49	F. Littlefield	R.W. Walden	Bertha B.*	Glendale
1889	**Buddhist**	2:17½	W. Anderson	J. Rogers	Japhet	(2-horse race)
1890	**Montague**	2:36¾	W. Martin	E. Feakes	Philosophy	Barrister
1891-93	Not held					
1894	**Assignee**	1:49¼	F. Taral	W. Lakeland	Potentate	Ed Kearney
1895	**Belmar**	1:50½	F. Taral	E. Feakes	April Fool	Sue Kittie
1896	**Margrave**	1:51	H. Griffin	Byron McClelland	Hamilton II	Intermission
1897	**Paul Kauvar**	1:51¼	T. Thorpe	T.P. Hayes	Elkins	On Deck
1898	**Sly Fox**	1:49¾	W. Simms	H. Campbell	The Huguenot	Nuto
1899	**Half Time**	1:47	R. Clawson	F. McCabe	Filigrane	Lackland
1900	**Hindus**	1:48⅖	H. Spencer	J.H. Morris	Sarmatian	Ten Candles
1901	**The Parader**	1:47⅕	F. Landry	T.J. Healey	Sadie S.	Dr. Barlow
1902	**Old England**	1:45⅘	L. Jackson	G.B. Morris	Maj. Daingerfield	Namtor
1903	**Flocarline**	1:44⅘	W. Gannon	H.C. Riddle	Mackey Dwyer	Rightful
1904	**Bryn Mawr**	1:44⅕	E. Hildebrand	W.F. Presgrave	Wotan	Dolly Spanker
1905	**Cairngorm**	1:45⅘	W. Davis	A.J. Joyner	Kiamesha	Coy Maid
1906	**Whimsical**	1:45	Walter Miller	T.J. Gaynor	Content	Larabie
1907	**Don Enrique**	1:45⅖	G. Mountain	J. Whalen	Ethon	Zambesi

Year		Time	Jockey	Trainer	2nd place	3rd place
1908	**Royal Tourist**	1:46⅖	Eddie Dugan	A.J. Joyner	Live Wire	Robert Cooper
1909	**Effendi**	1:39⅘	Willie Doyle	F.C. Frisbie	Fashion Plate	Hill Top
1910	**Layminster**	1:40⅗	R. Estep	J.S. Healy	Dalhousie	Sager
1911	**Watervale**	1:51	Eddie Dugan	J. Whalen	Zeus	The Nigger
1912	**Colonel Holloway**	1:56⅗	C. Turner	D. Woodford	Bwana Tumbo	Tipsand
1913	**Buskin**	1:53⅖	James Butwell	J. Whalen	Kleburne	Barnegat
1914	**Holiday**	1:53⅘	A. Schuttinger	J.S. Healy	Brave Cunarder	Defendum
1915	**Rhine Maiden**	1:58	Douglas Hoffman	F. Devers	Half Rock	Runes
1916	**Damrosch**	1:54⅘	Linus McAtee	A.G. Weston	Greenwood	Achievement
1917	**Kalitan**	1:54⅖	E. Haynes	Bill Hurley	Al M. Dick	Kentucky Boy
1918	**War Cloud**	1:53⅗	Johnny Loftus	W.B. Jennings	Sunny Slope	Lanius
1918	**Jack Hare Jr**	1:53⅖	Charles Peak	F.D. Weir	The Porter	Kate Bright
1919	**SIR BARTON**	1:53	Johnny Loftus	H. Guy Bedwell	Eternal	Sweep On
1920	**Man o' War**	1:51⅗	Clarence Kummer	L. Feustel	Upset	Wildair
1921	**Broomspun**	1:54⅕	F. Coltiletti	James Rowe Sr.	Polly Ann	Jeg
1922	**Pillory**	1:51⅗	L. Morris	Thomas Healey	Hea	June Grass
1923	**Vigil**	1:53⅗	B. Marinelli	Thomas Healey	General Thatcher	Rialto
1924	**Nellie Morse**	1:57⅕	John Merimee	A.B. Gordon	Transmute	Mad Play
1925	**Coventry**	1:59	Clarence Kummer	William Duke	Backbone	Almadel
1926	**Display**	1:59⅘	John Maiben	Thomas Healey	Blondin	Mars
1927	**Bostonian**	2:01⅗	Whitey Abel	Fred Hopkins	Sir Harry	Whiskery
1928	**Victorian**	2:00⅕	Sonny Workman	James Rowe Jr.	Toro	Solace
1929	**Dr. Freeland**	2:01⅗	Louis Schaefer	Thomas Healey	Minotaur	African
1930	**GALLANT FOX**	2:00⅗	Earl Sande	Jim Fitzsimmons	Crack Brigade	Snowflake
1931	**Mate**	1:59	George Ellis	J.W. Healy	Twenty Grand	Ladder
1932	**Burgoo King**	1:59⅘	Eugene James	Dick Thompson	Tick On	Boatswain
1933	**Head Play**	2:02	Charley Kurtsinger	Thomas Hayes	Ladysman	Utopian
1934	**High Quest**	1:58⅕	Robert Jones	Bob Smith	Cavalcade	Discovery
1935	**OMAHA**	1:58⅖	Willie Saunders	Jim Fitzsimmons	Firethorn	Psychic Bid
1936	**Bold Venture**	1:59	George Woolf	Max Hirsch	Granville	Jean Bart
1937	**WAR ADMIRAL**	1:58⅖	Charley Kurtsinger	George Conway	Pompoon	Flying Scot
1938	**Dauber**	1:59⅘	Maurice Peters	Dick Handlen	Cravat	Menow
1939	**Challedon**	1:59⅘	George Seabo	Louis Schaefer	Gilded Knight	Volitant
1940	**Bimelech**	1:58⅗	F.A. Smith	Bill Hurley	Mioland	Gallahadion
1941	**WHIRLAWAY**	1:58⅘	Eddie Arcaro	Ben Jones	King Cole	Our Boots
1942	**Alsab**	1:57	Basil James	Sarge Swenke	Requested & Sun Again (dead heat)	
1943	**COUNT FLEET**	1:57⅖	Johnny Longden	Don Cameron	Blue Swords	Vincentive
1944	**Pensive**	1:59⅕	Conn McCreary	Ben Jones	Platter	Stir Up
1945	**Polynesian**	1:58⅘	W.D. Wright	Morris Dixon	Hoop Jr.	Darby Dieppe
1946	**ASSAULT**	2:01⅖	Warren Mehrtens	Max Hirsch	Lord Boswell	Hampden
1947	**Faultless**	1:59	Doug Dodson	Jimmy Jones	On Trust	Phalanx
1948	**CITATION**	2:02⅖	Eddie Arcaro	Jimmy Jones	Vulcan's Forge	Bovard
1949	**Capot**	1:56	Ted Atkinson	J.M. Gaver	Palestinian	Noble Impulse
1950	**Hill Prince**	1:59⅕	Eddie Arcaro	Casey Hayes	Middleground	Dooly
1951	**Bold**	1:56⅖	Eddie Arcaro	Preston Burch	Counterpoint	Alerted
1952	**Blue Man**	1:57⅖	Conn McCreary	Woody Stephens	Jampol	One Count
1953	**Native Dancer**	1:57⅘	Eric Guerin	Bill Winfrey	Jamie K.	Royal Bay Gem
1954	**Hasty Road**	1:57⅖	Johnny Adams	Harry Trotsek	Correlation	Hasseyampa
1955	**Nashua**	1:54⅗	Eddie Arcaro	Jim Fitzsimmons	Saratoga	Traffic Judge
1956	**Fabius**	1:58⅖	Bill Hartack	Jimmy Jones	Needles	No Regrets
1957	**Bold Ruler**	1:56⅕	Eddie Arcaro	Jim Fitzsimmons	Iron Liege	Inside Tract
1958	**Tim Tam**	1:57⅕	Ismael Valenzuela	Jimmy Jones	Lincoln Road	Gone Fishin'
1959	**Royal Orbit**	1:57	William Harmatz	R. Cornell	Sword Dancer	Dunce
1960	**Bally Ache**	1:57⅗	Bobby Ussery	Jimmy Pitt	Victoria Park	Celtic Ash
1961	**Carry Back**	1:57⅗	Johnny Sellers	Jack Price	Globemaster	Crozier
1962	**Greek Money**	1:56⅕	John Rotz	V.W. Raines	Ridan	Roman Line
1963	**Candy Spots**	1:56⅕	Bill Shoemaker	Mesh Tenney	Chateaugay	Never Bend
1964	**Northern Dancer**	1:56⅘	Bill Hartack	Horatio Luro	The Scoundrel	Hill Rise
1965	**Tom Rolfe**	1:56⅕	Ron Turcotte	Frank Whiteley	Dapper Dan	Hail To All
1966	**Kauai King**	1:55⅖	Don Brumfield	Henry Forrest	Stupendous	Amberoid
1967	**Damascus**	1:55⅕	Bill Shoemaker	Frank Whiteley	In Reality	Proud Clarion
1968	**Forward Pass**	1:56⅘	Ismael Valenzuela	Henry Forrest	Out Of the Way	Nodouble
1969	**Majestic Prince**	1:55⅗	Bill Hartack	Johnny Longden	Arts and Letters	Jay Ray
1970	**Personality**	1:56⅕	Eddie Belmonte	John Jacobs	My Dad George	Silent Screen
1971	**Canonero II**	1:54	Gustavo Avila	Juan Arias	Eastern Fleet	Jim French
1972	**Bee Bee Bee**	1:55⅗	Eldon Nelson	Red Carroll	No Le Hace	Key To The Mint
1973	**SECRETARIAT**	1:54⅖	Ron Turcotte	Lucien Laurin	Sham	Our Native
1974	**Little Current**	1:54⅗	Miguel Rivera	Lou Rondinello	Neapolitan Way	Cannonade

Preakness Stakes (Cont.)

Year		Time	Jockey	Trainer	2nd place	3rd place
1975	**Master Derby**	1:56⅖	Darrel McHargue	Smiley Adams	Foolish Pleasure	Diabolo
1976	**Elocutionist**	1:55	John Lively	Paul Adwell	Play The Red	Bold Forbes
1977	**SEATTLE SLEW**	1:54⅖	Jean Cruguet	Billy Turner	Iron Constitution	Run Dusty Run
1978	**AFFIRMED**	1:54⅖	Steve Cauthen	Laz Barrera	Alydar	Believe It
1979	**Spectacular Bid**	1:54⅕	Ron Franklin	Bud Delp	Golden Act	Screen King
1980	**Codex**	1:54⅕	Angel Cordero Jr.	D. Wayne Lukas	Genuine Risk	Colonel Moran
1981	**Pleasant Colony**	1:54⅗	Jorge Velasquez	John Campo	Bold Ego	Paristo
1982	**Aloma's Ruler**	1:55⅖	Jack Kaenel	John Lenzini Jr.	Linkage	Cut Away
1983	**Deputed Testamony**	1:55⅖	Donald Miller Jr.	Bill Boniface	Desert Wine	High Honors
1984	**Gate Dancer**	1:53⅗	Angel Cordero Jr.	Jack Van Berg	Play On	Fight Over
1985	**Tank's Prospect**	1:53⅖	Pat Day	D. Wayne Lukas	Chief's Crown	Eternal Prince
1986	**Snow Chief**	1:54⅘	Alex Solis	Melvin Stute	Ferdinand	Broad Brush
1987	**Alysheba**	1:55⅘	Chris McCarron	Jack Van Berg	Bet Twice	Cryptoclearance
1988	**Risen Star**	1:56⅕	E. Delahoussaye	Louie Roussel III	Brian's Time	Winning Colors
1989	**Sunday Silence**	1:53⅘	Pat Valenzuela	Chas. Whittingham	Easy Goer	Rock Point
1990	**Summer Squall**	1:53⅗	Pat Day	Neil Howard	Unbridled	Mister Frisky
1991	**Hansel**	1:54	Jerry Bailey	Frank Brothers	Corporate Report	Mane Minister
1992	**Pine Bluff**	1:55⅗	Chris McCarron	Tom Bohannan	Alydeed	Casual Lies
1993	**Prairie Bayou**	1:56⅗	Mike Smith	Tom Bohannon	Cherokee Run	El Bakan
1994	**Tabasco Cat**	1:56⅖	Pat Day	D. Wayne Lukas	Go For Gin	Concern
1995	**Timber Country**	1:54⅖	Pat Day	D. Wayne Lukas	Oliver's Twist	Thunder Gulch
1996	**Louis Quatorze**	1:53⅖	Pat Day	Nick Zito	Skip Away	Editor's Note
1997	**Silver Charm**	1:54⅖	Gary Stevens	Bob Baffert	Free House	Captain Bodgit

* Later named Judge Murray.

Belmont Stakes

For three-year-olds. Held three weeks after Preakness Stakes at Belmont Park in Elmont, N.Y. Inaugurated in 1867 at Jerome Park, moved to Morris Park in 1890 and Belmont Park in 1905.

Originally run at 1 mile and 5 furlongs (1867-89), then 1¼ miles (1890-1905), 1⅜ miles (1906-25), and the present 1½ miles since 1926.

Trainers with most wins: James Rowe, Sr. (8); Sam Hildreth (7); Sunny Jim Fitzsimmons (6); Woody Stephens (5); Max Hirsch and Robert W. Walden (4); Elliott Burch, Lucien Laurin, D. Wayne Lukas, F. McCabe and D. McDaniel (3).

Jockeys with most wins: Eddie Arcaro and Jim McLaughlin (6); Earl Sande and Bill Shoemaker (5); Braulio Baeza, Laffit Pincay, Jr and James Stout (3).

Winning fillies: Ruthless (1867) and Tanya (1905).

Year		Time	Jockey	Trainer	2nd place	3rd place
1867	**Ruthless**	3:05	J. Gilpatrick	A.J. Minor	DeCourcey	Rivoli
1868	**General Duke**	3:02	Bobby Swim	A. Thompson	Northumberland	Fanny Ludlow
1869	**Fenian**	3:04¼	C. Miller	J. Pincus	Glenelg	Invercauld
1870	**Kingfisher**	2:59½	W. Dick	R. Colston	Foster	Midday
1871	**Harry Bassett**	2:56	W. Miller	D. McDaniel	Stockwood	By the Sea
1872	**Joe Daniels**	2:58¼	James Roe	D. McDaniel	Meteor	Shylock
1873	**Springbok**	3:01¾	James Roe	D. McDaniel	Count d'Orsay	Strachino
1874	**Saxon**	2:39½	G. Barbee	W. Prior	Grinstead	Aaron Pennington
1875	**Calvin**	2:42¼	Bobby Swim	A. Williams	Aristides	Milner
1876	**Algerine**	2:40½	Billy Donohue	Major Doswell	Fiddlesticks	Barricade
1877	**Cloverbrook**	2:46	C. Holloway	J. Walden	Loiterer	Baden-Baden
1878	**Duke of Magenta**	2:43½	L. Hughes	R.W. Walden	Bramble	Sparta
1879	**Spendthrift**	2:42¾	George Evans	T. Puryear	Monitor	Jericho
1880	**Grenada**	2:47	L. Hughes	R.W. Walden	Ferncliffe	Turenne
1881	**Saunterer**	2:47	T. Costello	R.W. Walden	Eole	Baltic
1882	**Forester**	2:43	Jim McLaughlin	L. Stuart	Babcock	Wyoming
1883	**George Kinney**	2:42½	Jim McLaughlin	James Rowe Sr.	Trombone	Renegade
1884	**Panique**	2:42	Jim McLaughlin	James Rowe Sr.	Knight of Ellerslie	Himalaya
1885	**Tyrant**	2:43	Paul Duffy	W. Claypool	St. Augustine	Tecumseh
1886	**Inspector B**	2:41	Jim McLaughlin	F. McCabe	The Bard	Linden
1887	**Hanover**	2:43½	Jim McLaughlin	F. McCabe	Oneko	(2-horse race)
1888	**Sir Dixon**	2:40¼	Jim McLaughlin	F. McCabe	Prince Royal	(2-horse race)
1889	**Eric**	2:47¼	W. Hayward	J. Huggins	Diablo	Zephyrus
1890	**Burlington**	2:07¾	Pike Barnes	A. Cooper	Devotee	Padishah
1891	**Foxford**	2:08¾	Ed Garrison	M. Donavan	Montana	Laurestan
1892	**Patron**	2:12	W. Hayward	L. Stuart	Shellbark	(2-horse race)
1893	**Commanche**	1:53¼	Willie Simms	G. Hannon	Dr. Rice	Rainbow
1894	**Henry of Navarre**	1:56½	Willie Simms	B. McClelland	Prig	Assignee

Year		Time	Jockey	Trainer	2nd place	3rd place
1895	**Belmar**	2:11½	Fred Taral	E. Feakes	Counter Tenor	Nanki Poo
1896	**Hastings**	2:24½	H. Griffin	J.J. Hyland	Handspring	Hamilton II
1897	**Scottish Chieftain**	2:23¼	J. Scherrer	M. Byrnes	On Deck	Octagon
1898	**Bowling Brook**	2:32	F. Littlefield	R.W. Walden	Previous	Hamburg
1899	**Jean Beraud**	2:23	R. Clawson	Sam Hildreth	Half Time	Glengar
1900	**Ildrim**	2:21¼	Nash Turner	H.E. Leigh	Petruchio	Missionary
1901	**Commando**	2:21	H. Spencer	James Rowe Sr.	The Parader	All Green
1902	**Masterman**	2:22⅗	John Bullman	J.J. Hyland	Renald	King Hanover
1903	**Africander**	2:21¾	John Bullman	R. Miller	Whorler	Red Knight
1904	**Delhi**	2:06⅗	George Odom	James Rowe Sr.	Graziallo	Rapid Water
1905	**Tanya**	2:08	E. Hildebrand	J.W. Rogers	Blandy	Hot Shot
1906	**Burgomaster**	2:20	Lucien Lyne	J.W. Rogers	The Quail	Accountant
1907	**Peter Pan**	N/A	G. Mountain	James Rowe Sr.	Superman	Frank Gill
1908	**Colin**	N/A	Joe Notter	James Rowe Sr.	Fair Play	King James
1909	**Joe Madden**	2:21⅗	E. Dugan	Sam Hildreth	Wise Mason	Donald MacDonald
1910	**Sweep**	2:22	James Butwell	James Rowe Sr.	Duke of Ormonde	(2-horse race)
1911-12	Not held					
1913	**Prince Eugene**	2:18	Roscoe Troxler	James Rowe Sr.	Rock View	Flying Fairy
1914	**Luke McLuke**	2:20	Merritt Buxton	J.F. Schorr	Gainer	Charlestonian
1915	**The Finn**	2:18⅖	George Byrne	E.W. Heffner	Half Rock	Pebbles
1916	**Friar Rock**	2:22	E. Haynes	Sam Hildreth	Spur	Churchill
1917	**Hourless**	2:17⅘	James Butwell	Sam Hildreth	Skeptic	Wonderful
1918	**Johren**	2:20⅖	Frank Robinson	A. Simons	War Cloud	Cum Sah
1919	**SIR BARTON**	2:17⅖	John Loftus	H. Guy Bedwell	Sweep On	Natural Bridge
1920	**Man o' War**	2:14⅕	Clarence Kummer	L. Feustel	Donnacona	(2-horse race)
1921	**Grey Lag**	2:16⅘	Earl Sande	Sam Hildreth	Sporting Blood	Leonardo II
1922	**Pillory**	2:18⅘	C.H. Miller	T.J. Healey	Snob II	Hea
1923	**Zev**	2:19	Earl Sande	Sam Hildreth	Chickvale	Rialto
1924	**Mad Play**	2:18⅘	Earl Sande	Sam Hildreth	Mr. Mutt	Modest
1925	**American Flag**	2:16⅘	Albert Johnson	G.R. Tompkins	Dangerous	Swope
1926	**Crusader**	2:32⅕	Albert Johnson	George Conway	Espino	Haste
1927	**Chance Shot**	2:32⅖	Earl Sande	Pete Coyne	Bois de Rose	Flambino
1928	**Vito**	2:33⅕	Clarence Kummer	Max Hirsch	Genie	Diavolo
1929	**Blue Larkspur**	2:32⅘	Mack Garner	C. Hastings	African	Jack High
1930	**GALLANT FOX**	2:31⅗	Earl Sande	Jim Fitzsimmons	Whichone	Questionnaire
1931	**Twenty Grand**	2:29⅗	Charley Kurtsinger	James Rowe Jr.	Sun Meadow	Jamestown
1932	**Faireno**	2:32⅘	Tom Malley	Jim Fitzsimmons	Osculator	Flag Pole
1933	**Hurryoff**	2:32⅗	Mack Garner	H. McDaniel	Nimbus	Union
1934	**Peace Chance**	2:29⅕	W.D. Wright	Pete Coyne	High Quest	Good Goods
1935	**OMAHA**	2:30⅗	Willie Saunders	Jim Fitzsimmons	Firethorn	Rosemont
1936	**Granville**	2:30	James Stout	Jim Fitzsimmons	Mr. Bones	Hollyrood
1937	**WAR ADMIRAL**	2:28⅗	Charley Kurtsinger	George Conway	Sceneshifter	Vamoose
1938	**Pasteurized**	2:29⅖	James Stout	George Odom	Dauber	Cravat
1939	**Johnstown**	2:29⅗	James Stout	Jim Fitzsimmons	Belay	Gilded Knight
1940	**Bimelech**	2:29⅗	Fred Smith	Bill Hurley	Your Chance	Andy K.
1941	**WHIRLAWAY**	2:31	Eddie Arcaro	Ben Jones	Robert Morris	Yankee Chance
1942	**Shut Out**	2:29⅕	Eddie Arcaro	John Gaver	Alsab	Lochinvar
1943	**COUNT FLEET**	2:28⅕	Johnny Longden	Don Cameron	Fairy Manhurst	Deseronto
1944	**Bounding Home**	2:32⅕	G.L. Smith	Matt Brady	Pensive	Bull Dandy
1945	**Pavot**	2:30⅕	Eddie Arcaro	Oscar White	Wildlife	Jeep
1946	**ASSAULT**	2:30⅘	Warren Mehrtens	Max Hirsch	Natchez	Cable
1947	**Phalanx**	2:29⅖	R. Donoso	Syl Veitch	Tide Rips	Tailspin
1948	**CITATION**	2:28⅕	Eddie Arcaro	Jimmy Jones	Better Self	Escadru
1949	**Capot**	2:30⅕	Ted Atkinson	John Gaver	Ponder	Palestinian
1950	**Middleground**	2:28⅗	William Boland	Max Hirsch	Lights Up	Mr. Trouble
1951	**Counterpoint**	2:29	David Gorman	Syl Veitch	Battlefield	Battle Morn
1952	**One Count**	2:30⅕	Eddie Arcaro	Oscar White	Blue Man	Armageddon
1953	**Native Dancer**	2:28⅗	Eric Guerin	Bill Winfrey	Jamie K.	Royal Bay Gem
1954	**High Gun**	2:30⅘	Eric Guerin	Max Hirsch	Fisherman	Limelight
1955	**Nashua**	2:29	Eddie Arcaro	Jim Fitzsimmons	Blazing Count	Portersville
1956	**Needles**	2:29⅘	David Erb	Hugh Fontaine	Career Boy	Fabius
1957	**Gallant Man**	2:26⅗	Bill Shoemaker	John Nerud	Inside Tract	Bold Ruler
1958	**Cavan**	2:30⅕	Pete Anderson	Tom Barry	Tim Tam	Flamingo
1959	**Sword Dancer**	2:28⅖	Bill Shoemaker	Elliott Burch	Bagdad	Royal Orbit
1960	**Celtic Ash**	2:29⅕	Bill Hartack	Tom Barry	Venetian Way	Disperse
1961	**Sherluck**	2:29⅕	Braulio Baeza	Harold Young	Globemaster	Guadalcanal
1962	**Jaipur**	2:28⅘	Bill Shoemaker	B. Mulholland	Admiral's Voyage	Crimson Satan
1963	**Chateaugay**	2:30⅕	Braulio Baeza	James Conway	Candy Spots	Choker

Belmont Stakes (Cont.)

Year		Time	Jockey	Trainer	2nd place	3rd place
1964	**Quadrangle**	2:28⅖	Manuel Ycaza	Elliott Burch	Roman Brother	Northern Dancer
1965	**Hail to All**	2:28⅖	John Sellers	Eddie Yowell	Tom Rolfe	First Family
1966	**Amberoid**	2:29⅗	William Boland	Lucien Laurin	Buffle	Advocator
1967	**Damascus**	2:28⅘	Bill Shoemaker	F.Y. Whiteley Jr.	Cool Reception	Gentleman James
1968	**Stage Door Johnny**	2:27⅕	Gus Gustines	John Gaver	Forward Pass	Call Me Prince
1969	**Arts and Letters**	2:28⅘	Braulio Baeza	Elliott Burch	Majestic Prince	Dike
1970	**High Echelon**	2:34	John Rotz	John Jacobs	Needles N Pens	Naskra
1971	**Pass Catcher**	2:30⅖	Walter Blum	Eddie Yowell	Jim French	Bold Reason
1972	**Riva Ridge**	2:28	Ron Turcotte	Lucien Laurin	Ruritania	Cloudy Dawn
1973	**SECRETARIAT**	2:24	Ron Turcotte	Lucien Laurin	Twice A Prince	My Gallant
1974	**Little Current**	2:29⅕	Miguel Rivera	Lou Rondinello	Jolly Johu	Cannonade
1975	**Avatar**	2:28⅕	Bill Shoemaker	Tommy Doyle	Foolish Pleasure	Master Derby
1976	**Bold Forbes**	2:29	Angel Cordero Jr.	Laz Barrera	McKenzie Bridge	Great Contractor
1977	**SEATTLE SLEW**	2:29⅗	Jean Cruguet	Billy Turner	Run Dusty Run	Sanhedrin
1978	**AFFIRMED**	2:26⅘	Steve Cauthen	Laz Barrera	Alydar	Darby Creek Road
1979	**Coastal**	2:28⅗	Ruben Hernandez	David Whiteley	Golden Act	Spectacular Bid
1980	**Temperence Hill**	2:29⅘	Eddie Maple	Joseph Cantey	Genuine Risk	Rockhill Native
1981	**Summing**	2:29	George Martens	Luis Barerra	Highland Blade	Pleasant Colony
1982	**Conquistador Cielo**	2:28⅕	Laffit Pincay Jr.	Woody Stephens	Gato Del Sol	Illuminate
1983	**Caveat**	2:27⅘	Laffit Pincay Jr.	Woody Stephens	Slew o' Gold	Barberstown
1984	**Swale**	2:27⅕	Laffit Pincay Jr.	Woody Stephens	Pine Circle	Morning Bob
1985	**Creme Fraiche**	2:27	Eddie Maple	Woody Stephens	Stephan's Odyssey	Chief's Crown
1986	**Danzig Connection**	2:29⅘	Chris McCarron	Woody Stephens	Johns Treasure	Ferdinand
1987	**Bet Twice**	2:28⅕	Craig Perret	Jimmy Croll	Cryptoclearance	Gulch
1988	**Risen Star**	2:26⅖	E. Delahoussaye	Louie Roussel III	Kingpost	Brian's Time
1989	**Easy Goer**	2:26	Pat Day	Shug McGaughey	Sunday Silence	Le Voyageur
1990	**Go And Go**	2:27⅕	Michael Kinane	Dermot Weld	Thirty Six Red	Baron de Vaux
1991	**Hansel**	2:28	Jerry Bailey	Frank Brothers	Strike the Gold	Mane Minister
1992	**A.P. Indy**	2:26	E. Delahoussaye	Neil Drysdale	My Memoirs	Pine Bluff
1993	**Colonial Affair**	2:29⅘	Julie Krone	Scotty Schulhofer	Kissin Kris	Wild Gale
1994	**Tabasco Cat**	2:26⅘	Pat Day	D. Wayne Lukas	Go For Gin	Strodes Creek
1995	**Thunder Gulch**	2:32	Gary Stevens	D. Wayne Lukas	Star Standard	Citadeed
1996	**Editor's Note**	2:28⅘	Rene Douglas	D. Wayne Lukas	Skip Away	My Flag
1997	**Touch Gold**	2:28⅘	Chris McCarron	David Hofmans	Silver Charm	Free House

Breeders' Cup Championship

Inaugurated on Nov. 10, 1984, the Breeders' Cup Championship consists of seven races on one track on one day late in the year to determine Thoroughbred racing's principle champions.

The Breeders' Cup has been held at the following tracks (in alphabetical order): Aqueduct Racetrack (N.Y.) in 1985; Belmont Park (N.Y.) in 1990 and '95; Churchill Downs (Ky.) in 1988, '91 and '94; Gulfstream Park (Fla.) in 1989 and '92; Hollywood Park (Calif.) in 1984, '87 and '97; Santa Anita Park (Calif.) in 1986 and '93 and Woodbine (Toronto) in 1996.

Trainers with most wins: D. Wayne Lukas (13); Shug McGaughey (7); Neil Drysdale (5); Ron McAnally (4); Francois Boutin and Bill Mott (3).

Jockeys with most wins: Pat Day (8); Eddie Delahoussaye and Laffit Pincay Jr. (7); Jerry Bailey, Chris McCarron, Mike Smith and Pat Valenzuela (6); Jose Santos (5); Angel Cordero, Craig Perret and Gary Stevens (4); Randy Romero (3).

Juvenile

Distances: one mile (1984-85, 87); 1$\frac{1}{16}$ miles (1986 and since 1988).

Year		Time	Jockey	Trainer	2nd place	3rd place
1984	**Chief's Crown**	1:36⅕	Don MacBeth	Roger Laurin	Tank's Prospect	Spend A Buck
1985	**Tasso**	1:36⅕	Laffit Pincay Jr.	Neil Drysdale	Storm Cat	Scat Dancer
1986	**Capote**	1:43⅘	Laffit Pincay Jr.	D. Wayne Lukas	Qualify	Alysheba
1987	**Success Express**	1:35⅕	Jose Santos	D. Wayne Lukas	Regal Classic	Tejano
1988	**Is It True**	1:46⅗	Laffit Pincay Jr.	D. Wayne Lukas	Easy Goer	Tagel
1989	**Rhythm**	1:43⅗	Craig Perret	Shug McGaughey	Grand Canyon	Slavic
1990	**Fly So Free**	1:43⅖	Jose Santos	Scotty Schulhofer	Take Me Out	Lost Mountain
1991	**Arazi**	1:44⅗	Pat Valenzuela	Francois Boutin	Bertrando	Snappy Landing
1992	**Gilded Time**	1:43⅖	Chris McCarron	Darrell Vienna	It'sali'lknownfact	River Special
1993	**Brocco**	1:42⅘	Gary Stevens	Randy Winick	Blumin Affair	Tabasco Cat
1994	**Timber Country**	1:44⅖	Pat Day	D. Wayne Lukas	Eltish	Tejano Run
1995	**Unbridled's Song**	1:41⅗	Mike Smith	James Ryerson	Hennessy	Editor's Note
1996	**Boston Harbor**	1:43⅖	Jerry Bailey	D. Wayne Lukas	Acceptable	Ordway

Juvenile Fillies

Distances: one mile (1984-85, 87); 1 1/16 miles (1986 and since 1988).

Year		Time	Jockey	Trainer	2nd place	3rd place
1984	**Outstandingly**	1:37⅘	Walter Guerra	Pancho Martin	Dusty Heart	Fine Spirit
1985	**Twilight Ridge**	1:35⅘	Jorge Velasquez	D. Wayne Lukas	Family Style	Steal A Kiss
1986	**Brave Raj**	1:43⅕	Pat Valenzuela	Melvin Stute	Tappiano	Saros Brig
1987	**Epitome**	1:36⅖	Pat Day	Phil Hauswald	Jeanne Jones	Dream Team
1988	**Open Mind**	1:46⅗	Angel Cordero Jr.	D. Wayne Lukas	Darby Shuffle	Lea Lucinda
1989	**Go for Wand**	1:44⅕	Randy Romero	Wm. Badgett, Jr.	Sweet Roberta	Stella Madrid
1990	**Meadow Star**	1:44	Jose Santos	LeRoy Jolley	Private Treasure	Dance Smartly
1991	**Pleasant Stage**	1:46⅖	Eddie Delahoussaye	Chris Speckert	La Spia	Cadillac Women
1992	**Liza**	1:42⅘	Pat Valenzuela	Alex Hassingfer	Educated Risk	Boots 'n Jackie
1993	**Phone Chatter**	1:43	Laffit Pincay Jr.	Richard Mandella	Sardula	Heavenly Prize
1994	**Flanders**	1:45⅕	Pat Day	D. Wayne Lukas	Serena's Song	Stormy Blues
1995	**My Flag**	1:42⅖	Jerry Bailey	Shug McGaughey	Cara Rafaela	Golden Attraction
1996	**Storm Song**	1:43⅗	Craig Perret	Nick Zito	Love That Jazz	Critical Factor

Note: In 1984, winner Fran's Valentine was disqualified for interference in the stretch and placed 10th.

Sprint

Distance: six furlongs (since 1984).

Year		Time	Jockey	Trainer	2nd place	3rd place
1984	**Eillo**	1:10⅕	Craig Perret	Budd Lepman	Commemorate	Fighting Fit
1985	**Precisionist**	1:08⅖	Chris McCarron	L.R. Fenstermaker	Smile	Mt. Livermore
1986	**Smile**	1:08⅖	Jacinto Vasquez	Scotty Schulhofer	Pine Tree Lane	Bedside Promise
1987	**Very Subtle**	1:08⅘	Pat Valenzuela	Melvin Stute	Groovy	Exclusive Enough
1988	**Gulch**	1:10⅖	Angel Cordero Jr.	D. Wayne Lukas	Play The King	Afleet
1989	**Dancing Spree**	1:09	Angel Cordero Jr.	Shug McGaughey	Safely Kept	Dispersal
1990	**Safely Kept**	1:09⅗	Craig Perret	Alan Goldberg	Dayjur	Black Tie Affair
1991	**Sheikh Albadou**	1:09⅕	Pat Eddery	Alexander Scott	Pleasant Tap	Robyn Dancer
1992	**Thirty Slews**	1:08⅕	Eddie Delahoussaye	Bob Baffert	Meafara	Rubiano
1993	**Cardmania**	1:08⅗	Eddie Delahoussaye	Derek Meredith	Meafara	Gilded Time
1994	**Cherokee Run**	1:09⅖	Mike Smith	Frank Alexander	Soviet Problem	Cardmania
1995	**Desert Stormer**	1:09	Kent Desormeaux	Frank Lyons	Mr. Greeley	Lit de Justice
1996	**Lit de Justice**	1:08⅗	Corey Nakatani	Jenine Sahadi	Paying Dues	Honour and Glory

Mile

Year		Time	Jockey	Trainer	2nd place	3rd place
1984	**Royal Heroine**	1:32⅗	Fernando Toro	John Gosden	Star Choice	Cozzene
1985	**Cozzene**	1:35	Walter Guerra	Jan Nerud	Al Mamoon	Shadeed
1986	**Last Tycoon**	1:35⅕	Yves St.-Martin	Robert Collet	Palace Music	Fred Astaire
1987	**Miesque**	1:32⅘	Freddie Head	Francois Boutin	Show Dancer	Sonic Lady
1988	**Miesque**	1:38⅗	Freddie Head	Francois Boutin	Steinlen	Simply Majestic
1989	**Steinlen**	1:37⅕	Jose Santos	D. Wayne Lukas	Sabona	Most Welcome
1990	**Royal Academy**	1:35⅕	Lester Piggott	M.V. O'Brien	Itsallgreektome	Priolo
1991	**Opening Verse**	1:37⅖	Pat Valenzuela	Dick Lundy	Val des Bois	Star of Cozzene
1992	**Lure**	1:32⅘	Mike Smith	Shug McGaughey	Paradise Creek	Brief Truce
1993	**Lure**	1:33⅖	Mike Smith	Shug McGaughey	Ski Paradise	Fourstars Allstar
1994	**Barathea**	1:34⅖	Frankie Dettori	Luca Cumani	Johann Quatz	Unfinished Symph
1995	**Ridgewood Pearl**	1:43⅗	John Murtagh	John Oxx	Fastness	Sayyedati
1996	**Da Hoss**	1:35⅘	Gary Stevens	Michael Dickinson	Spinning World	Same Old Wish

Note: In 1985, 2nd place finisher Palace Music was disqualified for interference and placed 9th.

Distaff

Distances: 1 1/4 miles (1984-87); 1 1/8 miles (since 1988).

Year		Time	Jockey	Trainer	2nd place	3rd place
1984	**Princess Rooney**	2:02⅖	Eddie Delahoussaye	Neil Drysdale	Life's Magic	Adored
1985	**Life's Magic**	2:02	Angel Cordero Jr.	D. Wayne Lukas	Lady's Secret	DontstopThemusic
1986	**Lady's Secret**	2:01⅕	Pat Day	D. Wayne Lukas	Fran's Valentine	Outstandingly
1987	**Sacahuista**	2:02⅘	Randy Romero	D. Wayne Lukas	Clabber Girl	Oueee Bebe
1988	**Personal Ensign**	1:52	Randy Romero	Shug McGaughey	Winning Colors	Goodbye Halo
1989	**Bayakoa**	1:47⅖	Laffit Pincay Jr.	Ron McAnally	Gorgeous	Open Mind
1990	**Bayakoa**	1:49⅕	Laffit Pincay Jr.	Ron McAnally	Colonial Waters	Valay Maid
1991	**Dance Smartly**	1:50⅘	Pat Day	Jim Day	Versailles Treaty	Brought to Mind
1992	**Paseana**	1:48	Chris McCarron	Ron McAnally	Versailles Treaty	Magical Maiden
1993	**Hollywood Wildcat**	1:48⅕	Eddie Delahoussaye	Neil Drysdale	Paseana	Re Toss
1994	**One Dreamer**	1:50⅗	Gary Stevens	Thomas Proctor	Heavenly Prize	Miss Dominique
1995	**Inside Information**	1:46	Mike Smith	Shug McGaughey	Heavenly Prize	Lakeway
1996	**Jewel Princess**	1:48⅕	Corey Nakatani	Wallace Dollase	Serena's Song	Different

Breeders' Cup Championship (Cont.)

Turf

Distance: 1½ miles (since 1984).

Year	Time	Jockey	Trainer	2nd place	3rd place
1984 **Lashkari**	2:25⅕	Yves St.-Martin	de Royer-Dupre	All Along	Raami
1985 **Pebbles**	2:27	Pat Eddery	Clive Brittain	StrawberryRoad II	Mourjane
1986 **Manila**	2:25⅖	Jose Santos	Leroy Jolley	Theatrical	Estrapade
1987 **Theatrical**	2:24⅖	Pat Day	Bill Mott	Trempolino	Village Star II
1988 **Gt. Communicator**	2:35⅕	Ray Sibille	Thad Ackel	Sunshine Forever	Indian Skimmer
1989 **Prized**	2:28	Eddie Delahoussaye	Neil Drysdale	Sierra Roberta	Star Lift
1990 **In The Wings**	2:29⅗	Gary Stevens	Andre Fabre	With Approval	El Senor
1991 **Miss Alleged**	2:30⅘	Eric Legrix	Pascal Bary	Itsallgreektome	Quest for Fame
1992 **Fraise**	2:24	Pat Valenzuela	Bill Mott	Sky Classic	Quest for Fame
1993 **Kotashaan**	2:25	Kent Desormeaux	Richard Mandella	Bien Bien	Luazur
1994 **Tikkanen**	2:26⅖	Mike Smith	Jonathan Pease	Hatoof	Paradise Creek
1995 **Northern Spur**	2:42	Chris McCarron	Ron McAnally	Freedom Cry	Carnegie
1996 **Pilsudski**	2:30⅕	Walter Swinburn	Michael Stoute	Singspiel	Swain

Classic

Distance: 1¼ miles (since 1984).

Year	Time	Jockey	Trainer	2nd place	3rd place
1984 **Wild Again**	2:03⅖	Pat Day	Vincent Timphony	Slew o' Gold	Gate Dancer
1985 **Proud Truth**	2:00⅘	Jorge Velasquez	John Veitch	Gate Dancer	Turkoman
1986 **Skywalker**	2:00⅖	Laffit Pincay Jr.	M. Whittingham	Turkoman	Precisionist
1987 **Ferdinand**	2:01⅖	Bill Shoemaker	C. Whittingham	Alysheba	Judge Angelucci
1988 **Alysheba**	2:04⅘	Chris McCarron	Jack Van Berg	Seeking the Gold	Waquoit
1989 **Sunday Silence**	2:00⅕	Chris McCarron	C. Whittingham	Easy Goer	Blushing John
1990 **Unbridled**	2:02⅕	Pat Day	Carl Nafzger	Ibn Bey	Thirty Six Red
1991 **Black Tie Affair**	2:02⅘	Jerry Bailey	Ernie Poulos	Twilight Agenda	Unbridled
1992 **A.P. Indy**	2:00⅕	Eddie Delahoussaye	Neil Drysdale	Pleasant Tap	Jolypha
1993 **Arcangues**	2:00⅘	Jerry Bailey	Andre Fabre	Bertrando	Kissin Kris
1994 **Concern**	2:02⅖	Jerry Bailey	Richard Small	Tabasco Cat	Dramatic Gold
1995 **Cigar**	1:59⅖	Chris McCarron	Ron McAnally	Freedom Cry	Carnegie
1996 **Alphabet Soup**	2:01	Chris McCarron	David Hofmans	Louis Quatorze	Cigar

Note: In 1984, 2nd place finisher Gate Dancer was disqualified for interference and placed 3rd.

Breeders' Cup Leaders

The all-time money-winning horses and race winning jockeys in the history of the Breeders' Cup through 1996.

Top 10 Horses

		Sts	1-2-3	Earnings
1	Alysheba	3	1-1-1	$2,133,000
2	Alphabet Soup	1	1-0-0	2,080,000
3	Cigar	2	1-0-1	2,040,000
4	Unbridled	2	1-0-1	1,710,000
5	Black Tie Affair (IRE)	3	1-0-1	1,668,000
6	A.P. Indy	1	1-0-0	1,560,000
7	Arcangues	1	1-0-0	1,560,000
	Concern	1	1-0-0	1,560,000
9	Ferdinand	1	1-0-0	1,350,000
	Proud Truth	1	1-0-0	1,350,000
	Skywalker	2	1-0-0	1,350,000
	Sunday Silence	1	1-0-0	1,350,000
	Theatrical (IRE)	3	1-1-0	1,350,000
	Wild Again	1	1-0-0	1,350,000

Top 5 Jockeys

		Sts	1-2-3	Earnings
1	Pat Day	69	8-13-7	$13,503,000
2	Chris McCarron	72	7-11-6	12,322,000
3	Jerry Bailey	38	6-3-3	8,887,000
4	Eddie Delahoussaye	58	7-3-5	7,499,000
5	Gary Stevens	57	4-10-7	7,249,000

Top 5 Trainers

		Sts	1-2-3	Earnings
1	D. Wayne Lukas	104	13-16-11	$12,456,000
2	Shug McGaughey	39	7-8-1	6,479,000
3	Andre Fabre	26	2-4-5	5,384,000
4	Bill Mott	19	3-3-2	5,042,000
5	Neil Drysdale	15	5-2-0	4,580,000

Annual Money Leaders

Horses

Annual money-leading horses since 1910, according to *The American Racing Manual.*

Multiple leaders: Round Table, Buckpasser, Alysheba and Cigar (2).

Year		Age	Sts	1st	Earnings
1910	Novelty	2	16	11	$72,630
1911	Worth	2	13	10	16,645
1912	Star Charter	4	17	6	14,655
1913	Old Rosebud	2	14	12	19,057
1914	Roamer	3	16	12	29,105
1915	Borrow	7	9	4	20,195
1916	Campfire	2	9	6	49,735
1917	Sun Briar	2	9	5	$59,505
1918	Eternal	2	8	6	56,173
1919	Sir Barton	3	13	8	88,250
1920	Man o' War	3	11	11	166,140
1921	Morvich	2	11	11	115,234
1922	Pillory	3	7	4	95,654
1923	Zev	3	14	12	272,008

Year		Age	Sts	1st	Earnings
1924	Sarzen	3	12	8	$ 95,640
1925	Pompey	2	10	7	121,630
1926	Crusader	3	15	9	166,033
1927	Anita Peabody	2	7	6	111,905
1928	High Strung	2	6	5	153,590
1929	Blue Larkspur	3	6	4	153,450
1930	Gallant Fox	3	10	9	308,275
1931	Gallant Flight	2	7	7	219,000
1932	Gusto	3	16	4	145,940
1933	Singing Wood	2	9	3	88,050
1934	Cavalcade	3	7	6	111,235
1935	Omaha	3	9	6	142,255
1936	Granville	3	11	7	110,295
1937	Seabiscuit	4	15	11	168,580
1938	Stagehand	3	15	8	189,710
1939	Challedon	3	15	9	184,535
1940	Bimelech	3	7	4	110,005
1941	Whirlaway	3	20	13	272,386
1942	Shut Out	3	12	8	238,872
1943	Count Fleet	3	6	6	174,055
1944	Pavot	2	8	8	179,040
1945	Busher	3	13	10	273,735
1946	Assault	3	15	8	424,195
1947	Armed	6	17	11	376,325
1948	Citation	3	20	19	709,470
1949	Ponder	3	21	9	321,825
1950	Noor	5	12	7	346,940
1951	Counterpoint	3	15	7	250,525
1952	Crafty Admiral	4	16	9	277,225
1953	Native Dancer	3	10	9	513,425
1954	Determine	3	15	10	328,700
1955	Nashua	3	12	10	752,550
1956	Needles	3	8	4	440,850
1957	Round Table	3	22	15	600,383
1958	Round Table	4	20	14	662,780
1959	Sword Dancer	3	13	8	537,004
1960	Bally Ache	3	15	10	445,045
1961	Carry Back	3	16	9	$565,349
1962	Never Bend	2	10	7	402,969
1963	Candy Spots	3	12	7	604,481
1964	Gun Bow	4	16	8	580,100
1965	Buckpasser	2	11	9	568,096
1966	Buckpasser	3	14	13	669,078
1967	Damascus	3	16	12	817,941
1968	Forward Pass	3	13	7	546,674
1969	Arts and Letters	3	14	8	555,604
1970	Personality	3	18	8	444,049
1971	Riva Ridge	2	9	7	503,263
1972	Droll Role	4	19	7	471,633
1973	Secretariat	3	12	9	860,404
1974	Chris Evert	3	8	5	551,063
1975	Foolish Pleasure	3	11	5	716,278
1976	Forego	6	8	6	401,701
1977	Seattle Slew	3	7	6	641,370
1978	Affirmed	3	11	8	901,541
1979	Spectacular Bid	3	12	10	1,279,334
1980	Temperence Hill	3	17	8	1,130,452
1981	John Henry	6	10	8	1,798,030
1982	Perrault (GB)	5	8	4	1,197,400
1983	All Along (FRA)	4	7	4	2,138,963
1984	Slew o' Gold	4	6	5	2,627,944
1985	Spend A Buck	3	7	5	3,552,704
1986	Snow Chief	3	9	6	1,875,200
1987	Alysheba	3	10	3	2,511,156
1988	Alysheba	4	9	7	3,808,600
1989	Sunday Silence	3	9	7	4,578,454
1990	Unbridled	3	11	4	3,718,149
1991	Dance Smartly	3	8	8	2,876,821
1992	A.P. Indy	3	7	5	2,622,560
1993	Kotashaan (FRA)	5	10	6	2,619,014
1994	Paradise Creek	5	11	8	2,610,187
1995	Cigar	5	10	10	4,819,800
1996	Cigar	6	8	5	4,910,000

Jockeys

Annual money-leading jockeys since 1910, according to *The American Racing Manual*.

Multiple leaders: Bill Shoemaker (10); Laffit Pincay Jr. (7); Eddie Arcaro (6); Braulio Baeza (5); Chris McCarron and Jose Santos (4); Angel Cordero Jr. and Earl Sande (3); Ted Atkinson, Jerry Bailey, Laverne Fator, Mack Garner, Bill Hartack, Charles Kurtsinger, Johnny Longden, Mike Smith, Sonny Workman and Wayne Wright (2).

Year		Mts	Wins	Earnings
1910	Carroll Shilling	506	172	$176,030
1911	Ted Koerner	813	162	88,308
1912	Jimmy Butwell	684	144	79,843
1913	Merritt Buxton	887	146	82,552
1914	J. McCahey	824	155	121,845
1915	Mack Garner	775	151	96,628
1916	John McTaggart	832	150	155,055
1917	Frank Robinson	731	147	148,057
1918	Lucien Luke	756	178	201,864
1919	John Loftus	177	65	252,707
1920	Clarence Kummer	353	87	292,376
1921	Earl Sande	340	112	263,043
1922	Albert Johnson	297	43	345,054
1923	Earl Sande	430	122	569,394
1924	Ivan Parke	844	205	290,395
1925	Laverne Fator	315	81	305,775
1926	Laverne Fator	511	143	361,435
1927	Earl Sande	179	49	277,877
1928	Linus McAtee	235	55	301,295
1929	Mack Garner	274	57	314,975
1930	Sonny Workman	571	152	420,438
1931	Charley Kurtsinger	519	93	392,095
1932	Sonny Workman	378	87	385,070
1933	Robert Jones	471	63	$226,285
1934	Wayne Wright	919	174	287,185
1935	Silvio Coucci	749	141	319,760
1936	Wayne Wright	670	100	264,000
1937	Charley Kurtsinger	765	120	384,202
1938	Nick Wall	658	97	385,161
1939	Basil James	904	191	353,333
1940	Eddie Arcaro	783	132	343,661
1941	Don Meade	1164	210	398,627
1942	Eddie Arcaro	687	123	481,949
1943	Johnny Longden	871	173	573,276
1944	Ted Atkinson	1539	287	899,101
1945	Johnny Longden	778	180	981,977
1946	Ted Atkinson	1377	233	1,036,825
1947	Douglas Dodson	646	141	1,429,949
1948	Eddie Arcaro	726	188	1,686,230
1949	Steve Brooks	906	209	1,316,817
1950	Eddie Arcaro	888	195	1,410,160
1951	Bill Shoemaker	1161	257	1,329,890
1952	Eddie Arcaro	807	188	1,859,591
1953	Bill Shoemaker	1683	485	1,784,187
1954	Bill Shoemaker	1251	380	1,876,760
1955	Eddie Arcaro	820	158	1,864,796

Year		Mts	Wins	Earnings	Year		Mts	Wins	Earnings
1956	Bill Hartack	1387	347	$2,343,955	1977	Steve Cauthen	2075	487	$6,151,750
1957	Bill Hartack	1238	341	3,060,501	1978	Darrel McHargue	1762	375	6,188,353
1958	Bill Shoemaker	1133	300	2,961,693	1979	Laffit Pincay Jr.	1708	420	8,183,535
1959	Bill Shoemaker	1285	347	2,843,133	1980	Chris McCarron	1964	405	7,666,100
1960	Bill Shoemaker	1227	274	2,123,961	1981	Chris McCarron	1494	326	8,397,604
1961	Bill Shoemaker	1256	304	2,690,819	1982	Angel Cordero Jr.	1838	397	9,702,520
1962	Bill Shoemaker	1126	311	2,916,844	1983	Angel Cordero Jr.	1792	362	10,116,807
1963	Bill Shoemaker	1203	271	2,526,925	1984	Chris McCarron	1565	356	12,038,213
1964	Bill Shoemaker	1056	246	2,649,553	1985	Laffit Pincay Jr.	1409	289	13,415,049
1965	Braulio Baeza	1245	270	2,582,702	1986	Jose Santos	1636	329	11,329,297
1966	Braulio Baeza	1341	298	2,951,022	1987	Jose Santos	1639	305	12,407,355
1967	Braulio Baeza	1064	256	3,088,888	1988	Jose Santos	1867	370	14,877,298
1968	Braulio Baeza	1089	201	2,835,108	1989	Jose Santos	1459	285	13,847,003
1969	Jorge Velasquez	1442	258	2,542,315	1990	Gary Stevens	1504	283	13,881,198
1970	Laffit Pincay Jr.	1328	269	2,626,526	1991	Chris McCarron	1440	265	14,456,073
1971	Laffit Pincay Jr.	1627	380	3,784,377	1992	Kent Desormeaux	1568	361	14,193,006
1972	Laffit Pincay Jr.	1388	289	3,225,827	1993	Mike Smith	1510	343	14,024,815
1973	Laffit Pincay Jr.	1444	350	4,093,492	1994	Mike Smith	1484	317	15,979,820
1974	Laffit Pincay Jr.	1278	341	4,251,060	1995	Jerry Bailey	1367	287	16,311,876
1975	Braulio Baeza	1190	196	3,674,398	1996	Jerry Bailey	1187	298	19,465,376
1976	Angel Cordero Jr.	1534	274	4,709,500					

Annual Money-Leading Female Jockeys

Annual money-leading female jockeys since 1979, according to *The American Racing Manual*.

Multiple leaders: Julie Krone (12); Patty Cooksey and Karen Rogers (2).

Year		Mts	Wins	Earnings	Year		Mts	Wins	Earnings
1979	Karen Rogers	550	77	$590,469	1988	Julie Krone	1958	363	$7,770,314
1980	Karen Rogers	622	65	894,878	1989	Julie Krone	1673	368	8,031,445
1981	Patty Cooksey	1469	197	895,951	1990	Julie Krone	649	144	2,846,237
1982	Mary Russ	952	84	1,319,363	1991	Julie Krone	1414	230	7,748,077
1983	Julie Krone	1024	151	1,095,622	1992	Julie Krone	1462	282	9,220,824
1984	Patty Cooksey	955	116	803,189	1993	Julie Krone	1012	212	6,415,462
1985	Abby Fuller	883	145	1,452,576	1994	Julie Krone	571	101	3,968,337
1986	Julie Krone	1442	199	2,357,136	1995	Julie Krone	866	147	7,759,878
1987	Julie Krone	1698	324	4,522,191	1996	Julie Krone	997	141	5,243,032

Trainers

Annual money-leading trainers since 1908, according to *The American Racing Manual*.

Multiple Leaders: D. Wayne Lukas (13); Sam Hildreth (9); Charlie Whittingham (7); Sunny Jim Fitzsimmons and Jimmy Jones (5); Laz Barrera, Ben Jones and Willie Molter (4); Hirsch Jacobs, Eddie Neloy and James Rowe Sr. (3); H. Guy Bedwell, Jack Gaver, John Schorr, Humming Bob Smith, Silent Tom Smith and Mesh Tenney (2).

Year		Wins	Earnings	Year		Wins	Earnings
1908	James Rowe Sr.	50	$284,335	1930	Sunny Jim Fitzsimmons	47	$397,355
1909	Sam Hildreth	73	123,942	1931	Big Jim Healy	33	297,300
1910	Sam Hildreth	84	148,010	1932	Sunny Jim Fitzsimmons	68	266,650
1911	Sam Hildreth	67	49,418	1933	Humming Bob Smith	53	135,720
1912	John Schorr	63	58,110	1934	Humming Bob Smith	43	249,938
1913	James Rowe Sr.	18	45,936	1935	Bud Stotler	87	303,005
1914	R.C. Benson	45	59,315	1936	Sunny Jim Fitzsimmons	42	193,415
1915	James Rowe Sr.	19	75,596	1937	Robert McGarvey	46	209,925
1916	Sam Hildreth	39	70,950	1938	Earl Sande	15	226,495
1917	Sam Hildreth	23	61,698	1939	Sunny Jim Fitzsimmons	45	266,205
1918	H. Guy Bedwell.	53	80,296	1940	Silent Tom Smith	14	269,200
1919	H. Guy Bedwell.	63	208,728	1941	Ben Jones	70	475,318
1920	Louis Feustal	22	186,087	1942	Jack Gaver	48	406,547
1921	Sam Hildreth	85	262,768	1943	Ben Jones	73	267,915
1922	Sam Hildreth	74	247,014	1944	Ben Jones	60	601,660
1923	Sam Hildreth	75	392,124	1945	Silent Tom Smith	52	510,655
1924	Sam Hildreth	77	255,608	1946	Hirsch Jacobs	99	560,077
1925	G.R. Tompkins	30	199,245	1947	Jimmy Jones	85	1,334,805
1926	Scott Harlan	21	205,681	1948	Jimmy Jones	81	1,118,670
1927	W.H. Bringloe	63	216,563	1949	Jimmy Jones	76	978,587
1928	John Schorr	65	258,425	1950	Preston Burch	96	637,754
1929	James Rowe Jr.	25	314,881	1951	Jack Gaver	42	616,392

Year		Wins	Earnings
1952	Ben Jones	29	$662,137
1953	Harry Trotsek	54	1,028,873
1954	Willie Molter	136	1,107,860
1955	Sunny Jim Fitzsimmons	66	1,270,055
1956	Willie Molter	142	1,227,402
1957	Jimmy Jones	70	1,150,910
1958	Willie Molter	69	1,116,544
1959	Willie Molter	71	847,290
1960	Hirsch Jacobs	97	748,349
1961	Jimmy Jones	62	759,856
1962	Mesh Tenney	58	1,099,474

Year		Sts	Wins	Earnings
1963	Mesh Tenney	192	40	860,703
1964	Bill Winfrey	287	61	1,350,534
1965	Hirsch Jacobs	610	91	1,331,628
1966	Eddie Neloy	282	93	2,456,250
1967	Eddie Neloy	262	72	1,776,089
1968	Eddie Neloy	212	52	1,233,101
1969	Elliott Burch	156	26	1,067,936
1970	Charlie Whittingham	551	82	1,302,354
1971	Charlie Whittingham	393	77	1,737,115
1972	Charlie Whittingham	429	79	1,734,020
1973	Charlie Whittingham	423	85	1,865,385

Year		Sts	Wins	Earnings
1974	Pancho Martin	846	166	$2,408,419
1975	Charlie Whittingham	487	3	2,437,244
1976	Jack Van Berg	2362	496	2,976,196
1977	Laz Barrera	781	127	2,715,848
1978	Laz Barrera	592	100	3,307,164
1979	Laz Barrera	492	98	3,608,517
1980	Laz Barrera	559	99	2,969,151
1981	Charlie Whittingham	376	74	3,993,302
1982	Charlie Whittingham	410	63	4,587,457
1983	D. Wayne Lukas	595	78	4,267,261
1984	D. Wayne Lukas	805	131	5,835,921
1985	D. Wayne Lukas	1140	218	11,155,188
1986	D. Wayne Lukas	1510	259	12,345,180
1987	D. Wayne Lukas	1735	343	17,502,110
1988	D. Wayne Lukas	1500	318	17,842,358
1989	D. Wayne Lukas	1398	305	16,103,998
1990	D. Wayne Lukas	1396	267	14,508,871
1991	D. Wayne Lukas	1497	289	15,942,223
1992	D. Wayne Lukas	1349	230	9,806,436
1993	Bobby Frankel	345	79	8,933,252
1994	D. Wayne Lukas	693	147	9,247,457
1995	D. Wayne Lukas	837	194	12,834,483
1996	D. Wayne Lukas	1006	192	15,966,344

All-Time Leaders

The all-time money-winning horses and race-winning jockeys of North America through 1996, according to *Thoroughbred Racing Communications, Inc.* Records include all available information on races in foreign countries.

Top 35 Horses — Money Won

Note that horses who raced in 1996 are in **bold** type.

		Sts	1st	2nd	3rd	Earnings
1	**Cigar**	33	19	4	5	$9,999,815
2	Alysheba	26	11	8	2	6,679,242
3	John Henry	83	39	15	9	6,597,947
4	Best Pal	47	18	11	4	5,668,245
5	Sunday Silence	14	9	5	0	4,968,554
6	Easy Goer	20	14	5	1	4,873,770
7	Unbridled	24	8	6	6	4,489,475
8	Spend A Buck	15	10	3	2	4,220,689
9	Creme Fraiche	64	17	12	13	4,024,727
10	Devil His Due	41	11	12	3	3,920,405
11	Ferdinand	29	8	9	6	3,777,978
12	Slew O'Gold	21	12	5	1	3,533,534
13	Precisionist	46	20	10	4	3,485,398
14	Strike the Gold	31	6	8	5	3,457,026
15	Paradise Creek	25	14	7	1	3,386,925
16	Snow Chief	24	13	3	5	3,383,210
17	Cryptoclearance	44	12	10	7	3,376,327
18	Black Tie Affair	45	18	9	6	3,370,694
19	Bet Twice	26	10	6	4	3,308,599
20	Steinlen	45	20	10	7	3,300,100
21	**Serena's Song**	38	18	11	3	3,283,388
22	Dance Smartly (f)	17	12	2	3	3,263,836
23	Sky Classic	29	15	6	1	3,240,398
24	Bertrando	24	9	6	2	3,185,610
25	**Paseana** (f)	36	19	10	2	3,173,203
26	**Siphon**	24	12	6	2	3,098,619
27	Gulch	32	13	8	4	3,095,521
28	**Concern**	30	7	7	11	3,079,350
29	Lady's Secret (f)	45	25	9	3	3,021,425
30	All Along (f)	21	9	6	2	3,015,764
31	**Alphabet Soup**	24	10	3	6	2,990,270
32	A.P. Indy	11	8	0	1	2,979,815
33	Theatrical	22	10	4	2	2,943,627
34	Hansel	14	7	2	3	2,936,586
35	Sea Hero	24	6	3	4	2,929,869

Top 35 Jockeys — Races Won

Note that jockeys active in 1996 are in **bold** type.

		Yrs	Wins	Earnings
1	Bill Shoemaker	42	8833	$123,375,524
2	**Laffit Pincay Jr.**	31	8497	194,212,231
3	Angel Cordero Jr.	35	7057	164,561,227
4	**David Gall**	40	6997	22,791,959
5	**Pat Day**	24	6821	174,639,847
6	Jorge Velasquez	32	6778	125,235,150
7	**Chris McCarron**	23	6427	203,438,047
8	**Sandy Hawley**	29	6402	87,052,722
9	Larry Snyder	35	6388	47,207,289
10	Carl Gambardella	39	6349	29,389,041
11	John Longden	41	6032	24,665,800
12	**Earlie Fires**	32	5863	70,456,814
13	**E. Delahoussaye**	29	5709	156,024,892
14	**Russell Baze**	23	5612	76,418,383
15	**Jacinto Vasquez**	37	5232	80,780,712
16	Eddie Arcaro	31	4779	30,039,543
17	Don Brumfield	37	4573	43,567,861
18	Steve Brooks	34	4451	18,239,817
19	**Ron Ardoin**	24	4387	43,092,012
20	Walter Blum	22	4382	26,497,189
21	**Eddie Maple**	32	4300	102,786,038
22	Bill Hartack	22	4272	26,466,758
23	**Rodolfo Baez**	23	4114	24,291,396
24	**Craig Perret**	30	4114	94,552,873
25	Avelino Gomez	34	4081	11,777,297
26	**Gary Stevens**	18	4050	144,691,251
27	**Randy Romero**	23	4046	69,656,674
28	Hugo Dittfach	33	4000	13,506,052
29	**Phil Grove**	30	3990	16,500,859
30	**Jerry Bailey**	23	3900	135,342,143
31	**Jeffrey Lloyd**	22	3888	28,824,382
32	**Rick Wilson**	24	3871	48,405,299
33	Ted Atkinson	22	3795	17,449,360
34	David Whited	36	3784	25,067,466
35	Ralph Neves	21	3772	13,786,239

Retired: Arcaro (1961), Atkinson (1959), Baird (1982), Blum (1975), Brooks (1975), Brumfield (1989), Cordero (1992), Dittfach (1989), Gambardella (1994), Gomez (1980), Hartack (1974), Hansen (1993), Longden (1966), Moyers (1992), Neves (1964), Shoemaker (1990), Snyder (1994) and Whited (1993).

Horse of the Year (1936-70)

In 1971, the *Daily Racing Form*, the Thoroughbred Racing Associations, and the National Turf Writers Assn. joined forces to create the Eclipse Awards. Before then, however, the *Racing Form* (1936-70) and the TRA (1950-70) issued separate selections for Horse of the Year. Their picks differed only four times from 1950-70 and are so noted. Horses listed in CAPITAL letters are Triple Crown winners; (f) indicates female.

Multiple winners: Kelso (5); Challedon, Native Dancer and Whirlaway (2).

Year	Year	Year	Year
1936 Granville	1946 ASSAULT	1955 Nashua	1964 Kelso
1937 WAR ADMIRAL	1947 Armed	1956 Swaps	1965 Roman Brother (DRF)
1938 Seabiscuit	1948 CITATION	1957 Bold Ruler (DRF)	Moccasin (TRA)
1939 Challedon	1949 Capot	Dedicate (TRA)	1966 Buckpasser
1940 Challedon	1950 Hill Prince	1958 Round Table	1967 Damascus
1941 WHIRLAWAY	1951 Counterpoint	1959 Sword Dancer	1968 Dr. Fager
1942 Whirlaway	1952 One Count (DRF)	1960 Kelso	1969 Arts and Letters
1943 COUNT FLEET	Native Dancer (TRA)	1961 Kelso	1970 Fort Marcy (DRF)
1944 Twilight Tear (f)	1953 Tom Fool	1962 Kelso	Personality (TRA)
1945 Busher (f)	1954 Native Dancer	1963 Kelso	

Eclipse Awards

The Eclipse Awards, honoring the Horse of the Year and other champions of the sport, are sponsored by the *Daily Racing Form*, the Thoroughbred Racing Associations and the National Turf Writers Assn.

The awards are named after the 18th century racehorse and sire, Eclipse, who began racing at age five and was unbeaten in 18 starts (eight wins were walkovers). As a stallion, Eclipse sired winners of 344 races, including three Epsom Derby champions.

Horses listed in CAPITAL letters won the Triple Crown that year. Age of horse in parentheses where necessary.

Multiple winners: (horses): Forego (8); John Henry (7); Affirmed and Secretariat (5); Cigar, Flatterer, Seattle Slew and Spectacular Bid (4); Ack Ack, Lonesome Glory, Susan's Girl and Zaccio (3); All Along, Alysheba, Bayakoa, Black Tie Affair, Cafe Prince, Conquistador Cielo, Desert Vixen, Ferdinand, Flawlessly, Go for Wand, Holy Bull, Housebuster, Kotashaan, Lady's Secret, Life's Magic, Miesque, Morley Street, Open Mind, Paseana, Riva Ridge, Slew o'Gold and Spend A Buck (2).

Multiple winners: (people): Laffit Pincay Jr. (5); Laz Barrera, Pat Day, John Franks and D. Wayne Lukas (4); Steve Cauthen, Pat Day, Harbor View Farm, Fred W. Hooper, Nelson Bunker Hunt, Mr. & Mrs. Gene Klein, Dan Lasater, Ogden Phipps, Bill Shoemaker, Edward Taylor and Charlie Whittingham (3); Braulio Baeza, Jerry Bailey, C.T. Chenery, Claiborne Farm, Angel Cordero Jr., Kent Desormeaux, John W. Galbreath, Chris McCarron, Paul Mellon, Bill Mott, Allen Paulson and Mike Smith (2).

Horse of the Year

Year	Year	Year	Year
1971 Ack Ack (5)	1978 AFFIRMED (3)	1985 Spend A Buck (3)	1991 Black Tie Affair (5)
1972 SECRETARIAT (2)	1979 Affirmed (4)	1986 Lady's Secret (4)	1992 A.P. Indy (3)
1973 SECRETARIAT (3)	1980 Spectacular Bid (4)	1987 Ferdinand (4)	1993 Kotashaan (5)
1974 Forego (4)	1981 John Henry (6)	1988 Alysheba (4)	1994 Holy Bull (3)
1975 Forego (5)	1982 Conquistador Cielo (3)	1989 Sunday Silence (3)	1995 Cigar (5)
1976 Forego (6)	1983 All Along (4)	1990 Criminal Type (5)	1996 Cigar (6)
1977 SEATTLE SLEW (3)	1984 John Henry (9)		

Older Male

Year	Year	Year	Year
1971 Ack Ack (5)	1978 Seattle Slew (4)	1985 Vanlandingham (4)	1991 Black Tie Affair (5)
1972 Autobiography (4)	1979 Affirmed (4)	1986 Turkoman (4)	1992 Pleasant Tap (5)
1973 Riva Ridge (4)	1980 Spectacular Bid (4)	1987 Ferdinand (4)	1993 Bertrando (4)
1974 Forego (4)	1981 John Henry (6)	1988 Alysheba (4)	1994 The Wicked North (4)
1975 Forego (5)	1982 Lemhi Gold (4)	1989 Blushing John (4)	1995 Cigar (5)
1976 Forego (6)	1983 Bates Motel (4)	1990 Criminal Type (5)	1996 Cigar (6)
1977 Forego (7)	1984 Slew o' Gold (4)		

Older Filly or Mare

Year	Year	Year	Year
1971 Shuvee (5)	1978 Late Bloomer (4)	1985 Life's Magic (4)	1991 Queena (5)
1972 Typecast (6)	1979 Waya (5)	1986 Lady's Secret (4)	1992 Paseana (5)
1973 Susan's Girl (4)	1980 Glorious Song (4)	1987 North Sider (5)	1993 Paseana (6)
1974 Desert Vixen (4)	1981 Relaxing (5)	1988 Personal Ensign (4)	1994 Sky Beauty (4)
1975 Susan's Girl (6)	1982 Track Robbery (6)	1989 Bayakoa (5)	1995 Inside Information (4)
1976 Proud Delta (4)	1983 Amb. of Luck (4)	1990 Bayakoa (6)	1996 Jewel Princess (4)
1977 Cascapedia (4)	1984 Princess Rooney (4)		

3-Year-Old Colt or Gelding

Year		Year		Year		Year	
1971	Canonero II	1978	AFFIRMED	1985	Spend A Buck	1991	Hansel
1972	Key to the Mint	1979	Spectacular Bid	1986	Snow Chief	1992	A.P. Indy
1973	SECRETARIAT	1980	Temperence Hill	1987	Alysheba	1993	Prairie Bayou
1974	Little Current	1981	Pleasant Colony	1988	Risen Star	1994	Holy Bull
1975	Wajima	1982	Conquistador Cielo	1989	Sunday Silence	1995	Thunder Gulch
1976	Bold Forbes	1983	Slew o' Gold	1990	Unbridled	1996	Skip Away
1977	SEATTLE SLEW	1984	Swale				

3-Year-Old Filly

Year		Year		Year		Year	
1971	Turkish Trousers	1978	Tempest Queen	1985	Mom's Command	1991	Dance Smartly
1972	Susan's Girl	1979	Davona Dale	1986	Tiffany Lass	1992	Saratoga Slew
1973	Desert Vixen	1980	Genuine Risk	1987	Sacahuista	1993	Hollywood Wildcat
1974	Chris Evert	1981	Wayward Lass	1988	Winning Colors	1994	Heavenly Prize
1975	Ruffian	1982	Christmas Past	1989	Open Mind	1995	Serena's Song
1976	Revidere	1983	Heartlight No. One	1990	Go for Wand	1996	Yanks Music
1977	Our Mims	1984	Life's Magic				

2-Year-Old Colt or Gelding

Year		Year		Year		Year	
1971	Riva Ridge	1978	Spectacular Bid	1985	Tasso	1991	Arazi
1972	Secretariat	1979	Rockhill Native	1986	Capote	1992	Gilded Time
1973	Protagonist	1980	Lord Avie	1987	Forty Niner	1993	Dehere
1974	Foolish Pleasure	1981	Deputy Minister	1988	Easy Goer	1994	Timber Country
1975	Honest Pleasure	1982	Roving Boy	1989	Rhythm	1995	Maria's Mon
1976	Seattle Slew	1983	Devil's Bag	1990	Fly So Free	1996	Boston Harbor
1977	Affirmed	1984	Chief's Crown				

2-Year-Old Filly

Year		Year		Year		Year	
1971	Numbered Account	1978	(tie) Candy Eclair	1984	Outstandingly	1991	Pleasant Stage
1972	La Prevoyante		& It's in the Air	1985	Family Style	1992	Eliza
1973	Talking Picture	1979	Smart Angle	1986	Brave Raj	1993	Phone Chatter
1974	Ruffian	1980	Heavenly Cause	1987	Epitome	1994	Flanders
1975	Dearly Precious	1981	Before Dawn	1988	Open Mind	1995	Golden Attraction
1976	Sensational	1982	Landaluce	1989	Go for Wand	1996	Storm Song
1977	Lakeville Miss	1983	Althea	1990	Meadow Star		

Champion Turf Horse

Year		Year		Year		Year	
1971	Run the Gantlet (3)	1973	SECRETARIAT(3)	1975	Snow Knight (4)	1977	Johnny D (3)
1972	Cougar II (6)	1974	Dahlia (4)	1976	Youth (3)	1978	Mac Diarmida (3)

Champion Male Turf Horse

Year		Year		Year		Year	
1979	Bowl Game (5)	1984	John Henry (9)	1989	Steinlen (6)	1993	Kotashaan (5)
1980	John Henry (5)	1985	Cozzene (4)	1990	Itsallgreektome (3)	1994	Paradise Creek (5)
1981	John Henry (6)	1986	Manila (3)	1991	Tight Spot (4)	1995	Northern Spur (4)
1982	Perrault (5)	1987	Theatrical (5)	1992	Sky Classic (5)	1996	Singspiel (4)
1983	John Henry (8)	1988	Sunshine Forever (3)				

Champion Female Turf Horse

Year		Year		Year		Year	
1979	Trillion (5)	1984	Royal Heroine (4)	1989	Brown Bess (7)	1993	Flawlessly (5)
1980	Just A Game II (4)	1985	Pebbles (4)	1990	Laugh and Be Merry (5)	1994	Hatoof (5)
1981	De La Rose (3)	1986	Estrapade (6)	1991	Miss Alleged (4)	1995	Possibly Perfect (5)
1982	April Run (4)	1987	Miesque (3)	1992	Flawlessly (4)	1996	Wandesta (5)
1983	All Along (4)	1988	Miesque (4)				

Eclipse Awards (Cont.)

Sprinter

Year		Year		Year		Year	
1971	Ack Ack (5)	1978	(tie) Dr. Patches (4)	1984	Eillo (4)	1991	Housebuster (4)
1972	Chou Croute (4)		& J.O. Tobin (4)	1985	Precisionist (4)	1992	Rubiano (5)
1973	Shecky Greene (3)	1979	Star de Naskra (4)	1986	Smile (4)	1993	Cardmania (7)
1974	Forego (4)	1980	Plugged Nickle (3)	1987	Groovy (4)	1994	Cherokee Run (4)
1975	Gallant Bob (3)	1981	Guilty Conscience (5)	1988	Gulch (4)	1995	Not Surprising (4)
1976	My Juliet (4)	1982	Gold Beauty (3)	1989	Safely Kept (3)	1996	Lit de Justice (6)
1977	What a Summer (4)	1983	Chinook Pass (4)	1990	Housebuster (3)		

Steeplechase or Hurdle Horse

Year		Year		Year		Year	
1971	Shadow Brook (7)	1978	Cafe Prince (8)	1985	Flatterer (6)	1991	Morley Street (7)
1972	Soothsayer (5)	1979	Martie's Anger (4)	1986	Flatterer (7)	1992	Lonesome Glory (4)
1973	Athenian Idol (5)	1980	Zaccio (4)	1987	Inlander (6)	1993	Lonesome Glory (5)
1974	Gran Kan (8)	1981	Zaccio (5)	1988	Jimmy Lorenzo (6)	1994	Warm Spell (6)
1975	Life's Illusion (4)	1982	Zaccio (6)	1989	Highland Bud (4)	1995	Lonesome Glory (7)
1976	Straight and True (6)	1983	Flatterer (4)	1990	Morley Street (6)	1996	Correggio (5)
1977	Cafe Prince (7)	1984	Flatterer (5)				

Outstanding Jockey

Year		Year		Year		Year	
1971	Laffit Pincay Jr.	1978	Darrel McHargue	1985	Laffit Pincay Jr.	1991	Pat Day
1972	Braulio Baeza	1979	Laffit Pincay Jr.	1986	Pat Day	1992	Kent Desormeaux
1973	Laffit Pincay Jr.	1980	Chris McCarron	1987	Pat Day	1993	Mike Smith
1974	Laffit Pincay Jr.	1981	Bill Shoemaker	1988	Jose Santos	1994	Mike Smith
1975	Braulio Baeza	1982	Angel Cordero Jr.	1989	Kent Desormeaux	1995	Jerry Bailey
1976	Sandy Hawley	1983	Angel Cordero Jr.	1990	Craig Perret	1996	Jerry Bailey
1977	Steve Cauthen	1984	Pat Day				

Outstanding Apprentice Jockey

Year		Year		Year		Year	
1971	Gene St. Leon	1978	Ron Franklin	1985	Art Madrid Jr.	1991	Mickey Walls
1972	Thomas Wallis	1979	Cash Asmussen	1986	Allen Stacy	1992	Rosemary Homeister
1973	Steve Valdez	1980	Frank Lovato Jr.	1987	Kent Desormeaux	1993	Juan Umana
1974	Chris McCarron	1981	Richard Migliore	1988	Steve Capanas	1994	Dale Beckner
1975	Jimmy Edwards	1982	Alberto Delgado	1989	Michael Luzzi	1995	Ramon B. Perez
1976	George Martens	1983	Declan Murphy	1990	Mark Johnston	1996	Neil Poznansky
1977	Steve Cauthen	1984	Wesley Ward				

Outstanding Trainer

Year		Year		Year		Year	
1971	Charlie Whittingham	1978	Laz Barrera	1985	D. Wayne Lukas	1991	Ron McAnally
1972	Lucien Laurin	1979	Laz Barrera	1986	D. Wayne Lukas	1992	Ron McAnally
1973	H. Allen Jerkens	1980	Bud Delp	1987	D. Wayne Lukas	1993	Bobby Frankel
1974	Sherill Ward	1981	Ron McAnally	1988	Shug McGaughey	1994	D. Wayne Lukas
1975	Steve DiMauro	1982	Charlie Whittingham	1989	Charlie Whittingham	1995	Bill Mott
1976	Laz Barrera	1983	Woody Stephens	1990	Carl Nafzger	1996	Bill Mott
1977	Laz Barrera	1984	Jack Van Berg				

Outstanding Owner

Year		Year		Year		Year	
1971	Mr. & Mrs. E.E. Fogleson	1979	Harbor View Farm	1985	Mr. & Mrs. Gene Klein	1991	Sam-Son Farms
1972-73	No award	1980	Mr. & Mrs. Bertram	1986	Mr. & Mrs. Gene Klein	1992	Juddmonta Farms
1974	Dan Lasater		Firestone	1987	Mr. & Mrs. Gene Klein	1993	John Franks
1975	Dan Lasater	1981	Dotsam Stable	1988	Ogden Phipps	1994	John Franks
1976	Dan Lasater	1982	Viola Sommer	1989	Ogden Phipps	1995	Allen Paulson
1977	Maxwell Gluck	1983	John Franks	1990	Frances Genter	1996	Allen Paulson
1978	Harbor View Farm	1984	John Franks				

Outstanding Breeder

Year		Year		Year		Year	
1971	Paul Mellon	1978	Harbor View Farm	1985	Nelson Bunker Hunt	1991	Mr. & Mrs. John Mabee
1972	C.T. Chenery	1979	Claiborne Farm	1986	Paul Mellon	1992	William S. Farish
1973	C.T. Chenery	1980	Mrs. Henry Paxson	1987	Nelson Bunker Hunt	1993	Allan Paulson
1974	John W. Galbreath	1981	Golden Chance Farm	1988	Ogden Phipps	1994	William T. Young
1975	Fred W. Hooper	1982	Fred W. Hooper	1989	North Ridge Farm	1995	Juddmonte Farms
1976	Nelson Bunker Hunt	1983	Edward P. Taylor	1990	Calumet Farm	1996	Farnsworth Farms
1977	Edward P. Taylor	1984	Claiborne Farm				

Outstanding Achievement

Year		Year	
1971	Charles Engelhard*	1972	Arthur B. Hancock Jr.*

*Awarded posthumously.

Man of the Year

Year		Year	
1972	John W. Galbreath	1974	William L. McKnight
1973	Edward P. Taylor	1975	John A. Morris

Award of Merit

Year		Year		Year		Year	
1976	Jack J. Dreyfus	1981	Bill Shoemaker	1987	J.B. Faulconer	1991	Fred W. Hooper
1977	Steve Cauthen	1984	John Gaines	1988	John Forsythe	1992	Joe Hirsch
1978	Dinny Phipps	1985	Keene Daingerfield	1989	Michael Sandler		& Robert P. Strub
1979	Jimmy Kilroe	1986	Herman Cohen	1990	Warner L. Jones	1995	James E. Bassett III
1980	John D. Shapiro						

Special Award

Year		Year		Year		Year	
1971	Robert J. Kleberg	1980	John T. Landry	1985	Arlington Park	1989	Richard Duchossois
1974	Charles Hatton		& Pierre E. Bellocq	1987	Anheuser-Busch	1995	Russell Baze
1976	Bill Shoemaker	1984	C.V. Whitney	1988	Edward J. DeBartolo Sr.		

HARNESS RACING

Triple Crown Winners

PACERS

Seven 3-year-olds have won the Cane Pace, Little Brown Jug and Messenger Stakes in the same year since the Pacing Triple Crown was established in 1956. No trainer or driver has won it more than once. This chapter was closed before the Oct. 10, 1997 running of the Messenger Stakes where a victory by Western Dreamer would give him the Triple Crown. See the updates section for results.

Year		Driver	Trainer	Owner
1959	**Adios Butler**	Clint Hodgins	Paige West	Paige West & Angelo Pellillo
1965	**Bret Hanover**	Frank Ervin	Frank Ervin	Richard Downing
1966	**Romeo Hanover**	Bill Myer & George Sholty*	Jerry Silverman	Lucky Star Stables & Morton Finder
1968	**Rum Customer**	Billy Haughton	Billy Haughton	Kennilworth Farms & L.C. Mancuso
1970	**Most Happy Fella** ...	Stanley Dancer	Stanley Dancer	Egyptian Acres Stable
1980	**Niatross**	Clint Galbraith	Clint Galbraith	Niagara Acres, Niatross Stables & Clint Galbraith
1983	**Ralph Hanover**	Ron Waples	Stew Firlotte	Waples Stable, Pointsetta Stable, Grant's Direct Stable & P.J. Baugh

*Myer drove Romeo Hanover in the Cane, Sholty in the other two races.

TROTTERS

Six 3-year-olds have won the Yonkers Trot, Hambletonian and Kentucky Futurity in the same year since the Trotting Triple Crown was established in 1955. Stanley Dancer is the only driver/trainer to win it twice.

Year		Driver/Trainer	Owner
1955	**Scott Frost**	Joe O'Brien	S.A. Camp Farms
1963	**Speedy Scot**	Ralph Baldwin	Castleton Farms
1964	**Ayres**	John Simpson Sr.	Charlotte Sheppard
1968	**Nevele Pride**	Stanley Dancer	Nevele Acres & Lou Resnick
1969	**Lindy's Pride**	Howard Beissinger	Lindy Farms
1972	**Super Bowl**	Stanley Dancer	Rachel Dancer & Rose Hild Breeding Farm

Triple Crown Near Misses

PACERS

Seven horses have won the first two legs of the Triple Crown, but not the third. The Cane Pace (CP), Little Brown Jug (LBJ), and Messenger Stakes (MS) have not always been run in the same order so numbers after races won indicate sequence for that year.

Year		CP	LBJ	MS
1957	**Torpid**	won, 1	won, 2	DNF
1960	**Countess Adios** ..	won, 2	NE	won, 1
1971	**Albatross**	won, 2	2nd*	won, 1
1976	**Keystone Ore** ...	won, 1	won, 2	2nd*
1986	**Barberry Spur** ...	won, 1	won, 2	2nd*
1990	**Jake and Elwood**	won, 1	NE	won, 2
1992	**Western Hanover**	won, 1	2nd*	won, 2
1993	**Rijadh**	won, 1	2nd*	won, 2

*Winning horses:** Nansemond (1971), Windshield Wiper (1976), Amity Chef (1986), Fake Left (1992), Life Sign (1993).
Note: Torpid (1957) scratched before the final heat; Countess Adios (1960) not eligible for Messenger; Jake and Elwood (1990) not eligible for Little Brown Jug.

TROTTERS

Seven horses have won the first two legs of the Triple Crown—the Yonkers Trot (YT) and the Hambletonian (Ham)—but not the third. The eventual winner of the Ky. Futurity (KF) is listed.

Year		YT	Ham	KF
1962	**A.C.'s Viking**	won	won	Safe Mission
1976	**Steve Lobell**	won	won	Quick Pay
1977	**Green Speed**	won	won	Texas
1978	**Speedy Somolli**	won	won	Doublemint
1987	**Mack Lobell**	won	won	Napoletano
1993	**American Winner**	won	won	Pine Chip
1996	**Continentalvictory**	won	won	Running Sea

Note: Green Speed (1977) not eligible for Ky. Futurity; Continentalvictory (1996) was withdrawn from the Ky. Futurity due to a leg injury.

The Hambletonian

For three-year-old trotters. Inaugurated in 1926 and has been held in Syracuse, N.Y.; Lexington, Ky.; Goshen, N.Y.; Yonkers, N.Y.; Du Quoin, Ill.; and, since 1981 at The Meadowlands in East Rutherford, N.J.

Run at one mile since 1947. Winning horse must win two heats.

Drivers with most wins: John Campbell, Stanley Dancer, Billy Haughton and Ben White (4); Howard Beissinger, Del Cameron, and Henry Thomas (3).

Year		Driver	Fastest Heat	Year		Driver	Fastest Heat
1926	**Guy McKinney**	Nat Ray	2:04¾	1963	**Speedy Scot**	Ralph Baldwin	1:57⅗
1927	**Iosola's Worthy** ..	Marvin Childs	2:03¾	1964	**Ayres**	John Simpson Sr.	1:56⅘
1928	**Spencer**	W.H. Lessee	2:02½	1965	**Egyptian Candor** ..	Del Cameron	2:03⅘
1929	**Walter Dear**	Walter Cox	2:02¾	1966	**Kerry Way**	Frank Ervin	1:58⅘
1930	**Hanover's Bertha**	Tom Berry	2:03	1967	**Speedy Streak** ...	Del Cameron	2:00
1931	**Calumet Butler** ..	R.D. McMahon	2:03¼	1968	**Nevele Pride**	Stanley Dancer	1:59⅖
1932	**The Marchioness** .	Will Caton	2:01¼	1969	**Lindys Pride**	Howard Beissinger	1:57⅗
1933	**Mary Reynolds** ...	Ben White	2:03¾	1970	**Timothy T**	John Simpson Jr.	1:58⅖
1934	**Lord Jim**	Doc Parshall	2:02¾	1971	**Speedy Crown**	Howard Beissinger	1:57⅖
1935	**Greyhound**	Sep Palin	2:02¼	1972	**Super Bowl**	Stanley Dancer	1:56⅖
1936	**Rosalind**	Ben White	2:01¾	1973	**Flirth**	Ralph Baldwin	1:57⅕
1937	**Shirley Hanover** ..	Henry Thomas	2:01½	1974	**Christopher T**	Billy Haughton	1:58⅜
1938	**McLin Hanover** ...	Henry Tomas	2:01¼	1975	**Bonefish**	Stanley Dancer	1:59
1939	**Peter Astra**	Doc Parshall	2:04¼	1976	**Steve Lobell**	Billy Haughton	1:56⅖
1940	**Spencer Scott**	Fred Egan	2:02	1977	**Green Speed**	Billy Haughton	1:55⅗
1941	**Bill Gallon**	Lee Smith	2:05	1978	**Speedy Somolli** ...	Howard Beissinger	1:55
1942	**The Ambassador** ..	Ben White	2:04	1979	**Legend Hanover** ..	George Sholty	1:56⅕
1943	**Volo Song**	Ben White	2:02½	1980	**Burgomeister**	Billy Haughton	1:56⅗
1944	**Yankee Maid**	Henry Thomas	2:04	1981	**Shiaway St. Pat** ...	Ray Remmen	2:01⅕
1945	**Titan Hanover**	Harry Pownall Sr.	2:04	1982	**Speed Bowl**	Tommy Haughton	1:56⅘
1946	**Chestertown**	Thomas Berry	2:02½	1983	**Duenna**	Stanley Dancer	1:57⅖
1947	**Hoot Mon**	Sep Palin	2:00	1984	**Historic Freight** ...	Ben Webster	1:56⅖
1948	**Demon Hanover** ..	Harrison Hoyt	2:02	1985	**Prakas**	Bill O'Donnell	1:54⅘
1949	**Miss Tilly**	Fred Egan	2:01⅖	1986	**Nuclear Kosmos** ..	Ulf Thoresen	1:55⅖
1950	**Lusty Song**	Del Miller	2:02	1987	**Mack Lobell**	John Campbell	1:53⅗
1951	**Mainliner**	Guy Crippen	2:02⅗	1988	**Armbro Goal**	John Campbell	1:54⅗
1952	**Sharp Note**	Bion Shively	2:02⅗	1989	**Park Avenue Joe** ..	Ron Waples	1:54⅗
1953	**Helicopter**	Harry Harvey	2:01⅗		& Probe	Bill Fahy	
1954	**Newport Dream** ..	Del Cameron	2:02⅖	1990	**Harmonious**	John Campbell	1:54⅕
1955	**Scott Frost**	Joe O'Brien	2:00⅗	1991	**Giant Victory**	Jack Moiseyev	1:54⅘
1956	**The Intruder**	Ned Bower	2:01⅖	1992	**Alf Palema**	Mickey McNichol	1:56⅖
1957	**Hickory Smoke** ...	John Simpson Sr.	2:00⅕	1993	**American Winner** ..	Ron Pierce	1:53⅕
1958	**Emily's Pride**	Flave Nipe	1:59⅘	1994	**Victory Dream**	Michel Lachance	1:54⅕
1959	**Diller Hanover** ...	Frank Ervin	2:01⅕	1995	**Tagliabue**	John Campbell	1:54⅘
1960	**Blaze Hanover** ...	Joe O'Brien	1:59⅗	1996	**Continentalvictory** .	Michel Lachance	1:52⅘
1961	**Harlan Dean**	James Arthur	1:58⅖	1997	**Malabar Man**	Mal Burroughs	1:55
1962	**A.C.'s Viking**	Sanders Russell	1:59⅗				

Note: In 1989, Park Avenue Joe and Probe finished in a dead heat in the race-off. They were later declared co-winners, but Park Avenue Joe was awarded 1st place money because his three-race summary (2-1-1) was better than Probe's (1-9-1).

The Little Brown Jug

Harness racing's most prestigious race for three-year-old pacers. Inaugurated in 1946 and held annually at the Delaware, Ohio County Fairgrounds. Winning horse must win two heats.

Drivers with most wins: Billy Haughton (5); Stanley Dancer and Michel Lachance (4); John Campbell, Frank Ervin and John Simpson Sr. (3); Adelbert Cameron, Herve Filion, Jack Moiseyev, Joe O'Brien, Bill O'Donnell, "Curly" Smart and Ron Waples (2).

Year		Driver	Fastest Heat	Year		Driver	Fastest Heat
1946	Ensign Hanover	"Curly" Smart	2:02	1972	Strike Out	Keith Waples	1:56⅗
1947	Forbes Chief	Adelbert Cameron	2:05	1973	Melvin's Woe	Joe O'Brien	1:57⅗
1948	Knight Dream	Frank Safford	2:07	1974	Armbro Omaha	Billy Haughton	1:57
1949	Good Time	Frank Ervin	2:03⅖	1975	Seatrain	Ben Webster	1:56⅘
1950	Dudley Hanover	Delvin Miller	2:02⅗	1976	Keystone Ore	Stanley Dancer	1:56⅘
1951	Tar Heel	Adelbert Cameron	2:00	1977	Governor Skipper	John Chapman	1:56⅕
1952	Meadow Rice	"Curly" Smart	2:01⅗	1978	Happy Escort	Bill Popfinger	1:55⅖
1953	Keystoner	Frank Ervin	2:02⅕	1979	Hot Hitter	Herve Filion	1:55⅗
1954	Adios Harry	Morris MacDonald	2:02⅘	1980	Niatross	Clint Galbraith	1:54⅘
1955	Quick Chief	Billy Haughton	2:00	1981	Fan Hanover (f)	Glen Garnsey	1:56
1956	Noble Adios	John Simpson, Sr.	2:00⅘	1982	Merger	John Campbell	1:54⅗
1957	Torpid	John Simpson, Sr.	2:00⅘	1983	Ralph Hanover	Ron Waples	1:55⅗
1958	Shadow Wave	Joe O'Brien	2:01	1984	Colt Fortysix	Chris Boring	1:53⅗
1959	Adios Butler	Clint Hodgkins	1:59⅖	1985	Nihilator	Bill O'Donnell	1:52⅕
1960	Bullet Hanover	John Simpson, Sr.	1:58⅗	1986	Barberry Spur	Bill O'Donnell	1:52⅘
1961	Henry T. Adios	Stanley Dancer	1:58⅘	1987	Jaguar Spur	Dick Stillings	1:54
1962	Lehigh Hanover	Stanley Dancer	1:58⅘	1988	B.J. Scoot	Michel Lachance	1:52⅗
1963	Overtrick	John Patterson, Sr.	1:57⅕	1989	Goalie Jeff	Michel Lachance	1:54⅕
1964	Vicar Hanover	Billy Haughton	2:00⅘	1990	Beach Towel	Ray Remmen	1:53⅗
1965	Bret Hanover	Frank Ervin	1:57	1991	Precious Bunny	Jack Moiseyev	1:53⅘
1966	Romeo Hanover	George Sholty	1:59⅗	1992	Fake Left	Ron Waples	1:53⅗
1967	Best Of All	Jim Hackett	1:59	1993	Life Sign	John Campbell	1:52
1968	Rum Customer	Billy Haughton	1:59⅗	1994	Magical Mike	Michel Lachance	1:52⅗
1969	Laverne Hanover	Billy Haughton	2:00⅖	1995	Nick's Fantasy	John Campbell	1:51⅖
1970	Most Happy Fella	Stanley Dancer	1:57⅕	1996	Armbro Operative	Jack Moiseyev	1:52⅗
1971	Nansemond	Herve Filion	1:57⅖	1997	Western Dreamer	Michel Lachance	1:51⅕

All-Time Leaders

The all-time winning trotters, pacers and drivers through 1996 according to *The Trotting and Pacing Guide*. Purses for horses include races in foreign countries. Earnings and wins for drivers include only races held in North America.

Top 10 Horses — Money Won

		T/P	Sts	1st	Earnings
1	Peace Corps	T	42	35	$5,506,443
2	Ourasi (FRA)	T	N/A	32	4,010,105
3	Mack Lobell	T	86	65	3,917,594
4	Reve d'Udon	T	23	18	3,611,351
5	Nihilator	P	38	35	3,225,653
6	Sea Cove	T	N/A	N/A	3,138,986
7	Artsplace	P	49	37	3,085,083
8	Presidential Ball	P	38	26	3,021,363
9	Matt's Scooter	P	61	37	2,944,591
10	On the Road Again	P	61	44	2,819,102

Top 10 Drivers — Races Won

		Yrs	1st	Earnings
1	Herve Filion	35	14,783	$85,044,328
2	Michel Lachance	29	7,639	91,200,742
3	Dave Magee	24	7,399	51,512,694
4	John Campbell	25	7,320	146,438,022
5	Walter Case Jr.	20	7,214	28,197,404
6	Carmine Abbatiello	41	7,159	50,201,484
7	Cat Manzi	29	7,146	59,978,674
8	Jack Moiseyev	21	6,810	63,414,029
9	Doug Brown	24	6,620	61,406,191
10	Eddie Davis	33	6,342	30,235,861

Annual Awards

Harness Horse of the Year

Selected since 1947 by U.S. Trotting Association and the U.S. Harness Writers Association; age of winning horse is noted; (t) indicates trotter and (p) indicates pacer. USTA added Trotter and Pacer of the Year awards in 1970.

Multiple winners: Bret Hanover and Nevele Pride (3); Adios Butler, Albatross, Cam Fella, Good Time, Mack Lobell, Niatross and Scott Frost (2).

Year		Year		Year		Year	
1947	Victory Song (4t)	1955	Scott Frost (3t)	1963	Speedy Scot (3t)	1971	Albatross (3p)
1948	Rodney (4t)	1956	Scott Frost (4t)	1964	Bret Hanover (2p)	1972	Albatross (4p)
1949	Good Time (3p)	1957	Torpid (3t)	1965	Bret Hanover (3p)	1973	Sir Dalrai (4p)
1950	Proximity (8t)	1958	Emily's Pride (3t)	1966	Bret Hanover (4p)	1974	Delmonica Hanover(5t)
1951	Pronto Don (6t)	1959	Bye Bye Byrd (4p)	1967	Nevele Pride (2t)	1975	Savoir (7t)
1952	Good Time (6t)	1960	Adios Butler (4p)	1968	Nevele Pride (3t)	1976	Keystone Ore (3p)
1953	Hi Lo's Forbes (5p)	1961	Adios Butler (5p)	1969	Nevele Pride (4t)	1977	Green Speed (3t)
1954	Stenographer (3t)	1962	Su Mac Lad (8t)	1970	Fresh Yankee (7t)	1978	Abercrombie (3p)

Harness Racing (Cont.)

Year		Year		Year		Year	
1979	Niatross (2p)	1984	Fancy Crown (3t)	1989	Matt's Scooter (4p)	1994	Cam's Card Shark (3p)
1980	Niatross (3p)	1985	Nihilator (3p)	1990	Beach Towel (3p)	1995	CR Kay Suzie (3t)
1981	Fan Hanover (3p)	1986	Forrest Skipper (4p)	1991	Precious Bunny (3p)	1996	Continentalvictory (3t)
1982	Cam Fella (3p)	1987	Mack Lobell (3t)	1992	Artsplace (4p)		
1983	Cam Fella (4p)	1988	Mack Lobell (4t)	1993	Staying Together (4p)		

Driver of the Year

Determined by Universal Driving Rating System (UDR) and presented by the Harness Tracks of America since 1968. Eligible drivers must have at least 1,000 starts for the season.

Multiple winners: Herve Filion (10); John Campbell and Michel Lachance (3); Walter Case Jr., Bill O'Donnell, Luc Ouellette and Ron Waples (2).

Year		Year		Year		Year	
1968	Stanley Dancer	1976	Herve Filion	1983	John Campbell	1991	Walter Case Jr.
1969	Herve Filion	1977	Donald Dancer	1984	Bill O'Donnell	1992	Walter Case Jr.
1970	Herve Filion	1978	Carmine Abbatiello & Herve Filion	1985	Michel Lachance	1993	Jack Moiseyev
1971	Herve Filion			1986	Michel Lachance	1994	Dave Magee
1972	Herve Filion	1979	Ron Waples	1987	Michel Lachance	1995	Luc Ouellette
1973	Herve Filion	1980	Ron Waples	1988	John Campbell	1996	Tony Morgan & Luc Ouellette
1974	Herve Filion	1981	Herve Filion	1989	Herve Filion		
1975	Joe O'Brien	1982	Bill O'Donnell	1990	John Campbell		

STEEPLECHASE RACING

Champion Horses

Annual horse of the year since 1956 based on vote of the National Turf Writers Association and other selected media.
Multiple Winners: Flatterer (4); Bon Nouvel, Lonesome Glory, Zaccio (3); Café Prince, Morley Street, Neji (2).

Year		Year		Year		Year	
1956	Shipboard	1967	Quick Pitch	1977	Café Prince	1987	Inlander
1957	Neji	1968	Bon Nouvel	1978	Café Prince	1988	Jimmy Lorenzo
1958	Neji	1969	L'Escargot	1979	Martie's Anger	1989	Highland Bud
1959	Ancestor	1970	Top Bid	1980	Zaccio	1990	Morley Street
1960	Benguala	1971	Shadow Brok	1981	Zaccio	1991	Morley Street
1961	Peal	1972	Soothsayer	1982	Zaccio	1992	Lonesome Glory
1962	Barnaby's Bluff	1973	Athenian Idol	1983	Flatterer	1993	Lonesome Glory
1963	Amber Diver	1974	Gran Kan	1984	Flatterer	1994	Warm Spell
1964	Bon Nouvel	1975	Life's Illusion	1985	Flatterer	1995	Lonesome Glory
1965	Bon Nouvel	1976	Fire Control & Straight and True	1986	Flatterer	1996	Correggio
1966	Tuscalee & Mako						

Champion Jockeys

Annual leading jockeys by races won since 1956, according to the National Steeplechase Association.
Multiple Winners: Joe Aitcheson Jr. (7); Jerry Fishback (5); John Cushman and Alfred P. Smithwick (4); Tom Skiffington and Jeff Teter (3); Ricky Hendriks, James Lawrence, Blythe Miller and Thomas Walsh (2).

Year		Year		Year		Year	
1956	Alfred P. Smithwick	1967	Joe Aitcheson Jr.	1977	Jerry Fishback	1987	Ricky Hendriks
1957	Alfred P. Smithwick	1968	Joe Aitcheson Jr.	1978	Tom Skiffington	1988	Jonathan Smart
1958	Alfred P. Smithwick	1969	Joe Aitcheson Jr.	1979	Tom Skiffington	1989	James Lawrence
1959	James Murphy	1970	Joe Aitcheson Jr.	1980	John Cushman	1990	Jeff Teter
1960	Thomas Walsh	1971	Jerry Fishback	1981	John Cushman	1991	Jeff Teter
1961	Joe Aitcheson Jr.	1972	Michael O'Brien	1982	John Cushman	1992	Craig Thornton
1962	Alfred P. Smithwick	1973	Jerry Fishback	1983	John Cushman	1993	James Lawrence
1963	Joe Aitcheson Jr.	1974	Jerry Fishback	1984	Jeff Teter	1994	Blythe Miller
1964	Joe Aitcheson Jr.	1975	Jerry Fishback	1985	Bernie Houghton	1995	Blythe Miller
1965	Doug Small Jr.	1976	Tom Skiffington	1986	Ricky Hendriks	1996	Chip Miller
1966	Thomas Walsh						

Tennis

Pete Sampras started off 1997 with a bang by winning the Australian Open, his ninth Grand Slam singles title.

Wide World Photos

Venus Rising

*For Martina Hingis, 1997 was a great year.
But Venus Williams has arrived.*

by
Sal Paolantonio

On an unusually cool, April morning in Eastern Switzerland, 16-year-old Martina Hingis made perhaps the most critical decision of her short, remarkable pro tennis career.

Instead of riding her horse, Montana, she wanted to see if she could handle a finicky foal named Tina, which belonged to a friend. She couldn't. Tina threw Hingis, who went sprawling to the dew-soaked turf.

After minor knee surgery, Hingis was forced to take seven weeks off, derailing her preparation for the French Open, where she lost in the finals to Iva Majoli of Croatia and missed her chance at becoming the youngest woman ever to win the Grand Slam of tennis.

Earlier in the year, with a sly grin and surgical ground strokes, Hingis had cruised through the Australian Open and then became the youngest Wimbledon champion since Lottie Dod in 1887. And she threatened to

dominate Flushing Meadows until 17-year-old Venus Williams suddenly decided to make the U.S. Open her coming out party.

With 1,800 red, white and blue beads glistening in New York's late summer sun, Williams singlehandedly put American tennis back on center stage. In week one, she was overpowering. In the second week, Williams—who until the Open had never advanced beyond a quarterfinal of any tournament—showed the savvy of an old pro developing an off-speed pitch. She cut back on her big forehand and serve to land in the semifinals against 11th seed Irina Spirlea, who had already ousted No. 2 Monica Seles.

Spirlea, a fiery Romanian who obviously learned a few tricks from her countryman Ilie Nastase, intentionally bumped Williams at the net, setting off a fresh round of criticism of Williams' aloofness on the women's tour.

Then, on the eve of her showdown in the finals with Hingis, Venus' father and coach, Richard, who chose to stay

Sal Paolantonio covers tennis for ESPN.

Nobody, anywhere, had a better year in 1997 than **Martina Hingis**. Hingis is shown with her trophy for winning the 1997 Australian Open, her first Grand Slam singles title.

in Florida throughout the Open, jumped into the fray by phone. He called Spirlea an "ugly, tall, white turkey," and charged that his daughter had been a victim of racism.

The next day, Hingis moved Williams around the court at the new Arthur Ashe Stadium like she was on skates and destroyed the American upstart in straight sets in little over an hour. And then the real fun began.

At her post-match press conference, several reporters repeatedly asked Williams to react to her father's comments. One black reporter from a local Queens weekly walked out in protest, yelling at his colleagues. In the end, it was Williams, again showing poise beyond her years, who put everyone in their place. "I think with this moment in the first year in Arthur Ashe Stadium, it all represents everyone being together, everyone having a chance to play," she said, perhaps sending a message to her dad in Florida, too. "So, I think this is definitely ruining the mood, these questions about racism."

The nationally televised soap opera couldn't have come at a better time for the tennis establishment, which had been reeling from bad TV ratings

The only thing standing between Martina Hingis and a Grand Slam sweep was **Iva Majoli**'s gritty victory at the 1997 French Open.

and declining American interest in the game. Thus, Williams' performance was quickly embraced. "Venus is the best thing that has happened to American tennis for the last 20 years," said USTA president Harry Marmion.

That may not sit well with Pete Sampras, who has been making some pretty startling history of his own. Sampras endured England's wettest summer to win Wimbledon, capturing his tenth Grand Slam title, just two short of Roy Emerson's record 12. But Sampras has been so methodically dominant that he has nearly put the sport to sleep. And with Andre Agassi fighting to come back after a long lay-off and Michael Chang playing perennial runner-up, it looks like the women's tour will have the charisma to usher the sport into the next century. The Hingis-Williams rivalry would be enough. But don't forget former No. 1 Steffi Graf, who promises to be back from knee surgery in time for the 1998 Australian Open. ∎

In 1997, **Gustavo Kuerten** of Brazil became the lowest-seeded player to win the French Open, which he entered ranked 66th in the world.

Sal Paolantonio's Top Ten Tennis Highlights of 1997

10. In the spirit of racial harmony, the new **Arthur Ashe Stadium** is dedicated at USTA Tennis Center in Flushing Meadows, on the day Althea Gibson celebrates her 70th birthday.

9. **Irina Spirlea** of Romania and Venus Williams bump at the net during U.S. Open semifinals.

8. After the bump, **Venus Williams' father** and coach, Richard, calls Irina Spirlea an "ugly, tall, white turkey," and claims on the eve of the U.S. Open finals that the women's tennis tour is rife with racism.

7. **Gustavo Kuerten** of Brazil, ranked 88th at the beginning of the year, wins the French Open title.

6. **Patrick Rafter** becomes the first Australian to win the U.S. Open since John Newcombe in 1973.

5. **Andre Agassi** marries actress Brooke Shields and takes a hiatus from the game.

4. **Iva Majoli** of Croatia wins the French Open title, denying Hingis a Grand Slam sweep.

3. **Pete Sampras** demolishes the field at Wimbledon to win his 10th Grand Slam title.

2. **Venus Williams** picks the U.S. Open to blossom, becoming the

first unseeded woman finalist in the open era.

1. **Martina Hingis**, 16, wins the U.S. Open, becoming the youngest woman ever to win three of the four Grand Slams in one year. ■

THE NUMBERS

INSIDE

by
Craig Wachs

HINGING ON GREATNESS

Martina Hingis is the youngest Wimbledon champion in the modern era. We checked on a random group of the best women's tennis players who won Wimbledon to see how old they were when they first took home the top prize from Centre Court.

Young Wimbledon Winners

	Year	Age
Lottie Dodd	1887	15.9 yrs
Martina Hingis	**1997**	**16.9 yrs**
Steffi Graf	1988	19.1 yrs
Chris Evert	1974	19.6 yrs
Margaret Court	1963	20.11 yrs
Martina Navratilova	1978	21.8
Billie Jean King	1966	22.7

This all bodes well for Hingis because the rest of these players, despite their relatively late starts, went on to win 33 Wimbledon singles titles between them.

LEGAL TENDER

1997 was a great year for young athletes. Tara Lipinski, who is an amateur, and Venus Williams, whose first great success came at the end of the tennis schedule, didn't win a ton of money but they certainly established themselves. The big three are Hingis, Woods and Gordon and here is how they rank, at press time, on the money board. Of course, if we figured in endorsements, Tiger might move up a bit.

Money won by October one

	Age	Earnings
Jeff Gordon	25	$3.9 million
Martina Hingis	**16**	**$3.1 million**
Tiger Woods	21	$1.9 million
Venus Williams	17	$426,861

TOURN FOR THE WORSE

After turning in a superhuman 1996, Steffi Graf had a very mortal 1997. After missing the 1996 Australian Open with bone spurs, she came back to win the rest of the Grand Slam events as well as four others. She hurt her knee at Wimbledon in 1996 and the injury essentially ruined this past year for her. This year was the first time since 1986 that Graf did not win at least one Grand Slam title.

What a difference a year makes

Steffi Graf	1996	1997
Record	54-4	16-3
Grand Slams/won	3/3	2/0
Tourney titles	7	1
Prize money	$2.7 mil	$200 k

■

THE 1998 · ESPN INFORMATION PLEASE SPORTS ALMANAC

TENNIS
STATISTICS

SEC A

THE SEASON IN REVIEW
1996-1997
MEN · WOMEN · LEADERS

PAGE 807

Tournament Results

Winners of men's and women's pro singles championships from Nov. 3, 1996 through Sept. 28, 1997. See Updates for later results.

Men's ATP Tour
LATE 1996

Finals	Tournament	Winner	Earnings	Runner-Up	Score
Nov. 3	Paris Open	Thomas Enqvist	$393,000	Y. Kafelnikov	62 64 75
Nov. 10	Stockholm Open	Thomas Enqvist	112,000	T. Martin	75 64 76
Nov. 10	Hellmann's Cup (Santiago)	Hernan Gumy	29,000	M. Rios	64 75
Nov. 10	Kremlin Cup (Moscow)	Goran Ivanisevic	157,000	Y. Kafelnikov	36 61 63
Nov. 17	ATP Doubles Champs. (Hartford)	Todd Woodbridge/ Mark Woodforde	165,000	S. Lareau/ A. O'Brien	64 57 62 76
Nov. 24	ATP World Championship (Hannover)	Pete Sampras	1,340,000	B. Becker	36 76 76 67 64
Dec. 8	ITF Grand Slam Cup (Munich)	Boris Becker	1,875,000	G. Ivanisevic	63 64 64

Note: The Grand Slam Cup, sponsored by the International Tennis Federation, is not an official ATP Tour event.

1997 (through Sept. 28)

Finals	Tournament	Winner	Earnings	Runner-Up	Score
Jan. 5	Qatar Mobil Open (Doha)	Jim Courier	$ 84,000	T. Henman	75 67 62
Jan. 5	Australian Hardcourt (Adelaide)	Todd Woodbridge	43,000	S. Draper	62 61
Jan. 11	Sydney International	Tim Henman	43,000	C. Moya	63 61
Jan. 12	BellSouth Open (Auckland)	Jonas Bjorkman	43,000	K. Carlsen	76 60
Jan. 26	**Australian Open** (Melbourne)	Pete Sampras	456,300	C. Moya	62 63 63
Feb. 2	Croatian Indoors (Zagreb)	Goran Ivanisevic	54,000	G. Rusedski	76 46 76
Feb. 2	Shanghai Open	Jan Kroslak	43,000	A. Volkov	62 76
Feb.16	Dubai Open	Thomas Muster	142,000	G. Ivanisevic	75 76
Feb. 16	Open 13 (Marseille)	Thomas Enqvist	72,000	M. Rios	64 10 (ret)
Feb. 16	Sybase Open (San Jose)	Pete Sampras	43,000	G. Rusedski	36 50 (ret)
Feb. 23	European Community Champs. (Antwerp)	Marc Rosset	162,500	T. Henman	62 75 64
Feb. 23	Kroger/St.Jude International (Memphis)	Michael Chang	120,000	T. Woodbridge	63 64
Mar. 2	Italian Indoors (Milan)	Goran Ivanisevic	128,000	S. Bruguera	62 62
Mar. 2	Advanta Champs.(Philadelphia)	Pete Sampras	110,000	P. Rafter	57 76 63
Mar. 9	ABN/AMRO World (Rotterdam)	Richard Krajicek	101,500	D. Vacek	76 76
Mar. 9	Franklin Templeton Classic (Scottsdale)	Mark Philippoussis	101,500	R. Reneberg	64 76
Mar. 16	Copenhagen Open	Thomas Johansson	29,000	M. Damm	64 36 62
Mar. 16	Newsweek Champions Cup (Indian Wells)	Michael Chang	337,000	B. Ulihrach	46 63 64 63
Mar. 23	St. Petersburg Open (Russia)	Thomas Johansson	43,000	R. Furlan	63 64
Mar. 30	Lipton Championships (Key Biscayne)	Thomas Muster	360,000	S. Bruguera	76 63 61
Mar. 30	Grand Prix Hassan II (Casablanca)	Hicham Arazi	29,000	F. Squillari	36 61 62
Apr. 13	Estoril Open (Lisbon)	Alex Corretja	84,000	F. Clavet	63 75
Apr. 13	Gold Flake Open (Chennai)	Mikael Tillstrom	58,000	A. Radulescu	64 46 75
Apr. 13	Salem Open (Hong Kong)	Michael Chang	43,000	P. Rafter	63 63
Apr. 20	Japan Open (Tokyo)	Richard Krajicek	154,000	L. Roux	62 36 61
Apr. 21	Open Seat - Godo (Barcelona)	Albert Costa	145,600	A. Portas	75 64 64
Apr. 27	Monte Carlo Open	Marcelo Rios	337,000	A. Corretja	64 63 63
Apr. 27	US Clay Court Champ. (Orlando)	Michael Chang	37,500	G. Stafford	46 62 61
May 4	BMW Open (Munich)	Mark Philippoussis	57,000	A. Corretja	76 16 64
May 4	AT&T Challenge (Atlanta)	Marcelo Filippini	43,000	J. Stoltenberg	76 64
May 4	Skoda Czech Open (Prague)	Cedric Pioline	48,200	B. Ulihrach	62 57 76
May 11	Panasonic German Open (Hamburg)	Andrei Medvedev	337,000	F. Mantilla	60 64 62
May 11	America's Red Clay Champ. (Coral Springs)	Jason Stoltenberg	34,800	J. Bjorkman	60 26 75
May 18	Italian Open (Rome)	Alex Corretja	325,000	M. Rios	75 75 63
May 25	Peugeot World Team Cup (Dusseldorf)	Spain	500,000	Australia	3-0
May 25	Raiffeisen Grand Prix (St. Polten)	Marcelo Filippini	57,000	P. Rafter	76 62
June 8	**French Open** (Paris)	Gustavo Kuerten	644,006	S. Bruguera	63 64 62
June 15	Stella Artois Grass Court (London)	Mark Philippoussis	80,000	G. Ivanisevic	75 63

Tournament Results (Cont.)

Men's ATP Tour

Finals	Tournament	Winner	Earnings	Runner-Up	Score
June 15	Gerry Weber Open (Halle)	Yevgeny Kafelnikov	122,000	P. Korda	76 67 76
June 15	Tennis International (Carisbo)	Felix Mantilla	21,000	G. Kuerten	46 62 61
June 21	The Nottingham Open	Greg Rusedski	43,000	K. Kucera	64 75
June 22	Heineken Open (Rosmalen)	Richard Krajicek	66,400	G. Raoux	64 76
July 6	**Wimbledon** (London)	Pete Sampras	702,471	C. Pioline	64 62 64
July 13	Hall of Fame Championships (Newport)	Sargis Sargsian	36,200	B. Steven	76 46 75
July 13	Swedish Open (Bastad)	Magnus Norman	43,000	J. Marin	75 62
July 13	Rado Swiss Open (Gstaad)	Felix Mantilla	74,000	J. Viloca	61 64 64
July 20	Mercedes Cup (Stuttgart)	Alex Corretja	157,000	K. Kucera	62 76
July 20	Legg Mason Classic (Washington, D.C.)	Michael Chang	90,000	P. Korda	57 62 61
July 27	EA Generali Open (Kitzbühel)	Filip Dewulf	62,400	J. Alonso	76 64 61
July 27	Croatia Open (Umag)	Felix Mantilla	54,000	S. Bruguera	63 75
July 27	Infiniti Open (Los Angeles)	Jim Courier	43,000	T. Enqvist	64 64
Aug 3	Grolsch Open (Amsterdam)	Slava Dosedel	66,400	C. Moya	76 76 67 62
Aug. 3	du Maurier Open (Montreal)	Chris Woodruff	337,000	G. Kuerten	75 46 63
Aug. 10	San Marino Open	Felix Mantilla	39,000	M. Gustafsson	64 61
Aug. 10	Great American Insurance (Cincinnati)	Pete Sampras	337,000	T. Muster	63 64
Aug. 17	RCA/U.S. Hardcourts (Indianapolis)	Jonas Bjorkman	150,000	C. Moya	63 76
Aug. 17	Pilot Pen International (New Haven)	Yevgeny Kafelnikov	150,000	P. Rafter	76 64
Aug. 24	Waldbaum's Hamlet Cup (Long Island)	Carlos Moya	43,000	P. Rafter	64 76
Aug. 24	MFS Pro Champs. (Boston)	Sjeng Schalken	43,000	M. Rios	75 63
Sept. 7	**U.S. Open** (New York)	Patrick Rafter	650,000	G. Rusedski	63 62 46 75
Sept. 14	Samsung Open (Bournemouth)	Felix Mantilla	54,000	C. Moya	62 62
Sept. 14	Marbella Open	Albert Costa	43,000	A. Berasategui	63 62
Sept. 14	President's Cup (Tashkent)	Tim Henman	54,000	M. Rosset	76 64
Sept. 28	Grand Slam Cup	Pete Sampras	1,500,000*	P. Rafter	62 64 75
Sept. 28	Toulouse Grand Prix	Nicolas Kiefer	54,000	M. Philippoussis	75 57 64
Sept. 28	Romanian Open (Bucharest)	Richard Fromberg	66,400	A. Gaudenzi	62 76

* Total does not include a $500,000 bonus Sampras earned for winning Wimbledon and the Australian Open.

Women's WTA Tour

LATE 1996

Finals	Tournament	Winner	Earnings	Runner-Up	Score
Nov. 3	Ameritech Cup	Jana Novotna	$79,000	J. Capriati	64 36 61
Nov. 3	Ladies Kremlin Cup	Conchita Martinez	67,000	B. Paulus	61 46 64
Nov. 10	Bank of the West Classic (Oakland)	Martina Hingis	79,000	M. Seles	62 60
Nov. 17	Advanta Championships (Philadelphia)	Jana Novotna	79,000	S. Graf	64 (ret.)
Nov. 24	Volvo Open (Pattaya)	Ruxandra Dragomir	17,700	T. Tanasugarn	46 75 (4-ret.)
Nov. 24	WTA Tour Championship (New York)	Steffi Graf	500,000	M. Hingis	63 46 60 46 60

1997 (through Sept. 28)

Finals	Tournament	Winner	Earnings	Runner-Up	Score
Jan. 4	ASB Bank Classic (Auckland)	Marion Maruska	$17,700	J. Wiesner	63 61
Jan. 4	Gold Coast Classic (Australia)	Elena Likhovtseva	27,000	A. Sugiyami	36 76 63
Jan. 11	Sydney International	Martina Hingis	59,500	J. Capriati	61 57 61
Jan. 11	Tasmanian International (Hobart)	Dominique Van Roost	17,700	M. Werdel-Witmeyer	63 63
Jan. 26	**Australian Open** (Melbourne)	Martina Hingis	428,126	M. Pierce	62 62
Feb. 2	Toray Pan Pacific Open (Tokyo)	Martina Hingis	150,000	S. Graf	Def.
Feb. 9	EA Generali (Linz)	Chanda Rubin	27,000	K. Habsudova	64 62
Feb. 16	Open Gaz de France (Paris)	Martina Hingis	79,000	A. Huber	63 36 63
Feb. 23	Faber Grand Prix (Hannover)	Iva Majoli	79,000	J. Novotna	46 76 64
Feb. 23	IGA Classic (Oklahoma City)	Lindsay Davenport	27,000	L. Raymond	64 62
Mar. 15	State Farm Evert Cup (Indian Wells)	Lindsay Davenport	205,000	I. Spirlea	62 61
Mar. 29	Lipton Championships (Key Biscayne)	Martina Hingis	215,000	M. Seles	62 61
Apr. 6	Family Circle Cup (Hilton Head)	Martina Hingis	150,000	M. Seles	36 63 76
Apr. 13	Bausch & Lomb Champs. (Amelia Island)	Lindsay Davenport	79,000	M. Pierce	62 63
Apr. 20	Japan Open (Tokyo)	Ai Sugiyama	27,000	A. Frazier	16 61 61
Apr. 27	Danamon Open (Jakarta)	Naoko Sawamatsu	17,700	Y. Yoshida	63 62
Apr. 27	Budapest Lotto Ladies Open	Amanda Coetzer	17,700	S. Appelmans	61 63
May 4	Rexona Cup (Hamburg)	Iva Majoli	79,000	R. Dragomir	63 62
May 4	Croatian Bol Ladies Open	Mirjana Lucic	17,700	C. Morariu	75 67 76
May 11	Italian Open (Rome)	Mary Pierce	150,000	C. Martinez	64 60
May 18	Welsh International Open (Cardiff)	V. Ruano-Pascual	17,700	A. Dechaume-Balleret	61 36 62
May 18	German Open (Berlin)	Mary Joe Fernandez	150,000	M. Pierce	64 62

Finals	Tournament	Winner	Earnings	Runner-Up	Score
May 24	Internationaux de Strasbourg	Steffi Graf	47,000	M. Lucic	62 75
May 24	Madrid Open	Jana Novotna	28,000	M. Seles	75 61
May 24	World Doubles Cup (Scotland)	Nicole Arendt/	65,200	R. McQuillan/	61 36 75
		Manon Bollegraf	65,200	N. Miyagi	
June 8	**French Open** (Paris)	Iva Majoli	673,302	M. Hingis	64 62
June 15	DFS Classic (Birmingham)	Nathalie Tauziat	27,000	Y. Basuki	26 62 62
June 21	Direct Line Insurance Int'l. (Eastbourne)	Final cancelled due to rain.			
June 21	Wilkinson Championships (Rosmalen)	Ruxandra Dragomir	27,000	M. Oremans	57 62 64
July 5	**Wimbledon** (London)	Martina Hingis	596,106	J. Novotna	26 63 63
July 20	Torneo Internazionale (Palermo)	Sandrine Testud	40,000	E. Makarova	75 63
July 20	Skoda Czech Open (Prague)	Joanette Kruger	26,000	M. Maruska	61 61
July 27	Bank of the West Classic (Stanford)	Martina Hingis	79,000	C. Martinez	60 62
July 27	Warsaw Cup	Barbara Paulus	27,000	H. Nagyova	64 64
Aug. 3	Toshiba Classic (San Diego)	Martina Hingis	79,000	M. Seles	76 64
Aug. 3	Styrian Open (Austria)	Barbara Schett	17,700	H. Nagyova	36 62 63
Aug. 10	Acura Classic (Los Angeles)	Monica Seles	79,000	L. Davenport	57 75 64
Aug. 17	du Maurier Open (Toronto)	Monica Seles	135,000	A. Huber	62 64
Aug. 23	U.S. Hardcourt Champs. (Atlanta)	Lindsay Davenport	79,000	S. Testud	64 61
Sept. 6	**U.S. Open** (New York)	Martina Hingis	650,000	V. Williams	60 64
Sept. 21	Nichirei Open (Tokyo)	Monica Seles	79,000	A. Sanchez Vicario	61 36 76
Sept. 28	Sparkassen Cup (Leipzig)	Jana Novotna	79,000	A. Coetzer	62 46 63
Sept. 28	Wismilak Int'l (Surabaya)	Dominique Van Roost	31,860	L. Nemeckova	61 63

1997 Grand Slam Tournaments

Australian Open

MEN'S SINGLES

FINAL EIGHT— #1 Pete Sampras; #2 Michael Chang; #3 Goran Ivanisevic; #5 Thomas Muster; #9 Marcelo Rios; #10 Alberto Costa; #14 Felix Mantilla; plus unseeded Carlos Moya

Quarterfinals

Sampras def. Costa . . . . .63 67(5) 61 36 62
Muster def. Ivanisevic 64 62 63
Moya def. Mantilla . . . . .75 62 67(5) 62
Chang def. Rios 75 61 64

Semifinals

Sampras def. Muster . . . . .61 76(3) 63
Moya def. Chang 75 62 64

Final

Sampras def. Moya 62 63 63

WOMEN'S SINGLES

FINAL EIGHT— #4 Martina Hingis; #8 Irina Spirlea; #12 Amanda Coetzer; #14 Mary Joe Fernandez; #16 Sabine Appelmans; plus unseeded Mary Pierce, Kimberly Po and Dominique van Roost.

Quarterfinals

Coetzer def. Po 64 61
Pierce def. Appelmans 16 64 64
Hingis def. Spirlea 75 62
Fernandez def. van Roost . . . . .75 40 (ret.)

Semifinals

Pierce def. Coetzer 75 61
Hingis def. Fernandez 61 63

Final

Hingis def. Pierce 62 62

DOUBLES FINALS

Men— #1 Todd Woodbridge & Mark Woodforde def. #7 Sebastien Lareau & Alex O'Brien, 4-6, 7-5, 7-5, 6-3.

Women— #4 Martina Hingis & Natasha Zvereva def. #3 Lindsay Davenport & Lisa Raymond, 6-2, 6-2.

Mixed— #3 Manon Bollegraf & Rick Leach def. Larisa Neiland & John De Jager, 6-3, 6-7 (5), 7-5.

French Open

MEN'S SINGLES

FINAL EIGHT— #3 Yevgeny Kafelnikov; #16 Sergei Bruguera; plus unseeded Hicham Arazi, Galo Blanco, Filip Dewulf, Gustavo Kuerten, Magnus Norman and Patrick Rafter.

Quarterfinals

Dewulf def. Norman . . . . .62 67(2) 64 63
Kuerten def. Kafelnikov 62 57 26 60 64
Rafter def. Blanco . . . . .63 76(3) 63
Bruguera def. Arazi 64 63 62 62

Semifinals

Kuerten def. Dewulf . . . . .61 36 61 76(4)
Bruguera def. Rafter . . . . .67(6) 61 75 76(1)

Final

Kuerten def. Bruguera 63 64 62

WOMEN'S SINGLES

FINAL EIGHT— #1 Martina Hingis; #2 Steffi Graf; #3 Monica Seles; #6 Arantxa Sanchez-Vicario; #9 Iva Majoli; #11 Amanda Coetzer; #12 Mary Joe Fernandez; plus unseeded Ruxandra Dragomir.

Quarterfinals

Hingis def. Sanchez-Vicario 62 62
Seles def. Fernandez 36 62 75
Majoli def. Dragomir 63 57 62
Coetzer Def. Graf 61 64

Semifinals

Hingis def. Seles . . . . .67(2) 75 64
Majoli def. Coetzer 63 46 75

Final

Majoli def. Hingis 64 62

DOUBLES FINALS

Men—#4 Yevgeny Kafelnikov & Daniel Vacek def. #1 Todd Woodbridge & Mark Woodeford 7-6(12), 4-6, 6-3.

Women—#1 Gigi Fernandez & Natasha Zvereva def. #5 Mary Joe Fernandez & Lisa Raymond 6-2, 6-3.

Mixed— #16 Rika Hiraki & Mahesh Bhupathi def. #1 Lisa Raymond & Patrick Galbraith 6-4, 6-1.

1997 Grand Slam Tournaments (Cont.)

Wimbledon

MEN'S SINGLES

FINAL EIGHT— #1 Pete Sampras; #8 Boris Becker; #14 Tim Henman; plus unseeded Nicolas Kiefer, Cedric Pioline, Greg Rusedski, Michael Stich and Todd Woodbridge.

Quarterfinals

Sampras def. Becker	.61 67(5) 61 64
Woodbridge def. Kiefer	.76(7) 26 60 64
Stich def. Henman	.63 62 64
Pioline def. Rusedski	.64 46 64 63

Semifinals

Sampras def. Woodbridge	.62 61 76(3)
Pioline def. Stich	.67(2) 62 61 57 64

Final

Sampras def. Pioline	.64 62 64

WOMEN'S SINGLES

FINAL EIGHT— #1 Martina Hingis; #3 Jana Novotna; #4 Iva Majoli; #8 Arantxa Sanchez-Vicario; plus unseeded Yayuk Basuki, Denisa Chladkova, Anna Kournikova and Nathalie Tauziat.

Quarterfinals

Hingis def. Chladkova	.63 62
Kournikova def. Majoli	.76(1) 64
Novotna def. Basuki	.63 63
Sanchez-Vicario def. Tauziat	.62 75

Semifinals

Hingis def. Kournikova	.63 62
Novotna def. Sanchez-Vicario	.64 62

Final

Hingis def. Novotna	.26 63 63

DOUBLES FINALS

Men— #1 Todd Woodbridge & Mark Woodforde def. #2 Jacco Eltingh & Paul Haarhuis 7-6(4), 7-6(7), 5-7, 6-3.

Women— #1 Gigi Fernandez & Natasha Zvereva def. #6 Nicole Arendt & Manon Bollegraf 7-6(4), 6-4.

Mixed— #4 Cyril Suk & Helena Sukova def. #3 Andrei Olhovskiy & Larisa Neiland 4-6, 6-3, 6-4.

U.S. Open

MEN'S SINGLES

FINAL EIGHT— #2 Michael Chang; #10 Marcelo Rios; #13 Patrick Rafter; # 15 Petr Korda; plus unseeded Jonas Bjorkman, Richard Krajicek, Magnus Larsson and Greg Rusedski.

Quarterfinals

Bjorkman def. Korda	.76(3) 62 1-0 (ret.)
Rusedski def. Krajicek	.75 76(5) 76(6)
Rafter def. Larsson	.76(4) 64 62
Chang def. Rios	.75 62 46 46 63

Semifinals

Rusedski def. Bjorkman	.61 36 36 63 75
Rafter def. Chang	.63 63 64

Final

Rafter def. Rusedski	.63 62 46 75

WOMEN'S SINGLES

FINAL EIGHT— #1 Martina Hingis; #2 Monica Seles; #3 Jana Novotna; #6 Lindsay Davenport; #10 Arantxa Sanchez-Vicario; #11 Irina Spirlea; plus unseeded Sandrine Testud and Venus Williams.

Quarterfinals

Hingis def. Sanchez-Vicario	.63 62
Davenport def. Novotna	.62 46 76(5)
Williams def. Testud	.75 75
Spirlea def. Seles	.67(5) 76(8) 63

Semifinals

Hingis def. Davenport	.62 64
Williams def. Spirlea	.76(5) 46 76(7)

Final

Hingis def. Williams	.60 64

DOUBLES FINALS

Men— #4 Yevgeny Kafelnikov & Daniel Vacek def. #11 Jonas Bjorkman & Nicklas Kulti 7-6(8), 6-3.

Women— #3 Lindsay Davenport & Jana Novotna def. #1 Gigi Fernandez & Natasha Zvereva 6-3, 6-4.

Mixed— #5 Manon Bollegraf & Rick Leach def. Mercedes Paz & Pablo Albano 3-6, 7-5, 7-6(3).

1997 Fed Cup

Originally the Federation Cup and started in 1963 by the International Tennis Federation as the Davis Cup of women's tennis. Played by 32 teams over one week at one site through 1994. Tournament changed in 1995 to Davis Cup-style format of four rounds and home sides.

Quarterfinals
(March 1-2)

Winner	Loser
Netherlands 3	USA 2
Czech Republic 3	Germany 2
France 4	Japan 1
Belgium 5	Spain 0

Semifinals

Netherlands 3, Czech Republic 2
at Prague, Czech Republic (July 12-13)

Day One— Brenda Schultz-McCarthy (NET) def. Sandra Kleinova (CZE), 6-1, 7-6 (7-5); Jana Novotna (CZE) def. Miriam Oremans (NET), 6-3, 60.

Day Two— Novotna (CZE) def. Schultz-McCarthy (NET), 7-6, 6-3; Oremans (NET) def. Adriana Gersi (CZE), 1-6, 6-2, 9-7; Oremans & Manon Bollegraf (NET) def. Novotna & Eva Martincova (CZE), 6-4, 7-6.

France 3, Belgium 2
at Nice, France (July 12-13)

Day One— Alexandra Fusai (FRA) def. Sabine Appelmans (BEL), 6-7(1), 6-3, 6-1; Dominique van Roost (BEL) def. Sandrine Testud (FRA), 6-4, 7-5, 6-4.

Day Two— Testud (FRA) def. Appelmans (BEL), 6-2, 6-4; van Roost (BEL) def. Fusai (FRA), 6-3, 6-3; Fusai & Nathalie Tauziat (FRA) def. Els Callens & Laurence Courtois (BEL), 3-6, 6-2, 7-5.

Finals

France 4, Netherlands 1
at Nice, France (Oct. 4-5).

Day One— Sandrine Testud (FRA) def. Brenda Schultz-McCarthy (NET), 6-4, 4-6, 6-3; Mary Pierce (FRA) def. Miriam Oremans (NET), 6-4, 6-1.

Day Two— Schultz-McCarthy (NET) def. Pierce (FRA), 4-6, 6-3, 6-4; Testud (FRA) def. Oremans (NET), 0-6, 6-3, 6-3; Alexandra Fusai & Nathalie Tauziat (FRA) def. Caroline Vis & Manon Bollegraf (NET), 6-3, 6-4.

Singles Leaders

Official Top 20 computer rankings and money leaders of men's and women's tours for 1996 and unofficial rankings and money leaders for 1997 (through Sept. 28), as compiled by the ATP Tour (Association of Tennis Professionals) and WTA (Women's Tennis Association). Note that money list includes doubles earnings.

Final 1996 Computer Rankings and Money Won

Listed are events won and times a finalist and semifinalist (Finish, 1-2-SF), match record (W-L), and earnings for the year.

MEN

		Finish 1-2-SF	W-L	Earnings
1	Pete Sampras	8-1-2	65-11	$3,702,919
2	Michael Chang	3-5-4	65-19	2,015,699
3	Yevgeny Kafelnikov	4-6-5	80-25	3,363,365
4	Goran Ivanisevic	5-5-3	77-26	3,007,985
5	Thomas Muster	7-0-4	68-20	2,875,496
6	Boris Becker	5-1-2	42-14	4,313,007
7	Richard Krajicek	1-2-1	46-28	1,861,761
8	Andre Agassi	3-1-2	38-14	1,629,928
9	Thomas Enqvist	3-0-2	58-29	1,668,547
10	Wayne Ferreira	2-1-3	49-28	961,020
11	Marcelo Rios	1-3-5	57-25	825,678
12	Todd Martin	1-2-4	55-21	868,636
13	Albert Costa	3-2-2	52-29	801,771
14	Stefan Edberg	0-1-2	45-24	651,137
15	Jan Siemerink	1-2-2	36-30	753,881
16	Michael Stich	1-1-0	25-14	778,795
17	Magnus Gustafsson	2-0-2	37-17	472,781
18	Felix Mantilla	1-4-2	48-27	497,701
19	Alberto Berasategui	3-0-4	46-26	529,732
20	MaliVai Washington	1-1-1	33-24	870,898

WOMEN

		Finish 1-2-SF	W-L	Earnings
1	Steffi Graf	7-1-2	54-4	$2,665,706
2*	Monica Seles	5-2-2	48-8	1,154,499
3	A. Sanchez-Vicario	2-6-2	57-22	1,858,444
4	Jana Novotna	4-1-5	54-13	1,354,307
5	Martina Hingis	3-3-3	51-16	1,330,996
6	Conchita Martinez	2-2-5	51-18	1,111,401
7	Anke Huber	3-3-2	49-17	691,335
8	Iva Majoli	2-2-4	41-17	962,855
9	Kimiko Date	3-0-4	36-16	449,181
10	Lindsay Davenport	2-1-3	51-15	871,393
11	Barbara Paulus	1-5-1	41-19	354,919
12	Irina Spirlea	1-0-2	35-19	476,059
13	Chanda Rubin	1-1-2	20-9	339,534
14	B. Schultz-McCarthy	1-0-3	40-20	321,994
15	Mary Joe Fernandez	0-1-1	32-17	553,771
16	Julie Halard-Decugis	2-1-1	31-11	220,299
17	Karina Habsudova	0-2-3	41-25	470,262
18	Amanda Coetzer	0-1-1	33-24	376,732
19	Magdalena Maleeva	0-1-1	23-17	197,849
20	Judith Wiesner	0-0-3	37-26	283,381
	Mary Pierce	0-1-1	19-13	195,570

* Seles was ranked co-No. 1 upon her return to the WTA Tour following her recovery from the on-court stabbing she suffered on April 13, 1993. She was provided with that ranking for the first six tournaments or 12 months from the date of her first tournament (Aug. 15. 1995). Then, Seles was co-ranked based upon her ranking average which was calculated using a reduced minimum divisor until she played 14 tournaments or 18 months from the date of her first tournament.

1997 Computer Rankings (through Sept. 28)

For Men's Tour, listed are tournaments won and times a finalist and semifinalist (Finish, 1-2-SF), match record (W-L), and computer points earned (Pts). For Women's Tour, listed are tournaments won and times a finalist and semifinalist (Finish, 1-2-SF), match record (W-L), and average computer points per game (Avg).

MEN

ATP Tour singles rankings based on total computer points from each player's 14 best tournaments covering the last 12 months. Tournaments, titles and match won-lost records, however, are for 1997 only.

Rank 97	(96)		Finish 1-2-SF	W-L	Pts
1	(1)	Pete Sampras	6-0-1	45-9	4291
2	(2)	Michael Chang	5-0-5	56-14	3442
3	(62)	Patrick Rafter	1-6-2	57-24	2889
4	(3)	Yevgeny Kafelnikov	2-0-3	38-20	2640
5	(28)	Carlos Moya	1-5-3	52-23	2451
6	(81)	Sergi Bruguera	0-4-2	46-21	2357
7	(11)	Marcelo Rios	1-3-0	52-22	2322
8	(4)	Goran Ivanisevic	2-2-4	46-19	2291
9	(23)	Alex Corretja	3-2-1	45-17	2284
10	(48)	Greg Rusedski	1-3-4	40-17	2277
11	(88)	Gustavo Kuerten	1-2-0	33-21	2230
12	(5)	Thomas Muster	2-1-2	39-18	2229
13	(69)	Jonas Bjorkman	2-1-6	54-21	2182
14	(18)	Felix Mantilla	5-1-1	51-17	2144
15	(9)	Thomas Enqvist	1-1-3	29-18	1983
16	(24)	Petr Korda	0-2-3	41-20	1947
17	(7)	Richard Krajicek	3-0-0	39-15	1903
18	(6)	Boris Becker	0-0-1	16-8	1882
19	(13)	Albert Costa	2-0-4	44-20	1819
20	(29)	Tim Henman	2-2-1	35-18	1729

WOMEN

Corel WTA Tour singles ranking system based on total Round and Quality Points for each tournament played during the last 12 months. Tournaments, titles and match won-lost records, however, are for 1997 only.

Rank 97	(96)		Finish 1-2-SF	W-L	Pts
1	(4)	Martina Hingis	10-1-2	65-3	6976
2	(3)	Jana Novotna	2-2-4	42-11	3881
3	(2)	Monica Seles	3-4-1	43-10	3429
4	(7)	Iva Majoli	3-2-6	42-18	3407
5	(9)	Lindsay Davenport	4-1-3	47-13	3120
6	(17)	Amanda Coetzer	1-1-9	52-22	2977
7	(6)	Anke Huber	0-2-2	33-19	2670
8	(20)	Mary Pierce	1-3-1	41-13	2400
9	(11)	Irina Spirlea	0-1-2	37-18	2236
10	(5)	Conchita Martinez	0-2-2	34-15	2198
11	(2)	Arantxa Sanchez-Vicario	0-1-3	40-19	2162
12	(14)	Mary Joe Fernandez	1-0-4	38-14	1902
13	(1)	Steffi Graf	1-1-0	16-3	1788
14	(40)	Sandrine Testud	1-1-0	41-19	1734
15	(13)	Brenda Schultz-McCarthy	0-0-3	29-21	1670
16	(25)	Ruxandra Dragomir	0-1-1	34-21	1474
17	(21)	Sabine Appelmans	0-1-0	33-21	1439
18	(10)	Barbara Paulus	1-1-0	32-14	1388
19	(28)	Kimberly Po	0-0-2	31-17	1315
20	(26)	Yayuk Basuki	0-1-1	28-18	1300

1997 Money Winners

Amounts include singles and doubles earnings through Sept. 29, 1997.

MEN

	Earnings			Earnings			Earnings
1 Pete Sampras	$3,905,078	10 Greg Rusedski	$1,121,473	18 Goran Ivanisevic	$848,797
2 Patrick Rafter	2,432,084	11 Alex Corretja	1,097,822	19 Carlos Moya	787,390
3 Gustavo Kuerten	1,505,213	12 Sergi Bruguera	1,058,808	20 Mark Philippoussis	775,311
4 Yevgeny Kafelnikov	1,421,392	13 Felix Mantilla	1,034,483	21 Richard Krajicek	745,364
5 Michael Chang	1,327,720	14 Mark Woodforde	1,021,697	22 Andrei Medvedev	704,578
6 Marcelo Rios	1,284,855	15 Petr Korda	978,333	23 Daniel Vacek	692,075
7 Jonas Bjorkman	1,215,130	16 Cedric Pioline	912,631	24 Paul Haarhuis	610,250
8 Thomas Muster	1,184,190	17 Albert Costa	849,784	25 Chris Woodruff	583,596
9 Todd Woodbridge	1,177,318				

WOMEN

	Earnings			Earnings			Earnings
1 Martina Hingis	$3,126,036	10 Amanda Coetzer	$609,884	18 Manon Bollegraf	$347,179
2 Iva Majoli	1,139,537	11 Irina Spirlea	550,798	19 Nicole Arendt	336,452
3 Lindsay Davenport	1,133,106	12 Gigi Fernandez	444,132	20 Lisa Raymond	336,110
4 Jana Novotna	966,215	13 Conchita Martinez	438,874	21 Yayuk Basuki	334,149
5 Monica Seles	862,580	14 Venus Williams	426,861	22 Nathalie Tauziat	328,682
6 Arantxa Sanchez-Vicario	718,442	15 Sandrine Testud	371,858	23 Helena Sukova	289,267
7 Mary Joe Fernandez	695,997	16 Ruxandra Dragomir	357,747	24 Anna Kournikova	286,362
8 Natasha Zvereva	687,228	17 Anke Huber	353,000	25 Sabine Appelmans	272,315
9 Mary Pierce	670,689				

Davis Cup

France defeated Sweden, 3-2, in Malmo, Sweden to capture the 1996 Davis Cup. It was the eighth championship for the French and their first since beating the Americans in 1991. The two matches on the dramatic final day each lasted five sets and a combined nine hours.

1996 Final
France 3, Sweden 2
(at Malmo, Nov. 29-Dec. 1)

Day One— Cedric Pioline (FRA) def. Stefan Edberg (SWE), 6-3, 6-4, 6-3; Thomas Enqvist (SWE) def. Arnaud Boetsch (FRA), 6-4, 6-3, 7-6(2).

Day Two— Guy Forget & Guillaume Raoux (FRA) def. Jonas Bjorkman & Nicklas Kulti (SWE), 6-3, 1-6, 6-3, 6-3.

Day Three— Enqvist (SWE) def. Pioline (FRA), 3-6, 6-7(8), 6-4, 6-4, 9-7; Boetsch (FRA) def. Kulti (SWE), 7-6(2), 2-6, 4-6, 7-6(5), 10-8.

1997 Early Rounds
Sweden plays host to the 1997 Davis Cup final from Nov. 28-30. Jonas Bjorkman leads the Swedes to their 11th Cup final against the United States and the world's best player, Pete Sampras. The United States has won the Cup a record 31 times since play began in 1900. Sweden, last year's runner-up, has won five times.

FIRST ROUND
(Feb. 7-9)

Winner	Loser
USA 4	at Brazil 1
Netherlands 3	at Romania 2
at Australia 4	France 1
at Czech Republic 3	India 2
at Italy 4	Mexico 1
at Spain 4	Germany 1
at South Africa 3	Russia 1
at Sweden 4	Switzerland 1

QUARTERFINALS
(Apr. 4-6)

Winner	Loser
at USA 4	Netherlands 1
at Australia 5	Czech Republic 0
at Italy 4	Spain 1
at Sweden 3	South Africa 2

SEMIFINALS
United States 4, Australia 1
at Washington, D.C. (Sept. 19-21)

Day One— Michael Chang (USA) def. Patrick Rafter (AUS), 6-4, 1-6, 6-3, 6-4; Pete Sampras (USA) def. Mark Philippoussis (AUS), 6-1, 6-2, 7-6(5).

Day Two— Todd Woodbridge & Mark Woodforde (AUS) def. Sampras & Todd Martin, 3-6, 7-6(5), 6-2, 6-4.

Day Three— Sampras (USA) def. Rafter (AUS), 6-7(6), 6-1, 6-1, 6-4; Chang (USA) def. Philippoussis (AUS), 7-6(5), 7-6(2).

Sweden 4, Italy 1
at Noorkoping, Sweden (Sept. 19-21)

Day One— Jonas Bjorkman (SWE) def. Omar Camporese (ITA), 6-7(5), 6-3, 6-2, 3-6, 6-3; Renzo Furlan (ITA) def. Thomas Enqvist (SWE), 3-6, 6-3, 6-4, 3-6, 6-3.

Day Two— Bjorkman & Nicklas Kulti (SWE) def. Camporese & Diego Nargiso (ITA), 6-1, 6-1, 6-2.

Day Three— Bjorkman (SWE) def. Furlan (ITA), 4-6, 6-4, 6-0, 6-4; Enqvist (SWE) def. Camporese (ITA), 6-3, 6-7(5), 6-3.

FINAL
at Sweden (Nov. 28-30)

1997 ATP Tour
Statistical Leaders (as of Sept. 29, 1997)

Service Game Leaders

	Aces	No	Mtchs		2nd Serve Points Won	Pct	Mtchs
1	Goran Ivanisevic	894	61	1	Michael Chang	54%	67
2	Richard Krajicek	799	54	2	Albert Costa	53%	56
3	Mark Philippoussis	757	54	3	Pete Sampras	53%	48
4	Greg Rusedski	665	52	4	Guillaume Raoux	53%	45
5	Marc-Kevin Goellner	544	46	5	Vincent Spadea	53%	37
6	Pete Sampras	510	48	6	Patrick Rafter	52%	71
7	Alex Radulescu	502	47	7	Jonas Bjorkman	52%	69
8	Patrick Rafter	488	71	8	Sergi Bruguera	52%	66
9	Magnus Norman	453	54		Marcelo Rios	52%	66
10	Tim Henman	422	51	10	Alex Corretja	52%	62
					Felix Mantilla	52%	62

	1st Serve	Pct	Mtchs		Service Games Won	Pct	Mtchs
1	Gilbert Schaller	77%	28	1	Richard Krajicek	91%	54
2	Alberto Berasategui	73%	56	2	Greg Rusedski	91%	52
3	Felix Mantilla	69%	62	3	Pete Sampras	91%	48
4	Albert Costa	69%	56	4	Goran Ivanisevic	88%	61
5	Marcelo Filippini	69%	37	5	Mark Philippoussis	86%	54
6	Jiri Novak	68%	31	6	Patrick Rafter	84%	71
	Albert Portas	68%	31	7	Thomas Enqvist	84%	41
8	Javier Sanchez	65%	57	8	Brett Steven	84%	37
9	Pete Sampras	65%	48	9	Magnus Larsson	83%	51
10	Slava Dosedel	65%	42	10	Michael Chang	82%	67

	1st Serve Points Won	Pct	Mtchs		Break Points Saved	Pct	Mtchs
1	Richard Krajicek	86%	54	1	Goran Ivanisevic	70%	61
2	Goran Ivanisevic	84%	61	2	Greg Rusedski	70%	52
3	Greg Rusedski	84%	52	3	Thomas Muster	68%	52
4	Pete Sampras	82%	48	4	Brett Steven	68%	37
5	Mark Philippoussis	81%	54	5	Galo Blanco	67%	31
6	Tim Henman	80%	51	6	Richard Krajicek	66%	54
7	Marc-Kevin Goellner	80%	46		Magnus Norman	66%	54
8	Jonathan Stark	79%	35		Mark Philippoussis	66%	54
9	Alex Radulescu	78%	47	9	Jan Siemerink	66%	36
10	Thomas Enqvist	78%	41	10	Patrick Rafter	65%	71

Return Of Serve Leaders

	Pts. Returning 1st Serve	Pct	Mtchs		Break Points Converted	Pct	Mtchs
1	Alex Corretja	35%	62	1	Grant Stafford	50%	36
2	Karol Kucera	34%	45	2	Pete Sampras	49%	48
3	Carlos Moya	33%	71	3	Alex Corretja	48%	62
4	Michael Chang	33%	67	4	Nicolas Kiefer	48%	31
5	Andrei Medvedev	33%	49	5	Carlos Moya	47%	71
6	Hicham Arazi	33%	48	6	Filip Dewulf	47%	36
7	Slava Dosedel	33%	42	7	Carlos Costa	47%	31
8	Arnaud Boetsch	33%	32	8	Jan Kroslak	47%	24
9	Jonas Bjorkman	32%	69	9	Michael Chang	46%	67
10	Alberto Berasategui	32%	56	10	Sergi Bruguera	46%	66

	Returning 2nd Serve	Pct	Mtchs		Return Games Won	Pct	Mtchs
1	Alberto Berasategui	59%	56	1	Michael Chang	35%	67
2	Felix Mantilla	58%	62	2	Alex Corretja	35%	62
3	Albert Portas	58%	31	3	Jonas Bjorkman	34%	69
4	Jonas Bjorkman	57%	69	4	Felix Mantilla	34%	62
5	Michael Chang	56%	67	5	Carlos Moya	33%	71
6	Byron Black	56%	42	6	Alberto Berasategui	32%	56
7	Grant Stafford	56%	36	7	Sergi Bruguera	31%	66
8	Carlos Moya	55%	71	8	Albert Portas	31%	31
9	Alex Corretja	55%	62	9	Francisco Clavet	30%	50
10	Albert Costa	55%	56	10	Todd Woodbridge	30%	46

1997 Serve Speed Rankings

(as of Sept. 29, 1997)

All serves recorded by Information & Display Systems, Inc. on Stadium Court and must be in play to count.

Wide World Photos

Britain's **Greg Rusedski** crushes another serve over the net at the 1997 U.S. Open in New York. Rusedski fell short in the finals to Patrick Rafter in four sets but did break the record for the fastest serve ever recorded when he launched one 143 MPH.

ATP

		MPH	Site (surface)
1	Greg Rusedski	143	U.S. Open (H)
	(Fastest male serve ever recorded)		
2	Mark Philippoussis	142.3	Dusseldorf (C)
3	Julian Alonso	140	Commack (H)
4	Richard Krajicek	139	U.S. Open (H)
5	Jonathan Stark	138	Indian Wells (H)
6	Marc Rosset	134.2	Tashkent (H)
7	Michael Stich	134	Wimbledon (G)
8	Carlos Moya	133	Scottsdale (H)
	Pete Sampras	133	Key Biscayne (H)
	Alex Radulescu	133	Chennai (H)
	Tim Henman	133	Cincinnati (H)
	Goran Ivanisevic	133	U.S. Open (H)

WTA

		MPH	Site (surface)
1	B. Schultz-McCarthy	123	Wimbledon (G)
	(Fastest female serve ever recorded)		
2	Venus Williams	119	U.S. Open (H)
3	Jana Novotna	116	Wimbledon (G)
4	Caroline Dhenin	113.1	French Open (C)
5	Kristie Boogert	111.2	French Open (C)
6	Debbie Graham	110	San Diego (H)
7	Ludmila Richterova	109.4	French Open (C)
8	Olga Barabanschikova	109	Hilton Head (C)
	Alexandra Stevenson	109	San Diego (H)
	Monica Seles	109	U.S. Open (H)
	Irina Spirlea	109	U.S. Open (H)

Annual Awards

The ATP and WTA held their first annual joint Awards Gala at the Jackie Gleason Theatre in Miami Beach on March 19, 1997. The ceremonies were hosted by comedian Dennis Miller and raised over $120,000 with all proceeds going to the Ashe-Buchholz Tennis Center and the greater Miami Partnership for the Homeless. Voting was done by a selection of worldwide media.

ATP

Player of the Year .... Pete Sampras
Doubles Team of the Year .... Todd Woodbridge/
Mark Woodforde
Most Improved Player .... Tim Henman
Arthur Ashe Humanitarian Award .... Paul Flory
Stefan Edberg Sportsmanship Award .... Alex Corretja
Comeback Player of the Year .... Stephane Simian
Rado Player to Watch .... Dominik Hrbaty
Senior Player of the Year .... Jimmy Connors
Ron Bookman Media Excellence Award .... Brett Haber
Championship Series
Tournament of the Year .... RCA Championships
World Series Tournament of the Year .... Rado Swiss Open

WTA

Player of the Year .... Steffi Graf
Doubles Team of the Year .... Arantxa Sanchez-Vicario/
Jana Novotna
Most Improved Player .... Martina Hingis
Most Impressive Newcomer .... Anna Kournikova
Comeback Player of the Year .... Jennifer Capriati
David Gray Service Award .... Martina Navratilova
Karen Krantzcke
Sportsmanship Award .... Yayuk Basuki
Corel WTA Tour Aces Award .... Gabriela Sabatini
David Gray Service Award .... Martina Navratilova
Corel WTA Tour Player Service Award ..... Katrina Adams
Ted Tingling Media Person of the Year .... Mary Carillo

THE 1998 — ESPN INFORMATION PLEASE SPORTS ALMANAC

T E N N I S   S T A T I S T I C S

THROUGH THE YEARS — 1877-1997

MAJOR TITLES • LEADERS

SEC B

PAGE 815

Grand Slam Championships

Australian Open

MEN

Became an Open Championship in 1969. Two tournaments were held in 1977; the first in January, the second in December. Tournament moved back to January in 1987, so no championship was decided in 1986.

Surface: Synpave Rebound Ace (hardcourt surface composed of polyurethane and synthetic rubber).

Multiple winners: Roy Emerson (6); Jack Crawford and Ken Rosewall (4); James Anderson, Rod Laver, Adrian Quist, Mats Wilander and Pat Wood (3); Boris Becker, Jack Bromwich, Ashley Cooper, Jim Courier, Stefan Edberg, Rodney Heath, Johan Kriek, Ivan Lendl, John Newcombe, Pete Sampras, Frank Sedgman, Guillermo Vilas and Tony Wilding (2).

Year	Winner	Loser	Score	Year	Winner	Loser	Score
1905	Rodney Heath	A. Curtis	46 63 64 64	1955	Ken Rosewall	L. Hoad	97 64 64
1906	Tony Wilding	H. Parker	60 64 64	1956	Lew Hoad	K. Rosewall	64 36 64 75
1907	Horace Rice	H. Parker	63 64 64	1957	Ashley Cooper	N. Fraser	63 9-11 64 62
1908	Fred Alexander	A. Dunlop	36 36 60 62 63	1958	Ashley Cooper	M. Anderson	75 63 64
1909	Tony Wilding	E. Parker	61 75 62	1959	Alex Olmedo	N. Fraser	61 62 36 63
1910	Rodney Heath	H. Rice	64 63 62	1960	Rod Laver	N. Fraser	57 36 63 86 86
1911	Norman Brookes	H. Rice	61 62 63	1961	Roy Emerson	R. Laver	16 63 75 64
1912	J. Cecil Parke	A. Beamish	36 63 16 61 75	1962	Rod Laver	R. Emerson	86 06 64 64
1913	Ernie Parker	H. Parker	26 61 62 63	1963	Roy Emerson	K. Fletcher	63 63 61
1914	Pat Wood	G. Patterson	64 63 57 61	1964	Roy Emerson	F. Stolle	63 63 62
1915	Francis Lowe	H. Rice	46 61 61 64	1965	Roy Emerson	F. Stolle	79 26 64 75 61
1916-18	Not held	World War I		1966	Roy Emerson	A. Ashe	64 68 62 63
1919	A.R.F. Kingscote	E. Pockley	64 60 63	1967	Roy Emerson	A. Ashe	64 61 61
1920	Pat Wood	R. Thomas	63 46 68 61 63	1968	Bill Bowrey	J. Gisbert	75 26 97 64
1921	Rhys Gemmell	A. Hedeman	75 61 64	1969	Rod Laver	A. Gimeno	63 64 75
1922	James Anderson	G. Patterson	60 36 36 63 62	1970	Arthur Ashe	D. Crealy	64 97 62
1923	Pat Wood	C.B. St. John	61 61 63	1971	Ken Rosewall	A. Ashe	61 75 63
1924	James Anderson	R. Schlesinger	63 64 36 57 63	1972	Ken Rosewall	M. Anderson	76 63 75
1925	James Anderson	G. Patterson	11-9 26 62 63	1973	John Newcombe	O. Parun	63 67 75 61
1926	John Hawkes	J. Willard	61 63 61	1974	Jimmy Connors	P. Dent	76 64 46 63
1927	Gerald Patterson	J. Hawkes	36 64 36 18-16 63	1975	John Newcombe	J. Connors	75 36 64 75
1928	Jean Borotra	R.O. Cummings	64 61 46 57 63	1976	Mark Edmondson	J. Newcombe	67 63 76 61
1929	John Gregory	R. Schlesinger	62 62 57 75	1977	Roscoe Tanner	G. Vilas	63 63 63
					Vitas Gerulaitis	J. Lloyd	63 76 57 36 62
1930	Gar Moon	H. Hopman	63 61 63	1978	Guillermo Vilas	J. Marks	64 64 36 63
1931	Jack Crawford	H. Hopman	64 62 26 61	1979	Guillermo Vilas	J. Sadri	76 63 62
1932	Jack Crawford	H. Hopman	46 63 36 63 61				
1933	Jack Crawford	K. Gledhill	26 75 63 62	1980	Brian Teacher	K. Warwick	75 76 63
1934	Fred Perry	J. Crawford	63 75 61	1981	Johan Kriek	S. Denton	62 76 67 64
1935	Jack Crawford	F. Perry	26 64 64 64	1982	Johan Kriek	S. Denton	63 63 62
1936	Adrian Quist	J. Crawford	62 63 46 36 97	1983	Mats Wilander	I. Lendl	61 64 64
1937	Viv McGrath	J. Bromwich	63 16 60 26 61	1984	Mats Wilander	K. Curren	67 64 76 62
1938	Don Budge	J. Bromwich	64 62 61	1985	Stefan Edberg	M. Wilander	64 63 63
1939	Jack Bromwich	A. Quist	64 61 63	1986	Not held		
1940	Adrian Quist	J. Crawford	63 61 62	1987	Stefan Edberg	P. Cash	63 64 36 57 63
1941-45	Not held	World War II		1988	Mats Wilander	P. Cash	63 67 36 61 86
1946	Jack Bromwich	D. Pails	57 63 75 36 62	1989	Ivan Lendl	M. Mecir	62 62 62
1947	Dinny Pails	J. Bromwich	46 64 36 75 86	1990	Ivan Lendl	S. Edberg	46 76 52 (ret.)
1948	Adrian Quist	J. Bromwich	64 36 63 26 63	1991	Boris Becker	I. Lendl	16 64 64 64
1949	Frank Sedgman	J. Bromwich	63 63 62	1992	Jim Courier	S. Edberg	63 36 64 62
1950	Frank Sedgman	K. McGregor	63 64 46 61	1993	Jim Courier	S. Edberg	62 61 26 75
1951	Dick Savitt	K. McGregor	63 26 63 61	1994	Pete Sampras	T. Martin	76 64 64
1952	Ken McGregor	F. Sedgman	75 12-10 26 62	1995	Andre Agassi	P. Sampras	46 61 76 64
1953	Ken Rosewall	M. Rose	60 63 64	1996	Boris Becker	M. Chang	62 64 26 62
1954	Mervyn Rose	R. Hartwig	62 06 64 62	1997	Pete Sampras	C. Moya	62 63 63

Australian Open (Cont.)

WOMEN

Became an Open Championship in 1969. Two tournaments were held in 1977, the first in January, the second in December. Tournament moved back to January in 1987, so no championship was decided in 1986.

Multiple winners: Margaret Smith Court (11); Nancye Wynne Bolton (6); Daphne Akhurst (5); Evonne Goolagong Cawley, Steffi Graf and Monica Seles (4); Jean Hartigan and Martina Navratilova (3); Coral Buttsworth, Chris Evert Lloyd, Thelma Long, Hana Mandlikova, Mall Molesworth and Mary Carter Reitano (2).

Year	Winner	Loser	Score	Year	Winner	Loser	Score
1922	Mall Molesworth	E. Boyd	63 10-8	1963	Margaret Smith	J. Lehane	62 62
1923	Mall Molesworth	E. Boyd	61 75	1964	Margaret Smith	L. Turner	63 62
1924	Sylvia Lance	E. Boyd	63 36 64	1965	Margaret Smith	M. Bueno	57 64 52 (ret)
1925	Daphne Akhurst	E. Boyd	16 86 64	1966	Margaret Smith	N. Richey	walkover
1926	Daphne Akhurst	E. Boyd	61 63	1967	Nancy Richey	L. Turner	61 64
1927	Esna Boyd	S. Harper	57 61 62	1968	Billie Jean King	M. Smith	61 62
1928	Daphne Akhurst	E. Boyd	75 62	1969	Margaret Court	B.J. King	64 61
1929	Daphne Akhurst	L. Bickerton	61 57 62				
1930	Daphne Akhurst	S. Harper	10-8 26 75	1970	Margaret Court	K. Melville	61 63
1931	Coral Buttsworth	M. Crawford	16 63 64	1971	Margaret Court	E. Goolagong	26 76 75
1932	Coral Buttsworth	K. Le Messurier	97 64	1972	Virginia Wade	E. Goolagong	64 64
1933	Joan Hartigan	C. Buttsworth	64 63	1973	Margaret Court	E. Goolagong	64 75
1934	Joan Hartigan	M. Molesworth	61 64	1974	Evonne Goolagong	C. Evert	76 46 60
1935	Dorothy Round	N. Lyle	16 61 63	1975	Evonne Goolagong	M. Navratilova	63 62
1936	Joan Hartigan	N. Bolton	64 64	1976	Evonne Cawley	R. Tomanova	62 62
1937	Nancye Wynne	E. Westacott	63 57 64	1977	Kerry Reid	D. Balestrat	75 62
1938	Dorothy Bundy	D. Stevenson	63 62		Evonne Cawley	H. Gourlay	63 60
1939	Emily Westacott	N. Hopman	61 62	1978	Chris O'Neill	B. Nagelsen	63 76
				1979	Barbara Jordan	S. Walsh	63 63
1940	Nancye Wynne	T. Coyne	57 64 60				
1941-45	Not held	World War II		1980	Hana Mandlikova	W. Turnbull	60 75
1946	Nancye Bolton	J. Fitch	64 64	1981	Martina Navratilova	C. Evert Lloyd	67 64 75
1947	Nancye Bolton	N. Hopman	63 62	1982	Chris Evert Lloyd	M. Navratilova	63 26 63
1948	Nancye Bolton	M. Toomey	63 61	1983	Martina Navratilova	K. Jordan	62 76
1949	Doris Hart	N. Bolton	63 64	1984	Chris Evert Lloyd	H. Sukova	67 61 63
				1985	Martina Navratilova	C. Evert Lloyd	62 46 62
1950	Louise Brough	D. Hart	64 36 64	1986	Not held		
1951	Nancye Bolton	T. Long	61 75	1987	Hana Mandlikova	M. Navratilova	75 76
1952	Thelma Long	H. Angwin	62 63	1988	Steffi Graf	C. Evert	61 76
1953	Maureen Connolly	J. Sampson	63 62	1989	Steffi Graf	H. Sukova	64 64
1954	Thelma Long	J. Staley	63 64				
1955	Beryl Penrose	T. Long	64 63	1990	Steffi Graf	M.J. Fernandez	63 64
1956	Mary Carter	T. Long	36 62 97	1991	Monica Seles	J. Novotna	57 63 61
1957	Shirley Fry	A. Gibson	63 64	1992	Monica Seles	M.J. Fernandez	62 63
1958	Angela Mortimer	L. Coghlan	63 64	1993	Monica Seles	S. Graf	46 63 62
1959	Mary Reitano	T. Schuurman	62 63	1994	Steffi Graf	A.S. Vicario	60 62
				1995	Mary Pierce	A.S. Vicario	63 62
1960	Margaret Smith	J. Lehane	75 62	1996	Monica Seles	A. Huber	64 61
1961	Margaret Smith	J. Lehane	61 64	1997	Martina Hingis	M. Pierce	62 62
1962	Margaret Smith	J. Lehane	60 62				

French Open

MEN

Prior to 1925, entry was restricted to members of French clubs. Became an Open Championship in 1968, but closed to contract pros in 1972.

Surface: Red clay.

First year: 1891. **Most wins:** Max Decugis (8).

Multiple winners (since 1925): Bjorn Borg (6); Henri Cochet (4); Rene Lacoste, Ivan Lendl and Mats Wilander (3); Sergi Bruguera, Jim Courier, Jaroslav Drobny, Roy Emerson, Jan Kodes, Rod Laver, Frank Parker, Nicola Pietrangeli, Ken Rosewall, Manuel Santana, Tony Trabert and Gottfried von Cramm (2).

Year	Winner	Loser	Score	Year	Winner	Loser	Score
1925	Rene Lacoste	J. Borotra	75 61 64	1935	Fred Perry	G. von Cramm	63 36 61 63
1926	Henri Cochet	R. Lacoste	62 64 63	1936	Gottfried von Cramm	F. Perry	60 26 62 26 60
1927	Rene Lacoste	B. Tilden	64 46 57 63 11-9	1937	Henner Henkel	H. Austin	61 64 63
1928	Henri Cochet	R. Lacoste	57 63 61 63	1938	Don Budge	R. Menzel	63 62 64
1929	Rene Lacoste	J. Borotra	63 26 60 26 86	1939	Don McNeill	B. Riggs	75 60 63
1930	Henri Cochet	B. Tilden	36 86 63 61	1941-45	Not held	World War II	
1931	Jean Borotra	C. Boussus	26 64 75 64	1946	Marcel Bernard	J. Drobny	36 26 61 64 63
1932	Henri Cochet	G. de Stefani	60 64 46 63	1947	Joseph Asboth	E. Sturgess	86 75 64
1933	Jack Crawford	H. Cochet	86 61 63	1948	Frank Parker	J. Drobny	64 75 57 86
1934	Gottfried von Cramm	J. Crawford	64 79 36 75 63	1949	Frank Parker	B. Patty	63 16 61 64

Year	Winner	Loser	Score	Year	Winner	Loser	Score
1950	Budge Patty	J. Drobny	61 62 36 57 75	1974	Bjorn Borg	M. Orantes	26 67 60 61 61
1951	Jaroslav Drobny	E. Sturgess	63 63 63	1975	Bjorn Borg	G. Vilas	62 63 64
1952	Jaroslav Drobny	F. Sedgman	62 60 36 64	1976	Adriano Panatta	H. Solomon	61 64 46 76
1953	Ken Rosewall	V. Seixas	63 64 16 62	1977	Guillermo Vilas	B. Gottfried	60 63 60
1954	Tony Trabert	A. Larsen	64 75 61	1978	Bjorn Borg	G. Vilas	61 61 63
1955	Tony Trabert	S. Davidson	26 61 64 62	1979	Bjorn Borg	V. Pecci	63 61 67 64
1956	Lew Hoad	S. Davidson	64 86 63				
1957	Sven Davidson	H. Flam	63 64 64	1980	Bjorn Borg	V. Gerulaitis	64 61 62
1958	Mervyn Rose	L. Ayala	63 64 64	1981	Bjorn Borg	I. Lendl	61 46 62 36 61
1959	Nicola Pietrangeli	I. Vermaak	36 63 64 61	1982	Mats Wilander	G. Vilas	16 76 60 64
				1983	Yannick Noah	M. Wilander	62 75 76
1960	Nicola Pietrangeli	L. Ayala	36 63 64 46 63	1984	Ivan Lendl	J. McEnroe	36 26 64 75 75
1961	Manuel Santana	N. Pietrangeli	46 61 36 60 62	1985	Mats Wilander	I. Lendl	36 64 62 62
1962	Rod Laver	R. Emerson	36 26 63 97 62	1986	Ivan Lendl	M. Pernfors	63 62 64
1963	Roy Emerson	P. Darmon	36 61 64 64	1987	Ivan Lendl	M. Wilander	75 62 36 76
1964	Manuel Santana	N. Pietrangeli	63 61 46 75	1988	Mats Wilander	H. Leconte	75 62 61
1965	Fred Stolle	T. Roche	36 60 62 63	1989	Michael Chang	S. Edberg	61 36 46 64 62
1966	Tony Roche	I. Gulyas	61 64 75				
1967	Roy Emerson	T. Roche	61 64 26 62	1990	Andres Gomez	A. Agassi	63 26 64 64
1968	Ken Rosewall	R. Laver	63 61 26 62	1991	Jim Courier	A. Agassi	36 64 26 61 64
1969	Rod Laver	K. Rosewall	64 63 64	1992	Jim Courier	P. Korda	75 62 61
				1993	Sergi Bruguera	J. Courier	64 26 62 36 63
1970	Jan Kodes	Z. Franulovic	62 64 60	1994	Sergi Bruguera	A. Berasategui	63 75 26 61
1971	Jan Kodes	I. Nastase	86 62 26 75	1995	Thomas Muster	M. Chang	75 62 64
1972	Andres Gimeno	P. Proisy	46 63 61 61	1996	Yevgeny Kafelnikov	M. Stich	76 75 76
1973	Ilie Nastase	N. Pilic	63 63 60	1997	Gustavo Kuerten	S. Bruguera	63 64 62

WOMEN

Prior to 1925, entry was restricted to members of French clubs. Became an Open Championship in 1968, but closed to contract pros in 1972.

First won: 1897. **Most wins:** Chris Evert Lloyd (7) and Suzanne Lenglen (6).

Multiple winners (since 1920): Chris Evert Lloyd (7); Margaret Smith Court and Steffi Graf (5); Helen Wills Moody (4); Monica Seles and Hilde Sperling (3); Maureen Connolly, Margaret Osborne duPont, Doris Hart, Ann Haydon Jones, Suzanne Lenglen, Simone Mathieu, Margaret Scriven, Martina Navratilova, Lesley Turner and Arantxa Sanchez Vicario (2).

Year	Winner	Loser	Score	Year	Winner	Loser	Score
1925	Suzanne Lenglen	K. McKane	61 62	1964	Margaret Smith	M. Bueno	57 61 62
1926	Suzanne Lenglen	M. Browne	61 60	1965	Lesley Turner	M. Smith	63 64
1927	Kea Bouman	I. Peacock	62 64	1966	Ann Jones	N. Richey	63 61
1928	Helen Wills	E. Bennett	61 62	1967	Francoise Durr	L. Turner	46 63 64
1929	Helen Wills	S. Mathieu	63 64	1968	Nancy Richey	A. Jones	57 64 61
				1969	Margaret Court	A. Jones	61 46 63
1930	Helen Moody	H. Jacobs	62 61				
1931	Cilly Aussem	B. Nuthall	86 61	1970	Margaret Court	H. Niessen	62 64
1932	Helen Moody	S. Mathieu	75 61	1971	Evonne Goolagong	H. Gourlay	63 75
1933	Margaret Scriven	S. Mathieu	62 46 64	1972	Billie Jean King	E. Goolagong	63 63
1934	Margaret Scriven	H. Jacobs	75 46 61	1973	Margaret Court	C. Evert	67 76 64
1935	Hilde Sperling	S. Mathieu	62 61	1974	Chris Evert	O. Morozova	61 62
1936	Hilde Sperling	S. Mathieu	63 64	1975	Chris Evert	M. Navratilova	26 62 61
1937	Hilde Sperling	S. Mathieu	62 64	1976	Sue Barker	R. Tomanova	62 06 62
1938	Simone Mathieu	N. Landry	60 63	1977	Mima Jausovec	F. Mihai	62 67 61
1939	Simone Mathieu	J. Jedrzejowska	63 86	1978	Virginia Ruzici	M. Jausovec	62 62
				1979	Chris Evert Lloyd	W. Turnbull	62 60
1940-45	Not held World War II						
1946	Margaret Osborne	P. Betz	16 86 75	1980	Chris Evert Lloyd	V. Ruzici	60 63
1947	Patricia Todd	D. Hart	63 36 64	1981	Hana Mandlikova	S. Hanika	62 64
1948	Nelly Landry	S. Fry	62 06 60	1982	Martina Navratilova	A. Jaeger	76 61
1949	Margaret duPont	N. Adamson	75 62	1983	Chris Evert Lloyd	M. Jausovec	61 62
				1984	Martina Navratilova	C. Evert Lloyd	63 61
1950	Doris Hart	P. Todd	64 46 62	1985	Chris Evert Lloyd	M. Navratilova	63 67 75
1951	Shirley Fry	D. Hart	63 36 63	1986	Chris Evert Lloyd	M. Navratilova	26 63 63
1952	Doris Hart	S. Fry	64 64	1987	Steffi Graf	M. Navratilova	64 46 86
1953	Maureen Connolly	D. Hart	62 64	1988	Steffi Graf	N. Zvereva	60 60
1954	Maureen Connolly	G. Bucaille	64 61	1989	A. Sanchez Vicario	S. Graf	76 36 75
1955	Angela Mortimer	D. Knode	26 75 10-8				
1956	Althea Gibson	A. Mortimer	60 12-10	1990	Monica Seles	S. Graf	76 64
1957	Shirley Bloomer	D. Knode	61 63	1991	Monica Seles	A.S. Vicario	63 64
1958	Susi Kormoczi	S. Bloomer	64 16 62	1992	Monica Seles	S. Graf	62 36 10-8
1959	Christine Truman	S. Kormoczi	64 75	1993	Steffi Graf	M.J. Fernandez	46 62 64
				1994	A. Sanchez Vicario	M. Pierce	64 64
1960	Darlene Hard	Y. Ramirez	63 64	1995	Steffi Graff	A.S. Vicario	76 46 60
1961	Ann Haydon	Y. Ramirez	62 61	1996	Steffi Graf	A.S. Vicario	63 61
1962	Margaret Smith	L. Turner	63 36 75	1997	Iva Majoli	M. Hingis	64 62
1963	Lesley Turner	A. Jones	26 63 75				

Wimbledon
MEN

Officially called "The Lawn Tennis Championships" at the All England Club, Wimbledon. Challenge round system (defending champion qualified for following year's final) used from 1877-1921. Became an Open Championship in 1968, but closed to contract pros in 1972.

Surface: Grass.

Multiple winners: Willie Renshaw (7); Bjorn Borg and Laurie Doherty (5); Reggie Doherty, Rod Laver, Pete Sampras and Tony Wilding (4); Wilfred Baddeley, Boris Becker, Arthur Gore, John McEnroe, John Newcombe, Fred Perry and Bill Tilden (3); Jean Borotra, Norman Brookes, Don Budge, Henri Cochet, Jimmy Connors, Stefan Edberg, Roy Emerson, John Hartley, Lew Hoad, Rene Lacoste, Gerald Patterson and Joshua Pim (2).

Year	Winner	Loser	Score
1877	Spencer Gore	W. Marshall	61 62 64
1878	Frank Hadow	S. Gore	75 61 97
1879	John Hartley	V. St. L. Gould	62 64 62
1880	John Hartley	H. Lawford	60 62 26 63
1881	Willie Renshaw	J. Hartley	60 62 61
1882	Willie Renshaw	E. Renshaw	61 26 46 62 62
1883	Willie Renshaw	E. Renshaw	26 63 63 46 63
1884	Willie Renshaw	H. Lawford	60 64 97
1885	Willie Renshaw	H. Lawford	75 62 46 75
1886	Willie Renshaw	H. Lawford	60 57 63 64
1887	Herbert Lawford	E. Renshaw	16 63 36 64 64
1888	Ernest Renshaw	H. Lawford	63 75 60
1889	Willie Renshaw	E. Renshaw	64 61 36 60
1890	William Hamilton	W. Renshaw	68 62 36 61 61
1891	Wilfred Baddeley	J. Pim	64 16 75 60
1892	Wilfred Baddeley	J. Pim	46 63 63 62
1893	Joshua Pim	W. Baddeley	36 61 63 62
1894	Joshua Pim	W. Baddeley	10-8 62 86
1895	Wilfred Baddeley	W. Eaves	46 26 86 62 63
1896	Harold Mahony	W. Baddeley	62 68 57 86 63
1897	Reggie Doherty	H. Mahony	64 64 63
1898	Reggie Doherty	L. Doherty	63 63 26 57 61
1899	Reggie Doherty	A. Gore	16 46 62 63 63
1900	Reggie Doherty	S. Smith	68 63 61 62
1901	Arthur Gore	R. Doherty	46 75 64 64
1902	Laurie Doherty	A. Gore	64 63 36 60
1903	Laurie Doherty	F. Riseley	75 63 60
1904	Laurie Doherty	F. Riseley	61 75 86
1905	Laurie Doherty	N. Brookes	86 62 64
1906	Laurie Doherty	F. Riseley	64 46 62 63
1907	Norman Brookes	A. Gore	64 62 62
1908	Arthur Gore	R. Barrett	63 62 46 36 64
1909	Arthur Gore	M. Ritchie	68 16 62 62 62
1910	Tony Wilding	A. Gore	64 75 46 62
1911	Tony Wilding	R. Barrett	64 46 26 62 (ret)
1912	Tony Wilding	A. Gore	64 64 46 64
1913	Tony Wilding	M. McLoughlin	86 63 10-8
1914	Norman Brookes	T. Wilding	64 64 75
1915-18	Not held	World War I	
1919	Gerald Patterson	N. Brookes	63 75 62
1920	Bill Tilden	G. Patterson	26 63 62 64
1921	Bill Tilden	B. Norton	46 26 61 60 75
1922	Gerald Patterson	R. Lycett	63 64 62
1923	Bill Johnston	F. Hunter	60 63 61
1924	Jean Borotra	R. Lacoste	61 36 61 36 64
1925	Rene Lacoste	J. Borotra	63 63 46 86
1926	Jean Borotra	H. Kinsey	86 61 63
1927	Henri Cochet	J. Borotra	46 46 63 64 75
1928	Rene Lacoste	H. Cochet	61 46 64 62
1929	Henri Cochet	J. Borotra	64 63 64
1930	Bill Tilden	W. Allison	63 97 64
1931	Sidney Wood	F. Shields	walkover
1932	Ellsworth Vines	H. Austin	64 62 60
1933	Jack Crawford	E. Vines	46 11-9 62 26 64
1934	Fred Perry	J. Crawford	63 60 75
1935	Fred Perry	G. von Cramm	62 64 64
1936	Fred Perry	G. von Cramm	61 61 60
1937	Don Budge	G. von Cramm	63 64 62
1938	Don Budge	H. Austin	61 60 63
1939	Bobby Riggs	E. Cooke	26 86 36 63 62
1940-45	Not held	World War II	
1946	Yvon Petra	G. Brown	62 64 79 57 64
1947	Jack Kramer	T. Brown	61 63 62
1948	Bob Falkenburg	J. Bromwich	75 06 62 36 75
1949	Ted Schroeder	J. Drobny	36 60 63 46 64
1950	Budge Patty	F. Sedgman	61 8-10 62 63
1951	Dick Savitt	K. McGregor	64 64 64
1952	Frank Sedgman	J. Drobny	46 62 63 62
1953	Vic Seixas	K. Nielsen	97 63 64
1954	Jaroslav Drobny	K. Rosewall	13-11 46 62 97
1955	Tony Trabert	K. Nielsen	63 75 61
1956	Lew Hoad	K. Rosewall	62 46 75 64
1957	Lew Hoad	A. Cooper	62 61 62
1958	Ashley Cooper	N. Fraser	36 63 64 13-11
1959	Alex Olmedo	R. Laver	64 63 64
1960	Neale Fraser	R. Laver	64 36 97 75
1961	Rod Laver	C. McKinley	63 61 64
1962	Rod Laver	M. Mulligan	62 62 61
1963	Chuck McKinley	F. Stolle	97 61 64
1964	Roy Emerson	F. Stolle	64 12-10 46 63
1965	Roy Emerson	F. Stolle	62 64 64
1966	Manuel Santana	D. Ralston	64 11-9 64
1967	John Newcombe	W. Bungert	63 61 61
1968	Rod Laver	T. Roche	63 64 62
1969	Rod Laver	J. Newcombe	64 57 64 64
1970	John Newcombe	K. Rosewall	57 63 62 36 61
1971	John Newcombe	S. Smith	63 57 26 64 64
1972	Stan Smith	I. Nastase	46 63 63 46 75
1973	Jan Kodes	A. Metreveli	61 98 63
1974	Jimmy Connors	K. Rosewall	61 61 64
1975	Arthur Ashe	J. Connors	61 61 57 64
1976	Bjorn Borg	I. Nastase	64 62 97
1977	Bjorn Borg	J. Connors	36 62 61 57 64
1978	Bjorn Borg	J. Connors	62 62 63
1979	Bjorn Borg	R. Tanner	67 61 36 63 64
1980	Bjorn Borg	J. McEnroe	16 75 63 67 86
1981	John McEnroe	B. Borg	46 76 76 64
1982	Jimmy Connors	J. McEnroe	36 63 67 76 64
1983	John McEnroe	C. Lewis	62 62 62
1984	John McEnroe	J. Connors	61 61 62
1985	Boris Becker	K. Curren	63 67 76 64
1986	Boris Becker	I. Lendl	64 63 75
1987	Pat Cash	I. Lendl	76 62 75
1988	Stefan Edberg	B. Becker	46 76 64 62
1989	Boris Becker	S. Edberg	60 76 64
1990	Stefan Edberg	B. Becker	62 62 36 36 64
1991	Michael Stich	B. Becker	64 76 64
1992	Andre Agassi	G. Ivanisevic	67 64 64 16 64
1993	Pete Sampras	J. Courier	76 76 36 63
1994	Pete Sampras	G. Ivanisevic	76 76 60
1995	Pete Sampras	B. Becker	67 62 64 62
1996	Richard Krajicek	M. Washington	63 64 63
1997	Pete Sampras	C. Pioline	64 62 64

WOMEN

Officially called "The Lawn Tennis Championships" at the All England Club, Wimbledon. Challenge round system (defending champion qualified for following year's final) used from 1877-1921. Became an Open Championship in 1968, but closed to contract pros in 1972.

Multiple winners: Martina Navratilova (9); Helen Willis Moody (8); Dorothea Douglass Chambers and Steffi Graf (7); Blanche Bingley Hillyard, Billie Jean King and Suzanne Lenglen (6); Lottie Dod and Charlotte Cooper Sterry (5); Louise Brough (4); Maria Bueno, Maureen Connolly, Margaret Smith Court and Chris Evert Lloyd (3); Evonne Goolagong Cawley, Althea Gibson, Dorothy Round, May Sutton and Maud Watson (2).

Year	Winner	Loser	Score
1884	Maud Watson	L. Watson	68 63 63
1885	Maud Watson	B. Bingley	61 75
1886	Blanche Bingley	M. Watson	63 63
1887	Lottie Dod	B. Bingley	62 60
1888	Lottie Dod	B. Hillyard	63 63
1889	Blanche Hillyard	L. Rice	46 86 64
1890	Lena Rice	M. Jacks	64 61
1891	Lottie Dod	B. Hillyard	62 61
1892	Lottie Dod	B. Hillyard	61 61
1893	Lottie Dod	B. Hillyard	68 61 64
1894	Blanche Hillyard	E. Austin	61 61
1895	Charlotte Cooper	H. Jackson	75 86
1896	Charlotte Cooper	W. Pickering	62 63
1897	Blanche Hillyard	C. Cooper	57 75 62
1898	Charlotte Cooper	L. Martin	64 64
1899	Blanche Hillyard	C. Cooper	62 63
1900	Blanche Hillyard	C. Cooper	46 64 64
1901	Charlotte Sterry	B. Hillyard	62 62
1902	Muriel Robb	C. Sterry	75 61
1903	Dorothea Douglass	E. Thomson	46 64 62
1904	Dorothea Douglass	C. Sterry	60 63
1905	May Sutton	D. Douglass	63 64
1906	Dorothea Douglass	M. Sutton	63 97
1907	May Sutton	D. Chambers	61 64
1908	Charlotte Sterry	A. Morton	64 64
1909	Dora Boothby	A. Morton	64 46 86
1910	Dorothea Chambers	D. Boothby	62 62
1911	Dorothea Chambers	D. Boothby	60 60
1912	Ethel Larcombe	C. Sterry	63 61
1913	Dorothea Chambers	R. McNair	60 64
1914	Dorothea Chambers	E. Larcombe	75 64
1915-18	Not held	World War I	
1919	Suzanne Lenglen	D. Chambers	10-8 46 97
1920	Suzanne Lenglen	D. Chambers	63 60
1921	Suzanne Lenglen	E. Ryan	62 60
1922	Suzanne Lenglen	M. Mallory	62 60
1923	Suzanne Lenglen	K. McKane	62 62
1924	Kathleen McKane	H. Wills	46 64 64
1925	Suzanne Lenglen	J. Fry	62 60
1926	Kathleen Godfree	L. de Alvarez	62 46 63
1927	Helen Wills	L. de Alvarez	62 64
1928	Helen Wills	L. de Alvarez	62 63
1929	Helen Wills	H. Jacobs	61 62
1930	Helen Moody	E. Ryan	62 62
1931	Cilly Aussem	H. Kranwinkel	62 75
1932	Helen Moody	H. Jacobs	63 61
1933	Helen Moody	D. Round	64 68 63
1934	Dorothy Round	H. Jacobs	62 57 63
1935	Helen Moody	H. Jacobs	63 36 75
1936	Helen Jacobs	H.K. Sperling	62 46 75
1937	Dorothy Round	J. Jedrzejowska	62 26 75
1938	Helen Moody	H. Jacobs	64 60
1939	Alice Marble	K. Stammers	62 60
1940-45	Not held	World War II	
1946	Pauline Betz	L. Brough	62 64
1947	Margaret Osborne	D. Hart	62 64
1948	Louise Brough	D. Hart	63 86
1949	Louise Brough	M. duPont	10-8 16 10-8
1950	Louise Brough	M. duPont	61 36 61
1951	Doris Hart	S. Fry	61 60
1952	Maureen Connolly	L. Brough	75 63
1953	Maureen Connolly	D. Hart	86 75
1954	Maureen Connolly	L. Brough	62 75
1955	Louise Brough	B. Fleitz	75 86
1956	Shirley Fry	A. Buxton	63 61
1957	Althea Gibson	D. Hard	63 62
1958	Althea Gibson	A. Mortimer	86 62
1959	Maria Bueno	D. Hard	64 63
1960	Maria Bueno	S. Reynolds	86 60
1961	Angela Mortimer	C. Truman	46 64 75
1962	Karen Susman	V. Sukova	64 64
1963	Margaret Smith	B.J. Moffitt	63 64
1964	Maria Bueno	M. Smith	64 79 63
1965	Margaret Smith	M. Bueno	64 75
1966	Billie Jean King	M. Bueno	63 36 61
1967	Billie Jean King	A. Jones	63 64
1968	Billie Jean King	J. Tegart	97 75
1969	Ann Jones	B.J. King	36 63 62
1970	Margaret Court	B.J. King	14-12 11-9
1971	Evonne Goolagong	M. Court	64 61
1972	Billie Jean King	E. Goolagong	63 63
1973	Billie Jean King	C. Evert	60 75
1974	Chris Evert	O. Morozova	60 64
1975	Billie Jean King	E. Cawley	60 61
1976	Chris Evert	E. Cawley	63 46 86
1977	Virginia Wade	B. Stove	46 63 61
1978	Martina Navratilova	C. Evert	26 64 75
1979	Martina Navratilova	C. Evert Lloyd	64 64
1980	Evonne Cawley	C. Evert Lloyd	61 76
1981	Chris Evert Lloyd	H. Mandlikova	62 62
1982	Martina Navratilova	C. Evert Lloyd	61 36 62
1983	Martina Navratilova	A. Jaeger	60 63
1984	Martina Navratilova	C. Evert Lloyd	76 62
1985	Martina Navratilova	C. Evert Lloyd	46 63 62
1986	Martina Navratilova	H. Mandlikova	76 63
1987	Martina Navratilova	S. Graf	75 63
1988	Steffi Graf	M. Navratilova	57 62 61
1989	Steffi Graf	M. Navratilova	62 67 61
1990	Martina Navratilova	Z. Garrison	64 61
1991	Steffi Graf	G. Sabatini	64 36 86
1992	Steffi Graf	M. Seles	62 61
1993	Steffi Graf	J. Novotna	76 16 64
1994	Conchita Martinez	M. Navratilova	64 36 63
1995	Steffi Graf	A.S. Vicario	46 61 75
1996	Steffi Graf	A.S. Vicario	63 75
1997	Martina Hingis	J. Novotna	26 63 63

U.S. Open
MEN

Challenge round system (defending champion qualified for following year's final) used from 1884-1911. Known as the Patriotic Tournament in 1917 during World War I. Amateur and Open Championships held in 1968 and '69. Became an exclusively Open Championship in 1970.

Surface: Decoturf II (acrylic cement).

Multiple winners: Bill Larned, Richard Sears and Bill Tilden (7); Jimmy Connors (5); John McEnroe, Pete Sampras and Robert Wrenn (4); Oliver Campbell, Ivan Lendl, Fred Perry and Malcolm Whitman (3); Don Budge, Stefan Edberg, Roy Emerson, Neale Fraser, Pancho Gonzales, Bill Johnston, Jack Kramer, Rene Lacoste, Rod Laver, Maurice McLoughlin, Lindley Murray, John Newcombe, Frank Parker, Bobby Riggs, Ken Rosewall, Frank Sedgman, Henry Slocum Jr., Tony Trabert, Ellsworth Vines and Dick Williams (2).

Year	Winner	Loser	Score	Year	Winner	Loser	Score
1881	Richard Sears	W. Glyn	60 63 62	1938	Don Budge	G. Mako	63 68 62 61
1882	Richard Sears	C. Clark	61 64 60	1939	Bobby Riggs	S.W. van Horn	64 62 64
1883	Richard Sears	J. Dwight	62 60 97	1940	Don McNeill	B. Riggs	46 68 63 63 75
1884	Richard Sears	H. Taylor	60 16 60 62	1941	Bobby Riggs	F. Kovacs	57 61 63 63
1885	Richard Sears	G. Brinley	63 46 60 63	1942	Fred Schroeder	F. Parker	86 75 36 46 62
1886	Richard Sears	R. Beeckman	46 61 63 64	1943	Joe Hunt	J. Kramer	63 68 10-8 60
1887	Richard Sears	H. Slocum Jr.	61 63 62	1944	Frank Parker	B. Talbert	64 36 63 63
1888	Henry Slocum Jr.	H. Taylor	64 61 60	1945	Frank Parker	B. Talbert	14-12 61 62
1889	Henry Slocum Jr.	Q. Shaw	63 61 46 62	1946	Jack Kramer	T. Brown, Jr.	97 63 60
1890	Oliver Campbell	H. Slocum Jr.	62 46 63 61	1947	Jack Kramer	F. Parker	46 26 61 60 63
1891	Oliver Campbell	C. Hobart	26 75 79 61 62	1948	Pancho Gonzales	E. Sturgess	62 63 14-12
1892	Oliver Campbell	F. Hovey	75 36 63 75	1949	Pancho Gonzales	F. Schroeder	16-18 26 61 62 64
1893	Robert Wrenn	F. Hovey	64 36 64 64	1950	Arthur Larsen	H. Flam	63 46 57 64 63
1894	Robert Wrenn	M. Goodbody	68 61 64 64	1951	Frank Sedgman	V. Seixas	64 61 61
1895	Fred Hovey	R. Wrenn	63 62 64	1952	Frank Sedgman	G. Mulloy	61 62 63
1896	Robert Wrenn	F. Hovey	75 36 60 16 61	1953	Tony Trabert	V. Seixas	63 62 63
1897	Robert Wrenn	W. Eaves	46 86 63 26 62	1954	Vic Seixas	R. Hartwig	36 62 64 64
1898	Malcolm Whitman	D. Davis	36 62 62 61	1955	Tony Trabert	K. Rosewall	97 63 63
1899	Malcolm Whitman	P. Paret	61 62 36 75	1956	Ken Rosewall	L. Hoad	46 62 63 63
1900	Malcolm Whitman	B. Larned	64 16 62 62	1957	Mal Anderson	A. Cooper	10-8 75 64
1901	Bill Larned	B. Wright	62 68 64 64	1958	Ashley Cooper	M. Anderson	62 36 46 10-8 86
1902	Bill Larned	R. Doherty	46 62 64 86	1959	Neale Fraser	A. Olmedo	63 57 62 64
1903	Laurie Doherty	B. Larned	60 63 10-8	1960	Neale Fraser	R. Laver	64 64 97
1904	Holcombe Ward	B. Clothier	10-8 64 97	1961	Roy Emerson	R. Laver	75 63 62
1905	Beals Wright	H. Ward	62 61 11-9	1962	Rod Laver	R. Emerson	62 64 57 64
1906	Bill Clothier	B. Wright	63 60 64	1963	Rafael Osuna	F. Froehling	75 64 62
1907	Bill Larned	R. LeRoy	62 62 64	1964	Roy Emerson	F. Stolle	64 62 64
1908	Bill Larned	B. Wright	61 62 86	1965	Manuel Santana	C. Drysdale	62 79 75 61
1909	Bill Larned	B. Clothier	61 62 57 16 61	1966	Fred Stolle	J. Newcombe	46 12-10 63 64
1910	Bill Larned	T. Bundy	61 57 60 68 61	1967	John Newcombe	C. Graebner	64 64 86
1911	Bill Larned	M. McLoughlin	64 64 62	1968	Am-Arthur Ashe	B. Lutz	46 63 8-10 60 64
1912	Maurice McLoughlin	W.F. Johnson	36 26 62 64 62		Op-Arthur Ashe	T. Okker	14-12 57 63 36 63
1913	Maurice McLoughlin	R. Williams	64 57 63 61	1969	Am-Stan Smith	B. Lutz	97 63 61
1914	Dick Williams	M. McLoughlin	63 86 10-8		Op-Rod Laver	T. Roche	79 61 63 62
1915	Bill Johnston	M. McLoughlin	16 60 75 10-8	1970	Ken Rosewall	T. Roche	26 64 76 63
1916	Dick Williams	B. Johnston	46 64 06 62 64	1971	Stan Smith	J. Kodes	36 63 62 76
1917	Lindley Murray	N. Niles	57 86 63 63	1972	Ilie Nastase	A. Ashe	36 63 67 64 63
1918	Lindley Murray	B. Tilden	63 61 75	1973	John Newcombe	J. Kodes	64 16 46 62 63
1919	Bill Johnston	B. Tilden	64 64 63	1974	Jimmy Connors	K. Rosewall	61 60 61
1920	Bill Tilden	B. Johnston	61 16 75 57 63	1975	Manuel Orantes	J. Connors	64 63 63
1921	Bill Tilden	W. Johnson	61 63 61	1976	Jimmy Connors	B. Borg	64 36 76 64
1922	Bill Tilden	B. Johnston	46 36 62 63 64	1977	Guillermo Vilas	J. Connors	26 63 76 60
1923	Bill Tilden	B. Johnston	64 61 64	1978	Jimmy Connors	B. Borg	64 62 62
1924	Bill Tilden	B. Johnston	61 97 62	1979	John McEnroe	V. Gerulaitis	75 63 63
1925	Bill Tilden	B. Johnston	46 11-9 63 46 63	1980	John McEnroe	B. Borg	76 61 67 57 64
1926	Rene Lacoste	J. Borotra	64 60 64	1981	John McEnroe	B. Borg	46 62 64 63
1927	Rene Lacoste	B. Tilden	11-9 63 11-9	1982	Jimmy Connors	I. Lendl	63 62 46 64
1928	Henri Cochet	F. Hunter	46 64 36 75 63	1983	Jimmy Connors	I. Lendl	63 67 75 60
1929	Bill Tilden	F. Hunter	36 63 46 62 64	1984	John McEnroe	I. Lendl	63 64 61
1930	John Doeg	F. Shields	10-8 16 64 16-14	1985	Ivan Lendl	J. McEnroe	76 63 64
1931	Ellsworth Vines	G. Lott Jr.	79 63 97 75	1986	Ivan Lendl	M. Mecir	64 62 60
1932	Ellsworth Vines	H. Cochet	64 64 64	1987	Ivan Lendl	M. Wilander	67 60 76 64
1933	Fred Perry	J. Crawford	63 11-13 46 60 61	1988	Mats Wilander	I. Lendl	64 46 63 57 64
1934	Fred Perry	W. Allison	64 63 16 86	1989	Boris Becker	I. Lendl	76 16 63 76
1935	Wilmer Allison	S. Wood	62 62 63	1990	Pete Sampras	A. Agassi	64 63 62
1936	Fred Perry	D. Budge	26 62 86 16 10-8	1991	Stefan Edberg	J. Courier	62 64 60
1937	Don Budge	G. von Cramm	61 79 61 36 61	1992	Stefan Edberg	P. Sampras	36 64 76 62

Year	Winner	Loser	Score	Year	Winner	Loser	Score
1993	Pete Sampras	C. Pioline	64 64 63	1996	Pete Sampras	M. Chang	61 64 76
1994	Andre Agassi	M. Stich	61 76 75	1997	Patrick Rafter	G. Rusedski	63 62 46 75
1995	Pete Sampras	A. Agassi	64 63 46 75				

WOMEN

Challenge round system used from 1887-1918. Five set final played from 1887-1901. Amateur and Open Championships held in 1968 and '69. Became an exclusively Open Championship in 1970.

Multiple winners: Molla Mallory Bjurstedt (8); Helen Wills Moody (7); Chris Everet Lloyd (6); Margaret Smith Court and Steffi Graf (5); Pauline Betz, Mario Bueno, Helen Jacobs, Billie Jean King, Alice Marble, Elisabeth Moore, Martina Navratilova and Hazel Hotchkiss Wightman (4); Juliette Atkinson, Mary Browne, Maureen Connolly and Margaret Osborne duPont (3); Tracy Austin, Mabel Cahill, Sarah Palfrey Cooke, Darlene Hard, Doris Hart, Althea Gibson, Monica Seles and Bertha Townsend (2).

Year	Winner	Loser	Score	Year	Winner	Loser	Score
1887	Ellen Hansell	L. Knight	61 60	1944	Pauline Betz	M. Osborne	63 86
1888	Bertha Townsend	E. Hansell	63 65	1945	Sarah Cooke	P. Betz	36 86 64
1889	Bertha Townsend	L. Voorhes	75 62	1946	Pauline Betz	P. Canning	11-9 63
1890	Ellen Roosevelt	B. Townsend	62 62	1947	Louise Brough	M. Osborne	86 46 61
1891	Mabel Cahill	E. Roosevelt	64 61 46 63	1948	Margaret duPont	L. Brough	46 64 15-13
1892	Mabel Cahill	E. Moore	57 63 64 46 62	1949	Margaret duPont	D. Hart	64 61
1893	Aline Terry	A. Schultz	61 63	1950	Margaret duPont	D. Hart	64 63
1894	Helen Hellwig	A. Terry	75 36 60 36 63	1951	Maureen Connolly	S. Fry	63 16 64
1895	Juliette Atkinson	H. Hellwig	64 62 61	1952	Maureen Connolly	D. Hart	63 75
1896	Elisabeth Moore	J. Atkinson	64 46 62 62	1953	Maureen Connolly	D. Hart	62 64
1897	Juliette Atkinson	E. Moore	63 63 46 36 63	1954	Doris Hart	L. Brough	68 61 86
1898	Juliette Atkinson	M. Jones	63 57 64 26 75	1955	Doris Hart	P. Ward	64 62
1899	Marion Jones	M. Banks	61 61 75	1956	Shirley Fry	A. Gibson	63 64
1900	Myrtle McAteer	E. Parker	62 62 60	1957	Althea Gibson	L. Brough	63 62
1901	Elizabeth Moore	M. McAteer	64 36 75 26 62	1958	Althea Gibson	D. Hard	36 61 62
1902	Marion Jones	E. Moore	61 10(ret)	1959	Maria Bueno	C. Truman	61 64
1903	Elizabeth Moore	M. Jones	75 86	1960	Darlene Hard	M. Bueno	64 10-12 64
1904	May Sutton	E. Moore	61 62	1961	Darlene Hard	A. Haydon	63 64
1905	Elizabeth Moore	H. Homans	64 57 61	1962	Margaret Smith	D. Hard	97 64
1906	Helen Homans	M. Barger-Wallach	64 63	1963	Maria Bueno	M. Smith	75 64
1907	Evelyn Sears	C. Neely	63 62	1964	Maria Bueno	C. Graebner	61 60
1908	Maud B. Wallach	Ev. Sears	63 16 63	1965	Margaret Smith	B.J. Moffitt	86 75
1909	Hazel Hotchkiss	M. Wallach	60 61	1966	Maria Bueno	N. Richey	63 61
1910	Hazel Hotchkiss	L. Hammond	64 62	1967	Billie Jean King	A. Jones	11-9 64
1911	Hazel Hotchkiss	F. Sutton	8-10 61 97	1968	Am-Margaret Court	M. Bueno	62 62
1912	Mary Browne	E. Sears	64 62		Op-Virginia Wade	B.J. King	64 62
1913	Mary Browne	D. Green	62 75	1969	Am-Margaret Court	V. Wade	46 63 60
1914	Mary Browne	M. Wagner	62 16 61		Op-Margaret Court	N. Richey	62 62
1915	Molla Bjurstedt	H. Wightman	46 62 60	1970	Margaret Court	R. Casals	62 26 61
1916	Molla Bjurstedt	L. Raymond	60 61	1971	Billie Jean King	R. Casals	64 76
1917	Molla Bjurstedt	M. Vanderhoef	46 60 62	1972	Billie Jean King	K. Melville	63 75
1918	Molla Bjurstedt	E. Goss	64 63	1973	Margaret Court	E. Goolagong	76 57 62
1919	Hazel Wightman	M. Zinderstein	61 62	1974	Billie Jean King	E. Goolagong	36 63 75
1920	Molla Mallory	M. Zinderstein	63 61	1975	Chris Evert	E. Cawley	57 64 62
1921	Molla Mallory	M. Browne	46 64 62	1976	Chris Evert	E. Cawley	63 60
1922	Molla Mallory	H. Wills	63 61	1977	Chris Evert	W. Turnbull	76 62
1923	Helen Wills	M. Mallory	62 61	1978	Chris Evert	P. Shriver	75 64
1924	Helen Wills	M. Mallory	61 63	1979	Tracy Austin	C. Evert Lloyd	64 63
1925	Helen Wills	K. McKane	36 60 62	1980	Chris Evert Lloyd	H. Mandlikova	57 61 61
1926	Molla Mallory	E. Ryan	46 64 97	1981	Tracy Austin	M. Navratilova	16 76 76
1927	Helen Wills	B. Nuthall	61 64	1982	Chris Evert Lloyd	H. Mandlikova	63 61
1928	Helen Wills	H. Jacobs	62 61	1983	Martina Navratilova	C. Evert Lloyd	61 63
1929	Helen Wills	P. Watson	64 62	1984	Martina Navratilova	C. Evert Lloyd	46 64 64
1930	Betty Nuthall	A. Harper	61 64	1985	Hana Mandlikova	M. Navratilova	76 16 76
1931	Helen Moody	E. Whitingstall	64 61	1986	Martina Navratilova	H. Sukova	63 62
1932	Helen Jacobs	C. Babcock	62 62	1987	Martina Navratilova	S. Graf	76 61
1933	Helen Jacobs	H. Moody	86 36 30(ret)	1988	Steffi Graf	G. Sabatini	63 36 61
1934	Helen Jacobs	S. Palfrey	61 64	1989	Steffi Graf	M. Navratilova	36 75 61
1935	Helen Jacobs	S. Fabyan	62 64	1990	Gabriela Sabatini	S. Graf	62 76
1936	Alice Marble	H. Jacobs	46 63 62	1991	Monica Seles	M. Navratilova	76 61
1937	Anita Lizana	J. Jedrzejowska	64 62	1992	Monica Seles	A.S. Vicario	63 63
1938	Alice Marble	N. Wynne	60 63	1993	Steffi Graf	H. Sukova	63 63
1939	Alice Marble	H. Jacobs	60 8-10 64	1994	A. Sanchez Vicario	S. Graf	16 76 64
1940	Alice Marble	H. Jacobs	62 63	1995	Steffi Graf	M. Seles	76 06 63
1941	Sarah Cooke	P. Betz	75 62	1996	Steffi Graf	M. Seles	75 64
1942	Pauline Betz	L. Brough	46 61 64	1997	Martina Hingis	V. Williams	60 64
1943	Pauline Betz	L. Brough	63 57 63				

Grand Slam Summary

Singles winners of the four Grand Slam tournaments–Australian, French, Wimbledon and United States–since the French was opened to all comers in 1925. Note that there were two Australian Opens in 1977 and none in 1986.

MEN

Three wins in one year: Jack Crawford (1933); Fred Perry (1934); Tony Trabert (1955); Lew Hoad (1956); Ashley Cooper (1958); Roy Emerson (1964); Jimmy Connors (1974); Mats Wilander (1988).

Two wins in one year: Roy Emerson and Pete Sampras (4 times); Bjorn Borg (3 times); Rene Lacoste, Ivan Lendl, John Newcombe and Fred Perry (twice); Boris Becker, Don Budge, Henri Cochet, Jimmy Connors, Jim Courier, Neale Fraser, Jack Kramer, John McEnroe, Alex Olmedo, Budge Patty, Bobby Riggs, Ken Rosewall, Dick Savitt, Frank Sedgman and Guillermo Vilas (once).

Year	Australian	French	Wimbledon	U.S.	Year	Australian	French	Wimbledon	U.S.
1925	Anderson	Lacoste	Lacoste	Tilden	1962	**Laver**	**Laver**	**Laver**	**Laver**
1926	Hawkes	Cochet	Borotra	Lacoste	1963	Emerson	Emerson	McKinley	Osuna
1927	Patterson	Lacoste	Cochet	Lacoste	1964	Emerson	Santana	Emerson	Emerson
1928	Borotra	Cochet	Lacoste	Cochet	1965	Emerson	Stolle	Emerson	Santana
1929	Gregory	Lacoste	Cochet	Tilden	1966	Emerson	Roche	Santana	Stolle
1930	Moon	Cochet	Tilden	Doeg	1967	Emerson	Emerson	Newcombe	Newcombe
1931	Crawford	Borotra	Wood	Vines	1968	Bowrey	Rosewall	Laver	Ashe
1932	Crawford	Cochet	Vines	Vines	1969	**Laver**	**Laver**	**Laver**	**Laver**
1933	Crawford	Crawford	Crawford	Perry	1970	Ashe	Kodes	Newcombe	Rosewall
1934	Perry	von Cramm	Perry	Perry	1971	Rosewall	Kodes	Newcombe	Smith
1935	Crawford	Perry	Perry	Allison	1972	Rosewall	Gimeno	Smith	Nastase
1936	Quist	von Cramm	Perry	Perry	1973	Newcombe	Nastase	Kodes	Newcombe
1937	McGrath	Henkel	Budge	Budge	1974	Connors	Borg	Connors	Connors
1938	**Budge**	**Budge**	**Budge**	**Budge**	1975	Newcombe	Borg	Ashe	Orantes
1939	Bromwich	McNeill	Riggs	Riggs	1976	Edmondson	Panatta	Borg	Connors
1940	Quist	—	—	McNeill	1977	Tanner & Gerulaitis	Vilas	Borg	Vilas
1941	—	—	—	Riggs	1978	Vilas	Borg	Borg	Connors
1942	—	—	—	Schroeder	1979	Vilas	Borg	Borg	McEnroe
1943	—	—	—	Hunt	1980	Teacher	Borg	Borg	McEnroe
1944	—	—	—	Parker	1981	Kriek	Borg	McEnroe	McEnroe
1945	—	—	—	Parker	1982	Kriek	Wilander	Connors	Connors
1946	Bromwich	Bernard	Petra	Kramer	1983	Wilander	Noah	McEnroe	Connors
1947	Pails	Asboth	Kramer	Kramer	1984	Wilander	Lendl	McEnroe	McEnroe
1948	Quist	Parker	Falkenburg	Gonzales	1985	Edberg	Wilander	Becker	Lendl
1949	Sedgman	Parker	Schroeder	Gonzales	1986	–	Lendl	Becker	Lendl
1950	Sedgman	Patty	Patty	Larsen	1987	Edberg	Lendl	Cash	Lendl
1951	Savitt	Drobny	Savitt	Sedgman	1988	Wilander	Wilander	Edberg	Wilander
1952	McGregor	Drobny	Sedgman	Sedgman	1989	Lendl	Chang	Becker	Becker
1953	Rosewall	Rosewall	Seixas	Trabert	1990	Lendl	Gomez	Edberg	Sampras
1954	Rose	Trabert	Drobny	Seixas	1991	Becker	Courier	Stich	Edberg
1955	Rosewall	Trabert	Trabert	Trabert	1992	Courier	Courier	Agassi	Edberg
1956	Hoad	Hoad	Hoad	Rosewall	1993	Courier	Bruguera	Sampras	Sampras
1957	Cooper	Davidson	Hoad	Anderson	1994	Sampras	Bruguera	Sampras	Agassi
1958	Cooper	Rose	Cooper	Cooper	1995	Agassi	Muster	Sampras	Sampras
1959	Olmedo	Pietrangeli	Olmedo	Fraser	1996	Becker	Kafelnikov	Krajicek	Sampras
1960	Laver	Pietrangeli	Fraser	Fraser	1997	Sampras	Kuerten	Sampras	Rafter
1961	Emerson	Santana	Laver	Emerson					

The Calendar Year Grand Slam

The tennis Grand Slam has only been accomplished nine times in the same calendar year in either singles or doubles. And only two players have managed to do it twice– Rod Laver in singles (1962 and '69) and Margaret Smith Court in singles (1970) and doubles (1963).

Men's Singles

1938	Don Budge, USA
1962	Rod Laver, Australia
1969	Rod Laver, Australia

Men's Doubles

1951	Frank Sedgman, Australia & Ken McGregor, Australia

Mixed Doubles

1963	Ken Fletcher, Australia & Margaret Smith, Australia
1967	Owen Davidson and two partners

Women's Singles

1953	Maureen Connolly, USA
1970	Margaret Smith Court, Australia
1988	Steffi Graf, West Germany*

*Also won gold medal at Seoul Olympics.

Women's Doubles

1960	Maria Bueno, Brazil & two partners
1984	Martina Navratilova, USA & Pam Shriver, USA

Note: In women's doubles, Bueno won Australia with Christine Truman, then took the French, Wimbledon and the U.S. with Darlene hard. In mixed Doubles–Davidson won Australia with Lesley Turner, then took the French, Wimbledon and the U.S. with Billie Jean King.

WOMEN

Three in one year: Helen Wills Moody (1928 and '29); Margaret Smith Court (1962, '65, '69 and '73); Billie Jean King (1972); Martina Navratilova (1983 and '84); Steffi Graf (1989, '93, '95 and '96); Monica Seles (1991 and '92); and Martina Hingis (1997).

Two in one year: Chris Evert Lloyd (5 times); Helen Wills Moody and Martina Navratilova (3 times); Maria Bueno, Maureen Connolly, Margaraet Smith Court, Althea Gibson, Billie Jean King (twice); Cilly Aussem, Pauleen Betz, Louise Brough, Evonne Goolagong Cawley, Shirley Fry, Darlene Hard, Margaret Osborne duPont, Suzanne Lenglen, Alice Marble and Arantxa Sanchez Vicario (once).

Year	Australian	French	Wimbledon	U.S.	Year	Australian	French	Wimbledon	U.S.
1925	Akhurst	Lenglen	Lenglen	Wills	1962	Smith	Smith	Susman	Smith
1926	Akhurst	Lenglen	Godfree	Mallory	1963	Smith	Turner	Smith	Bueno
1927	Boyd	Bouman	Wills	Wills	1964	Smith	Smith	Bueno	Bueno
1928	Akhurst	Wills	Wills	Wills	1965	Smith	Turner	Smith	Smith
1929	Akhurst	Wills	Wills	Wills	1966	Smith	Jones	King	Bueno
1930	Akhurst	Moody	Moody	Nuthall	1967	Richey	Durr	King	King
1931	Buttsworth	Aussem	Aussem	Moody	1968	King	Richey	King	Wade
1932	Buttsworth	Moody	Moody	Jacobs	1969	Court	Court	Jones	Court
1933	Hartigan	Scriven	Moody	Jacobs	1970	**Court**	**Court**	**Court**	**Court**
1934	Hartigan	Scriven	Round	Jacobs	1971	Court	Goolagong	Goolagong	King
1935	Round	Sperling	Moody	Jacobs	1972	Wade	King	King	King
1936	Hartigan	Sperling	Jacobs	Marble	1973	Court	Court	King	Court
1937	Bolton	Sperling	Round	Lizana	1974	Goolagong	Evert	Evert	King
1938	Bundy	Mathieu	Moody	Marble	1975	Goolagong	Evert	King	Evert
1939	Westacott	Mathieu	Marble	Marble	1976	Cawley	Barker	Evert	Evert
1940	Bolton	—	—	Marble	1977	Reid	Jausovec	Wade	Evert
1941	—	—	—	Cooke		& Cawley			
1942	—	—	—	Betz	1978	O'Neil	Ruzici	Navratilova	Evert
1943	—	—	—	Betz	1979	Jordan	Evert Lloyd	Navratilova	Austin
1944	—	—	—	Betz	1980	Mandlikova	Evert Lloyd	Cawley	Evert Lloyd
1945	—	—	—	Cooke	1981	Navratilova	Mandlikova	Evert Lloyd	Austin
1946	Bolton	Osborne	Betz	Betz	1982	Evert Lloyd	Navratilova	Navratilova	Evert Lloyd
1947	Bolton	Todd	Osborne	Brough	1983	Navratilova	Evert Lloyd	Navratilova	Navratilova
1948	Bolton	Landry	Brough	du Pont	1984	Evert Lloyd	Navratilova	Navratilova	Navratilova
1949	Hart	du Pont	Brough	du Pont	1985	Navratilova	Evert Lloyd	Navratilova	Mandlikova
1950	Brough	Hart	Brough	du Pont	1986	—	Evert Lloyd	Navratilova	Navratilova
1951	Bolton	Fry	Hart	Connolly	1987	Mandlikova	Graf	Navratilova	Navratilova
1952	Long	Hart	Connolly	Connolly	1988	**Graf**	**Graf**	**Graf**	**Graf**
1953	**Connolly**	**Connolly**	**Connolly**	**Connolly**	1989	Graf	Vicario	Graf	Graf
1954	Long	Connolly	Connolly	Hart	1990	Graf	Seles	Navratilova	Sabatini
1955	Penrose	Mortimer	Brough	Hart	1991	Seles	Seles	Graf	Seles
1956	Carter	Gibson	Fry	Fry	1992	Seles	Seles	Graf	Seles
1957	Fry	Bloomer	Gibson	Gibson	1993	Seles	Graf	Graf	Graf
1958	Mortimer	Kormoczi	Gibson	Gibson	1994	Graf	Vicario	Martinez	Vicario
1959	Reitano	Truman	Bueno	Bueno	1995	Pierce	Graf	Graf	Graf
1960	Smith	Hard	Bueno	Hard	1996	Seles	Graf	Graf	Graf
1961	Smith	Haydon	Mortimer	Hard	1997	Hingis	Majoli	Hingis	Hingis

All-Time Grand Slam Singles Titles

Men and women with the most singles championships in the Australian, French, Wimbledon and U.S. championships, through 1997. Note that (*) indicates player never played in that particular Grand Slam event; and players active in singles play in 1997 are in **bold** type.

Top 15 Men

		Aus	Fre	Wim	US	Total
1	Roy Emerson	6	2	2	2	12
2	Bjorn Borg	0	6	5	0	11
	Rod Laver	3	2	4	2	11
4	**Pete Sampras**	2	0	4	4	10
	Bill Tilden	*	0	3	7	10
6	Jimmy Connors	1	0	2	5	8
	Ivan Lendl	2	3	0	3	8
	Fred Perry	1	1	3	3	8
	Ken Rosewall	4	2	0	2	8
10	Henri Cochet	*	4	2	1	7
	Rene Lacoste	*	3	2	2	7
	Bill Larned	*	*	0	7	7
	John McEnroe	0	0	3	4	7
	John Newcombe	2	0	3	2	7
	Willie Renshaw	*	*	7	*	7
	Dick Sears	*	*	0	7	7

Top 15 Women

		Aus	Fre	Wim	US	Total
1	Margaret Smith Court	11	5	3	5	24
2	**Steffi Graf**	4	5	7	5	21
3	Helen Wills Moody	*	4	8	7	19
4	Chris Evert	2	7	3	6	18
	Martina Navratilova	3	2	9	4	18
6	Billie Jean King	1	1	6	4	12
	Suzanne Lenglen	*	6	6	0	12
8	Maureen Connolly	1	2	3	3	9
	Monica Seles	4	3	0	2	9
10	Molla Bjurstedt Mallory	*	*	0	8	8
11	Maria Bueno	0	0	3	4	7
	Evonne Goolagong	4	1	2	0	7
	Dorothea D. Chambers	*	*	7	0	7
14	Nancy Bolton	6	0	0	0	6
	Louise Brough	1	0	4	1	6
	Margaret duPont	*	2	1	3	6
	Doris Hart	1	2	1	2	6
	Blanche Bingley Hillyard	*	*	6	*	6

Overall Leaders

All-Time Grand Slam titleists including all singles and doubles championships at the four major tournaments. Titles listed under each heading are singles, doubles and mixed doubles. Players active in 1997 are in **bold** type.

MEN

		Career	Australian	French	Wimbledon	U.S.	S-D-M	Total Titles
1	Roy Emerson	1959-71	6-3-0	2-6-0	2-3-0	2-4-0	12-16-0	28
2	John Newcombe	1965-76	2-5-0	0-3-0	3-6-0	2-3-1	7-17-1	25
3	Frank Sedgman	1949-52	2-2-2	0-2-2	1-3-2	2-2-2	5-9-8	22
4	Bill Tilden	1913-30	*	0-0-1	3-1-0	7-5-4	10-6-5	21
5	Rod Laver	1959-71	3-4-0	2-1-1	4-1-2	2-0-0	11-6-3	20
6	Jack Bromwich	1938-50	2-8-1	0-0-0	0-2-2	0-3-1	2-13-4	19
7	Ken Rosewall	1953-72	4-3-0	2-2-0	0-2-0	2-2-1	8-9-1	18
	Neale Fraser	1957-62	0-3-1	0-3-0	1-2-0	2-3-3	3-11-4	18
	Jean Borotra	1925-36	1-1-1	1-5-2	2-3-1	0-0-1	4-9-5	18
	Fred Stolle	1962-69	0-3-1	1-2-0	0-2-3	1-3-2	2-10-6	18
11	John McEnroe	1977-93	0-0-0	0-0-1	3-5-0	4-4-0	7-9-1	17
	Jack Crawford	1929-35	4-4-3	1-1-1	1-1-1	0-0-0	6-6-5	17
	Adrian Quist	1936-50	3-10-0	0-1-0	0-2-0	0-1-0	3-14-0	17
14	Laurie Doherty	1897-1906	*	*	5-8-0	1-2-0	6-10-0	16
15	Henri Cochet	1922-32	*	4-3-2	2-2-0	1-0-1	7-5-3	15
	Vic Seixas	1952-56	0-1-0	0-2-1	1-0-4	1-2-3	2-5-8	15
	Bob Hewitt	1961-79	0-2-1	0-1-2	0-5-2	0-1-1	0-9-6	15

WOMEN

		Career	Australian	French	Wimbledon	U.S.	S-D-M	Total Titles
1	Margaret Court Smith	1960-75	11-8-2	5-4-4	3-2-5	5-5-8	24-19-19	62
2	Martina Navratilova	1974-95	3-8-0	2-7-2	9-7-2	4-9-2	18-31-6	55
3	Billie Jean King	1961-81	1-0-1	1-1-2	6-10-4	4-5-4	12-16-11	39
4	Margaret du Pont	1941-60	*	2-3-0	1-5-1	3-13-9	6-21-10	37
5	Louise Brough	1942-57	1-1-0	0-3-0	4-5-4	1-12-4	6-21-8	35
	Doris Hart	1948-55	1-1-2	2-5-3	1-4-5	2-4-5	6-14-15	35
7	Helen Wills Moody	1923-38	*	4-2-0	8-3-1	7-4-2	19-9-3	31
8	Elizabeth Ryan	1914-34	*	0-4-0	0-12-7	0-1-2	0-17-9	26
9	Suzanne Lenglen	1919-26	*	6-2-2	6-6-3	0-0-0	12-8-5	25
10	**Steffi Graf**	1982—	4-0-0	5-0-0	7-1-0	5-0-0	21-1-0	22
	Pam Shriver	1981—	0-7-0	0-4-1	0-5-0	0-5-0	0-21-1	22
12	Chris Evert	1974-89	2-0-0	7-2-0	3-1-0	6-0-0	18-3-0	21
	Darlene Hard	1958-69	*	1-3-2	0-4-3	2-6-0	3-13-5	21
14	**Natasha Zvereva**	1989—	0-3-2	0-6-0	0-5-0	0-4-0	0-18-2	20
	Nancye Wynne Bolton	1935-52	6-10-4	0-0-0	0-0-0	0-0-0	6-10-4	20

Annual Number One Players

Unofficial world rankings for men and women determined by the *London Daily Telegraph* from 1914-72. Since then, official world rankings computed by men's and women's tours. Rankings included only amateur players from 1914 until the arrival of open (professional) tennis in 1968. No rankings were released during World Wars I and II.

MEN

Multiple winners: Bill Tilden (6); Jimmy Connors (5); Henri Cochet, Rod Laver, Ivan Lendl, John McEnroe and Pete Sampras (4); John Newcombe and Fred Perry (3); Bjorn Borg, Don Budge, Ashley Cooper, Stefan Edberg, Roy Emerson, Neale Fraser, Jack Kramer, Rene Lacoste, Ilie Nastase, Frank Sedgman and Tony Trabert (2).

Year		Year		Year		Year	
1914	Maurice McLoughlin	1936	Fred Perry	1960	Neale Fraser	1979	Bjorn Borg
1915-18	No rankings	1937	Don Budge	1961	Rod Laver	1980	Bjorn Borg
1919	Gerald Patterson	1938	Don Budge	1962	Rod Laver	1981	John McEnroe
		1939	Bobby Riggs	1963	Rafael Osuna	1982	John McEnroe
1920	Bill Tilden			1964	Roy Emerson	1983	John McEnroe
1921	Bill Tilden	1940-45	No rankings	1965	Roy Emerson	1984	John McEnroe
1922	Bill Tilden	1946	Jack Kramer	1966	Manuel Santana	1985	Ivan Lendl
1923	Bill Tilden	1947	Jack Kramer	1967	John Newcombe	1986	Ivan Lendl
1924	Bill Tilden	1948	Frank Parker	1968	Rod Laver	1987	Ivan Lendl
1925	Bill Tilden	1949	Pancho Gonzales	1969	Rod Laver	1988	Mats Wilander
1926	Rene Lacoste					1989	Ivan Lendl
1927	Rene Lacoste	1950	Budge Patty	1970	John Newcombe		
1928	Henri Cochet	1951	Frank Sedgman	1971	John Newcombe	1990	Stefan Edberg
1929	Henri Cochet	1952	Frank Sedgman	1972	Ilie Nastase	1991	Stefan Edberg
1930	Henri Cochet	1953	Tony Trabert	1973	Ilie Nastase	1992	Jim Courier
1931	Henri Cochet	1954	Jaroslav Drobny	1974	Jimmy Connors	1993	Pete Sampras
1932	Ellsworth Vines	1955	Tony Trabert	1975	Jimmy Connors	1994	Pete Sampras
1933	Jack Crawford	1956	Lew Hoad	1976	Jimmy Connors	1995	Pete Sampras
1934	Fred Perry	1957	Ashley Cooper	1977	Jimmy Connors	1996	Pete Sampras
1935	Fred Perry	1958	Ashley Cooper	1978	Jimmy Connors		
		1959	Neale Fraser				

WOMEN

Multiple winners: Helen Wills Moody (9); Steffi Graf (8); Margaret Smith Court and Martina Navratilova (7); Chris Evert Lloyd (5); Margaret Osborne duPont and Billie Jean King (4); Maureen Connolly and Monica Seles (3); Maria Bueno, Althea Gibson, Suzanne Lenglen (2).

Year		Year		Year		Year	
1925	Suzanne Lenglen	1947	Margaret Osborne	1964	Margaret Smith	1981	Chris Evert Lloyd
1926	Suzanne Lenglen	1948	Margaret duPont	1965	Margaret Smith	1982	Martina Navratilova
1927	Helen Wills	1949	Margaret duPont	1966	Billie Jean King	1983	Martina Navratilova
1928	Helen Wills	1950	Margaret duPont	1967	Billie Jean King	1984	Martina Navratilova
1929	Helen Wills Moody	1951	Doris Hart	1968	Billie Jean King	1985	Martina Navratilova
1930	Helen Wills Moody	1952	Maureen Connolly	1969	Margaret Court	1986	Martina Navratilova
1931	Helen Wills Moody	1953	Maureen Connolly			1987	Steffi Graf
1932	Helen Wills Moody	1954	Maureen Connolly	1970	Margaret Court	1988	Steffi Graf
1933	Helen Wills Moody	1955	Louise Brough	1971	Evonne Goolagong	1989	Steffi Graf
1934	Dorothy Round	1956	Shirley Fry	1972	Billie Jean King		
1935	Helen Wills Moody	1957	Althea Gibson	1973	Margaret Court	1990	Steffi Graf
1936	Helen Jacobs	1958	Althea Gibson	1974	Billie Jean King	1991	Monica Seles
1937	Anita Lizana	1959	Maria Bueno	1975	Chris Evert	1992	Monica Seles
1938	Helen Wills Moody	1960	Maria Bueno	1976	Chris Evert	1993	Steffi Graf
1939	Alice Marble	1961	Angela Mortimer	1977	Chris Evert	1994	Steffi Graf
		1962	Margaret Smith	1978	Martina Navratilova	1995	Steffi Graf
1940-45	No rankings	1963	Margaret Smith	1979	Martina Navratilova		& Monica Seles
1946	Pauline Betz			1980	Chris Evert Lloyd	1996	Steffi Graf

Annual Top 10 World Rankings (since 1968)

Year by year Top 10 world computer rankings for Men (ATP Tour) and Women (WTA Tour) since the arrival of open tennis in 1968. Rankings from 1968-72 made by Lance Tingay of the London Daily Telegraph. Since 1973, computerized rankings by ATP Tour (men) and WTA Tour (women).

MEN

1968

1. Rod Laver
2. Arthur Ashe
3. Ken Rosewall
4. Tom Okker
5. Tony Roche
6. John Newcombe
7. Clark Graebner
8. Dennis Ralston
9. Cliff Drysdale
10. Pancho Gonzales

1969

1. Rod Laver
2. Tony Roche
3. John Newcombe
4. Tom Okker
5. Ken Rosewall
6. Arthur Ashe
7. Cliff Drysdale
8. Pancho Gonzales
9. Andres Gimeno
10. Fred Stolle

1970

1. John Newcombe
2. Ken Rosewall
3. Tony Roche
4. Rod Laver
5. Arthur Ashe
6. Ilie Nastase
7. Tom Okker
8. Roger Taylor
9. Jan Kodes
10. Cliff Richey

1971

1. John Newcombe
2. Stan Smith
3. Rod Laver
4. Ken Rosewall
5. Jan Kodes
6. Arthur Ashe
7. Tom Okker
8. Marty Riessen
9. Cliff Drysdale
10. Ilie Nastase

1972

1. Stan Smith
2. Ken Rosewall
3. Ilie Nastase
4. Rod Laver
5. Arthur Ashe
6. John Newcombe
7. Bob Lutz
8. Tom Okker
9. Marty Riessen
10. Andres Gimeno

1973

1. Ilie Nastase
2. John Newcombe
3. Jimmy Connors
4. Tom Okker
5. Stan Smith
6. Ken Rosewall
7. Manuel Orantes
8. Rod Laver
9. Jan Kodes
10. Arthur Ashe

1974

1. Jimmy Connors
2. John Newcombe
3. Bjorn Borg
4. Rod Laver
5. Guillermo Vilas
6. Tom Okker
7. Arthur Ashe
8. Ken Rosewall
9. Stan Smith
10. Ilie Nastase

1975

1. Jimmy Connors
2. Guillermo Vilas
3. Bjorn Borg
4. Arthur Ashe
5. Manuel Orantes
6. Ken Rosewall
7. Ilie Nastase
8. John Alexander
9. Roscoe Tanner
10. Rod Laver

1976

1. Jimmy Connors
2. Bjorn Borg
3. Ilie Nastase
4. Manuel Orantes
5. Raul Ramirez
6. Guillermo Vilas
7. Adriano Panatta
8. Harold Solomon
9. Eddie Dibbs
10. Brian Gottfried

1977

1. Jimmy Connors
2. Guillermo Vilas
3. Bjorn Borg
4. Vitas Gerulaitis
5. Brian Gottfried
6. Eddie Dibbs
7. Manuel Orantes
8. Raul Ramirez
9. Ilie Nastase
10. Dick Stockton

1978

1. Jimmy Connors
2. Bjorn Borg
3. Guillermo Vilas
4. John McEnroe
5. Vitas Gerulaitis
6. Eddie Dibbs
7. Brian Gottfried
8. Raul Ramirez
9. Harold Solomon
10. Corrado Barazzutti

1979

1. Bjorn Borg
2. Jimmy Connors
3. John McEnroe
4. Vitas Gerulaitis
5. Roscoe Tanner
6. Guillermo Vilas
7. Arthur Ashe
8. Harold Solomon
9. Jose Higueras
10. Eddie Dibbs

Annual Top 10 World Rankings (Cont.)

MEN

1980
1 Bjorn Borg
2 John McEnroe
3 Jimmy Connors
4 Gene Mayer
5 Guillermo Vilas
6 Ivan Lendl
7 Harold Solomon
8 Jose-Luis Clerc
9 Vitas Gerulaitis
10 Eliot Teltscher

1981
1 John McEnroe
2 Ivan Lendl
3 Jimmy Connors
4 Bjorn Borg
5 Jose-Luis Clerc
6 Guillermo Vilas
7 Gene Mayer
8 Eliot Teltscher
9 Vitas Gerulaitis
10 Peter McNamara

1982
1 John McEnroe
2 Jimmy Connors
3 Ivan Lendl
4 Guillermo Vilas
5 Vitas Gerulaitis
6 Jose-Luis Clerc
7 Mats Wilander
8 Gene Mayer
9 Yannick Noah
10 Peter McNamara

1983
1 John McEnroe
2 Ivan Lendl
3 Jimmy Connors
4 Mats Wilander
5 Yannick Noah
6 Jimmy Arias
7 Jose Higueras
8 Jose-Luis Clerc
9 Kevin Curren
10 Gene Mayer

1984
1 John McEnroe
2 Jimmy Connors
3 Ivan Lendl
4 Mats Wilander
5 Andres Gomez
6 Anders Jarryd
7 Henrik Sundstrom
8 Pat Cash
9 Eliot Teltscher
10 Yannick Noah

1985
1 Ivan Lendl
2 John McEnroe
3 Mats Wilander
4 Jimmy Connors
5 Stefan Edberg
6 Boris Becker
7 Yannick Noah
8 Anders Jarryd
9 Miloslav Mecir
10 Kevin Curren

1986
1 Ivan Lendl
2 Boris Becker
3 Mats Wilander
4 Yannick Noah
5 Stefan Edberg
6 Henri Leconte
7 Joakim Nystrom
8 Jimmy Connors
9 Miloslav Mecir
10 Andres Gomez

1987
1 Ivan Lendl
2 Stefan Edberg
3 Mats Wilander
4 Jimmy Connors
5 Boris Becker
6 Miloslav Mecir
7 Pat Cash
8 Yannick Noah
9 Tim Mayotte
10 John McEnroe

1988
1 Mats Wilander
2 Ivan Lendl
3 Andre Agassi
4 Boris Becker
5 Stefan Edberg

6 Kent Carlsson
7 Jimmy Connors
8 Jakob Hlasek
9 Henri Leconte
10 Tim Mayotte

1989
1 Ivan Lendl
2 Boris Becker
3 Stefan Edberg
4 John McEnroe
5 Michael Chang
6 Brad Gilbert
7 Andre Agassi
8 Aaron Krickstein
9 Alberto Mancini
10 Jay Berger

1990
1 Stefan Edberg
2 Boris Becker
3 Ivan Lendl
4 Andre Agassi
5 Pete Sampras
6 Andres Gomez
7 Thomas Muster
8 Emilio Sanchez
9 Goran Ivanisevic
10 Brad Gilbert

1991
1 Stefan Edberg
2 Jim Courier
3 Boris Becker
4 Michael Stich
5 Ivan Lendl
6 Pete Sampras
7 Guy Forget
8 Karel Novacek
9 Petr Korda
10 Andre Agassi

1992
1 Jim Courier
2 Stefan Edberg
3 Pete Sampras
4 Goran Ivanisevic
5 Boris Becker
6 Michael Chang
7 Petr Korda
8 Ivan Lendl

9 Andre Agassi
10 Richard Krajicek

1993
1 Pete Sampras
2 Michael Stich
3 Jim Courier
4 Sergi Bruguera
5 Stefan Edberg
6 Andrei Medvedev
7 Goran Ivanisevic
8 Michael Chang
9 Thomas Muster
10 Cedric Pioline

1994
1 Pete Sampras
2 Andre Agassi
3 Boris Becker
4 Sergi Brugera
5 Goran Ivanisevic
6 Michael Chang
7 Stefan Edberg
8 Alberto Berasategui
9 Michael Stich
10 Todd Martin

1995
1 Pete Sampras
2 Andre Agassi
3 Thomas Muster
4 Boris Becker
5 Michael Chang
6 Yevgeny Kafelnikov
7 Thomas Enqvist
8 Jim Courier
9 Wayne Ferreira
10 Goran Ivanisevic

1996
1 Pete Sampras
2 Michael Chang
3 Yevgeny Kafelnikov
4 Goran Ivanisevic
5 Thomas Muster
6 Boris Becker
7 Richard Krajicek
8 Andre Agassi
9 Thomas Enqvist
10 Wayne Ferreira

WOMEN

1968
1 Billie Jean King
2 Virginia Wade
3 Nancy Richey
4 Maria Bueno
5 Margaret Court
6 Ann Jones
7 Judy Tegart
8 Annette du Plooy
9 Leslie Bowrey
10 Rosie Casals

1969
1 Margaret Court
2 Ann Jones

3 Billie Jean King
4 Nancy Richey
5 Julie Heldman
6 Rosie Casals
7 Kerry Melville
8 Peaches Bartkowicz
9 Virginia Wade
10 Leslie Bowrey

1970
1 Margaret Court
2 Billie Jean King
3 Rosie Casals
4 Virginia Wade
5 Helga Niessen

6 Kerry Melville
7 Julie Heldman
8 Karen Krantzcke
9 Francoise Durr
10 Nancy R. Gunter

1971
1 Evonne Goolagong
2 Billie Jean King
3 Margaret Court
4 Rosie Casals
5 Kerry Melville
6 Virginia Wade
7 Judy Tagert
8 Francoise Durr

9 Helga N. Masthoff
10 Chris Evert

1972
1 Billie Jean King
2 Evonne Goolagong
3 Chris Evert
4 Margaret Court
5 Kerry Melville
6 Virginia Wade
7 Rosie Casals
8 Nancy R. Gunter
9 Francoise Durr
10 Linda Tuero

1973

1 Margaret S. Court
2 Billie Jean King
3 Evonne G. Cawley
4 Chris Evert
5 Rosie Casals
6 Virginia Wade
7 Kerry Reid
8 Nancy Richey
9 Julie Heldman
10 Helga Masthoff

1974

1 Billie Jean King
2 Evonne G. Cawley
3 Chris Evert
4 Virginia Wade
5 Julie Heldman
6 Rosie Casals
7 Kerry Reid
8 Olga Morozova
9 Lesley Hunt
10 Francoise Durr

1975

1 Chris Evert
2 Billie Jean King
3 Evonne G. Cawley
4 Martina Navratilova
5 Virginia Wade
6 Margaret S. Court
7 Olga Morozova
8 Nancy Richey
9 Francoise Durr
10 Rosie Casals

1976

1 Chris Evert
2 Evonne G. Cawley
3 Virginia Wade
4 Martina Navratilova
5 Sue Barker
6 Betty Stove
7 Dianne Balestrat
8 Mima Jausovec
9 Rosie Casals
10 Francoise Durr

1977

1 Chris Evert
2 Billie Jean King
3 Martina Navratilova
4 Virginia Wade
5 Sue Barker
6 Rosie Casals
7 Betty Stove
8 Dianne Balestrat
9 Wendy Turnbull
10 Kerry Reid

1978

1 Martina Navratilova
2 Chris Evert Lloyd
3 Evonne G. Cawley
4 Virginia Wade
5 Billie Jean King
6 Tracy Austin
7 Wendy Turnbull
8 Kerry Reid
9 Betty Stove
10 Dianne Balestrat

1979

1 Martina Navratilova
2 Chris Evert Lloyd
3 Tracy Austin
4 Evonne G. Cawley
5 Billie Jean King
6 Dianne Balestrat
7 Wendy Turnbull
8 Virginia Wade
9 Kerry Reid
10 Sue Barker

1980

1 Chris Evert Lloyd
2 Tracy Austin
3 Martina Navratilova
4 Hana Mandlikova
5 Evonne G. Cawley
6 Billie Jean King
7 Andrea Jaeger
8 Wendy Turnbull
9 Pam Shriver
10 Greer Stevens

1981

1 Chris Evert Lloyd
2 Tracy Austin
3 Martina Navratilova
4 Andrea Jaeger
5 Hana Mandlikova
6 Sylvia Hanika
7 Pam Shriver
8 Wendy Turnbull
9 Bettina Bunge
10 Barbara Potter

1982

1 Martina Navratilova
2 Chris Evert Lloyd
3 Andrea Jaeger
4 Tracy Austin
5 Wendy Turnbull
6 Pam Shriver
7 Hana Mandlikova
8 Barbara Potter
9 Bettina Bunge
10 Sylvia Hanika

1983

1 Martina Navratilova
2 Chris Evert Lloyd
3 Andrea Jaeger
4 Pam Shriver
5 Sylvia Hanika
6 Jo Durie
7 Bettina Bunge
8 Wendy Turnbull
9 Tracy Austin
10 Zina Garrison

1984

1 Martina Navratilova
2 Chris Evert Lloyd
3 Hana Mandlikova
4 Pam Shriver
5 Wendy Turnbull
6 Manuela Maleeva
7 Helena Sukova
8 Claudia Kohde-Kilsch
9 Zina Garrison
10 Kathy Jordan

1985

1 Martina Navratilova
2 Chris Evert Lloyd
3 Hana Mandlikova
4 Pam Shriver
5 Claudia Kohde-Kilsch
6 Steffi Graf
7 Manuela Maleeva
8 Zina Garrison
9 Helena Sukova
10 Bonnie Gadusek

1986

1 Martina Navratilova
2 Chris Evert Lloyd
3 Steffi Graf
4 Hana Mandlikova
5 Helena Sukova
6 Pam Shriver
7 Claudia Kohde-Kilsch
8 M. Maleeva-Fragniere
9 Zina Garrison
10 Claudia Kohde-Kilsch

1987

1 Steffi Graf
2 Martina Navratilova
3 Chris Evert
4 Pam Shriver
5 Hana Mandlikova
6 Gabriela Sabatini
7 Helena Sukova
8 M. Maleeva-Fragniere
9 Zina Garrison
10 Claudia Kohde-Kilsch

1988

1 Steffi Graf
2 Martina Navratilova
3 Chris Evert
4 Gabriela Sabatini
5 Pam Shriver
6 M. Maleeva-Fragniere
7 Natalia Zvereva
8 Helena Sukova
9 Zina Garrison
10 Barbara Potter

1989

1 Steffi Graf
2 Martina Navratilova
3 Gabriela Sabatini
4 Z. Garrison-Jackson
5 A. Sanchez Vicario
6 Monica Seles
7 Conchita Martinez
8 Helena Sukova
9 M. Maleeva-Fragniere
10 Chris Evert

1990

1 Steffi Graf
2 Monica Seles
3 Martina Navratilova
4 Mary Joe Fernandez
5 Gabriela Sabatini
6 Katerina Maleeva
7 A. Sanchez Vicario
8 Jennifer Capriati
9 M. Maleeva-Fragniere
10 Z. Garrison-Jackson

1991

1 Monica Seles
2 Steffi Graf
3 Gabriela Sabatini
4 Martina Navratilova
5 A. Sanchez Vicario
6 Jennifer Capriati
7 Jana Novotna
8 Mary Joe Fernandez
9 Conchita Martinez
10 M. Maleeva-Fragniere

1992

1 Monica Seles
2 Steffi Graf
3 Gabriela Sabatini
4 A. Sanchez Vicario
5 Martina Navratilova
6 Mary Joe Fernandez
7 Jennifer Capriati
8 Conchita Martinez
9 M. Maleeva-Fragniere
10 Jana Novotna

1993

1 Steffi Graf
2 A. Sanchez Vicario
3 Martina Navratilova
4 Conchita Martinez
5 Gabriela Sabatini
6 Jana Novotna
7 Mary Joe Fernandez
8 Monica Seles
9 Jennifer Capriati
10 Anke Huber

1994

1 Steffi Graf
2 A. Sanchez Vicario
3 Conchita Martinez
4 Jana Novotna
5 Mary Pierce
6 Lindsay Davenport
7 Gabriela Sabatini
8 Martina Navratilova
9 Kimiko Date
10 Natasha Zvereva

1995

1 Steffi Graf
  Monica Seles
2 Conchita Martinez
3 A. Sanchez Vicario
4 Kimiko Date
5 Mary Pierce
6 Magdalena Maleeva
7 Gabriela Sabatini
8 Mary Joe Fernandez
9 Iva Majoli
10 Anke Huber

1996

1 Steffi Graf
2 Monica Seles
  A. Sanchez Vicario
3 Jana Novotna
4 Martina Hingis
5 Conchita Martinez
6 Anke Huber
7 Iva Majoli
8 Kimiko Date
9 Lindsay Davenport
10 Barbara Paulus

All-Time Singles Leaders
Tournaments Won

All-time tournament wins from the arrival of open tennis in 1968 through 1996. Men's totals include ATP Tour, Grand Prix and WCT tournaments. Players active in singles play in 1997 are in **bold** type.

MEN

		Total			Total			Total
1	Jimmy Connors	109	11	Stefan Edberg	41	21	**Michael Chang**	26
2	Ivan Lendl	94	12	Stan Smith	39	22	Jose-Luis Clerc	25
3	John McEnroe	77	13	**Andre Agassi**	34		Brian Gottfried	25
4	Bjorn Borg	62	14	Arthur Ashe	33	24	Yannick Noah	23
	Guillermo Vilas	62		**Mats Wilander**	33	25	Eddie Dibbs	22
6	Ilie Nastase	57	16	John Newcombe	32		Harold Solomon	22
7	**Boris Becker**	49		Manuel Orantes	32	27	Andres Gomez	21
8	Rod Laver	47		Ken Rosewall	32	28	Brad Gilbert	20
9	**Pete Sampras**	44	19	Tom Okker	31	29	**Jim Courier**	19
10	**Thomas Muster**	42	20	Vitas Gerulaitis	27	30	**Michael Stich**	18

WOMEN

		Total			Total			Total
1	Martina Navratilova	167	12	Tracy Austin	29	23	Rosie Casals	18
2	Chris Evert	157	13	Hana Mandlikova	27	24	Virginia Ruzici	17
3	**Steffi Graf**	102		Gabriela Sabatini	27		Regina Marsikova	17
4	E. Goolagong Cawley	88	15	Nancy Richey	25		**Jana Novotna**	17
5	Margaret Court	79	16	**A. Sanchez Vicario**	24	27	Sue Barker	15
6	Billie Jean King	67	17	Kerry Melville Reid	22	28	Peaches Bartkowicz	14
7	Virginia Wade	55	18	Sue Barker	21		Andrea Jaeger	14
8	**Monica Seles**	38		Pam Shriver	21		**Sandra Cecchini**	14
9	Helga Masthoff	37	20	Julie Heldman	20		**Z. Garrison Jackson**	14
10	Olga Morozova	31	21	D. Fromholtz Balestrat	19			
	Conchita Martinez	31		M. Maleeva-Fragniere	19			

Money Won

All-time money winners from the arrival of open tennis in 1968 through 1996. Totals include doubles earnings.

MEN

		Earnings			Earnings			Earnings
1	Pete Sampras	$25,562,347	11	Sergi Bruguera	$9,520,901	21	Wayne Ferreira	$5,472,573
2	Boris Becker	23,841,402	12	Thomas Muster	9,474,064	22	Richard Krajicek	5,400,775
3	Ivan Lendl	21,262,417	13	Jimmy Connors	8,641,040	23	Anders Jarryd	5,377,067
4	Stefan Edberg	20,630,941	14	Mats Wilander	7,976,256	24	Emilio Sanchez	5,303,210
5	Goran Ivanisevic	14,748,280	15	Petr Korda	7,524,226	25	David Wheaton	5,048,829
6	Michael Chang	13,744,909	16	Yevgeny Kafelnikov	6,396,984	26	Guillermo Vilas	4,923,882
7	Andre Agassi	12,901,331	17	Jakob Hlasek	5,784,225	27	Todd Woodbridge	4,833,829
8	Jim Courier	12,734,485	18	Guy Forget	5,617,843	28	Paul Haarhuis	4,683,702
9	John McEnroe	12,539,622	19	Mark Woodforde	5,560,554	29	Todd Martin	4,663,699
10	Michael Stich	12,258,416	20	Brad Gilbert	5,507,745	30	Andres Gomez	4,385,040

WOMEN

		Earnings			Earnings			Earnings
1	Mart. Navratilova	$20,344,061	11	Natasha Zvereva	$5,336,043	21	Nathalie Tauziat	$2,414,222
2	Steffi Graf	19,846,316	12	Z. Garrison Jackson	4,587,816	22	Mary Pierce	2,337,870
3	A.S. Vicario	11,632,976	13	Gigi Fernandez	4,226,024	23	Claudia Kohde-Kilsch	2,227,043
4	Monica Seles	8,960,490	14	Mary Jo Fernandez	4,134,754	24	Katerina Maleeva	2,220,371
5	Chris Evert	8,896,195	15	Hana Madlikova	3,340,959	25	Lindsay Davenport	2,159,353
6	Gabriela Sabatini	8,785,850	16	M. Maleeva-Fragniere	3,244,811	26	B. Schulz-McCarthy	2,153,242
7	Jana Novotna	6,572,665	17	Larisa Neiland	3,226,139	27	Tracy Austin	1,992,380
8	Conchita Martinez	6,349,266	18	Lori McNeil	3,176,429	28	Kimiko Date	1,974,253
9	Helena Sukova	5,946,064	19	Wendy Turnbull	2,769,024	29	Billie Jean King	1,966,487
10	Pam Shriver	5,448,686	20	Anke Huber	2,708,585	30	Iva Majoli	1,945,900

Longest Matches

Singles

126 Games–Roger Taylor (GBR) def. Wieslaw Gasiorek (POL), 27-29,31-29, 6-4; King's Cup, Warsaw, 1966.

Doubles

147 Games–Dick Leach and Dick Dell (USA) def. Len Schloss and Tom Mazu (USA), 3-6,49-47, 22-20, 2nd round, Newport Casino, Newport, R.I., 1967.

Year-end Tournaments

MEN

Masters/ATP Tour World Championship

The year-end championship of the ATP men's tour since 1970. Contested by the year's top eight players. Originally a round-robin, the Masters was revised in 1972 to include a round-robin to decide the four semifinalists then a single elimination format after that. The tournament switched from December to January in 1977-78, then back to December in 1986. Held at Madison Square Garden in New York from 1978-89. Replaced by ATP Tour World Championship in 1990 and held in Frankfurt, Germany since then.

Multiple Winners: Ivan Lendl (5); Ilie Nastase (4); Boris Becker, John McEnroe and Pete Sampras (3); Bjorn Borg (2).

Year	Winner		Runner-Up	Year	Winner	Loser	Score
1970	Stan Smith (4-1)		Rod Laver (4-1)	1984	John McEnroe	I. Lendl	63 64 64
1971	Ilie Nastase (6-0)		Stan Smith (4-2)	1985	John McEnroe	I. Lendl	75 60 64

Year	Winner	Loser	Score	Year	Winner	Loser	Score
1972	Ilie Nastase	S. Smith	63 62 36 26 63	1986	Ivan Lendl	B. Becker	62 76 63
1973	Ilie Nastase	T. Okker	63 75 46 63	1986	Ivan Lendl	B. Becker	64 64 64
1974	Guillermo Vilas	I. Nastase	76 62 36 36 64	1987	Ivan Lendl	M. Wilander	62 62 63
1975	Ilie Nastase	B. Borg	62 62 61	1988	Boris Becker	I. Lendl	57 76 36 62 76
1976	Manuel Orantes	W. Fibak	57 62 06 76 61	1989	Stefan Edberg	B. Becker	46 76 63 61
1978	Jimmy Connors	B. Borg	64 16 64				
1979	John McEnroe	A. Ashe	67 63 75	1990	Andre Agassi	S. Edberg	57 76 75 62
				1991	Pete Sampras	J. Courier	36 76 63 64
1980	Bjorn Borg	V. Gerulaitis	62 62	1992	Boris Becker	J. Courier	64 63 75
1981	Bjorn Borg	I. Lendl	64 62 62	1993	Michael Stich	P. Sampras	76 26 76 62
1982	Ivan Lendl	V. Gerulaitis	67 26 76 62 64	1994	Pete Sampras	B. Becker	46 63 75 64
1983	Ivan Lendl	J. McEnroe	64 64 62	1995	Boris Becker	M. Chang	76 60 76
				1996	Pete Sampras	B. Becker	36 76 76 67 64

Note: In 1970, Smith was declared the winner because he beat Laver in their round-robin match (4-6, 6-3, 6-4).

WCT Championship (1971-89)

World Championship Tennis was established in 1967 to promote professional tennis and led the way into the open era. It's major singles and doubles championships were held every May among the top eight regular season finishers on the circuit from 1971 until the WCT folded in 1989.

Mutliple winners: John McEnroe (5), Jimmy Connors, Ivan Lendl and Ken Rosewall (2).

Year	Winner	Loser	Score	Year	Winner	Loser	Score
1971	Ken Rosewall	R. Laver	64 16 76 76	1981	John McEnroe	J. Kriek	61 62 64
1972	Ken Rosewall	R. Laver	46 60 63 67 76	1982	Ivan Lendl	J. McEnroe	62 36 63 63
1973	Stan Smith	A. Ashe	63 63 46 64	1983	John McEnroe	I. Lendl	62 46 63 67 76
1974	John Newcombe	B. Borg	46 63 63 62	1984	John McEnroe	J. Connors	61 62 63
1975	Arthur Ashe	B. Borg	36 64 64 60	1985	Ivan Lendl	T. Mayotte	76 64 61
1976	Bjorn Borg	G. Vilas	16 61 75 61	1986	Anders Jarryd	B. Becker	67 61 61 64
1977	Jimmy Connors	D. Stockton	67 61 64 63	1987	Miloslav Mercir	J. McEnroe	60 36 62 62
1978	Vitas Gerulaitis	E. Dibbs	63 62 61	1988	Boris Becker	S. Edberg	64 16 75 62
1979	John McEnroe	B. Borg	75 46 62 76	1989	John McEnroe	B. Gilbert	63 63 76
1980	Jimmy Connors	J. McEnroe	26 76 61 62				

WOMEN

WTA Tour Championship

Originally the Virginia Slims Championships from 1971-94. The WTA Tour's year-end tournament took place in March from 1972 until 1986 when the WTA decided to adopt a January-to-November playing season. Given the changeover, two championships were held in 1986. Held every year since 1979 at Madison Square Garden in New York.

Multiple winners: Martina Navratilova (8); Steffi Graf (5); Chris Evert (4); Monica Seles (3); Evonne Goolagong and Gabriela Sabatini (2).

Year	Winner	Loser	Score	Year	Winner	Loser	Score
1972	Chris Evert	K. Reid	75 64	1986	M. Navratilova	H. Mandlikova	62 60 36 61
1973	Chris Evert	N. Richey	63 63	1986	M. Navratilova	S. Graf	76 63 62
1974	Evonne Goolagong	C. Evert	63 64	1987	Steffi Graf	G. Sabatini	46 64 60 64
1975	Chris Evert	M. Navratilova	64 62	1988	Gabriela Sabatini	P. Shriver	75 62 62
1976	Evonne Goolagong	C. Evert	63 57 63	1989	Steffi Graf	M. Navratilova	64 75 26 62
1977	Chris Evert	S. Barker	26 61 61	1990	Monica Seles	G. Sabatini	64 57 36 64 62
1978	M. Navratilova	E. Goolagong	76 64	1991	Monica Seles	M. Navratilova	64 36 75 60
1979	M. Navratilova	T. Austin	63 36 62	1992	Monica Seles	M. Navratilova	75 63 61
1980	Tracy Austin	M. Navratilova	62 26 62	1993	Steffi Graf	A. S. Vicario	61 64 36 61
1981	M. Navratilova	A. Jaeger	63 76	1994	Gabriela Sabatini	L. Davenport	63 62 64
1982	Sylvia Hanika	M. Navratilova	16 63 64	1995	Steffi Graf	A. Huber	61 26 61 46 63
1983	M. Navratilova	C. Evert	62 60	1996	Steffi Graf	M. Hingis	63 46 60 46 60
1984	M. Navratilova	C. Evert	63 75 61				
1985	M. Navratilova	H. Sukova	63 75 64		*Two tournaments in 1986 due to change in playing season.		

Mike Powell/Allsport

The 1992 U.S. Davis Cup team that beat Switzerland in the final at Fort Worth, Texas (from left to right): singles players **Andre Agassi** and **Jim Courier**, doubles partners **John McEnroe** and **Pete Sampras**, and non-playing captain **Tom Gorman**. The Americans beat the Swiss, 3-1, for their 30th Davis Cup title since 1900.

Davis Cup

Established in 1900 as an annual international tournament by American player Dwight Davis. Originally called the International Lawn Tennis Challenge Trophy. Challenge round system until 1972. Since 1981, the top 16 nations in the world have played a straight knockout tournament over the course of a year. The format is a best-of-five match of two singles, one doubles and two singles over three days. Note that from 1900–24 Australia and New Zealand competed together as Australasia.

Multiple winners: USA (31); Australia (20); France (8); Australasia (6); British Isles and Sweden (5); Britain (4); Germany (3).

Challenge Rounds

Year	Winner	Loser	Score	Site	Year	Winner	Loser	Score	Site
1900	USA	British Isles	3-0	Boston	1929	France	USA	3-2	Paris
1901	Not held				1930	France	USA	4-1	Paris
1902	USA	British Isles	3-2	New York	1931	France	Britain	3-2	Paris
1903	British Isles	USA	4-1	Boston	1932	France	USA	3-2	Paris
1904	British Isles	Belgium	5-0	Wimbledon	1933	Britain	France	3-2	Paris
1905	British Isles	USA	5-0	Wimbledon	1934	Britain	USA	4-1	Wimbledon
1906	British Isles	USA	5-0	Wimbledon	1935	Britain	USA	5-0	Wimbledon
1907	Australasia	British Isles	3-2	Wimbledon	1936	Britain	Australia	3-2	Wimbledon
1908	Australasia	USA	3-2	Melbourne	1937	USA	Britain	4-1	Wimbledon
1909	Australasia	USA	5-0	Sydney	1938	USA	Australia	3-2	Philadelphia
1910	Not held				1939	Australia	USA	3-2	Philadelphia
1911	Australasia	USA	5-0	Christchurch, NZ	1940-45	Not held	World War II		
1912	British Isles	Australasia	3-2	Melbourne	1946	USA	Australia	5-0	Melbourne
1913	USA	British Isles	3-2	Wimbledon	1947	USA	Australia	4-1	New York
1914	Australasia	USA	3-2	New York	1948	USA	Australia	5-0	New York
1915-18	Not held	World War I			1949	USA	Australia	4-1	New York
1919	Australasia	British Isles	4-1	Sydney	1950	Australia	USA	4-1	New York
1920	USA	Australasia	5-0	Auckland, NZ	1951	Australia	USA	3-2	Sydney
1921	USA	Japan	5-0	New York	1952	Australia	USA	4-1	Adelaide
1922	USA	Australasia	4-1	New York	1953	Australia	USA	3-2	Melbourne
1923	USA	Australasia	4-1	New York	1954	USA	Australia	3-2	Sydney
1924	USA	Australia	5-0	Philadelphia	1955	Australia	USA	5-0	New York
1925	USA	France	5-0	Philadelphia	1956	Australia	USA	5-0	Adelaide
1926	USA	France	4-1	Philadelphia	1957	Australia	USA	3-2	Melbourne
1927	France	USA	3-2	Philadelphia	1958	USA	Australia	3-2	Brisbane
1928	France	USA	4-1	Paris	1959	Australia	USA	3-2	New York

Year	Winner	Loser	Score	Site	Year	Winner	Loser	Score	Site
1960	Australia	Italy	4-1	Sydney	1964	Australia	USA	3-2	Cleveland
1961	Australia	Italy	5-0	Melbourne	1965	Australia	Spain	4-1	Sydney
1962	Australia	Mexico	5-0	Brisbane	1966	Australia	India	4-1	Melbourne
1963	USA	Australia	3-2	Adelaide	1967	Australia	Spain	4-1	Brisbane

Final Rounds

Year	Winner	Loser	Score	Site	Year	Winner	Loser	Score	Site
1968	USA	Australia	4-1	Adelaide	1982	USA	France	4-1	Grenoble
1969	USA	Romania	5-0	Cleveland	1983	Australia	Sweden	3-2	Melbourne
1970	USA	W. Germany	5-0	Cleveland	1984	Sweden	USA	4-1	Göteborg
1971	USA	Romania	3-2	Charlotte	1985	Sweden	W. Germany	3-2	Munich
1972	USA	Romania	3-2	Bucharest	1986	Australia	Sweden	3-2	Melbourne
1973	Australia	USA	5-0	Cleveland	1987	Sweden	India	5-0	Göteborg
1974	So. Africa	India	walkover	Not held	1988	W. Germany	Sweden	4-1	Göteborg
1975	Sweden	Czech.	3-2	Stockholm	1989	W. Germany	Sweden	3-2	Stuttgart
1976	Italy	Chile	4-1	Santiago	1990	USA	Australia	3-2	St. Petersburg
1977	Australia	Italy	3-1	Sydney	1991	France	USA	3-1	Lyon
1978	USA	Britain	4-1	Palm Springs	1992	USA	Switzerland	3-1	Ft. Worth
1979	USA	Italy	5-0	San Francisco	1993	Germany	Australia	4-1	Dusseldorf
1980	Czech.	Italy	4-1	Prague	1994	Sweden	Russia	4-1	Moscow
1981	USA	Argentina	3-1	Cincinnati	1995	USA	Russia	3-2	Moscow
					1996	France	Sweden	3-2	Malmo

Note: In 1974, India refused to play the final as a protest against the South African government's policies of apartheid.

Fed Cup

Originally the Federation Cup and started in 1963 by the International Tennis Federation as the Davis Cup of women's tennis. Played by 32 teams over one week at one site through 1994. Tournament changed in 1995 to Davis Cup-style format of four rounds and home site.

Multiple winners: USA (15); Australia (7); Czechoslovakia (5); Spain (4); Germany (2).

Year	Winner	Loser	Score	Site	Year	Winner	Loser	Score	Site
1963	USA	Australia	2-1	London	1981	USA	Britain	3-0	Tokyo
1964	Australia	USA	2-1	Philadelphia	1982	USA	W. Germany	3-0	Santa Clara
1965	Australia	USA	2-1	Melbourne	1983	Czech.	W. Germany	2-1	Zurich
1966	USA	W. Germany	3-0	Italy	1984	Czech.	Australia	2-1	Brazil
1967	USA	Britain	2-0	W. Germany	1985	Czech.	USA	2-1	Japan
1968	Australia	Holland	3-0	Paris	1986	US	Czech.	3-0	Prague
1969	USA	Australia	2-1	Athens	1987	W. Germany	USA	2-1	Vancouver
1970	Australia	Britain	3-0	W. Germany	1988	Czech.	USSR	2-1	Melbourne
1971	Australia	Britain	3-0	Perth	1989	USA	Spain	3-0	Tokyo
1972	So. Africa	Britain	2-1	Africa	1990	USA	USSR	2-1	Atlanta
1973	Australia	So. Africa	3-0	W. Germany	1991	Spain	USA	2-1	Nottingham
1974	Australia	USA	2-1	Italy	1992	Germany	Spain	2-1	Frankfurt
1975	Czech.	Australia	3-0	France	1993	Spain	Australia	3-0	Frankfurt
1976	USA	Australia	2-1	Philadelphia	1994	Spain	USA	3-0	Frankfurt
1977	USA	Australia	2-1	Eastbourne	1995	Spain	USA	3-2	Valencia
1978	USA	Australia	2-1	Melbourne	1996	USA	Spain	5-0	Atlantic City
1979	USA	Australia	3-0	Spain	1997	France	Netherlands	4-1	Nice, France
1980	USA	Australia	3-0	W. Germany					

Maiden and Married Names of Women's Champions

Maiden Name	Married Name	Maiden Name	Married Name
Blanche Bingley	Blanche Hillyard	Hazel Hotchkiss	Hazel Wightman
Molla Bjurstedt	Molla Mallory	Hilde Krahwinkel	Hilde Sperling
Patricia Canning	Patricia Todd	Kerry Melville	Kerry Reid
Mary Carter	Mary Raitano	Kathleen McKane	Kathleen Godfrey
Charlotte Cooper	Charlotte Sterry	Billie Jean Moffitt	Billie Jean King
Thelma Coyne	Thelma Long	Margaret Osborne	Margaret duPont
Dorothea Douglass	Dorothea Lambert Chambers	Sarah Palfrey	Sarah Fabyan Cooke
Chris Evert	Chris Evert Lloyd	Margaret Smith	Margaret Smith Court
Evonne Goolagong	Evonne Cawley	Helen Wills	Helen Wills Moody
Louise Hammond	Louise Raymond	Nancye Wynne	Nancye Bolton
Ann Haydon	Ann Haydon Jones		

COLLEGES

NCAA team titles were not sanctioned until 1946. NCAA women's individual and team championships started in 1982.

Men's NCAA Individual Champions (1883-1945)

Multiple winners: Malcolm Chace and Pancho Segura (3); Edward Chandler, George Church, E.B. Dewhurst, Fred Hovey, Frank Guernsey, W.P. Knapp, Robert LeRoy, P.S. Sears, Cliff Sutter, Ernest Sutter and Richard Williams (2).

Year		Year		Year	
1883	J. Clark, Harvard (spring)	1903	E.B. Dewhurst, Penn	1925	Edward Chandler, Calif.
	H. Taylor, Harvard (fall)	1904	Robert LeRoy, Columbia	1926	Edward Chandler, Calif.
1884	W.P. Knapp, Yale	1905	E.B. Dewhurst, Penn	1927	Wilmer Allison, Texas
1885	W.P. Knapp, Yale	1906	Robert LeRoy, Columbia	1928	Julius Seligson, Lehigh
1886	G.M. Brinley, Trinity, CT	1907	G.P. Gardner Jr, Harvard	1929	Berkeley Bell, Texas
1887	P.S. Sears, Harvard	1908	Nat Niles, Harvard	1930	Cliff Sutter, Tulane
1888	P.S. Sears, Harvard	1909	Wallace Johnson, Penn	1931	Keith Gledhill, Stanford
1889	R.P. Huntington Jr, Yale	1910	R.A. Holden Jr, Yale	1932	Cliff Sutter, Tulane
1890	Fred Hovey, Harvard	1911	E.H. Whitney, Harvard	1933	Jack Tidball, UCLA
1891	Fred Hovey, Harvard	1912	George Church, Princeton	1934	Gene Mako, USC
1892	William Larned, Cornell	1913	Richard Williams, Harv.	1935	Wilbur Hess, Rice
1893	Malcolm Chace, Brown	1914	George Church, Princeton	1936	Ernest Sutter, Tulane
1894	Malcolm Chace, Yale	1915	Richard Williams, Harv.	1937	Ernest Sutter, Tulane
1895	Malcolm Chace, Yale	1916	G.C. Caner, Harvard	1938	Frank Guernsey, Rice
1896	Malcolm Whitman, Harvard	1917-1918	Not held	1939	Frank Guernsey, Rice
1897	S.G. Thompson, Princeton	1919	Charles Garland, Yale	1940	Don McNeill, Kenyon
1898	Leo Ware, Harvard	1920	Lascelles Banks, Yale	1941	Joseph Hunt, Navy
1899	Dwight Davis, Harvard	1921	Philip Neer, Stanford	1942	Fred Schroeder, Stanford
1900	Ray Little, Princeton	1922	Lucien Williams, Yale	1943	Pancho Segura, Miami-FL
1901	Fred Alexander, Princeton	1923	Carl Fischer, Phi. Osteo.	1944	Pancho Segura, Miami-FL
1902	William Clothier, Harvard	1924	Wallace Scott, Wash.	1945	Pancho Segura, Miami-FL

NCAA Men's Division I Champions

Multiple winners (Teams): Stanford, UCLA and USC (15); Georgia and William & Mary (2). (Players): Alex Olmedo, Mikael Pernfors, Dennis Ralston and Ham Richardson (2).

Year	Team winner	Individual Champion	Year	Team winner	Individual Champion
1946	USC	Bob Falkenburg, USC	1972	Trinity-TX	Dick Stockton, Trinity-TX
1947	Wm. & Mary	Garner Larned, Wm.& Mary	1973	Stanford	Alex Mayer, Stanford
1948	Wm. & Mary	Harry Likas, San Francisco	1974	Stanford	John Whitlinger, Stanford
1949	San Francisco	Jack Tuero, Tulane	1975	UCLA	Bill Martin, UCLA
1950	UCLA	Herbert Flam, UCLA	1976	USC & UCLA	Bill Scanlon, Trinity-TX
1951	USC	Tony Trabert, Cinncinati	1977	Stanford	Matt Mitchell, Stanford
1952	UCLA	Hugh Stewart, USC	1978	Stanford	John McEnroe, Stanford
1953	UCLA	Ham Richardson, Tulane	1979	UCLA	Kevin Curren, Texas
1954	UCLA	Ham Richardson, Tulane	1980	Stanford	Robert Van't Hof, USC
1955	USC	Jose Aguero, Tulane	1981	Stanford	Tim Mayotte, Stanford
1956	UCLA	Alex Olmedo, USC	1982	UCLA	Mike Leach, Michigan
1957	Michigan	Barry MacKay, Michigan	1983	Stanford	Greg Holmes, Utah
1958	USC	Alex Olmedo, USC	1984	UCLA	Mikael Pernfors, Georgia
1959	Tulane & Notre Dame	Whitney Reed, San Jose St.	1985	Georgia	Mikael Pernfors, Georgia
1960	UCLA	Larry Nagler, UCLA	1986	Stanford	Dan Goldie, Stanford
1961	UCLA	Allen Fox, UCLA	1987	Georgia	Andrew Burrow, Miami-FL
1962	USC	Rafael Osuna, USC	1988	Stanford	Robby Weiss, Pepperdine
1963	USC	Dennis Ralston, USC	1989	Stanford	Donni Leaycraft, LSU
1964	USC	Dennis Ralston, USC	1990	Stanford	Steve Bryan, Texas
1965	UCLA	Arthur Ashe, UCLA	1991	USC	Jared Palmer, Stanford
1966	USC	Charlie Pasarell, UCLA	1992	Stanford	Alex O'Brien Stanford
1967	USC	Bob Lutz, USC	1993	USC	Chris Woodruff, Tennessee
1968	USC	Stan Smith, USC	1994	USC	Mark Merklein, Florida
1969	USC	Joaquin Loyo-Mayo, USC	1995	Stanford	Sargis Sargisian, Ariz. St.
1970	UCLA	Jeff Borowiak, UCLA	1996	Stanford	Cecil Mamiit, USC
1971	UCLA	Jimmy Connors, UCLA	1997	Stanford	Luke Smith, UNLV

NCAA Women's Division I Champions

Multiple winners (Teams): Stanford (9); Florida, Texas and USC (2). (Players): Sandra Birch, Patty Fendick and Lisa Raymond (2).

Year	Team winner	Individual Champion	Year	Team winner	Individual Champion
1982	Stanford	Alycia Moulton, Stanford	1990	Stanford	Debbie Graham, Stanford
1983	USC	Beth Herr, USC	1991	Stanford	Sandra Birch, Stanford
1984	Stanford	Lisa Spain, Georgia	1992	Florida	Lisa Raymond, Florida
1985	USC	Linda Gates, Stanford	1993	Texas	Lisa Raymond, Florida
1986	Stanford	Patty Fendick, Stanford	1994	Georgia	Angela Lettiere, Georgia
1987	Stanford	Patty Fendick, Stanford	1995	Texas	Keri Phoebus, UCLA
1988	Stanford	Shaun Stafford, Florida	1996	Florida	Jill Craybas, Florida
1989	Stanford	Sandra Birch, Stanford	1997	Stanford	Lilia Osterloh, Stanford

Golf

1997 European Ryder Cup captain **Seve Ballesteros** kisses the Ryder Cup after his team beat the favored American team at Valderrama, Spain.

Wide World Photos

Youth Movement

Led by Tiger Woods, Ernie Els, and Justin Leonard, a new generation of golfers arrived in 1997.

by
Mike Tirico

From the twenty-somethings to Generation Next to Tiger-mania, 1997 will go down as a year in which golf's youth provided a profound boost in the sport's popularity. And while many contributed to this youth movement, which by the way is as cyclical as the American economy, one golfer personified the new frontier of the sport, Eldrick "Tiger" Woods.

As the season started in California, Woods was already armed with more than most professional golfers ever achieve. But in addition to two titles earned in his first professional season and more endorsement dollars than most established all-time greats ever garner, Woods also carried grandiose expectations. Many doubted that this tutored-since-youth son of a Vietnam Vet could dominate the pro game with the same aggressive and head-turning manner he conquered the amateur ranks. But with Team Tiger and that

quality that can be found in the greats of all sports, a percolating, intense, inner desire to be a champion, Woods amazed the sport.

The 21-year-old Woods became the fastest to reach one and two million dollars in career earnings by winning the season-opening Tournament of Champions, and then the Byron Nelson Classic and the Western Open.

He won with bravado, without his best game and with a month and half off between tournaments. But nothing will top the way Tiger Woods won the Masters.

Those of us privileged to be at Augusta will never forget that special week when the Masters was dominated like never before. Long-time and first-time observers were equally amazed. While racial inequality has always been a part of the story in golf, Woods' performance should go down in history only on its golf merits. Still, the combination of Tiger's multiracial background, his total dominance and

Mike Tirico covers golf for ESPN.

There is a youth movement afoot in professional golf and **Tiger Woods** (l) and **Ernie Els** (r) are in the forefront. The two stars are shown chatting before teeing off on the second hole of the first round of the 1997 PGA Championship at Winged Foot.

Augusta National's legacy led to the largest television audience ever for a golf broadcast.

Later in the year, Woods had bright moments in both the U.S. and British Opens, but was never a part of the equation on Sunday's back nine in any other major.

It was the other headline acts in the twenty-something gang that took those spotlights. South African Ernie Els won his second U.S. Open and followed it with a win the next week at the Buick Classic. Texan Justin Leonard equaled the greatest final-round comeback in the 125–year history of the British Open to bring the Claret Jug back to the States.

But Leonard's Open Championship victory was the only proud moment for the Yanks on European soil. Despite a big buildup and many pundits predicting that the young Americans would lead the U.S. over Europe in the Ryder Cup, Seve Ballesteros captained the European's successful effort to retain the Cup in a match played in his homeland at Valderrama, Spain. The golfing youth of Europe outperformed the Red, White, and Blue whiz kids. America's Ryder Cup disappointment will trace back to the paltry one and a half points earned by the three Americans who won Major Championships in '97, Woods, Leonard, and Davis Love III.

Australian **Karrie Webb** kisses the champion's trophy she won at the 1997 Weetabix Women's British Open at Sunningdale, England. Webb had a 19-under par final score of 269.

Love's win at the PGA Championship fit under several headings. It removed that un-desired tag of "best player never to win a major" from one of the most likable tour players. Love's victory also provided the golf image of the year as he holed his final putt on the 18th hole, with a rainbow framing the new champion. While Love, and two-time winners Greg Norman and Steve Elkington served as reminders that experience still counts for a lot in golf, it is clear that the game's future stars have arrived. There is depth in the young golf ranks, too, with Phil Mickelson, Jim Furyk, Paul Stankowski, Tommy Tolles and David Duval on the list with Woods and Leonard.

On the LPGA tour, the player of the year was the remarkable Annika Sorenstam who, at press time, had won five tournaments and over a million dollars in prize money. Karrie Webb also had a solid year with three victories including the Weetabix Women's British Open. At 26 and 24 respectively, Sorenstam and Webb constitute a youth movement of their own. The majors, however went to other golfers. Betsy King won the Nabisco Dinah Shore, Chris Johnson took the McDonald's LPGA Championship, Alison Nicholas won the U.S. Women's Open and Colleen Walker was victorious at the du Maurier Ltd Classic.

If it weren't for Tiger Woods, the hot, young golfer of 1997 would have been **Justin Leonard**, holding the Claret Jug he won at the 1997 British Open. Leonard also won the Kemper Open and earned over $1.5 million in prize money.

What is the impact of Woods and company? Consider the number of children who picked up a golf club for the first time this year. It is a number hard to quantify but most around the game will tell you attendance at their youth clinic's sky-rocketed after Woods' Masters victory. Go to one of these clinics and you notice one thing; in 1997 golf became cool. And cool is the youthful version of the Good Housekeeping Seal. One could theorize that this youthful approval will get more athletic children who were football, baseball, and basketball bound, more involved in golf. So, 1997's true impact on the sport may not be answered until 2017. ■

Mike Tirico's Top Highlights of the Year in Golf

10. **Terry-Jo Myers**, after dealing with painful bladder disease that nearly lead to her committing suicide, wins two LPGA events

9. **Steve Elkington** dominates March with two wins, one a runaway at the Players' Championship.

8. **Karrie Webb** shoots 62 to win Women's British Open

7. **Hale Irwin's** dominant senior tour season highlighted by lapping the field at PGA Seniors.

6. **Ernie Els** wins 2nd U.S. Open and wins the following week at

the Buick Classic in Westchester, NY, which he had won the year before by eight strokes.

5. **Davis Love III** wins an emotional first major at the PGA at Winged Foot in Mamaroneck, NY.

4. **Nancy Lopez** comes up 1 shot short of first U.S. Open title.

3. **A victorious Justin Leonard** equals best final day comeback in British Open history.

2. **Europeans** retain Ryder Cup with a superb second day at Valderrama, Spain.

1. **Tiger Woods** dominates the field at Masters. ■

THE **NUMBERS**

INSIDE

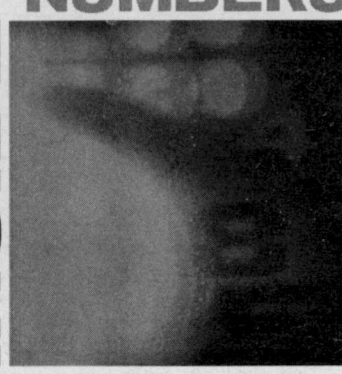

by
Craig Wachs and Steve Rutkowski

MASTERSFUL

Part of the attention drawn by Tiger Woods comes from the fact that he is not just another good white golfer. Woods' stunning victory at the 1997 Masters came 36 years after the first black man, Charles Sifford, played on the PGA tour and 22 years after Lee Elder became the first black to play at Augusta National Golf Course. So, the racial angle is legitimate, though perhaps overplayed. Remember that some of the hype developed because Woods also set some impressive Masters tournament records that weekend. It's the golf, stupid.

Tiger's Masters Marks

Youngest Masters winner	21 years
Widest victory margin	12 strokes
Lowest 72 hole score	270

KIDDING AROUND

While Tiger Woods is the youngest golfer ever to win the Masters, he is the oldest of the four youngsters who have won a major tournament. In any event, Woods is the youngest player to win a major since Tom Creavy won the PGA at 20 in 1931.

Youngest champions at each major

Major	Player	Age
1868 British Open	Young Tom Morris	17 yrs, 5 mos, 8 days
1911 U.S. Open	John J. McDermott	19 yrs, 10 mos, 14 days
1922 PGA	Gene Sarazen	20 yrs, 5 mos, 22 days
1997 Masters	**Tiger Woods**	**21 yrs, 3 mos, 14 days**

GREEN WITH ENVY

After missing the cut in 1996 as a 20 year-old amateur, Tiger Woods won the event in his first try as a pro. In 1963, Jack Nicklaus won his first Masters at 23 years and two months which was a record at the time and stood until Seve Ballesteros won in 1980 at 23 years and four days. Here is a look at how some golfers associated with Augusta performed the first time they played there as a pro.

My First Masters

Tiger Woods 1997	1st
Greg Norman 1981	4th
Tom Watson 1975	T-8th
Jack Nicklaus 1962	T-15th
Arnold Palmer 1955	T-10th

■

Tournament Results

Winners of PGA, European PGA, PGA Seniors and LPGA tournaments from Nov. 3, 1996 through Oct. 5, 1997.

PGA Tour

LATE 1996

Last Rd	Tournament	Winner	Earnings	Runner-Up
Nov. 3	World Open Championship	Frank Nobilo (272)	$342,000	S. Hoch (276)
Nov. 10	Kapalua International	Paul Stankowski (269)	216,000	F. Couples (270)
Nov. 13	PGA Grand Slam	Tom Lehman (134)	400,000	S. Jones (136)
Nov. 17	Shark Shootout	Jay Haas/ Tom Kite (187)	150,000 (each)	Stadler/Watkins & Irwin/Janzen (189)
Nov. 24	World Cup of Golf	S. AFR.—Ernie Els/ Wayne Westner (547)	200,000 (each)	USA—S. Jones/ T. Lehman (565)
Dec. 1	The Skins Game	Fred Couples (9 skins)	280,000	Tom Watson (7 skins)
Dec. 8	JC Penney Classic	Mile Hulbert/ Donna Andrews (197)#	375,000	Woods/Kuehne & Edwards/McGeorge (198)
Dec. 15	Diners Club Matches	Tom Lehman/ Duffy Waldorf (2 & 1)	110,000 (each)	Scott Hoch/ Kenny Perry

Weather shortened

1997 (through Oct. 5)

Last Rd	Tournament	Winner	Earnings	Runner-Up
Jan. 12	Mercedes Championship	Tiger Woods (202)#*	$216,000	T. Lehman (202)
Jan. 19	Bob Hope Chrysler Classic	John Cook (327)	270,000	M. Calcavecchia (328)
Jan. 26	Phoenix Open	Steve Jones (258)	270,000	J. Parnevik (269)
Feb. 2	AT&T Pebble Beach National Pro-Am	Mark O'Meara (268)	342,000	D. Duval & T. Woods (269)
Feb. 9	Buick Invitational	Mark O'Meara (275)	270,000	7-way tie (277)
Feb. 16	United Airlines Hawaii Open	Paul Stankowski (271)*	216,000	J. Furyk & M. Reid (271)
Feb. 23	Tucson Chrysler Classic	Jeff Sluman (275)	234,000	S. Jones (276)
Mar. 2	Nissan Open	Nick Faldo (272)	252,000	C. Stadler (275)
Mar. 9	Doral-Ryder Open	Steve Elkington (275)	324,000	L. Nelson & N. Price (277)
Mar. 16	Honda Classic	Stuart Appleby (274)	270,000	M. Bradley & P. Stewart (275)
Mar. 23	Bay Hill Invitational	Phil Mickelson (272)	270,000	S. Appleby (275)
Mar. 30	The Players Championship	Steve Elkington (272)	630,000	S. Hoch (279)
Apr. 6	Freeport-McDermott Classic	Brad Faxon (272)	270,000	B. Glasson & J. Parnevik (275)
Apr. 13	**The Masters** (Augusta)	Tiger Woods (270)	486,000	T. Kite (282)
Apr. 20	MCI Classic	Nick Price (269)	270,000	J. Parnevik & B. Faxon (275)
Apr. 27	Greater Greensboro Chrysler Classic	Frank Nobilo (274)*	342,000	B. Faxon (274)
May 4	Shell Houston Open	Phil Blackmar (276)*	288,000	K. Sutherland (276)
May 11	BellSouth Classic	Scott McCarron (274)	270,000	3-way tie (277)
May 18	GTE Byron Nelson Classic	Tiger Woods (263)	324,000	L. Rinker (265)
May 25	Mastercard Colonial	David Frost (265)	288,000	B. Faxon & D. Ogrin (267)
June 1	Memorial Tournament	Vijay Singh (202)#	324,000	G. Norman & J. Furyk (204)
June 8	Kemper Open	Justin Leonard (274)	270,000	M. Wiebe (275)
June 15	**U.S. Open** (Bethesda)	Ernie Els (276)	465,000	C. Montgomerie (277)
June 22	Buick Classic	Ernie Els (268)	270,000	J. Maggert (270)
June 29	FedEx St. Jude Classic	Greg Norman (268)	270,000	D. Hart (269)
July 6	Motorola Western Open	Tiger Woods (275)	360,000	F. Nobilo (278)
July 13	Quad City Classic	David Toms (265)	243,000	3-way tie (268)
July 20	**British Open** (Royal Troon)	Justin Leonard (272)	418,875	D. Clarke & J. Parnevik (275)
July 20	Deposit Guaranty Golf Classic	Billy Ray Brown (271)	180,000	M. Standly (272)

Tournament Results (Cont.)

Last Rd	Tournament	Winner	Earnings	Runner-Up
July 27	Canon Greater Hartford Open	Stewart Cink (267)	$270,000	3-way tie (268)
Aug. 3	The Sprint International	Phil Mickelson (48)†	306,000	S. Appleby (41)
Aug. 10	Buick Open	Vijay Singh (273)	270,000	6-way tie (277)
Aug. 17	**PGA Championship** (Mamaronek)	Davis Love III (269)	470,000	J. Leonard (274)
Aug. 24	NEC World Series of Golf	Greg Norman (273)	396,000	P. Mickelson (277)
Aug. 24	Greater Vancouver Open	Mark Calcavecchia (265)	270,000	A. Magee (266)
Aug. 31	Greater Milwaukee Open	Scott Hoch (268)	234,000	L. Roberts & D. Sutherland (269)
Sept. 7	Bell Canadian Open	Steve Jones (275)	270,000	G. Norman (276)
Sept. 14	CVS Charity Classic	Loren Roberts (266)	216,000	B. Glasson (267)
Sept. 21	LaCantera Texas Open	Tim Herron (271)	252,000	R. Fehr & B. Geiberger (273)
Sept. 28	B.C. Open	Gabriel Hjerstedt (275)	234,000	3-way tie (276)
Sept. 28	Ryder Cup (Valderrama)	Europe (14½)		USA (13½)
Oct. 5	Buick Challenge	Davis Love III (267)	216,000	S. Cink (271)

(See Updates Chapter for later results.)

#Weather-shortened.

†The scoring for the Sprint International was based on a modified Stableford system (8 points for a double eagle, 5 for an eagle, 2 for a birdie, 0 for a par, −1 for a bogey, −3 for double bogey or worse.

*Playoffs (4): Mercedes— Woods won on the 1st hole; **Hawaiian**— Stankowski beat Furyk on the 4th hole; Reid was eliminated on the 1st hole; **Greensboro**—Nobilo won on the 1st hole; **Shell Houston Open**—Blackmar won on the 1st hole.

Second place ties (3 players or more): 7-WAY— **Buick Inv.** (D. Ogrin, D. Waldorf, D. Hammond, L. Janzen, J. Parnevik, C. Stadler, M. Hulbert). 6-WAY— **Buick Open** (R, Cochran, T. Byrum, J. Ozaki, B. Fabel, E. Els, C. Strange). 3-WAY— **BellSouth** (L. Janzen, B. Henninger, D. Duval); **Quad City** (B. Chamblee, R. Gamez, J. Johnston); **Greater Hartford** (T. Byrum, B. Chamblee, J. Maggert); **B.C. Open** (L. Rinker, C. Perry, A. Magee).

PGA Majors

The Masters

Edition: 61st   **Dates:** April 10–13
Site: Augusta National GC, Augusta, Ga.
Par: 36-36—72 (6925 yards)   **Purse:** $2,500,000

		1	2	3	4	Tot	Earnings
1	Tiger Woods	70	66	65	69	270	$486,000
2	Tom Kite	77	69	66	70	282	291,600
3	Tommy Tolles	72	72	72	67	283	183,600
4	Tom Watson	75	68	69	72	284	129,600
5	Paul Stankowski	68	74	69	74	285	102,600
	Costantino Rocca	71	69	70	75	285	102,600
7	Jeff Sluman	74	67	72	73	286	78,570
	Fred Couples	72	69	73	72	286	78,570
	Davis Love III	72	71	72	71	286	78,570
	Justin Leonard	76	69	71	70	286	78,570
	Bernhard Langer	72	72	74	68	286	78,570

Early round leaders: 1st— John Huston (67); 2nd— Woods (136); 3rd— Woods (201).

Top amateur: none.

U.S. Open

Edition: 97th   **Dates:** June 12–15
Site: Congressional CC., Bethesda, MD
Par: 35-35—70 (7213 yards)   **Purse:** $2,600,000

		1	2	3	4	Tot	Earnings
1	Ernie Els	71	67	69	69	276	$465,000
2	Colin Montgomerie	65	76	67	69	277	275,000
3	Tom Lehman	67	70	68	73	278	172,828
4	Jeff Maggert	73	66	68	74	281	120,454
5	Bob Tway	71	71	70	70	282	79,875
	Olin Browne	71	71	69	71	282	79,875
	Jay Haas	73	69	68	72	282	79,875
	Tommy Tolles	74	67	69	72	282	79,875
9	Scott McCarron	73	71	69	70	283	56,949
	Scott Hoch	71	68	72	72	283	56,949
	Jim Furyk	74	68	69	72	283	56,949
	David Ogrin	70	69	71	73	283	56,949

Early round leaders: 1st— Montgomerie (65); 2nd— Lehman (137); 3rd— Lehman (205).

Top amateur: none.

British Open

Edition: 126th   **Dates:** July 17–20
Site: Royal Troon; Troon Ayrshire, Scotland
Par: 36-35—71 (7079 yards)   **Purse:** $2,699,680 (US)

		1	2	3	4	Tot	Earnings
1	Justin Leonard	69	66	72	65	272	$418,875
2	Jesper Parnevik	70	66	66	72	275	251,325
	Darren Clarke	67	66	71	68	275	251,325
4	Jim Furyk	67	72	70	70	279	150,795
5	Padraig Harrington	75	69	69	67	280	104,719
	Stephen Ames	74	69	66	71	280	104,719
7	Peter O'Malley	73	70	70	68	281	68,137
	Eduardo Romero	74	68	67	72	281	68,137
	Fred Couples	69	68	70	74	281	68,137
10	Ten tied at 282.						40,175

Early round leaders: 1st— Furyk and Clarke (67); 2nd— Clarke (133); 3rd— Parnevik (202).

Top amateur: D. Barclay Howard (293).

PGA Championship

Edition: 79th   **Dates:** Aug. 14–17
Site: Winged Foot GC, Mamaroneck, NY.
Par: 35-35—70 (6987 yards)   **Purse:** $2,400,000

		1	2	3	4	Tot	Earnings
1	Davis Love III	66	71	66	66	269	$470,000
2	Justin Leonard	68	70	65	71	274	280,000
3	Jeff Maggert	69	69	73	65	276	175,000
4	Lee Janzen	69	67	74	69	279	125,000
5	Tom Kite	68	71	71	70	280	105,000
6	Jim Furyk	69	72	72	68	281	85,000
	Phil Blackmar	70	68	74	69	281	85,000
	Scott Hoch	71	72	68	70	281	85,000
9	Tom Byrum	69	73	70	70	282	70,000
10	Joey Sindelar	72	71	71	69	283	60,000
	Tom Lehman	69	72	72	70	283	60,000
	Scott McCarron	74	71	67	71	283	60,000

Early round leaders: 1st— Love and John Daly (66); 2nd— Janzen (136); 3rd— Love and Leonard (203).

Top Amateur: none.

European PGA Tour

Earnings listed in pounds sterling (£) unless otherwise indicated.

LATE 1996

Last Rd	Tournament	Winner	Earnings	Runner-Up
Nov. 3	Sarazen World Open Championship	Frank Nobilo (272)	$342,000	S. Hoch (276)
Nov. 24	World Cup of Golf	S. AFR- Ernie Els/	$200,000	USA- T. Lehman/
		Wayne Westner (547)	(each)	S. Jones (565)

1997 (through Oct. 5)

Last Rd	Tournament	Winner	Earnings	Runner-Up
Jan. 26	Johnnie Walker Classic	Ernie Els (278)	£116,660	P. Lonard/
				& M. Long (279)
Feb. 2	Heineken Classic	Miguel Angel Martin (273)	107,547	F. Couples (274)
Feb. 9	South African Open	Vijay Singh (270)	71,476	N. Price (271)
Feb. 16	Dimenson Data Pro-Am	Nick Price (268)	63,384	D. Frost (276)
Feb. 23	Dunhill South Africa PGA	Nick Price (269)*	47,319	D. Frost (269)
Mar. 2	Dubai Desert Classic	Richard Green (272)*	116,660	I. Woosnam/
				& G. Norman (272)
Mar. 9	Moroccan Open	Clinton Whitelaw (277)	58,330	3-way tie (279)
Mar. 16	Portuguese Open	Michael Jonzon (269)	58,330	I. Garrido (272)
Mar. 23	Turespaña Masters	Jose Maria Olazabal (272)	61,965	L. Westwood (274)
Mar. 30	Madeira Island Open	Peter Mitchell (204)#	50,000	F. Jacobson (205)
Apr. 20	Cannes Open	Stuart Cage (270)	50,000	P. Broadhurst/
				& D. Carter (275)
Apr. 27	Peugeot Spanish Open	Mark James (277)*	84,843	G. Norman (277)
May 4	Conte of Florence Italian Open	Bernhard Langer (273)	77,898	J.M. Olazabal (274)
May 11	Benson & Hedges Intl. Open	Bernhard Langer (276)	116,660	I. Woosnam (278)
May 18	Alamo English Open	Per-Ulrik Johansson (269)	108,330	D. Edlund (271)
May 26	Volvo PGA Championship	Ian Woosnam (275)	183,340	3-way tie (277)
June 1	Deutsche Bank Open	Ross McFarlane (282)	125,000	A. Forsbrand/
				& G. Brand Jr. (283)
June 8	Slaley Hall European GP	Colin Montgomerie (270)	108,330	R. Goosen (275)
June 22	Volvo German Open	Ignacio Garrido (271)	116,660	R. Claydon (275)
June 29	Peugeot French Open	Retief Goosen (271)	100,000	J. Spence (274)
July 6	Murphy's Irish Open	Colin Montgomerie (269)	113,636	L. Westwood (276)
July 12	Loch Lomond World Invitational	Tom Lehman (265)	133,330	E. Els (270)
July 20	**British Open** (Royal Troon)	Justin Leonard (272)	250,000	D. Clarke/
				& J. Parnevik (275)
July 27	Sun Dutch Open	Sven Struver (266)	116,660	R. Claydon (269)
Aug. 3	Volvo Scandinavian Masters	Joakim Haeggman (270)	125,000	I. Garrido (274)
Aug. 10	Chemapol Trophy Czech Open	Bernhard Langer (264)	133,330	I. Garrido/
				& N. Fasth (268)
Aug. 24	Smurfit European Open	Per-Ulrik Johnasson (267)	141,660	P. Baker (273)
Aug. 31	BMW International Open	Robert Karlsson (264)*	125,000	C. Watts (264)
Sept. 7	Canon European Masters	Costantino Rocca (266)	133,330	R. Karlsson/
				& S. Henderson (267)
Sept. 14	Lancome Trophy	Mark O'Meara (271)	116,660	J. Sandelin (272)
Sept. 21	One 2 One British Masters	Greg Turner (275)	125,000	C. Montgomerie (276)
Sept. 28	Ryder Cup	Europe (14½)		USA (13½)
Oct. 5	Linde German Masters	Bernhard Langer (267)	125,000	C. Montgomerie (273)

(See Updates Chapter for later results.)

*Playoffs (4): **Dunhill—** Price won on the 1st hole; **Dubai—** Green won on the 1st hole; **Peugeot—** James won on the 3rd hole; **BMW International—** Karlsson won on the 3rd hole.
#Weather-shortened

Second place ties (3 players or more): 3-WAY **—** **Moroccan Open** (D. Cole, W. Riley, R. Chapman); **Volvo PGA** (D. Clarke, N. Faldo, E. Els).

Note: Ryder Cup qualifying points schedule began with the One 2 One British Masters (Aug. 28-31, 1996) up to the week ending Aug. 31, 1997.

Sony World Rankings

Begun in 1986, the Sony World Rankings combine the best golfers on the PGA and European PGA tours. Rankings are based on a rolling three-year period and weighted in favor of more recent results. Points are awarded after each world-wide tournament according to finish. Final point averages are determined by dividing a player's total points by the number of tournaments played in 1997 (through Oct. 5).

		Avg			Avg			Avg
1	Greg Norman	11.74	6	Tom Lehman	8.53	11	Justin Leonard	7.07
2	Tiger Woods	11.16	7	Jumbo Ozaki	8.22	12	Scott Hoch	6.87
3	Ernie Els	9.78	8	Mark O'Meara	8.06	13	Steve Elkington	6.48
4	Nick Price	9.27	9	Davis Love III	8.06	14	Fred Couples	6.48
5	Colin Montgomerie	8.80	10	Phil Mickelson	8.02	15	Nick Faldo	6.42

Tournament Results (Cont.)

Senior PGA Tour

LATE 1996

Last Rd	Tournament	Winner	Earnings	Runner-Up
Nov. 3	Emerald Coast Classic	Lee Trevino (207)*	$157,500	4-way tie (207)
Nov. 10	Senior Tour Championship	Jay Sigel (279)	280,000	K. Zarley (281)

*Playoffs (1): **Emerald Coast**— Trevino won on the 1st hole.

Second place ties (3 players or more): 4-WAY — **Emerald Coast** (D. Stockton, M. Hill, D. Graham, B. Eastwood).

1997 (through Oct. 5)

Last Rd	Tournament	Winner	Earnings	Runner-Up
Jan. 19	MasterCard Championship	Hale Irwin (209)	$186,000	G. Morgan (211)
Jan. 26	Senior Skins Game	Raymond Floyd (8 skins)	210,000	J. Nicklaus (5)
Feb. 2	Royal Caribbean Classic	Gibby Gilbert (202)	127,500	D. Graham (206)
Feb. 9	LG Championship	Hale Irwin (201)	150,000	B. Murphy (202)
Feb. 16	GTE Classic	David Graham (204)	135,000	B. Dickson (207)
Feb. 23	American Express Inviational	Bud Allin (205)	180,000	J. Colbert (206)
Feb. 25	Senior Slam	Hale Irwin (131)	250,000	D. Stockton (140)
Mar. 16	Toshiba Classic	Bob Murphy (207)*	150,000	J. Sigel (207)
Mar. 23	Liberty Mutual Legends of Golf	John Bland & Graham Marsh (192)	200,000	H. Green & G. Morgan (195)
Mar. 30	SBC Dominion Seniors	David Graham (206)	120,000	J. Jacobs (207)
Apr. 6	**The Tradition** (Scottsdale)	Gil Morgan (266)	180,000	I. Aoki (272)
Apr. 20	**PGA Seniors'** (Palm Beach Gardens)	Hale Irwin (274)	216,000	D. Douglass & J. Nicklaus (286)
Apr. 27	Las Vegas Senior Classic	Hale Irwin (207)	150,000	I. Aoki (208)
May 4	Bruno's Memorial Classic	Jay Sigel (205)	172,500	G. Morgan (208)
May 11	Home Depot Invitational	Jim Dent (208)*	135,000	L. Gilbert & L. Trevino (208)
May 18	Cadillac NFL Classic	Bruce Crampton (210)*	142,500	H. Baiocchi (210)
May 25	Bell Atlantic Classic	Bob Eastwood (135)#	150,000	B. Smith & J. Bland (136)
June 1	Ameritech Open	Gil Morgan (210)	180,000	H. Irwin (211)
June 8	BellSouth Classic at Opryland	Gil Morgan (202)	195,000	J. Bland (204)
June 15	du Maurier Champions	Jack Kiefer (269)	165,000	J. Colbert (271)
June 22	Nationwide Championship	Graham Marsh (205)	195,000	H. Irwin (206)
June 29	**U.S. Senior Open** (Olympia Fields)	Graham Marsh (280)	232,500	J. Bland (281)
July 6	Kroger Classic	Jay Sigel (195)	150,000	I. Aoki (202)
July 13	**Senior Players Champs.** (Dearborn)	Larry Gilbert (274)	270,000	4-way tie (277)
July 20	Burnet Classic	Hale Irwin (199)	202,500	L. Trevino (201)
July 27	Franklin Quest Classic	Dave Stockton (201)	150,000	K. Zarley (203)
Aug. 3	Bank of Boston Classic	Hale Irwin (203)	150,000	B. Wynn & J. McGee (205)
Aug. 10	Northville Long Island Classic	Dana Quigley (204)*	150,000	J. Sigel (204)
Aug. 17	First of America Classic	Gil Morgan (207)	150,000	B. Duval (208)
Aug. 24	Saint Luke's Classic	Bruce Summerhays (199)*	150,000	H. Baiocchi (199)
Aug. 31	Pittsburgh Classic	Hugh Baiocchi (206)*	165,000	B. Duval (206)
Sept. 7	Bank One Classic	Vicente Fernandez (203)	120,000	I. Aoki (204)
Sept. 14	Boone Valley Classic	Hale Irwin (200)	195,000	G. Morgan (202)
Sept. 21	Comfort Classic	David Graham (200)	157,500	L. Nelson & B. Allin (201)
Sept. 28	Emerald Coast Classic	Isao Aoki (196)*	165,000	G. Morgan (196)
Oct. 5	Vantage Championship	Hale Irwin (195)	225,000	D. Eichelberger (196)

(See Updates Chapter for later results.)

#Weather-shortened.

*Playoffs (7): **Toshiba**— Murphy won on the 9th hole; **Home Depot**— Dent won on the 2nd hole. Gilbert was eliminated on the 1st hole; **Cadillac NFL**— Crampton won on the 3rd hole; **Northville Long Island**— Quigley won on the 3rd hole; **Saint Luke's**— Summerhays won on the 2nd hole; **Pittsburgh**— Baiocchi won on the 6th hole; **Emerald Coast**— Aoki won on the 1st hole.

Second place ties (3 players or more): 4-WAY — **Ford Senior Players** (I. Aoki, J. Kiefer, B. Dickson, D. Stockton).

Senior PGA Majors

The Tradition

Edition: 9th   **Dates:** Apr. 3–6
Site: Desert Mt. Cochise Course, Scottsdale, Ariz.
Par: 36-36—72 (6954 yards)   **Purse:** $1,200,000

		1	2	3	4	Tot	Earnings
1	Gil Morgan	66	66	67	67	266	$180,000
2	Isao Aoki	66	68	70	68	272	105,600
3	John Jacobs	66	68	70	70	274	86,400
4	Larry Gilbert	70	71	68	67	276	72,000
5	Jay Sigel	72	70	68	67	277	57,600
6	Jim Dent	69	68	70	72	279	45,600
	Graham Marsh	68	69	69	73	279	45,600
8	Bob Eastwood	72	70	67	71	280	34,400
	George Archer	68	70	70	72	280	34,400
	Terry Dill	67	67	71	75	280	34,400

Early round leaders: 1st— Jacobs, J.C. Snead, Aoki, Morgan, Simon Hobday (66); 2nd— Morgan (132); 3rd— Morgan (199).

PGA Seniors' Championship

Edition: 60th   **Dates:** April 17–20
Site: PGA National GC, Palm Beach Gardens, Fla.
Par: 36-36—72 (6722 yards)   **Purse:** $1,200,000

		1	2	3	4	Tot	Earnings
1	Hale Irwin	69	65	72	68	274	$216,000
2	Dale Douglass	70	76	71	69	286	105,000
	Jack Nicklaus	71	72	73	70	286	105,000
4	Jack Kiefer	72	72	73	70	287	55,000
	Gibby Gilbert	69	73	74	71	287	55,000
	John Morgan	71	72	72	72	287	55,000
7	Bob Charles	71	70	75	72	288	40,000
	Larry Gilbert	74	69	70	75	288	40,000
	John Bland	67	77	71	73	288	40,000
10	Walt Morgan	74	75	69	71	289	30,000

Early round leaders: 1st— Bland (67); 2nd— Irwin (134); 3rd— Irwin (206).

U.S. Senior Open

Edition: 18th   **Dates:** June 26–29
Site: Olympia Fields (Ill.) CC
Par: 35-35—70 (6841 yards)   **Purse:** $1,300,000

		1	2	3	4	Tot	Earnings
1	Graham Marsh	72	67	67	74	280	$232,500
2	John Bland	69	70	69	73	281	137,500
3	Gil Morgan	69	74	71	68	282	73,321
	Tom Wargo	69	70	73	70	282	73,321
5	Hale Irwin	73	74	70	67	284	39,938
	Jack Nicklaus	73	72	70	69	284	39,938
	Hugh Baiocchi	73	71	69	71	284	39,938
	Leonard Thompson	70	72	70	72	284	39,938
	Dave Eichelberger	70	69	70	75	284	39,938
10	Jay Sigel	74	68	74	69	285	29,413
	Jose Maria Canizares	73	74	66	72	285	29,413

Early round leaders: 1st— Steve Veriato, Bland, Morgan, Kermit Zarley, Wargo (69); 2nd— Zarley (138); 3rd— Marsh (206).

PGA Sr. Players Championship

Edition: 15th   **Dates:** July 10–13
Site: TPC of Michigan, Dearborn, Mich.
Par: 36-36—72 (6876 yards)   **Purse:** $1,800,000

		1	2	3	4	Tot	Earnings
1	Larry Gilbert	67	68	72	67	274	$270,000
2	Isao Aoki	70	68	71	68	277	120,600
	Jack Kiefer	72	70	67	68	277	120,600
	Bob Dickson	72	66	69	70	277	120,600
	Dave Stockton	68	70	69	70	277	120,600
6	Gil Morgan	70	71	69	69	279	68,400
	John Jacobs	71	66	72	70	279	68,400
8	Jack Nicklaus	69	67	72	72	280	54,000
	Graham Marsh	70	69	69	72	280	54,000
10	Five players tied at 281.						39,960

Early round leaders: 1st— Gilbert, Dana Quigley (67); 2nd— Gilbert (135); 3rd—John Bland, Dickson, Stockton, Gilbert (207).

LPGA Tour

LATE 1996

Last Rd	Tournament	Winner	Earnings	Runner-Up
Nov. 3	Toray Japan Queens Cup	Mayumi Hirase (212)*	$112,500	L. Davies (212)
Nov. 24	ITT Tour Championship	Karrie Webb (272)	150,000	3-way tie (276)

*Playoffs (1): **Toray Japan**— Hirase won on 3rd hole.
Second place ties (3 players or more): 3–WAY — **ITT Tour Champs** (K. Robbins, N. Lopez, E. Klein).

1997 (through Oct. 5)

Last Rd	Tournament	Winner	Earnings	Runner-Up
Jan. 12	Chrysler-Plymouth Tourn. of Champions	Annika Sorenstam (272)	$115,000	K. Webb (276)
Jan. 19	HealthSouth Inaugural	Michelle McGann (207)*	90,000	K. Webb (207)
Feb. 9	Diet Dr. Pepper National Pro-Am	Kelly Robbins (271)*	75,000	E. Klein (271)
Feb. 16	Los Angeles Women's Championship	Terry-Jo Myers (206)	97,500	A. Sorenstam (208)
Feb. 22	Cup Noodles Hawaiian Open	Annika Sorenstam (206)	97,500	M. Mallon (207)
Mar. 2	Alpine Australian Ladies Masters	Gail Graham (273)	97,500	K. Webb (274)
Mar. 16	Welch's/Circle K Championship	Donna Andrews (273)	75,000	T. Barrett (274)
Mar. 23	Standard Register Ping	Laura Davies (277)*	127,500	K. Robbins (277)
Mar. 30	**Nabisco Dinah Shore** (Rancho Mirage)	Betsy King (276)	135,000	K. Tschetter (278)
Apr. 6	Longs Drugs Challenge	Annika Sorenstam (285)*	75,000	P. Kometani (285)
Apr. 20	Susan G. Komen International	Karrie Webb (276)	75,000	3-way tie (278)
Apr. 27	Chick-fil-A Charity Championship	Nancy Lopez (137)#	82,500	3-way tie (139)
May 4	Sprint Titleholders Championship	Tammie Green (274)	180,000	A. Sorenstam (276)
May 11	Sara Lee Classic	Terry-Jo Myers (207)*	101,250	N. Harvey & L. Kean (207)
May 18	**McDonald's LPGA Championship** (Wilmington)	Chris Johnson (281)*	180,000	L. Lindley (281)
May 25	Corning Classic	Rosie Jones (277)*	97,500	T. Green (277)
May 25	JCPenney Skins Game	Annika Sorenstam (8 skins)	220,000	L. Davies (5 skins)
June 1	Michelob Light Classic	Annika Sorenstam (277)	90,000	H. Kobayashi (280)
June 8	Oldsmobile Classic	Pat Hurst (279)	90,000	J. Inkster (280)

LPGA Tour (Cont.)

Last Rd	Tournament	Winner	Earnings	Runner-Up
June 15	Edina Realty Classic	Danielle Ammaccapane (208)	$90,000	4-way tie (209)
June 22	Rochester International	Penny Hammel (279)	90,000	3-way tie (280)
June 29	ShopRite Classic	Michelle McGann (201)	135,000	A. Sorenstam (204)
July 6	Jamie Farr Kroger Classic	Kelly Robbins (265)	105,000	T. Green (273)
July 13	**U.S. Women's Open** (Cornelius, OR)	Alison Nicholas (274)	232,500	N. Lopez (275)
July 20	JAL Big Apple Classic	Michele Redman (272)	112,500	A. Sorenstam (275)
July 27	Giant Eagle LPGA Classic	Tammie Green (203)*	90,000	L. Davies (203)
Aug. 3	**du Maurier Ltd. Classic** (Oakville, Ont.)	Colleen Walker (278)	180,000	L. Neumann (280)
Aug. 10	Friendly's Classic	Deb Richard (277)	82,500	C. Johnson (278)
Aug. 17	Weetabix Women's British Open	Karrie Webb (269)	129,938	R. Jones (277)
Aug. 24	Star Bank Classic	Colleen Walker (203)	82,500	T. Myers (205)
Sept. 1	State Farm Rail Classic	Cindy Figg-Currier (200)*	90,000	K. Tschetter & L. Kane (200)
Sept. 7	The Safeway Championship	Chris Johnson (206)	82,500	K. Saiki & L. Hackney (207)
Sept. 14	SAFECO Classic	Karrie Webb (272)	82,500	A. Sorenstam (273)
Sept. 21	Welch's Championship	Liselotte Neumann (276)	82,500	N. Harvey (279)
Sept. 28	Fieldcrest Cannon Classic	Wendy Ward (265)	82,500	J. Geddes & R. Jones (267)
Oct. 5	CoreStates Betsy King Classic	Annika Sorenstam (274)	90,000	K. Robbins (276)

(See Updates Chapter for later results.)
Rain-shortened

*Playoffs (9): HealthSouth— McGann won on the 1st hole; **Diet Dr. Pepper—** Robbins won on the 2nd hole; **Standard Register Ping—** Davies won on the 1st hole; **Longs Drugs—** Sorenstam won on the 2nd hole; **Sara Lee—** Myers won on the 5th hole. Harvey was eliminated in the 2nd hole; **McDonald's LPGA—** Johnson won on the 2nd hole; **Corning—** Jones won on the 1st hole; **Giant Eagle—** Green won on the 5th hole; **State Farm—** Figg-Currier won on the 1st hole.

Second Place ties: (3 players or more): 4-WAY — **Edina Realty** (H. Kobayashi, J. Geddes, C. Matthew, M. Hirase). 3-WAY — **Susan G. Komen** (L. Kane, C. Johnston-Forbes, N. Bowen); **Chick-fil-A** (T. Barrett, D. Richard, K. Webb); **Rochester** (T. Green, D. Pepper, N. Bowen).

LPGA Majors

Dinah Shore

Edition: 26th **Dates:** March 27–30
Site: Mission Hills CC, Rancho Mirage, Calif.
Par: 36-36—72 (6460 yards) **Purse:** $900,000

		1	2	3	4	Tot	Earnings
1	Betsy King	71	67	67	71	276	$135,000
2	Kris Tschetter	66	76	66	70	278	83,783
3	Amy Fruhwirth	69	70	68	72	279	54,346
	Kelly Robbisn	70	67	68	74	279	54,346
5	Nanci Bowen	70	74	70	68	282	35,097
	Lisa Hackney	70	72	72	68	282	35,097
7	Tina Barrett	70	71	70	72	283	26,720
8	Mary Beth Zimmerman	75	74	72	63	284	21,285
	Hiromi Kabayashi	72	69	71	72	284	21,285
	Annika Sorenstam	70	72	68	74	284	21,285

Early round leaders: 1st— Tschetter and Kathryn Marshall (66); 2nd— Robbins (137); 3rd— King and Robbins (205).

Top amateur: Marisa Baena (287).

LPGA Championship

Edition: 43rd **Dates:** May 15–18
Site: Du Pont CC, Wilmington, Del.
Par: 35-36—71 (6386 yards) **Purse:** $1,200,000

		1	2	3	4	Tot	Earnings
1	Chris Johnson	68	73	69	71	281	$180,000
2	Leta Lindley	72	69	69	71	281	111,711
3	Annika Sorenstam	70	73	74	68	285	81,519
4	Laura Davies	67	75	74	68	284	57,365
	Sherri Steinhauer	68	71	73	72	284	57,365
6	Gail Graham	69	79	71	66	285	38,947
	Dawn Coe-Jones	70	75	71	69	285	38,947
8	Trish Johnson	70	73	72	71	286	31,400
9	Karrie Webb	71	79	70	67	287	26,871
	Barb Mucha	68	73	72	74	287	26,871

Note: Johnson won on the 2nd playoff hole.
Early round leaders: 1st— Davies (67); 2nd— Steinhauer (139); 3rd— Johnson and Lindley (210).

Top amateur: none.

U.S. Women's Open

Edition: 52nd **Dates:** July 10–13
Site: Pumpkin Ridge GC, Cornelius, OR
Par: 36-35—71 (6365 yards) **Purse:** $1,300,000

		1	2	3	4	Tot	Earnings
1	Alison Nicholas	70	66	67	71	274	$232,500
2	Nancy Lopez	69	68	69	69	275	137,500
3	Kelly Robbins	68	69	74	66	277	86,708
4	Karrie Webb	73	72	65	68	278	60,432
5	Stefania Croce	72	69	71	67	279	46,159
	Lisa Hackney	71	70	67	71	279	46,159
7	Tammie Green	74	70	71	65	280	37,542
	Michele Redman	74	67	70	69	280	37,542
9	Five players tied at 282.						28,769

Early round leaders: 1st— Liselotte Neumann (67); 2nd—Nicholas (136); 3rd— Nicholas (203).

Top amateur: Jenny Chuasiriporn (297).

du Maurier Classic

Edition: 25th **Dates:** July 31–Aug. 3
Site: Glen Abbey GC, Oakville, Ontario, Canada
Par: 36-37—73 (6,367 yards) **Purse:** $1,200,000

		1	2	3	4	Tot	Earnings
1	Colleen Walker	68	72	73	65	278	$180,000
2	Liselotte Neumann	71	67	73	69	280	111,711
3	Betsy King	71	69	72	69	281	72,461
	Kelly Robbins	71	65	73	72	281	72,461
5	Cindy Figg-Currier	69	74	69	70	282	46,797
	Juli Inkster	70	69	71	72	282	46,797
7	Emilee Klein	73	70	71	69	283	33,513
	Rosie Jones	69	71	71	72	283	33,513
9	Lisa Hackney	73	69	75	67	284	26,871
10	Chris Johnson	70	72	72	70	284	26,871

Early round leaders: 1st— Walker, Vicki Fergon, Kathryn Marshall (68); 2nd— Robbins (136); 3rd— Robbins (209).

Top amateur: none.

1997 Ryder Cup

The 32nd Ryder Cup Tournament, Sept. 26-28, at Valderrama GC in Sotogrande, Spain.

ROSTERS

Selections for the 1996 United States team were determined by a special Ryder Cup points system that ranked players from the beginning of 1996 through the 1997 PGA Championship ending on August 17, 1997. The top ten players were joined by U.S. captain Tom Kite's two selections, Fred Couples and Lee Janzen.

The 1997 European squad was fielded via a points system that began with the One 2 One British Masters on August 28-31, 1996 and ended with the BMW International Open on August 28-31, 1997. The top ten players were joined by Europe captain Seve Ballesteros's two selections, Nick Faldo and Jesper Parnevik.

United States: Qualifiers— Brad Faxon, Jim Furyk, Scott Hoch, Tom Lehman, Justin Leonard, Davis Love III, Jeff Maggert, Phil Mickelson, Mark O'Meara, Mark O'Meara and Tiger Woods; Captain's Selections— Fred Couples and Lee Janzen.

Europe: Qualifiers— Thomas Bjorn (Denmark), Darren Clarke (N. Ireland), Ignacio Garrido (Spain), Per-Ulrik Johansson (Sweden), Bernhard Langer (Germany), Colin Montgomerie (Scotland), Jose Maria Olazabal (Spain), Costantino Rocca (Italy), Lee Westwood (England) and Ian Woosnam (Wales); Captain's Selections— Nick Faldo (England) and Jesper Parnevik (Sweden). Injured Miguel Angel Martin (Spain) qualified and is considered a non-playing member of the European team.

First Day

Four-Ball Match Results

Winner	Score	Loser
Olazabal/Rocca	1-up	Love/Mickelson
Couples/Faxon	1-up	Faldo/Westwood
Parnevik/Johansson	1-up	Lehman/Furyk
Woods/O'Meara	3 and 2	Langer/Montgomerie

Teams tie, 2-2

Foursome Match Results

Winner	Score	Loser
Hoch/Janzen	1-up	Olazabal/Rocca
Langer/Montgomerie	5&3	Woods/O'Meara
Faldo/Westwood	3&2	Leonard/Maggert
Garrido/Parnevik	halved	Lehman/Mickelson

Europe wins, 2½-1½
(Europe leads, 4½-3½)

Second Day

Four-Ball Match Results

Winner	Score	Loser
Montgomerie/Clarke	1-up	Couples/Love
Woosnam/Bjorn	2&1	Leonard/Faxon
Faldo/Westwood	2&1	Woods/O'Meara
Olazabal/Garrido	halved	Mickelson/Lehman

Europe wins, 3½-½
(Europe leads 8-4)

Foursome Match Results

Winner	Score	Loser
Montgomerie/Langer	1-up	Janzen/Furyk
Hoch/Maggert	2&1	Faldo/Westwood
Parnevik/Garrido	halved	Leonard/Woods
Olazabal/Rocca	5&4	Love/Couples

Europe wins, 2½-1½
(Europe leads, 10½-5½)

Third Day

Singles Match Results

Winner	Score	Loser
Fred Couples	8&7	Ian Woosnam
Per-Ulrik Johansson	3&2	Davis Love III
Costantino Rocca	4&2	Tiger Woods
Thomas Bjorn	halved	Justin Leonard
Phil Mickelson	2&1	Darren Clarke
Mark O'Meara	5&4	Jesper Parnevik
Lee Janzen	1-up	Jose Maria Olazabal
Bernhard Langer	2&1	Brad Faxon
Jeff Maggert	3&2	Lee Westwood
Colin Montgomerie	halved	Scott Hoch
Jim Furyk	3&2	Nick Faldo
Tom Lehman	7&6	Ignacio Garrido

USA wins day, 8-4

Europe wins Ryder Cup, 14½-13½

Overall Records

Team and Individual match play combined

United States	W-L-H	Pts		Europe	W-L-H	Pts
Scott Hoch	2-0-1	2½		Colin Montgomerie	3-1-1	3½
Jeff Maggert	2-1-0	2		Costantino Rocca	3-1-0	3
Lee Janzen	2-1-0	2		Bernhard Langer	3-1-0	3
Fred Couples	2-2-0	2		Jose Maria Olazabal	2-2-1	2½
Mark O'Meara	2-2-0	2		Per-Ulrik Johansson	2-0-0	2
Phil Mickelson	1-1-2	2		Jesper Parnevik	1-1-2	2
Tom Lehman	1-1-2	2		Nick Faldo	2-3-0	2
Tiger Woods	1-3-1	1½		Lee Westwood	2-3-0	2
Brad Faxon	1-2-0	1		Thomas Bjorn	1-0-1	1½
Jim Furyk	1-2-0	1		Ignacio Garrido	0-1-3	1½
Justin Leonard	0-2-2	1		Ian Woosnam	1-1-0	1
Davis Love III	0-4-0	0		Darren Clarke	1-1-0	1

Money Leaders

Official money leaders of PGA, European PGA, Senior PGA and LPGA tours for 1996 and unofficial money leaders for 1997 (through Oct. 5), as compiled by the PGA, European PGA and LPGA. All European amounts are in pound sterling (£).

PGA

Arnold Palmer Award standings: listed are tournaments played (TP); cuts made (CM); 1st, 2nd and 3rd place finishes; and earnings for the year.

Final 1996

		TP	CM	Finish 1-2-3	Earnings
1	Tom Lehman	22	20	2-2-1	$1,780,159
2	Phil Mickelson	21	19	4-1-1	1,697,799
3	Mark Brooks	29	23	3-1-0	1,429,396
4	Steve Strickler	22	19	2-1-4	1,383,739
5	Mark O'Meara	21	19	2-2-2	1,255,749
6	Fred Couples	18	ˉ16	1-1-0	1,248,694
7	Davis Love III	23	19	1-3-0	1,211,139
8	Brad Faxon	22	22	0-4-0	1,055,050
9	Scott Hoch	27	23	1-2-3	1,039,564
10	David Duval	23	16	0-2-3	977,079

1997 (through Oct. 5)

		TP	CM	Finish 1-2-3	Earnings
1	Tiger Woods	18	17	4-1-1	$1,949,920
2	Justin Leonard	27	24	2-1-1	1,463,531
3	Davis Love III	23	22	2-0-0	1,348,523
4	Greg Norman	14	12	2-2-1	1,248,256
5	Steve Elkington	16	13	2-0-1	1,240,411
6	Scott Hoch	19	19	1-1-1	1,213,555
7	Ernie Els	18	14	2-1-0	1,176,600
8	Jim Furyk	25	22	0-2-1	1,164,890
9	Phil Mickelson	19	17	2-1-0	1,121,990
10	Brad Faxon	22	16	1-3-0	1,093,505

EUROPEAN PGA

Volvo Order of Merit standings: listed are tournaments played (TP); cuts made (CM); 1st, 2nd and 3rd place finishes; and earnings for the year.

Final 1996

		TP	CM	Finish 1-2-3	Earnings
1	Colin Montgomerie	18	16	3-3-0	£1,034,752
2	Ian Woosnam	21	19	4-0-0	703,936
3	Ernie Els	7	7	2-2-0	596,725
4	Robert Allenby	17	17	3-0-1	533,332
5	Costantino Rocca	22	17	1-1-1	523,244
6	Mark McNulty	13	11	3-0-0	507,847
7	Frank Nobilo	17	12	2-0-1	495,356
8	Lee Westwood	33	25	1-1-1	449,960
9	Andrew Coltart	28	24	0-2-1	395,998
10	Sam Torrance	20	15	1-2-0	382,061

1997 (through Oct. 5)

		TP	CM	Finish 1-2-3	Earnings
1	Colin Montgomerie	18	18	2-2-1	£613,948
2	Bernhard Langer	16	12	4-0-0	568,698
3	Darren Clarke	22	18	0-2-2	467,709
4	Ian Woosnam	15	14	1-2-0	442,730
5	Ignacio Garrido	24	17	1-3-0	362,822
6	Retief Goosen	21	17	1-1-1	360,998
7	Lee Westwood	21	16	0-2-2	344,718
8	Per-Ulrik Johansson	15	13	2-0-0	322,880
9	Jose Maria Olazabal	15	14	1-1-1	301,649
10	Robert Karlsson	22	14	1-1-0	298,586

SENIOR PGA

Final 1996

		TP	CM	Finish 1-2-3	Earnings
1	Jim Colbert	32	32	5-5-1	$1,627,890
2	Hale Irwin	23	23	2-7-2	1,615,769
3	John Bland	35	35	4-1-2	1,357,987
4	Isao Aoki	26	26	2-4-1	1,162,581
5	Dave Stockton	29	29	2-3-1	1,117,685
6	Jay Sigel	32	32	1-3-0	1,094,630
7	Bob Murphy	30	30	2-2-2	1,067,188
8	Ray Floyd	23	23	1-0-4	1,043,051
9	Graham Marsh	28	28	2-2-2	1,024,290
10	Walter Morgan	37	37	2-0-0	848,303

1997 (through Oct. 5)

		TP	CM	Finish 1-2-3	Earnings
1	Hale Irwin	20	20	8-2-1	$2,003,864
2	Gil Morgan	22	22	4-4-2	1,665,762
3	Isao Aoki	24	24	1-5-3	1,203,728
4	Jay Sigel	28	28	2-2-1	1,173,581
5	David Graham	27	27	3-1-1	1,123,558
6	John Bland	29	29	0-3-2	1,108,397
7	Graham Marsh	25	25	2-0-1	1,047,976
8	Larry Gilbert	23	23	1-1-3	902,816
9	Dave Stockton	25	24	1-1-2	805,016
10	Hugh Baiocchi	20	20	1-2-1	770,468

LPGA

Final 1996

		TP	CM	Finish 1-2-3	Earnings
1	Karrie Webb	25	24	4-5-1	$1,002,000
2	Laura Davies	19	18	4-3-1	927,302
3	Annika Sorenstam	20	20	3-2-1	808,311
4	Liselotte Neumann	24	23	3-2-1	625,633
5	Dottie Pepper	23	21	4-1-1	589,401
6	Kelly Robbins	25	22	1-3-2	562,458
7	Meg Mallon	24	23	2-1-3	510,209
8	Michelle McGann	26	25	3-0-2	498,561
9	Emilee Klein	30	26	2-1-1	463,793
10	Val Skinner	27	26	0-2-1	413,419

1997 (through Oct. 5)

		TP	CM	Finish 1-2-3	Earnings
1	Annika Sorenstam	20	18	6-5-3	$1,055,039
2	Karrie Webb	23	23	3-4-3	929,981
3	Kelly Robbins	25	22	2-2-5	803,674
4	Chris Johnson	26	24	2-1-1	630,879
5	Tammie Green	24	20	2-3-1	580,813
6	Betsy King	28	25	1-0-3	444,305
7	Nancy Lopez	15	13	1-1-1	437,886
8	Laura Davies	18	16	1-1-2	436,921
9	Juli Inkster	22	22	0-1-3	401,988
10	Michelle McGann	24	20	2-0-0	399,056

1997 Tour Statistics (as of Oct. 5, 1997)

All-Around— Combined ranks in the other statistical categories; **Scoring Leaders**— The number is not a pure scoring average. It is adjusted to the average score of the field each week. If the field is under par, each player's score is adjusted upward a corresponding amount and vice versa if the field is above par. This keeps a player from receiving an advantage for playing easier-than-average courses. **Putting Leaders**— An average of the number of putts taken on greens hit in regulation. By using only greens hit in regulation, the stat no longer allows players who regularly miss greens to get up-and-down and then dominate the stat. **Eagle Leaders**— the average number of holes between each eagle. **Greens in Regulation**— A statistic based on number of greens reached in regulation out of total holes played. A hole is considered hit in regulation if any portion of the ball rest on the putting surface in two shots less than the par. A par five hit in two shots does not increase the statistic; it merely counts as one green hit in regulation. **Sand Saves**— a percentage of up-and-down efforts from greenside sand traps only. Fairway bunkers are not included. **Driving Distance**— Average computed by charting exact distances of two tee shots on the most open par four or five holes on both front and back nine. **Drive Accuracy**— Percentage of fairways hit on par four and five holes. Par threes are excluded. **Total Driving**— Drive distance rank + Drive Accuracy rank

PGA TOUR

Scoring Leaders

All-Around

		Rank
1	Greg Norman	265
2	Tom Byrum	280
3	Nick Price	284
4	Tom Lehman	303
5	Bill Glasson	317
6	Davis Love III	320
7	Tiger Woods	321
8	Phil Mickelson	326
9	Jay Haas	332
10	Scott Hoch	341
11	Andrew Magee	351
12	Jesper Parnevik	360
13	Jim Furyk	370
14	Bob Estes	378
15	Lee Janzen	390
16	Mark Calcavecchia	391
17	Paul Stankowski	409
18	Tommy Tolles	422
19	Brian Henninger	424
20	Fred Couples	426
21	Steve Lowery	430
22	Craig Stadler	440
	Brent Geiberger	440
24	Mark O'Meara	446
25	David Duval	467

Scoring Leaders

		Rnds	Avg
1	Nick Price	54	68.71
2	Tiger Woods	68	68.78
3	Greg Norman	47	69.03
4	Davis Love III	81	69.40
5	Tom Lehman	64	69.50
6	Jesper Parnevik	66	69.61
7	Jim Furyk	89	69.66
8	Phil Mickelson	67	69.67
9	Scott Hoch	75	69.68
10	Ernie Els	58	69.71

Top Tens

		Events	Top 10
1	Davis Love III	23	12
	Jim Furyk	25	12
3	Scott Hoch	19	9
	Tiger Woods	18	9
5	Tom Lehman	19	8
	Nick Price	15	8
	Tommy Tolles	22	8
	Jesper Parnevik	18	8
9	Six players tied at seven each.		

Consecutive Cuts Made

		Cuts
1	Vijay Singh	46
2	Scott Hoch	21
3	Justin Leonard	20
4	Tom Byrum	12
5	Mark Calcavecchia	10
	Phil Mickelson	10
7	Isao Aoki	8
	Russ Cochran	8
	Stuart Appleby	8
10	Skip Kendall	7
	Chris Smith	7
	Ernie Els	7
	Tommy Tolles	7

Putting Leaders

		Putts
1	Don Pooley	1.718
2	Lee Janzen	1.729
3	Brad Faxon	1.732
4	Loren Roberts	1.734
5	Tommy Tolles	1.736
6	Phil Blackmar	1.738
7	Mark O'Meara	1.743
	Charlie Rymer	1.743
9	Jim Furyk	1.746
10	Brian Claar	1.748
	Michael Christie	1.748

Eagle Leaders

		Holes
1	Steve Lowery	103.2
2	Fred Couples	108.0
	Tim Herron	108.0
4	Tiger Woods	111.3
5	Mark Calcavecchia	113.1
6	David Berganio Jr.	117.8
7	Charlie Rymer	118.3
8	John Daly	128.6
9	Davis Love III	132.5
10	Ken Green	136.3

Greens in Regulation

		Pct
1	Tom Lehman	71.9
2	John Cook	71.0
3	Hal Sutton	70.5
4	Peter Jacobsen	69.4
	Greg Norman	69.4
	Tiger Woods	69.4
7	Davis Love III	69.3
8	Skip Kendall	69.2
	Rocco Mediate	69.2
10	Mark Calcavecchia	69.1
	Bob Tway	69.1

1997 Tour Statistics (Cont.)

Sand Saves

		Pct
1	Bob Estes	.70.9
2	Jay Haas	.65.1
3	Loren Roberts	.64.7
4	John Morse	.64.2
5	Stewart Cink	.64.1
6	Stuart Appleby	.64.0
7	Ronnie Black	.63.9
8	Mark O'Meara	.63.8
9	Lanny Wadkins	.63.7
10	Frank Nobilo	.63.5

Birdies per Round Leaders

		Avg.
1	Tiger Woods	.4.22
2	Bill Glasson	.4.00
3	Jesper Parnevik	.3.98
4	David Duval	.3.94
5	Don Pooley	.3.90
	Tommy Tolles	.3.90
7	Greg Norman	.3.89
8	Lee Janzen	.3.87
	Nick Price	.3.87
10	Fred Couples	.3.81
	Phil Mickelson	.3.81
	Tom Watson	.3.81

Drive Accuracy

		Pct
1	Fred Funk	.80.2
2	Allen Doyle	.80.1
3	Nick Price	.79.9
4	Jim Furyk	.79.1
5	Larry Mize	.79.0
6	David Edwards	.78.8
	Loren Roberts	.78.8
8	Nick Faldo	.78.7
9	John Morse	.77.5
10	Olin Browne	.77.3
	Tom Byrum	.77.3

Driving Distance

		Yds
1	John Daly	.302.0
2	Tiger Woods	.293.9
3	Bill Glasson	.286.8
4	Davis Love III	.284.5
5	Chip Sullivan	.284.0
	Scott McCarron	.284.0
7	Fred Couples	.283.3
8	Phil Mickelson	.282.7
9	John Adams	.281.4
10	Vijay Singh	.280.8

Total Driving

		Rank				Rank
1	Kenny Perry	.71		6	Greg Norman	.94
2	Joe Durant	.76		7	Nick Price	.95
3	Hal Sutton	.77		8	Stuart Appleby	.96
4	Tom Byrum	.81		9	Tiger Woods	.98
5	Bill Glasson	.87		10	Grant Waite	.99

SENIORS

All-Around

		Rank
1	Gil Morgan	.58
2	Hale Irwin	.72
3	Graham Marsh	.107
4	David Graham	.123
5	Ray Floyd	.165
6	John Bland	.178
7	Jay Sigel	.187
8	Bob Eastwood	.194
9	Larry Gilbert	.201
10	Bob Duval	.206
11	Vicente Fernandez	.209
12	Hugh Baiocchi	.225
13	Mike Hill	.231
14	Lee Trevino	.233
15	Dave Stockton	.235
16	Jack Kiefer	.242
17	Walter Morgan	.244
18	Leonard Thompson	.246
19	Kermit Zarley	.248
20	Jim Dent	.252
	Jerry McGee	.252

Putting Leaders

		Putts
1	Hale Irwin	.1.738
2	Isao Aoki	.1.751
	Gil Morgan	.1.751
4	Graham Marsh	.1.752
5	Frank Conner	.1.754
6	Dave Stockton	.1.757
7	Gibby Gilbert	.1.767
8	Jerry McGee	.1.770
9	Lee Trevino	.1.771
10	Jim Dent	.1.774

Eagle Leaders

		Holes
1	David Graham	.103.2
2	Terry Dill	.120.0
3	Bob Duval	.128.0
4	Gil Morgan	.155.3
5	Leonard Thompson	.162.0
6	DeWitt Weaver	.163.8
7	Hale Irwin	.164.6
8	Dave Eichelberger	.165.6
9	Steven Veriato	.166.5
10	Jay Sigel	.174.0

Scoring Leaders

		Rnds	Avg				Rnds	Avg
1	Hale Irwin	.64	69.03		6	Jay Sigel	.87	70.30
2	Gil Morgan	.69	69.45		7	Graham Marsh	.80	70.41
3	Isao Aoki	.76	70.05		8	Hugh Baiocchi	.63	70.56
4	John Bland	.91	70.23		9	Dave Stockton	.76	70.64
5	David Graham	.86	70.28		10	Larry Gilbert	.73	70.71

Greens in Regulations Leaders

		Avg
1	Hale Irwin	.75.8
2	Jay Sigel	.73.6
3	Gil Morgan	.73.0
4	John Bland	.72.8
5	Hugh Baiocchi	.71.3
	David Graham	.71.3
7	Brian Barnes	.69.4
8	Vicente Fernandez	.69.0
	Graham Marsh	.69.0
10	Isao Aoki	.68.8

Sand Saves Leaders

		Pct
1	Isao Aoki	.64.5
2	John Schroeder	.62.3
3	Homero Blancas	.60.9
4	Bob Eastwood	.60.2
5	Gil Morgan	.58.2
6	Jerry McGee	.57.2
7	Don January	.56.7
8	Simon Hobday	.56.3
9	Dave Stockton	.55.9
10	Jimmy Powell	.55.8

Birdies per Round Leaders

		Avg
1	Hale Irwin	.4.28
2	Isao Aoki	.4.20
3	Gil Morgan	.4.13
4	David Graham	.3.83
5	Frank Conner	.3.72
6	Graham Marsh	.3.70
7	Larry Gilbert	.3.62
8	Jim Dent	.3.60
9	Kermit Zarley	.3.59
10	Jay Sigel	.3.57

Driving Distance

		Yds
1	John Jacobs	.290.0
2	Terry Dill	.287.0
3	Jay Sigel	.286.1
4	Gil Morgan	.282.5
5	Bob Duval	.280.5
6	Ray Floyd	.279.5
7	David Graham	.278.5
8	Dan Wood	.276.1
9	DeWitt Weaver	.273.8
10	Jim Dent	.273.2

Driving Accuracy

		Stat
1	John Bland	.81.0
2	Calvin Peete	.78.9
3	Bob E. Smith	.77.2
4	Bob Murphy	.77.0
5	David Oakley	.76.6
6	Hale Irwin	.76.0
7	Hubert Green	.75.7
8	Chi Chi Rodriguez	.75.5
9	David Ojala	.74.8
	Walter Zembriski	.74.8

Total Driving

		Stat
1	Hale Irwin	.31
2	Isao Aoki	.37
3	Gil Morgan	.39
4	Graham Marsh	.41
5	Jim Albus	.43
6	Larry Gilbert	.44
7	Jay Sigel	.47
8	David Graham	.49
9	Brian Barnes	.51
10	Hugh Baiocchi	.53

EUROPEAN

Scoring Leaders

		Avg
1	Ernie Els (S. Africa)	.68.96
2	Colin Montgomerie (Scotland)	.69.39
3	Jose Maria Olazabal (Spain)	.69.79
4	Bernhard Langer (Germany)	.69.88
	Nick Faldo (England)	.69.88
6	Eduardo Romero (Argentina)	.69.97
7	Patrik Sjoland (Sweden)	.70.13
8	Darren Clarke (N. Ireland)	.70.22
9	Ian Woosnam (Wales)	.70.26
10	Retief Goosen (S. Africa)	.70.42
11	Lee Westwood (England)	.70.44
	Jesper Parnevik (Sweden)	.70.44
13	Per-Ulrik Johansson (Sweden)	.70.63
	Thomas Bjorn (Denmark)	.70.63
15	Costantino Rocca (Italy)	.70.69
16	Sven Struver (Germany)	.70.71
17	Padraig Harrington (Ireland)	.70.76
18	Mark James (England)	.70.80
19	Robert Karlsson (Sweden)	.70.85
20	Clinton Whitelaw (S. Africa)	.70.86
21	Roger Chapman (England)	.70.90
22	Jose Coceres (Argentina)	.70.96
23	Joakim Haeggman (Sweden)	.70.97
24	Michael Long (New Zealand)	.70.98
25	David Carter (England)	.71.00

Eagle Leaders

		No
1	Retief Goosen (S. Africa)	.17
	Wayne Westner (S. Africa)	.17
	Carl Suneson (Spain)	.17
4	Patrik Sjoland (Sweden)	.13
	Dean Robertson (Scotland)	.13
	Colin Montgomerie (Scotland)	.13
	David Carter (England)	.13
8	Robert Karlsson (Sweden)	.11
	Ernie Els (S. Africa)	.11
	Jarmo Sandelin (Sweden)	.11
	Santiago Luna (Spain)	.11
	David Gilford (England)	.11
	Lee Westwood (England)	.11

Birdie Leaders

		No
1	Padraig Harrington (Ireland)	.372
2	Thomas Gogele (Germany)	.366
3	Daniel Chopra (Sweden)	.355
4	Carl Suneson (Spain)	.325
	Darren Clarke (N. Ireland)	.325
6	Andrew Coltart (Scotland)	.319
7	David Carter (England)	.313
8	Patrik Sjoland (Sweden)	.311
9	Raymond Russell (Scotland)	.310
10	Colin Montgomerie (Scotland)	.308

1997 Tour Statistics (Cont.)

LPGA

Scoring Average (Vare Trophy)

		Avg
1	Karrie Webb	.69.97
2	Annika Sorenstam	.70.04
3	Kelly Robbins	.70.36
4	Juli Inkster	.70.69
5	Nancy Lopez	.70.76
6	Laura Davies	.70.80
7	Chris Johnson	.70.92
8	Donna Andrews	.71.08
9	Tina Barrett	.71.17
10	Tammie Green	.71.24

Driving Accuracy

		Pct
1	Donna Andrews	.79.9
2	Stephanie Maynor	.79.7
3	Nancy Ramsbottom	.79.2
4	Amy Fruhwirth	.78.1
5	Caroline Pierce	.77.8
6	Penny Hammel	.77.1
7	Rosie Jones	.77.0
8	Joanne Morley	.76.9
9	Hiromi Kobayashi	.76.4
10	Michele Redman	.76.2

Driving Distance

		Yds
1	Smitri Mehra	.263.0
2	Jane Geddes	.261.5
3	Kris Tschetter	.257.7
4	Laura Davies	.257.4
5	Michelle McGann	.256.5
6	Kelly Robbins	.256.1
7	Karrie Webb	.254.8
8	Wendy Doolan	.253.7
9	Juli Inkster	.252.9
10	Dale Reid	.252.2

Total Eagles

		No
1	Kelly Robbins	.12
2	Chris Johnson	.10
	Karrie Webb	.10
4	Brandie Burton	.8
	Liselotte Neumann	.8
	Vickie Odegard	.8
7	Six tied with 7 each.	

Top 10s

		Top 10/Events	Pct.
1	Karrie Webb	.19/23	82.6
2	Annika Sorenstam	.14/20	70.0
	Kelly Robbins	.16/25	64.0
4	Nancy Lopez	.8/15	53.3
5	Chris Johnson	.12/26	46.2
6	Juli Inkster	.8/22	36.4
7	Lisa Hackney	.7/20	35.0
8	Donna Andrews	.8/24	33.3
	Brandie Burton	.8/24	33.3
	Tammie Green	.8/24	33.3

Greens In Regulation

		Pct
1	Kelly Robbins	.78.4
2	Karrie Webb	.74.5
3	Annika Sorenstam	.72.7
4	Nancy Lopez	.72.2
5	Dottie Pepper	.71.1
	Donna Andrews	.71.1
7	Sherri Steinhauer	.70.8
8	Barb Mucha	.70.1
9	Jane Geddes	.69.9
	Tina Barrett	.69.9

Putting Average

		Per Round
1	Liselotte Neumann	.29.19
2	Barb Bunkowsky-Scherbak	.29.26
3	Brandie Burton	.29.28
4	Juli Inkster	.29.34
5	Dana Dormann	.29.40
6	Caroline Pierce	.29.42
	Barb Whitehead	.29.42
8	Lucianna Bemvenuti	.29.45
9	Kathy Postlewait	.29.46
10	Betsy King	.29.51

Rounds Under Par/ # of Rounds

			Pct.
1	Karrie Webb	.62/87	71.3
2	Juli Inkster	.55/81	67.9
3	Nancy Lopez	.32/50	64.0
4	Annika Sorenstam	.44/70	62.9
5	Kelly Robbins	.53/85	62.4
6	Donna Andrews	.49/83	59.0
7	Chris Johnson	.54/93	58.1
8	Laura Davies	.34/61	55.7
9	Dottie Pepper	.44/82	53.7
10	Liselotte Neumann	.45/84	53.6

Sand Saves

		Pct
1	Caroline Pierce	.56.7
2	Nancy Ramsbottom	.53.3
3	Laurie Bower	.53.1
4	Sherrin Smyers	.52.5
5	Vicki Goetze-Ackerman	.52.3
6	Terry-Jo Myers	.51.9
7	Barb Whiehead	.51.3
8	Michele Redman	.51.1
9	Patty Sheehan	.50.8
10	Barb Bunkowsky-Scherbak	.50.0

Total Birdies

		Birds
1	Kelly Robbins	.347
2	Betsy King	.334
3	Karrie Webb	.330
4	Chris Johnson	.322
5	Lorie Kane	.308
6	Juli Inkster	.297
7	Brandie Burton	.294
	Karen Weiss	.294
9	Michelle McGann	.288
10	Donna Andrews	.287

THE 1998

ESPN
INFORMATION PLEASE
SPORTS
ALMANAC

GOLF
STATISTICS

SEC
B

THROUGH THE YEARS
1860-1997

MAJOR TITLES • LEADERS

PAGE
851

Major Golf Championships
MEN

The Masters

The Masters has been played every year since 1934 at the Augusta National Golf Club in Augusta, Ga. Both the course (6905 yards, par 72) and the tournament were created by Bobby Jones; (*) indicates playoff winner.

Multiple winners: Jack Nicklaus (6); Arnold Palmer (4); Jimmy Demaret, Nick Faldo, Gary Player and Sam Snead (3); Seve Ballesteros, Ben Hogan, Bernhard Langer, Byron Nelson, Horton Smith and Tom Watson (2).

Year	Winner	Score	Runner-up
1934	Horton Smith	284	Craig Wood (285)
1935	Gene Sarazen*	282	Craig Wood (282)
1936	Horton Smith	285	Harry Cooper (286)
1937	Byron Nelson	283	Ralph Guldahl (285)
1938	Henry Picard	285	Ralph Guldahl & Harry Cooper (287)
1939	Ralph Guldahl	279	Sam Snead (280)
1940	Jimmy Demaret	280	Lloyd Mangrum (284)
1941	Craig Wood	280	Byron Nelson (283)
1942	Byron Nelson*	280	Ben Hogan (280)
1943-45 Not held			World War II
1946	Herman Keiser	282	Ben Hogan (283)
1947	Jimmy Demaret	281	Frank Stranahan & Byron Nelson (283)
1948	Claude Harmon	279	Cary Middlecoff (284)
1949	Sam Snead	282	Lloyd Mangrum & Johnny Bulla (285)
1950	Jimmy Demaret	283	Jim Ferrier (285)
1951	Ben Hogan	280	Skee Riegel (282)
1952	Sam Snead	286	Jack Burke Jr. (290)
1953	Ben Hogan	274	Ed Oliver (279)
1954	Sam Snead*	289	Ben Hogan (289)
1955	Cary Middlecoff	279	Ben Hogan (286)
1956	Jack Burke Jr.	289	Ken Venturi (290)
1957	Doug Ford	283	Sam Snead (286)
1958	Arnold Palmer	284	Doug Ford, & Fred Hawkins (285)
1959	Art Wall Jr.	284	Cary Middlecoff (285)
1960	Arnold Palmer	282	Ken Venturi (283)
1961	Gary Player	280	Arnold Palmer & Charles R. Coe (281)
1962	Arnold Palmer*	280	Dow Finsterwald & Gary Player (280)
1963	Jack Nicklaus	286	Tony Lema (287)
1964	Arnold Palmer	276	Jack Nicklaus & Dave Marr (282)
1965	Jack Nicklaus	271	Arnold Palmer & Gary Player (280)
1966	Jack Nicklaus*	288	Gay Brewer Jr. & Tommy Jacobs (288)
1967	Gay Brewer Jr.	280	Bobby Nichols (281)
1968	Bob Goalby	277	Roberto DeVicenzo (278)
1969	George Archer	281	Billy Casper, George Knudson & Tom Weiskopf (282)
1970	Billy Casper*	279	Gene Littler (279)
1971	Charles Coody	279	Jack Nicklaus & Johnny Miller (281)
1972	Jack Nicklaus	286	Bruce Crampton, Bobby Mitchell & Tom Weiskopf (289)
1973	Tommy Aaron	283	J.C. Snead (284)
1974	Gary Player	278	Tom Weiskopf, & Dave Stockton (280)
1975	Jack Nicklaus	276	Johnny Miller & Tom Weiskopf (277)
1976	Ray Floyd	271	Ben Crenshaw (279)
1977	Tom Watson	276	Jack Nicklaus (278)
1978	Gary Player	277	Hubert Green, Rod Funseth & Tom Watson (278)
1979	Fuzzy Zoeller*	280	Ed Sneed & Tom Watson (280)
1980	Seve Ballesteros	275	Gibby Gilbert & Jack Newton (279)
1981	Tom Watson	280	Jack Nicklaus & Johnny Miller (282)
1982	Craig Stadler*	284	Dan Pohl (284)
1983	Seve Ballesteros	280	Ben Crenshaw, & Tom Kite (284)
1984	Ben Crenshaw	277	Tom Watson (279)
1985	Bernhard Langer	282	Curtis Strange, Seve Ballesteros & Ray Floyd (284)
1986	Jack Nicklaus	279	Greg Norman (280)
1987	Larry Mize*	285	Seve Ballesteros & Greg Norman (285)
1988	Sandy Lyle	281	Mark Calcavecchia (282)
1989	Nick Faldo*	283	Scott Hoch (283)
1990	Nick Faldo*	278	Ray Floyd (278)
1991	Ian Woosnam	277	J.M. Olazabal (278)
1992	Fred Couples	275	Ray Floyd (277)
1993	Bernhard Langer	277	Chip Beck (281)
1994	J.M. Olazabal	279	Tom Lehman (281)
1995	Ben Crenshaw	274	Davis Love III (275)
1996	Nick Faldo	276	Greg Norman (281)
1997	Tiger Woods	270	Tom Kite (282)

The Masters (Cont.)

*PLAYOFFS:

1935: Gene Sarazen (144) def. Craig Wood (149) in 36 holes. **1942:** Byron Nelson (69) def. Ben Hogan (70) in 18 holes. **1954:** Sam Snead (70) def. Ben Hogan (71) in 18 holes. **1962:** Arnold Palmer (68) def. Gary Player (71) and Dow Finsterwald (77) in 18 holes. **1966:** Jack Nicklaus (70 def. Tommy Jacobs (72) and Gay Brewer (78) in 18 holes. **1970:** Billy Casper (69) def. Gene Littler (74) in 18 holes. **1979:** Fuzzy Zoeller (4-3) def. Ed Sneed (4-4) and Tom Watson (4-4) on 2nd hole of sudden death. **1982:** Craig Stadler (4) def. Dan Pohl (5) on 1st hole of sudden death. **1987:** Larry Mize (4-3) def. Greg Norman (4-4) and Seve Ballesteros (5) on 2nd hole of sudden death. **1989:** Nick Faldo (5-3) def. Scott Hoch (5-4) on 2nd hole of sudden death. **1990:** Nick Faldo (4-4) def. Raymond Floyd (4-x) on second hole of sudden death.

U.S. Open

Played at a different course each year, the U.S. Open was launched by the new U.S. Golf Association in 1895. The Open was a 36-hole event from 1895-97 and has been 72 holes since then. It switched from a 3-day, 36-hole Saturday finish to 4 days of play in 1965. Note that (*) indicates playoff winner and (a) indicates amateur winner.

Multiple winners: Willie Anderson, Ben Hogan, Bobby Jones and Jack Nicklaus (4); Hale Irwin (3); Julius Boros, Billy Casper, Ernie Els, Ralph Guldahl, Walter Hagen, John McDermott, Cary Middlecoff, Andy Norht, Gene Sarazen, Alex Smith, Curtis Strange and Lee Trevino (2).

Year	Winner	Score	Runner-up	Course	Location
1895	Horace Rawlins	173	Willie Dunn (175)	Newport GC	Newport, R.I.
1896	James Foulis	152	Horace Rawlins (155)	Shinnecock Hills GC	Southampton, N.Y.
1897	Joe Lloyd	162	Willie Anderson (163)	Chicago GC	Wheaton, Ill.
1898	Fred Herd	328	Alex Smith (335)	Myopia Hunt Club	Hamilton, Mass.
1899	Willie Smith	315	George Low, W.H. Way & Val Fitzjohn (326)	Baltimore CC	Baltimore
1900	Harry Vardon*	313	J.H. Taylor (315)	Chicago GC	Wheaton, Ill.
1901	Willie Anderson*	331	Alex Smith (331)	Myopia Hunt Club	Hamilton, Mass.
1902	Laurie Auchterlonie	307	Stewart Gardner (313)	Garden City GC	Garden City, N.Y.
1903	Willie Anderson*	307	David Brown (307)	Baltusrol GC	Springfield, N.J.
1904	Willie Anderson	303	Gil Nicholls (308)	Glen View Club	Golf, Ill.
1905	Willie Anderson	314	Alex Smith (316)	Myopia Hunt Club	Hamilton, Mass.
1906	Alex Smith	295	Willie Smith (302)	Onwentsia Club	Lake Forest, Ill.
1907	Alec Ross	302	Gil Nicholls (304)	Phila. Cricket Club	Chestnut Hill, Pa.
1908	Fred McLeod*	322	Willie Smith (322)	Myopia Hunt Club	Hamilton, Mass.
1909	George Sargent	290	Tom McNamara (294)	Englewood GC	Englewood, N.J.
1910	Alex Smith*	298	Macdonald Smith & John McDermott (298)	Phila. Cricket Club	Chestnut Hill, Pa.
1911	John McDermott*	307	George Simpson & Mike Brady (307)	Chicago GC	Wheaton, Ill.
1912	John McDermott	294	Tom McNamara (296)	CC of Buffalo	Buffalo
1913	a-Francis Ouimet*	304	Harry Vardon & Ted Ray (304)	The Country Club	Brookline, Mass.
1914	Walter Hagen	290	a-Chick Evans (291)	Midlothian CC	Blue Island, Ill.
1915	a-John Travers	297	Tom McNamara (298)	Baltusrol GC	Springfield, N.J.
1916	a-Chick Evans	286	Jock Hutchinson (288)	Minikahda Club	Minneapolis
1917-18	Not held		World War I		
1919	Walter Hagen*	301	Mike Brady (301)	Brae Burn CC	West Newton, Mass.
1920	Ted Ray	295	Jock Hutchison, Jack Burke, Leo Diegel & Harry Vardon (296)	Inverness Club	Toledo, Ohio
1921	Jim Barnes	289	Walter Hagen & Fred McLeod (298)	Columbia CC	Chevy Chase, Md.
1922	Gene Sarazen	288	a-Bobby Jones & John Black (289)	Skokie CC	Glencoe, Ill.
1923	a-Bobby Jones*	296	Bobby Cruickshank (296)	Inwood CC	Far Rockaway, N.Y.
1924	Cyril Walker	297	a-Bobby Jones (300)	Oakland Hills CC	Birmingham, Mich.
1925	Willie Macfarlane*	291	a-Bobby Jones (291)	Worcester CC	Worcester, Mass.
1926	a-Bobby Jones	293	Joe Turnesa (294)	Scioto CC	Columbus, Ohio
1927	Tommy Armour*	301	Harry Cooper (301)	Oakmont CC	Oakmont, Pa.
1928	Johnny Farrell*	294	a-Bobby Jones (294)	Olympia Fields CC	Matteson, Ill.
1929	a-Bobby Jones*	294	Al Espinosa (294)	Winged Foot CC	Mamaroneck, N.Y.
1930	a-Bobby Jones	287	Macdonald Smith (289)	Interlachen CC	Hopkins, Minn.
1931	Billy Burke*	292	George Von Elm (292)	Inverness Club	Toledo, Ohio
1932	Gene Sarazen	286	Bobby Cruickshank & Phil Perkins (289)	Fresh Meadow CC	Flushing, N.Y.
1933	a-Johnny Goodman	287	Ralph Guldahl (288)	North Shore GC	Glenview, Ill.
1934	Olin Dutra	293	Gene Sarazen (294)	Merion Cricket Club	Ardmore, Pa.
1935	Sam Parks Jr.	299	Jimmy Thomson (301)	Oakmont CC	Oakmont, Pa.
1936	Tony Manero	282	Harry E. Cooper (284)	Baltusrol GC	Springfield, N.J.
1937	Ralph Guldahl	281	Sam Snead (283)	Oakland Hills CC	Birmingham, Mich.
1938	Ralph Guldahl	284	Dick Metz (290)	Cherry Hills CC	Denver

Year	Winner	Score	Runner-up	Course	Location
1939	Byron Nelson*	284	Craig Wood & Denny Shute (284)	Philadelphia CC	Philadelphia
1940	Lawson Little*	287	Gene Sarazen (287)	Canterbury GC	Cleveland
1941	Craig Wood	284	Denny Shute (287)	Colonial Club	Ft. Worth
1942-45 Not held			World War II		
1946	Lloyd Mangrum*	284	Byron Nelson & Vic Ghezzi (284)	Canterbury GC	Cleveland
1947	Lew Worsham*	282	Sam Snead (282)	St. Louis CC	Clayton, Mo.
1948	Ben Hogan	276	Jimmy Demaret (278)	Riviera CC	Los Angeles
1949	Cary Middlecoff	286	Clayton Heafner & Sam Snead (287)	Medinah CC	Medinah, Ill.
1950	Ben Hogan*	287	Lloyd Mangrum & George Fazio (287)	Merion Golf Club	Ardmore, Pa.
1951	Ben Hogan	287	Clayton Heafner (289)	Oakland Hills CC	Birmingham, Mich.
1952	Julius Boros	281	Ed Oliver (285)	Northwood Club	Dallas
1953	Ben Hogan	283	Sam Snead (289)	Oakmont CC	Oakmont, Pa.
1954	Ed Furgol	284	Gene Littler (285)	Baltusrol GC	Springfield, N.J.
1955	Jack Fleck*	287	Ben Hogan (287)	Olympic CC	San Francisco
1956	Cary Middlecoff	281	Ben Hogan & Julius Boros (282)	Oak Hill CC	Rochester, N.Y.
1957	Dick Mayer*	282	Cary Middlecoff (282)	Inverness Club	Toledo, Ohio
1958	Tommy Bolt	283	Gary Player (287)	Southern Hills CC	Tulsa
1959	Billy Casper	282	Bob Rosburg (283)	Winged Foot GC	Marmaroneck, N.Y.
1960	Arnold Palmer	280	Jack Nicklaus (282)	Cherry Hills CC	Denver
1961	Gene Littler	281	Doug Sanders & Bob Goalby (282)	Oakland Hills CC	Birmingham, Mich.
1962	Jack Nicklaus*	283	Arnold Palmer (283)	Oakmont CC	Oakmont, Pa.
1963	Julius Boros*	293	Arnold Palmer & Jacky Cupit (293)	The Country Club	Brookline, Mass.
1964	Ken Venturi	278	Tommy Jacobs (282)	Congressional CC	Bethesda, Md.
1965	Gary Player*	282	Kel Nagle (282)	Bellerive CC	St. Louis
1966	Billy Casper*	278	Arnold Palmer (278)	Olympic CC	San Francisco
1967	Jack Nicklaus	275	Arnold Palmer (279)	Baltusrol GC	Springfield, N.J.
1968	Lee Trevino	275	Jack Nicklaus (279)	Oak Hill CC	Rochester, N.Y.
1969	Orville Moody	281	Al Geiberger, Deane Beman & Bob Rosburg (282)	Champions GC	Houston
1970	Tony Jacklin	281	Dave Hill (288)	Hazeltine National GC	Chaska, Minn.
1971	Lee Trevino*	280	Jack Nicklaus (280)	Merion GC	Ardmore, Pa.
1972	Jack Nicklaus	290	Bruce Crampton (293)	Pebble Beach GL	Pebble Beach, Calif.
1973	Johnny Miller	279	John Schlee (280)	Oakmont CC	Oakmont, Pa.
1974	Hale Irwin	287	Forest Fezler (289)	Winged Foot GC	Mamaroneck, N.Y.
1975	Lou Graham*	287	John Mahaffey (287)	Medinah CC	Medinah, Ill.
1976	Jerry Pate	277	Al Geiberger & Tom Weiskopf (279)	Atlanta AC	Duluth, Ga.
1977	Hubert Green	278	Lou Graham (279)	Southern Hills CC	Tulsa
1978	Andy North	285	Dave Stockton & J.C. Snead (286)	Cherry Hills CC	Denver
1979	Hale Irwin	284	Gary Player & Jerry Pate (286)	Inverness Club	Toledo, Ohio
1980	Jack Nicklaus	272	Isao Aoki (274)	Baltusrol GC	Springfield, N.J.
1981	David Graham	273	George Burns & Bill Rogers (276)	Merion GC	Ardmore, Pa.
1982	Tom Watson	282	Jack Nicklaus (284)	Pebble Beach GL	Pebble Beach, Calif.
1983	Larry Nelson	280	Tom Watson (281)	Oakmont CC	Oakmont, Pa.
1984	Fuzzy Zoeller*	276	Greg Norman (276)	Winged Foot GC	Mamaroneck, N.Y.
1985	Andy North	279	Dave Barr, T.C. Chen & Denis Watson (280)	Oakland Hills CC	Birmingham, Mich.
1986	Ray Floyd	279	Lanny Wadkins & Chip Beck (281)	Shinnecock Hills GC	Southampton, N.Y.
1987	Scott Simpson	277	Tom Watson (278)	Olympic Club	San Francisco
1988	Curtis Strange*	278	Nick Faldo (278)	The Country Club	Brookline, Mass.
1989	Curtis Strange	278	Chip Beck, Ian Woosnam & Mark McCumber (279)	Oak Hill CC	Rochester, N.Y.
1990	Hale Irwin*	280	Mike Donald (280)	Medinah CC	Medinah, Ill.
1991	Payne Stewart*	282	Scott Simpson (282)	Hazeline National GC	Chaska, Minn.
1992	Tom Kite	285	Jeff Sluman (287)	Pebble Beach GL	Pebble Beach, Calif.
1993	Lee Janzen	272	Payne Stewart (274)	Baltusrol GC	Springfield, N.J.

U.S. Open (Cont.)

Year	Winner	Score	Runner-up	Course	Location
1994	Ernie Els*	279	Colin Montgomerie & Loren Roberts (279)	Oakmont CC	Oakmont, Pa.
1995	Corey Pavin	280	Greg Norman (282)	Shinnecock Hills GC	Southampton, N.Y.
1996	Steve Jones	278	Davis Love III & Tom Lehman (279)	Oakland Hills CC	Bloomfield Hills, Mich.
1997	Ernie Els	276	Colin Montgomerie (277)	Congressional CC	Bethesda, MD

*PLAYOFFS:

1901: Willie Anderson (85) def. Alex Smith (86) in 18 holes. **1903:** Willie Anderson (82) def. David Brown (84) in 18 holes. **1908:** Fred McLeod (77) def. Willie Smith (83) in 18 holes. **1910:** Alex Smith (71) def. John McDermott (75) & Macdonald Smith (77) in 18 holes. **1911:** John McDermott (80) def. Mike Brady (82) & George Simpson (85) in 18 holes. **1913:** Francis Ouimet (72) def. Harry Vardon (77) & Edward Ray (78) in 18 holes. **1919:** Walter Hagen (77) def. Mike Brady (78) in 18 holes. **1923:** Bobby Jones (76) def. Bobby Cruickshank (78) in 18 holes. **1925:** Willie Macfarlane (75-72—147) def. Bobby Jones (75-73—148) in 36 holes. **1927:** Tommy Armour (76) def. Harry Cooper (79) in 18 holes. **1928:** Johnny Farrell (70-73—143) def. Bobby Jones (73-71—144) in 36 holes. **1929:** Bobby Jones (141) def. Al Espinosa (164) in 36 holes. **1931:** Billy Burke (149-148) def. George Von Elm (149-149) in 72 holes. **1939:** Byron Nelson (68-70) def. Craig Wood (68-73) and Denny Shute (76) in 36 holes. **1940:** Lawson Little (70) def. Gene Sarazen (73) in 18 holes. **1946:** Lloyd Mangrum (72-72—144) def. Byron Nelson (72-73—145) and Vic Ghezzi (72-73—145) in 36 holes. **1947:** Lew Worsham (69) def. Sam Snead (70) in 18 holes. **1950:** Ben Hogan (69) def. Llyod Mangrum (73) & George Fazio (75) in 18 holes. **1955:** Jack Fleck (69) def. Ben Hogan (72) in 18 holes. **1957:** Dick Mayer (72) def. Cary Middlecoff (79) in 18 holes. **1962:** Jack Nicklaus (71) def. Arnold Palmer (74) in 18 holes. **1963:** Julius Boros (70) def. Jacky Cupit (73) & Arnold Palmer (76) in 18 holes. **1965:** Gary Player (71) def. Kel Nagle (74) in 18 holes. **1966:** Billy Casper (69) def. Arnold Palmer (73) in 18 holes. **1971:** Lee Trevino (68) def. Jack Nicklaus (71) in 18 holes. **1975:** Lou Graham (71) def. John Mahaffey (73) in 18 holes. **1984:** Fuzzy Zoeller (67) def. Greg Norman (75) in 18 holes. **1988:** Curtis Strange (71) def. Nick Faldo (75) in 18 holes. **1990:** Hale Irwin (74-3) def. Mike Donald (74-4) on 1st hole of sudden death after 18 holes. **1991:** Payne Stewart (75) def. Scott Simpson (77) in 18 holes. **1994:** Ernie Els (74-4-4) def. Loren Roberts (74-4-5) and Colin Montgomerie (78-x-x) on 2nd hole of sudden death after 18 holes.

British Open

The oldest of the Majors, The Open began in 1860 to determine "the champion golfer of the world." While only professional golfers participated in the first year of the tournament, amateurs have been invited ever since. Competition was extended from 36 to 72 holes in 1892. Conducted by the Royal and Ancient Golf Club of St. Andrews, The Open is rotated among select golf courses in England and Scotland. Note that (*) indicates playoff winner and (a) indicates amateur winner.

Multiple winners: Harry Vardon (6); James Braid, J.H. Taylor, Peter Thomson and Tom Watson (5); Walter Hagen, Bobby Locke, Tom Morris, Sr.; Tom Morris, Jr.; and Willie Park (4); Jamie Anderson, Seve Ballesteros, Henry Cotton, Nick Faldo, Robert Ferguson, Bobby Jones, Jack Nicklaus and Gary Player (3); Harold Hilton, Bob Martin, Greg Norman, Arnold Palmer, Willie Park, Jr.; and Lee Trevino (2).

Year	Winner	Score	Runner-up	Course	Location
1860	Willie Park	174	Tom Morris Sr. (176)	Prestwick Club	Ayrshire, Scotland
1861	Tom Morris Sr.	163	Willie Park (167)	Prestwick Club	Ayrshire, Scotland
1862	Tom Morris Sr.	163	Willie Park (176)	Prestwick Club	Ayrshire, Scotland
1863	Willie Park	168	Tom Morris Sr. (170)	Prestwick Club	Ayrshire, Scotland
1864	Tom Morris Sr.	167	Andrew Strath (169)	Prestwick Club	Ayrshire, Scotland
1865	Andrew Strath	162	Willie Park (164)	Prestwick Club	Ayrshire, Scotland
1866	Willie Park	169	David Park (171)	Prestwick Club	Ayrshire, Scotland
1867	Tom Morris Sr.	170	Willie Park (172)	Prestwick Club	Ayrshire, Scotland
1868	Tom Morris Jr.	157	Robert Andrew (159)	Prestwick Club	Ayrshire, Scotland
1869	Tom Morris Jr.	154	Tom Morris Sr. (157)	Prestwick Club	Ayrshire, Scotland
1870	Tom Morris Jr.	149	Bob Kirk (161)	Prestwick Club	Ayrshire, Scotland
1871	Not held				
1872	Tom Morris Jr.	166	David Strath (169)	Prestwick Club	Ayrshire, Scotland
1873	Tom Kidd	179	Jamie Anderson (180)	St. Andrews	St. Andrews, Scotland
1874	Mungo Park	159	Tom Morris Jr. (161)	Musselburgh	Musselburgh, Scotland
1875	Willie Park	166	Bob Martin (168)	Prestwick Club	Ayrshire, Scotland
1876	Bob Martin*	176	David Strath (176)	St. Andrews	St. Andrews, Scotland
1877	Jamie Anderson	160	Bob Pringle (162)	Musselburgh	Musselburgh, Scotland
1878	Jamie Anderson	157	Bob Kirk (159)	Prestwick Club	Ayrshire, Scotland
1879	Jamie Anderson	169	Andrew Kirkaldy & James Allan (172)	St. Andrews	St. Andrews, Scotland
1880	Bob Ferguson	162	Peter Paxton (167)	Musselburgh	Musselburgh, Scotland
1881	Bob Ferguson	170	Jamie Anderson (173)	Prestwick Club	Ayrshire, Scotland
1882	Bob Ferguson	171	Willie Fernie (174)	St. Andrews	St. Andrews, Scotland
1883	Willie Fernie*	159	Bob Ferguson (159)	Musselburgh	Musselburgh, Scotland
1884	Jack Simpson	160	David Rollan & Willie Fernie (164)	Prestwick Club	Ayrshire, Scotland
1885	Bob Martin	171	Archie Simpson (172)	St. Andrews	St. Andrews, Scotland
1886	David Brown	157	Willie Campbell (159)	Musselburgh	Musselburgh, Scotland
1887	Willie Park Jr.	161	Bob Martin (162)	Prestwick Club	Ayrshire, Scotland
1888	Jack Burns	171	David Anderson & Ben Sayers (172)	St. Andrews	St. Andrews, Scotland
1889	Willie Park Jr.*	155	Andrew Kirkaldy (155)	Musselburgh	Musselburgh, Scotland

Year	Winner	Score	Runner-up	Course	Location
1890	a-John Ball	164	Willie Fernie (167) & A. Simpson (167)	Prestwick Club	Ayrshire, Scotland
1891	Hugh Kirkaldy	166	Andrew Kirkaldy & Willie Fernie (168)	St. Andrews	St. Andrews, Scotland
1892	a-Harold Hilton	305	John Ball, Sandy Herd & Hugh Kirkaldy (308)	Muirfield	Gullane, Scotland
1893	Willie Auchterlonie	322	Johnny Laidlay (324)	Prestwick Club	Ayrshire, Scotland
1894	J.H. Taylor	326	Douglas Rolland (331)	Royal St. George's	Sandwich, England
1895	J.H. Taylor	322	Sandy Herd (326)	St. Andrews	St. Andrews, Scotland
1896	Harry Vardon*	316	J.H. Taylor (316)	Muirfield	Gullane, Scotland
1897	a-Harold Hilton	314	James Braid (315)	Hoylake	Hoylake, England
1898	Harry Vardon	307	Willie Park Jr. (308)	Prestwick Club	Ayrshire, Scotland
1899	Harry Vardon	310	Jack White (315)	Royal St. George's	Sandwich, England
1900	J.H. Taylor	309	Harry Vardon (317)	St. Andrews	St. Andrews, Scotland
1901	James Braid	309	Harry Vardon (312)	Muirfield	Gullane, Scotland
1902	Sandy Herd	307	Harry Vardon (308)	Hoylake	Hoylake, England
1903	Harry Vardon	300	Tom Vardon (306)	Prestwick Club	Ayrshire, Scotland
1904	Jack White	296	James Braid (297)	Royal St. George's	Sandwich, England
1905	James Braid	318	J.H. Taylor (323) & Rolland Jones (323)	St. Andrews	St. Andrews, Scotland
1906	James Braid	300	J.H. Taylor (304)	Muirfield	Gullane, Scotland
1907	Arnaud Massy	312	J.H. Taylor (314)	Hoylake	Hoylake, England
1908	James Braid	291	Tom Ball (299)	Prestwick Club	Ayrshire, Scotland
1909	J.H. Taylor	295	James Braid (299)	Deal	Deal, England
1910	James Braid	299	Sandy Herd (303)	St. Andrews	St. Andrews, Scotland
1911	Harry Vardon*	303	Arnaud Massy (303)	Royal St. George's	Sandwich, England
1912	Ted Ray	295	Harry Vardon (299)	Muirfield	Gullane, Scotland
1913	J.H. Taylor	304	Ted Ray (312)	Hoylake	Hoylake, England
1914	Harry Vardon	306	J.H. Taylor (309)	Prestwick Club	Ayrshire, Scotland
1915-19 Not held			World War I		
1920	George Duncan	303	Sandy Herd (305)	Deal	Deal, England
1921	Jock Hutchison*	296	Roger Wethered (296)	St. Andrews	St. Andrews, Scotland
1922	Walter Hagen	300	George Duncan & Jim Barnes (301)	Royal St. George's	Sandwich, England
1923	Arthur Havers	295	Walter Hagen (296)	Royal Troon	Troon, Scotland
1924	Walter Hagen	301	Ernest Whitcombe (302)	Hoylake	Hoylake, England
1925	Jim Barnes	300	Archie Compston & Ted Ray (301)	Prestwick Club	Ayrshire, Scotland
1926	a-Bobby Jones	291	Al Watrous (293)	Royal Lytham	Lytham, England
1927	a-Bobby Jones	285	Aubrey Boomer (291)	St. Andrews	St. Andrews, Scotland
1928	Walter Hagen	292	Gene Sarazen (294)	Royal St. George's	Sandwich, England
1929	Walter Hagen	292	Johnny Farrell (298)	Muirfield	Gullane, Scotland
1930	a-Bobby Jones	291	Macdonald Smith & Leo Diegel (293)	Hoylake	Hoylake, England
1931	Tommy Armour	296	Jose Jurado (297)	Carnoustie	Carnoustie, Scotland
1932	Gene Sarazen	283	Macdonald Smith (288)	Prince's	Prince's, England
1933	Denny Shute*	292	Craig Wood (292)	St. Andrews	St. Andrews, Scotland
1934	Henry Cotton	283	Sid Brews (288)	Royal St. George's	Sandwich, England
1935	Alf Perry	283	Alf Padgham (287)	Muirfield	Gullane, Scotland
1936	Alf Padgham	287	Jimmy Adams (288)	Hoylake	Hoylake, England
1937	Henry Cotton	290	Reg Whitcombe (292)	Carnoustie	Carnoustie, Scotland
1938	Reg Whitcombe	295	Jimmy Adams (297)	Royal St. George's	Sandwich, England
1939	Dick Burton	290	Johnny Bulla (292)	St. Andrews	St. Andrews, Scotland
1940-45 Not held			World War II		
1946	Sam Snead	290	Bobby Locke (294) & Johnny Bulla (294)	St. Andrews	St. Andrews, Scotland
1947	Fred Daly	293	Frank Stranahan (294) & Reg Horne (294)	Hoylake	Hoylake, England
1948	Henry Cotton	284	Fred Daly (289)	Muirfield	Gullane, Scotland
1949	Bobby Locke*	283	Harry Bradshaw (283)	Royal St. George's	Sandwich, England
1950	Bobby Locke	279	Roberto de Vicenzo (281)	Royal Troon	Troon, Scotland
1951	Max Faulkner	285	Tony Cerda (287)	Royal Portrush	Portrush, Ireland
1952	Bobby Locke	287	Peter Thomson (288)	Royal Lytham	Lytham, England
1953	Ben Hogan	282	Frank Stranahan Dai Rees, Tony Cerda & Peter Thomson (286)	Carnoustie	Carnoustie, Scotland
1954	Peter Thomson	283	Sid Scott, Dai Rees & Bobby Locke (284)	Royal Birkdale	Southport, England
1955	Peter Thomson	281	Johny Fallon (283)	St. Andrews	St. Andrews, Scotland

British Open (Cont.)

Year	Winner	Score	Runner-up	Course	Location
1956	Peter Thomson	286	Flory Van Donck (289)	Hoylake	Hoylake, England
1957	Bobby Locke	279	Peter Thomson (282)	St. Andrews	St. Andrews, Scotland
1958	Peter Thomson*	278	Dave Thomas (278)	Royal Lytham	Lytham, England
1959	Gary Player	284	Flory Van Donck & Fred Bullock (286)	Muirfield	Gullane, Scotland
1960	Kel Nagle	278	Arnold Palmer (279)	St. Andrews	St. Andrews, Scotland
1961	Arnold Palmer	284	Dai Rees (285)	Royal Birkdale	Southport, England
1962	Arnold Palmer	276	Kel Nagle (282)	Royal Troon	Troon, Scotland
1963	Bob Charles*	277	Phil Rodgers (277)	Royal Lytham	Lytham, England
1964	Tony Lema	279	Jack Nicklaus (284)	St. Andrews	St. Andrews, Scotland
1965	Peter Thomson	285	Christy O'Connor & Brian Huggett (287)	Royal Birkdale	Southport, England
1966	Jack Nicklaus	282	Doug Sanders & Dave Thomas (283)	Muirfield	Gullane, Scotland
1967	Roberto de Vicenzo	278	Jack Nicklaus (280)	Hoylake	Hoylake, England
1968	Gary Player	289	Jack Nicklaus & Bob Charles (291)	Carnoustie	Carnoustie, Scotland
1969	Tony Jacklin	280	Bob Charles (282)	Royal Lytham	Lytham, England
1970	Jack Nicklaus*	283	Doug Sanders (283)	St. Andrews	St. Andrews, Scotland
1971	Lee Trevino	278	Lu Liang Huan (279)	Royal Birkdale	Southport, England
1972	Lee Trevino	278	Jack Nicklaus (279)	Muirfield	Gullane, Scotland
1973	Tom Weiskopf	276	Johnny Miller & Neil Coles (279)	Royal Troon	Troon, Scotland
1974	Gary Player	282	Peter Oosterhuis (286)	Royal Lytham	Lytham, England
1975	Tom Watson*	279	Jack Newton (279)	Carnoustie	Carnoustie, Scotland
1976	Johnny Miller	279	Seve Ballesteros & Jack Nicklaus (285)	Royal Birkdale	Southport, England
1977	Tom Watson	268	Jack Nicklaus (269)	Turnberry	Turnberry, Scotland
1978	Jack Nicklaus	281	Tom Kite, Ray Floyd, Ben Crenshaw & Simon Owen (283)	St. Andrews	St. Andrews, Scotland
1979	Seve Ballesteros	283	Jack Nicklaus & Ben Crenshaw (286)	Royal Lytham	Lytham, England
1980	Tom Watson	271	Lee Trevino (275)	Muirfield	Gullane, Scotland
1981	Bill Rogers	276	Bernhard Langer (280)	Royal St. George's	Sandwich, England
1982	Tom Watson	284	Peter Oosterhuis & Nick Price (285)	Royal Troon	Troon, Scotland
1983	Tom Watson	275	Hale Irwin & Andy Bean (276)	Royal Birkdale	Southport, England
1984	Seve Ballesteros	276	Bernhard Langer & Tom Watson (278)	St. Andrews	St. Andrews, Scotland
1985	Sandy Lyle	282	Payne Stewart (283)	Royal St. George's	Sandwich, England
1986	Greg Norman	280	Gordon J. Brand (285)	Turnberry	Turnberry, Scotland
1987	Nick Faldo	279	Paul Azinger & Rodger Davis (280)	Muirfield	Gullane, Scotland
1988	Seve Ballesteros	273	Nick Price (275)	Royal Lytham	Lytham, England
1989	Mark Calcavecchia*	275	Greg Norman & Wayne Grady (275)	Royal Troon	Troon, Scotland
1990	Nick Faldo	270	Payne Stewart & Mark McNulty (275)	St. Andrews	St. Andrews, Scotland
1991	Ian Baker-Finch	272	Mike Harwood (274)	Royal Birkdale	Southport, England
1992	Nick Faldo	272	John Cook (273)	Muirfield	Gullane, Scotland
1993	Greg Norman	267	Nick Faldo (269)	Royal St. George's	Sandwich, England
1994	Nick Price	268	Jesper Parnevik (269)	Turnberry	Turnberry, Scotland
1995	John Daly*	282	Costantino Rocca (282)	St. Andrews	St. Andrews, Scotland
1996	Tom Lehman	271	Mark McCumber & Ernie Els (273)	Royal Lytham	Lytham, England
1997	Justin Leonard	272	Jesper Parnevik & Darren Clarke (275)	Royal Troon	Troon, Scotland

*PLAYOFFS:

1876: Bob Martin awarded title when David Strath refused playoff. **1883:** Willie Fernie (158) def. Robert Ferguson (159) in 36 holes. **1889:** Willie Park Jr. (158) def. Andrew Kirkaldy (163) in 36 holes. **1896:** Harry Vardon (157) def. John H. Taylor *161) in 36 holes. **1911:** Harry Bardon won when Arnaud Massy conceded at 35th hole. **1921:** Jack Hutchison (150) def. Roger Wethered (159) in 36 holes. **1933:** Denny Shute (149) def. Craig Wood (154) in 36 holes. **1949:** Bobby Locke (135) def. Harry Bradshaw (147) in 36 holes. **1958:** Peter Thomson (139) def. Dave Thomas (143) in 36 holes. **1963:** Bob Charles (140) def. Phil Rogers (148) in 36 holes. **1970:** Jack Nicklaus (72) def. Doug Sanders (73) in 18 holes. **1975:** Tom Watson (71) def. Jack Newton (72) in holes. **1989:** Mark Calcavecchia (4-3-3-3 — 13) def. Wayne Grady (4-4-4-4 — 16) and Greg Norman (3-3-4-x) in 4 holes. **1995:** John Daly (3-4-4-4 — 15) def. Costantino Rocca (4-5-7-3 — 19) in 4 holes.

PGA Championship

The PGA Championship began in 1916 as a professional golfers match play tournament, but switched to stroke play in 1958. Conducted by the PGA of America, the tournament is played on a different course each year.

Mulitple winners: Walter Hagen and Jack Nicklaus (5); Gene Sarazen and Same Snead (3); Jim Barnes, Leo Diegel, Raymond Floyd, Ben Hogan, Byron Nelson, Larry Nelson, Gary Player, Paul Runyan, Denny Shute, Dave Stockton and Lee Trevino (2).

Year	Winner	Score	Runner-up	Course	Location
1916	Jim Barnes	1-up	Jock Hutchison	Siwanoy CC	Bronxville, N.Y.
1917-18	Not held		World War I		
1919	Jim Barnes	6 & 5	Fred McLeod	Engineers CC	Roslyn, N.Y.
1920	Jock Hutchison	1-up	J. Douglas Edgar	Flossmoor CC	Flossmoor, Ill.
1921	Walter Hagen	3 & 2	Jim Barnes	Inwood CC	Far Rockaway, N.Y.
1922	Gene Sarazen	4 & 3	Emmet French	Oakmont CC	Oakmont, Pa.
1923	Gene Sarazen*	1-up/38	Walter Hagen	Pelham CC	Pelham, N.Y.
1924	Walter Hagen	2-up	Jim Barnes	French Lick CC	French Lick, Ind.
1925	Walter Hagen	6 & 5	Bill Mehlhorn	Olympia Fields CC	Matteson, Ill.
1926	Walter Hagen	5 & 3	Leo Diegel	Salisbury GC	Westbury, N.Y.
1927	Water Hagen	1-up	Joe Turnesa	Cedar Crest CC	Dallas
1928	Leo Diegel	6 & 5	Al Espinosa	Five Farms CC	Baltimore
1929	Leo Diegel	6 & 4	John Farrell	Hillcrest CC	Los Angeles
1930	Tommy Armour	1-up	Gene Sarazen	Fresh Meadow CC	Flushing, N.Y.
1931	Tom Creavy	2 & 1	Denny Shute	Wannamoisett CC	Rumford, R.I.
1932	Olin Dutra	4 & 3	Frank Walsh	Keller GC	St. Paul, Minn.
1933	Gene Sarazen	5 & 4	Willie Goggin	Blue Mound CC	Milwaukee
1934	Paul Runyan*	1-up/38	Craig Wood	Park CC	Williamsville, N.Y.
1935	Johnny Revolta	5 & 4	Tommy Armour	Twin Hills CC	Oklahoma City
1936	Denny Shute	3 & 2	Jimmy Thomson	Pinehurst CC	Pinehurst, N.C.
1937	Denny Shute*	1-up/37	Harold McSpaden	Pittsburgh FC	Aspinwall, Pa.
1938	Paul Runyan	8 & 7	Sam Snead	Shawnee CC	Shawnee-on-Del, Pa.
1939	Henry Picard*	1-up/37	Byron Nelson	Pomonok CC	Flushing, N.Y.
1940	Byron Nelson	1-up	Sam Snead	Hershey CC	Hershey, Pa.
1941	Vic Ghezzi*	1-up/38	Byron Nelson	Cherry Hills CC	Denver
1942	Sam Snead	2 & 1	Jim Turnesa	Seaview CC	Atlantic City, N.J.
1943	Not held		World War II		
1944	Bob Hamilton	1-up	Byron Nelson	Manito G & CC	Spokane, Wash.
1945	Byron Nelson	4 & 3	Sam Byrd	Morraine CC	Dayton, Ohio
1946	Ben Hogan	6 & 4	Porky Oliver	Portland GC	Portland, Ore.
1947	Jim Ferrier	2 & 1	Chick Harbert	Plum Hollow CC	Detroit
1948	Ben Hogan	7 & 6	Mike Turnesa	Norwood Hills CC	St. Louis
1949	Sam Snead	3 & 2	John Palmer	Hermitage CC	Richmond, Va.
1950	Chandler Harper	4 & 3	Henry Williams Jr.	Scioto CC	Columbus, Ohio
1951	Sam Snead	7 & 6	Walter Burkemo	Oakmont CC	Oakmont, Pa.
1952	Jim Turnesa	1-up	Chick Harbert	Big Spring CC	Louisville
1953	Walter Burkemo	2 & 1	Felice Torza	Birmingham CC	Birmingham, Mich.
1954	Chick Harbert	4 & 3	Walter Burkemo	Keller GC	St. Paul, Minn.
1955	Doug Ford	4 & 3	Cary Middlecoff	Meadowbrook CC	Detroit
1956	Jack Burke	3 & 2	Ted Kroll	Blue Hill CC	Boston
1957	Lionel Hebert	2 & 1	Dow Finsterwald	Miami Valley GC	Dayton, Ohio
1958	Dow Finsterwald	276	Billy Casper (278)	Llanerch CC	Havertown, Pa.
1959	Bob Rosburg	277	Jerry Barber & Doug Sanders (278)	Minneapolis GC	St. Louis Park, Minn.
1960	Jay Hebert	281	Jim Ferrier (282)	Firestone CC	Akron, Ohio
1961	Jerry Barber**	277	Don January (277)	Olympia Fields CC	Matteson, Ill.
1962	Gary Player	278	Bob Goalby (279)	Aronimink GC	Newtown Square, Pa.
1963	Jack Nicklaus	279	Dave Ragan (281)	Dallas AC	Dallas
1964	Bobby Nichols	271	Jack Nicklaus & Arnold Palmer (274)	Columbus CC	Columbus, Ohio
1965	Dave Marr	280	Jack Nicklaus & Billy Casper (282)	Laurel Valley GC	Ligonier, Pa.
1966	Al Geiberger	280	Dudley Wysong (284)	Firestone CC	Akron, Ohio
1967	Don January**	281	Don Massengale (281)	Columbine CC	Littleton, Colo.
1968	Julius Boros	281	Arnold Palmer & Bob Charles (282)	Pecan Valley CC	San Antonio
1969	Ray Floyd	276	Gary Player (277)	NCR GC	Dayton, Ohio
1970	Dave Stockton	279	Arnold Palmer & Bob Murphy (281)	Southern Hills CC	Tulsa
1971	Jack Nicklaus	281	Billy Casper (283)	PGA National GC	Palm Beach Gardens, Fla.
1972	Gary Player	281	Jim Jamieson & Tommy Aaron (283)	Oakland Hills GC	Birmingham, Mich.

PGA Championship (Cont.)

Year	Winner	Score	Runner-up	Course	Location
1973	Jack Nicklaus	277	Bruce Crampton (281)	Canterbury GC	Cleveland
1974	Lee Trevino	276	Jack Nicklaus (277)	Tanglewood GC	Winston-Salem, N.C.
1975	Jack Nicklaus	276	Bruce Crampton (278)	Firestone CC	Akron, Ohio
1976	Dave Stockton	281	Don January & Ray Floyd (282)	Congressional CC	Bethesda, Md.
1977	Lanny Wadkins**	282	Gene Littler (282)	Pebble Beach GL	Pebble Beach, Calif.
1978	John Mahaffey**	276	Jerry Pate & Tom Watson (276)	Oakmont CC	Oakmont, Pa.
1979	David Graham**	272	Ben Crenshaw (272)	Oakland Hills CC	Birmingham, Mich.
1980	Jack Nicklaus	274	Andy Bean (281)	Oak Hill CC	Rochester, N.Y.
1981	Larry Nelson	273	Fuzzy Zoeller (277)	Atlanta AC	Duluth, Ga.
1982	Ray Floyd	272	Lanny Wadkins (275)	Southern Hills CC	Tulsa
1983	Hal Sutton	274	Jack Nicklaus (275)	Riviera CC	Los Angeles
1984	Lee Trevino	273	Lanny Wadkins & Gary Player (277)	Shoal Creek	Birmingham, Ala.
1985	Hubert Green	278	Lee Trevino (280)	Cherry Hills CC	Denver
1986	Bob Tway	276	Greg Norman (278)	Inverness Club	Toledo, Ohio
1987	Larry Nelson**	287	Lanny Wadkins (287)	PGA National	Palm Beach Gardens, Fla.
1988	Jeff Sluman	272	Paul Azinger 275)	Oak Tree GC	Edmond, Okla.
1989	Payne Stewart	276	Andy Bean, Mike Reid & Curtis Strange (277)	Kemper Lakes GC	Hawthorn Woods, Ill.
1990	Wayne Grady	282	Fred Couples (285)	Shoal Creek	Birmingham, Ala.
1991	John Daly	276	Bruce Lietzke (279)	Crooked Stick GC	Carmel, Ind.
1992	Nick Price	278	Nick Faldo, John Cook, Jim Gallagher & Gene Sauers (281)	Bellerive CC	St. Louis
1993	Paul Azinger**	272	Greg Norman (272)	Inverness Club	Toledo, Ohio
1994	Nick Price	269	Corey Pavin (275)	Southern Hills CC	Tulsa
1995	Steve Elkington**	267	Colin Montgomerie (267)	Riviera CC	Pacific Palisades, Calif.
1996	Mark Brooks**	277	Kenny Perry (277)	Valhalla GC	Louisville, Ky.
1997	Davis Love III	269	Justin Leonard (274)	Winged Foot GC	Mamaroneck, NY

*While the PGA Championship was a match play tournament from 1916-57, the two finalists played 36 holes for the title. In the five years that a playoff was necessary, the match was decided on the 37th or 38th hole.

**PLAYOFFS:

1961: Jerry Barber (67) def. Don January (68) in 18 holes. **1967:** Don January (69) def. Don Massengale (71) in 18 holes. **1977:** Lanny Wadkins (4-4-4) def. Gene Littler (4-4-5) on 3rd hole of sudden death. **1978:** John Mahaffey (4-3) def. Jerry Pate (4-4) and Tom Watson (4-5) on 2nd hole of sudden death. **1979:** David Graham (4-4-2) def. Ben Crenshaw (4-4-4) on 3rd hole of sudden death. **1987:** Larry Nelson (4) def. Lanny Wadkins (5) on 1st hole of sudden death. **1993:** Paul Azinger (4-4) def. Greg Norman (4-5) on 2nd hole of sudden death. **1995:** Steve Elkington (3) def. Colin Montgomerie (4) on 1st hole of sudden death. **1996:** Mark Brooks (4) def. Kenny Perry (5) on 1st hole of sudden death.

Major Championship Leaders
Through 1997; active players in bold type.

	US Open	British Open	PGA	Masters	US Am	British Am	Total
Jack Nicklaus	4	3	5	6	2	0	**20**
Bobby Jones	4	3	0	0	5	1	13
Walter Hagen	2	4	5	0	0	0	11
Ben Hogan	4	1	2	2	0	0	9
Gary Player	1	3	2	3	0	0	9
John Ball	0	1	0	0	0	8	9
Arnold Palmer	1	2	0	4	1	0	8
Tom Watson	1	5	0	2	0	0	8
Harold Hilton	0	2	0	0	1	4	7
Gene Sarazen	2	1	3	1	0	0	7
Sam Snead	0	1	3	3	0	0	7
Harry Vardon	1	6	0	0	0	0	7
Nick Faldo	0	3	0	3	0	0	6
Lee Trevino	2	2	2	0	0	0	6

Tournaments: U.S. Open, British Open, PGA Championship, Masters, U.S. Amateur, and British Amateur.

Grand Slam Summary

The only golfer ever to win a recognized Grand Slam—four major championships in a single season—was Bobby Jones in 1930. That year, Jones won the U.S. and British Opens as well as the U.S. and British Amateurs.

The men's professional Grand Slam—the Masters, U.S. Open, British Open and PGA Championship—did not gain acceptance until 30 years later when Arnold Palmer won the 1960 Masters and U.S. Open. The media wrote that the popular Palmer was chasing the "new" Grand Slam and would have to win the British Open and the PGA to claim it. He did not, but then nobody has before or since.

Three wins in one year: Ben Hogan (1953). **Two wins in one year** (17): Jack Nicklaus (5 times); Ben Hogan, Arnold Palmer and Tom Watson (twice); Nick Faldo, Gary Player, Nick Price, Sam Snead, Lee Trevino and Craig Wood (once).

Year	Masters	US Open	Brit. Open	PGA	Year	Masters	US Open	Brit. Open	PGA
1934	H. Smith	Dutra	Cotton	Runyan	1966	Nicklaus	Casper	Nicklaus	Geiberger
1935	Sarazen	Parks	Perry	Revolta	1967	Brewer	Nicklaus	DeVicenzo	January
1936	H. Smith	Manero	Padgham	Shute	1968	Goalby	Trevino	Player	Boros
1937	B. Nelson	Guldahl	Cotton	Shute	1969	Archer	Moody	Jacklin	Floyd
1938	Picard	Guldahl	Whitcombe	Runyan	1970	Casper	Jacklin	Nicklaus	Stockton
1939	Guldahl	B. Nelson	Burton	Picard	1971	Coody	Trevino	Trevino	Nicklaus
1940	Demaret	Little	—	B. Nelson	1972	Nicklaus	Nicklaus	Trevino	Player
1941	Wood	Wood	—	Ghezzi	1973	Aaron	J. Miller	Weiskopf	Nicklaus
1942	B. Nelson	—	—	Snead	1974	Player	Irwin	Player	Trevino
1943	—	—	—	—	1975	Nicklaus	L. Graham	T. Watson	Nicklaus
1944	—	—	—	Hamilton	1976	Floyd	J. Pate	Miller	Stockton
1945	—	—	—	B. Nelson	1977	T. Watson	H. Green	T. Watson	L Wadkins
1946	Keiser	Mangrum	Snead	Hogan	1978	Player	North	Nicklaus	Mahaffey
1947	Demaret	Worsham	F. Daly	Ferrier	1979	Zoeller	Irwin	Ballesteros	D. Graham
1948	Harmon	Hogan	Cotton	Hogan	1980	Ballesteros	Nicklaus	T. Watson	Nicklaus
1949	Snead	Middlecoff	Locke	Snead	1981	T. Watson	D. Graham	Rogers	L. Nelson
1950	Demaret	Hogan	Locke	Harper	1982	Stadler	T. Watson	T. Watson	Floyd
1951	Hogan	Hogan	Faulkner	Snead	1983	Ballesteros	L. Nelson	T. Watson	Sutton
1952	Snead	Boros	Locke	Turnesa	1984	Crenshaw	Zoeller	Ballesteros	Trevino
1953	Hogan	Hogan	Hogan	Burkemo	1985	Langer	North	Lyle	H. Green
1954	Snead	Furgol	Thomson	Harbert	1986	Nicklaus	Floyd	Norman	Tway
1955	Middlecoff	Fleck	Thomson	Ford	1987	Mize	S. Simpson	Faldo	L. Nelson
1956	Burke	Middlecoff	Thomson	Burke	1988	Lyle	Strange	Ballesteros	Sluman
1957	Ford	Mayer	Locke	L. Hebert	1989	Faldo	Strange	Calcavecchia	Stewart
1958	Palmer	Bolt	Thomson	Finsterwald	1990	Faldo	Irwin	Faldo	Grady
1959	Wall	Casper	Player	Rosburg	1991	Woosnam	Stewart	Baker-Finch	J. Daly
1960	Palmer	Palmer	Nagle	J. Hebert	1992	Couples	Kite	Faldo	Price
1961	Player	Littler	Palmer	J. Barber	1993	Langer	Janzen	Norman	Azinger
1962	Palmer	Nicklaus	Palmer	Player	1994	Olazabal	Els	Price	Price
1963	Nicklaus	Boros	Charles	Nicklaus	1995	Crenshaw	Pavin	Daly	Elkington
1964	Palmer	Venturi	Lema	Nichols	1996	Faldo	S. Jones	Lehman	Brooks
1965	Nicklaus	Player	Thomson	Marr	1997	Woods	Els	Leonard	Love

Vardon Trophy

Awarded since 1937 by the PGA of America to the PGA Tour regular with the lowest scoring average. The award is named after Harry Vardon, the six-time British Open champion, who won the U.S. Open in 1900. A point system was used from 1937-41.

Multiple winners: Billy Casper and Lee Trevino (5); Arnold Palmer and Sam Snead (4); Ben Hogan, Greg Norman and Tom Watson (3); Fred Couples, Bruce Crampton, Tom Kite, and Lloyd Mangrum (2).

Year		Pts	Year		Avg	Year		Avg
1937	Harry Cooper	.500	1959	Art Wall	.70.35	1978	Tom Watson	.70.16
1938	Sam Snead	.520	1960	Billy Casper	.69.95	1979	Tom Watson	.70.27
1939	Byron Nelson	.473	1961	Arnold Palmer	.69.85	1980	Lee Trevino	.69.73
1940	Ben Hogan	.423	1962	Arnold Palmer	.70.27	1981	Tom Kite	.69.80
1941	Ben Hogan	.494	1963	Billy Casper	.70.58	1982	Tom Kite	.70.21
1942-46	No award		1964	Arnold Palmer	.70.01	1983	Ray Floyd	.70.61
Year		Avg	1965	Billy Casper	.70.85	1984	Calvin Peete	.70.56
1947	Jimmy Demaret	.69.90	1966	Billy Casper	.70.27	1985	Don Pooley	.70.36
1948	Ben Hogan	.69.30	1967	Arnold Palmer	.70.18	1986	Scott Hoch	.70.08
1949	Sam Snead	.69.37	1968	Billy Casper	.69.82	1987	Dan Pohl	.70.25
1950	Sam Snead	.69.23	1969	Dave Hill	.70.34	1988	Chip Beck	.69.46
1951	Lloyd Mangrum	.70.05	1970	Lee Trevino	.70.64	1989	Greg Norman	.69.49
1952	Jack Burke	.70.54	1971	Lee Trevino	.70.27	1990	Greg Norman	.69.10
1953	Lloyd Mangrum	.70.22	1972	Lee Trevino	.70.89	1991	Fred Couples	.69.59
1954	E.J. Harrison	.70.41	1973	Bruce Crampton	.70.57	1992	Fred Couples	.69.38
1955	Sam Snead	.69.86	1974	Lee Trevino	.70.53	1993	Nick Price	.69.11
1956	Cary Middlecoff	.70.35	1975	Bruce Crampton	.70.51	1994	Greg Norman	.68.81
1957	Dow Finsterwald	.70.30	1976	Don January	.70.56	1995	Steve Elkington	.69.62
1958	Bob Rosburg	.70.11	1977	Tom Watson	.70.32	1996	Tom Lehman	.69.32

U.S. Amateur

Match play from 1895-64, stroke play from 1965-72, match play since 1972.

Multiple winners: Bobby Jones (5); Jerry Travers (4); Walter Travis and Tiger Woods (3); Deane Beman, Charles Coe, Gary Cowan, H. Chandler Egan, Chick Evans, Lawson Little, Jack Nicklaus, Francis Ouimet, Jay Sigel, William Turnesa, Bud Ward, Harvie Ward, and H.J. Whigham (2).

Year		Year		Year		Year	
1895	Charles Macdonald	1921	Jesse Guilford	1949	Charles Coe	1974	Jerry Pate
1896	H.J. Whigham	1922	Jess Sweetser	1950	Sam Urzetta	1975	Fred Ridley
1897	H.J. Whigham	1923	Max Marston	1951	Billy Maxwell	1976	Bill Sander
1898	Findlay Douglas	1924	Bobby Jones	1952	Jack Westland	1977	John Fought
1899	H.M. Harriman	1925	Bobby Jones	1953	Gene Littler	1978	John Cook
1900	Walter Travis	1926	George Von Elm	1954	Arnold Palmer	1979	Mark O'Meara
1901	Walter Travis	1927	Bobby Jones	1955	Harvie Ward	1980	Hal Sutton
1902	Louis James	1928	Bobby Jones	1956	Harvie Ward	1981	Nathaniel Crosby
1903	Walter Travis	1929	Harrison Johnston	1957	Hillman Robbins	1982	Jay Sigel
1904	H. Chandler Egan	1930	Bobby Jones	1958	Charles Coe	1983	Jay Sigel
1905	H. Chandler Egan	1931	Francis Ouimet	1959	Jack Nicklaus	1984	Scott Verplank
1906	Eben Byers	1932	Ross Somerville	1960	Deane Beman	1985	Sam Randolph
1907	Jerry Travers	1933	George Dunlap	1961	Jack Nicklaus	1986	Buddy Alexander
1908	Jerry Travers	1934	Lawson Little	1962	Labron Harris	1987	Billy Mayfair
1909	Robert Gardner	1935	Lawson Little	1963	Deane Beman	1988	Eric Meeks
1910	W.C. Fownes Jr.	1936	John Fischer	1964	Bill Campbell	1989	Chris Patton
1911	Harold Hilton	1937	John Goodman	1965	Bob Murphy	1990	Phil Mickelson
1912	Jerry Travers	1938	William Turnesa	1966	Gary Cowan	1991	Mitch Voges
1913	Jerry Travers	1939	Bud Ward	1967	Bob Dickson	1992	Justin Leonard
1914	Francis Ouimet	1940	Richard Chapman	1968	Bruce Fleisher	1993	John Harris
1915	Robert Gardner	1941	Bud Ward	1969	Steve Melnyk	1994	Tiger Woods
1916	Chick Evans	1942-45	Not held	1970	Lanny Wadkins	1995	Tiger Woods
1917-18	Not held	1946	Ted Bishop	1971	Gary Cowan	1996	Tiger Woods
1919	Davidson Herron	1947	Skee Riegel	1972	Vinny Giles	1997	Matt Kuchar
1920	Chick Evans	1948	William Turnesa	1973	Craig Stadler		

British Amateur

Match play since 1885.

Multiple winners: John Ball (8); Michael Bonallack (5); Harold Hilton (4); Joe Carr (3); Horace Hutchinson, Ernest Holderness, Trevor Homer, Johnny Laidley, Lawson Little, Peter McEvoy, Dick Siderowf, Frank Stranahan, Freddie Tait and Cyril Tolley (2).

Year		Year		Year		Year	
1885	Allen MacFie	1911	Harold Hilton	1947	William Turnesa	1974	Trevor Homer
1886	Horace Hutchinson	1912	John Ball	1948	Frank Stranahan	1975	Vinny Giles
1887	Horace Hutchinson	1913	Harold Hilton	1949	Samuel McCready	1976	Dick Siderowf
1888	John Ball	1914	J.L.C. Jenkins	1950	Frank Stranahan	1977	Peter McEvoy
1889	Johnny Laidley	1915-19	Not held	1951	Richard Chapman	1978	Peter McEvoy
1890	John Ball	1920	Cyril Tolley	1952	Harvie Ward	1979	Jay Sigel
1891	Johnny Laidley	1921	William Hunter	1953	Joe Carr	1980	Duncan Evans
1892	John Ball	1922	Ernest Holderness	1954	Douglas Bachli	1981	Phillipe Ploujoux
1893	Peter Anderson	1923	Roger Wethered	1955	Joe Conrad	1982	Martin Thompson
1894	John Ball	1924	Ernest Holderness	1956	John Beharrell	1983	Philip Parkin
1895	Leslie Balfour-Melville	1925	Robert Harris	1957	Reid Jack	1984	Jose-Maria Olazabal
1896	Freddie Tait	1926	Jesse Sweetser	1958	Joe Carr	1985	Garth McGimpsey
1897	Jack Allan	1927	William Tweddell	1959	Deane Beman	1986	David Curry
1898	Freddie Tait	1928	Thomas Perkins	1960	Joe Carr	1987	Paul Mayo
1899	John Ball	1929	Cyril Tolley	1961	Michael Bonallack	1988	Christian Hardin
1900	Harold Hilton	1930	Bobby Jones	1962	Richard Davies	1989	Stephen Dodd
1901	Harold Hilton	1931	Eric Smith	1963	Michael Lunt	1990	Rolf Muntz
1902	Charles Hutchings	1932	John deForest	1964	Gordon Clark	1991	Gary Wolstenholme
1903	Robert Maxwell	1933	Michael Scott	1965	Michael Bonallack	1992	Stephen Dundas
1904	Walter Travis	1934	Lawson Little	1966	Bobby Cole	1993	Ian Pyman
1905	Arthur Barry	1935	Lawson Little	1967	Bob Dickson	1994	Lee James
1906	James Robb	1936	Hector Thomson	1968	Michael Bonallack	1995	Gordon Sherry
1907	John Ball	1937	Robert Sweeny Jr.	1969	Michael Bonallack	1996	Warren Bledon
1908	E.A. Lassen	1938	Charles Yates	1970	Michael Bonallack	1997	Craig Watson
1909	Robert Maxwell	1939	Alexander Kyle	1971	Steve Melnyk		
1910	John Ball	1940-45	Not held	1972	Trevor Homer		
		1946	James Bruen	1973	Dick Siderowf		

Major Championships
WOMEN
U.S. Women's Open

The U.S. Women's Open began under the direction of the defunct Women's Professional Golfers Assn. in 1946, passed to the LPGA in 1949 and to the USGA in 1953. The tournament used a match play format its first year then switched to stroke play; (*) indicates playoff winner and (a) indicates amateur winner.

Multiple winners: Betsy Rawls and Mickey Wright (4); Susie Maxwell Berning, Hollis Stacy and Babe Zaharis (3); JoAnne Carner, Donna Caponi, Betsy King, Patty Sheehan, Annika Sorenstam and Louise Suggs (2).

Year		Year		Year		Year	
1946	Patty Berg	1959	Mickey Wright	1972	Susie M. Berning	1985	Kathy Baker
1947	Betty Jameson	1960	Betsy Rawls	1973	Susie M. Berning	1986	Jane Geddes*
1948	Babe Zaharias	1961	Mickey Wright	1974	Sandra Haynie	1987	Laura Davies*
1949	Louise Suggs	1962	Murle Lindstrom	1975	Sandra Palmer	1988	Liselotte Neumann
1950	Babe Zaharias	1963	Mary Mills	1976	JoAnne Carner*	1989	Betsy King
1951	Betsy Rawls	1964	Mickey Wright*	1977	Hollis Stacy	1990	Betsy King
1952	Louise Suggs	1965	Carol Mann	1978	Hollis Stacy	1991	Meg Mallon
1953	Betsy Rawls*	1966	Sandra Spuzich	1979	Jerilyn Britz	1992	Patty Sheehan*
1954	Babe Zaharias	1967	a-Catherine Lacoste	1980	Amy Alcott	1993	Lauri Merten
1955	Fay Crocker	1968	Susie M. Berning	1981	Pat Bradley	1994	Patty Sheehan
1956	Kathy Cornelius*	1969	Donna Caponi	1982	Janet Anderson	1995	Annika Sorenstam
1957	Betsy Rawls	1970	Donna Caponi	1983	Jan Stephenson	1996	Annika Sorenstam
1958	Mickey Wright	1971	JoAnne Carner	1984	Hollis Stacy	1997	Alison Nicholas

*PLAYOFFS:

1953: Betsy Rawls (71) def. Jackie Pung (77) in 18 holes. **1956:** Kathy Cornelius (75) def. Barbara McIntire (82) in 18 holes. **1964:** Mickey Wright (70) def. Ruth Jessen (72) in 18 holes. **1976:** JoAnne Carner (76) def. Sandra Palmer (78) in 18 holes. **1986:** Jane Geddes (71) def. Sally Little (73) in 18 holes. **1987:** Laura Davies (71) def. Ayako Okamoto (73) and JoAnne Carner (74) in 18 holes. **1992:** Patty Sheehan (72) def. Juli Inkster (74) in 18 holes.

LPGA Championship

Officially the McDonald's LPGA Championship since 1994 (Mazda sponsored from 1987-93), the tournament began in 1955 and has had extended stays at the Stardust CC in Las Vegas (1961-66), Pleasant Valley CC in Sutton, Mass. (1967-68, 70-74); the Jack Nicklaus Sports Center at Kings Island, Ohio (1978-89) and Bethesda CC in Maryland (since 1990); (*) indicates playoff winner.

Multiple winners: Mickey Wright (4); Nancy Lopez, Patty Sheehan and Kathy Whitworth (3); Donna Caponi, Laura Davies, Sandra Haynie, Mary Mills and Betsy Rawls (2).

Year		Year		Year		Year	
1955	Beverly Hanson	1966	Gloria Ehret	1977	Chako Higuchi	1988	Sherri Turner
1956	Marlene Hagge*	1967	Kathy Whitworth	1978	Nancy Lopez	1989	Nancy Lopez
1957	Louise Suggs	1968	Sandra Post*	1979	Donna Caponi	1990	Beth Daniel
1958	Mickey Wright	1969	Betsy Rawls	1980	Sally Little	1991	Meg Mallon
1959	Betsy Rawls	1970	Shirley Englehorn*	1981	Donna Caponi	1992	Betsy King
1960	Mickey Wright	1971	Kathy Whitworth	1982	Jan Stephenson	1993	Patty Sheehan
1961	Mickey Wright	1972	Kathy Ahern	1983	Patty Sheehan	1994	Laura Davies
1962	Judy Kimball	1973	Mary Mills	1984	Patty Sheehan	1995	Kelly Robbins
1963	Mickey Wright	1974	Sandra Haynie	1985	Nancy Lopez	1996	Laura Davies
1964	Mary Mills	1975	Kathy Whitworth	1986	Pat Bradley	1997	Chris Johnson*
1965	Sandra Haynie	1976	Betty Burfeindt	1987	Jane Geddes		

*PLAYOFFS:

1956: Marlene Hagge def. Patti Berg in sudden death. **1968:** Sandra Post (68) def. Kathy Whitworth (75) in 18 holes. **1970:** Shirley Englehorn def. Kathy Whitworth in sudden death. **1997:** Chris Johnson def. Leta Lindley in sudden death.

Nabisco Dinah Shore

Formerly known as the Colgate Dinah Shore from 1972-81, the tournament become the LPGA's fourth designated major championship in 1983. Named after the entertainer, this tourney has been played at Mission Hills CC in Rancho Mirage, Calif., since it began; (*) indicates playoff winner.

Multiple winners: (as a major): Amy Alcott and Betsy King (3); Juli Inkster (2).

Year		Year		Year		Year	
1972	Jane Blalock	1979	Sandra Post	1986	Pat Bradley	1993	Helen Alfredsson
1973	Mickey Wright	1980	Donna Caponi	1987	Betsy King*	1994	Donna Andrews
1974	Jo Ann Prentice	1981	Nancy Lopez	1988	Amy Alcott	1995	Nanci Bowen
1975	Sandra Palmer	1982	Sally Little	1989	Juli Inkster	1996	Patty Sheehan
1976	Judy Rankin	1983	Amy Alcott	1990	Betsy King	1997	Betsy King
1977	Kathy Whitworth	1984	Juli Inkster*	1991	Amy Alcott		
1978	Sandra Post	1985	Alice Miller	1992	Dottie Mochrie*		

*PLAYOFFS:

1984: Juli Inkster def. Pat Bradley in sudden death. **1987:** Betsy King def. Patty Sheehan in sudden death. **1992:** Dottie Mochrie def. Juli Inkster in sudden death.

Major Championships (Cont.)
WOMEN
du Maurier Classic

Formerly known as La Canadienne in 1973 and the Peter Jackson Classic from 1974-83, this Canadian stop on the LPGA Tour became the third designated major championship in 1979; (*) indicates playoff winner.

Multiple winner (as a major): Pat Bradley (3).

Year		Year		Year		Year	
1973	Jocelyne Bourassa	1980	Pat Bradley	1987	Jody Rosenthal	1994	Martha Nause
1974	Carole Jo Skala	1981	Jan Stephenson	1988	Sally Little	1995	Jenny Lidback
1975	JoAnne Carner	1982	Sandra Haynie	1989	Tammie Green	1996	Laura Davies
1976	Donna Caponi	1983	Hollis Stacy	1990	Cathy Johnston	1997	Colleen Walker
1977	Judy Rankin	1984	Juli Inkster	1991	Nancy Scranton		
1978	JoAnne Carner	1985	Pat Bradley	1992	Sherri Steinhaur		
1979	Amy Alcott	1986	Pat Bradley*	1993	Brandie Burton*		

*PLAYOFFS:
1986: Pat Bradley def. Ayako Okamoto in sudden death. **1993:** Brandie Burton def. Betsy King in sudden death.

Titleholders Championship (1937-72)

The Titleholders was considered a major title on the women's tour until it was discontinued after the 1972 tournament.

Multiple winners: Patty Berg (7); Louise Suggs (4); Babe Zaharis (3); Dorothy Kirby, Marilynn Smith, Kathy Whitworth and Mickey Wright (2).

Year		Year		Year		Year	
1937	Patty Berg	1947	Babe Zaharias	1955	Patty Berg	1963	Marilynn Smith
1938	Patty Berg	1948	Patty Berg	1956	Louise Suggs	1964	Marilynn Smith
1939	Patty Berg	1949	Peggy Kirk	1957	Patty Berg	1965	Kathy Whitworth
1940	Betty Hicks	1950	Babe Zaharias	1958	Beverly Hanson	1966	Kathy Whitworth
1941	Dorothy Kirby	1951	Pat O'Sullivan	1959	Louise Suggs	1967-71	Not held
1942	Dorothy Kirby	1952	Babe Zaharias	1960	Fay Crocker	1972	Sandra Palmer
1943-45	Not held	1953	Patty Berg	1961	Mickey Wright		
1946	Louise Suggs	1954	Louise Suggs	1962	Mickey Wright		

Western Open (1930-67)

The Western Open was considered a major title on the women's tour until it was discontinued after the 1967 tournament.

Multiple winners: Patty Berg (7); Louise Suggs and Babe Zaharis (4); Mickey Wright (3); June Beebe, Opal Hill, Betty Jameson and Betsy Rawls (2).

Year		Year		Year		Year	
1930	Mrs. Lee Mida	1940	Babe Zaharias	1950	Babe Zaharias	1960	Joyce Ziske
1931	June Beebe	1941	Patty Berg	1951	Patty Berg	1961	Mary Lena Faulk
1932	Jane Weiller	1942	Betty Jameson	1952	Betsy Rawls	1962	Mickey Wright
1933	June Beebe	1943	Patty Berg	1953	Louise Suggs	1963	Mickey Wright
1934	Marian McDougall	1944	Babe Zaharias	1954	Betty Jameson	1964	Carol Mann
1935	Opal Hill	1945	Babe Zaharias	1955	Patty Berg	1965	Susie Maxwell
1936	Opal Hill	1946	Louise Suggs	1956	Beverly Hanson	1966	Mickey Wright
1937	Betty Hicks	1947	Louise Suggs	1957	Patty Berg	1967	Kathy Whitworth
1938	Bea Barrett	1948	Patty Berg	1958	Patty Berg		
1939	Helen Dettweiler	1949	Louise Suggs	1959	Betsy Rawls		

Major Championship Leaders
Through 1997; active players in bold type.

	US Open	LPGA	duM	Dinah	Title-holders	Western	US Am	Brit Am	Total
Patty Berg	1	0	0	0	7	7	1	0	16
Mickey Wright	4	4	0	0	2	3	0	0	13
Louise Suggs	2	1	0	0	4	4	1	1	13
Babe Zaharias	3	0	0	0	3	4	1	1	12
Betsy Rawls	4	2	0	0	0	2	0	0	8
JoAnne Carner	2	0	0	0	0	0	5	0	7
Kathy Whitworth	0	3	0	0	2	1	0	0	6
Pat Bradley	1	1	3	1	0	0	0	0	6
Juli Inkster	0	0	1	2	0	0	3	0	6
Betsy King	2	1	0	3	0	0	0	0	6
Patty Sheehan	2	3	0	1	0	0	0	0	6
Glenna C. Vare	0	0	0	0	0	0	6	0	6

Tournaments: U.S. Open, LPGA Championship, du Maurier Classic, Nabisco Dinah Shore, Titleholders (1937-72), Western Open (1937-67), U.S. Amateur, and British Amateur.

Grand Slam Summary

The Women's Grand Slam has consisted of four tournaments only 19 years. From 1955-66, the U.S. Open, LPGA Championship, Western Open and Titleholders tournaments served as the major events. Since 1983, the U.S. Open, LPGA, du Maurier Classic in Canada and Nabisco Dinah Shore have been the major events. No one has won a four-event Grand Slam on the women's tour.

Three wins in one year (3): Babe Zaharias (1950), Mickey Wright (1961) and Pat Bradley (1986).

Two wins in one year (15): Patty Berg and Mickey Wright (3 times); Louise Suggs (twice); Laura Davies, Sandra Haynie, Juli Inkster, Betsy King, Meg Mallon, Betsy Rawls and Kathy Whitworth (once).

Year	LPGA	US Open	T'holders	Western
1937	—	—	Berg	Hicks
1938	—	—	Berg	Barrett
1939	—	—	Berg	Dettweiler
1940	—	—	Hicks	Zaharias
1941	—	—	Kirby	Berg
1942	—	—	Kirby	Jameson
1943	—	—	—	Berg
1944	—	—	—	Zaharias
1945	—	—	—	Zaharias
1946	—	Berg	Suggs	Suggs
1947	—	Jameson	Zaharias	Suggs
1948	—	Zaharias	Berg	Berg
1949	—	Suggs	Kirk	Suggs
1950	—	Zaharias	Zaharias	Zaharias
1951	—	Rawls	O'Sullivan	Berg
1952	—	Suggs	Zaharias	Rawls
1953	—	Rawls	Berg	Suggs
1954	—	Zaharias	Suggs	Jameson
1955	Hanson	Crocker	Berg	Berg
1956	Hagge	Cornelius	Suggs	Hanson
1957	Suggs	Rawls	Berg	Berg
1958	Wright	Wright	Hanson	Berg
1959	Rawls	Wright	Suggs	Rawls
1960	Wright	Rawls	Crocker	Ziske
1961	Wright	Wright	Wright	Faulk
1962	Kimball	Lindstrom	Wright	Wright
1963	Wright	Mills	M.Smith	Wright
1964	Mills	Wright	M.Smith	Mann
1965	Haynie	Mann	Whitworth	Maxwell
1966	Ehret	Spuzich	Whitworth	Wright
1967	Whitworth	a-LaCoste	—	Whitworth
1968	Post	Berning	—	—

Year	LPGA	US Open	T'holders	Western
1969	Rawls	Caponi	—	—
1970	Englehorn	Caponi	—	—
1971	Whitworth	Carner	—	—
1972	Ahern	Berning	Palmer	—
1973	Mills	Berning	—	—
1974	Haynie	Haynie	—	—
1975	Whitworth	Palmer	—	—
1976	Burfeindt	Carner	—	—
1977	Higuchi	Stacy	—	—
1978	Lopez	Stacy	—	—

Year	LPGA	US Open	duMaurier	D. Shore
1979	Caponi	Britz	Alcott	—
1980	Little	Alcott	Bradley	—
1981	Caponi	Bradley	Stephenson	—
1982	Stephenson	Anderson	Haynie	—
1983	Sheehan	Stephenson	Stacy	Alcott
1984	Sheehan	Stacy	Inkster	Inkster
1985	Lopez	Baker	Bradley	Miller
1986	Bradley	Geddes	Bradley	Bradley
1987	Geddes	Davies	Rosenthal	King
1988	Turner	Neumann	Little	Alcott
1989	Lopez	King	Green	Inkster
1990	Daniel	King	Johnston	King
1991	Mallon	Mallon	Scranton	Alcott
1992	King	Sheehan	Steinhaur	Mochrie
1993	Sheehan	Merten	Burton	Alfredsson
1994	Davies	Sheehan	Nause	Andrews
1995	Robbins	Sorenstam	Lidback	Bowen
1996	Davies	Sorenstam	Davies	Sheehan
1997	Johnson	Nicholas	Walker	King

Vare Trophy

The Vare Trophy for best scoring average by a player on the LPGA Tour has been awarded since 1937 by the LPGA. The award is named after Glenna Collett Vare, winner of six U.S. women's amateur titles from 1922-35.

Multiple winners: Kathy Whitworth (7); JoAnne Carner and Mickey Wright (5); Patty Berg, Nancy Lopez and Judy Rankin (3); Pat Bradley, Beth Daniel, Betsy King and Annika Sorenstam (2).

Year		Avg	Year		Avg	Year		Avg
1953	Patty Berg	75.00	1968	Carol Mann	72.04	1982	JoAnne Carner	71.49
1954	Babe Zaharias	75.48	1969	Kathy Whitworth	72.38	1983	JoAnne Carner	71.41
1955	Patty Berg	74.47	1970	Kathy Whitworth	72.26	1984	Patty Sheehan	71.40
1956	Patty Berg	74.57	1971	Kathy Whitworth	72.88	1985	Nancy Lopez	70.73
1957	Louise Suggs	74.64	1972	Kathy Whitworth	72.38	1986	Pat Bradley	71.10
1958	Beverly Hanson	74.92	1973	Judy Rankin	73.08	1987	Betsy King	71.14
1959	Betsy Rawls	74.03	1974	JoAnne Carner	72.87	1988	Colleen Walker	71.26
1960	Mickey Wright	73.25	1975	JoAnne Carner	72.40	1989	Beth Daniel	70.38
1961	Mickey Wright	73.55	1976	Judy Rankin	72.25	1990	Beth Daniel	70.54
1962	Mickey Wright	73.67	1977	Judy Rankin	72.16	1991	Pat Bradley	70.66
1963	Mickey Wright	72.81	1978	Nancy Lopez	71.76	1992	Dottie Mochrie	70.80
1964	Mickey Wright	72.46	1979	Nancy Lopez	71.20	1993	Betsy King	70.85
1965	Kathy Whitworth	72.61	1980	Amy Alcott	71.51	1994	Beth Daniel	70.90
1966	Kathy Whitworth	72.60	1981	JoAnne Carner	71.75	1995	Annika Sorenstam	71.00
1967	Kathy Whitworth	72.74				1996	Annika Sorenstam	70.47

U.S. Women's Amateur

Stroke play in 1895, match play since 1896.

Multiple winners: Glenna Collett Vare (6); JoAnne Gunderson Carner (5); Margaret Curtis, Beatrix Hoyt, Dorothy Campbell Hurd, Juli Inkster, Alexa Stirling, Virginia Van Wie, Anne Quast Decker Welts (3); Kay Cockerill, Beth Daniel, Vicki Goetze, Katherine Harley, Genevieve Hecker, Betty Jameson, Kelli Kuehne and Barbara McIntire (2).

Year		Year		Year		Year	
1895	Mrs. C.S. Brown	1921	Marion Hollins	1949	Dorothy Porter	1974	Cynthia Hill
1896	Beatrix Hoyt	1922	Glenna Collett			1975	Beth Daniel
1897	Beatrix Hoyt	1923	Edith Cummings	1950	Beverly Hanson	1976	Donna Horton
1898	Beatrix Hoyt	1924	Dorothy C. Hurd	1951	Dorothy Kirby	1977	Beth Daniel
1899	Ruth Underhill	1925	Glenna Collett	1952	Jacqueline Pung	1978	Cathy Sherk
		1926	Helen Stetson	1953	Mary Lena Faulk	1979	Carolyn Hill
1900	Frances Griscom	1927	Miriam Burns Horn	1954	Barbara Romack		
1901	Genevieve Hecker	1928	Glenna Collett	1955	Patricia Lesser	1980	Juli Inkster
1902	Genevieve Hecker	1929	Glenna Collett	1956	Marlene Stewart	1981	Juli Inkster
1903	Bessie Anthony			1957	JoAnne Gunderson	1982	Juli Inkster
1904	Georgianna Bishop	1930	Glenna Collett	1958	Anne Quast	1983	Joanne Pacillo
1905	Pauline Mackay	1931	Helen Hicks	1959	Barbara McIntire	1984	Deb Richard
1906	Harriot Curtis	1932	Virginia Van Wie			1985	Michiko Hattori
1907	Margaret Curtis	1933	Virginia Van Wie	1960	JoAnne Gunderson	1986	Kay Cockerill
1908	Katherine Harley	1934	Virginia Van Wie	1961	Anne Quast Decker	1987	Kay Cockerill
1909	Dorothy Campbell	1935	Glenna Collett Vare	1962	JoAnne Gunderson	1988	Pearl Sinn
		1936	Pamela Barton	1963	Anne Quast Welts	1989	Vicki Goetze
1910	Dorothy Campbell	1937	Estelle Lawson	1964	Barbara McIntire		
1911	Margaret Curtis	1938	Patty Berg	1965	Jean Ashley	1990	Pat Hurst
1912	Margaret Curtis	1939	Betty Jameson	1966	JoAnne G. Carner	1991	Amy Fruhwirth
1913	Gladys Ravenscroft			1967	Mary Lou Dill	1992	Vicki Goetze
1914	Katherine Harley	1940	Betty Jameson	1968	JoAnne G. Carner	1993	Jill McGill
1915	Florence Vanderbeck	1941	Elizabeth Hicks	1969	Catherine Lacoste	1994	Wendy Ward
1916	Alexa Stirling	1942-45	Not held			1995	Kelli Kuehne
1917-18	Not held	1946	Babe D. Zaharias	1970	Martha Wilkinson	1996	Kelli Kuehne
1919	Alexa Stirling	1947	Louise Suggs	1971	Laura Baugh	1997	Silvia Cavalleri
1920	Alexa Stirling	1948	Grace Lenczyk	1972	Mary Budke		
				1973	Carol Semple		

British Women's Amateur Championship

Match play since 1893.

Multiple winners: Cecil Leitch and Joyce Wethered (4); May Hezlet, Lady Margaret Scott, Brigitte Varangot and Enid Wilson (3); Rhone Adair, Pam Barton, Dorothy Campbell, Elizabeth Chadwick, Helen Holm, Marley Spearman, Frances Stephens, Jessie Valentine and Michelle Walker (2).

Year		Year		Year		Year	
1893	Lady Margaret Scott	1921	Cecil Leitch	1950	Lally de St. Sauveur	1974	Carol Semple
1894	Lady Margaret Scott	1922	Joyce Wethered	1951	Catherine MacCann	1975	Nancy Roth Syms
1895	Lady Margaret Scott	1923	Doris Chambers	1952	Moira Paterson	1976	Cathy Panton
1896	Amy Pascoe	1924	Joyce Wethered	1953	Marlene Stewart	1977	Angela Uzielli
1897	Edith Orr	1925	Joyce Wethered	1954	Frances Stephens	1978	Edwina Kennedy
1898	Lena Thomson	1926	Cecil Leitch	1955	Jessie Valentine	1979	Maureen Madill
1899	May Hezlet	1927	Simone de la Chaume	1956	Wiffi Smith		
		1928	Nanette le Blan	1957	Philomena Garvey	1980	Anne Quast Sander
1900	Rhona Adair	1929	Joyce Wethered	1958	Jessie Valentine	1981	Belle Robertson
1901	Mary Graham			1959	Elizabeth Price	1982	Kitrina Douglas
1902	May Hezlet	1930	Diana Fishwick			1983	Jill Thornhill
1903	Rhona Adair	1931	Enid Wilson	1960	Barbara McIntire	1984	Jody Rosenthal
1904	Lottie Dod	1932	Enid Wilson	1961	Marley Spearman	1985	Lillian Behan
1905	Bertha Thompson	1933	Enid Wilson	1962	Marley Spearman	1986	Marnie McGuire
1906	Mrs. W. Kennion	1934	Helen Holm	1963	Brigitte Varangot	1987	Janet Collingham
1907	May Hezlet	1935	Wanda Morgan	1964	Carol Sorenson	1988	Joanne Furby
1908	Maud Titterton	1936	Pam Barton	1965	Brigitte Varangot	1989	Helen Dobson
1909	Dorothy Campbell	1937	Jessie Anderson	1966	Elizabeth Chadwick		
		1938	Helen Holm	1967	Elizabeth Chadwick	1990	Julie Wade Hall
1910	Elsie Grant-Suttie	1939	Pam Barton	1968	Brigitte Varangot	1991	Valerie Michaud
1911	Dorothy Campbell			1969	Catherine Lacoste	1992	Bernille Pedersen
1912	Gladys Ravenscroft	1940-45	Not held			1993	Catriona Lambert
1913	Muriel Dodd	1946	Jean Hetherington	1970	Dinah Oxley	1994	Emma Duggleby
1914	Cecil Leitch	1947	Babe Zaharias	1971	Michelle Walker	1995	Julie Wade Hall
1915-19	Not held	1948	Louise Suggs	1972	Michelle Walker	1996	Kelli Kuehne
1920	Cecil Leitch	1949	Frances Stephens	1973	Ann Irvin	1997	Alison Rose

Senior PGA
PGA Seniors' Championship

First played in 1937. Two championships played in 1979 and 1984.

Multiple winners: Sam Snead (6); Gary Player, Al Watrous and Eddie Williams (3); Julius Boros, Jock Hutchison, Hale Irwin, Don January, Arnold Palmer, Paul Runyan, Gene Sarazen and Lee Trevino (2).

Year		Year		Year		Year	
1937	Jock Hutchison	1954	Gene Sarazen	1970	Sam Snead	1984	Peter Thomson
1938	Fred McLeod*	1955	Mortie Dutra	1971	Julius Boros	1985	Not held
1939	Not held	1956	Pete Burke	1972	Sam Snead	1986	Gary Player
1940	Otto Hackbarth*	1957	Al Watrous	1973	Sam Snead	1987	Chi Chi Rodriguez
1941	Jack Burke	1958	Gene Sarazen	1974	Roberto de Vicenzo	1988	Gary Player
1942	Eddie Williams	1959	Willie Goggin	1975	Charlie Sifford*	1989	Larry Mowry
1943-44	Not held	1960	Dick Metz	1976	Pete Cooper	1990	Gary Player
1945	Eddie Williams	1961	Paul Runyan	1977	Julius Boros	1991	Jack Nicklaus
1946	Eddie Williams*	1962	Paul Runyan	1978	Joe Jiminez*	1992	Lee Trevino
1947	Jock Hutchison	1963	Herman Barron	1979	Jack Fleck*	1993	Tom Wargo*
1948	Charles McKenna	1964	Sam Snead	1979	Don January	1994	Lee Trevino
1949	Marshall Crichton	1965	Sam Snead	1980	Arnold Palmer*	1995	Ray Floyd
1950	Al Watrous	1966	Fred Haas	1981	Miller Barber	1996	Hale Irwin
1951	Al Watrous*	1967	Sam Snead	1982	Don January	1997	Hale Irwin
1952	Ernest Newnham	1968	Chandler Harper	1983	Not held		
1953	Harry Schwab	1969	Tommy Bolt	1984	Arnold Palmer		

*PLAYOFFS:

1938: Fred McLeod def. Otto Hackbarth in 18 holes. **1940:** Otto Hackbarth def. Jock Hutchison in 36 holes. **1946:** Eddie Williams def. Jock Hutchison in 18 holes. **1951:** Al Watrous def. Jock Hutchison in 18 holes. **1975:** Charlie Sifford def. Fred Wampler on 1st extra hole **1978:** Joe Jiminez def. Paul Harney on 1st extra hole. **1979:** Jack Fleck def. Bill Johnston on 1st extra hole. **1980:** Arnold Palmer def. Paul Harney on 1st extra hole. **1993:** Tom Wargo def. Bruce Crampton on 2nd extra hole.

U.S. Senior Open

Established in 1980 for senior players 55 years old and over, the minimum age was dropped to 50 (the PGA Seniors Tour entry age) in 1981. Arnold Palmer, Billy Casper, Orville Moody, Jack Nicklaus and Lee Trevino are the only golfers who have won both the U.S. Open and U.S. Senior Open.

Multiple winners: Miller Barber (3); Jack Nicklaus and Gary Player (2).

Year		Year		Year		Year	
1980	Roberto deVicenzo	1985	Miller Barber	1990	Lee Trevino	1995	Tom Weiskopf
1981	Arnold Palmer*	1986	Dale Douglass	1991	Jack Nicklaus*	1996	Dave Stockton
1982	Miller Barber	1987	Gary Player	1992	Larry Laoretti	1997	Graham Marsh
1983	Bill Casper*	1988	Gary Player*	1993	Jack Nicklaus		
1984	Miller Barber	1989	Orville Moody	1994	Simon Hobday		

*PLAYOFFS:

1981: Arnold Palmer (70) def. Bob Stone (74) and Billy Casper (77) in 18 holes. **1983:** Tied at 75 after 18-hole playoff, Casper def. Rod Funseth with a birdie on the 1st extra hole. **1988:** Gary Player (68) def. Bob Charles (70) in 18 holes. **1991:** Jack Nicklaus (65) def. Chi Chi Rodriquez (69) in 18 holes.

Senior Players Championship

First played in 1983 and contested in Cleveland (1983-86), Ponte Vedra, Fla. (1987-89), and Dearborn, Mich. (since 1990).

Multiple winners: Arnold Palmer and Dave Stockton (2).

Year		Year		Year		Year	
1983	Miller Barber	1987	Gary Player	1991	Jim Albus	1995	J.C. Snead*
1984	Arnold Palmer	1988	Billy Casper	1992	Dave Stockton	1996	Ray Floyd
1985	Arnold Palmer	1989	Orville Moody	1993	Jim Colbert	1997	Larry Gilbert
1986	Chi Chi Rodriguez	1990	Jack Nicklaus	1994	Dave Stockton		

*PLAYOFF:

1995: J.C. Snead def. Jack Nicklaus on 1st extra hole.

The Tradition

First played in 1989 and played every year since at the Golf Club at Desert Mountain in Scottsdale, Ariz.

Multiple winners: Jack Nicklaus (4).

Year		Year		Year		Year	
1989	Don Bies	1992	Lee Trevino	1994	Ray Floyd*	1996	Jack Nicklaus
1990	Jack Nicklaus	1993	Tom Shaw	1995	Jack Nicklaus*	1997	Gil Morgan
1991	Jack Nicklaus						

*PLAYOFFS:

1994: Ray Floyd def. Dale Douglas on 1st extra hole. **1995:** Jack Nicklaus def. Isao Aoki on 3rd extra hole.

Major Senior Championship Leaders
Through 1997. All players are still active.

	PGA Sr.	US Open	Senior Players	Trad	Total			PGA Sr.	US Open	Senior Players	Trad	Total
1 Jack Nicklaus	1	2	1	4	**8**	7	Billy Casper	0	1	1	0	**2**
2 Gary Player	3	2	1	0	**6**		Hale Irwin	2	0	0	0	**2**
3 Lee Trevino	2	1	0	1	**4**		Orville Moody	0	1	1	0	**2**
4 Arnold Palmer	1	0	2	0	**3**		Chi Chi					
Miller Barber	0	2	1	0	**3**		Rodriquez	1	0	1	0	**2**
Ray Floyd	1	0	1	1	**3**		Dave Stockton	0	0	2	0	**2**

Grand Slam Summary
The Senior Grand Slam has officially consisted of The Tradition, the PGA Senior Championship, the Senior Players Championship and the U.S. Senior Open since 1990. Jack Nicklaus won three of the four events in 1991, but no one has won all four in one season.

Three wins in one year: Jack Nicklaus (1991). **Two wins in one year:** Gary Player (twice); Orville Moody, Jack Nicklaus, Arnold Palmer and Lee Trevino (once).

Year	Tradition	PGA Sr.	Players	US Open	Year	Tradition	PGA Sr.	Players	US Open
1983	—	—	M. Barber	Casper	1991	Nicklaus	Nicklaus	Albus	Nicklaus
1984	—	Palmer	Palmer	M. Barber	1992	Trevino	Trevino	Stockton	Laoretti
1985	—	Thomson	Palmer	M. Barber	1993	Shaw	Wargo	Colbert	Nicklaus
1986	—	Player	Rodriguez	Douglass	1994	Floyd	Trevino	Stockton	Hobday
1987	—	Rodriguez	Player	Player	1995	Nicklaus	Floyd	Snead	Weiskopf
1988	—	Player	Casper	Player	1996	Nicklaus	Irwin	Floyd	Stockton
1989	Bies	Mowry	Moody	Moody	1997	Morgan	Irwin	Gilbert	Marsh
1990	Nicklaus	Player	Nicklaus	Trevino					

Annual Money Leaders
Official annual money leaders on the PGA, European PGA, Senior PGA and LPGA tours. European PGA earnings listed in pounds sterling (£).

PGA
Multiple leaders: Jack Nicklaus (8); Ben Hogan and Tom Watson (5); Arnold Palmer (4); Greg Norman, Sam Snead and Curtis Strange (3); Julius Boros, Billy Casper, Tom Kite, Byron Nelson and Nick Price (2).

Year		Earnings	Year		Earnings	Year		Earnings
1934	Paul Runyan	$ 6,767	1955	Julius Boros	$ 63,122	1976	Jack Nicklaus	$266,439
1935	Johnny Revolta	9,543	1956	Ted Kroll	72,836	1977	Tom Watson	310,653
1936	Horton Smith	7,682	1957	Dick Mayer	65,835	1978	Tom Watson	362,429
1937	Harry Cooper	14,139	1958	Arnold Palmer	42,608	1979	Tom Watson	462,636
1938	Sam Snead	19,534	1959	Art Wall	53,168			
1939	Henry Picard	10,303				1980	Tom Watson	530,808
			1960	Arnold Palmer	75,263	1981	Tom Kite	375,699
1940	Ben Hogan	10,655	1961	Gary Player	64,540	1982	Craig Stadler	446,462
1941	Ben Hogan	18,358	1962	Arnold Palmer	81,448	1983	Hal Sutton	426,668
1942	Ben Hogan	13,143	1963	Arnold Palmer	128,230	1984	Tom Watson	476,260
1943 No records kept			1964	Jack Nicklaus	113,285	1985	Curtis Strange	542,321
1944	Byron Nelson	37,968	1965	Jack Nicklaus	140,752	1986	Greg Norman	653,296
1945	Byron Nelson	63,336	1966	Billy Casper	121,945	1987	Curtis Strange	925,941
1946	Ben Hogan	42,556	1967	Jack Nicklaus	188,998	1988	Curtis Strange	1,147,644
1947	Jimmy Demaret	27,937	1968	Billy Casper	205,169	1989	Tom Kite	1,395,278
1948	Ben Hogan	32,112	1969	Frank Beard	164,707			
1949	Sam Snead	31,594				1990	Greg Norman	1,165,477
			1970	Lee Trevino	157,037	1991	Corey Pavin	979,430
1950	Sam Snead	35,759	1971	Jack Nicklaus	244,491	1992	Fred Couples	1,344,188
1951	Lloyd Mangrum	26,089	1972	Jack Nicklaus	320,542	1993	Nick Price	1,478,557
1952	Julius Boros	37,033	1973	Jack Nicklaus	308,362	1994	Nick Price	1,499,927
1953	Lew Worsham	34,002	1974	Johnny Miller	353,022	1995	Greg Norman	1,654,959
1954	Bob Toski	65,820	1975	Jack Nicklaus	298,149	1996	Tom Lehman	1,780,159

Note: In 1944-45, Nelson's winnings were in War Bonds.

Senior PGA
Multiple leaders: Don January (3); Miller Barber, Bob Charles, Jim Colbert, Dave Stockton and Lee Trevino (2).

Year		Earnings	Year		Earnings	Year		Earnings
1980	Don January	$44,100	1986	Bruce Crampton	$454,299	1992	Lee Trevino	$1,027,002
1981	Miller Barber	83,136	1987	Chi Chi Rodriguez	509,145	1993	Dave Stockton	1,175,944
1982	Miller Barber	106,890	1988	Bob Charles	533,929	1994	Dave Stockton	1,402,519
1983	Don January	237,571	1989	Bob Charles	725,887	1995	Jim Colbert	1,444,386
1984	Don January	328,597	1990	Lee Trevino	1,190,518	1996	Jim Colbert	1,627,890
1985	Peter Thomson	386,724	1991	Mike Hill	1,065,657			

European PGA

Multiple leaders: Seve Ballesteros (6); Colin Montgomerie (4); Sandy Lyle (3); Gay Brewer, Nick Faldo, Bernard Hunt, Bernhard Langer, Peter Thomson and Ian Woosnam (2).

Year		Earnings	Year		Earnings	Year		Earnings
1961	Bernard Hunt	£4,492	1973	Tony Jacklin	£24,839	1985	Sandy Lyle	£254,711
1962	Peter Thomson	5,764	1974	Peter Oosterhuis	32,127	1986	Seve Ballesteros	259,275
1963	Bernard Hunt	7,209	1975	Dale Hayes	20,507	1987	Ian Woosnam	439,075
1964	Neil Coles	7,890	1976	Seve Ballesteros	39,504	1988	Seve Ballesteros	502,000
1965	Peter Thomson	7,011	1977	Seve Ballesteros	46,436	1989	Ronan Rafferty	465,981
1966	Bruce Devlin	13,205	1978	Seve Ballesteros	54,348	1990	Ian Woosnam	737,977
1967	Gay Brewer	20,235	1979	Sandy Lyle	49,233	1991	Seve Ballesteros	790,811
1968	Gay Brewer	23,107	1980	Greg Norman	74,829	1992	Nick Faldo	1,220,540
1969	Billy Casper	23,483	1981	Bernhard Langer	95,991	1993	Colin Montgomerie	798,145
1970	Christy O'Connor	31,532	1982	Sandy Lyle	86,141	1994	Colin Montgomerie	920,647
1971	Gary Player	11,281	1983	Nick Faldo	140,761	1995	Colin Montgomerie	999,260
1972	Bob Charles	18,538	1984	Bernhard Langer	160,883	1996	Colin Montgomerie	1,034,752

LPGA

Multiple leaders: Kathy Whitworth (8); Mickey Wright (4); Patty Berg, JoAnne Carner, Betsy King and Nancy Lopez (3); Pat Bradley, Beth Daniel, Judy Rankin, Betsy Rawls, Louis Suggs and Babe Zaharis (2).

Year		Earnings	Year		Earnings	Year		Earnings
1950	Babe Zaharias	$14,800	1966	Kathy Whitworth	$33,517	1982	JoAnne Carner	$310,400
1951	Babe Zaharias	15,087	1967	Kathy Whitworth	32,937	1983	JoAnne Carner	291,404
1952	Betsy Rawls	14,505	1968	Kathy Whitworth	48,379	1984	Betsy King	266,771
1953	Louise Suggs	19,816	1969	Carol Mann	49,152	1985	Nancy Lopez	416,472
1954	Patty Berg	16,011	1970	Kathy Whitworth	30,235	1986	Pat Bradley	492,021
1955	Patty Berg	16,492	1971	Kathy Whitworth	41,181	1987	Ayako Okamoto	466,034
1956	Marlene Hagge	20,235	1972	Kathy Whitworth	65,063	1988	Sherri Turner	350,851
1957	Patty Berg	16,272	1973	Kathy Whitworth	82,864	1989	Betsy King	654,132
1958	Beverly Hanson	12,639	1974	JoAnne Carner	87,094	1990	Beth Daniel	863,578
1959	Betsy Rawls	26,774	1975	Sandra Palmer	76,374	1991	Pat Bradley	763,118
1960	Louise Suggs	16,892	1976	Judy Rankin	150,734	1992	Dottie Mochrie	693,335
1961	Mickey Wright	22,236	1977	Judy Rankin	122,890	1993	Betsy King	595,992
1962	Mickey Wright	21,641	1978	Nancy Lopez	189,814	1994	Laura Davies	687,201
1963	Mickey Wright	31,269	1979	Nancy Lopez	197,489	1995	Annika Sorenstam	666,533
1964	Mickey Wright	29,800	1980	Beth Daniel	231,000	1996	Karrie Webb	1,002,000
1965	Kathy Whitworth	28,658	1981	Beth Daniel	206,998			

All-Time Leaders

PGA, Senior PGA and LPGA leaders through 1996.

Tournaments Won

	PGA	No		Senior PGA	No		LPGA	No
1	Sam Snead	81	1	Lee Trevino	27	1	Kathy Whitworth	88
2	Jack Nicklaus	70	2	Miller Barber	24	2	Mickey Wright	82
3	Ben Hogan	63	3	Bob Charles	23	3	Patty Berg	57
4	Arnold Palmer	60	4	Don January	22	4	Betsy Rawls	55
5	Byron Nelson	52		Chi Chi Rodriguez	22	5	Louise Suggs	50
6	Billy Casper	51	6	Bruce Crampton	19	6	Nancy Lopez	47
7	Walter Hagan	40	7	Gary Player	18	7	JoAnne Carner	42
	Cary Middlecoff	40		Mike Hill	18		Sandra Haynie	42
9	Gene Sarazen	38		Jim Colbert	18	9	Carol Mann	38
10	Lloyd Mangrum	36	10	George Archer	17	10	Patty Sheehan	35
11	Tom Watson	33	11	Raymond Floyd	13	11	Beth Daniel	32
12	Horton Smith	32		Dave Stockton	13	12	Pat Bradley	31
13	Harry Cooper	31	13	Orville Moody	11		Babe Zaharias	31
	Jimmy Demaret	31		Peter Thomson	11	14	Betsy King	30
15	Leo Diegel	30		Dale Douglass	11	15	Amy Alcott	29
16	Gene Littler	29	16	Arnold Palmer	10		Jane Blalock	29
	Paul Runyan	29		Jim Dent	10	17	Judy Rankin	26
18	Lee Trevino	27		Al Geiberger	10	18	Marlene Hagge	25
19	Henry Picard	26		Bob Murphy	10	19	Donna Caponi	24
20	Tommy Armour	24		Jack Nicklaus	10	20	Marilynn Smith	22
	Macdonald Smith	24						
	Johnny Miller	24						

Note: Patty Berg's total includes 13 official pro wins prior to formation of LPGA in 1950.

All-Time Leaders (Cont.)
Money Won
PGA

#	Player	Earnings	#	Player	Earnings	#	Player	Earnings
1	Greg Norman	$10,564,662	10	Ben Crenshaw	$7,026,118	19	Hale Irwin	$5,890,364
2	Tom Kite	9,661,354	11	Curtis Strange	6,976,660	20	David Frost	5,841,119
3	Fred Couples	8,437,102	12	Davis Love III	6,835,029	21	Bruce Lietzke	5,837,203
4	Corey Pavin	8,031,052	13	Scott Hoch	6,505,462	22	Jack Nicklaus	5,500,051
5	Payne Stewart	7,926,773	14	Mark Calcavecchia	6,495,566	23	John Cook	5,293,214
6	Tom Watson	7,833,350	15	Craig Stadler	6,345,573	24	Mark McCumber	5,286,928
7	Nick Price	7,740,586	16	Lanny Wadkins	6,105,909	25	Ray Floyd	5,277,329
8	Mark O'Meara	7,382,215	17	Chip Beck	5,983,971			
9	Paul Azinger	7,189,365	18	Jay Haas	5,952,750			

Senior PGA

#	Player	Earnings	#	Player	Earnings	#	Player	Earnings
1	Lee Trevino	$6,715,649	10	Dale Douglass	$4,773,830	19	Rocky Thompson	$3,347,943
2	Bob Charles	6,621,207	11	Gary Player	4,269,992	20	Harold Henning	3,337,227
3	Jim Colbert	6,570,797	12	Bruce Crampton	4,000,892	21	Orville Moody	3,191,894
4	Dave Stockton	5,781,417	13	Bob Murphy	3,933,317	22	Charles Coody	3,183,235
5	Chi Chi Rodriguez	5,696,544	14	Al Geiberger	3,843,368	23	Tom Wargo	3,103,007
6	Mike Hill	5,658,265	15	Isao Aoki	3,719,638	24	Don January	3,016,549
7	George Archer	5,264,385	16	Miller Barber	3,627,184	25	Simon Hobday	2,905,280
8	Ray Floyd	4,995,515	17	Jim Albus	3,575,311			
9	Jim Dent	4,901,863	18	J.C. Snead	3,547,362			

European PGA

#	Player	Earnings	#	Player	Earnings	#	Player	Earnings
1	Bernhard Langer	£5,348,843	10	Ronan Rafferty	£2,574,510	19	Ernie Els	£2,155,980
2	Colin Montgomerie	5,194,708	11	Mark James	2,533,269	20	Rodger Davis	2,004,280
3	Nick Faldo	5,072,682	12	Sandy Lyle	2,521,705	21	Howard Clark	1,998,410
4	Ian Woosnam	4,880,723	13	Fred Couples	2,383,868	22	Vijay Singh	1,960,483
5	Seve Ballesteros	4,457,672	14	Anders Forsbrand	2,362,295	23	Jose Rivero	1,843,437
6	Sam Torrance	3,880,303	15	Gordon Brand Jr.	2,361,834	24	Miguel Angel Jimenez	1,786,439
7	Jose Maria Olazabal	3,140,347	16	Costantino Rocca	2,303,648	25	David Gilford	1,735,468
8	Mark McNulty	3,030,721	17	Frank Nobilo	2,238,343			
9	Barry Lane	2,736,011	18	Greg Norman	2,212,299			

LPGA

#	Player	Earnings	#	Player	Earnings	#	Player	Earnings
1	Betsy King	$5,510,482	10	Rosie Jones	$2,895,598	19	Hollis Stacy	$2,127,737
2	Pat Bradley	5,411,808	11	JoAnne Carner	2,885,708	20	Val Skinner	2,106,023
3	Beth Daniel	5,135,808	12	Meg Mallon	2,807,254	21	Judy Dickinson	2,102,049
4	Patty Sheehan	5,130,937	13	Ayako Okamoto	2,741,742	22	Chris Johnson	1,954,880
5	Nancy Lopez	4,538,136	14	Juli Inkster	2,525,817	23	Deb Richard	1,946,093
6	Dottie Pepper	3,685,117	15	Jan Stephenson	2,427,142	24	Michelle McGann	1,940,964
7	Amy Alcott	3,242,555	16	Liselotte Neumann	2,295,268	25	Dawn Coe-Jones	1,918,459
8	Laura Davies	3,143,308	17	Colleen Walker	2,281,471			
9	Jane Geddes	2,975,192	18	Tammie Green	2,208,218			

The Skins Game

The Skins Game is a made-for-TV, $540,000 shootout between four premier golfers playing 18 holes over two days (nine each day). Each hole is counted as a skin with the first six skins worth $20,000 apiece, the second six worth $30,000, and the last six worth $40,000. If a hole is tied, the money is added to the worth of the next hole. The PGA Skins Game was started in late November 1983, followed by the Senior Skins in late January 1988 and the LPGA Skins in late May 1990. Due to scheduling conflicts, the LPGA Skins was not played in 1991.

PGA Skins

Total winnings: 1. Fred Couples ($1,190,000); 2. Payne Stewart ($840,000); 3. Fuzzy Zoeller ($695,000); 4. Tom Watson ($660,000); 5. Jack Nicklaus ($650,000); 6. Curtis Strange ($605,000); 7. Lee Trevino ($435,000); 8. Ray Floyd ($350,000); 9. Arnold Palmer ($245,000); 10. Corey Pavin ($240,000); 11. Greg Norman ($200,000); 12. Gary Player ($170,000); 13. John Daly ($160,000); 14. Paul Azinger ($80,000); 15. Nick Faldo ($70,000); 16. Tiger Woods ($40,000); 17. Peter Jacobsen ($30,000); 18. Tom Kite ($0).

Year	Winner	Earnings	Outskinned		Year	Winner	Earnings	Outskinned	
1983	Gary Player	$170,000	Palmer	$140,000	1985	Fuzzy Zoeller	$255,000	Watson	$100,000
			Nicklaus	40,000				Palmer	80,000
			Watson	10,000				Nicklaus	15,000
1984	Jack Nicklaus	$240,000	Watson	$120,000	1986	Fuzzy Zoeller	$370,000	Trevino	$55,000
			Palmer	0				Palmer	25,000
			Player	0				Nicklaus	0

Year	Winner	Earnings	Outskinned		Year	Winner	Earnings	Outskinned	
1987	Lee Trevino	$310,000	Nicklaus	$70,000	1992	Payne Stewart	$220,000	Couples	$210,000
			Zoeller	70,000				Norman	110,000
			Palmer	0				Kite	0
1988	Ray Floyd	$290,000	Nicklaus	$125,000	1993	Payne Stewart	$280,000	Couples	$260,000
			Trevino	35,000				Palmer	0
			Strange	0				Azinger	0
1989	Curtis Strange	$265,000	Nicklaus	$90,000	1994	Tom Watson	$210,000	Couples	$170,000
			Floyd	60,000				Azinger	$80,000
			Trevino	35,000				Stewart	$80,000
1990	Curtis Strange	$220,000	Norman	$90,000	1995	Fred Couples	$270,000	Pavin	$240,000
			Faldo	70,000				Jacobsen	30,000
			Nicklaus	70,000				Watson	0
1991	Payne Stewart	$260,000	Daly	$160,000	1996	Fred Couples	$280,000	Watson	$220,000
			Strange	120,000				Woods	40,000
			Nicklaus	0				Daly	0

Senior Skins

Total winnings: 1. Ray Floyd ($1,170,000); 2. Jack Nicklaus ($945,000); 3. Arnold Palmer ($935,000); 4. Chi Chi Rodriguez ($685,000); 5. Lee Trevino ($305,000); 6. Jim Colbert and Gary Player ($180,000); 8. Hale Irwin ($160,000); 9. Billy Casper ($80,000); 10. Sam Snead ($0).

Year	Winner	Earnings	Outskinned		Year	Winner	Earnings	Outskinned	
1988	C.C. Rodriguez	$300,000	Player	$40,000	1993	Arnold Palmer	$190,000	Rodriguez	$145,000
			Palmer	20,000				Floyd	60,000
			Snead	0				Nicklaus	55,000
1989	C.C. Rodriguez	$120,000	Player	$90,000	1994	Ray Floyd	$240,000	Palmer	$115,000
			Casper	80,000				Trevino	80,000
			Palmer	70,000				Nicklaus	15,000
1990	Arnold Palmer	$240,000	Nicklaus	$140,000	1995	Ray Floyd	$420,000	Nicklaus	$120,000
			Trevino	70,000				Trevino	0
			Player	0				Palmer	0
1991	Jack Nicklaus	$310,000	Trevino	$125,000	1996	Ray Floyd	$240,000	Colbert	$180,000
			Palmer	15,000				Palmer	80,000
1992	Arnold Palmer	$205,000	Rodriguez	$120,000				Nicklaus	40,000
			Nicklaus	95,000	1997	Ray Floyd	$210,000	Nicklaus	$170,000
			Trevino	30,000				Irwin	160,000
								Trevino	0

LPGA Skins

Total winnings: 1. Laura Davies ($620,000); 2. Dottie (Mochrie) Pepper ($540,000); 3. Betsy King and Patty Sheehan ($395,000); 5. Nancy Lopez and Annika Sorenstam ($320,000); 7. Pat Bradley ($285,000); 8. Jan Stephenson ($270,000); 9. JoAnne Carner ($110,000); 10. Karrie Webb ($100,000); 11. Meg Mallon ($65,000); 12. Brandie Burton ($0).

Year	Winner	Earnings	Outskinned		Year	Winner	Earnings	Outskinned	
1990	Jan Stephenson	$200,000	Carner	$110,000	1994	Patty Sheehan	$285,000	King	$165,000
			Lopez	95,000				Burton	0
			King	45,000				Lopez	0
1991	Not held				1995	Dottie Mochrie	$290,000	Davies	$140,000
1992	Pat Bradley	$200,000	Lopez	$115,000				Sheehan	110,000
			Stephenson	70,000				Lopez	0
			Mallon	65,000	1996	Laura Davies	$340,000	Pepper	$100,000
1993	Betsy King	$185,000	Lopez	$110,000				Sorenstam	100,000
			Bradley	85,000				Daniel	0
			Mochrie	70,000	1997	A. Sorenstam	$220,000	Davies	$140,000
								Webb	100,000
								Pepper	80,000

Annual Awards

PGA of America Player of the Year

Awarded by the PGA of America; based on points scale that weighs performance in major tournaments, regular events, money earned and scoring average.

Multiple winners: Tom Watson (6); Jack Nicklaus (5); Ben Hogan (4); Julius Boros, Billy Casper, Arnold Palmer and Nick Price (2).

Year		Year		Year		Year	
1948	Ben Hogan	1957	Dick Mayer	1966	Billy Casper	1975	Jack Nicklaus
1949	Sam Snead	1958	Dow Finsterwald	1967	Jack Nicklaus	1976	Jack Nicklaus
1950	Ben Hogan	1959	Art Wall	1968	No award	1977	Tom Watson
1951	Ben Hogan	1960	Arnold Palmer	1969	Orville Moody	1978	Tom Watson
1952	Julius Boros	1961	Jerry Barber	1970	Billy Casper	1979	Tom Watson
1953	Ben Hogan	1962	Arnold Palmer	1971	Lee Trevino	1980	Tom Watson
1954	Ed Furgol	1963	Julius Boros	1972	Jack Nicklaus	1981	Bill Rogers
1955	Doug Ford	1964	Ken Venturi	1973	Jack Nicklaus	1982	Tom Watson
1956	Jack Burke	1965	Dave Marr	1974	Johnny Miller	1983	Hal Sutton

Annual Awards (Cont.)

Year		Year		Year		Year	
1984	Tom Watson	1988	Curtis Strange	1992	Fred Couples	1996	Tom Lehman
1985	Lanny Wadkins	1989	Tom Kite	1993	Nick Price		
1986	Bob Tway	1990	Nick Faldo	1994	Nick Price		
1987	Paul Azinger	1991	Corey Pavin	1995	Greg Norman		

PGA Tour Player of the Year

Award by the PGA Tour starting in 1990. Winner voted on by tour members from list of nominees.

Multiple winners: Fred Couples and Nick Price (2).

Year		Year		Year		Year	
1990	Wayne Levi	1992	Fred Couples	1994	Nick Price	1996	Tom Lehman
1991	Fred Couples	1993	Nick Price	1995	Greg Norman		

PGA Tour Rookie of the Year

Awarded by the PGA Tour in 1990. Winner voted on by tour members from list of first-year nominees.

Year		Year		Year		Year	
1990	Robert Gamez	1992	Mark Carnevale	1994	Ernie Els	1996	Tiger Woods
1991	John Daly	1993	Vijay Singh	1995	Woody Austin		

PGA Senior Player of the Year

Awarded by th PGA Seniors Tour starting in 1990. Winner voted on by tour members from list of nominees.

Multiple winner: Lee Trevino (3); Jim Colbert (2).

Year		Year		Year		Year	
1990	Lee Trevino	1992	Lee Trevino	1994	Lee Trevino	1996	Jim Colbert
1991	George Archer & Mike Hill	1993	Dave Stockton	1995	Jim Colbert		

PGA Senior Tour Rookie of the Year

Awarded by th PGA Tour starting in 1990. Winner voted on by tour members from list of first-year nominees.

Year		Year		Year		Year	
1990	Lee Trevino	1992	Dave Stockton	1994	Jay Sigel	1996	John Bland
1991	Jim Colbert	1993	Bob Murphy	1995	Hale Irwin		

European Golfer of the Year

Officially, the Johnnie Walker Trophy; voting done by panel of European golf writers and tour members.

Multiple winners; Seve Ballesteros and Nick Faldo (3); Bernhard Langer and Colin Montgomerie (2).

Year		Year		Year		Year	
1985	Bernhard Langer	1988	Seve Ballesteros	1991	Seve Ballesteros	1994	Ernie Els
1986	Seve Ballesteros	1989	Nick Faldo	1992	Nick Faldo	1995	Colin Montgomerie
1987	Ian Woosnam	1990	Nick Faldo	1993	Bernhard Langer	1996	Colin Montgomerie

LPGA Player of the Year

Awarded by the LPGA; based on performance points accumulated during the year.

Multiple winners: Kathy Whitworth (7); Nancy Lopez (4); JoAnne Carner, Beth Daniel and Betsy King (3); Pat Bradley and Judy Rankin (2).

Year		Year		Year		Year	
1966	Kathy Whitworth	1974	JoAnne Carner	1982	JoAnne Carner	1990	Beth Daniel
1967	Kathy Whitworth	1975	Sandra Palmer	1983	Patty Sheehan	1991	Pat Bradley
1968	Kathy Whitworth	1976	Judy Rankin	1984	Betsy King	1992	Dottie Mochrie
1969	Kathy Whitworth	1977	Judy Rankin	1985	Nancy Lopez	1993	Betsy King
1970	Sandra Haynie	1978	Nancy Lopez	1986	Pat Bradley	1994	Beth Daniel
1971	Kathy Whitworth	1979	Nancy Lopez	1987	Ayako Okamoto	1995	Annika Sorenstam
1972	Kathy Whitworth	1980	Beth Daniel	1988	Nancy Lopez	1996	Laura Davies
1973	Kathy Whitworth	1981	JoAnne Carner	1989	Betsy King		

Sony World Rankings

Begun in 1986, the Sony World Rankings combine the best golfers on the PGA and European PGA tours. Rankings are based on a rolling three-year period and weighed in favor of more recent results. While annual winners are not announced, certain players reaching No. 1 have dominated each year.

Multiple winners (at year's end): Greg Norman (6); Nick Faldo (3); Seve Ballesteros (2).

Year		Year		Year		Year	
1986	Seve Ballesteros	1990	Nick Faldo & Greg Norman	1992	Fred Couples & Nick Faldo	1994	Nick Price
1987	Greg Norman	1991	Ian Woosnam	1993	Nick Price	1995	Greg Norman
1988	Greg Norman					1996	Greg Norman
1989	Seve Ballesteros & Greg Norman						

National Team Competition
MEN

Ryder Cup

The Ryder Cup was presented by British seed merchant and businessman Samuel Ryder in 1927 for competition between professional golfers from Great Britain and the United States. The British team was expanded to include Irish players in 1973 and the rest of Europe in 1979. The United States leads the series 23-7-2 after 32 matches.

Year		Year		Year	
1927	United States, 9½-2½	1955	United States, 8-4	1977	United States, 12½-13½
1929	Britain-Ireland, 7-5	1957	Britain-Ireland, 7½-4½	1979	United States, 17-11
1931	United States, 9-3	1959	United States, 8½-3½	1981	United States, 18½-9½
1933	Great Britain, 6½-5½	1961	United States, 14½-9½	1983	United States, 14½-13½
1935	United States, 9-3	1963	United States, 23-9	1985	Europe, 16½-11½
1937	United States, 8-4	1965	United States, 19½-12½	1987	Europe, 15-13
1939-45	Not held	1967	United States, 23½-8½	1989	Draw, 14-14
1947	United States, 11-1	1969	Draw, 16-16	1991	United States, 14½-13½
1949	United States, 7-5	1971	United States, 18½-13½	1993	United States, 15-13
1951	United States, 9½-2½	1973	United States, 19-13	1995	Europe, 14½-13½
1953	United States, 6½-5½	1975	United States, 21-11	1997	Europe, 14½-13½

Playing Sites

1927—Worcester CC (Mass.); **1929**—Moortown, England; **1931**—Scioto CC (Ohio); **1933**—Southport & Ainsdale, England; **1935**—Ridgewood CC (N.J.); **1937**—Southport & Ainsdale, England; **1939-45**—Not held. **1947**—Portland CC (Ore.); **1949**—Ganton GC, England; **1951**—Pinehurst CC (N.C.); **1953**—Wentworth, England; **1955**—Thunderbird Ranch &CC (Calif.); **1957**—Lindrick GC, England; **1959**—Eldorado CC (Calif.); **1961**—Royal Lytham & St. Annes, England; **1963**—East Lake CC (Ga.); **1965**—Royal Birkdale, England; **1967**—Champions GC (Tex.); **1969**—Royal Birkdale, England; **1971**—Old Warson CC (Mo.); **1973**—Muirfield, Scotland; **1975**—Laurel Valley GC (Pa.); **1977**—Royal Lytham & St. Annes, England; **1979**—Greenbrier; **1981**—Walton Heath GC, England; **1983**—PGA National GC (Fla.); **1985**—The Belfry, England; **1987**—Muirfield Village GC (Ohio); **1989**—The Belfry, England; **1991**—Ocean Course (S.C.); **1993**—The Belfry, England; **1995**—Oak Hill CC (N.Y.); **1997**—Valderrama, Costa del Sol, Spain.

Walker Cup

The Walker Cup was presented by American businessman George Herbert Walker in 1922 for competition between amateur golfers from Great Britain and the United States. The U.S. leads the series with a 31-4-1 record after 36 matches.

Year		Year		Year	
1922	United States, 8-4	1951	United States, 7½-4½	1977	United States, 16-8
1923	United States, 6½-5½	1953	United States, 9-3	1979	United States, 15½-8½
1924	United States, 9-3	1955	United States, 10-2	1981	United States, 15-9
1926	United States, 6½-5½	1957	United States, 8½-3½	1983	United States, 13½-10½
1928	United States, 11-1	1959	United States, 9-3	1985	United States, 13-11
1930	United States, 10-2	1961	United States, 11-1	1987	United States, 16½-7½
1932	United States, 9½-2½	1963	United States, 14-10	1989	Britain-Ireland, 12½-11½
1934	United States, 9½-2½	1965	Draw, 12-12	1991	United States, 14-10
1936	United States, 10½-1½	1967	United States, 15-9	1993	United States, 19-5
1938	Britain-Ireland, 7½-4½	1969	United States, 13-11	1995	Britain-Ireland, 14-10
1940-46	Not held	1971	Britain-Ireland, 13-11	1997	United States, 18-6
1947	United States, 8-4	1973	United States, 14-10		
1949	United States, 10-2	1975	United States, 15½-8½		

WOMEN
Solheim Cup

The Solheim Cup was presented by the Karsten Manufacturing Co. in 1990 for competition between women professional golfers from Europe and the United States. The U.S. leads the series with a 3-1 record after four matches.

Year		Year		Year	
1990	United States, 11½-4½	1994	United States, 13-7	1996	United States, 17-11
1992	Europe, 11½-6½				

Curtis Cup

Named after British golfing sisters Harriot and Margaret Curtis, the Curtis Cup was first contested in 1932 between teams of women amateurs from the United States and the British Isles.

Competed for every other year since 1932 (except during World War II). The U.S. leads the series with a 20-6-3 record after 29 matches.

Year		Year		Year	
1932	United States, 5½-3½	1958	Draw, 4½-4½	1978	United States, 12-6
1934	United States, 6½-2½	1960	United States, 6½-2½	1980	United States, 13-5
1936	Draw, 4½-4½	1962	United States, 8-1	1982	United States, 14½-3½
1938	United States, 5½-3½	1964	United States, 10½-7½	1984	United States, 9½-8½
1940-46	Not held	1966	United States, 13-5	1986	British Isles, 13-5
1948	United States, 6½-2½	1968	United States, 10½-7½	1988	British Isles, 11-7
1950	United States, 7½-1½	1970	United States, 11½-6½	1990	United States, 14-4
1952	British Isles, 5-4	1972	United States, 10-8	1992	British Isles, 10-8
1954	United States, 6-3	1974	United States, 13-5	1994	Draw, 9-9
1956	British Isles, 5-4	1976	United States, 11½-6½	1996	British Isles, 11½-6½

COLLEGES

Men's NCAA Division I Champions

College championships decided by match play from 1897-1964, and stroke play since 1965.

Multiple winners (Teams): Yale (21); Houston (16); Oklahoma St. (8); Stanford (7); Harvard (6); LSU and North Texas (4); Florida and Wake Forest (3); Arizona St., Michigan, Ohio St. and Texas (2).

Multiple winners (Individuals): Ben Crenshaw and Phil Mickelson (3); Dick Crawford, Dexter Cummings, G.T. Dunlop, Fred Lamphrecht and Scott Simpson (2).

Year	Team winner	Individual champion	Year	Team winner	Individual champion
1897	Yale	Louis Bayard, Princeton	1947	LSU	Dave Barclay, Michigan
1898	Harvard (spring)	John Reid, Yale	1948	San Jose St.	Bob Harris, San Jose St.
1898	Yale (fall)	James Curtis, Harvard	1949	North Texas	Harvie Ward, N.Carolina
1899	Harvard	Percy Pyne, Princeton	1950	North Texas	Fred Wampler, Purdue
1900	Not held		1951	North Texas	Tom Nieporte, Ohio St.
1901	Harvard	H. Lindsley, Harvard	1952	North Texas	Jim Vichers, Oklahoma
1902	Yale (spring)	Chas. Hitchcock Jr., Yale	1953	Stanford	Earl Moeller, Oklahoma St.
1902	Harvard (fall)	Chandler Egan, Harvard	1954	SMU	Hillman Robbins, Memphis St.
1903	Harvard	F.O. Reinhart, Princeton	1955	LSU	Joe Campbell, Purdue
1904	Harvard	A.L. White, Harvard	1956	Houston	Rick Jones, Ohio St.
1905	Yale	Robert Abbott, Yale	1957	Houston	Rex Baxter Jr., Houston
1906	Yale	W.E. Clow Jr., Yale	1958	Houston	Phil Rodgers, Houston
1907	Yale	Ellis Knowles, Yale	1959	Houston	Dick Crawford, Houston
1908	Yale	H.H. Wilder, Harvard	1960	Houston	Dick Crawford, Houston
1909	Yale	Albert Seckel, Princeton	1961	Purdue	Jack Nicklaus, Ohio St.
1910	Yale	Robert Hunter, Yale	1962	Houston	Kermit Zarley, Houston
1911	Yale	George Stanley, Yale	1963	Oklahoma St.	R.H. Sikes, Arkansas
1912	Yale	F.C. Davison, Harvard	1964	Houston	Terry Small, San Jose St.
1913	Yale	Nathaniel Wheeler, Yale	1965	Houston	Marty Fleckman, Houston
1914	Princeton	Edward Allis, Harvard	1966	Houston	Bob Murphy, Florida
1915	Yale	Francis Blossom, Yale	1967	Houston	Hale Irwin, Colorado
1916	Princeton	J.W. Hubbell, Harvard	1968	Florida	Grier Jones, Oklahoma St.
1917-18 Not held			1969	Houston	Bob Clark, Cal St.-LA
1919	Princeton	A.L. Walker Jr., Columbia	1970	Houston	John Mahaffey, Houston
1920	Princeton	Jess Sweetster, Yale	1971	Texas	Ben Crenshaw, Texas
1921	Dartmouth	Simpson Dean, Princeton	1972	Texas	Ben Crenshaw & Tom Kite, Tex.
1922	Princeton	Pollack Boyd, Dartmouth	1973	Florida	Ben Crenshaw, Texas
1923	Princeton	Dexter Cummings, Yale	1974	Wake Forest	Curtis Strange, W.Forest
1924	Yale	Dexter Cummings, Yale	1975	Wake Forest	Jay Haas, Wake Forest
1925	Yale	Fred Lamprecht, Tulane	1976	Oklahoma St.	Scott Simpson, U.S.C
1926	Yale	Fred Lamprecht, Tulane	1977	Houston	Scott Simpson, U.S.C
1927	Princeton	Watts Gunn, Georgia Tech	1978	Oklahoma St.	David Edwards, Okla. St.
1928	Princeton	Maurice McCarthy, G'town	1979	Ohio St.	Gary Hallberg, Wake Forest
1929	Princeton	Tom Aycock, Yale	1980	Oklahoma St.	Jay Don Blake, Utah St.
1930	Princeton	G.T. Dunlap Jr., Princeton	1981	Brigham Young	Ron Commans, U.S.C
1931	Yale	G.T. Dunlap Jr., Princeton	1982	Houston	Billy Ray Brown, Houston
1932	Yale	J.W. Fischer, Michigan	1983	Oklahoma St.	Jim Carter, Arizona St.
1933	Yale	Walter Emery, Oklahoma	1984	Houston	John Inman, N.Carolina
1934	Michigan	Charles Yates, Ga.Tech	1985	Houston	Clark Burroughs, Ohio St.
1935	Michigan	Ed White, Texas	1986	Wake Forest	Scott Verplank, Okla. St.
1936	Michigan	Charles Kocsis, Michigan	1987	Oklahoma St.	Brian Watts, Oklahoma St.
1937	Princeton	Fred Haas Jr., LSU	1988	UCLA	E.J. Pfister, Oklahoma St.
1938	Stanford	John Burke, Georgetown	1989	Oklahoma	Phil Mickelson, Ariz. St.
1939	Stanford	Vincent D'Antoni, Tulane	1990	Arizona St.	Phil Mickelson, Ariz. St.
1940	Princeton & LSU	Dixon Brooke, Virginia	1991	Oklahoma St.	Warren Schuette, UNLV
1941	Stanford	Earl Stewart, LSU	1992	Arizona	Phil Mickelson, Ariz. St.
1942	LSU & Stanford	Frank Tatum Jr., Stanford	1993	Florida	Todd Demsey, Ariz. St.
1943	Yale	Wallace Ulrich, Carleton	1994	Stanford	Justin Leonard, Texas
1944	Notre Dame	Louis Lick, Minnesota	1995	Oklahoma St.	Chip Spratlin, Auburn
1945	Ohio State	John Lorms, Ohio St.	1996	Arizona St.	Tiger Woods, Stanford
1946	Stanford	George Hamer, Georgia	1997	Pepperdine	Charles Warren, Clemson

Women's NCAA Division I Champions

Decided by stroke play. **Multiple winners** (teams): Arizona St. (5); Florida, San Jose St. and Tulsa (2).

Year	Team winner	Individual champion	Year	Team winner	Individual champion
1982	Tulsa	Kathy Baker, Tulsa	1990	Arizona St.	Susan Slaughter, Arizona
1983	TCU	Penny Hammel, Miami	1991	UCLA	Annika Sorenstam, Arizona
1984	Miami-FL	Cindy Schreyer, Georgia	1992	San Jose St.	Vicki Goetze, Georgia
1985	Florida	Danielle Ammaccapane, Ariz.St.	1993	Arizona St.	Charlotta Sorenstam, Ariz. St.
1986	Florida	Page Dunlap, Florida	1994	Arizona St.	Emilee Klein, Ariz. St.
1987	San Jose St.	Caroline Keggi, New Mexico	1995	Arizona St.	K. Mourgue d'Algue, Ariz. St.
1988	Tulsa	Melissa McNamara, Tulsa	1996	Arizona	Marisa Baena, Arizona
1989	San Jose St.	Pat Hurst, San Jose St.	1997	Arizona St.	Heather Bowie, Texas

Auto Racing

1997 Indianapolis 500 winner
Arie Luyendyk relaxes during practice for the Pennzoil 200
at New Hampshire International
Speedway in Loudon, N.H. ——————————————————————

Mountain Do

*By winning his third straight Southern 500,
Jeff Gordon also won the Winston Million.*

by
Kenny Mayne

Not that he needed the money or anything, but Jeff Gordon's victory in the Mountain Dew Southern 500 gave him wins in 3 of the 4 Nascar Winston Cup majors and a million dollar bonus. Since a million doesn't go as far as it did back in 1985 when Bill Elliott became the only other driver to capture the Winston Million, the accomplishment was more about making history. Gordon became the first driver ever to win the Southern 500 three straight seasons.

Gordon's big run started with the opener, the Daytona 500. At the line, he had friends giving chase. Slow chase. The finish was under caution. Terry Labonte, the 1996 Winston Cup champion, was second and the third Hendrick Team member, Ricky Craven, was just that.

Gordon's Daytona win came about in part because of a wild crash on the back straightaway that sent Dale Earnhardt into the wall and then end over

end. He refused to leave the race (he probably intimidated the ambulance attendants) and climbed back in his battered car to finish the event he's never won.

What happened in Daytona was the beginning of a rough season for the 7-time champion. It reached a low point in the Southern 500 when he mysteriously crashed on the opening lap. He needed a series of medical tests before being allowed back on the track and as of this writing his winless streak had reached 56. Even so, he did run well enough for a likely top ten season finish.

Gordon's main threats all season for the title were Terry Labonte, Mark Martin and Dale Jarrett. Martin took over the points lead in late August when he finished second to Jarrett at Bristol, Tennessee. It was Jarrett's first-ever short track win. But Gordon regained the lead in the very next event when he raked in that Winston Million at Darlington. With four races left, Gordon had a 110 point lead over Martin. ∎

Kenny Mayne is the co-anchor of the ESPN 11 PM *SportsCenter*.

Wide World Photos

Jeff Gordon holds the Winston Million bonus check that he won by capturing the Mountain Dew Southern 500 on August 31, 1997.

Busch Series

Randy Lajoie became the first defending season champ ever to open the next season with a win when he took the opener at Daytona. Cup series regular Mark Martin then took three straight on his way to tying the record for Busch Series career wins held by Jack Ingram with 31. But as we went to print, Lajoie's consistency had him looking like a lock for a repeat and Steve Park was also a sure thing Rookie of the Year. He got win number one in just his 12th Busch start. ■

Craftsman Truck Series

It's still my contention that in the truck series the crew should ride in back and make repairs on the side of the road. As of our publication date, Jack Sprague was in the lead for his first Craftsman Truck series title but the most impressive run was made by the man in fifth. Ron Hornaday picked off 6 wins in one 8 race stretch and his first title was in reach. No matter the championship outcome, the season will be completed in honor of John Nemechek. He died after a crash in the third week of the season at Homestead. The younger brother of Cup series driver Joe Nemechek was just 27 years old. ■

CART Series

It took 16 races for the defending season champ Jimmy Vasser to score a win, but even as he did, the day belonged to his Target-Chip Ganassi teammate, Alex Zanardi. A year after being the CART Series top rookie, he wrapped up the title with a third place finish at Laguna Seca. Zanardi was

Wide World Photos

Alex Zanardi celebrates after placing third in the Texaco Havoline 300 at Laguna Seca. Zanardi wasn't overreacting to third place because that finish clinched the 1997 PPG Cup Championship for him.

great in his full-time job but no doubt lost his damage deposit in the IROC series. He actually wrecked *two* cars in the California IROC event. But the biggest dent he made was in the CART series going from number one rookie to number one of all.

Canadians Paul Tracy and Greg Moore ran to a combined five straight wins during the season but neither had the consistencey of Gil de Ferran, who finished second in the standings. ■

Formula One

It didn't take Michael Schumacher long to put Ferrari back on top of the F-1 world. With two races left, Schumacher trailed the favorite, Jacques Villeneuve, by nine points. However, at the Japanese Grand Prix, Villeneuve ignored a yellow flag during practice

and was disqualified but an appeal reinstated him for the race. Schumacher won and Villeneuve took fifth and saw his lead cut to one. The International Automobile Federation was discussing the case before the European Grand Prix in Jerez, Spain. As we went to press for this chapter, the IAF had yet to decide Villeneuve's fate. See the Updates chapter for the final result. ■

Kenny Mayne's Top Ten 1997 Auto Racing Highlights

10. **Daytona Go Kart Challenge** February 14, 1997. I beat Jeff Gordon on a five lap oval. He's pressed for time but not so much that he can't find another ten minutes to get revenge on a nearby

road course. Until he loses at Richmond in early March I'm the only man in the world who has beaten him.

9. **Grand Prix of Hungary** Damon Hill was tossed from the Williams team after winning the title in 1996. He gets to the line second with his new TWR Arrows Team. There's life after Williams.

8. **Autolite Platinum 250** Rookie Steve Park's the winner but sideshow is main attraction. After a wreck, Joe Bessey stands on the track and flings his helmet into the car of the guy he thought was to blame, Dale Shaw. Shaw had a helmet. He throws the extra one back at Bessey.

7. **Mopar Nationals** Kristin Powell skips her high school prom, wins her first top fuel drag race.

6. **Mopar Park** Tommy Kendall gets to the line first. What's new? It is his 11th straight Trans-Am Series win.

5. **Detroit Grand Prix** Greg Moore passes two who had no gas. Teammates Mauricio Gugelmin and Mark Blundell give up the lead one after the other when their tanks run empty on the last lap.

4. **Miller 400** Ernie Irvan beats the field and the track. Brooklyn, Michigan is the same place where he nearly lost his life in 1994.

3. **Budweiser/GI Joe's 200** Mark Blundell has enough gas this time and he stands on the pedal to beat Gil de Ferran in the closest CART Series finish ever.

2. **True Value 500** Arie Luyendyk takes punches from A.J. Foyt but counters with a successful protest over incorrect lap counting and is awarded the win.

1. **The (Mountain Dew) Southern 500** Jeff Gordon and Jeff Burton bang doors for the final two laps. Gordon banks a million dollar bonus, winning his third straight Southern 500. ■

THE NUMBERS

by
Paul Kinney

A CHAMPION'S PROFILE

1996 Winston Cup champion Terry Labonte also won that title in 1984. In a remarkable coincidence, Labonte's numbers in those two seasons are amazingly similar. One number, though, was a lot bigger. In '84, Labonte won $713,00 and in '96 he took home over $2 million.

It's Money that Matters

	1984	1996
Wins	2	2
Top 3's	14	14
Top 10's	24	24
DNF's	3	3

ANOTHER **HARDT** BREAKER

In 1996, Dale Earnhardt had another heart breaking Daytona 500. His crash continued a remarkable string of lousy luck. In 1996, he lost

Dale Earnhardt leans on his car as he waits his turn to qualify for the Exide 400 at Richmond International Raceway on September 5, 1997. The previous week Earnhardt fell asleep at the wheel at the Southern 500.

the lead with only 23 laps left. In 1994, he led until the final lap when he was bumped by Dale Jarrett. In 1990, he had the lead until he cut a tire and on the final lap and lost to Derrike Cope. We may all empathize with Earnhardt but only Greg Norman really knows what he feels like.

A FAST START

In 1997, Jeff Gordon won his 25th race on June 6 at the Pocono 500. In doing so, Gordon blew away the previous record for starts needed to win 25 races. On this list of active drivers with at least 25 wins, Darrell Waltrip is the all-time leader in wins with 84.

It's Always Something

Dale Earnhardt at Daytona	Result	Lap
1997	**Crash**	**188**
1996	Lost Lead	177
1993	Bumped	200*
1991	Lost Lead	195
1990	Cut Tire	200*

*Earnhardt was leading both races at time of mishap.

Here's A Quarter

Driver	Starts needed for 25th win
Jeff Gordon	137
Darrell Waltrip	198
Bill Elliott	243
Dale Earnhardt	252
Rusty Wallace	278

THE 1998

AUTO RACING
S T A T I S T I C S

THE SEASON IN REVIEW
1996-1997

NASCAR • INDYCAR • IRL • F1

SEC
A

PAGE
879

NASCAR RESULTS

Winston Cup Series

Winners of NASCAR Winston Cup races from Nov. 10, 1996 through Oct. 12, 1997 (see Updates chapter for later results).

LATE 1996

Date	Event	Location	Winner (Pos.)	Avg.mph	Earnings	Pole	Qual.mph
Nov. 10	NAPA 500 ....Atlanta		Bobby Labonte (1)	134.661	$274,900	B. Labonte	185.887

Winning cars (for entire season): CHEVY MONTE CARLO (17)— Gordon 10, Earnhardt 2, Marlin 2, T. Labonte 2, B. Labonte 1; FORD THUNDERBIRD (13)— Wallace 5, Jarrett 4, Irvan 2, Bodine 1, Rudd 1; PONTIAC GRAND PRIX (1)— Hamilton 1.

1997 SEASON (through Oct. 12)

Date	Event	Location	Winner (Pos.)	Avg.mph	Earnings	Pole	Qual.mph
Feb. 16	**Daytona 500** ....Daytona		Jeff Gordon (6)	148.295	$456,999	M. Skinner	189.813
Feb. 23	Goodwrench 400 ....Rockingham		Jeff Gordon (4)	125.927	93,115	M. Martin	157.885†
Mar. 2	Pontiac 400 ....Richmond		Rusty Wallace (7)	108.499	86,775	T. Labonte	—
Mar. 9	Primestar 500 ....Atlanta		Dale Jarrett (9)	132.730	137,650	R. Gordon	186.507†
Mar. 23	TranSouth 400 ....Darlington		Dale Jarrett (1)	121.162	142,860*	D. Jarrett	171.095
Apr. 6	Interstate 500 ....Texas		Jeff Burton (5)	125.105	354,350	J. Burton	—
Apr. 13	Food City 500 ....Bristol		Jeff Gordon (5)	75.035	83,640	R. Wallace	123.586
Apr. 20	Goody's 500 ....Martinsville		Jeff Gordon (4)	70.290	99,225	K. Wallace	93.961
May 4	Save Mart 300 ....Sonoma		Mark Martin (1)	75.788	113,995*	M. Martin	92.807†
May 10	**Winston 500** ....Talladega		Mark Martin (18)	188.354$	92,220	J. Andretti	193.627
May 17	The Winston Select .....Charlotte		Jeff Gordon (19)	157.895	207,500	B. Elliott	143.273
May 25	**Coca-Cola 600** ......Charlotte		Jeff Gordon (1)	136.745	432,400*	J. Gordon	184.300
June 1	Miller 500 ....Dover		Rick Rudd (13)	114.635	95,255	B. Labonte	152.788
June 8	Pocono 500 ....Pocono		Jeff Gordon (11)	139.828	166,080	B. Hamilton	168.089
June 15	Miller 400 ....Michigan		Ernie Irvan (20)	153.321	93,830	D. Jarrett	183.669
June 22	California 500 ....California		Jeff Gordon (3)	155.025	144,600	J. Nemecheck	183.015
July 5	Pepsi 400 ....Daytona		John Andretti (3)	157.791	109,525	M. Skinner	189.777
July 13	Jiffy Lube 300 ....Loudon		Jeff Burton (15)	117.194$	117,875	K. Schrader	129.423†
July 20	Pennsylvania 500 ......Pocono		Dale Jarrett (1)	142.068	104,570	J. Nemechek	168.881
Aug. 2	Brickyard 400 .....Indianapolis		Ricky Rudd (7)	130.828	571,000	E. Irvan	177.736†
Aug. 10	The Bud at the Glen .Watkins Glen		Jeff Gordon (11)	91.294	139,120	T. Bodine	120.505
Aug. 17	DeVilbiss 400 ....Michigan		Mark Martin (2)	126.880	93,045	J. Benson	183.332
Aug. 24	Goody's 500 ....Bristol		Dale Jarrett (3)	80.010	101,550	K. Wallace	123.039
Aug. 31	**Southern 500** ....Darlington		Jeff Gordon (7)	121.149	1,131,330**	B. Labonte	170.661
Sept. 6	Exide Select 400 ....Richmond		Dale Jarrett (23)	108.707$	91,490	B. Elliott	124.723
Sept. 14	CMT 300 ....Loudon		Jeff Gordon (13)	100.376	188,625	K. Schrader	129.182
Sept. 22	MBNA 400 ....Dover		Mark Martin (1)	132.719	195,305*	M. Martin	152.033
Sept. 29	Hanes 500 ....Martinsville		Jeff Burton (10)	73.072	78,675	W. Burton	93.410
Oct. 5	UAW-GM 500 ....Charlotte		Dale Jarrett (5)	144.323	130,000	G. Bodine	184.256
Oct. 12	Diehard 500 ....Talladega		Terry Labonte (6)	156.601	116,725	E. Irvan	193.271

Note: The Winston Select (May 17) is a 105-mile, non-points race.
†Track record. $Race record.
Coca Cola 600 was shortened to 333 laps instead of the scheduled 400 because of a 2½ rain delay.
*Includes carryover Unocal 76 bonus ($7,600 per race) for winning race from the pole: **TransSouth 400**— Jarrett ($38,000); **Save Mart 300**— Martin ($30,400); **Coca Cola 600**— Gordon ($22,800).
**Includes $1 million Winston Select Million bonus for winning three of four of NASCAR's "Crown Jewels" (Daytona 500, Winston Select, Coca-Cola 600 and Southern 500).
Winning Cars: CHEVY MONTE CARLO (12)— Gordon 11, T. Labonte 1; FORD THUNDERBIRD (10)— Jarrett 6, Rudd 2, Irvan 1, Wallace 1.
Remaining Races (3): AC-Delco 400 in Rockingham, N.C. (Oct. 26); Dura-Lube 500 in Phoenix (Nov. 2); NAPA 500 in Atlanta (Nov. 16).

1997 Race Locations

February— DAYTONA 500 at Daytona International Speedway in Daytona Beach, Fla.; GOODWRENCH 400 at North Carolina Motor Speedway in Rockingham, N.C. **March**— PONTIAC EXCITEMENT 400 at Richmond (Va.) International Raceway; PRIMESTAR 500 at Atlanta International Speedway in Atlanta, Ga.; TRANSOUTH FINANCIAL 400 at Darlington (S.C.) International Raceway. **April**— INTERSTATE BATTERIES 500 at Texas Motor Speedway in Ft. Worth, Tex.; FOOD CITY 500 at Bristol (Tenn.) Motor Speedway; GOODY'S HEADACHE POWDERS 500 at Martinsville (Va.) Speedway; **May**— SAVE MART SUPERMARKETS 300 at Sears Point International Raceway in Sonoma, Calif.; WINSTON SELECT 500 at Talladega (Ala.) Superspeedway; THE WINSTON SELECT at Charlotte Motor Speedway in Concord, N.C.; COCA-COLA 600 at Charlotte. **June**— Miller 500 at Dover (Del.) Downs International Speedway; Pocono 500 at Pocono (Pa.) International Raceway; MILLER 400 at Michigan International Speedway in Brooklyn, Mich; CALIFORNIA 500 by NAPA at California Speedway in Fontan, Calif. **July**— PEPSI 400 at Daytona; JIFFY LUBE 300 at New Hampshire International Speedway in Loudon, N.H.; PENNSYLVANIA 500 at Pocono. **August**— BRICKYARD 400 at Indianapolis Motor Speedway; THE BUD AT THE GLEN at Watkins Glen, (N.Y.) International; DEVILBISS 400 at Brooklyn, Mich.; GOODY'S HEADACHE POWDER 500 at Bristol; MOUNTAIN DEW SOUTHERN 500 at Darlington. **September**— EXIDE SELECT BATTERIES 400 at Richmond; CMT 300 at Loudon; MBNA 400 at Dover; HANES 500 at Martinsville. **October**— UAW-GM QUALITY 500 at Charlotte; SEARS DIE-HARD 500 at Talladega; ACDELCO 400 at Rockinham. **November**— DURA-LUBE 500 at Phoenix (Ariz.) International Raceway; NAPA 500 at Atlanta.

1997 Daytona 500

Date— Sunday, Feb. 16 ; 1997, at Daytona International Speedway. **Distance**— 500 miles; **Course**— 2.5 miles; **Field**— 42 cars; **Average speed**— 148.295 mph; **Margin of victory**— under caution; **Time of race**— 3 hours, 22 minutes, 18 seconds; **Caution flags**— 8 for 29 laps; **Lead changes**— 12 among 9 drivers; **Lap leaders**— M. Martin (52 laps), D. Earnhardt (48), J. Gordon (40), B. Elliott (30), E. Irvan (13), S. Marlin (8), M. Waltrip (8), G. Sacks (3), M. Skinner (1); **Pole sitter**— Mike Skinner at 189.813 mph; **Attendance**— 150,000 (estimated); **TV Rating**— 8.6/23 share (CBS). Note that (r) indicates circuit rookie driver.

	Driver (start pos.)	Team	Car	Laps	Ended	Earnings
1	Jeff Gordon (6)	DuPont Refinishes	Chevrolet Monte Carlo	200	Running	$456,999
2	Terry Labonte (18)	Kellogg's Corn Flakes	Chevrolet Monte Carlo	200	Running	194,925
3	Rick Craven (40)	Budweiser	Chevrolet Monte Carlo	200	Running	155,625
4	Bill Elliott (8)	McDonald's	Ford Thunderbird	200	Running	133,200
5	Sterling Marlin (9)	Kodak Film	Chevrolet Monte Carlo	200	Running	121,080
6	Jeremy Mayfield (21)	Kmart/RC Cola	Ford Thunderbird	200	Running	100,355
7	Mark Martin (11)	Valvoline	Ford Thunderbird	200	Running	105,515
8	Ward Burton (17)	MBNA America	Pontiac Grand Prix	200	Running	82,390
9	Rick Rudd (13)	Tide	Ford Thunderbird	200	Running	88,590
10	Darrell Waltrip (22)	Western Auto	Chevrolet Monte Carlo	200	Running	78,840
11	Jeff Burton (23)	Exide Batteries	Ford Thunderbird	200	Running	79,040
12	r-Mike Skinner (1)	Lowe's	Chevrolet Monte Carlo	200	Running	77,615
13	Ted Musgrave (41)	Family Channel/PRIMESTAR	Ford Thunderbird	200	Running	76,570
14	Kyle Petty (30)	Hot Wheels	Pontiac Grand Prix	200	Running	62,080
15	Bobby Hamilton (39)	STP	Pontiac Grand Prix	200	Running	77,415
16	r-Robby Gordon (20)	Coors Light	Chevrolet Monte Carlo	200	Running	76,570
17	Dave Marcis (24)	Realtree	Chevrolet Monte Carlo	200	Running	69,545
18	Brett Bodine (37)	Close Call Phone Card	Ford Thunderbird	200	Running	61,225
19	Hut Stricklin (28)	Circuit City	Ford Thunderbird	200	Running	67,155
20	Ernie Irvan (5)	Texaco-Havoline	Ford Thunderbird	200	Running	72,325
21	Bobby Labonte (15)	Interstate Batteries	Pontiac Grand Prix	200	Running	69,445
22	Kenny Wallace (36)	Square D	Ford Thunderbird	200	Running	65,465
23	Dale Jarrett (3)	Ford Quality Care	Ford Thunderbird	200	Running	70,510
24	Lake Speed (35)	Melling Engine Parts	Ford Thunderbird	199	Running	64,405
25	John Andretti (32)	RCA	Ford Thunderbird	198	Running	63,325
26	Loy Allen (33)	Child Support Recovery	Ford Thunderbird	198	Running	55,570
27	Joe Nemechek (38)	BellSouth	Chevrolet Monte Carlo	196	Accident	52,240
28	Johnny Benson (16)	Pennzoil	Pontiac Grand Prix	195	Accident	61,935
29	Morgan Shepherd (42)	Delco Remy America	Pontiac Grand Prix	195	Accident	61,655
30	Dick Trickle (27)	Heilig-Meyers	Ford Thunderbird	195	Accident	53,900
31	Dale Earnhardt (4)	GM Goodwrench	Chevrolet Monte Carlo	195	Running	72,945
32	Michael Waltrip (12)	Citgo	Ford Thunderbird	188	Running	57,990
33	Ken Schrader (10)	Skoal	Chevrolet Monte Carlo	173	Running	57,790
34	Geoff Bodine (25)	QVC	Ford Thunderbird	148	Accident	57,605
35	Jimmy Spencer (7)	Camel Cigarettes	Ford Thunderbird	145	Running	57,300
36	Derrike Cope (29)	Skittles	Pontiac Grand Prix	124	Handling	50,145
37	Greg Sacks (34)	Hardee's	Ford Thunderbird	120	Accident	50,040
38	Bobby Hillin (31)	Jasper Engines	Ford Thunderbird	111	Engine	49,605
39	Robert Pressley (19)	Cartoon Network	Chevrolet Monte Carlo	91	Accident	49,605
40	Steve Grissom (2)	Kodiak	Chevrolet Monte Carlo	88	Accident	57,565
41	Rusty Wallace (14)	Miller Lite	Ford Thunderbird	47	Engine	66,055
42	Wally Dallenbach (26)	First Union	Chevrolet Monte Carlo	32	Engine	49,605

Winston Cup Point Standings

Official Top 10 NASCAR Winston Cup point leaders and Top 15 money leaders for 1996 and unofficial Top 10 point leaders and Top 15 money leaders for 1997 (through Oct. 5). Points awarded for all qualifying drivers (winner receives 175) and lap leaders. Earnings include bonuses. Listed are starts (Sts), Top 5 finishes (1-2-3-4-5), poles won (PW) and points (Pts).

FINAL 1996

		Finishes		
	Sts	1-2-3-4-5	PW	Pts
1 Terry Labonte	31	2-7-5-1-6	4	4657
2 Jeff Gordon	31	10-3-4-2-2	15	4620
3 Dale Jarrett	31	4-7-4-2-0	2	4568
4 Dale Earnhardt	31	2-3-3-4-1	2	4327
5 Mark Martin	31	0-4-5-3-2	4	4278
6 Ricky Rudd	31	1-2-1-1-0	0	3845
7 Rusty Wallace	31	5-1-0-1-1	0	3717
8 Sterling Marlin	31	2-0-1-1-1	0	3682
9 Bobby Hamilton	31	1-0-1-0-1	0	3639
10 Ernie Irvan	31	2-2-0-6-2	1	3632

1997 SEASON (through Oct. 12)

		Finishes		
	Sts	1-2-3-4-5	PW	Pts
1 Jeff Gordon	29	10-3-2-3-3	1	4321
2 Mark Martin	29	4-2-3-2-4	3	4211
3 Dale Jarrett	29	6-2-4-2-3	3	4166
4 Jeff Burton	29	3-3-3-2-2	0	4041
5 Terry Labonte	29	1-3-2-2-0	0	3796
6 Dale Earnhardt	29	0-4-1-1-0	0	3794
7 Bobby Labonte	29	0-2-2-2-1	2	3687
8 Bill Elliott	29	0-1-0-3-1	1	3536
9 Ted Musgrave	29	0-1-1-3-0	0	3322
10 Rusty Wallace	29	1-2-2-0-2	1	3132

Top 5 Finishing Order + Pole

1997 SEASON (through Oct. 12)

No.	Event	Winner	2nd	3rd	4th	5th	Pole
1	Daytona 500	J. Gordon	T. Labonte	R. Craven	B. Elliott	S. Marlin	M. Skinner
2	Goodwrench 500	J. Gordon	D. Jarrett	J. Burton	R. Rudd	R. Craven	M. Martin
3	Pontiac 400	R. Wallace	G. Bodine	D. Jarrett	J. Gordon	B. Hamilton	T. Labonte
4	Primestar 500	D. Jarrett	E. Irvan	M. Shepherd	B. Labonte	J. Burton	R. Gordon
5	TranSouth 400	D. Jarrett	T. Musgrave	J. Gordon	J. Burton	B. Labonte	D. Jarrett
6	Interstate 500	J. Burton	D. Jarrett	B. Labonte	T. Labonte	R. Rudd	D. Jarrett
7	Food City 500	J. Gordon	R. Wallace	T. Labonte	D. Jarrett	M. Martin	R. Wallace
8	Goody's 500	J. Gordon	B. Hamilton	M. Martin	T. Labonte	R. Wallace	K. Wallace
9	Save Mart 300	M. Martin	J. Gordon	T. Labonte	D. Jarrett	D. Waltrip	M. Martin
10	Winston 500	M. Martin	D. Earnhardt	B. Labonte	J. Andretti	J. Gordon	J. Andretti
11	Coca-Cola 600	J. Gordon	R. Wallace	M. Martin	B. Elliott	J. Burton	J. Gordon
12	Miller 500	R. Rudd	M. Martin	J. Burton	J. Mayfield	K. Petty	B. Labonte
13	Pocono 500	J. Gordon	J. Burton	D. Jarrett	M. Martin	J. Mayfield	B. Hamilton
14	Miller 400	E. Irvan	B. Elliott	M. Martin	T. Musgrave	J. Gordon	D. Jarrett
15	California 500	J. Gordon	T. Labonte	R. Rudd	T. Musgrave	J. Spencer	J. Nemechek
16	Pepsi 400	J. Andretti	T. Labonte	S. Marlin	D. Earnhardt	D. Jarrett	M. Skinner
17	Jiffy Lube 300	J. Burton	D. Earnhardt	R. Wallace	S. Grissom	M. Martin	K. Schrader
18	Pennsylvania 500	D. Jarrett	J. Gordon	J. Burton	T. Musgrave	M. Martin	J. Nemechek
19	Brickyard 400	R. Rudd	B. Labonte	D. Jarrett	J. Gordon	J. Mayfield	E. Irvan
20	Bud at the Glen	J. Gordon	G. Bodine	R. Wallace	R. Gordon	M. Martin	T. Bodine
21	DeVilbiss 400	M. Martin	J. Gordon	T. Musgrave	E. Irvan	D. Jarrett	J. Benson
22	Goody's 500	D. Jarrett	M. Martin	D. Trickle	J. Burton	S. Grissom	K. Wallace
23	Southern 500	J. Gordon	J. Burton	D. Jarrett	B. Elliott	R. Rudd	B. Labonte
24	Exide Select 400	D. Jarrett	J. Burton	J. Gordon	G. Bodine	R. Wallace	B. Elliott
25	CMT 300	J. Gordon	E. Irvan	B. Hamilton	S. Grissom	R. Craven	K. Schrader
26	MBNA 400	M. Martin	D. Earnhardt	K. Petty	B. Labonte	D. Jarrett	M. Martin
27	Hanes 500	J. Burton	D. Earnhardt	B. Hamilton	J. Gordon	B. Elliott	W. Burton
28	UAW/GM 500	D. Jarrett	B. Labonte	D. Earnhardt	M. Martin	J. Gordon	G. Bodine
29	Diehard 500	T. Labonte	B. Labonte	J. Andretti	K. Schrader	E. Irvan	E. Irvan

Money Leaders

FINAL 1996

		Earnings
1	Terry Labonte	$4,030,648
2	Jeff Gordon	3,428,485
3	Dale Jarrett	2,985,418
4	Dale Earnhardt	2,285,926
5	Mark Martin	1,887,396
6	Ernie Irvan	1,683,313
7	Rusty Wallace	1,665,315
8	Sterling Marlin	1,588,425
9	Ricky Rudd	1,503,025
10	Bobby Labonte	1,475,196
11	Michael Waltrip	1,182,811
12	Bobby Hamilton	1,151,235
13	Jimmy Spencer	1,090,876
14	Ken Schrader	1,089,603
15	Geoff Bodine	1,031,762

1997 SEASON (through Oct. 12)

		Earnings
1	Jeff Gordon	$4,089,042
2	Dale Jarrett	2,267,177
3	Terry Labonte	1,832,869
4	Ricky Rudd	1,773,965
5	Jeff Burton	1,761,309
6	Mark Martin	1,751,174
7	Bobby Labonte	1,720,669
8	Dale Earnhardt	1,547,844
9	Ernie Irvan	1,396,759
10	Rusty Wallace	1,372,630
11	Bill Elliott	1,297,662
12	Sterling Marlin	1,185,425
13	Bobby Hamilton	1,170,930
14	Ted Musgrave	1,055,969
15	Ricky Craven	1,047,970

CART RESULTS

Winners of CART races from Mar. 2 through Sept. 28, 1997.

1997 SEASON

Date	Event	Location	Winner (Pos.)	Time	Avg.mph	Pole	Qual.mph
Mar. 2	GP of Miami	Miami	Michael Andretti (14)	1:38:45.666	135.478	A. Zanadri	195.043
Apr. 6	IndyCar Australia	Queensland	Scott Pruett (7)	2:01:04.678	78.948	A. Zanadri	104.878
Apr. 13	GP of Long Beach	Long Beach	Alex Zanardi (2)	1:46:17.792	93.999	G. de Ferran	111.313
Apr. 27	Bosch GP	Nazareth	Paul Tracy (1)	1:53:31.337	118.919	P. Tracy	191.174
May 11	Hollywood Rio 400	Rio de Janeiro	Paul Tracy (5)	2:10:47.996	113.721	M. Gugelmin	171.912
May 24	Motorola 300	Madison	Paul Tracy (2)	2:37:54.496	113.884	R. Boesel	187.963
June 1	Miller 200	Milwaukee	Greg Moore (5)	1:43:32.873	119.597	P. Tracy	184.286
June 8	Detroit GP	Belle Isle	Greg Moore (7)	1:52:45.143	86.047	G. de Ferran	109.483
June 22	Bud/G.I. Joe's 200	Portland	Mark Blundell (11)	2:00:12.982	76.575	S. Pruett	119.246
July 13	GP of Cleveland	Cleveland	Alex Zanardi (1)	1:41:40.861	111.848	A. Zanardi	133.048
July 20	Molson Indy	Toronto	Mark Blundell (2)	1:45:43.936	92.779	D. Franchitti	105.694
July 27	**U.S. 500**	Michigan	Alex Zanardi (7)	2:59:35.579	167.044	S. Pruett	233.857
Aug. 10	Miller 200	Mid-Ohio	Alex Zanardi (2)	1:41:16.682	110.456	B. Herta	122.649†
Aug. 17	Texaco/Havoline 200	Elkhart Lake	Alex Zanardi (3)	1:57:54.544	102.995	M. Gugelmin	142.342
Aug. 31	Molson Indy	Vancouver	Mauricio Gugelmin (5)	1:47:17.995	95.228	A. Zanardi	113.481
Sept. 7	GP of Monterey	Monterey	Jimmy Vasser (6)	1:41:38.813	109.647	B. Herta	118.666
Sept. 28	Marlboro 500	California	Mark Blundell (8)	3:02:42.620	166.575	M. Gugelmin	240.942

†Track record.

Note: IndyCar does not release per race winnings.

Winning cars: REYNARD/HONDA (6)— Zanardi 5, Vasser 1; REYNARD/MERCEDES-BENZ (6)— Blundell 3, Moore 2, Gugelmin 1; PENSKE/MERCEDES-BENZ (3)— Tracy 3; REYNARD/FORD COSWORTH (1)— Pruett 1; SWIFT/FORD COSWORTH (1)— Andretti 1.

1997 Race Locations

March— MARLBORO GRAND PRIX OF MIAMI Presented by Toyota at Metro-Dade Homestead Motorsports Complex. **April**— INDYCARNIVAL at Gold Coast, Queensland, Australia; TOYOTA GP OF LONG BEACH at Long Beach, Calif.; BOSCH SPARK PLUG GP Presented by Toyota at Nazareth (Pa.) Speedway. **May**— HOLLYWOOD RIO 400 at Nelson Piquet International Raceway; MOTOROLA 300 at Gateway International Raceway. **June**— MILLER 200 at the Milwaukee Mile in West Allis, Wisc.; ITT AUTOMOTIVE DETROIT GP at The Raceway at Belle Isle Park; BUDWEISER/G.I. JOE'S 200 Presented by Texaco/Havoline at Portland (Ore.) International Raceway. **July**— MEDIC DRUG GRAND PRIX OF CLEVELAND at Burke Lakefront Airport, Cleveland, Ohio; MOLSON INDY at Exhibition Place, Toronto, Ontario, Canada; U.S. 500 at Michigan International Speedway. **August**— MILLER 200 at Mid-Ohio Sports Car Course in Lexington; TEXACO/HAVOLINE 200 at Road America in Elkhart Lake, Wisc.; MOLSON INDY VANCOUVER at Concord Pacific Place. **September**— TOYOTA GRAND PRIX OF MONTEREY Featuring the Texaco/Havoline 300 at Laguna Seca (Calif.) Raceway; MARLBORO 500 Presented by Toyota at the California Speedway in Fontana, Calif.

1997 U.S. 500

Date— Sunday, July 27, 1997, at Michigan International Speedway. **Distance**— 500 miles; **Course**— 2 mile oval; **Field**—28 cars; **Winner's average speed**— 167.044 mph; **Margin of victory**— 31.737 seconds; **Time of race**— 2 hours, 59 minutes, 35.579 seconds; **Caution flags**— 6 for 55 laps; **Lead changes**— 13 by 9 drivers; **Lap leaders**—Zanardi (104 laps), Gugelmin (34), Pruett (32), Rahal (25), Ribeiro (21), Carpentier (14), Franchitti (12), de Ferran (5), Andretti (3); **Pole Sitter**—Scott Pruett at 233.857 mph; **Attendance**—70,000; **TV Rating**—1.8/5 share (ABC). Note that (r) indicates rookie driver.

	Driver (start pos.)	Country	Car	Laps	Ended
1	Alex Zanardi (7)	Italy	Reynard-Honda	250	Running
2	Mark Blundell (11)	England	Reynard-Ford Cosworth	250	Running
3	Gil de Ferran (10)	Brazil	Reynard-Honda	249	Running
4	Paul Tracy (18)	Canada	Penske-Mercedes	249	Running
5	Bryan Herta (8)	United States	Reynard-Mercedes	248	Running
6	Mauricio Gugelmin (2)	Brazil	Reynard-Ford Cosworth	244	Running
7	Dennis Vitolo (27)	United States	Lola-Ford Cosworth	242	Running
8	Max Papis (23)	Italy	Reynard-Toyota	241	Running
9	Hiro Matsushita (25)	Japan	Reynard-Toyota	241	Running
10	r-Gualter Salles (20)	Brazil	Reynard-Cosworth	240	Running
11	Juan Fangio II (25)	Argentina	Eagle-Toyota	226	Transmission
12	r-Arnd Meier (28)	Germany	Lola-Ford Cosworth	224	Running
13	Michel Jourdain Jr. (17)	Mexico	Lola-Ford Cosworth	182	Transmission
14	Scott Pruett (1)	United States	Lola-Ford Cosworth	174	Contact
15	r-Patrick Carpentier (12)	Canada	Reynard-Mercedes	144	Electrical
16	Christian Fittipaldi (14)	Brazil	Lola-Ford Cosworth	128	Lost Wheel
17	Bobby Rahal (6)	United States	Reynard-Mercedes	126	Contact
18	Raul Boesel (3)	Brazil	Reynard-Ford Cosworth	120	Transmission
19	r-Dario Franchitti (13)	Scotland	Reynard-Mercedes	101	Transmission
20	Al Unser Jr. (16)	United States	Penske-Mercedes	97	Engine
21	Michael Andretti (19)	United States	Lola-Ford Cosworth	79	Transmission
22	Richie Hearn (22)	United States	Lola-Ford Cosworth	60	Turbo Control
23	Andre Ribeiro (9)	Brazil	Lola-Honda	57	Transmission
24	Jimmy Vasser (4)	United States	Reynard-Honda	57	Transmission
25	Parker Johnstone (5)	United States	Reynard-Honda	53	Contact
26	Adrian Fernandez (15)	Mexico	Lola-Honda	46	Electrical
27	Greg Moore (21)	Canada	Reynard-Mercedes	19	Turbo Control
28	P.J. Jones (24)	United States	Reyanrd-Toyota	11	Engine

IndyCar Point Standings

Official Top 10 PPG Cup point leaders and Top 15 money leaders for 1996 and 1997. Points awarded for places 1 to 12, fastest qualifier and overall lap leader. Listed are starts (Sts), Top 5 finishes, poles won (PW) and points (Pts).

FINAL 1996

		Finishes		
	Sts	1-2-3-4-5	PW	Pts
1 Jimmy Vasser	16	4-1-0-1-0	4	154
2 Michael Andretti	16	5-0-1-0-0	0	132
3 Alex Zanardi	16	3-2-1-1-0	6	132
4 Al Unser Jr.	16	0-2-2-3-1	0	125
5 Christian Fittipaldi	16	0-1-2-0-2	0	110
6 Gil de Ferran	16	1-2-1-1-1	1	104
7 Bobby Rahal	16	0-2-1-0-1	0	102
8 Bryan Herta	16	0-2-0-1-2	0	86
9 Greg Moore	16	0-1-2-1-1	0	84
10 Scott Pruett	16	0-1-2-1-0	1	82

FINAL 1997

		Finishes		
	Sts	1-2-3-4-5	PW	Pts
1 Alex Zanardi	17	5-1-1-4-0	4	195
2 Gil de Ferran	17	0-2-5-1-2	2	162
3 Jimmy Vasser	17	1-2-2-1-3	0	144
4 Mauricio Gugelmin	17	1-2-0-1-1	3	132
5 Paul Tracy	17	3-1-0-1-0	2	121
6 Mark Blundell	17	3-2-0-0-0	0	115
7 Greg Moore	17	2-3-0-1-1	0	111
8 Michael Andretti	17	1-3-1-1-0	0	108
9 Scott Pruett	17	1-0-2-0-3	2	102
10 Raul Boesel	17	0-0-1-2-1	1	91

Top 5 Finishing Order + Pole

1997 Season

No. Event	Winner	2nd	3rd	4th	5th	Pole
1 Miami GP	M. Andretti	P. Tracy	J. Vasser	G. Moore	S. Pruett	A. Zanardi
2 Australian GP	S. Pruett	G. Moore	M. Andretti	A. Zanardi	G. de Ferran	A. Zanardi
3 Long Beach	A. Zanardi	M. Gugelmin	S. Pruett	A. Unser Jr.	P. Johnstone	G. de Ferran
4 Bosch GP	P. Tracy	M. Andretti	A. Unser Jr.	G. de Ferran	J. Vasser	P. Tracy
5 Rio 400	P. Tracy	G. Moore	S. Pruett	A. Zanardi	R. Boesel	M. Gugelmin
6 Madison	P. Tracy	P. Carpentier	G. de Ferran	A. Zanardi	J. Vasser	R. Boesel
7 Milwaukee	G. Moore	M. Andretti	J. Vasser	R. Boesel	M. Gugelmin	P. Tracy
8 Detroit	G. Moore	M. Andretti	G. de Ferran	J. Vasser	M. Moreno	G. de Ferran
9 Portland	M. Blundell	G. de Ferran	R. Boesel	C. Fittipaldi	G. Moore	S. Pruett
10 Cleveland	A. Zanardi	G. de Ferran	B. Herta	A. Unser Jr.	B. Rahal	A. Zanardi
11 Toronto	M. Blundell	A. Zanardi	A. Ribeiro	M. Andretti	S. Pruett	D. Franchitti
12 U.S. 500	A. Zanardi	M. Blundell	G. de Ferran	P. Tracy	B. Herta	S. Pruett
13 Mid-Ohio	A. Zanardi	G. Moore	B. Rahal	R. Boesel	J. Vasser	B. Herta
14 Road America	A. Zanardi	M. Gugelmin	G. de Ferran	C. Fittipaldi	S. Pruett	M. Gugelmin
15 Vancouver	M. Gugelmin	J. Vasser	G. de Ferran	A. Zanardi	A. Unser Jr.	A. Zanardi
16 Monterey	J. Vasser	M. Blundell	A. Zanardi	A. Ribeiro	G. de Ferran	B. Herta
17 California	M. Blundell	J. Vasser	A. Fernandez	M. Gugelmin	B. Rahal	M. Gugelmin

Money Leaders

FINAL 1996

	Earnings			Earnings			Earnings
1 Jimmy Vasser	$3,061,500	6 Greg Moore	$789,750	11 Bryan Herta	$642,250
2 Alex Zanardi	1,408,250	7 Mauricio Gugelmin	742,500	12 Scott Pruett	604,500
3 Michael Andretti	1,386,750	8 Gil de Ferran	694,000	13 Stefan Johansson	592,500
4 Al Unser Jr.	987,000	9 Andre Ribeiro	675,250	14 Paul Tracey	588,000
5 Christian Fittipaldi	913,750	10 Bobby Rahal	670,500	15 Robby Gordon	583,000

FINAL 1997

	Earnings			Earnings			Earnings
1 Alex Zanardi	$2,096,250	6 Mark Blundell	$949,750	11 Bryan Herta	$627,500
2 Gil de Ferran	1,355,250	7 Greg Moore	881,000	12 Al Unser Jr.	606,250
3 Jimmy Vasser	1,133,500	8 Scott Pruett	864,250	13 Andre Ribeiro	567,250
4 Mauricio Gugelmin	1,045,250	9 Michael Andretti	842,000	14 Parker Johnstone	557,000
5 Paul Tracy	977,250	10 Bobby Rahal	636,500	15 Patrick Carpentier	531,500

INDY RACING LEAGUE RESULTS

Winners of Indy Racing League events in the 1996-97 season that ran from Aug. 18, 1996 through Oct. 11, 1997. Beginning in 1998, the IRL will run on a calendar-year basis.

1996-97 SEASON

Date	Event	Location	Winner (Pos.)	Time	Avg.mph	Pole	Qual.mph
Aug. 18	True Value 200	Loudon	Scott Sharp (12)	1:36:57.912	130.934	R. Hearn	175.367
Sept. 15	Las Vegas 500K	Las Vegas	Richie Hearn (8)	2:36:17.345	115.171	A. Luyendyk	226.491
Jan. 25	Indy 200 at WDW	Orlando	Eddie Cheever Jr. (5)	1:06:43.145	133.995	T. Stewart	166.013
Mar. 23	Phoenix 200	Phoenix	Jim Guthrie (2)	2:14:32.000	89.120	T. Stewart	170.012

Indy Racing League Results (Cont.)

Date	Event	Location	Winner (Pos.)	Time	Avg.mph	Pole	Qual.mph
May 27	**Indianapolis 500**	.Indianapolis	Arie Luyendyk (1)	3:25:43.388	145.827	A. Luyendyk	218.263
June 7	True Value 500	Texas	Arie Luyendyk (11)	2:19:48.166	133.903	T. Stewart	167.133†
June 29	Samsonite 200	Pikes Peak	Tony Stewart (2)	1:59:50.000	100.128	S. Sharp	176.117†
July 26	VisionAire 500	Charlotte	Buddy Lazier (5)	1:55:29.000	152.096	T. Stewart	217.164†
Aug. 17	Pennzoil 200	Loudon	Robbie Buhl (7)	1:46:50.574	118.829	M. Greco	160.594
Oct. 11	Las Vegas 500K	Las Vegas	Eliseo Salazar (5)	2:11:07.915	142.757	B. Boat	207.413

†Track record

Winning cars: 1996—REYNARD/FORD (1)—Hearn 1; LOLA/FORD (1)— Sharp 1. 1997– G-FORCE/OLDSMOBILE (5)—Luyendyk 2, Buhl 1, Cheever 1, Stewart 1; DALLARA/OLDSMOBILE (3)—Guthrie 1, Lazier 1, Salazar 1.
Note: In 1997 IRl drivers started using new cars; chassis by Dallara of Italy and G-Force of England and engines by Oldsmobile and Nissan.

IRL Race Locations: August—TRUE VALUE 200 at New Hampshire International Speedway in Louden, NH. **September**—LAS VEGAS 500K at Las Vegas (Nev.) Motor Speedway. **January**— INDY 200 presented by Aurora at Walt Disney World, Orlando, Fla. **March**—PHOENIX 200 at Phoenix (Ari.) International Raceway. **May**—INDIANAPOLIS 500 at Indianapolis (Ind.) Motor Speedway. **June**— SAMSONITE 200 at Pikes Peak International Raceway in Colorado Springs, Colo. **July**— VISIONAIRE 500 at Charlotte (N.C.) Motor Speedway. **August**— PENZOIL 200 at Loudon. **October**— LAS VEGAS 500K at Las Vegas.

81st Indianapolis 500

Date— Tuesday, May 27, 1997, at Indianapolis Motor Speedway. The race was rained out Sunday and postponed one day. The race was started on Monday but then stopped after more rain and suspended again until Tuesday. It was the fifth time in history that the Indy 500 had been postponed overnight. The other postponements came in 1915, 1967, 1973 and 1986. **Distance**— 500 miles; **Course**— 2.5 mile oval; **Field**—35 cars; **Winner's average speed**—145.827 mph; **Margin of victory**— 0.570 seconds; **Time of race**— 3 hours, 25 minutes, 43.388 seconds; **Caution flags**— 10 for 59 laps; **Lead changes**— 15 by 5 drivers; **Lap leaders**— Stewart (64), Luyendyk (61), Ward (49), Buhl (16), Lazier (7), Goodyear (2), Boat (1); **Pole Sitter**—Arie Luyendyk at 218.263 mph; **Attendance**—100,000 (est.); **TV Rating**— 6.6/18 share on Mon., 5.0/18 share on Tues. (ABC). Note that (r) indicates rookie driver.

	Driver (start pos.)	Country	Car	Laps	Ended	Earnings
1	Arie Luyendyk (1)	Netherlands	G/A/F	200	Running	$1,568,150
2	Scott Goodyear (5)	Canada	G/A/F	200	Running	513,300
3	r-Jeff Ward (7)	Scotland	G/A/G	200	Running	414,250
4	Buddy Lazier (10)	United States	D/A/F	200	Running	279,250
5	Tony Stewart (1)	United States	G/A/F	200	Running	345,050
6	Davey Hamilton (8)	United States	G/A/G	199	Running	214,000
7	r-Billy Boat (22)	United States	D/A/G	199	Running	269,700
8	Robbie Buhl (4)	United States	G/A/F	199	Running	235,200
9	r-Robbie Groff (4)	United States	G/A/G	197	Running	222,350
10	Fermin Velez (29)	Spain	G/A/G	195	Running	216,400
11	Buzz Calkins (16)	United States	G/A/G	188	Rt Half Shaft	201,000
12	Mike Groff (18)	United States	G/I/F	188	Running	197,300
13	Lyn St. James (34)	United States	D/I/F	186	Accident	188,000
14	Steve Kinser (20)	United States	D/A/G	185	Accident	193,250
15	Dennis Vitolo (28)	United States	D/I/F	173	Running	210,000
16	Marco Greco (27)	Brazil	D/A/G	166	Gearbox	193,000
17	r-Vincenzo Sospiri (3)	Italy	D/A/G	163	Running	196,250
18	Johnny Unser (35)	United States	D/I/F	158	Oil Pressure	158,000
19	r-Tyce Carlson (26)	United States	D/A/G	156	Accident	173,250
20	r-Dr. Jack Miller (17)	United States	D/I/F	131	Accident	171,250
21	Paul Durant (33)'	United States	G/A/G	111	Accident	178,000
22	Billy Roe (24)	United States	D/A/F	110	Accident	150,250
23	Eddie Cheever Jr. (11)	United States	G/A/G	84	Timing Chain	176,000
24	Eliseo Salazar (9)	Chile	D/A/G	70	Accident	164,000
25	Greg Ray (30)	United States	D/A/F	48	Water Pump	171,250
26	r-Jim Guthrie (6)	United States	D/A/F	43	Engine	164,500
27	Roberto Guerrero (19)	Colombia	D/I/G	25	Steering Gear	160,000
28	Mark Dismore (25)	United States	D/A/G	24	Accident	159,000
29	Robby Gordon (12)	United States	G/A/G	19	Fire	139,500
30	Claude Bourbonnais (32)	Canada	D/A/F	9	Engine	152,250
31	Stephan Gregoire (13)	France	G/A/G	0	Accident	158,000
32	r-Alphonse Giaffone (14)	Brazil	D/A/G	0	Accident	158,250
33	r-Kenny Brack (15)	Sweden	G/A/G	0	Accident	202,250
34	r-Sam Schmidt (23)	United States	D/A/F	0	Engine	150,250
34	Alessandro Zampedri (31)	Italy	D/A/G	0	Oil Leak	145,000

Car Legend: Chassis/Engine/Tires. D-Dallara; G-G Force/A-Oldsmobile Aurora V-8; I-Nissan Infiniti V-8/F-Firestone; G-Goodyear.

Indy Racing League Point Standings

FINAL 1996

		Sts	Finishes 1-2-3-4-5	PW	Pts
1	Buzz Calkins	3	1-0-0-0-0	0	246
	Scott Sharp	3	0-1-0-0-0	0	246
3	Robbie Buhl	3	0-0-1-0-0	0	240
4	Richie Hearn	3	0-0-1-1-0	0	237
	Roberto Guerrero	3	0-0-0-0-2	0	237
6	Mike Groff	3	0-0-1-0-0	0	228
7	Arie Luyendyk	3	1-0-0-0-0	1	225
8	Tony Stewart	3	0-1-0-0-0	0	204
9	Davey Hamilton	3	0-0-0-0-0	0	192
	Johnny O'Connell	3	0-0-0-0-1	0	192

1996–97 SEASON (through Oct. 11)

		Sts	Finishes 1-2-3-4-5	PW	Pts
1	Tony Stewart	10	1-1-0-0-2	4	278
2	Davey Hamilton	10	0-0-3-0-1	0	272
3	Marco Greco	10	0-0-0-1-0	1	230
4	Eddie Cheever Jr.	10	1-0-0-1-0	0	226
5	Scott Goodyear	8	0-2-2-1-0	0	223
6	Arie Luyendyk	10	2-0-1-0-0	2	221
7	Roberto Guerrero	10	0-0-0-1-0	0	209
8	Buddy Lazier	10	1-0-0-1-1	0	204
9	Eliseo Salazar	8	1-0-0-1-0	0	192
10	Buzz Caulkins	9	0-1-0-0-1	0	186

Top 5 Finishing Order + Pole

1996–97 Season (through Oct. 11)

No.	Event	Winner	2nd	3rd	4th	5th	Pole
1	True Value 200	S. Sharp	B. Calkins	M. Alboreto	M. Groff	D. Hamilton	R. Hearn
2	Las Vegas 500K	R. Hearn	M. Jourdain Jr.	M. Groff	R. Guerrero	M. Alboreto	A. Luyendyk
3	Indy 200 at WDW	E. Cheever Jr.	M. Groff	S. Goodyear	S. Sharp	B. Lazier	T. Stewart
4	Phoenix 200	J. Guthrie	T. Stewart	D. Hamilton	M. Greco	S. Gregoire	T. Stewart
5	**Indy 500**	A. Luyendyk	S. Goodyear	J. Ward	B. Lazier	T. Stewart	A. Luyendyk
6	True Value 200	A. Luyendyk	B. Boat	D. Hamilton	S. Goodyear	T. Stewart	T. Stewart
7	Samsonite 200	T. Stewart	S. Gregoire	D. Hamilton	E. Cheever Jr.	B. Calkins	S. Sharp
8	VisionAire 500	B. Lazier	B. Boat	S. Goodyear	A. Giaffone	K. Brack	T. Stewart
9	Pennzoil 200	R. Buhl	V. Sospiri	A. Luyendyk	E. Salazar	K. Brack	M. Greco
10	Las Vegas 500K	E. Salazar	S. Goodyear	R. Buhl	J. Guthrie	M. Dismore	B. Boat

Money Leaders

FINAL 1996

		Earnings			Earnings			Earnings
1	Buddy Lazier	$1,446,854	6	Buzz Calkins	$376,553	11	Davey Hamilton	$286,503
2	Davy Jones	632,503	7	Tony Stewart	375,303	12	Michele Alboreto	283,703
3	Richie Hearn	512,203	8	Scott Sharp	361,303	13	Eddie Cheever	281,353
4	Roberto Guerrero	439,503	9	Robbie Buhl	351.153	14	Alessandro Zampedri	270,853
5	Arie Luyendyk	414,003	10	Mike Groff	306,253	15	Johnny O'Connell	269,303

1996–97 SEASON (through Oct. 11)

		Earnings			Earnings			Earnings
1	Arie Luyendyk	$2,079,150	6	Eddie Cheever Jr.	$725,400	11	Eliseo Salazar	$586,650
2	Tony Stewart	1,090,450	7	Jim Guthrie	627,200	12	Mike Groff	562,850
3	Scott Goodyear	953,350	8	Billy Boat	604,150	13	Marco Greco	554,850
4	Davey Hamilton	785,950	9	Roberto Guerrero	601,000	14	Robbie Buhl	528,400
5	Buddy Lazier	736,550	10	Buzz Caulkins	599,750	15	Jeff Ward	449,150

FORMULA ONE RESULTS

Winners of Formula One Grand Prix races from Mar. 9-Oct. 12, 1997. See Updates for later results.

1997 SEASON (through Oct. 12)

Date	Grand Prix	Location	Winner (Pos.)	Time	Avg.mph	Pole	Qual.mph
Mar. 9	Australian	Melbourne	David Coulthard (4)	1:30:28.718	126.735	J. Villeneuve	132.731†
Mar. 30	Brazilian	Interlagos	Jacques Villeneuve (1)	1:36:06.990	119.867	J. Villeneuve	126.323
Apr. 13	Argentine	Buenos Aires	Jacques Villeneuve (1)	1:52:01.715	102.003	J. Villeneuve	112.722†
Apr. 27	San Marino	Imola	Heinz-Harald Frentzen (2)	1:31:00.673	125.214	J. Villeneuve	132.327
May 11	Monaco	Monte Carlo	Michael Schumacher (2)	2:00:05.654	64.787	H.H. Frentzen	96.286†
May 25	Spanish	Barcelona	Jacques Villeneuve (1)	1:30:35.896	124.470	J. Villeneuve	138.205†
June 15	Canadian	Montreal	Michael Schumacher (1)	1:17:40.646	114.582	M. Schumacher	126.630†
June 29	French	Magny-Cours	Michael Schumacher (1)	1:38:50.492	115.351	M. Schumacher	127.537
July 13	British	Silverstone	Jacques Villeneuve (1)	1:28:01.665	128.439	J. Villeneuve	140.908
July 27	German	Hockenheim	Gerhard Berger (1)	1:20:59.046	141.348	G. Berger	149.820
Aug. 10	Hungarian	Budapest	Jacques Villeneuve (1)	1:45:47.149	107.681	M. Schumacher	118.868†
Aug. 24	Belgian	Spa-Francorchamps	Michael Schumacher (3)	1:33:46.717	121.881	J. Villeneuve	142.411†
Sept. 7	Italian	Monza	David Coulthard (6)	1:17:04.609	147.909	J. Alesi	155.513
Sept. 21	Austrian	A1-Ring	Jacques Villeneuve (2)	1:27:35.999	130.657	J. Villeneuve	137.549†
Sept. 28	Luxembourg	Nurburgring	Jacques Villeneuve (2)	1:31:27.843	120.139	M. Hakkinen	133.063†
Oct. 12	Japan	Suzuka	Michael Schumacher (2)	1:29:48.446	129.693	J. Villeneuve	219.737

†Track record.
Winning Constructors: WILLIAMS-RENAULT (8)— Villeneuve 7, Frentzen 1; FERRARI (5)— M. Schumacher (5); McLAREN-MERCEDES (2)— Coulthard (2); BENETTON-RENAULT (1)— Berger (1).
Remaining Races (1): European GP at Jerez, Spain (Oct. 26).

Formula One Results (Cont.)

1997 Race Locations

March— AUSTRALIAN GRAND PRIX at Melbourne; BRAZILIAN GP at Interlagos in Sao Paulo. **April**— ARGENTINE GP at Buenos Aires; SAN MARINO GP at Imola, Italy. **May**— GP of MONACO at Monte Carlo; SPANISH GRAND PRIX at Barcelona. **June**— CANADIAN GP at Circuit Gilles Villeneuve in Montreal; FRENCH GP at Magny-Cours. **July**—BRITISH GP at Silverstone in Towcester; GERMAN GP at Hockenheimring in Hockenheim. **August**— HUNGARIAN GP at Hungaroring in Budapest; BELGIAN GP at Spa-Francorchamps. **September**— ITALIAN GP at Monza in Milan; AUSTRIAN GP at Al-Ring in Spielberg; LUXEMBOURG GP at Nurburgring in Germany; **October**— JAPANESE GP at Suzuka; EUROPEAN GP at Jerez, Spain.

Formula One Point Standings

Official Top 10 Formula One World Championship point leaders for 1996 and unofficial Top 10 point leaders for 1997 (through Oct. 11). Points awarded for places 1 through 6 only (i.e., 10-6-4-3-2-1). Listed are starts (Sts), Top 6 finishes, poles won (PW) and points (Pts).

Note: Formula One does not keep Money Leader standings.

1996 SEASON

		Sts	Finishes 1-2-3-4-5-6	PW	Pts
1	Damon Hill	16	8-2-0-1-1-0	9	97
2	Jacques Villeneuve	16	4-5-2-0-0-0	3	78
3	Michael Schumacher	16	3-3-2-1-0-0	4	59
4	Jean Alesi	16	0-4-4-2-0-1	0	47
5	Mika Hakkinen	16	0-0-4-2-4-1	0	31
6	Gerhard Berger	16	0-1-1-3-0-2	0	21
7	David Coulthard	16	0-1-1-0-2-1	0	18
8	Rubens Barrichello	16	0-0-0-2-3-2	0	14
9	Olivier Panis	16	1-0-0-0-1-1	0	13
10	Eddie Irvine	16	0-0-1-1-2-0	0	11

1997 SEASON (through Oct. 12)

		Sts	Finishes 1-2-3-4-5-6	PW	Pts
1	Jacques Villeneuve	16	7-0-0-1-2-1	8	79
2	Michael Schumacher	16	5-3-0-2-1-3	3	78
3	Heinz-Harald Frentzen	16	1-2-3-2-0-0	1	41
4	Jean Alesi	16	0-4-1-0-2-3	1	35
5	David Coulthard	16	2-1-0-1-0-1	0	30
6	Gerhard Berger	15	1-1-0-2-0-1	1	24
7	Eddie Irvine	16	0-1-4-0-0-0	0	22
8	Giancarlo Fisichella	16	0-1-1-3-0-1	0	20
9	Mika Hakkinen	15	0-0-3-2-1-1	0	17
10	Olivier Panis	9	0-1-1-1-1-2	0	16

Top 5 + Pole Finishing Order

No.	Event	Winner	2nd	3rd	4th	5th	Pole
1	Australia	D. Coulthard	M. Schumacher	M. Hakkinen	G. Berger	O. Panis	J. Villeneuve
2	Brazil	J. Villeneuve	G. Berger	O. Panis	M. Hakkinen	M. Schumacher	J. Villeneuve
3	Argentina	J. Villeneuve	E. Irvine	R. Schumacher	J. Herbert	M. Hakkinen	J. Villeneuve
4	San Marino	H-H Frentzen	M. Schumacher	E. Irvine	G. Fisichella	J. Alesi	J. Villeneuve
5	Monaco	M. Schumacher	R. Barrichello	E. Irvine	O. Panis	M. Salo	H-H Frentzen
6	Spain	J. Villeneuve	O. Panis	J. Alesi	M. Schumacher	J. Herbert	J. Villeneuve
7	Canada	M. Schumacher	J. Alesi	G. Fisichella	H-H Frentzen	J. Herbert	M. Schumacher
8	France	M. Schumacher	H-H Frentzen	E. Irvine	J. Villeneuve	J. Alesi	M. Schumacher
9	Britain	J. Villeneuve	J. Alesi	A. Wurz	D. Coulthard	R. Schumacher	M. Schumacher
10	Germany	G. Berger	M. Schumacher	M. Hakkinen	J. Trulli	R. Schumacher	G. Berger
11	Hungary	J. Villeneuve	D. Hill	J. Herbert	M. Schumacher	R. Schumacher	M. Schumacher
12	Belgium	M. Schumacher	G. Fisichella	M. Hakkinen*	H-H Frentzen	J. Herbert	J. Villeneuve
13	Italy	D. Coulthard	J. Alesi	H-H Frentzen	G. Fisichella	J. Villeneuve	J. Alesi
14	Austrian	J. Villeneuve	D. Coulthard	H-H Frentzen	G. Fisichella	R. Schumacher	J. Villeneuve
15	Luxembourg	J. Villeneuve	J. Alesi	H-H Frentzen	G. Berger	P. Diniz	M. Hakkinen
16	Japan	M. Schumacher	H-H Frentzen	E. Irvine	M. Hakkinen	J. Villeneuve	J. Villeneuve

*Hakkinen was later disqualified from his third place finish in the Belgian GP for using non-conforming fuel.

Major 1997 Endurance Races

24 Hours of Daytona

Feb. 1-2, at Daytona Beach, Fla.

Officially the Rolex 24 at Daytona and first held in 1962 (as a 3-hour race). An IMSA Camel GT race for exotic prototype sports cars and contested over a 3.56-mile road course at Daytona International Speedway. Listed are qualifying position, drivers, chassis, class and laps completed.

1 (5) Rob Dyson, James Weaver, Butch Leitzinger, Andy Wallace, John Paul Jr., Eliot Forbes-Robinson, John Schneider; FORD R&S MK III; WSC; 690 laps (2456.4 miles) at 102.292 mph; 14.48691 margin of victory.

2 (1) Andrew Evans, Fermin Velez, Rob Morgan, Charles Morgan; FERRARI 333SP; WSC; 689 laps.

3 (10) Eduardo Dibos, Jim Pace, Barry Waddell; OLDSMOBILE R&S MK-III; WSC; 672 laps.

4 (20) Ralf Kellners, Patrice Goueslard, Andre Ahrle, Claudia Hurtgen; PORSCHE 911; GTS-2; 665 laps.

5 (18) Jochen Rohr, Andy Pilgrim, Harald Grohs, Arnd Meier; PORSCHE 911; GTS-2; 663 laps.

Fastest lap: Fermin Velez (lap #548), FERRARI 333 SP; WSC; 124.242 mph. **Top qualifier:** Velez, 127.578 mph (1:40.456).

Weather: sunny and hot. **Attendance:** 50,000 (est.).

24 Hours of Le Mans

June 14-15, at LeMans, France

Officially the Le Mans Grand Prix d'Endurance and first held in 1923. Contested over the 8.451-mile Circuit de la Sarthe in Le Mans, France. Listed are drivers, countries, car, and laps completed.

1 (1) Michele Alboreto (ITA), Stefan Johansson (SWE), Tom Kristensen (DEN); TWR Porsche; 361 laps (3050.726 miles) at 126.876 mph.

2 (19) Jean-Marc Gounon (FRA), Anders Olofsson (SWE), Pierre-Henri Raphanel (FRA); McLaren F1 GTR; 360 laps.

3 (16) Eric Helary (FRA), Peter Kox (NET), Roberto Ravaglia (ITA); McLaren BMW F1 GTR; 358 laps.

4 (13) Didier Cottaz (FRA), Mark Goossens (BEL), Jerome Policand (FRA); Courage C41; 336 laps.

5 (12) Patrice Gouseland (FRA), Armin Hahne (GER), Pedro Lamy (POR); Porsche 911 GT1; 331 laps.

Fastest lap: Tom Kristensen, (lap #210) TWR Porsche; 135.170 mph. **Top qualifier:** Michele Alboreto, TWR Porsche, 137.297 mph (3:41.581).

Weather: overcast, dry. **Attendance:** 174,000 (est.).

NHRA RESULTS

National Hot Rod Association Drag Racing champions in the Top Fuel, Funny Car and Pro Stock divisions from Feb. 2 through Sept. 28, 1977. All times are based on two cars racing head-to-head from a standing start over a straight line, quarter-mile course. Differences in reaction time account for apparently faster losing times. See updates for later results.

1997 Season (through Sept 28)

Date	Event	Event	Winner	Time	MPH	2nd Place	Time	MPH
Feb. 2	Winternationals	Top Fuel	Gary Scelzi	7.712	231.16	J. Amato	11.934	97.16
		Funny Car	John Force	4.958	287.26	A. Hofmann	18.048	46.62
		Pro Stock	Warren Johnson	6.964	197.75	K. Johnson	7.004	197.48
Feb. 23	ATSCO Nationals	Top Fuel	Gary Scelzi	4.626	305.70	K. Bernstein	4.061	315.23
		Funny Car	John Force	5.795	260.79	D. Skuza	6.578	154.55
		Pro Stock	Jim Yates	6.995	197.28	W. Johnson	7.000	197.71
Mar. 9	Gatornationals	Top Fuel	Joe Amato	4.650	312.60	M. Dunn	4.720	300.10
		Funny Car	Al Hofmann	5.058	287.35	M. Oswald	13.417	64.60
		Pro Stock	Jim Yates	6.964	197.19	M. Edwards	7.038	195.39
Mar. 23	Slick 50 Nationals	Top Fuel	Joe Amato	4.653	312.17	B. Vandergriff	4.694	302.62
		Funny Car	Tony Pedregon	5.054	288.00	C. Pedregon	6.231	151.05
		Pro Stock	Tom Martino	7.018	196.76	B. Allen	7.029	195.77
Apr. 13	Fram Nationals	Top Fuel	Kenny Bernstein	4.796	290.97	G. Scelzi	4.901	281.51
		Funny Car	Randy Anderson	5.385	271.90	J. Force	5.811	236.34
		Pro Stock	Jim Yates	6.988	196.76	K. Johnson	7.019	196.76
Apr. 27	Pennzoil Nationals	Top Fuel	Gary Scelzi	4.737	282.48	C. McClenathan	5.175	204.17
		Funny Car	Chuck Etchells	5.040	277.77	C. Pedregon	5.126	281.25
		Pro Stock	Warren Johnson	6.859	198.36	K. Johnson	8.498	113.80
May 4	Lone Star Nationals	Top Fuel	Joe Amato	4.638	316.01	L. Dixon	4.806	307.58
		Funny Car	Randy Anderson	5.056	284.36	J. Force	5.054	299.10
		Pro Stock	Warren Johnson	6.985	198.71	S. Geoffron	7.042	196.37
May 18	Mopar Nationals	Top Fuel	Cristen Powell	4.849	239.61	B. Sarvar	5.818	154.83
		Funny Car	Ken Okazaki	6.683	181.30	C. Etchells	10.316	88.62
		Pro Stock	Darrell Alderman	6.988	196.20	B. Allen	6.924	196.07
June 1	West. Auto Nationals	Top Fuel	Scott Kalitta	4.646	315.23	G. Scelzi	4.740	303.23
		Funny Car	Whit Bazemore	5.035	307.58	R. Anderson	5.638	189.99
		Pro Stock	Scott Geoffrion	7.077	194.25	L. Morgan	7.101	193.29
June 15	Pontiac Nationals	Top Fuel	Gary Scelzi	4.927	284.81	T. Schumacher	5.030	281.42
		Funny Car	Tom Hoover	5.349	270.35	W. Bazemore	5.445	275.14
		Pro Stock	Tom Martino	7.105	194.25	T. Coughlin	8.197	120.19
June 29	Sears Inagural Race	Top Fuel	Joe Amato	4.739	306.43	G. Scelzi	4.784	301.30
		Funny Car	Ron Capps	5.165	268.81	C. Pedregon	5.655	210.82
		Pro Stock	Warren Johnson	7.064	196.16	J. Yates	7.049	195.90
July 20	Mile-High Nationals	Top Fuel	Cory McClenathan	4.864	294.59	T. Schumacher	4.971	287.53
		Funny Car	Whit Bazemore	5.460	271.82	C. Etchells	5.496	276.15
		Pro Stock	Jim Yates	7.430	184.35	K. Johnson	114.02	79.33
July 27	Autolite Nationals	Top Fuel	Cory McClenathan	4.717	310.77	S. Kalitta	4.829	302.41
		Funny Car	Ron Capps	5.205	280.72	T. Pedregon	7.827	105.46
		Pro Stock	Jim Yates	7.020	195.52	D. Cambron	7.103	194.38
Aug. 3	Northwest Nationals	Top Fuel	Cory McClenathan	4.730	313.26	G. Scelzi	4.749	310.13
		Funny Car	Whit Bazemore	5.293	274.89	T. Pedregon	7.235	118.73
		Pro Stock	Mike Edwards	7.086	195.73	J. Yates	7.088	194.97
Aug. 17	Champion Nationals	Top Fuel	Cory McClenathan	4.785	315.01	B. Vandergriff	6.152	136.75
		Funny Car	John Force	4.974	310.55	R. Capps	28.451	33.03
		Pro Stock	Kurt Johnson	7.033	196.12	J. Yates	7.032	195.14
Sept. 1	U.S. Nationals	Top Fuel	Jim Head	4.738	300.00	C. McClenathan	5.333	258.91
		Funny Car	Whit Bazemore	4.996	306.85	T. Wilkerson	13.161	73.08
		Pro Stock	K. Johnson	7.046	195.82	V. Gaines	7.069	194.88
Sept. 14	Pioneer Nationals	Top Fuel	Cory McClenathan	4.753	305.28	K. Bernstein	4.790	299.90
		Funny Car	John Force	5.083	305.39	C. Etchells	5.282	224.66
		Pro Stock	Jim Yates	6.966	198.06	M. Belt	7.008	196.37
Sept. 28	Craftsman Nationals	Top Fuel	Kenny Bernstein	4.656	317.34	J. Amato	4.644	309.81
		Funny Car	John Force	4.988	308.74	R. Anderson	5.356	245.43
		Pro Stock	Jim Yates	7.026	195.48	M. Edwards	7.059	193.13

Winston Point Standings
1997 (through Oct. 5)
First place finishers in parentheses.

	Top Fuel	Pts		Funny Car	Pts		Pro Stock	Pts
1	Gary Scelzi (4)	1546	1	John Force (6)	1603	1	Jim Yates (8)	1753
2	Cory McClenathan (5)	1411	2	Whit Bazemore (4)	1265	2	Warren Johnson (4)	1405
3	Joe Amato (4)	1351	3	Chuck Etchells (1)	1169	4	Kurt Johnson (2)	1371
4	Scott Kalitta (1)	1136	4	Tony Pedregon (1)	1120	3	Buce Allen (0)	1036
5	Kenny Bernstein (2)	1123	5	Cruz Pedregon (0)	1048	5	Steve Schmidt (0)	960

AUTO RACING
STATISTICS
THE 1998
ESPN INFORMATION PLEASE SPORTS ALMANAC

SEC B

THROUGH THE YEARS
1911-1997

MAJOR RACES • LEADERS

PAGE 888

NASCAR Circuit
The Crown Jewels

The four biggest races on the NASCAR circuit are the Daytona 500, the Winston Select 500, the Coca-Cola 600 and the Mountain Dew Southern 500. The Winston Cup Media Guide lists them as the richest (Daytona), the fastest (Winston), the longest (Coca-Cola) and the oldest (Southern). Winston has offered a $1 million bonus since 1985 to any driver who can win three of the four races. The only drivers to win three of the races in a single year are Lee Roy Yarbrough (1969), David Pearson (1976), Bill Elliott (1985) and Jeff Gordon (1997).

Daytona 500

Held early in the NASCAR season; 200 laps around a 2.5-mile high-banked oval at Daytona International Speedway in Daytona Beach, FL. First race in 1959, although stock car racing at Daytona dates back to 1936. Winning drivers who started from pole positions are in **bold** type.

Multiple winners: Richard Petty (7); Cale Yarborough (4); Bobby Allison (3); Bill Elliott, Dale Jarrett and Sterling Marlin (2). **Multiple poles:** Buddy Baker and Cale Yarborough (4); Bill Elliott, Fireball Roberts and Ken Schrader (3); Donnie Allison (2).

Year	Winner	Car	Owner	MPH	Pole Sitter	MPH
1959	Lee Petty	Oldsmobile	Petty Enterprises	135.521	Bob Welborn	140.121
1960	Junior Johnson	Chevrolet	Ray Fox	124.740	Cotton Owens	149.892
1961	Marvin Panch	Pontiac	Smokey Yunick	149.601	Fireball Roberts	155.709
1962	**Fireball Roberts**	Pontiac	Smokey Yunick	152.529	Fireball Roberts	156.999
1963	Tiny Lund	Ford	Wood Brothers	151.566	Fireball Roberts	160.943
1964	Richard Petty	Plymouth	Petty Enterprises	154.334	Paul Goldsmith	174.910
1965-a	Fred Lorenzen	Ford	Holman-Moody	141.539	Darel Dieringer	171.151
1966-b	**Richard Petty**	Plymouth	Petty Enterprises	160.627	Richard Petty	175.165
1967	Mario Andretti	Ford	Holman-Moody	149.926	Curtis Turner	180.831
1968	**Cale Yarborough**	Mercury	Wood Brothers	143.251	Cale Yarborough	189.222
1969	Lee Roy Yarbrough	Ford	Junior Johnson	157.950	Buddy Baker	188.901
1970	Pete Hamilton	Plymouth	Petty Enterprises	149.601	Cale Yarborough	194.015
1971	Richard Petty	Plymouth	Petty Enterprises	144.462	A.J. Foyt	182.744
1972	A.J. Foyt	Mercury	Wood Brothers	161.550	Bobby Isaac	186.632
1973	Richard Petty	Dodge	Petty Enterprises	157.205	Buddy Baker	185.662
1974-c	Richard Petty	Dodge	Petty Enterprises	140.894	David Pearson	185.017
1975	Benny Parsons	Chevrolet	L.G. DeWitt	153.649	Donnie Allison	185.827
1976	David Pearson	Mercury	Wood Brothers	152.181	Ramo Stott	183.456
1977	Cale Yarborough	Chevrolet	Junior Johnson	153.218	Donnie Allison	188.048
1978	Bobby Allison	Ford	Bud Moore	159.730	Cale Yarborough	187.536
1979	Richard Petty	Oldsmobile	Petty Enterprises	143.977	Buddy Baker	196.049
1980	**Buddy Baker**	Oldsmobile	Ranier Racing	177.602*	Buddy Baker	194.099
1981	Richard Petty	Buick	Petty Enterprises	169.651	Bobby Allison	194.624
1982	Bobby Allison	Buick	DiGard Racing	153.991	Benny Parsons	196.317
1983	Cale Yarborough	Pontiac	Ranier Racing	155.979	Ricky Rudd	198.864
1984	**Cale Yarborough**	Chevrolet	Ranier Racing	150.994	Cale Yarborough	201.848
1985	**Bill Elliott**	Ford	Melling Racing	172.265	Bill Elliott	205.114
1986	Geoff Bodine	Chevrolet	Hendrick Motorsports	148.124	Bill Elliott	205.039
1987	**Bill Elliott**	Ford	Melling Racing	176.263	Bill Elliott	210.364†
1988	Bobby Allison	Buick	Stavola Brothers	137.531	Ken Schrader	198.823
1989	Darrell Waltrip	Chevrolet	Hendrick Motorsports	148.466	Ken Schrader	196.996
1990	Derrike Cope	Chevrolet	Bob Whitcomb	165.761	Ken Schrader	196.515
1991	Ernie Irvan	Chevrolet	Morgan-McClure	148.148	Davey Allison	195.955
1992	Davey Allison	Ford	Robert Yates	160.256	Sterling Martin	192.213
1993	Dale Jarrett	Chevrolet	Joe Gibbs Racing	154.972	Kyle Petty	189.426
1994	Sterling Marlin	Chevrolet	Morgan-McClure	156.931	Loy Allen	190.158
1995	Sterling Marlin	Chevrolet	Morgan-McClure	141.710	Dale Jarrett	193.498
1996	Dale Jarrett	Ford	Robert Yates	154.308	Dale Earnhardt	189.510
1997	Jeff Gordon	Chevrolet	Rick Hendrick	148.295	Mike Skinner	189.813

*Track and race record for Winning Speed. †Track and race record for Qualifying Speed.

Notes: a—rain shortened 1965 to 332+ miles; **b**—rain shortened 1966 race to 495 miles; **c**—in 1974, race shortened 50 miles due to energy crisis. **Also:** Pole sitters determined by pole qualifying race (1959-65); by two-lap average (1966-68); by fastest single lap (since 1969).

Winston Select 500

Held at Talladega (Ala.) Superspeedway. **Multiple winners:** Bobby Allison, Davey Allison, Buddy Baker and David Pearson (3); Dale Earnhardt, Mark Martin Darrell Waltrip and Cale Yarborough (2).

Year		Year		Year		Year	
1970	Pete Hamilton	1978	Cale Yarborough	1986	Bobby Allison	1994	Dale Earnhardt
1971	Donnie Allison	1979	Bobby Allison	1987	Davey Allison	1995	Mark Martin
1972	David Pearson	1980	Buddy Baker	1988	Phil Parsons	1996	Sterling Marlin
1973	David Pearson	1981	Bobby Allison	1989	Davey Allison	1997	Mark Martin
1974	David Pearson	1982	Darrell Waltrip	1990	Dale Earnhardt		
1975	Buddy Baker	1983	Richard Petty	1991	Harry Gant		
1976	Buddy Baker	1984	Cale Yarborough	1992	Davey Allison		
1977	Darrell Waltrip	1985	Bill Elliott	1993	Ernie Irvan		

Coca-Cola 600

Held at Charlotte (N.C.) Motor Speedway. **Multiple winners:** Darrell Waltrip (5); Bobby Allison, Buddy Baker, Dale Earnhardt and David Pearson (3); Neil Bonnett, Jeff Gordon, Fred Lorenzen, Jim Paschal and Richard Petty (2).

Year		Year		Year		Year	
1960	Joe Lee Johnson	1970	Donnie Allison	1980	Benny Parsons	1990	Rusty Wallace
1961	David Pearson	1971	Bobby Allison	1981	Bobby Allison	1991	Davey Allison
1962	Nelson Stacy	1972	Buddy Baker	1982	Neil Bonnett	1992	Dale Earnhardt
1963	Fred Lorenzen	1973	Buddy Baker	1983	Neil Bonnett	1993	Dale Earnhardt
1964	Jim Paschal	1974	David Pearson	1984	Bobby Allison	1994	Jeff Gordon
1965	Fred Lorenzen	1975	Richard Petty	1985	Darrell Waltrip	1995	Bobby Labonte
1966	Marvin Panch	1976	David Pearson	1986	Dale Earnhardt	1996	Dale Jarrett
1967	Jim Paschal	1977	Richard Petty	1987	Kyle Petty	1997	Jeff Gordon
1968	Buddy Baker	1978	Darrell Waltrip	1988	Darrell Waltrip		
1969	Lee Roy Yarbrough	1979	Darrell Waltrip	1989	Darrell Waltrip		

Southern 500

Held at Darlington (S.C.) International Raceway. Multiple winners: Cale Yarborough (5); Bobby Allison (4); Buck Baker, Dale Earnhardt, Bill Elliott, Jeff Gordon, David Pearson and Herb Thomas (3); Harry Gant and Fireball Roberts (2).

Year		Year		Year		Year	
1950	Johnny Mantz	1962	Larry Frank	1974	Cale Yarborough	1986	Tim Richmond
1951	Herb Thomas	1963	Fireball Roberts	1975	Bobby Allison	1987	Dale Earnhardt
1952	Fonty Flock	1964	Buck Baker	1976	David Pearson	1988	Bill Elliott
1953	Buck Baker	1965	Ned Jarrett	1977	David Pearson	1989	Dale Earnhardt
1954	Herb Thomas	1966	Darel Dieringer	1978	Cale Yarborough	1990	Dale Earnhardt
1955	Herb Thomas	1967	Richard Petty	1979	David Pearson	1991	Harry Gant
1956	Curtis Turner	1968	Cale Yarborough	1980	Terry Labonte	1992	Darrell Waltrip
1957	Speedy Thompson	1969	Lee Roy Yarbrough	1981	Neil Bonnett	1993	Mark Martin
1958	Fireball Roberts	1970	Buddy Baker	1982	Cale Yarborough	1994	Bill Elliott
1959	Jim Reed	1971	Bobby Allison	1983	Bobby Allison	1995	Jeff Gordon
1960	Buck Baker	1972	Bobby Allison	1984	Harry Gant	1996	Jeff Gordon
1961	Nelson Stacy	1973	Cale Yarborough	1985	Bill Elliott	1997	Jeff Gordon

All-Time Leaders

NASCAR's all-time Top 20 drivers in victories, pole positions and earnings based on records through 1996. Drivers active in 1997 are in **bold** type.

Victories

1	Richard Petty	200
2	David Pearson	105
3	**Darrell Waltrip**	84
	Bobby Allison	84
5	Cale Yarborough	83
6	**Dale Earnhardt**	70
7	Lee Petty	54
8	Ned Jarrett	50
	Junior Johnson	50
10	Herb Thomas	48
11	Buck Baker	46
	Rusty Wallace	46
13	**Bill Elliott**	40
	Tim Flock	40
15	Bobby Isaac	37
16	Fireball Roberts	34
17	Rex White	28
18	Fred Lorenzen	26
19	Jim Paschal	25
20	Joe Weatherly	24

Pole Positions

1	Richard Petty	127
2	David Pearson	113
3	Cale Yarborough	70
4	**Darrell Waltrip**	59
5	Bobby Allison	57
6	Bobby Isaac	51
7	**Bill Elliott**	48
8	Junior Johnson	47
9	Buck Baker	44
10	Buddy Baker	40
11	Herb Thomas	38
12	Tim Flock	37
	Fireball Roberts	37
14	Ned Jarrett	36
	Rex White	36
16	**Geoff Bodine**	35
17	Fred Lorenzen	33
18	**Mark Martin**	32
19	Fonty Flock	30
20	Marvin Panch	25
	Terry Labonte	25

Earnings

1	**Dale Earnhardt**	$28,234,471
2	**Bill Elliott**	16,256,985
3	**Darrell Waltrip**	15,182,051
4	**Terry Labonte**	14,485,403
5	**Rusty Wallace**	14,420,035
6	**Mark Martin**	11,918,208
7	**Ricky Rudd**	11,526,339
8	**Geoff Bodine**	10,444,550
9	**Jeff Gordon**	10,326,804
10	**Sterling Marlin**	8,940,657
11	**Ken Schrader**	8,792,786
12	Harry Gant	8,456,104
13	**Dale Jarrett**	8,052,820
14	**Kyle Petty**	7,876,740
15	Richard Petty	7,755,409
16	**Morgan Shepard**	7,401,249
17	**Ernie Irvan**	7,337,309
18	Bobby Allison	7,102,233
19	Davey Allison	6,726,974
20	**Michael Waltrip**	5,377,672

Wide World Photos   Wide World Photos

Richard Petty (left) and **Dale Earnhardt** are both NASCAR Rookies of the Year who went on to win a record seven Winston Cup driving championships. Earnhardt, who claimed his seventh title in 1994, is also the circuit's all-time money winner. Petty retired in 1992 with a record 200 victories, including seven wins in the Daytona 500.

Winston Cup Champions

Originally the Grand National Championship, 1949-70, and based on official NASCAR (National Association for Stock Car Auto Racing) records.

Multiple winners: Dale Earnhardt and Richard Petty (7); David Pearson, Lee Petty, Darrell Waltrip and Cale Yarborough (3); Buck Baker, Tim Flock, Ned Jarrett, Herb Thomas and Joe Weatherly (2).

Year		Year		Year		Year	
1949	Red Byron	1961	Ned Jarrett	1973	Benny Parsons	1985	Darrell Waltrip
1950	Bill Rexford	1962	Joe Weatherly	1974	Richard Petty	1986	Dale Earnhardt
1951	Herb Thomas	1963	Joe Weatherly	1975	Richard Petty	1987	Dale Earnhardt
1952	Tim Flock	1964	Richard Petty	1976	Cale Yarborough	1988	Bill Elliott
1953	Herb Thomas	1965	Ned Jarrett	1977	Cale Yarborough	1989	Rusty Wallace
1954	Lee Petty	1966	David Pearson	1978	Cale Yarborough	1990	Dale Earnhardt
1955	Tim Flock	1967	Richard Petty	1979	Richard Petty	1991	Dale Earnhardt
1956	Buck Baker	1968	David Pearson	1980	Dale Earnhardt	1992	Alan Kulwicki
1957	Buck Baker	1969	David Pearson	1981	Darrell Waltrip	1993	Dale Earnhardt
1958	Lee Petty	1970	Bobby Isaac	1982	Darrell Waltrip	1994	Dale Earnhardt
1959	Lee Petty	1971	Richard Petty	1983	Bobby Allison	1995	Jeff Gordon
1960	Rex White	1972	Richard Petty	1984	Terry Labonte	1996	Terry Labonte

NASCAR Rookie of the Year

Award presented to rookie driver who accumulates the most Winston Cup points based on his best 15 finishes.

Year		Year		Year		Year	
1958	Shorty Rollins	1968	Pete Hamilton	1978	Ronnie Thomas	1988	Ken Bouchard
1959	Richard Petty	1969	Dick Brooks	1979	Dale Earnhardt	1989	Dick Trickle
1960	David Pearson	1970	Bill Dennis	1980	Jody Ridley	1990	Rob Moroso
1961	Woodie Wilson	1971	Walter Ballard	1981	Ron Bouchard	1991	Bobby Hamilton
1962	Tom Cox	1972	Larry Smith	1982	Geoff Bodine	1992	Jimmy Hensley
1963	Billy Wade	1973	Lennie Pond	1983	Sterling Marlin	1993	Jeff Gordon
1964	Doug Cooper	1974	Earl Ross	1984	Rusty Wallace	1994	Jeff Burton
1965	Sam McQuagg	1975	Bruce Hill	1985	Ken Schrader	1995	Ricky Craven
1966	James Hylton	1976	Skip Manning	1986	Alan Kulwicki	1996	Johnny Benson
1967	Donnie Allison	1977	Ricky Rudd	1987	Davey Allison		

CART Circuit

Indianapolis 500

Held every Memorial Day weekend; 200 laps around a 2.5-mile oval at Indianapolis Motor Speedway. First race was held in 1911. Winning drivers are listed with starting positions. Winners who started from pole position are in **bold** type.

Multiple wins: A.J. Foyt, Rick Mears and Al Unser (4); Louis Meyer, Mauri Rose, Johnny Rutherford, Wilbur Shaw and Bobby Unser (3); Emerson Fittipaldi, Gordon Johncock, Arie Luyendyk, Tommy Milton, Al Unser Jr., Bill Vukovich and Rodger Ward (2).

Multiple poles: Rick Mears (6); Mario Andretti and A.J. Foyt (4); Rex Mays, Duke Nalon and Tom Sneva (3); Billy Arnold, Bill Cummings, Ralph DePalma, Leon Duray, Walt Faulkner, Parnelli Jones, Jack McGrath, Jimmy Murphy, Johnny Rutherford, Eddie Sachs and Jimmy Snyder (2).

Year	Winner (Pos.)	Car	MPH	Pole Sitter	MPH
1911	Ray Harroun (28)	Marmon Wasp	74.602	Lewis Strang	–
1912	Joe Dawson (7)	National	78.719	Gil Anderson	–
1913	Jules Goux (7)	Peugeot	75.933	Caleb Bragg	–
1914	Rene Thomas (15)	Delage	82.474	Jean Chassagne	–
1915	Ralph DePalma (2)	Mercedes	89.840	Howard Wilcox	98.90
1916-a	Dario Resta (4)	Peugeot	84.001	John Aitken	96.69
1917-18	Not held	World War I			
1919	Howdy Wilcox (2)	Peugeot	88.050	Rene Thomas	104.78
1920	Gaston Chevrolet (6)	Monroe	88.618	Ralph DePalma	99.15
1921	Tommy Milton (20)	Frontenac	89.621	Ralph DePalma	100.75
1922	**Jimmy Murphy** (1)	Murphy Special	94.484	Jimmy Murphy	100.50
1923	**Tommy Milton** (1)	H.C.S. Special	90.954	Tommy Milton	108.17
1924	L.L. Corum & Joe Boyer (21)	Duesenberg Special	98.234	Jimmy Murphy	108.037
1925	Peter DePaolo (2)	Duesenberg Special	101.127	Leon Duray	113.196
1926-b	Frank Lockhart (20)	Miller Special	95.904	Earl Cooper	111.735
1927	George Souders (22)	Duesenberg	97.545	Frank Lockhart	120.100
1928	Louie Meyer (13)	Miller Special	99.482	Leon Duray	122.391
1929	Ray Keech (6)	Simplex Piston Ring Special	97.585	Cliff Woodbury	120.599
1930	**Billy Arnold** (1)	Miller-Hartz Special	100.448	Billy Arnold	113.268
1931	Louis Schneider (13)	Bowes Seal Fast Special	96.629	Russ Snowberger	112.796
1932	Fred Frame (27)	Miller-Hartz Special	104.144	Lou Moore	117.363
1933	Louie Meyer (6)	Tydol Special	104.162	Bill Cummings	118.530
1934	Bill Cummings (10)	Boyle Products Special	104.863	Kelly Petillo	119.329
1935	Kelly Petillo (22)	Gilmore Speedway Special	106.240	Rex Mays	120.736
1936	Louie Meyer (28)	Ring Free Special	109.069	Rex Mays	119.644
1937	Wilbur Shaw (2)	Shaw-Gilmore Special	113.580	Bill Cummings	123.343
1938	**Floyd Roberts** (1)	Burd Piston Ring Special	117.200	Floyd Roberts	125.681
1939	Wilbur Shaw (3)	Boyle Special	115.035	Jimmy Snyder	130.138
1940	Wilbur Shaw (2)	Boyle Special	114.277	Rex Mays	127.850
1941	Floyd Davis & Mauri Rose (17)	Noc-Out Hose Clamp Special	115.117	Mauri Rose	128.691
1942-45	Not held	World War II			
1946	George Robson (15)	Thorne Engineering Special	114.820	Cliff Bergere	126.471
1947	Mauri Rose (3)	Blue Crown Spark Plug Special	116.338	Ted Horn	126.564
1948	Mauri Rose (3)	Blue Crown Spark Plug Special	119.814	Duke Nalon	131.603
1949	Bill Holland (4)	Blue Crown Spark Plug Special	121.327	Duke Nalon	132.939
1950-c	Johnnie Parsons (5)	Wynn's Friction Proofing	124.002	Walt Faulkner	134.343
1951	Lee Wallard (2)	Belanger Special	126.244	Duke Nalon	136.498
1952	Troy Ruttman (7)	Agajanian Special	128.922	Fred Agabashian	138.010
1953	**Bill Vukovich** (1)	Fuel Injection Special	128.740	Bill Vukovich	138.392
1954	Bill Vukovich (19)	Fuel Injection Special	130.840	Jack McGrath	141.033
1955	Bob Sweikert (14)	John Zink Special	128.213	Jerry Hoyt	140.045
1956	**Pat Flaherty** (1)	John Zink Special	128.490	Pat Flaherty	145.596
1957	Sam Hanks (13)	Belond Exhaust Special	135.601	Pat O'Connor	143.948
1958	Jimmy Bryan (7)	Belond AP Parts Special	133.791	Dick Rathmann	145.974
1959	Rodger Ward (6)	Leader Card 500 Roadster	135.857	Johnny Thomson	145.908
1960	Jim Rathmann (2)	Ken-Paul Special	138.767	Eddie Sachs	146.592
1961	A.J. Foyt (7)	Bowes Seal Fast Special	139.130	Eddie Sachs	147.481
1962	Rodger Ward (2)	Leader Card 500 Roadster	140.293	Parnelli Jones	150.370
1963	**Parnelli Jones** (1)	Agajanian-Willard Special	143.137	Parnelli Jones	151.153
1964	A.J. Foyt (5)	Sheraton-Thompson Special	147.350	Jim Clark	158.828
1965	Jim Clark (2)	Lotus Ford	150.686	A.J. Foyt	161.233
1966	Graham Hill (15)	American Red Ball Special	144.317	Mario Andretti	165.899
1967-d	A.J. Foyt (4)	Sheraton-Thompson Special	151.207	Mario Andretti	168.982
1968	Bobby Unser (3)	Rislone Special	152.882	Joe Leonard	171.559
1969	Mario Andretti (2)	STP Oil Treatment Special	156.867	A.J. Foyt	170.568

Year	Winner (Pos.)	Car	MPH	Pole Sitter	MPH
1970	**Al Unser** (1)	Johnny Lightning Special	155.749	Al Unser	170.221
1971	Al Unser (5)	Johnny Lightning Special	157.735	Peter Revson	178.696
1972	Mark Donohue (3)	Sunoco McLaren	162.962	Bobby Unser	195.940
1973-e	Gordon Johncock (11) ...	STP Double Oil Filters	159.036	Johnny Rutherford	198.413
1974	Johnny Rutherford (25) ...	McLaren	158.589	A.J. Foyt	191.632
1975-f	Bobby Unser (3)	Jorgensen Eagle	149.213	A.J. Foyt	193.976
1976-g	**Johnny Rutherford** (1)	Hy-Gain McLaren/Goodyear	148.725	Johnny Rutherford	188.957
1977	A.J. Foyt (4)	Gilmore Racing Team	161.331	Tom Sneva	198.884
1978	Al Unser (5)	FNCTC Chaparral Lola	161.363	Tom Sneva	202.156
1979	**Rick Mears** (1)	The Gould Charge	158.899	Rick Mears	193.736
1980	**Johnny Rutherford** (1)	Pennzoil Chaparral	142.862	Johnny Rutherford	192.256
1981-h	**Bobby Unser** (1)	Norton Spirit Penske PC-9B	139.084	Bobby Unser	200.546
1982	Gordon Johncock (5)	STP Oil Treatment	162.029	Rick Mears	207.004
1983	Tom Sneva (4)	Texaco Star	162.117	Teo Fabi	207.395
1984	Rick Mears (3)	Pennzoil Z-7	163.612	Tom Sneva	210.029
1985	Danny Sullivan (8)	Miller American Special	152.982	Pancho Carter	212.583
1986	Bobby Rahal (4)	Budweiser/Truesports/March	170.722	Rick Mears	216.828
1987	Al Unser (20)	Cummins Holset Turbo	162.175	Mario Andretti	215.390
1988	**Rick Mears** (1)	Pennzoil Z-7/Penske Chevy V-8	144.809	Rick Mears	219.198
1989	Emerson Fittipaldi (3)	Marlboro/Penske Chevy V-8	167.581	Rick Mears	223.885
1990	Arie Luyendyk (3)	Domino's Pizza Chevrolet	185.981*	Emerson Fittipaldi	225.301
1991	**Rick Mears** (1)	Marlboro Penske Chevy	176.457	Rick Mears	224.113
1992	Al Unser Jr. (12)	Valvoline Galmer '92	134.477	Roberto Guerrero	232.482†
1993	Emerson Fittipaldi (9)	Marlboro Penske Chevy	157.207	Arie Luyendyk	223.967
1994	**Al Unser Jr.** (1)	Marlboro Penske Mercedes	160.872	Al Unser Jr.	228.011
1995	Jacques Villeneuve (5)	Player's Ltd. Reynard Ford	153.616	Scott Brayton	231.604
1996	Buddy Lazier (5)	Reynard Ford	147.956	Tony Stewart	233.100&
1997	**Arie Luyendyk** (1)	G-Force Olds Aurora	145.827	Arie Luyendyk	218.263

*Track record for Winning Time.
†Track record for Qualifying Time.
& Scott Brayton won the pole position with an avg. mph of 233.718 but was killed in a practice run. Stewart was given pole position with the next fastest speed.
Notes: a–1916 race scheduled for 300 miles; **b**–rain shortened 1926 race to 400 miles; **c**–rain shortened 1950 race to 345 miles; **d**–1967 race postponed due to rain after 18 laps (May 30), resumed next day (May 31); **e**–rain shortened 1973 race to 332.5 miles; **f**–rain shortened 1975 race to 435 miles; **g**–rain shortened 1976 race to 255 miles; **h**–in 1981, runner-up Mario Andretti was awarded 1st place when winner Bobby Unser was penalized a lap after the race was completed for passing cars illegally under the caution flag. Unser and car-owner Roger Penske appealed the race stewards' decision to the U.S. Auto Club. Four months later, USAC overturned the ruling, saying that the penalty was too harsh and Unser should be fined $40,000 rather than stripped of his championship.

All-Time Leaders

IndyCar's all-time Top 20 drivers in victories, pole positions and earnings, based on records through 1996. Drivers active in 1997 are in **bold** type. Totals include victories, poles and earnings before CART was established in 1979.

Victories

1	A.J. Foyt	.67
2	Mario Andretti	.52
3	Al Unser	.39
4	Bobby Unser	.35
	Michael Andretti	.35
6	**Al Unser Jr.**	.31
7	Rick Mears	.29
8	Johnny Rutherford	.27
9	Roger Ward	.26
10	Gordon Johncock	.25
11	Ralph DePalma	.24
	Bobby Rahal	.24
13	Tommy Milton	.23
14	Tony Bettenhausen	.22
	Emerson Fittipaldi	.22
16	Earl Cooper	.20
17	Jimmy Bryan	.19
	Jimmy Murphy	.19
19	Ralph Mulford	.17
	Danny Sullivan	.17

Pole Positions

1	Mario Andretti	.67
2	A.J. Foyt	.53
3	Bobby Unser	.49
4	Rick Mears	.39
5	**Michael Andretti**	.30
6	Al Unser	.27
7	Johnny Rutherford	.23
8	Gordon Johncock	.20
9	Rex Mays	.19
	Danny Sullivan	.19
11	**Bobby Rahal**	.18
12	Emerson Fittipaldi	.17
13	Tony Bettenhausen	.14
	Don Branson	.14
	Tom Sneva	.14
16	Parnelli Jones	.12
17	Rodger Ward	.11
	Danny Ongais	.11
19	Johnny Thompson	.10
	Dan Gurney	.10
	Nigel Mansell	.10

Earnings

1	**Al Unser Jr.**	.....$17,735,906
2	**Bobby Rahal**	15,263,758
3	Emerson Fittipaldi	.14,293,625
4	**Michael Andretti**	.13,862,619
5	Mario Andretti	.11,552,154
6	Rick Mears	.11,050,807
7	Danny Sullivan	8,844,129
8	Arie Luyendyk*	7,732,188
9	Al Unser	6,740,843
10	**Raul Boesel**	6,509,137
11	**Jimmy Vasser**	5,421,494
12	A.J. Foyt	5,357,589
13	Teo Fabi*	5,045,881
14	**Paul Tracy**	4,990,770
15	Scott Brayton*	4,807,214
16	Scott Goodyear*	4,579,451
17	Tom Sneva	4,392,993
18	Roberto Guerrero	4,275,163
19	Johnny Rutherford	4,209,232
20	Jacques Villeneuve	4,097,732

*drivers active, but in IRL not CART.

PPG Cup Champions

Officially the PPG Indy Car World Series Championship since 1979 and based on official AAA (American Automobile Assn., 1909-55), USAC (U.S. Auto Club, 1956-79), and CART (Championship Auto Racing Teams, 1979-91). CART was renamed IndyCar in 1992.

Multiple titles: A.J. Foyt (7); Mario Andretti (4); Jimmy Bryan, Earl Cooper, Ted Horn, Rick Mears, Louie Meyer, Bobby Rahal, Al Unser (3); Tony Bettenhausen, Ralph DePalma, Peter DePaolo, Joe Leonard, Rex Mays, Tommy Milton, Jimmy Murphy, Wilbur Shaw, Tom Sneva, Al Unser Jr., Bobby Unser and Rodger Ward (2).

AAA

Year		Year		Year		Year	
1909	George Robertson	1920	Tommy Milton	1931	Louis Schneider	1942-45	No racing
1910	Ray Harroun	1921	Tommy Milton	1932	Bob Carey	1946	Ted Horn
1911	Ralph Mulford	1922	Jimmy Murphy	1933	Louie Meyer	1947	Ted Horn
1912	Ralph DePalma	1923	Eddie Hearne	1934	Bill Cummings	1948	Ted Horn
1913	Earl Cooper	1924	Jimmy Murphy	1935	Kelly Petillo	1949	Johnnie Parsons
1914	Ralph DePalma	1925	Peter DePaolo	1936	Mauri Rose		
1915	Earl Cooper	1926	Harry Hartz	1937	Wilbur Shaw	1950	Henry Banks
1916	Dario Resta	1927	Peter DePaolo	1938	Floyd Roberts	1951	Tony Bettenhausen
1917	Earl Cooper	1928	Louie Meyer	1939	Wilbur Shaw	1952	Chuck Stevenson
1918	Ralph Mulford	1929	Louie Meyer			1953	Sam Hanks
1919	Howard Wilcox	1930	Billy Arnold	1940	Rex Mays	1954	Jimmy Bryan
				1941	Rex Mays	1955	Bob Sweikert

USAC

Year		Year		Year		Year	
1956	Jimmy Bryan	1962	Rodger Ward	1968	Bobby Unser	1974	Bobby Unser
1957	Jimmy Bryan	1963	A.J. Foyt	1969	Mario Andretti	1975	A.J. Foyt
1958	Tony Bettenhausen	1964	A.J. Foyt	1970	Al Unser	1976	Gordon Johncock
1959	Rodger Ward	1965	Mario Andretti	1971	Joe Leonard	1977	Tom Sneva
1960	A.J. Foyt	1966	Mario Andretti	1972	Joe Leonard	1978	A.J. Foyt
1961	A.J. Foyt	1967	A.J. Foyt	1973	Roger McCluskey		

CART/IndyCar

Year		Year		Year		Year	
1979	Rick Mears	1984	Mario Andretti	1989	Emerson Fittipaldi	1994	Al Unser Jr.
1980	Johnny Rutherford	1985	Al Unser	1990	Al Unser Jr.	1995	Jacques Villeneuve
1981	Rick Mears	1986	Bobby Rahal	1991	Michael Andretti	1996	Jimmy Vasser
1982	Rick Mears	1987	Bobby Rahal	1992	Bobby Rahal	1997	Alex Zanardi
1983	Al Unser	1988	Danny Sullivan	1993	Nigel Mansell		

Indy 500 Rookie of the Year

Voted on by a panel of auto racing media. Award does not necessarily go to highest-finishing first-year driver. Graham Hill won the race on his first try in 1966, but the rookie award went to Jackie Stewart, who led with 10 laps to go only to lose oil pressure and finish 6th.

Father and son winners: Mario and Michael Andretti (1965 and 1984); Bill and Billy Vukovich (1968 and 1988).

Year		Year		Year		Year	
1952	Art Cross	1964	Johnny White	1977	Jerry Sneva	1988	Billy Vukovich III
1953	Jimmy Daywalt	1965	Mario Andretti	1978	Rick Mears	1989	Bernard Jourdain
1954	Larry Crockett	1966	Jackie Stewart		& Larry Rice		& Scott Pruett
1955	Al Herman	1967	Denis Hulme	1979	Howdy Holmes		
1956	Bob Veith	1968	Bill Vukovich			1990	Eddie Cheever
1957	Don Edmunds	1969	Mark Donohue	1980	Tim Richmond	1991	Jeff Andretti
1958	George Amick			1981	Josele Garza	1992	Lyn St. James
1959	Bobby Grim	1970	Donnie Allison	1982	Jim Hickman	1993	Nigel Mansell
		1971	Denny Zimmerman	1983	Teo Fabi	1994	Jacques Villeneuve
1960	Jim Hurtubise	1972	Mike Hiss	1984	Michael Andretti	1995	Christian Fittipaldi
1961	Parnelli Jones	1973	Graham McRae		& Roberto Guerrero	1996	Tony Stewart
	& Bobby Marshman	1974	Pancho Carter	1985	Arie Luyendyk	1997	Jeff Ward
1962	Jimmy McElreath	1975	Bill Puterbaugh	1986	Randy Lanier		
1963	Jim Clark	1976	Vern Schuppan	1987	Fabrizio Barbazza		

CART/IndyCar Rookie of the Year

Award presented to rookie who accumulates the most PPG Cup points among first year drivers. Originally the CART Rookie of the Year; CART was renamed IndyCar in 1992.

Year		Year		Year		Year	
1979	Bill Alsup	1984	Roberto Guerrero	1989	Bernard Jourdain	1994	Jacques Villeneuve
1980	Dennis Firestone	1985	Arie Luyendyk	1990	Eddie Cheever	1995	Gil de Ferran
1981	Bob Lazier	1986	Dominic Dobson	1991	Jeff Andretti	1996	Alex Zanardi
1982	Bobby Rahal	1987	Fabrizio Barbazza	1992	Stefan Johansson	1997	Patrick Carpentier
1983	Teo Fabi	1988	John Jones	1993	Nigel Mansell		

Formula One Circuit
United States Grand Prix

There have been 54 official Formula One races held in the United States since 1950, including the Indianapolis 500 from 1950-60. FISA sanctioned two annual U.S. Grand Prix–USA/East and USA/West–from 1976-80 and 1983. Phoenix was the site of the U.S. Grand Prix from 1989-91.

Indianapolis 500
Officially sanctioned as Grand Prix race from 1950-60 only. See IndyCar Circuit for details.

U.S. Grand Prix–East

Held from 1959-80 and 1981-88 at the following locations: Sebring, Fla. (1959); Riverside, Calif. (1960); Watkins Glen, N.Y. (1961-80); and Detroit (1982-88). There was no race in 1981. Race discontinued in 1989.

Multiple winners: Jim Clark, Graham Hill and Ayrton Senna (3); James Hunt, Carlos Reutemann and Jackie Stewart (2).

Year		Car	Year		Car
1959	Bruce McLaren, NZE	Cooper Climax	1974	Carlos Reutemann, ARG	Brabham Ford
1960	Stirling Moss, GBR	Lotus Climax	1975	Niki Lauda, AUT	Ferrari
1961	Innes Ireland, GBR	Lotus Climax	1976	James Hunt, GBR	McLaren Ford
1962	Jim Clark, GBR	Lotus Climax	1977	James Hunt, GBR	McLaren Ford
1963	Graham Hill, GBR	BRM	1978	Carlos Reutemann, ARG	Ferrari
1964	Graham Hill, GBR	BRM	1979	Gilles Villeneuve, CAN	Ferrari
1965	Graham Hill, GBR	BRM	1980	Alan Jones, AUS	Williams Ford
1966	Jim Clark, GBR	Lotus Climax	1981	Not held	
1967	Jim Clark, GBR	Lotus Ford	1982	John Watson, GBR	McLaren Ford
1968	Jackie Stewart, GBR	Matra Ford	1983	Michele Alboreto, ITA	Tyrrell Ford
1969	Jochen Rindt, AUT	Lotus Ford	1984	Nelson Piquet, BRA	Brabham BMW Turbo
1970	Emerson Fittipaldi, BRA	Lotus Ford	1985	Keke Rosberg, FIN	Williams Honda Turbo
1971	Francois Cevert, FRA	Tyrrell Ford	1986	Ayrton Senna, BRA	Lotus Renault Turbo
1972	Jackie Stewart, GBR	Tyrrell Ford	1987	Ayrton Senna, BRA	Lotus Honda Turbo
1973	Ronnie Peterson, SWE	Lotus Ford	1988	Ayrton Senna, BRA	McLaren Honda Turbo

U.S. Grand Prix–West

Held from 1976-83 at Long Beach, Calif. Races also held in Las Vegas (1981-82), Dallas (1984) and Phoenix (1989-91). Race discontinued in 1992.

Multiple winners: Alan Jones and Ayrton Senna (2).

Long Beach

Year		Car
1976	Clay Regazzoni, SWI	Ferrari
1977	Mario Andretti, USA	Lotus Ford
1978	Carlos Reutemann, ARG	Ferrari
1979	Gilles Villeneuve, CAN	Ferrari
1980	Nelson Piquet, BRA	Brabham Ford
1981	Alan Jones, AUS	Williams Ford
1982	Niki Lauda, AUT	McLaren Ford
1983	John Watson, GBR	McLaren Ford

Las Vegas

Year		Car
1981	Alan Jones, AUS	Williams Ford
1982	Michele Alboreto, ITA	Tyrrell Ford

Dallas

Year		Car
1984	Keke Rosberg, FIN	Williams Honda Turbo

Phoenix

Year		Car
1989	Alain Prost, FRA	McLaren Honda
1990	Ayrton Senna, BRA	McLaren Honda
1991	Ayrton Senna, BRA	McLaren Honda

All-Time Leaders

The all-time Top 20 Grand Prix winning drivers, based on records through 1996. Listed are starts (Sts), poles won (Pole), wins (1st), second place finishes (2nd), and thirds (3rd). Drivers active in 1997 and career victories in **bold** type.

		Sts	Pole	1st	2nd	3rd			Sts	Pole	1st	2nd	3rd
1	Alain Prost	199	33	**51**	35	20	12	Jack Brabham	126	13	**14**	10	7
2	Ayrton Senna	161	65	**41**	23	16	13	Emerson Fittipaldi	144	6	**14**	13	8
3	Nigel Mansell	187	32	**31**	17	11	14	Graham Hill	176	13	**14**	15	7
4	Jackie Stewart	99	17	**27**	11	5	15	Alberto Ascari	32	14	**13**	4	0
5	Jim Clark	72	33	**25**	1	6	16	Mario Andretti	128	18	**12**	2	5
6	Niki Lauda	171	24	**25**	20	9	17	Alan Jones	116	6	**12**	7	5
7	Juan-Manuel Fangio	51	28	**24**	10	1	18	Carlos Reutemann	146	6	**12**	13	20
8	Nelson Piquet	204	24	**23**	20	17	19	James Hunt	92	14	**10**	6	7
9	**M. Schumacher**	85	14	**22**	14	10		Ronnie Peterson	123	14	**10**	10	6
10	**Damon Hill**	67	20	**21**	14	5		Jody Scheckter	112	3	**10**	14	9
11	Stirling Moss	66	16	**16**	5	3							

Note: The following five drivers either died or were killed in their final year of competition—Clark in a Formula Two race in West Germany in 1968; Graham Hill in a plane crash in 1975; Ascari in a private practice run in 1955; Peterson following a crash in the 1978 Italian GP; and Senna following a crash in the 1994 San Marino GP.

World Champions

Officially called the World Championship of Drivers and based on Formula One (Grand Prix) records through the 1995 racing season.

Multiple winners: Juan-Manuel Fangio (5); Alain Prost (4); Jack Brabham, Niki Lauda, Nelson Piquet, Ayrton Senna and Jackie Stewart (3); Alberto Ascari, Jim Clark, Emerson Fittipaldi, Graham Hill and Michael Schumacher (2).

Year	Driver	Car	Year	Driver	Car
1950	Guiseppe Farina, ITA	Alfa Romeo	1974	Emerson Fittipaldi, BRA	McLaren Ford
1951	Juan-Manuel Fangio, ARG	Alfa Romeo	1975	Niki Lauda, AUT	Ferrari
1952	Alberto Ascari, ITA	Ferrari	1976	James Hunt, GBR	McLaren Ford
1953	Alberto Ascari, ITA	Ferrari	1977	Niki Lauda, AUT	Ferrari
1954	Juan-Manuel Fangio, ARG	Maserati/Mercedes	1978	Mario Andretti, USA	Lotus Ford
1955	Juan-Manuel Fangio, ARG	Mercedes	1979	Jody Scheckter, SAF	Ferrari
1956	Juan-Manuel Fangio, ARG	Ferrari	1980	Alan Jones, AUS	Williams Ford
1957	Juan-Manuel Fangio, ARG	Maserati	1981	Nelson Piquet, BRA	Brabham Ford
1958	Mike Hawthorn, GBR	Ferrari	1982	Keke Rosberg, FIN	Williams Ford
1959	Jack Brabham, AUS	Cooper Climax	1983	Nelson Piquet, BRA	Brabham BMW Turbo
1960	Jack Brabham, AUS	Cooper Climax	1984	Niki Lauda, AUT	McL. TAG Porsche Turbo
1961	Phil Hill, USA	Ferrari	1985	Alain Prost, FRA	McL. TAG Porsche Turbo
1962	Graham Hill, GBR	BRM	1986	Alain Prost, FRA	McL. TAG Porsche Turbo
1963	Jim Clark, GBR	Lotus Climax	1987	Nelson Piquet, BRA	Williams Honda Turbo
1964	John Surtees, GBR	Ferrari	1988	Ayrton Senna, BRA	McLaren Honda Turbo
1965	Jim Clark, GBR	Lotus Climax	1989	Alain Prost, FRA	McLaren Honda
1966	Jack Brabham, AUS	Brabham Repco	1990	Ayrton Senna, BRA	McLaren Honda
1967	Denis Hulme, NZE	Brabham Repco	1991	Ayrton Senna, BRA	McLaren Honda
1968	Graham Hill, GBR	Lotus Ford	1992	Nigel Mansell, GBR	Williams Renault
1969	Jackie Stewart, GBR	Matra Ford	1993	Alain Prost, FRA	Williams-Renault
1970	Jochen Rindt, AUT	Lotus Ford	1994	Michael Schumacher, GER	Benetton Ford
1971	Jackie Stewart, GBR	Tyrrell Ford	1995	Michael Schumacher, GER	Benetton Renault
1972	Emerson Fittipaldi, BRA	Lotus Ford	1996	Damon Hill, GBR	Williams-Renault
1973	Jackie Stewart, GBR	Tyrrell Ford			

ENDURANCE RACES

The 24 Hours of Le Mans

Officially, the Le Mans Grand Prix d'Endurance. First run May 22-23, 1923, and won by Andre Lagache and Rene Leonard in a 3-litre Chenard & Walcker. All subsequent races have been held in June, except in 1956 (July) and 1968 (September). Originally contested over a 10.73-mile track, the circuit was shortened to its present 8.451-mile distance in 1932. The original start of Le Mans, where drivers raced across the track to their unstarted cars, was discontinued in 1970.

Multiple winners: Jacky Ickx (6); Derek Bell (5); Oliver Gendebien and Henri Pescarolo (4); Woolf Barnato, Luigi Chinetti, Yannick Dalmas, Hurley Haywood, Phil Hill, Al Holbert and Klaus Ludwig (3); Sir Henry Birkin, Ivoe Bueb, Ron Flockhart, Jean-Pierre Jaussaud, Gerard Larrousse, Andre Rossignol, Raymond Sommer, Hans Stuck, Gijs van Lennep and Jean-Pierre Wimille (2).

Year	Drivers	Car	MPH	Year	Drivers	Car	MPH
1923	Andre Lagache & Rene Leonard	Chenard & Walcker	57.21	1937	Jean-Pierre Wimille & Robert Benoist	Bugatti 57G	85.13
1924	John Duff & Francis Clement	Bentley	53.78	1938	Eugene Chaboud & Jean Tremoulet	Delahaye	82.36
1925	Gerard de Courcelles & Andre Rossignol	La Lorraine	57.84	1939	Jean-Pierre Wimille & Pierre Veyron	Bugatti 57G	86.86
1926	Robert Bloch & Andre Rossignol	La Lorraine	66.08	1940-48	Not held	World War II	
1927	J.D. Benjafield & Sammy Davis	Bentley	61.35	1949	Luigi Chinetti & Lord Selsdon	Ferrari	82.28
1928	Woolf Barnato & Bernard Rubin	Bentley	69.11	1950	Louis Rosier & Jean-Louis Rosier	Talbot-Lago	89.71
1929	Woolf Barnato & Sir Henry Birkin	Bentley Speed 6	73.63	1951	Peter Walker & Peter Whitehead	Jaguar C	93.50
1930	Woolf Barnato & Glen Kidston	Bentley Speed 6	75.88	1952	Hermann Lang & Fritz Reiss	Mercedes-Benz	96.67
1931	Earl Howe & Sir Henry Birkin	Alfa Romeo	78.13	1953	Tony Rolt & Duncan Hamilton	Jaguar C	98.65
1932	Raymond Sommer & Luigi Chinetti	Alfa Romeo	76.48	1954	Froilan Gonzalez & Maurice Trintignant	Ferrari 375	105.13
1933	Raymond Sommer & Tazio Nuvolari	Alfa Romeo	81.40	1955	Mike Hawthorn & Ivor Bueb	Jaguar D	107.05
1934	Luigi Chinetti & Philippe Etancelin	Alfa Romeo	74.74	1956	Ron Flockhart & Ninian Sanderson	Jaguar D	104.47
1935	John Hindmarsh & Louis Fontes	Lagonda	77.85	1957	Ron Flockhart & Ivor Bueb	Jaguar D	113.83
1936	Not held			1958	Oliver Gendebien & Phil Hill	Ferrari 250	106.18

Wide World Photos

Mario Andretti (center), who retired from IndyCar racing after the 1994 season, with French teammates **Bob Wollek** (right) and **Eric Helary** (left) after their second place finish in the 1995 running of the 24 Hours of Le Mans. The 55-year-old Andretti has won the Indy 500, Daytona 500 and 24 Hours of Daytona in addition to driving championships in Indy-Car and Formula One racing.

Endurance Races (Cont.)

Year	Drivers	Car	MPH	Year	Drivers	Car	MPH
1959	Roy Salvadori & Carroll Shelby	Aston Martin	112.55	1977	Jacky Ickx, Jurgen Barth & Hurley Haywood	Porsche 936	120.95
1960	Oliver Gendebien & Paul Fräre	Ferrari 250	109.17	1978	Jean-Pierre Jaussaud & Didier Pironi	Renault-Alpine	130.60
1961	Oliver Gendebien & Phil Hill	Ferrari 250	115.88	1979	Klaus Ludwig, Bill Wittington & Don Whittington	Porsche 935	108.10
1962	Oliver Gendebien & Phil Hill	Ferrari 250	115.22	1980	Jean-Pierre Jaussaud & Jean Rondeau	Rondeau-Cosworth	119.23
1963	Lodovico Scarfiotti & Lorenzo Bandini	Ferrari 250	118.08	1981	Jacky Ickx & Derek Bell	Porsche 936	124.94
1964	Jean Guichel & Nino Vaccarella	Ferrari 275	121.54	1982	Jacky Ickx & Derek Bell	Porsche 956	126.85
1965	Masten Gregory & Jochen Rindt	Ferrari 250	121.07	1983	Vern Schuppan, Hurley Haywood & Al Holbert	Porsche 956	130.70
1966	Bruce McLaren & Chris Amon	Ford Mk. II	125.37	1984	Klaus Ludwig & Henri Pescarolo	Porsche 956	126.88
1967	A.J. Foyt & Dan Gurney	Ford Mk. IV	135.46	1985	Klaus Ludwig, Paolo Barilla & John Winter	Porsche 956	131.75
1968	Pedro Rodriguez & Lucien Bianchi	Ford GT40	115.27	1986	Derek Bell, Hans Stuck & Al Holbert	Porsche 962	128.75
1969	Jacky Ickx & Jackie Oliver	Ford GT40	129.38	1987	Derek Bell, Hans Stuck & Al Holbert	Porsche 962	124.06
1970	Hans Herrmann & Richard Attwood	Porsche 917	119.28	1988	Jan Lammers, Johnny Dumfries & Andy Wallace	Jaguar XJR	137.75
1971	Gijs van Lennep & Helmut Marko	Porsche 917	138.13	1989	Jochen Mass, Manuel Reuter & Stanley Dickens	Sauber-Mercedes	136.39
1972	Graham Hill & Henri Pescarolo	Matra-Simca	121.45	1990	John Nielsen, Price Cobb & Martin Brundle	Jaguar XJR-12	126.71
1973	Henri Pescarolo & Gerard Larrousse	Matra-Simca	125.67				
1974	Henri Pescarolo & Gerard Larrousse	Matra-Simca	119.27				
1975	Derek Bell & Jacky Ickx	Mirage-Ford	118.98				
1976	Jacky Ickx & Gijs van Lennep	Porsche 936	123.49				

Year	Drivers	Car	MPH
1991	Volker Weider, Johnny Herbert & Bertrand Gachof	Mazda 787B	127.31
1992	Derek Warwick, Yannick Dalmas & Mark Blundell	Peugeot 905B	123.89
1993	Geoff Brabham, Christophe Bouchut & Eric Helary	Peugeot 905	132.58
1994	Yannick Dalmas, Hurley Haywood & Mauro Baldi	Porsche 962LM	129.82
1995	Yannick Dalmas, J.J. Lehto & Masanori Sekiya	McLaren BMW	105.00
1996	Davy Jones, Manuel Reuter & Alexander Wurz	TWR Porsche	124.65
1997	Michele Alberto, Stefan Johansson & Tom Kristensen	TWR Porsche	126.88

The 24 Hours of Daytona

Officially, the Rolex 24 at Daytona. First run in 1962 as a three-hour race and won by Dan Gurney in a Lotus 19 Ford. Contested over a 3.56-mile course at Daytona (Fla.) International Speedway. There have been several distance changes since 1962: the event was a three-hour race (1962-63); a 2,000-kilometer race (1964-65); a 24-hour race (1966-71); a six-hour race (1972) and a 24-hour race again since 1973. The race was canceled in 1974 due to a national energy crisis.

Multiple winners: Hurley Haywood (5); Peter Gregg, Pedro Rodriguez and Bob Wollek (4); Derek Bell and Rolf Stommelen (3); A.J. Foyt, Al Holbert, Ken Miles, Brian Redman, Lloyd Ruby and Al Unser Jr. (2).

Year	Drivers	Car	MPH
1962	Dan Gurney	Lotus Ford	104.101
1963	Pedro Rodriguez	Ferrari GTO	102.074
1964	Pedro Rodriguez & Phil Hill	Ferrari GTO	98.230
1965	Ken Miles & Lloyd Ruby	Ford GT	99.944
1966	Ken Miles & Lloyd Ruby	Ford Mk. II	108.020
1967	Lorenzo Bandini & Chris Amon	Ferrari 330	105.688
1968	Vic Elford & Jochen Neerpasch	Porsche 907	106.697
1969	Mark Donohue & Chuck Parsons	Lola Chevrolet	99.268
1970	Pedro Rodriguez & Leo Kinnunen	Porsche 917	114.866
1971	Pedro Rodriguez & Jackie Oliver	Porsche 917K	109.203
1972	Mario Andretti & Jacky Ickx	Ferrari 312P	122.573
1973	Peter Gregg & Hurley Haywood	Porsche Carrera	106.225
1974	Not held		
1975	Peter Gregg & Hurley Haywood	Porsche Carrera	108.531
1976	Peter Gregg, Brian Redman & John Fitzpatrick	BMW CSL	104.040
1977	Hurley Haywood, John Graves & Dave Helmick	Porsche Carrera	108.801
1978	Peter Gregg, Rolf Stommelen & Antoine Hezemans	Porsche Turbo	108.743
1979	Hurley Haywood, Ted Field & Danny Ongais	Porsche Turbo	109.249
1980	Rolf Stommelen, Volkert Merl & Reinhold Joest	Porsche Turbo	114.303
1981	Bobby Rahal, Brian Redman & Bob Garretson	Porsche Turbo	113.153
1982	John Paul Sr., John Paul Jr. & Rolf Stommelen	Porsche Turbo	114.794
1983	A.J. Foyt, Preston Henn, Bob Wollek & Claude Ballot-Lena	Porsche Turbo	98.781
1984	Sarel van der Merwe, Tony Martin & Graham Duxbury	March Porsche	103.119
1985	A.J. Foyt, Bob Wollek, Al Unser Sr. & Thierry Boutsen	Porsche 962	104.162
1986	Al Holbert, Derek Bell & Al Unser Jr	Porsche 962	105.484
1987	Al Holbert, Derek Bell, Chip Robinson & Al Unser Jr	Porsche 962	111.599
1988	Raul Boesel, Martin Brundle & John Nielsen	Jaguar XJR-9	107.943
1989	John Andretti, Derek Bell & Bob Wollek	Porsche 962	92.009
1990	Davy Jones, Jan Lammers & Andy Wallace	Jaguar XJR-12	112.857
1991	Hurley Haywood, John Winter, Frank Jelinski, Henri Pescarolo & Bob Wollek	Porsche 962-C	106.633
1992	Masahiro Hasemi, Kazuyoshi Hoshino & Toshio Suzuki	Nissan R-91	112.897
1993	P.J. Jones, Mark Dismore & Rocky Moran	Toyota Eagle	103.537
1994	Paul Gentilozzi, Scott Pruett, Butch Leitzinger & Steve Millen	Nissan 300 ZXT	104.80
1995	Jurgen Lassig, Christophe Bouchut, Giovanni Lavaggi & Marco Werner	Porsche Spyder	102.280
1996	Wayne Taylor, Scott Sharp & Jim Pace	Oldsmobile Arness MK-III	103.32
1997	Rob Dyson, James Weaver, Butch Leitzinger, Andy Wallace, John Paul Jr., Eliot Forbes-Robinson & John Schneider	Ford R&S MK-III	102.29

NHRA Drag Racing
NHRA Winston Champions

Based on points earned during the NHRA Winston Drag Racing series. The series began for Top Fuel, Funny Car and Pro Stock in 1975.

Top Fuel

Multiple winners: Joe Amato (5); Don Garlits and Shirley Muldowney (3); Scott Kalitta (2).

Year		Year		Year		Year	
1975	Don Garlits	1981	Jeb Allen	1987	Dick LaHaie	1993	Eddie Hill
1976	Richard Tharp	1982	Shirley Muldowney	1988	Joe Amato	1994	Scott Kalitta
1977	Shirley Muldowney	1983	Gary Beck	1989	Gary Ormsby	1995	Scott Kalitta
1978	Kelly Brown	1984	Joe Amato	1990	Joe Amato	1996	Kenny Bernstein
1979	Rob Bruins	1985	Don Garlits	1991	Joe Amato		
1980	Shirley Muldowney	1986	Don Garlits	1992	Joe Amato		

Funny Car

Multiple winners: John Force (6); Don Prudhomme, Kenny Bernstein (4); Raymond Beadle (3); Frank Hawley (2).

Year		Year		Year		Year	
1975	Don Prudhomme	1981	Raymond Beadle	1987	Kenny Bernstein	1993	John Force
1976	Don Prudhomme	1982	Frank Hawley	1988	Kenny Bernstein	1994	John Force
1977	Don Prudhomme	1983	Frank Hawley	1989	Bruce Larson	1995	John Force
1978	Don Prudhomme	1984	Mark Oswald	1990	John Force	1996	John Force
1979	Raymond Beadle	1985	Kenny Bernstein	1991	John Force		
1980	Raymond Beadle	1986	Kenny Bernstein	1992	Cruz Pedregon		

Pro Stock

Multiple winners: Bob Glidden (9); Lee Shepherd (4); Warren Johnson (3); Darrell Alderman (2).

Year		Year		Year		Year	
1975	Bob Glidden	1981	Lee Shepherd	1987	Bob Glidden	1993	Warren Johnson
1976	Larry Lombardo	1982	Lee Shepherd	1988	Bob Glidden	1994	Darrell Alderman
1977	Don Nicholson	1983	Lee Shepherd	1989	Bob Glidden	1995	Warren Johnson
1978	Bob Glidden	1984	Lee Shepherd	1990	John Myers	1996	Jim Yates
1979	Bob Glidden	1985	Bob Glidden	1991	Darrell Alderman		
1980	Bob Glidden	1986	Bob Glidden	1992	Warren Johnson		

All-Time Leaders
Career Victories

Top Fuel		Funny Car		Pro Stock	
1 **Joe Amato**	40	1 **John Force**	67	1 Bob Glidden	85
2 Don Garlits	35	2 Don Prudhomme	35	2 **Warren Johnson**	63
3 Gary Beck	19	3 **Kenny Bernstein**	30	3 **Darrell Alderman**	27
4 Shirley Muldowney	18	4 Ed McCulloch	18	4 Lee Shepherd	26
Darrell Gwynn	18	Mark Oswald	18	5 Jim Yates	18

National-Event Victories (pro categories)
Drivers active in 1997 season are in **bold** type.
Totals as of Oct. 5, 1997.

1 **Bob Glidden**	85	12 Terry Vance	24		**Scott Kalitta**	15
2 **John Force**	67	13 Ed McCulloch	22	24	Gary Ormsby	14
3 **Warren Johnson**	63	14 **Mark Oswald**	20	25	Raymond Beadle	13
4 **Don Prudhomme**	49	15 Gary Beck	19		**Eddie Hill**	13
5 **Kenny Bernstein**	48	**Jim Yates**	19		**Al Hofmann**	13
6 **Dave Schultz**	41	17 Shirley Muldowney	18	28	**Bruce Allen**	12
7 **Joe Amato**	40	Darrell Gwynn	18		Billy Meyer	12
8 Don Garlits	35	19 **Cruz Pedregon**	17	30	**Frank Iaconio**	11
9 **John Myers**	30	20 **Mike Dunn**	16		Bill Jenkins	11
10 **Darrell Alderman**	27	**Cory McClenathan**	16	32	**Connie Kalitta**	10
11 Lee Shepherd	26	22 Dick LaHaie	15			

Fastest Mile-Per-Hour Speeds
Fastest performances in NHRA major event history as of Oct. 5, 1997.

Top Fuel	Funny Car	Pro Stock
MPH	MPH	MPH
318.69 ..Kenny Bernstein, 10/12/96	314.35 ....John Force, 10/5/97	200.53 ...Warren Johnson, 4/27/97
318.58 ..Cory McClenathan, 10/4/97	313.36 ....John Force, 10/5/97	200.13 ...Warren Johnson, 4/25/97
318.24 ....Joe Amato, 9/1/97	313.04 ...Whit Bazemore, 3/23/97	199.95 ....Warren Johnson, 3/7/97
317.90 ....Joe Amato, 8/30/97	312.93 ....John Force, 9/1/97	199.91 ...Warren Johnson, 5/18/97
317.80 ....Larry Dixon, 10/5/97	312.71 .....Cruz Pedregon, 5/2/97	199.77 ...Warren Johnson, 4/26/97

Boxing

A picture says a thousand words. **Mike Tyson** is shown biting the ear of **Evander Holyfield** during the most successful pay-per-view TV event ever.

Champ to Chomp to Chump

In 1997, Boxing Left a Bad Taste in Everyone's Mouth

by
Charley Steiner

Friends, Romans, Countrymen.

It was a miserable year for boxing. The worst. And in an industry with a sordid history of shooting itself in the foot, or giving itself a black eye, sports' red light district may have suffered the most embarrassing year in its history. Three heavyweight title fights all ended in disqualification, primarily because in boxing's rule book, there is no mention of biting. Or hugging, Or crying. There was a typical over-the-hill fighter, looking for one more shot at the limelight. But the harsh glare burned his dreams. There was a controversial decision involving two welterweights who fought for the mythical pound for pound championship. And there was a fighter, who has more talent than anyone else, but can't find a suitable dance partner to become a box office champion.

But 1997 will be remembered for the ex-champ. Turned chomp. Turned chump. Mike Tyson's place in boxing history is now secure, but not because he will be considered one of the great heavyweights in history, which once seemed an inevitable promise, but because of the bite. The bite. It was "no màs" all over again. But the difference between Roberto Duran quitting in the ring, and Mike Tyson quitting in the ring was simply this: Mike Tyson extracted his ounce of flesh.

Tyson was promptly disqualified, and subsequently had his occupational license revoked. On the very day that his license to fight was being confiscated, he was in New York, buying himself a quarter of a million dollar sports car. His sense of timing was as curious as his appetite.

Charley Steiner covers boxing for ESPN.

Oliver McCall is consoled by his trainers after his fight with Lennox Lewis on February 7, 1997 was stopped by referee Mills Lane. During the fifth round tears streamed down McCall's face.

Mike Tyson left even the most ardent defenders of a usually defense-less sport dismayed and disgusted. Only Evander Holyfield, who came out of this main event-turned side show survived with his dignity, if not a portion of his right ear.

Two other Don King heavyweights were also disqualified in title fights, a dubious triple crown honor to be sure. In February, Oliver McCall, coming off drug rehab, met Lennox Lewis and had a nervous breakdown in the ring. For the first time in history, a heavy-weight prize fight ended because one of the warriors was crying. There's no crying in boxing!

And there is no hugging in boxing, either, which is why Henry Akin-wande found himself disqualified, when he opted to embrace his opponent (the aforementioned), Lewis, instead of punching him. Even Roy Jones, Jr. found himself disqualified this year, when he continued to batter Montell Griffin even as Griffin had a knee on the ring floor. Griffin was awarded the light-heavyweight championship, no matter that he was face first on the canvas. Five months later, Jones knocked Griffin out, fair and square in one round, in a fight that lost promoters more than a million dollars.

A more conventional, but no less disturbing story took place in March, in Atlantic City, a city of broken dreams. And it was Sugar Ray Leonard's dream that was smashed in

Wide World Photos

Pernell Whitaker (r) taunts **Oscar De La Hoya** during their WBC Welterweight Championship bout, won by De La Hoya in a unanimous but controversial decision.

the sixth round, by the historically power-lite Hector "Macho" Camacho. Leonard was victimized by a conspiracy. Camacho. Mother Nature. Father Time.

Leonard never had a chance. ■

Charley Steiner's Top Ten Highlights of the Year in Boxing

10. **Johnny Tapia's unanimous decision over Danny Romero.** The Albuquerque street fight in Las Vegas may have been the most spirited championship bout of the year.

9. **Vince Phillips' upset over Kostya Tszyu.** A long, hard road traveled by the courageous Phillips to win the IBF Junior Welterweight title, in what was the upset of the year in boxing.

8. **Riddick Bowe's retirement.** The former heavyweight champion, and former (albeit briefly) Marine who got the boot from boot camp, left a career largely of unfulfilled promise and ability. He didn't have the stomach for discipline.

7. **Roy Jones Jr.'s first round knockout of Montell Griffin.** Jones proved his greatness, with a dominating performance. But if Jones is to be remembered as one

Wide World Photos

Montell Griffin avoids this punch from WBC light heavyweight champion **Roy Jones Jr**. but he didn't do that often enough as Jones went on to score a first round knockout to regain his title on August 7, 1997 at Foxwoods Resort in Connecticut.

of the true all-time greats, he needs a challenge . . . and a real challenger.

6. **Hector Camacho's knockout of Sugar Ray Leonard.** Leonard hadn't fought in five years and had fought only five times in the past ten years. At the age of 41, what could he (or anybody else) realistically have expected?

5. **Oscar De La Hoya's controversial decision over Pernell "Sweet Pea" Whitaker**. The argument still rages as to who really won that fight. If landing more punches, and being hit less than

the other guy wins fights, then Whitaker won it. If landing more "power" punches determines the winner then the Golden Boy won. And that's what the judges saw.

4. (tie) **Oliver McCall disqualified for crying. Henry Akinwande disqualified for hugging.** What do Tyson, McCall and Akinwande have in common? All are promoted by Don King. Their embarrassing losses effectively removes King from the heavyweight picture for the next year, although he remains the promoter of record for

Evander Holyfield, as long as Holyfield defends his WBA Heavyweight title.

2. **Mike Tyson's license to box is revoked.**

1. **The Bite.** ∎

THE NUMBERS

INSIDE

by

Todd Snyder and Andrew Villa

A **GOLDEN** ERA

Oscar De La Hoya and Sugar Ray Leonard are considered two of the best fighters, pound for pound, of the last three decades. Both of them won gold medals for the USA in the Olympics. Both have shown an ability to fight in different weight classes. While Leonard didn't win his first title until his 26th fight, he has won belts in a record five different weight classes. De La Hoya has said he would like to become the first fighter to win belts in six different classes. He's nearly there.

After 24 bouts	De La Hoya	Leonard
Age	24	23
Record (KO)	24-0 (20)	24-0 (15)
Title bouts	12	0
World Titles	5*	0

* Four different weight classes.

DE**BOX**LES

In the past year, boxing has had more than its fair share of bizarre events. The following five bouts ended under strange circumstances. Tyson wigged out during a fight he appeared to be losing but Andrew Golota was winning **both** of his fights when he hit Riddick Bowe below the belt.

Loser/Opp.	Result	Reason
Akinwande/Lewis	DQ-5	Holding
Tyson/Holyfield	DQ-3	Biting
McCall/Lewis	TKO-5	Reluctance
Golota/Bowe II	DQ-9	Low Blows
Golota/Bowe I	DQ-7	Low Blows

IN **LEW** OF A FIGHT

Lennox Lewis, the WBC heavyweight champion, was involved in two of the stranger fights of 1997, which is saying something. In Lewis' fights against Oliver McCall and Henry Akinwande, Lewis found himself with opponents who, essentially, didn't want to fight. As the chart below shows, McCall and Akinwande barely showed up. McCall lost on a TKO and he was seen crying openly in the ring. Akinwande was disqualified for excessive holding.

Put 'em up! . . . Put 'em up!	McCall and Akinwande	Lewis
Punches thrown	182	437*
Punches landed	56	191
Punches landed %	30.8	43.7

*Both fights ended in the fifth round. ∎

904

THE 1998

B O X I N G
S T A T I S T I C S

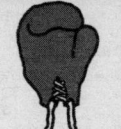

THE SEASON IN REVIEW
1996-1997
CHAMPIONS • TITLE BOUTS

SEC A

PAGE 905

Current Champions

WBA, WBC and IBF Titleholders (through Oct. 1, 1997)

The champions of professional boxing's 17 principal weight divisions, as recognized by the Word Boxing Association (WBA), World Boxing Council (WBC) and International Boxing Federation (IBF).

	Weight Limit	WBA Champion	WBC Champion	IBF Champion
Heavyweight	–	Evander Holyfield 34-3-0, 24 KOs	Lennox Lewis 31-1-0, 25 KOs	Michael Moorer 39-1-0, 31 KOs
Cruiserweight	190 lbs	Nate Miller 30-4-0, 26 KOs	Marcelo Dominguez 22-1-1, 12 KOs	Uriah Grant 26-12-0, 24 KOs
Light Heavyweight	175 lbs	Lou Del Valle 27-1-0, 19 KOs	Roy Jones Jr. 35-1-0, 30 KOs	William Guthrie 24-0-0, 21 KOs
Super Middleweight	168 lbs	Frank Liles 31-1-0, 19 KOs	Robin Reid 25-0-1 18 KOs	Charles Brewer 29-5-0, 20 KOs
Middleweight	160 lbs	Julio Cesar Green 22-2-0, 16 KOs	Keith Holmes 29-1-0, 19 KOs	Bernard Hopkins 32-2-1, 25 KOs
Jr. Middleweight	154 lbs	Laurent Boudouani 35-2-0, 31 KOs	Terry Norris 47-6-0, 31 KOs	Raul Marquez 28-0-0, 20 KOs
Welterweight	147 lbs	Ike Quartey 34-0-0, 29 KOs	Oscar De La Hoya 26-0-0, 21 KOs	Felix Trinidad 32-0-0, 28 KOs
Jr. Welterweight	140 lbs	Khalid Rahilou 30-2-0, 16 KOs	Vacant	Vince Phillips 37-3-1, 26 KOs
Lightweight	135 lbs	Orzubek Nazarov 24-0-0, 18 KOs	Steve Johnston 23-0-0, 13 KOs	Shane Mosley 24-0-0, 22 KOs
Jr. Lightweight	130 lbs	Choi Yong-Soo 23-2-0, 13 KOs	Genaro Hernandez 36-1-1, 17 KOs	Arturo Gatti 28-1-0, 23 KOs
Featherweight	126 lbs	Wilfredo Vasquez 49-7-3, 37 KOs	Luisito Espinoza 41-7-0, 21 KOs	Vacant
Jr. Featherweight	122 lbs	Antonio Cermeno 28-1-0, 17 KOs	Erik Moraies 27-0-0, 21 KOs	Vuyani Bungu 32-2-0, 18 KOs
Bantamweight	118 lbs	Nana Yaw Konadu 37-3-1, 29 KOs	Sirimongkol Singmanassak 16-0-0, 6 KOs	Tim Austin 16-0-1, 15 KOs
Jr. Bantamweight	115 lbs	Yokthai Sith Oar 14-0-1, 8 KOs	Gerry Penalosa 38-1-1, 23 KOs	Johnny Tapia 41-0-2, 24 KOs
Flyweight	112 lbs	Jose Bonilla 23-3-0, 11 KOs	Catchai Sasakul* 30-1-0, 23 KOs	Marc Johnson 33-1-0, 24 KOs
Jr. Flyweight	108 lbs	Phichitnoi C. Siriwat 17-1-0, 11 KOs	Saman Sor Jaturong 35-2-1, 28 KOs	Vacant
Minimumweight	105 lbs	Rosendo Alvarez 24-0-0, 16 KOs	Ricardo Lopez 46-0-0, 36 KOs	Ratan Voraphin 33-2-1, 26 KOs

Note: the following weight divisions are also known by these names—**Cruiserweight** as Jr. Heavyweight; **Jr. Middleweight** as Super Welterweight; **Jr. Welterweight** as Super Lightweight; **Jr. Lightweight** as Super Featherweight; **Jr. Featherweight** as Super Bantamweight; **Jr. Bantamweight** as Super Flyweight; **Jr. Flyweight** as Light Flyweight; and **Minimum** as Strawweight.

*Sasakul is the "interim" champion. The WBC sanctioned a bout for the interim championship because their regular flyweight champion, Yuri Arbachakov, had been sidelined with a broken wrist since August of 1996. The two will fight for the WBC flyweight belt when Arbachakov is back in action.

Major Bouts, 1996-97

Division by division, from Oct. 1, 1996 through Oct. 1, 1997.

WBA, WBC and IBF champions are listed in **bold** type. Note the following Result column abbreviations (in alphabetical order): **Disq.** (won by disqualification); **KO** (knockout); **MDraw** (majority draw); **NC** (no contest); **SDraw** (split draw); **TDraw** (technical draw); **TKO** (technical knockout); **TWs** (won by technical split decision); **TWu** (won by technical unanimous decision); **Wm** (won by majority decision); **Ws** (won by split decision) and **Wu** (won by unanimous decision).

Heavyweights

Date	Winner	Loser	Result	Title	Site
Oct. 15	Hasim Rahman	Trevor Berbick	Wu 10	Non-title	Atlantic City
Nov. 1	Lou Savarese	Buster Mathis Jr.	TKO 7	USBA	Indio, Calif.
Nov. 3	Tommy Morrison	Marcus Rhode	KO 1	Non-title	Tokyo
Nov. 3	George Foreman	Crawford Grimsley	Wu 12	WBU-IBA	Tokyo
Nov. 8	Ike Ibeabuchi	Anthony Wade	Wu 8	Non-title	Las Vegas
Nov. 9	Henry Akinwande	Alexandre Zolkin	TKO 10	WBO	Las Vegas
Nov. 9	Evander Holyfield	**Mike Tyson**	TKO 11	**WBA**	Las Vegas
Nov. 20	Vaughn Bean	Lou Turchiarelli	TKO 1	Non-title	Newark, N.J.
Dec. 7	Axel Schulz	Jose Ribalta	Wu 10	Non-title	Vienna, AUT
Dec. 14	Vaughn Bean	Earl Talley	TKO 1	Non-title	Atlantic City
Dec. 14	Ray Mercer	Tim Witherspoon	Wu 10	Non-title	Atlantic City
Dec. 14	Riddick Bowe	Andrew Golota	Disq. 9	Non-title	Atlantic City
Dec. 21	David Tua	David Izonritei	TKO 12	WBC Intl.	Uncasville, Conn.
Jan. 9	Ike Ibeabuchi	Calvin Jones	KO 3	Non-title	Beverly Hills, Calif.
Jan. 10	Buster Douglas	Rocky Pepeli	Wu 10	Non-title	Uncasville, Conn.
Jan. 11	Henry Akinwande	Scott Welch	Wu 12	WBO	Nashville, Tenn.
Jan. 24	Brian Nielsen	Larry Holmes	Ws 12	IBO	Copenhagen, DEN
Feb. 7	Lennox Lewis*	Oliver McCall	TKO 5	**WBC**	Las Vegas
Feb. 12	Buster Douglas	Dickie Ryan	Wu 10	Non-title	New York, City
Mar. 29	**Michael Moorer**	Vaughn Bean	Wm 12	**IBF**	Las Vegas
Mar. 30	Buster Douglas	Bryan Scott	TKO 6	Non-title	Uncasville, Conn.
Apr. 5	David Tua	Oleg Maskaev	TKO 11	WBC Intl.	Atlantic City
Apr. 15	Shannon Briggs	Melton Bowen	KO 1	Non-title	W. Orange, N.J.
Apr. 26	Axel Schulz	Jorge Valdez	Wu 10	Non-title	Leipzig, GER
May 10	Frans Botha	James Stanton	KO 10	Non-title	Coconut Grove, Fla.
May 13	Buster Douglas	Louis Monaco	Disq. 1	Non-title	Biloxi, Miss.
June 7	Ike Ibeabuchi	David Tua	Wu 12	WBC Intl.	Sacramento, Calif.
June 21	Frans Botha	Lee Gilbert	Wu 12	Non-title	Tampa, Fla.
June 24	Shannon Briggs	Jorge Valdez	TKO 10	Non-title	Baton Rouge, La.
June 28	Herbie Hide	Tony Tucker	TKO 2	WBO	Norwich, ENG
June 28	**Evander Holyfield**	Mike Tyson	Disq. 3	**WBA**	Las Vegas
July 12	**Lennox Lewis**	Henry Akinwande	Disq. 5	**WBC**	Stateline, Nev.
July 13	Buster Douglas	Quinn Navarre	TKO 4	Non-title	Biloxi, Miss.
July 29	Bert Cooper	Richie Melito	KO 1	WBF	New York City
July 29	Larry Holmes	Maurice Harris	Ws 10	Non-title	New York City

*Lewis won the vacant WBC Heavyweight title after the fight was stopped 55 seconds into round five because a visibly distraught McCall started crying and stopped punching. The title became vacant after the WBC stripped Mike Tyson of the heavyweight belt for not fighting Lewis, the mandatory challenger, and instead fighting Bruce Seldon in September of 1996.

Cruiserweights (190 lbs)
(Jr. Heavyweights)

Date	Winner	Loser	Result	Title	Site
Oct. 19	Juan C. Gomez	Brian LaSpada	TKO 11	WBC Intl.	Frankfurt, GER
Dec. 6	**Marcelo Dominguez**	Jose Arimateia	TKO 8	**WBC**	Buenos Aires, ARG
Dec. 7	Uriah Grant	Saul Montana	KO 3	Non-title	Indio, Calif.
Dec. 13	Ralf Rocchigiani	Stefan Anghern	Wu12	WBO	Hanover, GER
Dec. 21	Juan C. Gomez	Dan Ward	TKO 1	WBC Intl.	Franfurt, GER
Jan. 25	Juan C. Gomez	Mike Peak	Wu 8	Non-title	Stuttgart, GER
Feb. 22	**Nate Miller**	Alexandre Gurov	TKO 2	**WBA**	Ft. Lauderdale, Fla.
Feb. 22	James Toney	Mike McCallum	Wu 12	WBU	Uncasville, Conn.
Mar. 1	Fabrice Tiozzo	Mike Peak	Wu 10	Non-title	Paris
Mar. 8	Juan C. Gomez	Jose A. Da Silva	TKO 9	WBC Intl.	Cologne, GER
Apr. 26	Ralf Rocchigiani	Stefan Anghern	Wm 12	WBO	Zurich, SWI
May 10	Michael Nunn	Booker T. Word	TKO 7	Non-title	Moline, Ill.
June 14	Juan C. Gomez	Valerij Vikhor	TKO 5	WBC Intl.	Aachen, GER
June 14	James Toney	Steve Little	Wu 12	IBO	Biloxi, Miss.
June 21	Uriah Grant	**Adolpho Washington**	Wm 12	**IBF**	Tampa, Fla.
July 12	Juan C. Gomez	Ted Cofie	TKO 4	WBC Intl.	Hagen, GER
Aug. 16	**Marcelo Dominguez**	Akim Tafer	Wu 12	**WBC**	Le Cannet, FRA

Light Heavyweights (175 lbs)

Date	Winner	Loser	Result	Title	Site
Oct. 18	Montell Griffin	Russell Mitchell	TKO 1	Non-title	Dolton, Ill.
Oct. 29	Lou Del Valle	Thomas Reid	Wu 10	Non-title	Tunica, Miss.
Nov. 22	**Roy Jones Jr.**	Mike McCallum	Wu 12	**WBC**	Tampa, Fla.
Nov. 23	**Virgil Hill**	**Henry Maske**	Ws 12	**WBA/IBF**	Munich, GER
Nov. 29	Thomas Hearns	Karl Willis	TKO 5	Non-title	Roanoke, Va.
Dec. 6	Montell Griffin	James Toney	Wu 12	WBU	Reno, Nev.
Dec. 13	D. Michaelczewski	Christophe Girard	TKO 8	WBO	Hanover, GER
Jan. 17	Michael Nunn	Rudy Nix	TKO 2	NABF	Reseda, Calif.
Jan. 31	Thomas Hearns	Ed Dalton	TKO 5	Non-title	Inglewood, Calif.
Mar. 21	Montell Griffin	**Roy Jones Jr.**	Disq. 9	**WBC**	Atlantic City
Mar. 28	William Guthrie	Jamie Stevenson	KO 3	Non-title	Boston, Mass.
May 1	Louis Del Valle	Ken Payne	TKO 4	Non-title	Asbury Park, N.J.
May 14	Drake Thadzi	James Toney	Wm 12	IBO	Ledyard, Conn.
June 13	Louis Del Valle	Fermin Chirino	TKO 3	Non-title	Oberhausen, GER
June 13	**D. Michaelczewski**	**Virgil Hill**	Wu 12	**WBA/IBF**	Oberhausen, GER
July 19	William Guthrie*	Darrin Allen	KO 3	IBF	Indio, Calif.
Aug. 7	Roy Jones Jr.	**Montell Griffin**	KO 1	**WBC**	Ledyard, Conn.
Sept. 20	Louis Del Valle*	Eddy Smulders	TKO 8	**WBA**	Aachem, GER

*Guthrie won the vacant IBF light heavyweight title and Del Valle won the vacant WBA light heavyweight title after Michaelczewski was stripped of his belts for not fighting the mandatory challengers in each organization.

Super Middleweights (168 lbs)

Date	Winner	Loser	Result	Title	Site
Oct. 12	Robin Reid	Vincenzo Nardiello	TKO 7	**WBC**	Milan, ITA
Nov. 9	Steve Collins	Nigel Benn	TKO 7	WBO	Manchester, ENG
Feb. 8	**Robin Reid**	Giovanni Pretorius	KO 7	**WBC**	Millwall, ENG
Feb. 8	Steve Collins	Frederic Seillier	TKO 5	WBO	Millwall, ENG
Feb. 15	Jorge Castro	Roberto Duran	Wu 10	Non-title	Mar del Plata, ARG
Feb. 18	Charles Brewer	Greg Wright	Wu 12	USBA	Philadelphia
Apr. 19	**Frankie Liles**	Segundo Mercado	TKO 5	**WBA**	Shreveport, La.
May 3	**Robin Reid**	Henry Wharton	Wm 12	**WBC**	Manchester, ENG
June 14	Roberto Duran	Jorge Castro	Wu 10	Non-title	Panama City, PAN
June 21	Charles Brewer*	Gary Ballard	TKO 5	IBF	Tampa, Fla.
July 15	Steve Collins	Craig Cummings	TKO 3	WBO	Glasgow, SCOT
July 19	**Frankie Liles**	Zafarou Ballagou	Wu 12	**WBA**	Nashville, Tenn.
Sept. 6	**Robin Reid**	Hassine Cherifi	Ws 12	**WBC**	Widnes, ENG

*Brewer won the vacant IBF super middleweight title. The title was vacated when Roy Jones Jr. moved up in weight to become a light heavyweight.

Middleweights (160 lbs)

Date	Winner	Loser	Result	Title	Site
Oct. 19	Paul Vaden	Bernie Parker	Wu 10	Non-title	Upper Marlboro, Md.
Oct. 19	Andrew Council	Allen Watts	KO 10	Non-title	Upper Marlboro, Md.
Oct. 19	**Keith Holmes**	Richie Woodhall	TKO 12	**WBC**	Upper Marlboro, Md.
Oct. 19	**William Joppy**	Ray McElroy	TKO 6	**WBA**	Upper Marlboro, Md.
Jan. 5	Dana Rosenblatt	Glenwood Brown	Wu 10	Non-title	Boston, Mass.
Mar. 1	Hector Camacho	Sugar Ray Leonard	TKO 5	IBC	Atlantic City
Mar. 4	Lonnie Bradley	Otis Grant	Ws 12	WBO	Las Vegas
Mar. 29	Julio Cesar Green	Bernice Barber	KO 4	Non-title	Las Vegas
Apr. 19	Paul Vaden	Wayne Powell	TKO 8	Non-title	Shreveport, La.
Apr. 19	Robert Allen	Andrew Council	Wu 12	WBA N.A.	Shreveport, La.
Apr. 19	**Bernard Hopkins**	John David Jackson	TKO 7	**IBF**	Shreveport, La.
Apr. 23	Simon Brown	David Mendez	TKO 8	Non-title	Las Vegas
May 10	**William Joppy**	Peter Venancio	Wu 12	**WBA**	Coconut Grove, Fla.
June 21	Julio Cesar Green	Earl Allen	TKO 9	Non-title	Tampa, Fla.
June 28	Lonnie Bradley	John Williams	KO 8	WBO	Las Vegas
July 20	**Bernard Hopkins**	Glen Johnson	TKO 11	**IBF**	Indio, Calif.
Aug. 23	Julio Cesar Green	**William Joppy**	Wu 12	**WBA**	New York City

Junior Middleweights (154 lbs)
(Super Welterweights)

Date	Winner	Loser	Result	Title	Site
Oct. 25	Buddy McGirt	Kevin Tillman	Wu 12	IBC	Bay St. Louis, Miss.
Nov. 9	Ronald Wright	Ensley Bingham	Wu 12	WBO	Manchester, ENG
Dec. 6	Raul Marquez	Gregory Smith	KO 2	Non-title	Reno, Nev.
Dec. 14	Troy Waters	Luis Vasquez	TKO 6	Non-title	Ettalong, AUS
Dec. 14	**Laurent Boudouani**	Benji Singleton	TKO 4	Non-title	Atlantic City
Jan. 10	Raul Marquez	Rafael Williams	TKO 5	USBA	Uncasville, Conn.
Jan. 11	**Terry Norris**	Nick Rupa	TKO 10	**WBC/IBF**	Nashville, Tenn.
Feb. 15	Greg Haugen	Jesus Mayorga	Wu 10	Non-title	Tacoma, Wash.
Mar. 21	Mark Breland	Rick Haynes	Wu 10	Non-title	Jacksonville, Fla.
Mar. 29	**Laurent Boudouani**	Carl Daniels	Wu 15	**WBA**	Las Vegas
Apr. 12	Raul Marquez*	Anthony Stephens	TKO 9	**IBF**	Las Vegas
Apr. 25	Greg Haugen	Greg Johnson	Ws 10	Non-title	Tacoma, Wash.
May 3	Ronald Wright	Steve Foster	TKO 6	WBO	Manchester, ENG
June 14	Julio C. Vasquez	Ramon Britez	KO 1	Non-title	Buenos Aires, ARG
July 5	**Raul Marquez**	Romallis Ellis	TKO 4	**IBF**	Lake Charles, La.
Aug. 8	Terry Norris	Joaquin Velasquez	KO 2	Non-title	Kansas City, Mo.
Aug. 23	Felix Trinidad	Troy Waters	KO 1	Non-title	New York City
Sept. 13	**Raul Marquez**	Keith Mullings	Ws 12	**IBF**	Las Vegas

*Marquez won the vacant IBF Jr. middleweight title.

Welterweights (147 lbs)

Date	Winner	Loser	Result	Title	Site
Oct. 10	Meldrick Taylor	Tommy Small	Wu 10	Non-title	Washington, D.C.
Oct. 23	Vincent Pettway	Harold Bennett	TKO 4	Non-title	Baltimore, Md.
Jan. 10	Mark Breland	Bobby Butters	TKO 2	Non-title	Jacksonville, Fla.
Jan. 11	**Felix Trinidad**	Kevin Lueshing	TKO 3	**IBF**	Nashville, Tenn.
Jan. 24	**Pernell Whitaker**	Diobelys Hurtado	TKO 11	**WBC**	Atlantic City
Feb. 22	Michael Lowe	Santiago Samaniego	Wu 12	WBO	Hamburg, GER
Mar. 12	Roger Mayweather	Carlos Miranda	TKO 12	IBA	Grand Rapids, Mich.
Mar. 22	Wilfredo Rivera	Livingstone Bramble	KO 3	Non-title	San Juan, P.R.
Mar. 29	Julio Cesar Chavez	Tony Martin	Wu 10	Non-title	Las Vegas
Apr. 9	David Kamau	Juan C. Rodriguez	Wm 10	Non-title	Las Vegas
Apr. 12	Oscar de la Hoya	**Pernell Whitaker**	Wu 12	**WBC**	Las Vegas
Apr. 18	**Ike Quartey**	Ralph Jones	TKO 5	**WBA**	Las Vegas
Apr. 19	Wilfredo Rivera	Alex Lubo	TKO 5	Non-title	Condado, P.R.
June 14	**Oscar de la Hoya**	David Kamau	KO 2	**WBC**	San Antonio, Tex.
June 28	Julio Cesar Chavez	Daniel LaCoursiere	Wu 10	Non-title	Las Vegas
July 25	Wilfredo Rivera	Benji Marquez	KO 5	Non-title	Condado, P.R.
Sept. 13	**Oscar de la Hoya**	Hector Camacho	Wu 12	**WBC**	Las Vegas
Sept. 20	Michael Lowe	Michael Carruth	Ws 12	WBO	Aachen, GER

Junior Welterweights (140 lbs)
(Super Lightweights)

Date	Winner	Loser	Result	Title	Site
Oct. 12	Giovanni Parisi	Sergio Rey	TKO 4	WBO	Milan, ITA
Oct. 12	Julio Cesar Chavez	Joey Gamache	TKO 8	Non-title	Anaheim, Calif.
Oct. 28	Vincent Phillips	Juan C. Rodriguez	KO 5	Non-title	Inglewood, Calif.
Dec. 3	Rafael Ruelas	Jaime Balboa	TKO 5	Non-title	Indio, Calif.
Jan. 11	Khalid Rahilou	**Frankie Randall**	TKO 11	**WBA**	Nashville, Tenn.
Jan. 18	**Kostya Tszyu**	Leonardo Mas	TDraw 1	**IBF**	Las Vegas
Jan. 18	**Oscar de la Hoya**	Miguel A. Gonzalez	Wu 12	**WBC**	Las Vegas
Apr. 19	Giovanni Parisi	Harold Miller	TKO 8	WBO	Milan, ITA
May 31	Vincent Phillips	**Kostya Tszyu**	TKO 10	**IBF**	Atlantic City
June 14	Jesse James Leija	Jose Rodriguez	Wu 8	Non-title	San Antonio, Tex.
June 28	Miguel A. Gonzalez	Roberto Granciosa	TKO 4	Non-title	Las Vegas
July 5	**Khalid Rahilou**	Marty Jakubowski	TKO 7	**WBA**	Casablanca, MOR
July 19	Rafael Ruelas	Mike Griffith	TKO 2	Non-title	Indio, Calif.
Aug. 9	**Vincent Phillips**	Micky Ward	TKO 3	**IBF**	Boston, Mass.

Lightweights (135 lbs)

Date	Winner	Loser	Result	Title	Site
Oct. 19	**Phillip Holiday**	Joel Diaz	Wu 12	IBF	Johannesburg, S. Afr.
Nov. 1	Shane Mosley	Ramon Felix	TKO 1	Non-title	Indio, Calif.
Dec. 21	**Phillip Holiday**	Ivan Robinson	Wu 12	IBF	Uncasville, Conn.
Jan. 18	Steve Johnston	Jose Luis Baltazar	Wu 10	Non-title	Las Vegas
Feb. 14	Gabriel Ruelas	James Crayton	Wu 10	Non-title	Indio, Calif.
Feb. 22	Artur Grigorian	Raul H. Balbi	TKO 11	WBO	Hamburg, GER
Mar. 1	Steve Johnston	**Jean Baptiste Mendy**	Ws 12	WBC	Paris
Mar. 22	Jesse James Leija	Joel Perez	Wu 12	NABF	Corpus Christi, Tex.
Apr. 9	Shane Mosley	Mike Smith	KO 4	Non-title	Westmont, Ill.
May 4	Arturo Gatti	Calvin Grove	TKO 8	Non-title	Atlantic City
May 10	**Orzubek Nazarov**	Leavander Johnson	TKO 7	WBA	Coconut Grove, Fla.
May 16	**Phillip Holiday**	Pete Taliaferro	Ws 12	IBF	Hammanskraal, S. Afr
May 30	Juan Molina	Elias Quiroz	TKO 6	Non-title	Fajardo, P.R.
July 26	**Steve Johnston**	Hiroyuki Sakamoto	Ws 12	WBC	Yokohama, JPN
Aug. 2	Shane Mosley	**Phillip Holiday**	Wu 12	IBF	Uncasville, Conn.
Sept. 19	**Steve Johnson**	Saul Duran	Wu 12	WBC	Las Vegas

Junior Lightweights (130 lbs)
(Super Featherweights)

Date	Winner	Loser	Result	Title	Site
Oct. 13	**Yong-Soo Choi**	Yamato Mitani	Wu 12	WBA	Tokyo
Oct. 18	Troy Dorsey	Jimmy Bredahl	TKO 9	IBO	Vejle, DEN
Dec. 6	Tracy H. Patterson	Jose Aponte	TKO 10	Non-title	Atlantic City
Feb. 1	**Yong-Soo Choi**	Lakva Sim	Ws 12	WBA	Songnam, KOR
Feb. 22	**Arturo Gatti**	Tracy H. Pattterson	Wu 12	IBF	Atlantic City
Mar. 1	Julien Lorcy	Arnulfo Castillo	Wm 12	WBO	Paris
Mar. 22	**Genaro Hernandez**	Azumah Nelson	Ws 12	WBC	Corpus Christi, Tex.
May 24	**Yong-Soo Choi**	Koji Matsumoto	Wu 12	WBA	Suwon, KOR
June 14	**Genaro Hernandez**	Anatoli Alexandrov	Ws 12	WBC	San Antonio, Tex.

Featherweights (126 lbs)

Date	Winner	Loser	Result	Title	Site
Nov. 2	**Luisito Espinosa**	Nobutoshi Hiranaka	TKO 8	WBC	Fukuoka, JPN
Nov. 3	Orlando Canizales	Sergio Reyes	TKO 10	IBA	Tokyo, JPN
Nov. 9	Naseem Hamed	Remigio Molina	TKO 2	WBO	Manchester, ENG
Nov. 16	Kevin Kelley	Edwin Santana	Wu 12	WBU	Atlantic City
Dec. 7	**Wilfredo Vasquez**	Bernardo Mendoza	TKO 5	WBA	Indio, Calif.
Feb. 8	Naseem Hamed	**Tom Johnson**	TKO 8	IBF/WBO	Millwall, ENG
Mar. 1	Orlando Canizales	Roland Gomez	KO 3	Non-title	Atlantic City
Mar. 14	Kevin Kelley	Jesus Salud	Wu 12	WBU	Albany, N.Y.
Mar. 30	**Wilfredo Vasquez**	Yuji Watanabe	KO 5	WBA	Tokyo
May 3	**Naseem Hamed**	Billy Hardy	TKO 1	IBF/WBO	Manchester, ENG
May 17	**Luisito Espinosa**	Manuel Medina	TWu 8	WBC	Manila, PHI
July 12	Kevin Kelley	Orlando Fernandez	KO 10	WBU	Tunica, Miss.
July 19	**Naseem Hamed**	Juan Cabrera	TKO 2	IBF/WBO	Wembley, ENG
July 25	Orlando Canizales	Edwin Santana	Wm 12	IBA	Las Vegas
Aug. 23	**Wilfredo Vasquez**	Roque Cassiani	Wu 12	WBA	New York, N.Y.

Junior Featherweights (122 lbs)
(Super Bantamweights)

Date	Winner	Loser	Result	Title	Site
Oct. 12	Erik Morales	Pedro Javier Torres	TKO 2	NBAF	Anaheim, Calif.
Nov. 9	**Antonio Cermeno**	Eddy Saerz	TKO 6	WBA	Las Vegas
Nov. 22	Junior Jones	Marco A. Barrera	TKO 5	WBO	Tampa, Fla.
Dec. 21	**Antonio Cermeno**	Yuichi Kasai	Wu 12	WBA	Las Vegas
Jan. 11	**Daniel Zaragoza**	Wayne McCullough	Ws 12	WBC	Boston, Mass.
Apr. 5	**Vuyani Bungu**	Kennedy McKinney	Ws 12	IBF	Hammanskraal, S. Afr.
Apr. 14	**Daniel Zaragoza**	Joichiro Tatsuyoshi	Wu 12	WBC	Osaka, JPN
Apr. 18	Junior Jones	Marco A. Barrera	Wu 12	WBO	Las Vegas
May 10	**Antonio Cermeno**	Angel Chacon	Wu 12	WBA	Coconut Grove, Fla.
July 26	**Antonio Cermeno**	Yuichi Kasai	KO 12	WBA	Yokohama, JPN
Aug. 16	**Vuyani Bungu**	Enrique Jupiter	Wu 12	IBF	Hammanskraal, S. Afr.
Sept. 6	Erik Morales	**Daniel Zaragoza**	TKO 11	WBC	El Paso, Tex.

Bantamweights (118 lbs)

Date	Winner	Loser	Result	Title	Site
Oct. 27	Daorung Chuvatana	**Nana Yaw Konadu**	TWu 10	**WBA**	Uttaradit, THA
Nov. 26	**Mbulelo Botile**	Aristead Clayton	Wu 12	IBF	Baton Rouge, La.
Nov. 30	Johnny Bredahl	Harry Geier	TKO 5	Non-title	Vienna, AUT
Jan. 11	Paul Ayala	Cuauhtemoc Gomez	Wu 12	NABF	Las Vegas
Feb. 15	S. Singmanassak	Jesus Sarabia	Wu 12	**WBC**	N. Phanom, THA
Mar. 14	Johnny Bredahl	Drew Docherty	TKO 3	Non-title	Odense, DEN
Mar. 15	Daorung Chuvatana	Felix Machado	Ws 12	**WBA**	Satul, THA
Apr. 12	Paul Ayala	Nestor Lopez	Wu 10	Non-title	Las Vegas
Apr. 26	S. Singmanassak	Javier Campanario	TKO 4	**WBC**	Phuket, THA
June 13	Johnny Bredahl	Igor Gerasimov	TKO 5	IBO	Slagelse, DEN
June 21	Nana Yaw Konadu	**Daorung Chuvatana**	TKO 7	**WBA**	Tampa, Fla.
July 4	S. Singmanassak	Victor Rabanales	Wu 12	**WBC**	Pattani, THA
July 19	Tim Austin	**Mbulelo Botile**	TKO 8	IBF	Nashville, Tenn.
July 28	Jorge E. Julio	Oscar Maldonado	Ws 12	WBO	Inglewood, Calif.
Aug. 8	Paul Ayala	Roberto Suazo Lopez	TKO 5	NABF	Las Vegas

Junior Bantamweights (115 lbs)
(Super Flyweights)

Date	Winner	Loser	Result	Title	Site
Oct. 11	Johnny Tapia	Sammy Stewart	TKO 7	WBO	Las Vegas
Oct. 12	**Hiroshi Kawashima**	Domingo Sosa	TKO 2	**WBC**	Tokyo
Nov. 1	**Danny Romero**	Hipolito Saucedo	TKO 12	IBF	Indio, Calif.
Nov. 10	**Yokthai Sith-Oar**	Jack Siahaya	KO 2	**WBA**	Phichit, THA
Nov. 30	Johnny Tapia	Adonis Cruz	Wu 12	WBO	Albuquerque, N.M.
Feb. 20	Gerry Penalosa	**Hiroshi Kawashima**	Ws 12	**WBC**	Tokyo
Mar. 1	**Yokthai Sith-Oar**	Aquiles Guzman	Wu 12	**WBA**	Chachoensao, THA
Mar. 8	**Danny Romero**	Jaji Sibali	TKO 6	IBF	Albuquerque, N.M.
Mar. 8	Johnny Tapia	Jorge Barrera	TKO 3	WBO	Albuquerque, N.M.
Apr. 29	**Yokthai Sith-Oar**	Satoshi Iida	Wm 12	**WBA**	Nagoya, JPN
June 14	**Gerry Penalosa**	Seung-Koo Lee	KO 9	**WBC**	Lapu-Lapu, PHI
July 18	Johnny Tapia	**Danny Romero**	Wu 12	IBF/WBO	Las Vegas
Aug. 8	**Yokthai Sith-Oar**	Jesus (Kiki) Rojas	Wu 12	**WBA**	Bangkok, THA
Sept. 21	Cuahtemoc Gomez	Alimi Goitia	KO 2	Non-title	Miami, Fla.

Flyweights (112 lbs)

Date	Winner	Loser	Result	Title	Site
Nov. 24	Jose Bonilla	**Saen Sow Ploenchit**	Wu 12	**WBA**	U. Ratchathani, THA
Dec. 10	Michael Carbajal	Tomas Cordoba	TKO 3	Non-title	Corpus Christi, Tex.
Dec. 13	Carlos Salazar	Alberto Jimenez	TKO 10	WBO	Buenos Aires, ARG
Feb. 10	**Marc Johnson**	Alejandro Montiel	Wu 12	IBF	Inglewood, Calif.
Feb. 25	**Jose Bonilla**	Hiroki Ioka	TKO 7	**WBA**	Osaka, JPN
Mar. 8	Carlos Salazar	Antonio Ruiz	Wm 12	WBO	Mexicali, MEX
May 9	Chatchai Sasakul*	Ysaias Zamudio	Wu 12	**WBC**	Chantaburi, THA
May 23	Carlos Salazar	Antonio Ruiz	Wu 12	WBO	S. Pena, Chaco, ARG
June 1	**Marc Johnson**	Cecilio Espino	KO 2	IBF	Uncasville, Conn.
July 19	Carlos Salazar	Salvatore Fanni	Wu 12	WBO	P. Rotonde, SAR
Aug. 1	**Chatchai Sasakul**	Juan D. Cordoba	TKO 8	**WBC**	Chantaburi, THA
Sept. 16	**Marc Johnson**	Angel Almana	Wu 12	IBF	Nashville, Tenn.

*Sasakul won the WBC interim flyweight title. The "interim" bout was sanctioned because champion Yuri Arbachakov had been sidelined with a broken wrist since August of 1996.

Junior Flyweights (108 lbs)
(Light Flyweights)

Date	Winner	Loser	Result	Title	Site
Oct. 12	**Michael Carbajal**	Tomas Rivera	TKO 5	IBF	Anaheim, Calif.
Oct. 19	**Saman Sor Jaturong**	Alli Galvez	KO 2	**WBC**	Samut Prakam, THA
Dec. 3	Phichitnoi C. Siriwat	**Keiji Yamaguchi**	TKO 2	**WBA**	Osaka, Japan
Dec. 15	**Saman Sor Jaturong**	Manuel J. Herrera	Wu 12	**WBC**	Chiangrai, THA
Jan. 18	Mauricio Pastrana	**Michael Carbajal**	Ws 12	IBF	Las Vegas
Feb. 8	Jacob Matlala	Mickey Cantwell	Ws 12	WBO	Millwall, ENG
Mar. 22	Michael Carbajal	Scotty Olson	KO 10	IBA	Corpus Christi, Tex.
Apr. 13	**Saman Sor Jaturong**	Julio Coronel	TKO 7	**WBC**	Chaiyaphum, THA
May 31	**Saman Sor Jaturong**	Mzukisi Marali	TKO 4	**WBC**	Petchaboon, THA
May 31	Jesus Chong	Eric Griffin	TKO 2	WBO	Las Vegas
June 29	**Phichitnoi C. Siriwat**	Sang-Chul Lee	Wu 12	**WBA**	Ratchaburi, THA
July 18	Jacob Matlala	Michael Carbajal	TKO 9	IBA	Las Vegas

Minimumweights (105 lbs)
(Strawweights or Mini-Flyweights)

Date	Winner	Loser	Result	Title	Site
Nov. 9	**Ricardo Lopez**	Morgan Ndumo	TKO 6	WBC	Las Vegas
Nov. 24	**Ratan Voraphin**	Gustavo Vera	KO 2	IBF	Udonthani, THA
Dec. 7	**Ricardo Lopez**	Myung-Sup Park	TKO 1	WBC	Indio, Calif.
Jan. 11	**Rosendo Alvarez**	Songkram Porpaoin	KO 11	WBA	Sa Kaew, THA
Mar. 22	**Ratan Voraphin**	Luis Doria	TKO 4	IBF	Saraburi, THA
Mar. 29	Alex Sanchez	Victor Burgos	Wu 12	WBO	Las Vegas
Mar. 29	**Ricardo Lopez**	Mongkol Charoen	Wu 12	WBC	Las Vegas
June 14	**Ratan Voraphin**	Juan Herrera	Wu 12	IBF	Nakhon Ratch., THA
Aug. 23	**Ricardo Lopez**	Alex Sanchez	TKO 5	WBC/WBO	New York City

Heavyweight Records

The career pro records of heavyweights Riddick Bowe, Evander Holyfield, Michael Moorer and Mike Tyson, as of Oct. 1, 1997.

Riddick Bowe

Born: Aug. 10, 1967   **Pro record:** 40-1-0, 31 KOs
Height: 6'5"   **Manager:** Rock Newman
Weight: 247 lbs

Olympic medal: 1988 Silver as Super Heavyweight (lost to Lennox Lewis)

No	Date	Opponent, location	Result
1	3/6/89	Lionel Butler, Reno	TKO 2
2	4/14/89	Tracy Thomas, Atlantic City	TKO 3
3	5/9/89	Garing Lane, Atlantic City	Wu 4
4	7/2/89	Antonio Whiteside, Fayetteville	TKO 1
5	7/15/89	Lorenzo Canady, Atlantic City	TKO 2
6	9/3/89	Lee Moore, Pensacola, Fla	KO 1
7	9/15/89	Anthony Hayes, Brooklyn	KO 1
8	9/19/89	Earl Lewis, Jacksonville, Fla	KO 1
9	10/19/89	Mike Acey, Atlantic City	TKO 1
10	11/4/89	Garing Lane, Atlantic City	TKO 1
11	11/18/89	Don Askew, Washington, D.C	KO 1
12	11/28/89	Art Card, Buffalo	TKO 3
13	12/14/89	Charles Woodard, St.Joseph, Mo	TKO 2
14	2/20/90	Mike Robinson, Atlantic City	TKO 3
15	4/1/90	Robert Colay, Washington, D.C	TKO 2
16	4/14/90	Eddie Gonzales, Las Vegas	Wu 8
17	5/8/90	Manny Contreras, Atlantic City	KO 1
18	7/8/90	Art Tucker, Atlantic City	TKO 3
19	9/7/90	Pinklon Thomas, Wash, D.C	TKO 9
20	10/25/90	Bert Cooper, Las Vegas	TKO 2
21	12/14/90	Tony Morrison, Kansas City	KO 1
22	3/2/91	Tyrell Biggs, Atlantic City	TKO 8
23	4/20/91	Tony Tubbs, Atlantic City	Wu 10
24	6/28/91	Rodolfo Marin, Las Vegas	KO 2
25	7/23/91	Phillip Brown, Atlantic City	TKO 3
26	8/9/91	Bruce Seldon, Atlantic City	TKO 7
27	10/29/91	Elijah Tillery, Wash., D.C	W/disq 1
28	12/13/91	Elijah Tillery, Atlantic City	TKO 4
29	4/7/92	Conroy Nelson, Atlantic City	KO 1
30	5/8/92	Everett Martin, Las Vegas	TKO 5
31	7/18/92	Pierre Coetzer, Las Vegas	TKO 7
32	11/13/92	Evander Holyfield, Las Vegas	Wu 12
		(Won undisputed heavyweight title)	
33	2/6/93	Michael Dokes, New York	TKO 1
34	5/22/93	Jesse Ferguson, Wash., D.C	TKO 2
35	11/6/93	Evander Holyfield, Las Vegas	Lm 12
		(Lost IBF/WBA heavyweight titles)	
36	8/13/94	Buster Mathis Jr., Atl. City	NC 4
37	12/3/94	Larry Donald, Syracuse	Wu 12
38	3/11/95	Herbie Hide, Las Vegas	KO 6
		(Won WBO heavyweight title)	
39	6/17/95	Jorge Luis Gonzalez, Las Vegas	KO 2
40	11/4/95	Evander Holyfield, Las Vegas	TKO 8
41	7/11/96	Andrew Golota, New York	Disq 7
42	12/14/96	Andrew Golota, Atlantic City	Disq 9

Evander Holyfield

Born: Oct. 19, 1962   **Pro record:** 34-3-0, 23 KOs
Height: 6' 2½"   **Weight:** 217 lbs

Olympic medal: 1984 Bronze as light heavyweight (disqualifed for controversial late knockout punch in semifinal against Kevin Barry of New Zealand)

No	Date	Opponent, location	Result
1	11/15/84	Lionel Byarm, New York	Wu 6
2	1/20/85	Eric Winbush, Atlantic City	Wu 6
3	3/13/85	Freddie Brown, Norfolk	KO 1
4	4/20/85	Mark Rivera, Corpus Christi	KO 2
5	7/20/85	Tyrone Booze, Norfolk	Wu 8
6	8/29/85	Rick Myers, Atlanta	KO 1
7	10/30/85	Jeff Meachem, Atlantic City	KO 5
8	12/21/85	Anthony Davis, Virginia Beach	KO 4
9	3/1/86	Chisanda Mutti, Lancaster, Pa	KO 3
10	4/6/86	Jesse Shelby, Corpus Christi	KO 3
11	5/28/86	Terry Mims, Metairie, LA	KO 5
12	7/20/86	Dwight M. Qawi, Atlanta	Ws 15
		(won WBA cruiserweight title)	
13	12/8/86	Mike Brothers, Paris	KO 3
14	2/14/87	Henry Tillman, Reno	TKO 7
15	5/15/87	Rickey Parkey, Las Vegas	TKO 3
		(won IBF cruiserweight title)	
16	8/15/87	Ossie Ocasio, St.Topez, France	TKO 11
17	12/4/87	Dwight M. Qawi, Atlantic City	TKO 4
18	4/9/88	Carlos DeLeon, Las Vegas	KO 8
		(won WBC cruiserweight title)	
19	7/16/88	James Tillis, Lake Tahoe	KO 5
20	12/9/88	Pinklon Thomas, Atlantic City	TKO 7
21	3/11/89	Michael Dokes, Las Vegas	TKO 10
22	7/15/89	Adilson Rodrigues, Lake Tahoe	KO 2
23	11/4/89	Alex Stewart, Atlantic City	TKO 8
24	6/1/90	Seamus McDonagh, Atlantic City	TKO 4
25	10/25/90	Buster Douglas, Las Vegas	KO 3
		(won undisputed heavyweight title)	
26	4/19/91	George Foreman, Atlantic City	Wu 12
27	11/23/91	Bert Cooper, Atlanta	TKO 7
28	6/19/92	Larry Holmes, Las Vegas	Wu 12
29	11/13/92	Riddick Bowe, Las Vegas	Lu 12
		(lost undisputed heavyweight title)	
30	6/26/93	Alex Stewart, Atlantic City	Wu 12
31	11/6/93	Riddick Bowe, Las Vegas	Wm 12
		(won IBF/WBA heavyweight titles)	
32	4/22/94	Michael Moorer, Las Vegas	Lm 12
		(lost IBF/WBA heavyweight titles)	

Evander Holyfield (Cont.)

No	Date	Opponent, location	Result
33	5/20/95	Ray Mercer, Atlantic City	Wu 10
34	11/4/95	Riddick Bowe, Las Vegas	TKO by 8
35	5/10/96	Bobby Czyz, New York	TKO 5

No	Date	Opponent, location	Result
36	11/9/96	Mike Tyson, Las Vegas	TKO 11
		(won WBC heavyweight title)	
37	6/28/97	Mike Tyson, Las Vegas	W Disq. 3

Michael Moorer

Born: Nov. 12, 1967   **Pro record:** 38-1-0, 30 KOs
Height: 6'2"   **Manager:** John Davimos
Weight: 214 lbs

No	Date	Opponent, location	Result
1	3/4/88	Adrian Riggs, Las Vegas	TKO 1
2	3/25/88	Bill Lee, Detroit	TKO 1
3	4/29/88	Brett Zywcewinsk, Detroit	KO 1
4	5/10/88	Dennis Fikes, Phoenix	TKO 2
5	6/6/88	Keith McMurray, Las Vegas	TKO 2
6	6/25/88	Lavelle Stanley, Detroit	TKO 2
7	8/6/88	Terrance Walker, Las Vegas	KO 4
8	8/12/88	Jordan Keepers, Milwaukee	TKO 2
9	10/7/88	Jorge Suero, Auburn Hills	KO 2
10	10/17/88	Carl Williams, Tucson	TKO 1
11	11/4/88	Glenn Kennedy, Las Vegas	KO 1
12	12/3/88	Ramzi Hassan, Cleveland	TKO 4
13	12/8/88	Victor Claudio, Auburn Hills	TKO 2
14	1/14/89	Frankie Swindell, Monessen, Pa	TKO 6
15	2/19/89	Fred Delgado, Auburn Hills	TKO 1
16	6/25/89	Leslie Stewart, Atlantic City	TKO 8
17	11/16/89	Jeff Thompson, Atlantic City	TKO 1
18	12/22/89	Mike Sedillo, Auburn Hills	TKO 6
19	2/3/90	Marcellus Allen, Atlantic City	TKO 9
20	4/28/90	Mario Melo, Atlantic City	TKO 1

No	Date	Opponent, location	Result
21	8/21/90	Jim MacDonald, Auburn Hills	TKO 3
22	12/15/90	Danny Lindstrom, Pittsburgh	TKO 8
23	4/19/91	Terry Davis, Atlantic City	TKO 2
24	6/25/91	Levi Billups, Auburn Hills	TKO 3
25	7/27/91	Alex Stewart, Norfolk, Va	TKO 4
26	11/23/91	Bobby Crabtree, Atlanta	TKO 1
27	2/1/92	Mike White, Las Vegas	Wu 10
28	3/17/92	Big Foot Martin, Auburn Hills	Wu 10
29	5/15/92	Bert Cooper, Atlantic City	TKO 5
30	11/13/92	Billy Wright, Las Vegas	TKO 1
31	2/27/93	Bonecrusher Smith, Atl.City	Wu 10
32	4/26/93	Frankie Swindell, Detroit	TKO 3
33	6/22/93	James Pritchard, Atlantic City	TKO 3
34	12/4/93	Mike Evans, Reno	Wu 10
35	4/22/94	Evander Holyfield, Las Vegas	Wm 12
		(won IBF/WBA heavyweight titles)	
36	11/5/94	George Foreman, Las Vegas	L, KO 10
		(lost IBF/WBA heavyweight titles)	
37	5/13/95	Melvin Foster, Sacramento	Wu 10
38	6/22/96	Axel Shulz, Dortmund, GER	Ws 12
		(won IBF heavyweight title)	
39	3/29/97	Vaughn Bean, Las Vegas	Wm 12

Mike Tyson

Born: 6/30/66   **Pro record:** 45-3-0, 39 KOs
Height: 5'11"   **Manager:** Don King
Weight: 218

No	Date	Opponent, location	Result
1	3/6/85	Hector Mercedes, Albany, N.Y.	KO 1
2	4/10/85	Trent Singleton, Albany, N.Y.	TKO 1
3	5/23/85	Don Halpin, Albany, N.Y.	KO 4
4	6/20/85	Rick Spain, Atlantic City	KO 1
5	7/11/85	John Anderson, Atlantic City	TKO 2
6	7/19/85	Larry Sims, Poughkeepsie, N.Y.	KO 3
7	8/15/85	Lorenzo Canady, Atlantic City	TKO 1
8	9/5/85	Michael Johnson, Atlantic City	KO 1
9	10/9/85	Donnie Long, Atlantic City	KO 1
10	10/25/85	Robert Colay, Atlantic City	KO 1
11	11/1/85	Sterling Benjamin, Latham, N.Y.	TKO 1
12	11/13/85	Eddie Richardson, Houston	KO 1
13	11/22/85	Conroy Nelson, Latham, N.Y.	KO 2
14	12/6/85	Sammy Scaff, New York City	KO 1
15	12/27/85	Mark Young, Latham, N.Y.	KO 1
16	1/10/86	Dave Jaco, Albany, N.Y.	TKO 1
17	1/24/86	Mike Jameson, Atlantic City	TKO 5
18	2/16/86	Jesse Ferguson, Troy, N.Y.	TKO 6
19	3/10/86	Steve Zouski, Uniondale, N.Y.	KO 3
20	5/3/86	James Tillis, Glens Falls, N.Y.	Wu 10
21	5/20/86	Mitchell Green, New York City	Wu 10
22	6/13/86	Reggie Gross, New York City	TKO 1
23	6/28/86	William Hosea, Troy, N.Y.	KO 1
24	7/11/86	Lorenzo Boyd, Swan Lake, N.Y.	KO 2
25	7/26/86	Marvis Frazier, Glens Falls, N.Y.	KO 1
26	8/17/86	Jose Ribalta, Atlantic City	TKO 10
27	9/6/86	Alfonzo Ratliff, Las Vegas	TKO 2

No	Date	Opponent, location	Result
28	11/22/86	Trevor Berbick, Las Vegas	KO 2
		(won WBC heavyweight title)	
29	3/7/87	Bonecrusher Smith, Las Vegas	Wu 12
		(won WBA heavyweight title)	
30	5/30/87	Pinklon Thomas, Las Vegas	TKO 6
31	8/1/87	Tony Tucker, Las Vegas	Wu 12
		(won IBF heavyweight title)	
32	10/16/87	Tyrell Biggs, Atlantic City	TKO 7
33	1/22/88	Larry Holmes, Atlantic City	KO 4
34	3/21/88	Tony Tubbs, Tokyo	TKO 2
35	6/27/88	Michael Spinks, Atlantic City	KO 1
36	2/25/89	Frank Bruno, Las Vegas	TKO 5
37	7/21/89	Carl Williams, Atlantic City	TKO 1
38	2/10/90	Buster Douglas, Tokyo	KO by 10
		(lost world heavyweight title)	
39	6/16/90	Henry Tillman, Las Vegas	KO 1
40	12/8/90	Alex Stewart, Atlantic City	TKO 1
41	3/18/91	Razor Ruddock, Las Vegas	TKO 7
42	6/28/91	Razor Ruddock, Las Vegas	Wu 12
43	8/19/95	Peter McNeeley, Las Vegas	W disq. 1
		(first fight since release from prison)	
44	12/16/95	Buster Mathis Jr., Philadelphia	KO 3
45	3/16/96	Frank Bruno, Las Vegas	TKO 3
		(won WBC heavyweight title)	
46	9/7/96	Bruce Seldon, Las Vegas	TKO 1
		(won WBA heavyweight title)	
47	11/9/96	Evander Holyfield, Las Vegas	TKO by 11
		(lost WBA heavyweight title)	
48	6/28/97	Evander Holyfield, Las Vegas	L Disq 3
		(disqualified for biting Holyfield's ears)	

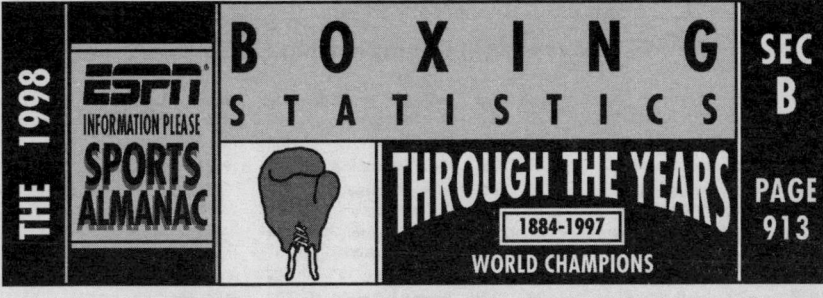

THE 1998 ESPN INFORMATION PLEASE SPORTS ALMANAC

B O X I N G
S T A T I S T I C S

THROUGH THE YEARS
1884-1997
WORLD CHAMPIONS

SEC **B**
PAGE
913

World Heavyweight Championship Fights

Widely accepted world champions in **bold** type. Note following result abbreviations: KO (knockout), TKO (technical knockout), Wu (unanimous decision), Wm (majority decision), Ws (split decision), Ref (referee's decision), ND (no decision), Disq (won on disqualification).

Year	Date	Winner	Age	Wgt	Loser	Wgt	Result	Location
1892	Sept. 7	James J. Corbett	26	178	John L. Sullivan	212	KO 21	New Orleans
1894	Jan. 25	**James J. Corbett**	27	184	Charley Mitchell	158	KO 3	Jacksonville, FL
1897	Mar. 17	Bob Fitzsimmons	34	167	**James J. Corbett**	183	KO 14	Carson City, Nev.
1899	June 9	James J. Jeffries	24	206	**Bob Fitzsimmons**	167	KO 11	Coney Island, NY
1899	Nov. 3	**James J. Jeffries**	24	215	Tom Sharkey	183	Ref 25	Coney Island, NY
1900	Apr. 6	**James J. Jeffries**	24	NA	Jack Finnegan	NA	KO 1	Detroit
1900	May 11	**James J. Jeffries**	25	218	James J. Corbett	188	KO 23	Coney Island, NY
1901	Nov. 15	**James J. Jeffries**	26	211	Gus Ruhlin	194	TKO 6	San Francisco
1902	July 25	**James J. Jeffries**	27	219	Bob Fitzsimmons	172	KO 8	San Francisco
1903	Aug. 14	**James J. Jeffries**	28	220	James J. Corbett	190	KO 10	San Francisco
1904	Aug. 25	**James J. Jeffries***	29	219	Jack Munroe	186	TKO 2	San Francisco
1905	July 3	Marvin Hart	28	190	Jack Root	171	KO 12	Reno, Nev.
1906	Feb. 23	Tommy Burns	24	180	**Marvin Hart**	188	Ref 20	Los Angeles
1906	Oct. 2	**Tommy Burns**	25	NA	Jim Flynn	NA	KO 15	Los Angeles
1906	Nov. 28	**Tommy Burns**	25	172	Phila. Jack O'Brien	163½	Draw 20	Los Angeles
1907	May 8	**Tommy Burns**	25	180	Phila. Jack O'Brien	167	Ref 20	Los Angeles
1907	July 4	**Tommy Burns**	26	181	Bill Squires	180	KO 1	Colma, CA
1907	Dec. 2	**Tommy Burns**	26	177	Gunner Moir	204	KO 10	London
1908	Feb. 10	**Tommy Burns**	26	NA	Jack Palmer	NA	KO 4	London
1908	Mar. 17	**Tommy Burns**	26	NA	Jem Roche	NA	KO 1	Dublin
1908	Apr. 18	**Tommy Burns**	26	NA	Jewey Smith	NA	KO 5	Paris
1908	June 13	**Tommy Burns**	26	184	Bill Squires	183	KO 8	Paris
1908	Aug. 24	**Tommy Burns**	27	181	Bill Squires	184	KO 13	Sydney
1908	Sept. 2	**Tommy Burns**	27	183	Bill Lang	187	KO 6	Melbourne
1908	Dec. 26	Jack Johnson	30	192	**Tommy Burns**	168	TKO 14	Sydney
1909	Mar. 10	**Jack Johnson**	30	NA	Victor McLaglen	NA	ND 6	Vancouver
1909	May 19	**Jack Johnson**	31	205	Phila. Jack O'Brien	161	ND 6	Philadelphia
1909	June 30	**Jack Johnson**	31	207	Tony Ross	214	ND 6	Pittsburgh
1909	Sept. 9	**Jack Johnson**	31	209	Al Kaufman	191	ND 10	San Francisco
1909	Oct. 16	**Jack Johnson**	31	205½	Stanley Ketchel	170¼	KO 12	Colma, Calif.
1910	July 4	**Jack Johnson**	32	208	James J. Jeffries	227	KO 15	Reno, Nev.
1912	July 4	**Jack Johnson**	34	195½	Jim Flynn	175	TKO 9	Las Vegas, N.M.
1913	Dec. 19	**Jack Johnson**	35	NA	Jim Johnson	NA	Draw 10	Paris
1914	June 27	**Jack Johnson**	36	221	Frank Moran	203	Ref 20	Paris
1915	Apr. 5	Jess Willard	33	230	**Jack Johnson**	205½	KO 26	Havana
1916	Mar. 25	**Jess Willard**	34	225	Frank Moran	203	ND 10	NYC (Mad.Sq. Garden)
1919	July 4	Jack Dempsey	24	187	**Jess Willard**	245	TKO 4	Toledo, Ohio
1920	Sept. 6	**Jack Dempsey**	25	185	Billy Miske	187	KO 3	Benton Harbor, Mich.
1920	Dec. 14	**Jack Dempsey**	25	188¼	Bill Brennan	197	KO 12	NYC (Mad. Sq. Garden)
1921	July 2	**Jack Dempsey**	26	188	Georges Carpentier	172	KO 4	Jersey City, N.J.
1923	July 4	**Jack Dempsey**	28	188	Tommy Gibbons	175½	Ref 15	Shelby, Montana
1923	Sept. 14	**Jack Dempsey**	28	192½	Luis Firpo	216½	KO 2	NYC (Polo Grounds)
1926	Sept. 23	Gene Tunney	29	189½	**Jack Dempsey**	190	Wu 10	Philadelphia
1927	Sept. 22	**Gene Tunney**	30	189½	Jack Dempsey	192½	Wu 10	Chicago
1928	July 26	**Gene Tunney***	31	192	Tom Heeney	203	TKO 11	NYC (Yankee Stadium)

*James J. Jeffries retired as champion on May 13, 1905, then came out of retirement to fight Jack Johnson for the title in 1910.
*Gene Tunney retired as undefeated champion in 1928.

World Heavyweight Championship Fights (Cont.)

Year	Date	Winner	Age	Wgt	Loser	Wgt	Result	Location
1930	June 12	Max Schmeling	24	188	Jack Sharkey	197	Foul 4	NYC (Yankee Stadium)
1931	July 3	**Max Schmeling**	25	189	Young Stribling	186½	TKO 15	Cleveland
1932	June 21	Jack Sharkey	29	205	**Max Schmeling**	188	Ws 15	Long Island City, N.Y.
1933	June 29	Primo Carnera	26	260½	**Jack Sharkey**	201	KO 6	Long Island City, N.Y.
1933	Oct. 22	**Primo Carnera**	26	259½	Paulino Uzcudun	229¼	Wu 15	Rome
1934	Mar. 1	**Primo Carnera**	27	270	Tommy Loughran	184	Wu 15	Miami
1934	June 14	Max Baer	25	209½	**Primo Carnera**	263¼	TKO 11	Long Island City, N.Y.
1935	June 13	James J. Braddock	29	193¾	**Max Baer**	209	Wu 15	Long Island City, N.Y.
1937	June 22	Joe Louis	23	197¼	**James J. Braddock**	197	KO 8	Chicago
1937	Aug. 30	Joe Louis	23	197	Tommy Farr	204¼	Wu 15	NYC (Yankee Stadium)
1938	Feb. 23	**Joe Louis**	23	200	Nathan Mann	193½	KO 3	NYC (Mad. Sq. Garden)
1938	Apr. 1	**Joe Louis**	23	202½	Harry Thomas	196	KO 5	Chicago
1938	June 22	**Joe Louis**	24	198¾	Max Schmeling	193	KO 1	NYC (Yankee Stadium)
1939	Jan. 25	**Joe Louis**	24	200¼	John Henry Lewis	180¾	KO 1	NYC (Mad. Sq. Garden)
1939	Apr. 17	**Joe Louis**	24	201¼	Jack Roper	204¾	KO 1	Los Angeles
1939	June 28	**Joe Louis**	25	200¾	Tony Galento	233¾	TKO 4	NYC (Yankee Stadium)
1939	Sept. 20	**Joe Louis**	25	200	Bob Pastor	183	KO 11	Detroit
1940	Feb. 9	**Joe Louis**	25	203	Arturo Godoy	202	Ws 15	NYC (Mad. Sq. Garden)
1940	Mar. 29	**Joe Louis**	25	201½	Johnny Paychek	187½	KO 2	NYC (Mad. Sq. Garden)
1940	June 20	**Joe Louis**	26	199	Arturo Godoy	201¼	TKO 8	NYC (Yankee Stadium)
1940	Dec. 16	**Joe Louis**	26	202¼	Al McCoy	180¾	TKO 6	Boston
1941	Jan. 31	**Joe Louis**	26	202½	Red Burman	188	KO 5	NYC (Mad. Sq. Garden)
1941	Feb. 17	**Joe Louis**	26	203½	Gus Dorazio	193½	KO 2	Philadelphia
1941	Mar. 21	**Joe Louis**	26	202	Abe Simon	254½	TKO 13	Detroit
1941	Apr. 8	**Joe Louis**	26	203½	Tony Musto	199½	TKO 9	St. Louis
1941	May 23	**Joe Louis**	27	201½	Buddy Baer	237½	Disq 7	Washington, D.C.
1941	June 18	**Joe Louis**	27	199½	Billy Conn	174	KO 13	NYC (Polo Grounds)
1941	Sept. 29	**Joe Louis**	27	202¼	Lou Nova	202½	TKO 6	NYC (Polo Grounds)
1942	Jan. 9	**Joe Louis**	27	206¾	Buddy Baer	250	KO 1	NYC (Mad. Sq. Garden)
1942	Mar. 27	**Joe Louis**	27	207½	Abe Simon	255½	KO 6	NYC (Mad. Sq. Garden)
1942–45 World War II								
1946	June 9	**Joe Louis**	32	207	Billy Conn	187	KO 8	NYC (Yankee Stadium)
1946	Sept. 18	**Joe Louis**	32	211	Tami Mauriello	198½	KO 1	NYC (Yankee Stadium)
1947	Dec. 5	**Joe Louis**	33	211½	Jersey Joe Walcott	194½	Ws 15	NYC (Mad. Sq. Garden)
1948	June 25	**Joe Louis****	34	213½	Jersey Joe Walcott	194¾	KO 11	NYC (Yankee Stadium)
1949	June 22	**Ezzard Charles**	27	181¾	Jersey Joe Walcott	195½	Wu 15	Chicago
1949	Aug. 10	**Ezzard Charles**	28	180	Gus Lesnevich	182	TKO 8	NYC (Yankee Stadium)
1949	Oct. 14	**Ezzard Charles**	28	182	Pat Valentino	188½	KO 8	San Francisco
1950	Aug. 15	**Ezzard Charles**	29	183¼	Freddie Beshore	184½	TKO 14	Buffalo
1950	Sept. 27	**Ezzard Charles**	29	184½	Joe Louis	218	Wu 15	NYC (Yankee Stadium)
1950	Dec. 5	**Ezzard Charles**	29	185	Nick Barone	178½	KO 11	Cincinnati
1951	Jan. 12	**Ezzard Charles**	29	185	Lee Oma	193	TKO 10	NYC (Mad. Sq. Garden)
1951	Mar. 7	**Ezzard Charles**	29	186	Jersey Joe Walcott	193	Wu 15	Detroit
1951	May 30	**Ezzard Charles**	29	182	Joey Maxim	181½	Wu 15	Chicago
1951	July 18	Jersey Joe Walcott	37	194	**Ezzard Charles**	182	KO 7	Pittsburgh
1952	June 5	**Jersey Joe Walcott**	38	196	Ezzard Charles	191½	Wu 15	Philadelphia
1952	Sept. 23	Rocky Marciano	29	184	**Jersey Joe Walcott**	196	KO 13	Philadelphia
1953	May 15	**Rocky Marciano**	29	184½	Jersey Joe Walcott	197¾	KO 1	Chicago
1953	Sept. 24	**Rocky Marciano**	30	185	Roland LaStarza	184¾	TKO 11	NYC (Polo Grounds)
1954	June 17	**Rocky Marciano**	30	187½	Ezzard Charles	185½	Wu 15	NYC (Yankee Stadium)
1954	Sept. 17	**Rocky Marciano**	31	187	Ezzard Charles	192½	KO 8	NYC (Yankee Stadium)
1955	May 16	**Rocky Marciano**	31	189	Don Cockell	205	TKO 9	San Francisco
1955	Sept. 21	**Rocky Marciano***	32	188¼	Archie Moore	188	KO 9	NYC (Yankee Stadium)
1956	Nov. 30	Floyd Patterson	21	182¼	Archie Moore	187¾	KO 5	Chicago
1957	July 29	**Floyd Patterson**	22	184	Tommy Jackson	192½	TKO 10	NYC (Polo Grounds)
1957	Aug. 22	**Floyd Patterson**	22	187¼	Pete Rademacher	202	KO 6	Seattle
1958	Aug. 18	**Floyd Patterson**	23	184½	Roy Harris	194	TKO 13	Los Angeles
1959	May 1	**Floyd Patterson**	24	182½	Brian London	206	KO 11	Indianapolis
1959	June 26	Ingemar Johansson	26	196	**Floyd Patterson**	182	TKO 3	NYC (Yankee Stadium)

**Joe Louis retired as undefeated champion on Mar. 1, 1949, then came out of retirement to fight Ezzard Charles for the title in 1950.

*Rocky Marciano retired as undefeated champion on Apr. 27, 1956.

Year	Date	Winner	Age	Wgt	Loser	Wgt	Result	Location
1960	June 20	Floyd Patterson	25	190	**Ingemar Johansson**	194¾	KO 5	NYC (Polo Grounds)
1961	Mar. 13	**Floyd Patterson**	26	194¾	Ingemar Johansson	206½	KO 6	Miami Beach
1961	Dec. 4	**Floyd Patterson**	26	188½	Tom McNeeley	197	KO 4	Toronto
1962	Sept. 25	Sonny Liston	30	214	**Floyd Patterson**	189	KO 1	Chicago
1963	July 22	**Sonny Liston**	31	215	Floyd Patterson	194½	KO 1	Las Vegas
1964	Feb. 25	Cassius Clay**	22	210½	**Sonny Liston**	218	TKO 7	Miami Beach
1965	Mar. 5	Ernie Terrell WBA	25	199	Eddie Machen	192	Wu 15	Chicago
1965	May 25	**Muhammad Ali**	23	206	Sonny Liston	215¼	KO 1	Lewiston, Me.
1965	Nov. 1	Ernie Terrell WBA	26	206	George Chuvalo	209	Wu 15	Toronto
1965	Nov. 22	**Muhammad Ali**	23	210	Floyd Patterson	196¾	TKO 12	Las Vegas
1966	Mar. 29	**Muhammad Ali**	24	214½	George Chuvalo	216	Wu 15	Toronto
1966	May 21	**Muhammad Ali**	24	201½	Henry Cooper	188	TKO 6	London
1966	June 28	Ernie Terrell WBA	27	209½	Doug Jones	187½	Wu 15	Houston
1966	Aug. 6	**Muhammad Ali**	24	209½	Brian London	201½	KO 3	London
1966	Sept. 10	**Muhammad Ali**	24	203½	Karl Mildenberger	194¼	TKO 12	Frankfurt, W. Ger.
1966	Nov. 14	**Muhammad Ali**	24	212¾	Cleveland Williams	210½	TKO 3	Houston
1967	Feb. 6	**Muhammad Ali**	25	212¼	Ernie Terrell WBA	212½	Wu 15	Houston
1967	Mar. 22	**Muhammad Ali**	25	211½	Zora Folley	202½	KO 7	NYC (Mad. Sq. Garden)
1968	Mar. 4	Joe Frazier	24	204½	Buster Mathis	243½	TKO 11	NYC (Mad. Sq. Garden)
1968	Apr. 27	Jimmy Ellis	28	197	Jerry Quarry	195	Wm 15	Oakland
1968	June 24	Joe Frazier NY	24	203½	Manuel Ramos	208	TKO 2	NYC (Mad. Sq. Garden)
1968	Aug. 14	Jimmy Ellis WBA	28	198	Floyd Patterson	188	Ref 15	Stockholm
1968	Dec. 10	Joe Frazier NY	24	203	Oscar Bonavena	207	Wu 15	Philadelphia
1969	Apr. 22	Joe Frazier NY	25	204½	Dave Zyglewicz	190½	KO 1	Houston
1969	June 23	Joe Frazier NY	25	203½	Jerry Quarry	198½	TKO 8	NYC (Mad. Sq. Garden)
1970	Feb. 16	Joe Frazier NY	26	205	Jimmy Ellis WBA	201	TKO 5	NYC (Mad. Sq. Garden)
1970	Nov. 18	Joe Frazier	26	209	Bob Foster	188	KO 2	Detroit
1971	Mar. 8	Joe Frazier	27	205½	**Muhammad Ali**	215	Wu 15	NYC (Mad. Sq. Garden)
1972	Jan. 15	**Joe Frazier**	28	215½	Terry Daniels	195	TKO 4	New Orleans
1972	May 26	**Joe Frazier**	28	217½	Ron Stander	218	TKO 5	Omaha, Neb.
1973	Jan. 22	George Foreman	24	217½	**Joe Frazier**	214	TKO 2	Kingston, Jamaica
1973	Sept. 1	**George Foreman**	24	219½	Jose (King) Roman	196½	KO 1	Tokyo
1974	Mar. 26	**George Foreman**	25	224¾	Ken Norton	212¾	TKO 2	Caracas, Venezuela
1974	Oct. 30	Muhammad Ali	32	216½	**George Foreman**	220	KO 8	Kinshasa, Zaire
1975	Mar. 24	**Muhammad Ali**	33	223½	Chuck Wepner	225	TKO 15	Cleveland
1975	May 16	**Muhammad Ali**	33	224½	Ron Lyle	219	TKO 11	Las Vegas
1975	July 1	**Muhammad Ali**	33	224½	Joe Bugner	230	Wu 15	Kuala Lumpur, Malaysia
1975	Oct. 1	**Muhammad Ali**	33	224½	Joe Frazier	215	TKO 15	Manila, Philippines
1976	Feb. 20	**Muhammad Ali**	34	226	Jean Pierre Coopman	206	KO 5	San Juan, P.R.
1976	Apr. 30	**Muhammad Ali**	34	230	Jimmy Young	209	Wu 15	Landover, Md.
1976	May 24	**Muhammad Ali**	34	220	Richard Dunn	206½	TKO 5	Munich, W. Ger.
1976	Sept. 28	**Muhammad Ali**	34	221	Ken Norton	217½	Wu 15	NYC (Yankee Stadium)
1977	May 16	**Muhammad Ali**	35	221¼	Alfredo Evangelista	209¼	Wu 15	Landover, Md.
1977	Sept. 29	**Muhammad Ali**	35	225	Earnie Shavers	211¼	Wu 15	NYC (Mad. Sq. Garden)
1978	Feb. 15	Leon Spinks	24	197¼	**Muhammad Ali**	224¼	Ws 15	Las Vegas
1978	June 9	Larry Holmes	28	209	Ken Norton WBC††	220	Ws 15	Las Vegas
1978	Sept. 15	Muhammad Ali†	36	221	**Leon Spinks**	201	Wu 15	New Orleans
1978	Nov. 10	Larry Holmes WBC	29	214	Alfredo Evangelista	208¼	KO 7	Las Vegas
1979	Mar. 23	Larry Holmes WBC	29	214	Osvaldo Ocasio	207	TKO 7	Las Vegas
1979	June 22	Larry Holmes WBC	29	215	Mike Weaver	202	TKO 12	NYC (Mad. Sq. Garden)
1979	Sept. 28	Larry Holmes WBC	29	210	Earnie Shavers	211	TKO 11	Las Vegas
1979	Oct. 20	John Tate	24	240	Gerrie Coetzee	222	Wu 15	Pretoria, S. Africa
1980	Feb. 3	Larry Holmes WBC	30	213½	Lorenzo Zanon	215	TKO 6	Las Vegas
1980	Mar. 31	Mike Weaver	27	232	John Tate WBA	232	KO 15	Knoxville, Tenn.
1980	Mar. 31	Larry Holmes WBC	30	211	Leroy Jones	254½	TKO 8	Las Vegas
1980	July 7	Larry Holmes WBC	30	214¼	Scott LeDoux	226	TKO 7	Minneapolis
1980	Oct. 2	Larry Holmes WBC	30	211½	Muhammad Ali	217½	TKO 11	Las Vegas
1980	Oct. 25	Mike Weaver WBA	28	210	Gerrie Coetzee	226½	KO 13	Sun City, Boph'swana

**After defeating Liston, Cassius Clay announced that he had changed his name to Muhammad Ali. He was later stripped of his title by the WBA and most state boxing commissions after refusing induction into the U.S. Army on Apr. 28, 1967.

† Muhammad Ali retired as champion on June 27, 1979, then came out of retirement to fight Larry Holmes for the title in 1980.

†† WBC recognized Ken Norton as world champion when Leon Spinks refused to meet Norton before Spinks' rematch with Muhammad Ali. Norton had scored a 15-round split decision over Jimmy Young on Nov. 5, 1977 in Las Vegas.

World Heavyweight Championship Fights (Cont.)

Year	Date	Winner	Age	Wgt	Loser	Wgt	Result	Location
1981	Apr. 11	**Larry Holmes**	31	215	Trevor Berbick	215½	Wu 15	Las Vegas
1981	June 12	**Larry Holmes**	31	212¼	Leon Spinks	200¼	TKO 3	Detroit
1981	Oct. 3	Mike Weaver WBA	29	215	Quick Tillis	209	Wu 15	Rosemont, Ill.
1981	Nov. 6	**Larry Holmes**	32	213¼	Renaldo Snipes	215¾	TKO 11	Pittsburgh
1982	June 11	**Larry Holmes**	32	212½	Gerry Cooney	225½	TKO 13	Las Vegas
1982	Nov. 26	**Larry Holmes**	33	217½	Randall (Tex) Cobb	234¼	Wu 15	Houston
1982	Dec. 10	Michael Dokes	24	216	Mike Weaver WBA	209¾	TKO 1	Las Vegas
1983	Mar. 27	**Larry Holmes**	33	221	Lucien Rodriguez	209	Wu 12	Scranton, Pa.
1983	May 20	Michael Dokes WBA	24	223	Mike Weaver	218½	Draw 15	Las Vegas
1983	May 20	**Larry Holmes**	33	213	Tim Witherspoon	219½	Ws 12	Las Vegas
1983	Sept. 10	**Larry Holmes**	33	223	Scott Frank	211¼	TKO 5	Atlantic City
1983	Sept. 23	Gerrie Coetzee	28	215	Michael Dokes WBA	217	KO 10	Richfield, Ohio
1983	Nov. 25	**Larry Holmes**	34	219	Marvis Frazier	200	TKO 1	Las Vegas
1984	Mar. 9	Tim Witherspoon*	26	220¼	Greg Page	239½	Wm 12	Las Vegas
1984	Aug. 31	Pinklon Thomas	26	216	Tim Witherspoon WBC	217	Wm 12	Las Vegas
1984	Nov. 9	**Larry Holmes** IBF	35	221½	Bonecrusher Smith	227	TKO 12	Las Vegas
1984	Dec. 1	Greg Page	26	236½	Gerrie Coetzee WBA	218	KO 8	Sun City, Boph'swana
1985	Mar. 15	**Larry Holmes**	35	223½	David Bey	233¼	TKO 10	Las Vegas
1985	Apr. 29	Tony Tubbs	26	229	Greg Page WBA	239½	Wu 15	Buffalo
1985	May 20	**Larry Holmes**	35	222¼	Carl Williams	215	Wu 15	Las Vegas
1985	June 15	Pinklon Thomas	27	220¼	Mike Weaver	221¼	KO 8	Las Vegas
1985	Sept. 21	Michael Spinks	29	200	**Larry Holmes** IBF	221½	Wu 15	Las Vegas
1986	Jan. 17	Tim Witherspoon	28	227	Tony Tubbs WBA	229	Wm 15	Atlanta
1986	Mar. 22	Trevor Berbick	33	218½	Pinklon Thomas WBC	223¾	Wu 15	Las Vegas
1986	Apr. 19	**Michael Spinks**	29	205	Larry Holmes	223	Ws 15	Las Vegas
1986	July 19	Tim Witherspoon WBA	28	234¾	Frank Bruno	228	TKO 11	Wembley, England
1986	Sept. 6	**Michael Spinks**	30	201	Steffen Tangstad	214¾	TKO 4	Las Vegas
1986	Nov. 22	Mike Tyson	20	221¼	Trevor Berbick WBC	218½	TKO 2	Las Vegas
1986	Dec. 12	Bonecrusher Smith	33	228½	Tim Witherspoon WBA	233½	TKO 1	NYC (Mad. Sq. Garden)
1987	Mar. 7	Mike Tyson WBC	20	219	Bonecrusher Smith WBA	233	Wu 12	Las Vegas
1987	May 30	Mike Tyson	20	218¾	Pinklon Thomas	217¾	Wu 6	Las Vegas
1987	May 30	Tony Tucker**	28	222¼	Buster Douglas	227¼	TKO 10	Las Vegas
1987	June 15	**Michael Spinks**	30	208¾	Gerry Cooney	238	TKO 5	Atlantic City
1987	Aug. 1	Mike Tyson	21	221	Tony Tucker IBF	221	Wu 12	Las Vegas
1987	Oct. 16	Mike Tyson	21	216	Tyrell Biggs	228¾	TKO 7	Atlantic City
1988	Jan. 22	Mike Tyson	21	215¾	Larry Holmes	225¾	TKO 4	Atlantic City
1988	Mar. 20	Mike Tyson	21	216¼	Tony Tubbs	238¼	KO 2	Tokyo
1988	June 27	Mike Tyson	21	218¼	**Michael Spinks**	212¼	KO 1	Atlantic City
1989	Feb. 25	**Mike Tyson**	22	218	Frank Bruno	228	TKO 5	Las Vegas
1989	July 21	**Mike Tyson**	23	219¼	Carl Williams	218	TKO 1	Atlantic City
1990	Feb. 10	Buster Douglas	29	231½	**Mike Tyson**	220½	KO 10	Tokyo
1990	Oct. 25	Evander Holyfield	28	208	**Buster Douglas**	246	KO 3	Las Vegas
1991	Apr. 19	**Evander Holyfield**	28	208	George Foreman	257	Wu 12	Atlantic City
1991	Nov. 23	**Evander Holyfield**	29	210	Bert Cooper	215	TKO 7	Atlanta
1992	June 19	**Evander Holyfield**	29	210	Larry Holmes	233	Wu 12	Las Vegas
1992	Nov. 13	Riddick Bowe	25	235	**Evander Holyfield**	205	Wu 12	Las Vegas
1993	Feb. 6	**Riddick Bowe**	25	243	Michael Dokes	244	TKO 1	NYC (Mad. Sq. Garden)
1993	May 8	Lennox Lewis WBC†	27	235	Tony Tucker	235	Wu 12	Las Vegas
1993	May 22	**Riddick Bowe**	25	244	Jesse Ferguson	224	TKO 2	Washington, D.C.
1993	Oct. 1	Lennox Lewis WBC	28	233	Frank Bruno	238	TKO 7	Cardiff, Wales
1993	Nov. 6	Evander Holyfield	31	217	**Riddick Bowe**	246	Wm 12	Las Vegas
1994	Apr. 22	Michael Moorer	26	214	**Evander Holyfield**	214	Wm 12	Las Vegas
1994	May 6	Lennox Lewis WBC	28	235	Phil Jackson	218	TKO 8	Atlantic City
1994	Sept. 25	Oliver McCall	29	231¼	**Lennox Lewis** WBC	238	TKO 2	London
1994	Nov. 5	George Foreman*	45	250	**Michael Moorer**	222	KO 10	Las Vegas

*WBC recognized winner of Mar. 9, 1984 fight between Tim Witherspoon and Greg Page as world champion after Larry Holmes relinquished title in dispute. IBF then recognized Holmes.

**IBF recognized winner of May 30, 1987 fight between Tony Tucker and James (Buster) Douglas as world champion after Michael Spinks relinquished title in dispute.

†WBC recognized Lennox Lewis as world champion when Riddick Bowe gave up that portion of his title on Dec. 14, 1992, rather than fight Lewis, the WBC's mandatory challenger.

*George Foreman won WBA and IBF championships when he beat Michael Moorer on Nov. 5, 1994. He was stripped of WBA title on Mar. 4, 1995, when he refused to fight No. 1 contender Tony Tucker, and he relinquished IBF title on June 29, 1995, rather than give Axel Schulz a rematch. Tucker lost to Bruce Seldon in their April 8 fight for vacant WBA title.

Year	Date	Winner	Age	Wgt	Loser	Wgt	Result	Location
1995	Apr. 8	Oliver McCall WBC	29	231	Larry Holmes	236	Wu 12	Las Vegas
1995	Apr. 8	Bruce Seldon*	28	236	Tony Tucker	240	TKO 7	Las Vegas
1995	Apr. 22	**George Foreman***	46	256	Axel Schulz	221	Wm 12	Las Vegas
1995	Aug. 19	Bruce Seldon WBA	28	234	Joe Hipp	223	TKO 10	Las Vegas
1995	Sept. 2	Frank Bruno	33	248	Oliver McCall WBC	235	Wu 12	London
1995	Dec. 9	Frans Botha**	27	227	Axel Schulz	222	Wu 12	Stuttgart, GER
1996	Mar. 16	Mike Tyson	29	220	Frank Bruno WBC	247	TKO 3	Las Vegas
1996	June 22	Michael Moorer**	28	222	Axel Schulz	223	Ws 12	Dortmund, GER
1996	Sept. 7	Mike Tyson WBC†	30	219	Bruce Seldon WBA	229	TKO 1	Las Vegas
1996	Nov. 9	Evander Holyfield	34	215	Mike Tyson WBA	222	TKO 11	Las Vegas
1997	Feb. 7	Lennox Lewis†	31	251	Oliver McCall	237	TKO 5	Las Vegas
1997	Mar. 29	Michael Moorer IBF	29	212	Vaughn Bean	212	Wm 12	Las Vegas
1997	June 28	Evander Holyfield WBA	34	218	Mike Tyson	218	Disq. 3	Las Vegas
1997	July 12	Lennox Lewis WBC	31	242	Henry Akinwande	237½	Disq. 5	Stateline, Nev.

**Botha won the vacant IBF title with a controversial 12–round decision over Azel Schulz on Dec. 9, 1995, but after legal sparring was eventually stripped of the IBF belt for using anabolic steroids.

†Mike Tyson won the WBC belt from Frank Bruno on Mar. 16 and still held it at the time of his Sept. 7 win over Bruce Seldon (although it was not at risk for that fight) but was forced to relinquish title after the bout for not fighting mandatory challenge Lennox Lewis. Tyson also paid Lewis $4 million to step aside and allow the Tyson-Seldon bout to take place. Lewis then fought Oliver McCall for the vacant WBC belt. The fight was stopped 55 seconds into round 5 because, inexplicably, McCall was visibly distraught and stopped throwing punches.

Holyfield won the bout by disqualification and retained the WBA belt after Tyson spit out his mouthpiece and bit off a piece of Holyfield's ear. Tyson received a two-point deduction from refereee Mills Lane and after a stern warning and a short delay the fight was allowed to continue. Shortly thereafter he bit Holyfield's other ear and Tyson was disqualified.

Wide World Photos

Cassius Clay (left) stunned the boxing world in 1964 when he beat champion **Sonny Liston** in a seventh round TKO. Clay changed his name to **Muhammad Ali** after winning the title.

All-Time Heavyweight Upsets

Buster Douglas was a 50-1 underdog when he defeated previously-unbeaten heavyweight champion Mike Tyson on Feb. 10, 1990. That 10th-round knockout ranks as the biggest upset in boxing history. By comparison, 45-year-old George Foreman was only a 3-1 underdog before he unexpectedly won the title from Michael Moorer on Nov. 5, 1994.

Here are the best-known upsets in the annals of the heavyweight division. All fights were for the world championship except the Max Schmeling-Joe Louis bout.

Date	Winner	Loser	Result	KO Time	Location
9/7/1892	James J. Corbett	John L. Sullivan	KO 21	1:30	Olympic Club, New Orleans
4/5/1915	Jess Willard	Jack Johnson	KO 26	1:26	Mariano Race Track, Havana
9/23/26	Gene Tunney	Jack Dempsey	Wu 10	–	Sesquicentennial Stadium, Phila.
6/13/35	James J. Braddock	Max Baer	Wu 15	–	Mad.Sq.Garden Bowl, L.I.City
6/19/36	Max Schmeling	Joe Louis	KO 12	2:29	Yankee Stadium, New York
7/18/51	Jersey Joe Walcott	Ezzard Charles	KO 7	0:55	Forbes Field, Pittsburgh
6/26/59	Ingemar Johansson	Floyd Patterson	TKO 3	2:03	Yankee Stadium, New York
2/25/64	Cassius Clay	Sonny Liston	TKO 7	*	Convention Hall, Miami Beach
10/30/74	Muhammad Ali	George Foreman	KO 8	2:58	20th of May Stadium, Zaire
2/15/78	Leon Spinks	Muhammad Ali	Ws 15	–	Hilton Pavilion, Las Vegas
9/21/85	Michael Spinks	Larry Holmes	Wu 15	–	Riviera Hotel, Las Vegas
2/10/90	Buster Douglas	Mike Tyson	KO 10	1:23	Tokyo Dome, Tokyo
11/5/94	George Foreman	Michael Moorer	KO 10	2:03	MGM Grand, Las Vegas
11/9/96	Evander Holyfield	Mike Tyson	TKO 11	0:37	MGM Grand, Las Vegas

*Liston failed to answer bell for Round 7.

Muhammad Ali's Career Pro Record

Born Cassius Marcellus Clay, Jr. on Jan. 17, 1942, in Louisville; Amateur record of 100-5; won light-heavyweight gold medal at 1960 Olympic Games; Pro record of 56-5-0 with 37 KOs in 61 fights.

1960

Date	Opponent (location)	Result
Oct. 29	Tunney Hunsaker, Louisville	Wu 6
Dec. 27	Herb Siler, Miami Beach	TKO 4

1961

Date	Opponent (location)	Result
Jan. 17	Tony Esperti, Miami Beach	TKO 3
Feb. 7	Jim Robinson, Miami Beach	TKO 1
Feb. 21	Donnie Fleeman, Miami Beach	TKO 7
Apr. 19	Lamar Clark, Louisville	KO 2
June 26	Duke Sabedong, Las Vegas	Wu 10
July 22	Alonzo Johnson, Louisville	Wu 10
Oct. 7	Alex Miteff, Louisville	TKO 6
Nov. 29	Willi Besmanoff, Louisville	TKO 7

1962

Date	Opponent (location)	Result
Feb. 10	Sonny Banks, New York	TKO 4
Feb. 28	Don Warner, Miami Beach	TKO 4
Apr. 23	George Logan, Los Angeles	TKO 4
May 19	Billy Daniels, Los Angeles	TKO 7
July 20	Alejandro Lavorante, Los Angeles	KO 5
Nov. 15	Archie Moore, Los Angeles	KO 4

1963

Date	Opponent (location)	Result
Jan. 24	Charlie Powell, Pittsburgh	KO 3
Mar. 13	Doug Jones, New York	Wu 10
June 18	Henry Cooper, London	TKO 5

1964

Date	Opponent (location)	Result
Feb. 25	Sonny Liston, Miami Beach	TKO 7

(won World Heavyweight title)

After the fight, Clay announces he is a member of the Black Muslim religious sect and has changed his name to Muhammad Ali.

1965

Date	Opponent (location)	Result
May 25	Sonny Liston, Lewiston, Me	KO 1
Nov. 22	Floyd Patterson, Las Vegas	TKO 12

1966

Date	Opponent (location)	Result
Mar. 29	George Chuvalo, Toronto	Wu 15
May 21	Henry Cooper, London	TKO 6
Aug. 6	Brian London, London	KO 3
Sept. 10	Karl Mildenberger, Frankfurt	TKO 12
Nov. 12	Cleveland Williams, Houston	TKO 3

1967

Date	Opponent (location)	Result
Feb. 6	Ernie Terrell, Houston	Wu 15
Mar. 22	Zora Folley, New York	KO 7
Apr. 28	Refuses induction into U.S. Army and is stripped of world title by WBA and most state commissions the next day.	
June 20	Found guilty of draft evasion in Houston; fined $10,000 and sentenced to 5 years; remains free pending appeals, but is barred from the ring.	

1968-69 (Inactive)

1970

Date	Opponent (location)	Result
Feb. 3	Announces retirement.	
Oct. 26	Jerry Quarry, Atlanta	TKO 3
Dec. 7	Oscar Bonavena, New York	TKO 15

1971

Date	Opponent (location)	Result
Mar. 8	Joe Frazier, New York	Lu 15

(for World Heavyweight title)

Date	Opponent (location)	Result
June 28	U.S. Supreme Court reverses Ali's 1967 conviction saying he had been drafted improperly.	
July 26	Jimmy Ellis, Houston	TKO 12

(won vacant NABF Heavyweight title)

Date	Opponent (location)	Result
Nov. 17	Buster Mathis, Houston	Wu 12
Dec. 26	Jurgen Blin, Zurich	KO 7

1972

Date	Opponent (location)	Result
Apr. 1	Mac Foster, Tokyo	Wu 15
May 1	George Chuvalo, Vancouver	Wu 12
June 27	Jerry Quarry, Las Vegas	TKO 7
July 19	Al (Blue) Lewis, Dublin, Ire	TKO 11
Sept. 20	Floyd Patterson, New York	TKO 7
Nov. 21	Bob Foster, Stateline, Nev	TKO 8

1973

Date	Opponent (location)	Result
Feb. 14	Joe Bugner, Las Vegas	Wu 12
Mar. 31	Ken Norton, San Diego	Ls 12

(lost NABF Heavyweight title)

Date	Opponent (location)	Result
Sept. 10	Ken Norton, Inglewood, Calif	Ws 12

(regained NABF Heavyweight title)

Date	Opponent (location)	Result
Oct. 20	Rudi Lubbers, Jakarta, Indonesia	Wu 12

1974

Date	Opponent (location)	Result
Jan. 28	Joe Frazier, New York	Wu 12
Oct. 30	George Foreman, Kinshasa, Zaire	KO 8

(regained World Heavyweight title)

1975

Date	Opponent (location)	Result
Mar. 24	Chuck Wepner, Cleveland	TKO 15
May 16	Ron Lyle, Las Vegas	TKO 11
June 30	Joe Bugner, Kuala Lumpur, Malaysia	Wu 15
Sept. 30	Joe Frazier, Manila	TKO 14

1976

Date	Opponent (location)	Result
Feb. 20	Jean-Pierre Coopman, San Juan	KO 5
Apr. 30	Jimmy Young, Landover, Md	Wu 15
May 24	Richard Dunn, Munich	TKO 5
Sept. 28	Ken Norton, New York	Wu 15

1977

Date	Opponent (location)	Result
May 16	Alfredo Evangelista, Landover	Wu 15
Sept. 29	Earnie Shavers, New York	Wu 15

1978

Date	Opponent (location)	Result
Feb. 15	Leon Spinks, Las Vegas	Ls 15

(lost World Heavyweight title)

Date	Opponent (location)	Result
Sept. 15	Leon Spinks, New Orleans	Wu 15

(regained World Heavyweight title)

1979

Date		
June 27	Announces retirement.	

1980

Date	Opponent (location)	Result
Oct. 2	Larry Holmes, Las Vegas	TKO 11

1981

Date	Opponent (location)	Result
Dec. 11	Trevor Berbick, Nassau	Lu 10

(retires after fight)

Foreman and Frazier
The career pro records of George Foreman and Joe Frazier as of Oct. 1, 1997

George Foreman
Born: Jan. 10, 1949 in Marshall, Tex.
Pro record: 74-4-0, 68 KO

No	Date	Opponent, location	Result
1	6/23/69	Don Waldhelm, New York	KO 3
2	7/1/69	Fred Ashew, Houston	KO 1
3	7/14/69	Sylvester Dullaire, Wash., D.C.	KO 1
4	8/18/69	Chuck Wepner, New York	TKO 3
5	9/18/69	John Carroll, Seattle	KO 1
6	9/23/69	Cookie Wallace, Houston	KO 2
7	10/7/69	Vernon Clay, Houston	TKO 2
8	10/31/69	Roberto Davila, New York	Wu 8
9	11/5/69	Leo Peterson, Scranton	KO 4
10	11/18/69	Max Martinez, Houston	KO 2
11	12/6/69	Bob Hazelton, Las Vegas	KO 1
12	12/16/69	Levi Forte, Miami Beach	Wu 10
13	12/18/69	Gary Wilder, Seattle	TKO 1
14	1/6/70	Charley Polite, Houston	KO 4
15	1/26/70	Jack O'Halloran, New York	KO 5
16	2/16/70	Gregorio Peralta, New York	Wu 10
17	3/31/70	Rufus Brassell, Houston	KO 1
18	4/17/70	James J. Woody, New York	TKO 3
19	4/29/70	Aaron Easting, Cleveland	TKO 4
20	5/16/70	George Johnson, Inglewood	TKO 7
21	7/20/70	Roger Russell, Philadelphia	TKO 1
22	8/4/70	George Chuvalo, New York	TKO 3
23	11/3/70	Lou Bailey, Oklahoma City	KO 3
24	11/18/70	Boone Kirkman, New York	TKO 2
25	12/19/70	Mel Turnbow, Seattle	TKO 1
26	2/8/71	Charlie Boston, St. Paul, Minn.	KO 1
27	4/3/71	Stanford Harris, Lake Geneva	KO 2
28	5/10/71	Gregorio Peralta, Oakland	TKO 10
29	9/14/91	Vic Scott, El Paso	KO 1
30	9/21/71	Leroy Caldwell, Beaumont, Tex.	KO 2
31	10/7/71	Ollie Wilson, San Antonio	TKO 2
32	10/29/71	Luis F. Pires, New York	TKO 5
33	2/29/72	Murphy Goodwin, Austin, Tex.	KO 2
34	3/7/72	Clarence Boone, Beaumont, Tex.	TKO 2
35	4/10/72	Ted Gullick, Inglewood	KO 2
36	5/11/72	Miguel A. Paez, Oakland	KO 2
37	10/10/72	Terry Sorrels, Salt Lake City	KO 2
38	1/22/73	Joe Frazier, Kingston, Jamaica	TKO 2
		(won World Heavyweight title)	
39	9/1/73	Jose Roman, Tokyo	KO 1
40	3/26/74	Ken Norton, Caracus, Venezuela	TKO 2
41	10/30/74	Muhammad Ali, Kinshasa, Zaire	KO by 8
		(lost World Heavyweight title)	
42	1/24/76	Ron Lyle, Las Vegas	KO 5
43	6/15/76	Joe Frazier, Uniondale, N.Y.	TKO 5
44	8/14/76	Scott Le Doux, Utica, N.Y.	KO 3
45	10/15/76	Dino Denis, Hollywood, Fla.	KO 4
46	1/22/77	Pedro Agosto, Pensacola, Fla.	TKO 4
47	3/17/77	Jimmy Young, Hato Rey, P.R.	Lu 12
		(retired after fight)	
48	3/9/87	Steve Zouski, Sacramento	TKO 4
		(first fight of comeback)	
49	7/9/87	Charles Hostetter, Oakland	KO 3
50	9/15/87	Bobby Crabree, Springfield, Mo.	TKO 6
51	11/21/87	Tim Anderson, Orlando	TKO 4
52	12/18/87	Rocky Sekorski, Las Vegas	TKO 3
53	1/23/88	Tom Trimm, Orlando	TKO 1
54	2/5/88	Guido Trane, Las Vegas	TKO 5
55	3/19/88	Dwight Qawi, Las Vegas	TKO 7
56	5/21/88	Frank Williams, Anchorage	TKO 3
57	6/26/88	Carlos Hernandez, Atlantic City	TKO 4
58	8/25/88	Ladislao Mijangos, Ft. Myers	TKO 2
59	9/10/88	Bobby Hitz, Auburn Hills, Mich.	KO 1
60	10/27/88	Tony Fulilangi, Marshall, Tex.	TKO 2

No	Date	Opponent, location	Result
61	12/28/88	David Jaco, Bakersfield, Calif.	KO 1
62	1/26/89	Mark Young, Rochester, N.Y.	TKO 7
63	2/16/89	Manuel de Almeida, Orlando	TKO 3
64	4/30/89	J.B. Williamson, Galveston, Tex.	TKO 5
65	6/1/89	Bert Cooper, Phoenix	TKO 3
66	7/20/89	Everett Martin, Tucson	Wu 10
67	1/15/90	Gerry Cooney, Atlantic City	KO 2
68	4/17/90	Mike Jameson, Stateline, Nev.	TKO 4
69	6/16/90	Adilson Rodrigues, Las Vegas	KO 2
70	7/31/90	Ken Lakusta, Edmonton	KO 3
71	9/25/90	Terry Anderson, Millwall, England	KO 1
72	4/19/91	Evander Holyfield, Atlantic City	Lu 12
		(for World Heavyweight title)	
73	12/7/91	Jimmy Ellis, Reno, Nev.	TKO 3
74	4/11/92	Alex Stewart, Las Vegas	Wm 10
75	1/16/93	Pierre Coetzer, Reno, Nev.	TKO 8
76	6/7/93	Tommy Morrison, Las Vegas	Lu 12
77	11/5/94	Michael Moorer, Las Vegas	KO 10
		(won WBA/IBF Heavyweight titles)	
78	4/22/95	Axel Schulz, Las Vegas	Wm 12
79	11/3/96	Crawford Grimsley, Tokyo	Wu 12

Joe Frazier
Born: Jan. 12, 1944 in Beaufort, S.C.
Pro record: 32-4-1, 27 KO

No	Date	Opponent	Result
1	8/16/65	Woody Gross	TKO 1
2	9/20/65	Michael Bruce	KO 3
3	9/28/65	Ray Staples	KO 2
4	11/11/65	Abe Davis	KO 1
5	1/17/66	Mel Turnbow	KO 1
6	3/4/66	Dick Wipperman	TKO 5
7	4/4/66	Charley Polite	TKO 2
8	4/28/66	Don Smith	KO 3
9	5/19/66	Chuck Leslie	KO 3
10	5/26/66	Memphis Jones	KO 1
11	7/25/66	Billy Daniels	TKO 6
12	9/21/66	Oscar Bonavena	Wu 10
13	11/21/66	Eddie Machen	TKO 10
14	2/21/67	Doug Jones	KO 5
15	4/11/67	Jeff Davis	KO 5
16	5/4/67	George Johnson	Wu 10
17	7/19/67	George Chuvalo	TKO 4
18	10/17/67	Tony Doyle	TKO 2
19	12/18/67	Marion Connors	KO 3
20	3/4/68	Buster Mathis	KO 11
21	6/24/68	Manuel Ramos	TKO 2
22	12/10/68	Oscar Bonavena	Wu 15
23	4/22/69	Dave Zyglewicz	KO 1
24	6/23/69	Jerry Quarry	TKO 7
25	2/6/70	Jimmy Ellis	TKO 5
		(won World Heavyweight title)	
26	11/18/70	Bob Foster	KO 2
27	3/8/71	Muhammad Ali	Wu 15
28	1/15/72	Terry Daniels	TKO 4
29	5/25/72	Ron Stander	TKO 5
30	1/22/73	George Foreman	TKO by 2
		(lost World Heavyweight title)	
31	7/2/73	Joe Bugner	Wu 12
32	1/28/74	Muhammad Ali	Lu 12
33	6/17/74	Jerry Quarry	TKO 5
34	4/1/75	Jimmy Ellis	TKO 9
35	9/30/75	Muhammad Ali	TKO by 14
		(for World Heavyweight title)	
36	6/15/76	George Foreman	KO by 5
37	3/12/81	Floyd Cummings	Draw 10

Major Titleholders

Note the following sanctioning body abbreviations: NBA (Bational Boxing Association), WBA (World Boxing Association), WBC (World Boxing Council), GBR (Great Britin), IBF (International Boxing Federation), plus other national and state commissions. Fighters who retired as champion are indicated by (*) and champions who abandoned or relinquished their titles are indicated by (†).

Heavyweights

Widely accepted champions in CAPITAL letters. Current champions in **bold** type (as of Oct. 1, 1997).

Note: that Muhammad Ali was stripped of his world title in 1967 after refusing induction into the Army (see Muhammad Ali's Career Pro Record). George Foreman was stripped of his WBA and IBF titles in 1995, but remained active as linear champin (see Boxing: Major Bouts 1996-97).

Champion	Held Title	Champion	Held Title
JOHN L. SULLIVAN	1885-92	MUHAMMAD ALI	1978-79*
JAMES J. CORBETT	1892-97	John Tate (WBA)	1979-80
BOB FITZSIMMONS	1897-99	Mike Weaver (WBA)	1980-82
JAMES J. JEFFRIES	1899-1905*	LARRY HOLMES	1980-85
MARVIN HART	1905-06	Michael Dokes (WBA)	1982-83
TOMMY BURNS	1906-08	Gerrie Coetzee (WBA)	1983-84
JACK JOHNSON	1908-15	Tim Witherspoon (WBC)	1984
JESS WILLARD	1915-19	Pinklon Thomas (WBC)	1984-86
JACK DEMPSEY	1919-26	Greg Page (WBA)	1984-85
GENE TUNNEY	1926-28*	MICHAEL SPINKS	1985-87
MAX SCHMELING	1930-32	Tim Witherspoon (WBA)	1986
JACK SHARKEY	1932-33	Trevor Berbick (WBC)	1986
PRIMO CARNERA	1933-34	Mike Tyson (WBC)	1986-87
MAX BAER	1934-35	James (Bonecrusher) Smith (WBA)	1986-87
JAMES J. BRADDOCK	1935-37	Tony Tucker (IBF)	1987
JOE LOUIS	1937-49*	MIKE TYSON (WBC, WBA, IBF)	1987-90
EZZARD CHARLES	1949-51	BUSTER DOUGLAS (WBC, WBA, IBF)	1990
JERSEY JOE WALCOTT	1951-52	EVANDER HOLYFIELD (WBC, WBA, IBF)	1990-92
ROCKY MARCIANO	1952-56*	Riddick Bowe (WBA, IBF)	1992-93
FLOYD PATTERSON	1956-59	Lennox Lewis (WBC)	1992-94
INGEMAR JOHANSSON	1959-60	EVANDER HOLYFIELD (WBA, IBF)	1993-94
FLOYD PATTERSON	1960-62	MICHAEL MOORER (WBA, IBF)	1994
SONNY LISTON	1962-64	Oliver McCall (WBC)	1994-95
CASSIUS CLAY (MUHAMMAD ALI)	1964-70	GEORGE FOREMAN (WBA, IBF)	1994-95
Ernie Terrell (WBA)	1965-67	Bruce Seldon (WBA)	1995-96
Joe Frazier (NY)	1968-70	GEORGE FOREMAN	1995-96
Jimmy Ellis (WBA)	1968-70	Frank Bruno (WBC)	1995-96
JOE FRAZIER	1970-73	Mike Tyson (WBC)	1996†
GEORGE FOREMAN	1973-74	**Michael Moorer** (IBF)	1996—
MUHAMMAD ALI	1974-78	Mike Tyson (WBC)	1996
LEON SPINKS	1978	**Evander Holyfield** (WBA)	1996—
Ken Norton (WBC)	1978	**Lennox Lewis** (WBC)	1997—
Larry Holmes (WBC)	1978-80		

Note: John L. Sullivan held the Bare Knuckle championship from 1882-85.

Light Heavyweights

Widely accepted champions in CAPITAL letters. Current champions in **bold** type.

Champion	Held Title	Champion	Held Title
JACK ROOT	1903	Len Harvey (GBR)	1939-42
GEORGE GARDNER	1903	BILLY CONN	1939-40†
BOB FITZSIMMONS	1903-05	ANTON CHRISTOFORIDIS (NBA)	1941
PHILADELPHIA JACK O'BRIEN	1905-12*	GUS LESNEVICH	1941-48
JACK DILLON	1914-16	Freddie Mills (GBR)	1942-46
BATTLING LEVINSKY	1916-20	FREDDIE MILLS	1948-50
GEORGES CARPENTIER	1920-22	JOEY MAXIM	1950-52
BATTLING SIKI	1922-23	ARCHIE MOORE	1952-62
MIKE McTIGUE	1923-25	Harold Johnson (NBA)	1961
PAUL BERLENBACH	1925-26	HAROLD JOHNSON	1962-63
JACK DELANEY	1926-27†	WILLIE PASTRANO	1963-65
Jimmy Slattery (NBA)	1927	Eddie Cotton (Mich.)	1963-64
TOMMY LOUGHRAN	1927-29	JOSE TORRES	1965-66
JIMMY SLATTERY	1930	DICK TIGER	1966-68
MAXIE ROSENBLOOM	1930-34	BOB FOSTER	1968-74*
George Nichols (NBA)	1932	Vicente Rondon (WBA)	1971-72
Bob Godwin (NBA)	1933	John Conteh (WBC)	1974-77
BOB OLIN	1934-35	Victor Galindez (WBA)	1974-78
JOHN HENRY LEWIS	1935-38	Miguel A. Cuello (WBC)	1977-78
MELIO BETTINA (NY)	1939	Mate Parlov (WBC)	1978

Champion	Held Title	Champion	Held Title
Mike Rossman (WBA)	1978-79	Sugar Ray Leonard (WBC)	1988
Marvin Johnson (WBC)	1978-79	Dennis Andries (WBC)	1989
Matthew (Franklin) Saad Muhammad (WBC)	1979-81	Jeff Harding (WBC)	1989-90
Marvin Johnson (WBA)	1979-80	Dennis Andries (WBC)	1990-91
Eddie (Gregory)		Jeff Harding (WBC)	1991-94
Mustapha Muhammad (WBA)	1980-81	Thomas Hearns (WBA)	1991-92
Michael Spinks (WBA)	1981-83	Iran Barkley (WBA)	1992†
Dwight (Braxton) Muhammad Qawi (WBC)	1981-83	Virgil Hill (WBA)	1992-97
MICHAEL SPINKS	1983-85†	Henry Maske (IBF)	1993-96
J.B.Williamson (WBC)	1985-86	Virgil Hill (WBA/IBF)	1996-97
Slobodan Kacar (IBF)	1985-86	Mike McCallum (WBC)	1994-95
Marvin Johnson (WBA)	1986-87	Fabrice Tiozzo (WBC)	1995-96
Dennis Andries (WBC)	1986-87	Roy Jones Jr. (WBC)	1996
Bobby Czyz (IBF)	1986-87	Montell Griffin (WBC)	1996
Leslie Stewart (WBA)	1987	D. Michaelczewski (WBA/IBF)	1997†
Virgil Hill (WBA)	1987-91	**William Guthrie** (IBF)	1997—
Prince Charles Williams (IBF)	1987-93	**Roy Jones Jr.** (WBC)	1997—
Thomas Hearns (WBC)	1987	**Lou Del Valle** (WBA)	1997—
Donny Lalonde (WBC)	1987-88		

Middleweights

Widely accepted champions in CAPITAL letters. Current champions in **bold** type.

Champion	Held Title	Champion	Held Title
JACK (NONPAREIL) DEMPSEY	1884-91	CARL (BOBO) OLSON	1953-55
BOB FITZSIMMONS	1891-97	SUGAR RAY ROBINSON	1955-57
CHARLES (KID) McCOY	1897-98	GENE FULLMER	1957
TOMMY RYAN	1898-1907	SUGAR RAY ROBINSON	1957
STANLEY KETCHEL	1908	CARMEN BASILIO	1957-58
BILLY PAPKE	1908	SUGAR RAY ROBINSON	1958-60
STANLEY KETCHEL	1908-10	Gene Fullmer (NBA)	1959-62
FRANK KLAUS	1913	PAUL PENDER	1960-61
GEORGE CHIP	1913-14	TERRY DOWNES	1961-62
AL McCOY	1914-17	PAUL PENDER	1962-63
Jeff Smith (AUS)	1914	Dick Tiger (WBA)	1962-63
Mick King (AUS)	1914	DICK TIGER	1963
Jeff Smith (AUS)	1914-15	JOEY GIARDELLO	1963-65
Lee Darcy (AUS)	1915-17	DICK TIGER	1965-66
MIKE O'DOWD	1917-20	EMILE GRIFFITH	1966-67
JOHNNY WILSON	1920-23	NINO BENVENUTI	1967
Wm. Bryan Downey (Ohio)	1921-22	EMILE GRIFFITH	1967-68
Dave Rosenberg (NY)	1922	NINO BENVENUTI	1968-70
Jock Malone (Ohio)	1922-23	CARLOS MONZON	1970-77*
Mike O'Dowd (NY)	1922	Rodrigo Valdez (WBC)	1974-76
Lou Bogash (NY)	1923	RODRIGO VALDEZ	1977-78
HARRY GREB	1923-26	HUGO CORRO	1978-79
TIGER FLOWERS	1926	VITO ANTUOFERMO	1979-80
MICKEY WALKER	1926-31†	ALAN MINTER	1980
GORILLA JONES	1931-32	MARVELOUS MARVIN HAGLER	1980-87
MARCEL THIL	1932-37	SUGAR RAY LEONARD	1987
Ben Jeby (NY)	1932-33	Frank Tate (IBF)	1987-88
Lou Brouillard (NBA, NY)	1933	Sumbu Kalambay (WBA)	1987-89
Vince Dundee (NBA, NY)	1933-34	Thomas Hearns (WBC)	1987-88
Teddy Yarosz (NBA, NY)	1934-35	Iran Barkley (WBC)	1988-89
Babe Risko (NBA, NY)	1935-36	Michael Nunn (IBF)	1988-91
Freddie Steele (NBA, NY)	1936-38	Roberto Duran (WBC)	1989-90*
FRED APOSTOLI	1937-39	Mike McCallum (WBA)	1989-91
Al Hostak (NBA)	1938	Julian Jackson (WBC)	1990-93
Solly Krieger (NBA)	1938-39	James Toney (IBF)	1991-93†
Al Hostak (NBA)	1939-40	Reggie Johnson (WBA)	1992-93
CEFERINO GARCIA	1939-40	Roy Jones Jr. (IBF)	1993-94†
KEN OVERLIN	1940-41	Gerald McClellan (WBC)	1993-95†
Tony Zale (NBA)	1940-41	John David Jackson (WBA)	1993-94
BILLY SOOSE	1941	Jorge Castro (WBA)	1994-97
TONY ZALE	1941-47	Julian Jackson (WBC)	1995
ROCKY GRAZIANO	1947-48	**Bernard Hopkins** (IBF)	1995—
TONY ZALE	1948	Quincy Taylor (WBC)	1995-96
MARCEL CERDAN	1948-49	Shinji Takehara (WBA)	1995-96
JAKE LA MOTTA	1949-51	William Joppy (WBA)	1996-97
SUGAR RAY ROBINSON	1951	**Keith Holmes** (WBC)	1996—
RANDY TURPIN	1951	**Julio Cesar Green** (WBA)	1997—
SUGAR RAY ROBINSON	1951-52*		

Welterweights

Widely accepted champions in CAPITAL letters. Current champions in **bold** type.

Champion	Held Title	Champion	Held Title
PADDY DUFFY	1888-90	CARMEN BASILIO	1955-56
MYSTERIOUS BILLY SMITH	1892-94	JOHNNY SAXTON	1956
TOMMY RYAN	1894-98	CARMEN BASILIO	1956-57†
MYSTERIOUS BILLY SMITH	1898-1900	VIRGIL AKINS	1958
MATTY MATTHEWS	1900	DON JORDAN	1958-60
EDDIE CONNOLLY	1900	BENNY (KID) PARET	1960-61
JAMES (RUBE) FERNS	1900	EMILE GRIFFITH	1961
MATTY MATHEWS	1900-01	BENNY (KID) PARET	1961-62
JAMES (RUBE) FERNS	1901	EMILE GRIFFITH	1962-63
JOE WALCOTT	1901-04	LUIS RODRIGUEZ	1963
THE DIXIE KID	1904-05	EMILE GRIFFITH	1963-66†
HONEY MELLODY	1906-07	Charlie Shipes (Calif.)	1966-67
Mike (Twin) Sullivan	1907-08†	CURTIS COKES	1966-69
Harry Lewis	1908-11	JOSE NAPOLES	1969-70
Jimmy Gardner	1908	BILLY BACKUS	1970-71
Jimmy Clabby	1910-11	JOSE NAPOLES	1971-75
WALDEMAR HOLBERG	1914	Hedgemon Lewis (NY)	1972-73
TOM McCORMICK	1914	Angel Espada (WBA)	1975-76
MATT WELLS	1914-15	JOHN H. STRACEY	1975-76
MIKE GLOVER	1915	CARLOS PALOMINO	1976-79
JACK BRITTON	1915	Pipino Cuevas (WBA)	1976-80
TED (KID) LEWIS	1915-16	WILFREDO BENITEZ	1979
JACK BRITTON	1916-17	SUGAR RAY LEONARD	1979-80
TED (KID) LEWIS	1917-19	ROBERTO DURAN	1980
JACK BRITTON	1919-22	Thomas Hearns (WBA)	1980-81
MICKEY WALKER	1922-26	SUGAR RAY LEONARD	1980-82
PETE LATZO	1926-27	Donald Curry (WBA)	1983-85
JOE DUNDEE	1927-29	Milton McCrory (WBC)	1983-85
JACKIE FIELDS	1929-30	DONALD CURRY	1985-86
YOUNG JACK THOMPSON	1930	LLOYD HONEYGHAN	1986-87
TOMMY FREEMAN	1930-31	JORGE VACA (WBC)	1987-88
YOUNG JACK THOMPSON	1931	LLOYD HONEYGHAN (WBC)	1988-89
LOU BROUILLARD	1931-32	Mark Breland (WBA)	1987
JACKIE FIELDS	1932-33	Marlon Starling (WBA)	1987-88
YOUNG CORBETT III	1933	Tomas Molinares (WBA)	1988-89
JIMMY McLARNIN	1933-34	Simon Brown (IBF)	1988-91
BARNEY ROSS	1934	Mark Breland (WBA)	1989-90
JIMMY McLARNIN	1934-35	MARLON STARLING (WBC)	1989-90
BARNEY ROSS	1935-38	Aaron Davis (WBA)	1990-91
HENRY ARMSTRONG	1938-40	Maurice Blocker (WBC)	1990-91
FRITZIE ZIVIC	1940-41	Meldrick Taylor (WBA)	1991-92
Izzy Jannazzo (Md.)	1940-41	Simon Brown (WBC)	1991
Freddie (Red) Cochrane	1941-46	Maurice Blocker (IBF)	1991-93
MARTY SERVO	1946*	Buddy McGirt (WBC)	1991-93
SUGAR RAY ROBINSON	1946-51†	Crisanto Espana (WBA)	1992-94
Johnny Bratton	1951	Pernell Whitaker (WBC)	1993-97
KID GAVILAN	1951-54	**Felix Trinidad** (IBF)	1993—
JOHNNY SAXTON	1954-55	**Ike Quartey** (WBA)	1994—
TONY DeMARCO	1955	**Oscar De La Hoya** (WBC)	1997—

Lightweights

Widely accepted champions in CAPITAL letters. Current champions in **bold** type.

Champion	Held Title	Champion	Held Title
JACK McAULIFFE	1886-94	SAMMY MANDELL	1926-30
GEORGE (KID) LAVIGNE	1896-99	AL SINGER	1930
FRANK ERNE	1899-02	TONY CANZONERI	1930-33
JOE GANS	1902-04	BARNEY ROSS	1933-35†
JIMMY BRITT	1904-05	TONY CANZONERI	1935-36
BATTLING NELSON	1905-06	LOU AMBERS	1936-38
JOE GANS	1906-08	HENRY ARMSTRONG	1938-39
BATTLING NELSON	1908-10	LOU AMBERS	1939-40
AD WOLGAST	1910-12	Sammy Angott (NBA)	1940-41
WILLIE RITCHIE	1912-14	LEW JENKINS	1940-41
FREDDIE WELSH	1915-17	SAMMY ANGOTT	1941-42
BENNY LEONARD	1917-25*	Beau Jack (NY)	1942-43
JIMMY GOODRICH	1925	Slugger White (Md.)	1943
ROCKY KANSAS	1925-26	Bob Montgomery (NY)	1943

Champion	Held Title	Champion	Held Title
Sammy Angott (NBA)	1943-44	Arturo Frias (WBA)	1981-82
Beau Jack (NY)	1943-44	Ray Mancini (WBA)	1982-84
Bob Montgomery (NY)	1944-47	ALEXIS ARGUELLO	1982-83
Juan Zurita (NBA)	1944-45	Edwin Rosario (WBC)	1983-84
IKE WILLIAMS	1947-51	Choo Choo Brown (IBF)	1984
JAMES CARTER	1951-52	Livingstone Bramble (WBA)	1984-86
LAURO SALAS	1952	Harry Arroyo (IBF)	1984-85
JAMES CARTER	1952-54	Jose Luis Ramirez (WBC)	1984-85
PADDY DeMARCO	1954	Jimmy Paul (IBF)	1985-86
JAMES CARTER	1954-55	Hector Camacho (WBC)	1985-86
WALLACE (BUD) SMITH	1955-56	Edwin Rosario (WBA)	1986-87
JOE BROWN	1956-62	Greg Haugen (IBF)	1986-87
CARLOS ORTIZ	1962-65	Julio Cesar Chavez (WBA)	1987-88
Kenny Lane (Mich.)	1963-64	Jose Luis Ramirez (WBC)	1987-88
ISMAEL LAGUNA	1965	JULIO CESAR CHAVEZ (WBC,WBA)	1988-89
CARLOS ORTIZ	1965-68	Vinny Pazienza (IBF)	1987-88
CARLOS TEO CRUZ	1968-69	Greg Haugen (IBF)	1988-89
MANDO RAMOS	1969-70	Pernell Whitaker (IBF,WBC)	1989-90
ISMAEL LAGUNA	1970	Edwin Rosario (WBA)	1989-90
KEN BUCHANAN	1970-72	Juan Nazario (WBA)	1990
Pedro Carrasco (WBC)	1971-72	PERNELL WHITAKER (IBF, WBC, WBA)	1990-92†
Mando Ramos (WBC)	1972	Joey Gamache (WBA)	1992
ROBERTO DURAN	1972-79†	Miguel A. Gonzalez (WBC)	1992-96
Chango Carmona (WBC)	1972	Tony Lopez (WBA)	1992-93
Rodolfo Gonzalez (WBC)	1972-74	Dingaan Thobela (WBA)	1993
Ishimatsu Suzuki (WBC)	1974-76	Fred Pendleton (IBF)	1993-94
Esteban De Jesus (WBC)	1976-78	**Gussie Nazarov** (WBA)	1993—
Jim Watt (WBC)	1979-81	Rafael Ruelas (IBF)	1994-95
Ernesto Espana (WBA)	1979-80	Oscar De La Hoya (IBF)	1995†
Hilmer Kenty (WBA)	1980-81	Phillip Holiday (IBF)	1995-97
Sean O'Grady (WBA,WAA)	1981	Jean-Baptiste Mendy (WBC)	1996-97
Alexis Arguello (WBC)	1981-82	**Steve Johnston** (WBC)	1997—
Claude Noel (WBA)	1981	**Shane Mosley** (IBF)	1997—
Andrew Ganigan (WAA)	1981-82		

Featherweights

Widely accepted champions in CAPITAL letters. Current champions in **bold** type.

Champion	Held Title	Champion	Held Title
TORPEDO BILLY MURPHY	1890	Leo Rodak (NBA)	1938-39
YOUNG GRIFFO	1890-92	JOEY ARCHIBALD	1939-40
GEORGE DIXON	1892-97	Petey Scalzo (NBA)	1940-41
SOLLY SMITH	1897-98	Jimmy Perrin (La.)	1940-41
Ben Jordan (GBR)	1898-99	HARRY JEFFRA	1940-41
Eddie Santry (GBR)	1899-1900	JOEY ARCHIBALD	1941
DAVE SULLIVAN	1898	Richie Lemos (NBA)	1941
GEORGE DIXON	1898-1900	CHALKY WRIGHT	1941-42
TERRY McGOVERN	1900-01	Jackie Wilson (NBA)	1941-43
YOUNG CORBETT II	1901-04	WILLIE PEP	1942-48
JIMMY BRITT	1904	Jackie Callura (NBA)	1943
ABE ATTELL	1904	Phil Terranova (NBA)	1943-44
BROOKLYN TOMMY SULLIVAN	1904-05	Sal Bartolo (NBA)	1944-46
ABE ATTELL	1906-12	SANDY SADDLER	1948-49
JOHNNY KILBANE	1912-23	WILLIE PEP	1949-50
Jem Driscoll (GBR)	1912-13	SANDY SADDLER	1950-57*
EUGENE CRIQUI	1923	HOGAN (KID) BASSEY	1957-59
JOHNNY DUNDEE	1923-24†	DAVEY MOORE	1959-63
LOUIS (KID) KAPLAN	1925-26†	ULTIMINIO (SUGAR) RAMOS	1963-64
Dick Finnegan (Mass.)	1926-27	VICENTE SALDIVAR	1964-67*
BENNY BASS	1927-28	Howard Winstone (GBR)	1968
TONY CANZONERI	1928	Raul Rojas (WBA)	1968
ANDRE ROUTIS	1928-29	Jose Legra (WBC)	1968-69
BATTLING BATTALINO	1929-32†	Shozo Saijyo (WBA)	1968-71
Tommy Paul (NBA)	1932-33	JOHNNY FAMECHON (WBC)	1969-70
Kid Chocolate (NY)	1932-33	VICENTE SALDIVAR (WBC)	1970
Freddie Miller (NBA)	1933-36	KUNIAKI SHIBATA (WBC)	1970-72
Baby Arizmendi (MEX)	1935-36	Antonio Gomez (WBA)	1971-72
Mike Belloise (NY)	1936-37	CLEMENTE SANCHEZ (WBC)	1972
Petey Sarron (NBA)	1936-37	Ernesto Marcel (WBA)	1972-74
HENRY ARMSTRONG	1937-38†	JOSE LEGRA (WBC)	1972-73
Joey Archibald (NY)	1938-39	EDER JOFRE (WBC)	1973-74

Champion	Held Title	Champion	Held Title
Ruben Olivares (WBA)	1974	Antonio Esparragoza (WBA)	1987-91
Bobby Chacon (WBC)	1974-75	Calvin Grove (IBF)	1988
ALEXIS ARGUELLO (WBA)	1974-76†	Jorge Paez (IBF)	1988-91†
Ruben Olivares (WBC)	1975	Jeff Fenech (WBC)	1988-90†
David (Poison) Kotey (WBC)	1975-76	Marcos Villasana (WBC)	1990-91
DANNY (LITTLE RED) LOPEZ (WBC)	1976-80	Yung-Kyun Park (WBA)	1991-93
Rafael Ortega (WBA)	1977	Troy Dorsey (IBF)	1991
Cecilio Lastra (WBA)	1977-78	Manuel Medina (IBF)	1991-93
Eusebio Pedroza (WBA)	1978-85	Paul Hodkinson (WBC)	1991-93
SALVADOR SANCHEZ (WBC)	1980-82	Tom Johnson (IBF)	1993-97
Juan LaPorte (WBC)	1982-84	Goyo Vargas (WBC)	1993
Wilfredo Gomez (WBC)	1984	Kevin Kelley (WBC)	1993-95
Min-Keun Oh (IBF)	1984-85	Eloy Rojas (WBA)	1993-96
Azumah Nelson (WBC)	1984-88	Alejandro Gonzalez (WBC)	1995
Barry McGuigan (WBA)	1985-86	Manuel Medina (WBC)	1995-96
Ki-Young Chung (IBF)	1985-86	**Wilfredo Vasquez** (WBA)	1996—
Steve Cruz (WBA)	1986-87	**Luisito Espinoza** (WBC)	1995—
Antonio Rivera (IBF)	1986-88	Naseem Hamed (IBF)	1997

Bantamweights

Widely accepted champions in CAPITAL letters. Current champions in **bold** type.

Champion	Held Title	Champion	Held Title
TOMMY (SPIDER) KELLY	1887	LOU SALICA	1940-42
HUGHEY BOYLE	1887-88	MANUEL ORTIZ	1942-47
TOMMY (SPIDER) KELLY	1889	HAROLD DADE	1947
CHAPPIE MORAN	1889-90	MANUEL ORTIZ	1947-50
Tommy (Spider) Kelly	1890-92	VIC TOWEEL	1950-52
GEORGE DIXON	1890-91	JIMMY CARRUTHERS	1952-54*
Billy Plummer	1892-95	ROBERT COHEN	1954-56
JIMMY BARRY	1894-99	Raul Macias (NBA)	1955-57
Pedlar Palmer	1895-99	MARIO D'AGATA	1956-57
TERRY McGOVERN	1899-1900	ALPHONSE HALIMI	1957-59
HARRY HARRIS	1901-02	JOE BECERRA	1959-60*
DANNY DOUGHERTY	1900-01	Johnny Caldwell (EBU)	1961-62
HARRY FORBES	1901-03	EDER JOFRE	1961-65
FRANKIE NEIL	1903-04	MASAHIKO FIGHTING HARADA	1965-68
JOE BOWKER	1904-05	LIONEL ROSE	1968-69
JIMMY WALSH	1905-06†	RUBEN OLIVARES	1969-70
OWEN MORAN	1907-08	CHUCHO CASTILLO	1970-71
MONTE ATTELL	1909-10	RUBEN OLIVARES	1971-72
FRANKIE CONLEY	1910-11	RAFAEL HERRERA	1972
JOHNNY COULON	1911-14	ENRIQUE PINDER	1972-73
Digger Stanley (GBR)	1910-12	ROMEO ANAYA	1973
Charles Ledoux (GBR)	1912-13	Rafael Herrera (WBC)	1973-74
Eddie Campi (GBR)	1913-14	ARNOLD TAYLOR	1973-74
KID WILLIAMS	1914-17	SOO-HWAN HONG	1974-75
Johnny Ertle	1915-18	Rodolfo Martinez (WBC)	1974-76
PETE HERMAN	1917-20	ALFONSO ZAMORA	1975-77
Memphis Pal Moore	1918-19	Carlos Zarate (WBC)	1976-79
JOE LYNCH	1920-21	JORGE LUJAN	1977-80
PETE HERMAN	1921	Lupe Pintor (WBC)	1979-83
JOHNNY BUFF	1921-22	JULIAN SOLIS	1980
JOE LYNCH	1922-24	JEFF CHANDLER	1980-84
ABE GOLDSTEIN	1924	Albert Davila (WBC)	1983-85
CANNONBALL EDDIE MARTIN	1924-25	RICHARD SANDOVAL	1984-86
PHIL ROSENBERG	1925-27	Satoshi Shingaki (IBF)	1984-85
Teddy Baldock (GBR)	1927	Jeff Fenech (IBF)	1985
BUD TAYLOR (NBA)	1927-28†	Daniel Zaragoza (WBC)	1985
Willie Smith (GBR)	1927-28	Miguel (Happy) Lora (WBC)	1985-88
Bushy Graham (NY)	1928-29	GABY CANIZALES	1986
PANAMA AL BROWN	1929-35	BERNARDO PINANGO	1986-87
Sixto Escobar (NBA)	1934-35	Wilfredo Vasquez (WBA)	1987-88
BALTAZAR SANGCHILLI	1935-36	Kevin Seabrooks (IBF)	1987-88
Lou Salica (NBA)	1935	Kaokor Galaxy (WBA)	1988
Sixto Escobar (NBA)	1935-36	Moon Sung-Kil (WBA)	1988-89
TONY MARINO	1936	Kaokor Galaxy (WBA)	1989
SIXTO ESCOBAR	1936-37	Raul Perez (WBC)	1988-91
HARRY JEFFRA	1937-38	Orlando Canizales (IBF)	1988-94†
SIXTO ESCOBAR	1938-39*	Luisito Espinosa (WBA)	1989-91
Georgie Pace (NBA)	1939-40	Greg Richardson	1991

Champion	Held Title	Champion	Held Title
Joichiro Tatsuyoshi (WBC)	1991-92	Harold Mestre (IBF)	1995
Israel Contreras (WBA)	1991-92	Mbulelo Botile (IBF)	1995-97
Eddie Cook (WBA)	1992	Wayne McCullough (WBC)	1995-96
Victor Rabanales (WBC)	1992-93	Veeraphol Sahaprom (WBA)	1995-96
Jorge Julio (WBA)	1992-93	Nana Yaw Konadu (WBA)	1996
Jung-Il Byun (WBC)	1993	Daorung Chuvatana (WBA)	1996-97
Junior Jones (WBA)	1993-94	**Nana Yaw Konadu** (WBA)	1997—
Yasuei Yakushiji (WBC)	1993-95	**Sirimongkol Singmanassak** (WBC)	1996—
John M. Johnson (WBA)	1994	**Tim Austin** (IBF)	1997—
Daorung Chuvatana (WBA)	1994-95		

Flyweights

Widely acceted champions in CAPITAL letters. Current champions in **bold** type.

Champion	Held Title	Champion	Held Title
Sid Smith (GBR)	1913	Erbito Salavarria (WBA)	1975-76
Bill Ladbury (GBR)	1913-14	Alfonso Lopez (WBA)	1976
Percy Jones (GBR)	1914	Guty Espadas (WBA)	1976-78
Joe Symonds (GBR)	1914-16	Betulio Gonzalez (WBA)	1978-79
JIMMY WILDE	1916-23	Chan-Hee Park (WBC)	1979-80
PANCHO VILLA	1923-25	Luis Ibarra (WBA)	1979-80
FIDEL LaBARBA	1925-27*	Tae-Shik Kim (WBA)	1980
FRENCHY BELANGER (NBA,IBU)	1927-28	Shoji Oguma (WBC)	1980-81
Izzy Schwartz (NY)	1927-29	Peter Mathebula (WBA)	1980-81
Johnny McCoy (Calif.)	1927-28	Santos Laciar (WBA)	1981
Newsboy Brown (Calif.)	1928	Antonio Avelar (WBC)	1981-82
FRANKIE GENARO (NBA,IBU)	1928-29	Luis Ibarra (WBA)	1981
Johnny Hill (GBR)	1928-29	Juan Herrera (WBA)	1981-82
SPIDER PLADNER (NBA,IBU)	1929	Prudencio Cardona (WBC)	1982
FRANKIE GENARO (NBA,IBU)	1929-31	Santos Laciar (WBA)	1982-85
Willie LaMorte (NY)	1929-30	Freddie Castillo (WBC)	1982
Midget Wolgast (NY)	1930-35	Eleoncio Mercedes (WBC)	1982-83
YOUNG PEREZ (NBA,IBU)	1931-32	Charlie Magri (WBC)	1983
JACKIE BROWN (NBA,IBU)	1932-35	Frank Cedeno (WBC)	1983-84
BENNY LYNCH	1935-38†	Soon-Chun Kwon (IBF)	1983-85
Small Montana (NY,Calif.)	1935-37	Koji Kobayashi (WBC)	1984
PETER KANE	1938-43	Gabriel Bernal (WBC)	1984
Little Dado (NBA,Calif.)	1938-40	Sot Chitalada (WBC)	1984-88
JACKIE PATERSON	1943-48	Hilario Zapate (WBA)	1985-87
RINTY MONAGHAN	1948-50*	Chong-Kwan Chung (IBF)	1985-86
TERRY ALLEN	1950	Bi-Won Chung (IBF)	1986
SALVADOR (DADO) MARINO	1950-52	Hi-Sup Shin (IBF)	1986-87
YOSHIO SHIRAI	1953-54	Dodie Penalosa (IBF)	1987
PASCUAL PEREZ	1954-60	Fidel Bassa (WBA)	1987-89
PONE KINGPETCH	1960-62	Choi Chang-Ho (IBF)	1987-88
MASAHIKO (FIGHTING) HARADA	1962-63	Rolando Bohol (IBF)	1988
PONE KINGPETCH	1963	Yong-Kang Kim (WBC)	1988-89
HIROYUKI EBIHARA	1963-64	Duke McKenzie (IBF)	1988-89
PONE KINGPETCH	1964-65	Dave McAuley (IBF)	1989-92
SALVATORE BURRINI	1965-66	Sot Chitalada (WBC)	1989-91
Horacio Accavallo (WBA)	1966-68	Jesus Rojas (WBA)	1989-90
WALTER McGOWAN	1966	Yul-Woo Lee (WBA)	1990
CHARTCHAI CHIONOI	1966-69	Leopard Tamakuma (WBA)	1990-91
EFREN TORRES	1969-70	Muangchai Kittikasem (WBC)	1991-92
Hiroyuki Ebihara (WBA)	1969	Yong-Kang Kim (WBA)	1991-92
Bernabe Villacampo (WBA)	1969-70	Rodolfo Blanco (IBF)	1992
CHARTCHAI CHIONOI	1970	**Yuri Arbachakov** (WBC)	1992—
Berkrerk Chartvanchai (WBA)	1970	Aquiles Guzman (WBA)	1992
Masao Ohba (WBA)	1970-73	Phichit Sithbangprachan (IBF)	1992-94†
ERBITO SALAVARRIA	1970-73	David Griman (WBA)	1992-94
Betulio Gonzalez (WBC)	1972	Saen Sor Ploenchit (WBA)	1994-96
Venice Borkorsor (WBC)	1972-73	Francisco Tejedor (IBF)	1995
VENICE BORKORSOR	1973	Danny Romero (IBF)	1995-96
Chartchai Chionoi (WBA)	1973-74	**Marc Johnson** (IBF)	1996—
Betulio Gonzalez (WBA)	1973-74	**Jose Bonilla** (WBA)	1996—
Shoji Oguma (WBC)	1974-75	**Catchai Sasakul** (WBC)*	1997—
Susumu Hanagata (WBA)	1974-75		
Miguel Canto (WBC)	1975-79		

*Sasakul is currently the WBC interim flyweight champion.

Wide World Photos

The middleweight championship fights between **Carmen Basilio** (left) and **Sugar Ray Robinson** in 1957 and '58 both earned Fight of the Year honors. Above, the two trade blows in the closing moments of their 15-round bout at Yankee Stadium on Sept. 23, 1957. Basilio won the title that night on a split decision. Robinson came back six months later at Chicago Stadium to reclaim the crown on a unanimous decision.

Annual Awards

Ring Magazine Fight of the Year

First presented in 1945 by Nat Fleischer, who started *The Ring* magazine in 1922.

Multiple matchups: Muhammad Ali vs. Joe Frazier, Carmen Basilio vs. Sugar Ray Robinson and Graziano vs. Tony Zale (2).

Multiple fights: Muhammad Ali (6); Carmen Basilio (5); George Foreman and Joe Frazier (4); Rocky Graziano, Rocky Marciano and Tony Zale (3); Nino Benvenuti, Bobby Chacon, Ezzard Charles, Marvin Hagler, Thomas Hearns, Sugar Ray Leonard, Floyd Patterson, Sugar Ray Robinson and Jersey Joe Walcott (2).

Year	Winner	Loser	Result	Year	Winner	Loser	Result
1945	Rocky Graziano	Red Cochrane	KO 10	1971	Joe Frazier	Muhammad Ali	W 15
1946	Tony Zale	Rocky Graziano	KO 6	1972	Bob Foster	Chris Finnegan	KO 14
1947	Rocky Graziano	Tony Zale	KO 6	1973	George Foreman	Joe Frazier	KO 2
1948	Marcel Cerdan	Tony Zale	KO 12	1974	Muhammad Ali	George Foreman	KO 8
1949	Willie Pep	Sandy Saddler	W 15	1975	Muhammad Ali	Joe Frazier	KO 14
1950	Jake LaMotta	Laurent Dauthuille	KO 15	1976	George Foreman	Ron Lyle	KO 4
1951	Jersey Joe Walcott	Ezzard Charles	KO 7	1977	Jimmy Young	George Foreman	W 12
1952	Rocky Marciano	Jersey Joe Walcott	KO 13	1978	Leon Spinks	Muhammad Ali	W 15
1953	Rocky Marciano	Roland LaStarza	KO 11	1979	Danny Lopez	Mike Ayala	KO 15
1954	Rocky Marciano	Ezzard Charles	KO 8	1980	Saad Muhammad	Yaqui Lopez	KO 14
1955	Carmen Basilio	Tony DeMarco	KO 12	1981	Sugar Ray Leonard	Thomas Hearns	KO 14
1956	Carmen Basilio	Johnny Saxton	KO 9	1982	Bobby Chacon	Rafael Limon	W 15
1957	Carmen Basilio	Sugar Ray Robinson	W 15	1983	Bobby Chacon	C. Boza-Edwards	W 12
1958	Sugar Ray Robinson	Carmen Basilio	W 15	1984	Jose Luis Ramirez	Edwin Rosario	KO 4
1959	Gene Fullmer	Carmen Basilio	KO 14	1985	Marvin Hagler	Thomas Hearns	KO 3
1960	Floyd Patterson	Ingemar Johansson	KO 5	1986	Stevie Cruz	Barry McGuigan	W 15
1961	Joe Brown	Dave Charnley	W 15	1987	Sugar Ray Leonard	Marvin Hagler	W 12
1962	Joey Giardello	Henry Hank	W 10	1988	Tony Lopez	Rocky Lockridge	W 12
1963	Cassius Clay	Doug Jones	W 10	1989	Roberto Duran	Iran Barkley	W 12
1964	Cassius Clay	Sonny Liston	KO 7	1990	Julio Cesar Chavez	Meldrick Taylor	KO 12
1965	Floyd Patterson	George Chuvalo	W 12	1991	Robert Quiroga	Akeem Anifowoshe	W 12
1966	Jose Torres	Eddie Cotton	W 15	1992	Riddick Bowe	Evander Holyfield	W 12
1967	Nino Benvenuti	Emile Griffith	W 15	1993	Michael Carbajal	Humberto Gonzalez	KO 7
1968	Dick Tiger	Frank DePaula	W 10	1994	Jorge Castro	John David Jackson	TKO 9
1969	Joe Frazier	Jerry Quarry	KO 7	1995	Saman Sorjaturong	Chiquita Gonzalez	KO 7
1970	Carlos Monzon	Nino Benvenuti	KO 12	1996	Evander Holyfield	Mike Tyson	TKO 11

Ring Magazine Fighter of the Year

First presented in 1928 by Nat Fleischer, who started *The Ring* magazine in 1922.

Multiple winners: Muhammad Ali (5); Joe Louis (4); Joe Frazier and Rocky Marciano (3); Ezzard Charles, George Foreman, Marvin Hagler, Thomas Hearns, Evander Holyfield, Ingemar Johansson, Sugar Ray Leonard, Tommy Loughran, Floyd Patterson, Sugar Ray Robinson, Barney Ross, Dick Tiger and Mike Tyson (2)

Year		Year		Year		Year	
1928	Gene Tunney	1945	Willie Pep	1963	Cassius Clay	1980	Thomas Hearns
1929	Tommy Loughran	1946	Tony Zale	1964	Emile Griffith	1981	Sugar Ray Leonard
1930	Max Schmeling	1947	Gus Lesnevich	1965	Dick Tiger		& Salvador Sanchez
1931	Tommy Loughran	1948	Ike Williams	1966	No award	1982	Larry Holmes
1932	Jack Sharkey	1949	Ezzard Charles	1967	Joe Frazier	1983	Marvin Hagler
1933	No award			1968	Nino Benvenuti	1984	Thomas Hearns
1934	Tony Canzoneri	1950	Ezzard Charles	1969	Jose Napoles	1985	Donald Curry
	& Barney Ross	1951	Sugar Ray Robinson				& Marvin Hagler
1935	Barney Ross	1952	Rocky Marciano	1970	Joe Frazier	1986	Mike Tyson
1936	Joe Louis	1953	Carl (Bobo) Olson	1971	Joe Frazier	1987	Evander Holyfield
1937	Henry Armstrong	1954	Rocky Marciano	1972	Muhammad Ali	1988	Mike Tyson
1938	Joe Louis	1955	Rocky Marciano		& Carlos Monzon	1989	Pernell Whitaker
1939	Joe Louis	1956	Floyd Patterson	1973	George Foreman		
		1957	Carmen Basilio	1974	Muhammad Ali	1990	Julio Cesar Chavez
1940	Billy Conn	1958	Ingemar Johansson	1975	Muhammad Ali	1991	James Toney
1941	Joe Louis	1959	Ingemar Johansson	1976	George Foreman	1992	Riddick Bowe
1942	Sugar Ray Robinson	1960	Floyd Patterson	1977	Carlos Zarate	1993	Michael Carbajal
1943	Fred Apostoli	1961	Joe Brown	1978	Muhammad Ali	1994	Roy Jones Jr.
1944	Beau Jack	1962	Dick Tiger	1979	Sugar Ray Leonard	1995	Oscar De La Hoya
						1996	Evander Holyfield

Note: Cassius Clay changed his name to Muhammad Ali after winning the heavyweight title in 1964.

Former Champions Who Have Won Back Heavyweight Title

Only eight times since 1892 has the heavyweight championship been lost by a fighter who was able to win it back. Seven men have done it and Muhammad Ali and Evander Holyfield have done it twice.

	Lost To	Won Back From		Lost To	Won Back From
Floyd Patterson	Johansson (1959)	Johansson (1960)	Michael Moorer	Foreman (1994)	Schulz (1996)*
Muhammad Ali	Frazier (1970)	Foreman (1974)	Mike Tyson	Douglas (1990)	Bruno (1996)
Muhammad Ali	L. Spinks (1978)	L. Spinks (1978)	Evander Holyfield	Moorer (1994)	Tyson (1996)
Tim Witherspoon	Thomas (1984)	Tubbs (1986)			
Evander Holyfield	Bowe (1992)	Bowe (1993)	*Moorer won the vacant IBF title in a fight with Germany's Axel Schulz		
George Foreman	Ali (1974)	Moorer (1994)			

All-Time Leaders

As compiled by *The Ring Record Book and Encyclopedia*.

Knockouts

		Division	Career	No
1	Archie Moore	Lt. Heavy	1936-63	130
2	Young Stribling	Heavy	1921-33	126
3	Billy Bird	Welter	1920-48	125
4	George Odwel	Welter	1930-45	114
5	Sugar Ray Robinson	Middle	1940-65	110
6	Sandy Saddle	Feather	1944-56	103
7	Sam Langford	Middle	1902-26	102
8	Henry Armstrong	Welter	1931-45	100
9	Jimmy Wilde	Fly	1911-23	98
10	Len Wickwar	Lt. Heavy	1928-47	93

Total Bouts

		Division	Career	No
1	Len Wickwar	Lt. Heavy	1928-47	463
2	Jack Britton	Welter	1905-30	350
3	Johnny Dundee	Feather	1910-32	333
4	Billy Bird	Welter	1920-48	318
5	George Marsden	n/a	1928-46	311
6	Maxie Rosenbloom	Lt. Heavy	1923-39	299
7	Harry Greb	Middle	1913-26	298
8	Young Stribling	Lt. Heavy	1921-33	286
9	Battling Levinsky	Lt. Heavy	1910-29	282
10	Ted (Kid) Lewis	Welter	1909-29	279

The only boxer in history to hold a world title in more weight classes than **Roberto Duran** is **Sugar Ray Leonard**. Leonard was a world champion in a record five divisions from 1979 to 1988.

Triple Champions

Fighters who have won widely-accepted world titles in more than one division. Henry Armstrong is the only fighter listed to hold three titles simultaneously. Note that (*) indicates title claimant.

Sugar Ray Leonard (5) WBC Welterweight (1979-80,80-82); WBA Jr. Middleweight (1981); WBC Middleweight (1987); WBC Super Middleweight (1988-90); WBC Light Heavyweight (1988).

Roberto Duran (4) Lightweight (1972-79); WBC Welterweight (1980); WBA Jr. Middleweight (1983-84); WBC Middleweight (1989-90).

Thomas Hearns (4) WBA Welterweight (1980-81); WBC Jr. Middleweight (1982-84); WBC Light Heavyweight (1987); WBA Light Heavyweight (1991); WBC Middleweight (1987-88).

Pernell Whitaker (4) IBF/WBC/WBA Lightweight (1989-92); IBF Jr. Welterweight (1992-93); WBC Welterweight (1993-97); WBC Jr. Middleweight (1995).

Alexis Arguello (3) WBA Featherweight (1974-77); WBC Jr. Lightweight (1978-80); WBC Lightweight (1981-83).

Henry Armstrong (3) Featherweight (1937-38); Welterweight (1938-40); Lightweight (1938-39).

Iran Barkley (3) WBC Middleweight (1988-89); IBF Super Middleweight (1992-93); WBA Light Heavyweight (1992).

Wilfredo Benitez (3) Jr. Welterweight (1976-79); Welterweight (1979); WBC Jr. Middleweight (1981-82).

Tony Canzoneri (3) Featherweight (1928); Lightweight (1930-33); Jr. Welterweight (1931-32,33).

Julio Cesar Chavez (3) WBC Jr. Lightweight (1984-87); WBA/WBC Lightweight (1987-89); WBC/IBF Jr. Welterweight (1989-91); WBC Jr. Welterweight (1991-94, 1994).

Jeff Fenech (3) IBF Bantamweight (1985); WBC Jr. Featherweight (1986-88); WBC Featherweight (1988-90).

Bob Fitzsimmons (3) Middleweight (1891-97); Light Heavyweight (1903-05); Heavyweight (1897-99).

Wilfredo Gomez (3) WBC Super Bantamweight (1977-83); WBC Featherweight (1984); WBA Jr. Lightweight (1985-86).

Emile Griffith (3) Welterweight (1961,62-63,63-66); Jr. Middleweight (1962-63); Middleweight (1966-67,67-68).

Roy Jones Jr. (3) IBF Middleweight (1993-94); IBF Super Middleweight (1994-96); WBC Light Heavyweight (1996, 1997—).

Terry McGovern (3) Bantamweight (1899-1900); Featherweight (1900-01); Lightweight* (1900-01).

Barney Ross (3) Lightweight (1933-35); Jr. Welterweight (1933-35); Welterweight (1934, 35-38).

Miscellaneous Sports

Emotions at the Little League World Series spill over for Mission Viejo shortstop and relief pitcher **Adam Sorgi**, who surrendered a game-tying three-run homer in the sixth inning. Guadalupe, Mexico went on to win 5-4.

World Wide Photos

CHESS

World Champions

PCA champion Garry Kasparov of Russia, fell to Deep Blue, IBM's RS-6000 supercomputer, in a six game match held in New York City during the first week of May. It was the first time that a computer defeated a world chess champion in a multi-game match. Kasparov beat Deep Blue in a six-game match 15 months previous, but the computer had since been upgraded and its programmers had been assisted on strategic nuances by chess grandmasters. Even still, Kasparov and Deep Blue traded wins in the first two games before playing to draws in the next three.

In the final game it seemed that Kasparov blundered and was forced to resign after just one hour and 19 moves. Each of the first five games last around four hours. After game six, an irate Kasparov complained that the match was unfair because he was unable to see records of Deep Blue's past games, while Deep Blue was programmed with all of his. After calming down, Kasparov admitted that he was tired and that the computer was playing above his comprehension. "When I see something that is beyond my understanding," he said, "I'm scared."

The match, widely touted as something more than a simple chess match, was billed by many as a battle of man and machine. The man took home the $400,000 loser's share of the $1.1 million prize fund, while spokesmen for the machine said they would use the winner's purse to fund further research.

The 34-year-old Kasparov suggested that Deep Blue enter the world of competitive chess tournaments. "It's time for Deep Blue to start playing real chess," said Kasparov. "I personally guarantee you I will tear it to pieces."

Unfortunately for Kasparov, he will never get that chance. IBM announced late in 1997 that it was retiring Deep Blue from chess to work on other projects.

Kasparov became the youngest man to win the world chess championship when he beat fellow Russian Anatoly Karpov in 1985 at age 22. In 1993, Kasparov and then-No. 1 challenger Nigel Short of England broke away from the established International Chess Federation (FIDE) to form the PCA. The FIDE retaliated by stripping Kasparov of their world title and arranging a playoff that was won by Karpov, the former title-holder.

Years		Years		Years	
1866-94	Wilhelm Steinitz, Austria	1948-57	Mikhail Botvinnik, USSR	1969-72	Boris Spassky, USSR
1894-1921	Emanuel Lasker, Germany	1957-58	Vassily Smyslov, USSR	1972-75	Bobby Fischer, USA*
1921-27	Jose Capablanca, Cuba	1958-59	Mikhail Botvinnik, USSR	1975-85	Anatoly Karpov, USSR
1927-35	Alexander Alekhine, France	1960-61	Mikhail Tal, USSR	1985—	Garry Kasparov, RUS
1935-37	Max Euwe, Holland	1961-63	Mikhail Botvinnik, USSR		*Fischer defaulted championship in 1975
1937-46	Alexander Alekhine, France	1963-69	Tigran Petrosian, USSR		

U.S. Champions

New Yorker Joel Benjamin, who served as the GM "trainer" for IBM's Deep Blue team (see above), won the 1997 U.S. Chess Championships in the 14-player, round robin tournament that ran Aug. 22-Sept. 12 in Chandler, Ariz. Benjamin defeated Larry Christiansen, 3.5-2.5 in the "best of six"finals match, and won the $10,000 first prize.

Years		Years		Years	
1857-71	Paul Morphy	1954-57	Arthur Bisguier	1984-85	Lev Alburt
1871-76	George Mackenzie	1957-61	Bobby Fischer	1986	Yasser Seirawan
1876-80	James Mason	1961-62	Larry Evans	1987	Joel Benjamin
1880-89	George Mackenzie	1962-68	Bobby Fischer		& Nick DeFirmian
1889-90	Samuel Lipschutz	1968-69	Larry Evans	1988	Michael Wilder
1890	Jackson Showalter	1969-72	Samuel Reshevsky	1989	Roman Dzindzichashvili,
1890-91	Max Judd	1972-73	Robert Byrne		Stuart Rachels
1891-92	Jackson Showalter	1973-74	Lubomir Kavalek		& Yasser Seirawan
1892-94	Samuel Lipschutz		& John Grefe	1990	Lev Alburt
1894	Jackson Showalter	1974-77	Walter Browne	1991	Gata Kamsky
1894-95	Albert Hodges	1978-80	Lubomir Kabalek	1992	Patrick Wolff
1895-97	Jackson Showalter	1980-81	Larry Evans,	1993	Alexander Shabalov
1897-1906	Harry Pillsbury		Larry Christiansen		& Alex Yermolinsky
1906-09	Vacant		& Walter Browne	1994	Boris Gulko
1909-36	Frank Marshall	1981-83	Walter Browne	1995	Alexander Ivanov
1936-44	Samuel Reshevsky		& Yasser Seirawan	1996	Alexander Yermolinsky
1944-46	Arnold Denker	1983	Roman Dzindzichashvili,	1997	Joel Benjamin
1946-48	Samuel Reshevsky		Larry Christiansen		
1948-51	Herman Steiner		& Walter Browne		
1951-54	Larry Evans				

DOGS

Iditarod Trail Sled Dog Race

Martin Buser became a three-time champion winning the 25th annual Iditarod Trail Sled Dog Race on Mar. 11. Buser held off a late charge from former winner Doug Swingley and crossed under the burled arch that marks the finish line in Nome 9 days, 8 hours, 31 minutes and 45 seconds after leaving the starting line in Anchorage. In odd-numbered years, the trail follows the 1,161-mile Southern Route, while in even-numbered years it takes the slightly-different 1,151-mile long Northern Route. Buser, Swingley and defending champ Jeff King swapped the lead several times early on until Buser made his move, only stopping for minutes at the Shageluk checkpoint and giving him a 90 minute lead that he never surrendered. Buser, who finished the course with 10 of his original 16 dogs, claimed the $50,000 first prize along with a new truck worth $38,000. Swingley, the 1995 champion and only Non-Alaskan ever to win the race, placed second.

Multiple winners: Rick Swenson (5); Susan Butcher (4); Martin Buser (3); Rick Mackey (2).

Year		Elapsed Time	Year		Elapsed Time
1973	Dick Wilmarth	20 days, 00:49:41	1986	Susan Butcher	11 days, 15:06:00
1974	Carl Huntington	20 days, 15:02:07	1987	Susan Butcher	11 days, 02:05:13
1975	Emmitt Peters	14 days, 14:43:45	1988	Susan Butcher	11 days, 11:41:40
1976	Gerald Riley	18 days, 22:58:17	1989	Joe Runyan	11 days, 05:24:34
1977	Rick Swenson	16 days, 16:27:13	1990	Susan Butcher	11 days, 01:53:23
1978	Dick Mackey	14 days, 18:52:24	1991	Rick Swenson	12 days, 16:34:39
1979	Rick Swenson	15 days, 10:37:47	1992	Martin Buser	10 days, 19:17:00
1980	Joe May	14 days, 07:11:51	1993	Jeff King	10 days, 15:38:15
1981	Rick Swenson	12 days, 08:45:02	1994	Martin Buser	10 days, 13:02:39
1982	Rick Swenson	16 days, 04:40:10	1995	Doug Swingley	9 days, 02:42:19*
1983	Rick Mackey	12 days, 14:10:44	1996	Jeff King	9 days, 05:43:13
1984	Dean Osmar	12 days, 15:07:33	1997	Martin Buser	9 days, 08:31:45
1985	Libby Riddles	18 days, 00:20:17	*Course record.		

Westminster Kennel Club

Best in Show

Ch. Parsifal di Casa Netzer, a standard schnauzer, won best in show at the 121st annual Westminster Kennel Club show on Feb. 11 at Madison Square Garden in New York. The schnauzer, owned by Rita Holloway and Gabrio Del Torre, was the first ever of its breed to win the best in show. The Westminster show is the most prestigious dog show in the country, and one of America's oldest annual sporting events.

Multiple winners: Ch. Warren Remedy (3); Ch. Chinoe's Adamant James, Ch. Comejo Wycollar Boy, Ch. Flornell Spicy Piece of Halleston; Ch. Matford Vic, Ch. My Own Brucie, Ch. Pendley Calling of Blarney, Ch. Rancho Dobe's Storm (2).

Year		Breed	Year		Breed
1907	Warren Remedy	Fox Terrier	1940	My Own Brucie	Cocker Spaniel
1908	Warren Remedy	Fox Terrier	1941	My Own Brucie	Cocker Spaniel
1909	Warren Remedy	Fox Terrier	1942	Wolvey Pattern of Edgerstoune	W. Highland Terrier
1910	Sabine Rarebit	Fox Terrier	1943	Pitter Patter of Piperscroft	Miniature Poodle
1911	Tickle Em Jock	Scottish Terrier	1944	Flornell Rarebit of Twin Ponds	Welsh Terrier
1912	Kenmore Sorceress	Airedale	1945	Shieling's Signature	Scottish Terrier
1913	Strathway Prince Albert	Bulldog	1946	Hetherington Model Rhythm	Fox Terrier
1914	Brentwood Hero	Old English Sheepdog	1947	Warlord of Mazelaine	Boxer
1915	Matford Vic	Old English Sheepdog	1948	Rock Ridge Night Rocket	Bedling. Terrier
1916	Matford Vic	Old English Sheepdog	1949	Mazelaine's Zazarac Brandy	Boxer
1917	Comejo Wycollar Boy	Fox Terrier	1950	Walsing Winning Trick of Edgerstoune	Scot. Terrier
1918	Haymarket Faultless	Bull Terrier	1951	Bang Away of Sirrah Crest	Boxer
1919	Briergate Bright Beauty	Airedale	1952	Rancho Dobe's Storm	Doberman
1920	Comejo Wycollar Boy	Fox Terrier	1953	Rancho Dobe's Storm	Doberman
1921	Midkiff Seductive	Cocker Spaniel	1954	Carmor's Rise and Shine	Cocker Spaniel
1922	Boxwood Barkentine	Airedale	1955	Kippax Fearnought	Bulldog
1923	No best-in-show award		1956	Wilber White Swan	Toy Poodle
1924	Barberryhill Bootlegger	Sealyham	1957	Shirkhan of Grandeur	Afghan Hound
1925	Governor Moscow	Pointer	1958	Puttencove Promise	Standard Poodle
1926	Signal Circuit	Fox Terrier	1959	Fontclair Festoon	Miniature Poodle
1927	Pinegrade Perfection	Sealyham	1960	Chick T'Sun of Caversham	Pekingese
1928	Talavera Margaret	Fox Terrier	1961	Cappoquin Little Sister	Toy Poodle
1929	Land Loyalty of Bellhaven	Collie	1962	Elfinbrook Simon	W. Highland Terrier
1930	Pendley Calling of Blarney	Fox Terrier	1963	Wakefield's Black Knight	English Springer Spaniel
1931	Pendley Calling of Blarney	Fox Terrier	1964	Courtenay Fleetfoot of Pennyworth	Whippet
1932	Nancolleth Markable	Pointer	1965	Carmichaels Fanfare	Scottish Terrier
1933	Warland Protector of Shelterock	Airedale	1966	Zeloy Mooremaides Magic	Fox Terrier
1934	Flornell Spicy Bit of Halleston	Fox Terrier	1967	Bardene Bingo	Scottish Terrier
1935	Nunsoe Duc de la Terrace of Blakeen	Stan. Poodle	1968	Stingray of Derryabah	Lakeland Terrier
1936	St. Margaret Magnificent of Clairedale	Sealyham	1969	Glamoor Good News	Skye Terrier
1937	Flornell Spicy Bit of Halleston	Fox Terrier	1970	Arriba's Prima Donna	Boxer
1938	Daro of Maridor	English Setter	1971	Chinoe's Adamant James	E.S. Spaniel
1939	Ferry v.Rauhfelsen of Giralda	Doberman	1972	Chinoe's Adamant James	E.S. Spaniel

Dogs (Cont.)

Year	Breed	Year	Breed
1973 Acadia Command Performance	Standard Poodle	1986 Marjetta National Acclaim	Pointer
1974 Gretchenhof Columbia River	German SH Pointer	1987 Covy Tucker Hill's Manhattan	German Shepherd
1975 Sir Lancelot of Barvan	Old Eng. Sheepdog	1988 Great Elms Prince Charming II	Pomeranian
1976 Jo Ni's Red Baron of Crofton	Lakeland Terrier	1989 Royal Tudor's Wild As The Wind	Doberman
1977 Dersade Bobby's Girl	Sealyham	1990 Wendessa Crown Prince	Pekingese
1978 Cede Higgens	Yorkshire Terrier	1991 Whisperwind on a Carousel	Stan. Poodle
1979 Oak Tree's Irishtocrat	Irish Water Spaniel	1992 Lonesome Dove	Fox Terrier
1980 Sierra Cinnar	Siberian Husky	1993 Salilyn's Condor	E.S. Spaniel
1981 Dhandy Favorite Woodchuck	Pug	1994 Chidley Willum	Norwich Terrier
1982 St. Aubrey Dragonora of Elsdon	Pekingese	1995 Gaelforce Post Script	Scottish Terrier
1983 Kabik's The Challenger	Afghan Hound	1996 Clussex Country Sunrise	Clumber Spaniel
1984 Seaward's Blackbeard	Newfoundland	1997 Parsifal di Casa Netzer	Standard Schnauzer
1985 Braeburn's Close Encounter	Scottish Terrier		

FISHING

IGFA All-Tackle World Records

All-tackle records are maintained for the heaviest fish of any species caught on any line up to 130-lb (60 kg) class and certified by the International Game Fish Association. Records logged through Aug. 4, 1997. **Address:** 3000 East Las Olas Blvd., Ft. Lauderdale, FL, 33316. **Telephone:** 954-941-3474.

FRESHWATER FISH

Species	Lbs-Oz	Where Caught	Date	Angler
Barramundi	63- 2	Queensland, Australia	Apr. 28, 1991	Scott Barnsley
Bass, Guadalupe	3-11	Lake Travis, TX	Sept. 25, 1983	Allen Christenson Jr.
Bass, largemouth	22- 4	Montgomery Lake, GA	June 2, 1932	George W. Perry
Bass, redeye	8-12	Apalachicola River, FL	Jan. 28, 1995	Carl W. Davis
Bass, Roanoke	1- 5	Nottoway River, VA	Nov. 11, 1991	Tom Elkins
Bass, rock	3- 0	York River, Ontario	Aug. 1, 1974	Peter Gulgin
Bass, smallmouth	10-14	Dale Hollow, TN	Apr. 24, 1969	John T. Gorman
Bass, spotted	9- 9	Pine Flat Lake, CA	Oct. 12, 1996	Kirk Sakamoto
Bass, striped (landlocked)	.67- 8	O'Neill Forebay, San Luis, CA	May 7, 1992	Hank Ferguson
Bass, Suwannee	3-14	Suwannee River, FL	Mar. 2, 1985	Ronnie Everett
Bass, white	6-13	Lake Orange, VA	July 31, 1989	Ronald L. Sprouse
Bass, whiterock	.25-15	Warrior River, AL	Sept. 13, 1996	E.H. (Sonny) Hodges
Bass, yellow	2- 4	Lake Monroe, IN	Mar. 27, 1977	Donald L. Stalker
Bass, yellow hybrid	2- 5	Kiamichi River, OK	Mar. 26, 1991	George Edwards
Bluegill	4-12	Ketona Lake, AL	Apr. 9, 1950	T.S. Hudson
Bowfin	21- 8	Florence, SC	Jan. 29, 1980	Robert L. Harmon
Buffalo, bigmouth	70- 5	Bussey Brake, Bastrop, LA	Apr. 21, 1980	Delbert Sisk
Buffalo, black	55- 8	Cherokee Lake, TN	May 3, 1984	Edward H. McLain
Buffalo, smallmouth	68- 8	Lake Hamilton, AR	May 16, 1984	Jerry L. Dolezal
Bullhead, black	8- 0	Lake Waccabuc, NY	Aug. 1, 1951	Kani Evans
Bullhead, brown	5- 11	Cedar Creek, FL	Mar. 28, 1995	Robert Bengis
Bullhead, yellow	4- 4	Mormon Lake, AZ	May 11, 1984	Emily Williams
Burbot	18- 11	Angenmanelren, Sweden	Oct. 22, 1996	Magit Agren
Carp	.75-11	Lac de St. Cassien, France	May 21, 1987	Leo van der Gugten
Catfish, blue	111- 0	Wheeler's Reservoir, TN	July 5, 1996	William McKinley
Catfish, channel	58- 0	Santee-Cooper Res., SC	July 7, 1964	W.B. Whaley
Catfish, flathead	91- 4	Lake Lewisville, TX	Mar. 28, 1982	Mike Rogers
Catfish, flatwhiskered	9- 4	Rio Paraquai, Brazil	Sept. 11, 1996	Cavour Pieranti
Catfish, gilded	85- 8	Amazon River, Brazil	Nov. 15, 1986	Gilberto Fernandes
Catfish, redtail	97- 7	Amazon River, Brazil	July 16, 1988	Gilberto Fernandes
Catfish, sharptoothed	.79- 5	Orange River, S. Africa	Dec. 5, 1992	Hennie Moller
Catfish, white	18-14	Inverness, FL	Sept. 21, 1991	Jim Miller
Char, Arctic	32- 9	Tree River, Canada	July 30, 1981	Jeffery Ward
Crappie, black	4- 8	Kerr Lake, VA	Mar. 1, 1981	L. Carl Herring Jr.
Crappie, white	5- 3	Enid Dam, MS	July 31, 1957	Fred L. Bright
Dolly Varden	18- 9	Mashutuk River, AK	July 13, 1993	Richard B. Evans
Dorado	51- 5	Corrientes, Argentina	Sept. 27, 1984	Armando Giudice
Drum, freshwater	54- 8	Nickajack Lake, TN	Apr. 20, 1972	Benny E. Hull
Gar, alligator	.279- 0	Rio Grande, TX	Dec. 2, 1951	Bill Valverde
Gar, Florida	21- 3	Boca Raton, FL	June 3, 1981	Jeff Sabol
Gar, longnose	50- 5	Trinity River, TX	July 30, 1954	Townsend Miller
Gar, shortnose	5-12	Rend Lake, Ill.	July 16, 1995	Donna K. Willmart
Gar, spotted	9-12	Lake Mevia, TX	Apr. 7, 1994	Rick Rivard
Goldfish	6-10	Lake Hodges, CA	Apr. 17, 1996	Florentino M. Abena
Grayling, Arctic	5-15	Katseyedie River, N.W.T.	Aug. 16, 1967	Jeanne P. Branson

Species	Lbs-Oz	Where Caught	Date	Angler
Inconnu	53- 0	Pah River, AK	Aug. 20, 1986	Lawrence E. Hudnall
Kokanee	9- 6	Okanagan Lake, Brit. Columbia	June 18, 1988	Norm Kuhn
Muskellunge	67- 8	Hayward, WI	July 24, 1949	Cal Johnson
Muskellunge, tiger	51- 3	Lac Vieux-Desert, WI-MI	July 16, 1919	John A. Knobla
Peacock, butterfly	9- 8	Kendale Lakes, FL	Mar. 11, 1993	Jerry Gomez
Peacock, speckled	27- 0	Rio Negro, Brazil	Dec. 4, 1994	Gerald (Doc) Lawson
Perch, Nile	191- 8	Lake Victoria, Kenya	Sept. 5, 1991	Andy Davison
Perch, white	4-12	Messalonskee Lake, ME	June 4, 1949	Mrs. Earl Small
Perch, yellow	4- 3	Bordentown, NJ	May, 1865	Dr. C.C. Abbot
Pickerel, chain	9- 6	Homerville, GA	Feb. 17, 1961	Baxley McQuaig Jr.
Pickerel, grass	1- 0	Dewart Lake, Indiana	June 9, 1990	Mike Berg
Pickerel, redfin	1-15	Redhook, NY	Oct. 16, 1988	Bill Stagias
Pike, northern	55- 1	Lake of Grefeern, W.Germany	Oct.16, 1986	Lothar Louis
Redhorse, greater	9- 3	Salmon River, Pulaski, NY	May 11, 1985	Jason Wilson
Redhorse, silver	11- 7	Plum Creek, WI	May 29, 1985	Neal D.G. Long
Salmon, Atlantic	79- 2	Tana River, Norway	1928	Henrik Henriksen
Salmon, chinook	97- 4	Kenai River, AK	May 17, 1985	Les Anderson
Salmon, chum	35- 0	Edye Pass, Brit. Columbia	July 11, 1995	Todd Johansson
Salmon, coho	33- 4	Salmon River, Pulaski, NY	Sept. 27, 1989	Jerry Lifton
Salmon, lake	18- 4	Lake Tanganyika, Zambia	Dec. 1, 1987	Steve Robinson
Salmon, pink	13- 1	St. Mary's River, Ontario	Sept. 23, 1992	Ray Higaki
Salmon, sockeye	15- 3	Kenai River, AK	Aug. 9, 1987	Stan Roach
Sauger	8-12	Lake Sakakawea, ND	Oct. 6, 1971	Mike Fischer
Shad, American	11- 4	Conn.River, S.Hadley, MA	May 19, 1986	Bob Thibodo
Shad, gizzard	4- 6	Lake Michigan, IN	Mar. 2, 1996	Mike Berg
Sturgeon, lake	168- 0	Georgian Bay, Canada	May 29, 1982	Edward Paszkowski
Sturgeon, white	468- 0	Benicia, CA	July 9, 1983	Joey Pallotta 3rd
Tigerfish, giant	97- 0	Zaire River, Kinshasa, Zaire	July 9, 1988	Raymond Houtmans
Tilapia	6- 5	Lake Arsenal, Costa Rica	Feb. 10, 1995	Marvin C. Smith
Trout, Apache	5- 3	White Mountain, AZ	May 29, 1991	John Baldwin
Trout, brook	14- 8	Nipigon River, Ontario	July, 1916	Dr. W.J. Cook
Trout, brown	40- 4	Little Red River, AR	May 9, 1992	Rip Collins
Trout, bull	32- 0	Lake Pend Orielle, ID	Oct. 27, 1949	N.L. Higgins
Trout, cutthroat	41- 0	Pyramid Lake, NV	Dec., 1925	John Skimmerhorn
Trout, golden	11- 0	Cooks Lake, WY	Aug. 5, 1948	Charles S. Reed
Trout, lake	66- 8	Great Bear Lake, N.W.T.	July 19, 1991	Rodney Harback
Trout, rainbow	42- 2	Bell Island, AK	June 22, 1970	David Robert White
Trout, tiger	20-13	Lake Michigan, WI	Aug. 12, 1978	Peter M. Friedland
Walleye	25- 0	Old Hickory Lake, TN	Apr. 1, 1960	Mabry Harper
Warmouth	2- 7	Guess Lake, Holt, FL	Oct. 19, 1985	Tony D. Dempsey
Whitefish, lake	14- 6	Meaford, Ontario	May 21, 1984	Dennis M. Laycock
Whitefish, mountain	5- 6	Rioh River, Saskatchewan	June 15, 1988	John R. Bell
Whitefish, round	6- 0	Putahow River, Manitoba	June 14, 1984	Allan J. Ristori
Zander	25- 2	Trosa, Sweden	June 12, 1986	Harry Lee Tennison

SALTWATER FISH

Species	Lbs-Oz	Where Caught	Date	Angler
Albacore	88- 2	Gran Canaria, Canary Islands	Nov. 19, 1977	Siegfried Dickemann
Amberjack, greater	155-10	Challenger Bank, Bermuda	June 24, 1981	Joseph Dawson
Amberjack, pacific	104- 0	Baja Calif., Mexico	July 4, 1984	Richard Cresswell
Barracuda, great	85- 0	Christmas Is., Rep. of Kiribati	Apr. 11, 1992	John W. Helfrich
Barracuda, Mexican	21- 0	Phantom Island, Costa Rica	Mar. 27, 1987	E. Greg Kent
Barracuda, pickhandle	25- 5	Scottburgh, South Africa	July 3, 1996	Demetrios Stamatis
Bass, barred sand	13- 3	Huntington Beach, CA	Aug. 29, 1988	Robert Halal
Bass, black sea	9- 8	Virginia Beach, VA	Jan. 9, 1987	Joe Mizelle Jr.
Bass, European	20-11	Stes Maries de la Mer, France	May 6, 1986	Jean Baptiste Bayle
Bass, giant sea	563- 8	Anacapa Island, CA	Aug. 20, 1968	J.D. McAdam Jr.
Bass, striped	78- 8	Atlantic City, NJ	Sept. 21, 1982	Albert R. McReynolds
Bluefish	31-12	Hatteras, NC	Jan. 30, 1972	James M. Hussey
Bonefish	19- 0	Zululand, South Africa	May 26, 1962	Brian W. Batchelor
Bonito, Atlantic	18- 4	Faial Island, Azores	July 8, 1953	D. Gama Higgs
Bonito, Pacific	14-12	San Benitos Is., Baja Calif., Mexico	Oct. 12, 1980	Jerome H. Rilling
Cabezon	23- 0	Juan de Fuca Strait, WA	Aug. 4, 1990	Wesley Hunter
Cobia	135-9	Shark Bay, W. Australia	July 9, 1985	Peter W. Goulding
Cod, Atlantic	98-12	Isle of Shoals, NH	June 8, 1969	Alphonse Bielevich
Cod, Pacific	30-0	Andrew Bay, AK	July 7, 1984	Donald R. Vaughn
Conger	133-4	South Devon, England	June 5, 1995	Vic Evans
Dolphin	87-0	Papagallo Gulf, Costa Rica	Sept. 25, 1976	Manuel Salazar
Drum, black	113-1	Lewes, DE	Sept. 15, 1975	Gerald M. Townsend
Drum, red	94-2	Avon, NC	Nov. 7, 1984	David G. Deuel

Fishing (Cont.)

Species	Lbs-Oz	Where Caught	Date	Angler
Eel, marbled	36-1	Durban, S. Africa	June 10, 1984	Ferdie van Nooten
Eel, American	9-4	Cape May, NJ	Nov. 9, 1995	Jeff Pennick
Flounder, southern	20-9	Nassau Sound, FL	Dec. 23, 1983	Larenza Mungin
Flounder, summer	22-7	Montauk, NY	Sept. 15, 1975	Charles Nappi
Grouper, warsaw	436-12	Gulf of Mexico, Destin, FL	Dec. 22, 1985	Steve Haeusler
Haddock	11-11	Perkins Cove, Ogunquit, ME	Sept. 12, 1991	Jim Mailea
Halibut, Atlantic	255-4	Gloucester, MA	July 28, 1989	Sonny Manley
Halibut, California	53-4	Santa Rosa Island, CA	July 7, 1988	Russell J. Harmon
Halibut, Pacific	459-0	Dutch Harbor, AK	June 11, 1996	Jack Tragis
Jack, almaco (Pacific)	132-0	La Paz, Baja Calif., Mexico	July 21, 1964	Howard H. Hahn
Jack, crevalle	57-5	Barra do Bwanza, Angola	Oct. 10, 1992	Cam Nicolson
Jack, horse-eye	24-8	Miami, FL	Dec. 20, 1982	Tito Schnau
Jewfish	680-0	Fernandina Beach, FL	May 20, 1961	Lynn Joyner
Kawakawa	29-0	Clarion Island, Mexico	Dec. 17, 1986	Ronald Nakamura
Lingcod	69-0	Langara Is., Brit. Columbia	June 16, 1992	Murray M.Romer
Mackerel, cero	17-2	Islamorada, FL	Apr. 5, 1986	G. Michael Mills
Mackerel, king	90-0	Key West, FL	Feb. 16, 1976	Norton I. Thomton
Mackerel, Spanish	13-0	Ocracoke Inlet, NC	Nov. 4, 1987	Robert Cranton
Marlin, Atlantic blue	1402-2	Vitoria, Brazil	Feb. 29, 1992	Paulo R.A. Amorim
Marlin, Black	1560-0	Cabo Blanco, Peru	Aug. 4, 1953	A.C. Glassell Jr.
Marlin, Pacific blue	1376-0	Kaaiwi Point, Kona, HI	May 31, 1982	Jay W. deBeaubien
Marlin, striped	494-0	Tutakaka, New Zealand	Jan. 16, 1986	Bill Boniface
Marlin, white	181-14	Vitoria, Brazil	Dec. 8, 1979	Evandro Luiz Coser
Permit	53-4	Lake Worth, FL	Mar. 25, 1994	Roy Brooker
Pollack	27-6	Salcombe, Devon, England	Jan. 16, 1986	Robert S. Milkins
Pollock	50-0	Salstraumen, Norway	Nov. 30, 1996	Thor-Magnus Ukang
Pompano, African	50-8	Daytona Beach, FL	Apr. 21, 1990	Tom Sargent
Roosterfish	114-0	La Paz, Baja Calif., Mexico	June 1, 1960	Abe Sackheim
Runner, blue	8-7	Port Arkansas, TX	Feb. 13, 1995	Allen E. Windecker
Runner, rainbow	37-9	Clarion Island, Mexico	Nov. 21, 1991	Tom Pfleger
Sailfish, Atlantic	141-10	Luanda, Angola	Feb. 19, 1994	Alfredo de Sousa Neves
Sailfish, Pacific	221-0	Santa Cruz Is., Ecuador	Feb. 12, 1947	C.W. Stewart
Seabass, white	83-12	San Felipe, Mexico	Mar. 31, 1953	L.C. Baumgardner
Seatrout, spotted	17-7	Ft. Pierce, FL	May 11, 1995	Craig F. Carson
Shark, blue	454-0	Martha's Vineyard, MA	July 19, 1996	Pete Bergin
Shark, great white	2664-0	Ceduna, S. Australia	Apr. 21, 1959	Alfred Dean
Shark, greenland	1708-9	Trondheimsfjord, Norway	Oct.18, 1987	Terje Nordtvedt
Shark, hammerhead	991-0	Sarasota, FL	May 30, 1982	Allen Ogle
Shark, shortfin mako	1115-0	Black River, Mauritius	Nov. 16, 1988	Patrick Guillanton
Shark, porbeagle	507-0	Pentland Firth, Scotland	Mar. 9, 1993	Christopher Bennet
Shark, bigeye thresher	802-0	Tutukaka, New Zealand	Feb. 8, 1981	Dianne North
Shark, tiger	1780-0	Cherry Grove, SC	June 14, 1964	Walter Maxwell
Snapper, cubera	121-8	Cameron, LA	July 5, 1982	Mike Hebert
Snapper, red	50-4	Gulf of Mexico, LA	June 23, 1996	Capt. Doc Kennedy
Snook	53-10	Parismina Ranch, Costa Rica	Oct. 18, 1978	Gilbert Ponzi
Spearfish, Mediterranean	90-13	Madeira Island, Portugal	June 2, 1980	Joseph Larkin
Swordfish	1182-0	Iquique, Chile	May 7, 1953	L. Marron
Tarpon	283-4	Sherbro Is., Sierra Leone	Apr. 16, 1991	Yvon Victor Sebag
Tautog	24-0	Wachapreague, VA	Aug. 25, 1987	Gregory R. Bell
Tuna, Atlantic bigeye	392-6	Gran Canaria, Puerto Rico	July 25, 1997	Dieter Vogel
Tuna, blackfin	45-8	Key West, FL	May 4, 1996	Sam J. Burnett
Tuna, bluefin	1496-0	Aulds Cove, Nova Scotia	Oct. 26, 1979	Ken Fraser
Tuna, longtail	79-2	Montague Is., NSW, Australia	Apr. 12, 1982	Tim Simpson
Tuna, Pacific bigeye	435-0	Cabo Blanco, Peru	Apr. 17, 1957	Dr. Russell Lee
Tuna, skipjack	45-4	Flathead Bank, Mexico	Nov. 16, 1996	Brian Evans
Tuna, southern bluefin	348-5	Whakatane, New Zealand	Jan. 16, 1981	Rex Wood
Tuna, yellowfin	388-12	San Benedicto Island, Mexico	Apr. 1, 1977	Curt Wiesenhutter
Tunny, little	35-2	Cape de Garde, Algeria	Dec. 14, 1988	Jean Yves Chatard
Wahoo	158-8	Lareto, CA	June 10, 1996	Keith Winter
Weakfish	19-2	Jones Beach, Long Island, NY	Oct. 11, 1984	Dennis R. Rooney
	19-2	Delaware Bay, DE	May 20, 1989	William E. Thomas

BASS Masters Classic

Dion Hibdon, 30, came from fourth place on Aug. 9 to win the 27th annual BASS Masters Classic Championship by a slim margin on Lake Logan Martin near Pell City, Ala. The professional angler from Stover, Mo., had a three-day catched of 34 pounds, 13 ounces earning him the $100,000 winner's check.

"I would have had an even better day if it had been a bluebird, bright sunny day," Hibdon said. "I got the right bites, but I broke off five times."

Hibdon, who has competed on the BASS Master Tournament trail since he was 18, became the second member of the Hibdon family to land the Classic championship. His father, Guido, won the title in 1988 on Virginia's James River.

The 1997 Classic set a record for the most limits of five bass caught in the event's history with 94. Dalton Bobo of Northport, Ala. was the runner-up, with a catch of 34 pounds, 12 ounces.

The BASS Masters Classic is fishing's version of the Masters golf tournament. Invitees to the three-day event include the 25 top-ranked pros on the BASS tour and the five top-ranked anglers from each BASSMASTER Invitational circuit. Anglers may weigh only seven bass per day and each bass must be at least 12 inches long. Competitors are allowed only seven rods and reels and are limited to the tackle they can pack into two tournament-approved tackleboxes. Only artificial lures are permitted. The first Classic, held at Lake Mead, Nevada in 1971, was a $10,000 winner-take-all event.

Multiple winners: Rick Clunn (4); George Cochran, Bobby Murray and Hank Parker (2).

Year		Weight	Year		Weight
1971	Bobby Murray, Hot Springs, Ark	43 -11	1985	Jack Chancellor, Phenix City, Ala	45 - 0
1972	Don Butler, Tulsa, Okla	38 -11	1986	Charlie Reed, Broken Bow, Okla	23 - 9
1973	Rayo Breckenridge, Paragould, Ark	52 - 8	1987	George Cochran, N. Little Rock, Ark	15 - 5
1974	Tommy Martin, Hemphill, Tex	33 -7	1988	Guido Hibdon, Gravois Mills, Mo	28 - 8
1975	Jack Hains, Rayne, La	45 - 4	1989	Hank Parker, Denver, N.C	31 - 6
1976	Rick Clunn, Montgomery, Tex	59 -15	1990	Rick Clunn, Montgomery, Tex	34 - 5
1977	Rick Clunn, Montgomery, Tex	27 -7	1991	Ken Cook, Meers, Okla	33 - 2
1978	Bobby Murray, Nashville, Tenn	37 - 9	1992	Robert Hamilton Jr., Brandon, Miss	59 - 6
1979	Hank Parker, Clover, S.C	31 - 0	1993	David Fritts, Lexington, N.C	48 - 6
1980	Bo Dowden, Natchitoches, La	54 -10	1994	Bryan Kerchal, Newtown, Conn	36 - 7
1981	Stanley Mitchell, Fitzgerald, Ga	35 - 2	1995	Mark Davis, Mount Ida, Ark.	47-14
1982	Paul Elias, Laurel, Miss	32 - 8	1996	George Cochran, Hot Springs, Ark.	31-14
1983	Larry Nixon, Hemphill, Tex	18 - 1	1997	Dion Hibdon, Stover, Mo.	34-13
1984	Rick Clunn, Montgomery, Tex	75 - 9			

POWER BOAT RACING

APBA Gold Cup

Dave Villwock repeated as the winning driver at the APBA Gold Cup but this year he did it in a different boat. In 1996, Villwock captured the coveted Cup at the helm of PICO/American Dream. In 1997, the 42-year-old veteran driver piloted Miss Budweiser to a win on the extremely choppy, 2.5-mile Detroit River course ahead of Mitch Evans in the Appian Jeronimo and Mike Hanson in the DeWALT Tools entry.

The American Power Boat Association Gold Cup for unlimited hydroplane racing is the oldest active motor sports trophy in North America. The first Gold Cup was competed for on the Hudson River in New York in June and September of 1904. Since then several cities have hosted the race, led by Detroit (28 times, including 1990) and Seattle (14). Note that (*) indicates driver was also owner of the winning boat.

Drivers with multiple wins: Chip Hanauer (10); Bill Muncey (8); Gar Wood (5); Dean Chenoweth (4); Caleb Bragg, Tom D'Eath, Lou Fageol, Ron Musson, George Reis and Jonathon Wainwright (3); Danny Foster, George Henley, Vic Kliesrath, E.J. Schroeder, Bill Schumacher, Zalmon G.Simmons Jr., Joe Taggart, Mark Tate, George Townsend and Dave Villwock (2).

Year	Boat	Driver	Avg.MPH	Year	Boat	Driver	Avg.MPH
1904	Standard (June)	Carl Riotte*	23.160	1924	Baby Bootlegger	Caleb Bragg*	45.302
1904	Vingt-Et-Un II (Sept.)	W. Sharpe Kilmer*	24.900	1925	Baby Bootlegger	Caleb Bragg*	47.240
				1926	Greenwich Folly	George Townsend*	47.984
1905	Chip I	J. Wainwright*	15.000	1927	Greenwich Folly	George Townsend*	47.662
1906	Chip II	J. Wainwright*	25.000	1928	Not held		
1907	Chip II	J. Wainwright*	23.903	1929	Imp	Richard Hoyt*	48.662
1908	Dixie II	E.J. Schroeder*	29.938	1930	Hotsy Totsy	Vic Kliesrath*	52.673
1909	Dixie II	E.J. Schroeder*	29.590	1931	Hotsy Totsy	Vic Kliesrath*	53.602
1910	Dixie III	F.K. Burnham*	32.473	1932	Delphine IV	Bill Horn	57.775
1911	MIT II	J.H. Hayden*	37.000	1933	El Lagarto	George Reis*	56.260
1912	P.D.Q. II	A.G. Miles*	39.462	1934	El Lagarto	George Reis*	55.000
1913	Ankle Deep	Cas Mankowski*	42.779	1935	El Lagarto	George Reis*	55.056
1914	Baby Speed Demon I	Jim Blackton & Bob Edgren	48.458	1936	Impshi	Kaye Don	45.735
				1937	Notre Dame	Clell Perry	63.675
1915	Miss Detroit	Johnny Milot & Jack Beebe	37.656	1938	Alagi	Theo Rossi*	64.340
				1939	My Sin	Z.G. Simmons Jr.*	66.133
1916	Miss Minneapolis	Bernard Smith	48.860	1940	Hotsy Totsy III	Sidney Allen*	48.295
1917	Miss Detroit II	Gar Wood*	54.410	1941	My Sin	Z.G. Simmons Jr.*	52.509
1918	Miss Detroit II	Gar Wood	51.619	1942-45	Not held		
1919	Miss Detroit III	Gar Wood*	42.748	1946	Tempo VI	Guy Lombardo*	68.132
1920	Miss America I	Gar Wood*	62.022	1947	Miss Peps V	Danny Foster	57.000
1921	Miss America I	Gar Wood*	52.825	1948	Miss Great Lakes	Danny Foster	46.845
1922	Packard Chriscraft	J.G. Vincent*	40.253	1949	My Sweetie	Bill Cantrell	73.612
1923	Packard Chriscraft	Caleb Bragg	43.867	1950	Slo-Mo-Shun IV	Ted Jones	78.216

Power Boat Racing (Cont.)

Year	Boat	Driver	Avg.MPH
1951	Slo-Mo-Shun V	Lou Fageol	90.871
1952	Slo-Mo-Shun IV	Stan Dollar	79.923
1953	Slo-Mo-Shun IV	Joe Taggart	99.108
		& Lou Fageol	
1954	Slo-Mo-Shun IV	Joe Taggart	92.613
		& Lou Fageol	
1955	Gale V	Lee Schoenith	99.552
1956	Miss Thriftaway	Bill Muncey	96.552
1957	Miss Thriftaway	Bill Muncey	101.787
1958	Hawaii Kai III	Jack Regas	103.000
1959	Maverick	Bill Stead	104.481
1960	Not held		
1961	Miss Century 21	Bill Muncey	99.678
1962	Miss Century 21	Bill Muncey	100.710
1963	Miss Bardahl	Ron Musson	105.124
1964	Miss Bardahl	Ron Musson	103.433
1965	Miss Bardahl	Ron Musson	103.132
1966	Tahoe Miss	Mira Slovak	93.019
1967	Miss Bardahl	Bill Shumacher	101.484
1968	Miss Bardahl	Bill Shumacher	108.173
1969	Miss Budweiser	Bill Sterett	98.504
1970	Miss Budweiser	Dean Chenoweth	99.562
1971	Miss Madison	Jim McCormick	98.043
1972	Atlas Van Lines	Bill Muncey	104.277
1973	Miss Budweiser	Dean Chenoweth	99.043

Year	Boat	Driver	Avg.MPH
1974	Pay 'n Pak	George Henley	104.428
1975	Pay 'n Pak	George Henley	108.921
1976	Miss U.S.	Tom D'Eath	100.412
1977	Atlas Van Lines	Bill Muncey*	111.822
1978	Atlas Van Lines	Bill Muncey*	111.412
1979	Atlas Van Lines	Bill Muncey*	100.765
1980	Miss Budweiser	Dean Chenoweth	106.932
1981	Miss Budweiser	Dean Chenoweth	116.932
1982	Atlas Van Lines	Chip Hanauer	120.050
1983	Atlas Van Lines	Chip Hanauer	118.507
1984	Atlas Van Lines	Chip Hanauer	130.175
1985	Miller American	Chip Hanauer	120.643
1986	Miller American	Chip Hanauer	116.523
1987	Miller American	Chip Hanauer	127.620
1988	Miss Circus Circus	Chip Hanauer	123.756
		& Jim Prevost	
1989	Miss Budweiser	Tom D'Eath	131.209
1990	Miss Budweiser	Tom D'Eath	143.176
1991	Winston Eagle	Mark Tate	137.771
1992	Miss Budweiser	Chip Hanauer	136.282
1993	Miss Budweiser	Chip Hanauer	141.296
1994	Smokin' Joe's	Mark Tate	145.532
1995	Miss Budweiser	Chip Hanauer	149.160
1996	Pico/American Dream	Dave Villwock	149.328
1997	Miss Budweiser	Dave Villwock	129.366

PRO RODEO

All-Around Champion Cowboy

Joe Beaver of Huntsville, Tex., beat incredible odds to repeat as the All-Around champion cowboy at the National Finals Rodeo on Dec. 15, 1996 in Las Vegas. Beaver, who broke his wrist that June at the Eastern Oregon Livestock and Rodeo, thought his chance at another title might be over. Against the advice of his doctor, Beaver returned to action early and managed to get back in the race. "The Beav," down by $25,000 in the standings entering the final two rounds at the NFR was able to overtake Herbert Theirot and hold off Roy Cooper to win his second gold buckle as the all-around champ.

The Professional Rodeo Cowboys Association (PRCA) title of All-Around World Champion Cowboy goes to the rodeo athlete who wins the most prize money in a single year in two or more events, earning a minimum of $2,000 in each event. Only prize money earned in sanctioned PRCA rodeos is counted. From 1929-44, All-Around champions were named by the Rodeo Association of America (earnings for those years is not available).

Multiple winners: Tom Ferguson, Larry Mahan and Ty Murray (6); Jim Shoulders (5); Lewis Feild and Dean Oliver (3); Joe Beaver, Everett Bowman, Louis Brooks, Clay Carr, Bill Linderman, Phil Lyne, Gerald Roberts, Casey Tibbs and Harry Tompkins (2).

Year		Year		Year		Year	
1929	Earl Thode	1934	Leonard Ward	1939	Paul Carney	1944	Louis Brooks
1930	Clay Carr	1935	Everett Bowman	1940	Fritz Truan	1945-46	No award
1931	John Schneider	1936	John Bowman	1941	Homer Pettigrew		
1932	Donald Nesbit	1937	Everett Bowman	1942	Gerald Roberts		
1933	Clay Carr	1938	Burel Mulkey	1943	Louis Brooks		

Year		Earnings	Year		Earnings	Year		Earnings
1947	Todd Whatley	$18,642	1964	Dean Oliver	$31,150	1981	Jimmie Cooper	$105,861
1948	Gerald Roberts	21,766	1965	Dean Oliver	33,163	1982	Chris Lybbert	123,709
1949	Jim Shoulders	21,495	1966	Larry Mahan	40,358	1983	Roy Cooper	153,391
1950	Bill Linderman	30,715	1967	Larry Mahan	51,996	1984	Dee Pickett	122,618
1951	Casey Tibbs	29,104	1968	Larry Mahan	49,129	1985	Lewis Feild	130,347
1952	Harry Tompkins	30,934	1969	Larry Mahan	57,726	1986	Lewis Feild	166,042
1953	Bill Linderman	33,674	1970	Larry Mahan	41,493	1987	Lewis Feild	144,335
1954	Buck Rutherford	40,404	1971	Phil Lyne	49,245	1988	Dave Appleton	121,546
1955	Casey Tibbs	42,065	1972	Phil Lyne	60,852	1989	Ty Murray	134,806
1956	Jim Shoulders	43,381	1973	Larry Mahan	64,447	1990	Ty Murray	213,772
1957	Jim Shoulders	33,299	1974	Tom Ferguson	66,929	1991	Ty Murray	244,231
1958	Jim Shoulders	32,212	1975	Tom Ferguson	50,300	1992	Ty Murray	225,992
1959	Jim Shoulders	32,905	1976	Tom Ferguson	87,908	1993	Ty Murray	297,896
1960	Harry Tompkins	32,522	1977	Tom Ferguson	65,981	1994	Ty Murray	246,170
1961	Benny Reynolds	31,309	1978	Tom Ferguson	83,734	1995	Joe Beaver	141,753
1962	Tom Nesmith	32,611	1979	Tom Ferguson	96,272	1996	Joe Beaver	166,103
1963	Dean Oliver	31,329	1980	Paul Tierney	105,568			

Guadalupe's **Gabriel Alvarez** gets set to score the tying run after beling a 250-foot three-run home run in the bottom of the sixth inning at the Little League World Series at Williamport, Pa. The team from Mexico overcame a 4-1 deficit in the final inning to beat Mission Viejo, Calif., 5-4, for the championship on August 23, 1997.

LITTLE LEAGUE BASEBALL

World Series

Multiple winners: Taiwan (16); California (5); Connecticut and Pennsylvania (4); Japan, Mexico and New Jersey (3); New York, South Korea and Texas (2).

Year	Winner	Score	Loser	Year	Winner	Score	Loser
1947	Williamsport, PA	16-7	Lock Haven, PA	1973	Tainan City, Taiwan	12-0	Tucson, AZ
1948	Lock Haven, PA	6-5	St. Petersburg, FL	1974	Kao Hsiung, Taiwan	12-1	Red Bluff, CA
1949	Hammonton, NJ	5-0	Pensacola, FL	1975	Lakewood, NJ	4-3*	Tampa, FL
1950	Houston, TX	2-1	Bridgeport, CT	1976	Tokyo, Japan	10-3	Campbell, CA
1951	Stamford, CT	3-0	Austin, TX	1977	Li-Teh, Taiwan	7-2	El Cajon, CA
1952	Norwalk, CT	4-3	Monongahela, PA	1978	Pin-Tung, Taiwan	11-1	Danville, CA
1953	Birmingham, AL	1-0	Schenectady, NY	1979	Hsien, Taiwan	2-1	Campbell, CA
1954	Schenectady, NY	7-5	Colton, CA	1980	Hua Lian, Taiwan	4-3	Tampa, FL
1955	Morrisville, PA	4-3	Merchantville, NJ	1981	Tai-Chung, Taiwan	4-2	Tampa, FL
1956	Roswell, NM	3-1	Merchantville, NJ	1982	Kirkland, WA	6-0	Hsien, Taiwan
1957	Monterrey, Mexico	4-0	La Mesa, CA	1983	Marietta, GA	3-1	Barahona, D. Rep.
1958	Monterrey, Mexico	10-1	Kankakee, IL	1984	Seoul, S. Korea	6-2	Altamonte, FL
1959	Hamtramck, MI	12-0	Auburn, CA	1985	Seoul, S. Korea	7-1	Mexicali, Mex.
1960	Levittown, PA	5-0	Ft. Worth, TX	1986	Tainan Park, Taiwan	12-0	Tucson, AZ
1961	El Cajon, CA	4-2	El Campo, TX	1987	Hua Lian, Taiwan	21-1	Irvine, CA
1962	San Jose, CA	3-0	Kankakee, IL	1988	Tai Ping, Taiwan	10-0	Pearl City, HI
1963	Granada Hills, CA	2-1	Stratford, CT	1989	Trumbull, CT	5-2	Kaohsiung, Taiwan
1964	Staten Island, NY	4-0	Monterrey, Mex.	1990	Taipei, Taiwan	9-0	Shippensburg, PA
1965	Windsor Locks, CT	3-1	Stoney Creek, Can.	1991	Taichung, Taiwan	11-0	Danville, CA
1966	Houston, TX	8-2	W. New York, NJ	1992	Long Beach, CA	6-0†	Zamboanga, Phil.
1967	West Tokyo, Japan	4-1	Chicago, IL	1993	Long Beach, CA	3-2	Panama
1968	Osaka, Japan	1-0	Richmond, VA	1994	Maracaibo, Venezuela	4-3	Northridge, CA
1969	Taipei, Taiwan	5-0	Santa Clara,CA	1995	Tainan, Taiwan	17-3	Spring, TX
1970	Wayne, NJ	2-0	Campbell, CA	1996	Taipei, Taiwan	13-3	Cranston, RI
1971	Tainan, Taiwan	12-3	Gary, IN				(called after 5th inn.)
1972	Taipei, Taiwan	6-0	Hammond, IN	1997	Guadalupe, Mexico	5-4	Mission Viejo, CA

*Foreign teams were banned from the tournament in 1975, but allowed back in the following year.

†In 1992, Zamboanga City of the Philippines beat Long Beach, 15-4, but was stripped of the title a month later when it was discovered that the team had used several players from outside the city limits. Long Beach was then awarded the title by forfeit, 6-0 (one run for each inning of the game).

SOAP BOX DERBY

All-American Soap Box Derby

Eleven-year-old Wade Wallace of Elk Hart, Indiana won the Master's division at the 60th annual All-American Soap Box Derby in Akron, Ohio on Aug. 9. Wallace edge out Akron's Loren Hurst with a time of 28.40 to win the Master's title. Dolline Vance of Salem, Ore. took the Super Stock, clocking a time of 28.67 and Mark Stephens of Waynesboro Suburban, Va. won the Stock division with a winning time of 28.94.

The All-American Soap Box Derby is a coasting race for small gravity-powered cars built by their drivers and assembled within strict guidelines on size, weight and cost. The Derby got its name in the 1930s when most cars were built from wooden soap boxes. Held every summer on the second Saturday of August at Derby Downs in Akron, the Soap Box Derby is open to all boys and girls from 9 to 16 years old who qualify.

There are three competitive divisions: 1. Stock (ages 9-16)— made up of generic, prefab racers that come from Derby-approved kits, can be assembled in four hours and don't exceed 200 pounds when driver, car and wheels are weighed together; 2. Super Stock (ages 10-16)— the same as Stock only with a weight limit of 220 pounds; 3. Masters (ages 11-16)— made up of racers designed by the drivers, but constructed with Derby-approved hardware. The racing ramp at Derby Downs is 953.75 feet with an 11 percent grade.

One champion reigned at the All-American Soap Box Derby each year from 1934-75; Junior and Senior division champions from 1976-87; Kit and Masters champions from 1988-91; Stock, Kit and Masters champions from 1992-94; Stock, Super Stock and Masters champions starting in 1995.

Year		Hometown	Age	Year		Hometown	Age
1934	Robert Turner	Muncie, IN	11	1979	JR: Russell Yurk	Flint, MI	10
1935	Maurice Bale Jr.	Anderson, IN	13		SR: Craig Kitchen	Akron, OH	14
1936	Herbert Muench Jr.	St. Louis	14	1980	JR: Chris Fulton	Indianapolis	11
1937	Robert Ballard	White Plains, NY	12		SR: Dan Porul	Sherman Oaks, CA	12
1938	Robert Berger	Omaha, NE	14	1981	JR: Howie Fraley	Portsmouth, OH	11
1939	Clifton Hardesty	White Plains, NY	11		SR: Tonia Schlegel	Hamilton, OH	13
1940	Thomas Fisher	Detroit	12	1982	JR: Carol A. Sullivan	Rochester, MN	10
1941	Claude Smith	Akron, OH	14		SR: Matt Wolfgang	Lehigh Val., PA	12
1942-45	Not held			1983	JR: Tony Carlini	Del Mar, CA	10
1946	Gilbert Klecan	San Diego	14		SR: Mike Burdgick	Flint, MI	14
1947	Kenneth Holmboe	Charleston, WV	14	1984	JR: Chris Hess	Hamilton, OH	11
1948	Donald Strub	Akron, OH	13		SR: Anita Jackson	St. Louis	15
1949	Fred Derks	Akron, OH	15	1985	JR: Michael Gallo	Danbury, CT	12
					SR: Matt Sheffer	York, PA	14
1950	Harold Williamson	Charleston, WV	15	1986	JR: Marc Behan	Dover, NH	9
1951	Darwin Cooper	Williamsport, PA	15		SR: Tami Jo Sullivan	Lancaster, OH	13
1952	Joe Lunn	Columbus, GA	11	1987	JR: Matt Margules	Danbury, CT	11
1953	Fred Mohler	Muncie, IN	14		SR: Brian Drinkwater	Bristol, CT	14
1954	Richard Kemp	Los Angeles	14	1988	KIT: Jason Lamb	Des Moines, IA	10
1955	Richard Rohrer	Rochester, NY	14		MAS: David Duffield	Kansas City	13
1956	Norman Westfall	Rochester, NY	14	1989	KIT: David Schiller	Dayton, OH	12
1957	Terry Townsend	Anderson, IN	14		MAS: Faith Chavarria	Ventura, CA	12
1958	James Miley	Muncie, IN	15				
1959	Barney Townsend	Anderson, IN	13	1990	MAS: Sami Jones	Salem, OR	13
					KIT: Mark Mihal	Valparaiso, IN	12
1960	Fredric Lake	South Bend, IN	11	1991	MAS: Danny Garland	San Diego, CA	14
1961	Dick Dawson	Wichita, KS	13		KIT: Paul Greenwald	Saginaw, MI	13
1962	David Mann	Gary, IN	14	1992	MAS: Bonnie Thornton	Redding, CA	14
1963	Harold Conrad	Duluth, MN	12		KIT: Carolyn Fox	Sublimity, OR	11
1964	Gregory Schumacher	Tacoma, WA	14		STK: Loren Hurst	Hudson, OH	14
1965	Robert Logan	Santa Ana, CA	12	1993	MAS: Dean Lutton	Delta, OH	14
1966	David Krussow	Tacoma, WA	12		KIT: D.M. Del Ferraro	Stow, OH	12
1967	Kenneth Cline	Lincoln, NE	13		STK: Owen Yuda	Boiling Springs, PA	10
1968	Branch Lew	Muncie, IN	11	1994	MAS: D.M. Del Ferraro	Akron, OH	13
1969	Steve Souter	Midland, TX	12		KIT: Joel Endres	Akron, OH	14
					STK: Kristina Damond	Jamestown, NY	13
1970	Samuel Gupton	Durham, NC	13	1995	MAS: J. Fensterbush	Kingman, AZ	11
1971	Larry Blair	Oroville, CA	13		SS: Darcie Davisson	Kingman, AZ	11
1972	Robert Lange Jr.	Boulder, CO	14		STK: Karen Thomas	Jamestown, NY	11
1973	Bret Yarborough	Elk Grove, CA	11	1996	MAS: Tim Scrofano	Conneaut, OH	12
1974	Curt Yarborough	Elk Grove, CA	11		SS: Jeremy Phillips	Charlestown, WV	14
1975	Karren Stead	Lower Bucks, PA	11		STK: Matt Perez	No. Canton, OH	12
1976	JR: Phil Raber	Sugarcreek, OH	11	1997	MAS: Wade Wallace	Elk Hart, IN	11
	SR: Joan Ferdinand	Canton, OH	14		SS: Dolline Vance	Salem, OR	13
1977	JR: Mark Ferdinand	Canton, OH	10		STK: Mark Stephens	Waynesboro, VA	13
	SR: Steve Washburn	Bristol, CT	15				
1978	JR: Darren Hart	Salem, OR	11				
	SR: Greg Cardinal	Flint, MI	13				

Welsh full back Justin Thomas, under pressure from the French pack, clears his lines in the early going of their **1996 Five Nations rugby** match at Cardiff Arms Park. Wales, holder of a record 33 Five Nations titles, would go on to win the match, 16-15.

Five Nations Rugby

The annual Five Nations rugby tournament, a.k.a. the International Championship, first contested in 1882 as a match between England and Wales. England, Ireland, Scotland and Wales competed in the early years. France made it five nations by joining the competition in 1910 and played until 1931 when they were expelled because of the sad state of French rugby. France rejoined the tournament in 1947. Each team plays each other once (two points are earned for a win and one for a tie) and the team with the most points is declared the winner. (*) indicates Grand Slam, meaning team won all four games.

Multiple Winners: Wales (33); England (32); Scotland (20); France (19); Ireland (18).

Year		Year		Year	
1882	England	1922	Wales	1964	Scotland & Wales
1883	England	1923	England*	1965	Wales
1884	England	1924	England*	1966	Wales
1885	Not completed	1925	Scotland*	1967	France
1886	England & Scotland	1926	Scotland & Ireland	1968	France*
1887	Scotland	1927	Scotland & Ireland	1969	Wales
1888	Not completed	1928	England*	1970	France & Wales
1889	Not completed	1929	Scotland	1971	Wales*
1890	England & Scotland	1930	England	1972	Not completed
1891	Scotland	1931	Wales	1973	Five way tie
1892	England	1932	England, Wales & Ireland	1974	Ireland
1893	Wales	1933	Scotland	1975	Wales
1894	Ireland	1934	England	1976	Wales*
1895	Scotland	1935	Ireland	1977	France*
1896	Ireland	1936	Wales	1978	Wales*
1897	Not completed	1937	England	1979	Wales
1898	Not completed	1938	Scotland	1980	England*
1899	Ireland	1939	England, Wales & Ireland	1981	France*
1900	Wales	1940-46	Not held—WW II	1982	Ireland
1901	Scotland	1947	Wales & England	1983	France & Ireland
1902	Wales	1948	Ireland*	1984	Scotland*
1903	Scotland	1949	Ireland	1985	Ireland
1904	Scotland	1950	Wales*	1986	France & Scotland
1905	Wales	1951	Ireland	1987	France*
1906	Ireland & Wales	1952	Wales*	1988	Wales & France
1907	Scotland	1953	England	1989	France
1908	Wales*	1954	England, France & Wales	1990	Scotland*
1909	Wales*	1955	France & Wales	1991	England*
1910	England	1956	Wales	1992	England*
1911	Wales*	1957	England*	1993	France
1912	England & Ireland	1958	England	1994	Wales
1913	England*	1959	France	1995	England*
1914	England*	1960	France & England	1996	England
1915-19	Not held—WW I	1961	France	1997	France*
1920	England, Scotland & Wales	1962	France		
1921	England*	1963	England		

SOFTBALL

Men's and women's national champions since 1933 in Major Fast Pitch, Major Slow Pitch and Super Slow Pitch (men only). Sanctioned by the Amateur Softball Association of America.

MEN
Major Fast Pitch

Multiple winners: Clearwater Bombers (10); Raybestos Cardinals (5); Sealmasters (4); Briggs Beautyware, Pay'n Pak and Zollner Pistons (3); Billard Barbell, Decatur Pride, Hammer Air Field, Kodak Park, National Health Care, Penn Corp and Peterbilt Western (2).

Year		Year		Year	
1933	J.L. Gill Boosters, Chicago	1957	Clearwater Bombers	1980	Peterbilt Western, Seattle
1934	Ke-Nash-A, Kenosha, WI	1958	Raybestos Cardinals	1981	Archer Daniels Midland,
1935	Crimson Coaches, Toledo, OH	1959	Sealmasters, Aurora, IL		Decatur, IL
1936	Kodak Park, Rochester, NY			1982	Peterbilt Western
1937	Briggs Body Team, Detroit	1960	Clearwater Bombers	1983	Franklin Cardinals,
1938	The Pohlers, Cincinnati	1961	Sealmasters		Stratford, C
1939	Carr's Boosters, Covington, KY	1962	Clearwater Bombers	1984	California Kings, Merced, CA
		1963	Clearwater Bombers	1985	Pay'n Pak, Seattle
1940	Kodak Park	1964	Burch Tool, Detroit	1986	Pay'n Pak
1941	Bendix Brakes, South Bend, IN	1965	Sealmasters	1987	Pay'n Pak
1942	Deep Rock Oilers, Tulsa, OK	1966	Clearwater Bombers	1988	TransAire, Elkhart, IN
1943	Hammer Air Field, Fresno, CA	1967	Sealmasters	1989	Penn Corp, Sioux City, IA
1944	Hammer Air Field	1968	Clearwater Bombers		
1945	Zollner Pistons, Ft. Wayne, IN	1969	Raybestos Cardinals	1990	Penn Corp
1946	Zollner Pistons			1991	Gianella Bros., Rohnert Park, CA
1947	Zollner Pistons	1970	Raybestos Cardinals	1992	National Health Care,
1948	Briggs Beautyware, Detroit	1971	Welty Way, Cedar Rapids, IA		Sioux City, IA
1949	Tip Top Tailors, Toronto	1972	Raybestos Cardinals	1993	National Health Care
		1973	Clearwater Bombers	1994	Decatur (IL) Pride
1950	Clearwater (FL) Bombers	1974	Gianella Bros., Santa Rosa, CA	1995	Decatur Pride
1951	Dow Chemical, Midland, MI	1975	Rising Sun Hotel, Reading, PA	1996	Green Bay All-Car,
1952	Briggs Beautyware	1976	Raybestos Cardinals		Green Bay, WI
1953	Briggs Beautyware	1977	Billard Barbell, Reading, PA	1997	Tampa Bay Smokers,
1954	Clearwater Bombers	1978	Billard Barbell		Tampa Bay, FL
1955	Raybestos Cardinals,	1979	McArdle Pontiac/Cadillac,		
1956	Clearwater Bombers		Midland, MI		

Super Slow Pitch

Multiple winners: Ritch's/Superior (4); Howard's/Western Steer and Steele's Sports (3).

Year		Year		Year	
1981	Howard's/Western Steer,	1987	Steele's Sports	1993	Ritch's/Superior
	Denver, NC	1988	Starpath, Monticello, KY	1994	Bellcorp., Tampa
1982	Jerry's Catering, Miami	1989	Ritch's Salvage, Harrisburg, NC	1995	Lighthouse/Worth, Stone Mt., GA
1983	Howard's/Western Steer	1990	Steele's Silver Bullets	1996	Ritch's/Superior
1984	Howard's/Western Steer	1991	Sun Belt/Worth, Atlanta	1997	Ritch's/Superior
1985	Steele's Sports, Grafton, OH	1992	Ritch's/Superior,		
1986	Steele's Sports		Windsor Locks, CT		

Major Slow Pitch

Multiple winners: Gatliff Auto Sales, Riverside Paving and Skip Hogan A.C. (3); Campbell Carpets, Hamilton Tailoring and Howard's Furniture (2).

Year		Year		Year	
1953	Shields Construction,	1966	Michael's Lounge, Detroit	1982	Triangle Sports, Minneapolis
	Newport, KY	1967	Jim's Sport Shop, Pittsburgh	1983	No.1 Electric & Heating,
1954	Waldneck's Tavern, Cincinnati	1968	County Sports, Levittown, NY		Gastonia, NC
1955	Lang Pet Shop, Covington, KY	1969	Copper Hearth, Milwaukee	1984	Lilly Air Systems, Chicago
1956	Gatliff Auto Sales,			1985	Blanton's Fayetteville, NC
	Newport, KY	1970	Little Caesar's, Southgate, MI	1986	Non-Ferrous Metals, Cleveland
1957	Gatliff Auto Sales	1971	Pile Drivers, Va. Beach, VA	1987	Stapath, Monticello, KY
1958	East Side Sports, Detroit	1972	Jiffy Club, Louisville, KY	1988	Bell Corp/FAF, Tampa, FL
1959	Yorkshire Restaurant,	1973	Howard's Furniture, Denver, NC	1989	Ritch's Salvage, Harrisburg, NC
	Newport, KY	1974	Howard's Furniture		
		1975	Pyramid Cafe, Lakewood, OH	1990	New Construction, Shelbyville, IN
1960	Hamilton Tailoring, Cincinnati	1976	Warren Motors, J'ville, FL	1991	Riverside Paving, Louisville
1961	Hamilton Tailoring	1977	Nelson Painting, Okla. City	1992	Vernon's, Jacksonville, FL
1962	Skip Hogan A.C., Pittsburgh	1978	Campbell Carpets, Concord, CA	1993	Back Porch/Destin (FL) Roofing
1963	Gatliff Auto Sales	1979	Nelco Mfg. Co., Okla. City	1994	Riverside Paving, Louisville
1964	Skip Hogan A.C.			1995	Riverside Paving
1965	Skip Hogan A.C.	1980	Campbell Carpets	1996	Bell II, Orlando, FL
		1981	Elite Coating, Gordon, CA	1997	Long Haul TPS, Albertville, MN

WOMEN

Major Fast Pitch

Multiple winners: Raybestos Brakettes (21); Orange Lionettes (9); Jax Maids (5); Arizona Ramblers and Redding Rebels (3); California Commotion, Hi-Ho Brakettes, J.J. Krieg's and National Screw & Manufacturing (2).

Year		Year		Year	
1933	Great Northerns, Chicago	1955	Orange Lionettes	1977	Raybestos Brakettes
1934	Hart Motors, Chicago	1956	Orange Lionettes	1978	Raybestos Brakettes
1935	Bloomer Girls, Cleveland	1957	Hacienda Rockets, Fresno, CA	1979	Sun City (AZ) Saints
1936	Nat'l Screw & Mfg., Cleveland	1958	Raybestos Brakettes, Stratford, CT	1980	Raybestos Brakettes
1937	Nat'l Screw & Mfg.	1959	Raybestos Brakettes	1981	Orlando (FL) Rebels
1938	J.J. Krieg's, Alameda, CA	1960	Raybestos Brakettes	1982	Raybestos Brakettes
1939	J.J. Krieg's	1961	Gold Sox, Whittier, CA	1983	Raybestos Brakettes
1940	Arizona Ramblers, Phoenix	1962	Orange Lionettes	1984	Los Angeles Diamonds
1941	Higgins Midgets, Tulsa, OK	1963	Raybestos Brakettes	1985	Hi-Ho Brakettes, Stratford, CT
1942	Jax Maids, New Orleans	1964	Erv Lind Florists, Portland, OR	1986	So. California Invasion, LA
1943	Jax Maids	1965	Orange Lionettes	1987	Orange County Majestics, Anaheim, CA
1944	Lind & Pomeroy, Portland, OR	1966	Raybestos Brakettes		
1945	Jax Maids	1967	Raybestos Brakettes	1988	Hi-Ho Brakettes
1946	Jax Maids	1968	Raybestos Brakettes	1989	Whittier (CA) Raiders
1947	Jax Maids	1969	Orange Lionettes	1990	Raybestos Brakettes
1948	Arizona Ramblers	1970	Orange Lionettes	1991	Raybestos Brakettes
1949	Arizona Ramblers	1971	Raybestos Brakettes	1992	Raybestos Brakettes
1950	Orange (CA) Lionettes	1972	Raybestos Brakettes	1993	Redding (CA) Rebels
1951	Orange Lionettes	1973	Raybestos Brakettes	1994	Redding Rebels
1952	Orange Lionettes	1974	Raybestos Brakettes	1995	Redding Rebels
1953	Betsy Ross Rockets, Fresno, CA	1975	Raybestos Brakettes	1996	California Commotion, Woodland Hills
1954	Leach Motor Rockets, Fresno, CA	1976	Raybestos Brakettes	1997	California Commotion

Major Slow Pitch

Multiple winners: Spooks (5); Dana Gardens (4); Universal Plastics (3); Cannan's Illusions, Bob Hoffman's Dots and Marks Brothers Dots (2).

Year		Year		Year	
1959	Pearl Laundry, Richmond, VA	1972	Riverside Ford, Cincinnati	1985	Key Ford Mustangs, Pensacola, FL
1960	Carolina Rockets, High Pt., NC	1973	Sweeney Chevrolet, Cincinnati	1986	Sur-Way Tomboys, Tifton, GA
1961	Dairy Cottage, Covington, KY	1974	Marks Brothers Dots, Miami	1987	Key Ford Mustangs
1962	Dana Gardens, Cincinnati	1975	Marks Brothers Dots	1988	Spooks
1963	Dana Gardens	1976	Sorrento's Pizza, Cincinnati	1989	Cannan's Illusions, Houston
1964	Dana Gardens	1977	Fox Valley Lassies, St. Charles, IL	1990	Spooks
1965	Art's Acres, Omaha, NE	1978	Bob Hoffman's Dots, Miami	1991	Cannan's Illusions, San Antonio
1966	Dana Gardens	1979	Bob Hoffman's Dots	1992	Universal Plastics, Cookeville, TN
1967	Ridge Maintenance, Cleveland	1980	Howard's Rubi-Otts, Graham, NC	1993	Universal Plastics
1968	Escue Pontiac, Cincinnati	1981	Tifton (GA) Tomboys	1994	Universal Plastics
1969	Converse Dots, Hialeah, FL	1982	Richmond (VA) Stompers	1995	Armed Forces, Sacramento
1970	Rutenschruder Floral, Cincinnati	1983	Spooks, Anoka, MN	1996	Spooks
1971	Gators, Ft. Lauderdale, FL	1984	Spooks	1997	Taylor's, Glendale, MD

Other 1997 Champions

Slow Pitch

MEN

Class A—Coffee Cup/DeMarini, Cottage Grove, Minn..
Major Industrial—Sikorsky, Shelton, Conn.
Class A Industrial—Shaw #1, Dalton, Ga..
35-Over—Winchell Chiropractic, Evansville, Ind..
40-Over—Maroadi Transfer, Pittsburgh, Pa.
45-Over—Maroadi Transfer, Pittsburgh, Pa.
55-Over—Florida Legens/Hudson Chriopractic, Ft. Myers, Fla..
60-Over—Wopac Masters, Cincinnati, Ohio
Major Church—Pathway Church of God, Mobile, Ala.
Class A Church—Second Baptist, Houston, Tex.

WOMEN

Class A—Fletch's Softball Club, Newark, Del.
Industrial—Walt Disney World, Orlando, Fla.
Church—North Gadsden, Gadsden, Ala.

Fast Pitch

MEN

Class A—D.C. Tire Roadrunners, Reading, Pa.
Class B—Kamphuis Pipeline, Wyoming, Mich.
Class C—Luna's Towing, Tucson, Ariz.
40-Over—Knoll Lumber Legends, Seattle, Wash.
45-Over—Super Sound Tapes, St. James, Minn.
23-Under—Hydraulics International, Salt Lake City, Utah

WOMEN

Class A—Diamonds, Montclair, Calif.
Class B—San Jose Strikkers, Santa Clara, Calif.
Class C—Cobo's, Atlanta, Ga.

COED

Major—Spaghetti/Station, Spokane, Wash.
Class A—Busch Road Warriors, Valley Park, Mo.

Modified Pitch

Women's Major—Thunderbolts, Troy, N.H.
Men's Major—D & S Roofing, Deer Park, N.Y.
Men's Class A—Legends, Fairhaven, Mass.

World Championship

Contested since 1989, the Triathlon World Championship consists of a 1.5 kilometer swim, a 40-kilometer bike ride and a 10-kilometer run. The 1997 championship was to take place November 16 in Perth, Australia.

Multiple winners: MEN— Simon Lessing (3); Spencer Smith (2). WOMEN— Michelle Jones and Karen Smyers (2).

MEN

Year		Time
1989	Mark Allen, United States	1:58:46
1990	Greg Welch, Australia	1:51:37
1991	Miles Stewart, Australia	1:48:20
1992	Simon Lessing, Great Britain	1:49:04
1993	Spencer Smith, Great Britain	1:51:20
1994	Spencer Smith, Great Britain	1:51:04
1995	Simon Lessing, Great Britain	1:48:29
1996	Simon Lessing, Great Britain	1:39:50

WOMEN

Year		Time
1989	Erin Baker, New Zealand	2:10:01
1990	Karen Smyers, United States	2:03:33
1991	Joanne Ritchie, Canada	2:02:04
1992	Michellie Jones, Australia	2:02:08
1993	Michellie Jones, Australia	2:07:41
1994	Emma Carney, Australia	2:03:19
1995	Karen Smyers, USA	2:04:58
1996	Jackie Gallagher, Australia	1:50:52

Ironman Championship

Contested in Hawaii since 1978, the Ironman Triathlon Championship consists of a 2.4-mile swim, a 112-mile bike ride and 26.2-mile run. The race begins at 7 a.m. and continues all day until the course is closed at midnight. The 1997 Ironman Championship was scheduled for Oct. 18.

MEN

Multiple winners: Mark Allen and Dave Scott (6); Scott Tinley (2).

Year	Date	Winner	Time	Runner-up	Margin	Start	Finish	Location
I	2/18/78	Gordon Haller	11:46	John Dunbar	34:00	15	12	Waikiki Beach
II	1/14/79	Tom Warren	11:15:56	John Dunbar	48:00	15	12	Waikiki Beach
III	1/10/80	Dave Scott	9:24:33	Chuck Neumann	1:08	108	95	Ala Moana Park
IV	2/14/81	John Howard	9:38:29	Tom Warren	26:00	326	299	Kailua-Kona
V	2/6/82	Scott Tinley	9:19:41	Dave Scott	17:16	580	541	Kailua-Kona
VI	10/9/82	Dave Scott	9:08:23	Scott Tinley	20:05	850	775	Kailua-Kona
VII	10/22/83	Dave Scott	9:05:57	Scott Tinley	0:33	964	835	Kailua-Kona
VIII	10/6/84	Dave Scott	8:54:20	Scott Tinley	24:25	1036	903	Kailua-Kona
IX	10/25/85	Scott Tinley	8:50:54	Chris Hinshaw	25:46	1018	965	Kailua-Kona
X	10/18/86	Dave Scott	8:28:37	Mark Allen	9:47	1039	951	Kailua-Kona
XI	10/10/87	Dave Scott	8:34:13	Mark Allen	11:06	1380	1284	Kailua-Kona
XII	10/22/88	Scott Molina	8:31:00	Mike Pigg	2:11	1277	1189	Kailua-Kona
XIII	10/15/89	Mark Allen	8:09:15	Dave Scott	0:58	1285	1231	Kailua-Kona
XIV	10/6/90	Mark Allen	8:28:17	Scott Tinley	9:23	1386	1255	Kailua-Kona
XV	10/19/91	Mark Allen	8:18:32	Greg Welch	6:01	1386	1235	Kailua-Kona
XVI	10/10/92	Mark Allen	8:09:08	Cristian Bustos	7:21	1364	1298	Kailua-Kona
XVII	10/30/93	Mark Allen	8:07:45	Paulli Kiuru	6:37	1438	1353	Kailua-Kona
XVIII	10/15/94	Greg Welch	8:20:27	Dave Scott	4:05	1405	1290	Kailua-Kona
XIX	10/7/95	Mark Allen	8:20:34	Thomas Hellriegel	2:25	1487	1323	Kailua-Kona
XX	10/26/96	Luc Van Lierde	8:04:08	Thomas Hellriegel	1:59	1420	1288	Kailua-Kona

WOMEN

Multiple winners: Paula Newby-Fraser (8); Erin Baker and Sylviane Puntous (2).

Year	Winner	Time	Runner-up	Year	Winner	Time	Runner-up
1978	No finishers			1987	Erin Baker	9:35:25	Sylviane Puntous
1979	Lyn Lemaire	12:55.00	None	1988	Paula Newby-Fraser	9:01:01	Erin Baker
				1989	Paula Newby-Fraser	9:00:56	Sylviane Puntous
1980	Robin Beck	11:21:24	Eve Anderson				
1981	Linda Sweeney	12:00:32	Sally Edwards	1990	Erin Baker	9:13:42	P. Newby-Fraser
1982	Kathleen McCartney	11:09:40	Julie Moss	1991	Paula Newby-Fraser	9:07:52	Erin Baker
1982	Julie Leach	10:54:08	Joann Dahlkoetter	1992	Paula Newby-Fraser	8:55:28	Julie Anne White
1983	Sylviane Puntous	10:43:36	Patricia Puntous	1993	Paula Newby-Fraser	8:58:23	Erin Baker
1984	Sylviane Puntous	10:25:13	Patricia Puntous	1994	Paula Newby-Fraser	9:20:14	Karen Smyers
1985	Joanne Ernst	10:25:22	Liz Bulman	1995	Karen Smyers	9:16:46	Isabelle Mouthon
1986	Paula Newby-Fraser	9:49:14	Sylviane Puntous	1996	Paula Newby-Fraser	9:06:49	Natascha Badmann

Triathlon Added To Olympics

The triathlon will be held for the first time in an Olympic Games at Sydney in 2000. It was developed as a combination of the longest Olympic swimming distance, 1500 meters, the 40 kilometer cycling time trial, and the longest athletic track event of 10,000 meters. The triathlon will start and finish at the Sydney Opera House.

YACHTING

The America's Cup

International yacht racing was launched in 1851 when England's Royal Yacht Squadron staged a 60-mile regatta around the Isle of Wight and offered a silver trophy to the winner. The 101-foot schooner *America*, sent over by the New York Yacht Club, won the race and the prize. Originally called the Hundred-Guinea Cup, the trophy was renamed The America's Cup after the winning boat's owners deeded it to the NYYC with instructions to defend it whenever challenged.

From 1870-1980, the NYYC successfully defended the Cup 25 straight times; first in large schooners and J-class boats that measured up to 140 feet in overall length, then in 12-meter boats. A foreign yacht finally won the Cup in 1983 when *Australia II* beat defender *Liberty* in the seventh and deciding race off Newport, R.I. Four years later, the San Diego Yacht Club's *Stars & Stripes* won the Cup back, sweeping the four races of the final series off Fremantle, Australia.

Then in 1988, New Zealand's Mercury Bay Boating Club, unwilling to wait the usual three- to four-year period between Cup defenses, challenged the SDYC to a match race, citing the Cup's 102-year-old Deed of Gift, which clearly stated that every challenge had to be honored. Mercury Bay announced it would race a 133-foot monohull. San Diego countered with a 60-foot catamaran. The resulting best-of-three series (Sept. 7-8) was a mismatch as the SDYC's catamaran *Stars & Stripes* won two straight by margins of better than 18 and 21 minutes. Mercury Bay syndicate leader Michael Fay protested the outcome and took the SDYC to court in New York State (where the Deed of Gift was first filed) claiming San Diego had violated the spirit of the deed by racing a catamaran instead of a monohull. N.Y. State Supreme Court judge Carmen Ciparick agreed and on March 28, 1989, ordered the SDYC to hand the Cup over to Mercury Bay. The SDYC refused, but did consent to the court's appointment of the New York Yacht Club as custodian of the Cup until an appeal was ruled on.

On Sept. 19, 1989, the Appellate Division of the N.Y. Supreme Court overturned Ciparick's decision and awarded the Cup back to the SDYC. An appeal by Mercury Bay was denied by the N.Y. Court of Appeals on April 26, 1990, ending three years of legal wrangling. To avoid the chaos of 1988-90, a new class of boat—75-foot monohulls with 110-foot masts—has been used by all competing countries since 1992.

The next America's Cup races will be held in New Zealand from Feb. 26-Mar. 11, 2000.

Note that (*) indicates skipper was also owner of the boat.

Schooners And J-Class Boats

Year	Winner	Skipper	Series	Loser	Skipper
1851	America	Richard Brown	—	—	
1870	Magic	Andrew Comstock	1-0	Cambria, GBR	J. Tannock
1871	Columbia (2-1)	Nelson Comstock	4-0	Livonia, GBR	J.R. Woods
	& Sappho (2-0)	Sam Greenwood			
1876	Madeleine	Josephus Williams	2-0	Countess of Dufferin, CAN	J.E. Ellsworth
1881	Mischief	Nathanael Clock	2-0	Atalanta, CAN	Alexander Cuthbert*
1885	Puritan	Aubrey Crocker	2-0	Genesta, GBR	John Carter
1886	Mayflower	Martin Stone	2-0	Galatea, GBR	Dan Bradford
1887	Volunteer	Henry Haff	2-0	Thistle, GBR	John Barr
1893	Vigilant	William Hansen	3-0	Valkyrie II, GBR	Wm. Granfield
1895	Defender	HenryHaff	3-0	Valkyrie III, GBR	Wm. Granfield
1899	Columbia	Charles Barr	3-0	Shamrock I, GBR	Archie Hogarth
1901	Columbia	Charles Barr	3-0	Shamrock II, GBR	E.A. Sycamore
1903	Reliance	Charles Barr	3-0	Shamrock III, GBR	Bob Wringe
1920	Resolute	Charles F. Adams	3-2	Shamrock IV, GBR	William Burton
1930	Enterprise	Harold Vanderbilt*	4-0	Shamrock V, GBR	Ned Heard
1934	Rainbow	Harold Vanderbilt*	4-2	Endeavour, GBR	T.O.M. Sopwith
1937	Ranger	Harold Vanderbilt*	4-0	Endeavour II, GBR	T.O.M. Sopwith

12–METER BOATS

Year	Winner	Skipper	Series	Loser	Skipper
1958	Columbia	Briggs Cunningham	4-0	Sceptre, GBR	Graham Mann
1962	Weatherly	Bus Mosbacher	4-1	Gretel, AUS	Jock Sturrock
1964	Constellation	Bob Bavier & Eric Ridder	4-0	Sovereign, AUS	Peter Scott
1967	Intrepid	Bus Mosbacher	4-0	Dame Pattie, AUS	Jock Sturrock
1970	Intrepid	Bill Ficker	4-1	Gretel II, AUS	Jim Hardy
1974	Courageous	Ted Hood	4-0	Southern Cross, AUS	John Cuneo
1977	Courageous	Ted Turner	4-0	Australia	Noel Robins
1980	Freedom	Dennis Conner	4-1	Australia	Jim Hardy
1983	Australia II	John Bertrand	4-3	Liberty, USA	Dennis Conner
1987	Stars & Stripes	Dennis Conner	4-0	Kookaburra III, AUS	Iain Murray

60–FT CATAMARAN VS 133–FT MONOHULL

Year	Winner	Skipper	Series	Loser	Skipper
1988	Stars & Stripes	Dennis Conner	2-0	New Zealand, NZE	David Barnes

75–FT INTERNATIONAL AMERICA'S CUP CLASS

Year	Winner	Skipper	Series	Loser	Skipper
1992	America[3]	Bill Koch* & Buddy Melges	4-1	Il Moro di Venezia, ITA	Paul Cayard
1995	Black Magic, NZE	Russell Coutts	5-0	Young America, USA	Dennis Conner & Paul Cayard

Other Champions

Championships decided in 1997, unless otherwise indicated.

ARCHERY

1997 World Outdoor Championship
at Victoria, Canada (Aug. 17-23)

MEN

Event	Championship
Olympic Indiv.	Kyung-Ho Kim, S. Kor. def. Christophe Peignois, BEL, 108-107
Olympic Team	South Korea def. Norway, 254-244
Compound Indiv.	Dee Wilde, USA def. Terry Ragsdale, USA, 109-105
Compound Team	Hungary def. Spain, 241-235

WOMEN

Event	Championship
Olympic Indiv.	Du-Ri Kim, S. Kor. def. Comelia Pfohl, GER, 105-102
Olympic Team	South Korea def. Ukraine, 242-231
Compound Indiv.	Fabiola Palazzini, ITA def. Catherine Pellen, FRA, 104-101
Compound Team	Italy def. United States, 243-237

1997 World Indoor Championship
at Istanbul, Turkey (Mar. 18-23)

MEN

Event	Championship
Olympic Indiv.	Jae-Hun Chung, S. Kor. def. Shane Parker, USA, 117-115
Olympic Team	Soauth Korea def. Sweden, 265-259
Compound Indiv.	Dee Wilde, USA def. Thomas Crowne, USA, 118-115
Compound Team	Sweden def. Denmark, 256-254

Note: Thomas Crowne had his second place finish vacated by FITA, the international governing body of archery, following a positive drug test.

WOMEN

Event	Championship
Olympic Indiv.	Tetyana Muntyan, UKR def. Hyun-Ji Kim, S. Kor., 118-113
Olympic Team	Germany def. Kazakhstan, 259-237
Compound Indiv.	Valerie Fabre, France def. Sylviane Lambelet, SWI, 114-113
Compound Team	United States def. France, 256-245

ARENA FOOTBALL

Final AFL Standings
(*) denotes division champion; (†) denotes playoff wild card.

American Conference

Central	W	L	Pct	PF	PA
*Iowa Barnstormers	11	3	.786	803	645
†Milwaukee Mustangs	8	6	.571	669	667
Texas Terror	6	8	.429	733	756
Portland Forest Dragons	2	12	.143	446	701

Western	W	L	Pct	PF	PA
*Arizona Rattlers	12	2	.857	713	540
†San Jose SaberCats	8	6	.571	548	563
Anaheim Piranhas	2	12	.143	615	735

National Conference

Eastern	W	L	Pct	PF	PA
*Nashville Kats	10	4	.714	740	660
†New Jersey Red Dogs	9	5	.643	660	596
Albany Firebirds	6	8	.429	745	714
New York CityHawks	2	12	.143	522	691

Southern	W	L	Pct	PF	PA
*Orlando Predators	10	4	.714	678	505
†Tampa Bay Storm	8	6	.571	548	521
Florida Bobcats	4	10	.286	519	645

Quarterfinals

at Orlando 45 . . . . .New Jersey 37
at Iowa 68 . . . . .San Jose 59
at Arizona 46 . . . . .Milwaukee 29
Tampa Bay 52 . . . . .at Nashville 49

Semifinals

at Arizona 49 . . . . OT . . . . .Tampa Bay 46
at Iowa 52 . . . . .Orlando 34

ArenaBowl XI
Aug. 25 at America West Arena,
Phoenix, Ariz; Att: 17,436

Arizona 55 . . . . .Iowa 33

MVP: Donnie Davis, Arizona QB, 13-for-21, 190 yards, 3 TDs.

LACROSSE

Women's 1997 World Cup
at Tokyo (Apr. 27-May 4)

First Round

	W	L	Pct	GF	GA
Australia	6	0	1.000	45	14
United States	5	1	.833	60	21
England	4	2	.667	42	19
Wales	3	3	.500	36	47
Scotland	2	4	.333	27	44
Canada	1	5	.167	28	49
Japan	0	6	.000	22	66

Medal Round

Championship . . . . .United States def. Australia, 3-2 OT
Third Place Game . . . . .England def. Wales, 18-4
Fifth Place Game . . . . .Canada def. Scotland, 6-5

Major Indoor Lacrosse League

Final MILL Regular Season Standings

	W	L	Pct	GF	GA
Philadelphia Wings	7	3	.700	137	115
Buffalo Bandits	6	4	.600	158	155
New York Saints	6	4	.600	136	117
Rochester Knighthawks	5	5	.500	156	136
Boston Blazers	4	6	.400	120	135
Baltimore Thunder	2	8	.200	125	165

Semifinals

Rochester 15 . . . . .at Philadelphia 13
at Buffalo 19 . . . . .New York 8

Finals
April 12 at Marine Midland Arena, in Buffalo, N.Y.
Att: 18,055

Rochester 15 . . . . .Buffalo 12

MOTORCYCLING

ROAD RACING

Speedway World Championship
Sept. 20 in Vojens, Denmark

		Pts
1	Greg Hancock, USA	118
2	Billy Hamill, USA	101
3	Tomasz Gollob, Poland	92
4	Tony Richardsson, Sweden	90

MOTOCROSS

Motorcross des Nations
Sept. 13 at Nismes, Belgium

1	Belgium
2	Italy
3	Great Britain
4	Sweden
5	France

Note: USA finsihed eighth

ROLLER HOCKEY

**Roller Hockey International
Regular Season Standings**

(*) denotes division champion; (†) denotes playoff qualifier.
Teams receive three points for a win and one point for overtime losses (OTL).

Eastern Conference

	W	L	OTL	Pts	GF	GA
*Orlando	20	4	0	40	229	145
†New Jersey	16	8	0	32	195	174
†Montreal	9	10	5	23	161	164
†Ottawa	10	12	2	22	162	181
Buffalo	6	18	0	12	127	208

Western Conference

	W	L	OTL	Pts	GF	GA
*San Jose	15	12	1	31	189	180
†Anaheim	18	7	3	39	217	162
†Los Angeles	15	11	2	32	187	181
†St. Louis	12	10	2	26	174	169
Sacramento	10	17	1	21	185	229

Playoffs

First Round(Best of 3)
Orlando def. Ottawa, 2 games to 0.
New Jersey def. Montreal, 2 games to 0.
San Jose def. St. Louis, 2 games to 1.
Anaheim def. Los Angeles, 2 games to 1.

Semifinals (Best of 3)
New Jersey def. Orlando , 2 games to 1.
Anaheim def. San Jose, 2 games to 1.

Championship(Best of 3)

	W-L	GF	GA
Anaheim	2-0	21	9
New Jersey	0-2	9	21

RESULTS: **Aug. 28**–Anaheim, 12-4; **Sept. 1**–Anaheim, 9-5.

**Australian Rules Football
AFL Grand Final**
at Melbourne Cricket Ground (Sept. 27)
Att: 99,645

Adelaide 125 .... St. Kilda 94

RUGBY

1996 EUROPEAN CUP
European Clubs Championship

Pool A

	W	L	PF	PA	Pts
Dax (France)	3	1	141	69	6
Bath (England)	3	1	135	88	6
Pontypridd (Wales)	3	1	97	60	6
Trevisio (Italy)	1	3	106	135	2
Edinburgh (Scotland)	0	4	71	199	0

RESULTS: **Oct. 12**— Bath 55, Edinburgh 26; Pontypridd 28, Trevisio 22; **Oct. 16**— Dax 34, Trevisio 14, Pontypridd 32, Edinburgh 10; **Oct. 19**— Pontypridd 19, Bath 6; **Oct. 20**— Dax 69, Edinburgh 12; **Oct. 26**— Bath 25, Dax 16; **Nov. 2**— Dax 22, Pontypridd 18; Bath 50, Trevisio 27.

Pool B

	W	L	PF	PA	Pts
Leicester (England)	4	0	114	43	8
Llanelli (Wales)	2	2	97	81	4
Leinster (Ireland)	2	2	86	109	4
Pau (France)	1	3	137	103	2
Borders (Scotland)	1	3	80	178	2

RESULTS: **Oct. 12**— Llanelli 34, Leinster 17; Pau 86, Borders 28; **Oct. 16**— Leicester 27, Leinster 10; Borders 24, Llanelli 16; **Oct. 19**— Leicester 43, Borders 3; Llanelli 31, Pau 15; **Oct. 26**— Leicester 19, Pau 14; Leinster 34, Borders 25; **Nov. 2**— Leicester 25, Llanelli 16; Leinster 25, Pau 23.

Pool C

	W	L	PF	PA	Pts
Brive (France)	4	0	106	65	8
Harlequins (England)	3	1	131	95	6
Neath (Wales)	2	2	83	109	4
Ulster (Ireland)	1	3	75	87	2
Caledonia (Scotland)	0	4	117	156	0

RESULTS: **Oct. 12**— Brive 34, Neath 19; **Oct. 13**— Ulster 41, Caledonia 34; **Oct. 16**— Harlequins 21, Ulster 15; Neath 27, Caledonia 18; **Oct. 19**— Harlequins 44, Neath 22; **Oct. 26**— Neath 15, Ulster 13; Brive 23, Harlequins 10; **Nov. 2**— Harlequins 56, Caledonia 35; Brive 17, Ulster 6.

Pool D

	W	L	PF	PA	Pts
Cardiff (Wales)	3	1	135	97	6
Toulouse (France)	3	1	157	142	6
Wasps (England)	2	2	156	115	4
Munster (Ireland)	2	2	109	135	4
Milan (Italy)	0	4	73	141	0

RESULTS: **Oct. 12**— Munster 23, Milan 5; **Oct. 13**— Cardiff 26, Wasps 24; **Oct. 16**— Toulouse 44, Milan 26; Cardiff 48, Munster 18; **Oct. 19**— Toulouse 36, Cardiff 20; Munster 49, Wasps 22; **Oct. 26**— Wasps 77, **Oct. 27**— Cardiff 41, Milan 19; **Nov. 2**— Toulouse 60, Munster 19; Wasps 33, Milan 23.

Quarterfinals

Toulousse 26	Dax 18
Leicester 23	Harlequins 13
Cardiff 22	Bath 19
Brive 35	Llanelli 14

Semifinals

Leicester 37	Toulouse 11
Brive 26	Cardiff 13

Final

Jan. 25 at Cardiff Arms Park, Wales. Att— 40,000

Brive 28 .... Leicester 9

U.S. CHAMPIONS

Club:	Men	Aspen, Colo.
	Women	Berkeley (Calif.) All-Blues
College:	Men	California (Berkeley)
	Women	Penn St.
High School:	Men	Highland H.S., Salt Lake City, UT
Military:	Men	Camp Pendleton

SHOOTING

U.S. Nationals
June 19-28 at Chino, Calif.

PISTOL
Men

Air Pistol	Daryl Szarenski, Ft. Benning, Ga.
Rapid Fire Pistol	Stan Hayes, Dallas, Tex.
Standard Pistol	Jerry Wilder, Lowell, Ind.
Center Fire Pistol	Steven King, Columbus, Ga.
Free Pistol	Daryl Szarenski, Ft. Benning, Ga..

Women

Sport Pistol	Elizabeth Callahan, Upper Marlboro, Md.

RIFLE
Men

Free Rifle, Prone	Glenn Dubis, Columbus, Ga.
Free Rifle, 3x40	Glenn Dubis, Columbus, Ga.
Air Rifle	Dan Jordan, Franktown, Colo.

Women

Standard Rifle, Prone	Stephanie Thomson, Salem, Ore.
Standard Rifle, 3x20	Elizabeth Bourland, Wichita Falls,. Tex.
Air Rifle	April Shea, Blackwood, N.J.

RUNNING TARGET
Men

10m Running Target	Lance Dement, Columbus, Ga.
50m Running Target	Roy Hill, Sun City, Calif.
10m Running Target, Mixed	Lance Dement, Columbus, Ga.
50m Running Target, Mixed	Armando Ayala, Ft. Benning, Ga.

Women

10m Running Target	Kelly Miltner, Colorado Springs, Colo.

VOLLEYBALL

FIVB Beach Volleyball World Championships
Sept. 10-13 at UCLA Tennis Center in Los Angeles, Calif.

2-on-2 Men's Finals	Para de Souza/Guilherme Marques, BRA def. Mike Whitmarsh/Canyon Cerman, USA 2-1 (5-12, 12-8, 12-10)
2-on-2 Women's Final	Jackie Silva/Sandra Pires, BRA def. Lisa Arce/Holly McPeak, USA 2-1 (12-11, 1-12, 12-10)
4-on-4 Men's Final	USA def. Brazil, 2-0 (12-5, 12-8)
4-on-4 Women's Final	USA def. Australia, 2-0 (12-3, 12-5)

USA Four Man Team: Bob Ctvrtlik, Doug Partie, Scott Fortune, Eric Sato, and Dan Hanan.
USA Four Woman Team: Gabrielle Reece, Stephanie Cox, Katy Eldridge, Jenny Johnson Jordan, and Annette Davis.

ESPN X GAMES

June 19-28 at San Diego and Oceanside, Calif.

Aggressive In-Line Skating

Men's Vert	Tim Ward, Melton, AUS
Women's Vert	Fabiola da Silva, Sao Paulo, BRA
Men's Street	Aaron Feinberg, Portland, Ore.
Women's Street	Sayaka Yabe, Tokyo, JPN

Waterskiing

Barefoot Jumping	Peter Fleck, Windermere, Fla.

Bicycle Stunt

Street	Dave Mirra, Greenville, N.C.
Flatland	Trevor Meyer, Spring Park, Minn.
Dirt Jumping	T.J. Lavin, Las Vegas, Nev.
Vert	Dave Mirra, Greenville, N.C.

Big Air Snowboarding

Men	Peter Line, Kirkland, Wash.
Women	Tina Dixon, Salt Lake City, Utah

Downhill In-line Skating

Men	Derek Downing, Cumming, Ga.
Women	Gypsy Tidwell, Waco, Tex.

Skateboarding

Street	Chris Senn, San Francisco, Calif.
Vert	Tony Hawk, Carlsbad, Calif.
Vert Doubles	Tony Hawk & Andy Macdonald, San Diego, Calif.

Skysurfing ..Troy Hartman/Vic Pappadato, Perris, Calif.

Sportclimbing

Men's Difficulty	Francois Legrand, Venelles, FRA
Women's Difficulty	Katie Brown, Lafayette, Ga..
Men's Speed	Hans Florine, Moraga, Calif.
Women's Speed	Elena Ovtchinnikova, Selenginsk, RUS

Street Luge

Dual	Biker Sherlock, San Diego, Calif.
Mass	Biker Sherlock, San Diego, Calif.
Super Mass	Chris Ponseti, Novato, Calif.

Wakeboarding

Men	Jeremy Kovak, Mill Grove, Ontario, CAN
Women	Tara Hamilton, Lanatan, Fla.

X-Venture Race ....Team Presidio
Ian Adamson, Denver, Colo.
John Howard, Christchurch, NZE
Andrea Spitzer, Los Angeles, Calif.

ESPN WINTER X GAMES

Jan. 30-Feb. 2 at Snow Summit Resort in Big Bear Lake, Calif.

Crossover ....Brian Patch, Huntington Beach, Calif.

Ice Climbing

Men's Difficulty	Jared Ogden, Telluride, Colo.
Women's Difficulty	Bird Lew, Truckee, Calif.
Men's Speed	Jared Ogden, Telluride, Colo.
Women's Speed	Bird Lew, Truckee, Calif.

Snowboarding

Men's Half-pipe	Todd Richards, Breckenridge, Colo.
Men's Boarder X	Shaun Palmer, S. Lake Tahoe, Calif.
Men's Slopestyle	Daniel Franck, Oslo, NOR
Men's Big Air	Jimmy Halopoff, S. Lake Tahoe, Calif.
Women's Half-pipe	Shannon Dunn, Steamboat Springs, Colo.
Women's Baorder X	Jennie Waara, Malmberge, SWE
Women's Slopestyle	Barrett Christy, Vail, Colo.
Women's Big Air	Barrett Christy, Vail, Colo.

Snow Mountain Bike Racing

Men's Downhill	Shaun Palmer, S. Lake Tahoe, Calif.
Men's Speed	Phil Tintsman, Phoenix, Ariz.
Women's Downhill	Missy Giove, Durango, Colo.
Women's Speed	Cheri Elliott, Cameron Park, Ill.

Super-modified Shovel Racing .Don Adkins, Holman, N.M.

Deaths

Golf legend **Ben Hogan**, who died on July 25, 1997, is shown after winning the 1951 U.S. Open in Birmingham, Mich. Hogan is one of only four golfers to win the U. S. Open four times, the others being Willie Anderson, Bobby Jones and Jack Nicklaus.

World Wide Photos

Wide World Photos

Richie Ashburn

Wide World Photos

Rex Barney

Wide World Photos

Denis Compton

John Akii-Bua, 47; winner of the gold medal in the 400m hurdles at the 1972 Olympics; set a world record in winning the event with a time of 47.82 seconds; remains the only Ugandan to win Olympic gold in track and field; unable to defend his title in 1976 because black African nations boycotted the Montreal Olympics; at his death Akii-Bua was a senior superintendent with the Ugandan police department; cause of death unknown; in Kampala, Uganda, June 20.

Cal Abrams, 72; probably best remembered for being thrown out at home plate as a Brooklyn Dodger in the last of the ninth in the final game of the 1950 World Series; had he scored on Duke Snider's hit it would have forced a playoff for the National League pennant which the Phillies would go on to win on a home run the next inning; of a heart attack; in Miami, Feb. 25.

Bobby Adams, 75; major league infielder who played with three teams between 1946–59; played on the Cincinnati Reds, Chicago White Sox and Chicago Cubs; started professional baseball career in 1939 with Ogden, Utah of the old Pioneer League; also served as secretary of the Association of Professional Baseball Players in 1959–60; joined Chicago Cubs coaching staff for five years in 1961; brother Dick played a year for the Philadelphia Phillies and his son Mike for three teams in a six year career; cause of death not announced; in Gig Harbor, Wash., Feb. 13.

Pokey Allen, 53; popular coach at Portland State from 1986–92 twice leading the Vikings to the NCAA Division II title game; rebuilt Boise State and led them to the 1994 NCAA 1–AA championship game; after receiving treatment in early 1995, rejoined Broncos and led them to a 7–4 record; named MVP of 1964 Liberty Bowl while a star at Utah; had a 86–41–2 record as a college coach; of rhabdomyosarcoma, a rare and aggressive muscle cancer; in Montana, Dec. 29, 1996.

Robert Anderson, 71; joined the New York Daily News in 1947 as a copy boy; worked as a sports reporter, makeup editor, deskman and night sports editor before being named sports editor in 1966; held the position for 10 years and guided coverage on such events as the 1969 Miracle Mets, Joe Namath and the Jets and the 1970 New York Knicks' championship season; also served as director of the city's Golden Gloves boxing competition; of a heart attack; in Massapequa, N.Y., Dec. 13, 1996.

Lynn Archibald, 52; former head basketball coach at the University of Utah and Idaho State; served as an assistant at Arizona St., Southern Cal, UNLV, Cal Poly-San Luis Obispo and Cal State-Long Beach during his career; most recently held position of assistant coach and director of basketball operations at BYU, which he joined in 1994; led Utah to two NCAA Tournaments, two NIT appearances and one WAC championship; of prostate cancer; in Provo, Utah, May 28.

Richie Ashburn, 70; member of the Baseball Hall of Fame, elected in 1995; center fielder for the Philadelphia Phillies from 1948–1959; finished his playing career with the Chicago Cubs and New York Mets; broadcaster for the Phillies for the past 35 years; nickname "Whitey," ended his first season as the Sporting News' Rookie of the Year, batting .333; won NL batting title in 1955 (.338) and 1958 (.350); finished second three times; batted over .300 nine times in his career; played solid defense, leading the NL in putouts for nine seasons; played in six All-Star games and one World Series; part of the 1950 pennant-winning "Whiz Kids"; holds Phillies record for consecutive games played with 731, singles with 1811; in his era he was overshadowed by his fellow center fielders Willie Mays, Mickey Mantle and Duke Snider; selected to the Hall of Fame by the veterans committee; a columnist for the Philadelphia Bulletin and Daily News from 1974–91; of an apparent heart attack; in Manhattan where the Phillies were staying, Sept. 9.

Rex Barney, 72; public address announcer for the Baltimore Orioles for more than 20 years and a former Dodgers pitcher who tossed a no-hitter on Sept. 9, 1948; a member of the team's hall of fame, Barney won 35 games for the Dodgers in the late 1940's; best known for broadcasting the line "give that fan a contract" when a fan made a nice play; cause of death not announced; in Baltimore, Md., Aug. 12.

Tim Bishop, 20; outfielder for the Columbia Mets, the New York Mets' South Atlantic League affiliate; in 1996 Bishop was an All-Star in the Appalachian League while batting .325 for Class A Kingsport; in a car accident; in Columbia, S.C., May 17.

Ewell Blackwell, 74; best remembered for coming within two outs of throwing consecutive no-hitters four days apart in 1947 against the Boston Braves; the 6-foot-6-inch right-hander was nicknamed "the Whip" and played 10 years with three teams; had a career ERA of 3.30 while posting an 82–78 career record; in 1947 won a league-high 22 games with a 2.47 ERA; pitched in six consecutive All-Star games from 1946–51; a member of the 1952 world champion New York Yankees; cause of death not released; in Hendersonville, N.C., Oct. 29, 1996.

Jim Bolus, 54; Kentucky Derby historian; was the former secretary of the National Turf Writers Association; worked for 23 years for the *Courier-Journal* and the *Louisville Times* before devoting all his time to free lance writing; author of seven books; also held the position of curator of the Kentucky Derby Museum in Louisville; of a heart attack after a jog with his wife; in Louisville, May 14.

Jack Kent Cooke

Bob Devaney

Carlo Fassi

Al Braverman, 78; fixture on the boxing scene, spending the last two decades as Don King's aide; unbeaten as a heavyweight from 1938–41; of complications from diabetes; in Yonkers, N.Y., July 5.

Paul Brechler, 86; first commissioner of the Western Athletic Conference; became the youngest athletic director in Big Ten history when Iowa hired him at the age of 37; became commissioner of the Skyline Conference in 1960 before moving to the WAC in 1961; after a brief term as the University of California's athletic director he presided over the Rocky Mountain Athletic Conference until 1990; cause of death undisclosed; in Denver, Sept. 13.

Roger Brown, 54; former Indiana Pacers guard who never played college basketball; at age 25 was the Pacers first player signed upon joining the ABA in 1967; led Pacers to three ABA championships, averaging 17.4 points and 6.5 rebounds during an eight-year career; Indiana's third leading scorer with 10,058 points, his No. 35 is one of three numbers retired by the Pacers; of liver cancer; in Indianapolis, March 4.

Peter Fredrick Bronfman, 68; co-owned the Montreal Canadiens from 1971–78 with his brother Edward; a shy and polite man who wanted to be known for his affection to family and friends instead of the billions of dollars he controlled in business; a major supporter of a home for single mothers, a local AIDS hostel, the Toronto Humane Society and many other charities; of cancer; in Toronto, Dec. 1, 1996.

Tyronee "Tiger" Bussey, 20; Colorado linebacker diagnosed with leukemia shortly after signing with the Buffaloes 1994 recruiting class; received first of two bone marrow transplants one month after Colorado's 1994 defeat of Michigan; able to practice in full pads in spring of 1996 but signs of the disease returned; Bussey was 6-foot-2, 240 pounds when he signed to play in Colorado, but was as low as 145 pounds the summer before his death, of leukemia; in Detroit, Jan. 3.

Bob Cain, 72; left-hander who pitched to dwarf Eddie Gaedel and walked him on four consecutive balls; Bill Veeck planned the gimmick of sending Gaedel to the plate as a pinch hitter to help the Browns who were drawing poor crowds; broke into the majors with the Chicago White Sox, also pitched for the Detroit Tigers and St. Louis Browns; of cancer; in Cleveland, April 7.

Guillermo Canedo, 76; FIFA senior vice-president was one of the architects of FIFA and football; head of FIFA World Cup Organizing Committee and masterminded two World Cup tournaments; created the FIFA Media Committee which he also chaired; of heart attack after long illness; in Zurich, Jan. 20.

Norman Cleveland, 96; won an Olympic gold medal as a member of the 1924 U.S. Rugby Team that beat heavily favored France in Paris; last year that rugby was an Olympic sport after rioting following the U.S. victory forced organizers to reconsider; officials had a special tunnel for the U.S. players to escape from the crowd, wanted to see rugby reinstated as an Olympic sport and had aspirations to throw out the first ball in the 2000 Summer Games in Sydney; of natural causes; in Santa Fe, N.M., June 8.

Denis Compton, 78; one of Britain's greatest cricket players; had a career of just over 20 years; set record after record, including, most runs scored 3,816 and most centuries (100–runs streaks) 18 — in a single season, first British cricketer to hire a business agent, credited with bringing style, joy and excitement to the game, played for Arsenal, a soccer team in North London, retired from cricket in 1957, scored 38,635 career runs, was a former sports commentator for the BBC; of complications from hip surgery; in Winsor, England, April 23.

Jack Kent Cooke, 84; majority owner of the NFL's Washington Redskins since 1974; oversaw the building of a new natural grass 78,600-seat stadium in Maryland which would later bear his name, Cooke invested $360 million of his own money in the project, in his 23 years since becoming majority owner, the Redskins are 223–151 with three Super Bowl victories, four NFC Championships and 11 playoff appearances, Cooke also owned the Los Angeles Lakers' team of the 1970's and 1980's and operated the Toronto Maple Leafs and a minor baseball team in the 1950's, Cooke built the Los Angeles Forum which was the first privately funded indoor arena in the United States, horses and horse racing were a passion of Cooke's, owned *The Los Angeles Daily News* and many other businesses, his son John Kent Cooke now has control of the Redskins, of cardiac arrest; in Washington, D.C., April 6.

Bob Cope, 58; former defensive coordinator for Kansas State University; on his second stint with the Wildcats; was on coach Bill Snyder's original staff from 1989–90, then left for Southern California and Baylor before returning to the Wildcats; of cancer; in Manhattan, Kan., Aug. 9.

Ted Darling, 61; former voice of the Buffalo Sabres for 22 years; Darling left the broadcast booth during the 1991–92 season, he was elected into the Sabres Hall of Fame with the Foster Hewitt Award for excellence in broadcasting in 1995; of complications arising from Pick's disease — a form of Alzheimer's; in Lockport, N.Y., Dec. 20, 1996.

Lorenzo "Piper" Davis, 79; a star infielder and manager for the Birmingham Black Barons of the Negro Leagues; helped develop the future superstar Willie Mays; received the nickname Piper for his birthplace, Piper, Ala., played first, second and shortstop for the Black Barons in the early 1940's and managed the team in 1948–49; became the first black player signed by the Red Sox organization in 1950, assigned to Class A but was never called up and never made it to the major leagues; he also played basketball with the Harlem Globetrotters, was a baseball scout in the 1970's and 1980's; of a heart attack; in Birmingham, Ala., May 21.

Fabrizio De Chiara, 25; Italian middleweight boxer, seventh Italian boxer to die from injuries sustained in the ring, of head injuries received during a title fight against Vincenzo Imparato, Nov. 18, 1996.

Bob Devaney, 82; former Nebraska Husker coach and Athletic Director, won two national championships and will be remembered for his excellence in building all his athletic programs, of a long illness; in Lincoln, Neb., May 9.

Jerry Diamond, 68; former executive director of the Women's Tennis Association; became executive director in 1974 and left in 1985, helped turn the fledgling sport into the largest and most lucrative professional sport for women; of colon cancer; in Stamford, Conn., Dec. 16, 1996.

Darold Dobs, 58; the executive director of the American Bowling Congress; of cancer; in Greendale, Wisc., Feb. 10.

Ed Donawick, 85; All-American halfback at Fordham during the 1932 and 1933 seasons; went on to play for the Giants from 1934 to 1939 and 1941; named to the All-NFL teams in 1935 and 1938, also led the NFL in passing during the 1935 and 1938 seasons; in the 1934 Championship game Donawski ran for a touchdown and threw for another for a 30–13 victory over the Chicago Bears, threw the game winning TD pass in New York's 23–17 victory over Green Bay in 1938; of complications due to Alzheimer's disease; in New York, Feb. 1.

Angelo Drossos, 68; founder of the San Antonio Spurs and owner until May 1988; responsible for bringing George Gervin and David Robinson to San Antonio, the two cornerstones of the franchise which was born in 1973; of a long illness associated with supra nuclear palsy; in San Antonio, Jan. 9.

Seth Dunscomb, 21; a senior at the University of Kansas and member of the swim team; was the captain of the 1995–96 season; placed fourth in the 200 individual medley and eight in the 200 butterfly at the Big 12 Conference Championships in 1996; set an Illinois state record for the 200–yard individual medley; had blacked out once before in practice but was cleared to compete; cause of death unknown after Dunscomb collapsed after getting out of the pool; in Lawrence, Kan., Jan. 22.

Yanick Dupre, 24; left wing for the Philadelphia Flyers; a second-round draft pick of the Flyers in 1991, Dupre played parts of three seasons with the team, scoring two career goals; played four seasons with Hershey of the American Hockey League; played junior hockey with Chicoutimi and Drummondville of the Quebec Major Junior Hockey League; will be remembered for his character and determination; of leukemia; in Montreal, Aug. 16.

Earle Edwards, 88; coached N.C. State football for 17 seasons, the longest tenure for any Wolfpack football coach; won three ACC titles and made two Liberty Bowl appearances; won four ACC Coach of the Year honors; of complications from a series of mild strokes; in Raleigh, N.C., Feb. 25.

Stephane Enjolras, 21; Indy car driver who was killed during pre-qualifications for the 24 Hours at Le Mans race when his Peugeot left the track and sailed into an adjoining area; Enjolras qualified for the race by winning the Autumn Cup last year; of injuries sustained in the crash; in Le Mans, France, May 3.

Jack "Tex" Evans, 68; was the last coach to lead the Hartford Whalers to a first place finish in the Adams Division (1987); broke into the NHL as a defenseman with the Rangers and won a Stanley Cup with Chicago in 1961; coaching career included stints with the California Seals and Cleveland Barons before taking the Whalers job in 1983; cause of death unavailable, but had been ill for several months; in Manchester, Conn., Nov. 10, 1996.

Robert Evans, 65; the first black captain of the Penn football team; the 6–foot-2, 215–pound lineman was named captain as a sophomore in 1952, but was declared academically ineligible during his junior year and never played another down; the day after the announcement Evans was hospitalized to treat a peptic ulcer which some believe Evans tried to hide to keep playing football; after falling two years behind because of football, Evans graduated and was elected to the Phi Beta Kappa and Sphinx academic honor societies; he served in the Navy and owned a funeral parlor; of a heart attack; in Philadelphia, Nov. 30, 1996.

Carlo Fassi, 67; respected Italian figure skating coach; coached Olympic champions Peggy Fleming and Dorothy Hamill; was European champion in 1953 and 1954 as well as a bronze medalist at the 1953 World Championships; also coached future Olympic champions John Curry (1976), Robin Cousins (1980) and Jill Trenary (1990); of a heart attack during the World Championships; in Lausanne, Switzerland, March 20.

Henri Filion, 55; harness racing driver/trainer who won 3,318 races and earned more than $21 million in his career; one of eight boys in his family to become harness drivers; younger brother of driver Herve Filion; of injuries sustained after a serious racing accident when he was thrown off his horse Bye Bye Angus; in Mississauga, Ontario, April 9.

Judith Marie Flannery, 57; four-time world champion and six-time U.S. champion triathlete; was killed when a car driven by an unlicensed man struck her as she rode her bike; in Chevy Chase, Md., April 2.

Curt Flood, 59; pioneer in baseball labor relations; traded to the Philadelphia Phillies by the St. Louis Cardinals in the offseason of 1969, he sat out the 1970 season and his case eventually went to the U.S. Supreme Court where he was defeated; baseball, however, was changed by Flood's opposition to the sport's reserve clause which bound players to organizations; free agency as we know it was created because of Flood's courageous efforts; on the field, Flood was a Gold-Glove outfielder for the Cardinals who was a six-time .300 hitter; of throat cancer; in Los Angeles, Jan. 20.

William Flynn, 82; former athletic director at Boston College who helped the Eagles build a competitive Div. 1–A sports program, increasing the number of varsity sports from six to 33 when he retired in 1991; Flynn entered B.C. as a student in 1935 and spent the next 60-plus years working with the school; of a long illness; in Boston, June 29.

Hans Froemming, 86; harness racing champion who won 5,592 races in a career spanning more than six decades; was German champion 15 times between 1934–53; was honored in 1964 for saving the lives of three Jewish-German horsemen during the Holocaust; of a stroke; in Hamburg, Germany, Nov. 8, 1996.

Ed Furgol, 79; former golfer who won the U.S. Open in 1954 by one stroke despite being unable to bend his left arm, which never healed properly when he broke his elbow at age 12; 1954 Player of the Year and a member of the 1957 Ryder Cup team; of a brief illness; in Miami Shores, Fla., March 6.

Hilliard Gates, 80; played the play-by-play announcer in the movie Hoosiers; announced games for the NBA Fort Wayne Pistons, Indiana University men's basketball and high school tournaments during his career; of a long illness, Nov. 20, 1996.

Abe Gibron, 72; head coach of the Chicago Bears from 1972–74 compiling an 11–30–1 record; known for his animated demeanor on the sidelines; also played in five Pro Bowls and was an all-pro three times during an 11–year pro career with Buffalo of the AAFC, the Cleveland Browns and finally, the Bears; won three NFL championships as a guard for the Browns; cause of death not announced; in Belle Air, Fla., Sept. 22.

Ben Gregory, 50; University of Colorado assistant football coach in charge of running backs since 1991; is credited with developing Heisman Trophy winner Rashaan Salaam; a two time All-Big Eight running back at Nebraska, he went on to play two seasons for the Buffalo Bills; of a massive heart attack; in Boulder, Colo., April 10.

Ron Grinker, 57; Cincinnati attorney and sports agent whose most famous client, Danny Manning, was selected first overall in the 1988 NBA Draft; he also represented Xavier coach Skip Prosser and former coach Pete Gillen of Cincinnati and current coach Bob Huggins and former coach Ed Badger; considered to be a mentor to many young sports agents; of cancer; in Cincinnati, Sept. 5.

Hilary Grivich, 19; member of the 1991 U.S. gymnastics team; considered one of America's most consistent and talented gymnasts; helped lead the U.S. to a silver-medal finish at the 1991 World Championships; earned a diving scholarship to the University of Houston and had dreams of one day making the U.S. diving team; of injuries sustained in an automobile accident; in Houston, May 4.

Kenneth Haas, 80; star two-way tackle who played at Missouri from 1937–39; captain of the 1939 team that played in the Orange Bowl; rejected an offer to play with the Detroit Lions, a decision he later called a mistake; named to the All-Mizzou Football Team, of kidney failure; in St. Louis, Mo., April 13.

David Hall, 49; respected baseball coach at many levels; coached at Rice University from 1981–91, posting a 338–267 record; coached at two other high schools before forming a special bond with the kids at Cypress Creek High School who watched him battle a form of non-smoking related cancer; as a player at Texas he led the Southwest Conference with a .364 average in 1970; of lung cancer; in Cypress Creek, Texas, May 4.

Terry Hall, 53; women's basketball coach at Wright State University the past seven years; her 20 year coaching career included tours with Eastern Kentucky, University of Kentucky, Louisville and Wright State; her best winning percentage came during a seven-year stretch at Kentucky where she coached the Lady Kats' first All-American Valerie Still and earned a 138–66 record plus an appearance in the NCAA Tournament; named the 1991–92 North Star Conference Coach of the Year; of cancer; in Jeffersonville, Ind., July 14.

Phil Hankinson, 45; reserve on the 1974 NBA Champion Boston Celtics; a second-round draft choice in 1973, Hankinson played less than two seasons in the NBA due to a knee injury; battled bouts of depression following the injury in college and went on to have a stellar career at Penn; of a gun shot wound to the right temple; in Shelbyville, Kent., Nov. 21, 1996.

Matthew Harding, 42; vice chairman of the Chelsea Soccer Club in the English premiere league; bought the club's Stamford Bridge ground in 1995 for $26 million and provided cash for stadium improvements and new players; from a helicopter crash; in Middlewich, England, Oct. 22, 1996.

I.H. "Sporty" Harvey, 71; boxing pioneer; was the first black boxer to oppose a white fighter in Texas; lost to Buddy Turman in a 10–round decision in 1955; Harvey sued the Texas state commissioner of labor statistics for permission to fight a white boxer and block a statute which prohibited interracial bouts; he won an appeal of his case in 1954; sparred with the likes of Joe Frazier and Sonny Liston during his career; of heart disease; in Los Angeles, June 5.

Terrence Harvey, 21; starting sophomore cornerback at Brigham Young, had transferred to BYU from Victor Valley CC three weeks previous; of injuries sustained in a highway car accident; near Provo, Utah., Nov. 17, 1996.

Buddy Hassett, 85; first baseman for the Brooklyn Dodgers, Boston Red Sox and New York Yankees; known as a fine hitter and fielder, Hassett never had more than 20 strike outs in a season; loved to entertain people by singing and sang between movies while a member of the Dodgers; served as a Naval officer in World War II then managed the Yankees' Newark, N.J. farm team; of bone cancer, Aug. 23.

Camille Henry, 64; star center in the 1950's and 60's for the New York Rangers; broke into the NHL in 1953 as a Ranger and played 727 career games with New York, Chicago and St. Louis; retired following the 1969–70 season; finished with 279 career goals and 249 assists; lived in poverty following his retirement; received $85,000 from the players association pension fund last year; of diabetes; in Quebec, Sept. 11.

Jay Hebert, 74; PGA Champion in 1960, played on two Ryder Cup teams and captained another; his PGA Championship came three years after his brother Lionel won the event, making them the only brothers to win that tournament; a member of the Louisiana Sports Hall of Fame, Hebert led the LSU Tigers to the 1947 NCAA College Golf Championships; a captain in the Marine Corps, he won a purple heart in World War II; was a club professional for eight years before he turned pro; of a heart condition; in Houston, May 25.

Bill Hewitt, 68; pioneer hockey broadcaster who called every play for the Toronto Maple Leafs from 1951–81; his father Foster Hewitt was also a broadcaster; cause of death not announced; in Port Perry, Ontario, Dec. 25, 1996.

Ben Hogan, 84; one of the greatest golfers ever to play the game; career numbers include 63 victories (second to only Sam Snead's 81 and Jack Nicklaus' 70), nine major championships, four U.S. Open titles and the only person to ever win three professional grand slam events in one year; overcame tremendous odds to become the legend he was; witnessed his father commit suicide when he was a child and neared bankruptcy many times as an adult; shattered his legs in a 1949 car/bus collision; was told he may not walk or live again; struggled back and won six of his nine major championships after the accident; although his legs limited him to only seven tournament appearances a year, he still managed to amass 13 more tournament victories; discovered golf as a 15–year-old caddie at Glen Garden Country Club where he lost the caddie championship in a playoff to another boy his age named Byron Nelson; turned pro at 17 and joined the tour full-time as a 19–year-old in 1931; by the age of 33 he was the top player in the world, earning nicknames like "Bantam Ben" and "the Hulk" for his stoic, small stature and ferocious play; of complications following a major stroke; in Ft. Worth, Texas, July 25.

Baskerville Holmes, 32; member of Memphis State's 1985 Final Four team; tied for the lead in games played at the school with 132, scoring 1,112 points in his four-year college career; of a gun shot from an apparent murder-suicide with his girlfriend; in Memphis, Tenn., March 18.

Mark Holtz, 51; longtime radio announcer for the Texas Rangers from 1981–94; had been the team's play-by-play television announcer since 1994; voted Texas sportscaster of the year eight times, Holtz was elected to the Texas Baseball Hall of Fame in 1990; broadcast his final game on May 22; of complications from a bone marrow transplant for treatment of leukemia; in Dallas, Sept. 7.

Wide World Photos

Curt Flood

Wide World Photos

Ron Grinker

Wide World Photos

Ben Hogan

Ralph Horween, 100; the first former NFL player to reach the age of 100; a member of the undefeated Harvard team that defeated Oregon in the 1920 Rose Bowl, Horween joined the NFL in its second year of existence; played in the backfield for the Chicago Cardinals under the name of McMahon for his mother who didn't think football was respectable; after retiring from football he returned to Harvard for a law degree and was a successful businessman; of natural causes; in Charlottesville, Va., May 26.

Chuck Howard, 63; former ABC Sports vice president of program production; was at ABC from 1960–86 before leaving for Trans World International; from a long battle with brain cancer; in Long Island, N.Y., Nov. 21, 1996.

Don Hutson, 84; a 1963 inductee into the Pro Football Hall of Fame and member of the NFL's 75th Anniversary team; considered the premiere receiver of the early days of the NFL, Hutson was also a kicker and a tenacious defender; he currently holds 11 NFL records; led the Green Bay Packers to three NFL Championships in 1936, 1939 and 1944; league MVP in both 1941 and 1942; led the NFL in receiving eight times; once scored 29 points in one quarter; an All-American at Alabama he earned the nickname "Alabama Antelope"; cause of death unknown; in Rancho Mirage, Calif., June 26.

Clarence Iba, 88; former Tulsa basketball coach credited with turning the program around shortly after arriving in 1949; won more games than any other Golden Hurricane coach (137) and guided the team to the 1955 NCAA Tournament; younger brother of longtime Oklahoma State Coach Henry Iba; a member of both the University of Tulsa Athletic Hall of Fame and the state of Missouri Basketball Hall of Fame; of an aneurysm; in Fort Worth, Texas, April 21.

Robert Irsay, 73; controversial NFL owner who moved the Colts from Baltimore to Indianapolis in 1984 overnight to avoid the media attention; became owner of the Baltimore team in 1972 by trading his new Los Angeles Rams organization; under his guidance in 1987 the Colts were involved in one of the largest player deals in NFL history which involved 10 players and sent Eric Dickerson to Indianapolis; the team's best success came when it advanced to the 1995 AFC Championship Game; Irsay's 37-year-old son, Jim, holds the titles of senior executive vice president, general manager and COO of the team; of heart and kidney failure; in Indianapolis, Jan. 14.

Bernard Jackson, 46; the starting free safety on the Denver Broncos' first Super Bowl team in 1977; the third member of that team to die including defensive end Lyle Alzado and backup quarterback Norris Weese; of inoperable liver cancer; in Lompoc, Calif, May 26.

Helen Jacobs, 88; winner of nine major tennis championships, including the U.S. national title four straight times from 1932–35; Wimbledon singles champ in 1936; was a regular on the U.S. Wightman Cup team from 1932–39; number one player in 1936 and ranked in the world top ten 12 straight times; her brilliant career was somewhat overshadowed by her one-sided rivalry with Helen Wills Moody; because she only beat Moody once in 11 matches Jacobs was often called "Helen the Second;" even her sole victory over Moody was not without controversy, it came when Moody decided to retire in the 1933 U.S. national final; also served as a commander in the U.S. Navy intelligence during World War II, one of only five women to achieve that rank in the Navy; of heart failure; in Easthampton, N.Y., June 2.

Frank Johnston, 67; former Notre Dame football player and longtime CFL assistant coach; a lineman for the undefeated 1949 Irish team; Johnston was an assistant coach with the British Columbia Lions and the Toronto Argonauts; of pneumonia; in Toronto, July 4.

Duane Josephson, 54; former Chicago White Sox (1965–70) and Boston Red Sox (1971–72) catcher; lifetime average was .258 with 23 home runs and 164 RBI; of a heart ailment; in New Hampton, Iowa, Jan. 30.

Jim Kensil, 66; former president of the New York Jets for 11 years and assistant to Commissioner Pete Rozelle; he began his career as a sports writer at the *Columbus Dispatch* and moved on to the Associated Press in 1952; in 1961 he became director of public relations for the NFL where he met Rozelle; his son Mike is currently the director of operations for the Jets; of complications from a heart condition; in Massapequa, N.Y., Jan. 16.

Artan Koka, 25; soccer player who played for Teuta in the Albanian first division; of gun shot wounds after he was shot while leaving a training session; in Tirana, Albania, Sept. 4.

Bernard C. "Bert" Kuczynski, 77; became the first athlete to play pro football and baseball in the same season when he suited up for the Philadelphia Athletics and the Detroit Lions in 1943; cause of death not announced; in Allentown, Penn., Jan. 19.

Gus Kyle, 75; former St. Louis Blues broadcaster; played three years in the NHL from 1949–52; worked the games with announcer and late Hall-of-Famer Dan Kelly; after several years battling heart trouble; in St. Louis, Nov. 17, 1996.

Wide World Photos

Don Hutson

Wide World Photos

Robert Irsay

Wide World Photos

Helen Jacobs

Elmo Langley, 68; NASCAR driver whose career lasted from the late 1950's until the early 1970's; career includes two wins in NASCAR's top stock car division; most recently a NASCAR official and pace car driver for the Winston Cup Series; had been a NASCAR official for the past six years; at time of death was in Japan to drive the pace car for the Suzuka Thunder Special 100 exhibition race; of apparent heart failure; in Suzuka, Japan, Nov. 21, 1996.

Jean-Pierre Leduc, 45; a French cyclist competing in the Dakar-Agades-Dakar rally; the rally claimed its 34th fatality since the inaugural event in 1979; of injuries when he fell from his KTM bike in the second stage of the rally; in Mali, Jan. 5.

Thorton Lee, 90; left-handed pitcher who lasted 16 years in the major leagues, 11 with Chicago White Sox teams that never finished higher than third; after a stint with Cleveland, Lee retired in 1948 as a member of the New York Giants; he spent 40 years as a major-league scout; he finished his career with a record of 117–124 and a 3.56 ERA; of complications related to Parkinsons disease; in Tucson, Ariz, June 9.

Dwight Lowry, 39; award winning minor league manager and former major league player; played catcher for the 1984 World Series Champion Detroit Tigers; named Tigers minor league manager of the year for his work with Fayetteville Generals; after collapsing outside his home; in Jamestown, N.Y., July 9.

Ray Mansfield, 55; former Pittsburgh Steelers center; played on two Super Bowl teams; love of outdoors earned him the nickname, Ranger; holds the Steelers record for consecutive games played with 182 from 1964–76; played on the University of Washington team that beat Minnesota in the 1961 Rose Bowl; drafted by the Philadelphia Eagles in 1963 and joined the Steelers the following year; a role model on and off the field by teammates; of natural causes; in the Grand Canyon National Park, Nov. 2, 1996.

Cliff Mapes, 74; former outfielder who played for the New York Yankees, St. Louis Browns and the Detroit Tigers; started career with the Yankees in 1948; he wore Babe Ruth's No. 3 until it was retired and switched to 13, then 7; was traded to St. Louis in 1951; the year Mantle came to New York and started wearing number 7; finished with a career .242 average with 38 home runs; cause of death not announced; in Pryor, Okla., Dec. 5, 1996.

Phil Marchildon, N/A; member of the Canadian Sports Hall of Fame; pitched for hometown team Penetanguishene to numerous Ontario finals in the 1930's; moved to Toronto and played two seasons for the Toronto Maple Leafs; in 1940 he signed to pitch for Connie Mack's Philadelphia Athletics; served three years of military service; returned to baseball and retired from the Boston Red Sox in 1950; cause of death not announced; in Toronto, Jan. 12.

Dave Marr, 63; professional golfer; won the 1965 PGA Championship at Laurel Valley in Pennsylvania; member of the Ryder Cup team and PGA player of the year in 1965; appointed captain of the Ryder Cup team in 1981, the same year he was elected to the College Golf Hall of Fame; longtime television golf analyst with ABC; after a long bout with stomach cancer; in Houston, Jan. 12.

Thomas Charles Mascaro, 81; credited with revolutionizing the world of golf course turf and maintenance; his work led to several products; including Grass-Cel which allows grass to grow despite foot traffic and also the battery operated greens mower, which is able to poke holes in the ground and help feed the greens; more interested in making green grass and the effect of the grass on the game instead of playing the game; of pneumonia complications; in Fort Lauderdale, Fla., May 6.

Bill McArthur, 78; former Western Oregon football coach who compiled a record of 180–124–6 over 36 seasons with the team; McArthur is a member of the NAIA Hall of Fame, University of Santa Barbara Hall of Fame and the Oregon Sports Hall of Fame; volunteered to coach Regis High School in the mid 1980's; cause of death not given; in Salem, Ore., April 24.

Hugh McLean, 84; longtime hockey referee who worked at all levels, including the NHL for 10 years; refereree in chief of the Canadian Amateur Hockey Association for 10 years; president of the Ontario Hockey Association from 1976–78; officiated more than 25 years of soccer; one of the three Canadians with credentials to ref a game anywhere in the world; coached the Hamilton Steelers pro soccer team; remembered for throwing Maurice Richard out of a game in Montreal; after a history of health problems; in London, Ontario, .

Rodrick McClure, 21; Eastern Washington point guard who started all nine games for the Eagles this year; averaged 7.7 points, 5.3 assists and 3.2 rebounds per game; a 1994 graduate of Cimarron Memorial High School in Las Vegas; played two seasons at Central Arizona College before transferring to Eastern Washington; from injuries sustained in a car accident; in Las Vegas, Dec. 26, 1996.

Bones McKinney, 78; former Wake Forest basketball coach who coached from 1958–65 and led the Deacons to two their first two ACC titles and an appearance in the Final Four in 1962; known for his showmanship and sideline antics; coached the Carolina Cougars of the American Basketball Association; returned to college basketball as a color commentator; cause of death not known but was receiving treatment for a stroke he suffered on May 2; in Raleigh, N.C., May 16.

Wide World Photos

Ray Mansfield

Wide World Photos

Jerry Neudecker

Archive Photos/The Sporting News

Pete Rozelle

Thomas "Shorty" McWilliams, 70; standout tailback at Mississippi State in the 1940's; began collegiate career in 1944 at Mississippi State and earned second team All-American and first team All-Southeastern Conference honors; after the outbreak of World War II McWilliams played for the 1945 undefeated Army team in the backfield with Heisman winners Doc Blanchard and Glenn Davis; inducted into the Mississippi Sports Hall of Fame in 1962; had a brief pro career with Los Angeles and Pittsburgh cut short by a knee injury; later purchased a restaurant in his home town which his family still owns; of a variety of medical problems after a month-long stay in the hospital; in Meridian, Miss, Jan. 9.

Maude Mildred McIntyre, 106; the United States' oldest active female bowler; she was granted that title by the Women's International Bowling Congress in 1993; started bowling when she was 69; of natural causes; in Fresno, Calif., March 6.

Jeff "Squeeky" Medlen, 43; caddie on the PGA Tour who carried Nick Price's bag during his British Open victory and two PGA Championships; began caddying on the tour in 1985 and rose to celebrity status in 1991 when he caddied for then unknown John Daly during his PGA Championship victory; got his nickname for his distinctive high-pitched voice; of chronic myelogenus leukemia; in Columbus, Ohio, June 16.

Veryl Miller, 28; center for the 1990 co-national champion Georgia Tech football team; of spiral meningitis; in Norcross, Ga., Mar. 22.

Jack Moran, 76; former Cincinnati Reds radio broadcaster; did Reds broadcasts for seven years with Hall-of-Famer Waite Hoyt; anchored the evening sports broadcasts and hosted the station's "King of TV Bowling" program; after leaving the station he formed a talent agency; of heart failure; in Cincinnati, Jan. 14.

Emil "Bus" Mosbacher, 75; skipper for two America's Cup winning yachts; defended the Cup successfully aboard the Weatherly, a 65-foot single masted sloop in 1962, winning the fourth race by 26 seconds, the slimmest margin in the event's history; defended the Cup again at the helm of Intrepid in 1967, beating Australian skipper Jock Sturrock for the second time; also served as the U.S. State Dept. chief of protocol under Nixon; of cancer; in Greenwich, Conn., Aug. 14.

Charlie Neal, 65; former Brooklyn and Los Angeles Dodger infielder; broke into the major leagues in 1956 and played eight seasons; cause of death not released; in Dallas, Nov. 8, 1996.

John Nemechek, 27; driver in the NASCAR Truck series; had 43 career starts; his best finish coming at the Homestead Facility in 1996 when he placed seventh; younger brother of NASCAR Winston Cup driver Joe Nemechek; of severe brain trauma after a high speed crash in a truck series race; in Miami, Jan. 11.

Jerry Neudecker, 66; last major league umpire to wear a balloon chest protector; American League umpire from 1956–86; his chest protector was sent to the Hall of Fame after his retirement; of cancer; in Fort Walton Beach, Fla, Jan. 11.

Harold Nichols, 79; a national champion wrestler who became one of the sport's most respected coaches; retired following the 1984–85 season; at Iowa St., where he coached for 32 years, he won six NCAA and seven Big Eight Championships; his career record of 492–93–14 includes five seasons at Arkansas St.; of complications following a stroke; in Ames, Iowa, Feb. 22.

Jim Pagel, 42; stock car driver; was beginning his sixth season on the local circuit; of injuries in a car accident during qualifying run; in Kaukauna, Wisc., May 2.

Jack Parkinson, 73; outstanding Kentucky basketball player who played under the legendary Adolph Rupp and earned All-American honors in 1946; left Kentucky for an 11-month stint in the Army before returning as a substitute two years later; Parkinson then was a pitcher-manager for a Middlesboro semipro baseball team; later played with two basketball teams — the Whiskered Wizards and the Toledo Mercurys; a member of both the Delaware County Athletic Hall of Fame and Indiana Basketball Hall of Fame; turned down a contract with the Cincinnati Reds to play for Kentucky; of complications from a brain tumor; in Yorktown, Ind., May 30.

Laura Patterson, 43; part of a 16–member professional bungee jumping team scheduled to be part of the Super Bowl halftime show; husband and sister on the team as well; of head injuries sustained on the final practice for the Super Bowl; in New Orleans, Jan. 23.

Eulace Peacock, 82; one of track and field's leading athletes considered to be Jesse Owens' rival who missed the 1936 Olympics due to injury; Peacock won seven of 10 meetings with Owen in 1935, including victories in the long jump and 100–meter dash at the Amateur Athletic Union National Championships; the following two Summer Games, scheduled for 1940 and 1944, were cancelled because of WWII, preventing Peacock from ever competing in an Olympics; won six national titles in the pentathlon; of Alzheimer's disease; in Yonkers, N.Y., Dec. 13, 1996.

Henry Picard, 90; former PGA Championship and Masters' winner who won 26 tournaments on the tour which puts him 19th on the all-time list; played on four U.S. Ryder teams; of a lengthy illness; in Charleston, S.C., April 30.

Wide World Photos

Shannon Smith

Wide World Photos

Joanie Weston

Wide World Photos

Tony Zale

Julie Reitan, 21; starting outfielder for the two-time defending national champion Arizona softball team; a standout in cross country and track as well as softball at Sahuaro High School; graduated from high school with perfect grade-point average as well; she hit .318 last season as a junior; cause of death unknown but believed to be associated with her diabetes; in Tuscon, Ariz., June 27.

Hedi Ben Rekhissa, 26; one of Africa's most gifted soccer players; a fullback that scored many crucial goals for the Tunisian National Team; played for the Tunis club Esperance; had won just about every Tunisian and African title, including Arab Footballer of the Year in 1995; of convulsions after falling in the closing minutes of a match; in Tunisia, Jan. 4.

Ray Renfro, 67; an NFL wide receiver, he spent his entire career with the Cleveland Browns between 1952–63; had 281 career receptions and played in five NFL Championship Games; served as an assistant coach for the Dallas Cowboys from 1968–72; son Mike played for the Houston Oilers and the Cowboys; cause of death not given; in Ft. Worth, Texas, Aug. 4.

Anthony Roberts, 42; star basketball player at Oral Roberts from 1973–77; his 2,341 points has him third on the Golden eagles career scoring list; set a state single-game scoring record with 66 points against North Carolina A&T on Feb. 19, 1977; holds the NIT single-game scoring record with 65 points; a first-round pick of the Denver Nuggets in 1977, he played less than three seasons before retiring; of gun shot wounds; in Tulsa, Okla, March 29.

Pete Rozelle, 70; former NFL Commissioner who introduced television to the sport and revolutionized the game; responsible for creating the Super Bowl and Monday Night Football; organized the AFL-NFL merger and watched the league grow from 12 to 28 teams during his tenure; elected commissioner in 1960 at the age of 33 as compromise choice to replace Bert Bell; set up plans for sharing television revenues to help support smaller-market teams; created NFL Films and NFL properties; was elected to the Pro Football Hall of Fame in 1985 while still in office; one of the premiere sports commissioners of all time; retired as commissioner on Mar. 22, 1989 after 29 years in office; former GM of LA Rams; of brain cancer; in Rancho Santa Fe, Calif, Dec. 6, 1996.

Ja'Mine Rozzell, 18; considered University of New Mexico's fullback of the future; played in five games as a freshman; rushed for 83 yards on nine carries; a standout at Texas' Albilene Cooper High School as an All-District running back and linebacker, rushing for 2,039 yards and 20 touchdowns in three years; from drowning after diving in the Jemez River; in Jemez Springs, N.M., Aug. 4.

Troy Ruttman, 67; became the youngest driver to win the Indianapolis 500 when he did so at the age of 22 in 1952; first raced at the Brickyard when he was 19, two years younger than the rules allow; also first Indy 500 winner to race Formula One when he drove at Reims, France; his son Troy Jr. died in a crash at the Pocono Raceway in 1969 and his younger brother is currently a driver on the NASCAR Craftsman Truck Series; of lung cancer; in Lake Havasu City, Ariz., May 19.

Ernie Sabayrac, 82; considered the father of golf merchandising, he introduced the concept of spiked golf shoes and apparel to golf shops across the nation in the 1940's; later introduced the Lacoste alligator featured on Izod shirts to the golf world; helped launch the PGA Merchandise Show in 1954; the PGA created the "Ernie Sabayrac Award for Lifetime Contributions to the Golf Industry" in his honor; after a brief illness; in Tampa, Fla, Feb. 6.

Leon M. Sandifer, 78; longtime baseball coach at Austin Peay who ran track and played football and baseball while a student at the school from 1937–39; member of the Austin Peay Hall of Fame; cause of death unannounced; in Clarksville, Tenn., March 24.

Eddie Sawyer, 87; major league baseball manager who led the Philadelphia Phillies' 1950 Whiz Kids to the franchises first NL pennant in 35 years, earning manager of the year kudos; hired as Phillies manager midway through the 1948 season and served until 1952 then again from 1958–59; quit after his team lost the first game of the 1960 season; long-time minor league outfielder in the NY Yankees' system, never played in majors; Phi Betta Kappa member and had a master's degree from Cornell; after a brief illness; in Phoenixville, Pa., Sept. 22.

Robert Schoonmaker, 64; last three-sport athlete at Missouri, lettering eight times in football, basketball and baseball between 1951 and 1954; captained the football team 1952–53 and was an All-Big Seven choice for baseball in 1954; 1991 inductee into the Missouri Intercollegiate Athletics Hall of Fame for baseball; of cancer; in Lebanon, Mo., Dec. 5, 1996.

William E. Schulz, 53; award-winning outdoor writer who spent 29 years writing for AP; best known for his writing on hunting, fishing and conservation issues; Ducks Unlimited honored Schulz with a national award in 1996 for his coverage of wetland conservation; got his start as a copy boy at the *Detroit Free Press*; of cancer; in Atlanta, Dec. 13, 1996.

Frank Slocum, 71; former major league baseball executive and award-winning television writer who was the first and only executive director of the Baseball Assistance Team, a non-profit organization formed in 1986 to help former players in need of financial assistance; has distributed more than $6 million to former players with medical and personal problems; he worked in the National League office and was an executive with the Brooklyn Dodgers during the late 1940's; he began a second career as a television and radio writer and author; he received the George Foster Peabody Award in 1973 for his meritorious service to broadcasting; of cancer; in Greenwich, Conn., May 18.

Shannon Smith, 20; kicker on the Hawaii football team; a Kauai resident, he played one year at Southern Oregon before transferring to Hawaii last season; police Sgt. Cecil Baliaris of Smith, "That young man was a hero. He gave up his own life to save that little boy,"; from drowning while trying to save coach Fred von Appen's 6-year-old son when the two were sucked into a whirlpool after going down a natural slide together; in Lihue, Hawaii, March 29.

Carey Spicer, 87; standout basketball and football player at the University of Kentucky; was the first of many All-American basketball players to suit up for coach Adolph Rupp; was the Wildcat's captain during Rupp's first season in 1930–31 and was the first two-time All-American at the school; he also quarterbacked the football team from 1928–30, setting then records for most touchdowns and points; coached Georgetown College basketball team for several years; of cancer; in Indianapolis, Dec. 6, 1996.

Angie Stevenson, 33; a cross-country skier and biathlete; won the U.S. Summer Biathlon Championships in 1991 and 1995; of a self-inflicted gunshot wound; in Bend, Ore., Feb. 13.

Valentin Sych, 59; president of Russia's Hockey Federation; elected to the position in 1994 and was working on assembling a team for the 1998 Winter Games; of gunshot wounds when after an apparent gunman opened fire; in Moscow, April 29.

Dan Swartz, 65; known as Dangerous Dan for his prowess on the basketball court; a transfer from Kentucky, Swartz had a standout career at what is now Morehead State University; he went on to play for the Boston Celtics where he was a member of their NBA championship teams in the 1960's; Swartz was sheriff in his native Bath County during the late 1970's and early 1980's; he had been a field representative for U.S. Rep Scotty Baesler for the last several years; of an apparent heart attack; in Mount Sterling, Ky., April 3.

Charles Taylor, 62; member of the Canadian Horse Racing Hall of Fame; a journalist and author who also served as chairman of the Jockey Club; responsible for bringing the Breeder's Cup to Toronto in 1996; of cancer; in Toronto, July 14.

Clayton Tonnemaker, 68; an All-American lineman at the University of Minnesota from 1946–49; a member of the College Football Hall of Fame; played professionally for the Green Bay Packers; of complications following heart and lung surgery; in St. Paul, Minn., Dec. 24, 1996.

Johnny Vander Meer, 82; pitcher who in 1938 at age 23 became the only man in major league history to throw two consecutive no-hit games; debuted in 1937 with Cincinnati Reds; extraordinary pitching run began Saturday afternoon, June 11 when he no-hit the Boston Braves at Reds' Crosley Field, a 3-0 Reds victory; second no-hitter came June 15 at the first night game ever at Ebbets Field, retiring Leo Durocher for the final out of the 6-0 Reds win; hitless streak finally ended at 21⅔ innings; went on to 15–10 record that season; led the NL in strikeouts in 1941, '42 and '43; four-time All-Star; career record of 119–121 with a ERA of 3.44 in 13 seasons; of an abdominal aneurysm; in Tampa, Fla., Oct. 6.

Daniel Paul VanEtten, 19; freshman lineman on the West Virginia football team; of injuries sustained when his sport-utility vehicle went out of control after a flat tire. Three other freshman players were injured in the accident; in Camden County, Ga., March 9.

Virginia Van Wie, 88; one of only five players to win golf's U.S. Women's Amateur Championship three consecutive years in 1932, 33 and 34; a member of the 1932 and 1934 Curtis Cup teams which defeated Great Britain and Ireland; taught golf in the Chicago area until she was 78; of natural causes, Feb 18.

Gigi Villoresi, 88; pioneering Formula One race car driver who began his career in 1950; he earned pole positions at five Grand Prix events, but didn't win one; he won the Mille Miglia in 1951, two Targa Florio and a Rally of the Acropolis in 1958; of heart failure; in Modena, Italy, Aug. 24.

Frank Wall, 78; former NFL Falcons' club president; played a major role in bringing the team to Atlanta; close friend of team owner Ranklin Smith Jr.; became vice president and treasurer for the Falcons since 1966; of a self-inflicted gunshot wound; in Atlanta, April 16.

Richard Weiss, 33; Olympic kayaker; finished sixth in the slalom event at the 1996 Summer Games and honored as Kayak Athlete of the Year by the U.S. Olympic Committee; of a kayak accident when the went over a 15-foot waterfall and did not resurface; in Trout Lake, Wash., June 25.

Corey Welch, 28; starting quarterback for Missouri football team in 1988; as a red-shirt freshman Welch rushed for 393 yards and passed for another 524; injured his knee, missed the last game of the year and was replaced before the 1989 season; of a gunshot to the head; in Kansas City, Mo., May 1.

Joanie Weston, 62; deemed the "Blonde Bomber" she became the biggest star of Roller Derby, skating for the Bay Bombers; married skater Nick Scopas; also a talented softball player; of Creutzfeld Jacob Disease, also known as Mad Cow disease; in Hayward, Calif., May 10.

John Williamson, 44; "Super John" played guard on two Nets' teams which won ABA championships; his No. 23 was retired by the team; traded to Indianapolis and reacquired by the Nets, Williamson scored 40 and 50 points in back-to-back games in 1977; of severe kidney problems; in New Haven, Conn., Nov. 30, 1996.

Arthur Michael Wirtz, 62; executive vice president of the Chicago Blackhawks; brother of team president William Wirtz; former general manager for Chicago Stadium and executive vice president of the United Center; of an undisclosed illness; in Chicago, Nov. 5, 1996.

Earl Young, 21; back-up defensive back on the Fresno State football team; played in nine of the team's 11 games last season, starting in one; in the final game of the season Young made his only career interception; of an undisclosed illness; in Fresno, Calif., Jan. 9.

Tony Zale, 83; middleweight champion from 1940–48, he battled Rocky Graziano for the world middleweight championship three times during the 1940's; Zale beat Graziano in the pair's first and last fights. Three months after recapturing the title in the final fight, Zale lost to French boxer Marcel Cerdan; he retired at the age of 35 and served with the U.S. Navy for four years; after struggles with Parkinson's and Alzheimer's diseases; in Portage, Ind., March 20.

RESEARCH MATERIAL

Many sources were used in the gathering of information for this almanac. Day to day material was almost always found in copies of *USA Today, The Boston Globe,* and *The New York Times* or online at various world wide web addresses (see below).

Several weekly and bi-weekly periodicals were also used in the past year's pursuit of facts and figures, among them— *Baseball America, International Boxing Digest, The European, FIFA News* (Soccer), *The Hockey News, The NCAA News, On Track, Soccer America, Sports Illustrated, The Sporting News, Track & Field News,* and *USA Today Baseball Weekly.*

In addition, the following books provided background material for one or more chapters of the almanac.

Auto Racing

1997 IndyCar Media Guide, edited by Bob Andrew; Championship Auto Racing Teams; Troy, Mich.

Indy: 75 Years of Racing's Greatest Spectacle, by Rich Taylor; St. Martin's Press (1991); New York.

Marlboro Grand Prix Guide, 1950-96 (1997 Edition), compiled by Jacques Deschenaux and Claude Michele Deschenaux; Charles Stewart & Company Ltd; Brentford, England.

1997 Winston Cup Media Guide, compiled and edited by Chris Powell; NASCAR Winston Cup Series; Winston-Salem, N.C.

NASCAR Online, produced by Starwave Corp. http://www.nascar.com

CART Online, maintained by USAInternet Direct. http://www.cart.com

Ballparks & Arenas

The Ballparks, by Bill Shannon and George Kalinsky; Hawthorn Books, Inc. (1975); New York.

Diamonds, by Michael Gershman; Houghton Mifflin Co. (1993); Boston.

Green Cathedrals (Revised Edition), by Philip Lowry; Addison-Wesley Publishing Co. (1992); Reading, Mass.

The NFL's Encyclopedic History of Professional Football, Macmillan Publishing Co. (1977); New York.

Take Me Out to the Ballpark, by Lowell Reidenbaugh; The Sporting News Publishing Co. (1983); St. Louis.

24 Seconds to Shoot (An Informal History of the NBA), by Leonard Koppett; Macmillan Publishing Co. (1968); New York.

Plus many major league baseball, NBA, NFL, NHL league and team guides, and college football and basketball guides.

Baseball

The All-Star Game (A Pictorial History, 1933 to Present), by Donald Honig; The Sporting News Publishing Co. (1987); St. Louis.

1996 American League Red Book, published by The Sporting News Publishing Co.; St. Louis.

The Baseball Chronology, edited by James Charlton; Macmillan Publishing Co. (1991); New York.

The Baseball Encyclopedia (Ninth Edition), editorial director, Rick Wolff; Macmillan Publishing Co. (1993); New York.

The Complete 1996 Baseball Record Book, edited by Craig Carter; The Sporting News Publishing Co.; St. Louis.

1996 National League Green Book, published by The Sporting News Publishing Co.; St. Louis.

The Scrapbook History of Baseball by Jordan Deutsch, Richard Cohen, Roland Johnson and David Neft; Bobbs-Merrill Company, Inc. (1975); Indianapolis/New York.

1996 Sporting News Official Baseball Guide, edited by Craig Carter and Dave Sloan; The Sporting News Publishing Co.; St. Louis.

1996 Sporting News Official Baseball Register, edited by Sean Stewart and Kyle Veltrop; The Sporting News Publishing Co.; St. Louis.

The Sports Encyclopedia: Baseball (1996 Edition), edited by David Neft and Richard Cohen; St. Martin's Press; New York.

Total Baseball (Fourth Edition), edited by John Thorn and Pete Palmer; HarperPerennial (1995); New York.

MLB@BAT, produced by Major League Baseball Properties, Inc. http://www.majorleaguebaseball.com

College Basketball

All the Moves (A History of College Basketball), by Neil D. Issacs; J.B. Lippincott Company (1975); New York.

College Basketball, U.S.A. (Since 1892), by John D. McCallum; Stein and Day (1978); New York.

Collegiate Basketball: Facts and Figures on the Cage Sport, by Edwin C. Caudle; The Paragon Press (1960); Montgomery, Ala.

The Encyclopedia of the NCAA Basketball Tournament, written and compiled by Jim Savage; Dell Publishing (1990); New York.

The Final Four (Reliving America's Basketball Classic), compiled by Billy Reed; Host Communications, Inc. (1988); Lexington, Ky.

1997 NCAA Final Four Records Book, compiled by Gary Johnson; edited by Stephen R. Hagwell; NCAA Books; Overland Park, Kan.

The Modern Encyclopedia of Basketball (Second Revised Edition), edited by Zander Hollander; Dolphins Books (1979); Doubleday & Company, Inc.; Garden City, N.Y.

1997 NCAA College Basketball Records Book, compiled by Gary Johnson, Richard Campbell, John Painter, Sean Straziscar and James Wright; edited by Laurie Bollig; NCAA Books; Overland Park, Kan.

NCAA Online, produced by National Collegiate Athletic Association. http://www.ncaa.org

Plus many 1996-97 NCAA Division I conference guides from America East to the WAC.

Pro Basketball

The Official NBA Basketball Encyclopedia (Second Edition), edited by Alex Sachare; Villard Books (1994); New York.

1996-97 Sporting News Official NBA Guide, edited by Mark Broussard and Craig Carter; The Sporting News Publishing Co.; St. Louis.

1996-97 Sporting News Official NBA Register, edited by Mark Bonavita, Mark Broussard and Sean Stewart; The Sporting News Publishing Co.; St. Louis.

NBA Online, produced by Starwave Corp. http://www.nba.com

Bowling

1995 Bowlers Journal Annual & Almanac; Luby Publishing; Chicago.

1997 LPBT Guide, Ladies Pro Bowlers Tour; Rockford, Ill.

1997 PBA Media Guide; Professional Bowlers Association; Akron, Ohio.

PBA Online, produced by the Pro Bowlers Association and Cadmus Interactive. http://www.pba.org

LPBT Online, produced by Bowling World Newspaper. http://www.lpbt.com

Boxing

The Boxing Record Book (1996), edited by Phill Marder; Fight Fax Inc.; Sicklerville, N.J.

The Ring 1985 Record Book & Boxing Encyclopedia, edited by Herbert G. Goldman; The Ring Publishing Corp.; New York.

The Ring: Boxing, The 20th Century, Steven Farhood, editor-in-chief; BDD Illustrated Books (1993); New York.

College Sports

1994-95 National Collegiate Championships, edited by Ted Breidenthal; NCAA Books; Overland Park, Kan.

1997 NCAA College Basketball Records Book, compiled by Gary Johnson, Richard Campbell, John Painter, Sean Straziscar and James Wright; edited by Laura Bollig; NCAA Books; Overland Park, Kan.

1996 NCAA College Football Records Book, compiled by Richard Campbell, John Painter and Sean Straziscar; edited by J. Gregory Summers; NCAA Books; Overland Park, Kan.

1996-97 NAIA Championships History and Records Book; National Assn. of Intercollegiate Athletics; Tulsa, Okla.

1996-97 National Directory of College Athletics, edited by Kevin Cleary; Collegiate Directories, Inc.; Cleveland.

NCAA Online, produced by National Collegiate Athletic Association. http://www.ncaa.org

College Football

Football: A College History, by Tom Perrin; McFarland & Company, Inc. (1987); Jefferson, N.C.

Football: Facts & Figures, by Dr. L.H. Baker; Farrar & Rinehart, Inc. (1945); New York.

Great College Football Coaches of the Twenties and Thirties, by Tim Cohane; Arlington House (1973); New Rochelle, N.Y.

1996 NCAA College Football Records Book, compiled by Richard Campbell, John Painter and Sean Straziscar; edited by J. Gregory Summers; NCAA Books; Overland Park, Kan.

Saturday Afternoon, by Richard Whittingham; Workman Publishing Co., Inc. (1985); New York.

Saturday's America, by Dan Jenkins; Sports Illustrated Books; Little, Brown & Company (1970); Boston.

Tournament of Roses, The First 100 Years, by Joe Hendrickson; Knapp Press (1989); Los Angeles.

NCAA Online, produced by National Collegiate Athletic Association. http://www.ncaa.org

Plus numerous college football team and conference guides, especially the 1996 guides compiled by the Atlantic Coast Conference, Big 12 and Southeastern Conference.

Pro Football

1996 Canadian Football League Guide, compiled by the CFL Communications Dept.; Toronto.

The Football Encyclopedia (The Complete History of NFL Football from 1892 to the Present), compiled by David Neft and Richard Cohen; St. Martin's Press (1994); New York.

The Official NFL Encyclopedia, by Beau Riffenburgh; New American Library (1986); New York.

Official NFL 1996 Record and Fact Book, compiled by the NFL Communications Dept. and Seymour Siwoff, Elias Sports Bureau; edited by Chris McCloskey and Chuck Garrity Jr.; produced by NFL Properties, Inc.; Los Angeles.

The Scrapbook History of Pro Football, by Richard Cohen, Jordan Deutsch, Roland Johnson and David Neft; Bobbs-Merrill Company, Inc. (1976); Indianapolis/New York.

1996 Sporting News Football Guide, edited by Craig Carter and Dave Sloan; The Sporting News Publishing Co.; St. Louis.

1996 Sporting News Football Register, edited Mark Bonavita and Sean Stewart; The Sporting News Publishing Co.; St. Louis.

1995 Sporting News Super Bowl Book, edited by Tom Dienhart, Joe Hoppel and Dave Sloan; The Sporting News Publishing Co.; St. Louis.

NFL.Com, produced by Starwave Corp. http://www.nfl.com

CFL Online, produced by SLAM! Sports. http://www.cfl.ca

Golf

The Encyclopedia of Golf (Revised Edition), compiled by Nevin H. Gibson; A.S. Barnes and Company (1964); New York.

Guinness Golf Records: Facts and Champions, by Donald Steel; Guinness Superlatives Ltd. (1987); Middlesex, England.

The History of the PGA Tour, by Al Barkow; Doubleday (1989); New York.

The Illustrated History of Women's Golf, by Rhonda Glenn, Taylor Publishing Co. (1991); Dallas.

1997 LPGA Player Guide, produced by LPGA Communications Dept.; Ladies Professional Golf Assn. Tour; Daytona Beach, Fla.

1997 PGA Tour Guide, produced by PGA Tour Creative Services; Professional Golfers Assn. Tour; Ponte Vedra, Fla.

Official Guide of the PGA Championships; Triumph Books (1994); Chicago.

The PGA World Golf Hall of Fame Book, by Gerald Astor, Prentice Hall Press (1991); New York.

1997 Senior PGA Tour Guide, produced by PGA Tour Creative Services; Professional Golfers Assn. Tour; Ponte Vedra, Fla.

Pro-Golf 1997, PGA European Tour Media Guide, Virginia Water, Surrey, England.

The Random House International Encyclopedia of Golf, by Malcolm Campbell; Random House (1991); New York.

USGA Record Books (1895-1959, 1960-80 and 1981-90); U.S. Golf Association; Far Hills, N.J.

LPGA.com, produced by the LPGA and Black Dog Design, http://www.lpga.com

PGA.com, produced by the PGA of America, http://www.pgaonline.com

Hockey

Canada Cup '87: The Official History, No.1 Publications Ltd.; Toronto.

The Complete Encyclopedia of Hockey; edited by Zander McFarlane; Visible Ink Press (1993); Detroit.

The Hockey Encyclopedia, by Stan Fischler and Shirley Walton Fischler; research editor, Bob Duff; Macmillan Publishing Co. (1983); New York.

Hockey Hall of Fame (The Official History of the Game and Its Greatest Stars), by Dan Diamond and Joseph Romain; Doubleday (1988); New York.

The National Hockey League, by Edward F. Dolan Jr.; W H Smith Publishers Inc. (1986); New York.

The Official National Hockey League 75th Anniversary Commemorative Book, edited by Dan Diamond; McClelland & Stewart, Inc. (1991); Toronto.

1996-97 Official NHL Guide & Record Book, compiled by the NHL Public Relations Dept.; New York/Montreal/Toronto.

1996-97 Sporting News Hockey Guide, edited by Craig Carter; The Sporting News Publishing Co.; St. Louis.

1996-97 Sporting News Hockey Register, edited by Mark Bonavita and Sean Stewart; The Sporting News Publishing Co.; St. Louis.

The Stanley Cup, by Joseph Romain and James Duplacey; Gallery Books (1989); New York.

The Trail of the Stanley Cup (Volumns I-III), by Charles L. Coleman; Progressive Publications Inc. (1969); Sherbrooke, Quebec.

NHL.com, produced by the NHL, http://www.nhl.com

Horse Racing

1997 American Racing Manual, compiled by the Daily Racing Form; Hightstown, N.J.

1997 Breeders' Cup Statistics; Breeders' Cup Limited; Lexington, Ky.

1996 Directory and Record Book, Thoroughbred Racing Associations of North America Inc.; Elkton, Md.

1996 Trotting and Pacing Guide, compiled and edited by John Pawlak; United States Trotting Association; Columbus, Ohio.

USTA online, produced by the USTA, http://www.ustrotting.com

International Sports

Athletics: A History of Modern Track and Field (1860-1990, Men and Women), by Roberto Quercetani; Vallardi & Associati (1990); Milan, Italy.

1995 International Track & Field Annual, Association of Track & Field Statisticians; edited by Peter Matthews; SportsBooks Ltd.; Surrey, England.

Track & Field News' Little Blue Book; Metric conversion tables; From the editors of Track & Field News (1989); Los Altos, Calif.

US Ski Team online, produced by US Ski Team and SportsLine USA, http://www.usskiteam.com

Miscellaneous

The America's Cup 1851-1987 (Sailing for Supremacy), by Gary Lester and Richard Sleeman; Lester-Townsend Publishing (1986); Sydney, Australia.

The Encyclopedia of Sports (Fifth Revised Edition), by Frank G. Menke; revisions by Suzanne Treat; A.S. Barnes and Co., Inc. (1975); Cranbury, N.J.

The Great American Sports Book, by George Gipe; Doubleday & Company, Inc. (1978); Garden City, N.Y.

The 1997 Information Please Almanac, edited by Otto Johnson; Houghton Mifflin Co.; Boston.

1997 Official PRCA Media Guide, edited by Steve Fleming; Professional Rodeo Cowboys Association; Colorado Springs.

The Sail Magazine Book of Sailing, by Peter Johnson; Alfred A. Knopf (1989); New York.

Ten Years of the Ironman, Triathlete Magazine; October, 1988; Santa Monica, Calif.

Iditarod online, produced by the Iditarod Trail Committtee and GCI, http://www.iditarod.com

Ironman online, produced by SportsLine USA, http://ironman.sportsline.com

PRCA online, produced by the Pro Rodeo Cowboys Association, http://www.prorodeo.com

Olympics

All That Glitters Is Not Gold (An Irreverent Look at the Olympic Games); by William O. Johnson, Jr.; G.P. Putnam's Sons (1972); New York.

Barcelona/Albertville 1992; edited by Lisa H. Albertson; for U.S. Olympic Committee by Commemorative Publications; Salt Lake City.

Chamonix to Lillehammer (The Glory of the Olympic Winter Games); edited by Lisa H. Albertson; for U.S. Olympic Committee by Commemorative Publication (1994); Salt Lake City.

The Complete Book of the Olympics (1992 Edition); by David Wallechinsky; Little, Brown and Co.; Boston.

The Games Must Go On (Avery Brundage and the Olympic Movement), by Allen Guttmann; Columbia University Press (1984); New York.

The Golden Book of the Olympic Games, edited by Erich Kamper and Bill Mallon; Vallardi & Associati (1992); Milan, Italy.

Hitler's Games (The 1936 Olympics), by Duff Hart-Davis; Harper & Row (1986); New York/London.

An Illustrated History of the Olympics (Third Edition); by Dick Schaap; Alfred A. Knopf (1975); New York.

The Nazi Olympics, by Richard D. Mandell; Souvenir Press (1972); London.

The Official USOC Book of the 1984 Olympic Games, by Dick Schaap; Random House/ABC Sports; New York.

The Olympics: A History of the Games, by William Oscar Johnson; Oxmoor House (1992); Birmingham, Ala.

Pursuit of Excellence (The Olympic Story), by The Associated Press and Grolier; Grolier Enterprises Inc. (1979); Danbury, Conn.

The Story of the Olympic Games (776 B.C. to 1948 A.D.), by John Kieran and Arthur Daley; J.B. Lippincott Company (1948); Philadelphia/New York.

United States Olympic Books (Seven Editions): 1936 and 1948-88; U.S. Olympic Association; New York.

The USA and the Olympic Movement, produced by the USOC Information Dept.; edited by Gayle Plant; U.S. Olympic Committee (1988); Colorado Springs.

Soccer

The American Encyclopedia of Soccer, edited by Zander Hollander; Everest House Publishers (1980); New York.

The European Football Yearbook (1994-95 Edition), edited by Mike Hammond; Sports Projects Ltd; West Midlands, England.

The Guinness Book of Soccer Facts & Feats, by Jack Rollin; Guinness Superlatives Ltd. (1978); Middlesex, England.

History of Soccer's World Cup, by Michael Archer; Chartwell Books, Inc. (1978); Secaucus, N.J.

The Simplest Game, by Paul Gardner; Collier Books (1994); New York.

The Story of the World Cup, by Brian Glanville; Faber and Faber Limited (1994); London/Boston.

1997 MLS Official Media Guide, edited by the MLS Communications staff; Los Angeles.

1991-92 MSL Official Guide, Major (Indoor) Soccer League; Overland Park, Kan.

U.S. Soccer 1996 Media Guide, edited by Tom Lang; U.S. Soccer Federation; Chicago.

FIFA online, produced by FIFA, http://www.fifa.com

France98 online, produced by the France 98 Organizing Committee, http://www.france98.com

MLSnet, produced by Major League Soccer and Boxtop Interactive, http://www.mlsnet.com

Tennis

Bud Collins' Modern Encyclopedia of Tennis, edited by Bud Collins and Zander Hollander; Visible Ink Press (1994); Detroit.

The Illustrated Encyclopedia of World Tennis, by John Haylett and Richard Evans; Exeter Books (1989); New York.

Official Encyclopedia of Tennis, edited by the staff of the U.S. Lawn Tennis Assn.; Harper & Row (1972); New York.

1997 ATP Tour Player Guide, compiled by ATP Tour Communications Dept.; Association of Tennis Professionals; Ponte Vedra Beach, Fla.

1997 Corel WTA Tour Media Guide, compiled by WTA Public Relations staff; edited by Renee Bloch Shallouf, Doug Clery and Toni Woods; St. Petersburg, Fla.

ATP Tour online, produced by ATP Tour, Inc., http://www.atptour.com

Corel WTA Tour Site, produced by the Corel WTA Tour, http://www.corelwtatour.com

Who's Who

The Guiness International Who's Who of Sport, edited by Peter Mathews, Ian Buchanan and Bill Mallon; Guiness Publishing (1993); Middlesex, England

101 Greatest Athletes of the Century, by Will Grimsley and the Associated Press Sports Staff; Bonanza Books (1987); Crown Publishers, Inc.; New York.

The New York Times Book of Sports Legends, edited by Joseph Vecchione; Simon & Shuster (1991); New York.

Superstars, by Frank Litsky; Vineyard Books, Inc. (1975); Secaucus, N.J.

A Who's Who of Sports Champions (Their Stories and Records), by Ralph Hickok, Houghton Mifflin Co. (1995); Boston.

Other Reference Books/Sites

Facts & Dates of American Sports, by Gorton Carruth & Eugene Ehrlich; Harper & Row, Publishers, Inc. (1988); New York.

Sports Market Place 1996 (July edition), edited by Richard A. Lipsey; Sportsguide Inc.; Princeton N.J.

The World Book Encyclopedia (1988 Edition); World Book, Inc.; Chicago.

The World Book Yearbook (Annual Supplements, 1954-95); World Book, Inc.; Chicago.

ESPNet SportsZone, produced by ESPN and Starwave Corp., http://espnet.sportszone.com

CBS SportsLine, produced by CBS and SportsLine USA, http://www.sportsline.com

JULY

S	M	T	W	T	F	S
			1	2	3	4
5	6	7	8	9	10	11
12	13	14	15	16	17	18
19	20	21	22	23	24	25
26	27	28	29	30	31	

Days
1 Canada Day
4 Independence Day

Events
2-5 U.S. Women's Open (Kohler, Wisc.)
4-26 Tour de France
7 Baseball All-Star Game (Denver)
9-12 U.S. Senior Open (Pacific Palisades, Calif.)
12 World Cup Soccer Final (Paris)
16-19 British Open (Royal Birkdale)
27 US 500 (Brooklyn, Mich.)

AUGUST

S	M	T	W	T	F	S
						1
2	3	4	5	6	7	8
9	10	11	12	13	14	15
16	17	18	19	20	21	22
23	24	25	26	27	28	29
30	31					

Events
6-8 Bass Masters Classic
8 All-America Soap Box Derby (Akron)
13-16 PGA Championship (Seattle)
24-29 Little League World Series (Williamsport, Pa.)
24-Sept.6 U.S. Open Tennis (Flushing, N.Y.)

SEPTEMBER

S	M	T	W	T	F	S
		1	2	3	4	5
6	7	8	9	10	11	12
13	14	15	16	17	18	19
20	21	22	23	24	25	26
27	28	29	30			

Days
7 Labor Day
21 First Day of Rosh Hashanah
23 First Day of Fall (1:37 am)
30 Yom Kippur

Events
6 NFL Regular Season Opens
18-20 Women's Golf Solheim Cup (Dublin, Ohio)
27 Baseball Regular Season Ends
30 Baseball Playoffs Begin (tentative)

OCTOBER

S	M	T	W	T	F	S
				1	2	3
4	5	6	7	8	9	10
11	12	13	14	15	16	17
18	19	20	21	22	23	24
25	26	27	28	29	30	31

Days
12 Columbus Day
Thanksgiving (Canada)
25 Daylight Savings Time Ends (Fall back)
31 Halloween

Events
11 Coll FB-Oklahoma vs Texas (Dallas)
16 ABL Regular Season Begins*
17 World Series Begins (AL city)*

*tentative date

NOVEMBER

S	M	T	W	T	F	S
1	2	3	4	5	6	7
8	9	10	11	12	13	14
15	16	17	18	19	20	21
22	23	24	25	26	27	28
29	30					

Days
3 Election Day
11 Veterans' Day
26 Thanksgiving

Events
1 New York City Marathon
8 Breeders' Cup (TBA)
16 CFL Grey Cup (Edmonton)
21 Coll FB-Auburn at Alabama (Birmingham)
Michigan at Ohio St.
UCLA at USC, Yale at Harvard

DECEMBER

S	M	T	W	T	F	S
		1	2	3	4	5
6	7	8	9	10	11	12
13	14	15	16	17	18	19
20	21	22	23	24	25	26
27	28	29	30	31		

Days
14 First Day of Hanukkah
21 First Day of Winter (8:56 pm)
25 Christmas Day
26 Boxing Day (Canada)

Events
4-13 National Finals Rodeo (Las Vegas)
5 Coll FB-Army vs Navy (Philadelphia)
Coll FB-SEC Title Game (Atlanta)
28 NFL Regular Season Ends
Jan. 2 NFL Playoffs Begin

JANUARY

S	M	T	W	T	F	S
					1	2
3	4	5	6	7	8	9
10	11	12	13	14	15	16
17	18	19	20	21	22	23
24	25	26	27	28	29	30
31						

FEBRUARY

S	M	T	W	T	F	S
	1	2	3	4	5	6
7	8	9	10	11	12	13
14	15	16	17	18	19	20
21	22	23	24	25	26	27
28						

MARCH

S	M	T	W	T	F	S
	1	2	3	4	5	6
7	8	9	10	11	12	13
14	15	16	17	18	19	20
21	22	23	24	25	26	27
28	29	30	31			

APRIL

S	M	T	W	T	F	S
				1	2	3
4	5	6	7	8	9	10
11	12	13	14	15	16	17
18	19	20	21	22	23	24
25	26	27	28	29	30	

MAY

S	M	T	W	T	F	S
						1
2	3	4	5	6	7	8
9	10	11	12	13	14	15
16	17	18	19	20	21	22
23	24	25	26	27	28	29
30	31					

JUNE

S	M	T	W	T	F	S
		1	2	3	4	5
6	7	8	9	10	11	12
13	14	15	16	17	18	19
20	21	22	23	24	25	26
27	28	29	30			

JULY

S	M	T	W	T	F	S
				1	2	3
4	5	6	7	8	9	10
11	12	13	14	15	16	17
18	19	20	21	22	23	24
25	26	27	28	29	30	31

AUGUST

S	M	T	W	T	F	S
1	2	3	4	5	6	7
8	9	10	11	12	13	14
15	16	17	18	19	20	21
22	23	24	25	26	27	28
29	30	31				

SEPTEMBER

S	M	T	W	T	F	S
			1	2	3	4
5	6	7	8	9	10	11
12	13	14	15	16	17	18
19	20	21	22	23	24	25
26	27	28	29	30		

OCTOBER

S	M	T	W	T	F	S
					1	2
3	4	5	6	7	8	9
10	11	12	13	14	15	16
17	18	19	20	21	22	23
24	25	26	27	28	29	30
31						

NOVEMBER

S	M	T	W	T	F	S
	1	2	3	4	5	6
7	8	9	10	11	12	13
14	15	16	17	18	19	20
21	22	23	24	25	26	27
28	29	30				

DECEMBER

S	M	T	W	T	F	S
			1	2	3	4
5	6	7	8	9	10	11
12	13	14	15	16	17	18
19	20	21	22	23	24	25
26	27	28	29	30	31	

ESPN, the worldwide leader in sports, joins forces with America's favorite sports reference book to create the most savvy, sophisticated, and informative sports almanac ever published.

1998 ESPN® Information Please®

Sports Almanac

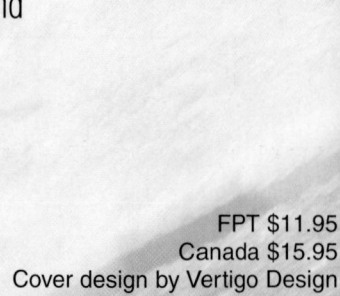

Essays and commentary by **top ESPN personalities**

Extensive statistics from ESPN's Inside the Numbers team

Fast access to the facts: Winners and losers, year by year, sport by sport

Hundreds of **photographs,** charts, and directories

Visit ESPN SportsZone at http://espn.com

FPT $11.95
Canada $15.95
Cover design by Vertigo Design
Cover photos © Tony Stone Images
Sports/ESPN tie-in

information please LLC

HYPERION

ESPN BOOKS®